continued . . .

The Pillars of the Earth

"Enormous and brilliant . . . crammed with characters unbelievably alive across the great gulf of centuries . . . touches all human emotion— love and hate, loyalty and treachery, hope and despair. See for yourself. This is truly a novel to get lost in." —*Cosmopolitan*

"Wonderful . . . will fascinate you, surround you."—*Chicago Sun-Times*

"A towering tale . . . a ripping read. . . . There's murder, arson, treachery, torture, love, and lust." —*New York Daily News*

"Ken Follett takes a giant step." —*San Francisco Chronicle*

"With this book, Follett risks all and comes out a clear winner . . . a historical novel of gripping readability, authentic atmosphere, and memorable characterization. Beginning with a mystery that casts its shadow, the narrative is a seesaw of tension, suspense, impeccable pacing . . . action, intrigue, violence, passion, greed, bravery, dedication, revenge, and love. A novel that entertains, instructs, and satisfies on a grand scale." —*Publishers Weekly*

"An extraordinary epic buttressed by suspense . . . a mystifying puzzle involving the execution of an innocent man . . . the erection of a magnificent cathedral . . . romance, rivalry, and spectacle. A monumental masterpiece . . . a towering triumph from a major talent." —*Booklist*

KEN FOLLETT

FALL *of* GIANTS

BOOK ONE OF THE CENTURY TRILOGY

 NEW AMERICAN LIBRARY

New American Library
Published by the Penguin Group
Penguin Group (USA) LLC, 375 Hudson Street,
New York, New York 10014

USA | Canada | UK | Ireland | Australia | New Zealand | India | South Africa | China
penguin.com
A Penguin Random House Company

Published by New American Library, a division of Penguin Group (USA) LLC. Previously published
in a Dutton edition.

First New American Library Printing, September 2011

Copyright © Ken Follett, 2010
Family tree illustration by Dave Hopkins
Map copyright © by David Atkinson, Hand Made Maps Ltd.
Penguin supports copyright. Copyright fuels creativity, encourages diverse voices, promotes free
speech, and creates a vibrant culture. Thank you for buying an authorized edition of this book and
for complying with copyright laws by not reproducing, scanning, or distributing any part of it in
any form without permission. You are supporting writers and allowing Penguin to continue to
publish books for every reader.

 REGISTERED TRADEMARK—MARCA REGISTRADA

New American Library Trade Paperback ISBN 978-0-451-23257-1

THE LIBRARY OF CONGRESS HAS CATALOGED THE HARDCOVER EDITION OF THIS TITLE AS
FOLLOWS:

Fall of Giants: book one of the century trilogy/by Ken Follett.
p. cm.—(Century: bk. 1)
ISBN 978-0-525-95165-0
1. Domestic Fiction. 1. Title
PR6056.O45F35 2010
823'.914—dc22 2010009279

Printed in the United States of America
7 9 10 8 6

Set in Warnock Pro
Designed by Amy Hill

To the memory of my parents,

Martin and Veenie Follett

Cast of Characters

American

DEWAR FAMILY

Senator Cameron Dewar
Ursula Dewar, his wife
Gus Dewar, their son

VYALOV FAMILY

Josef Vyalov, businessman
Lena Vyalov, his wife
Olga Vyalov, their daughter

OTHERS

Rosa Hellman, journalist
Chuck Dixon, school friend of Gus's
Marga, nightclub singer
Nick Forman, thief
Ilya, thug
Theo, thug
Norman Niall, crooked accountant
Brian Hall, union leader

REAL HISTORICAL CHARACTERS

Woodrow Wilson, twenty-eighth president
William Jennings Bryan, secretary of state
Josephus Daniels, secretary of the navy

English and Scottish

FITZHERBERT FAMILY

Earl Fitzherbert, called Fitz
Princess Elizaveta, called Bea, his wife
Lady Maud Fitzherbert, his sister
Lady Hermia, called Aunt Herm, their poor aunt
Duchess of Sussex, their rich aunt
Gelert, Pyrenean mountain dog
Grout, Fitz's butler
Sanderson, Maud's maid

OTHERS

Mildred Perkins, Ethel Williams's lodger
Bernie Leckwith, secretary of the Aldgate branch of the
    Independent Labour Party
Bing Westhampton, Fitz's friend
Marquis of Lowther, "Lowthie," rejected suitor of Maud
Albert Solman, Fitz's man of business
Dr. Greenward, volunteer at the baby clinic
Lord "Johnny" Remarc, junior War Office minister
Colonel Hervey, aide to Sir John French
Lieutenant Murray, aide to Fitz
Mannie Litov, factory owner
Jock Reid, treasurer of the Aldgate Independent Labour Party
Jayne McCulley, soldier's wife

REAL HISTORICAL CHARACTERS

King George V
Queen Mary
Mansfield Smith-Cumming, called "C," head of the Foreign
    Section of the Secret Service Bureau (later MI6)
Sir Edward Grey, M.P., foreign secretary
Sir William Tyrrell, private secretary to Grey
Frances Stevenson, mistress of Lloyd George
Winston Churchill, M.P.
H. H. Asquith, M.P., prime minister
Sir John French, commander of the British Expeditionary Force

French

Gini, a bar girl
Colonel Dupuys, aide to General Galliéni
General Lourceau, aide to General Joffre

REAL HISTORICAL CHARACTERS
General Joffre, commander in chief of French forces
General Galliéni, commander of the Paris garrison

German and Austrian

VON ULRICH FAMILY
Otto von Ulrich, diplomat
Susanne von Ulrich, his wife
Walter von Ulrich, their son, military attaché at the German
  embassy in London
Greta von Ulrich, their daughter
Graf (Count) Robert von Ulrich, Walter's second cousin, military
  attaché at the Austrian embassy in London

OTHERS
Gottfried von Kessel, cultural attaché at the German embassy in
  London
Monika von der Helbard, Greta's best friend

REAL HISTORICAL CHARACTERS
Prince Karl Lichnowsky, German ambassador to London
Field Marshal Paul von Hindenburg
General of Infantry Erich Ludendorff
Theobald von Bethmann-Hollweg, German chancellor
Arthur Zimmermann, German foreign minister

Russian

PESHKOV FAMILY
Grigori Peshkov, metalworker
Lev Peshkov, horse wrangler

PUTILOV MACHINE WORKS
Konstantin, lathe operator, chairman of the Bolshevik discussion
  group

Isaak, captain of the football team
Varya, female laborer, Konstantin's mother
Serge Kanin, supervisor of the casting section
Count Maklakov, director

OTHERS

Mikhail Pinsky, police officer
Ilya Kozlov, his sidekick
Nina, maid to Princess Bea
Prince Andrei, Bea's brother
Katerina, a peasant girl new to the city
Mishka, bar owner
Trofim, gangster
Fyodor, corrupt cop
Spirya, passenger on the *Angel Gabriel*
Yakov, passenger on the *Angel Gabriel*
Anton, clerk at the Russian embassy in London, also a spy for
    Germany
David, Jewish soldier
Sergeant Gavrik
Lieutenant Tomchak

REAL HISTORICAL CHARACTERS

Vladimir Ilyich Lenin, leader of the Bolshevik Party
Leon Trotsky

Welsh

WILLIAMS FAMILY

David Williams, union organizer
Cara Williams, his wife
Ethel Williams, their daughter
Billy Williams, their son
Gramper, Cara's father

GRIFFITHS FAMILY

Len Griffiths, atheist and Marxist
Mrs. Griffiths
Tommy Griffiths, their son, Billy Williams's best friend

PONTI FAMILY
Mrs. Minnie Ponti
Giuseppe "Joey" Ponti, her son
Giovanni "Johnny" Ponti, his younger brother

MINERS
David Crampton, "Dai Crybaby"
Harry "Suet" Hewitt
John Jones the Shop
Dai Chops, the butcher's son
Pat Pope, Main Level onsetter
Micky Pope, Pat's son
Dai Ponies, horse wrangler
Bert Morgan

MINE MANAGEMENT
Perceval Jones, chairman of Celtic Minerals
Maldwyn Morgan, colliery manager
Rhys Price, colliery manager's deputy
Arthur "Spotty" Llewellyn, colliery clerk

STAFF AT TŶ GWYN
Peel, butler
Mrs. Jevons, housekeeper
Morrison, footman

OTHERS
Dai Muck, sanitary worker
Mrs. Dai Ponies
Mrs. Roley Hughes
Mrs. Hywel Jones
Private George Barrow, B Company
Private Robin Mortimer, cashiered officer, B Company
Private Owen Bevin, B Company
Sergeant Elijah "Prophet" Jones, B Company
Second Lieutenant James Carlton-Smith, B Company
Captain Gwyn Evans, A Company
Second Lieutenant Roland Morgan, A Company

REAL HISTORICAL CHARACTERS
David Lloyd George, Liberal member of Parliament

FALL of GIANTS

BOOK ONE OF THE CENTURY TRILOGY

Circa 1914

PROLOGUE

INITIATION

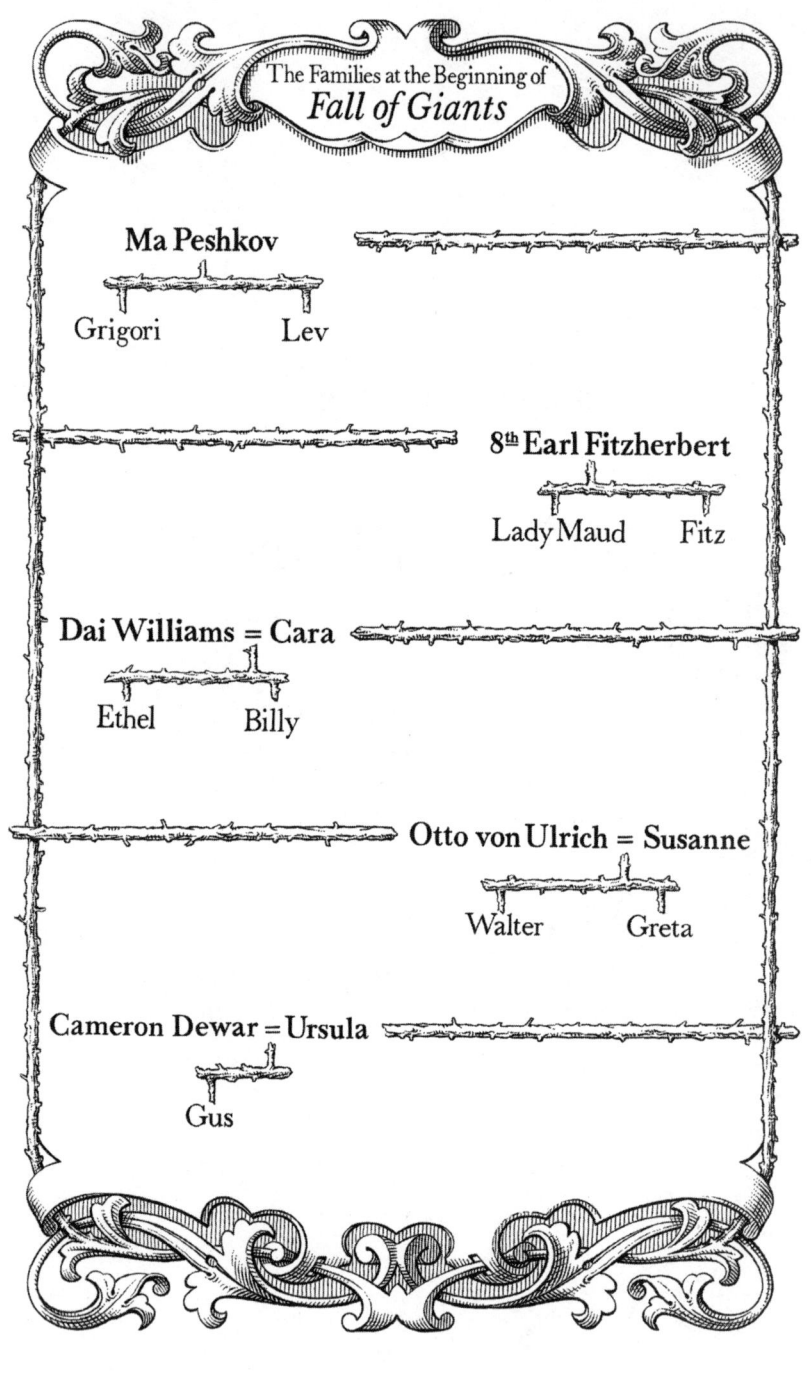

The Families at the Beginning of
Fall of Giants

Ma Peshkov

Grigori   Lev

8th Earl Fitzherbert

Lady Maud   Fitz

Dai Williams = Cara

Ethel   Billy

Otto von Ulrich = Susanne

Walter   Greta

Cameron Dewar = Ursula

Gus

CHAPTER ONE

June 22, 1911

O n the day King George V was crowned at Westminster Abbey in London, Billy Williams went down the pit in Aberowen, South Wales.

The twenty-second of June, 1911, was Billy's thirteenth birthday. He was woken by his father. Da's technique for waking people was more effective than it was kind. He patted Billy's cheek, in a regular rhythm, firmly and insistently. Billy was in a deep sleep, and for a second he tried to ignore it, but the patting went on relentlessly. Momentarily he felt angry; but then he remembered that he had to get up, he even wanted to get up, and he opened his eyes and sat upright with a jerk.

"Four o'clock," Da said; then he left the room, his boots banging on the wooden staircase as he went down.

Today Billy would begin his working life by becoming an apprentice collier, as most of the men in town had done at his age. He wished he felt more like a miner. But he was determined not to make a fool of himself. David Crampton had cried on his first day down the pit, and they still called him Dai Crybaby, even though he was twenty-five and the star of the town's rugby team.

It was the day after midsummer, and a bright early light came through the small window. Billy looked at his grandfather, lying beside him. Gramper's eyes were open. He was always awake, whenever Billy got up; he said old people did not sleep much.

Billy got out of bed. He was wearing only his underdrawers. In cold weather he wore his shirt to bed, but Britain was enjoying a hot summer, and the nights were mild. He pulled the pot from under the bed and took off the lid.

There was no change in the size of his penis, which he called his peter. It was still the childish stub it had always been. He had hoped it might have started to grow on the night before his birthday, or perhaps that he might see just one black hair sprouting somewhere near it, but he was disappointed. His best friend, Tommy Griffiths, who had been born on the same day, was different: he had a cracked voice and a dark fuzz on his upper lip, and his peter was like a man's. It was humiliating.

As Billy was using the pot, he looked out of the window. All he could see was the slag heap, a slate-gray mountain of tailings, waste from the coal mine, mostly shale and sandstone. This was how the world appeared on the second day of Creation, Billy thought, before God said: "Let the earth bring forth grass." A gentle breeze wafted fine black dust off the slag onto the rows of houses.

Inside the room there was even less to look at. This was the back bedroom, a narrow space just big enough for the single bed, a chest of drawers, and Gramper's old trunk. On the wall was an embroidered sampler that read:

BELIEVE ON THE
LORD JESUS CHRIST
AND THOU SHALT
BE SAVED

There was no mirror.

One door led to the top of the stairs, the other to the front bedroom, which could be accessed only through this one. It was larger and had space for two beds. Da and Mam slept there, and Billy's sisters had, too, years ago. The eldest, Ethel, had now left home, and the other three had died, one from measles, one from whooping cough, and one from diphtheria. There had been an older brother, too, who had shared Billy's bed before Gramper came. Wesley had been his name, and he had been killed underground by a runaway dram, one of the wheeled tubs that carried coal.

Billy pulled on his shirt. It was the one he had worn to school yesterday. Today was Thursday, and he changed his shirt only on Sunday. However, he did have a new pair of trousers, his first long ones, made of the thick water-repellent cotton called moleskin. They were the symbol of entry into the world of men, and he pulled them on proudly, enjoying the heavy masculine feel of the fabric. He put on a thick leather belt and the boots he had inherited from Wesley; then he went downstairs.

Most of the ground floor was taken up by the living room, fifteen feet square, with a table in the middle and a fireplace to one side, and a homemade rug on the stone floor. Da was sitting at the table reading an old copy of the *Daily Mail*, a pair of spectacles perched on the bridge of his long, sharp nose. Mam was making tea. She put down the steaming kettle, kissed Billy's forehead, and said: "How's my little man on his birthday?"

Billy did not reply. The "little" was wounding, because he was little, and the "man" was just as hurtful because he was not a man. He went into the scullery at the back of the house. He dipped a tin bowl into the water barrel, washed his face and hands, and poured the water away in the shallow stone sink. The scullery had a copper with a fire grate underneath, but it was used only on bath night, which was Saturday.

They had been promised running water soon, and some of the miners' houses already had it. It seemed a miracle to Billy that people could get a cup of cold clear water just by turning the tap, and not have to carry a bucket to the standpipe out in the street. But indoor water had not yet come to Wellington Row, where the Williamses lived.

He returned to the living room and sat at the table. Mam put a big cup of milky tea in front of him, already sugared. She cut two thick slices off a loaf of homemade bread and got a slab of dripping from the pantry under the stairs. Billy put his hands together, closed his eyes, and said: "Thank you, Lord, for this food. Amen." Then he drank some tea and spread dripping on his bread.

Da's pale blue eyes looked over the top of the paper. "Put salt on your bread," he said. "You'll sweat underground."

Billy's father was a miners' agent, employed by the South Wales Miners' Federation, which was the strongest trade union in Britain, as he said whenever he got the chance. He was known as Dai Union. A lot of men were called Dai, pronounced "die," short for David, or Dafydd in Welsh. Billy had learned in school that David was popular in Wales because it was the name of the country's patron saint, like Patrick in Ireland. All the Dais were distinguished one from another not by their surnames—almost everyone in town was Jones, Williams, Evans, or Morgan—but by a nickname. Real names were rarely used when there was a humorous alternative. Billy was William Williams, so they called him Billy Twice. Women were sometimes given their husband's nickname, so that Mam was Mrs. Dai Union.

Gramper came down while Billy was eating his second slice. Despite the warm weather he wore a jacket and waistcoat. When he had washed his hands he sat opposite Billy. "Don't look so nervous," he said. "I went down the pit when I was ten. And *my* father was carried to the pit on his father's back at the age of five, and worked from six in the morning until seven in the evening. He never saw daylight from October to March."

"I'm not nervous," Billy said. This was untrue. He was scared stiff.

However, Gramper was kindly, and he did not press the point. Billy liked Gramper. Mam treated Billy like a baby, and Da was stern and sarcastic, but Gramper was tolerant and talked to Billy as to an adult.

"Listen to this," said Da. He would never buy the *Mail*, a right-wing rag, but he sometimes brought home someone else's copy and read the paper aloud in a scornful voice, mocking the stupidity and dishonesty of the ruling class. "'Lady Diana Manners has been criticized for wearing the same dress to two different balls. The younger daughter of the Duke of Rutland won "best lady's costume" at the Savoy Ball for her off-the-shoulder boned bodice with full hooped skirt, receiving a prize of two hundred and fifty guineas.'" He lowered the paper and said: "That's at least five years' wages for you, Billy boy." He resumed: "'But she drew the frowns of the cognoscenti by wearing the same dress to Lord Winterton and F. E. Smith's party at Claridge's Hotel. One can have too much of a good thing, people said.'" He looked up from the paper. "You'd better change that frock, Mam," he said. "You don't want to draw the frowns of the cognoscenti."

Mam was not amused. She was wearing an old brown wool dress with patched elbows and stains under the armpits. "If I had two hundred and fifty guineas, I'd look better than Lady Diana Muck," she said, not without bitterness.

"It's true," Gramper said. "Cara was always the pretty one—just like her mother." Mam's name was Cara. Gramper turned to Billy. "Your grandmother was Italian. Her name was Maria Ferrone." Billy knew this, but Gramper liked to retell familiar stories. "That's where your mother gets her glossy black hair and lovely dark eyes—and your sister. Your gran was the most beautiful girl in Cardiff—and I got her!" Suddenly he looked sad. "Those were the days," he said quietly.

Da frowned with disapproval—such talk suggested the lusts of the flesh—but Mam was cheered by her father's compliments, and she smiled as she put his breakfast in front of him. "Oh, aye," she said. "Me and my sisters were considered beauties. We'd show those dukes what a pretty girl is, if we had the money for silk and lace."

Billy was surprised. He had never thought of his mother as beautiful or otherwise, though when she dressed for the chapel social on Saturday evening she did look striking, especially in a hat. He supposed she might once have been a pretty girl, but it was hard to imagine.

"Mind you," said Gramper, "your gran's family were clever, too. My brother-in-law was a miner, but he got out of the industry and opened a café in Tenby. Now there's a life for you—sea breezes, and nothing to do all day but make coffee and count your money."

Da read another item. "'As part of the preparations for the coronation, Buckingham Palace has produced a book of instructions two hundred and twelve pages long.'" He looked over the paper. "Mention that down the pit today, Billy. The men will be relieved to know that nothing has been left to chance."

Billy was not very interested in royalty. What he liked was the adventure stories the *Mail* often printed about tough rugby-playing public-school men catching sneaky German spies. According to the paper, such spies infested every town in Britain, although there did not seem to be any in Aberowen, disappointingly.

Billy stood up. "Going down the street," he announced. He left the house by the front door. "Going down the street" was a family euphemism: it meant going to the toilets, which stood halfway down Wellington Row. A low brick hut with a corrugated iron roof was built over a deep hole in the earth. The hut was divided into two compartments, one for men and one for women. Each compartment had a double seat, so that people went to the toilet two by two. No one knew why the builders had chosen this arrangement, but everyone made the best of it. Men looked straight ahead and said nothing, but—as Billy could often hear—women chatted companionably. The smell was suffocating, even when you experienced it every day of your life. Billy always tried to breathe as little as possible while he was inside, and came out gasping for air. The hole was shoveled out periodically by a man called Dai Muck.

When Billy returned to the house he was delighted to see his sister Ethel sitting at the table. "Happy birthday, Billy!" she cried. "I had to come and give you a kiss before you go down the pit."

Ethel was eighteen, and Billy had no trouble seeing *her* as beautiful. Her mahogany-colored hair was irrepressibly curly, and her dark eyes twinkled with mischief. Perhaps Mam had looked like this once. Ethel wore the plain black dress and white cotton cap of a housemaid, an outfit that flattered her.

Billy worshipped Ethel. As well as pretty, she was funny and clever and brave, sometimes even standing up to Da. She told Billy things no one else would explain, such as the monthly episode women called the curse, and what was the crime of public indecency that had caused the Anglican vicar to leave town in such a hurry. She had been top of the class all the way through school, and her essay "My Town or Village" had taken first prize in a contest run by the *South Wales Echo*. She had won a copy of *Cassell's Atlas of the World*.

She kissed Billy's cheek. "I told Mrs. Jevons the housekeeper that we were running out of boot polish and I'd better get some more from the town." Ethel lived and worked at Tŷ Gwyn, the vast home of Earl Fitzherbert, a mile away up the mountain. She handed Billy something wrapped in a clean rag. "I stole a piece of cake for you."

"Oh, thanks, Eth!" said Billy. He loved cake.

Mam said: "Shall I put it in your snap?"

"Aye, please."

Mam got a tin box from the cupboard and put the cake inside. She cut two more slabs of bread, spread them with dripping, sprinkled salt, and put them in the tin. All the miners had a "snap tin." If they took food underground wrapped in a rag, the mice would eat it before the midmorning break. Mam said: "When you bring me home your wages, you can have a slice of boiled bacon in your snap."

Billy's earnings would not be much, at first, but all the same they would make a difference to the family. He wondered how much Mam would allow him for pocket money and whether he would ever be able to save enough for a bicycle, which he wanted more than anything else in the world.

Ethel sat at the table. Da said to her: "How are things at the big house?"

"Nice and quiet," she said. "The earl and princess are in London for the coronation." She looked at the clock on the mantelpiece. "They'll be getting up soon—they need to be at the abbey early. *She* won't like it— she's not used to early hours—but she can't be late for the king." The earl's wife, Bea, was a Russian princess, and very grand.

Da said: "They'll want to get seats near the front, so they can see the show."

"Oh, no, you can't sit anywhere you like," Ethel said. "They've had six thousand mahogany chairs made special, with the names of the guests on the back in gold writing."

Gramper said: "Well, there's a waste! What will they do with them after?"

"I don't know. Perhaps everyone will take them home as souvenirs."

Da said dryly: "Tell them to send a spare one to us. There's only five of us here, and already your mam's got to stand."

When Da was being facetious there might be real anger underneath. Ethel leaped to her feet. "Oh, sorry, Mam. I didn't think."

"Stay where you are. I'm too busy to sit down," said Mam.

The clock struck five. Da said: "Best get there early, Billy boy. Start as you mean to go on."

Billy got to his feet reluctantly and picked up his snap.

Ethel kissed him again, and Gramper shook his hand. Da gave him two six-inch nails, rusty and a bit bent. "Put those in your trousers pocket."

"What for?" said Billy.

"You'll see," Da said with a smile.

Mam handed Billy a quart bottle with a screw top, full of cold tea with milk and sugar. She said: "Now, Billy, remember that Jesus is always with you, even down the pit."

"Aye, Mam."

He could see a tear in her eye, and he turned away quickly, because it made him feel weepy, too. He took his cap from the peg. "Bye, then," he said, as if he was only going to school; and he stepped out of the front door.

The summer had been hot and sunny so far, but today was overcast, and it even looked as if it might rain. Tommy was leaning against the wall of the house, waiting. "Aye, aye, Billy," he said.

"Aye, aye, Tommy."

They walked down the street side by side.

Aberowen had once been a small market town, serving hill farmers round about, Billy had learned in school. From the top of Wellington Row you could see the old commercial center, with the open pens of the cattle market, the wool exchange building, and the Anglican church, all on one side of the Owen River, which was little more than a stream.

Now a railway line cut through the town like a wound, terminating at the pithead. The miners' houses had spread up the slopes of the valley, hundreds of gray stone homes with roofs of darker gray Welsh slate. They were built in long serpentine rows that followed the contours of the mountainsides, the rows crossed by shorter streets that plunged headlong to the valley bottom.

"Who do you think you'll be working with?" said Tommy.

Billy shrugged. New boys were assigned to one of the colliery manager's deputies. "No way to know."

"I hope they put me in the stables." Tommy liked horses. About fifty ponies lived in the mine. They pulled the drams that the colliers filled, drawing them along railway tracks. "What sort of work do you want to do?"

Billy hoped he would not be given a task too heavy for his childish physique, but he was not willing to admit that. "Greasing drams," he said.

"Why?"

"It seems easy."

They passed the school where yesterday they had been pupils. It was a Victorian building with pointed windows like a church. It had been built by the Fitzherbert family, as the headmaster never tired of reminding the pupils. The earl still appointed the teachers and decided the curriculum. On the walls were paintings of heroic military victories, and the greatness of Britain was a constant theme. In the Scripture lesson with which every day began, strict Anglican doctrines were taught, even though nearly all the children were from Nonconformist families. There was a school management committee, of which Da was a member, but it had no power except to advise. Da said the earl treated the school as his personal property.

In their final year Billy and Tommy had been taught the principles of mining, while the girls learned to sew and cook. Billy had been surprised to discover that the ground beneath him consisted of layers of different kinds of earth, like a stack of sandwiches. A coal seam—a phrase he had heard all his life without really understanding it—was one such layer. He had also been told that coal was made of dead leaves and other vegetable matter, accumulated over thousands of years and compressed by the weight of earth above it. Tommy, whose father was an atheist, said this proved the Bible was not true; but Billy's da said that was only one interpretation.

The school was empty at this hour, its playground deserted. Billy felt proud that he had left school behind, although part of him wished he could go back there instead of down the pit.

As they approached the pithead, the streets began to fill with miners, each with his snap tin and bottle of tea. They all dressed the same, in old suits that they would take off once they reached their workplace. Some mines were cold but Aberowen was a hot pit, and the men worked in underwear and boots, or in the coarse linen shorts they called bannickers. Everyone wore a padded cap, all the time, because tunnel roofs were low and it was easy to bang your head.

Over the houses Billy could see the winding gear, a tower topped by two great wheels rotating in opposite directions, drawing the cables that raised and lowered the cage. Similar pithead structures loomed over most towns in the South Wales valleys, the way church spires dominated farming villages.

Other buildings were scattered around the pithead as if dropped by accident: the lamp room, the colliery office, the smithy, the stores. Railway lines snaked between the buildings. On the waste ground were broken drams, old cracked timbers, feed sacks, and piles of rusty disused machinery, all covered with a layer of coal dust. Da always said there would be fewer accidents if miners kept things tidy.

Billy and Tommy went to the colliery office. In the front room was Arthur "Spotty" Llewellyn, a clerk not much older than they were. His white shirt had a dirty collar and cuffs. They were expected—their fathers had previously arranged for them to start work today. Spotty wrote their names in a ledger, then took them into the colliery manager's office. "Young Tommy Griffiths and young Billy Williams, Mr. Morgan," he said.

Maldwyn Morgan was a tall man in a black suit. There was no coal dust on his cuffs. His pink cheeks were free of stubble, which meant he must shave every day. His engineering diploma hung in a frame on the wall, and his bowler hat—the other badge of his status—was displayed on the coat stand by the door.

To Billy's surprise, he was not alone. Next to him stood an even more formidable figure: Perceval Jones, chairman of Celtic Minerals, the company that owned and operated the Aberowen coal mine and several others. A small, aggressive man, he was called Napoleon by the miners. He wore morning dress, a black tailcoat and striped gray trousers, and he had not taken off his tall black top hat.

Jones looked at the boys with distaste. "Griffiths," he said. "Your father's a revolutionary socialist."

"Yes, Mr. Jones," said Tommy.

"And an atheist."

"Yes, Mr. Jones."

He turned his gaze on Billy. "And your father's an official of the South Wales Miners' Federation."

"Yes, Mr. Jones."

"I don't like socialists. Atheists are doomed to eternal damnation. And trade unionists are the worst of the lot."

He glared at them, but he had not asked a question, so Billy said nothing.

"I don't want troublemakers," Jones went on. "In the Rhondda Valley they've been on strike for forty-three weeks because of people like your fathers stirring them up."

Billy knew that the strike in the Rhondda had not been caused by troublemakers, but by the owners of the Ely Pit at Penygraig, who had locked out their miners. But he kept his mouth shut.

"Are you troublemakers?" Jones pointed a bony finger at Billy, making Billy shake. "Did your father tell you to stand up for your rights when you're working for me?"

Billy tried to think, though it was difficult when Jones looked so threatening. Da had not said much this morning, but last night he had given some advice. "Please, sir, he told me: 'Don't cheek the bosses. That's my job.'"

Behind him, Spotty Llewellyn sniggered.

Perceval Jones was not amused. "Insolent savage," he said. "But if I turn you away, I'll have the whole of this valley on strike."

Billy had not thought of that. Was he so important? No—but the miners might strike for the principle that the children of their officials must not suffer. He had been at work less than five minutes, and already the union was protecting him.

"Get them out of here," said Jones.

Morgan nodded. "Take them outside, Llewellyn," he said to Spotty. "Rhys Price can look after them."

Billy groaned inwardly. Rhys Price was one of the more unpopular deputy managers. He had set his cap at Ethel, a year ago, and she had turned him down flat. She had done the same to half the single men in Aberowen, but Price had taken it hard.

Spotty jerked his head. "Out," he said, and he followed them. "Wait outside for Mr. Price."

Billy and Tommy left the building and leaned on the wall by the door. "I'd like to punch Napoleon's fat belly," said Tommy. "Talk about a capitalist bastard."

"Yeah," said Billy, though he had had no such thought.

Rhys Price showed up a minute later. Like all the deputies, he wore a low round-crowned hat called a billycock, more expensive than a miner's cap but cheaper than a bowler. In the pockets of his waistcoat he had a notebook and a pencil, and he carried a yardstick. Price had dark stubble on his cheeks and a gap in his front teeth. Billy knew him to be clever but sly.

"Good morning, Mr. Price," Billy said.

Price looked suspicious. "What business have you got saying good morning to me, Billy Twice?"

"Mr. Morgan said we are to go down the pit with you."

"Did he, now?" Price had a way of darting looks to the left and right, and sometimes behind, as if he expected trouble from an unknown quarter. "We'll see about that." He looked up at the winding wheel, as if seeking an explanation there. "I haven't got time to deal with boys." He went into the office.

"I hope he gets someone else to take us down," Billy said. "He hates my family because my sister wouldn't walk out with him."

"Your sister thinks she's too good for the men of Aberowen," said Tommy, obviously repeating something he had heard.

"She *is* too good for them," Billy said stoutly.

Price came out. "All right, this way," he said, and headed off at a rapid walk.

The boys followed him into the lamp room. The lamp man handed Billy a shiny brass safety lamp, and he hooked it onto his belt as the men did.

He had learned about miners' lamps in school. Among the dangers of coal mining was methane, the inflammable gas that seeped out of coal seams. The men called it firedamp, and it was the cause of all underground explosions. Welsh pits were notoriously gassy. The lamp was ingeniously designed so that its flame would not ignite firedamp. In fact the flame would change its shape, becoming longer, thereby giving a warning—for firedamp had no smell.

If the lamp went out, the miner could not relight it himself. Carrying matches was forbidden underground, and the lamp was locked to discourage the breaking of the rule. An extinguished lamp had to be taken to a lighting station, usually at the pit bottom near the shaft. This might be a walk of a mile or more, but it was worth it to avoid the risk of an underground explosion.

In school the boys had been told that the safety lamp was one of the ways in which mine owners showed their care and concern for their employees—"as if," Da said, "there was no benefit to the bosses in preventing explosions and stoppage of work and damage to tunnels."

After picking up their lamps, the men stood in line for the cage. Cleverly placed alongside the queue was a notice board. Handwritten or crudely printed signs advertised cricket practice, a darts match, a lost penknife, a recital by the Aberowen Male Voice Choir, and a lecture on Karl Marx's theory of historical materialism at the Free Library. But deputies did not have to wait, and Price pushed his way to the front, with the boys tagging along.

Like most pits, Aberowen had two shafts, with fans placed to force air down one and up the other. The owners often gave the shafts whimsical names, and here they were Pyramus and Thisbe. This one, Pyramus, was the up shaft, and Billy could feel the draft of warm air coming from the pit.

Last year Billy and Tommy had decided they wanted to look down the shaft. On Easter Monday, when the men were not working, they had dodged the watchman and sneaked across the waste ground to the pithead, then climbed the guard fence. The shaft mouth was not completely enclosed by the cage housing, and they had lain on their bellies and looked over the rim. They had stared with dreadful fascination into that terrible hole, and Billy had felt his stomach turn. The blackness seemed infinite. He experienced a thrill that was half joy because he did not have to go down, half terror because one day he would. He had thrown a stone in, and they had listened as it bounced against the wooden cage-conductor and the brick lining of the shaft. It seemed a horrifically long time before they heard the faint, distant splash as it hit the pool of water at the bottom.

Now, a year later, he was about to follow the course of that stone.

He told himself not to be a coward. He had to behave like a man, even if he did not feel like one. The worst thing of all would be to disgrace himself. He was more afraid of that than of dying.

He could see the sliding grille that closed off the shaft. Beyond it was empty space, for the cage was on its way up. On the far side of the shaft he could see the winding engine that turned the great wheels high above. Jets of steam escaped from the mechanism. The cables slapped their guides with a whiplash sound. There was an odor of hot oil.

With a clash of iron, the empty cage appeared behind the gate. The banksman, in charge of the cage at the top end, slid the gate back. Rhys Price stepped into the empty cage and the two boys followed. Thirteen miners got in behind them—the cage held sixteen in total. The banksman slammed the gate shut.

There was a pause. Billy felt vulnerable. The floor beneath his feet was solid, but he might without much difficulty have squeezed through the widely spaced bars of the sides. The cage was suspended from a steel rope, but even that was not completely safe: everyone knew that the winding cable at Tirpentwys had snapped one day in 1902, and the cage had plummeted to the pit bottom, killing eight men.

He nodded to the miner beside him. It was Harry "Suet" Hewitt, a pudding-faced boy only three years older, though a foot taller. Billy remembered Harry in school: he had been stuck in Standard Three with the ten-year-olds, failing the exam every year, until he was old enough to start work.

A bell rang, signifying that the onsetter at the pit bottom had closed his gate. The banksman pulled a lever and a different bell rang. The steam engine hissed; then there was another bang.

The cage fell into empty space.

Billy knew that it went into free fall, then braked in time for a soft landing; but no theoretical foreknowledge could have prepared him for the sensation of dropping unhindered into the bowels of the earth. His feet left the floor. He screamed in terror. He could not help himself.

All the men laughed. They knew it was his first time and had been waiting for his reaction, he realized. Too late, he saw that they were all holding the bars of the cage to prevent themselves floating up. But the knowledge did nothing to calm his fear. He managed to stop screaming only by clamping his teeth together.

At last the brake engaged. The speed of the fall slowed, and Billy's feet touched the floor. He grabbed a bar and tried to stop shaking. After a minute the fear was replaced by a sense of injury so strong that tears threatened. He looked into the laughing face of Suet and shouted over the noise: "Shut your great gob, Hewitt, you shitbrain."

Suet's face changed in an instant and he looked furious, but the other men laughed all the more. Billy would have to say sorry to Jesus for swearing, but he felt a bit less of a fool.

He looked at Tommy, who was white-faced. Had Tommy screamed? Billy was afraid to ask in case the answer might be no.

The cage stopped, the gate was thrown back, and Billy and Tommy walked shakily out into the mine.

It was gloomy. The miners' lamps gave less light than the paraffin lights on the walls at home. The pit was as dark as a night with no moon. Perhaps they did not need to see well to hew coal, Billy thought. He splashed through a puddle, and looking down he saw water and mud everywhere, gleaming with the faint reflections of lamp flames. There was a strange taste in his mouth: the air was thick with coal dust. Was it possible that men breathed this all day? That must be why miners coughed and spat constantly.

Four men were waiting to enter the cage and go up to the surface. Each carried a leather case, and Billy realized they were the firemen. Every morning, before the miners started, the firemen tested for gas. If the concentration of methane was unacceptably high, they would order the men not to work until the ventilation fans cleared the gas.

In the immediate neighborhood Billy could see a row of stalls for ponies and an open door leading to a brightly lit room with a desk, presumably an office for deputies. The men dispersed, walking away along four tunnels that radiated from the pit bottom. Tunnels were called headings, and they led to the districts where the coal was won.

Price took them to a shed and undid a padlock. The place was a tool store. He selected two shovels, gave them to the boys, and locked up again.

They went to the stables. A man wearing only shorts and boots was shoveling soiled straw out of a stall, pitching it into a coal dram. Sweat ran down his muscular back. Price said to him: "Do you want a boy to help you?"

The man turned around, and Billy recognized Dai Ponies, an elder of the Bethesda Chapel. Dai gave no sign of recognizing Billy. "I don't want the little one," he said.

"Right," said Price. "The other is Tommy Griffiths. He's yours."

Tommy looked pleased. He had got his wish. Even though he would only be mucking out stalls, he was working in the stables.

Price said: "Come on, Billy Twice," and he walked into one of the headings.

Billy shouldered his shovel and followed. He felt more anxious now that Tommy was no longer with him. He wished he had been set to mucking out stalls alongside his friend. "What will I be doing, Mr. Price?" he said.

"You can guess, can't you?" said Price. "Why do you think I gave you a fucking shovel?"

Billy was shocked by the casual use of the forbidden word. He could not guess what he would be doing, but he asked no more questions.

The tunnel was round, its roof reinforced by curved steel supports. A two-inch pipe ran along its crown, presumably carrying water. Every night the headings were sprinkled in an attempt to reduce the dust. It was not merely a danger to men's lungs—if that were all, Celtic Minerals probably would not have cared—but it constituted a fire hazard. However, the sprinkler system was inadequate. Da had argued that a pipe of six inches' diameter was needed, but Perceval Jones had refused to spend the money.

After about a quarter of a mile they turned into a cross tunnel that sloped upward. This was an older, smaller passage, with timber props rather than steel rings. Price had to duck his head where the roof sagged. At intervals of about thirty yards they passed the entrances to workplaces where the miners were already hewing the coal.

Billy heard a rumbling sound, and Price said: "Into the manhole."

"What?" Billy looked at the ground. A manhole was a feature of town pavements, and he could see nothing on the floor but the railway tracks that carried the drams. He looked up to see a pony trotting toward him, coming fast down the slope, drawing a train of drams.

"In the manhole!" Price shouted.

Still Billy did not understand what was required of him, but he could see that the tunnel was hardly wider than the drams, and he would be crushed. Then Price seemed to step into the wall and disappear.

Billy dropped his shovel, turned, and ran back the way he had come. He tried to get ahead of the pony, but it was moving surprisingly fast. Then he saw a niche cut into the wall, the full height of the tunnel, and he realized that he had seen such niches, without remarking them, every twenty-five yards or so. This must be what Price meant by a manhole. He threw himself in, and the train rumbled past.

When it had gone he stepped out, breathing hard.

Price pretended to be angry, but he was smiling. "You'll have to be more alert than that," he said. "Otherwise you'll get killed down here—like your brother."

Most men enjoyed exposing and mocking the ignorance of boys, Billy found. He was determined to be different when he grew up.

He picked up his shovel. It was undamaged. "Lucky for you," Price commented. "If the dram had broken it, you would have had to pay for a new one."

They went on and soon entered an exhausted district where the workplaces were deserted. There was less water underfoot, and the ground was covered with a thick layer of coal dust. They took several turnings and Billy lost his sense of direction.

They came to a place where the tunnel was blocked by a dirty old dram. "This area has to be cleaned up," Price said. It was the first time he had bothered to explain anything, and Billy had a feeling he was lying. "Your job is to shovel the muck into the dram."

Billy looked around. The dust was a foot thick to the limit of the light cast by his lamp, and he guessed it went a lot farther. He could shovel for a week without making much impression. And what was the point? The district was worked out. But he asked no questions. This was probably some kind of test.

"I'll come back in a bit and see how you're getting on," Price said, and he retraced his steps, leaving Billy alone.

Billy had not expected this. He had assumed he would be working with older men and learning from them. But he could only do what he was told.

He unhooked the lamp from his belt and looked around for somewhere to put it. There was nothing he could use as a shelf. He put the lamp on the floor, but it was almost useless there. Then he remembered the nails Da had given him. So this was what they were for. He took one from his pocket. Using the blade of his shovel, he hammered it into a timber prop, then hung up his lamp. That was better.

The dram was chest high to a man but shoulder height to Billy, and when he started work he found that half the dust slipped off his shovel before he could get it over the lip. He developed an action that turned the blade to prevent this happening. In a few minutes he was bathed in sweat, and he realized what the second nail was for. He hammered it into another timber and hung up his shirt and trousers.

After a while he felt that someone was watching him. Out of the corner of his eye he saw a dim figure standing as still as a statue. "Oh, God!" he shrieked, and he turned around to face it.

It was Price. "I forgot to check your lamp," he said. He took Billy's lamp off the nail and did something to it. "Not so good," he said. "I'll leave you mine." He hung up the other lamp and disappeared.

He was a creepy character, but at least he seemed to have Billy's safety in mind.

Billy resumed work. Before long his arms and legs began to ache. He was used to shoveling, he told himself: Da kept a pig in the waste ground behind the house, and it was Billy's job to muck out the sty once a week. But that took about a quarter of an hour. Could he possibly keep this up all day?

Under the dust was a floor of rock and clay. After a while he had cleared an area four feet square, the width of the tunnel. The muck hardly covered the bottom of the dram, but he felt exhausted.

He tried to pull the dram forward so that he would not have to walk so far with his shovelful, but its wheels seemed to have locked with disuse.

He had no watch, and it was difficult to know how much time had passed. He began to work more slowly, conserving his strength.

Then his light went out.

The flame flickered first, and he looked anxiously at the lamp hanging on the nail, but he knew that the flame would lengthen if there was firedamp. This was not what he was seeing, so he felt reassured. Then the flame went out altogether.

He had never known darkness like this. He saw nothing, not even patches of gray, not even different shades of black. He lifted his shovel to face level and held it an inch from his nose, but he could not see it. This was what it must be like to be blind.

He stood still. What was he to do? He was supposed to take the lamp to the lighting station, but he could not have found his way back through the tunnels even if he had been able to see. In this blackness he might blunder about for hours. He had no idea how many miles the disused workings extended, and he did not want the men to have to send a search party for him.

He would just have to wait for Price. The deputy had said he would come back "in a bit." That could mean a few minutes, or an hour or more. And Billy suspected it would be later rather than sooner. Price had surely intended this. A safety lamp could not blow out, and anyway there was little wind here. Price had taken Billy's lamp and substituted one that was low on oil.

He felt a surge of self-pity, and tears came to his eyes. What had he done to deserve this? Then he pulled himself together. It was another test, like the cage. He would show them he was tough enough.

He should carry on working, even in the dark, he decided. Moving for the first time since the light went out, he put his shovel to the ground and ran it forward, trying to pick up dust. When he lifted it he thought, by its weight, that there was a load on the blade. He turned and walked two paces, then hefted it, trying to throw the muck into the dram, but he misjudged the height. The shovel clanged against the side of the dram and felt suddenly lighter as its load fell to the ground.

He would adjust. He tried again, lifting the shovel higher. When he had unloaded the blade he let it fall, and felt the wooden shaft bang against the lip of the dram. That was better.

As the work took him farther from the dram he continued to miss occasionally, until he began to count his paces aloud. He got into a rhythm, and although his muscles hurt he was able to carry on.

As the work became automatic, his mind was free to wander, which was not so good. He wondered how far the tunnel extended ahead of him and how long it had been disused. He thought of the earth above his head, extending for half a mile, and the weight being held up by these old timber props. He recalled his brother, Wesley, and the other men who had died in this mine. But their spirits were not here, of course.

Wesley was with Jesus. The others might be, too. If not they were in a different place.

He began to feel frightened and decided it was a mistake to think about spirits. He was hungry. Was it time for his snap? He had no idea, but he thought he might as well eat it. He made his way to the place where he had hung his clothes, fumbled on the ground below, and found his flask and tin.

He sat with his back against the wall and took a long drink of cold, sweet tea. As he was eating his bread-and-dripping, he heard a faint noise. He hoped it might be the creaking of Rhys Price's boots, but that was wishful thinking. He knew that squeak: it was rats.

He was not afraid. There were plenty of rats in the ditches that ran along every street in Aberowen. But they seemed bolder in the dark, and a moment later one ran over his bare legs. Transferring his food to his left hand, he picked up his shovel and lashed out. It did not even scare them, and he felt the tiny claws on his skin again. This time one tried to run up his arm. Obviously they could smell the food. The squeaking increased, and he wondered how many there were.

He stood up and crammed the last of his bread into his mouth. He drank some more tea, then ate his cake. It was delicious, full of dried fruit and almonds; but a rat ran up his leg, and he was forced to gobble the cake.

They seemed to know the food was gone, for the squeaking gradually died down and then stopped altogether.

Eating gave Billy renewed energy for a while, and he went back to work, but he had a burning ache in his back. He kept going more slowly, stopping for frequent rests.

To cheer himself up, he told himself it might be later than he thought. Perhaps it was noon already. Someone would come to fetch him at the end of the shift. The lamp man checked the numbers, so they always knew if a man had not come back up. But Price had taken Billy's lamp and substituted a different one. Could he be planning to leave Billy down here overnight?

It would never work. Da would raise the roof. The bosses were afraid of Da—Perceval Jones had more or less admitted it. Sooner or later, someone was sure to look for Billy.

But when he got hungry again he felt sure many hours must have passed. He started to get scared, and this time he could not shake it off. It was the darkness that unnerved him. He could have borne the waiting if he had been able to see. In the complete blackness he felt he was losing his mind. He had no sense of direction, and every time he walked back from the dram he wondered if he was about to crash into the tunnel side. Earlier he had worried about crying like a child. Now he had to stop himself screaming.

Then he recalled what Mam had said to him: "Jesus is always with you, even down the pit." At the time he had thought she was just telling him to behave well. But she had been wiser than that. Of course Jesus was with him. Jesus was everywhere. The darkness did not matter, nor the passage of time. Billy had someone taking care of him.

To remind him of that, he sang a hymn. He disliked his voice, which was still a treble, but there was no one to hear him, so he sang as loud as he could. When he had sung all the verses, and the scary feeling began to return, he imagined Jesus standing just the other side of the dram, watching, with a look of grave compassion on his bearded face.

Billy sang another hymn. He shoveled and paced to the time of the music. Most of the hymns went with a swing. Every now and then he suffered again the fear that he might have been forgotten, the shift might have ended and he might be alone down there; then he would just remember the robed figure standing with him in the dark.

He knew plenty of hymns. He had been going to the Bethesda Chapel three times every Sunday since he was old enough to sit quietly. Hymn books were expensive, and not all the congregation could read, so everyone learned the words.

When he had sung twelve hymns, he reckoned an hour had passed. Surely it must be the end of the shift? But he sang another twelve. After that it was hard to keep track. He sang his favorites twice. He worked slower and slower.

He was singing "Up from the Grave He Arose" at the top of his voice when he saw a light. The work had become so automatic that he did not stop, but picked up another shovelful and carried it to the dram, still singing, while the light grew stronger. When the hymn came to an end he leaned on his shovel. Rhys Price stood watching him, lamp at his belt, with a strange look on his shadowed face.

Billy would not let himself feel relief. He was not going to show Price how he felt. He put on his shirt and trousers, then took the unlit lamp from the nail and hung it on his belt.

Price said: "What happened to your lamp?"

"You know what happened," Billy said, and his voice sounded strangely grown-up.

Price turned away and walked back along the tunnel.

Billy hesitated. He looked the opposite way. Just the other side of the dram he glimpsed a bearded face and a pale robe, but the figure disappeared like a thought. "Thank you," Billy said to the empty tunnel.

As he followed Price, his legs ached so badly that he felt he might fall down, but he hardly cared if he did. He could see again, and the shift was over. Soon he would be home and he could lie down.

They reached the pit bottom and got into the cage with a crowd of black-faced miners. Tommy Griffiths was not among them, but Suet Hewitt was. As they waited for the signal from above, Billy noticed they were looking at him with sly grins.

Hewitt said: "How did you get on, then, on your first day, Billy Twice?"

"Fine, thank you," Billy said.

Hewitt's expression was malicious: no doubt he was remembering that Billy had called him shitbrain. He said: "No problems?"

Billy hesitated. Obviously they knew something. He wanted them to know that he had not succumbed to fear. "My lamp went out," he said, and he just about managed to keep his voice steady. He looked at Price, but decided it would be more manly not to accuse him. "It was a bit difficult shoveling in the dark all day," he finished. That was too understated—they might think his ordeal had been nothing much—but it was better than admitting to fear.

An older man spoke. It was John Jones the Shop, so called because his wife ran a little general store in their parlor. "All day?" he said.

Billy said: "Aye."

John Jones looked at Price and said: "You bastard, it's only supposed to be for an hour."

Billy's suspicion was confirmed. They all knew what had happened, and it sounded as if they did something similar to all new boys. But Price had made it worse than usual.

Suet Hewitt was grinning. "Weren't you scared, Billy boy, on your own in the dark?"

He thought about his answer. They were all looking at him, waiting to hear what he would say. Their sly smiles had gone, and they seemed a bit ashamed. He decided to tell the truth. "I was scared, yes, but I wasn't on my own."

Hewitt was baffled. "Not on your own?"

"No, of course not," Billy said. "Jesus was with me."

Hewitt laughed loudly, but no one else did. His guffaw resounded in the silence and stopped suddenly.

The hush lasted several seconds. Then there was a clang of metal and a jerk, and the cage lifted. Harry turned away.

After that, they called him Billy-with-Jesus.

PART ONE

THE
DARKENING
SKY

CHAPTER TWO

January 1914

Earl Fitzherbert, age twenty-eight, known to his family and friends as Fitz, was the ninth-richest man in Britain.

He had done nothing to earn his huge income. He had simply inherited thousands of acres of land in Wales and Yorkshire. The farms made little money, but there was coal beneath them, and by licensing mineral rights Fitz's grandfather had become enormously wealthy.

Clearly God intended the Fitzherberts to rule over their fellow men, and to live in appropriate style; but Fitz felt he had not done much to justify God's faith in him.

His father, the previous earl, had been different. A naval officer, he had been made admiral after the bombardment of Alexandria in 1882, had become the British ambassador to St. Petersburg, and finally had been a minister in the government of Lord Salisbury. The Conservatives lost the general election of 1906, and Fitz's father died a few weeks later—his end hastened, Fitz felt sure, by seeing irresponsible Liberals such as David Lloyd George and Winston Churchill take over His Majesty's government.

Fitz had taken his seat in the House of Lords, the upper chamber of the British Parliament, as a Conservative peer. He spoke good French and he could get by in Russian, and he would have liked one day to be his country's foreign secretary. Regrettably, the Liberals had continued to win elections, so he had had no chance yet of becoming a government minister.

His military career had been equally undistinguished. He had attended the army's officer training academy at Sandhurst, and had spent three years with the Welsh Rifles, ending as a captain. On marriage he had given up full-time soldiering, but had become honorary colonel of the South Wales Territorials. Unfortunately an honorary colonel never won medals.

However, he did have something to be proud of, he thought as the train steamed up through the South Wales valleys. In two weeks' time, the king was coming to stay at Fitz's country house. King George V and Fitz's father had been shipmates in their youth. Recently the king had expressed a wish to know what the younger men were thinking, and Fitz had organized a discreet house party for His Majesty to meet some of them. Now Fitz and his wife, Bea, were on their way to the house to get everything ready.

Fitz cherished traditions. Nothing known to mankind was superior to the comfortable order of monarchy, aristocracy, merchant, and peasant. But now, looking out of the train window, he saw a threat to the British way of life greater than any the country had faced for a hundred years. Covering the once-green hillsides, like a gray-black leaf blight on a rhododendron bush, were the terraced houses of the coal miners. In those grimy hovels there was talk of republicanism, atheism, and revolt. It was only a century or so since the French nobility had been driven in carts to the guillotine, and the same would happen here if some of those muscular black-faced miners had their way.

Fitz would gladly have given up his earnings from coal, he told himself, if Britain could go back to a simpler era. The royal family was a strong bulwark against insurrection. But Fitz felt nervous about the visit, as well as proud. So much could go wrong. With royalty, an oversight might be seen as a sign of carelessness, and therefore disrespectful. Every detail of the weekend would be reported, by the visitors' servants, to other servants and thence to those servants' employers, so that every woman in London society would quickly know if the king were given a hard pillow, a bad potato, or the wrong brand of champagne.

Fitz's Rolls-Royce Silver Ghost was waiting at Aberowen railway station. With Bea at his side he was driven a mile to Tŷ Gwyn, his country house. A light but persistent drizzle was falling, as it so often did in Wales.

"Tŷ Gwyn" was Welsh for White House, but the name had become ironic. Like everything else in this part of the world, the building was covered with a layer of coal dust, and its once-white stone blocks were now a dark gray color that smeared the skirts of ladies who carelessly brushed against its walls.

Nevertheless it was a magnificent building, and it filled Fitz with pride as the car purred up the drive. The largest private house in Wales, Tŷ Gwyn had two hundred rooms. Once when he was a boy he and his sister, Maud, had counted the windows and found 523. It had been built by his grandfather, and there was a pleasing order to the three-story design. The ground-floor windows were tall, letting plenty of light into the grand reception rooms. Upstairs were dozens of guest rooms, and in the attic countless small servants' bedrooms, revealed by long rows of dormer windows in the steep roofs.

The fifty acres of gardens were Fitz's joy. He supervised the gardeners personally, making decisions about planting and pruning and potting. "A house fit for a king to visit," he said as the car stopped at the grand portico. Bea did not reply. Traveling made her bad-tempered.

Getting out of the car, Fitz was greeted by Gelert, his Pyrenean mountain dog—a bear-sized creature that licked his hand, then raced joyously around the courtyard in celebration.

In his dressing room Fitz took off his traveling clothes and changed into a suit of soft brown tweed. Then he went through the communicating door into Bea's rooms.

The Russian maid, Nina, was unpinning the elaborate hat Bea had worn for the journey. Fitz caught sight of Bea's face in the dressing-table mirror, and his heart skipped a beat. He was taken back four years, to the St. Petersburg ballroom where he had first seen that impossibly pretty face framed by blond curls that could not quite be tamed. Then as now she had worn a sulky look that he found strangely alluring. In a heartbeat he had decided that she of all women was the one he wanted to marry.

Nina was middle-aged and her hand was unsteady—Bea often made her servants nervous. As Fitz watched, a pin pricked Bea's scalp, and she cried out.

Nina went pale. "I'm terribly sorry, Your Highness," she said in Russian.

Bea snatched up a hatpin from the dressing table. "See how you like it!" she cried, and jabbed the maid's arm.

Nina burst into tears and ran from the room.

"Let me help you," Fitz said to his wife in a soothing tone.

She was not to be mollified. "I'll do it myself."

Fitz went to the window. A dozen or so gardeners were at work trimming bushes, edging lawns, and raking gravel. Several shrubs were in flower: pink viburnum, yellow winter jasmine, witch hazel, and scented winter honeysuckle. Beyond the garden was the soft green curve of the mountainside.

He had to be patient with Bea, and remind himself that she was a foreigner, isolated in a strange country, away from her family and all that was familiar. It had been easy in the early months of their marriage, when he was still intoxicated by how she looked and smelled and the touch of her soft skin. Now it took an effort. "Why don't you rest?" he said. "I'll see Peel and Mrs. Jevons and find out how their plans are progressing." Peel was the butler and Mrs. Jevons the housekeeper. It was Bea's job to organize the staff, but Fitz was nervous enough about the king's visit to welcome an excuse to get involved. "I'll report back to you later, when you're refreshed." He took out his cigar case.

"Don't smoke in here," she said.

He took that for assent and went to the door. Pausing on his way out, he said: "Look, you won't behave like that in front of the king and queen, will you? Striking the servants, I mean."

"I didn't strike her. I stuck a pin in her as a lesson."

Russians did that sort of thing. When Fitz's father had complained about the laziness of the servants at the British embassy in St. Petersburg, his Russian friends had told him he did not beat them enough.

Fitz said to Bea: "It would embarrass the monarch to have to witness such a thing. As I've told you before, it's not done in England."

"When I was a girl, I was made to watch three peasants being hanged," she said. "My mother didn't like it, but my grandfather insisted. He said: 'This is to teach you to punish your servants. If you do not slap them or flog them for small offenses of carelessness and laziness, they will eventually commit larger sins and end up on the scaffold.' He taught me that indulgence to the lower classes is cruel, in the long run."

Fitz began to lose patience. Bea looked back to a childhood of limitless wealth and self-indulgence, surrounded by troops of obedient servants and thousands of happy peasants. If her ruthless, capable grandfather had still been alive, that life might have continued; but the family fortune had been frittered away by Bea's father, a drunk, and her weak brother, Andrei, who was always selling the timber without replanting the woods. "Times have changed," Fitz said. "I'm asking you—I'm ordering you—not to embarrass me in front of my king. I hope I have left no room for doubt in your mind." He went out and closed the door.

He walked along the wide corridor, feeling irritated and a bit sad. When they were first married, such spats had left him bewildered and regretful; now he was becoming inured to them. Were all marriages like that? He did not know.

A tall footman polishing a doorknob straightened up and stood with his back to the wall and his eyes cast down, as Tŷ Gwyn servants were trained to do when the earl went by. In some great houses the staff had to face the wall, but Fitz thought that was too feudal. Fitz recognized this man, having seen him play cricket in a match between Tŷ Gwyn staff and Aberowen miners. He was a good left-handed batsman. "Morrison," said Fitz, remembering his name. "Tell Peel and Mrs. Jevons to come to the library."

"Very good, my lord."

Fitz walked down the grand staircase. He had married Bea because he had been enchanted by her, but he had had a rational motive, too. He dreamed of founding a great Anglo-Russian dynasty that would rule vast tracts of the earth, much as the Habsburg dynasty had ruled parts of Europe for centuries.

But for that he needed an heir. Bea's mood meant she would not welcome him to her bed tonight. He could insist, but that was never very satisfactory. It was a couple of weeks since the last time. He did not wish for a wife who was vulgarly eager about that sort of thing but, on the other hand, two weeks was a long time.

His sister, Maud, was still single at twenty-three. Besides, any child of hers would probably be brought up a rabid socialist who would fritter away the family fortune printing revolutionary tracts.

He had been married three years, and he was beginning to worry. Bea had been pregnant just once, last year, but she had suffered a miscarriage at three months. It had happened just after a quarrel. Fitz had canceled a planned trip to St. Petersburg, and Bea had become terribly emotional, crying that she wanted to go home. Fitz had put his foot down—a man could not let his wife dictate to him, after all—but then, when she miscarried, he felt guiltily convinced it was his fault. If only she could get pregnant again he would make absolutely sure nothing was allowed to upset her until the baby was born.

Putting that worry to the back of his mind, he went into the library and sat down at the leather-inlaid desk to make a list.

A minute or two later, Peel came in with a housemaid. The butler was the younger son of a farmer, and there was an outdoor look about his freckled face and salt-and-pepper hair, but he had been a servant at Tŷ Gwyn all his working life. "Mrs. Jevons have been took poorly, my lord," he said. Fitz had long ago given up trying to correct the grammar of Welsh servants. "Stomach," Peel added lugubriously.

"Spare me the details." Fitz looked at the housemaid, a pretty girl of about twenty. Her face was vaguely familiar. "Who's this?"

The girl spoke for herself. "Ethel Williams, my lord. I'm Mrs. Jevons's assistant." She had the lilting accent of the South Wales valleys.

"Well, Williams, you look too young to do a housekeeper's job."

"If your lordship pleases, Mrs. Jevons said you would probably bring down the housekeeper from Mayfair, but she hopes I might give satisfaction in the meantime."

Was there a twinkle in her eye when she talked of giving satisfaction? Although she spoke with appropriate deference, she had a cheeky look. "Very well," said Fitz.

Williams had a thick notebook in one hand and two pencils in the other. "I visited Mrs. Jevons in her room, and she was well enough to go through everything with me."

"Why have you got two pencils?"

"In case one breaks," she said, and she grinned.

Housemaids were not supposed to grin at the earl, but Fitz could not help smiling back. "All right," he said. "Tell me what you've got written down in your book."

"Three subjects," she said. "Guests, staff, and supplies."

"Very good."

"From your lordship's letter, we understand there will be twenty guests. Most will bring one or two personal staff, say an average of two, therefore an extra forty in servants' accommodation. All arriving on the Saturday and leaving on the Monday."

"Correct." Fitz felt a mixture of pleasure and apprehension very like his emotions before making his first speech in the House of Lords: he was thrilled to be doing this and, at the same time, worried about doing it well.

Williams went on: "Obviously Their Majesties will be in the Egyptian Apartment."

Fitz nodded. This was the largest suite of rooms. Its wallpaper had decorative motifs from Egyptian temples.

"Mrs. Jevons suggested which other rooms should be opened up, and I've wrote it down by here."

The phrase "by here" was a local expression, pronounced like the Bayeux Tapestry. It was a redundancy, meaning exactly the same as "here." Fitz said: "Show me."

She came around the desk and placed her open book in front of him. House servants were obliged to bathe once a week, so she did not smell as bad as the working class generally did. In fact her warm body had a flowery fragrance. Perhaps she had been stealing Bea's scented soap. He read her list. "Fine," he said. "The princess can allocate guests to rooms—she may have strong opinions."

Williams turned the page. "This is a list of extra staff needed: six girls in the kitchen, for peeling vegetables and washing up; two men with clean hands to help serve at table; three extra chambermaids; and three boys for boots and candles."

"Do you know where we're going to get them?"

"Oh, yes, my lord, I've got a list of local people who've worked here before, and if that's not sufficient we'll ask them to recommend others."

"No socialists, mind," Fitz said anxiously. "They might try to talk to the king about the evils of capitalism." You never knew with the Welsh.

"Of course, my lord."

"What about supplies?"

She turned another page. "This is what we need, based on previous house parties."

Fitz looked at the list: a hundred loaves of bread, twenty dozen eggs, ten gallons of cream, a hundred pounds of bacon, fifty stone of potatoes . . . He began to feel bored. "Shouldn't we leave this until the princess has decided the menus?"

"It's all got to come up from Cardiff," Williams replied. "The shops in Aberowen can't cope with orders of this size. And even the Cardiff suppliers need notice, to be sure they have sufficient quantities on the day."

She was right. He was glad she was in charge. She had the ability to plan ahead—a rare quality, he found. "I could do with someone like you in my regiment," he said.

"I can't wear khaki. It doesn't suit my complexion," she replied saucily.

The butler looked indignant. "Now, now, Williams, none of your cheek."

"I beg your pardon, Mr. Peel."

Fitz felt it was his own fault for speaking facetiously to her. Anyway, he did not mind her impudence. In fact he rather liked her.

Peel said: "Cook have come up with some suggestions for the menus, my lord." He handed Fitz a slightly grubby sheet of paper covered with the cook's careful, childish handwriting. "Unfortunately we're too early for spring lamb, but we can get plenty of fresh fish sent up from Cardiff on ice."

"This looks very like what we had at our shooting party in November," Fitz said. "On the other hand, we don't want to attempt anything new on this occasion—better to stick with tried and tested dishes."

"Exactly, my lord."

"Now, the wines." He stood up. "Let's go down to the cellar."

Peel looked surprised. The earl did not often descend to the basement.

There was a thought at the back of Fitz's mind that he did not want to acknowledge. He hesitated, then said: "Williams, you come as well, to take notes."

The butler held the door, and Fitz left the library and went down the back stairs. The kitchen and servants' hall were in a semibasement. Etiquette was different here, and the skivvies and boot boys curtsied or touched their forelocks as he passed.

The wine cellar was in a subbasement. Peel opened the door and said: "With your permission, I'll lead the way." Fitz nodded. Peel struck a match and lit a candle lamp on the wall, then went down the steps. At the bottom he lit another lamp.

Fitz had a modest cellar, about twelve thousand bottles, much of it laid down by his father and grandfather. Champagne, port, and hock predominated, with lesser quantities of claret and white burgundy. Fitz was not an aficionado of wine, but he loved the cellar because it reminded him of his father. "A wine cellar requires order, forethought, and good taste," the old man used to say. "These are the virtues that made Britain great."

Fitz would serve the very best to the king, of course, but that required a judgment. The champagne would be Perrier-Jouët, the most expensive, but which vintage? Mature champagne, twenty or thirty years old, was less fizzy and had more flavor, but there was something cheerfully delicious about younger vintages. He took a bottle from a rack at random. It was filthy with dust and cobwebs. He used the white linen handkerchief from the breast pocket of his jacket to wipe the label. He still could not see the date in the dim candlelight. He showed the bottle to Peel, who had put on a pair of glasses.

"Eighteen fifty-seven," said the butler.

"My goodness, I remember this," Fitz said. "The first vintage I ever tasted, and probably the greatest." He felt conscious of the maid's presence, leaning close to him and peering at the bottle that was many years older than she. To his consternation, her nearness made him slightly out of breath.

"I'm afraid the fifty-seven may be past its best," said Peel. "May I suggest the eighteen ninety-two?"

Fitz looked at another bottle, hesitated, and made a decision. "I can't read in this light," he said. "Fetch me a magnifying glass, Peel, would you?"

Peel went up the stone steps.

Fitz looked at Williams. He was about to do something foolish, but he could not stop. "What a pretty girl you are," he said.

"Thank you, my lord."

She had dark curls escaping from under the maid's cap. He touched her hair. He knew he would regret this. "Have you ever heard of droit du seigneur?" He heard the throaty tone in his own voice.

"I'm Welsh, not French," she said, with the impudent lift of her chin that he was already seeing as characteristic.

He moved his hand from her hair to the back of her neck, and looked into her eyes. She returned his gaze with bold confidence. But did her expression mean that she wanted him to go further—or that she was ready to make a humiliating scene?

He heard heavy footsteps on the cellar stairs. Peel was back. Fitz stepped away from the maid.

She surprised Fitz by giggling. "You look so guilty!" she said. "Like a schoolboy."

Peel appeared in the dim candlelight, proffering a silver tray on which there was an ivory-handled magnifying glass.

Fitz tried to breathe normally. He took the glass and returned to his examination of the wine bottles. He was careful not to meet Williams's eye.

My God, he thought, what an extraordinary girl.

{ II }

Ethel Williams felt full of energy. Nothing bothered her; she could handle every problem, cope with any setback. When she looked in a mirror she could see that her skin glowed and her eyes sparkled. After chapel on Sunday her father had commented on it, with his usual sarcastic humor. "You're cheerful," he had said. "Have you come into money?"

She found herself running, not walking, along the endless corridors of Tŷ Gwyn. Every day she filled more pages of her notebook with shopping lists, staff timetables, schedules for clearing tables and laying them again, and calculations: numbers of pillowcases, vases, napkins, candles, spoons . . .

This was her big chance. Despite her youth, she was acting housekeeper, at the time of a royal visit. Mrs. Jevons showed no sign of rising from her sickbed, so Ethel bore the full responsibility of preparing Tŷ Gwyn for the king and queen. She had always felt she could excel, if only she were given the chance; but in the rigid hierarchy of the servants' hall there were few opportunities to show that you were better than the rest. Suddenly such an opening had appeared, and she was determined to use it. After this, perhaps the ailing Mrs. Jevons would be given a less demanding job, and Ethel would be made housekeeper, at double her present wages, with a bedroom to herself and her own sitting room in the servants' quarters.

But she was not there yet. The earl was obviously happy with the job she was doing, and he had decided not to summon the housekeeper from London, which Ethel took as a great compliment; but, she thought apprehensively, there was yet time for that tiny slip, that fatal error, that would spoil everything: the dirty dinner plate, the overflowing sewer, the dead mouse in the bathtub. And then the earl would be angry.

On the morning of the Saturday when the king and queen were due to arrive, she visited every guest room, making sure the fires were lit and the pillows were plumped. Each room had at least one vase of flowers, brought that morning from the hothouse. There was Tŷ Gwyn–headed writing paper at every desk. Towels, soap, and water were provided for washing. The old earl had not liked modern plumbing, and Fitz had not yet got around to installing running water in all rooms. There were only three water closets, in a house with a hundred bedrooms, so most rooms also needed chamber pots. Potpourri was provided, made by Mrs. Jevons to her own recipe, to take away the smell.

The royal party was due at teatime. The earl would meet them at Aberowen railway station. There would undoubtedly be a crowd there, hoping for a glimpse of royalty, but at this point the king and queen would not meet the people. Fitz would bring them to the house in his Rolls-Royce, a large closed car. The king's equerry, Sir Alan Tite, and the rest of the royal traveling staff would follow, with the luggage, in an assortment of horse-drawn vehicles. In front of Tŷ Gwyn a battalion from the Welsh Rifles was already assembling either side of the drive to provide a guard of honor.

The royal couple would show themselves to their subjects on Monday morning. They planned a progress around nearby villages in an open carriage, and a stop at Aberowen town hall to meet the mayor and councilors, before going to the railway station.

The other guests began to arrive at midday. Peel stood in the hall and assigned maids to guide them to their rooms and footmen to carry their bags. The first were Fitz's uncle and aunt, the Duke and Duchess of Sussex. The duke was a cousin of the king and had been invited to make the monarch feel more comfortable. The duchess was Fitz's aunt, and like most of the family she was deeply interested in politics. At their London house she held a salon that was frequented by cabinet ministers.

The duchess informed Ethel that King George V was a bit obsessed with clocks and hated to see different clocks in the same house telling different times. Ethel cursed silently: Tŷ Gwyn had more than a hundred clocks. She borrowed Mrs. Jevons's pocket watch and began to go around the house setting them all.

In the small dining room she came across the earl. He was standing at the window, looking distraught. Ethel studied him for a moment. He was the handsomest man she had ever seen. His pale face, lit by the soft winter sunlight, might have been carved in white marble. He had a square chin, high cheekbones, and a straight nose. His hair was dark but he had green eyes, an unusual combination. He had no beard or mustache or even side-whiskers. With a face like that, Ethel thought, why cover it with hair?

He caught her eye. "I've just been told that the king likes a bowl of oranges in his room!" he said. "There's not a single orange in the damn house."

Ethel frowned. None of the grocers in Aberowen would have oranges this early in the season—their customers could not afford such luxuries. The same would apply to every other town in the South Wales valleys. "If I might use the telephone, I could speak to one or two greengrocers in Cardiff," she said. "They might have oranges at this time of year."

"But how will we get them here?"

"I'll ask the shop to put a basket on the train." She looked at the clock she had been adjusting. "With luck the oranges will come at the same time as the king."

"That's it," he said. "That's what we'll do." He gave her a direct look. "You're astonishing," he said. "I'm not sure I've ever met a girl quite like you."

She stared back at him. Several times in the last two weeks he had spoken like this, overly familiar and a bit intense, and it gave Ethel a strange feeling, a sort of uneasy exhilaration, as if something dangerously exciting were about to happen. It was like the moment in a fairy tale when the prince enters the enchanted castle.

The spell was broken by the sound of wheels on the drive outside, then a familiar voice. "Peel! How delightful to see you."

Fitz looked out of the window. His expression was comical. "Oh, no," he said. "My sister!"

"Welcome home, Lady Maud," said Peel's voice. "Though we were not expecting you."

"The earl forgot to invite me, but I came anyway."

Ethel smothered a smile. Fitz loved his feisty sister, but he found her difficult to deal with. Her political opinions were alarmingly liberal: she was a suffragette, a militant campaigner for votes for women. Ethel thought Maud was wonderful—just the kind of independent-minded woman she herself would have liked to be.

Fitz strode out of the room, and Ethel followed him into the hall, an imposing room decorated in the Gothic style beloved of Victorians such as Fitz's father: dark paneling, heavily patterned wallpaper, and carved oak chairs like medieval thrones. Maud was coming through the door. "Fitz, darling, how are you?" she said.

Maud was tall like her brother, and they looked similar, but the sculpted features that made the earl seem like the statue of a god were not so flattering on a woman, and Maud was striking rather than pretty. Contrary to the popular image of feminists as frumpy, she was fashionably dressed, wearing a hobble skirt over button boots, a navy-blue coat with an oversize belt and deep cuffs, and a hat with a tall feather pinned to its front like a regimental flag.

She was accompanied by Aunt Herm. Lady Hermia was Fitz's other aunt. Unlike her sister, who had married a rich duke, Herm had wedded a thriftless baron who died young and broke. Ten years ago, after Fitz and Maud's parents had both died within a few months, Aunt Herm had moved in to mother the thirteen-year-old Maud. She continued to act as Maud's somewhat ineffectual chaperone.

Fitz said to Maud: "What are you doing here?"

Aunt Herm murmured: "I told you he wouldn't like it, dear."

"I couldn't be absent when the king came to stay," Maud said. "It would have been disrespectful."

Fitz's tone was fondly exasperated. "I don't want you talking to the king about women's rights."

Ethel did not think he needed to worry. Despite Maud's radical politics, she knew how to flatter and flirt with powerful men, and even Fitz's Conservative friends liked her.

"Take my coat, please, Morrison," Maud said. She undid the buttons and turned to allow the footman to remove it. "Hello, Williams. How are you?" she said to Ethel.

"Welcome home, my lady," Ethel said. "Would you like the Gardenia Suite?"

"Thank you. I love that view."

"Will you have some lunch while I'm getting the room ready?"

"Yes, please. I'm starving."

"We're serving it club style today, because guests are arriving at different times." Club style meant that guests were served whenever they came into the dining room, as in a gentlemen's club or a restaurant, instead of all at the same time. It was a modest lunch today: hot mulligatawny soup, cold meats and smoked fish, stuffed trout, lamb cutlets, and a few desserts and cheeses.

Ethel held the door and followed Maud and Herm into the large dining room. Already at lunch were the von Ulrich cousins. Walter von Ulrich, the younger one, was handsome and charming, and seemed delighted to be at Tŷ Gwyn. Robert was fussy: he had straightened the painting of Cardiff Castle on his wall, asked for more pillows, and discovered that the inkwell on his writing desk was dry—an oversight that made Ethel wonder fretfully what else she might have forgotten.

They stood up when the ladies walked in. Maud went straight up to Walter and said: "You haven't changed since you were eighteen! Do you remember me?"

His face lit up. "I do, although you *have* changed since you were thirteen."

They shook hands and then Maud kissed him on both cheeks, as if he were family. "I had the most agonizing schoolgirl passion for you at that age," she said with startling candor.

Walter smiled. "I was rather taken with you, too."

"But you always acted as if I was a terrible young pest!"

"I had to hide my feelings from Fitz, who protected you like a guard dog."

Aunt Herm coughed, indicating her disapproval of this instant intimacy. Maud said: "Aunt, this is Herr Walter von Ulrich, an old school friend of Fitz's who used to come here in the holidays. Now he's a diplomat at the German embassy in London."

Walter said: "May I present my cousin the Graf Robert von Ulrich." *Graf* was German for count, Ethel knew. "He is a military attaché at the Austrian embassy."

They were actually second cousins, Peel had explained gravely to Ethel: their grandfathers had been brothers, the younger of whom had married a German heiress and left Vienna for Berlin, which was how come Walter was German whereas Robert was Austrian. Peel liked to get such things right.

Everyone sat down. Ethel held a chair for Aunt Herm. "Would you like some mulligatawny soup, Lady Hermia?" she asked.

"Yes, please, Williams."

Ethel nodded to a footman, who went to the sideboard where the soup was being kept hot in an urn. Seeing that the new arrivals were comfortable, Ethel quietly left to arrange their rooms. As the door was closing behind her, she heard Walter von Ulrich say: "I remember how fond you were of music, Lady Maud. We were just discussing the Russian ballet. What do you think of Diaghilev?"

Not many men asked a woman for her opinion. Maud would like

that. As Ethel hurried down the stairs to find a couple of maids to do the rooms, she thought: That German is quite a charmer.

{ III }

The Sculpture Hall at Tŷ Gwyn was an anteroom to the dining room. The guests gathered there before dinner. Fitz was not much interested in art—it had all been collected by his grandfather—but the sculptures gave people something to talk about while they were waiting for their dinner.

As he chatted to his aunt the duchess, Fitz looked around anxiously at the men in white tie and tails and the women in low-cut gowns and tiaras. Protocol demanded that every other guest had to be in the room before the king and queen entered. Where was Maud? Surely she would not cause an incident! No, there she was, in a purple silk dress, wearing their mother's diamonds, talking animatedly to Walter von Ulrich.

Fitz and Maud had always been close. Their father had been a distant hero, their mother his unhappy acolyte; the two children had got the affection they needed from each other. After both parents died they had clung together, sharing their grief. Fitz had been eighteen then, and had tried to protect his little sister from the cruel world. She, in turn, had worshipped him. In adulthood, she had become independent-minded, whereas he continued to believe that as head of the family he had authority over her. However, their affection for each other had proved strong enough to survive their differences—so far.

Now she was drawing Walter's attention to a bronze cupid. Unlike Fitz, she understood such things. Fitz prayed she would talk about art all evening and keep off women's rights. George V hated liberals; everyone knew that. Monarchs were usually conservative, but events had sharpened this king's antipathy. He had come to the throne in the middle of a political crisis. Against his will he had been forced, by Liberal prime minister H. H. Asquith—strongly backed by public opinion—to curb the power of the House of Lords. This humiliation still rankled. His Majesty knew that Fitz, as a Conservative peer in the House of Lords, had fought to the last ditch against the so-called reform. All the same, if he were harangued by Maud tonight, he would never forgive Fitz.

Walter was a junior diplomat, but his father was one of the kaiser's oldest friends. Robert, too, was well-connected: he was close to the archduke Franz Ferdinand, the heir to the throne of the Austro-Hungarian Empire. Another guest who moved in exalted circles was the tall young American now talking to the duchess. His name was Gus Dewar, and his father, a senator, was intimate adviser to U.S. president Woodrow Wilson. Fitz felt he had done well in assembling such a group of young men, the ruling elite of the future. He hoped the king was pleased.

Gus Dewar was amiable but awkward. He stooped, as if he would have preferred to be shorter and less conspicuous. He seemed unsure of himself, but he was pleasantly courteous to everyone. "The American people are concerned with domestic issues more than foreign policy," he was saying to the duchess. "But President Wilson is a liberal, and as such he is bound to sympathize with democracies such as France and Britain more than with authoritarian monarchies such as Austria and Germany."

At that moment the double doors opened, the room fell silent, and the king and queen walked in. Princess Bea curtsied, Fitz bowed, and everyone else followed suit. There were a few moments of mildly embarrassed silence, for no one was allowed to speak until one of the royal couple had said something. At last the king said to Bea: "I stayed at this house twenty years ago, you know," and people began to relax.

The king was a neat man, Fitz reflected as the four of them made small talk. His beard and mustache were carefully barbered. His hair was receding, but he had enough left on top to comb with a parting as straight as a ruler. Close-fitting evening clothes suited his slim figure: unlike his father, Edward VII, he was not a gourmet. He relaxed with hobbies that required precision: he liked to collect postage stamps, sticking them meticulously into albums, a pastime that drew mockery from disrespectful London intellectuals.

The queen was a more formidable figure, with graying curls and a severe line to her mouth. She had a magnificent bosom, shown off to great advantage by the extremely low neckline that was currently de rigueur. She was the daughter of a German prince. Originally she had been engaged to George's older brother, Albert, but he had died of pneumonia before the wedding. When George became heir to the throne, he also took over his brother's fiancée, an arrangement that was regarded by some people as a bit medieval.

Bea was in her element. She was enticingly dressed in pink silk, and her fair curls were perfectly arranged to look slightly disordered, as if she had suddenly broken away from an illicit kiss. She talked animatedly to the king. Sensing that mindless chatter would not charm George V, she was telling him how Peter the Great had created the Russian navy, and he was nodding interestedly.

Peel appeared in the dining room door, an expectant look on his freckled face. He caught Fitz's eye and gave an emphatic nod. Fitz said to the queen: "Would you care to go in to dinner, Your Majesty?"

She gave him her arm. Behind them, the king stood arm in arm with Bea, and the rest of the party formed up in pairs according to precedence. When everyone was ready, they walked into the dining room in procession.

"How pretty," the queen murmured when she saw the table.

"Thank you," said Fitz, and breathed a silent sigh of relief. Bea had done a wonderful job. Three chandeliers hung low over the long table. Their reflections twinkled in the crystal glasses at each place. All the cutlery was gold, as were the salt and pepper containers and even the small boxes of matches for smokers. The white tablecloth was strewn with hothouse roses and, in a final dramatic touch, Bea had trailed delicate ferns from the chandeliers down to the pyramids of grapes on golden platters.

Everyone sat down, the bishop said grace, and Fitz relaxed. A party that began well almost always continued successfully. Wine and food made people less disposed to find fault.

The menu began with hors d'oeuvres *Russes,* a nod to Bea's home country: little blinis with caviar and cream, triangles of toast and smoked fish, crackers with soused herring, all washed down with the Perrier-Jouët 1892 champagne, which was as mellow and delicious as Peel had promised. Fitz kept an eye on Peel, and Peel watched the king. As soon as His Majesty put down his cutlery, Peel took away his plate, and that was the signal for the footmen to clear all the rest. Any guest who happened to be still tucking into the dish had to abandon it in deference.

Soup followed, a pot-au-feu, served with a fine dry oloroso sherry from Sanlúcar de Barrameda. The fish was sole, accompanied by a mature Meursault Charmes like a mouthful of gold. With the medallions of Welsh lamb Fitz had chosen the Château Lafite 1875—the 1870 was still not ready to drink. The red wine continued to be served with the parfait of goose liver that followed and with the final meat course, quails with grapes baked in pastry.

No one ate all this. The men took what they fancied and ignored the rest. The women picked at one or two dishes. Many plates went back to the kitchen untouched.

There was salad, a dessert, a savory, fruit, and petits fours. Finally, Princess Bea raised a discreet eyebrow to the queen, who replied with an almost imperceptible nod. They both got up, everyone else stood, and the ladies left the room.

The men sat down again, the footmen brought boxes of cigars, and Peel placed a decanter of Ferreira 1847 port at the king's right hand. Fitz drew thankfully on a cigar. Things had gone well. The king was famously unsociable, feeling comfortable only with old shipmates from his happy navy days. But this evening he had been charming and nothing had gone wrong. Even the oranges had arrived.

Fitz had spoken earlier with Sir Alan Tite, the king's equerry, a retired army officer with old-fashioned side-whiskers. They had agreed that tomorrow the king would have an hour or so alone with each of the men around the table, all of whom had inside knowledge of one government or another. This evening, Fitz was to break the ice with some general political conversation. He cleared his throat and addressed Walter von Ulrich. "Walter, you and I have been friends for fifteen years—we were together at Eton." He turned to Robert. "And I've known your cousin since the three of us shared an apartment in Vienna when we were students." Robert smiled and nodded. Fitz liked them both: Robert was a traditionalist, like Fitz; Walter, though not so conservative, was very clever. "Now we find the world talking about war between our countries," Fitz went on. "Is there really a chance of such a tragedy?"

Walter answered: "If talking about war can make it happen, then yes, we will fight, for everyone is getting ready for it. But is there a real reason? I don't see it."

Gus Dewar raised a tentative hand. Fitz liked Dewar, despite his liberal politics. Americans were supposed to be brash, but this one was well-mannered and a bit shy. He was also startlingly well-informed. Now he said: "Britain and Germany have many reasons to quarrel."

Walter turned to him. "Would you give me an example?"

Gus blew out cigar smoke. "Naval rivalry."

Walter nodded. "My kaiser does not believe there is a God-given law that the German navy should remain smaller than the British forever."

Fitz glanced nervously at the king. He loved the Royal Navy and might easily be offended. On the other hand, Kaiser Wilhelm was his cousin. George's father and Willy's mother had been brother and sister, both children of Queen Victoria. Fitz was relieved to see that His Majesty was smiling indulgently.

Walter went on: "This has caused friction in the past, but for two years now we have been in agreement, informally, about the relative size of our navies."

Dewar said: "How about economic rivalry?"

"It is true that Germany is daily growing more prosperous, and may soon catch up with Britain and the United States in economic production. But why should this be a problem? Germany is one of Britain's biggest customers. The more we have to spend, the more we buy. Our economic strength is good for British manufacturers!"

Dewar tried again. "It's said that Germany wants more colonies."

Fitz glanced at the king again, wondering if he minded the conversation being dominated by these two; but His Majesty appeared fascinated.

Walter said: "There have been wars over colonies, notably in your home country, Mr. Dewar. But nowadays we seem able to decide such squabbles without firing our guns. Three years ago Germany, Great Britain, and France quarreled about Morocco, but the argument was settled without war. More recently, Britain and Germany have reached agreement about the thorny issue of the Baghdad Railway. If we simply carry on as we are, we will not go to war."

Dewar said: "Would you forgive me if I used the term *German militarism*?"

That was a bit strong, and Fitz winced. Walter colored, but he spoke smoothly. "I appreciate your frankness. The German Empire is dominated by Prussians, who play something of the role of the English in Your Majesty's United Kingdom."

It was daring to compare Britain with Germany, and England with Prussia. Walter was right on the edge of what was permissible in a polite conversation, Fitz thought uneasily.

Walter went on: "The Prussians have a strong military tradition, but do not go to war for no reason."

Dewar said skeptically: "So Germany is not aggressive."

"On the contrary," said Walter. "I put it to you that Germany is the *only* major power on mainland Europe that is *not* aggressive."

There was a murmur of surprise around the table, and Fitz saw the king raise his eyebrows. Dewar sat back, startled, and said: "How do you figure that?"

Walter's perfect manners and amiable tone took the edge off his provocative words. "First, consider Austria," he went on. "My Viennese cousin Robert will not deny that the Austro-Hungarian Empire would like to extend its borders to the southeast."

"Not without reason," Robert protested. "That part of the world, which the British call the Balkans, has been part of the Ottoman domain for hundreds of years; but Ottoman rule has crumbled, and now the Balkans are unstable. The Austrian emperor believes it is his holy duty to maintain order and the Christian religion there."

"Quite so," said Walter. "But Russia, too, wants territory in the Balkans."

Fitz felt it was his job to defend the Russian government, perhaps because of Bea. "They, too, have good reasons," he said. "Half their foreign trade crosses the Black Sea, and passes from there through the straits to the Mediterranean Sea. Russia cannot allow any other great power to dominate the straits by acquiring territory in the eastern Balkans. It would be like a noose around the neck of the Russian economy."

"Exactly so," said Walter. "Turning to the western end of Europe, France has ambitions to take from Germany the territories of Alsace and Lorraine."

At this point the French guest, Jean-Pierre Charlois, bridled. "Stolen from France forty-three years ago!"

"I will not argue about that," Walter said. "Let us say that Alsace-Lorraine was joined to the German Empire in 1871, after the defeat of France in the Franco-Prussian War. Whether stolen or not, you allow, Monsieur le Comte, that France wants those lands back."

"Naturally." The Frenchman sat back and sipped his port.

Walter said: "Even Italy would like to take, from Austria, the territories of Trentino—"

"Where most people speak Italian!" cried Signor Falli.

"—plus much of the Dalmatian coast—"

"Full of Venetian lions, Catholic churches, and Roman columns!"

"—and Tyrol, a province with a long history of self-government, where most people speak German."

"Strategic necessity."

"Of course."

Fitz realized how clever Walter had been. Not rude, but discreetly provocative, he had stung the representatives of each nation into confirming, in more or less belligerent language, their territorial ambitions.

Now Walter said: "But what new territory is Germany asking for?" He looked around the table, but no one spoke. "None," he said triumphantly. "And the only other major country in Europe that can say the same is Britain!"

Gus Dewar passed the port and said in his American drawl: "I guess that's right."

Walter said: "So why, my old friend Fitz, should we ever go to war?"

{ IV }

On Sunday morning before breakfast Lady Maud sent for Ethel.

Ethel had to suppress an exasperated sigh. She was terribly busy. It was early, but the staff were already hard at work. Before the guests got up all the fireplaces had to be cleaned, the fires relit, and the scuttles filled with coal. The principal rooms—dining room, morning room, library, smoking room, and the smaller public rooms—had to be cleaned and tidied. Ethel was checking the flowers in the billiard room, replacing those that were fading, when she was summoned. Much as she liked Fitz's radical sister, she hoped Maud did not have some elaborate commission for her.

When Ethel had come to work at Tŷ Gwyn, at the age of thirteen, the Fitzherbert family and their guests were hardly real to her: they seemed like people in a story, or strange tribes in the Bible, Hittites perhaps, and they terrified her. She was frightened that she would do something wrong and lose her job, but also deeply curious to see these strange creatures close up.

One day a kitchen maid had told her to go upstairs to the billiard room and bring down the tantalus. She had been too nervous to ask what a tantalus was. She had gone to the room and looked around, hoping it would be something obvious like a tray of dirty dishes, but she could see nothing that belonged downstairs. She had been in tears when Maud walked in.

Maud was then a gangly fifteen-year-old, a woman in girl's clothes, unhappy and rebellious. It was not until later that she made sense of her life by turning her discontent into a crusade. But even at fifteen she had had the quick compassion that made her sensitive to injustice and oppression.

She had asked Ethel what was the matter. The tantalus turned out to be a silver container with decanters of brandy and whisky. It tantalized, because it had a locking mechanism to prevent servants stealing sips, she explained. Ethel thanked her emotionally. It was the first of many kindnesses and, over the years, Ethel had come to worship the older girl.

Ethel went up to Maud's room, tapped on the door, and walked in. The Gardenia Suite had elaborate flowery wallpaper of a kind that had gone out of fashion at the turn of the century. However, its bay window overlooked the most charming part of Fitz's garden, the West Walk, a long straight path through flower beds to a summerhouse.

Maud was pulling on boots, Ethel saw with displeasure. "I'm going for a walk—you must be my chaperone," she said. "Help me with my hat and tell me the gossip."

Ethel could hardly spare the time, but she was intrigued as well as bothered. Who was Maud going to walk with; where was her normal chaperone, Aunt Herm; and why was she putting on such a charming hat just to go into the garden? Could there be a man in the picture?

As she pinned the hat to Maud's dark hair, Ethel said: "There's a scandal below stairs this morning." Maud collected gossip the way the king collected stamps. "Morrison didn't get to bed until four o'clock. He's one of the footmen—tall with a blond mustache."

"I know Morrison. And I know where he spent the night." Maud hesitated.

Ethel waited a moment, then said: "Aren't you going to tell me?"

"You'll be shocked."

Ethel grinned. "All the better."

"He spent the night with Robert von Ulrich." Maud glanced at Ethel in the dressing-table mirror. "Are you horrified?"

Ethel was fascinated. "Well, I never! I knew Morrison wasn't much of a ladies' man, but I didn't think he might be one of *those*, if you see what I mean."

"Well, Robert is certainly one of *those*, and I saw him catch Morrison's eye several times during dinner."

"In front of the king, too! How do you know about Robert?"

"Walter told me."

"What a thing for a gentleman to say to a lady! People tell you everything. What's the gossip in London?"

"They're all talking about Mr. Lloyd George."

David Lloyd George was the chancellor of the Exchequer, in charge of the country's finances. A Welshman, he was a fiery left-wing orator. Ethel's da said Lloyd George should have been in the Labour Party. During the coal strike of 1912 he had even talked about nationalizing the mines. "What are they saying about him?" Ethel asked.

"He has a mistress."

"No!" This time Ethel was really shocked. "But he was brought up a Baptist!"

Maud laughed. "Would it be less outrageous if he were Anglican?"

"Yes!" Ethel refrained from adding *obviously*. "Who is she?"

"Frances Stevenson. She started as his daughter's governess, but she's a clever woman—she has a degree in classics—and now she's his private secretary."

"That's terrible."

"He calls her Pussy."

Ethel almost blushed. She did not know what to say to that. Maud stood up, and Ethel helped her with her coat. Ethel asked: "What about his wife, Margaret?"

"She stays here in Wales with their four children."

"Five, it was, only one died. Poor woman."

Maud was ready. They went along the corridor and down the grand staircase. Walter von Ulrich was waiting in the hall, wrapped in a long dark coat. He had a small mustache and soft hazel eyes. He looked dashing in a buttoned-up, German sort of way, the kind of man who would bow, click his heels, and then give you a little wink, Ethel thought. So this was why Maud did not want Lady Hermia as her chaperone.

Maud said to Walter: "Williams came to work here when I was a girl, and we've been friends ever since."

Ethel liked Maud, but it was going too far to say they were friends. Maud was kind, and Ethel admired her, but they were still mistress and servant. Maud was really saying that Ethel could be trusted.

Walter addressed Ethel with the elaborate politeness such people employed when speaking to their inferiors. "I'm pleased to make your acquaintance, Williams. How do you do?"

"Thank you, sir. I'll get my coat."

She ran downstairs. She did not really want to be going for a walk while the king was there—she would have preferred to be on hand to supervise the housemaids—but she could not refuse.

In the kitchen Princess Bea's maid, Nina, was making tea Russian style for her mistress. Ethel spoke to a chambermaid. "Herr Walter is up," she said. "You can do the Gray Room." As soon as the guests appeared, the maids needed to go into the bedrooms to clean, make the beds, empty the chamber pots, and put out fresh water for washing. She saw Peel, the butler, counting plates. "Any movement upstairs?" she asked him.

"Nineteen, twenty," he said. "Mr. Dewar has rung for hot water for shaving, and Signor Falli asked for coffee."

"Lady Maud wants me to go outside with her."

"That's inconvenient," Peel said crossly. "You're needed in the house."

Ethel knew that. She said sarcastically: "What shall I do, Mr. Peel, tell her to go and get knotted?"

"None of your sauce. Be back as quick as you can."

When she went back upstairs the earl's dog, Gelert, was standing at the front door, panting eagerly, having divined that a walk was in prospect. They all went out and crossed the East Lawn to the woods.

Walter said to Ethel: "I suppose Lady Maud has taught you to be a suffragette."

"It was the other way around," Maud told him. "Williams was the first person to introduce me to liberal ideas."

Ethel said: "I learned it all from my father."

Ethel knew they did not really want to talk to her. Etiquette did not permit them to be alone, but they wanted the next best thing. She called to Gelert, then ran ahead, playing with the dog, giving them the privacy they were probably longing for. Glancing back, she saw that they were holding hands.

Maud was a fast worker, Ethel thought. From what she had said yesterday, she had not seen Walter for ten years. Even then there had been no acknowledged romance, just an unspoken attraction. Something must have happened last night. Perhaps they had sat up late talking. Maud flirted with everyone—it was how she got information out of them—but clearly this was more serious.

A moment later, Ethel heard Walter sing a snatch of a tune. Maud joined in; then they stopped and laughed. Maud loved music, and could play the piano quite well, unlike Fitz, who was tone-deaf. It seemed Walter was also musical. His voice was a pleasant light baritone that would have been much appreciated, Ethel thought, in the Bethesda Chapel.

Her mind wandered to her work. She had not seen polished pairs of shoes outside any of the bedroom doors. She needed to chase the boot boys and hurry them up. She wondered fretfully what the time was. If this went on much longer she might have to insist on returning to the house.

She glanced back, but this time she could not see Walter or Maud. Had they stopped, or gone off in a different direction? She stood still for a minute or two, but she could not wait out there all morning, so she retraced her steps through the trees.

A moment later she saw them. They were locked in an embrace, kissing passionately. Walter's hands were on Maud's behind and he was pressing her to him. Their mouths were open, and Ethel heard Maud groan.

She stared at them. She wondered whether a man would ever kiss her that way. Spotty Llewellyn had kissed her on the beach during a chapel outing, but it had not been with mouths open and bodies pressed together, and it certainly had not made Ethel moan. Little Dai Chops, the son of the butcher, had put his hand up her skirt in the Palace Cinema in Cardiff, but she had pushed it away after a few seconds. She had really liked Llewellyn Davies, a schoolteacher's son, who had talked to her about the Liberal government, and told her she had breasts like warm baby birds in a nest; but he had gone away to college and never written. With them she had been intrigued, and curious to do more, but never passionate. She envied Maud.

Then Maud opened her eyes, caught a glimpse of Ethel, and broke the embrace.

Gelert whined suddenly and walked around in a circle with his tail between his legs. What was the matter with him?

A moment later Ethel felt a tremor in the ground, as if an express train were passing, even though the railway line ended a mile away.

Maud frowned and opened her mouth to speak; then there was a crack like a clap of thunder.

"What on earth was that?" said Maud.

Ethel knew.

She screamed, and began to run.

{ V }

Billy Williams and Tommy Griffiths were having a break.

They were working a seam called the Four-Foot Coal, only six hundred yards deep, not as far down as the Main Level. The seam was divided into five districts, all named after British racecourses, and they were in Ascot, the one nearest to the upcast shaft. Both boys were working as butties, assistants to older miners. The collier used his mandrel, a straight-bladed pick, to hew the coal away from the coal face, and his butty shoveled it into a wheeled dram. They had started work at six o'clock in the morning, as always, and now after a couple of hours they were taking a rest, sitting on the damp ground with their backs to the side of the tunnel, letting the soft breath of the ventilation system cool their skin, drinking long drafts of lukewarm sweet tea from their flasks.

They had been born on the same day in 1898, and were six months away from their sixteenth birthday. The difference in their physical development, so embarrassing to Billy when he was thirteen, had vanished. Now they were both young men, broad-shouldered and strong-armed, and they shaved once a week though they did not really need to. They were dressed only in their shorts and boots, and their bodies were black with a mixture of perspiration and coal dust. In the dim lamplight they gleamed like ebony statues of pagan gods. The effect was spoiled only by their caps.

The work was hard, but they were used to it. They did not complain of aching backs and stiff joints, as older men did. They had energy to spare, and on days off they found equally strenuous things to do, playing rugby or digging flower beds or even bare-knuckle boxing in the barn behind the Two Crowns pub.

Billy had not forgotten his initiation three years ago—indeed, he still burned with indignation when he thought of it. He had vowed then that he would never mistreat new boys. Only today he had warned little Bert Morgan: "Don't be surprised if the men play a trick on you. They may leave you in the dark for an hour or something stupid like that. Little things please little minds." The older men in the cage had glared at him, but he met their eyes: he knew he was in the right, and so did they.

Mam had been even angrier than Billy. "Tell me," she had said to Da, standing in the middle of the living room with her hands on her hips and her dark eyes flashing righteousness, "how is the Lord's purpose served by torturing little boys?"

"You wouldn't understand—you're a woman," Da had replied, an uncharacteristically weak response from him.

Billy believed that the world in general, and the Aberowen pit in particular, would be better places if all men led God-fearing lives. Tommy, whose father was an atheist and a disciple of Karl Marx, believed that the capitalist system would soon destroy itself, with a little help from a revolutionary working class. The two boys argued fiercely but continued best friends.

"It's not like you to work on a Sunday," Tommy said.

That was true. The mine was doing extra shifts to cope with the demand for coal but, in deference to religion, Celtic Minerals made the Sunday shifts optional. However, Billy was working despite his devotion to the Sabbath. "I think the Lord wants me to have a bicycle," he said.

Tommy laughed, but Billy was not joking. The Bethesda Chapel had opened a sister church in a small village ten miles away, and Billy was one of the Aberowen congregation who had volunteered to go across the mountain every other Sunday to encourage the new chapel. If he had a bicycle he could go there on weeknights as well, and help start a Bible class or a prayer meeting. He had discussed this plan with the elders, and they had agreed that the Lord would bless Billy's working on the Sabbath day for a few weeks.

Billy was about to explain this when the ground beneath him shook, there was a bang like the crack of doom, and his flask was blown out of his hand by a terrific wind.

His heart seemed to stop. Suddenly he remembered that he was half a mile underground, with millions of tons of earth and rock over his head, held up only by a few timber props.

"What the bloody hell was that?" said Tommy in a scared voice.

Billy jumped to his feet, shaking with fright. He lifted his lamp and looked both ways along the tunnel. He saw no flames, no fall of rock, and no more dust than was normal. When the reverberations died away, there was no noise.

"It was an explosion," he said, his voice unsteady. This was what every miner dreaded every day. A sudden release of firedamp could be produced by a fall of rock, or just by a collier hacking through to a fault in the seam. If no one noticed the warning signs—or if the concentration simply built up too quickly—the inflammable gas could be ignited by a spark from a pony's hoof, or from the electric bell of a cage, or by a stupid miner lighting his pipe against all regulations.

Tommy said: "But where?"

"It must be down on the Main Level—that's why we escaped."

"Jesus Christ, help us."

"He will," said Billy, and his terror began to ebb. "Especially if we help ourselves." There was no sign of the two colliers for whom the boys had been working—they had gone to spend their break in the Goodwood district. Billy and Tommy had to make their own decisions. "We'd better go to the shaft."

They pulled on their clothes, hooked their lamps to their belts, and ran to the upcast shaft, called Pyramus. The landing onsetter, in charge of the elevator, was Dai Chops. "The cage isn't coming!" he said with panic in his voice. "I've been ringing and ringing!"

The man's fear was infectious, and Billy had to fight down his own panic. After a moment he said: "What about the telephone?" The onsetter communicated with his counterpart on the surface by signals on an electric bell, but recently phones had been installed on both levels, connected with the office of the colliery manager, Maldwyn Morgan.

"No answer," said Dai.

"I'll try again." The phone was fixed to the wall beside the cage. Billy picked it up and turned the handle. "Come on, come on!"

A quavery voice answered. "Yes?" It was Arthur Llewellyn, the manager's clerk.

"Spotty, this is Billy Williams," Billy shouted into the mouthpiece. "Where's Mr. Morgan?"

"Not here. What was that bang?"

"It was an explosion underground, you clot! Where's the boss?"

"He have gone to Merthyr," Spotty said plaintively.

"Why's he gone—never mind, forget that. Here's what you got to do. Spotty, are you listening to me?"

"Aye." The voice seemed stronger.

"First of all, send someone to the Methodist chapel and tell Dai Crybaby to assemble his rescue team."

"Right."

"Then phone the hospital and get them to send the ambulance to the pithead."

"Is someone injured?"

"Bound to be, after a bang like that! Third, get all the men in the coal-cleaning shed to run out fire hoses."

"Fire?"

"The dust will be burning. Fourth, call the police station and tell Geraint there have been an explosion. He'll phone Cardiff." Billy could not think of anything else. "All right?"

"All right, Billy."

Billy put the earpiece back on the hook. He was not sure how effective his instructions would be, but speaking to Spotty had focused his mind. "There will be men injured on the Main Level," he said to Dai Chops and Tommy. "We must get down there."

Dai said: "We can't. The cage isn't here."

"There's a ladder in the shaft wall, isn't there?"

"It's two hundred yards down!"

"Well, if I was a sissy I wouldn't be a collier, now, would I?" His words were brave, but all the same he was scared. The shaft ladder was seldom used, and it might not have been well-maintained. One slip, or a broken rung, could cause him to fall to his death.

Dai opened the gate with a clang. The shaft was lined with brick, damp and moldy. A narrow shelf ran horizontally around the lining, outside the wooden cage housing. An iron ladder was fixed by brackets cemented into the brickwork. There was nothing reassuring about its thin side rails and narrow treads. Billy hesitated, regretting his impulsive bravado. But to back out now would be too humiliating. He took a deep breath and said a silent prayer, then stepped onto the shelf.

He edged around until he reached the ladder. He wiped his hands on his trousers, grasped the side rails, and put his feet on the treads.

He went down. The iron was rough to his touch, and rust flaked off on his hands. In places the brackets were loose, and the ladder shifted unnervingly under his feet. The lamp hooked to his belt was bright enough to illuminate the treads below him, but not to show the bottom of the shaft. He did not know whether that was better or worse.

Unfortunately, the descent gave him time to think. He remembered all the ways miners could die. To be killed by the explosion itself was a mercifully quick end for the luckiest. The burning of the methane produced suffocating carbon dioxide, which the miners called afterdamp. Many were trapped by falls of rock, and might bleed to death before rescue came. Some died of thirst, with their workmates just a few yards away trying desperately to tunnel through the debris.

Suddenly he wanted to go back, to climb upward to safety instead of down into destruction and chaos—but he could not, with Tommy immediately above him, following him down.

"Are you with me, Tommy?" he called.

Tommy's voice came from just above his head. "Aye!"

That strengthened Billy's nerve. He went down faster, his confidence returning. Soon he saw light, and a moment later he heard voices. As he approached the Main Level he smelled smoke.

Now he heard an eerie racket, screaming and banging, which he struggled to identify. It threatened to undermine his courage. He got a grip on himself: there had to be a rational explanation. A moment later he realized he was hearing the terrified whinnying of the ponies, and the sound of them kicking the wooden sides of their stalls, desperate to escape. Comprehension did not make the noise less disturbing: he felt the same way they did.

He reached the Main Level, sidled around the brick ledge, opened the gate from inside, and stepped gratefully onto muddy ground. The dim underground light was further reduced by traces of smoke, but he could see the main tunnels.

The pit bottom onsetter was Patrick O'Connor, a middle-aged man who had lost a hand in a roof collapse. A Catholic, he was inevitably known as Pat Pope. He stared with incredulity. "Billy-with-Jesus!" he said. "Where the bloody hell have you come from?"

"From the Four-Foot Coal," Billy answered. "We heard the bang."

Tommy followed Billy out of the shaft and said: "What's happened, Pat?"

"Far as I can make out, the explosion must have been at the other end of this level, near Thisbe," said Pat. "The deputy and everyone else have gone to see." He spoke calmly, but there was desperation in his look.

Billy went to the phone and turned the handle. A moment later he heard his father's voice. "Williams here. Who's that?"

Billy did not pause to wonder why a union official was answering the colliery manager's phone—anything could happen in an emergency. "Da, it's me, Billy."

"God in His mercy be thanked, you're all right," said his father, with a break in his voice; then he became his usual brisk self. "Tell me what you know, boy."

"Me and Tommy were in the Four-Foot Coal. We've climbed down Pyramus to the Main Level. The explosion was over toward Thisbe, we think. There's a bit of smoke, not much. But the cage isn't working."

"The winding mechanism have been damaged by the upward blast," Da said in a calm voice. "But we're working on it and we'll have it fixed in a few minutes. Get as many men as you can to the pit bottom so we can start bringing them up as soon as the cage is fixed."

"I'll tell them."

"The Thisbe shaft is completely out of action, so make sure no one tries to escape that way—they could get trapped by the fire."

"Right."

"There's breathing apparatus outside the deputies' office."

Billy knew that. It was a recent innovation, demanded by the union and made compulsory by the Coal Mines Act of 1911. "The air's not bad at the moment," he said.

"Where you are, perhaps, but it may be worse farther in."

"Right." Billy put the earpiece back on the hook.

He repeated to Tommy and Pat what his father had said. Pat pointed to a row of new lockers. "The key should be in the office."

Billy ran to the deputies' office, but he could see no keys. He guessed they were on someone's belt. He looked again at the row of lockers, each labeled: "Breathing Apparatus." They were made of tin. "Got a crowbar, Pat?" he said.

The onsetter had a tool kit for minor repairs. Pat handed him a stout screwdriver. Billy swiftly broke open the first locker.

It was empty.

Billy stared, unbelieving.

Pat said: "They tricked us!"

Tommy said: "Bastard capitalists."

Billy opened another locker. It, too, was empty. He broke open the others with angry savagery, wanting to expose the dishonesty of Celtic Minerals and Perceval Jones.

Tommy said: "We'll manage without."

Tommy was impatient to get going, but Billy was trying to think clearly. His eye fell on the fire dram. It was the management's pathetic excuse for a fire engine: a coal dram filled with water, with a hand pump strapped to it. It was not completely useless: Billy had seen it operate after what the miners called a "flash," when a small quantity of firedamp close to the roof of the tunnel would ignite, briefly, and they would all throw themselves to the floor. The flash would sometimes light the coal dust on the tunnel walls, which then had to be sprayed.

"We'll take the fire dram," he shouted to Tommy.

It was already on rails, and the two of them were able to push it along. Billy thought briefly of harnessing a pony to it, then decided it would take too long, especially as the beasts were all in a panic.

Pat Pope said: "My boy Micky is working in Marigold district, but I can't go and look for him. I've got to stay here." There was desperation in his face, but in an emergency the onsetter had to stay by the shaft—it was an inflexible rule.

"I'll keep an eye open for him," Billy promised.

"Thank you, Billy boy."

The two lads pushed the dram along the main road. Drams had no brakes: their drivers slowed them by sticking a stout piece of wood into the spokes. Many deaths and countless injuries were caused by runaway drams. "Not too fast," Billy said.

They were a quarter of a mile into the tunnel when the temperature rose and the smoke thickened. Soon they heard voices. Following the sound they turned into a branch tunnel. This part of the seam was currently being worked. On either side Billy could see, at regular intervals, the entrances to miners' workplaces, usually called gates, but sometimes just holes. As the noise grew, they stopped pushing the dram and looked ahead.

The tunnel was on fire. Flames licked up from walls and floor. A handful of men stood at the edge of the conflagration, silhouetted against the glow like souls in hell. One held a blanket and was batting it ineffectually at a blazing stack of timber. Others were shouting; no one was listening. In the distance, dimly visible, was a train of drams. The smoke had a strange whiff of roast meat, and Billy realized with a sick feeling that it must come from the pony that had been pulling the drams.

Billy spoke to one of the men. "What's happening?"

"There's men trapped in their gates—but we can't get to them."

Billy saw that the man was Rhys Price. No wonder nothing was being done. "We've brought the fire dram," he said.

Another man turned to him, and he was relieved to see John Jones the Shop, a more sensible character. "Good man!" said Jones. "Let's have the hose on this bloody lot."

Billy ran out the hose while Tommy connected the pump. Billy aimed the jet at the ceiling of the tunnel, so that the water would run down the walls. He soon realized that the mine's ventilation system, blowing down Thisbe and up Pyramus, was forcing the flames and smoke toward him. As soon as he got the chance he would tell the people on the surface to reverse the fans. Reversible fans were now mandatory— another requirement of the 1911 act.

Despite the difficulty, the fire began to die back, and Billy was able to go forward slowly. After a few minutes the nearest gate was clear of flame. Immediately two miners ran out, gasping the relatively good air of the tunnel. Billy recognized the Ponti brothers, Giuseppe and Giovanni, known as Joey and Johnny.

Some of the men ran into the gate. John Jones came out carrying the limp form of Dai Ponies, the horse wrangler. Billy could not tell whether he was dead or just unconscious. He said: "Take him to Pyramus, not Thisbe."

Price butted in: "Who are you to be giving orders, Billy-with-Jesus?"

Billy was not going to waste time arguing with Price. He addressed Jones. "I spoke on the phone to the surface. Thisbe is badly damaged but the cage should soon be operating in Pyramus. I was told to tell everyone to head for Pyramus."

"Right, I'll spread the word," said Jones, and he went off.

Billy and Tommy continued to fight the fire, clearing farther gates, freeing more trapped men. Some were bleeding, many were scorched, and a few had been hurt by falling rock. Those who could walk carried the dead and the seriously injured in a grim procession.

Too soon, their water was gone. "We'll push the dram back and fill it from the pond at the bottom of the shaft," Billy said.

Together they hurried back. The cage was still not working, and there were now a dozen or so rescued miners waiting, and several bodies on the ground, some groaning in agony, others ominously still. While Tommy filled the dram with muddy water, Billy picked up the phone. Once again his father answered. "The winding gear will be operating in five minutes," he said. "How is it down there?"

"We've got some dead and injured out of the gates. Send down drams full of water as soon as you can."

"What about you?"

"I'm all right. Listen, Da, you should reverse the ventilation. Blow down Pyramus and up Thisbe. That will drive the smoke and afterdamp away from the rescuers."

"Can't be done," said his father.

"But it's the law—pit ventilation *must* be reversible!"

"Perceval Jones told the inspectors a sob story, and they gave him another year to modify the blowers."

Billy would have cursed if anyone other than his father had been on the line. "How about turning on the sprinklers—can you do that?"

"Aye, we can," said Da. "Why didn't I think of that?" He spoke to someone else.

Billy replaced the earpiece. He helped Tommy refill the dram, taking turns with the hand pump. It took as long to fill as it had to empty. The flow of men from the afflicted district slowed while the fire raged unchecked. At last the tub was full and they started back.

The sprinklers came on, but when Billy and Tommy reached the fire, they found that the flow of water from the narrow overhead pipe was too slight to put out the flames. However, Jones the Shop had now got the men organized. He was keeping the uninjured survivors with him, for rescue work, and sending the walking wounded to the shaft. As soon as Billy and Tommy had connected the hose, he seized it and ordered another man to pump. "You two go back and get another dram of water!" he said. "That way we can keep on hosing."

"Right," said Billy, but before he turned to go something caught his eye. A figure came running through the flames with his clothes on fire. "Good God!" Billy said, horrified. As he watched, the runner stumbled and fell.

Billy shouted at Jones: "Hose me!" Without waiting for acknowledgment, he ran into the tunnel. He felt a jet of water strike his back. The heat was terrible. His face hurt and his clothes smoldered. He grabbed the prone miner under the shoulders and pulled, running backward. He could not see the face but he could tell it was a boy of his own age.

Jones kept the hose on Billy, soaking his hair, his back, and his legs, but the front of him was dry, and he could smell his skin scorching. He screamed in pain but managed to keep hold of the unconscious body. A second later he was out of the fire. He turned and let Jones spray his front. The water on his face was blessed relief: though he still hurt, it was bearable.

Jones sprayed the boy on the floor. Billy turned him over and saw that it was Michael O'Connor, known as Micky Pope, the son of Pat. Pat had asked Billy to look out for him. Billy said: "Dear Jesus, have mercy on Pat."

He bent down and picked Micky up. The body was limp and lifeless. "I'll take him to the shaft," Billy said.

"Aye," said Jones. He was staring at Billy with an odd expression. "You do that, Billy boy."

Tommy went with Billy. Billy felt light-headed, but he was able to carry Micky. On the main road they encountered a rescue team with a pony pulling a small train of drams filled with water. They must have come from the surface, which meant the cage was operating and the rescue was now being properly managed, Billy reasoned wearily.

He was right. As he reached the shaft, the cage arrived again and disgorged more rescuers in protective clothing and more drams of water. When the newcomers had dispersed, heading for the fire, the wounded began to board the cage, carrying the dead and unconscious.

When Pat Pope had sent the cage up, Billy went to him, holding Micky in his arms.

Pat stared at Billy with a terrified look, shaking his head in negation, as if he could deny the news.

"I'm sorry, Pat," said Billy.

Pat would not look at the body. "No," he said. "Not my Micky."

"I pulled him out of the fire, Pat," said Billy. "But I was too bloody late, that's all." Then he began to cry.

{ VI }

The dinner had been a great success in every way. Bea had been in a sparkling mood: she would have liked a royal party every week. Fitz had gone to her bed, and as he expected she had welcomed him. He stayed until morning, slipping away only just before Nina arrived with the tea.

He was afraid the debate amongst the men might have been too controversial for a royal dinner, but he need not have worried. The king thanked him at breakfast, saying: "Fascinating discussion, very illuminating, just what I wanted." Fitz had glowed with pride.

Thinking it over as he smoked his after-breakfast cigar, Fitz realized that the thought of war did not horrify him. He had spoken of it as a tragedy, in an automatic way, but it would not be entirely a bad thing. War would unite the nation against a common enemy, and dampen the fires of unrest. There would be no more strikes, and talk of republicanism would be seen as unpatriotic. Women might even stop demanding the vote. And in a personal way he found himself strangely drawn to the prospect. War would be his chance to be useful, to prove his courage, to serve his country, to do something in return for the wealth and privilege that had been lavished on him all his life.

The news from the pit, coming at midmorning, took the sparkle off the party. Only one of the guests actually went into Aberowen—Gus Dewar, the American. Nevertheless, they all had the feeling, unusual for them, of being far from the center of attention. Lunch was a subdued affair, and the afternoon's entertainments were canceled. Fitz feared the king would be displeased with him, even though he had nothing to do with the operation of the mine. He was not a director or shareholder of Celtic Minerals. He merely licensed the mining rights to the company, which paid him a royalty per ton. So he felt sure that no reasonable person could possibly blame him for what had happened. Still, the nobility could not be seen to indulge in frivolous pursuits while men were trapped underground, especially when the king and queen were visiting. That meant that reading and smoking were just about the only acceptable pursuits. The royal couple were sure to be bored.

Fitz was angered. Men died all the time: soldiers were killed in battle, sailors went down with their ships, railway trains crashed, hotels full of sleeping guests burned to the ground. Why did a pit disaster have to happen just when he was entertaining the king?

Shortly before dinner Perceval Jones, mayor of Aberowen and chairman of Celtic Minerals, came to the house to brief the earl, and Fitz asked Sir Alan Tite whether the king might like to hear the report. His Majesty would, came the reply, and Fitz was relieved: at least the monarch had something to do.

The male guests gathered in the small drawing room, an informal space with soft chairs and potted palms and a piano. Jones was wearing the black tailcoat he had undoubtedly put on for church this morning. A short, pompous man, he looked like a strutting bird in a double-breasted gray waistcoat.

The king was in evening dress. "Good of you to come," he said briskly.

Jones said: "I had the honor of shaking Your Majesty's hand in 1911, when you came to Cardiff for the investiture of the Prince of Wales."

"I'm glad to renew our acquaintanceship, though sorry it should happen in such distressing circumstances," the king replied. "Tell me what happened in plain words, just as if you were explaining it to one of your fellow directors, over a drink at your club."

That was clever, Fitz thought; it set just the right tone—though no one offered Jones a drink, and the king did not invite him to sit down.

"So kind of Your Majesty." Jones spoke with a Cardiff accent, harsher than the lilt of the valleys. "There were two hundred and twenty men down the pit when the explosion occurred, fewer than normal as this is a special Sunday shift."

"You know the exact figure?" the king asked.

"Oh, yes, sir. We note the name of each man going down."

"Forgive the interruption. Please carry on."

"Both shafts were damaged, but firefighting teams brought the blaze under control, with the help of our sprinkler system, and evacuated the men." He looked at his watch. "As of two hours ago, two hundred and fifteen had been brought up."

"It sounds as if you have dealt with the emergency very efficiently, Jones."

"Thank you very much, Your Majesty."

"Are all the two hundred and fifteen alive?"

"No, sir. Eight are dead. Another fifty have injuries sufficiently serious to require a doctor."

"Dear me," said the king. "How very sad."

As Jones was explaining the steps being taken to locate and rescue the remaining five men, Peel slipped into the room and approached Fitz. The butler was in evening clothes, ready to serve dinner. Speaking very low, he said: "Just in case it's of interest, my lord . . . "

Fitz whispered: "Well?"

"The maid Williams just came back from the pithead. Her brother was something of a hero, apparently. Whether the king might like to hear the story from her own lips . . . ?"

Fitz thought for a moment. Williams would be upset, and might say the wrong thing. On the other hand, the king would probably like to speak to someone directly affected. He decided to take a chance. "Your Majesty," he said. "One of my servants has just returned from the pithead, and may have more up-to-date news. Her brother was underground when the gas exploded. Would you care to question her?"

"Yes, indeed," said the king. "Send her in, please."

A few moments later Ethel Williams entered. Her uniform was smudged with coal dust, but she had washed her face. She curtsied, and the king said: "What is the latest news?"

"Please, Your Majesty, there are five men trapped in Carnation district by a fall of rock. The rescue team are digging through the debris but the fire is still burning."

Fitz noticed that the king's manners with Ethel were subtly different. He had hardly looked at Perceval Jones, and had tapped a finger restlessly on the arm of his chair while listening; but he gave Ethel a direct look, and seemed more interested in her. In a softer voice, he asked: "What does your brother say?"

"The explosion of firedamp set light to the coal dust, and that's what's burning. The fire trapped many of the men in their workplaces, and some suffocated. My brother and the others couldn't rescue them because they had no breathing apparatus."

"That's not so," Jones said.

"I think it is," Gus Dewar contradicted him. As always, the American was a bit diffident in his manner, but he made an effort to speak insistently. "I spoke to some of the men coming up. They said the lockers marked 'Breathing Apparatus' turned out to be empty." He seemed to be suppressing anger.

Ethel Williams said: "And they couldn't put out the flames because there was insufficient water kept underground." Her eyes flashed with fury in a way that Fitz found alluring, and his heart skipped a beat.

"There's a fire engine!" Jones protested.

Gus Dewar spoke again. "A coal dram filled with water, and a hand pump."

Ethel Williams went on: "They should have been able to reverse the flow of ventilation, but Mr. Jones has not modified the machinery in accordance with the law."

Jones looked indignant. "It wasn't possible—"

Fitz interrupted. "All right, Jones. This isn't a public inquiry. His Majesty just wants to get people's impressions."

"Quite so," said the king. "But there is one subject on which you might be able to advise me, Jones."

"I should be honored—"

"I was planning to visit Aberowen and some of the surrounding villages tomorrow morning, and indeed to call upon your good self at the town hall. But in these circumstances a parade seems inappropriate."

Sir Alan, sitting behind the king's left shoulder, shook his head and murmured: "Quite impossible."

"On the other hand," the king went on, "it seems wrong to go away without any acknowledgment of the disaster. People might think us indifferent."

Fitz guessed there was a clash between the king and his staff. They probably wanted to cancel the visit, imagining that was the least risky course; whereas the king felt the need to make some gesture.

There was a silence while Perceval considered the question. When he spoke, he said only: "It's a difficult choice."

Ethel Williams said: "May I make a suggestion?"

Peel was aghast. "Williams!" he hissed. "Speak only when spoken to!"

Fitz was startled by her impertinence in the presence of the king. He tried to keep his voice calm as he said: "Perhaps later, Williams."

But the king smiled. To Fitz's relief, he seemed quite taken with Ethel. "We might as well hear what this young person has to propose," he said.

That was all Ethel needed. Without further ado she said: "You and the queen should visit the bereaved families. No parade, just one carriage with black horses. It would mean a lot to them. And everybody would think you were wonderful." She bit her lip and subsided into silence.

That last sentence was a breach of etiquette, Fitz thought anxiously; the king did not need to make people think he was wonderful.

Sir Alan was horrified. "Never been done before," he said in alarm.

But the king seemed intrigued by the idea. "Visit the bereaved . . ." he said musingly. He turned to his equerry. "By Jove, I think that's capital, Alan. Commiserate with my people in their suffering. No cavalcade, just one carriage." He turned back to the maid. "Very good, Williams," he said. "Thank you for speaking up."

Fitz breathed a sigh of relief.

{ VII }

In the end there was more than one carriage, of course. The king and queen went in the first with Sir Alan and a lady-in-waiting; Fitz and Bea followed in a second with the bishop; and a pony-and-trap with assorted servants brought up the rear. Perceval Jones had wanted to be one of the party, but Fitz had squashed that idea. As Ethel had pointed out, the bereaved might have tried to take him by the throat.

It was a windy day, and a cold rain lashed the horses as they trotted down the long drive of Tŷ Gwyn. Ethel was in the third vehicle. Because of her father's job she was familiar with every mining family in Aberowen. She was the only person at Tŷ Gwyn who knew the names of all the dead and injured. She had given directions to the drivers, and it would be her job to remind the equerry who was who. She had her fingers crossed. This was her idea, and if it went wrong she would be blamed.

As they drove out of the grand iron gates, she was struck, as always, by the sudden transition. Inside the grounds all was order, charm, and beauty; outside was the ugliness of the real world. A row of agricultural laborers' cottages stood beside the road, tiny houses of two rooms, with odd bits of lumber and junk in front and a couple of dirty children playing in the ditch. Soon afterward the miners' terraces began, superior to the farm cottages but still ungainly and monotonous to an eye such as Ethel's, spoiled by the perfect proportions of Tŷ Gwyn's windows and doorways and roofs. The people out here had cheap clothes that quickly became shapeless and worn, and were colored with dyes that faded, so that all the men were in grayish suits and all the women brownish dresses. Ethel's maid's outfit was envied for its warm wool skirt and crisp cotton blouse, for all that some of the girls liked to say they would never lower themselves to be servants. But the biggest difference was in the people themselves. Out here they had blemished skin, dirty hair, and black fingernails. The men coughed, the women sniffed, and the children all had runny noses. The poor shambled and limped along roads where the rich strode confidently.

The carriages drove down the mountainside to Mafeking Terrace. Most of the inhabitants were lining the pavements, waiting, but there were no flags, and they did not cheer, just bowed and curtsied, as the cavalcade pulled up outside number 19.

Ethel jumped down and spoke quietly to Sir Alan. "Sian Evans, five children, lost her husband, David Evans, an underground horse wrangler." David Evans, known as Dai Ponies, had been familiar to Ethel as an elder of the Bethesda Chapel.

Sir Alan nodded, and Ethel stepped smartly back while he murmured in the ear of the king. Ethel caught Fitz's eye, and he gave her a nod of approval. She felt a glow. She was assisting the king—and the earl was pleased with her.

The king and queen went to the front door. Its paint was peeling, but the step was polished. I never thought I'd see this, Ethel thought, the king knocking on the door of a collier's house. The king wore a tailcoat and a tall black hat; Ethel had strongly advised Sir Alan that the people of Aberowen would not wish to see their monarch in the kind of tweed suit that they themselves might wear.

The door was opened by the widow in her Sunday best, complete with hat. Fitz had suggested that the king should surprise people, but Ethel had argued against that, and Sir Alan had agreed with her. On a surprise visit to a distraught family the royal couple might have been confronted with drunken men, half-naked women, and fighting children. Better to forewarn everyone.

"Good morning. I'm the king," said the king, raising his hat politely. "Are you Mrs. David Evans?"

She looked blank for a moment. She was more used to being called Mrs. Dai Ponies.

"I have come to say how very sorry I am about your husband, David," said the king.

Mrs. Dai Ponies seemed too nervous to feel any emotion. "Thank you very much," she said stiffly.

It was too formal, Ethel saw. The king was as uncomfortable as the widow. Neither was able to say how they really felt.

Then the queen touched Mrs. Dai's arm. "It must be very hard for you, my dear," she said.

"Yes, ma'am, it is," said the widow in a whisper, and then she burst into tears.

Ethel wiped a tear from her own cheek.

The king was embarrassed, but to his credit, he stood his ground, murmuring: "Very sad, very sad."

Mrs. Evans sobbed uncontrollably, but she seemed rooted to the spot, and did not turn her face away. There was nothing gracious about grief, Ethel saw: Mrs. Dai's face was blotched red, her open mouth showed that she had lost half her teeth, and her sobs were hoarse with desperation.

"There, there," said the queen. She pressed her handkerchief into Mrs. Dai's hand. "Take this."

Mrs. Dai was not yet thirty, but her big hands were knotted and lumpy with arthritis like an old woman's. She wiped her face with the queen's handkerchief. Her sobs subsided. "He was a good man, ma'am," she said. "Never raised a hand to me."

The queen did not know what to say about a man whose virtue was that he did not beat his wife.

"He was even kind to his ponies," Mrs. Dai added.

"I'm sure he was," said the queen, back on familiar ground.

A toddler emerged from the depths of the house and clung to its mother's skirt. The king tried again. "I believe you have five children," he said.

"Oh, sir, what are they going to do with no da?"

"It's very sad," the king repeated.

Sir Alan coughed, and the king said: "We're going on to see some other people in the same sad position as yourself."

"Oh, sir, it was kind of you to come. I can't tell you how much it means to me. Thank you, thank you."

The king turned away.

The queen said: "I will pray for you tonight, Mrs. Evans." Then she followed the king.

As they were getting into their carriage, Fitz gave Mrs. Dai an envelope. Inside, Ethel knew, were five gold sovereigns and a note, handwritten on blue crested Tŷ Gwyn paper, saying: "Earl Fitzherbert wishes you to have this token of his deep sympathy."

That, too, had been Ethel's idea.

{ VIII }

One week after the explosion Billy went to chapel with his da, mam, and gramper.

The Bethesda Chapel was a square whitewashed room with no pictures on the walls. The chairs were arranged in neat rows on four sides of a plain table. On the table stood a loaf of white bread on a Woolworth's china plate and a jug of cheap sherry—the symbolic bread and wine. The service was not called Communion or mass, but simply the breaking of the bread.

By eleven o'clock the congregation of a hundred or so worshippers were in their seats, the men in their best suits, the women in hats, the children scrubbed and fidgeting in the back rows. There was no set ritual: the men would do as the Holy Spirit moved them—extemporize a prayer, announce a hymn, read a passage from the Bible, or give a short sermon. The women would remain silent, of course.

In practice there was a pattern. The first prayer was always spoken by one of the elders, who would then break the loaf and hand the plate to the nearest person. Each member of the congregation, excluding the children, would take a small piece and eat it. Next the wine was passed around, and everyone drank from the jug, the women taking tiny sips, some of the men enjoying a good mouthful. After that they all sat in silence until someone was moved to speak.

When Billy had asked his father at what age he should begin taking a vocal part in the service, Da had said: "There's no rule. We follow where the Holy Spirit leads." Billy had taken him at his word. If the first line of a hymn came into his mind, at some point during the hour, he took that as a nudge from the Holy Spirit, and he would stand up and announce the hymn. He was precocious in doing so at his age, he knew, but the congregation accepted that. The story of how Jesus had appeared to him during his underground initiation had been retold in half the chapels in the South Wales coalfield, and Billy was seen as special.

This morning every prayer begged for consolation for the bereaved, especially Mrs. Dai Ponies, who was sitting there in a veil, her eldest son beside her looking scared. Da asked God for the greatness of heart to forgive the wickedness of the mine owners in flouting laws about breathing equipment and reversible ventilation. Billy felt something was missing. It was too simple just to ask for healing. He wanted help in understanding how the explosion fitted into God's plan.

He had never yet extemporized a prayer. Many of the men prayed with fine-sounding phrases and quotations from the Scriptures, almost as if they were sermonizing. Billy himself suspected God was not so easily impressed. He always felt most moved by simple prayers that seemed heartfelt.

Toward the end of the service, words and sentences began to take shape in his mind, and he felt a strong impulse to give voice to them. Taking that for the guidance of the Holy Spirit, he eventually stood up.

With his eyes shut tight he said: "Oh, God, we have asked Thee this morning to bring comfort to those who have lost a husband, a father, a son, especially our sister in the Lord Mrs. Evans, and we pray that the bereaved will open their hearts to receive Thy benison."

This had been said by others. Billy paused, then went on: "And now, Lord, we ask for one more gift: the blessing of understanding. We need to know, Lord, why this explosion have took place down the pit. All things are in Thy power, so why didst Thou allow firedamp to fill the Main Level, and why didst Thou permit it to catch alight? How come, Lord, that men are set over us, directors of Celtic Minerals, who in their greed for money become careless of the lives of Thy people? How can the deaths of good men, and the mangling of the bodies Thou didst create, serve Thy holy purpose?"

He paused again. He knew it was wrong to make demands of God, as if negotiating with the management, so he added: "We know that the suffering of the people of Aberowen must play a part in Thy eternal plan." He thought he should probably leave it there, but he could not refrain from adding: "But, Lord, we can't see how, so please explain it to us."

He finished: "In the name of the Lord Jesus Christ."

The congregation said: "Amen."

{ IX }

That afternoon the people of Aberowen were invited to view the gardens at Tŷ Gwyn. It meant a lot of work for Ethel.

A notice had gone up in the pubs on Saturday night, and the message was read in churches and chapels after services on Sunday morning. The gardens had been made especially lovely for the king, despite the winter season, and now Earl Fitzherbert wished to share their beauty with his neighbors, the invitation said. The earl would be wearing a black tie, and he would be glad to see his visitors wearing a similar token of respect for the dead. Although it would obviously be inappropriate to have a party, nevertheless refreshments would be offered.

Ethel had ordered three marquees to be pitched on the East Lawn. In one were half a dozen 108-gallon butts of pale ale brought by train from the Crown Brewery in Pontyclun. For teetotallers, of whom there were many in Aberowen, the next tent had trestle tables bearing giant tea urns and hundreds of cups and saucers. In the third, smaller tent, sherry was offered to the town's diminutive middle class, including the Anglican vicar, both doctors, and the colliery manager, Maldwyn Morgan, who was already being referred to as Gone-to-Merthyr Morgan.

By good luck it was a sunny day, cold but dry, with a few harmless-looking white clouds high in a blue sky. Four thousand people came—very nearly the entire population of the town—and almost everyone wore a black tie, ribbon, or armband. They strolled around the shrubbery, peered through the windows into the house, and churned up the lawns.

Princess Bea stayed in her room: this was not her kind of social event. All upper-class people were selfish, in Ethel's experience, but Bea had made an art of it. All her energy was focused on pleasing herself and getting her own way. Even when giving a party—something she did well—her motive was mainly to provide a showcase for her own beauty and charm.

Fitz held court in the Victorian-Gothic splendor of the Great Hall, with his huge dog lying on the floor beside him like a fur rug. He wore the brown tweed suit that made him seem more approachable, albeit with a stiff collar and black tie. He looked handsomer than ever, Ethel thought. She brought the relatives of the dead and injured to see him in groups of three or four, so that he was able to commiserate with every Aberowen resident who had suffered. He spoke to them with his usual charm, and sent each one away feeling special.

Ethel was now the housekeeper. After the king's visit, Princess Bea had insisted that Mrs. Jevons retire permanently: she had no time for tired old servants. In Ethel she had seen someone who would work hard to fulfill her wishes, and had promoted her despite her youth. So Ethel had achieved her ambition. She had taken over the housekeeper's little room off the servants' hall, and had hung up a photograph of her parents, in their Sunday best, taken outside the Bethesda Chapel the day it had opened.

When Fitz came to the end of the list, Ethel asked permission to spend a few minutes with her family.

"Of course," said the earl. "Take as much time as you like. You've been absolutely marvelous. I don't know how I would have managed without you. The king was grateful for your help, too. How do you remember all those names?"

She smiled. She was not sure why it gave her such a thrill to be praised by him. "Most of these people have been to our house, sometime or other, to see my father about compensation for an injury, or a dispute with an overseer, or a worry about some safety measure down the pit."

"Well, I think you're remarkable," he said, and he gave the irresistible smile that occasionally came over his face and made him seem almost like the boy next door. "Give my respects to your father."

She went out and ran across the lawn, feeling on top of the world. She found Da, Mam, Billy, and Gramper in the tea tent. Da looked distinguished in his black Sunday suit and a white shirt with a stiff collar. Billy had a nasty burn on his cheek. Ethel said: "How are you feeling, Billy boy?"

"Not bad. It looks horrible, but the doctor says it's better without a bandage."

"Everybody's talking about how brave you were."

"It wasn't enough to save Micky Pope, though."

There was nothing to say to that, but Ethel touched her brother's arm in sympathy.

Mam said proudly: "Billy led us in prayer this morning at Bethesda."

"Well done, Billy! I'm sorry I missed it." Ethel had not gone to chapel—there was too much to do in the house. "What did you pray about?"

"I asked the Lord to help us understand why He allowed the explosion down the pit." Billy cast a nervous glance at Da, who was not smiling.

Da said severely: "Billy might have done better to ask God to strengthen his faith, so that he can believe *without* understanding."

Clearly they had already argued about this. Ethel did not have the patience for theological disputes that made no difference to anything in the end. She tried to brighten the mood. "Earl Fitzherbert asked me to give you his respects, Da," she said. "Wasn't that nice of him?"

Da did not melt. "I was sorry to see you taking part in that farce on Monday," he said sternly.

"Monday?" she said incredulously. "When the king visited the families?"

"I saw you whispering the names to that flunky."

"That was Sir Alan Tite."

"I don't care what he calls himself. I know a lickspittle when I see one."

Ethel was shocked. How could Da be scornful of her great moment? She felt like crying. "I thought you'd be proud of me, helping the king!"

"How dare the king offer sympathy to our folk? What does a king know of hardship and danger?"

Ethel fought back tears. "But, Da, it meant so much to people that he went to see them!"

"It distracted everyone's attention from the dangerous and illegal actions of Celtic Minerals."

"But they need comfort." Why could he not see this?

"The king softened them up. Last Sunday afternoon this town was ready to revolt. By Monday evening all they could talk about was the queen giving her handkerchief to Mrs. Dai Ponies."

Ethel went swiftly from heartbreak to anger. "I'm sorry you feel that way," she said coldly.

"Nothing to be sorry for—"

"I'm sorry because you are wrong," she said, firmly overriding him.

Da was taken aback. It was rare for him to be told he was wrong by anyone, let alone a girl.

Mam said: "Now, Eth—"

"People have feelings, Da," she said recklessly. "That's what you always forget."

Da was speechless.

Mam said: "That's enough, now!"

Ethel looked at Billy. Through a mist of tears she saw his expression of awestruck admiration. That encouraged her. She sniffed and wiped her eyes with the back of her hand and said: "You and your union, and your safety regulations and your Scriptures—I know they're important, Da, but you can't do away with people's feelings. I hope that one day socialism will make the world a better place for working people, but in the meantime they need consolation."

Da found his voice at last. "I think we've heard enough from you," he said. "Being with the king has gone to your head. You're a slip of a girl, and you've no business lecturing your elders."

She was crying too much to argue further. "I'm sorry, Da," she said. After a heavy silence she added: "I'd better get back to work." The earl had told her to take all the time she liked, but she wanted to be alone. She turned away from her father's glare and walked back to the big house. She kept her eyes downcast, hoping the crowds would not notice her tears.

She did not want to meet anyone so she slipped into the Gardenia

Suite. Lady Maud had returned to London, so the room was empty and the bed was stripped. Ethel threw herself down on the mattress and cried.

She had been feeling so proud. How could Da undermine everything she had done? Did he want her to do a *bad* job? She worked for the nobility. So did every coal miner in Aberowen. Even though Celtic Minerals employed them, it was the earl's coal they were digging, and he was paid the same per ton as the miner who dug it out of the earth—a fact her father never tired of pointing out. If it was all right to be a good collier, efficient and productive, what was wrong with being a good housekeeper?

She heard the door open. Quickly she jumped to her feet. It was the earl. "What on earth is the matter?" he said kindly. "I heard you from outside the door."

"I'm very sorry, my lord. I shouldn't have come in here."

"That's all right." There was genuine concern on his impossibly handsome face. "Why are you crying?"

"I was so proud to have helped the king," she said woefully. "But my father says it was a farce, all done just to stop people feeling angry with Celtic Minerals." She burst into fresh tears.

"What nonsense," he said. "Anyone could tell that the king's concern was genuine. And the queen's." He took the white linen handkerchief from the breast pocket of his jacket. She expected him to hand it to her, but instead he wiped the tears from her cheeks with a gentle touch. "I was proud of you last Monday, even if your father wasn't."

"You're so kind."

"There, there," he said, and he bent down and kissed her lips.

She was dumbfounded. It was the last thing in the world she had expected. When he straightened up she stared at him uncomprehendingly.

He gazed back at her. "You are absolutely enchanting," he said in a low voice; then he kissed her again.

This time she pushed him away. "My lord, what are you doing?" she said in a shocked whisper.

"I don't know."

"But what can you be thinking of?"

"I'm not thinking at all."

She stared up at his chiseled face. The green eyes studied her intently, as if trying to read her mind. She realized that she adored him. Suddenly she was flooded with excitement and desire.

"I can't help myself," he said.

She sighed happily. "Kiss me again, then," she said.

CHAPTER THREE

February 1914

A t half past ten the looking glass in the hall of Earl Fitzherbert's Mayfair house showed a tall man immaculately dressed in the daytime clothing of an upper-class Englishman. He wore an upright collar, disliking the fashion for soft collars, and his silver tie was fastened with a pearl. Some of his friends thought it was undignified to dress well. "I say, Fitz, you look like a damn tailor, about to open his shop in the morning," the young Marquis of Lowther had said to him once. But Lowthie was a scruff, with crumbs on his waistcoat and cigar ash on the cuffs of his shirt, and he wanted everyone else to look as bad. Fitz hated to be grubby; it suited him to be spruce.

He put on a gray top hat. With his walking stick in his right hand and a new pair of gray suede gloves in his left, he went out of the house and turned south. In Berkeley Square a blond girl of about fourteen winked at him and said: "Suck you for a shilling?"

He crossed Piccadilly and entered Green Park. A few snowdrops clustered around the roots of the trees. He passed Buckingham Palace and entered an unattractive neighborhood near Victoria Station. He had to ask a policeman for directions to Ashley Gardens. The street turned out to be behind the Roman Catholic cathedral. Really, Fitz thought, if one is going to ask members of the nobility to call, one should have one's office in a respectable quarter.

He had been summoned by an old friend of his father's named Mansfield Smith-Cumming. A retired naval officer, Smith-Cumming was now doing something vague in the War Office. He had sent Fitz a rather short note. "I should be grateful for a word on a matter of national importance. Can you call on me tomorrow morning at, say, eleven o'clock?" The note was typewritten and signed, in green ink, with the single letter "C."

In truth Fitz was pleased that someone in the government wanted to talk to him. He had a horror of being thought of as an ornament, a wealthy aristocrat with no function other than to decorate social events. He hoped he was going to be asked for his advice, perhaps about his old regiment, the Welsh Rifles. Or there might be some task he could perform in connection with the South Wales Territorials, of which he was honorary colonel. Anyway, just being summoned to the War Office made him feel he was not completely superfluous.

If this really was the War Office. The address turned out to be a modern block of apartments. A doorman directed Fitz to an elevator. Smith-Cumming's flat seemed to be part home, part office, but a briskly efficient young man with a military air told Fitz that "C" would see him right away.

C did not have a military air. Podgy and balding, he had a nose like Mr. Punch and wore a monocle. His office was cluttered with miscellaneous objects: model aircraft, a telescope, a compass, and a painting of peasants facing a firing squad. Fitz's father had always referred to Smith-Cumming as "the seasick sea captain" and his naval career had not been brilliant. What was he doing here? "What exactly is this department?" Fitz asked as he sat down.

"This is the Foreign Section of the Secret Service Bureau," said C.

"I didn't know we had a Secret Service Bureau."

"If people knew, it wouldn't be secret."

"I see." Fitz felt a twinge of excitement. It was flattering to be given confidential information.

"Perhaps you'd be kind enough not to mention it to anyone."

Fitz was being given an order, albeit politely phrased. "Of course," he said. He was pleased to feel a member of an inner circle. Did this mean that C might ask him to work for the War Office?

"Congratulations on the success of your royal house party. I believe you put together an impressive group of well-connected young men for His Majesty to meet."

"Thank you. It was a quiet social occasion, strictly speaking, but I'm afraid word gets around."

"And now you're taking your wife to Russia."

"The princess is Russian. She wants to visit her brother. It's a long-postponed trip."

"And Gus Dewar is going with you."

C seemed to know everything. "He's on a world tour," Fitz said. "Our plans coincided."

C sat back in his chair and said conversationally: "Do you know why Admiral Alexeev was put in charge of the Russian army in the war against Japan, even though he knew nothing about fighting on land?"

Having spent time in Russia as a boy, Fitz had followed the progress of the Russo-Japanese War of 1904–1905, but he did not know this story. "Tell me."

"Well, it seems the grand duke Alexis was involved in a punch-up in a brothel in Marseilles and got arrested by the French police. Alexeev came to the rescue and told the gendarmes that it was he, not the grand duke, who had misbehaved. The similarity of their names made the story plausible and the grand duke was let out of jail. Alexeev's reward was command of the army."

"No wonder they lost."

"All the same, the Russians deploy the largest army the world has ever known—six million men, by some calculations, assuming they call up all their reserves. No matter how incompetent their leadership, it's a formidable force. But how effective would they be in, say, a European war?"

"I haven't been back since my marriage," Fitz said. "I'm not sure."

"Nor are we. That's where you come in. I would like you to make some inquiries while you're there."

Fitz was surprised. "But surely our embassy should do that."

"Of course." C shrugged. "But diplomats are always more interested in politics than military matters."

"Still, there must be a military attaché."

"An outsider such as yourself can offer a fresh perspective—in much the same way as your group at Tŷ Gwyn gave the king something he could not have got from the Foreign Office. But if you feel you can't . . . "

"I'm not refusing," Fitz said hastily. On the contrary, he was pleased to be asked to do a job for his country. "I'm just surprised that things should be done this way."

"We are a newish department with few resources. My best informants are intelligent travelers with enough military background to understand what they're looking at."

"Very well."

"I'd be interested to know whether you felt the Russian officer class has moved on since 1905. Have they modernized, or are they still attached to old ideas? You'll meet all the top men in St. Petersburg—your wife is related to half of them."

Fitz was thinking about the last time Russia went to war. "The main reason they lost against Japan was that the Russian railways were inadequate to supply their army."

"But since then they have been trying to improve their rail network—using money borrowed from France, their ally."

"Have they made much progress, I wonder?"

"That's the key question. You'll be traveling by rail. Do the trains run on time? Keep your eyes open. Are the lines still mostly single-track, or double? The German generals have a contingency plan for war that is based on a calculation of how long it will take to mobilize the Russian army. If there is a war, much will hang on the accuracy of that timetable."

Fitz was as excited as a schoolboy, but he forced himself to speak with gravity. "I'll find out all I can."

"Thank you." C looked at his watch.

Fitz stood up and they shook hands.

"When are you going, exactly?" C asked.

"We leave tomorrow," said Fitz. "Good-bye."

{ II }

Grigori Peshkov watched his younger brother, Lev, taking money off the tall American. Lev's attractive face wore an expression of boyish eagerness, as if his main aim was to show off his skill. Grigori suffered a familiar pang of anxiety. One day, he feared, Lev's charm would not be enough to keep him out of trouble.

"This is a memory test," Lev said in English. He had learned the words by rote. "Take any card." He had to raise his voice over the racket of the factory: heavy machinery clanking, steam hissing, people yelling instructions and questions.

The visitor's name was Gus Dewar. He wore a jacket, waistcoat, and trousers all in the same fine gray woollen cloth. Grigori was especially interested in him because he came from Buffalo.

Dewar was an amiable young man. With a shrug, he took a card from Lev's pack and looked at it.

Lev said: "Put it on the bench, facedown."

Dewar put the card on the rough wooden workbench.

Lev took a ruble note from his pocket and placed it on the card. "Now you put a dollar down." This could be done only with rich visitors.

Grigori knew that Lev had already switched the playing card. In his hand, concealed by the ruble note, there had been a different card. The skill—which Lev had practiced for hours—lay in picking up the first card, and concealing it in the palm of the hand, immediately after putting down the ruble note and the new card.

"Are you sure you can afford to lose a dollar, Mr. Dewar?" said Lev.

Dewar smiled, as the marks always did at that point. "I think so," he said.

"Do you remember your card?" Lev did not really speak English. He could say these phrases in German, French, and Italian, too.

"Five of spades," said Dewar.

"Wrong."

"I'm pretty sure."

"Turn it over."

Dewar turned over the card. It was the queen of clubs.

Lev scooped up the dollar bill and his original ruble.

Grigori held his breath. This was the dangerous moment. Would the American complain that he had been robbed, and accuse Lev?

Dewar grinned ruefully and said: "You got me."

"I know another game," Lev said.

It was enough: Lev was about to push his luck. Although he was twenty years old, Grigori still had to protect him. "Don't play against my brother," Grigori said to Dewar in Russian. "He always wins."

Dewar smiled and replied hesitantly in the same tongue. "That's good advice."

Dewar was the first of a small group of visitors touring the Putilov Machine Works. It was the largest factory in St. Petersburg, employing thirty thousand men, women, and children. Grigori's job was to show them his own small but important section. The factory made locomotives and other large steel artifacts. Grigori was foreman of the shop that made train wheels.

Grigori was itching to speak to Dewar about Buffalo. But before he could ask a question the supervisor of the casting section, Kanin, appeared. A qualified engineer, he was tall and thin with receding hair.

With him was a second visitor. Grigori knew from his clothes that this must be the British lord. He was dressed like a Russian nobleman, in a tailcoat and a top hat. Perhaps this was the clothing worn by the ruling class all over the world.

The lord's name, Grigori had been told, was Earl Fitzherbert. He was the handsomest man Grigori had ever seen, with black hair and intense green eyes. The women in the wheel shop stared as if at a god.

Kanin spoke to Fitzherbert in Russian. "We are now producing two new locomotives every week here," he said proudly.

"Amazing," said the English lord.

Grigori understood why these foreigners were so interested. He read the newspapers, and he went to lectures and discussion groups organized by the St. Petersburg Bolshevik Committee. The locomotives made here were essential to Russia's ability to defend itself. The visitors might pretend to be idly curious, but they were collecting military intelligence.

Kanin introduced Grigori. "Peshkov here is the factory's chess champion." Kanin was management, but he was all right.

Fitzherbert was charming. He spoke to Varya, a woman of about fifty with her gray hair in a head scarf. "Very kind of you to show us your workplace," he said, cheerfully speaking fluent Russian with a heavy accent.

Varya, a formidable figure, muscular and big-bosomed, giggled like a schoolgirl.

The demonstration was ready. Grigori had placed steel ingots in the hopper and fired up the furnace, and the metal was now molten. But there was one more visitor to come: the earl's wife, who was said to be Russian—hence his knowledge of the language, which was unusual in a foreigner.

Grigori wanted to question Dewar about Buffalo, but before he had a chance, the earl's wife came into the wheel shop. Her floor-length skirt was like a broom pushing a line of dirt and swarf in front of her. She wore a short coat over her dress, and she was followed by a manservant carrying a fur cloak, a maid with a bag, and one of the directors of the factory, Count Maklakov, a young man dressed like Fitzherbert. Maklakov was obviously very taken with his guest, smiling and talking in a low voice and taking her arm unnecessarily. She was extraordinarily pretty, with fair curls and a coquettish tilt to her head.

Grigori recognized her immediately. She was Princess Bea.

His heart lurched and he felt nauseated. He fiercely repressed the ugly memory that rose out of the distant past. Then, as in any emergency, he checked on his brother. Would Lev remember? He had been only six years old at the time. Lev was looking with curiosity at the princess, as if trying to place her. Then, as Grigori watched, Lev's face changed and he remembered. He went pale and looked ill; then suddenly he reddened with anger.

By that time Grigori was at Lev's side. "Stay calm," he murmured. "Don't say anything. Remember, we're going to America—nothing must interfere with that!"

Lev made a disgusted noise.

"Go back to the stables," Grigori said. Lev was a pony driver, working with the many horses used in the factory.

Lev glared a moment longer at the oblivious princess. Then he turned and walked away, and the moment of danger passed.

Grigori began the demonstration. He nodded to Isaak, a man of his own age, who was captain of the factory football team. Isaak opened up the mold. Then he and Varya picked up a polished wooden template of a flanged train wheel. This in itself was a work of great skill, with spokes that were elliptical in cross-section and tapered by one in twenty from hub to rim. The wheel was for a big 4-6-4 locomotive, and the template was almost as tall as the people lifting it.

They pressed it into a deep tray filled with damp sandy molding mixture. Isaak swung the cast-iron chill on top of that, to form the tread and the flange, and then finally the top of the mold.

They opened up the assemblage and Grigori inspected the hole made by the template. There were no visible irregularities. He sprayed the molding sand with a black oily liquid; then they closed the flask again. "Please stand well back now," he said to the visitors. Isaak moved the spout of the hopper to the funnel on top of the mold. Then Grigori pulled the lever that tilted the hopper.

Molten steel poured slowly into the mold. Steam from the wet sand hissed out of vents. Grigori knew by experience when to raise the hopper and stop the flow. "The next step is to perfect the shape of the wheel," he said. "Because the hot metal takes so long to cool, I have here a wheel that was cast earlier."

It was already set up on a lathe, and Grigori nodded to Konstantin, the lathe operator, who was Varya's son. A thin, gangling intellectual with wild black hair, Konstantin was chairman of the Bolshevik discussion group and Grigori's closest friend. He started the electric motor, turning the wheel at high speed, and began to shape it with a file.

"Please keep well away from the lathe," Grigori said to the visitors, raising his voice over the whine of the machine. "If you touch it, you may lose a finger." He held up his left hand. "As I did, here in this factory, at the age of twelve." His third finger, the ring finger, was an ugly stump. He caught a glance of irritation from Count Maklakov, who did not enjoy being reminded of the human cost of his profits. The look he got from Princess Bea mingled disgust with fascination, and he wondered whether she was weirdly interested in squalor and suffering. It was unusual for a lady to tour a factory.

He made a sign to Konstantin, who stopped the lathe. "Next, the dimensions of the wheel are checked with calipers." He held up the tool used. "Train wheels must be exactly sized. If the diameter varies by more than one-sixteenth of an inch—which is about the width of the lead in a pencil—the wheel must be melted down and remade."

Fitzherbert said in broken Russian: "How many wheels can you make per day?"

"Six or seven on average, allowing for rejects."

The American, Dewar, asked: "What hours do you work?"

"Six in the morning until seven in the evening, Monday through Saturday. On Sunday we are allowed to go to church."

A boy of about eight came racing into the wheel shop, pursued by a shouting woman—presumably his mother. Grigori made a grab for him, to keep him away from the furnace. The boy dodged and cannoned into

Princess Bea, his close-cropped head striking her in the ribs with an audible thump. She gasped, hurt. The boy stopped, apparently dazed. Furious, the princess drew back her arm and slapped his face so hard that he rocked on his feet, and Grigori thought he was going to fall over. The American said something abrupt in English, sounding surprised and indignant. In the next instant the mother swept the boy up in her strong arms and turned away.

Kanin, the supervisor, looked scared, knowing he might be blamed. He said to the princess: "Most High Excellency, are you hurt?"

Princess Bea was visibly enraged, but she took a deep breath and said: "It's nothing."

Her husband and the count went to her, looking concerned. Only Dewar stood back, his face a mask of disapproval and revulsion. He had been shocked by the slap, Grigori guessed, and he wondered whether all Americans were equally softhearted. A slap was nothing: Grigori and his brother had been flogged with canes as children in this factory.

The visitors began to move away. Grigori was afraid he might lose his chance of questioning the tourist from Buffalo. Boldly, he touched Dewar's sleeve. A Russian nobleman would have reacted with indignation, and shoved him away or struck him for insolence, but the American merely turned to him with a polite smile.

"You are from Buffalo, New York, sir?" said Grigori.

"That's right."

"My brother and I are saving to go to America. We will live in Buffalo."

"Why that city?"

"Here in St. Petersburg is a family who get the necessary papers—for a fee, of course—and promise us jobs with their relatives in Buffalo."

"Who are these people?"

"Vyalov is the name." The Vyalovs were a criminal gang, though they had lawful businesses, too. They were not the most trustworthy people in the world, so Grigori wanted their claims independently verified. "Sir, is the Vyalov family of Buffalo, New York, really an important rich family?"

"Yes," said Dewar. "Josef Vyalov employs several hundred people in his hotels and bars."

"Thank you." Grigori was relieved. "That is very good to know."

{ III }

Grigori's earliest memory was of the day the tsar came to Bulovnir. He was six.

The people of the village had talked of little else for days. Everyone got up at dawn, even though it was obvious the tsar would have his breakfast before setting out, so he could not possibly get there before midmorning. Grigori's father carried the table out of their one-room dwelling and set it beside the road. On it he placed a loaf of bread, a bunch of flowers, and a small container of salt, explaining to his elder son that these were the traditional Russian symbols of welcome. Most of the other villagers did the same. Grigori's grandmother had put on a new yellow head scarf.

It was a dry day in early autumn, before the onset of the hard winter cold. The peasants sat on their haunches to wait. The village elders walked up and down in their best clothes, looking important, but they were waiting just like everyone else. Grigori soon got bored and started to play in the dirt beside the house. His brother, Lev, was only a year old, and still being nursed by their mother.

Noon passed, but no one wanted to go indoors and make dinner for fear they might miss the tsar. Grigori tried to eat some of the loaf on the table and got his head smacked, but his mother brought him a bowl of cold porridge.

Grigori was not sure who or what the tsar was. He was frequently mentioned in church as loving all the peasants and watching over them while they slept, so he was clearly on a level with St. Peter and Jesus and the angel Gabriel. Grigori wondered if he would have wings or a crown of thorns, or just an embroidered coat like a village elder. Anyway, it was obvious that people were blessed just by seeing him, like the crowds that followed Jesus.

It was late afternoon when a cloud of dust appeared in the distance. Grigori could feel vibrations in the ground beneath his felt boots, and soon he heard the drumming of hooves. The villagers got down on their knees. Grigori knelt beside his grandmother. The elders lay facedown in the road with their foreheads in the dirt, as they did when Prince Andrei and Princess Bea came.

Outriders appeared, followed by a closed carriage drawn by four horses. The horses were huge, the biggest Grigori had ever seen, and they were being driven at speed, their flanks shining with sweat, their mouths foaming around their bits. The elders realized they were not going to stop and scrambled out of the way before they were trampled. Grigori screamed in fear, but his cry was inaudible. As the carriage passed, his father shouted: "Long live the tsar, father of his people!"

By the time he finished, the carriage was already leaving the village behind. Grigori had not been able to see the passengers because of the dust. He realized he had missed seeing the tsar, and therefore would receive no blessing, and he burst into tears.

His mother took the loaf from the table, broke off an end, and gave it to him to eat, and he felt better.

{ IV }

When the shift at the Putilov Machine Works finished at seven o'clock, Lev usually went off to play cards with his pals or drink with his easygoing girlfriends. Grigori often went to a meeting of some kind: a lecture on atheism, a socialist discussion group, a magic-lantern show about foreign lands, a poetry reading. But tonight he had nothing to do. He would go home, make a stew for supper, leave some in the pot for Lev to eat later, and go to bed early.

The factory was on the southern outskirts of St. Petersburg, its sprawl of chimneys and sheds covering a large site on the shore of the Baltic Sea. Many of the workers lived at the factory, some in barracks and some lying down to sleep beside their machines. That was why there were so many children running around.

Grigori was among those who had a home outside the factory. In a socialist society, he knew, houses for workers would be planned at the same time as factories, but haphazard Russian capitalism left thousands of people with nowhere to live. Grigori was well-paid, but he lived in a single room half an hour's walk from the factory. In Buffalo, he knew, factory hands had electricity and running water in their homes. He had been told that some had their own telephones, but that seemed ridiculous, like saying the streets were paved with gold.

Seeing Princess Bea had taken him back to his childhood. As he wound his way through the icy streets, he refused to allow himself to dwell on the unbearable memory she brought to mind. All the same he thought about the wooden hut where he had lived then, and he saw again the holy corner where the icons were hung, and opposite it the sleeping corner where he lay down at night, usually with a goat or calf beside him. What he remembered most distinctly was something he had hardly noticed at the time: the smell. It came from the stove, the animals, the black smoke of the kerosene lamp, and the homemade tobacco his father smoked rolled into newspaper cigarettes. The windows were shut tight with rags stuffed around the frames to keep the cold out, so the atmosphere was dense. He could smell it now in his imagination, and it made him nostalgic for the days before the nightmare, the last time in his life when he had felt secure.

Not far from the factory he came upon a sight that made him stop. In the pool of light thrown by a streetlamp two policemen, in black uniforms with green facings, were questioning a young woman. Her homespun coat, and the way she tied the head scarf with a knot at the back of the neck, suggested a peasant newly arrived in the city. At first glance he took her to be about sixteen—the age he had been when he and Lev were orphaned.

The stocky policeman said something and patted the girl's face. She flinched, and the other cop laughed. Grigori remembered being ill-treated by everyone in authority as a sixteen-year-old orphan, and his heart went out to this vulnerable girl. Against his better judgment, he approached the little group. Just to have something to say, he said: "If you're looking for the Putilov works, I can show you the way."

The stocky policeman laughed and said: "Get rid of him, Ilya."

His sidekick had a small head and a mean face. "Get lost, scum," he said.

Grigori was not afraid. He was tall and strong, his muscles hardened by constant heavy work. He had been in street fights ever since he was a boy and he had not lost one for many years. Lev was the same. Nevertheless, it was better not to annoy the police. "I'm a foreman at the works," he said to the girl. "If you're looking for a job, I can help you."

The girl shot him a grateful look.

"A foreman is nothing," said the stocky cop. As he spoke he looked directly at Grigori for the first time. In the yellow light from the kerosene streetlamp Grigori now recognized the round face with the look of stupid belligerence. The man was Mikhail Pinsky, the local precinct captain. Grigori's heart sank. It was madness to pick a fight with the precinct captain—but he had gone too far now to turn back.

The girl spoke, and her voice told Grigori that she was nearer to twenty than sixteen. "Thank you. I'll go with you, sir," she said to Grigori. She was pretty, he saw, with delicately molded features and a wide, sensual mouth.

Grigori looked around. Unfortunately, there was no one else about: he had left the factory a few minutes after the seven o'clock rush. He knew he should back down, but he could not abandon this girl. "I'll take you to the factory office," he said, though in fact it was now closed.

"She's coming with me—aren't you, Katerina?" Pinsky said, and he pawed her, squeezing her breasts through the thin coat and thrusting a hand between her legs.

She jumped back a pace and said: "Keep your filthy hands off."

With surprising speed and accuracy Pinsky punched her in the mouth.

She cried out, and blood spurted from her lips.

Grigori was angered. Throwing caution to the wind he stepped forward, put a hand to Pinsky's shoulder, and shoved hard. Pinsky staggered sideways and fell to one knee. Grigori turned to Katerina, who was crying. "Run like hell!" he said; then he felt an agonizing blow to the back of his head. The second policeman, Ilya, had deployed his nightstick faster than Grigori expected. The pain was excruciating, and he fell to his knees, but he did not black out.

Katerina turned and ran, but she did not get far. Pinsky reached out and grabbed her foot, and she fell full-length.

Grigori turned and saw the nightstick coming at him again. He dodged the blow and scrambled to his feet. Ilya swung and missed again. Grigori aimed a blow at the side of the man's head and punched with all his force. Ilya fell to the ground.

Grigori turned to see Pinsky standing over Katerina, kicking her repeatedly with his heavy boots.

A motorcar approached from the direction of the factory. As it passed, its driver braked hard, and it squealed to a stop under the streetlamp.

Two long strides brought Grigori to a position just behind Pinsky. He put both arms around the police captain, gripped him in a bear hug, and lifted him off the ground. Pinsky kicked his legs and waved his arms to no avail.

The car door opened and, to Grigori's surprise, the American from Buffalo got out. "What is happening?" he said. His youthful face, lit by the streetlight, showed outrage as he addressed the wriggling Pinsky. "Why do you kick a helpless woman?"

This was great good luck, Grigori thought. Only foreigners would object to a policeman kicking a peasant.

The long, thin figure of Kanin, the supervisor, unfolded out of the car behind Dewar. "Let the policeman go, Peshkov," he said to Grigori.

Grigori set Pinsky on the ground and released him. He spun around, and Grigori got ready to dodge a blow, but Pinsky restrained himself. In a voice full of poison he said: "I'll remember you, *Peshkov.*" Grigori groaned: the man knew his name.

Katerina got to her knees, moaning. Dewar gallantly helped her to her feet, saying: "Are you badly hurt, miss?"

Kanin looked embarrassed. No Russian would address a peasant so courteously.

Ilya got up, looking dazed.

From within the car came the voice of Princess Bea, speaking English, sounding annoyed and impatient.

Grigori addressed Dewar. "With your permission, Excellency, I will take this woman to a nearby doctor."

Dewar looked at Katerina. "Is that your wish?"

"Yes, sir," she said through bloody lips.

"Very well," he said.

Grigori took her arm and led her away before anyone could suggest otherwise.

At the corner he glanced back. The two cops stood arguing with Dewar and Kanin under the streetlamp.

Still holding Katerina's arm, he hurried her along, even though she was limping. They needed to put distance between themselves and Pinsky.

As soon as they had turned the corner, she said: "I have no money for a doctor."

"I could give you a loan," he said, with a pang of guilt: his money was for passage to America, not to soothe the bruises of pretty girls.

She gave him a calculating look. "I don't really want a doctor," she said. "What I need is a job. Could you take me to the factory office?"

She had guts, he thought admiringly. She had just been beaten up by a policeman, and all she could think about was getting a job. "The office is closed. I just said that to confuse the cops. But I can take you there in the morning."

"I have nowhere to sleep." She gave him a guarded look that he did not quite understand. Was she offering herself? Many peasant girls who came to the city ended up doing that. But perhaps her look meant the opposite, that she wanted a bed but was not prepared to pay with sexual favors.

"In the house where I live there's a room shared by a number of women," he said. "They sleep three or more to a bed, and they can always find space for another one."

"How far is it?"

He pointed ahead to a street that ran alongside a railway embankment. "Just here."

She nodded assent, and a few moments later they entered the house.

He had a back room on the first floor. The narrow bed that he shared with Lev stood against one wall. There was a fireplace with a hob, and a table and two chairs next to the window that overlooked the railway. An upended packing case served as a nightstand, with a jug and bowl for washing.

Katerina inspected the place with a long look that took everything in; then she said: "You have all this to yourself?"

"No—I'm not rich! I share with my brother. He'll be here later."

She looked thoughtful. Perhaps she was afraid she might be expected to have sex with both of them. To reassure her, Grigori said: "Shall I introduce you to the women in the house?"

"Plenty of time for that." She sat in one of the two chairs. "Let me rest a while."

"Of course." The fire was laid, ready to be lit: he always built it in the morning before going to work. He put a match to the kindling.

There was a thunderous noise, and Katerina looked frightened. "It's just a train," Grigori said. "We're right next to the railway."

He poured water from the jug into the bowl, then set the bowl on the hob to warm. He sat opposite Katerina and looked at her. She had straight fair hair and pale skin. At first he had judged her to be quite pretty, but now he saw that she was really beautiful, with an oriental cast to her bone structure that suggested Siberian ancestry. There was strength of character in her face, too: her wide mouth was sexy, but also determined, and there seemed to be iron purpose in her blue-green eyes.

Her lips were swelling up from Pinsky's punch. "How do you feel?" Grigori asked.

She ran her hands over her shoulders, ribs, hips, and thighs. "Bruised all over," she said. "But you pulled that animal off me before he could do any serious damage."

She was not going to feel sorry for herself. He liked that. He said: "When the water's warm, I'll wash away the blood."

He kept food in a tin box. He took out a knuckle of ham and dropped it in the saucepan, then added water from the jug. He rinsed a turnip and began to slice it into the pan. He caught Katerina's eye and saw a look of surprise. She said: "Did your father cook?"

"No," said Grigori, and in a blink he was transported back to the age of eleven. The nightmare memories of Princess Bea could no longer be resisted. He put the pan down heavily on the table, then sat on the edge of the bed and buried his head in his hands, overwhelmed by grief. "No," he repeated, "my father didn't cook."

{V}

They came to the village at dawn: the local land captain and six cavalrymen. As soon as Ma heard the trotting hoofbeats, she picked up Lev. He was a heavy burden at age six, but Ma was broad-shouldered and strong-armed. She grabbed Grigori's hand and ran out of the house. The horsemen were being led by the village elders, who must have met them at the outskirts. Because there was only one door, Grigori's family had no chance of concealment, and as soon as they appeared the soldiers spurred their mounts.

Ma pounded around the side of the house, scattering chickens and scaring the goat so that it broke its tether and bolted, too. She ran across the waste ground at the back toward the trees. They might have escaped, but Grigori suddenly realized that his grandmother was not with them. He stopped and pulled his hand free. "We forgot Gran!" he squealed.

"She can't run!" Ma yelled back.

Grigori knew that. Gran could hardly walk. But all the same he felt they must not leave her behind.

"Grishka, come on!" Ma shouted, and she ran ahead, still carrying Lev, who was now shrieking with fear. Grigori followed, but the delay had been fatal. The horsemen came closer, one approaching on either side. The path to the woods was cut off. In desperation Ma ran into the pond, but her feet sank into the mud, she slowed down, and at last she fell into the water.

The soldiers hooted with laughter.

They tied Ma's hands and marched her back. "Make sure the boys come, too," said the land captain. "Prince's orders."

Grigori's father had been taken away a week ago, along with two other men. Yesterday, Prince Andrei's household carpenters had built a scaffold in the north meadow. Now, as Grigori followed his mother into the meadow, he saw three men standing on the scaffold, bound hand and foot, with ropes around their necks. Beside the scaffold stood a priest.

Ma screamed: "No!" She began to struggle with the rope that bound her hands. A cavalryman drew a rifle from the holster fixed to his saddle and, reversing it, hit her in the face with its wooden stock. She stopped struggling and began to sob.

Grigori knew what this meant: his father was going to die here. He had seen horse thieves hanged by the village elders, though that had seemed different because the victims were men he did not know. He was seized by a terror that turned his entire body numb and feeble.

Perhaps something would happen to prevent the execution. The tsar might intervene, if he truly watched over his people. Or perhaps an angel. Grigori's face felt wet and he realized he was crying.

He and his mother were forced to stand right in front of the scaffold. The other villagers gathered around. Like Ma, the wives of the other two men had to be dragged there, screaming and crying, their hands bound, their children holding on to their skirts and howling in terror.

On the dirt track beyond the field gate stood a closed carriage, its matching chestnut horses cropping the roadside grass. When everyone was present, a black-bearded figure emerged from the carriage in a long dark coat: Prince Andrei. He turned and gave his hand to his little sister, Princess Bea, with furs around her shoulders against the morning cold. The princess was beautiful, Grigori could not help noticing, with pale skin and fair hair, just as he imagined angels to look, even though she was obviously a devil.

The prince addressed the villagers. "This meadow belongs to Princess Bea," he said. "No one may graze cattle here without her permission. To do so is to steal the princess's grass."

There was a murmur of resentment from the crowd. They did not believe in this kind of ownership, despite what they were told every Sunday in church. They adhered to an older, peasant morality, according to which the land was for those who worked it.

The prince pointed to the three men on the scaffold. "These fools broke the law—not once, but repeatedly." His voice was shrill with outrage, like a child whose toy has been snatched. "Worse, they told others that the princess had no right to stop them, and that fields the landowner is not using should be available to poor peasants." Grigori had heard his father say such things often. "As a result, men from other villages have started grazing cattle on land that belongs to the nobility. Instead of repenting their sins, these three have turned their neighbors into sinners, too! That is why they have been sentenced to death." He nodded to the priest.

The priest climbed the makeshift steps and spoke quietly to each man in turn. The first nodded expressionlessly. The second wept and began to pray aloud. The third, Grigori's father, spat in the priest's face. No one was shocked: the villagers had a low opinion of the clergy, and Grigori had heard his father say that they told the police everything they heard in the confessional.

The priest descended the steps, and Prince Andrei nodded to one of his servants, who was standing by with a sledgehammer. Grigori noticed for the first time that the three condemned men were standing on a crudely hinged wooden platform supported only by a single prop, and he realized with terror that the sledgehammer was to knock away the prop.

Now, he thought, this is when an angel should appear.

The villagers moaned. The wives began to scream, and this time the soldiers did not stop them. Little Lev was hysterical. He probably did not understand what was about to happen, Grigori thought, but he was scared by their mother's shrieks.

Pa showed no emotion. His face was stony. He looked into the distance and awaited his fate. Grigori wanted to be that strong. He struggled to maintain his self-control, even though he needed to howl like Lev. He could not hold back the tears, but he bit his lip and remained as silent as his father.

The servant hefted his sledgehammer, touched it to the prop to get his range, swung backward, and struck. The prop flew through the air. The hinged platform came down with a bang. The three men dropped, then jerked, their fall arrested by the ropes around their necks.

Grigori was unable to look away. He stared at his father. Pa did not die instantly. He opened his mouth, trying to breathe, or to shout, but could not do either. His face turned red and he struggled with the ropes that bound him. It seemed to go on for a long time. His face became redder.

Then his skin turned a bluish color and his movements became weaker. At last he was still.

Ma stopped screaming and began to sob.

The priest prayed aloud, but the villagers ignored him and, one by one, they turned away from the sight of the three dead men.

The prince and the princess got back into their carriage, and after a moment, the coachman cracked his whip and drove away.

{ VI }

Grigori was calm again by the time he finished telling the story. He dragged his sleeve across his face to dry his tears, then turned his attention back to Katerina. She had listened to him in compassionate silence, but she was not shocked. She must have seen similar sights herself: hanging, flogging, and mutilation were normal punishments in the villages.

Grigori put the bowl of warm water on the table and found a clean towel. Katerina tilted her head back, and Grigori hung the kerosene lamp from a hook on the wall so that he could see better.

There was a cut on her forehead and a bruise on her cheek, and her lips were puffy. Even so, staring at her close up took Grigori's breath away. She looked back at him with a candid, fearless gaze that he found enchanting.

He dipped a corner of the towel in warm water.

"Be gentle," she said.

"Of course." He began by wiping her forehead. Her injury there was only a graze, he saw when he had dabbed away the blood.

"That feels better," she said.

She watched his face while he worked. He washed her cheeks and her throat, then said: "I've left the painful part until last."

"It will be all right," she said. "You have such a light touch." All the same, she winced when his towel touched her swollen lips.

"Sorry," he said.

"Keep going."

The abrasions were already healing, he saw as he cleaned them. She had the even white teeth of a young girl. He wiped the corners of her wide mouth. As he bent closer, he could feel her warm breath on his face.

When he had finished he felt a sense of disappointment, as if he had been waiting for something that had not happened.

He sat back and rinsed the towel in the water, which was now dark with her blood.

"Thank you," she said. "You have very good hands."

His heart was racing. He had bathed people's wounds before, but he had never experienced this dizzy sensation. He felt he might be about to do something foolish.

He opened the window and emptied the bowl, making a pink splash on the snow in the yard.

The mad thought crossed his mind that Katerina might be a dream. He turned, half expecting her chair to be empty. But there she was, looking back at him with those blue-green eyes, and he realized he wanted her never to go away.

It occurred to him that he might be in love.

He had never thought that before. He was usually too busy looking after Lev to chase women. He was not a virgin: he had had sex with three different women. It had always been a joyless experience, perhaps because he had not much cared for any of them.

But now, he thought shakily, he wanted, more than anything else in the world, to lie down with Katerina on the narrow bed against the wall and kiss her hurt face and tell her—

And tell her that he loved her.

Don't be stupid, he said to himself. You met her an hour ago. What she wants from you is not love, but a loan and a job and a place to sleep.

He closed the window with a slam.

She said: "So you cook for your brother, and you have gentle hands, and yet you can knock a policeman to the ground with one punch."

He did not know what to say.

"You told me how your father died," she went on. "But your mother died, too, when you were young—didn't she?"

"How did you know?"

Katerina shrugged. "Because you had to become a mother."

{ VII }

She died on January 9, 1905, by the old Russian calendar. It was a Sunday, and in the days and years that followed it came to be known as Bloody Sunday.

Grigori was sixteen and Lev eleven. Like Ma, both boys worked at the Putilov factory. Grigori was an apprentice foundryman, Lev a sweep. That January all three of them were on strike, along with more than a hundred thousand other St. Petersburg factory workers, for an eight-hour day and the right to form trade unions. On the morning of the ninth they put on their best clothes and went out, holding hands and tramping through a fresh fall of snow, to a church near the Putilov factory. After the service they joined the thousands of workers marching from all points of the city toward the Winter Palace.

"Why do we have to march?" young Lev whined. He would have preferred to play soccer in an alleyway.

"Because of your father," said Ma. "Because princes and princesses are murdering brutes. Because we have to overthrow the tsar and all his kind. Because I will not rest until Russia is a republic."

It was a perfect St. Petersburg day, cold but dry, and Grigori's face was warmed by the sun just as his heart was warmed by the feeling of comradeship in a just cause.

Their leader, Father Gapon, was like an Old Testament prophet, with his long beard, his biblical language, and the light of glory in his eye. He was no revolutionary: his self-help clubs, approved by the government, started all meetings with the Lord's Prayer and ended with the national anthem. "I can see now what the tsar intended Gapon to be," Grigori said to Katerina nine years later, in his room overlooking the railway line. "A safety valve, designed to take the pressure for reform and release it harmlessly in tea drinking and country dancing. But it didn't work."

Wearing a long white robe and carrying a crucifix, Gapon led the procession along the Narva highway. Grigori, Lev, and Ma were right beside him: he encouraged families to march at the front, saying that the soldiers would never fire on infants. Behind them two neighbors carried a large portrait of the tsar. Gapon told them that the tsar was the father of his people. He would listen to their cries, overrule his hard-hearted ministers, and grant the workers' reasonable demands. "The Lord Jesus said: 'Suffer the little children to come unto me,' and the tsar says the same," Gapon cried, and Grigori believed him.

They had approached the Narva Gate, a massive triumphal arch, and Grigori remembered looking up at the statue of a chariot with six gigantic horses; then a squadron of cavalry charged the marchers, almost as if the copper horses atop the monument had come thunderously alive.

Some demonstrators fled; some fell to the hammer blows of the hooves. Grigori froze in place, terrified, as did Ma and Lev.

The soldiers did not draw weapons, and seemed intent simply on scaring people away; but there were too many workers, and a few minutes later the cavalry wheeled their horses and rode off.

The march resumed in a different spirit. Grigori sensed that the day might not end peacefully. He thought about the forces ranged against them: the nobility, the ministers, and the army. How far would they go to keep the people from speaking to their tsar?

His answer came almost immediately. Looking over the heads in front of him he saw a line of infantry and realized, with a shudder of dread, that they were in firing position.

The march slowed as people comprehended what they faced. Father Gapon, who was within touching distance of Grigori, turned and shouted to his followers: "The tsar will never allow his armies to shoot at his beloved people!"

There was a deafening rattle, like a hailstorm on a tin roof: the soldiers had fired a salvo. The acrid smell of gunpowder stung Grigori's nostrils, and fear clutched at his heart.

The priest shouted: "Don't worry—they're firing into the air!"

Another volley rang out, but no bullets seemed to land. All the same, Grigori's bowels clenched in terror.

Then there was a third salvo, and this time the bullets did not fly harmlessly up. Grigori heard screams and saw people fall. He stared around in confusion for a moment; then Ma shoved him violently, shouting: "Lie down!" He fell flat. At the same time Ma threw Lev to the ground and dropped on top of him.

We're going to die, Grigori thought, and his heart thudded louder than the guns.

The shooting continued relentlessly, a nightmare noise that could not be shut out. As people fled in panic, Grigori was trodden on by heavy boots, but Ma protected his head and Lev's. They lay there trembling while the shooting and screaming went on above them.

Then the firing stopped. Ma moved, and Grigori raised his head to look around. People were hurrying away in all directions, shouting to one another, but the screaming died down. "Get up, come on," said Ma, and they scrambled to their feet and hurried away from the road, jumping over still bodies and running around the bleeding wounded. They reached a side street and slowed down. Lev whispered to Grigori: "I've wet myself! Don't tell Ma!"

Ma's blood was up. "We WILL speak to the tsar!" she cried, and people stopped to look at her broad peasant face and intense gaze. She was deep-chested, and her voice boomed out across the street. "They cannot prevent us—we must go to the Winter Palace!" Some people cheered, and others nodded agreement. Lev started to cry.

Listening to the story, nine years later, Katerina said: "Why did she do that? She should have taken her children home to safety!"

"She used to say she did not want her sons to live as she had," Grigori replied. "I think she felt it would be better for us all to die than to give up the hope of a better life."

Katerina looked thoughtful. "I suppose that's brave."

"It's more than bravery," Grigori said stoutly. "It's heroism."

"What happened next?"

They had walked into the city center, along with thousands of others. As the sun rose higher over the snowy city, Grigori unbuttoned his coat and unwound his scarf. It was a long walk for Lev's short legs, but the boy was too shocked and scared to complain.

At last they reached Nevsky Prospekt, the broad boulevard that ran through the heart of the city. It was already thronged with people. Streetcars and omnibuses drove up and down, and horse cabs dashed dangerously in all directions—in those days, Grigori recalled, there had been no motor taxis.

They ran into Konstantin, a lathe operator from the Putilov works. He told Ma, ominously, that demonstrators had been killed in other parts of the city. But she did not break her pace, and the rest of the crowd seemed equally resolute. They moved steadily past shops selling German pianos, hats made in Paris, and special silver bowls to hold hothouse roses. In the jewelry stores there a nobleman could spend more on a bauble for his mistress than a factory worker would earn in a lifetime, Grigori had been told. They passed the Soleil Cinema, which Grigori longed to visit. Vendors were doing good business, selling tea from samovars and colored balloons for children.

At the end of the street they came to three great St. Petersburg landmarks standing side by side on the bank of the frozen Neva River: the equestrian statue of Peter the Great, always called *The Bronze Horseman*; the Admiralty building with its spire; and the Winter Palace. When he had first seen the palace, at the age of twelve, he had refused to believe that such a large building could be a place for people to actually live. It seemed inconceivable, like something in a story, a magic sword or a cloak of invisibility.

The square in front of the palace was white with snow. On the far side, ranged in front of the dark red building, were cavalry, riflemen in long coats, and cannon. The crowds massed around the edges of the square, keeping their distance, fearful of the military; but newcomers kept pouring in from the surrounding streets, like the waters of the tributaries emptying into the Neva, and Grigori was constantly pushed forward. Not all those present were workers, Grigori noted with surprise: many wore the warm coats of the middle classes on their way home from church, some looked like students, and a few even wore school uniforms.

Ma prudently moved them away from the guns and into the Alexandrovskii Garden, a park in front of the long yellow-and-white

Admiralty building. Other people had the same idea, and the crowd there became animated. The man who normally gave deer sled rides to middle-class children had gone home. Everyone there was talking of massacres: all over the city, marchers had been mown down by gunfire and hacked to death by Cossack sabres. Grigori spoke to a boy his own age and told him what had happened at the Narva Gate. As the demonstrators learned what had happened to others, they grew angrier.

Grigori stared up at the long façade of the Winter Palace, with its hundreds of windows. Where was the tsar?

"He was not at the Winter Palace that morning, as we found out later," Grigori told Katerina, and he could hear in his own voice the bitter resentment of a disappointed believer. "He was not even in town. The father of his people had gone to his palace at Tsarskoye Selo, to spend the weekend taking country walks and playing dominoes. But we did not know that then, and we called to him, begging him to show himself to his loyal subjects."

The crowd grew; the calls for the tsar became more insistent; some of the demonstrators started to jeer at the soldiers. Everyone was becoming tense and angry. Suddenly a detachment of guards charged into the gardens, ordering everyone out. Grigori watched, fearful and incredulous, as they lashed out indiscriminately with whips, some using the flat sides of their sabres. He looked at Ma for guidance. She said: "We can't give up now!" Grigori did not know what, exactly, they all expected the tsar to do: he just felt sure, as everyone did, that their monarch would somehow redress their grievances if only he knew about them.

The other demonstrators were as resolute as Ma and, although those who were attacked by guards cowered away, no one left the area.

Then the soldiers took up firing positions.

Near the front, several people fell to their knees, took off their caps, and crossed themselves. "Kneel down!" said Ma, and the three of them knelt, as did more of the people around them, until most of the crowd had assumed the position of prayer.

A silence descended that made Grigori scared. He stared at the rifles pointed at him, and the riflemen stared back expressionlessly, like statues.

Then Grigori heard a bugle call.

It was a signal. The soldiers fired their weapons. All around Grigori, people screamed and fell. A boy who had climbed a statue for a better view cried out and tumbled to the ground. A child fell out of a tree like a shot bird.

Grigori saw Ma go facedown. Thinking she was avoiding the gunfire, he did the same. Then, looking at her as they both lay on the ground, he saw the blood, bright red on the snow around her head.

"No!" he shouted. "No!"

Lev screamed.

Grigori grabbed Ma's shoulders and pulled her up. Her body was limp. He stared at her face. At first he was bewildered by the sight that met his eyes. What was he seeing? Where her forehead and her eyes should have been there was just a mass of unrecognizable pulp.

It was Lev who grasped the truth. "She's dead!" he screamed. "Ma's dead. My mother is dead!"

The firing stopped. All around, people were running, limping, or crawling away. Grigori tried to think. What should he do? He must take Ma away from here, he decided. He put his arms under her and picked her up. She was not light, but he was strong.

He turned around, looking for the way home. His vision was strangely blurred, and he realized he was weeping. "Come on," he said to Lev. "Stop screaming. We have to go."

At the edge of the square they were stopped by an old man, the skin of his face creased around watery eyes. He wore the blue tunic of a factory worker. "You're young," he said to Grigori. There was anguish and rage in his voice. "Never forget this," he said. "Never forget the murders committed here today by the tsar."

Grigori nodded. "I won't forget, sir," he said.

"May you live long," said the old man. "Long enough to take revenge on the bloodstained tsar for the evil he has done this day."

{ VIII }

"I carried her for about a mile. Then I got tired, so I boarded a streetcar, still holding her," Grigori told Katerina.

She stared at him. Her beautiful, bruised face was pale with horror. "You carried your dead mother home on a streetcar?"

He shrugged. "At the time I had no idea I was doing anything strange. Or, rather, everything that happened that day was so strange that nothing I did seemed odd."

"What about the people riding the car?"

"The conductor said nothing. I suppose he was too shocked to throw me off, and he didn't ask me for the fare—which I would not have been able to pay, of course."

"So you just sat down?"

"I sat there, with her body in my arms, and Lev beside me, crying. The passengers just stared at us. I didn't care what they thought. I was concentrating on what I had to do, which was to get her home."

"And so you became the head of your family, at the age of sixteen."

Grigori nodded. Although the memories were painful, he felt the most intense pleasure from her concentrated attention. Her eyes were fixed on him, and she listened with her mouth open and a look on her lovely face of mingled fascination and horror.

"What I remember most about that time is that no one helped us," he said, and he was revisited by the panicky feeling that he was alone in a hostile world. The memory never failed to fill his soul with rage. It's over now, he told himself; I've got a home and a job, and my brother has grown up strong and handsome. The bad times are over. But nevertheless he wanted to take someone by the neck—a soldier, a policeman, a government minister, or the tsar himself—and squeeze until there was no life left. He closed his eyes, shuddering, until the feeling passed.

"As soon as the funeral was over, the landlord threw us out, saying we would not be able to pay; and he took our furniture—for back rent, he said, although Ma was never behind with payments. I went to the church and told the priest we had nowhere to sleep."

Katerina laughed harshly. "I can guess what happened there."

He was surprised. "Can you?"

"The priest offered you a bed—his bed. That's what happened to me."

"Something like that," Grigori said. "He gave me a few kopeks and sent me to buy hot potatoes. The shop wasn't where he said, but instead of searching for it I hurried back to the church, because I didn't like the look of him. Sure enough, when I went into the vestry he was taking Lev's trousers down."

She nodded. "Priests have been doing that sort of thing to me since I was twelve."

Grigori was shocked. He had assumed that that particular priest was uniquely evil. Katerina obviously believed that depravity was the norm. "Are they all like that?" he said angrily.

"Most of them, in my experience."

He shook his head in disgust. "And you know what amazed me the most? When I caught him, he wasn't even ashamed! He just looked annoyed, as if I had interrupted him while he was meditating on the Bible."

"What did you do?"

"I told Lev to do up his trousers, and we left. The priest asked for his kopeks back, but I told him they were alms for the poor. I used them to pay for a bed in a lodging house that night."

"And then?"

"Eventually I got a good enough job, by lying about my age, and I found a room, and I learned, day by day, how to be independent."

"And now you're happy?"

"Certainly not. My mother intended us to have a better life, and I'm going to make sure of it. We're leaving Russia. I've saved up almost enough money. I'm going to America, and when I get there I'll send money back for a ticket for Lev. They have no tsar in America—no emperor or king of any kind. The army can't just shoot anyone they like. The people rule the country!"

She was skeptical. "Do you really believe that?"

"It's true!"

There was a tap at the window. Katerina was startled—they were on the second floor—but Grigori knew it was Lev. Late at night, when the door of the house was locked, Lev had to cross the railway line to the backyard, climb onto the washhouse roof, and come in through the window.

Grigori opened up and Lev climbed in. He was dressed smartly, in a jacket with mother-of-pearl buttons and a cap with a velvet band. His waistcoat sported a brass watch chain. His hair was cut in the fashionable "Polish" style with a parting at the side, instead of down the middle as the peasants wore it. Katerina looked surprised, and Grigori guessed she had not expected his brother to be so dashing.

Normally Grigori was pleased to see Lev, and relieved if he was sober and in one piece. Now he wished he could have had longer alone with Katerina.

He introduced them, and Lev's eyes gleamed with interest as he shook her hand. She wiped tears from her cheeks. "Grigori was telling me about the death of your mother," she explained.

"He has been mother and father to me for nine years," Lev said. He tilted his head and sniffed the air. "And he makes good stew."

Grigori got out bowls and spoons, and put a loaf of black bread on the table. Katerina explained to Lev about the fight with the policeman Pinsky. The way she told the story made Grigori seem braver than he felt, but he was happy to be a hero in her eyes.

Lev was enchanted by Katerina. He leaned forward, listening as if he had never heard anything so fascinating, smiling and nodding, looking amazed or disgusted, according to what she was saying.

Grigori spooned the stew into bowls and pulled the packing case up to the table for use as a third chair. The food was good: he had added an onion to the pot, and the ham bone gave a hint of meaty richness to the turnips. The atmosphere lightened as Lev talked of inconsequential matters, odd incidents at the factory and funny things people said. He kept Katerina laughing.

When they had finished, Lev asked Katerina how she came to be in the city.

"My father died and my mother remarried," she said. "Unfortunately, my stepfather seemed to like me better than my mother." She tossed her head, and Grigori could not tell whether she was ashamed or defiant. "At any rate, that's what my mother believed, and she threw me out."

Grigori said: "Half the population of St. Petersburg have come here from a village. Soon there will be no one left to till the soil."

Lev said: "What was your journey like?"

It was a familiar tale of third-class railway tickets and lifts begged on carts, but Grigori was mesmerized by her face as she talked.

Once again Lev listened with rapt attention, making amusing comments, asking the occasional question.

Soon, Grigori noticed, Katerina had turned in her seat and was talking exclusively to Lev.

Almost, Grigori thought, as if I was not even here.

CHAPTER FOUR

March 1914

"So," Billy said to his father, "all the books of the Bible were originally written in various languages and then translated into English."

"Aye," said Da. "And the Roman Catholic Church tried to ban translations—they didn't want people like us reading the Bible for ourselves and arguing with the priests."

Da was a bit un-Christian when he spoke of Catholics. He seemed to hate Catholicism more than atheism. But he loved an argument. "Well, then," said Billy, "where are the originals?"

"What originals?"

"The original books of the Bible, written in Hebrew and Greek. Where are they kept?"

They were sitting on opposite sides of the square table in the kitchen of the house in Wellington Row. It was midafternoon. Billy was home from the pit and had washed his hands and face, but still wore his work clothes. Da had hung up his suit jacket, and sat in his waistcoat and shirtsleeves, with a collar and tie—he would be going out again after dinner, to a union meeting. Mam was heating the stew on the fire. Gramper sat with them, listening to the discussion with a faint smile, as if he had heard it all before.

"Well, we don't have the actual originals," Da said. "They wore out, centuries ago. We have copies."

"Where are the copies, then?"

"All different places—monasteries, museums . . . "

"They should be kept in one place."

"But there's more than one copy of each book—and some are better than others."

"How can one copy be better than another? Surely they're not different."

"Yes. Over the years, human error crept in."

This startled Billy. "Well, how do we know which is right?"

"That's a study called textual scholarship—comparing the different versions and coming up with an agreed text."

Billy was shocked. "You mean there isn't an indisputable book that is the actual Word of God? Men argue about it and make a judgment?"

"Yes."

"Well, how do we know they're right?"

Da smiled knowingly, a sure sign that his back was to the wall. "We believe that if they work in prayerful humility, God will guide their labors."

"But what if they don't?"

Mam put four bowls on the table. "Don't argue with your father," she said. She cut four thick slices off a loaf of bread.

Gramper said: "Leave him be, Cara, my girl. Let the boy ask his questions."

Da said: "We have faith in God's power to ensure that His Word comes to us as He would wish."

"You're completely illogical!"

Mam interrupted again. "Don't speak to your father like that! You're still a boy—you don't know anything."

Billy ignored her. "Why didn't God guide the labors of the copiers, and stop them making mistakes, if He really wanted us to know His Word?"

Da said: "Some things are not given to us to understand."

That answer was the least convincing of all, and Billy ignored it. "If the copiers could make mistakes, obviously the textual scholars could, too."

"We must have faith, Billy."

"Faith in the Word of God, yes—not faith in a lot of professors of Greek!"

Mam sat at the table and pushed her graying hair out of her eyes. "So you are right, and everyone else is wrong, as usual, I suppose?"

This frequently used ploy always stung him, because it seemed justified. It was not possible that he was wiser than everyone else. "It's not me," he protested. "It's logic!"

"Oh, you and your old logic," said his mother. "Eat your dinner."

The door opened and Mrs. Dai Ponies walked in. This was normal in Wellington Row: only strangers knocked. Mrs. Dai wore a pinafore and a man's boots on her feet: whatever she had to say was so urgent that she had not even put on a hat before leaving her house. Visibly agitated, she brandished a sheet of paper. "I'm being thrown out!" she said. "What am I supposed to do?"

Da stood up and gave her his chair. "Sit down by here and catch your breath, Mrs. Dai Ponies," he said calmly. "Let me have a read of that letter, now." He took it from her red, knotted hand and laid it flat on the table.

Billy could see that it was typed on the letterhead of Celtic Minerals.

"'Dear Mrs. Evans,'" Da read aloud. "'The house at the above address is now required for a working miner.'" Celtic Minerals had built most of the houses in Aberowen. Over the years, some had been sold to their occupiers, including the one the Williams family lived in; but most were still rented to miners. "'In accordance with the terms of your lease, I—'" Da paused, and Billy could see he was shocked. "'I hereby give you two weeks' notice to quit!'" he finished.

Mam said: "Notice to quit—and her husband buried not six weeks ago!"

Mrs. Dai cried: "Where am I to go, with five children?"

Billy was shocked, too. How could the company do this to a woman whose husband had been killed in their pit?

"It's signed 'Perceval Jones, Chairman of the Board,' at the bottom," Da finished.

Billy said: "What lease? I didn't know miners had leases."

Da said to him: "There's no written lease, but the law says there's an implied contract. We've already fought that battle and lost." He turned to Mrs. Dai. "The house goes with the job, in theory, but widows are usually allowed to stay on. Sometimes they leave anyway, and go to live elsewhere, perhaps with their parents. Often they remarry, to another miner, and he takes over the lease. Usually they have at least one boy who becomes a miner when he's old enough. It's not really in the company's interest to throw widows out."

"So why do they want to get rid of me and my children?" wailed Mrs. Dai.

Gramper said: "Perceval Jones is in a hurry. He must think the price of coal is going up. That'll be why he started the Sunday shift."

Da nodded. "They want higher production, that's for sure, whatever the reason. But they're not going to get it by evicting widows." He stood up. "Not if I can help it."

{ II }

Eight women were being evicted, all widows of men who had died in the explosion. They had received identical letters from Perceval Jones, as Da established that afternoon when he visited each woman in turn, taking Billy with him. Their reactions varied from the hysterics of Mrs. Hywel Jones, who could not stop crying, to the grim fatalism of Mrs. Roley Hughes, who said this country needed a guillotine like they had in Paris for men like Perceval Jones.

Billy was boiling with outrage. Was it not enough that these women had lost their men to the pit? Must they be homeless as well as husbandless? "Can the company do this, Da?" he said as he and his father walked down the mean gray terraces to the pithead.

"Only if we let them, boy. The working class are more numerous than the ruling class, and stronger. They depend on us for everything. We provide their food and build their houses and make their clothes, and without us they die. They can't do *anything* unless we let them. Always remember that."

They went into the manager's office, stuffing their caps into their pockets. "Good afternoon, Mr. Williams," said Spotty Llewellyn nervously. "If you would just wait a minute, I'll ask if Mr. Morgan can see you."

"Don't be daft, boy—of course he'll see me," said Da, and without waiting he walked into the inner office. Billy followed.

Maldwyn Morgan was perusing a ledger, but Billy had a feeling he was only pretending. He looked up, his pink cheeks closely shaved as always. "Come in, Williams," he said unnecessarily. Unlike many men, he was not afraid of Da. Morgan was Aberowen-born, the son of a schoolmaster, and had studied engineering. He and Da were similar, Billy realized: intelligent, self-righteous, and stubborn.

"You know what I've come about, Mr. Morgan," said Da.

"I can guess, but tell me anyway."

"I want you to withdraw these eviction notices."

"The company needs the houses for miners."

"There will be trouble."

"Are you threatening me?"

"Don't get on your high horse," Da said mildly. "These women lost their husbands in your pit. Don't you feel responsible for them?"

Morgan tilted up his chin defensively. "The public inquiry found that the explosion was not caused by the company's negligence."

Billy wanted to ask him how an intelligent man could say such a thing and not feel ashamed of himself.

Da said: "The inquiry found a list of violations as long as the train to

Paddington—electrical equipment not shielded, no breathing apparatus, no proper fire engine—"

"But the violations did not cause the explosion, or the deaths of miners."

"The violations could not be *proved* to have caused the explosion or the deaths."

Morgan shifted uncomfortably in his chair. "You didn't come here to argue about the inquiry."

"I came here to get you to see reason. As we speak, the news of these letters is going around the town." Da gestured at the window, and Billy saw that the winter sun was going down behind the mountain. "Men are rehearsing with choirs, drinking in pubs, going to prayer meetings, playing chess—and they're all talking about the eviction of the widows. And you can bet your boots they're angry."

"I have to ask you again: are you trying to intimidate the company?"

Billy wanted to throttle the man, but Da sighed. "Look here, Maldwyn. We've known each other since school days. Be reasonable, now. You know there are men in the union who will be more aggressive than me." Da was talking about Tommy Griffiths's father. Len Griffiths believed in revolution, and he always hoped the next dispute would be the spark that lit the conflagration. He also wanted Da's job. He could be relied upon to propose drastic measures.

Morgan said: "Are you telling me you're calling a strike?"

"I'm telling you the men will be angry. What they will do I can't predict. But I don't want trouble and you don't want trouble. We're talking about eight houses out of, what, eight hundred? I've come here to ask you, is it worth it?"

"The company has made its decision," Morgan said, and Billy felt intuitively that Morgan did not agree with the company.

"Ask the board of directors to reconsider. What harm could that do?"

Billy was impatient with Da's mild words. Surely he should raise his voice, and point his finger, and accuse Morgan of the ruthless cruelty of which the company was obviously guilty? That was what Len Griffiths would have done.

Morgan was unmoved. "I'm here to carry out the board's decisions, not question them."

"So the evictions have already been approved by the board," Da said.

Morgan looked flustered. "I didn't say that."

But he had implied it, Billy thought, thanks to Da's clever questioning. Maybe mildness was not such a bad idea.

Da changed tack. "What if I could find you eight houses where the occupiers are prepared to take in new miners as lodgers?"

"These men have families."

Da said slowly and deliberately: "We *could* work out a compromise, *if* you were willing."

"The company must have the power to manage its own affairs."

"Regardless of the consequences to others?"

"This is our coal mine. The company surveyed the land, negotiated with the earl, dug the pit, and bought the machinery, and it built the houses for the miners to live in. We paid for all this and we own it, and we won't be told what to do with it by anyone else."

Da put his cap on. "You didn't put the coal in the earth, though, did you, Maldwyn?" he said. "God did that."

{ III }

Da tried to book the assembly rooms of the town hall for a gathering at seven thirty the following night, but the space was already taken by the Aberowen Amateur Dramatic Club, who were rehearsing *Henry IV, Part One,* so Da decided the miners would meet at Bethesda Chapel. Billy and Da, with Len and Tommy Griffiths and a few other active union members, went around the town announcing the meeting orally and pinning up handwritten notices in pubs and chapels.

By a quarter past seven the next evening, the chapel was packed. The widows sat in a row at the front, and everyone else stood. Billy was at the side near the front, where he could see the men's faces. Tommy Griffiths stood beside him.

Billy was proud of his da for his boldness, his cleverness, and the fact that he had put his cap back on before leaving Morgan's office. All the same he wished Da had been more aggressive. He should have talked to Morgan the way he talked to the congregation of Bethesda, predicting hellfire and brimstone for those who refused to see the plain truth.

At exactly seven thirty, Da called for quiet. In his authoritative preaching voice he read out the letter from Perceval Jones to Mrs. Dai Ponies. "The identical letter have been sent to eight widows of men killed in the explosion down the pit six weeks ago."

Several men called out: "Shame!"

"It is our rule that men speak when called upon by the chairman of the meeting, and not otherwise, so that each may be heard in his turn, and I will thank you for observing the rule, even on an occasion such as this when feelings run high."

Someone called out: "It's a bloody disgrace!"

"Now, now, Griff Pritchard, no swearing, please. This is a chapel and, besides, there are ladies present."

Two or three of the men said: "Hear, hear." They pronounced the word to rhyme with "fur."

Griff Pritchard, who had been in the Two Crowns since the shift ended that afternoon, said: "Sorry, Mr. Williams."

"I held a meeting yesterday with the colliery manager, and asked him formally to withdraw the eviction notices, but he refused. He implied that the board of directors had made the decision, and it was not in his power to change it, or even question it. I pressed him to discuss alternatives, but he said the company had the right to manage its affairs without interference. That is all the information I have for you." That was a bit low-key, Billy thought. He wanted Da to call for revolution. But Da just pointed to a man who had his hand up. "John Jones the Shop."

"I've lived in number twenty-three Gordon Terrace all my life," said Jones. "I was born there and I'm still there. But my father died when I was eleven. Very hard it was, too, for my mam, but she was allowed to stay. When I was thirteen I went down the pit, and now I pay the rent. That's how it's always been. No one said anything about throwing us out."

"Thank you, John Jones. Have you got a motion to propose?"

"No, I'm just saying."

"I have a motion," said a new voice. "Strike!"

There was a chorus of agreement.

Billy's father said: "Dai Crybaby."

"Here's how I see it," said the captain of the town's rugby team. "We can't let the company get away with this. If they're allowed to evict widows, none of us can feel that our families have any security. A man could work all his life for Celtic Minerals and die on the job, and two weeks later his family could be out on the street. Dai Union have been to the office and tried to talk sense to Gone-to-Merthyr Morgan, but it haven't done no good, so we got no alternative but to strike."

"Thank you, Dai," said Da. "Should I take that as a formal motion for strike action?"

"Aye."

Billy was surprised that Da had accepted that so quickly. He knew his father wanted to avoid a strike.

"Vote!" someone shouted.

Da said: "Before I put the proposal to a vote, we need to decide when the strike should take place."

Ah, Billy thought, he's not accepting it.

Da went on: "We might consider starting on Monday. Between now and then, while we work on, the threat of a strike might make the directors see sense—and we could get what we want without any loss of earnings."

Da was arguing for postponement as the next best thing, Billy realized.

But Len Griffiths had come to the same conclusion. "May I speak, Mr. Chairman?" he said. Tommy's father had a bald dome with a fringe of black hair, and a black mustache. He stepped forward and stood next to Da, facing the crowd, so that it looked as if the two of them had equal authority. The men went quiet. Len, like Da and Dai Crybaby, was among a handful of people they always heard in respectful silence. "I ask, is it wise to give the company four days' grace? Suppose they don't change their minds—which seems a strong possibility, given how stubborn they have been so far. Then we'll get to Monday with nothing achieved, and the widows will have that much less time left." He raised his voice slightly for rhetorical effect. "I say, comrades: don't give an inch!"

There was a cheer, and Billy joined in.

"Thank you, Len," said Da. "I have two motions on the table, then: Strike tomorrow, or strike Monday. Who else would like to speak?"

Billy watched his father manage the meeting. The next man called was Giuseppe "Joey" Ponti, top soloist with the Aberowen Male Voice Choir, older brother of Billy's schoolmate Johnny. Despite his Italian name, he had been born in Aberowen and spoke with the same accent as every other man in the room. He, too, argued for an immediate strike.

Da then said: "In fairness, may I have a speaker in favor of striking on Monday?"

Billy wondered why Da did not throw his personal authority into the balance. If he argued for Monday he might change their minds. But then, if he failed, he would be in an awkward position, leading a strike that he had argued against. Da was not completely free to say what he felt, Billy realized.

The discussion ranged widely. Coal stocks were high, so the management could hold out; but demand was high, too, and they would want to sell while they could. Spring was coming, so miners' families would soon be able to manage without their ration of free coal. The miners' case was well grounded in long-established practice, but the letter of the law was on the management's side.

Da let the discussion run on, and some of the speeches became tedious. Billy wondered what his father's motivation was, and guessed he was hoping that heads would cool. But in the end he had to put it to the vote.

"First, all those in favor of no strike at all."

A few men raised their hands.

"Next, those in favor of a strike starting Monday."

There was a strong vote for this, but Billy was not sure if it was enough to win. It would depend upon how many men abstained.

"Finally, those in favor of a strike starting tomorrow."

There was a cheer, and a forest of arms waved in the air. There could be no doubt about the result.

"The motion to strike tomorrow is passed," Da said. No one proposed a count.

The meeting broke up. As they went out, Tommy said brightly: "Day off, tomorrow, then."

"Aye," said Billy. "And no money to spend."

{ IV }

The first time Fitz went with a prostitute, he had tried to kiss her—not because he wanted to, but he assumed it was the done thing. "I don't kiss," she had said abruptly in her Cockney accent, and after that he had never tried it again. Bing Westhampton said a lot of prostitutes refused to kiss, which was odd, considering what other intimacies they permitted. Perhaps that trivial prohibition preserved a remnant of their dignity.

Girls of Fitz's social class were not supposed to kiss anyone before marriage. They did, of course, but only in rare moments of brief privacy, in a suddenly deserted side room at a ball, or behind a rhododendron bush in a country garden. There was never time for passion to develop.

The only woman Fitz had kissed properly was his wife, Bea. She gave him her body as a cook might present a special cake, fragrant and sugared and beautifully decorated for his enjoyment. She let him do anything, but made no demands. She offered her lips for him to kiss, and opened her mouth to his tongue, but he never felt she was hungry for his touch.

Ethel kissed as if she had one minute left to live.

They stood in the Gardenia Suite, beside the bed covered with its dust sheet, wrapped in each other's arms. She sucked his tongue and bit his lips and licked his throat, and at the same time she stroked his hair, clutched the back of his neck, and thrust her hands under his waistcoat so that she could rub her palms against his chest. When at last they broke apart, out of breath, she put her hands on either side of his face, holding his head still, staring at him, and said: "You are so beautiful."

He sat on the edge of the bed, holding her hands, and she stood in front of him. He knew that some men regularly seduced their servants, but he did not. When he was fifteen he had fallen in love with a parlor maid at the London house: his mother had guessed it within a few days and sacked the girl immediately. His father had smiled and said: "Good choice, though." Since then he had not touched an employee. But he could not resist Ethel.

She said: "Why have you come back? You were expected to stay in London all of May."

"I wanted to see you." He could tell that she found it hard to believe him. "I kept thinking about you, all day, every day, and I just had to come back."

She bent down and kissed him again. Holding the kiss, he slowly fell back on the bed, pulling her with him until she was lying on top of him. She was so slim that she weighed no more than a child. Her hair escaped from its pins and he buried his fingers in her glossy curls.

After a while she rolled off and lay beside him, panting. He leaned on his elbow and looked at her. She had said he was beautiful, but right now she was the prettiest thing he had ever seen. Her cheeks were flushed, her hair was mussed, and her red lips were moist and parted. Her dark eyes gazed at him with adoration.

He put his hand on her hip, then stroked her thigh. She covered his hand with her own, holding it still, as if afraid he was going too far. She said: "Why do they call you Fitz? Your name is Edward, isn't it?"

She was talking in an attempt to let their passion cool, he felt sure. "It started at school," he said. "All the boys had nicknames. Then Walter von Ulrich came home with me one vacation, and Maud picked it up from him."

"Before that, what did your parents call you?"

"Teddy."

"Teddy," she said, trying it on her tongue. "I like it better than Fitz."

He started to stroke her thigh again, and this time she let him. Kissing her, he slowly pulled up the long skirt of her black housekeeper's dress. She wore calf-length stockings, and he stroked her bare knees. Above the knee she had long cotton underdrawers. He touched her legs through the cotton, then moved his hand to the fork of her thighs. When he touched her there, she groaned and thrust upward against his hand.

"Take them off," he whispered.

"No!"

He found the drawstring at the waist. It was tied in a bow. He undid the knot with a tug.

She put her hand over his again. "Stop."

"I just want to touch you there."

"I want it more than you do," she said. "But, no."

He knelt up on the bed. "We won't do anything you don't want," he said. "I promise." Then he took the waist of her drawers in both hands and ripped the material apart. She gasped with shock, but she did not protest. He lay down again and explored her with his hand. She parted her legs immediately. Her eyes were closed and she was breathing hard, as if she had been running. He guessed that no one had done this to her before, and a faint voice told him he should not take advantage of her innocence, but he was too far gone in desire to listen.

He unbuttoned his trousers and lay on top of her.

"No," she said.

"Please."

"What if I fall for a baby?"

"I'll withdraw before the end."

"Promise?"

"I promise," he said, and he slid inside her.

He felt an obstruction. She was a virgin. His conscience spoke again, and this time its voice was not so faint. He stopped. But now it was she who was too far gone. She grasped his hips and pulled him into her, raising herself slightly at the same time. He felt something break, and she gave a sharp cry of pain; then the obstruction was gone. As he moved in and out, she matched his rhythm eagerly. She opened her eyes and looked at his face. "Oh, Teddy, Teddy," she said, and he saw that she loved him. The thought moved him almost to tears, and at the same time excited him beyond control, and his climax came unexpectedly soon. In desperate haste he withdrew, and spilled his seed on her thigh with a groan of passion mingled with disappointment. She put her hand behind his head and pulled his face to hers, kissing him wildly; then she closed her eyes and gave a small cry that sounded like surprise and pleasure; and then it was over.

I hope I pulled out in time, he thought.

{ V }

Ethel went about her work as usual, but all the time she felt as if she had a secret diamond in her pocket that she could touch from time to time, feeling its slick surfaces and its sharp edges when no one was looking.

In her more sober moments she worried about what this love meant and where it was going, and now and again she was horrified by the thought of what her God-fearing socialist father would think if he found out. But most of the time she just felt as if she was dropping through the air with no way to arrest her fall. She loved the way he walked, the way he smelled, his clothes, his careful good manners, his air of authority. She also loved the way he occasionally looked bewildered. And when he came out of his wife's room with that hurt look on his face, she could cry. She was in love and out of control.

Most days she spoke to him at least once, and they usually managed a few moments alone and a long, yearning kiss. Just kissing him made her wet, and she sometimes had to wash her drawers in the middle of the day. He took other liberties, too, whenever there was a chance, touching her body all over, which made her more excited. Twice more they had been able to meet in the Gardenia Suite and lie on the bed.

One thing puzzled Ethel: both times they had lain together, Fitz had bitten her, quite hard, once on her inner thigh and once on her breast. It had caused her to give a cry of pain, hastily muffled. The cry seemed to inflame him more. And, although it hurt, at the same time she, too, was aroused by the bite, or at least by the thought that his desire for her was so overwhelming that he was driven to express it that way. She had no idea whether this was normal, and no one she could ask.

But her main worry was that one day Fitz would fail to withdraw at the crucial moment. The tension was so high that it was almost a relief when he and Princess Bea had to go back to London.

Before he went she persuaded him to feed the children of the striking miners. "Not the parents, because you can't be seen to take sides," she said. "Just the little boys and girls. The strike has been on for two weeks now, and they're on starvation rations. It wouldn't cost you much. There would be about five hundred of them, I'd guess. They'd love you for it, Teddy."

"We could put up a marquee on the lawn," he said, lying on the bed in the Gardenia Suite with his trousers unbuttoned and his head in her lap.

"And we can make the food here in the kitchens," Ethel said enthusiastically. "A stew with meat and potatoes in it, and all the bread they can eat."

"And a suet pudding with currants in it, eh?"

Did he love her? she wondered. At that moment, she felt he would have done anything she asked: given her jewels, taken her to Paris, bought her parents a nice house. She did not want any of those things— but what *did* she want? She did not know, and she refused to let her happiness be blighted by unanswerable questions about the future.

A few days later she stood on the East Lawn at midday on a Saturday, watching the children of Aberowen tuck into their first free dinner. Fitz did not know that this was better food than they got when their fathers were working. Suet pudding with currants, indeed! The parents were not allowed in, but most of the mothers stood outside the gates, watching their lucky offspring. Glancing that way, she saw someone waving at her, and she walked down the drive.

The group at the gate was mostly women: men did not look after children, even during a strike. They gathered around Ethel, looking agitated.

"What's happened?" she said.

Mrs. Dai Ponies answered her. "Everyone have been evicted!"

"Everyone?" Ethel said, not understanding. "Who?"

"All the miners who rent their houses from Celtic Minerals."

"Good grief!" Ethel was horrified. "God save us all." Shock was followed by puzzlement. "But why? How does that help the company? They'll have no miners left."

"These men," said Mrs. Dai. "Once they get into a fight, all they care about is winning. They won't give in, whatever the cost. They're all the same. Not that I wouldn't have my Dai back, if I could."

"This is awful." How could the company find enough blacklegs to keep the pit going? she wondered. If they closed the mine, the town would die. There would be no customers left for the shops, no children to go to the schools, no patients for the doctors . . . Her father, too, would have no work. No one had expected Perceval Jones to be so obstinate.

Mrs. Dai said: "I wonder what the king would say, if he knew."

Ethel wondered, too. The king had seemed to show real compassion. But he probably did not know the widows had been evicted.

And then she was struck by a thought. "Perhaps you should tell him," she said.

Mrs. Dai laughed. "I will, next time I sees him."

"You could write him a letter."

"Don't talk daft, now, Eth."

"I mean it. You should do it." She looked around the group. "A letter signed by widows the king visited, telling him you are being thrown out of your homes and the town is on strike. He'd have to take notice, surely?"

Mrs. Dai looked scared. "I wouldn't like to get into trouble."

Mrs. Minnie Ponti, a thin blond woman of strong opinions, said to her: "You have no husband and no home and nowhere to go—how much more trouble could you be in?"

"That's true enough. But I wouldn't know what to say. Do you put 'Dear King,' or 'Dear George the Fifth,' or what?"

Ethel said: "You put: 'Sir, with my humble duty.' I know all that rubbish, from working here. Let's do it now. Come into the servants' hall."

"Will it be all right?"

"I'm the housekeeper now, Mrs. Dai. I'm the one who says what's all right."

The women followed her up the drive and around the back of the house to the kitchen. They sat around the servants' dining table, and the cook made a pot of tea. Ethel had a stock of plain writing paper that she used for correspondence with tradesmen.

"'Sir, with our humble duty,'" she said, writing. "What next?"

Mrs. Dai Ponies said: "'Forgive our cheek in writing to Your Majesty.'"

"No," Ethel said decisively. "Don't apologize. He's our king—we're entitled to petition him. Let's say: 'We are the widows Your Majesty visited in Aberowen after the pit explosion.'"

"Very good," said Mrs. Ponti.

Ethel went on: "'We were honored by your visit and comforted by your kind condolences, and the gracious sympathy of Her Majesty the queen.'"

Mrs. Dai said: "You've got the gift for this, like your father."

Mrs. Ponti said: "That's enough soft soap, though."

"All right. Now then. 'We are asking for your help as our king. Because our husbands are dead, we are being evicted from our homes.'"

"By Celtic Minerals," put in Mrs. Ponti.

"'By Celtic Minerals. The whole pit have gone on strike for us but now they are being evicted, too.'"

"Don't make it too long," said Mrs. Dai. "He might be too busy to read it."

"All right, then. Let's finish with: 'Is this the kind of thing that should be allowed in your kingdom?'"

Mrs. Ponti said: "It's a bit tame."

"No, it's good," said Mrs. Dai. "It appeals to his sense of right and wrong."

Ethel said: "'We have the honor to be, sir, Your Majesty's most humble and obedient servants.'"

"Do we have to have that?" said Mrs. Ponti. "I'm not a servant. No offense, Ethel."

"It's the normal thing. The earl puts it when he writes a letter to *The Times*."

"All right, then."

Ethel passed the letter around the table. "Put your addresses next to your signatures."

Mrs. Ponti said: "My writing's awful. You sign my name."

Ethel was about to protest; then it occurred to her that Mrs. Ponti might be illiterate, so she did not argue, but simply wrote: "Mrs. Minnie Ponti, 19 Wellington Row."

She addressed the envelope:

> *His Majesty the King*
> *Buckingham Palace*
> *London*

She sealed the letter and stuck on a stamp. "There we are, then," she said. The women gave her a round of applause.

She posted the letter the same day.

No reply was ever received.

{ VI }

The last Saturday in March was a gray day in South Wales. Low clouds hid the mountaintops and a tireless drizzle fell on Aberowen. Ethel and most of the servants at Tŷ Gwyn left their posts—the earl and princess were away in London—and walked into town.

Policemen had been sent from London to enforce the evictions, and they stood on every street, their heavy raincoats dripping. The Widows' Strike was national news, and reporters from Cardiff and London had come up on the first morning train, smoking cigarettes and writing in notebooks. There was even a big camera on a tripod.

Ethel stood with her family outside their house and watched. Da was employed by the union, not by Celtic Minerals, and he owned their house; but most of their neighbors were being thrown out. During the course of the morning, they brought their possessions out onto the streets: beds, tables and chairs, cooking pots and chamber pots, a framed picture, a clock, an orange box of crockery and cutlery, a few clothes wrapped in newspaper and tied with string. A small pile of near-worthless goods stood like a sacrificial offering outside each door.

Da's face was a mask of suppressed rage. Billy looked as if he wanted to have a fight with someone. Gramper kept shaking his head and saying: "I never seen the like, not in all my seventy years." Mam just looked grim.

Ethel cried and could not stop.

Some of the miners had got other jobs, but it was not easy: a miner could not adapt readily to the work of a shop assistant or a bus conductor, and employers knew this and turned them away when they saw the coal dust under their fingernails. Half a dozen had become merchant sailors, signing on as stokers and getting a pay advance to give to their wives before they left. A few were going to Cardiff or Swansea, hoping for jobs in the steelworks. Many were moving in with relatives in neighboring towns. The rest were simply crowding into another Aberowen house with a non-mining family until the strike was settled.

"The king never replied to the widows' letter," Ethel said to Da.

"You handled it wrong," he said bluntly. "Look at your Mrs. Pankhurst. I don't believe in votes for women, but she knows how to get noticed."

"What should I have done, got myself arrested?"

"You don't need to go that far. If I'd known what you were doing, I'd have told you to send a copy of the letter to the *Western Mail*."

"I never thought of that." Ethel was disheartened to think that she could have done something to prevent these evictions, and had failed.

"The newspaper would have asked the palace whether they had received the letter, and it would have been hard for the king to say he was just going to ignore it."

"Oh, dammo, I wish I'd asked your advice."

"Don't swear," her mother said.

"Sorry, Mam."

The London policemen looked on in bewilderment, not understanding the foolish pride and stubbornness that had led to this. Perceval Jones was nowhere to be seen. A reporter from the *Daily Mail* asked Da for an interview, but the newspaper was hostile to workers, and Da refused.

There were not enough handcarts in town, so people took it in turns to move their goods. The process took hours, but by midafternoon the last pile of possessions had gone, and the keys had been left sticking out of the locks on the front doors. The policemen went back to London.

Ethel stayed in the street for a while. The windows of the empty houses looked blankly back at her, and the rainwater ran down the street pointlessly. She looked across the wet gray slates of the roofs, downhill to the scattered pithead buildings in the valley bottom. She could see a cat walking along a railway line, but otherwise there was no movement. No smoke came from the engine room, and the great twin wheels of the winding gear stood on top of their tower, motionless and redundant in the soft relentless rain.

April 1914

The German embassy was a grand mansion in Carlton House Terrace, one of London's most elegant streets. It looked across a leafy garden to the pillared portico of the Athenaeum, the club for gentleman intellectuals. At the back, its stables opened on the Mall, the broad avenue that ran from Trafalgar Square to Buckingham Palace.

Walter von Ulrich did not live there—yet. Only the ambassador himself, Prince Lichnowsky, had that privilege. Walter, a mere military attaché, lived in a bachelor apartment ten minutes' walk away in Piccadilly. However, he hoped that one day he might inhabit the ambassador's grand private apartment within the embassy. Walter was not a prince, but his father was a close friend of Kaiser Wilhelm II. Walter spoke English like an Old Etonian, which he was. He had spent two years in the army and three years at the war academy before joining the Foreign Service. He was twenty-eight years old, and a rising star.

He was not attracted only by the prestige and glory of being an ambassador. He felt passionately that there was no higher calling than to serve his country. His father felt the same.

They disagreed about everything else.

They stood in the hall of the embassy and looked at each other. They were the same height, but Otto was heavier, and bald, and his mustache was the old-fashioned soup-strainer type, whereas Walter had a modern toothbrush. Today they were identically dressed in black velvet suits with knee breeches, silk stockings, and buckled shoes. Both wore swords and cocked hats. Amazingly, this was the normal costume for presentation at Britain's royal court. "We look as if we should be on the stage," Walter said. "Ridiculous outfits."

"Not at all," said his father. "It's a splendid old custom."

Otto von Ulrich had spent much of his life in the German army. A young officer in the Franco-Prussian War, he had led his company across a pontoon bridge at the Battle of Sedan. Later, Otto had been one of the friends the young Kaiser Wilhelm had turned to after he broke with Bismarck, the Iron Chancellor. Now Otto had a roving brief, visiting European capitals like a bee landing on flowers, sipping the nectar of diplomatic intelligence and taking it all back to the hive. He believed in the monarchy and the Prussian military tradition.

Walter was just as patriotic, but he thought Germany had to become modern and egalitarian. Like his father, he was proud of his country's achievements in science and technology, and of the hardworking and efficient German people; but he thought they had a lot to learn—democracy from the liberal Americans, diplomacy from the sly British, and the art of gracious living from the stylish French.

Father and son left the embassy and went down a broad flight of steps to the Mall. Walter was to be presented to King George V, a ritual that was considered a privilege even though it brought with it no particular benefits. Junior diplomats such as he were not normally so honored, but his father had no compunction about pulling strings to advance Walter's career.

"Machine guns make all handheld weapons obsolete," Walter said, continuing an argument they had begun earlier. Weapons were his specialty, and he felt strongly that the German army should have the latest in firepower.

Otto thought differently. "They jam, they overheat, and they miss. A man with a rifle takes careful aim. But give him a machine gun and he'll wield it like a garden hose."

"When your house is on fire, you don't throw water on it in cupfuls, no matter how accurate. You *want* a hose."

Otto wagged his finger. "You've never been in battle—you have no idea what it's like. Listen to me. I know."

This was how their arguments often ended.

Walter felt his father's generation was arrogant. He understood how they had got that way. They had won a war, they had created the German Empire out of Prussia and a group of smaller independent monarchies, and then they had made Germany one of the world's most prosperous countries. Of course they thought they were wonderful. But it made them incautious.

A few hundred yards along the Mall, Walter and Otto turned into St. James's Palace. This sixteenth-century brick pile was older and less impressive than neighboring Buckingham Palace. They gave their names to a doorman who was dressed as they were.

Walter was mildly anxious. It was so easy to make a mistake of etiquette—and there were no minor errors when you were dealing with royalty.

Otto spoke to the doorman in English. "Is Señor Diaz here?"

"Yes, sir, he arrived a few moments ago."

Walter frowned. Juan Carlos Diego Diaz was a representative of the Mexican government. "Why are you interested in Diaz?" he said in German as they walked on through a series of rooms decorated with wall displays of swords and guns.

"The British Royal Navy is converting its ships from coal power to oil."

Walter nodded. Most advanced nations were doing the same. Oil was cheaper, cleaner, and easier to deal with—you just pumped it in, instead of employing armies of black-faced stokers. "And the British get oil from Mexico."

"They have bought the Mexican oil wells in order to secure supplies for their navy."

"But if we interfere in Mexico, what would the Americans think?"

Otto tapped the side of his nose. "Listen and learn. And, whatever you do, don't say anything."

The men about to be presented were waiting in an anteroom. Most had on the same velvet court dress, though one or two were in the comic-opera costumes of nineteenth-century generals, and one—presumably a Scot—wore full-dress uniform with a kilt. Walter and Otto strolled around the room, nodding to familiar faces on the diplomatic circuit, until they came to Diaz, a thickset man with a mustache that curled up at the tips.

After the usual pleasantries Otto said: "You must be glad that President Wilson has lifted the ban on arms sales to Mexico."

"Arms sales to the rebels," said Diaz, as if correcting him.

The American president, always inclined to take a moral stand, had refused to recognize General Huerta, who had come to power after the assassination of his predecessor. Calling Huerta a murderer, Wilson was backing a rebel group, the Constitutionalists.

Otto said: "If arms may be sold to the rebels, surely they may be sold to the government?"

Diaz looked startled. "Are you telling me that Germany would be willing to do that?"

"What do you need?"

"You must already know that we are desperate for rifles and ammunition."

"We could talk further about it."

Walter was as startled as Diaz. This would cause trouble. He said: "But, Father, the United States—"

"One moment!" His father held up a hand to silence him.

Diaz said: "By all means let us talk further. But tell me: what other subjects might come up?" He had guessed that Germany would want something in return.

The door to the throne room opened, and a footman came out carrying a list. The presentation was about to start. But Otto continued unhurriedly: "In time of war, a sovereign country is entitled to withhold strategic supplies."

Diaz said: "You're talking about oil." It was the only strategic supply Mexico had.

Otto nodded.

Diaz said: "So you would give us guns—"

"Sell, not give," Otto murmured.

"You would sell us guns now, in exchange for a promise that we would withhold oil from the British in the event of war." Diaz was clearly not used to the elaborate waltz of normal diplomatic conversation.

"It might be worth discussing." In the language of diplomacy that was a yes.

The footman called out: "Monsieur Honoré de Picard de la Fontaine!" and the presentations began.

Otto gave Diaz a direct look. "What I'd like to know from you is how such a proposal might be received in Mexico City."

"I believe President Huerta would be interested."

"So, if the German minister to Mexico, Admiral Paul von Hintze, were to make a formal approach to your president, he would not receive a rebuff?"

Walter could tell that his father was determined to get an unequivocal answer to this. He did not want the German government to risk the embarrassment of having such an offer flung back in their faces.

In Walter's anxious view, embarrassment was not the greatest danger to Germany in this diplomatic ploy. It risked making an enemy of the United States. But it was frustratingly difficult to point this out in the presence of Diaz.

Answering the question, Diaz said: "He would not be rebuffed."

"You're sure?" Otto insisted.

"I guarantee it."

Walter said: "Father, may I have a word—"

But the footman cried: "Herr Walter von Ulrich!"

Walter hesitated, and his father said: "Your turn. Go on!"

Walter turned away and stepped into the Throne Room.

The British liked to overawe their guests. The high coffered ceiling had diamond-patterned coving, the red plush walls were hung with enormous portraits, and at the far end the throne was overhung by a high canopy with dark velvet drapes. In front of the throne stood the king in a naval uniform. Walter was pleased to see the familiar face of Sir Alan Tite at the king's side—no doubt whispering names in the royal ear.

Walter approached and bowed. The king said: "Good to see you again, von Ulrich."

Walter had rehearsed what he would say. "I hope Your Majesty found the discussions at Tŷ Gwyn interesting."

"Very! Although the party was dreadfully overshadowed, of course."

"By the pit disaster. Indeed, so tragic."

"I look forward to our next meeting."

Walter understood this was his dismissal. He walked backward, bowing repeatedly in the required manner, until he reached the doorway.

His father was waiting for him in the next room.

"That was quick!" Walter said.

"On the contrary, it took longer than normal," said Otto. "Usually the king says: 'I'm glad to see you in London,' and that's the end of the conversation."

They left the palace together. "Admirable people, the British, in many ways, but soft," said Otto as they walked up St. James's Street to Piccadilly. "The king is ruled by his ministers, the ministers are subject to Parliament, and members of Parliament are chosen by the ordinary men. What sort of way is that to run a country?"

Walter did not rise to that provocation. He believed that Germany's political system was out-of-date, with its weak parliament that could not stand up to the kaiser or the generals; but he had had that argument with his father many times, and besides, he was still worried by the conversation with the Mexican envoy. "What you said to Diaz was risky," he said. "President Wilson won't like us selling rifles to Huerta."

"What does it matter what Wilson thinks?"

"The danger is that we will make a friend of a weak nation, Mexico, by making an enemy of a strong nation, the United States."

"There's not going to be a war in America."

Walter supposed that was true, but all the same he was uneasy. He did not like the idea of his country being at odds with the United States.

In his apartment they took off their antiquated costumes and dressed in tweed suits with soft-collared shirts and brown trilby hats. Back in Piccadilly they boarded a motorized omnibus heading east.

Otto had been impressed by Walter's invitation to meet the king at Tŷ Gwyn in January. "Earl Fitzherbert is a good connection," he had said. "If the Conservative Party comes to power he may be a minister, perhaps foreign secretary one day. You must keep up the friendship."

Walter had been inspired. "I should visit his charity clinic, and make a small donation."

"Excellent idea."

"Perhaps you would like to come with me?"

His father had taken the bait. "Even better."

Walter had an ulterior motive, but his father was all unsuspecting.

The bus took them past the theaters of the Strand, the newspaper offices of Fleet Street, and the banks of the financial district. Then the streets became narrower and dirtier. Top hats and bowlers were replaced by cloth caps. Horse-drawn vehicles predominated, and motorcars were few. This was the East End.

They got off at Aldgate. Otto looked around disdainfully. "I didn't know you were taking me to the slums," he said.

"We're going to a clinic for the poor," Walter replied. "Where would you expect it to be?"

"Does Earl Fitzherbert himself come here?"

"I suspect he just pays for it." Walter knew perfectly well that Fitz had never been there in his life. "But he will of course hear about our visit."

They zigzagged through backstreets to a nonconformist chapel. A hand-painted wooden sign read: "Calvary Gospel Hall." Pinned to the board was a sheet of paper with the words:

Baby Clinic
Free of Charge
Today and
every Wednesday

Walter opened the door and they went in.

Otto made a disgusted noise, then took out a handkerchief and held it to his nose. Walter had been there before, so he had been expecting the smell, but even so it was startlingly unpleasant. The hall was full of ragged women and half-naked children, all filthy dirty. The women sat on benches and the children played on the floor. At the far end of the room were two doors, each with a temporary label, one saying "Doctor" and the other "Patroness."

Near the door sat Fitz's aunt Herm, listing names in a book. Walter introduced his father. "Lady Hermia Fitzherbert, my father, Herr Otto von Ulrich."

At the other end of the room, the door marked "Doctor" opened and a ragged woman came out carrying a tiny baby and a medicine bottle. A nurse looked out and said: "Next, please."

Lady Hermia consulted her list and called: "Mrs. Blatsky and Rosie!"

An older woman and a girl went into the doctor's surgery.

Walter said: "Wait here a moment, please, Father, and I'll fetch the boss."

He hurried to the far end, stepping around the toddlers on the floor. He tapped on the door marked "Patroness," and walked in.

The room was little more than a cupboard, and indeed there was a mop and bucket in a corner. Lady Maud Fitzherbert sat at a small table writing in a ledger. She wore a simple dove-gray dress and a broad-brimmed hat. She looked up, and the smile that lit up her face when she saw Walter was bright enough to bring tears to his eyes. She leaped out of her chair and threw her arms around him.

He had been looking forward to this all day. He kissed her mouth, which opened to him immediately. He had kissed several women, but she was the only one he had ever known to press her body against him this way. He felt embarrassed, fearing that she would feel his erection, and he arched his body away; but she only pressed more closely, as if she really wanted to feel it, so he gave in to the pleasure.

Maud was passionate about everything: poverty, women's rights, music—and Walter. He felt amazed and privileged that she had fallen in love with him.

She broke the kiss, panting. "Aunt Herm will become suspicious," she said.

Walter nodded. "My father is outside."

Maud patted her hair and smoothed her dress. "All right."

Walter opened the door and they went back into the hall. Otto was chatting amiably to Hermia: he liked respectable old ladies.

"Lady Maud Fitzherbert, may I present my father, Herr Otto von Ulrich."

Otto bowed over her hand. He had learned not to click his heels: the English thought it comical.

Walter watched them size each other up. Maud smiled as if amused, and Walter guessed she was wondering if this was what *he* would look like in years to come. Otto took in Maud's expensive cashmere dress and the fashionable hat with approval. So far, so good.

Otto did not know that they were in love. Walter's plan was that his father would get to know Maud first. Otto approved of wealthy women doing charitable work, and insisted that Walter's mother and his sister visit poor families at Zumwald, their country estate in East Prussia. He would find out what a wonderful and exceptional woman Maud was; then his defenses would be down by the time he learned that Walter wanted to marry her.

It was a little foolish, Walter knew, to be so nervous. He was twenty-eight years old: he had a right to choose the woman he loved. But eight years ago he had fallen in love with another woman. Tilde had been passionate and intelligent, like Maud, but she was seventeen and a

Catholic. The von Ulrichs were Protestants. Both sets of parents had been angrily hostile to the romance, and Tilde had been unable to defy her father. Now Walter had fallen in love with an unsuitable woman for the second time. It was going to be difficult for his father to accept a feminist and a foreigner. But Walter was older and craftier now, and Maud was stronger and more independent than Tilde had been.

All the same, he was terrified. He had never felt like this about a woman, not even Tilde. He wanted to marry Maud and spend his life with her; in fact he could not imagine being without her. And he did not want his father to make trouble about it.

Maud was on her best behavior. "It is very kind of you to visit us, Herr von Ulrich," she said. "You must be tremendously busy. For a trusted confidant of a monarch, as you are to your kaiser, I imagine work has no end."

Otto was flattered, as she had intended. "I'm afraid this is true," he said. "However your brother, the earl, is such a long-standing friend of Walter's that I was very keen to come."

"Let me introduce you to our doctor." Maud led the way across the room and knocked at the surgery door. Walter was curious: he had never met the doctor. "May we come in?" she called.

They stepped into what must normally have been the pastor's office, furnished with a small desk and a shelf of ledgers and hymn books. The doctor, a handsome young man with black eyebrows and a sensual mouth, was examining Rosie Blatsky's hand. Walter felt a twinge of jealousy: Maud spent whole days with this attractive fellow.

Maud said: "Dr. Greenward, we have a most distinguished visitor. May I present Herr von Ulrich?"

Otto said stiffly: "How do you do?"

"The doctor works here for no fee," Maud said. "We're most grateful to him."

Greenward nodded curtly. Walter wondered what was causing the evident tension between his father and the doctor.

The doctor returned his attention to his patient. There was an angry-looking cut across her palm, and the hand and wrist were swollen. He looked at the mother and said: "How did she do this?"

The child answered. "My mother doesn't speak English," she said. "I cut my hand at work."

"And your father?"

"My father's dead."

Maud said quietly: "The clinic is for fatherless families, though in practice we never turn anyone away."

Greenward said to Rosie: "How old are you?"

"Eleven."

Walter murmured: "I thought children were not allowed to work under thirteen."

"There are loopholes in the law," Maud replied.

Greenward said: "What work do you do?"

"I clean up at Mannie Litov's garment factory. There was a blade in the sweepings."

"Whenever you cut yourself, you must wash the wound and put on a clean bandage. Then you have to change the bandage every day so that it doesn't get too dirty." Greenward's manner was brisk, but not unkind.

The mother barked a question at the daughter in heavily accented Russian. Walter could not understand her, but he got the gist of the child's reply, which was a translation of what the doctor had said.

The doctor turned to his nurse. "Clean the hand and bandage it, please." To Rosie he said: "I'm going to give you some ointment. If your arm swells more you must come back and see me next week. Do you understand?"

"Yes, sir."

"If you let the infection get worse, you may lose your hand."

Tears came to Rosie's eyes.

Greenward said: "I'm sorry to frighten you, but I want you to understand how important it is to keep your hand clean."

As the nurse prepared a bowl of what was presumably antiseptic fluid, Walter said: "May I express my admiration and respect for your work here, Doctor."

"Thank you. I'm happy to give my time, but we need to buy medical supplies. Any help you can offer will be much appreciated."

Maud said: "We must leave the doctor to get on—there are at least twenty patients waiting."

The visitors left the surgery. Walter was bursting with pride. Maud had more than compassion. When told of young children working in sweatshops, many aristocratic ladies could wipe away a tear with an embroidered handkerchief; but Maud had the determination and the nerve to give real help.

And, he thought, she loves me!

Maud said: "May I offer you some refreshment, Herr von Ulrich? My office is cramped, but I do have a bottle of my brother's best sherry."

"Most kind, but we must be going."

That was a bit quick, Walter thought. Maud's charm had stopped working on Otto. He had a nasty feeling that something had gone wrong.

Otto took out his pocketbook and extracted a banknote. "Please accept a modest contribution to your excellent work here, Lady Maud."

"How generous!" she said.

Walter gave her a similar note. "Perhaps I may be allowed to donate something, too."

"I appreciate anything you can offer me," she said. Walter hoped he was the only one to notice the sly look she gave him as she said it.

Otto said: "Please be sure to give my respects to Earl Fitzherbert."

They took their leave. Walter felt worried about his father's reaction. "Isn't Lady Maud wonderful?" he said breezily as they walked back toward Aldgate. "Fitz pays for everything, of course, but Maud does all the work."

"Disgraceful," Otto said. "Absolutely disgraceful."

Walter had sensed he was grumpy, but this astonished him. "What on earth do you mean? You approve of well-born ladies doing something to help the poor!"

"Visiting sick peasants with a few groceries in a basket is one thing," Otto said. "But I am appalled to see the sister of an earl in a place like that with a Jew doctor!"

"Oh, God," Walter groaned. Of course; Dr. Greenward was Jewish. His parents had probably been Germans called Grunwald. Walter had not met the doctor before today, and anyway might not have noticed or cared about his race. But Otto, like most men of his generation, thought such things important. Walter said: "Father, the man is working for nothing—Lady Maud cannot afford to refuse the help of a perfectly good doctor just because he's Jewish."

Otto was not listening. "Fatherless families—where did she get that phrase?" he said with disgust. "The spawn of prostitutes is what she means."

Walter felt heartsick. His plan had gone horribly wrong. "Don't you see how brave she is?" he said miserably.

"Certainly not," said Otto. "If she were my sister, I'd give her a good thrashing."

{ II }

There was a crisis in the White House.

In the small hours of the morning of April 21, Gus Dewar was in the West Wing. This new building provided badly needed office space, leaving the original White House free to be used as a residence. Gus was sitting in the president's study near the Oval Office, a small, drab room lit by a dim bulb. On the desk was the battered Underwood portable typewriter used by Woodrow Wilson to write his speeches and press releases.

Gus was more interested in the phone. If it rang, he had to decide whether to wake the president.

A telephone operator could not make such a decision. On the other hand, the president's senior advisers needed their sleep. Gus was the lowliest of Wilson's advisers, or the highest of his clerks, depending on point of view. Either way, it had fallen to him to sit all night by the phone to decide whether to disturb the president's slumbers—or those of the first lady, Ellen Wilson, who was suffering from a mysterious illness. Gus was nervous that he might say or do the wrong thing. Suddenly all his expensive education seemed superfluous: even at Harvard there had never been a class in when to wake the president. He was hoping the phone would never ring.

Gus was there because of a letter he had written. He had described to his father the royal party at Tŷ Gwyn, and the after-dinner discussion about the danger of war in Europe. Senator Dewar had found the letter so interesting and amusing that he had shown it to his friend Woodrow Wilson, who had said: "I'd like to have that boy in my office." Gus had been taking a year off between Harvard, where he had studied international law, and his first job at a Washington law firm. He had been halfway through a world tour, but he had eagerly cut short his travels and rushed home to serve his president.

Nothing fascinated Gus so much as the relationships between nations—the friendships and hatreds, the alliances and the wars. As a teenager he had attended sessions of the Senate Committee on Foreign Relations—his father was a member—and he had found it more fascinating than a play at the theater. "This is how countries create peace and prosperity—or war, devastation, and famine," his father had said. "If you want to change the world, then foreign relations is the field in which you can do the most good—or evil."

And now Gus was in the middle of his first international crisis.

An overzealous Mexican government official had arrested eight American sailors in the port of Tampico. The men had already been released, the official had apologized, and the trivial incident might have ended there. But the squadron commander, Admiral Mayo, had demanded a twenty-one-gun salute. President Huerta had refused. Piling on the pressure, Wilson had threatened to occupy Veracruz, Mexico's biggest port.

And so America was on the brink of war. Gus greatly admired the high-principled Woodrow Wilson. The president was not content with the cynical view that one Mexican bandit was pretty much like another. Huerta was a reactionary who had killed his predecessor, and Wilson was looking for a pretext to unseat him. Gus was thrilled that a world leader would say it was not acceptable for men to achieve power through murder. Would there come a day when that principle was accepted by all nations?

The crisis had been cranked up a notch by the Germans. A German ship called the *Ypiranga* was approaching Veracruz with a cargo of rifles and ammunition for Huerta's government.

Tension had been high all day, but now Gus was struggling to stay awake. On the desk in front of him, illuminated by a green-shaded lamp, was a typewritten report from army intelligence on the strength of the rebels in Mexico. Intelligence was one of the army's smaller departments, with only two officers and two clerks, and the report was scrappy. Gus's mind kept wandering to Caroline Wigmore.

When he arrived in Washington he had called to see Professor Wigmore, one of his Harvard teachers who had moved to Georgetown University. Wigmore had not been at home, but his young second wife was there. Gus had met Caroline several times at campus events, and had been strongly drawn to her quietly thoughtful demeanor and her quick intelligence. "He said he needed to order new shirts," she said, but Gus could see the strain on her face, and then she added: "But I know he's gone to his mistress." Gus had wiped her tears with his handkerchief and she had kissed his lips and said: "I wish I were married to someone trustworthy."

Caroline had turned out to be surprisingly passionate. Although she would not allow sexual intercourse, they did everything else. She had shuddering orgasms when he did no more than stroke her.

Their affair had been going on for only a month, but already Gus knew that he wanted her to divorce Wigmore and marry him. But she would not hear of it, even though she had no children. She said it would ruin Gus's career, and she was probably right. It could not be done discreetly, for the scandal would be too juicy—the attractive wife leaving a well-known professor and rapidly marrying a wealthy younger man. Gus knew exactly what his mother would say about such a marriage: "It's understandable, if the professor was unfaithful, but one can't meet the woman socially, of course." The president would be embarrassed, and so would the kind of people a lawyer wanted for clients. It would certainly put paid to any hopes Gus might have had of following his father into the Senate.

Gus told himself he did not care. He loved Caroline and he would rescue her from her husband. He had plenty of money, and when his father died he would be a millionaire. He would find some other career. Perhaps he might become a journalist, reporting from foreign capitals.

All the same he felt a stabbing pain of regret. He had just got a job in the White House, something young men dreamed of. It would be agonizingly hard to give that up, along with all it might lead to.

The phone rang, and Gus was startled by its sudden jangling in the quiet of the West Wing at night. "Oh, my God," he said, staring at it. "Oh, my God, this is it." He hesitated several seconds, then at last picked up the handset. He heard the fruity voice of Secretary of State William Jennings Bryan. "I have Josephus Daniels on the line with me, Gus." Daniels was secretary of the navy. "And the president's secretary is listening on an extension."

"Yes, Mr. Secretary, sir," said Gus. He made his voice calm, but his heart was racing.

"Wake the president, please," said Secretary Bryan.

"Yes, sir."

Gus went through the Oval Office and out into the Rose Garden in the cool night air. He ran across to the old building. A guard let him in. He hurried up the main staircase and across the hall to the bedroom door. He took a deep breath and knocked hard, hurting his knuckles.

After a moment he heard Wilson's voice. "Who is it?"

"Gus Dewar here, Mr. President," he called. "Secretary Bryan and Secretary Daniels are on the telephone."

"Just a minute."

President Wilson came out of the bedroom putting on his rimless glasses, looking vulnerable in pajamas and a dressing gown. He was tall, though not as tall as Gus. At fifty-seven he had dark gray hair. He thought he was ugly, and he was not far wrong. He had a beak of a nose and sticking-out ears, but the thrust of his big chin gave his face a

CHAPTER FIVE

determined look that accurately reflected the strength of character that Gus respected. When he spoke, he showed bad teeth.

"Good morning, Gus," he said amiably. "What's the excitement?"

"They didn't tell me."

"Well, you'd better listen in on the extension next door."

Gus hurried into the next room and picked up the phone.

He heard Bryan's sonorous tones. "The *Ypiranga* is due to dock at ten this morning."

Gus felt a thrill of apprehension. Surely the Mexican president would cave in now? Otherwise there would be bloodshed.

Bryan read a cable from the American consul in Veracruz. "'Steamer *Ypiranga*, owned by Hamburg-Amerika line, will arrive tomorrow from Germany with two hundred machine guns and fifteen million cartridges; will go to pier four and start discharging at ten thirty.'"

"Do you realize what this means, Mr. Bryan?" said Wilson, and Gus thought his voice sounded querulous. "Daniels, are you there, Daniels? What do you think?"

Daniels replied: "The munitions should not be permitted to reach Huerta." Gus was surprised at this tough line from the peace-loving navy secretary. "I can wire Admiral Fletcher to prevent it and take the customs house."

There was a long pause. Gus was gripping the phone so hard that his hand hurt. At last the president spoke. "Daniels, send this order to Admiral Fletcher: Take Veracruz at once."

"Yes, Mr. President," said the navy secretary.

And America was at war.

{ III }

Gus did not go to bed that night or the following day.

Shortly after eight thirty, Secretary Daniels brought the news that an American warship had blocked the path of the *Ypiranga*. The German ship, an unarmed freighter, switched its engines to reverse and left the scene. American marines would go ashore at Veracruz later that morning, Daniels said.

Gus was dismayed by the rapidly developing crisis but thrilled to be at the heart of things.

Woodrow Wilson did not shrink from war. His favorite play was Shakespeare's *Henry V,* and he liked to quote the line "If it be a sin to covet honour, I am the most offending soul alive."

News came in by wireless and cable, and it was Gus's job to take the messages in to the president. At midday the marines took control of the Veracruz customs house.

Shortly afterward, he was told that there was someone to see him—a Mrs. Wigmore.

Gus frowned worriedly. This was indiscreet. Something must be wrong.

He hurried to the lobby. Caroline looked distraught. Although she wore a neat tweed coat and a plain hat, her hair was untidy and her eyes red with crying. Gus was shocked and distressed to see her in this state. "My darling!" he said in a low voice. "What on earth has happened?"

"This is the end," she said. "I can never see you again. I'm so sorry." She began to cry.

Gus wanted to hug her, but he could not do so there. He had no office of his own. He looked around. The guard at the door was staring at them. There was nowhere they could be private. It was maddening. "Come outside," he said, taking her arm. "We'll walk."

She shook her head. "No. I'll be all right. Stay here."

"What has upset you?"

She would not meet his eye, and looked at the floor. "I must be faithful to my husband. I have obligations."

"Let me be your husband."

She raised her face, and her yearning look broke his heart. "Oh, how I wish I could."

"But you can!"

"I have a husband already."

"He is not faithful to you—why should you be to him?"

She ignored that. "He's accepted a chair at Berkeley. We're moving to California."

"Don't go."

"I've made up my mind."

"Obviously," Gus said flatly. He felt as if he had been knocked down. His chest hurt and he found it hard to breathe. "California," he said. "Hell."

She saw his acceptance of the inevitable, and she began to recover her composure. "This is our last meeting," she said.

"No!"

"Please listen to me. There's something I want to tell you, and this is my only chance."

"All right."

"A month ago I was ready to kill myself. Don't look at me like that—it's true. I thought I was so worthless that no one would care if I died. Then you appeared on my doorstep. You were so affectionate, so courteous, so thoughtful, that you made me think it was worth staying alive. You cherished me." The tears were streaming down her cheeks, but she kept on. "And you were so happy when I kissed you. If I could give someone that much joy, I couldn't be completely useless, I realized; and that thought kept me going. You saved my life, Gus. May God bless you."

He almost felt angry. "What does that leave me with?"

"Memories," she said. "I hope you will treasure them as I will treasure mine."

She turned away. Gus followed her to the door, but she did not look back. She went out, and he let her go.

When she was out of sight he headed automatically for the Oval Office, then changed direction: his mind was in too much of a turmoil for him to be with the president. He went into the men's room for a moment's peace. Fortunately there was no one else there. He washed his face, then looked in the mirror. He saw a thin man with a big head: he was shaped like a lollipop. He had light brown hair and brown eyes, and was not very handsome, but women usually liked him, and Caroline loved him.

Or she had, at least, for a little while.

He should not have let her go. How could he have watched her walk away like that? He should have persuaded her to postpone her decision, think about it, talk to him some more. Perhaps they could have thought of alternatives. But in his heart he knew there were no alternatives. She had already been through all that in her mind, he guessed. She must have lain awake nights, with her husband sleeping beside her, going over and over the situation. She had made up her mind before coming here.

He needed to return to his post. America was at war. But how could he put this out of his mind? When he could not see her, he spent all day looking forward to the next time he could. Now he could not stop thinking about life without her. It already seemed a strange prospect. What would he do?

A clerk came into the men's room, and Gus dried his hands on a towel and returned to his station in the study next to the Oval Office.

A few moments later, a messenger brought him a cable from the American consul in Veracruz. Gus looked at it and said: "Oh, no!" It read: FOUR OF OUR MEN KILLED COMMA TWENTY WOUNDED COMMA FIRING ALL AROUND THE CONSULATE STOP.

Four men killed, Gus thought with horror: four good American men with mothers and fathers, and wives or girlfriends. The news seemed to put his sadness in perspective. At least, he thought, Caroline and I are alive.

He tapped on the door of the Oval Office and handed the cable to Wilson. The president read it and went pale.

Gus looked keenly at him. How did he feel, knowing they were dead because of the decision he had made in the middle of the night?

This was not supposed to happen. The Mexicans wanted freedom from tyrannical governments, didn't they? They should have welcomed the Americans as liberators. What had gone wrong?

Bryan and Daniels showed up a few minutes later, followed by the secretary of war, Lindley Garrison, a man normally more belligerent than Wilson, and Robert Lansing, the State Department counselor. They gathered in the Oval Office to wait for more news.

The president was wired tighter than a violin string. Pale, restless, and twitchy, he paced the floor. It was a pity, Gus thought, that Wilson did not smoke—it might have calmed him.

We all knew there might be violence, Gus thought, but somehow the reality is more shocking than we anticipated.

More details came in sporadically, and Gus handed the messages to Wilson. The news was all bad. Mexican troops had resisted, firing on the marines from their fort. The troops were supported by citizens, who took potshots at Americans from their upstairs windows. In retaliation the USS *Prairie*, anchored offshore, turned its three-inch guns on the city and shelled it.

Casualties mounted: six Americans killed, eight, twelve—and more wounded. But it was a hopelessly unequal contest, and more than a hundred Mexicans died.

The president seemed baffled. "We don't want to fight the Mexicans," he said. "We want to serve them, if we can. We want to serve mankind."

For the second time in a day, Gus felt knocked off his feet. The president and his advisers had had nothing but good intentions. How had things gone so wrong? Was it really so difficult to do good in international affairs?

A message came from the State Department. The German ambassador, Count Johann von Bernstorff, had been instructed by the kaiser to call on the secretary of state, and wished to know whether nine o'clock tomorrow morning would be convenient. Unofficially, his staff indicated that the ambassador would be lodging a formal protest against the halting of the *Ypiranga*.

"A protest?" said Wilson. "What the dickens are they talking about?"

Gus saw immediately that the Germans had international law on their side. "Sir, there had been no declaration of war, nor of a blockade, so, strictly speaking, the Germans are correct."

"What?" Wilson turned to Lansing. "Is that right?"

"We'll double-check, of course," said the State Department counselor.

"But I'm pretty sure Gus is right. What we did was contrary to international law."

"So what does that mean?"

"It means we'll have to apologize."

"Never!" said Wilson angrily.

But they did.

{ IV }

Maud Fitzherbert was surprised to find herself in love with Walter von Ulrich. On the other hand, she would have been surprised to find herself in love with any man. She rarely met one she even liked. Plenty had been attracted to her, especially during her first season as a debutante, but most had quickly been repelled by her feminism. Others had planned to take her in hand—like the scruffy Marquis of Lowther, who had told Fitz that she would see the error of her ways when she met a truly masterful man. Poor Lowthie, he had been shown the error of his.

Walter thought she was wonderful the way she was. Whatever she did, he marveled. If she espoused extreme points of view, he was impressed by her arguments; when she shocked society by helping unmarried mothers and their children, he admired her courage; and he loved the way she looked in daring fashions.

Maud was bored by wealthy upper-class Englishmen who thought the way society was currently arranged was pretty satisfactory. Walter was different. Coming as he did from a conservative German family, he was surprisingly radical. From where she sat, in the back row of seats in her brother's box at the opera, she could see Walter in the stalls, with a small group from the German embassy. He did not look like a rebel, with his carefully brushed hair, his trim mustache, and his perfectly fitting evening clothes. Even sitting down, he was upright and straight-shouldered. He looked at the stage with intense concentration as Don Giovanni, accused of trying to rape a simple country girl, brazenly pretended to have caught his servant, Leporello, committing the crime.

In fact, she mused, *rebel* was not the right word for Walter. Although unusually open-minded, Walter was sometimes conventional. He was proud of the great musical tradition of German-speaking people, and got cross with blasé London audiences for arriving late, chatting to their friends during the performance, and leaving early. He would be irritated at Fitz, now, for making comments about the soprano's figure to his pal Bing Westhampton, and at Bea for talking to the Duchess of Sussex about Madame Lucille's shop in Hanover Square, where they bought their gowns. She even knew what Walter would say: "They listen to the music only when they have run out of gossip!"

Maud felt the same, but they were in a minority. For most of London's high society, the opera was just one more opportunity to show off clothes and jewels. However, even they fell silent toward the end of act 1, as Don Giovanni threatened to kill Leporello, and the orchestra played a thunderstorm on drums and double basses. Then, with characteristic insouciance, Don Giovanni released Leporello and walked jauntily away, defying them all to stop him; and the curtain came down.

Walter stood up immediately, looking toward the box, and waved. Fitz waved back. "That's von Ulrich," he said to Bing. "All those Germans are pleased with themselves because they embarrassed the Americans in Mexico."

Bing was an impish, curly-haired Lothario distantly related to the royal family. He knew little of world affairs, being mainly interested in gambling and drinking in the capital cities of Europe. He frowned and said in puzzlement: "What do the Germans care about Mexico?"

"Good question," Fitz said. "If they think they can win colonies in South America, they're deceiving themselves—the United States will never allow it."

Maud left the box and went down the grand staircase, nodding and smiling to acquaintances. She knew something like half the people there: London society was a surprisingly small set. On the red-carpeted landing she encountered a group surrounding the slight, dapper figure of David Lloyd George, the chancellor of the Exchequer. "Good evening, Lady Maud," he said with the twinkle that appeared in his bright blue eyes whenever he spoke to an attractive woman. "I hear your royal house party went well." He had the nasal accent of North Wales, less musical than the South Wales lilt. "But what a tragedy in the Aberowen pit."

"The bereaved families were much comforted by the king's condolences," Maud said. Among the group was an attractive woman in her twenties. Maud said: "Good evening, Miss Stevenson. How nice to see you again." Lloyd George's political secretary and mistress was a rebel, and Maud felt drawn to her. In addition, a man was always grateful to people who were polite to his mistress.

Lloyd George spoke to the group. "That German ship delivered the guns to Mexico after all. It simply went to another port and quietly unloaded. So nineteen American troops died for nothing. It's a terrible humiliation for Woodrow Wilson."

Maud smiled and touched Lloyd George's arm. "Would you explain something to me, Chancellor?"

"If I can, my dear," he said indulgently. Most men were pleased to be asked to explain things, especially to attractive young women, Maud found.

She said: "Why does anyone care what happens in Mexico?"

"Oil, dear lady," Lloyd George replied. "Oil."

Someone else spoke to him, and he turned away.

Maud spotted Walter. They met at the foot of the staircase. He bowed over her gloved hand, and she had to resist the temptation to touch his fair hair. Her love for Walter had awakened within her a sleeping lion of physical desire, a beast that was both stimulated and tormented by their stolen kisses and furtive fumbles.

"How are you enjoying the opera, Lady Maud?" he said formally, but his hazel eyes said, *I wish we were alone.*

"Very much—the Don has a wonderful voice."

"For me the conductor goes a little too fast."

He was the only person she had ever met who took music as seriously as she did. "I disagree," she said. "It's a comedy, so the melodies need to bounce along."

"But not just a comedy."

"That's true."

"Perhaps he will slow down when things turn nasty in act two."

"You seem to have won some kind of diplomatic coup in Mexico," she said, changing the subject.

"My father is . . ." He searched for words, something that was unusual for him. "Cock-a-hoop," he said after a pause.

"And you are not?"

He frowned. "I worry that the American president may want to get his own back one day."

At that moment Fitz walked past and said: "Hello, von Ulrich. Come and join us in our box. We've got a spare seat."

"With pleasure!" said Walter.

Maud was delighted. Fitz was just being hospitable: he did not know his sister was in love with Walter. She would have to bring him up-to-date soon. She was not sure how he would take the news. Their countries were at odds, and although Fitz regarded Walter as a friend, that was a long step from welcoming him as a brother-in-law.

She and Walter walked up the stairs and along the corridor. The back row in Fitz's box had only two seats with a poor view. Without discussion, Maud and Walter took those seats.

A few minutes later the house lights went down. In the half dark, Maud could almost imagine herself alone with Walter. The second act began with the duet between the Don and Leporello. Maud liked the way Mozart made masters and servants sing together, showing the complex and intimate relationships between upper and lower orders. Many dramas dealt only with the upper classes, and portrayed servants as part of the furniture—as many people wished they were.

Bea and the duchess returned to the box during the trio "Ah! Taci, ingiusto core." Everyone seemed to have exhausted the available topics of conversation, for they talked less and listened more. No one spoke to Maud or Walter, or even turned to look at them, and Maud wondered excitedly whether she might take advantage of the situation. Feeling daring, she reached out and furtively took Walter's hand. He smiled, and stroked her fingers with the ball of his thumb. She wished she could kiss him, but that would be foolhardy.

When Zerina sang her aria "Vedrai, carino" in sentimental three-eight time, an irresistible impulse tempted Maud, and as Zerlina pressed Masetto's hand to her heart, Maud laid Walter's hand on her breast. He gave an involuntary gasp, but no one noticed because Masetto was making similar noises, having just been beaten up by the Don.

She turned his hand so that he could feel her nipple with his palm. He loved her breasts, and touched them whenever he could, which was seldom. She wished it were oftener: she loved it. This was another discovery. Other people had stroked them—a doctor, an Anglican priest, an older girl at dancing class, a man in a crowd—and she had been disturbed and at the same time flattered at the thought that she could arouse people's lust, but she had never enjoyed it until now. She glanced at Walter's face and saw that he was staring at the stage, but there was a glint of perspiration on his forehead. She wondered if she was wrong to excite him in this way, when she could not give him satisfaction; but he made no move to withdraw his hand, so she concluded that he liked what she was doing. So did she. But, as always, she wanted more.

What had changed her? She had never been like this. It was him, of course, and the connection she felt with him, an intimacy so intense that she felt she could say anything, do whatever she liked, suppress nothing. What made him so different from every other man who had ever taken a fancy to her? A man such as Lowthie, or even Bing, expected a woman to act like a well-behaved child: to listen respectfully when he was being ponderous, to laugh appreciatively at his wit, to obey when he was masterful, and to give him a kiss whenever he asked. Walter treated her as a grown-up. He did not flirt, or condescend, or show off, and he listened at least as much as he talked.

The music turned sinister as the statue came to life, and the Commendatore stalked into the Don's dining room to a discord that Maud recognized as a diminished seventh. This was the dramatic high point of the opera, and Maud was almost certain no one would look around. Perhaps she could give Walter satisfaction after all, she thought; and the idea made her breathless.

As the trombones blared over the deep bass voice of the Commendatore, she placed her hand on Walter's thigh. She could feel the warmth of his skin through the fine wool of his dress trousers. Still he did not look at her, but she could see that his mouth was open and he was breathing heavily. She slid her hand up his thigh and, as the Don bravely took the Commendatore's hand, she found Walter's stiff penis and grasped it.

She was excited and, at the same time, curious. She had never done this before. She explored it through the fabric of his trousers. It was bigger than she expected and harder, too, more like a piece of wood than a part of the body. How strange, she thought, that such a remarkable physical change should occur just because of a woman's touch. When she was aroused it showed in tiny changes: that almost imperceptible feeling of puffiness, and the dampness inside. For men it was like raising a flag.

She knew what boys did, for she had spied on Fitz when he was fifteen; and now she imitated the action she had seen him perform, the up-and-down movement of the hand, while the Commendatore called upon the Don to repent, and the Don repeatedly refused. Walter was panting, now, but no one could hear because the orchestra was so loud. She was overjoyed that she could please him so much. She watched the backs of the heads of the others in the box, terrified that one of them might look around, but she was too caught up in what she was doing to stop. Walter covered her hand with his own, teaching her how to do it, gripping harder on the downstroke and releasing the pressure on the up, and she imitated what he did. As the Don was dragged into the flames, Walter jerked in his seat. She felt a kind of spasm in his penis— once, twice, and a third time—and then, as the Don died of fright, Walter seemed to slump, exhausted.

Maud suddenly knew that what she had done was completely mad. She quickly withdrew her hand. She flushed with shame. She found she was panting, and tried to breathe normally.

The final ensemble began onstage, and Maud relaxed. She did not know what had possessed her, but she had got away with it. The release of tension made her want to laugh. She suppressed a giggle.

She caught Walter's eye. He was looking at her with adoration. She felt a glow of pleasure. He leaned over and put his lips to her ear. "Thank you," he murmured.

She sighed and said: "It was a pleasure."

CHAPTER SIX

June 1914

t the beginning of June Grigori Peshkov at last had enough money for a ticket to New York. The Vyalov family in St. Petersburg sold him both the ticket and the papers necessary for immigration into the United States, including a letter from Mr. Josef Vyalov in Buffalo promising to give Grigori a job.

Grigori kissed the ticket. He could hardly wait to leave. It was like a dream, and he was afraid he might wake up before the boat sailed. Now that departure was so close, he longed even more for the moment when he would stand on deck and look back to watch Russia disappear over the horizon and out of his life forever.

On the evening before his departure, his friends organized a party.

It was held at Mishka's, a bar near the Putilov Machine Works. There were a dozen workmates, most of the members of the Bolshevik Discussion Group on Socialism and Atheism, and the girls from the house where Grigori and Lev lived. They were all on strike—half the factories in St. Petersburg were on strike—so no one had much money, but they clubbed together and bought a barrel of beer and some herrings.

It was a warm summer evening, and they sat on benches in a patch of waste ground next to the bar.

Grigori was not a great party lover. He would have preferred to spend the evening playing chess. Alcohol made people stupid, and flirting with other men's wives and girlfriends just seemed pointless. His wild-haired friend Konstantin, the chairman of the discussion group, had a row about the strike with aggressive Isaak, the footballer, and they ended up in a shouting match. Big Varya, Konstantin's mother, drank most of a bottle of vodka, punched her husband, and passed out. Lev brought a crowd of friends—men Grigori had never met, and girls he did not want to meet—and they drank all the beer without paying for anything.

Grigori spent the evening staring mournfully at Katerina. She was in a good mood—she loved parties. Her long skirt whirled and her blue-green eyes flashed as she moved around, teasing the men and charming the women, that wide, generous mouth always smiling. Her clothes were old and patched, but she had a wonderful body, the kind of figure Russian men loved, with a full bust and broad hips. Grigori had fallen in love with her on the day he had met her, and he was still in love four months later. But she preferred his brother.

Why? It had nothing to do with looks. The two brothers were so alike that people sometimes mistook one for the other. They were the same height and weight, and could wear each other's clothes. But Lev had charm by the ton. He was unreliable and selfish, and he lived on the edge of the law, but women adored him. Grigori was honest and dependable, a hard worker and a serious thinker, and he was single.

It would be different in the United States. Everything would be different there. American landowners were not allowed to hang their peasants. American police had to put people on trial before punishing them. The government could not even jail socialists. There were no noblemen: everyone was equal, even Jews.

Could it be real? Sometimes America seemed too much of a fantasy, like the stories people told of South Seas islands where beautiful maidens gave their bodies to anyone who asked. But it must be true: thousands of immigrants had written letters home. At the factory a group of revolutionary socialists had started a series of lectures on American democracy, but the police had closed them down.

He felt guilty about leaving his brother behind, but it was the best way. "Look after yourself," he said to Lev toward the end of the evening. "I won't be here to get you out of trouble anymore."

"I'll be fine," Lev said carelessly. "You look after yourself."

"I'll send you the money for your ticket. It won't take long on American wages."

"I'll be waiting."

"Don't move house—we could lose touch."

"I'm not going anywhere, big brother."

They had not discussed whether Katerina, too, would eventually come to America. Grigori had left it to Lev to raise the subject, but he had not. Grigori did not know whether to hope or dread that Lev would want to bring her.

Lev took Katerina's arm and said: "We have to go now."

Grigori was surprised. "Where are you off to at this time of night?"

"I'm meeting Trofim."

Trofim was a minor member of the Vyalov family. "Why do you have to see him tonight?"

Lev winked. "Never mind. We'll be back before morning—in plenty of time to take you to Gutuyevsky Island." This was where the transatlantic steamers docked.

"All right," said Grigori. "Don't do anything dangerous," he added, knowing it was pointless.

Lev waved gaily and disappeared.

It was almost midnight. Grigori said his good-byes. Several of his friends wept, but he did not know whether it was from sorrow or just booze. He walked back to the house with some of the girls, and they all kissed him in the hall. Then he went to his room.

His secondhand cardboard suitcase stood on the table. Though small, it was half-empty. He was taking shirts, underwear, and his chess set. He had only one pair of boots. He had not accumulated much in the nine years since his mother died.

Before going to bed, he looked in the cupboard where Lev kept his revolver, a Belgian-made Nagant M1895. He saw, with a sinking feeling, that the gun was not in its usual place.

He unlatched the window so that he would not have to get out of bed to open it when Lev came in.

Lying awake, listening to the familiar thunder of passing trains, he wondered what it would be like, four thousand miles from here. He had lived with Lev all his life, and he had been a substitute mother and father. From tomorrow, he would not know when Lev was out all night and carrying a gun. Would it be a relief, or would he worry more?

As always, Grigori woke at five. His ship sailed at eight, and the dock was an hour's walk. He had plenty of time.

Lev had not come home.

Grigori washed his hands and face. Looking in a broken shard of mirror, he trimmed his mustache and beard with a pair of kitchen scissors. Then he put his best suit on. He would leave his other suit behind for Lev.

He was heating a pan of porridge on the fire when he heard a loud knocking at the door of the house.

It was sure to be bad news. Friends stood outside and shouted; only the authorities knocked. Grigori put on his cap, then stepped into the hall and looked down the staircase. The landlady was admitting two men in the black-and-green uniforms of the police. Looking more carefully, Grigori recognized the podgy moon-shaped face of Mikhail Pinsky and the small ratlike head of his sidekick, Ilya Kozlov.

He thought fast. Obviously someone in the house was suspected of a crime. The likeliest culprit was Lev. Whether it was Lev or another boarder, everyone in the building would be interrogated. The two cops would remember the incident back in February when Grigori had rescued Katerina from them, and they would seize the opportunity of arresting Grigori.

And Grigori would miss his ship.

The dreadful thought paralyzed him. To miss the ship! After all the saving and waiting and longing for this day. No, he thought; no, I won't let it happen.

He ducked back into his room as the two policemen started up the stairs. It would be no use to plead with them—quite the reverse: if Pinsky discovered that Grigori was about to emigrate he would take even more pleasure in keeping him incarcerated. Grigori would not even have a chance to cash his ticket and get the money back. All those years of saving would be wasted.

He had to flee.

He scanned the tiny room frantically. It had one door and one window. He would have to go out the way Lev came in at night. He looked out: the backyard was empty. The St. Petersburg police were brutal, but no one had ever accused them of being smart, and it had not occurred to Pinsky and Kozlov to cover the rear of the house. Perhaps they knew there was no exit from the yard except across the railway—but a railway line was not much of a barrier to a desperate man.

Grigori heard shouts and cries from the girls' room next door: the police had gone there first.

He patted the breast of his jacket. His ticket, papers, and money were in his pocket. All the rest of his worldly possessions were already packed in the cardboard suitcase.

Picking up his suitcase, he leaned as far as he could out of the window. He held the case out and threw it. It landed flat and seemed undamaged.

The door of his room burst open.

Grigori put his legs through the window, sat on the sill for a split second, then jumped to the roof of the washhouse. His feet slipped on the tiles and he sat down hard. He slid down the sloping roof to the gutter. He heard a shout behind him but he did not look back. He jumped from the washhouse roof to the ground and landed unhurt.

He picked up his suitcase and ran.

A shot rang out, scaring him into running faster. Most policemen could not hit the Winter Palace from three yards, but accidents sometimes happened. He scrambled up the railway embankment, conscious that as he climbed to the level of the window he was becoming an easier target. He heard the distinctive thud-and-gasp of a railway engine and looked to his right to see a goods train approaching fast. There was another shot, and he sensed a thump somewhere, but he felt no pain, and guessed the slug had hit his suitcase. He reached the top of the embankment, knowing his body was now outlined against the clear morning sky. The train was a few yards away. The driver sounded his klaxon loud and long. A third shot rang out. Grigori threw himself across the line just ahead of the train.

The locomotive howled past him, steel wheels clashing with steel rails, steam trailing as the klaxon faded. Grigori scrambled to his feet. Now he was shielded from gunfire by a train of open trucks loaded with coal. He ran across the remaining tracks. As the last of the coal wagons passed, he descended the far embankment and walked through the yard of a small factory into the street.

He looked at his suitcase. There was a bullet hole in one edge. It had been a near miss.

He walked briskly, catching his breath, and asked himself what he should do next. Now that he was safe—at least for the moment—he began to worry about his brother. He needed to know whether Lev was in trouble, and if so what kind.

He decided to start in the last place he had seen Lev, which was Mishka's Bar.

As he headed for the bar, he felt nervous about being spotted. It would be bad luck, but it was not impossible: Pinsky might be roaming the streets. He pulled his cap down over his forehead, not really believing it would disguise his identity. He came across some workers heading for the docks and attached himself to the group, but with his suitcase he did not look as if he belonged.

However, he reached Mishka's without incident. The bar was furnished with homemade wooden benches and tables. It smelled of last night's beer and tobacco smoke. In the morning Mishka served bread and tea to people who had nowhere at home to make breakfast, but business was slow because of the strike, and the place was almost empty.

Grigori intended to ask Mishka if he knew where Lev had been headed when he left, but before he could do so he saw Katerina. She looked as if she had been up all night. Her blue-green eyes were bloodshot, her fair hair was awry, and her skirt was crumpled and stained. She was visibly distressed, with shaking hands and tear streaks on her grimy cheeks. Yet that made her more beautiful to Grigori, and he longed to take her in his arms and comfort her. Since he could not, he would do the next best thing, and come to her aid. "What's happened?" he said. "What's the matter?"

"Thank God you're here," she said. "The police are after Lev."

Grigori groaned. So his brother *was* in trouble—today of all days. "What has he done?" Grigori did not bother to consider the possibility that Lev was innocent.

"There was a mess-up last night. We were supposed to unload some cigarettes from a barge." They would be stolen cigarettes, Grigori assumed. Katerina went on: "Lev paid for them. Then the bargeman said it wasn't enough money, and there was an argument. Someone started shooting. Lev fired back; then we ran away."

"Thank heaven neither of you got hurt!"

"Now we don't have the cigarettes or the money."

"What a mess." Grigori looked at the clock over the bar. It was a quarter past six. He still had plenty of time. "Let's sit down. Do you want some tea?" He beckoned to Mishka and asked for two glasses of tea.

"Thank you," said Katerina. "Lev thinks one of the wounded must have talked to the police. Now they're after him."

"And you?"

"I'm all right—no one knows my name."

Grigori nodded. "So what we have to do is keep Lev out of the hands of the police. He'll have to lie low for a week or so, then slip out of St. Petersburg."

"He hasn't got any money."

"Of course not." Lev never had any money for essentials, though he could always buy drinks, place a bet, and entertain girls. "I can give him something." Grigori would have to dip into the money he had saved for the journey. "Where is he?"

"He said he would meet you at the ship."

Mishka brought their tea. Grigori was hungry—he had left his porridge on the fire—and he asked for some soup.

Katerina said: "How much can you give Lev?"

She was looking earnestly at him, and that always made him feel he would do anything she asked. He looked away. "Whatever he needs," he said.

"You're so good."

Grigori shrugged. "He's my brother."

"Thank you."

It pleased Grigori when Katerina was grateful, but it embarrassed him, too. The soup came and he began to eat, glad of the diversion. The food made him feel more optimistic. Lev was always in and out of trouble. He would slip out of this difficulty as he had many times before. It did not mean Grigori had to miss his sailing.

Katerina watched him, sipping her tea. She had lost the frantic look. Lev puts you in danger, Grigori thought, and I come to the rescue, yet you prefer him.

Lev was probably at the dock now, skulking in the shadow of a derrick, nervously looking out for policemen as he waited. Grigori needed to get going. But he might never see Katerina again, and he could hardly bear the thought of saying good-bye to her forever.

He finished his soup and looked at the clock. It was almost seven. He was cutting things too fine. "I have to go," he said reluctantly.

Katerina walked with him to the door. "Don't be too hard on Lev," she said.

"Was I ever?"

She put her hands on his shoulders, stood on tiptoe, and kissed him briefly on the lips. "Good luck," she said.

Grigori walked away.

He went quickly through the streets of southwest St. Petersburg, an industrial quarter of warehouses, factories, storage yards, and overcrowded slums. The shameful impulse to weep left him after a few minutes. He walked on the shady side, kept his cap low and his head down, and avoided wide-open areas. If Pinsky had circulated a description of Lev, an alert policeman might easily arrest Grigori.

But he reached the docks without being spotted. His ship, the *Angel Gabriel,* was a small, rusty vessel that took both cargo and passengers. Right now it was being loaded with stoutly nailed wooden packing cases marked with the name of the city's largest fur trader. As he watched, the last box went into the hold and the crew fastened the hatch.

A family of Jews were showing their tickets at the head of the gangplank. All Jews wanted to go to America, in Grigori's experience. They had even more reason than he did. In Russia there were laws forbidding them to own land, to enter the civil service, to be army officers, and countless other prohibitions. They could not live where they liked, and there were quotas limiting the number who could go to universities. It was a miracle any of them made a living. And if they did prosper, against the odds, it would not be long before they were set upon by a crowd—usually egged on by policemen such as Pinsky—and beaten up, their families terrified, their windows smashed, their property set on fire. The surprise was that any of them stayed.

The ship's hooter sounded for "All aboard."

He could not see his brother. What had gone wrong? Had Lev changed plans again? Or had he been arrested already?

A small boy tugged at Grigori's sleeve. "A man wants to talk to you," the boy said.

"What man?"

"He looks like you."

Thank God, thought Grigori. "Where is he?"

"Behind the planks."

There was a stack of timber on the dock. Grigori hurried around it and found Lev hiding behind it, nervously smoking a cigarette. He was fidgety and pale—a rare sight, for he usually remained cheerful even in adversity.

"I'm in trouble," Lev said.

"Again."

"Those bargemen are liars!"

"And thieves, probably."

"Don't get sarcastic with me. There isn't time."

"No, you're right. We need to get you out of town until the fuss dies down."

Lev shook his head in negation, blowing out smoke at the same time. "One of the bargemen died. I'm wanted for murder."

"Oh, hell." Grigori sat down on a shelf of timber and buried his head in his hands. "Murder," he said.

"Trofim was badly wounded and the police got him to talk. He fingered me."

"How do you know all this?"

"I saw Fyodor half an hour ago." Fyodor was a corrupt policeman of Lev's acquaintance.

"This is bad news."

"There's worse. Pinsky has vowed to get me—as revenge on you."

Grigori nodded. "That's what I was afraid of."

"What am I going to do?"

"You'll have to go to Moscow. St. Petersburg won't be safe for you for a long time, maybe forever."

"I don't know that Moscow is far enough, now that the police have telegraph machines."

He was right, Grigori realized.

The ship's hooter sounded again. Soon the gangplanks would be withdrawn. "We only have a minute left," said Grigori. "What are you going to do?"

Lev said: "I could go to America."

Grigori stared at him.

Lev said: "You could give me your ticket."

Grigori did not want even to think about it.

But Lev went on with remorseless logic. "I could use your passport and papers for entering the United States—no one would know the difference."

Grigori saw his dream fading, like the ending of a motion picture at the Soleil Cinema in Nevsky Prospekt, when the house lights came up to show the drab colors and dirty floors of the real world. "Give you my ticket," he repeated, desperately postponing the moment of decision.

"You'd be saving my life," Lev said.

Grigori knew he had to do it, and the realization was like a pain in his heart.

He took the papers from the pocket of his best suit and gave them to Lev. He handed over all the money he had saved for the journey. Then he gave his brother the cardboard suitcase with the bullet hole.

"I'll send you the money for another ticket," Lev said fervently. Grigori made no reply, but his skepticism must have shown on his face, for Lev protested: "I really will. I swear it. I'll save up."

"All right," Grigori said.

They embraced. Lev said: "You always took care of me."

"Yes, I did."

Lev turned and ran for the ship.

The sailors were untying the ropes. They were about to pull up the gangplank, but Lev shouted and they waited a few seconds more for him.

He ran up onto the deck.

He turned, leaned on the rail, and waved to Grigori.

Grigori could not bring himself to wave back. He turned and walked away.

The ship hooted, but he did not look back.

His right arm felt strangely light without the burden of the suitcase. He walked through the docks, looking down at the deep black water, and the odd thought occurred to him that he could throw himself in. He shook himself: he was not prey to such foolish ideas. All the same he was depressed and bitter. Life never dealt him a winning hand.

He was unable to cheer himself up as he retraced his steps through the industrial district. He walked along with his eyes cast down, not even bothering to keep an eye open for the police: it hardly mattered if they arrested him now.

What was he going to do? He felt he could not summon the energy for anything. They would give him back his job at the factory, when the strike was over: he was a good worker and they knew it. He should probably go there now, and find out whether there had been any progress in the dispute—but he could not be bothered.

After an hour he found himself approaching Mishka's. He intended to go straight past but, glancing inside, he saw Katerina, sitting where he had left her two hours ago, with a cold glass of tea in front of her. He had to tell her what had happened.

He went inside. The place was empty except for Mishka, who was sweeping the floor.

Katerina stood up, looking scared. "Why are you here?" she said. "Did you miss your boat?"

"Not exactly." He could not think how to break the news.

"What, then?" she said. "Is Lev dead?"

"No, he's all right. But he's wanted for murder."

She stared at him. "Where is he?"

"He had to go away."

"Where?"

There was no gentle way to put it. "He asked me to give him my ticket."

"Your ticket?"

"And passport. He's gone to America."

"No!" she screamed.

Grigori just nodded.

"No!" she yelled again. "He wouldn't leave me! Don't you say that! Never say it!"

"Try to stay calm."

She slapped Grigori's face. She was only a girl, and he hardly flinched. "Swine!" she screeched. "You've sent him away!"

"I did it to save his life."

"Bastard! Dog! I hate you! I hate your stupid face!"

"Nothing you say could make me feel any worse," Grigori said, but she was not listening. Ignoring her curses, he walked away, her voice fading as he went out through the door.

The screaming stopped, and he heard footsteps running along the street after him. "Stop!" she cried. "Stop, please, Grigori. Don't turn your back on me. I'm so sorry."

He turned.

"Grigori, you have to look after me now that Lev's gone."

He shook his head. "You don't need me. The men of this city will form a queue to look after you."

"No, they won't," she said. "There's something you don't know."

Grigori thought: What now?

She said: "Lev didn't want me to tell you."

"Go on."

"I'm expecting a baby," she said, and she began to weep.

Grigori stood still, taking it in. Lev's baby, of course. And Lev knew. Yet he had gone to America. "A baby," Grigori said.

She nodded, crying.

His brother's child. His nephew or niece. His family.

He put his arms around her and drew her to him. She was shaking with sobs. She buried her face in his jacket. He stroked her hair. "All right," he said. "Don't worry. You'll be okay. So will your baby." He sighed. "I will take care of you both."

{ II }

Traveling on the *Angel Gabriel* was grim, even for a boy from the slums of St. Petersburg. There was only one class, steerage, and the passengers were treated as so much more cargo. The ship was dirty and unsanitary, especially when there were huge waves and people were seasick. It was impossible to complain because none of the crew spoke Russian. Lev was not sure what nationality they were, but he failed to get through to them with either his smattering of English or his even fewer words of German. Someone said they were Dutch. Lev had never heard of Dutch people.

Nevertheless the mood among the passengers was high optimism. Lev felt he had burst the walls of the tsar's prison and escaped, and now he was free. He was on his way to America, where there were no noblemen. When the sea was calm, passengers sat on the deck and told the stories they had heard about America: the hot water coming out of taps, the good-quality leather boots worn even by workers, and most of all the freedom to practice any religion, join any political group, state your opinion in public, and not be afraid of the police.

On the evening of the tenth day Lev was playing cards. He was dealer, but he was losing. Everyone was losing except Spirya, an innocent-looking boy of Lev's age who was also traveling alone. "Spirya wins every night," said another player, Yakov. The truth was that Spirya won when Lev was dealing.

They were steaming slowly through a fog. The sea was calm, and there was no sound but the low bass of the engines. Lev had not been able to find out when they would arrive. People gave different answers. The most knowledgeable said it depended on the weather. The crew were inscrutable as always.

As night fell, Lev threw in his hand. "I'm cleaned out," he said. In fact he had plenty more money inside his shirt, but he could see that the others were running low, all except Spirya. "That's it," he said. "When we get to America, I'm just going to have to catch the eye of a rich old woman and live like a pet dog in her marble palace."

The others laughed. "But why would anyone want you for a pet?" said Yakov.

"Old ladies get cold at night," he said. "She would need my heating appliance."

The game ended in good humor, and the players drifted away.

Spirya went aft and leaned on the rail, watching the wake disappear into the fog. Lev joined him. "My half comes to seven rubles even," Lev said.

Spirya took paper currency from his pocket and gave it to Lev, shielding the transaction with his body so that no one else could see money changing hands.

Lev pocketed the notes and filled his pipe.

Spirya said: "Tell me something, Grigori." Lev was using his brother's papers, so he had to tell people his name was Grigori. "What would you do if I refused to give you your share?"

This kind of talk was dangerous. Lev slowly put his tobacco away and put the unlit pipe back into his jacket pocket. Then he grabbed Spirya by the lapels and pushed him up against the rail so that he was bent backward and leaning out to sea. Spirya was taller than Lev but not as tough, by a long way. "I would break your stupid neck," Lev said. "Then I would take back all the money you've made with me." He pushed Spirya farther over. "Then I would throw you in the damn sea."

Spirya was terrified. "All right!" he said. "Let me go!"

Lev released his grip.

"Jesus!" Spirya gasped. "I only asked a question."

Lev lit his pipe. "And I gave you the answer," he said. "Don't forget it."

Spirya walked away.

When the fog lifted they were in sight of land. It was night, but Lev could see the lights of a city. Where were they? Some said Canada, some said Ireland, but no one knew.

The lights came nearer, and the ship slowed. They were going to make landfall. Lev heard someone say they had arrived in America already! Ten days seemed quick. But what did he know? He stood at the rail with his brother's cardboard suitcase. His heart beat faster.

The suitcase reminded him that Grigori should have been the one arriving in America now. Lev had not forgotten his vow to Grigori, to send him the price of a ticket. That was one promise he ought to keep. Grigori had probably saved his life—again. I'm lucky, Lev thought, to have such a brother.

He was making money on the ship, but not fast enough. Seven rubles went nowhere. He needed a big score. But America was the land of opportunity. He would make his fortune there.

Lev had been intrigued to find a bullet hole in the suitcase, and a slug embedded in a box containing a chess set. He had sold the chess set to one of the Jews for five kopeks. He wondered how Grigori had come to be shot at that day.

He was missing Katerina. He loved to walk around with a girl like that on his arm, knowing that every man envied him. But there would be plenty of girls here in America.

He wondered if Grigori knew about Katerina's baby yet. Lev suffered a pang of regret: would he ever see his son or daughter? He told himself not to worry about leaving Katerina to raise the child alone. She would find someone else to look after her. She was a survivor.

It was after midnight when at last the ship docked. The quay was dimly lit and there was no one in sight. The passengers disembarked with their bags and boxes and trunks. An officer from the *Angel Gabriel* directed them into a shed where there were a few benches. "You must wait here until the immigration people come for you in the morning," he said, demonstrating that he did, after all, speak a little Russian.

It was a bit of an anticlimax for people who had saved up for years to come here. The women sat on the benches and the children went to sleep while the men smoked and waited for morning. After a while they heard the ship's engines, and Lev went outside and saw it moving slowly away from its mooring. Perhaps the crates of furs had to be unloaded elsewhere.

He tried to recall what Grigori had told him, in casual conversation, about the first steps in the new country. Immigrants had to pass a medical inspection—a tense moment, for unfit people were sent back, their money wasted and their hopes dashed. Sometimes the immigration officers changed people's names, to make them easier for Americans to pronounce. Outside the docks, a representative of the Vyalov family would be waiting to take them by train to Buffalo. There they would get jobs in hotels and factories owned by Josef Vyalov. Lev wondered how far Buffalo was from New York. Would it take an hour to get there, or a week? He wished he had listened more carefully to Grigori.

The sun rose over miles of crowded docks, and Lev's excitement returned. Old-fashioned masts and rigging clustered side by side with steam funnels. There were grand dockside buildings and tumbledown sheds, tall derricks and squat capstans, ladders and ropes and carts. To landward, Lev could see serried ranks of railway trucks full of coal, hundreds of them—no, thousands—fading into the distance beyond the limit of his vision. He was disappointed that he could not see the famous Liberty statue with its torch: it must be out of sight around a headland, he guessed.

Dockworkers arrived, first in small groups, then in crowds. Ships departed and others arrived. A dozen women began to unload sacks of potatoes from a small vessel in front of the shed. Lev wondered when the immigration police would come.

Spirya came up to him. He seemed to have forgiven the way Lev had threatened him. "They've forgotten about us," he said.

"Looks that way," Lev said, puzzled.

"Shall we take a walk around—see if we can find someone who speaks Russian?"

"Good idea."

Spirya spoke to one of the older men. "We're going to see if we can find out what's happening."

The man looked nervous. "Maybe we should stay here as we were told."

They ignored him and walked over to the potato women. Lev gave them his best grin and said: "Does anyone speak Russian?" One of the younger women smiled back, but no one answered the question. Lev felt frustrated: his winning ways were useless with people who could not understand what he was saying.

Lev and Spirya walked in the direction from which most of the workers had come. No one took any notice of them. They came to a big set of gates, walked through, and found themselves in a busy street of shops and offices. The road was crowded with motorcars, electric trams, horses, and handcarts. Every few yards Lev spoke to someone, but no one responded.

Lev was mystified. What kind of place allowed anyone to walk off a ship and into the city without permission?

Then he spotted a building that intrigued him. It was a bit like a hotel, except that two poorly dressed men in sailors' caps were sitting on the steps, smoking. "Look at that place," he said.

"What about it?"

"I think it's a seamen's mission, like the one in St. Petersburg."

"We're not sailors."

"But there might be people there who speak foreign languages."

They went inside. A gray-haired woman behind a counter spoke to them.

Lev said in his own tongue: "We don't speak American."

She replied with a single word in the same language: "Russian?"

Lev nodded.

She made a beckoning sign with her finger, and Lev's hopes rose.

They followed her along a corridor to a small office with a window overlooking the water. Behind the desk was a man who looked, to Lev, like a Russian Jew, although he could not have said why he thought that. Lev said to him: "Do you speak Russian?"

"I am Russian," the man said. "Can I help you?"

Lev could have hugged him. Instead he looked the man in the eye and gave him a warm smile. "Someone was supposed to meet us off the ship and take us to Buffalo, but he didn't show up," he said, making his voice friendly but concerned. "There are about three hundred of us . . ." To gain sympathy he added: "Including women and children. Do you think you could help us find our contact?"

"Buffalo?" the man said. "Where do you think you are?"

"New York, of course."

"This is Cardiff."

Lev had never heard of Cardiff, but at least now he understood the problem. "That stupid captain set us down in the wrong port," he said. "How do we get to Buffalo from here?"

The man pointed out of the window, across the sea, and Lev had a sick feeling that he knew what was coming.

"It's that way," the man said. "About three thousand miles."

{ III }

Lev inquired the price of a ticket from Cardiff to New York. When converted to rubles it was ten times the amount of money he had inside his shirt.

He suppressed his rage. They had all been cheated by the Vyalov family, or the ship's captain—or both, most probably, since it would be easier to work the scam between them. All Grigori's hard-earned money had been stolen by those lying pigs. If he could have got the captain of the *Angel Gabriel* by the throat, he would have squeezed the life out of the man, and laughed when he died.

But there was no point in dreams of vengeance. The thing was not to give in. He would find a job, learn to speak English, and get into a high-stakes card game. It would take time. He would have to be patient. He must learn to be a bit more like Grigori.

That first night they all slept on the floor of the synagogue. Lev tagged along with the rest. The Cardiff Jews did not know, or perhaps did not care, that some of the passengers were Christian.

For the first time in his life he saw the advantage of being Jewish. In Russia Jews were so persecuted that Lev had always wondered why more of them did not abandon their religion, change their clothes, and mix in with everyone else. It would have saved a lot of lives. But now he realized that, as a Jew, you could go anywhere in the world and always find someone to treat you like family.

It turned out that this was not the first group of Russian immigrants to buy tickets to New York and end up somewhere else. It had happened before, in Cardiff and other British ports; and, as so many Russian migrants were Jewish, the elders of the synagogue had a routine. Next day the stranded travelers were given a hot breakfast and got their money changed to British pounds, shillings, and pence; then they were taken to boardinghouses where they were able to rent cheap rooms.

Like every city in the world, Cardiff had thousands of stables. Lev studied enough words to say he was an experienced worker with horses, then went around the city asking for a job. It did not take people long to see that he was good with the animals, but even well-disposed employers wanted to ask a few questions, and he could not understand or answer.

In desperation he learned more rapidly, and after a few days he could understand prices and ask for bread or beer. However, employers were asking complicated questions, presumably about where he had worked before and whether he had ever been in trouble with the police.

He returned to the seamen's mission and explained his problem to the Russian in the little office. He was given an address in Butetown, the neighborhood nearest the docks, and told to ask for Filip Kowal, pronounced "cole," known as Kowal the Pole. Kowal turned out to be a ganger who hired out foreign labor cheap and spoke a smattering of most European languages. He told Lev to be on the forecourt of the city's main railway station, with his suitcase, on the following Monday morning at ten o'clock.

Lev was so glad that he did not even ask what the job was.

He showed up along with a couple of hundred men, mostly Russian, but including Germans, Poles, Slavs, and one dark-skinned African. He was pleased to see Spirya and Yakov there, too.

They were herded onto a train, their tickets paid for by Kowal, and they steamed north through pretty mountain country. Between the green hillsides, the industrial towns lay pooled like dark water in the valleys. A feature of every town was at least one tower with a pair of giant wheels on top, and Lev learned that the main business of the region was coal mining. Several of the men with him were miners; some had other crafts such as metalworking; and many were unskilled laborers.

After an hour they got off the train. As they filed out of the station Lev realized this was no ordinary job. A crowd of several hundred men, all dressed in the caps and rough clothes of workers, stood waiting for them in the square. At first the men were ominously silent; then one of them shouted something, and the others quickly joined in. Lev had no idea what they were saying but there was no doubt it was hostile. There were also twenty or thirty policemen present, standing at the front of the crowd, keeping the men behind an imaginary line.

Spirya said in a frightened voice: "Who are these people?"

Lev said: "Short, muscular men with hard faces and clean hands—I'd say they are coal miners on strike."

"They look as if they want to kill us. What the hell is going on?"

"We're strikebreakers," Lev said grimly.

"God save us."

Kowal the Pole shouted: "Follow me!" in several languages, and they all marched up the main street. The crowd continued to shout, and men shook their fists, but no one broke the line. Lev had never before felt grateful to policemen. "This is awful," he said.

Yakov said: "Now you know what it's like to be a Jew."

They left the shouting miners behind and walked uphill through streets of row houses. Lev noticed that many of the houses appeared empty. People still stared as they went by, but the insults stopped. Kowal started to allocate houses to the men. Lev and Spirya were astonished to be given a house to themselves. Before leaving, Kowal pointed out the pithead—the tower with twin wheels—and told them to be there tomorrow morning at six. Those who were miners would be digging coal; the others would be maintaining tunnels and equipment or, in Lev's case, looking after ponies.

Lev gazed around his new home. It was no palace, but it was clean and dry. It had one big room downstairs and two up—a bedroom for each of them! Lev had never had a room to himself. There was no furniture, but they were used to sleeping on the floor, and in June they did not even need blankets.

Lev had no wish to leave, but eventually they became hungry. There was no food in the house, so, reluctantly, they went out to get their dinner. With trepidation they entered the first pub they came to, but the dozen or so customers glared angrily at them, and when Lev said in English: "Two pints of half-and-half, please," the bartender ignored him.

They walked downhill into the town center and found a café. Here at least the clientele did not appear to be spoiling for a fight. But they sat at a table for half an hour and watched the waitress serve everyone who came in after them. Then they left.

It was going to be difficult living here, Lev suspected. But it would not be for long. As soon as he had enough money he would go to America. Nevertheless, while he was here he had to eat.

They went into a bakery. This time Lev was determined to get what he wanted. He pointed to a rack of loaves and said in English: "One bread, please."

The baker pretended not to understand.

Lev reached across the counter and grabbed the loaf he wanted. Now, he thought, let him try to take it back.

"Hey!" cried the baker, but he stayed on his side of the counter.

Lev smiled and said: "How much, please?"

"Penny farthing," the baker said sulkily.

Lev put the coins on the counter. "Thank you very much," he said.

He broke the loaf and gave half to Spirya; then they walked down the street eating. They came to the railway station, but the crowd had dispersed. On the forecourt, a news vendor was calling his wares. His papers were selling fast, and Lev wondered if something important had happened.

A large car came along the road, going fast, and they had to jump out of the way. Looking at the passenger in the back, Lev was astonished to recognize Princess Bea.

"Good God!" he said. In a flash, he was transported back to Bulovnir, and the nightmare sight of his father dying on the gallows while this woman looked on. The terror he had felt then was unlike anything he had ever known. Nothing would ever scare him like that, not street fights nor policemen's nightsticks nor guns pointed at him.

The car pulled up at the station entrance. Hatred, disgust, and nausea overwhelmed Lev as Princess Bea got out. The bread in his mouth seemed like gravel and he spat it out.

Spirya said: "What's the matter?"

Lev pulled himself together. "That woman is a Russian princess," he said. "She had my father hanged fourteen years ago."

"Bitch. What on earth is she doing here?"

"She married an English lord. They must live nearby. Perhaps it's his coal mine."

The chauffeur and a maid busied themselves with luggage. Lev heard Bea speak to the maid in Russian, and the maid replied in the same tongue. They all went into the station; then the maid came back out and bought a newspaper.

Lev approached her. Taking off his cap, he gave a deep bow and said in Russian: "You must be the princess Bea."

She laughed merrily. "Don't be a fool. I'm her maid, Nina. Who are you?"

Lev introduced himself and Spirya and explained how they came to be there, and why they could not buy dinner.

"I'll be back tonight," Nina said. "We're only going to Cardiff. Come to the kitchen door of Tŷ Gwyn, and I'll give you some cold meat. Just follow the road north out of town until you come to a palace."

"Thank you, beautiful lady."

"I'm old enough to be your mother," she said, but she simpered just the same. "I'd better take the princess her paper."

"What's the big story?"

"Oh, foreign news," she said dismissively. "There's been an assassination. The princess is terribly upset. The archduke Franz Ferdinand of Austria was killed at a place called Sarajevo."

"That's frightening, to a princess."

"Yes," Nina said. "Still, I don't suppose it will make any difference to the likes of you and me."

"No," said Lev. "I don't suppose it will."

CHAPTER SEVEN

Early July 1914

The Church of St. James in Piccadilly had the most expensively dressed congregation in the world. It was the favorite place of worship for London's elite. In theory, ostentation was frowned upon; but a woman had to wear a hat, and these days it was almost impossible to buy one that did not have ostrich feathers, ribbons, bows, and silk flowers. From the back of the nave Walter von Ulrich looked at a jungle of extravagant shapes and colors. The men, by contrast, all looked the same, with their black coats and white stand-up collars, holding their top hats in their laps.

Most of these people did not understand what had happened in Sarajevo seven days ago, he thought sourly; some of them did not even know where Bosnia was. They were shocked by the murder of the archduke, but they could not work out what it meant for the rest of the world. They were vaguely bewildered.

Walter was not bewildered. He knew exactly what the assassination portended. It created a serious threat to the security of Germany, and it was up to people such as Walter to protect and defend their country in this moment of danger.

Today his first task was to find out what the Russian tsar was thinking. This was what everyone wanted to know: the German ambassador, Walter's father, the foreign minister in Berlin, and the kaiser himself. And Walter, like the good intelligence officer he was, had a source of information.

He scanned the congregation, trying to identify his man among the backs of heads, fearing he might not be there. Anton was a clerk at the Russian embassy. They met in Anglican churches because Anton could be sure there would be no one from his embassy there: most Russians belonged to the Orthodox Church, and those who did not were never employed in the diplomatic service.

Anton was in charge of the cable office at the Russian embassy, so he saw every incoming and outgoing telegram. His information was priceless. But he was difficult to manage, and caused Walter much anxiety. Espionage frightened Anton, and when he got scared he would fail to show up—often at moments of international tension, like this one, when Walter needed him most.

Walter was distracted by spotting Maud. He recognized the long, graceful neck rising out of a fashionable man-style wing collar, and his heart missed a beat. He kissed that neck whenever he got the chance.

When he thought about the danger of war, his mind went first to Maud, then to his country. He felt ashamed of this selfishness, but he could not do anything about it. His greatest fear was that she would be taken from him; the threat to the fatherland came second. For Germany's sake he was willing to die—but not to live without the woman he loved.

A head in the third row from the back turned, and Walter met the eye of Anton. The man had thinning brown hair and a patchy beard. Relieved, Walter walked to the south aisle, as if looking for a place, and after a moment's hesitation sat down.

Anton's soul was full of bitterness. Five years ago, a nephew whom he had loved had been accused, by the tsar's secret police, of revolutionary activities, and had been imprisoned in the Fortress of Peter and Paul, across the river from the Winter Palace in the heart of St. Petersburg. The boy had been a theology student, and quite innocent of subversion; but before he could be released he had contracted pneumonia and died. Anton had been wreaking his quiet, deadly revenge against the tsar's government ever since.

It was a pity the church was so well-lit. The architect, Christopher Wren, had put in long rows of huge round-arched windows. For this kind of work, a gloomy Gothic twilight would have been better. Still, Anton had chosen his position well, at the end of a row, with a child next to him and a massive wooden pillar behind.

"Good place to sit," Walter murmured.

"We can still be observed from the gallery," Anton fretted.

Walter shook his head. "They will all be looking toward the front."

Anton was a middle-aged bachelor. A small man, he was neat to the point of fussiness: the tie knotted tightly, every button done up on the jacket, the shoes gleaming. His well-worn suit was shiny from years of brushing and pressing. Walter thought this was a reaction against the grubbiness of espionage. After all, the man was there to betray his country. And I'm here to encourage him, Walter thought grimly.

Walter said nothing more during the hush before the service, but as soon as the first hymn started he said in a low voice: "What's the mood in St. Petersburg?"

"Russia does not want war," Anton said.

"Good."

"The tsar fears that war will lead to revolution." When Anton mentioned the tsar he looked as if he was going to spit. "Half St. Petersburg is on strike already. Of course, it does not occur to him that his own stupid brutality is what makes people want a revolution."

"Indeed." Walter always had to adjust for the fact that Anton's opinions were distorted by hate, but in this case the spy was not entirely wrong. Walter did not hate the tsar, but feared him. He had at his disposal the largest army in the world. Every discussion of Germany's security had to take that army into account. Germany was like a man whose next-door neighbor keeps a giant bear on a chain in the front garden. "What will the tsar do?"

"It depends on Austria."

Walter suppressed an impatient retort. Everyone was waiting to see what the Austrian emperor would do. He had to do *something*, because the assassinated archduke had been heir to his throne. Walter was hoping to learn about Austrian intentions from his cousin Robert later that day. That branch of the family was Catholic, like all the Austrian elite, and Robert would be at mass in Westminster Cathedral right now, but Walter would see him for lunch. Meanwhile Walter needed to know more about the Russians.

He had to wait for another hymn. He tried to be patient. He looked up and studied the extravagant gilding of Wren's barrel vaults.

The congregation broke into "Rock of Ages." "Suppose there is fighting in the Balkans," Walter murmured to Anton. "Will the Russians stay out of it?"

"No. The tsar cannot stand aside if Serbia is attacked."

Walter felt a chill. This was exactly the kind of escalation he was afraid of. "It would be madness to go to war over this!"

"True. But the Russians can't let Austria control the Balkan region— they have to protect the Black Sea route."

There was no arguing with that. Most of Russia's exports—grain from the southern cornfields and oil from the wells around Baku—were shipped to the world from Black Sea ports.

Anton went on: "On the other hand, the tsar is also urging everyone to tread carefully."

"In short, he can't make up his mind."

"If you call it a mind."

Walter nodded. The tsar was not an intelligent man. His dream was to return Russia to the golden age of the seventeenth century, and he was stupid enough to think that was possible. It was as if King George V were to try to re-create the Merrie England of Robin Hood. Since the tsar was barely rational, it was maddeningly difficult to predict what he would do.

During the last hymn Walter's gaze wandered to Maud, sitting two rows in front on the other side. He watched her profile fondly as she sang with gusto.

Anton's ambivalent report was unnerving. Walter felt more worried than he had been an hour ago. He said: "From now on, I need to see you every day."

Anton looked panicky. "Not possible!" he said. "Too risky."

"But the picture is changing hour by hour."

"Next Sunday morning, Smith Square."

That was the trouble with idealistic spies, Walter thought with frustration: you had no leverage. On the other hand, men who spied for money were never trustworthy. They would tell you what you wanted to hear in the hope of getting a bonus. With Anton, if he said the tsar was dithering, Walter could be confident that the tsar had not made a decision.

"Meet me once in the middle of the week, then," Walter pleaded as the hymn came to an end.

Anton did not reply. Instead of sitting down, he slipped away and left the church. "Damn," Walter said quietly, and the child in the next seat stared at him with disapproval.

When the service was over he stood in the paved churchyard greeting acquaintances until Maud emerged with Fitz and Bea. Maud looked supernaturally graceful in a stylish gray figured velvet dress with a darker gray crepe overdress. It was not a very feminine color, perhaps, but it heightened her sculptured beauty and seemed to make her skin glow. Walter shook hands all round, wishing desperately for a few minutes alone with her. He exchanged pleasantries with Bea, a confection in candy-pink and cream lace, and agreed with a solemn Fitz that the assassination was a "bad business." Then the Fitzherberts moved away, and Walter feared he had missed his chance; but, at the last moment, Maud murmured: "I'll be at the duchess's house for tea."

Walter smiled at her elegant back. He had seen Maud yesterday and he would see her tomorrow, yet he had been terrified that he might not get another chance to see her today. Was he really incapable of passing twenty-four hours without her? He did not think of himself as a weak man, but she had cast a spell over him. However, he had no wish to escape.

It was her independent spirit that he found so attractive. Most women of his generation seemed content to play the passive role that society gave them, dressing beautifully and organizing parties and obeying their husbands. Walter was bored by the doormat type. Maud was more like some of the women he had met in the United States, during a stint at the German embassy in Washington. They were elegant and charming but not subservient. To be loved by a woman like that was unbearably exciting.

He walked with a jaunty step along Piccadilly and stopped at a newsstand. Reading British papers was never pleasant: most were viciously anti-German, especially the rabid *Daily Mail.* They had the British believing they were surrounded by German spies. How Walter wished it were true! He had a dozen or so agents in coast towns, making notes of comings and goings at the docks, as the British had in German ports, but nothing like the thousands reported by hysterical newspaper editors.

He bought a copy of the *People.* The trouble in the Balkans was not big news here: the British were more worried about Ireland. A minority of Protestants had ruled the roost there for hundreds of years, with scant regard for the Catholic majority. If Ireland won independence the boot would be on the other foot. Both sides were heavily armed, and civil war threatened.

A single paragraph at the bottom of the front page referred to the "Austro-Servian Crisis." As usual, the newspapers had no idea what was really going on.

As Walter turned into the Ritz Hotel, Robert jumped out of a motor taxi. He was wearing a black waistcoat and a black tie in mourning for the archduke. Robert had been one of Franz Ferdinand's set— progressive thinkers by the standards of the Viennese court, albeit conservative by any other measure. He had liked and respected the murdered man and his family, Walter knew.

They left their top hats in the cloakroom and went into the dining room together. Walter felt protective toward Robert. Since they were boys he had known that his cousin was different. People called such men effeminate, but that was too crude: Robert was not a woman in a man's body. However, he had a lot of feminine traits, and this led Walter to treat him with a kind of understated chivalry.

He looked like Walter, with the same regular features and hazel eyes, but his hair was longer and his mustache waxed and curled. "How are things with Lady M?" he said as they sat down. Walter had confided in him: Robert knew all about forbidden love.

"She's wonderful, but my father can't get over her working in a slum clinic with a Jewish doctor."

"Oh, dear—that's harsh," Robert said. "His objection might be understandable if she herself were a Jew."

"I've been hoping he would warm to her gradually, meeting her socially now and again, and realizing that she is friendly with the most powerful men in the land; but it's not working."

"Unfortunately, the crisis in the Balkans is only going to increase tension in"—Robert smiled—"forgive me, international relations."

Walter forced a laugh. "We will work it out, whatever happens."

Robert said nothing, but looked as if he was not so confident.

Over Welsh lamb and potatoes with parsley sauce, Walter gave Robert the inconclusive information he had gleaned from Anton.

Robert had news of his own. "We have established that the assassins got their guns and bombs from Serbia."

"Oh, hell," said Walter.

Robert let his anger show. "The arms were supplied by the head of Serbian military intelligence. The murderers were given target practice in a park in Belgrade."

Walter said: "Intelligence officers sometimes act unilaterally."

"Often. And the secrecy of their work means they may get away with it."

"So this does not prove that the Serbian government organized the assassination. And, when you think logically about it, a small nation such as Serbia, trying desperately to preserve its independence, would be mad to provoke its powerful neighbor."

"It is even possible that Serbian intelligence acted in direct opposition to the wishes of the government," Robert conceded. But then he said firmly: "That makes absolutely no difference at all. Austria must take action against Serbia."

This was what Walter feared. The affair could no longer be regarded merely as a crime, to be dealt with by the police and the courts. It had escalated, and now an empire had to punish a small nation. Emperor Franz Joseph of Austria had been a great man in his time, conservative and devoutly religious but a strong leader. However, he was now eighty-four, and age had not made him any less authoritarian and narrow-minded. Such men thought they knew everything just because they were old. Walter's father was the same.

My fate is in the hands of two monarchs, Walter thought, the tsar and the emperor. One is foolish, the other geriatric; yet they control the destiny of Maud and me and countless millions more Europeans. What an argument against monarchy!

He thought hard while they ate dessert. When the coffee came he said optimistically: "I assume your aim will be to teach Serbia a sharp lesson without involving any other country."

Robert swiftly dashed his hopes. "On the contrary," he said. "My emperor has written a personal letter to your kaiser."

Walter was startled. He had heard nothing of this. "When?"

"It was delivered yesterday."

Like all diplomats, Walter hated it when monarchs talked directly to each other, instead of through their ministers. Anything could happen then. "What did he say?"

"That Serbia must be eliminated as a political power."

"No!" This was worse than Walter had feared. Shocked, he said: "Does he mean it?"

"Everything depends on the reply."

Walter frowned. Emperor Franz Joseph was asking for backing from Kaiser Wilhelm—that was the real point of the letter. The two countries were allies, so the kaiser was obliged to sound supportive, but his emphasis might be enthusiastic or reluctant, encouraging or cautious.

"I trust Germany will back Austria, whatever my emperor decides to do," Robert said severely.

"You can't possibly want Germany to attack Serbia!" Walter protested.

Robert was offended. "We want a reassurance that Germany will fulfill her obligations as our ally."

Walter controlled his impatience. "The problem with that way of thinking is that it raises the stakes. Like Russia making supportive noises about Serbia, it encourages aggression. What we ought to do is calm everyone down."

"I'm not sure I agree," Robert said stiffly. "Austria has suffered a terrible blow. The emperor cannot be seen to take it lightly. He who defies the giant must be crushed."

"Let's try to keep this in proportion."

Robert raised his voice. "The heir to the throne has been murdered!" A diner at the next table glanced up and frowned to hear German spoken in angry tones. Robert softened his speech but not his expression. "Don't talk to me about proportion."

Walter tried to suppress his own feelings. It would be stupid and dangerous for Germany to get involved in this squabble, but telling Robert that would serve no purpose. It was Walter's job to glean information, not have an argument. "I quite understand," he said. "Is your view shared by everyone in Vienna?"

"In Vienna, yes," said Robert. "Tisza is opposed." István Tisza was the prime minister of Hungary, but subordinate to the Austrian emperor. "His alternative proposal is diplomatic encirclement of Serbia."

"Less dramatic, perhaps, but also less risky," Walter observed carefully.

"Too weak."

Walter called for the bill. He was deeply unsettled by what he had heard. However, he did not want any ill feeling between himself and Robert. They trusted and helped each other, and he did not want that to change. On the pavement outside, he shook Robert's hand and clasped his elbow in a gesture of firm comradeship. "Whatever happens, we must stick together, cousin," he said. "We are allies, and always will be." He left it to Robert to decide whether he was talking about the two of them or their countries. They parted friends.

He walked briskly across Green Park. Londoners were enjoying the sunshine, but there was a cloud of gloom over Walter's head. He had hoped that Germany and Russia would stay out of the Balkan crisis, but what he had learned so far today ominously suggested the opposite. Reaching Buckingham Palace, he turned left and walked along the Mall to the back entrance of the German embassy.

His father had an office in the embassy: he spent about one week in three there. There was a painting of Kaiser Wilhelm on the wall and a framed photograph of Walter in lieutenant's uniform on the desk. Otto held in his hand a piece of pottery. He collected English ceramics, and loved to go hunting for unusual items. Looking more closely, Walter saw that this was a creamware fruit bowl, the edges delicately pierced and molded to mimic basketwork. Knowing his father's taste, he guessed it was eighteenth century.

With Otto was Gottfried von Kessel, a cultural attaché whom Walter disliked. Gottfried had thick dark hair combed with a side parting, and wore spectacles with thick lenses. He was the same age as Walter and also had a father in the diplomatic service, but despite having that much in common, they were not friends. Walter thought Gottfried was a toady.

He nodded to Gottfried and sat down. "The Austrian emperor has written to our kaiser."

"We know that," Gottfried said quickly.

Walter ignored him. Gottfried was always trying to start a pissing contest. "No doubt the kaiser's reply will be amicable," he said to his father. "But a lot may depend upon nuance."

"His Majesty has not yet confided in me."

"But he will."

Otto nodded. "It is the kind of thing he sometimes asks me about."

"And if he urges caution, he might persuade the Austrians to be less belligerent."

Gottfried said: "Why should he do that?"

"To avoid Germany's being dragged into a war over such a worthless piece of territory as Serbia!"

"What are you afraid of?" Gottfried said scornfully. "The Serbian army?"

"I am afraid of the Russian army, and so should you be," Walter replied. "It is the largest in history—"

"I know that," said Gottfried.

Walter ignored the interruption. "In theory, the tsar can put six million men into the field within a few weeks—"

"I know—"

"—and that is more than the total population of Serbia."

"I know."

Walter sighed. "You seem to know everything, von Kessel. Do you know where the assassins got their guns and bombs?"

"From Slav nationalists, I presume."

"Any *particular* Slav nationalists, do you presume?"

"Who knows?"

"The Austrians know, I gather. They believe the arms came from the head of Serbian intelligence."

Otto grunted in surprise. "That *would* make the Austrians vengeful."

Gottfried said: "Austria is still ruled by its emperor. In the end, the decision for war can be made only by him."

Walter nodded. "Not that a Habsburg emperor has ever needed much of an excuse to be ruthless and brutal."

"What other way is there to rule an empire?"

Walter did not rise to the bait. "Other than the Hungarian prime minister, who does not carry much weight, there seems to be no one urging caution. That role must fall to us." Walter stood up. He had reported his findings, and he did not want to stay any longer in the same room as the irritating Gottfried. "If you will excuse me, Father, I'll go to tea at the Duchess of Sussex's house and see what else is being said around town."

Gottfried said: "The English don't pay calls on Sundays."

"I have an invitation," Walter replied, and went out before he lost his temper.

He threaded his way through Mayfair to Park Lane, where the Duke of Sussex had his palace. The duke played no role in the British government, but the duchess held a political salon. When Walter had arrived in London in December Fitz had introduced him to the duchess, who had made sure he was invited everywhere.

He entered her drawing room, bowed, shook her plump hand, and said: "Everyone in London wants to know what will happen in Serbia, so, even though it is Sunday, I have come here to ask you, Your Grace."

"There will be no war," she said, showing no awareness that he was joking. "Sit down and have a cup of tea. Of course it is tragic about the poor archduke and his wife, and no doubt the culprits will be punished, but how silly to think that great nations such as Germany and Britain would go to war over Serbia."

Walter wished he could feel so confident. He took a chair near Maud, who smiled happily, and Lady Hermia, who nodded. There were a dozen people in the room, including the first lord of the Admiralty, Winston Churchill. The decor was grandly out of date: too much heavy carved furniture, rich fabrics of a dozen different patterns, and every surface covered with ornaments, framed photographs, and vases of dried grasses. A footman handed Walter a cup of tea and offered milk and sugar.

Walter was happy to be near Maud but, as always, he wanted more, and he immediately began to wonder whether there was any way they could contrive to be alone, even if only for a minute or two.

The duchess said: "The problem, of course, is the weakness of the Turks."

The pompous old bat was right, Walter thought. The Ottoman Empire was in decline, held back from modernization by a conservative

Muslim priesthood. For centuries the Turkish sultan had kept order in the Balkan peninsula, from the Mediterranean coast of Greece as far north as Hungary, but now, decade by decade, it was pulling back. The nearest Great Powers, Austria and Russia, were trying to fill the vacuum. Between Austria and the Black Sea were Bosnia, Serbia, and Bulgaria in a line. Five years ago Austria had taken control of Bosnia. Now Austria was in a quarrel with Serbia, the middle one. The Russians looked at the map and saw that Bulgaria was the next domino, and that the Austrians could end up controlling the west coast of the Black Sea, threatening Russia's international trade.

Meanwhile the subject peoples of the Austrian Empire were starting to think they might rule themselves—which was why the Bosnian nationalist Gavrilo Princip had shot Archduke Franz Ferdinand in Sarajevo.

Walter said: "It's a tragedy for Serbia. I should think their prime minister is ready to throw himself into the Danube."

Maud said: "You mean the Volga."

Walter looked at her, glad of the excuse to drink in her appearance. She had changed her clothes, and was wearing a royal blue tea gown over a pale pink lace blouse and a pink felt hat with a blue pompom. "I most certainly do not, Lady Maud," he said.

She said: "The Volga runs through Belgrade, which is the capital of Serbia."

Walter was about to protest again; then he hesitated. She knew perfectly well that the Volga hardly came within a thousand miles of Belgrade. What was she up to? "I am reluctant to contradict someone as well-informed as you, Lady Maud," he said. "All the same—"

"We will look it up," she said. "My uncle, the duke, has one of the greatest libraries in London." She stood. "Come with me, and I shall prove you wrong."

This was bold behavior for a well-bred young woman, and the duchess pursed her lips.

Walter mimed a helpless shrug and followed Maud to the door.

For a moment, Lady Hermia looked as if she might go, too, but she was comfortably sunk in deep velvet upholstery, with a cup and saucer in her hand and a plate in her lap, and it was too much effort to move. "Don't be long," she said quietly, and ate some more cake. Then they were out of the room.

Maud preceded Walter across the hall, where a couple of footmen stood like sentries. She stopped in front of a door and waited for Walter to open it. They went inside.

The big room was silent. They were alone. Maud threw herself into Walter's arms. He hugged her hard, pressing her body against his. She turned her face up. "I love you," she said, and kissed him hungrily.

After a minute she broke away, breathless. Walter looked at her adoringly. "You're outrageous," he said. "Saying the Volga runs through Belgrade!"

"It worked, didn't it?"

He shook his head in admiration. "I would never have thought of it. You're so clever."

"We need an atlas," she said. "In case anyone comes in."

Walter scanned the shelves. This was the library of a collector rather than a reader. All the books were in fine bindings, most looking as if they had never been opened. A few reference books lurked in a corner, and he pulled out an atlas and found a map of the Balkans.

"This crisis," Maud said anxiously. "In the long run . . . it's not going to split us up, is it?"

"Not if I can help it," Walter said.

He drew her behind a bookcase, so that they could not be seen immediately by someone coming in, and kissed her again. She was deliciously needy today, rubbing her hands over his shoulders and arms and back as she kissed him. She broke the kiss to whisper: "Lift my skirt."

He swallowed. He had daydreamed of this. He grasped the material and drew it up.

"And the petticoats," she said. He took a bunch of fabric in each hand. "Don't crease it," she said. He tried to raise the garments without crushing the silk, but everything slipped through his hands.

Impatient, she bent down, grasped skirt and petticoats by the hems, and lifted everything to her waist. "Feel me," she said, looking him in the eye.

He was nervous that someone would come in, but too overwhelmed with love and desire to restrain himself. He put his right hand on the fork of her thighs—and gasped with shock: she was naked there. The realization that she must have planned to give him this pleasure inflamed him further. He stroked her gently, but she thrust her hips forward against his hand, and he pressed harder. "That's right," she said. He closed his eyes, but she said: "Look at me, my darling—please, look at me while you're doing it," and he opened them again. Her face was flushed and she was breathing hard through open lips. She gripped his hand and guided him, as he had guided her in the opera box. She whispered: "Put your finger in." She leaned against his shoulder. He could feel the heat of her breath through his clothes. She thrust against him again and again. Then she made a small sound in the back of her throat, like the muted cry of someone dreaming; and at last she slumped against him.

He heard the door open, and then Lady Hermia's voice. "Come along, Maud, dear. We must take our leave."

Walter withdrew his hand and Maud hastily smoothed her skirt. In a shaky voice she said: "I'm afraid I was wrong, Aunt Herm, and Herr von Ulrich was right—it's the Danube, not the Volga, that runs through Belgrade. We've just found it in the atlas."

They bent over the book as Lady Hermia came around the end of the bookcase. "I never doubted it," she said. "Men are generally right about these things, and Herr von Ulrich is a diplomat, who has to know a great many facts with which women do not need to trouble themselves. You shouldn't argue, Maud."

"I expect you're right," said Maud with breathtaking insincerity.

They all left the library and crossed the hall. Walter opened the door to the drawing room. Lady Hermia went in first. As Maud followed, she met his eye. He raised his right hand, put the tip of his finger into his mouth, and sucked it.

{ II }

This could not go on, Walter thought as he made his way back to the embassy. It was like being a schoolboy. Maud was twenty-three years old and he was twenty-eight, yet they had to resort to absurd subterfuges in order to spend five minutes alone together. It was time they got married.

He would have to ask Fitz's permission. Maud's father was dead, so her brother was the head of the family. Fitz would undoubtedly have preferred her to marry an Englishman. However, he would probably come around: he must be worrying that he might never get his feisty sister married off.

No, the major problem was Otto. He wanted Walter to marry a well-behaved Prussian maiden who would be happy to spend the rest of her life breeding heirs. And when Otto wanted something he did all he could to get it, crushing opposition remorselessly—which was what had made him a good army officer. It would never occur to him that his son had a right to choose his own bride, without interference or pressure. Walter would have preferred to have his father's encouragement and support: he certainly did not look forward to the inevitable stand-up confrontation. However, his love was a force more powerful by far than filial deference.

It was Sunday evening, but London was not quiet. Although Parliament was not sitting, and the mandarins of Whitehall had gone to their suburban homes, politics continued in the palaces of Mayfair, the gentlemen's clubs of St. James's, and the embassies. On the streets Walter recognized several members of Parliament, a couple of junior ministers from Britain's Foreign Office, and some European diplomats. He wondered whether Britain's bird-watching foreign secretary, Sir Edward Grey, had stayed in town this weekend instead of going to his beloved country cottage in Hampshire.

Walter found his father at his desk, reading decoded telegrams. "This may not be the best time to tell you my news," Walter began.

Otto grunted and carried on reading.

Walter plunged on. "I'm in love with Lady Maud."

Otto looked up. "Fitzherbert's sister? I suspected as much. You have my profound sympathy."

"Be serious, please, Father."

"No, you be serious." Otto threw down the papers he was reading. "Maud Fitzherbert is a feminist, a suffragette, and a social maverick. She's not a fit wife for anyone, let alone a German diplomat from a good family. So let's hear no more of it."

Hot words came to Walter's lips, but he clenched his teeth and kept his temper. "She's a wonderful woman, and I love her, so you'd better speak politely of her, whatever your opinions."

"I'll say what I think," Otto said carelessly. "She's dreadful." He looked down at his telegrams.

Walter's eye fell on the creamware fruit bowl his father had bought. "No," he said. He picked up the bowl. "You will not say what you think."

"Be careful with that."

Walter had his father's full attention now. "I feel protective of Lady Maud, the way you feel protective of this trinket."

"Trinket? Let me tell you, it's worth—"

"Except, of course, that love is stronger than the collector's greed." Walter tossed the delicate object into the air and caught it one-handed. His father let out an anguished cry of inarticulate protest. Walter went on heedlessly: "So when you speak insultingly of her, I feel as you do when you think I'm going to drop this—only more so."

"Insolent pup—"

Walter raised his voice over his father's. "And if you continue to trample all over my sensibilities, I will crush this stupid piece of pottery beneath my heel."

"All right, you've made your point. Put it down, for God's sake."

Walter took that for acquiescence, and replaced the ornament on a side table.

Otto said maliciously: "But there is something else you need to take into account . . . if I may mention it without treading on your *sensibilities*."

"All right."

"She is English."

"For God's sake!" Walter cried. "Wellborn Germans have been marrying English aristocrats for years. Prince Albert of Saxe-Coburg and Gotha married Queen Victoria—his grandson is now king of England. And the queen of England was born a Württemberg princess!"

Otto raised his voice. "Things have changed! The English are determined to keep us a second-rate power. They befriend our adversaries, Russia and France. You would be marrying an enemy of your fatherland."

Walter knew this was how the old guard thought, but it was irrational. "We should not be enemies," he said in exasperation. "There's no reason for it."

"They will never allow us to compete on equal terms."

"That's just not true!" Walter heard himself shouting, and tried to be calmer. "The English believe in free trade—they allow us to sell our manufactures throughout the British Empire."

"Read that, then." Otto threw across the desk the telegram he had been reading. "His Majesty the kaiser has asked for my comments."

Walter picked it up. It was a draft reply to the Austrian emperor's personal letter. Walter read it with mounting alarm. It ended: "The Emperor Franz Joseph may, however, rest assured that His Majesty will faithfully stand by Austria-Hungary, as is required by the obligations of his alliance and of his ancient friendship."

Walter was horrified. "But this gives Austria carte blanche!" he said. "They can do anything they like and we will support them!"

"There are some qualifications."

"Not many. Has this been sent?"

"No, but it has been agreed. It will be sent tomorrow."

"Can we stop it?"

"No, and I would not want to."

"But it commits us to support Austria in a war against Serbia."

"No bad thing."

"We don't want war!" Walter protested. "We need science, and manufacturing, and commerce. Germany must modernize and become liberal and grow. We want peace and prosperity." And, he added silently, we want a world in which a man can marry the woman he loves without being accused of treason.

"Listen to me," Otto said. "We have powerful enemies on both sides, France to the west and Russia to the east—and they are hand in glove. We can't fight a war on two fronts."

Walter knew this. "That's why we have the Schlieffen Plan," he said. "If we are forced to go to war, we first invade France with an overwhelming force, achieve victory within a few weeks, and then, with the west secure, we turn east to face Russia."

"Our only hope," Otto said. "But when that plan was adopted by the German army nine years ago, our intelligence told us it would take the Russian army forty days to mobilize. That gave us almost six weeks in which to conquer France. Ever since then, the Russians have been improving their railways—with money loaned by France!" Otto banged the desk, as if he could squash France under his fist. "As the Russians' mobilization time gets shorter, so the Schlieffen Plan becomes more risky. Which means"—he pointed his finger dramatically at Walter—"the sooner we have this war, the better for Germany!"

"No!" Why could the old man not see how dangerous this thinking was? "It means we should be seeking peaceful solutions to petty disputes."

"Peaceful solutions?" Otto shook his head knowingly. "You're a young idealist. You think there is an answer to every question."

"You actually want war," Walter said incredulously. "You really do."

"No one wants war," said Otto. "But sometimes it's better than the alternative."

{ III }

Maud had inherited a pittance from her father—three hundred pounds a year, barely enough to buy gowns for the season. Fitz got the title, the lands, the houses, and nearly all the money. That was the English system. But it was not what angered Maud. Money meant little to her: she did not really need her three hundred. Fitz paid for anything she wanted without question: he thought it ungentlemanly to be careful with money.

Her great resentment was that she had had no education. When she was seventeen, she had announced that she was going to university—whereupon everyone had laughed at her. It turned out that you had to come from a good school, and pass examinations, before they would let you in. Maud had never been to school, and even though she could discuss politics with the great men of the land, a succession of governesses and tutors had completely failed to equip her to pass any sort of exam. She had cried and raged for days, and even now thinking about it could still put her in a foul mood. This was what made her a suffragette: she knew girls would never get a decent education until women had the vote.

She had often wondered why women married. They contracted themselves to a lifetime of slavery and, she had asked, what did they get in return? Now, however, she knew the answer. She had never felt anything as intensely as her love for Walter. And the things they did to express that love gave her the most exquisite pleasure. To be able to touch each other that way anytime you liked would be heaven. She would have enslaved herself three times over, if that were the price.

But slavery was not the price, at least not with Walter. She had asked him whether he thought a wife should obey her husband in all things, and he had answered: "Certainly not. I don't see that obedience comes into it. Two adults who love each other should be able to make decisions together, without one having to obey the other."

She spent a lot of time thinking about their life together. For a few years he would probably be posted from one embassy to another, and they would travel the world: Paris, Rome, Budapest, perhaps even farther afield to Addis Ababa, Tokyo, Buenos Aires. She thought of the story of Ruth in the Bible: "Whither thou goest, I will go." Their sons would be taught to treat women as equals, and their daughters would grow up independent and strong-willed. Perhaps they would eventually settle in a town house in Berlin, so that their children could go to good German schools. At some point, no doubt, Walter would inherit Zumwald, his father's country house in East Prussia. When they were old, and their children were adults, they would spend more time in the country, walking hand in hand around the estate, reading side by side in the evenings, and reflecting on how the world had changed since they were young.

Maud had trouble thinking about anything else. She sat in her office at the Calvary Gospel Hall, staring at a price list of medical supplies, and remembered how Walter had sucked his fingertip at the door to the duchess's drawing room. People were beginning to notice her absentmindedness: Dr. Greenward had asked if she was feeling all right, and Aunt Herm had told her to wake up.

She tried again to concentrate on the order form, and this time she was interrupted by a tap at the door. Aunt Herm looked in and said: "Someone to see you." She seemed a bit awestruck, and handed Maud a card.

General Otto von Ulrich
ATTACHÉ
EMBASSY OF THE EMPIRE OF GERMANY
CARLTON HOUSE TERRACE, LONDON

"Walter's father!" said Maud. "What on earth . . . ?"

"What shall I say?" whispered Aunt Herm.

"Ask him if he would like tea or sherry, and show him in."

Von Ulrich was formally dressed in a black frock coat with satin lapels, a white piqué waistcoat, and striped trousers. His red face was perspiring in the summer heat. He was rounder than Walter, and not as handsome, but they had the same straight-backed, chin-up military stance.

Maud summoned her habitual insouciance. "My dear Herr von Ulrich, is this a formal visit?"

"I want to talk to you about my son," he said. His English was almost as good as Walter's, though he had an accent where Walter did not.

"It's kind of you to come to the point so quickly," Maud replied with a touch of sarcasm that went right over his head. "Please sit down. Lady Hermia will order some refreshment."

"Walter comes from an old aristocratic family."

"As do I," said Maud.

"We are traditional, conservative, devoutly religious . . . perhaps a little old-fashioned."

"Just like my family," Maud said.

This was not going the way Otto had planned. "We are Prussians," he said with a touch of exasperation.

"Ah," said Maud as if trumped. "Whereas we, of course, are Anglo-Saxons."

She was fencing with him, as if this were nothing more than a battle of wits, but underneath she was frightened. Why was he here? What was his aim? She felt it could not be benign. He was against her. He would try to come between her and Walter, she felt bleakly certain.

Anyway, he was not to be put off by facetiousness. "Germany and Great Britain are at odds. Britain makes friends with our enemies, Russia and France. This makes Britain our adversary."

"I'm sorry to hear that you think that way. Many do not."

"The truth is not arrived at by majority vote." Again she heard a note of asperity in his voice. He was used to being heard uncritically, especially by women.

Dr. Greenward's nurse brought in tea on a tray and poured. Otto remained silent until she left. Then he said: "We may go to war in the next few weeks. If we do not fight over Serbia, there will be some other casus belli. Sooner or later, Britain and Germany must do battle for mastery of Europe."

"I'm sorry you feel so pessimistic."

"Many others think the same."

"But the truth is not arrived at by majority vote."

Otto looked annoyed. He evidently expected her to sit and listen to his pomposity in silence. He did not like to be mocked. He said angrily: "You should pay attention to me. I'm telling you something that affects you. Most Germans regard Britain as their enemy. If Walter were to marry an Englishwoman, think of the consequences."

"I have, of course. Walter and I have talked at length about this."

"First, he would suffer my disapproval. I could not welcome an English daughter-in-law into my family."

"Walter feels that your love for your son would help you get over your revulsion for me, in the end. Is there really no chance of that?"

"Second," he said, ignoring her question, "he would be regarded as disloyal to the kaiser. Men of his own class would no longer be his friends. He and his wife would not be received in the best houses."

Maud was becoming angry. "I find that hard to credit. Surely not *all* Germans are so narrow-minded?"

He appeared not to notice her rudeness. "Third, and finally, Walter's career is with the foreign ministry. He will distinguish himself. I sent him to schools and universities in different countries. He speaks perfect English and passable Russian. Despite his immature idealistic views, he is well thought of by his superiors, and the kaiser has spoken kindly to him more than once. He could be foreign minister one day."

"He's brilliant," Maud said.

"But if he marries you, his career is over."

"That's ridiculous," she said, shocked.

"My dear young lady, is it not obvious? A man who is married to one of the enemy cannot be trusted."

"We have talked about this. His loyalty would naturally lie with Germany. I love him enough to accept that."

"He might be too concerned about his wife's family to give total loyalty to his own country. Even if he ruthlessly ignored the connection, men would still ask the question."

"You're exaggerating," she said, but she was beginning to lose confidence.

"He certainly could not work in any area that required secrecy. Men would not speak of confidential matters in his presence. He would be finished."

"He doesn't have to be in military intelligence. He can switch to other areas of diplomacy."

"All diplomacy requires secrecy. And then there is my own position."

Maud was surprised by this. She and Walter had not considered Otto's career.

"I am a close confidant of the kaiser's. Would he continue to place absolute trust in me if my son were married to an enemy alien?"

"He ought to."

"He would, perhaps, if I took firm, positive action, and disowned my son."

Maud gasped. "You would not do that."

Otto raised his voice. "I would be obliged to!"

She shook her head. "You would have a choice," she said desperately. "A man always has a choice."

"I will not sacrifice everything I have earned—my position, my career, the respect of my countrymen—for a *girl*," he said contemptuously.

Maud felt as if she had been slapped.

Otto went on: "But Walter will, of course."

"What are you saying?"

"If Walter were to marry you he would lose his family, his country, and his career. But he will do it. He has declared his love for you without fully thinking through the consequences, and sooner or later he will understand what a catastrophic mistake he has made. But he undoubtedly considers himself unofficially engaged to you, and he will not back out of a commitment. He is too much of a gentleman. 'Go ahead, disown me,' he will say to me. He would consider himself a coward otherwise."

"That's true," Maud said. She felt bewildered. This horrible old man saw the truth more clearly than she did.

Otto went on: "So *you* must break off the engagement."

She felt stabbed. "No!"

"It is the only way to save him. You must give him up."

Maud opened her mouth to object again, but Otto was right, and she could not think of anything to say.

Otto leaned forward and spoke with pressing intensity. "Will you break with him?"

Tears ran down Maud's face. She knew what she had to do. She could not ruin Walter's life, even out of love. "Yes," she sobbed. Her dignity was gone, and she did not care; the pain was too much. "Yes, I will break with him."

"Do you promise?"

"Yes, I promise."

Otto stood up. "Thank you for your courtesy in listening to me." He bowed. "I bid you good afternoon." He went out.

Maud buried her face in her hands.

CHAPTER EIGHT

Mid-July 1914

T here was a cheval glass in Ethel's new bedroom at Tŷ
Gwyn. It was old, the woodwork cracked and the glass
misted, but she could see herself full-length. She
considered it a great luxury.

She looked at herself in her underwear. She seemed to
have become more voluptuous since falling in love. She had put on a
little weight around her waist and hips, and her breasts seemed fuller,
perhaps because Fitz stroked and squeezed them so much. When she
thought about him, her nipples hurt.

Fitz had arrived that morning, with Princess Bea and Lady Maud,
and had whispered that he would meet her in the Gardenia Suite after
lunch. Ethel had put Maud in the Pink Room, making up an excuse
about repairs to the floorboards in Maud's usual apartment.

Now Ethel had come to her room to wash and put on clean underwear.
She loved preparing herself for him like this, anticipating how he would
touch her body and kiss her mouth, hearing in advance the way he

would groan with desire and pleasure, thinking of the smell of his skin and the voluptuous texture of his clothes.

She opened a drawer to take out fresh stockings, and her eye fell on a pile of clean strips of white cotton, the rags she used when menstruating. It occurred to her that she had not washed them since she had moved into this room. Suddenly there was a tiny seed of pure dread in her mind. She sat down heavily on the narrow bed. It was now the middle of July. Mrs. Jevons had left at the beginning of May. That was ten weeks ago. In that time Ethel should have used the rags not once but twice. "Oh, no," she said aloud. "Oh, please, no!"

She forced herself to think calmly and worked it out again. The king's visit had taken place in January. Ethel had been made housekeeper immediately afterward, but Mrs. Jevons had been too ill to move then. Fitz had gone to Russia in February, and had come back in March, which was when they had first made love properly. In April Mrs. Jevons had rallied, and Fitz's man of business, Albert Solman, had come down from London to explain her pension to her. She had left at the beginning of May, and that was when Ethel had moved into this room and put that frightening little pile of white cotton strips into the drawer. It was ten weeks ago. Ethel could not make the arithmetic come out any differently.

How many times had they met in the Gardenia Suite? At least eight. Each time, Fitz withdrew before the end, but sometimes he left it a bit late, and she felt the first of his spasms while he was still inside her. She had been deliriously happy to be with him that way, and in her ecstasy she had closed her eyes to the risk. Now she had been caught.

"Oh, God forgive me," she said aloud.

Her friend Dilys Pugh had fallen for a baby. Dilys was the same age as Ethel. She had been working as a housemaid for Perceval Jones's wife and walking out with Johnny Bevan. Ethel recalled how Dilys's breasts had got larger around the time she realized that you could, in fact, get pregnant from doing it standing up. They were married now.

What was going to happen to Ethel? She could not marry the father of her child. Apart from anything else, he was already married.

It was time to go and meet him. There would be no rolling on the bed today. They would have to talk about the future. She put on her housekeeper's black silk dress.

What would he say? He had no children: would he be pleased, or horrified? Would he cherish his love child, or be embarrassed by it? Would he love Ethel more for conceiving, or would he hate her?

She left her attic room and went along the narrow corridor and down the back stairs to the west wing. The familiar wallpaper with its pattern of gardenias quickened her desire, in the same way that the sight of her knickers aroused Fitz.

He was already there, standing by the window, looking over the sunlit garden, smoking a cigar; and when she saw him, she was struck again by how beautiful he was. She threw her arms around his neck. His brown tweed suit was soft to the touch because, she had discovered, it was made of cashmere. "Oh, Teddy, my lovely, I'm so happy to see you," she said. She liked being the only person who called him Teddy.

"And I to see you," he said, but he did not immediately stroke her breasts.

She kissed his ear. "I got something to say to you," she said solemnly.

"And I have something to tell you! May I go first?"

She was about to say no, but he detached himself from her embrace and took a step back, and suddenly her heart filled with foreboding. "What?" she said. "What is it?"

"Bea is expecting a baby." He drew on his cigar and blew out smoke like a sigh.

At first she could make no sense of his words. "What?" she said in a bewildered tone.

"The princess Bea, my wife, is pregnant. She is going to have a baby."

"You mean you've been at it with her at the same time as with me?" Ethel said angrily.

He looked startled. It seemed he had not expected her to resent that. "I must!" he protested. "I need an heir."

"But you said you loved me!"

"I do, and in a way I always will."

"No, Teddy!" she cried. "Don't say it like that—please don't!"

"Keep your voice down!"

"Keep my voice down? You're throwing me over! What is it to me now if people know?"

"It's everything to me."

Ethel was distraught. "Teddy, please, I love you."

"But it's over now. I have to be a good husband and a father to my child. You must understand."

"Understand, hell!" she raged. "How can you say it so easily? I've seen you show more emotion over a dog that had to be shot!"

"It's not true," he said, and there was a catch in his voice.

"I gave myself to you, in this room, on that bed by there."

"And I shan't—" He stopped. His face, frozen until now in an expression of rigid self-control, suddenly showed anguish. He turned away, hiding from her gaze. "I shan't ever forget that," he whispered.

She moved closer to him, and saw tears on his cheeks, and her anger evaporated. "Oh, Teddy, I'm so sorry," she said.

He tried to pull himself together. "I care for you very much, but I must do my duty," he said. The words were cold, but his voice was tormented.

"Oh, God." She tried to stop crying. She had not told him her news yet. She wiped her eyes with her sleeve, sniffed, and swallowed. "Duty?" she said. "You don't know the half."

"What are you talking about?"

"I'm pregnant, too."

"Oh, my good God." He put his cigar to his lips, mechanically, then lowered it again without puffing on it. "But I always withdrew!"

"Not soon enough, then."

"How long have you known?"

"I just realized. I looked in my drawer and saw my clean rags." He winced. Evidently he did not like talk of menstruation. Well, he would have to put up with it. "I worked out that I haven't had the curse since I moved into Mrs. Jevons's old room, and that's ten weeks ago."

"Two cycles. That makes it definite. That's what Bea said. Oh, hell." He touched the cigar to his lips, found that it had gone out, and dropped it on the floor with a grunt of irritation.

A wry thought occurred to her. "You might have two heirs."

"Don't be ridiculous," he said sharply. "A bastard doesn't inherit."

"Oh," she said. She had not seriously intended to make a claim for her child. On the other hand, she had not until now thought of it as a bastard. "Poor little thing," she said. "My baby, the bastard."

He looked guilty. "I'm sorry," he said. "I didn't mean that. Forgive me."

She could see that his better nature was at war with his selfish instincts. She touched his arm. "Poor Fitz."

"God forbid that Bea should find out about this," he said.

She felt mortally wounded. Why should his main concern be the other woman? Bea would be all right: she was rich and married, and carrying the loved and honored child of the Fitzherbert clan.

Fitz went on: "The shock might be too much for her."

Ethel recalled a rumor that Bea had suffered a miscarriage last year. All the female servants had discussed it. According to Nina, the Russian maid, the princess blamed the miscarriage on Fitz, who had upset her by canceling a planned trip to Russia.

Ethel felt terribly rejected. "So your main concern is that the news of our baby might upset your wife."

He stared at her. "I don't want her to miscarry—it's important!"

He had no idea how callous he was being. "Damn you," Ethel said.

"What do you expect? The child Bea is carrying is one I have been hoping and praying for. Yours is not wanted by you, me, or anyone else."

"That's not how I see it," she said in a small voice, and she began to cry again.

"I've got to think about this," he said. "I need to be alone." He took her by the shoulders. "We'll talk again tomorrow. In the meantime, tell no one. Do you understand?"

She nodded.

"Promise me."

"I promise."

"Good girl," he said, and he left the room.

Ethel bent down and picked up the dead cigar.

{ II }

She told no one, but she was unable to pretend that everything was all right, so she feigned illness and went to bed. As she lay alone, hour after hour, grief slowly gave way to anxiety. How would she and her baby live?

She would lose her job here at Tŷ Gwyn—that was automatic, even if her baby had not been the earl's. That alone hurt. She had been so proud of herself when she was made housekeeper. Gramper was fond of saying that pride comes before a fall. He was right in this case.

She was not sure she could return to her parents' house: the disgrace would kill her father. She was almost as upset about that as she was about her own shame. It would wound him more than her, in a way; he was so rigid about this sort of thing.

Anyway, she did not want to live as an unmarried mother in Aberowen. There were two already: Maisie Owen and Gladys Pritchard. They were sad figures with no proper place in the town's social order. They were single, but no man was interested in them; they were mothers, but they lived with their parents as if they were still children; they were not welcome in any church, pub, shop, or club. How could she, Ethel Williams, who had always considered herself a cut above the rest, sink to the lowest level of all?

She had to leave Aberowen, then. She was not sorry. She would be glad to turn her back on the rows of grim houses, the prim little chapels, and the endless quarrels between miners and management. But where would she go? And would she be able to see Fitz?

As darkness fell she lay awake looking through the window at the stars, and at last she made a plan. She would start a new life in a new place. She would wear a wedding ring and tell a story about a dead husband. She would find someone to mind the baby, get a job of some kind, and earn money. She would send her child to school. It would be a girl, she felt, and she would be clever, a writer or a doctor, or perhaps a campaigner like Mrs. Pankhurst, championing women's rights and getting arrested outside Buckingham Palace.

She had thought she would not sleep, but emotion had drained her, and she drifted off around midnight and fell into a heavy, dreamless slumber.

The rising sun woke her. She sat upright, looking forward to the new day as always; then she remembered that her old life was over, ruined, and she was in the middle of a tragedy. She almost succumbed to grief again, but fought against it. She could not afford the luxury of tears. She had to start a new life.

She got dressed and went down to the servants' hall, where she announced that she was fully recovered from yesterday's malady and fit to do her normal work.

Lady Maud sent for her before breakfast. Ethel made up a coffee tray and took it to the Pink Room. Maud was at her dressing table in a purple silk negligee. She had been crying. Ethel had troubles of her own, but all the same her sympathy quickened. "What's the matter, my lady?"

"Oh, Williams, I've had to give him up."

Ethel assumed she meant Walter von Ulrich. "But why?"

"His father came to see me. I hadn't really faced the fact that Britain and Germany are enemies, and marriage to me would ruin Walter's career—and possibly his father's, too."

"But everyone says there's not going to be a war—Serbia's not important enough."

"If not now, it will be later; and even if it never happens, the threat is enough." There was a frill of pink lace around the dressing table, and Maud was picking at it nervously, tearing the expensive lace. It was going to take hours to mend, Ethel thought. Maud went on: "No one in the

German foreign ministry would trust Walter with secrets if he were married to an Englishwoman."

Ethel poured the coffee and handed Maud a cup. "Herr von Ulrich will give up his job if he really loves you."

"But I don't want him to!" Maud stopped tearing the lace and drank some coffee. "I can't be the person that ended his career. What kind of basis is that for marriage?"

He could have another career, Ethel thought; and if he really loved you, he would. Then she thought of the man *she* loved, and how quickly his passion had cooled when it became inconvenient. I'll keep my opinions to myself, she thought; I don't know a bloody thing. She asked: "What did Walter say?"

"I haven't seen him. I wrote him a letter. I stopped going to all the places where I usually meet him. Then he started to call at the house, and it became embarrassing to keep telling the servants I was not at home, so I came down here with Fitz."

"Why won't you talk to him?"

"Because I know what will happen. He will take me in his arms and kiss me, and I'll give in."

I know that feeling, Ethel thought.

Maud sighed. "You're quiet this morning, Williams. You've probably got worries of your own. Are things very hard with this strike?"

"Yes, my lady. The whole town is on short rations."

"Are you still feeding the miners' children?"

"Every day."

"Good. My brother is very generous."

"Yes, my lady." When it suits him, she thought.

"Well, you'd better get on with your work. Thank you for the coffee. I expect I'm boring you with my problems."

Impulsively, Ethel seized Maud's hand. "Please don't say that. You've always been good to me. I'm very sorry about Walter, and I hope you will always tell me your troubles."

"What a kind thing to say." Fresh tears came to Maud's eyes. "Thank you very much, Williams." She squeezed Ethel's hand, then released it.

Ethel picked up the tray and left. When she reached the kitchen, Peel, the butler, said: "Have you done something wrong?"

Little do you know, she thought. "Why do you ask?"

"His lordship wants to see you in the library at half past ten."

So it was to be a formal talk, Ethel thought. Perhaps that was better. They would be separated by a desk, and she would not be tempted to throw herself into his arms. That would help her keep back the tears. She would need to be cool and unemotional. The entire course of the rest of her life would be set by this discussion.

She went about her household duties. She was going to miss Tŷ Gwyn. In the years she had worked there she had come to love the gracious old furniture. She had picked up the names of the pieces, and learned to recognize a torchère, a buffet, an armoire, or a canterbury. As she dusted and polished she noticed the marquetry, the swags and scrolls, the feet shaped like lions' paws clasping balls. Occasionally, someone like Peel would say: "That's French—Louis Quinze," and she had realized that every room was decorated and furnished consistently in a style, baroque or neoclassical or Gothic. She would never live with such furniture again.

After an hour she made her way to the library. The books had been collected by Fitz's ancestors. Nowadays the room was not much used: Bea read only French novels, and Fitz did not read at all. Houseguests sometimes came here for peace and quiet, or to use the ivory chess set on the center table. This morning the blinds were pulled halfway down, on Ethel's instructions, to shade the room from the July sun and keep it cool. Consequently the room was gloomy.

Fitz sat in a green leather armchair. To Ethel's surprise, Albert Solman was there, too, in a black suit and a stiff-collared shirt. A lawyer by training, Solman was what Edwardian gentlemen called a man of business. He managed Fitz's money, checking his income from coal royalties and rents, paying the bills, and issuing cash for staff wages. He also dealt with leases and other contracts, and occasionally brought lawsuits against people who tried to cheat Fitz. Ethel had met him before and did not like him. She thought he was a know-all. Perhaps all lawyers were; she did not know: he was the only one she had ever met.

Fitz stood up, looking embarrassed. "I have taken Mr. Solman into my confidence," he said.

"Why?" said Ethel. She had had to promise to tell no one. Fitz's telling this lawyer seemed like a betrayal.

Fitz looked ashamed of himself—a rare sight. "Solman will tell you what I propose," he said.

"Why?" Ethel said again.

Fitz gave her a pleading look, as if to beg her not to make this any worse for him.

But she felt unsympathetic. It was not easy for her—why should it be easy for him? "What is it that you're frightened to tell me yourself?" she said, challenging him.

He had lost all his arrogant confidence. "I will leave him to explain," he said; and to her astonishment he left the room.

When the door closed behind him she stared at Solman, thinking: How can I talk about my baby's future with this stranger?

Solman smiled at her. "So, you've been naughty, have you?"

That stung her. "Did you say that to the earl?"

"Of course not!"

"Because he did the same thing, you know. It takes two people to make a baby."

"All right, there's no need to go into all that."

"Just don't speak as if I did this all on my own."

"Very well."

Ethel took a seat, then looked at him again. "You may sit down, if you wish," she said, just as if she were the lady of the house condescending to the butler.

He reddened. He did not know whether to sit, and look as if he had been waiting for permission, or remain standing, like a servant. In the end he paced up and down. "His lordship has instructed me to make you an offer," he said. Pacing did not really work, so he stopped and stood in front of her. "It is a generous offer, and I advise you to accept it."

Ethel said nothing. Fitz's callousness had one useful effect: it made her realize she was in a negotiation. This was familiar territory to her. Her father was always in negotiations, arguing and dealing with the mine management, always trying to get higher wages, shorter hours, and better safety precautions. One of his maxims was "Never speak unless you have to." So she remained silent.

Solman looked at her expectantly. When he gathered that she was not going to respond, he looked put out. He resumed: "His lordship is willing to give you a pension of twenty-four pounds a year, paid monthly in advance. I think that's very good of him. Don't you?"

The lousy rotten miser, Ethel thought. How could he be so mean to me? Twenty-four pounds was a housemaid's wage. It was half what Ethel was getting as housekeeper, and she would be losing her room and board.

Why did men think they could get away with this? Probably because they usually could. A woman had no rights. It took two people to make a baby, but only one was obliged to look after it. How had women let themselves get into such a weak position? It made her angry.

Still she did not speak.

Solman pulled up a chair and sat close to her. "Now, you must look on the bright side. You'll have ten shillings a week—"

"Not quite," she said quickly.

"Well, say we make it twenty-six pounds a year—that's ten shillings a week. What do you say?"

Ethel said nothing.

"You can find a nice little room in Cardiff for two or three shillings, and you can spend the rest on yourself." He patted her knee. "And, who knows, you may find another generous man to make life a little easier for you . . . eh? You're a very attractive girl, you know."

She pretended not to take his meaning. The idea of being the lover of a creepy lawyer such as Solman disgusted her. Did he really think he could take the place of Fitz? She did not respond to his innuendo. "Are there conditions?" she said coldly.

"Conditions?"

"Attached to the earl's offer."

Solman coughed. "The usual ones, of course."

"The usual? So you've done this before."

"Not for Earl Fitzherbert," he said quickly.

"But for someone else."

"Let us stick to the business at hand, please."

"You may go on."

"You must not put the earl's name on the child's birth certificate, or in any other way reveal to anyone that he is the father."

"And in your experience, Mr. Solman, do women usually accept these conditions of yours?"

"Yes."

Of course they do, she thought bitterly. What choice have they got? They are not entitled to anything, so they take what they can get. Of course they accept the conditions. "Are there any more?"

"After you leave Tŷ Gwyn, you must not attempt in any way to get in touch with his lordship."

So, Ethel thought, he doesn't want to see me or his child. Disappointment surged up inside her like a wave of weakness: if she had not been sitting down she might have fallen. She clenched her jaw to stop the tears. When she had herself under control, she said: "Anything else?"

"I believe that's all."

Ethel stood up.

Solman said: "You must contact me about where the monthly payments should be made." He took out a small silver box and extracted a card.

"No," she said when he offered it to her.

"But you will need to get in touch with me—"

"No, I won't," she said again.

"What do you mean?"

"The offer is not acceptable."

"Now, don't be foolish, Miss Williams—"

"I'll say it again, Mr. Solman, so there can be no doubt in your mind. The offer is not acceptable. My answer is no. I got nothing more to say to you. Good day." She went out and banged the door.

She returned to her room, locked her door, and cried her heart out.

How could Fitz be so cruel? Did he really never want to see her again? Or his baby? Did he think that everything that had happened between them could be wiped out by twenty-four pounds a year?

Did he really not love her any longer? Had he ever loved her? Was she a fool?

She had thought he loved her. She had felt sure that meant *something*. Perhaps he had been playacting all the time, and had deceived her—but she did not think so. A woman could tell when a man was faking.

So what was he doing now? He must be suppressing his feelings. Perhaps he was a man of shallow emotions. That was possible. He might have loved her, genuinely, but with a love that was easily forgotten when it became inconvenient. Such weakness of character might have escaped her notice in the throes of passion.

At least his hard-heartedness made it easier for her to bargain. She had no need to think of his feelings. She could concentrate on trying to get the best for herself and the baby. She must always think how Da would have handled things. A woman was not quite powerless, despite the law.

Fitz would be worried now, she guessed. He must have expected her to take the offer, or at worst hold out for a higher price; then he would have felt his secret was safe. Now he would be baffled as well as anxious.

She had not given Solman a chance to ask what she *did* want. Let them flounder around in the dark for a while. Fitz would begin to fear that Ethel intended to get revenge by telling Princess Bea about the baby.

She looked out of the window at the clock on the roof of the stable. It was a few minutes before twelve. On the front lawn, the staff would be getting ready to serve dinner to the miners' children. Princess Bea usually liked to see the housekeeper at about twelve. She often had complaints: she did not like the flowers in the hall, the footmen's uniforms were not pressed, the paintwork on the landing was flaking. In her turn the housekeeper had questions to ask about allocating rooms to guests, renewing china and glassware, hiring and firing maids and kitchen girls. Fitz usually came into the morning room at about half past twelve for a glass of sherry before lunch.

Then Ethel would turn the thumbscrews.

{ III }

Fitz watched the miners' children queuing up for their lunch—or "dinner," as they called it. Their faces were dirty, their hair was unkempt, and their clothes were ragged, but they looked happy. Children were amazing. These were among the poorest in the land, and their fathers were locked in a bitter dispute, but the children showed no sign of it.

Ever since marrying Bea he had longed for a child. She had miscarried once, and he was terrified she might do so again. Last time she had thrown a tantrum simply because he had canceled their trip to Russia. If she found out that he had made their housekeeper pregnant, her rage would be uncontrollable.

And the dreadful secret was in the hands of a servant girl.

He was tortured by worry. It was a terrible punishment for his sin. In other circumstances he might have taken some joy in having a child with Ethel. He could have put mother and baby into a little house in Chelsea and visited them once a week. He felt another stab of regret and longing at the poignancy of that daydream. He did not want to treat Ethel harshly. Her love had been sweet to him: her yearning kisses, her eager touch, the heat of her young passion. Even while he was telling her the bad news, he had wished he could run his hands over her lithe body and feel her kissing his neck in that hungry way that he found so exhilarating. But he had to harden his heart.

As well as being the most exciting woman he had ever kissed, she was intelligent and well-informed and funny. Her father always talked about current affairs, she had told him. And the housekeeper at Tŷ Gwyn was entitled to read the earl's newspapers after the butler had finished with them—a below-stairs rule that he had not known about.

Ethel asked him unexpected questions that he could not always answer, such as "Who ruled Hungary before the Austrians?" He was going to miss that, he thought sadly.

But she would not behave the way a discarded mistress was supposed to. Solman had been shaken by his conversation with her. Fitz had asked him: "What *does* she want?" but Solman did not know. Fitz harbored a dreadful suspicion that Ethel might tell Bea the whole story, just out of some twisted moral desire to let the truth come out. God help me keep her away from my wife, he prayed.

He was surprised to see the small round form of Perceval Jones, strutting across the lawn in green plus fours and walking boots. "Good morning, my lord," said the mayor, doffing his brown felt hat.

"Morning, Jones." As chairman of Celtic Minerals, Jones was the source of a great deal of Fitz's wealth, but all the same he did not like the man.

"The news is not good," Jones said.

"You mean from Vienna? I understand the Austrian emperor is still working on the wording of his ultimatum to Serbia."

"No, I mean from Ireland. The Ulstermen won't accept home rule, you know. It will make them a minority under a Roman Catholic government. The army is already mutinous."

Fitz frowned. He did not like to hear talk of mutiny in the British army. He said stiffly: "No matter what the newspapers may say, I don't believe that British officers will disobey the orders of their sovereign government."

"They already have!" said Jones. "What about the Curragh Mutiny?"

"No one disobeyed orders."

"Fifty-seven officers resigned when ordered to march on the Ulster Volunteers. You may not call that mutiny, my lord, but everyone else does."

Fitz grunted. Jones was unfortunately right. The truth was that English officers would not attack their fellow men in the defense of a mob of Irish Catholics. "Ireland should never have been promised independence," he said.

"I agree with you there," said Jones. "But I really came to talk to you about this." He indicated the children, seated on benches at trestle tables, eating boiled cod with cabbage. "I wish you'd put an end to it."

Fitz did not like to be told what to do by his social inferiors. "I don't care to let the children of Aberowen starve, even if it's the fault of their fathers."

"You're just prolonging the strike."

The fact that Fitz received a royalty on every ton of coal did not mean, in his view, that he was obliged to take the side of the mine owners against the men. Offended, he said: "The strike is your concern, not mine."

"You take the money quick enough."

Fitz was outraged. "I have no more to say to you." He turned away.

Jones was instantly contrite. "I beg your pardon, my lord, do forgive me—an overhasty remark, most ill-judged, but the matter is extremely tiresome."

It was hard for Fitz to refuse an apology. He was not mollified, but all the same he turned back and spoke to Jones courteously. "All right, but I shall continue to give the children dinner."

"You see, my lord, a coal miner may be stubborn on his own account, and suffer a good deal of hardship through foolish pride; but what breaks him, in the end, is to see his children go hungry."

"You're working the pit anyway."

"With third-rate foreign labor. Most of the men are not trained miners, and their output is small. Mainly we're using them to maintain the tunnels and keep the horses alive. We're not bringing up much coal."

"For the life of me I can't think why you evicted those wretched widows from their homes. There were only eight of them, and after all, they had lost their husbands in the damn pit."

"It's a dangerous principle. The house goes with the collier. Once we depart from that, we'll end up as nothing better than slum landlords."

Perhaps you should not have built slums, then, Fitz thought, but he held his tongue. He did not want to prolong the conversation with this pompous little tyrant. He looked at his watch. It was half past twelve: time for a glass of sherry. "It's no good, Jones," he said. "I shan't fight your battles for you. Good day." He walked briskly to the house.

Jones was the least of his worries. What was he going to do about Ethel? He had to make sure Bea was not upset. Apart from the danger to the unborn baby, he felt the pregnancy might be a new start for their marriage. The child might bring them together and re-create the warmth and intimacy they had had when they were first together. But that hope would be dashed if Bea learned he had been dallying with the housekeeper. She would be incandescent.

He was grateful for the cool of the hall, with its flagstones underfoot and hammer-beam ceiling. His father had chosen this feudal decor. The only book Papa had ever read, apart from the Bible, was Gibbon's *Decline and Fall of the Roman Empire.* He believed that the even greater British Empire would go the same way unless noblemen fought to preserve its institutions, especially the Royal Navy, the Church of England, and the Conservative Party.

He was right, Fitz had no doubt.

A glass of dry sherry was just the thing before lunch. It perked him up and sharpened his appetite. With a pleasant feeling of anticipation, he entered the morning room. There he was horrified to see Ethel talking to Bea. He stopped in the doorway and stared in consternation. What was she saying? Was he too late? "What's going on here?" he said sharply.

Bea looked at him in surprise and said coolly: "I am discussing pillowcases with my housekeeper. Did you expect something more dramatic?" Her Russian accent rolled the letter r in "dramatic."

For a moment he did not know what to say. He realized he was staring at his wife and his mistress. The thought of how intimate he had been with both these women was unsettling. "I don't know, I'm sure," he muttered, and he sat down at a writing desk with his back to them.

The two women carried on with their conversation. It was indeed about pillowcases: how long they lasted, how worn ones could be patched and used by servants, and whether it was best to buy them embroidered or get plain ones and have the housemaids do the embroidery. But Fitz was still shaken. The little tableau, mistress and servant in quiet conversation, reminded him of how terrifyingly easy it would be for Ethel to tell Bea the truth. This could not go on. He had to take action.

He took a sheet of blue crested writing paper from the drawer, dipped a pen in the inkwell, and wrote: "Meet me after lunch." He blotted the note and slipped it into a matching envelope.

After a couple of minutes, Bea dismissed Ethel. As she was leaving, Fitz spoke without turning his head. "Come here, please, Williams."

She came to his side. He noticed the light fragrance of scented soap—she had admitted stealing it from Bea. Despite his anger, he was uncomfortably aware of the closeness of her slim, strong thighs under the black silk of the housekeeper's dress. Without looking at her he handed her the envelope. "Send someone to the veterinary surgery in town to get a bottle of these dog pills. They're for kennel cough."

"Very good, my lord." She went out.

He would resolve the situation in a couple of hours' time.

He poured his sherry. He offered a glass to Bea but she declined. The wine warmed his stomach and eased his tension. He sat next to his wife, and she gave him a friendly smile. "How do you feel?" he said.

"Revolting, in the mornings," she said. "But that passes. I'm fine now."

His thoughts quickly returned to Ethel. She had him over a barrel. She had said nothing, but implicitly she was threatening to tell Bea everything. It was surprisingly crafty of her. He fretted impotently. He would have liked to settle the matter even sooner than this afternoon.

They had lunch in the small dining room, sitting at a square-legged oak table that might have come from a medieval monastery. Bea told him she had discovered there were some Russians in Aberowen. "More than a hundred, Nina tells me."

With an effort, Fitz put Ethel from his mind. "They will be among the strikebreakers brought in by Perceval Jones."

"Apparently they are being ostracized. They can't get service in the shops and cafés."

"I must get Reverend Jenkins to preach a sermon on loving your neighbor, even if he is a strikebreaker."

"Can't you just order the shopkeepers to serve them?"

Fitz smiled. "No, my dear, not in this country."

"Well, I feel sorry for them and I would like to do something for them."

He was pleased. "That's a kindly impulse. What do you have in mind?"

"I believe there is a Russian Orthodox church in Cardiff. I will get a priest up here to perform a service for them one Sunday."

Fitz frowned. Bea had converted to the Church of England when they married, but he knew that she hankered for the church of her childhood, and he saw it as a sign that she was unhappy in her adopted country. But he did not want to cross her. "Very well," he said.

"Then we could give them dinner in the servants' hall."

"It's a nice thought, my dear, but they might be a rough crowd."

"We'll feed only those who come to the service. That way we will exclude the Jews and the worst of the troublemakers."

"Shrewd. Of course, the townspeople may not like you for it."

"But that is of no concern to me or you."

He nodded. "Very well. Jones has been complaining that I am supporting the strike by feeding the children. If you entertain the strikebreakers, at least no one can say that we're taking sides."

"Thank you," she said.

The pregnancy had already improved their relationship, Fitz thought.

He had two glasses of hock with his lunch, but his anxiety came back when he left the dining room and made his way to the Gardenia Suite. Ethel held his fate in her hands. She had all of a woman's soft, emotional nature, but nevertheless she would not be told what to do. He could not control her, and that scared him.

But she was not there. He looked at his watch. It was a quarter past two. He had said "after lunch." Ethel would have known when coffee had been served and she should have been waiting for him. He had not specified the location, but surely she could work that out.

He began to feel apprehensive.

After five minutes he was tempted to leave. No one kept him waiting like this. But he did not want to leave the issue unresolved for another day, or even another hour, so he stayed.

She came in at half past two.

He said angrily: "What are you trying to do to me?"

She ignored the question. "What the hell were you thinking of, to make me talk to a lawyer from London?"

"I thought it would be less emotional."

"Don't be bloody daft." Fitz was shocked. No one had talked to him like this since he was a schoolboy. She went on: "I'm having your baby. How can it be unemotional?"

She was right; he had been foolish, and her words stung, but at the same time he could not help loving the music of her accent—the word "unemotional" having a different note for each of its five syllables, so that it sounded like a melody. "I'm sorry," he said. "I'll pay you double—"

"Don't make it worse, Teddy," she said, but her tone was softer. "Don't bargain with me, as if this was a matter of the right price."

He pointed an accusing finger. "You are not to speak to my wife, do you hear me? I won't have it!"

"Don't give me orders, Teddy. I've got no reason to obey you."

"How dare you speak to me like that?"

"Shut up and listen, and I'll tell you."

He was infuriated by her tone, but he remembered that he could not afford to antagonize her. "Go on, then," he said.

"You've behaved to me in a very unloving way."

He knew that was true, and he felt a stab of guilt. He was wretchedly sorry to have hurt her. But he tried not to show it.

She went on: "I still love you too much to want to spoil your happiness."

He felt even worse.

"I don't want to hurt you," she said. She swallowed and turned away, and he saw tears in her eyes. He began to speak, but she held up her hand to silence him. "You are asking me to leave my job and my home, so you must help me start a new life."

"Of course," he said. "If that's what you wish." Talking in more practical terms helped them both suppress their feelings.

"I'm going to London."

"Good idea." He could not help being pleased: no one in Aberowen would know she had a baby, let alone whose it was.

"You're going to buy me a little house. Nothing fancy—a working-class neighborhood will suit me very well. But I want six rooms, so that I can live on the ground floor and take in a lodger. The rent will pay for repairs and maintenance. I will still have to work."

"You've thought about this carefully."

"You're wondering how much it will cost, I expect, but you don't want to ask me, because a gentleman doesn't like to ask the price of things."

It was true.

"I looked in the newspaper," she said. "A house like that is about three hundred pounds. Probably cheaper than paying me two pounds a month for the rest of my life."

Three hundred pounds was nothing to Fitz. Bea could spend that much on clothes in one afternoon at the Maison Paquin in Paris. He said: "But you would promise to keep the secret?"

"And I promise to love and care for your child, and raise her—or him—to be happy and healthy and well-educated, even though you don't show any sign of being concerned about that."

He felt indignant, but she was right. He had hardly given a thought to the child. "I'm sorry," he said. "I'm too worried about Bea."

"I know," she said, her tone softening as it always did when he allowed his anxiety to show.

"When will you leave?"

"Tomorrow morning. I'm in just as much of a hurry as you. I'll get the train to London, and start looking for a house right away. When I've found the right place, I'll write to Solman."

"You'll have to stay in lodgings while you look for a house." He took his wallet from the inside pocket of his jacket and handed her two white five-pound notes.

She smiled. "You have no idea how much things cost, do you, Teddy?" She gave back one of the notes. "Five pounds is plenty."

He looked offended. "I don't want you to feel that I'm short-changing you."

Her manner changed, and he caught a glimpse of underlying rage. "Oh, you are, Teddy, you are," she said sourly. "But not in money."

"We both did it," he said defensively, glancing at the bed.

"But only one of us is going to have a baby."

"Well, let's not argue. I'll tell Solman to do what you have suggested."

She held out her hand. "Good-bye, Teddy. I know you'll keep your word." Her voice was even, but he could tell that she was struggling to maintain her composure.

He shook hands, even though it seemed odd for two people who had made passionate love. "I will," he said.

"Please leave now, quickly," she said, and she turned aside.

He hesitated a moment longer, then left the room.

As he walked away, he was surprised and ashamed to feel unmanly tears come to his eyes. "Good-bye, Ethel," he whispered to the empty corridor. "May God bless and keep you."

{ IV }

She went to the luggage store in the attic and stole a small suitcase, old and battered. No one would ever miss it. It had belonged to Fitz's father, and had his crest stamped in the leather: the gilding had worn off long ago, but the impression could still be made out. She packed stockings and underwear and some of the princess's scented soap.

Lying in bed that night, she decided she did not want to go to London after all. She was too frightened to go through this alone. She wanted to be with her family. She needed to ask her mother questions about pregnancy. She should be in a familiar place when the baby came. Her child would need its grandparents and its uncle Billy.

In the morning she put on her own clothing, left her housekeeper's dress hanging from its nail, and crept out of Tŷ Gwyn early. At the end of the drive she looked back at the house, its stones black with coal dust, its long rows of windows reflecting the rising sun, and she thought how much she had learned since she first came here to work as a thirteen-year-old fresh from school. Now she knew how the elite lived. They had strange food, prepared in complicated ways, and they wasted more than they ate. They all spoke with the same strangled accent, even some of the foreigners. She had handled rich women's beautiful underwear, fine cotton and slippery silk, hand-sewn and embroidered and trimmed with lace, twelve of everything piled in their chests of drawers. She could look at a sideboard and tell at a glance in what century it had been made. Most of all, she thought bitterly, she had learned that love is not to be trusted.

She walked down the mountainside into Aberowen and made her way to Wellington Row. The door of her parents' house was unlocked, as always. She went inside. The main room, the kitchen, was smaller than the Vase Room at Tŷ Gwyn, used only for arranging flowers.

Mam was kneading dough for bread, but when she saw the suitcase she stopped and said: "What's gone wrong?"

"I've come home," Ethel said. She put down the case and sat at the square kitchen table. She felt too ashamed to say what had happened.

However, Mam guessed. "You've been sacked!"

Ethel could not look at her mother. "Aye. I'm sorry, Mam."

Mam wiped her hands on a rag. "What have you done?" she said angrily. "Out with it, now!"

Ethel sighed. Why was she holding back? "I fell for a baby," she said.

"Oh, no—you wicked girl!"

Ethel fought back tears. She had hoped for sympathy, not condemnation. "I am a wicked girl," she said. She took off her hat, trying to keep her composure.

"It have all gone to your head—working at the big house, and meeting the king and queen. It have made you forget how you were raised."

"I expect you're right."

"It will kill your father."

"He doesn't have to give birth," Ethel said sarcastically. "I expect he'll be all right."

"Don't be cheeky. It's going to break his heart."

"Where is he?"

"Gone to another strike meeting. Think of his position in the town: elder of the chapel, miners' agent, secretary of the Independent Labour Party—how will he hold up his head at meetings, with everyone thinking his daughter's a slut?"

Ethel's control failed. "I'm very sorry to cause him shame," she said, and she began to cry.

Mam's expression changed. "Oh, well," she said. "It's the oldest story in the world." She came around the table and pressed Ethel's head to her breast. "Never mind, never mind," she said, just as she had when Ethel was a child and grazed her knees.

After a while, Ethel's sobs eased.

Mam released her and said: "We'd better have a cup of tea." There was a kettle kept permanently on the hob. She put tea leaves into a pot and poured boiling water in, then stirred the mixture with a wooden spoon. "When's the baby due?"

"February."

"Oh, my goodness." Mam turned from the fire to look at Ethel. "I'm going to be a grandmother!"

They both laughed. Mam set out cups and poured the tea. Ethel drank some and felt better. "Did you have easy births, or difficult?" she asked.

"There are no easy births, but mine were better than most, my mother said. I've had a bad back ever since Billy, all the same."

Billy came downstairs, saying: "Who's talking about me?" He could sleep late, Ethel realized, because he was on strike. Every time she saw him he seemed taller and broader. "Hello, Eth," he said, and kissed her with a bristly mustache. "Why the suitcase?" He sat down, and Mam poured him tea.

"I've done something stupid, Billy," said Ethel. "I'm having a baby."

He stared at her, too shocked to speak. Then he blushed, no doubt thinking of what she had done to get pregnant. He looked down, embarrassed. Then he drank some tea. At last he said: "Who's the father?"

"No one you know." She had thought about this and worked out a story of sorts. "He was a valet who came to Tŷ Gwyn with one of the guests, but he's gone in the army now."

"But he'll stand by you."

"I don't even know where he is."

"I'll find the beggar."

Ethel put a hand on his arm. "Don't get angry, my lovely. If I need your help, I'll ask for it."

Billy evidently did not know what to say. Threatening revenge was clearly no good, but he had no other response. He looked bewildered. He was still only sixteen.

Ethel remembered him as a baby. She had been only five years old when he arrived, but she had been completely fascinated by him, his perfection and his vulnerability. Soon I'll have a beautiful, helpless infant, she thought; and she did not know whether to feel happy or terrified.

Billy said: "Da's going to have something to say about it, I expect."

"That's what I'm worried about," said Ethel. "I wish there was something I could do to make it right for him."

Gramper came down. "Sacked, is it?" he said when he saw the suitcase. "Too cheeky, were you?"

Mam said: "Don't be cruel, now, Papa. She's expecting a baby."

"Oh, jowch," he said. "One of the toffs up there at the big house, was it? The earl himself, I wouldn't be surprised."

"Don't talk daft, Gramper," said Ethel, dismayed that he had guessed the truth so quickly.

Billy said: "It was a valet who came with a houseguest. Gone in the army now, he is. She doesn't want us to go after him."

"Oh, aye?" said Gramper. Ethel could tell he was not convinced, but he did not persist. Instead he said: "It's the Italian in you, my girl. Your grandmother was hot-blooded. She would have got into trouble if I hadn't married her. As it was she didn't want to wait for the wedding. In fact—"

Mam interrupted: "Papa! Not in front of the children."

"What's going to shock them, after this?" he said. "I'm too old for fairy tales. Young women want to lie with young men, and they want it so badly they'll do it, married or not. Anyone who pretends otherwise is a fool—and that includes your husband, Cara, my girl."

"You be careful what you say," Mam said.

"Aye, all right," said Gramper, and he subsided into silence and drank his tea.

A minute later Da came in. Mam looked at him in surprise. "You're back early!" she said.

He heard the displeasure in her voice. "You make it sound as if I'm not welcome."

She got up from the table, making a space for him. "I'll brew a fresh pot of tea."

Da did not sit down. "The meeting was canceled." His eye fell on Ethel's suitcase. "What's this?"

They all looked at Ethel. She saw fear on Mam's face, defiance on Billy's, and a kind of resignation on Gramper's. It was up to her to answer the question. "I've got something to tell you, Da," she said. "You're going to be cross about it, and all I can say is that I'm sorry."

His face darkened. "What have you done?"

"I've left my job at Tŷ Gwyn."

"That's nothing to be sorry for. I never liked you bowing and scraping to those parasites."

"I left for a reason."

He moved closer and stood over her. "Good or bad?"

"I'm in trouble."

He looked thunderous. "I hope you don't mean what girls sometimes mean when they say that."

She stared down at the table and nodded.

"Have you—" He paused, searching for appropriate words. "Have you been overtaken in moral transgression?"

"Aye."

"You wicked girl!"

It was what Mam had said. Ethel cringed away from him, although she did not really expect him to strike her.

"Look at me!" he said.

She looked up at him through a blur of tears.

"So you are telling me you have committed the sin of fornication."

"I'm sorry, Da."

"Who with?" he shouted.

"A valet."

"What's his name?"

"Teddy." It came out before she could think.

"Teddy what?"

"It doesn't matter."

"Doesn't matter? What on earth do you mean?"

"He came to the house on a visit with his master. By the time I found out my condition, he'd gone in the army. I've lost touch with him."

"On a visit? Lost touch?" Da's voice rose to an enraged roar. "You mean you're not even engaged to him? You committed this sin . . ." He spluttered, hardly able to get the disgusting words out. "You committed this foul sin *casually*?"

Mam said: "Don't get angry, now, Da."

"Don't get angry? When else should a man get angry?"

Gramper tried to calm him. "Take it easy, now, Dai boy. It does no good to shout."

"I'm sorry to have to remind you, Gramper, that this is my house, and I will be the judge of what does no good."

"Aye, all right," said Gramper pacifically. "Have it your way."

Mam was not ready to give in. "Don't say anything you might regret, now, Da."

These attempts to calm Da's wrath were only making him angrier. "I will not be ruled by women or old men!" he shouted. He pointed his finger at Ethel. "And I will not have a fornicator in my house! Get out!"

Mam began to cry. "No, please don't say that!"

"Out!" he shouted. "And never come back!"

Mam said: "But your grandchild!"

Billy spoke. "Will you be ruled by the Word of God, Da? Jesus said: 'I came not to call the righteous, but sinners to repentance.' Gospel of Luke, chapter five, verse thirty-two."

Da rounded on him. "Let me tell you something, you ignorant boy. My grandparents were never married. No one knows who my grandfather was. My grandmother sank as low as a woman can go."

Mam gasped. Ethel was shocked, and she could see that Billy was flabbergasted. Gramper seemed as if he already knew.

"Oh, yes," Da said, lowering his voice. "My father was brought up in a house of ill fame, if you know what that is; a place where sailors went, down the docks in Cardiff. Then one day, when his mother was in a drunken stupor, God led his childish footsteps into a chapel Sunday school, where he met Jesus. In the same place he learned to read and write and, eventually, to bring up his own children in the paths of righteousness."

Mam said softly: "You never told me this, David." She seldom called him by his Christian name.

"I hoped never to think of it again." Da's face was twisted into a mask of shame and rage. He leaned on the table and stared Ethel in the eye, and his voice sank to a whisper. "When I courted your mother, we held hands, and I kissed her cheek every evening until the wedding day." He banged his fist on the table, making the cups shake. "By the grace of our Lord Jesus Christ, my family dragged itself up out of the stinking gutter." His voice rose again to a shout. "We are not going back there! Never! Never! Never!"

There was a long moment of stunned silence.

Da looked at Mam. "Get Ethel out of here," he said.

Ethel stood up. "My case is packed and I've got some money. I'll get the train to London." She looked hard at her father. "I won't drag the family into the gutter."

Billy picked up her suitcase.

Da said: "Where are you going to, boy?"

"I'll walk her to the station," Billy said, looking frightened.

"Let her carry her own case."

Billy stooped to put it down, then changed his mind. An obstinate look came over his face. "I'll walk her to the station," he repeated.

"You'll do what you're told!" Da shouted.

Billy still looked scared, but now he was defiant, too. "What are you going to do, Da—throw me out of the house and all?"

"I'll put you across my knee and thrash you," Da said. "You're not too old."

Billy was white-faced, but he looked Da in the eye. "Yes, I am," he said. "I am too old." He shifted the case to his left hand and clenched his right fist.

Da took a step forward. "I'll teach you to make a fist at me, boy."

"No!" Mam screamed. She stood between them and pushed at Da's chest. "That's enough! I will not have a fight in my kitchen." She pointed her finger at Da's face. "David Williams, you keep your hands to yourself. Remember that you're an elder of Bethesda Chapel. What would people think?"

That calmed him.

Mam turned to Ethel. "You'd better go. Billy will go with you. Quick, now."

Da sat down at the table.

Ethel kissed her mother. "Good-bye, Mam."

"Write me a letter," Mam said.

Da said: "Don't you dare write to anyone in this house! The letters will be burned unopened!"

Mam turned away, weeping. Ethel went out and Billy followed.

They walked down the steep streets to the town center. Ethel kept her eyes on the ground, not wanting to speak to people she knew and be asked where she was off to.

At the station she bought a ticket to Paddington.

"Well," said Billy, as they stood on the platform, "two shocks in one day. First you, then Da."

"He have kept that bottled up inside him all these years," Ethel said. "No wonder he's so strict. I can almost forgive him for throwing me out."

"I can't," said Billy. "Our faith is about redemption and mercy, not about bottling things up and punishing people."

A train from Cardiff came in, and Ethel saw Walter von Ulrich get off. He touched his hat to her, which was nice of him: gentlemen did not do that to servants, normally. Lady Maud had said she had thrown him over. Perhaps he had come to win her back. She silently wished him luck.

"Do you want me to buy you a newspaper?" Billy said.

"No, thank you, my lovely," she said. "I don't think I could concentrate on it."

Waiting for her train she said: "Do you remember our code?" In childhood they had devised a simple way to write notes that their parents could not understand.

For a moment Billy looked puzzled; then his face cleared. "Oh, aye."

"I'll write to you in code, so Da can't read it."

"Right," he said. "And send the letter via Tommy Griffiths."

The train puffed into the station in clouds of steam. Billy hugged Ethel. She could see he was trying not to cry.

"Look after yourself," she said. "And take care of our mam."

"Aye," he said, and wiped his eyes with his sleeve. "We'll be all right. You be careful up there in London, now."

"I will."

Ethel boarded the train and sat by the window. A minute later it pulled out. As it picked up speed, she watched the pithead winding gear recede into the distance, and wondered if she would ever see Aberowen again.

{ V }

Maud had breakfast late with Princess Bea in the small dining room at Tŷ Gwyn. The princess was in high spirits. Normally she complained a lot about living in Britain—although Maud recalled, from her time as a child in the British embassy, that life in Russia was much more uncomfortable: the houses cold, the people surly, services unreliable, and government disorganized. But Bea had no complaints today. She was happy that she had at last conceived.

She even spoke generously of Fitz. "He saved my family, you know," she said to Maud. "He paid off the mortgages on our estate. But until now there has been no one to inherit it—my brother has no children. It would seem such a tragedy if all Andrei's land and Fitz's went to some distant cousin."

Maud could not see this as a tragedy. The distant cousin in question might well be a son of hers. But she had never expected to inherit a fortune and she gave little thought to such things.

Maud was not good company this morning, she realized as she drank coffee and toyed with toast. In fact she was miserable. She felt oppressed by the wallpaper, a Victorian riot of foliage that covered the ceiling as well as the walls, even though she had lived with it all her life.

She had not told her family about her romance with Walter, so now she could not tell them that it was over, and that meant she had no one to sympathize with her. Only the sparky little housekeeper, Williams, knew the story, and she seemed to have disappeared.

Maud read *The Times*'s report of Lloyd George's speech last night at the Mansion House dinner. He had been optimistic about the Balkan crisis, saying it could be resolved peacefully. She hoped he was right. Even though she had given Walter up, she was still horrified by the thought that he might have to put on a uniform and be killed or maimed in a war.

She read a short report in *The Times* datelined Vienna and headed THE SERVIAN SCARE. She asked Bea if Russia would defend Serbia against the Austrians. "I hope not!" Bea said, alarmed. "I don't want my brother to go to war."

Maud could remember having breakfast here in the small dining room with Fitz and Walter in the school holidays, when she was twelve and they were seventeen. The boys had had enormous appetites, she recalled, consuming eggs and sausages and great piles of buttered toast every morning before going off to ride horses or swim in the lake. Walter had been such a glamorous figure, handsome and foreign. He had treated her as courteously as if she were his age, which was flattering to a young girl—and, she could now see, a subtle way of flirting.

While she was reminiscing, the butler, Peel, came in and shocked her by saying to Bea: "Herr von Ulrich is here, Your Highness."

Walter could not possibly be here, Maud thought bewilderedly. Could it be Robert? Equally unlikely.

A moment later, Walter walked in.

Maud was too stupefied to speak. Bea said: "What a pleasant surprise, Herr von Ulrich."

Walter was wearing a lightweight summer suit of pale blue-gray tweed. His blue satin tie was the same color as his eyes. Maud wished she had put on something other than the plain cream-colored peg-top dress that had seemed perfectly adequate for breakfast with her sister-in-law.

"Forgive this intrusion, Princess," Walter said to Bea. "I had to visit our consulate in Cardiff—a tiresome business about German sailors who got into trouble with the local police."

That was rubbish. Walter was a military attaché: his job did not involve getting sailors out of jail.

"Good morning, Lady Maud," he said, shaking her hand. "What a delightful surprise to find you here."

More rubbish, she thought. He was here to see her. She had left London so that he could not badger her, but deep in her heart she could not help being pleased by his persistence in following her all this way. Flustered, she just said: "Hello, how are you?"

Bea said: "Do have some coffee, Herr von Ulrich. The earl is out riding, but he'll be back soon." She naturally assumed Walter was there to see Fitz.

"How kind you are." Walter sat down.

"Will you stay for lunch?"

"I would love to. Then I must catch a train back to London."

Bea stood up. "I should speak to the cook."

Walter jumped to his feet and pulled out her chair.

"Talk to Lady Maud," Bea said as she left the room. "Cheer her up. She's worried about the international situation."

Walter raised his eyebrows at the note of mockery in Bea's voice. "All sensible people are worried about the international situation," he said.

Maud felt awkward. Desperate for something to say, she pointed to *The Times*. "Do you think it's true that Serbia has called up seventy thousand reservists?"

"I doubt if they have seventy thousand reservists," Walter said gravely. "But they are trying to raise the stakes. They hope that the danger of a wider war will make Austria cautious."

"Why is it taking the Austrians so long to send their demands to the Serbian government?"

"Officially, they want to get the harvest in before doing anything which might require them to call men to the army. Unofficially, they know that the president of France and his foreign minister happen to be in Russia, which makes it dangerously easy for the two allies to agree on a concerted response. There will be no Austrian note until President Poincaré leaves St. Petersburg."

He was such a clear thinker, Maud reflected. She loved that about him.

His reserve failed him suddenly. His mask of formal courtesy fell away, and his face looked anguished. Abruptly, he said: "Please come back to me."

She opened her mouth to speak, but her throat seemed choked with emotion, and no words came out.

He said miserably: "I know you threw me over for my own sake, but it won't work. I love you too much."

Maud found words. "But your father . . . "

"He must work out his own destiny. I cannot obey him, not in this." His voice sank to a whisper. "I cannot bear to lose you."

"He might be right: perhaps a German diplomat can't have an English wife, at least not now."

"Then I'll follow another career. But I could never find another you."

Her resolve melted and her eyes flooded.

He reached across the table and took her hand. "May I speak to your brother?"

She bunched up her white linen napkin and blotted her tears. "Don't talk to Fitz yet," she said. "Wait a few days, until the Serbian crisis blows over."

"That may take more than a few days."

"In that case, we'll think again."

"I shall do as you wish, of course."

"I love you, Walter. Whatever happens, I want to be your wife."

He kissed her hand. "Thank you," he said solemnly. "You have made me very happy."

{ VI }

A strained silence descended on the house in Wellington Row. Mam made dinner, and Da and Billy and Gramper ate it, but no one said much. Billy was eaten up with a rage he could not express. In the afternoon he climbed the mountainside and walked for miles on his own.

Next morning he found his mind returning again and again to the story of Jesus and the woman taken in adultery. Sitting in the kitchen in his Sunday clothes, waiting to go with his parents and Gramper to the Bethesda Chapel for the service of the breaking of bread, he opened his Bible at the Gospel According to John and found chapter 8. He read the story over and over. It seemed to be about exactly the kind of crisis that had struck his family.

He continued to think of it in chapel. He looked around the room at his friends and neighbors: Mrs. Dai Ponies, John Jones the Shop, Mrs. Ponti and her two big sons, Suet Hewitt . . . They all knew that Ethel had left Tŷ Gwyn yesterday and bought a train ticket to Paddington; and although they did not know why, they could guess. In their minds, they were already judging her. But Jesus was not.

During the hymns and extempore prayers, he decided that the Holy Spirit was leading him to read those verses out. Toward the end of the hour he stood up and opened his Bible.

There was a little murmur of surprise. He was a bit young to be leading the congregation. Still, there was no age limit: the Holy Spirit could move anyone.

"A few verses from John's Gospel," he said. There was a slight shake in his voice, and he tried to steady it.

"'They say unto him: Master, this woman was taken in adultery, in the very act.'"

Bethesda Chapel went suddenly quiet: no one fidgeted, whispered, or coughed.

Billy read on: "'Now Moses in the Law commanded us that such should be stoned, but what sayest thou? This they said, tempting him, that they might have to accuse him. But Jesus stooped down, and with his finger wrote on the ground, as if he heard them not. So when they continued asking him, he lifted himself up, and said unto them'—"

Here Billy paused and looked up.

With careful emphasis he said: "'He that is without sin among you, let him first cast a stone at her.'"

Every face in the room stared back at him. No one moved.

Billy resumed: "'And again he stooped down, and wrote on the ground. And they which heard it, being convicted by their own conscience, went out one by one, beginning at the eldest, even unto the last: and Jesus was left alone, and the woman standing in the midst. When Jesus had lifted himself, and saw none but the woman, he said unto her: Woman, where are those thine accusers? Hath no man condemned thee? She said: No man, Lord.'"

Billy looked up from the book. He did not need to read the last verse: he knew it by heart. He looked at his father's stony face and spoke very slowly. "'And Jesus said unto her: Neither do I condemn thee. Go, and sin no more.'"

After a long moment he closed the Bible with a clap that sounded like thunder in the silence. "This is the Word of God," he said.

He did not sit down. Instead he walked to the exit. The congregation stared, rapt. He opened the big wooden door and walked out.

He never went back.

CHAPTER NINE

Late July 1914

Walter von Ulrich could not play ragtime.

He could play the tunes, which were simple. He could play the distinctive chords, which often used the interval of the flatted seventh. And he could play both together—but it did not sound like ragtime. The rhythm eluded him. His effort was more like something you might hear from a band in a Berlin park. For one who could play Beethoven sonatas effortlessly, this was frustrating.

Maud had tried to teach him, that Saturday morning at Tŷ Gwyn, at the upright Bechstein among the potted palms in the small drawing room, with the summer sun coming through the tall windows. They had sat hip to hip on the piano stool, their arms interlaced, and Maud had laughed at his efforts. It had been a moment of golden happiness.

His mood had darkened when she explained how his father had talked her into breaking with Walter. If he had seen his father on the evening when he returned to London, there would have been an explosion. But Otto had left for Vienna, and Walter had had to swallow his rage. He had not seen his father since.

He had agreed to Maud's proposal that they should keep their engagement secret until the Balkan crisis was over. It was still going on, though things had calmed down. Almost four weeks had passed since the assassination in Sarajevo, but the Austrian emperor still had not sent to the Serbians the note he had been mulling so long. The delay encouraged Walter to hope that tempers had cooled and moderate counsels had prevailed in Vienna.

Sitting at the baby grand piano in the compact drawing room of his bachelor flat in Piccadilly, he reflected that there was much the Austrians could do, short of war, to punish Serbia and soothe their wounded pride. For example, they could force the Serbian government to close anti-Austrian newspapers, and purge nationalists from the Serbian army and civil service. The Serbians could submit to that: it would be humiliating, but better than a war they could not win.

Then the leaders of the great European countries could relax and concentrate on their domestic problems. The Russians could crush their general strike, the English could pacify the mutinous Irish Protestants, and the French could enjoy the murder trial of Madame Caillaux, who had shot the editor of *Le Figaro* for printing her husband's love letters.

And Walter could marry Maud.

That was his focus now. The more he thought about the difficulties, the more determined he became to overcome them. Having looked, for a few days, at the joyless prospect of life without her, he was even more sure that he wanted to marry her, regardless of the price they might both have to pay. As he avidly followed the diplomatic game being played on the chessboard of Europe, he scrutinized every move to assess its effect first on him and Maud, and only second on Germany and the world.

He was going to see her tonight, at dinner and at the Duchess of Sussex's ball. He was already dressed in white tie and tails. It was time to leave. But as he closed the lid of the piano, the doorbell rang, and his manservant announced Count Robert von Ulrich.

Robert looked surly. It was a familiar expression. Robert had been a troubled and unhappy young man when they were students together in

Vienna. His feelings drew him irresistibly toward a group whom he had been brought up to regard as decadent. Then, when he came home after an evening with men like himself, he wore that look, guilty but defiant. In time he had discovered that homosexuality, like adultery, was officially condemned but—in sophisticated circles, at least—unofficially tolerated; and he had become reconciled to who he was. Today he wore that face for some other reason.

"I've just seen the text of the emperor's note," Robert said immediately.

Walter's heart leaped in hope. This might be the peaceful resolution he was waiting for. "What does it say?"

Robert handed him a sheet of paper. "I copied out the main part."

"Has it been delivered to the Serbian government?"

"Yes, at six o'clock Belgrade time."

There were ten demands. The first three followed the lines Walter had anticipated, he saw with relief: Serbia had to suppress liberal newspapers, break up the secret society called the Black Hand, and clamp down on nationalist propaganda. Perhaps the moderates in Vienna had won the argument after all, he thought gratefully.

Point four seemed reasonable at first—the Austrians demanded a purge of nationalists in the Serbian civil service—but there was a sting in the tail: the Austrians would supply the names. "That seems a bit strong," Walter said anxiously. "The Serbian government can't just sack everyone the Austrians tell them to."

Robert shrugged. "They will have to."

"I suppose so." For the sake of peace, Walter hoped they would.

But there was worse to come.

Point five demanded that Austria assist the Serbian government in crushing subversion, and point six, Walter read with dismay, insisted that Austrian officials take part in Serbia's judicial inquiry into the assassination. "But Serbia can't agree to this!" Walter protested. "It would amount to giving up their sovereignty."

Robert's face darkened further. "Hardly," he said peevishly.

"No country in the world could agree to it."

"Serbia will. It must, or be destroyed."

"In a war?"

"If necessary."

"Which could engulf all of Europe!"

Robert wagged his finger. "Not if other governments are sensible."

Unlike yours, Walter thought, but he bit back the retort and read on. The remaining points were arrogantly expressed, but the Serbs could probably live with them: arrest of conspirators, prevention of smuggling of weapons into Austrian territory, and a clampdown on anti-Austrian pronouncements by Serbian officials.

But there was a forty-eight-hour deadline for reply.

"My God, this is harsh," said Walter.

"People who defy the Austrian emperor must expect harshness."

"I know, I know, but he hasn't even given them room to save face."

"Why should he?"

Walter let his exasperation show. "For goodness' sake, does he *want* war?"

"The emperor's family, the Habsburg dynasty, has governed vast areas of Europe for hundreds of years. Emperor Franz Joseph knows that God intends him to rule over inferior Slavic peoples. This is his destiny."

"God spare us from men of destiny," Walter muttered. "Has my embassy seen this?"

"They will any minute now."

Walter wondered how others would react. Would they accept this, as Robert had, or be outraged like Walter? Would there be an international howl of protest or just a helpless diplomatic shrug? He would find out this evening. He looked at the clock on the mantelpiece. "I'm late for dinner. Are you going to the Duchess of Sussex's ball later?"

"Yes. I'll see you there."

They left the building and parted company in Piccadilly. Walter headed for Fitz's house, where he was to dine. He felt breathless, as if he had been knocked down. The war he dreaded had come dangerously closer.

He arrived with just enough time to bow to Princess Bea, in a lavender gown festooned with silk bows, and shake hands with Fitz, impossibly handsome in a wing collar and a white bow tie; then dinner was announced. He was glad to find himself assigned to escort Maud through to the dining room. She wore a dark red dress of some soft material that clung to her body the way Walter wanted to. As he held her chair he said: "What a very attractive gown."

"Paul Poiret," she said, naming a designer so famous that even Walter had heard of him. She lowered her voice a little. "I thought you might like it."

The remark was only mildly intimate, but all the same it gave him a thrill, rapidly followed by a shiver of fear at the thought that he could yet lose this enchanting woman.

Fitz's house was not quite a palace. Its long dining room, at the corner of the street, looked over two thoroughfares. Electric chandeliers burned despite the bright summer evening outside, and reflected lights glittered in the crystal glasses and silver cutlery marshaled at each place. Looking around the table at the other female guests, Walter marveled anew at the indecent amount of bosom revealed by upper-class Englishwomen at dinner.

Such observations were adolescent. It was time he got married.

As soon as he sat down, Maud slipped off a shoe and pushed her stockinged toe up the leg of his trousers. He smiled at her, but she saw immediately that he was distracted. "What's the matter?" she said.

"Start a conversation about the Austrian ultimatum," he murmured. "Say you've heard it has been delivered."

Maud addressed Fitz, at the head of the table. "I believe the Austrian emperor's note has at last been handed in at Belgrade," she said. "Have you heard anything, Fitz?"

Fitz put down his soup spoon. "The same as you. But no one knows what is in it."

Walter said: "I believe it is very harsh. The Austrians insist on taking a role in the Serbian judicial process."

"Taking a role!" said Fitz. "But if the Serbian prime minister agreed to that, he'd have to resign."

Walter nodded. Fitz foresaw the same consequences as he did. "It is almost as if the Austrians want war." He was perilously close to speaking disloyally about one of Germany's allies, but he felt anxious enough not to care. He caught Maud's eye. She was pale and silent. She, too, had immediately seen the threat.

"One has sympathy for Franz Joseph, of course," Fitz said. "Nationalist subversion can destabilize an empire if it is not firmly dealt with." Walter guessed he was thinking of Irish independence campaigners and South African Boers threatening the British Empire. "But you don't need a sledgehammer to crack a nut," Fitz finished.

Footmen took away the soup bowls and poured a different wine. Walter drank nothing. It was going to be a long evening, and he needed a clear head.

Maud said quietly: "I happened to see Prime Minister Asquith today. He said there could be a real Armageddon." She looked scared. "I'm afraid I did not believe him—but now I see he might have been right."

Fitz said: "It's what we're all afraid of."

Walter was impressed as always by Maud's connections. She hobnobbed casually with the most powerful men in London. Walter recalled that as a girl of eleven or twelve, when her father was a minister in a Conservative government, she would solemnly question his cabinet colleagues when they visited Tŷ Gwyn; and even then such men would listen to her attentively and answer her patiently.

She went on: "On the bright side, if there is a war Asquith thinks Britain need not be involved."

Walter's heart lifted. If Britain stayed out, the war need not separate him from Maud.

But Fitz looked disapproving. "Really?" he said. "Even if . . . " He looked at Walter. "Forgive me, von Ulrich—even if France is overrun by Germany?"

Maud replied: "We will be spectators, Asquith says."

"As I have long feared," Fitz said pompously, "the government does not understand the balance of power in Europe." As a Conservative, he mistrusted the Liberal government, and personally he hated Asquith, who had enfeebled the House of Lords; but, most important, he was not totally horrified by the prospect of war. In some ways, Walter feared, he might relish the thought, just as Otto did. And he certainly thought war preferable to any weakening of British power.

Walter said: "Are you quite sure, my dear Fitz, that a German victory over France *would* upset the balance of power?" This line of discussion was rather sensitive for a dinner party, but the issue was too important to be brushed under Fitz's expensive carpet.

Fitz said: "With all due respect to your honored country, and to His Majesty Kaiser Wilhelm, I fear Britain could not permit German control of France."

That was the trouble, Walter thought, trying hard not to show the anger and frustration he felt at these glib words. A German attack on Russia's ally France would, in reality, be defensive—but the English talked as if Germany was trying to dominate Europe. Forcing a genial smile, he said: "We defeated France forty-three years ago, in the conflict you call the Franco-Prussian War. Great Britain was a spectator then. And you did not suffer by our victory."

Maud added: "That's what Asquith said."

"There's a difference," Fitz said. "In 1871, France was defeated by Prussia and a group of minor German kingdoms. After the war, that coalition became one country, the modern Germany—and I'm sure you will agree, von Ulrich, my old friend, that Germany today is a more formidable presence than old Prussia."

Men like Fitz were so dangerous, Walter thought. With faultless good manners they would lead the world to destruction. He struggled to keep the tone of his reply light. "You're right, of course—but perhaps formidable is not the same as hostile."

"That's the question, isn't it?"

At the other end of the table, Bea coughed reproachfully. No doubt she thought this topic too contentious for polite conversation. She said brightly: "Are you looking forward to the duchess's ball, Herr von Ulrich?"

Walter felt reproved. "I feel sure the ball will be absolutely splendid," he gushed, and was rewarded with a grateful nod from Bea.

Aunt Herm put in: "You're such a good dancer!"

Walter smiled warmly at the old woman. "Perhaps you will grant me the honor of the first dance, Lady Hermia?"

She was flattered. "Oh, my goodness, I'm too old for dancing. Besides, you youngsters have steps that didn't even exist when I was a debutante."

"The latest craze is the czardas. It's a Hungarian folk dance. Perhaps I should teach you it."

Fitz said: "Would that constitute a diplomatic incident, do you think?" It was not very funny, but everyone laughed, and the conversation turned to other trivial but safe subjects.

After dinner the party boarded carriages to drive the four hundred yards to Sussex House, the duke's palace in Park Lane.

Night had fallen, and light blazed from every window: the duchess had at last given in and installed electricity. Walter climbed the grand staircase and entered the first of three grand reception rooms. The orchestra was playing the most popular tune of recent years, "Alexander's Ragtime Band." His left hand twitched: the syncopation was the crucial element.

He kept his promise and danced with Aunt Herm. He hoped she would have lots of partners: he wanted her to get tired and doze off in a side room, so that Maud would be left unchaperoned. He kept remembering what he and Maud had done in the library of this house a few weeks ago. His hands itched to touch her through that clinging dress.

But first he had work to do. He bowed to Aunt Herm, took a glass of pink champagne from a footman, and began to circulate. He moved through the Small Ballroom, the Salon, and the Large Ballroom, talking to the political and diplomatic guests. Every ambassador in London had been invited, and many had come, including Walter's boss, Prince Lichnowsky. Numerous members of Parliament were there. Most were Conservative, like the duchess, but there were some Liberals, including several government ministers. Robert was deep in conversation with Lord Remarc, a junior minister in the War Office. No Labour M.P.s were to be seen: the duchess considered herself an open-minded woman, but there were limits.

Walter learned that the Austrians had sent copies of their ultimatum to all the major embassies in Vienna. It would be cabled to London and translated overnight, and by morning everyone would know its contents. Most people were shocked by its demands, but no one knew what to do about it.

By one o'clock in the morning he had learned all he could, and he went to find Maud. He walked down the stairs and into the garden, where supper was laid out in a striped marquee. So much food was served in English high society! He found Maud toying with some grapes. Aunt Herm was happily nowhere to be seen.

Walter put his worries aside. "How can you English eat so much?" he said to Maud playfully. "Most of these people have had a hearty breakfast, a lunch of five or six courses, tea with sandwiches and cakes, and a dinner of at least eight courses. Do they now really need soup, stuffed quails, lobster, peaches, and ice cream?"

She laughed. "You think we're vulgar, don't you?"

He did not, but he teased her by pretending to. "Well, what culture do the English have?" He took her arm and, as if moving aimlessly, walked her out of the tent into the garden. The trees were decked with fairy lights that gave little illumination. On the winding paths between shrubs, a few other couples walked and talked, some holding hands discreetly in the gloom. Walter saw Robert with Lord Remarc again, and wondered if they, too, had found romance. "English composers?" he said, still teasing Maud. "Gilbert and Sullivan. Painters? While the French Impressionists were changing the way the world sees itself, the English were painting rosy-cheeked children playing with puppies. Opera? All Italian, when it's not German. Ballet? Russian."

"And yet we rule half the world," she said with a mocking smile.

He took her in his arms. "And you can play ragtime."

"It's easy, once you get the rhythm."

"That's the part I find difficult."

"You need lessons."

He put his mouth to her ear and murmured: "Teach me, please?" The murmur turned to a groan as she kissed him, and after that they did not speak for some time.

{ II }

That was in the small hours of Friday, July 24. On the following evening, when Walter attended another dinner and another ball, the rumor on everyone's lips was that the Serbians would concede every Austrian demand, except only for a request for clarification on points five and six. Surely, Walter thought elatedly, the Austrians could not reject such a cringing response? Unless, of course, they were determined to have a war regardless.

On his way home at daybreak on Saturday he stopped at the embassy to write a note about what he had learned during the evening. He was at his desk when the ambassador himself, Prince Lichnowsky, appeared in immaculate morning dress, carrying a gray top hat. Startled, Walter jumped to his feet, bowed, and said: "Good morning, Your Highness."

"You're here very early, von Ulrich," said the ambassador. Then, noting Walter's evening dress, he said: "Or rather, very late." He was handsome in a craggy way, with a big curved nose over his mustache.

"I was just writing you a short note on last night's gossip. Is there anything I can do for Your Highness?"

"I've been summoned by Sir Edward Grey. You can come with me and make notes, if you've got a different coat."

Walter was elated. The British foreign secretary was one of the most powerful men on earth. Walter had met him, of course, in the small world of London diplomacy, but had never exchanged more than a few words with him. Now, at Lichnowsky's characteristically casual invitation, Walter was to be present at an informal meeting of two men who were deciding the fate of Europe. Gottfried von Kessel would be sick with envy, he thought.

He reproved himself for being petty. This could be a critical meeting. Unlike the Austrian emperor, Grey might not want war. Would this be about preventing it? Grey was hard to predict. Which way would he jump? If he was against war, Walter would seize any chance to help him.

He kept a frock coat on a hook behind his door for just such emergencies as this. He pulled off his evening tailcoat and buttoned the daytime coat over his white waistcoat. He picked up a notebook and left the building with the ambassador.

The two men walked across St. James's Park in the cool of the early morning. Walter told his boss the rumor about the Serbian reply. The ambassador had a rumor of his own to report. "Albert Ballin dined with Winston Churchill last night," he said. Ballin, a German shipping magnate, was close to the kaiser, despite being Jewish. Churchill was in charge of the Royal Navy. "I'd love to know what was said," Lichnowsky finished.

He obviously feared the kaiser was bypassing him and sending messages to the British via Ballin. "I'll try to find out," said Walter, pleased at the opportunity.

They entered the Foreign Office, a neoclassical building that made Walter think of a wedding cake. They were shown to the foreign secretary's opulent room overlooking the park. The British are the richest people on earth, the building seemed to say, and we can do anything we like to the rest of you.

Sir Edward Grey was a thin man with a face like a skull. He disliked foreigners and almost never traveled abroad: in British eyes, that made him the perfect foreign secretary. "Thank you so much for coming," he said politely. He was alone but for an aide with a notebook. As soon as they were seated he got down to business. "We must do what we can to calm the situation in the Balkans."

Walter's hopes rose. That sounded pacific. Grey did not want war.

Lichnowsky nodded. The prince was part of the peace faction in the German government. He had sent a sharp telegram to Berlin urging that Austria be restrained. He disagreed with Walter's father and others who believed that war now was better, for Germany, than war later when Russia and France might be stronger.

Grey went on: "Whatever the Austrians do, it must not be so threatening to Russia as to provoke a military response from the tsar."

Exactly, Walter thought excitedly.

Lichnowsky obviously shared his view. "If I may say so, Foreign Secretary, you have hit the nail on the head."

Grey was oblivious to compliments. "My suggestion is that you and we, that is to say Germany and Britain, should together ask the Austrians to extend their deadline." He glanced reflexively at the clock on the wall: it was a little after six a.m. "They have demanded an answer by six tonight, Belgrade time. They could hardly refuse to give the Serbians another day."

Walter was disappointed. He had been hoping Grey had a plan to save the world. This postponement was such a small thing. It might make no difference. And in Walter's view the Austrians were so belligerent they easily *could* refuse the request, petty though it was. However, no one asked his opinion, and in this stratospherically elevated company he was not going to speak unless spoken to.

"A splendid idea," said Lichnowsky. "I will pass it to Berlin with my endorsement."

"Thank you," said Grey. "But, failing that, I have another proposal."

So, Walter thought, Grey was not really confident the Austrians would give Serbia more time.

Grey went on: "I propose that Britain, Germany, Italy, and France should together act as mediators, meeting at a four-power conference to produce a solution that would satisfy Austria without menacing Russia."

That was more like it, Walter thought.

"Austria would not agree in advance to be bound by the conference decision, of course," Grey continued. "But that's not necessary. We could ask the Austrian emperor at least to take no further action until he hears what the conference has to say."

Walter was delighted. It would be hard for Austria to refuse a plan that came from its allies as well as its rivals.

Lichnowsky looked pleased, too. "I will recommend this to Berlin most strongly."

Grey said: "It's good of you to come to see me so early in the morning."

Lichnowsky took that as dismissal and stood up. "Not at all," he said. "Will you get down to Hampshire today?"

Grey's hobbies were fly-fishing and bird-watching, and he was happiest at his cottage on the river Itchen in Hampshire.

"Tonight, I hope," said Grey. "This is wonderful fishing weather."

"I trust you will have a restful Sunday," said Lichnowsky, and they left.

Walking back across the park, Lichnowsky said: "The English are amazing. Europe is on the brink of war, and the foreign secretary is going fishing."

Walter felt elated. Grey might seem to lack a sense of urgency, but he was the first person to come up with a workable solution. Walter was grateful. I'll invite him to my wedding, he thought, and thank him in my speech.

When they got back to the embassy he was startled to find his father there.

Otto beckoned Walter into his office. Gottfried von Kessel was standing by the desk. Walter was bursting to confront his father about Maud, but he was not going to speak of such things in front of von Kessel, so he said: "When did you get here?"

"A few minutes ago. I came overnight on the boat train from Paris. What were you doing with the ambassador?"

"We were summoned to see Sir Edward Grey." Walter was gratified to see a look of envy cross von Kessel's face.

Otto said: "And what did he have to say?"

"He proposed a four-power conference to mediate between Austria and Serbia."

Von Kessel said: "Waste of time."

Walter ignored him and asked his father: "What do you think?"

Otto narrowed his eyes. "Interesting," he said. "Grey is crafty."

Walter could not hide his enthusiasm. "Do you think the Austrian emperor might agree?"

"Absolutely not."

Von Kessel snickered.

Walter was crushed. "But why?"

Otto said: "Suppose the conference proposes a solution and Austria rejects it?"

"Grey mentioned that. He said Austria would not be obliged to accept the conference recommendation."

Otto shook his head. "Of course not—but what then? If Germany is part of a conference that makes a peace proposal, and Austria rejects our proposal, how could we then back the Austrians when they go to war?"

"We could not."

"So Grey's purpose in making this suggestion is to drive a wedge between Austria and Germany."

"Oh." Walter felt foolish. He had seen none of this. His optimism was punctured. Dismally, he said: "So we won't support Grey's peace plan?"

"Not a chance," said his father.

{ III }

Sir Edward Grey's proposal came to nothing, and Walter and Maud watched, hour by hour, as the world lurched closer to disaster.

The next day was Sunday, and Walter met with Anton. Once again everyone was desperate to know what the Russians would do. The Serbians had given in to almost every Austrian demand, only asking for more time to discuss the two harshest clauses; but the Austrians had announced that this was unacceptable, and Serbia had begun to mobilize its little army. There would be fighting, but would Russia join in?

Walter went to the church of St. Martin-in-the-Fields, which was not in the fields but in Trafalgar Square, the busiest traffic junction in London. The church was an eighteenth-century building in the Palladian style, and Walter reflected that his meetings with Anton were giving him an education in the history of English architecture as well as information about Russian intentions.

He mounted the steps and passed through the great pillars into the nave. He looked around anxiously: at the best of times he was afraid Anton might not show up, and this would be the worst possible moment for the man to get cold feet. The interior was brightly lit by a big Venetian window at the east end, and he spotted Anton immediately. Relieved, he sat next to the vengeful spy a few seconds before the service began.

As always, they talked during the hymns. "The Council of Ministers met on Friday," Anton said.

Walter knew that. "What did they decide?"

"Nothing. They only make recommendations. The tsar decides."

Walter knew that, too. He controlled his impatience. "Excuse me. What did they *recommend*?"

"To permit four Russian military districts to prepare for mobilization."

"No!" Walter's cry was involuntary, and the hymn singers nearby turned and stared at him. This was the first preliminary to war. Calming himself with an effort, Walter said: "Did the tsar agree?"

"He ratified the decision yesterday."

Despairingly, Walter said: "Which districts?"

"Moscow, Kazan, Odessa, and Kiev."

During the prayers, Walter pictured a map of Russia. Moscow and Kazan were in the middle of that vast country, a thousand miles and more from its European borders, but Odessa and Kiev were in the southwest, near the Balkans. In the next hymn he said: "They are mobilizing against Austria."

"It's not mobilization—it's preparation for mobilization."

"I understand that," said Walter patiently. "But yesterday we were talking about Austria attacking Serbia, a minor Balkan conflict. Today we're talking about Austria and Russia, and a major European war."

The hymn ended, and Walter waited impatiently for the next one. He had been brought up by a devout Protestant mother, and he always suffered a twinge of conscience about using church services as a cover for his clandestine work. He said a brief prayer for forgiveness.

When the congregation began to sing again, Walter said: "Why are they in such a hurry to make these warlike preparations?"

Anton shrugged. "The generals say to the tsar: 'Every day you delay gives the enemy an advantage.' It's always the same."

"Don't they see that the preparations make the war more likely?"

"Soldiers want to win wars, not avoid them."

The hymn ended and the service came to a close. As Anton stood up, Walter held his arm. "I have to see you more often," he said.

Anton looked panicky. "We've been through that—"

"I don't care. Europe is on the brink of war. You say the Russians are *preparing* to mobilize in *some* districts. What if they authorize other districts to prepare? What other steps will they take? When does preparation turn into the real thing? I have to have daily reports. Hourly would be better."

"I can't take the risk." Anton tried to withdraw his arm.

Walter tightened his grip. "Meet me at Westminster Abbey every morning before you go to your embassy. Poet's Corner, in the south transept. The church is so big that no one will notice us."

"Absolutely not."

Walter sighed. He would have to threaten, which he did not like doing, not least because it risked the complete withdrawal of the spy. But he had to take the chance. "If you aren't there tomorrow, I'll come to your embassy and ask for you."

Anton went pale. "You can't do that! They will kill me!"

"I must have the information! I'm trying to prevent a war."

"I hope there *is* a war," the little clerk said savagely. His voice dropped to a hiss. "I hope my country is flattened and destroyed by the German army." Walter stared at him, astonished. "I hope the tsar is killed, brutally murdered, and all his family with him. And I hope they all go to hell, as they deserve."

He turned on his heel and scurried out of the church into the hubbub of Trafalgar Square.

{ IV }

Princess Bea was "at home" on Tuesday afternoons at teatime. This was when her friends called to discuss the parties they had been to and show off their daytime clothes. Maud was obliged to attend, as was Aunt Herm, both being poor relations who lived on Fitz's generosity. Maud found the conversation particularly stultifying today, when all she wanted to talk about was whether there would be a war.

The morning room at the Mayfair house was modern. Bea was attentive to decorating trends. Matching bamboo chairs and sofas were arranged in small conversational groups, with plenty of space between for people to move around. The upholstery had a quiet mauve pattern and the carpet was light brown. The walls were not papered, but painted a restful beige. There was no Victorian clutter of framed photographs, ornaments, cushions, and vases. One did not need to show off one's prosperity, fashionable people said, by cramming one's rooms full of stuff. Maud agreed.

Bea was talking to the Duchess of Sussex, gossiping about the prime minister's mistress, Venetia Stanley. Bea ought to be worried, Maud thought; if Russia joins in the war, her brother, Prince Andrei, will have to fight. But Bea appeared carefree. In fact she looked particularly bonny today. Perhaps she had a lover. It was not uncommon in the highest social circles, where many marriages were arranged. Some people disapproved of adulterers—the duchess would cross such a woman off her invitation list for all eternity—but others turned a blind eye. However, Maud did not really think Bea was the type.

Fitz came in for tea, having escaped from the House of Lords for an hour, and Walter was right behind him. They both looked elegant in their gray suits and double-breasted waistcoats. Involuntarily, in her imagination Maud saw them in army uniforms. If the war spread, both might have to fight—almost certainly on opposite sides. They would be officers, but neither would slyly wangle a safe job at headquarters: they would want to lead their men from the front. The two men she loved might end up shooting at each other. She shuddered. It did not bear thinking about.

Maud avoided Walter's eye. She had a feeling that the more intuitive women in Bea's circle had noticed how much time she spent talking to him. She did not mind their suspicions—they would learn the truth soon enough—but she did not want rumors to reach Fitz before he had been officially told. He would be mightily offended. So she was trying not to let her feelings show.

Fitz sat beside her. Casting about for a topic of conversation that did not involve Walter, she thought of Tŷ Gwyn, and asked: "Whatever happened to your Welsh housekeeper, Williams? She disappeared, and when I asked the other servants, they went all vague."

"I had to get rid of her," Fitz said.

"Oh!" Maud was surprised. "Somehow I had the impression you liked her."

"Not especially." He seemed embarrassed.

"What did she do to displease you?"

"She suffered the consequences of unchastity."

"Fitz, don't be pompous!" Maud laughed. "Do you mean she got pregnant?"

"Keep your voice down, please. You know what the duchess is like."

"Poor Williams. Who's the father?"

"My dear, do you imagine I asked?"

"No, of course not. I hope he's going to 'stand by her,' as they say."

"I have no idea. She's a servant, for goodness' sake."

"You're not normally callous about your servants."

"One mustn't reward immorality."

"I liked Williams. She was more intelligent and interesting than most of these society women."

"Don't be absurd."

Maud gave up. For some reason, Fitz was pretending he did not care about Williams. But he never liked explaining himself, and it was useless to press him.

Walter came over, balancing a cup and saucer and a plate with cake in one hand. He smiled at Maud, but spoke to Fitz. "You know Churchill, don't you?"

"Little Winston?" said Fitz. "I certainly do. He started out in my party, but switched to the Liberals. I think his heart is still with us Conservatives."

"Last Friday he had dinner with Albert Ballin. I'd love to know what Ballin had to say."

"I can enlighten you—Winston has been telling everyone. If there is a war, Ballin said that if Britain will stay out of it, Germany will promise to leave France intact afterward, taking no extra territory—by contrast with last time, when they helped themselves to Alsace and Lorraine."

"Ah," said Walter with satisfaction. "Thank you. I've been trying to find that out for days."

"Your embassy doesn't know?"

"This message was intended to bypass normal diplomatic channels, obviously."

Maud was intrigued. It seemed like a hopeful formula for keeping Britain out of any European war. Perhaps Fitz and Walter would not have to shoot at each other, after all. She said: "How did Winston respond?"

"Noncommittally," said Fitz. "He reported the conversation to the cabinet, but it was not discussed."

Maud was about to ask indignantly why not when Robert von Ulrich appeared, looking aghast, as if he had just learned of the death of a loved one. "What on earth is the matter with Robert?" Maud said as he bowed to Bea.

He turned to speak to everyone in the room. "Austria has declared war on Serbia," he announced.

For a moment Maud felt as if the world had stopped. No one moved and no one spoke. She stared at Robert's mouth under that curled mustache and willed him to unsay the words. Then the clock on the mantelpiece struck, and a buzz of consternation rose from the men and women in the room.

Tears welled up in Maud's eyes. Walter offered her a neatly folded white linen handkerchief. She said to Robert: "You will have to fight."

"I certainly will," Robert said. He said it briskly, as if stating the obvious, but he looked scared.

Fitz stood up. "I'd better get back to the Lords and find out what's going on."

Several others took their leave. In the general hubbub, Walter spoke quietly to Maud. "Albert Ballin's proposal has suddenly become ten times more important."

Maud thought so, too. "Is there anything we can do?"

"I need to know what the British government really thinks of it."

"I'll try to find out." She was glad of a chance to do something.

"I have to get back to the embassy."

Maud watched Walter go, wishing she could kiss him good-bye. Most of the guests went at the same time, and Maud slipped upstairs to her room.

She took off her dress and lay down. The thought of Walter going to war made her weep helplessly. After a while she cried herself to sleep.

When she woke up it was time to go out. She was invited to Lady Glenconner's musical soiree. She was tempted to stay home, then it struck her that there might be a government minister or two at the Glenconners' house. She might learn something useful to Walter. She got up and dressed.

She and Aunt Herm took Fitz's carriage through Hyde Park to Queen Anne's Gate, where the Glenconners lived. Among the guests was Maud's friend Johnny Remarc, a War Office minister; but, more important, Sir Edward Grey was there. She made up her mind to speak to him about Albert Ballin.

The music began before she had a chance, and she sat down to listen.

Campbell McInnes was singing selections from Handel—a German composer who had lived most of his life in London, Maud thought wryly.

She watched Sir Edward covertly during the recital. She did not like him much: he belonged to a political group called the Liberal Imperialists, more traditional and conservative than most of the party. However, she felt a pang of sympathy for him. He was never very jolly, but tonight his cadaverous face looked ashen, as if he had the weight of the world on his shoulders—which he did, of course.

McInnes sang well, and Maud thought with regret how much Walter would have enjoyed this, had he not been too busy to come.

As soon as the music finished, she buttonholed the foreign secretary. "Mr. Churchill tells me he gave you an interesting message from Albert Ballin," she said. She saw Grey's face stiffen, but she plowed on. "If we stay out of any European war, the Germans promise not to grab any French territory."

"Something like that," Grey said coldly.

Clearly she had raised a distasteful topic. Etiquette demanded that she abandon it instantly. But this was not just a diplomatic maneuver: it was about whether Fitz and Walter would have to go to war. She pressed on. "I understood that our main concern was that the balance of power in Europe should not be disturbed, and I imagined that Herr Ballin's proposal might satisfy us. Was I wrong?"

"You most certainly were," he said. "It is an infamous proposal." He was almost emotional.

Maud was downcast. How could he dismiss it? It offered a glimpse of hope! She said: "Will you explain, to a mere woman who does not grasp these matters as quickly as you, why you say that so definitely?"

"To do as Ballin suggested would be to pave the way for France to be invaded by Germany. We would be complicit. It would be a squalid betrayal of a friend."

"Ah," she said. "I think I see. It is as if someone said: 'I'm going to burgle your neighbor, but if you stand back and don't interfere, I promise not to burn his house down, too.' Is that it?"

Grey warmed up a little. "A good analogy," he said with a skeletal smile. "I shall use it myself."

"Thank you," said Maud. She felt dreadfully disappointed, and she knew it was showing on her face, but she could not help it. She said gloomily: "Unfortunately, this leaves us perilously close to war."

"I'm afraid it does," said the foreign secretary.

{ v }

Like most parliaments around the world, the British had two chambers. Fitz belonged to the House of Lords, which included the higher aristocracy, the bishops, and the senior judges. The House of Commons was made up of elected representatives known as members of Parliament, or M.P.s. Both chambers met in the Palace of Westminster, a purpose-built Victorian Gothic building with a clock tower. The clock was called Big Ben, although Fitz was fond of pointing out that that was actually the name of the great bell.

As Big Ben struck twelve noon on Wednesday, July 29, Fitz and Walter ordered a prelunch sherry on the terrace beside the smelly river Thames. Fitz looked at the palace with satisfaction, as always: it was extraordinarily large, rich, and solid, like the empire that was ruled from its corridors and chambers. The building looked as if it might last a thousand years—but would the empire survive? Fitz trembled when he thought of the threats to it: rabble-rousing trade unionists, striking coal miners, the kaiser, the Labour Party, the Irish, militant feminists—even his own sister.

However, he did not give utterance to such solemn thoughts, especially as his guest was a foreigner. "This place is like a club," he said lightheartedly. "It has bars, dining rooms, and a jolly good library; and only the right sort of people are allowed in." Just then a Labour M.P. walked past with a Liberal peer, and Fitz added: "Although sometimes the riffraff sneak past the doorman."

Walter was bursting with news. "Have you heard?" he said. "The kaiser has done a complete volte-face."

Fitz had not heard. "In what way?"

"He says the Serbian reply leaves no further reason for war, and the Austrians must halt at Belgrade."

Fitz was suspicious of peace plans. His main concern was that Britain should maintain its position as the most powerful nation in the world. He was afraid the Liberal government might let that position slip, out of some foolish belief that all nations were equally sovereign. Sir Edward Grey was fairly sound, but he could be ousted by the left wing of the party—led by Lloyd George, in all likelihood—and then anything could happen.

"Halt at Belgrade," he said musingly. The capital was on the border: to capture it, the Austrian army would have to venture only a mile inside Serbian territory. The Russians might be persuaded to regard that as a local police action that did not threaten them. "I wonder."

Fitz did not want war, but there was a part of him that secretly relished the prospect. It would be his chance to prove his courage. His father had won distinction in naval actions, but Fitz had never seen combat. There were certain things one had to do before one could really call oneself a man, and fighting for king and country was among them.

They were approached by a messenger wearing court dress—velvet knee breeches and white silk stockings. "Good afternoon, Earl Fitzherbert," he said. "Your guests have arrived and gone straight to the dining room, my lord."

When he had gone Walter said: "Why do you make them dress like that?"

"Tradition," said Fitz.

They drained their glasses and went inside. The corridor had a thick red carpet and walls with linenfold paneling. They walked to the Peers' Dining Room. Maud and Aunt Herm were already seated.

This lunch had been Maud's idea: Walter had never been inside the palace, she said. As Walter bowed, and Maud smiled warmly at him, a stray thought crossed Fitz's mind: could there be a little *tendresse* between them? No, it was ridiculous. Maud might do anything, of course, but Walter was much too sensible to contemplate an Anglo-German marriage at this time of tension. Besides, they were like brother and sister.

As they sat down, Maud said: "I was at your baby clinic this morning, Fitz."

He raised his eyebrows. "Is it *my* clinic?"

"You pay for it."

"My recollection is that you told me there ought to be a clinic in the East End for mothers and children who had no man to support them, and I said indeed there should, and the next thing I knew the bills were coming to me."

"You're so generous."

Fitz did not mind. A man in his position had to give to charity, and it was useful to have Maud do all the work. He did not broadcast the fact that most of the mothers were not married and never had been: he did not want his aunt the duchess to be offended.

"You'll never guess who came in this morning," Maud went on. "Williams, the housekeeper from Tŷ Gwyn." Fitz went cold. Maud added cheerfully: "We were talking about her only last night!"

Fitz tried to keep a look of stony indifference on his face. Maud, like most women, was quite good at reading him. He did not want her to suspect the true depth of his involvement with Ethel: it was too embarrassing.

He knew Ethel was in London. She had found a house in Aldgate, and Fitz had instructed Solman to buy it in her name. Fitz feared the embarrassment of meeting Ethel on the street, but it was Maud who had run into her.

Why had she gone to the clinic? He hoped she was all right. "I trust she's not ill," he said, trying to make it sound no more than a courteous inquiry.

"Nothing serious," Maud said.

Fitz knew that pregnant women suffered minor ailments. Bea had

had a little bleeding and had been worried, but Professor Rathbone had said it often happened at about three months and usually meant nothing, though she should not overexert herself—not that there was much danger of Bea's doing that.

Walter said: "I remember Williams—curly hair and a cheeky smile. Who is her husband?"

Maud answered: "A valet who visited Tŷ Gwyn with his master some months ago. His name is Teddy Williams."

Fitz felt a slight flush. So she was calling her fictional husband Teddy! He wished Maud had not met her. He wanted to forget Ethel. But she would not go away. To conceal his embarrassment he made a show of looking around for a waiter.

He told himself not to be so sensitive. Ethel was a servant girl and he was an earl. Men of high rank had always taken their pleasures where they found them. This kind of thing had been going on for hundreds of years, probably thousands. It was foolish to get sentimental about it.

He changed the subject by repeating, for the benefit of the ladies, Walter's news about the kaiser.

"I heard that, too," said Maud. "Goodness, I hope the Austrians will listen," she added fervently.

Fitz raised an eyebrow at her. "Why so passionate?"

"I don't want you to be shot at!" she said. "And I don't want Walter to be our enemy." There was a catch in her voice. Women were so emotional.

Walter said: "Do you happen to know, Lady Maud, how the kaiser's suggestion has been received by Asquith and Grey?"

Maud pulled herself together. "Grey says that in combination with his proposal of a four-power conference, it could prevent war."

"Excellent!" said Walter. "That was what I was hoping for." He was boyishly eager, and the look on his face reminded Fitz of their school days. Walter had looked like that when he won the Music Prize at Speech Day.

Aunt Herm said: "Did you see that that dreadful Madame Caillaux was found not guilty?"

Fitz was astonished. "Not guilty? But she shot the man! She went to a shop, bought a gun, loaded it, drove to the offices of *Le Figaro,* asked to see the editor, and shot him dead—how could she not be guilty?"

Aunt Herm replied: "She said: 'These guns go off by themselves.' Honestly!"

Maud laughed.

"The jury must have liked her," said Fitz. He was annoyed with Maud for laughing. Capricious juries were a threat to orderly society. It did not do to take murder lightly. "How very French," he said with disgust.

"I admire Madame Caillaux," Maud said.

Fitz grunted disapprovingly. "How can you say that about a murderess?"

"I think more people should shoot newspaper editors," Maud said gaily. "It might improve the press."

{ VI }

Walter was still full of hope the next day, Thursday, when he went to see Robert.

The kaiser was hesitating on the brink, despite pressure from men such as Otto. The war minister, Erich von Falkenhayn, had demanded a declaration *Zustand drohender Kriegsgefahr,* a preliminary that would light the fuse for war—but the kaiser had refused, believing that a general conflict might be avoided if the Austrians would halt at Belgrade. And when the Russian tsar had ordered his army to mobilize, Wilhelm had sent a personal telegram begging him to reconsider.

The two monarchs were cousins. The kaiser's mother and the tsar's mother-in-law had been sisters, both daughters of Queen Victoria. The kaiser and the tsar communicated in English, and called each other "Nicky" and "Willy." Tsar Nicholas had been touched by his cousin Willy's cable, and had countermanded his mobilization order.

If they could both just stand firm, then the future might be bright for Walter and Maud and millions of other people who just wanted to live in peace.

The Austrian embassy was one of the more imposing houses in prestigious Belgrave Square. Walter was shown to Robert's office. They always shared news. There was no reason not to: their two nations were close allies. "The kaiser seems determined to make his 'halt at Belgrade' plan work," Walter said as he sat down. "Then all remaining issues can be worked out."

Robert did not share his optimism. "It's not going to succeed," he said.

"But why should it not?"

"We're not willing to halt at Belgrade."

"For God's sake!" said Walter. "Are you sure?"

"It will be discussed by ministers in Vienna tomorrow morning, but I'm afraid the result is a foregone conclusion. We can't halt at Belgrade without reassurances from Russia."

"Reassurances?" Walter said indignantly. "You have to stop fighting and *then* talk about the problems. You can't demand assurances first!"

"I'm afraid we don't see it that way," Robert said stiffly.

"But we are your allies. How can you reject our peace plan?"

"Easily. Think about it. What can you do? If Russia mobilizes, you're threatened, so you have to mobilize, too."

Walter was about to protest, but he saw that Robert was right. The Russian army, when mobilized, was too big a threat.

Robert went on remorselessly. "You have to fight on our side, whether you want to or not." He made an apologetic face. "Forgive me if I sound arrogant. I'm just stating the reality."

"Hell," said Walter. He felt like crying. He had been holding on to hope, but Robert's grim words had shattered him. "This is going the wrong way, isn't it?" he said. "Those who want peace are going to lose the contest."

Robert's voice changed, and suddenly he looked sad. "I've known that from the start," he said. "Austria must attack."

Until now Robert had been sounding eager, not sad. Why the change? Probing, Walter said: "You may have to leave London."

"You, too."

Walter nodded. If Britain joined in the war, all Austrian and German embassy staff would have to go home at short notice. He lowered his voice. "Is there . . . someone you will especially miss?"

Robert nodded, and there were tears in his eyes.

Walter hazarded a guess. "Lord Remarc?"

Robert laughed mirthlessly. "Is it so obvious?"

"Only to someone who knows you."

"Johnny and I thought we were being so discreet." Robert shook his head miserably. "At least you can marry Maud."

"I wish I could."

"Why not?"

"A marriage between a German and an Englishwoman, when the two nations are at war? She would be shunned by everyone she knows. So would I. For myself I would hardly care, but I could never impose such a fate on her."

"Do it secretly."

"In London?"

"Get married in Chelsea. No one would know you there."

"Don't you have to be a resident?"

"You have to produce an envelope with your name and a local address. I live in Chelsea—I can give you a letter addressed to Mr. von Ulrich." He rummaged in a drawer of his desk. "Here you are. A bill from my tailor, addressed to Von Ulrich, Esquire. They think Von is my first name."

"There may not be time."

"You can get a special license."

"Oh, my God," Walter said. He felt stunned. "You're right, of course. I can."

"You have to go to the town hall."

"Yes."

"Shall I show you the way?"

Walter thought for a long moment, then said: "Yes, please."

{ VII }

"The generals won," said Anton, standing in front of the tomb of Edward the Confessor in Westminster Abbey on Friday, July 31. "The tsar gave in yesterday afternoon. The Russians are mobilizing."

It was a death sentence. Walter felt a cold chill around his heart.

"It is the beginning of the end," Anton went on, and Walter saw in his eyes the glitter of revenge. "The Russians think they are strong, because their army is the largest in the world. But they have weak leadership. It will be Armageddon."

It was the second time this week that Walter had heard that word. But this time he knew it was justified. In a few weeks' time the Russian army of six million men—six *million*—would be massed on the borders of Germany and Hungary. No leader in Europe could ignore such a threat. Germany would have to mobilize: the kaiser no longer had any choice.

There was nothing more Walter could do. In Berlin the General Staff were pressing for German mobilization and the chancellor, Theobald von Bethmann-Hollweg, had promised a decision by noon today. This news meant there was only one decision he could possibly make.

Walter had to inform Berlin immediately. He took an abrupt leave of Anton and went out of the great church. He walked as fast as he could through the little street called Storey's Gate, jogged along the eastern edge of St. James's Park, and ran up the steps by the Duke of York's memorial and into the German embassy.

The ambassador's door was open. Prince Lichnowsky sat at his desk, and Otto stood beside him. Gottfried von Kessel was using the telephone. There were a dozen other people in the room, with clerks hurrying in and out.

Walter was breathing hard. Panting, he spoke to his father. "What's happening?"

"Berlin has received a cable from our embassy in St. Petersburg that just says: 'First day of mobilization 31 July.' Berlin is trying to confirm the report."

"What is von Kessel doing?"

"Keeping the phone line to Berlin open so that we hear instantly."

Walter took a deep breath and stepped forward. "Your Highness," he said to Prince Lichnowsky.

"Yes?"

"I can confirm the Russian mobilization. My source told me less than an hour ago."

"Right." Lichnowsky reached for the phone and von Kessel gave it to him.

Walter looked at his watch. It was ten minutes to eleven—in Berlin, just short of the noon deadline.

Lichnowsky said into the phone: "Russian mobilization has been confirmed by a reliable source here."

He listened for a few moments. The room went quiet. No one moved. "Yes," Lichnowsky said at last. "I understand. Very well."

He hung up with a click that sounded like a thunderclap. "The chancellor has decided," he said; and then he repeated the words Walter had been dreading. "*Zustand drohender Kriegsgefahr.* Prepare for imminent war."

CHAPTER TEN

August 1–3, 1914

M aud was frantic with worry. On Saturday morning she sat in the breakfast room at the Mayfair house, eating nothing. The summer sun shone in through the tall windows. The decor was supposed to be restful—Persian rugs, eau-de-Nil paintwork, mid-blue curtains—but nothing could calm her. War was coming and no one seemed able to stop it: not the kaiser, not the tsar, not Sir Edward Grey.

Bea came in, wearing a filmy summer dress and a lace shawl. Grout, the butler, poured her coffee with gloved hands, and she took a peach from a bowl.

Maud looked at the newspaper but was unable to read beyond the headlines. She was too anxious to concentrate. She tossed the newspaper aside. Grout picked it up and folded it neatly. "Don't you worry, my lady," he said. "We'll give the Germans a bashing if we have to."

She glared at him but said nothing. It was foolish to argue with servants—they always ended up agreeing out of deference.

Aunt Herm tactfully got rid of him. "I'm sure you're right, Grout," she said. "Bring some more hot rolls, would you?"

Fitz came in. He asked Bea how she was feeling, and she shrugged. Maud sensed that something in their relationship had changed, but she was too distracted to think about that. She immediately asked Fitz: "What happened last night?" She knew he had been in conference with leading Conservatives at a country house called Wargrave.

"F.E. arrived with a message from Winston." F. E. Smith, a Conservative M.P., was close friends with the Liberal Winston Churchill. "He proposed a Liberal-Conservative coalition government."

Maud was shocked. She usually knew what was happening in Liberal circles, but Prime Minister Asquith had kept this secret. "That's outrageous!" she said. "It makes war *more* likely."

With irritating calmness, Fitz took some sausages from the hot buffet on the sideboard. "The left wing of the Liberal Party are little better than pacifists. I imagine that Asquith is afraid they will attempt to tie his hands. But he doesn't have enough support in his own party to overrule them. Who can he turn to for help? Only the Conservatives. Hence the proposal of a coalition."

That was what Maud feared. "What did Bonar Law say to the offer?" Andrew Bonar Law was the Conservative leader.

"He turned it down."

"Thank God."

"And I supported him."

"Why? Don't you want Bonar Law to have a seat in the government?"

"I'm hoping for more. If Asquith wants war, and Lloyd George leads a left-wing rebellion, the Liberals could be too divided to rule. Then what happens? We Conservatives have to take over—and Bonar Law becomes prime minister."

Furiously, Maud said: "You see how everything seems to conspire toward war? Asquith wants a coalition with the Conservatives because they are more aggressive. If Lloyd George leads a rebellion against Asquith, the Conservatives will take over anyway. Everyone is jockeying for position instead of struggling for peace!"

"What about you?" Fitz said. "Did you go to Halkyn House last night?" The home of the Earl of Beauchamp was the headquarters of the peace faction.

Maud brightened. There was a ray of hope. "Asquith has called a cabinet meeting this morning." This was unusual on a Saturday. "Morley and Burns want a declaration that Britain will in no circumstance fight Germany."

Fitz shook his head. "They can't prejudge the issue like that. Grey would resign."

"Grey is always threatening to resign, but never does."

"Still, you can't risk a split in the cabinet now, with my lot waiting in the wings, panting to take over."

Maud knew Fitz was right. She could have screamed with frustration.

Bea dropped her knife and made a strange noise.

Fitz said: "Are you all right, my dear?"

She stood up, holding her stomach. Her face was pale. "Excuse me," she said, and she rushed out of the room.

Maud stood up, concerned. "I'd better go to her."

"I'll go," said Fitz, surprising her. "You finish your breakfast."

Maud's curiosity would not let her leave it at that. As Fitz went to the door, she said: "Is Bea suffering from morning sickness?"

Fitz paused in the doorway. "Don't tell anyone," he said.

"Congratulations. I'm very happy for you."

"Thanks."

"But the child . . . " Maud's voice caught in her throat.

"Oh!" said Aunt Herm, cottoning on. "How lovely!"

Maud went on with an effort. "Will the child be born into a world at war?"

"Oh, dear me," said Aunt Herm. "I didn't think of that."

Fitz shrugged. "A newborn will not know the difference."

Maud felt tears come. "When is the baby due?"

"January," said Fitz. "Why are you so upset?"

"Fitz," Maud said, and she was weeping helplessly now. "Fitz, will you still be alive?"

{ II }

Saturday morning at the German embassy was frenzied. Walter was in the ambassador's room, fielding phone calls, bringing in telegrams, and taking notes. It would have been the most exciting time of his life, had he not been so worried about his future with Maud. But he could not enjoy the thrill of being a player in a great international power game, because he was tortured by the fear that he and the woman he loved would become enemies in war.

There were no more friendly messages between Willy and Nicky. Yesterday afternoon the German government had sent a cold ultimatum to the Russians, giving them twelve hours to halt the mobilization of their monstrous army.

The deadline had passed with no reply from St. Petersburg.

Yet Walter still believed the war could be confined to eastern Europe, so that Germany and Britain might remain friends. Ambassador Lichnowsky shared his optimism. Even Asquith had said that France and Britain could be spectators. After all, neither country was much involved in the future of Serbia and the Balkan region.

France was the key. Berlin had sent a second ultimatum yesterday afternoon, this one to Paris, asking the French to declare themselves neutral. It was a slender hope, though Walter clung to it desperately. The ultimatum expired at noon. Meanwhile, Chief of Staff Joseph Joffre had demanded immediate mobilization of the French army, and the cabinet was meeting this morning to decide. As in every country, Walter thought gloomily, army officers were pressing their political masters to take the first steps to war.

It was frustratingly difficult to guess which way the French would jump.

At a quarter to eleven, with seventy-five minutes to go before time ran out for France, Lichnowsky received a surprise visitor: Sir William Tyrrell. A key official with long experience in foreign affairs, he was private secretary to Sir Edward Grey. Walter showed him into the ambassador's room immediately. Lichnowsky motioned for Walter to stay.

Tyrrell spoke German. "The foreign secretary has asked me to let you know that a council of ministers taking place just now may result in his being able to make a statement to you."

This was obviously a rehearsed speech, and Tyrrell's German was perfectly fluent, but all the same his meaning escaped Walter. He glanced at Lichnowsky and saw that he, too, was baffled.

Tyrrell went on: "A statement that may, perhaps, prove helpful in preventing the great catastrophe."

That was hopeful but vague. Walter wanted to say, *Get to the point!*

Lichnowsky replied with the same strained diplomatic formality. "What indication can you give me of the subject of the statement, Sir William?"

For God's sake, Walter thought, we're talking about life and death here!

The civil servant spoke with careful precision. "It may be that, if Germany were to refrain from attacking France, then both France and Great Britain might consider whether they were truly obliged to intervene in the conflict in eastern Europe."

Walter was so shocked that he dropped his pencil. France and Britain staying out of the war—this was what he wanted! He stared at Lichnowsky. The ambassador, too, looked startled and delighted. "This is very hopeful," he said.

Tyrrell held up a cautionary hand. "Please understand that I make no promises."

Fine, Walter thought, but you didn't come here for a casual chat.

Lichnowsky said: "Then let me say quite simply that a proposal to confine the war to the east would be examined with great interest by His Majesty Kaiser Wilhelm and the German government."

"Thank you." Tyrrell stood up. "I shall report back to Sir Edward accordingly."

Walter showed Tyrrell out. He was elated. If France and Britain could be kept out of the war, there would be nothing to stop him marrying, Maud. Was this a pipe dream?

He returned to the ambassador's room. Before they had a chance to discuss Tyrrell's statement, the phone rang. Walter picked it up and heard a familiar English voice say: "This is Grey. May I speak to His Excellency?"

"Of course, sir." Walter handed the phone to the ambassador. "Sir Edward Grey."

"Lichnowsky here. Good morning . . . Yes, Sir William has just left . . . "

Walter stared at the ambassador, listening avidly to his half of the conversation and trying to read his face.

"A most interesting suggestion . . . Permit me to make our position clear. Germany has no quarrel with either France or Great Britain."

It sounded as if Grey was going over the same ground as Tyrrell. Clearly the English were very serious about this.

Lichnowsky said: "The Russian mobilization is a threat that clearly cannot be ignored, but it is a threat to our eastern border, and that of our ally Austria-Hungary. We have asked France for a guarantee of neutrality. If France can give us that—or, alternatively, if Britain can guarantee French neutrality—there will be no reason for war in western Europe . . . Thank you, Foreign Secretary. Perfect—I will call on you at half past three this afternoon." He hung up.

He looked at Walter. They both smiled triumphantly. "Well," said Lichnowsky, "I didn't expect that!"

{ III }

Maud was at Sussex House, where a group of influential Conservative M.P.s and peers had gathered in the duchess's morning room for tea, when Fitz came in boiling with rage. "Asquith and Grey are crumbling!" he said. He pointed to a silver cake stand. "Crumbling like that dashed scone. They're going to betray our friends. I feel ashamed to be British."

Maud had feared this. Fitz was no compromiser. He believed that

Britain should issue orders and the world should obey. The idea that the government might have to negotiate with others as equals was abhorrent to him. And there were distressingly many who agreed.

The duchess said: "Calm down, Fitz, dear, and tell us all what's happened."

Fitz said: "Asquith sent a letter this morning to Douglas." Maud presumed he meant General Sir Charles Douglas, chief of the Imperial General Staff. "Our prime minister wanted to put it on record that the government had never promised to send British troops to France in the event of a war with Germany!"

Maud, as the only Liberal present, felt obliged to defend the government. "But it's true, Fitz. Asquith is only making it clear that all our options are open."

"Then what on earth was the point of all the talks we've held with the French military?"

"To explore possibilities! To make contingency plans! Talks are not contracts—especially in international politics."

"Friends are friends. Britain is a world leader. A woman doesn't necessarily understand these things, but people expect us to stand by our neighbors. As gentlemen, we abhor the least hint of deceit, and we should do the same as a country."

That was the kind of talk that might yet get Britain embroiled in a war, Maud thought with a shiver of panic. She just could not get her brother to understand the danger. Their love for each other had always been stronger than their political differences, but now they were so angry that they might quarrel gravely. And when Fitz fell out with someone, he never made it up. Yet he was the one who would have to fight and perhaps die, shot or bayoneted or blown to pieces—Fitz, and Walter, too. Why could Fitz not see that? It made her want to scream.

While she struggled to find adequate words, one of the other guests spoke. Maud recognized him as the foreign editor of *The Times*, a man called Steed. "I can tell you that there is a dirty German-Jewish international financial attempt to bully my paper into advocating neutrality," he said.

The duchess pursed her lips: she disliked the language of the gutter press.

"What makes you say so?" Maud said coldly to Steed.

"Lord Rothschild spoke to our financial editor yesterday," the journalist said. "Wants us to moderate the anti-German tone of our articles in the interests of peace."

Maud knew Natty Rothschild, who was a Liberal. She said: "And what does Lord Northcliffe think of Rothschild's request?" Northcliffe was the proprietor of *The Times*.

Steed grinned. "He ordered us to print an even stiffer leading article today." He picked up a copy of the paper from a side table and waved it. "'Peace is not our strongest interest,'" he quoted.

Maud could not think of anything more contemptible than deliberately encouraging war. She could see that even Fitz was disgusted by the journalist's frivolous attitude. She was about to say something when Fitz, with his unfailing courtesy even to brutes, changed the subject. "I've just seen the French ambassador, Paul Cambon, coming out of the Foreign Office," he said. "He was as white as that tablecloth. He said: *'Ils vont nous lacher.'* 'They're going to let us down.' He had been with Grey."

The duchess asked: "Do you know what Grey had said, to upset Monsieur Cambon so?"

"Yes, Cambon told me. Apparently, the Germans are willing to leave France alone, if France promises to stay out of the war—and if the French refuse that offer, the British will not feel obliged to help defend France."

Maud felt sorry for the French ambassador, but her heart leaped with hope at the suggestion that Britain might stay out of the war.

"But France must refuse that offer," the duchess said. "She has a treaty with Russia, according to which each must come to the other's aid in war."

"Exactly!" said Fitz angrily. "What is the point of international alliances if they are to be broken at the moment of crisis?"

"Nonsense," Maud said, knowing she was being rude but not caring.

"International alliances are broken whenever convenient. That isn't the issue."

"And what is, pray?" Fitz said frostily.

"I think Asquith and Grey are simply trying to frighten the French with a dose of reality. France cannot defeat Germany without our help. If they think they might have to go it alone, perhaps the French will become peacemakers, and pressure their Russian allies to back off from war with Germany."

"And what about Serbia?"

Maud said: "Even at this stage, it's not too late for Russia and Austria to sit down at a table and work out a solution for the Balkans that both can live with."

There was a silence that lasted for a few seconds; then Fitz said: "I doubt very much that anything like that will happen."

"But surely," said Maud, and even as she spoke she could hear the desperation in her own voice, "surely we must keep hope alive?"

{ IV }

Maud sat in her room and could not summon the energy to change her clothes for dinner. Her maid had laid out a gown and some jewelry, but Maud just stared at them.

She went to parties almost every night during the London season, because much of the politics and diplomacy that fascinated her was done at social occasions. But tonight she felt she could not do it—could not be glamorous and charming, could not entice powerful men to tell her what they were thinking, could not play the game of changing their minds without their even suspecting that they were being persuaded.

Walter was going to war. He would put on a uniform and carry a gun, and enemy troops would fire shells and mortars and machine-gun rounds at him and try to kill him, or wound him so badly that he was no longer able to stand up. She found it hard to think about anything else, and she was constantly on the edge of tears. She had even had harsh words with her beloved brother.

There was a tap at the door. Grout stood outside. "Herr von Ulrich is here, my lady," he said.

Maud was shocked. She had not been expecting Walter. Why had he come?

Noticing her surprise, Grout added: "When I said my master was not at home, he asked for you."

"Thank you," said Maud, and she pushed past Grout and headed down the stairs.

Grout called after her: "Herr von Ulrich is in the drawing room. I will ask Lady Hermia to join you." Even Grout knew that Maud was not supposed to be left alone with a young man. But Aunt Herm did not move fast, and it would be several minutes before she arrived.

Maud rushed into the drawing room and threw herself into Walter's arms. "What are we going to do?" she wailed. "Walter, what are we going to do?"

He hugged her hard, then gazed at her gravely. His face was gray and drawn. He looked as if he had been told of a death. He said: "France has not replied to the German ultimatum."

"Have they said nothing at all?" she cried.

"Our ambassador in Paris insisted on a response. The message from Premier Viviani was: 'France will have regard to her own interests.' They will not promise neutrality."

"But there may still be time—"

"No. They have decided to mobilize. Joffre won the argument—as the military have in every country. The telegrams were sent at four o'clock this afternoon, Paris time."

"There must be something you can do!"

"Germany has run out of choices," he said. "We cannot fight Russia with a hostile France at our backs, armed and eager to win back Alsace-Lorraine. So we must attack France. The Schlieffen Plan has already been set in motion. In Berlin, the crowds are singing the 'Kaiserhymne' in the streets."

"You'll have to join your regiment," she said, and she could not hold back the tears.

"Of course."

She wiped her face. Her handkerchief was too small, a stupid scrap of embroidered lawn. She used her sleeve instead. "When?" she said. "When will you have to leave London?"

"Not for a few days." He was fighting back tears himself, she saw. He said: "Is there any chance at all that Britain can be kept out of the war? Then at least I wouldn't be fighting against your country."

"I don't know," she said. "Tomorrow will tell." She pulled him close. "Please hold me tight." She rested her head on his shoulder and closed her eyes.

{ V }

Fitz was angered to see an antiwar demonstration in Trafalgar Square on Sunday afternoon. Keir Hardie, the Labour M.P., was speaking, dressed in a tweed suit—like a gamekeeper, Fitz thought. He stood on the plinth of Nelson's Column, shouting hoarsely in his Scots accent, desecrating the memory of the hero who died for Britain at the Battle of Trafalgar.

Hardie said that the coming war would be the greatest catastrophe the world had ever seen. He represented a mining constituency— Merthyr, near Aberowen. He was the illegitimate son of a maidservant, and had been a coal miner until he went into politics. What did he know about war?

Fitz stalked off in disgust and went to the duchess's for tea. In the grand hall he came upon Maud deep in conversation with Walter. The crisis was driving him away from both of them, to his profound regret. He loved his sister and he was fond of Walter, but Maud was a Liberal and Walter a German, and in times like these it was hard even to speak to them. However, he did his best to seem amiable as he said to Maud: "I hear this morning's cabinet was stormy."

She nodded. "Churchill mobilized the fleet last night without asking anyone. John Burns resigned this morning in protest."

"I can't pretend to be sorry." Burns was an old radical, the most fervently antiwar cabinet minister. "So the rest must have endorsed Winston's action."

"Reluctantly."

"We must be grateful for small mercies." It was appalling, Fitz felt, that at this time of national danger the government should be in the hands of these leftist ditherers.

Maud said: "But they refused Grey's request for a commitment to defend France."

"Still acting like cowards, then," Fitz said. He knew he was being rude to his sister, but he felt too bitter to hold back.

"Not quite," Maud said evenly. "They agreed to prevent the German navy passing through the English Channel to attack France."

Fitz brightened a little. "Well, that's something."

Walter put in: "The German government has responded by saying we have no intention of sending ships into the English Channel."

Fitz said to Maud: "You see what happens when you stand firm?"

"Don't be so smug, Fitz," she said. "If we do go to war it will be because people such as you have not tried hard enough to prevent it."

"Oh, really?" He was offended. "Well, let me tell you something. I spoke to Sir Edward Grey last night at Brooks's Club. He has asked both the French and the Germans to respect the neutrality of Belgium. The French agreed immediately." Fitz looked challengingly at Walter. "The Germans have not responded."

"It's true." Walter gave an apologetic shrug. "My dear Fitz, you as a soldier will see that we couldn't answer that question, one way or the other, without giving away our war plans."

"I do see, but in the light of that, I want to know why my sister thinks I am a warmonger and you are a peacemaker."

Maud avoided the question. "Lloyd George thinks Britain should intervene only if the German army violates Belgian territory *substantially*. He may suggest it at tonight's cabinet."

Fitz knew what that meant. Furiously he said: "So we will give

Germany permission to attack France via the southern corner of Belgium?"

"I suppose that is exactly what it means."

"I knew it," Fitz said. "The traitors. They're planning to wriggle out of their duty. They will do anything to avoid war!"

"I wish you were right," said Maud.

{ VI }

Maud had to go to the House of Commons on Monday afternoon to hear Sir Edward Grey address members of Parliament. The speech would be a turning point, everyone agreed. Aunt Herm went with her. For once, Maud was glad of an old lady's reassuring company.

Maud's fate would be decided this afternoon, as well as the fate of thousands of men of fighting age. Depending on what Grey said, and how Parliament reacted, women all over Europe could become widows, their children orphans.

Maud had stopped being angry—worn-out with it, perhaps. Now she was just frightened. War or peace, marriage or loneliness, life or death: her destiny.

It was a holiday, so the city's huge population of bank clerks, civil servants, lawyers, stockbrokers, and merchants all had the day off. Most of them seemed to have gathered near the great departments of government in Westminster, hoping to be the first to hear news. The chauffeur steered Fitz's seven-passenger Cadillac limousine slowly through the vast crowds in Trafalgar Square, Whitehall, and Parliament Square. The weather was cloudy but warm, and the more fashionable young men wore straw boaters. Maud glimpsed a placard for the *Evening Standard* that read: ON THE BRINK OF CATASTROPHE.

The crowd cheered as the car drew up outside the Palace of Westminster; then there was a little groan of disappointment when it disgorged nothing more interesting than two ladies. The onlookers wanted to see their heroes, men such as Lloyd George and Keir Hardie.

The palace epitomized the Victorian mania for decoration, Maud thought. The stone was elaborately carved, there was linenfold paneling everywhere, the floor tiles were multicolored, the glass was stained, and the carpets were patterned.

Although it was a holiday, the House was sitting and the place was crowded with members and peers, most of them in the parliamentary uniform of black morning coat and black silk top hat. Only the Labour members defied the dress code by wearing tweeds or lounge suits.

The peace faction was still a majority in cabinet, Maud knew. Lloyd George had won his point last night, and the government would stand aside if Germany committed a merely technical violation of Belgian territory.

Helpfully, the Italians had declared neutrality, saying their treaty with Austria obliged them to join only in a defensive war, whereas Austria's action in Serbia was clearly aggressive. So far, Maud thought, Italy was the only country to have shown common sense.

Fitz and Walter were waiting in the octagonal Central Lobby. Maud immediately said: "I haven't heard what happened at this morning's cabinet—have you?"

"Three more resignations," Fitz said. "Morley, Simon, and Beauchamp."

All three were antiwar. Maud was discouraged, and also puzzled. "Not Lloyd George?"

"No."

"Strange." Maud felt a chill of foreboding. Was there a split in the peace faction? "What is Lloyd George up to?"

Walter said: "I don't know, but I can guess." He looked solemn. "Last night, Germany demanded free passage through Belgium for our troops."

Maud gasped.

Walter went on: "The Belgian cabinet sat from nine o'clock yesterday evening until four this morning, then rejected the demand and said they would fight."

This was dreadful.

Fitz said: "So Lloyd George was wrong—the German army is not going to commit a merely technical violation."

Walter said nothing, but spread his hands in a gesture of helplessness.

Maud feared that the brutal German ultimatum, and the Belgian government's foolhardy defiance, might have undermined the peace faction in the cabinet. Belgium and Germany looked too much like David and Goliath. Lloyd George had a nose for public opinion: had he sensed that the mood was about to change?

"We must take our places," said Fitz.

Full of apprehension, Maud passed through a small door and climbed a long staircase to emerge in the Strangers' Gallery overlooking the chamber of the House of Commons. Here sat the sovereign government of the British Empire. In this room, matters of life and death were decided for the 444 million people who lived under some form of British rule. Every time she came here Maud was struck by how small it was, with less room than the average London church.

Government and opposition faced each other on tiered rows of benches, separated by a gap that—according to legend—was two sword lengths, so that opponents could not fight. For most debates the chamber was almost empty, with no more than a dozen or so members sprawled comfortably on the green leather upholstery. Today, however, the benches were packed, and M.P.s who could not find seats were standing at the entrance. Only the front rows were vacant, those places being reserved by tradition for cabinet ministers, on the government side, and opposition leaders on the other.

It was significant, Maud thought, that today's debate was to take place in this chamber, not in the House of Lords. In fact many of the peers were, like Fitz, here in the gallery, watching. The House of Commons had the authority that came from being elected by the people—even though not many more than half of adult men and no women had the vote. Much of Asquith's time as prime minister had been spent fighting the Lords, especially over Lloyd George's plan to give all old people a small pension. The battles had been fierce but, each time, the Commons had won. The underlying reason, Maud believed, was that the English aristocracy were terrified that the French revolution would be repeated here, so in the end they always accepted a compromise.

The front-benchers came in, and Maud was immediately struck by the atmosphere among the Liberals. The prime minister, Asquith, was smiling at something said by the Quaker Joseph Pease, and Lloyd George was talking to Sir Edward Grey. "Oh, God," Maud muttered.

Walter, sitting next to her, said: "What?"

"Look at them," she said. "They're all pals together. They've made up their differences."

"You can't tell that just by looking."

"Yes, I can."

The speaker entered in an old-fashioned wig and sat on the raised throne. He called on the foreign secretary, and Grey stood up, his gaunt face pale and careworn.

He had no skill as a speaker. He was wordy and ponderous. Nevertheless, the members squeezed along the benches, and the visitors in the packed gallery listened in attentive silence, waiting patiently for the important part.

He spoke for three-quarters of an hour before mentioning Belgium. Then, at last, he revealed the details of the German ultimatum that Walter had told Maud about an hour earlier. The M.P.s were electrified. Maud saw that, as she had feared, this changed everything. Both sides of the Liberal Party—the right-wing imperialists and the left-wing defenders of the rights of small nations—were outraged.

Grey quoted Gladstone, asking "whether, under the circumstances of the case, this country, endowed as it is with influence and power, would quietly stand by and witness the perpetration of the direst crime that ever stained the pages of history, and thus become participators in the sin?"

This was rubbish, Maud thought. An invasion of Belgium would not be the direst crime in history—what about the Cawnpore Massacre? What about the slave trade? Britain did not intervene every time a country was invaded. It was ludicrous to say that such inaction made the British people participants in the sin.

But few present saw things her way. Members on both sides cheered. Maud stared in consternation at the government front bench. All the ministers who had been fervently against war yesterday were now nodding agreement: young Herbert Samuel; Lewis "Lulu" Harcourt; the Quaker Joseph Pease, who was president of the Peace Society; and, worst of all, Lloyd George himself. The fact that Lloyd George was supporting Grey meant that the political battle was over, Maud realized in despair. The German threat to Belgium had united the opposing factions.

Grey could not play on his audience's emotions, as Lloyd George did, nor could he sound like an Old Testament prophet, as Churchill did; but today he did not need such skills, Maud reflected: the facts were doing all the work. She turned to Walter and said in a fierce whisper: "Why? Why has Germany done this?"

His face twisted in an agonized expression, but he answered with his usual calm logic. "South of Belgium, the border between Germany and France is heavily fortified. If we attacked there, we would win, but it would take too long—Russia would have time to mobilize and attack us from behind. The only way for us to be sure of a quick victory is to go through Belgium."

"But it also ensures that Britain will go to war against you!"

Walter nodded. "But the British army is small. You rely on your navy, and this is not a sea war. Our generals think Britain will make little difference."

"Do you agree?"

"I believe it's never smart to make an enemy of a rich and powerful neighbor. But I lost that argument."

And that was what had happened repeatedly over the last two weeks, Maud thought despairingly. In every country, those who were against war had been overruled. The Austrians had attacked Serbia when they might have held back; the Russians had mobilized instead of negotiating; the Germans had refused to attend an international conference to settle the issue; the French had been offered the chance to remain neutral and had spurned it; and now the British were about to join in when they might easily have remained on the sidelines.

Grey had reached his peroration. "I have put the vital facts before the House, and if, as seems not improbable, we are forced, and rapidly forced, to take our stand upon these issues, then I believe, when the country realizes what is at stake, what the real issues are, the magnitude of the impending dangers in the west of Europe, which I have endeavored to describe to the House, we shall be supported throughout, not only by the House of Commons, but by the determination, the resolution, the courage, and the endurance of the whole country."

He sat down to cheers from all sides. There had been no vote, and Grey had not even proposed anything; but it was clear from the reaction that the M.P.s were ready for war.

The leader of the opposition, Andrew Bonar Law, got up to say that the government could rely on the support of the Conservatives. Maud was not surprised: they were always more warlike than the Liberals. But she was amazed, as was everyone else, when the Irish Nationalist leader said the same thing. Maud felt as if she was living in a madhouse. Was she the only person in the world who wanted peace?

Only the Labour Party leader dissented. "I think he is wrong," said Ramsay MacDonald, speaking of Grey. "I think the government which he represents and for which he speaks is wrong. I think the verdict of history will be that they are wrong."

But no one was listening. Some M.P.s were already leaving the chamber. The gallery was also emptying. Fitz stood up, and the rest of his group followed suit. Maud went along listlessly. Down in the chamber, MacDonald was saying: "If the right honorable gentleman had come here today and told us that our country is in danger, I do not care what party he appealed to, or to what class he appealed, we would be with him . . . What is the use of talking about coming to the aid of

Belgium, when, as a matter of fact, you are engaging in a whole European war?" Maud passed out of the gallery and heard no more.

This was the worst day of her life. Her country was going to fight an unnecessary war; her brother and the man she loved were going to risk their lives; and she was going to be separated from her fiancé, perhaps forever. All hope was lost and she was in total despair.

They went down the stairs, Fitz leading the way. "Most interesting, Fitz dear," said Aunt Herm politely, as if she had been taken to an art exhibition that had turned out better than expected.

Walter grasped Maud's arm and held her back. She let three or four other people get ahead of them, so that Fitz was out of earshot. But she was not prepared for what came next.

"Marry me," Walter said quietly.

Her heart raced. "What?" she whispered. "How?"

"Marry me, please, tomorrow."

"It can't be done—"

"I have a special license." He tapped the breast pocket of his coat. "I went to Chelsea Register Office on Friday."

Her mind was in a whirl. All she could think of to say was: "We agreed to wait." As soon as it was out, she wanted to take it back.

But he was already speaking. "We have waited. The crisis is over. Your country and mine will be at war tomorrow or the day after. I will have to leave Britain. I want to marry you before I go."

"We don't know what's going to happen!" she said.

"Indeed we don't. But, however the future turns out, I want you to be my wife."

"But—" Maud stopped speaking. Why was she voicing objections? He was right. No one knew what was going to happen, but that made no difference now. She wanted to be his wife, and no future that she could imagine would change that.

Before she could say more they reached the foot of the stairs and emerged into the Central Lobby, where a crowd was abuzz with excited conversation. Maud desperately wanted to ask Walter more questions, but Fitz gallantly insisted on escorting her and Aunt Herm out, because of the crowds. In Parliament Square Fitz handed the two

women into the car. The chauffeur activated the automatic crank, the
engine rumbled, and the car pulled smoothly away, leaving Fitz and
Walter standing on the pavement, with the crowd of bystanders waiting
to hear their fate.

{ VII }

Maud wanted to be Walter's wife. It was the only thing she was sure of.
She held on to that thought while questions and speculations buzzed
around her head. Should she fall in with Walter's plan, or would it be
better to wait? If she agreed to marry him tomorrow, whom would she
tell? Where would they go after the ceremony? Would they live together?
If so, where?

That evening before dinner her maid brought her an envelope on a
silver tray. It contained a single sheet of heavy cream-colored paper
covered with Walter's precise, upright handwriting in blue ink.

> Six o'clock p.m.
>
> My dearest love,
>
> At half past three tomorrow I will wait for you in a car
> across the road from Fitz's house. I will bring with me the
> requisite two witnesses. The registrar is booked for four
> o'clock. I have a suite at the Hyde Hotel. I have checked in
> already, so that we can go to our room without delaying in
> the lobby. We are to be Mr. and Mrs. Woolridge. Wear a veil.
>
> I love you, Maud.
>
> Your betrothed,
>
> W.

With a shaky hand, she put the sheet of paper down on the polished
mahogany top of her dressing table. Her breath was coming fast. She
stared at the floral wallpaper and tried to think calmly.

He had chosen the time well: midafternoon was a quiet moment when Maud might be able to slip out of the house unnoticed. Aunt Herm took a nap after lunch, and Fitz would be at the House of Lords.

Fitz must not know in advance, for he would try to stop her. He might simply lock her in her room. He could even get her committed to a lunatic asylum. A wealthy upper-class man could have a female relative put away without much difficulty. All Fitz would have to do was to find two doctors willing to agree with him that she must be mad to want to marry a German.

She would not tell *anyone*.

The false name and the veil indicated that Walter meant to be clandestine. The Hyde was a discreet hotel in Knightsbridge, where they were unlikely to meet anyone they knew. She shivered with a thrill of anticipation when she thought of spending the night with Walter.

But what would they do the next day? A marriage could not be secret forever. Walter would be leaving Britain in two or three days. Would she go with him? She was afraid she would blight his career. How could he be trusted to fight for his country if he was married to an Englishwoman? And if he did fight, he would be away from home—so what was the point of her going to Germany?

Despite all the unknowns, she was full of delicious excitement. "Mrs. Woolridge," she said to the bedroom, and she hugged herself with joy.

CHAPTER ELEVEN

August 4, 1914

At sunrise Maud got up and sat at her dressing table to write a letter. She had a stack of Fitz's blue paper in her drawer, and the silver inkwell was filled every day. *My darling,* she began; then she stopped to think.

She caught sight of herself in the oval mirror. Her hair was tousled and her nightdress rumpled. A frown creased her forehead and turned down the corners of her mouth. She picked a fragment of some green vegetable from between her teeth. If he could see me now, she thought, he might not want to marry me. Then she realized that if she went along with his plan he would see her exactly like this tomorrow morning. It was a strange thought, scary and thrilling at the same time.

She wrote:

> Yes, with all my heart, I want to marry you. But what is your plan? Where would we live?

She had been thinking about this half the night. The obstacles seemed immense.

If you stay in Britain they will put you in a prison camp.
If we go to Germany I will never see you because you will be
away from home, with the army.

Their relatives might create more trouble than the authorities.

When are we to tell our families about the marriage? Not
beforehand, please, because Fitz will find a way to stop us.
Even afterwards there will be difficulties with him and with
your father. Tell me what you are thinking.

I love you dearly.

She sealed the envelope and addressed it to his flat, which was a
quarter of a mile away. She rang the bell and a few minutes later her maid
tapped on the door. Sanderson was a plump girl with a big smile. Maud
said: "If Mr. Ulrich is out, go to the German embassy in Carlton House
Terrace. Either way, wait for his reply. Is that clear?"

"Yes, my lady."

"No need to tell any of the other servants what you're doing."

A worried look came over Sanderson's young face. Many maids were
party to their mistresses' intrigues, but Maud had never had secret
romances, and Sanderson was not used to deception. "What shall I say
when Mr. Grout asks me where I'm going?"

Maud thought for a moment. "Tell him you have to buy me certain
feminine articles." Embarrassment would curb Grout's curiosity.

"Yes, my lady."

Sanderson left and Maud got dressed.

She was not sure how she was going to maintain a semblance of
normality in front of her family. Fitz might not notice her mood—men
rarely did—but Aunt Herm was not completely oblivious.

She went downstairs at breakfast time, although she was too tense
to feel hungry. Aunt Herm was eating a kipper and the smell made
Maud feel rather ill. She sipped coffee.

Fitz appeared a minute later. He took a kipper from the sideboard and opened *The Times*. What do I normally do? Maud asked herself. I talk about politics. Then I must do that now. "Did anything happen last night?" she said.

"I saw Winston after cabinet," Fitz replied. "We are asking the German government to withdraw its ultimatum to Belgium." He gave a contemptuous emphasis to the word *asking*.

Maud did not dare to feel hope. "Does that mean we have not completely given up working for peace?"

"We might as well," he said scornfully. "Whatever the Germans may be thinking, they're not likely to change their minds because of a polite request."

"A drowning man may clutch at a straw."

"We're not clutching at straws. We're going through the ritual preliminaries to a declaration of war."

He was right, she thought dismally. All governments would want to say that they had not wanted war, but had been forced into it. Fitz showed no awareness of the danger to himself, no sign that this diplomatic fencing might result in a mortal wound to himself. She longed to protect him and at the same time she wanted to strangle him for his foolish obstinacy.

To distract herself she looked through *The Manchester Guardian*. It contained a full-page advertisement placed by the Neutrality League with the slogan "Britons, do your duty and keep your country out of a wicked and stupid war." Maud was glad to know there were still people who thought as she did. But they had no chance of prevailing.

Sanderson came in with an envelope on a silver tray. With a shock, Maud recognized Walter's handwriting. She was aghast. What was the maid thinking of? Did she not realize that if the original note was a secret, the reply must be, too?

She could not read Walter's note in front of Fitz. Heart racing, she took it with pretended carelessness and dropped it beside her plate, then asked Grout for more coffee.

She looked at her newspaper to hide her panic. Fitz did not censor her mail but, as the head of the family, he had the right to read any letter addressed to a female relative living in his house. No respectable woman would object.

She had to finish breakfast as fast as possible and take the note away unopened. She tried to eat a piece of toast, forcing the crumbs down her dry throat.

Fitz looked up from *The Times.* "Aren't you going to read your letter?" he said. And then, to her horror, he added: "That looks like von Ulrich's handwriting."

She had no choice. She slit the envelope with a clean butter knife and tried to fix her face in a neutral expression.

Nine o'clock a.m.

My dear love,

All of us at the embassy have been told to pack our bags, pay our bills, and be ready to leave Britain at a few hours' notice.

You and I should tell no one of our plan. After tonight I will return to Germany and you will remain here, living with your brother. Everyone agrees this war cannot last more than a few weeks or, at most, months. As soon as it is over, if we are both still alive, we will tell the world our happy tidings and start our new life together.

And in case we do not survive the war, oh, please, let us have one night of happiness as husband and wife.

I love you.

W.

P.S. Germany invaded Belgium an hour ago.

Maud's mind was in a whirl. Married secretly! No one would know. Walter's superiors would still trust him, not knowing about his marriage to an enemy, and he could fight as his honor demanded, and even work in secret intelligence. Men would continue to court Maud, thinking her single, but she could deal with that: she had been giving suitors the brush-off for years. They would live apart until the end of the war, which would come in a few months at most.

Fitz interrupted her thoughts. "What does he say?"

Maud's mind went blank. She could not tell Fitz any of this. How was she to answer his question? She looked down at the sheet of heavy cream-colored paper and the upright handwriting, and her eye fell on the P.S. "He says Germany invaded Belgium at eight o'clock this morning."

Fitz put down his fork. "That's it, then." For once even he looked shocked.

Aunt Herm said: "Little Belgium! I think those Germans are the most frightful bullies." Then she looked confused and said: "Except Herr von Ulrich, of course. He's charming."

Fitz said: "So much for the British government's polite request."

"It's madness," said Maud desolately. "Thousands of men are going to be killed in a war no one wants."

"I should have thought you might have supported the war," Fitz said argumentatively. "After all, we will be defending France, which is the only other real democracy in Europe. And our enemies will be Germany and Austria, whose elected parliaments are virtually powerless."

"But our ally will be Russia," Maud said bitterly. "So we will be fighting to preserve the most brutal and backward monarchy in Europe."

"I see your point."

"Everyone at the embassy has been told to pack," she said. "We may not see Walter again." She casually put the letter down.

It did not work. Fitz said: "May I see?"

Maud froze. She could not possibly show it to him. Not only would he lock her up: if he read the sentence about *one night of happiness*, he might take a gun and shoot Walter.

"May I?" Fitz repeated, holding out his hand.

"Of course," she said. She hesitated another second, then reached for the letter. At the last moment she was inspired, and she knocked over her cup, spilling coffee on the sheet of paper. "Oh, dash it," she said, noting with relief that the coffee had caused the blue ink to run and the words had already become illegible.

Grout stepped forward and began to clear up the mess. Pretending to be helpful, Maud picked up the letter and folded it, ensuring that any writing that might so far have escaped the coffee was now soaked. "I'm sorry, Fitz," she said. "But in fact there was no further information."

"Never mind," he said, and went back to his newspaper.

Maud put her hands in her lap to hide their shaking.

{ II }

That was only the beginning.

It was going to be difficult for Maud to get out of the house alone. Like all upper-class ladies, she was not supposed to go anywhere unescorted. Men pretended this was because they were so concerned to protect their women, but in truth it was a means of control. No doubt it would remain until women won the vote.

Maud had spent half her life finding ways to flout this rule. She would have to sneak out without being seen. This was quite difficult. Although only four family members lived in Fitz's Mayfair mansion, there were at least a dozen servants in the house at any time.

And then she had to stay out all night without anyone's knowledge.

She put her plan into place carefully.

"I have a headache," she said at the end of lunch. "Bea, will you forgive me if I don't come down to dinner tonight?"

"Of course," said Bea. "Is there anything I can do? Shall I send for Professor Rathbone?"

"No, thank you, it's nothing serious." A headache that was not serious was the usual euphemism for a menstrual period, and everyone accepted this without further comment.

So far, so good.

She went up to her room and rang for her maid. "I'm going to bed, Sanderson," she said, beginning a speech she had worked out carefully. "I'll probably stay there for the rest of the day. Please tell the other servants that I'm not to be disturbed for any reason. I may ring for a dinner tray, but I doubt it: I feel as if I could sleep the clock round."

That should ensure that her absence was not noticed for the rest of the day.

"Are you sick, my lady?" Sanderson asked, looking concerned. Some ladies took to their beds frequently, but it was rare for Maud.

"It's the normal female affliction, just worse than usual."

Sanderson did not believe her, Maud could tell. Already today the maid had been sent out with a secret message, something that had never happened before. Sanderson knew something unusual was going on. But maids were not permitted to cross-examine their mistresses. Sanderson would just have to wonder.

"And don't wake me in the morning," Maud added. She did not know what time she would get back, or how she would sneak unobserved into the house.

Sanderson left. It was a quarter past three. Maud undressed quickly, then looked in her wardrobe.

She was not used to getting her own clothes out—normally Sanderson did it. Her black walking dress had a hat with a veil, but she could not wear black for her wedding.

She looked at the clock above the fireplace: twenty past three. There was no time to dither.

She chose a stylish French outfit. She put on a tight-fitting white lace blouse with a high collar, to emphasize her long neck. Over it she wore a dress of a sky blue so pale it was almost white. In the latest daring fashion it ended an inch or two above her ankles. She added a broad-brimmed straw hat in dark blue with a veil the same color, and a gay blue parasol with a white lining. She had a blue velvet drawstring bag that matched the outfit. Into it she put a comb, a small vial of perfume, and a clean pair of drawers.

The clock struck half past three. Walter would be outside now, waiting. She felt her heart beating hard.

She pulled down the veil and examined herself in a full-length mirror. It was not quite a wedding dress, but it would look just right, she imagined, in a register office. She had never been to a civil wedding so she was not sure.

She took the key from the lock and stood by the closed door, listening. She did not want to meet anyone who might question her. It might not matter if she were seen by a footman or a boot boy, who would not care what she did, but all the maids would know by now that she was supposed to be unwell, and if she ran into one of the family her deception would be exposed instantly. She hardly cared about the embarrassment, but she was afraid they would try to stop her.

She was about to open the door when she heard heavy footsteps and caught a whiff of smoke. It must be Fitz, still finishing his after-lunch cigar, leaving for the House of Lords or perhaps White's Club. She waited impatiently.

After a few moments of silence she looked out. The broad corridor was deserted. She stepped out, closed the door, locked it, and dropped the key into her velvet bag. Now anyone trying the door would assume she was asleep inside.

She walked silently along the carpeted corridor to the top of the stairs and looked down. There was no one in the hall below. She went quickly down the steps. As she reached the half landing she heard a noise and froze. The door to the basement swung open and Grout emerged. Maud held her breath. She looked down at the bald dome of Grout's head as he crossed the hall carrying two decanters of port. He had his back to the stairs, and he entered the dining room without looking up.

As the door closed behind him, she ran down the last flight, throwing caution to the wind. She opened the front door, stepped out, and slammed it behind her. Too late, she wished she had thought to close it quietly.

The quiet Mayfair street baked in the August sun. She looked up and down and saw a horse-drawn fishmonger's cart, a nanny with a perambulator, and a cabbie changing the wheel of a motor taxi. A hundred yards along, on the opposite side of the road, stood a white car with a blue canvas canopy. Maud liked cars, and she recognized this as a Benz 10/30 belonging to Walter's cousin Robert.

As she crossed the road, Walter got out, and her heart filled with joy. He was wearing a light gray morning suit with a white carnation. He met her eye and she saw, from his expression, that until this moment he had not been sure she would come. The thought brought a tear to her eye.

Now, though, his face lit up with delight. How strange and wonderful it was, she thought, to be able to bring such happiness to another person.

She glanced anxiously back to the house. Grout was in the doorway, looking up and down the road with a puzzled frown. He had heard the door slam, she guessed. She turned her face resolutely forward, and the thought that came into her head was: Free at last!

Walter kissed her hand. She wanted to kiss him properly, but her veil was in the way. Besides, it was inappropriate before the wedding. There was no need to throw *all* the proprieties out of the window.

Robert was at the wheel, she saw. He touched his gray top hat to her. Walter trusted him. He would be one of the witnesses.

Walter opened the door and Maud got into the backseat. Someone was already there, and Maud recognized the housekeeper from Tŷ Gwyn. "Williams!" she cried.

Williams smiled. "You'd better call me Ethel now," she said. "I'm to be a witness at your wedding."

"Of course—I'm sorry." Impulsively, Maud hugged her. "Thank you for coming."

The car pulled away.

Maud leaned forward and spoke to Walter. "How did you find Ethel?"

"You told me she had come to your clinic. I got her address from Dr. Greenward. I knew you trusted her because you chose her to chaperone us at Tŷ Gwyn."

Ethel handed Maud a small posy of flowers. "Your bouquet."

They were roses, coral pink—the flower of passion. Did Walter know the language of flowers? "Who chose them?"

"It was my suggestion," said Ethel. "And Walter liked it when I explained the meaning." Ethel blushed.

Ethel knew how passionate they were because she had seen them kiss, Maud realized. "They're perfect," she said.

Ethel was wearing a pale pink dress that looked new and a hat decorated with more pink roses. Walter must have paid for that. How thoughtful he was.

They drove down Park Lane and headed for Chelsea. I'm getting married, Maud thought. In the past, whenever she had imagined her wedding, she had assumed it would be like those of all her friends, a long day of tedious ceremony. This was a better way to do things. There had been no planning, no guest list, and no caterer. There would be no hymns, no speeches, and no drunk relations trying to kiss her: just the bride and groom and two people they liked and trusted.

She thrust from her mind all thoughts about the future. Europe was at war, and anything might happen. She was just going to enjoy the day—and night.

They drove down King's Road and suddenly she felt nervous. She took Ethel's hand for courage. She had a nightmare vision of Fitz following behind in his Cadillac, shouting: "Stop that woman!" She glanced back. Of course neither Fitz nor his car was in sight.

They pulled up outside the classical façade of the Chelsea town hall. Robert took Maud's arm and led her up the steps to the entrance, and Walter followed with Ethel. Passersby stopped to watch: everyone loved a wedding.

Inside, the building was extravagantly decorated in the Victorian manner, with colored floor tiles and plaster moldings on the walls. It felt like the right sort of place to get married.

They had to wait in the lobby: another wedding had taken place at half past three and had not yet finished. The four of them stood in a little circle and no one could think of anything to say. Maud inhaled the scent of her roses, and the perfume went to her head, making her feel as if she had gulped a glass of champagne.

After a few minutes the earlier wedding party emerged, the bride wearing an everyday dress and the groom in the uniform of an army sergeant. Perhaps they, too, had made a sudden decision because of the war.

Maud and her party went in. The registrar sat at a plain table, wearing a morning coat and a silver tie. He had a carnation in his buttonhole, which was a nice touch, Maud thought. Beside him was a clerk in a lounge suit. They gave their names as Mr. von Ulrich and Miss Maud Fitzherbert. Maud raised her veil.

The registrar said: "Miss Fitzherbert, can you provide evidence of identity?"

She did not know what he was talking about.

Seeing her blank look, he said: "Your birth certificate, perhaps?"

She did not have her birth certificate. She had not known it was required, and even if she had she would not have been able to get hold of it, for Fitz kept it in the safe, along with other family documents such as his will. Panic seized her.

Then Walter said: "I think this will serve." He took from his pocket a stamped and franked envelope addressed to Miss Maud Fitzherbert at the street address of the baby clinic. He must have picked it up when he went to see Dr. Greenward. How clever of him.

The registrar handed the envelope back without comment. He said: "It is my duty to remind you of the solemn and binding nature of the vows you are about to take."

Maud felt mildly offended at the suggestion that she might not know what she was doing; then she realized that was something he had to say to everyone.

Walter stood more upright. This is it, Maud thought; no turning back. She felt quite sure she wanted to marry Walter—but, more than that, she was acutely aware that she had reached the age of twenty-three without meeting anyone else she would remotely have considered as a husband. Every other man she had ever met had treated her and all women like overgrown children. Only Walter was different. It was him or no one.

The registrar was speaking words for Walter to repeat. "I do solemnly declare that I know not of any lawful impediment why I, Walter von Ulrich, may not be joined in matrimony to Maud Elizabeth Fitzherbert." Walter pronounced his own name the English way, "Wall-ter," rather than the correct German "Val-ter."

Maud watched his face as he spoke. His voice was firm and clear.

In his turn he watched her solemnly as she made her declaration. She loved his seriousness. Most men, even quite clever ones, became silly when they talked to women. Walter spoke to her just as intelligently as he spoke to Robert or Fitz, and—even more unusually—he listened to her answers.

Next came the vows. Walter looked her in the eye as he took her for his wife, and this time she heard a little shake of emotion in his voice. That was the other thing she loved: she knew she could undermine his seriousness. She could make him tremble with love or happiness or desire.

She made the same vow. "I call upon these persons here present to witness that I, Maud Elizabeth Fitzherbert, do take thee, Walter von Ulrich, to be my lawful wedded husband." There was no unsteadiness in her voice, and she felt a little embarrassed that she was not visibly moved—but that was not her style. She preferred to appear cool even when she was not. Walter understood that, and he more than anyone knew about the storms of unseen passion that blew through her heart.

"Do you have a ring?" said the registrar. Maud had not even thought about it—but Walter had. He drew a plain gold wedding band from his waistcoat pocket, took her hand, and slipped it onto her finger. He must have guessed the size, but it was a near fit, perhaps just one size too big. As their marriage was to be secret, she would not be wearing it for a while after today.

"I now pronounce you man and wife," said the registrar. "You may kiss the bride."

Walter kissed her lips softly. She put her arm around his waist and drew him closer. "I love you," she whispered.

The registrar said: "And now for the marriage certificate. Perhaps you would like to sit down . . . Mrs. Ulrich."

Walter smiled, Robert giggled, and Ethel gave a little cheer. Maud guessed the registrar enjoyed being the first person to call the bride by her married name. They all sat down, and the registrar's clerk began to fill out the certificate. Walter gave his father's occupation as army officer and his place of birth as Danzig. Maud put her father down as George Fitzherbert, farmer—there was, in fact, a small flock of sheep at Tŷ Gwyn, so the description was not actually false—and her place of birth as London. Robert and Ethel signed as witnesses.

Suddenly it was over, and they were walking out of the room and through the lobby—where another pretty bride was waiting with a nervous groom to make a lifelong commitment. As they walked arm in arm down the steps to the car parked at the curb, Ethel threw a handful of confetti over them. Among the bystanders, Maud noticed a middle-class woman of her own age carrying a parcel from a shop. The woman looked hard at Walter, then turned her gaze on Maud, and what Maud saw in her eyes was envy. Yes, Maud thought, I'm a lucky girl.

Walter and Maud sat in the back of the car, and Robert and Ethel rode up front. As they drove away, Walter took Maud's hand and kissed it. They looked into each other's eyes and laughed. Maud had seen couples do that, and had always thought it was stupid and sentimental, but now it seemed the most natural thing in the world.

In a few minutes they arrived at the Hyde Hotel. Maud dropped her veil. Walter took her arm and they walked through the lobby to the stairs. Robert said: "I'll order the champagne."

Walter had taken the best suite and filled it with flowers. There must have been a hundred coral-pink roses. Tears came to Maud's eyes, and Ethel gasped in awe. On a sideboard was a big bowl of fruit and a box of chocolates. The afternoon sun shone through large windows onto chairs and sofas upholstered in gay fabrics.

"Let's make ourselves comfortable!" Walter said jovially.

While Maud and Ethel were inspecting the suite, Robert came in, followed by a waiter with champagne and glasses on a tray. Walter popped the cork and poured. When they each had a glass, Robert said:

"I would like to propose a toast." He cleared his throat, and Maud realized with amusement that he was going to make a speech.

"My cousin Walter is an unusual man," he began. "He has always seemed older than me, although in fact we are the same age. When we were students together in Vienna, he never got drunk. If a group of us went out in the evening, to visit certain houses in the city, he would stay home and study. I thought perhaps he was the type of man who does not love women." Robert gave a wry smile. "In fact it was I who was made that way—but that's another story, as the English say. Walter loves his family and his work, and he loves Germany, but he has never loved a woman—until now. He has changed." Robert grinned mischievously. "He buys new ties. He asks me questions—when do you kiss a girl, should men wear cologne, what colors flatter him—as if I knew anything about what women like. And—most terrible of all, in my view . . . " Robert paused dramatically. "He plays ragtime!"

The others laughed. Robert raised his glass. "Let us toast the woman who has wrought such changes—the bride!"

They drank and then, to Maud's surprise, Ethel spoke. "It falls to me to propose the toast to the groom," she said as if she had been making speeches all her life. How had a servant from Wales acquired such confidence? Then Maud remembered that her father was a preacher and a political activist, so she had an example to follow.

"Lady Maud is different from every other woman of her class I have ever met," Ethel began. "When I started work as a maid at Tŷ Gwyn, she was the only member of the family who even noticed me. Here in London, when young unmarried women have babies, most respectable ladies grumble about moral decay—but Maud offers them real practical help. In the East End of London, she is regarded as a saint. However, she has her faults, and they are grave."

Maud thought: What now?

"She is too serious to attract a normal man," Ethel went on. "All the most eligible men in London have been drawn to her by her striking good looks and vivacious personality, only to be frightened away by her brains and her tough political realism. Some time ago I realized it would take a rare man to win her. He would have to be clever, but open-minded; strictly moral, but not orthodox; strong, but not domineering." Ethel smiled. "I thought it was impossible. And then, January, he came up the hill from Aberowen in the station taxi and walked into Tŷ Gwyn, and the wait was over." She raised her glass. "To the groom!"

They all drank again; then Ethel took Robert's arm. "Now you can take me to the Ritz for dinner, Robert," she said.

Walter seemed surprised. "I assumed we would all have dinner together here," he said.

Ethel gave him an arch look. "Don't be daft, man," she said. She walked to the door, drawing Robert with her.

"Good night," Robert said, though it was only six o'clock. The two of them went out and closed the door.

Maud laughed. Walter said: "That housekeeper is extremely intelligent."

"She understands me," Maud said. She went to the door and turned the key. "Now," she said. "The bedroom."

"Would you prefer to undress in private?" Walter said, looking worried.

"Not really," Maud said. "Wouldn't you like to watch?"

He swallowed, and when he spoke he sounded a little hoarse. "Yes, please," he said. "I would." He held the bedroom door open and she passed through.

Despite her show of boldness, she felt nervous as she sat on the edge of the bed and took off her shoes. No one had seen her naked since she was eight years old. She did not know whether her body was beautiful because she had never seen anyone else's. By comparison with the nudes in museums, she had small breasts and wide hips. And there was a growth of hair between her legs that paintings never showed. Would Walter think her body was ugly?

He took off his coat and waistcoat and hung them up in a matter-of-fact way. She supposed they would get used to this one day. Everyone did it all the time. But somehow it felt strange, more intimidating than exciting.

She pulled down her stockings and took off her hat. She had nothing else superfluous. The next step was the big one. She stood up.

Walter stopped undoing his tie.

Quickly, Maud unfastened her dress and let it fall to the floor. Then she dropped her petticoat and pulled her lace blouse over her head. She stood in front of him in her underwear and watched his face.

"You are so beautiful," he said in a half whisper.

She smiled. He always said the right thing.

He took her in his arms and kissed her. She began to feel less nervous, almost relaxed. She savored the touch of his mouth on hers, the gentle lips and the bristles of the mustache. She stroked his cheek, squeezed his earlobe between her fingertips, and ran her hand around the column of his neck, feeling everything with heightened awareness, thinking: All this is mine now.

"Let's lie down," he said.

"No," she said. "Not yet." She stepped away from him. "Wait." She took off her chemise, revealing that she was wearing one of the newfangled brassieres. She reached behind her back, unfastened the clasp, and threw it to the floor. She looked at him defiantly, daring him not to like her breasts.

He said: "They are beautiful—may I kiss them?"

"You may do anything you like," she said, feeling deliciously wanton.

He bent his head to her chest and kissed one, then the other, letting his lips brush delicately across her nipples, which stood up suddenly as if the air had turned cold. She had a sudden yen to do the same to him, and wondered if he would think it odd.

He might have kissed her breasts forever. She pushed him away gently. "Take off the rest of your clothes," she said. "Quickly."

He pulled off shoes, socks, tie, shirt, undershirt, and trousers; then he hesitated. "I feel shy," he said, laughing. "I don't know why."

"I'll go first," she said. She untied the string of her drawers and pulled them off. When she looked up he was naked, too, and she saw with a shock that his penis was sticking up from the thatch of fair hair at his groin. She remembered grasping it through his clothes at the opera, and now she wanted to touch it again.

He said: "May we now lie down?"

He sounded so correct that she laughed. A hurt look crossed his face, and she was immediately apologetic. "I love you," she said, and his expression cleared. "Please let us lie down." She was so excited she felt she might burst.

At first they lay side by side, kissing and touching. "I love you," she said again. "How soon will you get bored with my saying that?"

"Never," he said gallantly.

She believed him.

After a while he said: "Now?" and she nodded.

She parted her legs. He lay on top of her, resting his weight on his elbows. She was taut with anticipation. Shifting his weight to his left arm, he reached between her thighs, and she felt his fingers opening her moist lips, then something larger. He pushed, and suddenly she felt a pain. She cried out.

"I'm sorry!" he said. "I hurt you. I'm so terribly sorry."

"Just wait a moment," she said. The pain was not very bad. She was more shocked than anything else. "Try again," she said. "Just gently."

She felt the head of his penis touch her lips again, and she knew that it would not go inside: it was too big, or the hole was too small, or both. But she let him push, hoping for the best. It hurt, but this time she gritted her teeth and stopped herself from crying out. Her stoicism did no good. After a few moments he stopped. "It won't go in," he said.

"What's wrong?" she said miserably. "I thought this was supposed to happen naturally."

"I don't understand it," he said. "I have no experience."

"And I certainly have none." She reached down and grasped his penis. She loved the feel of it in her hand, stiff but silky. She tried to maneuver it inside her, raising her hips to make it easier; but after a moment he pulled away, saying: "Ah! Sorry! It hurts me, too."

"Do you think you're bigger than usual?" she said tentatively.

"No. When I was in the army I saw many men naked. Some fellows have extra-large ones, and they are very proud, but I am average, and anyway I never heard even one of them complain of this difficulty."

Maud nodded. The only other penis she had ever seen was Fitz's, and as far as she could remember, it was about the same size as Walter's. "Perhaps I'm too small."

He shook his head. "When I was sixteen, I went to stay in Robert's family castle in Hungary. There was a maid there who was very . . . vivacious. We did not have sexual intercourse, but we did experiment. I touched her the way I touched you in the library at Sussex House. I hope I am not making you angry by telling you this."

She kissed his chin. "Not in the least."

"She was not very different from you in that area."

"Then what is wrong?"

He sighed and rolled off her. He put his arm under her head and pulled her to him, kissing her forehead. "I have heard that newly married couples may have difficulties. Sometimes the man is so nervous that he does not become erect. I have also heard of men who become overexcited and ejaculate even before intercourse takes place. I think we must be patient and love each other and see what happens."

"But we have only one night!" Maud began to cry.

Walter patted her and said: "There, there," but it did no good. She felt a complete failure. I believed I was so clever, she thought, escaping from my brother and marrying Walter secretly, and now it has all turned into a disaster. She was disappointed for herself but even more for Walter. How terrible for him to wait until the age of twenty-eight, then marry a woman who could not satisfy him!

She wished she could talk to someone about this, another woman— but who? The thought of discussing it with Aunt Herm was ludicrous. Some women shared secrets with their maids, but Maud had never had that kind of relationship with Sanderson. Perhaps she could talk to Ethel. Now that she came to think of it, it was Ethel who had told her it was normal to have hair between your legs. But Ethel had gone off with Robert.

Walter sat upright. "Let us order supper, and perhaps a bottle of wine," he said. "We will sit down together as man and wife, and talk of this and that for a while. Then, later, we will try again."

Maud had no appetite and could not imagine having a conversation about "this and that," but she did not have a better idea, so she consented. Miserably, she put her clothes back on. Walter dressed quickly, went to the next room, and rang the bell for a waiter. She heard him ordering cold meats, smoked fish, salads, and a bottle of hock.

She sat by an open window and looked down at the street below. A newspaper placard said BRITISH ULTIMATUM TO GERMANY. Walter might be killed in this war. She did not want him to die a virgin.

Walter called her when the food had arrived and she joined him in the next room. The waiter had spread a white cloth and laid out smoked salmon, sliced ham, lettuce, tomatoes, cucumber, and sliced white bread. She did not feel hungry, but sipped the white wine he poured, and nibbled some salmon to show she was willing.

In the end, they did talk of this and that. Walter reminisced about his childhood, his mother, and his time at Eton. Maud spoke about house parties at Tŷ Gwyn when her father was alive. The most powerful men in the land were guests, and her mother would have to arrange the allocation of bedrooms so that men could be near their mistresses.

At first, Maud found herself consciously making conversation, as if they were two people who hardly knew each other; but soon they relaxed into their normal intimacy, and she just said whatever came into her mind. The waiter cleared away the supper and they moved to the couch, where they continued to talk, holding hands. They speculated about the sex lives of other people: their parents, Fitz, Robert, Ethel, even the duchess. Maud was fascinated to learn about men such as Robert: where they met, how they recognized one another, and what they did. They kissed each other just as men kissed women, Walter told her, and they did what she had done to him at the opera, and other things . . . He said he was not sure of the details, but she thought he did know and just felt embarrassed to say.

She was surprised when the clock on the mantelpiece struck

midnight. "Let's go to bed," she said. "I want to lie in your arms, even if things don't happen the way they're supposed to."

"All right." He stood up. "Do you mind if I do something first? There is a telephone in the lobby for the use of guests. I'd like to phone the embassy."

"Of course."

He went out. Maud went to the bathroom along the corridor, then returned to the suite. She took off her clothes and got into bed naked. She almost felt she did not care what happened now. They loved each other, and they were together, and if that was all it would be enough.

Walter returned a few minutes later. His face was grim and she knew immediately that the news was bad. "Britain has declared war on Germany," he said.

"Oh, Walter, I'm so sorry!"

"The note was received at the embassy an hour ago. Young Nicolson brought it round from the Foreign Office and got Prince Lichnowsky out of bed."

They had known it was almost certain to happen, but even so the reality struck Maud like a blow. She could see that Walter was upset, too.

He took off his clothes automatically, as if he had been undressing in front of her for years. "We leave tomorrow," he said. He took off his underpants, and she saw that his penis in its normal state was small and wrinkled. "I must be at Liverpool Street station, with my bags packed, by ten o'clock." He turned off the electric light and got into bed with her.

They lay side by side, not touching, and for an awful moment Maud thought he was going to go to sleep like that; then he turned to her and took her in his arms and kissed her mouth. Despite everything she was flooded with desire for him; indeed, it was almost as if their troubles had made her love him more urgently and desperately. She felt his penis grow and harden against her soft belly. After a moment he got on top of her. As before, he leaned on his left arm and touched her with his right hand. As before, she felt the hard penis pressing her lips. As before, it hurt—but only for a moment. This time, it slipped inside her.

There was another moment of resistance; then she lost her virginity; and suddenly he was all the way in and they were locked together in the oldest embrace of all.

"Oh, thank heaven," she said; then relief gave way to delight, and she began to move in happy rhythm with him; and, at last, they made love.

PART TWO

THE WAR
of
GIANTS

Early to Late August 1914

Katerina was distraught. When the mobilization posters went up all over St. Petersburg, she sat in Grigori's room at the boardinghouse weeping, running her fingers distractedly through her long fair hair, and saying: "What am I going to do? What am I going to do?"

It made him long to take her in his arms and kiss her tears away and promise never to leave her side. But he could not make such a promise and, anyway, she loved his brother.

Grigori had done his military service and was therefore a reservist, theoretically ready for battle. In fact most of his training had consisted of marching and building roads. Nevertheless he expected to be among the first summoned.

It made him fume with rage. The war was as stupid and pointless as everything else Tsar Nicholas did. There had been a murder in Bosnia, and a month later Russia was at war with Germany! Thousands of working-class men and peasants would be killed on both sides, and nothing would be achieved. It proved, to Grigori and everyone he knew, that the Russian nobility were too stupid to govern.

Even if he survived, the war would ruin his plans. He was saving for another ticket to America. With his wages from the Putilov factory he might do it in two or three years, but on army pay it would take forever. How many more years must he suffer the injustice and brutality of tsarist rule?

He was even more worried about Katerina. What would she do if he had to go to war? She was sharing a room with three other girls at the boardinghouse, and working at the Putilov factory, packing rifle cartridges into cardboard boxes. But she would have to stop work when the baby was born, at least for a while. Without Grigori, how would she support herself and the child? She would be desperate, and he knew what country girls did in St. Petersburg when they were desperate for money. God forbid that she should sell her body on the streets.

However, he was not called up on the first day, or the first week. According to the newspapers, two and a half million reservists had been mobilized on the last day of July, but that was just a story. It was impossible for so many men to be marshaled, issued with uniforms, and put on trains to the front all in one day, or indeed one month. They were called in groups, some sooner, some later.

As the first hot days of August went by, Grigori began to think he might have been left out. It was a tantalizing possibility. The army was one of the worst-managed institutions in a hopelessly disorganized country, and there would probably be thousands of men who were overlooked through sheer incompetence.

Katerina had got into the habit of coming to his room early every morning, while he was making breakfast. It was the highlight of his day. He was always washed and dressed by then, but she appeared wearing the shift she slept in, her hair bewitchingly tousled, yawning. The garment was too small for her, now that she was putting on weight. He calculated that she must be four and a half months pregnant. Her breasts and hips were larger, and there was a small but noticeable bulge in her belly. Her voluptuousness was a delightful torture. Grigori tried not to stare at her body.

One morning she came in while he was scrambling two hen's eggs in a pan over the fire. He no longer made do with porridge for breakfast: his brother's unborn child needed good food to grow strong and healthy. Most days Grigori had something nourishing to share with Katerina: ham, or herrings, or her favorite, sausage.

Katerina was always hungry. She sat at the table, cut a thick slice of black bread from the loaf, and began to eat, too impatient to wait. With her mouth full she said: "When a soldier is killed, who gets his back pay?"

Grigori recalled giving the name and address of his next of kin. "In my case, Lev," he said.

"I wonder if he's in America yet."

"He must be. It doesn't take eight weeks to get there."

"I hope he's found a job."

"You don't need to worry. He'll be all right. Everyone likes him." Grigori suffered a pang of angry resentment at his brother. It should have been Lev here in Russia looking after Katerina and her unborn baby, and worrying about the draft, while Grigori started the new life he had saved and planned for. But Lev had snatched that opportunity. And still Katerina fretted about the man who had abandoned her, not the one who had stayed.

She said: "I'm sure he's doing well in America, but still I wish we'd had a letter from him."

Grigori shaved a heel of hard cheese over the eggs and added salt. He wondered sadly whether they would ever hear from America. Lev had never been sentimental, and he might have decided to shuck off his past, like a lizard crawling out of its old skin. But Grigori did not voice this thought, out of kindness to Katerina, who was still hoping Lev would send for her.

She said: "Do you think you will fight?"

"Not if I can help it. What are we fighting for?"

"For Serbia, they say."

Grigori spooned the eggs onto two plates and sat at the table. "The issue is whether Serbia will be tyrannized by the Austrian emperor or the Russian tsar. I doubt if the Serbs care one way or the other, and I certainly don't." He began to eat.

"For the tsar, then."

"I would fight for you, for Lev, for myself, or for your baby . . . but for the tsar? No."

Katerina ate her egg rapidly and wiped the plate with a fresh slice of bread. "What names do you like for a boy?"

"My father's name was Sergei, and his father was Tikhon."

"I like Mikhail," she said. "The same as the archangel."

"So do most people. That's why the name is so common."

"Perhaps I should call him Lev. Or even Grigori."

Grigori was touched by this. He would be thrilled to have a nephew named after him. But he did not like to make demands on her. "Lev would be nice," he said.

The factory whistle blew—a sound that could be heard all over the Narva district—and Grigori stood up to go.

"I'll wash the plates," Katerina said. Her job did not begin until seven, an hour later than Grigori's.

She turned her cheek up and Grigori kissed her. It was only a brief kiss, and he did not allow his lips to linger, but all the same he relished the soft smoothness of her skin and the warm, sleepy smell of her neck.

Then he put on his cap and went out.

The summer weather was warm and humid, despite the early hour. Grigori began to perspire as he walked briskly through the streets.

In the two months since Lev had left, Grigori and Katerina had settled into an uneasy friendship. She relied on him, and he looked after her, but it was not what either of them wanted. Grigori wanted love, not friendship. Katerina wanted Lev, not Grigori. But Grigori found a kind of fulfillment in making sure she ate well. It was the only way he had of expressing his love. It could hardly be a long-term arrangement, but right now it was difficult to think long-term. He still planned to escape from Russia and find his way to the promised land of America.

At the factory gate new mobilization posters had been stuck up, and men crowded around, those unable to read begging others to read aloud. Grigori found himself standing next to Isaak, the football captain. They were the same age and had been reservists together. Grigori scanned the notices, looking for the name of their unit.

Today it was there.

He looked again, but there was no mistake: Narva Regiment.

He looked down the list of names and found his own.

He had not really believed it could happen. But he had been fooling himself. He was twenty-five, fit and strong, perfect soldier material. Of course he was going to war.

What would happen to Katerina? And her baby?

Isaak cursed aloud. His name was also on the list.

A voice behind them said: "No need to worry."

They turned to see the long, thin shape of Kanin, the amiable supervisor of the casting section, an engineer in his thirties. "No need to worry?" said Grigori skeptically. "Katerina is having Lev's baby and there's no one to look after her. What am I going to do?"

"I've been to see the man in charge of mobilization for this district," Kanin said. "He promised me exemption for any of my workers. Only the troublemakers have to go."

Grigori's heart leaped with hope again. It sounded too good to be true.

Isaak said: "What do we have to do?"

"Just don't go to the barracks. You'll be all right. It's fixed."

Isaak was an aggressive character—no doubt that was why he made such a good sportsman—and he was not satisfied with Kanin's answer. "Fixed how?" he demanded.

"The army gives the police a list of men who fail to show, and the police have to round them up. Your name simply won't be on the list."

Isaak grunted with dissatisfaction. Grigori shared his dislike of such semiofficial arrangements—there was too much room for things to go wrong—but dealing with the government was always like this. Kanin had either bribed an official or performed some other favor. It was pointless to be churlish about it. "That's great," Grigori said to Kanin. "Thank you."

"Don't thank me," Kanin said mildly. "I did it for myself—and for Russia. We need skilled men like you two to make trains, not stop German bullets—an illiterate peasant can do that. The government hasn't worked this out yet, but they will in time, and then they'll thank me."

Grigori and Isaak passed through the gates. "We might as well trust him," Grigori said. "What have we got to lose?" They stood in line to check themselves in by each dropping a numbered metal square into a box. "It's good news," he said.

Isaak was not convinced. "I just wish I could feel surer," he said.

They headed for the wheel shop. Grigori put his worries out of his mind and prepared himself for the day's work. The Putilov plant was making more trains than ever. The army had to assume that locomotives and wagons would be destroyed by shelling, so they would be needing replacements as soon as the fighting started. The pressure was on Grigori's team to produce wheels faster.

He began to roll up his sleeves as he stepped into the wheel shop. It was a small shed, and the furnace made it hot in winter, a baking oven now at the height of summer. Metal screeched and rang as lathes shaped and polished it.

He saw Konstantin standing by his lathe, and his friend's stance made him frown. Konstantin's face telegraphed a warning: something was wrong. Isaak saw it, too. Reacting faster than Grigori, he stopped, grabbed Grigori's arm, and said: "What—?"

He did not finish the question.

A figure in a black-and-green uniform stepped from behind the furnace and hit Grigori in the face with a sledgehammer.

He tried to dodge the blow, but his reaction was a moment too slow and, although he ducked, the wooden head of the big hammer struck him high on the cheekbone and knocked him to the ground. An agonizing pain shot through his head and he cried out loud.

It took several moments for his vision to clear. At last he looked up and saw the stout figure of Mikhail Pinsky, the local police captain.

He should have expected this. He had got off too lightly after that fight back in February. Policemen never forgot such things.

He also saw Isaak fighting with Pinsky's sidekick, Ilya Kozlov, and two other cops.

Grigori remained on the ground. He was not going to fight back if he could help it. Let Pinsky take his revenge; then perhaps he would be satisfied.

In the next second he failed to keep that resolution.

Pinsky raised the sledgehammer. In a flash of redundant insight Grigori recognized the tool as his own, used for tapping templates into the molding sand. Then it came down at his head.

He lurched to the right but Pinsky slanted his swing, and the heavy oak tool landed on Grigori's left shoulder. He roared with pain and anger. While Pinsky was recovering his balance, Grigori leaped to his feet. His left arm was limp and useless, but there was nothing amiss with his right, and he drew back his fist to hit Pinsky, regardless of the consequences.

He never struck the blow. Two figures he had not noticed materialized either side of him in black-and-green uniforms, and his arms were grabbed and held firmly. He tried to shake off his captors but failed. Through a mist of rage he saw Pinsky draw back the hammer and strike. The blow hit him in the chest, and he felt ribs crack. The next blow was lower, and pounded his belly. He convulsed and vomited his breakfast. Then another blow struck the side of his head. He blacked out for a moment, and came around to find himself hanging limply in the grip of the two policemen. Isaak was similarly pinned by two others.

"Feeling calmer now?" said Pinsky.

Grigori spat blood. His body was a mass of pain and he could not think straight. What was going on? Pinsky hated him, but something must have happened to trigger this. And it was bold of Pinsky to act right here in the middle of the factory, surrounded by workers who had no reason to like the police. For some reason he must have been feeling sure of himself.

Pinsky hefted the sledgehammer and looked thoughtful, as if considering one more blow. Grigori braced himself and fought the temptation to beg for mercy. Then Pinsky said: "What is your name?"

Grigori tried to speak. At first nothing but blood came out of his mouth. At last he managed to say: "Grigori Sergeivich Peshkov."

Pinsky hit him in the stomach again. Grigori groaned and vomited blood. "Liar," said Pinsky. "What is your name?" He lifted the sledgehammer again.

Konstantin stepped from his lathe and came forward. "Officer, this man is Grigori Peshkov!" he protested. "All of us have known him for years!"

"Don't lie to me," Pinsky said. He lifted the hammer. "Or you'll get a taste of this."

Konstantin's mother, Varya, intervened. "It's no lie, Mikhail Mikhailovich," she said. Her use of the patronymic indicated that she knew Pinsky. "He is who he says he is." She stood with her arms folded over her large bosom as if defying the policeman to doubt her.

"Then explain this," said Pinsky, and he pulled from his pocket a sheet of paper. "Grigori Sergeivich Peshkov left St. Petersburg two months ago aboard the *Angel Gabriel.*"

Kanin, the supervisor, appeared and said: "What's going on here? Why is no one working?"

Pinsky pointed to Grigori. "This man is Lev Peshkov, Grigori's brother—wanted for the murder of a police officer!"

They all began to shout at once. Kanin held up his hand for quiet and said: "Officer, I know Grigori and Lev Peshkov, and have seen both men almost every day for several years. They look alike, as brothers generally do, but I can assure you that this is Grigori. And you are holding up the work of this section."

"If this is Grigori," said Pinsky with the air of one who plays a trump card, "then who left on the *Angel Gabriel?*"

As soon as he had asked the question, the answer became obvious. After a moment it dawned on Pinsky, too, and he looked foolish.

Grigori said: "My passport and ticket were stolen."

Pinsky began to bluster. "Why did you not report this to the police?"

"What was the point? Lev had left the country. You could not bring him back, nor my property."

"That makes you an accomplice in his escape."

Kanin intervened again. "Captain Pinsky, you began by accusing this man of murder. Perhaps that was a good enough reason to stop production in the wheel shop. But you have admitted that you were in error, and now you allege only that he failed to report the theft of some documents. Meanwhile, your country is at war, and you are delaying the manufacture of locomotives desperately needed by the Russian army. Unless you wish your name to be mentioned in our next report to the army high command, I suggest you finish your business here quickly."

Pinsky looked at Grigori. "What reserve unit are you in?"

Without thinking, Grigori replied: "Narva Regiment."

"Hah!" said Pinsky. "They were called up today." He looked at Isaak. "You, too, I'll bet."

Isaak said nothing.

"Release them," Pinsky said.

Grigori staggered when they let go of his arms, but he managed to stay upright.

"You'd better make sure you show up at the depot as ordered," Pinsky said to Grigori and Isaak. "Otherwise I'll be after you." He turned on his heel and exited with what little dignity he had left. His men followed him.

Grigori sat down heavily on a stool. He had a blinding headache, a pain in his ribs, and a bruised ache in his belly. He needed to curl up in a corner and pass out. The thought that kept him conscious was a scorching desire to destroy Pinsky and the entire system of which he was part. One of these days, he kept thinking, we will wipe out Pinsky and the tsar and everything they stand for.

Kanin said: "The army won't pursue you two—I've made sure of that—but I'm afraid I can't do anything about the police."

Grigori nodded grimly. It was as he had feared. Pinsky's most savage blow, worse than any he had struck with the sledgehammer, would be to make sure that Grigori and Isaak joined the army.

Kanin said: "I'll be sorry to lose you. You've been a good worker." He seemed genuinely moved, but he was impotent. He paused a moment longer, threw up his hands in a gesture of helplessness, and left the shop.

Varya appeared in front of Grigori with a bowl of water and a clean rag. She washed the blood from his face. She was a bulky woman but her broad hands had a gentle touch. "You should go to the factory barracks," she said. "Find an empty bed and lie down for an hour."

"No," Grigori said. "I'm going home."

Varya shrugged and moved to Isaak, who was not so badly injured.

With an effort, Grigori stood up. The factory spun around him for a while, and Konstantin held his arm when he staggered; but eventually he felt able to stand alone.

Konstantin picked up his cap from the floor and gave it to him.

He felt unsteady when he began to walk, but he waved away offers of support, and after a few steps he regained his normal stride. His head cleared with the effort, but the pain in his ribs forced him to tread carefully. He made his slow way through the maze of benches and lathes, furnaces and presses, to the outside of the building, and then to the factory gate.

There he met Katerina coming in.

"Grigori!" she said. "You've been called up—I saw the poster!" Then she noticed his damaged face. "What happened?"

"An encounter with your favorite police captain."

"That pig Pinsky. You're hurt!"

"The bruises will heal."

"I'll take you home."

Grigori was surprised. This was a switch of roles. Katerina had never before offered to take care of him. "I can make it on my own," he said.

"I'll come with you all the same."

She took his arm and they walked through the narrow streets against the tide of thousands of workers swarming to the factory. Grigori's body hurt and he felt ill, but all the same it was a joy to him to be walking arm in arm with Katerina as the sun rose over the dilapidated houses and the dirty streets.

However, the familiar walk tired him more than he expected, and when at last they got home he sat heavily on the bed and then, after a moment, lay down.

"I've got a bottle of vodka hidden in the girls' room," Katerina said.

"No, thanks, but I'd like some tea."

He did not have a samovar, but she made tea in a saucepan and gave him a cup with a lump of sugar. When he had drunk it, he felt a little better. He said: "The worst of it is, I could have avoided the draft—but Pinsky swore he would make sure I didn't."

She sat on the bed beside him and took from her pocket a pamphlet. "One of the girls gave me this."

Grigori glanced at it. It appeared dull and official, like a government publication. Its title was "Aid to Soldiers' Families."

Katerina said: "If you're the wife of a soldier you're entitled to a monthly allowance from the army. It's not just for the poor—everyone gets it."

Grigori vaguely remembered hearing about this. He had not taken much notice, as it did not apply to him.

Katerina went on: "There's more. You get cheap home fuel, cheap railway tickets, and help with children's schooling."

"That's good," Grigori said. He wanted to sleep. "Unusual for the army to be so sensible."

"But you have to be married."

Grigori became more alert. Surely she could not possibly be thinking . . . "Why are you telling me this?" he said.

"As it is I won't get anything."

Grigori lifted himself on one elbow and looked at her. Suddenly his heart was racing.

She said: "If I was married to a soldier I'd be better off. So would my baby."

"But . . . you love Lev."

"I know." She began to cry. "But Lev is in America and he doesn't care enough even to write and ask how I am."

"So . . . what do you want to do?" Grigori knew the answer, but he had to hear it.

"I want to get married," she said.

"Just so that you can get the soldier's wife's allowance."

She nodded, and with that nod she extinguished in him a faint, foolish hope that had flared briefly. "It would mean so much," she said. "To have a little money when the baby comes—especially as you'll be away with the army."

"I understand," he said with a heavy heart.

"Can we get married?" she said. "Please?"

"Yes," he said. "Of course."

{ II }

Five couples were married at the same time in the Church of the Blessed Virgin. The priest read the service fast, and Grigori observed with irritation that he did not look anyone in the eye. The man would hardly have noticed if one of the brides had been a gorilla.

Grigori did not much care. Whenever he passed a church, he remembered the priest who had tried to have some kind of sex with eleven-year-old Lev. Grigori's contempt for Christianity had later been reinforced by lectures on atheism at Konstantin's Bolshevik discussion group.

Grigori and Katerina were getting married at short notice, as were the other four couples. All the men were in uniform. Mobilization had caused a rush to matrimony, and the church was struggling to keep up. Grigori hated the uniform as a symbol of servitude.

He had told no one about the marriage. He did not feel it was a reason for celebration. Katerina had made it clear that it was a purely practical measure, a way for her to get an allowance. As such it was a very good idea, and Grigori would be less anxious, when he was away with the army, knowing that she had financial security. All the same he could not help feeling there was something horribly farcical about the wedding.

Katerina was not so shy, and all the girls from the boardinghouse were in the congregation, as well as several workers from the Putilov plant.

Afterward there was a party in the girls' room at the boardinghouse, with beer and vodka and a violinist who played folk tunes they all knew. When people started to get drunk, Grigori slipped out and went to his own room. He took off his boots and lay on the bed in his uniform trousers and shirt. He blew out the candle but he could see by the light from the street. He still ached from Pinsky's beating: his left arm hurt when he tried to use it and his cracked ribs gave him a stabbing pain every time he turned over in bed.

Tomorrow he would be on a train west. The shooting would start any day now. He was scared: only a mad person would feel otherwise. But he was smart and determined and he would try his best to stay alive, which was what he had done ever since his mother died.

He was still awake when Katerina came in. "You left the party early," she complained.

"I didn't want to get drunk."

She pulled up the skirt of her dress.

He was astonished. He stared at her body, outlined by the light from the streetlamps, the long curves of her thighs and the fair curls. He was aroused and confused. "What are you doing?" he said.

"Coming to bed, of course."

"Not here."

She kicked off her shoes. "What are you talking about? We're married."

"Just so that you can collect your allowance."

"Still, you deserve something in return." She lay on the bed and kissed his mouth with the smell of vodka on her breath.

He could not help the desire that rose within him, making him flush with passion and shame. All the same he managed to say a choked: "No."

She took his hand and pulled it to her breast. Against his will he caressed her, gently squeezing the soft flesh, his fingertips finding her nipple through the coarse fabric of her dress. "You see?" she said. "You want to."

The note of triumph angered him. "Of course I want to," he said. "I've loved you since the day I first saw you. But you love Lev."

"Oh, why do you always think about Lev?"

"It's a habit I got into when he was small and vulnerable."

"Well, he's a big man now, and he doesn't care two kopeks for you, or for me. He took your passport, your ticket, and your money, and left us with nothing except his baby."

She was right: Lev had always been selfish. "But you don't love your family because they're kind and considerate. You love them because they're your family."

"Oh, give yourself a treat," she said with irritation. "You're joining the army tomorrow. You don't want to die regretting that you didn't fuck me when you had the chance."

He was powerfully tempted. Even though she was half drunk, her body was warm and inviting beside him. Was he not entitled to one night of bliss?

She ran her hand up his leg and grasped his stiff penis. "Come on, you've married me. You might as well take what you're entitled to."

And that was the problem, he thought. She did not love him. She was offering herself in payment for what he had done. It was prostitution. He felt insulted to the point of anger, and the fact that he longed to give in only made the feeling worse.

She began to rub his penis up and down. Furious and inflamed, he pushed her away. The shove was rougher than he really intended, and she fell off the bed.

She cried out in surprise and pain.

He had not meant it to happen, but he was too angry to apologize.

For several long moments she lay on the floor, weeping and cursing at the same time. He resisted the temptation to help her. She struggled to her feet, staggering from the vodka. "You pig!" she said. "How can you be so cruel?" She straightened her dress, covering her beautiful legs. "What sort of wedding night is this for a girl—to be kicked out of her husband's bed?"

Grigori was stung by her words, but he lay still and said nothing.

"I never thought you could be so hard-hearted," she raved. "Go to hell! Go to hell!" She picked up her shoes, flung open the door, and stormed out of the room.

Grigori felt utterly miserable. On his last day as a civilian he had quarreled with the woman he adored. If he died in battle now, he would die unhappy. What a rotten world, he thought; what a lousy life.

He went to the door to close it. As he did so, he heard Katerina in the next room, speaking with forced gaiety. "Grigori can't get it up— too drunk!" she said. "Give me some more vodka and let's have another dance!"

He slammed the door and threw himself on the bed.

{ III }

Eventually he fell into a troubled sleep. Next morning he woke early. He washed and put on his uniform and ate some bread.

When he put his head around the door of the girls' room, he saw them all fast asleep, the floor littered with bottles, the air foul with stale tobacco smoke and spilled beer. He stared for a long minute at Katerina, sleeping with her mouth open. Then he left the house, not knowing if he would ever see her again, telling himself he did not care.

But his spirits lifted with the excitement and confusion of reporting to his regiment, being issued a gun and ammunition, finding the right train, and meeting his new comrades. He stopped thinking about Katerina and turned his mind to the future.

He boarded a train with Isaak and several hundred other reservists in their new gray-green uniform breeches and tunics. Like the rest of them, he carried a Russian-made Mosin-Nagant rifle, as tall as himself with its long spiked bayonet. The huge bruise that the sledgehammer had left, covering most of one side of his face, made the other men think he was some kind of thug, and they treated him with wary respect. The train steamed out of St. Petersburg and chuffed steadily through fields and forests.

The setting sun was generally ahead and to the right, so they were going southwest, toward Germany. That seemed obvious to Grigori, though when he said it his fellow soldiers were surprised and impressed: most of them did not know in which direction Germany lay.

This was only the second time he had been on a train, and he was reminded vividly of the first. When he was eleven his mother had brought him and little Lev to St. Petersburg. His father had been hanged a few days earlier, and Grigori's young head was full of fear and grief, but like any boy he had been thrilled by the ride: the oiled smell of the mighty locomotive, the huge wheels, the camaraderie of the peasants in the third-class carriage, and the intoxicating speed with which the countryside sped by. Some of that exhilaration came back to him now, and he could not help feeling that he was on an adventure that could be exciting as well as terrible.

This time, however, he was traveling in a cattle truck, as were all but the officers. The wagon contained about forty men: pale-skinned, sly-eyed St. Petersburg factory workers; long-bearded, slow-talking peasants who looked at everything with wondering curiosity; and half a dozen dark-eyed, dark-haired Jews.

One of the Jews sat next to Grigori and introduced himself as David. His father manufactured iron buckets in the backyard of their house, he said, and he went from village to village selling them. There were a lot of Jews in the army, he explained, because they found it more difficult to get exemption from military service.

They were all under the orders of a Sergeant Gavrik, a regular soldier who looked anxious, barked orders, and used a great deal of profanity.

He pretended to think all the men were peasants, and called them cowfuckers. He was about Grigori's age, too young to have been in the Japanese war of 1904–1905, and Grigori guessed that underneath the bluster he was scared.

Every few hours the train stopped at a country station and the men got out. Sometimes they were given soup and beer, sometimes just water. In between stops they sat on the floor of the wagon. Gavrik made sure they knew how to clean their rifles and reminded them of the different military ranks and how officers should be addressed. Lieutenants and captains were "Your Honor," but superior officers required a variety of honorifics all the way up to "Most High Radiance" for those who were also aristocrats.

By the second day, Grigori calculated they must be in the territory of Russian Poland.

He asked the sergeant which part of the army they were in. Grigori knew they were the Narva Regiment, but no one had told them how they fitted into the overall picture. Gavrik said: "None of your fucking business. Just go where you're sent and do as you're told." Grigori guessed he did not know the answer.

After a day and a half the train stopped at a town called Ostrolenka. Grigori had never heard of it, but he could see that it was the end of the railway line, and he guessed it must be near the German border. Here hundreds of railway wagons were being unloaded. Men and horses sweated and heaved to maneuver huge guns off the trains. Thousands of troops milled around as bad-tempered officers attempted to muster them in platoons and companies. At the same time tons of supplies had to be transferred to horse-drawn carts: sides of meat, sacks of flour, barrels of beer, crates of bullets, artillery shells in packing cases, and tons of oats for all the horses.

At one point Grigori saw the loathed face of Prince Andrei. He wore a gorgeous uniform—Grigori was not sufficiently familiar with badges and stripes to identify the regiment or rank—and rode on a tall chestnut horse. Behind him walked a corporal carrying a canary in a cage. I could shoot him now, Grigori thought, and avenge my father. It was a stupid idea, of course, but he stroked the trigger of his rifle as the prince and his caged bird disappeared into the crowd.

The weather was hot and dry. That night Grigori slept on the ground with the rest of the men from his wagon. He realized that they constituted a platoon, and would be together for the foreseeable future. The next morning they met their officer, an unnervingly young second lieutenant called Tomchak. He led them out of Ostrolenka on a road that headed northwest.

Lieutenant Tomchak told Grigori they were in 13 Corps, commanded by General Klyuev, which was part of the Second Army under General Samsonov. When Grigori relayed this information to the other men, they were spooked, because the number thirteen was unlucky, and Sergeant Gavrik said: "I told you it was none of your business, Peshkov, you cocksucking homo."

They were not far out of town when the metaled road ran out and became a sand track through a forest. The supply carts got stuck, and the drivers soon found out that a single horse could not pull a loaded army wagon through sand. All the horses had to be unhitched and reharnessed two to a cart, and every second wagon had to be abandoned at the roadside.

They marched all day and slept under the stars again. Each night when he went to bed Grigori said to himself: Another day, and I'm still alive to take care of Katerina and the baby.

That evening Tomchak received no orders, so they sat under the trees all the next morning. Grigori was glad: his legs ached from yesterday's march, and his feet hurt in the new boots. The peasants were used to walking all day, and they laughed at the weakness of the city dwellers.

At midday a runner brought orders commanding them to set out at eight a.m., four hours earlier.

There was no provision for supplying the marching men with water, so they had to drink from wells and streams they came across on the way. They soon learned to drink their fill at every opportunity, and keep their standard-issue water bottles topped up. There was no means of cooking, either, and the only food they got was the dry biscuits called hardtack. Every few miles they would be called upon to help pull a wheeled cannon out of a swamp or sandpit.

They marched until sundown and slept under the trees again.

Halfway through the third day they emerged from a wood to see a fine farmhouse set amid fields of ripening oats and wheat. It was a two-story building with a steeply pitched roof. In the yard was a concrete wellhead, and there was a low stone structure that seemed to be a pigsty, except that it was clean. The place looked like the home of a prosperous land captain, or perhaps the younger son of a nobleman. It was locked up and deserted.

A mile farther on, to everyone's astonishment, the road passed through an entire village of such places, all abandoned. The realization began to dawn on Grigori that he had crossed the border into Germany, and these luxurious houses were the homes of German farmers who had fled, with their families and livestock, to escape the oncoming Russian army. But where were the hovels of the poor peasants? What had been done with the filth of the pigs and cows? Why were there no tumbledown wooden cowsheds with patched walls and holes in the roofs?

The soldiers were jubilant. "They're running away from us!" said a peasant. "They're scared of us Russians. We'll take Germany without firing a shot!"

Grigori knew, from Konstantin's discussion group, that the German plan was to conquer France first and then deal with Russia. The Germans were not surrendering; they were choosing the best time to fight. Even so, it would be surprising if they were to give up this prime territory without a struggle.

"What part of Germany is this, Your Honor?" he asked Tomchak.

"They call it East Prussia."

"Is it the wealthiest part of Germany?"

"I don't think so," said the lieutenant. "I see no palaces."

"Are ordinary people in Germany rich enough to live in homes such as these?"

"I suppose they are."

Evidently Tomchak, who looked as if he was barely out of school, did not know much more than Grigori.

Grigori walked on, but he felt demoralized. He had thought himself a well-informed man, but he had had no idea that the Germans lived so well.

It was Isaak who voiced his doubts. "Our army is already having trouble feeding us, even though not a single shot has yet been fired," he said quietly. "How can we possibly fight against people who are so well organized that they keep their pigs in stone houses?"

{ IV }

Walter was elated by events in Europe. There was every prospect of a short war and a quick victory for Germany. He could be reunited with Maud by Christmas.

Unless he died, of course. But, if that happened, he would die happy.

He shuddered with joy whenever he remembered the night they had spent together. They had not wasted precious moments sleeping. They had made love three times. The initial, heartbreaking difficulty had in the end only intensified their euphoria. In between lovemaking they had lain side by side, talking and idly caressing each other. It was a conversation unlike any other. Anything Walter could say to himself, he could say to Maud. Never had he felt so close to another person.

Around dawn they had eaten all the fruit in the bowl and all the chocolates in the box. Then, at last, they had had to leave: Maud to sneak back into Fitz's house, pretending to the servants that she had been out for an early walk; Walter to his flat, to change his clothes, pack a bag, and leave his valet instructions to ship the rest of his possessions home to Berlin.

In the cab on the short ride from Knightsbridge to Mayfair they had held hands tightly and said little. Walter had stopped the driver around the corner from Fitz's house. Maud had kissed him once more, her tongue finding his in desperate passion; then she had gone, leaving him wondering if he would ever see her again.

The war had begun well. The German army was storming through Belgium. Farther south the French—led by sentiment rather than strategy—had invaded Lorraine, only to be mown down by German artillery. Now they were in full retreat.

Japan had sided with the French and British allies, which unfortunately freed up Russian soldiers in the far east to be switched to the European battlefield. But the Americans had confirmed their neutrality, to Walter's great relief. How small the world had become, he reflected: Japan was about as far east as you could go, and America as far west. This war encircled the globe.

According to German intelligence, the French had sent a stream of telegrams to St. Petersburg, begging the tsar to attack, in the hope that the Germans might be distracted. And the Russians had moved faster than anyone expected. Their First Army had astonished the world by marching across the German border a mere twelve days after mobilization began. Meanwhile the Second Army invaded farther south, from the railhead at Ostrolenka, on a trajectory that would close the teeth of the pincers near a town called Tannenberg. Both armies were unopposed.

The uncharacteristic German torpor that allowed this to happen soon came to an end. The commander in chief in the region, General Prittwitz, known as *der Dicke,* the Fat One, was smartly fired by the high command and replaced by the duo of Paul von Hindenburg, summoned out of retirement, and Erich Ludendorff, one of the few senior military men without an aristocratic "von" to his name. At forty-nine, Ludendorff was also among the younger generals. Walter admired him for having risen so high purely on merit, and was pleased to be his intelligence liaison.

On the way from Belgium to Prussia they stopped briefly on

Sunday, August 23, in Berlin, where Walter had a few moments with his mother on the station platform. Her sharp nose was reddened by a summer cold. She hugged him hard, shaking with emotion. "You are safe," she said.

"Yes, Mother, I'm safe."

"I'm terribly worried about Zumwald. The Russians are so close!" Zumwald was the von Ulrichs' country estate in the east.

"I'm sure it will be all right."

She was not so easily fobbed off. "I have spoken to the kaiserin." She knew the kaiser's wife well. "Several other ladies have done the same."

"You should not bother the royal family," Walter reproved her. "They already have so many worries."

She sniffed. "We cannot abandon our estates to the Russian army!"

Walter sympathized. He, too, hated the thought of primitive Russian peasants and their barbaric knout-wielding lords overrunning the well-kept pastures and orchards of the von Ulrich inheritance. Those hardworking German farmers, with their muscular wives and scrubbed children and fat cattle, deserved to be protected. Was that not what the war was about? And he planned to take Maud to Zumwald one day, and show the place off to his wife. "Ludendorff is going to stop the Russian advance, Mother," he said. He hoped it was true.

Before she could respond the whistle blew, and Walter kissed her and boarded the train.

Walter felt the sting of personal responsibility for the German reverses on the eastern front. He was one of the intelligence experts who had forecast that the Russians could not attack so soon after ordering mobilization. He was mortified with shame whenever he thought of it. But he suspected he had not been entirely wrong, and the Russians were sending ill-prepared troops forward with inadequate supplies.

This suspicion was reinforced, when he arrived in East Prussia later that Sunday with Ludendorff's entourage, by reports that the Russian First Army, in the north, had halted. They were only a few miles inside German territory, and military logic dictated that they should press forward. What were they waiting for? Walter guessed they were running out of food.

But the southern arm of the pincer was still advancing, and Ludendorff's priority was to stop it.

The following morning, Monday, August 24, Walter brought Ludendorff two priceless reports. Both were Russian wireless messages, intercepted and translated by German intelligence.

The first, sent at five thirty that morning by General Rennenkampf, gave marching orders for the Russian First Army. At last Rennenkampf was on the move again—but instead of turning south to close the pincers by meeting up with the Second Army, he was inexplicably heading west on a line that did not threaten any German forces.

The second message had been sent half an hour later by General Samsonov, the commander of the Russian Second Army. He ordered his 13 and 15 Corps to go after the German XX Corps, which he believed to be in retreat.

"This is astonishing!" said Ludendorff. "How did we get this information?" He looked suspicious, as if Walter might have been deceiving him. Walter had a feeling Ludendorff mistrusted him as a member of the old military aristocracy. "Do we know their codes?" Ludendorff demanded.

"They don't use codes," Walter told him.

"They send orders in clear? For heaven's sake, why?"

"Russian soldiers aren't sufficiently educated to deal with codes," Walter explained. "Our prewar intelligence estimates suggested that there are hardly enough literate men to operate the wireless transmitters."

"Then why don't they use field telephones? A phone call can't be intercepted."

"I think they have probably run out of telephone wire."

Ludendorff had a downturned mouth and a thrusting chin, and he always looked as if he were frowning aggressively. "This couldn't be a trick, could it?"

Walter shook his head. "The idea is inconceivable, sir. The Russians are barely able to organize normal communications. The use of phony wireless signals to deceive the enemy is as far beyond them as flying to the moon."

Ludendorff bent his balding head over the map on the table in front of him. He was a tireless worker, but he was often afflicted by terrible doubts, and Walter guessed he was driven by fear of failure. Ludendorff put his finger on the map. "Samsonov's 13 and 15 Corps form the center of the Russian line," he said. "If they move forward . . . "

Walter saw immediately what Ludendorff was thinking: the Russians could be drawn into an envelope trap, surrounded on three sides.

Ludendorff said: "On our right we have von François and his I Corps. At our center, Scholtz and the XX Corps, who have fallen back but are not on the run, contrary to what the Russians seem to think. And on our left, but fifty kilometers to the north, we have Mackensen and the XVII Corps. Mackensen is keeping an eye on the northern arm of the Russian pincer, but if those Russians are heading the wrong way, perhaps we can ignore them, for the moment, and turn Mackensen south."

"A classic maneuver," Walter said. It was simple, but he himself had not seen it until Ludendorff pointed it out. That, he thought admiringly, was why Ludendorff was the general.

Ludendorff said: "But it will work only if Rennenkampf and the Russian First Army continue in the wrong direction."

"You saw the intercept, sir. The Russian orders have gone out."

"Let's hope Rennenkampf doesn't change his mind."

{ V }

Grigori's battalion had no food, but a wagonload of spades had arrived, so they dug a trench. The men dug in shifts, relieving one another after half an hour, so it did not take long. The result was not very neat, but it would serve.

Earlier that day, Grigori and Isaak and their comrades had overrun a deserted German position, and Grigori had noticed that their trenches had a kind of zigzag at regular intervals, so that you could not see very far along. Lieutenant Tomchak said the zigzag was called a traverse, but he did not know what it was for. He did not order his men to copy the German design. But Grigori felt sure it must have a purpose.

Grigori had not yet fired his rifle. He had heard shooting, rifles and machine guns and artillery, and his unit had taken a good deal of German territory, but so far he had shot at no one, and no one had shot at him. Everywhere 13 Corps went, they found that the Germans had just left.

There was no logic to this. Everything in war was confusion, he was realizing. No one was quite sure where they were or where the enemy was. Two men from Grigori's platoon had been killed, but not by Germans: one had accidentally shot himself in the thigh with his own rifle and bled to death astonishingly quickly, and the other had been trampled by a runaway horse and never recovered consciousness.

They had not seen a cook wagon for days. They had finished their emergency rations, and even the hardtack had run out. None of them had eaten since yesterday morning. After digging the trench, they slept hungry. Fortunately it was summer, so at least they were not cold.

The shooting began at dawn the next day.

It started some distance away to Grigori's left, but he could see clouds of shrapnel burst in the air, and loose earth erupt suddenly where shells landed. He knew he ought to be scared, but he was not. He was hungry, thirsty, tired, aching, and bored, but he was not frightened. He wondered if the Germans felt the same.

There was heavy gunfire on his right, too, some miles to the north, but here it was quiet. "Like the eye of the storm," said David, the Jewish bucket salesman.

Soon enough, orders came to advance. Wearily, they climbed out of their trench and walked forward. "I suppose we should be grateful," Grigori said.

"For what?" Isaak demanded.

"Marching is better than fighting. We've got blisters, but we're alive."

In the afternoon they approached a town that Lieutenant Tomchak said was called Allenstein. They assembled in marching order on the outskirts, and entered the center in formation.

To their surprise, Allenstein was full of well-dressed German citizens going about their normal Thursday afternoon business, posting letters and buying groceries and walking babies in perambulators. Grigori's unit halted in a small park where the men sat in the shade of tall trees. Tomchak went into a nearby barbershop and came out shaved and with his hair cut. Isaak went to buy vodka, but returned saying the army had posted sentries outside all the wine shops with orders to keep soldiers out.

At last a horse and cart appeared with a barrel of freshwater. The men lined up to fill their canteens. As the afternoon cooled into evening, more carts arrived with loaves of bread, bought or requisitioned from the town's bakers. Night fell, and they slept under the trees.

At dawn there was no breakfast. Leaving a battalion behind to hold the town, Grigori and the rest of 13 Corps were marched out of Allenstein, heading southwest on the road to Tannenberg.

Although they had seen no action, Grigori noticed a change of mood among the officers. They cantered up and down the line and conferred in fretful huddles. Voices were raised in argument, with a major pointing one way and a captain gesturing in the opposite direction. Grigori continued to hear heavy artillery to the north and south, though it seemed to be moving eastward while 13 Corps went west. "Whose artillery is that?" said Sergeant Gavrik. "Ours or theirs? And why is it moving east when we're going west?" The fact that he used no profanity suggested to Grigori that he was seriously worried.

A few kilometers out of Allenstein, a battalion was left to guard the rear, which surprised Grigori, since he assumed the enemy was ahead, not behind. The 13 Corps was being stretched thin, he thought with a frown.

Around the middle of the day, his battalion was detached from the main march. While their comrades continued southwest, they were directed southeast, on a broad path through a forest.

There, at last, Grigori encountered the enemy.

They stopped for a rest by a stream, and the men filled their bottles. Grigori walked off into the trees to answer a call of nature. He was standing behind a thick pine trunk when he heard a noise off to his left and was astonished to see, a few meters away, a German officer, complete with spiked helmet, on a fine black horse. The German was looking through a telescope toward the place where the battalion had stopped. Grigori wondered what he was looking at: the man could not see far through the trees. Perhaps he was trying to make out whether the uniforms were Russian or German. He sat as motionless as a monument in a St. Petersburg square, but his horse was not so still, and it shifted and repeated the noise that had alerted Grigori.

Grigori carefully buttoned his trousers, picked up his rifle, and backed away, keeping the tree between himself and the German.

Suddenly the man moved. Grigori suffered a moment of fear, thinking he had been seen; but the German expertly turned his horse and headed west, breaking into a trot.

Grigori ran back to Sergeant Gavrik. "I saw a German!" he said.

"Where?"

Grigori pointed. "Over there—I was taking a leak."

"Are you sure it was a German?"

"He had a spiked helmet."

"What was he doing?"

"Sitting on his horse, looking at us through a telescope."

"A scout!" said Gavrik. "Did you shoot at him?"

Only then did Grigori remember that he was supposed to kill German soldiers, not run away from them. "I thought I should tell you," he said feebly.

"You great fairy, why do you think we gave you a fucking gun?" Gavrik yelled.

Grigori looked at the loaded rifle in his hand, with its vicious-looking bayonet. Of course he should have fired it. What was he thinking? "I'm sorry," he said.

"Now that you've let him get away, the enemy know where we are!"

Grigori was humiliated. This situation had never been mentioned during his time as a reservist, but he should have been able to work it out himself.

"Which way did he go?" Gavrik demanded.

At least Grigori could answer that. "West."

Gavrik turned and walked quickly to Lieutenant Tomchak, who was leaning against a tree, smoking. A moment later Tomchak threw down his cigarette and ran to Major Bobrov, a handsome older officer with flowing silver hair.

After that everything happened quickly. They had no artillery, but the machine-gun section unloaded its weapons. The six hundred men of the battalion were spread out in a ragged north-south line a thousand yards long. A few men were chosen to go ahead. Then the rest moved slowly west, toward the afternoon sun slanting through the leaves.

Minutes later the first shell landed. It made a screaming noise in the air, then crashed through the forest canopy, and finally hit the ground some distance behind Grigori and exploded with a deep bang that shook the ground.

"That scout gave them the range," said Tomchak. "They're firing at where we were. Good thing we moved."

But the Germans were logical, too, and they appeared to discover their mistake, for the next shell landed slightly in front of the advancing Russian line.

The men around Grigori became jumpy. They looked around them constantly, held their rifles at the ready, and cursed one another at the least provocation. David kept looking up as if he might be able to see a shell coming and dodge it. Isaak wore an aggressive expression, as he did on the football pitch when the other side started to play dirty. The knowledge that someone was trying his best to kill you was overwhelmingly oppressive, Grigori found. He felt as if he had received dreadfully bad news but could not quite remember what it was. He had a foolish fantasy of digging a hole in the ground and hiding in it.

He wondered what the gunners could see. Was there an observer stationed on a hill, raking the woods with powerful German binoculars?

You couldn't see one man in a forest, but perhaps you could see six hundred moving through the trees in a group.

Someone had decided the range was right, for in the next few seconds several shells landed, some of them dead on target. To both sides of Grigori there were deafening bangs, fountains of earth gushed up, men screamed, and parts of bodies flew through the air. Grigori shook with terror. There was nothing you could do, no way to protect yourself: either the shell got you or it missed. He quickened his pace, as if moving faster might help. The other men must have had the same thought because, without an order, they all broke into a jog-trot.

Grigori gripped his rifle with sweaty hands and tried not to panic. More shells fell, behind him and in front, to left and right. He ran faster.

The artillery fire became so heavy that he could no longer distinguish individual shells: there was just one continuous noise like a hundred express trains. Then the battalion seemed to get inside the gunners' range, for the shells began to land behind them. Soon the shelling petered out. A few moments later, Grigori realized why. Ahead of him a machine gun opened up, and he knew with a sickening feeling of dread that he was close to the enemy line.

Machine-gun rounds sprayed the forest, tearing up the foliage and splintering the pines. Grigori heard a scream beside him and saw Tomchak fall. Kneeling beside the lieutenant, he saw blood on his face and on the breast of his tunic. With horror, he saw that one eye had been destroyed. Tomchak tried to move, then screamed in pain. Grigori said: "What do I do? What do I do?" He could have bandaged a flesh wound, but how could he help a man who had been shot through the eye?

He felt a blow to his head and looked up to see Gavrik run past him, shouting: "Keep moving, Peshkov, you stupid cunt!"

He stared at Tomchak a moment longer. It seemed to him the officer was no longer breathing. He could not be sure, but all the same he stood up and ran forward.

The firing intensified. Grigori's fear turned to anger. The enemy's bullets produced a feeling of outrage. In the back of his mind he knew it was irrational, but he could not help it. Suddenly he wanted to kill those bastards. A couple of hundred yards ahead, across a clearing, he saw gray uniforms and spiked helmets. He dropped to one knee behind a tree, peeped around the trunk, raised his rifle, sighted on a German, and for the first time pulled the trigger.

Nothing happened, and he remembered the safety catch.

It was not possible to release the catch on a Mosin-Nagant while it was shouldered. He lowered the gun, sat on the ground behind the tree, and cradled the stock in the crook of his elbow, then turned the large knurled knob that unlocked the bolt.

He looked about him. His comrades had stopped running and taken cover as he had. Some were firing, some reloading, some writhing in the agony of wounds, some lying in the stillness of death.

Grigori peered around the trunk, shouldered his weapon, and squinted along the barrel. He saw a rifle poking out of a bush and a spiked helmet above it. His heart was filled with hatred, and he pulled the trigger five times fast. The rifle he was aiming at was hastily withdrawn, but did not fall, and Grigori guessed he had missed. He felt disappointed and frustrated.

The Mosin-Nagant held only five rounds. He opened his ammunition pack and reloaded. Now he wanted to kill Germans as fast as he could.

Looking around the tree again, he spotted a German running across a gap in the woods. He emptied his magazine, but the man kept running and disappeared behind a clump of saplings.

It was no good just shooting, Grigori decided. Hitting the enemy was difficult—much more difficult in a real fight than in the small amount of target practice he had had in training. He would have to try harder.

As he was reloading again, he heard a machine gun open up, and the vegetation around him was sprayed. He pressed his back against the tree and drew in his legs, making himself a smaller target. His hearing told him the gun must be a couple of hundred yards to his left.

When it paused he heard Gavrik shout: "Target that machine gun, you dumb pricks! Shoot them while they're reloading!" Grigori poked his head out and looked for the nest. He spotted the tripod standing between two large trees. He aimed his rifle, then paused. No good just shooting, he reminded himself. He breathed evenly, steadied the heavy barrel, and got a pointed helmet in his sight. He lowered the barrel slightly so that he could see the man's chest. The uniform tunic was open at the neck: the man was hot from his exertions.

Grigori pulled the trigger.

He missed. The German appeared not to have noticed the shot. Grigori had no idea where the bullet might have gone.

He fired again, emptying the magazine to no effect. It was maddening. Those pigs were trying to kill him and he was incapable of hitting even one of them. Perhaps he was too far away. Or perhaps he was just a lousy shot.

The machine gun opened up again, and everyone froze.

Major Bobrov appeared, crawling on hands and knees across the forest floor. "You men!" he yelled. "On my command, rush that machine gun!"

You must be mad, Grigori thought. Well, I'm not.

Sergeant Gavrik repeated the order. "Prepare to rush the machine-gun nest! Wait for the command!"

Bobrov stood upright and ran, crouching, along the line. Grigori heard him shout the same order a bit farther away. You're wasting your breath, Grigori thought. Do you imagine we're all suicidal?

The machine gun's chatter stopped, and the major stood up, exposing himself recklessly. He had lost his hat, and his silver hair made a highly visible target. "Go!" he screamed.

Gavrik repeated the order. "Go, go, go!"

Bobrov and Gavrik both led by example, running through the trees toward the machine-gun nest. Suddenly Grigori found himself doing the same, crashing through bushes and jumping over deadfalls, running in a half crouch, trying not to drop his unwieldy rifle. The machine gun remained silent but the Germans fired with everything else they had, and the effect of dozens of rifles shooting at the same time seemed almost as bad, but Grigori ran on as if it were the only thing he could do. He could see the machine-gun team desperately reloading, their hands fumbling the magazine, their faces white with fear. Some of the Russians were firing, but Grigori did not have that much presence of mind—he just ran. He was still some distance from the machine gun when he saw three Germans hiding behind a bush. They looked terribly young, and stared at him with frightened faces. He charged them with his bayoneted rifle held in front of him like a medieval lance. He heard someone screaming and realized it was himself. The three young soldiers ran away.

He went after them, but he was weak from hunger, and they easily outran him. After a hundred yards he stopped, exhausted. All around him the Germans were fleeing and the Russians giving chase. The machine-gun crew had abandoned their weapon. Grigori supposed he should be shooting, but for the moment he did not have the energy to raise his rifle.

Major Bobrov reappeared, running along the Russian line. "Forward!" he shouted. "Don't let them get away—kill them all, or they'll come back to shoot you another day! Go!"

Wearily, Grigori started to run. Then the picture changed. There was a commotion to his left: firing, shouting, cursing. Suddenly Russian soldiers appeared from that direction, running for their lives. Bobrov, standing next to Grigori, said: "What the hell?"

Grigori realized they were being attacked from the side.

Bobrov shouted: "Stand firm! Take cover and shoot!"

No one was listening. The newcomers poured through the woods in a panic, and Grigori's comrades began to join the stampede, turning right and running northward.

"Hold position, you men!" Bobrov yelled. He drew his pistol. "Hold position, I say!" He aimed at the crowd of Russian troops streaming past him. "I warn you, I will shoot deserters!" There was a crack, and blood stained his hair. He fell down. Grigori did not know whether he had been felled by a stray German bullet or one from his own side.

Grigori turned and ran with the rest.

There was firing on all sides now. Grigori did not know who was shooting whom. The Russians spread out through the woods, and gradually he seemed to be leaving the noise of battle behind. He kept running as long as he could, then at last collapsed on a carpet of leaves, unable to move. He lay there for a long time, feeling paralyzed. He still had his rifle, which surprised him: he did not know why he had not dropped it.

Eventually he rose sluggishly to his feet. For some time his right ear had been painful. He touched it, and cried out in pain. His fingers came away sticky with blood. Gingerly, he felt his ear again. To his horror he found that most of it had gone. He had been wounded without knowing it. At some point a bullet had taken away the top half of his ear.

He checked his rifle. The magazine was empty. He reloaded, though he was not sure why: he seemed incapable of hitting anyone. He set the safety knob.

The Russians had been caught in an ambush, he guessed. They had been lured forward until they were surrounded; then the Germans had closed the trap.

What should he do? There was no one in sight, so he could not ask an officer for orders. But he could not stay where he was. The corps was in retreat, that was certain, so he supposed he should head back. If there was any of the Russian force left, it was presumably to the east.

He turned so that the setting sun was at his back, and began to walk. He moved as quietly as he could through the forest, not knowing where the Germans might be. He wondered if the entire Second Army had been defeated and fled. He could starve to death in the forest.

After an hour he stopped to drink from a stream. He considered bathing his wound, and decided it might be best to leave it alone. When he had drunk his fill, he rested, squatting on the ground, eyes closed. Soon it would be dark. Fortunately the weather was dry, and he could sleep on the ground.

He was in a half doze when he heard a noise. Looking up, he was shocked to see a German officer on horseback moving slowly through the trees ten yards away. The man had passed without noticing Grigori crouching by the stream.

Stealthily, Grigori picked up his rifle and turned the safety knob. Kneeling, he shouldered it and took careful aim at the middle of the German's back. The man was now fifteen yards away, point-blank range for a rifle.

At the last moment the German was alerted by a sixth sense, and he turned in the saddle.

Grigori squeezed the trigger.

The bang was deafening in the quiet of the forest. The horse leaped forward. The officer fell sideways and hit the ground, but one foot remained caught in a stirrup. The horse dragged him through the undergrowth for a hundred yards, then slowed down and stopped.

Grigori listened carefully in case the sound of the shot had attracted anyone else. He heard nothing but a mild evening breeze riffling the leaves.

He walked toward the horse. As he got closer he shouldered his rifle and pointed it at the officer, but his caution was unnecessary. The man lay still, face upward, his eyes wide-open, his pointed helmet lying beside him. He had cropped blond hair and rather beautiful green eyes. It might have been the man Grigori had seen earlier: he could not be sure. Lev would have known—he would have remembered the horse.

Grigori opened the saddlebags. One contained maps and a telescope. The other held a sausage and a hunk of black bread. Grigori was starving. He bit off a piece of the sausage. It was strongly flavored with pepper, herbs, and garlic. The pepper made his cheeks hot and sweaty. He chewed rapidly, swallowed, then stuffed some of the bread into his mouth. The food was so good he could have wept. He stood there, leaning against the side of the big horse, eating as fast as he could, while the man he had killed stared up at him with dead green eyes.

{ VI }

Walter said to Ludendorff: "We estimate thirty thousand Russian dead, General." He was trying not to show his elation too obviously, but the German victory was overwhelming, and he could not get the smile off his face.

Ludendorff was coolly controlled. "Prisoners?"

"At the latest count about ninety-two thousand, sir."

It was an amazing statistic, but Ludendorff took it in his stride. "Any generals?"

"General Samsonov shot himself. We have his body. Martos, commander of the Russian 15 Corps, has been taken prisoner. We have captured five hundred artillery guns."

"In summary," said Ludendorff, at last looking up from his field desk, "the Russian Second Army has been wiped out. It no longer exists."

Walter could not help grinning. "Yes, sir."

Ludendorff did not return the smile. He waved the sheet of paper he had been studying. "Which makes this news all the more ironic."

"Sir?"

"They're sending us reinforcements."

Walter was astounded. "What? I beg your pardon, General— reinforcements?"

"I am as surprised as you. Three corps and a cavalry division."

"From where?"

"From France—where we need every last man if the Schlieffen Plan is to work."

Walter recalled that Ludendorff had worked on the details of the Schlieffen Plan, with his customary energy and meticulousness, and he knew what was needed in France, down to the last man, horse, and bullet. "But what has brought this about?" Walter said.

"I don't know, but I can guess." Ludendorff's tone became bitter. "It's political. Princesses and countesses in Berlin have been crying and sobbing to the kaiserin about their family estates being overrun by the Russians. The high command has bowed under the pressure."

Walter felt himself blush. His own mother was one of those who had pestered the kaiserin. For women to become worried and beg for protection was understandable, but for the army to give in to their pleas, and risk derailing the entire war strategy, was unforgivable. "Isn't this exactly what the Allies want?" he said indignantly. "The French persuaded the Russians to invade with a half-ready army, in the hope that we would panic and rush reinforcements to the eastern front, thereby weakening our army in France!"

"Exactly. The French are on the run—outnumbered, outgunned, defeated. Their only hope was that we might be distracted. And their wish has been granted."

"So," said Walter despairingly, "despite our great victory in the east, the Russians have achieved the strategic advantage their allies needed in the west!"

"Yes," said Ludendorff. "Exactly."

CHAPTER THIRTEEN

September to December 1914

The sound of a woman crying woke Fitz.

At first he thought it was Bea. Then he remembered that his wife was in London and he was in Paris. The woman in bed beside him was not a twenty-three-year-old pregnant princess, but a nineteen-year-old French bar girl with the face of an angel.

He raised himself on his elbow and looked at her. She had blond eyelashes that lay on her cheeks like butterflies on petals. Now they were wet with tears. *"J'ai peur,"* she sobbed. "I'm frightened."

He stroked her hair. *"Calme-toi,"* he said. "Relax." He had learned more French from women such as Gini than he ever had at school. Gini was short for Ginette, but even that sounded like a made-up name. She had probably been christened something prosaic such as Françoise.

It was a fine morning, and a warm breeze came through the open window of Gini's room. Fitz heard no gunfire, no stamp of marching boots on the cobblestones. "Paris has not yet fallen," he murmured in a reassuring tone.

It was the wrong thing to say, for it brought forth fresh sobs.

Fitz looked at his wristwatch. It was half past eight. He had to be back at his hotel by ten o'clock without fail.

Gini said: "If the Germans come, will you take care of me?"

"Of course, *chérie*," he said, suppressing a guilty pang. He would if he could, but she would not be his top priority.

"Will they come?" she asked in a small voice.

Fitz wished he knew. The German army was twice as numerous as predicted by French intelligence. It had stormed across northeast France, winning every battle. Now the avalanche had reached a line north of Paris—exactly how far north, Fitz would find out in the next couple of hours.

"Some say the city will not be defended," Gini sobbed. "Is it true?"

Fitz did not know that either. If Paris resisted, it would be mauled by German artillery. Its splendid buildings would be wrecked, its broad boulevards cratered, its bistros and boutiques turned to rubble. It was tempting to think the city *should* surrender, and escape all that. "It might be better for you," he said to Gini with false heartiness. "You will make love to a fat Prussian general who will call you his *Liebling*."

"I don't want a Prussian." Her voice sank to a whisper. "I love you."

Perhaps she did, he thought; or perhaps she just saw him as a ticket out of here. Everyone who could was leaving town, but it was not easy. Most private cars had been commandeered. Railway trains were liable to be requisitioned at any moment, their civilian passengers thrown out and stranded in the middle of nowhere. A taxi to Bordeaux cost fifteen hundred francs, the price of a small house.

"It may not happen," he told her. "The Germans must be exhausted by now. They've been marching and fighting for a month. They can't keep it up forever."

He half believed this. The French had fought hard in retreat. The soldiers were worn-out, starving and demoralized, but few had been taken prisoner and they had lost only a handful of guns. The unflappable commander in chief, General Joffre, had held the Allied forces together and withdrawn to a line southeast of Paris, where he was regrouping. He had also ruthlessly sacked senior French officers who did not come up to scratch: two army commanders, seven corps commanders, and dozens of others had been mercilessly dismissed.

The Germans did not know this. Fitz had seen decrypted German messages that suggested overconfidence. The German high command had actually removed troops from France and sent them as reinforcements to East Prussia. Fitz thought that might be a mistake. The French were not finished yet.

He was not so sure about the British.

The British Expeditionary Force was small—five and a half divisions, by contrast with the seventy French divisions in the field. They had fought bravely at Mons, making Fitz proud; but in five days they had lost fifteen thousand of their one hundred thousand men, and had gone into retreat.

The Welsh Rifles were part of the British force, but Fitz was not with them. At first he had been disappointed to be posted to Paris as a liaison officer: he yearned to be fighting with his regiment. He felt sure the generals were treating him as an amateur who had to be sent someplace where he could not do much harm. But he knew Paris and spoke French, so he could hardly deny that he was well-qualified.

As it turned out, the job was more important than he had thought. Relations between the French commanders and their British opposite numbers were dangerously bad. The British Expeditionary Force was commanded by a touchy fusspot whose name, slightly confusingly, was Sir John French. He had taken offense, early on, by what he saw as a lack of consultation by General Joffre, and had gone into a sulk. Fitz struggled to maintain a flow of information and intelligence between the two Allied commanders despite the atmosphere of hostility.

All this was embarrassing and a bit shameful, and Fitz as a representative of the British was mortified by the ill-disguised scorn of French officers. But it had got dramatically worse a week ago. Sir John had told Joffre that his troops required two days' rest. The next day he had changed his requirement to ten days. The French had been horrified, and Fitz had felt deeply ashamed of his own country.

He had remonstrated with Colonel Hervey, a sycophantic aide to Sir John, but his complaint had met with indignation and denial. In the end Fitz had spoken by phone to Lord Remarc, a junior minister in the War Office. They had been schoolboys at Eton together, and Remarc was one of Maud's gossipy friends. Fitz had not felt good about going behind the backs of his superior officers this way, but the struggle for Paris was so finely balanced that he felt he had to act. Patriotism was not so simple, he had learned.

The effect of his complaint had been explosive. Prime Minister Asquith had sent the new minister of war, Lord Kitchener, hotfoot to Paris, and Sir John had been carpeted by his boss the day before yesterday. Fitz had high hopes that he would shortly be replaced. Failing that, at least he might be jerked out of his lethargy.

Fitz would soon find out.

He turned away from Gini and put his feet on the floor.

"Are you leaving?" she said.

He stood up. "I have work to do."

She kicked off the sheet. Fitz looked at her perfect breasts. Catching his eye, she smiled through her tears and parted her legs invitingly.

He resisted temptation. "Make some coffee, *chérie,*" he said.

She put on a pale-green silk wrap and heated water while Fitz got dressed. Last night he had dined at the British embassy in his regimental mess kit, but after dinner he had shed the conspicuous scarlet military jacket and substituted a short tuxedo to go slumming.

She gave him strong coffee in a big cup like a bowl. "I will wait for you tonight at Albert's Club," she said. The nightclubs were officially closed, as were theaters and cinemas. Even the Folies Bergère was dark. Cafés closed at eight, and restaurants at nine thirty. But it was not so easy to shut down the nightlife of a great city, and enterprising types such as Albert had been quick to open illicit joints where they could sell champagne at extortionate prices.

"I'll try to get there by midnight," he said. The coffee was bitter but it washed away the last traces of sleepiness. He gave Gini a gold British sovereign. It was a generous payment for one night, and in such times gold was greatly preferred to paper money.

When he kissed her good-bye, she clung to him. "You will be there tonight, won't you?" she said.

He felt sorry for her. Her world was collapsing and she did not know what to do. He would have liked to take her under his wing and promise to look after her, but he could not. He had a pregnant wife, and if Bea was upset she could lose the baby. Even if he had been a single man, to have encumbered himself with a French tart would have made him a laughingstock. Anyway, Gini was only one of millions. Everyone was frightened, except those who were dead. "I'll do my best," he said, and extracted himself from her embrace.

His blue Cadillac was parked at the curb. A small Union Jack flew from the bonnet. There were few private cars on the streets, and most had a flag, usually a tricolor or a red cross, to show they were being used for essential war work.

Getting the car there from London had taken ruthless use of Fitz's connections and a small fortune in bribes, but he was glad he had taken the trouble. He needed to move daily between British and French headquarters, and it was a relief not to have to beg the loan of a car or a horse from the hard-pressed armies.

He pressed the automatic crank, and the engine turned over and fired. The streets were mostly empty of traffic. Even the buses had been commandeered for supplying the army at the front. He had to stop for a huge flock of sheep crossing town, presumably on their way to the Gare de l'Est to be sent by train to feed the troops.

He was intrigued to see a small crowd gathered around a poster freshly pasted to the wall of the Palais Bourbon. He pulled up and joined the people reading it.

ARMY OF PARIS
CITIZENS OF PARIS

Fitz's eye went to the foot of the notice and he saw that it was signed by General Galliéni, the military governor of the city. Galliéni, a crusty old soldier, had been brought out of retirement. He was famous for holding meetings at which no one was allowed to sit down: he believed people reached decisions faster that way.

The body of his message was characteristically terse.

The members of the Government of the Republic have left Paris to give new impetus to the national defense.

Fitz was dismayed. The government had fled! There had been rumors for the last few days that ministers would decamp to Bordeaux, but the politicians had hesitated, not wanting to abandon the capital. However, now they had gone. It was a very bad sign.

The rest of the announcement was defiant.

I have been entrusted with the duty of defending Paris against the invader.

So, Fitz thought, Paris will not surrender after all. The city will fight. Good! That was certainly in British interests. If the capital had to fall, at least the enemy should be made to pay heavily for their conquest.

This duty I shall carry out to the last extremity.

Fitz could not help smiling. Thank God for old soldiers.

The people around seemed to have mixed feelings. Some comments were admiring. Galliéni was a fighter, someone said with satisfaction; he would not let Paris be taken. Others were more realistic. The government has left us, a woman said; that means the Germans will be here today or tomorrow. A man with a briefcase said he had sent his wife and children to his brother's house in the country. A well-dressed woman said she had thirty kilos of dried beans in the kitchen cupboard.

Fitz just felt that the British contribution to the war effort, and his part in it, had become even more important.

With a strong sense of doom, he drove on to the Ritz.

He entered the lobby of his favorite hotel and went into a phone booth. There he called the British embassy and left a message for the ambassador, telling him about Galliéni's notice, just in case the news had not yet reached the rue du Faubourg St.-Honoré.

When he came out of the booth he ran into Sir John's aide Colonel Hervey.

Hervey looked at Fitz's tuxedo and said: "Major Fitzherbert! Why the devil are you dressed like that?"

"Good morning, Colonel," said Fitz, deliberately not answering the question. It was obvious that he had been out all night.

"It's nine o'clock in the bloody morning! Don't you know we're at war?"

This was another question that did not require an answer. Coolly Fitz said: "Is there something I can do for you, sir?"

Hervey was a bully who hated people he could not intimidate. "Less of your insolence, Major," he said. "We've got enough to do, with interfering bloody visitors from London."

Fitz raised an eyebrow. "Lord Kitchener *is* the minister of war."

"The politicians should leave us to do our job. But someone with friends in high places has stirred them up." He looked as if he suspected Fitz, but did not have the courage to say so.

"You can hardly have been surprised at the War Office being concerned," Fitz said. "Ten days' rest, with the Germans at the gates!"

"The men are exhausted!"

"In ten days the war might be over. What are we here for, if not to save Paris?"

"Kitchener took Sir John away from his headquarters on a crucial day of battle," Hervey blustered.

"Sir John wasn't in much of a hurry to get back to his troops, I noticed," Fitz rejoined. "I saw him dining here at the Ritz that evening." He knew he was being insolent but he could not help himself.

"Get out of my sight," said Hervey.

Fitz turned on his heel and went upstairs.

He was not as insouciant as he had pretended. Nothing would make him kowtow to idiots such as Hervey, but it was important to him to have a successful military career. He hated the thought that people might say he was not the man his father was. Hervey was not much use to the army because he spent all his time and energy patronizing his favorites and undermining his rivals, but by the same token he could ruin the careers of men who concentrated on other things, such as winning the war.

Fitz brooded as he bathed, shaved, and dressed in the khaki uniform of a major in the Welsh Rifles. Knowing that he might get nothing to eat until dinner, he ordered an omelette sent up to his suite with more coffee.

At ten o'clock sharp his working day began, and he put the malign Hervey out of his mind. Lieutenant Murray, a keen young Scot, arrived from British headquarters, bringing into Fitz's suite the dust of the road and the morning's aerial reconnaissance report.

Fitz rapidly translated the document into French and wrote it out in his clear, swooping script on pale blue Ritz paper. Every morning British planes overflew German positions and noted the direction in which enemy forces were moving. It was Fitz's job to get the information to General Galliéni as quickly as possible.

Going out through the lobby he was called by the head porter to take a phone call.

The voice that said: "Fitz, is that you?" was distant and distorted, but to his astonishment it was, unmistakably, that of his sister, Maud.

"How the devil did you manage this?" he said. Only the government and the military could phone Paris from London.

"I'm in Johnny Remarc's room at the War Office."

"I'm glad to hear your voice," Fitz said. "How are you?"

"Everyone's terribly worried here," she said. "At first the papers printed nothing but good news. Only people who knew their geography understood that after each gallant French victory the Germans seemed to be another fifty miles inside France. But on Sunday *The Times* published a special edition. Isn't that odd? The everyday paper is full of lies, so when they tell the truth they have to bring out a special edition."

She was trying to be witty and cynical, but Fitz could hear the fear and anger underneath. "What did the special edition say?"

"It spoke of our 'retreating and broken army.' Asquith is furious. Now everyone expects Paris to fall any day." Her façade cracked, and there was a sob in her voice as she said: "Fitz, are you going to be all right?"

He could not lie to her. "I don't know. The government has moved to Bordeaux. Sir John French has been told off, but he's still here."

"Sir John has complained to the War Office that Kitchener went to Paris in the uniform of a field marshal, which was a breach of etiquette because he is now a government minister and therefore a civilian."

"Good God. At a time like this he's thinking about etiquette! Why hasn't he been sacked?"

"Johnny says it would look like an admission of failure."

"What will it look like if Paris falls to the Germans?"

"Oh, Fitz!" Maud began to cry. "What about the baby Bea is expecting—your child?"

"How is Bea?" Fitz said, remembering guiltily where he had spent the night.

Maud sniffed and swallowed. More calmly, she said: "Bea looks bonny, and she no longer suffers from that tiresome morning sickness."

"Tell her I miss her."

There was a burst of interference, and another voice came on the line for a few seconds, then disappeared. That meant they might get cut off any second. When Maud spoke again, her voice was plaintive. "Fitz, when will it end?"

"Within the next few days," Fitz said. "One way or the other."

"Please look after yourself!"

"Of course."

The line went dead.

Fitz cradled the phone, tipped the head porter, and went out into the Place Vendôme.

He got into his car and drove off. Maud had upset him by speaking of Bea's pregnancy. Fitz was willing to die for his country, and hoped he would die bravely, but he wanted to see his baby. He had not yet been a parent and he was eager to meet his child, to watch him learn and grow, to help him become an adult. He did not want his son or daughter raised without a father.

He drove across the river Seine to the complex of army buildings known as Les Invalides. Galliéni had made his headquarters in a nearby school called the Lycée Victor-Duruy, set back behind trees. The entrance was closely guarded by sentries in bright blue tunics and red trousers with red caps, so much smarter than the mud-colored British khaki. The French had not yet grasped that accurate modern rifles meant that today's soldier wanted to disappear into the landscape.

Fitz was well known to the guards and walked straight in. It was a girls' school, with paintings of pets and flowers, and Latin verbs conjugated on blackboards that had been pushed out of the way. The rifles of the sentries and the boots of the officers seemed to offend against the gentility of what had gone before.

Fitz went straight to the staff room. As soon as he walked in he sensed an atmosphere of excitement. On the wall was a large map of central France on which the positions of the armies had been marked with pins. Galliéni was tall, thin, and upright despite the prostate cancer that had caused him to retire in February. Now back in uniform, he stared aggressively at the map through his pince-nez glasses.

Fitz saluted, then shook hands, French style, with his opposite number, Colonel Dupuys, and asked in a whisper what was going on.

"We're tracking von Kluck," said Dupuys.

Galliéni had a squadron of nine old aircraft that he was using to monitor the movements of the invading army. General von Kluck was in command of the First Army, the nearest German force to Paris.

"What have you got?" Fitz asked.

"Two reports." Dupuys pointed at the map. "Our aerial reconnaissance indicates that von Kluck is moving southeast, toward the river Marne."

This confirmed what the British had reported. On that trajectory, the First Army would pass to the east of Paris. And, since von Kluck commanded the German right wing, that meant their entire force would bypass the city. Would Paris escape after all?

Dupuys went on: "And we have a report from a cavalry scout that suggests the same."

Fitz nodded thoughtfully. "German military theory is to destroy the enemy's army first, and take possession of cities later."

"But don't you see?" said Dupuys excitedly. "They are exposing their flank!"

Fitz had not thought of that. His mind had been on the fate of Paris. Now he realized that Dupuys was right, and this was the reason for the air of exhilaration. If the intelligence was right, von Kluck had made a classic military error. The flank of an army was more vulnerable than its head. A flank attack was like a stab in the back.

Why had von Kluck made such a mistake? He must believe the French to be so weak that they were incapable of counterattack.

In which case, he was wrong.

Fitz addressed the general. "I think this will interest you greatly, sir," he said, and handed over his envelope. "It's our aerial reconnaissance report of this morning."

"Aha!" said Galliéni eagerly.

Fitz stepped up to the map. "If I may, General?"

The general nodded permission. The British were not popular, but all intelligence was welcome.

Consulting the English-language original, Fitz said: "Our people put von Kluck's army here." He stuck a new pin in the map. "And moving in this direction." It confirmed what the French already believed.

For a moment, the room was silent.

"It's true, then," said Dupuys quietly. "They have exposed their flank."

General Galliéni's eyes glittered behind his pince-nez. "So," he said, "this is our moment to attack."

{ II }

Fitz was at his most pessimistic at three o'clock in the morning, lying next to Gini's slim body, when sex was over and he found himself missing his wife. Then he thought dispiritedly that von Kluck must surely realize his mistake and reverse course.

But next morning, Friday, September 4, to the delight of the French defenders, von Kluck continued southeast. That was enough for General Joffre. He gave orders for the French Sixth Army to move out from Paris the following morning and strike at von Kluck's rearguard.

But the British continued to retreat.

Fitz was in despair that evening when he met Gini at Albert's. "This is our last chance," he explained to her over a champagne cocktail that did nothing to cheer him up. "If we can seriously rattle the Germans now, when they are exhausted and their supply lines are fully stretched, we may bring their advance to a halt. But if this counterattack fails, Paris will fall."

She was sitting on a barstool, and she crossed her long legs with a whisper of silk stockings. "But why are you so gloomy?"

"Because, at a time like this, the British are retreating. If Paris falls now, we will never live down the shame of it."

"General Joffre must confront Sir John and demand that the British fight! You must speak to Joffre yourself!"

"He doesn't give audience to British majors. Besides, he would probably think it was some kind of trick by Sir John. And I would be in deep trouble, not that I care about that."

"Then speak to one of his advisers."

"Same problem. I can't walk into French army headquarters and announce that the British are betraying them."

"But you could have a quiet word in the ear of General Lourceau, without anyone knowing about it."

"How?"

"He is sitting over there."

Fitz followed her gaze and saw a Frenchman of about sixty in civilian clothes sitting at a table with a young woman in a red dress.

"He is very amiable," Gini added.

"You know him?"

"We were friends for a while, but he preferred Lizette."

Fitz hesitated. Once again he was contemplating going behind the backs of his superiors. But this was no time for niceties. Paris was at stake. He had to do whatever he could.

"Introduce me," he said.

"Give me a minute." Gini slid elegantly off her stool and walked across the club, swaying slightly to the ragtime piano, until she came to the general's table. She kissed him on the lips, smiled at his companion, and sat down. After a few moments' earnest conversation she beckoned to Fitz.

Lourceau stood up and the two men shook hands. "I'm honored to meet you, sir," Fitz said.

"This is not the place for serious conversation," the general said. "But Gini assures me that what you have to say to me is terribly urgent."

"It most certainly is," Fitz said, and he sat down.

{ III }

Next day Fitz went to the British camp at Melun, twenty-five miles southeast of Paris, and learned to his dismay that the Expeditionary Force was still retreating.

Perhaps his message had not got through to Joffre. Or perhaps it had, and Joffre simply felt there was nothing he could do.

Fitz entered Vaux-le-Pénil, the magnificent Louis XV château Sir John was using as headquarters, and ran into Colonel Hervey in the hall. "May I ask, sir, why we are retreating when our allies are launching a counterattack?" he said as politely as he could.

"No, you may not ask," said Hervey.

Fitz persisted, suppressing his anger. "The French feel they and the Germans are evenly balanced, and even our small force may tip the scales."

Hervey laughed scornfully. "I'm sure they do." He spoke as if the French had no right to demand the help of their allies.

Fitz felt himself losing self-control. "Paris could be lost because of our timidity!"

"Do not dare to use such a word, Major."

"We were sent here to save France. This may be the decisive battle." Fitz could not help raising his voice. "If Paris is lost, and France with it, how will we explain, back home, that we were *resting* at the time?"

Instead of replying, Hervey stared over Fitz's shoulder. Fitz turned to see a heavy, slow-moving figure in French uniform: a black tunic that was unbuttoned over the large waist, ill-fitting red breeches, tight leggings, and the red-and-gold cap of a general pulled low over the forehead. Colorless eyes glanced at Fitz and Hervey from under salt-and-pepper eyebrows. Fitz recognized General Joffre.

When the general had lumbered past, followed by his entourage, Hervey said: "Are you responsible for this?"

Fitz was too proud to lie. "Possibly," he said.

"You haven't heard the last of it," Hervey said, and he turned and hurried after Joffre.

Sir John received Joffre in a small room with only a few officers present, and Fitz was not among them. He waited in the officers' mess, wondering what Joffre was saying and whether he could persuade Sir John to end the shameful British retreat and join in the assault.

He learned the answer two hours later from Lieutenant Murray. "They say Joffre tried everything," Murray reported. "He begged, he wept, and he insinuated that British honor was in danger of being forever besmirched. And he won his point. Tomorrow we turn north."

Fitz grinned broadly. "Hallelujah," he said.

A minute later Colonel Hervey approached. Fitz stood up politely.

"You've gone too far," Hervey said. "General Lourceau told me what you did. He thought he was paying you a compliment."

"I shan't deny it," Fitz said. "The outcome suggests that it was the right thing."

"You listen to me, Fitzherbert," Hervey said, lowering his voice. "You're fucking finished. You've been disloyal to a superior officer. There's a black mark against your name that will never be erased. You won't get a promotion, even if the war goes on for a year. Major you are and major you will always be."

"Thank you for your frankness, Colonel," said Fitz. "But I joined the army to win battles, not promotions."

{ IV }

Sir John's advance on Sunday was embarrassingly cautious, Fitz felt, but to his relief it was enough to force von Kluck to meet the threat by sending troops he could not easily spare. Now the German was fighting on two fronts, west and south, every commander's nightmare.

Fitz woke up on Monday morning, after a night on a blanket on the château floor, feeling optimistic. He had breakfast in the officers' mess, then waited impatiently for the spotter planes to return from their morning sortie. War was either a mad dash or futile inactivity. In the grounds of the château was a church said to date from the year 1000, and he went to look at it, but he had never really understood what people saw in old churches.

The reconnaissance debriefing took place in the magnificent salon overlooking the park and the river. The officers sat on camp chairs at a cheap board table with lavish eighteenth-century decor all around them. Sir John had a jutting chin and a mouth that seemed, underneath the white walrus mustache, to be permanently twisted into an expression of injured pride.

The aviators reported that there was open country ahead of the British force, because the German columns were marching away north.

Fitz was elated. The Allied counterattack had been unexpected, and the Germans had been caught napping, it seemed. Of course they would regroup soon, but for now they seemed to be in trouble.

He waited for Sir John to order a rapid advance but, disappointingly, the commander simply confirmed the limited objectives set earlier.

Fitz wrote his report in French, then got into his car. He drove the twenty-five miles to Paris as fast as he could against the flow of trucks, cars, and horse-drawn vehicles leaving the city, crammed with people and piled high with luggage, heading south to escape the Germans.

In Paris he was delayed by a formation of dark-skinned Algerian troops marching across the city from one railway station to another. Their officers rode mules and wore bright red cloaks. As they passed, women gave them flowers and fruit, and café proprietors brought them cold drinks.

When they had passed, Fitz drove on to Les Invalides and took his report into the school.

Once again, the British reconnaissance confirmed the French reports. Some German forces were retreating. "We must press the attack!" said the old general. "Where are the British?"

Fitz went to the map and pointed to the British position and the marching objectives given by Sir John for the end of the day.

"It's not enough!" said Galliéni angrily. "You must be more aggressive! We need you to attack, so that von Kluck will be too busy with you to reinforce his flank. When will you cross the river Marne?"

Fitz could not say. He felt ashamed. He agreed with every caustic word Galliéni uttered, but he could not admit it, so he merely said: "I will emphasize this to Sir John most strongly, General."

But Galliéni was already figuring out how to compensate for British lassitude. "We will send the 7th Division of the 4 Corps to reinforce Manoury's army on the Ourcq River this afternoon," he said decisively.

Immediately his staff began to write out orders.

Then Colonel Dupuys said: "General, we don't have enough trains to get them all there by this evening."

"Then use cars," said Galliéni.

"Cars?" Dupuys looked baffled. "Where would we get that many cars?"

"Hire taxis!"

Everyone in the room stared at him. Had the general gone off his head?

"Telephone the chief of police," said Galliéni. "Tell him to order his men to stop every taxi in the city, kick out the passengers, and direct the drivers here. We will fill them with soldiers and send them to the battlefield."

Fitz grinned when he realized Galliéni was serious. This was the kind of attitude he liked. Let's do whatever it takes, just so long as we win.

Dupuys shrugged and picked up a telephone. "Please get the chief of police on the phone immediately," he said.

Fitz thought: I have to see this.

He went outside and lit a cigar. He did not have long to wait. After a few minutes a red Renault taxi came across the Alexander III Bridge, drove around the large ornamental lawn, and parked in front of the main building. It was followed by two more, then a dozen, then a hundred.

In a couple of hours several hundred identical red taxis were parked at Les Invalides. Fitz had never seen anything like it.

The cabbies leaned against their cars, smoking pipes and talking animatedly, waiting for instructions. Every driver had a different theory as to why they were there.

Eventually Dupuys came out of the school and across the street with a megaphone in one hand and a sheaf of army requisition slips in the other. He climbed on the bonnet of a taxi, and the drivers fell quiet.

"The military commander of Paris requires five hundred taxis to go from here to Blagny," he shouted through the megaphone.

The drivers stared at him in incredulous silence.

"There each car will pick up five soldiers and drive them to Nanteuil."

Nanteuil was thirty miles east and very close to the front line. The drivers began to understand. They looked at one another, nodding and grinning. Fitz guessed they were pleased to be part of the war effort, especially in such an unusual way.

"Please take one of these forms before you leave and fill it out in order to claim payment on your return."

There was a buzz of reaction. They were going to get paid! That clinched their support.

"When five hundred cars have left, I will give instructions for the next five hundred. *Vive Paris! Vive la France!*"

The drivers broke into wild cheering. They mobbed Dupuys for the forms. Fitz, delighted, helped distribute the papers.

Soon the little cars began to leave, turning around in front of the great building and heading across the bridge in the sunshine, sounding their horns in enthusiasm, a long bright red lifeline to the forces on the battlefront.

{ V }

The British took three days to march twenty-five miles. Fitz was mortified. Their advance had been largely unopposed: if they had moved faster, they might have struck a decisive blow.

However, on the morning of Wednesday, September 9, he found Galliéni's men in an optimistic mood. Von Kluck was retreating. "The Germans are scared!" said Colonel Dupuys.

Fitz did not believe the Germans were scared, and the map offered a more plausible explanation. The British, slow and timid though they were, had marched into a gap that had appeared between the German First and Second armies, a gap made when von Kluck pulled his forces westward to face the attack from Paris. "We've found a weak point, and we're driving a wedge into it," Fitz said, and there was a tremor of hope in his voice.

He told himself to calm down. The Germans had won every battle so far. On the other hand, their supply lines were stretched, their men were exhausted, and their numbers had been reduced by the need to send reinforcements to East Prussia. By contrast the French in this zone had received heavy reinforcements and had virtually no supply lines to worry about, being on home ground.

Fitz's hopes went into reverse when the British halted five miles north of the river Marne. What was Sir John stopping for? He had encountered hardly any opposition!

But the Germans seemed not to notice the timidity of the Brits, for they continued to retreat, and hopes rose again in the lycée.

As the shadows of the trees lengthened outside the school windows, and the last reports of the day came in, a sense of suppressed jubilation began to permeate Galliéni's staff. By the end of the day the Germans were on the run.

Fitz could hardly believe it. The despair of a week ago had turned to hope. He sat on a chair that was too small for him and stared at the map on the wall. Seven days ago the German line had seemed like a springboard for the launch of their final attack; now it looked like a wall at which they had been turned back.

When the sun went down behind the Eiffel Tower, the Allies had not won a victory, exactly, but for the first time in weeks the German advance had ground to a halt.

Dupuys embraced Fitz, then kissed him on both cheeks; and for once Fitz did not mind at all.

"We have stopped them," said Galliéni, and to Fitz's surprise, tears gleamed behind the old general's pince-nez. "We have stopped them."

{ VI }

Soon after the Battle of the Marne, both sides began to dig trenches.

The heat of September turned into the cold, depressing rain of October. The stalemate at the eastern end of the line spread irresistibly west, like a paralysis creeping through the body of a dying man.

The decisive battle of the autumn was over the Belgian town of Ypres, at the westernmost end of the line, twenty miles from the sea. The Germans attacked fiercely in an all-out attempt to turn the flank of the British force. The fighting raged for four weeks. Unlike all previous battles this one was static, with both sides hiding in trenches from each other's artillery and coming out only for suicidal sorties against the enemy's machine guns. In the end the British were saved by reinforcements, including a corps of brown-faced Indians shivering in their tropical uniforms. When it was over, seventy-five thousand British soldiers had died, and the Expeditionary Force was broken; but the

Allies had completed a defensive barricade from the Swiss border to the English Channel, and the invading Germans had been stopped.

On December 24 Fitz was at British headquarters in the town of St.-Omer, not far from Calais, in a gloomy frame of mind. He remembered how glibly he and others had told the men they would be home for Christmas. Now it looked as if the war could go on for a year or even more. The opposing armies sat in their trenches day after day, eating bad food, getting dysentery and trench foot and lice, and desultorily killing the rats that thrived on the dead bodies littering no-man's-land. It had once seemed very clear to Fitz why Britain had to go to war, but he could no longer remember the reasons.

That day the rain stopped and the weather turned cold. Sir John sent a message to all units warning that the enemy was contemplating a Christmas attack. This was entirely imaginary, Fitz knew: there was no supporting intelligence. The truth was that Sir John did not want the men to relax their vigilance on Christmas Day.

Every soldier was to receive a gift from Princess Mary, the seventeen-year-old daughter of the king and queen. It was an embossed brass box containing tobacco and cigarettes, a picture of the princess, and a Christmas card from the king. There were different gifts for nonsmokers, Sikhs, and nurses, all of whom would get chocolate or candy instead of tobacco. Fitz helped distribute the boxes to the Welsh Rifles. At the end of the day, too late to return to the relative comfort of St.-Omer, he found himself at the headquarters of the Fourth Battalion, a damp dugout a quarter of a mile behind the front line, reading a Sherlock Holmes story and smoking the small, thin cigars he had taken to. They were not as good as his panatelas, but these days he hardly ever got time to smoke a big cigar. He was with Murray, who had been promoted to captain after Ypres. Fitz had not been promoted: Hervey was keeping his promise.

Soon after nightfall he was surprised to hear scattered rifle fire. It turned out that the men had seen lights and thought the enemy were trying a sneak attack. In fact the lights were colored lanterns with which the Germans were decorating their parapet.

Murray, who had been on the front line for a while, talked about the Indian troops defending the next sector. "Poor sods arrived in their summer uniforms, because someone told them the war would be over before the weather turned cold," he said. "But I'll tell you something, Fitz: your darkie soldier is an ingenious blighter. You know we've been asking the War Office to give us trench mortars like the ones the Germans have, that lob a grenade over the parapet? Well, the Indians have made their own out of odd pieces of cast-iron pipe. Looks like a bit of bodged plumbing in a pub toilet, but it works!"

In the morning there was a freezing fog and the ground underfoot was hard. Fitz and Murray gave out the princess's gifts at first light. Some of the men were huddled around braziers, trying to get warm, but they said they were grateful for the frost, which was better than the mud, especially for those suffering from trench foot. Some spoke to one another in Welsh, Fitz noticed, although they always used English with officers.

The German line, four hundred yards away, was hidden by a morning mist the same color as the German uniforms, a faded silver-blue called field gray. Fitz heard faint music: the Germans were singing carols. Fitz was not very musical, but he thought he recognized "Silent Night."

He returned to the dugout for a grim breakfast of stale bread and tinned ham with the other officers. Afterward he stepped outside to smoke. He had never been quite so miserable in all his life. He thought of the breakfast that was being served at that moment in Tŷ Gwyn: hot sausages, fresh eggs, deviled kidneys, smoky kippers, buttered toast, and fragrant coffee with cream in it. He longed for clean underwear, a crisply ironed shirt, and a soft wool suit. He wanted to sit by the blazing coal fire in the morning room with nothing better to do than read the stupid jokes in *Punch* magazine.

Murray followed him out of the dugout and said: "You're wanted on the telephone, Major. It's headquarters."

Fitz was surprised. Someone had gone to a lot of trouble to locate him. He hoped it was not on account of some quarrel that had flared up between the French and the British while he had been handing out

Christmas presents. With a worried frown he ducked inside and picked up the field telephone. "Fitzherbert."

"Good morning, Major," said a voice he did not recognize. "Captain Davies here. You don't know me, but I've been asked to pass you a message from home."

From home? Fitz hoped it was not bad news. "Very kind of you, Captain," he said. "What does the message say?"

"Your wife has given birth to a bouncing baby boy, sir. Mother and son are both doing fine."

"Oh!" Fitz sat down suddenly on a box. The baby was not due yet—it must be a week or two early. Premature babies were vulnerable. But the message said he was in good health. And so was Bea.

Fitz had a son, and the earldom had an heir.

"Are you there, Major?" said Captain Davies.

"Yes, yes," said Fitz. "Just a bit shocked. It's early."

"As it's Christmas, sir, we thought the news might cheer you up."

"It does, I can tell you!"

"May I be the first to offer my congratulations."

"Most kind," Fitz said. "Thank you." But Captain Davies had already hung up.

After a moment Fitz realized the other officers in the dugout were staring at him in silence. Finally one of them said: "Good news or bad?"

"Good!" said Fitz. "Wonderful, in fact. I have become a father."

They all shook his hand and slapped his back. Murray got out the whisky bottle, despite the early hour, and they drank the baby's health. "What'll he be called?" Murray asked.

"Viscount Aberowen, while I'm alive," Fitz said; then he realized that Murray was not asking about the baby's title, but his name. "George, for my father, and William for my grandfather. Bea's father was Petr Nikolaevich, so perhaps we'll add those as well."

Murray seemed amused. "George William Peter Nicholas Fitzherbert, Viscount Aberowen," he said. "Quite enough names to be going on with!"

Fitz nodded good-humoredly. "Especially as he probably weighs about seven pounds."

He was bursting with pride and good cheer, and he felt an urge to share his news. "I might go along to the front line," he said when they had finished their whisky. "Pass out a few cigars to the men."

He left the dugout and walked along the communication trench. He felt euphoric. There was no gunfire, and the air tasted crisp and clean, except when he passed the latrine. He found himself thinking not about Bea but about Ethel. Had she had her baby yet? Was she happy in her house, having extorted the money from Fitz to buy it? Although he was taken aback by the tough way she had bargained with him, he could not help remembering that it was his child she was carrying. He hoped she would deliver her baby safely, as Bea had.

All such thoughts flew from his mind when he reached the front. As he turned the corner into the frontline trench, he got a shock.

There was no one there.

He walked along the trench, zigzagging around one traverse, then another, and saw no one. It was like a ghost story, or one of those ships found floating undamaged with not a soul aboard.

There had to be an explanation. Had there been an attack that somehow Fitz had not been told about?

It occurred to him to look over the parapet.

This was not to be done casually. Many men were killed on their first day at the front because they took a quick look over the top.

Fitz picked up one of the short-handled spades called entrenching tools. He pushed the blade gradually up over the edge of the parapet. Then he climbed onto the fire step and slowly raised his head until he was looking out through the narrow gap between the parapet and the blade.

What he saw astonished him.

The men were all in the cratered desert of no-man's-land. But they were not fighting. They were standing around in groups, talking.

There was something odd about their appearance, and after a moment Fitz realized that some of the uniforms were khaki and others field gray.

The men were talking to the enemy.

Fitz dropped the entrenching tool, raised his head fully over the parapet, and stared. There were hundreds of soldiers in no-man's-land, stretching as far as he could see to left and right, British and Germans intermingled.

What the hell was going on?

He found a trench ladder and scrambled up over the parapet. He marched across the churned earth. The men were showing photographs of their families and sweethearts, offering cigarettes, and trying to communicate, saying things like: "Me Robert. Who you?"

He spotted two sergeants, one British and one German, deep in conversation. He tapped the Brit on the shoulder. "You!" he said. "What the devil are you doing?"

The man answered him in the flat guttural accent of the Cardiff docks. "I don't know how it happened, sir, exactly. Some of the Jerries got up on their parapet, unarmed, and shouted, 'Happy Christmas'; then one of our boys done the same, then they started walking toward one another and before you could say chips everyone was doing it."

"But there's no one in the trenches!" Fitz said angrily. "Don't you see this could be a trick?"

The sergeant looked up and down the line. "No, sir, if I'm honest, I can't say that I do see that," he said coolly.

The man was right. How could the enemy possibly take advantage of the fact that the frontline forces of both sides had become friends?

The sergeant pointed to the German. "This is Hans Braun, sir," he said. "Used to be a waiter at the Savoy Hotel in London. Speaks English!"

The German sergeant saluted Fitz. "Glad to make your acquaintance, Major," he said. "Happy Christmas." He had less of an accent than the sergeant from Cardiff. He proffered a flask. "Would you care for a drop of schnapps?"

"Good God," said Fitz, and walked away.

There was nothing he could do. This would have been difficult to stop even with the support of the noncommissioned officers such as that Welsh sergeant. Without their help it was impossible. He decided he had better report the situation to a superior and make it someone else's problem.

But before he could leave the scene he heard his name called. "Fitz! Fitz! Is that really you?"

The voice was familiar. He turned to see a German approaching. As the man came close, he recognized him. "Von Ulrich?" he said in amazement.

"The very same!" Walter smiled broadly and held out his hand. Automatically Fitz took it. Walter shook hands vigorously. He looked thinner, Fitz thought, and his fair skin was weathered. I suppose I've changed, too, Fitz thought.

Walter said: "This is amazing—what a coincidence!"

"I'm glad to see you fit and well," Fitz said. "Though I probably shouldn't be."

"Likewise!"

"What are we going to do about this?" Fitz waved a hand at the fraternizing soldiers. "I find it worrying."

"I agree. When tomorrow comes they may not wish to shoot at their new friends."

"And then what would we do?"

"We must have a battle soon to get them back to normal. If both sides start shelling in the morning, they'll soon start to hate each other again."

"I hope you're right."

"And how are you, my old friend?"

Fitz remembered his good news, and brightened. "I've become a father," he said. "Bea has given birth to a boy. Have a cigar."

They lit up. Walter had been on the eastern front, he revealed. "The Russians are corrupt," he said with disgust. "The officers sell supplies on the black market and let the infantry go hungry and cold. Half the population of East Prussia are wearing Russian army boots they bought cheap, while the Russian soldiers are barefoot."

Fitz said he had been in Paris. "Your favorite restaurant, Voisin's, is still open," he said.

The men started a football match, Britain versus Germany, piling up their uniform caps for goalposts. "I've got to report this," said Fitz.

"I, too," said Walter. "But first tell me, how is Lady Maud?"

"Fine, I think."

"I would most particularly like to be remembered to her."

Fitz was struck by the emphasis with which Walter uttered this otherwise routine remark. "Of course," he said. "Any special reason?"

Walter looked away. "Just before I left London . . . I danced with her at Lady Westhampton's ball. It was the last civilized thing I did before this *verdammten* war."

Walter seemed to be in the grip of emotion. There was a tremor in his voice, and it was highly unusual for him to mix German with English. Perhaps the Christmas atmosphere had got to him too.

Walter went on: "I should very much like her to know that I was thinking of her on Christmas Day." He looked at Fitz with moist eyes. "Would you be sure to tell her, old friend?"

"I will," said Fitz. "I'm sure she'll be very pleased."

CHAPTER FOURTEEN

February 1915

"I went to the doctor," said the woman next to Ethel. "I said to him, 'I've got an itchy twat.'"

A ripple of laughter ran around the room. It was on the top floor of a small house in East London, near Aldgate. Twenty women sat at sewing machines in close-packed rows either side of a long workbench. There was no fire, and the one window was closed tight against the February cold. The floorboards were bare. The whitewashed plaster on the walls was crumbling with age, and the laths beneath showed through in places. With twenty women breathing the same air the room became stuffy, but it never seemed to warm up, and the women all wore hats and coats.

They had just stopped for a break, and the treadles under their feet were briefly silent. Ethel's neighbor was Mildred Perkins, a Cockney of her own age. Mildred was also Ethel's lodger. She would have been beautiful but for protruding front teeth. Dirty jokes were her specialty. She went on: "The doctor says to me, he goes, 'You shouldn't say that. It's a rude word.'"

Ethel grinned. Mildred managed to create moments of cheer in the grim twelve-hour working day. Ethel had never known such talk before. At Tŷ Gwyn the staff had been genteel. These London women would say anything. They were all ages and several nationalities, and some barely spoke English, including two refugees from German-occupied Belgium. The only thing they all had in common was that they were desperate enough to want the job.

"I says to him, 'What should I say, then, Doctor?' He says to me, 'Say you've got an itchy finger.'"

They were sewing British army uniforms, thousands of them, tunics and trousers. Day after day the pieces of thick khaki cloth came in from a cutting factory in the next street, big cardboard boxes full of sleeves and backs and legs, and the women here sewed them together and sent them to another small factory to have the buttons and buttonholes added. They were paid according to how many they finished.

"He says to me, 'Do your finger itch you all the time, Mrs. Perkins, or just now and again?'"

Mildred paused, and the women were silent, waiting for the punch line.

"I says, 'No, Doctor, only when I piss through it.'"

The women hooted with laughter and cheered.

A thin girl of twelve came through the door with a pole on her shoulder. Hanging from it were large mugs and tankards, twenty of them. She put the pole down gingerly on the workbench. The mugs contained tea, hot chocolate, clear soup, or watery coffee. Each woman had her own mug. Twice a day, midmorning and midafternoon, they gave their pennies and halfpennies to the girl, Allie, and she got their mugs filled at the café next door.

The women sipped their drinks, stretched their arms and legs, and rubbed their eyes. The work was not hard like coal mining, Ethel thought, but it was tiring, bent over your machine hour after hour, peering at the stitching. And it had to be done right. The boss, Mannie Litov, checked each piece, and if it was wrong you did not get paid, even though Ethel suspected he sent the faulty uniforms off anyway.

After five minutes Mannie came into the workroom, clapping his hands and saying: "Come on now, back to work." They drained their cups and turned back to the bench.

Mannie was a slave driver, but not the worst, the women said. At least he did not paw the girls or demand sexual favors. He was about thirty, with dark eyes and a black beard. His father was a tailor who had come over from Russia and opened a shop in the Mile End Road, making cheap suits for bank clerks and stockbrokers' runners. Mannie had learned the trade from his father, then started a more ambitious enterprise.

The war was good for business. A million men had volunteered for the army between August and Christmas, and each one needed a uniform. Mannie was hiring every seamstress he could find. Fortunately Ethel had learned to use a sewing machine at Tŷ Gwyn.

Ethel needed a job. Although her house was paid for, and she was collecting rent from Mildred, she had to save money for when the baby came along. But the experience of looking for work had made her frustrated and irate.

All kinds of new jobs were opening up for women, but Ethel had quickly learned that men and women were still unequal. Jobs at which men earned three or four pounds were being offered to women at a pound a week. And even then the women had to put up with hostility and persecution. Male bus passengers would refuse to show their tickets to a woman conductor, male engineers would pour oil into a woman's tool box, and women workers were barred from the pub at the factory gate. What made Ethel even more furious was that the same men would call a woman lazy and shiftless if her children were dressed in rags.

In the end, reluctantly and angrily, she had opted for an industry in which women were traditionally employed, vowing she would change this unjust system before she died.

She rubbed her back. Her baby was due in a week or two, and she was going to have to stop work any day now. Sewing was awkward with a great distended belly, but what she found most difficult was the tiredness that threatened to overcome her.

Two more women came through the door, one with a bandage on her hand. The seamstresses frequently cut themselves with sewing needles or with the sharp scissors they used to trim their work.

Ethel said: "Look you, Mannie, you ought to keep a little medical kit here, with bandages and a bottle of iodine and a few other bits and pieces in a tin."

He said: "What am I, made of money?" It was his stock response to any demand by his workforce.

"But you must lose money every time one of us hurts herself," Ethel said in a tone of sweet reason. "Here's two women been away from their machines nearly an hour, because they had to go to the chemist's and get a cut seen to."

The woman with the bandage grinned and said: "Plus I had to stop at the Dog and Duck to steady my nerves."

Mannie said sarcastically to Ethel: "I suppose you want me to keep a bottle of gin in the medical kit as well."

Ethel ignored that. "I'll make you a list and find out what everything would cost. Then you can make up your mind, is it?"

"I'm not making any promises," said Mannie, which was as close as he ever came to making a promise.

"Right, then." Ethel turned back to her machine.

It was always she who asked Mannie for small improvements in the workplace, or protested when he made adverse changes such as asking them to pay to have their scissors sharpened. Without intending to, she seemed to have fallen into the kind of role her father played.

Outside the grimy window, the short afternoon was darkening. Ethel found the last three hours of the working day the hardest of all. Her back hurt, and the glare of the overhead lights made her head ache.

But, when seven o'clock came, she did not want to go home. The thought of spending the evening alone was too depressing.

When Ethel first came to London several young men had paid attention to her. She had not really fancied any of them, but she had accepted invitations to the cinema, the music hall, recitals, and evenings at pubs, and she had kissed one of them, though without much passion. However, as soon as her pregnancy began to show they had all lost interest. A pretty girl was one thing, and a woman with a baby quite another.

Fortunately, tonight there was a Labour Party meeting. Ethel had joined the Aldgate branch of the Independent Labour Party soon after buying her house. She often wondered what her father would have thought, had he known. Would he have wanted to exclude her from his party as he had from his house? Or would he have been secretly pleased? She would probably never know.

The scheduled speaker tonight was Sylvia Pankhurst, one of the leaders of the suffragettes, campaigners for votes for women. The war had split the famous Pankhurst family. Emmeline, the mother, had forsworn the campaign for the duration of the war. One daughter, Christabel, supported the mother, but the other, Sylvia, had broken with them and continued the campaign. Ethel was on Sylvia's side: women were oppressed in war as well as peace, and they would never get justice until they could vote.

On the pavement outside, she said good night to the other women. The gaslit street was busy with workers going home, shoppers putting together their evening meal, and revelers on the way to a night on the tiles. A breath of warm, yeasty air came from the open door of the Dog and Duck. Ethel understood the women who spent all evening in such places. Pubs were nicer than most people's homes, and there was friendly company and the cheap anesthetic of gin.

Next to the pub was a grocer's shop called Lippmann's, but it was closed: it had been vandalized by a patriotic gang because of its German name, and now it was boarded up. Ironically, the owner was a Jew from Glasgow with a son in the Highland Light Infantry.

Ethel caught a bus. It was two stops, but she was too tired to walk.

The meeting was at the Calvary Gospel Hall, the place where Lady Maud had her clinic. Ethel had come to Aldgate because it was the only district of London she had ever heard of, Maud having mentioned the name many times.

The hall was lit by cheerful gas mantels along the walls, and a coal stove in the middle of the room took the chill off the air. Cheap folding chairs had been put out in rows facing a table and a lectern. Ethel was greeted by the branch secretary, Bernie Leckwith, a studious, pedantic man with a good heart. Now he looked worried. "Our speaker has canceled," he said.

Ethel was disappointed. "What are we going to do?" she asked. She looked around the room. "You've already got more than fifty people here."

"They're sending a substitute, but she's not here yet, and I don't know if she'll be any good. She's not even a party member."

"Who is it?"

"Her name is Lady Maud Fitzherbert." Bernie added disapprovingly: "I gather she's from a coal-owning family."

Ethel laughed. "Fancy that!" she said. "I used to work for her."

"Is she a good speaker?"

"I've no idea."

Ethel was intrigued. She had not seen Maud since the fateful Tuesday when Maud had married Walter von Ulrich and Britain had declared war on Germany. Ethel still had the dress Walter had bought her, carefully wrapped in tissue paper and hanging in her wardrobe. It was pink silk with a gauzy overdress, and it was the most beautiful thing she had ever owned. Of course she could not fit into it now. Besides, it was too good for wearing to a Labour Party meeting. She still had the hat, too, in the original box from the shop in Bond Street.

She took her seat, grateful to get the weight off her feet, and settled to wait for the meeting to begin. She would never forget going to the Ritz, after the wedding, with Walter's handsome cousin Robert von Ulrich. Walking into the restaurant she had been the focus of hard looks from one or two of the women, and she guessed that, even though her dress was expensive, there was something about her that marked her as working class. But she hardly cared. Robert had made her laugh with catty comments about the other women's clothing and jewelry, and she had told him a bit about life in a Welsh mining town, which seemed stranger to him than the existence of the Eskimos.

Where were they now? Both Walter and Robert had gone to war, of course, Walter with the German army and Robert with the Austrian, and Ethel had no way of knowing whether they were dead or alive. She knew no more about Fitz. She presumed he had gone to France with the Welsh Rifles, but was not even sure of that. All the same, she scanned the casualty lists in the newspapers, fearfully looking for the name Fitzherbert. She hated him for the way he had treated her, but all the same she was deeply thankful when his name did not appear.

She could have remained in contact with Maud, simply by going to the Wednesday clinic, but how would she have explained her visit? Apart from a minor scare in July—a little spotting of blood in her underwear that Dr. Greenward had assured her was nothing to worry about—she had had nothing wrong with her.

However, Maud had not changed in six months. She walked into the hall as spectacularly well dressed as ever, in a huge wide-brimmed hat with a tall feather that stuck up out of the hatband like the mast of a yacht. Suddenly Ethel felt shabby in her old brown coat.

Maud caught her eye and came over. "Hello, Williams! Forgive me—I mean, Ethel. What a lovely surprise!"

Ethel shook her hand. "You'll excuse me if I don't get up," she said, patting her distended belly. "Just now I don't think I could manage to stand up for the king."

"Don't even think about it. Can we find a few minutes to chat after the meeting?"

"That would be lovely."

Maud went to the table, and Bernie opened the meeting. Bernie was a Russian Jew, like so many inhabitants of London's East End. In fact few East Enders were plain English. There were lots of Welsh, Scottish, and Irish. Before the war there had been many Germans; now there were thousands of Belgian refugees. The East End was where they got off the ship, so naturally they settled there.

Although they had a special guest, Bernie insisted on first going through apologies for absence, the minutes of the previous meeting, and other tedious routines. He worked for the local council in the libraries department, and he was a stickler for detail.

At last he introduced Maud. She spoke confidently and knowledgeably about the oppression of women. "A woman doing the same job as a man should be paid the same," she said. "But we are often told that the man has to support a family."

Several men in the audience nodded emphatically: that was what they always said.

"But what about the *woman* who has to support a family?"

This brought murmurs of agreement from the women.

"Last week in Acton I met a girl who is trying to feed and clothe her five children on two pounds a week, while her husband, who has run off and left her, is earning four pounds ten shillings making ships' propellers in Tottenham, and spending his money in the pub!"

"That's right!" said a woman behind Ethel.

"Recently I spoke to a woman in Bermondsey whose husband was killed at Ypres—she has to support his four children, yet she is paid a woman's wage."

"Shame!" said several women.

"If it's worth the employer's while to pay a man a shilling apiece to make gudgeon pins, it's worth his while to pay a woman at the same rate."

The men shifted uncomfortably in their seats.

Maud raked the audience with a steely gaze. "When I hear socialist men argue against equal pay, I say to them: Are you permitting greedy employers to treat women as cheap labor?"

Ethel thought it took a lot of courage and independence for a woman of Maud's background to have such views. She also envied Maud. She was jealous of her beautiful clothes and her fluent speaking style. On top of all that, Maud was married to the man she loved.

After the talk, Maud was questioned aggressively by the Labour Party men. The branch treasurer, a red-faced Scot called Jock Reid, said: "How can you keep on moaning about votes for women when our boys are dying in France?" There were loud sounds of agreement.

"I'm glad you asked me that, because it's a question that bothers many men and women, too," Maud said. Ethel admired the conciliatory tone of the answer, which contrasted nicely with the hostility of the questioner. "Should normal political activity go on during the war? Should you be attending a Labour Party meeting? Should trade unions continue to fight against exploitation of workers? Has the Conservative Party closed down for the duration? Have injustice and oppression been temporarily suspended? I say no, comrade. We must not permit the enemies of progress to take advantage of the war. It must not become an excuse for traditionalists to hold us back. As Mr. Lloyd George says, it's business as usual."

After the meeting, tea was made—by the women, of course—and Maud sat next to Ethel, taking off her gloves to hold a cup and saucer of thick blue earthenware pottery in her soft hands. Ethel felt it would be unkind to tell Maud the truth about her brother, so she gave her the latest version of her fictional saga, that "Teddy Williams" had been killed fighting in France. "I tell people we were married," she said, touching the cheap ring she wore. "Not that anyone cares these days. When boys are going off to war, girls want to please them, married or not." She lowered her voice. "I don't suppose you've heard from Walter."

Maud smiled. "The most amazing thing happened. You read in the newspapers about the Christmas truce?"

"Yes, of course—British and Germans exchanging presents and playing football in no-man's-land. It's a shame they didn't continue the truce, and refuse to fight on."

"Absolutely. But Fitz met Walter!"

"Well, now, that's marvelous."

"Of course, Fitz doesn't know we're married, so Walter had to be careful what he said. But he sent a message to say he was thinking of me on Christmas Day."

Ethel squeezed Maud's hand. "So he's all right!"

"He's been in the fighting in East Prussia, and now he's on the front line in France, but he hasn't been wounded."

"Thank heaven. But I don't suppose you'll hear from him again. Such luck doesn't repeat itself."

"No. My only hope is that for some reason he'll be sent to a neutral country, such as Sweden or the United States, where he can post a letter to me. Otherwise I'll have to wait until the war is over."

"And what about the earl?"

"Fitz is fine. He spent the first few weeks of the war living it up in Paris."

While I was looking for a job in a sweatshop, Ethel thought resentfully.

Maud went on: "Princess Bea had a baby boy."

"Fitz must be happy to have an heir."

"We're all pleased," Maud said, and Ethel remembered that she was an aristocrat as well as a rebel.

The meeting broke up. A cab was waiting for Maud, and they said good-bye. Bernie Leckwith got on the bus with Ethel. "She was better than I expected," he said. "Upper-class, of course, but quite sound. And friendly, especially to you. I suppose you get to know the family quite well when you're in service."

You don't know the half of it, Ethel thought.

Ethel lived on a quiet street of small terraced houses, old but well-built, mostly occupied by better-off workers, craftsmen and supervisors, and their families. Bernie walked her to her front door. He probably wanted to kiss her good night. She toyed with the idea of letting him, just because she was grateful there was one man in the world who still found her attractive. But common sense prevailed: she did not want to give him false hope. "Good night, comrade!" she said cheerfully, and she went inside.

There was no sound or light upstairs: Mildred and her children were already asleep. Ethel undressed and got into bed. She was weary, but her mind was active, and she could not fall asleep. After a while she got up and made tea.

She decided to write to her brother. She opened her writing pad and began.

My very dear young sister Libby,

In their childhood code, every third word counted, and familiar names were scrambled, so this meant simply *Dear Billy*.

She recalled that her method had been to write out the message she wanted to send, then fill in the spaces. She now wrote:

Sitting alone feeling proper miserable.

Then she turned it into code.

Where I'm sitting, if you're alone you're not feeling yourself either proper happy or miserable.

As a child she had loved this game, inventing an imaginary message to hide the real one. She and Billy had devised helpful tricks: crossed-out words counted, whereas underlined words did not.

She decided to write out the whole of her message, then go back and turn it into code.

The streets of London are not paved with gold, at least not in Aldgate.

She thought about writing a cheerful letter, making light of her troubles. Then she thought: To hell with that. I can tell my brother the truth.

I used to believe I was special, don't ask why. She thinks she's too good for Aberowen, they used to say, and they were right.

She had to blink back tears when she thought of those days: the crisp uniform, the hearty meals in the spotless servants' hall, and most of all the slim, beautiful body that had once been hers.

Now look at me. I work twelve hours a day in Mannie Litov's sweatshop. I have a headache every evening and a permanent pain in my back. I'm having a baby no one wants. No one wants me, either, except a boring librarian with glasses.

She sucked the end of her pencil for a long, thoughtful moment; then she wrote:

I might as well be dead.

{ II }

On the second Sunday of each month an Orthodox priest came from Cardiff on the train up the valley to Aberowen, carrying a suitcase full of carefully wrapped icons and candlesticks, to celebrate Divine Liturgy for the Russians.

Lev Peshkov hated priests, but he always attended the service—you had to, to get the free dinner afterward. The service took place in the reading room of the public library. It was a Carnegie library, built with a donation from the American philanthropist, according to a plaque in the lobby. Lev could read, but he did not really understand people who thought of it as a pleasure. The newspapers here were fixed to hefty wooden holders, so that they could not be stolen, and there were signs that read "Silence." How much fun could you have in such a place?

Lev disliked most things about Aberowen.

Horses were the same everywhere, but he hated working underground: it was always half dark, and the thick coal dust made him cough. Aboveground it rained all the time. He had never seen so much rain. It did not come in thunderstorms, or sudden cloudbursts, to be followed by the relief of clear skies and dry weather. Rather, it was a soft drizzle that drifted down all day, sometimes all week, creeping up the legs of his trousers and down the back of his shirt.

The strike had petered out in August, after the outbreak of war, and the miners had drifted back to work. Most had been rehired and given back their old houses. The exceptions were those the management branded troublemakers, most of whom had gone off to join the Welsh Rifles. The evicted widows had found places to live. The strikebreakers were no longer ostracized: the locals had come around to the view that the foreigners, too, had been manipulated by the capitalist system.

But it was not for this that Lev had escaped from St. Petersburg. Britain was better than Russia, of course: trade unions were allowed, the police were not completely out of control, and even Jews were free. All the same, he was not going to settle for a life of backbreaking work in a mining town on the edge of nowhere. This was not what he and Grigori had dreamed of. This was not America.

Even if he had been tempted to stay there, he owed it to Grigori to go on. He knew he had treated his brother badly, but he had sworn to send him the money for his own ticket. Lev had broken a lot of promises in his short life, but he intended to keep this one.

He had most of the price of a ticket from Cardiff to New York. The money was hidden under a flagstone in the kitchen of his house in Wellington Row, along with his gun and his brother's passport. He had not saved this out of his weekly wage, of course: that was barely enough to keep him in beer and tobacco. His savings came from the weekly card game.

Spirya was no longer his collaborator. The young man had left Aberowen after a few days and returned to Cardiff to seek easier work. But it was never difficult to find a greedy man, and Lev had befriended a colliery deputy called Rhys Price. Lev made sure Rhys won steadily, and afterward they shared the proceeds. It was important not to overdo things: other people had to win sometimes. If the miners worked out what was going on, not only would it be the end of the card school, but they would probably kill Lev. So the money accumulated slowly, and Lev could not afford to turn down a free meal.

The priest was always met at the station by the earl's car. He was driven to Tŷ Gwyn, where he was given sherry and cake. If Princess Bea was in residence, she accompanied him to the library and entered the room a few seconds before him, which saved her having to wait too long with the common people.

Today it was a few minutes after eleven by the large clock on the reading room wall when she entered, wearing a white fur coat and hat against the February cold. Lev repressed a shudder: he could not look at her without feeling again the sheer terror of a six-year-old seeing his father hanged.

The priest followed in a cream-colored robe with a gold sash. Today, for the first time, he was accompanied by another man in the garb of a novice priest—and Lev was shocked and horrified to recognize his former partner in crime Spirya.

Lev's mind was in turmoil as the two clergymen prepared the five loaves and watered the red wine for the service. Had Spirya found God and changed his ways? Or was the clerical outfit just another cover for stealing and cheating?

The older priest sang the blessing. A few of the more devout men had formed a choir—a development their Welsh neighbors approved of heartily—and now they sang the first *amen*. Lev crossed himself when the others did, but his mind was anxiously on Spirya. It would be just like a priest to blurt out the truth and ruin everything: no more card games, no ticket to America, no money for Grigori.

Lev recalled the last day on the *Angel Gabriel*, when he had brutally threatened to throw Spirya overboard for merely talking about double-crossing him. Spirya might well remember that now. Lev wished he had not humiliated the man.

Lev studied Spirya throughout the service, trying to read his face. When he went up to the front to receive communion, he tried to catch his old friend's eye, but he saw no sign even of recognition: Spirya was totally caught up in the rite, or pretending to be.

Afterward the two clergy left in the car with the princess, and the thirty or so Russian Christians followed on foot. Lev wondered if Spirya would speak to him at Tŷ Gwyn, and fretted about what he might say. Would he pretend their scam had never happened? Would he spill the beans and bring the wrath of the miners down on Lev's head? Would he demand a price for his silence?

Lev was tempted to leave town immediately. There were trains to Cardiff every hour or two. If he had had more money he might have cut and run. But he did not have enough for the ticket, so he trudged up the hill out of town to the earl's palace for the midday dinner.

They were fed in the staff quarters below stairs. The food was hearty: mutton stew with as much bread as you could eat, and ale to wash it down. The princess's middle-aged Russian maid, Nina, joined them and acted as interpreter. She had a soft spot for Lev, and made sure he got extra ale.

The priest ate with the princess but Spirya came to the servants' hall and sat next to Lev. Lev turned on his most welcoming smile. "Well, old friend, this is a surprise!" he said in Russian. "Congratulations!"

Spirya refused to be charmed. "Are you still playing cards, my son?" he replied.

Lev kept the smile but lowered his voice. "I'll shut up about that if you will. Is that fair?"

"We'll talk after dinner."

Lev was frustrated. Which way was Spirya going to jump— righteousness or blackmail?

When the meal was over, Spirya went out through the back door, and Lev followed. Without speaking, Spirya led him to a white rotunda like a miniature Greek temple. From its raised platform they could see anyone approaching. It was raining, and the water dripped down the marble pillars. Lev shook the rain off his cap and put it back on his head.

Spirya said: "Do you recall my asking you, on the ship, what you would do if I refused to give you your half of the money?"

Lev had pushed Spirya half over the rail and threatened to break his neck and throw his body in the sea. "No, I don't remember," he lied.

"It doesn't matter," Spirya said. "I simply wished to forgive you."

Righteousness, then, Lev thought with relief.

"What we did was sinful," Spirya said. "I have confessed and received absolution."

"I won't ask your priest to play cards with me, then."

"Don't joke."

Lev wanted to grab Spirya by the throat, as he had on the ship, but Spirya no longer looked as if he could be bullied. The robe had given him balls, ironically.

Spirya went on: "I ought to reveal your crime to those you robbed."

"They won't thank you. They may take revenge on you as well as me."

"My priestly garments will protect me."

Lev shook his head. "Most of the people you and I robbed were poor Jews. They probably remember priests looking on with a smile while the Cossacks beat them up. They might kick you to death all the more eagerly in your robe."

The shadow of anger passed over Spirya's young face, but he forced a benign smile. "I'm more concerned about you, my son. I would not like to provoke violence against you."

Lev knew when he was being threatened. "What are you going to do?"

"The question is what you're going to do."

"Will you keep your mouth shut if I stop?"

"If you confess, make a sincere contrition, and cease your sin, God will forgive you—and then it will not be for me to punish you."

And you'll get away with it, too, Lev thought. "All right, I'll do it," he said. As soon as he had spoken, he realized he had given in too quickly.

Spirya's next words confirmed that he was not so easily fooled. "I will check," he said. "And if I find you have broken your promise to me and to God, I will reveal your crime to your victims."

"And they will kill me. Good work, Father."

"As far as I can see, it's the best way out of a moral dilemma. And my priest agrees. So take it or leave it."

"I have no choice."

"God bless you, my son," said Spirya.

Lev walked away.

He left the grounds of Tŷ Gwyn and headed through the rain back into Aberowen, fuming. How like a priest, he thought resentfully, to take away a man's chance of bettering himself. Spirya was comfortable now, food and clothing and accommodation all provided, forever, by the church and the hungry worshippers who gave money they could not afford. For the rest of his life, Spirya would have nothing to do but sing the services and fiddle with the altar boys.

What was Lev to do? If he gave up the card games, it would take him forever to save enough for his passage. He would be doomed to spend years tending pit ponies half a mile underground. And he would never redeem himself by sending Grigori the price of a ticket to America.

He had never chosen the safe path.

He made his way to the Two Crowns pub. In Sabbath-observing Wales, pubs were not allowed to open on Sundays, but the rules were lightly regarded in Aberowen. There was only one policeman in the town and, like most people, he took Sundays off. The Two Crowns closed its front door, for the sake of appearances, but regulars went in through the kitchen, and business was done as usual.

At the bar were the Ponti brothers, Joey and Johnny. They were drinking whisky, unusually. The miners drank beer. Whisky was a rich man's potion, and a bottle probably lasted the Two Crowns from one Christmas to the next.

Lev ordered a pot of beer and addressed the elder brother. "Aye, aye, Joey."

"Aye, aye, Grigori." Lev was still using his brother's name, which was on the passport.

"Feeling flush today, Joey, is it?"

"Aye. Me and the kid went to Cardiff yesterday for the boxing."

The brothers looked like boxers themselves, Lev thought: two broad-shouldered, bull-necked men with big hands. "Good, was it?" he said.

"Darkie Jenkins versus Roman Tony. We bet on Tony, being Italian like us. Odds of thirteen to one, and he knocked Jenkins out in three rounds."

Lev sometimes struggled with formal English, but he knew the meaning of "thirteen to one." He said: "You should come and play cards. You are . . ." He hesitated, then remembered the phrase. "You are making a lucky streak."

"Oh, I don't want to lose it as quick as I won it," Joey said.

However, when the card school assembled in the barn half an hour later, Joey and Johnny were there. The rest of the players were a mixture of Russian and Welsh.

They played a local version of poker called three-card brag. Lev liked it. After the initial three, no further cards were dealt or exchanged, so the game went fast. If a player raised the bet, the next man in the circle had to match the raise immediately—he could not stay in the game by betting the original stake—so the pot grew quickly. Betting continued until there were only two players left, at which point one of them could end the round by doubling the previous bet, which forced his opponent to show his cards. The best hand was three of a kind, known as a prial, and the highest of all was a prial of treys, three threes.

Lev had a natural instinct for odds and would usually have won at cards without cheating, but that was too slow.

The deal moved to the left every hand, so Lev could fix the cards only once in a while. However, there were a thousand ways to cheat, and Lev had devised a simple code that enabled Rhys to indicate when he had a good hand. Lev would then stay in the betting, regardless of what he was holding, to force the stakes up and enlarge the pot. Most of the time everyone else would drop out, and Lev would then lose to Rhys.

As the first hand was dealt, Lev decided this would be his last game. If he cleaned out the Ponti brothers he would probably be able to buy his ticket. Next Sunday Spirya would make inquiries to find out whether Lev was still running a card school. By then Lev wanted to be at sea.

Over the next two hours Lev watched Rhys's winnings grow and told himself America was coming nearer with each penny. He did not usually like to clean anyone out, because he wanted them to come back next week. But today was the day to go for the jackpot.

As the afternoon began to darken outside he got the deal. He gave Joey Ponti three aces and Rhys three threes. In this game, threes beat aces. He gave himself a pair of kings, which justified him in betting high. He stayed in the betting until Joey was almost broke—he did not want to collect any IOUs. Joey used the last of his money to see Rhys's hand. The expression on Joey's face when Rhys showed a prial of treys was both comical and pitiful.

Rhys raked the money in. Lev stood up and said: "I'm cleaned out." The game broke up and they all returned to the bar, where Rhys bought a round of drinks to soothe the feelings of the losers. The Ponti brothers reverted to drinking beer, and Joey said: "Ah, well, easy come, easy go, isn't it?"

A few minutes later, Lev went back outside and Rhys followed. There was no toilet at the Two Crowns, so the men used the lane at the back of the barn. The only illumination came from a distant streetlight. Rhys quickly handed Lev his half of the winnings, partly in coins and partly in the new colored banknotes, green for a pound and brown for ten shillings.

Lev knew exactly what he was owed. Arithmetic came naturally to him, like figuring the odds at cards. He would count the money later, but he was sure Rhys would not cheat him. The man had tried, once. Lev had found his share to be five shillings short—an amount that a careless man might have overlooked. Lev had gone to Rhys's house, stuck the barrel of his revolver into the man's mouth, and cocked the hammer. Rhys had soiled himself in fear. After that the money had always been correct to a halfpenny.

Lev stuffed the money into his coat pocket and they returned to the bar.

As they walked in, Lev saw Spirya.

He had taken off his robes and put on the overcoat he had worn on the ship. He stood at the bar, not drinking, but talking earnestly to a small group of Russians, including some of the card school.

Momentarily, he met Lev's eye.

Lev turned on his heel and went out, but he knew he was too late.

He walked quickly away, heading up the hill to Wellington Row. Spirya would betray him, he felt sure. Even now he might be explaining how Lev managed to cheat at cards and yet seem the loser. The men would be furious, and the Ponti brothers would want their money back.

As he approached his house, he saw a man coming the other way with a suitcase, and in the lamplight he recognized a young neighbor known as Billy-with-Jesus. "Aye, aye, Billy," he said.

"Aye, aye, Grigori."

The boy looked as if he was leaving town, and Lev was curious. "Off somewhere?"

"London."

Lev's interest quickened. "What train?"

"Six o'clock to Cardiff." Passengers for London had to change trains at Cardiff.

"What is it now?"

"Twenty to."

"So long, then." Lev went into his house. He would catch the same train as Billy, he decided.

He turned on the electric light in the kitchen and lifted the flagstone. He took out his savings, the passport with his brother's name and photograph, a box of brass bullets, and his gun, a Nagant M1895 he had won from an army captain in a card game. He checked the cylinder to make sure there was a live round in each chamber: used rounds were not automatically ejected, but had to be removed manually when reloading. He put the money, the passport, and the gun in the pockets of his coat.

Upstairs he found Grigori's cardboard suitcase with the bullet hole. Into it he packed the ammunition plus his other shirt, his spare underwear, and two packs of cards.

He had no watch, but he calculated that five minutes had passed since he saw Billy. That gave him fifteen minutes to walk to the station, which was enough.

From the street outside he heard the voices of several men.

He did not want a confrontation. He was tough, but the miners were, too. Even if he won the fight he would miss his train. He could use the gun, of course, but in this country the police were serious about catching murderers even when the victims were nobodies. At a minimum they would check passengers at the docks in Cardiff and make it difficult for him to buy a ticket. In every way it would be best if he could leave town without violence.

He went out of the back door and hurried along the lane, walking as quietly as he could in his heavy boots. The ground underfoot was muddy, as it almost always was in Wales, so fortunately his footsteps made little noise.

At the end of the lane he turned down an alley and emerged into the lights of the street. The toilets in the middle of the road shielded him from the view of anyone outside his house. He hurried away.

Two streets farther on he realized that his route took him past the Two Crowns. He stopped and thought for a moment. He knew the layout of the town, and the only alternative route would require him to double back. But the men whose voices he had heard might still be near his house.

He had to risk the Two Crowns. He turned down another alley and took the back lane that passed behind the pub.

As he approached the barn where they had played cards, he heard voices and glimpsed two or more men, dimly outlined by the streetlamp at the far end of the lane. He was running out of time, but all the same he stopped and waited for them to go back inside. He stood close to a high wooden fence to make himself less visible.

They seemed to take forever. "Come on," he whispered. "Don't you want to get back into the warm?" The rain dripped off his cap and down the back of his neck.

At last they went inside, and Lev emerged from the shadows and hurried forward. He passed the barn without incident, but as he drew away from it he heard more voices. He cursed. The customers had been drinking beer since midday, and by this time of the afternoon they needed frequent visits to the lane. He heard someone call after him: "Aye, aye, butty." Their word for friend was "butty" or "butt." Its use meant he had not been recognized.

He pretended not to hear, and walked on.

He could hear a murmured conversation. Most of the words were unintelligible, but he thought one man said: "Looks like a Russky." Russian clothes were different from British, and Lev guessed they might be able to make out the cut of his coat and the shape of his cap by the light of the streetlamp, which he was quickly approaching. However, the call of nature was usually urgent for men coming out of a pub, and he thought they would not follow him before they had relieved themselves.

He turned down the next alley and disappeared from their view. Unfortunately, he doubted whether he had gone from their minds. Spirya must by now have told his story, and someone would soon realize the significance of a man in Russian clothes walking toward the town center with a suitcase in his hand.

He had to be on that train.

He broke into a run.

The railway line lay in the cleft of the valley, so the way to the station was all downhill. Lev ran easily, taking long strides. He could see, over the rooftops, the lights of the station and, as he came closer, the smoke from the funnel of a train standing at the platform.

He ran across the square and into the booking hall. The hands of the big clock stood at one minute to six. He hurried to the ticket window and fished money from his pocket. "Ticket, please," he said.

"Where would you like to go this evening?" the clerk said pleasantly.

Lev pointed urgently to the platform. "That train by there!"

"This train calls at Aberdare, Pontypridd—"

"Cardiff!" Lev glanced up and saw the minute hand click through its last segment and stop, trembling slightly, at the o'clock position.

"Single, or return?" said the clerk unhurriedly.

"Single, quickly!"

Lev heard the whistle. Desperately, he looked through the coins in his hand. He knew the fare—he had been to Cardiff twice in the last six months—and he put money on the counter.

The train began to move.

The clerk gave him his ticket.

Lev grabbed it and turned away.

"Don't forget your change!" said the clerk.

Lev strode the few paces to the barrier. "Ticket, please," said the collector, even though he had just watched Lev buy it.

Looking past the barrier, Lev saw the train gathering speed.

The collector punched his ticket and said: "Don't you want your change?"

The door of the booking hall burst open and the Ponti brothers rushed in. "There you are!" Joey cried, and he rushed at Lev.

Lev surprised him by stepping toward him and punching him directly in the face. Joey was stopped in his tracks. Johnny crashed into his older brother's back, and both fell to their knees.

Lev snatched his ticket from the collector and ran onto the platform. The train was moving quite fast. He ran alongside it for a moment. Suddenly a door opened, and Lev saw the friendly face of Billy-with-Jesus.

Billy shouted: "Jump!"

Lev leaped for the train and got one foot on the step. Billy grabbed his arm. They teetered for a moment as Lev tried desperately to haul himself aboard. Then Billy gave a heave and pulled Lev inside.

He sank gratefully into a seat.

Billy pulled the door shut and sat opposite him.

"Thank you," Lev said.

"You cut it fine," Billy said.

"I made it, though," said Lev with a grin. "That's all that counts."

{ III }

At Paddington Station the next morning, Billy asked for directions to Aldgate. A friendly Londoner gave him a rapid stream of detailed instructions, every word of which he found completely incomprehensible. He thanked the man and walked out of the station.

He had never been to London but he knew that Paddington was in the west and poor people lived in the east, so he walked toward the midmorning sun. The city was even bigger than he had imagined, a great deal busier and more confusing than Cardiff, but he relished it: the noise, the rushing traffic, the crowds, and most of all the shops. He had not known there were so many shops in the world. How much was spent in London's shops every day? he wondered. It must be thousands of pounds—maybe millions.

He felt a sense of freedom that was quite heady. No one here knew him. In Aberowen, or even on his occasional trips to Cardiff, he was always liable to be observed by friends or relations. In London he might walk along a street holding hands with a pretty girl and his parents would never find out. He had no intention of doing so, but the thought that he could—and the fact that there were so many pretty well-dressed girls walking around—was intoxicating.

After a while he saw a bus with "Aldgate" written on its front, and he jumped aboard. Ethel's letter had mentioned Aldgate.

When he decoded her letter he had been very worried. Of course he could not discuss it with his parents. He had waited until they left for the evening service at the Bethesda Chapel—which he no longer attended—then he had written a note.

> Dear Mam,
>   I am worried about our Eth and have gone to find her.
> Sorry to sneak off but I don't want a row.
>   Your loving son,
>   Billy

As it was Sunday, he was already bathed and shaved and dressed in his best clothes. His suit was a shabby hand-me-down from his father, but he had a clean white shirt and a black knitted tie. He had dozed in the waiting room at Cardiff station and caught the milk train in the early hours of Monday morning.

The bus conductor alerted him when they reached Aldgate, and he got off. It was a poor neighborhood, with crumbling slum houses, street stalls selling secondhand clothes, and barefoot children playing in noisome stairwells. He did not know where Ethel lived—her letter had not given an address. His only clue was *I work twelve hours a day in Mannie Litov's sweatshop.*

He looked forward to giving Eth all the news from Aberowen. She would know from the newspapers that the widows' strike had failed. Billy seethed when he thought of it. The bosses were able to behave outrageously because they held all the cards. They owned the mines and the houses, and they acted as if they owned the people. Because of various complex franchise rules, most miners did not have the vote, so Aberowen's member of Parliament was a Conservative who invariably sided with the company. Tommy Griffiths's father said nothing would ever change without a revolution like the one they had had in France. Billy's da said they needed a Labour government. Billy did not know who was right.

He went up to a friendly-looking young man and said: "Do you know the way to Mannie Litov's place?"

The man replied in a language that sounded like Russian.

He tried again, and this time got an English speaker who had never heard of Mannie Litov. Aldgate was not like Aberowen, where everyone on the street would know the way to every place of business in town. Had he come this far—and spent all that money on his train ticket—for nothing?

He was not yet ready to give up. He scanned the busy street for British-looking people who seemed to be about some kind of business, carrying tools or pushing carts. He questioned five more people without success, then came across a window cleaner with a ladder.

"Mannie Litov's?" the man repeated. He managed to say "Litov" without pronouncing the letter *t*, instead making a noise in his throat like a small cough. "Clouvin fectry?"

"Pardon me," Billy said politely. "What was that again?"

"Clouvin fectry. Plice where vey mikes clouvin—jickits an trahsies an at."

"Um . . . probably, yes," Billy said, feeling desperate.

The window cleaner nodded. "Strite on, quote of a ma, do a rye, Ark Rav Rahd."

"Straight on?" Billy replied. "Quarter of a mile?"

"Ass it. Ven do a rye."

"Turn right?"

"Ark Rav Rahd."

"Ark Rav Road?"

"Carn miss it."

The street name turned out to be Oak Grove Road. It had no grove of anything, let alone oaks. It was a narrow, winding lane of dilapidated brick buildings busy with people, horses, and handcarts. Two more inquiries brought Billy to a house squashed between the Dog and Duck pub and a boarded-up shop called Lippmann's. The front door stood open. Billy climbed the stairs to the top floor, where he found himself in a room with about twenty women sewing British army uniforms.

They continued working, operating their treadles, taking no apparent notice of him, until eventually one said: "Come in, love. We won't eat you—although, come to think of it, I might try a little taste." They all cackled with laughter.

"I'm looking for Ethel Williams," he said.

"She's not here," the woman said.

"Why not?" he said anxiously. "Is she ill?"

"What business is it of yours?" The woman got up from her machine. "I'm Mildred—who are you?"

Billy stared at her. She was pretty even though she had buckteeth. She wore bright red lipstick, and fair curls poked out from under her hat. She was wrapped in a thick, shapeless gray coat but, despite that, he could see the sway of her hips as she walked toward him. He was too taken with her to speak.

She said: "You're not the bastard who put her up the duff then scarpered, are you?"

Billy found his voice. "I'm her brother."

"Oh!" she said. "Fucking hell, are you Billy?"

Billy's jaw dropped. He had never heard a woman use that word.

She scrutinized him with a fearless gaze. "You are her brother, I can see it, though you look older than sixteen." Her tone softened in a way that made him feel warm inside. "You've got the same dark eyes and curly hair."

"Where can I find her?" he said.

She gave him a challenging look. "I happen to know that she doesn't want her family to find out where she's living."

"She's scared of my father," Billy said. "But she wrote me a letter. I was worried about her, so I came up on the train."

"All the way from that dump in Wales where she's from?"

"It's not a dump," Billy said indignantly. Then he shrugged and said: "Well, it is, really, I suppose."

"I love your accent," Mildred said. "To me it's like hearing someone sing."

"Do you know where she lives?"

"How did you find this place?"

"She said she worked at Mannie Litov's in Aldgate."

"Well, you're Sherlock bloody Holmes, aren't you?" she said, not without a note of reluctant admiration.

"If you don't tell me where she is, someone else will," he said with more confidence than he felt. "I'm not going home till I've seen her."

"She'll kill me, but all right," Mildred said. "Twenty-three Nutley Street."

Billy asked her for directions. He made her speak slowly.

"Don't thank me," she said as he took his leave. "Just protect me if Ethel tries to kill me."

"All right, then," said Billy, thinking how thrilling it would be to protect Mildred from something.

The other women shouted good-bye and blew kisses as he left, embarrassing him.

Nutley Street was an oasis of quiet. The terraced houses were built to a pattern that had become familiar to Billy after only one day in London. They were much larger than miners' cottages, with small front yards instead of a door opening onto the street. The effect of order and regularity was created by identical sash windows, each with twelve panes of glass, in rows all along the terrace.

He knocked at number 23 but no one answered.

He was worried. Why had she not gone to work? Was she ill? If not, why was she not at home?

He peered through the letterbox and saw a hallway with polished floorboards and a hat stand bearing an old brown coat that he recognized. It was a cold day: Ethel would not go out without her coat.

He stepped close to the window and tried to look inside, but he could not see through the net curtain.

He returned to the door and looked through the flap again. The scene inside was unchanged, but this time he heard a noise. It was a long, agonized groan. He put his mouth to the letterbox and shouted: "Eth! Is that you? It's Billy out here."

There was a long silence; then the groan was repeated.

"Bloody hell," he said.

The door had a Yale-type lock. That meant the catch was probably attached to the doorpost with two screws. He struck the door with the heel of his hand. It did not seem particularly stout, and he guessed the wood was cheap pine, many years old. He leaned back, lifted his right leg, and kicked the door with the heel of his heavy miner's boot. There was a sound of splintering. He kicked several more times, but the door did not open.

He wished he had a hammer.

He looked up and down the road, hoping to see a workman with tools, but the street was deserted except for two dirty-faced boys who were watching him with interest.

He walked down the short garden path to the gate, turned, and ran at the door, hitting it with his right shoulder. It burst open and he fell inside.

He picked himself up, rubbing his hurt shoulder, and pushed the ruined door to. The house seemed silent. "Eth?" he called. "Where are you?"

The groaning came again, and he followed the sound into the front room on the ground floor. It was a woman's bedroom, with china ornaments on the mantelpiece and flowered curtains at the window. Ethel was on the bed, wearing a gray dress that covered her like a tent. She was not lying down, but on her hands and knees, groaning.

"What's wrong with you, Eth?" said Billy, and his voice came out as a terrified squeak.

She caught her breath. "The baby's coming."

"Oh, hell. I'd better fetch a doctor."

"Too late, Billy. Dear Jesus, it hurts."

"You sound like you're dying!"

"No, Billy, this is what childbirth is like. Come by here and hold my hand."

Billy knelt by the bed, and Ethel took his hand. She tightened her grip and began to groan again. The groan was longer and more agonized than before, and she gripped his hand so hard he thought she might break a bone. Her groan ended with a shriek; then she panted as if she had run a mile.

After a minute she said: "I'm sorry, Billy, but you're going to have to look up my skirt."

"Oh!" he said. "Oh, right." He did not really understand, but he thought he had better do as he was told. He lifted the hem of Ethel's dress. "Oh, Christ!" he said. The bedsheet beneath her was soaked in blood. There in the middle of it was a tiny pink thing covered in slime. He made out a big round head with closed eyes, two tiny arms, and two legs. "It's a baby!" he said.

"Pick it up, Billy," said Ethel.

"What, me?" he said. "Oh, right, then." He leaned over the bed. He got one hand under the baby's head and one under its little bum. It was a boy, he saw. The baby was slippery and slimy, but Billy managed to pick him up. There was a cord still attaching him to Ethel.

"Have you got it?" she said.

"Aye," he said. "I've got him. It's a boy."

"Is he breathing?"

"I dunno. How can you tell?" Billy fought down panic. "No, he's not breathing, I don't think."

"Smack his bum, not too hard."

Billy turned the baby over, held him easily in one hand, and sharply smacked his bottom. Immediately the child opened his mouth, breathed in, and yelled in protest. Billy was delighted. "Hark at that!" he said.

"Hold him a minute while I turn over." Ethel got herself into a sitting position and straightened her dress. "Give him to me."

Billy carefully handed him over. Ethel held the baby in the crook of her arm and wiped his face with her sleeve. "He's beautiful," she said.

Billy was not sure about that.

The cord attached to the baby's navel had been blue and taut, but now it shriveled and turned pale. Ethel said: "Open that drawer over by there and pass me the scissors and a reel of cotton."

Ethel tied two knots in the cord, then snipped it between the knots. "There," she said. She unbuttoned the front of her dress. "I don't suppose you'll be embarrassed, after what you've seen," she said, and she took out a breast and put the nipple to the baby's mouth. He began to suck.

She was right: Billy was not embarrassed. An hour ago he would have been mortified by the sight of his sister's bare breast, but such a feeling seemed trivial now. All he felt was enormous relief that the baby was all right. He stared, watching him suckle, marveling at the tiny fingers. He felt as if he had witnessed a miracle. His face was wet with tears, and he wondered when he had cried: he had no memory of doing so.

Quite soon the baby fell asleep. Ethel buttoned her dress. "We'll wash him in a minute," she said. Then she closed her eyes. "My God," she said. "I didn't know it was going to hurt that much."

Billy said: "Who's his father, Eth?"

"Earl Fitzherbert," she said. Then she opened her eyes. "Oh, bugger, I never meant to tell you that."

"The bloody swine," said Billy. "I'll kill him."

CHAPTER FIFTEEN

June to September 1915

s the ship entered New York harbor, it occurred to Lev Peshkov that America might not be as wonderful as his brother, Grigori, said. He steeled himself for a terrible disappointment. But that was unnecessary. America was all the things he had hoped for: rich, busy, exciting, and free.

Three months later, on a hot afternoon in June, he was working at a hotel in Buffalo, in the stables, grooming a guest's horse. The place was owned by Josef Vyalov, who had put an onion dome on top of the old Central Tavern and renamed it the St. Petersburg Hotel, perhaps out of nostalgia for the city he had left when he was a child.

Lev worked for Vyalov, as did many of Buffalo's Russian immigrants, but he had never met the man. If he ever did, he was not sure what he would say. The Vyalov family in Russia had cheated Lev by dumping him in Cardiff, and that rankled. On the other hand, the papers supplied by the St. Petersburg Vyalovs had got Lev through U.S. immigration without a hitch. And mentioning the name of Vyalov in a bar on Canal Street had got him a job immediately.

He had been speaking English every day for a year now, ever since he landed in Cardiff, and he was becoming fluent. Americans said he had a British accent, and they were not familiar with some of the expressions he had learned in Aberowen, such as *by here* and *by there*, or *is it?* and *isn't it?* at the ends of sentences. But he could say just about anything he needed to, and girls were charmed when he called them *my lovely.*

At a few minutes to six o'clock, shortly before he finished work for the day, his friend Nick came into the stable yard, a cigarette between his lips. "Fatima brand," he said. He drew in smoke with exaggerated satisfaction. "Turkish tobacco. Beautiful."

Nick's full name was Nicolai Davidovich Fomek, but here he was called Nick Forman. He occasionally played the role previously taken by Spirya and Rhys Price in Lev's card games, though mostly he was a thief.

"How much?" said Lev.

"In the stores, fifty cents for a tin of a hundred cigarettes. To you, ten cents. Sell them for a quarter."

Lev knew that Fatima was a popular brand. It would be easy to sell them at half price. He looked around the yard. The boss was nowhere to be seen. "All right."

"How many do you want? I've got a trunkful."

Lev had one dollar in his pocket. "Twenty tins," he said. "I'll give you a dollar now and a dollar later."

"I don't give credit."

Lev grinned and put his hand on Nick's shoulder. "Come on, buddy, you can trust me. Are we pals, or not?"

"Twenty it is. I'll be right back."

Lev found an old feed sack in a corner. Nick returned with twenty long green tins, each with a picture of a veiled woman on the lid. Lev put the tins in the sack and gave Nick a dollar. "Always nice to give a helping hand to a fellow Russian," Nick said, and he sauntered away.

Lev cleaned his curry comb and hoofpick. At five past six he said good-bye to the chief ostler and headed for the First Ward. He felt a little conspicuous, carrying a feed sack through the streets, and he wondered what he would say if a cop stopped him and demanded to see what was in the sack. But he was not very worried: he could talk his way out of most situations.

He went to a large, popular bar called the Irish Rover. He pushed through the crowd, bought a tankard of beer, and downed half of it thirstily. Then he sat next to a group of workingmen speaking a mixture of Polish and English. After a few moments he said: "Anyone here smoke Fatimas?"

A bald man in a leather apron said: "Yeah, I'll smoke a Fatima now and again."

"Want to buy a tin at half price? Twenty-five cents for a hundred smokes."

"What's wrong with them?"

"They got lost. Someone found them."

"Sounds a little risky."

"I tell you what. Put your money on the table. I won't pick it up until you tell me to."

The men were interested now. The bald man fished in his pocket and came up with a quarter. Lev took a tin from his sack and handed it over. The man opened the tin. He took out a small rectangle of folded paper and opened it to disclose a photograph. "Hey, it's even got a baseball card!" he said. He put one of the cigarettes in his mouth and lit it. "All right," he said to Lev. "Pick up your quarter."

Another man was watching over Lev's shoulder. "How much?" he said. Lev told him, and he bought two tins.

In the next half hour Lev sold all the cigarettes. He was pleased: he had turned two dollars into five in less than an hour. At work it took him a day and a half to earn three dollars. Maybe he would buy some more stolen tins from Nick tomorrow.

He bought another beer, drank it, and went out, leaving the empty sack on the floor. Outside, he turned toward the Lovejoy district, a poor neighborhood of Buffalo where most of the Russians lived, along with many Italians and Poles. He could buy a steak on the way home and fry it with potatoes. Or he could pick up Marga and take her dancing. Or he could buy a new suit.

He ought to save it toward Grigori's fare to America, he thought, guiltily knowing he would do no such thing. Three dollars was a drop in the bucket. What he needed was a really big score. Then he could send Grigori the money all in one go, before he was tempted to spend it.

He was startled out of his reverie by a tap on his shoulder.

His heart gave a guilty leap. He turned, half expecting to see a police uniform. But the person who had stopped him was no cop. He was a heavily built man in overalls, with a broken nose and an aggressive scowl. Lev tensed: such a man had only one function.

The man said: "Who told you to sell smokes in the Irish Rover?"

"I'm just trying to make a few bucks," Lev said with a smile. "I hope I didn't offend anyone."

"Was it Nicky Forman? I heard Nick knocked over a truckload of cigarettes."

Lev was not going to give that information to a stranger. "I never met anyone by that name," he said, still using a pleasant tone of voice.

"Don't you know the Irish Rover belongs to Mister V?"

Lev felt a surge of anger. Mister V had to be Josef Vyalov. He dropped the conciliatory tone. "So put up a sign."

"You don't sell stuff in Mister V's bars 'less he tells you."

Lev shrugged. "I didn't know that."

"Here's something to help you remember," the man said, and he swung his fist.

Lev was expecting the blow, and he stepped back sharply. The thug's arm swept through empty space and he staggered, off balance. Lev stepped forward and kicked him in the shin. A fist was a poor weapon, generally, nowhere near as hard as a booted foot. Lev kicked as powerfully as he could, but it was not enough to break a bone. The man roared with anger, swung again, and missed again.

There was no point hitting such a man in the face—he had probably lost all feeling there. Lev kicked him in the groin. Both his hands went to his crotch and he gasped for breath, bending forward. Lev kicked him in the stomach. The man opened and closed his mouth like a goldfish, unable to breathe. Lev stepped to one side and kicked the man's legs from under him. He went down on his back. Lev aimed carefully and kicked his knee, so that when he got up he would not be able to move fast.

Panting with exertion, he said: "Tell Mister V he should be more polite."

He walked away, breathing hard. Behind him he heard someone say: "Hey, Ilya, what the fuck happened?"

Two streets away his breathing eased and his heartbeat slowed. To hell with Josef Vyalov, he thought. The bastard cheated me and I won't be bullied.

Vyalov would not know who had beaten up Ilya. No one in the Irish Rover knew Lev. Vyalov might get mad but there was nothing he could do about it.

Lev started to feel elated. I put Ilya on the ground, he thought, and there's not a mark on me!

He still had a pocket full of money. He stopped to buy two steaks and a bottle of gin.

He lived on a street of dilapidated brick houses subdivided into small apartments. Outside the house next door Marga was sitting on the stoop filing her nails. She was a pretty black-haired Russian girl of about nineteen with a sexy grin. She worked as a waitress but hoped for a career as a singer. He had bought her drinks a couple of times and kissed her once. She had kissed him back enthusiastically. "Hi, kid!" he shouted.

"Who are you calling a kid?"

"What are you doing tonight?"

"I've got a date," she said.

Lev did not necessarily believe her. She would never admit that she had nothing to do. "Throw him over," he said. "He has bad breath."

She grinned. "You don't even know who it is!"

"Come and see me." He hefted his paper bag. "I'm cooking steak."

"I'll think about it."

"Bring ice." He went into his building.

His apartment was a low-rent place, by American standards, but it seemed spacious and luxurious to Lev. It had a bed-sitting-room and a kitchen, with running water and electric light—and he had it all to himself! In St. Petersburg such an apartment would have housed ten or more people.

He took off his jacket, rolled up his sleeves, and washed his hands and face at the kitchen sink. He hoped Marga would come. She was his kind of girl, always ready to laugh or dance or have a party, never worrying too much about the future. He peeled and sliced some potatoes, then put a frying pan on the hot plate and dropped in a lump of lard. While the potatoes were frying, Marga came in with a tankard of chipped ice. She made drinks with gin and sugar.

Lev sipped his drink, then kissed her lightly on the lips. "Tastes good!" he said.

"You're fresh," she said, but it was not a serious protest. He began to wonder if he might get her into bed later.

He started to fry the steaks. "I'm impressed," she said. "Not many guys can cook."

"My father died when I was six, and my mother when I was eleven," Lev said. "I was raised by my brother, Grigori. We learned to do everything for ourselves. Not that we ever had steak, in Russia."

She asked him about Grigori, and he told her his life story over dinner. Most girls were touched by the tale of two motherless boys struggling to get by, working in a huge locomotive factory and renting space in a bed. He guiltily omitted the part of the story where he abandoned his pregnant girlfriend.

They had their second drink in the bed-sitting-room. By the time they started on the third it was getting dark outside and she was sitting on his lap. Between sips, Lev kissed her. When she opened her mouth to his tongue, he put his hand on her breast.

At that moment the door burst open.

Marga screamed.

Three men walked in. Marga jumped off Lev's lap, still screaming.

One of the men hit her backhanded across the mouth and said: "Shut the fuck up, bitch." She ran for the door, both hands to her bleeding lips. They let her go.

Lev sprang to his feet and lashed out at the man who had hit Marga. He got in one good punch, striking the man over the eye. Then the other two grabbed his arms. They were strong men, and he could not break free. While they held him the first man, who seemed to be their leader, punched him in the mouth, then in the stomach, several times. He spat blood and vomited his steak.

When he was weakened and in agony, they frog-marched him down the stairs and out of the building. A blue Hudson stood at the curb with its engine running. They threw him onto the floor in the back. Two of them sat with their feet on him and the other got in the front and drove.

He was in too much pain to think about where they were going. He assumed these men worked for Vyalov, but how had they found him? And what were they going to do with him? He tried not to give in to fear.

After a few minutes the car stopped and he was hauled out. They were outside a warehouse. The street was deserted and dark. He could smell the lake, so he knew they were near the waterfront. It was a good place to murder someone, he thought with grim fatalism. There would be no witnesses, and the body could go into Lake Erie, tied inside a sack, with a few bricks to make sure it sank to the bottom.

They dragged him into the building. He tried to pull himself together. This was the worst scrape he had ever been in. He was not sure he could talk his way out of it. Why do I do these things? he asked himself.

The warehouse was full of new tires piled fifteen or twenty high. They took him through the stacks to the back and stopped outside a door that was guarded by yet another heavyset man who held up an arm to stop them.

No words were spoken.

After a minute, Lev said: "Seems we have a few minutes to wait. Anybody got a pack of cards?"

No one even smiled.

Eventually the door opened and Nick Forman came out. His upper lip was swollen and one eye was closed. When he saw Lev he said: "I had to do it. They would have killed me."

So, Lev thought, they found me through Nick.

A thin man in spectacles came to the door of the office. Surely this could not be Vyalov, Lev thought; he was too weedy. "Bring him in, Theo," he said.

"Sure thing, Mr. Niall," said the leader of the thugs.

The office reminded Lev of the peasant hut in which he had been born. It was too warm and the air was full of smoke. In a corner was a little table with icons of saints.

Behind a steel desk sat a middle-aged man with unusually broad shoulders. He wore an expensive-looking lounge suit with a collar and tie, and there were two rings on the hand that held his cigarette. He said: "What is that fucking smell?"

"I'm sorry, Mister V—it's puke," said Theo. "He acted up, and we had to calm him down a little. Then he lunged up his lunch."

"Let him go."

They released Lev's arms, but stayed near.

Mister V looked at him. "I got your message," he said. "Telling me I should be more polite."

Lev summoned his courage. He was not going to die sniveling. He said: "Are you Josef Vyalov?"

"By Christ, you've got some nerve," the man said. "Asking me who I am."

"I been looking for you."

"*You* have been looking for *me*?"

"The Vyalov family sold me a ticket from St. Petersburg to New York, then dumped me in Cardiff," Lev said.

"So?"

"I want my money back."

Vyalov stared at him for a long moment; then he laughed. "I can't help it," he said. "I like you."

Lev held his breath. Did this mean Vyalov was not going to kill him?

"Do you have a job?" Vyalov said.

"I work for you."

"Where?"

"At the Hotel St. Petersburg, in the stables."

Vyalov nodded. "I think we can offer you something better than that," he said.

{ II }

In June 1915 America came one step closer to war.

Gus Dewar was appalled. He did not think the United States should join in the European war. The American people felt the same, and so did President Woodrow Wilson. But somehow the danger loomed closer.

The crisis came about in May when a German submarine torpedoed the *Lusitania,* a British ship carrying 173 tons of rifles, ammunition, and shrapnel shells. It also carried two thousand passengers, including 159 U.S. citizens.

Americans were as shocked as if there had been an assassination. The newspapers went into convulsions of indignation. "People are asking you to do the impossible!" Gus said indignantly to the president, standing in the Oval Office. "They want you to get tough with the Germans, but not to risk going to war."

Wilson nodded agreement. Looking up from his typewriter, he said: "There's no rule that says public opinion has to be consistent."

Gus found his boss's calm admirable, but a bit frustrating. "How the heck do you deal with that?"

Wilson smiled, showing his bad teeth. "Gus, did someone tell you politics was easy?"

In the end Wilson sent a stern note to the German government, demanding that they stop attacking shipping. He and his advisers, including Gus, hoped the Germans would agree to some compromise. But if they decided to be defiant, Gus did not see how Wilson could avoid escalation. It was a dangerous game to play, and Gus found he was not able to remain as coolly detached about the risk as Wilson appeared to be.

While the diplomatic telegrams crossed the Atlantic, Wilson went to his summer place in New Hampshire and Gus went to Buffalo, where he stayed at his parents' mansion on Delaware Avenue. His father had a house in Washington, but Gus lived in his own apartment there, and when he came home to Buffalo he relished the comforts of a house run by his mother: the silver bowl of cut roses on his nightstand; the hot rolls at breakfast; the crisp white linen tablecloth fresh at every meal; the way a suit would appear sponged and pressed in his wardrobe without his having noticed that it had been taken away.

The house was furnished in a consciously plain manner, his mother's reaction against the ornate fashions of her parents' generation. Much of the furniture was Biedermeier, a utilitarian German style that was enjoying a revival. The dining room had one good painting on each of the four walls, and a single three-branched candlestick on the table. At lunch on the first day, his mother said: "I suppose you're planning to go to the slums and watch prizefights?"

"There's nothing wrong with boxing," Gus said. It was his great enthusiasm. He had even tried it himself, as a foolhardy eighteen-year-old: his long arms had given him a couple of victories, but he lacked the killer instinct.

"So canaille," she said disdainfully. This was a snobby expression she had picked up in Europe that meant low-class.

"I'd like to take my mind off international politics, if I can."

"There's a lecture on Titian, with magic-lantern slides, at the Albright this afternoon," she said. The Albright Art Gallery, a white classical building set in Delaware Park, was one of Buffalo's most important cultural institutions.

Gus had grown up surrounded by Renaissance paintings, and he particularly liked Titian's portraits, but he was not very interested in going to a lecture. However, it was just the kind of event to be patronized by the city's wealthy young men and women, so there was a good chance he would be able to renew old friendships.

The Albright was a short drive up Delaware Avenue. He entered the pillared atrium and took a seat. As he had expected, there were several people he knew in the audience. He found himself sitting next to a strikingly pretty girl who seemed familiar.

He smiled vaguely at her, and she said brightly: "You've forgotten who I am, haven't you, Mr. Dewar?"

He felt foolish. "Ah . . . I've been out of town for a while."

"I'm Olga Vyalov." She held out a white-gloved hand.

"Of course," he said. Her father was a Russian immigrant whose first job had been throwing drunks out of a bar on Canal Street. Now he owned Canal Street. He was a city councilor and a pillar of the Russian Orthodox Church. Gus had met Olga several times, though he did not remember her looking quite so enchanting: perhaps she had suddenly grown up, or something. She was about twenty, he guessed, with pale skin and blue eyes, and she wore a pink jacket with a turned-up collar and a cloche hat with pink silk flowers.

"I hear you're working for the president," she said. "What do you think of Mr. Wilson?"

"I admire him enormously," Gus replied. "He's a practical politician who hasn't abandoned his ideals."

"How exciting to be at the center of power."

"It is exciting, but strangely enough it doesn't feel like the center of power. In a democracy the president is subject to the voters."

"But surely he doesn't just do what the public wants."

"Not exactly, no. President Wilson says a leader must treat public opinion the way a sailor deals with the wind, using it to blow the ship in one direction or another, but never trying to go directly against it."

She sighed. "I would have loved to study these things, but my father wouldn't let me go to college."

Gus grinned. "I suppose he thinks you would learn to smoke cigarettes and drink gin."

"And worse, I've no doubt," she said. It was a risqué remark for an unmarried woman, and the surprise must have shown on his face, for she said: "I'm sorry. I've shocked you."

"Not at all." In fact he was feeling captivated. To keep her talking he said: "What would you study if you could go to college?"

"History, I think."

"I love history. Any particular period?"

"I'd like to understand my own past. Why did my father have to leave Russia? Why is America so much better? There must be reasons for these things."

"Exactly!" Gus was thrilled that such a pretty girl should also share his intellectual curiosity. He saw a sudden vision of them as a married couple, in her dressing room after a party, talking about world affairs while they got ready for bed, himself in pajamas, sitting and watching while she unhurriedly took off her jewelry and slipped out of her clothes . . . Then he caught her eye, and got the feeling that she had guessed what he was thinking, and he felt embarrassed. He searched for something to say, but found himself tongue-tied.

Then the lecturer arrived, and the audience fell silent.

He enjoyed the talk more than he had expected. The speaker had made Autochrome color transparencies of some of Titian's canvases, and his magic lantern projected them onto a big white screen.

When it was over he wanted to talk some more to Olga, but he was prevented. Chuck Dixon, a man he knew from school, came up to them. Chuck had an easy charm that Gus envied. They were the same age, twenty-five, but Chuck made Gus feel like an awkward schoolboy. "Olga, you have to meet my cousin," he said jovially. "He's been staring at you across the room." He smiled amiably at Gus. "Sorry to deprive you of such bewitching company, Dewar, but you can't have her all afternoon, you know." He put a possessive arm around Olga's waist and led her away.

Gus felt bereft. He had been getting on so well with her, he felt. For him those first conversations with a girl were usually the hardest, but with Olga small talk had seemed easy. And now Chuck Dixon, who had always been bottom of the class at school, had just walked away with her as easily as he would have taken a drink from a waiter's tray.

While Gus was looking around for someone else he knew, he was approached by a girl with one eye.

The first time he met Rosa Hellman—at a fund-raising dinner for the Buffalo Symphony Orchestra, in which her brother played—he thought she was winking at him. In fact one eye was permanently closed. Her face was otherwise pretty, which made her disfigurement more striking. Furthermore, she always dressed stylishly, as if in defiance. Today she wore a straw boater set at a jaunty angle, and managed to look cute.

Last time he saw her she had been the editor of a small-circulation radical newspaper called the *Buffalo Anarchist*, and Gus said: "Are anarchists interested in art?"

"I work for the *Buffalo Advertiser* now," she said.

Gus was surprised. "Does the editor know about your political views?"

"My views aren't quite as extreme as they used to be, but he knows my history."

"I guess he figured that if you can make a success of an anarchist newspaper, you must be good."

"He says he gave me the job because I have more balls than any two of his male reporters."

Gus knew she liked to shock, but even so his mouth dropped open.

Rosa laughed. "But he still sends me to cover art exhibitions and fashion shows." She changed the subject. "What's it like working in the White House?"

Gus was conscious that anything he said might appear in her paper. "Tremendously exciting," he said. "I think Wilson is a great president, maybe the greatest ever."

"How can you say that? He's dangerously close to getting us involved in a European war."

Rosa's attitude was common among ethnic Germans, who naturally saw the German side of the story, and among left-wingers, who wanted to see the tsar defeated. However, plenty of people who were neither

German nor left-wing took the same view. Gus replied carefully: "When German submarines are killing American citizens, the president can't—" He was about to say *turn a blind eye.* He hesitated, flushed, and said: "Can't ignore it."

She did not seem to notice his embarrassment. "But the British are blockading German ports—in violation of international law—and German women and children are starving as a result. Meanwhile, the war in France is at a stalemate: neither side has changed its position by more than a few yards for the last six months. The Germans *have* to sink British ships. Otherwise they lose the war."

She had an impressive grasp of the complexities: that was why Gus always enjoyed talking to her. "I studied international law," he said. "Strictly speaking, the British aren't acting illegally. Naval blockades were banned by the Declaration of London of 1909, but that was never ratified."

She was not so easily sidetracked. "Never mind the legalities. The Germans warned Americans not to travel on British liners. They put an advertisement in the papers, for goodness' sake! What else can they do? Imagine that we were at war with Mexico, and the *Lusitania* had been a Mexican ship carrying armaments intended to kill American soldiers. Would we have let it pass?"

It was a good question, and Gus had no reasonable answer. He said: "Well, Secretary of State Bryan agreed with you." William Jennings Bryan had resigned over Wilson's note to the Germans. "He thought all we needed to do was warn Americans not to travel on the ships of combatant nations."

She was not willing to let him off the hook. "Bryan sees that Wilson has taken a grave risk," she said. "If the Germans don't back down now, we can hardly avoid war with them."

Gus was not going to admit to a journalist that he shared these misgivings. Wilson had demanded that the German government disavow the attacks on merchant shipping, make reparations, and prevent any recurrence—in other words, allow the British the freedom of the seas while accepting that Germany's own ships were trapped in dock by the blockade. It was hard to see any government agreeing to such demands. "But public opinion approves what the president has done."

"Public opinion can be wrong."

"But the president can't ignore it. Look, Wilson is walking a tightrope. He wants to keep us out of the war, but he doesn't want America to appear weak in international diplomacy. I think he's struck the right balance for the present."

"But in the future?"

That was the worrying question. "No one can predict the future," Gus said. "Not even Woodrow Wilson."

She laughed. "A politician's answer. You'll go far in Washington." Someone spoke to her, and she turned away.

Gus moved off, feeling a bit as if he had been in a boxing match that had ended in a draw.

Some of the audience were invited to take tea with the lecturer. Gus was among the privileged because his mother was a patron of the museum. He left Rosa and headed for a private room. When he entered, he was delighted to see Olga there. No doubt her father also gave money.

He got a cup of tea and then approached her. "If you're ever in Washington, I'd love to show you around the White House," he said.

"Oh! Could you introduce me to the president?"

He wanted to say, *Yes, anything!* But he hesitated to promise what he might not be able to deliver. "Probably," he said. "It would depend on how busy he happened to be. When he gets behind that typewriter and starts to write speeches or press releases, no one is allowed to disturb him."

"I was so sad when his wife passed away," Olga said. Ellen Wilson had died almost a year ago, shortly after the outbreak of war in Europe.

Gus nodded. "He was devastated."

"But I hear he's romancing a wealthy widow already."

Gus was discomfited. It was an open secret in Washington that Wilson had fallen passionately, boyishly in love, only eight months after the death of his wife, with the voluptuous Mrs. Edith Galt. The president was fifty-eight, his paramour forty-one. Right now they were together in New Hampshire. Gus was among a very small group who also knew that Wilson had proposed marriage a month ago, but Mrs. Galt had not yet given him an answer. He said to Olga: "Who told you that?"

"Is it true?"

He was desperate to impress her with his inside knowledge, but he managed to resist the temptation. "I can't talk about that sort of thing," he said reluctantly.

"Oh, how disappointing. I was hoping you'd give me the inside gossip."

"I'm sorry to be such a letdown."

"Don't be silly." She touched his arm, giving him a thrill like an electric shock. "I'm having a tennis party tomorrow afternoon," she said. "Do you play?"

Gus had long arms and legs, and was a fairly good player. "I do," he said. "I love the game."

"Will you come?"

"I'd be delighted," he said.

{ III }

Lev learned to drive in a day. The other main skill of a chauffeur, changing punctured tires, took him a couple of hours to master. By the end of a week he could also fill the tank, change the oil, and adjust the brakes. If the car would not go he knew how to check for a flat battery or a blocked fuel line.

Horses were the transport of the past, Josef Vyalov told him. Stablehands were low-paid: there were plenty of them. Chauffeurs were scarce, and earned high wages.

In addition, Vyalov liked to have a driver who was tough enough to double as a bodyguard.

Vyalov's car was a brand-new Packard Twin Six, a seven-passenger limousine. Other chauffeurs were impressed. The model had been launched only a few weeks ago, and its twelve-cylinder engine was the envy even of drivers of the Cadillac V8.

Lev was not so taken with Vyalov's ultramodern mansion. To him it looked like the world's largest cowshed. It was long and low, with broad overhanging eaves. The head gardener told him it was a "prairie house" in the latest fashion.

"If I had a house this big, I'd want it to *look* like a palace," Lev said.

He thought of writing to Grigori and telling him all about Buffalo and the job and the car; but he hesitated. He would want to say that he had put aside some money for Grigori's ticket, but in fact he had nothing saved. When he had a little stash he would write, he vowed. Meanwhile Grigori could not write because he did not know Lev's address.

There were three people in the Vyalov family: Josef himself; his wife, Lena, who rarely spoke; and Olga, a pretty daughter of about Lev's age with a bold look in her eye. Josef was attentive and courteous with his wife, even though he spent most evenings out with his cronies. To his daughter he was affectionate but strict. He often drove home at midday to have lunch with Lena and Olga. After lunch he and Lena would take a nap.

While Lev was waiting to drive Josef back downtown, he sometimes talked to Olga.

She liked to smoke cigarettes, something that was forbidden by her father, who was fiercely determined that she should be a respectable young lady and marry into the Buffalo social elite. There were a few places on the property where Josef never went, and the garage was one of them, so Olga came there to smoke. She would sit in the backseat of the Packard, her silk dress on the new leather, and Lev would lean on the door, with his foot up on the runningboard, and chat with her.

He was aware that he looked handsome in the chauffeur's uniform, and he wore the cap tilted jauntily back. He soon discovered that the way to please Olga was to compliment her on being high-class. She loved to be told that she walked like a princess, talked like a president's wife, and dressed like a Parisian socialite. She was a snob, and so was her father. Most of the time Josef was a bully and a thug, but Lev noticed how he became well-mannered, almost deferential, when talking to high-status men such as bank presidents and congressmen.

Lev had a quick intuition, and soon had Olga figured out. She was an overprotected rich girl who had no outlet for her natural romantic and sexual impulses. Unlike the girls Lev had known in the slums of St. Petersburg, Olga could not slip out to meet a boy at twilight and let him feel her up in the darkness of a shop doorway. She was twenty years old and a virgin. It was even possible she had never been kissed.

Lev watched the tennis party from a distance, drinking in the sight of Olga's strong, slim body, and the way her breasts moved under the light cotton of her dress as she flew across the court. She was playing against a very tall man in white flannel trousers. Lev felt a jolt of recognition. Staring at the man, he eventually recalled where he had seen him before. It was at the Putilov works. Lev had tricked him out of a dollar and Grigori had asked him if Josef Vyalov really was a big man in Buffalo. What was his name? It was the same as a brand of whisky. Dewar, that was it. Gus Dewar.

A group of half a dozen young people were watching the game, the girls in bright summer dresses, the men wearing straw boaters. Mrs. Vyalov looked out from under her parasol with a pleased smile. A uniformed maid was serving lemonade.

Gus Dewar defeated Olga and they left the court. Their places were immediately taken by another couple. Olga daringly accepted a cigarette from her opponent. Lev watched him light it for her. Lev ached to be one of them, playing tennis in beautiful clothes and drinking lemonade.

A wild stroke sent the ball his way. He picked it up and, instead of throwing it back, carried it to the court and handed it to one of the players. He looked at Olga. She was deep in conversation with Dewar, charming him in a flirtatious way, just as she did with Lev in the garage.

He felt a stab of jealousy and wanted to punch the tall guy in the mouth. He caught Olga's eye and gave her his most charming smile, but she looked away without acknowledging him. The other young people totally ignored him.

It was perfectly normal, he told himself: a girl could be friendly with the chauffeur while smoking in the garage, then treat him like a piece of furniture when she was with her friends. All the same, his pride was wounded.

He turned away—and saw her father walking down the gravel path toward the tennis court. Vyalov was dressed for business in a lounge suit with a waistcoat. He had come to greet his daughter's guests before returning downtown, Lev guessed.

Any second now he would see Olga smoking, and then there would be hell to pay.

Lev was inspired. In two strides he crossed to where Olga was sitting. With a swift motion he snatched the lighted cigarette from between her fingers.

"Hey!" she protested.

Gus Dewar frowned and said: "What the devil are you up to?"

Lev turned away, putting the cigarette between his lips. A moment later Vyalov spotted him. "What are you doing here?" he said crossly. "Get my car out."

"Yes, sir," said Lev.

"And put out that damned cigarette when you're talking to me."

Lev pinched out the coal and put the butt in his pocket. "Sorry, Mr. Vyalov, sir. I forgot myself."

"Don't let it happen again."

"Yes, sir."

"Now clear off."

Lev hurried away, then looked back over his shoulder. The young men had jumped to their feet, and Vyalov was jovially shaking hands all round. Olga, looking guilty, was introducing her friends. She had almost been caught. She met Lev's eye and shot him a grateful look.

Lev winked at her and walked on.

{ IV }

Ursula Dewar's drawing room contained a few ornaments, all precious in different ways: a marble head by Elie Nadelman, a first edition of the Geneva Bible, a single rose in a cut-glass vase, and a framed photograph of her grandfather, who had opened one of the first department stores in America. When Gus came into the room at six o'clock she was sitting in a silk evening dress, reading a new novel called *The Good Soldier.*

"How's the book?" he asked her.

"It is extraordinarily good, although I hear, paradoxically, that the author is a frightful cad."

He mixed an old-fashioned for her, the way she liked it, with bitters but no sugar. He felt nervous. At my age I shouldn't be afraid of my mother, he thought. But she could be scathing. He handed her the drink.

"Thank you," she said. "Are you enjoying your summer break?"

"Very much."

"I was afraid that by now you'd be itching to get back to the excitement of Washington and the White House."

Gus had expected that, too; but the holiday had brought unexpected pleasures. "I'll return as soon as the president does, but meanwhile I'm having a great time."

"Is Woodrow going to declare war on Germany, do you think?"

"I hope not. The Germans are willing to back down, but they want Americans to stop selling arms to the Allies."

"And will we stop?" Ursula was of German ancestry, as were some half the population of Buffalo, but when she said "we," she meant America.

"Absolutely not. Our factories are making too much money from British orders."

"Is it a deadlock, then?"

"Not yet. We're still dancing around one another. Meanwhile, as if to remind us of the pressures on neutral countries, Italy has joined the Allies."

"Will that make any difference?"

"Not enough." Gus took a deep breath. "I played tennis at the Vyalovs' place this afternoon," he said. His voice did not sound as casual as he had hoped.

"Did you win, dear?"

"Yes. They have a prairie house. It's very striking."

"So nouveau riche."

"I suppose we were nouveau riche once, weren't we? Perhaps when your grandfather opened his store?"

"I find it tiresome when you talk like a socialist, Angus, even though I know you don't mean it." She sipped her drink. "Mm, this is perfect."

He took a deep breath. "Mother, would you do something for me?"

"Of course, dear, if I can."

"You won't like it."

"What is it?"

"I want you to invite Mrs. Vyalov to tea."

His mother put her drink down slowly and carefully. "I see," she said.

"Aren't you going to ask why?"

"I know why," she said. "There is only one possible reason. I have met the ravishingly pretty daughter."

"You're not to be cross. Vyalov is a leading man in this city, and very wealthy. And Olga is an angel."

"Or, if not an angel, at least a Christian."

"The Vyalovs are Russian Orthodox," Gus said. Might as well get all the bad news on the table, he thought. "They go to the Church of Saints Peter and Paul on Ideal Street." The Dewars were Episcopalians.

"But not Jewish, thank God." Mother had once feared that Gus might marry Rachel Abramov, whom he had liked enormously but never loved. "And I suppose we can be grateful that Olga is not a fortune hunter."

"Indeed not. I should think Vyalov must be richer than Father."

"I'm sure I have no idea." Women such as Ursula were not supposed to know about money. Gus suspected they knew the net worth of their own and each others' husbands to the nearest dime, but they had to pretend ignorance.

She was not as cross as he had feared. "So you'll do it?" he said with trepidation.

"Of course. I'll send Mrs. Vyalov a note."

Gus felt elated, but a new fear struck him. "Mind you, you're not to invite your snobbish friends to make Mrs. Vyalov feel inferior."

"I have no snobbish friends."

That remark was too ludicrous even to be acknowledged. "Ask Mrs. Fischer—she's amiable. And Aunt Gertrude."

"Very well."

"Thank you, Mother." Gus felt great relief, as if he had survived an ordeal. "I know Olga is not the bride you may have dreamed of for me, but I feel sure you're going to become very fond of her in no time at all."

"My dear son, you're almost twenty-six years old. Five years ago I might have tried to talk you out of marriage to the daughter of a shady businessman. But lately I have been wondering if I'm ever to have grandchildren. If at this point you announced that you wanted to marry a divorced Polish waitress, I fear my first concern might be whether she were young enough to bear children."

"Don't jump the gun—Olga hasn't agreed to marry me. I haven't even asked her."

"How could she resist you?" She stood up and kissed him. "Now make me another drink."

{ V }

"You saved my life!" Olga said to Lev. "Father would have killed me."

Lev grinned. "I saw him coming. I had to act fast."

"I'm so grateful," Olga said, and she kissed his lips.

He was startled. She pulled away before he could take advantage, but he felt himself to be on a completely different footing with her immediately. He looked nervously around the garage, but they were alone.

She took out a pack of cigarettes and put one in her mouth. He lit it, copying what Gus Dewar had done yesterday. It was an intimate gesture, obliging the woman to dip her head and allowing the man to stare at her lips. It felt romantic.

She leaned back in the seat of the Packard and blew out smoke. Lev got into the car and sat beside her. She made no objection. He lit a cigarette for himself. They sat for a while in the half dark, their smoke mingling with the smells of oil and leather and a flowery perfume Olga was wearing.

To break the silence, Lev said: "I hope you enjoyed your tennis party."

She sighed. "All the boys in this town are frightened of my father," she said. "They think he'll shoot them if they kiss me."

"Will he shoot them?"

She laughed. "Probably."

"I'm not afraid of him." This was near to the truth. Lev was not really unafraid; he just ignored his fears, always hoping he could talk his way out of trouble.

But she looked skeptical. "Really?"

"That's why he hired me." This, too, was only one step removed from reality. "Ask him."

"I might do that."

"Gus Dewar really likes you."

"My father would love it if I married him."

"Why?"

"He's rich, his family are old Buffalo aristocracy, and his father is a senator."

"Do you always do what your pa wants?"

She drew thoughtfully on her cigarette. "Yes," she said, and blew out smoke.

Lev said: "I love to watch your lips when you smoke."

She made no reply, but gave him a speculative look.

That was invitation enough for Lev, and he kissed her.

She gave a little moan at the back of her throat, and pushed feebly at his chest with her hand, but neither protest was serious. He tossed his cigarette out of the car and put his hand on her breast. She grasped his wrist, as if to shove his hand away, then instead pressed it harder against her soft flesh.

Lev touched her closed lips with his tongue. She pulled away and gave him a startled look. He realized she did not know about kissing this way. She really was inexperienced. "It's okay," he said. "Trust me."

She threw away her cigarette, pulled him nearer, closed her eyes, and kissed him with her mouth open.

After that it happened very fast. There was a desperate urgency about her desire. Lev had been with several women, and he believed it was wise to let them set the pace. A hesitant woman could not be hurried, and an impatient one should not be held back. When he found his way through Olga's underwear and stroked the soft mound of her sex, she became so aroused that she sobbed with passion. If it were true that she had reached the age of twenty without being kissed by any of the timid boys of Buffalo, she must have a lot of stored-up frustration, he guessed. She lifted her hips eagerly for him to pull down her drawers. When he kissed her between her legs, she cried out with shock and excitement. She had to be a virgin, but he was too heated for such a thought to give him pause.

She lay back with one foot on the seat and the other on the floor, her skirt around her waist, her thighs spread ready for him. Her mouth was open and she was breathing hard. She watched him with wide eyes as he unbuttoned. He entered her cautiously, knowing how easy it was to hurt a girl there, but she grasped his hips and pulled him inside her impatiently, as if she feared she might be cheated at the last minute of what she wanted. He felt the membrane of her virginity resist him briefly, then break easily, with only a little gasp from her, as of a tinge of pain that went as quickly as it had come. She moved against him in a rhythm of her own, and again he let her take the lead, sensing that she was answering a call that would not be denied.

This was more thrilling, for him, than the act of love had ever been before. Some girls were knowing; some were innocent, but keen to please; some were careful to satisfy the man before seeking their own fulfillment. But Lev had never come across such raw need as Olga's, and it inflamed him beyond measure.

He held himself back. Olga cried out loud, and he put a hand over her mouth to muffle the sound. She bucked like a pony, then buried her face in his shoulder. With a stifled scream she reached her climax, and a moment later he did the same.

He rolled off her and sat on the floor. She lay still, panting. Neither of them spoke for a minute. Eventually she sat upright. "Oh, God," she said. "I didn't know it would be like that."

"Usually it's not," he replied.

There was a long, reflective pause; then she said in a quieter voice: "What have I done?"

He made no answer.

She picked up her drawers from the floor of the car and pulled them on. She sat still a moment longer, catching her breath; then she got out of the car.

Lev stared at her, waiting for her to say something, but she did not. She walked to the rear door of the garage, opened it, and went out.

But she came back the next day.

{ VI }

Edith Galt accepted President Wilson's proposal of marriage on June 29. In July the president returned to the White House temporarily. "I have to go back to Washington for a few days," Gus said to Olga as they strolled through the Buffalo Zoo.

"How many days?"

"As long as the president needs me."

"How thrilling!"

Gus nodded. "It's the best job in the world. But it does mean that I'm not my own master. If the crisis with Germany escalates, it could be a long time before I come back to Buffalo."

"We'll miss you."

"And I'll miss you. We've been such pals since I came back." They had gone boating on the lake in Delaware Park and bathing at Crystal Beach; they had taken steamers up the river to Niagara and across the lake to the Canadian side; and they had played tennis every other day—always with a group of young friends, and chaperoned by at least one watchful mother. Today Mrs. Vyalov was with them, walking a few paces behind and talking to Chuck Dixon. Gus went on: "I wonder if you have any idea how much I'll miss you."

Olga smiled, but made no reply.

Gus said: "This has been the happiest summer of my life."

"And mine!" she said, twirling her red-and-white polka-dot parasol.

That delighted Gus, although he was not sure it was his company that had made her happy. He still could not make her out. She always seemed pleased to see him, and was glad to talk to him hour after hour. But he had seen no emotion, no sign that her feelings for him might be passionate rather than merely friendly. Of course, no respectable girl ought to show such signs, at least until she was engaged; but all the same Gus felt at sea. Perhaps that was part of her appeal.

He recalled vividly that Caroline Wigmore had communicated her needs to him with unmistakable clarity. He found himself thinking a lot about Caroline, who was the only other woman he had ever loved. If she could say what she wanted, why not Olga? But Caroline had been a married woman, whereas Olga was a virgin who had had a sheltered upbringing.

Gus stopped in front of the bear pit, and they looked through the steel bars at a small brown bear sitting on its haunches staring back at them. "I wonder if all our days could be this happy," Gus said.

"Why not?" she said.

Was that encouragement? He looked at her. She did not return his gaze, but watched the bear. He studied her blue eyes, the soft curve of her pink cheek, the delicate skin of her neck. "I wish I were Titian," he said. "I'd paint you."

Her mother and Chuck went by and strolled on, leaving Gus and Olga behind. They were as alone as they would ever be.

She turned her gaze on him at last, and he thought he saw something like fondness in her eyes. That gave him courage. He thought: If a president who has been a widower less than a year can do it, surely I can?

He said: "I love you, Olga."

She said nothing, but continued to look at him.

He swallowed. Once again he could not make her out. He said: "Is there any chance . . . May I hope that one day you might love me, too?" He stared at her, holding his breath. At this moment she held his life in her hands.

There was a long pause. Was she thinking? Weighing him in the balance? Or just hesitating before a life-changing decision?

At last she smiled and said: "Oh, yes."

He could hardly believe it. "Really?"

She laughed happily. "Really."

He took her hand. "Do you love me?"

She nodded.

"You have to say it."

"Yes, Gus, I love you."

He kissed her hand. "I'll speak to your father before I go to Washington."

She smiled. "I think I know what he will say."

"After that we can tell everyone."

"Yes."

"Thank you," he said fervently. "You have made me very happy."

{ VII }

Gus called at Josef Vyalov's office in the morning and formally asked permission to propose to his daughter. Vyalov pronounced himself delighted. Although that was the answer Gus expected, he found himself weak with relief afterward.

Gus was on his way to the station to catch a train to Washington, so they agreed to celebrate as soon as he could get back. Meanwhile, Gus was happy to leave it to Olga's mother and his to plan the wedding.

Entering Central Station on Exchange Street with a spring in his step, he ran into Rosa Hellman coming out, wearing a red hat, carrying a small overnight bag. "Hello," he said. "May I help you with your luggage?"

"No, thanks, it's light," she said. "I was only away one night. I went for an interview with one of the wire services."

He raised his eyebrows. "For a job as a reporter?"

"Yes—and I got it."

"Congratulations! Forgive me if I sound surprised—I didn't think they employed women writers."

"It's unusual, but not unknown. *The New York Times* hired its first female reporter in 1869. Her name was Maria Morgan."

"What will you be doing?"

"I'll be the assistant to their Washington correspondent. The truth is, the president's love life has made them think they need a woman there. Men are liable to miss romantic stories."

Gus wondered if she had mentioned that she was friendly with one of Wilson's closest aides. He guessed she had: reporters were never coy. No doubt it had helped her get the job. "I'm on my way back," he said. "I guess we'll see each other there."

"I hope so."

"I have some good news, too," he said happily. "I proposed to Olga Vyalov—and she accepted me. We're getting married."

She gave him a long look; then she said: "You fool."

He could not have been more shocked if she had slapped him. He stared at her openmouthed.

"You goddamn fool," she said, and she walked away.

{ VIII }

Two more Americans died on August 19 when the Germans torpedoed another large British liner, the *Arabic.*

Gus was sorry for the victims but even more aghast at America's being pulled inexorably into the European conflict. He felt that the president was on the brink. Gus wanted to get married in a world of peace and happiness; he dreaded a future blighted by the mayhem and cruelty and destruction of war.

On Wilson's instructions, Gus told a few reporters, off the record, that the president was on the point of breaking off diplomatic relations with Germany. Meanwhile the new secretary of state, Robert Lansing, tried to make some kind of deal with the German ambassador, Count Johann von Bernstorff.

It could go horribly wrong, Gus thought. The Germans could call Wilson's bluff and defy him. Then what would he do? If he did nothing he would look stupid. He told Gus that breaking off diplomatic relations would not *necessarily* lead to war. Gus was left with the frightening feeling that the crisis was out of control.

But the kaiser did not want war with America and, to Gus's immense relief, Wilson's gamble paid off. At the end of August the Germans promised not to attack passenger ships without warning. It was not a fully satisfactory reassurance, but it ended the standoff.

The American newspapers, missing all the nuances, were ecstatic. On September 2 Gus triumphantly read aloud to Wilson a paragraph from a laudatory article in that day's New York *Evening Post*: "'Without mobilizing a regiment or assembling a fleet, by sheer, dogged, unwavering persistence in advocating the right, he has compelled the surrender of the proudest, the most arrogant, the best armed of nations.'"

"They haven't surrendered yet," said the president.

{ IX }

One evening in late September they took Lev to the warehouse, stripped him naked, and tied his hands behind his back. Then Vyalov came out of his office. "You dog," he said. "You mad dog."

"What have I done?" Lev pleaded.

"You know what you've done, you filthy cur," said Vyalov.

Lev was terrified. He could not talk his way out of this if Vyalov would not listen.

Vyalov took off his jacket and rolled up his shirtsleeves. "Bring it to me," he said.

Norman Niall, his weedy accountant, went into the office and returned with a knout.

Lev stared at it. It was the standard Russian pattern, traditionally used to punish criminals. It had a long wooden handle and three hardened leather thongs each terminating in a lead ball. Lev had never been flogged, but he had seen it done. In the countryside it was a common punishment for petty theft or adultery. In St. Petersburg the knout was often used on political offenders. Twenty lashes could cripple a man; a hundred would kill him.

Vyalov, still wearing his waistcoat with the gold watch chain, hefted the knout. Niall giggled. Ilya and Theo looked on with interest.

Lev cowered away, turning his back, pressing himself up against a stack of tires. The whip came down with a cruel swish, biting into his neck and shoulders, and he screamed in pain.

Vyalov brought the whip down again. This time it hurt more.

Lev could not believe what a fool he had been. He had fucked the virgin daughter of a powerful and violent man. What had he been thinking of? Why could he never resist temptation?

Vyalov lashed again. This time Lev flung himself away from the knout, trying to dodge the blow. Only the very ends of the thongs connected, but they still dug agonizingly into his flesh, and he cried out in pain again. He tried to get away, but Vyalov's men pushed him back, laughing.

Vyalov raised the whip again, started to bring it down, stopped in midswipe as Lev dodged, then struck. Lev's legs were slashed, and he saw blood pouring from the cuts. When Vyalov lashed again, Lev desperately flung himself away, then stumbled and fell to the concrete floor. As he lay on his back, losing strength rapidly, Vyalov whipped his front, striking his belly and thighs. Lev rolled over, too agonized and terror-struck to get to his feet, but the knout kept coming down. He summoned the energy to crawl a short way on his knees, like a baby, but he slipped in his own blood, and the whip came down again. He stopped screaming: he had no breath. Vyalov was going to flog him to death, he decided. He longed for oblivion to come.

But Vyalov denied him that relief. He dropped the knout, panting with exertion. "I ought to kill you," he said when he had caught his breath. "But I can't."

Lev was baffled. He lay in a pool of blood, staring at his torturer.

"She's pregnant," Vyalov said.

In a haze of fear and pain, Lev tried to think. They had used condoms. You could buy them in any big American city. He had always put one on—except for that first time, of course, when he had not been expecting anything . . . and the time she had been showing him around the empty house and they had done it on the big bed in the guest room . . . and once in the garden after dark . . .

There had been several times, he realized.

"She was going to marry Senator Dewar's boy," Vyalov said, and Lev could hear bitterness as well as rage in his harsh voice. "My grandson might have been a president."

It was hard for Lev to think straight, but he realized that the wedding would have to be called off. Gus Dewar would not marry a girl who was pregnant with someone else's baby, no matter how much he loved her. Unless . . .

Lev managed to croak a few words. "She doesn't have to have the baby. . . . There are doctors right here in town. . . ."

Vyalov snatched up the knout, and Lev cowered away. Vyalov screamed: "Never even think about that! It's against the will of God!"

Lev was amazed. Every Sunday he drove the Vyalov family to church, but he had assumed religion was a sham for Josef. The man lived by dishonesty and violence. Yet he could not bear to hear mention of abortion! Lev wanted to ask whether his church did not prohibit bribery and beating people up.

Vyalov said: "Can you imagine the humiliation you're causing me? Every newspaper in town reported the engagement." His face reddened and his voice rose to a roar. "What am I going to say to Senator Dewar? I've booked the church! I've hired caterers! The invitations are at the printers! I can just see Mrs. Dewar, that proud old cunt, laughing at me behind her wrinkled hand. And all because of a fucking chauffeur!"

He raised the knout again, then threw it away with a violent gesture. "I can't kill you." He turned to Theo. "Take this piece of shit to the doctor," he said. "Get him patched up. He's going to marry my daughter."

CHAPTER SIXTEEN

June 1916

Billy's father said: "Can we have a chat, boyo?"

Billy was astonished. For almost two years, ever since Billy had stopped attending the Bethesda Chapel, they had hardly spoken. There was always tension in the air at the little house in Wellington Row. Billy had almost forgotten what it was like to hear soft voices talking amiably in the kitchen—or even loud voices raised in the passionate arguments they used to have. The bad atmosphere was half the reason Billy had joined the army.

Da's tone now was almost humble. Billy looked carefully at his face. His expression told the same story: no aggression, no challenge, just a plea.

All the same, Billy was not prepared to dance to his tune. "What for?" he said.

Da opened his mouth to snap a retort, then visibly controlled himself. "I've acted proud," he said. "It's a sin. You may have been proud, too, but that's between you and the Lord, and it's no excuse for me."

"It's taken you two years to work that out."

"It would have took me longer if you hadn't gone in the army."

Billy and Tommy had volunteered last year, lying about their age. They had joined the Eighth Battalion of the Welsh Rifles, known as the Aberowen Pals. The Pals' battalions were a new idea. Men from the same town were kept together, to train and fight alongside people with whom they had grown up. It was thought to be good for morale.

Billy's group had done a year's training, mostly at a new camp outside Cardiff. He had enjoyed himself. It was easier than coal mining and a lot less dangerous. As well as a certain amount of grinding boredom—*training* often meant the same as *waiting*—there had been sports and games and the camaraderie of a group of young men learning new ways. During a long period with nothing to do he had picked up a book at random and found himself reading the play *Macbeth*. To his surprise he had found the story thrilling and the poetry strangely fascinating. Shakespeare's language was not difficult for someone who had spent so many hours studying the seventeenth-century English of the Protestant Bible. He had since gone through the complete works, rereading the best plays several times.

Now training was over, and the Pals had two days' leave before going to France. Da thought this might be the last time he saw Billy alive. That would be why he was humbling himself to talk.

Billy looked at the clock. He had come here only to say good-bye to his mother. He was planning to spend his leave in London, with his sister, Ethel, and her sexy lodger. Mildred's pretty face, with her red lips and bunny teeth, had remained vividly in his mind ever since she had shocked him by saying, *Fucking hell, are you Billy?* His kit bag stood on the floor by the door, packed and ready. His complete Shakespeare was in it. Tommy was waiting for him at the station. "I've got a train to catch," he said.

"There are plenty of trains," Da said. "Sit down, Billy . . . please."

Billy was not comfortable with his father in this mood. Da might be righteous, arrogant, and harsh, but at least he was strong. Billy did not want to see him weaken.

Gramper was in his usual chair, listening. "Be a good boy, now, Billy," he said persuasively. "Give your da a chance, is it?"

"All right, then." Billy sat at the kitchen table.

His mother came in from the scullery.

There was a moment of silence. Billy knew he might never enter this house again. Coming back from an army camp, he had seen for the first time that his home was small, the rooms dark, the air heavy with coal dust and cooking smells. Most of all, after the free-and-easy banter of the barracks, he understood that in this house he had been raised to a Bible-black respectability in which much that was human and natural found no expression. And yet the thought of going made him sad. It was not just the place; it was the life he was leaving. Everything had been simple here. He had believed in God, obeyed his father, and trusted his workmates down the pit. The coal owners were wicked, the union protected the men, and socialism offered a brighter future. But life was not that simple. He might return to Wellington Row, but he would never again be the boy who had lived here.

Da folded his hands, closed his eyes, and said: "Oh, Lord, help thy servant to be humble and meek as Jesus was." Then he opened his eyes and said: "Why did you do it, Billy? Why did you join up?"

"Because we're at war," Billy said. "Like it or not, we have to fight."

"But can't you see—" Da stopped and held up his hands in a pacific gesture. "Let me start again. You don't believe what you read in the newspapers about the Germans being evil men who rape nuns, do you?"

"No," said Billy. "Everything the papers ever said about coal miners was lies, so I don't suppose they're telling the truth about the Germans."

"The way I see it, this is a capitalist war that has got nothing to do with the workingman," Da said. "But you may disagree."

Billy was amazed by the effort his father was making to be conciliatory. Never before had he heard Da say, *You may disagree.* He replied: "I don't know much about capitalism, but I expect you're right. All the same, the Germans have got to be stopped. They think they're entitled to rule the world!"

Da said: "We're British. Our empire holds sway over more than four hundred million people. Hardly any of them are entitled to vote. They have no control over their own countries. Ask the average British man why, and he'll say it's our destiny to govern inferior peoples." Da spread both hands in a gesture that meant *Isn't it obvious?* "Billy boy, it's not the Germans who think they should rule the world—it's us!"

Billy sighed. He agreed with all this. "But we're under attack. The reasons for the war may be wrong, but we have to fight, regardless."

"How many have died in the last two years?" Da said. "Millions!" His voice went up a notch, but he was not angry so much as sad. "It will go on as long as young men are willing to kill one another *regardless,* as you say."

"It will go on until someone wins, I suppose."

His mother said: "I expect you're afraid people will think you're scared."

"No," he said, but she was right. His rational explanations for joining up were not the whole story. As usual, Mam saw into his heart. For almost two years he had been hearing and reading that able-bodied young men such as himself were cowards if they did not fight. It was in the newspapers; people said it in shops and pubs; in Cardiff city center pretty girls handed out white feathers to any boy not in uniform, and recruiting sergeants jeered at young civilians on the streets. Billy knew it was propaganda, but it affected him just the same. He found it hard to bear the thought that people believed him to be a coward.

He fantasized explaining, to those girls with white feathers, that coal mining was more dangerous than being in the army. Apart from frontline troops, most soldiers were less likely to be killed or injured than miners. And Britain needed the coal. It fueled half the navy. The government had actually said it did not want miners to join up. None of this made any difference. Since he had put on the itchy khaki tunic and trousers, the new boots and the peaked cap, he had felt better.

Da said: "People think there's a big push coming at the end of the month."

Billy nodded. "The officers won't say a word, but everyone else is talking about it. I expect that's why there's a sudden rush to get more men over there."

"The newspapers say this could be the battle that turns the tide—the beginning of the end."

"Let's hope so, anyhow."

"You should have enough ammunition now, thanks to Lloyd George."

"Aye." Last year there had been a shortage of shells. Newspaper agitation about the Shell Scandal had almost brought down Prime Minister Asquith. He had formed a coalition government, created the new post of minister of munitions, and given the job to the most popular man in the cabinet, David Lloyd George. Since then, production had soared.

"Try to take care of yourself," Da said.

Mam said: "Don't be a hero. Leave that to them that started the war—the upper classes, the Conservatives, the officers. Do as you're told and no more."

Gramper said: "War is war. There's no safe way to do it."

They were saying their good-byes. Billy felt an urge to cry, and repressed it harshly. "Right, then," he said, standing up.

Gramper shook his hand. Mam kissed him. Da shook hands, then yielded to an impulse and hugged him. Billy could not remember the last time his father had done that.

"God bless you and keep you, Billy," Da said. There were tears in his eyes.

Billy's self-control almost broke. "So long, then," he said. He picked up his kit bag. He heard his mother sob. Without looking back, he went out, closing the door behind him.

He took a deep breath and composed himself. Then he set off down the steep street toward the station.

{ II }

The river Somme meandered from east to west across France on its way to the sea. The front line, running north to south, crossed the river not far from Amiens. South of there, the Allied line was held by French troops all the way to Switzerland. To its north most of the forces were British and Commonwealth.

From this point a range of hills ran northwest for twenty miles. The German trenches in this sector had been dug into the slopes of the hills. From one such trench, Walter von Ulrich looked through powerful Zeiss *Doppelfernrohr* binoculars down to the British positions.

It was a sunny day in early summer, and he could hear birdsong. In a nearby orchard that had so far escaped shelling, apple trees were blossoming bravely. Men were the only animals that slaughtered their own kind by the million, and turned the landscape into a waste of shell craters and barbed wire. Perhaps the human race would wipe itself out completely, and leave the world to the birds and trees, Walter thought apocalyptically. Perhaps that would be for the best.

The high position had many advantages, he thought, coming back to practical matters. The British would have to attack uphill. Even more useful was the ability of the Germans to see everything the British were doing. And Walter felt sure that right now they were preparing a major assault.

Such activity could hardly be concealed. For months, ominously, the British had been improving the roads and railways in this previously sleepy area of the French countryside. Now they were using those supply lines to bring forward hundreds of heavy guns, thousands of horses, and tens of thousands of men. Behind the front lines, trucks and trains in constant streams were unloading crates of ammunition, barrels of fresh water, and bales of hay. Walter focused his lenses on a communications detail, digging a narrow trench and unspooling a huge reel of what was undoubtedly telephone wire.

They must have high hopes, he thought with cold apprehension. The expenditure of men, money, and effort was colossal. It could only be justified if the British thought this was the decisive attack of the war. Walter hoped it was—one way or the other.

Whenever he looked into enemy territory he thought of Maud. The picture he carried in his wallet, cut out of the *Tatler* magazine, showed her in a dramatically simple ball gown at the Savoy Hotel, over the caption *Lady Maud Fitzherbert is always dressed in the latest fashion.* He guessed she was not doing much dancing now. Had she found some role in the war effort, as Walter's sister, Greta, had in Berlin, bringing small luxuries to wounded men in army hospitals? Or had she retired to the country, like Walter's mother, and planted her flower beds with potatoes because of the food shortage?

He did not know whether the British were short of food. Germany's navy was trapped in port by the British blockade, so there had been no imports by sea for almost two years. But the British continued to get supplies from America. German submarines attacked transatlantic ships intermittently, but the high command held back from an all-out effort—what was called USW, for "unrestricted submarine warfare"—for fear of bringing the Americans into the war. So, Walter guessed, Maud was not as hungry as he was. And he was better off than German civilians. There had been strikes and demonstrations against the food shortage in some cities.

He had not written to her, nor she to him. There was no postal service between Germany and Britain. The only chance would come if one of them traveled to a neutral country, the United States or Sweden perhaps, and posted a letter from there; but that opportunity had not yet arisen for him nor, presumably, for her.

It was torment not to know anything about her. He was tortured by the fear that she might be ill in hospital without his knowledge. He longed for the end of the war so that he could be with her. He desperately wanted Germany to win, of course, but there were times when he felt he would not care about losing as long as Maud was all right. His nightmare was that the end came, and he went to London to find her, only to be told that she was dead.

He pushed the frightening thought to the back of his mind. He lowered his sights, focused his lenses nearer, and examined the barbed-wire defenses on the German side of no-man's-land. There were two belts of it, each fifteen feet wide. The wire was firmly fixed to the ground with iron stakes so that it could not easily be moved. It made a reassuringly formidable barrier.

He climbed down from the trench parapet and turned down a long flight of wooden steps to a deep dugout. The disadvantage of the hillside position was that the trenches were more visible to enemy artillery; so, to compensate, the dugouts in this sector had been cut far into the chalky soil, deep enough to provide protection from anything but a direct hit from the largest type of shell. There was room to shelter every man in the trench garrison during a bombardment. Some dugouts were interconnected, providing an alternative way out if shelling blocked the entrance.

Walter sat on a wooden bench and took out his notebook. For a few minutes he wrote abbreviated reminders of everything he had seen. His report would confirm other intelligence sources. Secret agents had been warning of what the British called a "big push."

He made his way through the maze of trenches to the rear. The Germans had constructed three lines of trenches two or three kilometers apart, so that if they were driven out of the front line, they could fall back on another trench and, failing that, a third. Whatever happened, he thought with considerable satisfaction, there would be no quick victory for the British.

Walter found his horse and rode back to Second Army headquarters, arriving at lunchtime. In the officers' mess he was surprised to encounter his father. The old man was a senior officer on the general staff, and now dashed from one battlefield to another just as, in peacetime, he had gone from one European capital to the next.

Otto looked older. He had lost weight—all Germans had lost weight. His monkish fringe was cut so short that he looked bald. But he seemed spry and cheerful. War suited him. He liked the excitement, the hurry, the quick decisions, and the sense of constant emergency.

He never mentioned Maud.

"What have you seen?" he asked.

"There will be a major assault in this area within the next few weeks," Walter said.

His father shook his head skeptically. "The Somme sector is the best-defended part of our line. We hold the upper ground and we have three lines of trenches. In war you attack at your enemy's weakest point, not his strongest—even the British know that."

Walter related what he had just seen: the trucks, the trains, and the communications detail laying telephone lines.

"I believe it's a ruse," said Otto. "If this were the real site of the attack, they would be doing more to conceal their efforts. There will be a feint here, followed by the real assault farther north, in Flanders."

Walter said: "What does von Falkenhayn believe?" Erich von Falkenhayn had been chief of staff for almost two years.

His father smiled. "He believes what I tell him."

{ III }

As coffee was served at the end of lunch, Lady Maud asked Lady Hermia: "In an emergency, Aunt, would you know how to get in touch with Fitz's lawyer?"

Aunt Herm looked mildly shocked. "My dear, what should I have to do with lawyers?"

"You never know." Maud turned to the butler as he put the coffeepot down on a silver trivet. "Grout, be so kind as to bring me a sheet of paper and a pencil." Grout went out and returned with writing materials. Maud wrote down the name and address of the family lawyer.

"Why do I need this?" Aunt Herm said.

"I may get arrested this afternoon," Maud said cheerfully. "If so, do please ask him to come and get me out of jail."

"Oh!" said Aunt Herm. "You can't mean it!"

"No, I'm sure it won't happen," Maud said. "But, you know, just in case . . . " She kissed her aunt and left the room.

Aunt Herm's attitude infuriated Maud, but most women were the same. It was unladylike even to know the name of your lawyer, let alone to understand your rights under the law. No wonder women were mercilessly exploited.

Maud put on her hat and gloves and a light summer coat, then went out and caught a bus to Aldgate.

She was alone. Chaperoning rules had relaxed since the outbreak of war. It was no longer scandalous for a single woman to go out unescorted in the daytime. Aunt Herm disapproved of the change, but she could not lock Maud up, and she could not appeal to Fitz, who was in France, so she had to accept the situation, albeit with a sour face.

Maud was editor of *The Soldier's Wife,* a small-circulation newspaper that campaigned for better treatment for the dependents of servicemen. A Conservative member of Parliament had described the journal as "a pestilential nuisance to the government," a quotation that was emblazoned on the masthead of every edition thereafter. Maud's campaigning rage was fueled by her indignation at the subjection of women combined with her horror at the pointless slaughter of war. Maud subsidized the newspaper out of her small inheritance. She hardly needed the money anyway: Fitz always paid for everything she needed.

Ethel Williams was the paper's manager. She had eagerly left the sweatshop for a better wage and a campaigning role. Ethel shared Maud's rage, but had a different set of skills. Maud understood politics at the top—she met cabinet ministers socially and talked to them about the issues of the day. Ethel knew a different political world: the National Union of Garment Workers, the Independent Labour Party, strikes and lockouts and street marches.

As appointed, Maud met Ethel across the road from the Aldgate office of the Soldiers' and Sailors' Families Association.

Before the war this well-meaning charity had enabled well-off ladies to graciously give help and advice to the hard-up wives of servicemen. Now it had a new role. The government paid one pound and one shilling to a soldier's wife with two children separated from her husband by the war. This was not much—about half what a coal miner earned—but it was enough to raise millions of women and children out of grinding poverty. The Soldiers' and Sailors' Families Association administered this separation allowance.

But the allowance was payable only to women of "good behavior" and the charity ladies sometimes withheld the government money from wives who rejected their advice about child rearing, household management, and the perils of visiting music halls and drinking gin.

Maud thought such women would be better off without the gin, but that did not give anyone the right to push them into penury. She was driven into a fury of outrage by comfortable middle-class people passing judgment on soldiers' wives and depriving them of the means to feed their children. Parliament would not permit such abuse, she thought, if women had the vote.

With Ethel were a dozen working-class women plus one man, Bernie Leckwith, secretary of the Aldgate Independent Labour Party. The party approved of Maud's paper and supported its campaigns.

When Maud joined the group on the pavement, Ethel was talking to a young man with a notebook. "The separation allowance is not a charitable gift," she said. "Soldiers' wives receive it as of right. Do you have to pass a good-conduct test before you get your wages as a reporter? Is Mr. Asquith questioned about how much Madeira he drinks before he can draw his salary as a member of Parliament? These women are entitled to the money just as if it was a wage."

Ethel had found her voice, Maud reflected. She expressed herself simply and vividly.

The reporter looked admiringly at Ethel: he seemed half in love with her. Rather apologetically he said: "Your opponents say that a woman should not receive support if she is unfaithful to her soldier husband."

"Are you checking on the husbands?" Ethel said indignantly. "I believe there are houses of ill fame in France and Mesopotamia and other places where our men are serving. Does the army take the names of married men entering such houses, and withdraw their wages? Adultery is a sin, but it is not a reason to impoverish the sinner and let her children starve."

Ethel was carrying her child, Lloyd, on her hip. He was now sixteen months old and able to walk, or at least stagger. He had fine dark hair and green eyes, and was as pretty as his mother. Maud put out her hands to take him, and he came to her eagerly. She felt a pang of longing: she almost wished she had become pregnant during her one night with Walter, despite all the trouble it would have caused.

She had heard nothing of Walter since the Christmas before last. She did not know whether he was alive or dead. She might already be a widow. She tried not to brood, but dreadful thoughts crept up on her unawares, sometimes, and then she had to keep from crying.

Ethel finished charming the reporter, then introduced Maud to a young woman with two children clinging to her skirts. "This is Jayne McCulley, who I told you about." Jayne had a pretty face and a determined look.

Maud shook hands. "I hope we can get justice for you today, Mrs. McCulley," she said.

"Very kind of you, I'm sure, ma'am." The habit of deference died hard even in egalitarian political movements.

"If we're all ready?" said Ethel.

Maud handed Lloyd back to Ethel, and together the group crossed the road and went in at the front door of the charity office. There was a reception area where a middle-aged woman sat behind a desk. She looked frightened by the crowd.

Maud said to her: "There's nothing to worry about. Mrs. Williams and I are here to see Mrs. Hargreaves, your manager."

The receptionist stood up. "I'll see if she's in," she said nervously.

Ethel said: "I know she's in—I saw her walk through the door half an hour ago."

The receptionist scurried out.

The woman who returned with her was less easily intimidated. Mrs. Hargreaves was a stout woman in her forties, wearing a French coat and skirt and a fashionable hat decorated with a large pleated bow. The ensemble lost all its continental chic on her stocky figure, Maud thought cattily, but the woman had the confidence that came with money. She also had a large nose. "Yes?" she said rudely.

In the struggle for female equality, Maud reflected, sometimes you had to fight women as well as men. "I have come to see you because I'm concerned about your treatment of Mrs. McCulley."

Mrs. Hargreaves looked startled, no doubt by Maud's upper-class accent. She gave Maud an up-and-down scrutiny. She was probably noting that Maud's clothes were as expensive as her own. When she spoke again, her tone was less arrogant. "I'm afraid I can't discuss individual cases."

"But Mrs. McCulley has asked me to speak to you—and she's here to prove it."

Jayne McCulley said: "Don't you remember me, Mrs. Hargreaves?"

"As a matter of fact, I do. You were very discourteous to me."

Jayne turned to Maud. "I told her to go and poke her nose into someone else's business."

The women giggled at the reference to the nose, and Mrs. Hargreaves blushed.

Maud said: "But you cannot refuse an application for a separation allowance on the grounds that the applicant was rude to you." Maud controlled her anger and tried to speak with icy disapproval. "Surely you know that?"

Mrs. Hargreaves tilted her chin defensively. "Mrs. McCulley was seen in the Dog and Duck public house, and at the Stepney Music Hall, on both occasions with a young man. The separation allowance is for wives of good conduct. The government does not wish to finance unchaste behavior."

Maud wanted to strangle her. "You seem to misunderstand your role," she said. "It is not for you to refuse payment on suspicion."

Mrs. Hargreaves looked a little less sure of herself.

Ethel put in: "I suppose Mr. Hargreaves is safe at home, is it?"

"No, he's not," the woman replied quickly. "He's with the army in Egypt."

"Oh!" said Ethel. "So you receive a separation allowance, too."

"That's neither here nor there."

"Does someone come to your house, Mrs. Hargreaves, to check on your conduct? Do they look at the level of the sherry in the decanter on your sideboard? Are you questioned about your friendship with your grocer's deliveryman?"

"How dare you!"

Maud said: "Your indignation is understandable—but perhaps now you will appreciate why Mrs. McCulley reacted as she did to your questioning."

Mrs. Hargreaves raised her voice. "That's ridiculous—there's no comparison!"

"No comparison?" Maud said angrily. "Her husband, like yours, is risking his life for his country. Both you and she claim the separation allowance. But you have the right to judge her behavior and refuse her the money—while no one judges you. Why not? Officers' wives sometimes drink too much."

Ethel said: "They commit adultery, too."

"That's it!" shouted Mrs. Hargreaves. "I refuse to be insulted."

"So does Jayne McCulley," said Ethel.

Maud said: "The man you saw with Mrs. McCulley was her brother. He was home on leave from France. He had only two days, and she wanted him to enjoy himself before going back to the trenches. That was why she took him to the pub and the music hall."

Mrs. Hargreaves looked abashed, but she put on a defiant air. "She should have explained that when I questioned her. And now I must ask you please to leave the premises."

"Now that you know the truth, I trust you will approve Mrs. McCulley's application."

"We'll see."

"I insist that you do it here and now."

"Impossible."

"We're not leaving until you do."

"Then I shall call the police."

"Very well."

Mrs. Hargreaves retreated.

Ethel turned to the admiring reporter. "Where is your photographer?"

"Waiting outside."

A few minutes later, a burly middle-aged police constable came in. "Now, now, ladies," he said. "No trouble, please. Just leave quietly."

Maud stepped forward. "I am refusing to leave," she said. "Never mind about the others."

"And who would you be, madam?"

"I am Lady Maud Fitzherbert, and if you want me to go you'll have to carry me out."

"If you insist," said the policeman, and he picked her up.

As they left the building, the photographer took a picture.

{ IV }

"Aren't you scared?" Mildred said.

"Aye," Billy admitted. "I am, a bit."

He could talk to Mildred. She seemed to know all about him anyway. She had been living with his sister for a couple of years, and women always told each other everything. However, there was something else about Mildred that made him feel comfortable. Aberowen girls were always trying to impress boys, saying things for effect and checking their appearance in mirrors, but Mildred was just herself. She said outrageous things sometimes, and made Billy laugh. He felt he could tell her anything.

He was almost overwhelmed by how attractive she was. It was not her fair curly hair or her blue eyes, but her devil-may-care attitude that mesmerized him. Then there was the age difference. She was twenty-three, and he was still not quite eighteen. She seemed very worldly-wise, yet she was frankly interested in him, and that was highly flattering. He looked longingly at her across the room, hoping he would get a chance to talk to her alone, wondering if he would dare to touch her hand, put his arm around her, and kiss her.

They were sitting around the square table in Ethel's kitchen: Billy, Tommy, Ethel, and Mildred. It was a warm evening, and the door was open to the backyard. On the flagstone floor Mildred's two little girls were playing with Lloyd. Enid and Lillian were three and four years old, but Billy had not yet worked out which was which. Because of the children, the women had not wanted to go out, so Billy and Tommy had fetched some bottles of beer from the pub.

"You'll be all right," Mildred said to Billy. "You've been trained."

"Aye." The training had not done much for Billy's confidence. There had been a lot of marching up and down, saluting, and doing bayonet drills. He did not feel he had been taught how to survive.

Tommy said: "If the Germans all turn out to be stuffed dummies tied to posts, we'll know how to stick our bayonets in them."

Mildred said: "You can shoot your guns, can't you?"

For a while they had trained with rusted and broken rifles stamped "D.P." for "drill purposes," which meant they were not on any account to be fired. But eventually each of them had been given a bolt-action Lee Enfield rifle with a detachable magazine holding ten rounds of .303 ammunition. It turned out that Billy could shoot well, being able to empty the magazine in under a minute and still hit a man-size target at three hundred yards. The Lee Enfield was renowned for its rapid rate of fire, the trainees had been told: the world record was thirty-eight rounds a minute.

"The equipment is all right," Billy said to Mildred. "It's the officers that worry me. So far I haven't met one I'd trust in an emergency down the pit."

"The good ones are all out in France, I expect," Mildred said optimistically. "They let the wankers stay home and do the training."

Billy laughed at her choice of words. She had no inhibitions. "I hope you're right."

What he was really afraid of was that when the Germans started shooting at him he might turn and run away. That scared him most of all. The humiliation would be worse than a wound, he thought. Sometimes he felt so wrought up about it that he longed for the terrible moment to come, so that he would know, one way or the other.

"Anyway, I'm glad you're going to shoot those wicked Germans," Mildred said. "They're all rapists."

Tommy said: "If I were you, I wouldn't believe everything you read in the *Daily Mail.* They'd have you think all trade unionists are disloyal. I know that's not true—most of the members of my union branch have volunteered. So the Germans may not be as bad as the *Mail* paints them."

"Yeah, you're probably right." Mildred turned back to Billy. "Have you seen *The Tramp*?"

"Aye, I love Charlie Chaplin."

Ethel picked up her son. "Say good night to Uncle Billy." The toddler wriggled in her arms, not wanting to go to bed.

Billy remembered him newborn, and the way he had opened his

mouth and wailed. How big and strong he seemed now. "Good night, Lloyd," he said.

Ethel had named him after Lloyd George. Billy was the only person who knew that he also had a middle name: Fitzherbert. It was on his birth certificate, but Ethel had not told anyone else.

Billy would have liked to get Earl Fitzherbert in the sights of his Lee Enfield.

Ethel said: "He looks like Gramper, doesn't he?"

Billy could not see the resemblance. "I'll let you know when he grows a mustache."

Mildred put her two to bed at the same time. Then the women announced that they wanted supper. Ethel and Tommy went to buy oysters, leaving Billy and Mildred alone.

As soon as they had gone, Billy said: "I really like you, Mildred."

"I like you, too," she said; so he moved his chair next to hers and kissed her.

She kissed him back with enthusiasm.

He had done this before. He had kissed several girls in the back row of the Majestic cinema in Cwm Street. They always opened their mouths straightaway, and he did the same now.

Mildred pushed him away gently. "Not so fast," she said. "Do this." And she kissed him with her mouth closed, her lips brushing his cheek and his eyelids and his neck, and then his lips. It was strange but he liked it. She said: "Do the same to me." He followed her instructions. "Now do this," she said, and he felt the tip of her tongue on his lips, touching them as lightly as possible. Once again he copied her. Then she showed him yet another way to kiss, nibbling his neck and his earlobes. He felt he could do this forever.

When they paused for breath she stroked his cheek and said: "You're a quick learner."

"You're lovely," he said.

He kissed her again and squeezed her breast. She let him do it for a while, but when he started to breathe heavily, she took his hand away. "Don't get too worked up," she said. "They'll be back any minute."

A moment later he heard the front door. "Oh, dammo," he said.

"Be patient," she whispered.

"Patient?" he said. "I'm going to France tomorrow."

"Well, it ain't tomorrow yet, is it?"

Billy was still wondering what she meant when Ethel and Tommy came into the room.

They ate their supper and finished the beer. Ethel told them the story of Jayne McCulley, and how Lady Maud had been carried out of the charity office by a policeman. She made it sound like a comedy, but Billy was bursting with pride for his sister and the way she stood up for the rights of poor women. And she was the manager of a newspaper and the friend of Lady Maud! He was determined that one day he, too, would be a champion for ordinary people. It was what he admired about his father. Da was narrow-minded and stubborn, but all his life he had fought for the workingman.

Darkness fell and Ethel announced it was bedtime. She used cushions to improvise beds on the kitchen floor for Billy and Tommy. They all retired.

Billy lay awake, wondering what Mildred had meant by *It ain't tomorrow yet.* Perhaps she was just promising to kiss him again in the morning, when he left to catch the train to Southampton. But she had seemed to imply more. Could it really be that she wanted to see him again tonight?

The thought of going to her room inflamed him so much that he could not sleep. She would be wearing a nightdress, and under the sheets her body would be warm to the touch, he thought. He imagined her face on the pillow, and envied the pillowcase because it was touching her cheek.

When Tommy's breathing seemed regular, Billy slipped out of his sheets.

"Where are you going?" said Tommy, not as fast asleep as Billy had thought.

"Toilet," Billy whispered. "All that beer."

Tommy grunted and turned over.

In his underwear, Billy crept up the stairs. There were three doors off the landing. He hesitated. What if he had misinterpreted Mildred? She might scream at the sight of him. How embarrassing that would be.

No, he thought; she's not the screaming type.

He opened the first door he came to. There was a faint light from the street, and he could see a narrow bed with the blond heads of two little girls on the pillow. He closed the door softly. He felt like a burglar.

He tried the next door. In this room, a candle was burning, and it took him a moment to adjust to its unsteady light. He saw a bigger bed, with one head on the pillow. Mildred's face was toward him, but he could not see whether her eyes were open. He waited for her protest, but no sound came.

He stepped inside and closed the door behind him.

He whispered hesitantly: "Mildred?"

In a clear voice she said: "About bloody time, Billy. Get into bed, quick."

He slipped between the sheets and put his arms around her. She was not wearing the nightdress he had expected. In fact, he realized with a thrilling shock, she was naked.

Suddenly he felt nervous. He said: "I've never . . . "

"I know," she said. "You'll be my first virgin."

{ V }

In June of 1916, Major the Earl Fitzherbert was assigned to the Eighth Battalion of the Welsh Rifles and put in charge of B Company, one hundred twenty-eight men and four lieutenants. He had never commanded men in battle, and he was secretly racked with anxiety.

He was in France, but the battalion was still in Britain. They were recruits who had just finished their training. They would be stiffened with a sprinkling of veterans, the brigadier explained to Fitz. The professional army that had been sent to France in 1914 no longer existed—more than half of them were dead—and this was Kitchener's New Army. Fitz's lot were called the Aberowen Pals. "You'll probably know most of them," said the brigadier, who seemed not to realize how wide was the gulf that separated earls from coal miners.

Fitz got his orders at the same time as half a dozen other officers, and he bought a round of drinks in the mess to celebrate. The captain who had been given A Company raised his whisky glass and said: "Fitzherbert? You must be the coal owner. I'm Gwyn Evans, the shopkeeper. You probably buy all your sheets and towels from me."

There were a lot of these cocky businessmen in the army now. It was typical of that type to speak as if he and Fitz were equals who just happened to be in different lines of business. But Fitz also knew that the organizational skills of commercial men were valued by the army. In calling himself a shopkeeper, the captain was indulging in a little false modesty. Gwyn Evans was the name over department stores in the larger towns of South Wales. There were many more people on his payroll than in A Company. Fitz himself had never organized anything more complicated than a cricket team, and the daunting complexity of the war machine made him vividly aware of his inexperience.

"This is the attack that was agreed upon in Chantilly, I presume," Evans said.

Fitz knew what he meant. Back in December Sir John French had at last been fired and Sir Douglas Haig had taken over as commander in chief of the British army in France, and a few days later Fitz— still doing liaison work—had attended an Allied conference at Chantilly. The French had proposed a massive offensive on the western front during 1916, and the Russians had agreed to a similar push in the east.

Evans went on: "What I heard then was that the French would attack with forty divisions and us with twenty-five. That's not going to happen now."

Fitz did not like this negative talk—he was already apprehensive enough—but unfortunately Evans was right. "It's because of Verdun," Fitz said. Since the December agreement, the French had lost a quarter of a million men defending the fortress city of Verdun, and they had few to spare for the Somme.

Evans said: "Whatever the reason, we're virtually on our own."

"I'm not sure it makes any difference," Fitz said with an air of detachment that he did not in the least feel. "We will attack along our stretch of the front, regardless of what they do."

"I disagree," said Evans, with a confidence that was not quite insolent. "The French withdrawal frees up a lot of German reserves. They can all be pulled into our sector as reinforcements."

"I think we'll move too fast for that."

"Do you, really, sir?" said Evans coolly, again remaining just the right side of disrespect. "If we get through the first line of German barbed wire, we've still got to fight our way through a second and third."

Evans was beginning to annoy Fitz. This kind of talk was bad for morale. "The barbed wire will be destroyed by our artillery," Fitz said.

"In my experience, artillery is not very effective against barbed wire. A shrapnel shell fires steel balls downward and forward—"

"I know what shrapnel is, thank you."

Evans ignored that. "—so it has to explode just a few yards above and before the target. Otherwise it has no effect. Our guns just aren't that accurate. And a high-explosive shell goes off when it hits the ground, so even a direct hit sometimes just throws the wire up in the air and down again without actually damaging it."

"You're underestimating the sheer scale of our barrage." Fitz's irritation with Evans was sharpened by a nagging suspicion that he might have a point. Worse, that suspicion fed Fitz's nervousness. "There will be nothing left afterward. The German trenches will be completely destroyed."

"I hope you're right. If they hide in their dugouts during the barrage, then come out again afterward with their machine guns, our men will be mown down."

"You don't seem to understand," Fitz said angrily. "There has never been a bombardment this intense in the history of warfare. We have one gun for every twenty yards of front line. We plan to fire more than a million shells! Nothing will be left alive."

"Well, we're in agreement about one thing, anyway," said Captain Evans. "This has never been done before, as you say; so none of us can be sure how it will work out."

{ VI }

Lady Maud appeared at Aldgate Magistrates Court in a large red hat with ribbons and ostrich feathers, and was fined one guinea for disturbing the peace. "I hope Prime Minister Asquith will take notice," she said to Ethel as they left the courtroom.

Ethel was not optimistic. "We have no way of compelling him to act," she said with exasperation. "This kind of thing will go on until women have the power to vote a government out of office." The suffragettes had planned to make women's votes the big issue of the general election of 1915, but the wartime Parliament had postponed elections. "We may have to wait until the war is over."

"Not necessarily," said Maud. They stopped to pose for a photograph on the courthouse steps, then headed for the office of *The Soldier's Wife.* "Asquith is struggling to hold the Liberal-Conservative coalition together. If it falls apart, there will have to be an election. And that's what gives us a chance."

Ethel was surprised. She had thought the issue of women's votes was moribund. "Why?"

"The government has a problem. Under the present system, serving soldiers can't vote because they aren't householders. That didn't matter much before the war, when there were only a hundred thousand men in the army. But today there are more than a million. The government wouldn't dare to hold an election and leave them out—these men are dying for their country. There would be a mutiny."

"And if they reform the system, how can they leave women out?"

"Right now the spineless Asquith is looking for a way to do just that."

"But he can't! Women are just as much part of the war effort as men: they make munitions, they take care of wounded soldiers in France, and they do so many jobs that used to be done only by men."

"Asquith is hoping to weasel his way out of having that argument."

"Then we must make sure he is disappointed."

Maud smiled. "Exactly," she said. "I think that's our next campaign."

{ VII }

"I joined up to get out of Borstal," said George Barrow, leaning on the rail of the troopship as it steamed out of Southampton. A Borstal was a jail for underage offenders. "I was done for housebreaking when I was sixteen, and got three years. After a year I got tired of sucking the warden's cock, so I said I wanted to volunteer. He marched me to the recruiting station and that was it."

Billy looked at him. He had a bent nose, a mutilated ear, and a scar on his forehead. He looked like a retired boxer. "How old are you now?" said Billy.

"Seventeen."

Boys were not allowed to join the army under eighteen, and had to be nineteen before they were sent overseas, officially. Both laws were constantly broken by the army. Recruiting sergeants and medical officers were each paid half a crown for every man passed, and they rarely questioned boys who claimed to be older than they seemed. There was a boy in the battalion called Owen Bevin who looked about fifteen.

"Was that an island we just passed?" said George.

"Aye," said Billy. "That's the Isle of Wight."

"Oh," said George. "I thought it was France."

"No, that's a lot farther."

The voyage took them until early the following morning, when they disembarked at Le Havre. Billy stepped off the gangplank and set foot on foreign soil for the first time in his life. In fact it was not soil but cobblestones, which proved difficult to march over in hobnailed boots. They passed through the town, watched listlessly by the French population. Billy had heard stories of pretty French girls gratefully embracing the arriving Brits, but he saw only apathetic middle-aged women in head scarves.

They marched to a camp, where they spent the night. Next morning they boarded a train. Being abroad was less exciting than Billy had hoped. Everything was different, but only slightly. Like Britain, France was mostly fields and villages, roads and railways. The fields had fences rather than hedges, and the cottages seemed larger and better built, but that was all. It was an anticlimax. At the end of the day they reached their billets in a huge new encampment of hastily built barracks.

Billy had been made a corporal, so he was in charge of his section, eight men including Tommy, young Owen Bevin, and George Barrow the Borstal boy. They were joined by the mysterious Robin Mortimer, who was a private despite looking thirty years old. As they sat down to tea with bread and jam in a long hall containing about a thousand men, Billy said: "So, Robin, we're all new here, but you seem more experienced. What's your story?"

Mortimer replied in the faintly accented speech of an educated Welshman, but he used the language of the pit. "None of your fucking business, Taffy," he said, and he went off to sit somewhere else.

Billy shrugged. "Taffy" was not much of an insult, especially coming from another Welshman.

Four sections made a platoon, and their platoon sergeant was Elijah Jones, age twenty, the son of John Jones the Shop. He was considered a hardened veteran because he had been at the front for a year. Jones belonged to the Bethesda Chapel and Billy had known him since they were both at school, where he had been dubbed Prophet Jones because of his Old Testament name.

Prophet overheard the exchange with Mortimer. "I'll have a word with him, Billy," he said. "He's a stuck-up old beggar, but he can't speak to a corporal like that."

"What's he so grumpy about?"

"He used to be a major. I dunno what he done, but he was court-martialed and cashiered, which means he lost his rank as an officer. Then, being eligible for war service, he was immediately conscripted as a private soldier. It's what they do to officers who misbehave."

After tea they met their platoon leader, Second Lieutenant James Carlton-Smith, a boy the same age as Billy. He was stiff and embarrassed, and seemed too young to be in charge of anyone. "Men," he said in a strangled upper-class accent, "I am honored to be your leader, and I know you will be brave as lions in the coming battle."

"Bloody wart," muttered Mortimer.

Billy knew that second lieutenants were called warts, but only by other officers.

Carlton-Smith then introduced the commander of B Company, Major the Earl Fitzherbert.

"Bloody hell," said Billy. He stared openmouthed as the man he hated most in the world stood on a chair to address the company. Fitz wore a well-tailored khaki uniform and carried the ash wood walking stick some officers affected. He spoke with the same accent as Carlton-Smith, and uttered the same kind of platitude. Billy could hardly believe his rotten luck. What was Fitz doing here—impregnating French maidservants? That this hopeless wastrel should be his commanding officer was hard to bear.

When the officers had gone, Prophet spoke quietly to Billy and Mortimer. "Lieutenant Carlton-Smith was at Eton until a year ago," he said. Eton was a posh school: Fitz had gone there too.

Billy said: "So why is he an officer?"

"He was a popper at Eton. It means a prefect."

"Oh, good," said Billy sarcastically. "We'll be all right, then."

"He doesn't know much about warfare, but he's got the sense not to throw his weight around, so he'll be fine so long as we keep an eye on him. If you see him about to do something really stupid, speak to me." He fixed his eye on Mortimer. "You know what it's like, don't you?"

Mortimer gave a surly nod.

"I'm counting on you, now."

A few minutes later it was lights-out. There were no cots, just straw palliasses in rows on the floor. Lying awake, Billy thought admiringly of what Prophet had done with Mortimer. He was dealing with a difficult subordinate by making an ally of him. That was the way Da would handle a troublemaker.

Prophet had given Billy and Mortimer the same message. Had Prophet also identified Billy as a rebel? He recalled that Prophet had been in the congregation the Sunday that Billy had read out the story of the woman taken in adultery. Fair enough, he thought; I am a troublemaker.

Billy did not feel drowsy, and it was still light outside, but he fell asleep immediately. He was awakened by a terrific noise like a thunderstorm overhead. He sat upright. A dull dawn light came in through the rain-streaked windows, but there was no storm.

The other men were equally startled. Tommy said: "Jesus H. Christ, what was that?"

Mortimer was lighting a cigarette. "Artillery fire," he said. "Our own guns. Welcome to France, Taffy."

Billy was not listening. He was looking at Owen Bevin, in the bed opposite. Owen was sitting up with a corner of the sheet in his mouth, crying.

{ VIII }

Maud dreamed that Lloyd George put his hand up her skirt, whereupon she told him she was married to a German, and he informed the police, who had come to arrest her and were banging on her bedroom window.

She sat up in bed, confused. After a moment she realized how unlikely it was that the police would bang on a second-floor bedroom window even if they did want to arrest her. The dream faded away, but the noise continued. There was also a deep bass rumble as of a distant railway train.

She turned on the bedside lamp. The art nouveau silver clock on her mantelpiece said it was four in the morning. Had there been an earthquake? An explosion in a munitions factory? A train crash? She threw back the embroidered coverlet and stood up.

She drew back heavy green-and-navy striped curtains and looked out of the window down to the Mayfair street. In the dawn light she saw a young woman in a red dress, probably a prostitute on her way home, speaking anxiously to the driver of a horse-drawn milk cart. There was no one else in sight. Maud's window continued to rattle for no apparent reason. It was not even windy.

She pulled a watered silk robe over her nightgown and glanced into her cheval glass. Her hair was untidy but otherwise she looked respectable enough. She stepped into the corridor.

Aunt Herm stood there in a nightcap, beside Sanderson, Maud's maid, whose round face was pale with fear. Then Grout appeared on the stairs. "Good morning, Lady Maud; good morning, Lady Hermia," he said with imperturbable formality. "No need for alarm. It's the guns."

"What guns?" said Maud.

"In France, my lady," said the butler.

{ IX }

The British artillery barrage went on for a week.

It was supposed to last five days, but only one of those days enjoyed fine weather, to Fitz's consternation. Even though it was summer, for the rest of the time there was low cloud and rain. This made it difficult for the gunners to fire accurately. It also meant the spotter planes could not survey the results and help the gunners adjust their aim. This made matters especially difficult for those dedicated to counter-battery—destroying the German artillery—because the Germans wisely kept moving their guns, so that the British shells would fall harmlessly on vacated positions.

Fitz sat in the damp dugout that was battalion headquarters, gloomily smoking cigars and trying not to listen to the unending boom. In the absence of aerial photographs, he and other company commanders organized trench raids. These at least allowed eyeball observation of the enemy. However, it was a hazardous business, and raiding parties that stayed too long never returned. So the men had to hastily observe a short section of the line and scurry home.

To Fitz's great annoyance, they brought back conflicting reports. Some German trenches were destroyed; others remained intact. Some barbed wire had been cut, but by no means all of it. Most worrying was that some patrols were driven back by enemy fire. If the Germans were still able to shoot, clearly the artillery had not succeeded in its task of wiping out their positions.

Fitz knew that exactly twelve German prisoners had been taken by the Fourth Army during the barrage. All had been interrogated but, infuriatingly, they gave conflicting evidence. Some said their dugouts had been destroyed, others that the Germans were sitting safe and sound beneath the earth while the British wasted their ammunition overhead.

So unsure were the British of the effects of their shells that Haig postponed the attack, which had been scheduled for June 29. But the weather continued poor.

"It will have to be canceled," said Captain Evans at breakfast on the morning of June 30.

"Unlikely," Fitz commented.

"We don't attack until we have confirmation that the enemy defenses have been destroyed," Evans said. "That's an axiom of siege warfare."

Fitz knew that this principle had been agreed upon early in the planning, but later dropped. "Be realistic," he said to Evans. "We've been preparing this offensive for six months. This is our major action for 1916. All our effort has been put into it. How could it be canceled? Haig would have to resign. It might even bring down Asquith's government."

Evans seemed angered by that remark. His cheeks flushed and his voice went up in pitch. "Better for the government to fall than for us to send our men up against entrenched machine guns."

Fitz shook his head. "Look at the millions of tons of supplies that have been shipped, the roads and railways we've built to bring them here, the hundreds of thousands of men trained and armed and brought here from all over Britain. What will we do—send them all home?"

There was a long silence; then Evans said: "You're right, of course, Major." His words were conciliatory but his tone was one of barely suppressed rage. "We won't send them home," he said through clenched teeth. "We will bury them here."

At midday the rain stopped and the sun came out. A little later, confirmation came down the line: we attack tomorrow.

CHAPTER SEVENTEEN

July 1, 1916

Walter von Ulrich was in hell.

The British bombardment had been going on for seven days and nights. Every man in the German trenches looked ten years older than he had a week ago. They huddled in their dugouts—man-made caves deep in the ground behind the trenches—but the noise was still deafening, and the earth beneath their feet shook continually. Worst of all, they knew that a direct hit from the largest-caliber shell might destroy even the strongest of dugouts.

Whenever it stopped they climbed out into the trenches, ready to repel the big attack that everyone expected. As soon as they were satisfied that the British were not yet advancing, they would look at the damage. They would find a trench caved in, a dugout entrance buried under a pile of earth, and—on one sorry afternoon—a smashed canteen full of broken crockery, dripping jam tins, and liquid soap. Wearily they would shovel away the soil, patch the revetment with new planks, and order more stores.

The ordered stores did not come. Very little came to the front line.

The bombardment made all approaches dangerous. The men were hungry and thirsty. Walter had gratefully drunk rainwater from a shell hole more than once.

The men could not stay in the dugouts between bombardments. They had to be in the trenches, ready for the British. Sentries kept constant watch. The rest sat in or near the dugout entrances, ready either to run down the steps and shelter underground when the big guns opened up, or to rush to the parapet to defend their position if the attack came. Machine guns had to be carried underground every time, then brought back up and returned to their emplacements.

In between barrages the British attacked with trench mortars. Although these small bombs made little noise when fired, they were powerful enough to splinter the timber of the revetment. However, they came across no-man's-land in a slow arc, and it was possible to see them coming and take cover. Walter had dodged one, getting far enough away to escape injury, although it had sprayed earth all over his dinner, forcing him to throw away a good bowlful of hearty pork stew. That had been the last hot meal he got, and if he had it now he would eat it, he thought, dirt, too.

Shells were not all. This sector had suffered a gas attack. The men had gas masks, but the bottom of the trench was littered with the bodies of rats, mice, and other small creatures killed by the chlorine. Rifle barrels had turned greenish-black.

Soon after midnight on the seventh night of the bombardment, the shelling eased up, and Walter decided to go out on a patrol.

He put on a wool cap and rubbed earth on his face to darken it. He drew his pistol, the standard nine-millimeter Luger issued to German officers. He ejected the magazine from the butt and checked the ammunition. It was fully loaded.

He climbed a ladder and went over the parapet, a death-defying act by daylight but relatively safe in the dark. He ran, bent double, down the gentle slope as far as the German barbed-wire entanglement. There was a gap in the wire, placed—by design—directly in front of a German machine-gun emplacement. He crawled through the gap on his knees.

It reminded him of the adventure stories he used to read as a schoolboy. Usually they featured square-jawed young Germans menaced by Red Indians, pygmies with blowpipes, or sly English spies. He recalled a lot of crawling through undergrowth, jungle, and prairie grass.

There was not much undergrowth here. Eighteen months of war had left only a few patches of grass and bushes and the occasional small tree dotted around a wasteland of mud and shell holes.

Which made it worse, because there was no cover. Tonight was moonless, but the landscape was occasionally lit by the flash of an explosion or the fierce bright light of a flare. All Walter could do then was fall flat and freeze. If he happened to be in a crater he might be hard to see. Otherwise he just had to hope no one was looking his way.

There were a lot of unexploded British shells on the ground. Walter calculated that something like a third of their ammunition were duds. He knew that Lloyd George had been put in charge of munitions, and guessed that the crowd-pleasing demagogue had prioritized volume over quality. Germans would never make such a mistake, he thought.

He reached the British wire, crawled laterally until he found a gap, and passed through.

As the British line began to appear, like the smear of a black paintbrush against a wash of dark gray sky, he dropped to his belly and tried to move silently. He had to get close: that was the point. He wanted to hear what the men in the trenches were saying.

Both sides sent out patrols every night. Walter usually dispatched a couple of bright-looking soldiers who were bored enough to relish an adventure, albeit a dangerous one. But sometimes he went himself, partly to show that he was willing to risk his own life, partly because his own observations were generally more detailed.

He listened, straining to hear a cough, a few muttered words, perhaps a fart followed by a sigh of satisfaction. He seemed to be in front of a quiet section. He turned left, crawled fifty yards, and stopped. Now he could hear an unfamiliar sound a bit like the hum of distant machinery.

He crawled on, trying hard to keep his bearings. It was easy to lose all sense of direction in the dark. One night, after a long crawl, he had come up against the barbed wire he had passed half an hour earlier, and realized he had gone around in a circle.

He heard a voice say quietly: "Over by here." He froze. A masked flashlight bobbed into his field of view, like a firefly. In its faint reflected light he made out three soldiers in British-style steel helmets thirty yards away. He was tempted to roll away from them, but decided the movement was more likely to give him away. He drew his pistol: if he was going to die he would take some of the enemy with him. The safety catch was on the left side just above the grip. He thumbed it up and forward. It made a click that sounded to him like a thunderclap, but the British soldiers did not appear to hear it.

Two of them were carrying a roll of barbed wire. Walter guessed they were going to renew a section that had been flattened by German artillery during the day. Maybe I should shoot them quickly, he thought, one-two-three. They will try to kill me tomorrow. But he had more important work to do, and he refrained from pulling the trigger as he watched them go by and recede into darkness.

He thumbed back the safety catch, holstered his gun, and crawled closer to the British trench.

Now the noise was louder. He lay still for a moment, concentrating. It was the sound of a crowd. They were trying to be quiet, but men in the mass could always be heard. It was a sound formed of shuffling feet, rustling clothes, sniffing and yawning and belching. Over that there was the occasional quiet word spoken in a voice of authority.

But what intrigued and startled Walter was that it seemed such a big crowd. He could not estimate how many. Lately the British had dug new, broader trenches, as if to hold vast quantities of stores, or very large artillery pieces. But perhaps they were for crowds.

Walter had to see.

He crawled forward. The sound grew. He had to look inside the trench, but how could he do so without being seen himself?

He heard a voice behind him, and his heart stopped.

He turned and saw the glowworm flashlight. The barbed-wire detail was returning. He pushed himself into the mud, then slowly drew his pistol.

They were hurrying, not troubling to be quiet, glad their task was done and keen to get back to safety. They came close, but did not look at him.

When they had passed, he was inspired, and leaped to his feet.

Now, if anyone should shine a light and see him, he would appear to be part of the group.

He followed them. He did not think they would hear his steps clearly enough to distinguish them from their own. None of them looked back.

He peered toward the source of the noise. He could see into the trench, now, but at first he could make out only a few points of light, presumably flashlights. But his eyes gradually adjusted, and at last he worked out what he was seeing, and then he was astonished.

He was looking at thousands of men.

He stopped. The broad trench, whose purpose had not been clear, was now revealed to be an assembly trench. The British were massing their troops for the big push. They stood waiting, fidgeting, the light from the officers' flashlights glinting off bayonets and steel helmets, line after line of them. Walter tried to count: ten lines of ten men was a hundred, the same again made two hundred, four hundred, eight . . . There were sixteen hundred men within his field of vision; then the darkness closed in over the others.

The assault was about to begin.

He had to get back as fast as possible with this information. If the German artillery opened up now, they could kill thousands of the enemy right here, behind British lines, before the attack got started. It was an opportunity sent by heaven, or perhaps by the devils who threw the cruel dice of war. As soon as he reached his own lines he would telephone headquarters.

A flare went up. In its light he saw a British sentry looking over the parapet, rifle at the ready, staring at him.

Walter dropped to the ground and buried his face in the mud.

A shot rang out. Then one of the barbed-wire detail shouted: "Don't shoot, you mad bastard. It's us!" The accent put Walter in mind of the staff at Fitz's house in Wales, and he guessed this was a Welsh regiment.

The flare died. Walter leaped to his feet and ran, heading for the German side. The sentry would be unable to see for a few seconds, his vision spoiled by the flare. Walter ran faster than he ever had, expecting the rifle to fire again at any moment. In half a minute he came to the British wire and dropped gratefully to his knees. He crawled rapidly forward through a gap. Another flare went up. He was still within rifle range, but no longer easily visible. He dropped to the ground. The flare was directly above him, and a dangerous lump of burning magnesium dropped a yard from his hand, but there were no more gunshots.

When the flare had burned out he got to his feet and ran all the way to the German line.

{ II }

Two miles behind the British front line, Fitz watched anxiously as the Eighth Battalion formed up shortly after two a.m. He was afraid these freshly trained men would disgrace him, but they did not. They were in a subdued mood and obeyed orders with alacrity.

The brigadier, sitting on his horse, addressed the men briefly. He was lit up from below by a sergeant's flashlight, and looked like the villain in an American moving picture. "Our artillery has wiped out the German defenses," he said. "When you reach the other side, you will find nothing but dead Germans."

A Welsh voice from somewhere nearby murmured: "Marvelous, isn't it, how these Germans can shoot back at us even when they're fucking dead."

Fitz raked the lines to identify the speaker but he could not in the dark.

The brigadier went on: "Take and secure their trenches, and the field kitchens will follow and give you a hot dinner."

B Company marched off toward the battlefield, led by the platoon sergeants. They went across the fields, leaving the roads clear for wheeled transport. As they left they started to sing "Guide Me O Thou Great Jehovah." Their voices lingered in the night air for some minutes after they disappeared into the darkness.

Fitz returned to battalion headquarters. An open truck was waiting to take the officers to the front line. Fitz sat next to Lieutenant Roland Morgan, son of the Aberowen colliery manager.

Fitz did all he could to discourage defeatist talk, but he could not help wondering if the brigadier had gone too far the other way. No army had ever mounted an offensive like this one, and nobody could be sure how it would turn out. Seven days of artillery bombardment had *not* obliterated the enemy's defenses: the Germans were still shooting back, as that anonymous soldier had sarcastically pointed out. Fitz had actually said the same thing in a report, whereupon Colonel Hervey had asked him if he was scared.

Fitz was worried. When the general staff closed their eyes to bad news, men died.

As if to prove his point, a shell exploded in the road behind. Fitz looked back and saw parts of a lorry just like this one flying through the air. A car following it swerved into a ditch, and in its turn was hit by another truck. It was a scene of carnage, but the driver of Fitz's truck quite correctly did not stop to help. The wounded had to be left to the medics.

More shells fell in the fields to the left and right. The Germans were targeting approaches to the front line, rather than the line itself. They must have worked out that the big assault was about to begin—such a huge movement of men could hardly be hidden from their intelligence branch—and with deadly efficiency they were killing men who had not yet even reached the trenches. Fitz fought down a feeling of panic, but his fear remained. B Company might not even make it to the battlefield.

He reached the marshaling area without further incident. Several thousand men were there already, leaning on their rifles and talking in low voices. Fitz heard that some groups had already been decimated by shelling. He waited, wondering grimly whether his company still existed. But eventually the Aberowen Pals arrived intact, to his relief, and formed up. Fitz led them the last few hundred yards to the frontline assembly trench.

Then they had nothing to do but wait for zero hour. There was water in the trench, and Fitz's puttees were soon soaked. No singing was permitted now: it might be heard at the enemy lines. Smoking was forbidden, too. Some of the men were praying. A tall soldier took out his pay book and began to fill out the "Last Will and Testament" page in the narrow beam of Sergeant Elijah Jones's flashlight. He wrote with his left hand, and Fitz recognized him as Morrison, a former footman at Tŷ Gwyn and left-handed bowler in the cricket team.

Dawn came early—midsummer was only a few days past. With the light, some men took out photographs and stared at them or kissed them. It seemed sentimental, and Fitz hesitated to copy the men, but after a while he did. His picture showed his son, George, whom they called Boy. He was now eighteen months old, but the photo had been taken on his first birthday. Bea must have taken him to a photographer's studio, for behind him there was a backdrop, in poor taste, of a flowery glade. He did not look much of a boy, dressed as he was in a white frock of some kind and a bonnet; but he was whole and healthy, and he was there to inherit the earldom if Fitz died today.

Bea and Boy would be in London now, Fitz assumed. It was July, and the social season went on, albeit in a lower key: girls had to make their debuts, for how else would they meet suitable husbands?

The light strengthened; then the sun appeared. The steel helmets of the Aberowen Pals shone, and their bayonets flashed reflections of the new day. Most of them had never been in battle. What a baptism they would have, win or lose.

A mammoth British artillery barrage began with the light. The gunners were giving their all. Perhaps this last effort would finally destroy the German positions. That must be what General Haig was praying for.

The Aberowen Pals were not in the first wave, but Fitz went forward to look at the battlefield, leaving the lieutenants in charge of B Company. He pushed through the crowds of waiting men to the frontline trench, where he stood on the fire step and looked through a peephole in the sandbagged parapet.

A morning mist was dispersing, chased by the rays of the rising sun. The blue sky was blotched by the dark smoke of exploding shells. It was going to be fine, Fitz saw, a beautiful French summer day. "Good weather for killing Germans," he said to no one in particular.

He remained at the front as zero hour approached. He wanted to see what happened to the first wave. There might be lessons to be learned. Although he had been an officer in France for almost two years, this would be the first time he commanded men in battle, and he was more nervous about that than about getting killed.

A ration of rum was given out to each man. Fitz drank some. Despite the warmth of the spirit in his stomach, he felt himself becoming more tense. Zero hour was seven thirty. When seven o'clock passed, the men grew still.

At seven twenty the British guns fell silent.

"No!" Fitz said aloud. "Not yet—this is too soon!" No one was listening, of course. But he was aghast. This would tell the Germans that an attack was imminent. They would now be piling out of their dugouts, hauling up their machine guns, and taking their positions. Our gunners had given the enemy a clear ten minutes to prepare! They should have kept up the fire until the last possible moment, seven twenty-nine and fifty-nine seconds.

But nothing could be done about it now.

Fitz wondered grimly how many men would die just because of that blunder.

Sergeants barked commands, and the men around Fitz climbed the scaling ladders and scrambled over the parapet. They formed up on the near side of the British wire. They were about a quarter of a mile from the German line, but no one fired at them yet. To Fitz's surprise the sergeants barked: "Dressing by numbers, right dress—one!" The men began to dress off as if on the parade ground, carefully adjusting the distances between them until they were ranged as perfectly as skittles in a bowling alley. To Fitz's mind this was madness—it just gave the Germans more time to get ready.

At seven thirty a whistle blew, all the signalers dropped their flags, and the first line moved forward.

They did not sprint, being weighed down by their equipment: extra ammunition, a waterproof sheet, food and water, and two Mills bombs per man, hand grenades weighing almost two pounds each. They moved at a jog, splashing through the shell holes, and passed through the gaps in the British wire. As instructed, they re-formed into lines and went on, shoulder-to-shoulder, across no-man's-land.

When they were halfway, the German machine guns opened up.

Fitz saw men begin to fall a second before his ears picked up the familiar rattling sound. One went down, then a dozen, then twenty, then more. "Oh, my God," Fitz said as they fell, fifty of them, a hundred more. He stared aghast at the slaughter. Some men threw up their hands when hit; others screamed, or convulsed; others just went limp and fell to the ground like dropped kit bags.

This was worse than the pessimistic Gwyn Evans had predicted, worse than Fitz's most terrible fears.

Before they reached the German wire, most of them had fallen.

Another whistle blew, and the second line advanced.

{ III }

Private Robin Mortimer was angry. "This is fucking stupid," he said when they heard the crackle of machine guns. "We should have gone over in the dark. You can't cross no-man's-land in broad fucking daylight. They're not even laying down a smoke screen. It's fucking suicide."

The men in the assembly trench were unnerved. Billy was worried by the fall in morale among the Aberowen Pals. On the march from their billet to the front line, they had experienced their first artillery attack. They had not suffered a direct hit, but groups ahead and behind had been massacred. Almost as bad, they had marched past a series of newly dug pits, all exactly six feet deep, and had worked out that these were mass graves, ready to receive the day's dead.

"The wind is wrong for a smoke screen," said Prophet Jones mildly. "That's why they're not using gas, either."

"Fucking insane," Mortimer muttered.

George Barrow said cheerfully: "The higher-ups know best. They been bred to rule. Leave it to them, I say."

Tommy Griffiths could not let that pass. "How can you believe that, when they sent you to Borstal?"

"They got to put people like me in jail," George said stoutly. "Otherwise everyone would be thieving. I might get robbed myself!"

Everyone laughed, except the morose Mortimer.

Major Fitzherbert reappeared, looking grim, carrying a jug of rum. The lieutenant gave them all a ration, pouring it into the mess tins they held out. Billy drank his without enjoyment. The fiery spirit cheered the men up, but not for long.

The only time Billy had felt like this was on his first day down the mine, when Rhys Price had left him alone and his lamp had gone out. A vision had helped him then. Unfortunately, Jesus appeared to boys with fevered imaginations, not sober, literal-minded men. Billy was on his own today.

The supreme test was almost on him, perhaps minutes away. Would he keep his nerve? If he failed—if he curled up in a ball on the ground and closed his eyes, or broke down in tears, or ran away—he would feel ashamed for the rest of his life. I'd rather die, he thought, but will I feel that way when the shooting starts?

They all moved a few steps forward.

He took out his wallet. Mildred had given him a photo of herself. She was dressed in a coat and hat: he would have preferred to remember her the way she had been the evening he went to her bedroom.

He wondered what she was doing now. Today was Saturday, so presumably she would be at Mannie Litov's, sewing uniforms. It was midmorning, and the women would be stopping for a break about now. Mildred might tell them all a funny story.

He thought about her all the time. Their night together had been an extension of the kissing lesson. She had stopped him going at things like a bull at a gate, and had taught him slower, more playful ways, caresses that had been exquisitely pleasurable, more so than he could have imagined. She had kissed his peter, and then asked him to do the equivalent to her. Even better, she had shown him how to do it so that it made her cry out in ecstasy. At the end, she had produced a condom from her bedside drawer. He had never seen one, though the boys talked about them, calling them rubber johnnies. She had put it on him, and even that had been thrilling.

It seemed like a daydream, and he had to keep reminding himself that it had really happened. Nothing in his upbringing had prepared him for Mildred's carefree, eager attitude to sex, and it had come to him like a revelation. His parents and most people in Aberowen would call her "unsuitable," with two children and no sign of a husband; but Billy would not have minded if she had six children. She had opened the gates of paradise to him, and all he wanted to do was go there again. More than anything else, he wanted to survive today so that he could see Mildred again and spend another night with her.

As the Pals shuffled forward, slowly getting nearer to the frontline trench, Billy found he was sweating.

Owen Bevin began to cry. Billy said gruffly: "Pull yourself together, now, Private Bevin. No good crying, is it?"

The boy said: "I want to go home."

"So do I, boyo. So do I."

"Please, Corporal, I didn't think it would be like this."

"How old are you anyway?"

"Sixteen."

"Bloody hell," said Billy. "How did you get recruited?"

"I told the doctor how old I was, and he said: 'Go away, and come back in the morning. You're tall for your age—you might be eighteen by tomorrow.' And he gave me a wink, see, so I knew I had to lie."

"Bastard," said Billy. He looked at Owen. The boy was not going to be any use on the battlefield. He was shaking and sobbing.

Billy spoke to Lieutenant Carlton-Smith. "Sir, Bevin is only sixteen, sir."

"Good God," said the lieutenant.

"He should be sent back. He'll be a liability."

"I don't know about that." Carlton-Smith looked baffled and helpless.

Billy recalled how Prophet Jones had tried to make an ally of Mortimer. Prophet was a good leader, thinking ahead and acting to prevent problems. Carlton-Smith, by contrast, seemed to be of no account, yet he was the superior officer. That's why it's called the class system, Da would have said.

After a minute, Carlton-Smith went to Fitzherbert and said something in a low voice. The major shook his head in negation, and Carlton-Smith shrugged helplessly.

Billy had not been brought up to look on cruelty without a protest. "The boy is only sixteen, sir!"

"Too late to say that now," said Fitzherbert. "And don't speak until you're spoken to, Corporal."

Billy knew that Fitzherbert did not recognize him. Billy was just one of hundreds of men who worked in the earl's pits. Fitzherbert did not know he was Ethel's brother. All the same, the casual dismissal angered Billy. "It's against the law," he said stubbornly. In other circumstances Fitzherbert would have been the first person to pontificate about respect for the law.

"I'll be the judge of that," said Fitz irritably. "That's why I'm the officer."

Billy's blood began to boil. Fitzherbert and Carlton-Smith stood there in their tailored uniforms, glaring at Billy in his itchy khaki, thinking that they could do anything. "The law is the law," Billy said.

Prophet spoke quietly. "I see you've forgotten your stick this morning, Major Fitzherbert. Shall I send Bevin back to headquarters to get it for you?"

It was a face-saving compromise, Billy thought. Well done, Prophet. But Fitzherbert was not buying it. "Don't be ridiculous," he said.

Suddenly Bevin darted away. He slipped into the crowd of men behind and disappeared from sight in a moment. It was so surprising that some of the men laughed.

"He won't get far," said Fitzherbert. "And when they catch him, it won't be very funny."

"He's a child!"

Fitzherbert fixed him with a look. "What's your name?" he said.

"Williams, sir."

Fitzherbert looked startled, but recovered fast. "There are hundreds of Williamses," he said. "What's your first name?"

"William, sir. They call me Billy Twice."

Fitzherbert gave him a hard stare.

He knows, Billy thought. He knows Ethel has a brother called Billy Williams. He stared straight back.

Fitzherbert said: "One more word out of you, Private William Williams, and you'll be on a charge."

There was a whistling sound above. Billy ducked. From behind him came a deafening bang. A hurricane blew all around him: clods of earth and fragments of planking flew past. He heard screams. Abruptly he found himself flat on the ground, not sure whether he had been knocked over or had thrown himself down. Something heavy hit his head, and he cursed. Then a boot thumped to the ground beside his face. There was a leg attached to the boot, but nothing else. "Oh, Christ," he said.

He got to his feet. He was uninjured. He looked around at the members of his section: Tommy, George Barrow, Mortimer . . . they were all standing up. Everyone pushed forward, suddenly seeing the front line as an escape route.

Major Fitzherbert shouted: "Hold your positions, men!"

Prophet Jones said: "As you were, as you were."

The surge forward was halted. Billy tried to brush mud off his uniform. Then another shell landed behind them. If anything, this one was farther back, but that made little difference. There was a bang, a hurricane, and a rain of debris and body parts. The men started scrambling out of the assembly trench at the front and to either side. Billy and his section joined in. Fitzherbert, Carlton-Smith, and Roland Morgan were screaming at the men to stay where they were, but no one was listening.

They ran forward, trying to get a safe distance from where the shells were landing. As they approached the British barbed wire, they slowed down, and stopped at the near edge of no-man's-land, realizing that ahead was a danger as great as the one from which they were fleeing.

Making the best of it, the officers joined them. "Form a line!" shouted Fitzherbert.

Billy looked at Prophet. The sergeant hesitated, then went along with it. "Line up, line up!" he called.

"Look at that," Tommy said to Billy.

"What?"

"Beyond the wire."

Billy looked.

"The bodies," Tommy said.

Billy saw what he meant. The ground was littered with corpses in khaki, some of them horribly mangled, some lying peacefully as if asleep, some intertwined like lovers.

There were thousands of them.

"Jesus help us," Billy whispered.

He felt sickened. What kind of world was this? What could be God's purpose in letting this happen?

A Company lined up, and Billy and the rest of B Company shuffled into place behind them.

Billy's horror turned to anger. Earl Fitzherbert and his like had planned this. They were in charge, and they were to blame for this slaughter. They should be shot, he thought furiously, every bloody one of them.

Lieutenant Morgan blew a whistle, and A Company ran on like

rugby forwards. Carlton-Smith blew his whistle, and Billy set off at a jog.

Then the German machine guns opened up.

The men of A Company started to fall, and Morgan was the first. They had not fired their weapons. This was not battle; it was massacre. Billy looked at the men around him. He felt defiant. The officers had failed. The men had to make their own decisions. To hell with orders. "Sod this," he shouted. "Take cover!" And he threw himself into a shell hole.

The sides were muddy and there was stinking water at the bottom, but he pressed himself gratefully to the clammy earth as the bullets flew over his head. A moment later Tommy landed by his side, then the rest of the section. Men from other sections copied Billy's.

Fitzherbert ran past their hole. "Keep moving, you men!" he shouted.

Billy said: "If he insists, I'm going to shoot the bastard."

Then Fitzherbert was hit by machine-gun fire. Blood spurted from his cheek, and one leg crumpled beneath him. He fell to the ground.

Officers were in as much danger as men. Billy was no longer angry. Instead he felt ashamed of the British army. How could it be so completely useless? After all the effort that had been put in, the money they had spent, the months of planning—the big assault was a fiasco. It was humiliating.

Billy looked around. Fitz lay still, unconscious. Neither Lieutenant Carlton-Smith nor Sergeant Jones was in sight. The other men in the section were looking at Billy. He was only a corporal, but they expected him to tell them what to do.

He turned to Mortimer, who had once been an officer. "What do you think—"

"Don't look at me, Taffy," said Mortimer sourly. "You're the fucking corporal."

Billy had to come up with a plan.

He was not going to lead them back. He hardly considered that option. It would be a waste of the lives of the men who had already died.

We must gain something from all this, he thought; we must give some kind of account of ourselves.

On the other hand, he was not going to run into machine-gun fire.

The first thing he needed to do was survey the scene.

He took off his steel helmet, held it at arm's length, and raised it over the lip of the crater as a decoy, just in case a German had his sights on this hole. But nothing happened.

He raised his head over the edge, expecting at any moment to be shot through the skull. He survived that, too.

He looked across the divide and up the hill, over the German barbed wire to their front line, dug into the hillside. He could see rifle barrels poking through gaps in the parapet. "Where's that fucking machine gun?" he said to Tommy.

"Not sure."

C Company ran past. Some took cover, but others held the line. The machine gun opened up again, raking the line, and the men fell like skittles. Billy was no longer shocked. He was searching for the source of the bullets.

"Got it," said Tommy.

"Where?"

"Take a straight line from here to that clump of bushes at the top of the hill."

"Right."

"See where that line crosses the German trench?"

"Aye."

"Then go a bit to your right."

"How far . . . Never mind. I see the bastards." Ahead and a little to Billy's right, something that might have been a protective iron shield stuck up above the parapet, and the distinctive barrel of a machine gun protruded over it. Billy thought he could make out three German helmets around it, but it was hard to be sure.

They must be concentrating on the gap in the British wire, Billy thought. They repeatedly fired on men as they surged forward from that point. The way to attack them might be from a different angle. If his section could work its way diagonally across no-man's-land, they could come at the gun from the Germans' left, while the Germans were looking right.

He plotted a route using three large craters, the third just beyond a flattened section of German wire.

He had no idea whether this was correct military strategy. But correct strategy had got thousands of men killed this morning, so to hell with that.

He ducked down again and looked at the men around him. George Barrow was a steady shot with the rifle despite his youth. "Next time that machine gun opens up, get ready to fire. As soon as it stops, you start. With a bit of luck, they'll take cover. I'll be running to that shell hole over by there. Shoot steady and empty your magazine. You've got ten shots—make them last half a minute. By the time the Germans raise their heads, I should be in the next hole." He looked at the others. "Wait for another pause. Then all of you run while Tommy covers you. Third time, I'll cover and Tommy can run."

D Company ran into no-man's-land. The machine gun opened up. Rifles and trench mortars fired at the same time. But the carnage was less because more men were taking cover in shell holes instead of running into the hail of bullets.

Any minute now, Billy thought. He had told the men what he was going to do, and it would be too shameful to back out. He gritted his teeth. Better to die than be a coward, he told himself again.

The machine-gun fire ceased.

In an instant Billy leaped to his feet. Now he was a clear target. He bent over and ran.

Behind him he heard Barrow shooting. His life was in the hands of a seventeen-year-old Borstal boy. George fired steadily: bang, two, three, bang, two, three, just as ordered.

Billy charged across the field as fast as he could, loaded down as he was with kit. His boots stuck in the mud, his breath came in ragged gasps, his chest hurt, but his mind was empty of all thought except the desire to go faster. He was as close to death as he had ever been.

When he was a couple of yards from the shell hole, he threw his gun into it and dived as if tackling a rugby opponent. He landed on the rim of the crater and tumbled forward into the mud. He could hardly believe he was still alive.

He heard a ragged cheer. His section was applauding his run. He was amazed they could be so upbeat amid such carnage. How strange men were.

When he had caught his breath, he cautiously looked over the rim. He had run about a hundred yards. It was going to take some time to cross no-man's-land this way. But the alternative was suicide.

The machine gun opened up again. When it stopped, Tommy started shooting. He followed George's example and paused between shots. How fast we learn when our lives are in danger, Billy thought. As the tenth and last bullet in Tommy's magazine was fired, the rest of the section fell into the pit beside Billy.

"Come this side," he shouted, beckoning them forward. The German position was uphill from here, and Billy feared the enemy might be able to see into the back half of the crater.

He rested his rifle on the rim and sighted at the machine gun. After a while the Germans opened up again. When they stopped, Billy fired. He willed Tommy to run fast. He cared more about Tommy than the rest of the section put together. He held his rifle steady and fired at intervals of about five seconds. It did not matter whether he hit anyone, as long as he forced the Germans to keep their heads down while Tommy ran.

His rifle clicked on empty, and Tommy landed beside him.

"Bloody hell," said Tommy. "How many times have we got to do that?"

"Two more, I reckon," Billy said, reloading. "Then we'll either be close enough to throw a Mills bomb . . . or we'll all be fucking dead."

"Don't swear, now, Billy, please," said Tommy straight-faced. "You know I finds it distasteful."

Billy chuckled. Then he wondered how he could. I'm in a shell hole with the German army shooting at me and I'm laughing, he thought. God help me.

They moved in the same way to the next shell hole, but it was farther off, and this time they lost a man. Joey Ponti was hit in the head while running. George Barrow picked him up and carried him, but he was dead, a bloody hole in his skull. Billy wondered where his kid brother, Johnny, was: he had not seen him since leaving the assembly trench. I'll have to be the one to tell him the news, Billy thought. Johnny worshipped his big brother.

There were other dead men in this hole. Three khaki-clad bodies floated in the scummy water. They must have been among the first to go over the top. Billy wondered how they had got this far. Perhaps it was just the odds. The guns were bound to miss a few in the first sweep, and mop them up on the return.

Other groups were coming closer to the German line now by following similar tactics. Either they were copying Billy's group or, more likely, they had gone through the same thought process, abandoning the foolish line charge ordered by the officers and devising their own more sensible tactics. The upshot was that the Germans no longer had things all their own way. Under fire themselves, they were not able to keep up the same relentless storm of gunfire. Perhaps for that reason, Billy's group made it to the last shell hole without further losses.

In fact they gained a man. A total stranger lay down next to Billy. "Where the fuck did you come from?" Billy said.

"I lost my group," the man said. "You seem to know what you're doing, so I followed you. I sure hope you don't mind."

He spoke with an accent Billy guessed might be Canadian. "Are you a good thrower?" Billy asked.

"Played for my high school baseball team."

"Right. When I give the word, see if you can hit that machine-gun emplacement with a Mills bomb."

Billy told Spotty Llewellyn and Alun Pritchard to throw their grenades while the rest of the section gave covering fire. Once again, they waited until the machine gun stopped. "Now!" Billy yelled, and he stood up.

There was a small flurry of rifle fire from the German trench. Spotty and Alun, spooked by the bullets, threw wildly. Neither bomb reached the trench, which was fifty yards away; they fell short and exploded harmlessly. Billy cursed: they had simply left the machine gun undamaged and, sure enough, it opened up again and, a moment later, Spotty convulsed horribly as a hail of bullets tore into his body.

Billy felt strangely calm. He took a second to focus on his target and draw his arm all the way back. He calculated the distance as if he were throwing a rugby ball. He was dimly aware that the Canadian, standing next to him, was equally cool. The machine gun rattled and spat and swung toward them.

They threw at the same time.

Both bombs went into the trench close to the emplacement. There was a double whump. Billy saw the barrel of the machine gun fly through the air, and he yelled in triumph. He pulled the pin from his second grenade and dashed up the slope, screaming: "Charge!"

Exhilaration ran in his veins like a drug. He hardly knew he was in danger. He had no idea how many Germans might be in that trench pointing their rifles at him. The others followed him. He threw his second grenade, and they copied him. Some flew wild, others landed in the trench and exploded.

Billy reached the trench. At that point he realized that his rifle was slung over his shoulder. By the time he could move it to the firing position, a German could shoot him dead.

But there were no Germans left alive.

The grenades had done terrible damage. The floor of the trench was littered with dead bodies and—worse to look at—parts of bodies. If any Germans had survived the onslaught, they had retreated. Billy jumped down into the trench and at last got his rifle in both hands in the ready stance. But he did not need it. There was no one left to shoot at.

Tommy leaped down beside him. "We done it!" he shouted ecstatically. "We took a German trench!"

Billy felt a savage glee. They had tried to kill him, but instead he had killed them. It was a feeling of profound satisfaction, like nothing he had known before. "You're right," he said to Tommy. "We done it."

Billy was struck by the quality of the German fortifications. He had a miner's eye for a secure structure. The walls were braced with planks, the traverses were square, and the dugouts were surprisingly deep, twenty and sometimes thirty feet down, with neatly framed doorways and wooden steps. That explained how so many Germans had survived seven days of relentless shelling.

The Germans presumably dug their trenches in networks, with communications trenches linking the front to storage and service areas in the rear. Billy needed to make sure there were no enemy troops waiting in ambush. He led the others on an exploratory patrol, rifles at the ready, but they found no one.

The network ended at the top of the hill. From there Billy looked around. Left of their position, beyond an area of heavy shell damage, other British troops had taken the next sector; to their right, the trench ended and the ground fell away into a little valley with a stream.

He looked east into enemy territory. He knew that a mile or two away was another trench system, the Germans' second line of defense. He was ready to lead his little group forward, but he hesitated. He could not see any other British troops advancing, and he guessed that his men had used up most of their ammunition. At any moment, he presumed, supply trucks would come bumping across the shell holes with more ammunition and orders for the next phase.

He looked up at the sky. It was midday. The men had not eaten since last night. "Let's see if the Germans left any food behind," he said. He stationed Suet Hewitt at the top of the hill as a lookout in case the Germans counterattacked.

There was not much to forage. It seemed the Germans were not very well-fed. They found stale black bread and hard salami-style sausage. There was not even any beer. The Germans were supposed to be famous for their beer.

The brigadier had promised that field kitchens would follow the advancing troops, but when Billy looked impatiently back over no-man's-land, he saw no sign of supplies.

They settled down to eat their rations of hard biscuits and bully beef.

He should send someone back to report. But before he could do so, the German artillery changed its aim. They had begun by shelling the British rear. Now they focused on no-man's-land. Volcanoes of earth were erupting between the British and German lines. The bombardment was so intense that no one could have got back alive.

Luckily, the gunners were avoiding their own front line. Presumably they did not know which sectors had been taken by the British and which remained in German hands.

Billy's group was stuck. They could not advance without ammunition, and they could not retreat because of the bombardment. But Billy seemed to be the only one worried by their position. The others started looking for souvenirs. They picked up pointed helmets, cap badges, and pocketknives. George Barrow examined all the dead Germans and took their watches and rings. Tommy took an officer's nine-millimeter Luger and a box of ammunition.

They began to feel lethargic. It was not surprising: they had been up all night. Billy posted two lookouts and let the rest of them doze. He felt disappointed. On his first day of battle he had won a little victory, and he wanted to tell someone about it.

In the evening the barrage let up. Billy considered whether to retreat. There seemed no point in doing anything else, but he was afraid of being accused of desertion in the face of the enemy. There was no telling what superior officers might be capable of.

However, the decision was made for him by the Germans. Suet Hewitt, the lookout on the ridge, saw them advancing from the east. Billy saw a large force—fifty or a hundred men—running across the valley toward him. His men could not defend the ground they had taken without fresh ammunition.

On the other hand, if they retreated they might be blamed.

He summoned his handful of men. "Right, boys," he said. "Fire at will. Then retreat when you run out of ammo." He emptied his rifle at the advancing troops, who were still half a mile out of range, then turned and ran. The others did the same.

They scrambled across the German trenches and back over no-man's-land toward the setting sun, jumping over the dead and dodging the stretcher parties who were picking up the wounded. But no one shot at them.

When Billy reached the British side he jumped into a trench that was crowded with dead bodies, wounded men, and exhausted survivors like himself. He saw Major Fitzherbert lying on a stretcher, his face bloody but his eyes open, alive and breathing. There's one I wouldn't have minded losing, he thought. Many men were just sitting or lying in the mud, staring into space, dazed by shock and paralyzed by weariness. The officers were trying to organize the return of men and bodies to the rear sections. There was no sense of triumph. No one was moving forward; the officers were not even looking at the battlefield. The great attack had been a failure.

The remaining men of Billy's section followed him into the trench.

"What a cock-up," Billy said. "What a God-almighty cock-up."

{ IV }

A week later Owen Bevin was court-martialed for cowardice and desertion.

He was given the option of being defended, at the trial, by an officer appointed to act as the "prisoner's friend," but he declined. Because the offense carried the death penalty, a plea of Not Guilty was automatically entered. However, Bevin said nothing in his defense. The trial took less than an hour. Bevin was convicted.

He was sentenced to death.

The papers were passed to general headquarters for review. The commander in chief approved the death sentence. Two weeks later, in a muddy French cow pasture at dawn, Bevin stood blindfolded before a firing squad.

Some of the men must have aimed to miss, because after they fired Bevin was still alive, though bleeding. The officer in charge of the firing squad then approached, drew his pistol, and fired two shots point-blank into the boy's forehead.

Then, at last, Owen Bevin died.

CHAPTER EIGHTEEN

Late July 1916

Ethel thought a lot about life and death after Billy went off to France. She knew she might never see him again. She was glad he had lost his virginity with Mildred. "I let your little brother have his wicked way with me," Mildred had said lightheartedly after he left. "Sweet boy. Have you got any more like that down there in Wales?" But Ethel suspected Mildred's feelings were not as superficial as she pretended, for in their nightly prayers Enid and Lillian now asked God to watch over Uncle Billy in France and bring him safely home again.

Lloyd developed a bad chest infection a few days later, and in an agony of desperation Ethel rocked him in her arms while he struggled to breathe. Fearing he might die, she bitterly regretted that her parents had never seen him. When he got better, she decided to take him to Aberowen.

She returned exactly two years after she had left. It was raining.

The place had not changed much, but it struck her as dismal. For the first twenty-one years of her life she had not seen it that way but now, after living in London, she noticed that Aberowen was all the same color. Everything was gray: the houses, the streets, the slag heaps, and the low rain clouds drifting disconsolately along the ridge of the mountain.

She felt tired as she emerged from the railway station in the middle of the afternoon. Taking a child of eighteen months on an all-day journey was hard work. Lloyd had been well-behaved, charming fellow passengers with his toothy grin. All the same he had to be fed in a rocking carriage, changed in a smelly toilet, and lulled to sleep when he became grizzly, and it was a strain with strangers looking on.

With Lloyd on her hip and a small suitcase in her hand, she set off across the station square and up the slope of Clive Street. Soon she was panting for breath. That was something else she had forgotten. London was mostly flat, but in Aberowen you could hardly go anywhere without walking up or down a steep hill.

She did not know what had happened here since she had left. Billy was her only source of news, and men were no good for gossip. No doubt she herself had been the main topic of conversation for some time. However, new scandals must have come along since.

Her return would be big news. Several women gave her frank stares as she walked up the street with her baby. She knew what they were thinking. Ethel Williams, believed she was better than us, coming back in an old brown dress with a toddler in her arms and no husband. Pride comes before a fall, they would say, their malice thinly disguised as pity.

She went to Wellington Row, but not to her parents' house. Her father had told her never to come back. She had written to Tommy Griffiths's mother, who was called Mrs. Griffiths Socialist on account of her husband's fiery politics. (In the same street there was a Mrs. Griffiths Church.) The Griffithses were not chapelgoers, and they disapproved of Ethel's father's hard line. Ethel had put Tommy up for the night in London, and Mrs. Griffiths was happy to reciprocate. Tommy was an only child, so while he was in the army there was a spare bed.

Da and Mam did not know Ethel was coming.

Mrs. Griffiths welcomed Ethel warmly and cooed over Lloyd. She had had a daughter of Ethel's age who had died of whooping cough—Ethel could just about remember her, a blond girl called Gwenny.

Ethel fed and changed Lloyd, then sat down in the kitchen for a cup of tea. Mrs. Griffiths noticed her wedding ring. "Married, is it?" she said.

"Widow," Ethel said. "He died at Ypres."

"Ah, pity."

"He was a Mr. Williams, so I didn't have to change my name."

This story would go all around the town. Some would question whether there really had been a Mr. Williams and if he had actually married Ethel. It did not matter whether they believed her. A woman who pretended to be married was acceptable; a mother who admitted to being single was a brazen hussy. The people of Aberowen had their principles.

Mrs. Griffiths said: "When are you going to see your mam?"

Ethel did not know how her parents would react to her. They might throw her out again, they might forgive everything, or they might find some way of condemning her sin without banishing her from their sight. "I dunno," she said. "I'm nervous."

Mrs. Griffiths looked sympathetic. "Aye, well, your da can be a Tartar. He loves you, though."

"People always think that. Your father loves you really, they say. But if he can throw me out of the house, I don't know why it's called love."

"People do things in haste, when their pride is hurt," Mrs. Griffiths said soothingly. "'Specially men."

Ethel stood up. "Well, no point in putting it off, I suppose." She scooped Lloyd up from the floor. "Come here, my lovely. Time you found out you've got grandparents."

"Good luck," said Mrs. Griffiths.

The Williams house was only a few doors away. Ethel was hoping her father would be out. That way she could at least have some time with her mother, who was less harsh.

She thought of knocking at the door, then decided that would be ridiculous, so she walked straight in.

She entered the kitchen where she had spent so many of her days. Neither of her parents was there, but Gramper was dozing in his chair. He opened his eyes, looked puzzled, then said warmly: "It's our Eth!"

"Hello, Gramper."

He stood up and came to her. He had become more frail: he leaned on the table just to cross the little room. He kissed her cheek and turned his attention to the baby. "Well, now, who is this?" he said with delight. "Could it be my first great-grandchild?"

"This is Lloyd," said Ethel.

"What a fine name!"

Lloyd hid his face in Ethel's shoulder. "He's shy," she said.

"Ah, he's scared of the strange old man with the white mustache. He'll get used to me. Sit down, my lovely, and tell me all about everything."

"Where's our mam?"

"Gone down the Co-op for a tin of jam." The local grocery was a cooperative store, sharing profits among its customers. Such shops were popular in South Wales, although no one knew how to pronounce *co-op*, variations ranging from *cop* to *quorp*. "She'll be back now in a minute."

Ethel put Lloyd on the floor. He began to explore the room, going unsteadily from one handhold to the next, a bit like Gramper. Ethel talked about her job as manager of *The Soldier's Wife:* working with the printer, distributing the bundles of newspapers, collecting unsold copies, getting people to place advertisements. Gramper wondered how she knew what to do, and she admitted that she and Maud just made it up as they went along. She found the printer difficult—he did not like taking instructions from women—but she was good at selling advertising space. While they talked, Gramper took off his watch chain and dangled it from his hand, not looking at Lloyd. The child stared at the bright chain, then reached for it. Gramper let him grab it. Soon Lloyd was leaning on Gramper's knees for support while he investigated the watch.

Ethel felt strange in the old house. She had imagined it would be comfortably familiar, like a pair of boots that have taken the shape of the feet that have worn them for years. But in fact she was vaguely uneasy. It seemed more like the home of familiar old neighbors. She kept looking at the faded samplers with their tired biblical verses and wondering why her mother had not changed them in decades. She did not feel that this was her place.

"Have you heard anything from our Billy?" she asked Gramper.

"No, have you?"

"Not since he left for France."

"I should think he's in this big battle by the river Somme."

"I hope not. They say it's bad."

"Aye, terrible, if you believe the rumors."

Rumors were all people had, for newspaper accounts were cheerfully vague. But many of the wounded were back in British hospitals, and their bloodcurdling accounts of incompetence and slaughter were passed from mouth to mouth.

Mam came in. "They stand talking in that shop as if they got nothing else to do— Oh!" She stopped short. "Oh, my heavens, is that our Eth?" She burst into tears.

Ethel hugged her.

Gramper said: "Look, Cara, here's your grandson, Lloyd."

Mam wiped her eyes and picked him up. "Isn't he beautiful?" she said. "Such curly hair! He looks just like Billy at that age." Lloyd stared fearfully at Mam for a long moment, then cried.

Ethel took him. "He's turned into a real mummy's boy lately," she said apologetically.

"They all do at that age," Mam said. "Make the most of it—he'll soon change."

"Where's Da?" Ethel said, trying not to sound too anxious.

Mam looked tense. "Gone to Caerphilly for a union meeting." She checked the clock. "He'll be home for his tea now in a minute, unless he's missed his train."

Ethel guessed Mam was hoping he would be late. She felt the same. She wanted more time with her mother before the crisis came.

Mam made tea and put a plate of sugary Welsh cakes on the table. Ethel took one. "I haven't had these for two years," she said. "They're lovely."

Gramper said happily: "Now, I call this nice. I got my daughter, my granddaughter, and my great-grandson, all in the same room. What more could a man ask of life?" He took a Welsh cake.

Ethel reflected that some people would think it was not much of a life Gramper led, sitting in a smoky kitchen all day in his only suit. But he was grateful for his lot, and she had made him happy today, at least.

Then her father came in.

Mam was halfway through a sentence. "I had a chance to go to London once, when I was your age, but your gramper said—" The door opened and she stopped dead. They all looked as Da came in from the street, wearing his meeting suit and a flat miner's cap, perspiring from the walk up the hill. He took a step into the room, then stopped, staring.

"Look who's here," Mam said with forced brightness. "Ethel, and your grandson." Her face was white with strain.

He said nothing. He did not take off his cap.

Ethel said: "Hello, Da. This is Lloyd."

He did not look at her.

Gramper said: "The little one resembles you, Dai boy—around the mouth, see what I mean?"

Lloyd sensed the hostility in the room and began to cry.

Still Da said nothing. Ethel knew then that she had made a mistake springing this on him. She had not wanted to give him the chance to forbid her to come. But now she saw that the surprise had put him on the defensive. He had a cornered look. It was always a mistake to back Da up against the wall, she remembered.

His face became stubborn. He looked at his wife and said: "I have no grandson."

"Oh, now," said Mam appealingly.

His expression remained rigid. He stood still, staring at Mam, not speaking. He was waiting for something, and he would not move until Ethel left. She began to cry.

Gramper said: "Oh, dammo."

Ethel picked up Lloyd. "I'm sorry, Mam," she sobbed. "I thought perhaps . . . " She choked up and could not finish the sentence. With Lloyd in her arms she pushed past her father. He did not meet her eye.

Ethel went out and slammed the door.

{ II }

In the morning, after the men had gone to work down the pit and the children had been sent to school, the women usually did jobs outside. They washed the pavement, polished the doorstep, or cleaned the windows. Some went to the shop or ran other errands. They needed to see the world beyond their small houses, Ethel thought, something to remind them that life was not bound within four jerry-built walls.

She stood in the sunshine outside the front door of Mrs. Griffiths Socialist, leaning against the wall. All up and down the street, women had found reasons to be out in the sun. Lloyd was playing with a ball. He had seen other children throw balls and he was trying to do the same, but failing. What a complicated action a throw was, Ethel reflected, using shoulder and arm, wrist and hand together. The fingers had to relax their grip just before the arm reached its longest stretch. Lloyd had not mastered this, and he released the ball too soon, sometimes dropping it behind his shoulder, or too late, so that it had no momentum. But he kept trying. He would get it right, eventually, Ethel supposed, and then he would never forget it. Until you had a child, you did not understand how much they had to learn.

She could not comprehend how her father could reject this little boy. Lloyd had done nothing wrong. Ethel herself was a sinner, but so were most people. God forgave their sins, so who was Da to sit in judgment? It made her angry and sad at the same time.

The boy from the post office came up the street on his pony and tied it up near the toilets. His name was Geraint Jones. His job was to bring parcels and telegrams, but today he did not appear to be carrying any packages. Ethel felt a sudden chill, as if a cloud had hidden the sun. In

Wellington Row telegrams were rare, and they usually brought bad news.

Geraint walked down the hill, away from Ethel. She felt relieved: the news was not for her family.

Her mind drifted to a letter she had received from Lady Maud. Ethel and Maud and other women had mounted a campaign to ensure that votes for women would be part of any discussion of franchise reform for soldiers. They had got enough publicity to ensure that Prime Minister Asquith could not duck the issue.

Maud's news was that he had sidestepped their thrust by handing the whole problem over to a committee called the Speaker's Conference. But this was good, Maud said. There would be a calm private debate instead of histrionic speeches in the chamber of the House of Commons. Perhaps common sense would prevail. All the same she was trying hard to find out whom Asquith was putting on the committee.

A few doors up, Gramper emerged from the Williams house, sat on the low windowsill, and lit his first pipe of the day. He spotted Ethel, smiled, and waved.

On the other side Minnie Ponti, the mother of Joey and Johnny, started beating a rug with a stick, knocking the dust out of it and making herself cough.

Mrs. Griffiths came out with a shovelful of ashes from the kitchen range and dropped them in a pothole in the dirt road.

Ethel said to her: "Can I do anything? I could go to the Co-op for you if you like." She had already made the beds and washed the breakfast dishes.

"All right," said Mrs. Griffiths. "I'll make you a list now in a minute." She leaned on the wall, panting. She was a heavy woman, and any exertion made her breathless.

Ethel became aware of a commotion at the bottom end of the street. Several voices were raised. Then she heard a scream.

She and Mrs. Griffiths looked at each other. Then Ethel picked up Lloyd and they hurried to find out what was happening on the far side of the toilets.

The first thing Ethel saw was a small group of women clustered around Mrs. Pritchard, who was wailing at the top of her voice. The other women were trying to calm her. But she was not the only one. Stumpy Pugh, an ex-miner who had lost a leg in a roof collapse, sat in the middle of the road as if knocked down, with two neighbors either side of him. Across the street Mrs. John Jones the Shop stood in her doorway sobbing, holding a sheet of paper.

Ethel saw Geraint the post office boy, white in the face and near to tears himself, cross the road and knock at another house.

Mrs. Griffiths said: "Telegrams from the War Office— Oh, God help us."

"The battle of the Somme," said Ethel. "The Aberowen Pals must be in it."

"Alun Pritchard must be dead, and Clive Pugh, and Prophet Jones. He was a sergeant. His parents were so proud . . . "

"Poor Mrs. Jones Shop—her other son died in the explosion down the pit."

"Let my Tommy be all right, please, God," Mrs. Griffiths prayed, even though her husband was a notorious atheist. "Oh, spare Tommy."

"And Billy," said Ethel; and then, whispering in Lloyd's tiny ear, she added: "And your daddy."

Geraint had a canvas sack slung across his shoulder. Ethel wondered fearfully how many more telegrams were in it. The boy crisscrossed the street, the angel of death in a post office cap.

By the time he passed the toilets and came to the upper half of the street, everyone was on the pavement. The women had stopped whatever work they were doing and stood waiting. Ethel's parents had come out—Da had not yet gone to work. They stood with Gramper, silent and afraid.

Geraint approached Mrs. Llewellyn. Her son Arthur must be dead. He was known as Spotty, Ethel recalled. The poor boy did not need to worry about his complexion now.

Mrs. Llewellyn held up her hands as if to ward Geraint off. "No!" she cried. "No, please!"

He held out her telegram. "I can't help it, Mrs. Llewellyn," he said. He was only about seventeen. "It's got your address on the front, see?"

Still she would not take the envelope. "No!" she said, turning her back and burying her face in her hands.

The boy's lip trembled. "Please take it," he said. "I got all these others to do. And there's more in the office, hundreds! It's ten o'clock now and I don't know how I'm going to get them all done before tonight. Please."

Her next-door neighbor, Mrs. Parry Price, said: "I'll take it for her. I haven't got any sons."

"Thank you very much, Mrs. Price," said Geraint, and he moved on.

He took another telegram from his sack, looked at the address, and walked past the Griffithses' house. "Oh, thank God," said Mrs. Griffiths. "My Tommy's all right, thank God." She began to cry with relief. Ethel switched Lloyd to her other hip and put an arm around her.

The boy approached Minnie Ponti. She did not scream, but tears ran down her face. "Which one?" she said in a cracked voice. "Joey or Johnny?"

"I dunno, Mrs. Ponti," said Geraint. "You'll have to read what it says by here."

She ripped open the envelope. "I can't see!" she cried. She rubbed her eyes, trying to clear her vision of tears, and looked again. "Giuseppe!" she said. "My Joey's dead. Oh, my poor little boy!"

Mrs. Ponti lived almost at the end of the street. Ethel waited, heart pounding, to see whether Geraint would go to the Williams house. Was Billy alive or dead?

The boy turned away from the weeping Mrs. Ponti. He looked across the street and saw Da, Mam, and Gramper staring at him in dreadful anticipation. He looked in his sack, then glanced up.

"No more for Wellington Row," he said.

Ethel almost collapsed. Billy was alive.

She looked at her parents. Mam was crying. Gramper was trying to light his pipe, but his hands were shaking.

Da was staring at her. She could not read the look on his face. He was in the grip of some emotion, but she could not tell what.

He took a step toward her.

It was not much, but it was enough. With Lloyd in her arms, she ran to Da.

He put his arms around both of them. "Billy's alive," he said. "And so are you."

"Oh, Da," she said. "I'm so sorry I let you down."

"Never mind that," he said. "Never mind, now." He patted her back as he had when she was a little girl and she fell down and scraped her knees. "There, there," he said. "Better now."

{ III }

An interdenominational service was a rare event among Aberowen's Christians, Ethel knew. To the Welsh, doctrinal differences were never minor. One group refused to celebrate Christmas, on the grounds that there was no biblical evidence of the date of Christ's birth. Another banned voting in elections, because the Apostle Paul wrote: "Our citizenship is in heaven." None of them liked to worship side by side with people who disagreed with them.

However, after Telegram Wednesday such differences came, briefly, to seem trivial.

The rector of Aberowen, the Reverend Thomas Ellis-Thomas, suggested a joint service of remembrance. When all the telegrams had been delivered there were two hundred and eleven dead and, as the battle was still going on, one or two more sad notifications arrived each day. Every street in town had lost someone, and in the close-packed rows of miners' hovels there was a bereavement every few yards.

The Methodists, the Baptists, and the Catholics agreed to the suggestion of the Anglican rector. The smaller groups might have preferred to remain aloof: the Full Gospel Baptists, the Jehovah's Witnesses, the Second Coming Evangelicals, and the Bethesda Chapel. Ethel saw her father wrestle with his conscience. But no one wanted to be left out of what promised to be the largest religious service in the town's history, and in the end they all joined in. There was no synagogue in Aberowen, but young Jonathan Goldman was among the dead, and the town's handful of practising Jews decided to attend, even though no concessions would be made to their religion.

The service was held on Sunday afternoon at half past two in a municipal park known as the Reck, short for Recreation Ground. A temporary platform was built by the town council for the clergy to stand on. It was a fine, sunny day, and three thousand people turned up.

Ethel scanned the crowd. Perceval Jones was there in a top hat. As well as being mayor of the town he was now its member of Parliament. He was also honorary commanding officer of the Aberowen Pals, and had led the recruiting drive. Several other directors of Celtic Minerals were with him—as if they had anything to do with the heroism of the dead, Ethel thought sourly. Maldwyn "Gone to Merthyr" Morgan showed up, with his wife, but they had a right, she thought, for their son Roland had died.

Then she saw Fitz.

At first she did not recognize him. She saw Princess Bea, in a black dress and hat, followed by a nurse carrying the young Viscount Aberowen, a boy the same age as Lloyd. With Bea was a man on crutches with his left leg in plaster and a bandage over one side of his head, covering his left eye. After a long moment Ethel realized it was Fitz, and she cried out in shock.

"What is it?" said her mam.

"Look at the earl!"

"Is that him? Oh, my word, the poor man."

Ethel stared at him. She was not in love with him anymore—he had been too cruel. But she could not be indifferent. She had kissed the face under that bandage, and caressed the long, strong body that was so woefully maimed. He was a vain man—it was the most pardonable of his weaknesses—and she knew that his mortification at looking in the mirror would hurt him more than his wounds.

"I wonder he didn't stay at home," Mam said. "People would have understood."

Ethel shook her head. "Too proud," she said. "He led the men to their deaths. He had to come."

"You know him well," Mam said, with a look that made Ethel wonder whether she suspected the truth. "But I expect he also wants people to see that the upper classes suffered, too."

Ethel nodded. Mam was right. Fitz was arrogant and high-handed, but paradoxically he also craved the respect of ordinary people.

Dai Chops, the butcher's son, came up. "It's very nice to see you back in Aberowen," he said.

He was a small man in a neat suit. "How are you, Dai?" she said.

"Very well, thank you. There's a new Charlie Chaplin film starting tomorrow. Do you like Chaplin?"

"I haven't got time to go to the pictures."

"Why don't you leave the little boy with your mam tomorrow night and come with me?"

Dai had put his hand up Ethel's skirt in the Palace Cinema in Cardiff. It was five years ago, but she could tell from the look in his eye that he had not forgotten. "No, thank you, Dai," she said firmly.

He was not ready to give up yet. "I'm working down the pit now, but I'll take over the shop when my da retires."

"You'll do very well, I know."

"There's some men wouldn't look at a girl with a baby," he said. "Not me, though."

That was a bit condescending, but Ethel decided not to take offense. "Good-bye, Dai. It was very nice of you to ask me."

He smiled ruefully. "You're still the prettiest girl I've ever met." He touched his cap and walked away.

Mam said indignantly: "What's wrong with him? You need a husband, and he's a catch!"

What *was* wrong with him? He was a bit short, but he made up for that with charm. He had good prospects and he was willing to take on another man's child. Ethel wondered why she was so unhesitatingly sure that she did not want to go to the pictures with him. Did she still think, in her heart, that she was too good for Aberowen?

There was a row of chairs at the front for the elite. Fitz and Bea took their seats alongside Perceval Jones and Maldwyn Morgan, and the service began.

Ethel believed vaguely in the Christian religion. She supposed there must be a God, but she suspected He was more reasonable than her father imagined. Da's ardent disagreements with the established churches had come down to Ethel merely as a mild dislike of statues, incense, and Latin. In London she occasionally went to the Calvary Gospel Hall on Sunday mornings, mainly because the pastor there was a passionate socialist who allowed his church to be used for Maud's clinic and Labour Party meetings.

There was no organ at the Reck, of course, so the puritans did not have to suppress their objection to musical instruments. Ethel knew, from Da, that there had been trouble about who was to lead the singing—a role that, in this town, was more important than preaching the sermon. In the end the Aberowen Male Voice Choir was placed at the front and its conductor, who belonged to no particular church, was put in charge of the music.

They began with Handel's "He Shall Feed His Flock Like a Shepherd," a popular anthem with elaborate part singing that the congregation performed faultlessly. As hundreds of tenor voices soared across the park with the line "And gather the lambs with his arm," Ethel realized that she missed this thrilling music when she was in London.

The Catholic priest recited Psalm 129, "De Profundis," in Latin. He shouted as loud as he could, but those at the edge of the crowd could hardly hear. The Anglican rector read the Collect Order for the Burial of the Dead from the *Book of Common Prayer.* Dilys Jones, a young Methodist, sang "Love Divine, All Loves Excelling," a hymn written by Charles Wesley. The Baptist pastor read I Corinthians 15 from verse 20 to the end.

One preacher had to represent the independent groups, and the choice had fallen on Da.

He began by reading a single verse from Romans 8: " 'If the spirit of Him that raised up Jesus from the dead dwell in you, He that raised up Christ from the dead shall also quicken your mortal bodies by His Spirit that dwelleth in you.'" Da had a big voice that carried strongly all across the park.

Ethel was proud of him. This honor acknowledged his status as one of the principal men of the town, a spiritual and political leader. He looked smart, too: Mam had bought him a new black tie, silk, from the Gwyn Evans department store in Merthyr.

He spoke about resurrection and the afterlife, and Ethel's attention drifted: she had heard it all before. She assumed there was life after death, but she was not sure, and anyway she would find out soon enough.

A stirring in the crowd alerted her that Da might have diverted from the usual themes. She heard him say: "When this country decided to go to war, I hope that every member of Parliament searched his conscience, sincerely and prayerfully, and sought the Lord's guidance. But who put those men in Parliament?"

He's going to get political, Ethel thought. Good for you, Da. That will take the smug look off the rector's face.

"Every man in this country is liable, in principle, for military service. But not every man is allowed a part in the decision to go to war."

There were shouts of agreement from the crowd.

"The rules of the franchise exclude more than half the men in this country!"

Ethel said loudly: "And all the women!"

Mam said: "Hush, now! It's your da that's preaching, not you."

"More than two hundred Aberowen men were killed on the first day of July, there on the banks of the Somme River. I have been told that the total of British casualties is over fifty thousand!"

There was a gasp of horror from the crowd. Not many people knew that figure. Da had got it from Ethel. Maud had been told by her friends in the War Office.

"Fifty thousand casualties, of which twenty thousand are dead," Da went on. "And the battle goes on. Day after day, more young men are being massacred." There were sounds of dissent from the crowd, but they were mostly drowned out by the shouts of agreement. Da held up his hand for quiet. "I do not say who is to blame. I say only this. Such slaughter cannot be right when men have been denied a part in the decision to go to war."

The rector stepped forward, trying to interrupt Da, and Perceval Jones tried unsuccessfully to climb up onto the platform.

But Da was almost done. "If ever we are asked again to go to war, it shall not be done without the consent of *all* the people."

"Women as well as men!" Ethel cried, but her voice was lost in the cheers of support from the miners.

Several men were now standing in front of Da, remonstrating with him, but his voice rang out over the commotion. "Never again will we wage war on the say-so of a minority!" he roared. "Never! Never! Never!"

He sat down, and the cheering was like thunder.

CHAPTER NINETEEN

July to October 1916

Kovel was a railway junction in the part of Russia that had once been in Poland, near the old border with Austria-Hungary. The Russian army assembled twenty miles east of the city, on the banks of the river Stokhod. The entire area was a swamp, hundreds of square miles of bog interlaced with footpaths. Grigori found a patch of drier ground and ordered his platoon to make camp. They had no tents: Major Azov had sold them all three months ago to a dressmaking factory in Pinsk. He said the men did not need tents in the summer, and by winter they would all be dead.

By some miracle, Grigori was still alive. He was a sergeant and his friend Isaak a corporal. Those few left of the 1914 intake were now mostly NCOs, noncommissioned officers. Grigori's battalion had been decimated, transferred, reinforced, and decimated again. They had been sent everywhere but home.

Grigori had killed many men in the last two years, with rifle, bayonet, or hand grenade, most of them close enough for him to see them die. Some of his comrades had nightmares about it, particularly the better-educated ones, but not Grigori. He had been born into the brutality of a peasant village and had survived as an orphan on the streets of St. Petersburg: violence did not give him bad dreams.

What had shocked him was the stupidity, callousness, and corruption of the officers. Living and fighting alongside the ruling class had made him a revolutionary.

He had to stay alive. There was no one else to take care of Katerina.

He wrote to her regularly, and received occasional letters, penned in a neat schoolgirl hand with many mistakes and crossings-out. He had kept every one, tied in a neat bundle in his kit bag, and when a long period went by with no letter, he reread the old ones.

In the first she had told him she had given birth to a boy, Vladimir, now eighteen months old—Lev's son. Grigori longed to see him. He vividly remembered his brother as a baby. Did Vladimir have Lev's irresistible gummy smile? he wondered. But he must have teeth by now, and be walking, and speaking his first words. Grigori wanted the child to learn to say "Uncle Grishka."

He often thought about the night Katerina had come to his bed. In his daydreams he sometimes changed the course of events so that, instead of throwing her out, he took her in his arms, kissed her generous mouth, and made love to her. But in real life he knew that her heart belonged to his brother.

Grigori had heard nothing from Lev, who had been gone more than two years. He feared that some catastrophe had befallen him in America. Lev's weaknesses often got him into scrapes, although somehow he seemed always to slip out of trouble. The problem stemmed from the way he had been brought up, living from hand to mouth with no proper discipline and only Grigori as a poor substitute for a parent. Grigori wished he had done better, but he had been only a boy himself.

The upshot was that Katerina had no one to look after her and her baby except Grigori. He was fiercely determined to keep himself alive, despite the chaotic inefficiency of the Russian army, so that he could one day return home to Katerina and Vladimir.

The commander in the zone was General Brusilov, a professional soldier—unlike so many of the generals who were courtiers. Under Brusilov's orders the Russians had made gains in June, driving the Austrians back in confusion. Grigori and his men fought hard when the orders made some kind of sense. Otherwise they devoted their energies to staying out of the line of fire. Grigori had become good at that, and in consequence had won the loyalty of his platoon.

In July the Russian advance had slowed, dragged back as always by lack of supplies. But now the Guard Army had arrived as reinforcements. The Guards were an elite group, the tallest and fittest of Russian soldiers. Unlike the rest of the army they had fine uniforms—dark green with gold braid—and new boots. But they had a poor commander, General Bezobrazov, another courtier. Grigori felt that Bezobrazov would not take Kovel, no matter how tall the Guards were.

It was Major Azov who brought the orders at dawn. He was a tall, heavy man in a tight uniform, and as usual his eyes were red this early in the morning. With him was Lieutenant Kirillov. The lieutenant summoned the sergeants and Azov told them to ford the river and follow the footpaths through the swamp toward the west. The Austrians were emplaced in the swamp, though not entrenched: the ground was too soggy for trenches.

Grigori could see a disaster in the making. The Austrians would be lying in wait, behind cover, in positions they had been able to choose with care. The Russians would be concentrated on the pathways and would not be able to move quickly on the boggy ground. They would be massacred.

In addition, they were low on bullets.

Grigori said: "Your Highness, we need an issue of ammunition."

Azov moved fast for a fat man. Without warning he punched Grigori in the mouth. Burning pain flared in Grigori's lips and he fell back. "That will keep you quiet for a while," Azov said. "You'll get ammunition when your officers say you need it." He turned to the others. "Form up in lines and advance when you hear the signal."

Grigori got to his feet, tasting blood. Touching his face gingerly, he found he had lost a front tooth. He cursed his carelessness. In an absentminded moment he had stood too close to an officer. He should have known better: they lashed out at the slightest provocation. He was lucky Azov had not been holding a rifle, or it would have been the butt that struck Grigori in the face.

He called his platoon together and got them in a ragged line. He planned to hold back and let others get ahead, but to his disappointment, Azov sent his company off early, and Grigori's platoon was among the leaders.

He would have to think of something else.

He waded into the river and the thirty-five men of his platoon followed. The water was cold but the weather was sunny and warm, so the men did not much mind getting wet. Grigori moved slowly, and his men did the same, staying behind him, waiting to see what he would do.

The Stokhod was broad and shallow, and they reached the far side without getting wet above their thighs. They had already been overtaken by keener men, Grigori saw with satisfaction.

Once on the narrow path through the swamp Grigori's platoon had to go at the same pace as everyone else, and he could not carry out his plan of falling behind. He began to worry. He did not want his men to be part of this crowd when the Austrians opened fire.

After they had gone a mile or so the path narrowed again and the pace slowed as the men ahead squeezed into single file. Grigori saw an opportunity. As if impatient with the delay, he moved off the path into the watery mud. The rest of his men quickly followed suit. The platoon behind moved up and closed the gap.

The water was up to Grigori's chest, and the mud was glutinous. Walking through the bog was very slow, and—as Grigori had anticipated—his platoon fell behind.

Lieutenant Kirillov saw what was happening and shouted angrily: "You men there! Get back on the path!"

Grigori called back: "Yes, Excellency." But he led his men farther away, as if searching for firmer ground.

The lieutenant cursed and gave up.

Grigori was scanning the terrain ahead as carefully as any of the officers, though for a different purpose. They were looking for the Austrian army; he was looking for a place to hide.

He kept moving forward while letting hundreds of troops overtake him. The Guards are so proud of themselves, he thought; let them do the fighting.

Around midmorning he heard the first shots from up ahead. The vanguard had engaged the enemy. It was time to take refuge.

Grigori came to a slight rise where the ground was drier. The rest of Major Azov's company was now out of sight far ahead. At the top of the rise Grigori shouted: "Take cover! Enemy emplacement ahead to the left!"

There was no enemy emplacement, and his men knew that, but they got down on the ground, behind bushes and trees, and aimed their rifles across the downside of the slope. Grigori shot one exploratory round into a clump of vegetation five hundred yards away, just in case he had unluckily picked a spot where there really were some Austrians; but no fire was returned.

They were safe, Grigori thought with satisfaction, as long as they stayed here. As the day wore on, one of two things would happen. Most likely, in a few hours' time Russian soldiers would come stumbling back through the swamp carrying their wounded, chased by the enemy—in which case Grigori's platoon would join the retreat. Alternatively, toward nightfall Grigori would conclude that the Russians had won the battle, and take his group forward to join the victory celebrations.

Meanwhile the only problem was forcing the men to maintain the pretense of engagement with an Austrian emplacement. It was boring to lie on the ground hour after hour staring ahead as if raking the landscape for enemy troops. The men tended to start eating and drinking, smoking, playing cards, or taking naps, which spoiled the illusion.

But before they had time to get comfortable, Lieutenant Kirillov appeared a couple of hundred yards to Grigori's right on the far side of a pond. Grigori groaned: this could ruin everything. "What are you men doing?" Kirillov shouted.

"Keep down, Excellency!" Grigori shouted back.

Isaak fired his rifle into the air, and Grigori ducked. Kirillov ducked, too, then retreated back the way he had come.

Isaak chuckled. "Works every time."

Grigori was not so sure. Kirillov had looked annoyed, not pleased, as if he knew he was being fooled but could not decide what to do about it.

Grigori listened to the boom and clatter and roar of battle up ahead. He thought it was about a mile away, and not moving in any direction.

The sun rose higher and dried his wet clothing. He began to feel hungry, and gnawed on a piece of hardtack from his ration tin, avoiding the sore place where Azov had knocked out his tooth.

After the mist had burned off, he saw German planes flying low about a mile ahead. Judging by the sound, Grigori could tell they were machine-gunning the troops on the ground. The Guards, crowded onto narrow paths or wading through mud, must have made dreadfully easy targets. Grigori was doubly glad he had made sure he and his men were not there.

Around the middle of the afternoon the sound of battle seemed to come nearer. The Russians were being pushed back. He got ready to order his men to join the fleeing forces—but not yet. He did not want to be conspicuous. Retreating slowly was almost as important as advancing slowly.

He saw a few scattered men away to his left and right, splashing through the swamp back toward the river, some evidently wounded. The retreat had begun, but the army was not yet in full flight.

From somewhere nearby he heard a neigh. A horse meant an officer. Grigori immediately fired at imaginary Austrians. His men followed suit, and there was a rattle of scattered fire. Then he looked around and saw Major Azov on a big gray hunter splashing through the mud. Azov was shouting at a group of retreating soldiers, telling them to return to the fray. They argued with him until he drew his pistol, a Nagant revolver—just like Lev's, Grigori thought irrelevantly—and pointed it at them, whereupon they turned around and reluctantly headed back the way they had come.

Azov holstered the gun and trotted up to Grigori's position. "What are you fools doing here?" he said.

Grigori remained lying on the ground but rolled over and reloaded his rifle, pushing his last five-round clip into place, making a show of haste. "Enemy emplacement in that clump of trees ahead, Your Highness," he said. "You'd better dismount, sir—they can see you."

Azov remained on his horse. "So what are you doing—hiding from them?"

"His Excellency Lieutenant Kirillov told us to take them out. I've sent a patrol to come at them from the side while we give covering fire."

Azov was not completely stupid. "They don't seem to be shooting back."

"We've got them pinned down."

He shook his head. "They've retreated—if they were ever there in the first place."

"I don't think so, Your Highness. They were blazing away at us a moment ago."

"There's no one there." Azov raised his voice. "Cease fire! You men, cease fire."

Grigori's platoon stopped shooting and looked at the major.

"On my signal, charge!" he said. He drew his pistol.

Grigori was not sure what to do. The battle had clearly been the disaster he had forecast. Having avoided it all day he did not want to risk lives when it was clearly over. But direct conflict with officers was dangerous.

At that moment, a group of soldiers broke through the vegetation in the place Grigori had been pretending was an enemy emplacement. Grigori stared in surprise. However, they were not Austrians, he saw as soon as he could make out their uniforms; they were retreating Russians.

But Azov did not change his mind. "Those men are cowardly deserters!" he screeched. "Charge them!" And he fired his pistol at the approaching Russians.

The men of the platoon were bewildered. Officers often threatened to shoot troops who seemed reluctant to go into battle, but Grigori's men had never before been ordered to attack their own side. They looked to him for guidance.

Azov aimed his pistol at Grigori. "Charge!" he screamed. "Shoot those traitors!"

Grigori made a decision. "Right, men!" he called. He scrambled to his feet. Turning his back to the approaching Russians, he looked to left and right and hefted his rifle. "You heard what the major said!" He swung his rifle, as if turning, then pointed it at Azov.

If he was going to shoot at his own side, he would kill an officer rather than a soldier.

Azov stared at him for a frozen moment, and in that second Grigori pulled the trigger.

His first shot hit Azov's horse, and it stumbled. That saved Grigori's life, for Azov fired at him, but the horse's sudden movement caused the shot to go wide. Automatically, Grigori worked the bolt of his rifle and fired again.

His second shot missed. Grigori swore. He was in real danger now. But so was the major.

Azov was struggling with his horse and unable to aim his weapon. Grigori followed his jerky movements with the sight of his rifle, fired a third time, and shot Azov in the chest. He stared as the major slowly fell off his horse. He felt a jolt of grim satisfaction as the heavy body plunged into a muddy puddle.

The horse walked away unsteadily, then suddenly sat down on its hindquarters like a dog.

Grigori went up to Azov. The major lay on his back in the mud, looking up, unmoving but still alive, bleeding from the right side of his chest. Grigori looked around. The retreating soldiers were still too far away to see clearly what was going on. His own men were completely trustworthy: he had saved their lives many times. He put the barrel of his rifle against Azov's forehead. "This is for all the good Russians you've killed, you murdering dog," he said. He grimaced, baring his teeth. "And for my front tooth," he added, and he pulled the trigger.

The major went limp and stopped breathing.

Grigori looked at his men. "The major has unfortunately been killed by enemy fire," he said. "Retreat!"

They cheered and began to run.

Grigori went up to the horse. It tried to rise, but Grigori could see it had a broken leg. He put his rifle to its ear and fired his last round. The horse fell sideways and lay still.

Grigori felt more pity for the horse than for Major Azov.

He ran after his retreating men.

{ II }

After the Brusilov Offensive slowed to a halt, Grigori was redeployed to the capital, now renamed Petrograd because "St. Petersburg" sounded too German. Battle-hardened troops were required to protect the tsar's family and his ministers from the angry citizens, it seemed. The remains of the battalion were merged with the elite First Machine Gun Regiment, and Grigori moved into their barracks in Samsonievsky Prospekt in the Vyborg district, a working-class neighborhood of factories and slums. The First Machine Guns were well fed and housed, in an attempt to keep them contented enough to defend the hated regime.

He was happy to be back, and yet the prospect of seeing Katerina filled him with apprehension. He longed to look at her, hear her voice, and hold her baby, his nephew. But his lust for her made him anxious. She was his wife, but that was a technicality. The reality was that she had chosen Lev, and her baby was Lev's child. Grigori had no right to love her.

He even toyed with the idea of not telling her he was back. In a city of more than two million people there was a good chance they would never meet by accident. But he would have found that too hard to bear.

On his first day back he was not allowed out of the barracks. He felt frustrated at not being able to go to Katerina. Instead, that evening he and Isaak made contact with other Bolsheviks at the barracks. Grigori agreed to start a discussion group.

Next morning his platoon became part of a squad assigned to guard the home of Prince Andrei, his former overlord, during a banquet. The prince lived in a pink-and-yellow palace on the English Embankment overlooking the Neva River. At midday the soldiers lined up on the steps. Low rain clouds darkened the city, but light shone from every window of the house. Behind the glass, framed by velvet curtains like a play at the theater, footmen and maids in clean uniforms hurried by, carrying bottles of wine, platters of delicacies, and silver trays piled with fruit. There was a small orchestra in the hall, and the strains of a symphony could be heard outside. The big shiny cars drew up at the foot of the steps, footmen hurried to open the car doors, and the guests emerged, the men in their black coats and tall hats, the women swathed in furs. A small crowd gathered on the other side of the street to watch.

It was a familiar scene, but there was a difference. Every time someone got out of a car the crowd booed and jeered. In the old days, the police would have broken up the mob with their nightsticks in a minute. Now there were no police, and the guests walked as quickly as they could up the steps between the two lines of soldiers and darted in through the grand doorway, clearly nervous of staying long in the open.

Grigori thought the bystanders were quite right to jeer at the nobility who had made such a mess of the war. If trouble broke out, he would be inclined to take the side of the crowd. He certainly did not intend to shoot at them, and he guessed many of the soldiers felt the same.

How could noblemen throw lavish parties at a time like this? Half Russia was starving and even the soldiers at the front were on short rations. Men like Andrei deserved to be murdered in their beds. If I see him, Grigori thought, I'm going to have to restrain myself from shooting him the way I shot Major Azov.

The procession of cars came to an end without incident, and the crowd got bored and drifted off. Grigori spent the afternoon looking hard at the faces of women passing by, eagerly hoping against the odds to see Katerina. By the time the guests began to leave it was getting dark and cold, and no one wanted to stand around on the street, so there was no more booing.

After the party the soldiers were invited to the back door to eat such of the leftovers as had not been consumed by the household staff: scraps of meat and fish, cold vegetables, half-eaten bread rolls, apples and pears. The food was thrown on a trestle table and unpleasantly mixed up, slices of ham smeared with fish pâté, fruit in gravy, bread dusted with cigar ash. But they had eaten worse in the trenches, and it was a long time since their breakfast of porridge and salt cod, so they tucked in hungrily.

At no time did Grigori see the hated face of Prince Andrei. Perhaps it was just as well.

When they had marched back to the barracks and handed in their weapons, they were given the evening off. Grigori was elated: it was his chance to visit Katerina. He went to the back door of the barracks kitchen and begged some bread and meat to take to her: a sergeant had his privileges. Then he shined his boots and went out.

Vyborg, where the barracks stood, was in the northeast of the city, and Katerina lived diagonally opposite in the southwestern district of Narva, assuming she still had his old room near the Putilov works.

He walked south along Samsonievsky Prospekt and over the Liteiny Bridge into the city center. Some of the swanky shops were still open, their windows bright with electric light, but many were closed. In the more mundane stores there was little for sale. A baker's window contained a single cake and a handwritten sign reading: "No bread until tomorrow."

The broad boulevard of Nevsky Prospekt reminded him of walking along here with his mother, on that fateful day in 1905 when he had seen her shot down by the tsar's soldiers. Now he was one of the tsar's soldiers. But he would not be shooting at women and children. If the tsar tried that now there would be trouble of a different kind.

He saw ten or twelve thuggish young men in black coats and black caps carrying a portrait of Tsar Nicholas as a young man, his dark hair not yet receding, his gingery beard luxuriant. One of them shouted: "Long live the tsar!" and they all stopped, raised their caps, and cheered. Several passersby raised their hats.

Grigori had encountered such bands before. They were called the Black Hundreds, part of the Union of the Russian People, a right-wing group that wanted to return to the golden age when the tsar was the unchallenged father of his people and Russia had no liberals, no socialists, and no Jews. Their newspapers were financed by the government and their pamphlets were printed in the basement of police headquarters, according to information the Bolsheviks got from their contacts in the police.

Grigori walked past with a glance of contempt, but one of them accosted him. "Hey, you! Why is your hat on?"

Grigori walked on without replying, but another member of the gang grabbed his arm. "What are you, a Jew?" the second man said. "Doff your cap!"

Grigori said quietly: "Touch me again and I'll tear your fucking head off, you loudmouthed schoolboy."

The man backed off, then offered Grigori a pamphlet. "Read this, friend," he said. "It explains how the Jews are betraying you soldiers."

"Get out of my way, or I'll shove that stupid pamphlet all the way up your arse," said Grigori.

The man looked to his comrades for support, but they had started beating up a middle-aged man in a fur hat. Grigori walked away.

As he passed the doorway of a boarded-up shop, a woman spoke to him. "Hey, big boy," she said. "You can fuck me for a ruble." Her words were standard prostitute's talk, but her voice surprised him: she sounded educated. He glanced her way. She was wearing a long coat, and when he looked at her, she opened it to show that she had nothing on underneath, despite the cold. She was in her thirties, with big breasts and a round belly.

Grigori felt a surge of desire. He had not been with a woman for years. The trench prostitutes were vile, dirty, and diseased. But this woman looked like someone he could embrace.

She closed her coat. "Yes or no?"

"I haven't got any money," Grigori said.

"What's in that bag?" She nodded at the sack he was carrying.

"A few scraps of food."

"I'll do you for a loaf of bread," the woman said. "My children are starving."

Grigori thought of those plump breasts. "Where?"

"In the back room of the shop."

At least, Grigori thought, I won't be mad with sexual frustration when I meet Katerina. "All right."

She opened the door, led him in, and closed and bolted it. They walked through the empty shop and into another room. Grigori saw, in the dim illumination from the streetlight, that there was a mattress on the floor covered with a blanket.

The woman turned to face him, letting her coat fall open again. He stared at the thatch of dark hair at her groin. She put out her hand. "The bread first, please, Sergeant."

He took a big loaf of black bread from his sack and gave it to her.

"I'll be back in a moment," she said.

She ran up a flight of stairs and opened a door. Grigori heard a child's voice. Then a man coughed, a hacking rasp from deep in his chest. There were muffled sounds of movement and low voices for a few moments. Then he heard the door again, and she came down the stairs.

She took off her coat, lay back on the mattress, and parted her legs. Grigori lay beside her and put his arms around her. She had an attractive, intelligent face lined with strain. She said: "Mm, you're so strong!"

He stroked her soft skin, but all desire had left him. The entire scene was too pathetic: the empty shop, the sick husband, the hungry children, and the woman's false coquetry.

She unbuttoned his trousers and grasped his limp penis. "Do you want me to suck it?"

"No." He sat upright and handed her the coat. "Put this back on."

In a frightened voice she said: "You can't have the bread back—it's already half-eaten."

He shook his head. "What happened to you?"

She put her coat on and fastened the buttons. "Have you got any cigarettes?"

He gave her a cigarette and took one himself.

She blew out smoke. "We had a shoe shop—high quality at reasonable prices for the middle class. My husband is a good businessman and we lived well." Her tone was bitter. "But no one in this town, apart from the nobility, has bought new shoes for two years."

"Couldn't you do something else?"

"Yes." Her eyes flashed anger. "We didn't just sit back and helplessly accept our fate. My husband found he could provide good boots for soldiers at half the price the army was paying. All the small factories that used to supply the shop were desperate for orders. He went to the War Industries Committee."

"What's that?"

"You've been away for a while, haven't you, Sergeant? Nowadays, everything that works here is run by independent committees: the government is too incompetent to do anything. The War Industries Committee supplies the army—or it did, while Polivanov was war minister."

"What went wrong?"

"We got the order, my husband put all his savings into paying the bootmakers, and then the tsar fired Polivanov."

"Why?"

"Polivanov allowed workers' elected representatives on the committee, so the tsaritsa thought he must be a revolutionist. Anyway, the order was canceled—and we went bankrupt."

Grigori shook his head in disgust. "And I thought it was just the commanders at the front who were mad."

"We tried other things. My husband was willing to do any job, waiter or streetcar driver or road mender, but no one was hiring, and then with the worry and lack of food he fell ill."

"So now you do this."

"I'm not very good at it. But some men are kind, like you. Others . . . " She shuddered and looked away.

Grigori finished his cigarette and got to his feet. "Good-bye. I won't ask your name."

She got up. "Because of you, my family is still alive." There was a catch in her voice. "And I don't need to go on the street again until tomorrow." She stood on tiptoe and kissed his lips lightly. "Thank you, Sergeant."

Grigori went out.

It was getting colder. He hurried through the streets to the Narva district. As he got farther away from the shopkeeper's wife, his libido returned, and he thought with regret of her soft body.

It occurred to him that like him, Katerina had physical needs. Two years was a long time to go without romance, for a young woman— she was still only twenty-three. She had little reason to be faithful to either Lev or Grigori. A woman with a baby was enough to scare off many men, but on the other hand she was very alluring, or she had been two years ago. She might not be alone this evening. How dreadful that would be.

He made his way to his old home by the railway line. Was it his imagination, or did the street appear shabbier than it had two years ago? In the interim nothing seemed to have been painted, repaired, or even cleaned. He noticed a queue outside the bakery on the corner, even though the shop was closed.

He still had his key. He entered the house.

He felt fearful as he went up the stairs. He did not want to find her with a man. Now he wished he had sent word in advance, so that she could have arranged to be alone.

He knocked on the door.

"Who is it?"

The sound of her voice nearly brought tears to his eyes. "A visitor," he said gruffly, and he opened the door.

She was standing by the fireplace holding a pan. She dropped the pan, spilling milk, and her hands went to her mouth. She let out a small scream.

"It's only me," said Grigori.

On the floor beside her sat a little boy with a tin spoon in his hand.

He appeared to have just stopped banging on an empty can. He stared at Grigori for a startled moment, then began to cry.

Katerina picked him up. "Don't cry, Volodya," she said, rocking him. "No need to be afraid." He quieted. Katerina said: "This is your daddy."

Grigori was not sure he wanted Vladimir to think he was his father, but this was not the moment to argue. He stepped into the room and closed the door behind him. He put his arms around them, kissed the child, then kissed Katerina's forehead.

He stood back and looked at them. She was no longer the fresh-faced kid he had rescued from the unwelcome attentions of Police Captain Pinsky. She was thinner and had a tired, strained look.

Strangely, the child did not look much like Lev. There was no sign of Lev's good looks, nor his winning smile. If anything, Vladimir had the intense blue-eyed gaze that Grigori saw when he looked in a mirror.

Grigori smiled. "He's beautiful."

Katerina said: "What happened to your ear?"

Grigori touched what remained of his right ear. "I lost most of it at the Battle of Tannenberg."

"And your tooth?"

"I displeased an officer. But he's dead now, so I got the better of him in the end."

"You're not so handsome."

She had never said he was handsome before. "They're minor wounds. I'm lucky to be alive."

He looked around his old room. It was subtly different. On the mantelpiece over the fireplace, where Grigori and Lev had kept pipes, tobacco in a jar, matches, and spills, Katerina had put a pottery vase, a doll, and a color postcard of Mary Pickford. There was a curtain at the window. It was made of scraps, like a quilt, but Grigori had never had any curtain. He also noticed the smell, or lack of it, and realized the place used to have a thick atmosphere of tobacco smoke, boiling cabbage, and unwashed men. Now it smelled fresh.

Katerina mopped up the spilled milk. "I've thrown away Volodya's supper," she said. "I don't know what I'll feed him. There's no milk in my breasts."

"Don't worry." From his sack Grigori took a length of sausage, a cabbage, and a tin of jam. Katerina stared in disbelief. "From the barracks kitchen," he explained.

She opened the jam and fed some to Vladimir on a spoon. He ate it and said: "More?"

Katerina ate a spoonful herself, then gave the child more. "This is like a fairy tale," she said. "All this food! I won't have to sleep outside the bakery."

Grigori frowned. "What do you mean?"

She swallowed more jam. "There's never enough bread. As soon as the bakery opens in the morning, it's all sold. The only way to get bread is to queue up. And if you don't join the queue before midnight, they'll be sold out before you get to the head of the line."

"My God." He hated the thought of her sleeping on the pavement. "What about Volodya?"

"One of the other girls listens for him while I'm out. He sleeps all night now anyway."

No wonder the shopkeeper's wife had been willing to have sex with Grigori for a loaf. He had probably overpaid her. "How do you manage?"

"I get twelve rubles a week at the factory."

He was puzzled. "But that's double what you were earning when I left!"

"But the rent for this room used to be four rubles a week—now it's eight. That leaves me four rubles for everything else. And a sack of potatoes used to be one ruble, but now it's seven."

"Seven rubles for a sack of potatoes!" Grigori was appalled. "How do people live?"

"Everyone is hungry. Children fall ill and die. Old people just fade away. It gets worse every day, and no one does anything."

Grigori felt heartsick. While he was suffering in the army, he had consoled himself with the thought that Katerina and the baby were better off, with a warm place to sleep and enough money for food. He had been fooling himself. It filled him with rage to think of her leaving Vladimir here while she slept outside the bakery.

They sat at the table and Grigori sliced the sausage with his knife. "Some tea would be nice," he said.

Katerina smiled. "I haven't had tea for a year."

"I'll bring some from the barracks."

Katerina ate the sausage. Grigori could see that she had to restrain herself from gobbling it. He picked up Vladimir and fed him more jam. The boy was still a bit young for sausage.

An easy contentment crept over Grigori. While at the front he had daydreamed this scene: the little room, the table with food, the baby, Katerina. Now it had come true. "This should not be so hard to find," he said ruminatively.

"What do you mean?"

"You and I are fit and strong and we work hard. All I want is this: a room, something to eat, rest at the end of the day. It should be ours every day."

"We've been betrayed by German-supporters at the royal court," she said.

"Really? How so?"

"Well, you know the tsaritsa is a German."

"Yes." The tsar's wife had been born Princess Alix of Hesse and Rhine in the German Empire.

"And Stürmer is obviously a German."

Grigori shrugged. Prime Minister Stürmer had been born in Russia, as far as Grigori knew. Many Russians had German names, and vice versa: inhabitants of the two countries had been crisscrossing the border for centuries.

"And Rasputin is pro-German."

"Is he?" Grigori suspected the mad monk was mainly interested in mesmerizing women at court and gaining influence and power.

"They're all in it together. Stürmer has been paid by the Germans to starve the peasantry. The tsar telephones his cousin Kaiser Wilhelm and tells him where our troops are going to be next. Rasputin wants us to surrender. And the tsaritsa and her lady-in-waiting Anna Vyrubova both sleep with Rasputin at the same time."

Grigori had heard most of these rumors. He did not believe the court was pro-German. They were just stupid and incompetent. But a lot of soldiers believed such stories, and to judge by Katerina some civilians did, too. It was the task of the Bolsheviks to explain the true reasons why Russians were losing the war and starving to death.

But not tonight. Vladimir yawned, so Grigori stood up and began to rock him, walking up and down, while Katerina talked. She told him about life at the factory, the other tenants in the house, and people he knew. Captain Pinsky was now a lieutenant with the secret police, ferreting out dangerous liberals and democrats. There were thousands of orphaned children on the streets, living by theft and prostitution or dying of starvation and cold. Konstantin, Grigori's closest friend at the Putilov works, was now a member of the Petrograd Bolshevik Committee. The Vyalov family were the only people getting richer: no matter how bad the shortages were, they could always sell you vodka, caviar, cigarettes, and chocolate. Grigori studied her wide mouth and full lips. It was a joy to watch her talk. She had a determined chin and bold blue eyes, yet to him she always looked vulnerable.

Vladimir fell asleep, lulled by Grigori's rocking and Katerina's voice. Grigori carefully put him down in a bed Katerina had improvised in a corner. It was just a sack filled with rags and covered by a blanket, but he curled up on it comfortably and put his thumb in his mouth.

A church clock struck nine, and Katerina said: "What time do you have to be back?"

"At ten," Grigori said. "I'd better go."

"Not just yet." She put her arms around his neck and kissed him.

It was a sweet moment. Her lips on his were soft and mobile. He closed his eyes for a second and inhaled the scent of her skin. Then he pulled away. "This is wrong," he said.

"Don't be stupid."

"You love Lev."

She looked him in the eye. "I was a peasant girl twenty years old and new to the city. I liked Lev's smart suits, his cigarettes and vodka, his openhandedness. He was charming and handsome and fun. But now I'm twenty-three and I have a child—and where is Lev?"

Grigori shrugged. "We don't know."

"But you're here." She stroked his cheek. He knew he should push her away, but he could not. "You pay the rent, and you bring food for my baby," she said. "Don't you think I see what a fool I was to love Lev instead of you? Don't you realize I know better now? Can't you understand that I've learned to love you?"

Grigori stared at her, unable to believe what he had heard.

Those blue eyes stared back at him candidly. "That's right," she said. "I love you."

He groaned, closed his eyes, took her in his arms, and surrendered.

CHAPTER TWENTY

November to December 1916

Ethel Williams anxiously scanned the casualty list in the newspaper. There were several Williamses, but no Corporal William Williams of the Welsh Rifles. With a silent prayer of thanks she folded the paper, handed it to Bernie Leckwith, and put the kettle on for cocoa.

She could not be sure Billy was alive. He might have been killed in the last few days or hours. She was haunted by the memory of Telegram Wednesday in Aberowen, and the women's faces twisted with fear and grief, faces that would carry forever the cruel marks of the news heard that day. She was ashamed of herself for feeling glad Billy was not among the dead.

The telegrams had kept coming to Aberowen. The Battle of the Somme did not end on that first day. Throughout July, August, September, and October the British army threw its young soldiers across no-man's-land to be mown down by machine guns. Again and again the newspapers hailed a victory, but the telegrams told another story.

Bernie was in Ethel's kitchen, as he was most evenings. Little Lloyd was fond of "Uncle" Bernie. Usually he sat on Bernie's lap, and Bernie read aloud to him from the newspaper. The child had little idea what the words meant but he seemed to like it anyway. Tonight, however, Bernie was on edge, for some reason, and paid no attention to Lloyd.

Mildred from upstairs came in carrying a teapot. "Lend us a spoonful of tea, Eth," she said.

"Help yourself. You know where it is. Do you want a cup of cocoa instead?"

"No, thanks. Cocoa makes me fart. Hello, Bernie. How's the revolution?"

Bernie looked up from the paper, smiling. He liked Mildred. Everyone did. "The revolution is slightly delayed," he said.

Mildred put tea leaves into her pot. "Any word from Billy?"

"Not lately," Ethel said. "You?"

"Not for a couple of weeks."

Ethel picked up the post from the hall floor in the morning, so she knew that Mildred received frequent letters from Billy. Ethel presumed they were love letters: why else would a boy write to his sister's lodger? Mildred apparently returned Billy's feelings: she asked regularly for news of him, assuming a casual air that failed to mask her anxiety.

Ethel liked Mildred, but she wondered whether Billy at eighteen was ready to take on a twenty-three-year-old woman and two stepchildren. True, Billy had always been extraordinarily mature and responsible for his age. And he might be a few years older before the war ended. Anyway, all Ethel wanted was for him to come home alive. After that, nothing mattered much.

Ethel said: "His name's not on the list of casualties in today's paper, thank God."

"I wonder when he'll get leave."

"He's only been gone five months."

Mildred put down the teapot. "Ethel, can I ask you something?"

"Of course."

"I'm thinking of going out on my own—as a seamstress, I mean."

Ethel was surprised. Mildred was the supervisor now at Mannie Litov's, so she was earning a better wage.

Mildred went on: "I've got a friend who can get me work trimming hats—putting on the veils, ribbons, feathers, and beads. It's skilled work and it pays a lot better than sewing uniforms."

"Sounds great."

"Only thing is, I'd have to work at home, at least at first. Long-term, I'd like to employ other girls and get a small place."

"You're really looking ahead!"

"Got to, haven't you? When the war's over they won't want no more uniforms."

"True."

"So you wouldn't mind me using upstairs as my workshop, for a while?"

"Of course not. Good luck to you!"

"Thanks." Impulsively she kissed Ethel's cheek; then she picked up the teapot and went out.

Lloyd yawned and rubbed his eyes. Ethel lifted him up and put him to bed in the front room. She watched him fondly for a minute or two as he drifted into sleep. As always, his helplessness tugged at her heart. It will be a better world when you grow up, Lloyd, she promised silently. We'll make sure of that.

When she returned to the kitchen, she tried to draw Bernie out of his mood. "There should be more books for children," she said.

He nodded. "I'd like every library to have a little section of children's books." He spoke without looking up from the paper.

"Perhaps if you librarians do that, it will encourage the publishers to bring out more."

"That's what I'm hoping."

Ethel put more coal on the fire and poured cocoa for them both. It was unusual for Bernie to be withdrawn. Normally she enjoyed these cozy evenings. They were two outsiders, a Welsh girl and a Jew, not that there was any scarcity of Welsh people or Jews in London. Whatever the reason, in the two years she had been living in London, he had become a close friend, along with Mildred and Maud.

She had an idea what was on his mind. Last night a bright young speaker from the Fabian Society had addressed the local Labour Party on the subject of "postwar socialism." Ethel had argued with him and he had obviously been rather taken with her. After the meeting he had flirted with her, even though everyone knew he was married, and she had enjoyed the attention, not taking it at all seriously. But perhaps Bernie was jealous.

She decided to leave him to be quiet if that was what he wanted. She sat at the kitchen table and opened a large envelope full of letters written by men on the front line. Readers of *The Soldier's Wife* sent their husbands' letters to the paper, which paid a shilling for each one published. They gave a truer picture of life at the front than anything in the mainstream press. Most of *The Soldier's Wife* was written by Maud, but the letters had been Ethel's idea and she edited that page, which had become the paper's most popular feature.

She had been offered a better-paid job, as a full-time organizer for the National Union of Garment Workers, but she had turned it down, wanting to stay with Maud and continue campaigning.

She read half a dozen letters, then sighed and looked at Bernie. "You would think people would turn against the war," she said.

"But they haven't," he replied. "Look at the results of that election."

Last month in Ayrshire there had been a by-election—a ballot in a single constituency, caused by the death of the sitting member of Parliament. The Conservative, Lieutenant-General Hunter-Weston, who had fought at the Somme, had been opposed by a Peace candidate, Reverend Chalmers. The army officer had won overwhelmingly, 7,149 votes to 1,300.

"It's the newspapers," Ethel said with frustration. "What can our little publication do to promote peace, against the propaganda put out by the bloody Northcliffe press?" Lord Northcliffe, a gung-ho militarist, owned *The Times* and the *Daily Mail*.

"It's not just the newspapers," Bernie said. "It's the money."

Bernie paid a lot of attention to government finance, which was odd in a man who had never had more than a few shillings. Ethel saw an opportunity to bring him out of his mood, and said: "What do you mean?"

"Before the war, our government used to spend about half a million pounds a day on everything—the army, courts and prisons, education, pensions, running the colonies, everything."

"So much!" She smiled at him affectionately. "That's the kind of statistic my father always knew."

He drank his cocoa, then said: "Guess how much we spend now."

"Double that? A million a day? It sounds impossible."

"You're nowhere near. The war costs five million pounds a day. That's ten times the normal cost of running the country."

Ethel was shocked. "Where does the money come from?"

"That's the problem. We borrow it."

"But the war has been going on for more than two years. We must have borrowed . . . nearly four thousand million pounds!"

"Something like that. Twenty-five years' normal expenditure."

"How will we ever pay it back?"

"We can never pay it back. A government that tried to bring in taxes sufficient to repay the loan would cause a revolution."

"So what will happen?"

"If we lose the war, our creditors—mainly Americans—will go bankrupt. And if we win, we'll make the Germans pay. 'Reparations' is the word they use."

"How will *they* manage it?"

"They will starve. But nobody cares what happens to the losers. Anyway, the Germans did the same to the French in 1871." He stood up and put his cup in the kitchen sink. "So you see why we can't make peace with Germany. Who then would pay the bill?"

Ethel was aghast. "And so we have to keep sending boys to die in the trenches. Because we can't pay the bill. Poor Billy. What a wicked world we live in."

"But we're going to change it."

I hope so, Ethel thought. Bernie believed it would take a revolution. She had read about the French Revolution and knew that such things did not always turn out the way people intended. All the same, she was determined that Lloyd would have a better life.

They sat in silence for a while; then Bernie stood up. He went to the door, as if to leave, then changed his mind. "That speaker last night was interesting."

"Aye," she said.

"Clever, too."

"Yes, he was clever."

Bernie sat down again. "Ethel . . . two years ago you told me you wanted friendship, not romance."

"I was very sorry to hurt your feelings."

"Don't be sorry. Our friendship is the best thing that ever happened to me."

"I like it, too."

"You said I'd soon forget all that lovey-dovey stuff, and we would just be pals. But you were wrong." He leaned forward in his chair. "As I've got to know you better, I've just come to love you more than ever."

Ethel could see the yearning in his eyes, and she felt desperately sorry that she could not return his feelings. "I'm very fond of you, too," she said. "But not in that way."

"What's the point of being alone? We like each other. We're such a good team! We have the same ideals, the same aims in life, similar opinions—we belong together."

"There's more to marriage than that."

"I know. And I long to take you in my arms." He moved his arm, as if about to reach out and touch her, but she crossed her legs and turned aside in her chair. He withdrew his hand, and a bitter smile twisted his usually amiable expression. "I'm not the handsomest man you've ever met. But I believe no one has ever loved you as I do."

He was right about that, she reflected sadly. Many men had fancied her, and one had seduced her, but none had shown the patient devotion of Bernie. If she married him she could be sure it would be forever. And somewhere in her soul she longed for that.

Sensing her hesitation, Bernie said: "Marry me, Ethel. I love you. I'll spend my life making you happy. It's all I want."

Did she need a man at all? She was not unhappy. Lloyd was a constant joy, with his stumbling walk, his attempts at speech, and his boundless curiosity. He was enough for her.

Bernie said: "Little Lloyd needs a father."

That gave her a pang of guilt. Bernie was already playing that role part-time. Should she marry Bernie for Lloyd's sake? It was not too late for him to start calling Bernie "Daddy."

It would mean giving up what little hope she had left of finding again the overwhelming passion she had felt with Fitz. She still suffered a spasm of longing when she thought about it. But, she asked herself, trying to think objectively despite her feelings, what did I get out of that love affair? I was disappointed by Fitz, rejected by my family, and exiled to another country. Why would I want that again?

Hard as she struggled, she could not bring herself to accept Bernie's proposal. "Let me think," she said.

He beamed. Clearly that was a more positive answer than he had dared to hope for. "Think as long as you want," he said. "I'll wait."

She opened the front door. "Good night, Bernie."

"Good night, Ethel." He leaned forward and she gave him her cheek to kiss. His lips lingered a moment on her skin. She drew back immediately. He caught her wrist. "Ethel . . ."

"Sleep well, Bernie," she said.

He hesitated, then nodded. "You, too," he said, and he went out.

{ II }

On election night in November 1916, Gus Dewar thought his career in politics had come to an end.

He was in the White House, fielding phone calls and passing messages to President Wilson, who was at Shadow Lawn, the new summer White House in New Jersey, with his second wife, Edith. Papers were sent from Washington to Shadow Lawn every day by the U.S. Postal Service, but sometimes the president needed to get the news faster.

By nine o'clock that evening it was clear that the Republican, a Supreme Court justice called Charles Evans Hughes, had won four swing states: New York, Indiana, Connecticut, and New Jersey.

But the reality did not hit Gus until a messenger brought him the early editions of the New York newspapers and he saw the headline:

PRESIDENT-ELECT HUGHES

He was shocked. He thought Woodrow Wilson was winning. Voters had not forgotten Wilson's deft handling of the *Lusitania* crisis: he had managed to get tough with the Germans while at the same time staying neutral. Wilson's campaign slogan was "He kept us out of war."

Hughes had accused Wilson of failing to prepare America for war, but this had backfired. Americans were more determined than ever to remain nonaligned after Britain's brutal suppression of the Easter Rising in Dublin. Britain's treatment of the Irish was no better than Germany's treatment of the Belgians, so why should America take sides?

When he had read the papers, Gus loosened his tie and napped on the couch in the study next to the Oval Office. He was unnerved by the prospect of leaving the White House. Working for Wilson had become his bedrock. His love life was a train wreck, but at least he knew he was valuable to the president of the United States.

His concern was not just selfish. Wilson was determined to create an international order in which wars could be avoided. Just as next-door neighbors no longer settled boundary disputes with six-guns, so the time must come when countries, too, submitted their quarrels to independent judgment. The British foreign secretary, Sir Edward Grey, had used the words "a league of nations" in a letter to Wilson, and the president had liked the phrase. If Gus could help bring that about his life would mean something.

But now it looked as if that dream was not going to come true, he thought, and he drifted into a disappointed sleep.

He was woken early in the morning by a cable saying that Wilson had won Ohio—a blue-collar state that had liked the president's stand on the eight-hour day—and Kansas, too. Wilson was back in the running. A little later he won Minnesota by fewer than a thousand votes.

It was not over after all, and Gus's spirits lifted.

By Wednesday evening Wilson was ahead with 264 electoral votes against 254, a lead of 10. But one state, California, had not yet declared a result, and it carried 13 electoral votes. Whoever won California would be president.

Gus's phone went quiet. There was nothing much for him to do. The counting in Los Angeles was slow. Every unopened box was guarded by armed Democrats, who believed that tampering had robbed them of a presidential victory in 1876.

The result was still hanging in the balance when the lobby called to tell Gus he had a visitor. To his surprise it was Rosa Hellman, the former editor of the *Buffalo Anarchist*. Gus was pleased: Rosa was always interesting to talk to. He recalled that an anarchist had assassinated President McKinley in Buffalo in 1901. However, President Wilson was far away in New Jersey, so he brought Rosa up to the study and offered her a cup of coffee.

She was wearing a red coat. When he helped her off with it, he towered over her. He caught the aroma of a light flowery perfume.

"Last time we met you told me I was a goddamn fool to get engaged to Olga Vyalov," he said as he hung her coat on the hat stand.

She looked embarrassed. "I apologize."

"Ah, but you were right." He changed the subject. "So now you're working for a wire service?"

"That's right."

"As their Washington correspondent."

"No, I'm his one-eyed girl assistant."

She had never before mentioned her deformity. Gus hesitated, then said: "I used to wonder why you didn't wear a patch. But now I'm glad you don't. You're just a beautiful woman with one closed eye."

"Thank you. You're a kind man. What sort of thing do you do for the president?"

"Apart from pick up the phone when it rings . . . I read the State Department's mealymouthed reports, then tell Wilson the truth."

"For example . . . ?"

"Our ambassadors in Europe say that the Somme Offensive is achieving some but not all its objectives, with heavy casualties on both sides. It's almost impossible to prove that statement wrong—and it tells the president nothing. So I tell him the Somme is a disaster for the British." He shrugged. "Or I used to. My job may be over." He was concealing his real feelings. The prospect that Wilson could lose was dreadful to him.

She nodded. "They're counting again in California. Almost a million people voted, and the difference is about five thousand."

"So much hangs on the decisions of a small number of poorly educated people."

"That's democracy."

Gus smiled. "A terrible way to run a country, but every other system is worse."

"If Wilson wins, what will be his top priority?"

"Off the record?"

"Of course."

"Peace in Europe," Gus said without hesitation.

"Really?"

"He was never really comfortable with the slogan 'He kept us out of war.' The matter isn't entirely in his hands. We may be dragged in whether we like it or not."

"But what can he do?"

"He'll put pressure on both sides to find a compromise."

"Can he succeed?"

"I don't know."

"Surely they can't go on slaughtering one another as they have been at the Somme."

"God knows." He changed the subject again. "Tell me the news from Buffalo."

She gave him a candid look. "Do you want to know about Olga, or is it too embarrassing?"

Gus looked away. What could be more embarrassing? First he had received a note from Olga, calling the engagement off. She had been abjectly apologetic but had given no explanation. Gus had been unwilling to accept this and had written back demanding to see her in person. He could not understand it and speculated that someone was putting pressure on her. But later that same day his mother had discovered, through her network of gossiping friends, that Olga was going to marry her father's driver. "But why?" Gus had said in anguish, and Mother had replied: "My darling boy, there is only one reason a girl marries the chauffeur." He had stared uncomprehendingly, and Mother had at last said: "She must be pregnant." It was the most humiliating moment of Gus's life, and even a year later he winced with pain every time he recalled it.

Rosa read his face. "I shouldn't have mentioned her. I'm sorry."

Gus felt he might as well know what everyone else knew. He touched Rosa's hand lightly. "Thank you for being direct. I prefer it. And yes, I'm curious about Olga."

"Well, they got married at that Russian Orthodox church on Ideal Street, and the reception took place at the Statler Hotel. Six hundred people were invited, and Josef Vyalov hired the ballroom *and* the dining room, and served caviar to everyone. It was the most lavish wedding in the history of Buffalo."

"And what is her husband like?"

"Lev Peshkov is handsome, charming, and completely untrustworthy. You know as soon as you look at him that he's a rogue. And now he's the son-in-law of one of the richest men in Buffalo."

"And the child?"

"A girl, Darya, but they call her Daisy. She was born in March. And Lev is no longer the chauffeur, of course. I think he runs one of Vyalov's nightclubs."

They talked for an hour; then Gus walked her downstairs and hailed a cab to take her home.

Early the next morning Gus got the California result by cable. Wilson had won by 3,777 votes. He had been reelected president.

Gus was elated. Four more years to try to achieve all they aimed for. They could change the world in four years.

While he was still staring at the telegram, his phone rang.

He picked it up and heard the switchboard operator say: "A call from Shadow Lawn. The president wants to speak to you, Mr. Dewar."

"Thank you."

A moment later he heard Wilson's familiar voice. "Good morning, Gus."

"Congratulations, Mr. President."

"Thank you. Pack a bag. I want you to go to Berlin."

{ III }

When Walter von Ulrich came home on leave, his mother gave a party.

There were not many parties in Berlin. It was difficult to buy food, even for a wealthy woman with an influential husband. Susanne von Ulrich was not well: she was thin, and had a permanent cough. However, she badly wanted to do something for Walter.

Otto had a cellar full of good wine he had bought before the war. Susanne decided to have an afternoon reception, so that she would not have to provide a full dinner. She served little snacks of smoked fish and cheese on triangles of toast, and made up for the poor food with unlimited magnums of champagne.

Walter was grateful for the thought, but he did not really want a party. He had two weeks away from the battlefield, and he just wanted a soft bed, dry clothes, and the chance to lounge all day in the elegant salon of his parents' town house, looking out of the window and thinking about Maud, or sitting at the Steinway grand piano and playing Schubert's "Frühlingsglaube": "Now everything, everything must change."

How glibly he and Maud had said, back in August 1914, that they would be reunited by Christmas! It was now more than two years since he had looked at her lovely face. And it was probably going to take Germany another two years to win the war. Walter's best hope was that

Russia would collapse, allowing the Germans to concentrate their forces on a massive final westward sweep.

Meanwhile Walter sometimes had trouble visualizing Maud, and had to look at the worn and fading magazine photograph he carried: *Lady Maud Fitzherbert is always dressed in the latest fashion.* He did not relish a party without her. As he got ready, he wished his mother had not troubled.

The house looked drab. There were not enough servants to keep the place spick-and-span. The men were in the army, the women had become streetcar conductors and mail deliverers, and the elderly staff who remained were struggling to maintain Mother's standards of cleanliness and polish. And the house was cold as well as grubby. The coal allowance was not enough to run the central heating, so Mother had put freestanding stoves in the hall, the dining room, and the drawing room, but they were inadequate against the chill of November in Berlin.

However, Walter cheered up when the cold rooms filled with young people and a small band began to play in the hall. His younger sister, Greta, had invited all her friends. He realized how much he missed social life. He liked seeing girls in beautiful gowns and men in immaculate suits. He enjoyed the joking and flirting and gossip. He had loved being a diplomat—the life suited him. It was easy for him to be charming and make small talk.

The von Ulrich house had no ballroom, but people began to dance on the tiled floor of the hall. Walter danced several times with Greta's best friend, Monika von der Helbard, a tall, willowy redhead with long hair who reminded him of pictures by the English artists who called themselves pre-Raphaelites.

He got her a glass of champagne and sat down with her. She asked him what it was like in the trenches, as they all did. He usually said it was a hard life but the men were in good spirits and they would win in the end. For some reason he told Monika the truth. "The worst thing about it is that it's pointless," he said. "We've been in the same positions, give or take a few yards, for two years, and I can't see how that will be changed by anything the high command is doing—or even by anything they might do. We're cold, hungry, sick with coughs and trench foot and stomachache, and bored to tears—all for nothing."

"That's not what we read in the newspapers," she said. "How very sad." She squeezed his arm sympathetically. The touch affected him like a mild electric shock. No woman outside his family had touched him for two years. He suddenly thought how wonderful it would be to take Monika in his arms, press her warm body to his, and kiss her lips. Her amber eyes looked back at him with a candid gaze, and after a moment he realized she had read his mind. Women often did know what men were thinking, he had found. He felt embarrassed, but clearly she did not care, and that thought made him more aroused.

Someone approached them, and Walter looked up irritably, guessing the man wanted to ask Monika to dance. Then he recognized a familiar face. "My God!" he said. The name came back to him: he had an excellent memory for people, like all good diplomats. He said in English: "Is it Gus Dewar?"

Gus replied in German. "It is, but we can speak German. How are you?"

Walter stood up and shook hands. "May I present Fräulein Monika von der Helbard? This is Gus Dewar, an adviser to President Woodrow Wilson."

"How delightful to meet you, Mr. Dewar," she said. "I shall leave you gentlemen to talk."

Walter watched her go with regret mingled with guilt. For a moment he had forgotten that he was a married man.

He looked at Gus. He had immediately liked the American when they met at Tŷ Gwyn. Gus was odd-looking, with a big head on a long thin body, but he was as sharp as a tack. Just out of Harvard then, Gus had had a charming shyness, but two years working in the White House had given him a degree of self-assurance. The shapeless style of lounge suit that Americans wore actually looked smart on him. Walter said: "I'm glad to see you. Not many people come here on holiday nowadays."

"It's not really a holiday," Gus said.

Walter waited for Gus to say more and, when he did not, prompted him. "What, then?"

"More like putting my toe in the water to see whether it's warm enough for the president to swim."

So this was official business. "I understand."

"To come to the point." Gus hesitated again, and Walter waited patiently. At last Gus spoke in a lowered voice. "President Wilson wants the Germans and the Allies to hold peace talks."

Walter's heart beat fast, but he raised a skeptical eyebrow. "He sent *you* to say this to *me*?"

"You know how it is. The president can't risk a public rebuff—it makes him look weak. Of course, he could tell our ambassador here in Berlin to speak to your foreign minister. But then the whole thing would become official, and sooner or later it would get out. So he asked his most junior adviser—me—to come to Berlin and use some of the contacts I made back in 1914."

Walter nodded. A lot was done in this fashion in the diplomatic world. "If we turn you down, no one needs to know."

"And even if the news gets out, it's just some low-ranking young men acting on their own initiative."

This made sense, and Walter began to feel excited. "What exactly does Mr. Wilson want?"

Gus took a deep breath. "If the kaiser were to write to the Allies suggesting a peace conference, then President Wilson would publicly support the proposal."

Walter suppressed a feeling of elation. This unexpected private conversation could have world-shaking consequences. Was it really possible that the nightmare of the trenches could be brought to an end? And that he might see Maud again in months rather than years? He told himself not to get carried away. Unofficial diplomatic feelers like this usually came to nothing. But he could not help being enthusiastic. "This is big, Gus," he said. "Are you sure Wilson means it?"

"Absolutely. It was the first thing he said to me after he won the election."

"What's his motivation?"

"He doesn't want to take America to war. But there's a danger we'll be dragged in anyway. He wants peace. And then he wants a new international system to make sure that a war like this never happens again."

"I'll vote for that," said Walter. "What do you want me to do?"

"Speak to your father."

"He may not like this proposal."

"Use your powers of persuasion."

"I'll do my best. Can I reach you at the American embassy?"

"No. This is a private visit. I'm staying at the Hotel Adlon."

"Of course you are, Gus," said Walter with a grin. The Adlon was the best hotel in the city and had once been called the most luxurious in the world. He felt nostalgic for those last years of peace. "Will we ever again be two young men with nothing on our minds except catching the waiter's eye to order another bottle of champagne?"

Gus took the question seriously. "No, I don't believe those days will ever come back, at least not in our lifetime."

Walter's sister, Greta, appeared. She had curly blond hair that shook fetchingly when she tossed her head. "What are you men looking so miserable about?" she said gaily. "Mr. Dewar, come and dance with me!"

Gus brightened. "Gladly!" he said.

She whisked him off.

Walter returned to the party, but as he chatted to friends and relations, half his mind was on Gus's proposal and how best to promote it. When he spoke to his father, he would try not to seem too keen. Father could be contrary. Walter would play the role of neutral messenger.

When the guests had gone, his mother cornered him in the salon. The room was decorated in the rococo style that was still the choice of old-fashioned Germans: ornate mirrors, tables with spindly curved legs, a big chandelier. "What a nice girl that Monika von der Helbard is," she said.

"Very charming," Walter agreed.

His mother wore no jewelry. She was chair of the gold-collection committee, and had given her baubles to be sold. All she had left was her wedding ring. "I must invite her again, with her parents next time. Her father is the Markgraf von der Helbard."

"Yes, I know."

"It's a very good family. They belong to the *Uradel*, the ancient nobility."

Walter moved to the door. "At what time do you expect Father to return home?"

"Soon. Walter, sit down and talk to me for a moment."

Walter had made it obvious he wanted to get away. The reason was that he needed to spend a quiet hour thinking about Gus Dewar's message. But he had been discourteous to his mother, whom he loved, and now he set about making amends. "With pleasure, Mother." He drew up a chair for her. "I imagined you might want to rest but, if not, I'd love to talk." He sat opposite her. "That was a super party. Thank you very much for organizing it."

She nodded acknowledgment, but changed the subject. "Your cousin Robert is missing," she said. "He was lost during the Brusilov Offensive."

"I know. He may have been taken prisoner by the Russians."

"And he may be dead. And your father is sixty years old. You could soon be the Graf von Ulrich."

Walter was not seduced by this possibility. Aristocratic titles mattered less and less nowadays. Perhaps he might be proud to be a count, but it might turn out to be a disadvantage in the postwar world.

Anyway, he did not have the title yet. "There has been no confirmation of Robert's death."

"Of course. But you must prepare yourself."

"In what way?"

"You should get married."

"Oh!" Walter was surprised. I should have seen that coming, he thought.

"You must have an heir, to assume the title when you die. And you may die soon, though I pray—" Her voice caught in her throat, and she stopped. She closed her eyes for a moment to regain her composure.

"Though I pray to heaven every day to protect you. It would be best if you were to father a son as soon as possible."

She was afraid of losing him, but he was just as fearful of losing her. He looked fondly at her. She was blond and pretty like Greta, and perhaps she had once been equally vivacious. Indeed, right now her eyes were bright and her cheeks were flushed from the excitement of the party and the champagne. However, just climbing the stairs made her breathless these days. She needed a holiday, and plenty of good food, and freedom from worry. Because of the war, she could have none of those things. It was not only soldiers who died, Walter thought worriedly.

"Please consider Monika," his mother said.

He longed to tell her about Maud. "Monika is a delightful girl, Mother, but I don't love her. I hardly know her."

"There isn't time for that! In war the proprieties may be overlooked. See her again. You've got ten more days of leave. See her every day. You could propose on your last day."

"What about her feelings? She may not want to marry me."

"She likes you." Mother looked away. "And she will do as her parents tell her."

Walter did not know whether to be annoyed or amused. "You two mothers have fixed this up, haven't you?"

"These are desperate times. You could get married three months from now. Your father will make sure you get special leave for the wedding and the honeymoon."

"He said that?" Normally, Father was angrily hostile to special privileges for well-connected soldiers.

"He understands the need for an heir to the title."

Father had been talked around. How long had that taken? He did not give in easily.

Walter tried not to squirm in his seat. He was in an impossible position. Married to Maud, he could not even pretend to be interested in marrying Monika—but he was not able to explain why. "Mother, I'm sorry to disappoint you, but I am not going to propose to Monika von der Helbard."

"But why not?" she cried.

He felt bad. "All I can say is that I wish I could make you happy."

She gave him a hard look. "Your cousin Robert never married. None of us were surprised, in his case. I hope there isn't a problem of that nature . . . "

Walter felt embarrassed by this reference to Robert's homosexuality. "Oh, Mother, please! I know exactly what you mean about Robert, and I'm not like him in that respect, so set your mind at rest."

She looked away. "I'm sorry to have mentioned it. But what is it? You're thirty years old!"

"It's hard to find the right girl."

"Not that hard."

"I'm looking for someone just like you."

"Now you're teasing me," she said crossly.

Walter heard a male voice outside the room. A moment later his father entered, in uniform, rubbing cold hands together. "It will snow," he said. He kissed his wife and nodded to Walter. "I trust the party was a success? I could not possibly attend—a whole afternoon of meetings."

"It was splendid," Walter said. "Mother conjured up tasty snacks out of nothing at all, and the Perrier-Jouët was superb."

"What vintage did you have?"

"The eighteen ninety-nine."

"You should have had the ninety-two."

"There's not much of it left."

"Ah."

"I had an intriguing conversation with Gus Dewar."

"I remember him—the American whose father is close to President Wilson."

"The son is even closer, now. Gus is working at the White House."

"What did he have to say?"

Mother stood up. "I'll leave you men to talk," she said.

They stood up.

"Please think about what I said, Walter, darling," she said as she went out.

A moment later the butler came in with a tray bearing a goblet with a stiff measure of golden-brown brandy. Otto took the glass. "One for you?" he said to Walter.

"No, thank you. I'm full of champagne."

Otto drank the brandy and stretched his legs toward the fire. "So, young Dewar appeared—with some kind of message?"

"In strictest confidence."

"Of course."

Walter could not feel much affection for his father. Their disagreements were too passionate, and Father was too flintily intransigent. He was narrow-minded, outdated, and deaf to reason, and he persisted in these faults with a kind of gleeful obstinacy that Walter found repellent. The consequence of his foolishness, and the foolishness of his generation in all European countries, was the slaughter of the Somme. Walter could not forgive that.

All the same, he spoke to his father with a soft voice and a friendly manner. He wanted this conversation to be as amiable and reasonable as possible. "The American president doesn't want to be drawn into the war," he began.

"Good."

"In fact, he would like us to make peace."

"Ha!" It was a shout of derision. "The cheap way to defeat us! What a nerve the man has."

Walter was dismayed by such immediate scorn, but he persisted, choosing his words with care. "Our enemies claim that German militarism and aggression caused this war, but of course that is not so."

"Indeed not," said Otto. "We were threatened by Russian mobilization on our eastern border and French mobilization to the west. The Schlieffen Plan was the only possible solution." As usual, Otto was speaking as if Walter were still twelve years old.

Walter answered patiently. "Exactly. I recall you saying that for us this was a defensive war, a response to an intolerable threat. We had to protect ourselves."

If Otto was surprised to hear Walter repeating the clichés of war justification, he did not show it. "Correct," he said.

"And we have done so," Walter said, playing his ace. "We have now achieved our aims."

His father was startled. "What do you mean?"

"The threat has been dealt with. The Russian army is destroyed, and the tsar's regime teeters on the brink of collapse. We have conquered Belgium, invaded France, and fought the French and their British allies to a standstill. We have done what we set out to do. We have protected Germany."

"A triumph."

"What more do we want, then?"

"Total victory!"

Walter leaned forward in his chair, looking intently at his father. "Why?"

"Our enemies must pay for their aggression! There must be reparations, perhaps border adjustments, colonial concessions."

"These were not our original war aims . . . were they?"

But Otto wanted to have it both ways. "No, but now that we have expended so much effort and money, and the lives of so many fine young Germans, we must have something in return."

It was a weak argument, but Walter knew better than to try to change his father's mind. Anyway, he had made the point that Germany's war aims had been achieved. Now he changed tack. "Are you quite sure that total victory is attainable?"

"Yes!"

"Back in February we launched an all-out assault on the French fortress of Verdun. We failed to take it. The Russians attacked us in the east, and the British threw everything into their offensive at the river Somme. These huge efforts by both sides have failed to end the stalemate." He waited for a response.

Grudgingly, Otto said: "So far, yes."

"Indeed, our own high command has acknowledged this. Since August, when von Falkenhayn was fired and Ludendorff became chief of staff, we have changed our tactics from attack to defense in depth. How do you imagine defense in depth will lead to total victory?"

"Unrestricted submarine warfare!" Otto said. "The Allies are being sustained by supplies from America, while our ports are blockaded by the British navy. We have to cut off their lifeline—then they'll give in."

Walter had not wanted to get into this, but now that he had begun, he had to go on. Gritting his teeth, he said as mildly as he could: "That would certainly draw America into the war."

"Do you know how many men there are in the United States Army?"

"It's only about a hundred thousand, but—"

"Correct. They can't even pacify Mexico! They're no threat to us."

Otto had never been to America. Few men of his generation had. They just did not know what they were talking about. "The United States is a big country with great wealth," Walter said, seething with frustration but keeping his tone conversational, trying to maintain the pretense of an amiable discussion. "They can build up their army."

"But not quickly. It will take them at least a year. By that time, the British and French will have surrendered."

Walter nodded. "We've had this discussion before, Father," he said in a conciliatory tone. "So has everyone connected with war strategy. There are arguments on both sides."

Otto could hardly deny that, so he just grunted disapprovingly.

Walter said: "Anyway, I'm sure it's not for me to decide Germany's response to this informal approach from Washington."

Otto took the hint. "Nor for me, of course."

"Wilson says that if Germany will write formally to the Allies proposing peace talks, he will publicly support the proposal. I suppose it's our duty to pass this message on to our sovereign."

"Indeed," said Otto. "The kaiser must decide."

{ IV }

Walter wrote a letter to Maud on a plain sheet of white paper with no letterhead.

My dearest darling,
It is winter in Germany and in my heart.

He wrote in English. He did not put his address at the top, nor did he use her name.

I cannot tell you how much I love you and how badly I miss you.

It was hard to know what to say. The letter might be read by inquisitive policemen, and he had to make sure neither Maud nor he could be identified.

I am one of a million men separated from the women we love, and the north wind blows through all our souls.

His idea was that this might be a letter from any soldier living away from his family because of the war.

It is a cold, bleak world for me, as it must be for you, but the hardest part to bear is our separation.

He wished he could tell her about his work in battlefield intelligence, about his mother trying to make him marry Monika, about the scarcity of food in Berlin, even about the book he was reading, a family saga called *Buddenbrooks*. But he was afraid that any specifics would put him or her in danger.

I cannot say much, but I want you to know that I am faithful to you—

He broke off, thinking guiltily of the urge he had felt to kiss Monika. But he had not yielded.

—and to the sacred promises we made to each other the
last time we were together.

It was as near as he could get to mentioning their marriage. He did
not want to risk someone at her end reading it and learning the truth.

I think every day of the moment when we will meet
again, and look into each other's eyes and say: "Hello, my
beloved."
Until then, remember me.

He did not sign his name.

He put the letter in an envelope and slipped it into the inside breast
pocket of his jacket.

There was no postal service between Germany and England.

He left his room, went downstairs, put on a hat and a heavy overcoat
with a fur collar, and went out into the shivering streets of Berlin.

He met Gus Dewar in the bar of the Adlon. The hotel maintained a
shadow of its prewar dignity, with waiters in evening dress and a string
quartet, but there were no imported drinks—no Scotch, no brandy, no
English gin—so they ordered schnapps.

"Well?" said Gus eagerly. "How was my message received?"

Walter was full of hope; but he knew that the grounds for optimism
were slight, and he wanted to play down his excitement. The news he
had for Gus was positive, but only just. "The kaiser is writing to the
president," he said.

"Good! What is he going to say?"

"I have seen a draft. I'm afraid the tone is not very conciliatory."

"What do you mean?"

Walter closed his eyes, remembering, then quoted: "'The most
formidable war in history has been raging for two and a half years.
In that conflict, Germany and her allies have given proof of our
indestructible strength. Our unshakable lines resist ceaseless attacks.
Recent events show that continuation of the war cannot break our
resisting power . . .' There's a lot more like that."

"I see why you say it's not very conciliatory."

"Eventually it gets to the point." Walter brought the next part to mind. "'Conscious of our military and economic strength and ready to carry on to the end, if we must, the struggle that is forced upon us, but animated at the same time by the desire to stem the flow of blood and bring the horrors of war to an end'—here comes the important part—'we propose even now to enter into peace negotiations.'"

Gus was elated. "That's great! He says yes!"

"Quietly, please!" Walter looked around nervously, but it seemed no one had noticed. The sound of the string quartet muffled their conversation.

"Sorry," Gus said.

"You're right, though." Walter smiled, allowing his feeling of sanguinity to show a little. "The tone is arrogant, combative, and scornful—but he proposes peace talks."

"I can't tell you how grateful I am."

Walter held up a warning hand. "Let me tell you something very frankly. Powerful men close to the kaiser who are against peace have supported this proposal cynically, merely to look good in the eyes of your president, feeling sure the Allies will reject it anyway."

"Let's hope they're wrong!"

"Amen to that."

"When will they send the letter?"

"They're still arguing about the wording. When that is agreed, the letter will be handed to the American ambassador here in Berlin, with a request that he pass it to the Allied governments." This diplomatic game of pass-the-parcel was necessary because enemy governments had no official means of communication.

"I'd better go to London," Gus said. "Perhaps I can do something to prepare for its reception."

"I thought you might say that. I have a request."

"After what you've done to help me? Anything!"

"It's strictly personal."

"No problem."

"It requires me to let you into a secret."

Gus smiled. "Intriguing!"

"I would like you to take a letter from me to Lady Maud Fitzherbert."

"Ah." Gus looked thoughtful. He knew there could be only one reason for Walter to be writing secretly to Maud. "I see the need for discretion. But that's okay."

"If your belongings are searched when you are leaving Germany or entering England, you will have to say that it is a love letter from an American man in Germany to his fiancée in London. The letter gives no names or addresses."

"All right."

"Thank you," Walter said fervently. "I can't tell you how much it means to me."

{ V }

There was a shooting party at Tŷ Gwyn on Saturday, December 2. Earl Fitzherbert and Princess Bea were delayed in London, so Fitz's friend Bing Westhampton acted as host, and Lady Maud as hostess.

Before the war, Maud had loved such parties. Women did not shoot, of course, but she liked the house full of guests, the picnic lunch at which the ladies joined the men, and the blazing fires and hearty food they all came home to at night. But she found herself unable to enjoy such pleasure when soldiers were suffering in the trenches. She told herself that one couldn't spend one's whole life being miserable, even in wartime; but it did not work. She pasted on her brightest smile, and encouraged everyone to eat and drink heartily, but when she heard the shotguns she could only think of the battlefields. Lavish food was left untouched on her plate, and glasses of Fitz's priceless old wines were taken away untasted.

She hated to be at leisure, these days, because all she did was think about Walter. Was he alive or dead? The Battle of the Somme was over, at last. Fitz said the Germans had lost half a million men. Was Walter one of them? Or was he lying in a hospital somewhere, maimed?

Perhaps he was celebrating victory. The newspapers could not quite conceal the fact that the British army's major effort for 1916 had gained a paltry seven miles of territory. The Germans might feel entitled to congratulate themselves. Even Fitz was saying, quietly and in private, that Britain's best hope now was that the Americans might join in. Was Walter lounging in a brothel in Berlin, with a bottle of schnapps in one hand and a pretty blond fräulein in the other? I'd rather he was wounded, she thought; then she felt ashamed of herself.

Gus Dewar was among the guests at Tŷ Gwyn, and at teatime he sought Maud out. All the men wore plus fours, tweed trousers buttoned just below the knee, and the tall American looked particularly foolish in them. He held a cup of tea precariously in one hand as he crossed the crowded morning room to where she sat.

She suppressed a sigh. When a single man approached her he usually had romance on his mind, and she had to fight him off without admitting she was married, which was sometimes difficult. Nowadays, so many eligible upper-class bachelors had been killed in the war that the most unprepossessing men fancied their chances with her: younger sons of bankrupt barons, weedy clergymen with bad breath, even homosexuals looking for a woman to give them respectability.

Not that Gus Dewar was such a poor prospect. He was not handsome, nor did he have the easy grace of such men as Walter and Fitz, but he had a sharp mind and high ideals, and he shared Maud's passionate interest in world affairs. And the combination of his slight awkwardness, physical and social, with a certain blunt honesty somehow amounted to a kind of charm. If she had been single he might even have had a chance.

He folded his long legs beside her on a yellow silk sofa. "Such a pleasure to be at Tŷ Gwyn again," he said.

"You were here shortly before the war," Maud recalled. She would never forget that weekend in January 1914, when the king had come to stay and there had been a terrible disaster at the Aberowen pit. What she remembered most vividly—she was ashamed to realize—was kissing Walter. She wished she could kiss him now. What fools they had been to do no more than kiss! She wished now that they had made love, and she had got pregnant, so that they were obliged to marry in undignified haste, and had been sent away to live in perpetual social disgrace somewhere frightful like Rhodesia or Bengal. All the considerations that had inhibited them—parents, society, career—seemed trivial by comparison with the awful possibility that Walter might be killed and she would never see him again. "How can men be so stupid as to go to war?" she said to Gus. "And to continue fighting when the dreadful cost in men's lives has long ago dwarfed any conceivable gain?"

He said: "President Wilson believes the two sides should consider peace without victory."

She was relieved that he did not want to tell her what fine eyes she had, or some such rubbish. "I agree with the president," she said. "The British army has already lost a million men. The Somme alone cost us four hundred thousand casualties."

"But what do the British people think?"

Maud considered. "Most of the newspapers are still pretending the Somme was a great victory. Any attempt at a realistic assessment is labeled unpatriotic. I'm sure Lord Northcliffe would really rather live under a military dictatorship. But most of our people know we're not making much progress."

"The Germans may be about to propose peace talks."

"Oh, I hope you're right."

"I believe a formal approach may be made soon."

Maud stared at him. "Pardon me," she said. "I assumed you were making polite conversation. But you're not." She felt excited. Peace talks? Could it happen?

"No, I'm not making conversation," Gus said. "I know you have friends in the Liberal government."

"It's not really a Liberal government anymore," she said. "It's a coalition, with several Conservative ministers in the cabinet."

"Excuse me. I misspoke. I did know about the coalition. All the same, Asquith is still prime minister, and he is a Liberal, and I know you are close to many leading Liberals."

"Yes."

"So I've come here to ask your opinion as to how the German proposal might be received."

She considered carefully. She knew who Gus represented. The president of the United States was asking her this question. She had better be exact. As it happened, she had a key item of information. "Ten days ago the cabinet discussed a paper by Lord Lansdowne, a former Conservative foreign secretary, arguing that we cannot win the war."

Gus lit up. "Really? I had no idea."

"Of course you didn't. It was secret. However, there have been rumors, and Northcliffe has been fulminating against what he calls defeatist talk of negotiated peace."

Gus said eagerly: "And how was Lansdowne's paper received?"

"I'd say there are four men inclined to sympathize with him: the foreign secretary, Sir Edward Grey; the chancellor, McKenna; the president of the Board of Trade, Runciman; and the prime minister himself."

Gus's face brightened with hope. "That's a powerful faction!"

"Especially now that the aggressive Winston Churchill has gone. He never recovered from the catastrophe of the Dardanelles expedition, which was his pet project."

"Who in the cabinet was against Lansdowne?"

"David Lloyd George, secretary for war, the most popular politician in the country. And Lord Robert Cecil, minister for blockade; Arthur Henderson, the paymaster general, who is also leader of the Labour Party; and Arthur Balfour, first lord of the Admiralty."

"I saw the interview Lloyd George gave to the papers. He said he wanted to see a fight to the knockout."

"Most people agree with him, unfortunately. Of course, they get little chance to hear any other point of view. People who argue against the war—such as the philosopher Bertrand Russell—are constantly harassed by the government."

"But what was the conclusion of the cabinet?"

"There was none. Asquith's meetings often end that way. People complain that he's indecisive."

"How frustrating. However, it seems a peace proposal won't fall on deaf ears."

It was so refreshing, Maud thought, to talk to a man who took her completely seriously. Even those who spoke intelligently to her tended to condescend a little. Walter was really the only other man who conversed with her as an equal.

At that moment Fitz came into the room. He was wearing black-and-gray London clothes, and had obviously just got off the train. He had an eye patch and walked with a stick. "I'm so sorry to have let you all down," he said, addressing everyone. "I had to stay last night in town. London is in a ferment over the latest political developments."

Gus spoke up. "What developments? We haven't seen today's newspapers yet."

"Yesterday Lloyd George wrote to Asquith demanding a change in the way we manage the war. He wants an all-powerful war council of three ministers to make all the decisions."

Gus said: "And will Asquith agree?"

"Of course not. He replied saying that if there were such a body, the prime minister would have to be its chairman."

Fitz's impish friend Bing Westhampton was sitting on a window seat with his feet up. "That defeats the object," he said. "Any council of which Asquith is the chair will be just as feeble and indecisive as the cabinet." He looked around apologetically. "Begging the pardon of government ministers here present."

"You're right, though," said Fitz. "The letter is really a challenge to Asquith's leadership, especially as Lloyd George's friend Max Aitken has given the story to all the newspapers. There's no possibility of compromise now. It's a fight to the knockout, as Lloyd George would say. If he doesn't get his way, he'll have to resign from the cabinet. And if he does get his way, Asquith will go—and then we'll have to choose a new prime minister."

Maud caught Gus's eye. They shared the same unspoken thought, she knew. With Asquith in Downing Street, the peace initiative had a chance. If the belligerent Lloyd George won this contest, everything would be different.

The gong rang in the hall, telling guests it was time to change into evening dress. The tea party broke up. Maud went to her room.

Her clothes had been laid out ready. The dress was one she had got in Paris for the London season of 1914. She had bought few clothes since. She took off her tea gown and slipped on a silk wrap. She would not ring for her maid yet: she had a few minutes to herself. She sat at the dressing table and looked at her face in the mirror. She was twenty-six, and it showed. She had never been pretty, but people had called her handsome. With wartime austerity she had lost what little she had of girlish softness, and the angles of her face had become more pronounced. What would Walter think when he saw her—if they ever met again? She touched her breasts. They were still firm, at least. He would be pleased about that. Thinking about him made her nipples stiffen. She wondered if she had time to—

There was a tap at the door, and she guiltily dropped her hands. "Who is it?" she called.

The door opened, and Gus Dewar stepped in.

Maud stood up, pulling the wrap tightly around her, and said in her most forbidding voice: "Mr. Dewar, please leave at once!"

"Don't be alarmed," he said. "I have to see you in private."

"I can't imagine what possible reason—"

"I saw Walter in Berlin."

Maud fell silent, shocked. She stared at Gus. How could he know about her and Walter?

Gus said: "He gave me a letter for you." He reached inside his tweed jacket and drew out an envelope.

Maud took it with a trembling hand.

Gus said: "He told me he had not used your name or his, for fear the letter might be read at the border, but in fact no one searched my baggage."

Maud held the letter uneasily. She had longed to hear from him, but now she feared bad news. Walter might have taken a lover, and the letter might beg her understanding. Perhaps he had married a German girl, and wrote to ask her to keep the earlier marriage secret forever. Worst of all, perhaps he had started divorce proceedings.

She tore open the envelope.

She read:

> My dearest darling,
>
> It is winter in Germany and in my heart. I cannot tell you how much I love you and how badly I miss you.

Her eyes filled with tears. "Oh!" she said. "Oh, Mr. Dewar, thank you for bringing this!"

He took a tentative step closer to her. "There, there," he said. He patted her arm.

She tried to read the rest of the letter but she could not see the words on the paper. "I'm so happy," she wept.

She dropped her head to Gus's shoulder, and he put his arms around her. "It's all right," he said.

Maud gave in to her feelings and began to sob.

CHAPTER TWENTY-ONE

December 1916

Fitz was working at the Admiralty in Whitehall. It was not the job he wanted. He longed to return to the Welsh Rifles in France. Much as he hated the dirt and discomfort of the trenches, he could not feel good about being safe in London while others were risking their lives. He had a horror of being thought a coward. However, the doctors insisted that his leg was not yet strong enough, and the army would not let him return.

Because Fitz spoke German, Smith-Cumming of the Secret Service Bureau—the man who called himself "C"—had recommended him to naval intelligence, and he had been temporarily posted to a department known as Room 40. The last thing he wanted was a desk job, but to his surprise, he found that the work was highly important to the war effort.

On the first day of the war a post office ship called the CS *Alert* had gone out into the North Sea, dredged up the Germans' heavy-duty seabed telecommunications cables, and severed them all. With that sly stroke the British had forced the enemy to use wireless for most messages. Wireless signals could be intercepted. The Germans were not stupid, and they sent all their messages in code. Room 40 was where the British tried to break the codes.

Fitz worked with an assortment of people—some of them quite odd, most not very military—who struggled to decipher the gibberish picked up by listening stations on the coast. Fitz was no good at the crossword-puzzle challenge of decoding—he could never even work out the murderer in a Sherlock Holmes mystery—but he was able to translate the decrypts into English and, more important, his battlefield experience enabled him to judge which were significant.

Not that it made much difference. At the end of 1916 the western front had hardly moved from its position at the beginning of the year, despite huge efforts by both sides—the relentless German assault at Verdun and the even more costly British attack at the Somme. The Allies desperately needed a boost. If the United States joined in they could tip the balance—but so far there was no sign of that.

Commanders in all armies issued their orders late at night or first thing in the morning, so Fitz started early and worked intensely until midday. On the Wednesday after the shooting party he left the Admiralty at half past twelve and took a taxi home. The uphill walk from Whitehall to Mayfair, though short, was too much for him.

The three women he lived with—Bea, Maud, and Aunt Herm—were just sitting down to lunch. He handed his walking stick and uniform cap to Grout and joined the ladies. After the utilitarian environment of his office, he took a warm pleasure in his home: the rich furnishings, the soft-footed servants, the French china on the snowy tablecloth.

He asked Maud what the political news was. A battle was raging between Asquith and Lloyd George. Yesterday Asquith had dramatically resigned as prime minister. Fitz was worried: he was no admirer of the Liberal Asquith, but what if the new man was seduced by facile talk of peace?

"The king has seen Bonar Law," Maud said. Andrew Bonar Law was the leader of the Conservatives. The last remnant of royal power in British politics was the monarch's right to appoint a prime minister—

although his chosen candidate still had to win the support of Parliament.

Fitz said: "What happened?"

"Bonar Law declined to be prime minister."

Fitz bridled. "How could he refuse the king?" A man should obey his monarch, Fitz believed, especially a Conservative.

"He thinks it has to be Lloyd George. But the king doesn't want Lloyd George."

Bea put in: "I should hope not. The man is not much better than a socialist."

"Indeed," said Fitz. "But he's got more aggression than the rest of them put together. At least he would inject some energy into the war effort."

Maud said: "I fear he won't make the most of any chance of peace."

"Peace?" said Fitz. "I don't think you need to worry too much about that." He tried not to sound heated, but defeatist talk of peace made him think of all the lives that had been lost: poor young Lieutenant Carlton-Smith, so many Aberowen Pals, even the wretched Owen Bevin, shot by a firing squad. Was their sacrifice to have been for nothing? The thought seemed blasphemous to him. Forcing himself to speak in a conversational tone, he said: "There won't be peace until one side or the other has won."

Anger flashed in Maud's eyes but she, too, controlled herself. "We might get the best of both worlds: energetic leadership of the war by Lloyd George as chairman of the War Council, and a statesmanlike prime minister such as Arthur Balfour to negotiate peace if we decide that's what we want."

"Hmm." Fitz did not like that idea at all, but Maud had a way of putting things that made it hard to disagree. Fitz changed the subject. "What are you planning to do this afternoon?"

"Aunt Herm and I are going to the East End. We host a soldiers' wives club. We give them tea and cake—paid for by you, Fitz, for which we thank you—and try to help them with their problems."

"Such as?"

Aunt Herm answered. "Getting a clean place to live and finding a reliable child minder are the usual ones."

Fitz was amused. "You surprise me, Aunt. You used to disapprove of Maud's adventures in the East End."

"It's wartime," Lady Hermia said defiantly. "We must all do what we can."

On impulse Fitz said: "Perhaps I'll come with you. It's good for them to see that earls get shot just as easily as stevedores."

Maud looked taken aback, but she said: "Well, of course, yes, if you'd like to."

He could tell she was not keen. No doubt there was a certain amount of left-wing rubbish talked at her club—votes for women and suchlike tosh. However, she could not refuse him, as he paid for the whole thing.

Lunch ended and they went off to get ready. Fitz went to his wife's dressing room. Bea's gray-haired maid, Nina, was helping her off with the dress she had worn at lunch. Bea murmured something in Russian, and Nina replied in the same language, which irritated Fitz as it seemed intended to exclude him. He spoke in Russian, hoping they would think he understood everything, and said to the maid: "Leave us alone, please." She curtsied and went out.

Fitz said: "I haven't seen Boy today." He had left the house early this morning. "I must go to the nursery before he's taken out for his walk."

"He's not going out at the moment," Bea said anxiously. "He's got a little cough."

Fitz frowned. "He needs fresh air."

To his surprise, she suddenly looked tearful. "I'm afraid for him," she said. "With you and Andrei both risking your lives in the war, Boy may be all I have left."

Her brother, Andrei, was married but had no children. If Andrei and Fitz died, Boy would be all the family Bea had. It explained why she was overprotective of the child. "All the same, it won't do him good to be mollycoddled."

"I don't know this word," she said sulkily.

"I think you know what I mean."

Bea stepped out of her petticoats. Her figure was more voluptuous than it used to be. Fitz watched her untie the ribbons that held up her stockings. He imagined biting the soft flesh of her inner thigh.

She caught his eye. "I'm tired," she said. "I must sleep for an hour."

"I could join you."

"I thought you were going slumming with your sister."

"I don't have to."

"I really need to rest."

He stood up to go, then changed his mind. He felt angry and rejected. "It's been a long time since you welcomed me into your bed."

"I haven't been counting the days."

"I have, and it's weeks, not days."

"I'm sorry. I feel so worried about everything." She was close to tears again.

Fitz knew she was fearful for her brother, and he sympathized with her helpless anxiety, but millions of women were going through the same agonies, and the nobility had a duty to be stoical. "I hear you started attending services at the Russian embassy while I was away in France." There was no Russian Orthodox church in London, but there was a chapel in the embassy.

"Who told you that?"

"Never mind who told me." It had been Aunt Herm. "Before we married, I asked you to convert to the Church of England, and you did."

She would not meet his eye. "I didn't think it would do any harm for me to go to one or two services," she said quietly. "I'm so sorry to have displeased you."

Fitz was suspicious of foreign clergymen. "Does the priest there tell you it's a sin to take pleasure in lying with your husband?"

"Of course not! But when you're away, and I feel so alone, so far away from everything I grew up with . . . it's a comfort to me to hear familiar Russian hymns and prayers."

Fitz felt sorry for her. It must be difficult. He certainly could not contemplate going to live permanently in a foreign country. And he knew, from conversations with other married men, that it was not unusual for a wife to resist her husband's advances after she had borne a child.

But he hardened his heart. Everyone had to make sacrifices. Bea should be grateful she did not have to run into machine-gun fire. "I think I have done my duty by you," he said. "When we married, I paid off your family's debts. I called in experts, Russian and English, to plan the reorganization of the estates." They had told Andrei to drain swamps to produce more farmland, and prospect for coal and other minerals, but he had never done anything. "It's not my fault that Andrei wasted every opportunity."

"Yes, Fitz," she said. "You did everything you promised."

"And I ask that you do your duty. You and I must produce heirs. If Andrei dies without fathering children, our son will inherit two huge estates. He will be one of the greatest landowners in the world. We must have more sons in case—God forbid—something should happen to Boy."

She kept her eyes cast down. "I know my duty."

Fitz felt dishonest. He talked about an heir—and everything he had said was true—but he was not telling her that he hungered to see her soft body spread-eagled for him on the bedsheets, white on white, and her fair hair spilling over the pillow. He repressed the vision. "If you know your duty, please do it. Next time I come into your room I shall expect to be welcomed like the loving husband that I am."

"Yes, Fitz."

He left. He was glad he had put his foot down, but he also felt an uneasy sense that he had done something wrong. It was ridiculous: he had pointed out to Bea the error of her ways, and she had accepted his reproof. That was how things ought to be between man and wife. But he could not feel as satisfied as he should.

He pushed Bea out of his mind when he met up with Maud and Aunt Herm in the hall. He put on his uniform cap and glanced in the mirror, then quickly looked away. He tried these days not to think much about his appearance. The bullet had damaged the muscles on the left side of his face, and his eyelid had a permanent droop. It was a minor disfigurement, but his vanity would never recover. He told himself to be grateful that his eyesight was unaffected.

The blue Cadillac was still in France, but he had managed to get hold of another. His chauffeur knew the way: he had obviously driven Maud to the East End before. Half an hour later they pulled up outside the Calvary Gospel Hall, a mean little chapel with a tin roof. It might have been transplanted from Aberowen. Fitz wondered if the pastor was Welsh.

The tea party was already under way and the place was packed with young women and their children. It smelled worse than a barracks, and Fitz had to resist the temptation to hold a handkerchief over his nose.

Maud and Herm went to work immediately, Maud seeing women one by one in the back office and Herm marshaling them. Fitz limped from one table to the next, asking the women where their husbands were serving and what their experiences had been, while their children rolled on the floor. Young women often became giggly and tongue-tied when Fitz spoke to them, but this group was not so easily flustered. They asked him what regiment he served in and how he had got his wounds.

It was not until he was halfway round the room that he saw Ethel.

He had noticed that there were two offices at the back of the hall, one Maud's, and he had vaguely wondered who was in the second. He happened to look up when the door opened and Ethel stepped out.

He had not seen her for two years, but she had not changed much. Her dark curls bounced as she walked, and her smile was a sunbeam. Her dress was drab and worn, like the clothes of all the women except Maud and Herm, but she had the same trim figure, and he could not help thinking about the petite body he had known so well. Without even looking at him she cast her spell. It was as if no time had passed since they had rolled around, giggling and kissing, on the bed in the Gardenia Suite.

She spoke to the only other man in the room, a stooped figure in a dark gray lounge suit of some heavy cloth, sitting at a table making notes in a ledger. He wore thick glasses, but even so Fitz could see the adoration in the man's eyes when he looked up at Ethel. She spoke to him with easy amiability, and Fitz wondered if they were married.

Ethel turned around and caught Fitz's eye. Her eyebrows went up and her mouth made an O of surprise. She took a step back, as if nervous, and bumped into a chair. The woman sitting in the chair looked up with an expression of irritation. Ethel mouthed: "Sorry!" without looking at her.

Fitz rose from his seat, not an easy matter with his busted leg, all the time gazing steadily at Ethel. She dithered visibly, not sure whether to approach him or flee to the safety of her office. He said: "Hello, Ethel." His words did not carry across the noisy room, but she could probably see his lips move and guess what he said.

She made a decision and walked toward him.

"Good afternoon, Lord Fitzherbert," she said, and her lilting Welsh accent made the routine phrase sound like a melody. She held out her hand and they shook. Her skin was rough.

He followed her in reverting to formality. "How are you, Mrs. Williams?"

She pulled up a chair and sat down. As he lowered himself into his seat he realized she had deftly put them on a footing of equality without intimacy.

"I seen you at the service in the Aberowen Reck," she said. "I was very sorry—" Her voice caught in her throat. She looked down and started again. "I was very sorry to see you wounded. I hope you're getting better."

"Slowly." He could tell that her concern was genuine. She did not hate him, it seemed, despite everything that had happened. His heart was touched.

"How did you get your injuries?"

He had told the story so often that it bored him. "It was the first day of the Somme. I hardly saw any fighting. We went over the top, got past our own barbed wire, and started across no-man's-land, and the next thing I remember is being carried on a stretcher, and hurting like hell."

"My brother saw you fall."

Fitz remembered the insubordinate Corporal William Williams. "Did he? What happened to him?"

"His section captured a German trench, then had to abandon it when they ran out of ammunition."

Fitz had missed all the debriefing, being in hospital. "Did he get a medal?"

"No. The colonel told him he should have defended his position to the death. Billy said: 'What, like you did?' and he was put on a charge."

Fitz was not surprised. Williams was trouble. "So what are you doing here?"

"I work with your sister."

"She didn't tell me."

Ethel gave him a level look. "She wouldn't think you'd be interested in news of your former servants."

It was a jibe, but he ignored it. "What do you do?"

"I'm managing editor of *The Soldier's Wife.* I arrange printing and distribution, and edit the letters page. And I take care of the money."

He was impressed. It was a big step up from housekeeper. But she had always been an extraordinarily capable organizer. "My money, I suppose?"

"I don't think so. Maud is careful. She knows you don't mind paying for tea and cake, and doctoring for soldiers' children, but she wouldn't use your money for antiwar propaganda."

He kept the conversation going just for the pleasure of watching her face as she talked. "Is that what is in the newspaper?" he asked. "Antiwar propaganda?"

"We discuss publicly what you speak of only in secret: the possibility of peace."

She was right. Fitz knew that senior politicians in both major parties had been talking about peace, and it angered him. But he did not want to have a row with Ethel. "Your hero, Lloyd George, is in favor of fighting harder."

"Will he become prime minister, do you think?"

"The king doesn't want him. But he may be the only candidate who can unite Parliament."

"I fear he may prolong the war."

Maud came out of her office. The tea party was breaking up, the women clearing up the cups and saucers and marshaling their children. Fitz marveled to see Aunt Herm carrying a stack of dirty plates. How the war had changed people!

He looked again at Ethel. She was still the most attractive woman he had ever met. He yielded to an impulse. Speaking in a lowered voice he said: "Will you meet me tomorrow?"

She looked shocked. "What for?" she said quietly.

"Yes or no?"

"Where?"

"Victoria Station. One o'clock. At the entrance to platform three."

Before she could reply the man in thick glasses came over, and Ethel introduced him. "Earl Fitzherbert, may I present Mr. Bernie Leckwith, chairman of the Aldgate branch of the Independent Labour Party."

Fitz shook hands. Leckwith was in his twenties. Fitz guessed that poor eyesight had kept him out of the armed forces.

"I'm sorry to see you wounded, Lord Fitzherbert," Leckwith said in a Cockney accent.

"I was one of thousands, and lucky to be alive."

"With hindsight, is there anything we could have done differently at the Somme, that would have greatly altered the outcome?"

Fitz thought for a moment. It was a damned good question.

While he considered, Leckwith said: "Did we need more men and ammunition, as the generals claim? Or more flexible tactics and better communications, as the politicians say?"

Fitz said thoughtfully: "All those things would have helped but, frankly, I don't think they would have brought us victory. The assault was doomed from the start. But we could not possibly have known that in advance. We had to try."

Leckwith nodded, as if his own view had been confirmed. "I appreciate your candor," he said, almost as if Fitz had made a confession.

They left the chapel. Fitz handed Aunt Herm and Maud into the waiting car, then got in himself, and the chauffeur drove away.

Fitz found himself breathing hard. He had suffered a small shock. Three years ago Ethel had been counting pillowcases at Tŷ Gwyn. Today she was the managing editor of a newspaper that, although small, was considered by senior ministers to be a thorn in the flesh of the government.

What was her relationship with the surprisingly intelligent Bernie Leckwith? "Who was that chap Leckwith?" he asked Maud.

"An important local politician."

"Is he Williams's husband?"

Maud laughed. "No, though everyone thinks he should be. He's a clever man who shares her ideals, and he's devoted to her son. I don't know why Ethel didn't marry him long ago."

"Perhaps he doesn't make her heart beat faster."

Maud raised her eyebrows, and Fitz realized he had been dangerously candid.

He added hastily: "Girls of that type want romance, don't they? She'll marry a war hero, not a librarian."

"She's not a *girl of that type* or any other type," Maud said rather frostily. "She's nothing if not exceptional. You don't meet two like her in a lifetime."

Fitz looked away. He knew that was true.

He wondered what the child was like. It must have been one of the dirty-faced toddlers playing on the floor of the chapel. He had probably seen his own son this afternoon. He was strangely moved by the thought. For some reason it made him want to cry.

The car was passing through Trafalgar Square. He told the driver to stop. "I'd better drop in at the office," he explained to Maud.

He limped into the Old Admiralty Building and up the stairs. His desk was in the diplomatic section, which inhabited Room 45. Sublieutenant Carver, a student of Latin and Greek who had come down from Cambridge to help decode German signals, told him that not many intercepts had come in during the afternoon, as usual, and there was nothing he needed to deal with. However, there was some political news. "Have you heard?" said Carver. "The king has summoned Lloyd George."

{ II }

All the next morning, Ethel told herself she was not going to meet Fitz. How dared he suggest such a thing? For more than two years she had heard nothing from him. Then when they met he had not even asked about Lloyd—his own child! He was the same selfish, thoughtless deceiver as always.

All the same, she had been thrown into a whirl. Fitz had looked at her with his intense green eyes, and asked her questions about her life that made her feel she was important to him—contrary to all the evidence. He was no longer the perfect godlike man he had once been: his beautiful face was marred by one half-closed eye, and he stooped over his walking stick. But his weakness only made her want to take care of him. She told herself she was a fool. He had all the care money could buy. She would not go to meet him.

At twelve noon she left the premises of *The Soldier's Wife*—two small rooms over a print shop, shared with the Independent Labour Party—and caught a bus. Maud was not at the office that morning, which saved Ethel the trouble of inventing an excuse.

It was a long journey by bus and underground train from Aldgate to Victoria, and Ethel arrived at the rendezvous a few minutes after one o'clock. She wondered if Fitz might have grown impatient and left, and the thought made her feel slightly ill; but he was there, wearing a tweed suit as if he were going into the country, and she immediately felt better.

He smiled. "I was afraid you weren't coming," he said.

"I don't know why I did," she replied. "Why did you ask me?"

"I want to show you something." He took her arm.

They walked out of the station. Ethel felt foolishly pleased to be arm in arm with Fitz. She wondered at his boldness. He was an easily recognizable figure. What if they ran into one of his friends? She supposed they would pretend not to see each other. In Fitz's social class, a man who had been married a few years was not expected to be faithful.

They rode a bus a few stops and got off in the raffish suburb of Chelsea, a low-rent neighborhood of artists and writers. Ethel wondered what he wanted her to see. They walked along a street of small villas. Fitz said: "Have you ever watched a debate in Parliament?"

"No," she said. "But I'd love to."

"You have to be invited by an M.P. or a peer. Shall I arrange it?"

"Yes, please!"

He looked happy that she had accepted. "I'll check when there's going to be something interesting. You might like to see Lloyd George in action."

"Yes!"

"He is putting his government together today. I should think he will kiss the king's hand as prime minister tonight."

Ethel gazed about her thoughtfully. In parts, Chelsea still looked like the country village it had been a hundred years ago. The older buildings were cottages and farmhouses, low-built with large gardens and orchards. There was not much greenery in December, but even so the neighborhood had a pleasant semirural feel. "Politics is a funny business," she said. "I've wanted Lloyd George for prime minister ever since I was old enough to read the newspaper, but now that it's happened, I'm dismayed."

"Why?"

"He's the most belligerent senior figure in the government. His appointment might kill off any chance of peace. On the other hand . . ."

Fitz looked intrigued. "What?"

"He's the only man who could agree to peace talks without being crucified by Northcliffe's bloodthirsty newspapers."

"That's a point," Fitz said, looking worried. "If anyone else did it, the headlines would scream: 'Fire Asquith—or Balfour, or Bonar Law—and bring in Lloyd George!' But if they attack Lloyd George there's no one left."

"So maybe there is a hope of peace."

He allowed his tone of voice to become testy. "Why aren't you hoping for victory, rather than peace?"

"Because that's how we got into this mess," she said equably. "What are you going to show me?"

"This." He unlatched a gate and held it open. They entered the grounds of a detached two-story house. The garden was overgrown and the place needed painting, but it was a charming medium-size home, the kind of place that might be owned by a successful musician, Ethel imagined, or perhaps a well-known actor. Fitz took a key from his pocket and opened the door. They stepped inside, and he closed the door and kissed her.

She gave herself up to it. She had not been kissed for a long time, and she felt like a thirsty traveler in a desert. She stroked his long neck and pressed her breasts against his chest. She sensed that he was as desperate as she. Before she lost control she pushed him away. "Stop," she said breathlessly. "Stop."

"Why?"

"Last time we did this I ended up talking to your bloody lawyer." She moved away from him. "I'm not as innocent as I used to be."

"It will be different this time," he said, panting. "I was a fool to let you go. I see that now. I was young, too."

To help her calm down she looked into the rooms. They were full of dowdy old furniture. "Whose house is this?" she said.

"Yours," he replied. "If you want it."

She stared at him. What did he mean?

"You could live here with the baby," he explained. "It was occupied for years by an old lady who used to be my father's housekeeper. She died a few months ago. You could redecorate it and buy new furniture."

"Live here?" she said. "As what?"

He could not quite bring himself to say it.

"As your mistress?" she said.

"You can have a nurse, and a couple of housemaids, and a gardener. Even a motorcar with a chauffeur, if that appeals to you."

The part of it that appealed to her was him.

He misinterpreted her thoughtful look. "Is the house too small? Would you prefer Kensington? Do you want a butler and a housekeeper? I'll give you anything you want, don't you understand? My life is empty without you."

He meant it, she saw. At least, he meant it now, when he was aroused and unsatisfied. She knew from bitter experience how fast he could change.

The trouble was, she wanted him just as badly.

He must have seen that in her face, for he took her in his arms again. She turned up her face to be kissed. I want more of this, she thought.

Once again she broke the embrace before she lost control.

"Well?" he said.

She could not make a sensible decision while he was kissing her. "I've got to be alone," she said. She forced herself to walk away from him before it was too late. "I'm going home," she said. She opened the door. "I need time to think." She hesitated on the doorstep.

"Think as long as you want," he said. "I'll wait."

She closed the door and ran away.

{ III }

Gus Dewar was in the National Gallery in Trafalgar Square, standing in front of Rembrandt's *Self-Portrait at the Age of Sixty-three,* when a woman standing next to him said: "Extraordinarily ugly man."

Gus turned and was surprised to recognize Maud Fitzherbert. He said: "Me, or Rembrandt?" and she laughed.

They strolled through the gallery together. "What a delightful coincidence," he said. "Meeting you here."

"As a matter of fact, I saw you and followed you in," she said. She lowered her voice. "I wanted to ask you why the Germans haven't yet made the peace offer you told me was coming."

He did not know the answer. "They may have changed their minds," he said gloomily. "There as here, there is a peace faction and a war faction. Perhaps the war faction has gained the upper hand, and succeeded in changing the kaiser's mind."

"Surely they must see that battles no longer make a difference!" she said with exasperation. "Did you read in this morning's papers that the Germans have taken Bucharest?"

Gus nodded. Rumania had declared war in August, and for a while the British had hoped their new partner might strike a mighty blow, but Germany had invaded back in September and now the Rumanian capital had fallen. "In fact the upshot is good for Germany, which now has Rumania's oil."

"Exactly," said Maud. "It's the same old one step forward, one step back. When will we learn?"

"The appointment of Lloyd George as prime minister isn't encouraging," Gus said.

"Ah. There you might be wrong."

"Really? He has built his political reputation on being more aggressive than everyone else. It would be hard for him to make peace after that."

"Don't be so sure. Lloyd George is unpredictable. He could do a volte-face. It would surprise only those naïve enough to have thought him sincere."

"Well, that's hopeful."

"All the same, I wish we had a woman prime minister."

Gus did not think that was ever likely to happen, but he did not say so.

"There's something else I want to ask you," she said, and she halted.

Gus turned to face her. Perhaps because the paintings had sensitized him, he found himself admiring her face. He noticed the sharp lines of her nose and chin, the high cheekbones, the long neck. The angularity of her features was softened by her full lips and large green eyes. "Anything you like," he said.

"What did Walter tell you?"

Gus's mind went back to that surprising conversation in the bar of the Adlon Hotel in Berlin. "He said he was obliged to let me into a secret. But then he didn't tell me what the secret was."

"He thought you would be able to guess."

"I guessed he must be in love with you. And from your reaction when I gave you the letter at Tŷ Gwyn, I could see that his love is returned." Gus smiled. "If I may say so, he's a lucky man."

She nodded, and Gus read something like relief on her face. There must be more to the secret, he realized; that was why she needed to find out how much he knew. He wondered what else they were hiding. Perhaps they were engaged.

They walked on. I understand why he loves you, Gus thought. I could fall for you in a heartbeat.

She surprised him again by suddenly saying: "Have you ever been in love, Mr. Dewar?"

It was an intrusive question, but he answered anyway. "Yes, I have—twice."

"But no longer."

He felt an urge to confide in her. "The year the war broke out, I was wicked enough to fall in love with a woman who was already married."

"Did she love you?"

"Yes."

"What happened?"

"I asked her to leave her husband for me. That was very wrong of me, and you will be shocked, I know. But she was a better person than I, and she rejected my immoral offer."

"I'm not so easily shocked. When was the second time?"

"Last year I became engaged to someone in my hometown, Buffalo; but she married someone else."

"Oh! I'm so sorry. Perhaps I should not have asked. I have revived a painful memory."

"Extremely painful."

"Forgive me if I say that makes me feel better. It's just that you know what sorrow love can bring."

"Yes, I do."

"But perhaps there will be peace after all, and my sorrow will soon be over."

"I very much hope so, Lady Maud," said Gus.

{ IV }

Ethel agonized for days over Fitz's proposition. As she stood freezing in her backyard, turning the mangle to wring out the washing, she imagined herself in that pretty house in Chelsea, with Lloyd running around the garden watched over by an attentive nurse. "I'll give you anything you want," Fitz had said, and she knew it was true. He would put the house in her name. He would take her to Switzerland and the south of France. If she set her mind to it, she could make him give her an annuity so that she would have an income until she died, even if he got bored with her—although she also knew she could make sure he never got bored.

It was shameful and disgusting, she told herself sternly. She would be a woman paid for sex, and what else did the word *prostitute* mean? She could never invite her parents to her Chelsea hideaway: they would know immediately what it meant.

Did she care about that? Perhaps not, but there were other things. She wanted more from life than comfort. As a millionaire's mistress she could hardly continue to campaign on behalf of working-class women.

Her political life would be over. She would lose touch with Bernie and Mildred, and it would be awkward even to see Maud.

But who was she, to ask for so much from life? She was Ethel Williams, born in a coal miner's cottage! How could she turn up her nose at a lifetime of ease? You should be so lucky, she told herself, using one of Bernie's sayings.

And then there was Lloyd. He would have a governess, and later Fitz would pay for him to go to a posh school. He would grow up among the elite and lead a life of privilege. Did Ethel have the right to deny him that?

She was no nearer an answer when she opened the newspapers in the office she shared with Maud and learned of another dramatic offer. On December 12 the German chancellor, Theobald von Bethmann-Hollweg, proposed peace talks with the Allies.

Ethel was elated. Peace! Was it really possible? Might Billy come home?

The French premier immediately described the note as a crafty move, and the Russian foreign minister denounced the Germans' "lying proposals," but Ethel believed it was the British reaction that would count.

Lloyd George was not making public speeches of any kind, claiming he had a sore throat. In London in December half the population had coughs and colds, but all the same Ethel suspected Lloyd George just wanted time to think. She took that as a good sign. An immediate response would have been a rejection; anything else was hopeful. He was at least considering peace, she thought optimistically.

Meanwhile President Wilson threw America's weight into the balance on the side of peace. He suggested that as a preliminary to talks all the warring powers state their aims—what they were trying to achieve by fighting.

"That's embarrassed them," said Bernie Leckwith that evening. "They've forgotten why they started it. They're fighting now just because they want to win."

Ethel remembered what Mrs. Dai Ponies had said about the strike:

These men—once they get into a fight, all they care about is winning. They won't give in, whatever the cost. She wondered how a woman prime minister might have reacted to a peace proposal.

But Bernie was right, she realized over the next few days. President Wilson's suggestion met with a strange silence. No country answered immediately. That made Ethel more angry. How could they carry on if they did not even know what they were fighting for?

At the end of the week Bernie organized a public meeting to debate the German note. On the day of the meeting, Ethel woke up to see her brother standing beside her bed in his khaki uniform. "Billy!" she cried. "You're alive!"

"And on a week's leave," he said. "Get out of bed, you lazy cow."

She jumped up, put on a dressing gown over her nightdress, and hugged him. "Oh, Billy, I'm so happy to see you." She noticed the stripes on his sleeve. "Sergeant, now, is it?"

"Aye."

"How did you get into the house?"

"Mildred opened the door. Actually, I been here since last night."

"Where did you sleep?"

He looked bashful. "Upstairs."

Ethel grinned. "Lucky lad."

"I really like her, Eth."

"So do I," Ethel said. "Mildred is solid gold. Are you going to marry her?"

"Aye, if I survive the war."

"You don't mind about the age difference?"

"She's twenty-three. It's not like she's really old, thirty or something."

"And the children?"

Billy shrugged. "They're nice kids, but even if they weren't I'd put up with them for her sake."

"You really do love her."

"It's not difficult."

"She's started a little business. You must have seen all the hats up there in her room."

"Aye. Going well, too, it is, she says."

"Very well. She's a hard worker. Is Tommy with you?"

"He come over on the boat with me, but now he've gone to Aberowen on the train."

Lloyd woke up, saw a strange man in the room, and began to cry. Ethel picked him up and quieted him. "Come in the kitchen," she said to Billy. "I'll make us some breakfast."

Billy sat and read the paper while she made porridge. After a moment he said: "Bloody hell."

"What?"

"Bloody Fitzherbert's been opening his big mouth, I see." He glanced at Lloyd, almost as if the baby might be offended at this scornful reference to his father.

Ethel looked over his shoulder. She read:

PEACE: A SOLDIER'S PLEA

"Don't Give Up on Us Now!"
Wounded Earl Speaks Out

A moving speech was made yesterday in the House of Lords against the current proposal of the German Chancellor for peace talks. The speaker was Earl Fitzherbert, a Major in the Welsh Rifles, who is in London recovering from wounds received at the Battle of the Somme.

Lord Fitzherbert said that to talk peace with the Germans would be a betrayal of all the men who have given their lives in the war. "We believe we are winning and can achieve complete victory provided you don't give up on us now," he said.

Wearing his uniform, with an eye patch, and leaning on a crutch, the earl made a striking figure in the debating chamber. He was listened to in absolute silence, and cheered when he sat down.

There was a lot more of the same. Ethel was aghast. It was sentimental claptrap, but it would be effective. Fitz did not normally wear the eye patch—he must have put it on for effect. The speech would prejudice a lot of people against the peace plan.

She ate breakfast with Billy, then dressed Lloyd and herself and went out. Billy was going to spend the day with Mildred, but he promised to come to the meeting that evening.

When Ethel arrived at the office of *The Soldier's Wife*, she saw that all the newspapers had reported Fitz's speech. Several made it the subject of a leading article. They took different views, but agreed he had struck a powerful blow.

"How can anyone be against the mere *discussion* of peace?" she said to Maud.

"You can ask him yourself," Maud said. "I invited him to tonight's meeting, and he accepted."

Ethel was startled. "He'll get a warm reception!"

"I certainly hope so."

The two women spent the day working on a special edition of the newspaper with the front-page headline SMALL DANGER OF PEACE. Maud liked the irony but Ethel thought it was too subtle. Late in the afternoon Ethel collected Lloyd from the child minder, took him home, fed him, and put him to bed. She left him in the care of Mildred, who did not go to political meetings.

The Calvary Gospel Hall was filling up when Ethel arrived, and soon there was standing room only. The audience included many soldiers and sailors in uniform. Bernie chaired the meeting. He opened with a speech of his own that managed to be dull even though short—he was no orator. Then he called on the first speaker, a philosopher from Oxford University.

Ethel knew the arguments for peace better than the philosopher did, and as he spoke she studied the two men on the platform who were wooing her. Fitz was the product of hundreds of years of wealth and culture. As always, he was beautifully dressed, his hair well-cut, his hands white, and his fingernails clean. Bernie came from a tribe of persecuted nomads who survived by being cleverer than those who tormented them. He was wearing his only suit, the heavy dark gray serge. Ethel had never seen him in anything else: when the weather was warm he simply took off the jacket.

The audience listened quietly. The Labour movement was divided over peace. Ramsay MacDonald, who had spoken against the war in Parliament on August 3, 1914, had resigned as Labour Party leader when war was declared two days later, and since then the party's M.P.s had supported the war, as did most of their voters. But Labour supporters tended to be the most skeptical of working-class people, and there was a strong minority in favor of peace.

Fitz began by speaking of Britain's proud traditions. For hundreds of years, he said, Britain had maintained the balance of power in Europe, generally by siding with weaker nations to make sure no one country dominated. "The German chancellor has not said anything about the terms of a peace settlement, but any discussion would have to start from the status quo," he said. "Peace now means that France is humiliated and robbed of territory and Belgium becomes a satellite. Germany would dominate the continent by sheer military force. We cannot allow that to happen. We must fight for victory."

When the discussion opened, Bernie said: "Earl Fitzherbert is here in a purely personal capacity, not as an army officer, and he has given me his word of honor that serving soldiers in the audience will not be disciplined for anything they say. Indeed, we would not have invited the earl to attend the meeting on any other basis."

Bernie himself asked the first question. As usual, it was a good one. "If France is humiliated and loses territory, then that will destabilize Europe, according to your analysis, Lord Fitzherbert."

Fitz nodded.

"Whereas if Germany is humiliated and loses the territories of Alsace and Lorraine—as she undoubtedly would—then that will stabilize Europe."

Fitz was momentarily stumped, Ethel could see. He had not expected to have to deal with such sharp opposition here in the East End. Intellectually he was no match for Bernie. She felt a bit sorry for him.

"Why the difference?" Bernie finished, and there was a murmur of approval from the peace faction in the audience.

Fitz recovered rapidly. "The difference," he said, "is that Germany is the aggressor, brutal, militaristic, and cruel, and if we make peace now we will be rewarding that behavior—and encouraging it in the future!"

That brought a cheer from the other section of the audience, and Fitz's face was saved, but it was a poor argument, Ethel thought, and Maud stood up to say so. "The outbreak of war was not the fault of any single nation!" she said. "It has become the conventional wisdom to blame Germany, and our militaristic newspapers encourage this fairy tale. We remember Germany's invasion of Belgium and talk as if it was completely unprovoked. We have forgotten the mobilization of six million Russian soldiers on Germany's border. We have forgotten the French refusal to declare neutrality." A few men booed her. You never get cheered for telling people the situation is not as simple as they think, Ethel reflected wryly. "I don't say Germany is innocent!" Maud protested. "I say no country is innocent. I say we are not fighting for the stability of Europe, or for justice for the Belgians, or to punish German militarism. We are fighting because we are too proud to admit we made a mistake!"

A soldier in uniform stood up to speak, and Ethel saw with pride that it was Billy. "I fought at the Somme," he began, and the audience went quiet. "I want to tell you why we lost so many men there." Ethel heard their father's strong voice and quiet conviction, and she realized Billy would have made a great preacher. "We were told by our officers"—here he stretched out his arm and pointed an accusing finger at Fitz—"that the assault would be a walk in the park."

Ethel saw Fitz shift uncomfortably in his chair on the platform.

Billy went on: "We were told that our artillery had destroyed the enemy positions, wrecked their trenches and demolished their dugouts, and when we got to the other side we would see nothing but dead Germans."

He was not addressing the people on the platform, Ethel observed, but looking all around him, sweeping the audience with an intense gaze, making sure all eyes were on him.

"Why did they tell us those things?" Billy said, and now he looked straight at Fitz and spoke with deliberate emphasis. "Things that were not true." There was a mutter of agreement from the audience.

Ethel saw Fitz's face darken. She knew that for men of Fitz's class an accusation of lying was the worst of all insults. Billy knew it, too.

Billy said: "The German positions had not been destroyed, as we discovered when we ran into machine-gun fire."

The audience reaction became less muted. Someone called out: "Shame!"

Fitz stood up to speak, but Bernie said: "One moment, please, Lord Fitzherbert. Let the present speaker finish." Fitz sat down, shaking his head vigorously from side to side.

Billy raised his voice. "Did our officers check, by aerial reconnaissance and by sending out patrols, how much damage the artillery had in fact done to the German lines? If not, why not?"

Fitz stood up again, furious. Some of the audience cheered, others booed. He began to speak. "You don't understand!" he said.

But Billy's voice prevailed. "If they knew the truth," he cried, "why did they tell us otherwise?"

Fitz began to shout, and half the audience were calling out, but Billy's voice could be heard over everything else. "I ask one simple question!" he roared. "Are our officers fools—or liars?"

{ V }

Ethel received a letter in Fitz's large, confident handwriting on his expensive crested notepaper. He did not mention the meeting in Aldgate, but invited her to the Palace of Westminster on the following day, Tuesday, December 19, to sit in the gallery of the House of Commons and hear Lloyd George's first speech as prime minister. She was excited. She had never thought she would see the inside of Westminster Palace, let alone hear her hero speak.

"Why do you suppose he's invited you?" said Bernie that evening, asking the key question as usual.

Ethel did not have a plausible answer. Sheer unadulterated kindness had never been part of Fitz's character. He could be generous when it suited him. Bernie was shrewdly wondering if he wanted something in return.

Bernie was cerebral rather than intuitive, but he had sensed some connection between Fitz and Ethel, and he had responded by becoming a bit amorous. It was nothing dramatic, for Bernie was not a dramatic man, but he held her hand an instant longer than he should have, stood an inch closer to her than was comfortable, patted her shoulder when speaking to her, and held her elbow as she went down a step. Suddenly insecure, Bernie was instinctively making gestures that said she belonged to him. Unfortunately, she found it hard not to flinch when he did so. Fitz had reminded her cruelly of what she did *not* feel about Bernie.

Maud came into the office at half past ten on Tuesday, and they worked side by side all morning. Maud could not write the front page of the next edition until Lloyd George had spoken, but there was a lot else in the paper: jobs, advertisements for child minders, advice on women's and children's health written by Dr. Greenward, recipes, and letters.

"Fitz is beside himself with rage after that meeting," Maud said.

"I told you they would give him a hard time."

"He doesn't mind that," she said. "But Billy called him a liar."

"You're sure it's not just that Billy got the better of the argument?"

Maud smiled ruefully. "Perhaps."

"I just hope he doesn't make Billy suffer for it."

"He won't do that," Maud said firmly. "It would be breaking his word."

"Good."

They had lunch in a café in the Mile End Road—"A Good Pull-In for Car Men," according to its signboard, and it was indeed full of lorry drivers. Maud was greeted cheerfully by the counter staff. They had beef and oyster pie, the cheap oysters added to eke out the scarce beef.

Afterward they took a bus across London to the West End. Ethel looked up at the giant dial of Big Ben and saw that it was half past three. Lloyd George was due to speak at four. He had it in his power to end the war and save millions of lives. Would he do it?

Lloyd George had always fought for the workingman. Before the war he had done battle with the House of Lords and the king to bring in old-age pensions. Ethel knew how much that meant to penniless old people. On the first day the pension was paid out she had seen retired miners—once-strong men now bent and trembling—come out of the Aberowen post office openly weeping for joy that they were no longer destitute. That was when Lloyd George had become a working-class hero. The Lords had wanted to spend the money on the Royal Navy.

I could write his speech today, she thought. I would say: "There are moments in the life of a man, and of a nation, when it is right to say: I have done my utmost, and I can do no more. Therefore I will cease my striving, and seek another road. Within the last hour I have ordered a cease-fire along the entire length of the British line in France. Gentlemen, the guns have fallen silent."

It could be done. The French would be furious, but they would have to join in the cease-fire, or take the risk that Britain might make a separate peace and leave them to certain defeat. The peace settlement would be hard on France and Belgium, but not as hard as the loss of millions more lives.

It would be an act of great statesmanship. It would also be the end of Lloyd George's political career: voters would not elect the man who lost the war. But what a way to go out!

Fitz was waiting in the Central Lobby. Gus Dewar was with him. No doubt he was as eager as everyone else to find out how Lloyd George would respond to the peace initiative.

They climbed the long staircase to the gallery and took their seats overlooking the debating chamber. Ethel had Fitz on her right and Gus on her left. Below them, the rows of green leather benches on both sides were already full of M.P.s, except for the few places in the front row traditionally reserved for the cabinet.

"Every M.P. a man," Maud said loudly.

An usher, wearing full formal court dress complete with velvet knee breeches and white stockings, officiously hissed: "Quiet, please!"

A backbencher was on his feet, but hardly anyone was listening to

him. They were all waiting for the new prime minister. Fitz spoke quietly
to Ethel. "Your brother insulted me."

"You poor thing," Ethel said sarcastically. "Are your feelings hurt?"

"Men used to fight duels for less."

"Now there's a sensible idea for the twentieth century."

He was unmoved by her scorn. "Does he know who is the father of
Lloyd?"

Ethel hesitated, not wanting to tell him but reluctant to lie.

Her hesitation told him what he wanted to know. "I see," he said.
"That would explain his vituperation."

"I don't think you need to look for an ulterior motive," she said.
"What happened at the Somme is enough to make soldiers angry, don't
you think?"

"He should be court-martialed for insolence."

"But you promised not to—"

"Yes," he said crossly. "Unfortunately, I did."

Lloyd George entered the chamber.

He was a small, slight figure in formal morning dress, the overlong
hair a bit unkempt, the bushy mustache now entirely white. He was
fifty-three, but there was a spring in his step, and as he sat down and
said something to a backbencher, Ethel saw the grin familiar from
newspaper photographs.

He began speaking at ten past four. His voice was a little hoarse, and
he said he had a sore throat. He paused, then said: "I appear before the
House of Commons today with the most terrible responsibility that can
fall on the shoulders of any living man."

That was a good start, Ethel thought. At least he was not going to
dismiss the German note as an unimportant trick or diversion, in the
way the French and Russians had.

"Any man or set of men who wantonly, or without sufficient cause,
prolonged a terrible conflict like this would have on his soul a crime that
oceans could not cleanse."

That was a biblical touch, Ethel thought, a Baptist-chapel reference
to sins being washed away.

But then, like a preacher, he made the contrary statement. "Any man or set of men who, out of a sense of weariness or despair, abandoned the struggle without the high purpose for which we had entered into it being nearly fulfilled, would have been guilty of the costliest act of poltroonery ever perpetrated by any statesman."

Ethel fidgeted anxiously. Which way was he going to jump? She thought of Telegram Wednesday in Aberowen, and saw again the faces of the bereaved. Surely Lloyd George—of all politicians—would not let heartbreak of that nature continue if he could help it? If he did, what was the point of his being in politics at all?

He quoted Abraham Lincoln. "'We accepted this war for an object, and a worthy object, and the war will end when that object is attained.'"

That was ominous. Ethel wanted to ask him what the object was. Woodrow Wilson had asked that question and as yet had got no reply. No answer was given now. Lloyd George said: "Are we likely to achieve that object by accepting the invitation of the German chancellor? That is the only question we have to put to ourselves."

Ethel felt frustrated. How could this question be discussed if no one knew what the object of the war was?

Lloyd George raised his voice, like a preacher about to speak of hell. "To enter at the invitation of Germany, proclaiming herself victorious, without any knowledge of the proposals she proposes to make, into a conference"—here he paused and looked around the chamber, first to the Liberals behind him and to his right, then across the floor to the Conservatives on the opposition side—"is to put our heads into a noose with the rope end in the hands of Germany!"

There was a roar of approval from the M.P.s.

He was rejecting the peace offer.

Beside Ethel, Gus Dewar buried his face in his hands.

Ethel said loudly: "What about Alun Pritchard, killed at the Somme?"

The usher said: "Quiet, there!"

Ethel stood up. "Sergeant Prophet Jones, dead!" she cried.

Fitz said: "Be quiet and sit down, for God's sake!"

Down in the chamber, Lloyd George continued speaking, though one or two M.P.s were looking up at the gallery.

"Clive Pugh!" she shouted at the top of her voice.

Two ushers came toward her, one from each side.

"Spotty Llewellyn!"

The ushers grabbed her arms and hustled her away.

"Joey Ponti!" she screamed, and then they dragged her out through the door.

CHAPTER TWENTY-TWO

January and February 1917

Walter von Ulrich dreamed he was in a horse-drawn carriage on his way to meet Maud. The carriage was going downhill, and began to travel dangerously fast, bouncing on the uneven road surface. He shouted, "Slow down! Slow down!" but the driver could not hear him over the drumming of hooves, which sounded oddly like the running of a motorcar engine. Despite this anomaly, Walter was terrified that the runaway carriage would crash and he would never reach Maud. He tried again to order the driver to slow down, and the effort of shouting woke him.

In reality he was in an automobile, a chauffeur-driven Mercedes 37/95 Double Phaeton, traveling at moderate speed along a bumpy road in Silesia. His father sat beside him, smoking a cigar. They had left Berlin in the early hours of the morning, both wrapped in fur coats—it was an open car—and they were on their way to the eastern headquarters of the high command.

The dream was easy to interpret. The Allies had scornfully rejected the peace offer that Walter had worked so hard to promote. The rejection

602 ↜ CHAPTER TWENTY-TWO

had strengthened the hand of the German military, who wanted to resume unrestricted submarine warfare, sinking every ship in the war zone, military or civilian, passenger or freight, combatant or neutral, in order to starve Britain and France into submission. The politicians, notably the chancellor, feared that was the way to defeat, for it was likely to bring the United States into the war, but the submariners were winning the argument. The kaiser had shown which way he leaned by promoting the aggressive Arthur Zimmermann to foreign minister. And Walter dreamed of charging downhill to disaster.

Walter believed that the greatest danger to Germany was the United States. The aim of German policy should be to keep America out of the war. True, Germany was being starved by the Allied naval blockade. But the Russians could not last much longer, and when they capitulated, Germany would overrun the rich western and southern regions of the Russian Empire, with their vast cornfields and bottomless oil wells. And the entire German army would then be able to concentrate on the western front. That was the only hope.

But would the kaiser see that?

The final decision would be made today.

A bleak winter daylight was breaking over countryside patchworked with snow. Walter felt like a shirker, being so far from the fighting. "I should have returned to the front line weeks ago," he said.

"Clearly the army wants you in Germany," said Otto. "You are valued as an intelligence analyst."

"Germany is full of older men who could do the job at least as well as I. Have you pulled strings?"

Otto shrugged. "I think if you were to marry and have a son, you could then be transferred anywhere you like."

Walter said incredulously: "You're keeping me in Berlin to make me marry Monika von der Helbard?"

"I don't have the power to do that. But it may be that there are men in the high command who understand the need to maintain noble bloodlines."

That was disingenuous, and a protest came to Walter's lips, but then the car turned off the road, passed through an ornamental gateway, and started up a long drive flanked by leafless trees and snow-covered lawn. At the end of the drive was a huge house, the largest Walter had ever seen in Germany. "Castle Pless?" he said.

"Correct."

"It's vast."

"Three hundred rooms."

They got out of the car and entered a hall like a railway station. The walls were decorated with boars' heads framed with red silk, and a massive marble staircase led up to the state rooms on the first floor. Walter had spent half his life in splendid buildings, but this was exceptional.

A general approached them, and Walter recognized von Henscher, a crony of his father's. "You've got time to wash and brush up, if you're quick," he said with amiable urgency. "You're expected in the state dining room in forty minutes." He looked at Walter. "This must be your son."

Otto said: "He's in the intelligence department."

Walter gave a brisk salute.

"I know. I put his name on the list." The general addressed Walter. "I believe you know America."

"I spent three years in our embassy in Washington, sir."

"Good. I have never been to the United States. Nor has your father. Nor, indeed, have most of the men here—with the notable exception of our new foreign minister."

Twenty years ago, Arthur Zimmermann had returned to Germany from China via the States, crossing from San Francisco to New York by train, and on the basis of this experience was considered an expert on America. Walter said nothing.

Von Henscher said: "Herr Zimmermann has asked me to consult you both on something." Walter was flattered but puzzled. Why would the new foreign minister want his opinion? "But we will have more time for that later." Von Henscher beckoned to a footman in old-fashioned livery, who showed them to a bedroom.

Half an hour later they were in the dining room, now converted to a conference room. Looking around, Walter was awestruck to see that just about every man who counted for anything in Germany was present, including the chancellor, Theobald von Bethmann-Hollweg, his close-cropped hair now almost white at age sixty.

Most of Germany's senior military commanders were sitting around a long table. For lesser men, including Walter, there were rows of hard chairs against the wall. An aide passed around a few copies of a two-hundred-page memorandum. Walter looked over his father's shoulder at the file. He saw charts of tonnage moving in and out of British ports, tables of freight rates and cargo space, the calorific value of British meals, even a calculation of how much wool there was in a lady's skirt.

They waited two hours; then Kaiser Wilhelm came in, wearing a general's uniform. Everyone sprang to their feet. His Majesty looked pale and ill-tempered. He was a few days from his fifty-eighth birthday. As ever, he held his withered left arm motionless at his side, attempting to make it inconspicuous. Walter found it difficult to summon up that emotion of joyous loyalty that had come so easily to him as a boy. He could no longer pretend the kaiser was the wise father of his people. Wilhelm II was too obviously an unexceptional man completely overwhelmed by events. Incompetent, bewildered, and miserably unhappy, he was a standing argument against hereditary monarchy.

The kaiser looked around, nodding to one or two special favorites, including Otto; then he sat down and made a gesture at Henning von Holtzendorff, white-bearded chief of the admiralty staff.

The admiral began to speak, quoting from his memorandum: the number of submarines the navy could maintain at sea at any one time, the tonnage of shipping required to keep the Allies alive, and the speed at which they could replace sunk vessels. "I calculate we can sink six hundred thousand tons of shipping per month," he said. It was an impressive performance, every statement backed up by a number. Walter was skeptical only because the admiral was too precise, too certain: surely war was never that predictable?

Von Holtzendorff pointed to a ribbon-tied document on the table, presumably the imperial order to begin unrestricted submarine warfare. "If Your Majesty approves my plan today, I guarantee the Allies will capitulate in precisely five months." He sat down.

The kaiser looked at the chancellor. Now, Walter thought, we will hear a more realistic assessment. Bethmann had been chancellor for seven years, and unlike the monarch he had a sense of the complexity of international relations.

Bethmann spoke gloomily of American entry into the war and the USA's uncounted resources of manpower, supplies, and money. In his support he quoted the opinions of every senior German who was familiar with the United States. But to Walter's disappointment he looked like a man going through the motions. He must believe the kaiser had already made up his mind. Was this meeting merely to ratify a decision already taken? Was Germany doomed?

The kaiser had a short attention span for people who disagreed with him, and while his chancellor was speaking he fidgeted, grunting impatiently and making disapproving faces. Bethmann began to dither. "If the military authorities consider the U-boat war essential, I am not in a position to contradict them. On the other hand—"

He never got to say what was on the other hand. Von Holtzendorff jumped to his feet and interrupted. "I guarantee on my word as a naval officer that no American will set foot upon the Continent!" he said.

That was absurd, Walter thought. What did his word as a naval officer have to do with anything? But it went down better than all his statistics. The kaiser brightened, and several other men nodded approval.

Bethmann seemed to give up. His body slumped in the chair, the tension went out of his face, and he spoke in a defeated voice. "If success beckons, we must follow," he said.

The kaiser made a gesture, and von Holtzendorff pushed the beribboned document across the table.

No, Walter thought, we can't possibly make this fateful decision on such inadequate grounds!

The kaiser picked up a pen and signed: "Wilhelm I.R."

He put down the pen and stood up.

Everyone in the room jumped to their feet.

This can't be the end, Walter thought.

The kaiser left the room. The tension was broken, and a buzz of talk broke out. Bethmann remained in his seat, staring down at the table. He looked like a man who has met his doom. He was muttering something, and Walter stepped closer to hear. It was a Latin phrase: *Finis Germaniae*— the end of the Germans.

General von Henscher appeared and said to Otto: "If you would care to come with me, we will have lunch privately. You, too, young man." He led them into a side room where a cold buffet was laid out.

Castle Pless served as a residence for the kaiser, so the food was good. Walter was angry and depressed, but like everyone else in Germany he was hungry, and he piled his plate high with cold chicken, potato salad, and white bread.

"Today's decision was anticipated by Foreign Minister Zimmermann," said von Henscher. "He wants to know what we can do to discourage the Americans."

Small chance of that, Walter thought. If we sink American ships and drown American citizens, there's not much we can do to soften the blow.

The general went on: "Can we, for example, foment a protest movement among the one point three million Americans who were born here in Germany?"

Walter groaned inwardly. "Absolutely not," he said. "It's a stupid fairy tale."

His father snapped: "Careful how you speak to your superiors."

Von Henscher made a calming gesture. "Let the boy speak his mind, Otto. I might as well have his frank opinion. Why do you say that, Major?"

Walter said: "They don't love the fatherland. Why do you think they left? They may eat wurst and drink beer, but they're Americans and they'll fight for America."

"What about the Irish-born?"

"Same thing. They hate the British, of course, but when our submarines kill Americans they'll hate us more."

Otto said irritably: "How can President Wilson declare war on us? He has just won reelection as the man who kept America out of war!"

Walter shrugged. "In some ways that makes it easier. People will believe he had no option."

Von Henscher said: "What might hold him back?"

"Protection for ships of neutral countries—"

"Out of the question," his father interrupted. "Unrestricted means unrestricted. That's what the navy wanted, and that's what His Majesty has given them."

Von Henscher said: "If domestic issues aren't likely to trouble Wilson, is there any chance he may be distracted by foreign affairs in his own hemisphere?" He turned to Otto. "Mexico, for example?"

Otto smiled, looking pleased. "You're remembering the *Ypiranga*. I must admit, that was a small triumph of aggressive diplomacy."

Walter had never shared his father's glee over the incident of the shipload of arms sent by Germany to Mexico. Otto and his cronies had made President Wilson look foolish, and they could yet come to regret it.

"And now?" said von Henscher.

"Most of the U.S. Army is either in Mexico or stationed on the border," said Walter. "Ostensibly they're chasing a bandit called Pancho Villa, who raids across the border. President Carranza is bursting with indignation at the violation of his sovereign territory, but there isn't much he can do."

"If he had help from us, would that change anything?"

Walter considered. This kind of diplomatic mischief-making struck him as risky, but it was his duty to answer the questions as accurately as he could. "The Mexicans feel they were robbed of Texas, New Mexico, and Arizona. They have a dream of winning those territories back, much like the French pipe dream of winning back Alsace and Lorraine. President Carranza may be stupid enough to believe it could be done."

Otto said eagerly: "In any event, the attempt would certainly take American attention away from Europe!"

"For a while," Walter agreed reluctantly. "In the long-term our interference might strengthen those Americans who would like to join in the war on the Allied side."

"The short term is what interests us. You heard von Holtzendorff—our submarines are going to bring the Allies to their knees in five months. All we want is to keep the Americans busy that long."

Von Henscher said: "What about Japan? Is there any chance the Japs might be persuaded to attack the Panama Canal, or even California?"

"Realistically, no," Walter said firmly. The discussion was venturing further into the land of fantasy.

But von Henscher persisted. "Nevertheless, the mere threat might tie up more American troops on the West Coast."

"I suppose it could, yes."

Otto patted his lips with his napkin. "This is all most interesting, but I must see whether His Majesty needs me."

They all stood up. Walter said: "If I may say so, General . . . "

His father sighed, but von Henscher said: "Please."

"I believe all this is very dangerous, sir. If word got out that German leaders were even talking about fomenting strife in Mexico, and encouraging Japanese aggression in California, American public opinion would be so outraged that the declaration of war could come much sooner, if not immediately. Forgive me if I am stating the obvious, but this conversation should remain highly secret."

"Quite all right," said von Henscher. He smiled at Otto. "Your father and I are the older generation, of course, but we still know a thing or two. You may rely on our discretion."

{ II }

Fitz was pleased that the German peace proposal had been spurned, and proud of his part in the process, but when it was over he had doubts.

He thought it over, walking—or, rather, limping—along Piccadilly on the morning of Wednesday, January 17, on his way to his office in the Admiralty. Peace talks would have been a sneaky way for the Germans to consolidate their gains, legitimizing their hold over Belgium, northeastern France, and parts of Russia. For Britain to take part in such talks would have amounted to an admission of defeat. But Britain still had not won.

Lloyd George's talk of a knockout went down well in the newspapers, but all sensible people knew it was a daydream. The war would go on, perhaps for a year, perhaps longer. And, if the Americans continued to remain neutral, it might end in peace talks after all. What if no one *could* win this war? Another million men would be killed for no purpose. The thought that haunted Fitz was that Ethel might have been right after all.

And what if Britain lost? There would be a financial crisis, unemployment, and destitution. Working-class men would take up Ethel's father's cry and say that they had never been allowed to vote for the war. The people's rage against their rulers would be boundless. Protests and marches would turn into riots. It was only a little more than a century ago that Parisians had executed their king and much of the nobility. Would Londoners do the same? Fitz imagined himself, bound hand and foot, carried on a cart to the place of execution, spat upon and jeered at by the crowd. Worse, he saw the same happening to Maud, and Aunt Herm, and Bea, and Boy. He pushed the nightmare out of his mind.

What a little spitfire Ethel was, he thought with mingled admiration and regret. He had been mortified with embarrassment when his guest was ejected from the gallery during Lloyd George's speech, but at the same time he found himself even more attracted to her.

Unfortunately, she had turned against him. He had followed her out and caught up with her in the Central Lobby, and she had berated him, blaming him and his kind for prolonging the war. From the way she talked you would think every soldier who died in France had been killed by Fitz personally.

That was the end of his Chelsea scheme. He had sent her a couple of notes but she had not replied. The disappointment hit him hard. When he thought of the delightful afternoons they might have spent in that love nest, he felt the loss like an ache in his chest.

However, he had some consolation. Bea had taken his reprimand to heart. She now welcomed him to her bedroom, dressed in pretty nightwear, offering him her scented body as she had when they were first married. In the end she was a well-brought-up aristocratic woman and she knew what a wife was for.

Musing on the compliant princess and the irresistible activist, he entered the Old Admiralty Building to find a partly decoded German telegram on his desk.

It was headed:

> Berlin zu Washington. W.158. 16 January 1917.

Fitz looked automatically at the foot of the decrypt to see who it was from. The name at the end was:

> Zimmermann.

His interest was piqued. This was a message from the German foreign minister to his ambassador in the United States. With a pencil Fitz wrote a translation, putting squiggles and question marks where code groups had not been decrypted.

> Most secret for Your Excellency's personal information and
> to be handed on to the imperial minister in (?Mexico?) with
> xxxx by a safe route.

The question marks indicated a code group whose meaning was not certain. The decoders were guessing. If they were right, this message was for the German ambassador in Mexico. It was simply being sent via the Washington embassy.

Mexico, Fitz thought. How odd.

The next sentence was completely decoded.

> We propose to begin on 1 February unrestricted submarine
> warfare.

"My God!" Fitz said aloud. It was fearfully expected, but this was firm confirmation—and with a date! The news would be a coup for Room 40.

> In doing so however we shall endeavor to keep America neutral xxxx. If we should not we propose to (?Mexico?) an alliance upon the following basis: conduct of war, conclusion of peace.

"An alliance with Mexico?" Fitz said to himself. "This is strong stuff. The Americans are going to be hopping mad!"

> Your Excellency should for the present inform the president secretly war with the USA xxxx and at the same time to negotiate between us and Japan xxxx our submarines will compel England to peace within a few months. Acknowledge receipt.

Fitz looked up and caught the eye of young Carver, who—he now saw—was bursting with excitement. "You must be reading the Zimmermann intercept," the sublieutenant said.

"Such as it is," Fitz said calmly. He was just as euphoric as Carver, but better at concealing it. "Why is the decrypt so scrappy?"

"It's in a new code that we haven't completely cracked. All the same, the message is hot stuff, isn't it?"

Fitz looked again at his translation. Carver was not exaggerating. This appeared very much like an attempt to get Mexico to ally with Germany against the United States. It was sensational.

It might even make the American president angry enough to declare war on Germany.

Fitz's pulse quickened. "I agree," he said. "And I'm going to take this straight to Blinker Hall." Captain William Reginald Hall, the director of naval intelligence, had a chronic facial tic, hence the nickname; but there was nothing wrong with his brain. "He will ask questions, and I need to have some answers ready. What are the prospects for getting a complete decrypt?"

"It's going to take us several weeks to master the new code."

Fitz gave a grunt of exasperation. The reconstruction of new codes from first principles was a painstaking business that could not be hurried.

Carver went on: "But I notice that the message is to be forwarded from Washington to Mexico. On that route, they're still using an old diplomatic code we broke more than a year ago. Perhaps we could get a copy of the forwarded cable?"

"Perhaps we could!" Fitz said eagerly. "We have an agent in the telegraph office in Mexico City." He thought ahead. "When we reveal this to the world . . . "

Carver said anxiously: "We can't do that."

"Why not?"

"The Germans would know we're reading their traffic."

Fitz saw that he was right. It was the perennial problem of secret intelligence: how to use it without compromising the source. He said: "But this is so important we might want to take the risk."

"I doubt it. This department has provided too much reliable information. They won't put that in jeopardy."

"Damn! Surely we can't come across something like this and then be powerless to use it?"

Carver shrugged. "It happens in this line of work."

Fitz was not prepared to accept that. The entry of America could win the war. That was surely worth any sacrifice. But he knew enough about the army to realize that some men would show more courage and resourcefulness defending a department than a redoubt. Carver's objection had to be taken seriously. "We need a cover story," he said.

"Let's say the Americans intercepted the cable," Carver said.

Fitz nodded. "It is to be forwarded from Washington to Mexico, so we could say the U.S. government got it from Western Union."

"Western Union may not like it . . . "

"To hell with them. Now: how, exactly, do we use this information to the maximum effect? Does our government make the announcement? Do we give it to the Americans? Do we get some third party to challenge the Germans?"

Carver put up both hands in a gesture of surrender. "I'm out of my depth."

"I'm not," said Fitz, suddenly inspired. "And I know just the person to help."

{ III }

Fitz met Gus Dewar at a south London pub called the Ring.

To Fitz's surprise, Dewar was a lover of boxing. As a teenager he had attended a waterfront arena in Buffalo, and in his travels across Europe, back in 1914, he had watched prizefights in every capital city. He kept his enthusiasm quiet, Fitz thought wryly: boxing was not a popular topic of conversation at teatime in Mayfair.

However, all classes were represented at the Ring. Gentlemen in evening dress mingled with dockers in torn coats. Illegal bookmakers took bets in every corner while waiters brought loaded trays of beer in pint glasses. The air was thick with the smoke of cigars, pipes, and cigarettes. There were no seats and no women.

Fitz found Gus deep in conversation with a broken-nosed Londoner, arguing about the American fighter Jack Johnson, the first black world heavyweight champion, whose marriage to a white woman had caused Christian ministers to call for him to be lynched. The Londoner had riled Gus by agreeing with the clergymen.

Fitz nourished a secret hope that Gus might fall for Maud. It would be a good match. They were both intellectuals, both liberals, both frightfully serious about everything, always reading books. The Dewars came from what Americans called Old Money, the nearest thing they had to an aristocracy.

In addition, both Gus and Maud were in favor of peace. Maud had always been strangely passionate about ending the war; Fitz had no idea why. And Gus revered his boss, Woodrow Wilson, who had made a speech a month ago calling for "peace without victory," a phrase that had infuriated Fitz and most of the British and French leadership.

But the compatibility Fitz had seen between Gus and Maud had not led anywhere. Fitz loved his sister, but he wondered what was wrong with her. Did she want to be an old maid?

When Fitz had detached Gus from the man with the broken nose, he raised the subject of Mexico.

"It's a mess," Gus said. "Wilson has withdrawn General Pershing and his troops, in an attempt to please President Carranza, but it hasn't worked—Carranza won't even discuss policing the border. Why do you ask?"

"I'll tell you later," Fitz said. "The next bout is starting."

As they watched a fighter called Benny the Yid pounding the brains out of Bald Albert Collins, Fitz resolved to avoid the topic of the German peace offer. He knew that Gus was heartbroken at the failure of Wilson's initiative. Gus asked himself constantly whether he could have handled matters better, or done something further to support the president's plan. Fitz thought the plan had been doomed from the start because neither side really wanted peace.

In the third round Bald Albert went down and stayed down.

"You caught me just in time," Gus said. "I'm about to head for home."

"Looking forward to it?"

"If I get there. I might be sunk by a U-boat on the way."

The Germans had resumed unrestricted submarine warfare on February 1, exactly as foretold in the Zimmermann intercept. This had angered the Americans, but not as much as Fitz had hoped. "President Wilson's reaction to the submarine announcement was surprisingly mild," he said.

"He broke off diplomatic relations with Germany. That's not mild."

"But he did not declare war." Fitz had been devastated by this. He had fought hard against peace talks, but Maud and Ethel and their pacifist friends were right to say there was no hope of victory in the foreseeable future—without extra help from somewhere. Fitz had felt sure that unrestricted submarine warfare would bring the Americans in. So far it had not.

Gus said: "Frankly, I think President Wilson was infuriated by the submarine decision, and is now ready to declare war. He's tried everything else, for goodness' sake. But he won reelection as the man who kept us out. The only way he can switch is if he is swept into war on a tide of public enthusiasm."

"In that case," said Fitz, "I believe I have something that might help him."

Gus raised an eyebrow.

"Since I was wounded, I've been working in a unit that decodes intercepted German wireless messages." Fitz took from his pocket a sheet of paper covered with his own handwriting. "Your government will be given this officially in the next few days. I'm showing it to you now because we need advice on how to handle it." He gave it to Gus.

The British spy in Mexico City had got hold of the relayed message in the old code, and the paper Fitz handed to Gus was a complete decrypt of the Zimmermann intercept. In full, it read:

Washington to Mexico, 19 January 1917

We intend to begin on 1 February unrestricted submarine warfare. We shall endeavour in spite of this to keep the USA neutral. In the event of this not succeeding we make Mexico a proposal of alliance on the following terms:

Make war together.

Make peace together.

Generous financial support and an undertaking on our part that Mexico is to reconquer the lost territory in Texas, New Mexico, and Arizona. The settlement in detail is left to you.

You will inform the president of the above most secretly as soon as the outbreak of war with the USA is certain, and add the suggestion that he should on his own initiative invite Japan to immediate adherence and at the same time mediate between Japan and ourselves.

Please call the president's attention to the fact that the ruthless employment of our submarines now offers the prospect of compelling England in a few months to make peace.

Gus read a few lines, holding the sheet close to his eyes in the low light of the boxing arena, and said: "Alliance? My God!"

Fitz glanced around. A new bout had begun, and the noise of the crowd was too loud for people nearby to overhear Gus.

Gus read on. "Reconquer Texas?" he said with incredulity. And then, angrily: "Invite Japan?" He looked up from the paper. "This is outrageous!"

This was the reaction Fitz had been hoping for, and he had to quell his elation. "Outrageous is the word," he said with forced solemnity.

"The Germans are offering to pay Mexico to invade the United States!"

"Yes."

"And they're asking Mexico to try to get Japan to join in!"

"Yes."

"Wait till this gets out!"

"That's what I want to talk to you about. We want to make sure it's publicized in a manner favorable to your president."

"Why doesn't the British government simply reveal it to the world?"

Gus was not thinking this through. "Two reasons," Fitz said. "One, we don't want the Germans to know we're reading their cables. Two, we may be accused of forging this intercept."

Gus nodded. "Pardon me. I was too angry to think. Let's look at this coolly."

"If possible, we would like you to say that the United States government obtained a copy of the cable from Western Union."

"Wilson won't tell a lie."

"Then get a copy from Western Union, and it won't be a lie."

Gus nodded. "That should be possible. As for the second problem, who could release the telegram without being suspected of forgery?"

"The president himself, I presume."

"That's one possibility."

"But you have a better idea?"

"Yes," Gus said thoughtfully. "I believe I do."

{ IV }

Ethel and Bernie got married in the Calvary Gospel Hall. Neither of them had strong views about religion, and they both liked the pastor.

Ethel had not communicated with Fitz since the day of Lloyd George's speech. Fitz's public opposition to peace had reminded her harshly of his true nature. He stood for everything she hated: tradition, conservatism, exploitation of the working class, unearned wealth. She could not be the lover of such a man, and she felt ashamed of herself for even being tempted by the house in Chelsea. Her true soul mate was Bernie.

Ethel wore the pink silk dress and flowered hat that Walter von Ulrich had bought her for Maud Fitzherbert's wedding. There were no bridesmaids, but Mildred and Maud served as matrons of honor. Ethel's parents came up from Aberowen on the train. Sadly, Billy was in France and could not get leave. Little Lloyd wore a pageboy outfit specially made for him by Mildred, sky blue with brass buttons and a cap.

Bernie surprised Ethel by producing a family no one knew about. His elderly mother spoke nothing but Yiddish and muttered under her breath all through the service. She lived with Bernie's prosperous older brother, Theo, who—Mildred discovered, flirting with him—owned a bicycle factory in Birmingham.

Afterward tea and cake were served in the hall. There were no alcoholic drinks, which suited Da and Mam, and smokers had to go outside. Mam kissed Ethel and said: "I'm glad to see you settled at last, anyway." That word *anyway* carried a lot of baggage, Ethel thought. It meant: "Congratulations, even though you're a fallen woman, and you've got an illegitimate child whose father no one knows, and you're marrying a Jew, and living in London, which is the same as Sodom and Gomorrah." But Ethel accepted Mam's qualified blessing and vowed never to say such things to her own child.

Mam and Da had bought cheap day-return tickets, and they left to catch their train. When the majority of guests had gone, the remainder went to the Dog and Duck for a few drinks.

Ethel and Bernie went home when it was Lloyd's bedtime. That morning, Bernie had put his few clothes and many books into a handcart and wheeled it from his rented lodgings to Ethel's house.

To give themselves one night alone, they put Lloyd to bed upstairs with Mildred's children, which Lloyd regarded as a special treat. Then Ethel and Bernie had cocoa in the kitchen and went to bed.

Ethel had a new nightdress. Bernie put on clean pajamas. When he got into bed beside her, he broke into a nervous sweat. Ethel stroked his cheek. "Although I'm a scarlet woman, I haven't got much experience," she said. "Just my first husband, and that was only for a few weeks before he went away." She had not told Bernie about Fitz and never would. Only Billy and the lawyer Albert Solman knew the truth.

"You're better off than me," Bernie said, but already she could feel him beginning to relax. "Just a few fumbles."

"What were their names?"

"Oh, you don't want to know."

She grinned. "Yes, I do. How many women? Six? Ten? Twenty?"

"Good God, no. Three. The first was Rachel Wright, in school. Afterward she said we would have to get married, and I believed her. I was so worried."

Ethel giggled. "What happened?"

"The next week she did it with Micky Armstrong, and I was off the hook."

"Was it nice with her?"

"I suppose it was. I was only sixteen. Mainly I just wanted to be able to say I had done it."

She kissed him gently, then said: "Who was next?"

"Carol McAllister. She was a neighbor. I paid her a shilling. It was a bit brief—I think she knew what to do and say to get it over quickly. The part she liked was taking the money."

Ethel frowned disapprovingly, then recalled the house in Chelsea, and realized she had contemplated doing the same as Carol McAllister. Feeling uncomfortable, she said: "Who was the other one?"

"An older woman. She was my landlady. She came to my bed at night when her husband was away."

"Was it nice with her?"

"Lovely. It was a happy time for me."

"What went wrong?"

"Her husband got suspicious and I had to leave."

"And then?"

"Then I met you, and I lost all interest in other women."

They began to kiss. Soon he pushed up the skirt of her nightdress and got on top of her. He was gentle, worried about hurting her, but he entered her easily. She felt a surge of affection for him, for his kindness and intelligence and devotion to her and her child. She put her arms around him and hugged his body to hers. Quite soon, his climax came. Then they both lay back, content, and went to sleep.

{ V }

Women's skirts had changed, Gus Dewar realized. They now showed the ankles. Ten years ago, a glimpse of ankle had been arousing; now it was mundane. Perhaps women covered their nakedness to make themselves more alluring, not less.

Rosa Hellman was wearing a dark-red coat that fell in pleats from the yoke at the back, rather fashionable. It was trimmed with black fur, which he guessed was welcome in Washington in February. Her gray hat was small and round with a red hatband and a feather, not very practical, but when was the last time American women's hats had been designed for practical purposes? "I'm honored by this invitation," she said. He could not be sure whether she was mocking him. "You're only just back from Europe, aren't you?"

They were having lunch in the dining room of the Willard Hotel, two blocks east of the White House. Gus had invited her for a specific purpose. "I've got a story for you," he said as soon as they had ordered.

"Oh, good! Let me guess. The president is going to divorce Edith and marry Mary Peck?"

Gus frowned. Wilson had had a dalliance with Mary Peck while he was married to his first wife. Gus doubted whether they had actually committed adultery, but Wilson had been foolish enough to write letters that showed more affection than was seemly. Washington gossips knew all about it, but nothing had been printed. "I'm talking about something serious," Gus said sternly.

"Oh, sorry," said Rosa. She composed her face in a solemn expression that made Gus want to laugh.

"The only condition is going to be that you can't say you got the information from the White House."

"Agreed."

"I'm going to show you a telegram from the German foreign minister, Arthur Zimmermann, to the German ambassador in Mexico."

She looked astonished. "Where did you get that?"

"From Western Union," he lied.

"Isn't it in code?"

"Codes can be broken." He handed her a typewritten copy of the full English translation.

"Is this off the record?" she said.

"No. The only thing I want you to keep to yourself is where you got it."

"Okay." She began to read. After a moment, her mouth dropped open. She looked up. "Gus," she said. "Is this real?"

"When did you know me to play a practical joke?"

"The last time was never." She read on. "The Germans are going to pay Mexico to invade Texas?"

"That's what Herr Zimmermann says."

"This isn't a story, Gus—this is the scoop of the century!"

He allowed himself a small smile, trying not to appear as triumphant as he felt. "That's what I thought you'd say."

"Are you acting independently, or on behalf of the president?"

"Rosa, do you imagine I would do a thing like this without approval from the very top?"

"I guess not. Wow. So this comes to me from President Wilson."

"Not officially."

"But how do I know it's true? I don't think I can write the story based only on a scrap of paper and your word."

Gus had anticipated this snag. "Secretary of State Lansing will personally confirm the authenticity of the telegram to your boss, provided the conversation is confidential."

"Good enough." She looked down at the sheet of paper again. "This changes everything. Can you imagine what the American people will say when they read it?"

"I think it will make them more inclined to join in the war and fight against Germany."

"Inclined?" she said. "They're going to be foaming at the mouth! Wilson will have to declare war."

Gus said nothing.

After a moment, Rosa interpreted his silence. "Oh, I see. That's why you're releasing the telegram. The president *wants* to declare war."

She was dead right. He smiled, enjoying this dance of wits with a bright woman. "I'm not saying that."

"But this telegram will anger the American people so much that they will demand war. And Wilson will be able to say he did not renege on his election promises—he was forced by public opinion to change his policy."

She was in fact a bit too bright for his purposes. He said anxiously: "That's not the story you'll write, is it?"

She smiled. "Oh, no. That's just me refusing to take anything at face value. I was an anarchist once, you know."

"And now?"

"Now I'm a reporter. And there's only one way to write this story."

He felt relieved.

The waiter brought their food: poached salmon for her, steak and mashed potatoes for him. Rosa stood up. "I have to get back to the office."

Gus was startled. "What about your lunch?"

"Are you serious?" she said. "I can't eat. Don't you understand what you've done?"

He thought he did, but he said: "Tell me."

"You've just sent America to war."

Gus nodded. "I know," he said. "Go write the story."

"Hey," she said. "Thanks for picking me."

A moment later she was gone.

CHAPTER TWENTY-THREE

March 1917

That winter in Petrograd was cold and hungry. The thermometer outside the barracks of the First Machine Gun Regiment stayed at minus fifteen degrees centigrade for a full month. Bakers stopped making pies, cakes, pastries, and anything else other than bread, but still there was not enough flour. Armed guards were posted at the barracks kitchen door because so many soldiers tried to beg or steal extra food.

One bitterly cold day early in March, Grigori got an afternoon pass and decided to go and see Vladimir, who would be with the landlady while Katerina was at work. He put on his army greatcoat and set off through icy streets. On Nevsky Prospekt he caught the eye of a child beggar, a girl of about nine, standing on a corner in an arctic wind. Something about her bothered him, and he frowned as he walked past. A minute later he realized what had struck him. She had given him a look of sexual invitation. He was so shocked that he stopped in his tracks. How could she be a whore at that age? He turned around, intending to question her, but she was gone.

He walked on with a troubled mind. He knew, of course, that there were men who wanted sex with children: he had learned that when he and little Lev sought help from a priest, all those years ago. But somehow the picture of that nine-year-old pathetically imitating a come-hither smile wrenched at his heart. It made him want to weep for his country. We are turning our children into prostitutes, he thought: can it possibly get any worse?

He was in a grim mood when he reached his old lodgings. As soon as he entered the house he heard Vladimir bawling. He went up to Katerina's room and found the child alone, his face red and contorted with crying. He picked him up and rocked him.

The room was clean and tidy, and smelled of Katerina. Grigori came here most Sundays. They had a routine: they went out in the morning, then came home and made lunch, with food Grigori brought from the barracks when he could get any. Afterward, while Vladimir had his nap, they made love. On Sundays when there was enough to eat, Grigori was blissfully happy in this room.

Vladimir's yelling became a droning discontented grizzle. With the child in his arms, Grigori went to look for the landlady, who was supposed to be watching Vladimir. He found her in the laundry, a low-built extension at the back of the house, running wet bedsheets through a mangle. She was a woman of about fifty with gray hair tied up in a scarf. She had been plump back in 1914 when Grigori left to go in the army, but now her throat was scraggy and her jowls hung loose. Even landladies were hungry these days.

She looked startled and guilty when she saw him. Grigori said: "Didn't you hear the child crying?"

"I can't rock him all day," she said defensively, and went on turning the handle of the wringer.

"Perhaps he's hungry."

"He's had his milk," she said quickly. Her response was suspiciously rapid, and Grigori guessed she had drunk the milk herself. He wanted to strangle her.

In the cold air of the unheated laundry he felt Vladimir's soft baby skin radiating heat. "I think he's got a fever," he said. "Didn't you notice his temperature?"

"Am I a doctor, now, too?"

Vladimir stopped crying and fell into a state of lassitude that Grigori found more worrying. He was normally an alert, busy child, curious and mildly destructive, but now he lay still in Grigori's arms, his face flushed, his eyes staring.

Grigori put him back on his bed in the corner of Katerina's room. He took a jug from Katerina's shelf, left the house, and hurried to the next street, where there was a general store. He bought some milk, a little sugar in a twist of paper, and an apple.

When he got back Vladimir was the same.

He warmed the milk, dissolved the sugar in it, and broke a crust of stale bread into the mixture, then fed morsels of soaked bread to Vladimir. He recalled his mother giving this to baby Lev when he was sick. Vladimir ate as if he was hungry and thirsty.

When all the bread and milk were gone, Grigori took out the apple. With his pocketknife he cut it into segments and peeled a slice. He ate the peel himself and offered the rest to Vladimir, saying: "Some for me, some for you." In the past the boy had been amused by this procedure, but now he was indifferent, and let the apple fall from his mouth.

There was no doctor nearby, and anyway Grigori could not afford the fee, but there was a midwife a few streets away. She was Magda, the pretty wife of Grigori's old friend Konstantin, the secretary of the Putilov Bolshevik Committee. Grigori and Konstantin played chess whenever they got the chance—Grigori usually won.

Grigori put a clean diaper on Vladimir, then wrapped him in the blanket from Katerina's bed, leaving only his eyes and nose visible. They went out into the cold.

Konstantin and Magda lived in a two-room apartment with Magda's aunt, who watched their three small children. Grigori was afraid Magda would be out delivering a baby, but he was in luck and she was at home.

Magda was knowledgeable and kindhearted, though a bit brisk. She felt Vladimir's forehead and said: "He has an infection."

"How bad?"

"Does he cough?"

"No."

"What are his stools like?"

"Runny."

She took off Vladimir's clothes and said: "I suppose Katerina's breasts have no milk."

"How did you know that?" Grigori said in surprise.

"It's common. A woman cannot feed a baby unless she herself is fed. Nothing comes from nothing. That's why the child is so thin."

Grigori did not know Vladimir was thin.

Magda poked Vladimir's belly and made him cry. "Inflammation of the bowels," she said.

"Will he be all right?"

"Probably. Children get infections all the time. They usually survive."

"What can we do?"

"Bathe his forehead with tepid water to bring down his temperature. Give him plenty to drink, all he wants. Don't worry about whether he eats. Feed Katerina, so that she can nurse him. Mother's milk is what he needs."

Grigori took Vladimir home. He bought more milk on the way, and warmed it up on the fire. He gave it to Vladimir on a teaspoon, and the boy drank it all. Then he warmed a pan of water and bathed Vladimir's face with a rag. It seemed to work: the child lost the flushed, staring look and began to breathe normally.

Grigori was feeling less anxious when Katerina came home at half past seven. She looked tired and cold. She had bought a cabbage and a few grams of pork fat, and Grigori put them in a saucepan to make stew while she rested. He told her about Vladimir's fever, the negligent landlady, and Magda's prescription. "What can I do?" Katerina said with weary despair. "I have to go to the factory. There is no one else to watch Volodya."

Grigori fed the child with the broth from the stew, then put him down to sleep. When Grigori and Katerina had eaten they lay on the bed together. "Don't let me sleep too long," Katerina said. "I have to join the bread queue."

"I'll go for you," Grigori said. "You rest." He would be late back to the barracks, but he could probably get away with that: the officers were too fearful of mutiny, these days, to make a fuss about minor transgressions.

Katerina took him at his word, and fell into a deep sleep.

When he heard the church clock strike two, he put on his boots and greatcoat. Vladimir seemed to be sleeping normally. Grigori left the house and walked to the bakery. To his surprise there was already a long queue, and he realized he had left it a bit late. There were about a hundred people in line, muffled up, stamping their feet in the snow. Some had brought chairs or stools. An enterprising young man with a brazier was selling porridge, washing the bowls in the snow when they were done with. A dozen more people joined the queue behind Grigori.

They gossiped and grumbled while they waited. Two women ahead of Grigori argued about who was to blame for the bread shortage: one said Germans at court, the other Jews hoarding flour. "Who rules?" Grigori said to them. "If a streetcar overturns, you blame the driver, because he was in charge. The Jews don't rule us. The Germans don't rule us. It's the tsar and the nobility." This was the Bolshevik message.

"Who would rule, if there was no tsar?" said the younger woman skeptically. She was wearing a yellow felt hat.

"I think we should rule ourselves," said Grigori. "As they do in France and America."

"I don't know," said the older woman. "It can't go on like this."

The shop opened at five. A minute later the news came down the line that customers were rationed to one loaf per person. "All night, just for one loaf!" said the woman in the yellow hat.

It took another hour to shuffle to the head of the queue. The baker's wife was admitting customers one at a time. The older of the two women ahead of Grigori went in; then the baker's wife said: "That's all. No more bread."

The woman in the yellow hat said: "No, please! Just one more!"

The baker's wife wore a stony expression. Perhaps this had happened before. "If he had more flour, he'd bake more bread," she said. "It's all gone—do you hear me? I can't sell you bread if I haven't got any."

The last customer came out of the shop with her loaf under her coat and hurried away.

The woman in the yellow hat began to cry.

The baker's wife slammed the door.

Grigori turned and walked away.

<h1 style="text-align:center">{ II }</h1>

Spring came to Petrograd on Thursday, March 8, but the Russian Empire clung obstinately to the calendar of Julius Caesar, so they called it February 23. The rest of Europe had been using the modern calendar for three hundred years.

The rise in temperature coincided with International Women's Day, and the female workers from the textile mills came out on strike and marched from the industrial suburbs into the city center to protest against the bread queues, the war, and the tsar. Bread rationing had been announced, but it seemed to have made the shortage worse.

The First Machine Gun Regiment, like all army units in the city, was detailed to help the police and the mounted Cossacks keep order. What would happen, Grigori wondered, if the soldiers were ordered to fire on the marchers? Would they obey? Or would they turn their rifles on their officers? In 1905 they had obeyed orders and shot workers. But since then the Russian people had suffered a decade of tyranny, repression, war, and hunger.

However, there was no trouble, and Grigori and his section returned to barracks that evening without having fired a shot.

On Friday more workers came out on strike.

The tsar was at army headquarters, four hundred miles away at

Mogilev. In charge of the city was the commander of the Petrograd Military District, General Khabalov. He decided to keep marchers out of the center by stationing soldiers at the bridges. Grigori's section was posted close to the barracks, guarding the Liteiny Bridge that led across the Neva River to Liteiny Prospekt. But the water was still frozen solid, and the marchers foiled the army by simply walking across the ice—to the delight of the watching soldiers, most of whom, like Grigori, sympathized with the marchers.

None of the political parties had organized the strike. The Bolsheviks, like the other leftist revolutionary parties, found themselves following rather than leading the working class.

Once again Grigori's section saw no action, but it was not the same everywhere. When he got back to barracks on Saturday night, he learned that police had attacked demonstrators outside the railway station at the far end of Nevsky Prospekt. Surprisingly, the Cossacks had defended the marchers against the police. Men were talking about the Comrade Cossacks. Grigori was skeptical. The Cossacks had never really been loyal to anyone but themselves, he thought; they just loved a fight.

On Sunday morning Grigori was awakened at five, long before first light. At breakfast there was a rumor that the tsar had instructed General Khabalov to put a stop to strikes and marches using whatever force was necessary. That was an ominous phrase, Grigori thought: *whatever force was necessary.*

After breakfast the sergeants were given their orders. Each platoon was to guard a different point in the city: not just bridges but intersections, railway stations, and post offices. The pickets would be connected by field telephones. The nation's capital was to be secured like a captured enemy city. Worst of all, the regiment was to set up machine guns at likely trouble spots.

When Grigori relayed the instructions to his men, they were horrified. Isaak said: "Is the tsar really going to order the army to machine-gun his own people?"

Grigori said: "If he does, will soldiers obey him?"

Grigori's mounting excitement was paralleled by fear. He was heartened by the strikes, for he knew the Russian people had to defy their rulers. Otherwise the war would drag on, the people would starve, and there was no prospect that Vladimir might live a better life than Grigori and Katerina. It was this conviction that had caused Grigori to join the party. On the other hand, he cherished a secret hope that if soldiers simply refused to obey orders, the revolution might go off without too much bloodshed. But when his own regiment was ordered to set up machine-gun emplacements on Petrograd street corners, he began to feel that his hope had been foolish.

Was it even possible that the Russian people could ever escape from the tyranny of the tsars? Sometimes it seemed like a pipe dream. Yet other nations had had revolutions, and overthrown their oppressors. Even the English had killed their king once.

Petrograd was like a pan of water on the fire, Grigori thought: there were wisps of steam and a few bubbles of violence, and the surface shimmered with intense heat, but the water seemed to hesitate, and the proverbial watched pot did not boil.

His platoon was sent to the Tauride Palace, the vast summer town house of Catherine II, now home to Russia's toothless parliament, the Duma. The morning was quiet: even starving people liked to sleep late on Sunday. But the weather continued sunny, and at midday they started to come in from the suburbs, on foot and in streetcars. Some gathered in the large garden of the Tauride Palace. They were not all factory workers, Grigori noticed. There were middle-class men and women, students, and a few prosperous-looking businessmen. Some had brought their children. Were they on a political demonstration, or just going for a walk in the park? Grigori guessed they themselves were not sure.

At the entrance to the palace he saw a well-dressed young man whose handsome face was familiar from photographs in the newspapers, and he recognized the Trudovik deputy Alexander Fedorovich Kerensky. The Trudoviks were a moderate breakaway faction from the Socialist Revolutionaries. Grigori asked him what was going on inside. "The tsar formally dissolved the Duma today," Kerensky told him.

Grigori shook his head in disgust. "A characteristic reaction," he said. "Repress those who complain, rather than address their discontents."

Kerensky looked at him sharply. Perhaps he had not been expecting such an analysis from a soldier. "Quite," he said. "Anyway, we deputies are ignoring the tsar's edict."

"What will happen?"

"Most people think the demonstrations will peter out as soon as the authorities manage to restore the supply of bread," Kerensky said, and he went inside.

Grigori wondered what made the moderates think that was going to happen. If the authorities were able to restore the supply of bread, would they not have done so, instead of rationing it? But moderates always seemed to deal in hopes rather than facts.

Early in the afternoon Grigori was surprised to see the smiling faces of Katerina and Vladimir. He normally spent Sunday with them, but had assumed he would not see them today. Vladimir looked well and happy, much to Grigori's relief. Evidently the boy had got over the infection. It was warm enough for Katerina to wear her coat open, showing her voluptuous figure. He wished he could caress her. She smiled at him, making him think of how she would kiss his face as they lay on the bed, and Grigori felt a stab of yearning that was almost unbearable. He hated to miss that Sunday afternoon embrace.

"How did you know I would be here?" he asked her.

"It was a lucky guess."

"I'm glad to see you, but it's dangerous for you to be in the city center."

Katerina looked at the crowds strolling through the park. "It seems safe enough to me."

Grigori could not dispute that. There was no sign of trouble.

Mother and child went off to walk around the frozen lake. Grigori's breath caught in his throat as he watched Vladimir toddle away and almost immediately fall over. Katerina picked him up, soothed him, and walked on. They looked so vulnerable. What was going to happen to them?

When they returned, Katerina said she was taking Vladimir home for his nap.

"Go by the backstreets," Grigori said. "Keep away from crowds. I don't know what might happen."

"All right," she said.

"Promise."

"I promise."

Grigori saw no bloodshed that day, but at the barracks in the evening he heard a different story from other groups. In Znamenskaya Square soldiers had been ordered to shoot demonstrators, and forty people had died. Grigori felt a cold hand on his heart. Katerina might have been killed just walking along the street!

Others were equally outraged, and in the mess hall feelings were running high. Sensing the mood of the men, Grigori stood on a table and took charge, calling for order and inviting soldiers to speak in turn. Supper turned rapidly into a mass meeting. He called first on Isaak, who was well known as the star of the regimental soccer team.

"I joined the army to kill Germans, not Russians," Isaak said, and there was a roar of approval. "The marchers are our brothers and sisters, our mothers and fathers—and their only crime is to ask for bread!"

Grigori knew all the Bolsheviks in the regiment, and he called on several of them to speak, but he was careful to point to others, too, not to seem overly biased. Normally the men were cautious about expressing their opinions, for fear their remarks would be reported and they would be punished; but today they did not seem to care.

The speaker who made the greatest impression was Yakov, a tall man with shoulders like a bear. He stood on the table beside Grigori with tears in his eyes. "When they told us to fire, I didn't know what to do," he said. He seemed unable to raise his voice, and the room went quiet as the other men strained to hear him. "I said: 'God, please guide me now,' and I listened in my heart, but God sent me no answer." The men were silent. "I raised my rifle," Yakov said. "The captain was screaming: 'Shoot! Shoot!' But who should I shoot at? In Galicia we knew who our enemies were because they were firing at us. But today in the square no one was attacking us. The people were mostly women, some with children. Even the men had no weapons."

He fell silent. The men were as still as stones, as if they feared that any movement might break the spell. After a moment Isaak prompted him. "What happened next, Yakov Davidovich?"

"I pulled the trigger," Yakov said, and the tears ran from his eyes into his bushy black beard. "I didn't even aim the gun. The captain was screaming at me and I fired just to shut him up. But I hit a woman. A girl, really—about nineteen, I suppose. She had a green coat. I shot her in the chest, and the blood went all over the coat, red on green. Then she fell down." He was weeping openly now, speaking in gasps. "I dropped my gun and tried to go to her, to help her, but the crowd went for me, punching and kicking, though I hardly felt it." He wiped his face with his sleeve. "I'm in trouble, now, for losing my rifle." There was another long pause. "Nineteen," he said. "I think she must have been about nineteen."

Grigori had not noticed the door opening, but suddenly Lieutenant Kirillov was there. "Get off that damn table, Yakov," he shouted. He looked at Grigori. "You, too, Peshkov, you troublemaker." He turned and spoke to the men, sitting on benches at their trestle tables. "Return to your barracks, all of you," he said. "Anyone still in this room one minute from now gets a flogging."

No one moved. The men stared surlily at the lieutenant. Grigori wondered if this was how a mutiny started.

But Yakov was too lost in his misery to realize what a moment of drama he had created; he got down clumsily from the table, and the tension was released. Some of the men close to Kirillov stood up, looking sullen but scared. Grigori remained defiantly standing on the table a few moments longer, but he sensed that the men were not quite angry enough to turn on an officer, so in the end he got down. The men started to leave the room. Kirillov remained where he was, glaring at everyone.

Grigori returned to barracks and soon the bell rang for lights-out. As a sergeant, he had the privilege of a curtained niche at the end of his platoon's dormitory. He could hear the men speaking in low voices.

"I won't shoot women," said one.

"Me neither."

A third voice said: "If you don't, some of these bastard officers will shoot you for disobedience!"

"I'm going to aim to miss," said another voice.

"They might see."

"You only have to aim a bit above the heads of the crowd. No one can be sure what you're doing."

"That's what I'm going to do," said another voice.

"Me, too."

"Me, too."

We'll see, Grigori thought as he drifted off to sleep. Brave words came easily in the dark. Daylight might tell a different story.

{ III }

On Monday Grigori's platoon was marched the short distance along Samsonievsky Prospekt to the Liteiny Bridge and ordered to prevent demonstrators crossing the river to the city center. The bridge was four hundred yards long, and rested on massive stone piers set into the frozen river like stranded icebreakers.

This was the same job they had had on Friday, but the orders were different. Lieutenant Kirillov briefed Grigori. He spoke these days as if he was in a constant bad temper, and perhaps he was: officers probably disliked being lined up against their own countrymen just as much as the men did. "No marchers are to cross the river, either by the bridge or on the ice, do you understand? You will shoot people who flout your instructions."

Grigori hid his contempt. "Yes, Excellency!" he said smartly.

Kirillov repeated the orders, then disappeared. Grigori thought the lieutenant was scared. Doubtless he feared being held responsible for what happened, whether his orders were obeyed or defied.

Grigori had no intention of obeying. He would allow the leaders of the march to engage him in discussion while their followers crossed the ice, exactly as it had played out on Friday.

However, early in the morning his platoon was joined by a detachment of police. To his horror, he saw that they were led by his old enemy Mikhail Pinsky. The man did not appear to be suffering from the shortage of bread: his round face was fatter than ever, and his police uniform was tight around the middle. He was carrying a megaphone. His weasel-faced sidekick, Kozlov, was nowhere in sight.

"I know you," Pinsky said to Grigori. "You used to work at the Putilov factory."

"Until you had me conscripted," Grigori said.

"Your brother is a murderer, but he escaped to America."

"So you say."

"No one is going to cross the river here today."

"We shall see."

"I expect full cooperation from your men. Is that understood?"

Grigori said: "Aren't you afraid?"

"Of the rabble? Don't be stupid."

"No, I mean of the future. Suppose the revolutionaries get their way. What do you think they will do to you? You've spent your life bullying the weak, beating people up, harassing women, and taking bribes. Don't you fear a day of retribution?"

Pinsky pointed a gloved finger at Grigori. "I'm reporting you as a damned subversive," he said, and he walked away.

Grigori shrugged. It was not as easy as it used to be for the police to arrest anyone they liked. Isaak and others might mutiny if Grigori was jailed, and the officers knew it.

The day started quietly, but Grigori noted that few workers were on the streets. Many factories were closed because they could not get fuel for their steam engines and furnaces. Other places were on strike, the employees demanding more money to pay inflated prices, or heating for ice-cold workshops, or safety rails around dangerous machinery. It looked as if almost no one was actually going to work today. But the sun rose cheerfully, and people were not going to stay indoors. Sure enough, at midmorning Grigori saw, coming along Samsonievsky Prospekt, a large crowd of men and women in the blue tunics and ragged coats of industrial workers.

Grigori had thirty men and two corporals. He had stationed them in four lines of eight across the road, blocking the end of the bridge. Pinsky had about the same number of men, half on foot and half on horseback, and he placed them at the sides of the road.

Grigori peered anxiously at the oncoming march. He could not predict what would happen. On his own he could have prevented bloodshed, by offering only token resistance, then letting the demonstrators pass. But he did not know what Pinsky was going to do.

The marchers came nearer. There were hundreds of people—no, thousands. Most wore red armbands or red ribbons. Their banners read *Down with the Tsar* and *Bread, Peace, and Land.* This was no longer merely a protest, Grigori concluded: it had become a political movement.

As the leaders came nearer, he sensed the tightening anxiety among his waiting men.

He walked forward to meet the marchers. At their head, to his surprise, was Varya, the mother of Konstantin. Her gray hair was tied up in a red scarf, and she carried a red flag on a hefty stick. "Hello, Grigori Sergeivich," she said amiably. "Are you going to shoot me?"

"No, I'm not," he replied. "But I can't speak for the police."

Although Varya stopped, the others came on, pressed from behind by thousands more. Grigori heard Pinsky urge his mounted men forward. These horseback policemen, called Pharaohs, were the most hated section of the force. They were armed with whips and clubs.

Varya said: "All we want is to make a living and feed our families. Isn't that what you want, too, Grigori?"

The marchers were not confronting Grigori's soldiers, or attempting to get past them onto the bridge. Instead they were spreading out along the embankment on both sides. Pinsky's Pharaohs nervously walked their horses along the towpath, as if to bar the way to the ice, but there were not enough of them to form a continuous barrier. However, no marcher wanted to be the first to make a dash for it, and there was a moment of stalemate.

Lieutenant Pinsky put his megaphone to his mouth. "Go back!" he shouted. The instrument was no more than a piece of tin shaped like a cone, and made his voice only a little louder. "You may not enter the city center. Return to your workplaces in orderly fashion. This is a police command. Go back."

Nobody went back—most people could not even hear—but the marchers started to jeer and boo. Someone deep in the crowd threw a stone. It struck the rump of a horse, and the beast started. Its rider, taken by surprise, almost fell off. Furious, he pulled himself upright, sawed on the reins, and lashed the horse with his whip. The crowd laughed, which made him angrier, but he brought his horse under control.

A brave marcher took advantage of the diversion, dodged past a Pharaoh on the embankment, and ran onto the ice. Several more people on both sides of the bridge did the same. The Pharaohs deployed their whips and clubs, wheeling and rearing their horses as they lashed out. Some of the marchers fell to the ground, but more got through, and others were emboldened to try. In seconds, thirty or more people were running across the frozen river.

For Grigori, that was a happy outcome. He could say that he had attempted to enforce the ban, and he had in fact kept people off the bridge, but the number of demonstrators was too great and it had proved impossible to stop people crossing the ice.

Pinsky did not see it that way.

He turned his megaphone to the armed police and said: "Take aim!"

"No!" Grigori shouted, but it was too late. The police took up the firing position, on one knee, and raised their rifles. Marchers at the front of the crowd tried to go back, but they were pushed forward by the thousands behind them. Some ran for the river, braving the Pharaohs.

Pinsky shouted: "Fire!"

There was a crackle of shots like fireworks, followed by shouts of fear and screams of pain as marchers fell dead and wounded.

Grigori was taken back twelve years. He saw the square in front of the Winter Palace, the hundreds of men and women kneeling in prayer, the soldiers with their rifles, and his mother lying on the ground with her blood spreading on the snow. In his mind he heard eleven-year-old Lev scream: "She's dead! Ma's dead, my mother is dead!"

"No," Grigori said aloud. "I will not let them do this again." He turned the safety knob on his Mosin-Nagant rifle, unlocking the bolt; then he raised the gun to his shoulder.

The crowd was screaming and running in all directions, trampling the fallen. The Pharaohs were out of control, lashing out at random. The police fired indiscriminately into the crowd.

Grigori aimed carefully at Pinsky, targeting the middle of the body. He was not a very good shot, and Pinsky was sixty yards away, but he had a chance of hitting him. He pulled the trigger.

Pinsky continued to yell through his megaphone.

Grigori had missed. He lowered his sights—the rifle kicked up a little when fired—and squeezed the trigger again.

He missed again.

The carnage went on, police shooting wildly into the crowd of fleeing men and women.

There were five rounds in the magazine of Grigori's rifle. He could usually hit something with one of the five. He fired a third time.

Pinsky gave a shout of pain that was amplified by his megaphone. His right knee seemed to fold under him. He dropped the megaphone and fell to the ground.

Grigori's men followed his example. They attacked the police, some firing and some using their rifles as clubs. Others pulled the Pharaohs off their horses. The marchers drew courage and joined in. Some of those on the ice turned around and came back.

The fury of the mob was ugly. For as long as anyone could remember, the Petrograd police had been sneering brutes, undisciplined and uncontrolled, and now the people took their revenge. Policemen on the ground were kicked and trampled, those on their feet were knocked down, and the Pharaohs had their horses shot from under them. The police resisted for only a few moments; then those who could fled.

Grigori saw Pinsky struggle to his feet. Grigori took aim again, eager now to finish the bastard off, but a Pharaoh got in the way, heaved Pinsky up onto his horse's neck, and galloped off.

Grigori stood back, watching the police run away.

He was in the worst trouble of his life.

His platoon had mutinied. In direct contravention of their orders, they had attacked the police, not the marchers. And he had led them, by shooting Lieutenant Pinsky, who had survived to tell the tale. There was no way to cover this up, no excuse he could offer that would make any difference, and no escape from punishment. He was guilty of treason. He could be court-martialed and executed.

Despite that, he felt happy.

Varya pushed through the crowd. There was blood on her face, but she was smiling. "What now, Sergeant?"

Grigori was not going to resign himself to his punishment. The tsar was murdering his people. Well, his people would shoot back. "To the barracks," Grigori said. "Let's arm the working class!" He snatched her red flag. "Follow me!"

He strode back along Samsonievsky Prospekt. His men came after him, marshaled by Isaak, and the crowd fell in behind them. Grigori was not sure exactly what he was going to do, but he did not feel the need of a plan: as he marched at the head of the crowd he had the sense that he could do anything.

The sentry opened the barracks gates for the soldiers, then was unable to close them on the marchers. Feeling invincible, Grigori led the procession across the parade ground to the arsenal. Lieutenant Kirillov came out of the headquarters building, saw the crowd, and turned toward them, breaking into a run. "You men!" he shouted. "Halt! Stop right there!"

Grigori ignored him.

Kirillov came to a standstill and drew his revolver. "Halt!" he said. "Halt, or I shoot!"

Two or three of Grigori's platoon raised their rifles and fired at Kirillov. Several bullets struck him and he fell to the ground, bleeding.

Grigori went on.

The arsenal was guarded by two sentries. Neither of them tried to stop Grigori. He used the last two rounds in his magazine to shoot out the lock on the heavy wooden doors. The crowd burst into the arsenal, pushing and shoving to get at the weapons. Some of Grigori's men took charge, opening wooden cases of rifles and revolvers and passing them out along with boxes of ammunition.

This is it, Grigori thought. This is a revolution. He was exhilarated and terrified at the same time.

He armed himself with two of the Nagant revolvers that were issued to officers, reloaded his rifle, and filled his pockets with ammunition. He was not sure what he intended to do, but now that he was a criminal he needed weapons.

The rest of the soldiers in the barracks joined in the looting of the arsenal, and soon everyone was armed to the teeth.

Carrying Varya's red flag, Grigori led the crowd out of the barracks. Demonstrations always went toward the city center. With Isaak, Yakov, and Varya he marched across the bridge to Liteiny Prospekt, heading for the affluent heart of Petrograd. He felt as if he were flying, or dreaming, as if he had drunk a large mouthful of vodka. For years he had talked about defying the authority of the regime, but today he was doing it, and that made him feel like a new man, a different creature, a bird of the air. He remembered the words of the old man who had spoken to him after his mother was shot dead. "May you live long," the man had said, as Grigori walked away from Palace Square with his mother's body in his arms. "Long enough to take revenge on the bloodstained tsar for the evil he has done this day." Your wish may come true, old man, he thought exultantly.

The First Machine Guns were not the only regiment to have mutinied this morning. When he reached the far side of the bridge he was even more elated to see that the streets were full of soldiers wearing their caps backward or their coats unbuttoned in merry defiance of regulations. Most sported red armbands or red lapel ribbons to show they were revolutionaries. Commandeered cars roared around, erratically driven, rifle barrels and bayonets sticking out of the windows, laughing girls sitting on the soldiers' knees inside. The pickets and checkpoints of yesterday had vanished. The streets had been taken over by the people.

Grigori saw a wine shop with its windows broken and its door battered down. A soldier and a girl came out, bottles in both hands, trampling over broken glass. Next door a café proprietor had put plates of smoked fish and sliced sausage on a table outside, and stood beside it with a red ribbon in his lapel, smiling nervously and inviting soldiers to help themselves. Grigori guessed he was trying to make sure his place was not broken into and looted like the wine shop.

The carnival atmosphere grew as they neared the center. Some people were already quite drunk, although it was only midday. Girls seemed happy to kiss anyone with a red armband, and Grigori saw a soldier openly fondling the large breasts of a smiling middle-aged woman. Some girls had dressed in soldiers' uniforms, and swaggered along the streets in caps and oversize boots, evidently feeling liberated.

A shiny Rolls-Royce car came along the street and the crowd tried to stop it. The chauffeur put his foot on the gas but someone opened the door and pulled him out. People shoved one another trying to get into the car. Grigori saw Count Maklakov, one of the directors of the Putilov works, scramble out of the backseat. Grigori recalled how Maklakov had been so entranced with Princess Bea the day she visited the factory. The crowd jeered but did not molest the count as he hurried away, pulling his fur collar up around his ears. Nine or ten people crammed into his car and someone drove it off, honking blithely.

At the next corner a handful of people were tormenting a tall man in the trilby hat and well-worn greatcoat of a middle-class professional. A soldier poked him with his rifle barrel, an old woman spat at him, and a young man in worker's overalls threw a handful of rubbish. "Let me pass!" the man said, trying to sound commanding, but they just laughed. Grigori recognized the thin figure of Kanin, supervisor of the casting section at the Putilov works. His hat fell off, and Grigori saw that he had gone bald.

Grigori pushed through the little crowd. "There's nothing wrong with this man!" he shouted. "He's an engineer. I used to work with him."

Kanin recognized him. "Thank you, Grigori Sergeivich," he said. "I'm just trying to make my way to my mother's house, to see if she's all right."

Grigori turned to the crowd. "Let him pass," he said. "I vouch for him." He saw a woman carrying a reel of red ribbon—looted, presumably, from a haberdashery—and asked her for a length. She cut some off with a pair of scissors, and Grigori tied it around Kanin's left sleeve. The crowd cheered.

"Now you'll be safe," Grigori said.

Kanin shook his hand and walked away, and they let him pass.

Grigori's group came out onto Nevsky Prospekt, the broad shopping street that ran from the Winter Palace to Nikolaevsky Station. It was full of people drinking from bottles, eating, kissing, and firing guns into the air. Those restaurants that were open had signs reading, "Free food for revolutionaries!" and "Eat what you like, pay what you can!" Many shops had been broken into, and there was smashed glass all over the cobblestones. One of the hated streetcars—priced too high for workers to use—had been overturned in the middle of the road, and a Renault automobile had crashed into it.

Grigori heard a rifle shot, but it was one of many, and he thought nothing of it for a second; but then Varya, by his side, staggered and fell down. Grigori and Yakov knelt either side of her. She seemed unconscious. They turned the heavy body over, not without difficulty, and saw immediately that she was beyond help: a bullet had entered her forehead, and her eyes stared up sightlessly.

Grigori did not allow himself to feel sorrow, either on his own account or for Varya's son, his best friend, Konstantin. He had learned on the battlefield to fight back first and grieve later. But was this a battlefield? Who could possibly want to kill Varya? Yet the wound was so exactly placed that he could hardly believe she was the victim of a stray bullet fired at random.

His question was answered a moment later. Yakov keeled over, bleeding from his chest. His heavy body hit the cobbles with a thump.

Grigori stepped away from the two bodies, saying: "What the hell?" He dropped into a crouch, making himself a smaller target, and rapidly looked around for somewhere he could take cover.

He heard another shot, and a passing soldier with a red scarf around his cap fell to the ground holding his stomach.

There was a sniper, and he was targeting revolutionaries.

Grigori ran three paces and dived behind the overturned streetcar.

A woman screamed, then another. People saw the bleeding bodies and began to run away.

Grigori lifted his head and scanned the surrounding buildings. The shooter had to be a police rifleman, but where was he? It seemed to Grigori that the crack of the rifle had come from the other side of the street and less than a block away. The buildings were bright in the afternoon sunlight. There was a hotel, a jewelry store with steel shutters closed, a bank, and on the corner, a church. He could see no open windows, so the sniper had to be on a roof. None of the roofs offered cover—except that of the church, which was a stone building in the baroque style with towers, parapets, and an onion dome.

Another shot rang out, and a woman in the clothes of a factory worker screamed and fell clutching her shoulder. Grigori felt sure the sound had come from the church, but he saw no smoke. That must mean the police had issued their snipers with smokeless ammunition. This really was war.

A whole block of Nevsky Prospekt was now deserted.

Grigori aimed his rifle at the parapet that ran along the top of the side wall of the church. That was the firing position he would have chosen, commanding the whole street. He watched carefully. Out of the corner of his eye he saw two more rifles pointing in the same direction as his, held by soldiers who had taken cover nearby.

A soldier and a girl came staggering along the street, both drunk. The girl was dancing a jig, raising the skirt of her dress to show her knees, while her boyfriend waltzed around her, holding his rifle to his neck and pretending to play it like a violin. Both wore red armbands. Several people shouted warnings, but the revelers did not hear. As they passed the church, happily oblivious to the danger, two shots rang out, and the soldier and his girl fell down.

Once again Grigori saw no wisp of smoke, but all the same he fired angrily at the parapet above the church door, emptying his magazine. His bullets chipped the stonework and sent up puffs of dust. The other two rifles cracked, and Grigori saw that they were shooting in the same direction, but there was no sign that either of them had hit anything.

It was impossible, Grigori thought as he reloaded. They were firing at an invisible target. The sniper must be lying flat, well back from the edge, so that no part of his gun needed to poke through the bars.

But he had to be stopped. He had already killed Varya, Yakov, two soldiers, and an innocent girl.

There was only one way to reach him, and that was to get up on the roof.

Grigori fired at the parapet again. As he expected, that caused the other two soldiers to do the same. Assuming the sniper must have put his head down for a few seconds, Grigori stood up, abandoning the shelter of the overturned streetcar, and ran to the far side of the street, where he flattened himself up against the window of a bookshop—one of the few stores that had not been looted.

Keeping within the afternoon shadow cast by the buildings, he made his way along the street to the church. It was separated by an alley from the bank next door. He waited patiently for several minutes, until the shooting started again, then darted across the alley and stood with his back to the east end of the church.

Had the sniper seen him run, and guessed what he was planning? There was no way to tell.

Staying close to the wall, he edged around the church until he came to a small door. It was unlocked. He slipped inside.

It was a rich church, gorgeously decorated with red, green, and yellow marble. There was no service taking place at that moment, but twenty or thirty worshippers stood or sat with bowed heads, holding their own private devotions. Grigori scanned the interior, looking for a door that might lead to a staircase. He hurried down the aisle, fearful that more people were being murdered every minute he delayed.

A young priest, dramatically handsome with black hair and white skin, saw his rifle and opened his mouth to voice a protest, but Grigori ignored him and hurried past.

In the vestibule he spotted a small wooden door set into a wall. He opened it and saw a spiral staircase leading up. Behind him, a voice said: "Stop there, my son. What are you doing?"

He turned to see the young priest. "Does this lead to the roof?"

"I am Father Mikhail. You can't bring that weapon into the house of God."

"There's a sniper on your roof."

"He is a police officer!"

"You know about him?" Grigori stared at the priest with incredulity. "He's killing people!"

The priest made no reply.

Grigori ran up the stairs.

A cold wind was coming from somewhere above. Clearly Father Mikhail was on the side of the police. Was there any way the priest could warn the sniper? Not short of running out into the street and waving—which would probably get him shot.

After a long climb in near-darkness, Grigori saw another door.

When his eyes were on a level with the bottom of the door, so that he presented a very small target, he opened it an inch, using his left hand, keeping his rifle in his right. Bright sunlight shone through the gap. He pushed it wide.

He could not see anyone.

He screwed up his eyes against the sun to scan the area visible through the small rectangle of doorway. He was in the bell tower. The door opened south. Nevsky Prospekt was on the north side of the church. The sniper was on the other side—unless he had moved to ambush Grigori.

Cautiously, Grigori ascended one step, then another, and put his head out.

Nothing happened.

He stepped through the door.

Under his feet the roof sloped gently to a gutter that ran alongside a decorative parapet. Wooden duckboards permitted workmen to move around without treading on the roof tiles. At his back the tower rose to a belfry.

Gun in hand, he edged around the tower.

At the first corner he found himself looking west the length of Nevsky Prospekt. In the clear light he could see the Alexander Garden and the Admiralty at the far end. In the middle distance the street was crowded, but nearby it was empty. The sniper must still be at work.

Grigori listened, but heard no shots.

He sidled farther around the tower until he could look around the next corner. Now he could see all along the north wall of the church. He had felt sure he would find the sniper there, flat on his belly, shooting between the uprights of the parapet—but there was no one in sight. Beyond the parapet he could see the wide street below, with people crouching in doorways and skulking around corners, waiting to see what would happen.

A moment later, the sniper's rifle rang out. A scream from the street told Grigori the man had hit his target.

The shot had come from above Grigori's head.

He looked up. The bell tower was pierced by glassless windows and flanked by open turrets placed diagonally at the corners. The shooter was up there somewhere, firing out of one of the many available openings. Fortunately, Grigori had remained hard up against the wall, where he could not have been seen by the sniper.

Grigori went back inside. Within the confined space of the stairwell his rifle felt big and clumsy. He put it down and took out one of his pistols. He knew by its weight that it was empty. He cursed: loading the

Nagant M1895 was slow. He took a box of cartridges from the pocket of his uniform coat and inserted seven of them, one by one, through the revolver's awkward loading gate into the cylinder. Then he cocked the hammer.

Leaving the rifle behind, he went up the spiral stairs, treading softly. He moved at a steady pace, not wanting to exert himself so much that his breathing would become audible. He kept his revolver in his right hand pointing up the stairs.

After a few moments he smelled smoke.

The sniper was having a cigarette. But the pungent smell of burning tobacco could travel a long way, and Grigori could not be sure how close the man was.

Ahead and above he saw reflected sunlight. He crept upward, ready to fire. The light was coming through a glassless window. The sniper was not there.

Grigori climbed farther and saw light again. The smell of smoke grew stronger. Was it his imagination, or could he sense the presence of the sniper just a little farther around the curve of the stairwell? And, if so, could the man sense him?

He heard a sharp intake of breath. It shocked him so much that he almost pulled the trigger. Then he realized it was the noise a man made when inhaling smoke. A moment later he heard the softer, satisfied sound of the smoker blowing out.

He hesitated. He did not know which way the sniper was looking or where his gun might be pointing. He wanted to hear the rifle fire again, for that would tell him that the sniper's attention was directed outward.

Waiting might mean another death, another Yakov or Varya bleeding on the cold cobblestones. On the other hand, if Grigori failed now how many more people would be brought down by the sniper this afternoon?

Grigori forced himself to be patient. It was like being on the battlefield. You did not rush to save a wounded comrade and thereby sacrifice your life. You took chances only when the reasons were overwhelming.

He heard another intake of breath, followed by a long exhalation, and a moment later a crushed cigarette stub came down the staircase, bouncing off the wall and landing at his feet. There was the sound of a man shifting position in a confined space. Then Grigori heard a low muttering, the words sounding mostly like imprecations: "Swine . . . revolutionaries . . . stinking Jews . . . diseased whores . . . retards . . . " The sniper was winding himself up to kill again.

If Grigori could stop him now it would save at least one life.

He went up a step.

The muttering continued: "Cattle . . . Slavs . . . thieves and criminals . . . " The voice was vaguely familiar, and Grigori wondered if this was a man he had met before.

He took another step, and saw the man's feet, shod in shiny new police-pattern black leather boots. They were small feet: the sniper was a diminutive man. He was down on one knee, the most stable position for shooting. Grigori could now see that he had positioned himself inside one of the corner turrets, so that he could fire in three different directions.

One more step, Grigori thought, and I will be able to shoot him dead.

He took another step, but tension caused him to miss his footing. He stumbled, fell, and dropped his gun. It hit the stone step with a clang.

The sniper uttered a loud, frightened curse and looked around.

With astonishment, Grigori recognized him as Pinsky's sidekick, Ilya Kozlov.

Grigori grabbed for his dropped gun and missed. The revolver fell down the stone staircase with agonizing slowness, one step at a time, until it came to rest well out of reach.

Kozlov began to turn, but he could not do so quickly from his kneeling position.

Grigori regained his balance and went up another step.

Kozlov tried to swing his rifle around. It was the standard Mosin-Nagant, but with a telescope attached. It was well over a yard long even without the bayonet, and Kozlov could not bring it to bear fast enough. Moving quickly, Grigori got close, so that the barrel of the rifle struck his left shoulder. Kozlov pulled the trigger uselessly, and a bullet ricocheted around the curved inside wall of the stairwell.

Kozlov sprang to his feet with surprising agility. Some part of Grigori's mind guessed that the ugly little man had become a sniper to get revenge on all the bigger boys—and girls—who had ever pushed him around.

Grigori got his hands on the rifle and the two men struggled for possession, face-to-face in the cramped little turret, next to the glassless window. Grigori heard excited shouting, and guessed they must be visible to people on the street.

Grigori was bigger and stronger, and knew that he would win possession of the gun. Kozlov realized it, too, and suddenly let go. Grigori staggered back. In a flash the policeman drew his short wooden club and struck out, hitting Grigori on the head. For a moment Grigori saw stars. In a blur, he saw Kozlov raise the club again. He lifted the rifle and the club landed on the barrel. Before the policeman could strike again, Grigori dropped the gun, grabbed the front of Kozlov's coat with both hands, and lifted him.

The man was slight and his weight was little. Grigori held him off the floor for a moment. Then, with all his might, he threw him out of the window.

Kozlov seemed to fall through the air very slowly. The sunlight picked out the green facings of his uniform as he sailed over the parapet of the church roof. A long scream of pure terror rang out in the silence. Then he hit the ground with a thump that could be heard in the bell tower, and the scream was abruptly cut off.

After a moment of quiet, a huge cheer went up.

Grigori realized the people were cheering him. They could see the police uniform on the ground and the army uniform in the turret, and they had worked out what had happened. As he watched, they came out of doorways and around corners and stood in the street, looking up at him, shouting and applauding. He was a hero.

He did not feel comfortable about that. He had killed several people in the war, and was no longer squeamish about it, but all the same he found it hard to celebrate another death, much as Kozlov had deserved to die. He stood there a few moments longer, letting them applaud but feeling uneasy. Then he ducked back inside and went down the spiral staircase.

He picked up his revolver and his rifle on the way down. When he emerged into the church, Father Mikhail was waiting, looking scared. Grigori pointed the revolver at him. "I ought to shoot you," he said. "That sniper you allowed onto your roof killed two of my friends and at least three other people, and you're a murdering devil for letting him do it." The priest was so shocked to be called a devil that he was lost for words. But Grigori could not bring himself to shoot an unarmed civilian, so he grunted in disgust and went outside.

The men of his platoon were waiting for him, and roared their approval as he stepped into the sunshine. He could not stop them lifting him onto their shoulders and carrying him in procession.

From his elevated viewpoint he saw that the atmosphere in the street had changed. People were more drunk, and on every block there were one or two passed out in doorways. He was startled to see men and women doing a lot more than just kissing in the alleyways. Everyone had a gun: clearly the mob had raided other arsenals and perhaps arms factories, too. At every intersection there were crashed cars, some with ambulances and doctors attending to the injured. Children as well as adults were on the streets, the small boys having a particularly good time, stealing food and smoking cigarettes and playing in abandoned automobiles.

Grigori saw a fur shop being looted with an efficiency that appeared professional, and he spotted Trofim, a former associate of Lev's, carrying armfuls of coats out of the store and loading them onto a handcart, watched by another crony of Lev's, the dishonest policeman Fyodor, now wearing a peasant-style overcoat to hide his uniform. The city's criminals saw the revolution as an opportunity.

After a while Grigori's men put him down. The afternoon light was growing dim, and several bonfires had been lit in the street. People gathered around them, drinking and singing songs.

Grigori was appalled to see a boy of about ten take a pistol from a soldier who had passed out. It was a long-barreled Luger P08 machine pistol, a gun issued to German artillery crew: the soldier must have taken it from a prisoner at the front. The boy held it in both hands, grinning, and pointed it at the man on the ground. As Grigori moved to take the gun away, the boy pulled the trigger, and a bullet thudded into the drunk soldier's chest. The boy screamed, but in his fright he kept the trigger pulled back, so that the machine pistol continued firing. The recoil jerked the boy's arms upward, and he sprayed bullets, hitting an old woman and another soldier, until the eight-round magazine was empty. Then he dropped the gun.

Before Grigori could react to this horror he heard a shout, and turned. In the doorway of a closed hat shop, a couple were having full sexual intercourse. The woman had her back to the wall and her skirt up around her waist, her legs spread apart and her booted feet firmly planted on the ground. The man, who wore the uniform of a corporal, stood between her legs, knees bent, trousers unbuttoned, thrusting. Grigori's platoon stood around them cheering.

The man appeared to reach his climax. He withdrew hastily, turned away, and buttoned his fly, while the woman pushed her skirts down. A soldier called Igor said: "Wait a minute—my turn!" He pulled up the woman's skirts, showing her white legs.

The others cheered.

"No!" the woman said, and tried to push him away. She was drunk, but not helpless.

Igor was a short, wiry man of unexpected strength. He pushed her up against the wall and grabbed her wrists. "Come on," he said. "One soldier's as good as another."

The woman struggled, but two other soldiers grabbed her and held her still.

Her original partner said: "Hey, leave her alone!"

"You've had your turn—now it's mine," said Igor, unbuttoning.

Grigori was revolted by this scene. "Stop it!" he shouted.

Igor gave him a challenging look. "Are you giving me an order as an officer, Grigori Sergeivich?"

"Not as an officer—as a human being!" Grigori said. "Come on, Igor, you can see she doesn't want you. There are plenty more women."

"I want this one." Igor looked around. "We all want this one—don't we, boys?"

Grigori stepped forward and stood with his hands on his hips. "Are you men, or dogs?" he cried. "The woman said no!" He put his arm around the angry Igor. "Tell me something, comrade," he said. "Is there anywhere around here where a man can get a drink?"

Igor grinned, the soldiers cheered, and the woman slipped away.

Grigori said: "I see a small hotel across the street. Shall we ask the proprietor whether, by any chance, he has any vodka?"

The men cheered again, and they all went into the hotel.

In the lobby a frightened proprietor was serving free beer. Grigori thought he was wise. It took men longer to drink beer than vodka, and they were less likely to become violent.

He accepted a glass and drank a mouthful. His elation had vanished. He felt as if he had been drunk and sobered up. The incident with the woman in the doorway had appalled him, and the small boy firing the machine pistol had been horrendous. Revolution was not a simple matter of throwing off your chains. There were dangers in arming the people. Allowing soldiers to commandeer the cars of the bourgeoisie was almost as lethal. Even the apparently harmless freedom to kiss anyone who took your fancy had led, in a few hours, to Grigori's platoon attempting a gang rape.

It could not go on.

There had to be order. Grigori did not want to go back to the old days, of course. The tsar had given them bread queues, brutal police, and soldiers without boots. But there had to be freedom without chaos.

Grigori mumbled an excuse about needing to piss and slipped away from his men. He walked back the way he had come along Nevsky Prospekt. The people had won today's battle. The tsar's police and army officers had been defeated. But if that led only to an orgy of violence, it would not be long before people clamored for a return of the old regime.

Who was in charge? The Duma had defied the tsar and refused to close, according to what Kerensky had told Grigori yesterday. The parliament was more or less impotent, but at least it symbolized democracy. Grigori decided to go to the Tauride Palace and see if anything was happening there.

He walked north to the river, then east to the Tauride Gardens. Night had fallen by the time he got there. The classical façade of the palace had dozens of windows, and they were all lit up. Several thousand people had had the same idea as Grigori, and the broad front courtyard was crammed with soldiers and workers milling around.

A man with a megaphone was making an announcement, repeating it over and over again. Grigori worked his way to the front so that he could hear.

"The Workers' Group of the War Industry Committee has been released from the Kresty Prison," the man shouted.

Grigori was not sure who they were, but their name sounded good.

"Together with other comrades, they have formed the provisional executive committee of the Soviet of Workers' Deputies."

Grigori liked that idea. A soviet was a council of representatives. There had been a St. Petersburg soviet in 1905. Grigori had been only sixteen at the time, but he knew the soviet had been elected by factory workers and had organized strikes. It had had a charismatic leader, Leon Trotsky, since exiled.

"All of this will be officially announced in a special edition of the newspaper *Izvestiia*. The executive committee has formed a food supply commission to ensure that workers and soldiers are fed. It has also created a military commission to defend the revolution."

There was no mention of the Duma. The crowd was cheering, but Grigori wondered whether soldiers would take orders from a self-elected military commission. Where was the democracy in all this?

His question was answered by the final sentence of the announcement.

"The committee appeals to workers and soldiers to elect representatives to the soviet as quickly as possible, and to send their representatives here to the palace to take part in the new revolutionary government!"

That was what Grigori had wanted to hear. The new revolutionary government—a soviet of workers and soldiers. Now there would be change without disorder. Full of enthusiasm, he left the courtyard and headed back toward the barracks. Sooner or later, the men would come back to their beds. He could hardly wait to tell them the news.

Then, for the first time, they would have an election.

{ IV }

On the morning of the next day, the First Machine Gun Regiment gathered on the parade ground to elect a representative to the Petrograd soviet. Isaak proposed Sergeant Grigori Peshkov.

He was elected unopposed.

Grigori was pleased. He knew what life was like for soldiers and workers, and he would bring the machine-oil smell of real life to the corridors of power. He would never forget his roots and put on a top hat. He would make sure that unrest led to improvements, not to random violence. Now he had a real chance to make a better life for Katerina and Vladimir.

He walked quickly across the Liteiny Bridge, alone this time, and headed for the Tauride Palace. His urgent priority had to be bread. Katerina, Vladimir, and the other two and a half million inhabitants of Petrograd had to eat. And now, as he assumed responsibility—at least in his imagination—he began to feel daunted. The farmers and the millers in the countryside had to send more flour to the Petrograd bakers immediately—but they would not do so unless they were paid. How was the soviet going to make sure there was enough money? He began to wonder whether overthrowing the government might have been the easy part.

The palace had a long central façade and two wings. Grigori discovered that both the Duma and the soviet were in session. Appropriately, the Duma—the old middle-class parliament—was in the right wing and the soviet in the left. But who was in charge? No one knew. That would have to be resolved first, Grigori thought impatiently, before they could start on the real problems.

On the steps of the palace Grigori spotted the broomstick figure and bushy black hair of Konstantin. He realized with a shock that he had not made any attempt to tell Konstantin of the death of Varya, his mother. But he saw immediately that Konstantin knew. As well as his red armband, Konstantin was wearing a black scarf tied around his hat.

Grigori embraced him. "I saw it happen," he said.

"Was it you who killed the police sniper?"

"Yes."

"Thank you. But her real revenge will be the revolution."

Konstantin had been elected as one of two deputies from the Putilov works. During the afternoon more and more deputies arrived until, by early evening, there were three thousand of them crammed into the huge Catherine Hall. Nearly all were soldiers. Troops were already organized into regiments and platoons, and Grigori guessed it had been easier for them to arrange elections than for the factory workers, many of whom were locked out of their workplaces. Some deputies had been elected by a few dozen people, others by thousands. Democracy was not as simple as it seemed.

Someone proposed that they should rename themselves the Petrograd Soviet of Workers' and Soldiers' Deputies, and the idea was approved by thunderous applause. There seemed to be no procedure. There was no agenda, no proposing or seconding of resolutions, no voting mechanism. People just stood up and spoke, often more than one at a time. On the platform, several suspiciously middle-class-looking men were scribbling notes, and Grigori guessed these were the members of the executive committee formed yesterday. At least someone was taking minutes.

Despite the worrying chaos, there was tremendous excitement. They all felt they had fought a battle and won. For better or worse, they were making a new world.

But no one was talking about bread. Frustrated by the inaction of the soviet, Grigori and Konstantin left the Catherine Hall during a particularly chaotic moment and walked across the palace to find out what the Duma was up to. On the way they saw troops with red armbands stockpiling food and ammunition in the hallway as if for a siege. Of course, Grigori thought, the tsar is not simply going to accept what has happened. At some point he will try to regain control by force. And that would mean attacking this building.

In the right wing they came across Count Maklakov, a director of the Putilov works. He was a delegate for a right-of-center party, but he spoke to them politely enough. He told them that yet another committee had been formed, the Temporary Committee of Duma Members for the Restoration of Order in the Capital and the Establishment of Relations with Individuals and Institutions. Despite its ludicrous title, Grigori felt it was an ominous attempt by the Duma to take control. He became more worried when Maklakov told him the committee had appointed a Colonel Engelhardt as commandant of Petrograd.

"Yes," said Maklakov with satisfaction. "And they have instructed all soldiers to return to barracks and obey orders."

"What?" Grigori was shocked. "But that would destroy the revolution. The tsar's officers would regain control!"

"The members of the Duma do not believe there is a revolution."

"The members of the Duma are idiots," Grigori said angrily.

Maklakov put his nose in the air and walked away.

Konstantin shared Grigori's anger. "This is a counterrevolution!" he said.

"And it must be stopped," said Grigori.

They hurried back to the left wing. In the big hall, a chairman was attempting to control a debate. Grigori leaped onto the platform. "I have an emergency announcement!" he shouted.

"Everyone has," said the chairman wearily. "But what the hell, go ahead."

"The Duma is ordering soldiers to return to barracks—and to accept the authority of their officers!"

A shout of protest went up from the delegates.

"Comrades!" Grigori shouted, trying to quiet them. "We are not going back to the old ways!"

They roared their agreement.

"The people of the city must have bread. Our women must feel safe on the streets. The factories must reopen and the mills must roll—but not in the same old way."

They were listening to him now, unsure where he was going.

"We soldiers must stop beating up the bourgeoisie, stop harassing women on the street, and stop looting wine shops. We must return to our barracks, sober up, and resume our duties, but"—he paused dramatically—"under our own conditions!"

There was a rumble of assent.

"What should those conditions be?"

Someone shouted: "Elected committees to issue orders, instead of officers!"

Another said: "No more 'Your Excellency' and 'Most High Radiance'— they should be called Colonel and General."

"No saluting!" cried another.

Grigori did not know what to do. Everyone had his own suggestion. He could not hear them all, let alone remember them.

The chairman came to his rescue. "I propose that all those with suggestions should form a group with Comrade Sokolov." Grigori knew that Nikolai Sokolov was a left-wing lawyer. That's good, he thought—we need someone to draft our proposal in correct legal terms. The chairman went on: "When you have agreed what you want, bring your proposal to the soviet for approval."

"Right." Grigori jumped off the platform. Sokolov was sitting at a small table to one side of the hall. Grigori and Konstantin approached him, along with a dozen or more deputies.

"Very well," said Sokolov. "Who is this addressed to?"

Grigori was baffled again. He was about so say *To the world.* But a soldier said: "To the Petrograd Garrison."

Another said: "And all the soldiers of the guard, army, and artillery."

"And the fleet," said someone else.

"Very good," said Sokolov, writing. "For immediate and precise execution, I presume?"

"Yes."

"And to the workers of Petrograd for information?"

Grigori became impatient. "Yes, yes," he said. "Now, who proposed elected committees?"

"That was me," said a soldier with a gray mustache. He sat on the edge of the table directly in front of Sokolov. As if giving dictation, he said: "All troops should set up committees of their elected representatives."

Sokolov, still writing, said: "In all companies, battalions, regiments . . . "

Someone added: "Depots, batteries, squadrons, warships . . . "

The gray mustache said: "Those who have not yet elected deputies must do so."

"Right," said Grigori impatiently. "Now. Weapons of all kinds, including armored cars, are under the control of the battalion and company committees, not the officers."

Several of the soldiers voiced their agreement.

"Very good," said Sokolov.

Grigori went on: "A military unit is subordinate to the Soviet of Workers' and Soldiers' Deputies and its committees."

For the first time, Sokolov looked up. "That would mean the soviet controls the army."

"Yes," said Grigori. "The orders of the military commission of the Duma are to be followed only when they do not contradict the decisions of the soviet."

Sokolov continued to look at Grigori. "This makes the Duma as powerless as it always was. Before, it was subject to the whim of the tsar. Now, every decision will require the approval of the soviet."

"Exactly," said Grigori.

"So the soviet is supreme."

"Write it down," said Grigori.

Sokolov wrote it down.

Someone said: "Officers are forbidden to be rude to other ranks."

"All right," said Sokolov.

"And must not address them as *tyi* as if we were animals or children."

Grigori thought these clauses were trivial. "The document needs a title," he said.

Sokolov said: "What do you suggest?"

"How have you headed previous orders by the soviet?"

"There are no previous orders," said Sokolov. "This is the first."

"That's it, then," said Grigori. "Call it 'Order Number One.'"

{ V }

It gave Grigori profound satisfaction to have passed his first piece of legislation as an elected representative. Over the next two days there were several more, and he became deeply absorbed in the minute-by-minute work of a revolutionary government. But he thought all the time about Katerina and Vladimir, and on Thursday evening he at last got a chance to slip away and check on them.

His heart was full of foreboding as he walked to the southwest suburbs. Katerina had promised to stay away from trouble, but the women of Petrograd believed this was their revolution as much as the men's. After all, it had started on International Women's Day. This was nothing new. Grigori's mother had died in the failed revolution of 1905. If Katerina had decided to go into the city center with Vladimir on her hip to see what was going on, she would not have been the only mother to do so. And many innocent people had died—shot by the police, trampled in crowds, run over by drunk soldiers in commandeered cars, or hit by stray bullets. As he entered the old house, he dreaded being met by one of the tenants, with a solemn face and tears in her eyes, saying *Something terrible has happened.*

He went up the stairs, tapped on her door, and walked in. Katerina leaped from her chair and threw herself into his arms. "You're alive!" she said. She kissed him eagerly. "I've been so worried! I don't know what we would do without you."

"I'm sorry I couldn't come sooner," Grigori said. "But I'm a delegate to the soviet."

"A delegate!" Katerina beamed with pride. "My husband!" She hugged him.

Grigori had actually impressed her. He had never done that before. "A delegate is only a representative of the people who elected him," he said modestly.

"But they always choose the cleverest and most reliable."

"Well, they try to."

The room was dimly lit by an oil lamp. Grigori put a parcel on the table. With his new status he had no trouble getting food from the barracks kitchen. "There are some matches and a blanket in there, too," he said.

"Thank you!"

"I hope you've been staying indoors as much as you can. It's still dangerous on the streets. Some of us are making a revolution, but others are just going wild."

"I've hardly been out. I've been waiting to hear from you."

"How's our little boy?" Vladimir was asleep in the corner.

"He misses his daddy."

She meant Grigori. It was not Grigori's wish that Vladimir should call him Daddy, but he had accepted Katerina's fancy. It was not likely that any of them would ever see Lev again—there had been no word from him for almost three years—so the child would never know the truth, and perhaps that was better.

Katerina said: "I'm sorry he's asleep. He loves to see you."

"I'll talk to him in the morning."

"You can stay the night? How wonderful!"

Grigori sat down, and Katerina knelt in front of him and pulled off his boots. "You look tired," she said.

"I am."

"Let's go to bed. It's late."

She began to unbutton his tunic, and he sat back and let her. "General Khabalov is hiding out in the Admiralty," he said. "We were afraid he might recapture the railway stations, but he didn't even try."

"Why not?"

Grigori shrugged. "Cowardice. The tsar ordered Ivanov to march on Petrograd and set up a military dictatorship, but Ivanov's men became mutinous and the expedition was canceled."

Katerina frowned. "Has the old ruling class just given up?"

"It seems that way. Strange, isn't it? But clearly there isn't going to be a counterrevolution."

They got into bed, Grigori in his underwear, Katerina with her dress still on. She had never stripped naked in front of him. Perhaps she felt she had to hold something back. It was a peculiarity of hers that he accepted, not without regret. He took her in his arms and kissed her. When he entered her, she said: "I love you," and he felt he was the luckiest man in the world.

Afterward she said sleepily: "What will happen next?"

"There's going to be a constituent assembly, elected by what they called the four-tail suffrage: universal, direct, secret, and equal. Meanwhile the Duma is forming a provisional government."

"Who will be its leader?"

"Lvov."

Katerina sat upright. "A prince! Why?"

"They want the confidence of all classes."

"To hell with all classes!" Indignation made her even more beautiful, bringing color to her face and a sparkle to her eyes. "The workers and soldiers have made the revolution—why do we need the confidence of anyone else?"

This question had bothered Grigori, too, but the answer had convinced him. "We need businessmen to reopen factories, wholesalers to recommence supplying the city, shopkeepers to open their doors again."

"And what about the tsar?"

"The Duma is demanding his abdication. They have sent two delegates to Pskov to tell him so."

Katerina was wide-eyed. "Abdication? The tsar? But that would be the end."

"Yes."

"Is it possible?"

"I don't know," said Grigori. "We'll find out tomorrow."

{ VI }

In the Catherine Hall of the Tauride Palace on Friday, the debate was desultory. Two or three thousand men and a few women packed the room, and the air was full of tobacco smoke and the smell of unwashed soldiers. They were waiting to hear what the tsar would do.

The debate was frequently interrupted for announcements. Often they were less than urgent—a soldier would stand up to say that his battalion had formed a committee and arrested the colonel. Sometimes they were not even announcements, but speeches calling for the defense of the revolution.

But Grigori knew something was different when a gray-haired sergeant jumped onto the platform, pink-faced and breathless, with a sheet of paper in his hand, and called for silence.

Slowly and loudly he said: "The tsar has signed a document . . ."

The cheering began after those few words.

The sergeant raised his voice: ". . . abdicating the crown . . ."

The cheer rose to a roar. Grigori was electrified. Had it really happened? Had the dream come true?

The sergeant held up his hand for quiet. He had not yet finished.

". . . and because of the poor health of his twelve-year-old son, Alexei, he has named as his successor the grand duke Mikhail, the tsar's younger brother."

The cheers turned to howls of protest. "No!" Grigori shouted, and his voice was lost among thousands.

When after several minutes they began to quieten, a greater roar was heard from outside. The crowd in the courtyard must have heard the same news, and were receiving it with the same indignation.

Grigori said to Konstantin: "The provisional government must not accept this."

"Agreed," said Konstantin. "Let's go and tell them so."

They left the soviet and crossed the palace. The ministers of the newly formed government were meeting in the room where the old temporary committee had met—indeed, they were to a worrying degree the same men. They were already discussing the tsar's statement.

Pavel Miliukov was on his feet. The monocled moderate was arguing that the monarchy had to be preserved as a symbol of legitimacy. "Horseshit," Grigori muttered. The monarchy symbolized incompetence, cruelty, and defeat, but not legitimacy. Fortunately, others felt the same way. Kerensky, who was now minister of justice, proposed that Grand Duke Mikhail should be told to refuse the crown, and to Grigori's relief the majority agreed.

Kerensky and Prince Lvov were mandated to go to see Mikhail immediately. Miliukov glared through his monocle and said: "And I should go with them, to represent the minority view!"

Grigori assumed this foolish suggestion would be trodden upon, but the other ministers weakly assented. At that point Grigori stood up. Without forethought he said: "And I shall accompany the ministers as an observer from the Petrograd soviet."

"Very well, very well," said Kerensky wearily.

They left the palace by a side door and got into two waiting Renault limousines. The former president of the Duma, the hugely fat Mikhail Rodzianko, also came. Grigori could not quite believe this was happening to him. He was part of a delegation going to order a crown prince to refuse to become tsar. Less than a week ago he had got down from a table because Lieutenant Kirillov had ordered him to. The world was changing so fast it was hard to keep up.

Grigori had never been inside the home of a wealthy aristocrat, and it was like entering a dream world. The large house was stuffed with possessions. Everywhere he looked there were gorgeous vases, elaborate clocks, silver candelabra, and jeweled ornaments. If he had grabbed a golden bowl and run out of the front door, he could have sold it for enough money to buy himself a house—except that right now no one was buying golden bowls. They just wanted bread.

Prince Georgy Lvov, a silver-haired man with a huge bushy beard, clearly was not impressed by the decor, nor intimidated by the solemnity of his errand, but everyone else seemed nervous. They waited in the drawing room, frowned upon by ancestral portraits, shuffling their feet on the thick rugs.

At last Grand Duke Mikhail appeared. He was a prematurely balding man of thirty-eight with a little mustache. To Grigori's surprise he appeared to be more nervous than the delegation. He seemed shy and bewildered, despite a haughty tilt to his head. He eventually summoned enough courage to say: "What do you have to tell me?"

Lvov replied: "We have come to ask you not to accept the crown."

"Oh, dear," said Mikhail, and seemed not to know what to do next.

Kerensky retained his presence of mind. He spoke clearly and firmly. "The people of Petrograd have reacted with outrage to the decision of His Majesty the tsar," he said. "Already a huge contingent of soldiers is marching on the Tauride Palace. There will be a violent uprising followed by a civil war unless we announce immediately that you have refused to take over as tsar."

"Oh, my goodness," said Mikhail mildly.

The grand duke was not very bright, Grigori realized. Why am I surprised? he thought. If these people were intelligent they would not be on the point of losing the throne of Russia.

The monocled Miliukov said: "Your Royal Highness, I represent the minority view in the provisional government. In our opinion, the monarchy is the only symbol of authority accepted by the people."

Mikhail looked even more bewildered. The last thing he needed was a choice, Grigori thought; that only made matters worse. The grand duke said: "Would you mind if I had a word alone with Rodzianko? No, don't all leave—we will just retire to a side room."

When the dithering tsar-designate and the fat president had left, the others talked in low voices. No one spoke to Grigori. He was the only working-class man in the room, and he sensed they were a bit frightened of him, suspecting—rightly—that the pockets of his sergeant's uniform were stuffed with guns and ammunition.

Rodzianko reappeared. "He asked me whether we could guarantee his personal safety if he became tsar," he said. Grigori was disgusted but not surprised that the grand duke was concerned about himself rather than his country. "I told him we could not," Rodzianko finished.

Kerensky said: "And . . . ?"

"He will rejoin us in a moment."

There was a pause that seemed endless; then Mikhail came back. They all fell silent. For a long moment, no one said anything.

At last Mikhail said: "I have decided to decline the crown."

Grigori's heart seemed to stop. Eight days, he thought. Eight days ago the women of Vyborg marched across the Liteiny Bridge. Today the rule of the Romanovs has ended.

He recalled the words of his mother on the day she died: "I will not rest until Russia is a republic." Rest now, Mother, he thought.

Kerensky was shaking the grand duke's hand and saying something pompous, but Grigori was not listening.

We have done it, he thought. We made a revolution.

We have deposed the tsar.

{ VII }

In Berlin, Otto von Ulrich opened a magnum of the 1892 Perrier-Jouët champagne.

The von Ulrichs had invited the von der Helbards to lunch. Monika's father, Konrad, was a *Graf*, or count, and her mother was therefore a *Gräfin*, or countess. Gräfin Eva von der Helbard was a formidable woman with gray hair piled in an elaborate coiffure. Before lunch she cornered Walter and told him that Monika was an accomplished violin player and had been top of her school class in all subjects. Out of the corner of his eye he saw his father talking to Monika, and guessed she was getting a school report about him.

He was irritated with his parents for persisting in foisting Monika on him. The fact that he found himself strongly attracted to her made matters worse. She was intelligent as well as beautiful. Her hair was always carefully dressed, but he could not help imagining her unpinning it at night and shaking her head to liberate her curls. Sometimes, these days, he found it hard to picture Maud.

Now Otto raised his glass. "Good-bye to the tsar!" he said.

"I'm surprised at you, Father," said Walter irritably. "Are you really celebrating the overthrow of a legitimate monarch by a mob of factory workers and mutinous soldiers?"

Otto went red in the face. Walter's sister, Greta, patted her father's arm soothingly. "Take no notice, Daddy," she said. "Walter just says these things to annoy you."

Konrad said: "I got to know Tsar Nicholas when I was at our embassy in Petrograd."

Walter said: "And what did you think of him, sir?"

Monika answered for her father. Giving Walter a conspiratorial grin, she said: "Daddy used to say that if the tsar had been born to a different station in life, he might, with an effort, have become a competent postman."

"This is the tragedy of inherited monarchy." Walter turned to his father. "But you must surely disapprove of democracy in Russia."

"Democracy?" said Otto derisively. "We shall see. All we know is that the new prime minister is a liberal aristocrat."

Monika said to Walter: "Do you think Prince Lvov will try to make peace with us?"

It was the question of the hour. "I hope so," said Walter, trying not to look at Monika's breasts. "If all our troops on the eastern front could be switched to France, we could overrun the Allies."

She raised her glass and looked over its rim into Walter's eyes. "Then let's drink to that," she said.

✳

In a cold, wet trench in northeastern France, Billy's platoon was drinking gin.

The bottle had been produced by Robin Mortimer, the cashiered officer. "I've been saving this," he said.

"Well, knock me down with a feather," said Billy, using one of Mildred's expressions. Mortimer was a surly beggar and had never been known to buy anyone a drink.

Mortimer splashed liquor into their mess tins. "Here's to bloody revolution," he said, and they all drank, then held out their tins for refills.

Billy had been in high spirits even before drinking the gin. The Russians had proved it was still possible to overthrow tyrants.

They were singing "The Red Flag" when Earl Fitzherbert came limping around the traverse, splashing through the mud. He was a colonel now, and more arrogant than ever. "Be quiet, you men!" he shouted.

The singing died down gradually.

Billy said: "We're celebrating the overthrow of the tsar of Russia!"

Fitz said angrily: "He was a legitimate monarch, and those who deposed him are criminals. No more singing."

Billy's contempt for Fitz went up a notch. "He was a tyrant who murdered thousands of his subjects, and all civilized men are rejoicing today."

Fitz looked more closely at him. The earl no longer wore an eye patch, but his left eyelid had a permanent droop. However, it did not seem to affect his eyesight. "Sergeant Williams—I might have guessed. I know you—and your family."

And how, Billy thought.

"Your sister's a peace agitator."

"So's yours, sir," said Billy, and Robin Mortimer laughed raucously, then shut up suddenly.

Fitz said to Billy: "One more insolent word out of you and you'll be on a charge."

"Sorry, sir," said Billy.

"Now calm down, all of you. And no more singing." Fitz walked away.

Billy said quietly: "Long live the revolution."

Fitz pretended not to hear.

❋

In London, Princess Bea screamed: "No!"

"Try to stay calm," said Maud, who had just told her the news.

"They cannot!" Bea screamed. "They cannot make our beloved tsar abdicate! He is the father of his people!"

"It may be for the best—"

"I don't believe you! It's a wicked lie!"

The door opened and Grout put his head in, looking worried.

Bea picked up a Japanese bottle-vase containing an arrangement of dried grasses and hurled it across the room. It hit the wall and smashed.

Maud patted Bea's shoulder. "There, there," she said. She was not sure what else to do. She herself was delighted that the tsar had been overthrown, but all the same she sympathized with Bea, for whom an entire way of life had been destroyed.

Grout crooked a finger and a maid came in, looking frightened. He pointed at the broken vase, and the maid began to pick up the pieces.

The tea things were on a table: cups, saucers, teapots, jugs of milk and cream, bowls of sugar. Bea swept them all violently to the floor. "Those revolutionaries are going to kill everyone!"

The butler knelt down and began to clear up the mess.

"Don't excite yourself," Maud said.

Bea began to cry. "The poor tsaritsa! And her children! What will become of them?"

"Perhaps you should lie down for a while," Maud said. "Come on, I'll walk you to your room." She took Bea's elbow, and Bea allowed herself to be led away.

"It's the end of everything," Bea sobbed.

"Never mind," said Maud. "Perhaps it's a new beginning."

Ethel and Bernie were in Aberowen. It was a sort of honeymoon. Ethel was enjoying showing Bernie the places of her childhood: the pithead, the chapel, the school. She even showed him around Tŷ Gwyn—Fitz and Bea were not in residence—though she did not take him to the Gardenia Suite.

They were staying with the Griffiths family, who had again offered Ethel Tommy's room, which saved disturbing Gramper. They were in Mrs. Griffiths's kitchen when her husband, Len, atheist and revolutionary socialist, burst in waving a newspaper. "The tsar have abdicated!" he said.

They all cheered and clapped. For a week they had been hearing of riots in Petrograd, and Ethel had been wondering how it would end.

Bernie asked: "Who's took over?"

"Provisional government under Prince Lvov," said Len.

"Not quite a triumph for socialism, then," said Bernie.

"No."

Ethel said: "Cheer up, you men—one thing at a time! Let's go to the Two Crowns and celebrate. I'll leave Lloyd with Mrs. Ponti for a while."

The women put on their hats and they all went to the pub. Within an hour the place was crammed. Ethel was astonished to see her mother and father come in. Mrs. Griffiths saw them, too, and said: "What the 'ell are they doing here?"

A few minutes later, Ethel's da stood on a chair and called for quiet. "I know some of you are surprised to see me here, but special occasions call for special actions." He showed them a pint glass. "I haven't changed my habits of a lifetime, but the landlord has been kind enough to give me a glass of tap water." They all laughed. "I'm here to share with my neighbors the triumph that have took place in Russia." He held up his glass. "A toast—to the revolution!"

They all cheered and drank.

"Well!" said Ethel. "Da in the Two Crowns! I never thought I'd see the day."

❋

In Josef Vyalov's ultramodern prairie house in Buffalo, Lev Peshkov helped himself to a drink from the cocktail cabinet. He no longer drank vodka. Living with his wealthy father-in-law, he had developed a taste for Scotch whisky. He liked it the way Americans drank it, with lumps of ice.

Lev did not like living with his in-laws. He would have preferred for Olga and him to have a place of their own. But Olga liked it this way, and her father paid for everything. Until Lev could build up a stash of his own he was stuck.

Josef was reading the paper and Lena was sewing. Lev raised his glass to them. "Long live the revolution!" he said exuberantly.

"Watch your words," said Josef. "It's going to be bad for business."

Olga came in. "Pour me a little glass of sherry, please, darling," she said.

Lev suppressed a sigh. She loved to ask him to perfom little services, and in front of her parents he could not refuse. He poured sweet sherry into a small glass and handed it to her, bowing like a waiter. She smiled prettily, missing the irony.

He drank a mouthful of Scotch and savored the taste and the burn of it.

Mrs. Vyalov said: "I feel sorry for the poor tsaritsa and her children. What will they do?"

Josef said: "They'll all be killed by the mob, I shouldn't wonder."

"Poor things. What did the tsar ever do to those revolutionaries, to deserve this?"

"I can answer that question," Lev said. He knew he should shut up, but he could not, especially with whisky warming his guts. "When I was eleven years old, the factory where my mother worked went on strike."

Mrs. Vyalov tutted. She did not believe in strikes.

"The police rounded up all the children of the strikers. I'll never forget it. I was terrified."

"Why would they do a thing like that?" said Mrs. Vyalov.

"The police flogged us all," Lev said. "On our bottoms, with canes. To teach our parents a lesson."

Mrs. Vyalov had gone white. She could not bear cruelty to children or animals.

"That's what the tsar and his regime did to me, Mother," said Lev. He clinked ice in his glass. "That's why I toast the revolution."

✳

"What do you think, Gus?" said President Wilson. "You're the only person around here who's actually been to Petrograd. What's going to happen?"

"I hate to sound like a State Department official, but it could go either way," said Gus.

The president laughed. They were in the Oval Office, Wilson behind the desk, Gus standing in front of it. "Come on," Wilson said. "Take a guess. Will the Russians pull out of the war or not? It's the most important question of the year."

"Okay. All the ministers in the new government belong to scary-sounding political parties with *socialist* and *revolutionary* in their names, but in fact they're middle-class businessmen and professionals. What they really want is a bourgeois revolution that gives them freedom to promote industry and commerce. But the people want bread, peace, and land: bread for the factory workers, peace for the soldiers, and land for the peasants. None of that really appeals to men like Lvov and

Kerensky. So, to answer your question, I think Lvov's government will try for gradual change. In particular, they will carry on fighting the war. But the workers will not be satisfied."

"And who will win in the end?"

Gus recalled his trip to St. Petersburg, and the man who had demonstrated the casting of a locomotive wheel in a dirty, tumbledown foundry at the Putilov factory. Later, Gus had seen the same man in a fight with a cop over some girl. He could not remember the man's name, but he could picture him now, his big shoulders and strong arms, one finger a stump, but most of all his fierce blue-eyed look of unstoppable determination. "The Russian people," Gus said. "They will win in the end."

CHAPTER TWENTY-FOUR

April 1917

On a mild day in early spring Walter walked with Monika von der Helbard in the garden of her parents' town house in Berlin. It was a grand house and the garden was large, with a tennis pavilion, a bowling green, a riding school for exercising horses, and a children's playground with swings and a slide. Walter remembered coming here as a child and thinking it was paradise. However, it was no longer an idyllic playground. All but the oldest horses had gone to the army. Chickens scratched on the flagstones of the broad terrace. Monika's mother was fattening a pig in the tennis pavilion. Goats grazed the bowling green, and it was rumored that the *Gräfin* milked them herself.

However, the old trees were coming into leaf, the sun was shining, and Walter was in his waistcoat and shirtsleeves with his coat slung over his shoulder—a state of undress that would have displeased his mother, but she was in the house, gossiping with the *Gräfin*. His sister, Greta, had been walking with Walter and Monika, but she had made an excuse and left them alone—another thing Mother would have deplored, at least in theory.

Monika had a dog called Pierre. It was a standard poodle, long-legged and graceful, with a lot of curly rust-colored hair and light brown eyes, and Walter could not help thinking that it looked a little like Monika, beautiful though she was.

He liked the way she acted with her dog. She did not pet it or feed it scraps or talk to it in a baby voice, as some girls did. She just let it walk at her heel, and occasionally threw an old tennis ball for it to fetch.

"It's so disappointing about the Russians," she said.

Walter nodded. Prince Lvov's government had announced they would continue to fight. Germany's eastern front was not to be relieved, and there would be no reinforcements for France. The war would drag on. "Our only hope now is that Lvov's government will fall and the peace faction will take over," Walter said.

"Is that likely?"

"It's hard to say. The left revolutionaries are still demanding bread, peace, and land. The government has promised a democratic election for a constituent assembly—but who will win?" He picked up a twig and threw it for Pierre. The dog bounded after it, and proudly brought it back. Walter bent down to pat its head, and when he straightened up Monika was very close to him.

"I like you, Walter," she said, looking very directly at him with her amber eyes. "I feel as if we would never run out of things to talk about."

He had the same feeling, and he knew that if he tried to kiss her now, she would let him.

He stepped away. "I like you, too," he said. "And I like your dog." He laughed, to show that he was speaking lightheartedly.

All the same he could see that she was hurt. She bit her lip and turned away. She had been about as bold as was possible for a well-brought-up girl, and he had rejected her.

They walked on. After a long silence Monika said: "What is your secret, I wonder?"

My God, he thought, she's sharp. "I have no secrets," he lied. "Do you?"

"None worth telling." She reached up and brushed something off his shoulder. "A bee," she said.

"It's too soon in the year for bees."

"Perhaps we shall have an early summer."

"It's not that warm."

She pretended to shiver. "You're right. It's chilly. Would you fetch me a wrap? If you go to the kitchen and ask a maid, she will find one."

"Of course." It was not chilly, but a gentleman never refused such a request, no matter how whimsical. She obviously wanted a minute alone. He strolled back to the house. He had to spurn her advances, but he was sorry to hurt her. They *were* well suited—their mothers were quite right— and clearly Monika could not understand why he kept pushing her away.

He entered the house and went down the back stairs to the basement, where he found an elderly housemaid in a black dress and a lace cap. She went off to look for a shawl.

Walter waited in the hall. The house was decorated in the up-to-date *Jugendstil*, which did away with the rococo flourishes loved by Walter's parents and favored well-lit rooms with gentle colors. The pillared hall was all cool gray marble and mushroom-colored carpet.

It seemed to him as if Maud was a million miles away on another planet. And in a way she was, for the prewar world would never come back. He had not seen his wife nor heard from her for almost three years, and he might never meet her again. Although she had not faded from his mind—he would never forget the passion they had shared—he did find, to his distress, that he could no longer recall the fine details of their times together: what she was wearing, where they were when they kissed or held hands, or what they ate and drank and talked about when they met at those endlessly similar London parties. Sometimes it crossed his mind that the war had in a way divorced them. But he pushed the thought aside: it was shamefully disloyal.

The maid brought him a yellow cashmere shawl. He returned to Monika, who was sitting on a tree stump with Pierre at her feet. Walter gave her the shawl and she put it around her shoulders. The color suited her, making her eyes gleam and her skin glow.

She had a strange look on her face, and she handed him his wallet. "This must have fallen out of your coat," she said.

"Oh, thank you." He returned it to the inside pocket of the coat that he still had slung over his shoulder.

She said: "Let's go back to the house."

"As you wish."

Her mood had changed. Perhaps she had simply decided to give up on him. Or had something else happened?

He was struck by a frightening thought. Had his wallet really fallen out of his coat? Or had she taken it, like a pickpocket, when she brushed that unlikely bee off his shoulder? "Monika," he said, and he stopped and turned to face her. "Did you look inside my wallet?"

"You said you had no secrets," she said, and she blushed bright red.

She must have seen the newspaper clipping he carried: *Lady Maud Fitzherbert is always dressed in the latest fashion.* "That was most ill-mannered of you," he said angrily. He was mainly angry with himself. He should not have kept the incriminating photo. If Monika could figure out its significance, so could others. Then he would be disgraced and drummed out of the army. He might be accused of treason and jailed or even shot.

He had been foolish. But he knew he would never throw the picture away. It was all he had of Maud.

Monika put a hand on his arm. "I have never done anything like that in my whole life, and I'm ashamed. But you must see that I was desperate. Oh, Walter, I could fall in love with you so easily, and I can tell that you could love me, too—I can see it, in your eyes and the way you smile when you see me. But you said nothing!" There were tears in her eyes. "It was driving me out of my mind."

"I'm sorry for that." He could no longer feel indignant. She had now gone beyond the bounds of propriety, and opened her heart to him. He felt terribly sad for her, sad for both of them.

"I just had to understand why you kept turning away from me. Now I do, of course. She's beautiful. She even looks a bit like me." She wiped her tears. "She found you before I did, that's all." She stared at him with those penetrating amber eyes. "I suppose you're engaged."

He could not lie to someone who was being so honest with him. He did not know what to say.

She guessed the reason for his hesitation. "Oh, my goodness!" she said. "You're married, aren't you?"

This was disastrous. "If people found out, I would be in serious trouble."

"I know."

"I hope I may trust you to keep my secret?"

"How can you ask?" she said. "You're the best man I've ever met. I wouldn't do anything to harm you. I will never breathe a word."

"Thank you. I know you'll keep your promise."

She looked away, fighting back the tears. "Let's go inside."

In the hall she said: "You go ahead. I must wash my face."

"All right."

"I hope—" Her voice broke into a sob. "I hope she knows how lucky she is," she whispered. Then she turned away and slipped into a side room.

Walter put on his coat and composed himself, then went up the marble staircase. The drawing room was done in the same understated style, with blond wood and pale blue-green curtains. Monika's parents had better taste than his, he decided.

His mother looked at him and knew instantly something was wrong. "Where is Monika?" she said sharply.

He raised an eyebrow at her. It was not like her to ask a question to which the answer might be *Gone to the toilet.* She was obviously tense. He said quietly: "She will join us in a few minutes."

"Look at this," said his father, waving a sheet of paper. "Zimmermann's office just sent it to me for my comments. Those Russian revolutionaries want to cross Germany. The nerve!" He had had a couple of glasses of schnapps, and was in an exuberant mood.

Walter said politely: "Which revolutionaries would those be, Father?" He did not really care, but was grateful for a topic of conversation.

"The ones in Zurich! Martov and Lenin and that crowd. There's supposed to be freedom of speech in Russia, now that the tsar has been deposed, so they want to go home. But they can't get there!"

Monika's father, Konrad von der Helbard, said thoughtfully: "I suppose they can't. There's no way to get from Switzerland to Russia without passing through Germany—any other overland route would involve crossing battle lines. But there are still steamers going from England across the North Sea to Sweden, aren't there?"

Walter said: "Yes, but they won't risk going via Britain. The British detained Trotsky and Bukharin. And France or Italy would be worse."

"So they're stuck!" said Otto triumphantly.

Walter said: "What will you advise Foreign Minister Zimmermann to do, Father?"

"Refuse, of course. We don't want that filth contaminating our folk. Who knows what kind of trouble those devils would stir up in Germany?"

"Lenin and Martov," Walter said musingly. "Martov is a Menshevik, but Lenin is a Bolshevik." German intelligence took a lively interest in Russian revolutionaries.

Otto said: "Bolsheviks, Mensheviks, socialists, revolutionaries, they're all the same."

"No, they're not," said Walter. "The Bolsheviks are the toughest."

Monika's mother said with spirit: "All the more reason to keep them out of our country!"

Walter ignored that. "More important, the Bolsheviks abroad tend to be more radical than those at home. The Petrograd Bolsheviks support the provisional government of Prince Lvov, but their comrades in Zurich do not."

His sister, Greta, said: "How do you know a thing like that?"

Walter knew because he had read intelligence reports from German spies in Switzerland who were intercepting the revolutionaries' mail. But he said: "Lenin made a speech in Zurich a few days ago in which he repudiated the provisional government."

Otto made a dismissive noise, but Konrad von der Helbard leaned forward in his chair. "What are you thinking, young man?"

Walter said: "By refusing the revolutionaries permission to pass through Germany, we are protecting Russia from their subversive ideas."

Mother looked bewildered. "Explain, please."

"I'm suggesting we should help these dangerous men get home. Once there, either they will try to undermine the Russian government and cripple its ability to make war, or alternatively they will take power and make peace. Either way, Germany gains."

There was a moment of silence while they all thought about that. Then Otto laughed loudly and clapped his hands. "My own son!" he said. "There is a bit of the old man in him after all!"

{ II }

My dearest darling,
    Zurich is a cold city by a lake,

Walter wrote,

> but the sun shines on the water, on the leafy hillsides all
> around, and on the Alps in the distance. The streets are laid
> out in a grid with no bends: the Swiss are even more orderly
> than the Germans! I wish you were here, my beloved friend,
> as I wish you were with me wherever I am!!!

The exclamation marks were intended to give the postal censor the impression that the writer was an excitable girl. Although Walter was in neutral Switzerland, he was still being careful that the text of the letter did not identify either the sender or the recipient.

> I wonder whether you suffer the embarrassment of
> unwanted attention from eligible bachelors. You are so
> beautiful and charming that you must. I have the same
> problem. I don't have beauty or charm, of course, but despite
> that I receive advances. My mother has chosen someone for
> me to marry, a chum of my sister's, a person I have always

known and liked. It was very difficult for a while, and I'm afraid that in the end the person discovered that I have a friendship that excludes marriage. However, I believe our secret is safe.

If a censor bothered to read this far, he would now conclude that the letter was from a lesbian to her lover. The same conclusion would be reached by anyone in England who read the letter. This hardly mattered: undoubtedly Maud, being a feminist and apparently single at twenty-six, was already suspected of Sapphic tendencies.

> In a few days' time I will be in Stockholm, another cold city beside the water, and you could send me a letter at the Grand Hotel there.

Sweden, like Switzerland, was a neutral country with a postal service to England.

> I would love to hear from you!!!
> > Until then, my wonderful darling,
> > remember your beloved—
> > Waltraud

{ III }

The United States declared war on Germany on Friday, April 6, 1917.

Walter had been expecting it, but all the same he felt the blow. America was rich, vigorous, and democratic: he could not imagine a worse enemy. The only hope now was that Russia would collapse, giving Germany a chance to win on the western front before the Americans had time to build up their forces.

Three days later, thirty-two exiled Russian revolutionaries met at the Zähringerhof Hotel in Zurich: men, women, and one child, a four-year-old boy called Robert. They walked from there to the baroque arch of the railway station to board a train for home.

Walter had been afraid they would not go. Martov, the Menshevik leader, had refused to leave without permission from the provisional government in Petrograd—an oddly deferential attitude for a revolutionary. Permission had not been given, but Lenin and the Bolsheviks decided to go anyway. Walter was keen that there should be no snags on the trip, and he accompanied the group to the riverside station and boarded the train with them.

This is Germany's secret weapon, Walter thought: thirty-two malcontents and misfits who want to bring down the Russian government. God help us.

Vladimir Ilyich Ulyanov, known as Lenin, was forty-six years old. He was a short, stocky figure, dressed neatly but without elegance, too busy to waste time on style. He had once been a redhead, but he had lost his hair early, and now he had a shiny dome with a vestigial fringe, and a carefully trimmed Vandyke beard, ginger streaked with gray. On first acquaintance Walter had found him unimpressive, without charm or good looks.

Walter was posing as a lowly official in the Foreign Office who had been given the job of making all the practical arrangements for the Bolsheviks' journey through Germany. Lenin had given him a hard, appraising look, clearly guessing that he was in reality some kind of intelligence operative.

They traveled to Schaffhausen, on the border, where they transferred to a German train. They all spoke some German, having been living in the German-speaking region of Switzerland. Lenin himself spoke it well. He was a remarkable linguist, Walter learned. He was fluent in French, spoke passable English, and read Aristotle in ancient Greek. Lenin's idea of relaxation was to sit down with a foreign-language dictionary for an hour or two.

At Gottmadingen they changed again, to a train with a sealed carriage specially prepared for them as if they were carriers of an infectious disease. Three of its four doors were locked shut. The fourth door was next to Walter's sleeping compartment. This was to reassure overanxious German authorities, but it was not necessary: the Russians had no desire to escape; they wanted to go home.

Lenin and his wife, Nadya, had a room to themselves, but the others were crowded four to a compartment. So much for egalitarianism, Walter thought cynically.

As the train crossed Germany from south to north, Walter began to sense the force of character beneath Lenin's dull exterior. Lenin had no interest in food, drink, comfort, or possessions. Politics consumed his entire day. He was always arguing about politics, writing about politics, or thinking about politics and making notes. In arguments, Walter noted, Lenin always appeared to know more than his comrades and to have thought longer and harder than they—unless the subject under discussion was nothing to do with Russia or politics, in which case he was rather ill-informed.

He was a real killjoy. The first evening, the bespectacled young Karl Radek was telling jokes in the next compartment. "A man was arrested for saying, 'Nicholas is a moron.' He told the policeman: 'I meant another Nicholas, not our beloved tsar.' The policeman said: 'Liar! If you say *moron* you obviously mean the tsar!'" Radek's companions hooted with laughter. Lenin came out of his compartment with a face like thunder and ordered them to keep quiet.

Lenin did not like smoking. He himself had given it up, on his mother's insistence, thirty years ago. In deference to him, people smoked in the toilet at the end of the carriage. As there was only one toilet for thirty-two people, this led to queues and squabbles. Lenin turned his considerable intellect to solving this problem. He cut up some paper and issued everyone with tickets of two kinds, some for normal use of the toilet and a smaller number for smoking. This reduced the queue and ended the arguments. Walter was amused. It worked, and everyone was happy, but there was no discussion, no attempt at collective decision-making. In this group, Lenin was a benign dictator. If he ever gained real power, would he manage the Russian Empire the same way?

But would he win power? If not, Walter was wasting his time.

There was only one way he could think of to improve Lenin's prospects, and he made up his mind to do something about it.

He left the train at Berlin, saying he would be back to rejoin the Russians for the last leg. "Don't be long," one of them said. "We leave again in an hour."

"I'll be quick," said Walter. The train would depart when Walter said, but the Russians did not know that.

The carriage was in a siding at the Potsdamer station, and it took him only a few minutes to walk from there to the Foreign Office at 76 Wilhelmstrasse in the heart of old Berlin. His father's spacious room had a heavy mahogany desk, a painting of the kaiser, and a glass-fronted cabinet containing his collection of ceramics, including the eighteenth-century creamware fruit bowl he had bought on his last trip to London. As Walter had hoped, Otto was at his desk.

"There's no doubt of Lenin's beliefs," he told his father over coffee. "He says they have got rid of the symbol of oppression—the tsar—without changing Russian society. The workers have failed to take control: the middle class still runs everything. On top of that, Lenin personally hates Kerensky for some reason."

"But can he overthrow the provisional government?"

Walter spread his hands in a helpless gesture. "He is highly intelligent, determined, and a natural leader, and he never does anything except work. But the Bolsheviks are just another little political party among a dozen or more vying for power, and there's no way to tell who will come out on top."

"So all this effort may have been for nothing."

"Unless we do something to help the Bolsheviks win."

"Such as?"

Walter took a deep breath. "Give them money."

"What?" Otto was outraged. "The government of Germany, to give money to socialist revolutionaries?"

"I suggest a hundred thousand rubles, initially," Walter said coolly. "Preferably in gold ten-ruble pieces, if you can get them."

"The kaiser would never agree."

"Does he have to be told? Zimmermann could approve this on his own authority."

"He would never do such a thing."

"Are you sure?"

Otto stared at Walter in silence for a long time, thinking. Then he said: "I'll ask him."

{ IV }

After three days on the train, the Russians left Germany. At Sassnitz, on the coast, they bought tickets for the ferry *Queen Victoria* to take them across the Baltic Sea to the southern tip of Sweden. Walter went with them. The crossing was rough and everyone was seasick except Lenin, Radek, and Zinoviev, who were on deck having an angry political argument and did not seem to notice the heavy seas.

They took an overnight train to Stockholm, where the socialist Borgmastare gave them a welcome breakfast. Walter checked into the Grand Hotel, hoping to find a letter from Maud waiting for him. There was nothing.

He was so disappointed that he wanted to throw himself into the cold water of the bay. This had been his only chance to communicate with his wife in almost three years, and something had gone wrong. Had she even received his letter?

Unhappy fantasies tormented him. Did she still care for him? Had she forgotten him? Was there perhaps a new man in her life? He was completely in the dark.

Radek and the well-dressed Swedish socialists took Lenin, somewhat against his will, to the menswear section of the PUB department store. The hobnailed mountain boots the Russian had been wearing vanished. He got a coat with a velvet collar and a new hat. Now, Radek said, he was at least dressed like someone who could lead his people.

That evening, as night fell, the Russians went to the station to board yet another train for Finland. Walter was leaving the group here, but he went with them to the station. Before the train left, he had a meeting alone with Lenin.

They sat in a compartment under a dim electric light that gleamed off Lenin's bald head. Walter was tense. He had to do this just right. It would be no good to beg or plead with Lenin, he felt sure. And the man certainly could not be bullied. Only cold logic would persuade him.

Walter had a prepared speech. "The German government is helping you to return home," he said. "You know we are not doing this out of goodwill—"

Lenin interrupted in fluent German. "You think it will be to the detriment of Russia!" he barked.

Walter did not contradict him. "And yet you have accepted our help."

"For the sake of the revolution! This is the only standard of right and wrong."

"I thought you would say that." Walter was carrying a heavy suitcase, and now he put it down on the floor of the railway carriage with a thump. "In the false bottom of this case you will find one hundred thousand rubles in notes and coins."

"What?" Lenin was normally imperturbable, but now he looked startled. "What is it for?"

"For you."

Lenin was offended. "A bribe?" he said indignantly.

"Certainly not," said Walter. "We have no need to bribe you. Your aims are the same as ours. You have called for the overthrow of the provisional government and an end to the war."

"What, then?"

"For propaganda. To help you spread your message. It is the message that we, too, would like to broadcast. Peace between Germany and Russia."

"So that you can win your capitalist-imperialist war against France!"

"As I said before, we are not helping you out of goodwill—nor would you expect us to. It's practical politics, that's all. For the moment, your interests coincide with ours."

Lenin looked as he had when Radek insisted on buying him new clothes: he hated the idea, but could not deny that it made sense.

Walter said: "We'll give you a similar amount of money once a month—as long, of course, as you continue to campaign effectively for peace."

There was a long silence.

Walter said: "You say that the success of the revolution is the only standard of right and wrong. If that is so, you should take the money."

Outside on the platform, a whistle blew.

Walter stood up. "I must leave you now. Good-bye, and good luck."

Lenin stared at the suitcase on the floor and did not reply.

Walter left the compartment and got off the train.

He turned and looked back at the window of Lenin's compartment. He half-expected the window to open and the suitcase to come flying out.

There was another whistle and a hoot. The carriages jerked and moved, and slowly the train steamed out of the station, with Lenin, the other Russian exiles, and the money on board.

Walter took the handkerchief from the breast pocket of his coat and wiped his forehead. Despite the cold, he was sweating.

{ V }

Walter walked from the railway station along the waterfront to the Grand Hotel. It was dark, and a cold east wind blew off the Baltic. He should have been rejoicing: he had bribed Lenin! But he felt a sense of anticlimax. And he was more depressed than he should have been over the silence from Maud. There were a dozen possible reasons why she had not sent him a letter. He should not assume the worst. But he had come dangerously close to falling for Monika, so why should Maud not do something similar? He could not help feeling she must have forgotten him.

He decided he would get drunk tonight.

At the front desk he was given a typewritten note: "Please call at suite 201, where someone has a message for you." He guessed it was an official from the Foreign Office. Perhaps they had changed their minds about supporting Lenin. If so, they were too late.

He walked up the stairs and tapped on the door of 201. From inside a muffled voice said in German: "Yes?"

"Walter von Ulrich."

"Come in. It's open."

He stepped inside and closed the door. The suite was lit by candles. "Someone has a message for me?" he said, peering into the gloom. A figure rose from a chair. It was a woman, and she had her back to him, but something about her made his heart skip. She turned to face him.

It was Maud.

His mouth fell open and he stood paralyzed.

She said: "Hello, Walter."

Then her self-control broke and she threw herself into his arms.

The familiar smell of her filled his nostrils. He kissed her hair and stroked her back. He could not speak for fear he might cry. He crushed her body to his own, hardly able to believe that this was really her, that he was really holding her and touching her, something he had longed for so painfully for almost three years. She looked up at him, her eyes full of tears, and he stared at her face, drinking it in. She was the same but different: thinner, with the faintest of lines under her eyes where there had been none before, yet with that familiar piercingly intelligent gaze.

She said in English: "'He falls to such perusal of my face, as he would draw it.'"

He smiled. "We're not Hamlet and Ophelia, so please don't go to a nunnery."

"Dear God, I've missed you."

"And I you. I was hoping for a letter—but this! How did you manage it?"

"I told the passport office I planned to interview Scandinavian politicians about votes for women. Then I met the home secretary at a party and had a word in his ear."

"How did you get here?"

"There are still passenger steamers."

"But it's so dangerous—our submarines are sinking everything."

"I know. I took the risk. I was desperate." She began to cry again.

"Come and sit down." With his arm still around her waist, he walked her across the room to the couch.

"No," she said when they were about to sit. "We waited too long, before the war." She took his hand and led him through an inner door to a bedroom. Logs crackled in the fireplace. "Let's not waste any more time. Come to bed."

{ VI }

Grigori and Konstantin were part of the delegation from the Petrograd soviet that went to the Finland Station late in the evening of Monday, April 16, to welcome Lenin home.

Most of them had never seen Lenin, who had been in exile for all but a few months of the last seventeen years. Grigori had been eleven years old when Lenin left. Nevertheless he knew him by reputation, and so, it seemed, did thousands more people, who gathered at the station to greet him. Why so many? Grigori wondered. Perhaps they, like him, were dissatisfied with the provisional government, suspicious of its middle-class ministers, and angry that the war had not ended.

The Finland Station was in the Vyborg district, close to the textile mills and the barracks of the First Machine Gun Regiment. There was a crowd in the square. Grigori did not expect treachery, but he had told Isaak to bring a couple of platoons and several armored cars to stand guard just in case. There was a searchlight on the station roof, and someone was playing it over the mass of people waiting in the dark.

Inside, the station was full of workers and soldiers, all carrying red flags and banners. A military band played. Twenty minutes before midnight, two sailors' units formed up on the platform as a guard of honor. The delegation from the soviet loitered in the grand waiting room formerly reserved for the tsar and the royal family, but Grigori went out onto the platform with the crowd.

It was about midnight when Konstantin pointed up the line and Grigori, following his finger, saw the distant lights of a train. A rumble of anticipation rose from those waiting. The train steamed into the station, puffing smoke, and hissed to a halt. It had the number 293 painted on its front.

After a pause a short, stocky man got off the train wearing a double-breasted wool coat and a Homburg hat. Grigori thought this could not be Lenin—surely he would not be wearing the clothes of the boss class? A young woman stepped forward and handed him a bouquet, which he accepted with an ungracious frown. This was Lenin.

Behind him was Lev Kamenev, who had been sent by the Bolshevik Central Committee to meet Lenin at the border in case of problems—though in fact Lenin had been admitted without trouble. Now Kamenev indicated with a gesture that they should go to the royal waiting room.

Lenin rather rudely turned his back on Kamenev and addressed the sailors. "Comrades!" he shouted. "You have been deceived! You have made a revolution—and its fruits have been stolen from you by the traitors of the provisional government!"

Kamenev went white. It was the policy of almost everyone on the left to support the provisional government, at least temporarily.

Grigori was delighted, however. He did not believe in bourgeois democracy. The parliament allowed by the tsar in 1905 had been a trick, disempowered when the unrest came to an end and everyone went back to work. This provisional government was headed the same way.

And now at last someone had the guts to say so.

Grigori and Konstantin followed Lenin and Kamenev into the reception room. The crowd squeezed in after them until the room was crammed. The chairman of the Petrograd soviet, the balding, rat-faced Nikolai Chkeidze, stepped forward. He shook Lenin's hand and said: "In the name of the Petrograd soviet and the revolution, we hail your arrival in Russia. But . . . "

Grigori raised his eyebrows at Konstantin. This "but" seemed inappropriately early in a speech of welcome. Konstantin shrugged his bony shoulders.

"But we believe that the main task of revolutionary democracy consists now of defending our revolution against all attacks . . . " Chkeidze paused, then said with emphasis: " . . . whether internal or external."

Konstantin murmured: "This is not a welcome—it's a warning."

"We believe that to accomplish this, not disunity but unity is necessary on the part of all revolutionists. We hope that, in agreement with us, you will pursue these aims."

There was polite applause from some of the delegation.

Lenin paused before replying. He looked at the faces around him and at the lavishly decorated ceiling. Then, in a gesture that seemed a deliberate insult, he turned his back on Chkeidze and spoke to the crowd.

"Comrades, soldiers, sailors, and workers!" he said, pointedly excluding middle-class parliamentarians. "I salute you as the vanguard of the world proletarian army. Today, or perhaps tomorrow, all of European imperialism may collapse. The revolution you have made has opened up a new epoch. Long live the world socialist revolution!"

They cheered. Grigori was startled. They had only just achieved a revolution in Petrograd—and the results of that were still in doubt. How could they think about a *world* revolution? But the idea thrilled him all the same. Lenin was right: all people should turn on the masters who had sent so many men to die in this pointless world war.

Lenin marched away from the delegation and out into the square.

A roar went up from the waiting crowd. Isaak's troops lifted Lenin onto the reinforced roof of an armored car. The searchlight was trained on him. He took off his hat.

His voice was a monotonous bark, but his words were electric. "The provisional government has betrayed the revolution!" he shouted.

They cheered. Grigori was surprised: he had not known how many people thought the way he did.

"The war is a predatory imperialist war. We want no part in this shameful imperialist slaughter of men. With the overthrow of the capital we can conclude a democratic peace!"

That got a bigger roar.

"We do not want the lies or frauds of a bourgeois parliament! The only possible form of government is a soviet of workers' deputies. All banks must be taken over and brought under the control of the soviet. All private land must be confiscated. And all army officers must be elected!"

That was exactly what Grigori thought, and he cheered and waved along with almost everyone else in the crowd.

"Long live the revolution!"

The crowd went wild.

Lenin clambered off the roof and got into the armored car. It drove off at a walking pace. The crowd surrounded and followed it, waving red flags. The military band joined in the procession, playing a march.

Grigori said: "This is the man for me!"

Konstantin said: "Me, too."

They followed the procession.

CHAPTER TWENTY-FIVE

May and June 1917

The Monte Carlo nightclub in Buffalo looked dreadful by daylight, but Lev Peshkov loved it just the same. The woodwork was scratched, the paint was chipped, the upholstery was stained, and there were cigarette butts all over the carpet; yet Lev thought it was paradise. As he walked in he kissed the hat-check girl, gave the doorman a cigar, and told the barman to be careful lifting a crate.

The job of nightclub manager was ideal for him. His main responsibility was to make sure no one was stealing. As a thief himself, he knew how to do that. Otherwise he just had to see that there was enough drink behind the bar and a decent band onstage. As well as his salary, he had free cigarettes and all the booze he could take without falling down. He always wore formal evening dress, which made him feel like a prince. Josef Vyalov left him alone to run the place. As long as the profits were coming in, his father-in-law had no other interest in the club, except to turn up occasionally with his cronies and watch the show.

Lev had only one problem: his wife.

Olga had changed. For a few weeks, back in the summer of 1915, she had been a sexpot, always hungry for his body. But that had been uncharacteristic, he now knew. Since they got married, everything he did displeased her. She wanted him to bathe every day and use a toothbrush and stop farting. She did not like dancing or drinking and she asked him not to smoke. She never came to the club. They slept in separate beds. She called him low-class. "I am low-class," he had said to her one day. "That's why I was the chauffeur." She continued dissatisfied.

So he had hired Marga.

His old flame was onstage now, rehearsing a new number with the band, while two black women in head scarves wiped the tables and swept the floor. Marga wore a tight dress and red lipstick. Lev had given her a job as a dancer, having no idea whether she was good. She had turned out to be not just good but a star. Now she was belting out a suggestive number about waiting all night for her man to come.

> *Though I suffer from frustrations*
> *The anticipation's*
> *A boost to our relations*
> *When he comes*

Lev knew exactly what she meant.

He watched her until she was done. She came offstage and kissed his cheek. He got two bottles of beer and followed her to her dressing room. "That's a great number," he said as he went in.

"Thanks." She put the bottle in her mouth and tilted it. Lev watched her red lips on the neck. She took a long drink. She caught him watching her, swallowed, and grinned. "That remind you of something?"

"You bet it does." He embraced her and ran his hands over her body. After a couple of minutes she knelt down, unbuttoned his pants, and took him into her mouth. She was good at this, the best he had ever known. Either she really liked it, or she was the greatest actor in America. He closed his eyes and sighed with pleasure.

The door opened and Josef Vyalov came in.

"So it's true!" he said furiously.

Two of his thugs, Ilya and Theo, followed him in.

Lev was scared half to death. He hastily tried to button his pants and apologize at the same time.

Marga stood up quickly and wiped her mouth. "You're in my dressing room!" she protested.

Vyalov said: "And you're in my nightclub. But not for much longer. You're fired." He turned to Lev. "When you're married to my daughter, you don't screw the help!"

Marga said defiantly: "He wasn't screwing me, Vyalov. Didn't you notice that?"

Vyalov punched her in the mouth. She cried out and fell back, her lip bleeding. "You've been fired," he said to her. "Fuck off."

She picked up her bag and left.

Vyalov looked at Lev. "You asshole," he said. "Haven't I done enough for you?"

Lev said: "I'm sorry, Pa." He was terrified of his father-in-law. Vyalov would do anything: people who displeased him might be flogged, tortured, maimed, or murdered. He had no mercy and no fear of the law. In his way he was as powerful as the tsar.

"Don't tell me it's the first time, either," said Vyalov. "I been hearing these rumors ever since I put you in charge here."

Lev said nothing. The rumors were true. There had been others, although not since Marga was hired.

"I'm moving you," Vyalov said.

"What do you mean?"

"I'm taking you out of the club. Too many goddamn girls here."

Lev's heart sank. He loved the Monte Carlo. "But what would I do?"

"I own a foundry down by the harbor. There are no women employees. The manager got sick—he's in the hospital. You can keep an eye on it for me."

"A foundry?" Lev was incredulous. "Me?"

"You worked at the Putilov factory."

"In the stables!"

"And in a coal mine."

"Same thing."

"So, you know the environment."

"And I hate it!"

"Did I ask you what you like? Jesus Christ, I just caught you with your pants down. You're lucky not to get worse."

Lev shut up.

"Go outside and get in the goddamn car," said Vyalov.

Lev left the dressing room and walked through the club, with Vyalov following. He could hardly believe he was leaving for good. The barman and the hat-check girl stared, sensing something wrong. Vyalov said to the barman: "You're in charge tonight, Ivan."

"Yes, boss."

Vyalov's Packard Twin Six was waiting at the curb. A new chauffeur stood proudly beside it, a kid from Kiev. The commissionaire hurried to open the rear door for Lev. At least I'm still riding in the back, Lev thought.

He was living like a Russian nobleman, if not better, he reminded himself for consolation. He and Olga had the nursery wing of the spacious prairie house. Rich Americans did not keep as many servants as the Russians, but their houses were cleaner and brighter than Petrograd palaces. They had modern bathrooms, iceboxes and vacuum cleaners, and central heating. The food was good. Vyalov did not share the Russian aristocracy's love of champagne, but there was always whisky on the sideboard. And Lev had six suits.

Whenever he felt oppressed by his bullying father-in-law, he cast his mind back to the old days in Petrograd: the single room he shared with Grigori, the cheap vodka, the coarse black bread, and the turnip stew. He remembered thinking what a luxury it would be to ride the streetcars instead of walking everywhere. Stretching out his legs in the back of Vyalov's limousine, he looked at his silk socks and shiny black shoes, and told himself to be grateful.

Vyalov got in after him and they drove to the waterfront. Vyalov's foundry was a small version of the Putilov works: same dilapidated buildings with broken windows, same tall chimneys and black smoke, same drab workers with dirty faces. Lev's heart sank.

"It's called the Buffalo Metal Works, but it makes only one thing," Vyalov said. "Fans." The car drove through the narrow gateway. "Before the war it was losing money. I bought it and cut the men's pay to keep it going. Lately business has picked up. We've got a long list of orders for airplane and ship propellers and fans for armored car engines. They want a pay raise now, but I need to get back some of what I've spent before I start giving money away."

Lev was dreading working here, but his fear of Vyalov was stronger, and he did not want to fail. He resolved that he would not be the one to give the men a raise.

Vyalov showed him around the factory. Lev wished he were not wearing his tuxedo. But the place was not like the Putilov works inside. It was a lot cleaner. There were no children running around. Apart from the furnaces, everything worked by electric power. Where the Russians would get twelve men hauling on a rope to lift a locomotive boiler, here a mighty ship's propeller was raised by an electric hoist.

Vyalov pointed to a bald man wearing a collar and tie under his overalls. "That's your enemy," he said. "Brian Hall, secretary of the local union branch."

Lev studied Hall. The man was adjusting a heavy stamping machine, turning a nut with a long-handled wrench. He had a pugnacious air and, when he glanced up and saw Lev and Vyalov, he gave them a challenging look, as if he might be about to ask whether they wanted to make trouble.

Vyalov shouted over the noise of a nearby grinder. "Come here, Hall."

The man took his time, replacing the wrench in a toolbox and wiping his hands on a rag before approaching.

Vyalov said: "This is your new boss, Lev; Peshkov."

"How do," Hall said to Lev; then he turned back to Vyalov. "Peter

Fisher got a nasty cut on his face from a flying shard of steel this morning. Had to be taken to the hospital."

"I'm sorry to hear that," Vyalov said. "Metalworking is a hazardous industry, but no one is forced to work here."

"It just missed his eye," Hall said indignantly. "We ought to have goggles."

"No one has lost an eye in my time here."

Hall became angry quickly. "Do we have to wait until someone is blinded before we get goggles?"

"How else will I know you need them?"

"A man who has never been robbed still puts a lock on the door of his house."

"But he's paying for it himself."

Hall nodded as if he had been expecting nothing better and, with an air of weary wisdom, returned to his machine.

"They're always asking for something," Vyalov said to Lev.

Lev gathered that Vyalov wanted him to be tough. Well, he knew how to do that. It was the way all factories were run in Petrograd.

They left the plant and drove up Delaware Avenue. Lev guessed they were going home to dinner. It would never occur to Vyalov to ask whether that was okay with Lev. Vyalov made decisions for everyone.

In the house Lev took off his shoes, which were dirty from the foundry, and put on a pair of embroidered slippers Olga had given him for Christmas; then he went to the baby's room. Olga's mother, Lena, was there with Daisy.

Lena said: "Look, Daisy, here's your father!"

Lev's daughter was now fourteen months old and just beginning to walk. She came staggering across the room toward him, smiling, then fell over and cried. He picked her up and kissed her. He had never before taken the least interest in babies or children, but Daisy had captured his heart. When she was fractious and did not want to go to bed, and no one else could soothe her, he would rock her, murmuring endearments and singing fragments of Russian folk songs, until her eyes closed, her tiny body went limp, and she fell asleep in his arms.

Lena said: "She looks just like her handsome daddy!"

Lev thought she looked like a baby, but he did not contradict his mother-in-law. Lena adored him. She flirted with him, touched him a lot, and kissed him at every opportunity. She was in love with him, though she undoubtedly thought she was showing nothing more than normal family affection.

On the other side of the room was a young Russian girl called Polina. She was the nurse, but she was not overworked: Olga and Lena spent most of their time taking care of Daisy. Now Lev handed the baby to Polina. As he did so, Polina gave him a direct look. She was a classic Russian beauty, with blond hair and high cheekbones. Lev wondered briefly whether he could have an affair with her and get away with it. She had her own tiny bedroom. Could he sneak in without anyone noticing? It might be worth the risk: that look had shown eagerness.

Olga came in, making him feel guilty. "What a surprise!" she said when she saw him. "I didn't expect you back until three in the morning."

"Your father has moved me," Lev said sourly. "I'm running the foundry now."

"But why? I thought you were doing well at the club."

"I don't know why," Lev lied.

"Maybe because of the draft," Olga said. President Wilson had declared war on Germany and was about to introduce conscription. "The foundry will be classified as an essential war industry. Daddy wants to keep you out of the army."

Lev knew from the newspapers that conscription would be run by local draft boards. Vyalov was sure to have at least one crony on the board who would fix anything he asked for. That was how this town worked. But Lev did not disabuse Olga. He needed a cover story that did not involve Marga, and Olga had invented one. "Sure," he said. "I guess that must be it."

Daisy said: "Dadda."

"Clever girl!" Polina said.

Lena said: "I'm sure you'll make a good job of managing the foundry."

Lev gave her his best aw-shucks American grin. "Guess I'll do my best," he said.

{ II }

Gus Dewar felt his European mission for the president had been a failure. "Failure?" said Woodrow Wilson. "Heck, no! You got the Germans to make a peace offer. It's not your fault the British and French told them to drop dead. You can lead a horse to water, but you can't make it drink." All the same, the truth was that Gus had not succeeded in bringing the two sides together even for preliminary discussions.

So he was all the more eager to succeed in the next major task Wilson gave him. "The Buffalo Metal Works has been closed by a strike," the president said. "We have ships and planes and military vehicles stuck on production lines waiting for the propellers and fans they make. You come from Buffalo—go up there and get them back to work."

On his first night back in his hometown, Gus went to dinner at the home of Chuck Dixon, once his rival for the affections of Olga Vyalov. Chuck and his new wife, Doris, had a Victorian mansion on Elmwood Avenue, which ran parallel to Delaware, and Chuck took the Belt Line railway every morning to work in his father's bank.

Doris was a pretty girl who looked a bit like Olga, and as Gus watched the newlyweds he wondered how much he would like this life of domesticity. He had once dreamed of waking up every morning next to Olga, but that was two years ago, and now that her enchantment had worn off he thought he might prefer his bachelor apartment on Sixteenth Street in Washington.

When they sat down to their steaks and mashed potatoes, Doris said: "What happened to President Wilson's promise to keep us out of the war?"

"You have to give him credit," Gus said mildly. "For three years he's been campaigning for peace. They just wouldn't listen."

"That doesn't mean we have to join in the fighting."

Chuck said impatiently: "Honey, the Germans are sinking American ships!"

"Then tell American ships to stay out of the war zone!" Doris looked cross, and Gus guessed they had had this argument before. No doubt her anger was fueled by the fear that Chuck would be conscripted.

To Gus, these issues were too nuanced for passionate declarations of right and wrong. He said gently: "Okay, that's an alternative, and the president considered it. But it means accepting Germany's power to tell us where American ships can and can't go."

Chuck said indignantly: "We can't be pushed around that way by Germany or anyone else!"

Doris was adamant. "If it saves lives, why not?"

Gus said: "Most Americans seem to feel the way Chuck does."

"That doesn't make it right."

"Wilson believes a president must treat public opinion the way a sailing ship treats the wind, using it but never going directly against it."

"Then why must we have conscription? That makes slaves of American men."

Chuck chipped in again. "Don't you think it's fair that we should all be equally responsible for fighting for our country?"

"We have a professional army. At least those men joined voluntarily."

Gus said: "We have an army of a hundred and thirty thousand men. That's nothing in this war. We're going to need at least a million."

"A lot more men to die," Doris said.

Chuck said: "We're damn glad at the bank, I can tell you. We have a lot of money out on loan to American companies supplying the Allies. If the Germans win, and the Brits and the Froggies can't pay their debts, we're in trouble."

Doris looked thoughtful. "I didn't know that."

Chuck patted her hand. "Don't worry about it, honey. It's not going to happen. The Allies are going to win, especially with the U.S. of A. helping out."

Gus said: "There's another reason for us to fight. When the war is over, the U.S. will be able to take part as an equal in the postwar settlement. That may not sound very important, but Wilson's dream is to set up a league of nations to resolve future conflicts without us killing one another." He looked at Doris. "You must be in favor of that, I guess."

"Certainly."

Chuck changed the subject. "What brings you home, Gus? Apart from the desire to explain the president's decisions to us common folk."

He told them about the strike. He spoke lightly, as this was dinner-party talk, but in truth he was worried. The Buffalo Metal Works was vital to the war effort, and he was not sure how to get the men back to work. Wilson had settled a national rail strike shortly before his reelection and seemed to think that intervention in industrial disputes was a natural element of political life. Gus found it a heavy responsibility.

"You know who owns that place, don't you?" said Chuck.

Gus had checked. "Vyalov."

"And who runs it for him?"

"No."

"His new son-in-law, Lev Peshkov."

"Oh," said Gus. "I didn't know that."

{ III }

Lev was furious about the strike. The union was trying to take advantage of his inexperience. He felt sure Brian Hall and the men had decided he was weak. He was determined to prove them wrong.

He had tried being reasonable. "Mr. V needs to make back some of the money he lost in the bad years," he had said to Hall.

"And the men need to make back some of what *they* lost in reduced wages!" Hall had replied.

"It's not the same."

"No, it's not," Hall had agreed. "You're rich and they're poor. It's harder for them." The man was infuriatingly quick-witted.

Lev was desperate to get back into his father-in-law's good books. It was dangerous to let a man such as Josef Vyalov remain displeased with you for long. The trouble was that charm was Lev's only asset, and it did not work on Vyalov.

However, Vyalov was being supportive about the foundry. "Sometimes you have to let them strike," he had said. "It doesn't do to give in. Just stick it out. They become more reasonable when they start to get hungry." But Lev knew how fast Vyalov could change his mind.

However, Lev had a plan of his own to hasten the collapse of the strike. He was going to use the power of the press.

Lev was a member of the Buffalo Yacht Club, thanks to his father-in-law, who had got him elected. Most of the town's leading businessmen belonged, including Peter Hoyle, editor of the *Buffalo Advertiser*. One afternoon Lev approached Hoyle in the clubhouse at the foot of Porter Avenue.

The *Advertiser* was a conservative newspaper that always called for stability and blamed all problems on foreigners, Negroes, and socialist troublemakers. Hoyle, an imposing figure with a black mustache, was a crony of Vyalov's. "Hello, young Peshkov," he said. His voice was loud and harsh, as if he was used to shouting over the noise of a printing press. "I hear the president has sent Cam Dewar's son up here to settle your strike."

"I believe so, but I haven't heard from him yet."

"I know him. He's naïve. You don't have much to worry about."

Lev agreed. He had taken a dollar from Gus Dewar in Petrograd in 1914, and more recently he had taken Gus's fiancée just as easily. "I wanted to talk to you about the strike," he said, sitting in the leather armchair opposite Hoyle.

"The *Advertiser* has already condemned the strikers as un-American socialists and revolutionaries," Hoyle said. "What more can we do?"

"Call them enemy agents," Lev said. "They're holding up the production of vehicles that our boys are going to need when they get to Europe—but the workers themselves are exempt from the draft!"

"That's an angle." Hoyle frowned. "But we don't yet know how the draft is going to work."

"It's sure to exclude war industries."

"That's true."

"And yet they're demanding more money. A lot of people would take less for a job that keeps them out of the army."

Hoyle took a notebook from his jacket pocket and began to write. "Take less money for a draft-exempt job," he muttered.

"Maybe you want to ask: whose side are they on?"

"Sounds like a headline."

Lev was surprised and pleased. It had been easy.

Hoyle looked up from his notebook. "I presume Mr. V knows we're having this conversation?"

Lev had not anticipated this question. He grinned to cover his confusion. If he said no, Hoyle would drop the whole thing immediately. "Yes, of course," he lied. "In fact it was his idea."

{ IV }

Vyalov asked Gus to meet him at the yacht club. Brian Hall proposed a conference at the Buffalo office of the union. Each wanted to meet on his own ground, where he would feel confident and in charge. So Gus took a meeting room at the Statler Hotel.

Lev Peshkov had attacked the strikers as draft dodgers, and the *Advertiser* had put his comments on the front page, under the headline WHOSE SIDE ARE THEY ON? When Gus saw the paper he had been dismayed: such aggressive talk could only escalate the dispute. But Lev's effort had backfired. This morning's papers reported a storm of protest from workers in other war industries, indignant at the suggestion that they should receive low wages on account of their privileged status, and furious at being labeled draft dodgers. Lev's clumsiness heartened Gus, but he knew that Vyalov was his real enemy, and that made him nervous.

Gus brought all the papers with him to the Statler and put them out on a side table in the meeting room. In a prominent position he placed a popular rag with the headline WILL *YOU* JOIN UP, LEV?

Gus had asked Brian Hall to get there a quarter of an hour before Vyalov. The union leader showed up on the dot. He wore a smart suit and a gray felt hat, Gus noted. That was good tactics. It was a mistake to look inferior, even if you represented the workers. Hall was as formidable, in his own way, as Vyalov.

Hall saw the newspapers and grinned. "Young Lev made a mistake," he said with satisfaction. "He's fetched himself a pile of trouble."

"Manipulating the press is a dangerous game," Gus said. He got right down to business. "You're asking for a dollar-a-day increase."

"It's only ten cents more than my men were getting before Vyalov bought the plant, and—"

"Never mind all that," Gus interrupted, showing more boldness than he felt. "If I can get you fifty cents, will you take it?"

Hall looked dubious. "I'd have to put it to the men—"

"No," Gus said. "You have to decide now." He prayed his nervousness was not showing.

Hall prevaricated. "Has Vyalov agreed to this?"

"I'll worry about Vyalov. Fifty cents, take it or leave it." Gus resisted an urge to wipe his forehead.

Hall gave Gus a long, appraising stare. Behind the pugnacious look there was a shrewd brain, Gus suspected. At last Hall said: "We'll take it—for now."

"Thank you." Gus managed not to let out his breath in a long sigh of relief. "Would you like coffee?"

"Sure."

Gus turned away, grateful to be able to hide his face, and pressed the bell for a waiter.

Josef Vyalov and Lev Peshkov walked in. Gus did not shake hands. "Sit down," he said curtly.

Vyalov's eyes went to the newspapers on the side table, and a look of anger crossed his face. Gus guessed that Lev was already in trouble over those headlines.

He tried not to stare at Lev. This was the chauffeur who had seduced Gus's fiancée—but that must not be allowed to cloud Gus's judgment. He would have liked to punch Lev in the face. However, if this meeting went according to plan, the result would be more humiliating to Lev than a punch—and much more satisfying to Gus.

A waiter appeared, and Gus said: "Bring coffee for my guests, please, and a plate of ham sandwiches." He deliberately did not ask them what they wanted. He had seen Woodrow Wilson act like this with people he wanted to intimidate.

He sat down and opened a folder. It contained a blank sheet of paper. He pretended to read it.

Lev sat down and said: "So, Gus, the president has sent you up here to negotiate with us."

Now Gus allowed himself to look at Lev. He stared at him for a long moment without speaking. Handsome, yes, he thought, but also untrustworthy and weak. When Lev began to look embarrassed, Gus spoke at last. "Are you out of your fucking mind?"

Lev was so shocked that he actually pushed his chair back from the table as if fearing a blow. "What the hell . . . ?"

Gus made his voice harsh. "America is at war," he said. "The president is not going to *negotiate* with you." He looked at Brian Hall. "Or you," he said, even though he had made a deal with Hall only ten minutes ago. Finally he looked at Vyalov. "Not even with you," he said.

Vyalov looked steadily back at him. Unlike his son-in-law, he was not intimidated. However, he had lost the look of amused contempt with which he began the meeting. After a long pause, he said: "So what are you here for?"

"I'm here to tell you what's going to happen," Gus said in the same voice. "And when I'm done, you'll accept it."

Lev said: "Huh!"

Vyalov said: "Shut up, Lev. Go on, Dewar."

"You're going to offer the men a raise of fifty cents a day," Gus said. He turned to Hall. "And you're going to accept his offer."

Hall kept his face blank and said: "Is that so?"

"And I want your men back at work by noon today."

Vyalov said: "And why the hell should we do what you tell us?"

"Because of the alternative."

"Which is?"

"The president will send an army battalion to the foundry to take it over, secure it, release all finished products to customers, and continue to run it with army engineers. After the war, he might give it back." He turned to Hall. "And your men can probably have their jobs back then, too." Gus wished he had run this past Woodrow Wilson first, but it was too late now.

Lev said with amazement: "Does he have the right to do that?"

"Under wartime legislation, yes," said Gus.

"So you say," said Vyalov skeptically.

"Challenge us in court," said Gus. "Do you think there's a judge in this country who will side with you—and our country's enemies?" He sat back and stared at them with an arrogance he did not feel. Would this work? Would they believe him? Or would they call his bluff, laugh at him, and walk out?

There was a long silence. Hall's face was expressionless. Vyalov was thoughtful. Lev looked sick.

At last Vyalov turned to Hall. "Are you willing to settle for fifty cents?"

Hall just said: "Yes."

Vyalov looked back at Gus. "Then we accept, too."

"Thank you, gentlemen." Gus closed his folder, trying to still the shaking of his hands. "I'll tell the president."

{ V }

Saturday was sunny and warm. Lev told Olga he was needed at the foundry; then he drove to Marga's place. She lived in a small room in

Lovejoy. They embraced, but when Lev started to unbutton her blouse, she said: "Let's go to Humboldt Park."

"I'd rather screw."

"Later. Take me to the park, and I'll show you something special when we come back. Something we haven't done before."

Lev's throat went dry. "Why do I have to wait?"

"It's such a beautiful day."

"What if we're seen?"

"There'll be a million people there."

"Even so . . . "

"I suppose you're afraid of your father-in-law?"

"Hell, no," Lev said. "Listen, I'm the father of his grandchild. What's he going to do, shoot me?"

"Let me change my dress."

"I'll wait in the car. If I watch you undress I might lose control."

He had a new Cadillac three-passenger coupe, not the swankiest car in town but a good place to start. He sat at the wheel and lit a cigarette. He *was* afraid of Vyalov, of course. But all his life he had taken risks. He was not Grigori, after all. And things had worked out pretty well for him so far, he thought, sitting in his car, wearing a summer-weight blue suit, about to take a pretty girl to the park. Life was good.

Before he had finished his smoke, Marga came out of the building and got into the car beside him. She was wearing a daring sleeveless dress and had her hair coiled over her ears in the latest fashion.

He drove to Humboldt Park, on the east side of town. They sat together on a slatted wooden park seat, enjoying the sunshine and watching the children playing in the pond. Lev could not stop touching Marga's bare arms. He loved the envious looks he got from other men. She's the prettiest girl in the park, he thought, and she's with me. How about that?

"I'm sorry about your lip," he said. Her lower lip was still swollen where Vyalov had punched her. It looked quite sexy.

"Not your fault," Marga said. "Your father-in-law is a pig."

"That's the truth."

"The Hot Spot offered me a job right away. I'll start there as soon as I can sing again."

"How does it feel?"

She tried a few bars.

> *I run my fingers through my hair*
> *Play a little solitaire*
> *Waiting for my millionaire*
> *To come*

She touched her mouth gingerly. "Still hurts," she said.

He leaned toward her. "Let me kiss it better." She turned her face up to his and he kissed her gently, hardly touching.

She said: "You can be a little firmer than that."

He grinned. "Okay, how about this?" He kissed her again, and this time he let the tip of his tongue caress the inside of her lips.

After a minute she said: "That's okay, too," and she giggled.

"In that case . . . " This time he put his tongue all the way inside her mouth. She responded eagerly—she always did. Her tongue and his met; then she put her hand behind his head and stroked his neck. He heard someone say: "Disgusting." He wondered whether people walking by could see his erection.

Smiling at Marga, he said: "We're shocking the townspeople." He glanced up to see whether anyone was watching, and met the eyes of his wife, Olga.

She was staring at him in shock, her mouth forming a silent O.

Beside her stood her father, in a suit with a vest and a straw boater. He was carrying Daisy. Lev's daughter had a white bonnet to shade her face from the sun. The nurse, Polina, was behind them.

Olga said: "Lev! What . . . Who is she?"

Lev felt he might have talked himself out of even this situation if Vyalov had not been there.

He got up. "Olga . . . I don't know what to say."

Vyalov said harshly: "Don't say a damn thing."

Olga began to cry.

Vyalov handed Daisy to the nurse. "Take my granddaughter to the car right away."

"Yes, Mr. Vyalov."

Vyalov grasped Olga's arm and moved her away. "Go with Polina, honey."

Olga put her hand over her eyes to hide her tears and followed the nurse.

"You piece of shit," Vyalov said to Lev.

Lev clenched his fists. If Vyalov struck him he would fight back. Vyalov was built like a bull, but he was twenty years older. Lev was taller, and had learned to fight in the slums of Petrograd. He was not going to take a beating.

Vyalov read his mind. "I'm not going to fight you," he said. "It's beyond that."

Lev wanted to say: *So what are you going to do?* He kept his mouth clamped shut.

Vyalov looked at Marga. "I should have hit you harder," he said.

Marga picked up her bag, opened it, put her hand inside, and left it there. "If you move one inch toward me, so help me God, I'll shoot you in the gut, you pig-faced Russian peasant," she said.

Lev could not help admiring her nerve. Few people had the balls to threaten Josef Vyalov.

Vyalov's face darkened in anger, but he turned away from Marga and spoke to Lev. "You know what you're going to do?"

What the hell was coming now?

Lev said nothing.

Vyalov said: "You're going in the goddamn army."

Lev went cold. "You don't mean it."

"When was the last time you heard me say something I didn't mean?"

"I'm not going in the army. How can you make me?"

"Either you'll volunteer, or you'll get conscripted."

Marga burst out: "You can't do that!"

"Yes, he can," Lev said in desolation. "He can fix anything in this town."

"And you know what?" said Vyalov. "You might be my son-in-law, but I hope to God you get killed."

{ VI }

Chuck and Doris Dixon gave an afternoon party in their garden at the end of June. Gus went with his parents. All the men wore suits, but the women dressed in summer outfits and extravagant hats, and the crowd looked colorful. There were sandwiches and beer, lemonade and cake. A clown gave out candy and a schoolteacher in shorts organized the children to run jokey races: a sack race, an egg-and-spoon race, a three-legged race.

Doris wanted to talk to Gus about the war, again. "There are rumors of mutiny in the French army," she said.

Gus knew that the truth was worse than the rumors: there had been mutinies in fifty-four French divisions, and twenty thousand men had deserted. "I assume that's why they've switched their tactics from offense to defense," he said neutrally.

"Apparently the French officers treat their men badly." Doris relished bad news about the war because it gave support to her opposition. "And the Nivelle Offensive has been a disaster."

"The arrival of American troops will buck them up." The first Americans had boarded ships to sail to France.

"But so far we have sent only a token force. I hope that means we're going to play only a small part in the fighting."

"No, it does not mean that. We have to recruit, train, and arm at least a million men. We can't do that instantly. But next year we will send them in the hundreds of thousands."

Doris looked over Gus's shoulder and said: "Goodness, here comes one of our new recruits."

Gus turned and saw the Vyalov family: Josef and Lena with Olga, Lev, and a little girl. Lev was wearing an army uniform. He looked dashing, but his handsome face was sulky.

Gus was embarrassed but his father, wearing his public persona as senator, shook hands cordially with Josef and said something that made him laugh. Mother spoke graciously to Lena and cooed over the baby. Gus realized his parents had anticipated this meeting and decided to act as if they had forgotten that he and Olga had once been engaged.

He caught Olga's eye and nodded politely. She blushed.

Lev was as brash as ever. "So, Gus, is the president pleased with you for settling the strike?"

The others heard this question and went quiet, listening to hear Gus's answer.

"He's pleased with you for being reasonable," Gus said tactfully. "I see you joined the army."

"I volunteered," Lev said. "I'm doing officer training."

"How are you finding it?"

Suddenly Gus was aware that he and Lev had an audience around them in a ring: the Vyalovs, the Dewars, and the Dixons. Since the engagement had been broken off, the two men had not been seen together in public. Everyone was curious.

"I'll get accustomed to the army," Lev said. "How about you?"

"What about me?"

"Are you going to volunteer? After all, you and your president got us into the war."

Gus said nothing, but he felt ashamed. Lev was right.

"You can always wait and see whether you get drafted," Lev said, turning the knife. "You never know—you could get lucky. Anyway, if you go back to Washington, I guess the president can get you exempted." He laughed.

Gus shook his head. "No," he said. "I've been thinking about this. You're right. I'm part of the government that brought in the draft. I could hardly evade it."

He saw his father nod, as if he had anticipated this; but his mother said: "But, Gus, you work for the president! What better way could there be for you to help the war effort?"

Lev said: "I guess it would seem kind of cowardly."

"Exactly," said Gus. "So I won't be going back to Washington. That part of my life is over for now."

He heard his mother say: "Gus, no!"

"I've already spoken to General Clarence of the Buffalo Division," he said. "I'm joining the National Army."

His mother began to cry.

CHAPTER TWENTY-SIX

Mid-June 1917

Ethel had never thought about women's rights until she stood in the library at Tŷ Gwyn, unmarried and pregnant, while the slimy lawyer Solman told her the facts of life. She was to spend her best years struggling to feed and care for Fitz's child, but there was no obligation upon the father to help in any way. The unfairness of it had made her want to murder Solman.

Her rage had been further inflamed by looking for work in London. A job would be open to her only if no man wanted it, and then she would be offered half a man's wages or less.

But her angry feminism had set as hard as concrete during years of living alongside the tough, hardworking, dirt-poor women of London's East End. Men often told a fairy tale in which there was a division of labor in families, the man going out to earn money, the woman looking after home and children. Reality was different. Most of the women Ethel knew worked twelve hours a day and looked after home and children as well. Underfed, overworked, living in hovels, and dressed in rags, they could still sing songs and laugh and love their children.

In Ethel's view one of those women had more right to vote than any ten men.

She had been arguing this for so long that she felt quite strange when votes for women became a real possibility in the middle of 1917. As a little girl she had asked: "What will it be like in heaven?" and had never got a satisfactory answer.

Parliament agreed to a debate in mid-June. "It's the result of two compromises," Ethel said excitedly to Bernie when she read the report in *The Times.* "The Speaker's Conference, which Asquith called to sidestep the issue, was desperate to avoid a row."

Bernie was giving Lloyd his breakfast, feeding him toast dipped in sweet tea. "I assume the government is afraid that women will start chaining themselves to railings again."

Ethel nodded. "And if the politicians get caught up in that kind of fuss, people will say they're not concentrating on winning the war. So the committee recommended giving the vote only to women over thirty who are householders or the wives of householders. Which means I'm too young."

"That was the first compromise," said Bernie. "And the second?"

"According to Maud, the cabinet was split." The War Cabinet consisted of four men plus the prime minister, Lloyd George. "Curzon is against us, obviously." Earl Curzon, the leader of the House of Lords, was proudly misogynist. He was president of the League for Opposing Woman Suffrage. "So is Milner. But Henderson supports us." Arthur Henderson was the leader of the Labour Party, whose M.P.s supported the women, even though many Labour Party men did not. "Bonar Law is with us, though lukewarm."

"Two in favor, two against, and Lloyd George as usual wanting to keep everyone happy."

"The compromise is that there will be a free vote." That meant the government would not order its supporters to vote one way or the other.

"So that whatever happens it won't be the government's fault."

"No one ever said Lloyd George was ingenuous."

"But he's given you a chance."

"A chance is all it is. We've got some campaigning work to do."

"I think you'll find attitudes have changed," Bernie said optimistically. "The government is desperate to get women into industry to replace all the men sent to France, so they've put out a lot of propaganda about how great women are as bus drivers and munitions workers. That makes it more difficult for people to say that women are inferior."

"I hope you're right," Ethel said fervently.

They had been married four months, and Ethel had no regrets. Bernie was clever, interesting, and kind. They believed in the same things and worked together to achieve them. Bernie would probably be the Labour candidate for Aldgate in the next general election—whenever that might be: like so much else, it had to wait for the end of the war. Bernie would make a good member of Parliament, hardworking and intelligent. However, Ethel did not know whether Labour could win Aldgate. The current M.P. was a Liberal, but much had changed since the last election in 1910. Even if the clause about votes for women did not pass, the other proposals of the Speaker's Conference would give the vote to many more working-class men.

Bernie was a good man, but to her shame Ethel still occasionally thought longingly of Fitz, who was not clever, nor interesting, nor kind, and whose beliefs were opposite to hers. When she had these thoughts she felt she was no better than the type of man that hankered after girls who danced the can-can. Such men were inflamed by stockings and petticoats and frilly knickers; she was entranced by Fitz's soft hands and clipped accent and the clean, slightly scented smell of him.

But she was Eth Leckwith now. Everyone spoke of Eth and Bernie the way they said horse-and-cart or bread-and-dripping.

She put Lloyd's shoes on and took him to the child minder, then walked to the office of *The Soldier's Wife*. The weather was fine and she felt hopeful. We *can* change the world, she thought. It's not easy, but it can be done. Maud's newspaper would whip up support for the bill among working-class women, and make sure all eyes were on M.P.s when they voted.

Maud was at their pokey office already, having come in early, no doubt because of the news. She sat at an old stained table, wearing a lilac summer gown and a hat like a fore-and-aft cap with one dramatically long feather stuck through its peak. Most of her clothes were prewar, but she still dressed elegantly. She looked too thoroughbred for this place, like a racehorse in a farmyard.

"We must bring out a special edition," she said, scribbling on a pad. "I'm writing the front page."

Ethel felt a wave of excitement. This was what she liked: action. She sat on the other side of the table and said: "I'll make sure the other pages are ready. How about a column on how readers can help?"

"Yes. Come to our meeting, lobby your member of Parliament, write a letter to a newspaper, that sort of thing."

"I'll draft something." She picked up a pencil and took a pad from a drawer.

Maud said: "We have to mobilize women against this bill."

Ethel froze, pencil in hand. "What?" she said. "Did you say against?"

"Of course. The government is going to *pretend* to give women the vote—but still withhold it from most of us."

Ethel looked across the table and saw the headline Maud had written: VOTE AGAINST THIS TRICK! "Just a minute." She did not see it as a trick. "This may not be all that we want, but it's better than nothing."

Maud looked at her angrily. "It's worse than nothing. This bill only pretends to make women equal."

Maud was being too theoretical. Of course it was wrong in principle to discriminate against younger women. But right now that was not important. This was about practical politics. Ethel said: "Look, sometimes reform has to go step by step. The vote has been extended to men very gradually. Even now only about half of men can vote—"

Maud interrupted her imperiously. "Have you thought about who the left-out women are?"

It was a fault of Maud's that she could occasionally seem high-handed. Ethel tried not to be offended. Mildly, she said: "Well, I'm one of them."

Maud did not soften her tone. "The majority of female munitions workers—such an essential part of the war effort—would be too young to vote. So would most of the nurses who have risked their lives caring for wounded soldiers in France. War widows could not vote, despite the terrible sacrifice they have made, if they happen to live in furnished lodgings. Can't you see that the purpose of this bill is to turn women into a minority?"

"So you want to campaign *against* the bill?"

"Of course!"

"That's crazy." Ethel was surprised and upset to find herself disagreeing violently with someone who had been a friend and colleague for so long. "I'm sorry. I just don't see how we can ask members of Parliament to vote against something we've been demanding for decades."

"That is *not* what we're doing!" Maud's anger mounted. "We've been campaigning for equality, and this is not it. If we fall for this ruse we'll be on the sidelines for another generation!"

"It's not a question of falling for a ruse," Ethel said tetchily. "I'm not being *fooled*. I understand the point you're making—it's not even particularly subtle. But your judgment is wrong."

"Is it, indeed?" Maud said stiffly, and Ethel suddenly saw her resemblance to Fitz: brother and sister held opposing opinions with a similar obstinacy.

Ethel said: "Just think of the propaganda the other side will put out! 'We always knew women couldn't make up their minds,' they'll say. 'That's why they can't vote.' They will make fun of us, yet again."

"Our propaganda must be better than theirs," Maud said airily. "We just have to explain the situation very clearly to everyone."

Ethel shook her head. "You're wrong. These things are too emotional. For years we've been campaigning against the rule that women can't vote. That's the barrier. Once it's broken down, people will see further concessions as mere technicalities. It will be relatively easy to get the voting age lowered and other restrictions eased. You must see that."

"No, I do not," Maud said icily. She did not like being told that she *must* see something. "This bill is a step backward. Anyone who supports it is a traitor."

Ethel stared at Maud. She felt wounded. She said: "You can't mean that."

"Please don't instruct me as to what I can and cannot mean."

"We've worked and campaigned together for two years," Ethel said, and tears came to her eyes. "Do you really believe that if I disagree with you I must be disloyal to the cause of women's suffrage?"

Maud was implacable. "I most certainly do."

"Very well," said Ethel; and, not knowing what else she could possibly do, she walked out.

{ II }

Fitz caused his tailor to make him six new suits. All the old ones hung loosely on his thin frame and made him look old. He put on his new evening clothes: black tailcoat, white waistcoat, and wing collar with white bow tie. He looked in the cheval glass in his dressing room and thought: That's better.

He went down to the drawing room. He could manage without a cane indoors. Maud poured him a glass of Madeira. Aunt Herm said: "How do you feel?"

"The doctors say the leg's getting better, but it's slow." Fitz had returned to the trenches earlier this year, but the cold and damp had proved too much for him, and he was back on the convalescent list, and working in intelligence.

Maud said: "I know you'd rather be over there, but we're not sorry you missed the spring fighting."

Fitz nodded. The Nivelle Offensive had been a failure, and the French general Nivelle had been fired. French soldiers were mutinous, defending their trenches but refusing to advance when ordered. So far this had been another bad year for the Allies.

But Maud was wrong to think Fitz would rather be on the front line. The work he was doing in Room 40 was probably even more important than the fighting in France. Many people had feared that German submarines would strangle Britain's supply lines. But Room 40 was able to find out where the U-boats were and forewarn ships. This information, combined with the tactic of sending ships in convoys escorted by destroyers, rendered the submarines much less effective. It was a triumph, albeit one that few people knew about.

The danger now was Russia. The tsar had been deposed, and anything could happen. So far, the moderates had remained in control, but could that last? It was not just Bea's family and Boy's inheritance that were in danger. If extremists took over the Russian government they might make peace, and free hundreds of thousands of German troops to fight in France.

Fitz said: "At least we haven't lost Russia."

"Yet," said Maud. "The Germans are hoping the Bolsheviks will triumph—everyone knows that."

As she spoke Princess Bea came in, wearing a low-cut dress in silver silk and a suite of diamond jewelry. Fitz and Bea were going to a dinner party, then a ball: it was the London season. Bea heard Maud's remark and said: "Don't underestimate the Russian royal family. There may yet be a counterrevolution. After all, what have the Russian people gained? The workers are still starving, the soldiers are still dying, and the Germans are still advancing."

Grout came in with a bottle of champagne. He opened it inaudibly and poured a glass for Bea. As always, she took one sip and set it down.

Maud said: "Prince Lvov has announced that women will be able to vote in the election for the Constituent Assembly."

"If it ever happens," Fitz said. "The provisional government is making a lot of announcements, but is anyone listening? As far as I can make out, every village has set up a soviet and is running its own affairs."

"Imagine it!" said Bea. "Those superstitious, illiterate peasants, pretending to govern!"

"It's very dangerous," Fitz said angrily. "People have no idea how easily they could slip into anarchy and barbarism." The subject made him irate.

Maud said: "How ironic it will be if Russia becomes more democratic than Great Britain."

"Parliament is about to debate votes for women," Fitz said.

"Only for women over thirty who are householders, or the wives of householders."

"Still, you must be pleased to have made progress. I read an article about it by your comrade Ethel in one of the journals." Fitz had been startled, sitting in the drawing room of his club looking at the *New Statesman*, to find he was reading the words of his former housekeeper. The uncomfortable thought had occurred to him that he might not be capable of writing such a clear and well-argued piece. "Her line is that women should accept this on the grounds that something is better than nothing."

"I'm afraid I disagree," Maud said frostily. "I will not wait until I am thirty to be considered a member of the human race."

"Have you two quarreled?"

"We have agreed to go our separate ways."

Fitz could see Maud was furious. To cool the atmosphere he turned to Lady Hermia. "If the British Parliament gives the vote to women, Aunt, for whom will you cast your ballot?"

"I'm not sure I shall vote at all," said Aunt Herm. "Isn't it a bit vulgar?"

Maud looked annoyed, but Fitz grinned. "If ladies of good family think that way, the only voters will be the working class, and they will put the socialists in," he said.

"Oh, dear," said Herm. "Perhaps I'd better vote, after all."

"Would you support Lloyd George?"

"A Welsh solicitor? Certainly not."

"Perhaps Bonar Law, the Conservative leader."

"I expect so."

"But he's Canadian."

"Oh, my goodness."

"This is the problem of having an empire. Riffraff from all over the world think they're part of it."

The nurse came in with Boy. He was two and a half years old now, a plump toddler with his mother's thick fair hair. He ran to Bea, and she sat him on her lap. He said: "I had porridge and Nursie dropped the sugar!" and laughed. That had been the big event of the day in the nursery.

Bea was at her best with the child, Fitz thought. Her face softened and she became affectionate, stroking and kissing him. After a minute he wriggled off her lap and waddled over to Fitz. "How's my little soldier?" said Fitz. "Going to grow up and shoot Germans?"

"Bang! Bang!" said Boy.

Fitz saw that his nose was running. "Has he got a cold, Jones?" he asked sharply.

The nurse looked frightened. She was a young girl from Aberowen, but she had been professionally trained. "No, my lord, I'm sure—it's June!"

"There's such a thing as a summer cold."

"He's been perfectly well all day. It's just a runny nose."

"It's certainly that." Fitz took a linen handkerchief from the inside breast pocket of his evening coat and wiped Boy's nose. "Has he been playing with common children?"

"No, sir, not at all."

"What about in the park?"

"There's none but children from good families in the parts we visit. I'm most particular."

"I hope you are. This child is heir to the Fitzherbert title, and may be a Russian prince, too." Fitz put Boy down and he ran back to the nurse.

Grout reappeared with an envelope on a silver tray. "A telegram, my lord," he said. "Addressed to the princess."

Fitz made a gesture indicating that Grout should give the cable to Bea. She frowned anxiously—telegrams made everyone nervous in wartime—and ripped it open. She scanned the sheet of paper and gave a cry of distress.

Fitz jumped up. "What is it?"

"My brother!"

"Is he alive?"

"Yes—wounded." She began to cry. "They have amputated his arm, but he is recovering. Oh, poor Andrei."

Fitz took the cable and read it. The only additional information was that Prince Andrei had been taken home to Bulovnir, his country estate in Tambov province southeast of Moscow. He hoped Andrei really was recovering. Many men died of infected wounds, and amputation did not always halt the spread of the gangrene.

"My dear, I'm most frightfully sorry," said Fitz. Maud and Herm stood on either side of Bea, trying to comfort her. "It says a letter will follow, but God knows how long it will take to get here."

"I must know how he is!" Bea sobbed.

Fitz said: "I will ask the British ambassador to make careful inquiries." An earl still had privileges, even in this democratic age.

Maud said: "Let us take you up to your room, Bea."

Bea nodded and stood up.

Fitz said: "I'd better go to Lord Silverman's dinner—Bonar Law is going to be there." Fitz wanted one day to be a minister in a Conservative government, and he was glad of any opportunity to chat with the party leader. "But I'll skip the ball and come straight home."

Bea nodded, and allowed herself to be taken upstairs.

Grout came in and said: "The car is ready, my lord."

During the short drive to Belgrave Square, Fitz brooded over the news. Prince Andrei had never been good at managing the family lands. He would probably use his disability as an excuse to take even less care of business. The estate would decline further. But there was nothing Fitz could do, fifteen hundred miles away in London. He felt frustrated and worried. Anarchy was always just around the corner, and slackness by noblemen such as Andrei was what gave revolutionists their chance.

When he reached the Silverman residence Bonar Law was already there—and so was Perceval Jones, the member of Parliament for Aberowen and chairman of Celtic Minerals. Jones was a turkey-cock at the best of times, and tonight he was bursting with pride at being in such distinguished company, talking to Lord Silverman with his hands in his pockets, a massive gold watch chain stretched across his wide waistcoat.

Fitz should not have been so surprised. This was a political dinner, and Jones was rising in the Conservative party: no doubt he, too, hoped to be a minister when and if Bonar Law should become prime minister. All the same, it was a bit like meeting your head groom at the Hunt Ball, and Fitz had an unnerving feeling that Bolshevism might be coming to London, not by revolution but by stealth.

At the table Jones shocked Fitz by saying he was in favor of votes for women. "For heaven's sake, why?" said Fitz.

"We have conducted a survey of constituency chairmen and agents," Jones replied, and Fitz saw Bonar Law nodding. "They are two to one in favor of the proposal."

"Conservatives are?" Fitz said incredulously.

"Yes, my lord."

"But why?"

"The bill will give the vote only to women over thirty who are householders or the wives of householders. Most women factory workers are excluded, because they tend to be younger. And all those dreadful female intellectuals are single women who live in other people's homes."

Fitz was taken aback. He had always regarded this as an issue of principle. But principle did not matter to jumped-up businessmen such as Jones. Fitz had never thought about electoral consequences. "I still don't see . . . "

"Most of the new voters will be mature middle-class mothers of families." Jones tapped the side of his nose in a vulgar gesture. "Lord Fitzherbert, they are the most conservative group of people in the country. This bill will give our party six million new votes."

"So you're going to support woman suffrage?"

"We must! We need those Conservative women. At the next election there will be three million new working-class male voters, a lot of them coming out of the army, most of them not on our side. But our new women will outnumber them."

"But the principle, man!" Fitz protested, though he sensed this was a losing battle.

"Principle?" said Jones. "This is practical politics." He gave a condescending smile that infuriated Fitz. "But then, if I may say so, you always were an idealist, my lord."

"We're all idealists," said Lord Silverman, smoothing over the conflict like a good host. "That's why we're in politics. People without ideals don't bother. But we have to confront the realities of elections and public opinion."

Fitz did not want to be labeled an impractical dreamer, so he quickly said: "Of course we do. Still, the question of a woman's place touches the heart of family life, something I should have thought dear to Conservatives."

Bonar Law said: "The issue is still open. Members of Parliament have a free vote. They will follow their consciences."

Fitz nodded submissively, and Silverman began speaking of the mutinous French army.

Fitz remained quiet for the rest of the dinner. He found it ominous that this bill had the support of both Ethel Leckwith and Perceval Jones. There was a dangerous possibility that it might pass. He thought Conservatives should defend traditional values, and not be swayed by short-term vote-winning considerations; but he had seen clearly that Bonar Law did not feel the same, and Fitz had not wanted to show himself out of step. The result was that he was ashamed of himself for not being completely honest, a feeling he hated.

He left Lord Silverman's house immediately after Bonar Law. He returned home and went upstairs. He took off his dress coat, put on a silk dressing gown, and went to Bea's room.

He found her sitting up in bed with a cup of tea. He could see that she had been crying, but she had put a little powder on her face and dressed in a flowered nightdress and a pink knitted bed jacket with puffed sleeves. He asked her how she was feeling.

"I am devastated," she said. "Andrei is all that is left of my family."

"I know." Both her parents were dead and she had no other close relatives. "It's worrying—but he will probably pull through."

She put down her cup and saucer. "I have been thinking very hard, Fitz."

That was an unusual thing for her to say.

"Please hold my hand," she said.

He took her left hand in both of his. She looked pretty, and despite the sad topic of conversation, he felt a stirring of desire. He could feel her rings, a diamond engagement ring and a gold wedding band. He had an urge to put her hand in his mouth and bite the fleshy part at the base of the thumb.

She said: "I want you to take me to Russia."

He was so startled that he dropped her hand. "What?"

"Don't refuse yet—think about it," she said. "You'll say it's dangerous—I know that. All the same there are hundreds of British people in Russia right now: diplomats at the embassy, businessmen, army officers and soldiers at our military missions there, journalists, and others."

"What about Boy?"

"I hate to leave him, but Nurse Jones is excellent, Hermia is devoted to him, and Maud can be relied upon to make sensible decisions in a crisis."

"We would need visas . . . "

"You could have a word in the right ear. My goodness, you've just dined with at least one member of the cabinet."

She was right. "The Foreign Office would probably ask me to write a report on the trip—especially as we'll be traveling through the countryside, where our diplomats rarely venture."

She took his hand again. "My only living relative is severely wounded and may die. I must see him. Please, Fitz. I'm begging you."

The truth was that Fitz was not as reluctant as she assumed. His perception of what was dangerous had been altered by the trenches. After all, most people survived an artillery barrage. A trip to Russia, though hazardous, was nothing by comparison. All the same he hesitated. "I understand your desire," he said. "Let me make some inquiries."

She took that for consent. "Oh, thank you!" she said.

"Don't thank me yet. Let me find out how practicable this is."

"All right," she said, but he could see that she was already assuming the outcome.

He stood up. "I must get ready for bed," he said, and went to the door.

"When you've put on your nightclothes . . . please come back. I want you to hold me."

Fitz smiled. "Of course," he said.

{ III }

On the day Parliament debated votes for women, Ethel organized a rally in a hall near the Palace of Westminster.

She was now employed by the National Union of Garment Workers, which had been eager to hire such a well-known activist. Her main job was recruiting women members in the sweatshops of the East End, but the union believed in fighting for its members in national politics as well as in the workplace.

She felt sad about the end of her relationship with Maud. Perhaps there had always been something artificial about a friendship between an earl's sister and his former housekeeper, but Ethel had hoped they could transcend the class divide. However, deep in her heart Maud had believed—without being conscious of it—that she was born to command and Ethel to obey.

Ethel hoped the vote in Parliament would take place before the end of the rally, so that she could announce the result, but the debate went on late, and the meeting had to break up at ten. Ethel and Bernie went to a pub in Whitehall used by Labour M.P.s and waited for news.

It was after eleven and the pub was closing when two M.P.s rushed in. One of them spotted Ethel. "We won!" he shouted. "I mean, you won. The women."

She could hardly believe it. "They passed the clause?"

"By a huge majority—three eighty-seven to fifty-seven!"

"We won!" Ethel kissed Bernie. "We won!"

"Well done," he said. "Enjoy your victory. You deserve it."

They could not have a drink to celebrate. New wartime rules forced pubs to stop serving at set hours. This was supposed to improve the productivity of the working class. Ethel and Bernie went out into Whitehall to catch a bus home.

Waiting at the bus stop, Ethel was euphoric. "I can't take it in. After all these years—votes for women!"

A passerby heard her, a tall man in evening dress walking with a cane.

She recognized Fitz.

"Don't be so sure," he said. "We'll vote you down in the House of Lords."

CHAPTER TWENTY-SEVEN

June to September 1917

Walter von Ulrich climbed out of the trench and, taking his life in his hands, began to walk across no-man's-land.

New grass and wildflowers were growing in the shell holes. It was a mild summer evening in a region that had once been Poland, then Russia, and was now partly occupied by German troops. Walter wore a nondescript coat over a corporal's uniform. He had dirtied his face and hands for authenticity. He wore a white cap, like a flag of truce, and carried on his shoulder a cardboard box.

He told himself there was no point being scared.

The Russian positions were dimly visible in the twilight. There had been no firing for weeks, and Walter thought his approach would be regarded with more curiosity than suspicion.

If he was wrong, he was dead.

The Russians were preparing an offensive. German reconnaissance aircraft and scouts reported fresh troops being deployed to the front lines and truckloads of ammunition being unloaded. This had been confirmed by starving Russian soldiers who had crossed the lines and surrendered in the hope of getting a meal from their German captors.

The evidence of the approaching offensive had come as a big disappointment to Walter. He had hoped that the new Russian government would be unable to fight on. In Petrograd, Lenin and the Bolsheviks were vociferously calling for peace, and pouring out a flood of newspapers and pamphlets—paid for with German money.

The Russian people did not want war. An announcement by Pavel Miliukov, the monocled foreign minister, that Russia was still aiming for "decisive victory" had brought enraged workers and soldiers out onto the streets again. The theatrical young war minister, Kerensky, who was responsible for the expected new offensive, had reinstated flogging in the army and restored the authority of officers. But would the Russian soldiers fight? That was what the Germans needed to know and Walter was risking his life to find out.

The signs were mixed. In some sections of the front, Russian soldiers had hoisted white flags and unilaterally declared an armistice. Other sections seemed quiet and disciplined. It was one such area that Walter had decided to visit.

He had at last got away from Berlin. Probably Monika von der Helbard had told her parents bluntly that there was not going to be a wedding. Anyway, Walter was on the front line again, gathering intelligence.

He shifted the box to the other shoulder. Now he could see half a dozen heads sticking up over the edge of a trench. They wore caps—Russian soldiers did not have helmets. They stared at him but did not point their weapons, yet.

He felt fatalistic about death. He thought he could die happy after his joyous night in Stockholm with Maud. Of course, he would prefer to live. He wanted to make a home with Maud and have children. And he hoped to do so in a prosperous, democratic Germany. But that meant winning the war, which in turn meant risking his life, so he had no choice.

All the same his stomach felt watery as he got within rifle range. It was so easy for a soldier to aim his gun and pull the trigger. That was what they were here for, after all.

He carried no rifle, and he hoped they had noticed that. He did have a nine-millimeter Luger stuffed into his belt at the back, but they could not see it. What they could see was the box he was carrying. He hoped it looked harmless.

He felt grateful for every step he survived, but conscious that each took him farther into danger. Any second now, he thought philosophically. He wondered whether a man heard the shot that killed him. What Walter feared most was being wounded and bleeding slowly to death, or succumbing to infection in a filthy field hospital.

He could now see the faces of the Russians, and he read amusement, astonishment, and lively wonderment in their expressions. He looked anxiously for signs of fear: that was the greatest danger. A scared soldier might shoot just to break the tension.

At last he had ten yards to go, then nine, eight . . . He came to the lip of the trench. "Hello, comrades," he said in Russian. He put down the box.

He held out his hand to the nearest soldier. Automatically, the man reached out and helped him jump into the trench. A small group gathered around him.

"I have come to ask you a question," he said.

Most educated Russians spoke some German, but the troops were peasants, and few understood any language other than their own. As a boy Walter had learned Russian as part of his preparation, rigidly enforced by his father, for a career in the army and the foreign ministry. He had never used his Russian much, but he thought he could remember enough for this mission.

"First a drink," he said. He brought the box into the trench, ripped open the top, and took out a bottle of schnapps. He pulled the cork, took a swig, wiped his mouth, and gave the bottle to the nearest soldier, a tall corporal of eighteen or nineteen. The man grinned, drank, and passed the bottle on.

Walter covertly studied his surroundings. The trench was poorly constructed. The walls slanted, and were not braced by timber. The floor was irregular and had no duckboards, so even now in summer it was muddy. The trench did not even follow a straight line—although that was probably a good thing, as there were no traverses to contain the blast of an artillery hit. There was a foul smell: obviously the men did not always bother to walk to the latrine. What was wrong with these Russians? Everything they did was slapdash, disorganized, and half-finished.

While the bottle was going around, a sergeant appeared. "What's going on, Feodor Igorovich?" he said, addressing the tall corporal. "Why are you talking to a cow-fucking German?"

Feodor was young, but his mustache was luxuriant and curled across his cheeks. For some reason he had a nautical cap, which he wore at a jaunty angle. His air of self-confidence bordered on arrogance. "Have a drink, Sergeant Gavrik."

The sergeant drank from the bottle like the rest, but he was not as nonchalant as his men. He gave Walter a mistrustful look. "What the fuck are you doing here?"

Walter had rehearsed what he would say. "On behalf of German workers, soldiers, and peasants, I come to ask why you are fighting us."

After a moment of surprised silence, Feodor said: "Why are *you* fighting *us*?"

Walter had his answer ready. "We have no choice. Our country is still ruled by the kaiser—we have not yet made our revolution. But you have. The tsar is gone, and Russia is now ruled by its people. So I have come to ask the people: Why are you fighting us?"

Feodor looked at Gavrik and said: "It's the question we keep asking ourselves!"

Gavrik shrugged. Walter guessed he was a traditionalist who was carefully keeping his opinions to himself.

Several more men came along the trench and joined the group. Walter opened another bottle. He looked around the circle of thin, ragged, dirty men who were rapidly getting drunk. "What do Russians want?"

Several men answered.

"Land."

"Peace."

"Freedom."

"More booze!"

Walter took another bottle from the box. What they really needed, he thought, was soap, good food, and new boots.

Feodor said: "I want to go home to my village. They're dividing up the prince's land, and I need to make sure my family gets its fair share."

Walter asked: "Do you support a political party?"

A soldier said: "The Bolsheviks!" The others cheered.

Walter was pleased. "Are you party members?"

They shook their heads.

Feodor said: "I used to support the Socialist Revolutionaries, but they have let us down." Others nodded agreement. "Kerensky has brought back flogging," Feodor added.

"And he has ordered a summer offensive," Walter said. He could see, in front of his eyes, a stack of ammunition boxes, but he did not refer to them, for fear of calling the Russians' attention to the obvious possibility that he was a spy. "We can see from our aircraft," he added.

Feodor said to Gavrik: "Why do we need to attack? We can make peace just as well from where we are now!" There was a mutter of agreement.

Walter said: "So what will you do if the order to advance is given?"

Feodor said: "There will have to be a meeting of the soldiers' committee to discuss it."

"Don't talk shit," said Gavrik. "Soldiers' committees are no longer allowed to debate orders."

There was a rumble of discontent, and someone at the edge of the circle muttered: "We'll see about that, comrade Sergeant."

The crowd continued to grow. Perhaps Russians could smell booze at a distance. Walter handed out two more bottles. By way of explanation to the new arrivals, he said: "German people want peace just as much as you. If you don't attack us, we won't attack you."

"I'll drink to that!" said one of the newcomers, and there was a ragged cheer.

Walter feared the noise would attract the attention of an officer, and wondered how he could get the Russians to keep their voices down despite the schnapps; but he was already too late. A loud, authoritative voice said: "What's going on here? What are you men up to?" The crowd parted to give passage to a big man in the uniform of a major. He looked at Walter and said: "Who the hell are you?"

Walter's heart sank. It was undoubtedly the officer's duty to take him prisoner. German intelligence knew how the Russians treated their POWs. Being captured by them was a sentence of lingering death by starvation and cold.

He forced a smile and offered the last unopened bottle. "Have a drink, Major."

The officer ignored him and turned to Gavrik. "What do you think you're doing?"

Gavrik was not intimidated. "The men have had no dinner today, Major, so I couldn't make them refuse a drink."

"You should have taken him prisoner!"

Feodor said: "We can't take him prisoner, now that we've drunk his booze." He was slurring already. "It wouldn't be fair!" he finished, and the others cheered.

The major said to Walter: "You're a spy, and I ought to blow your damned head off." He touched the holstered gun at his belt.

The soldiers shouted protests. The major continued to look angry, but he said no more, clearly not wanting a clash with the men.

Walter said to them: "I'd better leave you. Your major is a bit unfriendly. Besides, we have a brothel just behind our front line, and there's a blond girl with big tits who may be feeling a bit lonely . . ."

They laughed and cheered. It was half true: there was a brothel, but Walter had never visited it.

"Remember," he said. "We won't fight if you don't!"

He scrambled out of the trench. This was the moment of greatest danger. He got to his feet, walked a few paces, turned, waved, and walked on. They had satisfied their curiosity and all the schnapps was gone.

Now they might just take it into their heads to do their duty and shoot the enemy. He felt as if his coat had a target printed on the back.

Darkness was falling. Soon he would be out of sight. He was only a few yards from safety. It took all his willpower not to break into a sprint—but he felt that might provoke a shot. Gritting his teeth, he walked with even strides through the litter of unexploded shells.

He glanced back. He could not see the trench. That meant they could not see him. He was safe.

He breathed easier and walked on. It had been worth the risk. He had learned a lot. Although this section was showing no white flags, the Russians were in poor shape for battle. Clearly the men were discontented and rebellious, and the officers had only a weak hold on discipline. The sergeant had been careful not to cross them and the major had not dared to take Walter prisoner. In that frame of mind it was impossible for soldiers to put up a brave fight.

He came within sight of the German line. He shouted his name and a prearranged password. He dropped down into the trench. A lieutenant saluted him. "Successful sortie, sir?"

"Yes, thanks," said Walter. "Very successful indeed."

{ II }

Katerina lay on the bed in Grigori's old room, wearing only a thin shift. The window was open, letting in the warm July air and the thunder of the trains that passed a few steps away. She was six months pregnant.

Grigori ran a finger along the outline of her body, from her shoulder, over one swollen breast, down again to her ribs, up over the gentle hill of her belly, and down her thigh. Before Katerina he had never known this easygoing joy. His youthful relations with women had been hasty and short-lived. To him it was a new and thrilling experience to lie beside a woman after sex, touching her body gently and lovingly but without urgency or lust. Perhaps this was what marriage meant, he thought. "You're even more beautiful pregnant," he said, speaking in a low murmur so as not to wake Vlad.

For two and a half years he had acted as father to his brother's son, but now he was going to have a child of his own. He would have liked to name the baby after Lenin, but they already had a Vladimir. The pregnancy had made Grigori a hardliner in politics. He had to think about the country in which the child would grow up, and he wanted his son to be free. (For some reason he thought of the baby as a boy.) He had to be sure Russia would be ruled by its people, not by a tsar or a middle-class parliament or a coalition of businessmen and generals who would bring back the old ways in new disguises.

He did not really like Lenin. The man lived in a permanent rage. He was always shouting at people. Anyone who disagreed with him was a swine, a bastard, a cunt. But he worked harder than anyone else, he thought about things for a long time, and his decisions were always right. In the past, every Russian "revolution" had led to nothing but dithering. Grigori knew Lenin would not let that happen.

The provisional government knew it, too, and there were signs they wanted to target Lenin. The right-wing press had accused him of being a spy for Germany. The accusation was ridiculous. However, it was true that Lenin had a secret source of finance. Grigori, as one of those who had been Bolsheviks since before the war, was part of the inner circle, and he knew the money came from Germany. If the secret got out it would fuel suspicion.

He was dozing off when he heard footsteps in the hall followed by a loud, urgent knock at the door. Pulling on his trousers he shouted: "What is it?" Vlad woke up and cried.

A man's voice said: "Grigori Sergeivich?"

"Yes." Grigori opened the door and saw Isaak. "What's happened?"

"They've issued arrest warrants for Lenin, Zinoviev, and Kamenev."

Grigori went cold. "We have to warn them!"

"I've got an army car outside."

"I'll put my boots on."

Isaak went. Katerina picked up Vlad and comforted him. Grigori hastily pulled his clothes on, kissed them both, and ran down the stairs.

He jumped into the car beside Isaak and said: "Lenin is the most important." The government was right to target him. Zinoviev and Kamenev were sound revolutionaries, but Lenin was the engine that drove the movement. "We must warn him first. Drive to his sister's place. Fast as you can go."

Isaak headed off at top speed.

Grigori held tight while the car screeched around a corner. As it straightened up, he said: "How did you find out?"

"From a Bolshevik in the Ministry of Justice."

"When were the warrants signed?"

"This morning."

"I hope we're in time." Grigori was terrified that Lenin might already have been seized. No one else had his inflexible determination. He was a bully, but he had transformed the Bolsheviks into the leading party. Without him, the revolution could fall back into muddle and compromise.

Isaak drove to Shirokaya Street and pulled up outside a middle-class apartment building. Grigori jumped out, ran inside, and knocked at the Yelizarov flat. Anna Yelizarova, Lenin's elder sister, opened the door. She was in her fifties, with graying hair parted in the center. Grigori had met her before: she worked on *Pravda.* "Is he here?" Grigori said.

"Yes. Why? What's happened?"

Grigori felt a wave of relief. He was not too late. He stepped inside. "They're going to arrest him."

Anna slammed the door. "Volodya!" she called, using the familiar form of Lenin's first name. "Come quickly!"

Lenin appeared, dressed as always in a shabby dark suit with a collar and tie. Grigori explained the situation rapidly.

"I'll leave immediately," Lenin said.

Anna said: "Don't you want to throw a few things in your suitcase—"

"Too risky. Send everything later. I'll let you know where I am." He looked at Grigori. "Thank you for the warning, Grigori Sergeivich. Do you have a car?"

"Yes."

Without another word Lenin went out into the hall.

Grigori followed him to the street and hurried to open the car door. "They have also issued warrants for Zinoviev and Kamenev," Grigori said as Lenin got in.

"Go back to the apartment and telephone them," Lenin said. "Mark has a phone and he knows where they are." He slammed the door. He leaned forward and said something to Isaak that Grigori did not hear. Isaak drove off.

This was how Lenin was all the time. He barked orders at everyone, and they did what he said because he always made sense.

Grigori felt the pleasure of a great weight being lifted from his shoulders. He looked up and down the street. A group of men came out of a building on the other side. Some were dressed in suits, others wore army officers' uniforms. Grigori was shocked to recognize Mikhail Pinsky. The secret police had been abolished, in theory, but it seemed men such as Pinsky were continuing their work as part of the army.

These men must have come for Lenin—and just missed him by going into the wrong building.

Grigori ran back inside. The door to the Yelizarovs' apartment was still open. Just inside were Anna; her husband, Mark; her foster son, Gora; and the family servant, a country girl called Anyushka, all looking shocked. Grigori closed the door behind him. "He's safely away," he said. "But the police are outside. I have to telephone Zinoviev and Kamenev quickly."

Mark said: "The phone is there on the side table."

Grigori hesitated. "How does it work?" He had never used a telephone.

"Oh, sorry," said Mark. He picked up the instrument, holding one piece to his ear and the other to his mouth. "It's quite new to us, but we use it so much that we take it for granted already." Impatiently he jiggled the sprung bar on top of the stand. "Yes, please, operator," he said, and gave a number.

There was a banging at the door.

Grigori held his finger to his lips, telling the others to be quiet.

Anna took Anyushka and the child into the back of the apartment.

Mark spoke rapidly into the phone. Grigori stood at the apartment door. A voice said: "Open up or we'll break down the door! We have a warrant!"

Grigori shouted back: "Just a minute—I'm putting my pants on." The police came often to the kinds of buildings where he had lived most of his life, and he knew all the pretexts for keeping them waiting.

Mark jiggled the bar again and asked for another number.

Grigori shouted: "Who is it? Who's at the door?"

"Police! Open up this instant!"

"I'm just coming—I have to lock the dog in the kitchen."

"Hurry up!"

Grigori heard Mark say: "Tell him to go into hiding. The police are at my door now." He replaced the earpiece on its hook and nodded to Grigori.

Grigori opened the door and stood back.

Pinsky stepped in. "Where is Lenin?" he said.

Several army officers followed him in.

Grigori said: "There is no one here by that name."

Pinsky stared at him. "What are you doing here?" he said. "I always knew you were a troublemaker."

Mark stepped forward and said calmly: "Show me the warrant, please."

Reluctantly, Pinsky handed over a piece of paper.

Mark studied it for a few moments, then said: "High treason? That's ridiculous!"

"Lenin is a German agent," Pinsky said. He narrowed his eyes at Mark. "You're his brother-in-law, aren't you?"

Mark handed the paper back. "The man you are looking for is not here," he said.

Pinsky could sense he was telling the truth, and he looked angry. "Why the hell not?" he said. "He lives here!"

"Lenin is not here," Mark repeated.

Pinsky's face reddened. "Was he warned?" He grabbed Grigori by the front of his tunic. "What are you doing here?"

"I am a deputy to the Petrograd soviet, representing the First Machine Guns, and unless you want the regiment to pay a visit to your headquarters, you'd better take your fat hands off my uniform."

Pinsky let go. "We'll take a look around anyway," he said.

There was a bookcase beside the phone table. Pinsky took half a dozen books off the shelf and threw them to the floor. He waved the officers toward the interior of the flat. "Tear the place apart," he said.

{ III }

Walter went to a village within the territory won from the Russians and gave an astonished and delighted peasant a gold coin for all his clothes: a filthy sheepskin coat, a linen smock, loose coarse trousers, and shoes made of bast, the woven bark of a beech tree. Fortunately Walter did not have to buy his underwear, for the man wore none.

Walter cut his hair with a pair of kitchen scissors and stopped shaving.

In a small market town he bought a sack of onions. He put a leather bag containing ten thousand rubles in coins and notes in the bottom of the sack under the onions.

One night he smeared his hands and face with earth; then, dressed in the peasant's clothes and carrying the onion sack, he crossed no-man's-land, slipped through the Russian lines, and walked to the nearest railway station, where he bought a third-class ticket.

He adopted an aggressive attitude, and snarled at anyone who spoke to him, as if he feared they wanted to steal his onions, which they probably did. He had a large knife, rusty but sharp, clearly visible at his belt, and a Mosin-Nagant pistol, taken from a captured Russian officer, concealed under his smelly coat. On two occasions when a policeman spoke to him, he grinned stupidly and offered an onion, a bribe so contemptible that both times the policeman grunted with disgust and walked off. If a policeman had insisted on looking into the sack, Walter was ready to kill him, but it was never necessary. He bought tickets for short journeys, three or four stops at a time, for a peasant would not go hundreds of miles to sell his onions.

He was tense and wary. His disguise was thin. Anyone who spoke to him for more than a few seconds would know he was not really Russian. The penalty for what he was doing was death.

At first he was scared, but that eventually wore off, and by the second day he was bored. He had nothing to occupy his mind. He could not read, of course: indeed, he had to be careful not to look at timetables posted at stations, or do more than glance at advertisements, for most peasants were illiterate. As a series of slow trains rattled and shook through the endless Russian forests, he entered into an elaborate daydream about the apartment he and Maud would live in after the war. It would have modern decor, with pale wood and neutral colors, like that of the von der Helbard house, rather than the heavy, dark look of his parents' home. Everything would be easy to clean and maintain, especially in the kitchen and laundry, so that they could employ fewer servants. They would have a really good piano, a Steinway grand, for they both liked to play. They would buy one or two eye-catching modern paintings, perhaps by Austrian expressionists, to shock the older generation and establish themselves as a progressive couple. They would have a light, airy bedroom and lie naked on a soft bed, kissing and talking and making love.

In this way he journeyed to Petrograd.

The arrangement, made through a revolutionary socialist in the Swedish embassy, was that someone from the Bolsheviks would wait to collect the money from Walter at Petrograd's Warsaw Station every day at six p.m. for one hour. Walter arrived at midday, and took the opportunity to look around the city, with the aim of assessing the Russian people's ability to fight on.

He was shocked by what he saw.

As soon as he left the station, he was assailed by prostitutes, male and female, adult and child. He crossed a canal bridge and walked a couple of miles north into the city center. Most shops were closed, many boarded up, a few simply abandoned, with the smashed glass of their windows glittering on the street outside. He saw many drunks and two fistfights. Occasionally an automobile or a horse-drawn carriage dashed past, scattering pedestrians, its passengers hiding behind closed curtains. Most of the people were thin, ragged, and barefoot. It was much worse than Berlin.

He saw many soldiers, individually and in groups, most showing lapsed discipline: marching out of step or lounging at their posts, uniforms unbuttoned, chatting to civilians, apparently doing as they pleased. Walter was confirmed in the impression he had formed when he visited the Russian front line: these men were in no mood to fight.

This is all good news, he thought.

No one accosted him and the police ignored him. He was just another shabby figure shuffling about his own business in a city that was falling apart.

In high spirits, he returned to the station at six and quickly spotted his contact, a sergeant with a red scarf tied to the barrel of his rifle. Before making himself known, Walter studied the man. He was a formidable figure, not tall but broad-shouldered and thickset. He was missing his right ear, one front tooth, and the ring finger of his left hand. He waited with the patience of a veteran soldier, but he had a keen blue-eyed gaze that did not miss much. Although Walter intended to watch him covertly, the soldier met his eye, nodded, and turned and walked away. As was clearly intended, Walter followed him. They went into a large room full of tables and chairs and sat down.

Walter said: "Sergeant Grigori Peshkov?"

Grigori nodded. "I know who you are. Sit down."

Walter looked around the room. There was a samovar hissing in a corner, and an old woman in a shawl selling smoked and pickled fish.

Fifteen or twenty people were sitting at tables. No one gave a second glance to a soldier and a peasant who was obviously hoping to sell his sack of onions. A young man in the blue tunic of a factory worker followed them in. Walter caught the man's eye briefly and watched him take a seat, light a cigarette, and open *Pravda*.

Walter said: "May I have something to eat? I'm starving, but a peasant probably can't afford the prices here."

Grigori got a plate of black bread and herrings and two glasses of tea with sugar. Walter tucked into the food. After watching him for a minute, Grigori laughed. "I'm amazed you've passed for a peasant," he said. "I'd know you for a bourgeois."

"How?"

"Your hands are dirty, but you eat in small bites and dab your lips with a rag as if it was a linen napkin. A real peasant shovels the food in and slurps tea before swallowing."

Walter was irritated by his condescension. After all, I've survived three days on a damn train, he thought. I'd like to see you try that in Germany. It was time to remind Peshkov that he had to earn his money. "Tell me how the Bolsheviks are doing," he said.

"Dangerously well," said Grigori. "Thousands of Russians have joined the party in the last few months. Leon Trotsky has at last announced his support for us. You should hear him. Most nights he packs out the Cirque Moderne." Walter could see that Grigori hero-worshipped Trotsky. Even the Germans knew that Trotsky's oratory was enchanting. He was a real catch for the Bolsheviks. "Last February we had ten thousand members—today we have two hundred thousand," Grigori finished proudly.

"This is good, but can you change things?" Walter said.

"We have a strong chance of winning the election for the Constituent Assembly."

"When will it be held?"

"It has been much delayed—"

"Why?"

Grigori sighed. "First the provisional government called together a council of representatives which, after two months, finally agreed on the composition of a sixty-member second council to draft the electoral law—"

"Why? Why such an elaborate process?"

Grigori looked irate. "They say they want the election to be absolutely unchallengeable—but the real reason is that the conservative parties are dragging their feet, knowing they stand to lose."

He was only a sergeant, Walter thought, but his analysis seemed quite sophisticated. "So when will the election be held?"

"September."

"And why do you think the Bolsheviks will win?"

"We are still the only group firmly committed to peace. And everyone knows that—thanks to all the newspapers and pamphlets we've produced."

"Why did you say you were doing 'dangerously' well?"

"It makes us the government's prime target. There's a warrant out for Lenin's arrest. He's had to go into hiding. But he's still running the party."

Walter believed that, too. If Lenin could keep control of his party from exile in Zurich, he could certainly do so from a hideaway in Russia.

Walter had made the delivery and gathered the information he needed. He had accomplished his mission. A sense of relief came over him. Now all he had to do was get home.

With his foot he pushed the sack containing the ten thousand rubles across the floor to Grigori.

He finished his tea and stood up. "Enjoy your onions," he said, and he walked to the door.

Out of the corner of his eye, he saw the man in the blue tunic fold his copy of *Pravda* and get to his feet.

Walter bought a ticket to Luga and boarded the train. He entered a third-class compartment. He pushed through a group of soldiers smoking and drinking vodka, a family of Jews with all their possessions in string-tied bundles, and some peasants with empty crates who had

744 +~+ CHAPTER TWENTY-SEVEN

presumably sold their chickens. At the far end of the carriage he paused and looked back.

The blue tunic entered the carriage.

Walter watched for a second as the man pushed through the passengers, carelessly elbowing people out of his way. Only a policeman would do that.

Walter jumped off the train and hurriedly left the station. Recalling his tour of exploration that afternoon, he headed at a fast walk for the canal. It was the season of short summer nights, so the evening was light. He hoped he might have shaken his tail, but when he glanced over his shoulder he saw the blue tunic following him. He had presumably been following Peshkov, and had decided to investigate Grigori's onion-selling peasant friend.

The man broke into a jogging run.

If caught, Walter would be shot as a spy. He had no choice about what he had to do next.

He was in a low-rent neighborhood. All of Petrograd looked poor, but this district had the cheap hotels and dingy bars that clustered near railway stations all over the world. Walter started to run, and the blue tunic quickened his pace to keep up.

Walter came to a canalside brickyard. It had a high wall and a gate with iron bars, but next door was a derelict warehouse on an unfenced site. Walter turned off the street, raced across the warehouse site to the waterside, then scrambled over the wall into the brickyard.

There had to be a watchman somewhere, but Walter saw no one. He looked for a place of concealment. It was a pity the light was still so clear. The yard had its own quay with a small timber pier. All around him were stacks of bricks the height of a man, but he needed to see without being seen. He moved to a stack that was partly dismantled—some having been sold, presumably—and swiftly rearranged a few so that he could hide behind them and look through a gap. He eased the Mosin-Nagant revolver out of his belt and cocked the hammer.

A few moments later, he saw the blue tunic come over the wall.

The man was of medium height and thin, with a small mustache. He looked scared: he had realized he was no longer merely following a suspect. He was engaged in a manhunt, and he did not know whether he was the hunter or the quarry.

He drew a gun.

Walter pointed his own gun through the gap in the bricks and aimed at the blue tunic, but he was not close enough to be sure of hitting his target.

The man stood still for a moment, looking all around, clearly undecided about what to do next. Then he turned and walked hesitantly toward the water.

Walter followed him. He had turned the tables.

The man dodged from stack to stack, scanning the area. Walter did the same, ducking behind bricks whenever the man stopped, getting nearer all the time. Walter did not want a prolonged gunfight, which might attract the attention of other policemen. He needed to down his enemy with one or two shots and get away fast.

By the time the man reached the canal end of the site, they were only ten yards apart. The man looked up and down the canal, as if Walter might have rowed away in a boat.

Walter stepped out of cover and drew a bead on the middle of the man's back.

The man turned away from the water and looked straight at Walter.

Then he screamed.

It was a high-pitched, girlish scream of shock and terror. Walter knew, in that instant, that he would remember the scream all his life.

He squeezed the trigger, the revolver banged, and the scream was cut off instantly.

Only one shot was needed. The secret policeman crumpled to the ground, lifeless.

Walter bent over the body. The eyes stared upward sightlessly. There was no heartbeat, no breath.

Walter dragged the body to the edge of the canal. He put bricks in the pockets of the man's trousers and tunic, to weight the corpse. Then he slid it over the low parapet and let it fall into the water.

It sank below the surface, and Walter turned away.

{ IV }

Grigori was in a session of the Petrograd soviet when the counterrevolution began.

He was worried, but not surprised. As the Bolsheviks gained popularity, the backlash had become more ruthless. The party was doing well in local elections, winning control of one provincial soviet after another, and had gained 33 percent of the votes for the Petrograd city council. In response the government—now led by Kerensky—arrested Trotsky and again deferred the long-delayed national elections for the Constituent Assembly. The Bolsheviks had said all along that the provisional government would never hold a national election, and this further postponement only added to Bolshevik credibility.

Then the army made its move.

General Kornilov was a shaven-headed Cossack who had the heart of a lion and the brains of a sheep, according to a famous remark by General Alexeev. On September 9 Kornilov ordered his troops to march on Petrograd.

The soviet responded quickly. The delegates immediately resolved to set up the Committee for Struggle Against the Counterrevolution.

A committee was nothing, Grigori thought impatiently. He got to his feet, holding down anger and fear. As the delegate for the First Machine Gun Regiment, he was listened to respectfully, especially on military matters. "There is no point in a committee if its members are just going to make speeches," he said passionately. "If the reports we have just heard are true, some of Kornilov's troops are not far from the city limits of Petrograd. They can be halted only by force." He always wore his sergeant's uniform, and carried his rifle and a pistol. "The committee will be pointless unless it mobilizes the workers and soldiers of Petrograd against the mutiny of the army."

Grigori knew that only the Bolshevik party could mobilize the people. And all the other deputies knew it, too, regardless of what party they belonged to. In the end it was agreed that the committee would have three Mensheviks, three Socialist Revolutionaries, and three Bolsheviks including Grigori; but everyone knew the Bolsheviks were the only ones who counted.

As soon as that was decided, the Committee for Struggle left the debating hall. Grigori had been a politician for six months, and he had learned how to work the system. Now he ignored the formal composition of the committee and invited a dozen useful people to join them, including Konstantin from the Putilov works and Isaak from the First Machine Guns.

The soviet had moved from the Tauride Palace to the Smolny Institute, a former girls' school, and the committee reconvened in a classroom, surrounded by framed embroidery and girlish watercolors.

The chairman said: "Do we have a motion for debate?"

This was rubbish, but Grigori had been a deputy long enough to know how to get around it. He moved immediately to take control of the meeting and get the committee focused on action instead of words.

"Yes, comrade Chairman, if I may," he said. "I propose there are five things we need to do." A numbered list was always a good idea: people felt they had to listen until you got to the end. "First: Mobilize the Petrograd soldiers against the mutiny of General Kornilov. How can we achieve this? I suggest that Corporal Isaak Ivanovich should draw up a list of the principal barracks with the names of reliable revolutionary leaders in each. Having identified our allies, we should send a letter instructing them to put themselves under the orders of this committee and get ready to repel the mutineers. If Isaak begins now he can bring list and letter back to this committee for approval in a few minutes' time."

Grigori paused briefly to allow people to nod; then, taking that for approval, he went on.

"Thank you. Carry on, Comrade Isaak. Second, we must send a message to Kronstadt." The naval base at Kronstadt, an island twenty miles offshore, was notorious for its brutal treatment of sailors, especially young trainees. Six months ago the sailors had turned on their tormentors, and had tortured and murdered many of their officers. The place was now a radical stronghold. "The sailors must arm themselves, deploy to Petrograd, and put themselves under our orders." Grigori pointed to a Bolshevik deputy whom he knew to be close to the sailors. "Comrade Gleb, will you undertake that task, with the committee's approval?"

Gleb nodded. "If I may, I will draft a letter for our chairman to sign, then take it to Kronstadt myself."

"Please do."

The committee members were now looking a bit bewildered. Things were moving faster than usual. Only the Bolsheviks were unsurprised.

"Third, we must organize factory workers into defensive units and arm them. We can get the guns from army arsenals and from armaments factories. Most workers will need some training in firearms and military discipline. I suggest this task be carried out jointly by the trade unions and the Red Guards." The Red Guards were revolutionary soldiers and workers who carried firearms. Not all were Bolsheviks, but they usually obeyed orders from the Bolshevik committees. "I propose that Comrade Konstantin, the deputy from the Putilov works, take charge of this. He will know the leading union in each major factory."

Grigori knew that he was turning the population of Petrograd into a revolutionary army, and so did the other Bolsheviks on the committee, but would the rest of them figure that out? At the end of this process, assuming the counterrevolution was defeated, it was going to be very difficult for the moderates to disarm the force they had created and restore the authority of the provisional government. If they thought that far ahead they might try to moderate or reverse what Grigori was proposing. But at the moment they were focused on preventing a military takeover. As usual, only the Bolsheviks had a strategy.

Konstantin said: "Yes, indeed, I'll make a list." He would favor

Bolshevik union leaders, of course, but they were nowadays the most effective anyway.

Grigori said: "Fourth, the Railwaymen's Union must do all it can to hamper the advance of Kornilov's army." The Bolsheviks had worked hard to gain control of this union, and now had at least one supporter in every locomotive shed. Bolshevik trade unionists always volunteered for duty as treasurer, secretary, or chairman. "Although some troops are on the way here by road, the bulk of the men and their supplies will have to come by rail. The union can make sure they get held up and sent on long diversions. Comrade Viktor, may the committee rely on you to do this?"

Viktor, a railwaymen's deputy, nodded agreement. "I will set up an ad hoc committee within the union to organize the disruption of the mutineers' advance."

"Finally, we should encourage other cities to set up committees like this one," Grigori said. "The revolution must be defended everywhere. Perhaps other members of this committee could suggest which towns we should communicate with?"

This was a deliberate distraction, but they fell for it. Glad to have something to do, the committee members called out the names of towns that should organize Committees for Struggle. That ensured they did not pick over Grigori's more important proposals, but let them go unchallenged; and they never thought about the long-term consequences of arming the citizens.

Isaak and Gleb drafted their letters and got them signed by the chairman without further discussion. Konstantin made his list of factory leaders and started sending messages to them. Viktor left to organize the railwaymen.

The committee began to argue about the wording of a letter to neighboring towns. Grigori slipped away. He had what he wanted. The defense of Petrograd, and of the revolution, was well under way. And the Bolsheviks were in charge of it.

What he needed now was reliable information about the whereabouts of the counterrevolutionary army. Were there really troops approaching the southern suburbs of Petrograd? If so they might have to be dealt with faster than the Committee for Struggle could act.

He walked from the Smolny Institute across the bridge the short distance to his barracks. There he found the troops already preparing to fight Kornilov's mutineers. He took an armored car, a driver, and three reliable revolutionary soldiers, and drove across the city to the south.

In the darkening autumn afternoon they zigzagged through the southern suburbs, looking for the invading army. After a couple of fruitless hours Grigori decided there was a good chance the reports of Kornilov's progress had been exaggerated. In any event he was likely to come across nothing more than an advance party. All the same, it was important to check them, and he persisted with his search.

They eventually found an infantry brigade making camp at a school.

He considered returning to barracks and bringing the First Machine Guns here to attack. But he thought there might be a better way. It was risky, but it would save a lot of bloodshed if it worked.

He was going to try to win by talking.

They drove past an apathetic sentry into the playground and Grigori got out of the car. As a precaution, he unfolded the spike bayonet at the end of his rifle and fixed it in the attack position. Then he slung the rifle over his shoulder. Feeling vulnerable, he forced himself to look relaxed.

Several soldiers approached him. A colonel said: "What are you doing here, Sergeant?"

Grigori ignored him and addressed a corporal. "I need to speak to the leader of your soldiers' committee, comrade," he said.

The colonel said: "There are no soldiers' committees in this brigade, *comrade*. Get back in your car and clear off."

But the corporal spoke up with nervous defiance. "I was the leader of my platoon committee, Sergeant—before the committees were banned, of course."

The colonel's face darkened with anger.

This was the revolution in miniature, Grigori realized. Who would prevail—the colonel or the corporal?

More soldiers drew near to listen.

"Then tell me," Grigori said to the corporal, "why are you attacking the revolution?"

"No, no," said the corporal. "We're here to defend it."

"Someone has been lying to you." Grigori turned and raised his voice to address the bystanders. "The prime minister, Comrade Kerensky, has sacked General Kornilov, but Kornilov won't go, and that's why he has sent you to attack Petrograd."

There was a murmur of disapproval.

The colonel looked awkward: he knew Grigori was right. "Enough of these lies!" he blustered. "Get out of here now, Sergeant, or I'll shoot you down."

Grigori said: "Don't touch your weapon, Colonel. Your men have a right to the truth." He looked at the growing crowd. "Don't they?"

"Yes!" said several of them.

"I don't like everything Kerensky has done," said Grigori. "He has brought back the death penalty and flogging. But he is our revolutionary leader. Whereas your General Kornilov wants to destroy the revolution."

"Lies!" the colonel said angrily. "Don't you men understand? This sergeant is a Bolshevik. Everyone knows they are in the pay of Germany!"

The corporal said: "How do we know who to believe? You say one thing, Sergeant, but the colonel says another."

"Then don't believe either of us," Grigori said. "Go and find out for yourselves." He raised his voice to make sure everyone could hear him. "You don't have to hide in this school. Go to the nearest factory and ask any worker. Speak to soldiers you see in the streets. You'll soon learn the truth."

The corporal nodded. "Good idea."

"You'll do no such thing," said the colonel furiously. "I'm ordering you all to stay within the grounds."

That was a big mistake, Grigori thought. He said: "Your colonel doesn't want you to inquire for yourselves. Doesn't that show you that he must be telling you lies?"

The colonel put his hand on his pistol and said: "That's mutinous talk, Sergeant."

The men stared at the colonel and at Grigori. This was the moment of crisis, and death was as near to Grigori as it had ever been.

Suddenly Grigori realized that he was at a disadvantage. He had been so caught up in the argument that he had failed to plan what to do when it ended. He had his rifle over his shoulder, but the safety lock was engaged. It would take several seconds to swing it off his shoulder, turn the awkward knob that unlocked the safety catch, and lift the rifle into firing position. The colonel could draw and shoot his pistol a lot faster. Grigori felt a wave of fear, and had to suppress an urge to turn and run.

"Mutiny?" he said, playing for time, trying not to let fear weaken the assertive tone of his voice. "When a sacked general marches on the capital, but his troops refuse to attack their legitimate government, who's the mutineer? I say it's the general—and those officers who attempt to carry out his treasonable orders."

The colonel drew his pistol. "Get out of here, Sergeant." He turned to the others. "You men, go into the school and assemble in the hall. Remember, disobedience is a crime in the army—and the death penalty has been restored. I'll shoot anyone who refuses."

He pointed his gun at the corporal.

Grigori saw that the men were about to obey the authoritative, confident, armed officer. There was now only one way out, he saw in desperation. He had to kill the colonel.

He would have to be very quick indeed, but he thought he could probably do it.

If he was wrong he would die.

He slipped his rifle off his left shoulder and, without pausing to switch it to his right hand, he thrust it forward as hard as he could into the colonel's side. The sharp point of the long bayonet ripped through the cloth of the uniform, and Grigori felt it sink into the soft stomach. The colonel gave a shout of pain, but he did not fall. Despite his wound he turned, swinging his gun hand around in an arc. He pulled the trigger.

The shot went wild.

Grigori pushed on the rifle, thrusting the bayonet in and up, aiming for the heart. The colonel's face twisted in agony and his mouth opened, but no sound came out, and he fell to the ground, still clutching his pistol.

Grigori withdrew the bayonet with a jerk.

The colonel's pistol fell from his fingers.

Everyone stared at the officer writhing in silent torment on the parched grass of the playground. Grigori unlocked the safety on his rifle, aimed at the colonel's heart, and fired at close range twice. The man became still.

"As you said, Colonel," Grigori said. "It's the death penalty."

{ V }

Fitz and Bea took a train from Moscow accompanied only by Bea's Russian maid, Nina, and Fitz's valet, Jenkins, a former boxing champion who had been rejected by the army because he could not see farther than ten yards.

They got off the train at Bulovnir, the tiny station that served Prince Andrei's estate. Fitz's experts had suggested that Andrei build a small township here, with a timber yard and grain stores and a mill; but nothing had been done, and the peasants still took their produce by horse and cart twenty miles to the old market town.

Andrei had sent an open carriage to meet them, with a surly driver who looked on while Jenkins lifted the trunks onto the back of the vehicle. As they drove along a dirt road through farmland, Fitz recalled his previous visit, when he had come as the new husband of the princess, and the villagers had stood at the roadside and cheered. There was a different atmosphere now. Laborers in the fields barely looked up as the carriage passed, and in villages and hamlets the inhabitants deliberately turned their backs.

This kind of thing irritated Fitz and made him bad-tempered, but his spirits were soothed by the sight of the timeworn stones of the old house, colored a buttery yellow by the low afternoon sun. A little flock of immaculately dressed servants emerged from the front door like ducks coming to be fed, and bustled about the carriage opening doors and manhandling luggage. Andrei's steward, Georgi, kissed Fitz's hand and said, in an English phrase he had obviously learned by rote: "Welcome back to your Russian home, Earl Fitzherbert."

Russian houses were often grandiose but shabby, and Bulovnir was no exception. The double-height hall needed painting, the priceless chandelier was dusty, and a dog had peed on the marble floor. Prince Andrei and Princess Valeriya were waiting beneath a large portrait of Bea's grandfather frowning sternly down on them.

Bea rushed to Andrei and embraced him.

Valeriya was a classical beauty with regular features and dark hair in a neat coiffure. She shook hands with Fitz and said in French: "Thank you for coming. We're so happy to see you."

When Bea detached herself from Andrei, wiping her tears, Fitz offered his hand to shake. Andrei gave him his left hand: the right sleeve of his jacket hung empty. He was pale and thin, as if suffering from a wasting illness, and there was a little gray in his black beard, although he was only thirty-three. "I can't tell you how relieved I am to see you," he said.

Fitz said: "Is something wrong?" They were speaking French, in which they were all fluent.

"Come into the library. Valeriya will take Bea upstairs."

They left the women and went into a dusty room full of leather-bound books that looked as if they were not often read. "I've ordered tea. I'm afraid we've no sherry."

"Tea will be fine." Fitz eased himself into a chair. His wounded leg ached after the long journey. "What's going on?"

"Are you armed?"

"Yes, as a matter of fact, I am. My service revolver is in my luggage." Fitz had a Webley Mark V that had been issued to him in 1914.

"Please keep it close to hand. I wear mine constantly." Andrei opened his jacket to reveal a belt and holster.

"You'd better tell me why."

"The peasants have set up a land committee. Some Socialist Revolutionaries have talked to them and given them stupid ideas. They claim the right to take over any land I'm not cultivating and divide it up among themselves."

"Haven't you been through this before?"

"In my grandfather's time. We hanged three peasants and thought that was the end of the matter. But these wicked ideas lie dormant, and sprout again years later."

"What did you do this time?"

"I gave them a lecture and showed them I'd lost my arm defending them from the Germans, and they went quiet—until a few days ago, when half a dozen local men returned from service in the army. They claimed to have been discharged, but I'm sure they've deserted. Impossible to check, unfortunately."

Fitz nodded. The Kerensky Offensive had been a failure, and the Germans and Austrians had counterattacked. The Russians had fallen to pieces, and the Germans were now heading for Petrograd. Thousands of Russian soldiers had walked away from the battlefield and returned to their villages.

"They brought their rifles with them, and pistols they must have stolen from officers, or taken from German prisoners. Anyway, they're heavily armed, and full of subversive ideas. There's a corporal, Feodor Igorovich, who seems to be the ringleader. He told Georgi he did not understand why I was still claiming any land at all, let alone the fallow."

"I don't understand what happens to men in the army," said Fitz with exasperation. "You'd think it would teach them the value of authority and discipline—but it seems to do the opposite."

"I'm afraid things came to a head this morning," Andrei went on. "Corporal Feodor's younger brother, Ivan Igorovich, put his cattle to graze in my pasture. Georgi found out, and he and I went to remonstrate with Ivan. We started to turn his cattle out into the lane. He tried to close the gate to prevent us. I was carrying a shotgun, and I gave him a clout across the head with the butt end of it. Most of these damn peasants have heads like cannonballs, but this one was different, and the wretch fell down and died. The socialists are using that as an excuse to get everyone agitated."

Fitz politely concealed his distaste. He disapproved of the Russian practice of striking one's inferiors, and he was not surprised when it led to this kind of unrest. "Have you told anyone?"

"I sent a message to the town, reporting the death and asking for a detachment of police or troops to keep order, but my messenger hasn't returned yet."

"So for now, we're on our own."

"Yes. If things get any worse, I'm afraid we may have to send the ladies away."

Fitz was devastated. This was much worse than he had anticipated. They could all be killed. Coming here had been a dreadful mistake. He had to get Bea away as soon as possible.

He stood up. Conscious that Englishmen sometimes boasted to foreigners about their coolness in a crisis, he said: "I'd better go and change for dinner."

Andrei showed him up to his room. Jenkins had unpacked his evening clothes and pressed them. Fitz began to undress. He felt a fool. He had put Bea and himself into danger. He had gained a useful impression of the state of affairs in Russia, but the report he would write was hardly worth the risk he had taken. He had let himself be talked into it by his wife, and that was always a mistake. He resolved they would catch the first train in the morning.

His revolver was on the dresser with his cuff links. He checked the action, then broke it open and loaded it with .455 Webley cartridges. There was nowhere to put it in a dress suit. In the end he stuffed it into his trousers pocket, where it made an unsightly bulge.

He summoned Jenkins to put away his traveling clothes, then stepped into Bea's room. She stood at the mirror in her underwear, trying on a necklace. She looked more voluptuous than usual, her breasts and hips a little heavier, and Fitz suddenly wondered whether she might be pregnant. She had suffered an attack of nausea this morning in Moscow, he recalled, in the car going to the railway station. He was reminded of her first pregnancy, and that took him back to a time he now thought of as a golden moment, when he had Ethel and Bea, and there was no war.

He was about to tell her that they had to leave tomorrow when he glanced out of the window and stopped short.

The room was at the front of the house and had a view over the park and the fields beyond to the nearest village. What had caught Fitz's eye was a crowd of people. With deep foreboding he went to the window and peered across the grounds.

He saw a hundred or so peasants approaching the house across the park. Although it was still daylight, many carried blazing torches. Some, he saw, had rifles.

He said: "Oh, fuck."

Bea was shocked. "Fitz! Have you forgotten that I am here?"

"Look at this," he said.

Bea gasped. "Oh, no!"

Fitz shouted: "Jenkins! Jenkins, are you there?" He opened the communicating door and saw the valet, looking startled, putting the traveling suit on a hanger. "We're in mortal danger," Fitz said. "We have to leave in the next five minutes. Run to the stables, put the horses to a carriage, and bring it to the kitchen door as fast as you can."

Jenkins dropped the suit on the floor and dashed off.

Fitz turned to Bea. "Throw on a coat, any coat, and pick up a pair of sensible outdoor shoes, then go down the back stairs to the kitchen and wait for me there."

To her credit, there were no hysterics: she just did as she was told.

Fitz left the room and hurried, limping as fast as he could, to Andrei's bedroom. His brother-in-law was not there, nor was Valeriya.

Fitz went downstairs. Georgi and some of the male servants were in the hall, looking frightened. Fitz was scared, too, but he hoped he was not showing it.

Fitz found the prince and princess in the drawing room. There was an opened bottle of champagne on ice, and two glasses had been poured, but they were not drinking. Andrei stood in front of the fireplace and Valeriya was at the window, looking at the approaching crowd. Fitz stood beside her. The peasants were almost at the door. A few had firearms; most carried knives, hammers, and scythes.

Andrei said: "Georgi will attempt to reason with them, and if that fails I shall have to speak to them myself."

Fitz said: "For God's sake, Andrei, the time for talking is past. We have to leave now."

Before Andrei could reply, they heard raised voices in the hall.

Fitz went to the door and opened it a crack. He saw Georgi arguing with a tall young peasant who had a bushy mustache that stretched across his cheeks: Feodor Igorovich, he guessed. They were surrounded by men and a few women, some holding burning torches. More were pushing in through the front door. It was hard to understand their local accent, but one shouted phrase was repeated several times: "We *will* speak to the prince!"

Andrei heard it, too, and he stepped past Fitz and out into the hall. Fitz said: "No—" but it was too late.

The mob jeered and hissed when Andrei appeared in evening dress. Raising his voice, he said: "If you all leave quietly now, perhaps you won't be in such bad trouble."

Feodor shot back: "You're the one in trouble—you murdered my brother!"

Fitz heard Valeriya say quietly: "My place is beside my husband." Before he could stop her, she, too, had gone into the hall.

Andrei said: "I didn't intend Ivan to die, but he would be alive now if he had not broken the law and defied his prince!"

With a sudden quick movement, Feodor reversed his rifle and hit Andrei across the face with its butt.

Andrei staggered back, holding a hand to his cheek.

The peasants cheered.

Feodor shouted: "This is what you did to Ivan!"

Fitz reached for his revolver.

Feodor raised his rifle above his head. For a frozen moment the long Mosin-Nagant hovered in the air like an executioner's axe. Then he brought the rifle down, with a powerful blow, and hit the top of Andrei's head. There was a sickening crack, and Andrei fell.

Valeriya screamed.

Fitz, standing in the doorway with the door half closed, thumbed off the lock on the left side of his revolver's barrel and aimed at Feodor; but the peasants crowded around his target. They began to kick and beat Andrei, who lay on the floor unconscious. Valeriya tried to get to him to help him, but she could not push through the crowd.

A peasant with a scythe struck at the portrait of Bea's stern grandfather, slashing the canvas. One of the men fired a shotgun at the chandelier, which smashed into tinkling fragments. A set of drapes suddenly blazed up: someone must have put a torch to them.

Fitz had been on the battlefield and had learned that gallantry had to be tempered with cool calculation. He knew that on his own he could not save Andrei from the mob. But he might be able to rescue Valeriya.

He pocketed the gun.

He stepped into the hall. All attention was on the supine prince. Valeriya stood at the edge of the throng, beating ineffectually on the shoulders of the peasants in front of her. Fitz grabbed her by the waist, lifted her, and carried her away, stepping back into the drawing room. His bad leg hurt like fire under the burden, but he gritted his teeth.

"Let me go!" she screamed. "I must help Andrei!"

"We can't help Andrei!" Fitz said. He shifted his grip and slung his sister-in-law over his shoulder, easing the pressure on his leg. As he did so a bullet passed close enough for him to feel its wind. He glanced back and saw a grinning soldier in uniform aiming a pistol.

He heard a second shot, and sensed an impact. He thought for a moment that he had been hit, but there was no pain, and he dashed for the communicating door that led to the dining room.

He heard the soldier shout: "She's getting away!"

Fitz burst through the door as another bullet hit the woodwork. Ordinary soldiers were not trained with pistols and sometimes did not realize how much less accurate they were than rifles. Moving at a limping run, he went past the table elaborately laid with silver and crystal ready for four wealthy aristocrats to have dinner. Behind him he heard several pursuers. At the far end of the room a door led to the kitchen area. He passed into a narrow corridor and from there to the kitchen. A cook and several kitchen maids had stopped work and were standing around looking terrified.

Fitz's pursuers were too close behind him. As soon as they got a clear shot he would be killed. He had to do something to slow them down.

He set Valeriya on her feet. She swayed, and he saw blood on her dress. She had been hit by a bullet, but she was alive and conscious. He sat her in a chair, then turned to the corridor. The grinning soldier was running toward him, firing wildly, followed by several more in single file in the narrow space. Behind them, in the dining room and drawing room, Fitz saw flames.

He drew his Webley. It was a double-action gun so it did not need to be cocked. Shifting all his weight to his good leg, he aimed carefully at the belly of the soldier running at him. He squeezed the trigger, the gun banged, and the man fell on the stone floor in front of him. In the kitchen, Fitz heard women screaming in terror.

Fitz immediately fired again at the next man, who also went down. He fired a third time at a third man, with the same result. The fourth man ducked back into the dining room.

Fitz slammed the kitchen door. The pursuers would now hesitate, wondering how they could check whether he was lying in wait for them, and that might just give him the time he needed.

He picked up Valeriya, who seemed to be losing consciousness. He had never been in the kitchens of this house, but he moved toward the back. Another corridor took him past storerooms and laundries. At last he opened a door that led to the outside.

Stepping out, panting, his bad leg hurting like the very devil, he saw the carriage waiting, with Jenkins in the driver's seat and Bea inside with Nina, who was sobbing uncontrollably. A frightened-looking stable boy was holding the horses.

He manhandled the unconscious Valeriya into the carriage, climbed in after her, and shouted at Jenkins: "Go! Go!"

Jenkins whipped the horses, the stable boy leaped out of the way, and the carriage moved off.

Fitz said to Bea: "Are you all right?"

"No, but I'm alive and unhurt. You . . . ?"

"No damage. But I fear for your brother's life." In reality he was quite sure Andrei was dead by now, but he did not want to say that to her.

Bea looked at the princess. "What happened?"

"She must have been hit by a bullet." Fitz looked more closely. Valeriya's face was white and still. "Oh, dear God," he said.

"She's dead, isn't she?" Bea said.

"You must be brave."

"I will be brave." Bea took her sister-in-law's lifeless hand. "Poor Valeriya."

The carriage raced down the drive and past the small dowager house where Bea's mother had lived after Bea's father died. Fitz looked back at the big house. There was a small crowd of frustrated pursuers outside the kitchen door. One of them was aiming a rifle, and Fitz pushed Bea's head down and ducked himself.

When next he looked they were out of range. Peasants and the staff were pouring out of the house by all its doors. The windows were strangely bright, and Fitz realized that the place was on fire. As he looked, smoke drifted from the front door, and an orange flame licked up from an open window and set fire to the creeper growing up the wall.

Then the carriage topped a rise and rattled downhill, and the old house disappeared from view.

CHAPTER TWENTY-EIGHT

October and November 1917

W alter said angrily: "Admiral von Holtzendorff promised us the British would starve in five months. That was nine months ago."

"He made a mistake," said his father.

Walter suppressed a scornful retort.

They were in Otto's room at the Foreign Office in Berlin. Otto sat in a carved chair behind a big desk. On the wall behind him hung a painting of Kaiser Wilhelm I, grandfather of the present monarch, being proclaimed German emperor in the Hall of Mirrors at Versailles.

Walter was infuriated by his father's half-baked excuses. "The admiral gave his word as an officer that no American would reach Europe," he said. "Our intelligence is that fourteen thousand of them landed in France in June. So much for the word of an officer!"

That stung Otto. "He did what he believed was best for his country," he said irately. "What more can a man do?"

Walter raised his voice. "You ask me what more a man can do? He can avoid making false promises. When he doesn't know for sure, he can refrain from saying he knows for sure. He can tell the truth, or keep his stupid mouth shut."

"Von Holtzendorff gave the best advice he could."

The feebleness of these arguments maddened Walter. "Such humility would have been appropriate *before* the event. But there was none. You were there, at Castle Pless—you know what happened. Von Holtzendorff gave his word. *He misled the kaiser.* He brought the Americans into the war against us. A man could hardly serve his monarch worse!"

"I suppose you want him to resign—but then who would take his place?"

"Resign?" Walter was bursting with fury. "I want him to put the barrel of his revolver in his mouth and pull the trigger."

Otto looked severe. "That's a wicked thing to say."

"His own death would be small retribution for all those who have died because of his smug foolishness."

"You youngsters have no common sense."

"You dare to talk to me about common sense? You and your generation took Germany into a war that has crippled us and killed millions—a war that, after three years, we still have not won."

Otto looked away. He could hardly deny that Germany had not yet won the war. The opposing sides were deadlocked in France. Unrestricted submarine warfare had failed to choke off supplies to the Allies. Meanwhile, the British naval blockade was slowly starving the German people. "We have to wait and see what happens in Petrograd," said Otto. "If Russia drops out of the war, the balance will change."

"Exactly," said Walter. "Everything now depends on the Bolsheviks."

{ II }

Early in October, Grigori and Katerina went to see the midwife.

Grigori now spent most nights in the one-room apartment near the Putilov works. They no longer made love—she found it too uncomfortable. Her belly was huge. The skin was as taut as a football, and her navel stuck out instead of in. Grigori had never been intimate with a pregnant woman, and he found it frightening as well as thrilling. He knew that everything was normal, but all the same he dreaded the thought of a baby's head cruelly stretching the narrow passage he loved so much.

They set out for the home of the midwife, Magda, the wife of Konstantin. Vladimir rode on Grigori's shoulders. The boy was almost three, but Grigori still carried him without effort. His personality was emerging: in his childish way he was intelligent and earnest, more like Grigori than his charming, wayward father, Lev. A baby was like a revolution, Grigori thought: you could start one, but you could not control how it would turn out.

General Kornilov's counterrevolution had been crushed before it got started. The Railwaymen's Union had made sure most of Kornilov's troops got stuck in sidings miles from Petrograd. Those who came anywhere near the city were met by Bolsheviks who undermined them simply by telling them the truth, as Grigori had in the schoolyard. Soldiers then turned on officers who were in on the conspiracy and executed them. Kornilov himself was arrested and imprisoned.

Grigori became known as the man who turned back Kornilov's army. He protested that this was an exaggeration, but his modesty only increased his stature. He was elected to the Central Committee of the Bolshevik Party.

Trotsky got out of jail. The Bolsheviks won 51 percent of the vote in the Moscow city elections. Party membership reached 350,000.

Grigori had an intoxicating feeling that anything could happen, including total disaster. Every day the revolution might be defeated. That was what he dreaded, for then his child would grow up in a Russia that was no better. Grigori thought of the milestones of his own childhood: the hanging of his father, the death of his mother outside the Winter Palace, the priest who took little Lev's trousers down, the grinding work at the Putilov factory. He wanted a different life for his child.

"Lenin is calling for an armed uprising," he told Katerina as they walked to Magda's place. Lenin had been in hiding outside the city, but he had been sending a constant stream of furious letters urging the party to action.

"I think he's right," said Katerina. "Everyone is fed up with governments who speak about democracy but do nothing about the price of bread."

As usual, Katerina said what most Petrograd workers were thinking.

Magda was expecting them and had made tea. "I'm sorry there's no sugar," she said. "I haven't been able to get sugar for weeks."

"I can't wait to get this over with," said Katerina. "I'm so tired of carrying all this weight."

Magda felt Katerina's belly and said she had about two weeks to go.

Katerina said: "It was awful when Vladimir was born. I had no friends, and the midwife was a hard-faced Siberian bitch called Kseniya."

"I know Kseniya," said Magda. "She's competent, but a bit stern."

"I'll say."

Konstantin was leaving for the Smolny Institute. Although the soviet was not in session every day, there were constant meetings of committees and ad hoc groups. Kerensky's provisional government was now so weak that the soviet gained authority by default. "I hear Lenin is back in town," Konstantin said to Grigori.

"Yes, he got back last night."

"Where is he staying?"

"It's a secret. The police are still keen to arrest him."

"What made him return?"

"We'll find out tomorrow. He's called a meeting of the Central Committee."

Konstantin left to catch a streetcar to the city center. Grigori walked Katerina home. When he was about to leave for the barracks, she said: "I feel better, knowing Magda will be with me."

"Good." Grigori still felt that childbirth seemed more dangerous than an armed uprising.

"And you'll be there, too," Katerina added.

"Not actually in the room," Grigori said nervously.

"No, of course not. But you'll be outside, pacing up and down, and that will make me feel safe."

"Good."

"You will be there, won't you?"

"Yes," he said. "Whatever happens, I'll be there."

When he got to the barracks an hour later, he found the place in turmoil. On the parade ground, officers were trying to get guns and ammunition loaded onto wagons, with little success: every battalion committee was either holding a meeting or preparing to hold one. "Kerensky has done it now!" said Isaak jubilantly. "He's trying to send us to the front."

Grigori's heart sank. "Send who?"

"The entire Petrograd garrison! The orders have come down. We're to change places with soldiers at the front."

"What's their reason?"

"They say it's because of the German advance." The Germans had taken the islands in the Gulf of Riga and were heading toward Petrograd.

"Rubbish," said Grigori angrily. "It's an attempt to undermine the soviet." And it was a clever attempt, he realized as he thought it through. If the troops in Petrograd were replaced by others coming back from the front, it would take days, perhaps weeks of organization to form new soldiers' committees and elect new deputies to the soviet. Worse, the new men would lack the experience of the last six months' political battles—which would have to be fought all over again. "What do the soldiers say?"

"They're furious. They want Kerensky to negotiate peace, not send them to die."

"Will they refuse to leave Petrograd?"

"I don't know. It will help if they get the backing of the soviet."

"I'll take care of that."

Grigori took an armored car and two bodyguards and drove over the Liteiny Bridge to the Smolny. This looked like a setback, he reflected, but it might turn into an opportunity. Until now, not all troops had supported the Bolsheviks, but Kerensky's attempt to send them to the front might swing the waverers over. The more he thought about it, the more he believed this could be Kerensky's big mistake.

The Smolny was a grand building that had been a school for daughters of the wealthy. Two machine guns from Grigori's regiment guarded the entrance. Red Guards attempted to verify everyone's identity—but, Grigori noted uneasily, the crowds going in and out were so numerous that the check was not rigorous.

The courtyard was a scene of frenetic activity. Armored cars, motorcycles, trucks, and cars came and went constantly, competing for space. A broad flight of steps led up to a row of arches and a classical colonnade. In an upstairs room Grigori found the executive committee of the soviet in session.

The Mensheviks were calling on the garrison soldiers to prepare to move to the front. As usual, Grigori thought with disgust, the Mensheviks were surrendering without a fight; and he suffered a sudden panicky fear that the revolution was slipping away from him.

He went into a huddle with the other Bolsheviks on the executive to compose a more militant resolution. "The only way to defend Petrograd against the Germans is to mobilize the workers," Trotsky said.

"As we did at the time of the Kornilov Putsch," Grigori said with enthusiasm. "We need another Committee for Struggle to take charge of the defense of the city."

Trotsky scribbled a draft, then stood up to propose the motion.

The Mensheviks were outraged. "You would be creating a second military command center alongside army headquarters!" said Mark Broido. "No man can serve two masters."

To Grigori's disgust, most committeemen agreed with that. The Menshevik motion was passed and Trotsky's was defeated. Grigori left the meeting in despair. Could the soldiers' loyalty to the soviet survive such a rebuff?

That afternoon the Bolsheviks met in Room 36 and decided they could not accept this decision. They agreed to propose their motion again that evening, at the meeting of the full soviet.

The second time, the Bolsheviks won the vote.

Grigori was relieved. The soviet had backed the soldiers and set up an alternative military command.

They were one large step closer to power.

{ III }

Next day, feeling optimistic, Grigori and the other leading Bolsheviks slipped quietly away from the Smolny in ones and twos, careful not to attract the attention of the secret police, and made their way to the large apartment of a comrade, Galina Flakserman, for the meeting of the Central Committee.

Grigori was nervous about the meeting and arrived early. He circled the block, looking for idlers who might be police spies, but he saw no one suspicious. Inside the building he reconnoitered the different exits—there were three—and determined the fastest way out.

The Bolsheviks sat around a big dining table, many wearing the leather coats that were becoming a kind of uniform for them. Lenin was not there, so they started without him. Grigori fretted about him—he might have been arrested—but he arrived at ten o'clock, disguised in a wig that kept slipping and almost made him look foolish.

However, there was nothing laughable about the resolution he proposed, calling for an armed uprising, led by the Bolsheviks, to overthrow the provisional government and take power.

Grigori was elated. Everyone wanted an armed uprising, of course, but most revolutionaries said the time was not yet ripe. At last the most powerful of them was saying *now*.

Lenin spoke for an hour. As always he was strident, banging the table, shouting, and abusing those who disagreed with him. His style worked against him—you wanted to vote down someone who was so rude. But despite that he was persuasive. His knowledge was wide, his political instinct was unerring, and few men could stand firm against the hammer blows of his logical arguments.

Grigori was on Lenin's side from the start. The important thing was to seize power and end the dithering, he thought. All other problems could be solved later. But would the others agree?

Zinoviev spoke against. Normally a handsome man, he, too, had

OCTOBER AND NOVEMBER 1917   ↜   769

changed his appearance to confuse the police. He had grown a beard and cropped his luxuriant thatch of curly black hair. He thought Lenin's strategy was too risky. He was afraid an uprising would give the right wing an excuse for a military coup. He wanted the Bolshevik party to concentrate on winning the elections for the Constituent Assembly.

This timid argument infuriated Lenin. "The provisional government is *never* going to hold a national election!" he said. "Anyone who thinks otherwise is a fool and a dupe."

Trotsky and Stalin backed the uprising, but Trotsky angered Lenin by saying they should wait for the All-Russia Congress of Soviets, scheduled to begin in ten days' time.

That struck Grigori as a good idea—Trotsky was always reasonable— but Lenin surprised him by roaring: "No!"

Trotsky said: "We're likely to have a majority among the delegates—"

"If the congress forms a government, it is bound to be a coalition!" Lenin said angrily. "The Bolsheviks admitted to the government will be centrists. Who could wish for that—other than a counterrevolutionary traitor?"

Trotsky flushed at the insult, but he said nothing.

Grigori realized Lenin was right. As usual, Lenin had thought further ahead than anyone else. In a coalition, the Mensheviks' first demand would be that the prime minister must be a moderate—and they would probably settle for anyone but Lenin.

It dawned on Grigori—and at the same time on the rest of the committee, he guessed—that the only way Lenin could become prime minister was by a coup.

The dispute raged until the small hours. In the end they voted by ten to two in favor of an armed uprising.

However, Lenin did not get all his own way. No date was set for the coup.

When the meeting was over, Galina produced a samovar and put out cheese, sausage, and bread for the hungry revolutionaries.

{ IV }

As a child on Prince Andrei's estate, Grigori had once witnessed the climax of a deer hunt. The dogs had brought down a stag just outside the village, and everyone had gone to look. When Grigori got there the deer was dying, the dogs already greedily eating the intestines spilling out of its ripped belly while the huntsmen on their horses swigged brandy in celebration. Yet even then the wretched beast had made one last attempt to fight back. It had swung its mighty antlers, impaling one dog and slashing another, and had, for a moment, almost looked as if it might struggle to its feet; then it had sunk back to the bloodstained earth and closed its eyes.

Grigori thought Prime Minister Kerensky, the leader of the provisional government, was like that stag. Everyone knew he was finished—except him.

As the bitter cold of a Russian winter closed around Petrograd like a fist, the crisis came to a head.

The Committee for Struggle, soon renamed the Military Revolutionary Committee, was dominated by the charismatic figure of Trotsky. He was not handsome, with his big nose, high forehead, and bulging eyes staring through rimless glasses, but he was charming and persuasive. Where Lenin shouted and bullied, Trotsky reasoned and beguiled. Grigori suspected that Trotsky was as tough as Lenin but better at hiding it.

On Monday, November 5, two days before the All-Russia Congress was due to start, Grigori went to a mass meeting, called by the Military Revolutionary Committee, of all the troops in the Peter and Paul Fortress. The meeting started at noon and went on all afternoon, hundreds of soldiers debating politics in the square in front of the fort while their officers fumed impotently. Then Trotsky arrived, to thunderous applause, and after listening to him they voted to obey the committee rather than the government, Trotsky, not Kerensky.

Walking away from the square, Grigori reflected that the government could not possibly tolerate a key army unit declaring its loyalty to someone else. The cannon of the fortress were directly across the river from the Winter Palace, where the provisional government was headquartered. Surely, he thought, Kerensky would now admit defeat and resign.

Next day Trotsky announced precautions against a counterrevolutionary coup by the army. He ordered Red Guards and troops loyal to the soviet to take over the bridges, railway stations, and police stations, plus the post office, the telegraph office, the telephone exchange, and the state bank.

Grigori was at Trotsky's side, turning the great man's stream of commands into detailed instructions for specific military units and dispatching the orders around the city by messengers on horseback, on bicycles, and in cars. He thought Trotsky's "precautions" seemed very similar to a takeover.

To his amazement and delight, there was little resistance.

A spy at the Marinsky Palace reported that Prime Minister Kerensky had asked the preparliament—the body that had so miserably failed in its task of setting up the Constituent Assembly—for a vote of confidence. The preparliament refused. No one took much notice. Kerensky was history, just another inadequate man who had tried and failed to rule Russia. He returned to the Winter Palace, where his impotent government continued to pretend to rule.

Lenin was hiding at the apartment of a comrade, Margarita Fofanova. The Central Committee had ordered him not to move about the city, fearing he would be arrested. Grigori was one of the few people who knew his location. At eight o'clock in the evening Margarita arrived at the Smolny with a note from Lenin ordering the Bolsheviks to launch an armed insurrection immediately. Trotsky said tetchily: "What does he imagine we're doing?"

But Grigori thought Lenin was right. In spite of everything, the Bolsheviks had not quite seized power. Once the Congress of Soviets assembled it would have all authority—and then, even if the Bolsheviks were in a majority, the result would be yet another coalition government based on compromise.

The congress was scheduled to begin tomorrow afternoon at two o'clock. Only Lenin seemed to understand the urgency of the situation, Grigori thought with a sense of desperation. He was needed here, at the heart of things.

Grigori decided to go get him.

It was a freezing night, with a north wind that seemed to blow straight through the leather coat Grigori wore over his sergeant's uniform. The center of the city was shockingly normal: well-dressed middle-class people were coming out of theaters and walking to brightly lit restaurants, while beggars pestered them for change and prostitutes smiled on street corners. Grigori nodded to a comrade who was selling a pamphlet by Lenin called *Will the Bolsheviks Be Able to Hold the Power?* Grigori did not buy one. He already knew the answer to that question.

Margarita's flat was on the northern edge of the Vyborg district. Grigori could not drive there for fear of calling attention to Lenin's hideout. He walked to the Finland Station, then caught a streetcar. The journey was long, and he spent most of it wondering if Lenin would refuse to come.

However, to his great relief Lenin did not need much persuading. "Without you, I don't believe the other comrades will take the final decisive step," Grigori said, and that was all it took to convince Lenin to come.

He left a note on the kitchen table, so that Margarita would not imagine he had been arrested. It said: "I have gone where you wanted me not to go. Good-bye, Ilich." Party members called him Ilich, his middle name.

Grigori checked his pistol while Lenin put on his wig, a worker's cap, and a shabby overcoat. Then they set out.

Grigori kept a sharp lookout, fearful that they would run into a detachment of police or an army patrol and Lenin would be recognized. He made up his mind that, rather than let Lenin be arrested, he would shoot without hesitation.

They were the only passengers on the streetcar. Lenin questioned the conductress on what she thought of the latest political developments.

Walking from the Finland Station they heard hoofbeats and hid from what turned out to be a troop of loyalist cadets looking for trouble.

Grigori triumphantly delivered Lenin to the Smolny at midnight.

Lenin went at once to Room 36 and called a meeting of the Bolshevik Central Committee. Trotsky reported that Red Guards now controlled many of the city's key points. But that was not enough for Lenin. For symbolic reasons, he argued, the revolutionary troops had to seize the Winter Palace and arrest the ministers of the provisional government. That would be the act that convinced people that power had passed, finally and irrevocably, to the revolutionaries.

Grigori knew he was right.

So did everyone else.

Trotsky began to plan the taking of the Winter Palace.

Grigori did not get home to Katerina that night.

{ v }

There could be no mistakes.

The final act of the revolution had to be decisive, Grigori knew. He made sure the orders were clear and reached their destinations in good time.

The plan was not complicated, but Grigori worried that Trotsky's timetable was optimistic. The bulk of the attacking force would consist of revolutionary sailors. The majority were coming from Helsingfors, capital of the Finnish region, by train and ship. They left at three a.m. More were coming from Kronstadt, the island naval base twenty miles offshore.

The attack was scheduled to begin at twelve noon.

Like a battlefield operation, it would start with an artillery barrage: the guns of the Peter and Paul Fortress would fire across the river and batter down the walls of the palace. Then the sailors and soldiers would take over the building. Trotsky said it would be over by two o'clock, when the Congress of Soviets was due to start.

Lenin wanted to stand up at the opening and announce that the

Bolsheviks had *already* taken power. It was the only way to prevent another indecisive, ineffective compromise government, the only way to ensure that Lenin ended up in charge.

Grigori worried that things might not go as fast as Trotsky hoped.

Security was poor at the Winter Palace, and at dawn Grigori was able to send Isaak inside to reconnoiter. He reported that there were about three thousand loyalist troops in the building. If they were properly organized and fought bravely, there would be a mighty battle.

Isaak also discovered that Kerensky had left town. Because the Red Guards controlled the railway stations he had been unable to leave by train, and he had eventually departed in a commandeered car. "What kind of prime minister can't catch a train in his own capital?" Isaak said.

"Anyway, he's gone," Grigori said with satisfaction. "And I don't suppose he'll ever come back."

However, Grigori's mood turned pessimistic when noon came around and none of the sailors had appeared.

He crossed the bridge to the Peter and Paul Fortress to make sure the cannon were ready. To his horror he found that they were museum pieces, there only for show, and could not be fired. He ordered Isaak to find some working artillery.

He hurried back to the Smolny to tell Trotsky his plan was behind schedule. The guard at the door said: "There was someone here looking for you, comrade. Something about a midwife."

"I can't deal with that now," Grigori said.

Events were moving very fast. Grigori learned that the Red Guards had taken the Marinsky Palace and dispersed the preparliament without bloodshed. Those Bolsheviks in jail had been released. Trotsky had ordered all troops outside Petrograd to remain where they were, and they were obeying him, not their officers. Lenin was writing a manifesto that began: "To the citizens of Russia: The provisional government has been overthrown!"

"But the assault has not begun," Grigori told Trotsky miserably. "I don't see how it can be managed before three o'clock."

"Don't worry," said Trotsky. "We can delay the opening of the congress."

Grigori returned to the square in front of the Winter Palace. At two in the afternoon, at long last, he saw the minelayer *Amur* sail into the Neva with a thousand sailors from Kronstadt on its deck, and the workers of Petrograd lined the banks to cheer them.

If Kerensky had thought to put a few mines in the narrow channel, he could have kept the sailors out of the city and defeated the revolution. But there were no mines, and the sailors in their black pea jackets began to disembark, carrying their rifles. Grigori prepared to deploy them around the Winter Palace.

But the plan was still bedeviled by snags, to Grigori's immense exasperation. Isaak found a cannon and, with much effort, got it dragged into place, only to find that there were no shells for it. Meanwhile, loyalist troops at the palace were building barricades.

Maddened by frustration, Grigori drove back to the Smolny.

An emergency session of the Petrograd soviet was about to start. The spacious hall of the girls' school, painted a virginal white, was packed full with hundreds of delegates. Grigori went up onto the stage and sat beside Trotsky, who was about to open the session. "The assault has been delayed by a series of problems," he said.

Trotsky took the bad news calmly. Lenin would have thrown a fit. Trotsky said: "When can you take the palace?"

"Realistically, six o'clock."

Trotsky nodded calmly and stood up to address the meeting. "On behalf of the Military Revolutionary Committee, I declare that the provisional government no longer exists!" he shouted.

There was a storm of cheering and shouting. Grigori thought: I hope I can make that lie true.

When the noise died down, Trotsky listed the achievements of the Red Guards: the overnight seizure of railway stations and other key buildings, and the dispersal of the preparliament. He also announced that several government ministers had been individually arrested. "The Winter Palace has not been taken, but its fate will be decided momentarily!" There were more cheers.

A dissenter shouted: "You are anticipating the will of the Congress of Soviets!"

This was the soft democratic argument, one that Grigori himself would have advanced in the old days, before he became a realist.

Trotsky's response was so quick that he must have expected this criticism. "The will of the congress has already been anticipated by the uprising of workers and soldiers," he replied.

Suddenly there was a murmur around the hall. People began to stand up. Grigori looked toward the door, wondering why. He saw Lenin walking in. The deputies began to cheer. The noise became thunderous as Lenin came up onto the stage. He and Trotsky stood side by side, smiling and bowing in acknowledgment of the standing ovation, as the crowd acclaimed the coup that had not yet taken place.

The tension between the victory being proclaimed in the hall and the reality of muddle and delay outside was too much for Grigori to bear, and he slipped away.

The sailors still had not arrived from Helsingfors, and the cannon at the fortress were not yet ready to fire. As night fell, a cold drizzling rain began. Standing at the edge of Palace Square, with the Winter Palace in front of him and general staff headquarters behind, Grigori saw a force of cadets emerge from the palace. Their uniform badges said they were from the Mikhailovsky Artillery School, and they were leaving, taking four heavy guns with them. Grigori let them go.

At seven o'clock he ordered a force of soldiers and sailors to enter general staff headquarters and seize control. They did so without opposition.

At eight o'clock the two hundred Cossacks on guard at the palace decided to return to their barracks, and Grigori let them through the cordon. He realized that the irksome delays might not be a total catastrophe: the forces he had to overcome were diminishing with time.

Just before ten, Isaak reported that the cannon were finally ready at the Peter and Paul Fortress. Grigori ordered one blank round to be fired, followed by a pause. As he had expected, more troops fled the palace.

Could it be this easy?

Out on the water, an alarm sounded aboard the *Amur*. Seeking the cause, Grigori looked downriver and saw the lights of approaching ships. His heart went cold. Had Kerensky succeeded in sending loyal forces to save his government at the last gasp? But then a cheer went up on the deck of the *Amur,* and Grigori realized the newcomers were the sailors from Helsingfors.

When they were safely anchored, he gave the order for the shelling to begin—at last.

There was a thunder of guns. Some shells exploded in midair, lighting up the ships on the river and the besieged palace. Grigori saw a hit on a third-floor corner window, and wondered if there had been anyone in the room. To his amazement, the brightly lit streetcars continued without interruption to trundle across the nearby Troitsky Bridge and Palace Bridge.

It was nothing like the battlefield, of course. At the front there were hundreds of guns firing, perhaps thousands; here, just four. There were long intervals between shots, and it was shocking to see how many were wasted, falling short and dropping harmlessly into the river.

Grigori called a halt and sent small groups of troops into the palace to reconnoiter. They came back to say that those few guards left were offering no resistance.

Shortly after midnight, Grigori led a larger contingent inside. In accordance with prearranged tactics they spread through the palace, running along the grand dark corridors, neutralizing opposition and searching for government ministers. The palace looked like a disorderly barracks, with soldiers' mattresses on the parquet floors of the gilded staterooms, and everywhere a filthy litter of cigarette ends, crusts of bread, and empty bottles with French labels that the guards had presumably taken from the costly cellars of the tsar.

Grigori heard a few scattered shots but there was not much fighting. He found no government ministers on the ground floor. The thought occurred to him they might have sneaked away, and he suffered a panicky moment. He did not want to have to report to Trotsky and Lenin that the members of Kerensky's government had slipped through his fingers.

With Isaak and two other men he ran up a broad staircase to check the next floor. Together they burst through a pair of double doors into a meeting room and there found what was left of the provisional government: a small group of frightened men in suits and ties, sitting at a table and on armchairs around the room, wide-eyed with apprehension.

One of them mustered a remnant of authority. "The provisional government is here—what do you want?" he said.

Grigori recognized Alexander Konovalov, the wealthy textile manufacturer who was Kerensky's deputy prime minister.

Grigori replied: "You are all under arrest." It was a good moment, and he savored it.

He turned to Isaak. "Write down their names." He recognized all of them. "Konovalov, Maliantovich, Nikitin, Tereschenko . . . " When the list was complete, he said: "Take them to the Peter and Paul Fortress and put them in the cells. I'll go to the Smolny and give Trotsky and Lenin the good news."

He left the building. Crossing Palace Square, he stopped for a minute, remembering his mother. She had died on this spot twelve years ago, shot by the tsar's guards. He turned around and looked at the vast palace, with its rows of white columns and the moonlight glinting off hundreds of windows. In a sudden fit of rage, he shook his fist at the building. "That's what you get, you devils," he said aloud. "That's what you get for killing her."

He waited until he felt calm again. I don't even know who I'm talking to, he thought. He jumped into his dust-colored armored car, waiting beside a dismantled barricade. "To the Smolny," he told the driver.

As he rode the short distance he began to feel elated. Now we really have won, he told himself. We are the victors. The people have overthrown their oppressors.

He ran up the steps of the Smolny and into the hall. The place was packed, and the Congress of Soviets had opened. Trotsky had not been able to keep on postponing it. That was bad news. It would be just like the Mensheviks, and the other milquetoast revolutionaries, to demand a place in the new government even though they had done nothing to overthrow the old.

A fog of tobacco smoke hung around the chandeliers. The members of the presidium were seated on the platform. Grigori knew most of them, and he studied the composition of the group. The Bolsheviks occupied fourteen of the twenty-five seats, he noted. That meant the party had the largest number of delegates. But he was horrified to see that the chairman was Kamenev—a moderate Bolshevik who had voted against an armed uprising! As Lenin had warned, the congress was shaping up for another feeble compromise.

Grigori scanned the delegates in the hall and spotted Lenin in the front row. He went over and said to the man in the next seat: "I have to talk to Ilich—let me have your chair." The man looked resentful, but after a moment he got up.

Grigori spoke into Lenin's ear. "The Winter Palace is in our hands," he said. He gave the names of the ministers who had been arrested.

"Too late," said Lenin bleakly.

That was what Grigori had feared. "What's happening here?"

Lenin looked black. "Martov proposed the motion." Julius Martov was Lenin's old enemy. Martov had always wanted the Russian Social Democratic Labour Party to be like the British Labour Party, and fight for working people by democratic means; and his quarrel with Lenin over this issue had split the SDLP, back in 1903, into its two factions, Lenin's Bolsheviks and Martov's Mensheviks. "He argued for an end to street fighting followed by negotiations for a democratic government."

"Negotiations?" Grigori said incredulously. "We've seized power!"

"We supported the motion," Lenin said tonelessly.

Grigori was surprised. "Why?"

"We would have lost if we opposed it. We have three hundred of the six hundred and seventy delegates. We're the largest party by a big margin, but we don't have an overall majority."

Grigori could have wept. The coup had come too late. There would be another coalition, its composition dictated by deals and compromises, and the government would dither on while Russians starved at home and died at the front.

"But they're attacking us anyway," Lenin added.

Grigori listened to the current speaker, someone he did not know. "This congress was called to discuss the new government, yet what do we find?" the man was saying angrily. "An irresponsible seizure of power has already occurred and the will of the congress has been preempted! We must save the revolution from this mad venture."

There was a storm of protest from the Bolshevik delegates. Grigori heard Lenin saying: "Swine! Bastard! Traitor!"

Kamenev called for order.

But the next speech was also bitterly hostile to the Bolsheviks and their coup, and it was followed by more in the same vein. Lev Khinchuk, a Menshevik, called for negotiations with the provisional government, and the eruption of indignation among the delegates was so violent that Khinchuk could not continue for some minutes. Finally, shouting over the noise, he said: "We leave the present congress!" Then he walked out of the hall.

Grigori saw that their tactic would be to say that the congress had no authority once they had withdrawn. "Deserters!" someone shouted, and the cry was taken up around the hall.

Grigori was appalled. They had waited so long for this congress. The delegates represented the will of the Russian people. But it was falling apart.

He looked at Lenin. To Grigori's astonishment, Lenin's eyes glittered with delight. "This is wonderful," he said. "We're saved! I never imagined they would make such a mistake."

Grigori had no idea what he was talking about. Had Lenin become irrational?

The next speaker was Mikhail Gendelman, a leading Socialist Revolutionary. He said: "Taking cognizance of the seizure of power by the Bolsheviks, holding them responsible for this insane and criminal action, and finding it impossible to collaborate with them, the Socialist Revolutionary faction is leaving the congress!" And he walked out, followed by all the Socialist Revolutionaries. They were jeered, booed, and whistled at by the remaining delegates.

Grigori was mortified. How could his triumph have degenerated, so quickly, into this kind of rowdyism?

But Lenin looked even more pleased.

A series of soldier-delegates spoke in favor of the Bolshevik coup, and Grigori began to brighten, but he still did not understand Lenin's jubilation. Ilich was now scribbling something on a notepad. As speech followed speech he corrected and rewrote. Finally he handed two sheets of paper to Grigori. "This must be presented to the congress for immediate adoption," he said.

It was a long statement, full of the usual rhetoric, but Grigori homed in on the key sentence: "The congress hereby resolves to take governmental power into its own hands."

That was what Grigori wanted.

"For Trotsky to read out?" said Grigori.

"No, not Trotsky." Lenin scanned the men—and one woman—on the platform. "Lunacharsky," he said.

Grigori guessed Lenin felt Trotsky had already gained enough glory.

Grigori took the proclamation to Lunacharsky, who made a signal to the chairman. A few minutes later Kamenev called on Lunacharsky, who stood up and read out Lenin's words.

Every sentence was greeted with a roar of approval.

The chairman called for a vote.

And now, at last, Grigori began to see why Lenin was happy. With the Mensheviks and the Socialist Revolutionaries out of the room, the Bolsheviks had an overwhelming majority. They could do anything they liked. There was no need for compromise.

A vote was taken. Only two delegates were against.

The Bolsheviks had the power, and now they had the legitimacy.

The chairman closed the session. It was five a.m. on Thursday, November 8. The Russian revolution was victorious. And the Bolsheviks were in charge.

Grigori left the room behind Josef Stalin, the Georgian revolutionary, and another man. Stalin's companion wore a leather coat and a cartridge belt, as did many of the Bolsheviks, but something about him rang an alarm bell in Grigori's memory. When the man turned to say something to Stalin, Grigori recognized him, and a tremor of shock and horror ran through him.

It was Mikhail Pinsky.

He had joined the revolution.

{ VI }

Grigori was exhausted. He had not slept for two nights. There had been so much to do that he had hardly noticed the passage of days. The armored car was the most uncomfortable vehicle he had ever traveled in, but all the same he fell asleep as it drove him home. When Isaak woke him, he saw that they were outside the house. He wondered how much Katerina knew of what had happened. He hoped she had not heard too much, for that would give him the pleasure of telling her about the triumph of the revolution.

He went into the house and stumbled up the stairs. There was a light under the door. "It's me," he said, and went into the room.

Katerina was sitting up in bed with a tiny baby in her arms.

Grigori was suffused with delight. "The baby came!" he said. "He's beautiful."

"It's a girl."

"A girl!"

"You promised you would be here," Katerina said accusingly.

"I didn't know!" He looked at the baby. "She has dark hair, like me. What shall we call her?"

"I sent you a message."

Grigori recalled the guard who had told him someone was looking for him. *Something about a midwife*, the man had said. "Oh, my God," Grigori said. "I was so busy . . . "

"Magda was attending to another birth," Katerina said. "I had to have Kseniya."

Grigori was concerned. "Did you suffer?"

"Of course I suffered," Katerina snapped.

"I'm so sorry. But listen! There's been a revolution! A real one, this time—we've taken power! The Bolsheviks are forming a government." He bent down to kiss her.

"That's what I thought," she said, and she turned her face away.

CHAPTER TWENTY-NINE

March 1918

Walter stood on the roof of a small medieval church in the village of Villefranche-sur-Oise, not far from St.-Quentin. For a while this had been a rest-and-recreation area in the German rear echelon and the French inhabitants, making the best of it, had sold omelettes and wine, when they could get any, to their conquerors. *"Malheur la guerre,"* they said. *"Pour nous, pour vous, pour tout le monde."* "Miserable war—for us, for you, for everyone." Small advances by the Allies had since driven the French residents away, flattened half the buildings, and brought the village closer to the front line: now it was an assembly zone.

Down below, on the narrow road through the center, German soldiers marched four abreast. They had been passing through hour after hour, thousands of them. They looked weary but happy, even though they must have known they were heading for the front line. They had been transferred here from the eastern front. France in March was an improvement on Poland in February, Walter guessed, whatever else might be in store.

The sight gladdened his heart. These men had been freed up by the armistice between Germany and Russia. In the last few days the negotiators at Brest-Litovsk had signed a peace treaty. Russia was out of the war permanently. Walter had played a part in making that happen, by giving support to Lenin and the Bolsheviks, and this was the triumphant result.

The German army in France now had 192 divisions, up from 129 this time last year, most of the increase being units switched from the eastern front. For the first time they had more men here than the Allies, who had 173 divisions, according to German intelligence. Many times in the last three and a half years, the German people had been told they were on the brink of victory. This time Walter thought it was true.

He did not share his father's belief that the Germans were a superior type of human, but on the other hand he could see that German mastery of Europe would be no bad thing. The French had many brilliant talents—cooking, painting, fashion, wine—but they were not good at government. French officials saw themselves as some kind of aristocracy, and thought it was perfectly all right to keep citizens waiting hours. A dose of German efficiency would do them a world of good. The same went for the disorderly Italians. Eastern Europe would benefit most of all. The old Russian Empire was still in the Middle Ages, with ragged peasants starving in hovels, and women flogged for adultery. Germany would bring order, justice, and modern agricultural methods. They had just started their first scheduled air service. Planes went from Vienna to Kiev and back like railway trains. There would be a network of flights all over Europe after Germany won the war. And Walter and Maud would raise their children in a peaceful and well-ordered world.

But this moment of battlefield opportunity would not last long. Americans had started to arrive in greater numbers. It had taken them almost a year to build their army, but now there were three hundred thousand American soldiers in France, and more were landing every day. Germany had to win now, conquer France and drive the Allies into the sea before the American reinforcements tipped the scales.

The imminent assault had been named the *Kaiserschlacht,* the

Emperor's Battle. One way or another, it would be Germany's last offensive.

Walter had been reassigned to the battlefield. Germany needed every man to fight now, especially as so many officers had been killed. He had been given command of a *Sturmbataillon*—storm troopers— and had gone through a training course in the latest tactics with his men. Some were hardened veterans, others boys and old men recruited in desperation. Walter had grown to like them, in training, but he had to take care not to become too attached to men whom he might have to send to their deaths.

On the same training course had been Gottfried von Kessel, Walter's old rival from the German embassy in London. Despite his poor eyesight, Gottfried was a captain in Walter's battalion. War had done little to reduce his know-all pomposity.

Walter surveyed the surrounding countryside through his field glasses. It was a bright, cold day and he could see clearly. To the south the wide river Oise passed slowly through marshes. Northward, fertile land was dotted with hamlets, farmhouses, bridges, orchards, and small areas of woodland. A mile to the west was the network of German trenches, and beyond that the battleground. Here the same agricultural landscape had been devastated by war. Barren wheat fields were cratered like the moon; every village was a heap of stones; the orchards had been blasted and the bridges blown up. If he focused his binoculars carefully, he could see the rotting corpses of men and horses and the steel shells of burned-out tanks.

On the far side of this wasteland were the British.

A loud rumbling caused Walter to look eastward. The vehicle approaching was one he had never seen before, though he had heard talk. It was a self-propelled gun, with giant barrel and firing mechanism mounted on a chassis with its own one-hundred-horsepower engine. It was closely followed by a heavy-duty truck loaded, presumably, with proportionately huge ammunition. A second and a third gun came after. The artillery crews riding on the vehicles waved their caps as they passed by, as if they were on a victory parade.

Walter felt bucked. Such guns could be repositioned rapidly once the offensive got under way. They would give much better support to advancing infantry.

Walter had heard that an even bigger gun was shelling Paris from a distance of sixty miles. It hardly seemed possible.

The guns were followed by a Mercedes 37/95 Double Phaeton that looked distinctly familiar. It turned off the road and parked in the square in front of the church, and Walter's father got out.

What was he doing here?

Walter passed through the low doorway into the tower and hurried down the narrow spiral staircase to the ground. The nave of the disused church had become a dormitory. He picked his way through bedrolls and the upturned crates that served the men as tables and chairs.

Outside, the graveyard was packed with trench bridges, prefabricated wooden platforms that would enable artillery and supply trucks to cross captured British trenches in the wake of the storm troopers. They were stashed amid the tombstones so as not to be easily visible from the air.

The stream of men and vehicles passing through the village from east to west had now slowed to a trickle. Something was up.

Otto was in uniform, and saluted formally. Walter could see that his father was bursting with excitement. "A special visitor is coming!" Otto said immediately.

So that was it. "Who?"

"You'll see."

Walter guessed it was General Ludendorff, who was now in effect supreme commander. "What does he want to do?"

"Address the soldiers, of course. Please assemble the men in front of the church."

"How soon?"

"He's not far behind me."

"Right." Walter looked around the square. "Sergeant Schwab! Come here. You and Corporal Grunwald—and you men, come here." He dispatched messengers to the church, the canteen that had been set up in a large barn, and the tent village on the rise to the north. "I want every man in front of the church, properly dressed, in fifteen minutes. Quick!" They ran off.

Walter hurried around the village, informing the officers, ordering the men to the square, keeping an eye on the road from the east. He found his commanding officer, Generalmajor Schwarzkopf, in a cheese-smelling former dairy on the edge of the village, finishing a late breakfast of bread and tinned sardines.

Within a quarter of an hour two thousand men were assembled, and ten minutes later they looked respectable, uniforms buttoned and caps on straight. Walter brought up a flatbed truck and backed it up in front of the men. He improvised steps up to the back of the truck using ammunition crates.

Otto produced a length of red carpet from the Mercedes and placed it on the ground leading to the steps.

Walter took Grunwald out of the line. The corporal was a tall man with big hands and feet. Walter sent him up onto the church roof with his field glasses and a whistle.

Then they waited.

Half an hour went by, then an hour. The men fidgeted, the lines became ragged, and conversation broke out.

After another hour, Grunwald blew his whistle.

"Get ready!" Otto barked. "Here he comes!"

A cacophony of shouted orders burst out. The men came quickly to attention. A motorcade swept into the square.

The door of an armored car opened, and a man in a general's uniform got out. However, it was not the balding, bullet-headed Ludendorff. The special visitor moved awkwardly, holding his left hand in the pocket of his tunic as if his arm were injured.

After a moment, Walter saw that it was the kaiser himself.

Generalmajor Schwarzkopf approached him and saluted.

As the men realized who their visitor was, there was a rumble of reaction that grew rapidly into an explosion of cheering. The generalmajor at first looked angry at the indiscipline, but the kaiser smiled benignly and Schwarzkopf quickly recomposed his face into an expression of approval.

The kaiser mounted the steps, stood on the bed of the truck, and acknowledged the cheers. When the noise at last died down, he began to speak. "Germans!" he said. "This is the hour of victory!"

They cheered all over again, and this time Walter cheered with them.

{ II }

At one o'clock in the morning on Thursday, March 21, the brigade was disposed in its forward positions, ready for the attack. Walter and his battalion officers sat in a dugout in the frontline trench. They were talking to relieve the strain of waiting to go into battle.

Gottfried von Kessel was expounding Ludendorff's strategy. "This westward thrust will drive a wedge between the British and the French," he said, with all the ignorant confidence he used to display when they worked together at the German embassy in London. "Then we will swing north, turning the British right flank, and drive them into the English Channel."

"No, no," said Lieutenant von Braun, an older man. "The smart thing to do, once we've broken through their front line, will be to go all the way to the Atlantic coast. Imagine that—a German line stretching all the way across the middle of France, separating the French army from their allies."

Von Kessel protested: "But then we would have enemies to our north and south!"

A third man, Captain Kellerman, joined in. "Ludendorff will swing south," he predicted. "We need to take Paris. That's all that counts."

"Paris is just symbolic!" von Kessel said scornfully.

They were speculating—no one knew. Walter felt too tense to listen to pointless conversation, so he went outside. The men were sitting on the ground in the trench, still and calm. The few hours before battle were a time of reflection and prayer. There had been beef in their barley stew yesterday evening, a rare treat. Morale was good—they all felt the end of the war was coming.

It was a bright starry night. Field kitchens were giving out breakfast: black bread and a thin coffee that tasted of yellow turnips. There had been some rain, but that had passed, and the wind had dropped to almost nothing. This meant poison gas shells could be fired. Both sides used gas, but Walter had heard that this time the Germans would be using a new mixture: deadly phosgene plus tear gas. The tear gas was not lethal, but it could penetrate the standard-issue British gas mask. The theory was that the irritation of tear gas would cause enemy soldiers to pull off their masks in order to rub their eyes, whereupon they would inhale the phosgene and die.

The big guns were ranged all along the near side of no-man's-land. Walter had never seen so much artillery. Their crews were stacking ammunition. Behind them a second line of guns stood ready to move, the horses already in their traces; they would be the next wave of the rolling barrage.

At half past four everything went still. The field kitchens disappeared; the gun crews sat on the ground, waiting; the officers stood in the trenches, looking across no-man's-land into the darkness where the enemy slept. Even the horses became quiet. This is our last chance of victory, Walter thought. He wondered if he should pray.

At four forty a white flare shot up into the sky, its glare making the twinkling stars go out. A moment later, the big gun near Walter went off with a flash of flame and a bang so loud that he staggered back as if pushed. But that was nothing. Within seconds all the artillery were firing. The noise was much louder than a thunderstorm. The flashes lit up the faces of the gun crews as they manhandled the heavy shells and cordite charges. Fumes and smoke filled the air, and Walter tried to breathe only through his nose. The ground under his feet trembled in shock.

Soon Walter saw explosions and flames on the British side, as German shells hit ammunition dumps and petrol tanks. He knew what it was like to be under artillery fire, and he felt sorry for the enemy. He hoped Fitz was not over there.

The guns became so hot they would burn the skin of anyone foolish enough to touch them. The heat distorted the barrels enough to spoil their aim, so the crews used wet sacks to cool them. Walter's troopers volunteered to carry buckets of water from nearby shell holes to keep the sacking drenched. Infantry were always eager to help gun crews before an attack: every enemy soldier killed by the guns was one less man to shoot at the ground troops when they advanced.

Daylight brought fog. Near the guns, the explosion of charges burned the vapor away, but in the distance nothing could be seen. Walter was troubled. The gunners would have to aim "by the map." Fortunately they had detailed, accurate plans of the British positions, most of which had been German positions only a year ago. But there was no substitute for correction by observation. It was a bad start.

The mist mingled with the gun smoke. Walter tied a handkerchief over his nose and mouth. There was no return fire from the British, at least in this section. Walter felt encouraged. Perhaps their artillery had already been destroyed. The only German killed near Walter was a mortar operator whose gun blew up, presumably because the shell exploded in the barrel. A stretcher party took the body away, and a medical team bandaged the wounds of bystanders hit by shards.

At nine o'clock in the morning he moved his men into their jump-off positions, the storm troopers lying on the ground behind the guns, the regular infantry standing in the trenches. Behind them were massed the next wave of artillery, the medical teams, the telephonists, the ammunition resuppliers, and the messengers.

The storm troopers wore the modern "coal scuttle" helmet. They had been the first to abandon the old spiked *pickelhaube.* They were armed with the Mauser K98 carbine. Its short barrel made it inaccurate over distances, but it was less cumbersome than longer rifles in close-quarters trench fighting. Each man had a bag slung across his chest containing a dozen stick grenades. The Tommies called these "tatermashers" after the potato-mashing tool used by their wives. Apparently there was one in every British kitchen. Walter had learned this by interrogating prisoners of war: he had never actually been inside a British kitchen.

Walter put on his gas mask, and gestured to his men to follow suit, so that they would not be afflicted by their own poison fumes when they reached the other side. Then, at nine thirty, he stood up. He slung his rifle across his back and held a stick grenade in each hand, which was correct for advancing storm troopers. He could not shout orders, for no one could hear anything, so he gestured with his arm and then ran.

His men followed him into no-man's-land.

The ground was firm and dry: there had been no heavy rain for weeks. That was good for the attackers, making it easier to move men and vehicles.

They ran bent over. The German guns were firing over their heads. Walter's men understood the danger of being hit by their own shells falling short, especially in fog when artillery observers were unable to correct the gunners' aim. But it was worth the risk. This way they could get so close to the enemy trench that, when the bombardment ended, the British would not have time to get into position and set up their machine-gun posts before the storm troopers fell on them.

As they ran farther across no-man's-land, Walter hoped the other side's barbed wire had been destroyed by artillery. If not, his men would be delayed cutting it.

There was an explosion to his right, and he heard a scream. A moment later, a gleam on the ground caught his eye, and he spotted a trip wire. He was in a previously undetected minefield. A wave of pure panic swept over him as he realized that he might blow himself up with the next step. Then he got himself under control again. "Watch out underfoot!" he yelled, but his words were lost in the thunder of the guns. They ran on: the wounded had to be left for the medical teams, as always.

A moment later, at nine forty, the guns stopped.

Ludendorff had abandoned the old tactic of several days of artillery fire before an attack: it gave the enemy too much time to bring up reserves. Five hours was calculated to be enough to confuse and demoralize the enemy without permitting him to reorganize.

In theory, Walter thought.

He straightened up and ran faster. He was breathing hard but steadily, hardly sweating, alert but calm. Contact with the enemy was now seconds away.

He reached the British wire. It had not been destroyed, but there were gaps, and he led his men through.

The company and platoon commanders ordered the men to spread out again, using gestures rather than words: they might be near enough to be heard.

Now the fog was their friend, hiding them from the enemy, Walter thought with a little frisson of glee. At this point they might have expected to face the hell of machine-gun fire. But the British could not see them.

He came to an area where the ground had been completely churned up by German shells. At first he could see nothing but craters and mounds of earth. Then he saw a section of trench, and realized he had reached the British line. But it had been wrecked: the artillery had done a good job.

Was there anyone in the trench? No shots had been fired. But it was best to make sure. Walter pulled a pin from a grenade and tossed it into the trench as a precaution. After it had exploded he looked over the parapet. There were several men lying on the ground, none moving. Any who had not been killed earlier by the artillery had been finished off by the grenade.

Lucky so far, Walter thought. Don't expect it to last.

He ran along the line to check on the rest of his battalion. He saw half a dozen British soldiers surrendering, their hands on their steel soup-bowl helmets, their weapons abandoned. They looked well-fed by comparison with their German captors.

Lieutenant von Braun was pointing his rifle at the captives, but Walter did not want his officers wasting time dealing with prisoners. He pulled off his gas mask: the British were not wearing them. "Keep moving!" he shouted in English. "That way, that way." He pointed to the German lines. The British walked forward, eager to get away from the fighting and save their lives. "Let them go," he shouted at von Braun. "Rear echelons will deal with them. You must keep advancing." That was the whole idea of storm troopers.

He ran on. For several hundred yards the story was the same: destroyed trenches, enemy casualties, no real resistance. Then he heard machine-gun fire. A moment later he came upon a platoon that had taken cover in shell craters. He lay down beside the sergeant, a Bavarian called Schwab. "We can't see the emplacement," said Schwab. "We're shooting at the noise."

Schwab had not understood the tactics. Storm troopers were supposed to bypass strong points, leaving them to be mopped up by the following infantry. "Keep moving!" Walter ordered him. "Go around the machine gun." When there was a pause in the firing, he stood up and gestured to the men. "Come on! Up, up!" They obeyed. He led them away from the machine gun and across an empty trench.

He ran into Gottfried again. The lieutenant had a tin of biscuits and was stuffing them into his mouth as he ran along. "Incredible!" he shouted. "You should see the British food!"

Walter knocked the tin out of his hands. "You're here to fight, not eat, you damn fool," he yelled. "Get going."

He was startled by something running over his foot. He saw a rabbit disappearing into the fog. No doubt the artillery had destroyed their warrens.

He checked his compass to make sure he was still heading west. He did not know whether the trenches he was encountering might be communication or supply trenches, so their orientation did not tell him much.

He knew that the British had followed the Germans in creating multiple lines of trenches. Having passed the first he expected soon to come upon a well-defended trench they called the Red Line, then—if he could break through that—another trench a mile or so farther west called the Brown Line.

After that, there was nothing but open country all the way to the west coast.

Shells exploded in the mist ahead. Surely the British could not be responsible? They would be firing on their own defenses. It must be the next wave of the German rolling barrage. He and his men were in danger of outstripping their own artillery. He turned. Fortunately most of his people were behind him. He raised his arms. "Take cover!" he shouted. "Spread the word!"

They hardly needed telling, having come to the same conclusion as he. They ran back a few yards and jumped into some empty trenches.

Walter felt elated. This was going remarkably well.

There were three British soldiers lying on the trench floor. Two were motionless, one groaning. Where were the rest? Perhaps they had fled. Alternatively, this might be a suicide squad, left to defend an indefensible position in order to give their retreating comrades a better chance.

One of the dead Brits was an unusually tall man with big hands and feet. Grunwald immediately removed the corpse's boots. "My size!" he said to Walter by way of explanation. Walter did not have the heart to stop him: Grunwald's own boots had holes in them.

He sat down to catch his breath. Reviewing the first phase in his mind, he could not think how it could have gone better.

After an hour, the German guns fell silent again. Walter rallied the men and moved on.

Halfway up a long slope, he heard voices. He held up a hand to halt the men near him. Ahead, someone said in English: "I can't see a fucking dicky bird."

There was something familiar about the accent. Was it Australian? It sounded more like Indian.

Another voice said in the same accent: "If they can't see you, they can't bloody shoot you!"

In a flash Walter was transported back to 1914, and Fitz's big country house in Wales. This was how the servants there spoke. The men in front of him, here in this devastated French field, were Welsh.

Up above, the sky seemed to brighten a little.

{ III }

Sergeant Billy Williams peered into the fog. The artillery had stopped, mercifully, but that only meant the Germans were coming. What was he supposed to do?

He had no orders. His platoon occupied a redoubt, a defensive post on a rise some distance behind the front line. In normal weather their position commanded a wide view of a long, gradual downward slope to a pile of rubble that must once have been farm buildings. A trench linked them to other redoubts, now invisible. Orders normally came from the rear, but none had arrived today. The phone was dead, the line presumably cut by the barrage.

The men stood or sat in the trench. They had come out of the dugout when the shelling stopped. Sometimes the field kitchen sent a wheeled cart with a great urn of hot tea along the trench at midmorning, but there was no sign of refreshments today. They had eaten their iron rations for breakfast.

The platoon had an American-designed Lewis light machine gun. It stood on the back wall of the trench over the dugout. It was operated by nineteen-year-old George Barrow, the Borstal boy, a good soldier whose education was so poor he thought the last invader of England was called Norman the Conqueror. George was sitting behind his gun, protected from stray bullets by the steel breech assembly, smoking a pipe.

They also had a Stokes mortar, a useful weapon that fired a three-inch-diameter bomb up to eight hundred yards. Corporal Johnny Ponti, brother of the Joey Ponti who died at the Somme, had become lethally proficient with this.

Billy climbed up to the machine gun and stood beside George, but he could not see any farther.

George said to him: "Billy, do other countries have empires like us?"

"Aye," said Billy. "The French have most of North Africa. Then there's the Dutch East Indies, German South-West Africa . . . "

"Oh," said George, somewhat deflated. "I heard that, but I didn't think it could be true."

"Why not?"

"Well, what right have they got to rule over other people?"

"What right have *we* got to rule over Nigeria and Jamaica and India?"

"Because we're British."

Billy nodded. George Barrow, who evidently had never seen an atlas, felt superior to Descartes, Rembrandt, and Beethoven. And he was not unusual. They had all endured years of propaganda in school, telling them about every British military victory and none of the defeats. They were taught about democracy in London, not about tyranny in Cairo. When they learned about British justice, there was no mention of flogging in Australia, starvation in Ireland, or massacre in India. They learned that Catholics burned Protestants at the stake, and it came as a shock if they ever found out that Protestants did the same to Catholics whenever they got the chance. Few of them had a father like Billy's da to tell them that the world depicted by their schoolteachers was a fantasy.

But Billy had no time today to set George straight. He had other worries.

The sky brightened a little, and it seemed to Billy that the fog might be clearing; then, suddenly, it lifted completely. George said: "Bloody hell!" A split second later Billy saw what had shocked him. A quarter of a mile away, coming up the slope toward him, were several hundred German soldiers.

Billy jumped down into the trench. A number of men had spotted the enemy at the same time, and their surprised exclamations alerted the others. Billy looked through a slit in a steel panel set into the parapet. The Germans were slower to react, probably because the British in their trench were less conspicuous. One or two of them halted, but most came running on.

A minute later there was a crackle of rifle fire up and down the trench. Some of the Germans fell. The rest hurled themselves to the ground, seeking cover in shell holes and behind a few stunted bushes. Above Billy's head, the Lewis gun opened up with a noise like a football supporter's rattle. After a minute the Germans began to return fire. They appeared to have no machine guns or trench mortars, Billy noted gratefully. He heard one of his own men scream: a sharp-eyed German had spotted someone indiscreetly looking over the parapet, perhaps; or, more likely, a lucky shooter had hit an unlucky British head.

Tommy Griffiths appeared beside Billy. "Dai Powell got it," he said. "Wounded?"

"Dead. Shot through the head."

"Oh, bugger," said Billy. Mrs. Powell was a prodigious knitter who sent pullovers to her son in France. Who would she knit for now?

"I've took his collection from his pocket," Tommy said. Dai had a stack of pornographic postcards he had bought from a Frenchman. They showed plump girls with masses of pubic hair. Most of the men in the battalion had borrowed them at one time or another.

"Why?" said Billy distractedly as he surveyed the enemy.

"Don't want them sent home to Aberowen."

"Oh, aye."

"What shall I do with them?"

"Bloody hell, Tommy, ask me later, will you? I've got a few hundred fucking Germans to worry about at the moment."

"Sorry, Bill."

How many Germans were out there? Numbers were hard to estimate on the battlefield, but Billy thought he had seen at least two hundred, and presumably there were others out of sight. He guessed he was facing a battalion. His platoon of forty men was hopelessly outnumbered.

What was he supposed to do?

He had not seen an officer for more than twenty-four hours. He was the senior man here. He was in charge. He needed a plan.

He was long past getting angry about the incompetence of his superior officers. That was all part of the class system he had been brought up to despise. But on the rare occasions when the burden of command fell on him, he took little pleasure in it. Rather, he felt the weight of responsibility and the fear that he might make the wrong decisions and cause the deaths of his comrades.

If the Germans attacked frontally, his platoon would be overwhelmed. But the enemy did not know how weak he was. Could he make it look as if he had more men?

The thought of retreat crossed his mind. But soldiers were not supposed to run away the minute they were attacked. This was a defensive post, and he ought to try to hold it.

He would stand and fight, at least for now.

Once he had made that decision, others followed. "Give them another drum, George!" he shouted. As the Lewis gun opened up he ran along the trench. "Keep up a steady fire, boys," he said. "Make them think there's hundreds of us."

He saw Dai Powell's body lying on the ground, the blood already turning black around the hole in his head. Dai was wearing one of his mother's sweaters under his uniform tunic. It was a hideous brown thing, but it had probably kept him warm. "Rest in peace, boyo," Billy murmured.

Farther along the trench he found Johnny Ponti. "Deploy that Stokes mortar, Johnny bach," he said. "Make the buggers jump."

"Right," said Johnny. He set up his two-legged gun mount on the floor of the trench. "What's the range, five hundred yards?"

Johnny's partner was the pudding-faced boy called Suet Hewitt. He jumped up on the fire step and called back: "Aye, five to six hundred." Billy took a look for himself, but Suet and Johnny had worked together before and he left the decision to them.

"Two rings, then, at forty-five degrees," said Johnny. The self-propelling bombs could be fitted with additional charges of propellant in rings to extend their range.

Johnny jumped up on the fire step for another look at the Germans, then adjusted his aim. The other soldiers in the vicinity stood well to the side. Johnny dropped a bomb in the barrel. When it hit the bottom of the barrel, a firing pin ignited the propellant and it was fired.

The bomb fell short and exploded some distance from the nearest enemy soldiers. "Fifty yards farther, and a touch to your right," Suet shouted.

Johnny made the adjustments and fired again. The second bomb landed in a shell hole where some Germans were sheltering. "That's it!" shouted Suet.

Billy could not see whether any of the enemy had been hit, but the firing was forcing them to keep their heads down. "Give them a dozen like that!" he said.

He came up behind Robin Mortimer, the cashiered officer, who was on the fire step shooting rhythmically. Mortimer stopped to reload, and caught Billy's eye. "Get some more ammo, Taffy," he said. As always, his tone was surly even when he was being helpful. "You don't want everyone to run out at the same time."

Billy nodded. "Good idea. Thanks." The ammunition store was a hundred yards to the rear along a communication trench. He picked out two recruits who could hardly shoot straight anyway. "Jenkins and Nosey, bring up more ammo, double quick." The two lads hurried away.

Billy took another look through the parapet peephole. As he did so, one of the Germans stood up. Billy guessed it might be their commanding officer about to launch an attack. His heart sank. They must have guessed they were up against no more than a few dozen men, and realized they could easily overwhelm them.

But he was wrong. The officer gestured to rearward, then began to run downhill. His men followed suit. Billy's platoon cheered and fired wildly at the running men, bringing down a few more before they got out of range.

The Germans reached the ruined farm buildings and took cover in the rubble.

Billy could not help grinning. He had driven off a force ten times the size of his own! I should be a bloody general, he thought. "Hold your fire!" he shouted. "They're out of range."

Jenkins and Nosey reappeared, carrying ammunition boxes. "Keep going, lads," Billy said. "They may be back."

But, when he looked out again, he saw that the Germans had a different plan. They had split into two groups and were heading left and right away from the ruins. As Billy watched, they began to circle around his position, staying out of range. "Oh, bugger," he said. They were going to slip between his position and neighboring redoubts, then come at him from both sides. Or, alternatively, they might bypass him, leaving him to be mopped up by their rearguard.

Either way, this position was going to fall to the enemy.

"Take down the machine gun, George," Billy said. "And you, Johnny, dismantle the mortar. Pick up your stuff, everyone. We're falling back."

They slung their rifles and backpacks, hurried to the nearest communication trench, and began to run.

Billy looked into the dugout to make sure there was no one inside. He pulled the pin out of a grenade and threw it in, to deny any remaining supplies to the enemy.

Then he followed his men into retreat.

{ IV }

At the end of the afternoon, Walter and his battalion were in possession of a rearward line of British trenches.

He was weary but triumphant. The battalion had had a few fierce skirmishes but no sustained battle. The storm troopers' tactics had worked even better than expected, thanks to the fog. They had wiped out weak opposition, bypassed strong points, and taken a great deal of ground.

Walter found a dugout and ducked into it. Several of his men followed. The place had a homely look, as if the Brits had been living there for some months: there were magazine pictures nailed to the walls, a typewriter on an upturned box, cutlery and crockery in old cake tins, and even a blanket spread like a tablecloth on a stack of crates. Walter guessed this had been a battalion headquarters.

His men immediately found the food. There were crackers, jam, cheese, and ham. He could not stop them eating, but he did forbid them to open any of the bottles of whisky. They broke open a locked cupboard and found a jar of coffee, and one of the men made a small fire outside and brewed a pot. He gave Walter a cup, adding sweetened milk from a can. It tasted heavenly.

Sergeant Schwab said: "I read in the newspaper that the British were short of food, just as we are." He held up the tin of jam he was eating with a spoon. "Some shortage!"

Walter had been wondering how long it would take them to work that out. He had long suspected the German authorities of exaggerating the effect of submarine war on Allied supplies. Now he knew the truth, and so did the men. Food was rationed in Britain, but the Brits did not look as if they were starving to death. The Germans did.

He found a map carelessly left behind by the retreating forces. Comparing it with his own, he saw that he was not far from the Crozat Canal. That meant that in one day the Germans had taken back all the territory so painfully won by the Allies during the five months of the Battle of the Somme the year before last.

Victory really was within the Germans' grasp.

Walter sat down at the British typewriter and began to compose his report.

CHAPTER THIRTY

Late March and April 1918

Fitz held a house party at Tŷ Gwyn over the Easter weekend. He had an ulterior motive. The men he invited were as violently opposed as he was to the new regime in Russia.

His star guest was Winston Churchill.

Winston was a member of the Liberal Party, and might have been expected to sympathize with the revolutionaries; but he was also the grandson of a duke, and he had an authoritarian streak. Fitz had long thought of him as a traitor to his class, but was now inclined to forgive him because his hatred of the Bolsheviks was passionate.

Winston arrived on Good Friday. Fitz sent the Rolls-Royce to Aberowen Station to meet him. He came bouncing into the morning room, a small, slight figure with red hair and a pink complexion. There was rain on his boots. He wore a well-cut suit of wheat-colored tweed and a bow tie the same blue as his eyes. He was forty-three, but there was still something boyish about him as he nodded to acquaintances and shook hands with guests he did not know.

Looking around at the linenfold paneling, the patterned wallpaper, the carved stone fireplace, and the dark oak furniture, he said: "Your house is decorated like the Palace of Westminster, Fitz!"

He had reason to be ebullient. He was back in the government. Lloyd George had made him minister of munitions. There was much talk about why the prime minister had brought back such a troublesome and unpredictable colleague, and the consensus was that he preferred to have Churchill inside the tent spitting out.

"Your coal miners support the Bolsheviks," Winston said, half-amused and half-disgusted, as he sat down and stretched his wet boots to the roaring coal fire. "There were red flags flying from half the houses I passed."

"They have no idea what they're cheering for," Fitz said with contempt. Beneath his scorn he was deeply anxious.

Winston accepted a cup of tea from Maud and took a buttered muffin from a plate offered by a footman. "You've suffered a personal loss, I gather."

"The peasants killed my brother-in-law, Prince Andrei, and his wife."

"I'm very sorry."

"Bea and I happened to be there at the time, and escaped by the skin of our teeth."

"So I heard!"

"The villagers have taken over his land—a very large estate that is rightfully the inheritance of my son—and the new regime has endorsed such theft."

"I'm afraid so. The first thing Lenin did was to pass his Decree on Land."

Maud said: "In fairness, Lenin has also announced an eight-hour day for workers and universal free education for their children."

Fitz was annoyed. Maud had no tact. This was not the moment to defend Lenin.

But Winston was a match for her. "And a Decree on the Press that bans newspapers from opposing the government," he shot back. "So much for socialist freedom."

"My son's birthright is not the only reason, or even the main reason, why I'm so concerned," Fitz said. "If the Bolsheviks get away with what they've done in Russia, where next? Welsh miners already believe the coal found deep underground doesn't really belong to the man who owns the land on the surface. You can hear 'The Red Flag' sung in half the pubs in Wales on any given Saturday night."

"The Bolshevik regime should be strangled at birth," Winston said. He looked thoughtful. "Strangled at birth," he repeated, pleased with the expression.

Fitz controlled his impatience. Sometimes Winston imagined he had devised a policy when all he had done was coin a phrase. "But we're doing nothing!" Fitz said in exasperation.

The gong sounded to tell everyone it was time to change for dinner. Fitz did not persist with the conversation: he had all weekend to make his point.

On his way to his dressing room it struck him that, contrary to custom, Boy had not been brought down to the morning room at teatime. Before changing, he walked down a long corridor to the nursery wing.

Boy was now three years and three months old, no longer a baby or even a toddler, but a walking, talking boy with Bea's blue eyes and blond curls. He was sitting near the fire, wrapped in a blanket, and pretty, young Nurse Jones was reading to him. The rightful lord of thousands of acres of Russian farmland was sucking his thumb. He did not jump up and run to Fitz as he normally would. "What's wrong with him?" Fitz said.

"He's got a bad tummy, my lord."

Nurse Jones reminded Fitz a bit of Ethel Williams, but she was not as bright. "Try to be more exact," Fitz said impatiently. "What is wrong with his stomach?"

"He have got the diarrhea."

"How the dickens did he get that?"

"I don't know. The toilet on the train was not very clean . . ."

That made it Fitz's fault, for dragging his family down to Wales for this house party. He suppressed a curse. "Have you summoned a doctor?"

"Dr. Mortimer is on his way."

Fitz told himself not to be so fretful. Children suffered minor infections all the time. How often had he himself had a bad tummy as a child? Yet children did, sometimes, die of gastroenteritis.

He knelt in front of the sofa, bringing himself down to his son's level. "How's my little soldier?"

Boy's tone was lethargic. "I got the trots."

He must have picked up that vulgar expression from the servants— indeed, there was the hint of a Welsh lilt in the way he said it. But Fitz decided not to make a fuss about that now. "The doctor will be here soon," he said. "He'll make you better."

"I don't want a bath."

"Perhaps you can skip your bath tonight." Fitz got up. "Send for me when the doctor arrives," he said to Nurse. "I'd like to speak to the fellow myself."

"Very good, my lord."

He left the nursery and went to his dressing room. His valet had laid out his evening clothes, with the diamond studs in the shirtfront and the matching cuff links in the sleeves, a clean linen handkerchief in the coat pocket, and one silk sock placed inside each patent-leather shoe.

Before getting changed he went through to Bea's room.

She was eight months pregnant.

He had not seen her in this state when she was expecting Boy. He had left for France in August 1914, when she was only four or five months along, and he had not returned until after Boy had been born. He had not previously witnessed this spectacular swelling, nor marveled at the body's shocking ability to change and stretch.

She was sitting at her dressing table but not looking in the glass. She was leaning back, her legs apart, her hands resting on the bulge. Her eyes were closed and she looked pale. "I just can't get comfortable," she complained. "Standing, sitting, lying down, everything hurts."

"You ought to go along to the nursery and take a look at Boy."

"I will as soon as I can summon up the energy!" she snapped. "I should never have traveled to the country. It's ridiculous for me to host a house party in this state."

Fitz knew she was right. "But we need the support of these men if we're to do anything about the Bolsheviks."

"Is Boy's tummy still poorly?"

"Yes. The doctor is coming."

"You'd better send him to me while he's here—not that a country doctor is likely to know much."

"I'll tell the staff. I take it you won't be coming down to dinner."

"How can I, when I feel like this?"

"I was just asking. Maud can sit at the head of the table."

Fitz returned to his dressing room. Some men had abandoned tailcoats and white ties, and wore short tuxedo jackets and black ties at dinner, citing the war as their excuse. Fitz did not see the connection. Why should war oblige people to dress informally?

He put on his evening clothes and went downstairs.

{ II }

After dinner, as coffee was served in the drawing room, Winston said provocatively: "So, Lady Maud, you women have got the vote at last."

"Some of us have," she said.

Fitz knew she was disappointed that the bill had included only women over thirty who were householders or the wives of householders. Fitz himself was angry that it had passed at all.

Churchill went on mischievously: "You must thank, in part, Lord Curzon here, who surprisingly abstained when the bill went to the House of Lords."

Earl Curzon was a brilliant man whose stiffly superior air was made worse by a metal corset he wore for his back. There was a rhyme about him:

I am George Nathaniel Curzon
I am a most superior person

He had been viceroy of India and was now leader of the House of Lords and one of the five members of the War Cabinet. He was also president of the League for Opposing Woman Suffrage, so his abstention had astonished the political world and severely disappointed the opponents of votes for women, not least Fitz.

"The bill had been passed by the House of Commons," Curzon said. "I felt we could not defy elected members of Parliament."

Fitz was still annoyed about this. "But the Lords exist to scrutinize the decisions of the Commons, and to curb their excesses. Surely this was an exemplary case!"

"If we had voted down the bill, I believe the Commons would have taken umbrage and sent it back to us again."

Fitz shrugged. "We've had that kind of dispute before."

"But unfortunately the Bryce Committee is sitting."

"Oh!" Fitz had not thought of that. The Bryce Committee was considering the reform of the House of Lords. "So that was it?"

"They're due to report shortly. We can't afford a stand-up fight with the Commons before then."

"No." With great reluctance, Fitz had to concede the point. If the Lords made a serious attempt to defy the Commons, Bryce might recommend curbing the power of the upper chamber. "We might have lost all our influence—permanently."

"That is precisely the calculation that led me to abstain."

Sometimes Fitz found politics depressing.

Peel, the butler, brought Curzon a cup of coffee, and murmured to Fitz: "Dr. Mortimer is in the small study, my lord, awaiting your convenience."

Fitz had been worrying about Boy's stomachache, and welcomed the interruption. "I'd better see him," said Fitz. He excused himself and went out.

The small study was furnished with pieces that did not fit anywhere else in the house: an uncomfortable Gothic carved chair, a Scottish landscape no one liked, and the head of a tiger Fitz's father had shot in India.

Mortimer was a competent local physician who had a rather too confident air, as if he thought his profession made him in some way the equal of an earl. However, he was polite enough. "Good evening, my lord," he said. "Your son has a mild gastric infection, which will most likely do him no harm."

"Most likely?"

"I use the phrase deliberately." Mortimer spoke with a Welsh accent that had been moderated by education. "We scientists deal always in probabilities, never certainties. I tell your miners that they go down the pit every morning knowing there will *probably* be no explosion."

"Hmm." That was not much comfort to Fitz. "Did you see the princess?"

"I did. She, too, is not seriously ill. In fact she is not ill at all, but she is giving birth."

Fitz leaped up. "What?"

"She thought she was eight months pregnant, but she miscalculated. She is nine months pregnant, and happily will not continue pregnant many more hours."

"Who is with her?"

"Her servants are all around her. I have sent for a competent midwife, and I myself will attend the birth if you so wish."

"This is my fault," Fitz said bitterly. "I should not have persuaded her to leave London."

"Perfectly healthy babies are born outside London every day."

Fitz had a feeling he was being mocked, but he ignored it. "What if something should go wrong?"

"I know the reputation of your London doctor, Professor Rathbone. He is of course a physician of great distinction, but I think I can safely say that I have delivered more babies than he has."

"Miners' babies."

"Indeed, most of them; though at the moment of birth there is no apparent difference between them and the little aristocrats."

Fitz *was* being mocked. "I don't like your cheek," he said.

Mortimer was not intimidated. "I don't like yours," he said. "You've made it clear, without even a semblance of courtesy, that you consider me inadequate to treat your family. I will gladly take my leave." He picked up his bag.

Fitz sighed. This was a foolish quarrel. He was angry with the Bolsheviks, not with this touchy middle-class Welshman. "Don't be a fool, man."

"I try not to be." Mortimer went to the door.

"Aren't you supposed to put the interests of your patients first?"

Mortimer stopped at the door. "My God, you've got a bloody nerve, Fitzherbert."

Few people had ever talked to Fitz that way. But he suppressed the scathing retort that came to mind. It might take hours to find another doctor. Bea would never forgive him if he let Mortimer leave in a huff. "I'll forget you said that," Fitz said. "In fact I'll forget this whole conversation, if you will."

"I suppose that's the nearest thing to an apology that I'm likely to get."

It was, but Fitz said nothing.

"I'll go back upstairs," said the doctor.

{ III }

Princess Bea did not give birth quietly. Her screams could be heard throughout the principal wing of the house, where her room was. Maud played piano rags very loudly, to entertain the guests and drown out the noise, but one piano rag was much like the next, and she gave up after twenty minutes. Some of the guests went to bed, but as midnight struck, most of the men congregated in the billiard room. Peel offered cognac.

Fitz gave Winston an El Rey del Mundo cigar from Cuba. While Winston was getting it alight, Fitz said: "The government must do something about the Bolsheviks."

Winston glanced quickly around the room, as if to make sure that everyone present was completely trustworthy. Then he sat back in his chair and said: "Here is the situation. The British Northern Squadron is already in Russian waters off Murmansk. In theory their task is to make sure Russian ships there don't fall into German hands. We also have a small mission in Archangel. I'm pressing for troops to be landed at Murmansk. Longer-term, this could be the core of a counterrevolutionary force in northern Russia."

"It's not enough," Fitz said immediately.

"I agree. I'd like us to send troops to Baku, on the Caspian Sea, to make sure those vast oil fields are not taken over by the Germans, or indeed the Turks, and to the Black Sea, where there is already the nucleus of an anti-Bolshevik resistance in the Ukraine. Finally, in Siberia, we have thousands of tons of supplies at Vladivostok, worth perhaps a billion pounds, intended to support the Russians when they were our allies. We are entitled to send troops there to protect our property."

Fitz spoke half in doubt and half in hope. "Will Lloyd George do any of this?"

"Not publicly," said Winston. "The problem is those red flags flying from miners' houses. There is in our country a great well of support for the Russian people and their revolution. And I understand why, much as I loathe Lenin and his crew. With all due respect to the family of Princess Bea"—he glanced up at the ceiling as another scream began—"it cannot be denied that the Russian ruling class were slow to deal with their people's discontents."

Winston was an odd mix, Fitz thought: aristocrat and man of the people, a brilliant administrator who could never resist meddling in other people's departments, a charmer who was disliked by most of his political colleagues.

Fitz said: "The Russian revolutionaries are thieves and murderers."

"Indeed. But we have to live with the fact that not everyone sees them that way. So our prime minister cannot openly oppose the revolution."

"There's not much point in his opposing it in his mind," Fitz said impatiently.

"A certain amount may be done without his knowing about it, officially."

"I see." Fitz did not know whether that meant much.

Maud came into the room. The men stood up, a bit startled. In a country house women did not usually enter the billiard room. Maud ignored rules that did not suit her convenience. She came up to Fitz and kissed his cheek. "Congratulations, dear Fitz," she said. "You have another son."

The men cheered and clapped and gathered around Fitz, slapping him on the back and shaking his hand. "Is my wife all right?" he asked Maud.

"Exhausted but proud."

"Thank God."

"Dr. Mortimer has left, but the midwife says you may go and see the baby now."

Fitz went to the door.

Winston said: "I'll walk up with you."

As they left the room, Fitz heard Maud say: "Pour me some brandy, please, Peel."

In a lowered voice, Winston said: "You've been to Russia, of course, and you speak the language."

Fitz wondered where this was leading. "A bit," he said. "Nothing to boast about, but I can make myself understood."

"Have you come across a chap called Mansfield Smith-Cumming?"

"As it happens, I have. He runs . . . " Fitz hesitated to mention the Secret Intelligence Service out loud. "He runs a special department. I've written a couple of reports for him."

"Ah, good. When you get back to town, you might have a word with him."

Now that *was* interesting. "I'll see him at any time, of course," said Fitz, trying not to show his eagerness.

"I'll ask him to get in touch. He may have another mission for you."

They were at the door to Bea's rooms. From inside, there came the distinctive cry of a newborn baby. Fitz was ashamed to feel tears come to his eyes. "I'd better go in," he said. "Good night."

"Congratulations, and a good night to you, too."

{ IV }

They named him Andrew Alexander Murray Fitzherbert. He was a tiny scrap of life with a shock of hair as black as Fitz's. They took him to London wrapped in blankets, traveling in the Rolls-Royce with two other cars following in case of breakdowns. They stopped for breakfast in Chepstow and lunch in Oxford, and reached their home in Mayfair in time for dinner.

A few days later, on a mild April afternoon, Fitz walked along the Embankment, looking at the muddy water of the river Thames, heading for a meeting with Mansfield Smith-Cumming.

The Secret Service had outgrown its flat in Victoria. The man called "C" had moved his expanding organization into a swanky Victorian building called Whitehall Court, on the river within sight of Big Ben. A private lift took Fitz to the top floor, where the spymaster occupied two apartments linked by a walkway on the roof.

"We've been watching Lenin for years," said C. "If we fail to depose him, he will be one of the worst tyrants the world has ever known."

"I believe you're right." Fitz was relieved that C felt the same as he did about the Bolsheviks. "But what can we do?"

"Let's talk about what you might do." C took from his desk a pair of steel dividers such as were used for measuring distances on maps. As if absentmindedly, he thrust the point into his left leg.

Fitz was able to check the cry of shock that came to his lips. This was a test, of course. He recalled that C had a wooden leg as a result of a car crash. He smiled. "A good trick," he said. "I almost fell for it."

C put down the dividers and looked hard at Fitz through his monocle. "There is a Cossack leader in Siberia who has overthrown the local Bolshevik regime," he said. "I need to know if it's worth our while to support him."

Fitz was startled. "Openly?"

"Of course not. But I have secret funds. If we can sustain a kernel of counterrevolutionary government in the east, it will merit the expenditure of, say, ten thousand pounds a month."

"Name?"

"Captain Semenov, twenty-eight years old. He's based in Manchuli, which lies astride the Chinese Eastern Railway near its junction with the Trans-Siberian Express."

"So this Captain Semenov controls one railway line and could control another."

"Exactly. And he hates the Bolsheviks."

"So we need to find out more about him."

"Which is where you come in."

Fitz was delighted at the chance of helping to overthrow Lenin. He thought of many questions: How was he to find Semenov? The man was a Cossack, and they were notorious for shooting first and asking questions later: would he talk to Fitz, or kill him? Of course Semenov would claim he could defeat the Bolsheviks, but would Fitz be able to assess the reality? Was there any way to ensure he would be spending British money to good effect?

The question he asked was: "Am I the right choice? Forgive me, but I'm a conspicuous figure, hardly anonymous even in Russia . . . "

"Frankly, we don't have a wide choice. We need someone fairly high-level in case you get to the stage of negotiating with Semenov. And there aren't many thoroughly trustworthy men who speak Russian. Believe me, you're the best available."

"I see."

"It will be dangerous, of course."

Fitz recalled the crowd of peasants battering Andrei to death. That could be him. He repressed a fearful shudder. "I understand the danger," he said in a level voice.

"So tell me: will you go to Vladivostok?"

"Of course," said Fitz.

CHAPTER THIRTY-ONE

May to September 1918

G us Dewar did not take easily to soldiering. He was a gangling, awkward figure, and he had trouble marching and saluting and stamping his feet the army way. As for exercise, he had not done physical jerks since his school days. His friends, who knew of his liking for flowers on the dining table and linen sheets on his bed, had felt the army would come as a terrible shock. Chuck Dixon, who went through officer training with him, said: "Gus, at home you don't even run your own bath."

But Gus survived. At the age of eleven he had been sent to boarding school, so it was nothing new to him to be persecuted by bullies and ordered about by stupid superiors. He suffered a certain amount of mockery because of his wealthy background and careful good manners, but he bore it patiently.

In vigorous action, Chuck commented with surprise, Gus revealed a certain lanky grace, previously seen only on the tennis court. "You look like a goddamn giraffe," Chuck said, "but you run like one, too." Gus also did well at boxing, because of his long reach, although his sergeant instructor told him, regretfully, that he lacked the killer instinct.

Unfortunately, he turned out to be a terrible shot.

He wanted to do well in the army, partly because he knew people thought he could not hack it. He needed to prove to them, and perhaps to himself, that he was no wimp. But he had another reason. He believed in what he was fighting for.

President Wilson had made a speech, to Congress and the Senate, that had rung like a clarion around the world. He had called for nothing less than a new world order. "A general association of nations must be formed under specific covenants for the purpose of affording mutual guarantees of political independence and territorial integrity to great and small states alike."

A league of nations was a dream for Wilson, for Gus, and for many others—including, rather surprisingly, Sir Edward Grey, who had originated the idea while he was British foreign secretary.

Wilson had set out his program in fourteen points. He had spoken of reductions in armaments; the right of colonial people to a say in their own future; and freedom for the Balkan states, Poland, and the subject peoples of the Ottoman Empire. The speech had become known as Wilson's Fourteen Points. Gus envied the men who had helped the president write it. In the old days he would have had a hand in it himself.

"An evident principle runs through the whole program," Wilson had said. "It is the principle of justice to all peoples and nationalities, and their right to live on equal terms of liberty and safety with one another, whether they be strong or weak." Tears had come to Gus's eyes when he had read these words. "The people of the United States could act upon no other principle," Wilson had said.

Was it really possible that the nations could settle their arguments without war? Paradoxically, that was something worth fighting for.

Gus and Chuck and their machine-gun battalion traveled from Hoboken, New Jersey, on the *Corinna*, once a luxury liner, now converted to troop transport. The trip took two weeks. As second lieutenants, they shared a cabin on an upper deck. Although they had once been rivals for the affection of Olga Vyalov, they had become friends.

The ship was part of a convoy, with a navy escort, and the voyage was uneventful, except that several men died of Spanish flu, a new illness that was sweeping the world. The food was poor: the men said the Germans had given up submarine warfare and now aimed to win by poisoning them.

The *Corinna* waited a day and a half off Brest, on the northwest tip of France. They disembarked onto a dock crowded with men, vehicles, and stores, noisy with shouted orders and revving engines, busy with impatient officers and sweating stevedores. Gus made the mistake of asking a sergeant on the dock what the reason for the delay was. "Delay, sir?" he said, managing to make the word "sir" sound like an insult. "Yesterday we disembarked five thousand men, with their cars, guns, tents, and field kitchens, and transferred them to rail and road transport. Today we will disembark another five thousand, and the same tomorrow. There is no delay, sir. This is fucking fast."

Chuck grinned at Gus and murmured: "That's told you."

The stevedores were colored soldiers. Wherever black and white soldiers had to share facilities, there was trouble, usually caused by white recruits from the Deep South; so the army had given in. Rather than mix the races on the front line, the army assigned colored regiments to menial tasks in the rear. Gus knew that Negro soldiers complained bitterly about this: they wanted to fight for their country like everyone else.

Most of the regiment went on from Brest by train. They were not given passenger carriages, but crammed into a cattle truck. Gus amused the men by translating the sign on the side of a railcar: "Forty men or eight horses." However, the machine-gun battalion had its own vehicles, so Gus and Chuck went by road to their camp south of Paris.

In the States they had practiced trench warfare with wooden rifles, but now they had real weapons and ammunition. Gus and Chuck, as officers, had each been issued with a Colt M1911 semiautomatic pistol with a seven-round magazine in the grip. Before leaving the States they had thrown away their Mountie-style hats and replaced them with more practical caps with a distinctive fore-and-aft ridge. They also had steel helmets the same soup-bowl shape as the British.

Now blue-coated French instructors trained them to fight in cooperation with heavy artillery, a skill the United States Army had not previously needed. Gus could speak French, so inevitably he was assigned to liaison duties. Relations between the two nationalities were good, though the French complained that the price of brandy went up as soon as the doughboys arrived.

The German offensive had continued successfully through April. Ludendorff had advanced so fast in Flanders that General Haig said the British had their backs to the wall—a phrase that sent shock waves through the Americans.

Gus was in no hurry to see action, but Chuck became impatient in the training camp. What were they doing, he wanted to know, rehearsing mock battles when they ought to be fighting real ones? The nearest section of German front was at the champagne city of Rheims, northeast of Paris; but Gus's commanding officer, Colonel Wagner, told him that Allied intelligence was confident there would be no German offensive in that sector.

In that prediction, however, Allied intelligence was dead wrong.

{ II }

Walter was jubilant. Casualties were high, but Ludendorff's strategy was working. The Germans were attacking where the enemy was weak, moving fast, leaving strong points behind to be mopped up later. Despite some clever defensive moves by General Foch, the new supreme commander of the Allied armies, the Germans were gaining territory faster than at any time since 1914.

The biggest problem was that the advance was held up every time German troops overran stocks of food. They just stopped and ate, and Walter found it impossible to get them to move until they were full. It was the strangest thing to see men sitting on the ground, sucking raw eggs, stuffing their faces with cake and ham at the same time, or guzzling bottles of wine, while shells landed around them and bullets whistled over their heads. He knew that other officers had the same experience. Some tried threatening the men with handguns, but even that would not persuade them to leave the food and run on.

That aside, the spring offensive was a triumph. Walter and his men were exhausted, after four years of war, but so were the French and British soldiers they encountered.

After the Somme and Flanders, Ludendorff's third attack of 1918 was planned for the sector between Rheims and Soissons. Here the Allies held a ridge called the Chemin des Dames, the Ladies' Way—so named because the road along it had been built for the daughters of Louis XV to visit a friend.

The final deployment took place on Sunday, May 26, a sunny day with a fresh northeasterly breeze. Once again, Walter felt proud as he watched the columns of men marching to the front line, the thousands of guns being maneuvered into position under harassing fire from French artillery, the telephone lines being laid from the command dugouts to the battery positions.

Ludendorff's tactics remained the same. That night at two a.m. thousands of guns opened up, firing gas, shrapnel, and explosives into the French lines on the summit of the ridge. Walter noticed with satisfaction that the French firing slackened off immediately, indicating that the German guns were hitting their targets. The barrage was short, in line with the new thinking, and at five forty a.m. it stopped.

The storm troopers advanced.

The Germans were attacking uphill, but despite that they met little resistance, and to Walter's surprise and delight he reached the road along the top of the ridge in less than an hour. It was now clear daylight, and he could see the French retreating all along the downhill slope.

The storm troopers followed at a steady speed, keeping pace with the rolling barrage of the artillery, but all the same they reached the river Aisne, in the cleft of the valley, before midday. Some farmers had destroyed their reaping machines and burned the early crops in their barns, but most had left in too much of a hurry, and there were rich rewards for the requisition parties in the rear of the German forces. To Walter's astonishment, the retreating French had not even blown up the bridges over the Aisne. That suggested they were panicking.

Walter's five hundred men advanced across the next ridge during the afternoon, and made camp on the far side of the river Vesle, having advanced twelve miles in a single day.

Next day they paused, waiting for reinforcements, but on the third day they advanced again, and on the fourth day, Thursday, May 30, having gained an amazing thirty miles since Monday, they reached the north bank of the river Marne.

Here, Walter recalled ominously, the German advance had been halted in 1914.

He vowed it would not happen again.

{ III }

Gus was with the American Expeditionary Force at the Chateauvillain training area south of Paris on May 30 when the Third Division was ordered to help with the defense of the river Marne. Most of the division began to entrain, even though the battered French railway system might take several days to move them. However, Gus and Chuck and the machine guns set off by road immediately.

Gus was excited and fearful. This was not like boxing, where there was a referee to enforce the rules and stop the fight if it got dangerous. How would he act when someone actually fired a weapon at him? Would he turn and run away? What would prevent him? He generally did the logical thing.

Cars were as unreliable as trains, and numerous vehicles broke down or ran out of gas. In addition they were delayed by civilians traveling in the opposite direction, fleeing the battle, some driving herds of cows, others with their possessions in handcarts and wheelbarrows.

Seventeen machine guns arrived at the leafy small town of Château-

Thierry, fifty miles east of Paris, at six p.m. on Friday. It was a pretty little place in the evening sunshine. It straddled the Marne, with two bridges linking the southern suburb with the northern town center. The French held both banks, but the leading edge of the German advance had reached the northern city limits.

Gus's battalion was ordered to set up its armament along the south bank, commanding the bridges. Their crews were equipped with M1914 Hotchkiss heavy machine guns, each mounted on a sturdy tripod, fed by articulated metal cartridge belts holding 250 rounds. They also had rifle grenades, fired at a forty-five-degree angle from a bipod, and a few trench mortars of the British "Stokes" pattern.

As the sun set, Gus and Chuck were supervising the emplacement of their platoons between the two bridges. No training had prepared them to make these decisions: they just had to use their common sense. Gus picked a three-story building with a shuttered café on the ground floor. He broke in through the back door and climbed the stairs. There was a clear view from an attic window across the river and along a northward-leading street on the far side. He ordered a heavy machine-gun squad to set up there. He waited for the sergeant to tell him that was a stupid idea, but the man nodded approval and set about the task.

Gus placed three more machine guns in similar locations.

Looking for suitable cover for mortars, he found a brick boathouse on the riverbank, but was not sure whether it was in his sector or Chuck's, so he went looking for his friend to check. He spotted Chuck a hundred yards along the bank, near the east bridge, peering across the water through field glasses. He took two steps that way; then there was a terrific bang.

He turned in the direction of the noise, and in the next second there were several more deafening crashes. He realized the German artillery had opened up when a shell burst in the river, sending up a plume of water.

He looked again to where Chuck stood, just in time to see his friend disappear in an explosion of earth.

"Jesus Christ!" he said, and he ran toward the spot.

Shells and mortars burst all along the south bank. The men threw themselves flat. Gus reached the place where he had last seen Chuck and looked around in bewilderment. He saw nothing but piles of earth and stone. Then he spotted an arm poking out from the rubble. He moved a stone aside and found, to his horror, that the arm was not attached to a body.

Was it Chuck's arm? There had to be a way to tell, but Gus was too shocked to think how. He used the toe of his boot to push some loose earth aside ineffectually. Then he went down on his knees and began to dig with his hands. He saw a tan collar with a metal disc marked "US" and he groaned: "Oh, God." He quickly uncovered Chuck's face. There was no movement, no breath, no heartbeat.

He tried to remember what he was supposed to do next. Whom should he contact about a death? Something had to be done with the body, but what? Normally you would summon an undertaker.

He looked up to see a sergeant and two corporals staring at him. A mortar exploded on the street behind them, and they all ducked their heads reflexively, then looked at him again. They were waiting for his orders.

He stood up abruptly, and some of the training came back. It was not his job to deal with dead comrades, or even wounded ones. He was alive and well, and his duty was to fight. He felt a surge of irrational anger against the Germans who had killed Chuck. Hell, he thought, I'm going to fight back. He remembered what he had been doing: deploying the guns. He should get on with that. He would now have to take charge of Chuck's platoon as well.

He pointed at the sergeant in charge of the mortars. "Forget the boathouse—it's too exposed," he said. He pointed across the street to a narrow alleyway between a winery and livery stables. "Set up three mortars in that alley."

"Yes, sir." The sergeant hurried off.

Gus looked along the street. "See that flat roof, Corporal? Put a machine gun there."

"Sir, pardon me, that's an automobile repair shop—there may be a fuel tank below."

"Damn, you're right. Well spotted, Corporal. The tower of that church, then. Nothing but hymn books under that."

"Yes, sir, much better, thank you, sir."

"The rest of you, follow me. We'll take cover while I figure out where to put everything else."

He led them across the road and down a side street. A narrow pathway or lane ran along the backs of the buildings. A shell landed in the yard of an establishment selling farm supplies, showering Gus with clouds of powdered fertilizer, as if to remind him that he was not out of range.

He hurried along the lane, trying when he could to shelter from the barrage behind walls, barking orders at his NCOs, deploying his machine guns in the tallest and most solid-looking structures and his mortars in the gardens between houses. Occasionally his subordinates made suggestions or disagreed with him. He listened, then made quick decisions.

In no time it was dark, making the job harder. The Germans sent a storm of ordnance across the town, much of it accurately aimed at the American position on the south bank. Several buildings were destroyed, making the waterfront street look like a mouthful of bad teeth. Gus lost three machine guns to shelling in the first few hours.

It was midnight before he was able to return to battalion headquarters, in a sewing-machine factory a few streets south. Colonel Wagner was with his French opposite number, poring over a large-scale map of the town. Gus reported that all his guns and Chuck's were in position. "Good work, Dewar," the colonel said. "Are you all right?"

"Of course, sir," Gus said, puzzled and a bit offended, thinking the colonel might believe he did not have the nerve for this work.

"It's just that there's blood all over you."

"Is there?" Gus looked down and saw that there was indeed a good deal of congealed blood on the front of his uniform. "I wonder where that came from."

"From your face, by the look of it. You've got a nasty cut."

Gus felt his cheek, and winced as his fingers touched raw flesh. "I don't know when that happened," he said.

"Go along to the dressing station and get it cleaned up."

"It's nothing much, sir. I'd rather—"

"Do as you're told, Lieutenant. It will be serious if it gets infected." The colonel gave a thin smile. "I don't want to lose you. You seem to have the makings of a useful officer."

{ IV }

At four o'clock the next morning the Germans launched a gas barrage. Walter and his storm troopers approached the northern edge of the town at sunrise, expecting the resistance from the French forces to be as weak as it had been for the past two months.

They would have preferred to bypass Château-Thierry, but it was not possible. The railway line to Paris went through the town, and there were two key bridges. It had to be taken.

Farmhouses and fields gave way to cottages and smallholdings, then to paved streets and gardens. As Walter came close to the first of the two-story houses, a burst of machine-gun fire came from an upper window, dotting the road at his feet like raindrops on a pond. He threw himself over a low fence into a vegetable patch and rolled until he found cover behind an apple tree. His men scattered likewise, all but two who fell in the road. One lay still; the other moaned in pain.

Walter looked back and spotted Sergeant Schwab. "Take six men, find the back entrance to that house, and destroy that machine-gun emplacement," he said. He located his lieutenants. "Von Kessel, go west one block and enter the town from there. Von Braun, come east with me."

He kept off the streets and moved through alleys and backyards, but there were riflemen and machine gunners in about every tenth house.

Something had happened to give the French back their fighting spirit, Walter realized with trepidation.

All morning the storm troopers fought from house to house, taking heavy casualties. This was not how they were supposed to operate, bleeding for every yard. They were trained to follow the line of least resistance, penetrate deep behind enemy lines, and disrupt communications, so that the forces at the front would become demoralized and leaderless, and would quickly surrender to follow-up infantry. But that tactic had now failed, and they were slogging it out hand to hand with an enemy who seemed to have gained his second wind.

But they made progress, and at midday Walter stood on the ruins of the medieval castle that gave its name to the town. The castle was at the top of a hill, and the town hall stood at its foot. From there the main street ran in a straight line two hundred and fifty yards to a double-arched road bridge across the Marne. To the east, five hundred yards upriver, was the only other crossing, a railway bridge.

He could see all that with the naked eye. He took out his field glasses and focused on the enemy positions on the south bank. The men carelessly showed themselves, a sign that they were new to warfare: veterans stayed out of sight. They were young and energetic and well-fed and well-dressed, he noted. Their uniforms were not blue but tan, he saw with dismay.

They were Americans.

{ V }

During the afternoon, the French fell back to the north bank of the river, and Gus was able to bring his armament to bear, directing mortar and machine-gun fire over the heads of the French at the advancing Germans. The American guns sent a torrent of ammunition along the straight north-south avenues of Château-Thierry, turning them into killing lanes. All the same he could see the Germans advance fearlessly from bank to café, alley to shop doorway, overwhelming the French by sheer weight of numbers.

As afternoon turned to bloody evening, Gus watched from a high window and saw the tattered remnants of the blue-coated French falling back toward the west bridge. They made their last stand at the north end of the bridge and held it while the red sun went down behind the hills to the west. Then, in the dusk, they retreated across the bridge.

A small group of Germans saw what was happening and gave chase. Gus saw them run onto the bridge, barely visible in the twilight, gray moving on gray. Then the bridge exploded. The French had previously wired it for demolition, Gus realized. Bodies flew through the air and the northern arch of the bridge collapsed into a heap of rubble in the water.

Then it went quiet.

Gus lay down on a palliasse at headquarters and got some sleep, his first for almost forty-eight hours. He was awakened by the Germans' dawn barrage. Bleary-eyed, he hurried from the sewing-machine factory to the waterfront. In the pearly light of a June morning he saw that the Germans had occupied the entire north bank of the river and were shelling the American positions on the south bank at hellishly close range.

He arranged for the crews who had been up all night to be relieved by men who had got some rest. Then he went from position to position, always staying behind the waterfront buildings. He suggested ways of improving cover—moving a gun to a smaller window, using sheets of corrugated tin to protect crews from flying debris, or piling up rubble either side of the gun. But the best way for his men to protect themselves was to make life impossible for the enemy gunners. "Give the bastards hell," he said.

The men responded eagerly. The Hotchkiss fired four hundred and fifty rounds per minute, and its range was four thousand yards, so it was highly effective across the river. The Stokes mortar was less useful: its up-and-over trajectory was intended for trench warfare, where line-of-sight fire was ineffective. But the rifle grenades were highly destructive at short range.

The two sides pounded each other like bare-knuckle boxers fighting in a barrel. The noise of so much ammunition being fired was never less than deafening. Buildings collapsed, men screamed in the agony of wounds, bloodstained stretcher-bearers ran from the waterfront to the dressing station and back, and runners brought more ammunition and jugs of hot coffee to the weary soldiers manning the guns.

As the day wore on, Gus noticed, in a back-of-the-mind way, that he was not scared. He did not think about it often—there was too much to do. For a brief moment, in the middle of the day, as he stood in the canteen of the sewing-machine factory gulping down sweet milky coffee instead of lunch, he marveled at the strange person he had become. Could it really be Gus Dewar who ran from one building to the next through an artillery barrage, shouting at his men to give 'em hell? This man had been afraid he would lose his nerve and turn around and walk away from the battle. In the event, he hardly thought of his own safety, being too preoccupied with the danger to his men. How had that come about? Then a corporal came to tell him that his squad had lost the special wrench used to change overheated Hotchkiss barrels, and he swallowed the rest of his coffee and ran to deal with the problem.

He did suffer a moment of sadness that evening. It was dusk, and he happened to look out of a smashed kitchen window to the spot on the bank where Chuck Dixon had died. He no longer felt shocked by the way Chuck had disappeared in an explosion of earth: he had seen much more death and destruction in the last three days. What struck him now, with a different kind of shock, was the realization that one day he would have to speak about that awful moment to Chuck's parents, Albert and Emmeline, owners of a Buffalo bank, and to his young wife, Doris, who had been so against America's joining the war—probably because she feared exactly what had happened. What was Gus going to say to them? "Chuck fought bravely." Chuck had not fought at all: he had died in the first minute of his first battle, without firing a shot. It would hardly have mattered if he had been a coward—the result would have been the same. His life had just been wasted.

As Gus stared at the spot, lost in thought, his eye was caught by movement on the railway bridge.

His heart missed a beat. There were men coming onto the far end of the bridge. Their field-gray uniforms were only just visible in the half-light. They ran awkwardly along the rails, stumbling on the sleepers and the gravel. Their helmets were of the coal scuttle shape, and they carried their rifles slung. They were German.

Gus ran to the nearest machine-gun emplacement, behind a garden wall. The crew had not noticed the assault force. Gus tapped the gunner on the shoulder. "Fire at the bridge!" he shouted. "Look—Germans!" The gunner swung the barrel around to the new target.

Gus pointed to a soldier at random. "Run to headquarters and report an enemy incursion across the east bridge," he shouted. "Quick, quick!"

He found a sergeant. "Make sure everyone is firing at the bridge," he said. "Go!"

He headed west. Heavy machine guns could not be moved quickly—the Hotchkiss weighed eighty-eight pounds with its tripod—but he told all the rifle grenadiers and mortar crews to move to new positions from which they could defend the bridge.

The Germans began to be mown down, but they were determined, and kept coming. Through his glasses, Gus saw a tall man in the uniform of a major who looked familiar. He wondered if it was someone he had met before the war. As Gus looked, the major took a hit and fell to the ground.

The Germans were supported by a terrific barrage from their own artillery. It seemed as if every gun on the north bank had trained its sights on the south end of the railway bridge where the defending Americans were clustered. Gus saw his men fall one after another, but he replaced every killed or wounded gunner with a fresh man, and there was hardly a pause in the firing.

The Germans stopped running and began to take up positions, using the scant cover of dead comrades. The boldest of them advanced, but there was no place to hide, and they were swiftly brought down.

Darkness fell, but it made no difference: firing continued at maximum on both sides. The enemy became vague shapes lit by flashes of gunfire and exploding shells. Gus moved some of the heavy machine guns to new positions, feeling almost certain this incursion was not a feint to cover a river crossing somewhere else.

It was a stalemate, and at last the Germans began to retreat.

Seeing stretcher parties on the bridge, Gus ordered his men to stop firing.

In response, the German artillery went quiet.

"Christ Almighty," Gus said to no one in particular. "I think we've beaten them off."

{ VI }

An American bullet had broken Walter's shinbone. He lay on the railway line in agony, but he felt worse when he saw the men retreating and heard the guns fall silent. He knew then that he had failed.

He screamed when he was lifted onto the stretcher. It was bad for the men's morale to hear the wounded cry out, but he could not help it. They bumped him along the track and through the town to the dressing station, where someone gave him morphine and he passed out.

He woke up with his leg in a splint. He questioned everyone who passed his cot on the progress of the battle, but he got no details until Gottfried von Kessel came by to gloat over his wound. The German army had given up trying to cross the Marne at Château-Thierry, Gottfried told him. Perhaps they would try elsewhere.

Next day, just before he was put on a train home, he learned that the main body of the United States Third Division had arrived and taken up positions all along the south bank of the Marne.

A wounded comrade told him of a bloody battle in a wood near the town called the Bois de Belleau. There had been terrible casualties on both sides, but the Americans had won.

Back in Berlin, the papers continued to tell of German victories, but the lines on the maps got no nearer to Paris, and Walter came to the bitter conclusion that the spring offensive had failed. The Americans had arrived too soon.

He was released from the hospital to convalesce in his old room at his parents' house.

On August 8 an Allied attack at Amiens used almost five hundred of the new "tanks." These ironclad vehicles were plagued with problems but could be unstoppable, and the British gained eight miles in a single day.

It was only eight miles, but Walter suspected the tide had turned, and he could tell by his father's face that the old man felt the same. No one in Berlin now spoke of winning the war.

One night at the end of September, Otto came home looking as if someone had died. There was nothing left of his natural ebullience. Walter even wondered if he was going to cry.

"The kaiser has returned to Berlin," he said.

Walter knew that Kaiser Wilhelm had been at army headquarters in the Belgian hill resort called Spa. "Why has he come back?"

Otto's voice dropped to a near-whisper, as if he could not bear to say what he had to say in a normal voice. "Ludendorff wants an armistice."

CHAPTER THIRTY-TWO

October 1918

Maud had lunch at the Ritz with her friend Lord Remarc, who was a junior minister in the War Office. Johnny was wearing a new lavender waistcoat. Over the pot-au-feu she asked him: "Is the war really coming to an end?"

"Everyone thinks so," Johnny said. "The Germans have suffered seven hundred thousand casualties this year. They can't go on."

Maud wondered miserably if Walter was one of the seven hundred thousand. He might be dead, she knew; and the thought was like a cold lump inside her where her heart should be. She had had no word from him since their idyllic second honeymoon in Stockholm. She guessed that his work no longer took him to neutral countries from which he could write. The awful truth was that he had probably returned to the battlefield for Germany's last, all-or-nothing offensive.

Such thoughts were morbid, but realistic. So many women had lost their loved ones: husbands, brothers, sons, fiancés. They had all lived through four years during which such tragedies happened daily. It was no longer possible to be too pessimistic. Grief was the norm.

She pushed her soup dish away. "Is there any other reason to hope for peace?"

"Yes. Germany has a new chancellor, and he has written to President Wilson, suggesting an armistice based on Wilson's famous Fourteen Points."

"That is hopeful! Has Wilson agreed?"

"No. He said Germany must first withdraw from all conquered territories."

"What does our government think?"

"Lloyd George is hopping mad. The Germans treat the Americans as the senior partners in the alliance—and President Wilson acts as if they could make peace without consulting us."

"Does it matter?"

"I'm afraid it does. Our government doesn't necessarily agree with Wilson's Fourteen Points."

Maud nodded. "I suppose we're against point five, about colonial peoples having a say in their own government."

"Exactly. What about Rhodesia, and Barbados, and India? We can't be expected to ask the natives' permission before we civilize them. Americans are far too liberal. And we're dead against point two, freedom of the seas in war and peace. British power is based on the navy. We would not have been able to starve Germany into submission if we had not been allowed to blockade their seagoing trade."

"How do the French feel about it?"

Johnny grinned. "Clemenceau said Wilson was trying to outdo the Almighty. 'God himself only came up with ten points,' he said."

"I get the impression that most ordinary British people actually like Wilson and his points."

Johnny nodded. "And European leaders can hardly tell the American president to stop making peace."

Maud was so eager to believe it that she frightened herself. She told herself not to be happy yet. There could be such heavy disappointment in store.

A waiter brought them sole Waleska and cast an admiring eye at Johnny's waistcoat.

Maud turned to her other worry. "What do you hear from Fitz?" Her brother's mission in Siberia was secret, but he had confided in her, and Johnny gave her bulletins.

"That Cossack leader turned out to be a disappointment. Fitz made a pact with him, and we paid him for a while, but he was nothing more than a warlord, really. However, Fitz is staying on, hoping to encourage the Russians to overthrow the Bolsheviks. Meanwhile, Lenin has moved his government from Petrograd to Moscow, where he feels safer from invasion."

"Even if the Bolsheviks were deposed, would a new regime resume the war against Germany?"

"Realistically? No." Johnny took a sip of Chablis. "But a lot of very powerful people in the British government just hate the Bolsheviks."

"Why?"

"Lenin's regime is brutal."

"So was the tsar's, but Winston Churchill never plotted to overthrow him."

"Underneath, they're frightened that if Bolshevism is a success over there, it will come here next."

"Well, if it's a success, why not?"

Johnny shrugged. "You can't expect people such as your brother to see it that way."

"No," said Maud. "I wonder how he's getting on?"

{ II }

"We're in Russia!" Billy Williams said when the ship docked and he heard the voices of the longshoremen. "What are we doing in fucking Russia?"

"How can we be in Russia?" said Tommy Griffiths. "Russia's in the east. We've been sailing west for weeks."

"We've gone halfway round the world and come at it from the other side."

Tommy was not convinced. He leaned over the rail, staring. "The people look a bit Chinesey," he said.

"They're speaking Russian, though. They sound like that pony driver, Peshkov, the one who cheated the Ponti brothers at cards, then scarpered."

Tommy listened. "Aye, you're right. Well, I never."

"This must be Siberia," Billy said. "No wonder it's fucking cold."

A few minutes later they learned they were in Vladivostok.

People took little notice of the Aberowen Pals marching through the town. There were already thousands of soldiers in uniform here. Most were Japanese but there were also Americans and Czechs and others. The town had a busy port, trams running along broad boulevards, modern hotels and theaters, and hundreds of shops. It was like Cardiff, Billy thought, but colder.

When they reached their barracks they met a battalion of elderly Londoners who had been shipped there from Hong Kong. It made sense, Billy thought, to send old codgers to this backwater. But the Pals, though depleted by casualties, had a core of hardened veterans. Who had pulled strings to have them withdrawn from France and sent to the other side of the globe?

He soon found out. After dinner the brigadier, a comfortable-looking man evidently close to retirement, told them they were to be addressed by Colonel the Earl Fitzherbert.

Captain Gwyn Evans, the owner of the department stores, brought a wooden crate that had once held cans of lard, and Fitz climbed up on it, not without difficulty on account of his bad leg. Billy watched without sympathy. He reserved his compassion for Stumpy Pugh and the many other crippled ex-miners who had been injured digging the earl's coal. Fitz was smug, arrogant, and a merciless exploiter of ordinary men and women. It was a shame the Germans had not shot him in the heart rather than the leg.

"Our mission is fourfold," Fitz began, raising his voice to address six hundred men. "First, we're here to protect our property. On your way out of the docks, passing the railway sidings, you may have noticed a large supply dump guarded by troops. That ten-acre site contains six hundred thousand tons of munitions and other military equipment sent here by Britain and the United States when the Russians were our allies. Now that the Bolsheviks have made peace with Germany, we do not want bullets paid for by our people to fall into their hands."

"That doesn't make sense," Billy said loud enough for Tommy and the others around him to hear. "Instead of bringing us here, why didn't they ship the stores home?"

Fitz glanced irritably in the direction of the noise, but continued. "Second, there are many Czech nationalists in this country, some prisoners of war and others who were working here prewar, who have formed themselves into the Czech Legion and are trying to take ship from Vladivostok to join our forces in France. They are being harassed by the Bolsheviks and our job is to help them get away. Local Cossack community leaders will help us in this effort."

"Cossack community leaders?" Billy said. "Who is he trying to fool? They're bloody bandits."

Once again Fitz heard the dissident muttering. This time Captain Evans looked annoyed and walked down the mess hall to stand near Billy and his group.

"Here in Siberia there are eight hundred thousand Austrian and German prisoners of war who have been set free since the peace treaty. We must prevent them returning to the European battlefield. Finally, we suspect the Germans of eyeing up the oil fields of Baku, in the south of Russia. They must not be allowed to access that supply."

Billy said: "I've got a feeling Baku is quite a long way from here."

The brigadier said amiably: "Do any of you men have any questions?"

Fitz gave him a glare, but it was too late. Billy said: "I haven't read nothing about this in the papers."

Fitz replied: "Like many military missions, it is secret, and you will not be allowed to say where you are in your letters home."

"Are we at war with Russia, sir?"

"No, we are not." Fitz pointedly looked away from Billy. Perhaps he remembered how Billy had bested him at the peace talks meeting in the

Calvary Gospel Hall. "Does anyone other than Sergeant Williams have a question?"

Billy persisted. "Are we trying to overthrow the Bolshevik government?"

There was an angry murmur from the troops, many of whom sympathized with the revolution.

"There is no Bolshevik government," Fitz said with mounting exasperation. "The regime in Moscow has not been recognized by His Majesty the king."

"Have our mission been authorized by Parliament?"

The brigadier looked troubled—he had not been expecting *this* type of question—and Captain Evans said: "That's enough from you, Sergeant—let the others have a chance."

But Fitz was not smart enough to shut up. Apparently it did not occur to him that Billy's debating skills, learned from a radical nonconformist father, might be superior to his own. "Military missions are authorized by the War Office, not by Parliament," Fitz argued.

"So this have been kept secret from our elected representatives!" Billy said indignantly.

Tommy murmured anxiously: "Careful, now, butty."

"Necessarily," said Fitz.

Billy ignored Tommy's advice—he was too angry now. He stood up and said in a clear, loud voice: "Sir, is what we're doing legal?"

Fitz colored, and Billy knew he had scored a hit.

Fitz began: "Of course it is—"

"If our mission have not been approved by the British people or the Russian people," Billy interrupted, "how can it be legal?"

Captain Evans said: "Sit down, Sergeant. This isn't one of your bloody Labour Party meetings. One more word and you'll be on a charge."

Billy sat down, satisfied. He had made his point.

Fitz said: "We have been invited here by the All-Russia Provisional Government, whose executive arm is a five-man directory based at Omsk, at the western edge of Siberia. And that," Fitz finished, "is where you're going next."

{ III }

It was dusk. Lev Peshkov waited, shivering, in a freight yard in Vladivostok, the ass end of the Trans-Siberian Railway. He wore an army greatcoat over his lieutenant's uniform, but Siberia was the coldest place he had ever been.

He was furious to be in Russia. He had been lucky to escape, four years ago, and even luckier to marry into a wealthy American family. And now he was back—all because of a girl. What's wrong with me? he asked himself. Why can't I be satisfied?

A gate opened, and a cart drawn by a mule came out of the supply dump. Lev jumped onto the seat beside the British soldier who was driving it. "Aye, aye, Sid," said Lev.

"Wotcher," said Sid. He was a thin man of about forty with a perpetual cigarette and a prematurely lined face. A Cockney, he spoke English with an accent quite different from that of South Wales or upstate New York. At first Lev had found him hard to understand.

"Have you got the whisky?"

"Nah, just tins of cocoa."

Lev turned around, leaned into the cart, and pulled back a corner of the tarpaulin. He was almost certain Sid was joking. He saw a cardboard box marked: "Fry's Chocolate and Cocoa." He said: "Not much demand for that among the Cossacks."

"Look underneath."

Lev moved the box aside and saw a different legend: "Teacher's Highland Cream—Perfection of Old Scotch Whisky." He said: "How many?"

"Twelve cases."

He covered the box. "Better than cocoa."

He directed Sid away from the city center. He checked behind frequently to see if anyone was following them, and looked with apprehension when he saw a senior U.S. Army officer, but no one questioned them. Vladivostok was crammed with refugees from the Bolsheviks, most of whom had

OCTOBER 1918 ↶ 889

brought a lot of money with them. They were spending it as if there were no tomorrow, which there probably was not for many of them. In consequence the shops were busy and the streets full of carts like this one delivering goods. As everything was scarce in Russia, much of what was on sale had been smuggled in from China or, like Sid's Scotch, stolen from the military.

Lev saw a woman with a little girl, and thought of Daisy. He missed her. She was walking and talking now, and investigating the world. She had a pout that melted everyone's heart, even Josef Vyalov's. Lev had not seen her for six months. She was two and a half now, and she must have changed in the time he had been away.

He also missed Marga. She was the one he dreamed about, her naked body wriggling against his in bed. It was because of her that he had got into trouble with his father-in-law and ended up in Siberia, but all the same he longed to see her again.

"Have you got a weakness, Sid?" said Lev. He felt he needed a closer friendship with the taciturn Sid: partners in crime required trust.

"Nah," said Sid. "Only money."

"Does your love of money lead you to take risks?"

"Nah, just thieving."

"And does thieving ever get you into trouble?"

"Not really. Prison, once, but that was only for six months."

"My weakness is women."

"Is it?"

Lev was used to this British habit of asking the question after the answer had been given. "Yes," he said. "I can't resist them. I have to walk into a nightclub with a pretty girl on my arm."

"Do you?"

"Yes. I can't help myself."

The cart entered a dockland neighborhood of dirt roads and sailors' hostels, places that had neither names nor addresses. Sid looked nervous.

Lev said: "You're armed, yeah?"

"Nah," said Sid. "I just got this." He pulled back his coat to reveal a huge pistol with a foot-long barrel stuck into his belt.

Lev had never seen a gun like it. "What the fuck is that?"

"Webley-Mars. Most powerful handgun in the world. Very rare."

"No need to pull the trigger—just wave it about. It'll scare people to death."

In this area no one was paid to clear the streets of snow, and the cart followed the tracks of previous vehicles, or slid on the ice of little-used lanes. Being in Russia made Lev think of his brother. He had not forgotten his promise to send Grigori the fare to America. He was making good money selling stolen military supplies to the Cossacks. With today's deal he would have enough for Grigori's passage.

He had done a lot of wicked things in his short life, but if he could make amends to his brother, he would feel better about himself.

They drove into an alley and turned behind a low building. Lev opened a cardboard box and took out one bottle of Scotch. "Stay here and guard the load," he said to Sid. "Otherwise it will be gone when we come out."

"Don't worry," said Sid, but he looked apprehensive.

Lev reached under his greatcoat to touch the holstered Colt .45 semiautomatic pistol on his belt; then he went in through the back door.

The place was what passed for a tavern in Siberia. There was a small room with a few chairs and a table. It had no bar, but an open door revealed a dirty kitchen with a shelf of bottles and a barrel. Three men sat near the log fire, dressed in ragged furs. Lev recognized the one in the middle, a man he knew as Sotnik. He wore baggy trousers tucked into riding boots. He had high cheekbones and slanted eyes, and he sported an elaborate mustache and side-whiskers. His skin was reddened and lined by the weather. He might have been any age between twenty-five and fifty-five.

Lev shook hands all round. He uncorked the bottle, and one of the men—presumably the bar owner—brought four nonmatching glasses. Lev poured generous measures, and they all drank.

"This is the best whisky in the world," Lev said in Russian. "It comes from a cold country, like Siberia, where the water in the mountain streams is pure melted snow. What a pity it is so expensive."

Sotnik's face was expressionless. "How much?"

Lev was not going to let him reopen the bargaining. "The price you agreed to yesterday," he said. "Payable in gold rubles, nothing else."

"How many bottles?"

"One hundred and forty-four."

"Where are they?"

"Nearby."

"You should be careful. There are thieves in the neighborhood."

This might have been a warning or a threat: Lev guessed the ambiguity was intentional. "I know about thieves," he said. "I'm one of them."

Sotnik looked at his two comrades; then, after a pause, he laughed. They laughed, too.

Lev poured another round. "Don't worry," he said. "Your whisky is safe—behind the barrel of a gun." That, too, was ambiguous. It might have been a reassurance or a warning.

"That's good," said Sotnik.

Lev drank his whisky, then looked at his watch. "A military police patrol is due in this neighborhood soon," he lied. "I have to go."

"One more drink," said Sotnik.

Lev stood up. "Do you want the whisky?" He let his irritation show. "I can easily sell it to someone else." This was true. You could always sell liquor.

"I'll take it."

"Money on the table."

Sotnik picked up a saddlebag from the floor and began counting out five-ruble pieces. The agreed price was sixty rubles a dozen. Sotnik slowly put the coins in piles of twelve until he had twelve stacks. Lev guessed he could not actually count up to 144.

When Sotnik had finished he looked at Lev. Lev nodded. Sotnik put the coins back in the saddlebag.

They went outside, Sotnik carrying the bag. Night had fallen, but there was a moon, and they could see clearly. Lev said to Sid in English: "Stay on the cart. Be alert." In an illegal transaction, this was always the dangerous moment—the buyer's chance to grab the goods and keep the money. Lev was not taking any chances with Grigori's ticket money.

Lev pulled the cover off the cart, then moved three boxes of cocoa aside to reveal the Scotch. He took a case from the cart and put it on the ground at Sotnik's feet.

The other Cossack went to the cart and reached for another case.

"No," said Lev. He looked at Sotnik. "The bag."

There was a long pause.

On the driving seat, Sid pulled back his coat to reveal his weapon.

Sotnik gave Lev the bag.

Lev looked inside, but decided not to count the money again. He would have seen if Sotnik had slyly extracted a few coins. He handed the bag to Sid, then helped the others unload the cart.

He shook hands all round and was about to get up on the cart when Sotnik stopped him. "Look," he said. He pointed at an opened box. "There's a bottle missing."

That bottle was on the table in the tavern, and Sotnik knew it. Why was he trying to pick a quarrel at this stage? This was dangerous.

He said to Sid in English: "Give me one gold piece."

Sid opened the bag and handed him a coin.

Lev balanced it on his closed fist, then threw it in the air, spinning it. The coin flashed in the moonlight. As Sotnik reached out reflexively to catch it, Lev jumped onto the seat of the cart.

Sid cracked the whip.

"Go with God," Lev called out as the cart jerked into motion. "And let me know when you need more whisky."

The mule trotted out of the yard and turned onto the road, and Lev breathed easier.

"How much did we get?" said Sid.

"What we asked for. Three hundred and sixty rubles each. Minus five. I'll stand the loss of that last coin. Got a bag?"

Sid produced a large leather purse. Lev counted seventy-two coins into it.

He said good-bye to Sid and jumped off the cart near the U.S. officers' accommodation. As he was making his way to his room, he was accosted by Captain Hammond. "Peshkov! Where have you been?"

Lev wished he were not carrying 355 rubles in a Cossack saddlebag. "A little sightseeing, sir."

"It's dark!"

"That's why I came back."

"We've been looking for you. The colonel wants you."

"Right away, sir." Lev headed for his room, to drop off the saddlebag, but Hammond said: "The colonel's office is the other way."

"Yes, sir." Lev turned around.

Colonel Markham did not like Lev. The colonel was a career soldier, not a wartime recruit. He felt Lev did not share his commitment to excellence in the United States Army, and he was right—110 percent, as the colonel himself might have put it.

Lev considered parking the saddlebag on the floor outside the colonel's office door, but it was too much money to leave lying around.

"Where the hell were you?" said Markham as soon as Lev walked in.

"Taking a look around town, sir."

"I'm reassigning you. Our British allies need interpreters and they've asked me to second you to them."

It sounded like a soft option. "Yes, sir."

"You'll be going with them to Omsk."

That was not so soft. Omsk was four thousand miles away in the barbaric heartland of Russia. "What for, sir?"

"They will brief you."

Lev did not want to go. It was too far from home. "Are you asking me to volunteer, sir?"

The colonel hesitated, and Lev realized the assignment *was* voluntary, insofar as anything was in the army. "Are you refusing the assignment?" said Markham threateningly.

"Only if it's voluntary, sir, of course."

"I'll tell you the situation, Lieutenant," said the colonel. "If you volunteer, I won't ask you to open that bag and show me what's inside."

Lev cursed under his breath. There was nothing he could do. The colonel was too damn sharp. And Grigori's fare to America was in the saddlebag.

Omsk, he thought. Hell.

"I'd be glad to go, sir," he said.

{ IV }

Ethel went upstairs to Mildred's apartment. The place was clean but not tidy, with toys on the floor, a cigarette burning in an ashtray, and knickers drying in front of the fire. "Can you keep an eye on Lloyd tonight?" Ethel asked. She and Bernie were going to a Labour Party meeting. Lloyd was nearly four now and quite capable of getting out of bed and going for a walk on his own if not watched.

"Of course," said Mildred. They frequently watched each other's children in the evenings. "I've got a letter from Billy," Mildred said.

"Is he all right?"

"Yes. But I don't think he's in France. He doesn't say anything about the trenches."

"He must be in the Middle East, then. I wonder if he's seen Jerusalem." The Holy City had been taken by British forces at the end of last year. "Our da will be pleased if he has."

"There's a message for you. He says he'll write later, but to tell you . . ." She reached into the pocket of her apron. "Let me get it right. 'Believe me, I feel I am badly informed here about events in politics in Russia.' Funny bloody message, really."

"It's in code," Ethel said. "Every third word counts. The message says, *I am here in Russia.* What's he doing there?"

"I didn't know our army was in Russia."

"Nor did I. Does he mention a song, or a book title?"

"Yeah—how did you know?"

"That's code, too."

"He says to remind you of a song you used to sing called 'I'm with Freddie in the Zoo.' I've never heard of it."

"Nor have I. It's the initials. 'Freddie in the Zoo' means . . . Fitz."

Bernie came in wearing a red tie. "He's fast asleep," he said, meaning Lloyd.

Ethel said: "Mildred's got a letter from Billy. He seems to be in Russia with Earl Fitzherbert."

"Aha!" said Bernie. "I wondered how long it would take them."

"What do you mean?"

"We've sent troops to fight the Bolsheviks. I knew it would happen."

"We're at war with the new Russian government?"

"Not officially, of course." Bernie looked at his watch. "We need to go." He hated to be late.

On the bus, Ethel said: "We can't be *unofficially* at war. Either we are or we aren't."

"Churchill and that crowd know the British people won't support a war against the Bolsheviks, so they're trying to do it secretly."

Ethel said thoughtfully: "I'm disappointed in Lenin—"

"He's just doing what he's got to do!" Bernie interrupted. He was a passionate supporter of the Bolsheviks.

Ethel went on: "Lenin could become just as much of a tyrant as the tsar—"

"That's ridiculous!"

"—but even so, he should be given a chance to show what he can do for Russia."

"Well, we're in agreement about that, at least."

"I'm not sure what we can do about it, though."

"We need more information."

"Billy will write to me soon. He'll give me the details."

Ethel felt indignant about the government's secret war—if that was what it was—but she was in an agony of worry about Billy. He would not keep his mouth shut. If he thought the army was doing wrong, he would say so, and might get into trouble.

The Calvary Gospel Hall was full: the Labour Party had gained popularity during the war. This was partly because the Labour leader, Arthur Henderson, had been in Lloyd George's War Cabinet. Henderson had started work in a locomotive factory at the age of twelve, and his performance as a cabinet minister had killed off the Conservative argument that workers could not be trusted in government.

Ethel and Bernie sat next to Jock Reid, a red-faced Glaswegian who had been Bernie's best friend when he was single. The chairman of the meeting was Dr. Greenward. The main item on the agenda was the next general election. There were rumors that Lloyd George would call a national election as soon as the war ended. Aldgate needed a Labour candidate, and Bernie was the front runner.

He was proposed and seconded. Someone suggested Dr. Greenward as an alternative, but the doctor said he felt he should stick to medicine.

Then Jayne McCulley stood up. She had been a party member ever since Ethel and Maud had protested against the withdrawal of her separation allowance, and Maud had been carried off to jail in the arms of a policeman. Now Jayne said: "I read in the paper that women can stand in the next election, and I propose that Ethel Williams should be our candidate."

There was a moment of stunned silence; then everyone tried to speak at the same time.

Ethel was taken aback. She had not thought about this. Ever since she had known Bernie, he had wanted to be the local M.P. She had accepted that. Besides, it had never been possible for women to be elected. She was not sure it was possible now. Her first inclination was to refuse immediately.

Jayne had not finished. She was a pretty young woman, but the softness of her appearance was deceptive, and she could be formidable. "I respect Bernie, but he is an organizer and a meetings man," she said. "Aldgate has a Liberal M.P. who is quite well-liked and may be hard to defeat. We need a candidate who can win this seat for Labour, someone who can say to the people of the East End: 'Follow me to victory!' and they will. We need Ethel."

All the women cheered, and so did some of the men, though others muttered darkly. Ethel realized she would have a lot of support if she ran.

And Jayne was right: Bernie was probably the cleverest man in the room, but he was not an inspirational leader. He could explain how revolutions happened and why companies went bust, but Ethel could inspire people to join a crusade.

Jock Reid stood up. "Comrade Chairman, I believe the legislation does not permit women to stand."

Dr. Greenward said: "I can answer that question. The law that was passed earlier this year, giving the vote to certain women over thirty, did not provide for women to stand for election. But the government has admitted that this is an anomaly, and a further bill has been drafted."

Jock persisted. "But the law *as it stands today* forbids the election of women, so we can't nominate one." Ethel gave a wry smile: it was odd how men who called for world revolution could insist on following the letter of the law.

Dr. Greenward said: "The Parliament (Qualification of Women) Bill is clearly intended to become law before the next general election, so it seems perfectly in order for this branch to nominate a woman."

"But Ethel is under thirty."

"Apparently this new bill applies to women over twenty-one."

"Apparently?" said Jock. "How can we nominate a candidate if we don't know the rules?"

Dr. Greenward said: "Perhaps we should postpone nomination until the new legislation has been passed."

Bernie whispered something in Jock's ear, and Jock said: "Let's ask Ethel if she's willing to stand. If not, then there's no need to postpone the decision."

Bernie turned to Ethel with a confident smile.

"All right," said Dr. Greenward. "Ethel, if you were nominated, would you accept?"

Everyone looked at her.

Ethel hesitated.

This was Bernie's dream, and Bernie was her husband. But which of them would be the better choice for Labour?

As the seconds passed, a look of incredulity came over Bernie's face. He had expected her to decline the nomination instantly.

That hardened her resolve.

"I . . . I've never considered it," she said. "And, um, as the chairman said, it's not even a legal possibility yet. So it's a hard question to answer. I believe Bernie would be a good candidate . . . but all the same I'd like time to think about it. So perhaps we should accept the chairman's suggestion of a postponement."

She turned to Bernie.

He looked as if he could kill her.

CHAPTER THIRTY-THREE

November 11, 1918

A t two o'clock in the morning, the phone rang at Fitz's house in Mayfair.

Maud was still up, sitting in the drawing room with a candle, the portraits of dead ancestors looking down on her, the drawn curtains like shrouds, the pieces of furniture around her dimly visible, like beasts in a field at night. For the last few days she had hardly slept. A superstitious foreboding told her Walter would be killed before the war ended.

She sat alone, with a cold cup of tea in her hands, staring into the coal fire, wondering where he was and what he was doing. Was he sleeping in a damp trench somewhere, or preparing for tomorrow's fighting? Or was he already dead? She could be a widow, having spent only two nights with her husband in four years of marriage. All she could be sure of was that he was not a prisoner of war. Johnny Remarc checked every list of captured officers for her. Johnny did not know her secret: he believed she was concerned only because Walter had been a dear friend of Fitz's before the war.

The telephone bell startled her. At first she thought it might be a call about Walter, but that would not make sense. News of a friend taken prisoner could wait until morning. It must be Fitz, she thought with agony: could he have been wounded in Siberia?

She hurried out to the hall but Grout got there first. She realized with a guilty start that she had forgotten to give the staff permission to go to bed.

"I will inquire whether Lady Maud is at home, my lord," Grout said into the apparatus. He covered the mouthpiece with his hand and said to Maud: "Lord Remarc at the War Office, my lady."

She took the phone from Grout and said: "It is Fitz? Is he hurt?"

"No, no," said Johnny. "Calm down. It's good news. The Germans have accepted the armistice terms."

"Oh, Johnny, thank God!"

"They're all in the forest of Compiègne, north of Paris, on two trains in a railway siding. The Germans have just gone into the dining car of the French train. They're ready to sign."

"But they haven't signed yet?"

"No, not yet. They're quibbling about the wording."

"Johnny, will you phone me again when they've signed? I shan't go to bed tonight."

"I will. Good-bye."

Maud gave the handset back to the butler. "The war may end tonight, Grout."

"I'm very happy to hear it, my lady."

"But you should go to bed."

"With your ladyship's permission, I'd like to stay up until Lord Remarc telephones again."

"Of course."

"Would you like some more tea, my lady?"

{ II }

The Aberowen Pals arrived in Omsk early in the morning.

Billy would always remember every detail of the four-thousand-mile journey along the Trans-Siberian Railway from Vladivostok. It had taken twenty-three days, even with an armed sergeant posted in the locomotive to make sure the driver and fireman kept maximum speed. Billy was cold all the way: the stove in the center of the railcar hardly took the chill off the Siberian mornings. They lived on black bread and bully beef. But Billy found every day a revelation.

He had not known there were places in the world as beautiful as Lake Baikal. The lake was longer from one end to the other than Wales, Captain Evans told them. From the speeding train they watched the sun rise over the still blue water, lighting the tops of the mile-high mountains on the far side, the snow turning to gold on the peaks.

All his life he would cherish the memory of an endless caravan of camels alongside the railway line, the laden beasts plodding patiently through the snow, ignoring the twentieth century as it hurtled past them in a clash of iron and a shriek of steam. I'm a bloody long way from Aberowen, he thought at that moment.

But the most memorable incident was a visit to a high school in Chita. The train stopped there for two days while Colonel Fitzherbert parlayed with the local leader, a Cossack chieftain called Semenov. Billy attached himself to a party of American visitors on a tour. The principal of the school, who spoke English, explained that until a year ago he had taught only the children of the prosperous middle class, and that Jews had been banned even if they could afford the fees. Now, by order of the Bolsheviks, education was free to all. The effect was obvious. His classrooms were crammed to bursting with children in rags, learning to read and write and count, and even studying science and art. Whatever else Lenin might have done—and it was difficult to separate the truth from the conservative propaganda—at least, Billy thought, he was serious about educating Russian children.

On the train with him was Lev Peshkov. He had greeted Billy warmly, showing no sense of shame, as if he had forgotten being chased out of Aberowen as a cheat and a thief. Lev had made it to America and married a rich girl, and now he was a lieutenant, attached to the Pals as an interpreter.

The population of Omsk cheered the battalion as they marched from the railway station to their barracks. Billy saw numerous Russian officers on the streets, wearing fancy old-fashioned uniforms but apparently doing nothing military. There were also a lot of Canadian troops.

When the battalion was dismissed, Billy and Tommy strolled around town. There was not much to look at: a cathedral, a mosque, a brick fortress, and a river busy with freight and passenger traffic. They were surprised to see many locals wearing bits and pieces of British army uniform. A woman selling hot fried fish from a stall had on a khaki tunic; a deliveryman with a handcart wore thick army-issue serge trousers; a tall schoolboy with a satchel of books walked along the street in bright new British boots. "Where did they get them?" said Billy.

"We supply uniforms to the Russian army here, but Peshkov told me the officers sell them on the black market," Tommy said.

"Serves us bloody well right for supporting the wrong side," said Billy.

The Canadian YMCA had set up a canteen. Several of the Pals were already there: it seemed to be the only place to go. Billy and Tommy got hot tea and big wedges of apple tart, which North Americans called pie. "This town is the headquarters of the anti-Bolshevik reactionary government," Billy said. "I read it in *The New York Times*." The American papers, which had been available in Vladivostok, were more honest than the British.

Lev Peshkov came in. With him was a beautiful young Russian girl in a cheap coat. They all stared at him. How did he do it so fast?

Lev looked excited. "Hey, have you guys heard the rumor?"

Lev probably always heard rumors first, Billy thought.

Tommy said: "Yeah, we heard you're a homo."

They all laughed.

Billy said: "What rumor?"

"They've signed an armistice." Lev paused. "Don't you get it? The war is over!"

"Not for us," said Billy.

{ III }

Captain Dewar's platoon was attacking a small village called Aux Deux Eglises, east of the river Meuse. Gus had heard a rumor there would be a cease-fire at eleven a.m., but his commanding officer had ordered the assault, so he was carrying it out. He had moved his heavy machine guns forward to the edge of a spinney, and they were firing across a broad meadow at the outlying buildings, and giving the enemy plenty of time to retreat.

Unfortunately, the Germans were not taking the opportunity. They had set up mortars and light machine guns in the farmyards and orchards, and were shooting back energetically. One gun in particular, firing from the roof of a barn, was effectively keeping half of Gus's platoon pinned down.

Gus spoke to Corporal Kerry, the best shot in the unit. "Could you put a grenade into that barn roof?"

Kerry, a freckled youth of nineteen, said: "If I could get a bit closer."

"That's the problem."

Kerry surveyed the terrain. "There's a bit of a rise a third of the way across the meadow," he said. "From there I could do it."

"It's risky," Gus said. "Do you want to be a hero?" He looked at his watch. "The war could be over in five minutes, if the rumors are true."

Kerry grinned. "I'll give it a try, Captain."

Gus hesitated, reluctant to let Kerry risk his life. But this was the army, and they were still fighting, and orders were orders. "All right," Gus said. "In your own time."

He half hoped Kerry would delay, but the boy immediately shouldered his rifle and picked up a case of grenades.

Gus shouted: "All fire! Give Kerry as much cover as you can."

All the machine guns rattled, and Kerry began to run.

The enemy spotted him immediately, and their guns opened up. He zigzagged across the field like a hare chased by dogs. German mortars exploded around him but miraculously missed.

Kerry's "bit of a rise" was three hundred yards away.

He almost made it.

The enemy machine gunner got Kerry perfectly in his sights and let fly with a long burst. Kerry was struck by a dozen rounds within a heartbeat. He flung up his arms, dropped his mortars, and fell, momentum carrying him through the air until he landed a few paces from his rise. He lay quite still, and Gus thought he must have been dead before he hit the ground.

The enemy guns stopped. After a few moments, the Americans stopped firing, too. Gus thought he could hear the sound of distant cheering. All the men near him fell silent, listening. The Germans were cheering, too.

German soldiers began to appear, emerging from their shelters in the distant village.

Gus heard the sound of an engine. An Indian-brand American motorcycle came through the woods driven by a sergeant with a major on the pillion. "Cease fire!" the major yelled. The motorcyclist was driving him along the line from one position to the next. "Cease fire!" he shouted again. "Cease fire!"

Gus's platoon began to whoop. The men took off their helmets and threw them in the air. Some danced jigs; others shook one another's hands. Gus heard singing.

Gus could not take his eyes off Corporal Kerry.

He walked slowly across the meadow and knelt beside the body. He had seen many corpses and he had no doubt Kerry was dead. He wondered what the boy's first name was. He rolled the body over. There were small bullet holes all over Kerry's chest. Gus closed the boy's eyes and stood up.

"God forgive me," he said.

{IV}

As it happened, both Ethel and Bernie were home from work that day. Bernie was ill in bed with influenza, and so was Lloyd's child minder, so Ethel was looking after her husband and her son.

She felt very low. They had had a tremendous row about which of them was to be the parliamentary candidate. It was not merely the worst quarrel of their married life; it was the only one. And they had barely spoken to each other since.

Ethel knew she was justified, but she felt guilty all the same. She might well make a better M.P. than Bernie, and anyway the choice should be made by their comrades, not by themselves. Bernie had been planning this for years, but that did not mean the job was his by right. Although Ethel had not thought of it before, she was now eager to run. Women had won the vote, but there was more to be done. First, the age limit must be lowered so that it was the same as for men. Then women's pay and working conditions needed improvement. In most industries, women were paid less than men even when doing exactly the same work. Why should they not get the same?

But she was fond of Bernie, and when she saw the hurt on his face she wanted to give in immediately. "I expected to be undermined by my enemies," he had said to her one evening. "The Conservatives, the halfway-house Liberals, the capitalist imperialists, the bourgeoisie. I even expected opposition from one or two jealous individuals in the party. But there was one person I felt sure I could rely on. And she is the one who has sabotaged me." Ethel felt a pain in her chest when she thought about it.

She took him a cup of tea at eleven o'clock. Their bedroom was comfortable, if shabby, with cheap cotton curtains, a writing table, and a photograph of Keir Hardie on the wall. Bernie put down his novel, *The Ragged Trousered Philanthropists*, which all the socialists were reading. He said coldly: "What are you going to do tonight?" The Labour Party meeting was that evening. "Have you made a decision?"

She had. She could have told him two days ago, but she had not been able to bring herself to utter the words. Now that he had asked the question, she would answer it.

"It should be the best candidate," she said defiantly.

He looked wounded. "I don't know how you can do this to me and still say you love me."

She felt it was unfair of him to use such an argument. Why did it not apply in reverse? But that was not the point. "We shouldn't think of ourselves—we should think of the party."

"What about our marriage?"

"I'm not giving way to you just because I'm your wife."

"You've betrayed me."

"But I am giving way to you," she said.

"What?"

"I said, I am giving way to you."

Relief spread across his face.

She went on: "But it's not because I'm your wife. And it's not because you're the better candidate."

He looked mystified. "Why, then?"

Ethel sighed. "I'm pregnant."

"Oh, my word!"

"Yes. Just at the moment when a woman can become a member of Parliament, I've fallen for a baby."

Bernie smiled. "Well, then, everything's turned out for the best!"

"I knew you'd think that," Ethel said. At that moment she resented Bernie and the unborn baby and everything else about her life. Then she became aware that a church bell was ringing. She looked at the clock on the mantelpiece. It was five past eleven. Why were they ringing at this time on a Monday morning? Then she heard another. She frowned and went to the window. She could see nothing unusual in the street, but more bells began. To the west, in the sky over central London, she saw a red flare, the kind they called a maroon.

She turned back to Bernie. "It sounds as if every church in London is ringing its bells."

"Something's happened," he said. "I bet it's the end of the war. They must be ringing for peace!"

"Well," said Ethel sourly, "it's not for my bloody pregnancy."

{ V }

Fitz's hopes for the overthrow of Lenin and his bandits were centered on the All-Russia Provisional Government, based in Omsk. It was not just Fitz, but powerful men in most of the world's major governments, who looked to this town for the start of the counterrevolution.

The five-man directory was housed in a railway train on the outskirts of the city. A series of armored railcars guarded by elite troops contained, Fitz knew, the remains of the imperial treasury, many millions of rubles' worth of gold. The tsar was dead, killed by the Bolsheviks, but his money was here to give power and authority to the loyalist opposition.

Fitz felt he had a profound personal investment in the directory. The group of influential men he had assembled at Tŷ Gwyn back in April formed a discreet network within British politics, and they had managed to foster Britain's clandestine but weighty encouragement of the Russian resistance. That in turn had brought support from other nations, or at least discouraged them from helping Lenin's regime, he felt sure. But foreigners could not do everything: it was the Russians themselves who had to rise up.

How much could the directory achieve? Although it was anti-Bolshevik, its chairman was a Socialist Revolutionary, Nicholas D. Avkentsiev. Fitz deliberately ignored him. The Socialist Revoutionaries were almost as bad as Lenin's lot. Fitz's hopes lay with the right wing and the military. Only they could be relied upon to restore the monarchy and private property. He went to see General Boldyrev, commander in chief of the directory's Siberian army.

The rail carriages occupied by the government were furnished with fading tsarist splendor: worn velvet seats, chipped marquetry, stained lampshades, and elderly servants wearing dirty remnants of the elaborate braided and beaded livery of the old St. Petersburg court. In one carriage there was a lipsticked young woman in a silk dress smoking a cigarette.

Fitz was discouraged. He wanted to return to the old ways, but this setup seemed too backward-looking even for his taste. He thought with anger of Sergeant Williams's scornful mockery. "Is what we're doing legal?" Fitz knew the answer was doubtful. It was time he shut Williams up for good, he thought wrathfully: the man was practically a Bolshevik himself.

General Boldyrev was a big, clumsy-looking figure. "We have mobilized two hundred thousand men," he told Fitz proudly. "Can you equip them?"

"That's impressive," Fitz said, but he suppressed a sigh. This was the kind of thinking that had caused the Russian army of six million to be defeated by much smaller German and Austrian forces. Boldyrev even wore the absurd epaulets favored by the old regime, big round boards with fringes that made him look like a character in a comic opera by Gilbert and Sullivan. In his makeshift Russian Fitz went on: "But if I were you I'd send half the conscripts home."

Boldyrev was baffled. "Why?"

"At most we can equip a hundred thousand. And they must be trained. Better to have a small, disciplined army than a great rabble who will retreat or surrender at the first opportunity."

"Ideally, yes."

"The supplies we give you must be issued to men in the front line first, not to those in the rear."

"Of course. Very sensible."

Fitz had a dismal feeling that Boldyrev was agreeing without really listening. But he had to plow on. "Too much of what we send is going astray, as I can see by the number of civilians on the streets wearing articles of British army uniform."

"Yes, quite."

"I strongly recommend that all officers not fit to serve be deprived of their uniforms and asked to return to their homes." The Russian army was plagued by amateurs and elderly dilettantes who interfered with decisions but stayed away from the fighting.

"Hmm."

"And I suggest you give wider powers to Admiral Kolchak as minister of war." The Foreign Office thought Kolchak was the most promising of the members of the directory.

"Very good, very good."

"Are you willing to do all these things?" Fitz said, desperate to get some kind of commitment.

"Definitely."

"When?"

"All in good time, Colonel Fitzherbert, all in good time."

Fitz's heart sank. It was a good thing that men such as Churchill and Curzon could not see how unimpressive were the forces ranged against Bolshevism, he thought dismally. But perhaps they would shape up, with British encouragement. Anyway, he had to do his best with the materials to hand.

There was a knock at the door and his aide-de-camp, Captain Murray, came in holding a telegram. "Sorry to interrupt, sir," he said breathlessly. "But I feel sure you'll want to hear this news as soon as possible."

{ VI }

Mildred came downstairs in the middle of the day and said to Ethel: "Let's go up west." She meant the West End of London. "Everyone's going," she said. "I've sent my girls home." She was now employing two young seamstresses in her hat-trimming business. "The whole East End is shutting up shop. It's the end of the war!"

Ethel was eager to go. Her giving in to Bernie had not improved the atmosphere in the house much. He had cheered up but she had become more bitter. It would do her good to get out of the house. "I'll have to bring Lloyd," she said.

"That's all right. I'll take Enid and Lil. They'll remember it all their lives—the day we won the war."

Ethel made Bernie a cheese sandwich for his lunch; then she dressed Lloyd warmly and they set off. They managed to get on a bus, but soon it was full, with men and boys hanging on the outside. Every house seemed to be flying a flag, not just Union Jacks but Welsh dragons, French tricolors, and the American Stars and Stripes. People were embracing strangers, dancing in the streets, kissing. It was raining, but no one cared.

Ethel thought of all the young men who were now safe from harm, and she began to forget her troubles and share the joyous spirit of the moment.

When they passed the theaters and entered the government district, the traffic slowed to a crawl. Trafalgar Square was a heaving mass of rejoicing humanity. The bus could go no farther, and they got off. They made their way along Whitehall to Downing Street. They could not get near number 10, because of the crush of people hoping for a sight of Prime Minister Lloyd George, the man who won the war. They went into St. James's Park, which was full of couples embracing in the bushes. On the far side of the park, thousands of people stood outside Buckingham Palace. They were singing "Keep the Home Fires Burning." When the song ended they began "Now Thank We All Our God." Ethel saw that a slim young woman in a tweed suit was conducting the singing, standing on top of a lorry, and she reflected that a girl would not have dared to do such a thing before the war.

They crossed the street to Green Park, hoping to get nearer the palace. A young man smiled at Mildred, and when she smiled back, he put his arms around her and kissed her. She returned the kiss enthusiastically.

"You seemed to enjoy that," Ethel said a bit enviously as the boy walked away.

"I did," said Mildred. "I'd have sucked him off if he'd asked me."

"I won't tell Billy that," Ethel said with a laugh.

"Billy's not daft—he knows what I'm like."

They circled the crowd and reached the street called Constitution Hill. The crush thinned out here, but they were at the side of Buckingham Palace, so they would not be able to see the king if he decided to come out onto the balcony. Ethel was wondering where to go next when a troop of mounted police came down the road, causing people to scurry out of the way.

Behind them came a horse-drawn open carriage and inside, smiling and waving, were the king and queen. Ethel recognized them immediately, remembering them vividly from their visit to Aberowen almost five years ago. She could hardly believe her luck as the carriage came slowly toward her. The king's beard was gray, she saw: it had been dark when he came to Tŷ Gwyn. He looked exhausted but happy. Beside him, the queen was holding an umbrella to keep the rain off her hat. Her famous bosom seemed even larger than before.

"Look, Lloyd!" Ethel said. "It's the king!"

The carriage came within inches of where Ethel and Mildred stood. Lloyd called out loudly: "Hello, King!"

The king heard him and smiled. "Hello, young man," he said; and then he was gone.

{ VII }

Grigori sat in the dining car of the armored train and looked across the table. The man sitting opposite was chairman of the Revolutionary War Council and people's commissar for military and naval affairs. That meant he commanded the Red Army. His name was Lev Davidovich Bronstein, but like most of the leading revolutionaries he had adopted an alias, and he was known as Leon Trotsky. He was a few days past his thirty-ninth birthday, and he held the fate of Russia in his hands.

The revolution was a year old, and Grigori had never been so worried about it. The storming of the Winter Palace had seemed like a conclusion, but in fact it had been only the beginning of the struggle. The most powerful governments of the world were hostile to the Bolsheviks. Today's armistice meant they could now turn their full attention to destroying the revolution. And only the Red Army could stop them.

Many soldiers disliked Trotsky because they thought he was an aristocrat and a Jew. It was impossible to be both in Russia, but soldiers were not logical. Trotsky was no aristocrat, though his father had been a prosperous farmer, and Trotsky had had a good education. But his high-handed manners did him no favors, and he was foolish enough to travel with his own chef and clothe his staff in new boots and gold buttons. He looked older than his years. His great mop of curly hair was still black, but his face was now lined with strain.

He had worked miracles with the army.

The Red Guards who overthrew the provisional government had proved less effective on the battlefield. They were drunken and ill-disciplined. Deciding tactics by a show of hands at a soldiers' meeting had turned out to be a poor way to fight, even worse than taking orders from aristocratic dilettantes. The Reds had lost major battles against the counterrevolutionaries, who were beginning to call themselves the Whites.

Trotsky had reintroduced conscription, against howls of protest. He had drafted many former tsarist officers, called them "specialists," and put them back into their old posts. He had also brought back the death penalty for deserters. Grigori did not like these measures, but he saw the necessity. Anything was better than counterrevolution.

What kept the army together was a core of Bolshevik party members. They were carefully spread through all units to maximize their impact. Some were ordinary soldiers; some held command posts; some, such as Grigori, were political commissars, working alongside the military commanders and reporting back to the Bolshevik Central Committee in Moscow. They maintained morale by reminding soldiers they were fighting for the greatest cause in the history of humankind. When the army was obliged to be ruthless and cruel, requisitioning grain and horses from desperately poor peasant families, the Bolsheviks would explain to the soldiers why it was necessary for the greater good. And they reported rumblings of discontent early, so that such talk could be crushed before it spread.

But would all this be enough?

Grigori and Trotsky were bent over a map. Trotsky pointed to the Transcaucasia region between Russia and Persia. "The Turks are still in control of the Caspian Sea, with some German help," he said.

"Threatening the oil fields," Grigori muttered.

"Denikin is strong in the Ukraine." Thousands of aristocrats, officers, and bourgeoisie fleeing the revolution had ended up in Novocherkassk, where they had formed a counterrevolutionary force under the renegade General Denikin.

"The so-called Volunteer Army," said Grigori.

"Exactly." Trotsky's finger moved to the north of Russia. "The British have a naval squadron at Murmansk. There are three battalions of American infantry at Archangel. They are supplemented by just about every other country: Canada, China, Poland, Italy, Serbia . . . It might be quicker to list the nations that *don't* have troops in the frozen north of our country."

"And then Siberia."

Trotsky nodded. "The Japanese and Americans have forces in Vladivostok. The Czechs control most of the Trans-Siberian Railway. The British and Canadians are in Omsk, supporting the so-called All-Russia Provisional Government."

Grigori had known much of this, but he had not previously looked at the picture as a whole. "Why, we're surrounded!" he said.

"Exactly. And now that the capitalist-imperialist powers have made peace, they will have millions of troops free."

Grigori sought for a ray of hope. "On the other hand, in the last six months we have increased the size of the Red Army from three hundred thousand to a million men."

"I know." Trotsky was not cheered by this reminder. "But it's not enough."

{ VIII }

Germany was in the throes of a revolution—and to Walter it looked horribly like the Russian revolution of a year ago.

It started with a mutiny. Naval officers ordered the fleet at Kiel to put to sea and attack the British in a suicide mission, but the sailors knew an armistice was being negotiated and they refused. Walter had pointed out to his father that the officers were going against the wishes of the kaiser, so they were the mutineers, and the sailors were the loyal ones. This argument had made Otto apoplectic with rage.

After the government tried to suppress the sailors, the city of Kiel was taken over by a workers' and soldiers' council modeled on the Russian soviets. Two days later Hamburg, Bremen, and Cuxhaven were controlled by soviets. The day before yesterday, the kaiser had abdicated.

Walter was fearful. He wanted democracy, not revolution. But on the day of the abdication, workers in Berlin had marched in their thousands, waving red flags, and the extreme leftist Karl Liebknecht had declared Germany a free socialist republic. Walter did not know how it would end.

The armistice was a dreadfully low moment. He had always believed the war to be a terrible mistake, but there was no satisfaction in being right. The fatherland had been defeated and humiliated, and his fellow countrymen were starving. He sat in the drawing room of his parents' house in Berlin, leafing through the newspapers, too depressed even to play the piano. The wallpaper was faded and the picture rail dusty. There were loose blocks in the aging parquet floor, but no craftsmen to repair it.

Walter could only hope that the world would learn a lesson. President Wilson's Fourteen Points provided a gleam of light that might just herald the rising sun. Was it possible that the giants among nations would find a way to resolve their differences peacefully?

He was infuriated by an article in a right-wing paper. "This fool of a journalist says the German army was never defeated," he said as his father came into the room. "He claims we were betrayed by Jews and socialists at home. We must stamp out that kind of nonsense."

Otto was angrily defiant. "Why should we?" he said.

"Because we know it's not true."

"I think we *were* betrayed by Jews and socialists."

"What?" Walter said incredulously. "It wasn't Jews and socialists who turned us back at the Marne, twice. We lost the war!"

"We were weakened by the lack of supplies."

"That was the British blockade. And whose fault was it that the Americans came in? It was not Jews and socialists who demanded unrestricted submarine warfare and sank ships with American passengers."

"It is the socialists who have given in to the Allies' outrageous armistice terms."

Walter was almost incoherent with rage. "You know perfectly well that it was Ludendorff who asked for an armistice. Chancellor Ebert was appointed only the day before yesterday—how can you blame him?"

"If the army was still in charge we would never have signed today's document."

"But you're not in charge, because you lost the war. You told the kaiser you could win it, and he believed you, and in consequence he lost his crown. How will we learn from our mistakes if you let the German people believe such lies as these?"

"They will be demoralized if they think we were defeated."

"They *should* be demoralized! The leaders of Europe did something wicked and foolish, and ten million men died as a result. At least let the people understand that, so that they will never let it happen again!"

"No," said his father.

PART THREE

THE
WORLD
MADE NEW

CHAPTER THIRTY-FOUR

November to December 1918

Ethel woke early on the morning after Armistice Day. Shivering in the stone-floored kitchen, waiting for the kettle to boil on the old-fashioned range, she made a resolution to be happy. There was a lot to be happy about. The war was over and she was going to have a baby. She had a faithful husband who adored her. Things had not turned out exactly how she wanted, but she would not let that make her miserable. She would paint her kitchen a cheerful yellow, she decided. Bright colors in kitchens were a new fashion.

But first she had to try to mend her marriage. Bernie had been mollified by her surrender, but she had continued to feel bitter, and the atmosphere in the house had remained poisoned. She was angry, but she did not want the rift to be permanent. She wondered if she could make friends.

She took two cups of tea into the bedroom and got back into bed. Lloyd was still asleep in his cot in the corner. "How do you feel?" she said as Bernie sat up and put his glasses on.

"Better, I think."

"Stay in bed another day. Make sure you've got rid of it completely."

"I might do that." His tone was neutral, neither warm nor hostile.

She sipped hot tea. "What would you like, a boy or a girl?"

He was silent, and at first she thought he was sulkily refusing to answer; but in fact he was just thinking for a few moments, as he often did before answering a question. At last he said: "Well, we've got a boy, so it would be nice to have one of each."

She felt a surge of affection for him. He always talked as if Lloyd was his own child. "We've got to make sure this is a good country for them to grow up in," she said. "Where they can get good schooling and a job and a decent house to bring up their own children in. And no more wars."

"Lloyd George will call a snap election."

"Do you think so?"

"He's the man who won the war. He'll want to get reelected before that wears off."

"I think Labour will still do well."

"We've got a chance in places like Aldgate, anyway."

Ethel hesitated. "Would you like me to manage your campaign?"

Bernie looked doubtful. "I've asked Jock Reid to be my agent."

"Jock can deal with legal documents and finance," Ethel said. "I'll organize meetings and so on. I can do it much better." Suddenly she felt this was about their marriage, not just the campaign.

"Are you sure you want to?"

"Yes. Jock would just send you to make speeches. You'll have to do that, of course, but it's not your strong point. You're better sitting down with a few people, talking over a cup of tea. I'll get you into factories and warehouses where you can chat to the men informally."

"I'm sure you're right," Bernie said.

She finished her tea and put the cup and saucer on the floor beside the bed. "So you're feeling better?"

"Yes."

She took his cup and saucer, put them down, then pulled her nightdress over her head. Her breasts were not as perky as they had been before she got pregnant with Lloyd, but they were still firm and round. "How much better?" she said.

He stared. "A lot."

They had not made love since the evening Jayne McCulley had proposed Ethel as candidate. Ethel was missing it badly. She held her breasts in her hands. The cold air in the room was making her nipples stand up. "Do you know what these are?"

"I believe they're your bosoms."

"Some people call them tits."

"I call them beautiful." His voice had become a little hoarse.

"Would you like to play with them?"

"All day long."

"I'm not sure about that," she said. "But make a start, and we'll see how we go."

"All right."

Ethel sighed happily. Men were so simple.

An hour later she went to work, leaving Lloyd with Bernie. There were not many people on the streets: London had a hangover this morning. She reached the office of the National Union of Garment Workers and sat at her desk. Peace would bring new industrial problems, she realized as she thought about the working day ahead of her. Millions of men leaving the army would be looking for employment, and they would want to elbow aside the women who had been doing their jobs for four years. But those women needed their wages. They did not all have a man coming home from France: a lot of their husbands were buried there. They needed their union, and they needed Ethel.

Whenever the election came, the union would naturally be campaigning for the Labour Party. Ethel spent most of the day in planning meetings.

The evening papers brought surprising news about the election. Lloyd George had decided to continue the coalition government into peacetime. He would not campaign as leader of the Liberals, but as head of the coalition. That morning he had addressed two hundred Liberal M.P.s at Downing Street and won their support. At the same time Bonar Law had persuaded Conservative M.P.s to back the idea.

Ethel was baffled. What were people supposed to vote for?

When she got home she found Bernie furious. "It's not an election—

it's a bloody coronation," he said. "King David Lloyd George. What a traitor. He has a chance to bring in a radical left-wing government and what does he do? Sticks with his Conservative pals! He's a bloody turncoat."

"Let's not give up yet," said Ethel.

Two days later the Labour Party withdrew from the coalition and announced it would campaign against Lloyd George. Four Labour M.P.s who were government ministers refused to resign and were smartly expelled from the party. The date of the election was set for December 14. To give time for soldiers' ballots to be returned from France and counted, the results would not be announced until after Christmas.

Ethel started drawing up Bernie's campaigning schedule.

{ II }

On the day after Armistice Day, Maud wrote to Walter on her brother's crested writing paper and put the letter in the red pillar-box on the street corner.

She had no idea how long it would take for normal post to be resumed, but when it happened she wanted her envelope to be on top of the pile. Her message was carefully worded, just in case censorship continued: it did not refer to their marriage, but just said she hoped to resume their old relationship now that their countries were at peace. Perhaps the letter was risky all the same. But she was desperate to find out whether Walter was alive and, if he was, to see him.

She feared that the victorious Allies would want to punish the German people, but Lloyd George's speech to Liberal M.P.s that day was reassuring. According to the evening papers, he said the peace treaty with Germany must be fair and just. "We must not allow any sense of revenge, any spirit of greed, or any grasping desire to overrule the fundamental principles of righteousness." The government would set its face against what he called "a base, sordid, squalid idea of vengeance and avarice." That cheered her up. Life for the Germans now would be hard enough anyway.

However, she was horrified the following morning when she opened the *Daily Mail* at breakfast. The leading article was headed THE HUNS MUST PAY. The paper argued that food aid should be sent to Germany— only because "if Germany were starved to death she could not pay what she owes." The kaiser must be put on trial for war crimes, it added. The paper fanned the flames of revenge by publishing at the top of its letters column a diatribe from Viscountess Templetown headed KEEP OUT THE HUNS. "How long are we all supposed to go on hating one another?" Maud said to Aunt Herm. "A year? Ten years? Forever?"

But Maud should not have been surprised. The *Mail* had conducted a hate campaign against the thirty thousand Germans who had been living in Britain at the outbreak of war—most of them long-term residents who thought of this country as their home. In consequence families had been broken up and thousands of harmless people had spent years in British concentration camps. It was stupid, but people needed someone to hate, and the newspapers were always ready to supply that need.

Maud knew the proprietor of the *Mail*, Lord Northcliffe. Like all great press men, he really believed the drivel he published. His talent was to express his readers' most stupid and ignorant prejudices as if they made sense, so that the shameful seemed respectable. That was why they bought the paper.

She also knew that Lloyd George had recently snubbed Northcliffe personally. The self-important press lord had proposed himself as a member of the British delegation at the upcoming peace conference, and had been offended when the prime minister turned him down.

Maud was worried. In politics, despicable people sometimes had to be pandered to, but Lloyd George seemed to have forgotten that. She wondered anxiously how much effect the *Mail*'s malevolent propaganda would have on the election.

A few days later she found out.

She went to an election meeting in a municipal hall in the East End of London. Eth Leckwith was in the audience and her husband, Bernie, was on the platform. Maud had not made up her quarrel with Ethel, even though they had been friends and colleagues for years. In fact Maud still trembled with anger when she recalled how Ethel and others had encouraged Parliament to pass a law that kept women at a disadvantage to men in elections. All the same she missed Ethel's high spirits and ready smile.

The audience sat restlessly through the introductions. They were still mostly men, even though some women could now vote. Maud guessed that most women had not yet got used to the idea that they needed to take an interest in political discussions. But she also felt women would be put off by the tone of political meetings, in which men stood on a platform and ranted while the audience cheered or booed.

Bernie was the first speaker. He was no orator, Maud saw immediately. He spoke about the Labour Party's new constitution, in particular clause four, calling for public ownership of the means of production. Maud thought this was interesting, for it drew a clear line between Labour and the pro-business Liberals; but she soon realized she was in a minority. The man sitting next to her grew restless and eventually shouted: "Will you chuck the Germans out of this country?"

Bernie was thrown. He mumbled for a few moments, then said: "I would do whatever benefited the workingman." Maud wondered about the workingwoman, and guessed that Ethel must be thinking the same. Bernie went on: "But I don't see that action against Germans in Britain is a high priority."

That did not go down well; in fact it drew a few scattered boos.

Bernie said: "But to return to more important issues—"

From the other side of the hall, someone shouted: "What about the kaiser?"

Bernie made the mistake of replying to the heckler with a question. "What *about* the kaiser?" he rejoined. "He has abdicated."

"Should he be put on trial?"

Bernie said with exasperation: "Don't you understand that a trial means he will be entitled to defend himself? Do you really want to give the German emperor a platform to proclaim his innocence to the world?"

This was a compelling argument, Maud thought, but it was not what the audience wanted to hear. The booing grew louder, and there were shouts of "Hang the kaiser!"

British voters were ugly when riled, Maud thought; at least, the men were. Few women would ever want to come to meetings like this.

Bernie said: "If we hang our defeated enemies, we are barbarians."

The man next to Maud shouted again: "Will you make the Hun pay?"

That got the biggest reaction of all. Several people shouted out: "Make the Hun pay!"

"Within reason," Bernie began, but he got no further.

"Make the Hun pay!" The shout became common, and in a moment they were chanting in unison: "Make the Hun pay! Make the Hun pay!"

Maud got up from her seat and left.

{ III }

Woodrow Wilson was the first American president ever to leave the country during his term of office.

He sailed from New York on December 4. Nine days later Gus was waiting for him at the quayside in Brest, on the western tip of the Brittany panhandle. At midday the mist cleared and the sun came out, for the first time in days. In the bay, battleships from the French, British, and American navies formed an honor guard through which the president steamed in a U.S. Navy transport ship, the *George Washington*. Guns thundered a salute, and a band played "The Star-Spangled Banner."

It was a solemn moment for Gus. Wilson had come here to make sure there would never be another war like the one just ended. Wilson's Fourteen Points, and his League of Nations, were intended to change forever the way nations resolved their conflicts. It was a stratospheric ambition. In the history of human civilization, no politician had ever aimed so high. If he succeeded, the world would be made new.

At three in the afternoon the first lady, Edith Wilson, walked down the gangplank on the arm of General Pershing, followed by the president in a top hat.

The town of Brest received Wilson as a conquering hero. *Vive Wilson,* said the banners, *Defenseur du Droit des Peuples;* Long Live Wilson, Defender of People's Rights. Every building flew the Stars and Stripes. Crowds jammed the sidewalks, many of the women wearing the traditional Breton tall lace headdress. The sound of Breton bagpipes was everywhere. Gus could have done without the bagpipes.

The French foreign minister made a speech of welcome. Gus stood with the American journalists. He noticed a small woman wearing a big fur hat. She turned her head, and he saw that her pretty face was marred by one permanently closed eye. He smiled with delight: it was Rosa Hellman. He looked forward to hearing her view of the peace conference.

After the speeches, the entire presidential party boarded the night train for the four-hundred-mile journey to Paris. The president shook Gus's hand and said: "Glad to have you back on the team, Gus."

Wilson wanted familiar associates around him for the Paris Peace Conference. His main adviser would be Colonel House, the pale Texan who had been unofficially counseling him on foreign policy for years. Gus would be the junior member of the crew.

Wilson looked weary, and he and Edith retired to their suite. Gus was concerned. He had heard rumors that the president's health was poor. Back in 1906 a blood vessel had burst behind Wilson's left eye, causing temporary blindness, and the doctors had diagnosed high blood pressure and advised him to retire. Wilson had cheerfully ignored their advice and gone on to become president, of course—but lately he had been suffering from headaches that might be a new symptom of the same blood pressure problem. The peace conference would be taxing: Gus hoped Wilson could stand it.

Rosa was on the train. Gus sat opposite her on the brocaded upholstery in the dining car. "I wondered whether I might see you," she said. She seemed pleased they had met.

"I'm on detachment from the army," said Gus, who was still wearing the uniform of a captain.

"Back home, Wilson has been walloped for his choice of colleagues. Not you, of course—"

"I'm a small fish."

"But some people say he should not have brought his wife."

Gus shrugged. It seemed trivial. After the battlefield it was going to be difficult to take seriously some of the stuff people worried about in peacetime.

Rosa said: "More important, he hasn't brought any Republicans."

"He wants allies on his team, not enemies," Gus said indignantly.

"He needs allies back home, too," Rosa said. "He's lost Congress."

She had a point, and Gus was reminded how smart she was. The midterm elections had been disastrous for Wilson. The Republicans had gained control of the Senate and the House of Representatives. "How did that happen?" he said. "I've been out of touch."

"Ordinary people are fed up with rationing and high prices, and the end of the war came just a bit too late to help. And liberals hate the Espionage Act. It allowed Wilson to jail people who disagreed with the war. He used it, too—Eugene Debs was sentenced to ten years." Debs had been a presidential candidate for the Socialists. Rosa sounded angry as she said: "You can't put your opponents in jail and still pretend to believe in freedom."

Gus remembered how much he enjoyed the cut and thrust of an argument with Rosa. "Freedom sometimes has to be compromised in war," he said.

"Obviously American voters don't think so. And there's another thing: Wilson segregated his Washington offices."

Gus did not know whether Negroes could ever be raised to the level of white people but, like most liberal Americans, he thought the way to find out was to give them better chances in life and see what happened. However, Wilson and his wife were Southerners, and felt differently. "Edith won't take her maid to London, for fear the girl will get spoiled," Gus said. "She says British people are too polite to Negroes."

"Woodrow Wilson is no longer the darling of the left in America,"

Rosa concluded. "Which means he's going to need Republican support for his League of Nations."

"I suppose Henry Cabot Lodge feels snubbed." Lodge was a right-wing Republican.

"You know politicians," Rosa said. "They're as sensitive as schoolgirls, and more vengeful. Lodge is chairman of the Senate Foreign Relations Committee. Wilson should have brought him to Paris."

Gus protested: "Lodge is against the whole idea of the League of Nations!"

"The ability to listen to smart people who disagree with you is a rare talent—but a president should have it. And bringing Lodge here would have neutralized him. As a member of the team, he couldn't go home and fight against whatever is agreed in Paris."

Gus guessed she was right. But Wilson was an idealist who believed that the force of righteousness would overcome all obstacles. He underestimated the need to flatter, cajole, and seduce.

The food was good, in honor of the president. They had fresh sole from the Atlantic in a buttery sauce. Gus had not eaten so well since before the war. He was amused to see Rosa tuck in heartily. She had a petite figure: where did she put it all?

At the end of the meal they were served strong coffee in small cups. Gus found he did not want to leave Rosa and retire to his sleeping compartment. He was much too interested in talking to her. "Wilson will be in a strong position in Paris, anyway," he said.

Rosa looked skeptical. "How so?"

"Well, first of all we won the war for them."

She nodded. "Wilson said: 'At Château-Thierry we saved the world.'"

"Chuck Dixon and I were in that battle."

"Was that where he died?"

"Direct hit from a shell. First casualty I saw. Not the last, sadly."

"I'm very sorry, especially for his wife. I've known Doris for years—we used to have the same piano teacher."

"I don't know if we saved the world, though," Gus went on. "There are many more French and British and Russians among the dead than Americans. But we tipped the balance. That ought to mean something."

She shook her head, tossing her dark curls. "I disagree. The war is over, and the Europeans no longer need us."

"Men such as Lloyd George seem to think that American military power cannot be ignored."

"Then he's wrong," said Rosa. Gus was surprised and intrigued to hear a woman speak so forcefully about such a subject. "Suppose the French and British simply refuse to go along with Wilson," she said. "Would he use the army to enforce his ideas? No. Even if he wanted to, a Republican Congress wouldn't let him."

"We have economic and financial power."

"It's certainly true that the Allies owe us huge debts, but I'm not sure how much leverage that gives us. There's a saying: 'If you owe a hundred dollars, the bank has you in its power; but if you owe a million dollars, you have the bank in your power.'"

Gus began to see that Wilson's task might be more difficult than he had imagined. "Well, what about public opinion? You saw the reception Wilson got in Brest. All over Europe, people are looking to him to create a peaceful world."

"That's his strongest card. People are sick of slaughter. 'Never again' is their cry. I just hope Wilson can deliver what they want."

They returned to their compartments and said good night. Gus lay awake a long time, thinking about Rosa and what she had said. She really was the smartest woman he had ever met. She was beautiful, too. Somehow you quickly forgot about her eye. At first it seemed a terrible deformity, but after a while Gus stopped noticing it.

She had been pessimistic about the conference, however. And everything she said was true. Wilson had a struggle ahead, Gus now realized. He was overjoyed to be part of the team, and determined to do what he could to turn the president's ideals into reality.

In the small hours of the morning he looked out of the window as the train steamed eastward across France. Passing through a town, he was startled to see crowds on the station platforms and on the road beside the railway line, watching. It was dark, but they were clearly visible by lamplight. There were thousands of them, men and women and children. There was no cheering: they were quite silent. The men and boys took off their hats, Gus saw, and that gesture of respect moved him almost to tears. They had waited half the night to see the passing of the train that held the hope of the world.

CHAPTER THIRTY-FIVE

December 1918 to February 1919

The votes were counted three days after Christmas. Eth and Bernie Leckwith stood in Aldgate town hall to hear the results, Bernie on the platform in his best suit, Eth in the audience.

Bernie lost.

He was stoical, but Ethel cried. For him it was the end of a dream. Perhaps it had been a foolish dream, but all the same he was hurt, and her heart ached for him.

The Liberal candidate had supported the Lloyd George coalition, so there had been no Conservative candidate. Consequently the Conservatives had voted Liberal, and the combination had been too much for Labour to beat.

Bernie congratulated his winning opponent and came down off the platform. The other Labour Party members had a bottle of Scotch and wanted to hold a wake, but Bernie and Ethel went home.

"I'm not cut out for this, Eth," Bernie said as she boiled water for cocoa.

"You did a good job," she said. "We were outwitted by that bloody Lloyd George."

Bernie shook his head. "I'm not a leader," he said. "I'm a thinker and a planner. Time and again I tried to talk to people the way you do, and fire them with enthusiasm for our cause, but I never could do it. When you talk to them, they love you. That's the difference."

She knew he was right.

Next morning the newspapers showed that the Aldgate result had been mirrored all over the country. The coalition had won 525 of the 707 seats, one of the largest majorities in the history of Parliament. The people had voted for the man who won the war.

Ethel was bitterly disappointed. The old men were still running the country. The politicians who had caused millions of deaths were now celebrating, as if they had done something wonderful. But what had they achieved? Pain and hunger and destruction. Ten million men and boys had been killed to no purpose.

The only glimmer of hope was that the Labour Party had improved its position. They had won sixty seats, up from forty-two.

It was the anti–Lloyd George Liberals who had suffered. They had won only thirty constituencies, and Asquith himself had lost his seat. "This could be the end of the Liberal Party," said Bernie as he spread dripping on his bread for lunch. "They've failed the people, and Labour is the opposition now. That may be our only consolation."

Just before they left for work, the post arrived. Ethel looked at the letters while Bernie tied the laces of Lloyd's shoes. There was one from Billy, written in their code. She sat at the kitchen table to decode it.

She underlined the key words with a pencil and wrote them on a pad. As she deciphered the message she became more and more fascinated.

"You know Billy's in Russia," she said to Bernie.

"Yes."

"Well, he says our army is there to fight against the Bolsheviks. The American army is there, too."

"I'm not surprised."

"Yes, but listen, Bern," she said. "We know the Whites can't beat the Bolsheviks—but what if foreign armies join in? Anything could happen!"

Bernie looked thoughtful. "They could bring back the monarchy."

"The people of this country won't stand for that."

"The people of this country don't know what's going on."

"Then we'd better tell them," said Ethel. "I'm going to write an article."

"Who will publish it?"

"We'll see. Maybe the *Daily Herald*." The *Herald* was left-wing. "Will you take Lloyd to the child minder?"

"Yes, of course."

Ethel thought for a minute; then, at the top of a sheet of paper, she wrote:

> *Hands Off Russia!*

{ II }

Walking around Paris made Maud cry. Along the broad boulevards there were piles of rubble where German shells had fallen. Broken windows in the grand buildings were repaired with boards, reminding her painfully of her handsome brother with his disfigured eye. The avenues of trees were marred by gaps where an ancient chestnut or noble plane had been sacrificed for its timber. Half the women wore black for mourning, and on street corners crippled soldiers begged for change.

She was crying for Walter, too. She had received no reply to her letter. She had inquired about going to Germany, but that was impossible. It had been difficult enough to get permission to come to Paris. She had hoped Walter might come here with the German delegation, but there was no German delegation: the defeated countries were not invited to the peace conference. The victorious Allies intended to thrash out an agreement among themselves, then present the losers with a treaty for signing.

Meanwhile there was a shortage of coal, and all the hotels were freezing cold. She had a suite at the Majestic, where the British delegation was headquartered. To guard against French spies, the British had replaced all the staff with their own people. Consequently the food was dire: porridge for breakfast, overcooked vegetables, and bad coffee.

Wrapped in a prewar fur coat, Maud went to meet Johnny Remarc at Fouquet's on the Champs-Elysées. "Thank you for arranging for me to travel to Paris," she said.

"Anything for you, Maud. But why were you so keen to come here?"

She was not going to tell the truth, least of all to someone who loved to gossip. "Shopping," she said. "I haven't bought a new dress for four years."

"Oh, spare me," he said. "There's almost nothing to buy, and what there is costs a fortune. Fifteen hundred francs for a gown! Even Fitz might draw the line there. I think you must have a French paramour."

"I wish I did." She changed the subject. "I've found Fitz's car. Do you know where I might get petrol?"

"I'll see what I can do."

They ordered lunch. Maud said: "Do you think we're really going to make the Germans pay billions in reparations?"

"They're not in a good position to object," said Johnny. "After the Franco-Prussian War they made France pay five billion francs—which the French did in three years. And last March, in the Treaty of Brest-Litovsk, Germany made the Bolsheviks promise six billion marks, although of course it won't be paid now. All the same, the Germans' righteous indignation has the hollow ring of hypocrisy."

Maud hated it when people spoke harshly of the Germans. It was as if the fact that they had lost made them beasts. *What if we had been the losers,* Maud wanted to say—*would we have had to say the war was our fault, and pay for it all?* "But we're asking for so much more—twenty-four billion pounds, we say, and the French put it at almost double that."

"It's hard to argue with the French," Johnny said. "They owe us six hundred million pounds, and more to the Americans; but if we deny them German reparations, they'll say they can't pay us."

"Can the Germans pay what we're asking?"

"No. My friend Pozzo Keynes says they could pay about a tenth—two billion pounds—though it may cripple their country."

"Do you mean John Maynard Keynes, the Cambridge economist?"

"Yes. We call him Pozzo."

"I didn't know he was one of . . . your friends."

Johnny smiled. "Oh, yes, my dear, very much so."

Maud suffered a moment of envy for Johnny's cheerful depravity. She had fiercely suppressed her own need for physical love. It was almost two years since a man had touched her lovingly. She felt like an old nun, wrinkled and dried up.

"What a sad look!" Johnny did not miss much. "I hope you're not in love with Pozzo."

She laughed, then turned the conversation back to politics. "If we know the Germans can't pay, why is Lloyd George insisting?"

"I asked him that question myself. I've known him quite well since he was minister for munitions. He says all the belligerents will end up paying their own debts, and no one will get any reparations to speak of."

"So why this pretense?"

"Because in the end the taxpayers of every country will pay for the war—but the politician who tells them that will never win another election."

{ III }

Gus went to the daily meetings of the League of Nations Commission. This group had the job of drafting the covenant that would set up the league. Woodrow Wilson himself chaired the committee, and he was in a hurry.

Wilson had completely dominated the first month of the conference. He had swept aside a French agenda putting German reparations at the top and the league at the bottom, and insisted that the league must be part of any treaty signed by him.

The League Commission met at the luxurious Hotel Crillon on the Place de la Concorde. The hydraulic elevators were ancient and slow, and sometimes stopped between floors while the water pressure built up; Gus thought they were very like the European diplomats, who enjoyed nothing more than a leisurely argument, and never came to a decision until forced. He saw with secret amusement that both diplomats and lifts caused the American president to fidget and mutter in furious impatience.

The nineteen commissioners sat around a big table covered with a red cloth, their interpreters behind them whispering in their ears, their aides around the room with files and notebooks. Gus could tell that the Europeans were impressed by his boss's ability to drive the agenda forward. Some people had said the writing of the covenant would take months, if not years; and others said the nations would never reach agreement. However, to Gus's delight, after ten days they were close to completing a first draft.

Wilson had to return to the United States on February 14. He would be back soon, but he was determined to have a draft of the covenant to take home.

Unfortunately, the afternoon before he left, the French produced a major obstacle. They proposed that the League of Nations should have its own army.

Wilson's eyes rolled up in despair. "Impossible," he groaned.

Gus knew why. Congress would not allow American troops to be under someone else's control.

The French delegate, former prime minister Léon Bourgeois, argued that the league would be ignored if it had no means of enforcing its decisions.

Gus shared Wilson's frustration. There were other ways for the league to put pressure on rogue nations: diplomacy, economic sanctions, and in the last resort an ad hoc army, to be used for a specific mission, then disbanded when the job was done.

But Bourgeois said none of that would have protected France from Germany. The French could not focus on anything else. Perhaps it was understandable, Gus thought, but it was not the way to create a new world order.

Lord Robert Cecil, who had done a lot of the drafting, raised a bony finger to speak. Wilson nodded: he liked Cecil, who was a strong supporter of the league. Not everyone agreed: Clemenceau, the French prime minister, said that when Cecil smiled he looked like a Chinese dragon. "Forgive me for being blunt," Cecil said. "The French delegation seems to be saying that because the league may not be as strong as they hoped, they will reject it altogether. May I point out very frankly that in that case there will almost certainly be a bilateral alliance between Great Britain and the United States that would offer nothing to France."

Gus suppressed a smile. That's telling 'em, he thought.

Bourgeois looked shocked and withdrew his amendment.

Wilson shot a grateful look across the table at Cecil.

The Japanese delegate, Baron Makino, wanted to speak. Wilson nodded and looked at his watch.

Makino referred to the clause in the covenant, already agreed, that guaranteed religious freedom. He wished to add an amendment to the effect that all members would treat one another's citizens equally, without racial discrimination.

Wilson's face froze.

Makino's speech was eloquent, even in translation. Different races had fought side by side in the war, he pointed out. "A common bond of sympathy and gratitude has been established." The league would be a great family of nations. Surely they should treat one another as equals?

Gus was worried but not surprised. The Japanese had been talking about this for a week or two. It had already caused consternation among the Australians and the Californians, who wanted to keep the Japanese out of their territories. It had disconcerted Wilson, who did not for one moment think that American Negroes were his equals. Most of all it had upset the British, who ruled undemocratically over hundreds of millions of people of different races and did not want them to think they were as good as their white overlords.

Again it was Cecil who spoke. "Alas, this is a highly controversial matter," he said, and Gus could almost have believed in his sadness. "The mere suggestion that it might be discussed has already created discord."

There was a murmur of agreement around the table.

Cecil went on: "Rather than delay the agreement of a draft covenant, perhaps we should postpone discussion of, ah, racial discrimination to a later date."

The Greek prime minister said: "The whole question of religious liberty is a tricky subject, too. Perhaps we should drop that for the present."

The Portuguese delegate said: "My government has never yet signed a treaty that did not call on God!"

Cecil, a deeply religious man, said: "Perhaps this time we will all have to take a chance."

There was a ripple of laughter, and Wilson said with evident relief: "If that's agreed, let us move on."

{ IV }

Next day Wilson went to the French foreign ministry at the Quai d'Orsay and read the draft to a plenary session of the peace conference in the famous Clock Room under the enormous chandeliers that looked like stalactites in an Arctic cave. That evening he left for home. The following day was a Saturday, and in the evening Gus went dancing.

Paris after dark was a party town. Food was still scarce but there seemed to be plenty of booze. Young men left their hotel room doors open so that Red Cross nurses could wander in whenever they needed company. Conventional morality seemed to be put on hold. People did not try to hide their love affairs. Effeminate men cast off the pretense of masculinity. Larue's became the lesbian restaurant. It was said the coal shortage was a myth put about by the French so that everyone would keep warm at night by sleeping with their friends.

Everything was expensive, but Gus had money. He had other advantages, too: he knew Paris and could speak French. He went to the races at St. Cloud, saw *La Bohème* at the opera, and went to a risqué musical called *Phi Phi*. Because he was close to the president, he was invited to every party.

He found himself spending more and more time with Rosa Hellman. He had to be careful, when talking to her, to tell her only things that he would be happy to see printed, but the habit of discretion was automatic with him now. She was one of the smartest people he had ever met. He liked her, but that was as far as it went. She was always ready to go out with him, but what reporter would refuse an invitation from a presidential aide? He could never hold hands with her, or try to kiss her good night, in case she might think he was taking advantage of his position as someone she could not afford to offend.

He met her at the Ritz for cocktails. "What are cocktails?" she said.

"Hard liquor dressed up to be more respectable. I promise you, they're fashionable."

Rosa was fashionable, too. Her hair was bobbed. Her cloche hat came down over her ears like a German soldier's steel helmet. Curves and corsets had gone out of style, and her draped dress fell straight from the shoulders to a startlingly low waistline. By concealing her shape, paradoxically, the dress made Gus think about the body beneath. She wore lipstick and face powder, something European women still considered daring.

They had a martini each, then moved on. They drew a lot of stares as they walked together through the long lobby of the Ritz: the lanky man with the big head and his tiny one-eyed companion, him in white-tie-and-tails and her in silver-blue silk. They got a cab to the Majestic, where the British held Saturday night dances that everyone went to.

The ballroom was packed. Young aides from the delegations, journalists from all over the world, and soldiers freed from the trenches were "jazzing" with nurses and typists. Rosa taught Gus the fox-trot; then she left him and danced with a handsome dark-eyed man from the Greek delegation.

Feeling jealous, Gus drifted around the room chatting to acquaintances until he ran into Lady Maud Fitzherbert in a purple dress and pointed shoes. "Hello!" he said in surprise.

She seemed pleased to see him. "You look well."

"I was lucky. I'm all in one piece."

She touched the scar on his cheek. "Almost."

"A scratch. Shall we dance?"

He took her in his arms. She was thin: he could feel her bones through the dress. They did the hesitation waltz. "How is Fitz?" Gus asked.

"Fine, I think. He's in Russia. I'm probably not supposed to say that, but it's an open secret."

"I notice the British newspapers saying 'Hands Off Russia.'"

"That campaign is being led by a woman you met at Tŷ Gwyn, Ethel Williams, now Eth Leckwith."

"I don't remember her."

"She was the housekeeper."

"Good Lord!"

"She's becoming something of a force in British politics."

"How the world has changed."

Maud drew him closer and lowered her voice. "I don't suppose you have any news of Walter?"

Gus recalled the familiar-looking German officer he had seen fall at Château-Thierry, but he was far from certain that had been Walter, so he said: "Nothing, I'm sorry. It must be hard for you."

"No information is coming out of Germany and no one is allowed to go there!"

"I'm afraid you may have to wait until the peace treaty is signed."

"And when will that be?"

Gus did not know. "The league covenant is pretty much done, but they're a long way from agreement over how much Germany should pay in reparations."

"It's foolish," Maud said bitterly. "We need the Germans to be prosperous, so that British factories can sell them cars and stoves and carpet sweepers. If we cripple their economy, Germany will go Bolshevik."

"People want revenge."

"Do you remember 1914? Walter didn't want war. Nor did the majority of Germans. But the country wasn't a democracy. The kaiser was egged on by the generals. And once the Russians had mobilized, they had no choice."

"Of course I remember. But most people don't."

The dance ended. Rosa Hellman appeared, and Gus introduced the two women. They talked for a minute, but Rosa was uncharacteristically charmless, and Maud moved away.

"That dress cost a fortune," Rosa said grumpily. "It's by Jeanne Lanvin."

Gus was perplexed. "Didn't you like Maud?"

"You obviously do."

"What do you mean?"

"You were dancing very close."

Rosa did not know about Walter. All the same, Gus resented being falsely accused of flirting. "She wanted to talk about something rather confidential," he said with a touch of indignation.

"I bet she did."

"I don't know why you're taking this attitude," Gus said. "You went off with that oily Greek."

"He's very handsome, and not a bit oily. Why shouldn't I dance with other men? It's not as if you're in love with me."

Gus stared at her. "Oh," he said. "Oh, dear." He suddenly felt confused and uncertain.

"What's the matter now?"

"I've just realized something . . . I think."

"Are you going to tell me what it is?"

"I suppose I must," he said shakily. He paused.

She waited for him to speak. "Well?" she said impatiently.

"I am in love with you."

She looked back at him in silence. After a long pause she said: "Do you mean it?"

Although the thought had taken him by surprise, he had no doubt. "Yes. I love you, Rosa."

She smiled weakly. "Just fancy that."

"I think perhaps I've been in love with you for quite a long time without knowing it."

She nodded, as if having a suspicion confirmed. The band started a slow tune. She moved closer.

He took her in his arms automatically, but he was too wrought up to dance properly. "I'm not sure I can manage—"

"Don't worry." She knew what he was thinking. "Just pretend."

He shuffled a few steps. His mind was in turmoil. She had not said anything about her own feelings. On the other hand, she had not walked away. Was there any chance she might return his love? She obviously liked him, but that was not the same thing at all. Was she asking herself, at this very minute, how she felt? Or was she thinking up some gentle words of rejection?

She looked up at him, and he thought she was about to give him the answer; then she said: "Take me away from here, please, Gus."

"Of course."

She got her coat. The doorman summoned a red Renault taxi. "Maxim's," Gus said. It was a short drive, and they rode in silence. Gus longed to know what was in her mind, but he did not rush her. She would have to tell him soon.

The restaurant was packed, the few empty tables reserved for later customers. The headwaiter was *désolé*. Gus took out his wallet, extracted a hundred-franc note, and said: "A quiet table in a corner." A card saying *Réservée* was whipped away and they sat down.

They chose a light supper and Gus ordered a bottle of champagne. "You've changed so much," Rosa said.

He was surprised. "I don't think so."

"You were a diffident young man, back in Buffalo. I think you were even shy of me. Now you walk around Paris as if you own it."

"Oh, dear—that sounds arrogant."

"No, just confident. After all, you've worked for a president and fought a war—those things make a difference."

The food came but neither of them ate much. Gus was too tense. What was she thinking? Did she love him or not? Surely she must know? He put down his knife and fork, but instead of asking her the question on his mind he said: "You've always seemed self-confident."

She laughed. "Isn't that amazing?"

"Why?"

"I suppose I was confident until about the age of seven. And then . . . well, you know what schoolgirls are like. Everyone wants to be friends with the prettiest. I had to play with the fat girls and the ugly ones and those dressed in hand-me-downs. That went on into my teenage years. Even working for the *Buffalo Anarchist* was kind of an outsider thing to do. But when I became editor I started to get my self-esteem back." She took a sip of champagne. "You helped."

"I did?" Gus was surprised.

"It was the way you talked to me, as if I was the smartest and most interesting person in Buffalo."

"You probably were."

"Except for Olga Vyalov."

"Ah." Gus blushed. Remembering his infatuation with Olga made him feel foolish, but he did not want to say so, for that would be running her down, which was ungentlemanly.

When they had finished their coffee and he called for the bill, he still did not know how Rosa felt about him.

In the taxi he took her hand and pressed it to his lips. She said: "Oh, Gus, you are very dear." He did not know what she meant by that. However, her face was turned up toward him in a way that almost seemed expectant. Did she want him to . . . ? He screwed up his nerve and kissed her mouth.

There was a frozen moment when she did not respond, and he thought he had done the wrong thing. Then she sighed contentedly and parted her lips.

Oh, he thought happily; so that's all right, then.

He put his arms around her and they kissed all the way to her hotel. The journey was too short. Suddenly a commissionaire was opening the door of the cab. "Wipe your mouth," Rosa said as she got out. Gus pulled out a handkerchief and hastily rubbed at his face. The white linen came away red with her lipstick. He folded it carefully and put it back in his pocket.

He walked her to the door. "Can I see you tomorrow?" he said.

"When?"

"Early."

She laughed. "You never pretend, Gus, do you? I love that about you."

That was good. *I love that about you* was not the same as *I love you* but it was better than nothing. "Early it is," he said.

"What shall we do?"

"It's Sunday." He said the first thing that came into his head. "We could go to church."

"All right."

"Let me take you to Notre Dame."

"Are you Catholic?" she said in surprise.

"No, Episcopalian, if anything. You?"

"The same."

"It's all right—we can sit at the back. I'll find out what time mass is and phone your hotel."

She held out her hand and they shook like friends. "Thank you for a lovely evening," she said formally.

"It was such a pleasure. Good night."

"Good night," she said, and she turned away and disappeared into the hotel lobby.

CHAPTER THIRTY-SIX

March to April 1919

When the snow melted, and the iron-hard Russian earth turned to rich wet mud, the White armies made a mighty effort to rid their country of the curse of Bolshevism. Admiral Kolchak's force of one hundred thousand, patchily supplied with British uniforms and guns, came storming out of Siberia and attacked the Reds over a front that stretched seven hundred miles from north to south.

Fitz followed a few miles behind the Whites. He was leading the Aberowen Pals, plus some Canadians and a few interpreters. His job was to stiffen Kolchak by supervising communications, intelligence, and supply.

Fitz had high hopes. There might be difficulties, but it was unimaginable that Lenin and Trotsky would be allowed to steal Russia.

At the beginning of March he was in the city of Ufa on the European side of the Ural Mountains, reading a batch of week-old British newspapers. The news from London was mixed. Fitz was delighted that Lloyd George had appointed Winston Churchill as secretary for war. Of all the leading politicians, Winston was the most vigorous supporter of intervention in Russia. But some of the papers took the opposite side. Fitz was not surprised by the *Daily Herald* and the *New Statesman,* which in his view were more or less Bolshevik publications anyway. But even the Conservative *Daily Express* had a headline reading WITHDRAW FROM RUSSIA.

Unfortunately, they also had accurate details of what was going on. They even knew that the British had helped Kolchak with the coup that had abolished the directorate and made him supreme ruler. Where were they getting the information? He looked up from the paper. He was quartered in the city's commercial college, and his aide-de-camp sat at the opposite desk. "Murray," he said, "next time there's a batch of mail from the men to be sent home, bring it to me first."

This was irregular, and Murray looked dubious. "Sir?"

Fitz thought he had better explain. "I suspect information may be getting back from here. The censor must be asleep at the wheel."

"Perhaps they think they can slacken off now that the war in Europe has ended."

"No doubt. Anyway, I want to see whether the leak is in our section of the pipe."

The back page of the paper had a photograph of the woman leading the "Hands Off Russia" campaign, and Fitz was startled to see that it was Ethel. She had been a housemaid at Tŷ Gwyn but now, the *Express* said, she was general secretary of the National Garment Workers Union.

He had slept with many women since then—most recently, in Omsk, a stunning Russian blonde, the bored mistress of a fat tsarist general who was too drunk and lazy to fuck her himself. But Ethel shone out in his memory. He wondered what her child was like. Fitz probably had half a dozen bastards around the world, but Ethel's was the only one he knew of for sure.

And she was the one whipping up protest against intervention in Russia. Now Fitz knew where the information was coming from. Her damn brother was a sergeant in the Aberowen Pals. He had always been a troublemaker, and Fitz had no doubt he was briefing Ethel. Well, Fitz thought, I'll catch him out, and then there will be hell to pay.

Over the next few weeks the Whites raced ahead, driving before them the surprised Reds, who had thought the Siberian government a spent force. If Kolchak's armies could link up with their supporters in Archangel, in the north, and with Denikin's Volunteer Army in the south, they would form a semicircular force, a curved eastern scimitar a thousand miles long that would sweep irresistibly to Moscow.

Then, at the end of April, the Reds counterattacked.

By then Fitz was in Buguruslan, a grimly impoverished town in forest country a hundred miles or so east of the Volga River. The few dilapidated stone churches and municipal buildings poked up over the roofs of low-built wooden houses like weeds in a rubbish dump. Fitz sat in a large room in the town hall with the intelligence unit, sifting reports of prisoner interrogations. He did not know anything was wrong until he looked out of the window and saw the ragged soldiers of Kolchak's army streaming along the main road through the town in the wrong direction. He sent an American interpreter, Lev Peshkov, to question the retreating men.

Peshkov came back with a sorry story. The Reds had attacked in force from the south, striking the overstretched left flank of Kolchak's advancing army. To avoid his force being cut in two the local White commander, General Belov, had ordered them to retreat and regroup.

A few minutes later, a Red deserter was brought in for interrogation. He had been a colonel under the tsar. What he had to say dismayed Fitz. The Reds had been surprised by Kolchak's offensive, he said, but they had quickly regrouped and resupplied. Trotsky had declared that the Red Army must go on the offensive in the east. "Trotsky thinks that if the Reds falter, the Allies will recognize Kolchak as supreme ruler; and once they have done that, they will flood Siberia with men and supplies."

That was exactly what Fitz was hoping for. In his heavily accented Russian he asked: "So what did Trotsky do?"

The reply came fast, and Fitz could not understand what was said until he heard Peshkov's translation. "Trotsky drew on special levies of recruits from the Bolshevik party and the trade unions. The response was amazing. Twenty-two provinces sent detachments. The Novgorod Provincial Committee mobilized half its members!"

Fitz tried to imagine Kolchak summoning such a response from his supporters. It would never happen.

He returned to his quarters to pack his kit. He was almost too slow: the Pals got out only just ahead of the Reds, and a handful of men were left behind. By that evening Kolchak's Western Army was in full retreat and Fitz was on a train going back toward the Ural Mountains.

Two days later he was back in the commercial college at Ufa.

Over those two days, Fitz's mood turned black. He felt bitter with rage. He had been at war for five years, and he could recognize the turn of the tide—he knew the signs. The Russian civil war was as good as over.

The Whites were just too weak. The revolutionaries were going to win. Nothing short of an Allied invasion could turn the tables—and that was not going to happen: Churchill was in enough trouble for the little he was doing. Billy Williams and Ethel were making sure the needed reinforcements would never be sent.

Murray brought him a sack of mail. "You asked to see the men's letters home, sir," he said, with a hint of disapproval in his tone.

Fitz ignored Murray's scruples and opened the sack. He searched for a letter from Sergeant Williams. Someone, at least, could be punished for this catastrophe.

He found what he was looking for. Sergeant Williams's letter was addressed to E. Williams, her maiden name: no doubt he feared the use of her married name would call attention to his traitorous letter.

Fitz read it. Billy's handwriting was large and confident. At first sight the text seemed innocent, if a bit odd. But Fitz had worked in Room 40, and knew about codes. He settled down to crack this one.

Murray said: "On another matter, sir, have you seen the American interpreter, Peshkov, in the last day or two?"

"No," Fitz said. "What's happened to him?"

"We seem to have lost him, sir."

{ II }

Trotsky was immensely weary, but not discouraged. The lines of strain on his face did not diminish the light of hope in his eyes. Grigori thought admiringly that he was sustained by an unshakable belief in what he was doing. They all had that, Grigori suspected; Lenin and Stalin too. Each felt sure he knew the right thing to do, whatever the problem might be, from land reform to military tactics.

Grigori was not like that. With Trotsky, he tried to work out the best response to the White armies, but he never felt sure they had made the right decision until the results were known. Perhaps that was why Trotsky was world-famous and Grigori was just another commissar.

As he had many times before, Grigori sat in Trotsky's personal train with a map of Russia on the table. "We hardly need worry about the counterrevolutionaries in the north," Trotsky said.

Grigori agreed. "According to our intelligence, there are mutinies among the British soldiers and sailors there."

"And they have lost all hope of linking up with Kolchak. His armies are running as fast as they can back to Siberia. We could chase them over the Urals—but I think we have more important business elsewhere."

"In the West?"

"That's bad enough. The Whites are bolstered by reactionary nationalists in Latvia, Lithuania, and Estonia. Kolchak has appointed Yudenich commander in chief there, and he's supported by a British navy flotilla that is keeping our fleet bottled up in Kronstadt. But I'm even more worried about the South."

"General Denikin."

"He has about a hundred and fifty thousand men, supported by French and Italian troops, and supplied by the British. We think he's planning a dash for Moscow."

"If I may say so, I think the key to defeating him is political, not military."

Trotsky looked intrigued. "Go on."

"Everywhere he goes, Denikin makes enemies. His Cossacks rob everyone. Whenever he takes a town, he rounds up all the Jews and just shoots them. If the coal mines fail to meet production targets, he kills one in ten miners. And, of course, he executes all deserters from his army."

"So do we," said Trotsky. "And we kill villagers who harbor deserters."

"And peasants who refuse to give up their grain." Grigori had had to harden his heart to accept this brutal necessity. "But I know peasants—my father was one. What they care about most is land. A lot of these people gained considerable tracts of land in the revolution, and they want to hold on to it—whatever else happens."

"So?"

"Kolchak has announced that land reform should be based on the principle of private property."

"Which means the peasants giving back the fields they have taken from the aristocracy."

"And everyone knows that. I'd like to print his proclamation and post it outside every church. No matter what our soldiers do, the peasants will prefer us to the Whites."

"Do it," said Trotsky.

"One more thing. Announce an amnesty for deserters. For seven days, any who return to the ranks will escape punishment."

"Another political move."

"I don't believe it will encourage desertion, because it's only for a week; but it might bring men back to us—especially when they find out the Whites want to take their land."

"Give it a try," said Trotsky.

An aide came in and saluted. "A strange report, Comrade Peshkov, that I thought you would want to hear."

"All right."

"It's about one of the prisoners we took at Buguruslan. He was with Kolchak's army, but wearing an American uniform."

"The Whites have soldiers from all over the world. The capitalist imperialists support the counterrevolution, naturally."

"It's not that, sir."

"What, then?"

"Sir, he says he's your brother."

{ III }

The platform was long, and there was a heavy morning mist, so that Grigori could not see the far end of the train. There was probably some mistake, he thought; a confusion of names or an error of translation. He tried to steel himself for a disappointment, but he was not successful: his heart beat faster and his nerves seemed to tingle. It was almost five years since he had seen his brother. He had often thought Lev must be dead. That could still be the awful truth.

He walked slowly, peering into the swirling haze. If this really was Lev, he would naturally be different. In the last five years Grigori had lost a front tooth and most of one ear, and had probably changed in other ways he was not aware of. How would Lev have altered?

After a few moments two figures emerged from the white mist: a Russian soldier, in ragged uniform and homemade shoes; and, beside him, a man who looked American. Was that Lev? He had a short American haircut and no mustache. He had the round-faced look of the well-fed American soldiers, with meaty shoulders under the smart new uniform. It was an officer's uniform, Grigori saw with growing incredulity. Could his brother be an American officer?

The prisoner was staring back at him, and as Grigori came close he saw that it was, indeed, his brother. He did look different, and it was not just the general air of sleek prosperity. It was the way he stood, the expression on his face, and most of all the look in his eyes. He had lost his boyish cockiness and acquired an air of caution. He had, in fact, grown up.

As they came within touching distance, Grigori thought of all the ways Lev had let him down, and a host of recriminations sprang to his lips; but he uttered none of them, and instead opened his arms and hugged Lev. They kissed cheeks, slapped each other on the back, and hugged again, and Grigori found that he was weeping.

After a while he led Lev onto the train and took him to the carriage he used as his office. Grigori told his aide to bring tea. They sat in two faded armchairs. "You're in the army?" Grigori said incredulously.

"They have conscription in America," Lev said.

That made sense. Lev would never have joined voluntarily. "And you're an officer!"

"So are you," said Lev.

Grigori shook his head. "We've abolished ranks in the Red Army. I'm a military commissar."

"But there are still some men who order tea and others who bring it," Lev said as the aide came in with cups. "Wouldn't Ma be proud?"

"Fit to bust. But why did you never write to me? I thought you were dead!"

"Aw, hell, I'm sorry," said Lev. "I felt so bad about taking your ticket that I wanted to write and say I can pay for your passage. I kept putting off the letter until I had more money."

It was a feeble excuse, but characteristic of Lev. He would not go to a party unless he had a fancy jacket to put on, and he refused to enter a bar if he did not have the money to buy a round of drinks.

Grigori recalled another betrayal. "You didn't tell me Katerina was pregnant when you left."

"Pregnant! I didn't know."

"Yes, you did. You told her not to tell me."

"Oh. I guess I forgot." Lev looked foolish, caught in a lie, but it did not take him long to recover and come up with his own counteraccusation. "That ship you sent me on didn't even go to New York! It put us all ashore at a dump called Cardiff. I had to work for months to save up for another ticket."

Grigori even felt guilty for a moment, then recalled how Lev had begged for the ticket. "Maybe I shouldn't have helped you escape from the police," he said crisply.

"I suppose you did your best for me," Lev said reluctantly. Then he gave the warm smile that always caused Grigori to forgive him. "As you always have," he added. "Ever since Ma died."

Grigori felt a lump in his throat. "All the same," he said, concentrating to make his voice steady, "we ought to punish the Vyalov family for cheating us."

"I got my revenge," Lev said. "There's a Josef Vyalov in Buffalo. I fucked his daughter and made her pregnant, and he had to let me marry her."

"My God! You're part of the Vyalov family now?"

"He regretted it, which is why he arranged for me to be conscripted. He's hoping I'll be killed in battle."

"Hell, do you still go wherever your dick leads you?"

Lev shrugged. "I guess."

Grigori had some revelations of his own, and he was nervous about making them. He began by saying carefully: "Katerina had a baby boy, your son. She called him Vladimir."

Lev looked pleased. "Is that so? I've got a son!"

Grigori did not have the courage to say that Vladimir knew nothing of Lev, and called Grigori "Daddy." Instead he said: "I've taken good care of him."

"I knew you would."

Grigori felt a familiar stab of indignation at how Lev assumed that others would pick up the responsibilities he dropped. "Lev," he said, "I married Katerina." He waited for the outraged reaction.

But Lev remained calm. "I knew you'd do that, too."

Grigori was astonished. "What?"

Lev nodded. "You were crazy for her, and she needed a solid, dependable type to raise the child. It was in the cards."

"I went through agonies!" Grigori said. Had all that been for nothing? "I was tortured by the thought that I was being disloyal to you."

"Hell, no. I left her in the lurch. Good luck to you both."

Grigori was maddened by how casual Lev was about the whole thing. "Did you worry about us at all?" he asked pointedly.

"You know me, Grishka."

Of course Lev had not worried about them. "You hardly thought about us."

"Sure I thought about you. Don't be so holy. You wanted her. You held off for a while—maybe for years—but in the end you fucked her."

It was the crude truth. Lev had an annoying way of bringing everyone else down to his level. "You're right," Grigori said. "Anyway, we have another child now, a daughter, Anna. She's a year and a half old."

"Two adults and two children. It doesn't matter. I've got enough."

"What are you talking about?"

"I've been making money, selling whisky from British army stores to the Cossacks for gold. I've accumulated a small fortune." Lev reached inside his uniform shirt, unfastened a buckle, and pulled out a money belt. "There's enough here to pay for all four of you to come to America!" He gave the belt to Grigori.

Grigori was astonished and moved. Lev had not forgotten his family after all. He had saved up for a ticket. Naturally the handing over of the money had to be a flamboyant gesture—that was Lev's character. But he had kept his promise.

What a shame it was all for nothing.

"Thank you," Grigori said. "I'm proud of you for doing what you said you'd do. But, of course, it's not necessary now. I can get you released and help you return to normal Russian life." He handed the money belt back.

Lev took it and held it in his hands, staring at it. "What do you mean?"

Grigori saw that Lev looked hurt, and understood that he was wounded by the refusal of his gift. But there was a greater worry on Grigori's mind. What would happen when Lev and Katerina were reunited? Would she fall for the more attractive brother all over again? Grigori's heart was chilled by the thought that he could lose her, after all they had been through together. "We live in Moscow now," he said. "We have an apartment in the Kremlin, Katerina and Vladimir and Anna and me. I can get an apartment for you easily enough—"

"Wait a minute," said Lev, and there was a look of incredulity on his face. "You think I want to come back to Russia?"

"You already have," Grigori said.

"But not to stay!"

"You can't possibly want to return to America."

"Of course I do! And you should come with me."

"But there's no need! Russia's not like it used to be. The tsar is gone!"

"I like America," Lev said. "You'll like it, too, all of you, especially Katerina."

"But we're making history here! We've invented a new form of government, the soviet. This is the new Russia, the new world. You're missing everything!"

"You're the one who doesn't understand," Lev said. "In America I have my own car. There's more food than you can eat. All the booze I want, all the cigarettes I can smoke. I have five suits!"

"What's the point in having five suits?" Grigori said in frustration. "It's like having five beds. You can only use one at a time!"

"That's not how I see it."

What made the conversation so aggravating was that Lev clearly thought Grigori was the one who was missing the point. Grigori did not know what more he could say to change his brother's mind. "Is that really what you want? Cigarettes and too many clothes and a car?"

"It's what everyone wants. You Bolsheviks better remember that."

Grigori was not going to take lessons in politics from Lev. "Russians want bread, peace, and land."

"Anyway, I have a daughter in America. Her name is Daisy. She's three."

Grigori frowned doubtfully.

"I know what you're thinking," Lev said. "I didn't care about Katerina's child—what's his name?"

"Vladimir."

"I didn't care about him, you think, so why should I care about Daisy? But it's different. I never met Vladimir. He was just a speck when I left Petrograd. But I love Daisy, and what's more, she loves me."

Grigori could at least understand that. He was glad Lev had a good enough heart to feel attached to his daughter. And although he was bewildered by Lev's preference for America, in his heart he would be hugely relieved if Lev did not come home. For Lev would surely want to get to know Vladimir, and then how long would it be before Vladimir learned that Lev was his real father? And if Katerina decided to leave Grigori for Lev, and take Vladimir with her, what would happen to Anna? Would Grigori lose her, too? For himself, he thought guiltily, it was much better if Lev went back to America alone. "I believe you're making the wrong choice, but I'm not going to force you," he said.

Lev grinned. "You're afraid I'll take Katerina back, aren't you? I know you too well, brother."

Grigori winced. "Yes," he said. "Take her back, then discard her all over again, and leave me to pick up the pieces a second time. I know you, too."

"But you'll help me get back to America."

"No." Grigori could not help feeling a twitch of gratification at the look of fear that passed across Lev's face. But he did not prolong the agony. "I'll help you get back to the White Army. They can take you to America."

"What'll we do?"

"We'll drive to the front line, and a little beyond it. Then I'll release you into no-man's-land. After that you're on your own."

"I might get shot."

"We both might get shot. It's a war."

"I guess I'll have to take my chances."

"You'll be okay, Lev," said Grigori. "You always are."

{ IV }

Billy Williams was marched from the Ufa city jail, through the dusty streets of the city, to the commercial college being used as temporary accommodation by the British army.

The court-martial took place in a classroom. Fitz sat at the teacher's desk, with his aide-de-camp, Captain Murray, beside him. Captain Gwyn Evans was there with a notebook and pencil.

Billy was dirty and unshaven, and he had slept badly with the drunks and prostitutes of the town. Fitz wore a perfectly pressed uniform, as always. Billy knew he was in bad trouble. The verdict was a foregone conclusion: the evidence was clear. He had revealed military secrets in coded letters to his sister. But he was determined not to let his fear show. He was going to give a good account of himself.

Fitz said: "This is a field general court-martial, permitted when the accused is on active service or overseas and it is not possible to hold the more regular general court-martial. Only three officers are required to sit as judges, or two if no more are available. It may try a soldier of any rank on any offense, and has the power to impose the death penalty."

Billy's only chance was to influence the sentence. The possible punishments included penal servitude, hard labor, and death. No doubt Fitz would like to put Billy in front of a firing squad, or at least give him several years in prison. Billy's aim was to plant in the minds of Murray and Evans sufficient doubts about the fairness of the trial to make them plump for a short term in prison.

Now he said: "Where is my lawyer?"

"It is not possible to offer you legal representation," Fitz said.

"You're sure of that, are you, sir?"

"Speak when you're spoken to, Sergeant."

Billy said, "Let the record show that I was denied access to a lawyer." He stared at Gwyn Evans, the only one with a notebook. When Evans did nothing, Billy said: "Or will the record of this trial be a lie?" He put heavy emphasis on the word *lie,* knowing it would offend Fitz. It was part of the code of the English gentleman always to tell the truth.

Fitz nodded to Evans, who made a note.

First point to me, Billy thought, and he cheered up a bit.

Fitz said: "William Williams, you stand accused under part one of the Army Act. The charge is that you knowingly, while on active service, committed an act calculated to imperil the success of His Majesty's forces. The penalty is death, or such lesser punishment as the court shall impose."

The repeated emphasis on the death penalty chilled Billy, but he kept his face stiff.

"How do you plead?"

Billy took a deep breath. He spoke in a clear voice, and put into his tone as much scorn and contempt as he could muster. "I plead how dare you," he said. "How dare you pretend to be an objective judge? How dare you act as if our presence in Russia is a legitimate operation? And how dare you make an accusation of treason against a man who has fought alongside you for three years? That's how I plead."

Gwyn Evans said: "Don't be insolent, Billy boy. You'll only make it worse for yourself."

Billy was not going to let Evans pretend to be benevolent. He said: "And my advice to you is to leave now and have nothing more to do with this kangaroo court. When the news gets out—and believe you me, this is going to be on the front page of the *Daily Mirror*—you will find that you're the one in disgrace, not me." He looked at Murray. "Every man who had anything to do with this farce is going to be disgraced."

Evans looked troubled. Clearly he had not thought there might be publicity.

"Enough!" said Fitz loudly and angrily.

Good, Billy thought; I've got his goat already.

Fitz went on: "Let's have the evidence, please, Captain Murray."

Murray opened a folder and took out a sheet of paper. Billy recognized his own handwriting. It was, as he expected, a letter to Ethel.

Murray showed it to him and said: "Did you write this letter?"

Billy said: "How did it come to your attention, Captain Murray?"

Fitz barked: "Answer the question!"

Billy said, "You went to Eton school, didn't you, Captain? A gentleman would never read someone else's mail, or so we're told. But as I understand it, only the official censor has the right to examine soldiers' letters. So I assume this was brought to your attention by the censor." He paused. As he expected, Murray was unwilling to answer. He went on: "Or was the letter obtained illegally?"

Murray repeated: "Did you write this letter?"

"If it was obtained illegally, then it can't be used in a trial. I think that's what a lawyer would say. But there are no lawyers here. That's what makes this a kangaroo court."

"Did you write this letter?"

"I will answer that question when you have explained how it came into your possession."

Fitz said: "You can be punished for contempt of court, you know."

I'm already facing the death penalty, Billy thought; how stupid of Fitz to think he can threaten me! But he said: "I am defending myself by pointing out the irregularity of the court and the illegality of the prosecution. Are you going to forbid that . . . sir?"

Murray gave up. "The envelope is marked with a return address and the name of Sergeant Billy Williams. If the accused wishes to claim he did not write it, he should say so now."

Billy said nothing.

"The letter is a coded message," Murray went on. "It may be decoded by reading every third word, and the initial capital letters of titles of songs and films." Murray handed the letter to Evans. "When so decoded, it reads as follows."

Billy's letter described the incompetence of the Kolchak regime, saying that despite all their gold they had failed to pay the staff of the Trans-Siberian Railway, and so were continuing to have supply and transport problems. It also detailed the help the British army was trying to give. The information had been kept secret from the British public, who were paying for the army and whose sons were risking their lives.

Murray said to Billy: "Do you deny sending this message?"

"I cannot comment on evidence that has been obtained illegally."

"The addressee, E. Williams, is in fact Mrs. Ethel Leckwith, leader of the 'Hands Off Russia' campaign, is she not?"

"I cannot comment on evidence that has been obtained illegally."

"Have you written previous coded letters to her?"

Billy said nothing.

"And she has used the information you gave her to generate hostile newspaper stories bringing discredit on the British army and imperiling the success of our actions here."

"Certainly not," said Billy. "The army has been discredited by the men who sent us on a secret and illegal mission without the knowledge or consent of Parliament. The 'Hands Off Russia' campaign is the necessary first step in returning us to our proper role as the defenders of Great Britain, rather than the private army of a little conspiracy of right-wing generals and politicians."

Fitz's chiseled face was red with anger, Billy saw to his great satisfaction. "I think we've heard enough," Fitz said. "The court will now consider its verdict." Murray murmured something, and Fitz said: "Oh, yes. Does the accused have anything to say?"

Billy stood up. "I call as my first witness Colonel the Earl Fitzherbert."

"Don't be ridiculous," said Fitz.

"Let the record show that the court refused to allow me to question a witness even though he was present at the trial."

"Get on with it."

"If I had not been denied my right to call a witness, I would have asked the colonel what his relationship with my family was. Did he not bear a personal grudge against me because of my father's role as a miners' leader? What was his relationship with my sister? Did he not employ her as his housekeeper, then mysteriously sack her?" Billy was tempted to say more about Ethel, but it would have been dragging her name through the mud, and besides, the hint was probably enough. "I would ask him about his personal interest in this illegal war against the Bolshevik government. Is his wife a Russian princess? Is his son heir to property here? Is the colonel in fact here to defend his personal financial interest? And are all these matters the real explanation of why he has convened this sham of a court? And does that not completely disqualify him from being a judge in this case?"

Fitz stared stony-faced, but both Murray and Evans looked startled. They had not known all this personal stuff.

Billy said: "I have one more point to make. The German kaiser stands accused of war crimes. It is argued that he declared war, with the encouragement of his generals, against the will of the German people, as clearly expressed by their representatives in the Reichstag, the German parliament. By contrast, it is argued, Britain declared war on Germany only after a debate in the House of Commons."

Fitz pretended to be bored, but Murray and Evans were attentive.

Billy went on: "Now consider this war in Russia. It has never been debated in the British Parliament. The facts are hidden from the British people on the pretense of operational security—always the excuse for the army's guilty secrets. We are fighting, but war has never been declared. The British prime minister and his colleagues are in exactly the same position as the kaiser and his generals. They are the ones acting illegally—not me." Billy sat down.

The two captains went into a huddle with Fitz. Billy wondered if he had gone too far. He had felt the need to be trenchant, but he might have offended the captains instead of winning their support.

However, there seemed to be dissent among the judges. Fitz was speaking emphatically and Evans was shaking his head in negation. Murray looked awkward. That was probably a good sign, Billy thought. All the same he was as scared as he had ever been. When he had faced machine guns at the Somme and experienced an explosion down the pit, he had not been as frightened as he was now, with his life in the hands of malevolent officers.

At last they seemed to reach agreement. Fitz looked at Billy and said: "Stand up."

Billy stood.

"Sergeant William Williams, this court finds you guilty as charged." Fitz stared at Billy, as if hoping to see on his face the mortification of defeat. But Billy had been expecting a guilty verdict. It was the sentence he feared.

Fitz said: "You are sentenced to ten years' penal servitude."

Billy could no longer keep his face expressionless. It was not the death penalty—but ten years! When he came out he would be thirty. It would be 1929. Mildred would be thirty-five. Half their lives would be over. His façade of defiance crumbled, and tears came to his eyes.

A look of profound satisfaction came over Fitz's face. "Dismissed," he said.

Billy was marched away to begin his prison sentence.

CHAPTER THIRTY-SEVEN

May and June 1919

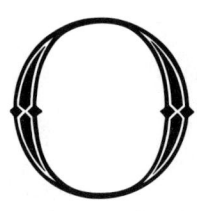n the first day of May, Walter von Ulrich wrote a letter to Maud and posted it in the town of Versailles.

He did not know whether she was dead or alive. He had heard no news of her since Stockholm. There was still no postal service between Germany and Britain, so this was his first chance of writing to her in two years.

Walter and his father had traveled to France the day before, with 180 politicians, diplomats, and foreign ministry officials, as part of the German delegation to the peace conference. The French railway had slowed their special train to walking pace as they crossed the devastated landscape of northeastern France. "As if we were the only ones who fired shells here," Otto said angrily. From Paris they had been bused to the small town of Versailles and dropped off at the Hotel des Réservoirs. Their luggage was unloaded in the courtyard and they were rudely told to carry it themselves. Clearly, Walter thought, the French were not going to be magnanimous in victory.

"They didn't win, that's their trouble," said Otto. "They may not have actually lost, not quite, because they were saved by the British and

Americans—but that's not much to boast about. We beat them, and they know it, and it hurts their pumped-up pride."

The hotel was cold and gloomy, but magnolias and apple trees were in blossom outside. The Germans were allowed to walk in the grounds of the great château and visit the shops. There was always a small crowd outside the hotel. The ordinary people were not as malign as the officials. Sometimes they booed, but mostly they were just curious to look at the enemy.

Walter wrote to Maud on the first day. He did not mention their marriage—he was not yet sure it was safe, and anyway the habit of secrecy was hard to break. He told her where he was, described the hotel and its surroundings, and asked her to write to him by return. He walked into the town, bought a stamp, and posted his letter.

He waited in anxious hope for the reply. If she were alive, did she still love him? He felt almost sure she would. But two years had passed since she had eagerly embraced him in a Stockholm hotel room. The world was full of men who had returned from the war to find that their girlfriends and wives had fallen in love with someone else during the long years of separation.

A few days later the leaders of the delegations were summoned to the Hotel Trianon Palace, across the park, and ceremonially handed printed copies of the peace treaty drafted by the victorious allies. It was in French. Back at the Hotel des Réservoirs, the copies were given to teams of translators. Walter was head of one such team. He divided his part into sections, passed them out, and sat down to read.

It was even worse than he expected.

The French army would occupy the border region of Rhineland for fifteen years. The Saar region of Germany was to become a League of Nations protectorate with the French controlling the coal mines. Alsace and Lorraine were returned to France without a plebiscite: the French government was afraid the population would vote to stay German. The new state of Poland was so large it took in the homes of three million Germans and the coalfields of Silesia. Germany was to lose all her colonies: the Allies had shared them out like thieves dividing the swag. And the Germans had to agree to pay reparations of an unspecified amount—in other words, to sign a blank check.

Walter wondered what kind of country they wanted Germany to be. Did they have in mind a giant slave camp where everyone lived on iron rations and toiled only so that the overlords could take the produce? If Walter was to be one such slave, how could he contemplate setting up home with Maud and having children?

But worst of all was the war guilt clause.

Article 231 of the treaty said: "The Allied and Associated Governments affirm, and Germany accepts, the responsibility of Germany and her allies for causing all the loss and damage to which the Allied and Associated Governments and their nationals have been subjected as a consequence of the war imposed upon them by the aggression of Germany and her allies."

"It's a lie," Walter said angrily. "A stupid, ignorant, wicked, vicious, damned lie." Germany was not innocent, he knew, and he had argued as much with his father, time and time again. But he had lived through the diplomatic crises of the summer of 1914; he had known about every small step on the road to war, and no single nation was guilty. Leaders on both sides had been mainly concerned to defend their own countries, and none of them had intended to plunge the world into the greatest war in history: not Asquith, nor Poincaré, nor the kaiser, nor the tsar, nor the Austrian emperor. Even Gavrilo Princip, the assassin of Sarajevo, had apparently been aghast when he understood what he had started. But even he was not responsible for "all the loss and damage."

Walter ran into his father shortly after midnight, when they were both taking a break, drinking coffee to stay awake and continue working. "This is outrageous!" Otto stormed. "We agreed to an armistice based on Wilson's Fourteen Points—but the treaty has nothing to do with the Fourteen Points!"

For once Walter agreed with his father.

By morning the translation had been printed and copies had been dispatched by special messenger to Berlin—a classic exercise in German efficiency, Walter thought, seeing his country's virtues more clearly when it was being denigrated. Too exhausted to sleep, he decided to walk until he felt relaxed enough to go to bed.

He left the hotel and went into the park. The rhododendrons were in bud. It was a fine morning for France, a grim one for Germany. What effect would the proposals have on Germany's struggling social-democratic government? Would the people despair and turn to Bolshevism?

He was alone in the great park except for a young woman in a light spring coat sitting on a bench beneath a chestnut tree. Deep in thought, he touched the brim of his trilby hat politely as he passed her.

"Walter," she said.

His heart stopped. He knew the voice, but it could not be her. He turned and stared.

She stood up. "Oh, Walter," she said. "Did you not know me?"

It was Maud.

His blood sang in his veins. He took two steps toward her and she threw herself into his arms. He hugged her hard. He buried his face in her neck and inhaled her fragrance, still familiar despite the years. He kissed her forehead and her cheek and then her mouth. He was speaking and kissing at the same time, but neither words nor kisses could say all that was in his heart.

At last she spoke. "Do you still love me?" she said.

"More than ever," he answered, and he kissed her again.

{ II }

Maud ran her hands over Walter's bare chest as they lay on the bed after making love. "You're so thin," she said. His belly was concave, and the bones of his hips jutted out. She wanted to fatten him on buttered croissants and foie gras.

They were in a bedroom at an auberge a few miles outside Paris. The window was open, and a mild spring breeze fluttered the primrose-yellow curtains. Maud had found out about this place many years ago when Fitz had been using it for assignations with a married woman, the Comtesse de Cagnes. The establishment, little more than a large house in a small village, did not even have a name. Men made a reservation for lunch and took a room for the afternoon. Perhaps there were such places on the outskirts of London but, somehow, the arrangement seemed very French.

They called themselves Mr. and Mrs. Woolridge, and Maud wore the wedding ring that had been hidden away for almost five years. No doubt the discreet proprietress assumed they were only pretending to be married. That was all right, as long as she did not suspect Walter was German, which would have caused trouble.

Maud could not keep her hands off him. She was so grateful that he had come back to her with his body intact. She touched the long scar on his shin with her fingertips.

"I got that at Château-Thierry," he said.

"Gus Dewar was in that battle. I hope it wasn't he who shot you."

"I was lucky that it healed well. A lot of men died of gangrene."

It was three weeks since they had been reunited. During that time Walter had been working around the clock on the German response to the draft treaty, only getting away for half an hour or so each day to walk with her in the park or sit in the back of Fitz's blue Cadillac while the chauffeur drove them around.

Maud had been as shocked as Walter by the harsh terms offered to the Germans. The object of the Paris conference was to create a just and peaceful new world—not to enable the winners to take revenge on the losers. The new Germany should be democratic and prosperous. She wanted to have children with Walter, and their children would be German. She often thought of the passage in the Book of Ruth that began "Whither thou goest, I will go." Sooner or later she would have to say that to Walter.

However, she had been comforted to learn that she was not the only person who disapproved of the treaty proposals. Others on the Allied side thought peace was more important than revenge. Twelve members of the American delegation had resigned in protest. In a British by-election, the candidate advocating a nonvengeful peace had won. The Archbishop of Canterbury had said publicly that he was "very uncomfortable" and claimed to speak for a silent body of opinion that was not represented in the Hun-hating newspapers.

Yesterday the Germans had submitted their counterproposal— more than a hundred closely argued pages based on Wilson's Fourteen Points. This morning the French press was apoplectic. Bursting with indignation, they called the document a monument of impudence and an odious piece of buffoonery. "They accuse us of arrogance—the French!" said Walter. "What is that phrase about a saucepan?"

"The pot calling the kettle black," said Maud.

He rolled onto his side and toyed with her pubic hair. It was dark and curly and luxuriant. She had offered to trim it, but he said he liked it the way it was. "What are we going to do?" he said. "It's romantic to meet in a hotel and go to bed in the afternoon, like illicit lovers, but we cannot do this forever. We have to tell the world we are man and wife."

Maud agreed. She was also impatient for the time when she could sleep with him every night, though she did not say so: she was a bit embarrassed by how much she liked sex with him. "We could just set up home, and let them draw their own conclusions."

"I'm not comfortable with that," he said. "It makes us look ashamed."

She felt the same. She wanted to trumpet her happiness, not hide it away. She was proud of Walter: he was handsome and brave and extraordinarily clever. "We could have another wedding," she said. "Get engaged, announce it, have a ceremony, and never tell anyone we've been married almost five years. It's not illegal to marry the same person twice."

He looked thoughtful. "My father and your brother would fight us. They could not stop us, but they could make things unpleasant—which would spoil the happiness of the event."

"You're right," she said reluctantly. "Fitz would say that some Germans may be jolly good chaps, but all the same you don't want your sister to marry one."

"So we must present them with a fait accompli."

"Let's tell them, then announce the news in the press," she said. "We'll say it's a symbol of the new world order. An Anglo-German marriage, at the same time as the peace treaty."

He looked dubious. "How would we manage that?"

"I'll speak to the editor of the *Tatler* magazine. They like me—I've provided them with lots of material."

Walter smiled and said: "Lady Maud Fitzherbert is always dressed in the latest fashion."

"What are you talking about?"

He reached for his billfold on the bedside table and extracted a magazine clipping. "My only picture of you," he said.

She took it from him. It was soft with age and faded to the color of sand. She studied the photo. "This was taken before the war."

"And it has been with me ever since. Like me, it survived."

Tears came to her eyes, blurring the faded image even more.

"Don't cry," he said, hugging her.

She pressed her face to his bare chest and wept. Some women cried at the drop of a hat, but she had never been that sort. Now she sobbed helplessly. She was crying for the lost years, and the millions of boys lying dead, and the pointless, stupid waste of it all. She was shedding all the tears stored up in five years of self-control.

When it was over, and her tears were dry, she kissed him hungrily, and they made love again.

{ III }

Fitz's blue Cadillac picked Walter up at the hotel on June 16 and drove him into Paris. Maud had decided that the *Tatler* magazine would want a photograph of the two of them. Walter wore a tweed suit made in London before the war. It was too wide at the waist, but every German man was walking around in clothes too big for him.

Walter had set up a small intelligence bureau at the Hotel des

Réservoirs, monitoring the French, British, American, and Italian newspapers and collating gossip picked up by the German delegation. He knew that there were bad-tempered arguments among the Allies about the German counterproposals. Lloyd George, a politician who was flexible to a fault, was willing to reconsider the draft treaty. But the French prime minister, Clemenceau, said he had already been generous and fumed with outrage at any suggestion of amendments. Surprisingly, Woodrow Wilson was also obdurate. He believed the draft was a just settlement, and whenever he had made up his mind he became deaf to criticism.

The Allies were also negotiating peace treaties to cover Germany's partners: Austria, Hungary, Bulgaria, and the Ottoman Empire. They were creating new countries such as Yugoslavia and Czechoslovakia, and carving up the Middle East into British and French zones. And they were arguing about whether to make peace with Lenin. In every country the people were tired of war, but a few powerful men were still keen to fight against the Bolsheviks. The British *Daily Mail* had discovered a conspiracy of international Jewish financiers supporting the Moscow regime—one of that newspaper's more implausible fantasies.

On the German treaty Wilson and Clemenceau overruled Lloyd George, and earlier that day the German team at the Hotel des Réservoirs had received an impatient note giving them three days to accept.

Walter thought gloomily about his country's future as he sat in the back of Fitz's car. It would be like an African colony, he thought, the primitive inhabitants working only to enrich their foreign masters. He would not want to raise children in such a place.

Maud was waiting in the photographer's studio, looking wonderful in a filmy summer dress that, she said, was by Paul Poiret, her favorite couturier.

The photographer had a painted backdrop that showed a garden in full flower, which Maud decided was in bad taste, so they posed in front of his dining room curtains, which were mercifully plain. At first they stood side by side, not touching, like strangers. The photographer proposed that Walter should kneel in front of Maud, but that was too sentimental. In the end they found a position they all liked, with the two of them holding hands and looking at each other rather than the camera.

Copies of the picture would be ready tomorrow, the photographer promised.

They went to their auberge for lunch. "The Allies can't just order Germany to sign," Maud said. "That's not negotiation."

"It is what they have done."

"What happens if you refuse?"

"They don't say."

"What are you going to do?"

"Some of the delegation are returning to Berlin tonight for consultations with our government." He sighed. "I'm afraid I have been chosen to go with them."

"Then this is the time to make our announcement. I'll go to London tomorrow after I've picked up the photographs."

"All right," he said. "I'll tell my mother as soon as I get to Berlin. She'll be nice about it. Then I'll tell Father. He won't."

"I'll speak to Aunt Herm and Princess Bea, and write to Fitz in Russia."

"So this will be the last time we meet for a while."

"Eat up, then, and let's go to bed."

{ IV }

Gus and Rosa met in the Tuileries Gardens. Paris was beginning to get back to normal, Gus thought happily. The sun was shining, the trees were in leaf, and men with carnations in their buttonholes sat smoking cigars and watching the best-dressed women in the world walk by. On one side of the park, the rue de Rivoli was busy with cars, trucks, and horse-drawn carts; on the other, freight barges plied the river Seine. Perhaps the world would recover, after all.

Rosa was ravishing in a red dress of light cotton and a wide-brimmed hat. If I could paint, Gus thought when he saw her, I'd paint her like this.

He had a blue blazer and a fashionable straw boater. When she saw him, she laughed.

"What is it?" he said.

"Nothing. You look nice."

"It's the hat, isn't it?"

She suppressed another giggle. "You're adorable."

"It looks stupid. I can't help it. Hats do that to me. It's because I'm shaped like a ball-peen hammer."

She kissed him lightly on the lips. "You're the most attractive man in Paris."

The amazing thing was that she meant it. Gus thought: How did I get so lucky?

He took her arm. "Let's walk." They strolled toward the Louvre.

She said: "Have you seen the *Tatler*?"

"The London magazine? No, why?"

"It seems that your intimate friend Lady Maud is married to a German."

"Oh!" he said. "How did they find out?"

"You mean you knew about this?"

"I guessed. I saw Walter in Berlin in 1916 and he asked me to carry a letter to Maud. I figured that meant they were either engaged or married."

"How discreet you are! You never said a word."

"It was a dangerous secret."

"It may still be dangerous. The *Tatler* is nice about them, but other papers may take a different line."

"Maud has been attacked by the press before now. She's pretty tough."

Rosa looked abashed. "I suppose this is what you were talking about that night I saw you tête-à-tête with her."

"Exactly. She was asking me if I had heard any news about Walter."

"I feel foolish for suspecting you of flirting."

"I forgive you, but reserve the right to recall the matter next time you criticize me unreasonably. Can I ask you something?"

"Anything you like, Gus."

"Three questions, in fact."

"How ominous. Like a folktale. If I get the answers wrong, will I be banished?"

"Are you still an anarchist?"

"Would it bother you?"

"I guess I'm asking myself if politics might divide us."

"Anarchism is the belief that no one has the right to rule. All political philosophies, from the divine right of kings to Rousseau's social contract, try to justify authority. Anarchists believe that all those theories fail, therefore no form of authority is legitimate."

"Irrefutable, in theory. Impossible to put into practice."

"You're quick on the uptake. In effect, all anarchists are anti-establishment, but they differ widely in their vision of how society should work."

"And what is your vision?"

"I don't see it as clearly as I used to. Covering the White House has given me a different slant on politics. But I still believe that authority needs to justify itself."

"I don't think we'll ever quarrel about that."

"Good. Next question?"

"Tell me about your eye."

"I was born like this. I could have an operation to open it. Behind my eyelid is nothing but a mass of useless tissue, but I could wear a glass eye. However, it would never shut. I figure this is the lesser evil. Does it bother you?"

He stopped walking and turned to face her directly. "May I kiss it?"

She hesitated. "All right."

He bent down and kissed her closed eyelid. There was nothing unusual about how it felt to his lips. It was just like kissing her cheek. "Thank you," he said.

She said quietly: "No one has ever done that before."

He nodded. He had guessed it might be some kind of taboo.

She said: "Why did you want to do it?"

"Because I love everything about you, and I want to make sure you know it."

"Oh." She was silent for a minute, in the grip of emotion; but then she grinned and reverted to the flip tone she preferred. "Well, if there's anything else weird you want to kiss, just let me know."

He was not sure how to respond to that vaguely exciting offer, so he filed it away for future consideration. "I have one more question."

"Shoot."

"Four months ago, I told you that I love you."

"I haven't forgotten."

"But you haven't said how you feel about me."

"Isn't it obvious?"

"Perhaps, but I'd like you to tell me. Do you love me?"

"Oh, Gus, don't you understand?" Her face changed and she looked anguished. "I'm not good enough for you. You were the most eligible bachelor in Buffalo, and I was the one-eyed anarchist. You're supposed to love someone elegant and beautiful and rich. I'm a doctor's daughter—my mother was a housemaid. I'm not the right person for you to love."

"Do you love me?" he said with quiet persistence.

She began to cry. "Of course I do, you dope. I love you with all my heart."

He put his arms around her. "Then that's all that matters," he said.

{ V }

Aunt Herm put down the *Tatler*. "It was very bad of you to get married secretly," she said to Maud. Then she smiled conspiratorially. "But so romantic!"

They were in the drawing room of Fitz's Mayfair house. Bea had redecorated after the end of the war, in the new art deco style, with utilitarian-looking chairs and modernistic silver gewgaws from Asprey. With Maud and Herm were Fitz's roguish friend Bing Westhampton and Bing's wife. The London season was in full swing, and they were going to the opera as soon as Bea was ready. She was saying good night to Boy, now three and a half, and Andrew, eighteen months.

Maud picked up the magazine and looked again at the article. The picture did not greatly please her. She had imagined that it would show two people in love. Unfortunately it looked like a scene from a moving picture show. Walter appeared predatory, holding her hand and gazing into her eyes like a wicked Lothario, and she seemed like the ingénue about to fall for his wiles.

However, the text was just what she had hoped for. The writer reminded readers that Lady Maud had been "the fashionable suffragette" before the war, she had started *The Soldier's Wife* newspaper to campaign for the rights of the women left at home, and she had gone to jail for her protest on behalf of Jayne McCulley. It said that she and Walter had intended to announce their engagement in the normal way, and had been prevented by the outbreak of war. Their hasty secret marriage was portrayed as a desperate attempt to do the right thing in abnormal circumstances.

Maud had insisted on being quoted exactly, and the magazine had kept its promise. "I know that some British people hate the Germans," she had said. "But I also know that Walter and many other Germans did all they could to prevent the war. Now that it is over, we must create peace and friendship between the former enemies, and I truly hope people will see our union as a symbol of the new world."

Maud had learned, in her years of political campaigning, that you could sometimes win support from a publication by giving it a good story exclusively.

Walter had returned to Berlin as planned. The Germans had been jeered by crowds as they drove to the railway station on their way home. A female secretary had been knocked out by a thrown rock. The French comment had been: "Remember what they did to Belgium." The secretary was still in the hospital. Meanwhile, the German people were angrily against signing the treaty.

Bing sat next to Maud on the sofa. For once he was not flirtatious. "I wish your brother were here to advise you about this," he said with a nod at the magazine.

Maud had written to Fitz to break the news of her marriage, and had enclosed the clipping from the *Tatler,* to show him that what she had done was being accepted by London society. She had no idea how long it would take for her letter to get to wherever Fitz was, and she did not expect a reply for months. By then it would be too late for Fitz to protest. He would just have to smile and congratulate her.

Now Maud bristled at the implication that she needed a man to tell her what to do. "What could Fitz possibly say?"

"For the foreseeable future, the life of a German wife is going to be hard."

"I don't need a man to tell me that."

"In Fitz's absence I feel a degree of responsibility."

"Please don't." Maud tried not to be offended. What advice could Bing possibly offer anyone, other than how to gamble and drink in the world's nightspots?

He lowered his voice. "I hesitate to say this, but . . . " He glanced at Aunt Herm, who took the hint and went to pour herself a little more coffee. "If you were able to say that the marriage had never been consummated, then there might be an annulment."

Maud thought of the room with the primrose-yellow curtains, and had to suppress a happy smile. "But I cannot—"

"Please don't tell me anything about it. I only want to make sure you understand your options."

Maud suppressed a growing indignation. "I know this is kindly meant, Bing—"

"There is also the possibility of divorce. There is always a way, you know, for a man to provide a wife with grounds."

Maud could no longer contain her outrage. "Please drop the subject instantly," she said in a raised voice. "I have not the slightest wish for either an annulment or a divorce. I love Walter."

Bing looked sulky. "I was just trying to say what I think Fitz, as the head of your family, might tell you if he were here." He stood up and spoke to his wife. "We'll go on, shall we? No need for all of us to be late."

A few minutes later, Bea came in wearing a new dress of pink silk. "I'm ready," she said, as if she had been waiting for them rather than the other way around. Her glance went to Maud's left hand and registered the wedding ring, but she did not comment. When Maud had told her the news her response had been carefully neutral. "I hope you will be happy," she had said without warmth. "And I hope Fitz will be able to accept the fact that you did not get his permission."

They went out and got into the car. It was the black Cadillac Fitz had bought after his blue one got stranded in France. Everything was provided by Fitz, Maud reflected: the house the three women lived in, the fabulously expensive gowns they were wearing, the car, and the box at the opera. Her bills at the Ritz in Paris had been sent to Albert Solman, Fitz's man of business here in London, and paid without question. Fitz never complained. Walter would never be able to keep her in such style, she knew. Perhaps Bing was right, and she would find it hard to do without her accustomed luxury. But she would be with the man she loved.

They reached Covent Garden at the last minute, because of Bea's tardiness. The audience had already taken their seats. The three women hurried up the red-carpeted staircase and made their way to the box. Maud suddenly remembered what she had done to Walter in this box during *Don Giovanni*. She felt embarrassed: what had possessed her to take such a risk?

Bing Westhampton was already there with his wife, and he stood up and held a chair for Bea. The auditorium was silent: the show was about to begin. People-watching was one of the attractions of the opera, and many heads turned to look as the princess took her seat. Aunt Herm sat in the second row, but Bing held a front-row seat for Maud. A murmur of comment rose from the stalls: most of the crowd would have seen the photograph and read the article in the *Tatler*. Many of them knew Maud personally: this was London society, the aristocrats and the politicians, the judges and the bishops, the successful artists and the wealthy businessmen—and their wives. Maud stood for a moment to let them get a good look at her, and see how pleased and proud she was.

That was a mistake.

The sound from the audience changed. The murmur became louder. No words could be made out, but all the same the voices took on a note of disapproval, like the change in the buzz of a fly when it encounters a closed window. Maud was taken aback. Then she heard another noise, and it sounded dreadfully like a hiss. Confused and dismayed, she sat down.

That made no difference. Everyone was staring at her now. The hissing spread through the stalls in seconds, then began in the circle, too. "I say," said Bing in feeble protest.

Maud had never encountered such hatred, even at the height of the suffragette demonstrations. There was a pain in her stomach like a cramp. She wished the music would start, but the conductor, too, was staring at her, his baton held at his side.

She tried to stare proudly back at them all, but tears came to her eyes and blurred her vision. This nightmare would not end of its own accord. She had to do something.

She stood up, and the hissing grew louder.

Tears ran down her face. Almost blind, she turned around. Knocking her chair over, she stumbled toward the door at the back of the box. Aunt Herm got up, saying: "Oh, dear, dear, dear."

Bing leaped up and opened the door. Maud went out, with Aunt Herm close behind. Bing followed them out. Behind her, Maud heard the hissing die away amid a few ripples of laughter; then, to her horror, the audience began to clap, congratulating themselves on having got rid of her; and their jeering applause followed her along the corridor, down the stairs, and out of the theater.

{ VI }

The drive from the park gate to the Palace of Versailles was a mile long. Today it was lined with hundreds of mounted French cavalrymen in blue uniforms. The summer sun glinted off their steel helmets. They held lances with red and white pennants that rippled in the warm breeze.

Johnny Remarc had been able to get Maud an invitation to the signing of the peace treaty, despite her disgrace at the opera; but she had to travel on the back of an open lorry, packed in with all the female secretaries from the British delegation, like sheep going to market.

At one moment it had looked as if the Germans would refuse to sign. The war hero Field Marshal von Hindenburg had said he would prefer honorable defeat to a disgraceful peace. The entire German cabinet had resigned rather than agree to the treaty. So had the head of their delegation to Paris. At last the National Assembly had voted for signing everything except the notorious war guilt clause. Even that was unacceptable, the Allies had said immediately.

"What will the Allies do if the Germans refuse?" Maud had said to Walter in their auberge, where they were now discreetly living together.

"They say they will invade Germany."

Maud shook her head. "Our soldiers would not fight."

"Nor would ours."

"So it would be a stalemate."

"Except that the British navy has not lifted the blockade, so Germany still cannot get supplies. The Allies would just wait until food riots broke out in every German city. Then they would walk in unopposed."

"So you have to sign."

"Sign or starve," said Walter bitterly.

Today was June 28, five years to the day since the archduke had been killed in Sarajevo.

The lorry took the secretaries into the courtyard, and they got down as gracefully as they could. Maud entered the palace and went up the grand staircase, flanked by more overdressed French soldiers, this time the Garde Républicaine in silver helmets with horsehair plumes.

Finally she entered the Hall of Mirrors. This was one of the most grandiose rooms in the world. It was the size of three tennis courts in a line. Along one side, seventeen long windows overlooked the garden; on the opposite wall, the windows were reflected by seventeen mirrored arches. More important, this was the room where in 1871, at the end of the Franco-Prussian War, the victorious Germans had crowned their first emperor and forced the French to sign away Alsace and Lorraine. Now the Germans were to be humiliated under the same barrel-vaulted ceiling. And no doubt some among them would be dreaming of the time in the future when they in turn would take their revenge. The degradation to which you subject others comes back, sooner or later, to haunt you, Maud thought. Would that reflection occur to men on either side at today's ceremony? Probably not.

She found her place on one of the red plush benches. There were dozens of reporters and photographers, and a film crew with huge movie cameras to record the event. The bigwigs entered in ones and twos and sat at a long table: Clemenceau relaxed and irreverent, Wilson stiffly formal, Lloyd George like an aging bantam cock. Gus Dewar appeared and spoke in Wilson's ear, then went over to the press section and spoke to a pretty young reporter with one eye. Maud remembered seeing her before. Gus was in love with her, Maud could tell.

At three o'clock someone called for silence, and a reverent hush fell. Clemenceau said something, a door opened, and the two German signatories came in. Maud knew from Walter that no one in Berlin had wanted to put his name to the treaty, and in the end they had sent the foreign minister and the postal minister. The two men looked pale and ashamed.

Clemenceau made a short speech, then beckoned the Germans forward. Both men took fountain pens from their pockets and signed the paper on the table. A moment later, at a hidden signal, guns boomed outside, telling the world that the peace treaty had been signed.

The other delegates came up to sign, not just from the major powers but from all the countries who were party to the treaty. It took a long time, and conversation broke out among the spectators. The Germans sat stiffly frozen until at last it was over and they were escorted out.

Maud was sick with disgust. We preached a sermon of peace, she thought, but all the time we were plotting revenge. She left the palace. Outside, Wilson and Lloyd George were being mobbed by rejoicing spectators. She skirted the crowd, made her way into the town, and went to the Germans' hotel.

She hoped Walter was not too cast down: it had been a dreadful day for him.

She found him packing. "We're going home tonight," he said. "The whole delegation."

"So soon!" She had hardly thought about what would happen after the signing. It was an event of such huge dramatic significance that she had been unable to look beyond it.

By contrast, Walter had thought about it, and he had a plan. "Come with me," he said simply.

"I can't get permission to go to Germany."

"Whose permission do you need? I've got you a German passport in the name of Frau Maud von Ulrich."

She felt bewildered. "How did you manage that?" she said, though that was hardly the most important question in her mind.

"It was not difficult. You are the wife of a German citizen. You are entitled to a passport. I used my special influence only to shorten the process to a matter of hours."

She stared at him. It was so sudden.

"Will you come?" he said.

She saw in his eyes a terrible fear. He thought she might back out at the last minute. His terror of losing her made her want to cry. She felt very fortunate to be loved so passionately. "Yes," she said. "Yes, I will come. Of course I will come."

He was not convinced. "Are you sure this is what you want?"

She nodded. "Do you remember the story of Ruth, in the Bible?"

"Of course. Why . . . ?"

Maud had read it several times in the last few weeks, and now she quoted the words that had so moved her. "'Whither thou goest I will go, and where thou lodgest I will lodge; thy people shall be my people, and thy God my God; where thou diest . . .'" She stopped, unable to speak for the constriction in her throat; then, after a moment, she swallowed hard and resumed. "'Where thou diest will I die, and there will I be buried.'"

He smiled, but there were tears in his eyes. "Thank you," he said.

"I love you," she said. "What time is the train?"

CHAPTER THIRTY-EIGHT

August to October 1919

us and Rosa returned to Washington at the same time as the president. In August they contrived to get simultaneous leave and went home to Buffalo. The day after they arrived, Gus brought Rosa to meet his parents.

He was nervous. He desperately wanted his mother to like Rosa. But Mother had an inflated opinion of how attractive her son was to women. She had found fault with every girl he had ever mentioned. No one was good enough, especially socially. If he wanted to marry the daughter of the king of England, she would probably say: "Can't you find a nice well-bred American girl?"

"The first thing you'll notice about her, Mother, is that she's very pretty," Gus said at breakfast that morning. "Second, you'll see that she has only one eye. After a few minutes, you'll realize that she's very smart. And when you get to know her well, you'll understand that she's the most wonderful young woman in the world."

"I'm sure I shall," said his mother with her accustomed breathtaking insincerity. "Who are her parents?"

Rosa arrived at midafternoon, when Mother was taking her nap and Father was still downtown. Gus showed her around the house and grounds. She said nervously: "You do know that I come from a more modest background?"

"You'll get used to it soon enough," he said. "Anyway, you and I won't be living in this kind of splendor. But we might buy an elegant small house in Washington."

They played tennis. It was an uneven match: Gus with his long arms and legs was too good for her, and her judgment of distance was erratic. But she fought back determinedly, going for every ball, and won a few games. And in a white tennis dress with the fashionable midcalf hemline she looked so sexy that Gus had to make a major effort of will to concentrate on his shots.

They went in for tea in a glow of perspiration. "Summon up your reserves of tolerance and goodwill," Gus said outside the drawing room. "Mother can be an awful snob."

But Mother was on her best behavior. She kissed Rosa on both cheeks and said: "How wonderfully healthy you both look, all flushed with exercise. Miss Hellman, I'm so glad to meet you, and I hope we're going to become friends."

"You're very kind," said Rosa. "It would be a privilege to be your friend."

Mother was pleased by the compliment. She knew she was a grand dame of Buffalo society, and she felt it was appropriate that young women should show her deference. Rosa had divined that in an instant. Clever girl, Gus thought. And generous, too, given that in her heart she hated all authority.

"I know Fritz Hellman, your brother," Mother said. Fritz played violin in the Buffalo Symphony Orchestra. Mother was on the board. "He has a wonderful talent."

"Thank you. We are very proud of him."

Mother made small talk, and Rosa let her take the lead. Gus could not help remembering that once before he had brought home a girl he planned to marry: Olga Vyalov. Mother's reaction then had been different: she had been courteous and welcoming, but Gus had known her heart was not in it. Today she seemed genuine.

He had asked his mother about the Vyalov family yesterday. Lev Peshkov had been sent to Siberia as an army interpreter. Olga did not go to many social events, and seemed taken up with raising their child. Josef had lobbied Gus's father, the senator, for more military aid to the Whites. "He seems to think the Bolsheviks will be bad for the Vyalov family business in Petrograd," Mother had said.

"That's the best thing I've heard about the Bolsheviks," Gus had replied.

After tea they went off to change. Gus was disturbed by the thought of Rosa showering in the next room. He had never seen her naked. They had spent passionate hours together in her Paris hotel room, but they had not gone as far as sexual intercourse. "I hate to be old-fashioned," she had said apologetically, "but somehow I feel we should wait." She was not much of an anarchist really.

Her parents were coming for dinner. Gus put on a short tuxedo jacket and went downstairs. He mixed a Scotch for his father but did not have one himself. He felt he might need his wits about him.

Rosa came down in a black dress and looked stunning. Her parents appeared on the dot of six o'clock. Norman Hellman was wearing white tie and tails, not quite right for a family dinner, but perhaps he did not own a tuxedo. He was an elf of a man with a charming grin, and Gus saw immediately that Rosa took after him. He drank two martinis rather quickly, the only sign that he might be tense, but then he refused any more alcohol. Rosa's mother, Hilda, was a slender beauty with lovely long-fingered hands. It was hard to imagine her as a housemaid. Gus's father took to her immediately.

As they sat down to eat, Dr. Hellman said: "What are your career plans, Gus?"

He was entitled to ask this, as the father of the woman Gus loved, but Gus did not have much of an answer. "I'll work for the president as long as he needs me," he said.

"He's got a tough job on his hands right now."

"That's true. The Senate is making trouble about approving the Versailles peace treaty." Gus tried not to sound too bitter. "After all Wilson did to persuade the Europeans to set up the League of Nations, I can hardly believe that Americans are turning up their noses at the whole idea."

"Senator Lodge is a formidable troublemaker."

Gus thought Senator Lodge was an egocentric son of a bitch. "The president decided not to take Lodge with him to Paris, and now Lodge is getting his revenge."

Gus's father, who was an old friend of the president as well as a senator, said: "Woodrow made the League of Nations part of the peace treaty, thinking we could not possibly reject the treaty, therefore we would have to accept the league." He shrugged. "Lodge told him to go to blazes."

Dr. Hellman said: "In fairness to Lodge, I think the American people are right to be concerned about article ten. If we join a league that guarantees to protect its members from aggression, we're committing American forces to unknown conflicts in the future."

Gus's reply was quick. "If the league is strong, no one will dare to defy it."

"I'm not as confident as you about that."

Gus did not want to have an argument with Rosa's father, but he felt passionately about the League of Nations. "I don't say there would never be another war," he said in a conciliatory tone. "I do think that wars would be fewer and shorter, and aggressors would gain little reward."

"And I believe you may be right. But many voters say: 'Never mind the world—I'm interested only in America. Are we in danger of becoming the world's policeman?' It's a reasonable question."

Gus struggled to hide his anger. The league was the greatest hope for peace that had ever been offered to humankind, and it was in danger of being stillborn because of this kind of narrow-minded quibble. He said: "The council of the league has to make unanimous decisions, so the United States would never find itself fighting a war against its will."

"Nevertheless, there's no point in having the league unless it is prepared to fight."

The enemies of the league were like this: first they complained that it would fight; then they complained it would not. Gus said: "These problems are minor by comparison with the deaths of millions!"

Dr. Hellman shrugged, too polite to press his point against such a passionate opponent. "In any case," he said, "I believe a foreign treaty requires the support of two-thirds of the Senate."

"And right now we don't even have half," said Gus gloomily.

Rosa, who was reporting on this issue, said: "I count forty in favor, including you, Senator Dewar. Forty-three have reservations, eight are implacably against, and five undecided."

Her father said to Gus: "So what will the president do?"

"He's going to reach out to the people over the heads of the politicians. He's planning a ten-thousand-mile tour of the entire country. He'll make more than fifty speeches in four weeks."

"A punishing schedule. He's sixty-two and has high blood pressure."

There was a touch of mischief in Dr. Hellman. Everything he said was challenging. Obviously he felt the need to test the mettle of a suitor for his daughter. Gus replied: "But at the end of it, the president will have explained to the people of America that the world needs the League of Nations to make sure we never fight another war like the one just ended."

"I pray you're right."

"If political complexities need to be explained to ordinary people, Wilson is the best."

Champagne was served with dessert. "Before we begin, I'd like to say something," Gus said. His parents looked startled: he never made speeches. "Dr. and Mrs. Hellman, you know that I love your daughter, who is the most wonderful girl in the world. It's old-fashioned, but I want to ask your permission"—he took from his pocket a small red leather box—"your permission to offer her this engagement ring." He opened the box. It contained a gold ring with a single one-carat diamond. It was not ostentatious, but the diamond was pure white, the most desirable color, in a round brilliant cut, and it looked fabulous.

Rosa gasped.

Dr. Hellman looked at his wife, and they both smiled. "You most certainly have our permission," he said.

Gus walked around the table and knelt beside Rosa's chair. "Will you marry me, dear Rosa?" he said.

"Oh, yes, my beloved Gus—tomorrow, if you like!"

He took the ring from the box and slid it onto her finger. "Thank you," he said.

His mother began to cry.

{ II }

Gus was aboard the president's train as it steamed out of Union Station in Washington, D.C., at seven o'clock in the evening on Wednesday, September 3. Wilson was dressed in a blue blazer, white pants, and a straw boater. His wife, Edith, went with him, as did Cary Travers Grayson, his personal physician. Also aboard were twenty-one newspaper reporters including Rosa Hellman.

Gus was confident Wilson could win this battle. He had always enjoyed the direct connection with voters. And he had won the war, hadn't he?

The train traveled overnight to Columbus, Ohio, where the president made his first speech of the tour. From there he went on—making whistle-stop appearances along the way—to Indianapolis, where he spoke to a crowd of twenty thousand people that evening.

But Gus was disheartened at the end of the first day. Wilson had spoken poorly. His voice was husky. He used notes—he was always better when he managed without them—and, as he got into the technicalities of the treaty that had so absorbed everyone in Paris, he seemed to ramble and lose the audience's attention. He had a bad headache, Gus knew, so bad that sometimes his vision blurred.

Gus was sick with worry. It was not just that his friend and mentor was ill. There was more at stake. America's future and the world's hung on what happened in the next few weeks. Only Wilson's personal commitment could save the League of Nations from its small-minded opponents.

After dinner Gus went to Rosa's sleeping compartment. She was the only female reporter on the trip, so she had a room to herself. She was almost as keen on the league as Gus, but she said: "It's hard to find much positive to say about today." They lay on her bunk, kissing and cuddling; then they said good night and parted. Their wedding was set for October, after the president's trip. Gus would have liked it to be even sooner, but the parents wanted time to prepare, and Gus's mother had muttered darkly about indecent haste, so he had given in.

Wilson worked on improvements to his speech, tapping on his old Underwood typewriter as the endless open plains of the Midwest sped by the windows. His performances got better over the next few days. Gus suggested he try to make the treaty relevant to each city. Wilson told business leaders in St. Louis that the treaty was needed to build up world trade. In Omaha he said the world without the treaty would be like a community with unsettled land titles, all the farmers sitting on fences with shotguns. Instead of long explanations, he rammed home the main points in short statements.

Gus also suggested that Wilson appeal to people's emotions. This was not just about policy, he said; it touched on their feelings about their country. At Columbus, Wilson spoke of the boys in khaki. In Sioux Falls, he said he wanted to redeem the sacrifices of mothers who had lost their sons on the battlefield. He rarely descended to scurrility, but in Kansas City, home of the vitriolic Senator Reed, he compared his opponents to the Bolsheviks. And he thundered out the message, again and again, that if the League of Nations failed there would be another war.

Gus smoothed relations with the reporters on board and the local men wherever the train stopped. When Wilson spoke without a prepared speech, his stenographer would produce an immediate transcript, which Gus distributed. He also persuaded Wilson to come forward to the club car now and again to chat informally with the press.

It worked. Audiences responded better and better. The press coverage continued mixed, but Wilson's message was repeated constantly even in papers that opposed him. And reports from Washington suggested that opposition was weakening.

But Gus could see how much the campaign was costing the president. His headaches became almost continuous. He slept badly. He could not digest normal food, and Dr. Grayson fed him liquids. He got a throat infection that developed into something like asthma, and he began to have trouble breathing. He tried to sleep sitting upright.

All of this was kept from the press, even Rosa. Wilson continued to give speeches, although his voice was weak. Thousands cheered him in Salt Lake City, but he looked drawn, and he clenched his hands repeatedly, in an odd gesture that made Gus think of a dying man.

Then, on the night of September 25, there was a commotion. Gus heard Edith calling for Dr. Grayson. He put on a dressing gown and went to the president's car.

What he saw there horrified and saddened him. Wilson looked dreadful. He could hardly breathe and had developed a facial twitch. Even so, he wanted to carry on; but Grayson was adamant that he call off the remainder of the tour, and in the end Wilson gave in.

Next morning Gus, with a heavy heart, told the press that the president had suffered a severe nervous attack, and the tracks were cleared to speed the 1,700-mile journey back to Washington. All presidential engagements were canceled for two weeks, notably a meeting with pro-treaty senators to plan the fight for confirmation.

That evening, Gus and Rosa sat in her compartment, disconsolately looking out of the window. People gathered at every station to watch the president go by. The sun went down, but still the crowds stood and stared in the twilight. Gus was reminded of the train from Brest to Paris, and the silent multitude that had stood beside the tracks in the middle of the night. It was less than a year ago, but already their hopes had been dashed. "We did our best," Gus said. "But we failed."

"Are you sure?"

"When the president was campaigning full-time, it was touch

and go. With Wilson sick, the chance of the treaty being ratified by the Senate is zero."

Rosa took his hand. "I'm sorry," she said. "For you, for me, for the world." She paused, then said: "What will you do?"

"I'd like to join a Washington law firm specializing in international law. I've got some relevant experience, after all."

"I should think they'll be lining up to offer you a job. And perhaps some future president will want your help."

He smiled. Sometimes she had an unrealistically high opinion of him. "And what about you?"

"I love what I'm doing. I hope I can carry on covering the White House."

"Would you like to have children?"

"Yes!"

"So would I." Gus stared meditatively out of the window. "I just hope Wilson is wrong about them."

"About our children?" She heard the note of solemnity in his tone, and she asked in a frightened voice: "What do you mean?"

"He says they will have to fight another world war."

"God forbid," Rosa said fervently.

Outside, night was falling.

CHAPTER THIRTY-NINE

January 1920

aisy sat at the table in the dining room of the Vyalov family's prairie house in Buffalo. She wore a pink dress. The large linen napkin tied around her neck swamped her. She was almost four years old, and Lev adored her.

"I'm going to make the world's biggest sandwich," he said, and she giggled. He cut two pieces of toast half an inch square, buttered them carefully, added a tiny portion of the scrambled eggs Daisy did not want to eat, and put the slices together. "It has to have one grain of salt," he said. He poured salt from the cellar onto his plate, then delicately picked up a single grain on the tip of his finger and put it on the sandwich. "Now I can eat it!" he said.

"I want it," said Daisy.

"Really? But isn't it a Daddy-size sandwich?"

"No!" she said, laughing. "It's a girl-size sandwich!"

"Oh, all right," he said, and popped it into her mouth. "You don't want another one, do you?"

"Yes."

"But that one was so big."

"No, it wasn't!"

"Okay, I guess I have to make another one."

Lev was riding high. Things were even better than he had told Grigori ten months ago when they had sat in Trotsky's train. He was living in great comfort in his father-in-law's house. He managed three Vyalov nightclubs, getting a good salary plus extras such as kickbacks from suppliers. He had installed Marga in a fancy apartment and he saw her most days. She had got pregnant within a week of his return, and she had just given birth to a boy, whom they had named Gregory. Lev had succeeded in keeping the whole thing secret.

Olga came into the dining room, kissed Daisy, and sat down. Lev loved Daisy, but he had no feelings for Olga. Marga was sexier and more fun. And there were plenty more girls, as he had found out when Marga was heavily pregnant.

"Good morning, Mommy!" Lev said gaily.

Daisy took her cue and repeated his words.

Olga said: "Is Daddy feeding you?"

These days they talked like this, mainly through the child. They had had sex a few times when Lev got back from the war, but they had soon reverted to their normal indifference, and now they had separate bedrooms, telling Olga's parents it was because of Daisy waking at night, though she rarely did. Olga wore the look of a disappointed woman, and Lev hardly cared.

Josef came in. "Here's Grandpa!" Lev said.

"Morning," Josef said curtly.

Daisy said: "Grandpa wants a sandwich."

"No," said Lev. "They're too big for him."

Daisy was delighted when Lev said things that were obviously wrong. "No, they're not," she said. "They're too small!"

Josef sat down. He had changed a lot, Lev had found on returning from the war. Josef was overweight, and his striped suit was tight. He panted just from the exertion of walking downstairs. Muscle had turned to fat, black hair had gone gray, a pink complexion had become an unhealthy flush.

Polina came in from the kitchen with a pot of coffee and poured a cup for Josef. He opened the *Buffalo Advertiser.*

Lev said: "How's business?" It was not an idle question. The Volstead Act had come into force at midnight on January 16, making it illegal to manufacture, transport, or sell intoxicating liquor. The Vyalov empire was based on bars, hotels, and liquor wholesaling. Prohibition was the serpent in Lev's paradise.

"We're dying," said Josef with unusual frankness. "I've closed five bars in a week, and there's worse to come."

Lev nodded. "I'm selling near-beer in the clubs, but nobody wants it." The act permitted beer that was less than half of one percent alcohol. "You have to drink a gallon to get a buzz."

"We can sell a little hooch under the counter, but we can't get enough, and anyway people are scared to buy."

Olga was shocked. She knew little about the business. "But, Daddy, what are you going to do?"

"I don't know," said Josef.

This was another change. In the old days, Josef would have planned ahead for such a crisis. Yet it was three months since the act had been passed, and in that time Josef had done nothing to prepare for the new situation. Lev had been waiting for him to pull a rabbit out of a hat. Now he began to see, with dismay, that it was not going to happen.

That was worrying. Lev had a wife, a mistress, and two children, all living off the proceeds of the Vyalov businesses. If the empire was going to collapse, Lev would need to make plans.

Polina called Olga to the phone and she went into the hallway. Lev could hear her speaking. "Hello, Ruby," she said. "You're up early." There was a pause. "What? I don't believe it." A long silence followed; then Olga began to cry.

Josef looked up from the newspaper and said: "What the hell . . . ?"

Olga hung up with a crash and came back into the dining room. With her eyes full of tears she pointed at Lev and said: "You bastard."

"What did I do?" he said, although he feared he knew.

"You—you—*fucking* bastard."

Daisy began to bawl.

Josef said: "Olga, honey, what is the matter?"

Olga answered: "She's had a baby!"

Under his breath, Lev said: "Oh, shit."

Josef said: "Who's had a baby?"

"Lev's whore. The one we saw in the park. Marga."

Josef reddened. "The singer from the Monte Carlo? She's had *Lev's* baby?"

Olga nodded, sobbing.

Josef turned to Lev. "You son of a bitch."

Lev said: "Let's all try to stay calm."

Josef stood up. "My God, I thought I'd taught you a damned lesson."

Lev pushed back his chair and got to his feet. He backed away from Josef, holding his arms out defensively. "Just calm the fuck down, Josef," he said.

"Don't you dare tell me to calm down," Josef said. With surprising agility he stepped forward and lashed out with a meaty fist. Lev was not quick enough to dodge the blow and it struck him high on his left cheekbone. It hurt like hell and he staggered back.

Olga snatched up the howling Daisy and retreated to the doorway. "Stop it!" she yelled.

Josef lashed out with his left.

It was a long time since Lev had been in a fistfight, but he had grown up in the slums of Petrograd, and the reflexes still operated. He blocked Josef's swing, moved in close, and punched his father-in-law's belly with both fists in turn. The breath whooshed out of Josef's chest. Then Lev struck at Josef's face with short jabs, hitting the nose and mouth and eyes.

Josef was a strong man and a bully, but people were too scared of him to fight back, and for a long time he had had no practice at defending himself. He staggered back, holding up his arms in a feeble attempt to protect himself from Lev's blows.

Lev's street-fighting instincts would not let him stop while his assailant was upright, and he kept after Josef, punching his body and head, until the older man fell backward over a dining chair and hit the carpet.

Olga's mother, Lena, came rushing into the room, screamed, and knelt beside her husband. Polina and the cook came to the doorway to the kitchen, looking scared. Josef's face was battered and bleeding, but he raised himself on his elbow and pushed Lena aside. Then, when he tried to get up, he cried out and fell back.

His skin turned gray and he stopped breathing.

Lev said: "Jesus Christ."

Lena started to wail: "Josef, oh, my Joe, open your eyes!"

Lev felt Josef's chest. There was no heartbeat. He picked up the wrist and could not find a pulse.

I'm in trouble now, he thought.

He stood up. "Polina, call an ambulance."

She went into the hall and picked up the phone.

Lev stared at the body. He had to make a big decision fast. Stay here, protest innocence, pretend grief, try to wriggle out of it? No. The chances were too slim.

He had to go.

He ran upstairs and stripped off his shirt. He had come home from the war with a lot of gold, accumulated by selling Scotch to the Cossacks. He had converted it to just more than five thousand U.S. dollars, stuffed the bills into his money belt, and taped the belt to the back of a drawer. Now he fastened the belt around his waist and put his shirt and jacket back on.

He put on his overcoat. On top of his wardrobe was an old duffel containing his U.S. Army officer's-issue Colt .45 model 1911 semiautomatic pistol. He stuffed the pistol into his coat pocket. He threw a box of ammunition and some underwear into the duffel; then he went downstairs.

In the dining room, Lena had put a cushion under Josef's head, but Josef looked deader than ever. Olga was on the phone in the hallway, saying: "Be quick, please, I think he may die!" Too late, baby, Lev thought.

He said: "The ambulance will take too long. I'm going to fetch Dr. Schwarz." No one asked why he was carrying a bag.

He went to the garage and started Josef's Packard Twin Six. He drove out of the property and turned north.

He was not going to fetch Dr. Schwarz.

He headed for Canada.

{ II }

Lev drove fast. As he left Buffalo's northern suburbs behind, he tried to figure out how much time he had. The ambulance crew would undoubtedly call the police. As soon as the cops arrived they would find out that Josef had died in a fistfight. Olga would not hesitate to tell them who had knocked her father down: if she had not hated Lev before, she would now. At that point, Lev would be wanted for murder.

There were normally three cars in the Vyalov garage: the Packard, Lev's Ford Model T, and a blue Hudson used by Josef's goons. It would not take the flatfoots very long to deduce that Lev had left in the Packard. In an hour, Lev calculated, the police would be looking for the car.

By then, with luck, he would be out of the country.

He had driven to Canada with Marga several times. It was only a hundred miles to Toronto, three hours in a fast car. They liked to check into a hotel as Mr. and Mrs. Peters and go out on the town, dressed to the nines, without having to worry about being spotted by someone who might tell Josef Vyalov. Lev did not have an American passport, but he knew several crossings where there were no border posts.

He reached Toronto at midday and checked into a quiet hotel.

He ordered a sandwich in the coffee shop and sat for a while contemplating his situation. He was wanted for murder. He had no home and he could not visit either of his two families without risking arrest. He might never see his children again. He had five thousand dollars in a money belt and a stolen car.

He thought back to the boasts he had made to his brother only ten months ago. What would Grigori think now?

He ate his sandwich, then wandered aimlessly around the center of town feeling depressed. He went into a liquor store and bought a bottle of vodka to take back to his room. Maybe he would just get drunk tonight. He noticed that rye whisky was four bucks a bottle. In Buffalo it cost ten, if you could get it at all; in New York City, fifteen or twenty. He knew because he had been trying to buy illicit liquor for the nightclubs.

He returned to the hotel and got some ice. His room was dusty, with faded furniture and a view of the backyards behind a row of cheap stores. As the early northern night fell outside, he felt more depressed than ever in his whole life. He thought of going out and picking up a girl, but he did not have the heart for it. Was he going to flee from every place he ever lived? He had quit Petrograd because of a dead policeman, and he had left Aberowen literally one step ahead of people he had cheated at cards; now he had fled Buffalo a fugitive.

He needed to do something about the Packard. The Buffalo police might cable a description to Toronto. He should either change the plates or change the car. But he could not summon the energy.

Olga was probably glad to get rid of him. She would have her inheritance all to herself. However, the Vyalov empire was worth less and less every day.

He wondered if he could bring Marga and baby Gregory to Canada. Would Marga even want to come? America was her dream, as it had been Lev's. Canada was not the fantasy destination of nightclub singers. She might follow Lev to New York or California, but not to Toronto.

He was going to miss his children. Tears came to his eyes as he thought of Daisy growing up without him. She was not quite four: she might forget him altogether. At best she would have a vague recollection. She would not remember the largest sandwich in the world.

After the third drink it struck him that he was a pitiable victim of injustice. He had not meant to kill his father-in-law. Josef had struck first. Anyway, Lev had not actually killed him: he had died of some kind of seizure or heart attack. It was really just bad luck. But no one was going to believe that. Olga was the only witness and she would want revenge.

He poured another vodka and lay on the bed. To hell with them all, he thought.

As he drifted into a restless alcoholic sleep, he thought of the bottles in the shop window. "Canadian Club, $4.00," read the sign. There was something important about that, he knew, but for the moment he could not put his finger on it.

When he woke up next morning his mouth was dry and his head ached, but he knew that Canadian Club at four bucks a bottle could be his salvation.

He rinsed his whisky glass and drank the melted ice at the bottom of the pail. By his third glassful he had a plan.

Orange juice, coffee, and aspirins made him feel better. He thought about the dangers ahead. But he had never allowed himself to be deterred by risks. If I did that, he thought, I'd be my brother.

There was one great drawback to his scheme. It depended on reconciliation with Olga.

He drove to a low-rent neighborhood and went into a cheap restaurant that was serving breakfast to workingmen. He sat at a table with a group of what looked like housepainters and said: "I need to trade my car for a truck. Do you know anyone who might be interested?"

One of the men said: "Is it legitimate?"

Lev gave his charming grin. "Give me a break, buddy," he said. "If it was legit, would I be selling it here?"

He found no takers there or at the next few places he tried, but eventually he ended up at an automobile repair shop run by a father and son. He exchanged the Packard for a two-ton Mack Junior van with two spare wheels in a no-cash, no-papers deal. He knew he was being robbed, but the garageman knew he was desperate.

Late that afternoon he went to a liquor wholesaler whose address he had found in the city directory. "I want a hundred cases of Canadian Club," he said. "What's your price?"

"For that quantity, thirty-six bucks a case."

"It's a deal." Lev took out his money. "I'm opening a tavern outside of town, and—"

"No need to explain, pal," said the wholesaler. He pointed out of the window. On the neighboring vacant lot, a team of building laborers were breaking ground. "My new warehouse, five times the size of this one. Thank God for Prohibition."

Lev realized he was not the first person to have this bright idea.

He paid the man and they loaded the whisky into the Mack van.

Next day Lev drove back to Buffalo.

{ III }

Lev parked the van full of whisky on the street outside the Vyalov house. The winter afternoon was turning to dusk. There were no cars on the driveway. He waited a while, tense, expectant, ready to flee, but he saw no activity.

His nerves stretched taut, he got out of the van, walked up to the front door, and let himself in with his own key.

The place was hushed. From upstairs he could hear Daisy's voice, and the murmured replies of Polina. There was no other sound.

Moving quietly on the thick carpet, he crossed the hall and looked into the drawing room. All the chairs had been pushed to the sides of the room. In the middle was a stand draped in black silk bearing a polished mahogany coffin with gleaming brass handles. In the casket was the corpse of Josef Vyalov. Death had softened the pugnacious lines of the face, and he looked harmless.

Olga sat alone beside the body. She wore a black dress. Her back was to the door.

Lev stepped into the room. "Hello, Olga," he said quietly.

She opened her mouth to scream, but he put his hand over her face and stopped her.

"Nothing to worry about," Lev said. "I just want to talk." Slowly, he eased his grip.

She did not scream.

He relaxed a little. He was over the first hurdle.

"You killed my father!" she said angrily. "What could there be to talk about?"

He took a deep breath. He had to handle this exactly right. Mere charm would not be enough. It would take brains too. "The future," he said. He spoke in a low, intimate tone. "Yours, mine, and little Daisy's. I'm in trouble, I know—but so are you."

She did not want to listen. "I'm not in any trouble." She turned away and looked at the body.

Lev pulled up a chair and sat close to her. "The business you've inherited is shot. It's falling apart, almost worthless."

"My father was very wealthy!" she said indignantly.

"He owned bars, hotels, and a liquor wholesaling business. They're all losing money, and Prohibition has been in force only two weeks. He's already closed five bars. Soon there will be nothing left." Lev hesitated, then used the strongest argument he had. "You can't just consider yourself. You have to think about how you're going to raise Daisy."

She looked shaken. "Is the business really going bust?"

"You heard what your father said to me at breakfast the day before yesterday."

"I don't really remember."

"Well, don't take my word for anything, please. Check it out. Ask Norman Niall, the accountant. Ask anyone."

She gave him a hard look and decided to take him seriously. "Why have you come to tell me this?"

"Because I've figured out how to save the business."

"How?"

"By importing liquor from Canada."

"It's against the law."

"Yes. But it's your only hope. Without booze, you have no business."

She tossed her head. "I can look after myself."

"Sure," he said. "You can sell this house for a good sum, invest the proceeds, and move into a little apartment with your mother. Probably you could salvage enough from the estate to keep yourself and Daisy alive for a few years, though you should consider going out to work—"

"I can't work!" she said. "I've never trained for anything. What would I do?"

"Oh, listen, you could be a salesgirl in a department store. You could work in a factory—"

He was not serious and she knew it. "Don't be ridiculous," she snapped.

"Then there's only one option." He reached out to touch her.

She flinched away. "Why do you care what happens to me?"

"You're my wife."

She gave him a strange look.

He put on his most sincere face. "I know I've mistreated you, but we loved each other once."

She made a scornful noise in her throat.

"And we have a daughter to worry about."

"But you're going to jail."

"Unless you tell the truth."

"What do you mean?"

"Olga, you saw what happened. Your father attacked me. Look at my face—I have a black eye to prove it. I had to fight back. He must have had a weak heart. He may have been ill for some time—it would explain why he failed to prepare the business for Prohibition. Anyway, he was killed by the effort of attacking me, not by the few blows I struck in self-defense. All you have to do is tell the police the truth."

"I've already told them you killed him."

Lev was heartened: he was making progress. "That's all right," he reassured her. "You made a statement in the heat of the moment when you were stricken with grief. Now that you're calmer, you realize that your father's death was a terrible accident, brought on by his bad health and his angry tantrum."

"Will they believe me?"

"A jury will. But if I hire a good lawyer there won't even be a trial. How could there be, if the only witness swears it wasn't murder?"

"I don't know." She changed tack. "How are you going to get the liquor?"

"Easy. Don't worry about it."

She turned in her chair to face him directly. "I don't believe you. You're saying all this just to make me change my story."

"Put your coat on and I'll show you something."

It was a tense moment. If she went with him, she was his.

After a pause, she stood up.

Lev hid a triumphant smile.

They left the room. Outside on the street, he opened the rear doors of the van.

She was silent for a long moment. Then she said: "Canadian Club?" Her tone had changed, he noted. It was practical. The emotion had faded into the background.

"A hundred cases," he said. "I bought it for three bucks a bottle. I can get ten here—more if we sell it by the shot."

"I have to think about this."

That was a good sign. She was ready to agree, but did not want to rush into anything. "I understand, but there's no time," he said. "I'm a wanted man with a truckload of illegal whisky and I have to have your decision right away. I'm sorry to hustle you, but you can see I have no choice."

She nodded thoughtfully, but did not say anything.

Lev went on: "If you turn me down I'll sell my booze, take a profit, and disappear. You'll be on your own, then. I'll wish you luck and say good-bye forever, with no hard feelings. I would understand."

"And if I say yes?"

"We'll go to the police right away."

There was a long silence.

At last she nodded. "All right."

Lev looked away to hide his face. You did it, he said to himself. You sat with her in the same room as her father's dead body, and you won her back.

You dog.

{ IV }

"I have to put on a hat," said Olga. "And you need a clean shirt. We want to make a favorable impression."

That was good. She was really on his side.

They went back into the house and got ready. While he was waiting for her he called the *Buffalo Advertiser* and asked for Peter Hoyle, the editor. A secretary asked him his business. "Tell him I'm the man who's wanted for the murder of Josef Vyalov."

A moment later a voice barked. "Hoyle here. Who are you?"

"Lev Peshkov, Vyalov's son-in-law."

"Where are you?"

Lev ignored the question. "If you can have a reporter on the steps of police headquarters in half an hour, I'll have a statement for you."

"We'll be there."

"Mr. Hoyle?"

"Yes?"

"Send a photographer, too." Lev hung up.

With Olga beside him in the open front of the van, he drove first to Josef's waterfront warehouse. Boxes of stolen cigarettes were stacked around the walls. In the office at the back they found Vyalov's accountant, Norman Niall, plus the usual group of thugs. Norman was crooked but persnickety, Lev knew. He was sitting in Josef's chair, behind Josef's desk.

They were all astonished to see Lev and Olga.

Lev said: "Olga has inherited the business. I'll be running things from now on."

Norman did not get up out of his chair. "We'll see about that," he said.

Lev gave him a hard stare and said nothing.

Norman spoke again with less assurance. "The will has to be proved, and so on."

Lev shook his head. "If we wait for the formalities there will be no business left." He pointed at one of the goons. "Ilya, go out in the yard, look in the van, come back here, and tell Norm what you see."

Ilya went out. Lev moved around the desk to stand next to Norman. They waited in silence until Ilya came back.

"A hundred cases of Canadian Club." He put a bottle on the table. "We can try it, see if it's the real thing."

Lev said: "I'm going to run the business with booze imported from Canada. Prohibition is the greatest business opportunity ever. People will pay anything for liquor. We're going to make a fortune. Get out of that chair, Norm."

"I don't think so, kid," said Norman.

Lev pulled his gun fast and pistol-whipped Norman on both sides of the face. Norman cried out. Lev held the Colt casually pointed in the direction of the thugs.

To her credit, Olga did not scream.

"You asshole," Lev said to Norman. "I killed Josef Vyalov—do you think I'm scared of a fucking accountant?"

Norman got up and scurried out of the room, holding a hand to his bleeding mouth.

Lev turned to the other men, still holding the pistol pointing in their general direction, and said: "Anyone else who doesn't want to work for me can leave now, and no hard feelings."

No one moved.

"Good," said Lev. "Because I was lying about no hard feelings." He pointed at Ilya. "You come with me and Mrs. Peshkov. You can drive. The rest of you, unload the van."

Ilya drove them downtown in the blue Hudson.

Lev felt he might have made a mistake back there. He should not have said *I killed Josef Vyalov* in front of Olga. She could yet change her mind. If she mentioned it, he decided he would say he didn't mean it, but just said it to scare Norm. However, Olga did not raise the matter.

Outside police headquarters, two men in overcoats and hats were waiting beside a big camera on a tripod.

Lev and Olga got out of the car.

Lev said to the reporter: "The death of Josef Vyalov is a tragedy for us, his family, and for this city." The man scribbled shorthand in a notebook. "I have come to give the police my account of what happened. My wife, Olga, the only other person present when he collapsed, is here to testify that I am innocent. The postmortem will show that my father-in-law died of a heart attack. My wife and I plan to continue to expand the great business Josef Vyalov started here in Buffalo. Thank you."

"Look at the camera, please?" said the photographer.

Lev put his arm around Olga, pulled her close, and looked at the camera.

The reporter said: "How did you get the shiner, Lev?"

"This?" he said, and pointed to his eye. "Oh, hell, that's another story." He smiled his most charming grin, and the photographer's magnesium flare went off with a blinding flash.

CHAPTER FORTY

February to December 1920

The Aldershot Military Detention Barracks was a grim place, Billy thought, but it was better than Siberia. Aldershot was an army town thirty-five miles southwest of London. The prison was a modern building with galleries of cells on three floors around an atrium. It was brightly lit by a glazed roof that gave the place its nickname of "the Glasshouse." With heat pipes and gas lighting, it was more comfortable than most of the places where Billy had slept during the past four years.

All the same, he was miserable. The war had been over for more than a year, yet he was still in the army. Most of his friends were out, earning good wages and taking girls to the pictures. He still wore the uniform and saluted, he slept in an army bed, and he ate army food. He worked all day at weaving mats, which was the prison industry. Worst of all, he never saw a woman. Somewhere out there, Mildred was waiting for him—probably. Everyone had a tale to tell of a soldier who had come home to find that his wife or girlfriend had gone off with another man.

He had no communication with Mildred or anyone else outside.

Prisoners—or "soldiers under sentence" as they were officially called— could normally send and receive letters, but Billy was a special case. Because he had been convicted of betraying army secrets in letters, his mail was confiscated by the authorities. This was part of the army's revenge. He no longer had any secrets to betray, of course. What was he going to tell his sister? "The boiled potatoes are always undercooked."

Did Mam and Da and Gramper even know about the court-martial? The soldier's next of kin had to be informed, he thought, but he was not sure and no one would answer his questions. Anyway, Tommy Griffiths would almost certainly have told them. He hoped Ethel had explained what he had really been doing.

He received no visitors. He suspected his family did not even know that he was back from Russia. He would have liked to challenge the ban on his receiving mail, but he had no way of contacting a lawyer—and no money to pay one. His only consolation was a vague feeling that this could not go on indefinitely.

His news of the outside world came from the papers. Fitz was back in London, making speeches urging more military aid for the Whites in Russia. Billy wondered if that meant the Aberowen Pals had come home.

Fitz's speeches were doing no good. Ethel's "Hands Off Russia" campaign had won support and been endorsed by the Labour Party. Despite colorful anti-Bolshevik speeches by the minister for war, Winston Churchill, Britain had withdrawn its troops from Arctic Russia. In mid-November the Reds had driven Admiral Kolchak out of Omsk. Everything Billy had said about the Whites, and Ethel had repeated in her campaign, turned out to be correct; everything Fitz and Churchill said was wrong. Yet Billy was in jail and Fitz was in the House of Lords.

He had little in common with his fellow inmates. They were not political prisoners. Most had committed real crimes, theft and assault and murder. They were hard men, but so was Billy and he was not afraid of them. They treated him with wary deference, apparently feeling that his offense was a cut above theirs. He talked to them amiably enough but none of them had any interest in politics. They saw nothing wrong with the society that had imprisoned them; they were just determined to beat the system next time.

During the half-hour lunch break he read the newspaper. Most of the others could not read. One day he opened the *Daily Herald* to see a photograph of a familiar face. After a moment of bewilderment he realized the picture was of him.

He recalled when it had been taken. Mildred had dragged him to a photographer in Aldgate and had him snapped in his uniform. "Every night I'll touch it to my lips," she had said. He had often thought of that ambiguous promise while he was away from her.

The headline said: WHY IS SERGEANT WILLIAMS IN JAIL? Billy read on with mounting excitement.

> William Williams of the Welsh Rifles (the "Aberowen Pals")
> 8th Battalion is serving ten years in a military prison, convicted
> of treason. Is this man a traitor? Did he betray his country, desert
> to the enemy, or run from battle? On the contrary. He fought
> bravely at the Somme and continued to serve in France for the
> next two years, winning promotion to sergeant.

Billy was excited. That's me, he thought, in the papers, and they say I fought bravely!

> Then he was sent to Russia. We are not at war with Russia.
> The British people do not necessarily approve of the Bolshevik
> regime, but we do not attack every regime of which we disapprove.
> The Bolsheviks present no threat to our country or our allies.
> Parliament has never agreed to military action against the
> government in Moscow. There is a serious question as to whether
> our mission there is not a breach of international law.
>
> Indeed, for some months the British people were not told that
> their army was fighting in Russia. The government made
> misleading statements to the effect that troops there were only

protecting our property, organizing orderly withdrawal, or on standby. The clear implication was that they were not in action against Red forces.

That this was exposed as a lie is in no small measure thanks to William Williams.

"Hey," he said to no one in particular. "Look at that. Thanks to William Williams."

The men at his table crowded around to look over his shoulder. His cellmate, a brute called Cyril Parks, said: "That's a picture of you! What are you doing in the paper?"

Billy read the rest of it aloud.

> His crime was to tell the truth, in letters to his sister that were written in a simple code to evade censorship. The British people owe him a debt of gratitude.
>
> But his action displeased those in the army and in government who were responsible for secretly using British soldiers for their own political ends. Williams was court-martialed and sentenced to ten years.
>
> He is not unique. A large number of servicemen who objected to being made part of the attempted counterrevolution were subjected to highly dubious trials in Russia and given scandalously long sentences.
>
> William Williams and others have been victimized by vengeful men in positions of power. This must be put right. Britain is a country of justice. That, after all, is what we fought for.

"How about that?" said Billy. "They say I've been victimized by powerful men."

"So have I," said Cyril Parks, who had raped a fourteen-year-old Belgian girl in a barn.

Suddenly the newspaper was snatched out of Billy's hands. He looked up to see the stupid face of Andrew Jenkins, one of the more unpleasant warders. "You may have friends in high fucking places, Williams," the man said. "But in here you're just another fucking con, so get back to fucking work."

"Right away, Mr. Jenkins," said Billy.

{ II }

Fitz was outraged, that summer of 1920, when a Russian trade delegation came to London and was welcomed by the prime minister, David Lloyd George, at number 10 Downing Street. The Bolsheviks were still at war with the newly reconstituted country of Poland, and Fitz thought Britain should be siding with the Poles, but he found little support. London dockers went on strike rather than load ships with rifles for the Polish army, and the Trades Union Congress threatened a general strike if the British army intervened.

Fitz reconciled himself to never taking possession of the late Prince Andrei's estates. His sons, Boy and Andrew, had lost their Russian birthright, and he had to accept that.

However, he could not keep quiet when he learned what the Russians Kamenev and Krassin were up to as they went around Britain. Room 40 still existed, albeit in a different form, and British intelligence was intercepting and deciphering the telegrams the Russians were sending home. Lev Kamenev, the chairman of the Moscow soviet, was shamelessly putting out revolutionary propaganda.

Fitz was so incensed that he berated Lloyd George, early in August, at one of the last dinner parties of the London season.

It was at Lord Silverman's house in Belgrave Square. The dinner was not as lavish as those Silverman had thrown before the war. There were fewer courses, with less food sent untasted back to the kitchen, and the table decoration was simpler. The food was served by maids instead of footmen: no one wanted to be a footman these days. Fitz guessed those extravagant Edwardian parties were gone for good. However, Silverman was still able to attract the most powerful men in the land to his house.

Lloyd George asked Fitz about his sister, Maud.

That was another topic that enraged Fitz. "I'm sorry to say that she has married a German and gone to live in Berlin," he said. He did not say that she had already given birth to her first child, a boy called Eric.

"I heard that," said Lloyd George. "I just wondered how she was getting on. Delightful young woman."

The prime minister's liking for delightful young women was well-known, not to say notorious.

"I'm afraid life in Germany is hard," said Fitz. Maud had written to him pleading for an allowance, but he had refused point-blank. She had not asked his permission for the marriage, so how could she expect his support?

"Hard?" said Lloyd George. "So it should be, after what they've done. All the same, I'm sorry for her."

"On another subject, Prime Minister," said Fitz, "this fellow Kamenev is a Jew Bolshevik—you ought to deport him."

The prime minister was in a mellow mood, with a glass of champagne in his hand. "My dear Fitz," he said amiably, "the government is not very worried about Russian misinformation, which is crude and violent. Please don't underestimate the British working class: they know claptrap when they hear it. Believe me, Kamenev's speeches are doing more to discredit Bolshevism than anything you or I could say."

Fitz thought this was complacent rubbish. "He's even given money to the *Daily Herald*!"

"It is discourteous, I agree, for a foreign government to subsidize one of our newspapers—but, really, are we frightened of the *Daily Herald*? It's not as if we Liberals and Conservatives don't have papers of our own."

"But he is contacting the most hard-line revolutionary groups in this country—maniacs dedicated to the overthrow of our entire way of life!"

"The more the British get to know about Bolshevism, the less they will like it, you mark my words. It is formidable only when seen at a distance, through impenetrable mists. Bolshevism is almost a safeguard to British society, for it infects all classes with a horror of what may happen if the present organization of society is overturned."

"I just don't like it."

"Besides," Lloyd George went on, "if we throw them out we may have to explain how we know what they're up to; and the news that we're spying on them may inflame working-class opinion against us more effectively than all their turgid speeches."

Fitz did not like being lectured on political realities, even by the prime minister, but he persisted with his argument because he felt so angry. "But surely we don't have to trade with the Bolsheviks!"

"If we refused to do business with all those who use their embassies here for propaganda, we wouldn't have many trading partners left. Come, come, Fitz, we trade with cannibals in the Solomon Islands!"

Fitz was not sure that was true—the cannibals of the Solomon Islands did not have much to offer, after all—but he let it pass. "Are we so badly off that we have to sell to these murderers?"

"I fear we are. I have talked to a good many businessmen, and they have rather frightened me about the next eighteen months. There are no orders coming in. Customers won't buy. We may be in for the worst period of unemployment that any of us have ever known. But the Russians want to buy—and they pay in gold."

"I would not take their gold!"

"Ah, but Fitz," said Lloyd George, "you have so much of your own."

{ III }

There was a party in Wellington Row when Billy took his bride home to Aberowen.

It was a summer Saturday, and for once there was no rain. At three o'clock in the afternoon Billy and Mildred arrived at the station with

Mildred's children, Billy's new stepdaughters, Enid and Lillian, aged eight and seven. By then the miners had come up from the pit, taken their weekly baths, and put on their Sunday suits.

Billy's parents were waiting at the station. They were older and seemed diminished, no longer dominating those around them. Da shook Billy's hand and said: "I'm proud of you, son. You stood up to them, just like I taught you to." Billy was glad, although he did not see himself as just another of Da's achievements in life.

They had met Mildred once before, at Ethel's wedding. Da shook Mildred's hand and Mam kissed her.

Mildred said: "It's lovely to see you again, Mrs. Williams. Should I call you Mam now?"

It was the best thing she could have said, and Mam was delighted. Billy felt sure Da would come to love her, provided she could keep from swearing.

Persistent questions by M.P.s in the House of Commons—fed with information by Ethel—had forced the government to announce reduced sentences for a number of soldiers and sailors court-martialed in Russia for mutiny and other offenses. Billy's prison term had been reduced to a year and he had been released and demobilized. He had married Mildred as quickly as possible after that.

Aberowen seemed strange to him. The place had not changed much, but his feelings were different. It was small and drab, and the mountains all around seemed like walls to keep the people in. He was no longer sure this was his home. As when he had put on his prewar suit, he found that, even though it still fit, he no longer felt right in it. Nothing that happened here would change the world, he thought.

They walked up the hill to Wellington Row to find the houses decorated with bunting: the Union Jack, the Welsh dragon, and the red flag. A banner across the street said WELCOME HOME, BILLY TWICE. All the neighbors were out in the street. There were tables with jugs of beer and urns of tea, and plates loaded with pies, cakes, and sandwiches. When they saw Billy they sang "We'll Keep a Welcome in the Hillsides."

It made Billy cry.

He was handed a pint of beer. A crowd of admiring young men gathered around Mildred. To them she was an exotic creature, with her London clothes and her Cockney accent and a hat with a huge brim that she had trimmed herself with silk flowers. Even when she was on her best behavior she could not help saying risqué things like "I had to get it off my chest, if you'll pardon the expression."

Gramper looked older, and could hardly stand up straight, but mentally he was still all right. He took charge of Enid and Lillian, producing sweets out of his waistcoat pockets and showing them how he could make a penny disappear.

Billy had to talk to all the bereaved families about his dead comrades: Joey Ponti, Prophet Jones, Spotty Llewellyn, and the others. He was reunited with Tommy Griffiths, whom he had last seen in Ufa, Russia. Tommy's father, Len, the atheist, was gaunt with cancer.

Billy was going to start down the pit again on Monday; and the miners all wanted to explain to him the changes underground since he had left: new roads driven deeper into the workings, more electric lights, better safety precautions.

Tommy stood on a chair and made a speech of welcome; then Billy had to respond. "The war has changed us all," he said. "I remember when people used to say the rich were put on this earth by God to rule over us lesser people." That was greeted by scornful laughs. "Many men were cured of that delusion by fighting under the command of upper-class officers who should not have been put in charge of a Sunday school outing." The other veterans nodded knowingly. "The war was won by men like us, ordinary men, uneducated but not stupid." They agreed, saying "Aye" and "Hear, hear."

"We've got the vote now—and so have our women, though not all of them yet, as my sister, Eth, will tell you quick enough." There was a little cheer from the women at that. "This is our country, and we must take control of it, just as the Bolsheviks have taken over in Russia and the Social Democrats in Germany." The men cheered. "We've got a working-class party, the Labour Party, and we've got the numbers to put our party in government. Lloyd George pulled a fast one at the last election, but he won't get away with that again."

Someone shouted: "No!"

"So here's what I've come home for. Perceval Jones's days as M.P. for Aberowen are almost over." There was a cheer. "I want to see a Labour man representing us in the House of Commons!" Billy caught his father's eye: Da's face was aglow. "Thank you for your wonderful welcome." He got down from the chair, and they clapped enthusiastically.

"Nice speech, Billy," said Tommy Griffiths. "But who's going to be that Labour M.P.?"

"I tell you what, Tommy boy," said Billy. "I'll give you three guesses."

{ IV }

The philosopher Bertrand Russell visited Russia that year and wrote a short book called *The Practice and Theory of Bolshevism*. In the Leckwith family it almost caused a divorce.

Russell came out strongly against the Bolsheviks. Worse, he did so from a left-wing perspective. Unlike Conservative critics, he did not argue that the Russian people had no right to depose the tsar, share out the lands of the nobility among the peasants, and run their own factories. On the contrary, he approved of all that. He attacked the Bolsheviks not for having the wrong ideals, but for having the right ideals and failing to live up to them. So his conclusions could not be dismissed out of hand as propaganda.

Bernie read it first. He had a librarian's horror of marking books, but in this case he made an exception, defacing the pages with angry comments, underlining sentences and writing "Rubbish!" or "Invalid argument!" with a pencil in the margins.

Ethel read it while nursing the baby, now just over a year old. She was named Mildred, but they always shortened it to Millie. The older Mildred had moved to Aberowen with Billy and was already pregnant with their first child. Ethel missed her, even though she was glad to have the use of the upstairs rooms in the house. Little Millie had curly hair and, already, a flirtatious twinkle in her eye that reminded everyone of Ethel.

Ethel enjoyed the book. Russell was a witty writer. With aristocratic insouciance, he had asked for an interview with Lenin, and had spent an hour with the great man. They had spoken English. Lenin had said that Lord Northcliffe was his best propagandist: the *Daily Mail*'s horror stories about Russians despoiling the aristocracy might terrify the bourgeoisie but they would have the opposite effect on the British working class, he thought.

But Russell made it clear that the Bolsheviks were completely undemocratic. The dictatorship of the proletariat was a real dictatorship, he said, but the rulers were middle-class intellectuals such as Lenin and Trotsky, assisted by only such proletarians who agreed with their views. "I think this is very worrying," said Ethel when she put the book down.

"Bertrand Russell is an aristocrat!" Bernie said angrily. "He's the third earl!"

"That doesn't make him wrong." Millie stopped sucking and went to sleep. Ethel stroked her soft cheek with a fingertip. "Russell is a socialist. His complaint is that the Bolsheviks are not implementing socialism."

"How can he say such a thing? The nobility has been crushed."

"But so has the opposition press."

"A temporary necessity—"

"How temporary? The Russian revolution is three years old!"

"You can't make an omelette without breaking eggs."

"He says there are arbitrary arrests and executions, and the secret police are more powerful now than they were under the tsar."

"But they act against counterrevolutionaries, not against socialists."

"Socialism means freedom, even for counterrevolutionaries."

"No, it doesn't!"

"It does to me."

Their raised voices woke Millie. Sensing the anger in the room, she started to cry.

"There," said Ethel resentfully. "Now look what you've done."

{ V }

When Grigori returned home from the civil war he joined Katerina, Vladimir, and Anna in their comfortable apartment within the government enclave in the old fort of the Kremlin. For his taste, it was too comfortable. The entire country was suffering shortages of food and fuel, but in the shops of the Kremlin there was plenty. The compound had three restaurants with French-trained chefs and, to Grigori's dismay, the waiters clicked their heels to the Bolsheviks as they had to the old nobility. Katerina put the children in the nursery while she visited the hairdresser. In the evening, members of the Central Committee went to the opera in chauffeur-driven cars.

"I hope we are not becoming the new nobility," he said to Katerina in bed one night.

She laughed scornfully. "If we are, where are my diamonds?"

"But, you know, we do have banquets, and travel first-class on the railway, and so on."

"The aristocrats never did anything useful. You all work twelve, fifteen, eighteen hours a day. You can't be expected to scavenge on rubbish tips for bits of wood to burn for warmth, as the poor do."

"But then, there's always an excuse for the elite to have their special privileges."

"Come here," she said. "I'll give you a special privilege."

After they had made love, Grigori lay awake. Despite his misgivings, he could not help feeling a secret satisfaction at seeing his family so well-off. Katerina had put on weight. When he first met her, she had been a voluptuous twenty-year-old girl; now she was a plump mother at twenty-six. Vladimir was five and learning to read and write in school with the other children of Russia's new rulers; Anna, usually called Anya, was a mischievous curly-headed three-year-old. Their home had formerly belonged to one of the tsaritsa's ladies-in-waiting. It was warm, dry, and spacious, with a second bedroom for the children and a kitchen and living room, too—enough accommodation for twenty people in

Grigori's old lodgings in Petrograd. There were curtains at the windows, china cups for tea, a rug in front of the fire, and an oil painting of Lake Baikal over the fireplace.

Grigori eventually fell asleep, to be wakened at six in the morning by a banging on the door. He opened it to a poorly dressed, skeletally thin woman who looked familiar. "I am sorry to bother you so early, Excellency," she said, using the old style of respectful address.

He recognized her as the wife of Konstantin. "Magda!" he said in astonishment. "You look so different—come in! What's the matter? Are you living in Moscow now?"

"Yes, we moved here, Excellency."

"Don't call me that, for God's sake. Where is Konstantin?"

"In prison."

"What? Why?"

"As a counterrevolutionary."

"Impossible!" said Grigori. "There must have been a terrible mistake."

"Yes, sir."

"Who arrested him?"

"The Cheka."

"The secret police. Well, they work for us. I'll find out about this. I'll make inquiries immediately after breakfast."

"Please, Excellency, I beg you, do something now—they are going to shoot him in one hour."

"Hell," said Grigori. "Wait while I get dressed."

He put on his uniform. Although it had no badges of rank, it was of a much better quality than that of an ordinary soldier, and marked him clearly as a commander.

A few minutes later he and Magda left the Kremlin compound. It was snowing. They walked the short distance to Lubyanka Square. The Cheka headquarters was a huge baroque building of yellow brick, formerly the office of an insurance company. The guard at the door saluted Grigori.

He began shouting as soon as he entered the building. "Who is in charge here? Bring me the duty officer this instant! I am Comrade

Grigori Peshkov, member of the Bolshevik Central Committee. I wish to see the prisoner Konstantin Vorotsyntsev immediately. What are you waiting for? Get on with it!" He had discovered that this was the quickest way to get things done, even though it reminded him horribly of the petulant behavior of a spoiled nobleman.

The guards ran around in panic for a few minutes; then Grigori suffered a shock. The duty officer was brought to the entrance hall. Grigori knew him. It was Mikhail Pinsky.

Grigori was horrified. Pinsky had been a bully and a brute in the tsarist police: was he now a bully and a brute for the revolution?

Pinsky gave an oily smile. "Comrade Peshkov," he said. "What an honor."

"You didn't say that when I knocked you down for pestering a poor peasant girl," Grigori said.

"How things have changed, comrade—for all of us."

"Why have you arrested Konstantin Vorotsyntsev?"

"Counterrevolutionary activities."

"That's ridiculous. He was chair of the Bolshevik discussion group at the Putilov works in 1914. He was one of the first deputies to the Petrograd soviet. He's more Bolshevik than I am!"

"Is that so?" said Pinsky, and there was the hint of a threat in his voice.

Grigori ignored it. "Bring him to me."

"Right away, comrade."

A few minutes later Konstantin appeared. He was dirty and unshaven, and he smelled like a pigsty. Magda burst into tears and threw her arms around him.

"I need to talk to the prisoner privately," Grigori said to Pinsky. "Take us to your office."

Pinsky shook his head. "My humble room—"

"Don't argue," Grigori said. "Your office." It was a way of emphasizing his power. He needed to keep Pinsky under his thumb.

Pinsky led them to an upstairs room overlooking the inner courtyard. He hastily swept a knuckle-duster off the desk into a drawer.

Looking out of the window, Grigori saw that it was daybreak. "Wait outside," he said to Pinsky.

They sat down and Grigori said to Konstantin: "What the hell is going on?"

"We came to Moscow when the government moved," Konstantin explained. "I thought I would become a commissar. But it was a mistake. I have no political support here."

"So what have you been doing?"

"I've gone back to ordinary work. I'm at the Tod factory, making engine parts, cogs and pistons and ball races."

"But why do the police imagine you're a counterrevolutionary?"

"The factory elects a deputy to the Moscow soviet. One of the engineers announced he would be a Menshevik candidate. He held a meeting, and I went to listen. There were only a dozen people there. I didn't speak, I left halfway through, and I didn't vote for him. The Bolshevik candidate won, of course. But, after the election, everyone who attended that Menshevik meeting was fired. Then, last week, we were all arrested."

"We can't do this," Grigori said in despair. "Not even in the name of the revolution. We can't arrest workers for listening to a different point of view."

Konstantin looked at him strangely. "Have you been away somewhere?"

"Of course," said Grigori. "Fighting the counterrevolutionary armies."

"Then that's why you don't know what's going on."

"You mean this has happened before?"

"Grishka, it happens every day."

"I can't believe it."

Magda said: "And last night I received a message—from a friend who is married to a policeman—saying Konstantin and the others were all to be shot at eight o'clock this morning."

Grigori looked at his army-issue wristwatch. It was almost eight. "Pinsky!" he shouted.

The policeman came in.

"Stop this execution."

"I fear it is too late, comrade."

"You mean these men have already been shot?"

"Not quite." Pinsky went to the window.

Grigori did the same. Konstantin and Magda stood beside him.

Down in the snow-covered courtyard, a firing squad had assembled in the clear early light. Opposite the soldiers, a dozen blindfolded men stood shivering in thin indoor clothes. A red flag flew above their heads.

As Grigori looked, the soldiers raised their rifles.

Grigori yelled: "Stop at once! Do not shoot!" But his voice was muffled by the window, and no one heard.

A moment later there was a crash of gunfire.

The condemned men fell to the ground. Grigori stared, aghast.

Around the slumped bodies, bloodstains appeared on the snow, bright red to match the flag flying above.

CHAPTER FORTY-ONE

November 11–12, 1923

Maud slept in the day and got up in the middle of the afternoon, when Walter brought the children home from Sunday school. Eric was three and Heike was two, and they looked so sweet in their best clothes that Maud thought her heart would burst with love.

She had never known an emotion like this. Even her mad passion for Walter had not been so overwhelming. The children also made her feel desperately anxious. Would she be able to feed them and keep them warm, and protect them from riot and revolution?

She gave them hot bread-and-milk to warm them; then she began to prepare for the evening. She and Walter were throwing a small family party to celebrate the thirty-eighth birthday of Walter's cousin Robert von Ulrich.

Robert had not been killed in the war, contrary to Walter's parents' fears—or were they hopes? Either way, Walter had not become the Graf von Ulrich. Robert had been held in a prisoner-of-war camp in Siberia. When the Bolsheviks had made peace with Austria, Robert and his wartime comrade, Jörg, had set out to walk, hitchhike, and ride freight trains home. It had taken them a year, but they had made it, and when they returned Walter had found them an apartment in Berlin.

Maud put on her apron. In the tiny kitchen of her little house she made a soup out of cabbage, stale bread, and turnips. She also baked a small cake, although she had to eke out her ingredients with more turnips.

She had learned to cook and much else besides. A kindly neighbor, an older woman, had taken pity on the bewildered aristocrat and taught her how to make a bed, iron a shirt, and clean a bathtub. It had all come as something of a shock.

They lived in a middle-class town house. They had not been able to spend any money on it, nor could they afford the servants Maud had always been used to, and they had a lot of secondhand furniture that Maud secretly thought was dreadfully suburban.

They had looked forward to better times, but in fact things had got worse: Walter's career in the foreign ministry had been dead-ended by his marriage to an Englishwoman, and he would have moved on to something else, but in the economic chaos he was lucky to have any job at all. And Maud's early dissatisfactions seemed petty now, four years of poverty later. There was patched upholstery where the children had torn it, broken windows covered with cardboard, and paintwork peeling everywhere.

But Maud had no regrets. Anytime she liked she could kiss Walter, slide her tongue into his mouth, unbutton his trousers, and lie with him on the bed or the couch or even the floor, and that made up for everything else.

Walter's parents came to the party bringing half a ham and two bottles of wine. Otto had lost his family estate, Zumwald, which was now in Poland. His savings had been reduced to nothing by inflation. However, the large garden of his Berlin house produced potatoes, and he still had a lot of prewar wine.

"How did you manage to find ham?" Walter said incredulously. Such things could normally be bought only with American dollars.

"I traded a bottle of vintage champagne for it," said Otto.

The grandparents put the children to bed. Otto told them a folktale. From what Maud could hear, it was about a queen who had her brother beheaded. She shuddered, but did not interfere. Afterward Susanne sang lullabies in a reedy voice and the children went to sleep, apparently none the worse for their grandfather's bloodthirsty story.

Robert and Jörg arrived, wearing identical red ties. Otto greeted them warmly. He seemed to have no idea of their relationship, apparently accepting that Jörg was simply Robert's flatmate. Indeed, that was how the men behaved when they were with older folk. Maud thought that Susanne probably guessed the truth. Women were harder to fool. Fortunately they were more accepting.

Robert and Jörg could be very different in liberal company. At parties in their own home they made no secret of their romantic love. Many of their friends were the same. Maud had been startled at first: she had never seen men kissing, admiring one another's outfits, and flirting like schoolgirls. But such behavior was no longer taboo, at least in Berlin. And Maud had read Proust's *Sodome et Gomorrhe,* which seemed to suggest that this kind of thing had always gone on.

Tonight, however, Robert and Jörg were on their best behavior. Over dinner everyone talked about what was happening in Bavaria. On Thursday an association of paramilitary groups called the Kampfbund had declared a national revolution in a beer hall in Munich.

Maud could hardly bear to read the news these days. Workers went on strike, so right-wing bullyboys beat up the strikers. Housewives marched to protest against the shortage of provisions, and their protests turned into food riots. Everyone in Germany was angry about the Versailles Treaty, yet the Social Democratic government had accepted it in full. People believed reparations were crippling the economy, even though Germany had paid only a fraction of the amount and obviously had no intention of trying to clear the total.

The Munich beer hall putsch had everyone worked up. The war hero Erich Ludendorff was its most prominent supporter. So-called storm troopers in their brown shirts and students from the Officers Infantry

School had seized control of key buildings. City councilors had been taken hostage and prominent Jews arrested.

On Friday the legitimate government had counterattacked. Four policemen and sixteen paramilitaries had been killed. Maud was not able to judge, from the news that had reached Berlin so far, whether the insurrection was over or not. If the extremists took control of Bavaria, would the whole country fall to them?

It made Walter angry. "We have a democratically elected government," he said. "Why can't people let them get on with the job?"

"Our government has betrayed us," said his father.

"In your opinion. So what? In America, when the Republicans won the last election, the Democrats didn't riot!"

"The United States is not being subverted by Bolsheviks and Jews."

"If you're worried about the Bolsheviks, tell people not to vote for them. And what is this obsession with Jews?"

"They are a pernicious influence."

"There are Jews in Britain. Father, don't you remember how Lord Rothschild in London tried his best to prevent the war? There are Jews in France, in Russia, in America. They're not conspiring to betray their governments. What makes you think ours are peculiarly evil? Most of them only want to earn enough to feed their families and send their children to school—just the same as everyone else."

Robert surprised Maud by speaking up. "I agree with Uncle Otto," he said. "Democracy is enfeebling. Germany needs strong leadership. Jörg and I have joined the National Socialists."

"Oh, Robert, for God's sake!" said Walter disgustedly. "How could you?"

Maud stood up. "Would anyone like a piece of birthday cake?" she said brightly.

{ II }

Maud left the party at nine to go to work. "Where's your uniform?" said her mother-in-law as she said good-bye. Susanne thought Maud was a night nurse for a wealthy old gentleman.

"I keep it there and change when I arrive," Maud said. In fact she played the piano in a nightclub called Nachtleben. However, it was true that she kept her uniform at work.

She had to earn money, and she had never been taught to do much except dress up and go to parties. She had had a small inheritance from her father, but she had converted it to marks when she moved to Germany, and now it was worthless. Fitz refused to give her money because he was still angry with her for marrying without his permission. Walter's salary at the Foreign Office was raised every month, but it never kept pace with inflation. In partial compensation, the rent they paid for their house was now negligible, and the landlord no longer bothered to collect it. But they had to buy food.

Maud got to the club at nine thirty. The place was newly furnished and decorated, and looked good even with the lights up. Waiters were polishing glasses, the barman was chipping ice, and a blind man was tuning the piano. Maud changed into a low-cut evening dress and fake jewelry, and made up her face heavily with powder, eyeliner, and lipstick. She was at the piano when the place opened at ten.

It rapidly filled up with men and women in evening clothes, dancing and smoking. They bought champagne cocktails and discreetly sniffed cocaine. Despite poverty and inflation, Berlin's nightlife was hot. Money was no problem to these people. Either they had income from abroad, or they had something better than money: stocks of coal, a slaughterhouse, a tobacco warehouse, or, best of all, gold.

Maud was part of an all-female band playing the new music called jazz. Fitz would have been horrified to see it, but she liked the job. She had always rebelled against the restrictions of her upbringing. Doing the same tunes every night could be tedious, but despite that it released something repressed within her. She wiggled on her piano stool and batted her eyelashes at the customers.

At midnight she had a spot of her own, singing and playing songs made popular by Negro singers such as Alberta Hunter, which she learned from American discs played on a gramophone that belonged to Nachtleben's owner. She was billed as Mississippi Maud.

Between numbers a customer staggered up to the piano and said: "Play 'Downhearted Blues,' will you?"

She knew the song, a big hit for Bessie Smith. She started to play blues chords in E flat. "I might," she said. "What's it worth?"

He held out a billion-mark note.

Maud laughed. "That won't buy you the first bar," she said. "Haven't you got any foreign currency?"

He handed her a dollar bill.

She took the money, stuffed it into her sleeve, and played "Downhearted Blues."

Maud was overjoyed to have a dollar, which was worth about a trillion marks. Nevertheless she felt a little down, and her heart was really in the blues. It was quite an achievement for a woman of her background to have learned to hustle tips, but the process was demeaning.

After her spot, the same customer accosted her on her way back to her dressing room. He put his hand on her hip and said: "Would you like to have breakfast with me, sweetheart?"

Most nights she was pawed, although at thirty-three she was one of the oldest women there: many were girls of nineteen and twenty. When this happened the girls were not allowed to make a fuss. They were supposed to smile sweetly, remove the man's hand gently, and say: "Not tonight, sir." But this was not always sufficiently discouraging, and the other girls had taught Maud a more effective line. "I've got these tiny insects in my cunt hair," she said. "Do you think it's anything to worry about?" The man disappeared.

Maud spoke German effortlessly after four years there, and working at the club she had learned all the vulgar words, too.

The club closed at four in the morning. Maud took off her makeup and changed back into her street clothes. She went to the kitchen and begged some coffee beans. A cook who liked her gave her a few in a twist of paper.

The musicians were paid in cash every night. All the girls brought large bags in which to carry the bundles of banknotes.

On the way out, Maud picked up a newspaper left behind by a customer. Walter would read it. They could not afford to buy papers.

She left the club and went straight to the bakery. It was dangerous to hold on to money: by evening your wages might not buy a loaf. Several women were already waiting outside the shop in the cold. At half past five the baker opened the door and chalked up his prices on a board. Today a loaf of black bread was 127 billion marks.

Maud bought four loaves. They would not eat it all today, but that did not matter. Stale bread could be used to thicken soup: banknotes could not.

She got home at six. Later she would dress the children and take them to their grandparents' house for the day, so that she could sleep. Right now she had an hour or so with Walter. It was the best part of the day.

She prepared breakfast and took a tray into the bedroom. "Look," she said. "New bread, coffee . . . and a dollar!"

"Clever girl!" He kissed her. "What shall we buy?" He shivered in his pajamas. "We need coal."

"No rush. We can keep it, if you want. It will be worth just as much next week. If you're cold, I'll warm you."

He grinned. "Come on, then."

She took off her clothes and got into bed.

They ate the bread, drank the coffee, and made love. Sex was still exciting, even though it did not take as long as it had when first they were together.

Afterward, Walter read the newspaper she had brought home. "The revolution in Munich is over," he said.

"For good?"

Walter shrugged. "They've caught the leader. It's Adolf Hitler."

"The head of the party Robert joined?"

"Yes. He's been charged with high treason. He's in jail."

"Good," said Maud with relief. "Thank God that's over."

CHAPTER FORTY-TWO

December 1923 to January 1924

Earl Fitzherbert got up on a platform outside Aberowen town hall at three o'clock in the afternoon on the day before the general election. He wore formal morning dress and a top hat. There was a burst of cheering from the Conservatives at the front, but most of the crowd booed. Someone threw a crumpled newspaper, and Billy said: "None of that, now, boys. Let him speak."

Low clouds darkened the winter afternoon, and the streetlights were already lit. It was raining, but there was a big crowd, two or three hundred people, mostly miners in their caps, with a few bowler hats at the front and a scatter of women under umbrellas. At the edges of the crowd, children played on the wet cobblestones.

Fitz was campaigning in support of the sitting M.P., Perceval Jones. He began to talk about tariffs. This was fine with Billy. Fitz could speak on this subject all day without touching the hearts of Aberowen people. In theory, it was the big election issue. The Conservatives proposed to end unemployment by raising the duty on imports to protect British manufactures. This had united the Liberals in opposition, for their oldest ideology was free trade. Labour agreed that tariffs were not the answer, and proposed a program of national work to employ the idle, together with extended years of education to prevent ever more youngsters coming into the overcrowded job market.

But the real issue was who was to rule.

"In order to encourage agricultural employment, the Conservative government will give a bounty of one pound per acre to every farmer—provided he is paying his laborers thirty shillings a week or more," said Fitz.

Billy shook his head, amused and disgusted at the same time. Why give money to farmers? They were not starving. Unemployed factory workers were.

Beside Billy, Da said: "This sort of talk isn't going to win votes in Aberowen."

Billy agreed. The constituency had once been dominated by hill farmers, but those days were over. Now that the working class had the vote, the miners would outnumber the farmers. Perceval Jones had held on to his seat, in the confused election of 1922, by a few votes. Surely this time he would be thrown out?

Fitz was winding up. "If you vote Labour, you will be voting for a man whose army record is stained," he said. The audience did not much like that: they knew Billy's story, and regarded him as a hero. There was a mutter of dissent, and Da shouted: "Shame on you!"

Fitz plowed on. "A man who betrayed his comrades-in-arms and his officers, a man who was court-martialed for disloyalty and sent to jail. I say to you: do not bring disgrace on Aberowen by electing to Parliament a man such as that."

Fitz got down to ragged applause and boos. Billy stared at him, but Fitz did not meet his eye.

Billy climbed onto the platform in his turn. "You're probably expecting me to insult Lord Fitzherbert the way he insulted me," he said.

In the crowd, Tommy Griffiths shouted: "Give him hell, Billy!"

Billy said: "But this isn't a pithead punch-up. This election is too important to be decided by cheap jibes." They became subdued. Billy knew they would not much like this reasonable approach. They enjoyed cheap jibes. But he saw his father nodding approval. Da understood what Billy was trying to do. Of course he understood. He had taught Billy.

"The earl has shown courage, coming here and stating his views to a crowd of coal miners," Billy went on. "He may be wrong—he is wrong—but he's no coward. He was like that in the war. Many of our officers were. They were brave, but wrongheaded. They had the wrong strategy and the wrong tactics, their communications were poor, and their thinking was out-of-date. But they wouldn't change their ideas until millions of men had been killed."

The audience had gone quiet. They were interested now. Billy saw Mildred, looking proud, with a baby in each arm—Billy's two sons, David and Keir, aged one and two. Mildred was not passionate about politics, but she wanted Billy to become an M.P. so that they could go back to London and she could restart her business.

"In the war, no working-class man was ever promoted above the rank of sergeant. And all public schoolboys entered the army as second lieutenants. Every veteran here today had his life needlessly put at risk by half-witted officers, and many of us had our lives saved by an intelligent sergeant."

There was a loud murmur of agreement.

"I'm here to say those days are over. In the army and in other walks of life, men should be promoted for brains, not birth." He raised his voice, and heard in his tone the thrill of passion that he knew from his father's sermons. "This election is about the future, and the kind of country our children will grow up in. We must make sure it's different from the one we grew up in. The Labour Party doesn't call for revolution—we've seen that in other countries, and it doesn't work. But we do call for change—serious change, major change, radical change."

He paused, then raised his voice again for his peroration. "No, I don't insult Lord Fitzherbert, nor Mr. Perceval Jones," he said, pointing at the two top hats in the front row. "I simply say to them: gentlemen, you are history." There was a cheer. Billy looked over the front row to the crowd of miners—strong, brave men who had been born with nothing but had nevertheless made lives for themselves and their families. "Fellow workers," he said. "We are the future!"

He got down from the platform.

When the votes were counted, he won by a landslide.

{ II }

So did Ethel.

The Conservatives formed the largest party in the new Parliament, but they did not have an overall majority. Labour came second, with 191 M.P.s, including Eth Leckwith from Aldgate and Billy Williams from Aberowen. The Liberals were third. The Scottish Prohibitionists won one seat. The Communist Party got none.

When the new Parliament assembled, Labour and Liberal members combined to vote the Conservative government out, and the king was obliged to ask the leader of the Labour Party, Ramsay MacDonald, to become prime minister. For the first time, Britain had a Labour government.

Ethel had not been inside the Palace of Westminster since the day in 1916 when she got thrown out for shouting at Lloyd George. Now she sat on the green leather bench in a new coat and hat, listening to the speeches, occasionally glancing up to the public gallery from which she had been ejected more than seven years ago. She went into the lobby and voted with the members of the cabinet, famous socialists she had admired from a distance: Arthur Henderson, Philip Snowden, Sidney Webb, and the prime minister himself. She had her own desk in a little office shared with another female Labour M.P. She browsed in the library, ate buttered toast in the tearoom, and picked up sacks of mail addressed to her. She walked around the vast building, learning its geography, trying to feel she was entitled to be there.

One day at the end of January she took Lloyd with her and showed him around. He was almost nine years old, and he had never been inside a building so large or so luxurious. She tried to explain the principles of democracy to him, but he was a little young.

On a narrow red-carpeted staircase on the border between the Commons and the Lords areas, they ran into Fitz. He, too, had a young guest—his son George, called Boy.

Ethel and Lloyd were going up, Fitz and Boy coming down, and they met on a half landing.

Fitz stared at her as if he expected her to give way.

Fitz's two sons, Boy and Lloyd, the heir to the title and the unacknowledged bastard, were the same age. They looked at each other with frank interest.

At Tŷ Gwyn, Ethel remembered, whenever she encountered Fitz in the corridor, she had had to stand aside, up against the wall, with her eyes cast down as he passed by.

Now she stood in the middle of the landing, holding Lloyd's hand firmly, and stared at Fitz. "Good morning, Lord Fitzherbert," she said, and she tilted her chin up defiantly.

He stared back. His face showed angry resentment. At last he said: "Good morning, Mrs. Leckwith."

She looked at his son. "You must be Viscount Aberowen," she said. "How do you do?"

"How do you do, ma'am," the child said politely.

She said to Fitz: "And this is my son, Lloyd."

Fitz refused to look at him.

Ethel was not going to let Fitz off lightly. She said: "Shake hands with the earl, Lloyd."

Lloyd stuck out his hand and said: "Pleased to meet you, Earl."

It would have been undignified to snub a nine-year-old. Fitz was forced to shake.

For the first time, he had touched his son Lloyd.

"And now we'll bid you good day," Ethel said dismissively, and she took a step forward.

Fitz's expression was thunderous. Reluctantly he stood aside, with his son, and they waited, backs to the wall, as Ethel and Lloyd walked past them and on up the stairs.

Historical Characters

Several real historical characters appear in these pages, and readers sometimes ask how I draw the line between history and fiction. It's a fair question, and here's the answer.

In some cases, for example when Sir Edward Grey addresses the House of Commons, my fictional characters are witnessing an event that really happened. What Sir Edward says in this novel corresponds to the parliamentary record, except that I have shortened his speech, without, I hope, losing anything important.

Sometimes a real person goes to a fictional location, as when Winston Churchill visits Tŷ Gwyn. In that case, I have made sure that it was not unusual for him to visit country houses, and that he could well have done so at around that date.

When real people have conversations with my fictional characters, they are usually saying things they really did say at some point. Lloyd George's explanation to Fitz of why he does not want to deport Lev Kamenev is based on what Lloyd George wrote, in a memo quoted in Peter Rowland's biography.

My rule is: either the scene did happen, or it might have; either these words were used, or they might have been. And if I find some reason why the scene could not have taken place in real life, or the words would not really have been said—if, for example, the character was in another country at the time—I leave it out.

Acknowledgments

My principal historical consultant for this book has been Richard Overy. Other historians who read drafts and made corrections, saving me from many errors, were: John M. Cooper, Mark Goldman, Holger Herwig, John Keiger, Evan Mawdsley, Richard Toye, and Christopher Williams. Susan Pedersen helped with the subject of soldiers' wives' separation allowances.

As always, many of these advisers were found for me by Dan Starer of Research for Writers in New York City.

Friends who helped include Tim Blythe, who gave me some essential books; Adam Brett-Smith, who advised on champagne; the sharp-eyed Nigel Dean; Tony McWalter and Chris Manners, two wise and perceptive critics; trainspotter Geoff Mann, who advised on locomotive wheels; and Angela Spizig, who read the first draft and commented from a German perspective.

Editors and agents who read and advised were Amy Berkower, Leslie Gelbman, Phyllis Grann, Neil Nyren, Imogen Taylor, and, as ever, Al Zuckerman.

Finally I thank family members who read the draft and gave me advice, especially Barbara Follett, Emanuele Follett, Marie-Claire Follett, Jann Turner, and Kim Turner.

About the Author

Ken Follett is one of the world's best-loved authors, selling more than 160 million copies of his thirty books. Follett's first bestseller was *Eye of the Needle*, a spy story set in the Second World War.

In 1989, *The Pillars of the Earth* was published and has since become Follett's most popular novel. It reached number one on bestseller lists around the world and was an Oprah's Book Club pick.

Its sequels, *World Without End* and *A Column of Fire*, proved equally popular, and the Kingsbridge series has sold 38 million copies worldwide.

Follett lives in Hertfordshire, England, with his wife, Barbara. Between them they have five children, six grandchildren, and three Labradors.

ALSO AVAILABLE

THE MODIGLIANI SCANDAL	A PLACE CALLED FREEDOM
PAPER MONEY	THE THIRD TWIN
EYE OF THE NEEDLE	THE HAMMER OF EDEN
TRIPLE	CODE TO ZERO
THE KEY TO REBECCA	JACKDAWS
THE MAN FROM ST. PETERSBURG	HORNET FLIGHT
ON WINGS OF EAGLES	WHITEOUT
LIE DOWN WITH LIONS	FALL OF GIANTS
NIGHT OVER WATER	WINTER OF THE WORLD
A DANGEROUS FORTUNE	EDGE OF ETERNITY

(P) PENGUIN BOOKS

WINTER OF THE WORLD

"GRIPPING...POWERFUL."
—*The New York Times*

"POLITICAL INTRIGUE, AMOROUS EPISODES,
SUSPENSE, AND DRAMA. HISTORY COMES TO LIFE."
—*The Louisville Courier-Journal*

"[FOLLETT] IS SO GOOD AT PLOTTING
A STORY, EVEN ONE THAT TAKES ON SUCH A COMPLEX
TOPIC AS THE WORLD WAR II ERA. THAT'S WHAT MAKES
WINTER OF THE WORLD SO HARD TO PUT DOWN. YOU
WANT TO KNOW WHAT HAPPENS NEXT."
—The Associated Press

"AN ENTERTAINING HISTORICAL SOAP OPERA."
—*Kirkus Reviews*

WINTER *of the* WORLD

EUROPEAN THEATER

BOOK TWO OF THE CENTURY TRILOGY

CIRCA 1939–1945

NORWAY

Bergen

SWEDEN

NORTH SEA

SCOTLAND

DENMARK

Glasgow • Edinburgh

Copenhagen

Newcastle

Belfast

Hamburg

IRELAND Liverpool Manchester

Berlin

Dublin

Hanover

ENGLAND

GERMANY

WALES Birmingham

Cambridge HOLLAND

Dresden

Aberowen

Frankfurt Prague

Cardiff London Dunkirk

BELGIUM

Königsberg

Southampton Calais

Bournemouth

Brussels

Lemberg

ENGLISH CHANNEL

Amiens SOMME RIVER

ALSACE-

WÜRT-

BAVARIA

Le Havre Rouen

Sedan

LORRAINE TEMBERG

Versailles Paris

Munich

SEINE RIVER

Belfort Basel

Brest

FRANCE

Berne Innsbruck AUSTR

SWITZERLAND

BAY OF

Geneva

BISCAY

LOIRE RIVER

Trieste

Lyons

Milan Venice

Bordeaux

Alessandria

ADRI

Toulouse

ITALY

RHONE RIVER

Perpignan Marseilles

Cerbère

Rome

EBRO RIVER Saragossa

Barcelona

ATLANTIC OCEAN

SPAIN

ALGERIA

TUNISIA

ALSO BY KEN FOLLETT

continued . . .

"*Winter of the World*, like its predecessor, should come with a warning label: 'Abandon your normal activities for a couple of days when you crack this one open, because you're likely to get hooked like a Copper River salmon.' . . . And, as in the previous book, Follett chooses his historical vignettes well, putting his major figures, essentially the children of the five international clusters of characters he created for *Fall of Giants*, in harm's way in the most spectacular and iconic fashion."
—*The Seattle Times*

"The man tells a story so well. . . . Follett can make things glow with some beautifully written episodes. . . . If you read Volume I, you'll have to read Volume II. And once you read Volume II, you'll be committed to reading Volume III. See you in a couple of years."
—*St. Louis Post-Dispatch*

"Follett's storytelling is unobtrusive and workmanlike, and he spins a reasonable and readable yarn that embraces dozens of characters and plenty of Big Picture history, with real historical figures bowing in now and then . . . an entertaining historical soap opera." —*Kirkus Reviews*

"Clips along at a brisk pace. . . . He knows how to keep the pages turning and how to make the reader feel a kinship with the characters' struggles. . . . No matter the ultimate destination, readers can expect to savor the journey—and agonize while waiting for the final book to arrive." —*The Christian Science Monitor*

PRAISE FOR
FALL OF GIANTS

"Follett is masterly in conveying so much drama and historical information so vividly . . . grippingly told."
—*The New York Times Book Review*

"*Fall of Giants*: Follett at his finest . . . sweeping epic that will thrill his fans for hours on end."   —The Huffington Post

"Follett conjures the winds of war."   —*The Washington Post*

"Tantalizing."   —*Newsday*

"A good read. . . . It's a book that will suck you in, consume you for days or weeks, depending upon how quick a reader you are, then let you out the other side both entertained and educated. That's quite the feat."
                    —*USA Today*

"Follett apparently intends to give readers the sweeping history of that century in the form of a novel that follows five families—one American, two British, one German, and one Russian. That's a big job. But *Fall of Giants* suggests that Follett is up to the task."   —*St. Louis Post-Dispatch*

"Follett entwines fiction and factual events well. . . . This is a dark novel, motivated by an unsparing view of human nature and a clear-eyed scrutiny of an ideal peace. It is not the least of Follett's feats that the reader finishes this near thousand-page book intrigued and wanting more."   —*Chicago Sun-Times*

"Follett once again creates a world at once familiar and fantastic . . . A guiltless pleasure, the book is impossible to put down. . . . Empires fall. Heroes rise. Love conquers. After going through a war with these characters, you're left hoping that Follett gets moving with the next giant installment."   —*Time Out New York*

"*Fall of Giants* grand in scope, scale, and story."
                    —The Associated Press

"Suspenseful, tightly constructed, sharply characterized, plot-driven."
                    —*The Seattle Times*

KEN FOLLETT

WINTER
of the
WORLD

BOOK TWO OF THE CENTURY TRILOGY

NEW AMERICAN LIBRARY

NEW AMERICAN LIBRARY
Published by the Penguin Group
Penguin Group (USA) Inc., 375 Hudson Street,
New York, New York 10014, USA

USA | Canada | UK | Ireland | Australia | New Zealand | India | South Africa | China

Penguin Books Ltd., Registered Offices: 80 Strand, London WC2R 0RL, England
For more information about the Penguin Group visit penguin.com.

Published by New American Library, a division of Penguin Group (USA) Inc.
Previously published in a Dutton edition.

First New American Library Printing, September 2013

 REGISTERED TRADEMARK—MARCA REGISTRADA

New American Library Trade Paperback ISBN: 978-0-451-41924-8

THE LIBRARY OF CONGRESS HAS CATALOGED THE HARDCOVER
EDITION OF THIS TITLE AS FOLLOWS:
Follett, Ken.
p. cm.—(Century trilogy; bk. 2)
ISBN 978-0-525-95292-3
1. Twentieth century—Fiction.   2. World War, 1939–1945—Fiction.
3. Spain—History—Civil War, 1936–1939—Fiction.   I. Title
PR6056.O45W56 2012
823'.914—dc23   2012004653

Printed in the United States of America
1 3 5 7 9 10 8 6 4 2

Set in Warnock Pro
Designed by Amy Hill
Maps copyright © David Atkinson, Hand Made Maps Ltd.

To the memory of my grandparents,

Tom and Minnie Follett,

Arthur and Bessie Evans

CAST OF CHARACTERS

American

DEWAR FAMILY

Senator Gus Dewar
Rosa Dewar, his wife
Woody Dewar, their elder son
Chuck Dewar, their younger son
Ursula Dewar, Gus's mother

PESHKOV FAMILY

Lev Peshkov
Olga Peshkov, his wife
Daisy Peshkov, their daughter
Marga, Lev's mistress
Greg Peshkov, son of Lev and Marga
Gladys Angelus, film star, also Lev's mistress

ROUZROKH FAMILY

Dave Rouzrokh
Joanne Rouzrokh, his daughter

BUFFALO SOCIALITES

Dot Renshaw
Charlie Farquharson

OTHERS

Joe Brekhunov, a thug
Brian Hall, union organizer
Jacky Jakes, starlet
Eddie Parry, sailor, friend of Chuck
Captain Vandermeier, Chuck's superior
Margaret Cowdry, beautiful heiress

REAL HISTORICAL CHARACTERS

President Franklin D. Roosevelt
Marguerite "Missy" LeHand, his assistant
Vice President Harry Truman
Cordell Hull, Secretary of State
Sumner Welles, Under-Secretary of State
Colonel Leslie Groves, Army Corps of Engineers

English

FITZHERBERT FAMILY

Earl Fitzherbert, called Fitz
Princess Bea, his wife
"Boy" Fitzherbert, Viscount Aberowen, their elder son
Andy, their younger son

LECKWITH-WILLIAMS FAMILY

Ethel Leckwith (née Williams), Member of Parliament for Aldgate
Bernie Leckwith, Ethel's husband
Lloyd Williams, Ethel's son, Bernie's stepson
Millie Leckwith, Ethel and Bernie's daughter

OTHERS

Ruby Carter, friend of Lloyd
Bing Westhampton, friend of Fitz
Lindy and Lizzie Westhampton, Bing's twin daughters
Jimmy Murray, son of General Murray
May Murray, his sister
Marquis of Lowther, called Lowthie

Naomi Avery, Millie's best friend
Abe Avery, Naomi's brother

REAL HISTORICAL CHARACTERS

Ernest Bevin, M.P., Foreign Secretary

German and Austrian

VON ULRICH FAMILY

Walter von Ulrich
Maud, his wife (née Lady Maud Fitzherbert)
Erik, their son
Carla, their daughter
Ada Hempel, their maid
Kurt, Ada's illegitimate son
Robert von Ulrich, Walter's second cousin
Jörg Schleicher, Robert's partner
Rebecca Rosen, an orphan

FRANCK FAMILY

Ludwig Franck
Monika, his wife (née Monika von der Helbard)
Werner, their elder son
Frieda, their daughter
Axel, their younger son
Ritter, chauffeur
Count Konrad von der Helbard, Monika's father

ROTHMANN FAMILY

Dr. Isaac Rothmann
Hannelore Rothmann, his wife
Eva, their daughter
Rudi, their son

VON KESSEL FAMILY

Gottfried von Kessel
Heinrich von Kessel, his son

GESTAPO

Commissar Thomas Macke
Inspector Kringelein, Macke's boss
Reinhold Wagner
Klaus Richter
Günther Schneider

OTHERS

Hermann Braun, Erik's best friend
Sergeant Schwab, gardener
Wilhelm Frunze, scientist

Russian

PESHKOV FAMILY

Grigori Peshkov
Katerina, his wife
Vladimir, always called Volodya, their son
Anya, their daughter

OTHERS

Zoya Vorotsyntsev, physicist
Ilya Dvorkin, officer of the secret police
Colonel Lemitov, Volodya's boss
Colonel Bobrov, Red Army officer in Spain

REAL HISTORICAL CHARACTERS

Lavrentiy Beria, head of the secret police
Vyacheslav Molotov, Foreign Minister

Spanish

Teresa, literacy teacher

Welsh

WILLIAMS FAMILY

Dai Williams, "Granda"
Cara Williams, "Grandmam"
Billy Williams, M.P. for Aberowen
Dave, Billy's elder son
Keir, Billy's younger son

GRIFFITHS FAMILY

Tommy Griffiths, Billy Williams's political agent
Lenny Griffiths, Tommy's son

PART ONE

THE OTHER CHEEK

CHAPTER ONE

1933

C arla knew her parents were about to have a row. The second she walked into the kitchen, she felt the hostility, like the bone-deep cold of the wind that blew through the streets of Berlin before a February snowstorm. She almost turned and walked back out again.

It was unusual for them to fight. Mostly they were affectionate—too much so. Carla cringed when they kissed in front of other people. Her friends thought it was strange: their parents did not do that. She had said that to her mother, once. Mother had laughed in a pleased way and said: "The day after our wedding, your father and I were separated by the Great War." She had been born English, though you could hardly tell. "I stayed in London while he came home to Germany and joined the army." Carla had heard this story many times, but Mother never tired of telling it. "We thought the war would last three months, but I didn't see him again for five years. All that time I longed to touch him. Now I never tire of it."

Father was just as bad. "Your mother is the cleverest woman I ever met," he had said here in the kitchen just a few days ago. "That's why I married her. It had nothing to do with . . ." He had trailed off, and Mother and he had giggled conspiratorially, as if Carla at the age of eleven knew nothing about sex. It was so embarrassing.

But once in a while they had a quarrel. Carla knew the signs. And a new one was about to erupt.

They were sitting at opposite ends of the kitchen table. Father was somberly dressed in a dark gray suit, starched white shirt, and black satin tie. He looked dapper, as always, even though his hair was receding and his waistcoat bulged a little beneath the gold watch chain. His face was frozen in an expression of false calm. Carla knew that look. He wore it when one of the family had done something that angered him.

He held in his hand a copy of the weekly magazine for which Mother worked, *The Democrat.* She wrote a column of political and diplomatic gossip under the name of Lady Maud. Father began to read aloud. "'Our new chancellor, Herr Adolf Hitler, made his debut in diplomatic society at President Hindenburg's reception.'"

The president was the head of state, Carla knew. He was elected, but he stood above the squabbles of day-to-day politics, acting as referee. The chancellor was the premier. Although Hitler had been made chancellor, his Nazi Party did not have an overall majority in the Reichstag—the German parliament—so, for the present, the other parties could restrain Nazi excesses.

Father spoke with distaste, as if forced to mention something repellent, like sewage. "'He looked uncomfortable in a formal tailcoat.'"

Carla's mother sipped her coffee and looked out of the window to the street, as if interested in the people hurrying to work in scarves and gloves. She, too, was pretending to be calm, but Carla knew she was just waiting for her moment.

The maid, Ada, was standing at the counter in an apron, slicing cheese. She put a plate in front of Father, but he ignored it. "'Herr Hitler was evidently charmed by Elisabeth Cerruti, the cultured wife of the Italian ambassador, in a rose-pink velvet gown trimmed with sable.'"

Mother always wrote about what people were wearing. She said it helped the reader picture them. She herself had fine clothes, but times were hard and she had not bought anything new for years. This morning she looked slim and elegant in a navy blue cashmere dress that was probably as old as Carla.

"'Signora Cerruti, who is Jewish, is a passionate Fascist, and they talked for many minutes. Did she beg Hitler to stop whipping up hatred of Jews?'" Father put the magazine down on the table with a slap.

Here it comes, Carla thought.

"You realize that will infuriate the Nazis," he said.

"I hope so," Mother said coolly. "The day they're pleased with what I write, I shall give it up."

"They're dangerous when riled."

Mother's eyes flashed anger. "Don't you dare condescend to me, Walter. I know they're dangerous—that's why I oppose them."

"I just don't see the point of making them irate."

"You attack them in the Reichstag." Father was an elected parliamentary representative for the Social Democratic Party.

"I take part in a reasoned debate."

This is typical, Carla thought. Father was logical, cautious, law-abiding. Mother had style and humor. He got his way by quiet persistence, she with charm and cheek. They would never agree.

Father added: "I don't drive the Nazis mad with fury."

"Perhaps that's because you don't do them much harm."

Father was irritated by her quick wit. His voice became louder. "And you think you damage them with jokes?"

"I mock them."

"And that's your substitute for argument."

"I believe we need both."

Father became angrier. "But, Maud, don't you see how you're putting yourself and your family at risk?"

"On the contrary. The real danger is *not* to mock the Nazis. What would life be like for our children if Germany became a Fascist state?"

This kind of talk made Carla feel queasy. She could not bear to hear that the family was in danger. Life must go on as it always had. She wished she could sit in this kitchen for an eternity of mornings, with her parents at opposite ends of the pine table, Ada at the counter, and her brother, Erik, thumping around upstairs, late again. Why should anything change?

She had listened to political talk every breakfast-time of her life and she thought she understood what her parents did, and how they planned to make Germany a better place for everyone. But lately they had begun to talk in a different way. They seemed to think that a terrible danger loomed, but Carla could not quite imagine what it was.

Father said: "God knows I'm doing everything I can to hold back Hitler and his mob."

"And so am I. But when you do it, you believe you're following a sensible course." Mother's face hardened in resentment. "And when I do it, I'm accused of putting the family at risk."

"And with good reason," said Father. The row was only just getting started, but at that moment Erik came down, clattering like a horse on the stairs, and lurched into the kitchen with his school satchel swinging from his shoulder. He was thirteen, two years older than Carla, and there were unsightly black hairs sprouting from his upper lip. When they were small, Carla and Erik had played together all the time; but those days were over, and since he had grown so tall, he had pretended to think she was stupid and childish. In fact she was smarter than he, and knew about a lot of things he did not understand, such as women's monthly cycles.

"What was that last tune you were playing?" he said to Mother.

The piano often woke them in the morning. It was a Steinway grand—inherited, like the house itself, from Father's parents. Mother played in the morning because, she said, she was too busy the rest of the day and too tired in the evening. This morning she had performed a Mozart sonata, then a jazz tune. "It's called 'Tiger Rag,'" she told Erik. "Do you want some cheese?"

"Jazz is decadent," Erik said.

"Don't be silly."

Ada handed Erik a plate of cheese and sliced sausage, and he began to shovel it in. Carla thought his manners were dreadful.

Father looked severe. "Who's been teaching you this nonsense, Erik?"

"Hermann Braun says that jazz isn't music, just Negroes making a noise." Hermann was Erik's best friend; his father was a member of the Nazi Party.

"Hermann should try to play it." Father looked at Mother, and his face softened. She smiled at him. He went on: "Your mother tried to teach me ragtime, many years ago, but I couldn't master the rhythm."

Mother laughed. "It was like trying to get a giraffe to roller-skate."

The fight was over, Carla saw with relief. She began to feel better. She took some black bread and dipped it in milk.

But now Erik wanted an argument. "Negroes are an inferior race," he said defiantly.

"I doubt that," Father said patiently. "If a Negro boy were brought up in a nice house full of books and paintings, and sent to an expensive school with good teachers, he might turn out to be smarter than you."

"That's ridiculous!" Erik protested.

Mother put in: "Don't call your father ridiculous, you foolish boy." Her tone was mild: she had used up her anger on Father. Now she just sounded wearily disappointed. "You don't know what you're talking about, and neither does Hermann Braun."

Erik said: "But the Aryan race must be superior—we rule the world!"

"Your Nazi friends don't know any history," Father said. "The Ancient Egyptians built the pyramids when Germans were living in caves. Arabs ruled the world in the Middle Ages—the Muslims were doing algebra when German princes could not write their own names. It's nothing to do with race."

Carla frowned and said: "What is it to do with, then?"

Father looked at her fondly. "That's a very good question, and you're a bright girl to ask it." She glowed with pleasure at his praise. "Civilizations rise and fall—the Chinese, the Aztecs, the Romans—but no one really knows why."

"Eat up, everyone, and put your coats on," Mother said. "It's getting late."

Father pulled his watch out of his waistcoat pocket and looked at it with raised eyebrows. "It's not late."

"I've got to take Carla to the Francks' house," Mother said. "The girls' school is closed for a day—something about repairing the furnace—so Carla's going to spend today with Frieda."

Frieda Franck was Carla's best friend. Their mothers were best friends, too. In fact, when they were young, Frieda's mother, Monika, had been in love with Father—a hilarious fact that Frieda's grandmother had revealed one day after drinking too much Sekt.

Father said: "Why can't Ada look after Carla?"

"Ada has an appointment with the doctor."

"Ah."

Carla expected Father to ask what was wrong with Ada, but he nodded as if he already knew, and put his watch away. Carla wanted to ask, but something told her she should not. She made a mental note to ask Mother later. Then she immediately forgot about it.

Father left first, wearing a long black overcoat. Then Erik put on his cap—perching it as far back on his head as it would go without falling off, as was the fashion among his friends—and followed Father out of the door.

Carla and her mother helped Ada clear the table. Carla loved Ada almost as much as she loved her mother. When Carla was little, Ada had taken care of her full-time, until she was old enough to go to school, for Mother had always worked. Ada was not married yet. She was twenty-nine and homely-looking, though she had a lovely kind smile. Last summer she had had a romance with a policeman, Paul Huber, but it had not lasted.

Carla and her mother stood in front of the mirror in the hall and put on their hats. Mother took her time. She chose a dark blue felt, with a round crown and a narrow brim, the type all the women were wearing, but she tilted hers at a different angle, making it look chic. As Carla put on her knitted wool cap, she wondered whether she would ever have Mother's sense of style. Mother looked like a goddess of war, her long neck and chin and cheekbones carved out of white marble; beautiful, yes, but definitely not pretty. Carla had the same dark hair and green eyes, but looked more like a plump doll than a statue. Carla had once accidentally overheard her grandmother say to Mother: "Your ugly duckling will grow into a swan, you'll see." Carla was still waiting for it to happen.

When Mother was ready, they went out. Their home stood in a row of tall, gracious town houses in the Mitte district, the old center of the city, built for high-ranking ministers and army officers such as Carla's grandfather, who had worked at the nearby government buildings.

Carla and her mother rode a tram along Unter den Linden, then took the S train from Friedrich Strasse to the Zoo Station. The Francks lived in the southwestern suburb of Schöneberg.

Carla was hoping to see Frieda's brother Werner, who was fourteen. She liked him. Sometimes Carla and Frieda imagined they each married the other's brother, and were next-door neighbors, and their children were best friends. It was just a game to Frieda, but Carla was secretly serious. Werner was handsome and grown-up and not a bit silly like Erik. In the dollhouse in Carla's bedroom, the mother and father sleeping side by side in the miniature double bed were called Carla and Werner, but no one knew that, not even Frieda.

Frieda had another brother, Axel, seven, but he had been born with spina bifida, and had to have constant medical care. He lived in a special hospital on the outskirts of Berlin.

Mother was preoccupied on the journey. "I hope this is going to be all right," she muttered, half to herself, as they got off the train.

"Of course it will," Carla said. "I'll have a lovely time with Frieda."

"I didn't mean that. I'm talking about my paragraph about Hitler."

"Are we in danger? Was Father right?"

"Your father is usually right."

"What will happen to us if we've annoyed the Nazis?"

Mother stared at her strangely for a long moment, then said: "Dear God, what kind of a world did I bring you into?" Then she went quiet.

After a ten-minute walk they arrived at a grand villa in a big garden. The Francks were rich: Frieda's father, Ludwig, owned a factory making radio sets. Two cars stood in the driveway. The large shiny black one belonged to Herr Franck. The engine rumbled, and a cloud of blue vapor rose from the tailpipe. The chauffeur, Ritter, with uniform trousers tucked into high boots, stood cap in hand ready to open the door. He bowed and said: "Good morning, Frau von Ulrich."

The second car was a little green two-seater. A short man with a gray beard came out of the house carrying a leather case, and touched his hat to Mother as he got into the small car. "I wonder what Dr. Rothmann is doing here so early in the morning," Mother said anxiously.

They soon found out. Frieda's mother, Monika, came to the door, a tall woman with a mass of red hair. Anxiety showed on her pale face. Instead of welcoming them in, she stood squarely in the doorway as if to bar their entrance. "Frieda has measles!" she said.

"I'm so sorry!" said Mother. "How is she?"

"Miserable. She has a fever and a cough. But Rothmann says she'll be all right. However, she's quarantined."

"Of course. Have you had it?"

"Yes—when I was a girl."

"And Werner has, too—I remember he had a terrible rash all over. But what about your husband?" Mother asked.

"Ludi had it as a boy."

Both women looked at Carla. She had never had measles. She realized this meant she could not spend the day with Frieda.

Carla was disappointed, but Mother was quite shaken. "This week's magazine is our election issue—I *can't* be absent." She looked distraught. All the grown-ups were apprehensive about the general election to be held next Sunday. Mother and Father both feared the Nazis might do well enough to take full control of the government. "Plus my oldest friend is visiting from London. I wonder whether Walter could be persuaded to take a day off to look after Carla?"

Monika said: "Why don't you telephone him?"

Not many people had phones in their homes, but the Francks did, and Carla and her mother stepped into the hall. The instrument stood on a spindly-legged table near the door. Mother picked it up and gave the number of Father's office at the Reichstag, the parliament building. She got through to him and explained the situation. She listened for a minute, then looked angry. "My magazine will urge a hundred thousand readers to campaign for the Social Democratic Party," she said. "Do you really have something more important than that to do today?"

Carla could guess how this argument would end. Father loved her dearly, she knew, but in all her eleven years he had never looked after her for a whole day. All her friends' fathers were the same. Men did not do that sort of thing. But Mother sometimes pretended not to know the rules women lived by.

"I'll just have to take her to the office with me, then," Mother said into the phone. "I dread to think what Jochmann will say." Herr Jochmann was her boss. "He's not much of a feminist at the best of times." She replaced the handset without saying good-bye.

Carla hated it when they fought, and this was the second time in a day. It made the whole world seem unstable. She was much more scared of quarrels than of the Nazis.

"Come on, then," Mother said to her, and she moved to the door.

I'm not even going to see Werner, Carla thought unhappily.

Just then Frieda's father appeared in the hall, a pink-faced man with a small black mustache, energetic and cheerful. He greeted Mother pleasantly, and she paused to speak politely to him while Monika helped him into a black topcoat with a fur collar.

He went to the foot of the stairs. "Werner!" he shouted. "I'm going without you!" He put on a gray felt hat and went out.

"I'm ready, I'm ready!" Werner ran down the stairs like a dancer. He was as tall as his father and more handsome, with red-blond hair worn too long. Under his arm he had a leather satchel that appeared to be full of books; in the other hand he held a pair of ice skates and a hockey stick. He paused in his rush to say: "Good morning, Frau von Ulrich," very politely. Then in a more informal tone: "Hello, Carla. My sister's got the measles."

Carla felt herself blush, for no reason at all. "I know," she said. She tried to think of something charming and amusing to say, but came up with nothing. "I've never had it, so I can't see her."

"I had it when I was a kid," he said, as if that was ever such a long time ago. "I must hurry," he added apologetically.

Carla did not want to lose sight of him so quickly. She followed him outside. Ritter was holding the rear door open. "What kind of car is that?" Carla said. Boys always knew the makes of cars.

"A Mercedes-Benz W10 limousine."

"It looks very comfortable." She caught a look from her mother, half surprised and half amused.

Werner said: "Do you want a lift?"

"That would be nice."

"I'll ask my father." Werner put his head inside the car and said something.

Carla heard Herr Franck reply: "Very well, but hurry up!"

She turned to her mother. "We can go in the car!"

Mother hesitated for only a moment. She did not like Herr Franck's politics—he gave money to the Nazis—but she was not going to refuse a lift in a warm car on a cold morning. "How very kind of you, Ludwig," she said.

They got in. There was room for four in the back. Ritter pulled away smoothly. "I assume you're going to Koch Strasse?" said Herr Franck. Many newspapers and book publishers had their offices in the same street in the Kreuzberg district.

"Please don't go out of your way. Leipziger Strasse would be fine."

"I'd be happy to take you to the door—but I suppose you don't want your leftist colleagues to see you getting out of the car of a bloated plutocrat." His tone was somewhere between humorous and hostile.

Mother gave him a charming smile. "You're not bloated, Ludi—just a little plump." She patted the front of his coat.

He laughed. "I asked for that." The tension eased. Herr Franck picked up the speaking tube and gave instructions to Ritter.

Carla was thrilled to be in a car with Werner, and she wanted to make the most of it by talking to him, but at first she could not think what to speak about. She really wanted to say: "When you're older, do you think you might marry a girl with dark hair and green eyes, about three years younger than yourself, and clever?" Eventually she pointed to his skates and said: "Do you have a match today?"

"No, just practise after school."

"What position do you play in?" She knew nothing about ice hockey, but there were always positions in team games.

"Right wing."

"Isn't it a rather dangerous sport?"

"Not if you're quick."

"You must be ever such a good skater."

"Not bad," he said modestly.

Once again Carla caught her mother watching her with an enigmatic little smile. Had she guessed how Carla felt about Werner? Carla felt another blush coming.

Then the car came to a stop outside a school building, and Werner got out. "Good-bye, everyone!" he said, and ran through the gates into the yard.

Ritter drove on, following the south bank of the Landwehr Canal. Carla looked at the barges, their loads of coal topped with snow like mountains. She felt a sense of disappointment. She had contrived to spend longer with Werner, by hinting that she wanted a lift; then she had wasted the time talking about ice hockey.

What would she have liked to talk to him about? She did not know.

Herr Franck said to Mother: "I read your column in *The Democrat*."

"I hope you enjoyed it."

"I was sorry to see you writing disrespectfully about our chancellor."

"Do you think journalists should write respectfully about politicians?" Mother replied cheerfully. "That's radical. The Nazi press would have to be polite about my husband! They wouldn't like that."

"Not all politicians, obviously," Franck said irritably.

They crossed the teeming junction of Potsdamer Platz. Cars and trams vied with horse-drawn carts and pedestrians in a chaotic melee.

Mother said: "Isn't it better for the press to be able to criticize everyone equally?"

"A wonderful idea," he said. "But you socialists live in a dream world. We practical men know that Germany cannot live on ideas. People must have bread and shoes and coal."

"I quite agree," Mother said. "I could use more coal myself. But I want Carla and Erik to grow up as citizens of a free country."

"You overrate freedom. It doesn't make people happy. They prefer leadership. I want Werner and Frieda and poor Axel to grow up in a country that is proud, and disciplined, and united."

"And in order to be united, we need young thugs in brown shirts to beat up elderly Jewish shopkeepers?"

"Politics is rough. Nothing we can do about it."

"On the contrary. You and I are leaders, Ludwig, in our different ways. It's our responsibility to make politics less rough—more honest, more rational, less violent. If we do not do that, we fail in our patriotic duty."

Herr Franck bristled.

Carla did not know much about men, but she realized they did not like to be lectured on their duty by women. Mother must have forgotten to press her charm switch this morning. But everyone was tense. The coming election had them all on edge.

The car reached Leipziger Platz. "Where may I drop you?" Herr Franck said coldly.

"Just here will be fine," said Mother.

Franck tapped on the glass partition. Ritter stopped the car and hurried to open the door.

Mother said: "I do hope Frieda gets better soon."

"Thank you."

They got out and Ritter closed the door.

The office was several minutes' walk away, but Mother clearly had not wanted to stay any longer in the car. Carla hoped Mother was not going to quarrel permanently with Herr Franck. That might make it difficult for her to see Frieda and Werner. She would hate that.

They set off at a brisk pace. "Try not to make a nuisance of yourself at the office," Mother said. The note of genuine pleading in her voice touched Carla, making her feel ashamed of causing her mother worry. She resolved to behave perfectly.

Mother greeted several people on the way: she had been writing her column for as long as Carla could remember, and was well known in the press corps. They all called her "Lady Maud" in English.

Near the building in which *The Democrat* had its office, they saw someone they knew: Sergeant Schwab. He had fought with Father in the Great War, and still wore his hair brutally short in the military style. After the war he had worked as a gardener, first for Carla's grandfather and later for her father, but he had stolen money from Mother's purse and Father had sacked him. Now he was wearing the ugly military uniform of the storm troopers, the Brownshirts, who were not soldiers but Nazis who had been given the authority of auxiliary policemen.

Schwab said loudly: "Good morning, Frau von Ulrich!" as if he felt no shame at all about being a thief. He did not even touch his cap.

Mother nodded coldly and walked past him. "I wonder what he's doing here," she muttered uneasily as they went inside.

The magazine had the first floor of a modern office building. Carla knew a child would not be welcome, and she hoped they could reach Mother's office without being seen. But they met Herr Jochmann on the stairs. He was a heavy man with thick spectacles. "What's this?" he said brusquely, speaking around the cigarette in his mouth. "Are we running a kindergarten now?"

Mother did not react to his rudeness. "I was thinking over your comment the other day," she said. "About how young people imagine journalism is a glamorous profession, and don't understand how much hard work is necessary."

He frowned. "Did I say that? Well, it's certainly true."

"So I brought my daughter here to see the reality. I think it will be good for her education, especially if she becomes a writer. She will make a report on the visit to her class. I felt sure you would approve."

Mother was making this up as she went along, but it sounded convincing, Carla thought. She almost believed it herself. The charm switch had been turned to the On position at last.

Jochmann said: "Don't you have an important visitor from London coming today?"

"Yes, Ethel Leckwith, but she's an old friend—she knew Carla as a baby."

Jochmann was somewhat mollified. "Hmm. Well, we have an editorial meeting in five minutes, as soon as I've bought some cigarettes."

"Carla will get them for you." Mother turned to her. "There is a tobacconist three doors down. Herr Jochmann likes the Roth-Händle brand."

"Oh, that will save me a trip." Jochmann gave Carla a one-mark coin.

Mother said to her: "When you come back, you'll find me at the top of the stairs, next to the fire alarm." She turned away and took Jochmann's arm confidentially. "I thought last week's issue was possibly our best ever," she said as they went up.

Carla ran out into the street. Mother had got away with it, using her characteristic mixture of boldness and flirting. She sometimes said: "We women have to deploy every weapon we have." Thinking about it, Carla realized she had used Mother's tactics to get a lift from Herr Franck. Perhaps she was like her mother after all. That might be why Mother had given her that curious little smile: she was seeing herself thirty years ago.

There was a queue in the shop. Half the journalists in Berlin seemed to be buying their supplies for the day. At last Carla got a pack of Roth-Händles and returned to the *Democrat* building. She found the fire alarm easily—it was a big lever fixed to the wall—but Mother was not in her office. No doubt she had gone to that editorial meeting.

Carla walked along the corridor. All the doors were open, and most of the rooms were empty but for a few women who might have been typists and secretaries. At the back of the building, around a corner, was a closed door marked CONFERENCE ROOM. Carla could hear male voices raised in argument. She tapped on the door, but there was no response. She hesitated, then turned the handle and went in.

The room was full of tobacco smoke. Eight or ten people sat around a long table. Mother was the only woman. They fell silent, apparently surprised, when Carla went up to the head of the table and handed Jochmann the cigarettes and change. Their silence made her think she had done wrong to come in.

But Jochmann just said: "Thank you."

"You're welcome, sir," she said, and for some reason she gave a little bow.

The men laughed. One said: "New assistant, Jochmann?" Then she knew it was all right.

She left the room quickly and returned to Mother's office. She did not take off her coat—the place was cold. She looked around. On the desk were a phone, a typewriter, and stacks of paper and carbon paper.

Next to the phone was a photograph in a frame, showing Carla and Erik with Father. It had been taken a couple of years ago on a sunny day at the beach by the Wannsee lake, fifteen miles from the center of Berlin. Father was wearing shorts. They were all laughing. That was before Erik started to pretend to be a tough, serious man.

The only other picture, hanging on the wall, showed Mother with the Social Democratic hero Friedrich Ebert, who had been the first president of Germany after the war. It had been taken about ten years ago. Carla smiled at Mother's shapeless, low-waisted dress and boyish haircut; they must have been fashionable at the time.

The bookshelf held social directories, phone books, dictionaries in several languages, and atlases, but nothing to read. In the desk drawer were pencils, several new pairs of formal gloves still wrapped in tissue paper, a packet of sanitary towels, and a notebook with names and phone numbers.

Carla reset the desk calendar to today's date, Monday, February 27, 1933. Then she put a sheet of paper into the typewriter. She typed her full name, Heike Carla von Ulrich. At the age of five she had announced that she did not like the name Heike and she wanted everyone to use her second name, and somewhat to her surprise her family had complied.

Each key of the typewriter caused a metal rod to rise up and strike the paper through an inky ribbon, printing a letter. When by accident she pressed two keys, the rods got stuck. She tried to prize them apart but she could not. Pressing another key did not help: now there were three jammed rods. She groaned: she was in trouble already.

A noise from the street distracted her. She went to the window. A dozen Brownshirts were marching along the middle of the road, shouting slogans: "Death to all Jews! Jews, go to hell!" Carla could not understand why they got so angry about Jews, who seemed the same as everyone else, apart from their religion. She was startled to see Sergeant Schwab at the head of the troop. She had felt sorry for him when he was sacked, for she knew he would find it hard to get another job. There were millions of men looking for jobs in Germany; Father said it was a depression. But Mother had said: "How can we have a man in our house who steals?"

Their chant changed. "Smash Jew papers!" they said in unison. One of them threw something, and a rotten vegetable splashed on the door of a national newspaper. Then, to Carla's horror, they turned toward the building she was in.

She drew back and peeped around the edge of the window frame, hoping they could not see her. They stopped outside, still chanting. One threw a stone. It hit Carla's window without breaking it, but all the same she gave a little scream of fear. A moment later one of the typists came in, a young woman in a red beret. "What's the matter?" she said; then she looked out of the window. "Oh, hell."

The Brownshirts entered the building, and Carla heard boots on the stairs. She was scared: What were they going to do?

Sergeant Schwab came into Mother's office. He hesitated, seeing the two females, then seemed to screw up his nerve. He picked up the typewriter and threw it through the window, shattering the glass. Carla and the typist both screamed.

More Brownshirts passed the doorway, shouting their slogans.

Schwab grabbed the typist by the arm and said: "Now, darling, where's the office safe?"

"In the file room!" she said in a terrified voice.

"Show me."

"Yes, anything!"

He marched her out of the room.

Carla started to cry, then stopped herself.

She thought of hiding under the desk, but hesitated. She did not want to show them how scared she was. Something inside her wanted to defy them.

But what should she do? She decided to warn Mother.

She stepped to the doorway and looked along the corridor. The Brownshirts were going in and out of the offices but had not reached the far end. Carla did not know whether the people in the conference room could hear the commotion. She ran along the corridor as fast as she could, but a scream stopped her. She looked into a room and saw Schwab shaking the typist with the red beret, yelling: "Where's the key?"

"I don't know. I swear I'm telling the truth!" the typist cried.

Carla was outraged. Schwab had no right to treat a woman that way. She shouted: "Leave her alone, Schwab, you thief!"

Schwab looked at her with hatred in his eyes, and suddenly she was ten times more frightened. Then his gaze shifted to someone behind her, and he said: "Get the kid out of the damn way."

She was picked up from behind. "Are you a little Jew?" said a man's voice. "You look it, with all that dark hair."

That terrified her. "I'm not Jewish!" she screamed.

The Brownshirt carried her back along the corridor and put her down in Mother's office. She stumbled and fell to the floor. "Stay in here," he said, and he went away.

Carla got to her feet. She was not hurt. The corridor was full of Brownshirts now, and she could not get to her mother. But she had to summon help.

She looked out of the smashed window. A small crowd was gathering on the street. Two policemen stood among the onlookers, chatting. Carla shouted at them: "Help! Help, police!"

They saw her and laughed.

That infuriated her, and anger made her less frightened. She looked outside the office again. Her gaze lit on the fire alarm on the wall. She reached up and grasped the handle.

She hesitated. You were not supposed to sound the alarm unless there was a fire, and a notice on the wall warned of dire penalties.

She pulled the handle anyway.

For a moment nothing happened. Perhaps the mechanism was not working.

Then there came a loud, harsh klaxon sound, rising and falling, that filled the building.

Almost immediately the people from the conference room appeared at the far end of the corridor. Jochmann was first. "What the devil is going on?" he said angrily, shouting over the noise of the alarm.

One of the Brownshirts said: "This Jew Communist rag has insulted our leader, and we're closing it down."

"Get out of my office!"

The Brownshirt ignored him and went into a side room. A moment later there was a female scream and a crash that sounded like a steel desk being overturned.

Jochmann turned to one of his staff. "Schneider—call the police immediately!"

Carla knew that would be no good. The police were there already, doing nothing.

Mother pushed through the knot of people and came running along the corridor. "Are you all right?" she cried. She threw her arms around Carla.

Carla did not want to be comforted like a child. Pushing her mother away, she said: "I'm fine. Don't worry."

Mother looked around. "My typewriter!"

"They threw it through the window." Carla realized that now she would not get into trouble for jamming the mechanism.

"We must get out of here." Mother snatched up the desk photo, then took Carla's hand, and they hurried out of the room.

No one tried to stop them running down the stairs. Ahead of them, a well-built young man who might have been one of the reporters had a Brownshirt in a headlock and was dragging him out of the building. Carla and her mother followed the pair out. Another Brownshirt came up behind them.

The reporter approached the two policemen, still dragging the Brownshirt. "Arrest this man," he said. "I found him robbing the office. You will find a stolen jar of coffee in his pocket."

"Release him, please," said the older of the two policemen.

Reluctantly, the reporter let the Brownshirt go.

The second Brownshirt stood beside his colleague.

"What is your name, sir?" the policeman asked the reporter.

"I am Rudolf Schmidt, chief parliamentary correspondent of *The Democrat*."

"Rudolph Schmidt, I am arresting you on a charge of assaulting the police."

"Don't be ridiculous. I caught this man stealing!"

The policeman nodded to the two Brownshirts. "Take him to the station house."

They grabbed Schmidt by the arms. He seemed about to struggle, then changed his mind. "Every detail of this incident will appear in the next edition of *The Democrat!*" he said.

"There will never be another edition," the policeman said. "Take him away."

A fire engine arrived and half a dozen firemen jumped out. Their leader spoke brusquely to the police. "We need to clear the building," he said.

"Go back to your fire station—there's no fire," said the older policeman. "It's just the storm troopers closing down a Communist magazine."

"That's no concern of mine," the fireman said. "The alarm has been sounded, and our first task is to get everyone out, storm troopers and all. We'll manage without your help." He led his men inside.

Carla heard her mother say: "Oh, no!" She turned and saw that Mother was staring at her typewriter, which lay on the pavement where it had fallen. The metal casing had dropped away, exposing the links between keys and rods. The keyboard was twisted out of shape, one end of the roller had become detached, and the bell that sounded for the end of a line lay forlornly on the ground. A typewriter was not a precious object, but Mother looked as if she might cry.

The Brownshirts and the staff of the magazine came out of the building, herded by firemen. Sergeant Schwab was resisting, shouting angrily: "There's no fire!" The firemen just shoved him on.

Jochmann came out and said to Mother: "They didn't have time to do much damage—the firemen stopped them. Whoever sounded the alarm did us a great service!"

Carla had been worried that she would be reprimanded for causing a false alarm. Now she realized she had done exactly the right thing.

She took her mother's hand. That seemed to jerk Mother out of her momentary fit of grief. She wiped her eyes with her sleeve, an unusual act that revealed how badly shaken she was: if Carla had done that, she would have been told to use her handkerchief. "What do we do now?" Mother never said that—she always knew what to do next.

Carla became aware of two people standing nearby. She looked up. One was a woman about the same age as Mother, very pretty, with an air of authority. Carla knew her, but could not place her. Beside her was a man young enough to be her son. He was slim, and not very tall, but he looked like a movie star. He had a handsome face that would have been almost too pretty except that his nose was flattened and misshapen. Both newcomers looked shocked, and the young man was white with anger.

The woman spoke first, and she used the English language. "Hello, Maud," she said, and the voice was distantly familiar to Carla. "Don't you recognize me?" she went on. "I'm Eth Leckwith, and this is Lloyd."

ii

Lloyd Williams found a boxing club in Berlin where he could do an hour's training for a few pennies. It was in a working-class district called Wedding, north of the city center. He exercised with the Indian clubs and the medicine ball, skipped rope, hit the punch bag, and then put on a helmet and did five rounds in the ring. The club coach found him a sparring partner, a German his own age and size—Lloyd was a welterweight. The German boy had a nice fast jab that came from nowhere and hurt Lloyd several times, until Lloyd hit him with a left hook and knocked him down.

Lloyd had been raised in a rough neighborhood, the East End of London. At the age of twelve he had been bullied at school. "Same thing happened to me," his stepfather, Bernie Leckwith, had said. "Cleverest boy in school, and you get picked on by the class *shlammer.*" Bernie, whom he called "Dad," was Jewish—his mother spoke only Yiddish. He had taken Lloyd to the Aldgate Boxing Club. Ethel had been against it, but Bernie had overruled her, something that did not happen often.

Lloyd had learned to move fast and punch hard, and the bullying had stopped. He had also got the broken nose that made him look less of a pretty boy. And he discovered a talent. He had quick reflexes and a combative streak, and he had won prizes in the ring. The coach was disappointed that he wanted to go to Cambridge University instead of turning professional.

He showered and put his suit back on, then went to a workingmen's bar, bought a glass of draft beer, and sat down to write to his half sister, Millie, about the incident with the Brownshirts. Millie was envious of his taking this trip with their mother, and he had promised to send her frequent bulletins.

Lloyd had been shaken by this morning's fracas. Politics was part of everyday life for him: his mother had been a member of Parliament, his father was a local councilor in London, and he himself was London chairman of the Labour League of Youth. But it had always been a matter of debating and voting—until today. He had never before seen an office trashed by uniformed thugs while the police looked on, smiling. It was politics with the gloves off, and it had shocked him.

"Could this happen in London, Millie?" he wrote. His first instinct was to think it could not. But Hitler had admirers among British industrialists and newspaper proprietors. Only a few months ago the rogue M.P. Sir Oswald Mosley had started the British Union of Fascists. Like the Nazis, they liked to strut up and down in military-style uniforms. What next?

He finished his letter and folded it, then caught the S train back into the city center. He and his mother were going to meet Walter and Maud von Ulrich for dinner. Lloyd had been hearing about Maud all his life. She and his mother were unlikely friends: Ethel had started her working life as a maid in a grand house owned by Maud's family. Later they had been suffragettes together, campaigning for votes for women. During the war they had produced a feminist newspaper, *The Soldier's Wife.* Then they had quarreled over political tactics and become estranged.

Lloyd could remember vividly the von Ulrich family's trip to London in 1925. He had been ten, old enough to feel embarrassed that he spoke no German while Erik and Carla, aged five and three, were bilingual. That was when Ethel and Maud had patched up their quarrel.

He made his way to the restaurant, Bistro Robert. The interior was art deco, with unforgivingly rectangular chairs and tables, and elaborate iron lamp stands with colored glass shades; but he liked the starched white napkins standing at attention beside the plates.

The other three were already there. The women were striking, he realized as he approached the table: both poised, well dressed, attractive, and confident. They were getting admiring glances from other diners. He wondered how much of his mother's modish dress sense had been picked up from her aristocratic friend.

When they had ordered, Ethel explained her trip. "I lost my parliamentary seat in 1931," she said. "I hope to win it back at the next election, but meanwhile I have to make a living. Fortunately, Maud, you taught me to be a journalist."

"I didn't teach you much," Maud said. "You had a natural talent."

"I'm writing a series of articles about the Nazis for the *News Chronicle,* and I have a contract to write a book for a publisher called Victor Gollancz. I brought Lloyd as my interpreter—he's studying French and German."

Lloyd observed her proud smile and felt he did not deserve it. "My translation skills have not been much tested," he said. "So far we've mostly met people like you, who speak perfect English."

Lloyd had ordered breaded veal, a dish he had never even seen in England. He found it delicious. While they were eating, Walter said to him: "Shouldn't you be at school?"

"Mam thought I would learn more German this way, and the school agreed."

"Why don't you come and work for me in the Reichstag for a while? Unpaid, I'm afraid, but you'd be speaking German all day."

Lloyd was thrilled. "I'd love to. What a marvelous opportunity!"

"If Ethel can spare you," Walter added.

She smiled. "Perhaps I can have him back now and again, when I really need him?"

"Of course."

Ethel reached across the table and touched Walter's hand. It was an intimate gesture, and Lloyd realized that the bond between these three was very close. "How kind you are, Walter," she said.

"Not really. I can always use a bright young assistant who understands politics."

Ethel said: "I'm not sure I understand politics anymore. What on earth is happening here in Germany?"

Maud said: "We were doing all right in the midtwenties. We had a democratic government and a growing economy. But everything was ruined by the Wall Street crash of 1929. Now we're in the depths of a depression." Her voice shook with an emotion that seemed close to grief. "You can see a hundred men standing in line for one advertised job. I look at their faces. They're desperate. They don't know how they're going to feed their children. Then the Nazis offer them hope, and they ask themselves: What have I got to lose?"

Walter seemed to think she might be overstating the case. In a more cheerful tone he said: "The good news is that Hitler has failed to win over a majority of Germans. In the last election the Nazis got a third of the votes. Nevertheless they were the largest party, but fortunately Hitler only leads a minority government."

"That's why he demanded another election," Maud put in. "He needs an overall majority to turn Germany into the brutal dictatorship he wants."

"Will he get it?" Ethel asked.

"No," said Walter.

"Yes," said Maud.

Walter said: "I don't believe the German people will ever actually vote for a dictatorship."

"But it won't be a fair election!" Maud said angrily. "Look what happened to my magazine today. Anyone who criticizes the Nazis is in danger. Meanwhile, their propaganda is everywhere."

Lloyd said: "Nobody seems to fight back!" He wished he had arrived a few minutes earlier at the *Democrat* office this morning, so that he could have punched a few Brownshirts. He realized he was making a fist, and forced himself to open his hand. But the indignation did not go away. "Why don't left-wingers raid the offices of Nazi magazines? Give them a taste of their own medicine!"

"We must not meet violence with violence!" Maud said emphatically. "Hitler is looking for an excuse to crack down—to declare a national emergency, sweep away civil rights, and put his opponents in jail." Her voice took on a pleading note. "We must avoid giving him that pretext—no matter how hard it is."

They finished their meal. The restaurant began to empty out. As their coffee was served, they were joined by the owner, Walter's second cousin Robert von Ulrich, and the chef, Jörg. Robert had been a diplomat at the Austrian embassy in London before the Great War, while Walter was doing the same thing at the German embassy there—and falling in love with Maud.

Robert resembled Walter, but was more fussily dressed, with a gold pin in his tie, seals on his watch chain, and heavily slicked hair. Jörg was younger, a blond man with delicate features and a cheerful smile. The two had been prisoners of war together in Russia. Now they lived in an apartment over the restaurant.

They reminisced about the wedding of Walter and Maud, held in great secrecy on the eve of the war. There had been no guests, but Robert and Ethel had been best man and bridesmaid. Ethel said: "We had champagne at the hotel. Then I tactfully said that Robert and I would leave, and Walter—" She suppressed a fit of giggles. "Walter said: 'Oh, I assumed we would all have dinner together!'"

Maud chuckled. "You can imagine how pleased I was about that!"

Lloyd looked into his coffee, feeling embarrassed. He was eighteen and a virgin, and honeymoon jokes made him uncomfortable.

More somberly, Ethel asked Maud: "Do you ever hear from Fitz these days?"

Lloyd knew that the secret wedding had caused a terrible rift between Maud and her brother, Earl Fitzherbert. Fitz had disowned her because she had not gone to him, as head of the family, and asked his permission to marry.

Maud shook her head sadly. "I wrote to him that time we went to London, but he refused even to see me. I hurt his pride by marrying Walter without telling him. My brother is an unforgiving man, I'm afraid."

Ethel paid the bill. Everything in Germany was cheap if you had foreign currency. They were about to get up and leave when a stranger came to the table and, uninvited, pulled up a chair. He was a heavy man with a small mustache in the middle of a round face.

He wore a Brownshirt uniform.

Robert said coldly: "What may I do for you, sir?"

"My name is Criminal Commissar Thomas Macke." He grabbed a passing waiter by the arm and said: "Bring me a coffee."

The waiter looked inquiringly at Robert, who nodded.

"I work in the political department of the Prussian police," Macke went on. "I am in charge of the Berlin intelligence section."

Lloyd translated for his mother in a low voice.

"However," said Macke, "I wish to speak to the proprietor of the restaurant about a personal matter."

Robert said: "Where did you work a month ago?"

The unexpected question startled Macke, and he replied immediately: "At the police station in Kreuzberg."

"And what was your job there?"

"I was in charge of records. Why do you ask?"

Robert nodded as if he had expected something like this. "So you have gone from a job as a filing clerk to head of the Berlin intelligence section. Congratulations on your rapid promotion." He turned to Ethel. "When Hitler became chancellor at the end of January, his henchman Hermann Göring took the role of interior minister of Prussia—in charge of the largest police force in the world. Since then, Göring has been firing policemen wholesale and replacing them with Nazis." He turned back to Macke and said sarcastically: "However, in the case of our surprise guest I'm sure the promotion was purely on merit."

Macke flushed, but kept his temper. "As I said, I wish to speak to the proprietor about something personal."

"Please come and see me in the morning. Would ten o'clock suit you?"

Macke ignored this suggestion. "My brother is in the restaurant business," he plowed on.

"Ah! Perhaps I know him. Macke is the name? What kind of establishment does he run?"

"A small place for workingmen in Friedrichshain."

"Ah. Then it isn't likely that I have met him."

Lloyd was not sure it was wise for Robert to be so waspish. Macke was rude, and did not deserve kindness, but he could probably make serious trouble.

Macke went on: "My brother would like to buy this restaurant."

"Your brother wants to move up in the world, as you have."

"We are prepared to offer you twenty thousand marks, payable over two years."

Jörg burst out laughing.

Robert said: "Permit me to explain something to you, Commissar. I am an Austrian count. Twenty years ago I had a castle and a large country estate in Hungary where my mother and sister lived. In the war I lost my family, my castle, my lands, and even my country, which was . . . miniaturized." His tone of amused sarcasm had gone, and his voice became gruff with emotion. "I came to Berlin with nothing but the address of Walter von Ulrich, my second cousin. Nevertheless I managed to open this restaurant." He swallowed. "It is all I have." He paused, and drank some coffee. The others around the table were silent. He regained his poise, and something of his superior tone of voice.

"Even if you offered a generous price—which you have not—I would still refuse, because I would be selling my whole life. I have no wish to be rude to you, even though you have behaved unpleasantly. But my restaurant is not for sale at any price." He stood up and held out his hand to shake. "Good night, Commissar Macke."

Macke automatically shook hands, then looked as if he regretted it. He stood up, clearly angry. His fat face was a purplish color. "We will talk again," he said, and he walked out.

"What an oaf," said Jörg.

Walter said to Ethel: "You see what we have to put up with? Just because he wears that uniform, he can do anything he likes!"

What had bothered Lloyd was Macke's confidence. He had seemed to feel sure he could buy the restaurant at the price he named. He reacted to Robert's refusal as if it were no more than a temporary setback. Were the Nazis already so powerful?

This was the kind of thing Oswald Mosley and his British Fascists wanted—a country in which the rule of law was replaced by bullying and beating. How could people be so damn stupid?

They put on their coats and hats and said good night to Robert and Jörg. As soon as they stepped outside, Lloyd smelled smoke—not tobacco, but something else. The four of them got into Walter's car, a BMW Dixi 3/15, which Lloyd knew was a German-manufactured Austin Seven.

As they drove through the Tiergarten park, two fire engines overtook them, bells clanging. "I wonder where the fire is," said Walter.

A moment later they saw the glow of flames through the trees. Maud said: "It seems to be near the Reichstag."

Walter's tone changed. "We'd better take a look," he said worriedly, and he made a sudden turn.

The smell of smoke grew stronger. Over the tops of the trees Lloyd could see flames shooting skyward. "It's a *big* fire," he said.

They emerged from the park onto the Königs Platz, the broad plaza between the Reichstag building and the Kroll Opera House opposite. The Reichstag was ablaze. Red and yellow light danced behind the classical rows of windows. Flame and smoke jetted up through the central dome. "Oh, no!" said Walter, and to Lloyd he sounded stricken with grief. "Oh, God in heaven, no."

He stopped the car and they all got out.

"This is a catastrophe," said Walter.

Ethel said: "Such a beautiful old building."

"I don't care about the building," Walter said surprisingly. "It's our democracy that's on fire."

A small crowd watched from a distance of about fifty yards. In front of the building, fire engines were lined up, their hoses already playing on the flames, water jetting in through broken windows. A handful of policemen stood around doing nothing. Walter spoke to one of them. "I am a Reichstag deputy," he said. "When did this start?"

"An hour ago," the policeman said. "We've got one of them that did it—a man with nothing on but his trousers! He used his clothes to start the fire."

"You should put up a rope cordon," Walter said with authority. "Keep people at a safe distance."

"Yes, sir," said the policeman, and went off.

Lloyd slipped away from the others and moved nearer to the building. The firemen were bringing the blaze under control: there was less flame and more smoke. He walked past the fire engines and approached a window. It did not seem very dangerous, and anyway his curiosity overcame his sense of self-protection—as usual.

When he peered through a window, he saw that the destruction was severe: walls and ceilings had collapsed into piles of rubble. As well as firemen he saw civilians in coats—presumably Reichstag officials—moving around in the debris, assessing the damage. Lloyd went to the entrance and climbed the steps.

Two black Mercedes cars roared up just as the police were erecting their cordon. Lloyd looked on with interest. Out of the second car jumped a man in a light-colored trench coat and a floppy black hat. He had a narrow mustache under his nose. Lloyd realized he was looking at the new chancellor, Adolf Hitler.

Behind Hitler followed a taller man in the black uniform of the Schutzstaffel, the SS, his personal bodyguard. Limping after them came the Jew-hating propaganda chief, Joseph Goebbels. Lloyd recognized them from newspaper photographs. He was so fascinated to see them close up that he forgot to be horrified.

Hitler ran up the steps two at a time, heading directly toward Lloyd. On impulse, Lloyd pushed open the big door and held it wide for the chancellor. With a nod to him, Hitler walked in, and his entourage followed.

Lloyd joined them. No one spoke to him. Hitler's people seemed to assume he was one of the Reichstag staff, and vice versa.

There was a foul smell of wet ashes. Hitler and his party stepped over charred beams and hosepipes, treading in mucky puddles. In the entrance hall stood Hermann Göring, a camel-hair coat covering his huge belly, his hat turned up in front Potsdam-fashion. This was the man who was packing the police force with Nazis, Lloyd thought, recalling the conversation in the restaurant.

As soon as Göring saw Hitler, he shouted: "This is the beginning of the Communist uprising! Now they'll strike out! There's not a minute to waste!"

Lloyd felt weirdly as if he were in the audience at the theater, and these powerful men were being played by actors.

Hitler was even more histrionic than Göring. "There will be no mercy now!" he shrieked. He sounded as if he were addressing a stadium. "Anyone who stands in our way will be butchered." He trembled as he worked himself up into a fury. "Every Communist functionary will be shot where he is found. The Communist deputies to the Reichstag must be hanged this very night." He looked as if he would burst.

But there was something artificial about it all. Hitler's hatred seemed real, but the outburst was also a performance, put on for the benefit of those around him, his own people and others. He was an actor, feeling a genuine emotion but amplifying it for the audience. And it was working, Lloyd saw: everyone within earshot was staring, mesmerized.

Göring said: "My Führer, this is my chief of political police, Rudolf

Diels." He indicated a slim, dark-haired man at his side. "He has already arrested one of the perpetrators."

Diels was not hysterical. Calmly he said: "Marinus van der Lubbe, a Dutch construction worker."

"And a Communist!" Göring said triumphantly.

Diels said: "Expelled from the Dutch Communist Party for starting fires."

"I knew it!" said Hitler.

Lloyd saw that Hitler was determined to blame the Communists, regardless of the facts.

Diels said deferentially: "From my first interrogation of the man, I have to say it is clear he is a lunatic, working alone."

"Nonsense!" Hitler cried. "This was planned long in advance. But they miscalculated! They don't understand that the people are on our side."

Göring turned to Diels. "The police are on emergency footing from this moment," he said. "We have lists of Communists—Reichstag deputies, local government elected representatives, Communist Party organizers and activists. Arrest them all—tonight! Firearms should be used ruthlessly. Interrogate them without mercy."

"Yes, Minister," said Diels.

Lloyd realized that Walter had been right to worry. This was the pretext the Nazis had been looking for. They were not going to listen to anyone who said the fire had been started by a lone madman. They wanted a Communist plot so that they could announce a crackdown.

Göring looked down with distaste at the muck on his shoes. "My official residence is only a minute away, but is fortunately unaffected by the fire, my Führer," he said. "Perhaps we should adjourn there?"

"Yes. We have much to discuss."

Lloyd held the door and they all went out. As they drove away, he stepped over the police cordon and rejoined his mother and the von Ulrichs.

Ethel said: "Lloyd! Where have you been? I was worried sick!"

"I went inside," he said.

"What? How?"

"No one stopped me. It's all chaos and confusion."

His mother threw her hands in the air. "He has no sense of danger," she said.

"I met Adolf Hitler."

Walter said: "Did he say anything?"

"He's blaming the Communists for the fire. There's going to be a purge."

"God help us," said Walter.

iii

Thomas Macke was still smarting from the sarcasm of Robert von Ulrich. "Your brother wants to move up in the world, as you have," von Ulrich had said.

Macke wished he had thought to reply: "And why should we not? We are as good as you, you arrogant popinjay." Now he yearned for revenge. But for a few days he was too busy to do anything about it.

The headquarters of the Prussian secret police were in a large, elegant building of classical architecture at no. 8 Prinz Albrecht Strasse in the government quarter. Macke felt proud every time he walked through the door.

It was a hectic time. Four thousand Communists had been arrested within twenty-four hours of the Reichstag fire, and more were being rounded up every hour. Germany was being cleansed of a plague, and to Macke the Berlin air already tasted purer.

But the police files were not up-to-date. People had moved house, elections had been lost and won, old men had died and young men had taken their places. Macke was in charge of a group updating the records, finding new names and addresses.

He was good at this. He liked registers, directories, street maps, news clippings, any kind of list. His talents had not been valued at the

Kreuzberg police station, where criminal intelligence was simply beating up suspects until they named names. He was hoping to be better appreciated here.

Not that he had any problem with beating up suspects. In his office at the back of the building he could hear the screams of men and women being tortured in the basement, but it did not bother him. They were traitors, subversives, and revolutionaries. They had ruined Germany with their strikes, and they would do worse if they got the chance. He had no sympathy for them. He only wished Robert von Ulrich was among them, groaning in agony and begging for mercy.

It was eight o'clock in the evening on Thursday, March 2, before he got a chance to check on Robert.

He sent his team home, and took a sheaf of updated lists upstairs to his boss, Criminal Inspector Kringelein. Then he returned to the files.

He was in no hurry to go home. He lived alone. His wife, an undisciplined woman, had gone off with a waiter from his brother's restaurant, saying she wanted to be free. There were no children.

He began to comb the files.

He had already established that Robert von Ulrich had joined the Nazi Party in 1923 and had left two years later. That in itself did not mean much. Macke needed more.

The filing system was not as logical as he would have liked. All in all, he was disappointed in the Prussian police. The rumor was that Göring was equally unimpressed, and planned to detach the political and intelligence departments from the regular force and form them into a new, more efficient secret police force. Macke thought that was a good idea.

Meanwhile, he failed to find Robert von Ulrich in any of the regular files. Perhaps that was not merely a sign of inefficiency. The man might be blameless. As an Austrian count, he was unlikely to be a Communist or a Jew. It seemed the worst that could be said of him was that his cousin Walter was a Social Democrat. That was not a crime—not yet.

Macke now realized he should have done this research before approaching the man. But he had gone ahead without full information.

He might have known that was a mistake. In consequence he had been forced to submit to condescension and sarcasm. He had felt humiliated. But he would get his own back.

He began to go through miscellaneous papers in a dusty cupboard at the back of the room.

The name of von Ulrich did not appear here either, but there was one document missing.

According to the list pinned to the inside of the cupboard door, there should have been a file of 117 pages entitled "Vice Establishments." It sounded like a survey of Berlin's nightclubs. Macke could guess why it was not here. It must have been in use recently: all the more decadent night spots had been closed down when Hitler became chancellor.

Macke went back upstairs. Kringelein was briefing uniformed police who were to raid the updated addresses Macke had provided for Communists and their allies.

Macke did not hesitate to interrupt his boss. Kringelein was not a Nazi, and would therefore be afraid to reprimand a storm trooper. Macke said: "I'm looking for the 'Vice Establishments' file."

Kringelein looked annoyed but made no protest. "On the side table," he said. "Help yourself."

Macke took the file and returned to his own room.

The survey was five years old. It detailed the clubs then in existence and stated what activities went on in them: gambling, indecent displays, prostitution, sale of drugs, homosexuality, and other depravities. The file named owners and investors, club members and employees. Macke patiently read each entry: perhaps Robert von Ulrich was a drug addict or a user of whores.

Berlin was famous for its homosexual clubs. Macke plowed through the dreary entry on the Pink Slipper, where men danced with men and the floor show featured transvestite singers. Sometimes, he thought, his work was disgusting.

He ran his finger down the list of members, and found Robert von Ulrich.

He gave a sigh of satisfaction.

Looking farther down, he saw the name of Jörg Schleicher.

"Well, well," he said. "Let's see how sarcastic you are now."

iv

The next time Lloyd saw Walter and Maud he found them angrier—and more scared.

It was the following Saturday, March 4, the day before the election. Lloyd and Ethel were planning to attend a Social Democratic Party rally organized by Walter, and they went to the von Ulrichs' home in Mitte for lunch beforehand.

It was a nineteenth-century house with spacious rooms and large windows, though much of the furniture was worn. The lunch was plain, pork chops with potatoes and cabbage, but there was good wine with it. Walter and Maud talked as if they were poor, and no doubt they were living more simply than their parents had, but all the same they were not going hungry.

However, they were frightened.

Hitler had persuaded Germany's aging president, Paul von Hindenburg, to approve the Reichstag Fire Decree, which gave the Nazis authority for what they were already doing, beating and torturing their political opponents. "Twenty thousand people have been arrested since Monday night!" Walter said, his voice shaking. "Not just Communists, but people the Nazis call 'Communist sympathizers.'"

"Which means anyone they dislike," said Maud.

Ethel said: "How can there be a democratic election now?"

"We must do our best," Walter said. "If we don't campaign, it will only help the Nazis."

Lloyd said impatiently: "When will you stop accepting this and start to fight back? Do you still believe it would be wrong to meet violence with violence?"

"Absolutely," said Maud. "Peaceful resistance is our only hope."

Walter said: "The Social Democratic Party has a paramilitary wing, the Reichsbanner, but it's weak. A small group of Social Democrats proposed a violent response to the Nazis, but they were outvoted."

Maud said: "Remember, Lloyd, the Nazis have the police and the army on their side."

Walter looked at his pocket watch. "We must get going."

Maud said suddenly: "Walter, why don't you cancel?"

He stared at her in surprise. "Seven hundred tickets have been sold."

"Oh, to blazes with the tickets," Maud said. "I'm worried about *you*."

"Don't worry. Seats have been carefully allocated, so there should be no troublemakers in the hall."

Lloyd was not sure Walter was as confident as he pretended.

Walter went on: "Anyway, I cannot let down people who are still willing to come to a democratic political meeting. They are all the hope that remains to us."

"You're right," Maud said. She looked at Ethel. "Perhaps you and Lloyd should stay home. It's dangerous, no matter what Walter says, and this isn't your country, after all."

"Socialism is international," Ethel said stoutly. "Like your husband, I appreciate your concern, but I'm here to witness German politics firsthand, and I'm not going to miss this."

"Well, the children can't go," Maud said.

Erik, the son, said: "I don't even want to go."

Carla looked disappointed but said nothing.

Walter, Maud, Ethel, and Lloyd got into Walter's little car. Lloyd was nervous but excited, too. He was getting a perspective on politics superior to anything his friends back home had. And if there was going to be a fight, he was not afraid.

They drove east, crossing Alexander Platz, into a neighborhood of poor houses and small shops, some of which had signs in Hebrew letters. The Social Democratic Party was working-class, but like the British Labour Party it had a few affluent supporters. Walter von Ulrich was in a small upper-class minority.

The car pulled up outside a marquee that said PEOPLE'S THEATER. A line had already formed outside. Walter crossed the pavement to the door, waving to the waiting crowd, who cheered. Lloyd and the others followed him inside.

Walter shook hands with a solemn young man of about eighteen. "This is Wilhelm Frunze, secretary of the local branch of our party." Frunze was one of those boys who looked as if they had been born middle-aged. He wore a blazer with buttoned pockets that had been fashionable ten years ago.

Frunze showed Walter how the theater doors could be barred from the inside. "When the audience is seated, we will lock up, so that no troublemakers can get in," he said.

"Very good," said Walter. "Well done."

Frunze ushered them into the auditorium. Walter went up onstage and greeted some other candidates who were already there. The public began to come in and take their seats. Frunze showed Maud, Ethel, and Lloyd to reserved places in the front row.

Two boys approached. The younger, who looked about fourteen but was taller than Lloyd, greeted Maud with careful good manners and made a little bow. Maud turned to Ethel and said: "This is Werner Franck, the son of my friend Monika." Then she said to Werner: "Does your father know you're here?"

"Yes—he said I should find out about Social Democracy myself."

"He's broad-minded, for a Nazi."

Lloyd thought this was a rather tough line to take with a fourteen-year-old, but Werner was a match for her. "My father doesn't really believe in Nazism, but he thinks Hitler is good for German business."

Wilhelm Frunze said indignantly: "How can it be good for business to throw thousands of people into jail? Apart from the injustice, they can't work!"

Werner said: "I agree with you. And yet Hitler's crackdown is popular."

"People think they're being saved from a Bolshevik revolution," Frunze said. "The Nazi press has them convinced that the Communists were about to launch a campaign of murder, arson, and poison in every town and village."

The boy with Werner, who was shorter but older, said: "And yet it is the Brownshirts, not the Communists, who drag people into basements and break their bones with clubs." He spoke German fluently with a slight accent that Lloyd could not place.

Werner said: "Forgive me. I forgot to introduce Vladimir Peshkov. He goes to the Berlin Boys' Academy, my school, and he's always called Volodya."

Lloyd stood up to shake hands. Volodya was about Lloyd's age, a striking young man with a frank blue-eyed gaze.

Frunze said: "I know Volodya Peshkov. I go to the Berlin Boys' Academy, too."

Volodya said: "Wilhelm Frunze is the school genius—top marks in physics and chemistry and math."

"It's true," said Werner.

Maud looked hard at Volodya and said: "Peshkov? Is your father Grigori?"

"Yes, Frau von Ulrich. He is a military attaché at the Soviet embassy."

So Volodya is Russian. He speaks German effortlessly, Lloyd thought with a touch of envy. No doubt that comes from living here.

"I know your parents well," Maud said to Volodya. She knew all the diplomats in Berlin, Lloyd had already gathered. It was part of her job.

Frunze checked his watch and said: "Time to begin." He went up onstage and called for order.

The theater went quiet.

Frunze announced that the candidates would make speeches and then take questions from the audience. Tickets had been issued only to Social Democratic Party members, he added, and the doors were now closed, so everyone could speak freely, knowing they were among friends.

It was like being a member of a secret society, Lloyd thought. This was not what he called democracy.

Walter spoke first. He was no demagogue, Lloyd observed. He had no rhetorical flourishes. But he flattered his audience, telling them they were intelligent and well-informed men and women who understood the complexity of political issues.

He had been speaking for only a few minutes when a Brownshirt walked onstage.

Lloyd cursed. How had he got in? He came from the wings: someone must have opened the stage door.

He was a huge brute with an army haircut. He stepped to the front of the stage and shouted: "This is a seditious gathering. Communists and subversives are not wanted in today's Germany. The meeting is closed."

The confident arrogance of the man outraged Lloyd. He wished he could get this great oaf in a boxing ring.

Wilhelm Frunze leaped to his feet, stood in front of the intruder, and yelled furiously: "Get out of here, you thug!"

The man shoved him in the chest powerfully. Frunze staggered back, stumbled, and fell over backward.

The audience were on their feet, some shouting in angry protest, some screaming in fear.

More Brownshirts appeared from the wings.

Lloyd realized with dismay that the bastards had planned this well.

The man who had shoved Frunze shouted: "Out!" The other Brownshirts took up the cry: "Out! Out! Out!" There were about twenty of them now, and more appearing all the time. Some carried police nightsticks or improvised clubs. Lloyd saw a hockey stick, a wooden sledgehammer, even a chair leg. They strutted up and down the stage, grinning fiendishly and waving their weapons as they chanted, and Lloyd had no doubt they were itching to start hitting people.

He was on his feet. Without thinking, he, Werner, and Volodya had formed a protective line in front of Ethel and Maud.

Half the audience were trying to leave, the other half shouting and shaking their fists at the intruders. Those attempting to get out were shoving others, and minor scuffles had broken out. Many of the women were crying.

Onstage, Walter grasped the lectern and shouted: "Everyone try to keep calm, please! There is no need for disorder!" Most people could not hear and the rest ignored him.

The Brownshirts began to jump off the stage and wade into the audience. Lloyd took his mother's arm, and Werner did the same with Maud. They moved toward the nearest exit in a group. But all the doors were already jammed with knots of panicking people trying to leave. That made no difference to the Brownshirts, who kept yelling at people to get out.

The attackers were mostly able-bodied, whereas the audience included women and old men. Lloyd wanted to fight back, but it was not a good idea.

A man in a Great War steel helmet shouldered Lloyd, and he lurched forward and bumped into his mother. He resisted the temptation to turn and confront the man. His priority was to protect Mam.

A spotty-faced boy carrying a truncheon put a hand on Werner's back and shoved energetically, yelling: "Get out, get out!" Werner turned quickly and took a step toward him. "Don't touch me, you Fascist pig," he said. The Brownshirt suddenly stopped dead and looked scared, as if he had not been expecting resistance.

Werner turned away again, concentrating like Lloyd on getting the two women to safety. But the huge man had heard the exchange and yelled: "Who are you calling a pig?" He lashed out at Werner, hitting the back of his head with his fist. His aim was poor and it was a glancing blow, but all the same Werner cried out and staggered forward.

Volodya stepped between them and hit the big man in the face, twice. Lloyd admired Volodya's rapid one-two, but turned his attention back to his task. Seconds later the four of them reached the doorway. Lloyd and Werner managed to help the women out into the theater foyer. Here the crush eased and the violence stopped—there were no Brownshirts.

Seeing the women safe, Lloyd and Werner looked back into the auditorium.

Volodya was fighting the big man bravely, but he was in trouble. He kept punching the man's face and body, but his blows had little effect, and the man shook his head as if pestered by an insect. The Brownshirt was heavy-footed and slow-moving, but he hit Volodya in the chest and then the head, and Volodya staggered. The big man drew back his fist for a massive punch. Lloyd was afraid it could kill Volodya.

Then Walter took a flying leap off the stage and landed on the big man's back. Lloyd wanted to cheer. They fell to the floor in a blur of arms and legs, and Volodya was saved, for the moment.

The spotty youth who had shoved Werner was now harassing the people trying to leave, hitting their backs and heads with his truncheon. "You fucking coward!" Lloyd yelled, stepping forward. But Werner was ahead of him. He shoved past Lloyd and grabbed the truncheon, trying to wrestle it away from the youth.

The older man in the steel helmet joined in and hit Werner with a pickax handle. Lloyd stepped forward and hit the older man with a straight right. The blow landed perfectly, next to the man's left eye.

But he was a war veteran, and not easily discouraged. He swung around and lashed out at Lloyd with his club. Lloyd dodged the blow easily and hit him twice more. He connected in the same area, around the man's eyes, breaking the skin. But the helmet protected the man's head, and Lloyd could not land a left hook, his knockout punch. He ducked a swing of the pickax handle and hit the man's face again, and the man backed away, blood pouring from cuts around his eyes.

Lloyd looked around. He saw that the Social Democrats were fighting back now, and he got a jolt of savage pleasure. Most of the audience had passed through the doors, leaving mainly young men in the auditorium, and they were coming forward, clambering over the theater seats to get at the Brownshirts; there were dozens of them.

Something hard struck his head from behind. It was so painful that he roared. He turned to see a boy of his own age holding a length of timber, raising it to strike again. Lloyd closed in on him and hit him hard in the stomach twice, first with his right fist, then with his left. The boy gasped for breath and dropped the wood. Lloyd hit him with an uppercut to the chin and he passed out.

Lloyd rubbed the back of his head. It hurt like hell but there was no blood.

The skin on his knuckles was raw and bleeding, he saw. He bent down and picked up the length of timber dropped by the boy.

When he looked around again, he was thrilled to see some of the Brownshirts retreating, clambering up onto the stage and disappearing into the wings, presumably aiming to leave through the stage door by which they had entered.

The big man who had started it all was on the floor, groaning and holding his knee as if he had dislocated something. Wilhelm Frunze stood over him, hitting him with a wooden shovel again and again, repeating at the top of his voice the words the man had used to start the riot: "Not! Wanted! In! Today's! Germany!" Helpless, the big man tried to roll away from the blows, but Frunze went after him, until two more Brownshirts grabbed the man's arms and dragged him away.

Frunze let them go.

Did we beat them? Lloyd thought with growing exultation. Maybe we did!

Several of the younger men chased their opponents up onto the stage, but they stopped there and contented themselves with shouting insults as the Brownshirts disappeared.

Lloyd looked at the others. Volodya had a swollen face and one closed eye. Werner's jacket was ripped, a big square of cloth dangling. Walter was sitting on a front-row seat, breathing hard and rubbing his elbow, but he was smiling. Frunze threw his shovel away, sailing it across the rows of empty seats to the back.

Werner, who was only fourteen, was exultant. "We gave them hell, didn't we?"

Lloyd grinned. "Yes, we certainly did."

Volodya put his arm around Frunze's shoulders. "Not bad for a bunch of schoolboys, eh?"

Walter said: "But they stopped our meeting."

The youngsters stared resentfully at him for spoiling their triumph.

Walter looked angry. "Be realistic, boys. Our audience has fled in terror. How long will it be before those people have the nerve to go to a political meeting again? The Nazis have made their point. It's dangerous even to listen to any party other than theirs. The big loser today is Germany."

Werner said to Volodya: "I hate those fucking Brownshirts. I think I might join you Communists."

Volodya looked at him hard with those intense blue eyes and spoke in a low voice. "If you're serious about fighting the Nazis, there might be something more effective you could do."

Lloyd wondered what Volodya meant.

Then Maud and Ethel came running back into the auditorium, both speaking at the same time, crying and laughing with relief, and Lloyd forgot Volodya's words and never thought of them again.

v

Four days later, Erik von Ulrich came home in a Hitler Youth uniform.

He felt like a prince.

He had a brown shirt just like the one worn by storm troopers, with various patches and a swastika armband. He also had the regulation black tie and black shorts. He was a patriotic soldier dedicated to the service of his country. At last he was one of the gang.

This was even better than supporting Hertha, Berlin's favorite soccer team. Erik was taken to matches occasionally, on Saturdays when his father did not have a political meeting to attend. That gave him the same sense of belonging to a great big crowd of people all feeling the same emotions.

But Hertha sometimes lost, and he came home disconsolate.

The Nazis were winners.

He was terrified of what his father was going to say.

His parents infuriated him by insisting on marching out of step. All the boys were joining the Hitler Youth. They had sports and singing and adventures in the fields and forests outside the city. They were smart and fit and loyal and efficient.

Erik was deeply troubled by the thought that he might have to fight in battle someday—his father and grandfather had—and he wanted to be ready for that, trained and hardened, disciplined and aggressive.

The Nazis hated Communists, but so did Mother and Father. So what if the Nazis hated Jews as well? The von Ulrichs were not Jewish; why should they care? But Mother and Father stubbornly refused to join in. Well, Erik was fed up with being left out, and he had decided to defy them.

He was scared stiff.

As usual, neither Mother nor Father was at the house when Erik and Carla came home from school. Ada pursed her lips disapprovingly as she served their tea, but she said: "You'll have to clear the table yourselves today—I've got a terrible backache. I'm going to lie down."

Carla looked concerned. "Is that what you had to see the doctor about?"

Ada hesitated before replying: "Yes, that's right."

She was obviously hiding something. The thought of Ada being ill— and lying about it—made Erik uneasy. He would never go as far as Carla and say he loved Ada, but she had been a kindly presence all his life, and he was more fond of her than he liked to say.

Carla was just as concerned. "I hope it gets better."

Lately Carla had become more grown-up, somewhat to Erik's bewilderment. Although he was two years older, he still felt like a kid, but she acted like an adult half the time.

Ada said reassuringly: "I'll be fine after a rest."

Erik ate some bread. When Ada left the room, he swallowed and said: "I'm only in the junior section, but as soon as I'm fourteen, I can move up."

Carla said: "Father's going to hit the roof! Are you mad?"

"Herr Lippmann said Father will be in trouble if he tries to make me leave."

"Oh, brilliant," said Carla. She had developed a streak of withering sarcasm that sometimes stung Erik. "So you'll get Father into a row with the Nazis," she said scornfully. "What a great idea. So good for the whole family."

Erik was taken aback. He had not thought of it that way. "But all the boys in my class are members," he said indignantly. "Except for Frenchy Fontaine and Jewboy Rothmann."

Carla spread fish paste on her bread. "Why do you have to be the same as the others?" she said. "Most of them are stupid. You told me Rudi Rothmann was the cleverest boy in the class."

"I don't want to be with Frenchy and Rudi!" Erik cried, and to his mortification he felt tears come to his eyes. "Why should I have to play with the boys no one likes?" This was what had given him the courage to defy his father: he could no longer bear to walk out of school with the Jews and the foreigners while all the German boys marched around the playing field in their uniforms.

They both heard a cry.

Erik looked at Carla and said: "What was that?"

Carla frowned. "It was Ada, I think."

Then, more distinctly, they heard: "Help!"

Erik got to his feet, but Carla was ahead of him. He went after her. Ada's room was in the basement. They ran down the stairs and into the small bedroom.

There was a narrow single bed up against the wall. Ada was lying there, her face screwed up in pain. Her skirt was wet and there was a puddle on the floor. Erik could hardly believe what he was seeing. Had she pissed herself? It was scary. There were no other grown-ups in the house. He did not know what to do.

Carla was scared, too—Erik could see it in her face—but she was not panicked. She said: "Ada, what's wrong?" Her voice sounded strangely calm.

"My waters broke," Ada said.

Erik had no idea what that meant.

Nor did Carla. "I don't understand," she said.

"It means my baby is coming."

"You're pregnant?" Carla said in astonishment.

Erik said: "But you're not married!"

Carla said furiously: "Shut up, Erik—don't you know anything?"

He did know, of course, that women could have babies when they were not married—but surely not Ada!

"That's why you went to the doctor last week," Carla said to Ada.

Ada nodded.

Erik was still trying to get used to the idea. "Do you think Mother and Father know?"

"Of course they do. They just didn't tell us. Fetch a towel."

"Where from?"

"The airing cupboard on the upstairs landing."

"A clean one?"

"Of course a clean one!"

Erik ran up the stairs, took a small white towel from the cupboard, and ran down again.

"That's not much good," Carla said, but she took it and dried Ada's legs.

Ada said: "The baby's coming soon. I can feel it. But I don't know what to do." She started to cry.

Erik was watching Carla. She was in charge now. It did not matter that he was the older one: he looked to her for leadership. She was being practical and staying calm, but he could tell that she was terrified, and her composure was fragile. She could crack at any minute, he thought.

Carla turned to Erik again. "Go and fetch Dr. Rothmann," she said. "You know where his office is."

Erik was hugely relieved to have been given a task he could manage. Then he thought of a snag. "What if he's out?"

"Then ask Frau Rothmann what you should do, you idiot!" Carla said. "Get going—run!"

Erik was glad to get out of the room. What was happening there was mysterious and frightening. He went up the stairs three at a time and flew out of the front door. Running was one thing he did know how to do.

The doctor's surgery was half a mile away. He settled into a fast trot. As he ran, he thought about Ada. Who was the father of her baby? He recalled that she had gone to the movies with Paul Huber a couple of times last summer. Had they had sexual intercourse? They must have! Erik and his friends talked about sex a lot, but they did not really know anything about it. Where had Ada and Paul done it? Not in a movie theater, surely? Didn't people have to lie down? He was baffled.

Dr. Rothmann's place was in a poorer street. He was a good doctor, Erik had heard Mother say, but he treated a lot of working-class people who could not pay high fees. The doctor's house had a consulting room and a waiting room on the ground floor, and the family lived upstairs.

Outside was parked a green Opel 4, an ugly little two-seater unofficially called the Tree Frog.

The front door of the house was unlatched. Erik walked in, breathing hard, and entered the waiting room. There was an old man coughing in a corner and a young woman with a baby. "Hello!" Erik called. "Dr. Rothmann?"

The doctor's wife stepped out of the consulting room. Hannelore Rothmann was a tall, fair woman with strong features, and she gave Erik a look like thunder. "How dare you come to this house in that uniform?" she said.

Erik was petrified. Frau Rothmann was not Jewish, but her husband was; Erik had forgotten that in his excitement. "Our maid is having a baby!" he said.

"And so you want a Jewish doctor to help you?"

Erik was taken completely by surprise. It had never occurred to him that the Nazis' attacks might cause the Jews to retaliate. But suddenly he saw that Frau Rothmann made total sense. The Brownshirts went around shouting, "Death to Jews!" Why should a Jewish doctor help such people?

Now he did not know what to do. There were other doctors, of course, plenty of them, but he did not know where, nor whether they would come out to see a total stranger. "My sister sent me," he said feebly.

"Carla's got a lot more sense than you."

"Ada said the waters have broken." Erik was not sure what that meant, but it sounded significant.

With a disgusted look, Frau Rothmann went back into the consulting room.

The old man in the corner cackled. "We're all dirty Jews until you need our help!" he said. "Then it's: 'Please come, Dr. Rothmann,' and 'What's your advice, Lawyer Koch?' and 'Lend me a hundred marks, Herr Goldman,' and—" He was overcome by a fit of coughing.

A girl of about sixteen came in from the hall. Erik thought she must be the Rothmanns' daughter, Eva. He had not seen her for years. She had breasts now, but she was still plain and dumpy. She said: "Did your father let you join the Hitler Youth?"

"He doesn't know," said Erik.

"Oh, boy," said Eva. "You're in trouble."

He looked from her to the consulting room door. "Do you think your father's going to come?" he said. "Your mother was awfully cross with me."

"Of course he'll come," Eva said. "If people are sick, he helps them." Her voice became scornful. "He doesn't check their race or politics first. We're not Nazis." She went out again.

Erik felt bewildered. He had not expected this uniform to get him into so much trouble. At school everyone thought it was wonderful.

A moment later Dr. Rothmann appeared. Speaking to the two waiting patients, he said: "I'll be back as soon as I can. I'm sorry, but a baby won't wait to be born." He looked at Erik. "Come on, young man, you'd better ride with me, despite that uniform."

Erik followed him out and got into the passenger seat of the Tree Frog. He loved cars and was desperate to be old enough to drive, and normally he enjoyed riding in any vehicle, watching the dials and studying the driver's technique. But now he felt as if he were on display, sitting beside a Jewish doctor in his brown shirt. What if Herr Lippmann should see him? The trip was agony.

Fortunately it was short: in a couple of minutes they were at the von Ulrich house.

"What's the young woman's name?" Rothmann said.

"Ada Hempel."

"Ah, yes, she came to see me last week. The baby's early. All right, take me to her."

Erik led the way into the house. He heard a baby cry. It had come already! He hurried down to the basement, the doctor following.

Ada lay on her back. The bed was soaked with blood and something else. Carla stood holding a tiny baby in her arms. The baby was covered in slime. Something that looked like thick string ran from the baby up Ada's skirt. Carla was wide-eyed with terror. "What must I do?" she cried.

"You're doing exactly the right thing," Dr. Rothmann reassured her. "Just hold that baby close a minute longer." He sat beside Ada. He listened to her heart, took her pulse, and said: "How do you feel, my dear?"

"I'm so tired," she said.

Rothmann gave a satisfied nod. He stood up again and looked at the baby in Carla's arms. "A little boy," he said.

Erik watched with a mixture of fascination and revulsion as the doctor opened his bag, took out some thread, and tied two knots in the cord. While he was doing so, he spoke to Carla in a soft voice. "Why are you crying? You've done a marvelous job. You've delivered a baby all on your own. You hardly needed me! You'd better be a doctor when you grow up."

Carla became calmer. Then she whispered: "Look at his head." The doctor had to lean toward her to hear. "I think there's something wrong with him."

"I know." The doctor took out a pair of sharp scissors and cut the cord between the two knots. Then he took the naked baby from Carla and held him at arm's length, studying him. Erik could not see anything wrong, but the baby was so red and wrinkled and slimy that it was hard to tell. However, after a thoughtful moment the doctor said: "Oh, dear."

Looking more carefully, Erik could see that there was something wrong. The baby's face was lopsided. One side was normal, but on the other the head seemed dented and there was something strange about the eye.

Rothmann handed the baby back to Carla.

Ada groaned again, and seemed to strain.

When she relaxed, Rothmann reached under her skirt and drew out a lump of something that looked disgustingly like meat. "Erik," he said. "Fetch me a newspaper."

Erik said: "Which one?" His parents took all the main papers every day.

"Any one, lad," said Rothmann gently. "I don't want to read it."

Erik ran upstairs and found yesterday's *Vossische Zeitung*. When he returned, the doctor wrapped the meaty thing in the paper and put it on the floor. "It's what we call the afterbirth," he said to Carla. "Best to burn it, later."

Then he sat on the edge of the bed again. "Ada, my dear girl, you must be very brave," he said. "Your baby is alive, but there may be something wrong with him. We're going to wash him and wrap him up warmly. Then we must take him to the hospital."

Ada looked frightened. "What's the matter?"

"I don't know. We need to have him checked."

"Will he be all right?"

"The hospital doctors will do everything they can. The rest we must leave to God."

Erik remembered that Jews worshipped the same God as Christians. It was easy to forget that.

Rothmann said: "Do you think you could get up and come to the hospital with me, Ada? Baby needs you to feed him."

"I'm so tired," she said again.

"Take a minute or two to rest, then. But not much more, because Baby needs to be looked at soon. Carla will help you get dressed. I'll wait upstairs." He addressed Erik with gentle irony. "Come with me, little Nazi."

Erik wanted to squirm. Dr. Rothmann's forbearance was even worse than Frau Rothmann's scorn.

As they were leaving, Ada said: "Doctor?"

"Yes, my dear."

"His name is Kurt."

"A very good name," said Dr. Rothmann. He went out, and Erik followed.

vi

Lloyd Williams's first day working as assistant to Walter von Ulrich was also the first day of the new parliament.

Walter and Maud were struggling frantically to save Germany's fragile democracy. Lloyd shared their desperation, partly because they were good people whom he had known off and on all his life, and partly because he feared that Britain could follow Germany down the road to hell.

The election had resolved nothing. The Nazis got 44 percent, an increase but still short of the 51 percent they craved.

Walter saw hope. Driving to the opening of the parliament, he said: "Even with massive intimidation, they failed to win the votes of most Germans." He banged his fist on the steering wheel. "Despite everything they say, they are *not* popular. And the longer they stay in government, the better people will get to know their wickedness."

Lloyd was not so sure. "They've closed opposition newspapers, thrown Reichstag deputies in jail, and corrupted the police," he said. "And yet forty-four percent of Germans approve? I don't find that reassuring."

The Reichstag building was badly fire-damaged and quite unusable, so the parliament assembled in the Kroll Opera House, on the opposite side of the Königs Platz. It was a vast complex with three concert halls and fourteen smaller auditoria, plus restaurants and bars.

When they arrived, they had a shock. The place was surrounded by Brownshirts. Deputies and their aides crowded around the entrances, trying to get in. Walter said furiously: "Is this how Hitler plans to get his way—by preventing us from entering the chamber?"

Lloyd saw that the doors were barred by Brownshirts. They admitted those in Nazi uniform without question, but everyone else had to produce credentials. A boy younger than Lloyd looked him up and down contemptuously before grudgingly letting him in. This was intimidation, pure and simple.

Lloyd felt his temper beginning to simmer. He hated to be bullied. He knew he could knock the Brownshirt boy down with one good left hook. He forced himself to remain calm, turn away, and walk through the door.

After the fight in the People's Theater, his mother had examined the egg-shaped lump on his head and ordered him to go home to England. He had talked her round, but it had been a close thing.

She said he had no sense of danger, but that was not quite right. He did get scared sometimes, but it always made him feel combative. His instinct was to go on the attack, not to retreat. This scared his mother.

Ironically, she was just the same. She was not going home. She was frightened, but she was also thrilled to be here in Berlin at this turning point in German history, and outraged by the violence and repression she was witnessing. She felt sure she could write a book that would forewarn democrats in other countries about Fascist tactics. "You're worse than me," Lloyd had said to her, and she had had no answer.

Inside, the opera house was swarming with Brownshirts and SS men, many of them armed. They guarded every door and showed, with looks and gestures, their hatred and contempt for anyone not supporting the Nazis.

Walter was late for a Social Democratic Party group meeting. Lloyd hurried around the building looking for the right room. Glancing into the debating chamber, he saw that a giant swastika hung from the ceiling, dominating the room.

The first matter to be discussed, when proceedings began that afternoon, was to be the Enabling Act, which would permit Hitler's cabinet to pass laws without the approval of the Reichstag.

The act offered a dreadful prospect. It would make Hitler a dictator. The repression, intimidation, violence, torture, and murder that

Germany had seen in the past few weeks would become permanent. It was unthinkable.

But Lloyd could not imagine that any parliament in the world would pass such a law. They would be voting themselves out of power. It was political suicide.

He found the Social Democrats in a small auditorium. Their meeting had already begun. Lloyd hurried Walter to the room; then he was sent for coffee.

Waiting in the queue, he found himself behind a pale, intense-looking young man dressed in funereal black. Lloyd's German had become more fluent and colloquial, and he now had the confidence to strike up a conversation with a stranger. The man in black was Heinrich von Kessel, he learned. He was doing the same sort of job as Lloyd, working as an unpaid aide to his father, Gottfried von Kessel, a deputy for the Centre Party, which was Catholic.

"My father knows Walter von Ulrich very well," Heinrich said. "They were both attachés at the German embassy in London in 1914."

The world of international politics and diplomacy was quite small, Lloyd reflected.

Heinrich told Lloyd that a return to the Christian faith was the answer to Germany's problems.

"I'm not much of a Christian," Lloyd said candidly. "I hope you don't mind my saying so. My grandparents are Welsh Bible-punchers, but my mother is indifferent and my stepfather's Jewish. Occasionally we go to the Calvary Gospel Hall in Aldgate, mainly because the pastor is a Labour Party member."

Heinrich smiled and said: "I'll pray for you."

Catholics were not proselytizers, Lloyd remembered. What a contrast with his dogmatic grandparents in Aberowen, who thought that people who did not believe as they did were willfully blinding themselves to the Gospel, and would be condemned to eternal damnation.

When Lloyd reentered the Social Democratic Party meeting, Walter was speaking. "It can't happen!" he said. "The Enabling Act is a constitutional amendment. Two-thirds of the representatives must be present, which would be 432 out of a possible 647. And two-thirds of those present must approve."

Lloyd added up the numbers in his head as he put the tray down on the table. The Nazis had 288 seats, and the Nationalists, who were their close allies, had 52, making 340—nearly 100 short. Walter was right. The act could not be passed. Lloyd was comforted, and sat down to listen to the discussion and improve his German.

But his relief was short-lived. "Don't be so sure," said a man with a working-class Berlin accent. "The Nazis are caucusing with the Centre Party." That was Heinrich's lot, Lloyd recalled. "That could give them another 74," the man finished.

Lloyd frowned. Why would the Centre Party support a measure that would take away all its power?

Walter voiced the same thought more bluntly. "How could the Catholics be so stupid?"

Lloyd wished he had known about this before he went for coffee— then he could have discussed it with Heinrich. He might have learned something useful. Damn.

The man with the Berlin accent said: "In Italy, the Catholics made a deal with Mussolini—a concordat to protect the Church. Why not here?"

Lloyd calculated that the Centre Party's support would bring the Nazis' votes up to 414. "It's still not two-thirds," he said to Walter with relief.

Another young aide heard him and said: "But that doesn't take into account the Reichstag president's latest announcement." The Reichstag president was Hermann Göring, Hitler's closest associate. Lloyd had not heard about an announcement. Nor had anyone else, it seemed. The deputies went quiet. The aide went on: "He has ruled that Communist deputies who are absent because they are in jail don't count."

There was an outburst of indignant protest all around the room. Lloyd saw Walter go red in the face. "He can't do that!" Walter said.

"It's completely illegal," said the aide. "But he has done it."

Lloyd was dismayed. Surely the law could not be passed by a trick? He did some more arithmetic. The Communists had 81 seats. If they were discounted, the Nazis needed only two-thirds of 566, which was 378. Even with the Nationalists they still did not have enough—but if they won the support of the Catholics, they could swing it.

Someone said: "This is all completely illegal. We should walk out in protest."

"No, no!" said Walter emphatically. "They would pass the act in our absence. We've got to talk the Catholics out of it. Wels must speak to Kaas immediately." Otto Wels was the leader of the Social Democratic Party, prelate Ludwig Kaas the head of the Centre Party.

There was a murmur of agreement around the room.

Lloyd took a deep breath and spoke up. "Herr von Ulrich, why don't you take Gottfried von Kessel to lunch? I believe you two worked together in London before the war."

Walter laughed mirthlessly. "That creep!" he said.

Maybe the lunch was not such a good idea. Lloyd said: "I didn't realize you disliked the man."

Walter looked thoughtful. "I hate him—but I'll try anything, by God."

Lloyd said: "Shall I find him and extend the invitation?"

"All right, give it a try. If he accepts, tell him to meet me at the Herrenklub at one."

"Very good."

Lloyd hurried back to the room into which Heinrich had disappeared. He stepped inside. A meeting was going on similar to the one he had left. He scanned the room, spotted the black-clad Heinrich, met his gaze, and beckoned him urgently.

They both stepped outside; then Lloyd said: "They're saying your party is going to support the Enabling Act!"

"It's not certain," said Heinrich. "They're divided."

"Who's against the Nazis?"

"Brüning and some others." Brüning was a former chancellor and a leading figure.

Lloyd felt more hopeful. "Which others?"

"Did you call me out of the room to pump me for information?"

"Sorry. No, I didn't. Walter von Ulrich wants to have lunch with your father."

Heinrich looked dubious. "They don't like each other—you know that, don't you?"

"I gathered as much. But they'll put their differences aside today!"

Heinrich did not seem sure. "I'll ask him. Wait here." He went back inside.

Lloyd wondered whether there was any chance this would work. It was a shame Walter and Gottfried were not bosom buddies. But he could hardly believe the Catholics would vote with the Nazis.

What bothered him most was the thought that if it could happen in Germany, it could happen in Britain. This grim prospect made him shiver with dread. He had his whole life in front of him, and he did not want to live it in a repressive dictatorship. He wanted to work in politics, like his parents, and make his country a better place for people such as the Aberowen coal miners. For that he needed political meetings where people could speak their minds, and newspapers that could attack the government, and pubs where men could have arguments without looking over their shoulders to see who was listening.

Fascism threatened all that. But perhaps Fascism would fail. Walter might be able to talk Gottfried around, and prevent the Centre Party supporting the Nazis.

Heinrich came out. "He'll do it."

"Great! Herr von Ulrich suggested the Herrenklub at one o'clock."

"Really? Is he a member?"

"I assume so—why?"

"It's a conservative institution. I suppose he is Walter *von* Ulrich, so he must come from a noble family, even if he is a socialist."

"I should probably book a table. Do you know where it is?"

"Just around the corner." Heinrich gave Lloyd directions.

"Shall I book for four?"

Heinrich grinned. "Why not? If they don't want you and me there, they can just ask us to leave." He went back into the room.

Lloyd left the building and walked quickly across the plaza, passing the burned-out Reichstag building, and made his way to the Herrenklub.

There were gentlemen's clubs in London, but Lloyd had never been inside one. This place was a cross between a restaurant and a funeral parlor, he thought. Waiters in full evening dress padded about, laying silent cutlery on tables shrouded in white. A headwaiter took his reservation and wrote down the name "von Ulrich" as solemnly as if he were making an entry in the Book of the Dead.

He returned to the opera house. The place was getting busier and noisier, and the tension seemed higher. Lloyd heard someone say excitedly that Hitler himself would open the proceedings this afternoon by proposing the act.

A few minutes before one, Lloyd and Walter walked across the plaza. Lloyd said: "Heinrich von Kessel was surprised to learn that you are a member of the Herrenklub."

Walter nodded. "I was one of the founders, a decade or more ago. In those days it was the Juniklub. We got together to campaign against the Versailles Treaty. It's become a right-wing bastion, and I'm probably the only Social Democrat, but I remain a member because it's a useful place to meet with the enemy."

Inside the club Walter pointed to a sleek-looking man at the bar. "That's Ludwig Franck, the father of young Werner, who fought alongside us at the People's Theater," Walter said. "I'm sure he's not a member here—he isn't even German-born—but it seems he's having lunch with his father-in-law, Count von der Helbard, the elderly man beside him. Come with me."

They went to the bar and Walter performed introductions. Franck said to Lloyd: "You and my son got into quite a scrap a couple of weeks back."

Lloyd touched the back of his head reflexively: the swelling had gone down, but the place was still painful to touch. "We had women to protect, sir," he said.

"Nothing wrong with a bit of a punch-up," Franck said. "Does you lads good."

Walter cut in impatiently: "Come on, Ludi. Busting up election meetings is bad enough, but your leader wants to completely destroy our democracy!"

"Perhaps democracy is not the right form of government for us," said Franck. "After all, we're not like the French or the Americans—thank God."

"Don't you care about losing your freedom? Be serious!"

Franck suddenly dropped his facetious air. "All right, Walter," he said coldly. "I will be serious, if you insist. My mother and I arrived here from Russia more than ten years ago. My father was not able to come with us. He had been found to be in possession of subversive literature, specifically a book called *Robinson Crusoe,* apparently a novel that promotes bourgeois individualism, whatever the hell that might be. He was sent to a prison camp somewhere in the Arctic. He may—" Franck's voice broke for a moment, and he paused, swallowed, and at last finished quietly: "He may still be there."

There was a moment of silence. Lloyd was shocked by the story. He knew that the Russian Communist government could be cruel, in general, but it was quite another thing to hear a personal account, told simply by a man who was clearly still grieving.

Walter said: "Ludi, we all hate the Bolsheviks—but the Nazis could be worse!"

"I'm willing to take that risk," said Franck.

Count von der Helbard said: "We'd better go in for lunch. I've got an afternoon appointment. Excuse us." The two men left.

"It's what they always say!" Walter raged. "The Bolsheviks! As if they were the only alternative to the Nazis! I could weep."

Heinrich walked in with an older man who was obviously his father: they had the same thick dark hair combed with a parting, except that Gottfried's was shorter and tweeded with silver. Although their features were similar, Gottfried looked like a fussy bureaucrat in an old-fashioned collar, whereas Heinrich was more like a romantic poet than a political aide.

The four of them went into the dining room. Walter wasted no time.

As soon as they had ordered, he said: "I can't understand what your party hopes to gain by supporting this Enabling Act, Gottfried."

Von Kessel was equally direct. "We are a Catholic party, and our first duty is to protect the position of the Church in Germany. That's what people hope for when they vote for us."

Lloyd frowned in disapproval. His mother had been a member of Parliament, and she always said it was her duty to serve the people who did *not* vote for her, as well as those who did.

Walter employed a different argument. "A democratic parliament is the best protection for all our churches—yet you're about to throw that away!"

"Wake up, Walter," Gottfried said testily. "Hitler won the election. He has come to power. Whatever we do, he's going to rule Germany for the foreseeable future. We have to protect ourselves."

"His promises are worth nothing!"

"We have asked for specific assurances in writing: the Catholic Church to be independent of the state, Catholic schools to operate unmolested, no discrimination against Catholics in the civil service." He looked inquiringly at his son.

Heinrich said: "They promised the agreement would be with us first thing this afternoon."

Walter said: "Weigh the options! A scrap of paper signed by a tyrant, against a democratic parliament—which is better?"

"The greatest power of all is God."

Walter rolled his eyes. "Then God save Germany," he said.

The Germans had not had time to develop faith in democracy, Lloyd reflected as the argument surged back and forth between Walter and Gottfried. The Reichstag had been sovereign for only fourteen years. They had lost a war, seen their currency devalued to nothing, and suffered mass unemployment: to them, the right to vote seemed inadequate protection.

Gottfried proved immovable. At the end of lunch his position was as firm as ever. His responsibility was to protect the Catholic Church. It made Lloyd want to scream.

They returned to the opera house and the deputies took their seats in the auditorium. Lloyd and Heinrich sat in a box looking down.

Lloyd could see the Social Democratic Party members in a group on the far left. As the hour approached, he noticed Brownshirts and SS men placing themselves at the exits and around the walls in a threatening arc behind the Social Democrats. It was almost as if they planned to prevent the deputies leaving the building until they had passed the act. Lloyd found it powerfully sinister. He wondered, with a shiver of fear, whether he, too, might find himself imprisoned here.

There was a roar of cheering and applause, and Hitler walked in, wearing a Brownshirt uniform. The Nazi deputies, most of them similarly dressed, rose to their feet in ecstasy as he mounted the rostrum. Only the Social Democrats remained seated, but Lloyd noticed that one or two looked uneasily over their shoulders at the armed guards. How could they speak and vote freely if they were nervous even about not joining in the standing ovation for their opponent?

When at last they became quiet, Hitler began to speak. He stood straight, his left arm at his side, gesturing only with his right. His voice was harsh and grating but powerful, reminding Lloyd of both a machine gun and a barking dog. His tone thrilled with feeling as he spoke of the "November traitors" of 1918 who had surrendered when Germany was about to win the war. He was not pretending: Lloyd felt he sincerely believed every stupid, ignorant word he spoke.

The November traitors were a well-worn topic for Hitler, but then he took a new tack. He spoke of the churches, and the important place of the Christian religion in the German state. This was an unusual theme for him, and his words were clearly aimed at the Centre Party, whose votes would determine today's result. He said that he saw the two main denominations, Protestant and Catholic, as the most important factors for upholding nationhood. Their rights would not be touched by the Nazi government.

Heinrich shot a triumphant look at Lloyd.

"I'd still get it in writing, if I were you," Lloyd muttered.

It was two and a half hours before Hitler reached his peroration.

He ended with an unmistakable threat of violence. "The government of the nationalist uprising is determined and ready to deal with the announcement that the act has been rejected—and with it, that resistance has been declared." He paused dramatically, letting the message sink in: voting against the act would be a declaration of resistance. Then he reinforced it. "May you, gentlemen, now take the decision yourselves as to whether it is to be peace or war!"

He sat down to roars of approval from the Nazi delegates, and the session was adjourned.

Heinrich was elated, Lloyd depressed. They went off in different directions: their parties would now hold desperate last-minute discussions.

The Social Democrats were gloomy. Their leader, Wels, had to speak in the chamber, but what could he say? Several deputies said that if he criticized Hitler he might not leave the building alive. They feared for their own lives, too. If the deputies were killed, Lloyd thought in a moment of cold dread, what would happen to their aides?

Wels revealed that he had a cyanide capsule in his waistcoat pocket. If arrested, he would commit suicide to avoid torture. Lloyd was horrified. Wels was an elected representative, yet he was forced to behave like some kind of saboteur.

Lloyd had started the day with false expectations. He had thought the Enabling Act a crazy idea that had no chance of becoming reality. Now he saw that most people expected the act to become a reality today. He had misjudged the situation badly.

Was he equally wrong to believe that something like this could not happen in his own country? Was he fooling himself?

Someone asked if the Catholics had made a final decision. Lloyd stood up. "I'll find out," he said. He left and ran to the Centre Party's meeting room. As before, he put his head around the door and beckoned Heinrich outside.

"Brüning and Ersing are wavering," Heinrich said.

Lloyd's heart sank. Ersing was a Catholic union leader. "How can a trade unionist even think about voting for this bill?" he said.

"Kaas says the Fatherland is in danger. They all think there will be bloody anarchy if we reject this act."

"There'll be bloody tyranny if you pass it."

"What about your lot?"

"They think they will all be shot if they vote against. But they're going to do it anyway."

Heinrich went back inside and Lloyd returned to the Social Democrats. "The diehards are weakening," Lloyd told Walter and his colleagues. "They're afraid of a civil war if the act is rejected."

The gloom deepened.

They all returned to the debating chamber at six o'clock.

Wels spoke first. He was calm, reasonable, and unemotional. He pointed out that life in a democratic republic had been good for Germans, overall, bringing freedom of opportunity and social welfare, and reinstating Germany as a normal member of the international community.

Lloyd noticed Hitler making notes.

At the end Wels bravely professed allegiance to humanity and justice, freedom and socialism. "No Enabling Law gives you the power to annihilate ideas that are eternal and indestructible," he said, gaining courage as the Nazis began to laugh and jeer.

The Social Democrats applauded, but they were drowned out.

"We greet the persecuted and oppressed!" Wels shouted. "We greet our friends in the Reich. Their steadfastness and loyalty deserve admiration."

Lloyd could just make out his words over the hooting and booing of the Nazis.

"The courage of their convictions and their unbroken optimism guarantee a brighter future!"

He sat down amid raucous heckling.

Would the speech make any difference? Lloyd could not tell.

After Wels, Hitler spoke again. This time his tone was quite different. Lloyd realized that in his earlier speech the chancellor had only been warming up. His voice was louder now, his phrases more intemperate, his tone full of contempt. He used his right arm constantly to make aggressive gestures—pointing, hammering, clenching his fist, putting his hand on his heart, and sweeping the air in a motion that seemed to brush all opposition aside. Every impassioned phrase was cheered uproariously by his supporters. Every sentence expressed the same emotion: a savage, all-consuming, murderous rage.

Hitler was also confident. He claimed he had not needed to propose the Enabling Act. "We appeal in this hour to the German Reichstag to grant us something we would have taken anyway!" he jeered.

Heinrich looked worried, and left the box. A minute later Lloyd saw him on the floor of the auditorium, whispering in his father's ear.

When he returned to the box, he looked stricken.

Lloyd said: "Have you got your written assurances?"

Heinrich could not meet Lloyd's eye. "The document is being typed up," he replied.

Hitler finished by scorning the Social Democrats. He did not want their votes. "Germany shall be free!" he screamed. "But not through you!"

The leaders of the other parties spoke briefly. Every one appeared crushed. Prelate Kaas said the Centre Party would support the bill. The rest followed suit. Everyone but the Social Democrats was in favor.

The result of the vote was announced, and the Nazis cheered wildly.

Lloyd was awestruck. He had seen naked power brutally wielded, and it was an ugly sight.

He left the box without speaking to Heinrich.

He found Walter in the entrance lobby, weeping. He was using a large white handkerchief to wipe his face, but the tears kept coming. Lloyd had not seen men cry like that except at funerals.

Lloyd did not know what to say or do.

"My life has been a failure," Walter said. "This is the end of all hope. German democracy is dead."

vii

Saturday, April 1, was Boycott Jews Day. Lloyd and Ethel walked around Berlin, staring in incredulity, Ethel making notes for her book. The Star of David was crudely daubed on the windows of Jewish-owned shops. Brownshirts stood at the doors of Jewish-owned department stores, intimidating people who wanted to go in. Jewish lawyers and doctors were picketed. Lloyd happened to see a couple of Brownshirts stopping patients going in to see the von Ulrichs' family physician, Dr. Rothmann, but then a hard-handed coal-heaver with a sprained ankle told the Brownshirts to fuck off out of it, and they went in search of easier prey. "How can people be so mean to each other?" Ethel said.

Lloyd was thinking of the stepfather he loved. Bernie Leckwith was Jewish. If Fascism came to Britain, Bernie would be the target of this kind of hatred. The thought made Lloyd shudder.

A sort of wake was held at Bistro Robert that evening. Apparently no one had organized it, but by eight o'clock the place was full of Social Democrats, Maud's journalistic colleagues, and Robert's theatrical friends. The more optimistic among them said that liberty had merely gone into hibernation for the duration of the economic slump, and one day it would awaken. The rest just mourned.

Lloyd drank little. He did not enjoy the effect of alcohol on his brain. It blurred his thinking. He was asking himself what German left-wingers could have done to prevent this catastrophe, and he did not have an answer.

Maud told them about Ada's baby, Kurt. "She's brought him home from the hospital, and he seems to be happy enough for now. But his brain is damaged and he will never be normal. When he's older, he will have to live in an institution, poor mite."

Lloyd had heard how the baby had been delivered by eleven-year-old Carla. That little girl had grit.

Commissar Thomas Macke arrived at half past nine, wearing his Brownshirt uniform.

Last time he was here, Robert had treated him as a figure of fun, but

Lloyd had sensed the menace of the man. He looked foolish, with the little mustache in the middle of the fat face, but there was a glint of cruelty in his eyes that made Lloyd nervous.

Robert had refused to sell the restaurant. What did Macke want now?

Macke stood in the middle of the dining area and shouted: "This restaurant is being used to promote degenerate behavior!"

The patrons went quiet, wondering what this was about.

Macke raised a finger in a gesture that meant *You'd better listen!* Lloyd felt there was something horribly familiar about the action, and realized Macke was mimicking Hitler.

Macke said: "Homosexuality is incompatible with the masculine character of the German nation!"

Lloyd frowned. Was he saying that Robert was queer?

Jörg came into the restaurant from the kitchen, wearing his tall chef's hat. He stood by the door, glaring at Macke.

Lloyd was struck by a shocking thought. Maybe Robert *was* queer.

After all, he and Jörg had been living together since the war.

Looking around at their theatrical friends, Lloyd noticed that they were all men in pairs, except for two women with short hair . . .

Lloyd felt bewildered. He knew that queers existed, and as a broad-minded person he believed they should not be persecuted but helped. However, he thought of them as perverts and creeps. Robert and Jörg seemed like normal men, running a business and living quietly—almost like a married couple!

He turned to his mother and said quietly: "Are Robert and Jörg really . . ."

"Yes, dear," she said.

Maud, sitting next to her, said: "Robert in his youth was a menace to footmen."

Both women giggled.

Lloyd was doubly shocked: not only was Robert queer, but Ethel and Maud thought it a matter for lighthearted banter.

Macke said: "This establishment is now closed!"

Robert said: "You have no right!"

Macke could not close the place on his own, Lloyd thought; then he remembered how the Brownshirts had crowded onto the stage at the People's Theater. He looked toward the entrance—and was aghast to see Brownshirts pushing through the door.

They went around the tables knocking over bottles and glasses. Some customers sat motionless and watched; others got to their feet. Several men shouted and a woman screamed.

Walter stood up and spoke loudly but calmly. "We should all leave quietly," he said. "There's no need for any rough stuff. Everybody just get your coats and hats and go home."

The customers began to leave, some trying to get their coats, others just fleeing. Walter and Lloyd ushered Maud and Ethel toward the door. The till was near the exit, and Lloyd saw a Brownshirt open it and begin stuffing money into his pockets.

Until then Robert had been standing still, watching miserably as a night's business hurried out of the door, but this was too much. He gave a shout of protest and shoved the Brownshirt away from the till.

The Brownshirt punched him, knocking him to the floor, and began to kick him as he lay there. Another Brownshirt joined in.

Lloyd leaped to Robert's rescue. He heard his mother shout, "No!" as he shoved the Brownshirts aside. Jörg was almost as quick, and the two of them bent to help Robert up.

They were immediately attacked by several more Brownshirts. Lloyd was punched and kicked, and something heavy hit him over the head, and as he cried out in pain, he thought: No, not again.

He turned on his attackers, punching with his left and right, making every blow connect hard, trying to punch *through* the target as he had been taught. He knocked two men down; then he was grabbed from behind and thrown off balance. A moment later he was on the floor with two men holding him down while a third kicked him.

Then he was rolled over onto his front, his arms were pulled behind his back, and he felt metal on his wrists. He had been handcuffed for the first time in his life. He felt a new kind of fear. This was not just another roughhouse. He had been beaten and kicked, but worse was in store.

"Get up," someone told him in German.

He struggled to his feet. His head hurt. Robert and Jörg were also in handcuffs, he saw. Robert's mouth was bleeding and Jörg had one closed eye. Half a dozen Brownshirts were guarding them. The rest were drinking from the glasses and bottles left on the tables, or standing at the dessert cart stuffing their faces with pastries.

All the customers seemed to have gone. Lloyd felt relieved that his mother had got away.

The restaurant door opened and Walter came back in. "Commissar Macke," he said, displaying a typical politician's facility for remembering names. With as much authority as he could muster he said: "What is the meaning of this outrage?"

Macke pointed to Robert and Jörg. "These two men are homosexuals," he said. "And that boy attacked an auxiliary policeman who was arresting them."

Walter pointed to the till, which was open, its drawer sticking out and empty except for a few small coins. "Do police officers commit robbery nowadays?"

"A customer must have taken advantage of the confusion created by those resisting arrest."

Some of the Brownshirts laughed knowingly.

Walter said: "You used to be a law enforcement officer, didn't you, Macke? You might have been proud of yourself, once. But what are you now?"

Macke was stung. "We enforce order, to protect the Fatherland."

"Where are you planning to take your prisoners, I wonder?" Walter persisted. "Will it be a properly constituted place of detention? Or some half-hidden unofficial basement?"

"They will be taken to the Friedrich Strasse Barracks," Macke said indignantly.

Lloyd saw a look of satisfaction pass briefly across Walter's face, and realized Walter had cleverly manipulated Macke, playing on whatever was left of his professional pride in order to get him to reveal his intentions. Now, at least, Walter knew where Lloyd and the others were being taken.

But what would happen at the barracks?

Lloyd had never been arrested. However, he lived in the East End of London, so he knew plenty of people who got into trouble with the police. Most of his life he had played street football with boys whose fathers were arrested frequently. He knew the reputation of Leman Street police station in Aldgate. Few men came out of that building uninjured. People said there was blood all over the walls. Was it likely the Friedrich Strasse Barracks would be any better?

Walter said: "This is an international incident, Commissar." Lloyd guessed he was using the title in the hope of making Macke behave more like an officer and less like a thug. "You have arrested three foreign citizens—two Austrians and one Englishman." He held up a hand as if to fend off a protest. "It is too late to back out now. Both embassies are being informed, and I have no doubt that their representatives will be knocking on the door of our Foreign Office in Wilhelm Strasse within the hour."

Lloyd wondered whether that was true.

Macke grinned unpleasantly. "The Foreign Office will not hasten to defend two queers and a young hooligan."

"Our foreign minister, von Neurath, is not a member of your party," Walter said. "He may well put the interests of the Fatherland first."

"I think you will find that he does what he's told. And now you are obstructing me in the course of my duty."

"I warn you!" Walter said bravely. "You had better follow procedure by the book—or there will be trouble."

"Get out of my sight," said Macke.

Walter left.

Lloyd, Robert, and Jörg were marched outside and bundled into the back of some kind of truck. They were forced to lie on the floor while Brownshirts sat on benches, guarding them. The vehicle moved off. It was painful being handcuffed, Lloyd discovered. He felt constantly that his shoulder was about to become dislocated.

The trip was mercifully short. They were shoved out of the truck and into a building. It was dark, and Lloyd saw little. At a desk, his name was written in a book and his passport was taken away. Robert lost his gold tiepin and watch chain. At last the handcuffs were removed and they were pushed into a room with dim lights and barred windows. About forty other prisoners were there already.

Lloyd hurt all over. He had a pain in his chest that felt like a cracked rib. His face was bruised and he had a blinding headache. He wanted an aspirin, a cup of tea, and a pillow. He had a feeling it might be some hours before he got any of those things.

The three of them sat on the floor near the door. Lloyd held his head in his hands while Robert and Jörg discussed how soon help would come. No doubt Walter would phone a lawyer. But all the usual rules had been suspended by the Reichstag Fire Decree, so they had no proper protection under the law. Walter would also contact the embassies: political influence was their main hope now. Lloyd thought his mother would probably try to place an international phone call to the British Foreign Office in London. If she could get through, the government would surely have something to say about the arrest of a British schoolboy. It would all take time—an hour at least, probably two or three.

But four hours passed, then five, and the door did not open.

Civilized countries had a law about how long the police could keep someone in custody without formalities: a charge, a lawyer, a court. Lloyd now realized that such a rule was no mere technicality. He could be here forever.

The other prisoners in the room were all political, he discovered: Communists, Social Democrats, trade union organizers, and one priest.

The night passed slowly. None of the three slept. To Lloyd sleep seemed unthinkable. The gray light of morning was coming through the barred windows when at last the cell door opened. But no lawyers or diplomats came in, just two men in aprons pushing a trolley on which stood a large urn. They ladled out a thin oatmeal. Lloyd did not eat any, but he drank a tin mug of coffee that tasted of burned barley.

He surmised that the staff on duty overnight at the British embassy were junior diplomats who carried little weight. This morning, as soon as the ambassador himself got up, action would be taken.

An hour after breakfast the door opened again, but this time only Brownshirts stood there. They marched all the prisoners out and loaded them onto a truck, forty or fifty men in one canvas-sided vehicle, packed so tightly that they had to remain standing. Lloyd managed to stay close to Robert and Jörg.

Perhaps they were going to court, even though it was Sunday. He hoped so. At least there would be lawyers, and some semblance of due process. He thought he was fluent enough to state his simple case in German, and he practised his speech in his head. He had been dining in a restaurant with his mother; he had seen someone robbing the till; he had intervened in the resulting fracas. He imagined his cross-examination. He would be asked if the man he attacked was a Brownshirt. He would answer: "I didn't notice his clothing—I just saw a thief." There would be laughter in court, and the prosecutor would look foolish.

They were driven out of town.

They could see through gaps in the canvas sides of the truck. It seemed to Lloyd that they had gone about twenty miles when Robert said: "We're in Oranienburg," naming a small town north of Berlin.

The truck came to a halt outside a wooden gate between brick pillars. Two Brownshirts with rifles stood guard.

Lloyd's fear rose a notch. Where was the court? This looked more like a prison camp. How could they put people in prison without a judge?

After a short wait, the truck drove in and stopped at a group of derelict buildings.

Lloyd was becoming even more anxious. Last night he at least had the consolation that Walter knew where he was. Today it was possible no one would know. What if the police simply said he was not in custody and they had no record of his arrest? How could he be rescued?

They got out of the truck and shuffled into what looked like a factory of some sort. The place smelled like a pub. Perhaps it had been a brewery.

Once again all their names were taken. Lloyd was glad there was some record of his movements. They were not tied up or handcuffed, but they were constantly watched by Brownshirts with rifles, and Lloyd had a grim feeling that those young men were only too eager for an excuse to shoot.

They were each given a canvas mattress filled with straw and a thin blanket. They were herded into a tumbledown building that might once have been a warehouse. Then the waiting began.

No one came for Lloyd all that day.

In the evening there was another trolley and another urn, this one containing a stew of carrots and turnips. Each man got a bowlful and a piece of bread. Lloyd was now ravenous, not having eaten for twenty-four hours, and he wolfed his meager supper and wished for more.

Somewhere in the camp there were three or four dogs that howled all night.

Lloyd felt dirty. This was the second night he had spent in the same clothes. He needed a bath and a shave and a clean shirt. The toilet facilities, two barrels in the corner, were absolutely disgusting.

But tomorrow was Monday. Then there would be some action.

Lloyd fell asleep around four. At six they were awakened by a Brownshirt bawling: "Schleicher! Jörg Schleicher! Which one is Schleicher?"

Maybe they were going to be released.

Jörg stood up and said: "Me, I'm Schleicher."

"Come with me," said the Brownshirt.

Robert said in a frightened voice: "Why? What do you want him for? Where is he going?"

"What are you, his mother?" said the Brownshirt. "Lie down and shut your mouth." He poked Jörg with his rifle. "Outside, you."

Watching them go, Lloyd asked himself why he had not punched the Brownshirt and snatched the rifle. He might have escaped. And if he had failed, what would they do to him—throw him in jail? But at the crucial moment the thought of escape had not even occurred to him. Was he already taking on the mentality of the prisoner?

He was even looking forward to the oatmeal.

Before breakfast, they were all taken outside.

They stood around a small wire-fenced area a quarter the size of a tennis court. It looked as if it might have been used to store something not very valuable, timber or tires perhaps. Lloyd shivered in the cold morning air: his overcoat was still at Bistro Robert.

Then he saw Thomas Macke approaching.

The police detective wore a black coat over his Brownshirt uniform. He had a heavy, flat-footed stride, Lloyd noticed.

Behind Macke were two Brownshirts holding the arms of a naked man with a bucket over his head.

Lloyd stared in horror. The prisoner's hands were tied behind his back, and the bucket was tightly tied with string under his chin so that it would not fall off.

He was a slight, youngish man with blond pubic hair.

Robert groaned: "Oh, sweet Jesus, it's Jörg."

All the Brownshirts in the camp had gathered. Lloyd frowned. What was this, some kind of cruel game?

Jörg was led into the fenced compound and left there, shivering. His two escorts withdrew. They disappeared for a few minutes, then returned, each of them leading two Alsatian dogs.

That explained the all-night barking.

The dogs were thin, with unhealthy bald patches in their tan fur. They looked starved.

The Brownshirts led them to the fenced compound.

Lloyd had a vague but dreadful premonition of what was to come.

Robert screamed: "No!" He ran forward. "No, no, no!" He tried to open the gate of the compound. Three or four Brownshirts pulled him away roughly. He struggled, but they were strong young thugs, and Robert was approaching fifty years old: he could not resist them. They threw him contemptuously to the ground.

"No," said Macke to his men. "Make him watch."

They lifted Robert to his feet and held him facing the wire fence.

The dogs were led into the compound. They were excited, barking and slavering. The two Brownshirts handled them expertly and without fear, clearly experienced. Lloyd wondered dismally how many times they had done this before.

The handlers released the dogs and hurried out of the compound.

The dogs dashed for Jörg. One bit his calf, another his arm, a third his thigh. From behind the metal bucket there was a muffled scream of agony and terror. The Brownshirts cheered and applauded. The prisoners looked on in mute horror.

After the first shock, Jörg tried to defend himself. His hands were tied and he was unable to see, but he could kick out randomly. However, his bare feet made little impact on the starving dogs. They dodged and came again, ripping his flesh with their sharp teeth.

He tried running. With the dogs at his heels he ran blindly in a straight line until he crashed into the wire fence. The Brownshirts cheered raucously. Jörg ran in a different direction with the same result. A dog took a chunk out of Jörg's behind, and they hooted with laughter.

A Brownshirt standing next to Lloyd was shouting: "His tail! Bite his tail!" Lloyd guessed that *tail* in German—der Schwanz—was slang for *penis*. The man was hysterical with excitement.

Jörg's white body was now running with blood from multiple wounds. He pressed himself up against the wire, face-first, protecting his genitals, kicking out backward and sideways. But he was weakening. His kicks became feeble. He was having trouble staying upright. The dogs became bolder, tearing at him and swallowing bloody chunks.

At last Jörg slid to the ground.

The dogs settled down to feed.

The handlers reentered the compound. With practised motions they reattached the dogs' leashes, pulled them off Jörg, and led them away.

The show was over, and the Brownshirts began to move away, chattering excitedly.

Robert ran into the compound, and this time no one stopped him. He bent over Jörg, moaning.

Lloyd helped him untie Jörg's hands and remove the bucket. Jörg was unconscious but breathing. Lloyd said: "Let's get him indoors. You take his legs." Lloyd grasped Jörg under the arms and the two of them carried him into the building where they had slept. They put him on a mattress. The other prisoners gathered around, frightened and subdued. Lloyd hoped one of them might announce that he was a doctor, but no one did.

Robert stripped off his jacket and waistcoat, then took off his shirt and used it to wipe the blood. "We need clean water," he said.

There was a standpipe in the yard. Lloyd went out, but he had no container. He returned to the compound. The bucket was still there on the ground. He washed it out, then filled it with water.

When he returned, the mattress was soaked in blood.

Robert dipped his shirt in the bucket and continued to wash Jörg's wounds, kneeling beside the mattress. Soon the white shirt was red.

Jörg stirred.

Robert spoke to him in a low voice. "Be calm, my beloved," he said. "It's over now, and I'm here." But Jörg seemed not to hear.

Then Macke came in, with four or five Brownshirts following. He grabbed Robert's arm and pulled him. "So!" he said. "Now you know what we think of homosexual perverts."

Lloyd pointed at Jörg and said angrily: "The pervert is the one who caused this to happen." Mustering all his rage and contempt, he said: "Commissar Macke."

Macke gave a slight nod to one of the Brownshirts. In a movement that was deceptively casual, the man reversed his rifle and hit Lloyd over the head with the butt.

Lloyd fell to the ground, holding his head in agony.

He heard Robert say: "Please, just let me look after Jörg."

"Perhaps," said Macke. "First come over here."

Despite his pain, Lloyd opened his eyes to see what was happening.

Macke pulled Robert across the room to a rough wooden table. From his pocket he drew a document and a fountain pen. "Your restaurant is now worth half of what I last offered you—ten thousand marks."

"Anything," said Robert, weeping. "Leave me to be with Jörg."

"Sign here," said Macke. "Then the three of you can go home."

Robert signed.

"This gentleman can be a witness," Macke said. He gave the pen to one of the Brownshirts. He looked across the room and met Lloyd's eye. "And perhaps our foolhardy English guest can be the second witness."

Robert said: "Just do what he wants, Lloyd."

Lloyd struggled to his feet, rubbed his sore head, took the pen, and signed.

Macke pocketed the contract triumphantly and went out.

Robert and Lloyd returned to Jörg.

But Jörg was dead.

viii

Walter and Maud came to the Lehrte Station, just north of the burned-out Reichstag, to see Ethel and Lloyd off. The station building was in the neo-Renaissance style and looked like a French palace. They were early, and they sat in a station café while they waited for the train.

Lloyd was glad to be leaving. In six weeks he had learned a lot, about the German language and about politics, but now he wanted to get home, tell people what he had seen, and warn them against the same thing happening to them.

All the same he felt strangely guilty about departing. He was going to a place where the law ruled, the press was free, and it was not a crime to be a Social Democrat. He was leaving the von Ulrich family to live on in a cruel dictatorship where an innocent man could be torn to pieces by dogs and no one would ever be brought to justice for the crime.

The von Ulrichs looked crushed, Walter even more than Maud. They were like people who have heard bad news, or suffered a death in the family. They seemed unable to think much about anything other than the catastrophe that had happened to them.

Lloyd had been released with profuse apologies from the German Foreign Ministry, and an explanatory statement that was abject yet at the same time mendacious, implying that he had got into a brawl through his own foolishness and then been held prisoner by an administrative error for which the authorities were deeply sorry.

Walter said: "I've had a telegram from Robert. He's arrived safely in London."

As an Austrian citizen Robert had been able to leave Germany without much difficulty. Getting his money out had been more tricky. Walter had demanded that Macke pay the money to a bank in Switzerland. At first Macke had said that was impossible, but Walter had put pressure on him, threatening to challenge the sale in court, saying that Lloyd was prepared to testify that the contract had been signed under duress, and in the end Macke had pulled some strings.

"I'm glad Robert got out," Lloyd said. He would be even happier when he himself was safe in London. His head was still tender and he got a pain in his ribs every time he turned over in bed.

Ethel said to Maud: "Why don't you come to London? Both of you. The whole family, I mean."

Walter looked at Maud. "Perhaps we should," he said. But Lloyd could tell that he did not really mean it.

"You've done your best," Ethel said. "You've fought bravely. But the other side won."

Maud said: "It's not over yet."

"But you're in danger."

"So is Germany."

"If you came to live in London, Fitz might soften his attitude, and help you."

Earl Fitzherbert was one of the wealthiest men in Britain, Lloyd knew, because of the coal mines beneath his land in South Wales.

"He wouldn't help me," Maud said. "Fitz doesn't relent. I know that, and so do you."

"You're right," Ethel said. Lloyd wondered how she could be so sure, but he did not get a chance to ask. Ethel went on: "Well, you could easily get a job on a London newspaper, with your experience."

Walter said: "And what would I do in London?"

"I don't know," Ethel said. "What are you going to do here? There's not much point in being an elected representative in an impotent parliament." She was being brutally frank, Lloyd felt, but characteristically she was saying what had to be said.

Lloyd sympathized, but felt the von Ulrichs should stay. "I know it will be hard," Walter said. "But if decent people flee from Fascism, it will spread all the faster."

"It's spreading anyway," Ethel rejoined.

Maud startled them all by saying vehemently: "I will not go. I absolutely refuse to leave Germany."

They all stared at her.

"I'm German, and have been for fourteen years," she said. "This is my country now."

"But you were born English," said Ethel.

"A country is mostly the people in it," Maud said. "I don't love England. My parents died a long time ago, and my brother has disowned me. I love Germany. For me, Germany is my wonderful husband, Walter; my misguided son, Erik; my alarmingly capable daughter, Carla; our maid, Ada, and her disabled son; my friend Monika and her family; my journalistic colleagues . . . I'm staying, to fight the Nazis."

"You've already done more than your share," Ethel said gently.

Maud's tone became emotional. "My husband has dedicated himself, his life, his entire being to making this country free and prosperous. I will not be the cause of his giving up his life's work. If he loses that, he loses his soul."

Ethel pushed the point in a way that only an old friend could. "Still," she said, "there must be a temptation to take your children to safety."

"A temptation? You mean a longing, a yearning, a desperate desire!" She began to cry. "Carla has nightmares about Brownshirts, and Erik puts on that shit-colored uniform every chance he gets." Lloyd was startled by her fervor. He had never heard a respectable woman say *shit*. She went on: "Of course I want to take them away." Lloyd could see how torn she was. She rubbed her hands together as if washing them, turned her head from side to side in distraction, and spoke in a voice that shook violently with her inner conflict. "But it's the wrong thing to do, for them as well as for us. I will not give in to it! Better to suffer evil than stand by and do nothing."

Ethel touched Maud's arm. "I'm sorry I asked. Perhaps it was silly of me. I might have known you wouldn't run away."

"I'm glad you asked," Walter said. He reached out and took Maud's slim hands in his own. "The question has been hanging in the air between Maud and me, unspoken. It was time we faced it." Their joined hands rested on the café table. Lloyd rarely thought about the emotional lives of his mother's generation—they were middle-aged and married, and that seemed to say it all—but now he saw that between Walter and Maud there was a powerful connection that was much more than the familiar habit of a mature marriage. They were under no illusions: they knew that by staying here they were risking their lives and the lives of their children. But they had a shared commitment that defied death.

Lloyd wondered whether he would ever have such a love.

Ethel looked at the clock. "Oh, my goodness!" she said. "We're going to miss the train!"

Lloyd picked up their bags and they hurried across the platform. A whistle blew. They boarded the train just in time. They both leaned out of the window as it pulled out of the station.

Walter and Maud stood on the platform, waving, getting smaller and smaller in the distance, until finally they disappeared.

CHAPTER TWO

1935

"Two things you need to know about girls in Buffalo," said Daisy Peshkov. "They drink like fish, and they're all snobs."

Eva Rothmann giggled. "I don't believe you," she said. Her German accent had almost completely vanished.

"Oh, it's true," said Daisy. They were in her pink-and-white bedroom, trying on clothes in front of a full-length three-way mirror. "Navy and white might look good on you," Daisy said. "What do you think?" She held a blouse up to Eva's face and studied the effect. The contrasting colors seemed to suit her.

Daisy was looking through her closet for an outfit Eva could wear to the beach picnic. Eva was not a pretty girl, and the frills and bows that decorated many of Daisy's clothes only made Eva look frumpy. Stripes better suited her strong features.

Eva's hair was dark, and her eyes deep brown. "You can wear bright colors," Daisy told her.

Eva had few clothes of her own. Her father, a Jewish doctor in Berlin, had spent his life savings to send her to America, and she had arrived a year ago with nothing. A charity paid for her to go to Daisy's boarding school—they were the same age, nineteen. But Eva had nowhere to go in the summer vacation, so Daisy had impulsively invited her home.

At first Daisy's mother, Olga, had resisted. "Oh, but you're away at school all year—I so look forward to having you to myself in the summer."

"She's really great, Mother," Daisy had said. "She's charming and easygoing and a loyal friend."

"I suppose you feel sorry for her because she's a refugee from the Nazis."

"I don't care about the Nazis. I just like her."

"That's fine, but does she have to live with us?"

"Mother, she has nowhere else to go!"

As usual, Olga let Daisy have her way in the end.

Now Eva said: "Snobs? No one would be snobby to you!"

"Oh, yes, they would."

"But you're so pretty and vivacious."

Daisy did not bother to deny it. "They hate that about me."

"And you're rich."

It was true. Daisy's father was wealthy, her mother had inherited a fortune, and Daisy herself would come into money when she was twenty-one. "It doesn't mean a thing. In this town it's about how long you've been rich. You're nobody if you work. The superior people are those who live on the millions left by their great-grandparents." She spoke in a tone of gay mockery to hide the resentment she felt.

Eva said: "And your father is famous!"

"They think he's a gangster."

Daisy's grandfather, Josef Vyalov, had owned bars and hotels. Her father, Lev Peshkov, had used the profits to buy ailing vaudeville theaters and convert them into cinemas. Now he owned a Hollywood studio, too.

Eva was indignant on Daisy's behalf. "How can they say such a thing?"

"They believe he was a bootlegger. They're probably right. I can't see how else he made money out of bars during Prohibition. Anyway, that's why Mother will never be invited to join the Buffalo Ladies' Society."

They both looked at Olga, sitting on Daisy's bed, reading the *Buffalo Sentinel*. In photographs taken when she was young, Olga was a willowy beauty. Now she was dumpy and drab. She had lost interest in her appearance, though she shopped energetically with Daisy, never caring how much she spent to make her daughter look fabulous.

Olga looked up from the newspaper to say: "I'm not sure they mind your father being a bootlegger, dear. But he's a Russian immigrant, and on the rare occasions he decides to attend divine service he goes to the Russian Orthodox Church on Ideal Street. That's almost as bad as being Catholic."

Eva said: "It's so unfair."

"I might as well warn you that they're not too fond of Jews, either," Daisy said. Eva was in fact half-Jewish. "Sorry to be blunt."

"Be as blunt as you like—after Germany, this country feels like the promised land."

"Don't get too comfortable," Olga warned her. "According to this paper, plenty of American business leaders hate President Roosevelt and admire Adolf Hitler. I know that's true, because Daisy's father is one of them."

"Politics is boring," said Daisy. "Isn't there something interesting in the *Sentinel*?"

"Yes, there is. Muffie Dixon is to be presented at the British court."

"Good for her," Daisy said sourly, failing to conceal her envy.

Olga read: "'Miss Muriel Dixon, daughter of the late Charles "Chuck" Dixon, who was killed in France during the war, will be presented at Buckingham Palace next Tuesday by the wife of the United States ambassador, Mrs. Robert W. Bingham.'"

Daisy had heard enough about Muffie Dixon. "I've been to Paris, but never London," she said to Eva. "What about you?"

"Neither," said Eva. "The first time I left Germany was when I sailed to America."

Olga suddenly said: "Oh, dear!"

"What's happened?" Daisy said.

Her mother crumpled the paper. "Your father took Gladys Angelus to the White House."

"Oh!" Daisy felt as if she had been slapped. "But he said he would take me!"

President Roosevelt had invited a hundred businessmen to a reception in an attempt to win them over to his New Deal. Lev Peshkov thought Franklin D. Roosevelt was the next thing to a Communist, but he had been flattered to be asked to the White House. However, Olga had refused to accompany him, saying angrily: "I'm not willing to pretend to the president that we have a normal marriage."

Lev officially lived here, in the stylish prewar prairie home built by Grandfather Vyalov, but he spent more nights at the swanky downtown apartment where he kept his mistress of many years, Marga. On top of that, everyone assumed he was having an affair with his studio's biggest star, Gladys Angelus. Daisy understood why her mother felt spurned. Daisy, too, felt rejected when Lev drove off to spend his evenings with his other family.

She had been thrilled when he asked her to accompany him to the White House instead of her mother. She had told everyone she was going. None of her friends had met the president except the Dewar boys, whose father was a senator.

Lev had not told her the exact date, and she assumed he would let her know at the last minute, which was his usual style. But he had changed his mind, or perhaps just forgotten. Either way, he had rejected Daisy again.

"I'm sorry, honey," said her mother. "But promises never did mean much to your father."

Eva was looking sympathetic. Her pity stung Daisy. Eva's father was thousands of miles away, and she might never see him again, but she felt sorry for Daisy, as if Daisy's plight were worse.

It made Daisy feel defiant. She would not let this ruin her day. "Well, I'll be the only girl in Buffalo who has been stood up for Gladys Angelus," she said. "Now, what shall I wear?"

Skirts were dramatically short this year in Paris, but the conservative Buffalo set followed fashion at a distance. However, Daisy had a knee-length tennis dress in a shade of baby blue the same as her eyes. Maybe today was the day to bring it out. She slipped off her dress and put on the new one. "What do you think?" she said.

Eva said: "Oh, Daisy, it's beautiful, but . . ."

Olga said: "That'll make their eyes pop." Olga liked it when Daisy dressed to kill. Perhaps it reminded her of her youth.

Eva said: "Daisy, if they're all so snobbish, why do you want to go to the party?"

"Charlie Farquharson will be there, and I'm thinking of marrying him," Daisy said.

"Are you serious?"

Olga said emphatically: "He's a great catch."

Eva said: "What's he like?"

"Absolutely adorable," Daisy said. "Not the handsomest boy in Buffalo, but sweet and kind, and rather shy."

"He sounds very different from you."

"It's the attraction of opposites."

Olga spoke again. "The Farquharsons are among the oldest families in Buffalo."

Eva raised her dark eyebrows. "Snobby?"

"Very," Daisy said. "But Charlie's father lost all his money in the Wall Street crash, then died—killed himself, some say—so they need to restore the family fortunes."

Eva looked shocked. "You're hoping he'll marry you for your money?"

"No. He'll marry me because I will bewitch him. But his mother will accept me for my money."

"You say you *will* bewitch him. Does he know about any of this?"

"Not yet. But I think I might make a start this afternoon. Yes, this is definitely the right dress."

Daisy wore the baby blue and Eva the navy-and-white stripes. By the time they got ready, they were late.

Daisy's mother would not have a chauffeur. "I married my father's chauffeur, and it ruined my life," she sometimes said. She was terrified Daisy might do something similar—that was why she was so keen on

Charlie Farquharson. If she needed to go anywhere in her creaking 1925 Stutz, she made Henry, the gardener, take off his rubber boots and put on a black suit. But Daisy had her own car, a red Chevrolet Sport Coupe.

Daisy liked driving, loved the power and speed of it. They headed south out of the city. She was almost sorry it was only five or six miles to the beach.

As she drove, she thought about life as Charlie's wife. With her money and his status they would become the leading couple in Buffalo society. At their dinner parties the table settings would be so elegant that people would gasp in delight. They would have the biggest yacht in the harbor, and throw onboard parties for other wealthy, fun-loving couples. People would yearn for an invitation from Mrs. Charles Farquharson. No charity function would be a success without Daisy and Charlie at the top table. In her head she watched a movie of herself, in a ravishing Paris gown, walking through a crowd of admiring men and women, smiling graciously at their compliments.

She was still daydreaming when they reached their destination.

The city of Buffalo was in upstate New York, near the Canadian border. Woodlawn Beach was a mile of sand on the shore of Lake Erie. Daisy parked and they walked across the dunes.

Fifty or sixty people were already there. These were the adolescent children of the Buffalo elite, a privileged group who spent their summers sailing and water-skiing in the daytime and going to parties and dances at night. Daisy greeted the people she knew, which was just about everyone, and introduced Eva around. They got glasses of punch. Daisy tasted it cautiously: some of the boys would think it hilarious to spike the drink with a couple of bottles of gin.

The party was for Dot Renshaw, a sharp-tongued girl whom no one wanted to marry. The Renshaws were an old Buffalo family, like the Farquharsons, but their fortune had survived the crash. Daisy made sure to approach the host, Dot's father, and thank him. "I'm sorry we're late," she said. "I lost track of time!"

Philip Renshaw looked her up and down. "That's a very short skirt." Disapproval vied with lasciviousness in his expression.

"I'm so glad you like it," Daisy replied, pretending he had paid her a straightforward compliment.

"Anyway, it's good that you're here at last," he went on. "A photographer from the *Sentinel* is coming and we must have some pretty girls in the picture."

Daisy muttered to Eva: "So that's why I was invited. How kind of him to let me know."

Dot came up. She had a thin face with a pointed nose. Daisy always thought she looked as if she might peck you. "I thought you were going with your father to meet the president," she said.

Daisy felt mortified. She wished she had not boasted to everyone about this.

"I see he took his, ahem, leading lady," Dot went on. "Unusual, that sort of thing, in the White House."

Daisy said: "I guess the president likes to meet movie stars occasionally. He deserves a little glamour, don't you think?"

"I can't imagine Eleanor Roosevelt approved. According to the *Sentinel*, all the other men took their wives."

"How thoughtful of them." Daisy turned away, desperate to escape.

She spotted Charlie Farquharson, trying to erect a net for beach tennis. He was too good-natured to mock her about Gladys Angelus. "How are you, Charlie?" she said brightly.

"Fine, I guess." He stood up, a tall man of about twenty-five, a little overweight, stooping slightly as if he feared his height might be intimidating.

Daisy introduced Eva. Charlie was sweetly awkward in company, especially with girls, but he made an effort and asked Eva how she liked America, and what she heard from her family back in Berlin.

Eva asked him if he was enjoying the picnic.

"Not much," he said candidly. "I'd rather be at home with my dogs."

No doubt he found pets easier to deal with than girls, Daisy thought. But the mention of dogs was interesting. "What kind of dogs do you have?" she asked.

"Jack Russell terriers."

Daisy made a mental note.

An angular woman of about fifty approached. "For goodness' sake, Charlie, haven't you got that net up yet?"

"Almost there, Mom," he said.

Nora Farquharson was wearing a gold tennis bracelet, diamond ear studs, and a Tiffany necklace—more jewelry than she really needed for a picnic. The Farquharsons' poverty was relative, Daisy reflected. They said they had lost everything, but Mrs. Farquharson still had a maid and a chauffeur and a couple of horses for riding in the park.

Daisy said: "Good afternoon, Mrs. Farquharson. This is my friend Eva Rothmann from Berlin."

"How do you do," said Nora Farquharson without offering her hand. She felt no need to be friendly toward arriviste Russians, much less their Jewish guests.

Then she seemed to be struck by a thought. "Ah, Daisy, you could go round and find out who wants to play tennis."

Daisy knew she was being treated somewhat as a servant, but she decided to be compliant. "Of course," she said. "Mixed doubles, I suggest."

"Good idea." Mrs. Farquharson held out a pencil stub and a scrap of paper. "Write the names down."

Daisy smiled sweetly and took a gold pen and a little beige leather notebook from her bag. "I'm equipped."

She knew who the tennis players were, good and bad. She belonged to the Racquet Club, which was not as exclusive as the Yacht Club. She paired Eva with Chuck Dewar, the fourteen-year-old son of Senator Dewar. She put Joanne Rouzrokh with the older Dewar boy, Woody, only fifteen but already as tall as his beanpole father. Naturally she herself would be Charlie's partner.

Daisy was startled to come across a somewhat familiar face and recognize her half brother, Greg, the son of Marga. They did not meet often, and she had not seen him for a year. In that time he seemed to have become a man. He was six inches taller, and although still only fifteen he had the dark shadow of a beard. As a child he had been disheveled, and that had not changed. He wore his expensive clothes carelessly: the sleeves of the blazer rolled up, the striped tie loose at the neck, the linen pants sea-wet and sandy at the cuffs.

Daisy was always embarrassed to run into Greg. He was a living reminder of how their father had rejected Daisy and her mother in favor of Greg and Marga. Many married men had affairs, she knew, but *her* father's indiscretion showed up at parties for everyone to see. Father should have moved Marga and Greg to New York, where nobody knew anybody, or to California, where no one saw anything wrong with adultery. Here they were a permanent scandal, and Greg was part of the reason people looked down on Daisy.

He asked her politely how she was, and she answered: "Angry as heck, if you want to know. Father's let me down—again."

Greg said guardedly: "What did he do?"

"Asked me to go to the White House with him—then took that tart Gladys Angelus. Now everyone's laughing at me."

"It must have been good publicity for *Passion,* her new film."

"You always take his side because he prefers you to me."

Greg looked irritated. "Maybe that's because I admire him instead of complaining about him all the time."

"I don't—" Daisy was about to deny complaining all the time when she realized it was true. "Well, maybe I do complain, but he should keep his promises, shouldn't he?"

"He has so much on his mind."

"Maybe he shouldn't have two mistresses as well as a wife."

Greg shrugged. "It's a lot to handle."

They both noticed the unintentional double entendre, and after a moment they giggled.

Daisy said: "Well, I guess I shouldn't blame you. You didn't ask to be born."

"And I should probably forgive you for taking my father away from me three nights a week—no matter how I cried and begged him to stay."

Daisy had never thought of it that way. In her mind Greg was the usurper, the illegitimate child who kept stealing her father. But now she realized he felt as hurt as she did.

She stared at him. Some girls might find him attractive, she guessed. He was too young for Eva, though. And he would probably turn out as selfish and unreliable as their father.

"Anyway," she said, "do you play tennis?"

He shook his head. "They don't let people like me into the Racquet Club." He forced an insouciant grin, and Daisy realized that, like her, Greg felt rejected by Buffalo society. "Ice hockey's my sport," he said.

"Too bad." She moved on.

When she had enough names, she returned to Charlie, who had finally got the net up. She sent Eva to round up the first foursome. Then she said to Charlie: "Help me make a competition tree."

They knelt side by side and drew a diagram in the sand with heats, semifinals, and a final. While they were entering the names, Charlie said: "Do you like the movies?"

Daisy wondered if he was about to ask her for a date. "Sure," she said.

"Have you seen *Passion*, by any chance?"

"No, Charlie, I haven't seen it," she said in a tone of exasperation. "It stars my father's mistress."

He was shocked. "The papers say they're just good friends."

"And why do you think Miss Angelus, who is barely twenty, is so *friendly* with my forty-year-old father?" Daisy asked sarcastically. "Do you think she likes his receding hairline? Or his little paunch? Or his fifty million dollars?"

"Oh, I see," said Charlie, looking abashed. "Sorry."

"You shouldn't be sorry. I'm being kind of bitchy. You're not like everyone else—you don't automatically think the worst of people."

"I guess I'm just dumb."

"No. You're just nice."

Charlie looked embarrassed, but pleased.

"Let's get on with this," Daisy said. "We have to rig it so the best players get through to the final."

Nora Farquharson reappeared. She looked at Charlie and Daisy kneeling side by side in the sand, then studied their drawing.

Charlie said: "Pretty good, Mom, don't you think?" He longed for approval from her; that was obvious.

"Very good." She gave Daisy an appraising look, like a mother dog seeing a stranger approach her puppies.

"Charlie did most of it," Daisy said.

"No, he didn't," Mrs. Farquharson said bluntly. Her gaze went to Charlie and back. "You're a smart girl," she said. She looked as if she were about to add something, but hesitated.

"What?" said Daisy.

"Nothing." She turned away.

Daisy stood up. "I know what she was thinking," she murmured to Eva.

"What?"

"You're a smart girl—almost good enough for my son, if you came from a better family."

Eva was skeptical. "You can't know that."

"I sure can. And I'll marry him if only to prove his mother wrong."

"Oh, Daisy, why do you care so much what these people think?"

"Let's watch the tennis."

Daisy sat on the sand beside Charlie. He might not have been handsome, but he would worship his wife and do anything for her. The mother-in-law would be a problem, but Daisy thought she could handle her.

Tall Joanne Rouzrokh was serving, in a white skirt that flattered her long legs. Her partner, Woody Dewar, who was even taller, handed her a tennis ball. Something in the way he looked at Joanne made Daisy think he was attracted to her, maybe even in love with her. But he was fifteen and she eighteen, so there was no future in that.

She turned to Charlie. "Maybe I should see *Passion* after all," she said.

He did not take the hint. "Maybe you should," he said indifferently. The moment had passed.

Daisy turned to Eva. "I wonder where I could buy a Jack Russell terrier."

ii

Lev Peshkov was the best father a guy could have—or, at least, he would have been, if he had been around more. He was rich and generous, he was smarter than anybody, he was even well dressed. He had probably been handsome when younger, and even now women threw themselves at him. Greg Peshkov adored him, and his only complaint was that he did not see enough of him.

"I should have sold this fucking foundry when I had the chance," Lev said as they walked around the silent, deserted factory. "It was losing money even before the goddamn strike. I should stick to cinemas and bars." He wagged a didactic finger. "People always buy booze, in good times and bad. And they go to the movies even when they can't afford to. Never forget that."

Greg was pretty sure his father did not often make mistakes in business. "So why did you keep it?" he said.

"Sentiment," Lev replied. "When I was your age, I worked in a place like this, the Putilov Machine Works in St. Petersburg." He looked around at the furnaces, molds, hoists, lathes, and workbenches. "Actually, it was a lot worse."

The Buffalo Metal Works made fans of all sizes, including huge propellers for ships. Greg was fascinated by the mathematics of the curved blades. He was top of his class in math. "Were you an engineer?" he asked.

Lev grinned. "I tell people that, if I need to impress them," he said. "But the truth is I looked after the horses. I was a stable boy. I was never good with machines. That was my brother Grigori's talent. You take after him. All the same, never buy a foundry."

"I won't."

Greg was to spend the summer shadowing his father, learning the business. Lev had just got back from Los Angeles, and Greg's lessons had begun today. But he did not want to know about the foundry. He was good at math but he was interested in power. He wished his father would take him on one of his frequent trips to Washington to lobby for the movie industry. That was where the real decisions were made.

He was looking forward to lunch. He and his father were to meet Senator Gus Dewar. Greg wanted to ask a favor of Senator Dewar. However, he had not yet cleared this with his father. He was nervous about asking, and instead he said: "Do you ever hear of your brother in Leningrad?"

Lev shook his head. "Not since the war. I wouldn't be surprised if he's dead. A lot of old Bolsheviks have disappeared."

"Speaking of family, I saw my half sister on Saturday. She was at the beach picnic."

"Did you have a good time?"

"She's mad at you—did you know that?"

"What have I done now?"

"You said you'd take her to the White House. Then you took Gladys Angelus."

"That's true. I forgot. But I wanted the publicity for *Passion*."

They were approached by a tall man whose striped suit was loud even by current fashions. He touched the brim of his fedora and said: "Morning, boss."

Lev said to Greg: "Joe Brekhunov is in charge of security here. Joe, this is my son Greg."

"Pleased to meet ya," said Brekhunov.

Greg shook his hand. Like most factories, the foundry had its own police force. But Brekhunov looked more like a hoodlum than a cop.

"All quiet?" Lev asked.

"A little incident in the night," Brekhunov said. "Two machinists tried to heist a length of fifteen-inch steel bar, aircraft quality. We caught them trying to manhandle it over the fence."

Greg said: "Did you call the police?"

"It wasn't necessary." Brekhunov grinned. "We gave them a little talk about the concept of private property, and sent them to the hospital to think about it."

Greg was not surprised to learn that his father's security men beat thieves so badly that they had to go to hospital. Although Lev had never struck him or his mother, Greg felt that violence was never far below his father's charming surface. It was because of Lev's youth in the slums of Leningrad, he guessed.

A portly man wearing a blue suit with a workingman's cap appeared from behind a furnace. "This is the union leader, Brian Hall," said Lev. "Morning, Hall."

"Morning, Peshkov."

Greg raised his eyebrows. People usually called his father Mr. Peshkov.

Lev stood with his feet apart and his hands on his hips. "Well, have you got an answer for me?"

Hall's face took on a stubborn expression. "The men won't come back to work with a pay cut, if that's what you mean."

"But I've improved my offer!"

"It's still a pay cut."

Greg began to feel nervous. His father did not like opposition, and he might explode.

"The manager tells me we aren't getting any orders, because he can't tender a competitive price at these wage levels."

"That's because you've got outdated machinery, Peshkov. Some of these lathes were here before the war! You need to reequip."

"In the middle of a depression? Are you out of your mind? I'm not going to throw away more money."

"That's how your men feel," said Hall, with the air of one who plays a trump card. "They're not going to give money to you when they haven't got enough for themselves."

Greg thought workers were stupid to strike during a depression, and he was angered by Hall's nerve. The man spoke as if he were Lev's equal, not an employee.

Lev said: "Well, as things are, we're all losing money. Where's the sense in that?"

"It's out of my hands now," said Hall. Greg thought he sounded smug. "The union is sending a team from headquarters to take over." He pulled a large steel watch out of his waistcoat pocket. "Their train should be here in an hour."

Lev's face darkened. "We don't need outsiders stirring up trouble."

"If you don't want trouble, you shouldn't provoke it."

Lev clenched a fist, but Hall walked away.

Lev turned to Brekhunov. "Did you know about these men from headquarters?" he said angrily.

Brekhunov looked nervous. "I'll get on it right away, boss."

"Find out who they are and where they're staying."

"Won't be difficult."

"Then send them back to New York in a fucking ambulance."

"Leave it to me, boss."

Lev turned away, and Greg followed him. Now, that was power, Greg thought with a touch of awe. His father gave the word, and union officials would be beaten up.

They walked outside and got into Lev's car, a Cadillac five-passenger sedan in the new streamlined style. Its long curving fenders made Greg think of a girl's hips.

Lev drove along Porter Avenue to the waterfront and parked at the Buffalo Yacht Club. Sunlight played prettily on the boats in the marina. Greg was pretty sure his father did not belong to this elite club. Gus Dewar must have been a member.

They walked onto the pier. The clubhouse was built on pilings over the water. Lev and Greg went inside and checked their hats. Greg immediately felt uneasy, knowing he was a guest in a club that would not have him as a member. The people here probably thought he must feel privileged to be allowed in. He put his hands in his pockets and slouched, so they would know he was not impressed.

"I used to belong to this club," Lev said. "But in 1921 the chairman told me I had to resign because I was a bootlegger. Then he asked me to sell him a case of Scotch."

"Why does Senator Dewar want to have lunch with you?" Greg asked.

"We're about to find out."

"Would you mind if I asked him a favor?"

Lev frowned. "I guess not. What are you after?"

But before Greg could answer, Lev greeted a man of about sixty. "This is Dave Rouzrokh," he said to Greg. "He's my main rival."

"You flatter me," the man said.

Roseroque Theatres was a chain of dilapidated movie houses in New York State. The owner was anything but decrepit. He had a patrician air: he was tall and white-haired, with a nose like a curved blade. He wore a blue cashmere blazer with the badge of the club on the breast pocket. Greg said: "I had the pleasure of watching your daughter, Joanne, play tennis on Saturday."

Dave was pleased. "Pretty good, isn't she?"

"Very."

Lev said: "I'm glad I ran into you, Dave—I was planning to call you."

"Why?"

"Your theaters need remodeling. They're very old-fashioned."

Dave looked amused. "You were planning to call me to give me this news?"

"Why don't you do something about it?"

He shrugged elegantly. "Why bother? I'm making enough money. At my age I don't want the strain."

"You could double your profits."

"By raising ticket prices. No, thanks."

"You're crazy."

"Not everyone is obsessed with money," Dave said with a touch of disdain.

"Then sell to me," Lev said.

Greg was surprised. He had not seen that coming.

"I'll give you a good price," Lev added.

Dave shook his head. "I like owning cinemas," he said. "They give people pleasure."

"Eight million dollars," Lev said.

Greg felt bemused. He thought: Did I just hear Father offer Dave eight million dollars?

"That is a fair price," Dave admitted. "But I'm not selling."

"No one else will give you as much," Lev said with exasperation.

"I know." Dave looked as if he had taken enough browbeating. He swallowed the rest of his drink. "Nice to see you both," he said, and he strolled out of the bar into the dining room.

Lev looked disgusted. "'Not everyone is obsessed with money,'" he quoted. "Dave's great-grandfather arrived here from Persia a hundred years ago with nothing but the clothes he wore and six rugs. He wouldn't have turned down eight million dollars."

"I didn't know you had that much money," Greg said.

"I don't, not in ready cash. That's what banks are for."

"So you'd take out a loan to pay Dave?"

Lev raised his forefinger again. "Never use your own money when you can spend someone else's."

Gus Dewar walked in, a tall figure with a large head. He was in his midforties, and his light brown hair was salted with silver. He greeted them with cool courtesy, shaking hands and offering them a drink. Greg saw immediately that Gus and Lev did not like one another. He feared that would mean Gus would not grant the favor Greg wanted to beg. Maybe he should give up the thought.

Gus was a big shot. His father had been a senator before him, a dynastic succession that Greg thought was un-American. Gus had helped Franklin Roosevelt become governor of New York and then president. Now he was on the powerful Senate Foreign Relations Committee.

His sons, Woody and Chuck, went to the same school as Greg. Woody was brainy; Chuck was a sportsman.

Lev said: "Has the president told you to settle my strike, Senator?"

Gus smiled. "No—not yet, anyway."

Lev turned to Greg. "Last time the foundry was on strike, twenty years ago, President Wilson sent Gus to strong-arm me into giving the men a raise."

"I saved you money," Gus said mildly. "They were asking for a dollar—I made them take half that."

"Which was exactly fifty cents more than I intended to give."

Gus smiled and shrugged. "Shall we have lunch?"

They went into the dining room. When they had ordered, Gus said: "The president was glad you could make it to the reception at the White House."

"I probably shouldn't have taken Gladys," Lev said. "Mrs. Roosevelt was a bit frosty with her. I guess she doesn't approve of movie stars."

She probably doesn't approve of movie stars who sleep with married men, Greg thought, but he kept his mouth shut.

Gus made small talk while they ate. Greg looked for an opportunity to ask his favor. He wanted to work in Washington one summer, to learn the ropes and make contacts. His father might have been able to get him an internship, but it would have been with a Republican, and they were out of power. Greg wanted to work in the office of the influential and respected Senator Dewar, personal friend and ally of the president.

He asked himself why he was nervous about asking. The worst that could happen was that Dewar would say no.

When the dessert was finished, Gus got down to business. "The president has asked me to speak to you about the Liberty League," he said.

Greg had heard of this organization, a right-wing group opposed to the New Deal.

Lev lit a cigarette and blew out smoke. "We have to guard against creeping socialism."

"The New Deal is all that is saving us from the kind of nightmare they're having in Germany."

"The Liberty League aren't Nazis."

"Aren't they? They have a plan for an armed insurrection to overthrow the president. It's not realistic, of course—not yet, anyway."

"I believe I have a right to my opinions."

"Then you're supporting the wrong people. The league is nothing to do with liberty, you know."

"Don't talk to me about liberty," Lev said with a touch of anger. "When I was twelve years old, I was flogged by the Leningrad police because my parents were on strike."

Greg was not sure why his father had said that. The brutality of the tsar's regime seemed like an argument for socialism, not against.

Gus said: "Roosevelt knows you give money to the league, and he wants you to stop."

"How does he know who I give money to?"

"The FBI told him. They investigate such people."

"We're living in a police state! You're supposed to be a liberal."

There was not much logic to Lev's arguments, Greg perceived. Lev was just trying everything he could think of to wrong-foot Gus, and he did not care if he contradicted himself in the process.

Gus remained cool. "I'm trying to make sure this doesn't become a matter for the police," he said.

Lev grinned. "Does the president know I stole your fiancée?"

This was news to Greg—but it had to be true, for Lev had at last succeeded in throwing Gus off balance. Gus looked shocked, turned his gaze aside, and reddened. Score one for our team, Greg thought.

Lev explained to Greg: "Gus was engaged to Olga, back in 1915," he said. "Then she changed her mind and married me."

Gus recovered his composure. "We were all terribly young."

Lev said: "You certainly got over Olga quickly enough."

Gus gave Lev a cool look and said: "So did you."

Greg saw that his father was embarrassed now. Gus's shot had hit home.

There was a moment of awkward silence; then Gus said: "You and I fought in a war, Lev. I was in a machine-gun battalion with my school friend Chuck Dixon. In a little French town called Château-Thierry he was blown to pieces in front of my eyes." Gus was speaking in a conversational tone, but Greg found himself holding his breath. Gus went on: "My ambition for my sons is that they should never have to go through what we went through. That's why groups such as the Liberty League have to be nipped in the bud."

Greg saw his chance. "I'm interested in politics, too, Senator, and I'd like to learn more. Might you be able to take me as an intern one summer?" He held his breath.

Gus looked surprised, but said: "I can always use a bright young man who's willing to work in a team."

That was neither a yes nor a no. "I'm top in math, and captain of ice hockey," Greg persisted, selling himself. "Ask Woody about me."

"I will." Gus turned to Lev. "And will you consider the president's request? It's really very important."

It almost seemed as if Gus was suggesting an exchange of favors. But would Lev agree?

Lev hesitated a long moment, then stubbed out his cigarette and said: "I guess we have a deal."

Gus stood up. "Good," he said. "The president will be pleased."

Greg thought: I did it!

They walked out of the club to their cars.

As they drove out of the parking lot, Greg said: "Thank you, Father. I really appreciate what you did."

"You chose your moment well," Lev said. "I'm glad to see you're so smart."

The compliment pleased Greg. In some ways he was smarter than his father—he certainly understood science and math better—but he feared he was not as shrewd and cunning as his old man.

"I want you to be a wise guy," Lev went on. "Not like some of these dummies." Greg had no idea who the dummies were. "You got to stay ahead of the curve, all the time. That's the way to get on."

Lev drove to his office, in a modern block downtown. As they walked through the marble lobby, Lev said: "Now I'm going to teach a lesson to that fool Dave Rouzrokh."

Going up in the elevator, Greg wondered how Lev would do that.

Peshkov Pictures occupied the top floor. Greg followed Lev along a broad corridor and through an outer office with two attractive young secretaries. "Get Sol Starr on the phone, will you?" Lev said as they walked into the inner office.

Lev sat behind the desk. "Solly owns one of the biggest studios in Hollywood," he explained.

The phone on the desk rang and Lev picked it up. "Sol!" he said.

"How are they hanging?" Greg listened to a minute or two of masculine joshing; then Lev got down to business. "Little piece of advice," he said. "Here in New York State we have a crappy chain of fleapits called Roseroque Theatres . . . Yeah, that's the one . . . Take my tip, don't send them your top-of-the-line first-run pictures this summer—you may not get paid." Greg realized that would hit Dave hard: without exciting new movies to show, his takings would tumble. "A word to the wise, right? Solly, don't thank me—you'd do the same for me . . . Bye."

Once again Greg was awestruck by his father's power. He could have people beaten up. He could offer eight million dollars of other people's money. He could scare a president. He could seduce another man's fiancée. And he could ruin a business with a single phone call.

"You wait and see," said his father. "In a month's time, Dave Rouzrokh will be begging me to buy him out—at half the price I offered him today."

iii

"I don't know what's wrong with this puppy," Daisy said. "He won't do anything I tell him. I'm going crazy." There was a shake in her voice and a tear in her eye, and she was exaggerating only a little.

Charlie Farquharson studied the dog. "There's nothing wrong with him," he said. "He's a lovely little fellow. What's his name?"

"Jack."

"Hmm."

They were sitting on lawn chairs in the well-kept two-acre garden of Daisy's home. Eva had greeted Charlie, then tactfully retired to write a letter home. The gardener, Henry, was hoeing a bed of purple and yellow pansies in the distance. His wife, Ella, the maid, brought a pitcher of lemonade and some glasses, and set them on a folding table.

The puppy was a tiny Jack Russell terrier, small and strong, white with tan patches. He had an intelligent look, as if he understood every word, but he seemed to have no inclination to obey. Daisy held him on her lap and stroked his nose with dainty fingers in a way that she hoped Charlie would find strangely disturbing. "Don't you like the name?"

"A bit obvious, perhaps?" Charlie stared at her white hand on the dog's nose and shifted uneasily in his chair.

Daisy did not want to overdo it. If she inflamed Charlie too much, he would just go home. This was why he was still single at twenty-five: several Buffalo girls, including Dot Renshaw and Muffie Dixon, had found it impossible to nail his foot to the floor. But Daisy was different. "Then you shall name him," she said.

"It's good to have two syllables, as in Bonzo, to make it easier for him to recognize the name."

Daisy had no idea how to name dogs. "How about Rover?"

"Too common. Rusty might be better."

"Perfect!" she said. "Rusty he shall be."

The dog wriggled effortlessly out of her grasp and jumped to the ground.

Charlie picked him up. Daisy noticed he had big hands. "You must show Rusty you're the boss," Charlie said. "Hold him tight, and don't let him jump down until you say so." He put the dog back on her lap.

"But he's so strong! And I'm afraid of hurting him."

Charlie smiled condescendingly. "You probably couldn't hurt him if you tried. Hold his collar tightly—twist it a bit if you need to—then put your other hand firmly on his back."

Daisy followed Charlie's orders. The dog sensed the increased pressure in her touch and became still, as if waiting to see what would happen next.

"Tell him to sit. Then press down on his rear end."

"Sit," she said.

"Say it louder, and pronounce the letter T very clearly. Then press down hard."

"Sit, Rusty!" she said, and pushed him down. He sat.

"There you are," said Charlie.

"You're so clever!" Daisy gushed.

Charlie looked pleased. "It's just a matter of knowing what to do," he said modestly. "You must always be emphatic and decisive with dogs. You have to almost bark at them." He sat back, looking content. He was quite heavy, and filled the chair. Talking about the subject in which he was expert had relaxed him, as Daisy had hoped.

She had called him that morning. "I'm in despair!" she had said. "I have a new puppy and I can't manage him at all. Can you give me any advice?"

"What breed of puppy?"

"It's a Jack Russell."

"Why, that's the kind of dog I like best—I have three!"

"What a coincidence!"

As Daisy had hoped, Charlie volunteered to come over and help her train the dog.

Eva had said doubtfully: "Do you really think Charlie is right for you?"

"Are you kidding?" Daisy had replied. "He's one of the most eligible bachelors in Buffalo!"

Now she said: "I bet you'd be really good with children, too."

"Oh, I don't know about that."

"You love dogs, but you're firm with them. I'm sure that works with children, too."

"I have no idea." He changed the subject. "Are you intending to go to college in September?"

"I might go to Oakdale. It's a two-year finishing college for ladies. Unless . . ."

"Unless what?"

Unless I get married, she meant, but she said: "I don't know. Unless something else happens."

"Such as what?"

"I'd like to see England. My father went to London and met the Prince of Wales. What about you? Any plans?"

"It was always assumed I would take over Father's bank, but now there is no bank. Mother has a little money from her family, and I manage that, but otherwise I'm kind of a loose wheel."

"You should raise horses," Daisy said. "I know you'd be good at it." She was a good rider and had won prizes when younger. She pictured herself and Charlie in the park on matching grays, with two children on ponies following behind. The vision gave her a warm glow.

"I love horses," Charlie said.

"So do I! I want to breed racehorses." Daisy did not have to feign this enthusiasm. It was her dream to raise a string of champions. She saw racehorse owners as the ultimate international elite.

"Thoroughbreds cost a lot of money," Charlie said lugubriously.

Daisy had plenty. If Charlie married her, he would never have to worry about money again. She naturally did not say so, but she guessed Charlie was thinking it, and she let the thought hang unspoken in the air for as long as possible.

Eventually Charlie said: "Did your father really have those two union organizers beaten up?"

"What a strange idea!" Daisy did not know whether Lev Peshkov had done any such thing, but in truth it would not have surprised her.

"The men who came from New York to take over the strike," Charlie persisted. "They were hospitalized. The *Sentinel* says they quarreled with local union leaders, but everyone thinks your father was responsible."

"I never talk about politics," Daisy said gaily. "When did you get your first dog?"

Charlie began a long reminiscence. Daisy considered what to do next. I've got him here, she thought, and put him at ease; now I have to get him aroused. But stroking the dog suggestively had unnerved him. What they needed was some casual physical contact.

"What should I do next with Rusty?" she asked when Charlie had finished his story.

"Teach him to walk to heel," Charlie said promptly.

"How do you do that?"

"Do you have some dog biscuits?"

"Sure." The kitchen windows were open, and Daisy raised her voice so that the maid could hear her. "Ella, would you kindly bring me that box of Milk-Bones?"

Charlie broke up one of the biscuits, then took the dog on his lap. He held a piece of biscuit in his closed fist, letting Rusty sniff it, then opened his hand and allowed the dog to eat the morsel. He took another piece, making sure the dog knew he had it. Then he stood up and put the dog at his feet. Rusty kept an alert gaze on Charlie's closed fist. "Walk to heel!" Charlie said, and walked a few steps.

The dog followed him.

"Good boy!" Charlie said, and gave Rusty the biscuit.

"That's amazing!" Daisy said.

"After a while you won't need the biscuit—he'll do it for a pat. Then eventually he'll do it automatically."

"Charlie, you are a genius!"

Charlie looked pleased. He had nice brown eyes, just like the dog, she observed. "Now you try," he said to Daisy.

She copied what Charlie had done, and achieved the same result.

"See?" said Charlie. "It's not so hard."

Daisy laughed with delight. "We should go into business," she said. "Farquharson and Peshkov, dog trainers."

"What a nice idea," he said, and he seemed to mean it.

This is going very well, Daisy thought.

She went to the table and poured two glasses of lemonade.

Standing beside her, he said: "I'm usually a bit shy with girls."

No kidding, she thought, but she kept her mouth firmly closed.

"But you're so easy to talk to," he went on. He imagined that was a happy accident.

As she handed a glass to him, she fumbled, spilling lemonade on him. "Oh, how clumsy!" she cried.

"It's nothing," he said, but the drink had wetted his linen blazer and his white cotton trousers. He pulled out a handkerchief and began to mop it.

"Here, let me," said Daisy, and she took the handkerchief from his large hand.

She moved intimately close to pat his lapel. He went still, and she knew he could smell her Jean Naté perfume—lavender notes on top, musk underneath. She brushed the handkerchief caressingly over the front of his jacket, though there was no spill there. "Almost done," she said as if she regretted having to stop soon.

Then she went down on one knee as if worshipping him. She began to blot the wet patches on his pants with butterfly lightness. As she stroked his thigh, she put on a look of alluring innocence and glanced up. He was staring down at her, breathing hard through his open mouth, mesmerized.

iv

Woody Dewar impatiently inspected the yacht *Sprinter*, checking that the kids had made everything shipshape. She was a forty-eight-foot racing ketch, long and slender like a knife. Dave Rouzrokh had loaned her to the Shipmates, a club Woody belonged to that took the sons of Buffalo's unemployed out on Lake Erie and taught them the rudiments of sailing. Woody was glad to see that the dock lines and fenders were set, the sails furled, the halyards tied off, and all the other lines neatly coiled.

His brother, Chuck, a year younger at fourteen, was on the dock already, joshing with a couple of colored kids. Chuck had an easygoing manner that enabled him to get on with everyone. Woody, who wanted to go into politics like their father, envied Chuck's effortless charm.

The boys wore nothing but shorts and sandals, and the three on the dock looked a picture of youthful strength and vitality. Woody would have liked to take a photograph, if he had had his camera with him. He was a keen photographer and had built a darkroom at home so that he could develop and print his own pictures.

Satisfied that the *Sprinter* was being left as they had found her that morning, Woody jumped onto the dock. A group of a dozen youngsters left the boatyard together, windswept and sunburned, aching pleasantly from their exertions, laughing as they relived the day's blunders and pratfalls and jokes.

The gap between the two rich brothers and the crowd of poor boys had vanished when they were out on the water, working together to control the yacht, but now it reappeared in the parking lot of the Buffalo Yacht Club. Two vehicles stood side by side: Senator Dewar's Chrysler Airflow, with a uniformed chauffeur at the wheel, for Woody and Chuck, and a Chevrolet Roadster pickup truck with two wooden benches in the back for the others. Woody felt embarrassed, saying good-bye as the chauffeur held the door for him, but the boys did not seem to care, thanking him and saying: "See you next Saturday!"

As they drove up Delaware Avenue, Woody said: "That was fun, though I'm not sure how much good it does."

Chuck was surprised. "Why?"

"Well, we're not helping their fathers find jobs, and that's the only thing that really counts."

"It might help the sons get work in a few years' time." Buffalo was a port city: in normal times there were thousands of jobs on merchant ships plying the Great Lakes and the Erie Canal, as well as on pleasure craft.

"Provided the president can get the economy moving again."

Chuck shrugged. "So go work for Roosevelt."

"Why not? Papa worked for Woodrow Wilson."

"I'll stick with the sailing."

Woody checked his wristwatch. "We've got time to change for the ball—just." They were going to a dinner-dance at the Racquet Club. Anticipation made his heart beat faster. "I want to be with humans that have soft skin, speak with high voices, and wear pink dresses."

"Huh," Chuck said derisively. "Joanne Rouzrokh never wore pink in her life."

Woody was taken aback. He had been dreaming about Joanne all day and half the night for a couple of weeks, but how did his brother know that? "What makes you think—"

"Oh, come on," Chuck said scornfully. "When she arrived at the beach party in a tennis skirt, you practically fainted. Everyone could see you were crazy about her. Fortunately *she* didn't seem to notice."

"Why was that fortunate?"

"For God's sake—you're fifteen, and she's eighteen. It's embarrassing! She's looking for a husband, not a schoolboy."

"Oh, gee, thanks. I forgot what an expert you are on women."

Chuck flushed. He had never had a girlfriend. "You don't have to be an expert to see what's under your goddamn nose."

They talked like this all the time. There was no malice in it: they were just brutally frank with each other. They were brothers, so there was no need to be nice.

They reached home, a mock-Gothic mansion built by their late grandfather, Senator Cam Dewar. They ran inside to shower and change.

Woody was now the same height as his father, and he put on one of Papa's old dress suits. It was a bit worn, but that was all right. The younger boys would be wearing school suits or blazers, but the college men would have tuxedos, and Woody was keen to look older. Tonight he would dance with her, he thought as he slicked his hair with brilliantine. He would be allowed to hold her in his arms. The palms of his hands would feel the warmth of her skin. He would look into her eyes as she smiled. Her breasts would brush against his jacket as they danced.

When he came down, his parents were waiting in the drawing room, Papa drinking a cocktail, Mama smoking a cigarette. Papa was long and thin, and looked like a coat hanger in his double-breasted tuxedo. Mama was beautiful, despite having only one eye, the other being permanently closed—she had been born that way. Tonight she looked stunning in a floor-length dress, black lace over red silk, and a short black velvet evening jacket.

Woody's grandmother was the last to arrive. At sixty-eight she was poised and elegant, as thin as her son but petite. She studied Mama's dress and said: "Rosa, dear, you look wonderful." She was always kind to her daughter-in-law. To everyone else she was waspish.

Gus made her a cocktail without being asked. Woody hid his impatience while she took her time drinking it. Grandmama could never be hurried. She assumed no social event would begin before she arrived: she was the grand old lady of Buffalo society, widow of a senator and mother of another, matriarch of one of the city's oldest and most distinguished families.

Woody asked himself when he had fallen for Joanne. He had known her most of his life, but he had always regarded girls as uninteresting spectators to the exciting adventures of boys—until two or three years ago, when girls had suddenly become even more fascinating than cars and speedboats. Even then he had been more interested in girls his own age or a little younger. Joanne for her part had always treated him as a kid—a bright kid, worth talking to now and again, but certainly not a possible boyfriend. But this summer, for no reason he could put a finger on, he had suddenly begun to see her as the most alluring girl in the world. Sadly, her feelings for him had not undergone a similar transformation.

Not yet.

Grandmama addressed a question to his brother. "How is school, Chuck?"

"Terrible, Grandmama, as you know perfectly well. I'm the family cretin, a throwback to our chimpanzee forbears."

"Cretins don't use phrases such as 'our chimpanzee forbears,' in my experience. Are you quite sure laziness plays no part?"

Rosa butted in. "Chuck's teachers say he works pretty hard at school, Mama."

Gus added: "And he beats me at chess."

"Then I ask what the problem is," Grandmama persisted. "If this goes on, he won't get into Harvard."

Chuck said: "I'm a slow reader, that's all."

"Curious," she said. "My father-in-law, your paternal great-grandfather, was the most successful banker of his generation, yet he could barely read or write."

Chuck said: "I didn't know that."

"It's true," she said. "But don't use it as an excuse. Work harder."

Gus looked at his watch. "If you're ready, Mama, we'd better go."

At last they got into the car and drove to the club. Papa had taken a table for the dinner and invited the Renshaws and their offspring, Dot and George. Woody looked around, but to his disappointment, he did not see Joanne. He checked the table plan, on an easel in the lobby, and was dismayed to see that there was no Rouzrokh table. Were they not coming? That would ruin his evening.

The talk over the lobster and steak was of events in Germany. Philip Renshaw thought Hitler was doing a good job. Woody's father said: "According to today's *Sentinel*, they jailed a Catholic priest for criticizing the Nazis."

"Are you Catholic?" said Mr. Renshaw in surprise.

"No, Episcopalian."

"It's not about religion, Philip," said Rosa crisply. "It's about freedom." Woody's mother had been an anarchist in her youth, and she was still a libertarian at heart.

Some people skipped the dinner and came later for the dancing, and more revelers appeared as the Dewars were served dessert. Woody kept his eyes peeled for Joanne. In the next room a band started to play "The Continental," a hit from last year.

He could not say what it was about Joanne that had so captivated him. Most people would not call her a great beauty, though she was certainly striking. She looked like an Aztec queen, with high cheekbones and the same knife-blade nose as her father, Dave. Her hair was dark and thick and her skin an olive shade, no doubt because of her Persian ancestry. There was a brooding intensity about her that made Woody long to know her better, to make her relax and hear her murmur softly about nothing in particular. He felt that her formidable presence must signify a capacity for deep passion. Then he thought: Now who's pretending to be an expert on women?

"Are you looking out for someone, Woody?" said Grandmama, who did not miss much.

Chuck sniggered knowingly.

"Just wondering who's coming to the dance," Woody replied casually, but he could not help blushing.

He still had not spotted her when his mother stood up and they all left the table. Disconsolate, he wandered into the ballroom to the strains of Benny Goodman's "Moonglow"—and there Joanne was: she must have come in when he was not looking. His spirits lifted.

Tonight she wore a dramatically simple silver-gray silk dress with a deep V-neck that showed off her figure. She had looked sensational in a tennis skirt that revealed her long brown legs, but this was even more arousing. As she glided across the room, graceful and confident, she made Woody's throat go dry.

He moved toward her, but the ballroom had filled up, and suddenly he was irritatingly popular: everyone wanted to talk to him. During his progress through the crowd he was surprised to see dull old Charlie Farquharson dancing with the vivacious Daisy Peshkov. He could not recall seeing Charlie dance with anyone, let alone a tootsie like Daisy. What had she done to bring him out of his shell?

By the time he reached Joanne, she was at the end of the room farthest from the band, and to his chagrin she was deep in discussion with a group of boys four or five years older than he. Fortunately he was taller than most of them, so the difference was not too obvious. They were all holding Coke glasses, but Woody could smell Scotch: one of them must have had a bottle in his pocket.

As he joined them, he heard Victor Dixon say: "No one's in favor of lynching, but you have to understand the problems they have in the South."

Woody knew that Senator Wagner had proposed a law to punish sheriffs who permitted lynchings—but President Roosevelt had refused to back the bill.

Joanne was outraged. "How can you say that, Victor? Lynching is murder! We don't have to understand their problems. We have to stop them killing people!"

Woody was pleased to learn how much Joanne shared his political values. But clearly this was not a good time to ask her to dance, which was unfortunate.

"You don't get it, Joanne, honey," said Victor. "Those Southern Negroes are not really civilized."

I might be young and inexperienced, Woody thought, but I wouldn't have made the mistake of speaking so condescendingly to Joanne.

"It's the people who carry out lynchings who are uncivilized!" she said.

Woody decided this was the moment to make his contribution to the argument. "Joanne is right," he said. He made his voice lower in pitch, to sound older. "There was a lynching in the hometown of our help, Joe and Betty, who have looked after me and my brother since we were babies. Betty's cousin was stripped naked and burned with a blowtorch, while a crowd watched. Then he was hanged." Victor glared at him, resentful of this kid who was taking Joanne's attention away, but the others in the group listened with horrified interest. "I don't care what his crime was," Woody said. "The white people who did that to him are savages."

Victor said: "Your beloved President Roosevelt didn't support the anti-lynch bill, though, did he?"

"No, and that was very disappointing," said Woody. "I know why he made that decision: he was afraid that angry Southern congressmen would retaliate by sabotaging the New Deal. All the same, I would have liked him to tell them to go to hell."

Victor said: "What do you know? You're just a kid." He took a silver flask from his jacket pocket and topped up his drink.

Joanne said: "Woody's political ideas are more grown-up than yours, Victor."

Woody glowed. "Politics is kind of the family business," he said. Then he was irritated by a tug at his elbow. Too polite to ignore it, he turned to see Charlie Farquharson, perspiring from his exertions on the dance floor.

"Can I talk to you for a minute?" said Charlie.

Woody resisted the temptation to tell him to buzz off. Charlie was a likable guy who did no harm to anyone. You had to feel sorry for a man with a mother like that. "What is it, Charlie?" he said with as much good grace as he could muster.

"It's about Daisy."

"I saw you dancing with her."

"Isn't she a great dancer?"

Woody had not noticed but, to be nice, he said: "You bet she is!"

"She's great at everything."

"Charlie," said Woody, trying to suppress a tone of incredulity, "are you and Daisy courting?"

Charlie looked bashful. "We've been horse riding in the park a couple of times, and so on."

"So you *are* courting." Woody was surprised. They seemed an unlikely pair. Charlie was such a lump, and Daisy was a poppet.

Charlie added: "She's not like other girls. She's so easy to talk to! And she loves dogs and horses. But people think her father is a gangster."

"I guess he is a gangster, Charlie. Everyone bought their liquor from him during Prohibition."

"That's what my mother says."

"So your mother doesn't like Daisy." Woody was not surprised.

"She likes Daisy fine. It's Daisy's family she objects to."

An even more surprising thought occurred to Woody. "Are you thinking of *marrying* Daisy?"

"Oh, God, yes," said Charlie. "And I think she might say yes, if I asked her."

Well, Woody thought, Charlie had class but no money, and Daisy was the opposite, so maybe they would complement one another. "Stranger things have happened," he said. This was kind of fascinating, but he wanted to concentrate on his own romantic life. He looked around, checking that Joanne was still there. "Why are you telling me this?" he asked Charlie. It was not as if they were great friends.

"My mother might change her mind if Mrs. Peshkov were invited to join the Buffalo Ladies' Society."

Woody had not been expecting that. "Why, it's the snobbiest club in town!"

"Exactly. If Olga Peshkov were a member, how could Mom object to Daisy?"

Woody did not know whether this scheme would work or not, but there was no doubting the earnest warmth of Charlie's feelings. "Maybe you're right," Woody said.

"Would you approach your grandmother for me?"

"Whoa! Wait a minute. Grandmama Dewar is a dragon. I wouldn't ask her for a favor for myself, let alone for you."

"Woody, listen to me. You know she's really the boss of that little clique. If she wants someone, they're in—and if she doesn't, they're out."

That was true. The society had a chairwoman and a secretary and a treasurer, but Ursula Dewar ran the club as if it belonged to her. All the same, Woody was reluctant to petition her. She might bite his head off. "I don't know," he said apologetically.

"Oh, come on, Woody, please. You don't understand." Charlie lowered his voice. "You don't know what it's like to love someone this much."

Yes, I do, Woody thought, and that changed his mind. If Charlie feels as bad as I do, how can I refuse him? I hope someone else would do the same for me, if it meant I had a better chance with Joanne. "Okay, Charlie," he said. "I'll talk to her."

"Thanks! Say—she's here, isn't she? Could you do it tonight?"

"Hell, no. I've got other things on my mind."

"Okay, sure . . . but when?"

Woody shrugged. "I'll do it tomorrow."

"You're a pal!"

"Don't thank me yet. She'll probably say no."

Woody turned back to speak to Joanne, but she had gone.

He began to look for her, then stopped himself. He must not appear desperate. A needy man was not sexy; he knew that much.

He danced dutifully with several girls: Dot Renshaw, Daisy Peshkov, and Daisy's German friend Eva. He got a Coke and went outside to where some of the boys were smoking cigarettes. George Renshaw poured some Scotch into Woody's Coke, which improved the taste, but he did not want to get drunk. He had done it before and he did not like it.

Joanne would want a man who shared her intellectual interests,

Woody believed—and that would rule out Victor Dixon. Woody had heard Joanne mention Karl Marx and Sigmund Freud. In the public library he had read *The Communist Manifesto,* but it just seemed like a political rant. He had had more fun with Freud's *Studies in Hysteria,* which made a kind of detective story out of mental illness. He was looking forward to letting Joanne know, in a casual way, that he had read these books.

He was determined to dance with Joanne at least once tonight, and after a while he went in search of her. She was not in the ballroom or the bar. Had he missed his chance? In trying not to show his desperation, had he been too passive? It was unbearable to think that the ball could end without his even having touched her shoulder.

He stepped outside again. It was dark, but he saw her almost immediately. She was walking away from Greg Peshkov, looking a little flushed, as if she had been arguing with him. "You might be the only person here who isn't a goddamn conservative," she said to Woody. She sounded a little drunk.

Woody smiled. "Thanks for the compliment—I think."

"Do you know about the march tomorrow?" she asked abruptly.

He did. Strikers from the Buffalo Metal Works planned a demonstration to protest against the beating up of union men from New York. Woody guessed that was the subject of her argument with Greg: his father owned the factory. "I was planning to go," he said. "I might take some photographs."

"Bless you," she said, and she kissed him.

He was so surprised that he almost failed to respond. For a second he stood there passively as she crushed her mouth to his, and he tasted whisky on her lips.

Then he recovered his composure. He put his arms around her and pressed her body to his, feeling her breasts and her thighs press delightfully against him. Part of him feared she would be offended, push him away, and angrily accuse him of treating her disrespectfully, but a deeper instinct told him he was on safe ground.

He had little experience of kissing girls—and none of kissing mature women of eighteen—but he liked the feel of her soft mouth so much that he moved his lips against hers in little nibbling motions that gave him exquisite pleasure, and he was rewarded by hearing her moan quietly.

He was vaguely aware that if one of the older generation should walk by there might be an embarrassing scene, but he was too aroused to care.

Joanne's mouth opened and he felt her tongue. This was new to him: the few girls he had kissed had not done that. But he figured she must know what she was doing, and anyway he really liked it. He imitated the motions of her tongue with his own. It was shockingly intimate and highly exciting. It must have been the right thing to do, because she moaned again.

Summoning his nerve, he put his right hand on her left breast. It was wonderfully soft and heavy under the silk of her dress. As he caressed it, he felt a small protuberance and thought, with a thrill of discovery, that it must be her nipple. He rubbed it with his thumb.

She pulled away from him abruptly. "Good God," she said. "What am I doing?"

"You're kissing me," Woody said happily. He rested his hands on her round hips. He could feel the heat of her skin through the silk dress. "Let's do it some more."

She pushed his hands away. "I must be out of my mind. This is the Racquet Club, for Christ's sake."

Woody could see that the spell had been broken, and sadly there would be no more kissing tonight. He looked around. "Don't worry," he said. "No one saw." He felt enjoyably conspiratorial.

"I'd better go home, before I do something even more stupid."

He tried not to be offended. "May I escort you to your car?"

"Are you crazy? If we walk in there together, everyone will guess what we've been doing—especially with that dumb grin all over your face."

Woody tried to stop grinning. "Then why don't you go inside and I'll wait out here for a minute?"

"Good idea." She walked away.

"See you tomorrow," he called after her.

She did not look back.

v

Ursula Dewar had her own small suite of rooms in the old Victorian mansion on Delaware Avenue. There was a bedroom, a bathroom, and a dressing room, and after her husband died, she had converted his dressing room into a little parlor. Most of the time she had the whole house to herself: Gus and Rosa spent a lot of time in Washington, and Woody and Chuck went to a boarding school. But when they came home, she spent a good deal of the day in her own quarters.

Woody went to talk to her on Sunday morning. He was still walking on air after Joanne's kiss, though he had spent half the night trying to figure out what it meant. It could signify anything from true love to true drunkenness. All he knew was that he could hardly wait to see Joanne again.

He walked into his grandmother's room behind the maid, Betty, as she took in the breakfast tray. He liked it that Joanne got angry about the way Betty's Southern relations were treated. In politics, dispassionate argument was overrated, he felt. People *should* get angry about cruelty and injustice.

Grandmama was already sitting up in bed, wearing a lace shawl over a mushroom-colored silk nightgown. "Good morning, Woodrow!" she said, surprised.

"I'd like to have a cup of coffee with you, Grandmama, if I may." He had already asked Betty to bring two cups.

"This is an honor," Ursula said.

Betty was a gray-haired woman of about fifty with the kind of figure that was sometimes called comfortable. She set the tray in front of Ursula, and Woody poured coffee into Meissen cups.

He had given some thought to what he would say, and had marshaled his arguments. Prohibition was over, and Lev Peshkov was now a legitimate businessman, he would contend. Furthermore, it was not fair to punish Daisy because her father had been a criminal—especially since most of the respectable families in Buffalo had bought his illegal booze.

"Do you know Charlie Farquharson?" he began.

"Yes."

Of course she did. She knew every family in *The Buffalo Blue Book*.

She said: "Would you like a piece of this toast?"

"No, thank you, I've had breakfast."

"Boys of your age never have enough to eat." She looked at him shrewdly. "Unless they're in love."

She was in good form this morning.

Woody said: "Charlie is kind of under the thumb of his mother."

"She kept her husband there, too," Ursula said drily. "Dying was the only way he could get free." She drank some coffee and started to eat her grapefruit with a fork.

"Charlie came to me last night and asked me to ask you a favor."

She raised an eyebrow, but said nothing.

Woody took a breath. "He wants you to invite Mrs. Peshkov to join the Buffalo Ladies' Society."

Ursula dropped her fork, and there was a chime of silver on fine porcelain. As if covering her discomposure, she said: "Pour me some more coffee, please, Woody."

He did her bidding, saying nothing for the moment. He could not recall ever seeing her discombobulated.

She sipped the coffee and said: "Why in the name of heaven would Charles Farquharson, or anyone else for that matter, want Olga Peshkov in the society?"

"He wants to marry Daisy."

"Does he?"

"And he's afraid his mother will object."

"He's got that part right."

"But he thinks he might be able to talk her around . . ."

"If I let Olga into the society."

"Then people might forget that her father was a gangster."

"A gangster?"

"Well, a bootlegger at least."

"Oh, that," Ursula said dismissively. "That's not it."

"Really?" It was Woody's turn to be surprised. "What is it, then?"

Ursula looked thoughtful. She was silent for such a long time that Woody wondered if she had forgotten he was there. Then she said: "Your father was in love with Olga Peshkov."

"Jesus!"

"Don't be vulgar."

"Sorry, Grandmama. You surprised me."

"They were engaged to be married."

"Engaged?" he said, astonished. He thought for a minute, then said: "I suppose I'm the only person in Buffalo who doesn't know about this."

She smiled at him. "There is a special mixture of wisdom and innocence that comes only to adolescents. I remember it so clearly in your father, and I see it in you. Yes, everyone in Buffalo knows, though your generation undoubtedly regard it as boring ancient history."

"Well, what happened?" Woody said. "I mean, who broke it off?"

"She did, when she got pregnant."

Woody's mouth fell open. "By Papa?"

"No, by her chauffeur—Lev Peshkov."

"He was the chauffeur?" This was one shock after another. Woody was silent, trying to take it in. "My goodness, Papa must have felt such a fool."

"Your Papa was never a fool," Ursula said sharply. "The only foolish thing he did in his life was propose to Olga."

Woody remembered his mission. "All the same, Grandmama, it was an awful long time ago."

"*Awfully.* You require an adverb, not an adjective. But your judgment is better than your grammar. It *is* a long time."

That sounded hopeful. "So you'll do it?"

"How do you think your father would feel?"

Woody considered. He could not bullshit Ursula—she would see through it in a heartbeat. "Would he care? I guess he might be embarrassed, if Olga were around as a constant reminder of a humiliating episode in his youth."

"You guess right."

"On the other hand, he's very committed to the ideal of behaving fairly to the people around him. He hates injustice. He wouldn't want to punish Daisy for something her mother did. Even less to punish Charlie. Papa has a pretty big heart."

"Bigger than mine, you mean," said Ursula.

"I didn't mean that, Grandmama. But I bet if you asked him, he wouldn't object to Olga joining the society."

Ursula nodded. "I agree. But I wonder whether you've worked out who is the real originator of this request."

Woody saw what she was driving at. "Oh, you're saying Daisy put Charlie up to it? I wouldn't be surprised. Does it make any difference to the rights and wrongs of the situation?"

"I guess not."

"So, will you do it?"

"I'm glad to have a grandson with a kind heart—even if I do suspect he's being used by a clever and ambitious girl."

Woody smiled. "Is that a yes, Grandmama?"

"You know I can't guarantee anything. I'll suggest it to the committee."

Ursula's suggestions were regarded by everyone else as royal commands, but Woody did not say so. "Thank you. You're very kind."

"Now give me a kiss and get ready for church."

Woody made his escape.

He quickly forgot about Charlie and Daisy. Sitting in the Cathedral of St. Paul in Shelton Square, he ignored the sermon—about Noah and the Flood—and thought about Joanne Rouzrokh. Her parents were in church, but she was not. Would she really show up at the demonstration? If she did, he was going to ask her for a date. But would she accept?

She was too smart to care about the age difference, he reckoned. She must have known she had more in common with Woody than with boneheads such as Victor Dixon. And that kiss! He was still tingling from it. What she had done with her tongue—did other girls do that? He wanted to try it again, as soon as he could.

Thinking ahead, if she did agree to date him, what would happen in September? She was going to Vassar College, in the town of Poughkeepsie; he knew that. He would return to school and not see her until Christmas. Vassar was for girls only but there must be men in Poughkeepsie. Would she date other guys? He was jealous already.

Outside the church he told his parents he was not coming home for lunch, but was going on the protest march.

"Good for you," his mother said. When young she had been the editor of the *Buffalo Anarchist*. She turned to her husband. "You should go, too, Gus."

"The union has brought charges," Papa said. "You know I can't prejudge the result of a court case."

She turned back to Woody. "Just don't get beaten up by Lev Peshkov's goons."

Woody got his camera out of the trunk of his father's car. It was a Leica III, so small he could carry it on a strap around his neck, yet it had shutter speeds as fast as one-five-hundredth of a second.

He walked a few blocks to Niagara Square, where the march was to begin. Lev Peshkov had tried to persuade the city to ban the demonstration on the grounds that it would lead to violence, but the union had insisted it would be peaceful. The union seemed to have won that argument, for several hundred people were milling around outside city hall. Many carried lovingly embroidered banners, red flags, and placards reading SAY NO TO BOSS THUGS. Woody looked around for Joanne but did not see her.

The weather was fine and the mood was sunny, and he took a few shots: workmen in their Sunday suits and hats; a car festooned with banners; a young cop biting his nails. There was still no sign of Joanne, and he began to think she would not appear. She might have a headache this morning, he guessed.

The march was due to move off at noon. It finally got going a few minutes before one. There was a heavy police presence along the route, Woody noted. He found himself near the middle of the procession.

As they walked south on Washington Street, heading for the city's industrial heartland, he saw Joanne join the march a few yards ahead, and his heart leaped. She was wearing tailored pants that flattered her figure. He hurried to catch up with her. "Good afternoon!" he said happily.

"Good grief, you're cheerful," she said.

It was an understatement. He was delirious with happiness. "Are you hungover?"

"Either that or I've contracted the Black Death. Which do you think it is?"

"If you have a rash, it's the Black Death. Are there any spots?" Woody hardly knew what he was saying. "I'm not a doctor, but I'd be happy to check you over."

"Stop being irrepressible. I know it's charming, but I'm not in the mood."

Woody tried to calm down. "We missed you in church," he said. "The sermon was about Noah."

To his consternation she burst out laughing. "Oh, Woody," she said. "I like you so much when you're funny, but please don't make me laugh today."

He thought this remark was probably favorable, but he was far from certain.

He spotted an open grocery store on a side street. "You need fluids," he said. "I'll be right back." He ran into the store and bought two bottles of Coke, ice-cold from the refrigerator. He got the clerk to open them, then returned to the march. When he handed a bottle to Joanne, she said: "Oh, boy, you're a lifesaver." She put the bottle to her lips and drank a long draft.

Woody felt he was ahead, so far.

The march was good-humored, despite the grim incident they were protesting about. A group of older men were singing political anthems and traditional songs. There were even a few families with children. And there was not a cloud in the sky.

"Have you read *Studies in Hysteria*?" Woody asked as they walked along.

"Never heard of it."

"Oh! It's by Sigmund Freud. I thought you were a fan of his."

"I'm interested in his ideas. I've never read one of his books."

"You should. *Studies in Hysteria* is amazing."

She looked curiously at him. "What made you read a book such as that? I bet they don't teach psychology at your expensively old-fashioned school."

"Oh, I don't know. I guess I heard you talking about psychoanalysis and thought it sounded really extraordinary. And it is."

"In what way?"

Woody had the feeling she was testing him, to see whether he had really understood the book or was merely pretending. "The idea that a crazy act, such as obsessively spilling ink on a tablecloth, can have a kind of hidden logic."

She nodded. "Yeah," she said. "That's it."

Woody knew instinctively that she did not understand what he was talking about. He had already overtaken her in his knowledge of Freud, but she was embarrassed to admit it.

"What's your favorite thing to do?" he asked her. "Theater? Classical music? I guess going to a film is no big treat to someone whose father owns about a hundred movie houses."

"Why do you ask?"

"Well . . ." He decided to be honest. "I want to ask you out, and I'd like to tempt you with something you really love to do. So name it, and we'll do it."

She smiled at him, but it was not the smile he was hoping for. It was friendly but sympathetic, and it told him that bad news was coming. "Woody, I'd like to, but you're fifteen."

"As you said last night, I'm more mature than Victor Dixon."

"I wouldn't go out with him, either."

Woody's throat seemed to constrict, and his voice came out hoarse. "Are you turning me down?"

"Yes, very firmly. I don't want to date a boy three years younger."

"Can I ask you again in three years? We'll be the same age then."

She laughed, then said: "Stop being witty. It hurts my head."

Woody decided not to hide his pain. What did he have to lose? Feeling anguished, he said: "So what was that kiss about?"

"It was nothing."

He shook his head miserably. "It was something to me. It was the best kiss I've ever had."

"Oh, God, I knew it was a mistake. Look, it was just a bit of fun. Yes, I enjoyed it—be flattered, you're entitled. You're a cute kid, and smart as a whip, but a kiss is not a declaration of love, Woody, no matter how much you enjoy it."

They were near the front of the march, and Woody saw their destination up ahead: the high wall around the Buffalo Metal Works. The gate was closed and guarded by a dozen or more factory police, thuggish men in light blue shirts that mimicked police uniforms.

"And I was drunk," Joanne added.

"Yeah, I was drunk, too," Woody said.

It was a pathetic attempt to salvage his dignity, but Joanne had the grace to pretend to believe him. "Then we both did something a little foolish, and we should just forget it," she said.

"Yeah," said Woody, looking away.

They were outside the factory now. Those at the head of the march stopped at the gates, and someone began to make a speech through a bullhorn. Looking more closely, Woody saw that the speaker was a local union organizer, Brian Hall. Woody's father knew and liked the man: at some time in the dim past they had worked together to resolve a strike.

The rear of the procession kept coming forward, and a crush developed across the width of the street. The factory police were keeping the entrance clear, though the gates were shut. Woody now saw that they were armed with police-type nightsticks. One of them was shouting: "Stay away from the gate! This is private property!" Woody lifted his camera and took a picture.

But the people at the front were being pushed forward by those behind. Woody took Joanne's arm and tried to steer her away from the focus of tension. However, it was difficult: the crowd was dense now, and no one wanted to move out of the way. Against his will, Woody found himself edging closer to the factory gate and the guards with nightsticks. "This is not a good situation," he said to Joanne.

But she was flushed with excitement. "Those bastards can't keep us back!" she cried.

A man next to her shouted: "Right! Damn right!"

The crowd was still ten yards or more from the gate, but just the same the guards unnecessarily began to push demonstrators away. Woody took a photograph.

Brian Hall had been yelling into his bullhorn about boss thugs and pointing an accusing finger at the factory police. Now he changed his tune and began to call for calm. "Move away from the gates, please, brothers," he said. "Move back, no rough stuff."

Woody saw a woman pushed by a guard hard enough to make her stumble. She did not fall over, but she cried out, and the man with her said to the guard: "Hey, buddy, take it easy, will you?"

"Are you trying to start something?" the guard said challengingly.

The woman yelled: "Just stop shoving!"

"Move back, move back!" the guard shouted. He raised his nightstick. The woman screamed.

As the nightstick came down, Woody took a picture.

Joanne said: "The son of a bitch hit that woman!" She stepped forward.

But most of the crowd began to move in the opposite direction, away from the factory. As they turned, the guards came after them, shoving, kicking, and lashing out with their truncheons.

Brian Hall said: "There is no need for violence! Factory police, step back! Do not use your clubs!" Then his bullhorn was knocked out of his hands by a guard.

Some of the younger men fought back. Half a dozen real policemen moved into the crowd. They did nothing to restrain the factory police, but began to arrest anyone fighting back.

The guard who had started the fracas fell to the ground, and two demonstrators started kicking him.

Woody took a picture.

Joanne was screaming with fury. She threw herself at a guard and scratched his face. He put out a hand to shove her away. Accidentally or otherwise, the heel of his hand connected sharply with her nose. She fell back with blood coming from her nostrils. The guard raised his nightstick. Woody grabbed her by the waist and jerked her back. The stick missed her. "Come on!" Woody yelled at her. "We have to get out of here!"

The blow to her face had deflated her fury, and she offered no resistance as he half-pulled, half-carried her away from the gates as fast as he could, his camera swinging on the strap around his neck. The crowd was panicking now, people falling over and others trampling them as everyone tried to flee.

Woody was taller than most and he managed to keep himself and Joanne upright. They fought their way through the crush, staying just ahead of the nightsticks. At last the crowd thinned out. Joanne detached herself from his grasp and they both began to run.

The noise of the fight receded behind them. They turned a couple of corners and, a minute later, found themselves on a deserted street of factories and warehouses, all closed on Sunday. They slowed to a walk, catching their breath. Joanne began to laugh. "That was so exciting!" she said.

Woody could not share her enthusiasm. "It was nasty," he said. "And it could have gotten worse." He had rescued her, and he half hoped that might cause her to change her mind about dating him.

But she did not feel she owed him much. "Oh, come on," she said in a tone of disparagement. "Nobody died."

"Those guards deliberately provoked a riot!"

"Of course they did! Peshkov wants to make union members look bad."

"Well, we know the truth." Woody tapped his camera. "And I can prove it."

They walked half a mile; then Woody saw a cruising cab and hailed it. He gave the driver the address of the Rouzrokh family home.

Sitting in the back of the taxi, he took a handkerchief from his pocket. "I don't want to bring you home to your father looking like this," he said. He unfolded the white cotton square and gently dabbed at the blood on her upper lip.

It was an intimate act, and he found it sexy, but she did not indulge him for long. After a second she said: "I've got it." She took the handkerchief from his grasp and cleaned herself up. "How's that?"

"You've missed a bit," he lied. He took the handkerchief back. Her mouth was wide, she had even white teeth, and her lips were enchantingly full. He pretended there was something under her lower lip. He wiped it gently, then said: "Better."

"Thanks." She looked at him with an odd expression, half fond, half annoyed. She knew he had been lying about the blood on her chin, he guessed, and she was not sure whether to be cross with him or not.

The cab halted outside her house. "Don't come in," she said. "I'm going to lie to my parents about where I've been, and I don't want you blabbing the truth."

Woody reckoned he was probably the more discreet of the two of them, but he did not say so. "I'll call you later."

"Okay." She got out of the taxi and walked up the driveway with a perfunctory wave.

"She's a doll," said the driver. "Too old for you, though."

"Take me to Delaware Avenue," Woody said. He gave the number and the cross street. He was not going to talk about Joanne to a goddamn cabby.

He pondered his rejection. He should not have been surprised: everyone from his brother to the taxi driver said he was too young for her. All the same it hurt. He felt as if he did not know what to do with his life now. How would he get through the rest of the day?

Back at home, his parents were taking their ritual Sunday afternoon nap. Chuck believed that was when they had sex. Chuck himself had gone swimming with a bunch of friends, according to Betty.

Woody went into the darkroom and developed the film from his camera. He ran warm water into the basin to bring the chemicals to the ideal temperature, then put the film into a black bag to transfer it into a light-trap tank.

It was a lengthy process that required patience, but he was happy to sit in the dark and think about Joanne. Their being together during a riot had not made her fall in love with him, but it had certainly brought them closer. He felt sure she was at least growing to like him more and more. Maybe her rejection was not final. Perhaps he should keep trying. He certainly had no interest in any other girls.

When his timer rang, he transferred the film into a stop bath to halt the chemical reaction, then to a bath of fixer to make the image permanent. Finally he washed and dried his film and looked at the negative black-and-white images on the reel.

He thought they were pretty good.

He cut the film into frames, then put the first into the enlarger. He laid a sheet of ten-by-eight photographic paper on the base of the enlarger, turned on the light, and exposed the paper to the negative image while he counted seconds. Then he put the paper into an open bath of developer.

This was the best part of the process. Slowly the white paper began to show patches of gray, and the image he had photographed began to appear. It always seemed to him like a miracle. The first print showed a Negro and a white man, both in Sunday suits and hats, holding a banner that said BROTHERHOOD in large letters. When the image was clear, he moved the paper to a bath of fixer, then washed it and dried it.

He printed all the shots he had taken, took them out into the light, and laid them out on the dining room table. He was pleased: they were vivid, active pictures that clearly showed a sequence of events. When he heard his parents moving about upstairs, he called his mother. She had been a journalist before she married, and she still wrote books and magazine articles. "What do you think?" he asked her.

She studied them thoughtfully with her one eye. After a while she said: "I think they're good. You should take them to a newspaper."

"Really?" he said. He began to feel excited. "Which paper?"

"They're all conservative, unfortunately. Maybe the *Buffalo Sentinel.* The editor is Peter Hoyle—he's been there since God was a boy. He knows your father well; he'll probably see you."

"When should I show him the photos?"

"Now. The march is hot news. It will be in all tomorrow's papers. They need the pictures tonight."

Woody was energized. "All right," he said. He picked up the glossy sheets and shuffled them into a neat stack. His mother produced a cardboard folder from Papa's study. Woody kissed her and left the house.

He caught a bus downtown.

The front entrance of the *Sentinel* office was closed, and he suffered a moment of dismay, but he reasoned that reporters must be able to get in and out today if they were to produce a Monday morning paper, and sure enough he found a side entrance. "I have some photographs for Mr. Hoyle," he said to a man sitting inside the door, and he was directed upstairs.

He found the editor's office, a secretary took his name, and a minute later he was shaking hands with Peter Hoyle. The editor was a tall, imposing man with white hair and a black mustache. He appeared to be finishing a meeting with a younger colleague. He spoke loudly, as if shouting over the noise of a printing press. "The hit-and-run-drivers story is fine, but the intro stinks, Jack," he said with a dismissive hand on the man's shoulder, moving him to the door. "Put a new nose on it. Move the mayor's statement to later and start with crippled children." Jack left, and Hoyle turned to Woody. "What have you got, kid?" he said without preamble.

"I was at the march today."

"You mean the riot."

"It wasn't a riot until the factory guards started hitting women with their clubs."

"I hear the marchers tried to break into the factory, and the guards repelled them."

"It's not true, sir, and the photos prove it."

"Show me."

Woody had arranged them in order while sitting on the bus. He put the first down on the editor's desk. "It started peacefully."

Hoyle pushed the photograph aside. "That's nothing," he said.

Woody brought out a picture taken at the factory. "The guards were waiting at the gate. You can see their nightsticks." His next picture had been taken when the shoving started. "The marchers were at least ten yards from the gate, so there was no need for the guards to try to move them back. It was a deliberate provocation."

"Okay," said Hoyle, and he did not push the pictures aside.

Woody brought out his best shot: a guard using a truncheon to beat a woman. "I saw this whole incident," Woody said. "All the woman did was tell him to stop shoving her, and he hit her like this."

"Good picture," said Hoyle. "Any more?"

"One," said Woody. "Most of the marchers ran away as soon as the fighting began, but a few fought back." He showed Hoyle the photograph of two demonstrators kicking a guard on the ground. "These men retaliated against the guard who hit the woman."

"You did a good job, young Dewar," said Hoyle. He sat at his desk and pulled a form from a tray. "Twenty bucks okay?"

"You mean you're going to print my photographs?"

"I assume that's why you brought them here."

"Yes, sir, thank you. Twenty dollars is okay. I mean fine. I mean plenty."

Hoyle scribbled on the form and signed it. "Take this to the cashier. My secretary will tell you where to go."

The phone on the desk rang. The editor picked it up and barked: "Hoyle." Woody gathered he was dismissed, and left the room.

He was elated. The payment was amazing, but he was more thrilled that the newspaper would use his photos. He followed the secretary's directions to a little room with a counter and a teller's window, and got his twenty bucks. Then he went home in a taxi.

His parents were delighted by his coup, and even his brother seemed pleased. Over dinner, Grandmama said: "As long as you don't consider journalism as a career. That would be lowering."

In fact Woody had been thinking that he might take up news photography instead of politics, and he was surprised to learn that his grandmother disapproved.

His mother smiled and said: "But, Ursula dear, I was a journalist."

"That's different—you're a girl," Grandmama replied. "Woodrow must become a man of distinction, like his father and grandfather before him."

Mother did not take offense at this. She was fond of Grandmama and listened with amused tolerance to her pronouncements of orthodoxy.

However, Chuck resented the traditional focus on the elder son. He said: "And what must I become, chopped liver?"

"Don't be vulgar, Charles," said Grandmama, having the last word as usual.

That night Woody lay awake a long time. He could hardly wait to see his photos in the paper. He felt the way he had as a kid on Christmas Eve: his longing for the morning kept him from sleep.

He thought about Joanne. She was wrong to think him too young. He was right for her. She liked him, they had a lot in common, and she had enjoyed the kiss. He still thought he might win her heart.

He fell asleep at last, and when he woke, it was daylight. He put on a dressing gown over his pajamas and ran downstairs. Joe, the butler, always went out early to buy the newspapers, and they were already laid out on the side table in the breakfast room. Woody's parents were there, his father eating scrambled eggs, his mother sipping coffee.

Woody picked up the *Sentinel*. His work was on the front page.

But it was not what he expected.

They had used only one of his shots—the last. It showed a factory guard lying on the ground being kicked by two workers. The headline was: METAL STRIKERS RIOT.

"Oh, no!" he said.

He read the report with incredulity. It said that marchers had attempted to break into the factory and had been bravely repelled by the factory police, several of whom had suffered minor injuries. The behavior of the workers was condemned by the mayor, the chief of police, and Lev Peshkov. At the foot of the article, like an afterthought, union spokesman Brian Hall was quoted as denying the story and blaming the guards for the violence.

Woody put the newspaper in front of his mother. "I told Hoyle that the guards started the riot—and I gave him the pictures to prove it!" he said angrily. "Why would he print the opposite of the truth?"

"Because he's a conservative," she said.

"Newspapers are supposed to tell the truth!" Woody said, his voice rising with furious indignation. "They can't just make up lies!"

"Yes, they can," she said.

"But it's not fair!"

"Welcome to the real world," said his mother.

vi

Greg Peshkov and his father were in the lobby of the Ritz-Carlton hotel in Washington, D.C., when they ran into Dave Rouzrokh.

Dave was wearing a white suit and a straw hat. He glared at them with hatred. Lev greeted him, but he turned away contemptuously without answering.

Greg knew why. Dave had been losing money all summer, because Roseroque Theatres was not able to get first-run hit movies. And Dave must have guessed that Lev was somehow responsible.

Last week Lev had offered Dave four million dollars for his movie houses—half the original bid—and Dave had again refused. "The price is dropping, Dave," Lev had warned him.

Now Greg said: "I wonder what he's doing here?"

"He's meeting with Sol Starr. He's going to ask why Sol won't give him good movies." Lev obviously knew all about it.

"What will Mr. Starr do?"

"String him along."

Greg marveled at his father's ability to know everything and stay on top of a changing situation. He was always ahead of the game.

They rode up in the elevator. This was the first time Greg had visited his father's permanent suite at the hotel. His mother, Marga, had never been here.

Lev spent a lot of time in Washington because the government was forever interfering with the movie business. Men who considered themselves to be moral leaders got very agitated about what was shown on the big screen, and they put pressure on the government to censor pictures. Lev saw this as a negotiation—he saw life as a negotiation—and his constant aim was to avoid formal censorship by adhering to a voluntary code, a strategy backed by Sol Starr and most other Hollywood big shots.

They entered a living room that was extremely fancy, much more so than the spacious apartment in Buffalo where Greg and his mother lived, and which Greg had always thought to be luxurious. This room had spindly-legged furniture that Greg imagined to be French, rich chestnut-brown velvet drapes at the windows, and a large phonograph.

In the middle of the room he was stunned to see, sitting on a yellow silk sofa, the movie star Gladys Angelus.

People said she was the most beautiful woman in the world.

Greg could see why. She radiated sex appeal, from her dark blue inviting eyes to the long legs crossed under her clinging skirt. As she put out a hand to shake, her red lips smiled and her round breasts moved alluringly inside a soft sweater.

He hesitated a split second before shaking her hand. He felt disloyal to his mother, Marga. She never mentioned the name of Gladys Angelus, a sure sign that she knew what people were saying about Gladys and Lev. Greg felt he was making friends with his mother's enemy. If Mom knew about this, she would cry, he thought.

But he had been taken by surprise. If he had been forewarned, if he had had time to think about his reaction, he might have prepared, and rehearsed a gracious withdrawal. But he could not bring himself to be clumsily rude to this overwhelmingly lovely woman.

So he took her hand, looked into her amazing eyes, and gave what people called a shit-eating grin.

She kept hold of his hand as she said: "I'm so happy to meet you at long last. Your father has told me all about you—but he didn't say how handsome you are!"

There was something unpleasantly proprietorial about this, as if she were a member of the family, rather than a whore who had usurped his mother. All the same he found himself falling under her spell. "I love your films," he said awkwardly.

"Oh, stop it—you don't have to say that," she said, but Greg thought she liked to hear it all the same. "Come and sit by me," she went on. "I want to get to know you."

He did as he was told. He could not help himself. Gladys asked him what school he attended, and while he was telling her, the phone rang. He vaguely heard his father say into the phone: "It was supposed to be tomorrow . . . Okay, if we have to, we can rush it . . . Leave it with me. I'll handle it."

Lev hung up and interrupted Gladys. "Your room is down the hall, Greg," he said. He handed over a key. "And you'll find a gift from me. Settle in and enjoy yourself. We'll meet for dinner at seven."

This was abrupt, and Gladys looked put out, but Lev could be peremptory sometimes, and it was best just to obey. Greg took the key and left.

In the corridor was a broad-shouldered man in a cheap suit. He reminded Greg of Joe Brekhunov, head of security at the Buffalo Metal Works. Greg nodded, and the man said: "Good afternoon, sir." Presumably he was a hotel employee.

Greg entered his room. It was pleasant enough, though not as swanky as his father's suite. He did not see the gift his father had mentioned, but his suitcase was there, and he began to unpack, thinking about Gladys. Was he being disloyal to his mother by shaking hands with his father's mistress? Of course, Gladys was only doing what Marga herself had done, sleeping with a married man. All the same he felt painfully uncomfortable. Was he going to tell his mother that he had met Gladys? Hell, no.

As he was hanging up his shirts, he heard a knock. It came from a door that looked as if it might lead to the neighboring room. Next moment the door opened and a girl walked through.

She was older than Greg, but not much. Her skin was the color of dark chocolate, and she wore a polka-dot dress and carried a clutch bag. She smiled broadly, showing white teeth, and said: "Hello, I've got the room next door."

"I figured that out," he said. "Who are you?"

"Jacky Jakes." She held out her hand. "I'm an actress."

Greg shook hands with the second beautiful actress in an hour. Jacky had a playful look that Greg found more attractive than Gladys's overpowering magnetism. Her mouth was a dark pink bow. He said: "My dad said he got me a gift—are you it?"

She giggled. "I guess I am. He said I would like you. He's going to get me into the movies."

Greg got the picture. His father had guessed he might feel bad about being friendly with Gladys. Jacky was his reward for not making a fuss. He thought he probably ought to reject such a bribe, but he could not resist. "You're a very nice gift," he said.

"Your father's real good to you."

"He's wonderful," Greg said. "And so are you."

"Aren't you sweet?" She put her purse down on the dresser, stepped closer to Greg, stood on tiptoe, and kissed his mouth. Her lips were soft and warm. "I like you," she said. She felt his shoulders. "You're strong."

"I play ice hockey."

"Makes a girl feel safe." She put both hands on his cheeks and kissed him again, longer; then she sighed and said: "Oh, boy, I think we're going to have fun."

"Are we?" Washington was a Southern city, still largely segregated. In Buffalo, white and black people could eat in the same restaurants and drink in the same bars, mostly, but here it was different. Greg was not sure what the laws were, but he felt certain that in practise a white man with a black woman would cause trouble. It was surprising to find Jacky occupying a room in this hotel; Lev must have fixed it. But there was certainly no question of Greg and Jacky swanning around town with Lev and Gladys in a foursome. So what did Jacky think they were going to do to have fun together? The amazing notion crossed his mind that she might be willing to go to bed with him.

He put his hands on her waist, to draw her to him for another kiss, but she pulled back. "I need to take a shower," she said. "Give me a few minutes." She turned and disappeared through the communicating door, closing it behind her.

He sat on the bed, trying to take it all in. Jacky wanted to act in movies, and it seemed she was willing to use sex to advance her career. She certainly was not the first actress, black or white, to use that strategy. Gladys was doing the same by sleeping with Lev. Greg and his father were the lucky beneficiaries.

He saw that she had left her clutch bag behind. He picked it up and tried the door. It was not locked. He stepped through.

She was on the phone, wearing a pink bathrobe. She said: "Yes, hunky-dory, no problem." Her voice seemed different, more mature, and he realized that with him she had been using a sexy little-girl tone that was not natural. Then she saw him, smiled, and reverted to the girly voice as she said into the phone: "Please hold my calls. I don't want to be disturbed. Thank you. Good-bye."

"You left this," said Greg, and handed her the purse.

"You just wanted to see me in my bathrobe," she said coquettishly. The front of the robe did not entirely hide her breasts, and he could see an enchanting curve of flawless brown skin.

He grinned. "No, but I'm glad I did."

"Go back to your room. I have to shower. I might let you see more later."

"Oh, my God," he said.

He returned to his room. This was astonishing. "I might let you see more later," he repeated to himself aloud. What a thing for a girl to say!

He had a hard-on, but he did not want to jerk off when the real thing seemed so close. To take his mind off it, he went on unpacking. He had an expensive shaving kit, a razor and brush with pearl handles, a present from his mother. He laid the things out in the bathroom, wondering whether they would impress Jacky if she saw them.

The walls were thin, and he heard the sound of running water from the next room. The thought of her body naked and wet possessed him. He tried to concentrate on arranging his underwear and socks in a drawer.

Then he heard her scream.

He froze. For a moment he was too surprised to move. What did it mean? Why would she yell out like that? Then she screamed again, and he was shocked into action. He threw open the communicating door and stepped into her room.

She was naked. He had never seen a naked woman in real life. She had pointed breasts with dark brown tips. At her groin was a thatch of wiry black hair. She was cowering back against the wall, trying ineffectually to cover her nakedness with her hands.

Standing in front of her was Dave Rouzrokh, with twin scratches down his aristocratic cheek, presumably caused by Jacky's pink-varnished nails. There was blood on the broad lapel of Dave's double-breasted white jacket.

Jacky screamed: "Get him away from me!"

Greg swung a fist. Dave was an inch taller, but he was an old man, and Greg was an athletic teenager. The blow connected with Dave's chin—more by luck than by judgment—and Dave staggered back, then fell to the floor.

The room door opened.

The broad-shouldered hotel employee Greg had seen earlier came in.

He must have a master key, Greg thought. "I'm Tom Cranmer, house detective," the man said. "What's going on here?"

Greg said: "I heard her scream and came in to find him here."

Jacky said: "He tried to rape me!"

Dave struggled to his feet. "That's not true," he said. "I was asked to come to this room for a meeting with Sol Starr."

Jacky began to sob. "Oh, now he's going to lie about it!"

Cranmer said: "Put something on, please, miss."

Jacky put on her pink bathrobe.

The detective picked up the room phone, dialed a number, and said: "There's usually a cop on the corner. Get him into the lobby, right now."

Dave was staring at Greg. "You're Peshkov's bastard, aren't you?"

Greg was about to hit him again.

Dave said: "Oh, my God, this is a setup."

Greg was thrown by this remark. He felt intuitively that Dave was telling the truth. He dropped his fist. This whole scene must have been scripted by Lev, he realized. Dave Rouzrokh was no rapist. Jacky was faking. And Greg himself was just an actor in the movie. He felt dazed.

"Please come with me, sir," said Cranmer, taking Dave firmly by the arm. "You two as well."

"You can't arrest me," said Dave.

"Yes, sir, I can," said Cranmer. "And I'm going to hand you over to a police officer."

Greg said to Jacky: "Do you want to get dressed?"

She shook her head quickly and decisively. Greg realized it was part of the plan that she would appear in her robe.

He took Jacky's arm and they followed Cranmer and Dave along the corridor and into the elevator. A cop was waiting in the lobby. Both he and the hotel detective must be in on the plot, Greg surmised.

Cranmer said: "I heard a scream from her room, found the old guy in there. She says he tried to rape her. The kid is a witness."

Dave looked bewildered, as if he thought this might be a bad dream. Greg found himself feeling sorry for Dave. He had been cruelly trapped. Lev was more pitiless than Greg had imagined. Half of him admired his father; the other half wondered if such ruthlessness was really necessary.

The cop snapped handcuffs on Dave and said: "All right, let's go."

"Go where?" Dave said.

"Downtown," said the cop.

Greg said: "Do we all have to go?"

"Yeah."

Cranmer spoke to Greg in a low voice. "Don't worry, son," he said. "You did a great job. We'll go to the precinct house and make our statements, and after that you can fuck her from here to Christmastime."

The cop led Dave to the door, and the others followed.

As they stepped outside, a photographer popped a flashgun.

vii

Woody Dewar got a copy of Freud's *Studies in Hysteria* mailed to him by a bookseller in New York. On the night of the Yacht Club ball—the climactic social event of the summer season in Buffalo—he wrapped it neatly in brown paper and tied a red ribbon around it. "Chocolates for a lucky girl?" said his mother, passing him in the hall. She had only one eye but she saw everything.

"A book," he said. "For Joanne Rouzrokh."

"She won't be at the ball."

"I know."

Mama stopped and gave him a searching look. After a moment she said: "You're serious about her."

"I guess. But she thinks I'm too young."

"Her pride is probably involved. Her friends would ask why she can't find a guy her own age to go out with. Girls are cruel like that."

"I'm planning to persist until she grows more mature."

Mama smiled. "I bet you make her laugh."

"I do. It's the best card I hold."

"Well, heck, I waited long enough for your father."

"Did you?"

"I loved him from the first time I met him. I pined for years. I had to watch him fall for that shallow cow Olga Vyalov, who wasn't worthy of him but had two working eyes. Thank God she got knocked up by her chauffeur." Mother's language could be a little coarse, especially when Grandmama was not around. She had picked up bad habits during the years she spent working on newspapers. "Then he went off to war. I had to follow him to France before I could nail his foot to the goddamn floor."

Nostalgia was mixed with pain in her reminiscence, Woody could tell. "But he realized you were the right girl for him."

"In the end, yes."

"Maybe that'll happen to me."

Mama kissed him. "Good luck, my son," she said.

The Rouzrokh house was less than a mile away and Woody walked there. None of the Rouzrokhs would be at the Yacht Club tonight. Dave had been all over the papers after a mysterious incident at the Ritz-Carlton hotel in Washington. A typical headline had read CINEMA MOGUL ACCUSED BY STARLET. Woody had recently learned to mistrust newspapers. However, gullible people said there must be something in it; otherwise, why would the police have arrested Dave?

None of the family had been seen at any social event since.

Outside the house an armed guard stopped Woody. "The family isn't seeing callers," he said brusquely.

Woody guessed the man had spent a lot of time repelling reporters, and he forgave the discourteous tone. He recalled the name of the Rouzrokhs' maid. "Please ask Miss Estella to tell Joanne that Woody Dewar has a book for her."

"You can leave it with me," said the guard, holding out his hand.

Woody held on firmly to the book. "Thanks, but no."

The guard looked annoyed, but he walked Woody up the drive and rang the doorbell. Estella opened it and said at once: "Hello, Mr. Woody, come in—Joanne will be so glad to see you!" Woody permitted himself a triumphant glance at the guard as he stepped inside.

Estella showed him into an empty drawing room. She offered him milk and cookies, as if he were still a kid, and he declined politely. Joanne came in a minute later. Her face was drawn and her olive skin looked washed out, but she smiled pleasantly at him and sat down to chat.

She was pleased with the book. "Now I'll have to read Dr. Freud instead of just gabbing about him," she said. "You're a good influence on me, Woody."

"I wish I could be a bad influence."

She let that pass. "Aren't you going to the ball?"

"I have a ticket, but if you're not there, I'm not interested. Would you like to go to a movie instead?"

"No, thanks, really."

"Or we could just get dinner. Somewhere really quiet. If you don't mind taking the bus."

"Oh, Woody, of course I don't mind the bus, but you're too young for me. Anyway, the summer's almost over. You'll be back at school soon, and I'm going to Vassar."

"Where you'll go on dates, I guess."

"I sure hope so!"

Woody stood up. "Okay, well, I'm going to take a vow of celibacy and enter a monastery. Please don't come and visit me—you'll distract the other brethren."

She laughed. "Thank you for taking my mind off my family's troubles."

It was the first time she had mentioned what had happened to her father. He had not been planning to raise the subject, but now that she had, he said: "You know we're all on your side. Nobody believes that actress's story. Everyone in town realizes it was a setup by that swine Lev Peshkov, and we're furious about it."

"I know," she said. "But the accusation alone is too shameful for my father to bear. I think my parents are going to move to Florida."

"I'm so sorry."

"Thank you. Now go to the ball."

"Maybe I will."

She walked him to the door.

"May I kiss you good-bye?" he said.

She leaned forward and kissed his lips. This was not like the last kiss, and he knew instinctively not to grab her and press his mouth to hers. It was a gentle kiss, her lips on his for a sweet moment that was over in a breath. Then she pulled away and opened the front door.

"Good night," Woody said as he stepped out.

"Good-bye," said Joanne.

viii

Greg Peshkov was in love.

He knew that Jacky Jakes had been bought for him by his father, as his reward for helping to entrap Dave Rouzrokh, but despite that it was real love.

He had lost his virginity a few minutes after they returned from the precinct house, and the two of them had then spent most of a week in bed at the Ritz-Carlton. Greg did not need to use birth control, she told him, because she was already "fixed up." He had only the vaguest idea what that meant, but he took her at her word.

He had never been so happy in his life, and he adored her, especially when she dropped the little-girl act and revealed a shrewd intelligence and a mordant sense of humor. She admitted she had seduced Greg on his father's orders, but confessed that against her will she had fallen in love. Her real name was Mabel Jakes and, although she pretended to be nineteen, she was in fact just sixteen, only a few months older than Greg.

Lev had promised her a part in a movie but, he said, he was still looking for just the right role. In a perfect imitation of Lev's vestigial Russian accent she said: "But I don't guess he's lookin' too fuckin' hard."

"I guess there aren't many parts written for Negro actors," Greg said.

"I know, I'll end up playing the maid, rolling my eyes and saying *lawdy*. There are Africans in plays and films—Cleopatra, Hannibal, Othello—but they're usually played by white actors." Her father, now dead, had been a professor in a Negro college, and she knew more about literature than Greg did. "Anyway, why should Negroes only play black people? If Cleopatra can be played by a white actress, why can't Juliet be black?"

"People would find it strange."

"People would get used to it. They get used to anything. Does Jesus have to be played by a Jew? Nobody cares."

She was right, Greg thought, but all the same it was never going to happen.

When Lev had announced their return to Buffalo—leaving it until the last minute, as usual—Greg had been devastated. He had asked his father if Jacky could come to Buffalo, but Lev had laughed and said: "Son, you don't shit where you eat. You can see her next time you come to Washington."

Despite that, Jacky had followed him to Buffalo a day later and moved into a cheap apartment near Canal Street.

Lev and Greg had been busy for the next couple of weeks with the takeover of Roseroque Theatres. Dave had sold for two million in the end, a quarter of the original offer, and Greg's admiration for his father went up another notch. Jacky had withdrawn her charges and hinted to the newspapers that she had accepted a cash settlement. Greg was awestruck by his father's callous nerve.

And he had Jacky. He told his mother he was out every night with male friends, but in fact he spent all his spare time with Jacky. He showed her around town, picnicked with her at the beach, even managed to take her out in a borrowed speedboat. No one connected her with the rather blurred newspaper photograph of a girl walking out of the Ritz-Carlton hotel in a bathrobe. But mostly they spent the warm summer evenings having sweaty, deliriously happy sex, tangling the worn sheets on the narrow bed in her small apartment. They decided to get married as soon as they were old enough.

Tonight he was taking her to the Yacht Club Ball.

It had been extraordinarily difficult to get tickets, but Greg had bribed a school friend.

He had bought Jacky a new dress, pink satin. He got a generous allowance from Marga, and Lev loved to slip him fifty bucks now and again, so he always had more money than he needed.

In the back of his mind a warning was sounding. Jacky would be the only Negro at the ball not serving drinks. She was very reluctant to go, but Greg had talked her around. The young men would envy him but the older ones might be hostile, he knew. There would be some muttering. Jacky's beauty and charm would overcome much prejudice, he felt: How could anyone resist her? But if some fool got drunk and insulted her, Greg would teach him a lesson with both fists.

Even as he thought this, he heard his mother telling him not to be a love-struck fool. But a man could not go through life listening to his mother.

As he walked along Canal Street in white tie and tails, he looked forward to seeing her in the new dress, and maybe kneeling to lift the hem up until he could see her panties and garter belt.

He entered her building, an old house now subdivided. There was a threadbare red carpet on the stairs and a smell of spicy cooking. He let himself into the apartment with his own key.

The place was empty.

That was odd. Where would she go without him?

With fear in his heart, he opened the closet. The pink satin ball dress hung there on its own. Her other clothes were gone.

"No!" he said aloud. How could this happen?

On the rickety pine table was an envelope. He picked it up and saw his name on the front in Jacky's neat, schoolgirl handwriting. A feeling of dread came over him.

He tore open the envelope with shaky hands and read the short message.

> My darling Greg,
> The last three weeks have been the happiest time of my entire
> life.

I knew in my heart that we couldn't ever get married but it was nice to pretend.

You are a lovely boy and will grow into a fine man, if you don't take after your father too much.

Had Lev found out that Jacky was living here, and somehow made her leave? He would not do that—would he?

Good-bye and don't forget me.

Your Gift,

Jacky

Greg crumpled the paper and wept.

ix

"You look wonderful," Eva Rothmann said to Daisy Peshkov. "If I was a boy, I'd fall in love with you in a minute."

Daisy smiled. Eva was already a little bit in love with her. And Daisy did look wonderful, in an ice-blue silk organdy ball gown that deepened the blue of her eyes. The skirt of the dress had a frilled hem that was ankle length in front but rose playfully to midcalf behind, giving a tantalizing glimpse of Daisy's legs in sheer stockings.

She wore a sapphire necklace of her mother's. "Your father bought me that, back in the days when he was still occasionally nice to me," Olga said. "But hurry up, Daisy, you're making us all late."

Olga was wearing matronly navy blue, and Eva was in red, which suited her dark coloring.

Daisy walked down the stairs on a cloud of happiness.

They stepped out of the house. Henry, the gardener, doubling as chauffeur tonight, opened the doors of the shiny old black Stutz.

This was Daisy's big night. Tonight Charlie Farquharson would formally propose to her. He would offer her a diamond ring that was a family heirloom—she had seen and approved it, and it had been altered to fit her. She would accept his proposal, and then they would announce their engagement to everyone at the ball.

She got into the car feeling like Cinderella.

Only Eva had expressed doubts. "I thought you'd go for someone who was more of a match for you," she had said.

"You mean a man who won't let me boss him around," Daisy had replied.

"No, but someone more like you, good-looking and charming and sexy."

This was unusually sharp for Eva: it implied that Charlie was homely and charmless and unglamorous. Daisy had been taken aback, and did not know how to reply.

Her mother had saved her. Olga had said: "I married a man who was good-looking and charming and sexy, and he made me utterly miserable."

Eva had said no more.

As the car approached the Yacht Club, Daisy vowed to restrain herself. She must not show how triumphant she felt. She must act as if there were nothing unexpected about her mother being asked to join the Buffalo Ladies' Society. As she showed the other girls her enormous diamond, she would be so gracious as to declare that she did not deserve someone as wonderful as Charlie.

She had plans to make him even more wonderful. As soon as the honeymoon was over, she and Charlie would start building their stable of racehorses. In five years they would be entering the most prestigious races around the world: Saratoga Springs, Longchamps, Royal Ascot.

Summer was turning to fall, and it was dusk when the car drew up at the pier. "I'm afraid we may be very late tonight, Henry," Daisy said gaily.

"Quite all right, Miss Daisy," he replied. He adored her. "You have a wonderful time, now."

At the door, Daisy noticed Victor Dixon following them in. Feeling well disposed toward everyone, she said: "So, Victor, your sister met the king of England. Congratulations!"

"Mm, yes," he said, looking embarrassed.

They entered the club. The first person they saw was Ursula Dewar, who had agreed to accept Olga into her snobby club. Daisy smiled warmly at her and said: "Good evening, Mrs. Dewar."

Ursula seemed distracted. "Excuse me just a moment," she said, and moved away across the lobby. She thought herself a queen, Daisy reflected, but did that mean she had no need of good manners? One day Daisy would rule over Buffalo society, but she would be unfailingly gracious to all, she vowed.

The three women went into the ladies' room, where they checked their appearance in the mirrors, in case anything had gone wrong in the twenty minutes since they left home. Dot Renshaw came in, looked at them, and went out again. "Stupid girl," Daisy said.

But her mother looked worried. "What's happening?" she said. "We've been here five minutes, and already three people have snubbed us!"

"Jealousy," Daisy said. "Dot would like to marry Charlie herself."

Olga said: "At this point Dot Renshaw would like to marry more or less anybody, I guess."

"Come on, let's enjoy ourselves," said Daisy, and she led the way out.

As she entered the ballroom, Woody Dewar greeted her. "At last, a gentleman!" Daisy said.

In a lowered voice he said: "I just want to say that I think it's wrong of people to blame you for anything your father might have done."

"Especially when they all bought their booze from him!" she replied.

Then she saw her future mother-in-law, in a ruched pink gown that did nothing for her angular figure. Nora Farquharson was not ecstatic about her son's choice of bride, but she had accepted Daisy and had been charming to Olga when they had exchanged visits. "Mrs. Farquharson!" Daisy said. "What a lovely dress!"

Nora Farquharson turned her back and walked away.

Eva gasped.

A feeling of horror came over Daisy. She turned back to Woody. "This isn't about bootlegging, is it?"

"No."

"What, then?"

"You must ask Charlie. Here he comes."

Charlie was perspiring, though it was not warm. "What's going on?" Daisy asked him. "Everyone's giving me the cold shoulder!"

He was terribly nervous. "People are so angry at your family," he said.

"What for?" she cried.

Several people nearby heard her raised voice and looked around. She did not care.

Charlie said: "Your father ruined Dave Rouzrokh."

"Are you talking about that incident in the Ritz-Carlton? What has that got to do with me?"

"Everyone likes Dave, even though he's Persian or something. And they don't believe he would rape anybody."

"I never said he did!"

"I know," Charlie said. He was clearly in agony.

People were frankly staring, now: Victor Dixon, Dot Renshaw, Chuck Dewar.

Daisy said to Charlie: "But I'm going to be blamed. Is that so?"

"Your father did a terrible thing."

Daisy was cold with fear. Surely she could not lose her triumph at the last minute? "Charlie," she said. "What are you telling me? Talk straight, for the love of God."

Eva put her arm around Daisy's waist in a gesture of support.

Charlie replied: "Mother says it's unforgivable."

"What does that mean, unforgivable?"

He stared miserably at her. He could not bring himself to speak.

But there was no need. She knew what he was going to say. "It's over, isn't it?" she said. "You're jilting me."

He nodded.

Olga said: "Daisy, we must leave." She was in tears.

Daisy looked around. She tilted her chin as she stared them all down: Dot Renshaw looking maliciously pleased, Victor Dixon admiring, Chuck Dewar with his mouth open in adolescent shock, and his brother, Woody, looking sympathetic.

"To hell with you all," Daisy said loudly. "I'm going to London to dance with the king!"

CHAPTER THREE

1936

I t was a sunny Saturday afternoon in May 1936, and Lloyd
Williams was at the end of his second year at Cambridge, when
Fascism reared its vile head among the white stone cloisters of
the ancient university.

Lloyd was at Emmanuel College—known as "Emma"—
doing modern languages. He was studying French and German, but he
preferred German. As he immersed himself in the glories of German
culture, reading Goethe, Schiller, Heine, and Thomas Mann, he looked
up occasionally from his desk in the quiet library to watch with sadness
as today's Germany descended into barbarism.

Then the local branch of the British Union of Fascists announced
that their leader, Sir Oswald Mosley, would address a meeting in
Cambridge. The news took Lloyd back to Berlin three years earlier. He
saw again the Brownshirt thugs wrecking Maud von Ulrich's magazine
office; heard again the grating sound of Hitler's hate-filled voice as
he stood in the parliament and poured scorn on democracy; shuddered
anew at the memory of the dogs' bloody muzzles savaging Jörg with a
bucket over his head.

Now Lloyd stood on the platform at Cambridge railway station, waiting to meet his mother off the train from London. With him was Ruby Carter, a fellow activist in the local Labour Party. She had helped him organize today's meeting on the subject of "the Truth about Fascism." Lloyd's mother, Eth Leckwith, was to speak. Her book about Germany had been a big success, she had stood for Parliament again in the 1935 election, and she was once again the member for Aldgate.

Lloyd was tense about the meeting. Mosley's new political party had gained many thousands of members, due in part to the enthusiastic support of the *Daily Mail,* which had run the infamous headline HURRAH FOR THE BLACKSHIRTS! Mosley was a charismatic speaker, and would undoubtedly recruit new members today. It was vital that there should be a bright beacon of reason to contrast with his seductive lies.

However, Ruby was chatty. She was complaining about the social life of Cambridge. "I'm so bored with local boys," she said. "All they want to do is go to a pub and get drunk."

Lloyd was surprised. He had imagined that Ruby had a well-developed social life. She wore inexpensive clothes that were always a bit tight, showing off her plump curves. Most men would find her attractive, he thought. "What do you like to do?" he asked. "Apart from organize Labour Party meetings."

"I love dancing."

"You can't be short of partners. There are twelve men for every woman at the university."

"No offense intended, but most of the university men are pansies."

There were a lot of homosexual men in Cambridge University, Lloyd knew, but it startled him to hear her mention the subject. Ruby was famously blunt, but this was shocking even from her. He had no idea how to respond, so he said nothing.

Ruby said: "You're not one of them, are you?"

"No! Don't be ridiculous."

"No need to be insulted. You're handsome enough for a pansy, except for that squashed nose."

He laughed. "That's what they call a backhanded compliment."

"You are, though. You look like Douglas Fairbanks Junior."

"Well, thanks, but I'm not a pansy."

"Have you got a girlfriend?"

This was becoming embarrassing. "No, not at the moment." He made a show of checking his watch and looking for the train.

"Why not?"

"I just haven't met Miss Right."

"Oh, thank you very much, I'm sure."

He looked at her. She was only half joking. He felt mortified that she had taken his remark personally. "I didn't mean . . ."

"Yes, you did. But never mind. Here's the train."

The locomotive drew into the station and came to a halt in a cloud of steam. The doors opened and passengers stepped out onto the platform: students in tweed jackets, farmers' wives going shopping, workingmen in flat caps. Lloyd scanned the crowd for his mother. "She'll be in a third-class carriage," he said. "Matter of principle."

Ruby said: "Would you come to my twenty-first-birthday party?"

"Of course."

"My friend's got a little flat in Market Street, and a deaf landlady."

Lloyd was not comfortable about this invitation, and hesitated over his reply; then his mother appeared, as pretty as a songbird in a red summer coat and a jaunty little hat. She hugged and kissed him. "You look very well, my lovely," she said. "But I must buy you a new suit for next term."

"This one is fine, Mam." He had a scholarship that paid his university fees and basic living expenses, but it did not run to suits. When he started at Cambridge, his mother had dipped into her savings and bought him a tweed suit for daytime and an evening suit for formal dinners. He had worn the tweed every day for two years, and it showed. He was particular about his appearance, and made sure he always had a clean white shirt, a perfectly knotted tie, and a folded white handkerchief in his breast pocket: there had to be a dandy somewhere in his ancestry. The suit was carefully pressed, but it was beginning to look shabby, and in truth he longed for a new one, but he did not want his mother to spend her savings.

"We'll see," she said. She turned to Ruby, smiled warmly, and held out her hand. "I'm Eth Leckwith," she said with the easy grace of a visiting duchess.

"Pleased to meet you. I'm Ruby Carter."

"Are you a student, too, Ruby?"

"No, I'm a maid at Chimbleigh, a big country house." Ruby looked a bit ashamed as she made this confession. "It's five miles out of town, but I can usually borrow a bike."

"Fancy that!" said Ethel. "When I was your age, I was a maid at a country house in Wales."

Ruby was amazed. "You, a housemaid? And now you're a member of Parliament!"

"That's what democracy means."

Lloyd said: "Ruby and I organized today's meeting together."

His mother said: "And how is it going?"

"Sold out. In fact we had to move to a bigger hall."

"I told you it would work."

The meeting was Ethel's idea. Ruby Carter and many others in the Labour Party had wanted to mount a protest demonstration, marching through the town. Lloyd had agreed at first. "Fascism must be publicly opposed at every opportunity," he had said.

Ethel had counseled otherwise. "If we march and shout slogans, we look just like them," she had said. "Show that we're different. Hold a quiet, intelligent meeting to discuss the reality of Fascism." Lloyd had been dubious. "I'll come and speak, if you like," she had said.

Lloyd had put that to the Cambridge party. There had been a lively discussion, with Ruby leading the opposition to Ethel's plan, but in the end the prospect of having an M.P. and famous feminist to speak had clinched it.

Lloyd was still not sure it had been the right decision. He recalled Maud von Ulrich in Berlin saying: "We must not meet violence with violence." That had been the policy of the German Social Democratic Party. For the von Ulrich family, and for Germany, the policy had been a catastrophe.

They walked out through the yellow-brick Romanesque arches of the station and hurried along leafy Station Road, a street of smug middle-class houses made of the same yellow brick. Ethel put her arm through Lloyd's. "How's my little undergraduate, then?" she said.

He smiled at the word *little*. He was four inches taller than she, and muscular because of his training with the university boxing team: he could have picked her up with one hand. She was bursting with pride, he knew. Few things in life had pleased her as much as his coming to this place. That was probably why she wanted to buy him suits.

"I love it here, you know that," he said. "I'll love it more when it's full of working-class boys."

"And girls," Ruby put in.

They turned into Hills Road, the main thoroughfare leading to the town center. Since the coming of the railway, the town had expanded south toward the station, and churches had been built along Hills Road to serve the new suburb. Their destination was a Baptist chapel whose left-wing pastor had agreed to loan it free of charge.

"I made a bargain with the Fascists," Lloyd said. "I said we'd refrain from marching if they would promise to do the same."

"I'm surprised they agreed," said Ethel. "Fascists love marching."

"They were reluctant. But I told the university authorities and the police what I was proposing, and the Fascists pretty much had to go along with it."

"That was clever."

"But, Mam, guess who is their local leader? Viscount Aberowen, otherwise known as Boy Fitzherbert, the son of your former employer Earl Fitzherbert!" Boy was twenty-one, the same age as Lloyd. He was at Trinity, the aristocratic college.

"What? My God!"

She seemed more shaken than he had expected, and he glanced at her. She had gone pale. "Are you shocked?"

"Yes!" She seemed to recover her composure. "His father is a junior minister in the Foreign Office." The government was a Conservative-dominated coalition. "Fitz must be embarrassed."

"Most Conservatives are soft on Fascism, I imagine. They see little wrong with killing Communists and persecuting Jews."

"Some of them, perhaps, but you exaggerate." She gave Lloyd a sideways look. "So, you went to see Boy?"

"Yes." Lloyd thought this seemed to have special significance for Ethel, but he could not imagine why. "I thought him perfectly frightful. In his room at Trinity he had a whole case of Scotch—twelve bottles!"

"You met him once before—do you remember?"

"No. When was that?"

"You were nine years old. I took you to the Palace of Westminster, shortly after I was elected. We met Fitz and Boy on the stairs."

Lloyd did vaguely remember. Then as now, the incident seemed to be mysteriously important to his mother. "That was him? How funny."

Ruby put in: "I know him. He's a pig. He paws maids."

Lloyd was shocked, but his mother seemed unsurprised. "Very unpleasant, but it happens all the time." Her grim acceptance made it more horrifying to him.

They reached the chapel and went in through the back door. There, in a kind of vestry, was Robert von Ulrich, looking startlingly British in a bold green-and-brown check suit and a striped tie. He stood up and Ethel hugged him. In faultless English Robert said: "My dear Ethel, what a perfectly charming hat."

Lloyd introduced his mother to the local Labour Party women who were preparing urns of tea and plates of biscuits to be served after the meeting. Having heard Ethel complain, many times, that people who organized political events seemed to think an M.P. never needed to go to the toilet, he said: "Ruby, before we start, would you show my mother where the ladies' facilities are?" The two women went off.

Lloyd sat down next to Robert and said conversationally: "How's business?"

Robert was now the proprietor of a restaurant much favored by the homosexuals about whom Ruby had been complaining. Somehow he had known that Cambridge in the 1930s was congenial to such men, just as Berlin had been in the 1920s. His new place had the same name as the old, Bistro Robert. "Business is good," he answered. A shadow crossed his face, a brief but intense look of real fear. "This time, I hope I can keep what I've built up."

"We're doing our best to fight off the Fascists, and meetings such as this are the way to do it," Lloyd said. "Your talk will be a big help—it will open people's eyes." Robert was going to speak about his personal experience of life under Fascism. "A lot of them say it couldn't happen here, but they're wrong."

Robert nodded in grim agreement. "Fascism is a lie, but an alluring one."

Lloyd's visit to Berlin three years ago was vivid in his mind. "I often wonder what happened to the old Bistro Robert," he said.

"I had a letter from a friend," Robert said in a voice full of sadness. "None of the old crowd go there anymore. The Macke brothers auctioned off the wine cellar. Now the clientele is mostly middle-ranking cops and bureaucrats." He looked even more pained as he added: "They no longer use tablecloths." He changed the subject abruptly. "Do you want to go to the Trinity Ball?"

Most of the colleges held summer dances to celebrate the end of exams. The balls, plus associated parties and picnics, constituted May Week, which illogically took place in June. The Trinity Ball was famously lavish. "I'd love to go, but I can't afford it," Lloyd said. "Tickets are two guineas, aren't they?"

"I've been given one. But you can have it. Several hundred drunk students dancing to a jazz band is actually my idea of hell."

Lloyd was tempted. "But I haven't got a tailcoat." College balls required white tie and tails.

"Borrow mine. It'll be too big at the waist, but we're the same height."

"Then I will. Thank you!"

Ruby reappeared. "Your mother is wonderful," she said to Lloyd. "I can't believe she used to be a maid!"

Robert said: "I have known Ethel for more than twenty years. She is truly extraordinary."

"I can see why you haven't met Miss Right," Ruby said to Lloyd. "You're looking for someone like her, and there aren't many."

"You're right about the last part, anyway," Lloyd said. "There's no one like her."

Ruby winced, as if in pain.

Lloyd said: "What's wrong?"

"Toothache."

"You must go to the dentist."

She looked at him as if he had said something stupid, and he realized that on a housemaid's wage she could not afford to pay a dentist. He felt foolish.

He went to the door and peeped through to the main hall. Like many nonconformist churches, this was a plain rectangular room with walls painted white. It was a warm day, and the clear glass windows were open. The rows of chairs were full and the audience was waiting expectantly.

When Ethel reappeared, Lloyd said: "If it's all right with everyone, I'll open the meeting. Then Robert will tell his personal story, and my mother will draw out the political lessons."

They all agreed.

"Ruby, will you keep an eye on the Fascists? Let me know if anything happens."

Ethel frowned. "Is that really necessary?"

"We probably shouldn't trust them to keep their promise."

Ruby said: "They're meeting a quarter of a mile up the road. I don't mind running in and out."

She left by the back door, and Lloyd led the others into the church. There was no stage, but a table and three chairs stood at the near end, with a lectern to one side. As Ethel and Robert took their seats, Lloyd went to the lectern. There was a brief round of subdued applause.

"Fascism is on the march," Lloyd began. "And it is dangerously attractive. It gives false hope to the unemployed. It wears a spurious patriotism, as the Fascists themselves wear imitation military uniforms."

The British government was keen to appease Fascist regimes, to

Lloyd's dismay. It was a coalition dominated by Conservatives, with a few Liberals and a sprinkling of renegade Labour ministers who had split with their party. Only a few days after it was reelected last November, the Foreign Secretary had proposed to yield much of Abyssinia to the conquering Italians and their Fascist leader Benito Mussolini.

Worse still, Germany was rearming and aggressive. Just a couple of months ago, Hitler had violated the Versailles Treaty by sending troops into the demilitarized Rhineland—and Lloyd had been horrified to see that no country had been willing to stop him.

Any hope he had that Fascism might be a temporary aberration had now vanished. Lloyd believed that democratic countries such as France and Britain must get ready to fight. But he did not say so in his speech today, for his mother and most of the Labour party opposed a buildup in British armaments and hoped the League of Nations would be able to deal with the dictators. They wanted at all costs to avoid repeating the dreadful slaughter of the Great War. Lloyd sympathized with that hope, but feared it was not realistic.

He was preparing himself for war. He had been an officer cadet at school and, when he came up to Cambridge, he had joined the Officer Training Corps—the only working-class boy and certainly the only Labour Party member to do so.

He sat down to muted applause. He was a clear and logical speaker, but he did not have his mother's ability to touch hearts—not yet, anyway.

Robert stepped to the lectern. "I am Austrian," he said. "In the war I was wounded, captured by the Russians, and sent to a prison camp in Siberia. After the Bolsheviks made peace with the Central Powers, the guards opened the gates and told us we were free to go. Getting home was our problem, not theirs. It is a long way from Siberia to Austria— more than three thousand miles. There was no bus, so I walked."

Surprised laughter rippled around the room, with a few appreciative hand-claps. Robert had already charmed them, Lloyd saw.

Ruby came up to him, looking annoyed, and spoke in his ear. "The

Fascists just went by. Boy Fitzherbert was driving Mosley to the railway station, and a bunch of hotheads in black shirts were running after the car, cheering."

Lloyd frowned. "They promised they wouldn't march. I suppose they'll say that running behind a car doesn't count."

"What's the difference, I'd like to know?"

"Any violence?"

"No."

"Keep a lookout."

Ruby retired. Lloyd was bothered. The Fascists had certainly broken the spirit of the agreement, if not the letter. They had appeared on the street in their uniforms—and there had been no counterdemonstration. The socialists were here, inside the church, invisible. All there was to show for their stand was a banner outside the church saying THE TRUTH ABOUT FASCISM in large red letters.

Robert was saying: "I am pleased to be here, honored to have been invited to address you, and delighted to see several patrons of Bistro Robert in the audience. However, I must warn you that the story I have to tell is most unpleasant, and indeed gruesome."

He related how he and Jörg had been arrested after refusing to sell the Berlin restaurant to a Nazi. He described Jörg as his chef and longtime business partner, saying nothing of their sexual relationship, though the more knowing people in the church probably guessed.

The audience became very quiet as he began to describe events in the concentration camp. Lloyd heard gasps of horror when he got to the part where the starving dogs appeared. Robert described the torture of Jörg in a low, clear voice that carried across the room. By the time he came to Jörg's death, several people were weeping.

Lloyd himself relived the cruelty and anguish of those moments, and he was possessed by rage against such fools as Boy Fitzherbert whose infatuation with marching songs and smart uniforms threatened to bring the same torment to England.

Robert sat down and Ethel went to the lectern. As she began to speak, Ruby reappeared, looking furious. "I told you this wouldn't work!" she hissed in Lloyd's ear. "Mosley has gone, but the boys are singing 'Rule, Britannia!' outside the station."

That certainly was a breach of the agreement, Lloyd thought angrily. Boy had broken his promise. So much for the word of an English gentleman.

Ethel was explaining how Fascism offered false solutions, simplistically blaming groups such as Jews and Communists for complex problems such as unemployment and crime. She made merciless fun of the concept of the triumph of the will, likening the Führer and the Duce to playground bullies. They claimed popular support, but banned all opposition.

Lloyd realized that when the Fascists returned from the railway station to the center of town they would have to pass this church. He began to listen to the sounds coming through the open windows. He could hear cars and lorries growling along Hills Road, punctuated now and again by the trill of a bicycle bell or the cry of a child. He thought he heard a distant shout, and it sounded ominously like the noise made by rowdy boys young enough still to be proud of their deep new voices. He tensed, straining to hear, and there were more shouts. The Fascists were marching.

Ethel raised her own voice as the bellowing outside got louder. She argued that working people of all kinds needed to band together in trade unions and the Labour Party to build a fairer society step by democratic step, not through the kind of violent upheaval that had gone so badly wrong in Communist Russia and Nazi Germany.

Ruby reentered. "They're marching up Hills Road now," she said in a low, urgent murmur. "We have to go out there and confront them!"

"No!" Lloyd whispered. "The party made a collective decision—no demonstration. We must stick to that. We must be a disciplined movement!" He knew the reference to party discipline would carry weight with her.

The Fascists were nearby now, raucously chanting. Lloyd guessed there must be fifty or sixty. He itched to go out there and face them. Two young men near the back stood up and went to the windows to look out. Ethel urged caution. "Don't react to hooliganism by becoming a hooligan," she said. "That will only give the newspapers an excuse to say that one side is as bad as the other."

There was a crash of breaking glass, and a stone came through the window. A woman screamed, and several people got to their feet. "Please remain seated," Ethel said. "I expect they will go away in a minute." She talked on in a calm and reassuring voice. Few people attended to her speech. Everyone was looking backward toward the church door, and listening to the hoots and jeers of the ruffians outside. Lloyd had to struggle to sit still. He looked toward his mother with a neutral expression fixed like a mask on his face. Every bone in his body wanted to rush outside and punch heads.

After a minute the audience quietened somewhat. They returned their attention to Ethel, though still fidgeting and looking back over their shoulders. Ruby muttered: "We're like a pack of rabbits, shaking in our burrow while the fox barks outside." Her tone was contemptuous, and Lloyd felt she was right.

But his mother's forecast proved true, and no more stones were thrown. The chanting receded.

"Why do the Fascists want violence?" Ethel asked rhetorically. "Those out there in Hills Road may be mere hooligans, but someone is directing them, and their tactics have a purpose. When there is fighting in the streets, they can claim that public order has broken down, and drastic measures are needed to restore the rule of law. Those emergency measures will include banning democratic political parties such as Labour, prohibiting trade union action, and jailing people without trial—people such as us, peaceful men and women whose only crime is to disagree with the government. Does this sound fantastic to you, unlikely, something that could never happen? Well, they used exactly those tactics in Germany—and it worked."

She went on to talk about how Fascism should be opposed: in discussion groups, at meetings such as this one, by writing letters to the newspapers, by using every opportunity to alert others to the danger. But even Ethel had trouble making this sound courageous and decisive.

Lloyd was cut to the quick by Ruby's talk of rabbits. He felt like a coward. He was so frustrated that he could hardly sit still.

Slowly the atmosphere in the hall returned to normal. Lloyd turned to Ruby. "The rabbits are safe, anyhow," he said.

"For now," she said. "But the fox will be back."

ii

"If you like a boy, you can let him kiss you on the mouth," said Lindy Westhampton, sitting on the lawn in the sunshine.

"And if you really like him, he can feel your breasts," said her twin sister, Lizzie.

"But nothing below the waist."

"Not until you're engaged."

Daisy was intrigued. She had expected English girls to be inhibited, but she had been wrong. The Westhampton twins were sex mad.

Daisy was thrilled to be a guest at Chimbleigh, the country house of Sir Bartholomew "Bing" Westhampton. It made her feel she had been accepted into English society. But she still had not met the king.

She recalled her humiliation at the Buffalo Yacht Club with a sense of shame that was still like a burn on her skin, continuing to give her agonizing pain long after the flame had gone away. But whenever she felt that pain, she thought about how she was going to dance with the king, and she imagined them all—Dot Renshaw, Nora Farquharson, Ursula Dewar—poring over her picture in the *Buffalo Sentinel,* reading every word of the report, envying her, and wishing they could honestly say they had always been her friends.

Things had been difficult at first. Daisy had arrived three months ago with her mother and her friend Eva. Her father had given them a handful of introductions to people who turned out not to be the crème de la crème of London's social scene. Daisy had begun to regret her overconfident exit from the Yacht Club Ball: What if it all came to nothing?

But Daisy was determined and resourceful, and she needed no more than a foot in the door. Even at entertainments that were more or less public, such as horse races and operas, she met high-ranking people. She flirted with the men, and she piqued the curiosity of the matrons by letting them know she was rich and single. Many aristocratic English families had been ruined by the Depression, and an American heiress would have been welcome even if she were not pretty and charming. They liked her accent, they tolerated her holding her fork in her right hand, and they were amused that she could drive a car—in England men did the driving. Many English girls could ride a horse as well as Daisy, but few looked so pertly assured in the saddle. Some older women still viewed Daisy with suspicion, but she would win them around eventually, she felt sure.

Bing Westhampton had been easy to flirt with. An elfin man with a winning smile, he had an eye for a pretty girl, and Daisy knew instinctively that more than his eye would be involved if he got the chance of a twilight fumble in the garden. Clearly his daughters took after him.

The Westhamptons' house party was one of several in Cambridgeshire held to coincide with May Week. The guests included Earl Fitzherbert, known as Fitz, and his wife, Bea. She was Countess Fitzherbert, of course, but she preferred her Russian title of princess. Their elder son, Boy, was at Trinity College.

Princess Bea was one of the social matriarchs who were doubtful about Daisy. Without actually telling a lie, Daisy had let people assume that her father was a Russian nobleman who had lost everything in the revolution, rather than a factory worker who had fled to America one step ahead of the police. But Bea was not taken in. "I can't recall a family called Peshkov in St. Petersburg or Moscow," she had said, hardly pretending to be puzzled, and Daisy had forced herself to smile as if it were of no consequence what the princess could remember.

There were three girls the same age as Daisy and Eva: the Westhampton twins plus May Murray, the daughter of a general. The balls went on all night, so everyone slept until midday, but the afternoons were dull. The five girls lazed in the garden or strolled in the woods. Now, sitting up in her hammock, Daisy said: "What can you do *after* you're engaged?"

Lindy said: "You can rub his thing."

"Until it squirts," said her sister.

May Murray, who was not as daring as the twins, said: "Oh, disgusting!"

That only encouraged the twins. "Or you can suck it," said Lindy. "They like that best of all."

"Stop it!" May protested. "You're just making this up."

They stopped, having teased May enough. "I'm bored," said Lindy. "What shall we do?"

An imp of mischief seized Daisy, and she said: "Let's come down to dinner in men's clothes."

She regretted it immediately. A stunt like that could ruin her social career when it had only just got started.

Eva's German sense of propriety was upset. "Daisy, you don't mean it!"

"No," she said. "Silly notion."

The twins had their mother's fine blond hair, not their father's dark curls, but they had inherited his streak of naughtiness, and they both loved the idea. "They'll all be in tailcoats tonight, so we can steal their dinner jackets," said Lindy.

"Yes!" said her twin. "We'll do it while they're having tea."

Daisy saw that it was too late to back out.

May Murray said: "We couldn't go to the ball like that!" The whole party was to attend the Trinity Ball after dinner.

"We'll change again before leaving," said Lizzie.

May was a timid creature, probably cowed by her military father, and she always went along with whatever the other girls decided. Eva as the only dissident was overruled, and the plan went ahead.

When the time came to dress for dinner, a maid brought two evening suits into the bedroom Daisy was sharing with Eva. The maid's name was Ruby. Yesterday she had been miserable with a toothache, so

Daisy had given her the money for a dentist, and she had had the tooth pulled out. Now Ruby was bright-eyed with excitement, toothache forgotten. "Here you are, ladies!" she said. "Sir Bartholomew's should be small enough for you, Miss Peshkov, and Mr. Andrew Fitzherbert's for Miss Rothmann."

Daisy took off her dress and put on the shirt. Ruby helped her with the unfamiliar studs and cuff links. Then she climbed into Bing Westhampton's trousers, black with a satin stripe. She tucked her slip in and pulled the suspenders over her shoulders. She felt a bit daring as she buttoned the fly.

None of the girls knew how to knot a tie, so the results were distinctly limp. But Daisy came up with the winning touch. Using an eyebrow pencil, she gave herself a mustache. "It's marvelous!" said Eva. "You look even prettier!" Daisy drew side-whiskers on Eva's cheeks.

The five girls met up in the twins' bedroom. Daisy walked in with a mannish swagger that made the others giggle hysterically.

May voiced the concern that remained in the back of Daisy's mind. "I hope we're not going to get into trouble over this."

Lindy said: "Oh, who cares if we do?"

Daisy decided to forget her misgivings and enjoy herself, and she led the way down to the drawing room.

They were the first to arrive, and the room was empty. Repeating something she had heard Boy Fitzherbert say to the butler, Daisy put on a man's voice and drawled: "Pour me a whisky, Grimshaw, there's a good chap—this champagne tastes like piss." The others squealed with shocked laughter.

Bing and Fitz came in together. Bing in his white waistcoat made Daisy think of a pied wagtail, a cheeky black-and-white bird. Fitz was a good-looking middle-aged man, his dark hair touched with gray. As a result of war wounds he walked with a slight limp, and one eyelid drooped, but this evidence of his courage in battle only made him more dashing.

Fitz saw the girls, looked twice, and said: "Good God!" His tone was sternly disapproving.

Daisy suffered a moment of sheer panic. Had she spoiled everything? The English could be frightfully straightlaced; everyone knew that. Would she be asked to leave the house? How terrible that would be. Dot Renshaw and Nora Farquharson would crow if she went home in disgrace. She would rather die.

But Bing burst out laughing. "I say, that's terribly good," he said. "Look at this, Grimshaw."

The elderly butler, coming in with a bottle of champagne in a silver ice bucket, observed them bleakly. In a tone of withering insincerity he said: "Most amusing, Sir Bartholomew."

Bing continued to regard them all with a delight mingled with lasciviousness, and Daisy realized—too late—that dressing like the opposite sex might misleadingly suggest, to some men, a degree of sexual freedom and a willingness to experiment—a suggestion that could obviously lead to trouble.

As the party assembled for dinner, most of the other guests followed the lead of their host in treating the girls' prank as an amusing piece of tomfoolery, though Daisy could tell they were not all equally charmed. Daisy's mother went pale with fright when she saw them, and sat down quickly as if she felt shaky. Princess Bea, a heavily corseted woman in her forties who might once have been pretty, wrinkled her powdered brow in a censorious frown. But Lady Westhampton was a jolly woman who reacted to life, as to her wayward husband, with a tolerant smile: she laughed heartily and congratulated Daisy on her mustache.

The boys, coming last, were also delighted. General Murray's son, Lieutenant Jimmy Murray, not as straightlaced as his father, roared with pleased laughter. The Fitzherbert sons, Boy and Andy, came in together, and it was Boy's reaction that was the most interesting of all. He stared at the girls with mesmeric fascination. He tried to cover up with jollity, haw-hawing like the other men, but it was clear he was weirdly captivated.

At dinner the twins picked up Daisy's joke and talked like men, in deep voices and hearty tones, making the others laugh. Lindy held up her wineglass and said: "How do you like this claret, Liz?"

Lizzie replied: "I think it's a bit thin, old boy. I've a notion Bing's been watering it, don't you know."

All through dinner Daisy kept catching Boy staring at her. He did not resemble his handsome father, but all the same he was good-looking, with his mother's blue eyes. She began to feel embarrassed, as if he was ogling her breasts. To break the spell she said: "And have you been taking exams, Boy?"

"Good Lord, no," he said.

His father said: "Too busy flying his plane to study much." This was phrased as a criticism, but it sounded as if Fitz was actually proud of his elder son.

Boy pretended to be outraged. "A slander!" he said.

Eva was mystified. "Why are you at the university if you don't wish to study?"

Lindy explained: "Some of the boys don't bother to graduate, especially if they're not academic types."

Lizzie added: "Especially if they're rich and lazy."

"I do study!" Boy protested. "But I don't intend actually to sit the exams. It's not as if I'm hoping to make a living as a doctor, or something." Boy would inherit one of the largest fortunes in England when Fitz died.

And his lucky wife would be Countess Fitzherbert.

Daisy said: "Wait a minute. Do you really have your own airplane?"

"Yes, I do. A Hornet Moth. I belong to the University Aero Club. We use a little airfield outside the town."

"But that's wonderful! You must take me up!"

Daisy's mother said: "Oh, dear, no!"

Boy said to Daisy: "Wouldn't you be nervous?"

"Not a bit!"

"Then I will take you." He turned to Olga. "It's perfectly safe, Mrs. Peshkov. I promise I'll bring her back in one piece."

Daisy was thrilled.

The conversation moved on to this summer's favorite topic: England's stylish new king, Edward VIII, and his romance with Wallis Simpson, an American woman separated from her second husband.

The London newspapers said nothing about it, except to include Mrs. Simpson on lists of guests at royal events, but Daisy's mother got the American papers sent over, and they were full of speculation that Wallis would divorce Mr. Simpson and marry the king.

"Completely out of the question," said Fitz severely. "The king is the head of the Church of England. He cannot possibly marry a divorcée."

When the ladies retired, leaving the men to port and cigars, the girls hurried to change. Daisy decided to emphasize how very feminine she really was, and chose a ball dress of pink silk patterned with tiny flowers that had a matching jacket with puffed short sleeves.

Eva wore a dramatically simple black silk gown with no sleeves. In the past year she had lost weight, changed her hair, and learned—under Daisy's tuition—to dress in an unfussy tailored style that flattered her. Eva had become like one of the family, and Olga delighted in buying clothes for her. Daisy regarded her as the sister she never had.

It was still light when they all climbed into cars and carriages and drove the five miles into the town center.

Daisy thought Cambridge was the quaintest place she had ever seen, with its winding little streets and elegant college buildings. They got out at Trinity and Daisy gazed up at the statue of its founder, King Henry VIII. When they passed through the sixteenth-century brick gatehouse, Daisy gasped with pleasure at the sight that met her eyes: a large quadrangle, its trimmed green lawn crossed by cobbled paths, with an elaborate architectural fountain in the middle. On all four sides, timeworn buildings of golden stone formed the backdrop against which young men in tailcoats danced with gorgeously dressed girls, and dozens of waiters in evening dress offered trays crowded with glasses of champagne. Daisy clapped her hands with joy: this was just the kind of thing she loved.

She danced with Boy, then Jimmy Murray, then Bing, who held her close and let his right hand drift from the small of her back down to the swell of her hips. She decided not to protest. The English band played a watery imitation of American jazz, but they were loud and fast, and they knew all the latest hits.

Night fell, and the quadrangle was illuminated with blazing torches.

Daisy took a break to check on Eva, who was not so self-confident and sometimes needed to be introduced around. However, she need not have worried: she found Eva talking to a strikingly handsome student in a suit too big for him. Eva introduced him as Lloyd Williams. "We've been talking about Fascism in Germany," Lloyd said, as if Daisy might want to join in the discussion.

"How extraordinarily dull of you," Daisy said.

Lloyd seemed not to hear that. "I was in Berlin three years ago, when Hitler came to power. I didn't meet Eva then, but it turns out we have some acquaintances in common."

Jimmy Murray appeared and asked Eva to dance. Lloyd was visibly disappointed to see her go, but summoned his manners and graciously asked Daisy, and they moved closer to the band. "What an interesting person your friend Eva is," he said.

"Why, Mr. Williams, that's what every girl longs to hear from her dancing partner," Daisy replied. As soon as the words were out of her mouth, she regretted sounding shrewish.

But he was amused. He grinned and said: "Dear me, you're so right. I am justly reproved. I must try to be more gallant."

She immediately liked him better for being able to laugh at himself. It showed confidence.

He said: "Are you staying at Chimbleigh, like Eva?"

"Yes."

"Then you must be the American who gave Ruby Carter the money for the dentist."

"How on earth do you know about that?"

"She's a friend of mine."

Daisy was surprised. "Do many undergraduates befriend housemaids?"

"My goodness, what a snobbish thing to say! My mother was a housemaid, before she became a member of Parliament."

Daisy felt herself blush. She hated snobbery and often accused others of it, especially in Buffalo. She thought she was totally innocent of such unworthy attitudes. "I've got off on the wrong foot with you, haven't I?" she said as the dance came to an end.

"Not really," he said. "You think it's dull to talk about Fascism, yet you take a German refugee into your home and even invite her to travel to England with you. You think housemaids have no right to be friends with undergraduates, yet you pay for Ruby to see the dentist. I don't suppose I'll meet another girl half as intriguing as you tonight."

"I'll take that as a compliment."

"Here comes your Fascist friend, Boy Fitzherbert. Do you want me to scare him off?"

Daisy sensed that Lloyd would relish the chance of a quarrel with Boy. "Certainly not!" she said, and turned to smile at Boy.

Boy nodded curtly to Lloyd. "Evening, Williams."

"Good evening," said Lloyd. "I was disappointed that your Fascists marched along Hills Road last Saturday."

"Ah, yes," Boy said. "They got a bit overenthusiastic."

"It surprised me, when you had given your word they would not." Daisy saw that Lloyd was angry about this, underneath his mask of cool courtesy.

Boy refused to take it seriously. "Sorry about that," he said lightly. He turned to Daisy. "Come and see the library," he said to her. "It's by Christopher Wren."

"With pleasure!" Daisy said. She waved good-bye to Lloyd and let Boy take her arm. Lloyd looked disappointed to see her go, which pleased her.

On the west side of the quadrangle a passage led to a courtyard with a single elegant building at the far end. Daisy admired the cloisters on the ground floor. Boy explained that the books were on the upper floor, because the river Cam was liable to flood. "Let's go and look at the river," he said. "It's pretty at night."

Daisy was twenty years old and, though she was inexperienced, she knew that Boy did not really care for gazing on rivers at night. But she wondered, after his reaction to seeing her in men's clothing, whether he might really prefer boys to girls. She guessed she was about to find out.

"Do you actually know the king?" she asked as he led her across a second courtyard.

"Yes. He's more my father's friend, obviously, but he comes to our house sometimes. And he's jolly keen on some of my political ideas, I can tell you."

"I'd love to meet him." She was sounding naïve, she knew, but this was her chance and she was not going to miss it.

They passed through a gateway and emerged onto a smooth lawn sloping down to a narrow walled-in river. "This area is called the Backs," Boy said. "Most of the older colleges own the fields on the other side of the water." He put his arm around her waist as they approached a little bridge. His hand moved up, as if accidentally, until his forefinger lay along the underside of her breast.

At the far end of the little bridge two college servants in uniform stood guard, presumably to repel gatecrashers. One of the men murmured: "Good evening, Viscount Aberowen," and the other smothered a grin. Boy responded with a barely perceptible nod. Daisy wondered how many other girls he had led across this bridge.

She knew Boy had a motive for giving her this tour, and sure enough, he stopped in the darkness and put his hands on her shoulders. "I say, you looked jolly fetching in that outfit at dinner." His voice was throaty with excitement.

"I'm glad you thought so." She knew the kiss was coming, and she felt aroused at the prospect, but she was not quite ready. She put a hand on his shirtfront, palm flat, holding him at a distance. "I really want to be presented at the royal court," she said. "Is it difficult to arrange?"

"Not difficult at all," he said. "Not for my family, at least. And not for someone as pretty as you." He dipped his head eagerly toward hers.

She leaned away. "Would you do that for me? Will you fix it for me to be presented?"

"Of course."

She moved in closer, and felt the erection bulging at the front of his trousers. No, she thought, he doesn't prefer boys. "Promise?" she said.

"I promise," he said breathlessly.

"Thank you," she said; then she let him kiss her.

iii

The little house in Wellington Row, Aberowen, South Wales, was crowded at one o'clock on Saturday afternoon. Lloyd's grandfather sat at the kitchen table looking proud. On one side he had his son, Billy Williams, a coal miner who had become member of Parliament for Aberowen. On the other was his grandson, Lloyd, the Cambridge University student. Absent was his daughter, also a member of Parliament. It was the Williams dynasty. No one here would ever say that—the notion of a dynasty was undemocratic, and these people believed in democracy the way the pope believed in God—but just the same Lloyd suspected Granda was thinking it.

Also at the table was Uncle Billy's lifelong friend and agent, Tom Griffiths. Lloyd was honored to sit with such men. Granda was a veteran of the miners' union; Uncle Billy had been court-martialed in 1919 for revealing Britain's secret war against the Bolsheviks; Tom had fought alongside Billy at the Battle of the Somme. This was more impressive than dining with royalty.

Lloyd's grandmother, Cara Williams, had served them stewed beef with homemade bread, and now they sat drinking tea and smoking. Friends and neighbors had come in, as they always did when Billy was here, and half a dozen of them stood leaning against the walls, smoking pipes and hand-rolled cigarettes, filling the little kitchen with the smell of men and tobacco.

Billy had the short stature and broad shoulders of many miners but, unlike the others, he was well dressed, in a navy blue suit with a clean white shirt and a red tie. Lloyd noticed that they all used his first name often, as if to emphasize that he was one of them, empowered by their votes. They called Lloyd "boyo," making it clear they were not overimpressed by a university student. But they addressed Granda as Mr. Williams: he was the one they truly respected.

Through the open back door Lloyd could see the slag heap from the mine, an ever-growing mountain that had now reached the lane behind the house.

Lloyd was spending the summer vacation as a low-paid organizer at a camp for unemployed colliers. Their project was to refurbish the Miners' Institute Library. Lloyd found the physical work of sanding and painting and building shelves a refreshing change from reading Schiller in German and Molière in French. He enjoyed the banter among the men: he had inherited from his mother a love of the Welsh sense of humor.

It was great, but it was not fighting Fascism. He winced every time he remembered how he had skulked in the Baptist chapel while Boy Fitzherbert and the other bullies chanted in the street and threw stones through the window. He wished he had gone outside and punched someone. It might have been stupid but he would have felt better. He thought about it every night before falling asleep.

He also thought about Daisy Peshkov in a pink silk jacket with puffed sleeves.

He had seen Daisy a second time in May Week. He had gone to a recital in the chapel of King's College, because the student in the room next to his at Emmanuel was playing the cello, and Daisy had been in the audience with the Westhamptons. She had been wearing a straw hat with a turned-up brim that made her look like a naughty schoolgirl. He had sought her out afterward, and asked her questions about America, where he had never been. He wanted to know about President Roosevelt's administration, and whether it had any lessons to teach Britain, but all Daisy talked about was tennis parties and polo matches and yacht clubs. Despite that, he had been captivated by her all over again. He liked her gay chatter all the more because it was punctuated, now and again, by unexpected darts of sarcastic wit. He had said: "I don't want to keep you from your friends—I just wanted to ask about the New Deal," and she had replied: "Oh, boy, you really know how to flatter a girl." But then, as they parted, she had said: "Call me when you come to London—Mayfair two four three four."

Today he had come to his grandparents' house for the midday meal, on his way to the railway station. He had a few days off from the work camp, and he was taking the train to London for a short break. He was vaguely hoping he might run into Daisy, as if London were a little town like Aberowen.

At the camp he was in charge of political education, and he told his grandfather he had organized a series of lectures by left-wing dons from Cambridge. "I tell them it's their chance to get out of the ivory tower and meet the working class, and they find it hard to refuse me."

Granda's pale blue eyes looked down his long, sharp nose. "I hope our lads teach them a thing or two about the real world."

Lloyd pointed to Tom Griffiths' son, standing in the open back door and listening. At sixteen Lenny already had the characteristic Griffiths shadow of a black beard that never went away even when his cheeks were freshly shaved. "Lenny had an argument with a Marxist lecturer."

"Good for you, Len," said Granda. Marxism was popular in South Wales, which was sometimes jokingly called Little Moscow, but Granda had always been fiercely anti-Communist.

Lloyd said: "Tell Granda what you said, Lenny."

Lenny grinned and said: "'In 1872 the anarchist leader Mikhail Bakunin warned Karl Marx that Communists in power would be as oppressive as the aristocracy they replaced. After what has happened in Russia, can you honestly say Bakunin was wrong?'"

Granda clapped his hands. A good debating point had always been relished around his kitchen table.

Lloyd's grandmother poured him a fresh cup of tea. Cara Williams was gray, lined, and bent, like all the women of her age in Aberowen. She asked Lloyd: "Are you courting yet, my lovely?"

The men grinned and winked.

Lloyd blushed. "Too busy studying, Grandmam." But an image of Daisy Peshkov came into his mind, together with the phone number: Mayfair two four three four.

His grandmother said: "Who's this Ruby Carter, then?"

The men laughed, and Uncle Billy said: "Caught out, boyo!"

Lloyd's mother had obviously been talking. "Ruby is membership officer of my local Labour Party in Cambridge, that's all," Lloyd protested.

Billy said sarcastically: "Oh, aye, very convincing," and the men laughed again.

"You wouldn't want me to go out with Ruby, Grandmam," Lloyd said. "You'd think she wears her clothes too tight."

"She doesn't sound very suitable," Cara said. "You're a university man, now. You must set your sights higher."

She was just as snobbish as Daisy, Lloyd perceived. "There's nothing wrong with Ruby Carter," he said. "But I'm not in love with her."

"You must marry an educated woman, a schoolteacher or a trained nurse."

The trouble was that she was right. Lloyd liked Ruby, but he would never love her. She was pretty enough, and intelligent, too, and Lloyd was as vulnerable as the next man to a curvy figure, but still he knew she was not right for him. Worse, Grandmam had put her wrinkled old finger precisely on the reason: Ruby's outlook was restricted, her horizons narrow. She was not exciting. Not like Daisy.

"That's enough women's chatter," Granda said. "Billy, tell us the news from Spain."

"It's bad," said Billy.

All Europe was watching Spain. The left-wing government elected last February had suffered an attempted military coup backed by Fascists and conservatives. The rebel general Franco had won support from the Catholic Church. The news had struck the rest of the continent like an earthquake. After Germany and Italy would Spain, too, fall under the curse of Fascism?

"The revolt was botched, as you probably know, and it almost failed," Billy went on. "But Hitler and Mussolini came to the rescue, and saved the insurrection by airlifting thousands of rebel troops from North Africa as reinforcements."

Lenny put in: "And the unions saved the government!"

"That's true," Billy said. "The government was slow to react, but the trade unions led the way in organizing workers and arming them with weapons they seized from military arsenals, ships, gun shops, and anywhere else they could find them."

Granda said: "At least someone is fighting back. Until now the Fascists have had it all their own way. In the Rhineland and Abyssinia, they just walked in and took what they wanted. Thank God for the Spanish people, I say. They've got the guts to say no."

There was a murmur of agreement from the men around the walls.

Lloyd again recalled that Saturday afternoon in Cambridge. He, too, had let the Fascists have it all their own way. He seethed with frustration.

"But can they win?" said Granda. "Weapons seem to be the issue now, aren't they?"

"Aye," said Billy. "The Germans and the Italians are supplying the rebels with guns and ammunition, as well as fighter planes and pilots. But no one is helping the elected Spanish government."

"And why the bloody hell not?" said Lenny angrily.

Cara looked up from the cooking range. Her dark Mediterranean eyes flashed disapproval, and Lloyd thought he glimpsed the beautiful girl she had once been. "None of that language in my kitchen!" she said.

"Sorry, Mrs. Williams."

"I can tell you the inside story," Billy said, and the men went quiet, listening. "The French prime minister, Léon Blum—a socialist, as you know—was all set to help. He's already got one Fascist neighbor, Germany, and the last thing he wants is a Fascist regime on his southern border, too. Sending arms to the Spanish government would enrage the French right wing, and French Catholic socialists, too, but Blum could withstand that, especially if he had British support and could say that arming the government was an international initiative."

Granda said: "So what went wrong?"

"Our government talked him out of it. Blum came to London and our foreign secretary, Anthony Eden, told him we would not support him."

Granda was angered. "Why does he need support? How can a socialist prime minister let himself be bullied by the conservative government of another country?"

"Because there's a danger of a military coup in France, too," said Billy. "The press there is rabidly right-wing, and they're whipping their own Fascists into a frenzy. Blum can fight them off with British support—but perhaps not without."

"So it's our Conservative government being soft on Fascism again!"

"All those Tories have investments in Spain—wine, textiles, coal, steel—and they're afraid the left-wing government will expropriate them."

"What about America? They believe in democracy. Surely they'll sell guns to Spain?"

"You'd think so, wouldn't you? But there's a well-financed Catholic lobby, led by a millionaire called Joseph Kennedy, opposing any help to the Spanish government. And a Democratic president needs Catholic support. Roosevelt won't do anything to jeopardize his New Deal."

"Well, there's something we can do," said Lenny Griffiths, and a look of adolescent defiance came over his face.

"What's that, Len boy?" said Billy.

"We can go to Spain and fight."

His father said: "Don't talk daft, Lenny."

"Lots of people are talking about going, all over the world, even in America. They want to form volunteer units to fight alongside the regular army."

Lloyd sat upright. "Do they?" This was the first he had heard of it. "How do you know?"

"I read about it in the *Daily Herald*."

Lloyd was electrified. Volunteers going to Spain to fight the Fascists!

Tom Griffiths said to Lenny: "Well, you're not going, and that's that."

Billy said: "Remember those boys who lied about their age to fight in the Great War? Thousands of them."

"And totally useless, most of them," Tom said. "I recall that kid who cried before the Somme. What was his name, Billy?"

"Owen Bevin. He ran away, didn't he?"

"Aye—to a firing squad. The bastards shot him for desertion. Fifteen, he was, poor little tyke."

Lenny said: "I'm sixteen."

"Aye," said his father. "Big difference, that."

Granda said: "Lloyd here is going to miss the train to London in about ten minutes."

Lloyd had been so struck by Lenny's revelation that he had not kept an eye on the clock. He jumped up, kissed his grandmother, and picked up his small suitcase.

Lenny said: "I'll walk with you to the station."

Lloyd said his good-byes and hurried down the hill. Lenny said nothing, seeming preoccupied. Lloyd was glad not to have to talk: his mind was in turmoil.

The train was in. Lloyd bought a third-class ticket to London. As he was about to board, Lenny said: "Tell me, now, Lloyd, how do you get a passport?"

"You're serious about going to Spain, aren't you?"

"Come on, man, don't muck about. I want to know."

The whistle blew. Lloyd climbed aboard, closed the door, and let down the window. "You go to the post office and ask for a form," he said.

Lenny said despondently: "If I went to the Aberowen Post Office and asked for a passport form, my mother would hear of it about thirty seconds later."

"Then go to Cardiff," said Lloyd, and the train pulled away.

He settled in his seat and took from his pocket a copy of *Le Rouge et le Noir* by Stendhal in French. He stared at the page without taking anything in. He could think of only one idea: going to Spain.

He knew he should be scared, but all he felt was excitement at the prospect of fighting—really fighting, not just holding meetings—against the kind of men who had set the dogs on Jörg. No doubt fear would come later. Before a boxing match he was not scared in the dressing room. But when he entered the ring and saw the man who wanted to beat him unconscious, looked at the muscular shoulders and the hard fists and the vicious face, then his mouth went dry and his heart pounded and he had to suppress the impulse to turn and run away.

Right now he was mainly worried about his parents. Bernie was so proud of having a stepson at Cambridge—he had told half the East End—and he would be devastated if Lloyd left before getting his degree.

Ethel would be frightened that her son might be wounded or killed. They would both be terribly upset.

There were other issues. How would he get to Spain? What city would he go to? How would he pay the fare? But only one snag really gave him pause.

Daisy Peshkov.

He told himself not to be ridiculous. He had met her twice. She was not even very interested in him. That was smart of her, because they were ill-suited. She was a millionaire's daughter and a shallow socialite who thought talking about politics was dull. She liked men such as Boy Fitzherbert; that alone proved she was wrong for Lloyd. Yet he could not get her out of his mind, and the thought of going to Spain and losing all chance of seeing her again filled him with sadness.

Mayfair two four three four.

He felt ashamed of his hesitation, especially when he recalled Lenny's simple determination. Lloyd had been talking about fighting Fascism for years. Now there was a chance to do it. How could he not go?

He reached London's Paddington station, took the Tube to Aldgate, and walked to the row house in Nutley Street where he had been born. He let himself in with his own key. The place had not changed much since he was a child, but one innovation was the telephone on a little table next to the hat stand. It was the only phone on the street, and the neighbors treated it as public property. Beside the phone was a box in which they placed the money for their calls.

His mother was in the kitchen. She had her hat on, ready to go out to address a Labour Party meeting—what else?—but she put the kettle on and made him tea. "How are they all in Aberowen?" she asked.

"Uncle Billy is there this weekend," he said. "All the neighbors came into Granda's kitchen. It's like a medieval court."

"Are your grandparents well?"

"Granda is the same as ever. Grandmam looks older." He paused. "Lenny Griffiths wants to go to Spain, to fight the Fascists."

She pursed her lips in disapproval. "Does he, now?"

"I'm considering going with him. What do you think?"

He was expecting opposition, but even so her reaction surprised him. "Don't you bloody dare," she said savagely. She did not share her mother's aversion to swear words. "Don't even speak of it!" She slammed the teapot down on the kitchen table. "I bore you in pain and suffering, and raised you, and put shoes on your feet and sent you to school, and I didn't go through all that for you to throw your life away in a bloody war!"

He was taken aback. "I wasn't thinking of throwing my life away," he said. "But I might risk it in a cause you brought me up to believe in."

To his astonishment she began to sob. She rarely cried—in fact Lloyd could not remember the last time.

"Mother, don't." He put his arm around her shaking shoulders. "It hasn't happened yet."

Bernie came into the kitchen, a stocky middle-aged man with a bald dome. "What's all this?" he said. He looked a bit scared.

Lloyd said: "I'm sorry, Dad. I've upset her." He stepped back and let Bernie put his arms around Ethel.

She wailed: "He's going to Spain! He'll be killed!"

"Let's all calm down and discuss it sensibly," Bernie said. He was a sensible man wearing a sensible dark suit and much-repaired shoes with sensible thick soles. No doubt that was why people voted for him: he was a local politician, representing Aldgate on the London County Council. Lloyd had never known his own father, but he could not imagine loving a real father more than he loved Bernie, who had been a gentle stepfather, quick to comfort and advise, slow to command or punish. He treated Lloyd no differently from his daughter, Millie.

Bernie persuaded Ethel to sit at the kitchen table, and Lloyd poured her a cup of tea.

"I thought my brother was dead, once," Ethel said, her tears still flowing. "The telegrams came to Wellington Row, and the wretched boy from the post office had to go from one house to the next, giving men and women the bits of paper that said their sons and husbands were dead. Poor lad, what was his name? Geraint, I think. But he didn't have a telegram for our house and, wicked woman that I am, I thanked God it was others that had died and not our Billy!"

"You're not a wicked woman," Bernie said, patting her.

Lloyd's half sister, Millie, appeared from upstairs. She was sixteen, but looked older, especially dressed as she was this evening, in a stylish black outfit and small gold earrings. For two years she had worked in a women's-wear shop in Aldgate, but she was bright and ambitious, and in the last few days she had got a job in a swanky West End department store. She looked at Ethel and said: "Mam, what's the matter?" She spoke with a cockney accent.

"Your brother wants to go to Spain and get himself killed!" Ethel cried.

Millie looked accusingly at Lloyd. "What have you been saying to her?" Millie was always quick to find fault with her older brother, who she felt was undeservedly adored.

Lloyd responded with fond tolerance. "Lenny Griffiths from Aberowen is going to fight the Fascists, and I told Mam I was thinking about going with him."

"Trust you," Millie said disgustedly.

"I doubt if you can get there," said Bernie, ever practical. "After all, the country is in the middle of a civil war."

"I can get a train to Marseilles. Barcelona's not far from the French border."

"Eighty or ninety miles. And it's a cold walk over the Pyrenees."

"There must be ships going from Marseilles to Barcelona. It's not so far by sea."

"True."

"Stop it, Bernie!" Ethel cried. "You sound as if you're discussing the quickest way to Piccadilly Circus. He's talking about going to war! I won't allow it."

"He's twenty-one, you know," Bernie said. "We can't stop him."

"I know how bloody old he is!"

Bernie looked at his watch. "We need to get to the meeting. You're the main speaker. And Lloyd's not going to Spain tonight."

"How do you know?" she said. "We might get home and find a note saying he's caught the boat train to Paris!"

"I tell you what," said Bernie. "Lloyd, promise your mother you won't go for a month at least. It's not a bad idea anyway—you need to check the lie of the land before you rush off. Set her mind at ease, just temporarily. Then we can talk about it again."

It was a typical Bernie compromise, calculated to let everyone back off without backing down, but Lloyd was reluctant to make a commitment. On the other hand he probably could not simply jump on a train. He had to find out what arrangements the Spanish government might be making to receive volunteers. Ideally he would go in company with Lenny and others. He would need visas, foreign currency, a pair of boots . . . "All right," he said. "I won't go for a month."

"Promise," his mother said.

"I promise."

Ethel became calm. After a minute she powdered her face and looked more normal. She drank her tea.

Then she put her coat on, and she and Bernie left.

"Right, I'm off, too," said Millie.

"Where are you going?" Lloyd asked her.

"The Gaiety."

It was a music hall in the East End. "Do they let sixteen-year-olds in?"

She gave him an arch look. "Who's sixteen? Not me. Anyway, Dave's going and he's only fifteen." She was speaking of their cousin David Williams, son of Uncle Billy and Aunt Mildred.

"Well, enjoy yourselves."

She went to the door and came back. "Just don't get killed in Spain, you stupid sod." She put her arms around him and hugged him hard, then went out without saying any more.

When he heard the front door slam, he went to the phone.

He did not have to think to recall the number. He could see Daisy in his mind's eye, turning as she left him, smiling winningly under the straw hat, saying: "Mayfair two four three four."

He picked up the phone and dialed.

What was he going to say? "You told me to phone, so here I am." That was feeble. The truth? "I don't admire you at all, but I can't get you off my mind." He should invite her to something, but what? A Labour Party meeting?

A man answered. "This is Mrs. Peshkov's residence. Good evening." The deferential tone made Lloyd think he was a butler. No doubt Daisy's mother had rented a London house complete with staff.

"This is Lloyd Williams . . ." He wanted to say something that would explain or justify his call, and he added the first thing that came to mind: ". . . of Emmanuel College." It meant nothing but he hoped it sounded impressive. "May I speak to Miss Daisy Peshkov?"

"No, I'm sorry, Professor Williams," said the butler, assuming Lloyd must be a don. "They've all gone to the opera."

Of course, Lloyd thought with disappointment. No socialite was home at this time of the evening, especially on a Saturday. "I remember," he lied. "She told me she was going, and I forgot. Covent Garden, isn't it?" He held his breath.

But the butler was not suspicious. "Yes, sir. *The Magic Flute,* I believe."

"Thank you." Lloyd hung up.

He went to his room and changed. In the West End most people wore evening dress, even to go to the cinema. But what would he do when he got there? He could not afford a ticket to the opera, and anyway it would be over soon.

He took the Tube. The Royal Opera House was incongruously located next to Covent Garden, London's wholesale fruit and vegetable market. The two institutions got along well because they kept different hours: the market opened for business at three or four o'clock in the morning, when London's most determined revelers were beginning to head for home, and it closed before the matinee.

Lloyd walked past the shuttered stalls of the market and looked through glazed doors into the opera house. Its bright lobby was empty, and he could hear muffled Mozart. He stepped inside. Adopting a careless upper-class manner, he said to an attendant: "What time does the curtain come down?"

If he had been wearing his tweed suit, he would probably have been told it was none of his business, but the dinner jacket was the uniform of authority, and the attendant said: "In about five minutes, sir."

Lloyd nodded curtly. To say "Thank you" would have given him away.

He left the building and walked around the block. It was a moment of quiet. In the restaurants, people were ordering coffee; in the cinemas, the big feature was approaching its melodramatic climax. Everything would change soon, and the streets would be thronged with people shouting for taxis, heading to nightclubs, kissing good-bye at bus stops, and hurrying for the last train back to the suburbs.

He returned to the opera house and went inside. The orchestra was silent, and the audience was just beginning to emerge. Released from long imprisonment in their seats, they were talking animatedly, praising the singers, criticizing the costumes, and making plans for late suppers.

He saw Daisy almost immediately.

She was wearing a lavender dress with a little cape of champagne-colored mink over her bare shoulders, and she looked ravishing. She emerged from the auditorium at the head of a small clutch of people her own age. Lloyd was sorry to recognize Boy Fitzherbert beside her, and to see her laugh gaily at something he murmured to her as they stepped down the red-carpeted stairs. Behind her was the interesting German girl, Eva Rothmann, escorted by a tall young man in the kind of military evening dress known as a mess kit.

Eva recognized Lloyd and smiled, and he spoke to her in German. "Good evening, Fräulein Rothmann, I hope you enjoyed the opera."

"Very much, thank you," she replied in the same language. "I didn't realize you were in the audience."

Boy said amiably: "I say, speak English, you lot." He sounded slightly drunk. He was good-looking in a dissipated way, like a sulkily handsome adolescent, or a pedigree dog that is fed too many scraps. He had a pleasant manner, and probably could be devastatingly charming when he chose.

Eva said in English: "Viscount Aberowen, this is Mr. Williams."

"We know each other," said Boy. "He's at Emma."

Daisy said: "Hello, Lloyd. We're going slumming."

Lloyd had heard this word before. It meant going to the East End to visit low pubs and watch working-class entertainment such as dogfights.

Boy said: "I bet Williams knows some places."

Lloyd hesitated only a fraction of a second. Was he willing to put up with Boy in order to be with Daisy? Of course he was. "As a matter of fact, I do," he said. "Do you want me to show you?"

"Splendid!"

An older woman appeared and wagged a finger at Boy. "You must have these girls home by midnight," she said in an American accent. "Not a second later, please." Lloyd guessed she must be Daisy's mother.

The tall man in the military outfit replied: "Leave it to the army, Mrs. Peshkov. We'll be on time."

Behind Mrs. Peshkov came Earl Fitzherbert with a fat woman who must have been his wife. Lloyd would have liked to question the earl about his government's policy on Spain.

Two cars were waiting for them outside. The earl, his wife, and Daisy's mother got into a black-and-cream Rolls-Royce Phantom III. Boy and his group piled into the other car, a dark blue Daimler E20 limousine, the royal family's favorite car. There were seven young people including Lloyd. Eva seemed to be with the soldier, who introduced himself to Lloyd as Lieutenant Jimmy Murray. The third girl was his sister, May, and the other boy—a slimmer, quieter version of Boy—turned out to be Andy Fitzherbert.

Lloyd gave the chauffeur directions to the Gaiety.

He noticed that Jimmy Murray discreetly slipped his arm around Eva's waist. Her reaction was to move slightly closer to him: obviously they were courting. Lloyd was happy for her. She was not a pretty girl, but she was intelligent and charming. He liked her, and he was glad she had found herself a tall soldier. He wondered, though, how others in this upper-class social set would react if Jimmy announced he was going to marry a half-Jewish German girl.

It occurred to him that the others formed two more couples: Andy and May, and—annoyingly—Boy and Daisy. Lloyd was the odd one out.

Not wanting to stare at them, he studied the polished mahogany window surrounds.

The car went up Ludgate Hill to St. Paul's Cathedral. "Take Cheapside," Lloyd said to the driver.

Boy took a long pull from a silver hip flask. Wiping his mouth, he said: "You know your way around, Williams."

"I live here," said Lloyd. "I was born in the East End."

"How splendid," said Boy, and Lloyd was not sure whether he was being thoughtlessly polite or unpleasantly sarcastic.

All the seats were taken at the Gaiety, but there was plenty of standing room, and the audience moved around constantly, greeting friends and going to the bar. They were dressed up, the women in brightly colored frocks, the men in their best suits. The air was warm and smoky, and there was a powerful odor of spilled beer. Lloyd found a place for his group near the back. Their clothes identified them as visitors from the West End, but they were not the only ones: music halls were popular with all classes.

Onstage a middle-aged performer in a red dress and blond wig was doing a double-entendre routine. "I said to him, 'I'm not letting you into my passage.'" The audience roared with laughter. "He said to me, 'I can see it from here, love.' I told him, 'You keep your nose out.'" She was pretending indignation. "He said, 'It looks to me like it needs a good clean-out.' Well! I ask you."

Lloyd saw that Daisy was grinning widely. He leaned over and murmured in her ear: "Do you realize it's a man?"

"No!" she said.

"Look at the hands."

"Oh, my God!" she said. "She's a man!"

Lloyd's cousin David walked past, spotted Lloyd, and came back. "What are you all dressed up for?" he said in a cockney accent. He was wearing a knotted scarf and a cloth cap.

"Hello, Dave, how's life?"

"I'm going to Spain with you and Lenny Griffiths," Dave said.

"No, you're not," said Lloyd. "You're fifteen."

"Boys my age fought in the Great War."

"But they were no use—ask your father. Anyway, who says I'm going?"

"Your sister, Millie," Dave said, and he walked on.

Boy said: "What do people usually drink in this place, Williams?"

Lloyd thought Boy did not need any more alcohol, but he replied: "Pints of best bitter for the men and port-and-lemon for the girls."

"Port-and-lemon?"

"It's port diluted with lemonade."

"How perfectly ghastly." Boy disappeared.

The comedian reached the climax of the act. "I said to him, 'You fool, *that's the wrong passage!*'" She, or he, went off to gales of applause.

Millie appeared in front of Lloyd. "Hello," she said. She looked at Daisy. "Who's your friend?"

Lloyd was glad Millie looked so pretty, in her sophisticated black dress, with a row of fake pearls and a discreet touch of makeup. He said: "Miss Peshkov, allow me to present my sister, Miss Leckwith. Millie, this is Daisy."

They shook hands. Daisy said: "I'm very glad to meet Lloyd's sister."

"Half sister, to be exact," said Millie.

Lloyd explained: "My father was killed in the Great War. I never knew him. My mother married again when I was still a baby."

"Enjoy the show," Millie said, turning away; then, as she left, she murmured to Lloyd: "Now I see why Ruby Carter has no chance."

Lloyd groaned inwardly. His mother had obviously told the whole family that he was romancing Ruby.

Daisy said: "Who's Ruby Carter?"

"She's a maid at Chimbleigh. You gave her the money to see a dentist."

"I remember. So her name is being romantically linked with yours."

"In the imagination of my mother, yes."

Daisy laughed at his discomfiture. "So you're not going to marry a housemaid."

"I'm not going to marry Ruby."

"She might suit you very well."

Lloyd gave her a direct look. "We don't always fall in love with the most suitable people, do we?"

She looked at the stage. The show was approaching its end, and the entire cast was beginning a familiar song. The audience joined in enthusiastically. The standing customers at the back linked arms and swayed in time, and Boy's party did likewise.

When the curtain came down, Boy still had not reappeared. "I'll look for him," Lloyd said. "I think I know where he might be." The Gaiety had a ladies' toilet, but the men's was a backyard with an earth closet and several halved oil drums. Lloyd found Boy puking into one of the drums.

He gave Boy a handkerchief to wipe his mouth, then took his arm and led him through the emptying theater and outside to the Daimler limousine. The others were waiting. They all got in and Boy immediately fell asleep.

When they got back to the West End, Andy Fitzherbert told the driver to go first to the Murray house, in a modest street near Trafalgar Square. Getting out of the car with May, he said: "You lot go on. I'll see May to her door, then walk home." Lloyd presumed that Andy was planning a romantic good night on May's doorstep.

They drove on to Mayfair. As the car was approaching Grosvenor Square, where Daisy and Eva were living, Jimmy told the chauffeur: "Just stop at the corner, please." Then he said quietly to Lloyd: "I say, Williams, would you mind taking Miss Peshkov to the door, and I'll follow with Fräulein Rothmann in half a minute?"

"Of course." Jimmy wanted to kiss Eva good night in the car, obviously. Boy would know nothing about it: he was snoring. The chauffeur would pretend to be oblivious in the expectation of a tip.

Lloyd got out of the car and handed Daisy out. When she grasped his hand, he got a thrill like a mild electric shock. He took her arm and they walked slowly along the pavement. At the midpoint between two streetlamps, where the light was dimmest, Daisy stopped. "Let's give them time," she said.

Lloyd said: "I'm so glad Eva has a paramour."

"Me, too."

He took a breath. "I can't say the same about you and Boy Fitzherbert."

"He got me presented at court!" Daisy said. "And I danced with the king in a nightclub—it was in all the American newspapers."

"And that's why you're courting him?" Lloyd said incredulously.

"Not only. He likes all the things I do—parties and racehorses and beautiful clothes. He's such fun! He even has his own airplane."

"None of that means anything," Lloyd said. "Give him up. Be my girlfriend instead."

She looked pleased, but she laughed. "You're crazy," she said. "But I like you."

"I mean it," he said desperately. "I can't stop thinking about you, even though you're the last person in the world I should marry."

She laughed again. "You say the rudest things! I don't know why I talk to you. I guess I think you're nice under your clumsy manners."

"I'm not really clumsy—only with you."

"I believe you. But I'm not going to marry a penniless socialist."

Lloyd had opened his heart only to be charmingly rejected, and now he felt miserable. He looked back at the Daimler. "I wonder how long they're going to be," he said disconsolately.

Daisy said: "I might kiss a socialist, though, just to see what it's like."

For a moment he did not react. He assumed she was speaking theoretically. But a girl would never say something like that theoretically. It was an invitation. He had almost been stupid enough to miss it.

He moved closer, putting his hands on her small waist. She tilted her face up, and her beauty took his breath away. He bent his head and kissed her mouth softly. She did not close her eyes, and neither did he. He felt tremendously aroused, staring into her blue eyes as he moved his lips against hers. She opened her mouth slightly, and he touched her parted lips with the tip of his tongue. A moment later he felt her tongue respond. She was still looking at him. He was in paradise, and he wanted to stay locked in this embrace for all eternity. She pressed her body to his. He had an erection, and he was embarrassed in case she might feel it, so he eased back—but she pushed forward again, and he understood, looking into her eyes, that she wanted to feel his penis pressed against her soft body. The realization heated him unbearably. He felt as if he was going to ejaculate, and it occurred to him that she might even want him to.

Then he heard the door of the Daimler open, and Jimmy Murray speaking with slightly unnatural loudness, as if giving a warning. Lloyd broke the embrace with Daisy.

"Well," she murmured in a surprised tone, "that was an unexpected pleasure."

Lloyd said hoarsely: "More than a pleasure."

Then Jimmy and Eva were beside them, and they all walked to the door of Mrs. Peshkov's house. It was a grand building with steps up to a covered porch. Lloyd wondered if the porch might give shelter enough for another kiss, but as they climbed the steps, the door was opened from the inside by a man in evening dress, probably the butler Lloyd had spoken to earlier. How glad he was that he had made that phone call!

The two girls said good night demurely, giving no hint that only seconds ago they had both been locked in passionate embraces; then the door closed and they were gone.

Lloyd and Jimmy went back down the steps.

"I'm going to walk from here," Jimmy said. "Shall I tell the chauffeur to drive you back to the East End? You must be three or four miles from home. And Boy won't care—he'll sleep until breakfast time, I should think."

"That's thoughtful of you, Murray, and I appreciate it; but, believe it or not, I feel like walking. Lots to think about."

"As you wish. Good night, then."

"Good night," said Lloyd, and, with his mind in a whirl and his erection slowly deflating, he turned east and headed for home.

iv

London's social season ended in the middle of August, and still Boy Fitzherbert had not proposed marriage to Daisy Peshkov.

Daisy was hurt and puzzled. Everyone knew they were courting. They saw one another almost every day. Earl Fitzherbert talked to Daisy like a daughter, and even the suspicious Princess Bea had warmed to her. Boy kissed her whenever he got the chance, but said nothing about the future.

The long series of lavish lunches and dinners, glittering parties and balls, traditional sporting events and champagne picnics that made up the London season came to an abrupt end. Many of the new friends Daisy had made suddenly left town. Most of them went to country houses where, as far as she could gather, they would spend their time hunting foxes, stalking deer, and shooting birds.

Daisy and Olga stayed for Eva Rothmann's wedding. Unlike Boy, Jimmy Murray was in a rush to marry the woman he loved. The ceremony was held at his parents' parish church in Chelsea.

Daisy felt she had done a great job with Eva. She had taught her friend how to choose clothes that suited her, smart styles without frills, in plain strong colors that flattered her dark hair and brown eyes. Gaining in confidence, Eva had learned how to use her natural warmth and quick intelligence to charm men and women. And Jimmy had fallen in love with her. He was no movie star, but he was tall and craggily attractive. He came from a military family with a modest fortune, so Eva would be comfortable, though not rich.

The British were as prejudiced as anyone else, and at first General Murray and Mrs. Murray had not been thrilled at the prospect of their son marrying a half-Jewish German refugee. Eva had won them over quickly, but many of their friends still expressed coded doubts. At the wedding Daisy had been told that Eva was "exotic," Jimmy was "courageous," and the Murrays were "marvelously broad-minded," all ways of making the best of an unsuitable match.

Jimmy had written formally to Dr. Rothmann in Berlin, and received permission to ask Eva for her hand in marriage, but the German authorities had refused to let the Rothmann family come to the wedding. Eva had said tearfully: "They hate Jews so much, you'd think they'd be happy to see them leave the country!"

Boy's father, Fitz, had heard this remark, and had later spoken to Daisy about it. "Tell your friend Eva not to say too much about Jews, if she can avoid it," he had said, in the tone of one who gives a friendly warning. "Having a half-Jewish wife is not going to help Jimmy's army career, you know." Daisy had not passed on this unpleasant counsel.

The happy couple went off to Nice for their honeymoon. Daisy realized with a pang of guilt that she was relieved to get Eva off her hands. Boy and his political pals disliked Jews so much that Eva was becoming a problem. Already the friendship between Boy and Jimmy had ended—Boy had refused to be Jimmy's best man.

After the wedding Daisy and Olga were invited by the Fitzherberts to a shooting party at their country house in Wales. Daisy's hopes rose. Now that Eva was out of the way, there was nothing to stop Boy proposing. The earl and princess must surely assume he was on the point of it. Perhaps they planned for him to do so this weekend.

Daisy and Olga went to Paddington station on a Friday morning and took a train west. They crossed the heart of England, rich rolling farmland dotted with hamlets, each with its stone church spire rising from a stand of ancient trees. They had a first-class carriage to themselves, and Olga asked Daisy what she thought Boy might do. "He must know I like him," Daisy said. "I've let him kiss me enough times."

"Have you shown any interest in anyone else?" her mother asked shrewdly.

Daisy suppressed the guilty memory of that brief moment of foolishness with Lloyd Williams. Boy could not possibly know about that, and anyway she had not seen Lloyd again, nor had she replied to the three letters he had sent her. "No one," she said.

"Then it's because of Eva," said Olga. "And now she's gone."

The train went through a long tunnel under the estuary of the river Severn, and when it emerged, they were in Wales. Bedraggled sheep grazed the hills, and in the cleft of each valley was a small mining town, its pithead winding gear rising from a scatter of ugly industrial buildings.

Earl Fitzherbert's black-and-cream Rolls-Royce was waiting for them at Aberowen station. The town was dismal, Daisy thought, with small gray stone houses in rows along the steep hillsides. They drove a mile or so out of town to the house, Tŷ Gwyn.

Daisy gasped with pleasure as they passed through the gates. Tŷ Gwyn was enormous and elegant, with long rows of tall windows in a perfectly classical façade. It was set in elaborate gardens of flowers, shrubs, and specimen trees that clearly were the pride of the earl himself. What a joy it would be to be mistress of this house, she thought. The British aristocracy might no longer rule the world, but they had perfected the art of living, and Daisy longed to be one of them.

Tŷ Gwyn meant "White House," but the place was actually gray, and Daisy learned why when she touched the stonework with her hand and got coal dust on her fingertips.

She was given a room called the Gardenia Suite.

That evening she and Boy sat on the terrace before dinner and watched the sun go down over the purple mountaintop, Boy smoking a cigar and Daisy sipping champagne. They were alone for a while, but Boy said nothing about marriage.

Over the weekend her anxiety grew. Boy had plenty more chances to speak to her alone—she made sure of that. On Saturday the men went shooting, but Daisy went out to meet them at the end of the afternoon, and she and Boy walked back through the woods together. On Sunday morning the Fitzherberts and most of their guests went to the Anglican church in the town. After the service, Boy took Daisy to a pub called the Two Crowns, where squat, broad-shouldered miners in flat caps stared at her in her lavender cashmere coat as if Boy had brought in a leopard on a leash.

She told him that she and her mother would soon have to go back to Buffalo, but he did not take the hint.

Could it simply be that he liked her, but not enough to marry her?

By lunch on Sunday she was desperate. Tomorrow she and her

mother were to return to London. If Boy had not proposed by then, his parents would begin to think he was not serious, and there would be no more invitations to Tŷ Gwyn.

That prospect frightened Daisy. She had made up her mind to marry Boy. She wanted to be Viscountess Aberowen, and then one day Countess Fitzherbert. She had always been rich, but she craved the respect and deference that went with social status. She longed to be addressed as "Your Ladyship." She coveted Princess Bea's diamond tiara. She wanted to count royalty among her friends.

She knew Boy liked her, and there was no doubt about his desire when he kissed her. "He needs something to spur him on," Olga murmured to Daisy as they drank their after-lunch coffee with the other ladies in the morning room.

"But what?"

"There is one thing that never fails with men."

Daisy raised her eyebrows. "Sex?" She and her mother talked about most things, but generally skirted around this subject.

"Pregnancy would do it," Olga said. "But that only happens for sure when you *don't* want it."

"What, then?"

"You need to give him a glimpse of the promised land, but not let him in."

Daisy shook her head. "I'm not certain, but I think he may have already been to the promised land with someone else."

"Who?"

"I don't know—a maid, an actress, a widow . . . I'm guessing, but he just doesn't have that virginal air."

"You're right. He doesn't. That means you have to offer him something he can't get from the others. Something he'd do anything for."

Daisy wondered briefly where her mother got this wisdom, having spent her life in a cold marriage. Perhaps she had done a lot of thinking about how her husband, Lev, had been stolen from her by his mistress Marga. Anyway, there was nothing Daisy could offer Boy that he couldn't get from another girl, was there?

The women were finishing their coffee and heading to their

bedrooms for the afternoon nap. The men were still in the dining room, smoking their cigars, but they would follow in a quarter of an hour. Daisy stood up.

Olga said: "What are you going to do?"

"I'm not sure," she said. "I'll think of something."

She left the room. She was going to go to Boy's room, she had decided, but she did not want to say so in case her mother objected. She would be waiting for him when he came for his nap. The servants also took a break at that time of day, so it was unlikely anyone would come into the room.

She would have Boy on his own then. But what would she say or do? She did not know. She would have to improvise.

She went to the Gardenia Suite, brushed her teeth, dabbed Jean Naté perfume on her neck, and walked quietly along the corridor to Boy's room.

No one saw her go in.

He had a spacious bedroom with a view of misty mountaintops. It felt as if it might have been his for many years. There were masculine leather chairs, pictures of airplanes and racehorses on the wall, a cedarwood humidor full of fragrant cigars, and a side table with decanters of whisky and brandy and a tray of crystal glasses.

She pulled open a drawer and saw Tŷ Gwyn writing paper, a bottle of ink, and pens and pencils. The paper was blue with the Fitzherbert crest. Would that one day be her crest?

She wondered what Boy would say when he found her here. Would he be pleased, take her in his arms, and kiss her? Or would he be angry that his privacy had been invaded, and accuse her of snooping? She had to take the risk.

She went into the adjoining dressing room. There was a small washbasin with a mirror over it. His shaving tackle was on the marble surround. Daisy thought she would like to learn to shave her husband. How intimate that would be.

She opened the wardrobe doors and looked at his clothes: formal morning dress, tweed suits, riding clothes, a leather pilot's jacket with a fur lining, and two evening suits.

That gave her an idea.

She recalled how aroused Boy had been, at Bing Westhampton's house back in June, by the sight of her and the other girls dressed as men. That evening had been the first time he kissed her. She was not sure why he had been so excited—such things were generally inexplicable. Lizzie Westhampton said some men liked women to spank their bottoms; how could you account for that?

Perhaps she should dress in his clothes now.

Something he'd do anything for, her mother had said. Was this it?

She stared at the row of suits on hangers, the stack of folded white shirts, the polished leather shoes each with its wooden tree inside. Would it work? Did she have time?

Did she have anything to lose?

She could pick the clothes she needed, take them to the Gardenia Suite, change there, and then hurry back, hoping no one saw her on the way . . .

No. There was no time for that. His cigar was not long enough. She had to change here, and fast—or not at all.

She made up her mind.

She pulled her dress off.

She was in danger now. Until this moment, she might have explained her presence here, just about plausibly, by pretending she had lost her bearings in Tŷ Gwyn's miles of corridors and gone into the wrong room by mistake. But no girl's reputation could survive being found in a man's room in her underwear.

She took the top shirt off the pile. The collar had to be attached with a stud, she saw with a groan. She found a dozen starched collars in a drawer with a box of studs, and fixed one to the shirt, then pulled the shirt over her head.

She heard a man's heavy footsteps in the corridor outside, and froze, her heart beating like a big drum, but the steps went by.

She decided to wear formal morning dress. The striped trousers had no suspenders attached, but she found some in another drawer. She figured out how to button the suspenders to the trousers, then pulled the trousers on. The waist was big enough for two of her.

She pushed her stockinged feet into a pair of shiny black shoes and laced them.

She buttoned the shirt and put on a silver tie. The knot was wrong, but it did not matter, and anyway she did not know the correct way to tie it, so she left it as it was.

She put on a fawn double-breasted waistcoat and a black tailcoat; then she looked in the full-length mirror on the inside of the wardrobe door.

The clothes were baggy but she looked cute anyway.

Now that she had time, she put gold links in the shirt cuffs and a white handkerchief in the breast pocket of the coat.

Something was missing. She stared at herself in the mirror until she figured out what else she needed.

A hat.

She opened another cupboard and saw a row of hatboxes on a high shelf. She found a gray top hat and perched it on the back of her head.

She remembered the mustache.

She did not have an eyebrow pencil with her. She returned to Boy's bedroom and bent over the fireplace. It was still summer, and there was no fire. She got some soot on her fingertip, returned to the mirror, and carefully drew a mustache on her upper lip.

She was ready.

She sat in one of the leather armchairs to wait for him.

Her instinct told her she was doing the right thing, but rationally it seemed bizarre. However, there was no accounting for arousal. She herself had got wet inside when he took her up in his plane. It had been impossible for them to canoodle while he was concentrating on flying the little aircraft, and that was just as well, for soaring through the air had been so exciting that she probably would have let him do anything he wanted.

However, boys could be unpredictable, and she feared he might be angry. When that happened, his handsome face would twist into an unattractive grimace, he would tap his foot very quickly, and he could become quite cruel. Once when a waiter with a limp had brought him the wrong drink, he had said: "Just hobble back to the bar and bring me the Scotch I ordered—being a cripple doesn't make you deaf, does it?" The wretched man had flushed with shame.

She wondered what Boy would say to her if he was angered by her being in his room.

He arrived five minutes later.

She heard his tread outside, and realized she already knew him well enough to recognize his step.

The door opened and he came in without seeing her.

She put on a deep voice and said: "Hello, old chap, how are you?"

He started and said: "Good God!" Then he looked again. "Daisy?"

She stood up. "The same," she said in her normal voice. He was still staring at her in surprise. She doffed the top hat, gave a little bow, and said: "At your service." She replaced the hat on her head at an angle.

After a long moment, he recovered from the shock and grinned.

Thank God, she thought.

He said: "I say, that topper does suit you."

She came closer. "I put it on to please you."

"Jolly nice of you, I must say."

She turned her face up invitingly. She liked kissing him. In truth, she liked kissing most men. She was secretly embarrassed by how much she liked it. She had even enjoyed kissing girls, at her boarding school where they did not see a boy for weeks on end.

He bent his head and touched his lips to hers. Her hat fell off, and they both giggled. Quickly he thrust his tongue into her mouth. She relaxed and enjoyed it. He was enthusiastic about all sensual pleasures, and she was excited by his eagerness.

She reminded herself that she had a purpose. Things were progressing nicely, but she wanted him to propose. Would he be satisfied with just a kiss? She needed him to want more. Often, if they had more than a few hasty moments, he would fondle her breasts.

A lot depended on how much wine he had drunk with lunch. He had a large capacity, but there came a point when he lost the urge.

She moved her body, pressing herself to him. He put a hand on her chest, but she was wearing a baggy waistcoat of woolen cloth and he could not find her small breasts. He grunted in frustration.

Then his hand roamed across her stomach and inside the waistband of the loose-fitting trousers.

She had never before let him touch her down there.

She still had on a silk petticoat and substantial cotton underdrawers, so he surely could not feel much, but his hand went to the fork of her thighs and pressed firmly against her through the layers. She felt a twinge of pleasure.

She pulled away from him.

Panting, he said: "Have I gone too far?"

"Lock the door," she said.

"Oh, my goodness." He went to the door, turned the key in the lock, and came back. They embraced again, and he resumed where he had left off. She touched the front of his trousers, found his erect penis through the cloth, and grasped it firmly. He groaned with pleasure.

She pulled away again.

The shadow of anger crossed his face. An unpleasant memory came back to her. Once, when she had made a boy called Theo Coffman take his hand off her breasts, he had turned nasty and called her a prick-teaser. She had never seen that boy again, but the insult had made her feel irrationally ashamed. Momentarily she feared that Boy might be about to make a similar accusation.

Then his face softened and he said: "I am dreadfully keen on you, y'know."

This was her moment. Sink or swim, she told herself. "We shouldn't be doing this," she said with a regret that was not greatly exaggerated.

"Why not?"

"We're not even engaged."

The word hung in the air for a long moment. For a girl to say that was tantamount to a proposal. She watched his face, terrified that he would take fright, turn away, mumble excuses, and ask her to leave.

He said nothing.

"I want to make you happy," she said. "But . . ."

"I do love you, Daisy," he said.

That was not enough. She smiled at him and said: "Do you?"

"Ever such a lot."

She said nothing, but looked at him expectantly.

At last he said: "Will you marry me?"

"Oh, yes," she said, and she kissed him again. With her mouth pressed to his she unbuttoned his fly, burrowed through his underclothing, found his penis, and took it out. The skin was silky and hot. She stroked it, remembering a conversation with the Westhampton twins. "You can rub his thing," Lindy had said, and Lizzie had added: "Until it squirts." Daisy was intrigued and excited by the idea of making a man do that. She grasped a bit harder.

Then she remembered Lindy's next remark. "Or you can suck it— they like that best of all."

She moved her lips away from Boy's and spoke into his ear. "I'll do anything for my husband," she said.

Then she knelt down.

v

It was the wedding of the year. Daisy and Boy were married at St. Margaret's Church, Westminster, on Saturday, October 3, 1936. Daisy was disappointed it was not Westminster Abbey, but she was told that was for the royal family only.

Coco Chanel made her wedding dress. Depression fashion was for simple lines and minimal extravagance. Daisy's floor-length bias-cut satin gown had pretty butterfly sleeves and a short train that could be carried by one page boy.

Her father, Lev Peshkov, came across the Atlantic for the ceremony. Her mother, Olga, agreed for the sake of appearances to sit beside him in church and generally pretend that they were a more or less happily married couple. Daisy's nightmare was that at some point Marga would show up with Lev's illegitimate son, Greg, on her arm, but it did not happen.

The Westhampton twins and May Murray were bridesmaids, and Eva Murray was matron of honor. Boy had been grumpy about Eva's being half-Jewish—he had not wanted to invite her at all—but Daisy had insisted.

She stood in the ancient church, conscious that she looked heartbreakingly beautiful, and happily gave herself to Boy Fitzherbert body and soul.

She signed the register "Daisy Fitzherbert, Viscountess Aberowen." She had been practising that signature for weeks, carefully tearing the paper into unreadable shreds afterward. Now she was entitled to it. It was her name.

Processing out of the church, Fitz took Olga's arm amiably, but Princess Bea put a yard of empty space between herself and Lev.

Princess Bea was not a nice person. She was friendly enough toward Daisy's mother, and if there was a heavy strain of condescension in her tone, Olga did not notice it, so relations were amiable. But Bea did not like Lev.

Daisy now realized that Lev lacked the veneer of social respectability. He walked and talked, ate and drank, smoked and laughed and scratched like a gangster, and he did not care what people thought. He did what he liked because he was an American millionaire, just as Fitz did what he liked because he was an English earl. Daisy had always known this, but it struck her with extra force when she saw her father with all these upper-class English people, at the wedding breakfast in the grand ballroom of the Dorchester Hotel.

But it did not matter now. She was Lady Aberowen, and that could not be taken away from her.

Nevertheless, Bea's constant hostility to Lev was an irritant, like a slightly bad smell or a distant buzzing noise, giving Daisy a feeling of dissatisfaction. Sitting beside Lev at the top table, Bea always turned slightly away. When he spoke to her, she replied briefly without meeting his eye. He seemed not to notice, smiling and drinking champagne, but

Daisy, seated on Lev's other side, knew he had not failed to read the signs. He was uncouth, not stupid.

When the toasts were over and the men began to smoke, Lev, who as the father of the bride was paying the bill, looked along the table and said: "Well, Fitz, I hope you enjoyed your meal. Were the wines up to your standards?"

"Very good, thank you."

"I must say, I thought it was a damn fine spread."

Bea tutted audibly. Men were not supposed to say *damn* in her hearing.

Lev turned to her. He was smiling, but Daisy knew the dangerous look in his eye. "Why, Princess, have I offended you?"

She did not want to reply, but he looked expectantly at her, and did not turn his gaze aside. At last she spoke. "I prefer not to hear coarse language," she said.

Lev took a cigar from his case. He did not light it at once, but sniffed it and rolled it between his fingers. "Let me tell you a story," he said, and he looked up and down the table to make sure they were all listening: Fitz, Olga, Boy, Daisy, and Bea. "When I was a kid, my father was accused of grazing livestock on someone else's land. No big deal, you might think, even if he was guilty. But he was arrested, and the land agent built a scaffold in the north meadow. Then the soldiers came and grabbed me and my brother and our mother and took us there. My father was on the scaffold with a noose around his neck. Then the landlord arrived."

Daisy had never heard this story. She looked at her mother. Olga seemed equally surprised.

The little group at the table were all very silent now.

"We were forced to watch while my father was hanged," Lev said. He turned to Bea. "And you know something strange? The landlord's sister was there as well." He put the cigar in his mouth, wetting the end, and took it out again.

Daisy saw that Bea had turned pale. Was this about her?

"The sister was about nineteen years old, and she was a princess,"

Lev said, looking at his cigar. Daisy heard Bea let out a small cry, and realized this story *was* about her. "She stood there and watched the hanging, cold as ice," Lev said.

Then he looked directly at Bea. "Now that's what I call coarse," he said.

There was a long moment of silence.

Then Lev put the cigar back in his mouth and said: "Has anyone got a light?"

vi

Lloyd Williams sat at the table in the kitchen of his mother's house in Aldgate, anxiously studying a map.

It was Sunday, October 4, 1936, and today there was going to be a riot.

The old Roman town of London, built on a hill beside the river Thames, was now the financial district, called the City. West of this hill were the palaces of the rich, and the theaters and shops and cathedrals that catered to them. The house in which Lloyd sat was to the east of the hill, near the docks and the slums. Here for centuries waves of immigrants had landed, determined to work their fingers to the bone so that their grandchildren could one day move from the East End to the West End.

The map Lloyd was looking at so intently was in a special edition of the *Daily Worker,* the Communist Party newspaper, and it showed the route of today's march by the British Union of Fascists. They planned to assemble outside the Tower of London, on the border between the City and the East End, then march east—

Straight into the overwhelmingly Jewish borough of Stepney.

Unless Lloyd and people who thought as he did could stop them.

There were 330,000 Jews in Britain, according to the newspaper, and half of them lived in the East End. Most were refugees from Russia, Poland, and Germany, where they had lived in fear that on any day the police, the army, or the Cossacks might ride into town, robbing families, beating old men and outraging young women, lining fathers and brothers up against the wall to be shot.

Here in the London slums those Jews had found a place where they had as much right to live as anyone else. How would they feel if they looked out of their windows to see, marching down their own streets, a gang of uniformed thugs sworn to wipe them all out? Lloyd felt that it just could not be allowed to happen.

The *Worker* pointed out that from the Tower there were really only two routes the marchers could take. One went through Gardiner's Corner, a five-way junction known as the Gateway to the East End; the other led along Royal Mint Street and the narrow Cable Street. There were a dozen other routes for an individual using side streets, but not for a march. St. George Street led to Catholic Wapping rather than Jewish Stepney, and was therefore no use to the Fascists.

The *Worker* called for a human wall to block Gardiner's Corner and Cable Street, and stop the march.

The paper often called for things that did not happen: strikes, revolutions, or—most recently—an alliance of all left parties to form a People's Front. The human wall might be just another fantasy. It would take many thousands of people to effectively close off the East End. Lloyd did not know whether enough would show up.

All he knew for sure was that there would be trouble.

At the table with Lloyd were his parents, Bernie and Ethel; his sister, Millie; and sixteen-year-old Lenny Griffiths from Aberowen, in his Sunday suit. Lenny was part of a small army of Welsh miners who had come to London to join the counterdemonstration.

Bernie looked up from his newspaper and said to Lenny: "The Fascists claim that the train fares for all you Welshmen to come to London have been paid by the big Jews."

Lenny swallowed a mouthful of fried egg. "I don't know any big Jews," he said. "Unless you count Mrs. Levy Sweetshop; she's quite big. Anyway, I came to London on the back of a lorry with sixty Welsh lambs going to Smithfield meat market."

Millie said: "That accounts for the smell."

Ethel said: "Millie! How rude."

Lenny was sharing Lloyd's bedroom, and he had confided that after the demonstration he was not planning to return to Aberowen. He and Dave Williams were going to Spain to join the International Brigades being formed to fight the Fascist insurrection.

"Did you get a passport?" Lloyd had asked. Getting a passport was not difficult, but the applicant did have to provide a reference from a clergyman, doctor, lawyer, or other person of status, so a young person could not easily keep it secret.

"No need," Lenny said. "We go to Victoria station and get a weekend return ticket to Paris. You can do that without a passport."

Lloyd had vaguely known that. It was a loophole intended for the convenience of the prosperous middle class. Now the anti-Fascists were taking advantage of it. "How much is the ticket?"

"Three pounds fifteen shillings."

Lloyd had raised his eyebrows. That was more money than an unemployed coal miner was likely to have.

Lenny had added: "But the Independent Labour Party is paying for my ticket, and the Communist Party for Dave's."

They must have lied about their ages. "Then what happens when you get to Paris?" Lloyd had asked.

"We'll be met by the French Communists at the Gare du Nord." He pronounced it *gair duh nord.* He did not speak a word of French. "From there we'll be escorted to the Spanish border."

Lloyd had delayed his own departure. He told people he wanted to soothe his parents' worries, but the truth was he could not give up on Daisy. He still dreamed of her throwing Boy over. It was hopeless—she did not even answer his letters—but he could not forget her.

Meanwhile Britain, France, and the USA had agreed with Germany and Italy to adopt a policy of nonintervention in Spain, which meant none of them would supply weapons to either side. This in itself was infuriating to Lloyd: surely the democracies should support the elected government? But what was worse, Germany and Italy were breaching the agreement every day, as Lloyd's mother and Uncle Billy pointed out at many public meetings held that autumn in Britain to discuss Spain. Earl Fitzherbert, as the government minister responsible, defended the policy stoutly, saying the Spanish government should not be armed for fear it would go Communist.

This was a self-fulfilling prophecy, as Ethel had argued in a scathing speech. The one nation willing to support the government of Spain was the Soviet Union, and the Spaniards would naturally gravitate toward the only country in the world that helped them.

The truth was that the Conservatives felt Spain had elected people who were dangerously left-wing. Men such as Fitzherbert would not be unhappy if the Spanish government was violently overthrown and replaced by right-wing extremists. Lloyd seethed with frustration.

Then had come this chance to fight Fascism at home.

"It's ridiculous," Bernie had said a week ago, when the march had been announced. "The Metropolitan Police must force them to change the route. They have the right to march, of course, but not in Stepney." However, the police said they did not have the power to interfere with a perfectly legal demonstration.

Bernie and Ethel and the mayors of eight London boroughs had been in a delegation that begged the home secretary, Sir John Simon, to ban the march or at least divert it, but he, too, claimed he had no power to act.

The question of what to do next had split the Labour Party, the Jewish community, and the Williams family.

The Jewish People's Council Against Fascism and Anti-Semitism, founded by Bernie and others three months ago, had called for a massive counterdemonstration that would keep the Fascists out of Jewish streets. Their slogan was the Spanish phrase *"No pasaran,"* meaning "They shall not pass," the cry of the anti-Fascist defenders of Madrid. The council was a small organization with a grand name. It occupied two upstairs rooms in a building on Commercial Road, and it owned a Gestetner duplicating machine and a couple of old typewriters. But it commanded huge support in the East End. In forty-eight hours it had collected an incredible one hundred thousand signatures on a

206 | CHAPTER THREE

petition calling for the march to be banned. Still the government did nothing.

Only one major political party supported the counterdemonstration, and that was the Communists. The protest was also backed by the fringe Independent Labour Party, to which Lenny belonged. The other parties were against.

Ethel said: "I see *The Jewish Chronicle* has advised its readers to stay off the streets today."

This was the problem, in Lloyd's opinion. A lot of people were taking the view that it was best to keep out of trouble. But that would give the Fascists a free hand.

Bernie, who was Jewish though not religious, said to Ethel: "How can you quote *The Jewish Chronicle* at me? It believes Jews should not be against Fascism, just anti-Semitism. What kind of political sense does that make?"

"I hear that the Board of Deputies of British Jews says the same as the *Chronicle*," Ethel persisted. "Apparently there was an announcement yesterday in all the synagogues."

"Those so-called deputies are alrightniks from Golders Green," Bernie said with contempt. "They've never been insulted on the streets by Fascist hooligans."

"You're in the Labour Party," Ethel said accusingly. "Our policy is not to confront the Fascists on the streets. Where's your solidarity?"

Bernie said: "What about solidarity with my fellow Jews?"

"You're only Jewish when it suits you. And you've never been abused on the street."

"All the same, the Labour Party has made a political mistake."

"Just remember, if you allow the Fascists to provoke violence, the press will blame the left for it, regardless of who really started it."

Lenny said rashly: "If Mosley's boys start a fight, they'll get what's coming to them."

Ethel sighed. "Think about it, Lenny: in this country, who's got the most guns—you and Lloyd and the Labour Party, or the Conservatives with the army and the police on their side?"

"Oh," said Lenny. Clearly he had not considered that.

Lloyd said angrily to his mother: "How can you talk like that? You were in Berlin three years ago—you saw how it was. The German left tried to oppose Fascism peacefully, and look what happened to them."

Bernie put in: "The German Social Democrats failed to form a popular front with the Communists. That allowed them to be picked off separately. Together they might have won." Bernie had been angry when the local Labour Party branch had refused an offer from the Communists to form a coalition against the march.

Ethel said: "An alliance with Communists is a dangerous thing."

She and Bernie disagreed on this. In fact it was an issue that split the Labour Party. Lloyd thought that Bernie was right and Ethel wrong. "We have to use every resource we've got to defeat Fascism," he said; then he added diplomatically: "But Mam's right, it will be best for us if today goes off without violence."

"It will be best if you all stay home, and oppose the Fascists through the normal channels of democratic politics," Ethel said.

"You tried to get equal pay for women through the normal channels of democratic politics," Lloyd said. "You failed." Only last April women Labour M.P.s had promoted a parliamentary bill to guarantee female government employees equal pay for equal work. It had been voted down by the male-dominated House of Commons.

"You don't give up on democracy every time you lose a vote," Ethel said crisply.

The trouble was, Lloyd knew, that these divisions could fatally weaken the anti-Fascist forces, as had happened in Germany. Today would be a harsh test. Political parties could try to lead, but the people would choose whom to follow. Would they stay at home, as urged by the timid Labour Party and *The Jewish Chronicle*? Or would they come out onto the streets in their thousands and say no to Fascism? By the end of the day he would know the answer.

There was a knock at the back door and their neighbor Sean Dolan came in dressed in his churchgoing suit. "I'll be joining you after Mass," he said to Bernie. "Where should we meet up?"

"Gardiner's Corner, not later than two o'clock," said Bernie. "We're hoping to have enough people to stop the Fascists there."

"You'll have every dockworker in the East End with you," said Sean enthusiastically.

Millie asked: "Why is that? The Fascists don't hate you, do they?"

"You're too young to remember, you darlin' girl, but the Jews have always supported us," Sean explained. "In the dock strike of 1912, when I was only nine years old, my father couldn't feed us, and me and my brother were taken in by Mrs. Isaacs the baker's wife in New Road, may God bless her great big heart. Hundreds of dockers' children were looked after by Jewish families then. It was the same in 1926. We're not going to let the bloody Fascists come down our streets—excuse my language, Mrs. Leckwith."

Lloyd was heartened. There were thousands of dockers in the East End: if they showed up en masse, it would hugely swell the ranks.

From outside the house came the sound of a loudspeaker. "Keep Mosley out of Stepney," said a man's voice. "Assemble at Gardiner's Corner at two o'clock."

Lloyd drank his tea and stood up. His role today was to be a spy, checking the position of the Fascists and calling in updates to Bernie's Jewish People's Council. His pockets were heavy with big brown pennies for public phones. "I'd better get started," he said. "The Fascists are probably assembling already."

His mother got up and followed him to the door. "Don't get into a fight," she said. "Remember what happened in Berlin."

"I'll be careful," Lloyd said.

She tried a light tone. "Your rich American girl won't like you with no teeth."

"She doesn't like me anyway."

"I don't believe it. What girl could resist you?"

"I'll be all right, Mam," Lloyd said. "Really I will."

"I suppose I should be glad you're not going to bloody Spain."

"Not today, anyway." Lloyd kissed his mother and went out.

It was a bright autumn morning, the sun unseasonably warm. In the middle of Nutley Street a temporary platform had been set up by a group of men, one of whom was speaking through a megaphone. "People of the East End, we do not have to stand quiet while a crowd of strutting anti-Semites insult us!" Lloyd recognized the speaker as a local official of the National Unemployed Workers' Movement. Because of the Depression there were thousands of unemployed Jewish tailors. They signed on every day at the Settle Street Labor Exchange.

Before Lloyd had gone ten yards, Bernie came after him and handed him a paper bag of the little glass balls that children called marbles. "I've been in a lot of demonstrations," he said. "If the mounted police charge the crowd, throw these under the horses' hooves."

Lloyd smiled. His stepfather was a peacemaker, almost all the time, but he was no softie.

All the same, Lloyd was dubious about the marbles. He had never had much to do with horses, but they seemed to him to be patient, harmless beasts, and he did not like the idea of causing them to crash to the ground.

Bernie read the look on his face and said: "Better a horse should fall than my boy should be trampled."

Lloyd put the marbles in his pocket, thinking that it did not commit him to using them.

He was pleased to see many people already on the streets. He noted other encouraging signs. The slogan "They shall not pass" in English and Spanish had been chalked on walls everywhere he looked. The Communists were out in force, handing out leaflets. Red flags draped many windowsills. A group of men wearing medals from the Great War carried a banner that read JEWISH EX-SERVICEMEN'S ASSOCIATION. Fascists hated to be reminded how many Jews had fought for Britain. Five Jewish soldiers had won the country's highest medal for bravery, the Victoria Cross.

Lloyd began to think that perhaps there would be enough people to stop the march after all.

Gardiner's Corner was a broad five-way junction, named for the Scottish clothing store, Gardiner and Company, that occupied a corner building with a distinctive clock tower. Lloyd saw when he got there that trouble was expected. There were several first-aid stations and hundreds of St. John Ambulance volunteers in their uniforms. Ambulances were parked in every side street. Lloyd hoped there would be no fighting, but better to risk violence, he thought, than to let the Fascists march unhindered.

He took a roundabout route and came toward the Tower of London from the northwest, in order not to be identified as an East Ender. Some minutes before he got there, he could hear the brass bands.

The Tower was a riverside palace that had symbolized authority and repression for eight hundred years. It was surrounded by a long wall of pale old stone that looked as if the color had been washed out of it by centuries of London rain. Outside the walls, on the landward side, was a park called Tower Gardens, and here the Fascists were assembling. He estimated there were already a couple of thousand of them, in a line that stretched back westward into the financial district. Every now and again they broke into a rhythmic chant:

> *One, two, three, four,*
> *We're gonna get rid of the Yids!*
> *The Yids! The Yids!*
> *We're gonna get rid of the Yids!*

They carried Union Jack flags. Why was it, Lloyd wondered, that the people who wanted to destroy everything good about their country were the quickest to wave the national flag?

They looked impressively military, in their wide black leather belts and black shirts, as they formed neat columns across the grass. Their officers wore a smart uniform: a black military-cut jacket, gray riding breeches, jackboots, a black cap with a shiny peak, and a red-and-white armband. Several motorcyclists in uniform roared around ostentatiously, delivering messages with Fascist salutes. More marchers were arriving, some of them in armored vans with wire mesh at the windows.

This was not a political party. It was an army.

The purpose of the display, Lloyd figured, was to give them false authority. They wanted to look as if they had the right to close meetings and empty buildings, to burst into homes and offices and arrest people, to drag them to jails and camps and beat them up, interrogate and torture them, as the Brownshirts did in Germany under the Nazi regime so admired by Mosley and the *Daily Mail*'s proprietor, Lord Rothermere.

They would terrify the people of the East End, people whose parents and grandparents had fled from repression and pogroms in Ireland and Poland and Russia.

Would East Enders come out on the streets and fight them? If not— if today's march went ahead as planned—what might the Fascists dare tomorrow?

He walked around the edge of the park, pretending to be one of the hundred or so casual onlookers. Side streets radiated from the hub like spokes. In one of them he noticed a familiar-looking black-and-cream Rolls-Royce drawing up. The chauffeur opened the rear door and, to Lloyd's shock and dismay, Daisy Peshkov got out.

There was no doubt why she was here. She was wearing a beautifully tailored female version of the uniform, with a long gray skirt instead of the breeches, her fair curls escaping from under the black cap. Much as he hated the outfit, Lloyd could not help finding her irresistibly alluring.

He stopped and stared. He should not have been surprised: Daisy had told him she liked Boy Fitzherbert, and Boy's politics clearly made no difference to that. But to see her obviously supporting the Fascists in their attack on Jewish Londoners rammed home to him how utterly alien she was from everything that mattered in his life.

He should simply have turned away, but he could not. As she hurried along the pavement, he blocked her way. "What the devil are you doing here?" he said brusquely.

She was cool. "I might ask you the same question, Mr. Williams," she said. "I don't suppose you're intending to march with us."

"Don't you understand what these people are like? They break up peaceful political meetings, they bully journalists, they imprison their political rivals. You're an American—how can you be against democracy?"

"Democracy is not necessarily the most appropriate political system for every country in all times." She was quoting Mosley's propaganda, Lloyd guessed.

He said: "But these people torture and kill everyone who disagrees with them!" He thought of Jörg. "I've seen it for myself, in Berlin. I was in one of their camps, briefly. I was forced to watch while a naked man was savaged to death by starving dogs. That's the kind of thing your Fascist friends do."

She was unintimidated. "And who, exactly, has been killed by Fascists here in England recently?"

"The British Fascists haven't got the power yet—but your Mosley admires Hitler. If they ever get the chance, they'll do exactly the same as the Nazis."

"You mean they will eliminate unemployment and give the people pride and hope."

Lloyd was drawn to her so powerfully that it broke his heart to hear her spouting this rubbish. "You know what the Nazis have done to the family of your friend Eva."

"Eva got married, did you know?" Daisy said, in the determinedly cheerful tone of one who tries to switch a dinner-table conversation to a more agreeable topic. "To nice Jimmy Murray. She's an English wife now."

"And her parents?"

Daisy looked away. "I don't know them."

"But you know what the Nazis have done to them." Eva had told Lloyd all about it at the Trinity Ball. "Her father is no longer allowed to practise medicine—he's working as an assistant in a pharmacy. He can't enter a park or a public library. *His* father's name has been scraped off the war memorial in his home village!" Lloyd realized he had raised his voice. More quietly he said: "How can you possibly stand side by side with people who do such things?"

She looked troubled, but she did not answer his question. Instead she said: "I'm late already. Please excuse me."

"What you're doing can't be excused."

The chauffeur said: "All right, sonny, that's enough."

He was a heavy middle-aged man who evidently took little exercise, and Lloyd was not in the least intimidated, but he did not want to start a fight. "I'm leaving," he said in a mild tone. "But don't call me sonny."

The chauffeur took his arm.

Lloyd said: "You'd better take your hand off me, or I'll knock you down before I go." He looked into the chauffeur's face.

The chauffeur hesitated. Lloyd tensed, preparing to react, watching for warning signs, as he would in the boxing ring. If the chauffeur tried to hit him, it would be a great swinging haymaker of a blow, easily dodged.

But the man either sensed Lloyd's readiness or felt the well-developed muscle in the arm he was holding; for one reason or the other he backed off and released his grip, saying: "No need for threats."

Daisy walked away.

Lloyd looked at her back in the perfectly fitting uniform as she hurried toward the ranks of the Fascists. With a deep sigh of frustration he turned and went in the other direction.

He tried to concentrate on the job at hand. What a fool he had been to threaten the chauffeur. If he had got into a fight, he would probably have been arrested; then he would have spent the day in a police cell—and how would that have helped defeat Fascism?

It was now half past twelve. He left Tower Hill, found a telephone box, called the Jewish People's Council, and spoke to Bernie. After he reported what he had seen, Bernie told him to make an estimate of the number of policemen in the streets between the Tower and Gardiner's Corner.

He crossed to the east side of the park and explored the radiating side streets. What he saw astonished him.

He had expected a hundred or so police. In fact there were thousands.

They stood lining the pavements, waited in dozens of parked buses, and sat astride huge horses in remarkably neat rows. Only a narrow gap was left for people who wanted to walk along the streets. There were more police than Fascists.

From inside one of the buses, a uniformed constable gave him the Hitler salute.

Lloyd was dismayed. If all these policemen sided with the Fascists, how could the counterdemonstrators resist them?

This was worse than a Fascist march: it was a Fascist march with police authority. What kind of message did that send to the Jews of the East End?

In Mansell Street he saw a beat policeman he knew, Henry Clarke. "Hello, Nobby," he said. For some reason all Clarkes were called Nobby. "A copper just gave me the Hitler salute."

"They're not from round here," Nobby said quietly, as if revealing a confidence. "They don't live with Jews like I do. I tell them Jews are the same as everyone else, mostly decent law-abiding people, a few villains and troublemakers. But they don't believe me."

"All the same . . . the Hitler salute?"

"Might have been a joke."

Lloyd did not think so.

He left Nobby and moved on. The police were forming cordons where the side streets entered the area around Gardiner's Corner, he saw.

He went into a pub with a phone—he had scouted all the available telephones the day before—and told Bernie there were at least five thousand policemen in the neighborhood. "We can't resist that many coppers," he said gloomily.

"Don't be so sure," Bernie said. "Have a look at Gardiner's Corner."

Lloyd found a way around the police cordon and joined the counterdemonstration. It was not until he got into the middle of the street outside Gardiner's that he could appreciate the full extent of the crowd.

It was the largest gathering of people he had ever seen.

The five-way junction was jammed, but that was the least of it. The crowd stretched east along Whitechapel High Street as far as the eye could see. Commercial Road, which ran southeast, was also crammed. Leman Street, where the police station stood, was impenetrable.

There must be a hundred thousand people here, Lloyd thought. He wanted to throw his hat in the air and cheer. East Enders had come out in force to repel the Fascists. There could be no doubt about their feelings now.

In the middle of the junction stood a stationary tram, abandoned by its driver and passengers.

Nothing could pass through this crowd, Lloyd realized with mounting optimism.

He saw his neighbor Sean Dolan climb a lamppost and fix a red flag to its top. The Jewish Lads' Brigade brass band was playing—probably without the knowledge of the respectable conservative organizers of the club. A police aircraft flew overhead, an autogyro of some kind, Lloyd thought.

Near the windows of Gardiner's he ran into his sister, Millie, and her friend Naomi Avery. He did not want Millie to become involved in any rough stuff; the thought chilled his heart. "Does Dad know you've come?" he said in a tone of reproof.

She was insouciant. "Don't be daft," she replied.

He was surprised she was there at all. "You're not usually very political," he said. "I thought you were more interested in making money."

"I am," she said. "But this is special."

Lloyd could imagine how upset Bernie would be if Millie got hurt. "I think you should go home."

"Why?"

He looked around. The crowd was amiable and peaceful. The police were some distance away, the Fascists nowhere to be seen. There would be no march today: that was clear. Mosley's people could not force their way through a crowd of a hundred thousand people determined to stop them, and the police would be insane to let them try. Millie was probably quite safe.

Just as he was thinking this, everything changed.

Several whistles shrilled. Looking in the direction of the sound, Lloyd saw the mounted police drawn up in an ominous line. The horses were stamping and blowing in agitation. The police had drawn long clubs shaped like swords.

They seemed to be getting ready to attack—but surely that could not be so.

Next moment, they charged.

There were angry shouts and terrified screams from the people. Everyone scrambled to get out of the way of the giant horses. The crowd made a path, but those at the edge fell under the pounding hooves. The police lashed out left and right with their long clubs. Lloyd was pushed helplessly backward.

He felt furious: What did the police think they were doing? Were they stupid enough to believe they could clear a path for Mosley to march along? Did they really imagine that two or three thousand Fascists chanting insults could pass through a crowd of a hundred thousand of their victims without starting a riot? Were the police led by idiots, or out of control? He was not sure which would be worse.

They backed away, wheeling their panting horses, and regrouped, forming a ragged line; then a whistle blew and they heeled the flanks of their mounts, urging them into another reckless charge.

Millie was scared now. She was only sixteen, and her bravado had gone. She screamed with fear as the crowd squeezed her up against the plate-glass window of Gardiner and Company. Tailor's dummies in cheap suits and winter coats stared out at the horrified crowd and the warlike riders. Lloyd was deafened by the roar of thousands of voices yelling in fearful protest. He got in front of Millie and pushed against the press with all his might, trying to protect her, but it was in vain. Despite his efforts he was crushed against her. Forty or fifty screaming people had their backs to the window, and the pressure was building dangerously.

Lloyd realized with rage that the police were determined to make a pathway through the crowd regardless of the cost.

A moment later there was a terrific crash of breaking glass and the window gave way. Lloyd fell on top of Millie, and Naomi fell on him. Dozens of people cried out in pain and panic.

Lloyd struggled to his feet. Miraculously, he was unhurt. He looked around frantically for his sister. It was maddeningly difficult to distinguish the people from the tailor's dummies. Then he spotted Millie lying in a mess of broken glass. He grasped her arms and pulled her to her feet. She was crying. "My back!" she said.

He turned her around. Her coat was cut to ribbons and there was blood all over her. He felt sick with anguish. He put his arm around her shoulders protectively. "There's an ambulance just around the corner," he said. "Can you walk?"

They had gone only a few yards when the police whistles blew again. Lloyd was terrified that he and Millie would be shoved back into Gardiner's window. Then he remembered what Bernie had given him. He took the paper bag of marbles from his pocket.

The police charged.

Drawing back his arm, Lloyd threw the paper bag over the heads of the crowd to land in front of the horses. He was not the only one so equipped, and several other people threw marbles. As the horses came at them, there was the sound of firecrackers. A police horse slipped on marbles and went down. Others stopped and reared at the banging of the fireworks. The police charge turned into chaos. Naomi Avery had somehow pushed to the front of the crowd, and he saw her burst a bag of pepper under the nose of a horse, causing it to veer away, shaking its head frantically.

The crush eased, and Lloyd led Millie around the corner. She was still in pain, but she had stopped crying.

A line of people were waiting for attention from the St. John Ambulance volunteers: a weeping girl whose hand appeared to have been crushed; several young men with bleeding heads and faces; a middle-aged woman sitting on the ground nursing a swollen knee. As Lloyd and Millie arrived, Sean Dolan walked away with a bandage around his head and went straight back into the crowd.

A nurse looked at Millie's back. "This is bad," she said. "You need to go to the London Hospital. We'll take you in an ambulance." She looked at Lloyd. "Do you want to go with her?"

Lloyd did, but he was supposed to be phoning in reports, and he hesitated.

Millie solved the dilemma for him with characteristic spunk. "Don't you dare come," she said. "You can't do anything for me, and you've got important work to do here."

She was right. He helped her into a parked ambulance. "Are you sure—?"

"Yes, I'm sure. Try not to end up in hospital yourself."

He was leaving her in the best hands, he decided. He kissed her cheek and returned to the fray.

The police had changed their tactics. The people had repelled the horse charges, but the police were still determined to make a path through the crowd. As Lloyd pushed his way to the front, they charged on foot, attacking with their batons. The unarmed demonstrators cowered back from them, like piled leaves in a wind, then surged forward in a different part of the line.

The police started to arrest people, perhaps hoping to weaken the crowd's determination by taking ringleaders away. In the East End, being arrested was no legal formality. Few people came back without a black eye or a few gaps in their teeth. Leman Street police station had a particularly bad reputation.

Lloyd found himself behind a vociferous young woman carrying a red flag. He recognized Olive Bishop, a neighbor in Nutley Street. A policeman hit her over the head with his truncheon, screaming: "Jewish whore!" She was not Jewish, and she certainly was not a whore; in fact she played the piano at the Calvary Gospel Hall. But she had forgotten the admonition of Jesus to turn the other cheek, and she scratched the cop's face, drawing parallel red lines on his skin. Two more officers grabbed her arms and held her while the scratched man hit her on the head again.

The sight of three strong men attacking one girl maddened Lloyd. He stepped forward and hit the woman's assailant with a right hook that had all of his rage behind it. The blow landed on the policeman's temple. Dazed, the man stumbled and fell.

More officers converged on the scene, lashing out randomly with their clubs, hitting arms and legs and heads and hands. Four of them picked up Olive, each taking an arm or a leg. She screamed and wriggled desperately but she could not get free.

But the bystanders were not passive. They attacked the police carrying the girl off, trying to pull the uniformed men away from her. The police turned on their attackers, yelling: "Jew bastards!" even though not all their assailants were Jews and one was a black-skinned Somali sailor.

The police let go of Olive, dropping her to the road, and began to defend themselves. Olive pushed through the crowd and vanished. The cops retreated, hitting out at anyone within reach as they backed away.

Lloyd saw with a thrill of triumph that the police strategy was not working. For all their brutality, the attacks had completely failed to make a way through the crowd. Another baton charge began, but the angry crowd surged forward to meet it, eager now for combat.

Lloyd decided it was time for another report. He worked his way backward through the crush and found a phone box. "I don't think they're going to succeed, Dad," he told Bernie excitedly. "They're trying to beat a path through us but they're making no progress. We're too many."

"We're redirecting people to Cable Street," Bernie said. "The police may be about to switch their thrust, thinking they have more chance there, so we're sending reinforcements. Go along there, see what's happening, and let me know."

"Right," said Lloyd, and he hung up before realizing he had not told his stepfather that Millie had been taken to hospital. But perhaps it was better not to worry him right now.

Getting to Cable Street was not going to be easy. From Gardiner's Corner, Leman Street led directly south to the near end of Cable Street, a distance of less than half a mile, but the road was jammed by demonstrators fighting with police. Lloyd had to take a less direct route.

He struggled eastward through the crowd into Commercial Road. Once there, further progress was not much easier. There were no police, therefore there was no violence, but the crowd was almost as dense. It was frustrating, but Lloyd was consoled for his difficulties by the reflection that the police would never force a way through so many.

He wondered what Daisy Peshkov was doing. Probably she was sitting in the car, waiting for the march to begin, tapping the toe of her expensive shoe impatiently on the Rolls-Royce's carpet. The thought that he was helping to frustrate her purpose gave him an oddly spiteful sense of satisfaction.

With persistence and a slightly ruthless attitude to those in his way, Lloyd pushed through the throng. The railway that ran along the north side of Cable Street obstructed his route, and he had to walk some distance before reaching a side road that tunneled beneath the line. He passed under the tracks and entered Cable Street.

The crowd here was not so close packed, but the street was narrow, and passage was still difficult. That was a good thing: it would be even more difficult for the police to get through. But there was another obstruction, he saw. A lorry had been parked across the road and turned on its side. At either end of the vehicle, the barricade had been extended the full width of the street with old tables and chairs, odd lengths of timber, and other assorted rubbish piled high.

A barricade! It made Lloyd think of the French Revolution. But this was no revolution. The people of the East End did not want to overthrow the British government. On the contrary, they were deeply attached to their elections and their borough councils and their Houses of Parliament. They liked their system of government so much that they were determined to defend it against Fascism even if it would not defend itself.

He had emerged behind the barrier, and now he moved toward it to see what was happening. He stood on a wall to get a better view. He saw a lively scene. On the far side, police were trying to dismantle the blockage, picking up broken furniture and dragging old mattresses away. But they were not having an easy time of it. A hail of missiles fell on their helmets, some hurled from behind the barricade, some thrown from the upstairs windows of the houses packed closely on either side of the street: stones, milk bottles, broken pots, and bricks that came, Lloyd saw, from a nearby builder's yard. A few daring young men stood on top of the barricade, lashing out at the police with sticks, and occasionally a fight would break out as the police tried to pull one down and give him a kicking. With a start Lloyd recognized two of the figures standing on the barricade as Dave Williams, his cousin, and Lenny Griffiths, from Aberowen. Side by side they were fighting policemen off with shovels.

But as the minutes passed, Lloyd saw that the police were winning. They were working systematically, picking up the components of the barricade and taking them away. On this side a few people reinforced the wall, replacing what the police removed, but they were less organized and did not have an infinite supply of materials. It looked to Lloyd as if the police would soon prevail. And if they could clear Cable Street, they would let the Fascists march down here, past one Jewish shop after another.

Then, looking behind him, he saw that whoever was organizing the defense of Cable Street was thinking ahead. Even while the police dismantled the barricade, another was going up a few hundred yards farther along the street.

Lloyd retreated and began enthusiastically to help build the second wall. Dockers with pickaxes were prizing up paving stones, housewives dragged dustbins from their yards, and shopkeepers brought empty crates and boxes. Lloyd helped carry a park bench, then pulled down a notice board from outside a municipal building. Learning from experience, the builders did a better job this time, using their materials economically and making sure the structure was sturdy.

Looking behind him again, Lloyd saw that a third barricade was beginning to rise farther east.

The people began to retreat from the first one and regroup behind the second. A few minutes later the police at last made a gap in the first barricade and poured through it. The first of them went after the few young men remaining, and Lloyd saw Dave and Lenny chased down an alley. The houses on either side were swiftly shut up, doors slamming and windows closing.

Then, Lloyd saw, the police did not know what to do next. They had broken through the barricade only to be confronted with another, stronger one. They seemed not to have the heart to begin dismantling the second. They milled around in the middle of Cable Street, talking desultorily, looking resentfully at the residents watching them from upstairs windows.

It was too early to proclaim victory, but all the same, Lloyd could not suppress a happy feeling of success. It was beginning to look as if the anti-Fascists were going to win the day.

He remained at his post for another quarter of an hour, but the police did nothing more, so he left the scene, found a telephone kiosk, and called in.

Bernie was cautious. "We don't know what's happening," he said. "There seems to be a lull everywhere, but we need to find out what the Fascists are up to. Can you get back to the Tower?"

Lloyd certainly could not fight his way through the massed police, but perhaps there was another way. "I could try going via St. George Street," he said doubtfully.

"Do the best you can. I want to know their next move."

Lloyd worked his way south through a maze of alleys. He hoped he was right about St. George Street. It was outside the contested area, but the crowds might have spilled over.

However, as he had hoped, there were no crowds there, even though he was still within earshot of the counterdemonstration, and could hear shouting and police whistles. A few women stood in the street talking, and a gaggle of little girls skipped a rope in the middle of the road. Lloyd headed west, breaking into a jog-trot, expecting to see crowds of demonstrators or police around every bend. He came across a few people who had strayed from the fracas—two men with bandaged heads, a woman in a ripped coat, a bemedaled veteran with his arm in a sling—but no crowds. He ran all the way to where the street ended at the Tower. He was able to walk unhindered into Tower Gardens.

The Fascists were still there.

That in itself was an achievement, Lloyd felt. It was now half past three: the marchers had been kept waiting here, not marching, for hours. He saw that their high spirits had evaporated. They were no longer singing or chanting but stood quiet and listless, lined up but not so neatly, their banners drooping, their bands silent. They already looked beaten.

However, there was a change a few minutes later. An open car emerged from a side street and drove alongside the Fascist lines. Cheers went up. The lines straightened, the officers saluted, the Fascists stood at attention. In the backseat of the car sat their leader, Sir Oswald Mosley, a handsome man with a mustache, wearing the uniform complete with cap. Rigidly straight-backed, he saluted repeatedly as his car went by at walking pace, as if he were a monarch inspecting his troops.

His presence reinvigorated his forces and worried Lloyd. This probably meant they were going to march as planned—otherwise why was he here? The car followed the Fascist line along a side street into the financial district. Lloyd waited. Half an hour later Mosley returned, this time on foot, again saluting and acknowledging cheers.

When he reached the head of the line, he turned and, accompanied by one of his officers, entered a side street.

Lloyd followed.

Mosley approached a group of older men standing in a huddle on the pavement. Lloyd was surprised to recognize Sir Philip Game, the commissioner of police, in a bow tie and trilby hat. The two men began an intense conversation. Sir Philip must surely be telling Sir Oswald that the crowd of counterdemonstrators was too huge to be dispersed. But what then would be his advice to the Fascists? Lloyd longed to get close enough to eavesdrop, but he decided not to risk arrest, and remained at a discreet distance.

The police commissioner did most of the talking. The Fascist leader nodded briskly several times and asked a few questions. Then the two men shook hands and Mosley walked away.

He returned to the park and conferred with his officers. Among them Lloyd recognized Boy Fitzherbert, wearing the same uniform as Mosley. Boy did not look so well in it: the trim military outfit did not suit his soft body and the lazy sensuality of his stance.

Mosley seemed to be giving orders. The other men saluted and moved away, no doubt to carry out his commands. What had he told them to do? Their only sensible option was to give up and go home. But if they had been sensible, they would not have been Fascists.

Whistles blew, orders were shouted, bands began to play, and the men stood to attention. They were going to march, Lloyd realized. The police must have assigned them a route. But what route?

Then the march began—and they went in the opposite direction. Instead of heading into the East End, they went west, into the financial district, deserted on a Sunday afternoon.

Lloyd could hardly believe it. "They've given up!" he said aloud, and a man standing near him said: "Looks like it, don't it?"

He watched for five minutes as the columns slowly moved off. When there was absolutely no doubt what was happening, he ran to a phone box and called Bernie. "They're marching away!" he said.

"What, into the East End?"

"No, the other way! They're going west, into the City. We've won!"

"Good God!" Bernie spoke to the other people with him. "Everybody! The Fascists are marching west. They've given up!"

Lloyd heard a burst of wild cheering in the room.

After a minute Bernie said: "Keep an eye on them. Let us know when they've all left Tower Gardens."

"Absolutely." Lloyd hung up.

He walked around the perimeter of the park in high spirits. It became clearer every minute that the Fascists were defeated. Their bands played, and they marched in time, but there was no spring in their step, and they no longer chanted that they were going to get rid of the Yids. The Yids had got rid of them.

As he passed the end of Byward Street, he saw Daisy again.

She was heading toward the distinctive black-and-cream Rolls-Royce, and she had to walk past Lloyd. He could not resist the temptation to gloat. "The people of the East End have rejected you and your filthy ideas," he said.

She stopped and looked at him, cool as ever. "We've been obstructed by a gang of thugs," she said with disdain.

"Still, you're marching in the other direction now."

"One battle doesn't make a war."

That might be true, Lloyd thought, but it was a pretty big battle. "You're not marching home with your boyfriend?"

"I prefer to drive," she said. "And he's not my boyfriend."

Lloyd's heart leaped in hope.

Then she said: "He's my husband."

Lloyd stared at her. He had never really believed she would be so stupid. He was speechless.

"It's true," she said, reading the disbelief in his face. "Didn't you see our engagement reported in the newspapers?"

"I don't read the society pages."

She showed him her left hand, with a diamond engagement ring and a gold wedding band. "We were married yesterday. We postponed our honeymoon to join the march today. Tomorrow we're flying to Deauville in Boy's plane."

She walked the few steps to the car and the chauffeur opened the door. "Home, please," she said.

"Yes, my lady."

Lloyd was so angry he wanted to hit someone.

Daisy looked back over her shoulder. "Good-bye, Mr. Williams."

He found his voice. "Good-bye, Miss Peshkov."

"Oh, no," she said. "I'm Viscountess Aberowen now."

She just loved saying it, Lloyd could tell. She was a titled lady, and it meant the world to her.

She got into the car and the chauffeur closed the door.

Lloyd turned away. He was ashamed to realize he had tears in his eyes. "Hell," he said aloud.

He sniffed, swallowing tears. He squared his shoulders and headed back toward the East End at a brisk walk. Today's triumph had been soured. He knew he was a fool to care about Daisy—clearly she did not care about him—but all the same it broke his heart that she was throwing herself away on Boy Fitzherbert.

He tried to put her out of his mind.

The police were getting back into their buses and leaving the scene. Lloyd had not been surprised by their brutality—he had lived in the East End all his life, and it was a rough neighborhood—but their anti-Semitism had shocked him. They had called every woman a Jewish whore, every man a Jew bastard. In Germany the police had supported the Nazis and sided with the Brownshirts. Would they do the same here? Surely not!

The crowd at Gardiner's Corner had begun to rejoice. The Jewish Lads' Brigade band was playing a jazz tune for men and women to dance to, and bottles of whisky and gin were passed from hand to hand. Lloyd decided to go to the London Hospital and check on Millie. Then he decided he should probably go to the Jewish Council headquarters and break the news to Bernie that Millie had been hurt.

Before he got any farther, he ran into Lenny Griffiths. "We sent the buggers packing!" Lenny said excitedly.

"We did, too." Lloyd grinned.

Lenny lowered his voice. "We beat the Fascists here, and we're going to beat them in Spain, too."

"When are you leaving?"

"Tomorrow. Me and Dave are catching a train to Paris in the morning."

Lloyd put his arm around Lenny's shoulders. "I'll come with you," he said.

CHAPTER FOUR

1937

Volodya Peshkov bent his head against the driving snow as he walked across the bridge over the Moscow River. He wore a heavy greatcoat, a fur hat, and a stout pair of leather boots. Few Muscovites were so well dressed. Volodya was lucky.

He always had good boots. His father, Grigori, was an army commander. Grigori was not a high flyer: although he was a hero of the Bolshevik revolution and a personal acquaintance of Stalin, his career had stalled at some point in the twenties. All the same, the family had always lived comfortably.

Volodya himself *was* a high flyer. After university he had got into the prestigious Military Intelligence Academy. A year later he had been posted to Red Army Intelligence headquarters.

His greatest piece of luck had been meeting Werner Franck in Berlin, while his father was a military attaché at the Soviet embassy there. Werner had been at the same school in a more junior class. Learning that young Werner hated Fascism, Volodya had suggested to him that he could best oppose the Nazis by spying for the Russians.

Werner had been only fourteen years old then, but now he was eighteen, he worked at the Air Ministry, he hated the Nazis even more, and he had a powerful radio transmitter and a codebook. He was resourceful and courageous, taking dreadful risks and gathering priceless information. And Volodya was his contact.

Volodya had not seen Werner for four years, but he remembered him vividly. Tall with striking red-blond hair, Werner looked and acted older than he was, and even at fourteen he had been enviably successful with women.

Werner had recently tipped him off about Markus, a diplomat at the German embassy in Moscow who was secretly a Communist. Volodya had sought Markus out and recruited him as a spy. For some months now Markus had been supplying a stream of reports that Volodya translated into Russian and passed to his boss. The latest was a fascinating account of how pro-Nazi American business leaders were supplying the right-wing Spanish rebels with trucks, tires, and oil. Texaco's chairman, the Hitler-admiring Torkild Rieber, was using the company's tankers to smuggle oil to the rebels in defiance of a specific request from President Roosevelt.

Volodya was on his way to meet Markus now.

He walked along Kutuzovsky Prospekt and turned toward the Kiev Station. Their rendezvous today was a workingmen's bar near the station. They never used the same place twice, but finished each meeting by arranging the next one: Volodya was meticulous about tradecraft. They always used cheap bars or cafés where Markus's diplomatic colleagues would never dream of going. If somehow Markus were to fall under suspicion and be followed by a German counterespionage agent, Volodya would know, for such a man would stand out from the other customers.

This place was called the Ukraine Bar. Like most buildings in Moscow, it was a timber structure. The windows were steamed up, so at least it would be warm inside. But Volodya did not go in immediately. There were further precautions to be taken. He crossed the street and ducked into the entrance of an apartment house. He stood in the cold hallway, looking out through a small window, watching the bar.

He wondered if Markus would show up. He always had, in the past, but Volodya could not feel sure. If he did show up, what information would he bring? Spain was the hot issue in international politics, but Red Army Intelligence was also passionately interested in German armaments. How many tanks were they producing per month? How many Mauser M34 machine guns per day? How good was the new Heinkel He 111 bomber? Volodya longed for such information to pass to his boss, Major Lemitov.

Half an hour went by, and Markus did not come.

Volodya began to worry. Had Markus been found out? He worked as assistant to the ambassador, and therefore saw everything that crossed the ambassador's desk, but Volodya had been urging him to seek access to other documents, especially the correspondence of military attachés. Had that been a mistake? Had someone noticed Markus sneaking a peek at cables that were none of his business?

Then Markus came along the street, a professorial figure in spectacles and an Austrian-style loden coat, white snowflakes spotting the green felt cloth. He turned into the Ukraine Bar. Volodya waited, watching. Another man followed Markus in, and Volodya frowned anxiously, but the second man was obviously a Russian worker, not a German counterespionage agent. He was a small, rat-faced man in a threadbare coat, his boots wrapped in rags, and he wiped the wet end of his pointed nose with his sleeve.

Volodya crossed the street and went into the bar.

It was a smoky place, none too clean, and it smelled of men who did not often bathe. On the walls were fading watercolors of Ukrainian scenery in cheap frames. It was midafternoon, and there were not many customers. The only woman in the place looked like an aging prostitute recovering from a hangover.

Markus was at the back of the room, hunched over an untasted glass of beer. He was in his thirties but looked older, with a neat fair beard and mustache. He had thrown open his coat, revealing a fur lining. The rat-faced Russian sat two tables away, rolling a cigarette.

As Volodya approached, Markus stood up and punched him in the mouth.

"You cowfucker!" he screamed in German. "You pig's cunt!"

Volodya was so shocked that for a moment he did nothing. His lips hurt and he tasted blood. Reflexively, he raised his arm to hit back. But he restrained himself.

Markus swung at him again, but this time Volodya was ready, and he easily dodged the wild blow.

"Why did you do it?" Markus yelled. "Why?"

Then, just as suddenly, he crumpled, falling back into his chair, burying his face in his hands, and beginning to sob.

Volodya spoke through bleeding lips. "Shut up, you fool," he said. He turned around and spoke to the other customers, who were all staring. "It's nothing—he's upset."

They all looked away, and one man left. Muscovites never voluntarily got involved in trouble. It was dangerous even to separate two scrapping drunks, in case one of them was powerful in the party. And they knew that Volodya was such a man: they could tell by his good coat.

Volodya turned back to Markus. In a lowered voice he said angrily: "What the hell was that for?" He spoke German; Markus's Russian was poor.

"You arrested Irina," the man replied, weeping. "You fucking bastard, you burned her nipples with a cigarette."

Volodya winced. Irina was Markus's Russian girlfriend. Volodya began to see what this might be about and he had a bad feeling. He sat down opposite Markus. "I didn't arrest Irina," he said. "And I'm sorry if she's been hurt. Just tell me what happened."

"They came for her in the middle of the night. Her mother told me. They wouldn't say who they were, but they weren't regular police detectives—they had better clothes. She doesn't know where they took her. They questioned her about me and accused her of being a spy. They tortured her and raped her. Then they threw her out."

"Fuck," said Volodya. "I'm really sorry."

"You're sorry? It must have been you that did it—who else?"

"This is nothing to do with Army Intelligence, I swear."

"Makes no difference," Markus said. "I'm finished with you, and I'm finished with Communism."

"There are sometimes casualties in the war against capitalism." It sounded glib even to Volodya as he said it.

"You young fool," Markus said savagely. "Don't you understand that socialism means freedom from this kind of shit?"

Volodya glanced up and saw a burly man in a leather coat come through the door. He was not here for a drink, Volodya knew instinctively.

Something was going on, and Volodya did not know what it was. He was new to this game, and right now he felt his lack of experience like a missing limb. He thought he might be in danger but he did not know what to do.

The newcomer approached the table where Volodya sat with Markus.

Then the rat-faced man stood up. He was about the same age as Volodya. Surprisingly, he spoke with an educated accent. "You two are under arrest."

Volodya cursed.

Markus jumped to his feet. "I am commercial attaché at German embassy!" he screamed in ungrammatical Russian. "You cannot arrest! I have diplomatic immunity!"

The other customers left the bar in a rush, shoving at each other as they squeezed through the door. Only two people remained: the bartender, nervously swiping at the counter with a filthy rag, and the prostitute, smoking a cigarette and staring into an empty vodka glass.

"You can't arrest me, either," Volodya said calmly. He took his identification card from his pocket. "I'm Lieutenant Peshkov, Army Intelligence. Who the fuck are you?"

"Dvorkin, NKVD."

The man in the leather coat said: "Berezovsky, NKVD."

The secret police. Volodya groaned; he might have known. The NKVD overlapped with Army Intelligence. He had been warned that the two organizations were always treading on each other's toes, but this was his first experience of it. He said to Dvorkin: "I suppose it was you who tortured this man's girlfriend."

Dvorkin wiped his nose on his sleeve; apparently that unpleasant habit was not part of his disguise. "She had no information."

"So you burned her nipples for nothing."

"Lucky for her. If she had been a spy, it would have been worse."

"It didn't occur to you to check with us first?"

"When did you ever check with us?"

Markus said: "I'm leaving."

Volodya felt desperate. He was about to lose a valuable asset. "Don't go," he pleaded. "We'll make this up to Irina somehow. We'll get her the best hospital treatment—"

"Fuck you," said Markus. "You'll never see me again." He walked out of the bar.

Dvorkin evidently did not know what to do. He did not want to let Markus go, but clearly he could not arrest him without looking foolish. In the end he said to Volodya: "You shouldn't let people speak to you that way. It makes you look weak. They should respect you."

"You prick," Volodya said. "Can't you see what you've done? That man was a good source of reliable intelligence—but now he'll never work for us again, thanks to your blundering."

Dvorkin shrugged. "As you said to him, sometimes there are casualties."

"God spare me," Volodya said, and he went out.

He felt vaguely nauseated as he walked back across the river. He was sickened by what the NKVD had done to an innocent woman, and downcast by the loss of his source. He boarded a tram; he was too junior to have a car. He brooded as the vehicle trundled through the snow to his place of work. He had to report to Major Lemitov, but he hesitated, wondering how to tell the story. He needed to make it clear that he was not to blame, yet avoid seeming to make excuses.

Army Intelligence headquarters stood on one edge of the Khodynka airfield, where a patient snowplow crawled up and down, keeping the runway clear. The architecture was peculiar: a two-story building with no windows in its outer walls surrounded a courtyard in which stood the nine-story head office, sticking up like a pointed finger out of a brick fist. Cigarette lighters and fountain pens could not be brought in, as they might set off the metal detectors at the entrance, so the army provided its staff with one of each inside. Belt buckles were a problem, too, so most people wore suspenders. The security was superfluous, of course. Muscovites would do anything to stay out of such a building; no one was mad enough to want to sneak inside.

Volodya shared an office with three other subalterns, their steel desks side by side on opposite walls. There was so little space that Volodya's desk prevented the door from opening fully. The office wit, Kamen, looked at his swollen lips and said: "Let me guess—her husband came home early."

"Don't ask," said Volodya.

On his desk was a decrypt from the radio section, the German words penciled letter by letter under the code groups.

The message was from Werner.

Volodya's first reaction was fear. Had Markus already reported what had happened to Irina, and persuaded Werner, too, to withdraw from espionage? Today seemed a sufficiently unlucky day for such a disaster.

But the message was the opposite of disastrous.

Volodya read with growing amazement. Werner explained that the German military had decided to send spies to Spain posing as anti-Fascist volunteers wanting to fight for the government side in the civil war. They would report clandestinely from behind the lines to German-manned listening stations in the rebel camp.

That in itself was red-hot information.

But there was more.

Werner had the names.

Volodya had to restrain himself from whooping with joy. A coup like this could happen only once in the lifetime of an intelligence man, he thought. It more than made up for losing Markus. Werner was solid gold. Volodya dreaded to think what risks he must have taken to purloin this list of names and smuggle it out of Air Ministry headquarters in Berlin.

He was tempted to run upstairs to Lemitov's office right away, but he restrained himself.

The four subalterns shared a typewriter. Volodya lifted the heavy old machine off Kamen's desk and put it on his own. Using the forefinger of each hand, he typed out a Russian translation of the message from Werner. While he was doing so, the daylight faded and powerful security lights came on outside the building.

Leaving a carbon copy in his desk drawer, he took the top copy and went upstairs. Lemitov was in. A good-looking man of about forty, he had dark hair slicked down with brilliantine. He was shrewd, and had a knack of thinking one step ahead of Volodya, who strove to emulate his forethought. He did not subscribe to the orthodox military view that army organization was about shouting and bullying, yet he was merciless with incompetent people. Volodya respected him and feared him.

"This might be tremendously useful information," Lemitov said when he had read the translation.

"Might be?" Volodya did not see any reason for doubt.

"It could be disinformation," Lemitov pointed out.

Volodya did not want to believe that, but he realized with a surge of disappointment that he had to acknowledge the possibility that Werner had been caught and turned into a double agent. "What kind of disinformation?" he asked dispiritedly. "Are these false names, to send us on a wild goose chase?"

"Perhaps. Or they might be the real names of genuine volunteers, Communists and socialists who have escaped from Nazi Germany and gone to Spain to fight for freedom. We could end up arresting real anti-Fascists."

"Hell."

Lemitov smiled. "Don't look so miserable! The information is still very good. We have our own spies in Spain—young Russian soldiers and officers who have 'volunteered' to join the International Brigades. They can investigate." He picked up a red pencil and wrote on the sheet of paper in small, neat handwriting. "Well done," he said.

Volodya took that for dismissal and went to the door.

Lemitov said: "Did you meet Markus today?"

Volodya turned back. "There was a problem."

"I guessed, by your mouth."

Volodya told the story. "So I lost a good source," he finished. "But I don't know what I could have done differently. Should I have told the NKVD about Markus and warned them off?"

"Fuck, no," said Lemitov. "They're completely untrustworthy. Never tell them anything. But don't worry—you haven't lost Markus. You can get him back easily."

"How?" Volodya said uncomprehendingly. "He hates us all now."

"Arrest Irina again."

"What?" Volodya was horrified. Had she not suffered enough? "Then he'll hate us even more."

"Tell him that if he doesn't continue to cooperate with us, we'll interrogate her all over again."

Volodya tried desperately to hide his revulsion. It was important not to appear squeamish. And he could see that Lemitov's plan would work. "Yes," he managed to say.

"Only this time," Lemitov went on, "tell him we'll put the lighted cigarettes up her cunt."

Volodya felt as if he might vomit. He swallowed hard and said: "Good idea. I'll pick her up now."

"Tomorrow is soon enough," said Lemitov. "Four in the morning. Maximum shock."

"Yes, sir." Volodya went out and closed the door behind him.

He stood in the corridor for a moment, feeling unsteady. Then a passing clerk looked strangely at him and he forced himself to walk away.

He was going to have to do this. He would not torture Irina, of course: the threat would be enough. But she would surely *think* she was going to be tortured all over again, and that would terrify her out of her wits. Volodya felt that in her place he might go insane. He had never imagined, when he joined the Red Army, that he might have to do such things. Of course the army was about killing people—he knew that—but torturing girls?

The building was emptying, lights being switched off in offices, men with hats on in the corridors. It was time to go home. Returning to his office, Volodya called the military police and arranged to meet a squad at three thirty in the morning to arrest Irina. Then he put on his coat and went to catch a tram home.

Volodya lived with his parents, Grigori and Katerina, and his sister, Anya, nineteen, who was still at university. On the tram he wondered if he could talk to his father about this. He imagined saying: "Do we have to torture people in a Communist society?" But he knew what the answer would be. It was a temporary necessity, essential to defend the revolution against spies and subversives in the pay of the capitalist imperialists. Perhaps he could ask: "How long will it be until we can abandon such dreadful practises?" Of course his father would not know, nor would anyone else.

On their return from Berlin, the Peshkov family had moved into Government House, sometimes called the House on the Embankment, an apartment block across the river from the Kremlin, occupied by members of the Soviet elite. It was a huge building in the Constructivist style, with more than five hundred flats.

Volodya nodded at the military policeman at the door, then passed through the grand lobby—so large that some evenings there was dancing to a jazz band—and went up in the elevator. The apartment was luxurious by Soviet standards, with constant hot water and a phone, but it was not as pleasant as their home in Berlin.

His mother was in the kitchen. Katerina was an indifferent cook and an unenthusiastic housekeeper, but Volodya's father adored her. Back in 1914, in St. Petersburg, he had rescued her from the unwelcome attentions of a bullying policeman, and he had been in love with her ever since. She was still attractive at forty-three, Volodya guessed, and while the family had been on the diplomatic circuit, she had learned how to dress more stylishly than most Russian women—though she was careful not to look Western, a serious offense in Moscow.

"Did you hurt your mouth?" she said to him after he kissed her hello.

"It's nothing." Volodya smelled chicken. "Special dinner?"

"Anya is bringing a boyfriend home."

"Ah! A fellow student?"

"I don't think so. I'm not sure what he does."

Volodya was pleased. He was fond of his sister, but he knew she was not beautiful. She was short and stumpy, and wore dull clothes in drab colors. She had not had many boyfriends, and it was good news that one liked her enough to come home with her.

He went to his room, took off his jacket, and washed his face and hands. His lips were almost back to normal: Markus had not hit him very hard. While he was drying his hands, he heard voices, and gathered that Anya and her boyfriend had arrived.

He put on a knitted cardigan, for comfort, and left his room. He went into the kitchen. Anya was sitting at the table with a small, rat-faced man Volodya recognized. "Oh, no!" Volodya said. "You!"

It was Ilya Dvorkin, the NKVD agent who had arrested Irina. His disguise had gone, and he was dressed in a normal dark suit and decent boots. He stared at Volodya in surprise. "Of course—Peshkov!" he said. "I didn't make the connection."

Volodya turned to his sister. "Don't tell me this is your boyfriend."

Anya said in dismay: "What's the matter?"

Volodya said: "We met earlier today. He screwed up an important army operation by sticking his nose in where it didn't belong."

"I was doing my job," said Dvorkin. He wiped the end of his nose on his sleeve.

"Some job!"

Katerina stepped in to rescue the situation. "Don't bring your work home," she said. "Volodya, please pour a glass of vodka for our guest."

Volodya said: "Really?"

His mother's eyes flashed anger. "Really!"

"Okay." Reluctantly, he took the bottle from the shelf. Anya got glasses from a cupboard and Volodya poured.

Katerina took a glass and said: "Now, let's start again. Ilya, this is my son, Vladimir, who we always call Volodya. Volodya, this is Anya's friend Ilya, who has come to dinner. Why don't you shake hands."

Volodya had no option but to shake the man's hand.

Katerina put snacks on the table: smoked fish, pickled cucumber, sliced sausage. "In summer we have salad that I grow at the dacha, but at this time of year of course there is nothing," she said apologetically. Volodya realized she was keen to impress Ilya. Did his mother really want Anya to marry this creep? He supposed she must.

Grigori came in, wearing his army uniform, all smiles, sniffing the chicken and rubbing his hands together. At forty-eight he was red-faced and corpulent: it was hard to imagine him storming the Winter Palace as he had in 1917. He must have been thinner then.

He kissed his wife with relish. Volodya thought his mother was thankful for his father's unabashed lust without actually returning it. She would smile when he patted her bottom, hug him when he embraced her, and kiss him as often as he wanted, but she was never the initiator. She liked him, respected him, and seemed happy being married to him; but clearly she did not burn with desire. Volodya would want more than that from marriage.

The matter was purely hypothetical: Volodya had had a dozen or so short-term girlfriends but had not yet met a woman he wanted to marry.

Volodya poured his father a shot of vodka, and Grigori tossed it back with relish, then took some smoked fish. "So, Ilya, what work do you do?"

"I'm with the NKVD," Ilya said proudly.

"Ah! A very good organization to belong to!"

Grigori did not really think this, Volodya suspected; he was just trying to be friendly. Volodya thought the family should be unfriendly, in the hope that they could drive Ilya away. He said: "I suppose, Father, that when the rest of the world follows the Soviet Union in adopting the Communist system, there will no longer be a need for the secret police, and the NKVD can then be abolished."

Grigori chose to treat the question lightly. "No police at all!" he said jovially. "No criminal trials, no prisons. No counterespionage department, as there will be no spies. No army, either, since we will have no enemies! What will we all do for a living?" He laughed heartily. "This, however, may still be some distance in the future."

Ilya looked suspicious, as if he felt something subversive was being said but could not put his finger on it.

Katerina brought to the table a plate of black bread and five bowls of hot borscht, and they all began to eat. "When I was a boy in the countryside," Grigori said, "all winter long my mother would save vegetable peelings, apple cores, the discarded outer leaves of cabbages, the hairy part of the onion, anything like that, in a big old barrel outside the house, where it all froze. Then, in the spring, when the snow melted, she would use it to make borscht. That's what borscht really is, you know—soup made from peelings. You youngsters have no idea how well off you are."

There was a knock at the door. Grigori frowned, not expecting anyone, but Katerina said: "Oh, I forgot! Konstantin's daughter is coming."

Grigori said: "You mean Zoya Vorotsyntsev? The daughter of Magda the midwife?"

"I remember Zoya," said Volodya. "Skinny kid with blond ringlets."

"She's not a kid anymore," Katerina said. "She's twenty-four and a scientist." She stood up to go to the door.

Grigori frowned. "We haven't seen her since her mother died. Why has she suddenly made contact?"

"She wants to talk to you," Katerina replied.

"To me? About what?"

"Physics." Katerina went out.

Grigori said proudly: "Her father, Konstantin, and I were delegates to the Petrograd Soviet in 1917. We issued the famous Order Number One." His face darkened. "He died, sadly, after the Civil War."

Volodya said: "He must have been young—what did he die of?"

Grigori glanced at Ilya and quickly looked away. "Pneumonia," he said, and Volodya knew he was lying.

Katerina returned, followed by a woman who took Volodya's breath away.

She was a classic Russian beauty, tall and slim, with light blond hair, blue eyes so pale they were almost colorless, and perfect white skin. She wore a simple Nile-green dress whose plainness only drew attention to her slender figure.

She was introduced all around; then she sat at the table and accepted a bowl of borscht. Grigori said: "So, Zoya, you're a scientist."

"I'm a graduate student, doing my doctorate, and I teach undergraduate classes," she said.

"Volodya here works in Red Army Intelligence," Grigori said proudly.

"How interesting," she said, obviously meaning the opposite.

Volodya realized that Grigori saw Zoya as a potential daughter-in-law. He hoped his father would not hint at this too heavily. He had already made up his mind to ask her for a date before the end of the evening. But he could manage that by himself. He did not need his father's help. On the contrary: unsubtle parental boasting might put her off.

"How is the soup?" Katerina asked Zoya.

"Delicious, thank you."

Volodya was already getting the impression of a matter-of-fact personality behind the gorgeous exterior. It was an intriguing combination: a beautiful woman who made no attempt to charm.

Anya cleared away the soup bowls while Katerina brought the main course, chicken and potatoes cooked in a pot. Zoya tucked in, stuffing the food into her mouth, chewing and swallowing and eating more. Like most Russians, she did not often see food this good.

Volodya said: "What kind of science do you do, Zoya?"

With evident regret she stopped eating to answer. "I'm a physicist," she said. "We're trying to understand the atom: what its components are, what holds them together."

"Is that interesting?"

"Completely fascinating." She put down her fork. "We're finding out what the universe is really made of. There's nothing so exciting." Her eyes lit up. Apparently physics was the one thing that could distract her from her dinner.

Ilya spoke up for the first time. "Ah, but how does all this theoretical stuff help the revolution?"

Zoya's eyes blazed anger, and Volodya liked her even more. "Some comrades make the mistake of undervaluing pure science, preferring practical research," she said. "But technical developments, such as improved aircraft, are ultimately based on theoretical advances."

Volodya concealed a grin. Ilya had been demolished with one casual swipe.

But Zoya had not finished. "This is why I wanted to talk to you, sir," she said to Grigori. "We physicists read all the scientific journals published in the West—they foolishly reveal their results to the whole world. And we have lately realized that they are making alarming forward leaps in their understanding of atomic physics. Soviet science is in grave danger of falling behind. I wonder if Comrade Stalin is aware of this."

The room went quiet. The merest hint of a criticism of Stalin was dangerous. "He knows most things," Grigori said.

"Of course," Zoya said automatically. "But perhaps there are times when loyal comrades such as yourself need to draw important matters to his attention."

"Yes, that's true."

Ilya said: "Undoubtedly Comrade Stalin believes that science should be consistent with Marxist-Leninist ideology."

Volodya saw a flash of defiance in Zoya's eyes, but she dropped her gaze and said humbly: "There can be no question that he is right. We scientists must clearly redouble our efforts."

This was horseshit, and everyone in the room knew it, but no one would say so. The proprieties had to be observed.

"Indeed," said Grigori. "Nevertheless, I will mention it next time I get a chance to talk to the comrade general secretary of the party. He may wish to look into it further."

"I hope so," said Zoya. "We want to be ahead of the West."

"And how about after work, Zoya?" said Grigori cheerily. "Do you have a boyfriend, a fiancé perhaps?"

Anya protested: "Dad! That's none of our business."

Zoya did not seem to mind. "No fiancé," she said mildly. "No boyfriend."

"As bad as my son, Volodya! He, too, is single. He is twenty-three years old, well educated, tall, and handsome—yet he has no fiancée!"

Volodya squirmed at the heavy-handedness of this hint.

"Hard to believe," Zoya said, and as she glanced at Volodya, he saw a gleam of humor in her eyes.

Katerina put a hand on her husband's arm. "Enough," she said. "Stop embarrassing the poor girl."

The doorbell rang.

"Again?" said Grigori.

"This time I have no idea who it might be," said Katerina as she left the kitchen.

She returned with Volodya's boss, Major Lemitov.

Startled, Volodya jumped to his feet. "Good evening, sir," he said. "This is my father, Grigori Peshkov. Dad, may I present Major Lemitov?"

Lemitov saluted smartly.

Grigori said: "At ease, Lemitov. Sit down and have some chicken. Has my son done something wrong?"

That was precisely the thought that was making Volodya's hands shake.

"No, sir—rather the contrary. But . . . I was hoping for a private word with you and him."

Volodya relaxed a little. Perhaps he was not in trouble after all.

"Well, we've just about finished dinner," Grigori said, standing up. "Let's go into my study."

Lemitov looked at Ilya. "Aren't you with the NKVD?" he said.

"And proud of it. Dvorkin is the name."

"Oh! You tried to arrest Volodya this afternoon."

"I thought he was behaving like a spy. I was right, wasn't I?"

"You must learn to arrest enemy spies, not our own." Lemitov went out.

Volodya grinned. That was the second time Dvorkin had been put down.

Volodya, Grigori, and Lemitov crossed the hallway. The study was a small room, sparsely furnished. Grigori took the only easy chair.

Lemitov sat at a small table. Volodya closed the door and remained standing.

Lemitov said to Volodya: "Does your comrade father know about this afternoon's message from Berlin?"

"No, sir."

"You'd better tell him."

Volodya related the story of the spies in Spain. His father was delighted. "Well done!" he said. "Of course this might be disinformation, but I doubt it; the Nazis aren't that imaginative. However, we are. We can arrest the spies and use their radios to send misleading messages to the right-wing rebels."

Volodya had not thought of that. Dad may play the fool with Zoya, he thought, but he still has a sharp mind for intelligence work.

"Exactly," said Lemitov.

Grigori said to Volodya: "Your school friend Werner is a brave man." He turned back to Lemitov. "How do you plan to handle this?"

"We'll need some good intelligence men in Spain to investigate these Germans. It shouldn't be too difficult. If they really are spies, there will be evidence: codebooks, wireless sets, and so on." He hesitated. "I've come here to suggest we send your son."

Volodya was astonished. He had not seen that coming.

Grigori's face fell. "Ah," he said thoughtfully. "I must confess, the prospect fills me with dismay. We would miss him so much." Then a look of resignation came over his face, as if he realized he did not really have a choice. "The defense of the revolution must come first, of course."

"An intelligence man needs field experience," Lemitov said. "You and I have seen action, sir, but the younger generation have never been on the battlefield."

"True, true. How soon would he go?"

"In three days' time."

Volodya could see that his father was trying desperately to think of a reason to keep him at home, but finding none. Volodya himself was excited. Spain! He thought of bloodred wine, black-haired girls with strong brown legs, and hot sunshine instead of Moscow snow. It would be dangerous, of course, but he had not joined the army to be safe.

Grigori said: "Well, Volodya, what do you think?"

Volodya knew his father wanted him to come up with an objection. The only drawback he could think of was that he would not have time to get to know the stunning Zoya. "It is a wonderful opportunity," he said. "I'm honored to have been chosen."

"Very well," said his father.

"There is one small problem," Lemitov said. "It has been decided that Army Intelligence will investigate but not actually carry out the arrests. That will be the prerogative of the NKVD." His smile was humorless. "I'm afraid you will be working with your friend Dvorkin."

ii

It was amazing, Lloyd Williams thought, how quickly you could come to love a place. He had been in Spain for only ten months, but already his passion for the country was almost as strong as his attachment to Wales. He loved to see a rare flower blooming in the scorched landscape; he enjoyed sleeping in the afternoon; he liked the way there was wine to drink even when there was nothing to eat. He had experienced flavors he had never tasted before: olives, paprika, chorizo, and the fiery spirit they called *orujo*.

He stood on a rise, staring across a heat-hazed landscape with a map in his hand. There were a few meadows beside a river, and some trees on distant mountainsides, but in between was a barren, featureless desert of dusty soil and rock. "Not much cover for our advance," he said anxiously.

Beside him, Lenny Griffiths said: "It's going to be a bloody hard battle."

Lloyd looked at his map. Saragossa straddled the Ebro River about a hundred miles from its Mediterranean end. The town dominated communications in the Aragon region. It was a major crossroads, a rail junction, and the meeting of three rivers. Here the Spanish army confronted the antidemocratic rebels across an arid no-man's-land.

Some people called the government forces Republicans and the rebels Nationalists, but these were misleading names. Many people on both sides were republicans, in that they did not want to be ruled by a king. And they were all nationalist, in that they loved their country and were willing to die for it. Lloyd thought of them as the government and the rebels.

Right now Saragossa was held by Franco's rebels, and Lloyd was looking toward the town from a vantage point fifty miles south. "Still, if we can take the town, the enemy will be bottled up in the north for another winter," he said.

"If," said Lenny.

It was a grim prognosis, Lloyd thought gloomily, when the best he could wish for was that the rebel advance might be halted. But no victory was in sight this year for the government.

All the same, a part of Lloyd was looking forward to the fight. He had been in Spain for ten months, and this would be his first taste of action. Until now he had been an instructor in a base camp. As soon as the Spaniards discovered he had been in Britain's Officer Training Corps, they had speeded him through his induction, made him a lieutenant, and put him in charge of new arrivals. He had to drill them until obeying orders became a reflex, march them until their feet stopped bleeding and their blisters turned to calluses, and show them how to strip down and clean what few rifles were available.

But the flood of volunteers had now slowed to a trickle, and the instructors had been moved to fighting battalions.

Lloyd wore a beret, a zipped blouson with his badge of rank roughly hand-sewn to the sleeve, and corduroy breeches. He carried a short Spanish Mauser rifle, firing seven-millimeter ammunition that had presumably been stolen from some Civil Guard arsenal.

Lloyd, Lenny, and Dave had been split up for a while, but the three had been reunited in the British battalion of the Fifteenth International

Brigade for the coming battle. Lenny now had a black beard and looked a decade older than his seventeen years. He had been made a sergeant, though he had no uniform, just blue dungarees and a striped bandana. He looked more like a pirate than a soldier.

Now Lenny said: "Anyway, this attack has nothing to do with bottling up the rebels. It's political. This region has always been dominated by the anarchists."

Lloyd had seen anarchism in action during a brief spell in Barcelona. It was a cheerfully fundamentalist form of Communism. Officers and men got the same pay. The dining rooms of the grand hotels had been turned into canteens for the workers. Waiters would hand back a tip, explaining amiably that the practise of tipping was demeaning. Posters everywhere condemned prostitution as exploitation of female comrades. There had been a wonderful atmosphere of liberation and camaraderie. The Russians hated it.

Lenny went on: "Now the government has brought Communist troops from the Madrid area and amalgamated us all into the new Army of the East—under overall Communist command, of course."

This kind of talk made Lloyd despair. The only way to win was for all the left-wing factions to work together, as they had—in the end, at least—at the Battle of Cable Street. But anarchists and Communists had been fighting each other in the streets of Barcelona. He said: "Prime Minister Negrín isn't a Communist."

"He might as well be."

"He understands that without the support of the Soviet Union we're finished."

"But does that mean we abandon democracy and let the Communists take over?"

Lloyd nodded. Every discussion about the government ended the same way: Do we have to do everything the Soviets want just because they are the only people who will sell us guns?

They walked down the hill. Lenny said: "We'll have a nice cup of tea, now, is it?"

"Yes, please. Two lumps of sugar in mine."

It was a standing joke. Neither of them had had tea for months.

They came to their camp by the river. Lenny's platoon had taken over a little cluster of crude stone buildings that had probably been cowsheds until the war drove the farmers away. A few yards upriver a boathouse had been occupied by some Germans from the Eleventh International Brigade.

Lloyd and Lenny were met by Lloyd's cousin Dave Williams. Like Lenny, Dave had aged ten years in one. He looked thin and hard, his skin tanned and dusty, his eyes wrinkled with squinting into the sun. He wore the khaki tunic and trousers, leather belt pouches, and ankle-buckled boots that formed the standard-issue uniform—though few soldiers had a complete set. He had a red cotton scarf around his neck. He carried a Russian Mosin-Nagant rifle with the old-fashioned spike bayonet reversed, making the weapon less clumsy. At his belt he had a German nine-millimeter Luger that he must have taken from the corpse of a rebel officer. Apparently he was very accurate with rifle or pistol.

"We've got a visitor," he said excitedly.

"Who is he?"

"She!" said Dave, and pointed.

In the shade of a misshapen black poplar tree, a dozen British and German soldiers were talking to a startlingly beautiful woman.

"Oh, *Duw*," said Lenny, using the Welsh word for *God*. "She's a sight for sore eyes."

She looked about twenty-five, Lloyd thought, and she was petite, with big eyes and a mass of black hair pinned up and topped by a fore-and-aft army cap. Somehow her baggy uniform seemed to cling to her like an evening gown.

A volunteer called Heinz who knew that Lloyd understood German spoke to him in that language. "This is Teresa, sir. She has come to teach us to read."

Lloyd nodded understanding. The International Brigades consisted of foreign volunteers mixed with Spanish soldiers, and literacy was a problem with the Spanish. They had spent their childhood chanting the catechism in village schools run by the Catholic Church. Many priests did not teach the children to read, for fear that in later life they would get hold of socialist books. As a result, only about half the population had been literate under the monarchy. The republican government elected in 1931 had improved education, but there remained millions of Spaniards who could not read or write, and classes for soldiers continued even in the front line.

"I'm illiterate," said Dave, who was not.

"Me, too," said Joe Eli, who taught Spanish literature at Columbia University in New York.

Teresa spoke in Spanish. Her voice was low and calm and very sexy. "How many times do you think I have heard this joke?" she said, but she did not seem very cross.

Lenny moved closer. "I'm Sergeant Griffiths," he said. "I'll do anything I can to help you, of course." His words were practical, but his tone of voice made them sound like an amorous invitation.

She gave him a dazzling smile. "That would be most helpful," she said.

Lloyd spoke formally to her in his best Spanish. "I'm so very glad you're here, señorita." He had spent much of the last ten months studying the language. "I am Lieutenant Williams. I can tell you exactly which members of the group require lessons . . . and which do not."

Lenny said dismissively: "But the lieutenant has to go to Bujaraloz to get our orders." Bujaraloz was the small town where government forces had set up headquarters. "Perhaps you and I should look around here for a suitable place to hold classes." He might have been suggesting a walk in the moonlight.

Lloyd smiled and nodded agreement. He was happy to let Lenny romance Teresa. He himself was in no mood for flirting, whereas Lenny seemed already in love. In Lloyd's opinion Lenny's chances were close to zero. Teresa was an educated twenty-five-year-old who probably got a dozen propositions a day, and Lenny was a seventeen-year-old coal miner who had not taken a bath for a month. But he said nothing: Teresa seemed capable of looking after herself.

A new figure appeared, a man of Lloyd's age who looked vaguely familiar. He was dressed better than the soldiers, in wool breeches and a cotton shirt, and had a handgun in a buttoned holster. His hair was cut so short it looked like stubble, a style favored by Russians. He was only a lieutenant, but had an air of authority, even power. He said in fluent German: "I am looking for Lieutenant Garcia."

"He's not here," said Lloyd in the same language. "Where have you and I met before?"

The Russian seemed shocked and irritated at the same time, like one who finds a snake in his bedroll. "We have never met," he said firmly. "You are mistaken."

Lloyd snapped his fingers. "Berlin," he said. "Nineteen thirty-three. We were attacked by Brownshirts."

A look of relief came briefly over the man's face, as if he had been expecting something worse. "Yes, I was there," he said. "My name is Vladimir Peshkov."

"But we called you Volodya."

"Yes."

"At that scrap in Berlin you were with a boy called Werner Franck."

Volodya looked panicked for a moment, then hid his feelings with an effort. "I know no one of that name."

Lloyd decided not to press the point. He could guess why Volodya was jumpy. The Russians were as terrified as everyone else of their secret police, the NKVD, who were operating in Spain and had a reputation for brutality. To them, any Russian who was friendly with foreigners might be a traitor. "I'm Lloyd Williams."

"I do remember." Volodya looked at him with a penetrating blue-eyed stare. "How strange that we should meet again here."

"Not so strange, really," Lloyd said. "We fight the Fascists wherever we can."

"Can I have a quiet word?"

"Of course."

They walked a few yards away from the others. Peshkov said: "There is a spy in Garcia's platoon."

Lloyd was astonished. "A spy? Who?"

"A German called Heinz Bauer."

"Why, that's him in the red shirt. A spy? Are you sure?"

Peshkov did not bother to answer that question. "I'd like you to summon him to your dugout, if you have one, or some other private place." Peshkov looked at his wristwatch. "In one hour, an arrest unit will be here to pick him up."

"I'm using that little shed as my office," said Lloyd, pointing. "But I need to speak to my commanding officer about this." The CO was a Communist, and unlikely to interfere, but Lloyd wanted time to think.

"If you wish." Volodya clearly did not care what Lloyd's commanding officer thought. "I want the spy taken quietly, without any fuss. I have explained to the arrest unit the importance of discretion." He sounded as if he was not sure his wishes would be obeyed. "The fewer people who know, the better."

"Why?" said Lloyd, but before Volodya could reply, he figured out the answer for himself. "You're hoping to turn him into a double agent, sending misleading reports to the enemy. But if too many people know he has been caught, then other spies may warn the rebels, and they will not believe the disinformation."

"It is better not to speculate about such matters," Peshkov said severely. "Now let us go to your shed."

"Wait a minute," said Lloyd. "How do you know he is a spy?"

"I can't tell you without compromising security."

"That's a bit unsatisfactory."

Peshkov looked exasperated. Clearly he was not used to being told that his explanations were unsatisfactory. Discussion of orders was a feature of the Spanish Civil War that the Russians particularly detested.

Before Peshkov could say anything further, two more men appeared and approached the group under the tree. One of the newcomers wore a leather jacket despite the heat. The other, who seemed to be in charge, was a scrawny man with a long nose and a receding chin.

Peshkov let out an exclamation of anger. "Too early!" he said; then he called out something indignant in Russian.

The scrawny man made a dismissive gesture. In rough Spanish he said: "Which one is Heinz Bauer?"

No one answered. The scrawny man wiped the end of his nose with his sleeve.

Then Heinz moved. He did not immediately flee, but cannoned into the man in the leather jacket, knocking him down. Then he dashed away—but the scrawny man stuck out a leg and tripped him up.

Heinz fell hard, his body skidding on the dry soil. He lay stunned—only for a moment, but it was a moment too long. As he got to his knees, the two men pounced on him and knocked him down again.

He lay still, but all the same they started to beat him up. They drew wooden clubs. Standing either side of him they took turns to hit his head and body, raising their arms above their heads and striking down in a vicious ballet. In a few seconds there was blood all over Heinz's face. He tried desperately to escape, but when he got to his knees, they pushed him down again. Then he curled up in a ball, whimpering. He was clearly finished, but they were not. They clubbed the helpless man again and again.

Lloyd found himself shouting a protest and pulling the scrawny man off. Lenny did the same to the other one. Lloyd grabbed his man in a bear hug and lifted him; Lenny knocked his man to the ground. Then Lloyd heard Volodya say in English: "Stand still, or I'll shoot!"

Lloyd let go of his man and turned, incredulous. Volodya had drawn his sidearm, a standard-issue Russian Nagant M1895 revolver, and cocked it. "Threatening an officer with a weapon is a court-martial offense in every army in the world," Lloyd said. "You're in deep trouble, Volodya."

"Don't be a fool," said Volodya. "When was the last time a Russian was in trouble in this army?" But he lowered the gun.

The man in the leather jacket raised his club as if to hit Lenny, but Volodya barked: "Back off, Berezovsky!" and the man obeyed.

Other soldiers appeared, drawn by the mysterious magnetism that attracts men to a fight, and in seconds there were twenty of them.

The scrawny man pointed a finger at Lloyd. Speaking English with a heavy accent, he said: "You have interfered in matters that do not concern you!"

Lloyd helped Heinz to his feet. He was groaning in pain and covered in blood.

"You people can't just march in and start beating people up!" Lloyd said to the scrawny man. "Where's your authority?"

"This German is a Trotsky-Fascist spy!" the man screeched.

Volodya said: "Shut up, Ilya."

Ilya took no notice. "He has been photographing documents!" he said.

"Where is your evidence?" Lloyd said calmly.

Ilya clearly did not know or care about the evidence. But Volodya sighed and said: "Look in his kit bag."

Lloyd nodded to Mario Rivera, a corporal. "Go and check," he said.

Corporal Rivera ran to the boathouse and disappeared inside.

But Lloyd had a dreadful feeling Volodya was telling the truth. He said: "Even if you're right, Ilya, you could use a little courtesy."

Ilya said: "Courtesy? This is a war, not an English tea party."

"It might save you from getting into unnecessary fights."

Ilya said something contemptuous in Russian.

Rivera emerged from the building carrying a small, expensive-looking camera and a sheaf of official papers. He showed them to Lloyd. The top document was yesterday's general order for deployment of troops ahead of the coming assault. The paper bore a wine stain of familiar shape, and Lloyd realized with a shock that it was his own copy, and must have been purloined from his shed.

He looked at Heinz, who straightened, gave the Fascist salute, and said: "*Heil* Hitler!"

Ilya looked triumphant.

Volodya said: "Well, Ilya, you have now ruined the prisoner's value as a double agent. Another coup for the NKVD. Congratulations." And he walked off.

iii

Lloyd went into battle for the first time on Tuesday, August 24.

His side, the elected government, had eighty thousand men. The antidemocratic rebels had fewer than half that. The government also had two hundred aircraft against the rebels' fifteen.

To make the most of this superiority, the government advanced over a wide front, a north-south line sixty miles long, so that the rebels could not concentrate their limited numbers.

It was a good plan—so why, Lloyd asked himself two days later, was it not working?

It had started well enough. On the first day the government had taken two villages north of Saragossa and two to the south. Lloyd's group, in the south, had overcome fierce resistance to take a village called Codo. The only failure was the central push, up the river valley, which had stalled at a place called Fuentes de Ebro.

Lloyd had been scared, before the battle, and spent the night awake, imagining what was to come, as he sometimes did before a boxing match. But once the fighting started, he was too busy to worry. The worst moment was advancing across the barren scrubland, with no cover but stunted bushes, while the defenders fired from inside stone buildings. Even then, what he had felt was not fear but a kind of desperate cunning, zigzagging as he ran, crawling and rolling when the bullets came too near, then getting up and running, bent double, a few more yards. The main problem was shortage of ammunition: they had to make every shot count. They took Codo by force of numbers, and Lloyd, Lenny, and Dave ended the day unhurt.

The rebels were tough and brave—but so were the government forces. The foreign brigades were made up of idealistic volunteers who had come to Spain knowing they might have to give their lives. Because of their reputation for courage they were often chosen to spearhead attacks.

The assault began to go wrong on the second day. The northern forces had stayed put, reluctant to advance because of lack of intelligence about rebel defenses—a feeble excuse, Lloyd thought. The central group still could not take Fuentes de Ebro, despite being reinforced on the third day, and Lloyd was appalled to hear that they had lost nearly all their tanks to devastating defensive fire. In the south Lloyd's group, instead of pushing forward, was directed to make a sideways move, to the riverside village of Quinto. Once again they had to overcome determined defenders in house-to-house fighting. When the enemy surrendered, Lloyd's group took a thousand prisoners.

Now Lloyd sat in the evening light outside a church that had been wrecked by artillery fire, surrounded by the smoking ruins of houses and the strangely still bodies of the recently dead. A group of exhausted men gathered around him: Lenny, Dave, Joe Eli, Corporal Rivera, and a Welshman called Muggsy Morgan. There were so many Welshmen in Spain that someone had made up a limerick poking fun at the similarity in their names:

> *There was a young fellow named Price*
> *And another young fellow named Price*
> *And a fellow named Roberts*
> *And a fellow named Roberts*
> *And another young fellow named Price.*

The men were smoking, waiting quietly to see whether there would be any dinner, too weary even to banter with Teresa, who was, remarkably, still with them, as the transport due to take her to the rear had failed to appear. They could hear occasional bursts of shooting as mopping up continued a few streets away.

"What have we gained?" Lloyd said to Dave. "We used scarce ammunition, we lost a lot of men, and we're no farther forward. Worse, we've given the Fascists time to bring up reinforcements."

"I can tell you the fucking reason," Dave said in his East End accent. His soul had hardened even more than his body, and he had become cynical and contemptuous. "Our officers are more afraid of their commissars than of the fucking enemy. At the least excuse they can be branded as Trotsky-Fascist spies and tortured to death, so they're terrified of sticking their necks out. They'd rather sit still than move, they won't do anything on their own initiative, and they never take risks. I bet they don't shit without an order in writing."

Lloyd wondered whether Dave's scornful analysis was right. The Communists never ceased to talk about the need for a disciplined army with a clear chain of command. By that they meant an army following Russian orders, but all the same Lloyd saw their point. However, too much discipline could stifle thinking. Was that what was going wrong?

Lloyd did not want to believe it. Surely Social Democrats and Communists and anarchists could fight in their common cause without one group tyrannizing the others; they all hated Fascism, and they all believed in a future society that was fairer to everyone.

He wondered what Lenny thought, but Lenny was sitting next to Teresa, talking to her in a low voice. She giggled at something he said, and Lloyd guessed he must be making progress. It was a good sign when you could make a girl laugh. Then she touched his arm, said a few words, and stood up. Lenny said: "Hurry back." She smiled over her shoulder.

Lucky Lenny, thought Lloyd, but he felt no envy. A passing romance held no appeal for him: he did not see the point. He was an all-or-nothing man, he supposed. The only girl he had ever really wanted had been Daisy. She was now Boy Fitzherbert's wife, and Lloyd still had not met the girl who might take her place in his heart. He would, one day, he felt sure, but, meanwhile, he was not much attracted to temporary substitutes even when they were as alluring as Teresa.

Someone said: "Here come the Russians." The speaker was Jasper Johnson, a black American electrician from Chicago. Lloyd looked up to see a dozen or so military advisers walking through the village like conquerors. The Russians were recognizable by their leather jackets and buttoned holsters. "Strange thing, I didn't see them while we were fighting," Jasper went on sarcastically. "I guess they must have been in a different part of the battlefield."

Lloyd looked around, making sure that no political commissars were nearby to hear this subversive talk.

As the Russians passed through the graveyard of the ruined church, Lloyd spotted Ilya Dvorkin, the weaselly secret policeman he had clashed with a week ago. The Russian crossed paths with Teresa and stopped to speak to her. Lloyd heard him say something in bad Spanish about dinner.

She replied, he spoke again, and she shook her head, evidently refusing. She turned to walk away, but he took hold of her arm, detaining her.

Lloyd saw Lenny sit upright, looking alertly at the tableau, the two figures framed by a stone archway that no longer led anywhere.

"Oh, shit," said Lloyd.

Teresa tried again to move away, and Ilya seemed to tighten his grip.

Lenny moved to get up, but Lloyd put a hand on his shoulder and pushed him down. "Let me deal with this," he said.

Dave murmured a low warning. "Careful, mate—he's in the NKVD. Best not to mess with those fucking bastards."

Lloyd walked over to Teresa and Ilya.

The Russian saw him and said in Spanish: "Get lost."

Lloyd said: "Hello, Teresa."

She said: "I can handle this. Don't worry."

Ilya looked more closely at Lloyd. "I know you," he said. "You tried to prevent the arrest of a dangerous Trotsky-Fascist spy last week."

Lloyd said: "And is this young lady also a dangerous Trotsky-Fascist spy? I thought I just heard you ask her to have dinner with you."

Ilya's sidekick Berezovsky appeared and stood aggressively close to Lloyd.

Out of the corner of his eye, Lloyd saw Dave draw the Luger from his belt.

This was getting out of control.

Lloyd said: "I came to tell you, señorita, that Colonel Bobrov wants to see you in his headquarters immediately. Please follow me and I'll take you to him." Bobrov was a senior Russian military "adviser." He had not invited Teresa, but it was a plausible story, and Ilya did not know it was a lie.

For a frozen moment Lloyd could not tell which way it was going to go. Then the bang of a nearby gunshot was heard, perhaps from the next street. It seemed to return the Russians to reality. Teresa again moved away from Ilya, and this time he let her go.

Ilya pointed a finger aggressively at Lloyd's face. "I'll see you again," he said, and he made a dramatic exit, followed doglike by Berezovsky.

Dave said: "Stupid prick."

Ilya pretended not to hear.

They all sat down. Dave said: "You've made a bad enemy, Lloyd."

"I didn't have much choice."

"All the same, watch your back from now on."

"An argument about a girl," Lloyd said dismissively. "Happens a thousand times a day."

As darkness fell, a handbell summoned them to a field kitchen. Lloyd got a bowl of thin stew, a slab of dry bread, and a big cup of red wine so harsh tasting that he imagined it taking the enamel off his teeth. He dipped his bread in the wine, improving both.

When the food was gone, he was still hungry, as usual. He said: "We'll have a nice cup of tea, shall we?"

"Aye," said Lenny. "Two lumps of sugar, please."

They unrolled their thin blankets and prepared to sleep. Lloyd went in search of a latrine, found none, and relieved himself in a small orchard on the edge of the village. There was a three-quarter moon, and he could see the dusty leaves on olive trees that had survived the shelling.

As he buttoned up, he heard a footstep. He turned around slowly—too slowly. By the time he saw Ilya's face, the club was coming down on his head. He felt an agonizing pain and fell to the ground. Dazed, he looked up. Berezovsky held a short-barreled revolver pointed at his head. Beside him, Ilya said: "Don't move or you'll be dead."

Lloyd was terrified. Desperately he shook his head to clear it. This was insane. "Dead?" he said incredulously. "And how will you explain the murder of a lieutenant?"

"Murder?" said Ilya. He smiled. "This is the front line. A stray bullet got you." He switched to English. "Jolly bad luck."

Lloyd realized with despair that Ilya was right. When his body was found, it would look as if he had been killed in the battle.

What a way to die.

Ilya said to Berezovsky: "Finish him off."

There was a bang.

Lloyd felt nothing. Was this death? Then Berezovsky crumpled and fell to the ground. At the same moment Lloyd realized that the shot had come from behind him. He turned, incredulous, to look. In the moonlight he saw Dave holding his stolen Luger. Relief swamped him like a tidal wave. He was alive!

Ilya, too, had seen Dave, and he ran like a startled rabbit.

Dave tracked him with the pistol for several seconds, and Lloyd willed him to shoot, but Ilya dodged frantically between the olive trees, like a rat in a maze, then disappeared into the darkness.

Dave lowered the gun.

Lloyd looked down at Berezovsky. He was not breathing. Lloyd said: "Thanks, Dave."

"I told you to watch your back."

"You watched it for me. But it's a pity you didn't get Ilya, too. Now you're in trouble with the NKVD."

"I wonder," said Dave. "Will Ilya want people to know that he got his sidekick killed in a squabble over a woman? Even the NKVD people are frightened of the NKVD. I think he'll keep it quiet."

Lloyd looked again at the body. "How do we explain this?"

"You heard the man," Dave said. "This is the front line. No explanation needed."

Lloyd nodded. Dave and Ilya were both right. No one would ask how Berezovsky had died. A stray bullet got him.

They walked away, leaving the body where it lay.

"Jolly bad luck," said Dave.

iv

Lloyd and Lenny spoke to Colonel Bobrov and complained that the attack on Saragossa was stalemated.

Bobrov was an older Russian with a cropped fuzz of white hair, nearing retirement and rigidly orthodox. In theory he was there only to help and advise the Spanish commanders. In practise the Russians called the shots.

"We're wasting time and energy on these little villages," Lloyd said, translating into German what Lenny and all the experienced men were saying. "Tanks are supposed to be armored fists, used for deep penetration, striking far into enemy territory. The infantry should follow, mopping up and securing after the enemy has been scattered."

Volodya was standing nearby, listening, and seemed by his expression to agree, though he said nothing.

"Small strongpoints like this wretched one-horse town should not be allowed to delay the advance, but should be bypassed and dealt with later by a second line," Lloyd finished.

Bobrov looked shocked. "This is the theory of the discredited Marshal Tuchachevsky!" he said in hushed tones. It was as if Lloyd had told a bishop to pray to Buddha.

"So what?" said Lloyd.

"He has confessed to treason and espionage, and has been executed."

Lloyd stared incredulously. "Are you telling me that the Spanish government cannot use modern tank tactics because some general has been purged in Moscow?"

"Lieutenant Williams, you are becoming disrespectful."

Lloyd said: "Even if the charges against Tuchachevsky are true, that doesn't mean his methods are wrong."

"That will do!" Bobrov thundered. "This conversation is over."

Any hope Lloyd might have had remaining was crushed when his battalion was moved from Quinto back in the direction they had come, another sideways maneuver. On September 1 they were part of the attack on Belchite, a well-defended but strategically worthless small town twenty-five miles wide of their objective.

It was another hard battle.

Some seven thousand defenders were well dug in at the town's largest church, San Agustin, and atop a nearby hill, with trenches and earthworks. Lloyd and his platoon reached the outskirts of town without casualties, but then came under withering fire from windows and rooftops.

Six days later they were still there.

The corpses were stinking in the heat. As well as humans, there were dead animals, for the town's water supply had been cut off and livestock were dying of thirst. Whenever they could, the engineers stacked the bodies up, doused them with gasoline, and set fire to them, but the smell of roasting humans was worse than the stink of corruption. It seemed hard to breathe, and some of the men wore their gas masks.

The narrow streets around the church were killing fields, but Lloyd had devised a way to make progress without going outside. Lenny had found some tools in a workshop. Now two men were making a hole in the wall of the house in which they were sheltering. Joe Eli was using a pickax, sweat gleaming on his bald head. Corporal Rivera, who wore a striped shirt in the anarchist colors of red and black, wielded a sledgehammer. The wall was made of flat, yellow local bricks, roughly mortared. Lenny directed the operation to make sure they did not bring the entire house down: as a miner, he had an instinct for the trustworthiness of a roof.

When the hole was big enough for a man to pass through, Lenny nodded to Jasper, also a corporal. Jasper took one of his few remaining grenades from his belt pouch, drew the pin, and threw it into the next house, just in case there was an ambush. As soon as it had exploded, Lloyd crawled quickly through the hole, rifle at the ready.

He found himself in another poor Spanish home, with whitewashed walls and a floor of beaten earth. There was no one here, dead or alive.

The thirty-five men of his platoon followed him through the hole and ran through the place to flush out any defenders. The house was small and empty.

In this way they were moving slowly but safely through a row of cottages toward the church.

They started work on the next hole, but before they broke through, they were halted by a major called Marquez who came along the row of houses by the route they had made through the walls. "Forget all that," he said in Spanish-accented English. "We're going to rush the church."

Lloyd went cold. It was suicidal. He said: "Is that Colonel Bobrov's idea?"

"Yes," said Major Marquez noncommittally. "Wait for the signal: three sharp blows on the whistle."

"Can we get more ammunition?" Lloyd said. "We're low, especially for this kind of action."

"No time," said the major, and he went away.

Lloyd was horrified. He had learned a lot in a few days of battle, and he knew that the only way to rush a well-defended position was under a hail of covering fire. Otherwise the defenders would just mow the attackers down.

The men looked mutinous, and Corporal Rivera said: "It is impossible."

Lloyd was responsible for maintaining their morale. "No complaints, you lot," he said breezily. "You're all volunteers. Did you think war wasn't dangerous? If it was safe, your sisters could do it for you." They laughed, and the moment of danger passed, for now.

He moved to the front of the house, opened the door a crack, and peeped out. The sun glared down on a narrow street with houses and shops on both sides. The buildings and the ground were the same pale tan color, like undercooked bread, except where shelling had gouged up red earth. Right outside the door a militiaman lay dead, a cloud of flies feasting on the hole in his chest. Looking toward the square, Lloyd saw that the street widened toward the church. The gunmen in the high twin towers had a clear view and an easy shot at anyone approaching. On the ground there was only minimal cover: some rubble, a dead horse, a wheelbarrow.

We're all going to die, he thought.

But why else did we come here?

He turned back to his men, wondering what to say. He had to keep them thinking positively. "Just hug the sides of the street, close to the houses," he said. "Remember, the slower you go, the longer you're exposed—so wait for the whistle, then run like fuck."

Sooner than expected, he heard the three sharp chirrups of Major Marquez's whistle.

"Lenny, you're last out," he said.

"Who's first?" said Lenny.

"I am, of course."

Good-bye, world, Lloyd thought. At least I'll die fighting Fascists.

He threw the door wide. "Let's go!" he yelled, and he ran out.

Surprise gave him a few seconds' grace, and he ran freely along the street toward the church. He felt the scorch of the midday sun on his face and heard the pounding of his men's boots behind him, and noted with a weird sentiment of gratitude that such sensations meant he was still alive. Then gunfire broke out like a hailstorm. For a few more heartbeats he ran, hearing the zip and thwack of bullets, then there was a feeling in his left arm as if he had banged it against something, and inexplicably he fell down.

He realized he had been hit. There was no pain, but his arm was numb and hung lifeless. He managed to roll sideways until he hit the wall of the nearest building. Shots continued to fly, and he was terribly vulnerable, but a few feet ahead he saw a dead body. It was a rebel soldier, propped against the house. He looked as if he had been sitting on the ground, resting with his back against the wall, and had gone to sleep, except that there was a bullet wound in his neck.

Lloyd wriggled forward, moving awkwardly, rifle in his right hand, left arm dragging behind, then crouched behind the body, trying to make himself small.

He rested his rifle barrel on the dead man's shoulder and took aim at a high window in the church tower. He fired all five rounds in his magazine in rapid succession. He could not tell whether he had hit anyone.

He looked back. To his horror he saw the street littered with the corpses of his platoon. The still body of Mario Rivera in his red-and-black shirt looked like a crumpled anarchist flag. Next to Mario was

Jasper Johnson, his black curls soaked in blood. All the way from a factory in Chicago, Lloyd thought, to die on the street in a small town in Spain, because he believed in a better world.

Worse were those who still lived, moaning and crying on the ground. Somewhere a man was screaming in agony, but Lloyd could not see who or where. A few of his men were still running, but as he watched, more fell and others threw themselves down. Seconds later no one was moving except the writhing wounded.

What a slaughter, he thought, and a bile of anger and sorrow rose chokingly in his throat.

Where were the other units? Surely Lloyd's platoon was not the only one involved in the attack? Perhaps others were advancing along parallel streets leading to the square. But a rush required overwhelming numbers. Lloyd and his thirty-five were obviously too few. The defenders had been able to kill and wound nearly all of them, and the few who remained of Lloyd's platoon had been forced to take cover before reaching the church.

He caught the eye of Lenny, peering from behind the dead horse. At least he was still alive. Lenny held up his rifle and made a helpless gesture, pantomiming "no ammunition." Lloyd was out, too. In the next minute, firing from the street died away as the others also ran out of bullets.

That was the end of the attack on the church. It had been impossible anyway. With no ammunition it would have been pointless suicide.

The hail of fire from the church had lessened as the easier targets were eliminated, but sporadic sniping continued at those remaining behind cover. Lloyd realized that all his men would be killed eventually. They had to withdraw.

They would probably all be killed in the retreat.

He caught Lenny's eye again and waved emphatically toward the rear, away from the church. Lenny looked around, repeating the gesture to the few others left alive. They would have a better chance if they all moved at the same time.

When as many as possible had been forewarned, Lloyd struggled to his feet.

"Retreat!" he yelled at the top of his voice.

Then he began to run.

It was no more than two hundred yards, but it was the longest journey of his life.

The rebels in the church opened fire as soon as they saw the government troops move. Out of the corner of his eye Lloyd thought he saw five or six of his men retreating. He ran with a ragged gait, his wounded arm putting him off balance. Lenny was ahead of him, apparently unhurt. Bullets scored the masonry of the buildings that Lloyd staggered past. Lenny made it to the house they had come from, dashed in, and held the door open. Lloyd ran in, panting hoarsely, and collapsed on the floor. Three more followed them in.

Lloyd stared at the survivors: Lenny, Dave, Muggsy Morgan, and Joe Eli. "Is that all?" he said.

Lenny said: "Yes."

"Jesus. Five of us left, out of thirty-six."

"What a great military adviser Colonel Bobrov is."

They stood panting, catching their breath. The feeling returned to Lloyd's arm and it hurt like hell. He found he could move it, painfully, so perhaps it was not broken. Looking down, he saw that his sleeve was soaked with blood. Dave took off his red scarf and improvised a sling.

Lenny had a head wound. There was blood on his face, but he said it was a scratch, and he seemed all right.

Dave, Muggsy, and Joe were miraculously unhurt.

"We'd better go back for fresh orders," Lloyd said when they had lain down a few minutes. "We can't accomplish anything without ammunition anyway."

"Let's have a nice cup of tea first, is it?" said Lenny.

Lloyd said: "We can't. We haven't got teaspoons."

"Oh, all right, then."

Dave said: "Can't we rest here a bit longer?"

"We'll rest in the rear," Lloyd said. "It's safer."

They made their way back along the row of houses, using the holes they had made in the walls. The repeated bending made Lloyd dizzy. He wondered if he was weak from loss of blood.

They emerged out of sight of the church of San Agustin, and hurried along a side street. Lloyd's relief at still being alive was rapidly giving way to a feeling of rage at the waste of the lives of his men.

They came to the barn on the outskirts where the government forces had made their headquarters. Lloyd saw Major Marquez behind a stack of crates, giving out ammunition. "Why couldn't we have had some of that?" he said furiously.

Marquez just shrugged.

"I'm reporting this to Bobrov," Lloyd said.

Colonel Bobrov was outside the barn, sitting on a chair at a table, both of which looked as if they had been taken from a village house. His face was reddened with sunburn. He was talking to Volodya Peshkov. Lloyd went straight up to them. "We rushed the church, but we had no support," he said. "And we ran out of ammunition because Marquez refused to supply us!"

Bobrov looked coldly at Lloyd. "What are you doing here?" he said.

Lloyd was puzzled. He expected Bobrov to congratulate him for a brave effort and at least commiserate with him over the lack of support. "I just told you," he said. "There was no support. You can't rush a fortified building with one platoon. We did our best, but we were slaughtered. I've lost thirty-one of my thirty-six men." He pointed at his four companions. "This is all that's left of my platoon!"

"Who ordered you to retreat?"

Lloyd was fighting off dizziness. He felt close to collapse, but he had to explain to Bobrov how bravely his men had fought. "We came back for fresh orders. What else could we do?"

"You should have fought to the last man."

"What should we have fought with? We had no bullets!"

"Silence!" Bobrov barked. "Stand to attention!"

Automatically, they all stood to attention: Lloyd, Lenny, Dave, Muggsy, and Joe in a line. Lloyd feared he was about to faint.

"About-face!"

They turned their backs. Lloyd thought: What now?

"Those who are wounded, fall out."

Lloyd and Lenny stepped back.

Bobrov said: "The walking wounded are transferred to prisoner escort duty."

Dimly, Lloyd perceived that this meant he would probably be guarding prisoners of war on a train to Barcelona. He swayed on his feet. Right now I couldn't guard a flock of sheep, he thought.

Bobrov said: "Retreating under fire without orders is desertion."

Lloyd turned and looked at Bobrov. To his astonishment and horror he saw that Bobrov had drawn his revolver from its buttoned holster.

Bobrov stepped forward so that he was immediately behind the three men standing to attention. "You three are found guilty and sentenced to death." He raised the gun until the barrel was three inches from the back of Dave's head.

Then he fired.

There was a bang. A bullet hole appeared in Dave's head, and blood and brains exploded from his brow.

Lloyd could not believe what he was seeing.

Next to Dave, Muggsy began to turn, his mouth open to shout, but Bobrov was quicker. He swung the gun to Muggsy's neck and fired again. The bullet entered behind Muggsy's right ear and came out through his left eye, and he crumpled.

At last Lloyd's voice came, and he shouted: "No!"

Joe Eli turned, roaring with shock and rage, and raised his hands to grab Bobrov. The gun banged again and Joe got a bullet in the throat. Blood spurted like a fountain from his neck and splashed Bobrov's Red Army uniform, causing the colonel to curse and jump back a pace. Joe fell to the ground but did not die immediately. Lloyd watched, helpless, as the blood pumped out of Joe's carotid artery into the parched Spanish earth. Joe seemed to try to speak, but no words came, and then his eyes closed and he went limp.

"There's no mercy for cowards," Bobrov said, and he walked away.

Lloyd looked at Dave on the ground: thin, grimy, brave as a lion, sixteen years old, and dead. Killed not by the Fascists but by a stupid and brutal Soviet officer. What a waste, Lloyd thought, and tears came to his eyes.

A sergeant came running out of the barn. "They've given up!" he shouted joyfully. "The town hall has surrendered—they've raised the white flag. We've taken Belchite!"

The dizziness overwhelmed Lloyd at last, and he fainted.

v

London was cold and wet. Lloyd walked along Nutley Street in the rain, heading for his mother's house. He still wore his zipped Spanish army blouson and corduroy breeches, and boots with no socks. He carried a small backpack containing his spare underwear, a shirt, and a tin cup. Around his neck he had the red scarf Dave had turned into an improvised sling for his wounded arm. The arm still hurt, but he no longer needed the sling.

It was late on an October afternoon.

As expected, he had been put on a supply train returning to Barcelona crammed with rebel prisoners. The journey was not much more than a hundred miles, but it had taken three days. In Barcelona he had been separated from Lenny and lost contact. He had got a lift in a lorry going north. After the trucker dropped him off, he had walked, hitchhiked, and ridden in railway wagons full of coal or gravel or—on one lucky occasion—cases of wine. He had slipped across the border into France at night. He had slept rough, begged food, done odd jobs for a few coins, and, for two glorious weeks, earned his cross-channel boat fare picking grapes in a Bordeaux vineyard. Now he was home.

He inhaled the damp, soot-smelling Aldgate air as if it were perfume. He stopped at the garden gate and looked up at the terraced house in which he had been born more than twenty-two years ago. Lights glowed behind the rain-streaked windows: someone was at home. He walked up to the front door. He still had his key: he had kept it with his passport. He let himself in.

He dropped his backpack on the floor in the hall, by the hat stand.

From the kitchen he heard: "Who's that?" It was the voice of his stepfather, Bernie.

Lloyd found he could not speak.

Bernie came into the hall. "Who . . . ?" Then he recognized Lloyd. "My life!" he said. "It's you."

Lloyd said: "Hello, Dad."

"My boy," said Bernie. He put his arms around Lloyd. "Alive," Bernie said. Lloyd could feel him shaking with sobs.

After a minute Bernie rubbed his eyes with the sleeve of his cardigan, then went to the bottom of the stairs. "Eth!" he called.

"What?"

"Someone to see you."

"Just a minute."

She came down the stairs a few seconds later, pretty as ever in a blue dress. Halfway down she saw his face and turned pale. "Oh, *Duw*," she said. "It's Lloyd." She came down the rest of the stairs in a rush and threw her arms around him. "You're alive!" she said.

"I wrote to you from Barcelona—"

"We never got that letter."

"Then you don't know . . ."

"What?"

"Dave Williams died."

"Oh, no!"

"Killed at the Battle of Belchite." Lloyd had decided not to tell the truth about how Dave died.

"What about Lenny Griffiths?"

"I don't know. I lost touch with him. I was hoping he might have got home before me."

"No, there's no word."

Bernie said: "What was it like over there?"

"The Fascists are winning. And it's mainly the fault of the Communists, who are more interested in attacking the other left parties."

Bernie was shocked. "Surely not."

"It's true. If I've learned one thing in Spain, it's that we have to fight the Communists just as hard as the Fascists. They're both evil."

His mother smiled wryly. "Well, just fancy that." She had figured out the same thing long ago, Lloyd realized.

"Enough politics," he said. "How are you, Mam?"

"Oh, I'm the same, but look at you—you're so thin!"

"Not much to eat in Spain."

"I'd better make you something."

"No rush. I've been hungry for twelve months—I can keep going a few more minutes. I tell you what would be nice, though."

"What? Anything!"

"I'd love a nice cup of tea."

CHAPTER FIVE

1939

Thomas Macke was watching the Soviet embassy in Berlin when Volodya Peshkov came out.

The Prussian secret police had been transformed into the new, more efficient Gestapo six years ago, but Commissar Macke was still in charge of the section that monitored traitors and subversives in the city of Berlin. The most dangerous of them were undoubtedly getting their orders from this building at 63–65 Unter den Linden. So Macke and his men watched everyone who went in and came out.

The embassy was an art deco fortress made of a white stone that painfully reflected the glare of the August sun. A pillared lantern stood watchful above the central block, and to either side the wings had rows of tall, narrow windows like guardsmen at attention.

Macke sat at a pavement café opposite. Berlin's most elegant boulevard was busy with cars and bicycles; the women shopped in their summer dresses and hats; the men walked briskly by in suits or smart uniforms. It was hard to believe there were still German Communists. How could anyone possibly be against the Nazis? Germany was transformed. Hitler had wiped out unemployment—something no other European leader had achieved. Strikes and demonstrations were a distant memory of the bad old days. The police had no-nonsense powers to stamp out crime. The country was prospering: many families had a radio, and soon they would have people's cars to drive on the new autobahns.

And that was not all. Germany was strong again. The military was well armed and powerful. In the last two years both Austria and Czechoslovakia had been absorbed into Greater Germany, which was now the dominant power in Europe. Mussolini's Italy was allied with Germany in the Pact of Steel. Earlier this year Madrid had at last fallen to Franco's rebels, and Spain now had a Fascist-friendly government. How could any German wish to undo all that and bring the country under the heel of the Bolsheviks?

In Macke's eyes such people were scum, vermin, filth that had to be ruthlessly sought out and utterly destroyed. As he thought about them, his face twisted into a scowl of anger, and he tapped his foot on the pavement as if preparing to stomp a Communist.

Then he saw Peshkov.

He was a young man in a blue serge suit, carrying a light coat over his arm as if expecting a change in the weather. His close-cropped hair and quick march indicated the army, despite his civilian clothes, and the way he scanned the street, deceptively casual but thorough, suggested either Red Army Intelligence or the NKVD, the Russian secret police.

Macke's pulse quickened. He and his men knew everyone at the embassy by sight, of course. Their passport photographs were on file and the team watched them all the time. But he did not know much about Peshkov. The man was young—twenty-five, according to his file, Macke recalled—so he might be a junior staffer of no importance. Or he could be good at seeming unimportant.

Peshkov crossed Unter den Linden and walked toward where Macke sat, near the corner of Friedrich Strasse. As Peshkov came closer, Macke noted that the Russian was quite tall, with the build of an athlete. He had an alert look and an intense gaze.

Macke looked away, suddenly nervous. He picked up his cup and sipped the cold dregs of his coffee, partly covering his face. He did not want to meet those blue eyes.

Peshkov turned onto Friedrich Strasse. Macke nodded to Reinhold Wagner, standing on the opposite corner, and Wagner followed Peshkov. Macke then got up from his table and followed Wagner.

Not everyone in Red Army Intelligence was a cloak-and-dagger spy, of course. They got most of their information legitimately, mainly by reading the German newspapers. They did not necessarily believe everything they read, but they took note of clues such as an advertisement by a gun factory needing to recruit ten skilled lathe operators. Furthermore, Russians were free to travel Germany and look around— unlike diplomats in the Soviet Union, who were not allowed to leave Moscow unescorted. The young man whom Macke and Wagner were now tailing might be the tame, newspaper-reading kind of intelligence gatherer; all that was required for such a job was fluent German and the ability to summarize.

They followed Peshkov past Macke's brother's restaurant. It was still called Bistro Robert, but it had a different clientele. Gone were the wealthy homosexuals, the Jewish businessmen with their mistresses, and the overpaid actresses calling for pink champagne. Such people kept their heads down nowadays, if they were not already in concentration camps. Some had left Germany—and good riddance, Macke thought, even if it did, unfortunately, mean that the restaurant no longer made much money.

He wondered idly what had become of the former owner, Robert von Ulrich. He vaguely remembered the man had gone to England. Perhaps he had opened a restaurant for perverts there.

Peshkov went into a bar.

Wagner followed him in a minute or two later, while Macke watched the outside. It was a popular place. While Macke waited for Peshkov to reappear, he saw a soldier and a girl enter, and a couple of well-dressed women and an old man in a grubby coat come out and walk away. Then Wagner came out alone, looked directly at Macke, and spread his arms in a gesture of bewilderment.

Macke crossed the street. Wagner was distressed. "He's not there!"

"Did you look everywhere?"

"Yes, including the toilets and the kitchen."

"Did you ask if anyone had gone out the back way?"

"They said not."

Wagner was scared, with reason. This was the new Germany, and errors were no longer dealt with by a slap on the wrist. He could be severely punished.

But not this time. "That's all right," said Macke.

Wagner could not hide his relief. "Is it?"

"We've learned something important," Macke said. "The fact that he shook us off so expertly tells us that he's a spy—and a very good one."

ii

Volodya entered the Friedrich Strasse station and boarded a U-Bahn train. He took off the cap, glasses, and dirty raincoat that had helped him look like an old man. He sat down, took out a handkerchief, and wiped away the powder he had put on his shoes to make them appear shabby.

He had been unsure about the raincoat. It was such a sunny day that he feared the Gestapo might have noticed it and realized what he was up to. But they had not been that clever, and no one had followed him from the bar after he had done his quick change in the men's room.

He was about to do something highly dangerous. If they caught him contacting a German dissident, the best that he could expect was to be deported back to Moscow with his career in ruins. If he was less lucky, he and the dissident would both vanish into the basement of Gestapo headquarters in Prinz-Albrecht-Strasse, never to be seen again. The Soviets would complain that one of their diplomats had disappeared, and the German police would pretend to do a missing-persons search, then regretfully report no success.

Volodya had never been to Gestapo headquarters, of course, but he

knew what it would be like. The NKVD had a similar facility in the
Soviet Trade Mission at 11 Lietsenburger Strasse: steel doors, an
interrogation room with tiled walls so that the blood could be washed
off easily, a tub for cutting up the bodies, and an electrical furnace for
burning the parts.

Volodya had been sent to Berlin to expand the network of Soviet
spies there. Fascism was triumphant in Europe, and Germany was more
of a threat to the USSR now than ever. Stalin had fired his foreign
minister, Litvinov, and replaced him with Vyacheslav Molotov. But
what could Molotov do? The Fascists seemed unstoppable. The Kremlin
was haunted by the humiliating memory of the Great War, in which the
Germans had defeated a Russian army of six million men. Stalin had
taken steps to form a pact with France and Britain to restrain Germany,
but the three powers had been unable to agree, and the talks had broken
down in the last few days.

Sooner or later, war was expected between Germany and the Soviet
Union, and it was Volodya's job to gather military intelligence that
would help the Soviets win that war.

He got off the train in the poor working-class district of Wedding,
north of Berlin's center. Outside the station he stood and waited,
watching the other passengers as they left, pretending to study a
timetable pasted on the wall. He did not move off until he was quite
sure no one had followed him there.

Then he made his way to the cheap restaurant that was his chosen
rendezvous. As was his regular practise, he did not go in, but stood at a
bus stop on the other side of the road and watched the entrance. He was
confident he had shaken off any tail, but now he needed to make sure
Werner had not been followed.

He was not sure he would recognize Werner Franck, who had been
a fourteen-year-old boy when Volodya last saw him, and was now
twenty. Werner felt the same, so they had agreed they would both carry
today's edition of the *Berliner Morgenpost* open to the sports page.
Volodya read a preview of the new soccer season as he waited, glancing
up every few seconds to look for Werner. Ever since he was a schoolboy

in Berlin, Volodya had followed the city's top team, Hertha. He had often chanted: "Ha! Ho! He! Hertha B-S-C!" He was interested in the team's prospects, but anxiety spoiled his concentration, and he read the same report over and over again without taking anything in.

His two years in Spain had not boosted his career in the way he had hoped—rather the reverse. Volodya had uncovered numerous Nazi spies like Heinz Bauer among the German "volunteers." But then the NKVD had used that as an excuse to arrest genuine volunteers who had merely expressed mild disagreement with the Communist line. Hundreds of idealistic young men had been tortured and killed in the NKVD's prisons. At times it had seemed as if the Communists were more interested in fighting their anarchist allies than their Fascist enemies.

And all for nothing. Stalin's policy was a catastrophic failure. The upshot was a right-wing dictatorship, the worst imaginable outcome for the Soviet Union. But the blame was put on those Russians who had been in Spain, even though they had faithfully carried out Kremlin instructions. Some of them had disappeared soon after returning to Moscow.

Volodya had gone home in fear after the fall of Madrid. He had found many changes. In 1937 and 1938 Stalin had purged the Red Army. Thousands of commanders had disappeared, including many of the residents of Government House, where his parents lived. But previously neglected men such as Grigori Peshkov had been promoted to take the places of those purged, and Grigori's career had a new impetus. He was in charge of the defense of Moscow against air raids, and was frantically busy. His enhanced status was probably the reason why Volodya was not among those scapegoated for the failure of Stalin's Spanish policy.

The unpleasant Ilya Dvorkin had also somehow avoided punishment. He was back in Moscow and married to Volodya's sister, Anya, much to Volodya's regret. There was no accounting for women's choices in such matters. She was already pregnant, and Volodya could not repress a nightmare image of her nursing a baby with the head of a rat.

After a brief leave Volodya had been posted to Berlin, where he had to prove his worth all over again.

He looked up from his paper to see Werner walking along the street.

Werner had not changed much. He was a little taller and broader, but he had the same strawberry blond hair falling over his forehead in a way girls had found irresistible, the same look of tolerant amusement in his blue eyes. He wore an elegant light blue summer suit, and gold links glinted at his cuffs.

There was no one following him.

Volodya crossed the road and intercepted him before he reached the café. Werner smiled broadly, showing white teeth. "I wouldn't have recognized you with that army haircut," he said. "It's good to see you, after all these years."

He had not lost any of his warmth and charm, Volodya noted. "Let's go inside."

"You don't really want to go into that dump, do you?" Werner said. "It will be full of plumbers eating sausages with mustard."

"I want to get off the street. Here we could be seen by anyone passing."

"There's an alley three doors down."

"Good."

They walked a short distance and turned into a narrow passage between a coal yard and a grocery store. "What have you been doing?" Werner said.

"Fighting the Fascists, just like you." Volodya considered whether to tell him more. "I was in Spain." It was no secret.

"Where you had no more success than we did here in Germany."

"But it's not over yet."

"Let me ask you something," Werner said, leaning against the wall. "If you thought Bolshevism was wicked, would you be a spy working against the Soviet Union?"

Volodya's instinct was to say *No, absolutely not!* But before the words came out, he realized how tactless that would be—for the prospect that revolted him was precisely what Werner was doing, betraying his country for the sake of a higher cause. "I don't know," he said. "I think it must be very difficult for you to work against Germany, even though you hate the Nazis."

"You're right," Werner said. "And what happens if war breaks out? Am I going to help you kill our soldiers and bomb our cities?"

Volodya was worried. It seemed that Werner was weakening. "It's the only way to defeat the Nazis," he said. "You know that."

"I do. I made my decision a long time ago. And the Nazis have done nothing to change my mind. It's hard, that's all."

"I understand," Volodya said sympathetically.

Werner said: "You asked me to suggest other people who might do for you what I do."

Volodya nodded. "People like Willi Frunze. Remember him? Cleverest boy in school. He was a serious socialist—he chaired that meeting the Brownshirts broke up."

Werner shook his head. "He went to England."

Volodya's heart sank. "Why?"

"He's a brilliant physicist and he's studying in London."

"Shit."

"But I've thought of someone else."

"Good!"

"Did you ever know Heinrich von Kessel?"

"I don't think so. Was he at our school?"

"No, he went to a Catholic school. And in those days he didn't share our politics, either. His father was a big shot in the Centre Party—"

"Which put Hitler in power in 1933!"

"Correct. Heinrich was then working for his father. The father has now joined the Nazis, but the son is racked by guilt."

"How do you know?"

"He got drunk and told my sister, Frieda. She's seventeen. I think he fancies her."

This was promising. Volodya's spirits lifted. "Is he a Communist?"

"No."

"What makes you think he'll work for us?"

"I asked him, straight out. 'If you got a chance to fight against the Nazis by spying for the Soviet Union, would you do it?' He said he would."

"What's his job?"

"He's in the army, but he has a weak chest, so they made him a pen pusher—which is lucky for us, because now he works for the Supreme High Command in the economic planning and procurement department."

Volodya was impressed. Such a man would know exactly how many trucks and tanks and machine guns and submarines the German military was acquiring month by month—and where they were being deployed. He began to feel excited. "When can I meet him?"

"Now. I've arranged to have a drink with him in the Hotel Adlon after work."

Volodya groaned. The Adlon was Berlin's swankiest hotel. It was located on Unter den Linden. Because it was in the government and diplomatic district, the bar was a favorite haunt of journalists hoping to pick up gossip. It would not have been Volodya's choice of rendezvous. But he could not afford to miss this chance. "All right," he said. "But I'm not going to be seen talking to either of you in that place. I'll follow you in, identify Heinrich, then follow him out and accost him later."

"Okay. I'll drive you there. My car's around the corner."

As they walked to the other end of the alley, Werner told Volodya Heinrich's work and home addresses and phone numbers, and Volodya committed them to memory.

"Here we are," said Werner. "Jump in."

The car was a Mercedes 540K Autobahnkurier, a model that was head-turningly beautiful, with sensually curved fenders, a bonnet longer than an entire Ford Model T, and a sloping fastback rear end. It was so expensive that only a handful had ever been sold.

Volodya stared aghast. "Shouldn't you have a less ostentatious car?" he said incredulously.

"It's a double bluff," Werner said. "They think no real spy would be so flamboyant."

Volodya was going to ask how he could afford it, but then he recalled that Werner's father was a wealthy manufacturer.

"I'm not getting into that thing," Volodya said. "I'll go by train."

"As you wish."

"I'll see you at the Adlon, but don't acknowledge me."

"Of course."

Half an hour later Volodya saw Werner's car carelessly parked in front of the hotel. This cavalier attitude of Werner's seemed foolish to him, but now he wondered whether it was a necessary element of Werner's courage. Perhaps Werner had to pretend to be carefree in order to take the appalling risks required to spy on the Nazis. If he acknowledged the danger he was in, maybe he would not be able to carry on.

The bar of the Adlon was full of fashionable women and well-dressed men, many in smartly tailored uniforms. Volodya spotted Werner right away, at a table with another man who was presumably Heinrich von Kessel. Passing close to them, Volodya heard Heinrich say argumentatively: "Buck Clayton is a much better trumpeter than Hot Lips Page." He squeezed in at the counter, ordered a beer, and discreetly studied the new potential spy.

Heinrich had pale skin and thick dark hair that was long by army standards. Although they were talking about the relatively unimportant topic of jazz, he seemed very intense, arguing with gestures and repeatedly running his fingers through his hair. He had a book stuffed into the pocket of his uniform tunic, and Volodya would have bet it contained poetry.

Volodya drank two beers slowly and pretended to read the *Morgenpost* from cover to cover. He tried not to get too keyed up about Heinrich. The man was thrillingly promising, but there was no guarantee he would cooperate.

Recruiting informers was the hardest part of Volodya's work. Precautions were difficult to take because the target was not yet on his side. The proposition often had to be made in inappropriate places, usually somewhere public. It was impossible to know how the target would react: he might be angry and shout his refusal, or be terrified and literally run away. But there was not much the recruiter could do to control the situation. At some point he just had to ask the simple, blunt question: "Do you want to be a spy?"

He thought about how to approach Heinrich. Religion was probably the key to his personality. Volodya recalled his boss, Lemitov, saying: "Lapsed Catholics make good agents. They reject the total authority of the Church only to accept the total authority of the party." Heinrich might need to seek forgiveness for what he had done. But would he risk his life?

At last Werner paid the bill and the two men left. Volodya followed. Outside the hotel they parted company, Werner driving off with a squeal of tires and Heinrich going on foot across the park. Volodya went after Heinrich.

Night was falling, but the sky was clear and he could see well. There were many people strolling in the warm evening air, most of them in couples. Volodya looked back repeatedly, to make sure no one had followed him or Heinrich from the Adlon. When he was satisfied, he took a deep breath, steeled his nerve, and caught up with Heinrich.

Walking alongside him, Volodya said: "There is atonement for sin."

Heinrich looked at him warily, as at someone who might be mad. "Are you a priest?"

"You could strike back at the wicked regime you helped to create."

Heinrich kept walking, but he looked worried. "Who are you? What do you know about me?"

Volodya continued to ignore Heinrich's questions. "The Nazis will be defeated, one day. That day could come sooner, with your help."

"If you're a Gestapo agent hoping to entrap me, don't bother. I'm a loyal German."

"Do you notice my accent?"

"Yes—you sound Russian."

"How many Gestapo agents speak German with a Russian accent? Or have the imagination to fake it?"

Heinrich laughed nervously. "I know nothing about Gestapo

agents," he said. "I shouldn't have mentioned the subject—very foolish of me."

"Your office produces reports of the quantities of armaments and other supplies ordered by the military. Copies of those reports could be immeasurably useful to the enemies of the Nazis."

"To the Red Army, you mean."

"Who else is going to destroy this regime?"

"We keep careful track of all copies of such reports."

Volodya suppressed a surge of triumph. Heinrich was thinking about practical difficulties. That meant he was inclined to agree in principle. "Make an extra carbon," Volodya said. "Or write out a copy in longhand. Or take someone's file copy. There are ways."

"Of course there are. And any of them could get me killed."

"If we do nothing about the crimes that are being committed by this regime . . . is life worth living?"

Heinrich stopped and stared at Volodya. Volodya could not guess what the man was thinking, but instinct told him to remain quiet. After a long pause, Heinrich sighed and said: "I'll think about it."

I have him, Volodya thought exultantly.

Heinrich said: "How do I contact you?"

"You don't," Volodya said. "I will contact you." He touched the brim of his hat, then walked back the way he had come.

He felt exultant. If Heinrich had not meant to accept the proposition, he would have rejected it firmly. His promising to think about it was almost as good as acceptance. He would sleep on it. He would run over the dangers. But he would do it, eventually. Volodya felt almost certain.

He told himself not to be overconfident. A hundred things could go wrong.

All the same he was full of hope as he left the park and walked in bright lights past the shops and restaurants of Unter den Linden. He had had no dinner, but he could not afford to eat on this street.

He took a tram eastward into the low-rent neighborhood called Friedrichshain and made his way to a small apartment in a tenement. The door was opened by a short, pretty girl of eighteen with fair hair.

She wore a pink sweater and dark slacks, and her feet were bare. Although she was slim, she had delightfully generous breasts.

"I'm sorry to call unexpectedly," Volodya said. "Is it inconvenient?"

She smiled. "Not at all," she said. "Come in."

He stepped inside. She closed the door, then threw her arms around him. "I'm always happy to see you," she said, and kissed him eagerly.

Lili Markgraf was a girl with a lot of affection to give. Volodya had been taking her out about once a week since he got back to Berlin. He was not in love with her, and he knew that she dated other men, including Werner, but when they were together, she was passionate.

After a moment she said: "Have you heard the news? Is that why you've come?"

"What news?" Lili worked as a secretary in a press agency, and always heard things first.

"The Soviet Union has made a pact with Germany!" she said.

That made no sense. "You mean with Britain and France, against Germany."

"No, I don't! That's the surprise—Stalin and Hitler have made friends."

"But . . ." Volodya trailed off, baffled. Friends with Hitler? It seemed crazy. Was this the solution devised by the new Soviet foreign minister, Molotov? We have failed to stop the tide of world Fascism—so we give up trying?

Did my father fight a revolution for that?

iii

Woody Dewar saw Joanne Rouzrokh again after four years.

No one who knew her father actually believed he had tried to rape a starlet in the Ritz-Carlton hotel. The girl had dropped the charges, but that was dull news, and the papers had given it little prominence. Consequently Dave was still a rapist in the eyes of Buffalo people. So Joanne's parents had moved to Palm Beach, and Woody lost touch.

Next time he saw her it was in the White House.

Woody was with his father, Senator Gus Dewar, and they were going to see the president. Woody had met Franklin D. Roosevelt several times. His father and the president had been friends for many years. But those had been social occasions, when FDR had shaken Woody's hand and asked him how he was getting along at school. This would be the first time Woody attended a real political meeting with the president.

They went in through the main entrance of the West Wing, passed through the entrance lobby, and stepped into a large waiting room—and there she was.

Woody stared at her in delight. She had hardly changed. With her narrow, haughty face and curved nose she still looked like the high priestess of an ancient religion. As ever, she wore simple clothes to dramatic effect: today she had on a dark blue suit of some cool fabric and a straw hat the same color with a big brim. Woody was glad he had put on a clean white shirt and his new striped tie this morning.

She seemed pleased to see him. "You look great!" she said. "Are you working in D.C. now?"

"Just helping out in my father's office for the summer," he replied. "I'm still at Harvard."

She turned to his father and said deferentially: "Good afternoon, Senator."

"Hello, Joanne."

Woody was thrilled to run into her. She was as alluring as ever. He wanted to keep the conversation going. "What are you doing here?" Woody said.

"I work at the State Department."

Woody nodded. That explained her deference to his father. She had joined a world in which people kowtowed to Senator Dewar. Woody said: "What's your job?"

"I'm assistant to an assistant. My boss is with the president now, but I'm too lowly to go in with him."

"You were always interested in politics. I recall an argument about lynching."

284 I CHAPTER FIVE

"I miss Buffalo. What fun we used to have!"

Woody remembered kissing her at the Racquet Club Ball, and he felt himself blush.

His father said: "Please give my best regards to your father," indicating that they needed to move on.

Woody considered asking for her phone number, but she preempted him. "I'd love to see you again, Woody," she said.

He was delighted. "Sure!"

"Are you free tonight? I'm having a few friends for cocktails."

"Sounds great!"

She gave him the address, an apartment building not far away; then his father hurried him out of the other end of the room.

A guard nodded familiarly to Gus, and they stepped into another waiting room.

Gus said: "Now, Woody, don't say anything unless the president addresses you directly."

Woody tried to concentrate on the imminent meeting. There had been a political earthquake in Europe: the Soviet Union had signed a peace pact with Nazi Germany, upsetting everyone's calculations. Woody's father was a key member of the Senate Foreign Relations Committee, and the president wanted to know what he thought.

Gus Dewar had another subject to discuss. He wanted to persuade Roosevelt to revive the League of Nations.

It would be a tough sell. The USA had never joined the league and Americans did not much like it. The league had failed dismally to deal with the crises of the 1930s: Japanese aggression in the Far East, Italian imperialism in Africa, Nazi takeovers in Europe, the ruin of democracy in Spain. But Gus was determined to try. It had always been his dream, Woody knew: a world council to resolve conflicts and prevent war.

Woody was 100 percent behind him. He had made a speech about this in a Harvard debate. When two nations had a quarrel, the worst possible procedure was for men to kill people on the other side. That seemed to him pretty obvious. "I understand why it happens, of course," he had said in the debate. "Just like I understand why drunks get into fistfights. But that doesn't make it any less irrational."

But now Woody found it hard to think about the threat of war in Europe. All his old feelings about Joanne came back in a rush. He wondered if she would kiss him again—maybe tonight. She had always liked him, and it seemed she still did—why else would she have invited him to her party? She had refused to date him, back in 1935, because he had been fifteen and she eighteen, which was understandable, though he had not thought so at the time. But now that they were both four years older, the age difference would not seem so stark—would it? He hoped not. He had dated girls in Buffalo and at Harvard, but he had not felt for any of them the overwhelming passion he had had for Joanne.

"Have you got that?" his father said.

Woody felt foolish. His father was about to make a proposal to the president that could bring world peace, and all Woody could think about was kissing Joanne. "Sure," he said. "I won't say anything unless he speaks to me first."

A tall, slim woman in her early forties came into the room, looking relaxed and confident, as if she owned the place, and Woody recognized Marguerite LeHand, nicknamed Missy, who managed Roosevelt's office. She had a long, masculine face with a big nose, and there was a touch of gray in her dark hair. She smiled warmly at Gus. "What a pleasure to see you again, Senator."

"How are you, Missy? You remember my son, Woodrow."

"I do. The president is ready for you both."

Missy's devotion to Roosevelt was famous. FDR was more fond of her than a married man was entitled to be, according to Washington gossip. Woody knew, from guarded but revealing remarks his parents made to one another, that Roosevelt's wife, Eleanor, had refused to sleep with him since she gave birth to their sixth child. The paralysis, which had struck him five years later, did not extend to his sexual equipment. Perhaps a man who had not slept with his wife for twenty years was entitled to an affectionate secretary.

She showed them through another door and across a narrow corridor; then they were in the Oval Office.

The president sat at a desk with his back to three tall windows in a curving bay. The blinds were drawn to filter the August sun coming through the south-facing glass. Roosevelt used an ordinary office chair, Woody saw, not his wheelchair. He wore a white suit and he was smoking a cigarette in a holder.

He was not really handsome. He had a receding hairline and a jutting chin, and he wore pince-nez glasses that made his eyes seem too close together. All the same there was something immediately attractive about his engaging smile, his hand extended to shake, and the amiable tone of voice in which he said: "Good to see you, Gus. Come on in."

"Mr. President, you remember my elder son, Woodrow."

"Of course. How's Harvard, Woody?"

"Just fine, sir, thank you. I'm on the debating team." He knew that politicians often had the knack of seeming to know everyone intimately. Either they had remarkable memories, or their secretaries reminded them efficiently.

"I was at Harvard myself. Sit down, sit down." Roosevelt removed the end of his cigarette from the holder and stubbed it in a full ashtray. "Gus, what the heck is happening in Europe?"

The president knew what was happening in Europe, of course, thought Woody. He had an entire State Department to tell him. But he wanted Gus Dewar's analysis.

Gus said: "Germany and Russia are still mortal enemies, in my opinion."

"That's what we all thought. But then why have they signed this pact?"

"Short-term convenience for both. Stalin needs time. He wants to build up the Red Army, so they can defeat the Germans if it comes to that."

"And the other guy?"

"Hitler is clearly on the point of doing something to Poland. The German press is full of ridiculous stories about how the Poles are mistreating their German-speaking population. Hitler doesn't stir up hatred without a purpose. Whatever he's planning, he doesn't want the Soviets to stand in his way. Hence the pact."

"That's pretty much what Hull says." Cordell Hull was secretary of state. "But he doesn't know what will happen next. Will Stalin let Hitler do anything he wants?"

"My guess is they'll carve up Poland between them in the next couple of weeks."

"And then what?"

"A few hours ago the British signed a new treaty with the Poles promising to come to their aid if they're attacked."

"But what can they do?"

"Nothing, sir. The British army, navy, and air force have no power to prevent the Germans overrunning Poland."

"What do you think we should do, Gus?" said the president.

Woody knew that this was his father's chance. He had the president's attention for a few minutes. It was a rare opportunity to make something happen. Woody discreetly crossed his fingers.

Gus leaned forward. "We don't want our sons to go to war as we did." Roosevelt had four boys in their twenties and thirties. Woody suddenly understood why he was here: he had been brought to the meeting to remind the president of his own sons. Gus said quietly: "We can't send American boys to be slaughtered in Europe again. The world needs a police force."

"What do you have in mind?" Roosevelt said noncommittally.

"The League of Nations isn't such a failure as people think. In the 1920s it resolved a border dispute between Finland and Sweden, and another between Turkey and Iraq." Gus was ticking items off on his fingers. "It stopped Greece and Yugoslavia from invading Albania, and persuaded Greece to pull out of Bulgaria. And it sent a peacekeeping force to keep Colombia and Peru from hostilities."

"All true. But in the thirties . . ."

"The league was not strong enough to deal with Fascist aggression. It's not surprising. The league was crippled from the start because Congress refused to ratify the covenant, so the United States was never a member. We need a new, American-led version, with teeth." Gus paused. "Mr. President, it's too soon to give up on a peaceful world."

Woody held his breath. Roosevelt nodded, but then he always nodded, Woody knew. It was rare for him to disagree openly. He hated confrontation. You had to be careful, Woody had heard his father say, not to take his silence for consent. Woody did not dare look at his father, sitting beside him, but he could sense the tension.

At last the president said: "I believe you're right."

Woody had to restrain himself from whooping aloud. The president had consented! He looked at his father. The normally imperturbable Gus was barely concealing his surprise. It had been such a quick victory.

Gus moved rapidly to consolidate it. "In that case, may I suggest that Cordell Hull and I draft a proposal for your consideration?"

"Hull has a lot on his plate. Talk to Welles."

Sumner Welles was under-secretary of state. He was both ambitious and flamboyant, and Woody knew he would not have been Gus's first choice. But he was a longtime friend of the Roosevelt family—he had been a page boy at FDR's wedding.

Anyway, Gus was not going to make difficulties at this point. "By all means," he said.

"Anything else?"

That was clearly a dismissal. Gus stood up, and Woody followed suit. Gus said: "What about Mrs. Roosevelt, your mother, sir? Last I heard she was in France."

"Her ship left yesterday, thank goodness."

"I'm glad to hear it."

"Thank you for coming in," Roosevelt said. "I really value your friendship, Gus."

Gus said: "Nothing could give me more pleasure, sir." He shook hands with the president, and Woody did the same.

Then they left.

Woody half-hoped that Joanne would still be hanging around, but she had gone.

As they made their way out of the building, Gus said: "Let's go for a celebratory drink."

Woody looked at his watch. It was five o'clock. "Sure," he said.

They went to Old Ebbitt, on Fifteenth Street near F: stained glass, green velvet, brass lamps, and hunting trophies. The place was full of congressmen, senators, and the people who followed them around: aides, lobbyists, and journalists. Gus ordered a dry martini straight up with a twist for himself and a beer for Woody. Woody smiled: maybe he would have liked a martini. In fact he would not—to him it just tasted like cold gin—but it would have been nice to be asked. However, he raised his glass and said: "Congratulations. You got what you wanted."

"What the world needs."

"You argued brilliantly."

"Roosevelt hardly needed convincing. He's a liberal, but a pragmatist. He knows you can't do everything—you have to pick the battles you can win. The New Deal is his number one priority—getting unemployed men back to work. He won't do anything that interferes with the main mission. If my plan becomes controversial enough to upset his supporters, he'll drop it."

"So we haven't won anything yet."

Gus smiled. "We've taken the important first step. But no, we haven't won anything."

"A pity he forced Welles on you."

"Not entirely. Sumner strengthens the project. He's closer to the president than I am. But he's unpredictable. He might pick it up and run in a different direction."

Woody looked across the room and saw a familiar face. "Guess who's here. I might have known."

His father looked in the same direction.

"Standing at the bar," Woody said. "With a couple of older guys in hats, and a blond girl. It's Greg Peshkov." As usual, Greg looked a mess despite his expensive clothes: his silk tie was awry, his shirt was coming out of his waistband, and there was a smear of cigarette ash on his ice-cream-colored trousers. Nevertheless the blonde was looking adoringly at him.

"So it is," said Gus. "Do you see much of him at Harvard?"

"He's a physics major, but he doesn't hang around with the

scientists—too dull for him, I guess. I run into him at the *Crimson*." *The Harvard Crimson* was the student newspaper. Woody took photographs for the paper and Greg wrote articles. "He's doing an internship at the State Department this summer—that's why he's here."

"In the press office, I imagine," said Gus. "The two men he's with are reporters, the one in the brown suit for the *Chicago Tribune* and the pipe smoker for the Cleveland *Plain Dealer*."

Woody saw that Greg was talking to the journalists as if they were old friends, taking the arm of one as he leaned forward to say something in a low voice, patting the other on the back in mock congratulation. They seemed to like him, Woody thought, as they laughed loudly at something he said. Woody envied that talent. It was useful to politicians—though perhaps not essential: his father did not have that hail-fellow-well-met quality, and he was one of the most senior statesmen in America.

Woody said: "I wonder how his half sister, Daisy, feels about the threat of war. She's over there in London. She married some English lord."

"To be exact, she married the elder son of Earl Fitzherbert, whom I used to know quite well."

"She's the envy of every girl in Buffalo. The king went to her wedding."

"I also knew Fitzherbert's sister, Maud—a wonderful woman. She married Walter von Ulrich, a German. I would have married her myself if Walter hadn't got to her first."

Woody raised his eyebrows. It was not like Papa to talk this way.

"That was before I fell in love with your mother, of course."

"Of course." Woody smothered a grin.

"Walter and Maud dropped out of sight after Hitler banned the Social Democrats. I hope they're all right. If there's a war . . ."

Woody saw that talk of war had put his father in a reminiscent mood. "At least America isn't involved."

"That's what we thought last time." Gus changed the subject. "What do you hear from your kid brother?"

Woody sighed. "He's not going to change his mind, Papa. He won't go to Harvard, or any other university."

This was a family crisis. Chuck had announced that as soon as he was eighteen he was going to join the navy. Without a college degree he would be an enlisted man, with no prospect of ever becoming an officer. This horrified his high-achieving parents.

"He's bright enough for college, damn it," said Gus.

"He beats me at chess."

"He beats me, too. So what's his problem?"

"He hates to study. And he loves boats. Sailing is the only thing he cares about." Woody looked at his wristwatch.

"You've got a party to go to," his father said.

"There's no hurry—"

"Sure there is. She's a very attractive girl. Get the hell out of here."

Woody grinned. His father could be surprisingly smart. "Thanks, Papa." He got up.

Greg Peshkov was leaving at the same time, and they went out together. "Hello, Woody, how are things?" Greg said amiably, turning in the same direction.

There had been a time when Woody wanted to punch Greg for his part in what had been done to Dave Rouzrokh. His feelings had cooled over the years, and in truth it was Lev Peshkov who had been responsible, not his son, who had then been only fifteen. All the same Woody was no more than polite. "I'm enjoying Washington," he said, walking along one of the city's wide Parisian boulevards. "How about you?"

"I like it. They soon get over their surprise at my name." Seeing Woody's inquiring look, Greg explained: "The State Department is all Smiths, Fabers, Jensens, and McAllisters. No one called Kozinsky or Cohen or Papadopoulos."

Woody realized it was true. Government was carried on by a rather exclusive little ethnic group. Why had he not noticed that before? Perhaps because it had been the same in school, in church, and at Harvard.

Greg went on: "But they're not narrow-minded. They'll make an exception for someone who speaks fluent Russian and comes from a wealthy family."

Greg was being flippant, but there was an undertone of real resentment, and Woody saw that the guy had a serious chip on his shoulder.

"They think my father is a gangster," Greg said. "But they don't really mind. Most rich people have a gangster somewhere in their ancestry."

"You sound as if you hate Washington."

"On the contrary! I wouldn't be anywhere else. The power is here."

Woody felt he was more high-minded. "I'm here because there are things I want to do, changes I want to make."

Greg grinned. "Same thing, I guess—power."

"Hmm." Woody had not thought of it that way.

Greg said: "Do you think there will be war in Europe?"

"You should know: you're in the State Department!"

"Yeah, but I'm in the press office. All I know is the fairy tales we tell reporters. I have no idea what the truth is."

"Heck, I don't know, either. I've just been with the president and I don't think even he knows."

"My sister, Daisy, is over there."

Greg's tone had changed. His worry was evidently genuine, and Woody warmed to him. "I know."

"If there's bombing, even women and children won't be safe. Do you think the Germans will bomb London?"

There was only one honest answer. "I guess they will."

"I wish she'd come home."

"Maybe there won't be a war. Chamberlain, the British premier, made a last-minute deal with Hitler over Czechoslovakia last year—"

"A last-minute sellout."

"Right. So perhaps he'll do the same over Poland—although time is running out."

Greg nodded glumly and changed the subject. "Where are you headed?"

"To Joanne Rouzrokh's apartment. She's giving a party."

"I heard about it. I know one of her roommates. But I'm not invited, as you could probably guess. Her building is—good God!" Greg stopped in midsentence.

Woody stopped, too. Greg was staring ahead. Following his gaze, Woody saw that he was looking at an attractive black woman walking toward them on E Street. She was about their age, and pretty, with wide pinky-brown lips that made Woody think about kissing. She had on a plain black dress that might have been part of a waitress uniform, but she wore it with a cute hat and fashionable shoes that gave her a stylish look.

She saw the two of them, caught Greg's eye, and looked away.

Greg said: "Jacky? Jacky Jakes?"

The girl ignored him and kept walking, but Woody thought she looked troubled.

Greg said: "Jacky, it's me, Greg Peshkov."

Jacky—if it were she—did not respond, but she looked as if she might be about to burst into tears.

"Jacky—real name Mabel. You know me!" Greg stood in the middle of the sidewalk with his arms spread in a gesture of appeal.

She deliberately went around him, not speaking or meeting his eye, and walked on.

Greg turned. "Wait a minute!" he called after her. "You ran out on me, four years ago—you owe me an explanation!"

This was uncharacteristic of Greg, Woody thought. He had always been such a smooth operator with girls, at school and at Harvard. Now he seemed genuinely upset: bewildered, hurt, almost desperate.

Four years ago, Woody reflected. Could this be the girl in the scandal? It had taken place here in Washington. No doubt she lived here.

Greg ran after her. A cab had stopped at the corner and the passenger, a man in a tuxedo, was standing at the curb paying the driver. Jacky jumped in, slamming the door.

Greg went to the window and shouted through it: "Talk to me, please!"

The man in the tuxedo said: "Keep the change," and walked away.

The cab moved off, leaving Greg staring after it.

He slowly returned to where Woody stood waiting, intrigued. "I don't understand it," Greg said.

Woody said: "She looked frightened."

"What of? I never did her any harm. I was crazy about her."

"Well, she was scared of something."

Greg seemed to shake himself. "Sorry," he said. "Not your problem anyway. My apologies."

"Not at all."

Greg pointed to an apartment block a few steps away. "That's Joanne's building," he said. "Have a good time." Then he walked away.

Somewhat bemused, Woody went to the entrance. But he soon forgot about Greg's romantic life and started to think about his own. Did Joanne really like him? She might not kiss him this evening, but maybe he could ask her for a date.

This was a modest apartment house, with no doorman or hall porter. A list in the lobby revealed that Rouzrokh shared her place with Stewart and Fisher, presumably two other girls. Woody went up in the elevator. He realized he was empty-handed: he should have brought candy or flowers. He thought about going back to buy something, then decided that would be taking good manners too far. He rang the bell.

A girl in her early twenties opened the door.

Woody said: "Hello, I'm—"

"Come on in," she said, not waiting to hear his name. "The drinks are in the kitchen, and there's food on the table in the living room, if there's any left." She turned away, clearly thinking she had given him sufficient welcome.

The small apartment was packed with people drinking, smoking, and shouting at one another over the noise of the phonograph. Joanne had said "a few friends" and Woody had imagined eight or ten young people sitting around a coffee table discussing the crisis in Europe. He was disappointed: this overcrowded bash would give him little opportunity to demonstrate to Joanne how much he had grown up.

He looked around for her. He was taller than most people and could see over the heads. She was not in sight. He pushed through the crowd, searching for her. A girl with plump breasts and nice brown eyes looked up at him as he squeezed past and said: "Hello, big guy. I'm Diana Taverner. What's your name?"

"I'm looking for Joanne," he said.

She shrugged. "Good luck with that." She turned away.

He made his way into the kitchen. The noise level dropped a fraction. Joanne was nowhere to be seen, but he decided to get a drink while he was there. A broad-shouldered man of about thirty was rattling a cocktail shaker. Well dressed in a tan suit, pale blue shirt, and dark blue tie, he clearly was not a barman, but was acting like a host. "Scotch is over there," he said to another guest. "Help yourself. I'm making martinis, for anyone who's interested."

Woody said: "Got any bourbon?"

"Right here." The man passed him a bottle. "I'm Bexforth Ross."

"Woody Dewar." Woody found a glass and poured bourbon.

"Ice in that bucket," said Bexforth. "Where are you from, Woody?"

"I'm an intern in the Senate. You?"

"I work in the State Department. I'm in charge of the Italy desk." He started passing martinis around.

Clearly a rising star, Woody thought. The man had so much self-confidence it was irritating. "I was looking for Joanne."

"She's somewhere around. How do you know her?"

Here Woody felt he could show clear superiority. "Oh, we're old friends," he said airily. "In fact I've known her all my life. We were kids together in Buffalo. How about you?"

Bexforth took a long sip of martini and gave a satisfied sigh. Then he looked speculatively at Woody. "I haven't known Joanne as long as you have," he said. "But I guess I know her better."

"How so?"

"I'm planning to marry her."

Woody felt as if he had been slapped. "Marry her?"

"Yes. Isn't that great?"

Woody could not hide his dismay. "Does she know about this?"

Bexforth laughed, and patted Woody's shoulder condescendingly. "She sure does, and she's all for it. I'm the luckiest guy in the world."

Clearly Bexforth had divined that Woody was attracted to Joanne. Woody felt a fool. "Congratulations," he said dispiritedly.

"Thank you. And now I must circulate. Good talking to you, Woody."

"My pleasure."

Bexforth moved away.

Woody put his drink down untasted. "Fuck it," he said quietly. Then he left.

iv

The first day of September was sultry in Berlin. Carla von Ulrich woke up sweaty and uncomfortable, her bedsheets thrown off during the warm night. She looked out of her bedroom window to see low gray clouds hanging over the city, keeping heat in like a saucepan lid.

Today was a big day for her. In fact it would determine the course of her life.

She stood in front of the mirror. She had her mother's coloring, the dark hair and green eyes of the Fitzherberts. She was prettier than Maud, who had an angular face, striking rather than beautiful. Yet there was a bigger difference. Her mother attracted just about every man she met. Carla, by contrast, could not flirt. She watched other eighteen-year-old girls doing it—simpering, pulling their sweaters tight over their breasts, tossing their hair, and batting their eyelashes—and she just felt embarrassed. Her mother was more subtle, of course, so that men hardly knew they were being enchanted, but it was essentially the same game.

Today, however, Carla did not want to appear sexy. On the contrary, she needed to look practical, sensible, and capable. She put on a plain stone-colored cotton dress that came to midcalf, stepped into her flat unglamorous school sandals, and wove her hair into two plaits in the approved German-maiden fashion. The mirror showed her an ideal girl student: conservative, dull, sexless.

She was up and dressed before the rest of the family. The maid, Ada, was in the kitchen, and Carla helped her set out the breakfast things.

Her brother appeared next. Erik, nineteen and sporting a clipped black mustache, supported the Nazis, infuriating the rest of his family. He was a student at the Charité, the medical school of the University of Berlin, as was his best friend and fellow Nazi, Hermann Braun. The von Ulrichs could not afford tuition fees, of course, but Erik had won a scholarship.

Carla had applied for the same scholarship to study at the same institution. Her interview was today. If she was successful, she would study and become a doctor. If not . . .

She had no idea what else she would do.

The coming to power of the Nazis had ruined her parents' lives. Her father was no longer a deputy in the Reichstag, having lost his job when the Social Democratic Party became illegal, along with all other parties except for the Nazis. There was no work her father could do that would use his expertise as a politician and a diplomat. He scraped a living translating German newspaper articles for the British embassy, where he still had a few friends. Mother had once been a famous left-wing journalist, but newspapers were no longer allowed to publish her articles.

Carla found it heartbreaking. She was deeply devoted to her family, which included Ada. She was saddened by the decline in her father, who in her childhood had been a hardworking and politically powerful man and was now simply defeated. Even worse was the brave face put on by her mother, a famous suffragette leader in England before the war, now scraping a few marks by giving piano lessons.

But they said they could bear anything as long as their children grew up to lead happy and fulfilled lives.

Carla had always taken it for granted that she would spend her life making the world a better place, as her parents had. She did not know whether she would have followed her father into politics or her mother into journalism, but both were out of the question now.

What else was she to do, under a government that prized ruthlessness and brutality above all else? Her brother had given her the clue. Doctors made the world a better place regardless of the government. So she had made it her ambition to go to medical school. She had studied harder than any other girl in her class, and she had passed every exam with top marks, especially the sciences. She was better qualified than her brother to win a scholarship.

"There are no girls at all in my year," Erik said. He sounded grumpy. Carla thought he disliked the idea of her following in his footsteps. Their parents were proud of his achievements, despite his repellent politics. Perhaps he was afraid of being outshone.

Carla said: "All my grades are better than yours: biology, chemistry, math—"

"All right, all right."

"And the scholarship is available to female students, in principle—I checked."

Their mother came in at the end of this exchange, dressed in a gray watered-silk bathrobe with the cord doubled around her narrow waist. "They should follow their own rules," she said. "This is Germany, after all." Mother said she loved her adopted country, and perhaps she did, but since the coming of the Nazis she had taken to making wearily ironic remarks.

Carla dipped bread into milky coffee. "How will you feel, Mother, if England attacks Germany?"

"Miserably unhappy, as I felt last time," she replied. "I was married to your father throughout the Great War, and every day for more than four years I was terrified that he would be killed."

Erik said in a challenging tone: "But whose side will you take?"

"I'm German," she said. "I married for better or worse. Of course, we never foresaw anything as wicked and oppressive as this Nazi regime. No one did." Erik grunted in protest and she ignored him. "But a vow is a vow, and anyway I love your father."

Carla said: "We're not at war yet."

"Not quite," said Mother. "If the Poles have any sense, they will back down and give Hitler what he asks for."

"They should," said Erik. "Germany is strong now. We can take what we want, whether they like it or not."

Mother rolled her eyes up. "God spare us."

A car horn sounded outside. Carla smiled. A minute later her friend Frieda Franck entered the kitchen. She was going to accompany Carla to the interview, just to give moral support. She, too, was dressed in sober-schoolgirl fashion, though she, unlike Carla, had a wardrobe full of stylish clothes.

She was followed in by her older brother. Carla thought Werner Franck was wonderful. Unlike so many handsome boys, he was kind and thoughtful and funny. He had once been very left-wing, but all that seemed to have faded away, and he was nonpolitical now. He had had a string of beautiful and stylish girlfriends. If Carla had known how to flirt, she would have started with him.

Mother said: "I'd offer you coffee, Werner, but ours is ersatz, and I know you have the real thing at home."

"Shall I steal some from our kitchen for you, Frau von Ulrich?" he said. "I think you deserve it."

Mother blushed slightly, and Carla realized, with a twinge of disapproval, that even at forty-eight Mother was susceptible to Werner's charm.

Werner glanced at a gold wristwatch. "I have to go," he said. "Life is completely frantic at the Air Ministry these days."

Frieda said: "Thank you for the lift."

Carla said to Frieda: "Wait a minute—if you came in Werner's car, where's your bike?"

"Outside. We strapped it to the back of the car."

The two girls belonged to the Mercury Cycling Club and went everywhere by bike.

Werner said: "Best wishes for the interview, Carla. Bye, everyone."

Carla swallowed the last of her bread. As she was about to leave, her father came down. He had not shaved or put on a tie. He had been quite plump, when Carla was a girl, but now he was thin. He kissed Carla affectionately.

Mother said: "We haven't listened to the news!" She turned on the radio that stood on the shelf.

While the set was warming up, Carla and Frieda left the house, so they did not hear the news.

The University Hospital was in Mitte, the central area of Berlin where the von Ulrichs lived, so Carla and Frieda had a short bicycle ride. Carla began to feel nervous. The fumes from car exhausts nauseated her, and she wished she had not eaten breakfast. They reached the hospital, a new building put up in the twenties, and found their way to the room of Professor Bayer, who had the job of recommending a student for the scholarship. A haughty secretary said they were early and told them to wait.

Carla wished she had worn a hat and gloves. That would have made her look older and more authoritative, like someone sick people would trust. The secretary might have been polite to a girl in a hat.

The wait was long, but Carla was sorry when it came to an end and the secretary said the professor was ready to see her.

Frieda whispered: "Good luck!"

Carla went in.

Bayer was a thin man in his forties with a small gray mustache. He sat behind a desk, wearing a tan linen jacket over the waistcoat of a gray business suit. On the wall was a photograph of him shaking hands with Hitler.

He did not greet Carla, but barked: "What is an imaginary number?"

She was taken aback by his abruptness, but at least it was an easy question. "The square root of a negative real number; for example, the square root of minus one," she said in a shaky voice. "It cannot be assigned a real numerical value but can, nevertheless, be used in calculations."

He seemed a bit surprised. Perhaps he had expected to floor her completely. "Correct," he said after a momentary hesitation.

She looked around. There was no chair for her. Was she to be interviewed standing up?

He asked her some questions in chemistry and biology, all of which she answered easily. She began to feel a bit less nervous. Then he suddenly said: "Do you faint at the sight of blood?"

"No, sir."

"Aha!" he said triumphantly. "How do you know?"

"I delivered a baby when I was eleven years old," she said. "That was quite bloody."

"You should have sent for a doctor!"

"I did," she said indignantly. "But babies don't wait for doctors."

"Hmm." Bayer stood up. "Wait there." He left the room.

Carla stayed where she was. She was being subjected to a harsh test, but so far she thought she was doing all right. Fortunately, she was used to give-and-take arguments with men and women of all ages: combative discussions were commonplace in the von Ulrich house, and she had been holding her own with her parents and brother for as long as she could remember.

Bayer was gone for several minutes. What was he doing? Had he gone to fetch a colleague to meet this unprecedentedly brilliant girl applicant? That seemed too much to hope for.

She was tempted to pick up one of the books on his shelf and read, but she was scared of offending him, so she stood still and did nothing.

He came back after ten minutes with a pack of cigarettes. Surely he had not kept her standing in the middle of the room all this time while he went to the tobacconist's shop? Or was that another test? She began to feel angry.

He took his time lighting up, as if he needed to collect his thoughts. He blew out smoke and said: "How would you, as a woman, deal with a man who had an infection of the penis?"

She was embarrassed, and felt herself blush. She had never discussed the penis with a man. But she knew she had to be robust about such things if she wanted to be a doctor. "In the same way that you, as a man, would deal with a vaginal infection," she said. He looked horrified, and she feared she had been insolent. Hastily she went on: "I would examine the infected area carefully, try to establish the nature of the infection, and probably treat it with sulfonamide, although I have to admit we did not cover this in my school biology course."

He said skeptically: "Have you ever seen a naked man?"

"Yes."

He affected to be outraged. "But you are a single girl!"

"When my grandfather was dying, he was bedridden and incontinent. I helped my mother keep him clean—she could not manage on her own. He was too heavy." She tried a smile. "Women do these things all the time, Professor, for the very young and the very old, the sick and the helpless. We're used to it. It's only men who find such tasks embarrassing."

He was looking more and more cross, even though she was answering well. What was going wrong? It was almost as if he would have been happier for her to be intimidated by his manner and to give stupid replies.

He put out his cigarette thoughtfully in the ashtray on his desk. "I'm afraid you are not suitable as a candidate for this scholarship," he said.

She was astonished. How had she failed? She had answered every question! "Why not?" she said. "My qualifications are irreproachable."

"You are unwomanly. You talk freely of the vagina and the penis."

"It was you who started that! I merely answered your question."

"You have clearly been brought up in a coarse environment where you saw the nakedness of your male relatives."

"Do you think old people's diapers should be changed by men? I'd like to see you do it!"

"Worst of all you are disrespectful and insolent."

"You asked me challenging questions. If I had given you timid replies, you would have said I wasn't tough enough to be a doctor— wouldn't you?"

He was momentarily speechless, and she realized that was exactly what he would have done.

"You've wasted my time," she said, and she went to the door.

"Get married," he said. "Produce children for the Führer. That's your role in life. Do your duty!"

She went out and slammed the door.

Frieda looked up in alarm. "What happened?"

Carla headed for the exit without replying. She caught the eye of the secretary, who looked pleased, clearly knowing what had happened. Carla said to her: "You can wipe that smirk off your face, you dried-up old bitch." She had the satisfaction of seeing the woman's shock and horror.

Outside the building she said to Frieda: "He had no intention of recommending me for the scholarship, because I'm a woman. My qualifications were irrelevant. I did all that work for nothing." Then she burst into tears.

Frieda put her arms around her.

After a minute she felt better. "I'm not going to raise children for the damned Führer," she muttered.

"What?"

"Let's go home. I'll tell you when we get there." They climbed onto their bikes.

There was a strange air in the streets, but Carla was too full of her own woes to wonder what was going on. People were gathering around the loudspeakers that sometimes broadcast Hitler's speeches from the Kroll Opera, the building that was being used instead of the burned-out Reichstag. Presumably he was about to speak.

When they got back to the von Ulrich town house, Mother and Father were still in the kitchen, Father sitting next to the radio with a frown of concentration.

"They turned me down," Carla said. "Regardless of what their rules say, they don't want to give a scholarship to a girl."

"Oh, Carla, I'm so sorry," said Mother.

"What's on the radio?"

"Haven't you heard?" said Mother. "We invaded Poland this morning. We're at war."

v

The London season was over, but most people were still in town because of the crisis. Parliament, normally in recess at this time of year, had been specially recalled. But there were no parties, no royal receptions, no balls. It was like being at a seaside resort in February, Daisy thought. Today was Saturday, and she was getting ready to go to dinner at the home of her father-in-law, Earl Fitzherbert. What could be more dull?

She sat at her dressing table wearing an evening gown in eau-de-nil silk with a V-neck and a pleated skirt. She had silk flowers in her hair and a fortune in diamonds around her neck.

Her husband, Boy, was getting ready in his dressing room. She was pleased he was here. He spent many nights elsewhere. Although they lived in the same Mayfair house, sometimes several days would go by without their meeting. But he was at home tonight.

She held in her hand a letter from her mother in Buffalo. Olga had divined that Daisy was discontented in her marriage. There must have been hints in Daisy's letters home. Mother had good intuition. "I only want you to be happy," she wrote. "So listen when I tell you not to give up too soon. You're going to be Countess Fitzherbert one day, and your son, if you have one, will be the earl. You might regret throwing all that away just because your husband didn't pay you enough attention."

She might be right. People had been addressing Daisy as "my lady" for almost three years, yet it still gave her a little jolt of pleasure every time, like a puff on a cigarette.

But Boy seemed to think that marriage need make no great difference to his life. He spent evenings with his men friends, traveled all over the country to go horse racing, and rarely told his wife what his plans were. Daisy found it embarrassing to go to a party and be surprised to meet her husband there. But if she wanted to know where he was going, she had to ask his valet, and that was too demeaning.

Would he gradually grow up, and start to behave as a husband should, or would he always be like this?

He put his head around her door. "Come on, Daisy, we're late."

She put Mother's letter in a drawer, locked it, and went out. Boy was waiting in the hall, wearing a tuxedo. Fitz had at last succumbed to fashion and permitted informal short dinner jackets for family dinners at home.

They could have walked to Fitz's house, but it was raining, so Boy had had the car brought around. It was a Bentley Airline saloon, cream-colored with whitewall tires. Boy shared his father's love of beautiful cars.

Boy drove. Daisy hoped he would let her drive back. She enjoyed it, and anyway he was not safe after dinner, especially on wet roads.

London was preparing for war. Barrage balloons floated over the city at a height of two thousand feet, to impede bombers. In case that failed, sandbags were stacked outside important buildings. Alternate curbstones had been painted white, for the benefit of drivers in the blackout, which had begun yesterday. There were white stripes on large trees, street statues, and other obstacles that might cause accidents.

Princess Bea welcomed Boy and Daisy. In her fifties she was quite fat, but she still dressed like a girl. Tonight she wore a pink gown embroidered with beads and sequins. She never spoke about the story Daisy's father had told at the wedding, but she had stopped hinting that Daisy was socially inferior, and now always spoke to Daisy with courtesy, if not warmth. Daisy was cautiously friendly, and treated Bea like a slightly dotty aunt.

Boy's younger brother, Andy, was there. He and May had two children and May looked, to Daisy's interested eye, as if she might be expecting a third.

Boy wanted a son, of course, to be heir to the Fitzherbert title and fortune, but so far Daisy had failed to get pregnant. It was a sore point, and the evident fecundity of Andy and May made it worse. Daisy would have had a better chance if Boy spent more nights at home.

She was delighted to see her friend Eva Murray there—but without her husband. Jimmy Murray, now a captain, was with his unit and had not been able to get away, for most troops were in barracks and their officers were with them. Eva was family now, because Jimmy was May's brother and therefore an in-law. So Boy had been forced to overcome his prejudice against Jews and be polite to Eva.

Eva adored Jimmy as much now as she had three years ago when she married him. They, too, had produced two children in three years. But Eva looked worried tonight, and Daisy could guess why. "How are your parents?" she said.

"They can't get out of Germany," Eva said miserably. "The government won't give them exit visas."

"Can't Fitz help?"

"He's tried."

"What have they done to deserve this?"

"It's not them, particularly. There are thousands of German Jews in the same position. Only a few get visas."

"I'm so sorry." Daisy was more than sorry. She squirmed with embarrassment when she recalled how she and Boy had supported the Fascists in the early days. Her doubts had grown rapidly as the brutality of Fascism at home and abroad had become more and more obvious, and in the end she had been relieved when Fitz had complained that they were embarrassing him and had begged them to leave Mosley's party. Now Daisy felt she had been an utter fool ever to join in the first place.

Boy was not quite so repentant. He still thought that upper-class white Europeans formed a superior species, chosen by God to rule the earth. But he no longer believed that was a practical political philosophy. He was often infuriated by British democracy, but he did not advocate abolishing it.

They sat down to dinner early. "Neville is making a statement in the House of Commons at half past seven," Fitz said. Neville Chamberlain was prime minister. "I want to see it—I shall sit in the peers' gallery. I may have to leave you before dessert."

Andy said: "What do you think will happen, Papa?"

"I really don't know," Fitz said with a touch of exasperation. "Of course we would all like to avoid a war, but it's important not to give an impression of indecision."

Daisy was surprised: Fitz believed in loyalty and rarely criticized his government colleagues, even as obliquely as this.

Princess Bea said: "If there is a war, I shall go and live in Tŷ Gwyn."

Fitz shook his head. "If there is a war, the government will ask owners of large country houses to put them at the disposal of the military for the duration. As a member of the government I must set an example. I shall have to lend Tŷ Gwyn to the Welsh Rifles for use as a training center, or possibly a hospital."

Bea was outraged. "But it is my country house!"

"We may reserve a small part of the premises for private use."

"I don't choose to live in a small part of the premises—I am a princess!"

"It might be cozy. We could use the butler's pantry as a kitchen, and the breakfast room as a dining room, plus three or four of the smaller bedrooms."

"Cozy!" Bea looked disgusted, as if something unpleasant had been set before her, but she said no more.

Andy said: "Presumably Boy and I will have to join the Welsh Rifles."

May made a noise in her throat like a sob.

Boy said: "I shall join the air force."

Fitz was shocked. "But you can't. The Viscount Aberowen has always been in the Welsh Rifles."

"They haven't got any planes. The next war will be an air war. The RAF will be desperate for pilots. And I've been flying for years."

Fitz was about to argue, but the butler came in and said: "The car is ready, my lord."

Fitz looked at the clock on the mantelpiece. "Dash it, I've got to go. Thank you, Grout." He looked at Boy. "Don't make a final decision until we've talked some more. This is not right."

"Very well, Papa."

Fitz looked at Bea. "Forgive me, my dear, for leaving in the middle of dinner."

"Of course," she said.

Fitz got up from the table and walked to the door. Daisy noticed his limp, a grim reminder of what the last war had done.

The rest of dinner was gloomy. They were all wondering whether the prime minister would declare war.

When the ladies got up to withdraw, May asked Andy to take her arm. He excused himself to the two remaining men, saying: "My wife is in a delicate condition." It was the usual euphemism for pregnancy.

Boy said: "I wish my wife were as quick to get delicate."

It was a cheap shot, and Daisy felt herself blush bright red. She repressed a retort, then asked herself why she should be silent. "You know what footballers say, Boy," she said loudly. "You have to shoot to score."

It was Boy's turn to blush. "How dare you!" he said furiously.

Andy laughed. "You asked for it, brother."

Bea said: "Stop it, both of you. I expect my sons to wait until the ladies are out of earshot before indulging in such disgusting talk." She swept out of the room.

Daisy followed, but she parted company from the other women on the landing and went on upstairs, still feeling angry, wanting to be alone. How could Boy say such a thing? Did he really believe it had to be her fault that she was not pregnant? It could just as easily be his! Perhaps he knew that, and tried to blame her because he was afraid people would think he was infertile. That was probably the truth, but it was no excuse for a public insult.

She went to his old room. After they got married, the two of them had lived here for three months while their own house was being redecorated. They had used Boy's old bedroom and the one next door, although in those days they had slept together every night.

She went in and turned on the light. To her surprise she saw that Boy appeared not to have completely moved out. There was a razor on the washstand and a copy of *Flight* magazine on the bedside table. She opened a drawer and found a tin of Leonard's Liver-Aid, which he took every morning before breakfast. Did he sleep here when he was too disgustingly drunk to face his wife?

The lower drawer was locked, but she knew he kept the key in a pot on the mantelpiece. She had no qualms about prying: in her view a husband should have no secrets from his wife. She opened the drawer.

The first thing she found was a book of photographs of naked women. In artistic paintings and photographs, the women generally posed to half-conceal their private parts, but these girls were doing the opposite: legs akimbo, buttocks held open, even the lips of their vaginas spread to show the inside. Daisy would pretend to be shocked if anyone caught her, but in truth she was fascinated. She looked through the entire book with great interest, comparing the women with herself: the size and shape of their breasts, the amount of hair, their sexual organs. What a wonderful variety there was in women's bodies!

Some of the girls were stimulating themselves, or pretending to, and some were photographed in pairs, doing it to each other. Daisy was not really surprised that men liked this sort of thing.

She felt like an eavesdropper. It reminded her of the time she had gone to his room at Tŷ Gwyn, before they were married. Then she had been desperate to learn more about him, to gain intimate knowledge of the man she loved, to find a way to make him her own. What was she doing now? Spying on a husband who seemed no longer to love her, trying to understand where she had failed.

Beneath the book was a brown paper bag. Inside were several small, square paper envelopes, white with red lettering on the front. She read:

"Prentif" Reg. Trade Mark

SERVISPAK

NOTICE
Do not leave the envelope
or contents in public places
as this is likely to cause offense

BRITISH MADE
Latex rubber
Withstands all climates

None of it made any sense. Nowhere did it say what the package actually contained. So she opened it.

Inside was a piece of rubber. She unfolded it. It was shaped like a tube, closed at one end. She took a few seconds to figure out what it was.

She had never seen one, but she had heard people talk about such things. Americans called it a Trojan, the British a rubber johnny. The correct term was *condom,* and it was to stop you getting pregnant.

Why did her husband have a bag of them? There could be only one answer. They were to be used with another woman.

She felt like crying. She had given him everything he wanted. She had never told him she was too tired to make love—even when she was—nor had she refused anything he suggested in bed. She would even have posed like the women in the book of photographs, if he had asked her to.

What had she done wrong?

She decided to ask him.

Sorrow turned to anger. She stood up. She would take the paper packets down to the dining room and confront him with them. Why should she protect his feelings?

At that moment he walked in.

"I saw the light from the hall," he said. "What are you doing in here?" He looked at the open drawers of the bedside cupboard and said: "How dare you spy on me?"

"I suspected you of being unfaithful," she said. She held up the condom. "And I was right."

"Damn you for a sneak."

"Damn you for an adulterer."

He raised his hand. "I should beat you like a Victorian husband."

She snatched a heavy candlestick from the mantelpiece. "Try it, and I'll bop you like a twentieth-century wife."

"This is ridiculous." He sat down heavily on a chair by the door, looking defeated.

His evident unhappiness deflated Daisy's rage, and she just felt sad. She sat on the bed. But she had not lost her curiosity. "Who is she?"

He shook his head. "Never mind."

"I want to know!"

He shifted uncomfortably. "Does it matter?"

"It sure does." She knew she would get it out of him eventually.

He would not meet her eye. "Nobody you know, or would ever know."

"A prostitute?"

He was stung by this suggestion. "No!"

She goaded him further. "Do you pay her?"

"No. Yes." He was clearly ashamed enough to wish to deny it. "Well, an allowance. It's not the same thing."

"Why do you pay, if she's not a prostitute?"

"So they don't have to see anyone else."

"They? You have several mistresses?"

"No! Only two. They live in Aldgate. Mother and daughter."

"What? You can't be serious."

"Well, one day Joanie was . . . the French say *elle avait les fleurs*."

"American girls call it the curse."

"So Pearl offered to . . ."

"Act as a substitute? This is the most sordid arrangement imaginable! So you go to bed with them both?"

"Yes."

She thought of the book of photographs, and an outrageous possibility occurred to her. She had to ask. "Not at the same time?"

"Occasionally."

"How utterly foul."

"You don't need to worry about disease." He pointed to the condom in her hand. "Those things prevent infection."

"I'm overwhelmed by your thoughtfulness."

"Look, most men do this sort of thing, you know. At least, most men of our class."

"No, they don't," she said, but she thought of her father, who had a wife and a longtime mistress and still felt the need to romance Gladys Angelus.

Boy said: "My father isn't a faithful husband. He has bastards all over the place."

"I don't believe you. I think he loves your mother."

"He has one bastard for certain."

"Where?"

"I don't know."

"Then you can't be sure."

"I heard him say something to Bing Westhampton once. You know what Bing is like."

"I do," said Daisy. This seemed a moment for telling the truth, so she added: "He feels my bottom every chance he gets."

"Dirty old man. Anyway, we were all a bit drunk, and Bing said: 'Most of us have got one or two bastards hidden away, haven't we?' and Papa said: 'I'm pretty sure I've only got one.' Then he seemed to realize what he'd said, and he coughed and looked foolish and changed the subject."

"Well, I don't care how many bastards your father has. I'm a modern American girl and I won't live with an unfaithful husband."

"What can you do about it?"

"I'll leave you." She put on a defiant expression, but she felt in pain, as if he had stabbed her.

"And go back to Buffalo with your tail between your legs?"

"Perhaps. Or I could do something else. I've got plenty of money." Her father's lawyers had made sure Boy did not get his hands on the Vyalov-Peshkov fortune when they married. "I could go to California. Act in one of Father's movies. Become a film star. I bet you I could." This was all pretense. She wanted to burst into tears.

"Leave me, then," he said. "Go to hell, for all I care." She wondered if that was true. Looking at his face, she thought not.

They heard a car. Daisy pulled the blackout curtain aside an inch and saw Fitz's black-and-cream Rolls-Royce outside, its headlights dimmed by slit masks. "Your father's back," she said. "I wonder if we're at war."

"We'd better go down."

"I'll follow you."

Boy went out and Daisy looked in the mirror. She was surprised to see that she looked no different from the woman who had walked in here half an hour ago. Her life had been turned upside down, but there was no sign of it on her face. She felt terribly sorry for herself, and wanted to cry, but she repressed the urge. Steeling herself, she went downstairs.

Fitz was in the dining room, with raindrops on the shoulders of his dinner jacket. Grout, the butler, had set out cheese and fruit, as Fitz had skipped dessert. The family sat around the table as Grout poured a glass of claret for Fitz. He drank some and said: "It was absolutely dreadful."

Andy said: "What on earth happened?"

Fitz ate a corner of cheddar cheese before answering. "Neville spoke for four minutes. It was the worst performance by a prime minister that I have ever seen. He mumbled and prevaricated and said Germany might withdraw from Poland, which no one believes. He said nothing about war, or even an ultimatum."

Andy said: "But why?"

"Privately, Neville says he's waiting for the French to stop dithering and declare war simultaneously with us. But a lot of people suspect that's just a cowardly excuse."

Fitz took another draft of wine. "Arthur Greenwood spoke next." Greenwood was deputy leader of the Labour Party. "As he stood up, Leo Amery—a Conservative member of Parliament, mind you—shouted out: 'Speak for England, Arthur!' To think that a damned socialist might speak for England where a Conservative prime minister has failed! Neville looked as sick as a dog."

Grout refilled Fitz's glass.

"Greenwood was quite mild, but he did say: 'I wonder how long we are prepared to vacillate?' and, at that, M.P.s on both sides of the house roared their approval. I should think Neville wanted the earth to swallow him up." Fitz took a peach and sliced it with a knife and fork.

Andy said: "How were things left?"

"Nothing is resolved! Neville has gone back to Number Ten Downing Street. But most of the cabinet is holed up in Simon's room at the Commons." Sir John Simon was Chancellor of the Exchequer. "They're saying they won't leave the room until Neville sends the Germans an ultimatum. Meanwhile, Labour's National Executive Committee is in session, and discontented backbenchers are meeting in Winston's flat."

Daisy had always said she did not like politics, but since becoming part of Fitz's family, and seeing everything from the inside, she had become interested, and she found this drama fascinating and scary. "Then the prime minister must act!" she said.

"Oh, certainly," said Fitz. "Before Parliament meets again—which should be at noon tomorrow—I think Neville must either declare war or resign."

The phone rang in the hall and Grout went out to answer it. A minute later he came back and said: "That was the Foreign Office, my lord. The gentleman would not wait for you to come to the telephone, but insisted on giving a message." The old butler looked disconcerted, as if he had been spoken to rather sharply. "The prime minister has called an immediate meeting of the cabinet."

"Movement!" said Fitz. "Good."

Grout went on. "The foreign secretary would like you to be in attendance, if convenient." Fitz was not in the cabinet, but junior ministers were sometimes asked to attend meetings on their area of specialization, sitting at the side of the room rather than at the central table, so that they could answer questions of detail.

Bea looked at the clock. "It's almost eleven. I suppose you must go."

"Indeed I must. The phrase 'if convenient' is an empty courtesy." He patted his lips with a snowy napkin and limped out again.

Princess Bea said: "Make some more coffee, Grout, and bring it to the drawing room. We may be up late tonight."

"Yes, Your Highness."

They all returned to the drawing room, talking animatedly. Eva was in favor of war: she wanted to see the Nazi regime destroyed. She would worry about Jimmy, of course, but she had married a soldier and had always known he would have to risk his life in battle. Bea was pro-war, too, now that the Germans were allied with the Bolsheviks she hated. May feared that Andy would be killed, and could not stop crying. Boy did not see why two great nations such as England and Germany should go to war over a half-barbaric wasteland such as Poland.

As soon as she could, Daisy got Eva to go with her to another room where they could talk privately. "Boy's got a mistress," she said immediately. She showed Eva the condoms. "I found these."

"Oh, Daisy, I'm so sorry," Eva said.

Daisy thought of giving Eva the grisly details—they normally told each other everything—but this time Daisy felt too humiliated, so she just said: "I confronted him, and he admitted it."

"Is he sorry?"

"Not very. He says all men of his class do it, including his father."

"Jimmy doesn't," Eva said decisively.

"No, I'm sure you're right."

"What will you do?"

"I'm going to leave him. We can get divorced. Then someone else can be the viscountess."

"But you can't if there's a war!"

"Why not?"

"It's too cruel, when he's on the battlefield."

"He should have thought of that before he slept with a pair of prostitutes in Aldgate."

"But it would be cowardly, as well. You can't dump a man who is risking his life to protect you."

Reluctantly, Daisy saw Eva's point. War would transform Boy from a despicable adulterer who deserved rejection into a hero defending his wife, his mother, and his country from the terror of invasion and conquest. It was not just that everyone in London and Buffalo would see Daisy as a coward for leaving him. She would feel that way herself. If there was a war, she wanted to be brave, even though she was not sure what that might involve.

"You're right," she said grudgingly. "I can't leave him if there's a war."

There was a clap of thunder. Daisy looked at the clock: it was midnight. The rain altered in sound as a torrential downpour began.

Daisy and Eva returned to the drawing room. Bea was asleep on a couch. Andy had his arm around May, who was still sniveling. Boy was smoking a cigar and drinking brandy. Daisy decided she would definitely be driving home.

Fitz came in at half past midnight, his evening suit soaking wet. "The dithering is over," he said. "Neville will send the Germans an ultimatum in the morning. If they do not begin to withdraw their troops from Poland by midday—eleven o'clock our time—we will be at war."

They all got up and prepared to leave. In the hall, Daisy said: "I'll drive," and Boy did not argue with her. They got into the cream Bentley and Daisy started the engine. Grout closed the door of Fitz's house. Daisy turned on the windscreen wipers but did not pull away.

"Boy," she said, "let's try again."

"What do you mean?"

"I don't really want to leave you."

"I certainly don't want you to go."

"Give up those women in Aldgate. Sleep with me every night. Let's really try for a baby. It's what you want, isn't it?"

"Yes."

"Then will you do as I ask?"

There was a long pause. Then he said: "All right."

"Thank you."

She looked at him, hoping for a kiss, but he sat still, looking straight ahead through the windscreen, as the rhythmic wipers swept away the relentless rain.

vi

On Sunday the rain stopped and the sun came out. Lloyd Williams felt as if London had been washed clean.

During the course of the morning, the Williams family gathered in the kitchen of Ethel's house in Aldgate. There was no prior arrangement:

they turned up spontaneously. They wanted to be together, Lloyd guessed, if war was declared.

Lloyd longed for action against the Fascists, and at the same time dreaded the prospect of war. In Spain he had seen enough bloodshed and suffering for a lifetime. He wished never to take part in another battle. He had even given up boxing. Yet he hoped with all his heart that Chamberlain would not back down. He had seen for himself what Fascism meant in Germany, and the rumors coming out of Spain were equally nightmarish: the Franco regime was murdering former supporters of the elected government in their hundreds and thousands, and the priests were in control of the schools again.

This summer, after he graduated, he had immediately joined the Welsh Rifles, and as a former member of the Officer Training Corps he had been given the rank of lieutenant. The army was energetically preparing for combat: it was only with the greatest difficulty that he had got a twenty-four-hour pass to visit his mother this weekend. If the prime minister declared war today, Lloyd would be among the first to go.

Billy Williams came to the house in Nutley Street after breakfast on Sunday morning. Lloyd and Bernie were sitting by the radio, newspapers open on the kitchen table, while Ethel prepared a leg of pork for dinner. Uncle Billy almost wept when he saw Lloyd in uniform. "It makes me think of our Dave, that's all," he said. "He'd be a conscript now, if he'd come back from Spain."

Lloyd had never told Billy the truth about how Dave had died. He pretended he did not know the details, just that Dave had been killed in action at Belchite and was presumably buried there. Billy had been in the Great War and knew how haphazardly bodies were dealt with on the battlefield, and that probably made his grief worse. His great hope was to visit Belchite one day, when Spain was freed at last, and pay his respects to the son who died fighting in that great cause.

Lenny Griffiths was another who had never returned from Spain. No one had any idea where he might be buried. It was even possible he was still alive, in one of Franco's prison camps.

Now the radio reported Prime Minister Chamberlain's statement to the House of Commons last night, but nothing further.

"You'd never know what a stink there was afterwards," said Billy.

"The BBC doesn't report stinks," said Lloyd. "They like to sound reassuring."

Both Billy and Lloyd were members of the Labour Party's National Executive Committee—Lloyd as the representative of the party's youth section. After he came back from Spain, he had managed to gain readmission to Cambridge University, and while finishing his studies he had toured the country addressing Labour Party groups, telling people how the elected Spanish government had been betrayed by Britain's Fascist-friendly government. It had done no good—Franco's antidemocracy rebels had won anyway—but Lloyd had become a well-known figure, even something of a hero, especially among young left-wingers, hence his election to the Executive.

So both Lloyd and Uncle Billy had been at last night's committee meeting. They knew that Chamberlain had bowed to pressure from the cabinet and sent the ultimatum to Hitler. Now they were waiting on tenterhooks to see what would happen.

As far as they knew, no response had yet been received from Hitler.

Lloyd recalled his mother's friend Maud and her family in Berlin. Those two little children would be eighteen and nineteen now, he calculated. He wondered if they were sitting around a radio wondering whether they were going to war against England.

At ten o'clock Lloyd's half sister, Millie, arrived. She was now nineteen, and married to her friend Naomi Avery's brother Abe, a leather wholesaler. She earned good money as a salesgirl on commission in an expensive dress shop. She had ambitions to open her own shop, and Lloyd had no doubt that she would do it one day. Although it was not the career Bernie would have chosen for her, Lloyd could see how proud he was of her brains and ambition and smart appearance.

But today her poised self-assurance had collapsed. "It was awful when you were in Spain," she said tearfully to Lloyd. "And Dave and Lenny never did come back. Now it will be you and my Abie off somewhere, and us women waiting every day for news, wondering if you're dead yet."

Ethel put in: "And your cousin Keir. He's almost eighteen now."

Lloyd said to his mother: "Which regiment was my real father in?"

"Oh, does it matter?" She was never keen to talk about Lloyd's father, perhaps out of consideration for Bernie.

But Lloyd wanted to know. "It matters to me," he said.

She threw a peeled potato into a pan of water with unnecessary vigor. "He was in the Welsh Rifles."

"The same as me! Why didn't you tell me before?"

"The past is the past."

There might be another reason for her caginess, Lloyd knew. She had probably been pregnant when she married. This did not bother Lloyd, but to her generation it was shameful. All the same, he persisted. "Was my father Welsh?"

"Yes."

"From Aberowen?"

"No."

"Where, then?"

She sighed. "His parents moved around—something to do with his father's job—but I think they were from Swansea originally. Satisfied now?"

"Yes."

Lloyd's aunt Mildred came in from church, a stylish middle-aged woman, pretty except for protruding front teeth. She wore a fancy hat—she was a milliner with a small factory. Her two daughters by her first marriage, Enid and Lillian, both in their late twenties, were married with children of their own. Her elder son was the Dave who died in Spain. Her younger son, Keir, followed her into the kitchen. Mildred insisted on taking her children to church, even though her husband, Billy, would have nothing to do with religion. "I had a lifetime's worth of that when I was a child," he often said. "If I'm not saved, no one is."

Lloyd looked around. This was his family: mother, stepfather, half sister, uncle, aunt, cousin. He did not want to leave them and go away to die somewhere.

Lloyd looked at his watch, a stainless-steel model with a square face that Bernie had given him as a graduation present. It was eleven o'clock. On the radio, the fruity voice of newsreader Alvar Liddell said the prime minister was expected to make an announcement shortly. Then there was some solemn classical music.

"Hush, now, everyone," said Ethel. "I'll make you all a cup of tea after."

The kitchen went quiet.

Alvar Liddell announced the prime minister, Neville Chamberlain.

The appeaser of Fascism, Lloyd thought; the man who gave Czechoslovakia to Hitler; the man who had stubbornly refused to help the elected government of Spain even after it became indisputably obvious that the Germans and Italians were arming the rebels. Was he about to cave in yet again?

Lloyd noticed that his parents were holding hands, Ethel's small fingers digging into Bernie's palm.

He checked his watch again. It was a quarter past eleven.

Then they heard the prime minister say: "I am speaking to you from the Cabinet Room at Ten Downing Street."

Chamberlain's voice was reedy and overprecise. He sounded like a pedantic schoolmaster. What we need is a warrior, Lloyd thought.

"This morning the British ambassador in Berlin handed the German government a final note, stating that unless we heard from them by eleven o'clock that they were prepared at once to withdraw their troops from Poland, a state of war would exist between us."

Lloyd found himself feeling impatient with Chamberlain's verbiage. *A state of war would exist between us:* what a strange way to put it. Get on with it, he thought; get to the point. This is life and death.

Chamberlain's voice deepened and became more statesmanlike. Perhaps he was no longer looking at the microphone, but instead seeing millions of his countrymen in their homes, sitting by their radio sets, waiting for his fateful words. "I have to tell you now that no such undertaking has been received . . ."

Lloyd heard his mother say: "Oh, God, spare us." He looked at her. Her face was gray.

Chamberlain uttered his next, dreadful words quite slowly. ". . . and that, consequently, this country is at war with Germany."

Ethel began to cry.

PART TWO

A SEASON
OF
BLOOD

CHAPTER SIX

1940 (I)

Aberowen had changed. There were cars, trucks, and buses on the streets. When Lloyd had come here as a child in the 1920s to visit his grandparents, a parked car had been a rarity that would draw a crowd.

But the town was still dominated by the twin towers of the pithead, with their majestically revolving wheels. There was nothing else: no factories, no office blocks, no industry other than coal. Almost every man in town worked down the pit. There were a few dozen exceptions: some shopkeepers, numerous clergymen of all denominations, a town clerk, a doctor. Whenever the demand for coal slumped, as it had in the thirties, and men were laid off, there was nothing else for them to do. That was why the Labour Party's most passionate demand was help for the unemployed, so that such men would never again suffer the agony and humiliation of being unable to feed their families.

Lieutenant Lloyd Williams arrived by train from Cardiff on a Sunday in April 1940. Carrying a small suitcase, he walked up the hill to Tŷ Gwyn. He had spent eight months training new recruits—the same work he had done in Spain—and coaching the Welsh Rifles boxing team, but the army had at last realized he spoke fluent German, transferred him to intelligence duties, and sent him on a training course.

Training was all the army had done so far. No British forces had yet fought the enemy in an engagement of any significance. Germany and the USSR had overrun Poland and divided it between them, and the Allied guarantee of Polish independence had proved worthless.

British people called it the Phoney War, and they were impatient for the real thing. Lloyd had no sentimental illusions about warfare— he had heard the piteous voices of dying men begging for water on the battlefields of Spain—but even so he was eager to get started on the final showdown with Fascism.

The army was expecting to send more forces to France, assuming the Germans would invade. It had not happened, and they remained at the ready, but meanwhile they did a lot of training.

Lloyd's initiation into the mysteries of military intelligence was to take place in the stately home that had featured in his family's destiny for so long. The wealthy and noble owners of many such palaces had loaned them to the armed forces, perhaps for fear that otherwise they might be confiscated permanently.

The army had certainly made Tŷ Gwyn look different. There were a dozen olive-drab vehicles parked on the lawn, and their tires had chewed up the earl's lush turf. The gracious entrance courtyard, with its curved granite steps, had become a supply dump, and giant cans of baked beans and cooking lard stood in teetering stacks where, formerly, bejeweled women and men in tailcoats had stepped out of their carriages. Lloyd grinned: he liked the leveling effect of war.

Lloyd entered the house. He was greeted by a podgy officer in a creased and stained uniform. "Here for the intelligence course, Lieutenant?"

"Yes, sir. My name is Lloyd Williams."

"I'm Major Lowther."

Lloyd had heard of him. He was the Marquis of Lowther, known to his pals as Lowthie.

Lloyd looked around. The paintings on the walls had been shrouded with huge dust sheets. The ornate carved marble fireplaces had been boxed in with rough planking, leaving only a small space for a grate. The dark old furniture that his mother sometimes mentioned fondly had all disappeared, to be replaced by steel desks and cheap chairs. "My goodness, the place looks different," he said.

Lowther smiled. "You've been here before. Do you know the family?"

"I was up at Cambridge with Boy Fitzherbert. I met the viscountess there, too, although they weren't married then. But I suppose they've moved out for the duration."

"Not entirely. A few rooms have been reserved for their private use. But they don't bother us at all. So you came here as a guest?"

"Goodness, no, I don't know them well. No, I was shown around the place as a boy, one day when the family weren't in residence. My mother worked here at one time."

"Really? What, looking after the earl's library, or something?"

"No, as a housemaid." As soon as the words were out of Lloyd's mouth, he knew he had made a mistake.

Lowther's face changed to an expression of distaste. "I see," he said. "How very interesting."

Lloyd knew he had instantly been pigeonholed as a proletarian upstart. He would now be treated as a second-class citizen throughout his time here. He should have kept quiet about his mother's past: he knew how snobbish the army was.

Lowthie said: "Show the lieutenant to his room, Sergeant. Attic floor."

Lloyd had been assigned a room in the old servants' quarters. He did not really mind. It was good enough for my mother, he thought.

As they walked up the back stairs, the sergeant told Lloyd he had no obligations until dinner in the mess. Lloyd asked whether any of the Fitzherberts happened to be in residence right now, but the man did not know.

It took Lloyd two minutes to unpack. He combed his hair, put on a clean uniform shirt, and went to visit his grandparents.

The house in Wellington Row seemed smaller and more drab than ever, though it now had hot water in the scullery and a flushing toilet in the outhouse. The decor had not altered within Lloyd's memory: same rag rug on the floor, same faded paisley curtains, same hard oak chairs in the single ground-floor room that served as living room and kitchen.

His grandparents had changed, though. Both were about seventy now, he guessed, and looking frail. Granda had pains in his legs, and had reluctantly retired from his job with the miners' union. Grandmam had a weak heart: Dr. Mortimer had told her to put her feet up for a quarter of an hour after meals.

They were pleased to see Lloyd in his uniform. "Lieutenant, is it?" said Grandmam. A class warrior all her life, she nevertheless could not conceal her pride that her grandson was an officer.

News traveled fast in Aberowen, and the fact that Dai Williams's grandson was visiting probably went halfway round the town before Lloyd had finished his first cup of Grandmam's strong tea. So he was not really surprised when Tommy Griffiths dropped in.

"I expect my Lenny would be a lieutenant, like you, if he'd come back from Spain," Tommy said.

"I should think so," Lloyd said. He had never met an officer who had been a coal miner in civilian life, but anything might happen once the war got going properly. "He was the best sergeant in Spain, I can tell you that."

"You two went through a lot together."

"We went through hell," Lloyd said. "And we lost. But the Fascists won't win this time."

"I'll drink to that," said Tommy, and emptied his mug of tea.

Lloyd went with his grandparents to the evening service at the Bethesda Chapel. Religion was not a big part of his life, and he certainly did not go along with Granda's dogmatism. The universe was mysterious, Lloyd thought, and people might as well admit it. But it pleased his grandparents that he sat with them in chapel.

The extempore prayers were eloquent, knitting biblical phrases seamlessly into colloquial language. The sermon was a bit tedious. But the singing thrilled Lloyd. Welsh chapelgoers automatically sang in four-part harmony, and when they were in the mood, they could raise the roof.

As he joined in, Lloyd felt this was the beating heart of Britain, here in this whitewashed chapel. The people around him were poorly dressed and ill-educated, and they lived lives of unending hard work, the men winning the coal underground, the women raising the next generation of miners. But they had strong backs and sharp minds, and all on their own they had created a culture that made life worth living. They gained hope from nonconformist Christianity and left-wing politics, they found joy in rugby football and male voice choirs, and they were bonded together by generosity in good times and solidarity in bad. This was what he would be fighting for, these people, this town. And if he had to give his life for them, it would be well spent.

Granda gave the closing prayer, standing up with his eyes shut, leaning on a walking stick. "You see among us, O Lord, your young servant Lloyd Williams, sitting by here in his uniform. We ask you, in your wisdom and grace, to spare his life in the conflict to come. Please, Lord, send him back home to us safe and whole. If it be your will, O Lord."

The congregation gave a heartfelt amen, and Lloyd wiped away a tear.

He walked the old folks home as the sun went down behind the mountain and an evening gloom settled on the rows of gray houses. He refused the offer of supper and hurried back to Tŷ Gwyn, arriving in time for dinner in the mess.

They had braised beef, boiled potatoes, and cabbage. It was no better or worse than most army food, and Lloyd tucked in, aware that it had been paid for by people such as his grandparents who were having bread-and-dripping for their supper. There was a bottle of whisky on the table, and Lloyd took some to be convivial. He studied his fellow trainees and tried to remember their names.

On his way up to bed he passed through the Sculpture Room, now empty of art and furnished with a blackboard and twelve cheap desks.

There he saw Major Lowther talking to a woman. At a second glance he saw that the woman was Daisy Fitzherbert.

He was so surprised that he stopped. Lowther looked around with an irritated expression. He saw Lloyd and reluctantly said: "Lady Aberowen, I believe you know Lieutenant Williams."

If she denies it, Lloyd thought, I shall remind her of the time she kissed me, long and hard, on a Mayfair street in the dark.

"How nice to see you again, Mr. Williams," she said, and put out her hand to shake.

Her skin was warm and soft to his touch. His heart beat faster.

Lowther said: "Williams tells me his mother worked at this house as a maid."

"I know," Daisy said. "He told me that at the Trinity Ball. He was reproving me for being a snob. I'm sorry to say that he was quite right."

"You're generous, Lady Aberowen," said Lloyd, feeling embarrassed. "I don't know what business I had to say such a thing to you." She seemed less brittle than he remembered; perhaps she had matured.

Daisy said to Lowther: "Mr. Williams's mother is a member of Parliament now, though."

Lowther was taken aback.

Lloyd said to Daisy: "And how is your Jewish friend Eva? I know she married Jimmy Murray."

"They have two children now."

"Did she get her parents out of Germany?"

"How kind of you to remember—but no, sadly, the Rothmanns can't get exit visas."

"I'm so sorry. It must be hell for her."

"It is."

Lowther was visibly impatient with this talk of housemaids and Jews. "To get back to what I was saying, Lady Aberowen . . ."

Lloyd said: "I'll bid you good night." He left the room and ran upstairs.

As he got ready for bed, he found himself singing the last hymn from the service:

No storm can shake my inmost calm
While to that rock I'm clinging
Since Love is Lord of heaven and earth
How can I keep from singing?

ii

Three days later Daisy was finishing writing to her half brother, Greg. When war broke out, he had sent her a sweetly anxious letter, and since then they had corresponded every month or so. He had told her about seeing his old flame, Jacky Jakes, on E Street in Washington, and asked Daisy what would make a girl run away like that. Daisy had no idea. She said so, and wished him luck, then signed off.

She looked at the clock. It was an hour before the trainees' dinnertime, so lessons had ended and she had a good chance of catching Lloyd in his room.

She went up to the old servants' quarters on the attic floor. The young officers were sitting or lying on their beds, reading or writing. She found Lloyd in a narrow room with an old cheval glass, sitting by the window, studying an illustrated book. She said: "Reading something interesting?"

He sprang to his feet. "Hello, this is a surprise."

He was blushing. He probably still had a crush on her. It had been very cruel of her to kiss him, when she had no intention of letting the relationship go any further. But that was four years ago, and they had both been kids. He should have gotten over it by now.

She looked at the book in his hands. It was in German, and had color pictures of badges.

"We have to know German insignia," he explained. "A lot of military intelligence comes from interrogation of prisoners of war immediately after their capture. Some won't talk, of course; so the interrogator needs to be able to tell, just by looking at the prisoner's uniform, what his rank is, what army corps he belongs to, whether he is from infantry, cavalry, artillery, or a specialist unit such as veterinarian, and so on."

"That's what you're learning here?" she said skeptically. "The meanings of German badges?"

He laughed. "It's one of the things we're learning. One I can tell you about without giving away military secrets."

"Oh, I see."

"Why are you here in Wales? I'm surprised you're not doing something for the war effort."

"There you go again," she said. "Moral reproof. Did someone tell you this was a way to charm women?"

"Pardon me," he said stiffly. "I didn't mean to rebuke you."

"Anyway, there is no war effort. Barrage balloons float in the air as a hazard to German planes that never come."

"At least you'd have a social life in London."

"Do you know, that used to be the most important thing in the world, and now it's not?" she said. "I must be getting old."

There was another reason she had left London, but she was not going to tell him.

"I imagined you in a nurse's uniform," he said.

"Not likely. I hate sick people. But before you give me another of those disapproving frowns, take a look at this." She handed him the framed photograph she was carrying.

He studied it, frowning. "Where did you get it?"

"I was looking through a box of old pictures in the basement junk room."

It was a group photo taken on the east lawn of Tŷ Gwyn on a summer morning. In the center was the young Earl Fitzherbert, with a big white dog at his feet. The girl next to him was probably his sister, Maud, whom Daisy had never met. Lined up on either side of them were forty or fifty men and women in a variety of servants' uniforms.

"Look at the date," she said.

"Nineteen twelve," Lloyd read aloud.

She watched him, studying his reactions to the photo he was holding. "Is your mother in it?"

"Goodness! She might be." Lloyd looked closer. "I believe she is," he said after a minute.

"Show me."

Lloyd pointed. "I think that's her."

Daisy saw a slim, pretty girl of about nineteen, with curly black hair under a maid's white cap, and a smile that had more than a hint of mischief in it. "Why, she's enchanting!" she said.

"She was then, anyway," Lloyd said. "Nowadays people are more likely to call her formidable."

"Have you ever met Lady Maud? Do you think that's her next to Fitz?"

"I suppose I've known her all my life, off and on. She and my mother were suffragettes together. I haven't seen her since I left Berlin in 1933, but this is definitely her in the picture."

"She's not so pretty."

"Perhaps, but she's very poised, and wonderfully well dressed."

"Anyway, I thought you might like to have the picture."

"To keep?"

"Of course. No one else wants it—that's why it was in a box in the basement."

"Thank you!"

"You're welcome." Daisy went to the door. "Go back to your studies."

Going down the back stairs she hoped she had not flirted. She probably should not have gone to see him at all. She had succumbed to a generous impulse. Heaven forbid that he should misinterpret it.

She felt a sharp pain in her tummy, and stopped on the half landing. She had had a slight backache all day—which she attributed to the cheap mattress she was sleeping on—but this was different. She thought back over what she had eaten today, but could not identify anything that might have made her ill: no undercooked chicken, no unripe fruit. She had not eaten oysters—no such luck! The pain went as quickly as it had come and she told herself to forget about it.

She returned to her quarters in the basement. She was living in what had been the housekeeper's flat: a tiny bedroom, a sitting room, a small kitchen, and an adequate bathroom with a tub. An old footman called Morrison was acting as caretaker to the house, and a young woman from Aberowen was her maid. The girl was called Little Maisie Owen, although she was quite big. "My mother's Maisie, too, so I've always been Little Maisie, even though I'm taller than her now," she had explained.

The phone rang as Daisy entered. She picked it up and heard her husband's voice. "How are you?" he said.

"I'm fine. What time will you be here?" He had flown to RAF St. Athan, a large air base outside Cardiff, on some mission, and he had promised to visit her and spend the night.

"I'm not going to make it. I'm sorry."

"Oh, how disappointing!"

"There's a ceremonial dinner at the base that I'm required to attend."

He did not sound particularly dispirited that he would not see her, and she felt spurned. "How nice for you," she said.

"It will be boring, but I can't get out of it."

"Not half as boring as living here on my own."

"It must be dull. But you're better off there, in your condition."

Thousands of people had left London after war was declared, but most of them had drifted back when the expected bombing raids and gas attacks did not materialize. However, Bea and May and even Eva were agreed that Daisy's pregnancy meant she should live at Tŷ Gwyn. Many women gave birth safely every day in London, Daisy had pointed out, but of course the heir to the earldom was different.

In truth she did not mind as much as she had expected. Perhaps pregnancy had made her uncharacteristically passive. But there was a halfhearted quality about London social life since the declaration of war, as if people felt they did not have the right to enjoy themselves. They were like vicars in a pub, knowing it was supposed to be fun but unable to enter into the spirit.

"I wish I had my motorcycle here, though," she said. "Then at least I could explore Wales." Petrol was rationed, but not severely.

"Really, Daisy!" he said censoriously. "You can't ride a motorcycle—the doctor absolutely forbade it."

"Anyway, I've discovered literature," she said. "The library here is wonderful. A few rare and valuable editions have been packed away, but nearly all the books are still on the shelves. I'm getting the education I worked so hard to avoid at school."

"Excellent," he said. "Well, curl up with a good murder mystery and enjoy your evening."

"I had a slight tummy pain earlier."

"Probably indigestion."

"I expect you're right."

"Give my regards to that slob Lowthie."

"Don't drink too much port at your dinner."

Just as Daisy hung up, she got the tummy cramp again. This time it lasted longer. Maisie came in, saw her face, and said: "Are you all right, my lady?"

"Just a twinge."

"I have came to ask if you are ready for your supper."

"I don't feel hungry. I think I'll skip supper tonight."

"I done you a lovely cottage pie," Maisie said reproachfully.

"Cover it and put it in the larder. I'll eat it tomorrow."

"Shall I make you a nice cup of tea?"

Just to get rid of her Daisy said: "Yes, please." Even after four years she had not grown to like strong British tea with milk and sugar in it.

The pain went away, and she sat down and opened *The Mill on the Floss*. She forced herself to drink Maisie's tea and felt a little better. When she had finished the drink, and Maisie had washed the cup and saucer, she sent Maisie home. The girl had to walk a mile in the dark, but she carried a flashlight, and said she did not mind.

An hour later the pain returned, and this time it did not go away. Daisy went to the toilet, vaguely hoping to relieve pressure in her abdomen. She was surprised and worried to see spots of dark red blood in her underwear.

She put on clean panties, and, seriously worried now, she went to the phone. She got the number of RAF St. Athan and called the base. "I need to speak to Flight Lieutenant the Viscount Aberowen," she said.

"We can't connect personal calls to officers," said a pedantic Welshman.

"This is an emergency. I must speak to my husband."

"There are no phones in the rooms—this isn't the Dorchester Hotel." Perhaps it was her imagination, but he sounded quite pleased that he could not help her.

"My husband will be at the ceremonial banquet. Please send an orderly to bring him to the phone."

"I haven't got any orderlies, and anyway there's no banquet."

"No banquet?" Daisy was momentarily at a loss.

"Just the usual dinner in the mess," the operator said. "And that was finished an hour ago."

Daisy slammed the phone down. No banquet? Boy had distinctly said he had to attend a ceremonial dinner at the base. He must have lied. She wanted to cry. He had chosen not to see her, preferring to go drinking with his comrades, or perhaps to visit some woman. The reason did not matter. Daisy was not his priority.

She took a deep breath. She needed help. She did not know the phone number of the Aberowen doctor, if there was one. What was she to do?

Last time Boy had left he had said: "You'll have a hundred or more army officers to look after you if necessary." But she could not tell the Marquis of Lowther that she was bleeding from her vagina.

The pain was getting worse, and she could feel something warm and sticky between her legs. She went to the bathroom again and washed herself. There were clots in the blood, she saw. She did not have any sanitary towels—pregnant women did not need them, she had thought. She cut a length off a hand towel and stuffed it in her panties.

Then she thought of Lloyd Williams.

He was kind. He had been brought up by a strong-minded feminist woman. He adored Daisy. He would help her.

She went up to the hall. Where was he? The trainees would have finished their dinner by now. He might be upstairs. Her stomach hurt so much that she did not think she could make it all the way to the attic.

Perhaps he was in the library. The trainees used the room for quiet study. She went in. A sergeant was poring over an atlas. "Would you be very kind," she said to him, "and find Lieutenant Lloyd Williams for me?"

"Of course, my lady," said the man, closing the book. "What's the message?"

"Ask him if he would come down to the basement for a moment."

"Are you all right, ma'am? You look a bit pale."

"I'll be fine. Just fetch Williams as quickly as you can."

"Right away."

Daisy returned to her rooms. The effort of seeming normal had exhausted her, and she lay on the bed. Before long she felt the blood soaking through her dress, but she hurt too much to care. She looked at her watch. Why had Lloyd not come? Perhaps the sergeant could not find him. It was such a big house. Perhaps she would just die here.

There was a tap at the door, and then to her immense relief she heard his voice. "It's Lloyd Williams."

"Come in," she called. He was going to see her in a dreadful state. Perhaps it would put him off her for good.

She heard him enter the next room. "It took me a while to find your quarters," he said. "Where are you?"

"Through here."

He stepped into the bedroom. "Good God!" he exclaimed. "What on earth has happened?"

"Get help," she said. "Is there a doctor in this town?"

"Of course. Dr. Mortimer. He's been here for centuries. But there may not be time. Let me . . ." He hesitated. "You may be hemorrhaging, but I can't tell unless I look."

She closed her eyes. "Go ahead." She was almost too scared to be embarrassed.

She felt him raise the skirt of her dress. "Oh, dear," he said. "Poor you." Then he ripped her underpants. "I'm sorry," he said. "Is there some water . . . ?"

"Bathroom," she said, pointing.

He stepped into the bathroom and ran a tap. A moment later she felt a warm, damp cloth being used to clean her.

Then he said: "It's just a trickle. I've seen men bleed to death, and you're not in that danger." She opened her eyes to see him pulling her skirt back down. "Where's the phone?" he said.

"Sitting room."

She heard him say: "Put me through to Dr. Mortimer, quick as you can." There was a pause. "This is Lloyd Williams. I'm at Tŷ Gwyn. May I speak to the doctor? . . . Oh, hello, Mrs. Mortimer, when do you expect him back? . . . It's a woman with abdominal pain and vaginal bleeding . . . Yes, I do realize most women suffer that every month, but this is clearly abnormal . . . She's twenty-four . . . yes, married . . . no children . . . I'll ask." He raised his voice. "Could you be pregnant?"

"Yes," Daisy replied. "Three months."

He repeated her answer; then there was a long silence. Eventually he hung up the phone and returned to her.

He sat on the edge of the bed. "The doctor will come as soon as he can, but he's operating on a miner crushed by a runaway dram. However, his wife is quite sure that you've suffered a miscarriage." He took her hand. "I'm sorry, Daisy."

"Thank you," she whispered. The pain seemed less, but she felt terribly sad. The heir to the earldom was no more. Boy would be so upset.

Lloyd said: "Mrs. Mortimer says it's quite common, and most women suffer one or two miscarriages between pregnancies. There's no danger, provided the bleeding isn't copious."

"What if it gets worse?"

"Then I must drive you to Merthyr Hospital. But going ten miles in an army lorry would be quite bad for you, so it's to be avoided unless your life is in danger."

She was not frightened anymore. "I'm so glad you were here."

"May I make a suggestion?"

"Of course."

"Do you think you can walk a few steps?"

"I don't know."

"Let me run you a bath. If you can manage it, you'll feel so much better when you're clean."

"Yes."

"Then perhaps you can improvise a bandage of some kind."

"Yes."

He returned to the bathroom, and she heard water running. She sat upright. She felt dizzy, and rested for a minute; then her head cleared. She swung her feet to the floor. She was sitting in congealing blood, and felt disgusted with herself.

The taps were turned off. He came back in and took her arm. "If you feel faint, just tell me," he said. "I won't let you fall." He was surprisingly strong, and half-carried her as he walked her into the bathroom. At some point her ripped underwear fell to the floor. She stood beside the bath and let him undo the buttons at the back of her dress. "Can you manage the rest?" he said.

She nodded, and he went out.

Leaning on the linen basket, she took off her clothes slowly, leaving them on the floor in a bloodstained heap. Gingerly, she got into the bath. The water was just hot enough. The pain eased as she lay back and relaxed. She felt overwhelmed with gratitude to Lloyd. He was so kind that it made her want to cry.

After a few minutes, the door opened a crack and his hand appeared holding some clothes. "A nightdress, and so on," he said. He placed them on top of the linen basket and closed the door.

When the water began to cool, she stood up. She felt dizzy again, but only for a moment. She dried herself with a towel, then put on the nightdress and underwear he had brought. She placed a hand towel inside her panties to soak up the blood that continued to seep.

When she returned to the bedroom, her bed was made up with clean sheets and blankets. She climbed in and sat upright, pulling the covers to her neck.

He came in from the sitting room. "You must be feeling better," he said. "You look embarrassed."

"*Embarrassed* isn't the word," she said. "Mortified, perhaps, though even that seems understated." The truth was not so simple. She winced when she thought of how he had seen her—but, on the other hand, he had not seemed disgusted.

He went into the bathroom and picked up her discarded clothes. Apparently he was not squeamish about menstrual blood.

She said: "Where have you put the sheets?"

"I found a big sink in the flower room. I left them to soak in cold water. I'll do the same with your clothes, shall I?"

She nodded.

He disappeared again. Where had he learned to be so competent and self-sufficient? In the Spanish Civil War, she supposed.

She heard him moving around the kitchen. He reappeared with two cups of tea. "You probably hate this stuff, but it will make you feel better." She took the tea. He showed her two white pills in the palm of his hand. "Aspirin? May ease the stomach cramps a bit."

She took them and swallowed them with hot tea. He had always struck her as being mature beyond his years. She remembered how confidently he had gone off to find the drunken Boy at the Gaiety Theatre. "You've always been like this," she said. "A real grown-up, when the rest of us were just pretending."

She finished the tea and felt sleepy. He took the cups away. "I may just close my eyes for a moment," she said. "Will you stay here, if I go to sleep?"

"I'll stay as long as you like," he said. Then he said something else, but his voice seemed to fade away, and she slept.

iii

After that Lloyd began to spend his evenings in the little housekeeper's flat.

He looked forward to it all day.

He would go downstairs a few minutes after eight, when dinner in the mess was over and Daisy's maid had left for the night. They would sit opposite one another in the two old armchairs. Lloyd would bring a book to study—there was always "homework," with tests in the morning—and Daisy would read a novel, but mostly they talked. They related what had happened during the day, discussed whatever they were reading, and told each other the story of their lives.

He recounted his experiences at the Battle of Cable Street. "Standing there in a peaceful crowd, we were charged by mounted policemen screaming about dirty Jews," he told her. "They beat us with their truncheons and pushed us through the plate-glass windows."

She had been quarantined with the Fascists in Tower Gardens, and had seen none of the fighting. "That wasn't the way it was reported," she said. She had believed the newspapers that said it had been a street riot organized by hooligans.

Lloyd was not surprised. "My mother watched the newsreel at the Aldgate Essoldo a week later," he recalled. "That plummy-voiced commentator said: 'From impartial observers the police received nothing but praise.' Mam said the entire audience burst out laughing."

Daisy was shocked by his skepticism about the news. He told her that most British papers had suppressed stories of atrocities by Franco's army in Spain, and exaggerated any report of bad behavior by government forces. She admitted she had swallowed Earl Fitzherbert's view that the rebels were high-minded Christians liberating Spain from the threat of Communism. She knew nothing of mass executions, rape, and looting by Franco's men.

It seemed never to have occurred to her that newspapers owned by capitalists might play down news that reflected badly on the Conservative government, the military, or businessmen, and would seize upon any incident of bad behavior by trade unionists or left-wing parties.

Lloyd and Daisy talked about the war. There was action at last. British and French troops had landed in Norway, and were contending for control with the Germans who had done the same. The newspapers could not quite conceal the fact that it was going badly for the Allies.

Her attitude to him had changed. She no longer flirted. She was always pleased to see him, and complained if he was late arriving in the evening, and she teased him sometimes, but she was never coquettish. She told him how disappointed everyone was about the baby she had lost: Boy, Fitz, Bea, her mother in Buffalo, even her father, Lev. She could not shake the irrational feeling that she had done something shameful, and she asked if he thought that was foolish. He did not. Nothing she did was foolish to him.

Their conversation was personal but they kept their distance from one another physically. He would not exploit the extraordinary intimacy of the night she miscarried. Of course the scene would live in his heart forever. Wiping the blood from her thighs and her belly had not been sexy—not in the least—but it had been unbearably tender. However, it had been a medical emergency, and it did not give him permission to take liberties later. He was so afraid of giving the wrong impression about this that he was careful never to touch her.

At ten o'clock she would make them cocoa, which he loved and she said she liked, though he wondered if she was just being nice. Then he would say good night and go upstairs to his attic bedroom.

They were like old friends. It was not what he wanted, but she was a married woman, and this was the best he was going to get.

He tended to forget Daisy's status. He was startled, one evening, when she announced that she was going to pay a visit to the earl's retired butler, Peel, who was living in a cottage just outside the grounds. "He's eighty!" she told Lloyd. "I'm sure Fitz has forgotten all about him. I should check on him."

Lloyd raised his eyebrows in surprise, and she added: "I need to make sure he's all right. It's my duty as a member of the Fitzherbert clan. Taking care of your old retainers is an obligation of wealthy families—didn't you know that?"

"It had slipped my mind."

"Will you come with me?"

"Of course."

The next day was a Sunday, and they went in the morning, when Lloyd had no lectures. They were both shocked by the state of the little house. The paint was flaking, the wallpaper was peeling, and the curtains were gray with coal dust. The only decoration was a row of photographs cut from magazines and tacked to the wall: the king and queen, Fitz and Bea, and other assorted members of the nobility. The place had not been properly cleaned for years, and there was a smell of urine and ash and decay. But Lloyd guessed it was not unusual for an old man on a small pension.

Peel had white eyebrows. He looked at Lloyd and said: "Good morning, my lord—I thought you were dead!"

Lloyd smiled. "I'm just a visitor."

"Are you, sir? My poor brain is scrambled eggs. The old earl died, what, thirty-five or forty years ago? Well, then, who are you, young sir?"

"I'm Lloyd Williams. You knew my mother, Ethel, years ago."

"You're Eth's boy? Well, in that case, of course . . ."

Daisy said: "In that case, what, Mr. Peel?"

"Oh, nothing. My brain's scrambled eggs!"

They asked him if he needed anything, and he insisted he had everything a man could want. "I don't eat much, and I rarely drink beer. I've got enough money to buy pipe tobacco, and the newspaper. Will Hitler invade us, do you think, young Lloyd? I hope I don't live to see that."

Daisy cleaned up his kitchen a bit, though housekeeping was not her forte. "I can't believe it," she said to Lloyd in a low voice. "Living here, like this, he says he's got everything—he thinks he's lucky!"

"Many men his age are worse off," Lloyd said.

They talked to Peel for an hour. Before they left, he thought of something he did want. He looked at the row of pictures on the wall. "At the funeral of the old earl, there was a photograph took," he said. "I was a mere footman, then, not the butler. We all lined up alongside the hearse. There was a big old camera with a black cloth over it, not like the little modern ones. That was in 1906."

"I bet I know where that photograph is," said Daisy. "We'll go and look."

They returned to the big house and went down to the basement. The junk room, next to the wine cellar, was quite large. It was full of boxes and chests and useless ornaments: a ship in a bottle, a model of Tŷ Gwyn made of matchsticks, a miniature chest of drawers, a sword in an ornate scabbard.

They began to sort through old photographs and paintings. The dust made Daisy sneeze, but she insisted on continuing.

They found the photograph Peel wanted. In the box with it was an even older photo of the previous earl. Lloyd stared at it in some astonishment. The sepia picture was five inches high and three inches wide, and showed a young man in the uniform of a Victorian army officer.

He looked exactly like Lloyd.

"Look at this," he said, handing the photo to Daisy.

"It could be you, if you had side-whiskers," she said.

"Perhaps the old earl had a romance with one of my ancestors," Lloyd said flippantly. "If she was a married woman, she might have passed off the earl's child as her husband's. I wouldn't be very pleased, I can tell you, to learn that I was illegitimately descended from the aristocracy—a red-hot socialist like me!"

Daisy said: "Lloyd, how stupid are you?"

He could not tell whether she was serious. Besides, she had a smear of dust on her nose that looked so sweet that he longed to kiss it. "Well," he said, "I've made a fool of myself more than once, but—"

"Listen to me. Your mother was a maid in this house. Suddenly in 1914 she went to London and married a man called Teddy whom no one knows anything about except that his surname was Williams, the same as hers, so she did not have to change her name. The mysterious Mr. Williams died before anyone met him and his life insurance bought her the house she still lives in."

"Exactly," he said. "What are you getting at?"

"Then, after Mr. Williams died, she gave birth to a son who happens to look remarkably like the late Earl Fitzherbert."

He began to get a glimmer of what she might be saying. "Go on."

"Has it never occurred to you that there might be a completely different explanation for this whole story?"

"Not until now . . ."

"What does an aristocratic family do when one of their daughters gets pregnant? It happens all the time, you know."

"I suppose it does, but I don't know how they handle it. You never hear about it."

"Exactly. The girl disappears for a few months—to Scotland, or Brittany, or Geneva—with her maid. When the two of them reappear, the maid has a little baby, which, she says, she gave birth to during the holiday. The family treat her surprisingly kindly, even though she has admitted fornication, and send her to live a safe distance away, with a small pension."

It seemed like a fairy story, nothing to do with real life, but all the same Lloyd was intrigued and troubled. "And you think I was the baby in some such pretense?"

"I think Lady Maud Fitzherbert had a love affair with a gardener, or a coal miner, or perhaps a charming rogue in London, and she got pregnant. She went away somewhere to give birth in secret. Your mother agreed to pretend the baby was hers, and in exchange she was given a house."

Lloyd was struck by a corroborating thought. "She's always been evasive whenever I've asked about my real father." That now seemed suspicious.

"There you are! There never was a Teddy Williams. To maintain her respectability, your mother said she was a widow. She called her fictional late husband Williams to avoid the problem of changing her name."

Lloyd shook his head in disbelief. "It seems too fantastic."

"She and Maud continued to be friends, and Maud helped raise you. In 1933 your mother took you to Berlin because your real mother wanted to see you again."

Lloyd felt as if he were either dreaming or just waking up. "You think I'm Maud's child?" he said incredulously.

Daisy tapped the frame of the picture she was still holding. "And you look just like your grandfather!"

Lloyd was bewildered. It could not be true—yet it made sense. "I'm used to Bernie not being my real father," he said. "Is Ethel not my real mother?"

Daisy must have seen a look of helplessness on his face, for she leaned forward and touched him—something she did not generally do—and said: "I'm sorry. Have I been brutal? I just want you to see what's in front of your eyes. If Peel suspects the truth, don't you think others may, too? It's the kind of news you want to hear from someone who . . . from a friend."

A gong sounded distantly. Lloyd said mechanically: "I'd better go to the mess for lunch." He took the photograph out of its frame and slipped it into a pocket of his uniform jacket.

"You're upset," Daisy said anxiously.

"No, no. Just . . . astonished."

"Men always deny that they're upset. Please come and see me later."

"All right."

"Don't go to bed without talking to me again."

"I won't."

He left the junk room and made his way upstairs to the grand dining room, now the mess. He ate his canned beef mince automatically, his mind in turmoil. He took no part in the discussion at the table about the battle raging in Norway.

"Having a daydream, Williams?" said Major Lowther.

"Sorry, sir," Lloyd said mechanically. He improvised an excuse. "I was trying to remember which was the higher German rank, *Generalleutnant* or *Generalmajor*."

Lowther said: "*Generalleutnant* is higher." Then he added quietly: "Just don't forget the difference between *meine Frau* and *deine Frau*."

Lloyd felt himself blush. So his friendship with Daisy was not as discreet as he had imagined. It had even come to Lowther's notice. He felt indignant: he and Daisy had done nothing improper. Yet he did not protest. He felt guilty, even though he was not. He could not put his hand on his heart and swear that his intentions were pure. He knew what Granda would say: "Whosoever looketh on a woman to lust after her hath committed adultery with her already in his heart."

That was the no-bullshit teaching of Jesus and there was a lot of truth in it.

Thinking of his grandparents led him to wonder if they knew about his real parents. Being in doubt about his real father and mother gave him a lost feeling, like a dream about falling from a height. If he had been told lies about that, he might have been misled about anything.

He decided he would question Granda and Grandmam. He could do it today, as it was Sunday. As soon as he could decently excuse himself from the mess, he walked downhill to Wellington Row.

It occurred to him that if he asked them outright whether he was Maud's son they might simply deny everything point-blank. Perhaps a more gradual approach would be more likely to elicit information.

He found them sitting in their kitchen. To them Sunday was the Lord's Day, devoted to religion, and they would not read newspapers or listen to the radio. But they were pleased to see him, and Grandmam made tea, as always.

Lloyd began: "I wish I knew more about my real father. Mam says that Teddy Williams was in the Welsh Rifles. Did you know that?"

Grandmam said: "Oh, why do you want to go digging up the past? Bernie's your father."

Lloyd did not contradict her. "Bernie Leckwith has been everything a father should be to me."

Granda nodded. "A Jew, but a good man, there's no doubt." He imagined he was being magnanimously tolerant.

Lloyd let it pass. "All the same, I'm curious. Did you meet Teddy Williams?"

Granda looked angry. "No," he said. "And it was a sorrow to us."

Grandmam said: "He came to Tŷ Gwyn as a valet to a guest. We never knew your mother was sweet on him till she went to London to marry him."

"Why didn't you go to the wedding?"

They were both silent. Then Granda said: "Tell him the truth, Cara. No good ever comes of lies."

"Your mother yielded to temptation," Grandmam said. "After the valet left Tŷ Gwyn, she found she was with child." Lloyd had suspected that, and thought it might account for her evasiveness. "Your Granda was very angry," Grandmam added.

"Too angry," Granda said. "I forgot that Jesus said: 'Judge not, that ye be not judged.' Her sin was lust, but mine was pride." Lloyd was astonished to see tears in his grandfather's pale blue eyes. "God forgave her, but I didn't, not for a long time. By then my son-in-law was dead, killed in France."

Lloyd was more bewildered than before. Here was another detailed story, somewhat different from what he had been told by his mother and completely different from Daisy's theory. Was Granda weeping for a son-in-law who had never existed?

He persisted. "And the family of Teddy Williams? Mam said he came from Swansea. He probably had parents, brothers and sisters . . ."

Grandmam said: "Your mother never talked about his family. I think she was ashamed. Whatever the reason, she didn't want to know them. And it wasn't our place to go against her in that."

"But I might have two more grandparents in Swansea. And uncles and aunts and cousins I've never met."

"Aye," said Granda. "But we don't know."

"My mother knows, though."

"I suppose she does."

"I'll ask her, then," said Lloyd.

iv

Daisy was in love.

She knew now that she had never loved anyone before Lloyd. She had never truly loved Boy, though she had been excited by him. As for poor Charlie Farquharson, she had been at most fond of him. She had believed that love was something she could bestow upon whomever she liked, and that her main responsibility was to choose cleverly. Now she knew that was all wrong. Cleverness had nothing to do with it, and she had no choice. Love was an earthquake.

Life was empty but for the two hours she spent with Lloyd each evening. The rest of the day was anticipation; the night was recollection.

Lloyd was the pillow she put her cheek on. He was the towel with which she patted her breasts when she got out of the bathtub. He was the knuckle she put into her mouth and sucked thoughtfully.

How could she have ignored him for four years? The love of her life had appeared before her at the Trinity Ball, and she had noticed only that he appeared to be wearing someone else's dress clothes! Why had she not taken him in her arms and kissed him and insisted they get married immediately?

He had known all along, she surmised. He must have fallen in love with her from the start. He had begged her to throw Boy over. "Give him up," he had said the night they went to the Gaiety Theatre. "Be my girlfriend instead." And she had laughed at him. But he had seen the truth to which she had been blind.

However, some intuition deep within her had told her to kiss him, there on the Mayfair pavement in the darkness between two streetlights. At the time she had regarded it as a self-indulgent whim, but in fact it was the smartest thing she had ever done, for it had probably sealed his devotion.

Now, at Tŷ Gwyn, she refused to think about what would happen next. She was living from day to day, walking on air, smiling at nothing. She got an anxious letter from her mother in Buffalo, worrying about her health and her state of mind after the miscarriage, and she sent back a reassuring reply. Olga included tidbits of news: Dave Rouzrokh had died in Palm Beach; Muffie Dixon had married Philip Renshaw; Senator Dewar's wife, Rosa, had written a bestseller called *Behind the Scenes at the White House,* with photographs by Woody. A month ago this would have made her homesick; now she was just mildly interested.

She felt sad only when she thought of the baby she had lost. The pain had gone immediately, and the bleeding had stopped after a week, but the loss grieved her. She no longer cried about it, but occasionally she found herself staring into empty space, thinking about whether it would have been a girl or a boy, and what it would have looked like—and then realized with a shock that she had not moved for an hour.

Spring had come, and she walked on the windy mountainside, in waterproof boots and a raincoat. Sometimes, when she was sure there was no one to hear but the sheep, she shouted at the top of her voice: "I love him!"

She worried about his reaction to her questions about his parentage. Perhaps she had done wrong to raise the issue: it had only made him unhappy. Yet her excuse had been valid: sooner or later the truth would probably come out, and it was better to hear such things from someone who loves you. His pained bafflement touched her heart, and made her love him even more.

Then he told her he had arranged leave. He was going to a south-coast resort called Bournemouth for the Labour Party's annual conference on the second weekend in May, which was a British holiday called Whitsun.

His mother would also be at Bournemouth, he said, so he would have a chance to question her about his parentage; and Daisy thought he looked eager and afraid at the same time.

Lowther would certainly have refused to let him go, but Lloyd had spoken to Colonel Ellis-Jones back in March, when he had been assigned to this course, and the colonel either liked Lloyd or sympathized with the party, or both, and gave him permission that Lowther could not countermand. Of course, if the Germans invaded France, then nobody would be able to take leave.

Daisy was strangely frightened by the prospect of Lloyd's leaving Aberowen without knowing that she loved him. She was not sure why, but she had to tell him before he went.

Lloyd was to leave on Wednesday and return six days later. By coincidence, Boy had announced he would come to visit, arriving on Wednesday evening. Daisy was glad, for reasons she could not quite figure out, that the two men would not be there at the same time.

She decided to make her confession to Lloyd on Tuesday, the day before he left. She had no idea what she was going to say to her husband a day later.

Imagining the conversation she would have with Lloyd, she realized that he would surely kiss her, and when they kissed, they would be overwhelmed by their feelings, and they would make love. And then they would lie all night in each other's arms.

At this point in her thinking, the need for discretion intruded into her daydream. Lloyd must not be seen emerging from her quarters in the morning, for both their sakes. Lowthie already had his suspicions: she could tell by his attitude toward her, which was both disapproving and roguish, almost as if he felt that he rather than Lloyd should be the one she should fall for.

How much better it would be if she and Lloyd could meet somewhere else for their fateful conversation. She thought of the unused bedrooms in the west wing, and she felt breathless. He could leave at dawn, and if anyone saw him, they would not know he had been with her. She could emerge later, fully dressed, and pretend to be looking for some lost piece of family property, a painting perhaps. In fact, she thought, elaborating on the lie she would tell if necessary, she could take some object from the junk room and place it in the bedroom in advance, ready to be used as concrete evidence of her story.

At nine o'clock on Tuesday, when the students were all in classes, she walked along the upper floor, carrying a set of perfume vials with tarnished silver tops and a matching hand mirror. She felt guilty already. The carpet had been taken up, and her footsteps rang loud on the floorboards, as if announcing the approach of a scarlet woman. Fortunately there was no one in the bedrooms.

She went to the Gardenia Suite, which she vaguely thought was being used for storage of bed linen. There was no one in the corridor as she stepped inside. She closed the door quickly behind her. She was panting. I haven't done anything yet, she told herself.

She had remembered aright: all around the room, piled up against the gardenia-printed wallpaper, were neat stacks of sheets and blankets and pillows, wrapped in covers of coarse cotton and tied with string like large parcels.

The room smelled musty, and she opened a window. The original furniture was still here: a bed, a wardrobe, a chest of drawers, a writing table, and a kidney-shaped dressing table with three mirrors. She put the perfume vials on the dressing table; then she made the bed up with some of the stored linen. The sheets were cold to her touch.

Now I've done something, she thought. I've made a bed for my lover and me.

She looked at the white pillows and the pink blankets with their satin edging, and she saw herself and Lloyd, locked in a clinging embrace, kissing with mad desperation. The thought aroused her so much that she felt faint.

She heard footsteps outside, ringing on the floorboards as hers had. Who could that be? Morrison, perhaps, the old footman, on his way to look at a leaking gutter or a cracked windowpane. She waited, heart pounding with guilt, as the footsteps came nearer, then receded.

The scare calmed her excitement and cooled the heat she felt inside. She took one last look around the scene and left.

There was no one in the corridor.

She walked along, her shoes heralding her progress, but she looked perfectly innocent now, she told herself. She could go anywhere she wanted; she had more right to be here than anyone else; she was at home; her husband was heir to the whole place.

The husband she was carefully planning to betray.

She knew she should be paralyzed by guilt, but in fact she was eager to do it, consumed by longing.

Next she had to brief Lloyd. He had come to her apartment last night, as usual, but she could not have made this assignation with him then, for he would have expected her to explain herself and then, she knew, she would have told him everything and taken him to her bed and ruined the whole plan. So she had to speak to him briefly today.

She did not normally see him in the daytime, unless she ran into him by accident, in the hall or library. How could she make sure of meeting him? She went up the back stairs to the attic floor. The trainees were not in their rooms, but at any moment one of them might appear, returning to his room for something he had forgotten. So she had to be quick.

She went into Lloyd's room. It smelled of him. She could not say exactly what the fragrance was. She did not see a bottle of cologne in the room, but there was a jar of some kind of hair lotion beside his razor. She opened it and sniffed: yes, that was it, citrus and spice. Was he vain? she asked herself. Perhaps a little bit. He usually looked well dressed, even in his uniform.

She would leave him a note. On top of the dresser was a pad of cheap writing paper. She opened it and tore out a sheet. She looked around for something to write with. He had a black fountain pen with his name engraved on the barrel, she knew, but he would have that with him, for writing notes in class. She found a pencil in the top drawer.

What could she write? She had to be careful in case someone else should read the note. In the end she just wrote: "Library." She left the pad open on the dresser where he could hardly fail to see it. Then she left.

No one saw her.

He would probably come to his room at some point, she speculated, perhaps to fill his pen with ink from the bottle on the dresser. Then he would see the note and come to her.

She went to the library to wait.

The morning was long. She was reading Victorian authors—they seemed to understand how she felt right now—but today Mrs. Gaskell could not hold her attention, and she spent most of the time looking out of the window. It was May, and there would normally have been a brilliant display of spring flowers on the grounds of Tŷ Gwyn, but most of the gardeners had joined the armed forces, and the rest were growing vegetables, not flowers.

Several trainees came into the library just before eleven, and settled down in the green leather chairs with their notebooks, but Lloyd was not among them.

The last lecture of the morning ended at half past twelve, she knew. At that point the men got up and left the library, but Lloyd did not appear.

Surely he would go to his room now, she thought, just to put down his books and wash his hands in the nearby bathroom.

The minutes passed, and the gong sounded for lunch.

Then he came in, and her heart leaped.

He looked worried. "I just saw your note," he said. "Are you all right?"

His first concern was for her. A problem of hers was not a nuisance to him, but an opportunity to help her, and he would seize it eagerly. No man had cared for her this way, not even her father.

"Everything is all right," she said. "Do you know what a gardenia looks like?" She had rehearsed this speech all morning.

"I suppose so. A bit like a rose. Why?"

"In the west wing there's an apartment called the Gardenia Suite. It has a white gardenia painted on the door, and it's full of stored linen. Do you think you could find it?"

"Of course."

"Meet me there tonight, instead of coming to the flat. Usual time."

He stared at her, trying to figure out what was going on. "I will," he said. "But why?"

"I want to tell you something."

"How exciting," he said, but he looked puzzled.

She could guess what was going through his mind. He was electrified by the thought that she might intend a romantic assignation, and at the same time he was telling himself that was a hopeless dream.

"Go to lunch," she said.

He hesitated.

She said: "I'll see you tonight."

"I can't wait," he said, and went out.

She returned to her flat. Maisie, who was not much of a cook, had made her a sandwich with two slabs of bread and a slice of canned ham. Daisy's stomach was full of butterflies; she could not have eaten if it had been peach ice cream.

She lay down to rest. Her thoughts about the night to come were so explicit she felt embarrassed. She had learned a lot about sex from Boy, who clearly had much experience with other women, and she knew a great deal about what men liked. She wanted to do everything with Lloyd, to kiss every part of his body, to do what Boy called *soixante-neuf*, to swallow his semen. The thoughts were so arousing that it took all her willpower to resist the temptation to pleasure herself.

She had a cup of coffee at five, then washed her hair and took a long bath, shaving her underarms and trimming her pubic hair, which grew too abundantly. She dried herself and rubbed in a light body lotion all over. She perfumed herself and began to get dressed.

She put on new underwear. She tried on all her dresses. She liked the look of one with fine blue-and-white stripes, but all down the front it had little buttons that would take forever to undo, and she knew she would want to undress quickly. I'm thinking like a whore, she realized, and she did not know whether to be amused or ashamed. In the end she decided on a simple peppermint green cashmere knee-length that showed off her shapely legs.

She studied herself in the narrow mirror on the inside of the wardrobe door. She looked good.

She perched on the edge of the bed to put her stockings on, and Boy came in.

Daisy felt faint. If she had not been sitting, she would have fallen down. She stared at him in disbelief.

"Surprise!" he said with jollity. "I came a day early."

"Yes," she said when at last she was able to speak. "Surprise."

He bent down and kissed her. She had never much liked his tongue in her mouth, because he always tasted of booze and cigars. He did not mind her distaste; in fact he seemed to enjoy forcing the issue. But now, out of guilt, she tongued him back.

"Gosh!" he said when he ran out of breath. "You're frisky."

You have no idea, Daisy thought; at least, I hope you don't.

"The exercise was brought forward by a day," he explained. "No time to warn you."

"So you're here for the night," she said.

"Yes."

And Lloyd was leaving in the morning.

"You don't seem very pleased," Boy said. He looked at her dress. "Did you have something else planned?"

"Such as what?" she said. She had to regain her composure. "A night out at the Two Crowns pub, perhaps?" she asked sarcastically.

"Speaking of that, let's have a drink." He left the room in search of booze.

Daisy buried her face in her hands. How could this be? Her plan was ruined. She would have to find some way of alerting Lloyd. And she could not declare her love for him in a hurried whisper with Boy around the corner.

She told herself that the whole scheme would simply be postponed. It was only for a few days: he was due back next Tuesday. The delay would be agonizing, but she would survive, and so would her love. All the same, she almost cried with disappointment.

She finished putting on her stockings and shoes; then she went into the little sitting room.

Boy had found a bottle of Scotch and two glasses. She took some to be convivial. He said: "I see that girl is making a fish pie for supper. I'm starving. Is she a good cook?"

"Not really. Her food is edible, if you're hungry."

"Oh, well, there's always whisky," he said, and he poured himself another drink.

"What have you been doing?" She was desperate to get him to talk so that she would not have to. "Did you fly to Norway?" The Germans were winning the first land battle of the war there.

"No, thank God. It's a disaster. There's a big debate in the House of Commons tonight." He began to talk about the mistakes the British and French commanders had made.

When supper was ready, Boy went down to the cellar to get some wine. Daisy saw a chance to alert Lloyd. But where would he be? She looked at her wristwatch. It was half past seven. He would be having dinner in the mess. She could not walk into that room and whisper in his ear as he sat at the table with his fellow officers: it would be as good as telling everyone they were lovers. Was there some way she could get him out of there? She racked her brains, but before she could think of anything, Boy returned, triumphantly carrying a bottle of 1921 Dom Pérignon. "The first vintage they made," he said. "Historic."

They sat at the table and ate Maisie's fish pie. Daisy drank a glass of the champagne but she found it difficult to eat. She pushed her food around the plate in an attempt to look normal. Boy had a second helping.

For dessert Maisie served canned peaches with condensed milk. "War has been bad for British cuisine," Boy said.

"Not that it was great before," Daisy commented, still working on seeming normal.

By now Lloyd must be in the Gardenia Suite. What would he do if she were unable to get a message to him? Would he remain there all night, waiting and hoping for her to arrive? Would he give up at midnight and return to his own bed? Or would he come down here looking for her? That might be awkward.

Boy took out a large cigar and smoked it with satisfaction, occasionally dipping the unlit end into a glass of brandy. Daisy tried to think of an excuse to leave him and go upstairs, but nothing came. What pretext could she possibly cite for visiting the trainees' quarters at this time of night?

She still had done nothing when he put out his cigar and said: "Well, time for bed. Do you want to use the bathroom first?"

Not knowing what else to do, she got up and went into the bedroom. Slowly, she took off the clothes she had put on so carefully for Lloyd. She washed her face and put on her least alluring nightdress. Then she got into bed.

Boy was moderately drunk when he climbed in beside her, but he still wanted sex. The thought appalled her. "I'm sorry," she said. "Dr. Mortimer said no marital relations for three months." This was not true. Mortimer had said it would be all right when the bleeding stopped.

She felt horribly dishonest. She had been planning to do it with Lloyd tonight.

"What?" Boy said indignantly. "Why?"

Improvising, she said: "If we do it too soon, it might affect my chances of getting pregnant again, apparently."

That convinced him. He was desperate for an heir. "Ah, well," he said, and turned away.

In a minute he was asleep.

Daisy lay awake, her mind buzzing. Could she slip away now? She would have to get dressed—she certainly could not walk around the house in her nightdress. Boy slept heavily, but often woke to go to the bathroom. What if he did that while she was gone, and saw her return with her clothes on? What story could she tell that had a chance of being believed? Everyone knew there was only one reason why a woman went creeping around a country house at night.

Lloyd would have to suffer. And she suffered with him, thinking of him alone and disappointed in that musty room. Would he lie down in his uniform and fall asleep? He would be cold, unless he pulled a blanket around him. Would he assume some emergency, or just think she had carelessly stood him up? Perhaps he would feel let down, and be angry with her.

Tears rolled down her face. Boy was snoring, so he would never know.

She dozed off in the small hours, and dreamed she was catching a train, but silly things kept happening to delay her: the taxi took her to the wrong place, she had to walk unexpectedly far with her suitcase, she could not find her ticket, and when she reached the platform, she found waiting for her an old-fashioned stagecoach that would take days to get to London.

When she woke from the dream, Boy was in the bathroom, shaving.

She lost heart. She got up and dressed. Maisie prepared breakfast, and Boy had eggs and bacon and buttered toast. By the time they had finished, it was nine o'clock. Lloyd had said he was leaving at nine. He might be in the hall now, with his suitcase in his hand.

Boy got up from the table and went into the bathroom, taking the newspaper with him. Daisy knew his morning habits: he would be there five or ten minutes. Suddenly her apathy left her. She went out of the flat and ran up the stairs to the hall.

Lloyd was not there. He must already have left. Her heart sank.

But he would be walking to the railway station: only the wealthy and infirm took taxis to go a mile. Perhaps she could catch him up. She went out through the front door.

She saw him four hundred yards down the drive, walking smartly, carrying his case, and her heart leaped. Throwing caution to the wind, she ran after him.

A light army pickup truck of the kind they called a Tilly was bowling down the drive ahead of her. To her dismay it slowed alongside Lloyd. "No!" Daisy said, but Lloyd was too far away to hear her.

He threw his suitcase into the back and jumped into the cab beside the driver.

She kept running, but it was hopeless. The little truck pulled away and picked up speed.

Daisy stopped. She stood and watched as the Tilly passed through the gates of Tŷ Gwyn and disappeared from view. She tried not to cry.

After a moment she turned around and went back inside the house.

v
___

On the way to Bournemouth Lloyd spent a night in London, and that evening, Wednesday, May 8, he was in the visitors' gallery of the House of Commons, watching the debate that would decide the fate of the prime minister, Neville Chamberlain.

It was like being in the gods at the theater: the seats were cramped and hard, and you looked vertiginously down on the drama unfolding below. The gallery was full tonight. Lloyd and his stepfather, Bernie, had got tickets only with difficulty, through the influence of his mother,

Ethel, who was now sitting with his uncle Billy among the Labour M.P.s down in the packed chamber.

Lloyd had had no chance yet to ask about his real father and mother: everyone was too preoccupied with the political crisis. Both Lloyd and Bernie wanted Chamberlain to resign. The appeaser of Fascism had little credibility as a war leader, and the debacle in Norway only underlined that.

The debate had begun the night before. Chamberlain had been furiously attacked, not just by Labour M.P.s but by his own side, Ethel had reported. The Conservative Leo Amery had quoted Cromwell at him: "You have sat too long here for any good you have been doing. Depart, I say, and let us have done with you. In the name of God, go!" It was a cruel speech to come from a colleague, and it was made more wounding by the chorus of "Hear, hear!" that arose from both sides of the chamber.

Lloyd's mother and the other female M.P.s had got together in their own room in the palace of Westminster and agreed to force a vote. The men could not stop them and so joined them instead. When this was announced on Wednesday, the debate was transformed into a ballot on Chamberlain. The prime minister accepted the challenge, and—in what Lloyd felt was a sign of weakness—appealed to his friends to stand by him.

The attacks continued tonight. Lloyd relished them. He hated Chamberlain for his policy on Spain. For two years, from 1937 to 1939, Chamberlain had continued to enforce "nonintervention" by Britain and France, while Germany and Italy poured arms and men into the rebel army, and American ultraconservatives sold oil and trucks to Franco. If any one British politician bore guilt for the mass murders now being carried out by Franco, it was Neville Chamberlain.

"And yet," said Bernie to Lloyd during a lull, "Chamberlain isn't really to blame for the fiasco in Norway. Winston Churchill is first lord of the Admiralty, and your mother says he was the one who pushed for this invasion. After all Chamberlain has done—Spain, Austria, Czechoslovakia—it will be ironic if he falls from power because of something that isn't really his fault."

"Everything is ultimately the prime minister's fault," said Lloyd. "That's what it means to be the leader."

Bernie smiled wryly, and Lloyd knew he was thinking that young people saw everything too simply, but to his credit Bernie did not say it.

It was a noisy debate, but the house went quiet when the former prime minister David Lloyd George stood up. Lloyd had been named after him. Seventy-seven years old now, a white-haired elder statesman, he spoke with the authority of the man who had won the Great War.

He was merciless. "It is not a question of who are the prime minister's friends," he said, stating the obvious with withering sarcasm. "It is a far bigger issue."

Once again, Lloyd was heartened to see that the chorus of approval came from the Conservative side as well as the opposition.

"He has appealed for sacrifices," Lloyd George said, his nasal North Wales accent seeming to sharpen the edge of his contempt. "There is nothing which can contribute more to victory, in this war, than that he should sacrifice the seals of office."

The opposition shouted their approval, and Lloyd could see his mother cheering.

Churchill closed the debate. As a speaker he was the equal of Lloyd George, and Lloyd feared that his oratory might rescue Chamberlain. But the House was against him, interrupting and jeering, sometimes so loudly that he could not be heard over the clamor.

He sat down at eleven P.M. and the vote was taken.

The voting system was cumbersome. Instead of raising their hands, or ticking slips of paper, M.P.s had to leave the chamber and be counted as they walked through one of two lobbies, for ayes or noes. The process took fifteen or twenty minutes. It could have been devised only by men who did not have enough to do, Ethel said. She felt sure it would be modernized soon.

Lloyd waited on tenterhooks. The fall of Chamberlain would give him profound satisfaction, but it was by no means certain.

To distract himself he thought about Daisy, always a pleasant occupation. How strange his last twenty-four hours at Tŷ Gwyn had been: first the one-word note, "Library"; then the rushed conversation, with her tantalizing summons to the Gardenia Suite; then a whole night of waiting, cold and bored and bewildered, for a woman who did not show up. He had stayed there until six o'clock in the morning, miserable but unwilling to give up hope until the moment when he was obliged to wash and shave and change his clothes and pack his suitcase for the trip.

Clearly something had gone wrong, or she had changed her mind, but what had she intended in the first place? She had said she wanted to tell him something. Had she planned to say something earth-shaking, to merit all that drama? Or something so trivial that she had forgotten all about it and the rendezvous? He would have to wait until next Tuesday to ask her.

He had not told his family that Daisy had been at Tŷ Gwyn. That would have required him to explain to them what his relationship with Daisy was now, and he could not do that, for he did not really understand it himself. Was he in love with a married woman? He did not know. How did she feel about him? He did not know. Most likely, he thought, Daisy and he were two good friends who had missed their chance at love. And somehow he did not want to admit that to anyone, for it seemed unbearably final.

He said to Bernie: "Who will take over, if Chamberlain goes?"

"The betting is on Halifax." Lord Halifax was currently the foreign secretary.

"No!" said Lloyd indignantly. "We can't have an earl for prime minister at a time like this. Anyway, he's an appeaser, just as bad as Chamberlain!"

"I agree," said Bernie. "But who else is there?"

"What about Churchill?"

"You know what Stanley Baldwin said about Churchill?" Baldwin, a Conservative, had been prime minister before Chamberlain. "When Winston was born, lots of fairies swooped down on his cradle with gifts—imagination, eloquence, industry, ability—and then came a fairy who said: 'No person has a right to so many gifts,' picked him up, and gave him such a shake and a twist that he was denied judgment and wisdom."

Lloyd smiled. "Very witty, but is it true?"

"There's something in it. In the last war he was responsible for the Dardanelles campaign, which was a terrible defeat for us. Now he's pushed us into the Norwegian adventure, another failure. He's a fine orator, but the evidence suggests he has a tendency to wishful thinking."

Lloyd said: "He was right about the need to rearm in the thirties—when everyone else was against it, including the Labour Party."

"Churchill will be calling for rearmament in paradise, when the lion lies down with the lamb."

"I think we need someone with an aggressive streak. We want a prime minister who will bark, not whimper."

"Well, you may get your wish. The tellers are coming back."

The votes were announced. The ayes had 280, the noes 200. Chamberlain had won. There was uproar in the chamber. The prime minister's supporters cheered, but others yelled at him to resign.

Lloyd was bitterly disappointed. "How can they want to keep him, after all that?"

"Don't jump to conclusions," said Bernie as the prime minister left and the noise subsided. Bernie was making calculations with a pencil in the margin of the *Evening News*. "The government usually has a majority of about two hundred and forty. That's dropped to eighty." He scribbled numbers, adding and subtracting. "Taking a rough guess at the number of M.P.s absent, I reckon about forty of the government's supporters voted against Chamberlain, and another sixty abstained. That's a terrible blow to a prime minister—a hundred of his colleagues don't have confidence in him."

"But is it enough to force him to resign?" Lloyd said impatiently.

Bernie spread his arms in a gesture of surrender. "I don't know," he said.

vi

Next day Lloyd, Ethel, Bernie, and Billy went to Bournemouth by train.

The carriage was full of delegates from all over Britain. They all spent the entire journey discussing last night's debate and the future of the prime minister, in accents ranging from the harsh chop of Glasgow to the swerve and swoop of cockney. Once again Lloyd had no chance to raise with his mother the subject that was haunting him.

Like most delegates, they could not afford the swanky hotels on the cliff tops, so they stayed in a boardinghouse on the outskirts. That evening the four of them went to a pub and sat in a quiet corner, and Lloyd saw his chance.

Bernie bought a round of drinks. Ethel wondered aloud what was happening to her friend Maud in Berlin; she no longer got news, for the war had ended the postal service between Germany and Britain.

Lloyd sipped his pint of beer, then said firmly: "I'd like to know more about my real father."

Ethel said sharply: "Bernie is your father."

Evasion again! Lloyd suppressed the anger that immediately rose in him. "You don't need to tell me that," he said. "And I don't need to tell Bernie that I love him like a father, because he already knows."

Bernie patted him on the shoulder, an awkward but genuine gesture of affection.

Lloyd made his voice insistent. "But I'm curious about Teddy Williams."

Billy said: "We need to talk about the future, not the past—we're at war."

"Exactly," said Lloyd. "So I want answers to my questions *now*. I'm not willing to wait, because I will be going into battle soon, and I don't want to die in ignorance." He did not see how they could deny that argument.

Ethel said: "You know all there is to know," but she was not meeting his eye.

"No, I don't," he said, forcing himself to be patient. "Where are my other grandparents? Do I have uncles and aunts and cousins?"

"Teddy Williams was an orphan," Ethel said.

"Raised in what orphanage?"

She said irritably: "Why are you so stubborn?"

Lloyd allowed his voice to rise in reciprocal annoyance. "Because I'm like you!"

Bernie could not repress a grin. "That's true, anyway."

Lloyd was not amused. "What orphanage?"

"He might have told me, but I don't remember. In Cardiff, I think."

Billy intervened. "You're touching a sore place, now, Lloyd, boy. Drink your beer and drop the subject."

Lloyd said angrily: "I've got a bloody sore place, too, Uncle Billy, thank you very much, and I'm fed up with lies."

"Now, now," said Bernie. "Let's not have talk of lies."

"I'm sorry, Dad, but it's got to be said." Lloyd held up a hand to stave off interruption. "Last time I asked, Mam told me Teddy Williams's family came from Swansea but they moved around a lot because of his father's job. Now she says he was raised in an orphanage in Cardiff. One of those stories is a lie—if not both."

At last Ethel looked him in the eye. "Me and Bernie fed you and clothed you and sent you to school and university," she said indignantly. "You've got nothing to complain about."

"And I'll always be grateful to you, and I'll always love you," Lloyd said.

Billy said: "Why has this come up now, anyhow?"

"Because of something somebody said to me in Aberowen."

His mother did not respond, but there was a flash of fear in her eyes. Someone in Wales knows the truth, Lloyd thought.

He went on relentlessly: "I was told that perhaps Maud Fitzherbert fell pregnant in 1914, and her baby was passed off as yours, for which you were rewarded with the house in Nutley Street."

Ethel made a scornful noise.

Lloyd held up a hand. "That would explain two things," he said. "One, the unlikely friendship between you and Lady Maud." He reached into his jacket pocket. "Two, this picture of me in side-whiskers." He showed them the photograph.

Ethel stared at the picture without speaking.

Lloyd said: "It could be me, couldn't it?"

Billy said testily: "Yes, Lloyd, it could. But obviously it's not, so stop mucking about and tell us who it is."

"It's Earl Fitzherbert's father. Now *you* stop mucking about, Uncle Billy, and you, Mam. Am I Maud's son?"

Ethel said: "The friendship between me and Maud was a political alliance, foremost. It was broken off when we disagreed about strategy for suffragettes, then resumed later. I like her a lot, and she gave me important chances in life, but there is no secret bond. She doesn't know who your father is."

"All right, Mam," said Lloyd. "I could believe that. But this photo . . ."

"The explanation of that resemblance . . ." She choked up.

Lloyd was not going to let her escape. "Come on," he said remorselessly. "Tell me the truth."

Billy intervened again. "You're barking up the wrong tree, boyo," he said.

"Am I? Well, then, set me straight, why don't you?"

"It's not for me to do that."

That was as good as an admission. "So you *were* lying before."

Bernie looked gobsmacked. He said to Billy: "Are you saying the Teddy Williams story isn't true?" Clearly he had believed it all these years, just as Lloyd had.

Billy did not reply.

They all looked at Ethel.

"Oh, bugger it," she said. "My father would say: 'Be sure your sins will find you out.' Well, you've asked for the truth, so you shall have it, though you won't like it."

"Try me," Lloyd said recklessly.

"You're not Maud's child," she said. "You're Fitz's."

vii

Next day, Friday, May 10, Germany invaded Holland, Belgium, and Luxembourg.

Lloyd heard the news on the radio as he sat down to breakfast with his parents and Uncle Billy in the boardinghouse. He was not surprised: everyone in the army had believed the invasion was imminent.

He was much more stunned by the revelations of the previous evening. Last night he had lain awake for hours, angry that he had been misled so long, dismayed that he was the son of a right-wing aristocratic appeaser who was also, weirdly, the father-in-law of the enchanting Daisy.

"How could you fall for him?" he had said to his mother in the pub.

Her reply had been sharp. "Don't be a hypocrite. You used to be crazy about your rich American girl, and she was so right-wing she married a Fascist."

Lloyd had wanted to argue that that was different, but quickly realized it was the same. Whatever his relationship with Daisy now, there was no doubt he had once felt in love with her. Love was not logical. If he could succumb to an irrational passion, so could his mother; indeed, they had been the same age, twenty-one, when it had happened.

He had said she should have told him the truth from the start, but she had an argument for that, too. "How would you have reacted, as a little boy, if I had told you that you were the son of a rich man, an earl? How long would it have been before you boasted to the other boys at school? Think how they would have mocked your childish fantasy. Think how they would have hated you for being superior to them."

"But later . . ."

"I don't know," she had said wearily. "There never seemed to be a good time."

Bernie had at first gone white with shock, but soon recovered and became his usual phlegmatic self. He said he understood why Ethel had not told him the truth. "A secret shared is a secret no more."

Lloyd wondered about his mother's relationship with the earl now. "I suppose you must see him all the time, in Westminster."

"Just occasionally. Peers have a separate section of the palace, with their own restaurants and bars, and when we see them, it's usually by arrangement."

That night Lloyd was too shocked and bewildered to know how he felt. His father was Fitz—the aristocrat, the Tory, the father of Boy, the father-in-law of Daisy. Should he be sad about it, angry, suicidal? The revelation was so devastating that he felt numbed. It was like an injury so grave that at first there was no pain.

The morning news gave him something else to think about.

In the early hours the German army had made a lightning westward strike. Although it was anticipated, Lloyd knew that the best efforts of Allied intelligence had been unable to discover the date in advance, and the armies of those small states had been taken by surprise. Nevertheless, they were fighting back bravely.

"That's probably true," said Uncle Billy, "but the BBC would say it anyway."

Prime Minister Chamberlain had called a cabinet meeting that was going on at that very moment. However, the French army, reinforced by ten British divisions already in France, had long ago agreed on a plan for dealing with such an invasion, and that plan had automatically gone into operation. Allied troops had crossed the French border into Holland and Belgium from the west and were rushing to meet the Germans.

With the momentous news heavy on their hearts, the Williams family caught the bus into the town center and made their way to Bournemouth Pavilion, where the party conference was being held.

There they heard the news from Westminster. Chamberlain was clinging to power. Billy learned that the prime minister had asked Labour Party leader Clement Attlee to become a cabinet minister, making the government a coalition of the three main parties.

All three of them were aghast at this prospect. Chamberlain the appeaser would remain prime minister, and the Labour Party would be obliged to support him in a coalition government. It did not bear thinking about.

"What did Attlee say?" asked Lloyd.

"That he would have to consult his National Executive Committee," Billy replied.

"That's us." Both Lloyd and Billy were members of the committee, which had a meeting scheduled for four o'clock that afternoon.

"Right," said Ethel. "Let's start canvassing, and find out how much support Chamberlain's plan might have on our Executive."

"None, I should think," said Lloyd.

"Don't be so sure," said his mother. "There will be some who want to keep Churchill out at any price."

Lloyd spent the next few hours in constant political activity, talking to members of the committee and their friends and assistants, in cafés and bars in the pavilion and along the seafront. He ate no lunch, but drank so much tea he felt he might have floated.

He was disappointed to find that not everyone shared his view of Chamberlain and Churchill. There were a few pacifists left over from the last war, who wanted peace at any price, and approved of Chamberlain's appeasement. On the other side, Welsh M.P.s still thought of Churchill as the home secretary who sent the troops in to break a strike in Tonypandy. That had been thirty years ago, but Lloyd was learning that memories could be long in politics.

At half past three Lloyd and Billy walked along the seafront in a fresh breeze and entered the Highcliff Hotel, where the meeting was to be held. They thought that a majority of the committee were against accepting Chamberlain's offer, but they could not be completely sure, and Lloyd was still worried about the result.

They went into the room and sat at the long table with the other committee members. Promptly at four the party leader came in.

Clem Attlee was a slim, quiet, unassuming man, neatly dressed, with a bald head and a mustache. He looked like a solicitor—which his father was—and people tended to underestimate him. In his dry, unemotional way he summarized, for the committee, the events of the last twenty-four hours, including Chamberlain's offer of a coalition with Labour.

Then he said: "I have two questions to ask you. The first is: Would you serve in a coalition government with Neville Chamberlain as prime minister?"

There was a resounding "No!" from the people around the table, more vehement than Lloyd had expected. He was thrilled. Chamberlain, friend of the Fascists, the betrayer of Spain, was finished. There was some justice in the world.

Lloyd also noted how subtly the unassertive Attlee had controlled the meeting. He had not opened the subject for general discussion. His question had not been: What shall we do? He had not given people the chance to express uncertainty or dither. In his understated way he had put them all up against the wall and made them choose. And Lloyd felt sure the answer he got was the one he had wanted.

Attlee said: "Then the second question is: Would you serve in a coalition under a different prime minister?"

The answer was not so vocal, but it was yes. As Lloyd looked around the table, it was clear to him that almost everyone was in favor. If there were any against, they did not bother to ask for a vote.

"In that case," said Attlee, "I shall tell Chamberlain that our party will serve in a coalition but only if he resigns and a new prime minister is appointed."

There was a murmur of agreement around the table.

Lloyd noted how cleverly Attlee had avoided asking who they thought the new prime minister should be.

Attlee said: "I shall now go and telephone Number Ten Downing Street."

He left the room.

viii

That evening Winston Churchill was summoned to Buckingham Palace, in accordance with tradition, and the king asked him to become prime minister.

Lloyd had high hopes for Churchill, even if the man was a Conservative. Over the weekend Churchill made his dispositions. He formed a five-man War Cabinet including Clem Attlee and Arthur Greenwood, respectively leader and deputy leader of the Labour Party. Union leader Ernie Bevin became minister of labor. Clearly, Lloyd thought, Churchill intended to have a genuine cross-party government.

Lloyd packed his case ready to catch the train back to Aberowen. Once there, he expected to be quickly redeployed, probably to France. But he only needed an hour or two. He was desperate to learn the explanation of Daisy's behavior last Tuesday. Knowing he was going to see her soon increased his impatience to understand.

Meanwhile, the German army rolled across Holland and Belgium, overcoming spirited opposition with a speed that shocked Lloyd. On Sunday evening Billy spoke on the phone to a contact in the War Office, and afterward he and Lloyd borrowed an old school atlas from the boardinghouse proprietress and studied the map of northwest Europe.

Billy's forefinger drew an east-west line from Dusseldorf through Brussels to Lille. "The Germans are thrusting at the softest part of the French defenses, the northern section of the border with Belgium." His finger moved down the page. "Southern Belgium is bordered by the Ardennes forest, a huge strip of hilly, wooded terrain virtually impassable to modern motorized armies. So my friend in the War Office says." His finger moved on. "Yet farther south, the French-German border is defended by a series of heavy fortifications called the Maginot Line, stretching all the way to Switzerland." His finger returned up the page. "But there are no fortifications between Belgium and northern France."

Lloyd was puzzled. "Did no one think of this until now?"

"Of course we did. And we have a strategy to deal with it." Billy lowered his voice. "Called Plan D. It can't be a secret anymore, since we're already implementing it. The best part of the French army, plus all of the British Expeditionary Force already over there, are pouring across the border into Belgium. They will form a solid line of defense at the Dyle River. That will stop the German advance."

Lloyd was not much reassured. "So we're committing half our forces to Plan D?"

"We need to make sure it works."

"It better."

They were interrupted by the proprietress, who brought Lloyd a telegram.

It had to be from the army. He had given Colonel Ellis-Jones this address before going on leave. He was surprised he had not heard sooner. He ripped open the envelope. The cable said:

```
DO NOT RETURN ABEROWEN STOP REPORT SOUTHAMPTON
DOCKS IMMEDIATELY STOP A BIENTOT
SIGNED ELLISJONES
```

He was not going back to Tŷ Gwyn. Southampton was one of Britain's largest ports, a common embarkation point for the Continent, and it was located just a few miles along the coast from Bournemouth, an hour perhaps by train or bus.

Lloyd would not be seeing Daisy tomorrow, he realized with an ache in his heart. Perhaps he might never learn what she had wanted to tell him.

Colonel Ellis-Jones's "A BIENTOT" confirmed the obvious inference.

Lloyd was going to France.

CHAPTER SEVEN

1940 (II)

E rik von Ulrich spent the first three days of the Battle of France in a traffic jam.

Erik and his friend Hermann Braun were part of a medical unit attached to the Second Panzer Division. They saw no action as they passed through southern Belgium, just mile after mile of hills and trees. They were in the Ardennes forest, they reckoned. They traveled on narrow roads, many not even paved, and a broken-down tank could cause a fifty-mile tailback in no time. They were stationary, stuck in queues, more than they were moving.

Hermann's freckled face was set in a grimace of anxiety, and he muttered to Erik in an undertone no one else could hear: "This is stupid!"

"You should know better than to say that—you were in the Hitler Youth," said Erik quietly. "Have faith in the Führer." But he was not angry enough to denounce his friend.

When they did move, it was painfully uncomfortable. They sat on the hard wooden floor of an army truck as it bounced over tree roots and swerved around potholes. Erik longed for battle just so that he could get out of the damn truck.

Hermann said more loudly: "What are we doing here?"

Their boss, Dr. Rainer Weiss, was sitting on a real seat beside the driver. "We are following the orders of the Führer, which are of course always correct." He said it straight-faced, but Erik felt sure he was being sarcastic. Major Weiss, a thin man with black hair and spectacles, often spoke cynically about the government and the military, but always in this enigmatic way, so that nothing could be proved against him. Anyway, the army could not afford to get rid of a good doctor at this point.

There were two other medical orderlies in the truck, both older than Erik and Hermann. One of them, Christof, had a better answer to Hermann's question. "Perhaps the French aren't expecting us to attack here, because the terrain is so difficult."

His friend Manfred said: "We will have the advantage of surprise, and will encounter light defenses."

Weiss said sarcastically: "Thanks for that lesson in tactics, you two— most enlightening." But he did not say they were wrong.

Despite all that had happened, there were still people who lacked faith in the Führer, to Erik's amazement. His own family continued to close their eyes to the triumphs of the Nazis. His father, once a man of status and power, was now a pathetic figure. Instead of rejoicing in the conquest of barbarian Poland, he just moaned about ill treatment of the Poles—which he must have heard about by listening illegally to a foreign radio station. Such behavior could get them all into trouble— including Erik, who was guilty of not reporting it to the local Nazi block supervisor.

Erik's mother was just as bad. Every now and again she disappeared with small packages of smoked fish or eggs. She said nothing in explanation, but Erik felt sure she was taking them to Frau Rothmann, whose Jewish husband was no longer allowed to practise as a doctor.

Despite that, Erik sent home a large slice of his army pay, knowing his parents would be cold and hungry if he did not. He hated their politics, but he loved them. They undoubtedly felt the same about his politics and him.

Erik's sister, Carla, had wanted to be a doctor, like Erik, and had been furious when it was made clear to her that in today's Germany this was a man's job. She was now training as a nurse, a much more appropriate role for a German girl. And she, too, was supporting their parents with her meager pay.

Erik and Hermann had wanted to join infantry units. Their idea of battle was to run at the enemy firing a rifle, and kill or be killed for the fatherland. But they were not going to be killing anyone. Both had had one year of medical school, and such training was not to be wasted; so they were made medical orderlies.

The fourth day in Belgium, Monday, May 13, was like the first three until the afternoon. Above the roar and snarl of hundreds of tank and truck engines, they began to hear another, louder sound. Aircraft were flying low over their heads and, not too far away, dropping bombs on someone. Erik's nose twitched with the smell of high explosives.

They stopped for their midafternoon break on high ground overlooking a meandering river valley. Major Weiss said the river was the Meuse, and they were west of the city of Sedan. So they had entered France. The planes of the Luftwaffe roared past them, one after another, diving toward the river a couple of miles away, bombing and strafing the scattered villages on the banks, where, presumably, there were French defensive positions. Smoke rose from countless fires among the ruined cottages and farm buildings. The barrage was relentless, and Erik almost felt pity for anyone trapped in that inferno.

This was the first action he had seen. Before long he would be in it, and perhaps some young French soldier would look from a safe vantage point and feel sorry for the Germans being maimed and killed. The thought made Erik's heart thud with excitement like a big drum in his chest.

Looking to the east, where the details of the landscape were obscured by distance, he could nevertheless see aircraft like specks, and columns of smoke rising through the air, and he realized that the battle had been joined along several miles of this river.

As he watched, the air bombardment came to an end, the planes turning and heading north, waggling their wings to say "Good luck" as they passed overhead on their way home.

Nearer to where Erik stood, on the flat plain leading to the river, the German tanks were going into action.

They were two miles from the enemy, but already the French artillery was shelling them from the town. Erik was surprised that so many gunners had survived the air bombardment. But fire flashed in the ruins, the boom of cannon was heard across the fields, and fountains of French soil spurted where the shells landed. Erik saw a tank explode with a direct hit, smoke and metal and body parts spewing out of the volcano's mouth, and he felt sick.

But the French shelling did not stop the advance. The tanks crawled on relentlessly toward the stretch of river to the east of the town, which Weiss said was called Donchery. Behind them followed the infantry, in trucks and on foot.

Hermann said: "The air attack wasn't enough. Where's our artillery? We need them to take out the big guns in the town, and give our tanks and infantry a chance to cross the river and establish a bridgehead."

Erik wanted to punch him to shut his whining mouth. They were about to go into action—they had to be positive now!

But Weiss said: "You're right, Braun—but our artillery ammunition is gridlocked in the Ardennes forest. We've only got forty-eight shells."

A red-faced major came running past, yelling: "Move out! Move out!"

Major Weiss pointed and said: "We'll set up our field dressing station over to the east, where you see that farmhouse." Erik made out a low gray roof about eight hundred yards from the river. "All right, get moving!"

They jumped into the truck and roared down the hill. When they reached level ground, they swerved left along a farm track. Erik wondered what they would do with the family that presumably lived in the building that was about to become an army hospital. Throw them out of their home, he guessed, and shoot them if they made trouble. But where would they go? They were in the middle of a battlefield.

He need not have worried: they had already left.

The building was half a mile from the worst of the fighting, Erik observed. He guessed there was no point setting up a dressing station within range of enemy guns.

"Stretcher bearers, get going," Weiss shouted. "By the time you get back here, we'll be ready."

Erik and Hermann took a rolled-up stretcher and first-aid kit from the medical supply truck and headed toward the battle. Christof and Manfred were just ahead of them, and a dozen of their comrades followed. This is it, Erik thought exultantly; this is our chance to be heroes. Who will keep his nerve under fire, and who will lose control and crawl into a hole and hide?

They ran across the fields to the river. It was a long jog, and it was going to seem longer coming back, carrying a wounded man.

They passed burned-out tanks but there were no survivors, and Erik averted his eyes from the scorched human remains smeared across the twisted metal. Shells fell around them, though not many: the river was lightly defended, and many of the guns had been taken out by the air attack. All the same, it was the first time in his life Erik had been shot at, and he felt the absurd, childish impulse to cover his eyes with his hands, but he kept running forward.

Then a shell landed right in front of them.

There was a terrific thud, and the earth shook as if a giant had stamped his foot. Christof and Manfred were hit directly, and Erik saw their bodies fly up into the air as if weightless. The blast threw Erik off his feet. As he lay on the ground, faceup, he was showered with dirt from the explosion, but he was not injured. He struggled to his feet. Right in front of him were the mangled bodies of Christof and Manfred. Christof lay like a broken doll, as if all his limbs were disjointed. Manfred's head had somehow been severed from his body and lay next to his booted feet.

Erik was paralyzed with horror. In medical school he had not had to deal with maimed and bleeding bodies. He was used to corpses in anatomy class—they had had one between two students, and he and Hermann had shared the cadaver of a shriveled old woman—and he had watched living people being cut open on the operating table. But none of that had prepared him for this.

He wanted nothing but to run away.

He turned around. His mind was blank of every thought but fear. He started to walk back the way they had come, toward the forest, away from the battle, taking long, determined strides.

Hermann saved him. He stood in front of Erik and said: "Where are you going? Don't be a fool!" Erik kept moving, and tried to walk past him. Hermann punched him in the stomach, really hard, and Erik folded over and fell to his knees.

"Don't run away!" Hermann said urgently. "You'll be shot for desertion! Pull yourself together!"

While Erik was trying to catch his breath, he came to his senses. He could not run away, he must not desert, he had to stay here, he realized. Slowly his willpower overcame his terror. Eventually he got to his feet.

Hermann looked at him warily.

"Sorry," said Erik. "I panicked. I'm all right now."

"Then pick up the stretcher and keep going."

Erik picked up the rolled stretcher, balanced it on his shoulder, turned around, and ran on.

Closer to the river, Erik and Hermann found themselves among infantry. Some were manhandling inflated rubber dinghies out of the backs of trucks and carrying them to the water's edge, while the tanks tried to cover them by firing at the French defenses. But Erik, rapidly recovering his mental powers, soon saw that it was a losing battle: the French were behind walls and inside buildings, while the German infantry were exposed on the bank of the river. As soon as they got a dinghy into the water, it came under intense machine-gun fire.

Upstream, the river turned a right-angled bend, so the infantry could not move out of range of the French without retreating a long distance.

There were already many dead and wounded men on the ground.

"Let's pick this one up," Hermann said decisively, and Erik bent to the task. They unrolled their stretcher on the ground next to a groaning infantryman. Erik gave him water from a flask, as he had learned in training. The man seemed to have numerous superficial wounds on his face and one limp arm. Erik guessed he had been hit by machine-gun fire that had luckily missed his vital areas. He saw no gush of blood, so they did not attempt to staunch his wounds. They lifted the man onto the stretcher, picked it up, and began to jog back to the dressing station.

The wounded man cried out in agony as they moved; then, when they stopped, he shouted: "Keep going, keep going!" and gritted his teeth.

Carrying a man on a stretcher was not as easy as it might seem. Erik thought his arms would fall off when they were only halfway. But he could see that the patient was in greater pain by far, and he just kept running.

Shells no longer fell around them, he noticed gratefully. The French were concentrating all their fire on the riverbank, trying to prevent the Germans from crossing.

At last Erik and Hermann reached the farmhouse with their burden. Weiss had the place organized, the rooms cleared of superfluous furniture, places marked on the floor for patients, the kitchen table set up for operations. He showed Erik and Hermann where to put the wounded man. Then he sent them back for another.

The run back to the river was easier. They were unburdened and going slightly downhill. As they approached the bank, Erik wondered fearfully whether he would panic again.

He saw with trepidation that the battle was going badly. There were several deflated vessels in midstream and many more bodies on the bank—and still no Germans on the far side.

Hermann said: "This is a catastrophe. We should have waited for our artillery!" His voice was shrill.

Erik said: "Then we would have lost the advantage of surprise, and the French would have had time to bring up reinforcements. There would have been no point in that long trek through the Ardennes."

"Well, this isn't working," said Hermann.

Deep in his heart Erik was beginning to wonder whether the Führer's plans really were infallible. The thought undermined his resolution and threatened to throw him completely off balance. Fortunately there was no more time for reflection. They stopped beside a man with most of one leg blown off. He was about their age, twenty, with pale, freckled skin and copper red hair. His right leg ended at midthigh in a ragged stump. Amazingly, he was conscious, and he stared at them as if they were angels of mercy.

Erik found the pressure point in his groin and stopped the bleeding while Hermann got out a tourniquet and applied it. Then they put him on the stretcher and began the run back.

Hermann was a loyal German, but he sometimes allowed negative feelings to get the better of him. If Erik ever had such feelings, he was careful not to voice them. That way he did not lower anyone else's morale—and he stayed out of trouble.

But he could not help thinking. It seemed the approach through the Ardennes had not given the Germans the expected walkover victory. The Meuse defenses were light but the French were fighting back fiercely. Surely, he thought, his first experience of battle was not going to destroy his faith in his Führer? The idea made him feel panicky.

He wondered whether the German forces farther east were faring any better. The First Panzer and the Tenth Panzer had been alongside Erik's division, the Second, as they approached the border, and it must be they who were attacking upstream.

His arm muscles were now in constant agony.

They arrived back at the dressing station for the second time. The place was now frantically busy, the floor crowded with men groaning and crying, bloody bandages everywhere, Weiss and his assistants moving quickly from one maimed body to the next. Erik had never imagined there could be so much suffering in one small place. Somehow, when the Führer spoke of war, Erik never thought of this kind of thing.

Then he noticed that his own patient's eyes were closed.

Major Weiss felt for a pulse, then said harshly: "Put him in the barn—and for fuck's sake don't waste time bringing me corpses!"

Erik could have cried with frustration, and with the pain in his arms, which was beginning to afflict his legs, too.

They put the body in the barn, and saw that there were already a dozen dead young men there.

This was worse than anything he had envisaged. When he had thought about battle, he had foreseen courage in the face of danger, stoicism in suffering, heroism in adversity. What he saw now was agony, screaming, blind terror, broken bodies, and a complete lack of faith in the wisdom of the mission.

They went back again to the river.

The sun was low in the sky now, and something had changed on the battlefield. The French defenders in Donchery were being shelled from the far side of the river. Erik guessed that farther upstream the First Panzers had had better luck, and had secured a bridgehead on the south bank, and now they were coming to the aid of the comrades on their flanks. Clearly *they* had not lost their ammunition in the forest.

Heartened, Erik and Hermann rescued another wounded man. When they got back to the dressing station this time, they were given tin bowls of a tasty soup. Resting for ten minutes while he drank the soup made Erik want to lie down and go to sleep for the night. It took a mighty effort to stand up and pick up his end of the stretcher and jog back to the battlefield.

Now they saw a different scene. Tanks were crossing the river on rafts. The Germans on the far side were coming under heavy fire, but they were shooting back, with the help of reinforcements from the First Panzers.

Erik saw that his side had a chance of winning their objective after all. He was heartened, and he began to feel ashamed that he had doubted the Führer.

He and Hermann kept on retrieving the wounded, hour after hour, until they forgot what it was like to be free from pain in their arms and legs. Some of their charges were unconscious; some thanked them, some cursed them; many just screamed; some lived and some died.

By eight o'clock that evening there was a German bridgehead on the far side of the river, and by ten it was secure.

The fighting came to an end at nightfall. Erik and Hermann

continued to sweep the battlefield for wounded men. They brought back the last one at midnight. Then they lay down under a tree and fell into a sleep of utter exhaustion.

Next day Erik and Hermann and the rest of the Second Panzers turned west and broke through what remained of the French defenses.

Two days later they were fifty miles away, at the river Oise, and moving fast through undefended territory.

By May 20, a week after emerging unexpectedly from the Ardennes forest, they had reached the coast of the English Channel.

Major Weiss explained their achievement to Erik and Hermann. "Our attack on Belgium was a feint, you see. Its purpose was to draw the French and British into a trap. We Panzer divisions formed the jaws of the trap, and now we have them between our teeth. Much of the French army and nearly all of the British Expeditionary Force are in Belgium, encircled by the German army. They are cut off from supplies and reinforcements, helpless—and defeated."

Erik said triumphantly: "This was the Führer's plan all along!"

"Yes," said Weiss, and as ever Erik could not tell whether he was sincere. "No one thinks like the Führer!"

ii

Lloyd Williams was in a football stadium somewhere between Calais and Paris. With him were another thousand or more British prisoners of war. They had no shelter from the blazing June sun, but they were grateful for the warm nights as they had no blankets. There were no toilets and no water for washing.

Lloyd was digging a hole with his hands. He had organized some of the Welsh miners to make latrines at one end of the soccer pitch, and he was working alongside them to show he was willing. Other men joined in, having nothing else to do, and soon there were a hundred or so helping. When a guard strolled over to see what was going on, Lloyd explained.

"You speak good German," said the guard amiably. "What's your name?"

"Lloyd."

"I'm Dieter."

Lloyd decided to exploit this small expression of friendliness. "We could dig faster if we had tools."

"What's the hurry?"

"Better hygiene would benefit you as well as us."

Dieter shrugged and went away.

Lloyd felt awkwardly unheroic. He had seen no fighting. The Welsh Rifles had gone to France as reserves, to relieve other units in what was expected to be a long battle. But it had taken the Germans only ten days to defeat the bulk of the Allied army. Many of the defeated British troops had then been evacuated from Calais and Dunkirk, but thousands had missed the boat, and Lloyd was among them.

Presumably the Germans were now pushing south. As far as he knew, the French were still fighting, but their best troops had been annihilated in Belgium, and there was a triumphant look about the German guards, as if they knew victory was assured.

Lloyd was a prisoner of war, but how long would he remain so? At this point there must be powerful pressure on the British government to make peace. Churchill would never do so, but he was a maverick, different from all other politicians, and he could be deposed. Men such as Lord Halifax would have little difficulty signing a peace treaty with the Nazis. The same was true, Lloyd thought bitterly, of the junior Foreign Office minister Earl Fitzherbert, whom he now shamefully knew to be his father.

If peace came soon, his time as a prisoner of war could be short. He might spend all of it here, in this French arena. He would go home scrawny and sunburned, but otherwise whole.

But if the British fought on, it would be a different matter. The last war had continued more than four years. Lloyd could not bear the thought of wasting four years of his life in a prisoner-of-war camp. To avoid that, he decided, he would try to escape.

Dieter reappeared carrying half a dozen spades.

Lloyd gave them to the strongest men, and the work went faster.

At some point the prisoners would have to be moved to a permanent camp. That would be the time to make a run for it. Based on his experience in Spain, Lloyd guessed the army would not prioritize the guarding of prisoners. If one tried to get away, he might succeed, or he might be shot dead; either way, it was one less mouth to feed.

They spent the rest of the day completing the latrines. Apart from the improvement in hygiene, this project had boosted morale, and Lloyd lay awake that night, looking at the stars, trying to think of other communal activities he might organize. He decided on a grand athletics contest, a prison-camp Olympic Games.

But he did not have the chance to put this into practise, for the next morning they were marched away.

At first he was not sure of the direction they were taking, but before long they got onto a Route Napoléon two-lane road and began to go steadily east. In all probability, Lloyd thought, they were intended to walk all the way to Germany.

Once there, he knew, escape would be much more difficult. He had to seize this opportunity. And the sooner the better. He was scared— those guards had guns—but determined.

There was not much motor traffic other than the occasional German staff car, but the road was busy with people on foot, heading in the opposite direction. With their possessions in handcarts and wheelbarrows, some driving their livestock ahead of them, they were clearly refugees whose homes had been destroyed in battle. That was a heartening sign, Lloyd told himself. An escaped prisoner might hide himself among them.

The prisoners were lightly guarded. There were only ten Germans in charge of this moving column of a thousand men. The guards had one car and a motorcycle; the rest were on foot and on civilian bicycles that they must have commandeered from the locals.

All the same, escape seemed hopeless at first. There were no English-style hedgerows to provide cover, and the ditches were too shallow to hide in. A man running away would provide an easy target for a competent rifleman.

Then they entered a village. Here it was a little harder for the guards to keep an eye on everyone. Local men and women stood at the edges of the column, staring at the prisoners. A small flock of sheep got mixed up with them. There were cottages and shops beside the road. Lloyd watched hopefully for his opportunity. He needed a place to hide instantly, an open door or a passage between houses or a bush to hide behind. And he needed to be passing it at a moment when none of the guards was in sight.

In a couple of minutes he had left the village behind without spotting his opportunity.

He felt annoyed, and told himself to be patient. There would be more chances. It was a long way to Germany. On the other hand, with every day that passed the Germans would tighten their grip on conquered territory, improve their organization, impose curfews and passes and checkpoints, stop the movement of refugees. Being on the run would be easier at first, harder as time went on.

It was hot, and he took off his uniform jacket and tie. He would get rid of them as soon as he could. Close up he probably still looked like a British soldier, in his khaki trousers and shirt, but at a distance he hoped he would not be so conspicuous.

They passed through two more villages, then came to a small town. This should present some possible escape routes, Lloyd thought nervously. He realized that a part of him hoped he would not see a good opportunity, would not have to put himself in danger of those rifles. Was he getting accustomed to captivity already? It was too easy to continue marching, footsore but safe. He had to snap out of it.

The road through the town was unfortunately broad. The column kept to the middle of the street, leaving wide aisles either side that would have to be crossed before an escaper could find concealment. Some shops were closed, and a few buildings were boarded up, but Lloyd could see promising-looking alleys, cafés with open doors, a church—but he could not get to any of them unobserved.

He studied the faces of the townspeople as they stared at the passing prisoners. Were they sympathetic? Would they remember that these men had fought for France? Or would they be understandably terrified of the Germans, and refuse to put themselves in danger? Half and half, probably. Some would risk their lives to help, others would hand him over to the Germans in a heartbeat. And he would not be able to tell the difference until it was too late.

They reached the town center. I've lost half my opportunities already, he told himself. I have to act.

Up ahead he saw a crossroads. An oncoming line of traffic was waiting to turn left, its way blocked by the marching men. Lloyd saw a civilian pickup truck in the queue. Dusty and battered, it looked as if it might belong to a builder or a road mender. The back was open, but Lloyd could not see inside, for its sides were high.

He thought he might be able to pull himself up the side and scramble over the edge into the truck.

Once inside he could not be seen by anyone standing or walking on the street, nor by the guards on their bikes. But he would be plainly visible to people looking out of the upstairs windows of the buildings that lined the streets. Would they betray him?

He came closer to the truck.

He looked back. The nearest guard was two hundred yards behind.

He looked ahead. A guard on a bicycle was twenty yards in front.

He said to the man beside him: "Hold this for me, would you?" and gave him his jacket.

He drew level with the front of the truck. At the wheel was a bored-looking man in overalls and a beret with a cigarette dangling from his lip. Lloyd passed him. Then he was level with the side of the truck. There was no time to check the guards again.

Without breaking step, Lloyd put both hands on the side of the truck; heaved himself up; threw one leg over, then the other; and fell inside, hitting the bed of the truck with a crash that seemed terribly loud despite the tramp of a thousand pairs of feet. He flattened himself immediately. He lay still, listening for a clamor of shouted German, the roar of a motorcycle approaching, the crack of a rifle shot.

He heard the irregular snore of the truck's engine, the stamp and shuffle of the prisoners' feet, the background noises of a small town's traffic and people. Had he got away with it?

He looked around him, keeping his head low. In the truck with him were buckets, planks, a ladder, and a wheelbarrow. He had been hoping for a few sacks with which to cover himself, but there were none.

He heard a motorcycle. It seemed to come to a halt nearby. Then, a few inches from his head, someone spoke French with a strong German accent. "Where are you going?" A guard was talking to the truck driver, Lloyd figured with a racing heart. Would the guard try to look into the back?

He heard the driver reply, an indignant stream of fast French that Lloyd could not decipher. The German soldier almost certainly could not understand it, either. He asked the question again.

Looking up, Lloyd saw two women at a high window overlooking the street. They were staring at him, mouths open in surprise. One was pointing, her arm sticking out through the open window.

Lloyd tried to catch her eye. Lying still, he moved one hand from side to side in a gesture that meant no.

She got the message. She withdrew her arm suddenly and covered her mouth with her hand as if realizing, with horror, that her pointing could be a sentence of death.

Lloyd wanted both women to move away from the window, but that was too much to hope for, and they continued to stare.

Then the motorcycle guard seemed to decide not to pursue his inquiry, for, a moment later, the motorcycle roared away.

The sound of feet receded. The body of prisoners had passed. Was Lloyd free?

There was a crash of gears and the truck moved. Lloyd felt it turn the corner and pick up speed. He lay still, too scared to move.

He watched the tops of buildings pass by, alert in case anyone else should spot him, though he did not know what he would do if it happened. Every second was taking him away from the guards, he told himself encouragingly.

To his disappointment, the truck came to a halt quite soon. The engine was turned off; then the driver's door opened and slammed shut. Then nothing. Lloyd lay still for a while, but the driver did not return.

Lloyd looked at the sky. The sun was high: it must be after midday. The driver was probably having lunch.

The trouble was, Lloyd continued to be visible from high windows on both sides of the street. If he remained where he was, he would be noticed sooner or later. And then there was no telling what might happen.

He saw a curtain twitch in an attic, and that decided him.

He stood up and looked over the side. A man in a business suit walking along the pavement stared in curiosity but did not stop.

Lloyd scrambled over the side of the truck and dropped to the ground. He found himself outside a bar-restaurant. No doubt that was where the driver had gone. To Lloyd's horror there were two men in German army uniforms sitting at a window table with glasses of beer in their hands. By a miracle they did not look at Lloyd.

He walked quickly away.

He looked around alertly as he walked. Everyone he passed stared at him: they knew exactly what he was. One woman screamed and ran away. He realized he needed to change his khaki shirt and trousers for something more French in the next few minutes.

A young man took him by the arm. "Come with me," he said in English with a heavy accent. "I will 'elp you 'ide."

He turned down a side street. Lloyd had no reason to trust this man, but he had to make a split-second decision, and he went along.

"This way," the young man said, and steered Lloyd into a small house.

In a bare kitchen was a young woman with a baby. The young man introduced himself as Maurice, the woman as his wife, Marcelle, and the baby as Simone.

Lloyd allowed himself a moment of grateful relief. He had escaped from the Germans! He was still in danger, but he was off the streets and in a friendly house.

The stiffly correct French Lloyd had learned in school and at Cambridge had become more colloquial during his escape from Spain, and especially in the two weeks he spent picking grapes in Bordeaux. "You're very kind," he said. "Thank you."

Maurice replied in French, evidently relieved not to have to speak English. "I guess you'd like something to eat."

"Very much."

Marcelle rapidly cut several slices off a long loaf and put them on the table with a round of cheese and a wine bottle with no label. Lloyd sat down and tucked in ravenously.

"I'll give you some old clothes," said Maurice. "But also, you must try to walk differently. You were striding along looking all around you, so alert and interested, you might as well have a sign around your neck saying 'Visitor from England.' Better to shuffle with your eyes on the ground."

With his mouth full of bread and cheese, Lloyd said: "I'll remember that."

There was a small shelf of books, including French translations of Marx and Lenin. Maurice noticed Lloyd looking at them and said: "I was a Communist—until the Hitler-Stalin pact. Now—it's finished." He made a swift cutting-off gesture with his hand. "All the same, we have to defeat Fascism."

"I was in Spain," said Lloyd. "Before that, I believed in a united front of all left parties. Not anymore."

Simone cried. Marcelle lifted a large breast out of her loose dress and began to feed the baby. French women were more relaxed about this than the prudish British, Lloyd remembered.

When he had eaten, Maurice took him upstairs. From a wardrobe that had very little in it he took a pair of dark blue overalls, a light blue shirt, underwear, and socks, all worn but clean. The kindness of this evidently poor man overwhelmed Lloyd, and he had no idea how to say thank you.

"Just leave your army clothes on the floor," Maurice said. "I'll burn them."

Lloyd would have liked a wash, but there was no bathroom. He guessed it was in the backyard.

He put on the fresh clothes and studied his reflection in a mirror hanging on the wall. French blue suited him better than army khaki, but he still looked British.

He went back downstairs.

Marcelle was burping the baby. "Hat," she said.

Maurice produced a typical French beret, dark blue, and Lloyd put it on.

Then Maurice looked anxiously at Lloyd's stout black leather British army boots, dusty but unmistakably good quality. "They give you away," he said.

Lloyd did not want to give up his boots. He had a long way to walk. "Perhaps we can make them look older?" he said.

Maurice looked doubtful. "How?"

"Do you have a sharp knife?"

Maurice took a clasp knife from his pocket.

Lloyd took his boots off. He cut holes in the toecaps, then slashed the ankles. He removed the laces and re-threaded them untidily. Now they looked like something a down-and-out would wear, but they still fit well and had thick soles that would last many miles.

Maurice said: "Where will you go?"

"I have two options," Lloyd said. "I can head north, to the coast, and hope to persuade a fisherman to take me across the English Channel. Or I can go southwest, across the border into Spain." Spain was neutral, and still had British consuls in major cities. "I know the Spanish route— I've traveled it twice."

"The channel is a lot nearer than Spain," Maurice said. "But I think the Germans will close all the ports and harbors."

"Where's the front line?"

"The Germans have taken Paris."

Lloyd suffered a moment of shock. Paris had fallen already!

"The French government has moved to Bordeaux." Maurice shrugged. "But we are beaten. Nothing can save France now."

"All Europe will be Fascist," Lloyd said.

"Except for Britain. So you must go home."

Lloyd mused. North or southwest? He could not tell which would be better.

Maurice said: "I have a friend, a former Communist, who sells cattle feed to farmers. I happen to know he's delivering this afternoon to a place southwest of here. If you decide to go to Spain, he could take you twenty miles."

That helped Lloyd make up his mind. "I'll go with him," he said.

iii

Daisy had been on a long journey that had brought her around in a circle.

When Lloyd was sent to France, she was heartbroken. She had missed her chance of telling him she loved him—she had not even kissed him!

And now there might never be another opportunity. He was reported missing in action after Dunkirk. That meant his body had not been found and identified, but neither was he registered as a prisoner of war. Most likely he was dead, blown up into unidentifiable fragments by a shell, or perhaps lying unmarked beneath the debris of a destroyed farmhouse. She cried for days.

For another month she moped about Tŷ Gwyn, hoping to hear more, but no further news came. Then she began to feel guilty. There were many women as badly off as she or worse. Some had to face the prospect of raising two or three children with no man to support the family. She had no right to feel sorry for herself just because the man with whom she had been contemplating an adulterous affair was missing.

She had to pull herself together and do something positive. Fate did not intend her to be with Lloyd, that was clear. She already had a husband, one who was risking his life every day. It was her duty, she told herself, to take care of Boy.

She returned to London. She opened up the Mayfair house, as best she could with limited servants, and made it into a pleasant home for Boy to come to when on leave.

She needed to forget Lloyd and be a good wife. Perhaps she would even get pregnant again.

Many women signed up for war work, joining the Women's Auxiliary

Air Force, or doing agricultural labor with the Women's Land Army. Others worked for no pay in the Women's Voluntary Service for Air Raid Precautions. But there was not enough for most such women to do, and *The Times* published letters to the editor complaining that air raid precautions were a waste of money.

The war in Continental Europe appeared to be over. Germany had won. Europe was Fascist from Poland to Sicily and from Hungary to Portugal. There was no fighting anywhere. Rumors said the British government had discussed peace terms.

But Churchill did not make peace with Hitler, and that summer the Battle of Britain began.

At first civilians were not much affected. Church bells were silenced, their peal reserved to warn of the expected German invasion. Daisy followed government instructions and placed buckets of sand and water on every landing in the house, for firefighting, but they were not needed. The Luftwaffe bombed harbors, hoping to cut Britain's supply lines. Then they started on air bases, trying to destroy the Royal Air Force. Boy was flying a Spitfire, engaging enemy aircraft in sky battles that were watched by openmouthed farmers in Kent and Sussex. In a rare letter home he said proudly that he had shot down three German planes. He had no leave for weeks on end, and Daisy sat alone in the house she filled with flowers for him.

At last, on the morning of Saturday, September 7, Boy showed up with a weekend pass. The weather was glorious, hot and sunny, a late spell of warmth that people called an Indian summer.

As it happened, that was the day the Luftwaffe changed their tactics.

Daisy kissed her husband and made sure there were clean shirts and fresh underwear in his dressing room.

From what other women said, she believed that fighting men on leave wanted sex, booze, and decent food, in that order.

Boy and she had not slept together since the miscarriage. This would be the first time. She felt guilty that she did not really relish the prospect. But she certainly would not refuse to do her duty.

She half-expected him to tumble her into bed the minute he arrived, but he was not that desperate. He took off his uniform, bathed and washed his hair, and dressed again in a civilian suit. Daisy ordered the cook to spare no ration coupons in the preparation of a good lunch, and Boy brought up from the cellar one of his oldest bottles of claret.

She was surprised and hurt after lunch when he said: "I'm going out for a few hours. I'll be back for dinner."

She wanted to be a good wife, but not a passive one. "This is your first leave for months!" she protested. "Where the heck are you going?"

"To look at a horse."

That was all right. "Oh, fine—I'll come with you."

"No, don't. If I show up with a woman in tow, they'll think I'm a softie and put the price up."

She could not hide her disappointment. "I always dreamed this would be something we did together—buying and breeding racehorses."

"It's not really a woman's world."

"Oh, stink on that!" she said indignantly. "I know as much about horseflesh as you do."

He looked irritated. "Perhaps you do, but I still don't want you hanging around when I'm bargaining with these blighters—and that's final."

She gave in. "As you please," she said, and she left the dining room.

Her instinct told her that he was lying. Fighting men on leave did not think about buying horses. She intended to find out what he was up to. Even heroes had to be true to their wives.

In her room she put on trousers and boots. As Boy went down the main staircase to the front door, she ran down the back stairs, through the kitchen, across the yard, and into the old stables. There she put on a leather jacket, goggles, and a crash helmet. She opened the garage door into the mews and wheeled out her motorcycle, a Triumph Tiger 100, so called because its top speed was one hundred miles per hour. She kicked it into life and drove out of the mews effortlessly.

She had taken quickly to motorcycling when petrol rationing was introduced back in September 1939. It was like bicycling, but easier. She loved the freedom and independence it gave her.

She turned into the street just in time to see Boy's cream-colored Bentley Airline disappear around the next corner.

She followed.

He drove across Trafalgar Square and through the theater district. Daisy stayed a discreet distance behind, not wanting to be conspicuous. There was still plenty of traffic in central London, where there were hundreds of cars on official business. In addition, the petrol ration for private vehicles was not unreasonably small, especially for people who only wanted to drive around town.

Boy continued east, through the financial district. There was little traffic here on a Saturday afternoon, and Daisy became more concerned about being noticed. But she was not easily recognizable, in her goggles and helmet. And Boy was paying little attention to his surroundings, driving with the window open, smoking a cigar.

He headed into Aldgate, and Daisy had a dreadful feeling she knew why.

He turned into one of the East End's less squalid streets and parked outside a pleasant eighteenth-century house. There were no stables in sight: this was not a place where racehorses were bought and sold. So much for his story.

Daisy stopped her motorcycle at the end of the street and watched. Boy got out of the car and slammed the door. He did not look around, or study the house numbers; clearly he had been here before and knew exactly where he was going. Walking with a jaunty air, cigar in his mouth, he went up to the front door and opened it with a key.

Daisy wanted to cry.

Boy disappeared into the house.

Somewhere to the east, there was an explosion.

Daisy looked in that direction and saw planes in the sky. Had the Germans chosen today to begin bombing London?

If so, she did not care. She was not going to let Boy enjoy his infidelity in peace. She drove up to the house and parked her bike behind his car. She took off her helmet and goggles, marched up to the front door of the house, and knocked.

She heard another explosion, this one closer; then the air raid sirens began their mournful song.

The door came open a crack, and she shoved it hard. A young woman in a maid's black dress cried out and staggered backward, and Daisy walked in. She slammed the door behind her. She was in the hallway of a standard middle-class London house, but it was decorated in exotic fashion with Oriental rugs, heavy curtains, and a painting of naked women in a bathhouse.

She threw open the nearest door and stepped into the front parlor. It was dimly lit, velvet drapes keeping out the sunlight. There were three people in the room. Standing up, staring at her in shock, was a woman of about forty, dressed in a loose silk wrap, but carefully made up with bright red lipstick: the mother, she assumed. Behind her, sitting on a couch, was a girl of about sixteen wearing only underwear and stockings, smoking a cigarette. Next to the girl sat Boy, his hand on her thigh above the top of the stocking. He snatched his hand away guiltily. It was a ludicrous gesture, as if taking his hand off her could make this tableau look innocent.

Daisy fought back tears. "You promised me you would give them up!" she said. She wanted to be coldly angry, like the avenging angel, but she could hear that her voice was just wounded and sad.

Boy reddened and looked panicked. "What the devil are you doing here?"

The older woman said: "Oh, fuck, it's his wife."

Her name was Pearl, Daisy recalled, and the daughter was Joanie. How dreadful that she should know the names of such women.

The maid came to the door of the room and said: "I didn't let the bitch in—she just shoved past me!"

Daisy said to Boy: "I tried so hard to make our home beautiful and welcoming for you—and yet you prefer this!"

He started to say something, but had trouble finding his words. He sputtered incoherently for a moment or two. Then a big explosion nearby shook the floor and rattled the windows.

The maid said: "Are you all deaf? There's a fucking air raid on!" No one looked at her. "I'm going down to the basement," she said, and she disappeared.

They all needed to seek shelter. But Daisy had something to say to Boy before she left. "Don't come to my bed again, ever, please. I refuse to be contaminated."

The girl on the couch—Joanie—said: "It's only a bit of fun, love. Why don't you join in? You might like it."

Pearl, the older one, looked Daisy up and down. "She's got a nice little figure."

Daisy realized they would humiliate her further if she gave them the chance. Ignoring them, she spoke to Boy. "You've made your choice," she said. "And I've made my decision." She left the room, holding her head high even though she felt debased and spurned.

She heard Boy say: "Oh, damn, what a mess."

A mess? she thought. Is that all?

She went out of the front door.

Then she looked up.

The sky was full of planes.

The sight made her shake with fear. They were high, about ten thousand feet, but all the same they seemed to block the sun. There were hundreds of them, fat bombers and waspish fighters, a fleet that seemed twenty miles wide. To the east, in the direction of the docks and Woolwich Arsenal, palls of smoke rose from the ground where the bombs were landing. The explosions ran together into a continuous tidal roar like an angry sea.

Daisy recalled that Hitler had made a speech in the German parliament, just last Wednesday, ranting about the wickedness of RAF bombing raids on Berlin, and threatening to erase British cities in retaliation. Apparently he had meant it. They were intending to flatten London.

This was already the worst day of Daisy's life. Now she realized it might be the last.

But she could not bring herself to go back into that house and share their basement shelter. She had to get away. She needed to be at home where she could cry in private.

Hurriedly, she put on helmet and goggles. She resisted an irrational but nonetheless powerful impulse to throw herself behind the nearest wall. She jumped on her motorcycle and drove away.

She did not get far.

Two streets away, a bomb landed on a house directly in her line of vision, and she braked suddenly. She saw the hole in the roof, felt the thump of the explosion, and a few seconds later saw flames inside, as if kerosene from a heater had spilled and caught fire. A moment later, a girl of about twelve came out, screaming, with her hair on fire, and ran straight at Daisy.

Daisy jumped off the bike, pulled off her leather jacket, and used it to cover the girl's head, wrapping it tightly over the hair, denying oxygen to the flames.

The screaming stopped. Daisy removed the jacket. The girl was sobbing. She was no longer in agony, but she was bald.

Daisy looked up and down the street. A man wearing a steel helmet and an Air Raid Precautions armband came running up carrying a tin case with a white first-aid cross painted on its side.

The girl looked at Daisy, opened her mouth, and screamed: "My mother's in there!"

The ARP warden said: "Calm down, love. Let's have a look at you."

Daisy left the girl with him and ran to the front door of the building. It seemed to be an old house subdivided into cheap apartments. The upper floors were burning but she was able to enter the hall. Taking a guess, she ran to the back and found herself in a kitchen. There she saw a woman unconscious on the floor and a toddler in a cot. She picked up the child and ran out again.

The girl with the burned hair yelled: "That's my sister!"

Daisy thrust the toddler into the girl's arms and ran back inside.

The unconscious woman was too heavy for her to lift. Daisy got behind her, raised her to a sitting position, took hold of her under the arms, and dragged her across the kitchen floor and through the hallway into the street.

An ambulance had arrived, a converted saloon car, its rear bodywork replaced by a canvas roof with a back opening. The ARP warden was helping the burned girl into the vehicle. The driver came running over to Daisy. Between them, they lifted the mother into the ambulance.

The driver said to Daisy: "Is there anyone else inside?"

"I don't know!"

He ran into the hall. At that moment the entire building sagged. The burning upper stories crashed through to the ground floor. The ambulance driver disappeared into an inferno.

Daisy heard herself scream.

She covered her mouth with her hand and stared into the flames, searching for him, even though she could not have helped him, and it would have been suicide to try.

The ARP warden said: "Oh, my God, Alf's been killed."

There was another explosion as a bomb landed a hundred yards along the street.

The warden said: "Now I've got no driver, and I can't leave the scene." He looked up and down the street. There were little knots of people standing outside some of the houses, but most were probably in shelters.

Daisy said: "I'll drive it. Where should I go?"

"Can you drive?"

Most British women could not drive: it was still a man's job here. "Don't ask stupid questions," Daisy said. "Where am I taking the ambulance?"

"St. Bart's. Do you know where it is?"

"Of course." St. Bartholomew's was one of the biggest hospitals in London, and Daisy had been living here for four years. "West Smithfield," she added, to make sure he believed her.

"Emergency ward is around the back."

"I'll find it." She jumped in. The engine was still running.

The warden shouted: "What's your name?"

"Daisy Fitzherbert. What's yours?"

"Nobby Clarke. Take care of my ambulance."

The car had a standard gearshift with a clutch. Daisy put it into first and drove off.

The planes continued to roar overhead, and the bombs fell

relentlessly. Daisy was desperate to get the injured people to the hospital, and St. Bart's was not much more than a mile away, but the journey was maddeningly difficult. She drove along Leadenhall Street, Poultry, and Cheapside, but several times she found the road blocked, and had to reverse away and find another route. There seemed to be at least one destroyed house in every street. Everywhere was smoke and rubble, people bleeding and crying.

With huge relief she reached the hospital and followed another ambulance to the emergency entrance. The place was frantically busy, with a dozen vehicles discharging maimed and burned patients into the care of hurrying porters with bloodstained aprons. Perhaps I've saved the mother of these children, Daisy thought. I'm not completely worthless, even if my husband doesn't want me.

The girl with no hair was still carrying her baby sister. Daisy helped them both out of the back of her ambulance.

A nurse helped Daisy lift the unconscious mother and carry her in.

But Daisy could see that the woman had stopped breathing.

She said to the nurse: "These two are her children!" She heard the edge of hysteria in her own voice. "What will happen now?"

"I'll deal with it," the nurse said briskly. "You have to go back."

"Must I?" said Daisy.

"Pull yourself together," said the nurse. "There will be a lot more dead and injured before this night is over."

"All right," said Daisy, and she got back behind the wheel and drove off.

iv

On a warm Mediterranean afternoon in October, Lloyd Williams arrived in the sunlit French town of Perpignan, only twenty miles from the border with Spain.

He had spent the month of September in the Bordeaux area,

picking grapes for the wine harvest, just as he had in the terrible year of 1937. Now he had money in his pockets for buses and trams, and could eat in cheap restaurants instead of living on unripe vegetables he dug up in people's gardens or raw eggs stolen from hen coops. He was going back along the route he had taken when he left Spain three years ago. He had come south from Bordeaux through Toulouse and Béziers, occasionally riding freight trains, mostly begging lifts from truck drivers.

Now he was at a roadside café on the main highway running southeast from Perpignan toward the Spanish border. Still dressed in Maurice's blue overalls and beret, he carried a small canvas bag containing a rusty trowel and a mortar-spattered spirit level, evidence that he was a Spanish bricklayer making his way home. God forbid that anyone should offer him work: he had no idea how to build a wall.

He was worried about finding his way across the mountains. Three months ago, back in Picardy, he had told himself glibly that he could find the route over the Pyrenees along which his guides had led him into Spain in 1936, parts of which he had retraced in the opposite direction when he left a year later. But as the purple peaks and green passes came into distant view on the horizon, the prospect seemed more daunting. He had thought that every step of the journey must be engraved on his memory, but when he tried to recall specific paths and bridges and turning points, he found that the pictures were blurred, and the exact details slipped infuriatingly from his mind's grasp.

He finished his lunch—a peppery fish stew—then spoke quietly to a group of drivers at the next table. "I need a lift to Cerbère." It was the last village before the Spanish border. "Anyone going that way?"

They were probably all going that way: it was the only reason for being here on this southeast route. All the same they hesitated. This was Vichy France, technically an independent zone, in practise under the thumb of the Germans occupying the other half of the country. No one was in a hurry to help a traveling stranger with a foreign accent.

"I'm a mason," he said, hefting his canvas bag. "Going home to Spain. Leandro is my name."

A fat man in an undershirt said: "I can take you halfway."

"Thank you."

"Are you ready now?"

"Of course."

They went outside and got into a grimy Renault van with the name of an electrical goods store on the side. As they pulled away, the driver asked Lloyd if he was married. A series of unpleasantly personal inquiries followed, and Lloyd realized the man had a fascination with other people's sex lives. No doubt that was why he had agreed to take Lloyd: it gave him the chance to ask intrusive questions. Several of the men who had given Lloyd lifts had had some such creepy motive.

"I'm a virgin," Lloyd told him, which was true, but that only led to an interrogation about heavy petting with schoolgirls. Lloyd did have considerable experience of that, but he was not going to share it. He refused to give details while trying not to be rude, and eventually the driver despaired. "I have to turn off here," he said, and pulled over.

Lloyd thanked him for the ride and walked on.

He had learned not to march like a soldier, and had developed what he thought was a fairly realistic peasant slouch. He never carried a newspaper or a book. His hair had last been cut by a brutally incompetent barber in the poorest quarter of Toulouse. He shaved about once a week, so that he normally had a growth of stubble, which was surprisingly effective in making him look like a nobody. He had stopped washing, and acquired a ripe odor that discouraged people from talking to him.

Few working-class people had watches, in France or Spain, so the steel wristwatch with the square face that Bernie had given him as a graduation present had to go. He could not give it to one of the many French people who had helped him, for a British watch could have incriminated them, too. In the end, with great sadness, he had thrown it into a pond.

His greatest weakness was that he had no identity papers.

He had tried to buy papers from a man who looked vaguely like him, and schemed to steal them from two others, but people were cautious about such things just now, not surprisingly. His strategy was therefore to steer clear of situations in which he might be asked to identify himself. He made himself inconspicuous, he walked across fields rather than take roads when he had the choice, and he never traveled by passenger train because there were often checkpoints at stations. So far he had been lucky. One village gendarme had demanded his papers, and when he explained that they had been stolen from him after he got drunk and passed out in a bar in Marseilles, the policeman had believed him and sent him on his way.

Now, however, his luck ran out.

He was passing through poor agricultural terrain. He was in the foothills of the Pyrenees, close to the Mediterranean, and the soil was sandy. The dusty road ran through struggling smallholdings and poor villages. The landscape was sparsely populated. To his left, through the hills, he got blue glimpses of the distant sea.

The last thing he expected was the green Citroën that pulled up alongside him with three gendarmes inside.

It happened very suddenly. He heard the car approaching—the only car he had heard since the fat man dropped him off. He carried on shuffling like a tired worker going home. Either side of the road were dry fields with sparse vegetation and stunted trees. When the car stopped, he thought for a second of making a run for it across the fields. He dropped the idea when he saw the holstered pistols of the two gendarmes who jumped out of the car. They were probably not very good shots, but they might get lucky. His chances of talking his way out of this were better. These were country constables, more amiable than the hard-nosed French city police.

"Papers?" said the nearest gendarme in French.

Lloyd spread his hands in a helpless gesture. "Monsieur, I am so unfortunate. My papers were stolen in Marseilles. I am Leandro, Spanish mason, going—"

"Get in the car."

Lloyd hesitated, but it was hopeless. The odds of his getting away were now worse than before.

A gendarme took him firmly by the arm, hustled him into the backseat, and got in beside him.

His spirits sank as the car pulled away.

The gendarme next to him said: "Are you English, or what?"

"I am a Spanish mason. My name—"

The gendarme made a waving-away gesture and said: "Don't bother."

Lloyd saw that he had been wildly optimistic. He was a foreigner without papers heading for the Spanish border: they simply assumed he was an escaping British soldier. If they had any doubt, they would find proof when they ordered him to strip, for they would see the identity tag around his neck. He had not thrown it away, for without it he would automatically be shot as a spy.

And now he was stuck in a car with three armed men, and the likelihood that he would find a way to escape was zero.

They drove on, in the direction in which he had been heading, as the sun went down over the mountains on their right-hand side. There were no big towns between here and the border, so he assumed they intended to put him in a village jail for the night. Perhaps he could escape from there. Failing that, they would undoubtedly take him back to Perpignan tomorrow and hand him over to the city police. What then? Would he be interrogated? The prospect made him cold with fear. The French police would beat him up; the Germans would torture him. If he survived, he would end up in a prisoner-of-war camp, where he would remain until the end of the war, or until he died of malnutrition. And yet he was only a few miles from the border!

They drove into a small town. Could he escape between the car and the jail? He could make no plan; he did not know the terrain. There was nothing he could do but remain alert and seize any opportunity.

The car turned off the main street and into an alley behind a row of shops. Were they going to shoot him here and dump his body?

The car stopped at the back of a restaurant. The yard was littered with boxes and giant cans. Through a small window Lloyd could see a brightly lit kitchen.

The gendarme in the front passenger seat got out, then opened

Lloyd's door, on the side of the car nearest the building. Was this his chance? He would have to run around the car and along the alley. It was dusk: after the first few yards he would not be an easy target.

The gendarme reached into the car and grasped Lloyd's arm, holding him as he got out and stood up. The second one got out immediately behind Lloyd. The opportunity was not good enough.

But why had they brought him here?

They walked him into the kitchen. A chef was beating eggs in a bowl and an adolescent boy was washing up in a big sink. One of the gendarmes said: "Here's an Englishman. He calls himself Leandro."

Without pausing in his work, the chef lifted his head and bawled: "Teresa! Come here!"

Lloyd remembered another Teresa, a beautiful Spanish anarchist who had taught soldiers to read and write.

The kitchen door swung wide and she walked in.

Lloyd stared at her in astonishment. There was no possibility of mistake: he would never forget those big eyes and that mass of black hair, even though she wore the white cotton cap and apron of a waitress.

At first she did not look at him. She put a pile of plates on the counter next to the young washer-up, then turned to the gendarmes with a smile and kissed each on both cheeks, saying: "Pierre! Michel! How are you?" Then she turned to Lloyd, stared at him, and said in Spanish: "No—it's not possible. Lloyd—is it really you?"

He could only nod dumbly.

She put her arms around him, embraced him, and kissed him on both cheeks.

One of the gendarmes said: "There we are. All is well. We have to go. Good luck!" He handed Lloyd his canvas bag; then they left.

Lloyd found his tongue. "What's going on?" he said to Teresa in Spanish. "I thought I was being taken to jail!"

"They hate the Nazis, so they help us," she said.

"Who is *us*?"

"I'll explain later. Come with me." She opened a door that gave onto a staircase and led him to an upper story, where there was a sparsely furnished bedroom. "Wait here. I'll bring you something to eat."

Lloyd lay down on the bed and contemplated his extraordinary fortune. Five minutes ago he had been expecting torture and death. Now he was waiting for a beautiful woman to bring him supper.

It could change again just as quickly, he reflected.

She returned half an hour later with an omelette and fried potatoes on a thick plate. "We've been busy, but we close soon," she said. "I'll be back in a few minutes."

He ate the food quickly.

Night fell. He listened to the chatter of customers leaving and the clang of pots being put away; then Teresa reappeared with a bottle of red wine and two glasses.

Lloyd asked her why she had left Spain.

"Our people are being murdered by the thousands," she said. "For those they don't kill, they have passed the Law of Political Responsibilities, making criminals of everyone who supported the government. You can lose all your assets if you opposed Franco even by 'grave passivity.' You are innocent only if you can prove you supported him."

Lloyd thought bitterly of Chamberlain's reassurance to the House of Commons, back in March, that Franco had renounced political reprisals. What an evil liar Chamberlain had been.

Teresa went on: "Many of our comrades are in filthy prison camps."

"I don't suppose you have any idea what happened to Sergeant Lenny Griffiths, my friend?"

Teresa shook her head. "I never saw him again after Belchite."

"And you . . . ?"

"I escaped from Franco's men, came here, got a job as a waitress . . . and found there was other work for me to do."

"What work?"

"I take escaping soldiers across the mountains. That's why the gendarmes brought you to me."

Lloyd was heartened. He had been planning to do it alone, and he had been worried about finding the way. Now perhaps he would have a guide.

"I have two others waiting," she said. "A British gunner and a Canadian pilot. They are in a farmhouse in the hills."

"When are you planning to go across?"

"Tonight," she said. "Don't drink too much wine."

She went away again and returned half an hour later carrying an old, ripped brown overcoat for him. "It's cold where we're going," she explained.

They slipped out of the kitchen door and threaded their way through the small town by starlight. Leaving the houses behind, they followed a dirt track steadily uphill. After an hour they came to a small group of stone buildings. Teresa whistled, then opened the door to a barn, and two men came out.

"We always use false names," she said in English. "I am Maria and these two are Fred and Tom. Our new friend is Leandro." The men shook hands. She went on: "No talking, no smoking, and anyone who falls behind will be left. Are we ready?"

From here the path was steeper. Lloyd found himself slipping on stones. Now and again he clutched at stunted bushes of heather beside the path and pulled himself upward with their aid. The petite Teresa set a pace that soon had the three men puffing and blowing. She was carrying a flashlight, but she refused to use it while the stars were bright, saying she had to conserve the battery.

The air got colder. They waded across an icy stream, and Lloyd's feet did not get warm again afterward.

An hour later, Teresa said: "Take care to stay in the middle of the path here." Lloyd looked down and realized he was on a ridge between steep slopes. When he saw how far he could fall, he felt a little giddy, and quickly looked up and ahead at Teresa's swiftly moving silhouette. In normal circumstances he would have enjoyed every minute of walking behind a figure like that, but now he was so tired and cold he did not have the energy even to ogle.

The mountains were not uninhabited. At one point a distant dog barked; at another they heard a tinkling of eerie bells, which spooked the men until Teresa explained that mountain shepherds hung bells on their sheep so they could find their flocks.

Lloyd thought about Daisy. Was she still at Tŷ Gwyn? Or had she gone back to her husband? Lloyd hoped she had not returned to London, for London was being bombed every night, the French newspapers said. Was she alive or dead? Would he ever see her again? If he did, how would she feel about him?

They stopped every two hours to rest, drink water, and take a few mouthfuls from a bottle of wine Teresa was carrying.

It started to rain around dawn. The ground underfoot instantly became treacherous, and they all stumbled and slipped, but Teresa did not slow down. "Be glad it's not snow," she said.

Daylight revealed a landscape of scrubby vegetation in which rocky outcrops stuck up like tombstones. The rain continued, and a cold mist obscured the distance.

After a while, Lloyd realized they were walking downhill. At the next rest stop, Teresa announced: "We are now in Spain." Lloyd should have been relieved, but he just felt exhausted.

Gradually the landscape softened, rocks giving way to coarse grass and shrubs.

Suddenly Teresa dropped to the ground and lay flat.

The three men instantly did the same, not needing to be prompted. Following Teresa's gaze, Lloyd saw two men in green uniforms and peculiar hats: Spanish border guards, presumably. He realized that being in Spain did not mean he was out of trouble. If he was caught entering the country illegally, he might just be sent back. Worse, he could disappear into one of Franco's prison camps.

The border guards were walking along a mountain track toward the fugitives. Lloyd prepared himself for a fight. He would have to move fast, in order to overcome them before they could draw their guns. He wondered how good the other two men would be in a fracas.

But his trepidation was unnecessary. The two guards reached some unmarked boundary and then turned back. Teresa acted as if she had known this would happen. When the guards disappeared from sight, she stood up and the four of them walked on.

Soon afterward the mist lifted. Lloyd saw a fishing village around a sandy bay. He had been here before, when he came to Spain in 1936. He even remembered that there was a railway station.

They walked into the village. It was a sleepy place, with no signs of officialdom: no police, no town hall, no soldiers, no checkpoints. Doubtless that was why Teresa had chosen it.

They went to the station and Teresa bought tickets, flirting with the vendor as if they were old friends.

Lloyd sat on a bench on the shady platform, footsore, weary, grateful, and happy.

An hour later they caught a train to Barcelona.

V

Daisy had never before understood the meaning of *work*.

Or *tiredness*.

Or *tragedy*.

She sat in a school classroom, drinking sweet English tea out of a cup with no saucer. She wore a steel helmet and rubber boots. It was five o'clock in the afternoon, and she was still weary from the night before.

She was part of the Aldgate district Air Raid Precautions sector. Theoretically she worked an eight-hour shift followed by eight hours on standby and eight hours off duty. In practise she worked as long as the air raid continued and there were wounded people to be driven to the hospital.

London was bombed every single night of October 1940.

Daisy always worked with one other woman, the driver's attendant, and four men, forming a first-aid party. Their headquarters was in a school, and now they were sitting at the children's desks, waiting for the planes to come and the sirens to wail and the bombs to fall.

The ambulance she drove was a converted American Buick. They also had a normal car and driver to transport what they called sitting cases—injured people who could nevertheless sit upright without assistance while being transported to hospital.

Her attendant was Naomi Avery, an attractive blond cockney who liked men and enjoyed the camaraderie of the team. Now she bantered with the post warden, Nobby Clarke, a retired policeman. "The chief warden is a man," she said. "The district warden is a man. You're a man."

"I hope so," Nobby said, and the others chuckled.

"There are plenty of women in ARP," Naomi went on. "How come none of them are officials?"

The men laughed. A bald man with a big nose called Gorgeous George said: "Here we go, women's rights again." He had a misogynist streak.

Daisy joined in. "You don't really think all you men are smarter than all of us women, do you?"

Nobby said: "Matter of fact, there are some women senior wardens."

"I've never met one," said Naomi.

"It's tradition, isn't it," Nobby said. "Women have always been homemakers."

"Like Catherine the Great of Russia," Daisy said sarcastically.

Naomi put in: "Or Queen Elizabeth of England."

"Amelia Earhart."

"Jane Austen."

"Marie Curie, the only scientist ever to win the Nobel Prize twice."

"Catherine the Great?" said Gorgeous George. "Isn't there a story about her and her horse?"

"Now, now, ladies present," said Nobby in a tone of reproof. "Anyway, I can answer Daisy's question," he went on.

Daisy, willing to be his foil, said: "Go on, then."

"I grant you that some women may be just as clever as a man," he said with the air of one who makes a remarkably generous concession. "But there is one very good reason why almost all ARP officials are men, nevertheless."

"And what would that reason be, Nobby?"

"It's very simple. Men won't take orders from a woman." He sat back with a triumphant expression, confident that he had won the argument.

The irony was that when the bombs were falling, and they were digging through the rubble to rescue the injured, they *were* equals. There was no hierarchy then. If Daisy shouted at Nobby to pick up the other end of a roof beam, he would do it without demur.

Daisy loved these men, even George. They would give their lives for her, and she for them.

She heard a low hooting sound outside. Slowly it rose in pitch until it became the tiresomely familiar siren of an air raid warning. Seconds later there was the boom of a distant explosion. The warning was often late; sometimes it sounded after the first bombs had fallen.

The phone rang and Nobby picked it up.

They all stood up. George said wearily: "Don't the Germans ever take a ruddy day off?"

Nobby put the phone down and said: "Nutley Street."

"I know where that is," said Naomi as they all hurried out. "Our M.P. lives there."

They jumped into the cars. As Daisy put the ambulance in gear and drove off, Naomi, sitting beside her, said: "Happy days."

Naomi was being ironic but, strangely, Daisy *was* happy. It was very odd, she thought as she careered around a bend. Every night she saw destruction, tragic bereavement, and horribly maimed bodies. There was a good chance she herself would die in a blazing building tonight. Yet she felt wonderful. She was working and suffering for a cause, and paradoxically that was better than pleasing herself. She was part of a group that would risk everything to help others, and it was the best feeling in the world.

Daisy did not hate the Germans for trying to kill her. She had been told by her father-in-law, Earl Fitzherbert, why they were bombing London. Until August the Luftwaffe had raided only ports and airfields. Fitz had explained, in an unusually candid moment, that the British were not so scrupulous: the government had approved bombing of targets in German cities back in May, and all through June and July the RAF had dropped bombs on women and children in their homes. The German public had been enraged by this and demanded retaliation. The Blitz was the result.

Daisy and Boy were keeping up appearances, but she locked her bedroom door when he was at home, and he made no objection. Their marriage was a sham, but they were both too busy to do anything about it. When Daisy thought about it, she felt sad, for she had lost both Boy and Lloyd now. Fortunately she hardly had time to think.

Nutley Street was on fire. The Luftwaffe dropped incendiary bombs and high explosive together. Fire did the most damage, but the high explosive helped the blaze to spread by blowing out windows and ventilating the flames.

Daisy brought the ambulance to a screeching halt and they all went to work.

People with minor injuries were helped to the nearest first-aid station. Those more seriously hurt were driven to St. Bart's or the London Hospital in Whitechapel. Daisy made one trip after another. When darkness fell, she switched on her headlights. They were masked, with only a slit of light, as part of the blackout, though it seemed a superfluous precaution when London was burning like a bonfire.

The bombing went on until dawn. In full daylight the bombers were too vulnerable to being shot down by the fighter aircraft piloted by Boy and his comrades, so the air raid petered out. As the cold gray light washed over the wreckage, Daisy and Naomi returned to Nutley Street to find there were no more victims to be taken to hospital.

They sat down wearily on the remains of a brick garden wall. Daisy took off her steel helmet. She was filthy dirty and worn out. I wonder what the girls in the Buffalo Yacht Club would think of me now, she thought; then she realized she no longer cared much what they thought. The days when their approval was all-important to her seemed a long time in the past.

Someone said: "Would you like a cup of tea, my lovely?"

She recognized the accent as Welsh. She looked up to see an

attractive middle-aged woman carrying a tray. "Oh, boy, that's what I need," she said, and helped herself. She had now grown to like this beverage. It tasted bitter but it had a remarkable restorative effect.

The woman kissed Naomi, who explained: "We're related. Her daughter, Millie, is married to my brother, Abie."

Daisy watched the woman take the tray around the little crowd of ARP wardens and firemen and neighbors. She must be a local dignitary, Daisy decided: she had an air of authority. Yet at the same time she was clearly a woman of the people, speaking to everyone with an easy warmth, making them smile. She knew Nobby and Gorgeous George, and greeted them as old friends.

She took the last cup on the tray for herself and came to sit beside Daisy. "You sound American," she said pleasantly.

Daisy nodded. "I'm married to an Englishman."

"I live in this street—but my house escaped the bombs last night. I'm the member of Parliament for Aldgate. My name is Eth Leckwith."

Daisy's heart skipped a beat. This was Lloyd's famous mother! She shook hands. "Daisy Fitzherbert."

Ethel's eyebrows went up. "Oh!" she said. "You're the Viscountess Aberowen."

Daisy blushed and lowered her voice. "They don't know that in the ARP."

"Your secret is safe with me."

Hesitantly, Daisy said: "I knew your son, Lloyd." She could not help the tears that came to her eyes when she thought of their time at Tŷ Gwyn, and the way he had looked after her when she miscarried. "He was very kind to me, once when I needed help."

"Thank you," said Ethel. "But don't talk as if he's dead."

The reproof was mild, but Daisy felt she had been dreadfully tactless. "I'm so sorry!" she said. "He's missing in action, I know. How frightfully stupid of me."

"But he's not missing any longer," Ethel said. "He escaped through Spain. He arrived home yesterday."

"Oh, my God!" Daisy's heart was racing. "Is he all right?"

"Perfectly. In fact he looks very well, despite what he's been through."

"Where . . ." Daisy swallowed. "Where is he now?"

"Why, he's here somewhere." Ethel looked around. "Lloyd?" she called.

Daisy scanned the crowd wildly. Could it be true?

A man in a ripped brown overcoat turned around and said: "Yes, Mam?"

Daisy stared at him. His face was sunburned, and he was as thin as a stick, but he looked more attractive than ever.

"Come here, my lovely," said Ethel.

Lloyd took a step forward, then saw Daisy. Suddenly his face was transformed. He smiled happily. "Hello," he said.

Daisy sprang to her feet.

Ethel said: "Lloyd, there's someone here you may remember—"

Daisy could not restrain herself. She ran to Lloyd and threw herself into his arms. She hugged him. She looked into his green eyes, then kissed his brown cheeks and his broken nose and then his mouth. "I love you, Lloyd," she said madly. "I love you, I love you, I love you."

"I love you, too, Daisy," he said.

Behind her, Daisy heard Ethel's wry voice. "You do remember, I see."

vi

Lloyd was eating toast and jam when Daisy entered the kitchen of the house in Nutley Street. She sat at the table, looking exhausted, and took off her steel helmet. Her face was smudged and her hair was dirty with ash and dust, and Lloyd thought she looked irresistibly beautiful.

She came in most mornings when the bombing ended and the last victim had been driven to the hospital. Lloyd's mother had told her she did not need an invitation, and Daisy had taken her at her word.

Ethel poured Daisy a cup of tea and said: "Hard night, my lovely?"

Daisy nodded grimly. "One of the worst. The Peabody building on Orange Street burned down."

"Oh, no!" Lloyd was horrified. He knew the place: a big overcrowded tenement full of poor families with numerous children.

Bernie said: "That's a big building."

"It was," said Daisy. "Hundreds of people were burned and God knows how many children are orphans. Nearly all my patients died on the way to the hospital."

Lloyd reached across the little table and took her hand.

She looked up from her cup of tea. "You don't get used to it. You think you'll become hardened, but you don't." She was stricken with sadness.

Ethel put a hand on her shoulder for a moment in a gesture of compassion.

Daisy said: "And we're doing the same to families in Germany."

Ethel said: "Including my old friends Maud and Walter and their children, I presume."

"Isn't that terrible?" Daisy shook her head despairingly. "What's wrong with us?"

Lloyd said: "What's wrong with the human race?"

Bernie, ever practical, said: "I'll go over to Orange Street later and make sure everything's being done for the children."

"I'll come with you," said Ethel.

Bernie and Ethel thought alike and acted together effortlessly, often seeming to read each other's minds. Lloyd had been observing them carefully, since he got home, worrying that their marriage might have been affected by the shocking revelation that Ethel had never had a husband called Teddy Williams, and that Lloyd's father was Earl Fitzherbert. He had discussed this at length with Daisy, who now knew the whole truth. How did Bernie feel about having been lied to for twenty years? But Lloyd saw no sign that it had made any difference. In his unsentimental way Bernie adored Ethel, and to him she could do no wrong. He believed she would never do anything to hurt him, and he was right. It made Lloyd hope that he, too, might one day have such a marriage.

Daisy noticed that Lloyd was in uniform. "Where are you off to this morning?"

"I've had a summons from the War Office." He looked at the clock on the mantelpiece. "I'd better get going."

"I thought you'd already been debriefed."

"Come to my room and I'll explain while I'm putting on my tie. Bring your tea."

They went upstairs. Daisy looked around with interest, and he realized she had not been in his bedroom before. He looked at the single bed, the bookshelf of novels in German, French, and Spanish, and the writing table with the row of sharpened pencils, and wondered what she thought of it.

"What a nice little room," she said.

It was not little. It was the same size as the other bedrooms in the house. But she had different standards.

She picked up a framed photograph. It showed the family at the seaside: little Lloyd in shorts, toddling Millie in a swimsuit, young Ethel in a big floppy hat, Bernie wearing a gray suit with a white shirt open at the neck and a knotted handkerchief on his head.

"Southend," Lloyd explained. He took her cup, put it on the dressing table, and folded her into his arms. He kissed her mouth. She kissed him back with weary tenderness, stroking his cheek, letting her body slump against his.

After a minute he released her. She was really too tired to canoodle, and he had an appointment.

She took off her boots and lay down on his bed.

"The War Office have asked me to go in and see them again," he said as he tied his tie.

"But you were there for hours last time."

It was true. He had had to dredge his memory for every last detail of his time on the run in France. They wanted to know the rank and regiment of every German he had encountered. He could not remember them all, of course, but he had done his homework meticulously for the Tŷ Gwyn course and he was able to give them a great deal of information.

That was standard military intelligence debriefing. But they had also asked about his escape, the roads he had taken and who had helped him. They were even interested in Maurice and Marcelle, and reproved him for not knowing their surname. They had got very excited about Teresa, who clearly could be a major asset to future escapers.

"I'm seeing a different lot today." He glanced at a typed note on his dressing table. "At the Metropole Hotel in Northumberland Avenue. Room four twenty-four." The address was off Trafalgar Square in a neighborhood of government offices. "Apparently it's a new department dealing with British prisoners of war." He put on his peaked cap and looked in the mirror. "Am I smart enough?"

There was no answer. He looked at the bed. She had fallen asleep.

He pulled a blanket over her, kissed her forehead, and went out.

He told his mother that Daisy was asleep on his bed, and she said she would check on her later to make sure she was all right.

He took the Tube to central London.

He had told Daisy the true story of his parentage, disabusing her of the theory that he was Maud's child. She believed him readily, for she suddenly recalled Boy telling her that Fitz had an illegitimate child somewhere. "This is creepy," she had said, looking thoughtful. "The two Englishmen I've fallen for turn out to be half brothers." She had looked appraisingly at Lloyd. "You inherited your father's good looks. Boy just got his selfishness."

Lloyd and Daisy had not yet made love. One reason was that she never had a night off. Then, on the single occasion they had had a chance to be alone together, things had gone wrong.

It had been last Sunday, at Daisy's home in Mayfair. Her servants had Sunday afternoon off, and she had taken him to her bedroom in the empty house. But she had been nervous and ill at ease. She had kissed him, then turned her head aside. When he put his hands on her breasts, she had pushed them away. He had been confused: If he was not supposed to behave this way, why were they in her bedroom?

"I'm sorry," she had said at last. "I love you, but I can't do this. I can't betray my husband in his own house."

"But he betrayed you."

"At least he went somewhere else."

"All right."

She had looked at him. "Do you think I'm being silly?"

He shrugged. "After all we've been through together, this seems overly fastidious of you, yes—but, look, you feel the way you feel. What a rotter I would be if I tried to bully you into doing it when you're not ready."

She put her arms around him and hugged him hard. "I said it before," she said. "You're a grown-up."

"Don't let's spoil the whole afternoon," he said. "We'll go to the pictures."

They saw Charlie Chaplin in *The Great Dictator* and laughed their heads off; then she went back on duty.

Pleasant thoughts of Daisy occupied Lloyd all the way to Embankment station; then he walked up Northumberland Avenue to the Metropole. The hotel had been stripped of its reproduction antiques and furnished with utilitarian tables and chairs.

After a few minutes' wait Lloyd was taken to see a tall colonel with a brisk manner. "I've read your account, Lieutenant," he said. "Well done."

"Thank you, sir."

"We expect more people to follow in your footsteps, and we'd like to help them. We're especially interested in downed airmen. They're expensive to train, and we want them back so they can fly again."

Lloyd thought that was harsh. If a man survived a crash landing, should he really be asked to risk going through the whole thing again? But wounded men were sent back into battle as soon as they recovered. That was war.

The colonel said: "We're setting up a kind of underground railroad, all the way from Germany to Spain. You speak German, French, and Spanish, I see, but, more importantly, you've been at the sharp end. We'd like to second you to our department."

Lloyd had not been expecting this, and he was not sure how he felt about it. "Thank you, sir. I'm honored. But is it a desk job?"

"Not at all. We want you to go back to France."

Lloyd's heart raced. He had not thought he would have to face those perils again.

The colonel saw the dismay on his face. "You know how dangerous it is."

"Yes, sir."

In an abrupt tone the colonel said: "You can refuse if you like."

Lloyd thought of Daisy in the Blitz, and of the people burned to death in the Peabody tenement, and realized he did not even want to refuse. "If you think it's important, sir, then I will go back most willingly, of course."

"Good man," said the colonel.

Half an hour later Lloyd was dazedly walking back to the Tube station. He was now part of a department called MI9. He would return to France with false papers and large sums in cash. Already dozens of German, Dutch, Belgian, and French people in occupied territory had been recruited to the deadly dangerous task of helping British and Commonwealth airmen return home. He would be one of numerous MI9 agents expanding the network.

If he were caught, he would be tortured.

Although he was scared, he was also excited. He was going to fly to Madrid; it would be his first time up in an airplane. He would reenter France across the Pyrenees and make contact with Teresa. He would be moving in disguise among the enemy, rescuing people under the noses of the Gestapo. He would make sure that men following in his footsteps would not be as alone and friendless as he had been.

He got back to Nutley Street at eleven o'clock. There was a note from his mother: "Not a peep from Miss America." After visiting the bomb site, Ethel would have gone to the House of Commons, Bernie to County Hall. Lloyd and Daisy had the house to themselves.

He went up to his room. Daisy was still asleep. Her leather jacket and heavy-duty wool trousers were carelessly tossed on the floor. She was in his bed wearing only her underwear. This had never happened before.

He took off his jacket and tie.

A sleepy voice from the bed said: "And the rest."

He looked at her. "What?"

"Take off your clothes and get into bed."

The house was empty: no one would disturb them.

He took off his boots, trousers, shirt, and socks; then he hesitated.

"You're not going to feel cold," she said. She wriggled under the blankets, then threw a pair of silk camiknickers at him.

He had expected this to be a solemn moment of high passion, but Daisy seemed to think it should be a matter of laughter and fun. He was willing to be guided by her.

He took off his undershirt and pants and slipped into bed beside her. She was warm and languid. He felt nervous: he had never actually told her that he was a virgin.

He had always heard that the man should take the initiative, but it seemed Daisy did not know that. She kissed and caressed him; then she grasped his penis. "Oh, boy," she said. "I was hoping you'd have one of these."

After that, he stopped being nervous.

CHAPTER EIGHT

1941 (I)

On a cold winter Sunday, Carla von Ulrich went with the maid, Ada, to visit Ada's son, Kurt, at the Wannsee Children's Nursing Home, by the lake on the western outskirts of Berlin. It took an hour to get there on the train. Carla made a habit of wearing her nurse's uniform on these visits, because the staff at the home talked more frankly about Kurt to a fellow professional.

In summer the lakeside would be crowded with families and children playing on the beach and paddling in the shallows, but today there were just a few walkers, well wrapped up against the chill, and one hardy swimmer with an anxious wife waiting at the waterside.

The home, which specialized in caring for severely handicapped children, was a once-grand house whose elegant reception rooms had been subdivided and painted pale green and furnished with hospital beds and cots.

Kurt was now eight years old. He could walk and feed himself about as well as a two-year-old, but he could not talk and still wore diapers. He had shown no sign of improvement for years. However, there was no doubt of his joy at seeing Ada. He beamed with happiness, burbled excitedly, and held out his arms to be picked up and hugged and kissed.

He recognized Carla, too. Whenever she saw him, she remembered the frightening drama of his birth, when she had delivered him while her brother, Erik, ran to fetch Dr. Rothmann.

They played with him for an hour or so. He liked toy trains and cars, and books with highly colored pictures. Then the time for his afternoon nap drew near, and Ada sang to him until he went to sleep.

On their way out a nurse spoke to Ada. "Frau Hempel, please come with me to the office of Herr Professor Doctor Willrich. He would like to speak to you."

Willrich was director of the home. Carla had never met him and she was not sure Ada had, either.

Ada said nervously: "Is there some problem?"

The nurse said: "I'm sure the director just wants to talk to you about Kurt's progress."

Ada said: "Fräulein von Ulrich will come with me."

The nurse did not like that idea. "Professor Willrich asked only for you."

But Ada could be stubborn when necessary. "Fräulein von Ulrich will come with me," she repeated firmly.

The nurse shrugged and said curtly: "Follow me."

They were shown into a pleasant office. This room had not been subdivided. A coal fire burned in the grate, and a bay window gave a view of the Wannsee lake. Someone was sailing, Carla saw, slicing through the wavelets before a stiff breeze. Willrich sat behind a leather-topped desk. He had a jar of tobacco and a rack of different-shaped pipes. He was about fifty, tall and heavily built. All his features seemed large: big nose, square jaw, huge ears, and a domed bald head. He looked at Ada and said: "Frau Hempel, I presume?" Ada nodded. Willrich turned to Carla. "And you are Fräulein . . . ?"

"Carla von Ulrich, Professor. I'm Kurt's godmother."

He raised his eyebrows. "A little young to be a godmother, surely?"

Ada said indignantly: "She delivered Kurt! She was only eleven, but she was better than the doctor, because he wasn't there!"

Willrich ignored that. Still looking at Carla, he said disdainfully: "And hoping to become a nurse, I see."

Carla wore a beginner's uniform, but she considered herself to be more than just hopeful. "I am a trainee nurse," she said. She did not like Willrich.

"Please sit." He opened a thin file. "Kurt is eight years old, but has reached the developmental stage of only two years."

He paused. Neither woman said anything.

"This is unsatisfactory," he said.

Ada looked at Carla. Carla did not know what he was getting at, and indicated as much with a shrug.

"There is a new treatment available for cases of this type. However, it will necessitate moving Kurt to another hospital." Willrich closed the file. He looked at Ada, and for the first time, he smiled. "I'm sure you would like Kurt to undergo a therapy that might improve his condition."

Carla did not like his smile: it seemed creepy. She said: "Could you tell us more about the treatment, Professor?"

"I'm afraid it would be beyond your understanding," he said. "Even though you are a trainee nurse."

Carla was not going to let him get away with that. "I'm sure Frau Hempel would like to know whether it would involve surgery, or drugs, or electricity, for example."

"Drugs," he said with evident reluctance.

Ada said: "Where would he have to go?"

"The hospital is in Akelberg, in Bavaria."

Ada's geography was weak, and Carla knew she had no sense of how far that was. "It's two hundred miles," she said.

"Oh, no!" said Ada. "How would I visit him?"

"By train," said Willrich impatiently.

Carla said: "It would take four or five hours. She would probably have to stay overnight. And what about the cost of the fare?"

"I cannot concern myself with such things!" said Willrich angrily. "I am a doctor, not a travel agent!"

Ada was close to tears. "If it means Kurt will get better, and learn to say a few words, and not to soil himself . . . one day we might perhaps bring him home."

"Exactly," said Willrich. "I felt sure you would not wish to deny him the chance of getting better just for your own selfish reasons."

"Is that what you're telling us?" said Carla. "That Kurt might be able to live a normal life?"

"Medicine offers no guarantees," he said. "Even a trainee nurse should know that."

Carla had learned, from her parents, to be impatient with prevarication. "I don't ask you for a guarantee," she said crisply. "I ask you for a prognosis. You must have one. Otherwise you would not be proposing the treatment."

He reddened. "The treatment is new. We hope it will improve Kurt's condition. That is what I am telling you."

"Is it experimental?"

"All medicine is experimental. All therapies work on some patients but not on others. You must listen to what I tell you: medicine offers no guarantees."

Carla wanted to oppose him just because he was so arrogant, but she realized that was not the basis on which to make a judgment. Besides, she was not sure Ada really had a choice. Doctors could go against the wishes of parents if the child's health was at risk: in effect they could do what they liked. Willrich was not asking Ada's permission—he had no real need of it. He was speaking to her only in order to avoid a fuss.

Carla said: "Can you tell Frau Hempel how long it might be before Kurt returns from Akelberg to Berlin?"

"Quite soon," said Willrich.

It was no answer at all, but Carla felt that if she pressed him he would become angry again.

Ada was looking helpless. Carla sympathized; she herself found it difficult to know what to say. They had not been given enough information. Doctors were often like this, Carla had noticed: they seemed to want to hug their knowledge to themselves. They preferred to fob patients off with platitudes, and became defensive when questioned.

Ada had tears in her eyes. "Well, if there's a chance he could get better . . ."

"That's the attitude," Willrich said.

But Ada had not finished. "What do you think, Carla?"

Willrich looked outraged at this appeal to the opinion of a mere nurse.

Carla said: "I agree with you, Ada. This opportunity must be seized, for Kurt's sake, even though it will be hard for you."

"Very sensible," said Willrich, and he got to his feet. "Thank you for coming to see me." He went to the door and opened it. Carla felt he could not get rid of them quickly enough.

They left the home and walked back to the station. As their nearly empty train pulled away, Carla picked up a leaflet that had been left on the seat. It was headed HOW TO OPPOSE THE NAZIS, and it listed ten things people could do to hasten the end of the regime, starting with slowing down their rate of work.

Carla had seen such flyers before, though not often. They were placed by some underground resistance movement.

Ada snatched it from her, crumpled it, and threw it out of the window. "You can be arrested for reading such things!" she said. She had been Carla's nanny, and sometimes she behaved as though Carla had not grown up. Carla did not mind her occasional bossiness, for she knew it came from love.

However, in this case Ada was not overreacting. People could be imprisoned not just for reading such things but even for failing to report that they had found one. Ada could be in trouble merely for throwing it out of the window. Fortunately there was no one else in the carriage to see what she had done.

Ada was still troubled by what she had been told at the home. "Do you think we did the right thing?" she said to Carla.

"I don't really know," Carla said candidly. "I think so."

"You're a nurse—you understand these things better than I do."

Carla was enjoying nursing, though she still felt frustrated that she had not been allowed to train as a doctor. Now, with so many young men in the army, the attitude toward female medical students had changed, and more women were going to medical school. Carla could have applied again for a scholarship—except that her family was so desperately poor that they depended on her meager wages. Her father had no work at all, her mother gave piano lessons, and Erik sent home as much as he could afford out of his army pay. The family had not paid Ada for years.

Ada was a naturally stoical person, and by the time they got home, she was getting over her upset. She went into the kitchen, put on her apron, and began to prepare dinner for the family, and the comfortable routine seemed to console her.

Carla was not having dinner. She had plans for the evening. She felt she was abandoning Ada to her sadness, and she was a bit guilty, but not guilty enough to sacrifice her night out.

She put on a knee-length tennis dress she had made herself by shortening the frayed hem of an old frock of her mother's. She was not going to play tennis. She was going to dance, and her aim was to look American. She put on lipstick and face powder, and combed out her hair in defiance of the government's preference for braids.

The mirror showed her a modern girl with a pretty face and a bold air. She knew that her confidence and self-possession put a lot of boys off her. Sometimes she wished she could be seductive as well as capable, a trick her mother had always been able to pull off; but it was not in her nature. She had long ago given up trying to be winsome: it just made her feel silly. Boys had to accept her as she was.

Some boys were scared of her, but others were attracted, and at parties she often ended up with a small cluster of admirers. She in turn liked boys, especially when they forgot about trying to impress people and started to talk normally. Her favorites were the ones who made her laugh. So far she had not had a serious boyfriend, though she had kissed quite a few.

To complete her outfit she put on a striped blazer she had bought from a secondhand clothing cart. She knew her parents would disapprove of her appearance, and try to make her change, saying it was dangerous to defy the Nazis' prejudices. So she needed to get out of the house without seeing them. It should be easy enough. Mother was giving a piano lesson: Carla could hear the painfully hesitant playing of her pupil. Father would be reading the newspaper in the same room, for they could not afford to heat more than one room of the house. Erik was away with the army, though he was now stationed near Berlin and due home on leave shortly.

She covered up with a conventional raincoat and put her white shoes in her pocket.

She went down to the hall, opened the front door, shouted: "Good-bye, back soon!" and hurried out.

She met Frieda at the Friedrich Strasse station. She was dressed similarly with a stripy dress under a plain tan coat, her hair hanging loose—the main difference being that Frieda's clothes were new and expensive. On the platform, two boys in Hitler Youth outfits stared at them with a mixture of disapproval and desire.

They got off the train in the northern suburb of Wedding, a working-class district that had once been a left-wing stronghold. They headed for the Pharus Hall, where in the past Communists had held their conferences. Now there was no political activity at all, of course. Nevertheless the building had become the center of the movement called Swing Kids.

Kids between fifteen and twenty-five were already gathering in the streets around the hall. Swing boys wore check jackets and carried an umbrella, to look English. They let their hair grow long to show their contempt for the military. Swing girls had heavy makeup and American sports clothes. They all thought the Hitler Youth were stupid and boring, with their folk music and community dances.

Carla thought it was ironic. When she was little, she had been teased by the other kids and called a foreigner because her mother was English; now the same children, a little older, thought English was the fashionable thing to be.

Carla and Frieda went into the hall. There was a conventional, innocent youth club there, with girls in pleated skirts and boys in short trousers playing table tennis and drinking sticky orange cordial. But the action was in the side rooms.

Frieda quickly led Carla to a large storeroom with stacked chairs around the walls. There her brother, Werner, had plugged in a record player. Fifty or sixty boys and girls were dancing the jitterbug jive. Carla recognized the tune that was playing: "Ma, He's Making Eyes at Me." She and Frieda started to dance.

Jazz records were banned because most of the best musicians were Negroes. The Nazis had to denigrate anything that was done well by non-Aryans; it threatened their theories of superiority. Unfortunately for them, Germans loved jazz just as much as everyone else. People who visited other countries brought records home, and you could buy them from American sailors in Hamburg. There was a lively black market.

Werner had lots of discs, of course. He had everything: a car, modern clothes, cigarettes, money. He was still Carla's dream boy, though he always went for girls older than she—women, really. Everyone assumed he went to bed with them. Carla was a virgin.

Werner's earnest friend Heinrich von Kessel immediately came up to them and started to dance with Frieda. He wore a black jacket and waistcoat, which looked dramatic with his longish dark hair. He was devoted to Frieda. She liked him—she enjoyed talking to clever men— but she would not go out with him because he was too old, twenty-five or twenty-six.

Soon a boy Carla did not know came and danced with her, and the evening was off to a good start.

She abandoned herself to the music: the irresistible sexual drumbeat, the suggestively crooned lyrics, the exhilarating trumpet solos, the joyous flight of the clarinet. She whirled and kicked, let her skirt flare outrageously high, fell into the arms of her partner and sprang out again.

When they had danced for an hour or so, Werner put on a slow tune. Frieda and Heinrich began dancing cheek to cheek. There was no one available whom Carla liked enough for slow dancing, so she left the room and went to get a Coke. Germany was not at war with America, so Coca-Cola syrup was imported and bottled in Germany.

To her surprise Werner followed her out, leaving someone else to put on records for a while. She was flattered that the most attractive man in the room wanted to talk to her.

She told him about Kurt being moved to Akelberg, and Werner said the same thing had happened to his brother, Axel, who was fifteen. Axel had been born with spina bifida. "Could the same treatment work for both of them?" he said with a frown.

"I doubt it, but I don't really know," Carla said.

"Why is it that medical men never explain what they're doing?" Werner said irritably.

She laughed humorlessly. "They think that if ordinary people understand medicine they won't hero-worship doctors any longer."

"Same principle as a conjurer: it's more impressive if you don't know how it's done," said Werner. "Doctors are as egocentric as anyone else."

"More so," said Carla. "As a nurse, I know."

She told him about the leaflet she had read on the train. Werner said: "How did you feel about it?"

Carla hesitated. It was dangerous to speak honestly about such things. But she had known Werner all her life, he had always been left-wing, and he was a Swing Kid. She could trust him. She said: "I'm pleased someone is opposing the Nazis. It shows that not all Germans are paralyzed by fear."

"There are lots of things you can do against the Nazis," he said quietly. "Not just wearing lipstick."

She assumed he meant she could distribute such leaflets. Could he be involved in such activity? No, he was too much of a playboy. Heinrich might be different: he was very intense.

"No, thanks," she said. "I'm too scared."

They finished their Cokes and returned to the storeroom. It was packed now, with hardly room enough to dance.

To Carla's surprise, Werner asked her for the last dance. He put on Bing Crosby singing "Only Forever." Carla was thrilled. He held her close and they swayed, rather than danced, to the slow ballad.

At the end, by tradition, someone turned off the light for a minute, so that couples could kiss. Carla was embarrassed: she had known Werner since they were children. But she had always been attracted to him, and now she turned her face up eagerly. As she had expected, he kissed her expertly, and she returned the kiss with enthusiasm. To her delight she felt his hand gently grasp her breast. She encouraged him by opening her mouth. Then the light came on and it was all over.

"Well," she said breathlessly, "that was a surprise."

He gave his most charming smile. "Perhaps I can surprise you again sometime."

ii

Carla was passing through the hall, on her way to the kitchen for breakfast, when the phone rang. She picked up the handset. "Carla von Ulrich."

She heard Frieda's voice. "Oh, Carla, my little brother's dead!"

"What?" Carla could hardly believe it. "Frieda, I'm so sorry! Where did it happen?"

"In that hospital." Frieda was sobbing.

Carla recalled Werner telling her that Axel had been sent to the same Akelberg hospital as Kurt. "How did he die?"

"Appendicitis."

"That's terrible." Carla was sad for her friend, but also suspicious. She had had a bad feeling when Professor Willrich spoke to them a month ago about the new treatment for Kurt. Had it been more experimental than he had let on? Could it have actually been dangerous? "Do you know any more?"

"We just got a short letter. My father is enraged. He phoned the hospital but he wasn't able to speak to the senior people."

"I'll come round to your house. I'll be there in a few minutes."

"Thanks."

Carla hung up and went into the kitchen. "Axel Franck has died at that hospital in Akelberg," she said.

Her father, Walter, was looking at the morning post. "Oh!" he said. "Poor Monika." Carla recalled that Axel's mother, Monika Franck, had once been in love with Walter, according to family legend. The look of concern on Walter's face was so pained that Carla wondered if he had had a slight tendresse for Monika, despite being in love with Maud. How complicated love was.

Carla's mother, who was now Monika's best friend, said: "She must be devastated."

Walter looked down at the post again and said in a tone of surprise: "Here's a letter for Ada."

The room went quiet.

Carla stared at the white envelope as Ada took it from Walter.

Ada did not receive many letters.

Erik was home—it was the last day of his short leave—so there were four people watching as Ada opened the envelope.

Carla held her breath.

Ada drew out a typed letter on headed paper. She read the message quickly, gasped, then screamed.

"No!" said Carla. "It can't be!"

Maud jumped up and put her arms around Ada.

Walter took the letter from Ada's fingers and read it. "Oh, dear, how terribly sad," he said. "Poor little Kurt." He put the paper down on the breakfast table.

Ada began to sob. "My little boy, my dear little boy, and he died without his mother—I can't bear it!"

Carla fought back tears. She felt bewildered. "Axel *and* Kurt?" she said. "At the same time?"

She picked up the letter. It was printed with the name of the hospital and its address in Akelberg. It read:

Dear Mrs. Hempel,

I regret to inform you of the sad death of your son, Kurt

Walter Hempel, age eight years. He passed away on 4 April at
this hospital as a result of a burst appendix. Everything
possible was done for him but to no avail. Please accept my
deepest condolences.

It was signed by the senior physician.

Carla looked up. Her mother was sitting next to Ada, arm around
her, holding her hand as she sobbed.

Carla was grief-stricken, but more alert than Ada. She spoke to her
father in a shaky voice. "There's something wrong."

"What makes you say that?"

"Look again." She handed him the letter. "Appendicitis."

"What is the significance?"

"Kurt had had his appendix removed."

"I remember," her father said. "He had an emergency operation, just
after his sixth birthday."

Carla's sorrow was mixed with angry suspicion. Had Kurt been
killed by a dangerous experiment that the hospital was now trying to
cover up? "Why would they lie?" she said.

Erik banged his fist on the table. "Why do you say it is a lie?" he
cried. "Why do you always accuse the establishment? This is obviously
a mistake! Some typist has made a copying error!"

Carla was not so sure. "A typist working in a hospital is likely to
know what an appendix is."

Erik said furiously: "You will seize upon even this personal tragedy
as a way of attacking those in authority!"

"Be quiet, you two," said their father.

They looked at him. There was a new tone in his voice. "Erik may be
right," he said. "If so, the hospital will be perfectly happy to answer
questions and give further details of how Kurt and Axel died."

"Of course they will," said Erik.

Walter went on: "And if Carla is right, they will try to discourage
inquiries, withhold information, and intimidate the parents of the dead
children by suggesting that their questions are somehow illegitimate."

Erik looked less comfortable about that.

Half an hour ago Walter had been a shrunken man. Now somehow he seemed to fill his suit again. "We will find out as soon as we start asking questions."

Carla said: "I'm going to see Frieda."

Her mother said: "Don't you have to go to work?"

"I'm on the late shift."

Carla phoned Frieda, told her that Kurt was dead, too, and said she was coming to talk about it. She put on her coat, hat, and gloves, then wheeled her bicycle outside. She was a fast rider and it took her only a quarter of an hour to get to the Francks' villa in Schöneberg.

The butler let her in and told her the family were still in the dining room. As soon as she walked in, Frieda's father, Ludwig Franck, bellowed at her: "What did they tell you at the Wannsee children's home?"

Carla did not much like Ludwig. He was a right-wing bully and he had supported the Nazis in the early days. Perhaps he had changed his views: many businessmen had by now, though they showed little sign of the humility that ought to go with having been so wrong.

She did not answer immediately. She sat down at the table and looked at the family: Ludwig, Monika, Werner, and Frieda, and the butler hovering in the background. She collected her thoughts.

"Come on, girl, answer me!" Ludwig demanded. He had in his hand a letter that looked very like Ada's, and he was waving it angrily.

Monika put a restraining hand on her husband's arm. "Take it easy, Ludi."

"I want to know!" he said.

Carla looked at his pink face and little black mustache. He was in an agony of grief, she saw. In other circumstances she would have refused to speak to someone so rude. But he had an excuse for his bad manners, and she decided to overlook them. "The director, Professor Willrich, told us there was a new treatment for Kurt's condition."

"The same as he told us," said Ludwig. "What kind of treatment?"

"I asked him that question. He said I would not be able to understand it. I persisted, and he said it involved drugs, but he did not give any further information. May I see your letter, Herr Franck?"

Ludwig's expression said he was the one who should be asking questions, but he handed the sheet of paper to Carla.

It was exactly the same as Ada's, and Carla had a queer feeling that the typist had done several of them, just changing the names.

Franck said: "How can two boys have died of appendicitis at the same time? It's not a contagious illness."

Carla said: "Kurt certainly did not die of appendicitis, for he had no appendix. It was removed two years ago."

"Right," said Ludwig. "That's enough talk." He snatched the letter from Carla's hand. "I'm going to see someone in the government about this." He went out.

Monika followed him, and so did the butler.

Carla went over to Frieda and took her hand. "I'm so sorry," she said.

"Thank you," Frieda whispered.

Carla went to Werner. He stood up and put his arms around her. She felt a tear fall on her forehead. She was gripped by she did not know what intense emotion. Her heart was full of grief, yet she thrilled to the pressure of his body against hers, and the gentle touch of his hands.

After a long moment Werner stepped back. He said angrily: "My father has phoned the hospital twice. The second time, they told him they had no more information and hung up on him. But I'm going to find out what happened to my brother, and I won't be brushed off."

Frieda said: "Finding out won't bring him back."

"I still want to know. If necessary I'll go to Akelberg."

Carla said: "I wonder if there's anyone in Berlin who could help us."

"It would have to be someone in the government," Werner said.

Frieda said: "Heinrich's father is in the government."

Werner snapped his fingers. "The very man. He used to belong to the Centre Party, but he's a Nazi now, and something important in the Foreign Office."

Carla said: "Will Heinrich take us to see him?"

"He will if Frieda asks him," said Werner. "Heinrich will do anything for Frieda."

Carla could believe that. Heinrich had always been intense about everything he did.

"I'll phone him now," said Frieda.

She went into the hall, and Carla and Werner sat down side by side. He put his arm around her, and she leaned her head on his shoulder. She did not know whether these signs of affection were merely a side effect of the tragedy, or something more.

Frieda came back in and said: "Heinrich's father will see us right away if we go over there now."

They all got into Werner's sports car, squeezing onto the front seat. "I don't know how you keep this car going," Frieda said as he pulled away. "Even Father can't get petrol for private use."

"I tell my boss it's for official business," he said. Werner worked for an important general. "But I don't know how much longer I can get away with it."

The von Kessel family lived in the same suburb. Werner drove there in five minutes.

The house was luxurious, though smaller than the Francks'. Heinrich met them at the door and showed them into a living room with leather-bound books and an old German wood carving of an eagle.

Frieda kissed him. "Thank you for doing this," she said. "It probably wasn't easy—I know you don't get on so well with your father."

Heinrich beamed with pleasure.

His mother brought them coffee and cake. She seemed a warm, simple person. When she had served them, she left, like a maid.

Heinrich's father, Gottfried, came in. He had the same thick straight hair, but it was silver instead of black.

Heinrich said: "Father, here are Werner and Frieda Franck, whose father manufactures People's Radios."

"Ah, yes," said Gottfried. "I have seen your father in the Herrenklub."

"And this is Carla von Ulrich—I believe you know her father, too."

"We were colleagues at the German embassy in London," Gottfried said carefully. "That was in 1914." Clearly he was not so pleased to be reminded of his association with a Social Democrat. He took a piece of cake, clumsily dropped it on the rug, tried ineffectually to pick up the crumbs, then abandoned the effort and sat back.

Carla thought: What is he afraid of?

Heinrich got straight down to the purpose of the visit. "Father, I expect you've heard of Akelberg."

Carla was watching Gottfried closely. There was a split-second flash of something in his expression, but he quickly adopted a pose of indifference. "A small town in Bavaria?" he said.

"There is a hospital there," said Heinrich. "For handicapped people."

"I don't think I was aware of that."

"We think something strange is going on there, and we wondered if you might know about it."

"I certainly don't. What seems to be happening?"

Werner broke in. "My brother died there, apparently of appendicitis. Herr von Ulrich's maid's child died at the same time in the same hospital of the same illness."

"Very sad—but a coincidence, surely?"

Carla said: "My maid's child did not have an appendix. It was removed two years ago."

"I understand why you are keen to ascertain the facts," said Gottfried. "This is deeply unsatisfactory. However, the likeliest explanation would seem to be clerical error."

Werner said: "If so, we would like to know."

"Of course. Have you written to the hospital?"

Carla said: "I wrote to ask when my maid could visit her son. They never replied."

Werner said: "My father telephoned the hospital this morning. The senior physician slammed the phone down on him."

"Oh, dear. Such bad manners. But, you know, this is hardly a Foreign Office matter."

Werner leaned forward. "Herr von Kessel, is it possible that both boys were involved in a secret experiment that went wrong?"

Gottfried sat back. "Quite impossible," he said, and Carla had a feeling he was telling the truth. "That is definitely not happening." He sounded relieved.

Werner looked as if he had run out of questions, but Carla was not satisfied. She wondered why Gottfried seemed so happy about the assurance he had just given. Was it because he was concealing something worse?

She was struck by a possibility so appalling that she could hardly contemplate it.

Gottfried said: "Well, if that's all . . ."

Carla said: "You're very sure, sir, that they were not killed by an experimental therapy that went wrong?"

"Very sure."

"To know for certain that is *not* true, you must have some knowledge of what *is* being done at Akelberg."

"Not necessarily," he said, but all his tension had returned, and she knew she was on to something.

"I remember seeing a Nazi poster," she went on. It was this memory that had triggered her dreadful thought. "There was a picture of a male nurse and a mentally handicapped man. The text said something like: 'Sixty thousand reichsmarks is what this person suffering from hereditary defects costs the people's community during his lifetime. Comrade, that is your money, too!' It was an advertisement for a magazine, I think."

"I have seen some of that propaganda," Gottfried said disdainfully, as if it were nothing to do with him.

Carla stood up. "You're a Catholic, Herr von Kessel, and you brought up Heinrich in the Catholic faith."

Gottfried made a scornful noise. "Heinrich says he's an atheist now."

"But you're not. And you believe that human life is sacred."

"Yes."

"You say that the doctors at Akelberg are not testing dangerous new therapies on handicapped people, and I believe you."

"Thank you."

"But are they doing something else? Something worse?"

"No, no."

"Are they deliberately *killing* the handicapped?"

Gottfried shook his head silently.

Carla moved closer to Gottfried and lowered her voice, as if they were the only two people in the room. "As a Catholic who believes that human life is sacred, will you put your hand on your heart and tell me that mentally ill children are not being murdered at Akelberg?"

Gottfried smiled, made a reassuring gesture, and opened his mouth to speak, but no words came out.

Carla knelt on the rug in front of him. "Would you do that, please? Right now? Here in your house with you are four young Germans, your son and his three friends. Just tell us the truth. Look me in the eye and say that our government does not kill handicapped children."

The silence in the room was total. Gottfried seemed about to speak, but changed his mind. He squeezed his eyes shut, twisted his mouth into a grimace, and bowed his head. The four young people watched his facial contortions in amazement.

At last he opened his eyes. He looked at them one by one, ending with his gaze on his son.

Then he stood up and walked out of the room.

<u>iii</u>

The next day, Werner said to Carla: "This is awful. We've talked of the same thing for more than twenty-four hours. We'll go mad if we don't do something else. Let's see a movie."

They went to the Kurfürstendamm, a street of theaters and shops, always called the Ku'damm. Most of the good German filmmakers had gone to Hollywood years ago, and the domestic movies were now second-rate. They saw *Three Soldiers*, set during the invasion of France.

The three soldiers were a tough Nazi sergeant, a sniveling complainer who looked a bit Jewish, and an earnest young man. The earnest one asked naïve questions like: "Do the Jews really do us any harm?" and in answer received long, stern lectures from the sergeant. When battle was joined, the sniveler admitted to being a Communist, deserted, and was blown up in an air raid. The earnest young man fought bravely, was promoted to sergeant, and became an admirer of the Führer. The script was dire but the battle scenes were exciting.

Werner held Carla's hand all the way through. She hoped he would kiss her in the dark, but he did not.

As the lights came up, he said: "Well, it was terrible, but it took my mind off things for a couple of hours."

They went outside and found his car. "Shall we go for a drive?" he said. "It could be our last chance. This car goes up on blocks next week."

He drove out to the Grunewald. On the way Carla's thoughts inevitably returned to yesterday's conversation with Gottfried von Kessel. No matter how many times she went over it in her mind, there was no way she could escape the terrible conclusion all four of them had reached at the end of it. Kurt and Axel had not been accidental victims of a dangerous medical experiment, as she had at first thought. Gottfried had denied that convincingly. But he had not been able to bring himself to deny that the government was deliberately killing the handicapped, and lying to their families about it. It was hard to believe, even of people as ruthless and brutal as the Nazis. Yet Gottfried's response had been the clearest example of guilty behavior that Carla had ever witnessed.

When they were in the forest, Werner pulled off the road and drove along a track until the car was hidden by shrubbery. Carla guessed he had brought other girls to this spot.

He turned out the lights, and they were in deep darkness. "I'm going to speak to General Dorn," he said. Dorn was his boss, an important officer in the air force. "What about you?"

"My father says there's no political opposition left, but the churches are still strong. No one who is sincere about their religious beliefs could condone what's being done."

"Are you religious?" Werner asked.

"Not really. My father is. For him, the Protestant faith is part of the German heritage he loves. Mother goes to church with him, though I suspect her theology might be a bit unorthodox. I believe in God, but I can't imagine he cares whether people are Protestant or Catholic or Muslim or Buddhist. And I like singing hymns."

Werner's voice fell to a whisper. "I can't believe in a God who allows the Nazis to murder children."

"I don't blame you."

"What is your father going to do?"

"Speak to the pastor of our church."

"Good."

They were silent for a while. He put his arm around her. "Is this all right?" he said in a half whisper.

She was tense with anticipation, and her voice seemed to fail. Her reply came out as a grunt. She tried again, and managed to say: "If it stops you feeling so sad . . . yes."

Then he kissed her.

She kissed him back eagerly. He stroked her hair, then her breasts. At this point, she knew, a lot of girls would call a halt. They said if you went any further you would lose control of yourself.

Carla decided to risk it.

She touched his cheek while he was kissing her. She caressed his throat with her fingertips, enjoying the feel of the warm skin. She put her hand under his jacket and explored his body, her hand on his shoulder blades and his ribs and his spine.

She sighed when she felt his hand on her thigh, under her skirt. As soon as he touched her between her legs, she parted her knees. Girls said a boy would think you cheap for doing that, but she could not help herself.

He touched her in just the right place. He did not try to put his hand inside her underwear, but stroked her lightly through the cotton. She heard herself making noises in her throat, quietly at first but then louder. Eventually she cried out with pleasure, burying her face in his neck to muffle the sound. Then she had to push his hand away because she felt too sensitive.

She was panting. As she began to get her breath back, she kissed his neck. He touched her cheek lovingly.

After a minute she said: "Can I do something for you?"

"Only if you want to."

She was embarrassed by how much she wanted to. "The only thing is, I've never . . ."

"I know," he said. "I'll show you."

iv

Pastor Ochs was a portly, comfortable clergyman with a large house, a nice wife, and five children, and Carla feared he would refuse to get involved. But she underestimated him. He had already heard rumors that were troubling his conscience, and he agreed to go with Walter to the Wannsee children's home. Professor Willrich could hardly refuse a visit from an interested clergyman.

They decided to take Carla with them, because she had witnessed the interview with Ada. The director might find it more difficult to change his story in front of her.

On the train, Ochs suggested he should do the talking. "The director is probably a Nazi," he said. Most people in senior jobs nowadays were party members. "He will naturally see a former Social Democrat deputy as an enemy. I will play the role of unbiased arbitrator. That way, I believe, we may learn more."

Carla was not sure about that. She felt her father would be a more expert questioner. But Walter went along with the pastor's suggestion.

It was spring, and the weather was warmer than on Carla's last visit. There were boats on the lake. Carla decided to ask Werner to come out here for a picnic. She wanted to make the most of him before he drifted off to another girl.

Professor Willrich had a fire blazing, but a window was open, letting in a fresh breeze off the water.

The director shook hands with Pastor Ochs and Walter. He gave Carla a brief glance of recognition, then ignored her. He invited them to sit down, but Carla saw there was angry hostility behind his superficial courtesy. Clearly he did not relish being questioned. He picked up one of his pipes and played with it nervously. He was less arrogant today, confronted by two mature men rather than a couple of young women.

Ochs opened the discussion. "Herr von Ulrich and others in my congregation are concerned, Professor Willrich, about the mysterious deaths of several handicapped children known to them."

"No children have died mysteriously here," Willrich shot back. "In fact no child has died here in the last two years."

Ochs turned to Walter. "I find that very reassuring, Walter. Don't you?"

"Yes," said Walter.

Carla did not, but she kept her mouth shut for the moment.

Ochs went on unctuously: "I feel sure that you give your charges the best possible care."

"Yes." Willrich looked a little less anxious.

"But you do send children from here to other hospitals?"

"Of course, if another institution can offer a child some treatment not available here."

"And when a child is transferred, I suppose you are not necessarily kept informed about his treatment or his condition thereafter."

"Exactly!"

"Unless they come back."

Willrich said nothing.

"Have any come back?"

"No."

Ochs shrugged. "Then you cannot be expected to know what happened to them."

"Precisely."

Ochs sat back and spread his hands in a gesture of openness. "So you have nothing to hide!"

"Nothing at all."

"Some of those transferred children have died."

Willrich said nothing.

Ochs gently persisted. "That's true, isn't it?"

"I cannot answer you with any certain knowledge, Herr Pastor."

"Ah!" said Ochs. "Because even if one of those children died, you would not be notified."

"As we said before."

"Forgive me the repetition, but I simply want to establish beyond doubt that you cannot be asked to shed light on those deaths."

"Not at all."

Once again Ochs turned to Walter. "I think we're clearing matters up splendidly."

Walter nodded.

Carla wanted to say *Nothing has been cleared up!*

But Ochs was speaking again. "Approximately how many children have you transferred in, say, the last twelve months?"

"Ten," said Willrich. "Exactly." He smiled complacently. "We scientific men prefer not to deal in approximations."

"Ten patients, out of . . . ?"

"Today we have one hundred and seven children here."

"A very small proportion!" said Ochs.

Carla was getting angry. Ochs was obviously on Willrich's side! Why was her father swallowing this?

Ochs said: "And did those children suffer from one common condition, or a variety?"

"A variety." Willrich opened a folder on his desk. "Idiocy; Down's syndrome; microcephaly; hydrocephaly; malformations of limbs, head, and spinal column; and paralysis."

"These are the types of patients you were instructed to send to Akelberg."

That was a jump. It was the first mention of Akelberg, and the first suggestion that Willrich had received instructions from a higher authority. Perhaps Ochs was more subtle than he had seemed.

Willrich opened his mouth to say something, but Ochs forestalled him with another question. "Were they all to receive the same special treatment?"

Willrich smiled. "Again, I was not informed, so I cannot tell you."

"You simply complied—"

"With my instructions, yes."

Ochs smiled. "You're a judicious man. You choose your words carefully. Were the children all ages?"

"Initially the program was restricted to children under three, but later it was expanded to benefit all ages, yes."

Carla noted the mention of a "program." That had not been admitted before. She began to realize that Ochs was cleverer than he might have at first appeared.

Ochs spoke his next sentence as if confirming something already stated. "And all handicapped Jewish children were included, irrespective of their particular disability."

There was a moment of silence. Willrich looked shocked. Carla wondered how Ochs knew that about Jewish children. Perhaps he did not; he might have been guessing.

After a pause, Ochs added: "Jewish children, and those of mixed race, I should have said."

Willrich did not speak, but gave a slight nod.

Ochs went on: "It's unusual, in this day and age, for Jewish children to be given preference, isn't it?"

Willrich looked away.

The pastor stood up, and when he spoke again, his voice rang with anger. "You have told me that ten children suffering from a range of illnesses, who could not possibly all benefit from the same treatment, were sent away to a special hospital from which they never returned; and that Jews got priority. What did you think happened to them, Herr Professor Doctor Willrich? In God's name, *what did you think*?"

Willrich looked as if he would cry.

"You may say nothing, of course," Ochs said more quietly. "But one day you will be asked the same question by a higher authority, in fact by the highest of all authorities."

He stretched out his arm and pointed a condemning finger.

"And on that day, my son, you *will* answer."

With that he turned around and left the room.

Carla and Walter followed him out.

V

Inspector Thomas Macke smiled. Sometimes the enemies of the state did his job for him. Instead of working in secret, and hiding away where they were difficult to find, they identified themselves to him and generously provided irrefutable evidence of their crimes. They were like fish that did not require bait and a hook but simply jumped out of the river into the fisherman's basket and begged to be fried.

Pastor Ochs was one such.

Macke read his letter again. It was addressed to the justice minister, Franz Gürtner.

> Dear Minister,
> Is the government killing handicapped children? I ask you
> this question bluntly because I must have a plain answer.

What a fool! If the answer was no, this was a criminal libel; if yes, Ochs was guilty of revealing state secrets. Could he not figure that out for himself?

> After it became impossible to ignore rumors circulating
> in my congregation, I visited the Wannsee Children's
> Nursing Home and spoke to its director, Professor Willrich.
> His responses were so unsatisfactory that I became
> convinced something terrible is going on, something that is
> presumably a crime and unquestionably a sin.

The man had the nerve to write of crimes! Did it not occur to him that accusing government agencies of illegal acts was itself an illegal act? Did he imagine he was living in a degenerate liberal democracy?

Macke knew what Ochs was complaining about. The program was called Aktion T4 after its address, 4 Tiergarten Strasse. The agency was officially the Charitable Foundation for Cure and Institutional Care, though it was supervised by Hitler's personal office, the Chancellery of the Führer. Its job was to arrange the painless deaths of handicapped people who could not survive without costly care. It had done splendid work in the last couple of years, disposing of tens of thousands of useless people.

The problem was that German public opinion was not yet sophisticated enough to understand the need for such deaths, so the program had to be kept quiet.

Macke was in on the secret. He had been promoted to inspector and had at last been admitted to the Nazi Party's elite paramilitary Schutzstaffel, the SS. He had been briefed on Aktion T4 when he was assigned to the Ochs case. He felt proud: he was a real insider now.

Unfortunately, people had been careless, and there was a danger that the secret of Aktion T4 would get out.

It was Macke's job to plug the leak.

Preliminary inquiries had swiftly revealed that there were three men to be silenced: Pastor Ochs, Walter von Ulrich, and Werner Franck.

Franck was the elder son of a radio manufacturer who had been an important early supporter of the Nazis. The manufacturer himself, Ludwig Franck, had initially made furious demands for information about the death of his disabled younger son, but had quickly fallen silent after a threat to close his factories. Young Werner, a fast-rising officer in the Air Ministry, had persisted in asking troubling questions, trying to involve his influential boss, General Dorn.

The Air Ministry, said to be the largest office building in Europe, was an ultramodern edifice occupying an entire block of Wilhelm Strasse, just around the corner from Gestapo headquarters in Prinz Albrecht Strasse. Macke walked there.

In his SS uniform he was able to ignore the guards. At the reception desk he barked: "Take me to Lieutenant Werner Franck immediately."

The receptionist took him up in an elevator and along a corridor to an open door leading into a small office. The young man at the desk did not at first look up from the papers in front of him. Observing him, Macke guessed he was about twenty-two years old. Why was he not with a front-line unit, bombing England? The father had probably pulled strings, Macke thought resentfully. Werner looked like a son of privilege: tailored uniform, gold rings, and overlong hair that was distinctly unmilitary. Macke despised him already.

Werner wrote a note with a pencil, then looked up. The amiable expression on his face died quickly when he saw the SS uniform, and Macke noted with interest a flash of fear. The boy immediately tried to cover up with a show of bonhomie, standing up deferentially and smiling a welcome, but Macke was not fooled.

"Good afternoon, Inspector," said Werner. "Please be seated."

"*Heil* Hitler," said Macke.

"*Heil* Hitler. How can I help you?"

"Sit down and shut up, you foolish boy," Macke spat.

Werner struggled to hide his fear. "My goodness, what can I have done to incur such wrath?"

"Don't presume to question me. Speak when you're spoken to."

"As you wish."

"From this moment on you will ask no further questions about your brother, Axel."

Macke was surprised to see a momentary look of relief pass over Werner's face. That was puzzling. Had he been afraid of something else, something more frightening than the simple order to stop asking questions about his brother? Could Werner be involved in other subversive activities?

Probably not, Macke thought on reflection. Most likely Werner was relieved he was not being arrested and taken to the basement in Prinz Albrecht Strasse.

Werner was not yet completely cowed. He summoned the nerve to say: "Why should I not ask how my brother died?"

"I told you not to question me. Be aware that you are being treated gently only because your father has been a valued friend of the Nazi Party. Were it not for that, *you* would be in *my* office." That was a threat everyone understood.

"I'm grateful for your forbearance," Werner said, struggling to retain a shred of dignity. "But I want to know who killed my brother, and why."

"You will learn no more, regardless of what you do. But any further inquiries will be regarded as treason."

"I hardly need to make further inquiries, after this visit from you. It is now clear that my worst suspicions were right."

"I require you to drop your seditious campaign immediately."

Werner stared defiantly back but said nothing.

Macke said: "If you do not, General Dorn will be informed that there are questions about your loyalty." Werner could be in no doubt about what that meant. He would lose his cozy job here in Berlin and be dispatched to a barracks on an airstrip in northern France.

Werner looked less defiant, more thoughtful.

Macke stood up. He had spent enough time here. "Apparently General Dorn finds you a capable and intelligent assistant," he said. "If you do the right thing, you may continue in that role." He left the room.

He felt edgy and dissatisfied. He was not sure he had succeeded in crushing Werner's will. He had sensed a bedrock defiance that remained untouched.

He turned his mind to Pastor Ochs. A different approach would be required for him. Macke returned to Gestapo headquarters and collected a small team: Reinhold Wagner, Klaus Richter, and Günther Schneider. They took a black Mercedes 260D, the Gestapo's favorite car, unobtrusive because many Berlin taxis were the same model and color. In the early days, the Gestapo had been encouraged to make themselves visible and let the public see the brutal way they dealt with opposition. However, the terrorization of the German people had been accomplished long ago, and open violence was no longer necessary. Nowadays the Gestapo acted discreetly, always with a cloak of legality.

They drove to Ochs's house next to the large Protestant church in

Mitte, the central district. In the same way that Werner might think he was protected by his father, so Ochs probably imagined his church made him safe. He was about to learn otherwise.

Macke rang the bell; in the old days they would have kicked the door down, just for effect.

A maid opened the door, and he walked into a broad, well-lit hallway with polished floorboards and heavy rugs. The other three followed him in. "Where is your master?" Macke said pleasantly to the maid.

He had not threatened her, but all the same she was frightened. "In his study, sir," she said, and she pointed to a door.

Macke said to Wagner: "Get the women and children together in the next room."

Ochs opened the study door and looked into the hall, frowning. "What on earth is going on?" he said indignantly.

Macke walked directly toward him, forcing him to step back and allow Macke to enter the room. It was a small, well-appointed den, with a leather-topped desk and shelves of biblical commentaries. "Close the door," said Macke.

Reluctantly, Ochs did as he was told; then he said: "You'd better have a very good explanation for this intrusion."

"Sit down and shut up," said Macke.

Ochs was dumbfounded. Probably he had not been told to shut up since he was a boy. Clergymen were not normally insulted, even by policemen. But the Nazis ignored such enfeebling conventions.

"This is an outrage!" Ochs managed at last. Then he sat down.

Outside the room, a woman's voice was raised in protest: the wife, presumably. Ochs paled when he heard it, and rose from his chair.

Macke pushed him back down. "Stay where you are."

Ochs was a heavy man, and taller than Macke, but he did not resist.

Macke loved to see these pompous types deflated by fear.

"Who are you?" said Ochs.

Macke never told them. They could guess, of course, but it was more frightening if they did not know for sure. Afterward, in the unlikely event that anyone asked questions, the whole team would swear that they had begun by identifying themselves as police officers and showing their badges.

He went out. His men were hustling several children into the parlor. Macke told Reinhold Wagner to go into the study and keep Ochs there. Then he followed the children into the other room.

There were flowered curtains, family photographs on the mantelpiece, and a set of comfortable chairs upholstered in a checked fabric. It was a nice home and a nice family. Why could they not be loyal to the Reich and mind their own business?

The maid was by the window, hand over her mouth as if to stop herself crying out. Four children clustered around Ochs's wife, a plain, heavy-breasted woman in her thirties. She held a fifth child in her arms, a girl of about two years with blond ringlets.

Macke patted the girl's head. "And what is this one's name?" he said.

Frau Ochs was terrified. She whispered: "Lieselotte. What do you want with us?"

"Come to Uncle Thomas, little Lieselotte," said Macke, holding out his arms.

"No!" Frau Ochs cried. She clutched the child closer and turned away.

Lieselotte began to cry loudly.

Macke nodded to Klaus Richter.

Richter grabbed Frau Ochs from behind, pulling her arms back, forcing her to let go of the child. Macke took Lieselotte before she fell. The child wriggled like a fish, but he just held her tighter, as he would have held a cat. She wailed louder.

A boy of about twelve flung himself at Macke, small fists pounding ineffectually. It was about time he learned to respect authority, Macke decided. He put Lieselotte on his left hip, then, with his right hand, picked the boy up by his shirtfront and threw him across the room, making sure he landed in an upholstered chair. The boy yelled in fear and Frau Ochs screamed. The chair went over backward and the boy tumbled to the floor. He was not really hurt but he began to cry.

Macke took Lieselotte out into the hall. She screamed at the top of her voice for her mother. Macke put her down. She ran to the parlor door and banged on it, screeching in terror. She had not yet learned to turn doorknobs, Macke noted.

Leaving the child in the hallway, Macke reentered the study. Wagner was by the door, guarding it; Ochs was standing in the middle of the room, white with fear. "What are you doing to my children?" he said. "Why is Lieselotte screaming?"

"You will write a letter," Macke said.

"Yes, yes, anything," Ochs said, going to the leather-topped desk.

"Not now, later."

"All right."

Macke was enjoying this. Ochs's collapse was complete, unlike Werner's. "A letter to the justice minister," he went on.

"So that's what this is about."

"You will say you now realize there is no truth in the allegations you made in your first letter. You were misled by secret Communists. You will apologize to the minister for the trouble you have caused by your incautious actions, and assure him that you will never again speak of the matter to anyone."

"Yes, yes, I will. What are they doing to my wife?"

"Nothing. She is screaming because of what will happen to her if you fail to write the letter."

"I want to see her."

"It will be worse for her if you annoy me with stupid demands."

"Of course, I'm sorry. I beg your pardon."

The opponents of Nazism were so weak. "Write the letter this evening, and mail it in the morning."

"Yes. Should I send you a copy?"

"It will come to me anyway, you idiot. Do you think the minister himself reads your insane scribbling?"

"No, no, of course not. I see that."

Macke went to the door. "And stay away from people like Walter von Ulrich."

"I will, I promise."

Macke went out, beckoning Wagner to follow. Lieselotte was sitting on the floor screaming hysterically. Macke opened the parlor door and summoned Richter and Schneider.

They left the house.

"Sometimes violence is quite unnecessary," Macke said reflectively as they got into the car.

Wagner took the wheel and Macke gave him the address of the von Ulrich house.

"And then again, sometimes it's the simplest way," he added.

Von Ulrich lived in the neighborhood of the church. His house was a spacious old building that he evidently could not afford to maintain. The paint was peeling, the railings were rusty, and a broken window had been patched with cardboard. This was not unusual: wartime austerity meant that many houses were not kept up.

The door was opened by a maid. Macke presumed this was the woman whose handicapped child had started the whole problem—but he did not bother to inquire. There was no point in arresting girls.

Walter von Ulrich stepped into the hall from a side room.

Macke remembered him. He was the cousin of the Robert von Ulrich whose restaurant Macke and his brother had bought eight years ago. In those days he had been proud and arrogant. Now he wore a shabby suit, but his manner was still bold. "What do you want?" he said, attempting to sound as if he still had the power to demand explanations.

Macke did not intend to waste much time here. "Cuff him," he said.

Wagner stepped forward with the handcuffs.

A tall, handsome woman appeared and stood in front of von Ulrich. "Tell me who you are and what you want," she demanded. She was obviously the wife. She had the hint of a foreign accent. No surprise there.

Wagner slapped her face, hard, and she staggered back.

"Turn around and put your wrists together," Wagner said to von Ulrich. "Otherwise I'll knock her teeth down her throat."

Von Ulrich obeyed.

A pretty young woman dressed in a nurse's uniform came rushing down the stairs. "Father!" she said. "What's happening?"

Macke wondered how many more people there might be in the house. He felt a twinge of anxiety. An ordinary family could not overcome trained police officers, but a crowd of them might create enough of a fracas for von Ulrich to slip away.

However, the man himself did not want a fight. "Don't confront them!" he said to his daughter in a voice of urgency. "Stay back!"

The nurse looked terrified and did as she was told.

Macke said: "Put him in the car."

Wagner walked von Ulrich out of the door.

The wife began to sob.

The nurse said: "Where are you taking him?"

Macke went to the door. He looked at the three women: the maid, the wife, and the daughter. "All this trouble," he said, "for the sake of an eight-year-old moron. I will never understand you people."

He went out and got into the car.

They drove the short distance to Prinz Albrecht Strasse. Wagner parked at the back of the Gestapo headquarters building alongside a dozen identical black cars. They all got out.

They took von Ulrich in through a back door and down the stairs to the basement, and put him in a white-tiled room.

Macke opened a cupboard and took out three long, heavy clubs like American baseball bats. He gave one to each of his assistants.

"Beat the shit out of him," he said, and he left them to it.

vi

Captain Volodya Peshkov, head of the Berlin section of Red Army Intelligence, met Werner Franck at the Invalids' Cemetery beside the Berlin-Spandau Ship Canal.

It was a good choice. Looking around the graveyard carefully,

Volodya was able to confirm that no one followed him or Werner in. The only other person present was an old woman in a black head scarf, and she was on her way out.

Their rendezvous was the tomb of General von Scharnhorst, a large pedestal bearing a slumbering lion made of melted-down enemy cannons. It was a sunny day in spring, and the two young spies took off their jackets as they walked among the graves of German heroes.

After the Hitler-Stalin pact almost two years ago, Soviet espionage had continued in Germany, and so had surveillance of Soviet embassy staff. Everyone saw the treaty as temporary, though no one knew how temporary. So counterintelligence agents were still tailing Volodya everywhere.

They ought to be able to tell when he was going out on a genuine secret intelligence mission, he thought, for that was when he shook them off. If he went out to buy a frankfurter for lunch, he let them shadow him. He wondered whether they were smart enough to figure that out.

"Have you seen Lili Markgraf lately?" said Werner.

She was a girl they had both dated at different times in the past. Volodya had now recruited her, and she had learned to encode and decode messages in the Red Army Intelligence cipher. Of course Volodya would not tell Werner that. "I haven't seen her for a while," he lied. "How about you?"

Werner shook his head. "Someone else has won my heart." He seemed bashful. Perhaps he was embarrassed about belying his playboy reputation. "Anyway, why did you want to see me?"

"We have received devastating information," Volodya said. "News that will change the course of history—if it is true."

Werner looked skeptical.

Volodya went on: "A source has told us that Germany will invade the Soviet Union in June." He thrilled again as he said it. It was a huge triumph for Red Army Intelligence, and a terrible threat to the USSR.

Werner pushed a lock of hair out of his eyes in a gesture that probably made girls' hearts beat faster. He said: "A reliable source?"

It was a journalist in Tokyo who was in the confidence of the German ambassador there, but was in fact a secret Communist. Everything he had said so far had turned out to be true. But Volodya could not tell Werner that. "Reliable," he said.

"So you believe it?"

Volodya hesitated. That was the problem. Stalin did not believe it. He thought it was Allied disinformation intended to sow mistrust between himself and Hitler. Stalin's skepticism about this intelligence coup had devastated Volodya's superiors, souring their jubilation. "We seek verification," he said.

Werner looked around at the trees in the graveyard coming into leaf. "I hope to God it's true," he said with sudden savagery. "It will finish the damned Nazis."

"Yes," said Volodya. "If the Red Army is prepared."

Werner was surprised. "Are you not prepared?"

Once again Volodya was not able to tell Werner the whole truth. Stalin believed the Germans would not attack before they had defeated the British, fearing a war on two fronts. While Britain continued to defy Germany, the Soviet Union was safe, he thought. In consequence the Red Army was nowhere near prepared for a German invasion.

"We *will be* prepared," Volodya said, "if you can get me verification of the invasion plan."

He could not help enjoying a moment of self-importance. His spy could be the key.

Werner said: "Unfortunately, I can't help you."

Volodya frowned. "What do you mean?"

"I can't get verification, or otherwise, of this information, nor can I get you anything else. I'm about to be fired from my job at the Air Ministry. I'll probably be posted to France—or, if your intelligence is correct, sent to invade the Soviet Union."

Volodya was horrified. Werner was his best spy. It was Werner's information that had won Volodya promotion to captain. He found he could hardly breathe. With an effort he said: "What the hell happened?"

"My brother died in a home for the handicapped, and the same thing happened to my girlfriend's godson, and we're asking too many questions."

"Why would you be demoted for that?"

"The Nazis are killing off handicapped people, but it's a secret program."

Volodya was momentarily diverted from his mission. "What? They just murder them?"

"So it seems. We don't know the details yet. But if they had nothing to hide, they wouldn't have punished me—and others—for asking questions."

"How old was your brother?"

"Fifteen."

"God! Still a child!"

"They're not going to get away with it. I refuse to shut up."

They stopped in front of the tomb of Manfred von Richthofen, the air ace. It was a huge slab, six feet high and twice as wide. On it was carved, in elegant capital letters, the single word RICHTHOFEN. Volodya always found its simplicity moving.

He tried to recover his composure. He told himself that the Soviet secret police murdered people, after all, especially anyone suspected of disloyalty. The head of the NKVD, Lavrentiy Beria, was a torturer whose favorite trick was to have his men pull a couple of pretty girls off the street for him to rape as his evening's entertainment, according to rumor. But the thought that Communists could be as bestial as Nazis was no consolation. One day, he reminded himself, the Soviets would get rid of Beria and his kind; then they could begin to build true Communism. Meanwhile, the priority was to defeat the Nazis.

They came to the canal wall and stood there, watching a barge make its slow progress along the waterway, belching oily black smoke. Volodya mulled over Werner's alarming confession. "What would happen if you stopped investigating these deaths of handicapped children?" he asked.

"I'd lose my girlfriend," Werner said. "She's as angry about it as I am."

Volodya was struck by the scary thought that Werner might reveal the truth to his girlfriend. "You certainly couldn't tell her the real reason for your change of mind," he said emphatically.

Werner looked stricken, but he did not argue.

Volodya realized that by persuading Werner to abandon his campaign he would be helping the Nazis hide their crimes. He pushed the uncomfortable thought aside. "But would you be allowed to keep your job with General Dorn if you promised to drop the matter?"

"Yes. That's what they want. But I'm not letting them murder my brother, then cover it up. They'll send me to the front line, but I won't shut up."

"What do you think they'll do to you when they realize how determined you are?"

"They'll throw me in some camp."

"And what good will that do?"

"I just can't lie down for this."

Volodya had to get Werner back on his side, but so far he had failed to get through. Werner had an answer for everything. He was a smart guy. That was why he was such a valuable spy.

"What about the others?" Volodya said.

"What others?"

"There must be thousands more handicapped adults and children. Are the Nazis going to kill them all?"

"Probably."

"You certainly won't be able to stop them, if you're in a prison camp."

For the first time, Werner did not have a comeback.

Volodya turned away from the water and surveyed the cemetery. A young man in a suit was kneeling at a small tombstone. Was he a tail? Volodya watched carefully. The man was shaking with sobs. He seemed genuine: counterintelligence agents were not good actors.

"Look at him," Volodya said to Werner.

"Why?"

"He's grieving. Which is what you're doing."

"So what?"

"Just watch."

After a minute the man got up, wiped his face with a handkerchief, and walked away.

Volodya said: "Now he's happy. That's what grieving is about. It doesn't achieve anything. It just makes you feel better."

"You think my asking questions is just to make me feel better."

Volodya turned and looked him in the eye. "I don't criticize you," he said. "You want to discover the truth, and shout it out loud. But think about it logically. The only way to end this is to bring down the regime. And the only way that's going to happen is if the Nazis are defeated by the Red Army."

"Maybe."

Werner was weakening, Volodya perceived with a surge of hope. "Maybe?" he said. "Who else is there? The British are on their knees, desperately trying to fight off the Luftwaffe. The Americans are not interested in European squabbles. Everyone else supports the Fascists." He put his hands on Werner's shoulders. "The Red Army is your only hope, my friend. If we lose, those Nazis will be murdering handicapped children—and Jews, and Communists, and homosexuals—for a thousand more blood-soaked years."

"Hell," said Werner. "You're right."

vii

Carla and her mother went to church on Sunday. Maud was distraught about Walter's arrest and desperate to find out where he had been taken. Of course the Gestapo refused to give out any information. But Pastor Ochs's church was a fashionable one, people came in from the wealthier suburbs to attend, and the congregation included some powerful men, one or two of whom might be able to make inquiries.

Carla bowed her head and prayed that her father might not be beaten or tortured. She did not really believe in prayer but she was desperate enough to try anything.

She was glad to see the Franck family, sitting a few rows in front. She studied the back of Werner's head. He wore his hair curled a little at the neck, in contrast with most of the men, who were close-cropped. She had touched his neck and kissed his throat. He was adorable. He was easily the nicest boy who had ever kissed her. Every night before sleeping she relived that evening when they had driven to the Grunewald.

But she was not in love with him, she told herself.

Not yet.

When Pastor Ochs entered, she saw at once that he had been crushed. The change in him was horrifying. He walked slowly to the lectern, head bent and shoulders slumped, causing a few in the congregation to exchange concerned whispers. He recited the prayers without expression, then read the sermon from a book. Carla had been a nurse for two years now and she recognized in him the symptoms of depression. She guessed that he, too, had received a visit from the Gestapo.

She noticed that Frau Ochs and the five children were not in their usual places in the front pew.

As they sang the last hymn, Carla vowed that she would not give up, scared though she was. She still had allies: Frieda and Werner and Heinrich. But what could they do?

She wished she had solid proof of what the Nazis were doing. She had no doubts, herself, that they were exterminating the handicapped—this Gestapo crackdown made it obvious. But she could not convince others without concrete evidence.

How could she get it?

After the service she walked out of the church with Frieda and Werner. Drawing them away from their parents, she said: "I think we have to get evidence of what's going on."

Frieda immediately saw what she meant. "We should go to Akelberg," she said. "Visit the hospital."

Werner had proposed that, right at the start, but they had decided to begin their inquiries here in Berlin. Now Carla considered the idea afresh. "We'd need permits to travel."

"How could we manage that?"

Carla snapped her fingers. "We both belong to the Mercury Cycling Club. They can get permits for bicycle holidays." It was just the kind of thing the Nazis were keen on, healthy outdoor exercise for young people.

"Could we get inside the hospital?"

"We could try."

Werner said: "I think you should drop the whole thing."

Carla was startled. "What do you mean?"

"Pastor Ochs has obviously been scared half to death. This is a very dangerous business. You could be imprisoned, tortured. And it won't bring back Axel or Kurt."

She stared at him incredulously. "You want us to give it up?"

"You must give it up. You're talking as if Germany were a free country! You'll get yourselves killed, both of you."

"We have to take risks!" Carla said angrily.

"Leave me out of this," he said. "I've had a visit from the Gestapo, too."

Carla was immediately concerned. "Oh, Werner—what happened?"

"Just threats, so far. If I ask any more questions, I'll be sent to the front line."

"Oh, well, thank God it's not worse."

"It's bad enough."

The girls were silent for a few moments; then Frieda said what Carla was thinking. "This is more important than your job—you must see that."

"Don't tell me what I must see," Werner replied. He was superficially angry, but underneath that, Carla could tell he was in fact ashamed. "It's not your career that's at stake," he went on. "And you haven't met the Gestapo yet."

Carla was astonished. She thought she knew Werner. She would have been sure he would see this the way she did. "Actually, I have met them," she said. "They arrested my father."

Frieda was appalled. "Oh, Carla!" she said, and put her arm around Carla's shoulders.

"We can't find out where he is," Carla added.

Werner showed no sympathy. "Then you should know better than to defy them!" he said. "They would have arrested you, too, except that Inspector Macke thinks girls aren't dangerous."

Carla wanted to cry. She had been on the point of falling in love with Werner, and now he turned out to be a coward.

Frieda said: "Are you saying you won't help us?"

"Yes."

"Because you want to keep your job?"

"It's pointless—you can't beat them!"

Carla was furious with him for his cowardice and defeatism. "We can't just let this happen!"

"Open confrontation is insane. There are other ways to oppose them."

Carla said: "How, by working slowly, like those leaflets say? That won't stop them killing handicapped children!"

"Defying the government is suicidal!"

"Anything else is cowardice!"

"I refuse to be judged by two girls!" With that he stalked off.

Carla fought back tears. She could not cry in front of two hundred people standing outside the church in the sunshine. "I thought he was different," she said.

Frieda was upset, but baffled, too. "He *is* different," she said. "I've known him all my life. Something else is going on, something he's not telling us about."

Carla's mother approached. She did not notice Carla's distress, which was unusual. "Nobody knows anything!" she said despairingly. "I can't find out where your father might be."

"We'll keep trying," Carla said. "Didn't he have friends at the American embassy?"

"Acquaintances. I've asked them already, but they haven't come up with any information."

"We'll ask them again tomorrow."

"Oh, God, I suppose there are a million German wives in the same situation as me."

Carla nodded. "Let's go home, Mother."

They walked back slowly, not talking, each with her own thoughts. Carla was angry with Werner, the more so because she had badly mistaken his character. How could she have fallen for someone so weak?

They reached their street. "I shall go to the American embassy in the morning," Maud said as they approached the house. "I'll wait in the lobby all day if necessary. I'll beg them to do something. If they really want to, they can make a semiofficial inquiry about the brother-in-law of a British government minister. Oh! Why is our front door open?"

Carla's first thought was that the Gestapo had paid them a second visit. But there was no black car parked at the curb. And a key was sticking out of the lock.

Maud stepped into the hall and screamed.

Carla rushed in after her.

There was a man lying on the floor covered in blood.

Carla managed to stop herself screaming. "Who is it?" she said.

Maud knelt beside the man. "Walter," she said. "Oh, Walter, what have they done to you?"

Then Carla saw that it was her father. He was so badly injured he was almost unrecognizable. One eye was closed, his mouth was swollen into a single huge bruise, and his hair was covered with congealed blood. One arm was twisted oddly. The front of his jacket was stained with vomit.

Maud said: "Walter, speak to me, speak to me!"

He opened his ruined mouth and groaned.

Carla suppressed the hysterical grief that bubbled up inside her by shifting into professional gear. She fetched a cushion and propped up his head. She got a cup of water from the kitchen and dribbled a little on his lips. He swallowed and opened his mouth for more. When he seemed to have had enough, she went into his study and got a bottle of schnapps and gave him a few drops. He swallowed them and coughed.

"I'm going for Dr. Rothmann," Carla said. "Wash his face and give him more water. Don't try to move him."

Maud said: "Yes, yes—hurry!"

Carla wheeled her bike out of the house and pedaled away. Dr. Rothmann was not allowed to practise any longer—Jews could not be doctors—but, unofficially, he still attended poor people.

Carla pedaled furiously. How had her father got home? She guessed they had brought him in a car, and he had managed to stagger from the curbside into the house, then collapsed.

She reached the Rothmann house. Like her own home, it was in bad repair. Most of the windows had been broken by Jew-haters. Frau Rothmann opened the door. "My father has been beaten," Carla said breathlessly. "The Gestapo."

"My husband will come," said Frau Rothmann. She turned and called up the stairs. "Isaac!"

The doctor came down.

"It's Herr von Ulrich," said Frau Rothmann.

The doctor picked up a canvas shopping bag that stood near the door. Because he was banned from practising medicine, Carla guessed he could not carry anything that looked like an instrument case.

They left the house. "I'll cycle on ahead," Carla said.

When she got home, she found her mother sitting on the doorstep, weeping.

"The doctor's on his way!" Carla said.

"He is too late," said Maud. "Your father's dead."

viii

Volodya was outside the Wertheim department store, just off the Alexander Platz, at half past two in the afternoon. He patrolled the area several times, looking for men who might be plainclothes police officers. He was sure he had not been followed here, but it was not impossible that a passing Gestapo agent might recognize him and wonder what he was up to. A busy place with crowds was the best camouflage, but it was not perfect.

Was the invasion story true? If so, Volodya would not be in Berlin much longer. He would kiss good-bye to Gerda and Sabine. He would presumably return to Red Army Intelligence headquarters in Moscow. He looked forward to spending some time with his family. His sister, Anya, had twin babies whom he had never seen. And he felt he could do with a rest. Undercover work meant continual stress: losing Gestapo shadows, holding clandestine meetings, recruiting agents, and worrying about betrayal. He would welcome a year or two at headquarters, assuming the Soviet Union survived that long. Alternatively, he might be sent on another foreign posting. He fancied Washington. He had always had a yen to see America.

He took from his pocket a ball of crumpled tissue paper and dropped it into a litter bin. At one minute to three he lit a cigarette, although he did not smoke. He dropped the lighted match carefully into the bin so that it landed in the nest of tissue paper. Then he walked away.

Seconds later, someone cried: "Fire!"

Just when everyone in the vicinity was looking at the fire in the litter bin, a taxi drew up at the entrance to the store, a regular black Mercedes 260D. A handsome young man in the uniform of an air force lieutenant jumped out. As the lieutenant was paying the driver, Volodya jumped into the cab and slammed the door.

On the floor of the cab, where the driver could not see it, was a copy of *Neues Volk,* the Nazi magazine of racial propaganda. Volodya picked it up, but did not read it.

"Some idiot has set fire to a litter bin," said the driver.

"Hotel Adlon," Volodya said, and the car pulled away.

He riffled the pages of the magazine and verified that a buff-colored envelope was concealed within.

He longed to open it, but he waited.

He got out of the cab at the hotel, but did not go inside. Instead he walked through the Brandenburg Gate and into the park. The trees were showing bright new leaves. It was a warm spring day and there were plenty of afternoon strollers.

The magazine seemed to burn the skin of Volodya's hand. He found an unobtrusive bench and sat down.

He unfolded the magazine and, behind its screen, he opened the buff-colored envelope.

He drew out a document. It was a carbon copy, typed and a bit faint, but legible. It was headed:

Directive No. 21: Case "Barbarossa"

Friedrich Barbarossa was the German emperor who had led the Third Crusade in the year 1189.

The text began: "The German Wehrmacht must be prepared, even before the completion of the war against England, to overthrow Russia in a rapid campaign."

Volodya found himself gasping for breath. This was dynamite. The Tokyo spy had been right, and Stalin wrong. And the Soviet Union was in mortal danger.

Heart pounding, Volodya looked at the end of the document. It was signed: "Adolf Hitler."

He scanned the pages, looking for a date, and found one. The invasion was scheduled for May 15, 1941.

Next to this was a penciled note in Werner Franck's handwriting: "The date has now been changed to 22 June."

"Oh, my God, he's done it," Volodya said aloud. "He's confirmed the invasion."

He put the document back into the envelope and the envelope into the magazine.

This changed everything.

He got up from the bench and walked back to the Soviet embassy to give them the news.

ix

There was no railway station at Akelberg, so Carla and Frieda got off at the nearest stop, ten miles away, and wheeled their bicycles off the train.

They wore shorts, sweaters, and utilitarian sandals, and they had put their hair up in plaits. They looked like members of the League of German Girls, the Bund Deutscher Mädel, or BDM. Such girls often took cycling holidays. Whether they did anything other than cycle, especially during the evenings in the spartan hostels at which they stayed, was the subject of much speculation. Boys said BDM stood for "Bubi Drück Mir," "Baby, Do Me."

Carla and Frieda consulted their map, then rode out of town in the direction of Akelberg.

Carla thought about her father every hour of every day. She knew she would never get over the horror of finding him savagely beaten and dying. She had cried for days. But alongside her grief was another emotion: rage. She was not merely going to be sad. She was going to do something about it.

Maud, distraught with grief, had at first tried to persuade Carla not to go to Akelberg. "My husband is dead. My son is in the army. I don't want my daughter to put her life on the line, too!" she had wailed.

After the funeral, when horror and hysteria gave way to a calmer, more profound mourning, Carla had asked her what Walter would have wanted. Maud had thought for a long time. It was not until the next day that she answered. "He would have wanted you to carry on the fight."

It was hard for Maud to say it, but they both knew it was true.

Frieda had had no such discussion with her parents. Her mother, Monika, had once loved Walter, and was devastated by his death; nonetheless she would have been horrified if she knew what Frieda was doing. Her father, Ludi, would have locked her in the cellar. But they believed she was going bicycling. If anything, they might have suspected she was meeting some unsuitable boyfriend.

The countryside was hilly, but they were both in good shape, and an hour later they coasted down a slope into the small town of Akelberg. Carla felt apprehensive: they were entering enemy territory.

They went into a café. There was no Coca-Cola. "This isn't Berlin!" said the woman behind the counter, with as much indignation as if they had asked to be serenaded by an orchestra. Carla wondered why someone who disliked strangers would run a café.

They got glasses of Fanta, a German product, and took the opportunity to refill their water bottles.

They did not know the precise location of the hospital. They needed to ask directions, but Carla was concerned about arousing suspicion. The local Nazis might take an interest in strangers asking questions. As they were paying, Carla said: "We're supposed to meet the rest of our group at the crossroads by the hospital. Which way is that?"

The woman would not meet her eye. "There's no hospital here."

"The Akelberg Medical Institution," Carla persisted, quoting from the letterhead.

"Must be another Akelberg."

Carla thought she was lying. "How strange," she said, keeping up the pretense. "I hope we're not in the wrong place."

They wheeled their bikes along the high street. There was nothing else for it, Carla thought: she had to ask the way.

A harmless-looking old man was sitting on a bench outside a bar, enjoying the afternoon sunshine. "Where's the hospital?" Carla asked him, covering her anxiety with a cheery veneer.

"Through the town and up the hill on your left," he said. "Don't go inside, though—not many people come out!" He cackled as if he had made a joke.

The directions were a bit vague, but might suffice, Carla thought. She decided she would not draw further attention by asking again.

A woman in a head scarf took the arm of the old man. "Pay no attention to him—he doesn't know what he's saying," she said, looking worried. She jerked him to his feet and hustled him along the sidewalk. "Keep your mouth shut, you old fool," she muttered.

It seemed these people had an inkling of what was going on in their neighborhood. Fortunately their main reaction was to act surly and not get involved. Perhaps they would not be in a hurry to give information to the police or the Nazi Party.

Carla and Frieda went farther along the street and found the youth hostel. There were thousands of such places in Germany, designed to cater to exactly such people as they were pretending to be, athletic youngsters on a vigorous open-air holiday. They checked in. The facilities were primitive, with three-tiered bunk beds, but the place was cheap.

It was late afternoon when they cycled out of town. After a mile they came to a left turn. There was no signpost, but the road led uphill, so they took it.

Carla's apprehension intensified. The nearer they got, the harder it would be to seem innocent under questioning.

A mile later they saw a large house in a park. It did not seem to be walled or fenced, and the road led up to the door. Once again there were no signs.

Unconsciously, Carla had been expecting a hilltop castle of forbidding gray stone, with barred windows and ironbound oak doors. But this was a Bavarian country house, with steep overhanging roofs, wooden balconies, and a little bell tower. Surely nothing as horrible as child murder could go on here? It also seemed small, for a hospital. Then she saw that a modern extension had been added to one side, with a tall chimney.

They dismounted and leaned their bikes against the side of the building. Carla's heart was in her mouth as they walked up the steps to the entrance. Why were there no guards? Because no one would be so foolhardy as to try to investigate the place?

There was no bell or knocker, but when Carla pushed the door, it opened. She stepped inside, and Frieda followed. They found themselves in a cool hall with a stone floor and bare white walls. There were several rooms off the hall, but all the doors were closed. A middle-aged woman in spectacles was coming down a broad staircase. She wore a smart gray dress. "Yes?" she said.

"Hello," said Frieda casually.

"What are you doing? You can't come in here."

Frieda and Carla had prepared a story. "I just wanted to visit the place where my brother died," Frieda said. "He was fifteen—"

"This isn't a public facility!" the woman said indignantly.

"Yes, it is." Frieda had been brought up in a wealthy family, and was not cowed by minor functionaries.

A nurse of about nineteen appeared from a side door and stared at them. The woman in the gray dress spoke to her. "Nurse König, fetch Herr Römer immediately."

The nurse hurried away.

The woman said: "You should have written in advance."

"Did you not get my letter?" said Frieda. "I wrote to the senior physician." This was not true; Frieda was improvising.

"No such letter has been received!" Clearly the woman felt that Frieda's outrageous request could not possibly have gone unnoticed.

Carla was listening. The place was strangely quiet. She had dealt with physically and mentally handicapped people, adults and children, and they were not often silent. Even through these closed doors she should have been able to hear shouts, laughter, crying, voices raised in protest, and nonsensical ravings. But there was nothing. It was more like a morgue.

Frieda tried a new tack. "Perhaps you can tell me where my brother's grave is. I'd like to visit it."

"There are no graves. We have an incinerator." She immediately corrected herself. "A cremation facility."

Carla said: "I noticed the chimney."

Frieda said: "What happened to my brother's ashes?"

"They will be sent to you in due course."

"Don't mix them up with anyone else's, will you?"

The woman's neck reddened in a blush, and Carla guessed they did mix up the ashes, figuring that no one would know.

Nurse König reappeared, followed by a burly man in the white uniform of a male nurse. The woman said: "Ah, Römer. Please escort these girls off the premises."

"Just a minute," said Frieda. "Are you quite sure you're doing the right thing? I only wanted to see the place where my brother died."

"Quite sure."

"Then you won't mind letting me know your name."

There was a second's hesitation. "Frau Schmidt. Now please leave us."
Römer moved toward them in a menacing way.

"We're going," Frieda said frostily. "We have no intention of giving
Herr Römer an excuse to molest us."

The man changed course and opened the door for them.

They went out, climbed on their bikes, and rode down the drive.
Frieda said: "Do you think she believed our story?"

"Totally," said Carla. "She didn't even ask our names. If she had
suspected the truth, she would have called the police right away."

"But we didn't learn much. We saw the chimney. But we didn't find
anything we could call proof."

Carla felt a bit down. Getting evidence was not as easy as it sounded.

They returned to the hostel. They washed and changed and went out
in search of something to eat. The only café was the one with the
grumpy proprietress. They ate potato pancakes with sausage. Afterward
they went to the town's bar. They ordered beers and spoke cheerfully to
the other customers, but no one wanted to talk to them. This in itself
was suspicious. People everywhere were wary of strangers, for anyone
might be a Nazi snitch, but even so Carla wondered how many towns
there were where two young girls could spend an hour in a bar without
anyone even trying to flirt with them.

They returned to the hostel for an early night. Carla could not think
what else to do. Tomorrow they would return home empty-handed. It
seemed incredible that she should know about these awful killings yet
be unable to stop them. She felt so frustrated she wanted to scream.

It occurred to her that Frau Schmidt—if that really was her name—
might have further thoughts about her visitors. At the time, she had
taken Carla and Frieda for what they claimed to be, but she might
develop suspicions later, and call the police just to be safe. If that
happened, Carla and Frieda would not be hard to find. There were just
five people at the hostel tonight and they were the only girls. She
listened in fear for the fatal knock on the door.

If they were questioned, they would tell part of the truth, saying that
Frieda's brother and Carla's godson had died at Akelberg, and they

wanted to visit their graves, or at least see the place where they died and spend a few minutes in remembrance. The local police might buy that story. But if they checked with Berlin, they would swiftly learn the connection with Walter von Ulrich and Werner Franck, two men who had been investigated by the Gestapo for asking disloyal questions about Akelberg. Then Carla and Frieda would be deep in trouble.

As they were getting ready to go to bed in the uncomfortable-looking bunks, there was a knock at the door.

Carla's heart stopped. She thought of what the Gestapo had done to her father. She knew she could not withstand torture. In two minutes she would name every Swing Kid she knew.

Frieda, who was less imaginative, said: "Don't look so scared!" and opened the door.

It was not the Gestapo but a small, pretty blond girl. It took Carla a moment to recognize her as Nurse König, out of uniform.

"I have to speak to you," she said. She was distressed, breathless and tearful.

Frieda invited her in. She sat on a bunk bed and wiped her eyes on the sleeve of her dress. Then she said: "I can't keep it inside any longer."

Carla glanced at Frieda. They were thinking the same thing. Carla said: "Keep what inside, Nurse König?"

"My name is Ilse."

"I'm Carla and this is Frieda. What's on your mind, Ilse?"

Ilse spoke in a voice so low they could hardly hear her. She said: "We kill them."

Carla could hardly breathe. She managed to say: "At the hospital?"

Ilse nodded. "The poor people who come in on the gray buses. Children, even babies, and old people, grandmothers. They're all more or less helpless. Sometimes they're horrid, dribbling and soiling themselves, but they can't help it, and some of them are really sweet and innocent. It makes no difference—we kill them all."

"How do you do it?"

"An injection of morphium-scopolamin."

Carla nodded. It was a common anesthetic, fatal in overdose. "What about the special treatments they're supposed to have?"

Ilse shook her head. "There are no special treatments."

Carla said: "Ilse, let me get this clear. Do they kill every patient that comes here?"

"Every one."

"As soon as they arrive?"

"Within a day, no more than two."

It was what Carla had suspected, but even so, the stark reality was horrifying, and she felt nauseated.

After a minute she said: "Are there any patients there now?"

"Not alive. We were giving injections this afternoon. That's why Frau Schmidt was so frightened when you walked in."

"Why don't they make it harder for strangers to get into the building?"

"They think guards and barbed wire around a hospital would make it obvious that something sinister was going on. Anyway, no one ever tried to visit before you."

"How many people died today?"

"Fifty-two."

Carla's skin crawled. "The hospital killed fifty-two people this afternoon, around the time we were there?"

"Yes."

"So they're all dead now?"

Ilse nodded.

An intention had been germinating in Carla's mind, and now she resolved to carry it out. "I want to see," she said.

Ilse looked frightened. "What do you mean?"

"I want to go inside the hospital and see those corpses."

"They're burning them already."

"Then I want to see that. Can you sneak us in?"

"Tonight?"

"Right now."

"Oh, God."

Carla said: "You don't have to do anything. You've already been brave, just by talking to us. If you don't want to do any more, it's okay. But if we're going to put a stop to this, we need proof."

"Proof?"

"Yes. Look, the government is ashamed of this project—that's why it's secret. The Nazis know that ordinary Germans won't tolerate the killing of children. But people prefer to believe it's not happening, and it's easy for them to dismiss a rumor, especially if they hear it from a young girl. So we have to prove it to them."

"I see." Ilse's pretty face took on a look of grim determination. "All right, then. I'll take you."

Carla stood up. "How do you normally get there?"

"Bicycle. It's outside."

"Then we'll all ride."

They went out. Darkness had fallen. The sky was partly cloudy, and the starlight was faint. They used their cycle lights as they rode out of town and up the hill. When they came in sight of the hospital, they switched off their lights and continued on foot, pushing their bikes. Ilse took them by a forest path that led to the rear of the building.

Carla smelled an unpleasant odor, somewhat like a car's exhaust. She sniffed.

Ilse whispered: "The incinerator."

"Oh, no!"

They hid the bikes in a shrubbery and walked silently to the back door. It was unlocked. They went in.

The corridors were bright. There were no shadowy corners: the place was lit like the hospital it pretended to be. If they met someone, they would be seen clearly. Their clothes would give them away immediately as intruders. What would they do then? Run, probably.

Ilse walked quickly along a corridor, turned a corner, and opened a door. "In here," she whispered.

They walked in.

Frieda let out a squeal of horror and covered her mouth.

Carla whispered: "Oh, my soul."

In a large, cold room were about thirty dead people, all lying faceup on tables, naked. Some were fat, some thin; some old and withered, some children, and one a baby of about a year. A few were bent and twisted, but most appeared physically normal.

Each one had a small adhesive bandage on the upper left arm, where the needle had gone in.

Carla heard Frieda crying softly.

She steeled her nerves. "Where are the others?" she whispered.

"Already gone to the furnace," Ilse replied.

They heard voices coming from behind the double door at the far end of the room.

"Back outside," Ilse said.

They stepped into the corridor. Carla closed the door all but a crack, and peeped through. She saw Herr Römer and another man push a hospital trolley through the doors.

The men did not look in Carla's direction. They were arguing about soccer. She heard Römer say: "It's only nine years ago that we won the national championship. We beat Eintracht Frankfurt two–nil."

"Yes, but half your best players were Jews, and they've all gone."

Carla realized they were talking about the Bayern Munich team.

Römer said: "The old days will come back, if only we play the right tactics."

Still arguing, the two men went to a table where a fat woman lay dead. They took her by the shoulders and knees, then unceremoniously swung her onto the trolley, grunting with the effort.

They moved the trolley to another table and put a second corpse on top of the first.

When they had three, they wheeled the trolley out.

Carla said: "I'm going to follow them."

She crossed the morgue to the double doors, and Frieda and Ilse followed her. They passed into an area that felt more industrial than medical: the walls were painted brown, the floor was concrete, and there were store cupboards and tool racks.

They looked around a corner.

They saw a large room like a garage, with harsh lighting and deep shadows. The atmosphere was warm, and there was a faint smell of cooking. In the middle of the space was a steel box large enough to hold a motorcar. A metal canopy led from the top of the box through the roof. Carla realized she was looking at a furnace.

The two men lifted a body off the trolley and shifted it to a steel conveyor belt. Römer pushed a button on the wall. The belt moved, a door opened, and the corpse passed into the furnace.

They put the next corpse on the belt.

Carla had seen enough.

She turned and motioned the others back. Frieda bumped into Ilse, who let out an involuntary cry. They all froze.

They heard Römer say: "What was that?"

"A ghost," the other replied.

Römer's voice was shaky. "Don't joke about such things!"

"Are you going to pick up the other end of this stiff, or what?"

"All right, all right."

The three girls hurried back to the morgue. Seeing the remaining bodies, Carla suffered a wave of grief about Ada's Kurt. He had lain here, with an adhesive bandage on his arm, and had been thrown onto the conveyor belt and disposed of like a bag of garbage. But you're not forgotten, Kurt, she thought.

They went out into the corridor. As they turned toward the back door, they heard footsteps and the voice of Frau Schmidt. "What is taking those two men so long?"

They hurried along the corridor and through the door. The moon was out, and the park was brightly lit. Carla could see the shrubbery where they had hidden the bikes, two hundred yards away across the grass.

Frieda came out last, and in her rush she let the door bang.

Carla thought fast. Frau Schmidt was likely to investigate the noise. The three girls might not reach the shrubbery before she opened the door. They had to hide. "This way!" Carla hissed, and she ran around the corner of the building. The others followed.

They flattened themselves against the wall. Carla heard the door open. She held her breath.

There was a long pause. Then Frau Schmidt muttered something unintelligible, and the door banged again.

Carla peeped around the corner. Frau Schmidt had gone.

The three girls ran across the lawn and retrieved their bicycles.

They pushed the bikes along the forest path and emerged onto the road. They switched on their lights, mounted up, and pedaled away. Carla felt euphoric. They had got away with it!

As they approached the town, triumph gave way to more practical considerations. What had they achieved, exactly? What would they do next?

They must tell someone what they had seen. She was not sure whom. In any event they had to convince someone. Would they be believed? The more she thought about it, the less sure she was.

When they reached the hostel and dismounted, Ilse said: "Thank goodness that's over. I've never been so scared in all my life."

"It's not over," said Carla.

"What do you mean?"

"It won't be over until we've closed that hospital, and any others like it."

"How can you do that?"

"We need you," Carla said to her. "You're the proof."

"I was afraid you were going to say that."

"Will you come with us, tomorrow, when we go back to Berlin?"

There was a long pause; then Ilse said: "Yes, I will."

x
<hr>

Volodya Peshkov was glad to be home. Moscow was at its summery best, sunny and warm. On Monday, June 30, he returned to Red Army Intelligence headquarters beside the Khodynka airfield.

Both Werner Franck and the Tokyo spy had been right: Germany had invaded the Soviet Union on June 22. Volodya and all the personnel at the Soviet embassy in Berlin had returned to Moscow, by ship and train. Volodya had been prioritized, and made it back faster than most: some were still traveling.

Volodya now realized how much Berlin had been getting him down. The Nazis were tedious in their self-righteousness and triumphalism. They were like a winning soccer team at the after-match party, getting drunker and more boring and refusing to go home. He was sick of them.

Some people might say that the USSR was similar, with its secret police, its rigid orthodoxy, and its puritan attitudes to such pleasures as abstract painting and fashion. They were wrong. Communism was a work in progress, with mistakes being made on the road to a fair society. The NKVD with its torture chambers was an aberration, a cancer in the body of Communism. One day it would be surgically removed. But probably not in wartime.

Anticipating the outbreak of war, Volodya had long ago equipped his Berlin spies with clandestine radios and codebooks. Now it was more vital than ever that the handful of brave anti-Nazis should continue to pass information to the Soviets. Before leaving he had destroyed all records of their names and addresses, which now existed only in his head.

He had found both his parents fit and well, although his father looked harassed. It was his responsibility to prepare Moscow for air raids. Volodya had gone to see his sister, Anya, her husband, Ilya Dvorkin, and the twins, now eighteen months old: Dmitriy, called Dimka, and Tatiana, called Tania. Unfortunately their father struck Volodya as being just as ratlike and contemptible as ever.

After a pleasant day at home, and a good night's sleep in his old room, he was ready to start work again.

He passed through the metal detector at the entrance to the intelligence building. The familiar corridors and staircases touched a nostalgic chord, even if they were drab and utilitarian. Walking through the building he half-expected people to come up and congratulate him: many of them must have known he had been the one to confirm Barbarossa. But no one did; perhaps they were being discreet.

He entered a large open area of typists and file clerks and spoke to the middle-aged woman receptionist. "Hello, Nika—are you still here?"

"Good morning, Captain Peshkov," she said, not as warmly as he might have hoped. "Colonel Lemitov would like to see you right away."

Like Volodya's father, Lemitov had not been important enough to suffer in the great purge of the late thirties, and now he had been promoted to fill the place of an unlucky former superior. Volodya did not know much about the purge, but he found it hard to believe that so many senior men had been disloyal enough to merit such punishment. Not that Volodya knew exactly what the punishment was. They could be in exile in Siberia, or in prison somewhere, or dead. All he knew was that they had vanished.

Nika added: "He has the big office at the end of the main corridor now."

Volodya walked through the open room, nodding and smiling at one or two acquaintances, but again he got the feeling that he was not the hero he had expected to be. He tapped on Lemitov's door, hoping the boss might shed some light.

"Come in."

Volodya entered, saluted, and closed the door behind him.

"Welcome back, Captain." Lemitov came around his desk. "Between you and me, you did a great job in Berlin. Thank you."

"I'm honored, sir," said Volodya. "But why is this between you and me?"

"Because you contradicted Stalin." He held up a hand to forestall protest. "Stalin doesn't know it was you, of course. But all the same, people around here are nervous, after the purge, of associating with anyone who takes the wrong line."

"What should I have done?" Volodya said incredulously. "Faked wrong intelligence?"

Lemitov shook his head emphatically. "You did exactly the right thing—don't get me wrong. And I've protected you. But just don't expect people around here to treat you like a champion."

"Okay," said Volodya. Things were worse than he had imagined.

"You have your own office now, at least—three doors down. You'll need to spend a day or so catching up."

Volodya took that for dismissal. "Yes, sir," he said. He saluted and left.

His office was not luxurious—a small room with no carpet—but he had it to himself. He was out of touch with the progress of the German invasion, having been busy trying to get home as fast as possible. Now he put his disappointment aside and began to read the reports of the battlefield commanders for the first week of the war.

As he did so, he became more and more desolate.

The invasion had taken the Red Army by surprise.

It seemed impossible, but the evidence covered his desk.

On June 22, when the Germans attacked, many forward units of the Red Army had had *no live ammunition*.

That was not all. Planes had been lined up neatly on airstrips with no camouflage, and the Luftwaffe had destroyed twelve hundred Soviet aircraft in the first few hours of the war. Army units had been thrown at the advancing Germans without adequate weapons, with no air cover, and lacking intelligence about enemy positions—and in consequence had been annihilated.

Worst of all, Stalin's standing order to the Red Army was that retreat was forbidden. Every unit had to fight to the last man, and officers were expected to shoot themselves to avoid capture. Troops were never allowed to regroup at a new, stronger defensive position. This meant that every defeat turned into a massacre.

Consequently the Red Army was hemorrhaging men and equipment.

The warning from the Tokyo spy, and Werner Franck's confirmation, had been ignored by Stalin. Even when the attack began, Stalin had at first insisted it was a limited act of provocation, done by German army officers without the knowledge of Hitler, who would put a stop to it as soon as he found out.

By the time it became undeniable that it was not a provocation but the largest invasion in the history of warfare, the Germans had overwhelmed the Soviets' forward positions. After a week they had pushed three hundred miles inside Soviet territory.

It was a catastrophe—but what made Volodya want to scream out loud was that it could have been avoided.

There was no doubt whose fault it was. The Soviet Union was an autocracy. Only one person made the decisions: Josef Stalin. He had been stubbornly, stupidly, disastrously wrong. And now his country was in mortal danger.

Until now Volodya had believed that Soviet Communism was the true ideology, marred only by the excesses of the secret police, the NKVD. Now he saw that the failure was at the very top. Beria and the NKVD existed only because Stalin permitted them. It was Stalin who was preventing the march to true Communism.

Late that afternoon, as Volodya was staring out of the window over the sunlit airstrip, brooding over what he had learned, he was visited by Kamen. They had been lieutenants together four years ago, fresh out of the Military Intelligence Academy, and had shared a room with two others. In those days Kamen had been the clown, making fun of everyone, daringly mocking pious Soviet orthodoxy. Now he was heavier and seemed more serious. He had grown a small black mustache like that of the foreign minister, Molotov, perhaps to make himself look more mature.

Kamen closed the door behind him and sat down. He took from his pocket a toy, a tin soldier with a key in its back. He wound up the key and placed the toy on Volodya's desk. The soldier swung his arms as if marching, and the clockwork mechanism made a loud ratcheting sound as it wound down.

In a lowered voice Kamen said: "Stalin has not been seen for two days."

Volodya realized that the clockwork soldier was there to swamp any listening device that might be hidden in his office.

He said: "What do you mean, he hasn't been seen?"

"He has not come to the Kremlin, and he is not answering the phone."

Volodya was baffled. The leader of a nation could not just disappear. "What's he doing?"

"No one knows." The soldier ran down. Kamen wound it up and set it going again. "On Saturday night, when he heard that the Soviet Western Army Group had been encircled by the Germans, he said: 'Everything's lost. I give up. Lenin founded our state and we've fucked it up.' Then he went to Kuntsevo." Stalin had a country house near the town of Kuntsevo on the outskirts of Moscow. "Yesterday he didn't show up at the Kremlin at his usual time of midday. When they phoned Kuntsevo, no one answered. Today, the same."

Volodya leaned forward. "Is he suffering"—his voice fell to a whisper—"a mental breakdown?"

Kamen made a helpless gesture. "It wouldn't be surprising. He insisted, against all the evidence, that Germany would not attack us, and now look."

Volodya nodded. It made sense. Stalin had allowed himself to be officially called Father, Teacher, Great Leader, Transformer of Nature, Great Helmsman, Genius of Mankind, the Greatest Genius of All Times and Peoples. But now it had been proved, even to him, that he had been wrong and everyone else right. Men committed suicide in such circumstances.

The crisis was even worse than Volodya had thought. Not only was the Soviet Union under attack and losing; it was also leaderless. This had to be its most perilous moment since the revolution.

But was it also an opportunity? Could it be a chance to get rid of Stalin?

The last time Stalin had appeared vulnerable was in 1924, when Lenin's Testament had said that Stalin was not fit to hold power. Since Stalin had survived that crisis, his power had seemed unassailable, even—Volodya could now see clearly—when his decisions had verged on madness: the purges, the blunders in Spain, the appointment of the sadist Beria as head of the secret police, the pact with Hitler. Was this emergency the occasion, at last, to break his hold?

Volodya hid his excitement from Kamen and everyone else. He hugged his thoughts to himself as he rode the bus home through the soft light of a summer evening. His journey was delayed by a slow-moving convoy of lorries towing antiaircraft guns—presumably being deployed by his father, who was in charge of Moscow's air raid defenses.

Could Stalin be deposed?

He wondered how many Kremlin insiders were asking themselves the same question.

He entered his parents' apartment building, the ten-story Government House, across the Moskva River from the Kremlin. They were out, but his sister was there with the twins, Dimka and Tania. The boy, Dimka, had dark eyes and hair. He held a red pencil and was scribbling messily on an old newspaper. The girl had the same intense blue-eyed stare that Grigori had—and so did Volodya, people said. She immediately showed Volodya her doll.

Also there was Zoya Vorotsyntsev, the astonishingly beautiful physicist Volodya had last seen four years earlier when he was about to leave for Spain. She and Anya had discovered a shared interest in Russian folk music: they went to recitals together, and Zoya played the *gudok*, a three-stringed fiddle. Neither could afford a phonograph, but Grigori had one, and they were listening to a record of a balalaika orchestra. Grigori was not a great music lover but he thought the record sounded jolly.

Zoya was wearing a short-sleeved summer dress the pale color of her blue eyes. When Volodya asked her the conventional question about how she was, she replied sharply: "I'm very angry."

There were lots of reasons for Russians to be angry just now. Volodya asked: "Why's that?"

"My research into nuclear physics has been canceled. All the scientists I work with have been reassigned. I myself am working on improvements to the design of bomb sights."

That seemed very reasonable to Volodya. "We are at war, after all."

"You don't understand," she said. "Listen. When uranium metal undergoes a process called fission, enormous quantities of energy are released. I mean *enormous*. We know this, and Western scientists do, too—we have read their papers in scientific journals."

"Still, the question of bomb sights seems more immediate."

Zoya said angrily: "This process, fission, could be used to create bombs that would be a hundred times more powerful than anything anyone has now. One nuclear explosion could flatten Moscow. What if the Germans make such a bomb and we don't have it? It will be as if they had rifles and we only had swords!"

Volodya said skeptically: "But is there any reason to believe that scientists in other countries are working on a fission bomb?"

"We're sure they are. The concept of fission leads automatically to the idea of a bomb. We thought of it—why shouldn't they? But there's another reason. They published all their early results in the journals—and then they stopped, suddenly, one year ago. There have been no new scientific papers on fission since this time last year."

"And you believe the politicians and generals in the West realized the military potential of the research and made it secret?"

"I can't think of another reason. And yet here in the Soviet Union we have not even begun to prospect for uranium."

"Hmm." Volodya was pretending to be doubtful, but in truth he found it all too credible. Even Stalin's greatest admirers—a group that included Volodya's father, Grigori—did not claim he understood science. And it was all too easy for an autocrat to ignore anything that made him uncomfortable.

"I've told your father," Zoya went on. "He listens to me, but no one listens to him."

"So what are you going to do?"

"What can I do? I'm going to make a damn good bomb sight for our airmen, and hope for the best."

Volodya nodded. He liked that attitude. He liked this girl. She was smart and feisty and a joy to look at. He wondered if she would go to a movie with him.

Talk of physics reminded him of Willi Frunze, who had been his friend at the Berlin Boys' Academy. According to Werner Franck, Willi was a brilliant physicist now studying in England. He might know something about the fission bomb Zoya was so exercised about. And if he was still a Communist, he might be willing to tell what he knew.

Volodya made a mental note to send a cable to the Red Army Intelligence desk in the London embassy.

His parents came in. Father was in full dress uniform, Mother in a coat and hat. They had been to one of the many interminable ceremonies the army loved: Stalin insisted such rituals continue, despite the German invasion, because they were so good for morale.

They cooed over the twins for a few minutes, but Father looked distracted. He muttered something about a phone call and went immediately to his study. Mother began to make supper.

Volodya talked to the three women in the kitchen, but he was desperate to speak to his father. He thought he could guess the subject of Father's urgent phone call: the overthrow of Stalin was being either planned or prevented right now, probably here in this building.

After a few minutes he decided to risk the old man's wrath and interrupt him. He excused himself and went to the study. But his father was just coming out. "I have to go to Kuntsevo," he said.

Volodya longed to know what was going on. "Why?" he said.

Grigori ignored the question. "I've called down for my car, but my chauffeur has gone home. You can drive me."

Volodya was thrilled. He had never been to Stalin's dacha. Now he was going there at a moment of profound crisis.

"Come on," his father said impatiently.

They shouted good-byes from the hallway and went out.

Grigori's car was a black ZIS 101-A, a Soviet copy of an American Packard, with three-speed automatic transmission. Its top speed was about eighty miles per hour. Volodya got behind the wheel and pulled away.

He drove through the Arbat, a neighborhood of craftsmen and intellectuals, and out onto the westward Mozhaisk Highway. "Have you been summoned by Comrade Stalin?" he asked his father.

"No. Stalin has been incommunicado for two days."

"That's what I heard."

"Did you? It's supposed to be secret."

"You can't keep something like that secret. What's happening now?"

"A group of us are going to Kuntsevo to see him."

Volodya asked the key question. "For what purpose?"

"Primarily to find out whether he's alive or dead."

Could he really be dead already, and no one know about it? Volodya wondered. It seemed unlikely. "And if he's alive?"

"I don't know. But whatever happens, I'd rather be there to see it than find out later."

Listening devices did not work in moving cars, Volodya knew—the microphone just picked up engine noise—so he was confident he could not be overheard. Nevertheless he felt fearful as he said the unthinkable. "Could Stalin be overthrown?"

His father answered irritably: "I told you, I don't know."

Volodya was electrified. Such a question demanded a confident negative. Anything else was a yes. His father had admitted the possibility that Stalin could be finished.

Volodya's hopes rose volcanically. "Think what that could be like!" he said joyously. "No more purges! The labor camps will be closed. Young girls will no longer be pulled off the street to be raped by the secret police." He half-expected his father to interrupt, but Grigori just listened with half-closed eyes. Volodya went on: "The stupid phrase 'Trotsky-Fascist spy' will disappear from our language. Army units who find themselves outnumbered and outgunned could retreat, instead of sacrificing themselves uselessly. Decisions will be made rationally, by groups of intelligent men working out what's best for everyone. It's the Communism you dreamed of thirty years ago!"

"Young fool," his father said contemptuously. "The last thing we want at this point is to lose our leader. We're at war and retreating! Our sole aim must be to defend the revolution—whatever it takes. We need Stalin now more than ever."

Volodya felt as if he had been slapped. It was many years since his father had called him a fool.

Was the old man right? Did the Soviet Union need Stalin? The leader had made so many disastrous decisions that Volodya did not see how the country could possibly be worse off with someone else in charge.

They reached their destination. Stalin's home was conventionally called a dacha, but it was not a country cottage. A long, low building with five tall windows each side of a grand entrance, it stood in a pine forest and was painted dull green, as if to hide it. Hundreds of armed troops guarded the gates and the double barbed-wire fence. Grigori pointed to an antiaircraft battery partly concealed by camouflage netting. "I put that there," he said.

The guard at the gate recognized Grigori, but nevertheless asked for their identification documents. Even though Grigori was a general and Volodya a captain in intelligence, they were both patted down for weapons.

Volodya drove up to the door. There were no other cars in front of the house. "We'll wait for the others," his father said.

A few moments later three more ZIS limousines drew up. Volodya recalled that ZIS stood for Zavod Imeni Stalina, Factory Called Stalin. Had the executioners arrived in cars named after their victim?

They all got out, eight middle-aged men in suits and hats, holding in their hands the future of their country. Among them Volodya recognized Foreign Minister Molotov and secret police chief Beria.

"Let's go," said Grigori.

Volodya was astonished. "I'm coming in there with you?"

Grigori reached under his seat and handed Volodya a Tokarev TT-33 pistol. "Put this in your pocket," he said. "If that prick Beria tries to arrest me, you shoot the fucker."

Volodya took it gingerly: the TT-33 had no safety catch. He slipped the gun into his jacket pocket—it was about seven inches long—and got out of the car. There were eight rounds, he recalled, in the magazine of the gun.

They all went inside. Volodya feared he would be patted down again, and his gun discovered, but there was no second check.

The house was painted dark colors and poorly lit. An officer showed the group into what looked like a small dining room. Stalin sat there in an armchair.

The most powerful man in the Eastern Hemisphere appeared

haggard and depressed. Looking up at the group entering the room he said: "Why have you come?"

Volodya gasped. Clearly he thought they were there either to arrest him or to execute him.

There was a long pause, and Volodya realized the group had not planned what to do. How could they, not even knowing whether Stalin was alive?

But what would they do now? Shoot him? There might never be another chance.

At last Molotov stepped forward. "We're asking you to come back to work," he said.

Volodya had to suppress the urge to protest.

But Stalin shook his head. "Can I live up to people's hopes? Can I lead the country to victory?"

Volodya was flabbergasted. Would he really refuse?

Stalin added: "There may be better candidates."

He was giving them a second chance to fire him!

Another member of the group spoke up, and Volodya recognized Marshal Voroshilov. "There's none more worthy," he said.

How did that help? This was hardly the time for naked flattery.

Then his father joined in, saying: "That's right!"

Were they not going to let Stalin go? How could they be so stupid?

Molotov was the first to say something sensible. "We propose to form a war cabinet called the State Defense Committee, a kind of ultra-politburo with a very small membership and sweeping powers."

Stalin quickly interposed: "Who will be its head?"

"You, Comrade Stalin!"

Volodya wanted to shout *No!*

There was another long silence.

At last Stalin spoke. "Very well," he said. "Now, who else shall we have on the committee?"

Beria stepped forward and began to propose the members.

It was all over, Volodya realized, feeling dizzy with frustration and disappointment. They had lost their chance. They could have deposed a tyrant, but they had lacked the nerve. Like the children of a violent father, they feared they could not manage without him.

In fact it was worse than that, he saw with growing despondency. Perhaps Stalin really had had a breakdown—it had certainly seemed real—but he had also made a brilliant political move. All the men who might replace him were here in this room. At the moment when his catastrophically poor judgment had been exposed for all to see, he had forced his rivals to come out and beg him to be their leader again. He had drawn a line under his appalling mistake and given himself a new start.

Stalin was not just back.

He was stronger than ever.

xi

Who would have the courage to make a public protest about what was going on at Akelberg? Carla and Frieda had seen it with their own eyes, and they had Ilse König as a witness, but now they needed an advocate. There were no elected representatives anymore: all Reichstag deputies were Nazis. There were no real journalists, either, just scribbling sycophants. The judges were all Nazi appointees subservient to the government. Carla had never before realized how much she had been protected by politicians, newspapermen, and lawyers. Without them, she saw now, the government could do anything it liked, even kill people.

Who could they turn to? Frieda's admirer Heinrich von Kessel had a friend who was a Catholic priest. "Peter was the cleverest boy in my class," he told them. "But he wasn't the most popular. A bit upright and stiff-necked. I think he'll listen to us, though."

Carla thought it was worth a try. Her Protestant pastor had been sympathetic, until the Gestapo terrified him into silence. Perhaps the same would happen again. But she did not know what else to do.

Heinrich took Carla, Frieda, and Ilse to Peter's church in Schöneberg early on a Sunday morning in July. Heinrich was handsome in a black suit; the girls all wore their nurses' uniforms, symbols of trustworthiness. They entered by a side door and went into a small, dusty room with a few old chairs and a large wardrobe. They found Father Peter alone, praying. He must have heard them come in, but he remained on his knees for a minute before getting up and turning to greet them.

Peter was tall and thin, with regular features and a neat haircut. He was twenty-seven, Carla calculated, if he was Heinrich's contemporary. He frowned at them, not troubling to conceal his irritation at being disturbed. "I am preparing myself for Mass," he said severely. "I am pleased to see you in church, Heinrich, but you must leave me now. I will see you afterward."

"This is a spiritual emergency, Peter," said Heinrich. "Sit down. We have something important to tell you."

"It could hardly be more important than Mass."

"Yes, it could, Peter, believe me. In five minutes' time you will agree."

"Very well."

"This is my girlfriend, Frieda Franck."

Carla was surprised. Was Frieda his girlfriend now?

Frieda said: "I had a younger brother who was born with spina bifida. Earlier this year he was transferred to a hospital at Akelberg in Bavaria for special treatment. Shortly afterward we got a letter saying he had died of appendicitis."

She turned to Carla, who took up the tale. "My maid had a son born brain-damaged. He, too, was transferred to Akelberg. The maid got an identical letter on the same day."

Peter spread his hands in a so-what gesture. "I have heard this kind of thing before. It's antigovernment propaganda. The Church does not interfere in politics."

What rubbish that was, Carla thought. The Church was up to its neck in politics. But she let it pass. "My maid's son did not have an appendix," she went on. "He had had it removed two years earlier."

"Please," said Peter. "What does this prove?"

Carla felt discouraged. Peter was obviously biased against them.

Heinrich said: "Wait, Peter. You haven't heard it all. Ilse here worked at the hospital in Akelberg."

Peter looked at her expectantly.

"I was raised Catholic, Father," Ilse said.

Carla had not known that.

"I'm not a good Catholic," Ilse went on.

"God is good, not us, my daughter," said Peter piously.

Ilse said: "But I knew that what I was doing was a sin. Yet I did it, because they told me to, and I was frightened." She began to cry.

"What did you do?"

"I killed people. Oh, Father, will God forgive me?"

The priest stared at the young nurse. He could not dismiss this as propaganda: he was looking at a soul in torment. He went pale.

The others were silent. Carla held her breath.

Ilse said: "The handicapped people are brought to the hospital in gray buses. They don't have special treatment. We give them an injection, and they die. Then we cremate them." She looked up at Peter. "Will I ever be forgiven for what I have done?"

He opened his mouth to speak. His words caught in his throat, and he coughed. At last he said quietly: "How many?"

"Usually four. Buses, I mean. There are about twenty-five patients in a bus."

"A hundred people?"

"Yes. Every week."

Peter's proud composure had vanished. His face was pale gray, and his mouth hung open. "A hundred handicapped people a week?"

"Yes, Father."

"What sort of handicap?"

"All sorts, mental and physical. Some senile old people, some deformed babies, men and women, paralyzed or retarded or just helpless."

He had to keep repeating it. "And the staff of the hospital kill them all?"

Ilse sobbed. "I'm sorry. I'm sorry. I knew it was wrong."

Carla watched Peter. His supercilious air had gone. It was a remarkable transformation. After years of hearing the prosperous Catholics of this sylvan suburb confess their little sins, he had suddenly been confronted with raw evil. And he was shocked to his core.

But what would he do?

Peter stood up. He took Ilse by the hands and raised her from her seat. "Come back to the Church," he said. "Confess to your priest. God will forgive you. This much I know."

"Thank you," she whispered.

He released her hands and looked at Heinrich. "It may not be so simple for the rest of us," he said.

Then he turned his back on them and knelt to pray again.

Carla looked at Heinrich, who shrugged. They got up and left the little room, Carla with her arm around the weeping Ilse.

Carla said: "We'll stay for the service. Perhaps he'll speak to us again afterward."

The four of them walked into the nave of the church. Ilse stopped crying and became calmer. Frieda held Heinrich's arm. They took seats among the gathering congregation, prosperous men and plump women and restless children in their best clothes. People such as these would never kill the handicapped, Carla thought. Yet their government did, on their behalf. How had this happened?

She did not know what to expect of Father Peter. Clearly he had believed what they had told him, in the end. He had wanted to dismiss them as politically motivated, but Ilse's sincerity had convinced him. He had been horrified. But he had not made any promises, except that God would forgive Ilse.

Carla looked around the church. The decoration was more colorful than what she was used to in Protestant churches. There were more statues and paintings, more marble and gilding and banners and candles. Protestants and Catholics had fought wars about such trivia, she recalled. How strange it seemed, in a world where children could be murdered, that anyone should care about candles.

The service began. The priests entered in their robes, Father Peter the tallest among them. Carla could not read anything in his facial expression except stern piety.

She sat indifferent through the hymns and prayers. She had prayed for her father, and two hours later had found him cruelly beaten and dying on the floor of their home. She missed him every day, sometimes every hour. Praying had not saved him, nor would it protect those deemed useless by the government. Action was needed, not words.

Thinking of her father brought her brother, Erik, to mind. He was somewhere in Russia. He had written a letter home, jubilantly celebrating the rapid progress of the invasion, and angrily refusing to believe that Walter had been murdered by the Gestapo. Their father had obviously been released unharmed by the Gestapo and then attacked in the street by criminals or Communists or Jews, he asserted. He was living in a fantasy, beyond the reach of reason.

Was the same true of Father Peter?

Peter mounted the pulpit. Carla had not known he was due to preach a sermon. She wondered what he would say. Would he be inspired by what he had heard this morning? Would he speak of something irrelevant, the virtue of modesty or the sin of envy? Or would he close his eyes and devoutly thank God for the German army's continuing victories in Russia?

He stood tall in the pulpit and swept the church with a gaze that might have been arrogant, or proud, or defiant.

"The fifth commandment says: 'Thou shalt not kill.'"

Carla met Heinrich's eyes. What was Peter going to say?

His voice rang out between the echoing stones of the nave. "There is a place in Akelberg, Bavaria, where our government is breaking the commandment a hundred times a week!"

Carla gasped. He was doing it—he was preaching a sermon against the program! This could change everything.

"It makes no difference that the victims are handicapped, or mentally ill, or incapable of feeding themselves, or paralyzed." Peter was letting his anger show. "Helpless babies and senile old people are all God's children, and their lives are as sacred as yours and mine." His voice rose in volume. "To kill them is a mortal sin!" He lifted his right arm and made a fist, and his voice shook with emotion. "I say to you that if we do nothing about it, we sin just as much as the doctors and nurses who administer the lethal injections. If we remain silent . . ." He paused. "If we remain silent, we are murderers, too!"

xii

Inspector Thomas Macke was furious. He had been made to look a fool in the eyes of Superintendent Kringelein and the rest of his superiors. He had assured them he had plugged the leak. The secret of Akelberg—and hospitals of the same kind in other parts of the country—was safe, he had said. He had tracked down the three troublemakers, Werner Franck, Pastor Ochs, and Walter von Ulrich, and in different ways he had silenced each of them.

And yet the secret had come out.

The man responsible was an arrogant young priest called Peter.

Father Peter was in front of Macke now, naked, strapped by wrists and ankles to a specially constructed chair. He was bleeding from the ears, nose, and mouth, and had vomit all down his chest. Electrodes were attached to his lips, his nipples, and his penis. A strap around his forehead prevented him from breaking his neck while the convulsions shook him.

A doctor sitting beside the priest checked his heart with a stethoscope and looked dubious. "He can't stand much more," he said in a matter-of-fact tone.

Father Peter's seditious sermon had been taken up elsewhere. The bishop of Münster, a much more important clergyman, had preached a similar sermon, denouncing the T4 program. The bishop had called upon Hitler to save the people from the Gestapo, cleverly implying that the Führer could not possibly know about the program, thereby offering Hitler a ready-made alibi.

His sermon had been typed out and duplicated and passed from hand to hand all over Germany.

The Gestapo had arrested every person found in possession of a copy, but to no avail. It was the only time in the history of the Third Reich that there had been a public outcry against any government action.

The clampdown was savage, but it did no good: the duplicates of the sermon continued to proliferate, more clergymen prayed for the handicapped, and there was even a protest march in Akelberg. It was out of control.

And Macke was to blame.

He bent over Peter. The priest's eyes were closed and his breathing was shallow, but he was conscious. Macke shouted in his ear: "Who told you about Akelberg?"

There was no reply.

Peter was Macke's only lead. Investigations in the town of Akelberg had turned up nothing of significance. Reinhold Wagner had been told a story about two girl cyclists who had visited the hospital, but no one knew who they were, and another story about a nurse who had resigned suddenly, writing a letter saying she was getting married in haste, but not revealing who the husband was. Neither clue led anywhere. In any case, Macke felt sure this calamity could not be the work of a gaggle of girls.

Macke nodded to the technician operating the machine. He turned a knob.

Peter screamed in agony as the electrical current coursed through his body, torturing his nerves. He shook as if in a fit, and the hair on his head stood up.

The operator turned the current off.

Macke screamed: "Give me his name!"

At last Peter opened his mouth.

Macke leaned closer.

Peter whispered: "No man."

"A woman, then! Give me the name!"

"It was an angel."

"Damn you to hell!" Macke seized the knob and turned it. "This goes on until you tell me!" he yelled, as Peter shuddered and screamed.

The door opened. A young detective looked in, turned pale, and beckoned to Macke.

The technician turned the current off, and the screaming stopped. The doctor leaned forward to check Peter's heart.

The detective said: "Excuse me, Inspector Macke, but you're wanted by Superintendent Kringelein."

"Now?" said Macke irritably.

"That's what he said, sir."

Macke looked at the doctor, who shrugged. "He's young," he said. "He'll be alive when you get back."

Macke left the room and went upstairs with the detective. Kringelein's office was on the first floor. Macke knocked and went in. "The damn priest hasn't talked yet," he said without preamble. "I need more time."

Kringelein was a slight man with spectacles, clever but weak-willed. A late convert to Nazism, he was not a member of the elite SS. He lacked the fervor of enthusiasts such as Macke. "Don't bother any further with that priest," he said. "We're no longer interested in any of the clergymen. Throw them in camps and forget them."

Macke could not believe his ears. "But these people have conspired to undermine the Führer!"

"And they have succeeded," said Kringelein. "Whereas you have failed."

Macke suspected that Kringelein was privately pleased about this.

"A decision has been made at the top," the superintendent went on. "Aktion T4 has been canceled."

Macke was flabbergasted. The Nazis never allowed their decisions to be swayed by the misgivings of the ignorant. "We didn't get where we are by kowtowing to public opinion!" he said.

"We have this time."

"Why?"

"The Führer neglected to explain his decision to me personally,"

Kringelein said sarcastically. "But I can guess. The program has attracted remarkably angry protests from a normally passive public. If we persist with it, we risk an open confrontation with churches of all denominations. That would be a bad thing. We must not weaken the unity and determination of the German people—particularly right now, when we are at war with the Soviet Union, our strongest enemy yet. So the program is canceled."

"Very good, sir," said Macke, controlling his anger. "Will there be anything else?"

"Dismissed," said Kringelein.

Macke went to the door.

"Macke."

He turned. "Yes, sir."

"Change your shirt."

"My shirt?"

"There's blood on it."

"Yes, sir. Sorry, sir."

Macke stamped down the stairs, boiling. He returned to the basement chamber. Father Peter was still alive.

Raging, he yelled again: "Who told you about Akelberg?"

There was no reply.

He turned the current up to maximum.

Father Peter screamed for a long time; then, at last, he fell into a final silence.

xiii

The villa where the Franck family lived was set in a small park. Two hundred yards from the house, on a slight rise, was a little pagoda, open on all sides, with seats. As children Carla and Frieda had pretended it was their country house, and had played for hours pretending to have grand parties where dozens of servants waited on their glamorous guests. Later it became their favorite place to sit and talk where no one could hear them.

"The first time I sat on this bench, my feet didn't reach the floor," Carla said.

Frieda said: "I wish we could go back to those days."

It was a sultry afternoon, overcast and humid, and they both wore sleeveless dresses. They were in a somber mood. Father Peter was dead: he had committed suicide in custody, having become depressed about his crimes, according to the police. Carla wondered if he had been beaten as her father had. It seemed dreadfully likely.

There were dozens more in police cells all over Germany. Some had protested publicly about the killing of the handicapped; others had done no more than pass round copies of Bishop von Galen's sermon. She wondered if all of them would be tortured. She wondered how long she would escape such a fate.

Werner came out of the house with a tray. He carried it across the lawn to the pagoda. Cheerily he said: "How about some lemonade, girls?"

Carla looked away. "No, thank you," she said coldly. She did not understand how he could pretend to be her friend after the cowardice he had shown.

Frieda said: "Not for me."

"I hope we're still friends," Werner said, looking at Carla.

How could he say such a thing? Of course they were not friends.

Frieda said: "Father Peter is dead, Werner."

Carla added: "Probably tortured to death by the Gestapo, because he refused to accept the murder of people such as your brother. My father is dead, too, for the same reason. Lots of other people are in jail or in camps. But you kept your cushy desk job, so that's all right."

Werner looked hurt. That surprised Carla. She had expected defiance, or at least an effort at insouciance. But he seemed genuinely upset. He said: "Don't you think we each have our different ways of doing what we can?"

This was feeble. "You did nothing!" Carla said.

"Perhaps," he said sadly. "No lemonade, then?"

Neither girl answered, and he went back to the house.

Carla was indignant and angry, but she could not help also feeling regret. Before she discovered that Werner was a coward, she had been embarking on a romance with him. She had liked him a lot, ten times more than any other boy she had kissed. She was not quite heartbroken, but she was deeply disappointed.

Frieda was luckier. This thought was prompted by the sight of Heinrich coming out of the house. Frieda was glamorous and fun-loving, and Heinrich was brooding and intense, but somehow they made a good pair. "Are you in love with him?" Carla said while he was still out of earshot.

"I don't know yet," Frieda replied. "He's terribly sweet, though. I kind of adore him."

That might not be love, Carla thought, but it was well on the way.

Heinrich was bursting with news. "I had to come and tell you right away," he said. "My father told me after lunch."

"What?" said Frieda.

"The government has canceled the project. It was called Aktion T4. The killing of the handicapped. They're stopping."

Carla said: "You mean we won?"

Heinrich nodded vigorously. "My father is amazed. He says he has never known the Führer to give in to public opinion before."

Frieda said: "And we forced him to!"

"Thank God no one knows that," Heinrich said fervently.

Carla said: "They're just going to close the hospitals and end the whole program?"

"Not exactly."

"What do you mean?"

"My father says all those doctors and nurses are being transferred."

Carla frowned. "Where?"

"To Russia," said Heinrich.

CHAPTER NINE

1941 (II)

The phone rang on Greg Peshkov's desk on a hot morning in July. He had finished his penultimate year at Harvard and was once again interning at the State Department for the summer, working in the information office. He was good at physics and math, and passed exams effortlessly, but he had no interest in becoming a scientist. Politics was what excited him. He picked up the phone. "Greg Peshkov."

"Morning, Mr. Peshkov. This is Tom Cranmer."

Greg's heart beat a little faster. "Thank you for returning my call. You obviously remember me."

"The Ritz-Carlton hotel, 1935. Only time I ever got my picture in the paper."

"Are you still the hotel detective?"

"I moved to retail. I'm a store detective now."

"Do you ever do any freelance work?"

"Sure. What did you have in mind?"

"I'm in my office now. I'd like to talk privately."

"You work in the Old Executive Office Building, across the street from the White House."

"How did you know that?"

"I'm a detective."

"Of course."

"I'm around the corner, at Aroma Coffee on F Street and Nineteenth."

"I can't come now." Greg looked at his watch. "In fact I have to hang up right away."

"I'll wait."

"Give me an hour."

Greg hurried down the stairs. He arrived at the main entrance just as a Rolls-Royce motorcar came silently to a stop outside. An overweight chauffeur clambered out and opened the rear door. The passenger who emerged was tall, lean, and handsome, with a full head of silver hair. He wore a perfectly cut double-breasted suit of pearl gray flannel that draped him in a style only London tailors could achieve. As he ascended the granite steps to the huge building, his fat chauffeur hurried after him, carrying his briefcase.

He was Sumner Welles, under-secretary of state, number two at the State Department, and personal friend of President Roosevelt.

The chauffeur was about to hand the briefcase to a waiting State Department usher when Greg stepped forward. "Good morning, sir," he said, and he smoothly took the briefcase from the chauffeur and held the door open. Then he followed Welles into the building.

Greg had got into the information office because he was able to show factual, well-written articles he had produced for *The Harvard Crimson*. However, he did not want to end up a press attaché. He had higher ambitions.

Greg admired Sumner Welles, who reminded him of his father. The good looks, the fine clothes, and the charm concealed a ruthless operator. Welles was determined to take over from his boss, Secretary of State Cordell Hull, and never hesitated to go behind his back and speak directly to the president—which infuriated Hull. Greg found it exciting to be close to someone who had power and was not afraid to use it. That was what he wanted for himself.

Welles had taken a shine to him. People often did take a shine to

Greg, especially when he wanted them to, but in the case of Welles there was another factor. Though Welles was married—apparently happily, to an heiress—he had a fondness for attractive young men.

Greg was heterosexual to a fault. He had a steady girl at Harvard, a Radcliffe student named Emily Hardcastle, who had promised to acquire a birth control device before September, and here in Washington he was dating Rita, the voluptuous daughter of Congressman Lawrence of Texas. He walked a tightrope with Welles. He avoided all physical contact while being amiable enough to remain in favor. Also, he stayed away from Welles any time after the cocktail hour, when the older man's inhibitions weakened and his hands began to stray.

Now, as the senior staff gathered in the office for the ten o'clock meeting, Welles said: "You can stay for this, my boy. It will be good for your education." Greg was thrilled. He wondered if the meeting would give him a chance to shine. He wanted people to notice him and be impressed.

A few minutes later Senator Dewar arrived with his son Woody. Father and son were lanky and large-headed, and wore similar dark blue single-breasted linen summer suits. However, Woody differed from his father in being artistic: his photographs for *The Harvard Crimson* had won prizes. Woody nodded to Welles's senior assistant, Bexforth Ross; they must have met before. Bexforth was an excessively self-satisfied guy who called Greg "Russkie" because of his Russian name.

Welles opened the meeting by saying: "I now have to tell you all something highly confidential that must not be repeated outside this room. The president is going to meet with the British prime minister early next month."

Greg just stopped himself from saying *Wow*.

"Good!" said Gus Dewar. "Where?"

"The plan is to rendezvous by ship somewhere in the Atlantic, for security and to reduce Churchill's travel time. The president wants me to attend, while Secretary of State Hull stays here in Washington to mind the store. He also wants you there, Gus."

"I'm honored," said Gus. "What's the agenda?"

"The British seem to have beaten off the threat of invasion, for now, but they're too weak to attack the Germans on the European continent—unless we help. Therefore Churchill will ask us to declare war on Germany. We will refuse, of course. Once we've got past that, the president wants a joint statement of aims."

"Not war aims," Gus said.

"No, because the United States is not at war and has no intention of going to war. But we are nonbelligerently allied with the British, we're supplying them with just about everything they need on unlimited credit, and when peace comes at last, we expect to have a say in how the postwar world is run."

"Will that include a strengthened League of Nations?" Gus asked. He was keen on this idea, Greg knew, and so was Welles.

"That's why I wanted to talk to you, Gus. If we want our plan implemented, we need to be prepared. We have to get FDR and Churchill to commit to it as part of their statement."

Gus said: "We both know that the president is in favor, theoretically, but he's nervous about public opinion."

An aide came in and passed a note to Bexforth, who read it and said: "Oh! My goodness."

Welles said testily: "What is it?"

"The Japanese imperial council met last week, as you know," Bexforth said. "We have some intelligence on their deliberations."

He was being vague about the source of information, but Greg knew what he meant. The Signal Intelligence Service of the U.S. Army was able to intercept and decode wireless messages from the Foreign Ministry in Tokyo to its embassies abroad. The data from these decrypts was code-named MAGIC. Greg knew about this, even though he was not supposed to—in fact there would have been a hell of a stink if the army found out he was in on the secret.

"The Japanese discussed extending their empire," Bexforth went on. They had already annexed the vast region of Manchuria, Greg knew, and had moved troops into much of the rest of China. "They do not favor the option of westward expansion, into Siberia, which would mean war with the Soviet Union."

"That's good!" said Welles. "It means the Russians can concentrate on fighting the Germans."

"Yes, sir. But the Japs are planning instead to extend southward, by taking full control of Indochina, then the Dutch East Indies."

Greg was shocked. This was hot news—and he was among the first to hear it.

Welles was indignant. "Why, that's nothing less than an imperialist war!"

Gus interposed: "Technically, Sumner, it's not war. The Japanese already have some troops in Indochina, with formal permission from the incumbent colonial power, France, as represented by the Vichy government."

"Puppets of the Nazis!"

"I did say 'technically.' And the Dutch East Indies are theoretically ruled by the Netherlands, which is now occupied by the Germans, who are perfectly happy for their Japanese allies to take over a Dutch colony."

"That's a quibble."

"It's a quibble that others will raise with us—the Japanese ambassador, for one."

"You're right, Gus, and thanks for forewarning me."

Greg was alert for an opportunity to make a contribution to the discussion. He wanted above all else to impress the senior men around him. But they all knew so much more than he did.

Welles said: "What are the Japanese after, anyway?"

Gus said: "Oil, rubber, and tin. They're securing their access to natural resources. It's hardly surprising, since we keep interfering with their supplies." The United States had embargoed exports of materials such as oil and scrap iron to Japan, in a failed attempt to discourage the Japanese from taking over ever-larger tracts of Asia.

Welles said irritably: "Our embargoes have never been applied very effectively."

"No, but the threat is obviously sufficient to panic the Japanese, who have almost no natural resources of their own."

"Clearly we need to take more effective measures," Welles snapped. "The Japanese have a lot of money in American banks. Can we freeze their assets?"

The officials around the room looked disapproving. This was a radical idea. After a moment Bexforth said: "I guess we could. That would be more effective than any embargoes. They would be unable to buy oil or any other raw materials here in the States because they couldn't pay for them."

Gus Dewar said: "The secretary of state will be concerned, as usual, to avoid any action that might lead to war."

He was right. Cordell Hull was cautious to the point of timidity, and frequently clashed with his more aggressive deputy, Welles.

"Mr. Hull has always followed that course, and very wisely," said Welles. They all knew he was insincere, but etiquette required it. "However, the United States must walk tall on the international stage. We're prudent, not cowardly. I'm going to put this idea of an asset freeze to the president."

Greg was awestruck. This was what power meant. In a heartbeat, Welles could propose something that would rock an entire nation.

Gus Dewar frowned. "Without imported oil, the Japanese economy will grind to a halt, and their military will be powerless."

"Which is good!" said Welles.

"Is it? What do you imagine Japan's military government will do, faced with such a catastrophe?"

Welles did not much like to be challenged. He said: "Why don't you tell me, Senator?"

"I don't know. But I think we should have an answer before we take the action. Desperate men are dangerous. And I do know that the United States is not ready to go to war against Japan. Our navy isn't ready and our air force isn't ready."

Greg saw his chance to speak and took it. "Mr. Under-Secretary, sir, it may help you to know that public opinion favors war with Japan, rather than appeasement, by a factor of two to one."

"Good point, Greg, thank you. Americans don't want to let Japan get away with murder."

"They don't really want war, either," said Gus. "No matter what the poll says."

Welles closed the folder on his desk. "Well, Senator, we agree about the League of Nations and disagree about Japan."

Gus stood up. "And in both cases the decision will be made by the president."

"Good of you to come in to see me."

The meeting broke up.

Greg left on a high. He had been invited into the briefing, he had learned startling news, and he had made a comment that Welles had thanked him for. It was a great start to the day.

He slipped out of the building and headed for Aroma Coffee.

He had never hired a private detective before. It felt vaguely illegal. But Cranmer was a respectable citizen. And there was nothing criminal about trying to get in contact with an old girlfriend.

At Aroma Coffee there were two girls who looked like secretaries taking a break, an older couple out shopping, and Cranmer, a broad man in a rumpled seersucker suit, dragging on a cigarette. Greg slid into the booth and asked the waitress for coffee.

"I'm trying to reconnect with Jacky Jakes," he said to Cranmer.

"The black girl?"

She had been a girl, back then, Greg thought nostalgically; sweet sixteen, though she was pretending to be older. "It's six years ago," he said to Cranmer. "She's not a girl anymore."

"It was your father who hired her for that little drama, not me."

"I don't want to ask him. But you can find her, right?"

"I expect so." Cranmer took out a little notebook and a pencil. "I guess Jacky Jakes was an assumed name?"

"Mabel Jakes is her real name."

"Actress, right?"

"Would-be. I don't know that she made it." She had had good looks and charm in abundance, but there were not many parts for black actors.

"Obviously she's not in the phone book, or you wouldn't need me."

"Could be unlisted, but more likely she can't afford a phone."

"Have you seen her since 1935?"

"Twice. First time two years ago, not far from here, on E Street. Second time, two weeks ago, two blocks away."

"Well, she sure as hell doesn't live in this swanky neighborhood, so she must work nearby. You have a photo?"

"No."

"I remember her vaguely. Pretty girl, dark skin, big smile."

Greg nodded, remembering that thousand-watt smile. "I just want her address, so I can write her a letter."

"I don't need to know what you want the information for."

"Suits me." Is it really this easy? Greg thought.

"I charge ten bucks a day, with a two-day minimum, plus expenses."

It was less than Greg had expected. He took out his billfold and gave Cranmer a twenty.

"Thanks," said the detective.

"Good luck," said Greg.

ii

Saturday was hot, so Woody went to the beach with his brother, Chuck.

The whole Dewar family was in Washington. They had a nine-room apartment near the Ritz-Carlton hotel. Chuck was on leave from the navy, Papa was working twelve hours a day planning the summit meeting he referred to as the Atlantic Conference, and Mama was writing a new book, about the wives of presidents.

Woody and Chuck put on shorts and polo shirts, grabbed towels and sunglasses and newspapers, and caught a train to Rehoboth Beach, on the Delaware coast. The journey took a couple of hours, but this was the only place to go on a summer Saturday. There was a wide stretch of sand and a refreshing breeze off the Atlantic Ocean. And there were a thousand girls in swimsuits.

The two brothers were different. Chuck was shorter, with a compact, athletic figure. He had their mother's attractive looks and winning smile. He had been a poor student at school, but he also displayed Mama's quirky intelligence, always taking an off-center view of life. He was better than Woody at all sports except running, where Woody's long legs gave him speed, and boxing, in which Woody's long arms made him nearly impossible to hit.

At home, Chuck had not said much about the navy, no doubt because the parents were still angry with him for not going to Harvard. But alone with Woody he opened up a bit. "Hawaii is great, but I'm really disappointed to have a shore job," he said. "I joined the navy to go to sea."

"What are you doing, exactly?"

"I'm part of the signal intelligence unit. We listen to radio messages, mainly from the Imperial Japanese Navy."

"Aren't they in code?"

"Yes, but you can learn a lot even without breaking the codes. It's called traffic analysis. A sudden increase in the number of messages indicates that some action is imminent. And you learn to recognize patterns in the traffic. An amphibious landing has a distinctive configuration of signals, for example."

"That's fascinating. And I bet you're good at it."

Chuck shrugged. "I'm just a clerk, annotating and filing the transcripts. But you can't help picking up the basics."

"How's the social life in Hawaii?"

"Lots of fun. Navy bars can get pretty riotous. The Black Cat Café is the best. I have a good pal, Eddie Parry, and we go surfboarding on Waikiki Beach every chance we get. I've had some good times. But I wish I was on a ship."

They swam in the cold Atlantic, ate hot dogs for lunch, took photos of each other with Woody's camera, and studied the swimsuits until the sun began to go down. As they were leaving, picking their way through the crowd, Woody saw Joanne Rouzrokh.

He did not need to look twice. She was like no other girl on the beach, nor indeed in Delaware. There was no mistaking those high cheekbones, that scimitar nose, the luxuriant dark hair, the skin the color and smoothness of café au lait.

Without hesitation he walked straight toward her.

She looked absolutely sensational. Her black one-piece swimsuit had spaghetti straps that revealed the elegant bones of her shoulders. It was cut straight across her upper thighs, showing almost all of her long, brown legs.

He could hardly believe that he had once taken this fabulous woman in his arms and smooched her like there was no tomorrow.

She looked up at him, shading her eyes from the sun. "Woody Dewar! I didn't know you were in Washington."

That was all the invitation he needed. He knelt on the sand beside her. Just being this close made him breathe harder. "Hello, Joanne." He glanced briefly at the plump brown-eyed girl beside her. "Where's your husband?"

She burst out laughing. "Whatever made you think I was married?"

He was flustered. "I came to your apartment for a party, a couple of summers back."

"You did?"

Joanne's companion said: "I remember. I asked you your name, but you didn't answer."

Woody had no memory of her at all. "I'm sorry I was so impolite," he said. "I'm Woody Dewar, and this is my brother, Chuck."

The brown-eyed girl shook hands with both of them and said: "I'm Diana Taverner." Chuck sat beside her on the sand, which seemed to please her: Chuck was good-looking, much more handsome than Woody.

Woody went on. "Anyway, I went into the kitchen, looking for you, and a man called Bexforth Ross introduced himself to me as your fiancé. I assumed you'd be married by now. Is it an extraordinarily long engagement?"

"Don't be silly," she said with a touch of irritation, and he remembered that she did not respond well to teasing. "Bexforth told people we were engaged, because he was practically living at our apartment."

Woody was startled. Did that mean that Bexforth had been sleeping there? With Joanne? It was not uncommon, of course, but few girls admitted it.

"He was the one who talked about marriage," she went on. "I never agreed to it."

So she was single. Woody could not have been happier if he had won the lottery.

There might be a boyfriend, he warned himself. He would have to find out. But anyway, a boyfriend was not the same as a husband.

"I was at a meeting with Bexforth a few days back," Woody said. "He's a great man in the State Department."

"He'll go far, and he'll find a woman more suitable than I to be the wife of a great man in the State Department."

It seemed from her tone that she did not have warm feelings toward her former lover. Woody found that he was pleased about that, although he could not have said why.

He reclined on his elbow. The sand was hot. If she had a serious boyfriend, she would find a reason to mention him before too long, he felt sure. He said: "Speaking of the State Department, are you still working there?"

"Yes. I'm assistant to the under-secretary for Europe."

"Exciting."

"Right now it is."

Woody was looking at the line where her swimsuit crossed her thighs, and thinking that no matter how little a girl was wearing, a man was always thinking about the parts of her that were hidden. He began to get an erection, and rolled onto his front to conceal it.

Joanne saw the direction of his gaze and said: "You like my swimsuit?" She was always frank. It was one of the many things he found attractive about her.

He decided to be equally candid. "I like *you*, Joanne. I always did."

She laughed. "Don't beat about the bush, Woody—come right out with it!"

All around them, people were packing up. Diane said: "We'd better get going."

"We were just leaving," Woody said. "Shall we travel together?"

This was the moment for her to give him the polite brush-off. She could easily say *Oh, no, thanks. You guys go on ahead.* But instead she said: "Sure, why not?"

The girls pulled dresses over their swimsuits and threw their stuff into a couple of bags, and they all walked up the beach.

The train was crowded with trippers like them, sunburned and hungry and thirsty. Woody bought four Cokes at the station and produced them as the train pulled out. Joanne said: "You once bought me a Coke on a hot day in Buffalo. Do you remember?"

"During that demonstration. Of course I remember."

"We were just kids."

"Buying Cokes is a technique I use with beautiful women."

She laughed. "Is it successful?"

"It has never got me a single smooch."

She raised her bottle in a toast. "Well, keep trying."

He thought that was encouraging, so he said: "When we get back to the city, do you want to get a hamburger, or something, and maybe see a movie?"

This was the moment for her to say *No, thanks, I'm meeting my boyfriend.*

Diana said quickly: "I'd like that. How about you, Joanne?"

Joanne said: "Sure."

No boyfriend—and a date! Woody tried to hide his elation. "We could see *The Bride Came C.O.D.*," he said. "I hear it's pretty funny."

Joanne said: "Who's in it?"

"James Cagney and Bette Davis."

"I'd like to see that."

Diana said: "Me, too."

"That's settled, then," said Woody.

Chuck said: "How about you, Chuck? Would you like that? Oh, sure, I'd like it swell, but nice of you to ask, big brother."

It was not all that funny, but Diana giggled appreciatively.

Soon afterward, Joanne fell asleep with her head on Woody's shoulder.

Her dark hair tickled his neck, and he could feel her warm breath on his skin below the cuff of his short-sleeved shirt. He felt blissfully contented.

They parted company at Union Station, went home to change, and met up again at a Chinese restaurant downtown.

Over chow mein and beer they talked about Japan. Everyone was talking about Japan. "Those people have to be stopped," said Chuck. "They're Fascists."

"Maybe," said Woody.

"They're militaristic and aggressive, and the way they treat the Chinese is racialist. What else do they have to do to be Fascists?"

"I can answer that," said Joanne. "The difference is in their vision of the future. Real Fascists want to kill off all their enemies, then create a radically new type of society. The Japanese are doing all the same things in defense of traditional power groups, the military caste and the emperor. For the same reason, Spain is not really Fascist: Franco is murdering people for the sake of the Catholic Church and the old aristocracy, not to create a new world."

"Either way, the Japs must be stopped," said Diana.

"I see it differently," said Woody.

Joanne said: "Okay, Woody, how do you see it?"

She was seriously political, and would appreciate a thoughtful answer, he knew. "Japan is a trading nation, with no natural resources: no oil, no iron, just some forests. The only way they can make a living is by doing business. For example, they import raw cotton, weave it, and sell it to India and the Philippines. But in the Depression the two great economic empires—Britain and the USA—put up tariff walls to protect our own industries. That was the end of Japanese trade with the British Empire, including India, and the American zone, including the Philippines. It hit them pretty hard."

Diana said: "Does that give them the right to conquer the world?"

"No, but it makes them think that the only way to economic security is to have your own empire, as the British do, or at least to dominate your hemisphere, as the U.S. does. Then nobody else can close down your business. So they want the Far East to be their backyard."

Joanne agreed. "And the weakness of our policy is that every time we impose economic sanctions, to punish the Japanese for their aggression, it only reinforces their feeling that they've got to be self-sufficient."

"Maybe," said Chuck. "But they still have to be stopped."

Woody shrugged. He did not have an answer to that.

After dinner they went to the cinema. The movie was great. Then Woody and Chuck walked the girls back to their apartment. On the way, Woody took Joanne's hand. She smiled at him and squeezed his hand, and he took that for encouragement.

Outside the girls' building he took her in his arms. Out of the corner of his eye he saw Chuck do the same with Diana.

Joanne kissed Woody's lips briefly, almost chastely, then said: "The traditional good-night kiss."

"There was nothing traditional about it last time I kissed you," he said. He bent his head to kiss her again.

She put a forefinger on his chin and pushed him away.

Surely, he thought, that little peck was not all he was going to get?

"I was drunk that night," she said.

"I know." He saw what the problem was. She was afraid he was going to think she was easy. He said: "You're even more alluring when you're sober."

She looked thoughtful for a moment. "That was the right thing to say," she said eventually. "You win the prize." Then she kissed him again, softly, lingering, not with the urgency of passion but with a concentration that suggested tenderness.

All too soon he heard Chuck sing out: "Good night, Diana!"

Joanne broke the kiss with Woody.

Woody said in dismay: "My brother was a bit quick!"

She laughed softly. "Good night, Woody," she said; then she turned and walked to the building.

Diana was already at the door, looking distinctly disappointed.

Woody blurted out: "Can we have another date?" He sounded needy, even to himself, and he cursed his haste.

But Joanne did not seem to mind. "Call me," she said, and went inside.

Woody watched until the two girls disappeared; then he rounded on his brother. "Why didn't you kiss Diana longer?" he said crossly. "She seems really nice."

"Not my type," said Chuck.

"Really?" Woody was more mystified than annoyed. "Nice round tits, pretty face—what's not to like? I'd have kissed her, if I wasn't with Joanne."

"We all have different tastes."

They started to walk back toward their parents' apartment. "Well, what is your type, then?" Woody asked Chuck.

"There's something I should probably explain to you, before you plan any more double dates."

"Okay, what?"

Chuck stopped, forcing Woody to do the same. "You have to swear never to tell Papa and Mama."

"I swear." Woody studied his brother in the yellow light of the streetlamps. "What's the big secret?"

"I don't like girls."

"A pain in the ass, I agree, but what are you going to do?"

"I mean, I don't like to hug and kiss them."

"What? Don't be stupid."

"We're all made differently, Woody."

"Yeah, but you'd have to be some kind of pansy."

"Yes."

"Yes, what?"

"Yes, I'm some kind of pansy."

"You're such a kidder."

"I'm not kidding, Woody. I'm dead serious."

"You're *queer*?"

"That's exactly what I am. I didn't choose to be. When we were kids, and we started jerking off, you used to think about bouncy tits and hairy cunts. I never told you that I used to think about big stiff cocks."

"Chuck, this is disgusting!"

"No, it's not. It's the way some guys are made. More guys than you think—especially in the navy."

"There are pansies in the navy?"

Chuck nodded vigorously. "A lot."

"Well . . . how do you know?"

"We usually recognize one another. Like Jews always know who's Jewish. For example, the waiter in the Chinese restaurant."

"He was one?"

"Didn't you hear him say he liked my jacket?"

"Yes, but I didn't think anything of it."

"There you are."

"He was attracted to you?"

"I guess."

"Why?"

"Same reason Diana liked me, probably. Hell, I'm better-looking than you."

"This is weird."

"Come on, let's go home."

They continued on their way. Woody was still reeling. "You mean there are Chinese pansies?"

Chuck laughed. "Of course!"

"I don't know. You never think of Chinese guys being that way."

"Remember, not a word to anyone, especially the parents. God knows what Papa would say."

After a while, Woody put his arm around Chuck's shoulders. "Well, what the hell," he said. "At least you're not a Republican."

iii

Greg Peshkov sailed with Sumner Welles and President Roosevelt on a heavy cruiser, the *Augusta,* to Placentia Bay, off the coast of Newfoundland. Also in the convoy were the battleship *Arkansas,* the cruiser *Tuscaloosa,* and seventeen destroyers.

They anchored in two long lines, with a broad sea passage down the middle. At nine o'clock in the morning of Saturday, August 9, in bright sunshine, the crews of all twenty vessels mustered at the rails in their dress whites as the British battleship *Prince of Wales* arrived, escorted by three destroyers, and steamed majestically down the middle, bearing Prime Minister Churchill.

It was the most impressive show of power Greg had ever seen, and he was delighted to be part of it.

He was also worried. He hoped the Germans did not know about this rendezvous. If they found out, one U-boat could kill the two leaders of what remained of Western civilization—and Greg Peshkov.

Before leaving Washington Greg had met with the detective, Tom Cranmer, again. Cranmer had produced an address, a house in a low-rent neighborhood on the far side of Union Station. "She's a waitress at the University Women's Club near the Ritz-Carlton, which is why you saw her in that neighborhood twice," he had said as he pocketed the balance of his fee. "I guess acting didn't work out for her—but she still goes by Jacky Jakes."

Greg had written her a letter.

> Dear Jacky,
> I just want to know why you ran out on me six years ago. I thought we were so happy, but I must have been wrong. It bugs me, that's all.
> You act scared when you see me, but there's nothing to be afraid of. I'm not angry, just curious. I would never do anything to hurt you. You were the first girl I ever loved.
> Can we meet, just for a cup of coffee or something, and talk?
>
> Very sincerely,
Greg Peshkov

He had added his phone number and mailed the note the day he left for Newfoundland.

The president was keen that the conference should result in a joint statement. Greg's boss, Sumner Welles, wrote a draft, but Roosevelt refused to use it, saying it was better to let Churchill produce the first draft.

Greg immediately saw that Roosevelt was a smart negotiator. Whoever produced the first draft would need, in all fairness, to put in some of what the other side wanted alongside his own demands. His statement of the other side's wishes then became an irreducible minimum, while all of his own demands were still up for negotiation. So the drafter always started at a disadvantage. Greg vowed to remember never to write the first draft.

On Saturday the president and the prime minister enjoyed a convivial lunch on board the *Augusta*. On Sunday they attended a church service on the deck of the *Prince of Wales*, with the Stars and Stripes and the Union Jack draping the altar red, white, and blue. On Monday morning, by which time they were firm friends, they got down to brass tacks.

Churchill produced a five-point plan that delighted Sumner Welles and Gus Dewar by calling for an effective international organization to assure the security of all states—in other words, a strengthened League of Nations. But they were disappointed to find that that was too much for Roosevelt. He was in favor, but he feared the isolationists, people who still believed America did not need to get involved with the troubles of the rest of the world. He was extraordinarily sensitive to public opinion, and made ceaseless efforts not to provoke opposition.

Welles and Dewar did not give up, nor did the British. They got together to seek a compromise acceptable to both leaders. Greg took notes for Welles. The group came up with a clause that called for disarmament "pending the establishment of a wider and more permanent system of general security."

They put it to the two great men, who accepted it.

Welles and Dewar were jubilant.

Greg could not see why. "It seems so little," he said. "All that effort— the leaders of two great countries brought together across thousands of miles, dozens of staffers, twenty-four ships, three days of talks—and all for a few words that don't quite say what we want."

"We move by inches, not miles," said Gus Dewar with a smile. "That's politics."

iv

Woody and Joanne had been dating for five weeks.

Woody wanted to go out with her every night, but he held back. Nevertheless, he had seen her on four of the last seven days. Sunday they had gone to the beach; Wednesday they had dinner; Friday they saw a movie; and today, Saturday, they were spending the whole day together.

He never tired of talking to her. She was funny and intelligent and sharp-tongued. He loved the way she was so definite about everything. They jawed for hours about the things they liked and hated.

The news from Europe was bad. The Germans were still thrashing the Red Army. East of Smolensk they had wiped out the Russian Sixteenth and Twentieth Armies, taking three hundred thousand prisoners, leaving few Soviet forces between the Germans and Moscow. But bad news from afar could not dampen Woody's elation.

Joanne probably was not as crazy about him as he was about her. But she was fond of him, he could tell. They always kissed good night, and she seemed to enjoy it, though she did not show the kind of passion he knew she was capable of. Perhaps it was because they always had to kiss in public places, such as the cinema, or a doorway on the street near her building. When they were in her apartment, there was always at least one of her two roommates in the living room, and she had not yet invited him to her bedroom.

Chuck's leave had ended weeks ago, and he was back in Hawaii. Woody still did not know what to think about Chuck's confession. Sometimes he felt as shocked as if the world had turned upside down;

other times he asked himself what difference it made to anything. But he kept his promise not to tell anyone, not even Joanne.

Then Woody's father went off with the president, and his mother went to Buffalo to spend a few days with her parents. So Woody had the Washington apartment—all nine rooms—to himself for a few days. He decided he would look out for an opportunity to invite Joanne Rouzrokh there, in the hope of getting a real kiss.

They had lunch together and went to an exhibition called "Negro Art," which had been attacked by conservative writers who said there was no such thing as Negro art—despite the unmistakable genius of such people as the painter Jacob Lawrence and the sculptor Elizabeth Catlett.

As they left the exhibition, Woody said: "Would you like to have cocktails while we decide where to go for dinner?"

"No, thanks," she said in her usual decisive manner. "I'd really like a cup of tea."

"Tea?" He was not sure where you could get good tea in Washington. Then he had a brainwave. "My mother has English tea," he said. "We could go to the apartment."

"Okay."

The building was a few blocks away on Twenty-second Street NW, near L Street. They breathed easier as they stepped out of the summer heat into the air-conditioned lobby. A porter took them up in the elevator.

As they entered the apartment, Joanne said: "I see your papa around Washington all the time, but I haven't talked to your mama for years. I must congratulate her on her bestseller."

"She's not here right now," Woody said. "Come into the kitchen."

He filled the kettle from the tap and put it on the heat. Then he put his arms around Joanne and said: "Alone at last."

"Where are your parents?"

"Out of town, both of them."

"And Chuck is in Hawaii."

"Yes."

She moved away from him. "Woody, how could you do this to me?"

"Do what? I'm making you tea!"

"You've got me up here on false pretenses! I thought your parents were at home."

"I never said that."

"Why didn't you tell me they were away?"

"You didn't ask!" he said indignantly, though there was a grain of truth in her complaint. He would not have lied to her, but he had been hoping he would not have to tell her in advance that the apartment was empty.

"You got me up here to make a pass! You think I'm a cheap broad."

"I do not! It's just that we're never really private. I was hoping for a kiss, that's all."

"Don't try to kid me."

Now she really was being unjust. Yes, he hoped to go to bed with her one day, but no, he had not expected to do so today. "We'll go," he said. "We'll get tea somewhere else. The Ritz-Carlton is right down the street. All the British stay there—they must have tea."

"Oh, don't be stupid. We don't need to leave. I'm not afraid of you. I can fight you off. I'm just mad at you. I don't want a man who goes out with me because he thinks I'm easy."

"Easy?" he said, his voice rising. "Hell! I've waited six years for you to condescend to go out with me. Even now, all I'm asking for is a kiss. If you're easy, I'd hate to be in love with a girl who's difficult!"

To his astonishment, she started to laugh.

"Now what?" he said irritably.

"I'm sorry—you're right," she said. "If you wanted a girl who was easy, you would have given up on me long ago."

"Exactly!"

"After I kissed you like that when I was drunk, I thought you must have a low opinion of me. I assumed you were chasing me for a cheap thrill. I've even been worrying about that in the last few weeks. I misjudged you. I'm sorry."

He was bewildered by her rapid changes of mood, but he figured this latest phase was an improvement. "I was crazy about you even before that kiss," he said. "I guess you didn't notice."

"I hardly noticed *you*."

"I'm pretty tall."

"It's your only attractive feature, physically."

He smiled. "I won't get swollen-headed talking to you, will I?"

"Not if I can help it."

The kettle boiled. He put tea in a china pot and poured water on top. Joanne looked thoughtful. "You said something else a minute ago."

"What?"

"You said: 'I'd hate to be in love with a girl who's difficult.' Did you mean it?"

"Did I mean what?"

"The part about being in love."

"Oh! I didn't intend to say that." He threw caution to the wind. "But hell, yes, if you want to know the truth, I'm in love with you. I think I've loved you for years. I adore you. I want—"

She put her arms around his neck and kissed him.

This time it was the real thing, her mouth moving urgently against his, the tip of her tongue touching his lips, her body pressing against his. It was like 1935 except that she did not taste of whisky. This was the girl he loved, the real Joanne, he thought ecstatically: a woman of strong passions. And she was in his arms and kissing him for all she was worth.

She pushed her hands up inside his summer sports shirt and rubbed his chest, pressing her fingers into his ribs, grazing his nipples with her palms, grasping his shoulders, as if she wanted to sink her hands deep into his flesh. He realized that she, too, had a store of frustrated desire that was now overflowing like a busted dam, out of control. He did the same to her, stroking her sides and grasping her breasts, with a feeling of happy liberation, like a child let out of school for an unexpected holiday.

When he pressed his eager hand between her thighs, she pulled away.

But what she said surprised him. "Have you got any birth control?"

"No! I'm sorry—"

"It's okay. In fact it's good. It proves you really didn't plan to seduce me."

"I wish I had."

"Never mind. I know a woman doctor who'll fix me up on Monday. Meanwhile we'll improvise. Kiss me again."

As he did so, he felt her unbuttoning his pants.

"Oh," she said a moment later. "How nice."

"That's just what I was thinking," he whispered.

"I may need two hands, though."

"What?"

"I guess it goes with being so tall."

"I don't know what you're talking about."

"Then I'll shut up and kiss you."

A few minutes later she said: "Handkerchief."

Fortunately he had one.

He opened his eyes, a few moments before the end, and saw her looking at him. In her expression he read desire and excitement and something else that he thought might even be love.

When it was over, he felt blissfully calm. I love her, he thought, and I'm happy. How good life is. "That was wonderful," he said. "I'd like to do the same for you."

"Would you?" she said. "Really?"

"You bet."

They were still standing, there in the kitchen, leaning against the door of the refrigerator, but neither of them wanted to move. She took his hand and guided it under her summer dress and inside her cotton underwear. He felt hot skin, crisp hair, and a wet cleft. He tried to push his finger inside, but she said: "No." Grasping his fingertip, she guided it between the soft folds. He felt something small and hard, the size of a pea, just under the skin. She moved his finger in a little circle. "Yes," she said, closing her eyes. "Just like that." He watched her face adoringly as she abandoned herself to the sensation. In a minute or two she gave a little cry, and repeated it two or three times. Then she withdrew his hand and slumped against him.

After a while he said: "Your tea will be cold."

She laughed. "I love you, Woody."

"Do you really?"

"I hope you're not spooked by me saying that."

"No." He smiled. "It makes me very happy."

"I know girls aren't supposed to come right out with it, just like that. But I can't pretend to dither. Once I make up my mind, that's it."

"Yes," said Woody. "I'd noticed that."

v

Greg Peshkov was living in his father's permanent apartment at the Ritz-Carlton. Lev came and went, stopping off for a few days between Buffalo and Los Angeles. At present Greg had the place to himself—except that the congressman's curvy daughter, Rita Lawrence, had stayed overnight, and now looked adorably tousled in a man's red silk dressing gown.

A waiter brought them breakfast, the newspapers, and a message envelope.

The joint statement by Roosevelt and Churchill had caused more of a stir than Greg expected. It was still the main news more than a week later. The press called it the Atlantic Charter. It had seemed, to Greg, to be all cautious phrases and vague commitments, but the world saw it otherwise. It was hailed as a trumpet blast for freedom, democracy, and world trade. Hitler was reported to be furious, saying it amounted to a declaration of war by the United States against Germany.

Countries that had not been at the conference nevertheless wanted to sign the charter, and Bexforth Ross had suggested the signatories should be called the United Nations.

Meanwhile the Germans were overrunning the Soviet Union. In the north they were closing in on Leningrad. In the south the retreating Russians had blown up the Dnieper Dam, the biggest hydroelectric power complex in the world and their pride and joy, in order to deny its power to the conquering Germans—a heartbreaking sacrifice. "The Red Army has slowed the invasion a bit," Greg said to Rita, reading from *The Washington Post*. "But the Germans are still advancing five miles a day. And they claim to have killed three and a half million Soviet soldiers. Is it possible?"

"Do you have any relatives in Russia?"

"As a matter of fact, I do. My father told me, one time when he was a little drunk, that he left a pregnant girl behind."

Rita made a disapproving face.

"That's him, I'm afraid," Greg said. "He's a great man, and great men don't obey the rules."

She said nothing, but he could read her expression. She disagreed with his view, but was not willing to quarrel with him about it.

"Anyway, I have a Russian half brother, illegitimate like me," Greg went on. "His name is Vladimir, but I don't know anything else about him. He may be dead by now. He's the right age to fight. He's probably one of those three and a half million." He turned the page.

When he had finished the paper, he read the message the waiter had brought.

It was from Jacky Jakes. It gave a phone number and just said *Not between 1 and 3.*

Suddenly Greg could not wait to get rid of Rita. "What time are you expected home?" he asked unsubtly.

She looked at her watch. "Oh, my gosh, I should be there before my mother starts looking for me." She had told her parents she was staying over with a girlfriend.

They got dressed together and left in two cabs.

Greg figured the phone number must be Jacky's place of work, and she would be busy between one o'clock and three. He would phone her around midmorning.

He wondered why he was so excited. After all, he was only curious.

Rita Lawrence was great-looking and very sexy, but with her and several others he had never recaptured the excitement of that first affair with Jacky. No doubt that was because he could never again be fifteen years old.

He got to the Old Executive Office Building and began his main task for the day, which was drafting a press release on advice to Americans living in North Africa, where British, Italians, and Germans fought backward and forward, mostly on a coastal strip two thousand miles long and forty miles wide.

At ten thirty he phoned the number on the message.

A woman's voice answered: "University Women's Club." Greg had never been there: men went only as guests of female members.

He said: "Is Jacky Jakes there?"

"Yes, she's expecting a call. Please hold on." She probably had to get special permission to receive a phone call at work, he reflected.

A few moments later he heard: "This is Jacky. Who's that?"

"Greg Peshkov."

"I thought so. How did you get my address?"

"I hired a private detective. Can we meet?"

"I guess we have to. But there's one condition."

"What?"

"You have to swear by all that's holy not to tell your father. Never, ever."

"Why?"

"I'll explain later."

He shrugged. "Okay."

"Do you swear?"

"Sure."

She persisted. "Say it."

"I swear it, okay?"

"All right. You can buy me lunch."

Greg frowned. "Are there any restaurants in this neighborhood that will serve a white man and a black woman together?"

"Only one that I know of—the Electric Diner."

"I've seen it." He had noticed the name, but he had never been inside: it was a cheap lunch counter used by janitors and messengers. "What time?"

"Half past eleven."

"So early?"

"What time do you think waitresses have lunch—one o'clock?"

He grinned. "You're as sassy as ever."

She hung up.

Greg finished his press release and took the typed sheets into his boss's office. Dropping the draft into the in-tray, he said: "Would it be convenient for me to take an early lunch, Mike? Around eleven thirty?"

Mike was reading *The New York Times.* "Yeah, no problem," he said without looking up.

Greg walked past the White House in the sunshine and reached the diner at eleven twenty. It was empty but for a handful of people taking a midmorning break. He sat in a booth and ordered coffee.

He wondered what Jacky would have to say. He looked forward to the solution of a puzzle that had mystified him for six years.

She arrived at eleven thirty-five, wearing a black dress and flat shoes—her waitress uniform without the apron, he presumed. Black suited her, and he remembered vividly the sheer pleasure of looking at her, with her bow-shaped mouth and her big brown eyes. She sat opposite him and ordered a salad and a Coke. Greg had more coffee; he was too tense to eat.

Her face had lost the childish plumpness he remembered. She had been sixteen when they met, so she was twenty-two now. They had been kids playing at being grown up; now they really were adults. In her face he read a story that had not been there six years ago: disappointment and suffering and hardship.

"I work the day shift," she told him. "Come in at nine, set the tables, dress the room. Wait at lunch, clear away, leave at five."

"Most waitresses work in the evening."

"I like to have evenings and weekends free."

"Still a party girl!"

"No, mostly I stay home and listen to the radio."

"I guess you have lots of boyfriends."

"All I want."

It took him a moment to realize that could mean anything.

Her lunch came. She drank her Coke and picked at the salad.

Greg said: "So why did you run out, back in 1935?"

She sighed. "I don't want to tell you this, because you're not going to like it."

"I have to know."

"I got a visit from your father."

Greg nodded. "I figured he must have something to do with it."

"He had a goon with him—Joe something."

"Joe Brekhunov. He's a thug." Greg began to feel angry. "Did he hurt you?"

"He didn't need to, Greg. I was scared to death just looking at him. I was ready to do anything your father wanted."

Greg suppressed his fury. "What did he want?"

"He said I had to leave, right then. I could write you a note but he would read it. I had to come back here to Washington. I was so sad to leave you."

Greg remembered his own anguish. "Me, too," he said. He was tempted to reach across the table and take her hand, but he was not sure she would want that.

She went on: "He said he would give me a weekly allowance just to keep away from you. He's still paying me. It's only a few bucks but it takes care of the rent. I promised—but somehow I managed to summon up the nerve to make one condition."

"What?"

"That he would never make a pass at me. If he did, I would tell you everything."

"And he agreed?"

"Yes."

"Not many people get away with threatening him."

She pushed her plate away. "Then he said if I broke my word, Joe would cut my face. Joe showed me his straight razor."

It all fell into place. "That's why you're still scared."

Her dark skin was bloodless with fear. "You bet your goddamn life."

Greg's voice fell to a whisper. "Jacky, I'm sorry."

She forced a smile. "Are you sure he was so wrong? You were fifteen. It's not a good age to get married."

"If he had said that to me, it might be different. But he decides what's going to happen and just does it, as if no one else is entitled to an opinion."

"Still, we had good times."

"You bet."

"I was your gift."

He laughed. "Best present I ever got."

"So what are you doing these days?"

"Working in the press office at the State Department for the summer."

She made a face. "Sounds boring."

"It's the opposite! It's so exciting to watch powerful men make earth-shaking decisions, just sitting there at their desks. They run the world!"

She looked skeptical, but said: "Well, it probably beats waitressing."

He began to see how far apart they had moved. "In September I'm going back to Harvard for my last year."

"I bet you're a gift to the coeds."

"There are lots of men and not many girls."

"You do all right, though, don't you?"

"I can't lie to you." He wondered whether Emily Hardcastle had kept her promise and got herself fitted with a contraceptive device.

"You'll marry one of them and have beautiful children and live in a house on the edge of a lake."

"I'd like to be something in politics, maybe secretary of state, or a senator like Woody Dewar's father."

She looked away.

Greg thought about that house on the edge of a lake. It must be her dream. He felt sad for her.

"You'll make it," she said. "I know. You have that air about you. Even when you were fifteen, you had it. You're like your father."

"What? Come on!"

She shrugged. "Think about it, Greg. You knew I didn't want to see you. But you set a private dick on me. 'He decides what's going to happen and just does it, as if no one else is entitled to an opinion.' That's what you said about him a minute ago."

Greg was dismayed. "I hope I'm not completely like him."

She gave him an appraising look. "The jury's still out."

The waitress took her plate. "Some dessert?" she said. "Peach pie's good."

Neither of them wanted dessert, so the waitress gave Greg the check.

Jacky said: "I hope I've satisfied your curiosity."

"Thank you, I appreciate it."

"Next time you see me on the street, just walk on by."

"If that's what you want."

She stood up. "Let's leave separately. I'd feel more comfortable."

"Whatever you say."

"Good luck, Greg."

"Good luck to you."

"Tip the waitress," she said, and she walked away.

CHAPTER TEN

1941 (III)

I n October the snow fell and melted, and the streets of Moscow were cold and wet. Volodya was searching in the store cupboard for his *valenki,* the traditional felt boots that warmed the feet of Muscovites in winter, when he was astonished to see six cases of vodka.

His parents were not great drinkers. They rarely took more than one small glass. Now and again his father went to one of Stalin's long, boozy dinners with old comrades, and staggered in through the door in the early hours of the morning as drunk as a skunk. But in this house a bottle of vodka lasted a month or more.

Volodya went into the kitchen. His parents were having breakfast, canned sardines with black bread and tea. "Father," he said, "why do we have six years' supply of vodka in the store cupboard?"

His father looked surprised.

Both men looked at Katerina, who blushed. Then she switched on the radio and turned the volume down to a low mutter. Did she suspect their apartment had concealed listening devices? Volodya wondered.

She spoke quietly but angrily. "What are you going to use for money when the Germans get here?" she said. "We won't belong to the privileged elite any longer. We'll starve unless we can buy food on the black market. I'm too damn old to sell my body. Vodka will be better than gold."

Volodya was shocked to hear his mother talking this way.

"The Germans aren't going to get here," his father said.

Volodya was not so sure. They were advancing again, closing the jaws of a pincer around Moscow. They had reached Kalinin in the north and Kaluga to the south, both cities only about a hundred miles away. Soviet casualties were unimaginably high. A month ago eight hundred thousand Red Army troops had held the line, but only ninety thousand were left, according to the estimates reaching Volodya's desk. He said to his father: "Who the hell is going to stop them?"

"Their supply lines are stretched. They're unprepared for our winter weather. We will counterattack when they're weakened."

"So why are you moving the government out of Moscow?"

The bureaucracy was in the process of being transported two thousand miles east, to the city of Kuibyshev. The citizens of the capital had been unnerved by the sight of government clerks carrying boxes of files out of their office buildings and packing them into trucks.

"That's just a precaution," Grigori said. "Stalin is still here."

"There is a solution," Volodya argued. "We have hundreds of thousands of men in Siberia. We need them here as reinforcements."

Grigori shook his head. "We can't leave the east undefended. Japan is still a threat."

"Japan is not going to attack us—we know that!" Volodya glanced at his mother. He knew he should not talk about secret intelligence in front of her, but he did anyway. "The Tokyo source that warned us— correctly—that the Germans were about to invade has now told us the Japanese will not. Surely we're not going to disbelieve him again!"

"Evaluating intelligence is never easy."

"We don't have a choice!" Volodya said angrily. "We have twelve armies in reserve—a million men. If we deploy them, Moscow might survive. If we don't, we're finished."

Grigori looked troubled. "Don't speak like that, even in private."

"Why not? I'll probably be dead soon anyway."

His mother started to cry.

His father said: "Now look what you've done."

Volodya left the room. Putting on his boots, he asked himself why he had shouted at his father and made his mother cry. He saw that it was because he now believed that Germany would defeat the Soviet Union. His mother's stash of vodka to be used as currency during a Nazi occupation had forced him to confront the reality. We're going to lose, he said to himself. The end of the Russian Revolution is in sight.

He put on his coat and hat. Then he returned to the kitchen. He kissed his mother and embraced his father.

"What's this for?" said his father. "You're only going to work."

"It's just in case we never meet again," Volodya said. Then he went out.

When he crossed the bridge into the city center, he found that all public transport had stopped. The metro was closed and there were no buses or trams.

It seemed there was nothing but bad news.

This morning's bulletin from SovInformBuro, broadcast on the radio and from black-painted loudspeaker posts on street corners, had been uncharacteristically honest. "During the night of October 14 to 15, the position on the western front became worse," it had said. "Large numbers of German tanks broke through our defenses." Everyone knew that SovInformBuro always lied, so they assumed the real situation was even worse.

The city center was clogged with refugees. They were pouring in from the west, with their possessions in handcarts, driving herds of skinny cows and filthy pigs and wet sheep through the streets, heading for the countryside east of Moscow, desperate to get as far away as possible from the advancing Germans.

Volodya tried to hitch a lift. There was not much civilian traffic in Moscow these days. Fuel was being saved for the endless military convoys driving around the Garden Ring orbital road. He was picked up by a new GAZ-64 jeep.

Looking from the open vehicle, he saw a good deal of bomb damage.

Diplomats returning from England said this was nothing by comparison with the London Blitz, but Muscovites thought it was bad enough. Volodya passed several wrecked buildings and dozens of burned-out wooden houses.

Grigori, in charge of air raid defense, had mounted antiaircraft guns on the tops of the tallest buildings, and launched barrage balloons to float below the snow clouds. His most bizarre decision had been to order the golden onion domes of the churches to be painted in camouflage green and brown. He had admitted to Volodya that this would make no difference to the accuracy—or otherwise—of the bombing but, he said, it gave citizens the feeling that they were being protected.

If the Germans won, and the Nazis ruled Moscow, then Volodya's nephew and niece, the twin children of his sister, Anya, would be brought up not as patriotic Communists but as slavish Nazis, saluting Hitler. Russia would be like France, a country in servitude, perhaps partly ruled by an obedient pro-Fascist government that would round up Jews to be sent to concentration camps. It hardly bore thinking about. Volodya wanted a future in which the Soviet Union could free itself from the malign rule of Stalin and the brutality of the secret police and begin to build true Communism.

When Volodya reached the headquarters building at the Khodynka airfield, he found the air full of grayish flakes that were not snow but ash. Red Army Intelligence was burning its records to prevent their falling into enemy hands.

Shortly after he arrived, Colonel Lemitov came into his office. "You sent a memo to London about a German physicist called Wilhelm Frunze. That was a very smart move. It turned out to be a great lead. Well done."

What does it matter? Volodya thought. The Panzers were only a hundred miles away. It was too late for spies to help. But he forced himself to concentrate. "Frunze, yes. I was at school with him in Berlin."

"London contacted him and he is willing to talk. They met at a safe house." As Lemitov talked, he fiddled with his wristwatch. It was unusual for him to fidget. He was clearly tense. Everyone was tense.

Volodya said nothing. Obviously some information had come out of the meeting; otherwise Lemitov would not be talking about it.

"London says that Frunze was wary at first, and suspected our man of belonging to the British secret police," Lemitov said with a smile. "In fact, after the initial meeting he went to Kensington Palace Gardens and knocked on the door of our embassy and demanded confirmation that our man was genuine!"

Volodya smiled. "A real amateur."

"Exactly," said Lemitov. "A disinformation decoy wouldn't do anything so stupid."

The Soviet Union was not finished yet, not quite, so Volodya had to carry on as if Willi Frunze mattered. "What did he give us, sir?"

"He says he and his fellow scientists are collaborating with the Americans to make a superbomb."

Volodya, startled, recalled what Zoya Vorotsyntsev had told him. This confirmed her worst fears.

Lemitov went on. "There's a problem with the information."

"What?"

"We've translated it, but we still can't understand a word." Lemitov handed Volodya a sheaf of typewritten sheets.

Volodya read a heading aloud. "Isotope separation by gaseous diffusion."

"You see what I mean."

"I did languages at university, not physics."

"But you once mentioned a physicist you know." Lemitov smiled. "A gorgeous blonde who declined to go to a movie with you, if I remember."

Volodya blushed. He had told Kamen about Zoya, and Kamen must have repeated the gossip. The trouble with having a spy for a boss was that he knew everything. "She's a family friend. She told me about an explosive process called fission. Do you want me to question her?"

"Unofficially and informally. I don't want to make a big thing of this until I understand it. Frunze may be a crackpot, and he could make us look foolish. Find out what the reports are about, and whether Frunze is making scientific sense. If he's genuine, can the British and Americans really make a superbomb? And the Germans, too?"

"I haven't seen Zoya for two or three months."

Lemitov shrugged. It did not really matter how well Volodya knew Zoya. In the Soviet Union, answering questions put by the authorities was never optional.

"I'll track her down."

Lemitov nodded. "Do it today." He went out.

Volodya frowned thoughtfully. Zoya was sure the Americans were making a superbomb, and she had been convincing enough to persuade Grigori to mention it to Stalin, but Stalin had scorned the idea. Now a spy in England was saying what Zoya had said. It looked as if she had been right. And Stalin had been wrong—again.

The leaders of the Soviet Union had a dangerous tendency to deny the truth of bad news. Only last week, an air reconnaissance mission had spotted German armored vehicles just eighty miles from Moscow. The General Staff had refused to believe it until the sighting had been confirmed twice. Then they had ordered the reporting air officer to be arrested and tortured by the NKVD for "provocation."

It was difficult to think long-term when the Germans were so close, but the possibility of a bomb that could flatten Moscow could not be disregarded, even at this moment of extreme peril. If the Soviets beat the Germans, they might afterward be attacked by Britain and America: something similar had happened after the 1914–18 war. Would the USSR find itself helpless against a capitalist-imperialist superbomb?

Volodya detailed his assistant, Lieutenant Belov, to find out where Zoya was.

While waiting for the address Volodya studied Frunze's reports, in the original English and in translation, memorizing what seemed to be key phrases, as he could not take the papers out of the building. At the end of an hour he understood enough to ask further questions.

Belov discovered that Zoya was not at the university nor at the nearby apartment building for scientists. However, the building administrator told him that all the younger residents had been requested to help with the construction of new inner defenses for the city, and gave him the location where Zoya was working.

Volodya put on his coat and went out.

He felt excited, but he was not sure whether that was on account of Zoya or the superbomb. Maybe both.

He was able to get an army ZIS and driver.

Passing the Kazan station—for trains to the east—he saw what looked like a full-blown riot. It seemed that people could not get into the station, let alone board the trains. Affluent men and women were struggling to reach the entrance doors with their children and pets and suitcases and trunks. Volodya was shocked to see some of them punching and kicking one another shamelessly. A few policemen looked on, helpless: it would have taken an army to impose order.

Military drivers were normally taciturn, but this one was moved to comment. "Fucking cowards," he said. "Running away, leaving us to fight the Nazis. Look at them, in their fur fucking coats."

Volodya was surprised. Criticism of the ruling elite was dangerous. Such remarks could cause a man to be denounced. Then he would spend a week or two in the basement of the NKVD's headquarters in Lubyanka Square. He might come out crippled for life.

Volodya had an unnerving sense that the rigid system of hierarchy and deference that sustained Soviet Communism was beginning to weaken and disintegrate.

They found the barricade party just where the building administrator had predicted. Volodya got out of the car, told the driver to wait, and studied the work.

A main road was strewn with antitank "hedgehogs." A hedgehog consisted of three pieces of steel railway track, each a yard long, welded together at their centers, forming an asterisk that stood on three feet and stuck three arms up. Apparently they wreaked havoc with caterpillar tracks.

Behind the hedgehog field an antitank ditch was being dug with pickaxes and shovels, and beyond that a sandbag wall was going up, with gaps for defenders to shoot through. A narrow zigzag path had been left between the obstacles so that the road could continue to be used by Muscovites until the Germans arrived.

Almost all the workers digging and building were women.

Volodya found Zoya beside a sand mountain, filling sacks with a shovel. For a minute he watched her from a distance. She wore a dirty coat, woolen mittens, and felt boots. Her blond hair was pulled back and covered with a colorless rag tied under her chin. Her face was smeared with mud, but she still looked sexy. She wielded the shovel in a steady rhythm, working efficiently. Then the supervisor blew a whistle and work stopped.

Zoya sat on a stack of sandbags and took from her coat pocket a small packet wrapped in newspaper. Volodya sat beside her and said: "You could have got exemption from this work."

"It's my city," she said. "Why wouldn't I help to defend it?"

"So you're not fleeing to the east."

"I'm not running away from the motherfucking Nazis."

Her vehemence surprised him. "Plenty of people are."

"I know. I thought you'd be long gone."

"You have a low opinion of me. You think I belong to a selfish elite."

She shrugged. "Those who are able to save themselves generally do."

"Well, you're wrong. All my family are still here in Moscow."

"Perhaps I misjudged you. Would you like a pancake?" She opened her packet to reveal four pale-colored patties wrapped in cabbage leaves. "Try one."

He accepted and took a bite. It was not very tasty. "What is it?"

"Potato peelings. You can get a bucketful free at the back door of any party canteen or officers' mess. You mince them small in the kitchen grinder, boil them until they're soft, mix them with a little flour and milk, add salt if you've got any, and fry them in lard."

"I didn't know you were so badly off," he said, feeling embarrassed. "You can always get a meal at our place, you know."

"Thank you. What brings you here?"

"A question. What is isotope separation by gaseous diffusion?"

She stared at him. "Oh, my God—what's happened?"

"Nothing has happened. I'm simply trying to evaluate some dubious information."

"Are we building a fission bomb at last?"

Her reaction told him that the information from Frunze was

probably sound. She had immediately understood the significance of what he said. "Please answer the question," Volodya said sternly. "Even though we're friends, this is official business."

"Okay. Do you know what an isotope is?"

"No."

"Some elements exist in slightly different forms. Carbon atoms, for example, always have six protons, but some have six neutrons and others have seven or eight. The different types are isotopes, called carbon-12, carbon-13, and carbon-14."

"Simple enough, even for a student of languages," Volodya said. "Why is it important?"

"Uranium has two isotopes, U-235 and U-238. In natural uranium the two are mixed up. But only U-235 is explosive."

"So we need to separate them."

"Gaseous diffusion would be one way, theoretically. When a gas is diffused through a membrane, the lighter molecules pass through faster, so the emerging gas is richer in the lower isotope. Of course I've never seen it done."

Frunze's report said that the British were building a gaseous diffusion plant in Wales, in the west of the United Kingdom. The Americans were also building one. "Would there be any other purpose for such a plant?"

"I know of no other reason for separating isotopes." She shook her head. "Figure the odds. Anyone who prioritizes this kind of process in wartime is either going crazy or building a weapon."

Volodya saw a car approach the barricade and begin to negotiate the zigzag passage. It was a KIM-10, a small two-door car designed for affluent families. It had a top speed of sixty miles per hour, but this one was so overloaded it probably would not do forty.

A man in his sixties was at the wheel, wearing a hat and a Western-style cloth coat. Beside him was a young woman in a fur hat. The backseat of the car was piled with cardboard boxes. There was a piano strapped precariously to the roof.

This was clearly a senior member of the ruling elite trying to get out of town with his wife, or mistress, and as many of his valuables as he could take—the kind of person Zoya assumed Volodya to be, which was perhaps why she had declined to go out with him. He wondered if she might be revising her opinion of him.

One of the barricade volunteers moved a hedgehog in front of the KIM-10, and Volodya saw that there was going to be trouble.

The car inched forward until its bumper touched the hedgehog. Perhaps the driver thought he could nudge it out of the way. Several more women came closer to watch. The device was designed to resist being pushed out of the way. Its legs dug into the ground, jamming, and it stuck fast. There was a sound of bending metal as the car's front bumper deformed. The driver put it in reverse and backed off.

He stuck his head out of the window and yelled: "Move that thing, right now!" He sounded as if he were used to being obeyed.

The volunteer, a chunky middle-aged woman wearing a man's checked cap, folded her arms. She shouted: "Move it yourself—deserter!"

The driver got out, red-faced with anger, and Volodya was surprised to recognize Colonel Bobrov, whom he had known in Spain. Bobrov had been famous for shooting his own men in the back of the head if they retreated. "No mercy for cowards" had been his slogan. At Belchite Volodya had personally seen him kill three International Brigade troops for retreating when they ran out of ammunition. Now Bobrov was in civilian clothes. Volodya wondered if he would shoot the woman who had blocked his way.

Bobrov walked to the front of the car and took hold of the hedgehog. It was heavier than he expected, but with an effort he was able to drag it out of the way.

As he was walking back to his car, the woman in the cap replaced the hedgehog in front of the car.

The other volunteers were now crowding around, watching the confrontation, grinning and making jokes.

Bobrov walked up to the woman, taking from his coat pocket an identification card. "I am General Bobrov!" he said. He must have been promoted since returning from Spain. "Let me pass!"

"You call yourself a soldier?" the woman sneered. "Why aren't you fighting?"

Bobrov flushed. He knew her contempt was justified. Volodya wondered if the brutal old soldier had been talked into fleeing by his younger wife.

"I call you a traitor," said the volunteer in the cap. "Trying to run away with your piano and your young tart." Then she knocked his hat off.

Volodya was flabbergasted. He had never seen such defiance of authority in the Soviet Union. Back in Berlin, before the Nazis came to power, he had been surprised by the sight of ordinary Germans fearlessly arguing with police officers, but it did not happen here.

The crowd of women cheered.

Bobrov still had short-cropped white hair all over his head. He looked at his hat as it rolled across the wet road. He took one step in pursuit, then thought better of it.

Volodya was not tempted to intervene. There was nothing he could do against the mob, and anyway he had no sympathy for Bobrov. It seemed just that Bobrov should be treated with the brutality he had always shown to others.

Another volunteer, an older woman wrapped in a filthy blanket, opened the car's trunk. "Look at all this!" she said. The trunk was full of leather luggage. She pulled out a suitcase and thumbed its catches. The lid came open, and the contents fell out: lacy underwear, linen petticoats and nightdresses, silk stockings and camisoles, all obviously made in the West, finer than anything ordinary Russian women ever saw, let alone bought. The filmy garments dropped into the filthy slush of the street and stuck there like petals on a dunghill.

Some of the women started to pick them up. Others seized more suitcases. Bobrov ran to the back of his car and started to shove the women away. This was turning very nasty, Volodya thought. Bobrov probably carried a gun, and he would draw it any second now. But then the woman in the blanket lifted a spade and hit Bobrov hard over the head. A woman who could dig a trench with a spade was no weakling, and the blow made a sickeningly loud thud as it connected. The general fell to the ground, and the woman kicked him.

The young mistress got out of the car.

The woman in the cap shouted: "Coming to help us dig?" and the others laughed.

The general's girlfriend, who looked about thirty, put her head down and walked back along the road the way the car had come. The volunteer in the checked cap shoved her, but she dodged between the hedgehogs and started to run. The volunteer ran after her. The mistress was wearing tan suede shoes with high heels, and she slipped in the wet and fell down. Her fur hat came off. She struggled to her feet and started to run again. The volunteer went after the hat, letting the mistress go.

All the suitcases now lay open around the abandoned car. The workers pulled the boxes from the backseat and turned them upside down, emptying the contents onto the road. Cutlery spilled out, china broke, and glassware smashed. Embroidered bedsheets and white towels were dragged through the slush. A dozen pretty pairs of shoes were scattered across the tarmac.

Bobrov got to his knees and tried to stand. The woman in the blanket hit him with the spade again. Bobrov collapsed on the ground. She unbuttoned Bobrov's fine wool coat and tried to pull it off him. Bobrov struggled, resisting. The woman became furious and hit Bobrov again and again until he lay still, his cropped white head covered with blood. Then she discarded her old blanket and put Bobrov's coat on.

Volodya walked across to Bobrov's unmoving body. The eyes stared lifelessly. Volodya knelt down and checked for breathing, a heartbeat, or a pulse. There was none. The man was dead.

"No mercy for cowards," Volodya said, but he closed Bobrov's eyes.

Some of the women unstrapped the piano. The instrument slid off the car roof and hit the ground with a discordant clang. They began gleefully to smash it up with picks and shovels. Others were quarreling over the scattered valuables, snatching up the cutlery, bundling the bedsheets, tearing the fine underwear as they struggled for possession. Fights broke out. A china teapot came flying through the air and just missed Zoya's head.

Volodya hurried back to her. "This is developing into a full-scale riot," he said. "I've got an army car and a driver. I'll get you out of here."

She hesitated only for a second. "Thanks," she said, and they ran to the car, jumped in, and drove away.

ii

Erik von Ulrich's faith in the Führer was vindicated by the invasion of the Soviet Union. As the German armies raced across the vastness of Russia, sweeping the Red Army aside like chaff, Erik rejoiced in the strategic brilliance of the leader to whom he had given his allegiance.

Not that it was easy. During rainy October the countryside had been a mud bath: they called it the *rasputitsa*, the time of no roads. Erik's ambulance had plowed through a quagmire. A wave of mud built up in front of the vehicle, gradually slowing it, until he and Hermann had to get out and clear it away with shovels before they could drive any farther. It was the same for the entire German army, and the dash for Moscow had slowed to a crawl. Furthermore, the swamped roads meant that supply trucks never caught up. The army was low on ammunition, fuel, and food, and Erik's unit was dangerously short of drugs and other medical necessities.

So Erik had at first rejoiced when the frost had set in at the beginning of November. The freeze seemed a blessing, making the roads hard again and allowing the ambulance to move at normal speed. But Erik shivered in his summer coat and cotton underwear—winter uniforms had not yet arrived from Germany. Nor had the low-temperature lubricants needed to keep the engine of his ambulance operating— and the engines of all the army's trucks, tanks, and artillery. While on the road, Erik got up every two hours in the night to start his engine and run it for five minutes, the only way to keep the oil from congealing and the coolant from freezing solid. Even then he cautiously lit a fire under the vehicle every morning an hour before moving off.

Hundreds of vehicles broke down and were abandoned. The planes of the Luftwaffe, left outside all night on makeshift airfields, froze solid and refused to start, and air cover for the troops simply disappeared.

Despite all that, the Russians were retreating. They fought hard, but they were always pushed back. Erik's unit stopped continually to clear away Russian bodies, and the frozen dead stacked by the roadside made a grisly embankment. Relentlessly, remorselessly, the German army was closing in on Moscow.

Soon, Erik felt sure, he would see Panzers majestically rolling across Red Square, while swastika banners fluttered jubilantly from the towers of the Kremlin.

Meanwhile, the temperature was minus ten degrees centigrade, and falling.

Erik's field hospital unit was in a small town beside a frozen canal, surrounded by spruce forest. Erik did not know the name of the place. The Russians often destroyed everything as they retreated, but this town had survived more or less intact. It had a modern hospital, which the Germans had taken over. Dr. Weiss had briskly instructed the local doctors to send their patients home, regardless of condition.

Now Erik studied a frostbite patient, a boy of about eighteen. The skin of his face was a waxy yellow, and frozen hard to the touch. When Erik and Hermann cut away the flimsy summer uniform, they saw that the arms and legs were covered with purple blisters. The torn and broken boots had been stuffed with newspaper in a pathetic attempt to keep out the cold. When Erik took them off, he smelled the characteristic rotting stink of gangrene.

Nevertheless he thought they might yet save the boy from amputation.

They knew what to do. They were treating more men for frostbite than for combat wounds.

He filled a bathtub; then he and Hermann Braun lowered the patient into the warm water.

Erik studied the body as it thawed. He saw the black color of gangrene on one foot and the toes of the other.

When the water began to cool, they took him out, patted him dry, put him in a bed, and covered him with blankets. Then they surrounded him with hot stones wrapped in towels.

The patient was conscious and alert. He said: "Am I going to lose my foot?"

"That's up to the doctor," Erik said automatically. "We're just orderlies."

"But you see a lot of patients," he persisted. "What's your best guess?"

"I think you might be all right," Erik said. If not, he knew what would happen. On the foot less badly affected, Weiss would amputate the toes, cutting them off with a big pair of clippers like bolt cutters. The other leg would be amputated below the knee.

Weiss came a few minutes later and examined the boy's feet. "Prepare the patient for amputation," he said brusquely.

Erik was desolate. Another strong young man was going to spend the rest of his life a cripple. What a shame.

But the patient saw it differently. "Thank God," he said. "I won't have to fight anymore."

As they got the boy ready for surgery, Erik reflected that the patient was one of many who persisted in a defeatist attitude—his own family among them. He thought a lot about his late father, and felt deep rage mingled with his grief and loss. The old man would not have joined in with the majority and celebrated the triumph of the Third Reich, he thought bitterly. He would have complained about something, questioned the Führer's judgment, undermined the morale of the armed forces. Why had he had to be such a rebel? Why had he been so attached to the outdated ideology of democracy? Freedom had done nothing for Germany, whereas Fascism had saved the country!

He was angry with his father, yet hot tears came to his eyes when he thought about how he had died. Erik had at first denied that the Gestapo had killed him, but he soon realized it was probably true. They were not Sunday school teachers: they beat people who told wicked lies about the government. Father had persisted in asking whether the government was killing handicapped children. He had been foolish to listen to his English wife and his overemotional daughter. Erik loved them, which made it all the more painful to him that they were so misguided and obstinate.

While on leave in Berlin Erik had gone to see Hermann's father, the man who had first revealed the exciting Nazi philosophy to him when he and Hermann were boys. Herr Braun was in the SS now. Erik said he had met a man in a bar who claimed the government killed disabled people in special hospitals. "It is true that the handicapped are a costly drag on the forward march to the new Germany," Herr Braun had said to Erik. "The race must be purified, by repressing Jews and other degenerate types, and preventing mixed marriages that produce mongrel people. But euthanasia has never been Nazi policy. We are determined, tough, even brutal sometimes, but we do not murder people. That is a Communist lie."

Father's accusations had been wrong. Still Erik wept sometimes.

Fortunately, he was frantically busy. There was always a morning rush of patients, mostly men injured the day before. Then there was a short lull before the first new casualties of the day. When Weiss had operated on the frostbitten boy, he and Erik and Hermann took a midmorning break in the cramped staff room.

Hermann looked up from a newspaper. "In Berlin they're saying we've already won!" he exclaimed. "They ought to come here and see for themselves."

Dr. Weiss spoke with his usual cynicism. "The Führer made a most interesting speech at the Sportpalast," he said. "He spoke of the bestial inferiority of the Russians. I find that reassuring. I had the impression that the Russians were the toughest fighters we have yet come across. They have fought longer and harder than the Poles, the Belgians, the Dutch, the French, or the British. They may be underequipped and badly led and half-starved, but they come running at our machine guns, waving their obsolete rifles, as if they don't care whether they live or die. I'm glad to hear that this is no more than a sign of their bestiality. I was beginning to fear that they might be courageous and patriotic."

As always, Weiss pretended to agree with the Führer, while meaning the opposite. Hermann just looked confused, but Erik understood and was infuriated. "Whatever the Russians may be, they're losing," he said. "We're forty miles from Moscow. The Führer has been proved right."

"And he is much smarter than Napoléon," said Dr. Weiss.

"In Napoléon's time nothing could move faster than a horse," said Erik. "Today we have motor vehicles and wireless telegraphy. Modern communications have enabled us to succeed where Napoléon failed."

"Or they will have, when we take Moscow."

"Which we will do in a few days, if not hours. You can hardly doubt that!"

"Can I not? I believe some of our own generals have suggested we halt where we are and build a defense line. We could secure our positions, resupply over the winter, and go back on the offensive when the spring comes."

"That sounds to me like treacherous cowardice!" Erik said hotly.

"You are right—you must be, because that is exactly what Berlin told the generals, I understand. Headquarters people obviously have a better perspective than the men on the front line."

"We have almost wiped out the Red Army!"

"But Stalin seems to produce more armies from nowhere, like a magician. At the beginning of this campaign we thought he had two hundred divisions. Now we think he has more than three hundred. Where did he find another hundred divisions?"

"The Führer's judgment will be proved right—again."

"Of course it will, Erik."

"He has never yet been wrong!"

"A man thought he could fly, so he jumped off the top of a ten-story building, and as he fell past the fifth floor, flapping his arms uselessly in the air, he was heard to say: 'So far, so good.'"

A soldier rushed into the staff room. "There's been an accident," he said. "At the quarry north of the town. A collision, three vehicles. Some SS officers are injured."

The SS, or Schutzstaffel, had originally been Hitler's personal guard, and now formed a powerful elite. Erik admired their superb discipline, their ultrasmart uniforms, and their specially close relationship with Hitler.

"We'll send an ambulance," said Weiss.

The soldier said: "It's the Einsatzgruppe, the Special Group."

Erik had heard of the Special Groups, vaguely. They followed the army into conquered territory and rounded up troublemakers and potential saboteurs such as Communists. They were probably setting up a prison camp outside the town.

"How many hurt?" asked Weiss.

"Six or seven. They're still getting people out of the cars."

"Okay. Braun and von Ulrich, you go."

Erik was pleased. He would be glad to rub shoulders with the Führer's most fervent supporters, even happier if he could be of service to them.

The soldier handed him a message slip with directions.

Erik and Hermann gulped their tea, stubbed their cigarettes, and left the room. Erik put on a fur coat he had taken from a dead Russian officer, but left it open to show his uniform. They hurried down to the garage, and Hermann drove the ambulance out into the street. Erik read out the directions, peering through a light snowfall.

The road led out of town and snaked through the forest. They passed several buses and trucks coming the other way. The snow on the road was packed hard, and Hermann could not go fast on the glossy surface. Erik could easily imagine how there had been a collision.

It was the afternoon of the short day. At this time of year, daylight began at ten and ended at five. A gray light came through the snow clouds. The tall pine trees crowding in on either side darkened the road further. Erik felt as if he were in one of the fairy tales of the Brothers Grimm, following the path into the deep wood where evil lurked.

They looked out for a turning to the left, and found it guarded by a soldier who pointed the way. They bumped along a treacherous path between the trees until they were waved down by a second guard, who said: "Don't go faster than walking pace. That's how the crash happened."

A minute later they came upon the accident. Three damaged vehicles stood as if welded together: a bus, a jeep, and a Mercedes limousine with snow chains on the tires. Erik and Hermann jumped out of their ambulance.

The bus was empty. There were three men on the ground, perhaps the occupants of the jeep. Several soldiers gathered around the car sandwiched between the other two vehicles, apparently trying to get the people out of it.

Erik heard a volley of rifle fire, and wondered for a moment who was shooting, but he put the thought aside and concentrated on the job.

He and Hermann went from one man to the next assessing the gravity of the injuries. Of the three people on the ground one was dead, another had a broken arm, and the third appeared to be no worse than bruised. In the car, one man had bled to death, another was unconscious, and a third was screaming.

Erik gave the screamer a shot of morphine. When the drug took effect, he and Hermann were able to get the patient out of the car and into the ambulance. With him out of the way, the soldiers could begin to free the unconscious man, who was trapped by the deformed bodywork of the Mercedes. The man had a head injury that was going to kill him anyway, Erik thought, but he did not tell them that. He turned his attention to the men from the jeep. Hermann put a splint on the broken arm, and Erik walked the bruised man to the ambulance and sat him inside.

He returned to the Mercedes. "We'll have him out in five to ten minutes," said a captain. "Just hold on."

"Okay," said Erik.

He heard shooting again, and walked a little farther into the forest, curious about what the Special Group might be doing here. The snow on the ground between the trees was heavily trodden and littered with cigarette ends, apple cores, discarded newspapers, and other litter, as if a factory outing had passed this way.

He entered a clearing where lorries and buses were parked. A lot of people had been brought here. Some buses were leaving, skirting the accident; another arrived as Erik passed through. Beyond the parking lot, he came upon a hundred or so Russians of all ages, apparently prisoners, though many had suitcases, boxes, and sacks that they clutched as if guarding precious possessions. One man held a violin. A little girl with a doll caught Erik's eye, and he felt in his guts a sensation of sick foreboding.

The prisoners were being guarded by local policemen armed with truncheons. Clearly the Special Group had collaborators for whatever they were doing. The policemen looked at him, noted the German army uniform visible beneath the unbuttoned coat, and said nothing.

As he walked by, a well-dressed Russian prisoner spoke to him in German. "Sir, I am the director of the tire factory in this town. I have never believed in Communism, but only paid lip service, as all managers had to. I can help you—I know where everything is. Please take me away from here."

Erik ignored him and walked in the direction of the shooting.

He came upon the quarry. It was a large, irregular hole in the ground, its edge fringed by tall spruce trees like guardsmen in dark green uniforms laden with snow. At one end a long slope led into the pit. As he watched, a dozen prisoners began to walk down, two by two, marshaled by soldiers, into the shadowed valley.

Erik noticed three women and a boy of about eleven among them. Was their prison camp somewhere in that quarry? But they were no longer carrying luggage. Snow fell on their bare heads like a benison.

Erik spoke to an SS sergeant standing nearby. "Who are these prisoners, Sarge?"

"Communists," said the man. "From the town. Political commissars, and so on."

"What, even that little boy?"

"Jews, too," said the sergeant.

"Well, what are they, Communists or Jews?"

"What's the difference?"

"It's not the same thing."

"Balls. Most Communists are Jews. Most Jews are Communists. Don't you know anything?"

The tire factory director who had spoken to Erik seemed to be neither, he thought.

The prisoners reached the rocky floor of the quarry. Until this moment they had shuffled along like sheep in a herd, not speaking or looking around, but now they became animated, pointing at something on the ground. Peering through the snowflakes, Erik saw what looked like bodies scattered among the rocks, snow dusting their garments.

For the first time Erik noticed twelve riflemen standing on the lip of the ravine, among the trees. Twelve prisoners, twelve riflemen: he realized what was happening here, and incredulity mixed with horror rose like bile inside him.

They raised their guns and aimed at the prisoners.

"No," Erik said. "No, you can't." Nobody heard him.

A woman prisoner screamed. Erik saw her grab the eleven-year-old boy and clasp him to herself, as if her arms around him could stop bullets. She seemed to be his mother.

An officer said: "Fire."

The rifles cracked. The prisoners staggered and fell. The noise dislodged a little snow from the pines, and it fell on the riflemen, a sprinkling of pure white.

Erik saw the boy and his mother drop, still locked together in an embrace. "No," he said. "Oh, no!"

The sergeant looked at him. "What's the matter with you?" he said irritably. "Who are you, anyway?"

"Medical orderly," said Erik, without taking his eyes off the dread scene in the pit.

"What are you doing here?"

"I brought an ambulance for the officers hurt in the collision." Erik saw that another twelve prisoners were already being marched down the slope into the quarry. "Oh, God, my father was right," he moaned. "We're murdering people."

"Stop whining and fuck off back to your ambulance."

"Yes, Sergeant," said Erik.

iii

At the end of November Volodya asked for a transfer to a fighting unit. His intelligence work no longer seemed important: the Red Army did not need spies in Berlin to discover the intentions of a German army that was already on the outskirts of Moscow. And he wanted to fight for his city.

His misgivings about the government came to seem trivial. Stalin's stupidity, the brutishness of the secret police, the way nothing in the Soviet Union worked the way it was supposed to work—all that faded away. He felt nothing but a blazing need to repel the invader who threatened to bring violence, rape, starvation, and death to his mother, his sister, the twins Dimka and Tania, and Zoya.

He was sharply aware that if everyone thought that way he would have no spies. His German informants were people who had decided that patriotism and loyalty were outweighed by the terrible wickedness of the Nazis. He was grateful to them for their courage and the stern morality that drove them. But he felt differently.

So did many of the younger men in Red Army Intelligence, and a small company of them joined a rifle battalion at the beginning of December. Volodya kissed his parents, wrote a note to Zoya saying he hoped to survive to see her again, and moved into barracks.

At long last, Stalin brought reinforcements from the east to Moscow. Thirteen Siberian divisions were deployed against the ever-nearer Germans. On their way to the front line some of them stopped briefly in Moscow, and Muscovites on the streets stared at them in their white padded coats and warm sheepskin boots, with their skis and goggles and hardy steppe ponies. They arrived in time for the Russian counterattack.

This was the Red Army's last chance. Time and time again, in the last five months, the Soviet Union had hurled hundreds of thousands of men at the invaders. Each time the Germans had paused, dealt with the attack, and continued their relentless advance. But if this attempt failed, there would be no more. The Germans would have Moscow, and when they had Moscow, they would have the USSR. And then his mother would be trading vodka for black-market milk for Dimka and Tania.

On the fourth day of December the Soviet forces moved out of the city to the north, west, and south and took up their positions for the last effort. They went without lights, to avoid alerting the enemy. They were not allowed to have fires or smoke tobacco.

That evening the front line was visited by NKVD agents. Volodya did not see his rodent-faced brother-in-law, Ilya Dvorkin, who must have been among them. A pair he did not recognize came to the bivouac where Volodya and a dozen men were cleaning their rifles. Have you heard anyone criticizing the government? they asked. What do the fellows say about Comrade Stalin? Who among your comrades questions the wisdom of the army's strategy and tactics?

Volodya was incredulous. What did it matter at this point? In the next few days Moscow would be saved or lost. Who cared if soldiers bitched about their officers? He cut the questioning short, saying that he and his men were under a rule of silence, and he had orders to shoot anyone who broke it, but—he added recklessly—he would let the secret policemen off if they left immediately.

That worked, but Volodya had no doubt that the NKVD was undermining the morale of the troops all along the line.

On Friday, December 5, in the evening, the Russian artillery thundered into action. Next morning at dawn Volodya and his battalion moved off in a blizzard. Their orders were to take a small town on the far side of a canal.

Volodya ignored orders to attack the German defenses frontally—that was the old-fashioned Russian tactic, and this was no moment to stick obstinately to wrongheaded ideas. With his company of a hundred men he went upstream and crossed the ice to the north of the town, then moved in on the Germans' flank. He could hear the crash and roar of battle off to his left, so he knew he was behind the enemy's front line.

Volodya was almost blinded by the blizzard. The occasional blaze of gunfire lit up the clouds for a moment, but at ground level visibility was only a few yards. However, he thought optimistically, that would help the Russians creep up on the Germans and take them by surprise.

It was viciously cold, down to minus thirty-five degrees centigrade in places, and while this was bad for both sides, it was worse for the Germans, who lacked cold-weather supplies.

Somewhat to his surprise Volodya found that the normally efficient Germans had not consolidated their line. There were no trenches, no antitank ditches, no dugouts. Their front was no more than a series of strongpoints. It was easy to slip through the gaps into the town and look for soft targets, barracks and canteens and ammunition dumps.

His men shot three sentries to take a soccer field in which were parked fifty tanks. Could it be so easy? Volodya wondered. Was the force that had conquered half Russia now depleted and spent?

The corpses of Soviet soldiers, killed in previous skirmishes and left to freeze where they had died, were without their boots and coats, which had presumably been taken by shivering Germans.

The streets of the town were littered with abandoned vehicles— empty trucks with open doors, snow-covered tanks with cold engines, and jeeps with their bonnet lids propped up as if to show that mechanics had tried to fix them but had given up in despair.

Crossing a main road, Volodya heard a car engine and made out, through the snowfall, a pair of headlights approaching on his left. At first he assumed it was a Soviet vehicle that had pushed through the German lines. Then he and his group were fired on, and he yelled at them to take cover. The car turned out to be a Kübelwagen, a Volkswagen jeep with the spare wheel on the hood in front. It had an air-cooled engine, which was why it had not frozen up. It rattled past them at top speed, the Germans firing from their seats.

Volodya was so surprised that he forgot to fire back. Why was a vehicle full of armed Germans driving away from the battle?

He took his company across the road. He had expected that by now they would be fighting their way from house to house, but they met little opposition. The buildings of the occupied town were locked up, shuttered, dark. Any Russians inside were hiding under their beds, if they had any sense.

More cars came along the road, and Volodya decided that officers must be fleeing the battlefield. He detailed a section with a Degtyarev

DP-28 light machine gun to take cover in a café and fire on them. He did not want them to live to kill Russians tomorrow.

Just off the main road he spotted a low brick building with bright lights behind skimpy curtains. Creeping past a sentry who could not see far in the snowstorm, he was able to peer in and discern officers inside. He guessed he was looking at a battalion headquarters.

He gave whispered instructions to his sergeants. They shot out the windows, then tossed grenades through. A few Germans came out with their hands on their heads. A minute later Volodya had taken the building.

He heard a new noise. He listened, frowning in puzzlement. More than anything else, it sounded like a football crowd. He stepped out of the headquarters building. The sound was coming from the front line, and it was growing louder.

There was a rattle of machine-gun fire; then, a hundred yards away on the main road, a truck slewed sideways and careered off the road into a brick wall, then burst into flames—hit, presumably, by the DP-28 Volodya had deployed. Two more vehicles followed immediately behind it and escaped.

Volodya ran to the café. The machine gun stood on its bipod on a dining table. This model was nicknamed Record Player because of the disc-shaped magazine that sat atop the barrel. The men were enjoying themselves. "It's like shooting pigeons in the yard, sir!" said a gunner. "Easy!" One of the men had raided the kitchen and found a big canister of ice cream, miraculously unspoiled, and they were taking turns to scoff it.

Volodya looked out through the smashed window of the café. He saw another vehicle coming, a jeep he thought, and behind it some men running. As they got nearer, he recognized German uniforms. More followed behind, dozens, perhaps hundreds. They were responsible for the football-crowd sound.

The gunner trained the barrel on the oncoming car, but Volodya put a hand on his shoulder. "Wait," he said.

He stared into the blizzard, making his eyes sting. All he could see were more vehicles and more running men, plus a few horses.

A soldier raised a rifle. "Don't shoot," Volodya said. The crowd came closer. "We can't stop this lot—we'd be overrun in a minute," he said. "Let them pass. Take cover." The men lay down. The gunner lifted the DP-28 off the table. Volodya sat on the floor and peered over the windowsill.

The noise rose to a roar. The leading men drew level with the café and passed. They were running, stumbling, and limping. Some carried rifles; most seemed to have lost their weapons; some had coats and hats, others nothing but their uniform tunics. Many were wounded. Volodya saw a man with a bandaged head fall down, crawl a few yards, and collapse. No one took any notice. A cavalryman on horseback trampled an infantryman and galloped on, heedless. Jeeps and staff cars drove dangerously through the crowd, skidding on the ice, honking madly and scattering men to both sides.

It was a rout, Volodya realized. They went by in the thousands. It was a stampede. They were on the run.

At last, the Germans were in retreat.

CHAPTER ELEVEN

1941 (IV)

Woody Dewar and Joanne Rouzrokh flew from
Oakland, California, to Honolulu on a Boeing B-314
flying boat. The Pan Am flight took fourteen hours.
Just before arriving they had a massive row.

Perhaps it was spending so long in a small space.
The flying boat was one of the biggest planes in the world, but passengers
sat in one of six small cabins, each of which had two facing rows of four
seats. "I prefer the train," said Woody, awkwardly crossing his long legs,
and Joanne had the grace not to point out that you could not go to
Hawaii by train.

The trip was Woody's parents' idea. They had decided to take a
vacation in Hawaii so they could see Woody's younger brother, Chuck,
who was stationed there. Then they invited Woody and Joanne to join
them for the second week of the holiday.

Woody and Joanne were engaged. Woody had proposed at the end
of the summer, after four weeks of hot weather and passionate love in
Washington. Joanne had said it was too soon, but Woody had pointed
out that he had been in love with her for six years, and asked how long

would be enough. She had given in. They would get married next June, as soon as Woody graduated from Harvard. Meanwhile, their engaged status entitled them to go on family holidays together.

She called him Woods, and he called her Jo.

The plane began to lose altitude as they approached Oahu, the main island. They could see forested mountains, a sparse scatter of villages in the lowlands, and a fringe of sand and surf. "I bought a new swimsuit," Joanne said. They were sitting side by side, and the roar of the four Wright Twin Cyclone fourteen-cylinder engines was too loud for her to be overheard.

Woody was reading *The Grapes of Wrath* but he put it down willingly. "I can't wait to see you in it." He meant it. She was a swimsuit manufacturer's dream, making all their products look sensational.

She glanced at him from under half-closed eyelids. "I wonder if your parents booked us adjoining rooms at the hotel." Her dark brown eyes seemed to smolder.

Their engaged status did not allow them to sleep together, at least not officially, though Woody's mother did not miss much and she might have guessed they were lovers.

Woody said: "I'll find you, wherever you are."

"You'd better."

"Don't talk like that. I'm already uncomfortable enough in this seat."

She smiled contentedly.

The American naval base came into view. A lagoon shaped like a palm leaf formed a large natural harbor. Half the Pacific Fleet was here, about a hundred ships. The rows of fuel storage tanks looked like checkers on a board.

In the middle of the lagoon was an island with an airstrip. At the western end of the island, Woody saw a dozen or more seaplanes moored.

Right next to the lagoon was Hickam air base. Several hundred aircraft were parked with military precision, wingtip to wingtip, on the tarmac.

Banking for its approach, the plane flew over a beach with palm trees and gaily striped umbrellas—which Woody guessed must be Waikiki—then a small town that had to be Honolulu, the capital.

Joanne was owed some leave by the State Department, but Woody had had to skip a week of classes in order to take this vacation. "I'm kind of surprised at your father," Joanne said. "He's usually against anything that interrupts your education."

"I know," said Woody. "But you know the real reason for this trip, Jo? He thinks it could be the last time we see Chuck alive."

"Oh, my God, really?"

"He thinks there's going to be a war, and Chuck is in the navy."

"I think he's right. There will be a war."

"What makes you so sure?"

"The whole world is hostile to freedom." She pointed to the book in her lap, a bestseller called *Berlin Diary* by the radio broadcaster William Shirer. "The Nazis have Europe," she said. "The Bolsheviks have Russia. And now the Japanese are taking control of the Far East. I don't see how America can survive in such a world. We have to trade with somebody!"

"That's pretty much what my father thinks. He believes we'll go to war against Japan next year." Woody frowned thoughtfully. "What's happening in Russia?"

"The Germans don't seem quite able to take Moscow. Just before I left, there was a rumor of a massive Russian counterattack."

"Good news!"

Woody looked out. He could see Honolulu airport. The plane would splash down in a sheltered inlet alongside the runway, he presumed.

Joanne said: "I hope nothing major happens while I'm away."

"Why?"

"I want a promotion, Woods—so I don't want someone bright and promising to shine in my absence."

"Promotion? You didn't say."

"I don't have it yet, but I'm aiming for research officer."

He smiled. "How high do you want to go?"

"I'd like to be ambassador to someplace fascinating and complex, Nanking or Addis Ababa."

"Really?"

"Don't look skeptical. Frances Perkins is the first woman secretary of labor—and a damn good one."

Woody nodded. Perkins had been labor secretary from the start of Roosevelt's presidency eight years ago, and had won union support for the New Deal. An exceptional woman could aspire to almost anything nowadays. And Joanne was truly exceptional. But somehow it came as a shock to him that she was so ambitious. "But an ambassador has to live overseas," he said.

"Wouldn't it be great? Foreign culture, weird weather, exotic customs."

"But . . . how does that fit in with marriage?"

"Excuse me?" she said with asperity.

He shrugged. "It's a natural question, don't you think?"

Her expression did not change, except that her nostrils flared—a sign, he knew, that she was getting angry. "Have I asked *you* that question?" she said.

"No, but . . ."

"Well?"

"I'm just wondering, Jo—do you expect me to live wherever your career takes you?"

"I'll try to fit in with your needs, and I think you should try to fit in with mine."

"But it's not the same."

"Isn't it?" She was openly annoyed now. "This is news to me."

He wondered how the conversation had become so acrimonious so quickly. With an effort at making his tone of voice reasonable and amiable, he said: "We've talked about having children, haven't we?"

"You'll have them, as well as me."

"Not in exactly the same way."

"If children are going to make me a second-class citizen in this marriage, then we're not having any."

"That's not what I mean!"

"What the heck do you mean?"

"If you're appointed ambassador somewhere, do you expect me to drop everything and go with you?"

"I expect you to say: 'My darling, this is a wonderful opportunity for you, and I'm certainly not going to stand in your way.' Is that unreasonable?"

"Yes!" Woody was baffled and angry. "What's the point of being married, if we're not together?"

"If war breaks out, will you volunteer?"

"I guess I might."

"And the army would send you wherever they need you—Europe, the Far East."

"Well, yes."

"So you'll go where your duty takes you, and leave me at home."

"If I have to."

"But I can't do that."

"It's not the same! Why are you pretending it is?"

"Strangely enough, my career and my service to my country seem important to me—just as important as yours to you."

"You're just being perverse!"

"Well, Woods, I'm really sorry you think that, because I've been talking very seriously about our future together. Now I have to ask myself whether we even have one."

"Of course we do!" Woody could have screamed with frustration. "How did this happen? How did we get to this?"

There was a bump, and the plane splashed down in Hawaii.

ii

Chuck Dewar was terrified that his parents would learn his secret.

Back home in Buffalo he had never had a real love affair, just a few hasty fumbles in dark alleys with boys he hardly knew. Half the reason he had joined the navy was to go places where he could be himself without his parents finding out.

Since he got to Hawaii it had been different. Here he was part of an underground community of similar people. He went to bars and restaurants and dance halls where he did not have to pretend to be heterosexual. He had had some affairs, and then he had fallen in love. A lot of people knew his secret.

And now his parents were here.

His father was invited to visit the signal intelligence unit at the naval base, known as Station HYPO. As a member of the Senate Foreign Relations Committee, Senator Dewar was let into many military secrets, and he had already been shown around signal intelligence headquarters, called Op-20-G, in Washington.

Chuck picked him up at his hotel in Honolulu in a navy car, a Packard LeBaron limousine. Papa was wearing a white straw hat. As they drove around the rim of the harbor, he whistled. "The Pacific Fleet," he said. "A beautiful sight."

Chuck agreed. "Quite something, isn't it?" he said. Ships were beautiful, especially in the U.S. Navy, where they were painted and scrubbed and shined. Chuck thought the navy was great.

"All those battleships in a perfect straight line," Gus marveled.

"We call it Battleship Row. Moored off the island are *Maryland, Tennessee, Arizona, Nevada, Oklahoma,* and *West Virginia.*" Battleships were named after states. "We also have *California* and *Pennsylvania* in harbor, but you can't see them from here."

At the main gate to the navy yard, the marine on sentry duty recognized the official car and waved them in. They drove to the submarine base and stopped in the parking lot behind headquarters, the Old Administration Building. Chuck took his father into the recently opened new wing.

Captain Vandermeier was waiting for them.

Vandermeier was Chuck's greatest fear. He had taken a dislike to Chuck, and he had guessed the secret. He was always calling Chuck a powder puff or a pantywaist. If he could, he would spill the beans.

Vandermeier was a short, stocky man with a gravelly voice and bad breath. He saluted Gus and shook hands. "Welcome, Senator. It'll be my privilege to show you the Communications Intelligence Unit of the

Fourteenth Naval District." This was the deliberately vague title for the group monitoring the radio signals of the Imperial Japanese Navy.

"Thank you, Captain," said Gus.

"A word of warning, first, sir. It's an informal group. This kind of work is often done by eccentric people, and correct naval uniform is not always worn. The officer in charge, Commander Rochefort, wears a red velvet jacket." Vandermeier gave a man-to-man grin. "You may think he looks like a goddamn homo."

Chuck tried not to wince.

Vandermeier said: "I won't say any more until we're in the secure zone."

"Very good," said Gus.

They went down the stairs and into the basement, passing through two locked doors on the way.

Station HYPO was a windowless neon-lit cellar housing thirty men. As well as the usual desks and chairs, it had oversize chart desks, racks of exotic IBM machine printers, sorters and collators, and two cots where the cryptanalysts took naps during their marathon codebreaking sessions. Some of the men wore neat uniforms but others, as Vandermeier had warned, were in scruffy civilian clothing, unshaven, and—to judge by the smell—unwashed.

"Like all navies, the Japanese have many different codes, using the simplest for less secret signals, such as weather reports, and saving the complex ones for the most highly sensitive messages," Vandermeier said. "For example, call signs identifying the sender of a message and its destination are in a primitive cipher, even when the text itself is in a high-grade cipher. They recently changed the code for call signs, but we cracked the new one in a few days."

"Very impressive," said Gus.

"We can also figure out where the signal originated, by triangulation. Given locations and the call signs, we can build up a pretty good picture of where most of the ships of the Japanese Navy are, even if we can't read the messages."

"So we know where they are, and what direction they're taking, but not what their orders are," said Gus.

"Frequently, yes."

"But if they wanted to hide from us, all they would have to do is impose radio silence."

"True," said Vandermeier. "If they go quiet, this whole operation becomes useless, and we are well and truly fucked up the ass."

A man in a smoking jacket and carpet slippers approached, and Vandermeier introduced the head of the unit. "Commander Rochefort is fluent in Japanese, as well as being a master cryptanalyst," Vandermeier said.

"We were making good progress decrypting the main Japanese cipher until a few days ago," Rochefort said. "Then the bastards changed it and undid all our work."

Gus said: "Captain Vandermeier was telling me you can learn a lot without actually reading the messages."

"Yes." Rochefort pointed to a wall chart. "Right now, most of the Japanese fleet has left home waters and is heading south."

"Ominous."

"It sure is. But tell me, Senator, what's your reading of Japanese intentions?"

"I believe they will declare war on the United States. Our oil embargo is really hurting them. The British and the Dutch are refusing to supply them, and right now they're trying to ship it from South America. They can't survive like this indefinitely."

Vandermeier said: "But what would they achieve by attacking us? A little country such as Japan can't invade the USA!"

Gus said: "Great Britain is a little country, but they achieved world domination just by ruling the seas. The Japanese don't have to conquer America. They just need to defeat us in a naval war so that they can control the Pacific, and no one can stop them trading."

"So, in your opinion, what might they be doing, heading south?"

"Their likeliest target has to be the Philippines."

Rochefort nodded agreement. "We've already reinforced our base there. But one thing bothers me: the commander of the Japanese aircraft carrier fleet hasn't received any signals for several days."

Gus frowned. "Radio silence. Has that ever happened before?"

"Yes. Aircraft carriers go quiet when they return to home waters. So we assume that's the explanation this time."

Gus nodded. "It sounds reasonable."

"Yes," said Rochefort. "I just wish I could be sure."

iii

The Christmas lights were ablaze on Fort Street in Honolulu. It was Saturday night, December 6, and the street was thronged with sailors in white tropical uniform, each with a round white cap and a crossed black scarf, all out for a good time.

The Dewar family strolled along enjoying the atmosphere, Rosa on Chuck's arm and Gus and Woody on either side of Joanne.

Woody had patched up his quarrel with his fiancée. He apologized for making wrong assumptions about what Joanne expected in their marriage. Joanne admitted she had flown off the handle. Nothing was truly resolved, but it was enough of a rapprochement for them to tear off their clothes and jump into bed.

Afterward the quarrel seemed less important, and nothing really mattered except how much they loved each other. Then they vowed that in the future they would discuss such agreements in a loving and tolerant way. As they got dressed, Woody felt they had passed a milestone. They had had an acrimonious quarrel about a serious difference of view, but they had survived it. It could even be a good sign.

Now they were heading out for dinner, Woody carrying his camera, snapping photos of the scene as they walked along. Before they had gone far, Chuck stopped and introduced another sailor. "This is my pal Eddie Parry. Eddie, meet Senator Dewar; Mrs. Dewar; my brother, Woody; and Woody's fiancée, Miss Joanne Rouzrokh."

Rosa said: "I'm pleased to meet you, Eddie. Chuck has mentioned you several times in his letters home. Won't you join us for dinner? We're only going to eat Chinese."

Woody was surprised. It was not like his mother to invite a stranger to a family meal.

Eddie said: "Thank you, ma'am. I'd be honored." He had a Southern accent.

They went into the Heavenly Delight restaurant and sat down at a table for six. Eddie had formal manners, calling Gus "sir" and the women "ma'am," but he seemed relaxed. After they had ordered, he said: "I've heard so much about this family, I feel as if I know y'all." He had a freckled face and a big smile, and Woody could tell that everyone liked him.

Eddie asked Rosa how she liked Hawaii. "To tell you the truth, I'm a little disappointed," she said. "Honolulu is just like any small American town. I expected it to be more Asian."

"I agree," said Eddie. "It's all diners and motor courts and jazz bands."

He asked Gus if there was going to be a war. Everyone asked Gus that question. "We've tried our darnedest to reach a modus vivendi with Japan," Gus said. Woody wondered if Eddie knew what a modus vivendi was. "Secretary of State Hull had a whole series of talks with Ambassador Nomura that lasted all summer long. But we can't seem to agree."

"What's the problem?" said Eddie.

"American business needs a free trade zone in the Far East. Japan says okay, fine, we love free trade, let's have it, not just in our backyard, but all over the world. The United States can't deliver that, even if we wanted it. So Japan says that as long as other countries have their own economic zone, they need one, too."

"I still don't see why they had to invade China."

Rosa, who always tried to see the other side, said: "The Japanese want troops in China and Indochina and the Dutch East Indies to protect their interests, just as we Americans have troops in the Philippines, and the British have theirs in India, and the French in Algeria, and so on."

"When you put it that way, the Japs don't seem so unreasonable!"

Joanne said firmly: "They're not unreasonable, but they're wrong. Conquering an empire is the nineteenth-century solution. The world is changing. We're moving away from empires and closed economic zones. To give them what they want would be a backward step."

Their food arrived. "Before I forget," Gus said, "we're having breakfast tomorrow morning aboard the *Arizona*. Eight o'clock sharp."

Chuck said: "I'm not invited, but I've been detailed to get you there. I'll pick you up at seven thirty and drive you to the navy yard, then take you across the harbor in a launch."

"Fine."

Woody tucked into fried rice. "This is great," he said. "We should have Chinese food at our wedding."

Gus laughed. "I don't think so."

"Why not? It's cheap, and it tastes good."

"A wedding is more than a meal. It's an occasion. Speaking of which, Joanne, I must call your mother."

Joanne frowned. "About the wedding?"

"About the guest list."

Joanne put down her chopsticks. "Is there a problem?" Woody saw her nostrils flare, and knew there was going to be trouble.

"Not really a problem," said Gus. "I have a rather large number of friends and allies in Washington who would be offended if they were not invited to the wedding of my son. I'm going to suggest that your mother and I share the cost."

Papa was being thoughtful, Woody guessed. Because Dave had sold his business for a bargain price before he died, Joanne's mother might not have a lot of money to spare for a swanky wedding. But Joanne disliked the idea of the two parents making wedding arrangements over her head.

"Who are the friends and allies you're thinking about?" Joanne said coolly.

"Senators and congressmen, mostly. We must invite the president, but he won't come."

"Which senators and congressmen?" Joanne said.

Woody saw his mother hide a grin. She was amused at Joanne's insistence. Not many people had the nerve to push Gus up against the wall like this.

Gus began a list of names.

Joanne interrupted him. "Did you say Congressman Cobb?"

"Yes."

"He voted against the anti-lynching law!"

"Peter Cobb is a good man. But he's a Mississippi politician. We live in a democracy, Joanne; we have to represent our voters. Southerners won't support an anti-lynching law." He looked at Chuck's friend. "I hope I'm not treading on any toes here, Eddie."

"Don't mince your words on my account, sir," Eddie said. "I'm from Texas, but I feel ashamed when I think of Southern politics. I hate prejudice. A man's a man, whatever his color."

Woody glanced at Chuck. He looked so proud of Eddie he might have burst.

At that moment, Woody realized Eddie was more than just Chuck's pal.

That was weird.

There were three loving couples around the table: Papa and Mama, Woody and Joanne, and Chuck and Eddie.

He stared at Eddie. Chuck's lover, he thought.

Damn weird.

Eddie caught him staring, and smiled amiably.

Woody tore his gaze away. Thank God Papa and Mama haven't figured it out, he thought.

Unless that was why Mama had invited Eddie to join in a family dinner. Did she know? Did she even approve? No, that was beyond the bounds of possibility.

"Anyway, Cobb has no choice," Papa was saying. "And in everything else he's a liberal."

"There's nothing democratic about it," Joanne said hotly. "Cobb doesn't represent the people of the South. Only white people are allowed to vote there."

Gus said: "Nothing is perfect in this life. Cobb supported Roosevelt's New Deal."

"That doesn't mean I have to invite him to my wedding."

Woody put in: "Papa, I don't want him, either. He has blood on his hands."

"That's unfair."

"It's how we feel."

"Well, the decision is not entirely up to you. Joanne's mother will be throwing the party, and if she'll let me, I'll share the cost. I guess that gives us at least a say in the guest list."

Woody sat back. "Heck, it's our wedding."

Joanne looked at Woody. "Maybe we should have a quiet town hall wedding, with just a few friends."

Woody shrugged. "Suits me."

Gus said severely: "That would upset a lot of people."

"But not us," said Woody. "The most important person of the day is the bride. I just want her to have what she wants."

Rosa spoke up. "Listen to me, everyone," she said. "Don't let's go overboard. Gus, my darling, you may have to take Peter Cobb aside and explain to him, gently, that you are lucky enough to have an idealistic son, who is marrying a wonderful and equally idealistic girl, and they have stubbornly refused your impassioned request to invite Congressman Cobb to the wedding. You're sorry, but you cannot follow your own inclinations in this any more than Peter can follow his when voting on anti-lynching bills. He will smile and say he understands, and he has always liked you because you're as straight as a die."

Gus hesitated for a long moment, then decided to give in graciously. "I guess you're right, my dear," he said. He smiled at Joanne. "Anyway, I'd be a fool to quarrel with my delightful daughter-in-law on account of Pete Cobb."

Joanne said: "Thank you . . . Should I start calling you Papa yet?"

Woody almost gasped. It was the perfect thing to say. She was so damn smart!

Gus said: "I would really like that."

Woody thought he saw the glint of a tear in his father's eye.

Joanne said: "Then, thank you, Papa."

How about that? thought Woody. She stood up to him—and she won. What a girl!

iv

On Sunday morning, Eddie wanted to go with Chuck to pick up the family at their hotel.

"I don't know, baby," said Chuck. "You and I are supposed to be friendly, not inseparable."

They were in bed in a motel at dawn. They had to sneak back into barracks before sunup.

"You're ashamed of me," said Eddie.

"How can you say that? I took you to dinner with my family!"

"That was your mama's idea, not yours. But your papa liked me, didn't he?"

"They all adored you. Who wouldn't? But they don't know you're a filthy homo."

"I am not a filthy homo. I'm a very clean homo."

"True."

"Please take me. I want to know them better. It's really important to me."

Chuck sighed. "Okay."

"Thank you." Eddie kissed him "Do we have time . . . ?"

Chuck grinned. "If we're quick."

Two hours later they were outside the hotel in the navy's Packard. Their four passengers appeared at seven thirty. Rosa and Joanne wore hats and gloves, Gus and Woody white linen suits. Woody had his camera.

Woody and Joanne were holding hands. "Look at my brother," Chuck murmured to Eddie. "He's so happy."

"She's a beautiful girl."

They held the doors open and the Dewars climbed into the back of the limousine. Woody and Joanne folded down the jump seats. Chuck pulled away and headed for the naval base.

It was a fine morning. On the car radio, station KGMB was playing hymns. The sun shone over the lagoon and glinted off the glass portholes and polished brass rails of a hundred ships. Chuck said: "Isn't that a pretty sight?"

They entered the base and drove to the navy yard, where a dozen ships were in floating docks and dry docks for repair, maintenance, and refueling. Chuck pulled up at the officers' landing. They all got out and looked across the lagoon at the mighty battleships standing proud in the morning light. Woody took a photo.

It was a few minutes before eight o'clock. Chuck could hear the tolling of church bells in nearby Pearl City. On the ships, the forenoon watch was being piped to breakfast, and color parties were assembling to hoist ensigns at eight precisely. A band on the deck of the *Nevada* was playing "The Star-Spangled Banner."

They walked to the jetty, where a launch was tied up ready for them. The boat was big enough to take a dozen passengers and had an inboard motor under a hatch in the stern. Eddie started the engine while Chuck handed the guests into the boat. The small motor burbled cheerfully. Chuck stood in the bows while Eddie eased the launch away from the dockside and turned toward the battleships. The prow lifted as the launch picked up speed, throwing off twin curves of foam like a seagull's wings.

Chuck heard a plane and looked up. It was coming in from the west, so low it looked as if it might be in danger of crashing. He assumed it was about to land at the naval airstrip on Ford Island.

Woody, sitting near Chuck in the bows, frowned and said: "What kind of plane is that?"

Chuck knew every aircraft of both the army and the navy, but he had trouble identifying this one. "It almost looks like a Type 97," he said. That was the carrier-based torpedo bomber of the Imperial Japanese Navy.

Woody pointed his camera.

As the plane came nearer, Chuck saw large red suns painted on its wings. "It is a Jap plane!" he said.

Eddie, steering the boat from the stern, heard him. "They must have faked it up for an exercise," he said. "A surprise drill to spoil everyone's Sunday morning."

"I guess so," said Chuck.

Then he saw a second plane behind the first.

And another.

He heard his father say anxiously: "What the heck is going on?"

The planes banked over the navy yard and passed low over the launch, their noise rising to a roar like Niagara Falls. There were about ten of them, Chuck saw; no, twenty; no, more.

They headed straight for Battleship Row.

Woody stopped taking pictures to say: "It can't be a real attack, can it?" There was fear as well as doubt in his voice.

"How could they be Japanese?" Chuck said incredulously. "Japan is nearly four thousand miles away! No plane can fly that far."

Then he remembered that the aircraft carriers of the Japanese navy had gone into radio silence. The signal intelligence unit had assumed they were in home waters, but had never been able to confirm that.

He caught his father's eye, and guessed he was remembering the same conversation.

Everything suddenly became clear, and incredulity turned to fear.

The lead plane flew low over the *Nevada*, the stern marker in Battleship Row. There was a burst of cannon fire. On deck, seamen scattered and the band left off in a ragged diminuendo of abandoned notes.

In the launch, Rosa screamed.

Eddie said: "Christ Jesus in heaven, it is an attack."

Chuck's heart pounded. The Japanese were bombing Pearl Harbor, and he was in a small boat in the middle of the lagoon. He looked at the scared faces of the others—both parents, his brother, and Eddie—and realized that all the people he loved were in the boat with him.

Long bullet-shaped torpedoes began to fall from the underbellies of the planes and splash into the tranquil waters of the lagoon.

Chuck yelled: "Turn back, Eddie!" But Eddie was already doing it, swinging the launch around in a tight arc.

As it turned, Chuck saw, over Hickam air base, another flight of aircraft with the big red discs on their wings. These were dive-bombers, and they were streaming down like birds of prey on the rows of American aircraft perfectly lined up on the runways.

How the hell many of the bastards were there? Half the Japanese air force seemed to be in the sky over Pearl.

Woody was still taking pictures.

Chuck heard a deep bang like an underground explosion, then another immediately after. He spun around. There was a flash of flame aboard the *Arizona*, and smoke began to rise from her.

The stern of the launch squatted farther into the water as Eddie opened the throttle. Chuck said unnecessarily: "Hurry, hurry!"

From one of the ships Chuck heard the insistent rhythmic hoot of a klaxon sounding general quarters, calling the crew to battle stations, and he realized that this *was* a battle, and his family was in the middle of it. A moment later on Ford Island the air raid siren began with a low moan and wailed higher in pitch until it struck its frantic top note.

There was a long series of explosions from Battleship Row as torpedoes found their targets. Eddie yelled: "Look at the *Wee Vee*!" It was what they called the *West Virginia*. "She's listing to port!"

He was right, Chuck saw. The ship had been holed on the side nearest the attacking planes. Millions of tons of water must have poured into her in a few seconds to make such a huge vessel tilt sideways.

Next to her, the same fate was overtaking the *Oklahoma*, and to his horror Chuck could see sailors slipping helplessly, sliding across the tilted deck and falling over the side into the water.

Waves from the explosions rocked the launch. Everyone clung to the sides.

Chuck saw bombs rain down on the seaplane base at the near end of Ford Island. The planes were moored close together, and the fragile aircraft were blown to pieces, fragments of wings and fuselages flying into the air like leaves in a hurricane.

Chuck's intelligence-trained mind was trying to identify aircraft types, and now he spotted a third model among the Japanese attackers, the deadly Mitsubishi "Zero," the best carrier-based fighter in the world. It had only two small bombs, but was armed with twin machine guns and a pair of 20 mm cannon. Its role in this attack must be to escort the bombers, defending them from American fighters—but all the American fighters were still on the ground, where many of them had already been destroyed. That left the Zeroes free to strafe buildings, equipment, and troops.

Or, Chuck thought fearfully, to strafe a family crossing the lagoon, desperately trying to get to shore.

At last the United States began to shoot back. On Ford Island, and on the decks of the ships that had not yet been hit, antiaircraft guns and regular machine guns came to life, adding their rattle to the cacophony of lethal noise. Antiaircraft shells burst in the sky like black flowers blossoming. Almost immediately, a machine gunner on the island scored a direct hit on a dive-bomber. The cockpit burst into flames and the plane hit the water with a mighty splash. Chuck found himself cheering savagely, shaking his fists in the air.

The listing *West Virginia* began to return to the vertical, but continued to sink, and Chuck realized that the commander must have opened the starboard seacocks, to ensure that she remained upright while she went down, giving the crew a better chance of survival. But the *Oklahoma* was not so fortunate, and they all watched in terrified awe as the great ship began to turn over. Joanne said: "Oh, God, look at the crew." The sailors were frantically scrambling up the steeply banked deck and over the starboard rail in a desperate attempt to save themselves. But they were the lucky ones, Chuck realized, as at last the mighty vessel turned turtle with a terrible crash and began to sink, for how many hundreds of men were trapped belowdecks?

"Hold on, everyone!" Chuck yelled. A huge wave created by the capsizing of the *Oklahoma* was approaching. Papa grabbed Mama and Woody held on to Joanne. The wave reached them and lifted the launch impossibly high. Chuck staggered but kept hold of the rail. The launch stayed afloat. Smaller waves followed, rocking them, but everyone was safe.

They were still a long quarter of a mile offshore, Chuck saw with consternation.

Astonishingly the *Nevada,* which had been strafed at the start, began to move off. Someone must have had the presence of mind to signal all ships to sail. If they could get out of the harbor, they could scatter and present less easy targets.

Then from Battleship Row came a bang ten times bigger than anything that had gone before. The explosion was so violent that Chuck felt the blast like a blow to his chest, though he was now almost half a mile away. A spurt of flame spewed out of the no. 2 gun turret of the *Arizona.* A split second later the forward half of the ship seemed to burst. Debris flew into the air, twisted steel girders and warped plates drifting up through the smoke with a nightmare slowness, like scraps of charred paper from a bonfire. Flames and smoke enveloped the front of the ship. The lofty mast tipped forward drunkenly.

Woody said: "What was *that?*"

"The ship's ammunition store must have gone up," Chuck said, and he realized with heartfelt grief that hundreds of his fellow seamen must have been killed in that mammoth detonation.

A column of dark red smoke rose into the air as from a funeral pyre.

There was a crash and the boat lurched as something hit it. Everyone ducked. Falling to his knees, Chuck thought it must have been a bomb, then realized it could not be, for he was still alive. When he recovered, he saw that a heavy scrap of metal debris a yard long had pierced the deck over the engine. It was a miracle it had not hit anyone.

However, the engine died.

The boat slowed and was becalmed. It wallowed in the choppy waves while Japanese planes rained hellfire on the lagoon.

Gus said tightly: "Chuck, we have to get out of here right now."

"I know." Chuck and Eddie examined the damage. They grabbed the metal scrap and tried to wrestle it out of the teak deck, but it was firmly stuck.

"We don't have time for this!" Gus said.

Woody said: "The engine is blitzed anyway, Chuck."

They were still a quarter of a mile from shore. However, the launch was equipped for an emergency such as this. Chuck unshipped a pair of oars. He took one and Eddie took the other. The boat was large for rowing, and their progress was slow.

Luckily for them there was a lull in the attack. The sky was no longer swarming with planes. Vast billows of smoke rose from the damaged ships, including a column a thousand feet high from the fatally wounded *Arizona,* but there were no new explosions. The amazingly plucky *Nevada* was now heading for the mouth of the harbor.

The water around the ships was crowded with life rafts, motor launches, and seamen swimming or clinging to floating wreckage. Drowning was not their only fear: oil from the holed ships had spread across the surface and caught fire. The cries for help of those who could not swim mingled horrifyingly with the screams of the burned.

Chuck stole a glance at his watch. He thought the attack had been going on for hours, but amazingly, it was only thirty minutes.

Just as he was thinking that, the second wave began.

This time the planes came from the east. Some of them chased the escaping *Nevada*; others targeted the navy yard, where the Dewars had boarded the launch. Almost immediately the destroyer *Shaw* in a floating dock exploded with great gouts of flame and billows of smoke. Oil spread across the water and caught fire. Then in the largest dry dock the battleship *Pennsylvania* was hit. Two destroyers in the same dry dock blew up as their ammunition stores were ignited.

Chuck and Eddie strained at the oars, sweating like racehorses.

At the navy yard, marines appeared—presumably from the nearby barracks—and broke out firefighting gear.

At last the launch reached the officers' landing. Chuck leaped out and swiftly tied up while Eddie helped the passengers out. They all ran to the car.

Chuck jumped into the driver's seat and started the engine. The car radio came on automatically, and he heard the KGMB announcer say: "All army, navy, and marine personnel report for duty immediately." Chuck had not had a chance to report to anyone, but he felt sure that his orders would be first to ensure the safety of the four civilians in his care, especially as two were women and one was a senator.

As soon as everyone was in the car, he pulled away.

The second wave of the attack seemed to be ending. Most of the Japanese planes were heading away from the harbor. All the same, Chuck drove fast: there might be a third wave.

The main gate was open. If it had been shut, he would have been tempted to crash it.

There was no other traffic.

He raced away from the harbor along Kamehameha Highway. The farther he got from Pearl Harbor, the safer his family would be, he figured.

Then he saw a lone Zero coming toward him.

It was flying low and following the highway, and after a moment he realized it was targeting the car.

The cannon were in the wings, and there was a good chance they would miss the narrow target of the car, but the machine guns were set close together, either side of the engine cowling. That was what the pilot would use if he was smart.

Chuck looked frantically at both sides of the road. There was no hiding place, nothing but cane fields.

He began to zigzag. The approaching pilot sensibly did not attempt to track him. The road was not wide, and if Chuck drove into the cane field, the car would be slowed to a walking pace. He stepped on the gas, realizing that the faster he was going, the better his chances of not being hit.

Then it was too late for forethought. The plane was so close Chuck could see the round black holes in the wings through which the cannon fired. But, as he had guessed, the pilot opened up with machine guns, and bullets spat dust from the road ahead.

Chuck moved left, to the crown of the road; then instead of continuing left, he swerved right. The pilot corrected. Bullets hit the hood. The windscreen smashed. Eddie roared with pain, and in the back one of the women screamed.

Then the Zero was gone.

The car began to zigzag of its own accord. A forward wheel must have been damaged. Chuck fought with the steering wheel, trying to stay on the road. The car slewed sideways, skidded across the tarmac, crashed into the field at the side of the road, and bumped to a stop.

Flames rose from the engine, and Chuck smelled gasoline.

"Everybody out!" Chuck yelled. "Before the fuel tank blows!" He opened his door and leaped out. He yanked open the rear door and his father jumped out, pulling his mother along. Chuck could see the others getting out on the far side. "Run!" he shouted, but it was superfluous. Eddie was already heading into the cane field, limping as though wounded. Woody was half-pulling, half-carrying Joanne, who also seemed to have been hit. His parents charged into the field, apparently unhurt. He joined them. They all ran a hundred yards, then threw themselves flat.

There was a moment of stillness. The sounds of planes had become a distant buzz. Glancing up, Chuck saw oily smoke from the harbor rising thousands of feet into the air. Above that, the last few high-level bombers were heading away to the north.

Then there was a bang that stunned his eardrums. Even with closed eyes he saw the bright flash of exploding gasoline. A wave of heat passed over him.

He lifted his head and looked back. The car was ablaze.

He jumped to his feet. "Mama! Are you okay?"

"Miraculously unhurt," she said coolly as his father helped her up.

He scanned the field and spotted the others. He ran to Eddie, who was sitting upright, clutching his thigh. "Are you hit?"

"Hurts like fuck," Eddie said. "But there's not much blood." He managed a grin. "Top of my thigh, I think, but no vital organs damaged."

"We'll get you to the hospital."

At that moment Chuck heard a terrible noise.

His brother was crying.

Woody was weeping not like a baby but like a lost child: a loud, sobbing noise of utter wretchedness.

Chuck knew immediately that it was the sound of a broken heart.

He ran to his brother. Woody was on his knees, his chest shaking, his mouth open, his eyes running with tears. There was blood all over his white linen suit, but he was not wounded. Between sobs he moaned: "No, no."

Joanne lay on the ground in front of him, faceup.

Chuck could see right away that she was dead. Her body was still and her eyes were open, staring at nothing. The front of her gaily striped cotton dress was soaked with bright red arterial blood, already darkening in patches. Chuck could not see the wound but he guessed she had taken a bullet to the shoulder that had opened her axillary artery. She would have bled to death in minutes.

He did not know what to say.

The others came and stood by him: Mama, Papa, and Eddie. Mama knelt on the ground beside Woody and put her arms around him. "My poor boy," she said, as if he were a child.

Eddie put his arm around Chuck's shoulders and gave him a discreet hug.

Papa knelt by the body. He reached out and took Woody's hand.

Woody's sobs quieted a little.

Papa said: "Close her eyes, Woody."

Woody's hand was shaking. With an effort, he steadied it.

He stretched out his fingertips to her eyelids.

Then, with infinite gentleness, he closed her eyes.

CHAPTER TWELVE

1942 (I)

On the first day of 1942 Daisy got a letter from her former fiancé, Charlie Farquharson.

When she opened it, she was at the breakfast table in the Mayfair house, alone except for the aged butler, who poured her coffee, and the fifteen-year-old maid, who brought her hot toast from the kitchen.

Charlie wrote not from Buffalo but from RAF Duxford, an air base in the east of England. Daisy had heard of the place: it was near Cambridge, where she had met both her husband, Boy Fitzherbert, and the man she loved, Lloyd Williams.

She was pleased to hear from Charlie. He had jilted her, of course, and she had hated him then, but it was a long time ago. She felt like a different person now. In 1935 she had been an American heiress called Miss Peshkov; today she was Viscountess Aberowen, an English aristocrat. All the same, she was pleased she was still in Charlie's mind. A woman would always prefer to be remembered rather than forgotten.

Charlie wrote with a heavy black pen. His handwriting was untidy, the letters large and jagged. Daisy read:

> Before anything else, I need of course to apologize
> for the way I treated you back in Buffalo. I shudder with
> mortification every time I think of it.

Good Lord, thought Daisy, he seems to have grown up.

> What snobs we all were, and how weak I was to allow my
> late mother to bully me into behaving shabbily.

Ah, she thought, his *late* mother. So the old bitch is dead. That might explain the change.

> I have joined No. 133 Eagle Squadron. We fly Hurricanes,
> but we're getting Spitfires any day now.

There were three Eagle squadrons, Royal Air Force units manned by American volunteers. Daisy was surprised: she would not have expected Charlie to go to war voluntarily. When she knew him, he had been interested in nothing but dogs and horses. He really had grown up.

> If you can find it in your heart to forgive me, or at least
> put the past behind you, I would love to see you and meet
> your husband.

The mention of a husband was a tactful way of saying he had no romantic intentions, Daisy guessed.

> I will be in London on leave next weekend. May I take the
> two of you to dinner? Do say yes.
>> With affectionate good wishes,
>> Charles H. B. Farquharson

Boy was not at home that weekend, but Daisy accepted for herself. She was starved of male companionship, like many women in wartime London. Lloyd had gone to Spain and disappeared. He said he was going to be a military attaché at the British embassy in Madrid. Daisy wished it might be true that he had such a safe job, but she did not believe it. When she asked why the government would send an able-bodied young officer to do a desk job in a neutral country, he had explained how important it was to discourage Spain from joining in the war on the Fascist side. But he said it with a rueful smile that told her plainly she was not to be fooled. She feared that in reality he was slipping across the border to work with the French resistance, and she had nightmares about his being captured and tortured.

She had not seen him for more than a year. His absence was like an amputation: she felt it every hour of the day. But she was glad of the chance to spend an evening out with a man, even if it was the awkward, unglamorous, overweight Charlie Farquharson.

Charlie booked a table in the Grill Room of the Savoy Hotel.

In the lobby of the hotel, as a waiter was helping her take off her mink coat, she was approached by a tall man in a well-cut dinner jacket who looked vaguely familiar. He stuck out his hand and said shyly: "Hello, Daisy. What a pleasure to see you after all these years."

When she heard his voice, she realized it was Charlie. "Good Lord!" she said. "You've changed!"

"I lost a little weight," he admitted.

"You sure did." Forty or fifty pounds, she guessed. It made him better-looking. His features now seemed craggy rather than ugly.

"But you haven't changed at all," he said, looking her up and down.

She had made an effort with her clothes. She had bought nothing new for years, because of wartime austerity, but for tonight she had exhumed an off-the-shoulder sapphire blue silk evening gown by Lanvin that she had acquired on her last prewar trip to Paris. "In a couple of months I'll be twenty-six," she said. "I can't believe I look the same as I did when I was nineteen."

He glanced down at her décolletage, blushed, and said: "Believe me, you do."

They went into the restaurant and sat down. "I was afraid you weren't coming," he said.

"My watch stopped. I'm sorry I'm late."

"Only by twenty minutes. I would have waited an hour."

A waiter asked if they would like a drink. Daisy said: "This is one of the few places in England where you can get a decent martini."

"Two of those, please," Charlie said.

"I like mine straight up with an olive."

"So do I."

She studied him, intrigued by the way he had altered. His old awkwardness had softened to a charming shyness. It was still hard to imagine him as a fighter pilot, shooting down German planes. Anyway, the Blitz on London had come to an end half a year ago, and there were no longer air battles in the skies over southern England. "What kind of flying do you do?" she said.

"Mainly daytime circus operations over northern France."

"What's a circus operation?"

"A bomber attack with a heavy escort of fighters, the main object being to lure enemy planes into an air battle in which they're outnumbered."

"I hate bombers," she said. "I lived through the Blitz."

He was surprised. "I would have thought you'd want to give the Germans a taste of their own medicine."

"Not at all." Daisy had thought about this a lot. "I could weep for all the innocent women and children who were burned and maimed in London—and it doesn't help at all to know that German women and children are suffering the same."

"I never looked at it that way."

They ordered dinner. Wartime regulations restricted them to three courses, and their meal could not cost more than five shillings. On the menu were special austerity dishes such as Mock Duck—made out of pork sausages—and Woolton Pie, which contained no meat at all.

Charlie said: "I can't tell you how good it is to hear a girl speak real American. I like English girls, and I've even dated one, but I miss American voices."

"Me, too," she said. "This is my home now, and I don't guess I'll ever go back, but I know how you feel."

"I'm sorry I missed meeting Viscount Aberowen."

"He's in the air force, like you. He's a pilot trainer. He gets home now and again—but not this weekend."

Daisy was sleeping with Boy again, on his occasional visits home. She had sworn she never would after catching him with those awful women in Aldgate. But he had put pressure on her. He said that fighting men needed consolation when they came home, and he had promised never to visit prostitutes again. She did not really believe his promises, but all the same she gave in, albeit against her inclination. After all, she told herself, I did marry him for better or worse.

However, she no longer took any pleasure in sex with him, unfortunately. She could go to bed with Boy but she could not fall back in love with him. She had to use cream for lubrication. She had tried to summon again the fond feelings she had once had for him, when she had found him an exciting young aristocrat with the world at his feet, full of fun and capable of enjoying life thoroughly. But he was not really exciting, she now realized: he was just a selfish and rather limited man with a title. When he was on top of her, all she could think about was that he might be passing her some disgusting infection.

Charlie said carefully: "I'm sure you don't want to talk too much about the Rouzrokh family . . ."

"No."

". . . but did you hear that Joanne died?"

"No!" Daisy was shocked. "How?"

"At Pearl Harbor. She was engaged to Woody Dewar, and she went with him to visit his brother, Chuck, who is stationed there. They were in a car that was strafed by a Zero—that's a Jap fighter plane—and she was hit."

"I'm so sorry. Poor Joanne. Poor Woody."

Their food came, and a bottle of wine. They ate in silence for a while. Daisy discovered that Mock Duck did not taste much like duck.

Charlie said: "Joanne was one of twenty-four hundred people killed at Pearl Harbor. We lost eight battleships and ten other vessels. Goddamn sneaky Japs."

"People here are secretly pleased, because the U.S. is in the fight now. God alone knows why Hitler was dumb enough to declare war on the States. But the British think they have a chance of winning at last, with the Russians and us on their side."

"Americans are very angry about Pearl Harbor."

"People here don't see why."

"The Japanese kept on negotiating right up until the last minute—long after they must have made the decision. That's deceitful!"

Daisy frowned. "It seems sensible to me. If agreement had been reached at the last minute, they could have called off the attack."

"But they didn't declare war!"

"Would that have made any difference? We were expecting them to attack the Philippines. Pearl Harbor would have taken us by surprise even after a declaration of war."

Charlie spread his hands in a gesture of bafflement. "Why did they have to attack us anyway?"

"We stole their money."

"Froze their assets."

"They can't see the difference. And we cut off their oil. We had them up against the wall. They were facing ruin. What were they to do?"

"They should have given in, and agreed to withdraw from China."

"Yes, they should. But if it was America that was being pushed around and told what to do by some other country, would you want us to give in?"

"Maybe not." He grinned. "I said you hadn't changed. I'd like to take that back."

"Why?"

"You never used to talk like this. In the old days you wouldn't discuss politics at all."

"If you don't take an interest, then what happens is your fault."

"I guess we've all learned that."

They ordered dessert. Daisy said: "What's going to happen to the world, Charlie? All Europe is Fascist. The Germans have conquered much of Russia. The USA is an eagle with a broken wing. Sometimes I'm glad I don't have children."

"Don't underestimate the USA. We're wounded, not crushed. Japan is cock of the walk now, but the day will come when the Japanese people shed bitter tears of regret for Pearl Harbor."

"I hope you're right."

"And the Germans aren't having things all their own way any longer. They failed to take Moscow, and they're on the retreat. Do you realize the battle of Moscow was Hitler's first real defeat?"

"Is it a defeat, or just a setback?"

"Either way, it's the worst military result he's ever had. The Bolsheviks gave the Nazis a bloody nose."

Charlie had discovered vintage port, a British taste. In London men drank it after the ladies had retired from the dinner table, a tiresome practise that Daisy had tried to abolish in her own house, without success. They had a glass each. On top of the martini and the wine, it made Daisy feel a little drunk and happy.

They reminisced about their adolescence in Buffalo, and laughed about the foolish things they and others had done. "You told us all you were going to London to dance with the king," Charlie said. "And you did!"

"I hope they were jealous."

"And how! Dot Renshaw went into spasm."

Daisy laughed happily.

"I'm glad we got back in contact," Charlie said. "I like you so much."

"I'm glad, too."

They left the restaurant and got their coats. The doorman summoned a taxi. "I'll take you home," Charlie said.

As they drove along the Strand, he put his arm around her. She was about to protest; then she thought: What the hell. She snuggled up to him.

"What a fool I am," he said. "I wish I'd married you when I had the chance."

"You would have made a better husband than Boy Fitzherbert," she said. But then she would never have met Lloyd.

She realized she had not said anything to Charlie about Lloyd.

As they turned into her street, Charlie kissed her.

It felt nice to be wrapped in a man's arms and kissing his lips, but she knew it was the booze making her feel that way, and in truth the only man she wanted to kiss was Lloyd. All the same she did not push him away until the cab came to a halt.

"How about a nightcap?" he said.

For a moment she was tempted. It was a long time since she had touched a man's hard body. But she did not really want Charlie. "No," she said. "I'm sorry, Charlie, but I love someone else."

"We don't have to go to bed together," he whispered. "But if we could just, you know, smooch awhile . . ."

She opened the door and stepped out. She felt like a heel. He was risking his life for her every day, and she would not even give him a cheap thrill. "Good night, Charlie, and good luck," she said. Before she could change her mind, she slammed the car door and went into her house.

She went straight upstairs. A few minutes later, alone in bed, she felt wretched. She had betrayed two men: Lloyd, because she had kissed Charlie; and Charlie, because she had sent him away dissatisfied.

She spent most of Sunday in bed with a hangover.

On Monday evening she got a phone call. "I'm Hank Bartlett," said a young American voice. "Friend of Charlie Farquharson, at Duxford. He talked to me about you, and I found your number in his book."

Her heart stopped. "Why are you calling me?"

"Bad news, I'm afraid," he said. "Charlie died today, shot down over Abbeville."

"No!"

"It was his first mission in his new Spitfire."

"He talked about that," she said dazedly.

"I thought you might like to know."

"Thank you, yes," she whispered.

"He just thought you were the bee's knees."

"Did he?"

"You should have heard him go on about how great you are."

"I'm sorry," she said. "I'm so sorry." Then she could no longer speak, and she hung up the phone.

ii

Chuck Dewar looked over the shoulder of Lieutenant Bob Strong, one of the cryptanalysts. Some of them were chaotic but Strong was the tidy kind, and he had nothing on his desk but a single sheet of paper on which he had written:

YO—LO—KU—TA—WA—NA

"I can't get it," Strong said in frustration. "If the decrypt is right, it says they have struck yolokutawana. But it doesn't mean anything. There's no such word."

Chuck stared at the six Japanese syllables. He felt sure they ought to mean something to him, even though he knew only a smattering of the language. But he could not figure it out, and he got on with his work.

The atmosphere in the Old Administration Building was grim.

For weeks after the raid, Chuck and Eddie saw bloated bodies from sunken ships floating on the oily surface of Pearl Harbor. At the same time, the intelligence they were handling reported more devastating attacks by the Japanese. Only three days after Pearl Harbor, Japanese planes hit the American base at Luzon in the Philippines and destroyed the Pacific Fleet's entire stock of torpedoes. The same day in the South China Sea they sank two British battleships, the *Repulse* and the *Prince of Wales,* leaving the British helpless in the Far East.

They seemed unstoppable. Bad news just kept coming. In the first few months of the New Year Japan defeated U.S. forces in the Philippines and beat the British in Hong Kong, Singapore, and Rangoon, the capital of Burma.

Many of the place names were unfamiliar even to seamen such as Chuck and Eddie. To the American public they sounded like distant planets in a science-fiction yarn: Guam, Wake, Bataan. But everyone knew the meaning of *retreat, submit,* and *surrender.*

Chuck felt bewildered. Could Japan really beat America? He could hardly believe it.

By May the Japanese had what they wanted: an empire that gave them rubber, tin, and—most important of all—oil. Information leaking out indicated that they were ruling their empire with a brutality that would have made Stalin blush.

But there was a fly in their ointment, and it was the U.S. Navy. The thought made Chuck proud. The Japanese had hoped to destroy Pearl Harbor completely, and gain control of the Pacific Ocean, but they had failed. American aircraft carriers and heavy cruisers were still afloat. Intelligence suggested the Japanese commanders were infuriated that the Americans refused to lie down and die. After their losses at Pearl Harbor the Americans were outnumbered and outgunned, but they did not flee and hide. Instead they launched hit-and-run raids on Japanese ships, doing minor damage but boosting American morale and giving the Japanese the unshakable feeling that they had not yet won. Then, on April 25, planes launched from a carrier bombed the center of Tokyo, inflicting a terrible wound on the pride of the Japanese military. The celebrations in Hawaii were ecstatic. Chuck and Eddie got drunk that night.

But there was a showdown coming. Every man Chuck spoke to in the Old Administration Building said the Japanese would launch a major attack early in the summer to tempt American ships to come out in force for a final battle. The Japanese hoped the superior strength of their navy would be decisive, and the American Pacific Fleet would be wiped out. The only way the Americans could win was to be better prepared and have better intelligence, to move faster and be smarter.

During those months, Station HYPO worked day and night to crack JN-25b, the new code of the Imperial Japanese Navy. By May they had made progress.

The U.S. Navy had wireless intercept stations all around the Pacific Rim, from Seattle to Australia. There, men known as the On the Roof Gang sat with headsets and radio receivers listening to Japanese radio traffic. They scanned the airwaves and wrote what they heard on message pads.

The signals were in Morse code, but the dots and dashes of naval signals translated into five-digit number groups, each representing a letter, word, or phrase in a codebook. The apparently random numbers were relayed by secure cable to teleprinters in the basement of the Old Administration Building. Then the difficult part began: cracking the code.

They always started with small things. The last word of any signal was often *owari*, meaning "end." The cryptanalyst would look for other appearances of that number group in the same signal, and write "END?" above any he found.

The Japanese helped them by making an uncharacteristically careless mistake.

Delivery of the new codebooks for JN-25b was delayed to some far-flung units. So, for a fatal few weeks, the Japanese high command sent out some messages *in both codes.* Since the Americans had broken much of the original JN-25, they were able to translate the message in the old code, set the decrypt alongside the message in the new code, and figure out the meanings of the five-digit groups of the new code. For a while they progressed by leaps and bounds.

The original eight cryptanalysts were supplemented, after Pearl Harbor, by some of the musicians from the band of the sunken battleship *California.* For reasons no one understood, musicians were good at decoding.

Every signal was kept and every decrypt filed. Comparison of one with another was crucial to the work. An analyst might ask for all the signals from a particular day, or all the signals to one ship, or all the signals that mentioned Hawaii. Chuck and the other clerical staff developed ever-more-complex systems of cross-indexing to help them find whatever the analysts needed.

The unit predicted that in the first week of May the Japanese would attack Port Moresby, the Allied base in Papua. They were right, and the U.S. Navy intercepted the invasion fleet in the Coral Sea. Both sides claimed victory, but the Japanese did not take Port Moresby. And Admiral Nimitz, commander in chief of the Pacific, began to trust his codebreakers.

The Japanese did not use regular names for locations in the Pacific Ocean. Every important place had a designation consisting of two letters—in fact two characters, or kanas, of the Japanese alphabet, although the codebreakers usually used equivalents from the Roman A to Z. The men in the basement struggled to figure out the meaning of each of these two-kana designators. They made slow progress: MO was Port Moresby, AH was Oahu, but many were unknown.

In May evidence was fast building up of a major Japanese assault at a location they called AF.

The best guess of the unit was that AF meant Midway, the atoll at the western end of the fifteen-hundred-mile-long chain of islands that started at Hawaii. Midway was halfway between Los Angeles and Tokyo.

A guess was not enough, of course. Given the numerical superiority of the Japanese navy, Admiral Nimitz had to *know*.

Day by day, the men Chuck was working with built up an ominous picture of the Japanese order of battle. New planes were delivered to aircraft carriers. An "occupation force" was embarked: the Japanese were planning to hold on to whatever territory they won.

It looked as if this was the big one. But where would the attack come?

The men in the basement were particularly proud of decoding a signal from the Japanese fleet urging Tokyo: "Expedite delivery of fueling hose." They were pleased partly because of the specialized language but mainly because the signal proved that a long-range midocean maneuver was imminent.

But the American high command thought the attack might come at Hawaii, and the army feared an invasion of the West Coast of the United States. Even the team at Pearl Harbor had a nagging suspicion it could be Johnston Island, an airstrip a thousand miles south of Midway.

They had to be 100 percent certain.

Chuck had a notion how it might be done, but he hesitated to say anything. The cryptanalysts were so clever, and he was not. He had never done well in school. In third grade a classmate had called him Chucky the Chump. He had cried, and that had guaranteed that the nickname would stick. He still thought of himself as Chucky the Chump.

At lunchtime he and Eddie got sandwiches and coffee from the commissary and sat on the dockside, looking across the harbor. It was returning to normal. Most of the oil had gone, and some of the wrecks had been raised.

While they were eating, a wounded aircraft carrier appeared around Hospital Point and steamed slowly into harbor, trailing an oil slick that stretched all the way out to sea. Chuck identified the vessel as the *Yorktown*. Her hull was blackened with soot and she had a huge hole in the flight deck, presumably caused by a Japanese bomb in the Battle of the Coral Sea. Sirens and hooters sounded a congratulatory fanfare as she approached the navy yard, and tugs assembled to nudge her through the open gates of No. 1 Dry Dock.

"She needs three months' work, I hear," Eddie said. He was based in the same building as Chuck, but in the naval intelligence office upstairs, so he got to hear more gossip. "But she's putting to sea again in three days."

"How are they going to manage that?"

"They've started already. The master shipfitter flew to meet her—he's on board already, with a team. And look at the dry dock."

Chuck saw that the vacant dock was already swarming with men and equipment: he could not count the number of welding machines waiting at the quayside.

"All the same," Eddie said, "they'll just be patching her up. They'll repair the deck and make her seaworthy, and everything else will have to wait."

Something about the name of the ship bugged Chuck. He could not shake the nagging feeling. What did Yorktown mean? The siege of Yorktown was the last big battle of the War of Independence. Did that have some significance?

Captain Vandermeier walked by. "Get back to work, you two girlie boys," he said.

Eddie said under his breath: "One of these days I'm going to punch him out."

"After the war, Eddie," said Chuck.

When he returned to the basement and saw Bob Strong at his desk, Chuck realized he had solved Strong's problem.

Looking over the cryptanalyst's shoulder again, he saw the same sheet of paper with the same six Japanese syllables:

YO—LO—KU—TA—WA—NA

He tactfully tried to make it sound as if Strong himself had solved it. "But you have got it, Lieutenant!" he said.

Strong was disconcerted. "Do I?"

"It's an English name, so the Japanese have spelled it out phonetically."

"Yolokutawana is an English name?"

"Yes, sir. That's how the Japanese pronounce Yorktown."

"What?" Strong looked baffled.

For a dreadful moment, Chucky the Chump wondered if he was completely wrong.

Then Strong said: "Oh, my God, you're right! Yolokutawana—Yorktown, with a Japanese accent!" He laughed delightedly. "Thank you!" he enthused. "Well done!"

Chuck hesitated. He had another idea. Should he say what was on his mind? It was not his job to solve codes. But America was an inch away from defeat. Maybe he should take a chance. "Can I make another suggestion?" he said.

"Fire away."

"It's about the designator AF. We need definite confirmation that it's Midway, right?"

"Yup."

"Couldn't we write a message about Midway that the Japanese would want to rebroadcast in code? Then when we intercepted the broadcast, we could find out how they encode the name."

Strong looked thoughtful. "Maybe," he said. "We might have to send our message in clear, to be sure they understood it."

"We could do that. It would have to be something not very confidential—like, say: 'There is an outbreak of venereal disease on Midway, please send medicine,' or something like that."

"But why would the Japs rebroadcast that?"

"Okay, so it has to be something of military significance, but not top secret—something like the weather."

"Even weather forecasts are secret nowadays."

The cryptanalyst at the next desk put in: "How about a water shortage? If they're planning to occupy the place, that would be important information."

"Hell, this could work." Strong was getting excited. "Suppose Midway sends a message in clear to Hawaii, saying their desalination plant has broken down."

Chuck said: "And Hawaii replies, saying we're sending a water barge."

"The Japanese would be sure to rebroadcast that, if they're planning to attack Midway. They would need to make plans to ship fresh water there."

"And they would broadcast in code to avoid alerting us to their interest in Midway."

Strong stood up. "Come with me," he said to Chuck. "Let's put this to the boss, see what he thinks of the idea."

The signals were exchanged that day.

Next day, a Japanese radio signal reported a water shortage at AF.

The target was Midway.

Admiral Nimitz commenced to set a trap.

iii

That evening, while more than a thousand workmen swarmed over the crippled aircraft carrier *Yorktown*, repairing the damage under arc lights, Chuck and Eddie went to the Band Round the Hat, a bar down a dark alley in Honolulu. It was packed, as always, with sailors and locals. Almost all the customers were men, though there were a few nurses in pairs. Chuck and Eddie liked the place because the other men were their kind. The lesbians liked it because the men did not hit on them.

There was nothing overt, of course. You could be thrown out of the navy and put in jail for homosexual acts. All the same the place was congenial. The bandleader wore makeup. The Hawaiian singer was in drag, although he was so convincing that some people did not realize he was a man. The owner was as queer as a three-dollar bill. Men could dance together. And no one would call you a wimp for ordering vermouth.

Since the death of Joanne, Chuck felt he loved Eddie even more. Of course he had always known that Eddie could be killed, in theory, but the danger had never seemed real. Now, after the attack on Pearl Harbor, Chuck never passed a day without visualizing that beautiful girl lying on the ground covered in blood, and his brother sobbing his heart out beside her. It could so easily have been Chuck kneeling next to Eddie, and feeling the same unbearable grief. Chuck and Eddie had cheated death on December 7, but they were at war now, and life was cheap. Every day together was precious because it might be the last.

Chuck was leaning on the bar with a beer in his hand, and Eddie was sitting on a high stool. They were laughing at a navy pilot called Trevor Paxman—known as Trixie—who was talking about the time he tried to have sex with a girl. "I was horrified!" Trixie said. "I thought it would be all tidy down there, and kind of sweet, like girls in paintings—but she had more hair than me!" They roared with laughter. "She was like a gorilla!" At that point Chuck saw, out of the corner of his eye, the stocky figure of Captain Vandermeier entering the bar.

Few officers went into enlisted men's bars. It was not forbidden, merely thoughtless and inconsiderate, like wearing muddy boots in the restaurant of the Ritz-Carlton. Eddie turned his back, hoping Vandermeier would not see him.

No such luck. Vandermeier came right up to them and said: "Well, well, all girls together, are we?"

Trixie turned away and melted into the crowd. Vandermeier said: "Where did he go?" He was already drunk enough to slur his words.

Chuck saw Eddie's face darken. Chuck said stiffly: "Good evening, Captain, may I buy you a beer?"

"Scotch onna rocks."

Chuck got him a drink. Vandermeier took a swallow and said: "So, I hear the action in this place is out the back—is that right?" He looked at Eddie.

"No idea," Eddie said coldly.

"Aw, come on," said Vandermeier. "Off the record." He patted Eddie's knee.

Eddie stood up abruptly and pushed his stool back. "Don't you touch me," he said.

Chuck said: "Take it easy, Eddie."

"There's no rule in the navy says I have to be pawed by this old queen!"

Vandermeier said drunkenly: "What did you call me?"

Eddie said: "If he touches me again, I swear I'll knock his ugly head off."

Chuck said: "Captain Vandermeier, sir, I know a much better place than this. Would you like to go there?"

Vandermeier looked confused. "What?"

Chuck improvised: "A smaller, quieter place—like this, but more intimate. Do you know what I mean?"

"Sounds good!" The captain drained his glass.

Chuck took Vandermeier's right arm and gestured to Eddie to take the left. They led the drunk captain outside.

Luckily, a taxi was waiting in the gloom of the alley. Chuck opened the car door.

At that point, Vandermeier kissed Eddie.

The captain threw his arms around him, pressed his lips to Eddie's, then said: "I love you."

Chuck's heart filled with fear. There was no good ending to this now.

Eddie punched Vandermeier in the stomach, hard. The captain grunted and gasped. Eddie hit him again, in the face this time. Chuck stepped between them. Before Vandermeier could fall down, Chuck bundled him into the backseat of the taxi.

He leaned through the window and gave the driver a ten-dollar bill. "Take him home, and keep the change," he said.

The taxi pulled away.

Chuck looked at Eddie. "Oh, boy," he said. "Now we're in trouble."

iv

But Eddie Parry was never charged with the crime of assaulting an officer.

Captain Vandermeier showed up at the Old Administration Building next morning with a black eye, but he made no accusation. Chuck figured it would ruin the man's career if he admitted he had got into a fight at the Band Round the Hat. All the same everyone was talking about his bruise. Bob Strong said: "Vandermeier claims he slipped on a patch of oil in his garage, and hit his face on the lawn mower, but I think his wife socked him. Have you seen her? She looks like Jack Dempsey."

That day, the cryptanalysts in the basement told Admiral Nimitz that the Japanese would attack Midway on June 4. More specifically, the Japanese force would be one hundred and seventy-five miles north of the atoll at seven A.M.

They were almost as confident as they sounded.

Eddie was gloomy. "What can we do?" he said when he and Chuck met for lunch. He worked in naval intelligence, too, and he knew the Japanese strength as revealed by the codebreakers. "The Japs have two hundred ships at sea—practically their entire navy—and how many do we have? Thirty-five!"

Chuck was not so glum. "But their strike force is only a quarter of their strength. The rest are the occupation force, the diversion force, and the reserves."

"So? A quarter of their strength is still more than our entire Pacific Fleet!"

"The actual Japanese strike force has only four aircraft carriers."

"But we have just three." Eddie pointed with his ham sandwich at the smoke-blackened carrier in the dry dock, with workmen swarming all over her. "And that includes the broken-down *Yorktown*."

"Well, we know they're coming, and they don't know we're lying in wait."

"I sure hope that makes as much difference as Nimitz thinks."

"Yeah, so do I."

When Chuck returned to the basement, he was told that he no longer worked there. He had been reassigned—to the *Yorktown*.

"It's Vandermeier's way of punishing me," Eddie said tearfully that evening. "He thinks you'll die."

"Don't be pessimistic," Chuck said. "We might win the war."

A few days before the attack, the Japanese changed to new codebooks. The men in the basement sighed and started again from scratch, but they produced little new intelligence before the battle. Nimitz had to make do with what he already had, and hope the Japanese did not revise the whole plan at the last minute.

The Japanese expected to take Midway by surprise and overwhelm it easily. They hoped the Americans would then attack in full force in a bid to win the atoll back. At that point, the Japanese reserve fleet would pounce and wipe out the entire American fleet. Japan would rule the Pacific.

And the USA would ask for peace talks.

Nimitz planned to nip the scheme in the bud by ambushing the strike force before they could take Midway.

Chuck was now part of the ambush.

He packed his kit bag and kissed Eddie good-bye; then they went together to the dockside.

There they ran into Vandermeier.

"There was no time to repair the watertight compartments," he told them. "If she's holed, she'll go down like a lead coffin."

Chuck put a restraining hand on Eddie's shoulder and said: "How's your eye, Captain?"

Vandermeier's mouth twisted in a grimace of malice. "Good luck, faggot." He walked away.

Chuck shook hands with Eddie and went on board.

He forgot about Vandermeier instantly, for at long last he had his wish: he was at sea—and on one of the greatest ships ever made.

The *Yorktown* was the lead ship of the carrier class. She was longer than two football pitches and had a crew of more than two thousand.

She carried ninety aircraft: elderly Douglas Devastator torpedo bombers with folding wings, newer Douglas Dauntless dive-bombers, and Grumman Wildcat fighters to escort the bombers.

Almost everything was below, apart from the island structure, which stood up thirty feet from the flight deck. It contained the ship's command and communications heart, with the bridge, the radio room just below it, the chart house, and the aviators' ready room. Behind these was a huge smokestack containing three funnels in a row.

Some of the repairmen were still aboard, finishing their work, when she left the dry dock and steamed out of Pearl Harbor. Chuck thrilled to the throb of her colossal engines as she put to sea. When she reached deep water and began to rise and fall with the swell of the Pacific Ocean, he felt as if he were dancing.

Chuck was assigned to the radio room, a sensible posting that made use of his experience in handling signals.

The carrier steamed to a rendezvous northeast of Midway, her welded patches creaking like new shoes. The ship had a soda fountain, known as the Gedunk, that served freshly made ice cream. There on the first afternoon Chuck ran into Trixie Paxman, whom he had last seen at the Band Round the Hat. He was glad to have a friend aboard.

On Wednesday, June 3, the day before the predicted attack, a navy flying boat on reconnaissance west of Midway spotted a convoy of Japanese transport ships—presumably carrying the occupation force that was to take over the atoll after the battle. The news was broadcast to all U.S. ships, and Chuck in the radio room of the *Yorktown* was among the first to know. It was hard confirmation that his comrades in the basement had been right, and he felt a sense of relief that they had been vindicated. That was ironic, he realized: he would not be in such danger if they had been wrong and the Japanese were elsewhere.

He had been in the navy for a year and a half, but until now he had never gone into battle. The hastily repaired *Yorktown* was going to be the target of Japanese torpedoes and bombs. She was steaming toward people who would do everything in their power to sink her, and sink

Chuck, too. It was a weird feeling. Most of the time he was strangely calm, but every now and again he felt an impulse to dive over the side and start swimming back toward Hawaii.

That night he wrote to his parents. If he died tomorrow, he and the letter would probably go down with the ship, but he wrote it anyway. He said nothing about why he had been reassigned. It crossed his mind to confess that he was queer, but he quickly dismissed that idea. He told them he loved them and was grateful for everything they had done for him. "If I die fighting for a democratic country against a cruel military dictatorship, my life will not have been wasted," he wrote. When he read it over, it sounded a bit pompous, but he left it as it was.

It was a short night. Aircrew were piped to breakfast at one thirty A.M. Chuck went to wish Trixie Paxman good luck. In recompense for the early start, the airmen were eating steak and eggs.

Their planes were brought up from the belowdecks hangars in the ship's huge elevators, then maneuvered by hand to their parking slots on deck to be fueled and armed. A few pilots took off and went looking for the enemy. The rest sat in the briefing room, wearing their flying gear, waiting for news.

Chuck went on duty in the radio room. Just before six he picked up a signal from a reconnaissance flying boat:

MANY ENEMY PLANES HEADING MIDWAY

A few minutes later he got a partial signal:

ENEMY CARRIERS

It had started.

When the full report came in a minute later, it placed the Japanese strike force almost exactly where the cryptanalysts had forecast. Chuck felt proud—and scared.

The three American aircraft carriers—*Yorktown, Enterprise,* and *Hornet*—set a course that would bring their planes within striking distance of the Japanese ships.

On the bridge was the long-nosed Admiral Frank Fletcher, a fifty-seven-year-old veteran who had won the Navy Cross in the First World War. Carrying a signal to the bridge, Chuck heard him say: "We haven't seen a Japanese plane yet. That means they still don't know we're here."

That was all the Americans had going for them, Chuck knew: the advantage of better intelligence.

The Japanese undoubtedly hoped to catch Midway napping, in a repeat of the Pearl Harbor scenario, but it was not going to happen, thanks to the cryptanalysts. The American planes at Midway were not sitting targets parked on their runways. By the time the Japanese bombers arrived, they were all in the air and spoiling for a fight.

Tensely listening to the crackling wireless traffic from Midway and the Japanese ships, the officers and men in the radio room of the *Yorktown* had no doubt that there was a terrific air battle going on over the tiny atoll, but they did not know who was winning.

Soon afterward, American planes from Midway took the fight to the enemy and attacked the Japanese aircraft carriers.

In both battles, as far as Chuck could make out, the antiaircraft guns had the best of it. Only moderate damage was done to the base at Midway, and almost all the bombs and torpedoes aimed at the Japanese fleet missed, but in both encounters a lot of aircraft were shot down.

The score seemed even—but that bothered Chuck, for the Japanese had more in reserve.

Just before seven the *Yorktown,* the *Enterprise,* and the *Hornet* swung around to the southeast. It was a course that unfortunately took them away from the enemy, but their planes had to take off into the southeasterly wind.

Every corner of the mighty *Yorktown* trembled to the thunder of the aircraft as their engines rose to full throttle and they powered along the deck, one after another, and shot up into the air. Chuck noticed the tendency of the Wildcat to lift its right wing and wander left as it accelerated along the deck, a characteristic much complained of by pilots.

By half past eight the three carriers had sent 155 American planes to attack the enemy strike force.

The first planes arrived in the target area, with perfect timing, when the Japanese were busy refueling and rearming their own planes returning from Midway. The flight decks were littered with ammunition cases scattered in a snakes' nest of fuel hoses, all ready to blow up in an instant. There should have been carnage.

But it did not happen.

Almost all the American aircraft in the first wave were destroyed.

The Devastators were obsolete. The Wildcats that escorted them were better, but no match for the fast, maneuverable Japanese Zeroes. Those planes that survived to deliver their ordnance were decimated by devastating antiaircraft fire from the carriers.

Dropping a bomb from a moving aircraft onto a moving ship, or dropping a torpedo where it would hit a ship, was extraordinarily difficult, especially for a pilot who was under fire from above and below.

Most of the airmen gave their lives in the attempt.

And not one of them scored a hit.

No American bomb or torpedo found its target. The first three waves of attacking planes, one from each American carrier, did no damage at all to the Japanese strike force. The ammunition on their decks did not explode, and their fuel lines did not catch fire. They were unharmed.

Listening to the radio chatter, Chuck despaired.

He saw with new vividness the genius of the attack on Pearl Harbor seven months earlier. The American ships had been at anchor, static targets crowded together, relatively easy to hit. The fighter planes that might have protected them were destroyed on their airstrips. And by the time the Americans had armed and deployed their antiaircraft guns, the attack was almost over.

However, this battle was still going on, and not all the American planes had yet reached the target area. He heard an air officer on the *Enterprise* radio shout: "Attack! Attack!" and the laconic response from a pilot: "Wilco, as soon as I can find the bastards."

The good news was that the Japanese commander had not yet sent aircraft to attack the American ships. He was sticking to his plan and concentrating on Midway. He might by now have figured out that he must be under attack from carrier-borne planes, but perhaps he was not sure where the American ships were located.

Despite this advantage, the Americans were not winning.

Then the picture changed. A flight of thirty-seven Dauntless dive-bombers from the *Enterprise* sighted the Japanese. The Zeroes protecting the ships had come down almost to sea level in their dogfights with previous attackers, so the bombers found themselves fortunately above the fighters, and able to come down at them out of the sun. Just minutes later another eighteen Dauntlesses from the *Yorktown* reached the target area. One of the pilots was Trixie.

The radio exploded with excited chatter. Chuck closed his eyes and concentrated, trying to make sense of the distorted sounds. He could not identify Trixie's voice.

Then, behind the talk, he began to hear the characteristic scream of bombers diving. The attack had begun.

Suddenly, for the first time, there were cries of triumph from the pilots.

"Got you, you bastard!"

"Shit, I felt that go up!"

"Eat that, you sons of bitches!"

"Bull's-eye!"

"Look at her burn!"

The men in the radio room cheered wildly, but they were not sure what was happening.

It was over in a few minutes, but it took a long time to get a clear report. The pilots were incoherent with the joy of victory. Gradually, as they calmed down and headed back toward their ships, the picture emerged.

Trixie Paxman was among the survivors.

Most of their bombs had missed, as previously, but about ten had scored direct hits, and those few had done tremendous damage.

Three mighty Japanese aircraft carriers were burning out of control: *Kaga, Soryu,* and the flagship *Akagi.* The enemy had only one left, the *Hiryu.*

"Three out of the four!" Chuck said elatedly. "And they still haven't come anywhere near our ships!"

That soon changed.

Admiral Fletcher sent out ten Dauntlesses to scout for the surviving Japanese carrier. But it was the *Yorktown*'s radar that picked up a flight of planes, presumably from the *Hiryu,* fifty miles away and approaching. At noon Fletcher sent up twelve Wildcats to meet the attackers. The rest of the planes were also ordered up so they would not be on deck and vulnerable when the attack came. Meanwhile the *Yorktown*'s fuel lines were flooded with carbon dioxide as a fire precaution.

The attacking flight included fourteen "Vals," Aichi D3A dive-bombers, plus escorting Zeroes.

Here it comes, Chuck thought, my first action. He wanted to throw up. He swallowed hard.

Before the attackers could be seen, the *Yorktown*'s gunners opened up. The ship had four pairs of large antiaircraft guns with five-inch-diameter barrels that could send their shells several miles. Plotting the enemy's position with the aid of radar, gunnery officers sent a salvo of giant fifty-four-pound shells toward the approaching aircraft, setting the timers to explode when they reached their target.

The Wildcats got above the attackers and, according to the pilots' radio reports, shot down six bombers and three fighters.

Chuck ran to the flag bridge with a signal to say the remainder of the attack force were diving in. Admiral Fletcher said coolly: "Well, I've got my tin hat on—I can't do anything else."

Chuck looked out of the window and saw the dive-bombers screaming out of the sky toward him at an angle so steep they seemed to be falling straight down. He resisted the impulse to throw himself to the floor.

The ship made a sudden full-rudder turn to port. Anything that might throw the attacking aircraft off course was worth a try.

602 | CHAPTER TWELVE

The *Yorktown* deck also had four "Chicago pianos"—smaller, short-range antiaircraft guns with four barrels each. Now these opened up, and so did the guns of *Yorktown*'s escort of cruisers.

As Chuck stared forward from the bridge, terrified and helpless to do anything to defend himself, a deck gunner found his range and hit a Val. The plane seemed to break into three pieces. Two fell into the sea and one crashed into the side of the ship. Then another Val blew up. Chuck cheered.

But that left six.

The *Yorktown* made a sudden turn to starboard.

The Vals braved the hail of death from the deck guns to chase after the ship.

As they got closer, the machine guns on the catwalks either side of the flight deck also opened up. Now the *Yorktown*'s guns played a lethal symphony, with deep booms from the five-inch barrels, midrange sounds from the Chicago pianos, and the urgent rattle of machine guns.

Chuck saw the first bomb.

Many Japanese bombs had a delayed fuse. Instead of exploding on impact, they went off a second or so later, the idea being that they would crash through the deck and explode deep in the interior, causing maximum devastation.

But this bomb rolled along the *Yorktown*'s deck.

Chuck watched in mesmerized horror. For a moment it looked as if it might do no harm. Then it went off with a boom and a flash of flame. The two Chicago pianos aft were destroyed in an instant. Small fires appeared on deck and in the towers.

To Chuck's amazement the men around him remained as cool as if they were attending a war game in a conference room. Admiral Fletcher issued orders even as he staggered across the shuddering deck of the flag bridge. Moments later, damage control teams were dashing across the flight deck with fire hoses, and stretcher parties were picking up the wounded and carrying them down steep companionways to dressing stations below.

There were no major fires: the carbon dioxide in the fuel lines had prevented that. And there were no bomb-loaded planes on deck to blow up.

A moment later another Val screamed down at the *Yorktown* and a bomb hit the smokestack. The explosion rocked the mighty ship. A huge pall of oily black smoke gouted from the funnels. The bomb must have damaged the engines, Chuck realized, because the ship lost speed immediately.

More bombs missed their targets, landing in the sea, sending up geysers that splashed onto the deck, where seawater mingled with the blood of the wounded.

The *Yorktown* slowed to a halt. When the crippled ship was dead in the water, the Japanese scored a third hit, and a bomb crashed through the forward elevator and exploded somewhere below.

Then, suddenly, it was over, and the surviving Vals climbed into the clear blue Pacific sky.

I'm still alive, Chuck thought.

The ship was not lost. Fire-control parties were at work before the Japanese were out of sight. Down below, the engineers said they could get the boilers going within an hour. Repair crews patched the hole in the flight deck with six-by-four planks of Douglas fir.

But the radio gear had been destroyed, so Admiral Fletcher was deaf and blind. With his personal staff he transferred to the cruiser *Astoria*, and he handed over tactical command to Spruance on the *Enterprise*.

Under his breath, Chuck said: "Fuck you, Vandermeier—I survived."

He spoke too soon.

The engines throbbed back to life. Now under the command of Captain Buckmaster, the *Yorktown* began once again to cut through the Pacific waves. Some of her planes had already taken refuge on the *Enterprise,* but others were still in the air, so she turned into the wind, and they began to touch down and refuel. As she had no working radio, Chuck and his colleagues became a semaphore team to communicate with other ships using old-fashioned flags.

At half past two, the radar of a cruiser escorting the *Yorktown* revealed planes coming in low from the west—an attack flight from the

Hiryu, presumably. The cruiser signaled the news to the carrier. Buckmaster sent up twelve Wildcats to intercept.

The Wildcats must have been unable to stop the attack, for ten torpedo bombers appeared, skimming the waves, heading straight for the *Yorktown.*

Chuck could see the planes clearly. They were Nakajima B5Ns, called Kates by the Americans. Each carried a torpedo slung under its fuselage, the weapon almost half the length of the entire plane.

The four heavy cruisers escorting the carrier shelled the sea around her, throwing up a screen of foamy water, but the Japanese pilots were not so easily deterred, and they flew straight through the spray.

Chuck saw the first plane drop its torpedo. The long bomb splashed into the water, pointed at the *Yorktown.*

The plane flashed past the ship so close that Chuck saw the pilot's face. He was wearing a white-and-red headband as well as his flight helmet. He shook a triumphant fist at the crew on deck. Then he was gone.

More planes roared by. Torpedoes were slow, and ships could sometimes dodge them, but the crippled *Yorktown* was too cumbersome to zigzag. There was a tremendous bang, shaking the ship: torpedoes were several times more powerful than regular bombs. It felt to Chuck as if she had been struck on the port stern. Another explosion followed close behind, and this one actually lifted the ship, throwing half the crew to the deck. Immediately afterward, the mighty engines faltered.

Once again the damage parties were at work before the attacking planes were out of sight. But this time the men could not cope. Chuck joined the teams manning the pumps, and saw that the steel hull of the great ship was ripped like a tin can. A Niagara of seawater poured through the gash. Within minutes Chuck could feel that the deck had tilted. The *Yorktown* was listing to port.

The pumps could not cope with the inward rush of water, especially as the ship's watertight compartments had been damaged at the Coral Sea and not fixed during her rush repairs.

How long could it be before she capsized?

At three o'clock Chuck heard the order: "Abandon ship!"

Sailors dropped ropes over the high edge of the sloping deck. On the hangar deck, by jerking a few strings crewmen released thousands of life jackets from overhead stowage to fall like rain. The escort vessels moved closer and launched their boats. The crew of the *Yorktown* took off their shoes and swarmed over the side. For some reason, they put their shoes on the deck in neat lines, hundreds of pairs, like some ritual sacrifice. Wounded men were lowered on stretchers to waiting whaleboats. Chuck found himself in the water, swimming as fast as he could to get away from the *Yorktown* before she turned over. A wave took him by surprise and washed away his cap. He was glad he was in the warm Pacific: the Atlantic might have killed him with cold while he was waiting to be rescued.

He was picked up by a lifeboat. The boat continued to retrieve men from the sea. Dozens of other boats were doing the same. Many of the crew climbed down from the main deck, which was lower than the flight deck. The *Yorktown* somehow managed to stay afloat.

When all the crew were safe, they were taken aboard the escorting vessels.

Chuck stood on deck, looking across the water as the sun went down behind the slowly sinking *Yorktown*. It occurred to him that during the whole day he had not seen a Japanese ship. The entire battle had been fought by aircraft. He wondered if this was the first of a new kind of naval battle. If so, aircraft carriers would be the key vessels in the future. Nothing else would count for much.

Trixie Paxman appeared beside him. Chuck was so pleased to see him alive that he hugged him.

Trixie told Chuck that the last flight of Dauntless dive-bombers, from the *Enterprise* and the *Yorktown*, had set alight the *Hiryu*, the surviving Japanese carrier, and destroyed her.

"So all four Japanese carriers are out of action," Chuck said.

"That's right. We got them all, and lost only one of our own."

"So," said Chuck, "does that mean we won?"

"Yes," said Trixie. "I guess it does."

V

After the Battle of Midway it was clear that the Pacific war would be won by planes launched from ships. Both Japan and the United States began crash programs to build aircraft carriers as fast as possible.

During 1943 and 1944, Japan produced seven of these huge, costly vessels.

In the same period, the United States produced ninety.

CHAPTER THIRTEEN

1942 (II)

Nursing Sister Carla von Ulrich wheeled a cart into the supply room and closed the door behind her.

She had to work quickly. What she was about to do would get her sent to a concentration camp if she were caught.

She took a selection of wound dressings from a cupboard, plus a roll of bandage and a jar of antiseptic cream. Then she unlocked the drug cabinet. She took morphine for pain relief, sulfonamide for infections, and aspirin for fever. She added a new hypodermic syringe, still in its box.

She had already falsified the register, over a period of weeks, to look as if what she was stealing had been used legitimately. She had rigged the register before taking the stuff, rather than afterward, so that any spot check would reveal a surplus, suggesting mere carelessness, instead of a deficit, which indicated theft.

She had done all this twice before, but she felt no less frightened.

As she wheeled the cart out of the store, she hoped she looked innocent: a nurse bringing medical necessities to a patient's bedside.

She walked into the ward. To her dismay she saw Dr. Ernst there, sitting beside a bed, taking a patient's pulse.

All the doctors should have been at lunch.

It was now too late to change her mind. Trying to assume an air of confidence that was the opposite of what she felt, she held her head high and walked through the ward, pushing her cart.

Dr. Ernst glanced up at her and smiled.

Berthold Ernst was the nurses' dreamboat. A talented surgeon with a warm bedside manner, he was tall, handsome, and single. He had romanced most of the attractive nurses, and had slept with many of them, if hospital gossip could be credited.

She nodded to him and went briskly past.

She pushed the trolley out of the ward, then suddenly turned into the nurses' cloakroom.

Her outdoor coat was on a hook. Beneath it was a basketwork shopping bag containing an old silk scarf, a cabbage, and a box of sanitary towels in a brown paper bag. Carla removed the contents, then swiftly transferred the medical supplies from the trolley to the bag. She covered the supplies with the scarf, a blue-and-gold geometric design that her mother must have bought in the twenties. Then she put the cabbage and the sanitary towels on top, hung the bag on a hook, and arranged her coat to cover it.

I got away with it, she thought. She realized she was trembling a little. She took a deep breath, got herself under control, opened the door—and saw Dr. Ernst standing just outside.

Had he been following her? Was he about to accuse her of stealing? His manner was not hostile; in fact he looked friendly. Perhaps she had got away with it.

She said: "Good afternoon, Doctor. Can I help you with something?"

He smiled. "How are you, Sister? Is everything going well?"

"Perfectly, I think." Guilt made her add ingratiatingly: "But it is you, Doctor, who must say whether things are going well."

"Oh, I have no complaints," he said dismissively.

Carla thought: So what is this about? Is he toying with me, sadistically delaying the moment when he makes his accusation?

She said nothing, but stood waiting, trying not to shake with anxiety.

He looked down at the cart. "Why did you take that into the cloakroom?"

"I wanted something," she said, improvising desperately. "Something from my raincoat." She tried to suppress the frightened tremor in her voice. "A handkerchief, from my pocket." Stop gabbling, she told herself. He's a doctor, not a Gestapo agent. But he scared her all the same.

He looked amused, as if he enjoyed her nervousness. "And the trolley?"

"I'm returning it to its place."

"Tidiness is essential. You're a very good nurse . . . Fräulein von Ulrich . . . or is it Frau?"

"Fräulein."

"We should talk some more."

The way he smiled told her this was not about stealing medical supplies. He was about to ask her to go out with him. She would be the envy of dozens of nurses if she said yes.

But she had no interest in him. Perhaps it was because she had loved one dashing Lothario, Werner Franck, and he had turned out to be a self-centered coward. She guessed that Berthold Ernst was similar.

However, she did not want to risk annoying him, so she just smiled and said nothing.

"Do you like Wagner?" he said.

She could see where this was going. "I have no time for music," she said firmly. "I take care of my elderly mother." In fact Maud was fifty-one and enjoyed robust good health.

"I have two tickets for a recital tomorrow evening. They're playing the *Siegfried Idyll*."

"A chamber piece!" she said. "Unusual." Most of Wagner's work was on a grand scale.

He looked pleased. "You know about music, I see."

She wished she had not said it. She had just encouraged him. "My family is musical—my mother gives piano lessons."

"Then you must come. I'm sure someone else could take care of your mother for an evening."

"It's really not possible," Carla said. "But thank you very much for the invitation." She saw anger in his eyes: he was not used to rejection. She turned and started to push the cart away.

"Another time, perhaps?" he called after her.

"You're very kind," she replied, without slowing her pace.

She was afraid he would come after her, but her ambiguous reply to his last question seemed to have mollified him. When she looked back over her shoulder, he had gone.

She stowed the trolley and breathed easier.

She returned to her duties. She checked on all the patients in her ward and wrote her reports. Then it was time to hand over to the evening shift.

She put on her raincoat and slung her bag over her arm. Now she had to walk out of the building with stolen property, and her fear mounted again.

Frieda Franck was going at the same time, and they left together. Frieda had no idea Carla was carrying contraband. They walked in June sunshine to the tram stop. Carla wore a coat mainly to keep her uniform clean.

She thought she was giving a convincing impression of normality until Frieda said: "Are you worried about something?"

"No, why?"

"You seem nervous."

"I'm fine." To change the subject, she pointed at a poster. "Look at that."

The government had opened an exhibition in Berlin's Lustgarten, the park in front of the cathedral. "The Soviet Paradise" was the ironic title of a show about life under Communism, portraying Bolshevism as a Jewish trick and the Russians as subhuman Slavs. But even today the Nazis did not have everything their own way, and someone had gone around Berlin pasting up a spoof poster that read:

Permanent Installation
The NAZI PARADISE
War Hunger Lies Gestapo
How much longer?

There was one such poster stuck to the tram shelter, and it warmed Carla's heart. "Who puts these things up?" she said.

Frieda shrugged.

Carla said: "Whoever they are, they're brave. They would be killed if caught." Then she remembered what was in her bag. She, too, could be killed if caught.

Frieda just said: "I'm sure."

Now it was Frieda who seemed a little jumpy. Could she be one of those who put up the posters? Probably not. Maybe her boyfriend, Heinrich, was. He was the intense, moralistic type who would do that sort of thing. "How's Heinrich?" said Carla.

"He wants to get married."

"Don't you?"

Frieda lowered her voice. "I don't want to have children." This was a seditious remark: young women were supposed to produce children gladly for the Führer. Frieda nodded at the illegal poster. "I wouldn't like to bring a child into this paradise."

"I guess I wouldn't, either," said Carla. Maybe that was why she had turned down Dr. Ernst.

A tram arrived and they got on. Carla perched the basket on her lap nonchalantly, as if it contained nothing more sinister than cabbage. She scanned the other passengers. She was relieved to see no uniforms.

Frieda said: "Come home with me. Let's have a jazz night. We can play Werner's records."

"I'd love to, but I can't," Carla said. "I've got a call to pay. Remember the Rothmann family?"

Frieda looked around warily. Rothmann might or might not be a Jewish name. But no one was near enough to hear them. "Of course—he used to be our doctor."

"He's not supposed to practise anymore. Eva Rothmann went to London before the war and married a Scottish soldier. But the parents can't get out of Germany, of course. Their son, Rudi, was a violin maker—quite brilliant, apparently—but he lost his job, and now he repairs instruments and tunes pianos." He came to the von Ulrich house four times a year to tune the Steinway grand. "Anyway, I said I'd go round there this evening and see them."

"Oh," said Frieda. It was the long drawn-out *oh* of someone who has just seen the light.

"Oh, what?" said Carla.

"Now I understand why you're clutching that basket as if it contained the Holy Grail."

Carla was thunderstruck. Frieda had guessed her secret! "How did you know?"

"You said he's not *supposed* to practise. That suggests he does."

Carla saw that she had given Dr. Rothmann away. She should have said that he was not *allowed* to practise. Fortunately it was only to Frieda that she had betrayed him. She said: "What is he to do? They come to his door and beg him to help them. He can't turn sick people away! It's not as if he makes any money—all his patients are Jews and other poor folk who pay him with a few potatoes or an egg."

"You don't have to defend him to me," said Frieda. "I think he's brave. And you're heroic, stealing supplies from the hospital to give to him. Is this the first time?"

Carla shook her head. "Third. But I feel such a fool for letting you find out."

"You're not a fool. It's just that I know you too well."

The tram approached Carla's stop. "Wish me luck," she said, and she got off.

When she entered her house, she heard hesitant notes on the piano upstairs. Maud had a pupil. Carla was glad. It would cheer her mother up as well as provide a little money.

Carla took off her raincoat, then went into the kitchen and greeted Ada. When Maud had announced that she could no longer pay Ada's wages, Ada had asked if she could stay on anyway. Now she had a job cleaning an office in the evening, and she did housework for the von Ulrich family in exchange for her room and board.

Carla kicked off her shoes under the table and rubbed her feet together to ease their ache. Ada made her a cup of grain coffee.

Maud came into the kitchen, eyes sparkling. "A new pupil!" she said. She showed Carla a handful of banknotes. "And he wants a lesson every day!" She had left him practising scales, and his novice fingering sounded in the background like a cat walking along the keyboard.

"That's great," said Carla. "Who is he?"

"A Nazi, of course. But we need the money."

"What's his name?"

"Joachim Koch. He's quite young and shy. If you meet him, for goodness' sake bite your tongue and be polite."

"Of course."

Maud disappeared.

Carla drank her coffee gratefully. She had got used to the taste of burned acorns, as most people had.

She chatted idly to Ada for a few minutes. Ada had once been plump, but now she was thin. Few people were fat in today's Germany, but there was something wrong with Ada. The death of her handicapped son, Kurt, had hit her hard. She had a lethargic air. She did her job competently, but then she sat staring out of the window for hours, her expression blank. Carla was fond of her, and felt her anguish, but did not know what to do to help her.

The sound of the piano ceased and, a little later, Carla heard two voices in the hallway, her mother's and a man's. She assumed Maud was seeing Herr Koch out, and she was horrified, a moment later, when her mother entered the kitchen, closely followed by a man in an immaculate lieutenant's uniform.

"This is my daughter," Maud said cheerfully. "Carla, this is Lieutenant Koch, a new pupil."

Koch was an attractive, shy-looking man in his twenties. He had a fair mustache, and reminded Carla of pictures of her father when young.

Carla's heart raced with fear. The basket containing the stolen medical supplies was on the kitchen chair next to her. Would she accidentally betray herself to Lieutenant Koch, as she had to Frieda?

She could hardly speak. "I—I—I am pleased to make your acquaintance," she said.

Maud looked at her with curiosity, surprised at her nervousness. All Maud wanted was for Carla to be nice to the new pupil in the hope that he would continue his studies. She saw no harm in bringing an army officer into the kitchen. She had no idea that Carla had stolen medicines in her shopping basket.

Koch made a formal bow and said: "The pleasure is mine."

"And Ada is our maid."

Ada shot him a hostile look, but he did not see it: maids were beneath his notice. He put his weight on one leg and stood lopsided, trying to seem at ease but giving the opposite impression.

He acted younger than he looked. There was an innocence about him that suggested an overprotected child. All the same he was a danger.

Changing his stance, he rested his hands on the back of the chair on which Carla had put her basket. "I see you are a nurse," he said to her.

"Yes." Carla tried to think calmly. Did Koch have any idea who the von Ulrichs were? He might be too young to know what a Social Democrat was. The party had been illegal for nine years. Perhaps the infamy of the von Ulrich family had faded away with the death of Walter. At any rate, Koch seemed to take them for a respectable German family who were poor simply because they had lost the man who had supported them, a situation in which many well-bred women found themselves.

There was no reason he should look in the basket.

Carla made herself speak pleasantly to him. "How are you getting on with the piano?"

"I believe I am making rapid progress!" He glanced at Maud. "So my teacher tells me."

Maud said: "He shows evidence of talent, even at this early stage." She always said that, to encourage them to pay for a second lesson, but it seemed to Carla that she was being more charming than usual. She was entitled to flirt, of course; she had been a widow for more than a year. But she could not possibly have romantic feelings for someone half her age.

"However, I have decided not to tell my friends until I have mastered the instrument," Koch added. "Then I will astonish them with my skill."

"Won't that be fun?" said Maud. "Please sit down, Lieutenant, if you have a few minutes to spare." She pointed to the chair on which Carla's basket stood.

Carla reached out to grab the basket, but Koch beat her to it. He picked it up, saying: "Allow me." He glanced inside. Seeing the cabbage, he said: "Your supper, I presume?"

Carla said: "Yes." Her voice came out as a squeak.

He sat on the chair and placed the basket on the floor by his feet, on the side away from Carla. "I always fancied I might be musical. Now I have decided it is time to find out." He crossed his legs, then uncrossed them.

Carla wondered why he was so fidgety. He had nothing to fear. The thought crossed her mind that his unease might be sexual. He was alone with three single women. What was going through his mind?

Ada put a cup of coffee in front of him. He took out cigarettes. He smoked like a teenager, as if he were trying it out. Ada gave him an ashtray.

Maud said: "Lieutenant Koch works at the Ministry of War on Bendler Strasse."

"Indeed!" That was the headquarters of the Supreme Staff. It was just as well Koch was telling no one there about learning the piano. All the greatest secrets of the German military were in that building. Even if Koch himself was ignorant, some of his colleagues might remember that Walter von Ulrich had been an anti-Nazi. And that would be the end of his lessons with Frau von Ulrich.

"It is a great privilege to work there," said Koch.

Maud said: "My son is in Russia. We're terribly worried about him."

"That is natural in a mother, of course," Koch said. "But please do not be pessimistic! The recent Russian counteroffensive has been decisively beaten back."

That was rubbish. The propaganda machine could not conceal the fact that the Russians had won the battle of Moscow and pushed the German line back a hundred miles.

Koch went on: "We are now in a position to resume our advance."

"Are you sure?" Maud looked anxious. Carla felt the same. They were both tortured by fear of what might happen to Erik.

Koch tried a superior smile. "Believe me, Frau von Ulrich, I am certain. Of course I cannot reveal all that I know. However, I can assure you that a very aggressive new operation is being planned."

"I am sure our troops have everything they need—enough food, and so on." She put a hand on Koch's arm. "All the same, I worry. I shouldn't say that, I know, but I feel I can trust you, Lieutenant."

"Of course."

"I haven't heard from my son for months. I don't know if he's dead or alive."

Koch reached into his pocket and took out a pencil and a small notebook. "I can certainly find out for you," he said.

"Could you?" said Maud, wide-eyed.

Carla thought this might be her reason for flirting.

Koch said: "Oh, yes. I am on the General Staff, you know—albeit in a humble role." He tried to look modest. "I can inquire about . . ."

"Erik."

"Erik von Ulrich."

"That would be wonderful. He's a medical orderly. He was studying to be a doctor, but he was impatient to fight for the Führer."

It was true. Erik had been a gung-ho Nazi—although his last few letters home had taken a more subdued tone.

Koch wrote down the name.

Maud said: "You're a wonderful man, Lieutenant Koch."

"It is nothing."

"I'm so glad we're about to counterattack on the eastern front. But you mustn't tell me when the attack will begin. Though I'm desperate to know."

Maud was fishing for information. Carla could not imagine why. She had no use for it.

Koch lowered his voice, as if there might be a spy outside the open kitchen window. "It will be very soon," he said. He looked around at the three women. Carla saw that he was basking in their attention. Perhaps it was unusual for him to have women hanging on his words. Prolonging the moment, he said: "Case Blue will begin very soon."

Maud flashed her eyes at him. "Case Blue—how tremendously thrilling!" she said in the tone a woman might use if a man offered to take her to the Ritz in Paris for a week.

He whispered: "The twenty-eighth of June."

Maud put her hand on her heart. "So soon! That's marvelous news."

"I should not have said anything."

Maud put her hand over his. "I'm so glad you did, though. You've made me feel so much better."

He stared at her hand. Carla realized he was not used to being touched by women. He looked up from her hand to her eyes. She smiled warmly—so warmly that Carla could hardly believe it was 100 percent fake.

Maud withdrew her hand. Koch stubbed out his cigarette and stood up. "I must go," he said.

Thank God, Carla thought.

He bowed to her. "A pleasure to meet you, Fräulein."

"Good-bye, Lieutenant," she replied neutrally.

Maud saw him to the door, saying: "Same time tomorrow, then."

When she came back into the kitchen, she said: "What a find—a foolish boy who works for the General Staff!"

Carla said: "I don't understand why you're so excited."

Ada said: "He's very handsome."

Maud said: "He gave us secret information!"

"What good is it to us?" Carla asked. "We're not spies."

"We know the date of the next offensive—surely we can find a way to pass it to the Russians?"

"I don't know how."

"We're supposed to be surrounded by spies."

"That's just propaganda. Everything that goes wrong is blamed on subversion by Jewish-Bolshevik secret agents, instead of Nazi bungling."

"All the same, there must be some real spies."

"How would we get in touch with them?"

Mother looked thoughtful. "I'd speak to Frieda."

"What makes you say that?"

"Intuition."

Carla recalled the moment at the bus stop, when she had wondered aloud who put up the anti-Nazi posters, and Frieda had gone quiet. Carla's intuition agreed with her mother's.

But that was not the only problem. "Even if we could, do we want to betray our country?"

Maud was emphatic. "We have to defeat the Nazis."

"I hate the Nazis more than anyone, but I'm still German."

"I know what you mean. I don't like the idea of turning traitor, even though I was born English. But we aren't going to get rid of the Nazis unless we lose the war."

"But suppose we could give the Russians information that would ensure we lost a battle. Erik might die in that battle! Your son—my brother! We might be the cause of his death."

Maud opened her mouth to answer, but found she could not speak. Instead she began to cry. Carla stood up and put her arms around her.

After a minute, Maud whispered: "He might die anyway. He might die fighting for Nazism. Better he should be killed losing a battle than winning it."

Carla was not sure about that.

She released her mother. "Anyway, I wish you'd warn me before bringing someone like that into the kitchen," she said. She picked up her basket from the floor. "It's a good thing Lieutenant Koch didn't look any further into this."

"Why, what have you got in there?"

"Medicines stolen from the hospital for Dr. Rothmann."

Maud smiled proudly through her tears. "That's my girl."

"I nearly died when he picked up the bag."

"I'm sorry."

"You couldn't know. But I'm going to get rid of the stuff right now."

"Good idea."

Carla put her raincoat back on over her uniform and went out.

She walked quickly to the street where the Rothmanns lived. Their house was not as big as the von Ulrich place, but it was a well-proportioned town dwelling with pleasant rooms. However, the windows were now boarded up and there was a crude sign on the front door that said: SURGERY CLOSED.

The Rothmanns had once been prosperous. Dr. Rothmann had had a flourishing practise with many wealthy patients. He had also treated poor people at cheaper prices. Now only the poor were left.

Carla went around the back, as the patients did.

She knew immediately that something was wrong. The back door was open, and when she stepped into the kitchen, she saw a guitar with a broken neck lying on the tiled floor. The room was empty, but she could hear sounds from elsewhere in the house.

She crossed the kitchen and entered the hall. There were two main rooms on the ground floor. They had been the waiting room and the consulting room. Now the waiting room was disguised as a family sitting room, and the surgery had become Rudi's workshop, with a bench and woodworking tools, and usually half a dozen mandolins, violins, and cellos in various states of repair. All medical equipment was stashed out of sight in locked cupboards.

But not anymore, she saw when she walked in.

The cupboards had been opened and their contents thrown out. The floor was littered with smashed glass and assorted pills, powders, and liquids. In the debris Carla saw a stethoscope and a blood pressure gauge. Parts of several instruments were strewn around, evidently having been thrown on the floor and stamped upon.

Carla was shocked and disgusted. All that waste!

Then she looked into the other room. Rudi Rothmann lay in a corner.

He was twenty-two years old, a tall man with an athletic build. His eyes were closed, and he was moaning in agony.

His mother, Hannelore, knelt beside him. Once a handsome blonde, Hannelore was now gray and gaunt.

"What happened?" said Carla, fearing the answer.

"The police," said Hannelore. "They accused my husband of treating Aryan patients. They have taken him away. Rudi tried to stop them smashing the place up. They have . . ." She choked up.

Carla put down her basket and knelt beside Hannelore. "What have they done?"

Hannelore recovered the power of speech. "They broke his hands," she whispered.

Carla saw it at once. Rudi's hands were red and horribly twisted. The police seemed to have broken his fingers one by one. No wonder he was moaning. She was sickened. But she saw horror every day, and she knew how to suppress her personal feelings and give practical help. "He needs morphine," she said.

Hannelore indicated the mess on the floor. "If we had any, it's gone."

Carla felt a spasm of pure rage. Even the hospitals were short of supplies—and yet the police had wasted precious drugs in an orgy of destruction. "I brought you morphine." She took from her basket a vial of clear fluid and the new syringe. Swiftly, she took the syringe from its box and charged it with the drug. Then she injected Rudi.

The effect was almost instant. The moaning stopped. He opened his eyes and looked at Carla. "You angel," he said. Then he closed his eyes and seemed to sleep.

"We must try to set his fingers," Carla said. "So that the bones heal straight." She touched Rudi's left hand. There was no reaction. She grasped the hand and lifted it. Still he did not stir.

"I've never set bones," said Hannelore. "Though I've seen it done often enough."

"Same here," said Carla. "But we'd better try. I'll do his left hand. You do the right. We must finish before the drug wears off. God knows he'll be in enough pain."

"All right," said Hannelore.

Carla paused a moment longer. Her mother was right. They had to do anything they could to end this Nazi regime, even if it meant betraying their own country. She was no longer in any doubt.

"Let's get it done," Carla said.

Gently, carefully, the two women began to straighten Rudi's broken hands.

ii

Thomas Macke went to the Tannenberg Bar every Friday afternoon.

It was not much of a place. On one wall was a framed photograph of the proprietor, Fritz, in a First World War uniform, twenty-five years younger and without a beer belly. He claimed to have killed nine Russians at the Battle of Tannenberg. There were a few tables and chairs, but the regulars all sat at the bar. A menu in a leather cover was almost entirely fantasy: the only dishes served were sausages with potatoes or sausages without potatoes.

But the place stood across the street from the Kreuzberg police station, so it was a cop bar. That meant it was free to break all the rules. Gambling was open, street girls gave blow jobs in the bathroom, and the food inspectors of the Berlin city government never entered the kitchen. It opened when Fritz got up and closed when the last drinker went home.

Macke had been a lowly police officer at the Kreuzberg station years ago, before the Nazis took over and men such as he were suddenly given a break. Some of his former colleagues still drank at the Tannenberg, and he could be sure of seeing a familiar face or two. He still liked to talk to old friends, even though he had risen so far above them, becoming an inspector and a member of the SS.

"You've done well, Thomas. I'll give you that," said Bernhardt Engel, who had been a sergeant over Macke in 1932 and was still a sergeant.

"Good luck to you, son." He raised to his lips the stein of beer that Macke had bought him.

"I won't argue with you," Macke replied. "Though I will say, Superintendent Kringelein is a lot worse to work for than you were."

"I was too soft on you boys," Bernhardt admitted.

Another old comrade, Franz Edel, laughed scornfully. "I wouldn't say soft!"

Glancing out of the window, Macke saw a motorcycle pull up outside, driven by a young man in the light blue belted jacket of an air force officer. He looked familiar: Macke had seen him somewhere before. He had overlong red-blond hair flopping onto a patrician forehead. He crossed the pavement and came into the Tannenberg.

Macke remembered the name. He was Werner Franck, spoiled son of the radio manufacturer Ludi Franck.

Werner came to the bar and asked for a pack of Kamel cigarettes. How predictable, Macke thought, that the playboy should smoke American-style cigarettes, even if they were a German imitation.

Werner paid, opened the pack, took out a cigarette, and asked Fritz for a light. Turning to leave, cigarette in his mouth tilted at a rakish angle, he caught Macke's eye and, after a moment's thought, said: "Inspector Macke."

The men in the bar all stared at Macke to see what he would say.

He nodded casually. "How are you, young Werner?"

"Very well, sir, thank you."

Macke was pleased, but surprised, by the respectful tone. He recalled Werner as an arrogant whippersnapper with insufficient respect for authority.

"I'm just back from a visit to the eastern front with General Dorn," Werner added.

Macke sensed the cops in the bar become alert to the conversation. A man who had been to the eastern front merited respect. Macke could not help feeling pleased that they were all impressed that he moved in such elevated circles.

Werner offered Macke the cigarette pack, and Macke took one. "A beer," Werner said to Fritz. Turning back to Macke, he said: "May I buy you a drink, Inspector?"

"The same, thank you."

Fritz filled two steins. Werner raised his glass to Macke and said: "I want to thank you."

That was another surprise. "For what?" said Macke.

His friends were all listening intently.

Werner said: "A year ago you gave me a good telling-off."

"You didn't seem grateful at the time."

"And for that I apologize. But I thought very hard about what you said to me, and eventually I realized you were right. I had allowed personal emotion to cloud my judgment. You set me straight. I'll never forget that."

Macke was touched. He had disliked Werner, and had spoken harshly to him, but the young man had taken his words to heart and changed his ways. It gave Macke a warm glow to feel that he had made such a difference in a young man's life.

Werner went on: "In fact I thought of you the other day. General Dorn was talking about catching spies, and asking if we could track them down by their radio signals. I'm afraid I couldn't tell him much."

"You should have asked me," said Macke. "It's my specialty."

"Is that so?"

"Come and sit down."

They carried their drinks to a grubby table.

"These men are all police officers," Macke said. "But still, one should not talk publicly about such matters."

"Of course." Werner lowered his voice. "But I know I may confide in you. You see, some of the battlefield commanders told Dorn they believe the enemy often knows our intentions in advance."

"Ah!" said Macke. "I feared as much."

"What can I tell Dorn about radio signal detection?"

"The correct term is goniometry." Macke collected his thoughts. This was an opportunity to impress an influential general, albeit indirectly. He needed to be clear, and emphasize the importance of what he was doing without exaggerating its success. He imagined General Dorn saying casually to the Führer: "There's a very good man in the Gestapo—name of Macke—only an inspector, at the moment, but most impressive . . ."

"We have an instrument that tells us the direction from which the signal is coming," he began. "If we take three readings from widely separated locations, we can draw three lines on the map. Where they intersect is the address of the transmitter."

"That's fantastic!"

Macke raised a cautionary hand. "In theory," he said. "In practise, it's more difficult. The pianist—that's what we call the radio operator—does not usually stay in the location long enough for us to find him. A careful pianist never broadcasts from the same place twice. And our instrument is housed in a van with a conspicuous aerial on its roof, so they can see us coming."

"But you have had some success."

"Oh, yes. But perhaps you should come out in the van with us one evening. Then you could see the whole process for yourself—and make a firsthand report to General Dorn."

"That's a good idea," said Werner.

iii

Moscow in June was sunny and warm. At lunchtime Volodya waited for Zoya at a fountain in the Alexander Gardens behind the Kremlin. Hundreds of people strolled by, many in pairs, enjoying the weather. Life was hard, and the water in the fountain had been turned off to save power, but the sky was blue, the trees were in leaf, and the German army was a hundred miles away.

Volodya was full of pride every time he thought back to the Battle of Moscow. The dreaded German army, master of blitzkrieg attack, had been at the gates of the city—and had been thrown back. Russian soldiers had fought like lions to save their capital.

Unfortunately the Russian counterattack had petered out in March. It had won back much territory, and made Muscovites feel safer, but the Germans had licked their wounds and were now preparing to try again.

And Stalin was still in charge.

Volodya spotted Zoya walking through the crowd toward him. She was wearing a red-and-white checked dress. There was a spring in her step, and her pale blond hair seemed to bounce with her stride. Every man stared at her.

Volodya had dated some beautiful women, but he was surprised to find himself courting Zoya. For years she had treated him with cool indifference, and talked to him about nothing but nuclear physics. Then one day, to his astonishment, she had asked him to go to a movie.

It was shortly after the riot in which General Bobrov had been killed. Her attitude to him had changed that day—he was not sure he understood why; somehow the shared experience had created an intimacy. Anyway, they had gone to see *George's Dinky Jazz Band,* a knockabout comedy starring an English banjolele player called George Formby. It was a popular movie, and had been running for months in Moscow. The plot was about as unrealistic as could be: unknown to George, his instrument was sending messages to German U-boats. It was so silly that they had both laughed their socks off.

Since then they had been dating regularly.

Today they were to have lunch with his father. He had arranged to meet her beforehand at the fountain in order to have a few minutes alone with her.

Zoya gave him her thousand-candlepower smile and stood on tiptoe to kiss him. She was tall, but he was taller. He relished the kiss. Her lips were soft and moist on his. It was over too soon.

Volodya was not completely sure of her yet. They were still "walking out," as the older generation termed it. They kissed a lot, but they had not yet gone to bed together. They were not too young: he was twenty-seven, she twenty-eight. All the same, Volodya sensed that Zoya was not going to sleep with him until she was ready.

Half of him did not believe he would ever spend a night with this dream girl. She seemed too blond, too intelligent, too tall, too self-possessed, too sexy ever to give herself to a man. Surely he would never be allowed to watch her take off her clothes, to gaze at her naked body, to touch her all over, to lie on top of her . . . ?

They walked through the long, narrow park. On one side was a busy road. All along the other side, the towers of the Kremlin loomed over a high wall. "To look at it, you'd think our leaders in there were being held prisoner by the Russian people," Volodya said.

"Yes," Zoya agreed. "Instead of the other way round."

He looked behind them, but no one had heard. All the same it was foolhardy to talk like that. "No wonder my father thinks you're dangerous."

"I used to think you were like your father."

"I wish I was. He's a hero. He stormed the Winter Palace! I don't suppose I'll ever change the course of history."

"Oh, I know, but he's so narrow-minded and conservative. You're not like that."

Volodya thought he was pretty much like his father, but he was not going to argue.

"Are you free this evening?" she said. "I'd like to cook for you."

"You bet!" She had never invited him to her place.

"I've got a piece of steak."

"Great!" Good beef was a treat even in Volodya's privileged home.

"And the Kovalevs are out of town."

That was even better news. Like many Muscovites, Zoya lived in someone else's apartment. She had two rooms and shared the kitchen and bathroom with another scientist, Dr. Kovalev, and his wife and child. But the Kovalevs had gone away, so Zoya and Volodya would have the place to themselves. His pulse quickened. "Should I bring my toothbrush?" he said.

She gave him an enigmatic smile and did not answer the question.

They left the park and crossed the road to a restaurant. Many were closed, but the city center was full of offices whose workers had to eat lunch somewhere, and a few cafés and bars survived.

Grigori Peshkov was at a pavement table. There were better

restaurants inside the Kremlin, but he liked to be seen in places used by ordinary Russians. He wanted to show that he was not above the common people just because he wore a general's uniform. All the same, he had chosen a table well away from the rest, so that he could not be overheard.

He disapproved of Zoya, but he was not immune to her enchantment, and he stood up and kissed her on both cheeks.

They ordered potato pancakes and beer. The only alternatives were pickled herrings and vodka.

"Today I am not going to speak to you about nuclear physics, General," said Zoya. "Please take my word for it that I still believe everything I said last time we talked about the subject. I don't want to bore you."

"That's a relief," he said.

She laughed, showing white teeth. "Instead you can tell me how much longer we will be at war."

Volodya shook his head in mock despair. She always had to challenge his father. If she had not been a beautiful young woman, Grigori would have had her arrested long ago.

"The Nazis are beaten, but they won't admit it," Grigori said.

Zoya said: "Everyone in Moscow is wondering what will happen this summer—but you two probably know."

Volodya said: "If I did, I certainly could not tell my girlfriend, no matter how crazy I am about her." Apart from anything else, it could get her shot, he thought, but he did not say it.

The potato pancakes came and they began to eat. As always, Zoya tucked in hungrily. Volodya loved the relish with which she attacked food. But he did not much like the pancakes. "These potatoes taste suspiciously like turnips," he said.

His father shot him a disapproving look.

"Not that I'm complaining," Volodya added hastily.

When they had finished, Zoya went to the ladies' room. As soon as she was out of earshot, Volodya said: "We think the German summer offensive is imminent."

"I agree," said his father.

"Are we ready?"

"Of course," said Grigori, but he looked anxious.

"They will attack in the south. They want the oilfields of the Caucasus."

Grigori shook his head. "They will come back to Moscow. It's all that matters."

"Stalingrad is equally symbolic. It bears the name of our leader."

"Fuck symbolism. If they take Moscow, the war is over. If they don't, they haven't won, no matter what else they gain."

"You're just guessing," Volodya said with irritation.

"So are you."

"On the contrary, I have evidence." He looked around, but there was no one nearby. "The offensive is code-named Case Blue. It will start on the twenty-eighth of June." He had learned that much from Werner Franck's network of spies in Berlin. "And we found partial details in the briefcase of a German officer who crash-landed a reconnaissance plane near Kharkov."

"Officers on reconnaissance do not carry battle plans in briefcases," Grigori said. "Comrade Stalin thinks that was a ruse to deceive us, and I agree. The Germans want us to weaken our central front by sending forces south to deal with what will turn out to be no more than a diversion."

This was the problem with intelligence, Volodya thought with frustration. Even when you had the information, stubborn old men would believe what they wanted.

He saw Zoya coming back, all eyes on her as she walked across the plaza. "What would convince you?" he said to his father before she arrived.

"More evidence."

"Such as?"

Grigori thought for a moment, taking the question seriously. "Get me the battle plan."

Volodya sighed. Werner Franck had not yet succeeded in obtaining the document. "If I get it, will Stalin reconsider?"

"If you get it, I'll ask him to."

"It's a deal," said Volodya.

He was being rash. He had no idea how he was going achieve this. Werner, Heinrich, Lili, and the others already took horrendous risks. Yet he would have to put even more pressure on them.

Zoya reached their table and Grigori stood up. They were going in three different directions, so they said good-bye.

"I'll see you tonight," Zoya said to Volodya.

He kissed her. "I'll be there at seven."

"Bring your toothbrush," she said.

He walked away a happy man.

iv

A girl knows when her best friend has a secret. She may not know what the secret is, but she knows it is there, like an unidentifiable piece of furniture under a dust sheet. She realizes, from guarded and unforthcoming answers to innocent questions, that her friend is seeing someone she shouldn't; she just doesn't know the name, although she may guess that the forbidden lover is a married man, or a dark-skinned foreigner, or another woman. She admires that necklace, and knows from her friend's muted reaction that it has shameful associations, though it may not be until years later that she discovers it was stolen from a senile grandmother's jewel box.

So Carla thought when she reflected on Frieda.

Frieda had a secret, and it was connected with resistance to the Nazis. She might be deeply, criminally involved: perhaps she went through her brother Werner's briefcase every night, copied secret papers, and handed the copies to a Russian spy. More likely it was not so dramatic: she probably helped print and distribute those illegal posters and leaflets that criticized the government.

So Carla was going to tell Frieda about Joachim Koch. However, she did not immediately get a chance. Carla and Frieda were nurses in different departments of a large hospital, and had different rotas, so they did not necessarily meet every day.

Meanwhile, Joachim came to the house daily for lessons. He made no more indiscreet revelations, but Maud continued to flirt with him. "You do realize that I'm almost forty years old?" Carla heard her say one day, although she was in fact fifty-one. Joachim was completely infatuated. Maud was enjoying the power she still had to fascinate an attractive young man, albeit a very naïve one. The thought crossed Carla's mind that her mother might be developing deeper feelings for this boy with a fair mustache who looked a bit like the young Walter, but that seemed ridiculous.

Joachim was desperate to please her, and soon brought news of her son. Erik was alive and well. "His unit is in the Ukraine," Joachim said. "That's all I can tell you."

"I wish he could get leave to come home," Maud said wistfully.

The young officer hesitated.

She said: "A mother worries so much. If I could just see him, even for only a day, it would be such a comfort to me."

"I *might* be able to arrange that."

Maud pretended to be astonished. "Really? You're that powerful?"

"I'm not sure. I could try."

"Thank you for even trying." She kissed his hand.

It was a week before Carla saw Frieda again. When she did, she told her all about Joachim Koch. She told the story as if simply retelling an interesting piece of news, but she felt sure Frieda would not regard it in that innocent light. "Just imagine," she said. "He told us the code name of the operation and the date of the attack!" She waited to see how Frieda would respond.

"He could be executed for that," Frieda said.

"If we knew someone who could get in touch with Moscow, we might turn the course of the war," Carla went on, as if still talking about the gravity of Joachim's crime.

"Perhaps," said Frieda.

That proved it. Frieda's normal reaction to such a story would include expressions of surprise, lively interest, and further questions. Today she offered nothing but neutral phrases and noncommittal grunts. Carla went home and told her mother that her intuition had been correct.

Next day at the hospital, Frieda appeared in Carla's ward looking frantic. "I have to talk to you urgently," she said.

Carla was changing a dressing for a young woman who had been badly burned in a munitions factory explosion. "Go to the cloakroom," she said. "I'll be there as soon as I can."

Five minutes later she found Frieda in the little room, smoking by an open window. "What is it?" she said.

Frieda put out the cigarette. "It's about your Lieutenant Koch."

"I thought so."

"You have to find out more from him."

"I *have* to? What are you talking about?"

"He has access to the entire battle plan for Case Blue. We know something about it, but Moscow needs the details."

Frieda was making a bewildering set of assumptions, but Carla went along with it. "I can ask him . . ."

"No. You have to *make* him bring you the battle plan."

"I'm not sure that's possible. He's not completely stupid. Don't you think—"

Frieda was not even listening. "Then you have to photograph it," she interrupted. She produced from the pocket of her uniform a stainless-steel box about the size of a pack of cigarettes but longer and narrower. "This is a miniature camera specially designed for photographing documents." Carla noticed the name *Minox* on the side. "You'll get eleven pictures on one film. Here are three films." She brought out three cassettes, the shape of dumbbells but small enough to fit into the little camera. "This is how you load the film." Frieda demonstrated. "To take a picture, you look through this window. If you're not sure, read this manual."

Carla had never known Frieda to be so domineering. "I really need to think about this."

"There's no time. This is your raincoat, isn't it?"

"Yes, but—"

Frieda stuffed the camera, films, and booklet into the pockets of the coat. She seemed relieved they were out of her hands. "I've got to go." She went to the door.

"But, Frieda!"

At last Frieda stopped and looked directly at Carla. "What?"

"Well . . . You're not behaving like a friend."

"This is more important."

"You've backed me into a corner."

"You created this situation when you told me about Joachim Koch. Don't pretend you didn't expect me to do something with the information."

It was true. Carla had triggered this emergency herself. But she had not envisaged things turning out this way. "What if he says no?"

"Then you'll probably be living under the Nazis the rest of your life." Frieda went out.

"Hell," said Carla.

She stood alone in the cloakroom, thinking. She could not even get rid of the little camera without risk. It was in her raincoat, and she could hardly throw it into a hospital rubbish bin. She would have to leave the building with it in her pocket, and try to find a place where she could dispose of it secretly.

But did she want to?

It seemed unlikely that Koch, naïve though he was, could be talked into smuggling a copy of a battle plan out of the War Ministry and bringing it to show his inamorata. However, if anyone could persuade him, Maud could.

But Carla was scared. There would be no mercy for her if she was caught. She would be arrested and tortured. She thought of Rudi Rothmann, moaning in the agony of broken bones. She recalled her father after they released him, so brutally beaten that he had died. Her crime would be worse than theirs, her punishment correspondingly bestial. She would be executed, of course—but not for a long time.

She told herself she was willing to risk that.

What she could not accept was the danger that she would help kill her brother.

He was there, on the eastern front; Joachim had confirmed it. He would be involved in Case Blue. If Carla enabled the Russians to win that battle, Erik could die as a result. She could not bear that.

She went back to her work. She was distracted and made mistakes, but fortunately the doctors did not notice and the patients could not tell. When at last her shift ended, she hurried away. The camera was burning a hole in her pocket but she did not see a safe place to dump it.

She wondered where Frieda had got it. Frieda had plenty of money, and could easily have bought it, though she would have had to come up with a story about why she needed such a thing. More likely she could have got it from the Russians before they closed their embassy a year ago.

The camera was still in Carla's coat pocket when she arrived home.

There was no sound from the piano upstairs; Joachim was having his lesson later today. Her mother was sitting at the kitchen table. When Carla walked in, Maud beamed and said: "Look who's here!"

It was Erik.

Carla stared at him. He was painfully thin, but apparently uninjured. His uniform was grimy and ripped, but he had washed his face and hands. He stood up and put his arms around her.

She hugged him hard, careless of dirtying her spotless uniform. "You're safe," she said. There was so little flesh on him that she could feel his bones, his ribs and hips and shoulders and spine, through the thin material.

"Safe for the moment," he said.

She released her hold. "How are you?"

"Better than most."

"You weren't wearing this flimsy uniform in the Russian winter?"

"I stole a coat from a dead Russian."

She sat down at the table. Ada was there, too. Erik said: "You were right. About the Nazis, I mean. You were right."

She was pleased, but not sure exactly what he meant. "In what way?"

"They murder people. You told me that. Father told me, too, and Mother. I'm sorry I didn't believe you. I'm sorry, Ada, that I didn't believe they killed your poor little Kurt. I know better now."

This was a big reversal. Carla said: "What changed your mind?"

"I saw them doing it, in Russia. They round up all the important people in town, because they must be Communists. And they get the Jews, too. Not just men, but women and children. And old people too frail to do anyone any harm." Tears were streaming down his face now. "Our regular soldiers don't do it—there are special groups. They take the prisoners out of town. Sometimes there's a quarry, or some other kind of pit. Or they make the younger ones dig a great hole. Then . . ."

He choked up, but Carla had to hear him say it. "Then what?"

"They do them twelve at a time. Six pairs. Sometimes the husbands and wives hold hands as they walk down the slope. The mothers carry the babies. The riflemen wait until the prisoners are in the right spot. Then they shoot." Erik wiped his tears with his dirty uniform sleeve. "Bang," he said.

There was a long silence in the kitchen. Ada was crying. Carla was aghast. Only Maud was stony-faced.

Eventually Erik blew his nose, then took out cigarettes. "I was surprised to get leave and a ticket home," he said.

Carla said: "When do you have to go back?"

"Tomorrow. I have only twenty-four hours here. All the same I'm the envy of all my comrades. They'd give anything for a day at home. Dr. Weiss said I must have friends in high places."

"You do," said Maud. "Joachim Koch, a young lieutenant who works at the War Ministry and comes to me for piano lessons. I asked him to arrange leave for you." She glanced at her watch. "He'll be here in a few minutes. He has grown fond of me—he's in need of a mother figure, I think."

Mother, hell, Carla thought. There was nothing maternal about Maud's relationship with Joachim.

Maud went on: "He's very innocent. He told us there's going to be a new offensive on the eastern front starting on the twenty-eighth of June. He even mentioned the code name: Case Blue."

Erik said: "He's going to get himself shot."

Carla said: "Joachim is not the only one who might be shot. I told someone what I learned. Now I've been asked to persuade Joachim, somehow, to get me the battle plan."

"Good God!" Erik was rocked. "This is serious espionage—you're in more danger than I am on the eastern front!"

"Don't worry. I can't imagine Joachim would do it," Carla said.

"Don't be so sure," said Maud.

They all looked at her.

"He might do it for me," she said. "If I asked him the right way."

Erik said: "He's *that* naïve?"

She looked defiant. "He's in love with me."

"Oh." Erik was embarrassed at the idea of his mother being involved in a romance.

Carla said: "All the same, we can't do it."

Erik said: "Why not?"

"Because if the Russians win the battle you might die!"

"I'll probably die anyway."

Carla heard her own voice rise in pitch agitatedly. "But we'd be helping the Russians kill you!"

"I still want you to do it," Erik said fiercely. He looked down at the checkered oilcloth on the kitchen table, but what he was seeing was a thousand miles away.

Carla felt torn. If he *wanted* her to . . . She said: "But why?"

"I think of those people walking down the slope into the quarry, holding hands." His own hands on the table grasped each other hard enough to bruise. "I'll risk my life, if we can put a stop to that. I *want* to risk my life—I'll feel better about myself, and my country, if I do. Please, Carla, if you can, send the Russians that battle plan."

Still she hesitated. "Are you sure?"

"I'm begging you."

"Then I will," said Carla.

V

Thomas Macke told his men—Wagner, Richter, and Schneider—to be on their best behavior. "Werner Franck is only a lieutenant, but he works for General Dorn. I want him to have the best possible impression of our team and our work. No swearing, no jokes, no eating, and no rough stuff unless it's really necessary. If we catch a Communist spy, you can give him a good kicking. But if we fail, I don't want you to pick on someone else just for fun." Normally he would turn a blind eye to that sort of thing. It all helped to keep people in fear of the displeasure of the Nazis. But Franck might be squeamish.

Werner turned up punctually at Gestapo headquarters in Prinz Albrecht Strasse on his motorcycle. They all got into the surveillance van with the revolving aerial on the roof. With so much radio equipment inside it was cramped. Richter took the wheel and they drove around the city in the early evening, the favored time for spies to send messages to the enemy.

"Why is that, I wonder?" said Werner.

"Most spies have a regular job," Macke explained. "It's part of their cover story. So they go to an office or a factory in the daytime."

"Of course," said Werner. "I never thought of that."

Macke was worried they might not pick up anything at all tonight. He was terrified that he would get the blame for the reverses the German army was suffering in Russia. He had done his best, but there were no prizes for effort in the Third Reich.

It sometimes happened that the unit picked up no signals. On other occasions there would be two or three, and Macke would have to choose which to follow up on and which to ignore. He felt sure there was more than one spy network in the city, and they probably did not know of each other's existence. He was trying to do an impossible job with inadequate tools.

They were near the Potsdamer Platz when they heard a signal. Macke recognized the characteristic sound. "That's a pianist," he said with relief. At least he could prove to Werner that the equipment worked.

Someone was broadcasting five-digit numbers, one after the other. "Soviet intelligence uses a code in which pairs of numbers stand for letters," Macke explained to Werner. "So, for example, 11 might stand for A. Transmitting them in groups of five is just a convention."

The radio operator, an electrical engineer named Mann, read off a set of coordinates, and Wagner drew a line on a map with a pencil and rule. Richter put the van in gear and set off again.

The pianist continued to broadcast, his beeps sounding loud in the van. Macke hated the man, whoever he was. "Bastard Communist swine," he said. "One day he'll be in our basement, begging me to let him die so the pain will come to an end."

Werner looked pale. He was not used to police work, Macke thought.

After a moment the young man pulled himself together. "The way you describe the Soviet code, it sounds as if it might not be too difficult to break," he said thoughtfully.

"Correct!" Macke was pleased that Werner caught on so fast. "But I was simplifying. They have refinements. After encoding the message as a series of numbers, the pianist then writes a key word underneath it repeatedly—it might be *Kurfürstendamm*, say—and encodes that. Then he subtracts the second numbers from the first and broadcasts the result."

"Almost impossible to decipher if you don't know the key word!"

"Exactly."

They stopped again near the burned-out Reichstag building and drew another line on the map. The two met in Friedrichshain, to the east of the city center.

Macke told the driver to swing northeast, taking them nearer to the likely spot while giving them a third line from a different angle. "Experience shows that it's best to take three bearings," Macke told Werner. "The equipment is only approximate, and the extra measurement reduces error."

"Do you always catch him?" said Werner.

"By no means. In most cases we don't. Often we're just not quick enough. He may change frequency halfway through, so that we lose him. Sometimes he breaks off in midtransmission and resumes at another location. He may have lookouts who see us coming and warn him to flee."

"A lot of snags."

"But we catch them, sooner or later."

Richter stopped the van and Mann took the third bearing. The three pencil lines on Wagner's map met to form a small triangle near the East Station. The pianist was somewhere between the railway line and the canal.

Macke gave Richter the location and added: "Quick as you can."

Werner was perspiring, Macke noticed. Perhaps it was rather hot in the van. And the young lieutenant was not accustomed to action. He was learning what life was like in the Gestapo. All the better, Macke thought.

Richter headed south on Warschauer Strasse, crossed the railway, then turned into a cheap industrial neighborhood of warehouses, yards, and small factories. There was a group of soldiers toting kit bags outside a back entrance to the station, no doubt embarking for the eastern front. And a fellow countryman somewhere in this neighborhood is doing his best to betray them, Macke thought angrily.

Wagner pointed down a narrow street leading away from the station. "He's in the first few hundred yards, but could be either side," he said. "If we take the van any closer, he'll see us."

"All right, men, you know the drill," Macke said. "Wagner and Richter take the left-hand side. Schneider and I will take the right." They all picked up long-handled sledgehammers. "Come with me, Franck."

There were few people on the street—a man in a worker's cap walking briskly toward the railway station, an older woman in shabby clothes probably on her way to clean offices—and they hurried quickly past, not wanting to attract the attention of the Gestapo.

Macke's team entered each building, one man leapfrogging his partner. Most businesses were closed for the day, so they had to rouse a janitor. If he took more than a minute to come to the door, they knocked it down. Once inside they raced through the building checking every room.

The pianist was not in the first block.

The first building on the right-hand side of the next block had a fading sign that said: FASHION FURS. It was a two-story factory that stretched along the side street. It looked disused, but the front door was steel and the windows were barred: a fur coat factory naturally had heavy security.

Macke led Werner down the side street, looking for a way in. The adjacent building was bomb-damaged and derelict. The rubble had been cleared from the street and there was a hand-painted sign saying: DANGER—NO ENTRY. The remains of a name board identified it as a furniture warehouse.

They stepped over a pile of stones and splintered timbers, going as fast as they could but forced to tread carefully. A surviving wall concealed the rear of the building. Macke went behind it and found a hole through to the factory next door.

He had a strong feeling the pianist was in here.

He stepped through the hole, and Werner followed.

They found themselves in an empty office. There was an old steel desk with no chair, and a file cabinet opposite. The calendar pinned to the wall was for 1939, probably the last year during which Berliners could afford such frivolities as fur coats.

Macke heard a footstep on the floor above.

He drew his gun.

Werner was unarmed.

They opened the door and stepped into a corridor.

Macke noted several open doors, a staircase up, and a door under the staircase that might lead to a basement.

Macke crept along the corridor toward the foot of the stairs, then noticed that Werner was checking the door to the basement.

"I thought I heard a noise from below," Werner said. He turned the handle but the door had a flimsy lock. He stepped back and raised his right foot.

Macke said: "No—"

"Yes—I hear them!" Werner said, and he kicked the door open.

The crash resounded throughout the empty factory.

Werner burst through the door and disappeared. A light came on, showing a stone staircase. "Don't move!" Werner yelled. "You are under arrest!"

Macke went down the stairs after him.

He reached the basement. Werner stood at the foot of the stairs, looking baffled.

The room was empty.

Suspended from the ceiling were rails on which coats had probably been hung. An enormous roll of brown paper stood on end in one corner, probably intended for wrapping. But there was no radio and no spy tapping messages to Moscow.

"You fucking idiot," Macke said to Werner.

He turned and ran back up the stairs. Werner ran after him. They traversed the hallway and went up to the next floor.

There were rows of workbenches under a glass roof. At one time the place must have been full of women working at sewing machines. Now there was nobody.

A glass door led to a fire escape, but the door was locked. Macke looked out and saw nobody.

He put his gun away. Breathing hard, he leaned on a workbench.

On the floor he noticed a couple of cigarette ends, one with lipstick on it. They did not look very old. "They were here," he said to Werner, pointing at the floor. "Two of them. Your shout warned them, and they escaped."

"I was a fool," Werner said. "I'm sorry, but I'm not used to this kind of thing."

Macke went to the corner window. Along the street he saw a young man and woman walking briskly away. The man was carrying a tan leather suitcase. As he watched, they disappeared into the railway station. "Shit," he said.

"I don't think they were spies," Werner said. He pointed to something on the floor, and Macke saw a crumpled condom. "Used, but empty," Werner said. "I think we caught them in the act."

"I hope you're right," said Macke.

vi

The day Joachim Koch promised to bring the battle plan, Carla did not go to work.

She probably could have done her usual morning shift and been home in time—but "probably" was not enough. There was always a risk that there might be a major fire or a road accident obliging her to work after the end of her shift to deal with an inrush of injured people. So she stayed home all day.

In the end Maud had not had to ask Joachim to bring the plan. He had said he needed to cancel his lesson; then, unable to resist the temptation to boast, he had explained that he had to carry a copy of the plan across town. "Come for your lesson on the way," Maud had said, and he had agreed.

Lunch was strained. Carla and Maud ate a thin soup made with a ham bone and dried peas. Carla did not ask what Maud had done, or promised to do, to persuade Koch. Perhaps she had told him he was making marvelous progress on the piano but could not afford to miss a lesson. She might have asked whether he was so junior that he was monitored every minute: such a remark would sting him, for he pretended constantly to be more important than he was, and it might easily provoke him into showing up just to prove her wrong. However, the ploy most likely to have succeeded was the one Carla did not want to think about: sex. Her mother flirted outrageously with Koch, and he responded with slavish devotion. Carla suspected that this was the irresistible temptation that had made Joachim ignore the voice in his head saying: "Don't be so damn stupid."

Or perhaps not. He might see sense. He could show up this

afternoon, not with a carbon copy in his bag, but with a Gestapo squad and a set of handcuffs.

Carla loaded a film cassette into the Minox camera, then put the camera and the two remaining cassettes in the top drawer of a low kitchen cupboard, under some towels. The cupboard stood next to the window, where the light was bright. She would photograph the document on the cupboard top.

She did not know how the exposed film would reach Moscow, but Frieda had assured her it would, and Carla imagined a traveling salesman—in pharmaceuticals, perhaps, or German-language Bibles—who had permission to sell his wares in Switzerland and could discreetly pass the film to someone from the Soviet embassy in Bern.

The afternoon was long. Maud went to her room to rest. Ada did laundry. Carla sat in the dining room, which they rarely used nowadays, and tried to read, but she could not concentrate. The newspaper was all lies. She needed to cram for her next nursing exam, but the medical terms in her textbook swam before her eyes. She was reading an old copy of *All Quiet on the Western Front,* a German bestseller about the First World War, now banned because it was too honest about the hardships of soldiers, but she found herself holding the book in her hand and gazing out of the window at the June sunlight beating down on the dusty city.

At last he came. Carla heard a footstep on the path and jumped up to look out. There was no Gestapo squad, just Joachim Koch in his pressed uniform and shiny boots, his movie-star face as full of eager anticipation as that of a child arriving for a birthday party. He had his canvas bag over his shoulder as usual. Had he kept his promise? Did that bag hold a copy of the battle plan for Case Blue?

He rang the bell.

Carla and Maud had premeditated every move from now on. In accordance with their plan, Carla did not answer the door. A few moments later she saw her mother walk across the hall wearing a purple silk dressing gown and high-heeled slippers—almost like a prostitute, Carla thought with shame and embarrassment. She heard the front door open, then close again. From the hall there was a whisper of silk and a murmured endearment that suggested an embrace. Then the purple robe and the field gray uniform passed the dining room door and disappeared upstairs.

Maud's first priority was to make sure he had the document. She was to look at it, say something admiring, then put it down. She would lead Joachim to the piano. Then she would find some pretext—Carla tried not to think what—for taking the young man through the double doors that led from the drawing room into the neighboring study, a smaller, more intimate room with red velvet curtains and a big, sagging old couch. As soon as they were there, Maud would give the signal.

Because it was hard to know in advance the exact choreography of their movements, there were several possible signals, all of which meant the same thing. The simplest was that she would slam the door loud enough to be heard throughout the house. Alternatively, she would use the bell-push beside the fireplace that sounded a ring in the kitchen, part of the obsolete system for summoning servants. But any other noise would do, they had decided: in desperation she would knock the marble bust of Goethe to the floor or "accidentally" smash a vase.

Carla stepped out of the dining room and stood in the hall, looking up the stairs. There was no sound.

She looked into the kitchen. Ada was washing the iron pot in which she had made the soup, scrubbing with an energy that was undoubtedly fueled by tension. Carla gave her what she hoped was an encouraging smile. Carla and Maud would have liked to keep this whole affair secret from Ada, not because they did not trust her—quite the contrary; her hostility to the Nazis was fanatical—but because the knowledge made her complicit in treachery, and liable to the most extreme punishment. However, they lived too much together for secrecy to be possible, and Ada knew everything.

Carla faintly heard Maud give a tinkling laugh. She knew that sound. It struck an artificial note, and indicated that she was straining her powers of fascination to the limit.

Did Joachim have the document, or not?

A minute or two later Carla heard the piano. It was undoubtedly Joachim playing. The tune was a simple children's song about a cat in the snow: "*ABC, die Katze lief im Schnee.*" Carla's father had sung it to her a hundred times. She felt a lump in her throat now when she thought of that. How dare the Nazis play such songs when they had made orphans of so many children?

The song stopped abruptly in the middle. Something had happened. Carla strained to hear—voices, footsteps, anything—but there was nothing.

A minute went by, then another.

Something had gone wrong—but what?

She looked through the kitchen doorway at Ada, who stopped scrubbing to spread her hands in a gesture that signified *I have no idea.*

Carla had to find out.

She went quietly up the stairs, treading noiselessly on the threadbare carpet.

She stood outside the drawing room. Still she could hear nothing: no piano music, no movement, no voices.

She opened the door as quietly as possible.

She peeped in. She could see no one. She stepped inside and looked all around. The room was empty.

There was no sign of Joachim's canvas bag.

She looked at the double door that led to the study. One of the two doors stood half open.

Carla tiptoed across the room. There was no carpet here, just polished wood blocks, and her footsteps were not completely silent, but she had to take the risk.

As she got nearer, she heard whispers.

She reached the doorway. She flattened herself against the wall, then risked a look inside.

They were standing up, embracing, kissing. Joachim had his back to the door and to Carla: no doubt Maud had taken care to move him into that position. As Carla watched, Maud broke the kiss, looked over his shoulder, and caught Carla's eye. She took her hand away from Joachim's neck and made an urgent pointing gesture.

Carla saw the canvas bag on a chair.

She understood immediately what had gone wrong. When Maud had inveigled Joachim into the study, he had not obliged them by leaving his bag in the drawing room, but had nervously taken it with him.

Now Carla had to retrieve it.

Heart thudding, she stepped into the room.

Maud murmured: "Oh, yes, keep doing that, my sweet boy."

Joachim groaned: "I love you, my darling."

Carla took two paces forward, picked up the canvas bag, turned around, and stepped silently out of the room.

The bag was light.

She walked quickly across the drawing room and ran down the stairs, breathing hard.

In the kitchen she put the bag on the table and unbuckled its straps. Inside were today's edition of the Berlin newspaper *Der Angriff,* a fresh pack of Kamel cigarettes, and a plain buff-colored cardboard folder. With trembling hands she took out the folder and opened it. It contained a carbon copy of a document.

The first page was headed:

DIRECTIVE NO. 41

On the last page was a dotted line for a signature. Nothing was penned there, no doubt because this was a copy, but the name typed beside the line was Adolf Hitler.

In between was the plan for Case Blue.

Exultation rose in her heart, mingled with the tension she already felt and the terrible dread of discovery.

She put the document on the low cupboard next to the kitchen window. She jerked open the drawer and took out the Minox camera and the two spare films. She positioned the document carefully, then began to photograph it page by page.

It did not take long. There were just ten pages. She did not even have to reload film. She was done. She had stolen the battle plan.

That was for you, Father.

She put the camera back in the drawer, closed the drawer, slipped the document into the cardboard folder, put the folder back in the canvas bag, and closed the bag, fastening the straps.

Moving as quietly as she could, she carried the bag back upstairs.

As she crept into the drawing room, she heard her mother's voice. Maud was speaking clearly and emphatically, as if she wanted to be overheard, and Carla immediately sensed a warning. "Please don't worry," she was saying. "It's because you were so excited. We were both excited."

Joachim's voice came in reply, low and embarrassed. "I feel a fool," he said. "You only touched me, and it was all over."

Carla could guess what had happened. She had no experience of it, but girls talked, and nurses' conversations were brutally detailed. Joachim must have ejaculated prematurely. Frieda had told her that Heinrich had done the same, several times, when they were first together, and had been mortified with embarrassment, though he had soon got over it. It was a sign of nervousness, she said.

The fact that Maud and Joachim's embraces were over so early created a difficulty for Carla. Joachim would be more alert now, no longer blind and deaf to everything going on around him.

All the same, Maud must be doing her best to keep his back to the doorway. If Carla could just slip in for a second and replace the bag on the chair without being seen by Joachim, they could still get away with it.

Heart pounding, Carla crossed the drawing room and paused at the open door.

Maud said reassuringly: "It happens often—the body becomes impatient. It's nothing."

Carla put her head around the door.

The two of them were still standing in the same place, still close together. Maud looked past Joachim and saw Carla. She put her hand on Joachim's cheek, keeping his gaze away from Carla, and said: "Kiss me again, and tell me you don't hate me for this little accident."

Carla stepped inside.

Joachim said: "I need a cigarette."

As he turned around, Carla stepped back outside.

She waited by the door. Did he have cigarettes in his pocket, or would he look for the new pack in his bag?

The answer came a second later. "Where's my bag?" he said.

Carla's heart stopped.

Maud's voice came clearly. "You left it in the drawing room."

"No, I didn't."

Carla crossed the room, dropped the bag on a chair, and stepped outside. Then she paused on the landing, listening.

She heard them move from the study to the drawing room.

Maud said: "There it is. I told you so."

"I did not leave it there," he said stubbornly. "I vowed I would not let it out of my sight. But I did—when I was kissing you."

"My darling, you're upset about what happened between us. Try to relax."

"Someone must have come into the room, while I was distracted . . ."

"How absurd."

"I don't think so."

"Let's sit at the piano, side by side, the way you like to," she said, but she was beginning to sound desperate.

"Who else is in this house?"

Guessing what would happen next, Carla ran down the stairs and into the kitchen. Ada stared at her in alarm, but there was no time to explain.

She heard Joachim's boots on the stairs.

A moment later he was in the kitchen. He had the canvas bag in his hand. His face was angry. He looked at Carla and Ada. "One of you has been looking inside this bag!" he said.

Carla spoke as calmly as she could. "I don't know why you should think that, Joachim," she said.

Maud appeared behind Joachim and came past him into the kitchen. "Let's have coffee, please, Ada," she said brightly. "Joachim, do sit down, please."

He ignored her and scrutinized the kitchen. His eye lit upon the top of the low cupboard by the window. Carla saw, to her horror, that although she had put the camera away, she had left the two spare film cassettes out.

"Those are eight-millimeter film cassettes, aren't they?" Joachim said. "Have you got a miniature camera?"

Suddenly he did not seem such a little boy.

"Is that what those things are?" said Maud. "I've been wondering. They were left behind by another pupil, a Gestapo officer in fact."

It was a clever improvisation, but Joachim was not buying it. "And did he also leave behind his camera, I wonder?" he said. He pulled open the drawer.

The neat little stainless-steel camera lay there on a white towel, guilty as a bloodstain.

Joachim looked shocked. Perhaps he had not really believed he was the victim of treachery, but had been blustering to compensate for his sexual failure, and now he was facing the truth for the first time. Whatever the reason, he was momentarily stunned. Still holding the knob of the drawer, he stared at the camera as if hypnotized. In that short moment Carla saw that a young man's dream of love had been defiled, and his rage was going to be terrible.

At last he raised his eyes. He looked at the three women around him, and his gaze rested on Maud. "You have done this," he said. "You tricked me. But you will be punished." He picked up the camera and films and put them in his pocket. "You are under arrest, Frau von Ulrich." He took a step forward and grabbed her arm. "I am taking you to Gestapo headquarters."

Maud jerked her arm free of his grasp and took a step back.

Joachim drew back his arm and punched her with all his might. He was tall, strong, and young. The blow landed on her face and knocked her down.

Joachim stood over her. "You made a fool of me!" he screeched. "You lied, and I believed you!" He was hysterical now. "We will both be tortured by the Gestapo, and we both deserve it!" He began to kick her where she lay. She tried to roll away, but came up against the cooker. His right boot thudded into her ribs, her thigh, her belly.

Ada rushed at him and scratched his face with her nails. He batted her away with a swipe. Then he kicked Maud in the head.

Carla moved.

She knew that people recovered from all kinds of trauma to the body, but a head injury often did irreparable damage. However, the reasoning was barely conscious. She acted without forethought. She picked up from the kitchen table the iron soup pot that Ada had so energetically scrubbed clean. Holding it by its long handle, she raised it high, then brought it down with all her might on top of Joachim's head.

He staggered, stunned.

She hit him again, even harder.

He slumped to the floor, unconscious. Maud moved out of the way of his falling body, and sat upright against the wall, holding her chest.

Carla raised the pot again.

Maud screamed: "No! Stop!"

Carla put the pot down on the kitchen table.

Joachim moved, trying to rise.

Ada seized the pot and hit him again, furiously. Carla tried to grab her arm but she was in a mad rage. She battered the unconscious man's head again and again until she was exhausted, and then she dropped the pot to the floor with a clang.

Maud struggled to her knees and stared at Joachim. His eyes were wide and staring. His nose was twisted sideways. His skull seemed to be out of shape. Blood came from his ear. He did not appear to be breathing.

Carla knelt beside him, put her fingertips to his neck, and felt for a pulse. There was none. "He's dead," she said. "We've killed him. Oh, my God."

Maud said: "You poor, stupid boy." She was crying.

Ada, panting with effort, said: "What do we do now?"

Carla realized they had to get rid of the body.

Maud struggled to her feet with difficulty. The left side of her face was swelling. "Dear God, it hurts," she said, holding her side. Carla guessed she had a cracked rib.

Looking down at Joachim, Ada said: "We could hide him in the attic."

Carla said: "Yes, until the neighbors start to complain about the smell."

"Then we'll bury him in the back garden."

"And what will people think when they see three women digging a hole six feet long in the yard of a Berlin town house? That we are prospecting for gold?"

"We could dig at night."

"Would that seem less suspicious?"

Ada scratched her head.

Carla said: "We have to take the body somewhere and dump it. A park, or a canal."

"But how will we carry it?" said Ada.

"He doesn't weigh much," said Maud sadly. "So slim and strong."

Carla said: "It's not the weight that's the problem. Ada and I can carry him. But somehow we have to do it without arousing suspicion."

Maud said: "I wish we had a car."

Carla shook her head. "No one can get petrol anyway."

They were silent. Outside, dusk was falling. Ada got a towel and wrapped it around Joachim's head, to prevent his blood staining the floor. Maud cried silently, the tears rolling down a face twisted in anguish. Carla wanted to sympathize but first she had to solve this problem.

"We could put him in a box," she said.

Ada said: "The only box that size is a coffin."

"How about a piece of furniture? A sideboard?"

"Too heavy." Ada looked thoughtful. "But the wardrobe in my room is not so weighty."

Carla nodded. A maid was assumed not to have many clothes, nor to need mahogany furniture, she realized with a touch of embarrassment, so Ada's room had a narrow hanging cupboard made of flimsy deal wood. "Let's get it," she said.

Ada had originally lived in the basement, but that was now an air raid shelter, and her room was upstairs. Carla and Ada went up. Ada opened her cupboard and pulled all the clothes off the rail. There were not many: two sets of uniforms, a few dresses, one winter coat, all old. She laid them neatly on the single bed.

Carla tilted the wardrobe and took its weight; then Ada picked up the other end. It was not heavy, but it was awkward, and it took them some time to manhandle it out of the door and down the stairs.

At last they laid it on its back in the hall. Carla opened the door. Now it looked like a coffin with a hinged lid.

Carla went back into the kitchen and bent over the body. She took the camera and films from Joachim's pocket, and replaced them in the kitchen drawer.

Carla took his arms, Ada took his legs, and they lifted the body. They carried it out of the kitchen into the hall and lowered it into the wardrobe. Ada rearranged the towel about the head, though the bleeding had stopped.

Should they take off his uniform? Carla wondered. It would make the body harder to identify—but it would give her two problems of disposal instead of one. She decided against.

She picked up the canvas bag and dropped it into the wardrobe with the corpse.

She closed the wardrobe door and turned the key, to make sure it did not fall open by accident. She put the key in the pocket of her dress.

She went into the dining room and looked out through the window. "It's getting dark," she said. "That's good."

Maud said: "What will people think?"

"That we're moving a piece of furniture—selling it, perhaps, to get money for food."

"Two women, moving a wardrobe?"

"Women do this sort of thing all the time, now that so many men are in the army or dead. It's not as if we could get a removal van—they can't buy petrol."

"Why would you be doing it in the half dark?"

Carla let her frustration show. "I don't know, Mother. If we're asked, I'll have to make something up. But the body can't stay here."

"They'll know he's been murdered, when they find the body. They'll examine the injuries."

Carla, too, was worried about that. "Nothing we can do."

"They may try to investigate where he went today."

"He said he had not told anyone about his piano lessons. He wanted to astonish his friends with his skill. With luck, no one knows he came here." And without luck, Carla thought, we're all dead.

"What will they guess to be the motive for the murder?"

"Will they find traces of semen in his underwear?"

Maud looked away, embarrassed. "Yes."

"Then they will imagine a sexual encounter, perhaps with another man, that ended in a quarrel."

"I hope you're right."

Carla was not at all sure, but she could not think of anything they could do about it. "The canal," she said. The body would float, and be found sooner or later, and there would be a murder investigation. They would just have to hope it did not lead to them.

Carla opened the front door.

She stood at the front of the wardrobe on its left, and Ada positioned herself at the back on the right. They bent down.

Ada, who undoubtedly had more experience of heavy lifting than her employers, said: "Tilt it sideways and get your hands under it."

Carla did as she said.

"Now lift your end a little."

Carla did so.

Ada got her hands underneath her end and said: "Bend your knees. Take the weight. Straighten up."

They raised the wardrobe to hip height. Ada bent down and got her shoulder underneath. Carla did the same.

The two women straightened up.

The weight tilted to Carla as they went down the steps from the front door, but she could bear it. When they reached the street, she turned toward the canal, a few blocks away.

It was now full dark, with no moon but a few stars shedding a faint light. With the blackout, there was a good chance no one would see them tip the wardrobe into the water. The disadvantage was that Carla could hardly see where she was going. She was terrified she would stumble and fall, and the wardrobe would smash to splinters, revealing the murdered man inside.

An ambulance drove by, its headlights covered by slit masks. It was probably hurrying to a road accident. There were many during the blackout. That meant there would be police cars in the vicinity.

Carla recalled a sensational murder case from the beginning of the blackout. A man had killed his wife, forced her body into a packing case, and carried it across town on the seat of his bicycle in the dark before dropping it in the Havel River. Would the police remember the case and suspect anyone transporting a large object?

As she thought that, a police car drove by. A cop stared out at the two women with their wardrobe, but the car did not stop.

The burden seemed to get heavier. It was a warm night, and soon Carla was running with perspiration. The wood hurt her shoulder, and she wished she had thought of putting a folded handkerchief inside her blouse as a cushion.

They turned a corner and came upon the accident.

An eight-wheeler articulated truck carrying timber had collided head-on with a Mercedes saloon car, which had been badly crushed. The police car and the ambulance were shining their headlights onto the wreckage. In a little pool of faint light, a group of men gathered around the car. The crash must have happened in the last few minutes, for there were still people inside the car. An ambulance man was leaning in at the back door, probably examining the injuries to see whether the passengers could be moved.

Carla was momentarily terrified. Guilt froze her and she stopped in her tracks. But no one had noticed her and Ada and the wardrobe, and after a moment she realized she just needed to steal away, double back, and take a different route to the canal.

She began to turn, but just then an alert policeman shone a flashlight her way.

She was tempted to drop the wardrobe and run, but she held her nerve.

The cop said: "What are you up to?"

"Moving a wardrobe, officer," she said. Recovering her presence of mind, she faked a grisly curiosity to cover her guilty nervousness. "What happened here?" she said. For good measure she added: "Is anyone dead?"

Professionals disliked this kind of vampire inquisitiveness, she knew—she was a professional herself. As she expected, the policeman reacted dismissively. "None of your business," he said. "Just keep out of the way." He turned back and shone his light into the crashed car.

The pavement on this side of the street was clear. Carla made a snap decision and walked straight on. She and Ada carried the wardrobe containing the dead man toward the wreckage.

She kept her eyes on the little knot of emergency workers in the small circle of light. They were intensely focused on their task and no one looked up as Carla passed the car.

It seemed to take forever to pass along the length of the eight-wheel trailer. Then, when at last she drew level with the back end, she had a flash of inspiration.

She stopped.

Ada hissed: "What is it?"

"This way." Carla stepped into the road at the back of the truck. "Put the wardrobe down," she hissed. "No noise."

They placed the wardrobe gently on the pavement.

Ada whispered: "Are we leaving it here?"

Carla drew the key from her pocket and unlocked the wardrobe door. She looked up: as far as she could tell, the men were still gathered around the car, twenty feet away on the other side of the truck.

She opened the wardrobe door.

Joachim Koch stared up sightlessly, his head wrapped in a bloody towel.

"Tip him out," Carla said. "By the wheels."

They tilted the wardrobe, and the body rolled out, coming to rest up against the tires.

Carla retrieved the bloody towel and threw it into the wardrobe. She left the canvas bag lying beside the corpse; she was glad to get rid of it. She closed and locked the wardrobe door; then they picked it up and walked away.

It was easy to carry now.

When they were fifty yards away in the dark, Carla heard a distant voice say: "My God, there's another casualty—looks like a pedestrian was run over!"

Carla and Ada turned a corner, and relief washed over Carla like a tidal wave. She had got rid of the corpse. If only she could get home without attracting further attention—and without anyone looking inside the wardrobe and seeing the bloody towel—she would be safe. There would be no murder investigation. Joachim had become a pedestrian killed in a blackout accident. If he had really been dragged along the cobbled street by the wheels of the truck, he might have received injuries similar to those caused by the heavy base of Ada's soup pot. Perhaps a skilled autopsy doctor could tell the difference—but no one would consider an autopsy necessary.

Carla thought about dumping the wardrobe, and decided against. Even without the towel it had bloodstains inside, and might spark a police investigation on its own. They had to take it home and scrub it clean.

They got home without meeting anyone else.

They put the wardrobe down in the hall. Ada took out the towel, put it in the kitchen sink, and ran the cold tap. Carla felt a mixture of elation and sadness. She had stolen the Nazis' battle plan, but she had killed a young man who was more foolish than wicked. She would think about that for many days, perhaps years, before she could be sure how she felt about it. For now she was just too tired.

She told her mother what they had done. Maud's left cheek was so puffed up that her eye was almost closed. She was pressing her left side as if to ease a pain. She looked terrible.

Carla said: "You were terribly brave, Mother. I admire you so much for what you did today."

Maud said wearily: "I don't feel admirable. I'm so ashamed. I despise myself."

"Because you didn't love him?" said Carla.

"No," said Maud. "Because I did."

CHAPTER FOURTEEN

1942 (III)

Greg Peshkov graduated from Harvard summa cum laude, the highest honor. He could have gone on effortlessly to take a doctorate in physics, his major, and thus have avoided military service. But he did not want to be a scientist. His ambition was to wield a different kind of power. And, after the war was over, a military record would be a huge plus for a rising young politician. So he joined the army.

On the other hand, he did not want actually to have to fight.

He followed the European war with heightened interest at the same time as he pressured everyone he knew in Washington—which was a lot of people—to get him a desk job at War Department headquarters.

The German summer offensive had started on June 28, and they had swiftly pushed east, meeting relatively light opposition, until they reached the city of Stalingrad, formerly called Tsaritsyn, where they were halted by fierce Russian resistance. Now they were stalled, with overstretched supply lines, and it was looking more and more as if the Red Army had drawn them into a trap.

Greg had not long been in basic training when he was summoned to the colonel's office. "The Army Corps of Engineers needs a bright young officer in Washington," the colonel said. "You've interned in Washington, but all the same you wouldn't have been my first choice—you can't even keep your goddamn uniform clean; look at you—but the job requires a knowledge of physics, and the field is kind of limited."

Greg said: "Thank you, sir."

"Try that kind of sarcasm on your new boss and you'll regret it. You're going to be an assistant to a Colonel Groves. I was at West Point with him. He's the biggest son of a bitch I ever met, in the army or out. Good luck."

Greg called Mike Penfold in the State Department press office and found out that until recently Leslie Groves had been chief of construction for the entire U.S. Army, and had been responsible for the military's new Washington headquarters, the vast five-sided building they were beginning to call the Pentagon. But he had been moved to a new project that no one knew much about. Some said he had offended his superiors so often that he had been effectively demoted, others that his new role was even more important but top secret. They all agreed he was egotistical, arrogant, and ruthless.

"Does *everybody* hate him?" Greg asked.

"Oh, no," Mike said. "Only those who have met him."

Lieutenant Greg Peshkov was full of trepidation when he arrived at Groves's office in the striking new War Department Building, a pale tan art deco palace on Twenty-first Street and Virginia Avenue. Right away he learned that he was part of a group called the Manhattan Engineer District. This deliberately uninformative name camouflaged a team who were trying to invent a new kind of bomb using uranium as an explosive.

Greg was intrigued. He knew there was incalculable energy locked up in uranium's lighter isotope, U-235, and he had read several papers on the subject in scientific journals. But news of the research had dried up a couple of years ago, and now Greg knew why.

He learned that President Roosevelt felt the project was moving too slowly, and Groves had been appointed to crack the whip.

Greg arrived six days after Groves had been reassigned. His first task for Groves was to help him pin stars to the collar of his khaki shirt: he had just been promoted to brigadier general. "It's mainly to impress all these civilian scientists we have to work with," Groves growled. "I have a meeting in the secretary of war's office in ten minutes. You'd better come with me. It'll serve you for a briefing."

Groves was heavy. An inch under six feet tall, he had to weigh two hundred and fifty pounds, maybe three hundred. He wore his uniform pants high, and his belly bulged under his webbing belt. He had chestnut-colored hair that might have curled if it had been grown long enough. He had a narrow forehead, fat cheeks, and a jowly chin. His small mustache was all but invisible. He was an unattractive man in every way, and Greg was not looking forward to working for him.

Groves and his entourage, including Greg, left the building and walked down Virginia Avenue to the National Mall. On the way, Groves said to Greg: "When they gave me this job, they told me it could win the war. I don't know if that's true, but my plan is to act as if it is. You'd better do the same."

"Yes, sir," said Greg.

The secretary of war had not yet moved into the unfinished Pentagon, and War Department headquarters were still in the old Munitions Building, a long, low, out-of-date "temporary" structure on Constitution Avenue.

Secretary of War Henry Stimson was a Republican, brought in by the president to keep that party from undermining the war effort by making trouble in Congress. At seventy-five Stimson was an elder statesman, a dapper old man with a white mustache, but the light of intelligence still gleamed in his gray eyes.

The meeting was a full-dress performance, and the room was full of bigwigs, including Army Chief of Staff George Marshall. Greg felt nervous, and he thought admiringly that Groves was remarkably calm for someone who had been a mere colonel yesterday.

Groves began by outlining how he intended to impose order on the hundreds of civilian scientists and dozens of physics laboratories involved in the Manhattan Project. He made no attempt to defer to the high-ranking men who might well have thought they were in charge.

He outlined his plans without troubling to use such mollifying phrases as "with your permission" and "if you agree." Greg wondered whether the man was trying to get himself fired.

Greg learned so much new information that he wanted to take notes, but no one else did, and he guessed it would not look right.

When Groves had done, one of the group said: "I believe supplies of uranium are crucial to the project. Do we have enough?"

Groves answered: "There are twelve hundred fifty tons of pitchblende—that's the ore that contains uranium oxide—in a yard on Staten Island."

"Then we'd better acquire some of that," said the questioner.

"I bought it all on Friday, sir."

"Friday? The day after you were appointed?"

"Correct."

The secretary of war smothered a smile. Greg's surprise at Groves's arrogance began to turn to admiration of his nerve.

A man in admiral's uniform said: "What about the priority rating of this project? You need to clear the decks with the War Production Board."

"I saw Donald Nelson on Saturday, sir," said Groves. Nelson was the civilian head of the board. "I asked him to raise our rating."

"What did he say?"

"He said no."

"That's a problem."

"Not any longer. I told him I would have to recommend to the president that the Manhattan Project be abandoned because the War Production Board was unwilling to cooperate. Then he gave us a triple-A."

"Good," said the secretary of war.

Greg was impressed again. Groves was a real pistol.

Stimson said: "Now, you'll be supervised by a committee that will report to me. Nine members have been suggested—"

"Hell, no," said Groves.

The secretary of war said: "What did you say?"

Surely, Greg thought, Groves has gone too far this time.

Groves said: "I can't report to a committee of nine, Mr. Secretary. I'll never get 'em off my back."

Stimson grinned. He was too old a hand to get offended by this kind of talk, it seemed. He said mildly: "What number would you suggest, General?"

Greg could see that Groves wanted to say *None,* but what came out was: "Three would be perfect."

"All right," said the secretary of war, to Greg's amazement. "Anything else?"

"We're going to need a large site, something like sixty thousand acres, for a uranium enrichment plant and associated facilities. There's a suitable area in Oak Ridge, Tennessee. It's a ridge valley, so that if there should be an accident the explosion will be contained."

"An accident?" said the admiral. "Is that likely?"

Groves did not hide his feeling that this was a dumb question. "We're making an experimental bomb, for Christ's sake," he said. "A bomb so powerful that it promises to flatten a medium-size city with one detonation. We'd be pretty goddamn dumb if we ignored the possibility of accidents."

The admiral looked as if he wanted to protest, but Stimson intervened, saying: "Carry on, General."

"Land is cheap in Tennessee," Groves said. "So is electricity—and our plant will use huge quantities of power."

"So you're proposing to buy this land."

"I'm proposing to view it today." Groves looked at his watch. "In fact I need to leave now to catch my train to Knoxville." He stood up. "If you will excuse me, gentlemen, I don't want to lose any time."

The other men in the room were flabbergasted. Even Stimson looked startled. No one in Washington dreamed of leaving a secretary's office before he indicated he was through. It was a major breach of etiquette. But Groves seemed not to care.

And he got away with it. "Very well," said Stimson. "Don't let us hold you up."

"Thank you, sir," said Groves, and he left the room.

Greg hurried out after him.

ii

The most attractive civilian secretary in the New War Office Building was Margaret Cowdry. She had big dark eyes and a wide, sensual mouth. When you saw her sitting behind her typewriter, and she glanced up at you and smiled, you felt as if you were already making love to her.

Her father had turned baking into a mass-production industry: "Cowdry's Cookies crumble just like Ma's!" She had no need to work, but she was doing her bit for the war effort. Before inviting her to lunch Greg made sure she knew that he, too, was the child of a millionaire. An heiress usually preferred to date a rich boy: she could feel confident he was not after her money.

It was October and cold. Margaret wore a stylish navy blue coat with padded shoulders and a nipped-in waist. Her matching beret had a military look.

They went to the Ritz-Carlton, but when they got to the dining room, Greg saw his father having lunch with Gladys Angelus. He did not want to make it a foursome. When he explained this to Margaret, she said: "No problem. We'll have lunch at the University Women's Club around the corner. I'm a member there."

Greg had never been there, but he had a feeling he knew something about it. For a moment he chased the thought around his memory, but it eluded him, so he put it out of his mind.

At the club Margaret removed her coat to reveal a royal blue cashmere dress that clung to her alluringly. She kept on her hat and gloves, as all respectable women did when eating out.

As always, Greg loved the sensation of walking into a place with a beautiful woman on his arm. In the dining room of the University Women's Club there was only a handful of men, but they all envied him. Although he might not admit it to anyone else, he enjoyed this as much as sleeping with women.

He ordered a bottle of wine. Margaret mixed hers with mineral water, French-style, saying: "I don't want to spend the afternoon correcting my typing mistakes."

He told her about General Groves. "He's a real go-getter. In some ways he's a badly dressed version of my father."

"Everyone hates him," Margaret said.

Greg nodded. "He rubs people the wrong way."

"Is your father like that?"

"Sometimes, but mostly he uses charm."

"Mine's the same! Maybe all successful men are that way."

The meal went quickly. Service in Washington restaurants had speeded up. The nation was at war and men had urgent work to do.

A waitress brought them the dessert menu. Greg glanced at her and was startled to recognize Jacky Jakes. "Hello, Jacky!" he said.

"Hi, Greg," she replied, familiarity overlaying nervousness. "How have you been?"

Greg recalled the detective telling him that she worked at the University Women's Club. That was the memory that had eluded him before. "I'm just fine," he said. "How about you?"

"Real good."

"Everything going on just the same?" He was wondering if his father was still paying her an allowance.

"Pretty much."

Greg guessed that some lawyer was paying out the money and Lev had forgotten all about it. "That's good," he said.

Jacky remembered her job. "Can I offer you some dessert today?"

"Yes, thank you."

Margaret asked for fruit salad and Greg had ice cream.

When Jacky had gone, Margaret said: "She's very pretty," then looked expectant.

"I guess," he said.

"No wedding ring."

Greg sighed. Women were so perceptive. "You're wondering how come I'm friendly with a pretty black waitress who isn't married," he said. "I might as well tell you the truth. I had an affair with her when I was fifteen. I hope you're not shocked."

"Of course I am," she said. "I'm morally outraged." She was neither serious nor joking, but something in between. She was not really scandalized, he felt sure, but perhaps she did not want to give him the impression that she was easygoing about sex—not on their first lunch date, anyway.

Jacky brought the desserts and asked if they wanted coffee. They did not have time—the army did not believe in long lunch hours—and Margaret asked for the check. "Guests aren't allowed to pay here," she explained.

When Jacky had gone, Margaret said: "What's nice is that you're so fond of her."

"Am I?" Greg was surprised. "I have fond memories, I guess. I wouldn't mind being fifteen again."

"And yet she's scared of you."

"She is not!"

"Terrified."

"I don't think so."

"Take my word. Men are blind, but a woman sees these things."

Greg looked hard at Jacky when she brought the bill, and he realized that Margaret was right. Jacky was still scared. Every time she saw Greg, she was reminded of Joe Brekhunov and his straight razor.

It made Greg angry. The girl had a right to live in peace.

He was going to have to do something about this.

Margaret, who was as sharp as a tack, said: "I think you know why she's scared."

"My father frightened her off. He was worried I might marry her."

"Is your father scary?"

"He does like to get his own way."

"My father's the same," she said. "Sweet as cherry pie, until you cross him. Then he turns mean."

"I'm so glad you understand."

They returned to work. Greg felt angry all afternoon. Somehow his father's curse still lay like a blight over Jacky's life. But what could he do?

What would his father do? That was a good way to look at it. Lev would be completely single-minded about getting his way, and would not care whom he hurt in the process. General Groves would be similar. I can be like that, Greg thought; I'm my father's son.

The beginning of a plan began to form in his mind.

He spent the afternoon reading and summarizing an interim report from the University of Chicago Metallurgical Laboratory. The scientists there included Leo Szilard, the man who first conceived of the nuclear chain reaction. Szilard was a Hungarian Jew who had studied at the University of Berlin—until the fatal year of 1933. The research team in Chicago was led by Enrico Fermi, the Italian physicist. Fermi, whose wife was Jewish, had left Italy when Mussolini published his *Manifesto of Race.*

Greg wondered whether the Fascists realized that their racism had brought such a windfall of brilliant scientists to their enemies.

He understood the physics perfectly well. The theory of Fermi and Szilard was that when a neutron struck a uranium atom, the collision could produce two neutrons. Those two neutrons could then collide with further uranium atoms to make four, then eight, and so on. Szilard had called this a chain reaction—a brilliant insight.

That way, a ton of uranium could produce as much energy as three million tons of coal—in theory.

In practise, it had never been done.

Fermi and his team were building a pile of uranium at Stagg Field, a disused football stadium belonging to the University of Chicago. To prevent the stuff exploding spontaneously, they buried the uranium in graphite, which absorbed the neutrons and killed the chain reaction. Their aim was to bring the radioactivity up, very gradually, to the level at which more was being created than absorbed—which would prove that a chain reaction was a reality—then close it down, fast, before it blew up the pile, the stadium, the campus of the university, and quite possibly the city of Chicago.

So far they had not succeeded.

Greg wrote a favorable précis of the report, asked Margaret Cowdry to type it right away, then took it in to Groves.

The general read the first paragraph and said: "Will it work?"

"Well, sir—"

"You're the goddamn scientist. Will it work?"

"Yes, sir, it will work," Greg said.

"Good," said Groves, and threw the summary in his wastepaper bin.

Greg returned to his desk and sat for a while, staring at the representation of the Periodic Table of the Elements on the wall opposite his desk. He was pretty sure the nuclear pile would work. He was more worried about how to force his father to withdraw the threat to Jacky.

Earlier, he had thought about handling the problem as Lev would have done. Now he began to think about practical details. He needed to take a dramatic stand.

His plan began to take shape.

But did he have the guts to confront his father?

At five he left for the day.

On the way home he stopped at a barbershop and bought a straight razor, the folding kind where the blade slid into the handle. The barber said: "You'll find it better than a safety razor, with your beard."

Greg was not going to shave with it.

His home was his father's permanent suite at the Ritz-Carlton. When Greg arrived, Lev and Gladys were having cocktails.

He remembered meeting Gladys for the first time in this room seven years ago, sitting on the same yellow silk couch. She was an even bigger star now. Lev had put her in a series of shamelessly gung-ho war movies in which she defied sneering Nazis, outwitted sadistic Japanese, and nursed square-jawed American pilots back to health. She was not quite as beautiful as she had been at twenty, Greg observed. The skin of her face did not have the same perfect smoothness; her hair did not seem so luxuriant; and she was wearing a brassiere, which she would undoubtedly have scorned before. But she still had dark blue eyes that seemed to issue an irresistible invitation.

Greg accepted a martini and sat down. Was he really going to defy his father? He had not done it in the seven years since he had first shaken Gladys's hand. Perhaps it was time.

I'll do it just the way he would, Greg thought.

He sipped his drink and set it down on a side table with spidery legs. Speaking conversationally, he said to Gladys: "When I was fifteen, my father introduced me to an actress called Jacky Jakes."

Lev's eyes widened.

"I don't think I know her," said Gladys.

Greg took the razor from his pocket, but did not open it. He held it in his hand as if feeling its weight. "I fell in love with her."

Lev said: "Why are you dragging this ancient history up now?"

Gladys sensed the tension and looked anxious.

Greg went on: "Father was afraid I might want to marry her."

Lev laughed mockingly. "That cheap tart?"

"Was she a cheap tart?" Greg said. "I thought she was an actress." He looked at Gladys.

Gladys flushed at the implied insult.

Greg said: "Father paid her a visit, and took with him a colleague, Joe Brekhunov. Have you met him, Gladys?"

"I don't believe so."

"Lucky you. Joe has a razor like this." Greg snapped the razor open, showing the gleaming sharp blade.

Gladys gasped.

Lev said: "I don't know what game you think you're playing—"

"Just a minute," Greg said. "Gladys wants to hear the rest of the story." He smiled at her. She looked terrified. He said: "My father told Jacky that if she ever saw me again, Joe would cut her face with his razor."

He jerked the knife, just a little, and Gladys gave a small scream.

"The hell with this," Lev said, and took a step toward Greg. Greg raised the hand holding the razor. Lev stopped.

Greg did not know whether he would be able to cut his father. But Lev did not know, either.

"Jacky lives right here in Washington," Greg said.

His father said crudely: "Are you fucking her again?"

"No. I'm not fucking anyone, though I have plans for Margaret Cowdry."

"The cookie heiress?"

"Why, do you want Joe to threaten her, too?"

"Don't be stupid."

"Jacky is a waitress now—she never got the movie part she was hoping for. I run into her on the street sometimes. Today she served me in a restaurant. Every time she sees my face, she thinks Joe is going to come after her."

"She's out of her mind," Lev said. "I'd forgotten all about her until five minutes ago."

"Can I tell her that?" Greg said. "I think by now she's entitled to her peace of mind."

"Tell her whatever the hell you like. For me she doesn't exist."

"That's great," said Greg. "She'll be pleased to hear it."

"Now put that damn blade away."

"One more thing. A warning."

Lev looked angry. "You're warning *me*?"

"If anything bad happens to Jacky—anything at all . . ." Greg moved the razor side to side, just a little.

Lev said scornfully: "Don't tell me you're going to cut Joe Brekhunov."

"No."

Lev showed a hint of fear. "You'd cut me?"

Greg shook his head.

Angrily, Lev said: "What, then, for Christ's sake?"

Greg looked at Gladys.

She took a second to catch his drift. Then she jerked back in her silk-upholstered chair, put both hands on her cheeks as if to protect them, and gave another little scream, louder this time.

Lev said to Greg: "You little asshole."

Greg folded the razor and stood up. "It's how you would have handled it, Father," he said.

Then he went out.

He slammed the door and leaned against the wall, breathing as hard as if he had been running. He had never felt so scared in his life. Yet he also felt triumphant. He had stood up to the old man, used his own tactics back on him, even scared him a little.

He walked to the elevator, pocketing the razor. His breathing eased. He looked back along the hotel corridor, half-expecting his father to come running after him. But the door of the suite remained closed, and Greg boarded the elevator and went down to the lobby.

He entered the hotel bar and ordered a dry martini.

iii

On Sunday Greg decided to visit Jacky.

He wanted to tell her the good news. He remembered the address— the only piece of information he had ever paid a private detective for. Unless she had moved, she lived just the other side of Union Station. He had promised her he would not go there, but now he could explain to her that such caution was no longer necessary.

He went by cab. Crossing town, he told himself he would be glad to draw a line at last under his affair with Jacky. He had a soft spot for his first lover, but he did not want to be involved in her life in any way. It would be a relief to get her off his conscience. Then, next time he ran into her, she would not look scared to death. They could say hello, chat for a while, and walk on.

The cab took him to a poor neighborhood of one-story homes with low chain-link fences around small yards. He wondered how Jacky lived these days. What did she do during those evenings she was so keen to have to herself? No doubt she saw movies with her girlfriends. Did she go to Washington Redskins football games, or follow the Nats baseball team? When he had asked her about boyfriends, she had been enigmatic. Perhaps she was married and could not afford a ring. By his calculation she was twenty-four. If she was looking for Mr. Right, she should have found him by now. But she had never mentioned a husband, nor had the detective.

He paid off the taxi outside a small, neat house with flower pots in a concrete front yard—more domesticated than he had expected. As soon as he opened the gate, he heard a dog bark. That made sense: a woman living alone might feel safer with a dog. He stepped onto the porch and rang the doorbell. The barking got louder. It sounded like a big dog, but that could be deceptive, Greg knew.

No one came to the door.

When the dog paused for breath, Greg heard the distinctive silence of an empty house.

There was a wooden bench on the stoop. He sat and waited a few minutes. No one came, and no helpful neighbor appeared to tell him whether Jacky was away for a few minutes, all day, or two weeks.

He walked a few blocks, bought the Sunday edition of *The Washington Post,* and returned to the bench to read it. The dog continued to bark intermittently, knowing he was still there. It was the first of November, and he was glad he had worn his olive green uniform greatcoat and cap: the weather was wintry. Midterm elections would be held on Tuesday, and the *Post* was predicting that the Democrats would take a beating because of Pearl Harbor. That incident had transformed America, and it came as a surprise to Greg to realize that it had happened less than a year ago. Now American men of his own age were dying on an island no one had ever heard of called Guadalcanal.

He heard the gate click, and looked up.

At first Jacky did not notice him, and he had a moment to study her. She looked dowdily respectable in a dark coat and a plain felt hat, and she carried a book with a black cover. If he had not known her better, Greg would have thought she was coming home from church.

With her was a little boy. He wore a tweed coat and a cap, and he was holding her hand.

The boy saw Greg first, and said: "Look, Mommy, there's a soldier!"

Jacky looked at Greg, and her hand flew to her mouth.

Greg stood up as they mounted the steps to the stoop. A child! She had kept that secret. It explained why she needed to be home in the evenings. He had never thought of it.

"I told you never to come here," she said as she put the key in the lock.

"I wanted to tell you that you need not be afraid of my father anymore. I didn't know you had a son."

She and the boy stepped into the house. Greg stood expectantly at the door. A German shepherd growled at him, then looked up at Jacky for guidance. Jacky glared at Greg, evidently thinking about slamming the door in his face, but after a moment she gave an exasperated sigh and turned away, leaving it open.

Greg walked in and offered his left fist to the dog. It sniffed warily and gave him provisional approval. He followed Jacky into a small kitchen.

"It's All Saints' Day," Greg said. He was not religious, but at his boarding school he had been forced to learn all the Christian festivals. "Is that why you went to church?"

"We go every Sunday," she replied.

"This is a day of surprises," Greg murmured.

She took off the boy's coat, sat him at the table, and gave him a cup of orange juice. Greg sat opposite and said: "What's your name?"

"Georgy." He said it quietly, but with confidence: he was not shy. Greg studied him. He was as pretty as his mother, with the same bow-shaped mouth, but his skin was lighter than hers, more like coffee with cream, and he had green eyes, unusual in a Negro face. He reminded Greg a little of his half sister, Daisy. Meanwhile Georgy looked at Greg with an intense gaze that was almost intimidating.

Greg said: "How old are you, Georgy?"

He looked at his mother for help. She gave Greg a strange look and said: "He's six."

"Six!" said Greg. "You're quite a big boy, aren't you? Why . . . ?"

A bizarre thought crossed his mind, and he fell silent. Georgy had been born six years ago. Greg and Jacky had been lovers seven years ago. His heart seemed to falter.

He stared at Jacky. "Surely not," he said.

She nodded.

"He was born in 1936," said Greg.

"May," she said. "Eight and a half months after I left that apartment in Buffalo."

"Does my father know?"

"Heck, no. That would have given him even more power over me."

Her hostility had vanished, and now she just looked vulnerable. In her eyes he saw a plea, though he was not sure what she was pleading for.

He looked at Georgy with new eyes: the light skin, the green eyes, the odd resemblance to Daisy. Are you mine? he thought. Can it be true?

But he knew it was.

His heart filled with a strange emotion. Suddenly Georgy seemed terribly vulnerable, a helpless child in a cruel world, and Greg needed to take care of him, make sure he came to no harm. He had an impulse to take the boy in his arms, but he realized that might scare him, so he held back.

Georgy put down his orange juice. He got off his chair and came around the table to stand close to Greg. With a remarkably direct look, he said: "Who are you?"

Trust a kid to ask the toughest question of all, Greg thought. What the hell was he going to say? The truth was too much for a six-year-old to take. I'm just a former friend of your mother's, he thought; I was just passing the door, thought I'd say hello. Nobody special. May see you again, most likely not.

He looked at Jacky, and saw that pleading expression intensified. He realized what was on her mind: she was desperately afraid he was going to reject Georgy.

"I tell you what," Greg said, and he lifted Georgy onto his knees. "Why don't you call me Uncle Greg?"

iv

Greg stood shivering in the spectators' gallery of an unheated squash court. Here, under the west stand of the disused stadium on the edge of the University of Chicago campus, Fermi and Szilard had built their atomic pile. Greg was impressed and scared.

The pile was a cube of gray bricks reaching the ceiling of the court, standing just shy of the end wall, which still bore the polka-dot marks of hundreds of squash balls. The pile had cost a million dollars, and it could blow up the entire city.

Graphite was the material of which pencil leads were made, and it gave off a filthy dust that covered the floor and walls. Everyone who had been in the room awhile was as black-faced as a coal miner. No one had a clean lab coat.

Graphite was not the explosive material—on the contrary, it was there to suppress radioactivity. But some of the bricks in the stack were drilled with narrow holes stuffed with uranium oxide, and this was the material that radiated the neutrons. Running through the pile were ten channels for control rods. These were thirteen-foot strips of cadmium, a metal that absorbed neutrons even more hungrily than graphite. Right now the rods were keeping everything calm. When they were withdrawn from the pile, the fun would start.

The uranium was already throwing off its deadly radiation, but the graphite and the cadmium were soaking it up. Radiation was measured by counters that clicked menacingly and a cylindrical pen recorder that was mercifully silent. The array of controls and meters near Greg in the gallery gave off the only heat in the place.

Greg visited on Wednesday, December 2, a bitterly cold, windy day in Chicago. Today for the first time the pile was supposed to go critical. Greg was there to observe the experiment on behalf of his boss, General Groves. He hinted jovially to anyone who asked that Groves feared an explosion and had deputed Greg to take the risk for him. In fact Greg had a more sinister mission. He was making an initial assessment of the scientists with a view to deciding who might be a security risk.

Security on the Manhattan Project was a nightmare. The top scientists were foreigners. Most of the rest were left-wingers, either Communists themselves or liberals who had Communist friends. If everyone suspicious was fired, there would be hardly any scientists left. So Greg was trying to figure out which ones were the worst risks.

Enrico Fermi was about forty. A small, balding man with a long nose, he smiled engagingly while supervising this terrifying experiment. He was smartly dressed in a suit with a waistcoat. It was midmorning when he ordered the trial to begin.

He instructed a technician to withdraw all but one of the control rods from the pile. Greg said: "What, all at once?" It seemed frighteningly precipitate.

The scientist standing next to him, Barney McHugh, said: "We took it this far last night. It worked fine."

"I'm glad to hear it," said Greg.

McHugh, bearded and podgy, was low down on Greg's list of suspects. He was American, with no interest in politics. The only black mark against him was a foreign wife: she was British—never a good sign, but not in itself evidence of treachery.

Greg had assumed there would be some sophisticated mechanism for moving the rods in and out, but it was simpler than that. The technician just put a ladder up against the pile, climbed halfway up it, and pulled out the rods by hand.

Speaking conversationally, McHugh said: "We were originally going to do this in the Argonne Forest."

"Where's that?"

"Twenty miles southwest of Chicago. Pretty isolated. Fewer casualties."

Greg shivered. "So why did you change your minds and decide to do it right here on Fifty-seventh Street?"

"The builders we hired went on strike, so we had to build the damn thing ourselves, and we couldn't be that far away from the laboratories."

"So you took the risk of killing everyone in Chicago."

"We don't think that will happen."

Greg had not thought so, either, but he did not feel so sure now, standing a few feet away from the pile.

Fermi was checking his monitors against a forecast he had prepared of radiation levels at every stage of the experiment. Apparently the initial stage went according to plan, for he now ordered the last rod to be pulled halfway out.

There were some safety measures. A weighted rod hung poised to be dropped into the pile automatically if the radiation rose too high. In case that did not work, a similar rod was tied to the gallery railing with a rope, and a young physicist, looking as if he felt a bit silly, stood holding an axe, ready to cut the rope in an emergency. Finally three more scientists called the suicide squad were positioned near the ceiling, standing on the platform of the elevator used during construction, holding large jugs of cadmium sulfate solution, which they would throw onto the pile, as if dousing a bonfire.

Greg knew that neutron generation multiplied in thousandths of a second. However, Fermi argued that some neutrons took longer, perhaps several seconds. If Fermi was right, there would be no problem. But if he was wrong, the squad with the jugs and the physicist with the axe would be vaporized before they could blink.

Greg heard the clicking become more rapid. He looked anxiously at Fermi, who was doing calculations with a slide rule. Fermi looked pleased. Anyway, Greg thought, if things go wrong, it will probably happen so fast that we'll never know anything about it.

The rate of clicking leveled off. Fermi smiled and gave the order for the rod to be pulled out another six inches.

More scientists were arriving, climbing the stairs to the gallery in their heavyweight Chicago-winter clothing, coats and hats and scarves and gloves. Greg was appalled at the lack of security. No one was checking credentials: any one of these men could have been a spy for the Japanese.

Among them Greg recognized the great Szilard, tall and heavy, with a round face and thick curly hair. Leo Szilard was an idealist who had imagined nuclear power liberating the human race from toil. It was with a heavy heart that he had joined the team designing the atom bomb.

Another six inches, another increase in the pace of the clicking.

Greg looked at his watch. It was eleven thirty.

Suddenly there was a loud crash. Everyone jumped. McHugh said: "Fuck."

Greg said: "What happened?"

"Oh, I see," said McHugh. "The radiation level activated the safety mechanism and released the emergency control rod, that's all."

Fermi announced: "I'm hungry. Let's go to lunch." In his Italian accent it came out "I'm hungary. Les go to luncha."

How could they think about food? But no one argued. "You never know how long an experiment is going to take," said McHugh. "Could be all day. Best to eat when you can." Greg could have screamed.

All the control rods were reinserted into the pile and locked into position, and everyone left.

Most of them went to a campus canteen. Greg got a grilled cheese sandwich and sat next to a solemn physicist called Wilhelm Frunze. Most scientists were badly dressed but Frunze was notably so, in a green suit with tan suede trimmings: buttonholes, collar lining, elbow patches, pocket flaps. This guy was high on Greg's suspect list. He was German, though he had left in the mid-1930s and gone to London. He was an anti-Nazi but not a Communist: his politics were Social Democrat. He was married to an American girl, an artist. Talking to him over lunch, Greg found no reason for suspicion: he seemed to love living in America and to be interested in little but his work. But with foreigners you could never be quite sure where their ultimate loyalty lay.

After lunch he stood in the derelict stadium, looking at thousands of empty stands, and thought about Georgy. He had told no one he had a son—not even Margaret Cowdry, with whom he was now enjoying delightfully carnal relations—but he longed to tell his mother. He felt proud, for no reason—he had made no contribution to bringing Georgy into the world apart from making love to Jacky, probably about the easiest thing he had ever done. Most of all he felt excited. He was at the beginning of some kind of adventure. Georgy was going to grow, and learn, and change, and one day become a man, and Greg would be there, watching and marveling.

The scientists reassembled at two o'clock. Now there were about forty people crowded into the gallery with the monitoring equipment. The experiment was carefully reset in the position at which they had left off, Fermi checking his instruments constantly.

Then he said: "This time, withdraw the rod twelve inches."

The clicks became rapid. Greg waited for the increase to level off, as it had before, but it did not. Instead the clicking became faster and faster until it was a continuous roar.

The radiation level was above the maximum of the counters, Greg realized when he noticed that everyone's attention had switched to the pen recorder. Its scale was adjustable. As the level rose, the scale was changed, then changed again, and again.

Fermi raised a hand. They all went silent. "The pile has gone critical," he said. He smiled—and did nothing.

Greg wanted to scream *So turn the fucker off!* But Fermi remained silent and still, watching the pen, and such was his authority that no one challenged him. The chain reaction was happening, but it was under control. He let it run for a minute, then another.

McHugh muttered: "Jesus Christ."

Greg did not want to die. He wanted to be a senator. He wanted to sleep with Margaret Cowdry again. He wanted to see Georgy go to college. I haven't had half a life yet, he thought.

At last Fermi ordered the control rods to be pushed in.

The noise of the counters reverted to a clicking that gradually slowed and stopped.

Greg breathed normally.

McHugh was jubilant. "We proved it!" he said. "The chain reaction is real!"

"And it's controllable, more importantly," said Greg.

"Yes, I suppose that is more important, from the practical point of view."

Greg smiled. Scientists were like this, he knew from Harvard: for them theory was reality, and the world a rather inaccurate model.

Someone produced a bottle of Italian wine in a straw basket and some paper cups. The scientists all drank a tiny share. This was another reason Greg was not a scientist: they had no idea how to party.

Someone asked Fermi to sign the basket. He did so; then all the others signed it.

The technicians shut down the monitors. Everyone began to drift away. Greg stayed, observing. After a while he found himself alone in the gallery with Fermi and Szilard. He watched as the two intellectual giants shook hands. Szilard was a big, round-faced man; Fermi was elfin. For a moment Greg was inappropriately reminded of Laurel and Hardy.

Then he heard Szilard speak. "My friend," he said, "I think this will go down as a black day in the history of mankind."

Greg thought: Now what the hell did he mean by that?

V

Greg wanted his parents to accept Georgy.

It would not be easy. No doubt it would be unnerving for them to be told they had a grandson who had been concealed from them for six years. They might be angry. On top of that, they might look down on Jacky. They had no right to take a moralistic attitude, he thought wryly: they themselves had an illegitimate child—himself. But people were not rational.

He was not sure how much difference it would make that Georgy was black. Greg's parents were laid-back about race, and never talked viciously about niggers or kikes as some people of their generation did, but they might change when they learned there was a Negro in the family.

His father would be the more difficult one, he guessed, so he spoke to his mother first.

He got a few days' leave at Christmas and went home to her place in Buffalo. Marga had a large apartment in the best building in town. She lived mostly alone, but she had a cook, two maids, and a chauffeur. She had a safe full of jewelry and a dress closet the size of a two-car garage. But she did not have a husband.

Lev was in town, but traditionally he took Olga out on Christmas Eve. He was still married to her, technically, though he had not spent a night at her house for years. As far as Greg knew, Olga and Lev hated one another, but for some reason they met once a year.

That evening, Greg and his mother had dinner together in the apartment. He put on a tuxedo to please her. "I love to see my men dressed up," she often said. They had fish soup, roast chicken, and Greg's boyhood favorite, peach pie.

"I have some news for you, Mother," he said nervously as the maid poured coffee. He feared she would be angry. He was not frightened for himself, but for Georgy, and he wondered if this was what parenthood was about—worrying about someone else more than you worried about yourself.

"Good news?" she said.

She had become heavier in recent years, but she was still glamorous at forty-six. If there was any gray in her dark hair, it had been carefully camouflaged by her hairdresser. Tonight she wore a simple black dress and a diamond choker.

"Very good news, but I guess a little surprising, so please don't fly off the handle."

She raised a black eyebrow but said nothing.

He reached inside his dinner jacket and took out a photograph. It showed Georgy on a red bicycle with a ribbon around the handlebars. The rear wheel of the bike had a pair of stabilizing wheels so that it would not fall over. The expression on the boy's face was ecstatic. Greg was kneeling beside him, looking proud.

He handed the picture to his mother.

She studied it thoughtfully. After a minute she said: "I'm assuming you gave this little boy a bicycle for Christmas."

"That's right."

She looked up. "Are you telling me you have a child?"

Greg nodded. "His name is Georgy."

"Are you married?"

"No."

She threw down the photo. "For God's sake!" she said angrily. "What is the matter with you Peshkov men?"

Greg was dismayed. "I don't know what you mean!"

"Another illegitimate child! Another woman bringing him up alone!"

He realized that she saw Jacky as a younger version of herself. "Mother, I was fifteen . . ."

"Why can't you be normal?" she stormed. "For the love of Jesus Christ, what's wrong with having a regular family?"

Greg looked down. "There's nothing wrong with it."

He felt ashamed. Until this moment he had seen himself as a passive player in this drama, even a victim. Everything that had happened had been done to him by his father and Jacky. But his mother did not view it that way, and now he saw that she was right. He had not thought twice about sleeping with Jacky, he had not questioned her when she had said airily that there was no need to worry about contraception, and he had not confronted his father when Jacky left. He had been very young, yes, but if he was old enough to fuck her, he was old enough to take responsibility for the consequences.

His mother was still raging. "Don't you remember how you used to carry on? 'Where is my daddy? Why doesn't he sleep here? Why can't we go with him to Daisy's house?' And then later, the fights you had at school when the boys called you a bastard. And you were so angry to be refused membership of that goddamn yacht club."

"Of course I remember."

She banged a beringed fist on the table, causing crystal glasses to shake. "Then how can you put another little boy through the same torture?"

"I didn't know he existed until two months ago. Father scared the mother away."

"Who is she?"

"Her name is Jacky Jakes. She's a waitress." He took out another photo.

His mother sighed. "A pretty Negress." She was calming down.

"She was hoping to be an actress, but I guess she gave that up when Georgy came along."

Marga nodded. "A baby will ruin your career faster than a dose of the clap."

Mother assumed that an actress had to sleep with the right people to progress, Greg noted. How the hell would she know? But then, she had been a nightclub singer when his father met her . . .

He did not want to go down that road.

She said: "What did you give her for Christmas?"

"Medical insurance."

"Good choice. Better than a fluffy bear."

Greg heard a step in the hall. His father was home. Hastily, he said: "Mother, will you meet Jacky? Will you accept Georgy as your grandson?"

Her hand went to her mouth. "Oh, my God, I'm a grandmother." She did not know whether to be shocked or pleased.

Greg leaned forward. "I don't want Father to reject him. Please!"

Before she could reply, Lev came into the room.

Marga said: "Hello, darling, how was your evening?"

He sat at the table, looking grumpy. "Well, I've had my shortcomings explained to me in full detail, so I guess I had a great time."

"You poor thing. Did you get enough to eat? I can make you an omelette in a minute."

"The food was fine."

The photographs were on the table, but Lev had not noticed them yet.

The maid came in and said: "Would you like coffee, Mr. Peshkov?"

"No, thank you."

Marga said: "Bring the vodka, in case Mr. Peshkov would like a drink later."

"Yes, ma'am."

Greg noticed how solicitous Marga was about Lev's comfort and pleasure. He guessed that was why Lev was here, not at Olga's, for the night.

The maid brought a bottle and three small glasses on a silver tray. Lev still drank vodka the Russian way, warm and neat.

Greg said: "Father, you know Jacky Jakes—"

"Her again?" Lev said irritably.

"Yes, because there's something you don't know about her."

That got his attention. He hated to think other people knew things he did not. "What?"

"She has a child." He pushed the photographs across the polished table.

"Is it yours?"

"He's six years old. What do you think?"

"She kept this pretty damned quiet."

"She was scared of you."

"What did she think I might do, cook the baby and eat it?"

"I don't know, Father—you're the expert at scaring people."

Lev gave him a hard look. "You're learning, though."

He was talking about the scene with the razor. Maybe I am learning to scare people, Greg thought.

Lev said: "Why are you showing me these photos?"

"I thought you might like to know that you have a grandson."

"By a goddamn two-bit actress who was hoping to snag herself a rich man!"

Marga said: "Darling! Please remember that I was a two-bit nightclub singer hoping to snag myself a rich man."

He looked furious. For a moment he glared at Marga. Then his expression changed. "You know what?" he said. "You're right. Who am I to judge Jacky Jakes?"

Greg and Marga stared at him, astonished at this sudden humility.

He said: "I'm just like her. I was a two-kopek hoodlum from the slums of St. Petersburg until I married Olga Vyalov, my boss's daughter."

Greg caught his mother's eye, and she gave an almost imperceptible shrug that simply said *You never can tell.*

Lev looked again at the photo. "Apart from the color, this kid looks like my brother, Grigori. There's a surprise. Until now I thought all these picaninnies looked the same."

Greg could hardly breathe. "Will you see him, Father? Will you come with me and meet your grandson?"

"Hell, yes." Lev uncorked the bottle, poured vodka into three glasses, and passed them round. "What's the boy's name, anyway?"

"Georgy."

Lev raised his glass. "So here's to Georgy."

They all drank.

CHAPTER FIFTEEN

1943 (I)

L loyd Williams walked along a narrow uphill path at the tail end of a line of desperate fugitives.

He breathed easily. He was used to this. He had now crossed the Pyrenees several times. He wore rope-soled espadrilles that gave his feet a better grip on the rocky ground. He had a heavy coat on top of his blue overalls. The sun was hot now but later, when the party reached higher altitudes and the sun went down, the temperature would drop below freezing.

Ahead of him were two sturdy ponies, three local people, and eight weary, bedraggled escapers, all loaded with packs. There were three American airmen, the surviving crew of a B-24 Liberator bomber that had crash-landed in Belgium. Two more were British officers who had escaped from the Oflag 65 prisoner-of-war camp in Strasbourg. The others were a Czech Communist, a Jewish woman with a violin, and a mysterious Englishman called Watermill who was probably some kind of spy.

They had all come a long way and suffered many hardships. This was the last leg of their journey, and the most dangerous. If captured now, they would all be tortured until they betrayed the brave men and women who had helped them en route.

Leading the party was Teresa. The climb was hard work for people who were not used to it, but they had to keep up a brisk pace to minimize their exposure, and Lloyd had found that the refugees were less likely to fall behind when they were led by a small, ravishingly pretty woman.

The path leveled and broadened into a small clearing. Suddenly a loud voice rang out. Speaking French with a German accent, it shouted: "Halt!"

The column came to an abrupt halt.

Two German soldiers emerged from behind a rock. They carried standard Mauser bolt-action rifles, each holding five rounds of ammunition.

Reflexively Lloyd touched the overcoat pocket that contained his loaded 9 mm Luger pistol.

Escaping from mainland Europe had become harder, and Lloyd's job had grown even more dangerous. At the end of last year the Germans had occupied the southern half of France, contemptuously ignoring the Vichy French government like the flimsy sham it had always been. A forbidden zone ten miles deep was declared all along the frontier with Spain. Lloyd and his party were in that zone now.

Teresa addressed the soldiers in French. "Good morning, gentlemen. Is everything all right?" Lloyd knew her well, and he could hear the tremor of fear in her voice, but he hoped it was too faint for the sentries to notice.

Among the French police there were many Fascists and a few Communists, but all of them were lazy, and none wanted to chase refugees across the icy passes of the Pyrenees. However, the Germans did. German troops had moved into border towns and begun to patrol the hill paths and mule trails Lloyd and Teresa used. The occupiers were not crack troops; those were fighting in Russia, where they had recently surrendered Stalingrad after a long and murderous struggle. Many of the Germans in France were old men, boys, and the walking wounded. But that seemed to make them more determined to prove themselves. Unlike the French, they rarely turned a blind eye.

Now the older of the two soldiers, cadaverously thin with a gray mustache, said to Teresa: "Where are you going?"

"To the village of Lamont. We have groceries for you and your comrades."

This particular German unit had moved into a remote hill village, kicking out the local inhabitants. Then they had realized how difficult it was to supply troops in that location. It had been a stroke of genius on Teresa's part to undertake to carry food to them—at a healthy profit—and thereby get permission to enter the prohibited zone.

The thin soldier looked suspiciously at the men with their backpacks. "All this is for German soldiers?"

"I hope so," Teresa said. "There's no one else up here to sell it to." She took a piece of paper from her pocket. "Here's the order, signed by your Sergeant Eisenstein."

The man read it carefully and handed it back. Then he looked at Lieutenant Colonel Will Donelly, a beefy American pilot. "Is he French?"

Lloyd put his hand on the gun in his pocket.

The appearance of the fugitives was a problem. In this part of the world the local people, French and Spanish, were usually small and dark. And everyone was thin. Both Lloyd and Teresa fitted that description, as did the Czech and the violinist. But the British were pale and fair-haired, and the Americans were huge.

Teresa said: "Guillaume was born in Normandy. All that butter."

The younger of the two soldiers, a pale boy with glasses, smiled at Teresa. She was easy to smile at. "Do you have wine?" he said.

"Of course."

The two sentries brightened visibly.

Teresa said: "Would you like some right now?"

The older man said: "It's thirsty in the sun."

Lloyd opened a pannier on one of the ponies, took out four bottles of Roussillon white wine, and handed them over. The Germans took two each. Suddenly everyone was smiling and shaking hands. The older sentry said: "Carry on, friends."

The fugitives went on. Lloyd had not really expected trouble, but you could never be sure, and he was relieved to have got past the sentry post.

It took them two more hours to reach Lamont. A dirt-poor hamlet with a handful of crude houses and some empty sheep pens, it stood on the edge of a small upland plain where the new spring grass was just beginning to show. Lloyd pitied the people who had lived here. They had had so little, and even that had been taken from them.

The party walked into the center of the village and gratefully unshouldered their burdens. They were surrounded by German soldiers.

This was the most dangerous moment, Lloyd thought.

Sergeant Eisenstein was in charge of a platoon of fifteen or twenty men. Everyone helped to unload the supplies: bread, sausage, fresh fish, condensed milk, canned food. The soldiers were pleased to get supplies and glad to see new faces. They merrily attempted to engage their benefactors in conversation.

The fugitives had to say as little as possible. This was the moment when they could so easily betray themselves by a slip. Some Germans spoke French well enough to detect an English or American accent. Even those who had passable accents, such as Teresa and Lloyd, could give themselves away with a grammatical error. It was so easy to say *"sur le table"* instead of *"sur la table,"* but it was a mistake no French person would ever make.

To compensate, the two genuine Frenchmen in the party went out of their way to be voluble. Any time a soldier began to talk to a fugitive, someone would jump into the conversation.

Teresa presented the sergeant with a bill, and he took a long time to check the numbers, then count out the money.

At last they were able to take their leave, with empty backpacks and lighter hearts.

They walked back down the mountain half a mile; then they split up. Teresa went on down with the Frenchmen and the horses. Lloyd and the fugitives turned onto an upward path.

The German sentries at the clearing would probably be too drunk by now to notice that fewer people were coming down than went up. But if they asked questions, Teresa would say some of the party had started a card game with the soldiers, and would be following later.

Then there would be a change of shift and the Germans would lose track.

Lloyd made his group walk for two hours; then he allowed them a ten-minute break. They had all been given bottles of water and packets of dried figs for energy. They were discouraged from bringing anything else: Lloyd knew from experience that treasured books, silverware, ornaments, and gramophone records would become too heavy and be thrown into a snow-filled ravine long before the footsore travelers crested the pass.

This was the hard part. From now on it would only get darker and colder and rockier.

Just before the snow line, he instructed them to refill their water bottles at a clear cold stream.

When night fell, they kept going. It was dangerous to let people sleep: they might freeze to death. They were tired, and they slipped and stumbled on the icy rocks. Inevitably their pace slowed. Lloyd could not let the line spread: stragglers might lose their way, and there were precipitate ravines for the careless to fall into. But he had never lost anyone, yet.

Many of the fugitives were officers, and this was the point where they would sometimes challenge Lloyd, arguing when he ordered them to keep going. Lloyd had been promoted to major to give him more authority.

In the middle of the night, when their morale was at rock bottom, Lloyd announced: "You are now in neutral Spain!" and they raised a ragged cheer. In truth he did not know exactly where the border was, and always made the announcement when they seemed most in need of a boost.

Their spirits lifted again when dawn broke. They still had some way to go, but the route now led downhill, and their cold limbs gradually thawed.

At sunrise they skirted a small town with a dust-colored church at the top of a hill. Just beyond, they reached a large barn beside the road. Inside was a green Ford flatbed truck with a grimy canvas cover. The

lorry was large enough to carry the whole party. At the wheel was
Captain Silva, a middle-aged Englishman of Spanish descent who
worked with Lloyd.

Also there, to Lloyd's surprise, was Major Lowther, who had been in
charge of the intelligence course at Tŷ Gwyn, and had been snootily
disapproving—or perhaps just envious—of Lloyd's friendship with
Daisy.

Lloyd knew that Lowthie had been posted to the British embassy in
Madrid, and guessed he worked for MI6, the Secret Intelligence Service,
but he would not have expected to see him this far from the capital.

Lowther wore an expensive white flannel suit that was crumpled
and grubby. He stood beside the truck looking proprietorial. "I'll take
over from here, Williams," he said. He looked at the fugitives. "Which
one of you is Watermill?"

Watermill could have been a real name or a code.

The mysterious Englishman stepped forward and shook hands.

"I'm Major Lowther. I'm taking you straight to Madrid." Turning
back to Lloyd he said: "I'm afraid your party will have to make your way
to the nearest railway station."

"Just a minute," said Lloyd. "That truck belongs to my organization."
He had purchased it with his budget from MI9, the department that
helped escaping prisoners. "And the driver works for me."

"Can't be helped," Lowther said briskly. "Watermill has priority."

The Secret Intelligence Service always thought they had priority. "I
don't agree," Lloyd said. "I see no reason why we can't all go to Barcelona
in the truck, as planned. Then you can take Watermill on to Madrid by
train."

"I didn't ask for your opinion, laddie. Just do as you're told."

Watermill himself interjected, in a reasonable tone: "I'm perfectly
happy to share the truck."

"Leave this to me, please," Lowther told him.

Lloyd said: "All these people have just walked across the Pyrenees.
They're exhausted."

"Then they'd better have a rest before going on."

Lloyd shook his head. "Too dangerous. The town on the hill has a sympathetic mayor—that's why we rendezvous here. But farther down the valley their politics are different. The Gestapo are everywhere—you know that—and most of the Spanish police are on their side, not ours. My group will be in serious danger of arrest for entering the country illegally. And you know how difficult it is to get people out of Franco's jails even when they're innocent."

"I'm not going to waste my time arguing with you. I outrank you."

"No, you don't."

"What?"

"I'm a major. So don't call me 'laddie' ever again, unless you want a punch on the nose."

"My mission is urgent!"

"So why didn't you bring your own vehicle?"

"Because this one was available!"

"But it wasn't."

Will Donelly, the big American, stepped forward. "I'm with Major Williams," he drawled. "He's just saved my life. You, Major Lowther, haven't done shit."

"That's got nothing to do with it," said Lowther.

"Well, the situation here seems pretty clear," Donelly said. "The truck is under the authority of Major Williams. Major Lowther wants it, but he can't have it. End of story."

Lowther said: "You keep out of this."

"I happen to be a lieutenant colonel, so I guess I outrank you both."

"But this isn't under your jurisdiction."

"Nor yours, evidently." Donelly turned to Lloyd. "Should we get going?"

"I insist!" spluttered Lowther.

Donelly turned back to him. "Major Lowther," he said. "Shut the fuck up. And that's an order."

Lloyd said: "All right, everybody—climb aboard."

Lowther glared furiously at Lloyd. "I'll get you for this, you little Welsh bastard," he said.

ii

The daffodils were out in London on the day Daisy and Boy went for their medical.

The visit to the doctor was Daisy's idea. She was fed up with Boy blaming her for not getting pregnant. He constantly compared her to his brother Andy's wife, May, who now had three children. "There must be something wrong with you," he had said aggressively.

"I got pregnant once before." She winced at the remembered pain of her miscarriage; then she recalled how Lloyd had taken care of her, and she felt a different kind of pain.

Boy said: "Something could have happened since then to make you infertile."

"Or you."

"What do you mean?"

"There might just as easily be something wrong with you."

"Don't be absurd."

"Tell you what. I'll make a deal." The thought flashed through her mind that she was negotiating rather as her father, Lev, might have done. "I'll go for an examination—if you will."

That had surprised him, and he had hesitated, then said: "All right. You go first. If they say there's nothing wrong with you, I'll go."

"No," she said. "You go first."

"Why?"

"Because I don't trust you to keep your promises."

"All right, then, we'll go together."

Daisy was not sure why she was bothering. She did not love Boy— had not loved him for a long time. She was in love with Lloyd Williams, still in Spain on a mission he could not say much about. But she was married to Boy. He had been unfaithful to her, of course, with numerous women. But she had committed adultery, too, albeit with only one man. She had no moral ground to stand on, and in consequence she was paralyzed. She just felt that if she did her duty as a wife she might retain the last shreds of her self-respect.

The doctor's office was in Harley Street, not far from their house though in a less expensive neighborhood. Daisy found the examination unpleasant. The doctor was a man, and he was grumpy about her being ten minutes late. He asked her a lot of questions about her general health, her menstrual periods, and what he called her "relations" with her husband, not looking at her but making notes with a fountain pen. Then he put a series of cold metal instruments up her vagina. "I do this every day, so you don't need to worry," he said; then he gave her a grin that told her the opposite.

When she came out of the doctor's office, she half-expected Boy to renege on their deal and refuse to take his turn. He looked sour about it, but he went in.

While she was waiting, Daisy reread a letter from her half brother, Greg. He had discovered he had a child, from an affair he had with a black girl when he was fifteen. To Daisy's astonishment the playboy Greg was excited about his son and keen to be part of the child's life, albeit as an uncle rather than a father. Even more surprising, Lev had met the child and announced that he was smart.

It was ironic, she thought, that Greg had a son even though he had never wanted one, and Boy had no son even though he longed for one so badly.

Boy came out of the doctor's office an hour later. The doctor promised to give them their results in a week. They left at twelve noon.

"I need a drink after that," Boy said.

"So do I," said Daisy.

They looked up and down the street of identical row houses. "This neighborhood is a bloody desert. Not a pub in sight."

"I'm not going to a pub," said Daisy. "I want a martini, and they don't know how to make them in pubs." She spoke from experience. She had asked for a dry martini at the King's Head in Chelsea and had been served a glass of disgustingly warm vermouth. "Take me to Claridge's hotel, please. It's only five minutes' walk."

"Now that's a damn good idea."

The bar at Claridge's was full of people they knew. There were austerity rules about the meals restaurants could sell, but Claridge's had found a loophole: there were no restrictions on giving food away, so they offered a free buffet, charging only their usual high prices for drinks.

Daisy and Boy sat in art deco splendor and sipped perfect cocktails, and Daisy began to feel better.

"The doctor asked me if I'd had mumps," Boy said.

"But you have." It was mainly a childhood illness, but Boy had caught it a couple of years back. He had been briefly billeted at a vicarage in East Anglia, and had picked up the infection from the vicar's three small sons. It had been very painful. "Did he say why?"

"No. You know what these chaps are like. Never tell you a bloody thing."

It occurred to Daisy that she was not as happy-go-lucky as she had once been. In the old days she would never have brooded about her marriage this way. She had always liked what Scarlett O'Hara said in *Gone With the Wind:* "I'll think about that tomorrow." Not anymore. Perhaps she was growing up.

Boy was ordering a second cocktail when Daisy looked toward the door and saw the Marquis of Lowther walking in, dressed in a creased and stained uniform.

Daisy disliked him. Ever since he had guessed at her relationship with Lloyd, he had treated her with oily familiarity, as if they shared a secret that made them intimates.

Now he sat at their table uninvited, dropping cigar ash on his khaki trousers, and asked for a Manhattan.

Daisy knew at once that he was up to no good. There was a look of malignant relish in his eye that could not be explained merely as anticipation of a good cocktail.

Boy said: "I haven't seen you for a year or so, Lowthie. Where have you been?"

"Madrid," Lowthie said. "Can't say much about it. Hush-hush, you know. How about you?"

"I spend a lot of time training pilots, though I've flown a few missions lately, now that we've stepped up the bombing of Germany."

"Jolly good thing, too. Give the Germans a taste of their own medicine."

"You may say that, but there's a lot of muttering among the pilots."

"Really—why?"

"Because all this stuff about military targets is absolute rubbish. There's no point in bombing German factories, because they just re-build them. So we're targeting large areas of dense working-class housing. They can't replace the workers so fast."

Lowther looked shocked. "That would mean it's our policy to kill civilians."

"Exactly."

"But the government assures us—"

"The government lies," Boy said. "And the bomber crews know it. Many of them don't give a damn, of course, but some feel bad. They believe that if we're doing the right thing, then we should say so, and if we're doing the wrong thing, we should stop."

Lowther looked uneasy. "I'm not sure we should be talking like this here."

"You're probably right," Boy said.

The second round of cocktails came. Lowther turned to Daisy. "And what about the little woman?" he said. "You must have some war work. The devil finds mischief for idle hands, according to the proverb."

Daisy replied in a neutral matter-of-fact tone. "Now that the Blitz is over, they don't need women ambulance drivers, so I'm working with the American Red Cross. We have an office in Pall Mall. We do what we can to help American servicemen over here."

"Men lonely for a bit of feminine company, eh?"

"Mostly they're just homesick. They like to hear an American accent."

Lowthie leered. "I expect you're very good at consoling them."

"I do what I can."

"I bet you do."

Boy said: "Look here, Lowthie, are you a bit drunk? Because this sort of talk is awfully bad form, you know."

Lowther's expression turned spiteful. "Oh, come on, Boy, don't tell me you don't know. What are you, blind?"

Daisy said: "Take me home, please, Boy."

He ignored her and spoke to Lowther. "What the devil do you mean?"

"Ask her about Lloyd Williams."

Boy said: "Who the hell is Lloyd Williams?"

Daisy said: "I'm going home alone, if you won't take me."

"Do you know a Lloyd Williams, Daisy?"

He's your brother, Daisy thought, and she felt a powerful impulse to reveal the secret, and knock him sideways, but she resisted the temptation. "You know him," she said. "He was up at Cambridge with you. He took us to a music hall in the East End, years ago."

"Oh!" said Boy, remembering. Then, puzzled, he said to Lowther: "Him?" It was difficult for Boy to see someone such as Lloyd as a rival. With growing incredulity he added: "A man who can't even afford his own dress clothes?"

Lowther said: "Three years ago he was on my intelligence course down at Tŷ Gwyn while Daisy was living there. You were risking your life in a Hawker Hurricane over France at the time, I seem to remember. She was dallying with that Welsh weasel—in your family's house!"

Boy was getting red in the face. "If you're making this up, Lowthie, by God I'll thrash you."

"Ask your wife!" said Lowther with a confident grin.

Boy turned to Daisy.

She had not slept with Lloyd at Tŷ Gwyn. She had slept with him in his own bed at his mother's house during the Blitz. But she could not explain that to Boy in front of Lowther, and anyway it was a detail. The accusation of adultery was true, and she was not going to deny it. The secret was out. All she wanted now was to retain some semblance of dignity.

She said: "I will tell you everything you want to know, Boy—but not in front of this leering slob."

Boy raised his voice in astonishment. "So you don't deny it?"

The people at the next table looked around, seemed embarrassed, and returned their attention to their drinks.

Daisy raised her own voice. "I refused to be cross-examined in the bar of Claridge's hotel."

"You admit it, then?" he shouted.

The room went quiet.

Daisy stood up. "I don't admit or deny anything here. I'll tell you everything in private at home, which is where civilized couples discuss such matters."

"My God, you did it. You slept with him!" Boy roared.

Even the waiters had paused in their work and were standing still, watching the row.

Daisy walked to the door.

Boy yelled: "You slut!"

Daisy was not going to exit on that line. She turned around. "You know about sluts, of course. I had the misfortune to meet two of yours, remember?" She looked around the room. "Joanie and Pearl," she said contemptuously. "How many wives would put up with that?" She went out before he could reply.

She stepped into a waiting taxi. As it pulled away, she saw Boy emerge from the hotel and get into the next cab in line.

She gave the driver her address.

In a way she felt relieved that the truth was out. But she also felt terribly sad. Something had ended, she knew.

The house was only a quarter of a mile away. As she arrived, Boy's taxi pulled up behind hers.

He followed her into the hall.

She could not stay here with him, she realized. That was over. She would never again share his home or his bed. "Bring me a suitcase, please," she said to the butler.

"Very good, my lady."

She looked around. It was an eighteenth-century town house of perfect proportions, with an elegantly curving staircase, but she was not really sorry to leave it.

Boy said: "Where are you going?"

"To a hotel, I suppose. Probably not Claridge's."

"To meet your lover!"

"No, he's overseas. But, yes, I do love him. I'm sorry, Boy. You have no right to judge me—your offenses are worse—but I judge myself."

"That's it," he said. "I'm going to divorce you."

Those were the words she had been waiting for, she realized. Now they had been said, and everything was over. Her new life began from this moment.

She sighed. "Thank God," she said.

iii

Daisy rented an apartment in Piccadilly. It had a large American-style bathroom with a shower. There were two separate toilets, one for guests—a ridiculous extravagance in the eyes of most English people.

Fortunately money was not an issue for Daisy. Her grandfather Vyalov had left her rich, and she had had control of her own fortune since she was twenty-one. And it was all in American dollars.

New furniture was difficult to buy, so she shopped for antiques, of which there were plenty for sale cheap. She hung modern paintings for a gay, youthful look. She hired an elderly laundress and a girl to clean, and found it was easy to manage the place without a butler or a cook, especially when you did not have a husband to mollycoddle.

The servants at the Mayfair house packed all her clothes and sent them to her in a pantechnicon. Daisy and the laundress spent an afternoon opening the boxes and putting everything away tidily.

She had been both humiliated and liberated. On balance, she thought she was better off. The wound of rejection would heal, but she would be free of Boy forever.

After a week she wondered what had been the results of the medical examination. The doctor would have reported to Boy, of course, as the husband. She did not want to ask him, and anyway it did not seem important any longer, so she forgot about it.

She enjoyed making a new home. For a couple of weeks she was too busy to socialize. When she had fixed up the apartment, she decided to see all the friends she had been ignoring.

She had a lot of friends in London. She had been there seven years. For the last four years Boy had been away more than he was home, and she had gone to parties and balls on her own, so being without a husband would not make much difference to her life, she figured. No doubt she would be crossed off the Fitzherbert family's invitation lists, but they were not the only people in London society.

She bought crates of whisky, gin, and champagne, scouring London for what little was available legitimately and buying the rest on the black market. Then she sent out invitations to a flat-warming party.

The responses came back with ominous promptness, and they were all declines.

In tears, she phoned Eva Murray. "Why won't anyone come to my party?" she wailed.

Eva was at her door ten minutes later.

She arrived with three children and a nanny. Jamie was six, Anna four, and baby Karen two.

Daisy showed her around the apartment, then ordered tea while Jamie turned the couch into a tank, using his sisters as crew.

Speaking English with a mixture of German, American, and Scots accents, Eva said: "Daisy, dear, this isn't Rome."

"I know. Are you sure you're comfortable?"

Eva was heavily pregnant with her fourth child. "Would you mind if I put my feet up?"

"Of course not." Daisy fetched a cushion.

"London society is respectable," Eva went on. "Don't imagine I approve of it. I have been excluded often, and poor Jimmy is snubbed sometimes for having married a half-Jewish German."

"That's awful."

"I wouldn't wish it on anyone, whatever the reason."

"Sometimes I hate the British."

"You're forgetting what Americans are like. Don't you remember telling me that all the girls in Buffalo were snobs?"

Daisy laughed. "What a long time ago it seems."

"You've left your husband," Eva said. "And you did so in undeniably spectacular fashion, hurling insults at him in the bar of Claridge's hotel."

"And I'd only had one martini!"

Eva grinned. "How I wish I'd been there!"

"I kind of wish I hadn't."

"Needless to say, everyone in London society has talked about little else for the last three weeks."

"I guess I should have anticipated that."

"Now, I'm afraid, anyone who appears at your party will be seen as approving of adultery and divorce. Even I wouldn't like my mother-in-law to know I'd come here and had tea with you."

"But it's so unfair—Boy was unfaithful first!"

"And you thought women were treated equally?"

Daisy remembered that Eva had a great deal more to worry about than snobbery. Her family were still in Nazi Germany. Fitz had made inquiries through the Swiss embassy and learned that her doctor father was now in a concentration camp, and her brother, a violin maker, had been beaten up by the police, his hands smashed. "When I think about your troubles, I'm ashamed of myself for complaining," Daisy said.

"Don't be. But cancel the party."

Daisy did.

But it made her miserable. Her work for the Red Cross filled her days, but in the evenings she had nowhere to go and nothing to do. She went to the movies twice a week. She tried to read *Moby-Dick* but found it tedious. One Sunday she went to church. St. James's, the Wren church opposite her apartment building in Piccadilly, had been bombed, so she went to St. Martin-in-the-Fields. Boy was not there, but Fitz and Bea were, and Daisy spent the service looking at the back of Fitz's head, reflecting that she had fallen in love with two of this man's sons. Boy had his mother's looks and his father's single-minded selfishness. Lloyd had Fitz's good looks and Ethel's big heart. Why did it take me so long to see that? she wondered.

The church was full of people she knew, and after the service none of them spoke to her. She was lonely and almost friendless in a foreign country in the middle of a war.

One evening she took a taxi to Aldgate and knocked at the Leckwith house. When Ethel opened the door, Daisy said: "I've come to ask for your son's hand in marriage." Ethel let out a peal of laughter and hugged her.

She had brought a gift, an American tin of ham she had got from a USAF navigator. Such things were luxuries to British families on rations. She sat in the kitchen with Ethel and Bernie, listening to dance tunes on the radio. They all sang along with "Underneath the Arches" by Flanagan and Allen. "Bud Flanagan was born right here in the East End," Bernie said proudly. "Real name Chaim Reuben Weintrop."

The Leckwiths were excited about the Beveridge Report, a government paper that had become a bestseller. "Commissioned under a Conservative prime minister and written by a Liberal economist," said Bernie. "Yet it proposes what the Labour Party has always wanted! You know you're winning, in politics, when your opponents steal your ideas."

Ethel said: "The idea is that everyone of working age should pay a weekly insurance premium, then get benefits when they are sick, unemployed, retired, or widowed."

"A simple proposal, but it will transform our country," Bernie said enthusiastically. "Cradle to grave, no one will ever be destitute again."

Daisy said: "Has the government accepted it?"

"No," said Ethel. "Clem Attlee pressed Churchill very hard, but Churchill won't endorse the report. The Treasury thinks it will cost too much."

Bernie said: "We'll have to win an election before we can implement it."

Ethel and Bernie's daughter, Millie, dropped in. "I can't stay long," she said. "Abie's watching the children for half an hour." She had lost her job—women were not buying expensive gowns now, even if they could afford them—but fortunately her husband's leather business was flourishing, and they had two babies, Lennie and Pammie.

They drank cocoa and talked about the young man they all adored. They had little real news of Lloyd. Every six or eight months Ethel received a letter on the headed paper of the British embassy in Madrid, saying he was safe and well and doing his bit to defeat Fascism. He had been promoted to major. He had never written to Daisy, for fear Boy might see the letters, but he could now. Daisy gave Ethel the address of her new flat, and took down Lloyd's address, which was a British Forces Post Office number.

They had no idea when he might come home on leave.

Daisy told them about her half brother, Greg, and his son, Georgy. She knew that the Leckwiths of all people would not be censorious, and would be able to rejoice in such news.

She also told the story of Eva's family in Berlin. Bernie was Jewish, and tears came to his eyes when he heard about Rudi's broken hands. "They should have fought the bastard Fascists on the street, when they had the chance," he said. "That's what we did."

Millie said: "I've still got the scars on my back, where the police pushed us through Gardiner's plate-glass window. I used to be ashamed of them—Abie never saw my back until we'd been married six months, but he says they make him proud of me."

"It wasn't pretty, the fighting in Cable Street," said Bernie. "But we put a stop to their bloody nonsense." He took off his glasses and wiped his eyes with his handkerchief.

Ethel put her arm around his shoulders. "I told people to stay home that day," she said. "I was wrong, and you were right."

He smiled ruefully. "Doesn't happen often."

"But it was the Public Order Act, brought in after Cable Street, that finished the British Fascists," Ethel said. "Parliament banned the wearing of political uniforms in public. That finished them. If they couldn't strut up and down in their black shirts, they were nothing. The Conservatives did that—credit where credit's due."

Always a political family, the Leckwiths were planning the postwar reform of Britain by the Labour Party. Their leader, the quietly brilliant Clement Attlee, was now deputy prime minister under Churchill, and union hero Ernie Bevin was minister of labour. Their vision made Daisy feel excited about the future.

Millie left and Bernie went to bed. When they were alone, Ethel said to Daisy: "Do you really want to marry my Lloyd?"

"More than anything in the world. Do you think it will be all right?"

"I do. Why not?"

"Because we come from such different backgrounds. You're all such good people. You live for public service."

"Except for our Millie. She's like Bernie's brother—she wants to make money."

"Even she has scars on her back from Cable Street."

"True."

"Lloyd is like you. Political work isn't something extra he does, like a hobby—it's the center of his life. And I'm a selfish millionaire."

"I think there are two kinds of marriage," Ethel said thoughtfully. "One is a comfortable partnership, where two people share the same hopes and fears, raise children as a team, and give each other comfort and help." She was talking about herself and Bernie, Daisy realized. "The other is a wild passion, madness and joy and sex, possibly with someone completely unsuitable, maybe someone you don't admire or don't even really like." She was thinking about her affair with Fitz, Daisy felt sure. She held her breath: she knew Ethel was now telling her the raw truth. "I've been lucky. I've had both," Ethel said. "And here's my advice to you. If you get the chance of the mad kind of love, grab it with both hands, and to hell with the consequences."

"Wow," said Daisy.

She left a few minutes later. She felt privileged that Ethel had given her a glimpse into her soul. But when she got back to her empty apartment, she felt depressed. She made a cocktail and poured it away. She put the kettle on and took it off again. The radio went off the air. She lay between cold sheets and wished Lloyd were there.

She compared Lloyd's family with her own. Both had troubled histories, but Ethel had forged a strong, supportive family out of unfavorable materials, which Daisy's own mother had been unable to do—though that was more Lev's fault than Olga's. Ethel was a remarkable woman, and Lloyd had many of her qualities.

Where was he now, and what was he doing? Whatever the answer, he was sure to be in danger. Would he be killed now, when at last she was free to love him without restraint and, eventually, to marry him? What would she do if he died? Her own life would be at an end, she felt: no husband, no lover, no friends, no country. In the early hours of the morning she cried herself to sleep.

Next day she slept late. At midday she was drinking coffee in her little dining room, dressed in a black silk wrap, when her fifteen-year-old maid came in and said: "Major Williams is here, my lady."

"What?" she screeched. "He can't be!"

Then he came through the door with his kit bag over his shoulder.

He looked tired and had several days' growth of beard, and he had evidently slept in his uniform.

She threw her arms around him and kissed his bristly face. He kissed her back, inhibited somewhat by being unable to stop grinning. "I must stink," he said between kisses. "I haven't changed my clothes for a week."

"You smell like a cheese factory," she said. "I love it." She pulled him into her bedroom and started to take his clothes off.

"I'll take a quick shower," he said.

"No," she said. She pushed him back on the bed. "I'm in too much of a hurry." Her longing for him was frantic. And the truth was that she relished the strong smell. It should have repelled her, but it had the opposite effect. It was him, the man she had thought might be dead, and he was filling her nostrils and her lungs. She could have wept with joy.

Taking off his trousers would require removing his boots, and she could see that would be complicated, so she did not bother. She just unbuttoned his fly. She threw off her black silk robe and hiked her nightdress up to her waist, all the time staring with happy lust at the white penis sticking up out of the rough khaki cloth. Then she straddled him, easing herself down, and leaned forward and kissed him. "Oh, God," she said. "I can't tell you how much I've been longing for you."

She lay on him, not moving much, kissing him again and again. He held her face in his hands and stared at her. "This is real, isn't it?" he said. "Not just another happy dream?"

"It's real," she said.

"Good. I wouldn't like to wake up now."

"I want to stay like this forever."

"Nice idea, but I can't keep still much longer." He began to move under her.

"If you do that, I'll come," she said.

And she did.

Afterward they lay on her bed for a long time, talking.

He had two weeks' leave. "Live here," she said. "You can visit your parents every day, but I want you at night."

"I wouldn't like you to get a bad reputation."

"That ship has sailed. I've already been shunned by London society."

"I know." He had telephoned Ethel from Waterloo station, and she had told him about Daisy's separation from Boy and given him the address of the flat.

"We must do something about contraception," he said. "I'll get some rubber johnnies. But you might want to get fixed up with a device. What do you think?"

"You want to make sure I don't get pregnant?" she said.

There was a note of sadness in her voice, she realized, and he heard it. "Don't get me wrong," he said. He raised himself on his elbow. "I'm illegitimate. I was told lies about my parentage, and when I found out the truth, it was a terrible shock." His voice shook a little with emotion. "I'll never put my children through that. Never."

"We wouldn't have to lie to them."

"Would we tell them that we're not married? That in fact you're married to someone else?"

"I don't see why not."

"Think how they would be teased at school."

She was not convinced, but clearly the issue was a profound one for him. "So, what's your plan?" she said.

"I want us to have children. But not until we're married. To each other."

"I get that," she said. "So . . ."

"We have to wait."

Men were slow to pick up hints. "I'm not much of a girl for tradition," she said. "But, still, there are some things . . ."

At last he saw what she was getting at. "Oh! Okay. Just a minute." He knelt upright on the bed. "Daisy, dear—"

She burst out laughing. He looked comical, in full uniform with his limp dick hanging out of his fly. "Can I take a photo of you like that?" she said.

He looked down and saw what she meant. "Oh, sorry."

"No—don't you dare put it away! Stay just as you are, and say what you were going to say."

He grinned. "Daisy, dear, will you be my wife?"

"In a heartbeat," she said.

They lay down again, embracing.

Soon the novelty of his odor wore off. They got into the shower together. She soaped him all over, taking merry pleasure in his embarrassment when she washed his most intimate places. She put shampoo on his hair and scrubbed his grimy feet with a brush.

When he was clean, he insisted on washing her, but he had only got as far as her breasts when they had to make love again. They did it standing in the shower with the hot water coursing down their bodies. Clearly he had momentarily forgotten his aversion to illegitimate pregnancy, and she did not care.

Afterward he stood at her mirror, shaving. She wrapped a large towel around herself and sat on the lid of the toilet, watching him. He asked: "How long will it take you to get divorced?"

"I don't know. I'd better speak to Boy."

"Not today, though. I want you to myself all day."

"When will you go to see your parents?"

"Tomorrow, maybe."

"Then I'll go to Boy at the same time. I want to get this over as soon as possible."

"Good," he said. "That's settled, then."

iv

Daisy felt strange going into the house where she had lived with Boy. A month ago it had been hers. She had been free to come and go as she wished, and enter any room without asking permission. The servants had obeyed her every order without question. Now she was a stranger in the same house. She kept her hat and gloves on, and she had to follow the old butler as he led her to the morning room.

Boy did not shake hands or kiss her cheek. He looked full of righteous indignation.

"I haven't hired a lawyer yet," Daisy said as she sat down. "I wanted to talk to you personally first. I'm hoping we can do this without hating one another. After all, there are no children to fight over, and we both have plenty of money."

"You betrayed me!" he said.

Daisy sighed. Clearly it was not going to go the way she had hoped. "We both committed adultery," she said. "You first."

"I've been humiliated. Everyone in London knows!"

"I did try to stop you making a fool of yourself in Claridge's—but you were too busy humiliating me! I hope you've thrashed the loathsome marquis."

"How could I? He did me a favor."

"He might have done you a bigger favor by having a quiet word at the club."

"I don't understand how you could fall for such a low-class oik as Williams. I've found out a few things about him. His mother was a housemaid!"

"She's probably the most impressive woman I've ever met."

"I hope you realize that no one really knows who his father is."

That was about as ironic as you could get, Daisy thought. "I know who his father is," she said.

"Who?"

"I'm certainly not telling you."

"There you are, then."

"This isn't getting us anywhere, is it?"

"No."

"Perhaps I should just have a lawyer write to you." She stood up. "I loved you once, Boy," she said sadly. "You were fun. I'm sorry I wasn't enough for you. I wish you happiness. I hope you marry someone who suits you better, and that she gives you lots of sons. I would be happy for you if that came about."

"Well, it won't," he said.

She had turned toward the door, but now she looked back. "Why do you say that?"

"I got the report from that doctor we went to."

She had forgotten about the medical. It had seemed irrelevant after they split. "What did he say?"

"There's nothing wrong with you—you can have a whole litter of pups. But I can't father children. Mumps in adult men sometimes causes infertility, and I copped it." He laughed bitterly. "All those bloody Germans shooting at me for years, and I've been downed by a vicar's three little brats."

She felt sad for him. "Oh, Boy, I'm really sorry to hear that."

"Well, you're going to be sorrier, because I'm not divorcing you."

She suddenly felt cold. "What do you mean? Why not?"

"Why should I bother? I don't want to marry again. I can't have children. Andy's son will inherit."

"But I want to marry Lloyd!"

"Why should I care about that? Why should he have children if I can't?"

Daisy was devastated. Would happiness be snatched away from

her just when it seemed to be within her reach? "Boy, you can't mean this!"

"I've never been more serious in my life."

Her voice was anguished. "But Lloyd wants children of his own!"

"He should have thought of that before he f-f-fucked another man's wife."

"Very well, then," she said defiantly. "I'll divorce you."

"On what grounds?"

"Adultery, of course."

"But you have no evidence." She was about to say that that shouldn't be a problem when he grinned maliciously and added: "And I'll take care you don't get any."

He could do that, if he was discreet about his liaisons, she realized with growing horror. "But you threw me out!" she said.

"I shall tell the judge you're welcome to come home anytime."

She tried to stop herself crying. "I never thought you'd hate me this much," she said miserably.

"Didn't you?" said Boy. "Well, now you bloody well know."

V

Lloyd Williams went to Boy Fitzherbert's house in Mayfair at midmorning, when Boy would be sober, and told the butler he was Major Williams, a distant relative. He thought a man-to-man conversation was worth a try. Surely Boy did not really want to dedicate the rest of his life to revenge? Lloyd was in uniform, hoping to appeal to Boy as one fighting man to another. Good sense must surely prevail.

He was shown into the morning room, where Boy sat reading the paper and smoking a cigar. It took Boy a moment to recognize him. "You!" he said when comprehension dawned. "You can piss off right away."

"I've come to ask you to give Daisy a divorce," Lloyd said.

"Get out." Boy got to his feet.

Lloyd said: "I can see that you're toying with the idea of taking a swing at me, so in fairness I should tell you that it won't be as easy as you imagine. I'm a bit smaller than you, but I box at welterweight, and I've won quite a lot of contests."

"I'm not going to soil my hands on you."

"Good decision. But will you reconsider the divorce?"

"Absolutely not."

"There's something you don't know," Lloyd said. "I wonder if it might change your mind."

"I doubt it," Boy said. "But go on, now that you're here, give it a shot." He sat down, but did not offer Lloyd a chair.

Be it on your own head, Lloyd thought.

He took from his pocket a faded sepia photograph. "If you'd be so kind, glance at this picture of me." He put it on the side table next to Boy's ashtray.

Boy picked it up. "This isn't you. It looks like you, but the uniform is Victorian. It must be your father."

"My grandfather, in fact. Turn it over."

Boy read the inscription on the back. "Earl Fitzherbert?" he said scornfully.

"Yes. The previous earl, your grandfather—and mine. Daisy found that photo at Tŷ Gwyn." Lloyd took a deep breath. "You told Daisy that no one knows who my father is. Well, I can tell you. It's Earl Fitzherbert. You and I are brothers." He waited for Boy's response.

Boy laughed. "Ridiculous!"

"My reaction, exactly, when I was first told."

"Well, I must say, you have surprised me. I would have thought you could come up with something better than this absurd fantasy."

Lloyd had been hoping the revelation would shock Boy into a different frame of mind, but so far it was not working. Nevertheless he continued to reason. "Come on, Boy—how unlikely is it? Doesn't it happen all the time in great houses? Maids are pretty, young noblemen are randy, and nature takes its course. When a baby is born, the matter is hushed up. Please don't pretend you had no idea such things could occur."

"No doubt it's common enough." Boy's confidence was shaken, but still he blustered. "However, lots of people pretend they have connections with the aristocracy."

"Oh, please," Lloyd said disparagingly. "I don't want connections with the aristocracy. I'm not a draper's assistant with daydreams of grandeur. I come from a distinguished family of socialist politicians. My maternal grandfather was one of the founders of the South Wales Miners' Federation. The last thing I need is a wrong-side-of-the-blanket link with a Tory peer. It's highly embarrassing to me."

Boy laughed again, but with less conviction. "*You're* embarrassed! Talk about inverted snobbery."

"Inverted? I'm more likely to become prime minister than you are." Lloyd realized they had got into a pissing contest, which was not what he wanted. "Never mind that," he said. "I'm trying to persuade you that you can't spend the rest of your life taking revenge on me—if only because we're brothers."

"I still don't believe it," Boy said, putting the photo down on the side table and picking up his cigar.

"Nor did I, at first." Lloyd kept trying: his whole future was at stake. "Then it was pointed out to me that my mother was working at Tŷ Gwyn when she fell pregnant, that she had always been evasive about my father's identity, and that shortly before I was born she somehow acquired the funds to buy a three-bedroom house in London. I confronted her with my suspicions and she admitted the truth."

"This is laughable."

"But you know it's true, don't you?"

"I know no such thing."

"You do, though. For the sake of our brotherhood, won't you do the decent thing?"

"Certainly not."

Lloyd saw that he was not going to win. He felt downcast. Boy had the power to blight Lloyd's life, and he was determined to use it.

He picked up the photograph and put it back in his pocket. "You'll ask our father about this. You won't be able to restrain yourself. You'll have to find out."

Boy made a scornful noise.

Lloyd went to the door. "I believe he will tell you the truth. Goodbye, Boy."

He went out and closed the door behind him.

CHAPTER SIXTEEN

1943 (II)

C olonel Albert Beck got a Russian bullet in his right lung at Kharkov in March 1943. He was lucky: a field surgeon put in a chest drain and reinflated the lung, saving his life, just. Weakened by blood loss and the almost inevitable infection, Beck was put on a train home and ended up in Carla's hospital in Berlin.

He was a tough, wiry man in his early forties, prematurely bald, with a protruding jaw like the prow of a Viking longboat. The first time he spoke to Carla, he was drugged and feverish and wildly indiscreet. "We're losing the war," he said.

She was immediately alert. A discontented officer was a potential source of information. She said lightly: "The newspapers say we're shortening the line on the eastern front."

He laughed scornfully. "That means we're retreating."

She continued to draw him out. "And Italy looks bad." The Italian dictator Benito Mussolini—Hitler's greatest ally—had fallen.

"Remember 1939, and 1940?" Beck said nostalgically. "One brilliant lightning victory after another. Those were the days."

Clearly he was not ideological, perhaps not even political. He was a normal patriotic soldier who had stopped kidding himself.

Carla led him on. "It can't be true that the army is short of everything from bullets to underpants." This kind of mildly risky talk was not unusual in Berlin nowadays.

"Of course we are." Beck was radically disinhibited but quite articulate. "Germany simply can't produce as many guns and tanks as the Soviet Union, Great Britain, and the United States combined—especially when we're being bombed constantly. And no matter how many Russians we kill, the Red Army seems to have an inexhaustible supply of new recruits."

"What do you think will happen?"

"The Nazis will never admit defeat, of course. So more people will die. Millions more, just because they're too proud to yield. Insanity. Insanity." He drifted off to sleep.

You had to be sick—or crazy—to voice such thoughts, but Carla believed that more and more people were thinking that way. Despite relentless government propaganda it was becoming clear that Hitler was losing the war.

There had been no police investigation of the death of Joachim Koch. It had been reported in the newspaper as a road accident. Carla had got over the initial shock, but every now and again the realization hit her that she had killed a man, and she would relive his death in her imagination. It made her shake and she had to sit down. This had happened only once when she was on duty, fortunately, and she had passed that off as a faint due to hunger—highly plausible in wartime Berlin. Her mother was worse. It was strange that Maud had loved Joachim, weak and foolish as he was, but there was no explaining love. Carla herself had completely misjudged Werner Franck, thinking he was strong and brave, only to learn that he was selfish and weak.

She talked to Beck a lot before he was discharged, probing to find out what kind of man he was. Once recovered, he never again spoke indiscreetly about the war. She learned that he was a career soldier, his wife was dead, and his married daughter lived in Buenos Aires. His father had been a Berlin city councilor; he did not say for which party, so clearly it was not the Nazis or any of their allies. He never said anything bad about Hitler, but he never said anything good, either, nor did he speak disparagingly of Jews or Communists. These days that in itself was close to insubordination.

His lung would heal, but he would never again be strong enough for active service, and he told her he was being posted to the General Staff. He could become a diamond mine of vital secrets. She would be risking her life if she tried to recruit him—but she had to try.

She knew he would not remember their first conversation. "You were very candid," Carla told him in a low voice. There was no one nearby. "You said we were losing the war."

His eyes flashed fear. He was no longer a woozy patient in a hospital gown with stubble on his cheeks. He was washed and shaved, sitting upright in dark blue pajamas buttoned to the throat. "I suppose you're going to report me to the Gestapo," he said. "I don't think a man should be held to account for what he says when he's sick and raving."

"You weren't raving," she said. "You were very clear. But I'm not going to report you to anyone."

"No?"

"Because you are right."

He was surprised. "Now I should report *you*."

"If you do, I'll say that you insulted Hitler in your delirium, and when I threatened to report it, you made up a story about me in self-defense."

"If I denounce you, you'll denounce me," he said. "Stalemate."

"But you're not going to denounce me," she said. "I know that, because I know you. I've nursed you. You're a good man. You joined the army for love of your country, but you hate the war and you hate the Nazis." She was 99 percent sure of this.

"It's very dangerous to talk like that."

"I know."

"So this isn't just a casual conversation."

"Correct. You said that millions of people are going to die just because the Nazis are too proud to surrender."

"Did I?"

"You can help save some of those millions."

"How?"

Carla paused. This was where she put her life on the line. "Any information you have, I can pass it to the appropriate quarters." She held her breath. If she was wrong about Beck, she was dead.

She read amazement in his look. He could hardly imagine that this briskly efficient young nurse was a spy. But he believed her, she could see that. He said: "I think I understand you."

She handed him a green hospital file folder, empty.

He took it. "What's this for?" he said.

"You're a soldier—you understand camouflage."

He nodded. "You're risking your life," he said, and she saw something like admiration in his eyes.

"So are you, now."

"Yes," said Colonel Beck. "But I'm used to it."

ii

Early in the morning, Thomas Macke took young Werner Franck to the Plötzensee Prison in the western suburb of Charlottenburg. "You should see this," he said. "Then you can tell General Dorn how effective we are."

He parked in the Königsdamm and led Werner to the rear of the main prison. They entered a room twenty-five feet long and about half as wide. Waiting there was a man dressed in a tailcoat, a top hat, and white gloves. Werner frowned at the peculiar costume. "This is Herr Reichhart," said Macke. "The executioner."

Werner swallowed. "So we're going to witness an execution?"

"Yes."

With a casual air that might have been faked, Werner said: "Why the fancy dress outfit?"

Macke shrugged. "Tradition."

A black curtain divided the room in two. Macke drew it back to show eight hooks attached to an iron girder that ran across the ceiling.

716 | CHAPTER SIXTEEN

Werner said: "For hanging?"

Macke nodded.

There was also a wooden table with straps for holding someone down. At one end of the table was a high device of distinctive shape. On the floor was a heavy basket.

The young lieutenant was pale. "A guillotine," he said.

"Exactly," said Macke. He looked at his watch. "We shan't be kept waiting long."

More men filed into the room. Several nodded in a familiar way to Macke. Speaking quietly into Werner's ear, Macke said: "Regulations demand that the judges, the court officers, the prison governor, and the chaplain all attend."

Werner swallowed. He was not liking this, Macke could see.

He was not meant to. Macke's motive in bringing him here had nothing to do with impressing General Dorn. Macke was worried about Werner. There was something about him that did not ring true.

Werner worked for Dorn; that was not in question. He had accompanied Dorn on a visit to Gestapo headquarters, and subsequently Dorn had written a note saying that the Berlin counterespionage effort was most impressive, and mentioning Macke by name. For weeks afterward Macke had walked around in a miasma of warm pride.

But Macke could not forget Werner's behavior on that evening, nearly a year ago now, when they had almost caught a spy in a disused fur coat factory near the East Station. Werner had panicked—or had he? Accidentally or otherwise, he had given the pianist enough warning to get away. Macke could not shake the suspicion that the panic had been an act, and Werner had in fact been coolly and deliberately sounding the alarm.

Macke did not quite have the nerve to arrest and torture Werner. It could be done, of course, but Dorn might well kick up a fuss, and then Macke would be questioned. His boss, Superintendent Kringelein, who did not much like him, would ask what hard evidence he had against Werner—and he had none.

But this ought to reveal the truth.

The door opened again, and two prison guards entered either side of a young woman called Lili Markgraf.

He heard Werner gasp. "What's the matter?" Macke said.

Werner said: "You didn't tell me it was going to be a girl."

"Do you know her?"

"No."

Lili was twenty-two, Macke knew, though she looked younger. Her fair hair had been cut this morning, and it was now as short as a man's. She was limping, and walked bent over as if she had an abdominal injury. She wore a plain blue dress of heavy cotton with no collar, just a round neckline. Her eyes were red with crying. The guards held her arms firmly, not taking any chances.

"This woman was denounced by a relative who found a codebook hidden in her room," Macke said. "The five-digit Russian code."

"Why is she walking like that?"

"The effects of interrogation. But we didn't get anything from her."

Werner's face was impassive. "What a shame," he said. "She might have led us to other spies."

Macke saw no sign that he was faking. "She knew her associate only as Heinrich—no last name—and he may have used a pseudonym anyway. I find we rarely profit by arresting women—they don't know enough."

"But at least you have her codebook."

"For what it's worth. They change the key word regularly, so we still face a challenge in decrypting their signals."

"Pity."

One of the men cleared his throat and spoke loudly enough for everyone to hear. He said he was the president of the court, then read out the death sentence.

The guards walked Lili to the wooden table. They gave her the chance of lying on it voluntarily, but she took a step backward, so they picked her up forcibly. She did not struggle. They laid her facedown and strapped her in.

The chaplain began a prayer.

Lili began to plead. "No, no," she said, without raising her voice. "No, please, let me go. Let me go." She spoke coherently, as if she were merely asking someone for a favor.

The man in the top hat looked at the president, who shook his head and said: "Not yet. The prayer must be finished."

Lili's voice rose in pitch and urgency. "I don't want to die! I'm afraid to die! Don't do this to me, please!"

The executioner looked again at the court president. This time the president just ignored him.

Macke studied Werner. He looked sick, but so did everybody else in the room. As a test, this was not really working. Werner's reaction showed that he was sensitive, not that he was a traitor. Macke might have to think of something else.

Lili began to scream.

Even Macke felt impatient.

The pastor hurried through the rest of the prayer.

When he said "Amen," she stopped screaming, as if she knew it was all over.

The president gave the nod.

The executioner moved a lever, and the weighted blade fell.

It made a whispering sound as it sliced through Lili's pale neck. Her head with its short-cropped hair fell forward and there was a gush of blood. The head hit the basket with a loud thump that seemed to resound in the room.

Absurdly, Macke wondered if the head felt any pain.

iii

Carla bumped into Colonel Beck in the hospital corridor. He was in uniform. She looked at him in sudden fear. Ever since he was discharged, she had lived every day in fear that he had betrayed her, and that the Gestapo were on their way.

But he smiled and said: "I came back for a checkup with Dr. Ernst."

Was that all? Had he forgotten their conversation? Was he pretending to have forgotten it? Was there a black Gestapo Mercedes waiting outside?

Beck was carrying a green hospital file folder.

A cancer specialist in a white coat approached. As he went by, Carla said brightly to Beck: "How are things?"

"I'm as fit as I'm ever going to be. I'll never lead a battalion into battle again, but aside from athletics I can lead a normal life."

"I'm glad to hear that."

People kept walking by. Carla feared Beck would never get the chance to say anything to her privately.

But he remained unruffled. "I'd just like to thank you for your kindness and professionalism."

"You're welcome."

"Good-bye, Sister."

"Good-bye, Colonel."

When Beck left, Carla was holding the file folder.

She walked briskly to the nurses' cloakroom. It was empty. She stood with her heel firmly wedged against the door so no one could come in.

Inside the folder was a large envelope made of the cheap buff-colored paper used in offices everywhere. Carla opened the envelope. It contained several typewritten sheets. She looked at the first without removing it from the envelope. It was headed:

Operational Order No. 6
Code Zitadelle

It was the battle plan for the summer offensive on the eastern front. Her heart raced. This was gold dust.

She had to pass the envelope to Frieda. Unfortunately Frieda was not working at the hospital today: it was her day off. Carla considered leaving the hospital right away, in the middle of her shift, and going to Frieda's house, but she swiftly rejected that idea. Better to behave normally, not to attract attention.

She slipped the envelope into the shoulder bag hanging on her coat hook. She covered it with the blue-and-gold silk scarf that she always carried for hiding things. She stood still for a few moments, letting her breathing return to normal. Then she went back to the ward.

She worked the rest of her shift as best she could; then she put on her coat, left the hospital, and walked to the station. Passing a bomb site, she saw graffiti on the remains of the building. A defiant patriot had written: "Our walls might break, but not our hearts." But someone else had ironically quoted Hitler's 1933 election slogan: "Give me four years, and you will not recognize Germany."

She bought a ticket to the Zoo.

On the train she felt like an alien. All the other passengers were loyal Germans, and she was the one with secrets in her bag to betray to Moscow. She did not like the feeling. No one looked at her, but that only made her think they were all deliberately avoiding her eye. She could hardly wait to hand over the envelope to Frieda.

The Zoo Station was on the edge of the Tiergarten. The trees were dwarfed now by a huge flak tower. One of three in Berlin, this square concrete block was more than a hundred feet high. At the corners of the roof were four giant 128 mm antiaircraft guns weighing twenty-five tons each. The raw concrete was painted green in a hopelessly optimistic attempt to make the monstrosity less of an eyesore in the park.

Ugly though it was, Berliners loved it. When the bombs were falling, its thunder reassured them that someone was shooting back.

Still in a state of high tension, Carla walked from the station to Frieda's house. It was midafternoon, so the Franck parents would probably be out, Ludi at his factory and Monika seeing a friend, possibly Carla's mother. Werner's motorcycle was parked on the drive.

The manservant opened the door. "Miss Frieda is out, but she won't be long," he said. "She went to KaDeWe to buy gloves. Mr. Werner is in bed with a heavy cold."

"I'll wait for Frieda in her room, as usual."

Carla took off her coat and went upstairs, still carrying her bag. In

Frieda's room she kicked off her shoes and lay on the bed to read the battle plan for Operation Zitadelle. She was as stressed as an overwound clock, but she would feel better when she had given the purloined document to someone else.

From the next room she heard the sound of sobbing.

She was surprised. That was Werner's room. Carla found it hard to imagine the suave playboy in tears.

But the sound definitely came from a man, and he seemed to be trying and failing to suppress his grief.

Against her will, Carla felt pity. She told herself that some feisty woman had thrown Werner over, probably for very good reasons. But she could not help responding to the real distress she was hearing.

She got off the bed, put the battle plan back in her bag, and stepped outside.

She listened at Werner's door. She could hear it even more clearly. She was too softhearted to ignore it. She opened the door and went in.

Werner was sitting on the edge of the bed, head in hands. When he heard the door, he looked up, startled. His face was red with emotion and wet with tears. His tie was pulled down and his collar undone. He looked at Carla with misery in his eyes. He was bowled over, devastated, and too wretched to care who knew it.

Carla could not pretend to be heartless. "What is it?" she said.

"I can't do this anymore," he said.

She closed the door behind her. "What happened?"

"They cut off Lili Markgraf's head—and I had to watch."

Carla stared, openmouthed. "What on earth are you talking about?"

"She was twenty-two." He took a handkerchief from his pocket and wiped his face. "You're already in danger, but if I tell you this, it will be a lot worse."

Her mind was full of amazing surmises. "I think I can guess, but tell me," she said.

He nodded. "You'll figure it out soon anyway. Lili helped Heinrich broadcast to Moscow. It's much quicker if someone reads you the code groups. And the faster you go, the less likely you are to be caught. But

Lili's cousin stayed at the apartment for a few days and found her codebooks. Nazi bitch."

His words confirmed her astonishing suspicions. "You know about the spying?"

He looked at her with an ironic smile. "I'm in charge of it."

"Good God!"

"That's why I had to drop the whole business of the murdered children. Moscow ordered me to. And they were right. If I'd lost my job at the Air Ministry, I would have had no access to secret papers, nor to other people who could bring me secrets."

She needed to sit down. She perched on the edge of the bed beside him. "Why didn't you tell me?"

"We work on the assumption that everyone talks under torture. Knowing nothing, you can't betray others. Poor Lili was tortured, but she only knew Volodya, who's back in Moscow now, and Heinrich, and she never knew Heinrich's second name or anything else about him."

Carla was chilled to the bone. *Everyone talks under torture.*

Werner finished: "I'm sorry I've told you, but after seeing me like this, you were on the point of guessing it all anyway."

"So I've completely misjudged you."

"Not your fault. I deliberately misled you."

"I feel a fool just the same. I've despised you for two years."

"All the while I was desperate to explain to you."

She put her arm around him.

He took her other hand and kissed it. "Can you forgive me?"

She was not sure how she felt, but she did not want to reject him when he was so down, so she said: "Yes, of course."

"Poor Lili," he said. His voice fell to a whisper. "She had been so badly beaten, she could hardly walk to the guillotine. Yet she begged for life, right up to the end."

"How come you were there?"

"I've befriended a Gestapo man, Inspector Thomas Macke. He took me."

"Macke? I remember him—he arrested my father." She vividly

recalled a round-faced man with a small black mustache, and she experienced again her rage at the arrogant power Macke had to take her father away, and her grief when he died of the injuries he suffered at Macke's hands.

"I think he suspects me, and taking me to the execution was a test. Perhaps he thought I might lose my self-control and try to intervene. Anyway, I think I passed the test."

"But if you were arrested . . ."

Werner nodded. "Everyone talks under torture."

"And you know everything."

"Every agent, every code . . . The only thing I don't know is where they broadcast from. I leave it up to them to pick the locations, and they don't tell me."

They held hands in silence. After a while, Carla said: "I came to give it to Frieda, but I might as well give it to you."

"Give what?"

"The battle plan for Operation Zitadelle."

Werner was electrified. "But I've been trying to put my hands on that for weeks! Where did you get it?"

"From an officer on the General Staff. Perhaps I shouldn't say his name."

"Quite right, don't tell me. But is it authentic?"

"You'd better take a look." She went to Frieda's room and returned with the buff envelope. It had never occurred to her that the document might not be genuine. "It looks all right to me, but what do I know?"

He took out the typewritten sheets. After a minute he said: "This is the real thing. Fantastic!"

"I'm so glad."

He stood up. "I have to take this to Heinrich right away. We must get this encrypted and broadcast tonight."

Carla felt disappointed that their moment of intimacy was over so soon, though she could not have said what she had been expecting. She followed him through the door. She picked up her bag from Frieda's room and went downstairs.

With his hand on the front door, Werner said: "I'm so glad we're friends again."

"Me, too."

"Do you think we'll be able to forget this period of estrangement?"

She did not know what he was trying to say. Did he want to be her lover again—or was he telling her that was out of the question? "I think we can put it behind us," she said neutrally.

"Good." He bent and kissed her lips very quickly. Then he opened the door.

They left the house together, and he climbed on his motorcycle.

Carla walked down the driveway to the street and headed for the station. A moment later, Werner drove past her with a honk and a wave.

Now that she was alone, she could begin to think about his revelation. How did she feel? For two years she had hated him. But in that time she had not had a serious boyfriend. Had she remained in love with him all along? At a minimum she had retained, in her heart of hearts, a fondness for him despite everything. Today, when she heard him in such distress, her hostility had melted away. Now she felt a glow of affection.

Did she love him still?

She did not know.

iv

Macke sat in the rear seat of the black Mercedes with Werner beside him. Around Macke's neck was a bag like a school satchel, except that he wore it in front instead of behind. It was small enough to be covered by a buttoned overcoat. A thin wire ran from the bag to a small earphone. "It's the latest thing," Macke said. "As you get closer to the broadcaster, the sound gets louder."

Werner said: "More discreet than a van with a big aerial on its roof."

"We have to use both—the van to discover the general area, and this to pinpoint the exact location."

Macke was in trouble. Operation Zitadelle had been a catastrophe. Even before the offensive opened, the Red Army had attacked the airfields where the Luftwaffe were assembling. Zitadelle had been called off after a week, but even that was too late to prevent irreparable damage to the German army.

Germany's leaders were always quick to blame Jewish-Bolshevik conspirators whenever things went wrong, but in this case they were right. The Red Army had appeared to know the entire battle plan in advance. And that, according to Superintendent Kringelein, was Thomas Macke's fault. He was head of counterespionage for the city of Berlin. His career was on the line. He faced dismissal and worse.

His only hope now was a tremendous coup, a massive operation to round up the spies who were undermining the German war effort. So tonight he had set a trap for Werner Franck.

If Franck turned out to be innocent, he did not know what he would do.

In the front seat of the car, a walkie-talkie crackled. Macke's pulse quickened. The driver picked up the handset. "Wagner here." He started the engine. "We're on our way," he said. "Over and out."

It had started.

Macke asked him: "Where are we headed?"

"Kreuzberg." It was a densely populated low-rent neighborhood south of the city center.

As they pulled away, the air raid siren sounded.

That was an unwelcome complication. Macke looked out of the window. The searchlights came on, waving like giant wands. Macke supposed they must have found planes sometimes, but he had never seen it happen. When the sirens ceased their howling, he could hear the thunder of approaching bombers. In the early years of the war, a British bombing mission had consisted of a few dozen aircraft—which was bad enough—but now they were sending hundreds at a time. The noise was terrifying even before they dropped their bombs.

Werner said: "I suppose we'd better call off our mission tonight."

"Hell, no," said Macke.

The roar of the planes grew.

Flares and small incendiary bombs began to fall as the car approached Kreuzberg. The neighborhood was a typical target for the RAF's current strategy of killing as many civilian factory workers as possible. With staggering hypocrisy Churchill and Attlee were claiming they attacked only military targets, and civilian casualties were a regrettable side effect. Berliners knew better.

Wagner drove as fast as he could along streets lit fitfully by flames. There were no people around apart from air raid officials: everyone else was legally obliged to take shelter. The only other vehicles were ambulances, fire engines, and police cars.

Macke covertly studied Werner. The boy was edgy, never quite still, staring out of the window anxiously, tapping his foot in unconscious tension.

Macke had not confided his suspicions to anyone but his immediate team. It was going to be difficult for him if he had to admit that he had demonstrated Gestapo operations to someone whom he now thought was a spy. He could end up under interrogation in his own basement torture chamber. He was not going to do it until he was sure. The only way he might get away with it would be if at the same time he could present his superiors with a captured spy.

But then, if his suspicion turned out to be true, he would arrest not just Werner but his family and friends, and announce the destruction of a massive spy ring. That would transform the picture. He might even be promoted.

As the raid progressed, the type of bombs changed, and Macke heard the profound thudding sound of high explosive. Once the target was illuminated, the RAF liked to drop a mixture of large oil bombs to start fires and high explosive to ventilate the flames and hamper the emergency services. It was cruel, but Macke knew that the Luftwaffe's bombing pattern was similar.

The sound in Macke's earphone started up as they drove cautiously along a street of five-story tenements. The area was taking a terrific pounding and several buildings were newly demolished. Werner said shakily: "We're in the middle of the target area, for Christ's sake."

Macke did not care: tonight was already life or death to him. "All the better," he said. "The pianist will imagine he doesn't need to worry about the Gestapo, in the middle of an air raid."

Wagner stopped the car next to a burning church and pointed along a side street. "Down there," he said.

Macke and Werner jumped out.

Macke walked quickly along the street with Werner beside him and Wagner behind. Werner said: "Are you sure it's a spy? Could it be anything else?"

"Broadcasting a radio signal?" Macke said. "What else could it be?"

Macke could still hear his earphone, but only just, for the air raid was cacophonous: the planes, the bombs, the antiaircraft guns, the crash of falling buildings, and the roar of huge fires.

They passed a stable where horses were neighing in terror, the signal growing ever stronger. Werner was glancing from side to side anxiously. If he was a spy, he would now be fearing that one of his colleagues was about to be arrested by the Gestapo—and wondering what the hell he could do about it. Would he repeat the trick he used last time, or think of some new way of giving a warning? If he was not a spy, this whole farce was a waste of time.

Macke took out the earpiece and handed it to Werner. "Listen," he said, continuing to walk.

Werner nodded. "Getting stronger," he said. The look in his eyes was almost frantic. He handed the earpiece back.

I believe I've got you, Macke thought triumphantly.

There was a thunderous crash as a bomb landed in a building they had just passed. They turned to see flames already licking up beyond the smashed windows of a bakery. Wagner said: "Christ, that was close."

They came to a school, a low brick building in an asphalt yard. "In there, I think," said Macke.

The three men walked up a short flight of stone steps to the entrance. The door was not locked. They went in.

They were at one end of a broad corridor. At its far end was a large door that probably led to the school hall. "Straight ahead," said Macke.

He drew his gun, a 9 mm Luger pistol.

Werner was not armed.

There was a crash, a thud, and the roar of an explosion, all terrifyingly close. All the windows in the corridor smashed, and shards of glass rained on the tiled floor. A bomb must have landed in the playground.

Werner shouted: "Clear out, everyone! The building is about to collapse."

There was no danger of the building collapsing, Macke could see. This was Werner's ruse for giving the alarm to the pianist.

Werner broke into a run, but instead of heading back the way they had come, he went on down the corridor toward the hall.

To warn his friends, Macke thought.

Wagner drew his gun, but Macke said: "No! Don't shoot!"

Werner reached the end of the corridor and flung open the door to the hall. "Run, everyone!" he yelled. Then he fell silent and stood still.

Inside the hall Macke's colleague Mann, the electrical engineer, was tapping out nonsense on a suitcase radio.

Beside him stood Schneider and Richter, both holding drawn guns.

Macke smiled triumphantly. Werner had fallen straight into his trap.

Wagner walked forward and put his gun to Werner's head.

Macke said: "You're under arrest, you subhuman Bolshevik."

Werner acted fast. He jerked his head away from Wagner's gun, seized Wagner's arm, and pulled him into the hall. For a moment Wagner shielded Werner from the guns in the hall. Then he thrust Wagner away from him, causing Wagner to stumble and fall. In the next moment he stepped out of the hall and slammed the door.

For a few seconds it was just Macke and Werner in the corridor.

Werner walked toward Macke.

Macke pointed his Luger. "Stop, or I'll shoot."

"No, you won't." Werner came closer. "You need to interrogate me, and find out who the others are."

Macke pointed his gun at Werner's legs. "I can interrogate you with a bullet in your knee," he said, and he fired.

The shot missed.

Werner lunged and knocked Macke's gun hand aside. Macke dropped the weapon. As he stooped to retrieve it, Werner ran past.

Macke picked up the gun.

Werner reached the school door. Macke took careful aim at his legs and fired.

His first three shots missed, and Werner went through the door.

Macke fired one more shot through the still-open door, and Werner cried out and fell down.

Macke ran along the corridor. Behind him, he heard the others coming out of the school hall.

Then the roof opened with a crash, there was another noise like a thud, and liquid fire splashed like a fountain. Macke screamed in terror, then in agony as his clothes caught alight. He fell to the ground; then there was silence, then darkness.

V

The doctors were triaging patients in the hospital lobby. Those merely bruised and cut were sent into the outpatients' waiting area, where the most junior nurses cleaned their cuts and consoled them with aspirins. The serious cases were given emergency treatment right there in the lobby, then sent to specialists upstairs. The dead were taken into the yard and laid on the cold ground until someone claimed them.

Dr. Ernst examined a screaming burn victim and prescribed morphine. "Then get his clothes off and put some gel on those burns," he said, and moved on to the next one.

Carla loaded a syringe while Frieda cut the patient's blackened clothes away. He had severe burns all down his right side, but the left was not so bad. Carla found an intact patch of skin and flesh on his left thigh. She was about to inject the patient when she looked at his face and froze.

She knew that fat round countenance with the mustache like a dirt mark under the nose. Two years ago he had come into the hall of her house and arrested her father. Next time she saw her father, he had been dying. This was Inspector Thomas Macke of the Gestapo.

You killed my father, she thought.

Now I can kill you.

It would be simple. She would give him four times the maximum dose of morphine. No one would notice, especially on a night like tonight. He would fall unconscious immediately and die in a few minutes. A doctor who was almost asleep on his feet would assume his heart had failed. No one would doubt the diagnosis, and no one would ask skeptical questions. He would be one of thousands killed in a massive air raid. Rest in peace.

She knew that Werner feared Macke might be on to him. Any day now Werner could be arrested. *Everyone talks under torture.* Werner would give away Frieda, and Heinrich, and others—and Carla. She could save them all, now, in a minute.

But she hesitated.

She asked herself why. Macke was a torturer and a killer. He deserved to die a thousand deaths.

Carla had killed Joachim, or at least helped to kill him. But that had been a fight. Joachim had been kicking Carla's mother to death when she hit him over the head with a soup cauldron. This was different.

Macke was a patient.

Carla was not very religious, but she did believe that some things were sacred. She was a nurse, and patients put their trust in her. She knew that Macke would torture and kill her without hesitation—but she was not like Macke; she was not that kind. This was nothing to do with him: it was about her.

If she killed a patient, she felt, she would have to leave the profession and never again dare to care for sick people. She would be like a banker who steals money, or a politician who takes bribes, or a priest who feels up the young girls who come to him for first communion classes. She would have betrayed herself.

Frieda said: "What are you waiting for? I can't gel him until he calms down."

Carla stuck the needle in Thomas Macke, and he stopped screaming.

Frieda started to put gel on his burned skin.

"This one's only concussed," Dr. Ernst was saying of another patient. "But he's got a bullet in his backside." He raised his voice to talk to the patient. "How did you get shot? Bullets are about the only things the RAF isn't throwing at us tonight."

Carla turned to look. The patient was lying on his front. His trousers had been cut off, showing his rear. He had white skin and fine, fair hair on the small of his back. He was woozy, but he muttered something.

Ernst said: "Policeman's gun went off by accident, did you say?"

The patient spoke more clearly. "Yes."

"I'm going to take the bullet out. It will hurt, but we're short of morphine, and there are worse cases than you."

"Go ahead."

Carla swabbed the wound. Ernst picked up a long, narrow pair of forceps. "Bite the pillow," he said.

He inserted the forceps into the wound. A muffled cry of pain came from the patient.

Dr. Ernst said: "Try not to tense your muscles. It makes it worse."

Carla thought that was a stupid thing to say. No one could relax their muscles while a wound was being probed.

The patient roared: "Ah, shit!"

"I've got it," Dr. Ernst said. "Try to keep still!"

The patient lay still, and Ernst drew the slug out and dropped it into a tray.

Carla wiped the blood from the hole and slapped a dressing on the wound.

The patient rolled over.

"No," Carla said. "You must lie on your—"

She stopped. The patient was Werner.

"Carla?" he said.

"It's me," she said happily. "Putting a bandage on your bum."

"I love you," he said.

She threw her arms around him in the most unprofessional way possible and said: "Oh, my dearest, I love you, too."

vi

Thomas Macke came around slowly. At first he was in a dreamlike state. Then he became more aware, and realized he was in a hospital and drugged. He knew why, too: his skin hurt intensely, especially down his right side. He was able to figure out that the drugs must be reducing the pain but not completely eliminating it.

Slowly he remembered how he had come here. He had been bombed. He would be dead if he had not been running away from the blast, chasing a fugitive. Those behind him were certainly dead: Mann, Schneider, Richter, and young Wagner. His whole team.

But he had caught Werner.

Or had he? He had shot Werner, and Werner had fallen; then the bomb had dropped. Macke had survived, so Werner might have, too.

Macke was now the only man living who knew that Werner was a spy. He had to speak to his boss, Superintendent Kringelein. He tried to sit upright, but found he did not have the strength to move. He decided to call a nurse, but when he opened his mouth, no sound came out. The effort exhausted him and he went back to sleep.

The next time he awoke, he sensed it was night. The place was quiet, no one moving. He opened his eyes to see a face hovering over him.

It was Werner.

"You're leaving here now," Werner said.

Macke tried to call for help, but found he could not speak.

"You're going to a new place," Werner said. "You won't be a torturer anymore—in fact you'll be the one who gets tortured there."

Macke opened his mouth to scream.

A pillow descended on his face. It was pressed firmly over his mouth and nose. He found he could not breathe. He tried to struggle, but there was no strength in his limbs. He tried to gasp for air, but there was no air. He started to panic. He managed to move his head from side to side, but the pillow was pressed down more firmly. At last he made a noise, but it was only a whimper in his throat.

The universe became a disc of light that shrank slowly until it was a pinpoint.

Then it went out.

CHAPTER SEVENTEEN

1943 (III)

"Will you marry me?" said Volodya Peshkov, and held his breath.

"No," said Zoya Vorotsyntsev. "But thank you."

She was remarkably matter-of-fact about everything, but this was unusually brisk even for her.

They were in bed at the lavish Hotel Moskva, and they had just made love. Zoya had come twice. Her preferred type of sex was cunnilingus. She liked to recline on a pile of pillows while he knelt worshipfully between her legs. He was a willing acolyte, and she returned the favor with enthusiasm.

They had been a couple for more than a year, and everything seemed to be going wonderfully well. Her refusal baffled him.

He said: "Do you love me?"

"Yes. I adore you. Thank you for loving me enough to propose marriage."

That was a bit better. "So why won't you accept?"

"I don't want to bring children into a world at war," she said.

"Okay, I can understand that."

"Ask me again when we've won."

"By then I may not want to marry you."

"If that's how inconstant you are, it's a good thing I refused you today."

"Sorry. For a moment there, I forgot that you don't understand teasing."

"I have to pee." She got off the bed and walked naked across the hotel room. Volodya could hardly believe he was allowed to see this. She had the body of a fashion model or a movie star. Her skin was milk white and her hair pale blond—all of it. She sat on the toilet without closing the bathroom door, and he listened to her peeing. Her lack of modesty was a perpetual delight.

He was supposed to be working.

The Moscow intelligence community was thrown into disarray every time Allied leaders visited, and Volodya's normal routine had been disrupted again for the Foreign Ministers' Conference that had opened on October 18.

The visitors were the American secretary of state, Cordell Hull, and the British foreign secretary, Anthony Eden. They had a harebrained scheme for a four-power pact including China. Stalin thought it was all nonsense and did not understand why they were wasting time on it. The American, Hull, was seventy-two years old and coughing blood—his doctor had come to Moscow with him—but he was no less forceful for that, and he was insistent on the pact.

There was so much to do during the conference that the NKVD— the secret police—were forced to cooperate with their hated rivals in Red Army Intelligence, Volodya's outfit. Microphones had to be concealed in hotel rooms—there was one in here, only Volodya had disconnected it. The visiting ministers and all their aides had to be kept under minute-by-minute surveillance. Their luggage had to be clandestinely opened and searched. Their phone calls had to be tape-recorded and transcribed and translated into Russian and read and summarized. Most of the people they met, including waiters and chambermaids, were NKVD agents, but anyone else they happened to speak to, in the hotel lobby or on the street, had to be checked out, perhaps arrested and imprisoned and interrogated under torture. It was a lot of work.

Volodya was riding high. His spies in Berlin were producing remarkable intelligence. They had given him the battle plan for the Germans' main summer offensive, Zitadelle, and the Red Army had inflicted a tremendous defeat.

Zoya was happy, too. The Soviet Union had resumed nuclear research, and Zoya was part of the team trying to design a nuclear bomb. They were a long way behind the West, because of the delay caused by Stalin's skepticism, but in compensation they were getting invaluable help from Communist spies in England and America, including Volodya's old school friend Willi Frunze.

She came back to bed. Volodya said: "When we first met, you didn't seem to like me much."

"I didn't like men," she replied. "I still don't. Most of them are drunks and bullies and fools. It took me a while to figure out that you were different."

"Thanks, I think," he said. "But are men really so bad?"

"Look around you," she said. "Look at our country."

He reached over her and turned on the bedside radio. Even though he had disconnected the listening device behind the headboard, you couldn't be too careful. When the radio had warmed up, a military band played a march. Satisfied that he could not be overheard, Volodya said: "You're thinking of Stalin and Beria. But they won't always be around."

"Do you know how my father fell from favor?" she said.

"No. My parents never mentioned it."

"There's a reason for that."

"Go on."

"According to my mother, there was an election at my father's factory for a deputy to attend the Moscow Soviet. A Menshevik candidate stood against the Bolshevik, and my father went to a meeting to hear him speak. He did not support the Menshevik, nor vote for him, but everyone who went to that meeting was sacked, and a few weeks later my father was arrested and taken to the Lubyanka."

She meant the NKVD headquarters and prison in Lubyanka Square.

She went on: "My mother went to your father and begged him to help. He immediately went with her to the Lubyanka. They saved my father, but they saw twelve other workers shot."

"That's terrible," Volodya said. "But it was Stalin—"

"No. This was 1920. Stalin was just a Red Army commander fighting in the Soviet-Polish War. Lenin was leader."

"This happened under Lenin?"

"Yes. So, you see, it's not just Stalin and Beria."

Volodya's view of Communist history was badly shaken. "What is it, then?"

The door opened.

Volodya reached for his gun in the bedside table drawer.

But the person who came in was a girl wearing a fur coat and, as far as he could see, nothing else.

"Sorry, Volodya," she said. "I didn't know you had company."

Zoya said: "Who the fuck is she?"

Volodya said: "Natasha, how did you open my door?"

"You gave me a passkey. It opens every door in the hotel."

"Well, you might have knocked!"

"Sorry. I just came to tell you the bad news."

"What?"

"I went into Woody Dewar's room, just as you told me. But I didn't succeed."

"What did you do?"

"This." Natasha opened her coat to show her naked body. She had a voluptuous figure and a luxuriant bush of dark pubic hair.

"All right, I get the picture. Close your coat," said Volodya. "What did he say?"

She switched to English. "He just said: 'No.' I said: 'What do you mean, no?' He said: 'It's the opposite of yes.' Then he just held the door wide open until I went out."

"Bugger," said Volodya. "I'll have to think of something else."

ii

Chuck Dewar knew there was going to be trouble when Captain Vandermeier came into the enemy land section in the middle of the afternoon, red-faced from a beery lunch.

The intelligence unit at Pearl Harbor had expanded. Formerly called Station HYPO, it now had the grand title of Joint Intelligence Center, Pacific Ocean Area, or JICPOA.

Vandermeier had a marine sergeant in tow. "Hey, you two powder puffs," Vandermeier said. "You got a customer complaint here."

As the operation had grown, everyone began to specialize, and Chuck and Eddie had become experts at mapping the territory where American forces were about to land as they fought their way island by island across the Pacific.

Vandermeier said: "This is Sergeant Donegan." The marine was very tall and looked as hard as a rifle. Chuck guessed that the sexually troubled Vandermeier was smitten.

Chuck stood up: "Good to meet you, Sergeant. I'm Chief Petty Officer Dewar."

Chuck and Eddie had both been promoted. As thousands of conscripts poured into the U.S. military, there was a shortage of officers, and prewar enlisted men who knew the ropes rose fast. Chuck and Eddie were now permitted to live off base. They had rented a small apartment together.

Chuck put out his hand, but Donegan did not shake it.

Chuck sat down again. He slightly outranked a sergeant, and he was not going to be polite to one who was rude. "Something I can do for you, Captain Vandermeier?"

There were many ways a captain could torment petty officers in the navy, and Vandermeier knew them all. He adjusted rotas so that Chuck and Eddie never had the same day off. He marked their reports "adequate," knowing full well that anything less than "excellent" was in fact a black mark. He sent confusing messages to the pay office, so that Chuck and Eddie were paid late or got less than they should have, and had to spend hours straightening things out. He was a royal pain. And now he had thought up some new mischief.

Donegan pulled from his pocket a grubby sheet of paper and unfolded it. "Is this your work?" he said aggressively.

Chuck took the paper. It was a map of New Georgia, a group in the Solomon Islands. "Let me check," he said. It was his work, and he knew it, but he was playing for time.

He went to a filing cabinet and pulled open a drawer. He took out the file for New Georgia and shut the drawer with his knee. He returned to his desk, sat down, and opened the file. It contained a duplicate of Donegan's map. "Yes," Chuck said. "That's my work."

"Well, I'm here to tell you it's shit," said Donegan.

"Is it?"

"Look, right here. You show the jungle coming down to the sea. In fact there's a beach a quarter of a mile wide."

"I'm sorry to hear that."

"Sorry!" Donegan had drunk about the same amount of beer as Vandermeier, and he was spoiling for a fight. "Fifty of my men died on that beach."

Vandermeier belched and said: "How could you make a mistake like that, Dewar?"

Chuck was shaken. If he was responsible for an error that had killed fifty men, he deserved to be shouted at. "This is what we had to work on," he said. The file contained an inaccurate map of the islands that might have been Victorian, and a more recent naval chart that showed sea depths but almost no terrain features. There were no on-the-spot reports and no wireless decrypts. The only other item in the file was a blurred black-and-white aerial reconnaissance photograph. Putting his finger on the relevant spot in the photo, Chuck said: "It sure looks as if the trees come all the way to the waterline. Is there a tide? If not, the sand might have been covered with algae when the photograph was taken. Algae can bloom suddenly, and die off just as fast."

Donegan said: "You wouldn't be so goddamn casual about it if you had to fight over the terrain."

Maybe that was true, Chuck thought. Donegan was aggressive and rude, and he was being egged on by the malicious Vandermeier, but that did not mean he was wrong.

Vandermeier said: "Yeah, Dewar. Maybe you and your nancy-boy friend should go with the marines on their next assault. See how your maps are used in action."

Chuck was trying to think of a smart retort when it occurred to him to take the suggestion seriously. Maybe he ought to see some action. It *was* easy to be blasé behind a desk. Donegan's complaint deserved to be taken seriously.

On the other hand, it would mean risking his life.

Chuck looked Vandermeier in the eye. "That sounds like a good idea, Captain," he said. "I'd like to volunteer for that duty."

Donegan looked startled, as if he were beginning to think he might have misjudged the situation.

Eddie spoke for the first time. "So would I. I'll go, too."

"Good," said Vandermeier. "You'll come back wiser—or not at all."

iii

Volodya could not get Woody Dewar drunk.

In the bar of the Hotel Moskva he thrust a glass of vodka in front of the young American and said in schoolboy English: "You'll like this— it's the very best."

"Thank you very much," said Woody. "I appreciate it." And he left the glass untouched.

Woody was tall and gangly and seemed straightforward to the point of naïveté, which was why Volodya had targeted him.

Speaking through the interpreter, Woody said: "Is Peshkov a common Russian name?"

"Not especially," Volodya replied in Russian.

"I'm from Buffalo, where there is a well-known businessman called Lev Peshkov. I wonder if you're related."

Volodya was startled. His father's brother was called Lev Peshkov and had gone to Buffalo before the First World War. But caution made him prevaricate. "I must ask my father," he said.

"I was at Harvard with Lev Peshkov's son, Greg. He could be your cousin."

"Possibly." Volodya glanced nervously at the police spies around the table. Woody did not understand that any connection with someone in America could bring down suspicion on a Soviet citizen. "You know, Woody, in this country it's considered an insult to refuse to drink."

Woody smiled pleasantly. "Not in America," he said.

Volodya picked up his own glass and looked around the table at the assorted secret policemen pretending to be civil servants and diplomats. "A toast!" he said. "To friendship between the United States and the Soviet Union!"

The others raised their glasses high. Woody did the same. "Friendship!" they all echoed.

Everyone drank except Woody, who put his glass down untasted.

Volodya began to suspect that he was not as naïve as he seemed.

Woody leaned across the table. "Volodya, you need to understand that I don't know any secrets. I'm too junior."

"So am I," said Volodya. It was far from the truth.

Woody said: "What I'm trying to explain is that you can just ask me questions. If I know the answers, I'll tell you. I can do that, because anything I know can't possibly be secret. So you don't need to get me drunk or send prostitutes to my room. You can just ask me."

It was some kind of trick, Volodya decided. No one could be so innocent. But he decided to humor Woody. Why not? "All right," he said. "I need to know what you're after. Not you personally, of course. Your delegation, and Secretary Hull, and President Roosevelt. What do you want from this conference?"

"We want you to back the Four-Power Pact."

It was the standard answer, but Volodya decided to persist. "This is what we don't understand." He was being candid now, perhaps more than he should have, but instinct was telling him to take the risk of opening up a little. "Who cares about a pact with China? We need to defeat the Nazis in Europe. We want you to help us do that."

"And we will."

"So you say. But you said you would invade Europe this summer."

"Well, we did invade Italy."

"It's not enough."

"France next year. We've promised that."

"So why do you need the pact?"

"Well." Woody paused, collecting his thoughts. "We have to show the American people how it's in their interests to invade Europe."

"Why?"

"Why what?"

"Why do you need to explain this to the public? Roosevelt is president, isn't he? He should just do it!"

"Next year is election year. He wants to get reelected."

"So?"

"American people won't vote for him if they think he's involved them unnecessarily in the war in Europe. So he wants to put it to them as part of his overall plan for world peace. If we have the Four-Power Pact, showing that we're serious about the United Nations organization, then American voters are more likely to accept that the invasion of France is a step on the road to a more peaceful world."

"This is amazing," Volodya said. "He's the president, yet he has to make excuses all the time for what he does!"

"Something like that," Woody said. "We call it democracy."

Volodya had a sneaking suspicion that this incredible story might actually be the truth. "So the pact is necessary to persuade American voters to support the invasion of Europe."

"Exactly."

"Then why do we need China?" Stalin was particularly scornful of the Allies' insistence that China should be included in the pact.

"China is a weak ally."

"So ignore China."

"If the Chinese are left out, they will become discouraged, and may fight less enthusiastically against the Japanese."

"So?"

"So we will have to bolster our forces in the Pacific theater, and that will take away from our strength in Europe."

That alarmed Volodya. The Soviet Union did not want Allied forces diverted from Europe to the Pacific. "So you are making a friendly gesture to China simply in order to conserve more forces for the invasion of Europe."

"Yes."

"You make it seem simple."

"It is," said Woody.

iv

In the early hours of the morning on November 1, Chuck and Eddie ate a steak breakfast with the U.S. Marine Third Division just off the South Sea island of Bougainville.

The island was about 125 miles long. It had two Japanese naval air bases, one in the north and one in the south. The marines were getting ready to land halfway along the lightly defended west coast. Their object was to establish a beachhead and win enough territory to build an airstrip from which to launch attacks on the Japanese bases.

Chuck was on deck at twenty-six minutes past seven when marines in helmets and backpacks began to swarm down the rope nets hanging over the sides of the ship and jump into high-sided landing craft. With them were a small number of war dogs, Doberman pinschers that made tireless sentries.

As the boats approached land, Chuck could already see a flaw in the map he had prepared. Tall waves crashed onto a steeply sloping beach. As he watched, a boat turned sideways to the waves and capsized. The marines swam for shore.

"We have to show surf conditions," Chuck said to Eddie, who was standing beside him on the deck.

"How do we find them out?"

"Reconnaissance aircraft will have to fly low enough for whitecaps to register on their photographs."

"They can't risk coming that low when there are enemy air bases so close."

Eddie was right. But there had to be a solution. Chuck filed it away as the first question to be considered as a result of this mission.

For this landing they had benefited from more information than usual. As well as the normal unreliable maps and hard-to-decipher aerial photographs, they had a report from a reconnaissance team landed by submarine six weeks earlier. The team had identified twelve beaches suitable for landing along a four-mile stretch of coast. But they had not warned of the surf. Perhaps it was not so high that day.

In other respects Chuck's map was right, so far. There was a sandy beach about a hundred yards wide, then a tangle of palm trees and other vegetation. Just beyond the brush line, according to the map, there should be a swamp.

The coast was not completely undefended. Chuck heard the roar of artillery fire, and a shell landed in the shallows. It did no harm, but the gunner's aim would improve. The marines were galvanized with a new urgency as they leaped from the landing craft to the beach and ran for the brush line.

Chuck was glad he had decided to come. He had never been careless or slack about his maps, but it was salutary to see firsthand how correct mapping could save men's lives, and how the smallest errors could be deadly. Even before they embarked, he and Eddie had become a lot more demanding. They asked for blurred photographs to be taken again, they interrogated reconnaissance parties by phone, and they cabled all over the world for better charts.

He was glad for another reason. He was at sea, which he loved. He was on a ship with seven hundred young men, and he relished the camaraderie, the jokes, the songs, and the intimacy of crowded berths and shared showers. "It's like being a straight guy in a girls' boarding school," he said to Eddie one evening.

"Except that that never happens, and this does," Eddie said. He felt the same as Chuck. They loved each other, but they did not mind looking at naked sailors.

Now all seven hundred marines were getting off the ship and onto land as fast as they could. The same was happening at eight other locations along this stretch of coast. As soon as a landing craft emptied out, it lost no time in turning around and coming back for more, but the process still seemed desperately slow.

The Japanese artillery gunner, hidden somewhere in the jungle, found his range at last, and to Chuck's shock a well-aimed shell exploded in a knot of marines, sending men and rifles and body parts flying through the air to litter the beach and stain the sand red.

Chuck was staring in horror at the carnage when he heard the roar of a plane, and looked up to see a Japanese Zero flying low, following the coast. The red suns painted on the wings struck fear into his heart. Last time he saw that sight had been at the Battle of Midway.

The Zero strafed the beach. Marines who were in the process of disembarking from landing craft were caught defenseless. Some threw themselves flat in the shallows, some tried to get behind the hull of the boat, some ran for the jungle. For a few seconds blood spurted and men fell.

Then the plane was gone, leaving the beach scattered with American dead.

Chuck heard it open up a moment later, strafing the next beach.

It would be back.

There were supposed to be U.S. planes in attendance, but he could not see any. Air support was never where you wanted it to be, which was directly above your head.

When all the marines were ashore, alive and dead, the boats transported medics and stretcher parties to the beach. Then they began landing supplies: ammunition, drinking water, food, drugs, and dressings. On the return trip the landing craft brought the wounded back to the ship.

Chuck and Eddie, as nonessential personnel, went ashore with the supplies.

The boat skippers had got used to the swell now, and their craft held a stable position, with its ramp on the sand and the waves breaking on its stern, while the boxes were unloaded and Chuck and Eddie jumped into the surf to wade to shore.

They reached the waterline together.

As they did so, a machine gun opened up.

It seemed to be in the jungle about four hundred yards along the beach. Had it been there all along, the gunner biding his time, or had it just been moved into position from another location? Eddie and Chuck bent double and ran for the tree line.

A sailor with a crate of ammunition on his shoulder gave a shout of pain and fell, dropping the box.

Then Eddie cried out.

Chuck ran on two paces before he could stop. When he turned, Eddie was rolling on the sand clutching his knee, yelling: "Ah, fuck!"

Chuck came back and knelt beside him. "It's okay, I'm here!" he shouted. Eddie's eyes were closed, but he was alive, and Chuck could see no wounds other than the knee.

He glanced up. The boat that had brought them was still close to shore, being unloaded. He could get Eddie back to the ship in minutes. But the machine gun was still firing.

He got into a crouching position. "This is going to hurt," he said. "Yell as much as you like."

He got his right arm under Eddie's shoulder, then slid his left under Eddie's thighs. He took the weight and straightened up. Eddie screamed with pain as his smashed leg swung free. "Hang in there, buddy," Chuck said. He turned toward the water.

He felt sudden, unbearably sharp pains in his legs, his back, and finally his head. In the next fraction of a second he thought he must not drop Eddie. A moment later he knew he was going to. There was a flash of light behind his eyes that rendered him blind.

And then the world came to an end.

V

On her day off, Carla worked at the Jewish Hospital.

Dr. Rothmann had persuaded her. He had been released from the camp—no one knew why, except the Nazis, and they did not tell anyone. He had lost one eye and he walked with a limp, but he was alive, and capable of practising medicine.

The hospital was in the northern working-class district of Wedding, but there was nothing proletarian about the architecture. It had been built before the First World War, when Berlin's Jews had been prosperous and proud. There were seven elegant buildings set in a large garden. The different departments were linked by tunnels, so that patients and staff could move from one to another without braving the weather.

It was a miracle there was still a Jewish hospital. Very few Jews were left in Berlin. They had been rounded up in their thousands and sent away in special trains. No one knew where they had gone or what happened to them. There were incredible rumors about extermination camps.

The few Jews still in Berlin could not be treated, if they were sick, by Aryan doctors and nurses. So, by the tangled logic of Nazi racism, the hospital was allowed to remain. It was mainly staffed by Jews and other unfortunate people who did not count as properly Aryan: Slavs from eastern Europe, people of mixed ancestry, and those married to Jews. But there were not enough nurses, so Carla helped out.

The hospital was harassed constantly by the Gestapo; critically short of supplies, especially drugs; understaffed; and almost completely without funds.

Carla was breaking the law as she took the temperature of an eleven-year-old boy whose foot had been crushed in an air raid. It was also a crime for her to smuggle medicines out of her everyday hospital and bring them here. But she wanted to prove, if only to herself, that not everyone had given in to the Nazis.

As she finished her ward round, she saw Werner outside the door, in his air force uniform.

748 | CHAPTER SEVENTEEN

For several days he and Carla had lived in fear, wondering whether anyone had survived the bombing of the school and lived to condemn Werner, but it was now clear they had all died, and no one else knew of Macke's suspicions. They had got away with it, again.

Werner had recovered quickly from his bullet wound.

And they were lovers. Werner had moved into the von Ulrichs' large, half-empty house, and he slept with Carla every night. Their parents made no objection; everyone felt they could die any day, and people should take what joy they could from a life of hardship and suffering.

But Werner looked more solemn than usual as he waved to Carla through the glass panel in the door to the ward. She beckoned him inside and kissed him. "I love you," she said. She never tired of saying it.

He was always happy to say: "I love you, too."

"What are you doing here?" she said. "Did you just want a kiss?"

"I've got bad news. I've been posted to the eastern front."

"Oh, no!" Tears came to her eyes.

"It's really a miracle I've avoided it this long. But General Dorn can't keep me any longer. Half our army consists of old men and schoolboys, and I'm a fit twenty-four-year-old officer."

She whispered: "Please don't die."

"I'll do my best."

Still whispering, she said: "But what will happen to the network? You know everything. Who else could run it?"

He looked at her without speaking.

She realized what was in his mind. "Oh, no—not me!"

"You're the best person. Frieda's a follower, not a leader. You've shown the ability to recruit new people and motivate them. You've never been in trouble with the police and you have no record of political activity. No one knows the role you played in opposing Aktion T4. As far as the authorities are concerned, you are a blameless nurse."

"But, Werner, I'm scared!"

"You don't have to do it. But no one else can."

Just then they heard a commotion.

The neighboring ward was for mental patients, and it was not unusual to hear shouting and even screaming, but this seemed different. A cultured voice was raised in anger. Then they heard a second voice, this one with a Berlin accent and the insistent, bullying tone that outsiders said was typical of Berliners.

Carla stepped into the corridor, and Werner followed.

Dr. Rothmann, wearing a yellow star on his jacket, was arguing with a man in SS uniform. Behind them, the double doors to the psychiatric ward, normally locked, were wide open. The patients were leaving. Two more policemen and a couple of nurses were herding a ragged line of men and women, most in pajamas, some walking upright and apparently normal, others shambling and mumbling as they followed one another down the staircase.

Carla was immediately reminded of Ada's son, Kurt, and Werner's brother, Axel, and the so-called hospital in Akelberg. She did not know where these patients were going, but she was quite sure they would be killed there.

Dr. Rothmann was saying indignantly: "These people are sick! They need treatment!"

The SS officer replied: "They're not sick, they're lunatics, and we're taking them where lunatics belong."

"To a hospital?"

"You will be informed in due course."

"That's not good enough."

Carla knew she should not intervene. If they found out she was not Jewish, she would be in deep trouble. She did not look particularly Aryan or otherwise, with dark hair and green eyes. If she kept quiet, probably they would not bother her. But if she protested about what the SS were doing, she would be arrested and questioned, and then it would come out that she was working illegally. So she clamped her teeth together.

The officer raised his voice. "Hurry up—get those cretins in the bus."

Rothmann persisted. "I must be informed where they are going. They are my patients."

They were not really his patients—he was not a psychiatrist.

The SS man said: "If you're so concerned about them, you can go with them."

Dr. Rothmann paled. He would almost certainly be going to his death.

Carla thought of his wife, Hannelore; his son, Rudi; and his daughter in England, Eva, and she felt sick with fear.

The officer grinned. "Suddenly not so concerned?" he jeered.

Rothmann straightened up. "On the contrary," he said. "I accept your offer. I swore an oath, many years ago, to do all I can to help sick people. I'm not going to break my oath now. I hope to die at peace with my conscience." He limped down the stairs.

An old woman went by wearing nothing but a robe open at the front, showing her nakedness.

Carla could not remain silent. "It's November out there!" she cried. "They have no outdoor clothing!"

The officer gave her a hard look. "They'll be all right on the bus."

"I'll get some warm clothing." Carla turned to Werner. "Come and help me. Grab blankets from anywhere."

The two of them ran around the emptying psychiatric ward, pulling blankets off beds and out of the cupboards. Each carrying a pile, they hurried down the stairs.

The garden of the hospital was frozen earth. Outside the main door was a gray bus, its engine idling, its driver smoking at the wheel. Carla saw that he was wearing a heavy coat plus a hat and gloves, which told her that the bus was not heated.

A small group of Gestapo and SS men stood in a knot, watching the proceedings.

The last few patients were climbing aboard. Carla and Werner boarded the bus and began to distribute the blankets.

Dr. Rothmann was standing at the back. "Carla," he said. "You . . . you'll tell my Hannelore how it was. I have to go with the patients. I have no choice."

"Of course." Her voice was choked.

"I may be able to protect these people."

Carla nodded, though she did not really believe it.

"In any event, I cannot abandon them."

"I'll tell her."

"And say that I love her."

Carla could no longer stop the tears.

Rothmann said: "Tell her that was the last thing I said. I love her."

Carla nodded.

Werner took her arm. "Let's go."

They got off the bus.

An SS man said to Werner: "You, in the air force uniform, what the hell do you think you're doing?"

Werner was so angry that Carla was frightened he would start a fight. But he spoke calmly. "Giving blankets to old people who are cold," he said. "Is that against the law now?"

"You should be fighting on the eastern front."

"I'm going there tomorrow. How about you?"

"Take care what you say."

"If you would be kind enough to arrest me before I go, you might save my life."

The man turned away.

The gears of the bus crashed and its engine note rose. Carla and Werner turned to look. At every window was a face, and they were all different: babbling, drooling, laughing hysterically, distracted, or distorted with spiritual distress—all insane. Psychiatric patients being taken away by the SS. The mad leading the mad.

The bus pulled away.

vi

"I might have liked Russia, if I'd been allowed to see it," Woody said to his father.

"I feel the same."

"I didn't even get any decent photographs."

They were sitting in the grand lobby of the Hotel Moskva, near the entrance to the subway station. Their bags were packed and they were on their way home.

Woody said: "I have to tell Greg Peshkov that I met a Volodya Peshkov. Though Volodya was not so pleased about it. I guess anyone with connections in the West might fall under suspicion."

"You bet your socks."

"Anyway, we got what we came for—that's the main thing. The allies are committed to the United Nations organization."

"Yes," said Gus with satisfaction. "Stalin took some persuading, but he saw sense in the end. You helped with that, I think, by your straight-talking to Peshkov."

"You've fought for this all your life, Papa."

"I don't mind admitting that this is a pretty good moment."

A worrying thought crossed Woody's mind. "You're not going to retire now, are you?"

Gus laughed. "No. We've won agreement in principle, but the job has only just begun."

Cordell Hull had already left Moscow, but some of his aides were still there, and now one of them approached the Dewars. Woody knew him, a young man called Ray Baker. "I have a message for you, Senator," he said. He seemed nervous.

"Well, you just caught me in time—I'm about to leave," said Gus. "What is it?"

"It's about your son Charles—Chuck."

Gus went pale and said: "What is the message, Ray?"

The young man was having trouble speaking. "Sir, it's bad news. He's been in a battle in the Solomon Islands."

"Is he wounded?"

"No, sir, it's worse."

"Oh, Christ," said Gus, and he began to cry.

Woody had never seen his father cry.

"I'm sorry, sir," said Ray. "The message is that he's dead."

CHAPTER EIGHTEEN

1944

Woody stood in front of the mirror in his bedroom at his parents' Washington apartment. He was wearing the uniform of a second lieutenant in the 510th Parachute Regiment of the United States Army.

He had had the suit made by a good Washington tailor, but it did not look good on him. Khaki made his complexion sallow, and the badges and flashes on the tunic jacket just seemed untidy.

He could probably have avoided the draft, but he had decided not to. Part of him wanted to continue to work with his father, who was helping President Roosevelt plan a new global order that would avoid any more world wars. They had won a triumph in Moscow, but Stalin was inconstant, and seemed to relish creating difficulties. At the Tehran Conference in December, the Soviet leader had revived the halfway-house idea of regional councils, and Roosevelt had had to talk him out of it. Clearly the United Nations organization was going to require tireless vigilance.

But Gus could do that without Woody. And Woody was feeling worse and worse about letting other men fight the war for him.

He was looking as good as he ever would in the uniform, so he went into the drawing room to show his mother.

Rosa had a visitor, a young man in navy whites, and after a moment Woody recognized the freckled good looks of Eddie Parry. He was sitting on the couch with Rosa, holding a walking stick. He got to his feet with difficulty to shake Woody's hand.

Mama had a sad face. She said: "Eddie was telling me about the day Chuck died."

Eddie sat down again, and Woody sat opposite. "I'd like to hear about that," Woody said.

"It doesn't take long to tell," Eddie began. "We were on the beach at Bougainville for about five seconds when a machine gun opened up from somewhere in the swamp. We ran for cover, but I got a couple of bullets in my knee. Chuck should have gone on to the tree line. That's the drill—you leave the wounded to be picked up by the medics. Of course, Chuck disobeyed that rule. He stopped and came back for me."

Eddie paused. There was a cup of coffee on the small table beside him, and he took a gulp.

"He picked me up in his arms," he went on. "Darn fool. Made himself a target. But I guess he wanted to get me back in the landing craft. Those boats have high sides, and they're made of steel. We would have been safe, and I could have gotten medical attention right away on the ship. But he shouldn't have done it. Soon as he stood upright, he got hit by a spray of bullets—legs, back, and head. I think he must have died before he hit the sand. Anyway, by the time I was able to lift my head and look at him, he just wasn't there anymore."

Woody saw that his mother was controlling herself with difficulty. He was afraid that if she cried, he would too.

"I lay on that beach beside his body for an hour," Eddie said. "I held his hand all the time. Then they brought a stretcher for me. I didn't want to go. I knew I'd never see him again." He buried his face in his hands. "I loved him so much," he said.

Rosa put her arm around his big shoulders and hugged him. He laid his head on her chest and sobbed like a child. She stroked his hair. "There, there," she said. "There, there."

Woody realized that his mother knew what Chuck and Eddie were.

After a minute Eddie began to pull himself together. He looked at Woody. "You know what this is like," he said.

He was talking about the death of Joanne. "Yes, I do," Woody said. "It's the worst thing in the world—but it hurts a little less every day."

"I sure hope so."

"Are you still in Hawaii?"

"Yes. Chuck and I work in the enemy land unit. Used to work." He swallowed. "Chuck decided we needed to get a better feel for how our maps were used in action. That's why we went to Bougainville with the marines."

"You must be doing a good job," Woody said. "We seem to be beating the Japs in the Pacific."

"Inch by inch," Eddie said. He glanced at Woody's uniform. "Where are you stationed?"

"I've been at Fort Benning, in Georgia, doing parachute training," Woody said. "Now I'm on my way to London. I leave tomorrow."

He caught his mother's eye. Suddenly she looked older. He realized her face was lined. Her fiftieth birthday had passed with no big fuss. However, he guessed that talking about Chuck's death while her other son stood there in army uniform had struck her a hard blow.

Eddie did not pick that up. "People say we'll invade France this year," he said.

"I assume that's why my training was accelerated," Woody said.

"You should see some action."

Rosa muffled a sob.

Woody said: "I hope I'll be as brave as my brother."

Eddie said: "I hope you never find out."

ii

Greg Peshkov took dark-eyed Margaret Cowdry to an afternoon symphony concert. Margaret had a wide, generous mouth that loved kissing. But Greg had something else on his mind.

He was following Barney McHugh.

So was an FBI agent called Bill Bicks.

Barney McHugh was a brilliant young physicist. He was on leave from the U.S. Army's secret laboratory at Los Alamos, New Mexico, and had brought his British wife to Washington to see the sights.

The FBI had found out in advance that McHugh was coming to the concert, and Special Agent Bicks had managed to get Greg two seats a few rows behind McHugh's. A concert hall, with hundreds of strangers crowding together to come in and go out, was the perfect location for a clandestine rendezvous, and Greg wanted to know what McHugh might be up to.

It was a pity they had met before. Greg had talked to McHugh in Chicago on the day the nuclear pile was tested. It had been a year and a half ago, but McHugh might remember. So Greg had to make sure McHugh did not see him.

When Greg and Margaret arrived, McHugh's seats were empty. Either side were two ordinary-looking couples, a middle-aged man in a cheap gray chalk-stripe suit and his dowdy wife on the left, and two elderly ladies on the right. Greg hoped McHugh was going to show up. If the guy was a spy, Greg wanted to nail him.

They were going to hear Tchaikovsky's first symphony. "So, you like classical music," said Margaret chattily as the orchestra tuned up. She had no idea of the real reason she had been brought here. She knew that Greg was working in weapons research, which was secret, but like almost all Americans she had no inkling of the nuclear bomb. "I thought you only listened to jazz," she said.

"I love Russian composers—they're so dramatic," Greg told her. "I expect it's in my blood."

"I was raised listening to classical. My father likes to have a small orchestra at dinner parties." Margaret's family were rich enough to make Greg feel a pauper by comparison. But he still had not met her parents, and he suspected they would disapprove of the illegitimate son of a famous Hollywood womanizer. "What are you looking at?" she said.

"Nothing." The McHughs had arrived. "What's your perfume?"

"Chichi by Renoir."

"I love it."

The McHughs looked happy, a bright and prosperous young couple on holiday. Greg wondered if they were late because they had been making love in their hotel room.

Barney McHugh sat next to the man in the gray chalk stripe. Greg knew it was a cheap suit by the unnatural stiffness of the padded shoulders. The man did not look at the newcomers. The McHughs started to do a crossword, their heads leaning together intimately as they studied the newspaper Barney was holding. A few minutes later the conductor appeared.

The opening piece was by Saint-Saëns. German and Austrian composers had declined in popularity since war broke out, and concertgoers were discovering alternatives. There was a revival of Sibelius.

McHugh was probably a Communist. Greg knew this because J. Robert Oppenheimer had told him. Oppenheimer, a leading theoretical physicist from the University of California, was director of the Los Alamos laboratory and scientific leader of the entire Manhattan Project. He had strong Communist ties, though he insisted he had never joined the party.

Special Agent Bicks had said to Greg: "Why does the army have to have all these pinkos? Whatever it is you're trying to achieve out there in the desert, aren't there enough bright young conservative scientists in America to do it?"

"No, there aren't," Greg had told him. "If there were, we would have hired them."

Communists were sometimes more loyal to their cause than to their country, and might think it right to share the secrets of nuclear research with the Soviet Union. This would not be like giving information to the enemy. The Soviets were America's allies against the Nazis—in fact they had done more of the fighting than all the other allies put together. All the same it was dangerous. Information intended for Moscow might find its way to Berlin. And anyone who thought about the postwar world for more than a minute could guess that the USA and the USSR might not always be friends.

The FBI thought Oppenheimer was a security risk and kept trying to persuade Greg's boss, General Groves, to fire him. But Oppenheimer was the outstanding scientist of his generation, so the general insisted on keeping him.

In an attempt to prove his loyalty, Oppenheimer had named McHugh as a possible Communist, and that was why Greg was tailing him.

The FBI was skeptical. "Oppenheimer is blowing smoke up your ass," Bicks had said.

Greg said: "I can't believe it. I've known him for a year now."

"He's a fucking Communist, like his wife and his brother and his sister-in-law."

"He's working nineteen hours a day to build better weapons for American soldiers—what kind of traitor does that?"

Greg hoped McHugh did turn out to be a spy, for that would lift suspicion from Oppenheimer, bolster General Groves's credibility, and boost Greg's own status, too.

He watched McHugh constantly throughout the first half of the concert, not wanting to take his eyes off. The physicist did not look at the people either side of him. He seemed absorbed in the music, and only moved his gaze from the stage to look lovingly at Mrs. McHugh, who was a pale English rose. Had Oppenheimer simply been wrong about McHugh? Or, more subtly, was Oppenheimer's accusation a distraction to divert suspicion away from himself?

Bicks was watching, too, Greg knew. He was upstairs in the dress circle. Perhaps he had seen something.

During the intermission, Greg followed the McHughs out and stood in the same line for coffee. Neither the dowdy couple nor the two old ladies were anywhere nearby.

Greg felt thwarted. He did not know what to conclude. Were his suspicions unfounded? Or was it simply that this visit by the McHughs was innocent?

As he and Margaret were returning to their seats, Bill Bicks came up beside him. The agent was middle-aged, a little overweight, and losing his hair. He wore a light gray suit that had sweat stains under the armpits. He said in a low voice: "You were right."

"How do you know?"

"That guy sitting next to McHugh."

"In a gray striped suit?"

"Yeah. He's Nikolai Yenkov, a cultural attaché at the Soviet embassy."

Greg said: "Good God!"

Margaret turned around. "What?"

"Nothing," Greg said.

Bicks moved away.

"You've got something on your mind," she said as they took their seats. "I don't believe you heard a single bar of the Saint-Saëns."

"Just thinking about work."

"Tell me it's not another woman, and I'll forget it."

"It's not another woman."

In the second half he began to feel anxious. He had seen no contact between McHugh and Yenkov. They did not speak, and Greg saw nothing pass from one to the other: no file, no envelope, no roll of film.

The symphony came to an end and the conductor took his bows. The audience began to file out. Greg's spy hunt was a washout.

In the lobby, Margaret went to the ladies' room. While Greg was waiting, Bicks approached him.

"Nothing," Greg said.

"Me, neither."

"Maybe it's a coincidence, McHugh sitting by Yenkov."

"There are no coincidences."

"Perhaps there was a snag. A wrong code word, say."

Bicks shook his head. "They passed something. We just didn't see it."

Mrs. McHugh also went to the ladies' room and, like Greg, McHugh waited nearby. Greg studied him from behind a pillar. He had no briefcase, no raincoat under which to conceal a package or a file. But all the same, something about him was wrong. What was it?

Then Greg realized. "The newspaper!" he said.

"What?"

"When Barney came in, he was carrying a newspaper. They did the crossword while waiting for the show. Now he doesn't have it!"

"Either he threw it away—or he passed it to Yenkov, with something concealed inside."

"Yenkov and his wife have left already."

"They may still be outside."

Bicks and Greg ran for the door.

Bicks shoved his way through the crowd still filing out of the exits. Greg stayed close behind. They reached the sidewalk outside and looked both ways. Greg could not see Yenkov, but Bicks had sharp eyes. "Across the street!" he cried.

The attaché and his dowdy wife were standing at the curb, and a black limousine was approaching them slowly.

Yenkov was holding a folded newspaper.

Greg and Bicks ran across the road.

The limousine stopped.

Greg was faster than Bicks and reached the far sidewalk first.

Yenkov had not noticed them. Unhurriedly, he opened the car door, then stepped back to let his wife get in.

Greg threw himself at Yenkov. They both fell to the ground. Mrs. Yenkov screamed.

Greg scrambled to his feet. The chauffeur had got out of the car and was coming around it, but Bicks yelled: "FBI!" and held up his badge.

Yenkov had dropped the newspaper. Now he reached for it. But Greg was faster. He picked it up, stepped back, and opened it.

Inside was a sheaf of papers. The top one was a diagram. Greg recognized it immediately. It showed the working of an implosion trigger for a plutonium bomb. "Jesus Christ," he said. "This is the very latest stuff!"

Yenkov jumped into the car, slammed the door, and locked it from the inside.

The chauffeur got back in and drove away.

iii

It was Saturday night, and Daisy's apartment in Piccadilly was heaving. There had to be a hundred people there, she thought, feeling pleased.

She had become the leader of a social group based on the American Red Cross in London. Every Saturday she gave a party for American servicemen, and invited nurses from St. Bart's Hospital to meet them. RAF pilots came, too. They drank her unlimited Scotch and gin, and danced to Glenn Miller records on her gramophone. Conscious that it might be the last party the men ever attended, she did everything she could to make them happy—except kiss them, but the nurses did plenty of that.

Daisy never drank liquor at her own parties. She had too much to think about. Couples were always locking themselves in the toilet, and having to be dragged out because the room was needed for its regular purpose. If a really important general got drunk, he had to be seen safely home. She often ran out of ice—she could not make her British staff understand how much ice a party needed.

For a while after she split up with Boy Fitzherbert, her only friends had been the Leckwith family. Lloyd's mother, Ethel, had never judged her. Although Ethel was the height of respectability now, she had mistakes in her past, and that made her more understanding. Daisy still went to Ethel's house in Aldgate every Wednesday evening, and drank cocoa around the radio. It was her favorite night of the week.

She had now been socially rejected twice, once in Buffalo and again in London, and the depressing thought occurred to her that it might be her fault. Perhaps she did not really belong in those prissy high-society groups, with their strict rules of conduct. She was a fool to be attracted to them.

The trouble was that she loved parties and picnics and sporting events and any gathering where people dressed up and had fun.

However, she now knew she did not need British aristocrats or old-money Americans to have fun. She had created her own society, and it was a lot more exciting than theirs. Some of the people who had refused to speak to her after she left Boy now hinted heavily that they would like an invitation to one of her famous Saturday nights. And many guests came to her apartment to let their hair down after an excruciatingly grand dinner in a palatial Mayfair residence.

Tonight was the best party so far, for Lloyd was home on leave.

He was openly living with her at the flat. She did not care what people thought: her reputation in respectable circles was already so bad that no further damage could be done. Anyway, the urgency of wartime love had driven many people to break the rules in similar ways. Domestic staff could sometimes be as rigid as duchesses about such things, but all Daisy's employees adored her, so she and Lloyd did not even pretend to be occupying separate bedrooms.

She loved sleeping with him. He was not as experienced as Boy, but he made up for that in enthusiasm—and he was eager to learn. Every night was a voyage of exploration in a double bed.

As they looked at their guests talking and laughing, drinking and smoking, dancing and smooching, Lloyd smiled at her and said: "Happy?"

"Almost," she said.

"Almost?"

She sighed. "I want to have children, Lloyd. I don't care that we're not married. Well, I do care, of course, but I still want a baby."

His face darkened. "You know how I feel about illegitimacy."

"Yes, you explained it to me. But I want some part of you to cherish if you die."

"I'll do my best to stay alive."

"I know." But if her suspicion was correct, and he was working undercover in occupied territory, he could be executed, as German spies were executed in Britain. He would be gone, and she would have nothing left. "It's the same for a million women, I realize that, but I can't face the thought of life without you. I think I'll die."

"If I could make Boy divorce you, I would."

"Well, this is no kind of talk for a party." She looked across the room. "What do you know? I believe that's Woody Dewar!"

Woody was wearing a lieutenant's uniform. She went over and greeted him. It was strange to see him again after nine years—though he did not look much different, just older.

"There are thousands of American soldiers here now," Daisy said as they foxtrotted to "Pennsylvania Six-Five Thousand." "We must be about to invade France. What else?"

"The top brass certainly don't share their plans with greenhorn lieutenants," Woody said. "But like you I can't think of any other reason why I'm here. We can't leave the Russians to bear the brunt of the fighting much longer."

"When do you think it will happen?"

"Offensives always begin in the summer. Late May or early June is everyone's best guess."

"That soon!"

"But no one knows where."

"Dover-to-Calais is the shortest sea crossing," Daisy said.

"And for that reason the German defenses are concentrated around Calais. So maybe we'll try to surprise them—say, by landing on the south coast, near Marseilles."

"Perhaps then it will be over at last."

"I doubt it. Once we have a bridgehead, we still have to conquer France, then Germany. There's a long road ahead."

"Oh, dear." Woody seemed to need cheering up. And Daisy knew just the girl to do it. Isabel Hernandez was a Rhodes scholar doing a master's in history at St. Hilda's College, Oxford. She was gorgeous, but the boys called her a ball-buster because she was so fiercely intellectual. However, Woody would be oblivious to that. "Come over here," she called to Isabel. "Woody, this is my friend Bella. She's from San Francisco. Bella, meet Woody Dewar from Buffalo."

They shook hands. Bella was tall, with thick dark hair and olive skin just like Joanne Rouzrokh's. Woody smiled at her and said: "What are you doing here in London?" Daisy left them.

She served supper at midnight. When she could get American supplies, it was ham and eggs; otherwise, cheese sandwiches. It provided a lull when people could talk, a bit like the intermission at the theater. She noticed that Woody Dewar was still with Bella Hernandez, and they seemed to be deep in conversation. She made sure everyone had what they needed, then sat in a corner with Lloyd.

"I've decided what I'd like to do after the war, if I'm still alive," he said. "As well as marry you, that is."

"What?"

"I'm going to try for Parliament."

Daisy was thrilled. "Lloyd, that's wonderful!" She put her arms around his neck and kissed him.

"It's too early for congratulations. I've put my name down for Hoxton, the constituency next to Mam's. But the local Labour Party may not pick me. And if they do, I may not win. Hoxton has a strong Liberal M.P. at the moment."

"I want to help you," she said. "I could be your right-hand woman. I'll write your speeches—I bet I'd be good at that."

"I'd love you to help me."

"Then it's settled!"

The older guests left after supper, but the music continued and the drink never ran out, so the party became even more uninhibited. Woody was now slow-dancing with Bella: Daisy wondered if this was his first romance since Joanne.

The petting got heavier, and people began disappearing into the two bedrooms. They could not lock the doors—Daisy took the keys out—so there were sometimes several couples in the same room, but no one seemed to mind. Daisy had once found two people in the broom cupboard, fast asleep in each other's arms.

At one o'clock her husband arrived.

She had not invited Boy, but he showed up in the company of a couple of American pilots, and Daisy shrugged and let him in. He was amiably squiffy, and danced with several nurses, then politely asked her.

Was he just drunk, she wondered, or had he softened toward her? And if so, might he reconsider the divorce?

She consented, and they did the jitterbug. Most of the guests had no idea they were a separated husband and wife, but those who knew were amazed.

"I read in the papers that you bought another racehorse," she said, making small talk.

"Lucky Laddie," he said. "Cost me eight thousand guineas—a record price."

"I hope he's worth it." She loved horses, and she had thought they would buy and train racehorses together, but he had not wanted to share that enthusiasm with his wife. It had been one of the frustrations of her marriage.

He read her mind. "I disappointed you, didn't I?" he said.

"Yes."

"And you disappointed me."

That was a new thought to her. After a minute's reflection she said: "By not turning a blind eye to your infidelities?"

"Exactly." He was drunk enough to be honest.

She saw her opportunity. "How long do you think we should punish one another?"

"Punish?" he said. "Who's punishing anyone?"

"We're punishing each other by staying married. We should get divorced, as sensible people do."

"Perhaps you're right," he said. "But this time on a Saturday night is not the best moment to discuss it."

Her hopes rose. "Why don't I come and see you?" she said. "When we're both fresh—and sober."

He hesitated. "All right."

She pressed her advantage eagerly. "How about tomorrow?"

"All right."

"I'll see you after church. Say, twelve noon?"

"All right," said Boy.

iv

As Woody was walking Bella home through Hyde Park, to a friend's flat in South Kensington, she kissed him.

He had not done this since Joanne died. At first he froze. He liked Bella a lot: she was the smartest girl he had met since Joanne. And the way she had clung to him while they were slow-dancing had let him know he could kiss her if he wanted to. All the same he had been holding back. He kept thinking about Joanne.

Then Bella took the initiative.

She opened her mouth and he tasted her tongue, but that only made him think of Joanne kissing him that way. It was only two and a half years since she died.

His brain was forming words of polite rejection when his body took over. He was suddenly consumed with desire. He began to kiss her back hungrily.

She responded eagerly to his access of passion. She took both his hands and put them on her breasts, which were large and soft. He groaned helplessly.

It was dark and he could hardly see but he realized, by half-smothered sounds coming from the surrounding vegetation, that there were numerous couples doing similar things nearby.

She pressed her body against his, and he knew she could feel his erection. He was so excited he felt he would ejaculate any second. She seemed as madly aroused as he was. He felt her unbuttoning his pants with frantic fingers. Her hands were cool on his hot penis. She eased it out of his clothing; then, to his surprise and delight, she knelt down. As soon as her lips closed over the head, he spurted uncontrollably into her mouth. She sucked and licked feverishly as he did so.

When the climax was over, she continued to kiss it until it softened. Then she gently put it away and stood up.

"That was exciting," she whispered. "Thank you."

He had been about to thank her. Instead he put his arms around her and pulled her close. He felt so grateful to her that he could have wept. He had not realized how badly he needed a woman's affection tonight. Some kind of shadow had been lifted from him. "I can't tell you . . ." he began, but he could not find words to explain how much it meant to him.

"Then don't," she said. "I know, anyway. I could feel it."

They walked to her building. At the door he said: "Can we—"

She put a finger on his lips to silence him. "Go and win the war," she said.

Then she went inside.

v

When Daisy went to a Sunday service, which was not often, she now avoided the elite churches of the West End, whose congregations had snubbed her, and instead caught the Tube to Aldgate and attended the Calvary Gospel Hall. The doctrinal differences were wide, but they did not matter to her. The singing was better in the East End.

She and Lloyd arrived separately. People in Aldgate knew who she was, and they liked having a rogue aristocrat sitting on one of their cheap seats, but it would have been pushing their tolerance too far for a married-and-separated woman to walk in on the arm of her paramour. Ethel's brother Billy had said: "Jesus did not condemn the adulteress, but he did tell her to sin no more."

During the service she thought about Boy. Had he really meant last night's conciliatory words, or were they just the softness of the drunken moment? Boy had even shaken hands with Lloyd as he left. Surely that meant forgiveness? But she told herself not to let her hopes rise. Boy was the most completely self-absorbed person she had ever known, worse than his father or her brother Greg.

After church Daisy often went to Eth Leckwith's house for Sunday dinner, but today she left Lloyd to his family and hurried away.

She returned to the West End and knocked on the door of her husband's house in Mayfair. The butler showed her into the morning room.

Boy came in shouting. "What the hell is this?" he roared, and he threw a newspaper at her.

She had seen him in this mood plenty of times, and she was not afraid of him. Only once had he raised a hand to strike her. She had seized a heavy candlestick and threatened to bop him. It did not happen again.

Though not scared, she was disappointed. He had been in such a good mood last night. But perhaps he might still listen to reason.

"What has happened to displease you?" she said calmly.

"Look at that bloody paper."

She bent and picked it up. It was today's edition of the *Sunday Mirror*, a popular left-wing tabloid. On the front page was a photograph of Boy's new horse, Lucky Laddie, and the headline:

LUCKY LADDIE—
Worth 28
Coal Miners

The story of Boy's record-breaking purchase had appeared in yesterday's press, but today the *Mirror* had an outraged opinion piece, pointing out that the price of the horse, £8,400, was exactly twenty-eight times the £300 standard compensation paid to the widow of a miner who died in a pit accident.

And the Fitzherbert family wealth came from coal mines.

Boy said: "My father is furious. He was hoping to be foreign secretary in the postwar government. This has probably ruined his chances."

Daisy said in exasperation: "Boy, kindly explain why this is my fault?"

"Look who wrote the damned thing!"

Daisy looked.

By Billy Williams
Member of Parliament for Aberowen

Boy said: "Your boyfriend's uncle!"

"Do you imagine he consults me before writing his articles?"

He wagged a finger. "For some reason, that family hates us!"

"They think it's unfair that you should make so much money from coal, when the miners themselves get such a raw deal. There is a war on, you know."

"You live on inherited money," he said. "And I didn't see much sign of wartime austerity at your Piccadilly apartment last night."

"You're right," she said. "But I gave a party for the troops. You spent a fortune on a horse."

"It's my money!"

"But you got it from coal."

"You've spent so much time in bed with that Williams bastard that you've become a bloody Bolshevik."

"And that's one more thing that's driving us apart. Boy, do you really want to stay married to me? You could find someone who suits you. Half the girls in London would love to be Viscountess Aberowen."

"I won't do anything for that damned Williams family. Anyway, I heard last night that your boyfriend wants to be a member of Parliament."

"He'll make a great one."

"Not with you in tow. He won't even get elected. He's a bloody socialist. You're an ex-Fascist."

"I've thought about this. I know it's a bit of a problem—"

"Problem? It's an insuperable barrier. Wait till the papers get that story! You'll be crucified the way I've been today."

"I suppose you'll give the story to the *Daily Mail*."

"I won't need to—his opponents will do that. You mark my words. With you by his side, Lloyd Williams doesn't stand a bloody chance."

vi

For the first five days of June, Lieutenant Woody Dewar and his platoon of paratroopers, plus a thousand or so others, were isolated at an airfield somewhere northwest of London. An aircraft hangar had been converted into a giant dormitory with hundreds of cots in long rows. There were movies and jazz records to entertain them while they waited.

Their objective was Normandy. By means of elaborate deception plans, the Allies had tried to convince the German High Command that the target would be two hundred miles northeast, at Calais. If the Germans had been fooled, the invasion force would meet relatively light resistance, at least for the first few hours.

The paratroopers were to be the first wave, in the middle of the night. The second wave would be the main force of one hundred and thirty thousand men, aboard a fleet of five thousand vessels, landing on the beaches of Normandy at dawn. By then, the paratroopers should have already destroyed inland strongpoints and taken control of key transport links.

Woody's platoon had to capture a bridge across a river in a small town called Eglise-des-Soeurs, ten miles inland. When they had done so, they had to keep control of the bridge, blocking any German units that might be sent to reinforce the beach, until the main invasion force caught up with them. At all costs they must prevent the Germans from blowing up the bridge.

While they waited for the green light, Ace Webber ran a marathon poker game, winning a thousand dollars and losing it again. Lefty Cameron obsessively cleaned and oiled his lightweight M1 semiautomatic carbine, the paratrooper model with a folding stock. Lonnie Callaghan and Tony Bonanio, who did not like one another, went to Mass together every day. Sneaky Pete Schneider sharpened the commando knife he had bought in London until he could have shaved with it. Patrick Timothy, who looked like Clark Gable and had a similar mustache, played a ukulele, the same tune over and over again, driving everybody crazy. Sergeant Defoe wrote long letters to his wife, then tore them up and started again. Mack Trulove and Smoking Joe Morgan cropped and shaved each other's hair, believing that would make it easier for the medics to deal with head injuries.

Most of them had nicknames. Woody had discovered that his own was Scotch.

D-day was set for Sunday, June 4, then postponed because of bad weather.

On Monday, June 5, in the evening, the colonel made a speech. "Men!" he shouted. "Tonight is the night we invade France!"

They roared their approval. Woody thought it was ironic. They were safe and warm here, but they could hardly wait to get over there, jump out of airplanes, and land in the arms of enemy troops who wanted to kill them.

They were given a special meal, all they could eat: steak, pork, chicken, fries, ice cream. Woody did not want any. He had more idea than the other men of what was ahead of him, and he did not want to do it on a full stomach. He got coffee and a donut. The coffee was American, fragrant and delicious, unlike the frightful brew served up by the British, when they had any coffee at all.

He took off his boots and lay down on his cot. He thought about Bella Hernandez, her lopsided smile and her soft breasts.

Next thing he knew, a hooter was sounding.

For a moment, Woody thought he was waking from a bad dream in which he was going into battle to kill people. Then he realized it was true.

They all put on their jumpsuits and assembled their equipment. They had too much. Some of it was essential: a carbine with 150 rounds of .30 ammunition; antitank grenades; a small bomb known as a Gammon grenade; K rations; water purifying tablets; a first-aid kit with morphine. Other things they might have done without: an entrenching tool, a shaving kit, a French phrase book. They were so overloaded that the smaller men struggled to walk to the planes lined up on the runway in the dark.

Their transport aircraft were C-47 Skytrains. To Woody's surprise, he saw by the dim lights that they had all been painted with distinctive black-and-white stripes. The pilot of his aircraft, a bad-tempered Midwesterner called Captain Bonner, said: "That's to prevent us being shot down by our own goddamn side."

Before boarding, the men were weighed. Callaghan and Bonanio both had disassembled bazookas packed in bags that dangled from their legs, adding eighty pounds to their weight. As the total mounted, Captain Bonner became angry. "You're overloading me!" he snarled at Woody. "I won't get this motherfucker off the ground!"

"Not my decision, Captain," Woody said. "Talk to the colonel."

Sergeant Defoe boarded first and went to the front of the plane, taking a seat beside the open arch leading to the flight deck. He would be the last to jump. Any man who developed a last-minute reluctance to leap into the night would be helped along with a good shove from Defoe.

Callaghan and Bonanio, carrying the leg bags holding their bazookas as well as everything else, had to be helped up the steps. Woody as platoon commander boarded last. He would be first out, and first on the ground.

The interior was a tube with a row of simple metal seats on either side. The men had trouble fastening seat belts around their equipment, and some did not bother. The door closed and the engines roared into life.

Woody felt excited as well as scared. Against all reason, he felt eager for the battle to come. To his surprise he found himself impatient to get down on the ground, meet the enemy, and fire his weapons. He wanted the waiting to be over.

He wondered if he would ever see Bella Hernandez again.

He thought he could feel the plane straining as it lumbered down the runway. Painfully, it picked up speed. It seemed to rumble along on the ground forever. Woody found himself wondering how long the damn runway was anyhow. Then at last it lifted. There was little sensation of flying, and he thought the plane must be remaining just a few feet above the ground. Then he looked out. He was sitting by the rearmost of the seven windows, next to the door, and he could see the shrouded lights of the base dropping away. They were airborne.

The sky was overcast, but the clouds were faintly luminous, presumably because the moon had risen beyond them. There was a blue light at the tip of each wing, and Woody could see as his plane moved into formation with others, forming a giant V shape.

The cabin was so noisy that men had to shout into one another's ears to be heard, and conversation soon ceased. They all shifted in their hard seats, trying in vain to get comfortable. Some closed their eyes, but Woody doubted that anyone actually slept.

They were flying low, not much above a thousand feet, and occasionally Woody saw the dull pewter gleam of rivers and lakes. At one point he glimpsed a crowd of people, hundreds of faces all staring up at the planes roaring overhead. Woody knew that more than a thousand aircraft were flying over southern England at the same time, and he realized it must be a remarkable sight. It occurred to him that those people were watching history being made, and he was part of it.

After half an hour they crossed the English beach resorts and were over the sea. For a moment the moon shone through a break in the clouds, and Woody saw the ships. He could hardly believe what he was looking at. It was a floating town, vessels of all sizes sailing in ragged rows like assorted houses in city streets, thousands of them, as far as the eye could see. Before he could call the attention of his comrades to the remarkable sight, the clouds covered the moon again and the vision was gone like a dream.

The planes headed right in a long curve, aiming to hit France to the west of the drop area and then follow the coastline eastward, checking position by terrain features to ensure the paratroopers landed where they should.

The Channel Islands, British though closer to France, had been occupied by Germany at the end of the Battle of France in 1940, and now, as the armada overflew the islands, German antiaircraft guns opened fire. At such a low altitude the Skytrains were terribly vulnerable. Woody realized he could be killed even before he reached the battlefield. He would hate to die pointlessly.

Captain Bonner zigzagged to avoid the flak. Woody was glad he did, but the effect on the men was unfortunate. They all felt airsick, Woody included. Patrick Timothy was the first to succumb, and vomited on the floor. The foul smell made the others feel worse. Sneaky Pete threw up next, then several men all at once. They had stuffed themselves with steak and ice cream, all of which now came back up. The stink was appalling and the floor became disgustingly slippery.

The flight path straightened as they left the islands behind. A few minutes later the French coast appeared. The plane banked and turned left. The copilot got up from his seat and spoke in the ear of Sergeant Defoe, who turned to the platoon and held up ten fingers. Ten minutes to drop.

The plane slowed from its cruising speed of 160 mph to the approximate speed for a parachute jump, about 100 mph.

Suddenly they entered fog. It was heavy enough to blot out the blue light at the tip of the wing. Woody's heart raced. For planes flying in close formation this was very dangerous. How tragic it would be to die in a plane crash, not even in combat. But Bonner could do nothing but fly straight and level and hope for the best. Any change of direction would cause a collision.

The plane left the fog bank as suddenly as it had entered it. To either side, the other planes were still miraculously in formation.

Almost immediately, antiaircraft fire broke out, the flak exploding in deadly blossoms among the serried planes. In these circumstances, Woody knew, the pilot's orders were to maintain speed and fly straight to the target zone. But Bonner defied orders and broke formation. The roar of the engines went to full throttle. He began to zigzag again. The nose of the plane dipped as he tried for more speed. Looking out of the window, Woody saw that many other pilots had been equally undisciplined. They could not control the urge to save their own lives.

The red light went on over the door: four minutes to go.

Woody felt certain the crew had put the light on too soon, desperate to dump their troops and fly to safety. But they had the charts and he could not argue.

He got to his feet. "Stand up and hook!" he yelled. Most of the men could not hear him, but they knew what he was saying. They got up, and each man clipped his static line to the overhead cable, so that he could not be thrown through the door accidentally. The door opened, and the wind roared in. The plane was still going too fast. Jumping at this speed was unpleasant, but that was not the main problem. They would land farther apart, and it would take Woody much longer to find his men on the ground. His approach to his objective would be delayed. He would begin his mission behind schedule. He cursed Bonner.

The pilot continued to bank one way, then the other, dodging flak. The men struggled to keep their footing on a floor that was slimy with vomit.

Woody looked out of the open door. Bonner had lost height while trying to gain speed, and the plane was now at about five hundred feet— too low. There might not be enough time for the parachutes to open fully before the men hit the ground. He hesitated, then beckoned his sergeant forward.

Defoe stood beside him and looked down, then shook his head. He put his mouth to Woody's ear and shouted: "Half our men will break their ankles if we jump at this height. The bazooka carriers will kill themselves."

Woody made a decision.

"Make sure no one jumps!" he yelled at Defoe.

Then he unhooked his static line and went forward, pushing through the double row of standing men, to the flight deck. There were three crew. Yelling at the top of his voice, Woody said: "Climb! Climb!"

Bonner yelled: "Get back there and jump!"

"No one is going to jump at this altitude!" Woody leaned over and pointed at the altimeter, which showed 480 feet. "It's suicide!"

"Get off the flight deck, Lieutenant. That's an order."

Woody was outranked, but he stood his ground. "Not until you gain height."

"We'll be past your target zone if you don't jump now!"

Woody lost his temper. "Climb, you dumb fuck! Climb!"

Bonner looked furious, but Woody did not move. He knew the pilot would not want to return home with a full plane. He would face a military inquiry into what had gone wrong. Bonner had disobeyed too many orders tonight for that. With a curse, he jerked the control lever back. The nose went up immediately, and the aircraft began to gain height and lose speed.

"Satisfied?" Bonner snarled.

"Hell, no." Woody was not going to go aft now and give Bonner the chance to reverse the maneuver. "We jump at a thousand feet."

Bonner went to full throttle. Woody kept his eyes on the altimeter.

When it touched one thousand, he went aft. He pushed through his men, reached the door, looked out, gave the men the thumbs-up, and jumped.

His chute opened immediately. He dropped fast through the air while it spread its dome; then his fall was arrested. Seconds later he hit water. He suffered a split second of panic, fearing that the cowardly Bonner had dropped them all in the sea. Then his feet touched solid ground, or at least soft mud, and he understood that he had come down in a flooded field.

The silk of the parachute fell around him. He struggled out of its folds and unfastened his harness.

Standing in two feet of water, he looked around. This was either a water meadow or, more likely, a field that had been flooded by the Germans to impede an invasion force. He saw no one, enemy or friend, and no animals, either, but the light was poor.

He checked his watch—it was three forty A.M.—then looked at his compass and oriented himself.

Next he took his M1 carbine out of its case and unfolded the stock. He snapped a fifteen-round magazine into the slot, then worked the slide to chamber a round. Finally he rotated the safety lever into the disengaged position.

He reached into a pocket and took out a small tin object like a child's toy. When pressed, it made a distinctive clicking sound. It had been issued to everyone so that they could recognize each other in the dark without resorting to giveaway English passwords.

When he was ready, he looked around again.

Experimentally, he pressed the click twice. After a moment, an answering click came from directly ahead.

He splashed through the water. He smelled vomit. In a low voice he said: "Who's there?"

"Patrick Timothy."

"Lieutenant Dewar here. Follow me."

Timothy had been second to jump, so Woody figured if he continued in the same direction he had a good chance of finding the others.

Fifty yards along he bumped into Mack and Smoking Joe, who had found one another.

They emerged from the water onto a narrow road, and found their first casualties. Lonnie and Tony, with their bazookas in leg bags, had both landed too hard. "I think Lonnie's dead," said Tony. Woody checked: he was right. Lonnie was not breathing. He looked as if he had broken his neck. Tony himself could not move, and Woody thought the man's leg was broken. He gave him a shot of morphine, then dragged him off the road into the next field. Tony would have to wait there for the medics.

Woody ordered Mack and Smoking Joe to hide Lonnie's body, for fear it might lead the Germans to Tony.

He tried to see the landscape around him, straining to recognize something that corresponded to his map. The task seemed impossible, especially in the dark. How was he going to lead these men to the objective if he did not know where he was? The only thing of which he could be reasonably sure was that they had not landed where they were supposed to.

He heard a strange noise, and a moment later he saw a light.

He motioned for the others to duck down.

The paratroopers were not supposed to use flashlights, and French people were subject to a curfew, so the person approaching was probably a German soldier.

In the dim light Woody saw a bicycle.

He stood up and aimed his carbine. He thought of shooting the rider immediately, but could not bring himself to do it. Instead he shouted: "Halt! *Arretez!*"

The cycle stopped. "Hello, Lieut," said the rider, and Woody recognized the voice of Ace Webber.

Woody lowered his weapon. "Where did you get the bike?" he said incredulously.

"Outside a farmhouse," Ace said laconically.

Woody led the group the way Ace had come, figuring that the others were more likely to be in that direction than any other. He looked anxiously for terrain features to match his map, but it was too dark. He felt useless and stupid. He was the officer. He had to solve such problems.

He picked up more of his platoon on the road; then they came to a windmill. Woody decided he could not blunder around any longer, so he went to the mill house and hammered on the door.

An upstairs window opened, and a man said in French: "Who is it?"

"The Americans," Woody said. "*Vive la France!*"

"What do you want?"

"To set you free," Woody said in schoolboy French. "But first I need some help with my map."

The miller laughed and said: "I'm coming down."

A minute later Woody was in the kitchen, spreading his silk map over the table under a bright light. The miller showed him where he was. It was not as bad as Woody had feared. Despite Captain Bonner's panic, they were only four miles northeast of Eglise-des-Soeurs. The miller traced the best route on the map.

A girl of about thirteen crept into the room in a nightdress. "Maman says you're American," she said to Woody.

"That's right, mademoiselle," he said.

"Do you know Gladys Angelus?"

Woody laughed. "As it happens, I did meet her once, at the apartment of a friend's father."

"Is she really, really beautiful?"

"Even more beautiful than she looks in the movies."

"I knew it!"

The miller offered him wine. "No, thanks," said Woody. "Maybe after we've won." The miller kissed him on both cheeks.

Woody went back outside and led his platoon away, heading in the direction of Eglise-des-Soeurs. Including himself, nine of the original eighteen were now together. They had suffered two casualties, Lonnie dead and Tony wounded, and seven more had not yet appeared. His orders were not to spend too much time trying to find everyone. As soon as he had enough men to do the job, he was to proceed to the target.

One of the missing seven showed up right away. Sneaky Pete emerged from a ditch and joined the group with a casual "Hi, gang," as if it was the most natural thing in the world.

"What were you doing in there?" Woody asked him.

"I thought you were German," Pete said. "I was hiding."

Woody had seen the pale gleam of parachute silk in the ditch. Pete must have been hiding there since he landed. He had obviously suffered panic, and curled up in a ball. But Woody pretended to accept his story.

The one Woody really wanted to find was Sergeant Defoe. He was an experienced soldier, and Woody had been planning to rely heavily on him. But he was nowhere to be seen.

They were approaching a crossroads when they heard noises. Woody identified the sound of an engine idling, and two or three voices in conversation. He ordered everyone down on their hands and knees, and the platoon advanced crawling.

Up ahead, he saw that a motorcycle rider had stopped to talk to two men on foot. All three were in uniform. They were speaking German. There was a building at the crossroads, perhaps a small tavern or a bakery.

He decided to wait. Perhaps they would leave. He wanted his group to move silently and unobserved for as long as possible.

After five minutes he ran out of patience. He turned around. "Patrick Timothy!" he hissed.

Someone else said: "Pukey Pat! Scotch wants you."

Timothy crawled forward. He still smelled of vomit, and now it had become his name.

Woody had seen Timothy play baseball, and knew he could throw hard and accurately. "Hit that motorcycle with a grenade," Woody said.

Timothy took a grenade from his pack, pulled the pin, and lobbed it.

There was a clang. One of the men said in German: "What was that?" Then the grenade detonated.

There were two explosions. The first knocked all three Germans to the ground. The second was the motorcycle's fuel tank blowing up, and it sent a starburst of flame that burned the men, leaving a stink of scorched flesh.

"Stay where you are!" Woody shouted to his platoon. He watched the building. Was there anyone inside? During the next five minutes, no one opened a window or a door. Either the place was empty, or the occupants were hiding under their beds.

Woody got to his feet and waved the platoon on. He felt strange as he stepped over the grisly bodies of the three Germans. He had ordered their deaths—men who had mothers and fathers, wives or girlfriends, perhaps sons and daughters. Now each man was an ugly mess of blood and burned flesh. Woody should have felt triumphant. It was his first encounter with the enemy, and he had vanquished them. But he just felt a bit sick.

Past the crossroads, he set a brisk pace, and ordered no talking or smoking. To keep up his strength he ate a bar of D-ration chocolate, which was a bit like builder's putty with sugar added.

After half an hour he heard a car and ordered everyone to hide in the fields. The vehicle was traveling fast, with its headlights on. It was probably German, but the Allies were sending over jeeps by glider, along with antitank guns and other artillery, so it was just possible this was a friendly vehicle. He lay under a hedge and watched it go by.

It went too fast for him to identify it. He wondered whether he should have ordered the platoon to shoot it up. No, he thought, on balance they did better to focus on their mission.

They passed through three hamlets that Woody was able to identify on his map. Dogs barked occasionally but no one came to investigate. Doubtless the French had learned to mind their own business under enemy occupation. It was eerie, creeping along foreign roads in the dark, armed to the teeth, passing quiet houses where people slept unconscious of the deadly firepower outside their windows.

At last they came to the outskirts of Eglise-des-Soeurs. Woody ordered a short rest. They entered a little stand of trees and sat on the ground. They drank from their canteens and ate rations. Woody still would not permit smoking: the glow of a cigarette could be seen from surprisingly far.

The road they were on should lead straight to the bridge, he reckoned. There was no hard information about how the bridge was guarded. Since the Allies had decided it was important, he assumed the Germans thought the same; therefore some security was likely, but it might be anything from one man with a rifle to a whole platoon. Woody could not plan the assault until he saw the target.

After ten minutes he moved them on. The men did not have to be nagged about silence now: they sensed the danger. They trod quietly along the street, past houses and churches and shops, keeping to the sides, peering into the gloomy night, jumping at the least sound. A sudden loud cough from an open bedroom window almost caused Woody to fire his carbine.

Eglise-des-Soeurs was a large village rather than a small town, and Woody saw the silver glint of the river sooner than he expected. He raised a hand for them all to halt. The main street led gently downhill at a slight angle to the bridge, so he had a good view. The waterway was about a hundred feet wide, and the bridge had a single curved span. It must be an old structure, he guessed, because it was so narrow that two cars could not have passed.

The bad news was that there was a pillbox at each end, twin concrete domes with horizontal shooting slits. A pair of sentries patrolled the bridge between the pillboxes. They stood one at each end. The nearer one was speaking through a firing slit, presumably chatting to whomever was inside. Then they both walked to the middle, where they looked over the parapet at the black water flowing beneath. They did not appear very tense, so Woody deduced they had not yet learned that the invasion had begun. On the other hand they were not slacking. They were awake and moving and looking about them with some degree of alertness.

Woody could not guess how many men were inside, nor how they were armed. Were there machine guns behind those slits, or just rifles? It would make a big difference.

Woody wished he had some experience of battle. How was he supposed to deal with this situation? He guessed there must be thousands of men like him, new junior officers who just had to make it up as they went along. If only Sergeant Defoe were here.

The easy way to neutralize a pillbox was to sneak up and put a grenade through one of the slits. A good man could probably crawl to the nearer one unobserved. But Woody needed to take out both at the same time—otherwise the attack on the first would forewarn the occupants of the second.

How could he reach the farther pillbox without being seen by the patrolling sentries?

He sensed his men getting restless. They did not like to think their leader might be unsure what to do next.

"Sneaky Pete," he said. "You'll crawl up to that nearest pillbox and put a grenade through the slit."

Pete looked terrified, but he said: "Yes, sir."

Next, Woody named the two best shots in the platoon. "Smoking Joe and Mack," he said. "Choose one each of the sentries. As soon as Pete deploys his grenade, take the sentries out."

The two men nodded and hefted their weapons.

In the absence of Defoe, he decided to make Ace Webber his deputy. He named four others and said: "Go with Ace. As soon as the shooting starts, run like hell across the bridge and storm the pillbox on the other side. If you're quick enough, you'll catch them napping."

"Yes, sir," said Ace. "The bastards won't know what's hit them." His aggression was masking fear, Woody guessed.

"Everyone not in Ace's group, follow me into the near pillbox."

Woody felt bad about giving Ace and those with him the more dangerous assignment, and himself the relative safety of the nearer pillbox, but it had been drummed into him that an officer must not risk his life unnecessarily, for then he might leave his men leaderless.

They walked toward the bridge, Pete in the lead. This was a dangerous moment. Ten men going along a street together could not remain unnoticed for long even at night. Anyone looking carefully in their direction would sense movement.

If the alarm was raised too soon, Sneaky Pete might not get to the pillbox, and then the platoon would lose the advantage of surprise.

It was a long walk.

Pete reached a corner and stopped. Woody guessed he was waiting for the near sentry to leave his post outside the pillbox and walk to the middle.

The two sharpshooters found cover and settled in.

Woody dropped to one knee and signaled the others to do likewise. They all watched the sentry.

The man took a long pull on his cigarette, dropped it, trod on the end to put it out, and blew a long cloud of smoke. Then he eased himself upright, settled his rifle strap on his shoulder, and started walking.

The sentry on the far side did the same.

Pete ran the next block and came to the end of the street. He got down on his hands and knees and crawled rapidly across the road. He reached the pillbox and stood up.

No one had noticed. The two sentries were still approaching one another.

Peter took out a grenade and pulled the pin. Then he waited a few seconds. Woody guessed he did not want the men inside to have time to throw the grenade out again.

Pete reached around the curve of the dome and gently dropped the grenade inside.

Joe's and Mack's carbines barked. The nearer sentry fell, but the farther one was unhurt. To his credit he did not turn and run, but courageously went down on one knee and unslung his rifle. He was too slow, though: the carbines spoke again, almost simultaneously, and he fell without firing.

Then Pete's grenade exploded inside the nearer pillbox with a muffled thump.

Woody was already running full pelt, and the men were close behind him. Within seconds he reached the bridge.

The pillbox had a low wooden door. Woody flung it open and stepped inside. Three men in German uniforms were dead on the floor.

He moved to a firing slit and looked out. Ace and his four men were haring across the short bridge, shooting at the farther pillbox as they ran. The bridge was only a hundred feet long, but that proved to be fifty feet too much. As they reached the middle, a machine gun opened up. The Americans were trapped in a narrow corridor with no cover. The machine gun clacked insanely and in seconds all five of them had fallen. The gun continued to rake them for several seconds, to be certain they were dead—and, in the process, making sure of the two German sentries, too.

When it stopped, they were all still.

Silence fell.

Beside Woody, Lefty Cameron said: "Jesus Christ Almighty."

Woody could have wept. He had sent ten men to their deaths, five Americans and five Germans, yet he had failed to achieve his objective. The enemy still held the far end of the bridge and could stop Allied forces crossing it.

He had four men left. If they tried again, and ran across the bridge together, they would all be killed. He needed a new plan.

He studied the townscape. What could he do? He wished he had a tank.

He had to act fast. There might well be enemy troops elsewhere in the town. They would have been alerted by the gunfire. They would respond soon. He could deal with them if he had both pillboxes. Otherwise he would be in trouble.

If his men could not cross the bridge, he thought desperately, perhaps they could swim the river. He decided to take a quick look at the bank. "Mack and Smoking Joe," he said. "Fire at the other pillbox. See if you can get a bullet through the slit. Keep them busy while I scout around."

The carbines opened up and he went out through the door.

He was able to shelter behind the near pillbox while he looked over the parapet at the upstream bank. Then he had to scuttle across the road to see the other edge. However, no fire came from the enemy position.

There was no river wall. Instead an earth slope went down to the water. It looked the same on the far bank, he thought, though there was not enough light to be sure. A good swimmer might get across. Under the span of the arch he would not be easy to see from the enemy position. Then he could repeat on the far side what Sneaky Pete had done this side, and grenade the pillbox.

Looking at the structure of the bridge, he had a better idea. Below the level of the parapet was a stone ledge a foot wide. A man with steady nerves could crawl across, all the time remaining out of sight.

He returned to the captured pillbox. The smallest man was Lefty Cameron. He was also feisty, not the type to get the shakes. "Lefty," said Woody. "There's a hidden ledge that runs across the outside of the bridge below the parapet. Probably used by workmen doing repairs. I want you to crawl across and grenade the other pillbox."

"You bet," said Lefty.

It was a gutsy response from someone who had just seen five comrades killed.

Woody turned to Mack and Smoking Joe and said: "Give him cover." They began to shoot.

Lefty said: "What if I fall in?"

"It's only fifteen or twenty feet above the water at most," Woody said. "You'll be fine."

"Okay," said Lefty. He went to the door. "I can't swim, though," he said. Then he was gone.

Woody saw him dart across the road. He looked over the parapet, then straddled it and eased down the other side until he was lost to view.

"Okay," he said to the others. "Hold your fire. He's on his way."

They all stared out. Nothing moved. It was dawn, Woody realized: the town was coming more clearly into view. But none of the inhabitants showed themselves: they knew better. Perhaps German troops were mobilizing in some neighboring street, but he could hear nothing. He realized he was listening for a splash, fearful that Lefty would fall in the river.

A dog came trotting across the bridge, a medium-size mongrel with a curled tail that stuck up jauntily. It sniffed the dead bodies with curiosity, then moved on purposefully, as if it had an important rendezvous elsewhere. Woody watched it pass the far pillbox and continue into the other side of the town.

Dawn meant the main force was now landing on the beaches. Someone had said it was the largest amphibious attack in the history of warfare. He wondered what kind of resistance they were meeting. There was no one more vulnerable than an infantryman loaded with gear splashing through the shallows, the flat beach ahead of him offering a clear field of fire to gunners in the dunes. Woody felt grateful for this concrete pillbox.

Lefty was taking a long time. Had he fallen in the water quietly? Could something else have gone wrong?

Then Woody saw him, a slim khaki form bellying over the parapet of the bridge at the far end. Woody held his breath. Lefty dropped to his knees, crawled to the pillbox, and came upright with his back flat against the curved concrete. With his left hand he drew out a grenade. He pulled the pin, waited a couple of seconds, then reached around and threw the grenade through the slit.

Woody heard the boom of the explosion and saw a flash of lurid light from the firing slits. Lefty raised his arms above his head like a champion.

"Get back under cover, asshole," Woody said, though Lefty could not hear him. There could be a German soldier hiding in a nearby building waiting to avenge the deaths of his friends.

But no shot rang out, and after a brief victory dance Lefty went inside the pillbox, and Woody breathed easier.

However, he was not yet fully secure. At this point a sudden sally by a couple of dozen Germans could win the bridge back. Then it would all have been in vain.

He forced himself to wait another minute to see if any enemy troops showed themselves. Still nothing moved. It was beginning to look as if there were no Germans in Eglise-des-Soeurs other than those manning the bridge: they were probably relieved every twelve hours from a barracks a few miles away.

"Smoking Joe," he said. "Get rid of the dead Germans. Throw them in the river."

Joe dragged the three bodies out of the pillbox and disposed of them, then did the same with the two sentries.

"Pete and Mack," Woody said. "Go over to the other pillbox and join Lefty. Make sure the three of you stay alert. We haven't killed all the Germans in France yet. If you see enemy troops approaching your position, don't hesitate, don't negotiate, just shoot them."

The two men left the pillbox and walked briskly across the bridge to the far end.

There were now three Americans in the far pillbox. If the Germans tried to retake the bridge, they would have a hard time of it, especially in the growing light.

Woody realized that the dead Americans on the bridge would forewarn any approaching enemy forces that the pillboxes had been captured. Otherwise he might retain an element of surprise.

That meant he had to get rid of the American corpses too.

He told the others what he was going to do, then stepped outside.

The morning air tasted fresh and clean.

He walked to the middle of the bridge. He checked each body for a pulse, but there was no doubt: they were all dead.

One by one, he picked up his comrades and dropped them over the parapet.

The last one was Ace Webber. As he hit the water, Woody said: "Rest in peace, buddies." He stood still for a minute with his head bent and his eyes closed.

When he turned around, the sun was coming up.

vii

The great fear of Allied planners was that the Germans would rapidly reinforce their troops in Normandy, and mount a powerful counterattack that would drive the invaders back into the sea, in a repeat of the Dunkirk disaster.

Lloyd Williams was one of the people trying to make sure that did not happen.

His job helping escaped prisoners get home had low priority after the invasion, and he was now working with the French Resistance.

At the end of May the BBC broadcast coded messages that triggered a campaign of sabotage in German-occupied France. During the first few days of June hundreds of telephone lines were cut, usually in hard-to-find places. Fuel depots were set on fire, roads were blocked by trees, and tires were slashed.

Lloyd was assisting the railwaymen, who were strongly Communist and called themselves Résistance-Fer. For years they had maddened the Nazis with their sly subversion. German troop trains somehow got diverted down obscure branch lines and sent many miles out of their way. Engines broke down unaccountably and carriages were derailed. It was so bad that the occupiers brought railwaymen from Germany to run the system. But the disruption got worse. In the spring of 1944 the railwaymen began to damage their own network. They blew up tracks and sabotaged the heavy lifting cranes required for moving crashed trains.

The Nazis did not take this lying down. Hundreds of railwaymen were executed, and thousands deported to camps. But the campaign escalated, and by D-day rail traffic in some parts of France had come to a halt.

Now, on D-day plus one, Lloyd lay at the summit of an embankment beside the main line to Rouen, capital city of Normandy, at a point where the track entered a tunnel. From his vantage point he could see approaching trains a mile away.

With Lloyd were two others, code-named Legionnaire and Cigare. Legionnaire was leader of the resistance in this neighborhood. Cigare was a railwayman. Lloyd had brought the dynamite. Supplying weaponry was the main role played by the British in the French Resistance.

The three men were half hidden by long grass dotted with wild-flowers. It was the kind of place to bring a girl on a fine day such as this, Lloyd thought. Daisy would like it.

A train appeared in the distance. Cigare scrutinized it as it came nearer. He was about sixty, wiry and small, with the lined face of a heavy smoker. When the train was still a quarter of a mile away, he shook his head in negation. This was not the one they were waiting for. The engine passed them, puffing smoke, and entered the tunnel. It was hauling four passenger coaches, all full, carrying a mixture of civilians and uniformed men. Lloyd had more important prey in his sights.

Legionnaire looked at his watch. He had dark skin and a black mustache, and Lloyd guessed he might have a North African somewhere in his ancestry. Now he was jumpy. They were exposed here, in the open air and in daylight. The longer they stayed, the higher the chance they would be spotted. "How much longer?" he said worriedly.

Cigare shrugged. "We'll see."

Lloyd said in French: "You can leave now, if you wish. Everything is set."

Legionnaire did not reply. He was not going to miss the action. For the sake of his prestige and authority he had to be able to say: "I was there."

Cigare tensed, peering into the distance, the skin around his eyes creasing with the effort. "So," he said cryptically. He raised himself to his knees.

Lloyd could hardly see the train, let alone identify it, but Cigare was alert. It was moving a lot faster than the previous one, Lloyd could tell. As it came closer, he observed that it was longer, too: twenty-four carriages or more, he thought.

"This is it," said Cigare.

Lloyd's pulse quickened. If Cigare was right, this was a German troop train carrying more than a thousand officers and men to the Normandy battlefield—perhaps the first of many such trains. It was Lloyd's job to make sure neither this train nor any following passed through the tunnel.

Then he saw something else. A plane was tracking the train. As he watched, the aircraft matched course with the train and began to lose height.

The plane was British.

Lloyd recognized it as a Hawker Typhoon, nicknamed a Tiffy, a one-man fighter-bomber. Tiffies were often given the dangerous mission of penetrating deep behind enemy lines to harass communications. There was a brave man at the controls, Lloyd thought.

But this formed no part of Lloyd's plan. He did not want the train to be wrecked before it reached the tunnel.

"Shit," he said.

The Tiffy fired a machine-gun burst at the carriages.

Legionnaire said: "But what is this?"

Lloyd replied in English: "Fucked if I know."

He could see now that the engine was hauling a mixture of passenger coaches and cattle trucks. However, the cattle trucks probably also contained men.

The plane, traveling faster, strafed the carriages as it overhauled the train. It had four belt-fed 20 mm cannon, and they made a fearsome rattling sound that could be heard over the roar of the plane's engine and the energetic puffing of the train. Lloyd could not help feeling sorry for the trapped soldiers, unable to get out of the way of the lethal hail of bullets. He wondered why the pilot did not fire his rockets. They were highly destructive against trains and cars, though difficult to fire accurately. Perhaps they had been used up in an earlier encounter.

Some of the Germans bravely put their heads out of the windows and fired pistols and rifles at the plane, with no effect.

But Lloyd now saw a light antiaircraft battery emplaced on a flatbed car immediately behind the engine. Two gunners were hastily deploying the big gun. It swiveled on its base and the barrel lifted to aim at the British plane.

The pilot did not appear to have seen it, for he held his course, rounds from his cannon tearing through the roofs of the carriages as he overhauled them.

The big gun fired and missed.

Lloyd wondered if he knew the flyer. There were only about five thousand pilots on active service in the UK at any one time. Quite a lot of them had been to Daisy's parties. Lloyd thought of Hubert St. John, a brilliant Cambridge graduate with whom he had been reminiscing about student days a few weeks ago; of Dennis Chaucer, a West Indian from Trinidad who complained bitterly about tasteless English food, especially the mashed potatoes that seemed to be served with every meal; and of Brian Mantel, an amiable Australian he had brought across the Pyrenees on his last trip. The brave man in the Tiffy could easily be someone Lloyd had met.

The antiaircraft gun fired again, and missed again.

Either the pilot still had not seen the gun, or he felt it could not hit him, for he took no evasive action, but continued to fly dangerously low and wreak carnage on the troop train.

The engine was just a few seconds from the tunnel when the plane was hit.

Flame flared from the plane's engine, and black smoke billowed. Too late, the pilot veered away from the railway track.

The train entered the tunnel, and the carriages flashed past Lloyd's position. He saw that every one was packed full with dozens, hundreds of German soldiers.

The Tiffy flew directly at Lloyd. For a moment he thought it would crash where he lay. He was already flat on the ground, but he stupidly put his hands over his head, as if that could protect him.

The Tiffy roared by a hundred feet above him.

Then Legionnaire pressed the plunger of the detonator.

There was a roar like thunder inside the tunnel as the track blew up, followed by a terrible screeching of tortured steel as the train crashed.

At first the carriages full of soldiers continued to flash by, but a second later their charge was arrested. The ends of two linked carriages rose in the air, forming an inverted V. Lloyd heard the men inside screaming. All the carriages came off the rails and tumbled like dropped matchsticks around the dark O of the tunnel's mouth. Iron crumpled like paper, and broken glass rained on the three saboteurs watching from the top of the embankment. They were in danger of being killed by their own explosion, and without a word they all leaped to their feet and ran.

By the time they had reached a safe distance, it was all over. Smoke was billowing out of the tunnel: in the unlikely event that any men in there had survived the crash, they would burn to death.

Lloyd's plan was a success. Not only had he killed hundreds of enemy troops and wrecked a train, he had also blocked a main railway line. Crashes in tunnels took weeks to clear. He had made it much more difficult for the Germans to reinforce their defenses in Normandy.

He was horrified.

He had seen death and destruction in Spain, but nothing like this. And he had caused it.

There was another crash, and when he looked in the direction of the sound, he saw that the Tiffy had hit the ground. It was burning, but the fuselage had not broken up. The pilot might be alive.

He ran toward the plane, and Cigare and Legionnaire followed.

The downed aircraft lay on its belly. One wing had snapped in half.

Smoke came from the single engine. The Perspex dome was blackened by soot and Lloyd could not see the pilot.

He stepped on the wing and unfastened the hood catch. Cigare did the same on the other side. Together, they slid the dome back on its rails.

The pilot was unconscious. He wore a helmet and goggles, and an oxygen mask over his nose and mouth. Lloyd could not tell whether it was someone he knew.

He wondered where the oxygen tank was, and whether it had yet burst.

Legionnaire had a similar thought. "We have to get him out before the plane blows up," he said.

Lloyd reached inside and unfastened the safety harness. Then he put his hands under the pilot's arms and pulled. The man was completely limp. Lloyd had no way of knowing what his injuries might be. He was not even sure the man was alive.

He dragged the pilot out of the cockpit, then got him over his shoulder in a fireman's lift and carried him a safe distance from the burning wreckage. As gently as he could, he laid the man on the ground faceup.

He heard a noise that was a cross between a whoosh and a thump, and looked back to see that the whole plane was ablaze.

He bent over the pilot and carefully removed the goggles and the oxygen mask, revealing a face that was shockingly familiar.

The pilot was Boy Fitzherbert.

And he was breathing.

Lloyd wiped blood from Boy's nose and mouth.

Boy opened his eyes. At first there seemed to be no intelligence behind them. Then, after a minute, his expression altered and he said: "You."

"We blew up the train," Lloyd said.

Boy seemed unable to move anything but his eyes and mouth. "Small world," he said.

"Isn't it?"

Cigare said: "Who is he?"

Lloyd hesitated, then said: "My brother."

"My God."

Boy's eyes closed.

Lloyd said to Legionnaire: "We have to bring a doctor."

Legionnaire shook his head. "We must get out of here. The Germans will be coming to investigate the train crash within minutes."

Lloyd knew he was right. "We'll have to take him with us."

Boy opened his eyes and said: "Williams."

"What is it, Boy?"

Boy seemed to grin. "You can marry the bitch now," he said.

Then he died.

viii

Daisy cried when she heard. Boy had been a rotter, and treated her badly, but she had loved him once, and he had taught her a lot about sex; she felt sad that he had been killed.

His brother, Andy, was now a viscount and heir to the earldom; Andy's wife, May, was a viscountess; and Daisy's name, according to the elaborate rules of the aristocracy, was the Dowager Viscountess Aberowen—until she married Lloyd, when she would be relieved to become plain Mrs. Williams.

However, that might be a long time coming, even now. Over the summer, hopes of a quick end to the war came to nothing. A plot by German army officers to kill Hitler on July 20 failed. The German army was in full retreat on the eastern front, and the Allies took Paris in August, but Hitler was determined to fight on to the terrible end. Daisy had no idea when she would see Lloyd, let alone marry him.

One Wednesday in September, when she went to spend the evening in Aldgate, she was greeted by a jubilant Eth Leckwith. "Great news!" Ethel said when Daisy walked into the kitchen. "Lloyd has been selected as prospective parliamentary candidate for Hoxton!"

Lloyd's sister, Millie, was there with her two children, Lennie and Pammie. "Isn't it wonderful?" she said. "He'll be prime minister, I bet."

"Yes," said Daisy, and she sat down heavily.

"Well, I can see you're not happy about that," said Ethel. "As my friend Mildred would say, it went down like a cup of cold sick. What's the matter?"

"It's just that having me as a wife isn't going to help him get elected." It was because she loved him so much that she felt so bad. How could she blight his prospects? But how could she give him up? When she thought like this, her heart felt heavy and life seemed desolate.

"Because you're an heiress?" said Ethel.

"Not just that. Before Boy died, he told me Lloyd would never get elected with an ex-Fascist as his wife." She looked at Ethel, who always told the truth, even when it hurt. "He was right, wasn't he?"

"Not entirely," Ethel said. She put the kettle on for tea, then sat opposite Daisy at the kitchen table. "I'm not going to say it doesn't matter. But I don't think you should despair."

You're just like me, Daisy thought. You say what you think. No wonder he loves me: I'm a younger version of his mother!

Millie said: "Love conquers all, doesn't it?" She noticed that four-year-old Lennie was hitting two-year-old Pammie with a wooden soldier. "Don't bash your sister!" she said. Turning back to Daisy, she went on: "And my brother loves you to bits. I don't think he's ever loved anyone else, to tell you the truth."

"I know," said Daisy. She wanted to cry. "But he's determined to change the world, and I can't bear the thought that I'm standing in his way."

Ethel took the crying two-year-old onto her knee, and the toddler calmed down immediately. "I'll tell you what to do," she said to Daisy. "Be prepared for questions, and expect hostility, but don't dodge the issue and don't hide your past."

"What should I say?"

"You might say you were fooled by Fascism, as millions of others were, but you drove an ambulance in the Blitz, and you hope you've paid your dues. Work out the exact words with Lloyd. Be confident, be your irresistibly charming self, and don't let it get you down."

"Will it work?"

Ethel hesitated. "I don't know," she said after a pause. "I really don't. But you have to try."

"It would be awful if he had to give up what he loves most for my sake. Something like that could destroy a marriage."

Daisy was half hoping Ethel would deny this, but she did not. "I don't know," she said again.

CHAPTER NINETEEN

1945 (I)

Woody Dewar got used to the crutches quickly.

He was wounded at the end of 1944, in Belgium, in the Battle of the Bulge. The Allies pushing toward the German border had been surprised by a powerful counterattack. Woody and others of the 101st Airborne Division had held out at a vital crossroads town called Bastogne. When the Germans sent a formal letter demanding surrender, General McAuliffe sent back a one-word message that became famous: "Nuts!"

Woody's right leg was smashed up by machine-gun bullets on Christmas Day. It hurt like hell. Even worse, it was a month before he got out of the besieged town and into a real hospital.

His bones would mend, and he might even lose the limp, but his leg would never again be strong enough for parachuting.

The Battle of the Bulge was the last offensive of Hitler's army in the west. After that they would never counterattack again.

Woody returned to civilian life, which meant he could live at his parents' apartment in Washington and enjoy being fussed over by his mother. When the plaster cast came off, he went back to work at his father's office.

On Thursday, April 12, 1945, he was in the Capitol building, the home of the Senate and the House of Representatives, hobbling slowly through the basement, talking to his father about refugees. "We think about twenty-one million people in Europe have been driven from their homes," said Gus. "The United Nations Relief and Rehabilitation Administration is ready to help them."

"I guess that will start any day now," said Woody. "The Red Army is almost in Berlin."

"And the U.S. Army is only fifty miles away."

"How much longer can Hitler hold out?"

"A sane man would have surrendered by now."

Woody lowered his voice. "Somebody told me the Russians found what seems to have been an extermination camp. The Nazis killed hundreds of people a day there. A place called Auschwitz, in Poland."

Gus nodded grimly. "It's true. The public don't know yet, but they'll find out sooner or later."

"Someone should be put on trial for that."

"The UN War Crimes Commission has been at work for a couple of years now, making lists of war criminals and collecting evidence. Someone will be put on trial, provided we can keep the United Nations going after the war."

"Of course we can," Woody said indignantly. "Roosevelt campaigned on that basis last year, and he won the election. The United Nations conference opens in San Francisco in a couple of weeks." San Francisco had a special significance for Woody, because Bella Hernandez lived there, but he had not yet told his father about her. "The American people want to see international cooperation, so that we never have another war like this one. Who could be against that?"

"You'd be surprised. Look, most Republicans are decent men who simply have a view of the world that is different from ours. But there is a hard core of fucking nutcases."

Woody was startled. His father rarely swore.

"The types who planned an insurrection against Roosevelt in the thirties," Gus went on. "Businessmen like Henry Ford, who thought

Hitler was a good strong anti-Communist leader. They sign up for right-wing groups such as America First."

Woody could not remember him speaking this angrily before.

"If these fools have their way, there will be a third world war even worse than the first two," Gus said. "I've lost a son to war, and if I ever have a grandson, I don't want to lose him, too."

Woody suffered a stab of grief: Joanne would have given Gus grandchildren, if she had lived.

Right now Woody was not even dating, so grandchildren were a distant prospect—unless he could track down Bella in San Francisco . . .

"We can't do anything about complete idiots," Gus went on. "But perhaps we can deal with Senator Vandenberg."

Arthur Vandenberg was a Republican from Michigan, a conservative, and an opponent of Roosevelt's New Deal. He was on the Senate Foreign Relations Committee with Gus.

"He's our greatest danger," Gus said. "He may be self-important and vain, but he commands respect. The president has been wooing him, and he's come around to our point of view, but he could backslide."

"Why would he do that?"

"He's strongly anti-Communist."

"Nothing wrong with that. We are, too."

"Yes, but Arthur is kind of rigid about it. He'll get riled if we do anything he thinks is kowtowing to Moscow."

"Such as?"

"God knows what kind of compromises we might have to make in San Francisco. We've already agreed to admit Belorussia and the Ukraine as separate states, which is just a way of giving Moscow three votes in the General Assembly. We have to keep the Soviets on board—but if we go too far, Arthur could turn against the whole United Nations project. Then the Senate may refuse to ratify it, exactly the way they rejected the League of Nations in 1919."

"So our job in San Francisco is to keep the Soviets happy without offending Senator Vandenberg."

"Exactly."

They heard running footsteps, an unusual sound in the dignified hallways of the Capitol. They both looked around. Woody was surprised to see the vice president, Harry Truman, running through the hallway. He was dressed normally, in a gray double-breasted suit and a polka-dot tie, though he had no hat. He seemed to have lost his normal escort of aides and Secret Service guards. He was running steadily, breathing hard, not looking at anyone, going somewhere in a terrific hurry.

Woody and Gus watched in astonishment. So did everyone else.

When Truman disappeared around a corner, Woody said: "What the heck . . . ?"

Gus said: "I think the president must have died."

ii

Volodya Peshkov entered Germany in a ten-wheeler Studebaker US6 army truck. Made in South Bend, Indiana, the truck had been carried by rail to Baltimore, shipped across the Atlantic and around the Cape of Good Hope to the Persian Gulf, then sent by train from Persia to central Russia. Volodya knew it was one of two hundred thousand Studebaker trucks given to the Red Army by the American government. The Russians liked them: they were tough and reliable. The men said the letters "USA" stenciled on the side stood for *Ubit Sukina syna Adolf,* which meant "Kill that son of a bitch Adolf."

They also liked the food the Americans were sending, especially the cans of compressed meat called Spam, strangely bright pink in color but gloriously fatty.

Volodya had been posted to Germany because the intelligence he was getting from spies in Berlin was now not as up-to-date as information that could be gained by interviewing German prisoners of war. His fluent German made him a first-class frontline interrogator.

When he crossed the border, he had seen a Soviet government poster that said: RED ARMY SOLDIER: YOU ARE NOW ON GERMAN SOIL. THE

HOUR OF REVENGE HAS STRUCK! It was among the milder pieces of propaganda. The Kremlin had been whipping up hatred of Germans for some time, believing it would make soldiers fight harder. Political commissars had calculated—or said they had—the number of men killed in battle, the number of houses torched, the number of civilians murdered for being Communists or Slavs or Jews, in every village and town overrun by the German army. Many frontline soldiers could quote the figures for their own neighborhoods, and were eager to do the same kind of damage in Germany.

The Red Army had reached the river Oder, which snaked north-south across Prussia, the last barrier before Berlin. A million Soviet soldiers were within fifty miles of the capital, poised to strike. Volodya was with the 5th Shock Army. Waiting for the fighting to begin, he was studying the army newspaper, *Red Star*.

What he read horrified him.

The hate propaganda went further than anything he had read before. "If you have not killed at least one German a day, you have wasted that day," he read. "If you are waiting for the fighting, kill a German before combat. If you kill one German, kill another—there is nothing more amusing for us than a heap of German corpses. Kill the German—this is your old mother's prayer. Kill the German—this is what your children beseech you to do. Kill the German—this is the cry of your Russian earth. Do not waver. Do not let up. Kill."

It was a bit sickening, Volodya thought. But worse was implied. The writer made light of looting: "German women are only losing fur coats and silver spoons that were stolen in the first place." And there was a sidelong joke about rape: "Soviet soldiers do not refuse the compliments of German women."

Soldiers were not the most civilized of men in the first place. The way the invading Germans had behaved in 1941 had enraged all Russians. The government was fueling their wrath with talk of revenge. And now the army newspaper was making it clear they could do anything they liked to the defeated Germans.

It was a recipe for Armageddon.

iii

Erik von Ulrich was consumed by a yearning that the war should be over.

With his friend Hermann Braun and their boss Dr. Weiss, Erik set up a field hospital in a small Protestant church; then they sat in the nave with nothing to do but wait for the horse-drawn ambulances to arrive loaded with horribly torn and burned men.

The German army had reinforced Seelow Heights, overlooking the Oder River where it passed closest to Berlin. Erik's aid station was in a village a mile back from the line.

Dr. Weiss, who had a friend in army intelligence, said there were 110,000 Germans defending Berlin against a million Soviets. With his usual sarcasm he said: "But our morale is high, and Adolf Hitler is the greatest genius in military history, so we are certain to win."

There was no hope, but German soldiers were still fighting fiercely. Erik believed this was because of the stories filtering back about how the Red Army behaved. Prisoners were killed, homes were looted and wrecked, women were raped and nailed to barn doors. The Germans believed they were defending their own families from Communist brutality. The Kremlin's hate propaganda was backfiring.

Erik was looking forward to defeat. He longed for the killing to stop. He just wanted to go home.

He would have his wish soon—or he would be dead.

Sleeping on a wooden pew, Erik was awakened at three o'clock in the morning on Monday, April 16, by the Russian guns. He had heard artillery bombardments before, but this was ten times as loud as anything in his experience. For the men on the front line it must have been literally deafening.

The wounded started to arrive at dawn, and the team went wearily to work, amputating limbs, setting broken bones, extracting bullets, and cleaning and bandaging wounds. They were short of everything from drugs to clean water, and they gave morphine only to those who were screaming in agony.

Men who could still walk and hold a gun were sent back to the line.

The German defenders held out longer than Dr. Weiss expected. At the end of the first day they were still in position, and as darkness fell, the rush of wounded slowed. The medical unit got some sleep that night.

Early on the next day Werner Franck was brought in, his right wrist horribly crushed.

He was a captain now. He had been in charge of a section of the line with thirty 88 mm flak guns. "We only had eight shells for each gun," he said while Dr. Weiss's clever fingers worked slowly and meticulously to set his smashed bones. "Our orders were to fire seven at the Russian tanks, then use the eighth to destroy our own gun so that it could not be used by the Reds." He had been standing by an 88 when it suffered a direct hit from the Soviet artillery and turned over on him. "I was lucky it was only my hand," he said. "It might have been my damn head."

When his wrist had been taped up, he said to Erik: "Have you heard from Carla?"

Erik knew that his sister and Werner were now a couple. "I haven't had any letters for weeks."

"Nor me. I hear things are pretty grim in Berlin. I hope she's all right."

"I worry, too," said Erik.

Surprisingly, the Germans held the Seelow Heights for another day and night.

The dressing station got no warning that the line had collapsed. They were triaging a fresh cartload of wounded when seven or eight Soviet soldiers crashed into the church. One fired a machine-gun burst at the vaulted ceiling and Erik threw himself to the ground, as did everyone else capable of moving.

Seeing that no one was armed, the Russians relaxed. They went around the room taking watches and rings from those who had them. Then they left.

Erik wondered what would happen next. This was the first time he had been trapped behind enemy lines. Should they abandon the field hospital and try to catch up with their retreating army? Or were their patients safer here?

Dr. Weiss was decisive. "Carry on with your work, everyone," he said.

A few minutes later a Soviet soldier came in with a comrade over his shoulder. Pointing his gun at Weiss, he spoke a rapid stream of Russian. He was in a panic, and his friend was covered in blood.

Weiss replied calmly. In halting Russian he said: "No need for the gun. Put your friend on this table."

The soldier did so, and the team went to work. The soldier kept his rifle pointed at the doctor.

Later in the day, the German patients were marched or carried out and put into the back of a truck, which drove away east. Erik watched Werner Franck disappear, a prisoner of war. As a boy, Erik had often been told the story of his uncle Robert, who had been imprisoned by the Russians during the First World War, and had walked home from Siberia, a journey of four thousand miles. Erik wondered now where Werner would end up.

More wounded Russians were brought in, and the Germans took care of them as they would have for their own men.

Later, as Erik fell into an exhausted sleep, he realized that now he, too, was a prisoner of war.

iv

As the Allied armies closed in on Berlin, the victorious countries began squabbling among themselves at the United Nations conference in San Francisco. Woody would have found it depressing, except that he was more interested in trying to reconnect with Bella Hernandez.

She had been on his mind all through the D-day invasion and the fighting in France, his time in the hospital, and his convalescence. A year ago she had been at the end of her period at Oxford University and planning to do a doctorate at Berkeley, right here in San Francisco. She would probably be living at her parents' home in Pacific Heights, unless she had an apartment near the campus.

Unfortunately, he was having trouble getting a message to her.

His letters were not answered. When he called the number listed in the phone book, a middle-aged woman who he suspected was Bella's mother said with icy courtesy: "She's not at home right now. May I give her a message?" Bella never called back.

She probably had a serious boyfriend. If so he wanted her to tell him. But perhaps her mother was intercepting her mail and not passing on messages.

He should probably give up. He might be making a fool of himself. But that was not his way. He recalled his long, stubborn courtship of Joanne. There seems to be a pattern here, he thought; is it something about me?

Meanwhile, every morning he went with his father to the penthouse at the top of the Fairmont Hotel, where Secretary of State Edward Stettinius held a briefing for the American team at the conference. Stettinius had taken over from Cordell Hull, who was in the hospital. The USA also had a new president, Harry Truman, who had been sworn in on the death of the great Franklin D. Roosevelt. It was a pity, Gus Dewar observed, that at such a crucial moment in world history the United States should be led by two inexperienced newcomers.

Things had begun badly. President Truman had clumsily offended Soviet foreign minister Molotov at a preconference meeting at the White House. Consequently Molotov arrived in San Francisco in a foul mood. He announced he was going home unless the conference agreed immediately to admit Belorussia, Ukraine, and Poland.

No one wanted the USSR to pull out. Without the Soviets, the United Nations were not the United Nations. Most of the American delegation were in favor of compromising with the Communists, but the bow-tied Senator Vandenberg prissily insisted that nothing should be done under pressure from Moscow.

One morning when Woody had a couple of hours to spare, he went to Bella's parents' house.

The swanky neighborhood where they lived was not far from the

Fairmont Hotel on Nob Hill, but Woody was still walking with a cane, so he took a taxi. Their home was a yellow-painted Victorian mansion on Gough Street. The woman who came to the door was too well dressed to be a maid. She gave him a lopsided smile just like Bella's: she had to be the mother. He said politely: "Good morning, ma'am. I'm Woody Dewar. I met Bella Hernandez in London last year and I'd sure like to see her again, if I may."

The smile disappeared. She gave him a long look and said: "So you're him."

Woody had no idea what she was talking about.

"I'm Caroline Hernandez, Isabel's mother," she said. "You'd better come in."

"Thank you."

She did not offer to shake hands, and she was clearly hostile, though there was no clue as to why. However, he was inside the house.

Mrs. Hernandez led Woody into a large, pleasant parlor with a breathtaking ocean view. She pointed to a chair, indicating that he should sit down with a gesture that was barely polite. She sat opposite him and gave him another hard look. "How much time did you spend with Bella in England?" she asked.

"Just a few hours. But I've been thinking about her ever since."

There was another pregnant pause; then she said: "When she went to Oxford, Bella was engaged to be married to Victor Rolandson, a splendid young man she has known most of her life. The Rolandsons are old friends of my husband's and mine—or, at least, they were, until Bella came home and broke off the engagement abruptly."

Woody's heart leaped with hope.

"She would only say she had realized she did not love Victor. I guessed she'd met someone else, and now I know who."

Woody said: "I had no idea she was engaged."

"She was wearing a diamond ring that was pretty hard to miss. Your poor powers of observation have caused a tragedy."

"I'm very sorry," Woody said. Then he told himself to stop being a pussy. "Or rather, I'm not," he said. "I'm very glad she's broken off her engagement, because I think she's absolutely wonderful and I want her for myself."

Mrs. Hernandez did not like that. "You're mighty fresh, young man."

Woody suddenly felt resentful of her condescension. "Mrs. Hernandez, you used the word *tragedy* just now. My fiancée, Joanne, died in my arms at Pearl Harbor. My brother, Chuck, was killed by machine-gun fire on the beach at Bougainville. On D-day I sent Ace Webber and four other young Americans to their deaths for the sake of a bridge in a one-horse town called Eglise-des-Soeurs. I know what tragedy is, ma'am, and it's not a broken engagement."

She was taken aback. He guessed young people did not often stand up to her. She did not reply, but looked a little pale. After a moment she got up and left the room without explanation. Woody was not sure what she expected him to do, but he had not yet seen Bella so he sat tight.

Five minutes later, Bella came in.

Woody stood up, his pulse quickening. Just the sight of her made him smile. She wore a plain pale yellow dress that set off her lustrous dark hair and coffee skin. She would always look good in dramatically simple clothing, he guessed, just like Joanne. He wanted to put his arms around her and crush her soft body to his own, but he waited for a sign from her.

She looked anxious and uncomfortable. "What are you doing here?" she said.

"I came looking for you."

"Why?"

"Because I can't get you out of my mind."

"We don't even know each other."

"Let's put that right, starting today. Will you have dinner with me?"

"I don't know."

He crossed the room to where she stood.

She was startled to see him using the walking stick. "What happened to you?"

"My knee got shot up in France. It's getting better, slowly."

"I'm so sorry."

"Bella, I think you're wonderful. I believe you like me. We're both free of commitments. What's worrying you?"

She gave that lopsided grin that he liked so much. "I guess I'm embarrassed. About what I did, that night in London."

"Is that all?"

"It was a lot, for a first date."

"That kind of thing went on all the time. Not to me, necessarily, but I heard about it. You thought I was going to die."

She nodded. "I've never done anything like that, not even with Victor. I don't know what came over me. And in a public park! I feel like a whore."

"I know exactly what you are," Woody said. "You're a smart, beautiful woman with a big heart. So why don't we forget that mad moment in London, and start getting to know one another like the respectable well-brought-up young people that we are?"

She began to soften. "Can we, really?"

"You bet."

"Okay."

"I'll pick you up at seven?"

"Okay."

That was an exit line, but he hesitated. "I can't tell you how glad I am that I found you again," he said.

She looked him in the eye for the first time. "Oh, Woody, so am I," she said. "So glad!" Then she put her arms around his waist and hugged him.

It was what he had been longing for. He embraced her and put his face into her wonderful hair. They stayed like that for a long minute.

At last she pulled away. "I'll see you at seven," she said.

"You bet."

He left the house in a cloud of happiness.

He went from there straight to a meeting of the steering committee in the Veterans Building next to the opera house. There were forty-six members around the long table, with aides such as Gus Dewar sitting behind them. Woody was an aide to an aide, and sat up against the wall.

The Soviet foreign minister, Molotov, made the first speech. He was not impressive to look at, Woody reflected. With his receding hair, neat mustache, and glasses, he looked like a store clerk, which was what his father had been. But he had survived a long time in Bolshevik politics. A friend of Stalin's since before the revolution, he was the architect of the Nazi-Soviet pact of 1939. He was a hard worker, and was nicknamed Stone Arse because of the long hours he spent at his desk.

He proposed that Belorussia and Ukraine be admitted as original members of the United Nations. These two Soviet republics had borne the brunt of the Nazi invasion, he pointed out, and each had contributed more than a million men to the Red Army. It had been argued that they were not fully independent of Moscow, but the same argument could be applied to Canada and Australia, dominions of the British Empire that had each been given separate membership.

The vote was unanimous. It had all been fixed up in advance, Woody knew. The Latin American countries had threatened to dissent unless Hitler-supporting Argentina was admitted, and that concession had been granted to secure their votes.

Then came a bombshell. The Czech foreign minister, Jan Masaryk, stood up. He was a famous liberal and anti-Nazi who had been on the cover of *Time* magazine in 1944. He proposed that Poland should also be admitted to the UN.

The Americans were refusing to admit Poland until Stalin permitted elections there, and Masaryk as a democrat should have supported that stand, especially as he, too, was trying to create a democracy with Stalin looking over his shoulder. Molotov must have put terrific pressure on Masaryk to get him to betray his ideals in this way. And, indeed, when Masaryk sat down, he wore the expression of one who has eaten something disgusting.

Gus Dewar also looked grim. The prearranged compromises over Belorussia, Ukraine, and Argentina should have ensured that this session went smoothly. But now Molotov had thrown them a curve ball.

Senator Vandenberg, sitting with the American contingent, was outraged. He took out a pen and notepad and began writing furiously.

After a minute he tore the sheet off, beckoned Woody, gave him the note, and said: "Take that to the secretary of state."

Woody went to the table, leaned over Stettinius's shoulder, put the note in front of him, and said: "From Senator Vandenberg, sir."

"Thank you."

Woody returned to his chair up against the wall. My part in history, he thought. He had glanced at the note as he handed it over. Vandenberg had drafted a short, passionate speech rejecting the Czech proposal. Would Stettinius follow the senator's lead?

If Molotov got his way over Poland, then Vandenberg might sabotage the United Nations in the Senate. But if Stettinius took Vandenberg's line now, Molotov might walk out and go home, which would kill off the UN just as effectively.

Woody held his breath.

Stettinius stood up with Vandenberg's note in his hand. "We've just honored our Yalta engagements in behalf of Russia," he said. He meant the commitment made by the USA to support Belorussia and Ukraine. "There are other Yalta obligations which equally require allegiance." He was using the words Vandenberg had written. "One calls for a new and representative Polish provisional government."

There was a murmur of shock around the room. Stettinius was going up against Molotov. Woody glanced at Vandenberg. He was purring.

"Until that happens," Stettinius went on, "the conference cannot, in good conscience, recognize the Lublin government." He looked directly at Molotov and quoted Vandenberg's exact words. "It would be a sordid exhibition of bad faith."

Molotov looked incandescent.

The British foreign secretary, Anthony Eden, unfolded his lanky figure and stood up to support Stettinius. His tone was faultlessly courteous, but his words were scathing. "My government has no way of knowing whether the Polish people support their provisional government," he said, "because our Soviet allies refuse to let British observers into Poland."

Woody sensed the meeting turning against Molotov. The Russian clearly had the same impression. He was conferring with his aides loudly enough for Woody to hear the fury in his voice. But would he walk out?

The Belgian foreign minister, bald and podgy with a double chin, proposed a compromise, a motion expressing the hope that the new Polish government might be organized in time to be represented here in San Francisco before the end of the conference.

Everyone looked at Molotov. He was being offered a face-saver. But would he accept it?

He still looked angry. However, he gave a slight but unmistakable nod of assent.

And the crisis was over.

Well, Woody thought, two victories in one day. Things are looking up.

V

Carla went out to queue for water.

There had been no water in the taps for two days. Luckily, Berlin's housewives had discovered that every few blocks there were old-fashioned street pumps, long disused, connected to underground wells. They were rusty and creaky but, amazingly, they still worked. So every morning now the women stood in line, holding their buckets and jugs.

The air raids had stopped, presumably because the enemy was on the point of entering the city. But it was still dangerous to be on the street, because the Red Army's artillery was shelling. Carla was not sure why they bothered. Much of the city had gone. Whole blocks and even larger areas had been completely flattened. All utilities were cut off. No trains or buses ran. Thousands were homeless, perhaps millions. The city was one huge refugee camp. But the shelling went on. Most people spent all day in their cellars or in public air raid shelters, but they had to come out for water.

On the radio, shortly before the electricity went off permanently, the

BBC had announced that the Sachsenhausen concentration camp had been liberated by the Red Army. Sachsenhausen was north of Berlin, so clearly the Soviets, coming from the east, were encircling the city instead of marching straight in. Carla's mother, Maud, deduced that the Russians wanted to keep out the American, British, French, and Canadian forces rapidly approaching from the west. She had quoted Lenin: "Who controls Berlin, controls Germany; and who controls Germany, controls Europe."

Yet the German army had not given up. Outnumbered, outgunned, short of ammunition and fuel, and half-starved, they slogged on. Again and again their leaders hurled them at overwhelming enemy forces, and again and again they obeyed orders, fought with spirit and courage, and died in their hundreds of thousands. Among them were the two men Carla loved: her brother, Erik, and her boyfriend, Werner. She had no idea where they were fighting or even whether they were alive.

Carla had wound up the spy ring. The fighting was deteriorating into chaos. Battle plans meant little. Secret intelligence from Berlin was of small value to the conquering Soviets. It was no longer worth the risk. The spies had burned their codebooks and hidden their radio transmitters in the rubble of bombed buildings. They had agreed never to speak of their work. They had been brave, they had shortened the war, and they had saved lives, but it was too much to expect the defeated German people to see things that way. Their courage would remain forever secret.

While Carla waited her turn at the tap, a Hitler Youth tank-hunting squad went past, heading east, toward the fighting. There were two men in their fifties and a dozen teenage boys, all on bicycles. Strapped to the front of each bicycle were two of the new one-shot antitank weapons called *Panzerfäuste*. The uniforms were too large for the boys, and their oversize helmets would have looked comical if their plight had not been so pathetic. They were off to fight the Red Army.

They were going to die.

Carla looked away as they passed: she did not want to remember their faces.

As she was filling her bucket, the woman behind her in line, Frau Reichs, spoke to her quietly, so that no one else could hear: "You're a friend of the doctor's wife, aren't you?"

Carla tensed. Frau Reichs was obviously talking about Hannelore Rothmann. The doctor had disappeared along with the mental patients from the Jewish Hospital. Hannelore's son, Rudi, had thrown away his yellow star and joined those Jews living clandestinely, called U-boats in Berlin slang. But Hannelore, not herself Jewish, was still at the old house.

For twelve years a question such as the one just asked—are you a friend of a Jew's wife?—had been an accusation. What was it today? Carla did not know. Frau Reichs was only a nodding acquaintance: she could not be trusted.

Carla turned off the tap. "Dr. Rothmann was our family physician when I was a child," she said guardedly. "Why?"

The other woman took her place at the standpipe and began to fill a large can that had once held cooking oil. "Frau Rothmann has been taken away," she said. "I thought you'd like to know."

It was commonplace. People were "taken away" all the time. But when it happened to someone close to you, it came as a blow to the heart.

There was no point in trying to find out what had happened to them—in fact it was downright dangerous: people who inquired about disappearances tended to disappear themselves. All the same, Carla had to ask. "Do you know where they took her?"

This time there was an answer. "The Schul Strasse transit camp." Carla felt hopeful. "It's in the old Jewish Hospital, in Wedding. Do you know it?"

"Yes, I do." Carla sometimes worked at the hospital, unofficially and illegally, so she knew that the government had taken over one of the hospital buildings, the pathology lab, and surrounded it with barbed wire.

"I hope she's all right," said the other woman. "She was good to me when my Steffi was ill." She turned off the tap and walked away with her can of water.

Carla hurried away in the opposite direction, heading for home.

She had to do something about Hannelore. It had always been nearly impossible to get anyone out of a camp, but now that everything was breaking down, perhaps there might be a way.

She took the bucket into the house and gave it to Ada.

Maud had gone to queue for food rations. Carla changed into her nurse's uniform, thinking it might help. She explained to Ada where she was going and left again.

She had to walk to Wedding. It was two or three miles. She wondered if it was worth it. Even if she found Hannelore, she probably would not be able to help her. But then she thought of Eva in London and Rudi in hiding somewhere here in Berlin: how terrible it would be if they lost their mother in the last hours of the war. She had to try.

The military police were on the streets, stopping people and demanding papers. They worked in threes, forming summary courts, and were mainly interested in men of fighting age. They did not bother Carla in her nurse's uniform.

It was strange that in this blasted cityscape the apple and cherry trees were gorgeous with white and pink blossoms, and that in the quiet moments between explosions she could hear the birds singing as optimistically as they did every spring.

To her horror she saw several men hanged from lampposts, some in uniform. Most of the bodies had a card hanging around the neck saying COWARD or DESERTER. These had been found guilty by those three-man street courts, she knew. Was there not already enough killing to satisfy the Nazis? It made her want to weep.

She was forced to take shelter from artillery bombardments three times. On the last occasion, when she was only a few hundred yards from the hospital, the Soviets and the Germans seemed to be fighting only a few streets away. The shooting was so heavy that Carla was tempted to turn back. Hannelore was probably doomed, and might already be dead: Why should Carla add her own life to the toll? But she went on anyway.

It was evening when she reached her destination. The hospital was in Iranische Strasse, on the corner of Schul Strasse. The trees lining the streets were in new leaf. The laboratory building, which had been turned into a transit camp, was guarded. Carla considered going up to the guard and explaining her mission, but it seemed an unpromising strategy. She wondered if she might slip inside from the tunnel system.

She went into the main building. The hospital was functioning. All the patients had been moved into the basements and tunnels. The staff were working by the light of oil lamps. Carla could tell by the smell that the toilets were not flushing. Water was being carried in buckets from an old well in the garden.

Surprisingly, soldiers were bringing wounded comrades in for help. Suddenly they did not care that the doctors and nurses might be Jewish.

She followed a tunnel under the garden to the basement of the laboratory. As she expected, the door was guarded. However, the young Gestapo man looked at her uniform and waved her through without questioning her. Perhaps he no longer saw any point in his job.

She was inside the camp now. She wondered whether it would be as easy to get out.

The smell here was worse, and she soon saw why. The basement was overcrowded. Hundreds of people were packed into four storerooms. They sat or lay on the floor, the lucky ones having a wall to lean against. They were dirty, smelly, and exhausted, and they looked at her with dull uninterested gazes.

She found Hannelore after a few minutes.

The doctor's wife had never been beautiful, but she had once been a statuesque woman with a strong face. Now she was gaunt, like most people, and her hair was gray and lifeless. She was hollow-cheeked and lined with strain.

She was talking to an adolescent who was at the age when a girl can seem too voluptuous for her years, having womanly breasts and hips but the face of a child. The girl was sitting on the floor, crying, and Hannelore was kneeling beside her, holding her hand and speaking in a low, soothing voice.

When Hannelore saw Carla, she stood up, saying: "Good God! Why are you in here?"

"I thought maybe if I tell them you're not Jewish, they might let you go."

"That was brave."

"Your husband saved many lives. Someone ought to save yours."

For a moment, Carla thought Hannelore was going to cry. Her face seemed about to crumple. Then she blinked and shook her head. "This is Rebecca Rosen," she said in a controlled voice. "Her parents were killed by a shell today."

Carla said: "I'm so sorry, Rebecca."

The girl did not speak.

Carla said: "How old are you, Rebecca?"

"Nearly fourteen."

"You're going to have to be a grown-up now."

"Why didn't I die, too?" Rebecca said. "I was right beside them. I should have died. Now I'm all alone."

"You're not alone," Carla said briskly. "We're with you." She turned back to Hannelore. "Who's in charge here?"

"His name is Walter Dobberke."

"I'm going to tell him he must let you go."

"He's left for the day. And his second-in-command is a sergeant with the brains of a warthog. But look, here comes Gisela. She's Dobberke's mistress."

The young woman walking into the room was pretty, with long fair hair and creamy skin. No one looked at her. She wore a defiant expression.

Hannelore said: "She has sex with him on the bed in the electrocardiogram room upstairs. She gets extra food in exchange. No one will speak to her except me. I just don't think we can judge people for the compromises they make. We are living in hell, after all."

Carla was not so sure. She would not befriend a Jewish girl who slept with a Nazi.

Gisela met Hannelore's eye and came over. "He's had new orders," she said, speaking so quietly that Carla had to strain to hear her. Then she hesitated.

Hannelore said: "Well? What are the orders?"

Gisela's voice fell to a whisper. "To shoot everyone here."

Carla felt a cold hand grasp her heart. All these people—including Hannelore and young Rebecca.

"Walter doesn't want to do it," Gisela said. "He's not a bad man, really."

Hannelore spoke with fatalistic calm. "When is he supposed to kill us?"

"Immediately. But he wants to destroy the records first. Hans-Peter and Martin are putting the files into the furnace right now. It's a long job, so we have a few hours left. Maybe the Red Army will get here in time to save us."

"And maybe they won't," Hannelore said crisply. "Is there any way we can persuade him to disobey his orders? For God's sake, the war is almost over!"

"I used to be able to talk him into anything," Gisela said sadly. "But he's getting tired of me now. You know what men are like."

"But he should be thinking of his own future. Any day now the Allies will be in charge here. They will punish Nazi crimes."

Gisela said: "If we're all dead, who's going to accuse him?"

"I will," said Carla.

The other two stared at her, not speaking.

Carla realized that even though she was not Jewish, she, too, would be shot, to prevent her bearing witness.

Casting about for ideas, she said: "Perhaps, if Dobberke spared us, it would help him with the Allies."

"That's a thought," said Hannelore. "We could all sign a declaration saying that he saved our lives."

Carla looked inquiringly at Gisela. Her expression was dubious, but she said: "He might do it."

Hannelore looked around. "There's Hilde," she said. "She acts as a secretary for Dobberke." She called the woman over and explained the plan.

"I'll type out release documents for everyone," Hilde said. "We'll ask him to sign them before we give him the declaration."

There were no guards within the basement area, just at the ground-floor door and the tunnel, so the prisoners could move around freely inside. Hilde went into the room that served as Dobberke's underground office. She typed the declaration first. Hannelore and Carla went around the basement explaining the plan and getting everyone to sign. Meanwhile Hilde typed the release documents.

By the time they finished, it was the middle of the night. There was no more they could do until Dobberke showed up in the morning.

Carla lay on the floor next to Rebecca Rosen. There was nowhere else to sleep.

After a while Rebecca began to cry quietly.

Carla was not sure what to do. She wanted to give comfort, but no words came. What did you say to a child who had just seen both her parents killed? The muffled weeping continued. In the end Carla rolled over and put her arms around Rebecca.

She knew immediately that she had done the right thing. Rebecca cuddled up to her, head on her breast. Carla patted her back as if she were a baby. Slowly the sobs eased and eventually Rebecca fell asleep.

Carla did not sleep. She spent the night making imaginary speeches to the camp commandant. Sometimes she appealed to his better nature, sometimes she threatened him with Allied justice, sometimes she argued from his own self-interest.

She tried not to think about the process of being shot. Erik had explained to her how the Nazis executed people twelve at a time in Russia. She supposed they would have an efficient system here, too. It was hard to imagine. Perhaps that was just as well.

She could probably escape shooting if she left the camp right now, or first thing in the morning. She was not an inmate, nor a Jew, and her papers were perfectly in order. She could go out the way she came in, dressed in her nurse's uniform. But that would mean abandoning both Hannelore and Rebecca. She could not bring herself to do that, no matter how badly she longed to get out of here.

The fighting in the streets outside continued until the small hours; then there was a short pause. It began again at dawn. Now it was close enough for her to hear machine-gun fire as well as artillery.

Early in the morning the guards brought an urn of watery soup and a sack of bread, all discarded parts of stale loaves. Carla drank the soup and ate the bread and then, reluctantly, used the toilet, which was unspeakably dirty.

With Hannelore, Gisela, and Hilde she went up to the ground floor to wait for Dobberke. The shelling had resumed, and they were in danger every second, but they wanted to confront him the moment he arrived.

He did not appear at his usual hour. He was normally punctual, Hilde said. Perhaps he had been delayed by the fighting in the streets. He might have been killed, of course. Carla hoped not. His second-in-command, Sergeant Ehrenstein, was too stupid to argue with.

When Dobberke was an hour late, Carla began to lose hope.

After another hour, he arrived.

"What's this?" he said when he saw the four women waiting in the hall. "A mothers' meeting?"

Hannelore replied: "All the prisoners have signed a declaration saying you saved their lives. It may save *your* life, if you accept our terms."

"Don't be ridiculous," he said.

Carla spoke up. "According to the BBC, the United Nations has a list of the names of Nazi officers who have taken part in mass murders. In a week's time you could be on trial. Wouldn't you like to have a signed declaration that you spared people?"

"Listening to the BBC is a crime," he said.

"Though not as serious as murder."

Hilde had a file folder in her hand. She said: "I have typed release orders for all the prisoners here. If you sign them, you can have the declaration."

"I could just take it from you."

"No one will believe in your innocence if we're all dead."

Dobberke was angered by the situation he found himself in, but not confident enough just to walk away. "I could shoot the four of you for insolence," he said.

Carla spoke impatiently. "This is what defeat is like," she said. "Get used to it."

His face darkened with anger, and she realized she had gone too far. She wished she could take back her words. She stared at Dobberke's furious expression, trying not to let her fear show.

At that moment a shell landed outside the building. The doors rattled and a window smashed. They all ducked instinctively, but no one was hurt.

When they straightened up, Dobberke's face had changed. Rage was replaced by something like disgusted resignation. Carla's heartbeat quickened. Had he given up?

Sergeant Ehrenstein ran in. "No one hurt, sir," he reported.

"Very good, Sergeant."

Ehrenstein was about to go out again when Dobberke called him back. "This camp is now closed," Dobberke said.

Carla held her breath.

"Closed, sir?" There was aggression as well as surprise in the sergeant's voice.

"New orders. Tell the men to go . . ." Dobberke hesitated. "Tell them to report to the railway bunker at Friedrich Strasse station."

Carla knew Dobberke was making this up, and Ehrenstein seemed to suspect it, too. "When, sir?"

"Immediately."

"Immediately." Ehrenstein paused, as if the word *immediately* required further elucidation.

Dobberke stared him out.

"Very good, sir," said the sergeant. "I'll tell the men." He went out.

Carla felt a surge of triumph, but told herself she was not yet free.

Dobberke said to Hilde: "Show me the declaration."

Hilde opened her folder. There were a dozen sheets, all with the same wording typed at the top, the rest of the space covered with signatures. She handed them over.

Dobberke folded the papers and stuffed them in his pocket.

Hilde placed the release orders in front of him. "Sign these, please."

"You don't need release orders," Dobberke said. "And I don't have time to sign my name hundreds of times."

Carla said: "The police are on the streets. They're hanging people from the lampposts. We need papers."

He patted his pocket. "They'll hang me if they find this declaration." He went to the door.

Gisela cried: "Take me with you, Walter!"

He turned to her. "Take you?" he said. "What would my wife say?" He went out and slammed the door.

Gisela burst into tears.

Carla went to the door, opened it, and watched Dobberke stride away. There were no other Gestapo men in sight: they had already obeyed his orders and abandoned the camp.

The commandant reached the street and broke into a run.

He left the gate open.

Hannelore was standing beside Carla, looking out with incredulity.

"We're free, I think," said Carla.

"We must tell the others."

Hilde said: "I'll tell them." She went down the basement stairs.

Carla and Hannelore walked fearfully along the path that led from the laboratory entrance to the open gate. There they hesitated and looked at one another.

Hannelore said: "We're frightened of freedom."

Behind them a girlish voice said: "Carla, don't go without me!" It was Rebecca, running down the path, her breasts bouncing under a grubby blouse.

Carla sighed. I've acquired a child, she thought. I don't feel ready to be a mother. But what can I do?

"Come on, then," she said. "But be ready to run." She realized she did not need to worry about Rebecca's agility: the girl could undoubtedly run faster than either Carla or Hannelore.

They crossed the hospital garden to the main gate. There they paused and looked up and down Iranische Strasse. It seemed quiet. They crossed the road and ran to the corner. As Carla looked along Schul Strasse, she heard a burst of machine-gun fire and saw that farther up the street there was a firefight. She saw German troops retreating toward her and Red Army soldiers coming after them.

She looked around. There was nowhere to hide except behind trees, and that was hardly any protection at all.

A shell landed in the middle of the road fifty yards away and exploded. Carla felt the blast, but she was not hurt.

Without conferring, all three women ran back inside the hospital grounds.

They returned to the laboratory building. Some of the other prisoners were standing just inside the barbed wire, as if not quite daring to come out.

Carla said to them: "The basement stinks, but right now it's the safest place." She went inside the building and down the stairs, and most of the others followed.

She wondered how long she would have to stay here. The German army must give up, but when? Somehow she could not imagine Hitler agreeing to surrender under any circumstances. The man's whole life had been based on arrogantly shouting that he was the boss. How could such a man admit that he had been wrong, stupid, and wicked? That he had murdered millions and caused his country to be bombed to ruins? That he would go down in history as the most evil man who had ever lived? He could not. He would go mad, or die of shame, or put a pistol in his mouth and pull the trigger.

But how long would it take? Another day? Another week? Longer?

There was a shout from upstairs. "They're here! The Russians are here!"

Then Carla heard heavy boots clattering down the steps. Where had the Russians got such good boots? From the Americans?

Then they were in the room, four, six, eight, nine men with dirty faces, carrying submachine guns with drum magazines, ready to kill as quick as look at you. They seemed to take up a lot of room. People shrank away from them, even though they were the liberators.

The soldiers took in their surroundings. They saw that they were in no danger from the emaciated prisoners, mainly female. They lowered their guns. Some moved into the adjoining rooms.

A tall soldier pulled up his left sleeve. He was wearing six or seven wristwatches. He shouted something in Russian, pointing at the watches with the stock of his gun. Carla thought she knew what he was saying, but she could hardly believe it. The man then grabbed an elderly woman, took her hand, and pointed to her wedding ring.

Hannelore said: "Are they going to rob us of what little the Nazis didn't steal?"

They were. The tall soldier looked frustrated and tried to pull off the woman's ring. When she realized what he wanted, she took it off herself and gave it to him.

The Russian took it, nodded, then pointed all around the room.

Hannelore stepped forward. "These people are prisoners!" she said in German. "Jews, and families of Jews, persecuted by the Nazis!"

Whether he understood her or not, he took no notice, but just pointed insistently at the watches on his arm.

Those few who had any valuables that had not been stolen or traded for food handed them over.

Liberation by the Red Army was not going to be the happy event many people had been looking forward to.

But there was worse to come.

The tall soldier pointed at Rebecca.

She cringed away from him and tried to hide behind Carla.

A second man, small with fair hair, grabbed Rebecca and pulled her away. Rebecca screamed, and the small man grinned as if he liked the sound.

Carla had a dreadful feeling she knew what was going to happen next.

The short man held Rebecca firmly while the tall man squeezed her breasts roughly, then said something that made them both laugh.

There were cries of protest from the people all around.

The tall man leveled his gun. Carla was terrified he would fire. He would kill and wound dozens of people if he pulled the trigger of a submachine gun in a crowded room.

Everyone else realized the danger, and they went quiet.

The two soldiers backed toward the door, taking Rebecca with them. She yelled and struggled, but she could not break the small soldier's grip.

When they reached the door, Carla stepped forward and cried: "Wait!"

Something in her voice made them stop.

"She's too young," Carla said. "Only thirteen!" She did not know whether they understood her. She held up two hands, showing ten fingers, then one hand showing three. "Thirteen!"

The tall soldier seemed to understand her. He grinned and said in German: "*Frau ist Frau*." A woman is a woman.

Carla found herself saying: "You need a real woman." She walked slowly forward. "Take me, instead." She tried to smile seductively. "I'm not a child. I know what to do." She came close, close enough to smell the rank odor of a man who had not bathed for months. Trying to conceal her distaste, she lowered her voice and said: "I understand what a man wants." She touched her own breast suggestively. "Forget the child."

The tall soldier looked again at Rebecca. Her eyes were red with weeping and her nose was running, which helpfully made her look more like a child, less like a woman.

He looked back at Carla.

She said: "There's a bed upstairs. Shall I show you where?"

Again she was not sure he understood the words, but she took him by the hand and he followed her up the steps to the ground floor.

The fair one let go of Rebecca and came after.

Now that she had succeeded, Carla regretted her bravado. She wanted to break away from the Russians and run. But they would probably shoot her down, then go back to Rebecca. Carla thought of the devastated child who had lost both parents yesterday. To be raped the next day would surely destroy her spirit forever. Carla had to save her.

I will not be smashed by this, Carla thought. I can live through it. I will be myself again afterward.

She led them to the electrocardiogram room. She felt cold, as if her heart were freezing and her thoughts becoming sluggish. Next to the bed was a can of the grease used by the doctors to improve the conductivity of the terminals. She pulled off her underpants, then took a large dab of grease and pushed it into her vagina. That might save her from bleeding.

She had to keep her act up. She turned back to the two soldiers. To her horror, three more followed them into the room. She tried to smile, but she could not.

She lay on her back and parted her legs.

The tall one knelt between her knees. He ripped open her uniform blouse to expose her breasts. She could see that he was manipulating himself, making his penis erect. He lay on top and entered her. She told herself this had no connection with what she and Werner had done together.

She turned her head to the side, but the soldier grasped her chin and turned her face back, making her look at him as he thrust inside her. She closed her eyes. She felt him kissing her, trying to force his tongue into her mouth. His breath smelled like rotting meat. When she clamped her mouth shut, he punched her face. She cried out and opened her bruised lips to him. She tried to think how much worse this would have been for a thirteen-year-old virgin.

The soldier grunted and ejaculated inside her. She tried not to let her disgust show on her face.

He climbed off, and the fair-haired one took his place.

Carla tried to close down her mind, to make her body into something detached, a machine, an object that had nothing to do with her. This one did not want to kiss her, but he sucked her breasts and bit her nipples, and when she cried out in pain, he seemed pleased and did it harder.

Time passed, and he ejaculated.

Then another one got on top.

She realized that when this was over, she would not be able to bathe or shower, for there was no running water in the city. That thought pushed her over the top. Their fluids would be inside her, their smell would be on her skin, their saliva in her mouth, and she would have no effective way to wash. Somehow that was worse than everything else. Her courage failed her, and she started to cry.

The third soldier satisfied himself; then the fourth lay on her.

CHAPTER TWENTY

1945 (II)

Adolf Hitler killed himself on Monday, April 30, 1945, in his bunker in Berlin. Exactly a week later in London, at twenty to eight in the evening, the Ministry of Information announced that Germany had surrendered. A holiday was declared for the following day, Tuesday, May 8.

Daisy sat at the window of her apartment in Piccadilly, watching the celebrations. The street was thronged with people, making it almost impassable to cars and buses. The girls would kiss any man in uniform, and thousands of lucky servicemen were taking full advantage. By early afternoon many people were drunk. Through the open window Daisy could hear distant singing, and guessed that the crowd outside Buckingham Palace was doing "Land of Hope and Glory." She shared their happiness, but Lloyd was somewhere in France or Germany, and he was the only soldier she wanted to kiss. She prayed he had not been killed in the last few hours of the war.

Lloyd's sister, Millie, showed up with her two children. Millie's husband, Abe Avery, was also with the army somewhere. She and the children had come to the West End to join in the celebrations, and they took a break from the crowds at Daisy's place. The Leckwith home in Aldgate had long been a place of refuge for Daisy, and she was glad to have a chance to reciprocate. She made tea for Millie—her staff were out there celebrating—and poured orange juice for the children. Lennie was five now and Pammie three.

Since Abe had been conscripted, Millie had been running his leather wholesaling business. His sister, Naomi Avery, was the bookkeeper, but Millie did the selling. "It's going to change now," Millie said. "For the past five years the demand has been for tough hides for boots and shoes. Now we're going to need softer leathers, calf and pigskin, for handbags and briefcases. When the luxury market comes back, there'll be decent money to be made at last."

Daisy recalled that her father had the same way of thinking as Millie. Lev, too, was always looking ahead, searching out the opportunities.

Eva Murray appeared next, with her four children in tow. Jamie, aged eight, organized a game of hide-and-seek, and the apartment became like a kindergarten. Eva's husband, Jimmy, now a colonel, was also somewhere in France or Germany, and Eva was suffering the same agonies of anxiety as Daisy and Millie.

"We'll hear from them, any day now," Millie said. "And then it will really be all over."

Eva was also desperate for news of her family in Berlin. However, she thought it might be weeks or months before anyone could learn the fates of individual Germans in the postwar chaos. "I wonder whether my children will ever know my parents," she said sadly.

At five o'clock Daisy made a pitcher of martinis. Millie went into the kitchen and, with characteristic speed and efficiency, produced a plate of sardines on toast to eat with the drinks. Eth and Bernie arrived just as Daisy was making a second round.

Bernie told Daisy that Lennie could read already, and Pammie could sing the national anthem. Ethel said: "Typical grandfather, thinks there have never been bright children before," but Daisy could tell that in her heart she was just as proud of them.

Feeling relaxed and happy halfway down her second martini, she looked around at the disparate group gathered in her home. They had paid her the compliment of coming to her door without an invitation, knowing they would be welcomed. They belonged to her, and she to them. They were, she realized, her family.

She felt very blessed.

ii

Woody Dewar sat outside Leo Shapiro's office, looking through a sheaf of photographs. They were the pictures he had taken at Pearl Harbor, in the hour before Joanne died. The film had stayed in his camera for months, but eventually he had developed it and printed the pictures. Looking at them had made him so sad that he had put them in a drawer in his bedroom at the Washington apartment and left them there.

But this was a time for change.

He would never forget Joanne, but he was in love again, at last. He adored Bella and she felt the same. When they parted, at the Oakland train station outside San Francisco, he had told her that he loved her, and she had said: "I love you, too." He was going to ask her to marry him. He would have done so already but it seemed too soon—less than three months—and he did not want to give her hostile parents a pretext for objecting.

Also, he needed to make a decision about his future.

He did not want to go into politics.

This was going to shock his parents, he knew. They had always assumed he would follow in his father's footsteps and end up as the third Senator Dewar. He had gone along with this assumption unthinkingly. But in the war, and especially while in hospital, he had asked himself what he *really* wanted to do, if he survived, and the answer was not politics.

This was a good time to leave. His father had achieved his life's ambition. The Senate had debated the United Nations. It was at a similar point in history that the old League of Nations had foundered, a painful memory for Gus Dewar. But Senator Vandenberg had spoken passionately in favor, speaking of "the dearest dream of mankind," and the UN Charter had been ratified by eighty-nine votes to two. The job was done. Woody would not be letting his father down by quitting now.

He hoped Gus would see it that way, too.

Shapiro opened his office door and beckoned. Woody stood up and went in.

Shapiro was younger than Woody had expected, somewhere in his thirties. He was Washington bureau chief for the National Press Agency. He sat behind his desk and said: "What can I do for Senator Dewar's son?"

"I'd like to show you some photographs, if I may."

"All right."

Woody spread his pictures on Shapiro's desk.

"Is this Pearl Harbor?" Shapiro said.

"Yes. December seventh, nineteen forty-one."

"My God."

Woody was looking at them upside down, but still they brought tears to his eyes. There was Joanne, looking so beautiful, and Chuck, grinning happily to be with his family and Eddie. Then the planes coming over, the bombs and torpedoes dropping from their bellies, the black-smoke explosions on the ships, and the sailors scrambling over the sides, dropping into the sea, swimming for their lives.

"This is your father," Shapiro said. "And your mother. I recognize them."

"And my fiancée, who died a few minutes later. My brother, who was killed at Bougainville. And my brother's best friend."

"These are fantastic photographs! How much do you want for them?"

"I don't want money," Woody said.

Shapiro looked up in surprise.

Woody said: "I want a job."

iii

Fifteen days after VE Day, Winston Churchill called a general election.

The Leckwith family were taken by surprise. Like most people, Ethel and Bernie had thought Churchill would wait until the Japanese surrendered. The Labour leader, Clement Attlee, had suggested an election in October. Churchill wrong-footed them all.

Major Lloyd Williams was released from the army to stand as Labour candidate for Hoxton, in the East End of London. He was full of eager enthusiasm for the future envisioned by his party. Fascism had been vanquished, and now British people could create a society that combined freedom with welfare. Labour had a well-thought-out plan for avoiding the catastrophes of the last twenty years: universal comprehensive unemployment insurance to help families through hard times, economic planning to prevent another Depression, and the United Nations organization to keep the peace.

"You don't stand a chance," said his stepfather, Bernie, in the kitchen of the house in Aldgate on Monday, June 4. Bernie's pessimism was the more convincing for being so uncharacteristic. "They'll vote Tory because Churchill won the war," he went on gloomily. "It was the same with Lloyd George in 1918."

Lloyd was about to reply, but Daisy got in first. "The war wasn't won by the free market and capitalist enterprise," she said indignantly. "It was people working together and sharing the burdens, everybody doing his bit. That's socialism!"

Lloyd loved her most when she was passionate, but he was more deliberate. "We already have measures that the old Tories would have condemned as Bolshevism: government control of railways, mines, and shipping, for example, all brought in by Churchill. And Ernie Bevin has been in charge of economic planning all through the war."

Bernie shook his head knowingly, an old-man gesture that irritated Lloyd. "People vote with their hearts, not brains," he said. "They'll want to show their gratitude."

"Well, no point sitting here arguing with you," Lloyd said. "I'm going to argue with voters instead."

He and Daisy took a bus a few stops north to the Black Lion pub in Shoreditch, where they met up with a canvassing team from the Hoxton Constituency Labour Party. In fact canvassing was not about arguing with voters, Lloyd knew. Its main purpose was to identify supporters, so that on election day the party machine could make sure they all went to the polling station. Firm Labour supporters were noted; firm supporters of other parties were crossed off. Only people who had not yet made up their minds were worth more than a few seconds: they were offered the chance to speak to the candidate.

Lloyd got some negative reactions. "Major, eh?" one woman said. "My Alf is a corporal. He says the officers nearly lost us the war."

There were also accusations of nepotism. "Aren't you the son of the M.P. for Aldgate? What is this, a hereditary monarchy?"

He remembered his mother's advice. "You never win a vote by proving the constituent a fool. Be charming, be modest, and don't lose your temper. If a voter is hostile and rude, thank him for his time and go away. You'll leave him thinking maybe he misjudged you."

Working-class voters were strongly Labour. A lot of people told Lloyd that Attlee and Bevin had done a good job during the war. The waverers were mostly middle-class. When people said that Churchill had won the war, Lloyd quoted Attlee's gentle put-down: "It wasn't a one-man government, and it wasn't a one-man war."

Churchill had described Attlee as a modest man with much to be modest about. Attlee's wit was less brutal, and for that reason more effective—at least, Lloyd thought so.

A couple of constituents mentioned the sitting M.P. for Hoxton, a Liberal, and said they would vote for him because he had helped them solve some problem. Members of Parliament were often called upon by constituents who felt they were being treated unjustly by the government, an employer, or a neighbor. It was time-consuming work but it won votes.

Overall, Lloyd could not tell which way public opinion was leaning.

Only one constituent mentioned Daisy. The man came to the door with his mouth full of food. Lloyd said: "Good evening, Mr. Perkinson, I understand you wanted to ask me something."

"Your fiancée was a Fascist," the man said, chewing.

Lloyd guessed he had been reading the *Daily Mail,* which had run a spiteful story about Lloyd and Daisy under the headline THE SOCIALIST AND THE VISCOUNTESS.

Lloyd nodded. "She was briefly fooled by Fascism, like many others."

"How can a socialist marry a Fascist?"

Lloyd looked around, spotted Daisy, and beckoned her. "Mr. Perkinson here is asking me about my fiancée being an ex-Fascist."

"Pleased to meet you, Mr. Perkinson." Daisy shook the man's hand. "I quite understand your concern. My first husband was a Fascist in the thirties, and I supported him."

Perkinson nodded. He probably believed a wife should take her views from her husband.

"How foolish we were," Daisy went on. "But, when the war came, my first husband joined the RAF and fought against the Nazis as bravely as anyone."

"Is that a fact?"

"Last year he was flying a Typhoon over France, strafing a German troop train, when he was shot down and killed. So I'm a war widow."

Perkinson swallowed his food. "I'm sorry to hear that, of course."

But Daisy had not finished. "For myself, I lived in London throughout the war. I drove an ambulance all through the Blitz."

"Very brave of you, I'm sure."

"Well, I just hope you think that my late husband and I both paid our dues."

"I don't know about that," Perkinson said sulkily.

"We won't take up any more of your time," said Lloyd. "Thank you for explaining your views to me. Good evening."

As they walked away, Daisy said: "I don't think we won him around."

"You never do," Lloyd said. "But he's seen both sides of the story now, which might make him a bit less vociferous about it, later this evening, when he talks about us in the pub."

"Hmm."

Lloyd sensed he had failed to reassure Daisy.

Canvassing finished early, for tonight the first of the radio election broadcasts would be aired on the BBC, and all party workers would be listening. Churchill had the privilege of making the first one.

On the bus home, Daisy said: "I'm worried. I'm an election liability to you."

"No candidate is perfect," Lloyd said. "It's how you deal with your weaknesses that matters."

"I don't want to be your weakness. Perhaps I should stay out of the way."

"On the contrary, I want everyone to know all about you from the start. If you are a liability, I will get out of politics."

"No, no! I'd hate to think I made you give up your ambitions."

"It won't come to that," he said, but once again he could see that he had not succeeded in assuaging her anxiety.

Back in Nutley Street, the Leckwith family sat around the radio in the kitchen. Daisy held Lloyd's hand. "I came here a lot while you were away," she said. "We used to listen to swing music and talk about you."

The thought made Lloyd feel very lucky.

Churchill came on. The familiar rasp was stirring. For five grim years that voice had given people strength and hope and courage. Lloyd felt despairing: even he was tempted to vote for this man.

"My friends," the prime minister said. "I must tell you that a socialist policy is abhorrent to the British ideas of freedom."

Well, that was routine knockabout stuff. All new ideas were condemned as foreign imports. But what would Churchill offer people? Labour had a plan, but what did the Conservatives propose?

"Socialism is inseparably interwoven with totalitarianism," Churchill said.

Lloyd's mother, Ethel, said: "Surely he's not going to pretend we're like the Nazis?"

"I think he is, though," Bernie said. "He'll say we've defeated the enemy abroad, now we must defeat the enemy in our midst. Standard conservative tactic."

"People won't believe that," Ethel said.

Lloyd said: "Hush!"

Churchill said: "A socialist state, once thoroughly completed in all its details and its aspects, could not afford to suffer opposition."

"This is outrageous," said Ethel.

"But I will go farther," said Churchill. "I declare to you, from the bottom of my heart, that no socialist system can be established without a political police."

"Political police?" Ethel said indignantly. "Where is he getting this stuff from?"

Bernie said: "This is good, in a way. He can't find anything to criticize in our manifesto. Therefore he's attacking us for things we aren't actually proposing to do. Bloody liar."

Lloyd shouted: "Listen!"

Churchill said: "They would have to fall back on some form of Gestapo."

Suddenly they were all on their feet, shouting protests. The prime minister was drowned out. "Bastard!" Bernie yelled, shaking his fist at the Marconi radio set. "Bastard, bastard!"

When they had quietened down, Ethel said: "Is that going to be their campaign? Just lies about us?"

"It bloody well is," said Bernie.

Lloyd said: "But will people believe it?"

iv

In southern New Mexico, not far from El Paso, there is a desert called Jornada del Muerto, the Voyage of the Dead. All day long the cruel sun beats down on needle-thorn mesquite and sword-leafed yucca plants. The inhabitants are scorpions and rattlesnakes and fire ants and tarantula spiders. Here the men of the Manhattan Project tested the most dreadful weapon the human race had ever devised.

Greg Peshkov was with the scientists watching from ten thousand yards away. He had two hopes: first, that the bomb would work, and second, that ten thousand yards was far enough.

The countdown started at nine minutes past five in the morning, Mountain War Time, on Monday, July 16. It was dawn, and there were streaks of gold in the sky to the east.

The test was code-named Trinity. When Greg had asked why, the senior scientist, the pointy-eared Jewish New Yorker J. Robert Oppenheimer, had quoted a poem by John Donne: "Batter my heart, three-person'd God."

"Oppie" was the cleverest person Greg had ever met. The most brilliant physicist of his generation, he also spoke six languages. He had read Karl Marx's *Capital* in the original German. The kind of thing he did for fun was learn Sanskrit. Greg liked and admired him. Most physicists were geeks, but Oppie, like Greg himself, was an exception: tall, handsome, charming, and a real lady-killer.

In the middle of the desert, Oppie had instructed the Army Corps of Engineers to build a one-hundred-foot tower of steel struts in concrete footings. On top was an oak platform. The bomb had been winched up to the platform on Saturday.

The scientists never used the word *bomb*. They called it "the gadget." At its heart was a ball of plutonium, a metal that did not exist in nature but was created as a by-product in nuclear piles. The ball weighed ten pounds and contained all the plutonium in the world. Someone had calculated that it was worth a billion dollars.

Thirty-two detonators on the surface of the ball would go off simultaneously, creating such powerful inward pressure that the plutonium would become more dense and go critical.

No one really knew what would happen next.

The scientists were running a betting pool, a dollar a ticket, on the force of the explosion measured in equivalent tons of TNT. Edward Teller bet 45,000 tons. Oppie bet 300 tons. The official forecast was 20,000 tons. The night before, Enrico Fermi had offered to take side bets on whether the blast would wipe out the entire state of New Mexico. General Groves had not found it funny.

The scientists had had a perfectly serious discussion about whether the explosion would ignite the atmosphere of the entire earth, and destroy the planet, but they had come to the conclusion that it would not. If they were wrong, Greg just hoped it would happen fast.

The trial had originally been scheduled for July 4. However, every time they tested a component, it failed, so the big day had been postponed several times. Back at Los Alamos, on Saturday, a mock-up they called the Chinese Copy had refused to ignite. In the betting pool, Norman Ramsey had picked zero, gambling that the bomb would be a dud.

Today detonation had been scheduled for two A.M., but at that time there had been a thunderstorm—in the desert! Rain would bring the radioactive fallout down on the heads of the watching scientists, so the blast was postponed.

The storm had ended at dawn.

Greg was at a bunker called S-10000, which was the control room. Like most of the scientists, he was standing outside for a better view. Hope and fear struggled for mastery of his heart. If the bomb was a dud, the efforts of hundreds of people—plus about two billion dollars— would have gone for nothing. And if the bomb was not a dud, they might all be killed in the next few minutes.

Beside him was Wilhelm Frunze, a young German scientist he had first met in Chicago. "What would have happened, Will, if lightning had struck the bomb?"

Frunze shrugged. "No one knows."

A green Verey rocket shot into the sky, startling Greg.

"Five-minute warning," Frunze said.

Security had been haphazard. Santa Fe, the nearest town to Los Alamos, was crawling with well-dressed FBI agents. Leaning nonchalantly against walls in their tweed jackets and neckties, they were obvious to local residents, who wore blue jeans and cowboy boots.

The bureau was also illegally tapping the phones of hundreds of people involved in the Manhattan Project. This bewildered Greg. How could the nation's premier law enforcement agency systematically commit criminal acts?

Nevertheless, army security and the FBI had identified some spies and quietly removed them from the project, including Barney McHugh. But had they found them all? Greg did not know. Groves had been forced to take risks. If he had fired everyone the FBI asked him to, there would not have been enough scientists left to build the bomb.

Unfortunately, most scientists were radicals, socialists, and liberals. There was hardly a conservative among them. And they believed that the truths discovered by science were for humankind to share, and should never be kept secret in the service of one regime or country. So while the American government was keeping this huge project top secret, the scientists held discussion groups about sharing nuclear technology with all the nations of the world. Oppie himself was suspect: the only reason he was not in the Communist Party was that he never joined clubs.

Right now Oppie was lying on the ground next to his kid brother, Frank, also an outstanding physicist, also a Communist. They both held pieces of welding glass through which to observe the explosion. Greg and Frunze had similar pieces of glass. Some of the scientists were wearing sunglasses.

Another rocket went off. "One minute," said Frunze.

Greg heard Oppie say: "Lord, these affairs are hard on the heart."

He wondered if those would be Oppie's last words.

Greg and Frunze lay on the sandy earth near Oppie and Frank. They all held their visors of welding glass in front of their eyes and gazed toward the test site.

Facing death, Greg thought about his mother, his father, and his sister, Daisy, in London. He wondered how much they would miss him. He thought, with mild regret, of Margaret Cowdry, who had dumped him for a guy who was willing to marry her. But most of all he thought of Jacky Jakes and Georgy, now nine years old. He passionately wanted to watch Georgy grow up. He realized Georgy was the main reason he was hoping to stay alive. Stealthily, the child had crept into his soul and stolen his love. The strength of this feeling surprised Greg.

A gong chimed, a strangely inappropriate sound in the desert.

"Ten seconds."

Greg suffered an impulse to get up and run away. Silly though it was—how far could he get in ten seconds?—he had to force himself to lie still.

The bomb went off at five twenty-nine and forty-five seconds.

First there was an awesome flash, impossibly bright, the fiercest glare Greg had ever seen, stronger than the sun.

Then a weird dome of fire seemed to come out of the ground. With terrifying speed it grew monstrously high. It reached the level of the mountains and continued to rise, rapidly dwarfing the peaks.

Greg whispered: "Jesus . . ."

The dome morphed into a square. The light was still brighter than noonday, and the distant mountains were so vividly illuminated that Greg could see every fold and crevice and rock.

Then the shape changed again. A pillar appeared below, seeming to push miles into the sky, like the fist of God. The cloud of boiling fire above the pillar spread like an umbrella, until the whole thing looked like a mushroom seven miles tall. The colors in the cloud were hellish orange, green, and purple.

Greg was hit by a wave of heat as if the Almighty had opened a giant oven. At the same moment the bang of the explosion reached his ears like the crack of doom. But that was only the beginning. A noise like supernaturally loud thunder rolled over the desert, drowning all other sound.

The blazing cloud began to diminish but the thunder went on and on, impossibly sustained, until Greg wondered if this was the sound of the end of the world.

At last it faded away, and the mushroom cloud began to disperse.

Greg heard Frank Oppenheimer say: "It worked."

Oppie said: "Yes, it worked."

The two brothers shook hands.

And the world is still here, Greg thought.

But it has been forever changed.

V

Lloyd Williams and Daisy went to Hoxton Town Hall on the morning of July 26 to watch the votes being counted.

If Lloyd lost, Daisy was going to break off the engagement.

He fervently denied that she was a political liability, but she knew better. Lloyd's political enemies made a point of calling her "Lady Aberowen." Voters reacted to her American accent by looking indignant, as if she had no right to take part in British politics. Even Labour Party members treated her differently, asking if she would prefer coffee when they were all drinking tea.

As Lloyd had forecast, she was often able to overcome people's initial hostility by being natural and charming, and helping the other women wash up the teacups. But was that enough? The election results would give the only definite answer.

She was not going to marry him if it meant his giving up his life's work. He said he was willing to do it, but it was a hopeless foundation for marriage. Daisy shuddered with horror as she imagined him doing some other job, working at a bank or in the civil service, miserably unhappy and trying to pretend it was not her fault. It did not bear thinking about.

Unfortunately, everyone thought the Conservatives were going to win the election.

Some things had gone Labour's way in the campaign. Churchill's "Gestapo" speech had backfired. Even Conservatives had been dismayed. Clement Attlee, broadcasting the following evening for Labour, had been coolly ironic. "When I listened to the prime minister's speech last night, in which he gave such a travesty of the policy of the Labour Party, I realized at once what was his object. He wanted the voters to understand how great was the difference between Winston Churchill, the great leader in war of a united nation, and Mr. Churchill, the party leader of the Conservatives. He feared lest those who had accepted his leadership in war might be tempted out of gratitude to follow him further. I thank him for having disillusioned them so thoroughly."

Attlee's magisterial disdain had made Churchill seem a rabble-rouser. People had had too much of bloodred passion, Daisy thought; they would surely prefer temperate common sense in peacetime.

A Gallup poll taken the day before voting showed Labour winning, but no one believed it. The idea that you could forecast the result by asking a small number of electors seemed a bit unlikely. The *News Chronicle*, which had published the poll, was predicting a tie.

All the other papers said the Conservatives would win.

Daisy had never before taken any interest in the mechanics of democracy, but her fate was in the balance now, and she watched, mesmerized, as the voting papers were taken out of the boxes, sorted, counted, bundled, and counted again. The man in charge was called the returning officer, as if he had been away for a while. He was in fact the town clerk. Observers from each of the parties monitored the proceedings to make sure there was no carelessness or dishonesty. The process was long, and Daisy felt tortured by suspense.

At half past ten they heard the first result from elsewhere. Harold Macmillan, a protégé of Churchill's and a wartime cabinet minister, had lost Stockton-on-Tees to Labour. Fifteen minutes later there was news of a huge swing to Labour in Birmingham. No radios were allowed into the hall, so Daisy and Lloyd were relying on rumors filtering in from outside, and Daisy was not sure what to believe.

It was midday when the returning officer called the candidates and their agents into a corner of the room, to give them the result before making the announcement publicly. Daisy wanted to go with Lloyd but she was not permitted.

The man spoke quietly to all of them. As well as Lloyd and the sitting M.P., there was a Conservative and a Communist. Daisy studied their faces, but could not guess who had won. They all went up onto the platform, and the room fell silent. Daisy felt nauseated.

"I, Michael Charles Davies, being the duly appointed returning officer for the parliamentary constituency of Hoxton . . ."

Daisy stood with the Labour Party observers and stared at Lloyd. Was she about to lose him? The thought squeezed her heart and made her breathless with fear. In her life she had twice chosen a man who was disastrously wrong. Charlie Farquharson had been the opposite of her father, nice but weak. Boy Fitzherbert had been much like her father, willful and selfish. Now, at last, she had found Lloyd, who was both strong and kind. She had not picked him for his social status or for what he could do for her, but simply because he was an extraordinarily good man. He was gentle, he was smart, he was trustworthy, and he adored her. It had taken her a long time to realize that he was what she was looking for. How foolish she had been.

The returning officer read out the number of votes cast for each candidate. They were listed alphabetically, so Williams came last. Daisy was so anxious that she could not keep the numbers in her head. "Reginald Sidney Blenkinsop, five thousand four hundred and twenty-seven . . ."

When Lloyd's vote was read out, the Labour Party people all around Daisy burst out cheering. It took her a moment to realize that meant he had won. Then she saw his solemn expression turn into a broad grin. Daisy began to clap and cheer louder than anyone. He had won! And she did not have to leave him! She felt as if her life had been saved.

"I therefore declare that Lloyd Williams is duly elected member of Parliament for Hoxton."

Lloyd was a member of Parliament. Daisy watched proudly as he stepped forward and made an acceptance speech. There was a formula for such speeches, she realized, and he tediously thanked the returning officer and his staff, then thanked his losing opponents for a fair fight. She was impatient to hug him. He finished with a few sentences about the task that lay ahead, of rebuilding war-torn Britain and creating a fairer society. He stood down to more applause.

Coming off the stage, he walked straight to Daisy, put his arms around her, and kissed her.

She said: "Well done, my darling." Then she found she could no longer speak.

After a while they went outside and caught a bus to Labour Party headquarters at Transport House. There they learned that Labour had already won 106 seats.

It was a landslide.

Every pundit had been wrong, and everyone's expectations were confounded. When all the results were in, Labour had 393 seats, the Conservatives 210. The Liberals had twelve and the Communists one—Stepney. Labour had an overwhelming majority.

At seven o'clock in the evening Winston Churchill, Britain's great war leader, went to Buckingham Palace and resigned as prime minister.

Daisy thought of one of Churchill's jibes about Attlee: "An empty car drew up and Clem got out." The man he called a nonentity had thrashed him.

At half past seven Clement Attlee went to the palace in his own car, driven by his wife, Violet, and King George VI asked him to become prime minister.

In the house in Nutley Street, after they had all listened to the news on the radio, Lloyd turned to Daisy and said: "Well, that's that. Can we get married now?"

"Yes," said Daisy. "As quick as you like."

vi

Volodya and Zoya's wedding reception was held in one of the smaller banqueting halls in the Kremlin.

The war with Germany was over, but the Soviet Union was still battered and impoverished, and a lavish celebration would have been frowned upon. Zoya had a new dress, but Volodya wore his uniform. However, there was plenty to eat, and the vodka flowed freely.

Volodya's nephew and niece were there, the twin children of his sister, Anya, and her unpleasant husband, Ilya Dvorkin. They were not yet six years old. Dimka, the dark-haired boy, sat quietly reading a book, while blue-eyed Tania was running around the room crashing into tables and annoying the guests, in a reversal of the expected behavior of boys and girls.

Zoya looked so desirable in pink that Volodya would have liked to leave right away and take her to bed. That was out of the question, of course. His father's circle of friends included some of the most senior generals and politicians in the country, and many of them had come to toast the happy couple. Grigori was hinting that one extremely distinguished guest might arrive later; Volodya hoped it was not the depraved NKVD boss Beria.

Volodya's happiness did not quite let him forget the horrors he had seen and the profound misgivings he had developed about Soviet Communism. The unspeakable brutality of the secret police, the blunders of Stalin that had cost millions of lives, and the propaganda that had encouraged the Red Army to behave like crazed beasts in Germany had all caused him to doubt the most fundamental things he had been brought up to believe. He wondered uneasily what kind of country Dimka and Tania would grow up in. But today was not the day to think about that.

The Soviet elite were in a good mood. They had won the war and defeated Germany. Their old enemy Japan was being crushed by the USA. The insane honor code of Japan's leaders made it difficult for them to surrender, but it was only a matter of time now. Tragically, while they clung to their pride, more Japanese and American troops would die, and more Japanese women and children would be bombed out of their homes, but the end result would be the same. Sadly, it seemed there was nothing the Americans could do to hasten the process and prevent unnecessary deaths.

Volodya's father, drunk and happy, made a speech. "The Red Army has occupied Poland," he said. "Never again will that country be used as a springboard for a German invasion of Russia."

All the old comrades cheered and thumped the tables.

"In Western Europe, Communist parties are being endorsed by the masses as never before. In the Paris municipal elections last March, the Communist Party won the largest share of the vote. I congratulate our French comrades."

They cheered again.

"As I look around the world today, I see that the Russian Revolution, in which so many brave men fought and died . . ." He trailed off as drunken tears came to his eyes. A hush descended on the room. He recovered himself. "I see that the revolution has never been as secure as it is today!"

They raised their glasses. "The revolution! The revolution!" Everyone drank.

The doors flew open, and Comrade Stalin walked in.

Everyone stood up.

His hair was gray, and he looked tired. He was about sixty-five, and he had been ill: there were rumors that he had suffered a series of strokes or minor heart attacks. But his mood today was ebullient. "I have come to kiss the bride!" he said.

He walked up to Zoya and put his hands on her shoulders. She was a good three inches taller than he, but she managed to stoop discreetly. He kissed her on both cheeks, allowing his gray-mustached mouth to linger just long enough to make Volodya feel resentful. Then he stepped back and said: "How about a drink for me?"

Several people hastened to get him a glass of vodka. Grigori insisted on giving Stalin his chair in the center of the head table. The buzz of conversation resumed, but it was subdued: they were thrilled he was here, but now they had to be careful of every word and every move. This man could have a person killed with a snap of his fingers, and he frequently had.

More vodka was brought, the band began to play Russian folk dances, and slowly people relaxed. Volodya, Zoya, Grigori, and Katerina did a four-person dance called a *kadril*, which was intended to be comic and always made people laugh. After that more couples danced, and the men started to do the *barynya*, in which they had to squat and kick up their legs, which caused many of them to fall over. Volodya kept checking on Stalin out of the corner of his eye—as did everyone else in the room—and he seemed to be enjoying himself, tapping his glass on the table in time with the balalaikas.

Zoya and Katerina were dancing a troika with Zoya's boss, Vasili, a senior physicist working on the bomb project, and Volodya was sitting out, when the atmosphere changed.

An aide in a civilian suit came in, hurried around the edge of the room, and went right up to Stalin. Without ceremony, he leaned over the leader's shoulder and spoke to him quietly but urgently.

Stalin at first looked puzzled, and asked a sharp question, then another. Then his face changed. He went pale, and seemed to stare at the dancers without seeing them.

Volodya said under his breath: "What the hell has happened?"

The dancers had not yet noticed, but those sitting at the head table looked frightened.

After a moment Stalin stood up. Those around him deferentially did the same. Volodya saw that his father was still dancing. People had been shot for less.

But Stalin had no eyes for the wedding guests. With the aide at his side he left the table. He walked toward the door, crossing the dance floor. Terrified revelers jumped out of his way. One couple fell over. Stalin did not seem to notice. The band ground to a halt. Saying nothing, looking at nobody, Stalin left the room.

Some of the generals followed him out, looking scared.

Another aide appeared, then two more. They all sought out their bosses and spoke to them. A young man in a tweed jacket went up to Vasili. Zoya seemed to know the man, and listened intently to him. She looked shocked.

Vasili and the aide left the room. Volodya went to Zoya and said: "For God's sake, what's going on?"

Her voice was shaky. "The Americans have dropped a nuclear bomb on Japan." Her beautifully pale face seemed even whiter than normal. "At first the Japanese government couldn't figure out what had happened. It took them hours to realize what it was."

"Are we sure?"

"It flattened five square miles of buildings. They estimate that seventy-five thousand people were killed instantly."

"How many bombs?"

"One."

"One bomb?"

"Yes."

"Good God. No wonder Stalin turned pale."

They both stood silent. The news was spreading around the room visibly. Some people sat stunned; others got up and left, heading for their offices, their telephones, their desks, and their staffs.

"This changes everything," Volodya said.

"Including our honeymoon plans," said Zoya. "My leave is sure to be canceled."

"We thought the Soviet Union was safe."

"Your father has just made a speech about how the revolution has never been so secure."

"Now nothing is secure."

"No," said Zoya. "Not until we have a bomb of our own."

vii

Jacky Jakes and Georgy were in Buffalo, staying at Marga's apartment for the first time. Greg and Lev were there, too, and on Victory in Japan Day—Wednesday, August 15—they all went to Humboldt Park. The paths were crowded with jubilant couples and there were hundreds of children splashing in the pond.

Greg was happy and proud. The bomb had worked. The two devices dropped on Hiroshima and Nagasaki had wreaked sickening devastation, but they had brought the war to a quick end and saved thousands of American lives. Greg had played a role in that. Because of what they had all done, Georgy was going to grow up in a free world.

"He's nine," Greg said to Jacky. They were sitting on a bench, talking, while Lev and Marga took Georgy to buy ice cream.

"I can hardly believe it."

"What will he be, I wonder?"

Jacky said fiercely: "He's not going to do something stupid like acting or playing the goddamn trumpet. He's got brains."

"Would you like him to be a college professor, like your father?"

"Yes."

"In that case"—Greg had been leading up to this, and was nervous about how Jacky might react—"he ought to go to a good school."

"What did you have in mind?"

"How about boarding school? He could go where I went."

"He'd be the only black pupil."

"Not necessarily. When I was there, we had a colored guy, an Indian from Delhi called Kamal."

"Just one."

"Yes."

"Was he teased?"

"Sure. We called him Camel. But the boys got used to him, and he made some friends."

"What happened to him, do you know?"

"He became a pharmacist. I hear he already owns two drugstores in New York."

Jacky nodded. Greg could tell that she was not opposed to this plan. She came from a cultured family. Although she herself had rebelled and dropped out, she believed in the value of education. "What about the school fees?"

"I could ask my father."

"Would he pay?"

"Look at them." Greg pointed along the path. Lev, Marga, and Georgy were returning from the ice-cream vendor's cart. Lev and Georgy were walking side by side, eating ice-cream cones, holding hands. "My conservative father, holding the hand of a colored child in a public park. Trust me, he'll pay the school fees."

"Georgy doesn't really fit anywhere," Jacky said, looking troubled. "He's a black boy with a white daddy."

"I know."

"People in your mother's apartment building think I'm the maid—did you know that?"

"Yes."

"I've been careful not to set them straight. If they thought Negroes were in the building as guests, there might be trouble."

Greg sighed. "I'm sorry, but you're right."

"Life is going to be tough for Georgy."

"I know," said Greg. "But he's got us."

Jacky gave him a rare smile. "Yeah," she said. "That's something."

PART THREE

THE
COLD PEACE

CHAPTER TWENTY-ONE

1945 (III)

After the wedding Volodya and Zoya moved into an apartment of their own. Few Russian newlyweds were so lucky. For four years the industrial might of the Soviet Union had been directed to making weapons. Hardly any homes had been built, and many had been destroyed. But Volodya was a major in Red Army Intelligence, as well as the son of a general, and he was able to pull strings.

It was a compact space: a living room with a dining table, a bedroom so small the bed almost filled it, a kitchen that was crowded with two people in it, a cramped toilet with a washbasin and shower, and a tiny hall with a closet for their clothes. When the radio was on in the living room, they could hear it all over the flat.

They quickly made it their own. Zoya bought a bright yellow coverlet for the bed. Volodya's mother produced a set of crockery that she had bought in 1940, in anticipation of his wedding, and saved all through the war. Volodya hung a picture on the wall, a graduation photograph of his class at the Military Intelligence Academy.

They made love more now. Being alone made a difference Volodya had not anticipated. He had never felt particularly inhibited when sleeping with Zoya at his parents' place, or in the apartment she used to share, but now he realized it had an influence. You had to keep your voice down, you listened in case the bed squeaked, and there was always the possibility, albeit remote, that somebody would walk in on you. Other people's homes were never completely private.

They often woke early, made love, then lay kissing and talking for an hour before getting dressed for work. Lying with his head on her thighs on one such morning, the smell of sex in his nostrils, Volodya said: "Do you want some tea?"

"Yes, please." She stretched luxuriously, reclining on the pillows.

Volodya put on a robe and crossed the tiny hallway to the little kitchen, where he lit the gas under the samovar. He was displeased to see the pots and dishes from last night's dinner stacked in the sink. "Zoya!" he said. "This kitchen's in a mess!"

She could hear him easily in the small apartment. "I know," she said.

He went back to the bedroom. "Why didn't you clean up last night?"

"Why didn't you?"

It had not occurred to him that it might be his responsibility. But he said: "I had a report to write."

"And I was tired."

The suggestion that it was his fault irritated him. "I hate a filthy kitchen."

"So do I."

Why was she being so obtuse? "If you don't like it, clean it!"

"Let's do it together, right away." She sprang out of bed. She pushed past him with a sexy smile and went into the kitchen.

Volodya followed.

She said: "You wash. I'll dry." She took a clean towel from a drawer.

She was still naked. He could not help but smile. Her body was long and slim, and her skin was white. She had flat breasts and pointed nipples, and the hair of her groin was fine and blond. One of the joys of being married to her was her habit of moving around the apartment in the nude. He could stare at her body for as long as he liked. She seemed to enjoy it. If she caught his eye, she showed no embarrassment, but just smiled.

He rolled up the sleeves of his robe and began to wash the dishes, passing them to Zoya to dry. Washing up was not a very manly activity—Volodya had never seen his father do it—but Zoya seemed to think such chores should be shared. It was an eccentric idea. Did Zoya have a highly developed sense of fairness in marriage? Or was he being emasculated?

He thought he heard something outside. He glanced into the hall: the apartment door was only three or four steps from the kitchen sink. He could see nothing out of the ordinary.

Then the door was smashed open.

Zoya screamed.

Volodya picked up the carving knife he had just washed. He stepped past Zoya and stood in the kitchen doorway. A uniformed policeman holding a sledgehammer was just outside the ruined door.

Volodya was filled with fear and rage. He said: "What the fuck is this?"

The policeman stepped back, and a small, thin man with a face like a rodent entered the flat. It was Volodya's brother-in-law, Ilya Dvorkin, an agent of the secret police. He was wearing leather gloves.

"Ilya!" said Volodya. "You stupid weasel."

"Speak respectfully," said Ilya.

Volodya was baffled as well as angry. The secret police did not normally arrest the staff of Red Army Intelligence, and vice versa. Otherwise it would have been gang warfare. "Why the hell have you busted my door? I would have opened it!"

Two more agents stepped into the hall and stood behind Ilya. They wore their trademark leather coats, despite the mild late-summer weather.

Volodya was fearful. What was going on?

Ilya said in a shaky voice: "Put the knife down, Volodya."

"No need to be afraid," said Volodya. "I was just washing up." He handed the knife to Zoya, standing behind him. "Please step into the living room. We can talk while Zoya gets dressed."

"Do you imagine this is a social call?" Ilya said indignantly.

"Whatever kind of call it is, I'm sure you don't want the embarrassment of seeing my wife naked."

"I am here on official police business!"

"Then why did they send my brother-in-law?"

Ilya lowered his voice. "Don't you understand that it would be much worse for you if someone else had come?"

This looked like bad trouble. Volodya struggled to keep up the façade of bravado. "Exactly what do you and these other assholes want?"

"Comrade Beria has taken over the direction of the nuclear physics program."

Volodya knew that. Stalin had set up a new committee to direct the work and made Beria chairman. Beria knew nothing about physics and was completely unqualified to organize a scientific research project. But Stalin trusted him. It was the usual problem of Soviet government: incompetent but loyal people were promoted into jobs they could not cope with.

Volodya said: "And Comrade Beria needs my wife in her laboratory, developing the bomb. Have you come to drive her to work?"

"The Americans created their nuclear bomb before the Soviets."

"Indeed. Could they perhaps have given research physics higher priority than we did?"

"It is not possible that capitalist science should be superior to Communist science!"

"This is a truism." Volodya was puzzled. Where was this heading? "So what do you conclude?"

"There must have been sabotage."

That was exactly the kind of ludicrous fantasy the secret police would dream up. "What kind of sabotage?"

"Some of the scientists deliberately delayed the development of the Soviet bomb."

Volodya began to understand, and he felt afraid. But he continued to respond belligerently: it was always a mistake to show weakness with these people. "Why the hell would they do that?"

"Because they are traitors—and your wife is one!"

"You'd better not be serious, you piece of shit—"

"I am here to arrest your wife."

"What?" Volodya was flabbergasted. "This is insane!"

"It is the view of my organization."

"There is no evidence."

"For evidence, go to Hiroshima!"

Zoya spoke for the first time since she had screamed. "I'll have to go with them, Volodya. Don't get yourself arrested, too."

Volodya pointed a finger at Ilya. "You are in so much fucking trouble."

"I'm carrying out my orders."

"Step out of the way. My wife is going into the bedroom to get dressed."

"No time for that," said Ilya. "She must come as she is."

"Don't be ridiculous."

Ilya put his nose in the air. "A respectable Soviet citizen would not walk around the apartment with no clothes on."

Volodya wondered briefly how his sister felt being married to this creep. "You, the secret police, morally disapprove of nudity?"

"Her nakedness is evidence of her degradation. We will take her as she is."

"No, you fucking won't."

"Stand aside."

"You stand aside. She's going to get dressed." Volodya stepped into the hall and stood in front of the three agents, holding his arms out so that Zoya could pass behind him.

As she moved, Ilya reached past Volodya and grabbed her arm.

Volodya punched him in the face, twice. Ilya cried out and staggered back. The two men in leather coats stepped forward. Volodya aimed a punch at one, but the man dodged it. Then each man took one of Volodya's arms. He struggled, but they were strong and seemed to have done this before. They slammed him against the wall.

While they held him, Ilya punched him in the face with leather-gloved fists, twice, three times, four, then in the stomach, again and again until Volodya puked blood. Zoya tried to intervene, but Ilya punched her, too, and she screamed and fell back.

Volodya's bathrobe came open in front. Ilya kicked him in the balls, then kicked his knees. Volodya sagged, unable to stand, but the two men in leather coats held him up, and Ilya punched him some more.

At last Ilya turned away, rubbing his knuckles. The other two released Volodya, and he crumpled to the floor. He could hardly breathe and felt unable to move, but he was conscious. Out of the corner of his eye he saw the two heavies grab Zoya and march her naked out of the apartment. Ilya followed.

As the minutes went by, the pain changed from sharp agony to deep, dull ache, and Volodya's breathing began to return to normal.

Motion eventually returned to his limbs, and he dragged himself upright. He made it to the phone and dialed his father's number, hoping the old man had not yet left for work. He was relieved to hear his father's voice. "They've arrested Zoya," he said.

"Fucking bastards," Grigori said. "Who was it?"

"It was Ilya."

"What?"

"Make some calls," Volodya said. "See if you can find out what the fuck is going on. I have to wash off the blood."

"What blood?"

Volodya hung up.

It was only a couple of steps to the bathroom. He dropped his bloodstained robe and got into the shower. The warm water brought some relief to his bruised body. Ilya was mean but not strong, and he had not broken any bones.

Volodya turned off the water. He looked in the bathroom mirror. His face was covered with cuts and bruises.

He did not bother to dry himself. With considerable effort, he got dressed in his Red Army uniform. He wanted the symbol of authority.

His father arrived as he was trying to tie the laces of his boots. "What the fucking hell happened here?" Grigori roared.

Volodya said: "They were looking for a fight, and I was foolish enough to give them one."

His father was unsympathetic at first. "I'd have expected you to know better."

"They insisted on taking her away naked."

"Fucking creeps."

"Did you find out anything?"

"Not yet. I talked to a couple of people. No one knows anything." Grigori looked worried. "Either someone has made a really stupid mistake . . . or for some reason they're very sure of themselves."

"Drive me to my office. Lemitov is going to be mad as hell. He won't let them get away with this. If they are allowed to do it to me, they'll do it to all of Red Army Intelligence."

Grigori's car and driver were waiting outside. They drove to the Khodynka airfield. Grigori stayed in the car while Volodya limped into Red Army Intelligence headquarters. He went straight to the office of his boss, Colonel Lemitov.

He tapped on the door, walked in, and said: "The fucking secret police have arrested my wife."

"I know," said Lemitov.

"You know?"

"I okayed it."

Volodya's jaw dropped. "What the fuck?"

"Sit down."

"What is going on?"

"Sit down and shut up, and I'll tell you."

Volodya eased himself painfully into a chair.

Lemitov said: "We have to have a nuclear bomb, and fast. At the moment, Stalin is playing it tough with the Americans, because we're fairly sure they don't have a big enough arsenal of nuclear weapons to wipe us out. But they're building a stockpile, and at some point they will use them—unless we are in a position to retaliate."

This made no sense. "My wife can't design the bomb while the secret police are punching her in the face. This is insane."

"Shut the fuck up. Our problem is that there are several possible designs. The Americans took five years to figure out which would work. We don't have that much time. We have to steal their research."

"We'll still need Russian physicists to copy the design—and for that they have to be in their laboratories, not locked in the basement of the Lubyanka."

"You know a man called Wilhelm Frunze."

"I was at school with him. The Berlin Boys' Academy."

"He gave us valuable information about British nuclear research. Then he moved to the States, where he worked on the nuclear bomb project. The Washington staff of the NKVD contacted him, scared him by their incompetence, and fucked up the relationship. We need to win him back."

"What has all this got to do with me?"

"He trusts you."

"I don't know that. I haven't seen him for twelve years."

"We want you to go to America and talk to him."

"But why did you arrest Zoya?"

"To make sure you come back."

ii

Volodya told himself he knew how to do this. In Berlin, before the war, he had shaken off Gestapo tails, met with potential spies, recruited them, and made them into reliable sources of secret intelligence. It was never easy—especially the part where he had to talk someone into turning traitor—but he was an expert.

However, this was America.

The Western countries he had visited, Germany and Spain in the thirties and forties, were nothing like this.

He was overwhelmed. All his life he had been told that Hollywood movies gave an exaggerated impression of prosperity, and that in reality most Americans lived in poverty. But it was clear to Volodya, from the day he arrived in the USA, that the movies hardly exaggerated at all. And poor people were hard to find.

New York was jammed with cars, many driven by people who clearly were not important government officials: youngsters, men in work clothes, even women out shopping. And everybody was so well dressed! All the men appeared to be wearing their best suits. The women's calves were clad in sheer stockings. Everyone seemed to have new shoes.

He had to keep reminding himself of the bad side of America. There was poverty, somewhere. Negroes were persecuted, and in the South they could not vote. There was a lot of crime—Americans themselves said that it was rampant—although, strangely, Volodya did not actually see any evidence of it, and he felt quite safe walking the streets.

He spent a few days exploring New York. He worked on his English, which was not good, but it hardly mattered: the city was full of people who spoke broken English with heavy accents. He got to know the faces of some of the FBI agents assigned to tail him, and identified several convenient locations where he would be able to lose them.

One sunny morning he left the Soviet consulate in New York, hatless and wearing only gray slacks and a blue shirt, as if he were going to run a few errands. A young man in a dark suit and tie followed him.

He went to the Saks Fifth Avenue department store and bought underwear and a shirt with a small brown checked pattern. Whoever was tailing him had to think he was probably just shopping.

The NKVD chief at the consulate had announced that a Soviet team would shadow Volodya throughout his American visit, to make sure of his good behavior. He could barely contain his rage at the organization that had imprisoned Zoya, and he had to repress the urge to take the man by the throat and strangle him. But he had remained calm. He had pointed out sarcastically that in order to fulfill his mission he would have to evade FBI surveillance, and in doing so he might inadvertently also lose his NKVD tail, but he wished them luck. Most days he shook them off in five minutes.

So the young man tailing him was almost certainly an FBI agent. His crisply conservative clothes corroborated that.

Carrying his purchases in a paper bag, Volodya left the store by a side entrance and hailed a cab. He left the FBI man at the curb waving his arm. When the cab had turned two corners, Volodya threw the driver a bill and jumped out. He darted into a subway station, left again by a different entrance, and waited in the doorway of an office building for five minutes.

The young man in the dark suit was nowhere to be seen.

Volodya walked to Penn Station.

There he double-checked that he was not being followed, then bought his ticket. With nothing but that and his paper bag he boarded a train.

The journey to Albuquerque took three days.

The train sped through mile after endless mile of rich farmland, mighty factories belching smoke, and great cities with skyscrapers pointing arrogantly at the heavens. The Soviet Union was bigger, but apart from the Ukraine it was mostly pine forests and frozen steppes. He had never imagined wealth on this scale.

And wealth was not all. For several days something had been nagging at the back of Volodya's mind, something strange about life in America. Eventually he realized what it was: no one asked for his papers. After he had passed through immigration control in New York, he had not shown his passport again. In this country, it seemed, anyone could walk into a railway station or a bus terminus and buy a ticket to any place without having to get permission or explain the purpose of the trip to an official. It gave him a dangerously exhilarating sense of freedom. He could go anywhere!

America's wealth also heightened Volodya's sense of the danger his country faced. The Germans had almost destroyed the Soviet Union, and this country was three times as populous and ten times as rich. The thought that Russians might become underlings, frightened into subservience, softened Volodya's doubts about Communism, despite what the NKVD had done to him and his wife. If he had children, he did not want them to grow up in a world tyrannized by America.

He traveled via Pittsburgh and Chicago and attracted no attention en route. His clothes were American, and his accent was not noticed for the simple reason that he spoke to no one. He bought sandwiches and coffee by pointing and paying. He flicked through newspapers and magazines that other travelers left behind, looking at the pictures and trying to work out the meanings of the headlines.

The last part of the journey took him through a desert landscape of desolate beauty, with distant snowy peaks stained red by the sunset, which probably explained why they were called the Blood of Christ Mountains.

He went to the toilet, where he changed his underwear and put on the new shirt he had bought in Saks.

He expected the FBI or army security to be watching the train station in Albuquerque, and sure enough he spotted a young man whose check jacket—too warm for the climate of New Mexico in September—did not quite conceal the bulge of a gun in a shoulder holster. However, the agent was undoubtedly interested in long-distance travelers who might be arriving from New York or Washington. Volodya, with no hat or jacket and no luggage, looked like a local man coming back from a short trip. He was not followed as he walked to the bus station and boarded a Greyhound for Santa Fe.

He reached his destination late in the afternoon. He noted two FBI men at the Santa Fe bus station, and they scrutinized him. However, they could not tail everyone who got off the bus, and once again his casual appearance caused them to dismiss him.

Doing his best to look as if he knew where he was going, he strolled along the streets. The low flat-roofed pueblo-style houses and squat churches baking in the sun reminded him of Spain. The storefront buildings overhung the sidewalks, creating pleasantly shady arcades.

He avoided La Fonda, the big hotel on the town square next to the cathedral, and checked into the St. Francis. He paid cash and gave his name as Robert Pender, which might have been American or one of several European nationalities. "My suitcase will be delivered later," he said to the pretty girl behind the reception desk. "If I'm out when it comes, can you make sure it gets sent up to my room?"

"Oh, sure, that won't be a problem," she said.

"Thank you," he said; then he added a phrase he had heard several times on the train: "I sure appreciate it."

"If I'm not here, someone else will deal with the bag, so long as it has your name on it."

"It does." He had no luggage, but she would never realize that.

She looked at his entry in the book. "So, Mr. Pender, you're from New York."

There was a touch of skepticism in her voice, no doubt because he did not sound like a New Yorker. "I'm from Switzerland originally," he explained, naming a neutral country.

"That accounts for the accent. I haven't met a Switzerland person before. What's it like there?"

Volodya had never been to Switzerland, but he had seen photographs. "It snows a lot," he said.

"Well, enjoy our New Mexico weather!"

"I will."

Five minutes later he went out again.

Some of the scientists lived at the Los Alamos laboratory, he had learned from his colleagues in the Soviet embassy, but it was a shantytown with few civilized comforts, and they preferred to rent houses and apartments nearby if they could. Willi Frunze could afford it easily: he was married to a successful artist who drew a syndicated cartoon strip called *Slack Alice*. His wife, also called Alice, could work anywhere, so they had a place in the historic downtown neighborhood.

The New York office of the NKVD had provided this information. They had researched Frunze carefully, and Volodya had his address and phone number and a description of his car, a prewar Plymouth convertible with whitewall tires.

The Frunzes' building had an art gallery on the ground floor. The apartment upstairs had a large north-facing window that would appeal to an artist. A Plymouth convertible was parked outside.

Volodya preferred not to go in: the place might be bugged.

The Frunzes were an affluent childless couple, and he guessed they would not stay at home listening to the radio on a Friday night. He decided to wait around and see if they came out.

He spent some time in the art gallery, looking at the paintings for sale. He liked clear, vivid pictures and would not have wanted to own any of these messy daubs. He found a coffee shop down the block and got a window seat from which he could just see the Frunzes' door. He left there after an hour, bought a newspaper, and stood at a bus stop pretending to read it.

The long wait permitted him to establish that no one was watching the Frunze apartment. That meant that the FBI and army security had not tagged Frunze as a high risk. He was a foreigner, but so were many of the scientists, and presumably nothing else was known against him.

This was a downtown commercial district, not a residential neighborhood, and there were plenty of people on the streets, but all the same after a couple of hours Volodya began to worry that someone might notice him hanging around.

Then the Frunzes came out.

Frunze was heavier than he had been twelve years ago—there was no shortage of food in America. His hairline was beginning to recede, although he was only thirty. He still had that solemn look. He wore a sports shirt and khaki pants, a common American combination.

His wife was not so conservatively dressed. Her fair hair was pinned up under a beret, and she wore a shapeless cotton dress in an indistinct brown color, but she had an assortment of bangles on both wrists, and numerous rings. Artists had dressed like that in Germany before Hitler, Volodya remembered.

The couple set off along the street, and Volodya followed.

He wondered what the wife's politics were, and what difference her presence would make in the difficult conversation he was about to have. Frunze had been a staunch Social Democrat back in Germany, so it was not likely his wife would be a conservative, a speculation that was borne out by her appearance. On the other hand, she probably did not know he had given secrets to the Soviets in London. She was an unknown quantity.

He would prefer to deal with Frunze alone, and he considered leaving them and trying again tomorrow. But the hotel receptionist had noticed his foreign accent, so by the morning he might have an FBI tail.

He could deal with that, he thought, though not as easily in this small town as in New York or Berlin. And tomorrow was Saturday, so the Frunzes would probably spend the day together. How long might Volodya have to wait before catching Frunze alone?

There was never an easy way to do this. On balance he decided to go ahead tonight.

The Frunzes went into a diner.

Volodya walked past the place and glanced through the window. It was an inexpensive restaurant with booths. He thought of going in and sitting down with them, but he decided to let them eat first. They would be in a good mood when full of food.

He waited half an hour, watching the door from a distance. Then, full of trepidation, he went in.

They were finishing their dinner. As he crossed the restaurant, Frunze glanced up, then looked away, not recognizing him.

He slid into the booth next to Alice and spoke quietly in German. "Hello, Willi, don't you remember me from school?"

Frunze looked hard at him for several seconds; then his face broke into a smile. "Peshkov? Volodya Peshkov? Is it really you?"

A wave of relief washed over Volodya. Frunze was still friendly. There was no barrier of hostility to overcome. "It's really me," Volodya said. He offered his hand and they shook. Turning to Alice, he said in English: "I am very bad speaking your language. Sorry."

"Don't bother to try," she replied in fluent German. "My family were immigrants from Bavaria."

Frunze said in amazement: "I've been thinking about you lately, because I know another guy with the same surname—Greg Peshkov."

"Really? My father had a brother called Lev who came to America in about 1915."

"No, Lieutenant Peshkov is much younger. Anyway, what are you doing here?"

Volodya smiled. "I came to see you." Before Frunze could ask why, he said: "Last time I saw you, you were secretary of the Neukölln Social Democratic Party." This was his second step. Having established a friendly footing, he was reminding Frunze of his youthful idealism.

"That experience convinced me that democratic socialism doesn't work," Frunze said. "Against the Nazis we were completely impotent. It took the Soviet Union to stop them."

That was true, and Volodya was pleased Frunze realized it, but, more importantly, the comment showed that Frunze's political ideas had not been softened by life in affluent America.

Alice said: "We were planning to have a couple of drinks at a bar around the corner. A lot of the scientists go there on a Friday night. Would you like to join us?"

The last thing Volodya wanted was to be seen in public with the Frunzes. "I don't know," he said. In fact he had been too long with them in this restaurant. It was time for step three: reminding Frunze of his terrible guilt. He leaned forward and lowered his voice. "Willi, did you know the Americans were going to drop nuclear bombs on Japan?"

There was a long pause. Volodya held his breath. He was gambling that Frunze would be racked by remorse.

For a moment he feared he had gone too far. Frunze looked as if he might burst into tears.

Then the scientist took a deep breath and got control of himself. "No, I didn't know," he said. "None of us did."

Alice interjected angrily: "We assumed the American military would give *some* demonstration of the power of the bomb, as a threat to make the Japanese surrender earlier." So she had known about the bomb beforehand, Volodya noted. He was not surprised. Men found it hard to keep such things from their wives. "So we expected a detonation sometime, somewhere," she went on. "But we imagined they would destroy an uninhabited island, or maybe a military facility with a lot of weapons and very few people."

"That might have been justifiable," Frunze said. "But . . ." His voice fell to a whisper. "Nobody thought they would drop it on a city and kill eighty thousand men, women, and children."

Volodya nodded. "I thought you might feel this way." He had been hoping for it with all his heart.

Frunze said: "Who wouldn't?"

"Let me ask you an even more important question." This was step four. "Will they do it again?"

"I don't know," Frunze said. "They might. Christ forgive us all, they might."

Volodya concealed his satisfaction. He had made Frunze feel responsible for future use of nuclear weapons, as well as past.

Volodya nodded. "That's what we think."

Alice said sharply: "Who's *we*?"

She was shrewd, and probably more worldly-wise than her husband. She would be hard to fool, and Volodya decided not to try. He had to risk leveling with her. "A fair question," he said. "And I didn't come all this way to deceive an old friend. I'm a major in Red Army Intelligence."

They stared at him. The possibility must have crossed their minds already, but they were surprised by the stark admission.

"I have something I need to say to you," Volodya went on. "Something hugely important. Is there somewhere we can go to talk privately?"

They both looked uncertain. Frunze said: "Our apartment?"

"It has probably been bugged by the FBI."

Frunze had some experience of clandestine work, but Alice was shocked. "You think so?" she said incredulously.

"Yes. Could we drive out of town?"

Frunze said: "There's a place we go sometimes, around this time of the evening, to watch the sunset."

"Perfect. Go to your car, sit in, and wait for me. I'll be a minute behind you."

Frunze paid the check and left with Alice, and Volodya followed. During the short walk he established that no one was tailing him. He reached the Plymouth and got in. They sat three across the front seat, American-style. Frunze drove out of town.

They followed a dirt road to the top of a low hill. Frunze stopped the car. Volodya motioned for them all to get out, and led them a hundred yards away, just in case the car was bugged, too.

They looked across the landscape of stony soil and low bushes toward the setting sun, and Volodya took step five. "We think the next nuclear bomb will be dropped somewhere in the Soviet Union."

Frunze nodded. "God forbid, but you're probably right."

"And there's absolutely nothing we can do about it," Volodya went on, pressing home his point relentlessly. "There are no precautions we can take, no barriers we can erect, no way we can protect our people. There is no defense against the nuclear bomb—the bomb that you made, Willi."

"I know it," said Frunze miserably. Clearly he felt it would be his fault if the USSR was attacked with nuclear weapons.

Step six. "The only protection would be our own nuclear bomb."

Frunze did not want to believe that. "It's not a defense," he said.

"But it's a deterrent."

"It might be," he conceded.

Alice said: "We don't want these bombs to spread."

"Nor do I," said Volodya. "But the only sure way to stop the Americans flattening Moscow the way they flattened Hiroshima is for the Soviet Union to have a nuclear bomb of its own, and threaten retaliation."

Alice said: "He's right, Willi. Hell, we all know it."

She was the tough one, Volodya saw.

Volodya made his voice light for step seven. "How many bombs do the Americans have right now?"

This was a crucial moment. If Frunze answered this question, he would have crossed a line. So far the conversation had been general. Now Volodya was requesting secret information.

Frunze hesitated for a long moment. Finally he glanced at Alice.

Volodya saw her give an almost imperceptible nod.

Frunze said: "Only one."

Volodya concealed his triumph. Frunze had betrayed trust. It was the difficult first move. A second secret would come more easily.

Frunze added: "But they'll have more soon."

"It's a race, and if we lose, we die," Volodya said urgently. "We have to build at least one bomb of our own before they have enough to wipe us out."

"Can you do that?"

That gave Volodya the cue for step eight. "We need help."

He saw Frunze's face harden, and guessed he was remembering whatever it was that had made him refuse to cooperate with the NKVD.

Alice said to Volodya: "What if we say we can't help you? That it's too dangerous?"

Volodya followed his instinct. He held up his hands in a gesture of surrender. "I go home and report failure," he said. "I can't make you do anything you don't want to do. I wouldn't want to pressure you or coerce you in any way."

Alice said: "No threats?"

That confirmed Volodya's guess that the NKVD had tried to bully Frunze. They tried to bully everyone: it was all they knew. "I'm not even trying to persuade you," Volodya said to Frunze. "I'm laying out the facts. The rest is up to you. If you want to help, I'm here as your contact. If you see things differently, that's the end of it. You're both smart people. I couldn't fool you even if I wanted to."

Again they looked at each other. He hoped they were thinking how different he was from the last Soviet agent who had approached them.

The moment stretched out agonizingly.

It was Alice who spoke at last. "What kind of help do you need?"

That was not a yes, but it was better than rejection, and it led logically to step nine. "My wife is one of the physicists on the team," he said, hoping this would humanize him at a moment when they might be in danger of seeing him as manipulative. "She tells me there are several routes to a nuclear bomb, and we don't have time to try them all. We can save years if we know what worked for you."

"That makes sense," Willi said.

Step ten, the big one. "We have to know what type of bomb was dropped on Japan."

Frunze's expression was agonized. He looked at his wife. This time she did not give him the nod, but neither did she shake her head. She seemed as torn as he did.

Frunze sighed. "Two kinds," he said.

Volodya was thrilled and startled. "Two different designs?"

Frunze nodded. "For Hiroshima they used a uranium device with a gun ignition. We called it Little Boy. For Nagasaki, Fat Man, a plutonium bomb with an implosion trigger."

Volodya could hardly breathe. This was red-hot data. "Which is better?"

"They both worked, obviously, but Fat Man is easier to make."

"Why?"

"It takes years to produce enough U-235 for a bomb. Plutonium is quicker, once you have a nuclear pile."

"So the USSR should copy Fat Man."

"Definitely."

"There is one more thing you could do to help save Russia from destruction," Volodya said.

"What?"

Volodya looked him in the eye. "Get me the design drawings," he said.

Willi paled. "I'm an American citizen," he said. "You're asking me to commit treason. The penalty is death. I could go to the electric chair."

So could your wife, Volodya thought; she's complicit. Thank God you haven't thought of that.

He said: "I've asked a lot of people to put their lives at risk in the last few years. People like yourselves, Germans who hated the Nazis, men and women who took terrible risks to send us information that helped us win the war. And I have to say to you what I said to them: a lot more people will be killed if you don't do it." He fell silent. That was his best shot. He had nothing more to offer.

Frunze looked at his wife.

Alice said: "You made the bomb, Willi."

Frunze said to Volodya: "I'll think about it."

iii

Two days later he handed over the plans.

Volodya took them to Moscow.

Zoya was released from jail. She was not as angry about her imprisonment as he was. "They did it to protect the revolution," she said. "And I wasn't hurt. It was like staying in a really bad hotel."

On her first day at home, after they made love, he said: "I have something to show you, something I brought back from America." He rolled off the bed, opened a drawer, and took out a book. "It's called the Sears Roebuck Catalogue," he said. He sat beside her on the bed and opened the book. "Look at this."

The catalogue fell open at a page of women's dresses. The models were impossibly slender, but the fabrics were bright and cheerful, stripes and checks and solid colors, some with ruffles, pleats, and belts. "That's attractive," Zoya said, putting her finger on one. "Is two dollars ninety-eight a lot of money?"

"Not really," Volodya said. "The average wage is about fifty dollars a week. Rent is about a third of that."

"Really?" Zoya was amazed. "So most people could easily afford these dresses?"

"That's right. Maybe not peasants. On the other hand, these catalogues were invented for farmers who lived a hundred miles from the nearest store."

"How does it work?"

"You pick what you want from the book and send them the money. Then a couple of weeks later the mailman brings you whatever you ordered."

"It must be like being a tsar." Zoya took the book from him and turned the page. "Oh! Here are some more." The next page showed jacket-and-skirt combinations for four dollars and ninety-eight cents. "These are elegant, too," she said.

"Keep turning the pages," Volodya said.

Zoya was astonished to see page after page of women's coats, hats, shoes, underwear, pajamas, and stockings. "People can have *any* of these?" she said.

"That's right."

"But there's more choice on one of these pages than there is in the average Russian shop!"

"Yes."

She carried on slowly leafing through the book. There was a similar range of clothing for men, and again for children. Zoya put her finger on a heavy woolen winter coat for boys that cost fifteen dollars. "At that price, I suppose every boy in America has one."

"They probably do."

After the clothes came furniture. You could buy a bed for twenty-five dollars. Everything was cheap if you had fifty dollars a week. And it went on and on. There were hundreds of things that could not be bought for any money in the Soviet Union: toys and games, beauty products, guitars, elegant chairs, power tools, novels in colorful jackets, Christmas decorations, and electric toasters.

There was even a tractor. "Do you think," Zoya said, "that any farmer in America who wants a tractor can have one *right away*?"

"Only if he has the money," said Volodya.

"He doesn't have to put his name down on a list and wait for a few years?"

"No."

Zoya closed the book and looked at him solemnly. "If people can have all this," she said, "why would they want to be Communist?"

"Good question," said Volodya.

CHAPTER TWENTY-TWO

1946

The children of Berlin had a new game called Komm, Frau—Come, Woman. It was one of a dozen games in which boys chased girls, but it had a new twist, Carla noticed. The boys would team up and target one of the girls. When they caught her, they would shout: "*Komm, Frau!*" and throw her to the ground. Then they would hold her down while one of their number lay on top of her and simulated sexual intercourse. Children of seven and eight, who ought not to know what rape was, played this game because they had seen what Red Army soldiers did to German women. Every Russian knew that one phrase of the German language: "*Komm, Frau.*"

What was it about the Russians? Carla had never met anyone who had been raped by a French, British, American, or Canadian soldier, though she supposed it must happen. By contrast, every woman she knew between fifteen and fifty-five had been raped by at least one Soviet soldier: her mother, Maud; her friend Frieda; Frieda's mother, Monika; Ada, the maid; all of them.

Yet they were lucky, for they were still alive. Some women, abused by dozens of men, hour after hour, had died. Carla had heard of a girl who had been bitten to death.

Only Rebecca Rosen had escaped. After Carla had protected her, the day the Jewish Hospital was liberated, Rebecca moved into the von Ulrich town house. It was in the Soviet zone, but she had nowhere else to go. She hid for months like a criminal in the attic, coming down only late at night when the bestial Russians had fallen into drunken sleep. Carla spent a couple of hours up there with her when she could, and they played card games and told each other their life stories. Carla wanted to be like an older sister, but Rebecca treated her like a mother.

Then Carla found she was going to be a mother for real.

Maud and Monika were in their fifties, and too old to have babies, mercifully, and Ada was lucky, but both Carla and Frieda were pregnant by their rapists.

Frieda had an abortion.

It was illegal, and a Nazi law that threatened the death penalty was still in force. So Frieda went to an elderly "midwife" who did it for five cigarettes. Frieda contracted a severe infection, and would have died but that Carla was able to steal scarce penicillin from the hospital.

Carla decided to have her baby.

Her feelings about it swung violently from one extreme to another. When suffering morning sickness she raged against the beasts who had violated her body and left her with this burden. At other times she found herself sitting with her hands on her belly, staring into space and thinking dreamily about baby clothes. Then she would wonder if the baby's face would remind her of one of the men, and cause her to hate her own child. But surely it would have some von Ulrich features, too? She felt anxious and frightened.

She was eight months pregnant in January 1946. Like most Germans she was also cold, hungry, and destitute. When her pregnancy became obvious, she had to give up nursing and join the millions of unemployed. Food rations were issued every ten days. The daily amount, for those without special privileges, was fifteen hundred calories. It still had to be paid for, of course. And even for customers with cash and ration cards, sometimes there was simply no food to buy.

Carla had considered asking the Soviets for special treatment because of her wartime work as a spy. But Heinrich had tried that and suffered a frightening experience. Red Army Intelligence had expected him to continue to spy for them, and asked him to infiltrate the U.S. military. When he said he would rather not, they became nasty and threatened to send him to a labor camp. He got out of it by saying he spoke no English, therefore was no use to them. But Carla was well warned, and decided it was safest to keep quiet.

Today Carla and Maud were happy because they had sold a chest of drawers. It was a Jugendstil piece in burled light oak that Walter's parents had bought when they got married in 1889. Carla, Maud, and Ada had loaded it onto a borrowed handcart.

There were still no men in their house. Erik and Werner were among millions of German soldiers who had disappeared. Perhaps they were dead. Colonel Beck had told Carla that almost three million Germans had died in battle on the eastern front, and more had died as prisoners of the Soviets—killed by hunger, cold, and disease. But another two million were still alive and working in labor camps in the Soviet Union. Some had come back: they had either escaped from their guards or had been released because they were too ill to work, and they had joined the thousands of displaced persons on the tramp all over Europe, trying to find their way home. Carla and Maud had written letters and sent them care of the Red Army, but no replies had ever come.

Carla felt torn about the prospect of Werner's return. She still loved him, and hoped desperately that he was alive and well, but she dreaded meeting him when she was pregnant with a rapist's baby. Although it was not her fault, she felt irrationally ashamed.

So the three women pushed the handcart through the streets. They left Rebecca behind. The Red Army orgy of rape and looting had passed its nightmare peak, and Rebecca no longer lived in the attic, but it was still not safe for a pretty girl to walk the streets.

Huge photographs of Lenin and Stalin now hung over Unter den Linden, once the promenade of Germany's fashionable elite. Most Berlin roads had been cleared, and the rubble of destroyed buildings stood in stacks every few hundred yards, ready to be reused, perhaps, if ever Germans were able to rebuild their country. Acres of houses had been flattened, often entire city blocks. It would take years to deal with the wreckage. There were thousands of bodies rotting in the ruins, and the sickly-sweet smell of decaying human flesh had been in the air all summer. Now it smelled only after rain.

Meanwhile, the city had been divided into four zones: Russian, American, British, and French. Many of the buildings still standing had been commandeered by the occupying troops. Berliners lived where they could, often seeking inadequate shelter in the surviving rooms of half-demolished houses. The city had running water again, and electric power came on fitfully, but it was hard to find fuel for heating and cooking. The chest of drawers might be almost as valuable chopped up for firewood.

They took it to Wedding, in the French zone, where they sold it to a charming Parisian colonel for a carton of Gitanes. The occupation currency had become worthless, because the Soviets printed too much of it, so everything was bought and sold for cigarettes.

Now they were returning triumphant, Maud and Ada steering the empty cart while Carla walked alongside. She ached all over from pushing the cart, but they were rich: a whole carton of cigarettes would go a long way.

Night fell and the temperature dropped to freezing. Their route home took them briefly into the British sector. Carla sometimes wondered whether the British might help her mother if they knew the hardship she was suffering. On the other hand, Maud had been a German citizen for twenty-six years. Her brother, Earl Fitzherbert, was wealthy and influential, but he had refused to support her after her marriage to Walter von Ulrich, and he was a stubborn man: it was not likely he would change his attitude.

They came across a small crowd, thirty or forty ragged people, outside a house that had been taken over by the occupying power. Stopping to find out what they were staring at, the three women saw a party going on inside. Through the windows they could observe brightly lit rooms, laughing men and women holding drinks, and waitresses moving through the throng with trays of food. Carla looked around her. The crowd was mostly women and children—there were not many men left in Berlin, or indeed in Germany—and they were all staring longingly at the windows, like rejected sinners outside the gates of paradise. It was a pathetic sight.

"This is obscene," said Maud, and she marched up the path to the door of the house.

A British sentry stood in her way and said: "*Nein, nein,*" probably the only German he knew.

Maud addressed him in the crisp upper-class English she had spoken as a girl. "I must see your commanding officer immediately."

Carla admired her mother's nerve and poise, as always.

The sentry looked doubtfully at Maud's threadbare coat, but after a moment he tapped on the door. It opened, and a face looked out. "English lady wants the CO," said the sentry.

A moment later the door opened again and two people looked out. They might have been caricatures of a British officer and his wife: he in his mess kit with a black bow tie, she in a long dress and pearls.

"Good evening," Maud said. "I'm frightfully sorry to disturb your party."

They stared at her, astonished to be spoken to that way by a woman in rags.

Maud went on: "I just thought you should see what you're doing to these wretched people outside."

The couple looked at the crowd.

Maud said: "You might draw the curtains, for pity's sake."

After a moment the woman said: "Oh, dear, George, have we been terribly unkind?"

"Unintentionally, perhaps," the man said gruffly.

"Could we possibly make amends by sending some food out to them?"

"Yes," Maud said quickly. "That would be a kindness as well as an apology."

The officer looked dubious. It was probably against some kind of regulation to give canapés to starving Germans.

The woman pleaded: "George, darling, may we?"

"Oh, very well," said her husband.

The woman turned back to Maud. "Thank you for alerting us. We really didn't mean to do this."

"You're welcome," Maud said, and she retreated down the path.

A few minutes later, guests began to emerge from the house with plates of sandwiches and cakes, which they offered to the starving crowd. Carla grinned. Her mother's impudence had paid off. She took a large piece of fruitcake, which she wolfed in a few starved bites. It contained more sugar than she had eaten in the past six months.

The curtains were drawn, the guests returned to the house, and the crowd dispersed. Maud and Ada grasped the handles of the cart and recommenced pushing it home. "Well done, Mother," said Carla. "A carton of Gitanes *and* a free meal, all in one afternoon!"

Apart from the Soviets, few of the occupying soldiers were cruel to Germans, Carla reflected. She found it surprising. American GIs gave out chocolate bars. Even the French, whose own children had gone hungry under German occupation, often showed kindness. After all the misery we Germans have inflicted on our neighbors, Carla thought, it's astonishing they don't hate us more. On the other hand, what with the Nazis, the Red Army, and the air raids, perhaps they think we've been punished enough.

It was late when they got home. They left the cart with the neighbors who had loaned it, giving them half a pack of Gitanes as payment. They entered their house, which was luckily still intact. There was no glass in most of the windows, and the stonework was pocked with craters, but the place had not suffered structural damage, and it still kept the weather out.

All the same, the four women now lived in the kitchen, sleeping there on mattresses they dragged in from the hall at night. It was hard enough to warm that one room, and they certainly did not have fuel to heat the rest of the house. The kitchen stove had burned coal, in the old days, but that was now virtually unobtainable. However, they had found the stove would burn many other things: books, newspapers, broken furniture, even net curtains.

They slept in pairs, Carla with Rebecca and Maud with Ada. Rebecca often cried herself to sleep in Carla's arms, as she had the night after her parents were killed.

The long walk had exhausted Carla, and she immediately lay down. Ada built up the fire in the stove with old news magazines Rebecca had brought down from the attic. Maud added water to the remains of the lunchtime bean soup and reheated it for their supper.

Sitting up to drink her soup, Carla suffered a sharp abdominal pain. This was not a result of pushing the handcart, she realized. It was something else. She checked the date and counted back to the date of the liberation of the Jewish Hospital.

"Mother," she said fearfully, "I think the baby's coming."

"It's too soon!" Maud said.

"I'm thirty-six weeks pregnant, and I'm getting cramps."

"Then we'd better get ready."

Maud went upstairs to fetch towels.

Ada brought a wooden chair from the dining room. She had a useful length of twisted steel from a bomb site that served her as a sledgehammer. She smashed the chair into manageable pieces, then built up the fire in the stove.

Carla put her hands on her distended belly. "You might have waited for warmer weather, Baby," she said.

Soon she was in too much pain to notice the cold. She had not known anything could hurt this much.

Nor that it could go on so long. She was in labor all night. Maud and Ada took turns holding her hand while she moaned and cried. Rebecca looked on, white-faced and scared.

The gray light of morning was filtering through the newspaper taped over the glassless kitchen window when at last the baby's head emerged. Carla was overwhelmed by a feeling of relief like nothing she had ever experienced, even though the pain did not immediately cease.

After one more agonizing push, Maud took the baby from between her legs.

"A boy," she said.

She blew on his face, and he opened his mouth and cried.

She gave the baby to Carla, and propped her upright on the mattress with some cushions from the drawing room.

He had lots of dark hair all over his head.

Maud tied off the cord with a piece of cotton, then cut it. Carla unbuttoned her blouse and put the baby to her breast.

She was worried she might have no milk. Her breasts should have swollen and leaked toward the end of her pregnancy, but they had not, perhaps because the baby was early, perhaps because the mother was undernourished. But, after a few moments of sucking, she felt a strange pain, and the milk began to flow.

Soon he fell asleep.

Ada brought a bowl of warm water and a rag, and gently washed the baby's face and head, then the rest of him.

Rebecca whispered: "He's so beautiful."

Carla said: "Mother, shall we call him Walter?"

She had not intended to be dramatic, but Maud fell apart. Her face crumpled and she bent double, racked by terrible sobs. She recovered herself sufficiently to say, "I'm sorry." Then she was convulsed by grief again. "Oh, Walter, my Walter," she wept.

Eventually her crying subsided. "I'm sorry," she said again. "I didn't mean to make a fuss." She wiped her face with her sleeve. "I just wish your father could see the baby, that's all. It's so unfair."

Ada surprised them both by quoting the book of Job: "'The Lord giveth and the Lord taketh away,'" she said. "'Blessed be the name of the Lord.'"

Carla did not believe in God—no holy being worthy of the name could have allowed the Nazi death camps to happen—but all the same she found comfort in the quotation. It was about accepting everything in human life, including the pain of birth and the sorrow of death. Maud seemed to appreciate it, too, and she became calmer.

Carla looked adoringly at baby Walter. She would care for him and feed him and keep him warm, she vowed, no matter what difficulties stood in the way. He was the most wonderful child that had ever been born, and she would love and cherish him forever.

He woke up, and Carla gave him her nipple again. He sucked

contentedly, making small smacking noises with his mouth, while four women watched him. For a little while, in the warm, dim-lit kitchen, there was no other sound.

ii

The first speech made by a new member of Parliament is called a maiden speech, and is usually dull. Certain things have to be said, stock phrases are used, and the convention is that the subject must not be controversial. Colleagues and opponents alike congratulate the newcomer, the traditions are observed, and the ice is broken.

Lloyd Williams made his first *real* speech a few months later, during the debate on the national insurance bill. That was more scary.

In preparing it he had two orators in mind. His grandfather Dai Williams used the language and rhythms of the Bible, not just in chapel but also—perhaps especially—when speaking of the hardship and injustice of the life of a coal miner. He relished short words rich in meaning: *toil, sin, greed.* He spoke of the hearth and the pit and the grave.

Churchill did the same, but had humor that Dai Williams lacked. His long, majestic sentences often ended with an unexpected image or a reversal of meaning. Having been editor of the government newspaper the *British Gazette* during the General Strike of 1926, he had warned trade unionists: "Make your minds perfectly clear: if ever you let loose upon us again a general strike, we will loose upon you another *British Gazette.*" A speech needed such surprises, Lloyd believed; they were like the raisins in a bun.

But when he stood up to speak, he found that his carefully wrought sentences suddenly seemed unreal. His audience clearly felt the same, and he could sense that the fifty or sixty M.P.s in the chamber were only half listening. He suffered a moment of panic: How could he be boring about a subject that mattered so profoundly to the people he represented?

On the government front bench he could see his mother, now minister for schools, and his uncle Billy, minister for coal. Billy Williams had started work down the pit at the age of thirteen, Lloyd knew. Ethel had been the same age when she began scrubbing the floors of Tŷ Gwyn. This debate was not about fine phrases; it was about their lives.

After a minute he abandoned his script and spoke extempore. He recalled instead the misery of working-class families made penniless by unemployment or disability, scenes he had witnessed firsthand in the East End of London and the South Wales coalfield. His voice betrayed the emotion he felt, somewhat to his embarrassment, but he plowed on. He sensed his audience beginning to pay attention. He spoke of his grandfather and others who had started the Labour movement with the dream of comprehensive employment insurance to banish forever the fear of destitution. When he sat down, there was a roar of approval.

In the visitors' gallery his wife, Daisy, smiled proudly and gave him a thumbs-up sign.

He listened to the rest of the debate in a glow of satisfaction. He felt he had passed his first real test as an M.P.

Afterward, in the lobby, he was approached by a Labour whip, one of the people responsible for making sure M.P.s voted the right way. After congratulating Lloyd on his speech, the whip said: "How would you like to be a parliamentary private secretary?"

Lloyd was thrilled. Each minister and secretary of state had at least one PPS. In truth a PPS was often little more than a bag-carrier, but the job was the usual first step on the way to a ministerial appointment. "I'd be honored," Lloyd said. "Who would I be working for?"

"Ernie Bevin."

Lloyd could hardly believe his luck. Bevin was foreign secretary and the closest colleague of Prime Minister Attlee. The intimate relationship between the two men was a case of the attraction of opposites. Attlee was middle-class: the son of a lawyer, an Oxford graduate, an officer in the First World War. Bevin was the illegitimate child of a housemaid, never knew his father, started work at the age of eleven, and founded the mammoth Transport and General Workers' Union. They were physical opposites, too: Attlee slim and dapper, quiet, solemn; Bevin a huge man, tall and strong and overweight, with a loud laugh. The foreign secretary referred to the prime minister as "little Clem." All the same they were staunch allies.

Bevin was a hero to Lloyd and to millions of ordinary British people. "There's nothing I'd like more," Lloyd said. "But hasn't Bevin already got a PPS?"

"He needs two," the whip said. "Go to the Foreign Office tomorrow morning at nine and you can get started."

"Thank you!"

Lloyd hurried along the oak-paneled corridor, heading for his mother's office. He had arranged to meet Daisy there after the debate. "Mam!" he said as he entered. "I've been made PPS to Ernie Bevin!"

Then he saw that Ethel was not alone. Earl Fitzherbert was with her.

Fitz stared at Lloyd with a mixture of surprise and distaste.

Even in his shock Lloyd noticed that his father was wearing a perfectly cut light gray suit with a double-breasted waistcoat.

He looked back at his mother. She was quite calm. This encounter was not a surprise to her. She must have contrived it.

The earl came to the same conclusion. "What the devil is this, Ethel?"

Lloyd stared at the man whose blood ran in his veins. Even in this embarrassing situation, Fitz was poised and dignified. He was handsome, despite the drooping eyelid that resulted from the Battle of the Somme. He leaned on a walking stick, another consequence of the Somme. A few months short of sixty years old, he was immaculately groomed, his gray hair neatly trimmed, his silver tie tightly knotted, his black shoes shining. Lloyd, too, always liked to look well turned out. That's where I get it from, he thought.

Ethel went and stood close to the earl. Lloyd knew his mother well enough to understand this move. She frequently used her charm when she wanted to persuade a man. All the same, Lloyd did not like to see her being so warm to one who had exploited her, then let her down.

"I was so sorry when I heard about the death of Boy," she said to Fitz. "Nothing is as precious to us as our children, is it?"

"I must go," Fitz said.

Until this moment, Lloyd had met Fitz only in passing. He had never before spent this much time with him or heard him speak this number of words. Despite feeling uncomfortable, Lloyd was fascinated. Grumpy though he was right now, Fitz had a kind of allure.

"Please, Fitz," said Ethel. "You have a son whom you have never acknowledged—a son you should be proud of."

"You shouldn't do this, Ethel," said Fitz. "A man is entitled to forget the mistakes of his youth."

Lloyd cringed with embarrassment, but his mother pressed on. "Why should you want to forget? I know he was a mistake, but look at him now—a member of Parliament who has just made a thrilling speech and been appointed PPS to the foreign secretary."

Fitz pointedly did not look at Lloyd.

Ethel said: "You want to pretend that our affair was a meaningless dalliance, but you know the truth. Yes, we were young and foolish, and randy, too—me as much as you—but we loved each other. We *really* loved each other, Fitz. You should admit it. Don't you know that if you deny the truth about yourself you lose your soul?"

Fitz's face was no longer merely impassive, Lloyd saw. He was struggling to maintain control. Lloyd understood that his mother had put her finger on the real problem. It was not so much that Fitz was ashamed of having an illegitimate son. But he was too proud to accept that he had loved a housemaid. He probably loved Ethel more than his wife, Lloyd guessed. And that upset all his most fundamental beliefs about the social hierarchy.

Lloyd spoke for the first time. "I was with Boy at the end, sir. He died bravely."

For the first time, Fitz looked at him. "My son doesn't require your approval," he said.

Lloyd felt as if he had been slapped.

Even Ethel was shocked. "Fitz!" she said. "How can you be so mean?"

At that point Daisy came in.

"Hello, Fitz!" she said gaily. "You probably thought you'd got rid of me, but now you're my father-in-law again. Isn't that amusing?"

Ethel said: "I'm just trying to persuade Fitz to shake Lloyd's hand."

Fitz said: "I try to avoid shaking hands with socialists."

Ethel was fighting a losing battle, but she would not give up. "See how much of yourself there is in him! He resembles you, dresses like you, shares your interest in politics—he'll probably end up foreign secretary, which you always wanted to be!"

Fitz's expression darkened further. "It is now most unlikely that I shall ever be foreign secretary." He went to the door. "And it would not please me in the least if that great office of state were to be held by my Bolshevik bastard!" With that he walked out.

Ethel burst into tears.

Daisy put her arm around Lloyd. "I'm so sorry," she said.

"Don't worry," Lloyd said. "I'm not shocked or disappointed." This was not true, but he did not want to appear pathetic. "I was rejected by him a long time ago." He looked at Daisy with adoration. "I'm lucky to have plenty of other people who love me."

Ethel said tearfully: "It's my fault. I shouldn't have asked him to come here. I might have known it would turn out badly."

"Never mind," said Daisy. "I have some good news."

Lloyd smiled at her. "What's that?"

She looked at Ethel. "Are you ready for this?"

"I think so."

"Come on," said Lloyd. "What is it?"

Daisy said: "We're going to have a baby."

iii

Carla's brother, Erik, came home that summer, near to death. He had contracted tuberculosis in a Soviet labor camp, and they had released him when he became too ill to work. He had been sleeping rough for weeks, traveling on freight trains and begging lifts on lorries. He arrived at the von Ulrich house barefoot and wearing filthy clothes. His face was like a skull.

However, he did not die. It might have been being with people who loved him, or the warmer weather as winter turned into spring, or perhaps just rest, but he coughed less and regained enough energy to do some work around the house, boarding up smashed windows, repairing roof tiles, unblocking pipes.

Fortunately, at the beginning of the year Frieda Franck had struck gold.

Ludwig Franck had been killed in the air raid that destroyed his factory, and for a while Frieda and her mother had been as destitute as everyone else. But she got a job as a nurse in the American zone, and soon afterward, she explained to Carla, a little group of American doctors had asked her to sell their surplus food and cigarettes on the black market in exchange for a cut of the proceeds. Thereafter she turned up at Carla's house once a week with a little basket of supplies: warm clothing, candles, flashlight batteries, matches, soap, and food—bacon, chocolate, apples, rice, canned peaches. Maud divided the food into portions and gave Carla double. Carla accepted without hesitation, not for her own sake, but to help her feed baby Walli.

Without Frieda's illicit groceries, Walli might not have made it.

He was changing fast. The dark hair with which he had been born had now gone, and instead he had fine, fair hair. At six months he had Maud's wonderful green eyes. As his face took shape, Carla noticed a fold of flesh in the outer corners of his eyes that gave him a slant-eyed look, and she wondered if his father had been a Siberian. She could not remember all the men who had raped her. Most of the time she had closed her eyes.

She no longer hated them. It was strange, but she was so happy to have Walli that she could hardly bring herself to regret what had happened.

Rebecca was fascinated by Walli. Now just fifteen, she was old enough to have the beginnings of maternal feelings, and she eagerly helped Carla bathe and dress the baby. She played with him constantly, and he gurgled with delight when he saw her.

As soon as Erik felt well enough, he joined the Communist Party.

Carla was baffled. After what he had suffered at the hands of the

Soviets, how could he? But she found that he talked about Communism in the same way he had talked about Nazism a decade earlier. She just hoped that this time his disillusionment would not be so long coming.

The Allies were keen for democracy to return to Germany, and city elections were scheduled for Berlin later in 1946.

Carla felt sure the city would not return to normal until its own people took control, so she decided to stand for the Social Democratic Party. But Berliners quickly discovered that the Soviet occupiers had a curious notion of what democracy meant.

The Soviets had been shocked by the results of elections in Austria last November. The Austrian Communists had expected to run neck and neck with the socialists, but had won only four seats out of 165. It seemed that voters blamed Communism for the brutality of the Red Army. The Kremlin, unused to genuine elections, had not anticipated that.

To avoid a similar result in Germany, the Soviets proposed a merger between the Communists and the Social Democrats in what they called a united front. The Social Democrats refused, despite heavy pressure. In East Germany the Russians started arresting Social Democrats, just as the Nazis had in 1933. There the merger was forced through. But the Berlin elections were supervised by the four Allies, and the Social Democrats survived.

Once the weather warmed up, Carla was able to take her turn queuing for food. She carried Walli with her wrapped in a pillowcase— she had no baby clothes. Standing in line for potatoes one morning, a few blocks from home, she was surprised to see an American jeep pull up with Frieda in the passenger seat. The balding, middle-aged driver kissed her on the lips, and she jumped out. She was wearing a sleeveless blue dress and new shoes. She walked quickly away, heading for the von Ulrich house, carrying her little basket.

Carla saw everything in a flash. Frieda was not trading on the black market, and there was no syndicate of doctors. She was the paid mistress of an American officer.

It was not unusual. Thousands of pretty German girls had been faced with the choice: see your family starve, or sleep with a generous officer. French women had done the same under German occupation; officers' wives back here in Germany had spoken bitterly about it.

All the same, Carla was horrified. She believed that Frieda loved Heinrich. They were planning to get married as soon as life returned to some semblance of normality. Carla felt sick at heart.

She reached the head of the line and bought her ration of potatoes, then hurried home.

She found Frieda upstairs in the drawing room. Erik had cleaned up the room and put newspaper in the windows, the next best thing to glass. The curtains had long ago been recycled as bed linen, but most of the chairs had survived so far, their upholstery faded and worn. The grand piano was still there, miraculously. A Russian officer had discovered it and announced that he would return next day with a crane to lift it out through the window, but he had never come back.

Frieda immediately took Walli from Carla and began to sing to him. "*A, B, C, die Katze lief im Schnee.*" The women who had not yet had children, Rebecca and Frieda, could hardly get enough of Walli, Carla observed. Those who had had children of their own, Maud and Ada, adored him but dealt with him in a briskly practical way.

Frieda opened the lid of the piano and encouraged Walli to bang on the keys as she sang. The instrument had not been played for years: Maud had not touched it since the death of her last pupil, Joachim Koch.

After a few minutes Frieda said to Carla: "You're a bit solemn. What is it?"

"I know how you get the food you bring us," Carla said. "You're not a black marketeer, are you?"

"Of course I am," Frieda said. "What are you talking about?"

"I saw you this morning, getting out of a jeep."

"Colonel Hicks gave me a lift."

"He kissed you on the lips."

Frieda looked away. "I knew I should have got out earlier. I could have walked from the American zone."

"Frieda, what about Heinrich?"

"He'll never know! I'll be more careful, I swear."

"Do you still love him?"

"Of course! We're going to get married."

"Then why . . . ?"

"I've had enough of hard times! I want to put on pretty clothes and go to nightclubs and dance."

"No, you don't," Carla said confidently. "You can't lie to me, Frieda—we've been friends too long. Tell me the truth."

"The truth?"

"Yes, please."

"You're sure?"

"I'm sure."

"I did it for Walli."

Carla gasped with shock. That had never occurred to her, but it made sense. She could believe Frieda would make such a sacrifice for her and her baby.

But she felt dreadful. This made her responsible for Frieda's prostituting herself. "This is terrible!" Carla said. "You shouldn't have done it—we would have managed somehow."

Frieda sprang up from the piano stool with the baby still in her arms. "No, you wouldn't!" she blazed.

Walli was frightened, and cried. Carla took him and rocked him, patting his back.

"You wouldn't have managed," Frieda said more quietly.

"How do you know?"

"All last winter, babies were brought into the hospital naked, wrapped in newspapers, dead of hunger and cold. I could hardly bear to look at them."

"Oh, God." Carla held Walli tight.

"They turn a peculiar bluish color when they freeze to death."

"Stop it."

"I have to tell you. Otherwise you won't understand what I did. Walli would have been one of those blue frozen babies."

"I know," Carla whispered. "I know."

"Percy Hicks is a kind man. He has a frumpy wife back in Boston and I'm the sexiest thing he's ever seen. He's nice and quick about intercourse and always uses a condom."

"You should stop," Carla said.

"You don't mean that."

"No, I don't," Carla confessed. "And that's the worst part. I feel so guilty. I am guilty."

"You're not. It's my choice. German women have to make hard choices. We're paying for the easy choices German men made fifteen years ago. Men such as my father, who thought Hitler would be good for business, and Heinrich's father, who voted for the Enabling Act. The sins of the fathers are visited on the daughters."

There was a loud knock at the front door. A moment later they heard scampering steps as Rebecca hurried upstairs to hide, just in case it was the Red Army.

Then Ada's voice said: "Oh! Sir! Good morning!" She sounded surprised and a bit worried, though not scared. Carla wondered who would induce that particular mixture of reactions in the maid.

There was a heavy masculine tread on the stairs; then Werner walked in.

He was dirty and ragged and thin as a rail, but there was a broad smile on his handsome face. "It's me!" he said ebulliently. "I'm back!"

Then he saw the baby. His jaw dropped and the happy smile disappeared. "Oh," he said. "What . . . who . . . whose baby is that?"

"Mine, my darling," said Carla. "Let me explain."

"Explain?" he said angrily. "What explanation is necessary? You've had someone else's baby!" He turned to go.

Frieda said: "Werner! In this room are two women who love you. Don't walk out without listening to us. You don't understand."

"I think I understand everything."

"Carla was raped."

He went pale. "Raped? Who by?"

Carla said: "I never knew their names."

"Names?" Werner swallowed. "There . . . there was more than one?"

"Five Red Army soldiers."

His voice fell to a whisper. "Five?"

Carla nodded.

"But . . . couldn't you . . . I mean . . ."

Frieda said: "I was raped, too, Werner. And so was Mother."

"Dear God, what has been going on here?"

"Hell," said Frieda.

Werner sat down heavily in a worn leather chair. "I thought hell was where I've been," he said. He buried his face in his hands.

Carla crossed the room, still holding Walli, and stood in front of Werner's chair. "Look at me, Werner," she said. "Please."

He looked up, his face twisted with emotion.

"Hell is over," she said.

"Is it?"

"Yes," she said firmly. "Life is hard, but the Nazis have gone, the war is finished, Hitler is dead, and the Red Army rapists have been brought under control, more or less. The nightmare has ended. And we're both alive, and together."

He reached out and took her hand. "You're right."

"We've got Walli, and in a minute you'll meet a fifteen-year-old girl called Rebecca who has somehow become my child. We have to make a new family out of what the war has left us, just as we have to build new houses with the rubble in the streets."

He nodded acceptance.

"I need your love," she said. "So do Rebecca and Walli."

He stood up slowly. She looked at him expectantly. He said nothing, but after a long moment, he put his arms around her and the baby, gently embracing them both.

iv

Under wartime regulations still in force, the British government had a right to open a coal mine anywhere, regardless of the wishes of the owner of the land. Compensation was paid only for loss of earnings on farmland or commercial property.

Billy Williams, as minister for coal, authorized an open-cast mine on the grounds of Tŷ Gwyn, the palatial residence of Earl Fitzherbert on the outskirts of Aberowen.

No compensation was payable, as the land was not commercial.

There was uproar on the Conservative benches in the House of Commons. "Your slag heap will be right under the bedroom windows of the countess!" said one indignant Tory.

Billy Williams smiled. "The earl's slag heap has been under my mother's window for fifty years," he said.

Lloyd Williams and Ethel both traveled to Aberowen with Billy the day before the engineers began to dig the hole. Lloyd was reluctant to leave Daisy, who was due to give birth in two weeks, but it was a historic moment, and he wanted to be there.

Both his grandparents were now in their late seventies. Granda was almost blind despite his pebble-lensed glasses, and Grandmam was bent-backed. "This is nice," Grandmam said when they all sat around the old kitchen table. "Both my children here." She served stewed beef with mashed turnips and thick slices of homemade bread spread with the butcher's fat called dripping. She poured large mugs of sweetened milky tea to go with it.

Lloyd had eaten like this frequently as a child, but now he found it coarse. He knew that even in hard times French and Spanish women managed to serve up tasty dishes delicately flavored with garlic and garnished with herbs. He was ashamed of his fastidiousness, and pretended to eat and drink with relish.

"Pity about the gardens at Tŷ Gwyn," Grandmam said tactlessly.

Billy was stung. "What do you mean? Britain needs the coal."

"But people love those gardens. Beautiful, they are. I've been there at least once every year since I was a girl. Shame it is to see them go."

"There's a perfectly good recreation ground right in the middle of Aberowen!"

"It's not the same," said Grandmam imperturbably.

Granda said: "Women will never understand politics."

"No," said Grandmam. "I don't suppose we will."

Lloyd caught his mother's eye. She smiled and said nothing.

Billy and Lloyd shared the second bedroom, and Ethel made up a bed on the kitchen floor. "I slept in this room every night of my life until I went in the army," Billy said as they lay down. "And I looked out the window every morning at that fucking slag heap."

"Keep your voice down, Uncle Billy," Lloyd said. "You don't want your mother to hear you swear."

"Aye, you're right," said Billy.

Next morning after breakfast they all walked up the hill to the big house. It was a mild morning, and for a change there was no rain. The ridge of mountains at the skyline was softened with summer grass. As Tŷ Gwyn came into view, Lloyd could not help seeing it more as a beautiful building than as a symbol of oppression. It was both, of course; nothing was simple in politics.

The great iron gates stood open. The Williams family passed onto the grounds. A crowd had gathered already: the contractor's men with their machinery, a hundred or so miners and their families, Earl Fitzherbert with his son Andrew, a handful of reporters with notebooks, and a film crew.

The gardens were breathtaking. The avenue of ancient chestnut trees was in full leaf, there were swans on the lake, and the flower beds blazed with color. Lloyd guessed the earl had made sure the place looked its best. He wanted to brand the Labour government as wreckers in the eyes of the world.

Lloyd found himself sympathizing with Fitz.

The mayor of Aberowen was giving an interview. "The people of this town are against the open-cast mine," he said. Lloyd was surprised; the town council was Labour, and it must have gone against the grain for them to oppose the government. "For more than a hundred years, the beauty of these gardens has refreshed the souls of people who live in a grim industrial landscape," the mayor went on. Switching from prepared speech to personal reminiscence, he added: "I proposed to my wife under that cedar tree."

He was interrupted by a loud clanking sound like the footsteps of an iron giant. Turning to look back along the drive, Lloyd saw a huge machine approaching. It looked like the biggest crane in the world. It had an enormous boom ninety feet long and a bucket into which a lorry could easily fit. Most astonishing of all, it moved along on rotating steel shoes that made the earth shake every time they hit the ground.

Billy said proudly to Lloyd: "That's a walking monighan dragline excavator. Picks up six tons of earth at a time."

The camera rolled as the monstrous machine stomped up the drive.

Lloyd had only one misgiving about the Labour Party. There was a streak of puritan authoritarianism in many socialists. His grandfather had it, and so did Billy. They were not comfortable with sensual pleasures. Sacrifice and self-denial suited them better. They dismissed the ravishing beauty of these gardens as irrelevant. They were wrong.

Ethel was not that way, nor was Lloyd. Perhaps the killjoy strain had been bred out of their line. He hoped so.

Fitz gave an interview on the pink gravel path while the digger driver maneuvered his machine into position. "The minister for coal has told you that when the mine is exhausted, the garden will be subject to what he calls an effective restoration program," he said. "I say to you that that promise is worthless. It has taken more than a century for my grandfather and my father and me to bring the garden to its present pitch of beauty and harmony. It would take another hundred years to restore it."

The boom of the excavator was lowered until it stood at a forty-five-degree angle over the shrubbery and flower beds of the west garden. The bucket was positioned over the croquet lawn. There was a long moment of waiting. The crowd fell silent. Billy said loudly: "Get on with it, for God's sake."

An engineer in a bowler hat blew a whistle.

The bucket was dropped to the earth with a massive thud. Its steel teeth dug into the flat green lawn. The dragrope tautened, there was a loud creak of straining machinery, and then the bucket began to move back. As it was dragged across the ground, it dug up a bed of huge yellow sunflowers, the rose garden, a shrubbery of summersweet and bottlebrush buckeye, and a small magnolia tree. At the end of its travel the bucket was full of earth, flowers, and plants.

The bucket was then lifted to a height of twenty feet, dribbling loose earth and blossoms.

The boom swung sideways. It was taller than the house, Lloyd saw. He almost thought the bucket would smash the upstairs windows, but the operator was skilled, and stopped it just in time. The dragrope slackened, the bucket tilted, and six tons of garden fell to the ground a few feet from the entrance.

The bucket was returned to its original position, and the process was repeated.

Lloyd looked at Fitz and saw that he was crying.

CHAPTER TWENTY-THREE

1947

A t the beginning of 1947 it seemed possible that all Europe might go Communist.

Volodya Peshkov was not sure whether to hope for that or its opposite.

The Red Army dominated Eastern Europe, and Communists were winning elections in the west. Communists had gained respect for their role in resisting the Nazis. Five million people had voted Communist in the first French postwar election, making the Communists the most popular party. In Italy a Communist-socialist alliance won 40 percent of the vote. In Czechoslovakia the Communists on their own won 38 percent and led the democratically elected government.

It was different in Austria and Germany, where voters had been robbed and raped by the Red Army. In the Berlin city elections, the Social Democrats won 63 of 130 seats, the Communists only 26. However, Germany was ruined and starving, and the Kremlin still hoped that the people might turn to Communism in desperation, just as they had turned to Nazism in the Depression.

Britain was the great disappointment. Only one Communist had been sent to Parliament in the postwar election there. And the Labour government was delivering everything Communism promised: welfare, free health care, education for all, even a five-day week for coal miners.

But in the rest of Europe, capitalism was failing to lift people out of the postwar slump.

And the weather was on Stalin's side, Volodya thought as the layers of snow grew thick on the onion domes. The winter of 1946–47 was the coldest in Europe for more than a century. Snow fell in St.-Tropez. British roads and railways became impassable, and industry ground to a halt—something that had never happened in the war. In France, food rations fell below wartime levels. The United Nations organization calculated that one hundred million Europeans were living on fifteen hundred calories a day—the level at which health begins to suffer from malnutrition. As the engines of production ran slower and slower, people began to feel they had nothing to lose, and revolution came to seem the only way out.

Once the USSR had nuclear weapons, no other country would be able to stand in its way. Volodya's wife, Zoya, and her colleagues had built a nuclear pile, at Laboratory No. 2 of the Academy of Sciences, a deliberately vague name for the powerhouse of Soviet nuclear research. The pile had gone critical on Christmas Day, six months after the birth of their son, Konstantin, who was at the time sleeping in the laboratory's crèche. If the experiment went wrong, Zoya had whispered to Volodya, it would do little Kotya no good to be a mile or two away: all central Moscow would be flattened.

Volodya's conflicting feelings about the future took on a new intensity with the birth of his son. He wanted Kotya to grow up a citizen of a proud and powerful country. The Soviet Union deserved to dominate Europe, he felt. It was the Red Army that had defeated the Nazis, in four cruel years of total warfare; the other Allies had stood on the sidelines, fighting minor wars, joining in only for the last eleven months. All their casualties put together were only a fraction of those suffered by the Soviet people.

But then he would think of what Communism meant: arbitrary

purges, torture in the basements of the secret police, conquering soldiers urged on to excesses of bestiality, the whole vast country forced to obey the wayward decisions of a tyrant more powerful than a tsar. Did Volodya really want to extend that brutal system to the rest of the continent?

He remembered walking into Penn Station in New York and buying a ticket to Albuquerque, without asking anyone's permission or showing any papers, and the exhilarating sense of total freedom that had given him. He had long ago burned the Sears Roebuck Catalogue, but it lived in his memory, with its hundreds of pages of good things available for everyone to have. Russian people believed that stories of Western freedom and prosperity were just propaganda, but Volodya knew better. A part of him longed for Communism to be defeated.

The future of Germany, and therefore of Europe, was to be decided at the Conference of Foreign Ministers held in Moscow in March 1947.

Volodya, now a colonel, was in charge of the intelligence team assigned to the conference. Meetings were held in an ornate room at Aviation Industry House, conveniently close to the Hotel Moskva. As always, the delegates and their interpreters sat around a table, with their aides on several rows of chairs behind them. The Soviet foreign minister, Vyacheslav Molotov, Old Stone Arse, demanded that Germany pay ten billion dollars to the USSR in war reparations. The Americans and British protested that this would be a deathblow to Germany's sickly economy. That was probably what Stalin wanted.

Volodya renewed his acquaintance with Woody Dewar, who was now a news photographer assigned to cover the conference. He was married, too, and showed Volodya a photo of a striking dark-haired woman holding a baby. Sitting in the back of a ZIS-110B limousine, returning from a formal photo session at the Kremlin, Woody said to Volodya: "You realize that Germany doesn't have the money to pay your reparations, don't you?"

Volodya's English had improved, and they could manage without an interpreter. He said: "Then how are they feeding their people and rebuilding their cities?"

"With handouts from us, of course," said Woody. "We're spending a fortune in aid. Any reparations the Germans paid you would be, in reality, our money."

"Is that so wrong? The United States prospered in the war. My country was devastated. Maybe you should pay."

"American voters don't think so."

"American voters may be wrong."

Woody shrugged. "True—but it's their money."

There it was again, Volodya thought: the deference to public opinion. He had remarked it before in Woody's conversation. Americans talked about voters the way Russians talked about Stalin: they had to be obeyed, right or wrong.

Woody wound down the window. "You don't mind if I take a cityscape, do you? The light is wonderful." His camera clicked.

He knew he was supposed to take only approved shots. However, there was nothing sensitive on the street, just some women shoveling snow. All the same, Volodya said: "Please don't." He leaned past Woody and wound up the window. "Official photos only."

He was about to ask for the film out of Woody's camera when Woody said: "Do you remember me mentioning my friend Greg Peshkov, with the same surname as you?"

Volodya certainly did. Willi Frunze had said something similar. It was probably the same man. "No, I don't remember," Volodya lied. He wanted nothing to do with a possible relative in the West. Such connections brought suspicion and trouble to Russians.

"He's on the American delegation. You should talk to him. See if you're related."

"I will," said Volodya, resolving to avoid the man at all costs.

He decided not to insist on taking Woody's film. It was not worth the fuss for a harmless street scene.

At the next day's conference the American secretary of state, George Marshall, proposed that the four Allies should abolish the separate sectors of Germany and unify the country, so that it could once again become the beating economic heart of Europe, mining and manufacturing and buying and selling.

That was the last thing the Soviets wanted.

Molotov refused to discuss unification until the question of reparations had been settled.

The conference was stalemated.

And that, Volodya thought, was exactly where Stalin wanted it.

ii

The world of international diplomacy was a small one, Greg Peshkov reflected. One of the young aides in the British delegation at the Moscow conference was Lloyd Williams, the husband of Greg's half sister, Daisy. At first Greg did not like the look of Lloyd, who was dressed like a prissy English gentleman, but he turned out to be a regular guy. "Molotov is a prick," Lloyd said in the bar of the Hotel Moskva over a couple of vodka martinis.

"So what are we going to do about him?"

"I don't know, but Britain can't live with these delays. The occupation of Germany is costing money we can't afford, and the hard winter has turned the problem into a crisis."

"You know what?" said Greg, thinking aloud. "If the Soviets won't play ball, we should just go ahead without them."

"How could we do that?"

"What do we want?" Greg counted points on his fingers. "We want to unify Germany and hold elections."

"So do we."

"We want to scrap the worthless reichsmark and introduce a new currency, so that Germans can start to do business again."

"Yes."

"And we want to save the country from Communism."

"Also British policy."

"We can't do it in the east because the Soviets won't come to the party. So fuck them! We control three-quarters of Germany—let's do it in our zone, and let the eastern part of the country go to blazes."

Lloyd looked thoughtful. "Is this something you've discussed with your boss?"

"Hell, no. I'm just running off at the mouth. But listen, why not?"

"I might suggest it to Ernie Bevin."

"And I'll put it to George Marshall." Greg sipped his drink. "Vodka is the only thing the Russians do well," he said. "So, how's my sister?"

"She's expecting our second baby."

"What is Daisy like as a mother?"

Lloyd laughed. "You think she's probably terrible."

Greg shrugged. "I never saw her as the domestic type."

"She's patient, calm, and organized."

"She didn't hire six nurses to do all the work?"

"Just one, so that she can come out with me in the evenings, usually to political meetings."

"Wow, she's changed."

"Not completely. She still loves parties. What about you—still single?"

"There's a girl called Nelly Fordham that I'm pretty serious about. And I guess you know that I have a godson."

"Yes," said Lloyd. "Daisy told me all about him. Georgy."

Greg felt sure, from the slightly embarrassed look on Lloyd's face, that he knew Georgy was Greg's child. "I'm very fond of him."

"That's great."

A member of the Russian delegation came up to the bar, and Greg caught his eye. There was something very familiar about him. He was in his thirties, handsome apart from a brutally short military haircut, and he had a slightly intimidating blue-eyed gaze. He nodded in a friendly way, and Greg said: "Have we met before?"

"Perhaps," the Russian said. "I was at school in Germany—the Berlin Boys' Academy."

Greg shook his head. "Ever been to the States?"

"No."

Lloyd said: "This is the guy with the same surname as you, Volodya Peshkov."

Greg introduced himself. "We might be related. My father, Lev

Peshkov, emigrated in 1914, leaving behind a pregnant girlfriend, who then married his older brother, Grigori Peshkov. Could we be half brothers?"

Volodya's manner altered immediately. "Definitely not," he said. "Excuse me." He left the bar without buying a drink.

"That was abrupt," Greg said to Lloyd.

"It was," said Lloyd.

"He looked kind of shocked."

"It must have been something you said."

iii

It could not be true, Volodya told himself.

Greg claimed that Grigori had married a girl who was already pregnant by Lev. If that was the case, the man Volodya had always called Father was not his father but his uncle.

Perhaps it was a coincidence. Or the American could just be stirring up trouble.

All the same Volodya was reeling with shock.

He returned home at his usual time. He and Zoya were rising fast and had been given an apartment in Government House, the luxury block where his parents lived. Grigori and Katerina came to the apartment at Kotya's suppertime, as they did most evenings. Katerina bathed her grandson; then Grigori sang to him and told him Russian fairy tales. Kotya was nine months old and not yet talking, but he seemed to like bedtime stories just the same.

Volodya followed the evening routine as if sleepwalking. He tried to behave normally, but he found he could hardly speak to either of his parents. He did not believe Greg's story, but he could not stop thinking about it.

When Kotya was asleep, and the grandparents were about to leave, Grigori said to Volodya: "Have I got a boil on my nose?"

"No."

"Then why have you been staring at me all evening?"

Volodya decided to tell the truth. "I met a man called Greg Peshkov. He's part of the American delegation. He thinks we're related."

"It's possible." Grigori's tone was light, as if it did not much matter, but Volodya saw that his neck had reddened, a giveaway sign of suppressed emotion in his father. "I last saw my brother in 1919. Since then I haven't heard from him."

"Greg's father is called Lev, and Lev had a brother called Grigori."

"Then Greg could be your cousin."

"He said brother."

Grigori's blush deepened and he said nothing.

Zoya put in: "How could that be?"

Volodya said: "According to this American Peshkov, Lev had a pregnant girlfriend in St. Petersburg who married his brother."

Grigori said: "Ridiculous!"

Volodya looked at Katerina. "You haven't said anything, Mother."

There was a long pause. That in itself was significant. What did they have to think about, if there was no truth in Greg's story? A weird coldness descended on Volodya like a freezing fog.

At last his mother said: "I was a flighty girl." She looked at Zoya. "Not sensible, like your wife." She sighed deeply. "Grigori Peshkov fell in love with me, more or less at first sight, poor idiot." She smiled fondly at her husband. "But his brother, Lev, had fancy clothes, cigarettes, money for vodka, gangster friends. I liked Lev better. More fool me."

Volodya said amazedly: "So it's true?" Part of him still hoped desperately for a denial.

"Lev did what such men always do," Katerina said. "He made me pregnant, then left me."

"So Lev is my father." Volodya looked at Grigori. "And you're just my uncle!" He felt as if he might fall over. The ground under his feet had shifted. It was like an earthquake.

Zoya stood beside Volodya's chair and put her hand on his shoulder, as if to calm him, or perhaps restrain him.

Katerina went on: "And Grigori did what men such as Grigori always do: he took care of me. He loved me, he married me, and he provided for me and my children." Sitting on the couch next to Grigori, she took his hand. "I didn't want him, and I certainly didn't deserve him, but God gave him to me anyway."

Grigori said: "I have dreaded this day. Ever since you were born, I have dreaded it."

Volodya said: "Then why did you keep the secret? Why didn't you just speak the truth?"

Grigori was choked up, and spoke with difficulty. "I couldn't bear to tell you that I wasn't your father," he managed to say. "I loved you too much."

Katerina said: "Let me tell you something, my beloved son. Listen to me, now, and I don't care if you never listen to your mother again, but hear this. Forget the stranger in America who once seduced a foolish girl. Look at the man sitting in front of you with tears in his eyes."

Volodya looked at Grigori and saw a pleading expression that tugged at his heart.

Katerina went on: "This man has fed you and clothed you and loved you unfailingly for three decades. If the word *father* means anything at all, this is your father."

"Yes," Volodya said. "I know that."

iv

Lloyd Williams got on well with Ernie Bevin. They had a lot in common, despite the age difference. During the four-day train journey across snowy Europe, Lloyd had confided that he, like Bevin, was the illegitimate son of a housemaid. They were both passionate anti-Communists: Lloyd because of his experiences in Spain, Bevin because he had seen Communist tactics in the trade union movement. "They're slaves to the Kremlin and tyrants over everyone else," Bevin said, and Lloyd knew exactly what he meant.

Lloyd had not warmed to Greg Peshkov, who always looked as if he had dressed in a rush: shirtsleeves unbuttoned, coat collar twisted, shoelaces untied. Greg was shrewd, and Lloyd tried to like him, but he felt that underneath Greg's casual charm there was a core of ruthlessness. Daisy had said that Lev Peshkov was a gangster, and Lloyd could imagine that Greg had the same instincts.

However, Bevin jumped at Greg's idea for Germany. "Was he speaking for Marshall, do you suppose?" said the portly foreign secretary in his broad West Country accent.

"He said not," Lloyd replied. "Do you think it could work?"

"I think it's the best idea I've heard in three bloody weeks in bloody Moscow. If he's serious, arrange an informal lunch, just Marshall and this youngster with you and me."

"I'll do it right away."

"But tell nobody. We don't want the Soviets to get a whisper of this. They'll accuse us of conspiring against them, and they'll be right."

They met the following day at no. 10 Spasopeskovskaya Square, the American ambassador's residence, an extravagant neoclassical mansion built before the revolution. Marshall was tall and lean, every inch a soldier; Bevin rotund, nearsighted, a cigarette frequently dangling from his lips; but they clicked immediately. Both were plain-speaking men. Bevin had once been accused of ungentlemanly speech by Stalin himself, a distinction of which the foreign secretary was very proud. Beneath the painted ceilings and chandeliers they got down to the task of reviving Germany without the help of the USSR.

They agreed rapidly on the principles: the new currency; the unification of the British, American, and—if possible—French zones; the demilitarization of West Germany; elections; and a new transatlantic military alliance. Then Bevin said bluntly: "None of this will work, you know."

Marshall was taken aback. "Then I fail to understand why we're discussing it," he said sharply.

"Europe's in a slump. This scheme will fail if people are starving. The best protection against Communism is prosperity. Stalin knows that— which is why he wants to keep Germany impoverished."

"I agree."

"Which means we've got to rebuild. But we can't do it with our bare hands. We need tractors, lathes, excavators, rolling stock—all of which we can't afford."

Marshall saw where he was going. "Americans aren't willing to give Europeans any more handouts."

"Fair enough. But there must be a way the USA can lend us the money we need to buy equipment from you."

There was a silence.

Marshall hated to waste words, but this was a long pause even by his standards.

Then at last he spoke. "It makes sense," he said. "I'll see what I can do."

The conference lasted six weeks, and when they all went home again, nothing had been decided.

v

Eva Williams was a year old when she got her back teeth. The others had come fairly easily, but these hurt. There was not much Lloyd and Daisy could do for her. She was miserable, she could not sleep, she would not let them sleep, and they were miserable, too.

Daisy had a lot of money, but they lived unostentatiously. They had bought a pleasant row house in Hoxton, where their neighbors were a shopkeeper and a builder. They got a small family car, a new Morris Eight with a top speed of almost sixty miles per hour. Daisy still bought pretty clothes, but Lloyd had just three suits: evening dress, a chalk stripe for the House of Commons, and tweeds for constituency work on the weekends.

Lloyd was in his pajamas late one evening, trying to rock the grizzling Evie to sleep, and at the same time leafing through *Life* magazine. He noticed a striking photograph taken in Moscow. It showed a Russian woman, wearing a head scarf and a coat tied with string like a parcel, her old face deeply lined, shoveling snow on the street.

Something about the way the light struck her gave her a look of timelessness, as if she had been there for a thousand years. He looked for the photographer's name and found it was Woody Dewar, whom he had met at the conference.

The phone rang. He picked it up and heard the voice of Ernie Bevin. "Turn your wireless on," Bevin said. "Marshall's made a speech." He hung up without waiting for a reply.

Lloyd went downstairs to the living room, still carrying Evie, and switched on the radio. The show was called *American Commentary*. The BBC's Washington correspondent, Leonard Miall, was reporting from Harvard University in Cambridge, Massachusetts. "The secretary of state told alumni that the rebuilding of Europe is going to take a longer time, and require a greater effort, than was originally foreseen," said Miall.

That was promising, Lloyd thought with excitement. "Hush, Evie, please," he said, and for once she quietened.

Then Lloyd heard the low, reasonable voice of George C. Marshall. "Europe's requirements, for the next three or four years, of foreign food and other essential products—principally from America—are so much greater than her present ability to pay that she must have substantial additional help . . . or face economic, social, and political deterioration of a very grave character."

Lloyd was electrified. "Substantial additional help" was what Bevin had asked for.

"The remedy lies in breaking the vicious circle and restoring the confidence of the European people in the economic future," Marshall said. "The United States should do whatever it is able to assist in the return of normal economic health in the world."

"He's done it!" Lloyd said triumphantly to his uncomprehending baby daughter. "He's told America they have to give us aid! But how much? And how, and when?"

The voice changed, and the reporter said: "The secretary of state did not outline a detailed plan for aid to Europe, but said it was up to the Europeans to draft the program."

"Does that mean we have carte blanche?" Lloyd eagerly asked Evie.

Marshall's voice returned to say: "The initiative, I think, must come from Europe."

The report ended, and the phone rang again. "Did you hear that?" said Bevin.

"What does it mean?"

"Don't ask!" said Bevin. "If you ask questions, you'll get answers you don't want."

"All right," Lloyd said, baffled.

"Never mind what he meant. The question is, what do we do? The initiative must come from Europe, he said. That means me and you."

"What can I do?"

"Pack a bag," said Bevin. "We're going to Paris."

CHAPTER TWENTY-FOUR

1948

Volodya was in Prague as part of a Red Army delegation holding talks with the Czech military. They were staying in art deco splendor at the Imperial Hotel.

It was snowing.

He missed Zoya and little Kotya. His son was two years old and learning new words at bewildering speed. The child was changing so fast that he seemed different every day. And Zoya was pregnant again. Volodya resented having to spend two weeks apart from his family. Most of the men in the group saw the trip as a chance to get away from their wives, drink too much vodka, and maybe fool around with loose women. Volodya just wanted to go home.

The military talks were genuine, but Volodya's part in them was a cover for his real assignment, which was to report on the activities in Prague of the ham-fisted Soviet secret police, perennial rivals of Red Army Intelligence.

Volodya had little enthusiasm for his work nowadays. Everything he had once believed in had been undermined. He no longer had faith in Stalin, Communism, or the essential goodness of the Russian people. Even his father was not his father. He would have defected to the West if he could have found a way of getting Zoya and Kotya out with him.

However, he did have his heart in his mission here in Prague. It was a rare chance to do something he believed in.

Two weeks before, the Czech Communist Party had taken full control of the government, ousting their coalition partners. Foreign Minister Jan Masaryk, a war hero and democratic anti-Communist, had become a prisoner on the top floor of his official residence, the Czernin Palace. The Soviet secret police had undoubtedly been behind the coup. In fact Volodya's brother-in-law, Colonel Ilya Dvorkin, was also in Prague, staying at the same hotel, and had almost certainly been involved.

Volodya's boss, General Lemitov, saw the coup as a public relations catastrophe for the USSR. Masaryk had constituted proof, to the world, that east European countries could be free and independent in the shadow of the USSR. He had enabled Czechoslovakia to have a Communist government friendly to the Soviet Union and at the same time wear the costume of bourgeois democracy. This had been the perfect arrangement, for it gave the USSR everything it wanted while reassuring the Americans. But that equilibrium had been upset.

However, Ilya was crowing. "The bourgeois parties have been smashed!" he said to Volodya in the hotel bar one night.

"Did you see what happened in the American Senate?" Volodya said mildly. "Vandenberg, the old isolationist, made an eighty-minute speech in favor of the Marshall Plan, and he was cheered to the rafters."

George Marshall's vague ideas had become a plan. This was mainly thanks to the ratlike cunning of British foreign secretary Ernie Bevin. In Volodya's opinion, Bevin was the most dangerous kind of anti-Communist: a working-class Social Democrat. Despite his bulk he moved fast. With lightning speed he had organized a conference in Paris that had given a resounding collective European welcome to George Marshall's Harvard speech.

Volodya knew, from spies in the British Foreign Office, that Bevin was determined to bring Germany into the Marshall Plan and keep the USSR out. And Stalin had fallen straight into Bevin's trap, by commanding the east European countries to repudiate Marshall Aid.

Now the Soviet secret police seemed to be doing all they could to assist the passage of the bill through Congress. "The Senate was all set to reject Marshall," Volodya said to Ilya. "American taxpayers don't want to foot the bill. But the coup here in Prague has persuaded them that they have to, because European capitalism is in danger of collapse."

Ilya said indignantly: "The bourgeois Czech parties wanted to take the American bribe."

"We should have let them," said Volodya. "It might have been the quickest way to sabotage the whole scheme. Congress would then have rejected the Marshall Plan—they don't want to give money to Communists."

"The Marshall Plan is an imperialist trick!"

"Yes, it is," said Volodya. "And I'm afraid it's working. Our wartime allies are forming an anti-Soviet bloc."

"People who obstruct the forward march of Communism must be dealt with appropriately."

"Indeed they must." It was amazing how consistently people such as Ilya made the wrong political judgments.

"And I must go to bed."

It was only ten, but Volodya went, too. He lay awake thinking about Zoya and Kotya and wishing he could kiss them both good night.

His thoughts drifted to his mission. He had met Jan Masaryk, the symbol of Czech independence, two days earlier, at a ceremony at the grave of his father, Thomas Masaryk, the founder and first president of Czechoslovakia. Dressed in a coat with a fur collar, head bared to the falling snow, the second Masaryk had seemed beaten and depressed.

If he could be persuaded to stay on as foreign minister, some compromise might be possible, Volodya mused. Czechoslovakia could have a thoroughly Communist domestic government, but in its international relations it might be neutral, or at least minimally anti-American. Masaryk had both the diplomatic skills and the international credibility to walk that tightrope.

Volodya decided he would suggest it to Lemitov tomorrow.

He slept fitfully and woke before six o'clock with a mental alarm ringing in his imagination. It was something about last night's conversation with Ilya. Volodya ran over it again in his mind. When Ilya had said "people who obstruct the forward march of Communism," he had been talking about Masaryk, and when a secret policeman said someone had to be "dealt with appropriately," he always meant "killed."

Then Ilya had gone to bed early, which suggested an early start this morning.

I'm a fool, Volodya thought. The signs were there and it took me all night to read them.

He leaped out of bed. Perhaps he was not too late.

He dressed quickly and put on a heavy overcoat, scarf, and hat. There were no taxis outside the hotel—it was too early. He could have called a Red Army car, but by the time a driver was awakened and the car brought, it would have taken the best part of an hour.

He set out to walk. The Czernin Palace was only a mile or two away. He headed west out of Prague's gracious city center, crossed the Charles Bridge, and hurried uphill toward the castle.

Masaryk was not expecting him, nor was the foreign minister obliged to give audience to a Red Army colonel. But Volodya felt sure Masaryk would be curious enough to see him.

He walked fast through the snow and reached the Czernin Palace at six forty-five. It was a huge baroque building with a grandiose row of Corinthian half columns on the three upper stories. The place was lightly guarded, he found to his surprise. A sentry pointed to the front door. Volodya walked unchallenged through an ornate hall.

He had expected to find the usual secret police moron behind a reception desk, but there was no one. This was a bad sign, and he was filled with foreboding.

The hall led to an inner courtyard. Glancing through a window, he saw what looked like a man sleeping in the snow. Perhaps he had fallen there drunk: if so, he was in danger of freezing to death.

Volodya tried the door and found it open.

He ran across the quadrangle. A man in blue silk pajamas lay facedown on the ground. There was no snow covering him, so he could not have been there many minutes. Volodya knelt beside him. The man was quite still and did not appear to be breathing.

Volodya looked up. Rows of identical windows like soldiers on parade looked into this courtyard. All were closed tightly against the freezing weather—except one, high above the man in pajamas, that stood wide open.

As if someone had been thrown out of it.

Volodya turned the lifeless head and looked at the man's face.

It was Jan Masaryk.

ii

Three days later in Washington, the Joint Chiefs of Staff presented to President Truman an emergency war plan to meet a Soviet invasion of Western Europe.

The danger of a third world war was a hot topic in the press. "We just *won* the war," Jacky Jakes said to Greg Peshkov. "How come we're about to have another?"

"That's what I keep asking myself," said Greg.

They were sitting on a park bench while Greg took a breather from throwing a football with Georgy.

"I'm glad he's too young to fight," Jacky said.

"Me, too."

They both looked at their son, standing talking to a blond girl about his age. The laces of his Keds were undone and his shirt was untucked. He was twelve years old and growing up. He had a few soft black hairs on his upper lip, and he seemed three inches taller than last week.

"We've been bringing our troops home as fast as we can," Greg said. "So have the British and the French. But the Red Army stayed put. Result: they now have three times as many soldiers in Germany as we do."

"Americans don't want another war."

"You can say that again. And Truman hopes to win the presidential election in November, so he's going to do everything he can to avoid war. But it may happen anyway."

"You're getting out of the army soon. What are you going to do?"

There was a quaver in her voice that made him suspect the question was not as casual as she pretended. He looked at her face, but her expression was unreadable. He answered: "Assuming America is not at war, I'm going to run for Congress in 1950. My father has agreed to finance my campaign. I'll start as soon as the presidential election is over."

She looked away. "Which party?" She asked the question mechanically.

He wondered if he had said something to upset her. "Republican, of course."

"What about marriage?"

Greg was taken aback. "Why do you ask that?"

She was looking hard at him now. "Are you getting married?" she persisted.

"As it happens, I am. Her name is Nelly Fordham."

"I thought so. How old is she?"

"Twenty-two. What do you mean, you thought so?"

"A politician needs a wife."

"I love her!"

"Sure you do. Is her family in politics?"

"Her father is a Washington lawyer."

"Good choice."

Greg felt annoyed. "You're being very cynical."

"I know you, Greg. Good Lord, I fucked you when you weren't much older than Georgy is now. You can fool everyone except your mother and me."

She was perceptive, as always. His mother had also been critical of his engagement. They were right: it was a career move. But Nelly was pretty and charming and she adored Greg, so what was so wrong? "I'm meeting her for lunch near here in a few minutes," he said.

Jacky said: "Does Nelly know about Georgy?"

"No. And we must keep it that way."

"You're right. Having an illegitimate child is bad enough; a black one could ruin your career."

"I know."

"Almost as bad as a black wife."

Greg was so surprised that he came right out with it. "Did you think I was going to marry *you*?"

She looked sour. "Hell, no, Greg. If I was given a choice between you and the Acid Bath Murderer, I'd ask for time to think about it."

She was lying, he knew. For a moment he contemplated the idea of marrying Jacky. Interracial marriages were unusual, and attracted a good deal of hostility from blacks as well as whites, but some people did it and put up with the consequences. He had never met a girl he liked as much as Jacky, not even Margaret Cowdry, whom he had dated for a couple of years, until she got fed up waiting for him to propose. Jacky was sharp-tongued, but he liked that, maybe because his mother was the same. There was something deeply attractive about the idea of the three of them being together all the time. Georgy would learn to call him Dad. They could buy a house in a neighborhood where people were broad-minded, someplace that had a lot of students and young professors, maybe Georgetown.

Then he saw Georgy's blond friend being called away by her parents, a cross white mother wagging a finger in admonition, and he realized that marrying Jacky was the worst idea in the world.

Georgy returned to where Greg and Jacky sat. "How's school?" Greg asked him.

"I like it better than I used to," the boy said. "Math is getting more interesting."

"I was good at math," Greg said.

Jacky said: "Now there's a coincidence."

Greg stood up. "I have to go." He squeezed Georgy's shoulder. "Keep working on the math, buddy."

"Sure," said Georgy.

Greg waved at Jacky and left.

She had been thinking about marriage at the same time as he, no doubt. She knew that coming out of the army was a decisive moment for him. It forced him to think about his future. She could not really have thought he would marry her, but all the same she must have harbored a secret fantasy. Now he had shattered it. Well, that was too bad. Even if she had been white, he would not have married her. He was fond of her, and he loved the kid, but he had his whole life ahead of him, and he wanted a wife who would bring him connections and support. Nelly's father was a powerful man in Republican politics.

He walked to the Napoli, an Italian restaurant a few blocks from the park. Nelly was already there, her copper red curls escaping from under a little green hat. "You look great!" he said. "I hope I'm not late." He sat down.

Nelly's face was stony. "I saw you in the park," she said.

Greg thought: Oh, shit.

"I was a little early, so I sat for a while," she said. "You didn't notice me. Then I started to feel like a snoop, so I left."

"So you saw my godson?" he said with forced cheerfulness.

"Is that who he is? You're a surprising choice for a godfather. You never even go to church."

"I'm good to the kid!"

"What's his name?"

"Georgy Jakes."

"You've never mentioned him before."

"Haven't I?"

"How old is he?"

"Twelve."

"So you were sixteen when he was born. That's young to be a godfather."

"I guess it is."

"What does his mother do for a living?"

"She's a waitress. Years ago she was an actress. Her stage name was Jacky Jakes. I met her when she was under contract to my father's studio." That was more or less true, Greg thought uncomfortably.

"And his father?"

Greg shook his head. "Jacky is single." A waiter approached. Greg said: "How about a cocktail?" Perhaps it might ease the tension. "Two martinis," he said to the waiter.

"Right away, sir."

As soon as the waiter had left, Nelly said: "You're the boy's father, aren't you?"

"Godfather."

Her voice became contemptuous. "Oh, stop it."

"What makes you so sure?"

"He may be black, but he looks like you. He can't keep his shoelaces tied or his shirt tucked in, and neither can you. And he was charming the pants off that little blond girl he was talking to. Of course he's yours."

Greg gave in. He sighed and said: "I was going to tell you."

"When?"

"I was waiting for the right moment."

"Before you proposed would have been a good time."

"I'm sorry." He was embarrassed, but not really contrite: he thought she was making an unnecessary fuss.

The waiter brought menus and they both looked at them. "The spaghetti Bolognese is great," said Greg.

"I'm going to get a salad."

Their martinis arrived. Greg raised his glass and said: "To forgiveness in marriage."

Nelly did not pick up her drink. "I can't marry you," she said.

"Honey, come on, don't overreact. I've apologized."

She shook her head. "You don't get it, do you?"

"What don't I get?"

"That woman sitting on the park bench with you—she loves you."

"Does she?" Greg would have denied it yesterday, but after today's conversation he was not sure.

"Of course she does. Why hasn't she married? She's pretty enough. By now she could have found a man willing to take on a stepson, if she'd really been trying. But she's in love with you, you rotter."

"I'm not so sure."

"And the boy adores you, too."

"I'm his favorite uncle."

"Except that you're not." She pushed her glass across the table. "You have my drink."

"Honey, please relax."

"I'm leaving." She stood up.

Greg was not used to girls walking out on him. He found it unnerving. Was he losing his allure?

"I want to marry you!" he said. He sounded desperate even to himself.

"You can't marry me, Greg," she said. She slipped the diamond ring off her finger and put it down on the red-checked tablecloth. "You already have a family."

She walked out of the restaurant.

iii

The world crisis came to a head in June, and Carla and her family were at the center of it.

The Marshall Plan had been signed into law by President Truman, and the first shipments of aid were arriving in Europe, to the fury of the Kremlin.

On Friday, June 18, the Western Allies alerted Germans that they would make an important announcement at eight o'clock that evening. Carla's family gathered around the radio in the kitchen, tuned to Radio Frankfurt, and waited anxiously. The war had been over for three years, yet still they did not know what the future held: capitalism or Communism, unity or fragmentation, freedom or subjugation, prosperity or destitution.

Werner sat beside Carla with Walli, now two and a half, on his knee. They had married quietly a year ago. Carla was working as a nurse again. She was also a Berlin city councilor for the Social Democrats. So was Frieda's husband, Heinrich.

In East Germany the Russians had banned the Social Democratic

Party, but Berlin was an oasis in the Soviet sector, ruled by a council of the four main Allies called the Kommandatura, which had vetoed the ban. As a result, the Social Democrats had won, and the Communists had come a poor third after the conservative Christian Democrats. The Russians were incensed and did everything they could to obstruct the elected council. Carla found it frustrating, but she could not give up the hope of independence from the Soviets.

Werner had managed to start a small business. He had searched through the ruins of his father's factory and scavenged a small hoard of electrical supplies and radio parts. Germans could not afford to buy new radios, but everyone wanted their old ones repaired. Werner had found some engineers formerly employed at the factory and set them to work fixing broken wireless sets. He was the manager and salesman, going to houses and apartment buildings, knocking on doors, drumming up business.

Maud, also at the kitchen table this evening, worked as an interpreter for the Americans. She was one of the best, and often translated at meetings of the Kommandatura.

Carla's brother, Erik, was wearing the uniform of a policeman. Having joined the Communist Party—to the dismay of his family—he had got a job as a police officer in the new East German force organized by the Russian occupiers. Erik said the Western Allies were trying to split Germany in two. "You Social Democrats are secessionists," he said, quoting the Communist line in the same way he had parroted Nazi propaganda.

"The Western Allies haven't divided anything," Carla retorted. "They've opened the borders between their zones. Why don't the Soviets do the same? Then we would be one country again." He seemed not to hear her.

Rebecca was almost seventeen. Carla and Werner had legally adopted her. She was doing well at school and good at languages.

Carla was pregnant again, though she had not told Werner. She was thrilled. He had an adopted daughter and a stepson, but now he would have a child of his own as well. She knew he would be delighted when she told him. She was waiting a little longer to be sure.

But she yearned to know in what kind of country her three children were going to live.

An American officer called Robert Lochner came on the air. He had been raised in Germany and spoke the language effortlessly. Beginning at seven o'clock on Monday morning, he explained, West Germany would have a new currency, the deutsche mark.

Carla was not surprised. The reichsmark was worth less every day. Most people were paid in reichsmarks, if they had a job at all, and the currency could be used for basics such as food rations and bus fares, but everyone preferred to get groceries or cigarettes. Werner charged people in reichsmarks in his business but offered overnight service for five cigarettes and delivery anywhere in the city for three eggs.

Carla knew from Maud that the new currency had been discussed at the Kommandatura. The Russians had demanded plates so that they could print it. But they had debased the old currency by printing too much, and there was no point in a new currency if the same thing was going to happen. Consequently the West refused and the Soviets sulked.

Now the West had decided to go ahead without the cooperation of the Soviets. Carla was pleased, for the new currency would be good for Germany, but she felt apprehensive about the Soviet reaction.

People in West Germany could exchange sixty inflated old reichsmarks for three deutsche marks and ninety new pennies, said Lochner.

Then he said that none of this would apply in Berlin, at least at first, whereupon there was a collective groan in the kitchen.

Carla went to bed wondering what the Soviets would do. She lay beside Werner, part of her brain listening in case Walli, in the next room, should cry. The Soviet occupiers had been getting angrier for the last few months. A journalist called Dieter Friede had been kidnapped in the American zone by the Soviet secret police, then held captive; the Soviets at first denied all knowledge, then said they had arrested him as a spy. Three students had been expelled from university for criticizing the Russians in a magazine. Worst of all, a Soviet fighter aircraft buzzed a British European Airways passenger plane landing at Gatow airport and clipped its wing, causing both planes to crash and killing four BEA crew, ten passengers, and the Soviet pilot. When the Russians got angry, someone else always suffered.

Next morning the Soviets announced it would be a crime to import deutsche marks into East Germany. This included Berlin, the statement said, "which is part of the Soviet zone." The Americans immediately denounced this phrase and affirmed that Berlin was an international city, but the temperature was rising, and Carla remained anxious.

On Monday, West Germany got the new currency.

On Tuesday, a Red Army courier came to Carla's house and summoned her to city hall.

She had been summoned this way before, but all the same she was fearful as she left home. There was nothing to stop the Soviets imprisoning her. The Communists had all the same arbitrary powers the Nazis had assumed. They were even using the old concentration camps.

The famous Red City Hall had been damaged by bombing, and the city government was based in the New City Hall in Parochial Strasse. Both buildings were in the Mitte district, where Carla lived, which was in the Soviet zone.

When she got there, she found that Acting Mayor Louise Schroeder and others had also been called for a meeting with the Soviet liaison officer, Major Otshkin. He informed them that the East German currency was to be reformed, and in future only the new ostmark would be legal in the Soviet zone.

Acting Mayor Schroeder immediately saw the crucial point. "Are you telling us that this will apply in all sectors of Berlin?"

"Yes."

Frau Schroeder was not easily intimidated. "Under the city constitution, the Soviet occupying power cannot make such a rule for the other sectors," she said firmly. "The other Allies must be consulted."

"They will not object." He handed over a sheet of paper. "This is Marshal Sokolovsky's decree. You will bring it before the city council tomorrow."

Later that evening, as Carla got into bed with Werner, she said: "You can see what the Soviet tactic is. If the city council were to pass the decree, it would be difficult for the democratically minded Western Allies to overturn it."

"But the council won't pass it. The Communists are a minority, and no one else will want the ostmark."

"No. Which is why I'm wondering what Marshal Sokolovsky has up his sleeve."

The next morning's newspapers announced that from Friday there would be two competing currencies in Berlin, the ostmark and the deutsche mark. It turned out that the Americans had secretly flown in 250 million in the new currency in wooden boxes marked "Clay" and "Bird Dog," which were now stashed all over Berlin.

During the day Carla began to hear rumors from West Germany. The new money had brought about a miracle there. Overnight, more goods had appeared in shop windows: baskets of cherries and neatly tied bundles of carrots from the surrounding countryside, butter and eggs and pastries, and long-hoarded luxuries such as new shoes, handbags, and even stockings at four deutsche marks the pair. People had been waiting until they could sell things for real money.

That afternoon Carla set off for city hall to attend the council meeting scheduled for four o'clock. As she drew near, she saw dozens of Red Army trucks parked in the streets around the building, their drivers lounging around, smoking. They were mostly American vehicles that must have been given to the USSR as Lend-Lease aid during the war. She got an inkling of their purpose when she began to hear the sound of an unruly mob. What the Soviet governor had up his sleeve, she suspected, was a truncheon.

In front of city hall, red flags fluttered above a crowd of several thousand, most of them wearing Communist Party badges. Loudspeaker trucks blared angry speeches, and the crowd chanted: "Down with the secessionists."

Carla did not see how she was going to reach the building. A handful of policemen looked on uninterestedly, making no attempt to help councilors get through. It reminded Carla painfully of the attitude of police on the day the Brownshirts had trashed her mother's office, fifteen years ago. She was quite sure the Communist councilors were already inside, and that if Social Democrats did not get into the building, the minority would pass the decree and claim it to be valid.

She took a deep breath and began to push through the crowd.

For a few steps she made progress unnoticed. Then someone recognized her. "American whore!" he yelled, pointing at her. She pressed on determinedly. Someone else spat at her, and a gob of saliva smeared her dress. She kept going, but she felt panicky. She was surrounded by people who hated her, something she had never experienced, and it made her want to run away. She was shoved, but managed to keep her feet. A hand grasped her dress, and she pulled free with a tearing sound. She wanted to scream. What would they do, rip all her clothes off?

Someone else was fighting his way through the crowd behind her, she realized, and she looked back and saw Heinrich von Kessel, Frieda's husband. He drew level with her and they barreled on together. Heinrich was more aggressive, stamping on toes and vigorously elbowing everyone within range. Together they moved faster, and at last reached the door and went in.

But their ordeal was not over. There were Communist demonstrators inside, too, hundreds of them. They had to fight through the corridors. In the meeting hall the demonstrators were everywhere—not just in the visitors' gallery but on the floor of the chamber. Their behavior here was just as aggressive as outside.

Some Social Democrats were here, and others arrived after Carla. Somehow most of the sixty-three had been able to fight their way through the mob. She was relieved. The enemy had not managed to scare them off.

When the speaker of the assembly called for order, a Communist assemblyman standing on a bench urged the demonstrators to stay. When he saw Carla, he yelled: "Traitors stay outside!"

It was all grimly reminiscent of 1933: bullying, intimidation, and democracy being undermined by rowdyism. Carla was in despair.

Glancing up to the gallery, she was appalled to see her brother, Erik, among the yelling mob. "You're German!" she screamed at him. "You lived under the Nazis. Have you learned *nothing*?"

He seemed not to hear her.

Frau Schroeder stood on the platform, calling for calm. She was jeered and booed by the demonstrators. Raising her voice to a shout, she said: "If the city council cannot hold an orderly debate in this building, I will move the meeting to the American sector."

There was renewed abuse, but the twenty-six Communist councilors saw that this move would not suit their purpose. If the council met outside the Soviet zone once, it might do so again, and even move permanently out of the range of Communist intimidation. After a short discussion, one of them stood up and told the demonstrators to leave. They filed out, singing "The Internationale."

"It's obvious whose command they're under," Heinrich said.

At last there was quiet. Frau Schroeder explained the Soviet demand, and said that it could not apply outside the Soviet sector of Berlin unless it was ratified by the other Allies.

A Communist deputy made a speech accusing her of taking orders directly from New York.

Accusations and abuse raged to and fro. Eventually they voted. The Communists unanimously backed the Soviet decree—after accusing others of being controlled from outside. Everyone else voted against, and the motion was defeated. Berlin had refused to be bullied. Carla felt wearily triumphant.

However, it was not yet over.

By the time they left, it was seven o'clock in the evening. Most of the mob had disappeared, but there was a thuggish hard core still hanging around the entrance. An elderly woman councilor was kicked and punched as she left. The police looked on with indifference.

Carla and Heinrich left by a side door with a few friends, hoping to depart unobserved, but a Communist on a bicycle was monitoring the exit. He rode off quickly.

As the councilors hurried away, he returned at the head of a small gang. Someone tripped Carla, and she fell to the ground. She was kicked painfully once, twice, three times. Terrified, she covered her belly with her hands. She was almost three months pregnant—the stage at which most miscarriages occurred, she knew. Will Werner's baby die, she thought desperately, kicked to death on a Berlin street by Communist thugs?

Then they disappeared.

The councilors picked themselves up. No one was badly injured. They moved off together, fearful of a recurrence, but it seemed the Communists had roughed up enough people for one day.

Carla got home at eight o'clock. There was no sign of Erik.

Werner was shocked to see her bruises and torn dress. "What happened?" he said. "Are you all right?"

She burst into tears.

"You're hurt," Werner said. "Should we go to the hospital?"

She shook her head vigorously. "It's not that," she said. "I'm just bruised. I've had worse." She slumped in a chair. "Christ, I'm tired."

"Who did this?" he asked angrily.

"The usual people," she said. "They call themselves Communists instead of Nazis, but they're the same type. It's 1933 all over again."

Werner put his arms around her.

She could not be consoled. "The bullies and the thugs have been in power for so long!" she sobbed. "Will it ever end?"

iv

That night the Soviet news agency put out an announcement. From six o'clock in the morning, all passenger and freight transport in and out of West Berlin—trains, cars, and canal barges—would be stopped. No supplies of any kind would get through: no food, no milk, no medicines, no coal. Because the electricity generating stations would therefore be shut down, they were switching off the supply of electricity—to western sectors only.

The city was under siege.

Lloyd Williams was at British military headquarters. There was a short parliamentary recess, and Ernie Bevin had gone on holiday to Sandbanks, on the south coast of England, but he was worried enough to send Lloyd to Berlin to observe the introduction of the new currency and keep him informed.

Daisy had not accompanied Lloyd. Their new baby, Davey, was only six months old, and anyway Daisy and Eva Murray were organizing a birth-control clinic for women in Hoxton that was about to open its doors.

Lloyd was desperately afraid that this crisis would lead to war. He had fought in two wars, and he never wanted to see a third. He had two small children who he hoped would grow up in a peaceful world. He was married to the prettiest, sexiest, most lovable woman on the planet and he wanted to spend many long decades with her.

General Clay, the workaholic American military governor, ordered his staff to plan an armored convoy that would barrel down the autobahn from Helmstedt, in the west, straight through Soviet territory to Berlin, sweeping all before it.

Lloyd heard about this plan at the same time as the British governor, Sir Brian Robertson, and heard him say in his clipped soldierly tones: "If Clay does that, it will be war."

But nothing else made any sense. The Americans came up with other suggestions, Lloyd heard, talking to Clay's younger aides. The secretary of the army, Kenneth Royall, wanted to halt the currency reform. Clay told him it had gone too far to be reversed. Next, Royall proposed evacuating all Americans. Clay told him that was exactly what the Soviets wanted.

Sir Brian wanted to supply the city by air. Most people thought that was impossible. Someone calculated that Berlin required four thousand tons of fuel and food per day. Were there enough airplanes in the *world* to move that much stuff? No one knew. Nevertheless, Sir Brian ordered the Royal Air Force to make a start.

On Friday afternoon Sir Brian went to see Clay, and Lloyd was invited to be part of the entourage. Sir Brian said to Clay: "The Russians might block the autobahn ahead of your convoy, and wait and see if you have the nerve to attack them, but I don't think they'll shoot planes down."

"I don't see how we can deliver enough supplies by air," Clay said again.

"Nor do I," said Sir Brian. "But we're going to do it until we think of something better."

Clay picked up the phone. "Get me General LeMay in Wiesbaden," he said. After a minute he said: "Curtis, have you got any planes there that can carry coal?"

There was a pause.

"Coal," said Clay more loudly.

Another pause.

"Yes, that is what I said—coal."

A moment later, Clay looked up at Sir Brian. "He says the U.S. Air Force can deliver anything."

The British returned to their headquarters.

On Saturday, Lloyd got an army driver and went into the Soviet zone on a personal mission. He drove to the address at which he had visited the von Ulrich family fifteen years ago.

He knew that Maud was still living there. His mother and Maud had resumed correspondence at the end of the war. Maud's letters put a brave face on what was undoubtedly severe hardship. She did not ask for help, and anyway there was nothing Ethel could do for her— rationing was still in force in Britain.

The place looked very different. In 1933 it had been a fine town house, a little run-down but still gracious. Now it looked like a dump. Most of the windows had boards or paper instead of glass. There were bullet holes in the stonework, and the garden wall had collapsed. The woodwork had not been painted for many years.

Lloyd sat in the car for a few moments, looking at the house. Last time he came here, he had been eighteen, and Hitler had only just become chancellor of Germany. The young Lloyd had not dreamed of the horrors the world was going to see. Neither he nor anyone else had suspected how close Fascism would come to triumphing over all Europe, and how much they would have to sacrifice to defeat it. He felt a bit like the von Ulrich house looked, battered and bombed and shot at but still standing.

He walked up the path and knocked.

He recognized the maid who opened the door. "Hello, Ada, do you remember me?" he said in German. "I'm Lloyd Williams."

The house was better inside than out. Ada showed him up to the drawing room, where there were flowers in a glass tumbler on the piano. A brightly patterned blanket had been thrown over the sofa, no doubt to hide holes in the upholstery. The newspapers in the windows let in a surprising amount of light.

A two-year-old boy walked into the room and inspected him with frank curiosity. He was dressed in clothes that were evidently homemade, and he had an Oriental look. "Who are you?" he said.

"My name is Lloyd. Who are you?"

"Walli," he said. He ran out again, and Lloyd heard him say to someone outside: "That man talks funny!"

So much for my German accent, Lloyd thought.

Then he heard the voice of a middle-aged woman. "Don't make such remarks! It's impolite."

"Sorry, Grandma."

Next moment Maud walked in.

Her appearance shocked Lloyd. She was in her midfifties, but looked seventy. Her hair was gray, her face was gaunt, and her blue silk dress was threadbare. She kissed his cheek with shrunken lips. "Lloyd Williams, what a joy to see you!"

She's my aunt, Lloyd thought with a rather queer feeling. But she did not know that: Ethel had kept the secret.

Maud was followed by Carla, who was unrecognizable, and her husband. Lloyd had met Carla as a precocious eleven-year-old; now, he calculated, she was twenty-six. Although she looked half-starved—most Germans did—she was pretty, and had a confident air that surprised Lloyd. Something about the way she stood made him think she might be pregnant. He knew from Maud's letters that Carla had married Werner, who had been a handsome charmer back in 1933 and was still the same.

They spent an hour catching up. The family had been through unimaginable horror, and said so frankly, yet Lloyd still had a sense that they were editing out the worst details. He told them about Daisy, Evie, and Davey. During the conversation a teenage girl came in and asked Carla if she could go to her friend's house.

"This is our daughter, Rebecca," Carla said to Lloyd.

She was about sixteen, so Lloyd supposed she must be adopted.

"Have you done your homework?" Carla asked the girl.

"I'll do it tomorrow morning."

"Do it now, please," Carla said firmly.

"Oh, Mother!"

"No argument," said Carla. She turned back to Lloyd, and Rebecca stomped out.

They talked about the crisis. Carla was deeply involved, as a city councilor. She was pessimistic about the future of Berlin. She thought the Russians would simply starve the population until the West gave in and handed the city over to total Soviet control.

"Let me show you something that may make you feel differently," Lloyd said. "Will you come with me in the car?"

Maud stayed behind with Walli, but Carla and Werner went with Lloyd. He told the driver to take them to Tempelhof, the airport in the American zone. When they arrived, he led them to a high window from which they could look down on the runway.

There on the tarmac were a dozen C-47 Skytrain aircraft lined up nose to tail, some with the American star, some with the RAF roundel. Their cargo doors were open, and a truck stood at each one. German porters and American airmen were unloading the aircraft. There were sacks of flour, big drums of kerosene, cartons of medical supplies, and wooden crates containing thousands of bottles of milk.

While they watched, empty aircraft were taking off and more were coming in to land.

"This is amazing," said Carla, her eyes glistening. "I've never seen anything like it."

"There has never *been* anything like it," Lloyd replied.

She said: "But can the British and Americans keep it up?"

"I think we have to."

"But for how long?"

"As long as it takes," said Lloyd firmly.

And they did.

CHAPTER TWENTY-FIVE

1949

Almost halfway through the twentieth century, on August 29, 1949, Volodya Peshkov was on the Ustyurt Plateau, east of the Caspian Sea in Kazakhstan. It was a stony desert in the deep south of the USSR, where nomads herded goats in much the same way as they had in biblical times. Volodya was in a military truck that bounced uncomfortably along a rough track. Dawn was breaking over a landscape of rock, sand, and low thorny bushes. A bony camel, alone beside the road, stared malevolently at the truck as it passed.

In the dim distance, Volodya saw the bomb tower, lit by a battery of spotlights.

Zoya and the other scientists had built their first nuclear bomb according to the design Volodya had got from Willi Frunze in Santa Fe. It was a plutonium device with an implosion trigger. There were other designs, but this one had worked twice before, once in New Mexico and once at Nagasaki.

So it should work today.

The test was code-named RDS-1, but they called it First Lightning.

Volodya's truck pulled up at the foot of the tower. Looking up, he saw a clutch of scientists on the platform, doing something with a snake's nest of cables that led to detonators on the skin of the bomb. A figure in blue overalls stepped back, and there was a toss of blond hair: Zoya. Volodya felt a flush of pride. My wife, he thought, top physicist *and* mother of two.

She conferred with two men, the three heads close together, arguing. Volodya hoped nothing was wrong.

This was the bomb that would save Stalin.

Everything else had gone wrong for the Soviet Union. Western Europe had turned decisively democratic, scared off Communism by bully-boy Kremlin tactics and bought off by Marshall Plan bribes. The USSR had not even been able to take control of Berlin: when the airlift had gone on relentlessly day after day for almost a year, the Soviet Union had given up and reopened the roads and railways. In Eastern Europe, Stalin had retained control only by brute force. Truman had been reelected president, and considered himself leader of the world. The Americans had stockpiled nuclear weapons, and had stationed B-29 bombers in Britain, ready to turn the Soviet Union into a radioactive wasteland.

But everything would change today.

If the bomb exploded as it should, the USSR and the USA would be equals again. When the Soviet Union could threaten America with nuclear devastation, American domination of the world would be over.

Volodya no longer knew whether that would be good or bad.

If it did not explode, both Zoya and Volodya would probably be purged, sent to labor camps in Siberia or just shot. Volodya had already talked to his parents, and they had promised to take care of Kotya and Galina.

As they would if Volodya and Zoya were killed by the test.

In the strengthening light Volodya saw, at various distances around the tower, an odd variety of buildings: houses of brick and wood, a bridge over nothing, and the entrance to some kind of underground structure. Presumably the army wanted to measure the effect of the blast. Looking more carefully he saw trucks, tanks, and obsolete aircraft, placed for the same purpose, he imagined. The scientists were also going to assess the impact of the bomb on living creatures: there were horses, cattle, sheep, and dogs in kennels.

The confab on the platform ended with a decision. The three scientists nodded and resumed their work.

A few minutes later Zoya came down and greeted her husband.

"Is everything all right?" he said.

"We think so," Zoya replied.

"You *think* so?"

She shrugged. "We've never done this before, obviously."

They got into the truck and drove, across country that was already a wasteland, to the distant control bunker.

The other scientists were close behind.

At the bunker they all put on welders' goggles as the countdown ticked away.

At sixty seconds, Zoya held Volodya's hand.

At ten seconds, he smiled at her and said: "I love you."

At one second, he held his breath.

Then it was as if the sun had suddenly risen. A light stronger than noon flooded the desert. In the direction of the bomb tower, a ball of fire grew impossibly high, reaching for the moon. Volodya was startled by the lurid colors in the fireball: green, purple, and orange.

The ball turned into a mushroom whose umbrella kept rising. At last the sound arrived, a bang as if the largest artillery piece in the Red Army had been fired a foot away, followed by rolling thunder that reminded Volodya of the terrible bombardment of the Seelow Heights.

At last the cloud began to disperse and the noise faded.

There was a long moment of stunned silence.

Someone said: "My God, I didn't expect *that*."

Volodya embraced his wife. "You did it," he said.

She looked solemn. "I know," she said. "But *what* did we do?"

"You saved Communism," said Volodya.

ii

"The Russian bomb was based on Fat Man, the one we dropped on Nagasaki," said Special Agent Bill Bicks. "Someone gave them the plans."

"How do you know?" Greg asked him.

"From a defector."

They were sitting in Bicks's carpeted office in the Washington headquarters of the FBI at nine o'clock in the morning. Bicks had his jacket off. His shirt was stained in the armpits with sweat, though the building was comfortably air-conditioned.

"According to this guy," Bicks went on, "a Red Army Intelligence colonel got the plans from one of the scientists on the Manhattan Project team."

"Did he say who?"

"He doesn't know which scientist. That's why I called you in. We need to find the traitor."

"The FBI checked them all out at the time."

"And most of them were security risks! There was nothing we could do. But you knew them personally."

"Who was the Red Army colonel?"

"I was coming to that. You know him. His name is Vladimir Peshkov."

"My half brother!"

"Yes."

"If I were you, I'd suspect me." Greg said it with a laugh, but he was very uneasy.

"Oh, we did, believe me," Bicks said. "You've been subjected to the most thorough investigation I have seen in twenty years with the bureau."

Greg gave him a skeptical look. "No kidding."

"Your kid's doing well in school, isn't he?"

Greg was shocked. Who could have told the FBI about Georgy? "You mean my godson?" he said.

"Greg, I said *thorough*. We know he's your son."

Greg was annoyed, but he suppressed the feeling. He had probed the personal secrets of numerous suspects during his time in army security. He had no right to object.

"You're clean," Bicks went on.

"I'm relieved to hear it."

"Anyway, our defector insisted the plans came from a scientist, rather than any of the normal army personnel working on the project."

Greg said thoughtfully: "When I met Volodya in Moscow, he told me he had never been to the United States."

"He lied," said Bicks. "He came here in September 1945. He spent a week in New York. Then we lost him for eight days. He resurfaced briefly, then went home."

"Eight days?"

"Yeah. We're embarrassed."

"It's enough time to go to Santa Fe, stay a couple of days, and come back."

"Right." Bicks leaned forward across his desk. "But think. If the scientist had already been recruited as a spy, why wasn't he contacted by his regular controller? Why bring someone from Moscow to talk to him?"

"You think the traitor was recruited on this two-day visit? It seems too quick."

"Possibly he had worked for them before but lapsed. Either way, we're guessing the Soviets needed to send *someone who the scientist already knew*. That means there ought to be a connection between Volodya and one of the scientists." Bicks gestured at a side table covered with tan file folders. "The answer is in there somewhere. Those are our files on every one of the scientists who had access to those plans."

"What do you want me to do?"

"Go through them."

"Isn't that your job?"

"We've already done it. We didn't find anything. We're hoping you'll spot something we've missed. I'll sit here and keep you company, do some paperwork."

"It's a long job."

"You've got all day."

Greg frowned. Did they know . . . ?

Bicks said confidently: "You have no plans for the rest of the day."

Greg shrugged. "Got any coffee?"

He had coffee and donuts, then more coffee, then a sandwich at lunchtime, then a banana midafternoon. He read every known detail about the lives of the scientists, their wives and families: childhood, education, career, love and marriage, achievements and eccentricities and sins.

He was eating the last bite of banana when he said: "Jesus fucking Christ."

"What?" said Bicks.

"Willi Frunze went to the Berlin Boys' Academy." Greg slapped the file triumphantly down on the desk.

"And . . . ?"

"So did Volodya—he told me."

Bicks thumped his desk in excitement. "School friends! That's it! We've got the bastard!"

"It's not proof," said Greg.

"Oh, don't worry. He'll confess."

"How can you be sure?"

"Those scientists believe that knowledge should be shared with everyone, not kept secret. He'll try to justify himself by arguing that he did it for the good of humanity."

"Maybe he did."

"He'll go to the electric chair all the same," said Bicks.

Greg was suddenly chilled. Willi Frunze had seemed a nice guy. "Will he?"

"You bet your ass. He's going to fry."

Bicks was right. Willi Frunze was found guilty of treason and sentenced to death, and he died in the electric chair.

So did his wife.

Daisy watched her husband tie his white bow tie and slip into the tailcoat of his perfectly fitting dress suit. "You look like a million dollars," she said, and she meant it. He should have been a movie star.

She remembered him thirteen years earlier, wearing borrowed clothes at the Trinity Ball, and she felt a pleasant frisson of nostalgia. He had looked pretty good then, she recalled, even though his suit was two sizes too big.

They were staying in her father's permanent suite at the Ritz-Carlton hotel in Washington. Lloyd was now a junior minister in the British Foreign Office, and he had come here on a diplomatic visit. Lloyd's parents, Ethel and Bernie, were thrilled to be looking after two grandchildren for a week.

Tonight Daisy and Lloyd were going to a ball at the White House.

She was wearing a drop-dead dress by Christian Dior, pink satin with a dramatically spreading skirt made of endless folds of flaring tulle. After the years of wartime austerity she was delighted to be able to buy gowns in Paris again.

She thought of the Yacht Club Ball of 1935 in Buffalo, the event that she imagined, at the time, had ruined her life. The White House was obviously a lot more prestigious, but she knew that nothing that happened tonight could ruin her life. She reflected on that while Lloyd helped her put on her mother's necklace of rose-colored diamonds with matching earrings. At the age of nineteen she had desperately wanted high-status people to accept her. Now she could hardly imagine worrying about such a thing. As long as Lloyd said she looked fabulous, she did not care what anyone else thought. The only other person whose approval she might seek was her mother-in-law, Eth Leckwith, who had little social status and had certainly never worn a Paris gown.

Did every woman look back and think how foolish she had been when young? Daisy thought again about Ethel, who had certainly behaved foolishly—getting pregnant by her married employer—but never spoke regretfully about it. Maybe that was the right attitude.

Daisy contemplated her own mistakes: becoming engaged to Charlie Farquharson, rejecting Lloyd, marrying Boy Fitzherbert. She was not quite able to look back and think about the good that had come of those choices. It was really not until she had been decisively rejected by high society, and had found consolation at Ethel's kitchen in Aldgate, that her life had taken a turn for the better. She had stopped yearning for social status and had learned what real friendship was, and she had been happy ever since.

Now that she no longer cared, she enjoyed parties even more.

"Ready?" said Lloyd.

She was ready. She put on the matching evening coat that Dior had made to go with the dress. They went down in the elevator, left the hotel, and stepped into the waiting limousine.

iv

Carla persuaded her mother to play the piano on Christmas Eve.

Maud had not played for years. Perhaps it saddened her by bringing back memories of Walter: they had always played and sung together, and she had often told the children how she had tried, and failed, to teach him to play ragtime. But she no longer told that story, and Carla suspected that nowadays the piano made Maud think of Joachim Koch, the young officer who had come to her for piano lessons, whom she had deceived and seduced, and whom Carla and Ada had killed in the kitchen. Carla herself was not able to shut out the recollection of that nightmare evening, especially getting rid of the body. She did not regret it—they had done the right thing—but, all the same, she would have preferred to forget it.

However, Maud at last agreed to play "Silent Night" for them all to sing along. Werner, Ada, Erik, and the three children, Rebecca, Walli, and the new baby, Lili, gathered around the old Steinway in the drawing room. Carla put a candle on the piano, and studied the faces of her family in its moving shadows as they sang the familiar German carol.

Walli, in Werner's arms, would be four years old in a few weeks' time, and he tried to sing along, alertly guessing the words and the melody. He had the Oriental eyes of his rapist father; Carla had decided that her revenge would be to raise a son who treated women with tenderness and respect.

Erik sang the words of the hymn sincerely. He supported the Soviet regime as blindly as he had supported the Nazis. Carla had at first been baffled and infuriated, but now she saw a sad logic to it. Erik was one of those inadequate people who were so scared by life that they preferred to live under harsh authority, to be told what to do and what to think by a government that allowed no dissent. They were foolish and dangerous, but there were an awful lot of them.

Carla gazed fondly at her husband, still handsome at thirty. She recalled kissing him, and more, in the front of his sexy car, parked in the Grunewald, when she was nineteen. She still liked kissing him.

When she thought over the time that had passed since then, she had a thousand regrets, but the biggest was her father's death. She missed him constantly and still cried when she remembered him lying in the hall, beaten so cruelly that he did not live until the doctor arrived.

But everyone had to die, and Father had given his life for the sake of a better world. If more Germans had had his courage, the Nazis would not have triumphed. She wanted to do all the things he had done: to raise her children well, to make a difference to her country's politics, to love and be loved. Most of all, when she died, she wanted her children to be able to say, as she said of her father, that her life had meant something, and that the world was a better place for it.

The carol came to an end; Maud held the final chord; and little Walli leaned forward and blew the candle out.

ACKNOWLEDGMENTS

My principal history adviser for the Century Trilogy is Richard Overy. I am grateful also to historians Evan Mawdsley, Tim Rees, Matthias Reiss, and Richard Toye for reading the typescript of *Winter of the World* and making corrections.

As always I had invaluable help from my editors and agents, especially Amy Berkower, Leslie Gelbman, Phyllis Grann, Neil Nyren, Susan Opie, and Jeremy Treviathan.

I met my agent Al Zuckerman in about 1975 and he has been my most critical and inspiring reader ever since.

Several friends made helpful comments. Nigel Dean has an eye for detail like no one else. Chris Manners and Tony McWalter were as sharply perceptive as ever. Angela Spizig and Annemarie Behnke saved me from numerous errors in the German sections.

We always thank our families, and so we should. Barbara Follett, Emanuele Follett, Jann Turner, and Kim Turner read the first draft and made useful criticisms, as well as giving me the matchless gift of their love.

ABOUT THE AUTHOR

Ken Follett burst into the book world with *Eye of the Needle*, an award-winning thriller and international bestseller. After several more successful thrillers, he surprised everyone with *The Pillars of the Earth* and its long-awaited sequel, *World Without End*, a national and international bestseller. Follett's new, magnificent historical epic, the Century Trilogy, opened with the bestselling *Fall of Giants*. He lives in England with his wife, Barbara.

CONNECT ONLINE

www.ken-follett.com

ABOUT THE AUTHOR

KEN FOLLETT burst into the book world with *Eye of the Needle*, an award-winning thriller and international bestseller. After several more successful thrillers, he surprised everyone with *The Pillars of the Earth* and its long-awaited sequel, *World Without End*, a national and international bestseller. Follett's new, magnificent historical epic, the Century Trilogy, opened with the bestselling *Fall of Giants*. He lives in England with his wife, Barbara.

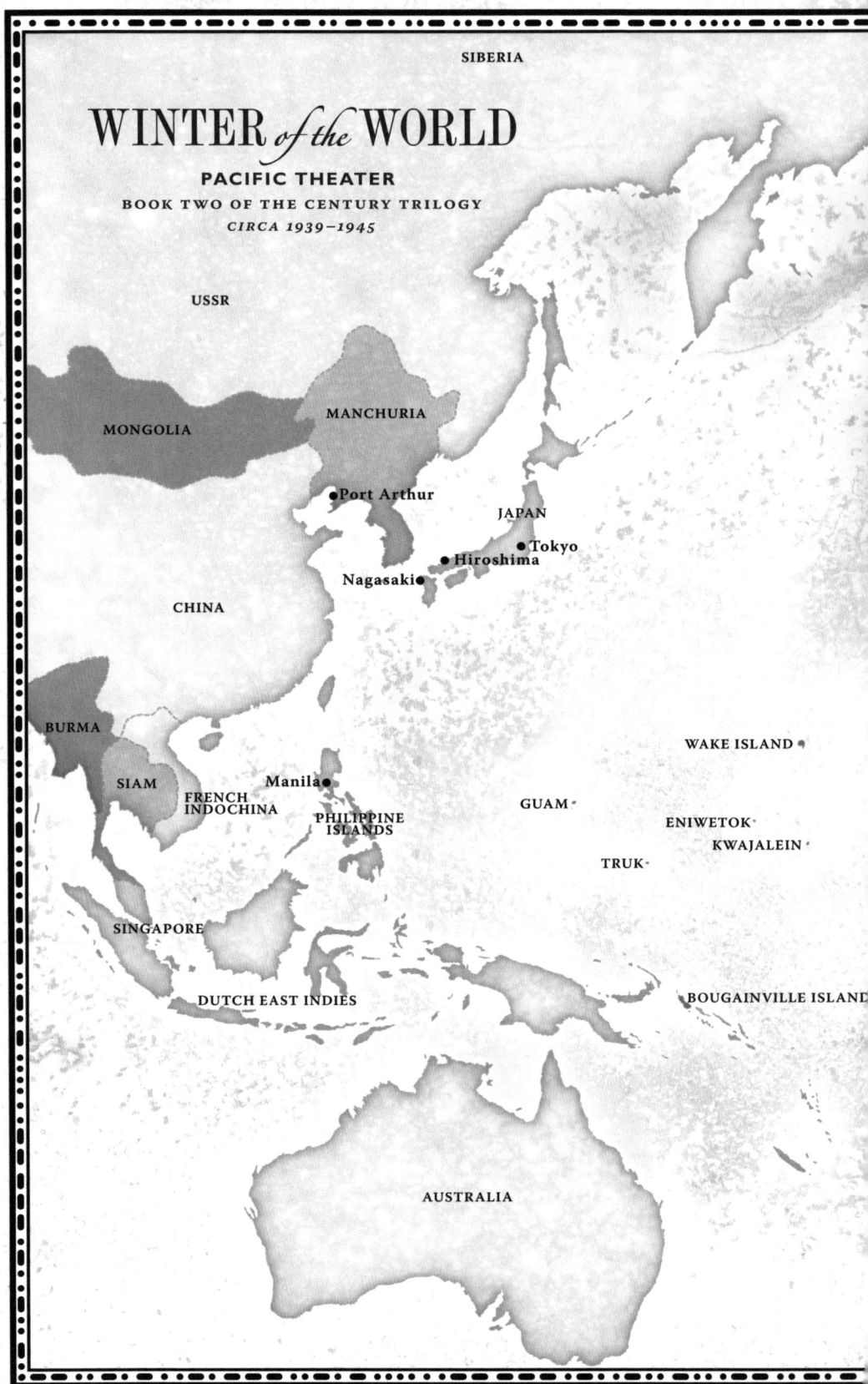

WINTER *of the* WORLD

PACIFIC THEATER

BOOK TWO OF THE CENTURY TRILOGY

CIRCA 1939–1945

SIBERIA

USSR

MONGOLIA

MANCHURIA

●Port Arthur

JAPAN

●Tokyo

● Hiroshima

Nagasaki●

CHINA

BURMA

SIAM

FRENCH
INDOCHINA

Manila●

PHILIPPINE
ISLANDS

GUAM ·

WAKE ISLAND ◗

ENIWETOK·

KWAJALEIN ·

TRUK·

SINGAPORE

DUTCH EAST INDIES

BOUGAINVILLE ISLAND

AUSTRALIA

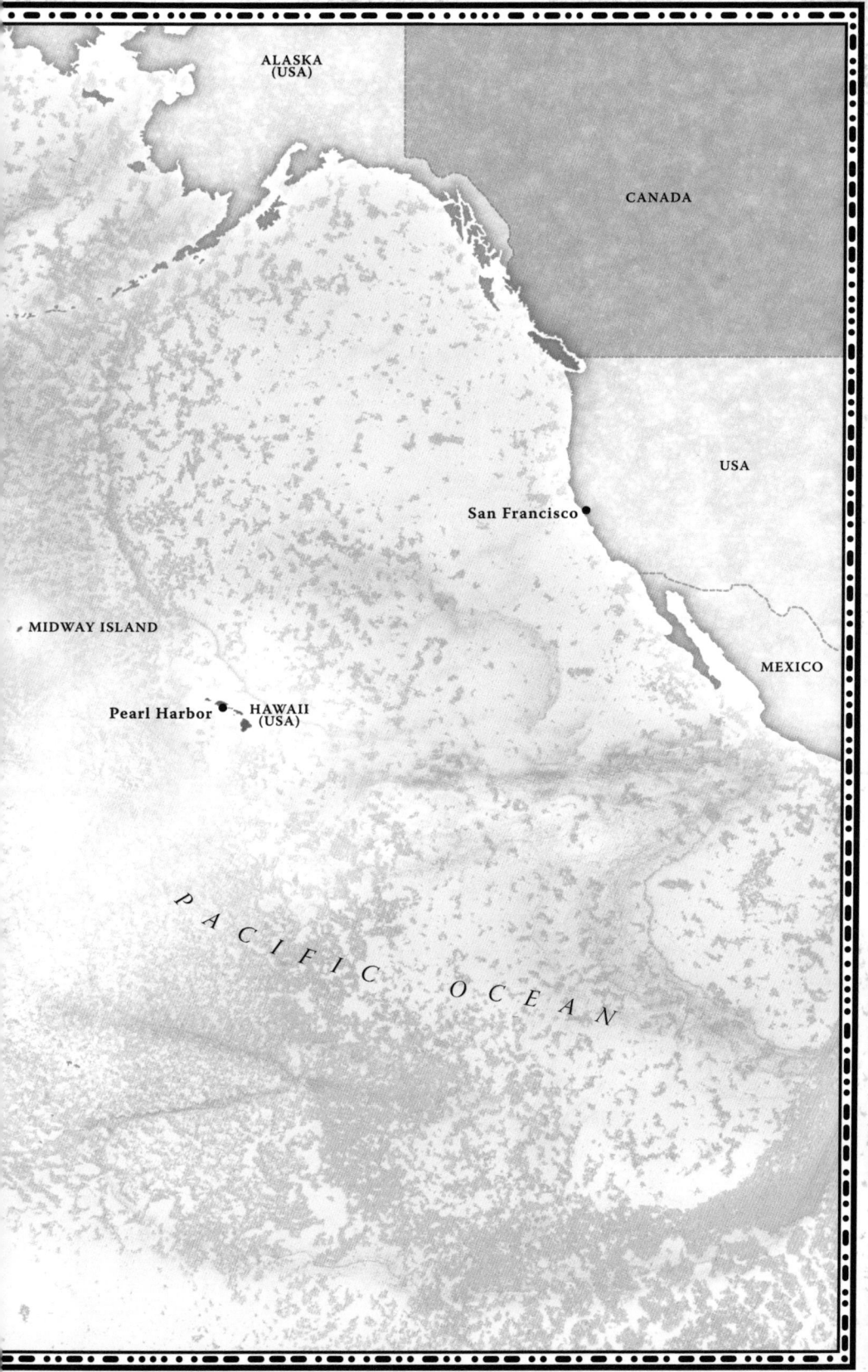

★ BOOK THREE OF ★
THE CENTURY TRILOGY

EDGE OF ETERNITY

FALL 2014

Dutton, A member of Penguin Group (USA) Inc.

PRAISE FOR THE NOVELS
OF KEN FOLLETT

Edge of Eternity

"[Follett] is a commanding storyteller who has taken on an impossibly large task and accomplished it with passion, intelligence, and skill. Like its predecessors, *Edge of Eternity* is a solid, rigorously researched work of popular fiction. It's an honest entertainment that brings back vivid, sometimes painful, memories of the not-too-distant past."
—*The Washington Post*

"*Edge of Eternity* is as compulsively readable a mighty page-turner as its two predecessors."
—*The Seattle Times*

"Hugely ambitious, the trilogy serves as a massive history lesson as well as an example of good old-fashioned storytelling."
—*New York Daily News*

"Follett never forgets he is telling a story. The historical events are the backdrop but the characters are the focal point. Good storytellers know this, and Follett is an excellent one."
—The Huffington Post

"Mesmerizing . . . flowing with spicy, expertly paced melodrama, character-rich exploits, familial histrionics, and international intrigue."
—*Publishers Weekly* (starred review)

"Worth the wait. . . . Once again, Follett has written pitch-perfect popular fiction that readers will devour."
—*Library Journal* (starred review)

"A glorious conclusion to a remarkable trilogy that is wonderful, exhilarating reading for all ages. Fine, fine historical fiction."
—Historical Novel Society

"Follett does an outstanding job of interweaving and personalizing complicated narratives set on a multicultural stage."
—*Booklist*

continued . . .

"Follett . . . knows how to turn in a robust yarn without too much slack . . . a well-written entertainment." —*Kirkus Reviews*

Winter of the World

"This book is truly epic. . . . The reader will probably wish there were a thousand more pages." —The Huffington Post

"Some of the biggest-picture fiction being written today." —*The Seattle Times*

"Follett's real gifts are those of a natural storyteller: swift, cinematic pacing, the ability to juggle multiple narratives coherently, and an eye for the telling detail . . . a consistently compelling portrait of a world in crisis." —*The Washington Post*

"Gripping . . . powerful." —*The New York Times*

"Masterfully sweeping stories . . . political intrigue, amorous episodes, suspense, and drama. History comes to life." —*The Louisville Courier-Journal*

"[Follett] is so good at plotting a story, even one that takes on such a complex topic as the World War II era. That's what makes *Winter of the World* so hard to put down. You want to know what happens next." —The Associated Press

"An entertaining historical soap opera." —*Kirkus Reviews*

"The man tells a story so well. . . . Follett can make things glow with some beautifully written episodes. . . . If you read Volume I, you'll have to read Volume II. And once you read Volume II, you'll be committed to reading Volume III. See you in a couple of years." —*St. Louis Post-Dispatch*

"Clips along at a brisk pace. . . . He knows how to keep the pages turning and how to make the reader feel a kinship with the characters' struggles. . . . No matter the ultimate destination, readers can expect to savor the journey—and agonize while waiting for the final book to arrive." —*The Christian Science Monitor*

Fall of Giants

"Follett is masterly in conveying so much drama and historical information so vividly . . . grippingly told."   —*The New York Times Book Review*

"*Fall of Giants*: Follett at his finest. . . . [a] sweeping epic that will thrill his fans for hours on end."   —The Huffington Post

"Follett conjures the winds of war."   —*The Washington Post*

"Tantalizing."   —*Newsday*

"A good read. . . . It's a book that will suck you in, consume you for days or weeks, depending upon how quick a reader you are, then let you out the other side both entertained and educated. That's quite the feat."   —*USA Today*

"Follett apparently intends to give readers the sweeping history of that century in the form of a novel that follows five families—one American, two British, one German, and one Russian. That's a big job. But *Fall of Giants* suggests that Follett is up to the task."   —*St. Louis Post-Dispatch*

"Follett entwines fiction and factual events well. . . . This is a dark novel, motivated by an unsparing view of human nature and a clear-eyed scrutiny of an ideal peace. It is not the least of Follett's feats that the reader finishes this near thousand-page book intrigued and wanting more."   —*Chicago Sun-Times*

"Follett once again creates a world at once familiar and fantastic. . . . A guiltless pleasure, the book is impossible to put down. . . . Empires fall. Heroes rise. Love conquers. After going through a war with these characters, you're left hoping that Follett gets moving with the next giant installment."   —*Time Out*

"*Fall of Giants* grand in scope, scale, and story."   —The Associated Press

"Suspenseful, tightly constructed, sharply characterized, plot-driven."   —*The Seattle Times*

KEN FOLLETT

EDGE
of
ETERNITY

BOOK THREE OF THE CENTURY TRILOGY

 NEW AMERICAN LIBRARY

NEW AMERICAN LIBRARY
Published by New American Library,
an imprint of Penguin Random House LLC
375 Hudson Street, New York, New York 10014

This book is a publication of New American Library.
Previously published in a Dutton edition.

First New American Library Printing, September 2015

NEW AMERICAN LIBRARY TRADE PAPERBACK ISBN: 978-0-451-47401-8

THE LIBRARY OF CONGRESS HAS CATALOGUED THE HARDCOVER EDITION OF
THIS BOOK AS FOLLOWS:
Follett, Ken.
Edge of eternity/Ken Follett.
p. cm.—(Century trilogy; book three)
ISBN 978-0-525-95309-8
1. World politics—1945–1989—Fiction.   2. Political fiction.   I. Title.
PR0656.O45E46 2014   823'.914—dc23   2014005306

Printed in the United States of America
3   5   7   9   10   8   6   4   2

Set in Warnock Pro, Bodoni Svntytwo ITC, and Gill Sans Infant
Designed by Amy Hill

Penguin
Random
House

To all the freedom fighters,

especially Barbara

CAST OF CHARACTERS

American

DEWAR FAMILY

Cameron Dewar
Ursula "Beep" Dewar, his sister
Woody Dewar, his father
Bella Dewar, his mother

PESHKOV-JAKES FAMILY

George Jakes
Jacky Jakes, his mother
Greg Peshkov, his father
Lev Peshkov, his grandfather
Marga, his grandmother

MARQUAND FAMILY

Verena Marquand
Percy Marquand, her father
Babe Lee, her mother

CIA

Florence Geary
Tony Savino
Tim Tedder, semiretired
Keith Dorset

OTHERS

Maria Summers
Joseph Hugo, FBI
Larry Mawhinney, Pentagon
Nelly Fordham, old flame of Greg Peshkov
Dennis Wilson, aide to Bobby Kennedy
Skip Dickerson, aide to Lyndon Johnson
Leopold "Lee" Montgomery, reporter
Herb Gould, television journalist on *This Day*
Suzy Cannon, gossip reporter
Frank Lindeman, television network owner

REAL HISTORICAL CHARACTERS

John F. Kennedy, thirty-fifth U.S. president
Jackie, his wife
Bobby Kennedy, his brother
Dave Powers, assistant to President Kennedy
Pierre Salinger, President Kennedy's press officer
Rev. Dr. Martin Luther King Jr., president of the Southern
   Christian Leadership Conference
Lyndon B. Johnson, thirty-sixth U.S. president
Richard Nixon, thirty-seventh U.S. president
Jimmy Carter, thirty-ninth U.S. president
Ronald Reagan, fortieth U.S. president
George H. W. Bush, forty-first U.S. president

British

LECKWITH-WILLIAMS FAMILY

Dave Williams
Evie Williams, his sister
Daisy Williams, his mother
Lloyd Williams, M.P., his father
Eth Leckwith, Dave's grandmother

MURRAY FAMILY

Jasper Murray
Anna Murray, his sister
Eva Murray, his mother

MUSICIANS IN THE GUARDSMEN AND PLUM NELLIE

Lenny, Dave Williams's cousin
Lew, drummer
Buzz, bass player
Geoffrey, lead guitarist

OTHERS

Earl Fitzherbert, called Fitz
Sam Cakebread, friend of Jasper Murray
Byron Chesterfield (real name Brian Chesnowitz), music agent
Hank Remington (real name Harry Riley), pop star
Eric Chapman, record company executive

German

FRANCK FAMILY

Rebecca Hoffmann
Carla Franck, Rebecca's adoptive mother
Werner Franck, Rebecca's adoptive father
Walli Franck, son of Carla
Lili Franck, daughter of Werner and Carla
Maud von Ulrich, née Fitzherbert, Carla's mother
Hans Hoffmann, Rebecca's husband

OTHERS

Bernd Held, schoolteacher
Karolin Koontz, folksinger
Odo Vossler, clergyman

REAL HISTORICAL PEOPLE

Walter Ulbricht, first secretary of the Socialist Unity Party
   (Communist)
Erich Honecker, Ulbricht's successor
Egon Krenz, successor to Honecker

Polish

Stanislaw "Staz" Pawlak, army officer
Lidka, girlfriend of Cam Dewar
Danuta Gorski, Solidarity activist

REAL HISTORICAL PEOPLE

Anna Walentynowicz, crane driver
Lech Wałęsa, leader of the trade union Solidarity
General Jaruzelski, prime minister

Russian

DVORKIN-PESHKOV FAMILY

Tanya Dvorkin, journalist
Dimka Dvorkin, Kremlin aide, Tanya's twin brother
Anya Dvorkin, their mother
Grigori Peshkov, their grandfather
Katerina Peshkov, their grandmother
Vladimir, always called Volodya, their uncle
Zoya, Volodya's wife
Nina, Dimka's girlfriend

OTHERS

Daniil Antonov, features editor at TASS
Pyotr Opotkin, features editor in chief
Vasili Yenkov, dissident
Natalya Smotrov, official in the Foreign Ministry
Nik Smotrov, Natalya's husband
Yevgeny Filipov, aide to Defense Minister Rodion Malinovsky
Vera Pletner, Dimka's secretary
Valentin, Dimka's friend
Marshal Mikhail Pushnoy

REAL HISTORICAL CHARACTERS

Nikita Sergeyevitch Khrushchev, first secretary of the Communist
    Party of the Soviet Union
Andrei Gromyko, foreign minister under Khrushchev

Rodion Malinovsky, defense minister under Khrushchev
Alexei Kosygin, chairman of the Council of Ministers
Leonid Brezhnev, Khrushchev's successor
Yuri Andropov, successor to Brezhnev
Konstantin Chernenko, successor to Andropov
Mikhail Gorbachev, successor to Chernenko

Other Nations

Paz Oliva, Cuban general
Frederik Bíró, Hungarian politician
Enok Andersen, Danish accountant

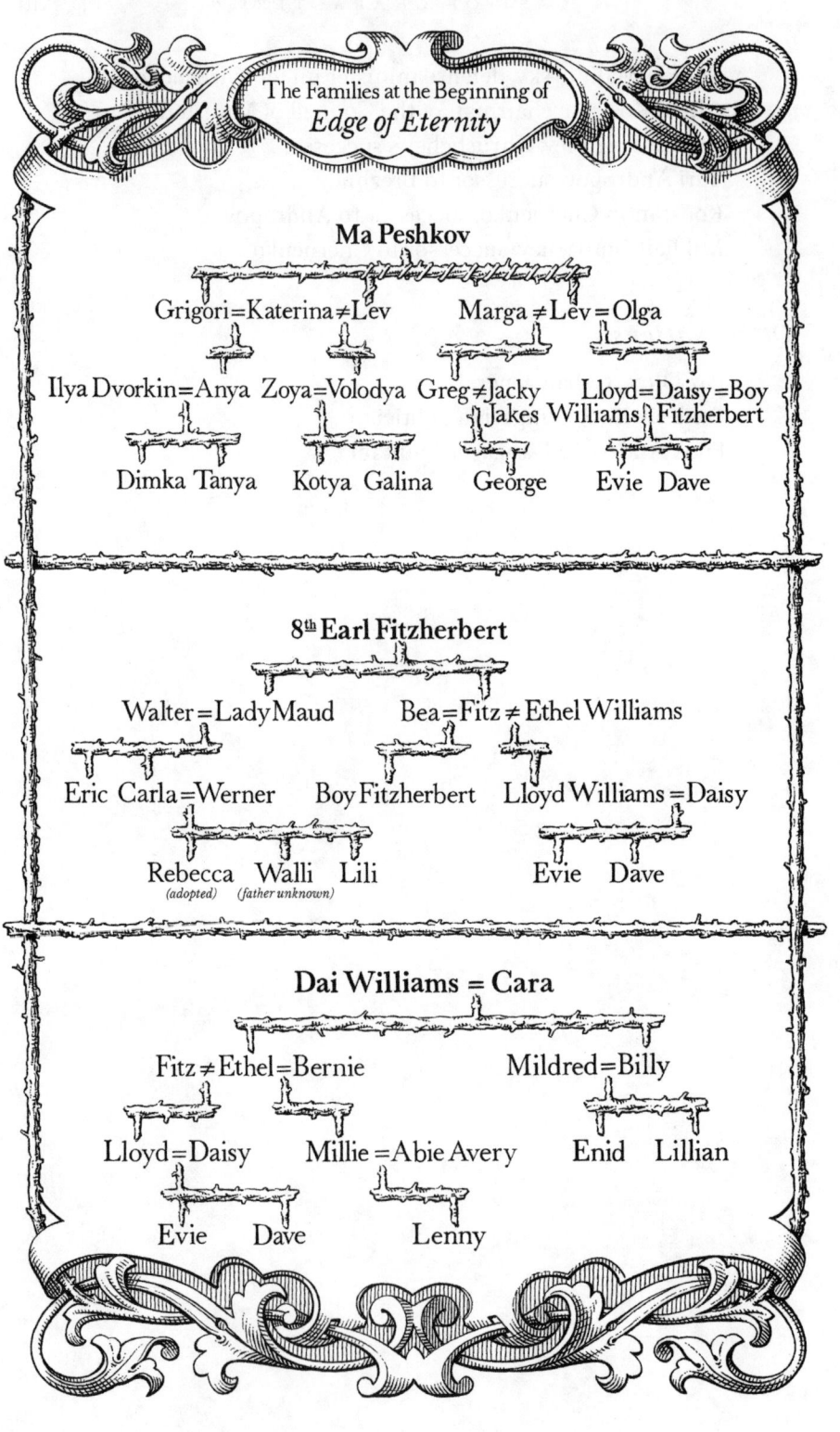

The Families at the Beginning of
Edge of Eternity

Ma Peshkov

Grigori = Katerina ≠ Lev   Marga ≠ Lev = Olga

Ilya Dvorkin = Anya Zoya = Volodya Greg ≠ Jacky Lloyd = Daisy = Boy
Jakes Williams Fitzherbert

Dimka Tanya   Kotya Galina   George   Evie Dave

8ᵗʰ Earl Fitzherbert

Walter = Lady Maud   Bea = Fitz ≠ Ethel Williams

Eric Carla = Werner   Boy Fitzherbert   Lloyd Williams = Daisy

Rebecca Walli Lili   Evie   Dave
(adopted) *(father unknown)*

Dai Williams = Cara

Fitz ≠ Ethel = Bernie   Mildred = Billy

Lloyd = Daisy   Millie = Abie Avery   Enid Lillian

Evie   Dave   Lenny

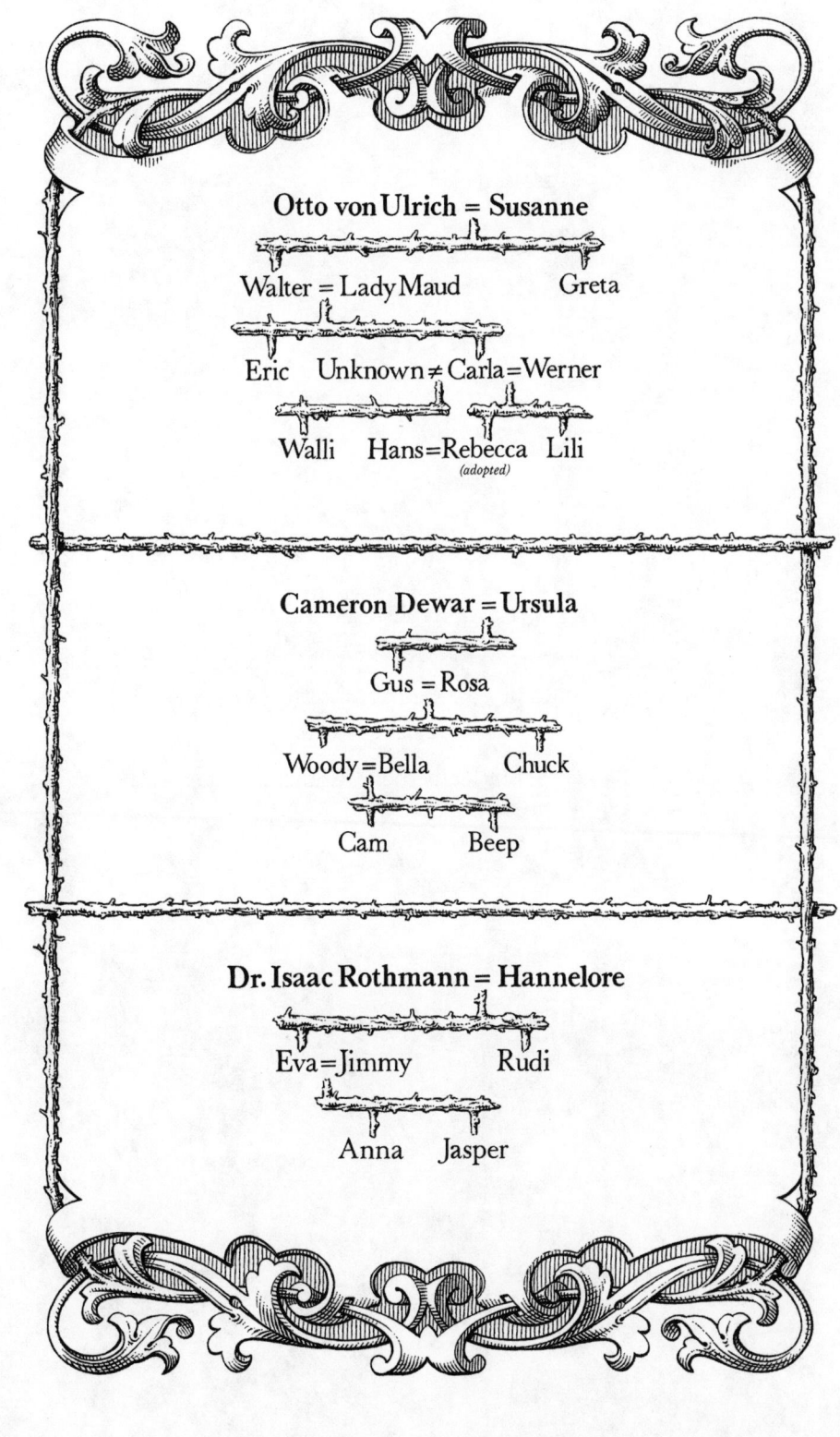

Otto von Ulrich = Susanne

Walter = Lady Maud   Greta

Eric   Unknown ≠ Carla = Werner

Walli   Hans = Rebecca   Lili
                (adopted)

Cameron Dewar = Ursula

Gus = Rosa

Woody = Bella   Chuck

Cam   Beep

Dr. Isaac Rothmann = Hannelore

Eva = Jimmy   Rudi

Anna   Jasper

EDGE OF ETERNITY

PART ONE

WALL

1961

Rebecca Hoffmann was summoned by the secret police on a rainy Monday in 1961.

It began as an ordinary morning. Her husband drove her to work in his tan Trabant 500. The graceful old streets of central Berlin still had gaps from wartime bombing, except where new concrete buildings stood up like ill-matched false teeth. Hans was thinking about his job as he drove. "The courts serve the judges, the lawyers, the police, the government—everyone except the victims of crime," he said. "This is to be expected in Western capitalist countries, but under Communism the courts ought surely to serve the people. My colleagues don't seem to realize that." Hans worked for the Ministry of Justice.

"We've been married almost a year, and I've known you for two, but I've never met one of your colleagues," Rebecca said.

"They would bore you," he said immediately. "They're all lawyers."

"Any women among them?"

"No. Not in my section, anyway." Hans's job was administration: appointing judges, scheduling trials, managing courthouses.

"I'd like to meet them, all the same."

Hans was a strong man who had learned to rein himself in. Watching him, Rebecca saw in his eyes a familiar flash of anger at her insistence. He controlled it by an effort of will. "I'll arrange something," he said. "Perhaps we'll all go to a bar one evening."

Hans had been the first man Rebecca met who matched up to her father. He was confident and authoritative, but he always listened to her. He had a good job—not many people had a car of their own in East Germany—and men who worked in the government were usually hard-line Communists, but Hans, surprisingly, shared Rebecca's political skepticism. Like her father he was tall, handsome, and well dressed. He was the man she had been waiting for.

Only once during their courtship had she doubted him, briefly. They had been in a minor car crash. It had been wholly the fault of the other driver, who had come out of a side street without stopping. Such things happened every day, but Hans had been mad with rage. Although the damage to the two cars was minimal, he had called the police, shown them his Ministry of Justice identity card, and had the other driver arrested for dangerous driving and taken off to jail.

Afterward he had apologized to Rebecca for losing his temper. She had been scared by his vindictiveness, and had come close to ending their relationship. But he had explained that he had not been his normal self, due to pressure at work, and she had believed him. Her faith had been justified: he had never done such a thing again.

When they had been dating for a year, and sleeping together most weekends for six months, Rebecca wondered why he did not ask her to marry him. They were not kids: she had then been twenty-eight, he thirty-three. So she had proposed to him. He had been startled, but said yes.

Now he pulled up outside her school. It was a modern building, and well equipped: the Communists were serious about education. Outside the gates, five or six older boys were standing under a tree, smoking cigarettes. Ignoring their stares, Rebecca kissed Hans on the lips. Then she got out.

The boys greeted her politely, but she felt their yearning adolescent eyes on her figure as she splashed through the puddles in the school yard.

Rebecca came from a political family. Her grandfather had been a Social Democrat member of the Reichstag, the national parliament, until Hitler came to power. Her mother had been a city councilor, also for the Social Democrats, during East Berlin's brief postwar period of democracy. But East Germany was a Communist tyranny now, and Rebecca saw no point in engaging in politics. So she channeled her idealism into teaching, and hoped that the next generation would be less dogmatic, more compassionate, smarter.

In the staff room she checked the emergency timetable on the notice board. Most of her classes were doubled today, two groups of pupils crammed into one room. Her subject was Russian, but she also had to teach an English class. She did not speak English, though she had picked up a smattering from her British grandmother, Maud, still feisty at seventy.

This was the second time Rebecca had been asked to teach an English class, and she began to think about a text. The first time, she had used a leaflet handed out to American soldiers, telling them how to get on with Germans: the pupils had found it hilarious, and they had learned a lot too. Today perhaps she would write on the blackboard the words of a song they knew, such as "The Twist"—played all the time on American Forces Network radio—and get them to translate it into German. It would not be a conventional lesson, but it was the best she could do.

The school was desperately short of teachers because half the staff had emigrated to West Germany, where salaries were three hundred marks a month higher and people were free. The story was the same in most schools in East Germany. And it was not just teachers. Doctors could double their earnings by moving west. Rebecca's mother, Carla, was head of nursing at a large East Berlin hospital, and she was tearing her hair out at the scarcity of both nurses and doctors. The story was the same in industry and even the armed forces. It was a national crisis.

As Rebecca was scribbling the lyrics of "The Twist" in a notebook, trying to remember the line about "my little sis," the deputy head came into the staff room. Bernd Held was probably Rebecca's best friend outside her family. He was a slim, dark-haired man of forty, with a livid scar across his forehead where a shard of flying shrapnel had struck him while he was defending the Seelow Heights in the last days of the war. He taught physics, but he shared Rebecca's interest in Russian literature, and they ate their lunchtime sandwiches together a couple of times a week. "Listen, everybody," Bernd said. "Bad news, I'm afraid. Anselm has left us."

There was a murmur of surprise. Anselm Weber was the head teacher. He was a loyal Communist—heads had to be. But it seemed his principles had been overcome by the appeal of West German prosperity and liberty.

Bernd went on: "I will be taking his place until a new head can be appointed." Rebecca and every other teacher in the school knew that

Bernd himself should have got the job, if ability had been what counted; but Bernd was ruled out because he would not join the Socialist Unity Party, the SED—the Communist Party in all but name.

For the same reason, Rebecca would never be a head teacher. Anselm had pleaded with her to join the party, but it was out of the question. For her it would be like checking herself into a lunatic asylum and pretending all the other inmates were sane.

As Bernd detailed the emergency arrangements, Rebecca wondered when the school would get its new head. A year from now? How long would this crisis go on? No one knew.

Before the first lesson she glanced into her pigeonhole, but it was empty. The mail had not yet arrived. Perhaps the postman had gone to West Germany, too.

The letter that would turn her life upside down was still on its way.

She taught her first class, discussing the Russian poem "The Bronze Horseman" with a large group seventeen and eighteen years old. This was a lesson she had given every year since she started teaching. As always, she guided the pupils to the orthodox Soviet analysis, explaining that the conflict between personal interest and public duty was resolved, by Pushkin, in favor of the public.

At lunchtime she took her sandwich to the head's office and sat down across the big desk from Bernd. She looked at the shelf of cheap pottery busts: Marx, Lenin, and East German Communist leader Walter Ulbricht. Bernd followed her gaze and smiled. "Anselm is a sly one," he said. "For years he pretended to be a true believer, and now— zoom, he's off."

"Aren't you tempted to leave?" Rebecca asked Bernd. "You're divorced, no children—you have no ties."

He looked around, as if wondering whether someone might be listening; then he shrugged. "I've thought about it—who hasn't?" he said. "How about you? Your father works in West Berlin anyway, doesn't he?"

"Yes. He has a factory making television sets. But my mother is determined to stay in the East. She says we must solve our problems, not run away from them."

"I've met her. She's a tiger."

"That's the truth. And the house we live in has been in her family for generations."

"What about your husband?"

"He's dedicated to his job."

"So I don't have to worry about losing you. Good."

Rebecca said: "Bernd—" Then she hesitated.

"Spit it out."

"Can I ask you a personal question?"

"Of course."

"You left your wife because she was having an affair."

Bernd stiffened, but he answered: "That's right."

"How did you find out?"

Bernd winced, as if at a sudden pain.

"Do you mind me asking?" Rebecca said anxiously. "Is it too personal?"

"I don't mind telling *you*," he said. "I confronted her, and she admitted it."

"But what made you suspicious?"

"A lot of little things—"

Rebecca interrupted him. "The phone rings, you pick it up, there's a silence for a few seconds, then the person at the other end hangs up."

He nodded.

She went on: "Your spouse tears a note up small and flushes the shreds down the toilet. At the weekend he's called to an unexpected meeting. In the evening he spends two hours writing something he won't show you."

"Oh, dear," said Bernd sadly. "You're talking about Hans."

"He's got a lover, hasn't he?" She put down her sandwich: she had no appetite. "Tell me honestly what you think."

"I'm so sorry."

Bernd had kissed her once, four months ago, on the last day of the autumn term. They had been saying good-bye, and wishing one another a happy Christmas, and he had lightly grasped her arm, and bent his head, and kissed her lips. She had asked him not to do it again, ever, and said she would still like to be his friend; and when they had returned to school in January both had pretended it had never happened. He had even told her, a few weeks later, that he had a date with a widow his own age.

Rebecca did not want to encourage hopeless aspirations, but Bernd was the only person she could talk to, except for her family, and she did not want to worry them, not yet. "I was so sure that Hans loved me," she said, and tears came to her eyes. "And I love him."

"Perhaps he does love you. Some men just can't resist temptation."

Rebecca did not know whether Hans found their sex life satisfactory. He never complained, but they made love only about once a week, which she believed to be infrequent for newlyweds. "All I want is a family of my own, just like my mother's, in which everyone is loved and supported and protected," she said. "I thought I could have that with Hans."

"Perhaps you still can," said Bernd. "An affair isn't necessarily the end of the marriage."

"In the first year?"

"It's bad, I agree."

"What should I do?"

"You must ask him about it. He may admit it, he may deny it; but he'll know that you know."

"And then what?"

"What do you want? Would you divorce him?"

She shook her head. "I would never leave. Marriage is a promise. You can't keep a promise only when it suits you. You have to keep it against your inclination. That's what it means."

"I did the opposite. You must disapprove of me."

"I don't judge you or anyone else. I'm just talking about myself. I love my husband and I want him to be faithful."

Bernd's smile was admiring but regretful. "I hope you get your wish."

"You're a good friend."

The bell rang for the first lesson of the afternoon. Rebecca stood up and put her sandwich back in its paper wrapping. She was not going to eat it, now or later, but she had a horror of throwing food away, like most people who had lived through the war. She touched her damp eyes with a handkerchief. "Thank you for listening," she said.

"I wasn't much comfort."

"Yes, you were." She went out.

As she approached the classroom for the English lesson, she realized she had not worked out the lyrics to "The Twist." However, she had been a teacher long enough to improvise. "Who's heard a record called 'The Twist'?" she asked loudly as she walked through the door.

They all had.

She went to the blackboard and picked up a stub of chalk. "What are the words?"

They all began to shout at once.

On the board she wrote: "Come on, baby, let's do the Twist." Then she said: "What's that in German?"

For a while she forgot about her troubles.

She found the letter in her pigeonhole at the midafternoon break. She carried it with her into the staff room and made a cup of instant coffee before opening it. When she read it she dropped her coffee.

The single sheet of paper was headed: "Ministry for State Security." This was the official name for the secret police: the unofficial name was the Stasi. The letter came from a Sergeant Scholz, and it ordered her to present herself at his headquarters office for questioning.

Rebecca mopped up her spilled drink, apologized to her colleagues, pretended nothing was wrong, and went to the ladies' room, where she locked herself in a cubicle. She needed to think before confiding in anyone.

Everyone in East Germany knew about these letters, and everyone dreaded receiving one. It meant she had done something wrong—perhaps something trivial, but it had come to the attention of the watchers. She knew, from what other people said, that there was no point protesting innocence. The police attitude would be that she must be guilty of something, or why would they be questioning her? To suggest they might have made a mistake was to insult their competence, which was another crime.

Looking again, she saw that her appointment was for five this afternoon.

What had she done? Her family was deeply suspect, of course. Her father, Werner, was a capitalist, with a factory that the East German government could not touch because it was in West Berlin. Her mother,

Carla, was a well-known Social Democrat. Her grandmother Maud was the sister of an English earl.

However, the authorities had not bothered the family for a couple of years, and Rebecca had imagined that her marriage to an official in the Justice Ministry might have gained them a ticket of respectability. Obviously not.

Had she committed any crimes? She owned a copy of George Orwell's anti-Communist allegory *Animal Farm,* which was illegal. Her kid brother, Walli, who was fifteen, played the guitar and sang American protest songs such as "This Land Is Your Land." Rebecca sometimes went to West Berlin to see exhibitions of abstract painting. Communists were as conservative about art as Victorian matrons.

Washing her hands, she glanced in the mirror. She did not *look* scared. She had a straight nose and a strong chin and intense brown eyes. Her unruly dark hair was sharply pulled back. She was tall and statuesque, and some people found her intimidating. She could face a classroom full of boisterous eighteen-year-olds and silence them with a word.

But she *was* scared. What frightened her was the knowledge that the Stasi could do anything. There were no real restraints on them: complaining about them was a crime in itself. And that reminded her of the Red Army at the end of the war. The Soviet soldiers had been free to rob, rape, and murder Germans, and they had used their freedom in an orgy of unspeakable barbarism.

Rebecca's last class of the day was on the construction of the passive voice in Russian grammar, and it was a shambles, easily the worst lesson she had given since she qualified as a teacher. The pupils could not fail to know that something was wrong and, touchingly, they gave her an easy ride, even making helpful suggestions when she found herself lost for the right word. With their indulgence she got through it.

When school ended, Bernd was closeted in the head's office with officials from the Education Ministry, presumably discussing how to keep the school open with half the staff gone. Rebecca did not want to go to Stasi headquarters without telling anyone, just in case they decided to keep her there, so she wrote him a note telling him of the summons.

Then she caught a bus through the wet streets to Normannen Strasse in the suburb of Lichtenberg.

The Stasi headquarters there was an ugly new office block. It was not finished, and there were bulldozers in the car park and scaffolding at one end. It showed a grim face in the rain, and would not look much more cheerful in sunshine.

When she went through the door she wondered if she would ever come out.

She crossed the vast atrium, presented her letter at a reception desk, and was escorted upstairs in an elevator. Her fear rose with the lift. She emerged into a corridor painted a nightmarish shade of mustard yellow. She was shown into a small, bare room with a plastic-topped table and two uncomfortable chairs made of metal tubing. There was a pungent smell of paint. Her escort left.

She sat alone for five minutes, shaking. She wished she smoked: it might steady her. She struggled not to cry.

Sergeant Scholz came in. He was a little younger than Rebecca—about twenty-five, she guessed. He carried a thin file. He sat down, cleared his throat, opened the file, and frowned. Rebecca thought he was trying to seem important, and she wondered whether this was his first interrogation.

"You are a teacher at Friedrich Engels Polytechnic Secondary School," he said.

"Yes."

"Where do you live?"

She answered him, but she was puzzled. Did the secret police not know her address? That might explain why the letter had come to her at school rather than at home.

She had to give the names and ages of her parents and grandparents. "You're lying to me!" Scholz said triumphantly. "You say your mother is thirty-nine and you are twenty-nine. How could she have given birth to you when she was ten years old?"

"I'm adopted," Rebecca said, relieved to be able to give an innocent explanation. "My real parents were killed at the end of the war, when our house suffered a direct hit." She had been thirteen. Red Army shells were falling and the city was in ruins and she was alone, bewildered, terrified. A plump adolescent, she had been singled out for rape by a group of soldiers. She had been saved by Carla, who had offered herself instead. Nevertheless that terrifying experience had left Rebecca hesitant and nervous about sex. If Hans was dissatisfied, she felt sure it must be her fault.

She shuddered and tried to put the memory away. "Carla Franck saved me from . . ." Just in time, Rebecca stopped herself. The Communists denied that Red Army soldiers had committed rape, even though every woman who had been in East Germany in 1945 knew the horrible truth. "Carla saved me," she said, skipping the contentious details. "Later, she and Werner legally adopted me."

Scholz was writing everything down. There could not be much in that file, Rebecca thought. But there must be something. If he knew little about her family, what was it that had attracted his interest?

"You are an English teacher," he said.

"No, I'm not. I teach Russian."

"You are lying again."

"I'm not lying, and I have not lied previously," she said crisply. She was surprised to find herself speaking to him in this challenging way. She was no longer as frightened as she had been. Perhaps this was foolhardy. He may be young and inexperienced, she told herself, but he still has the power to ruin my life. "My degree is in Russian language and literature," she went on, and she tried a friendly smile. "I'm head of the department of Russian at my school. But half our teachers have gone to the West, and we have to improvise. So, in the past week, I have given two English lessons."

"So, I was right! And in your lessons you poison the children's minds with American propaganda."

"Oh, hell," she groaned. "Is this about the advice to American soldiers?"

He read from a sheet of notes. "It says here: 'Bear in mind that there is no freedom of speech in East Germany.' Is that not American propaganda?"

"I explained to the pupils that Americans have a naïve pre-Marxist concept of freedom," she said. "I suppose your informant failed to mention that." She wondered who the snitch was. It must have been a pupil, or perhaps a parent who had been told about the lesson. The Stasi had more spies than the Nazis.

"It also says: 'When in East Berlin, do not ask police officers for directions. Unlike American policemen, they are not there to help you.' What do you say to that?"

"Isn't it true?" Rebecca said. "When you were a teenager, did you ever ask a Vopo to tell you the way to a U-Bahn station?" The Vopos were the *Volkspolizei*, the East German police.

"Couldn't you find something more appropriate for teaching children?"

"Why don't you come to our school and give an English lesson?"

"I don't speak English!"

"Nor do I!" Rebecca shouted. She immediately regretted raising her voice. But Scholz was not angry. In fact he seemed a little cowed. He was definitely inexperienced. But she should not get careless. "Nor do I," she said more quietly. "So I'm making it up as I go along, and using whatever English-language materials come to hand." It was time for some phony humility, she thought. "I've obviously made a mistake, and I'm very sorry, Sergeant."

"You seem like an intelligent woman," he said.

She narrowed her eyes. Was this a trap? "Thank you for the compliment," she said neutrally.

"We need intelligent people, especially women."

Rebecca was mystified. "What for?"

"To keep their eyes open, see what's happening, let us know when things are going wrong."

Rebecca was flabbergasted. After a moment she said incredulously: "Are you asking me to be a Stasi informant?"

"It's important, public-spirited work," he said. "And vital in schools, where young people's attitudes are formed."

"I see that." What Rebecca saw was that this young secret policeman had blundered. He had checked her out at her place of work, but he knew nothing about her notorious family. If Scholz had looked into Rebecca's background he would never have approached her.

She could imagine how it had happened. "Hoffmann" was one of the commonest surnames, and "Rebecca" was not unusual. A raw beginner could easily make the mistake of investigating the wrong Rebecca Hoffmann.

He went on: "But the people who do this work must be completely honest and trustworthy."

That was so paradoxical that she almost laughed. "Honest and trustworthy?" she repeated. "To spy on your friends?"

"Absolutely." He seemed unaware of the irony. "And there are advantages." He lowered his voice. "You would become one of us."

"I don't know what to say."

"You don't have to decide now. Go home and think about it. But don't discuss it with anyone. It must be secret, obviously."

"Obviously." She was beginning to feel relieved. Scholz would soon find out that she was unsuitable for his purpose, and he would withdraw his proposal. But at that point he could hardly go back to pretending that she was a propagandist for capitalist imperialism. Perhaps she might come out of this unscathed.

Scholz stood up, and Rebecca followed suit. Was it possible that her visit to Stasi headquarters could end so well? It seemed too good to be true.

He held the door for her politely, then escorted her along the yellow corridor. A group of five or six Stasi men stood near the elevator doors, talking animatedly. One was startlingly familiar: a tall, broad-shouldered man with a slight stoop, wearing a light gray flannel suit that Rebecca knew well. She stared at him uncomprehendingly as she walked up to the elevator.

It was her husband, Hans.

Why was he here? Her first frightened thought was that he, too, was under interrogation. But a moment later she realized, from the way they were all standing, that he was not being treated as a suspect.

What, then? Her heart pounded with fear, but what was she afraid of?

Perhaps his job at the Ministry of Justice brought him here from time to time, she thought. Then she heard one of the other men say to him: "But, with all due respect, Lieutenant . . ." She did not hear the rest of the sentence. Lieutenant? Civil servants did not hold military ranks— unless they were in the police . . .

Then Hans saw Rebecca.

She watched the emotions cross his face: men were easy to read. At first he had the baffled frown of one who sees a familiar sight in an alien context, such as a turnip in a library. Then his eyes widened in shock as he accepted the reality of what he was seeing, and his mouth opened a fraction. But it was the next expression that struck her hardest: his cheeks darkened with shame and his eyes shifted away from her in an unmistakable look of guilt.

Rebecca was silent for a long moment, trying to take this in. Still not understanding what she was seeing, she said: "Good afternoon, *Lieutenant* Hoffmann."

Scholz looked puzzled and scared. "Do you know the lieutenant?"

"Quite well," she said, struggling to keep her composure as a dreadful suspicion began to dawn on her. "I'm beginning to wonder whether he has had me under surveillance for some time." But it was not possible—was it?

"Really?" said Scholz, stupidly.

Rebecca stared hard at Hans, watching for his reaction to her surmise, hoping he would laugh it off and immediately come out with the true, innocent explanation. His mouth was open, as if he were about to speak, but she could see that he was not intending to tell the truth: instead, she thought, he had the look of a man desperately trying to think of a story and failing to come up with something that would meet all the facts.

Scholz was on the brink of tears. "I didn't know!"

Still watching Hans, Rebecca said: "I am Hans's wife."

Hans's face changed again, and as guilt turned to anger his face became a mask of fury. He spoke at last, but not to Rebecca. "Shut your mouth, Scholz," he said.

Then she knew, and her world crashed around her.

Scholz was too astonished to heed Hans's warning. He said to Rebecca: "You're *that* Frau Hoffmann?"

Hans moved with the speed of rage. He lashed out with a meaty right fist and punched Scholz in the face. The young man staggered back, lips bleeding. "You fucking fool," Hans said. "You've just undone two years of painstaking undercover work."

Rebecca muttered to herself: "The funny phone calls, the sudden meetings, the ripped-up notes . . ." Hans did not have a lover.

It was worse than that.

She was in a daze, but she knew this was the moment to find out the truth, while everyone was off balance, before they began to tell lies and concoct cover stories. With an effort she stayed focused. She said coolly: "Did you marry me just to spy on me, Hans?"

He stared at her without answering.

Scholz turned and staggered away along the corridor. Hans said: "Go after him." The elevator came and Rebecca stepped in just as Hans called out: "Arrest the fool and throw him in a cell." He turned to speak to Rebecca, but the elevator doors closed and she pressed the button for the ground floor.

She could hardly see through her tears as she crossed the atrium. No one spoke to her: doubtless it was commonplace to see people weeping here. She found her way across the rain-swept car park to the bus stop.

Her marriage was a sham. She could hardly take it in. She had slept with Hans, loved him, and married him, and all the time he had been deceiving her. Infidelity might be considered a temporary lapse, but Hans had been false to her from the start. He must have begun dating her in order to spy on her.

No doubt he had never intended actually to marry her. Originally, he had probably intended no more than a flirtation as a way of getting inside the house. The deception had worked too well. It must have come as a shock to him when she proposed marriage. Maybe he had been forced to make a decision: refuse her, and abandon the surveillance, or marry her and continue it. His bosses might even have ordered him to accept her. How could she have been so completely deceived?

A bus pulled up and she jumped on. She walked with lowered gaze to a seat near the back and covered her face with her hands.

She thought about their courtship. When she had raised the issues that had got in the way of her previous relationships—her feminism, her anti-Communism, her closeness to Carla—he had given all the right answers. She had believed that he and she were like-minded, almost miraculously so. It had never occurred to her that he was putting on an act.

The bus crawled through the landscape of old rubble and new concrete toward the central district of Mitte. Rebecca tried to think about her future but she could not. All she could do was run over the past in her mind. She remembered their wedding day, the honeymoon, and their year of marriage, seeing it all now as a play in which Hans had been performing. He had stolen two years from her, and it made her so angry that she stopped crying.

She recalled the evening when she had proposed. They had been strolling in the People's Park at Friedrichshain, and they had stopped in front of the old Fairy Tale Fountain to look at the carved stone turtles. She had worn a navy blue dress, her best color. Hans had a new tweed jacket: he managed to find good clothes even though East Germany was a fashion desert. With his arm around her, Rebecca had felt safe, protected, cherished. She wanted one man, forever, and he was the man. "Let's get married, Hans," she had said with a smile, and he had kissed her and replied: "What a wonderful idea."

I was a fool, she thought furiously; a stupid fool.

One thing was explained. Hans had not wanted to have children yet. He had said he wanted to get another promotion and a home of their own, first. He had not mentioned this before the wedding, and Rebecca had been surprised, given their ages: she was now twenty-nine and he thirty-four. Now she knew the real reason.

By the time she got off the bus she was in a rage. She walked quickly through the wind and rain to the tall old town house where she lived. From the hall she could see, through the open door of the front room, her mother deep in conversation with Heinrich von Kessel, who had been a Social Democrat city councilor with her after the war. Rebecca walked quickly past without speaking. Her twelve-year-old sister, Lili, was doing homework at the kitchen table. She could hear the grand piano in the drawing room: her brother, Walli, was playing a blues. Rebecca went upstairs to the two rooms she and Hans shared.

The first thing she saw when she walked into the room was Hans's model. He had been working on this throughout their year of marriage. He was making a scale model of the Brandenburg Gate out of matchsticks and glue. Everyone he knew had to save their spent matches. The model was almost done, and stood on the small table in the middle of the room. He had made the central arch and its wings, and was working on the quadriga, the four-horse chariot on the top, which was much more difficult.

He must have been bored, Rebecca thought bitterly. No doubt the project was a way of passing the evenings he was obliged to spend with a woman he did not love. Their marriage was like the model, a flimsy copy of the real thing.

She went to the window and stared out at the rain. After a minute, a tan Trabant 500 pulled up at the curb, and Hans got out.

How dare he come here now?

Rebecca flung open the window, heedless of the rain blowing in, and yelled: "Go away!"

He stopped on the wet sidewalk and looked up.

Rebecca's eye lit on a pair of his shoes on the floor beside her. They had been hand-made by an old shoemaker Hans had found. She picked one up and threw it at him. It was a good shot and, although he dodged, it hit the top of his head.

"You mad cow!" he yelled.

Walli and Lili came into the room. They stood in the doorway, staring at their grown-up sister as if she had become a different person, which she probably had.

"You got married on the orders of the Stasi!" Rebecca shouted out of the window. "Which of us is mad?" She threw the other shoe and missed.

Lili said in awestruck tones: "What are you doing?"

Walli grinned and said: "This is crazy, man."

Outside, two passersby stopped to watch, and a neighbor appeared on a doorstep, gazing in fascination. Hans glared at them. He was proud, and it was agony for him to be made a fool of in public.

Rebecca looked around for something else to throw at him, and her gaze fell on the matchstick model of the Brandenburg Gate.

It stood on a plywood board. She picked it up. It was heavy, but she could manage.

Walli said: "Oh, wow."

Rebecca carried the model to the window.

Hans shouted: "Don't you dare! That belongs to me!"

She rested the plywood base on the windowsill. "You ruined my life, you Stasi bully!" she shouted.

One of the women bystanders laughed, a scornful, jeering cackle that rang out over the sound of the rain. Hans flushed with rage and looked around, trying to identify its source, but he could not. To be laughed at was the worst form of torture for him.

He roared: "Put that model back, you bitch! I worked on it for a year!"

"That's how long I worked on our marriage," Rebecca replied, and she lifted the model.

Hans yelled: "I'm ordering you!"

Rebecca heaved the model through the window and let it go.

It turned over in midair, so that the board was uppermost and the quadriga below. It seemed to take a long time to drop, and Rebecca felt suspended in a moment of time. Then it hit the paved front yard with a sound like paper being crumpled. The model exploded and the matchsticks scatted outward in a spray, then came down on the wet stones and stuck, forming a sunburst of destruction. The board lay flat, everything on it crushed to nothing.

Hans stared at it for a long moment, his mouth open in shock.

He recovered himself and pointed a finger up at Rebecca. "You listen to me," he said, and his voice was so cold that suddenly she felt afraid. "You'll regret this, I tell you," he said. "You and your family. You'll regret it for the rest of your lives. And that's a promise."

Then he got back into his car and drove away.

For breakfast, George Jakes's mother made him blueberry pancakes and bacon with grits on the side. "If I eat all this I'll have to wrestle heavyweight," he said. George weighed a hundred and seventy pounds and had been the welterweight star of the Harvard wrestling team.

"Eat hearty, and give up that wrestling," she said. "I didn't raise you to be a dumb jock." She sat opposite him at the kitchen table and poured cornflakes into a dish.

George was not dumb, and she knew it. He was about to graduate from Harvard Law School. He had finished his final exams, and was as sure as he could be that he had passed. Now he was here at his mother's modest suburban home in Prince George's County, Maryland, outside Washington, DC. "I want to stay fit," he said. "Maybe I'll coach a high school wrestling team."

"Now that would be worth doing."

He looked at her fondly. Jacky Jakes had once been pretty, he knew: he had seen photographs of her as a teenager, when she had aspired to be a movie star. She still looked young: she had the kind of dark-chocolate-colored skin that did not wrinkle. "Good black don't crack," the Negro women said. But the wide mouth that smiled so broadly in those old photos was now turned down at the corners in an expression of grim determination. She had never become an actress. Perhaps she had never had a chance: the few roles for Negro women generally went to light-skinned beauties. Anyway, her career had ended before it began when, at the age of sixteen, she had become pregnant with George. She had gained that careworn face raising him alone for the first six years of his life, working as a waitress and living in a tiny house at the back of Union Station, and drilling him in the need for hard work and education and respectability.

He said: "I love you, Mom, but I'm still going on the Freedom Ride."

She pressed her lips together disapprovingly. "You're twenty-five years old," she said. "You please yourself."

"No, I don't. Every important decision I've ever made, I've discussed with you. I probably always will."

"You don't do what I say."

"Not always. But you're still the smartest person I've ever met, and that includes everyone at Harvard."

"Now you're just buttering me up," she said, but she was pleased, he could tell.

"Mom, the Supreme Court has ruled that segregation on interstate buses and bus stations is unconstitutional—but those Southerners just defy the law. We have to do something!"

"How do you think it's going to help, this bus ride?"

"We're going to board here in Washington and travel south. We'll sit at the front, use the whites-only waiting rooms, and ask to be served in the whites-only diners; and when people object we're going to tell them that the law is on our side, and they are the criminals and troublemakers."

"Son, I know you're *right*. You don't have to tell me that. I understand the Constitution. But what do you think will happen?"

"I guess we'll get arrested sooner or later. Then there'll be a trial, and we'll argue our case in front of the world."

She shook her head. "I sure hope you get off that easy."

"What do you mean?"

"You grew up privileged," she said. "At least, you did after your white father came back into our lives when you were six years old. You don't know what the world is like for most colored folk."

"I wish you wouldn't say that." George was stung: he got this accusation from black activists, and it annoyed him. "Having a rich white grandfather pay for my education doesn't make me blind. I know what goes on."

"Then maybe you know that getting arrested might be the least bad thing that could happen to you. What if things get rough?"

George knew she was right. The Freedom Riders might be risking worse than jail. But he wanted to reassure his mother. "I've had lessons in passive resistance," he said. All those chosen for the Freedom Ride were experienced civil rights activists, and they had been put through a special training program that included role-playing exercises. "A white man pretending to be a redneck called me nigger, pushed and shoved me, and dragged me out of the room by my heels—and I let him, even though I could have thrown him out the window with one arm."

"Who was he?"

"A civil rights campaigner."

"Not the real thing."

"Of course not. He was acting a part."

"Okay," she said, and he knew from her tone that she meant the opposite.

"It's going to be all right, Mom."

"I'm not saying any more. Are you going to eat those pancakes?"

"Look at me," George said. "Mohair suit, narrow tie, hair close-cropped, and shoes shined so bright I could use the toe caps for a shaving mirror." He usually dressed smartly anyway, but the Riders had been instructed to look ultra-respectable.

"You look fine, except for that cauliflower ear." George's right ear was deformed from wrestling.

"Who would want to hurt such a nice colored boy?"

"You have no idea," she said with sudden anger. "Those Southern whites, they—" To his dismay, tears came to her eyes. "Oh, God, I'm just so afraid they'll kill you."

He reached across the table and took her hand. "I'll be careful, Mom, I promise."

She dried her eyes on her apron. George ate some bacon, to please her, but he had little appetite. He was more anxious than he pretended. His mother was not exaggerating. Some civil rights activists had argued against the Freedom Ride idea on the grounds that it would provoke violence.

"You're going to be a long time on that bus," she said.

"Thirteen days, here to New Orleans. We're stopping every night for meetings and rallies."

"What have you got to read?"

"The autobiography of Mahatma Gandhi." George felt he ought to know more about Gandhi, whose philosophy had inspired the civil rights movement's nonviolent protest tactics.

She took a book from on top of the refrigerator. "You might find this a little more entertaining. It's a bestseller."

They had always shared books. Her father had been a literature professor at a Negro college, and she had been a reader from childhood. When George was a boy he and his mother had read the Bobbsey Twins and the Hardy Boys together, even though all the heroes were white. Now they regularly passed each other books they had enjoyed. He looked at the volume in his hand. Its transparent plastic cover told him it was borrowed from the local public library. "*To Kill a Mockingbird*," he read. "This just won a Pulitzer Prize, didn't it?"

"And it's set in Alabama, where you're going."

"Thanks."

A few minutes later he kissed his mother good-bye, left the house with a small suitcase in his hand, and caught a bus to Washington. He got off at the downtown Greyhound station. A small group of civil rights activists had gathered in the coffee shop. George knew some of them from the training sessions. They were a mixture of black and white, male and female, old and young. As well as a dozen or so Riders, there were some organizers from the Congress of Racial Equality, a couple of journalists from the Negro press, and a few supporters. CORE had decided to split the group in two, and half would leave from the Trailways bus station across the street. There were no placards and no television cameras: it was all reassuringly low-key.

George greeted Joseph Hugo, a fellow law student, a white guy with prominent blue eyes. Together they had organized a boycott of the Woolworth's lunch counter in Cambridge, Massachusetts. Woolworth's was integrated in most states but segregated in the South, like the bus service. But Joe had a way of disappearing just before a confrontation, and George had him pegged as a well-meaning coward. "Are you coming with us, Joe?" he asked, trying to keep the skepticism out of his voice.

Joe shook his head. "I just came by to say good luck." He smoked long mentholated cigarettes with white filter tips, and he was twitchily tapping one on the edge of a tin ashtray.

"Pity. You're from the South, aren't you?"

"Birmingham, Alabama."

"They're going to call us outside agitators. It would have been useful to have a Southerner on the bus to prove them wrong."

"I can't. I have stuff to do."

George did not press Joe. He was scared enough himself. If he started to discuss the dangers he might talk himself out of going. He looked around the group. He was pleased to see John Lewis, a quietly impressive theology student who was a founding member of the Student Nonviolent Coordinating Committee, the most radical of the civil rights groups.

Their leader called for attention and began a short statement to the press. While he was speaking George saw, slipping into the coffee shop, a tall white man of forty in a crumpled linen suit. He was handsome though heavy, his face showing the flush of a drinker. He looked like a bus passenger, and no one paid him any attention. He sat next to George and, putting one arm around his shoulders, gave him a brief hug.

This was Senator Greg Peshkov, George's father.

Their relationship was an open secret, known to Washington insiders but never publicly acknowledged. Greg was not the only politician to have such a secret. Senator Strom Thurmond had paid for the college education of a daughter of his family's maid: the girl was rumored to be his child—which did not stop Thurmond being a rabid segregationist. When Greg had appeared, a total stranger to his six-year-old son, he had asked George to call him Uncle Greg, and they had never found a better euphemism.

Greg was selfish and unreliable but, in his own way, he cared for George. As a teenager George had gone through a long phase of anger with his father, but then he had come to accept him for what he was, figuring that half a father was better than none.

"George," Greg said now in a low voice, "I'm worried."

"You and Mom too."

"What did she say?"

"She thinks those Southern racists are going to kill us all."

"I don't think that'll happen, but you could lose your job."

"Has Mr. Renshaw said something?"

"Heck, no, he doesn't know anything about this, yet. But he'll find out soon enough if you get arrested."

Renshaw, who was from Buffalo, was a childhood friend of Greg's, and senior partner in a prestigious Washington law firm, Fawcett Renshaw. Last summer Greg had got George a vacation job as a law clerk at the firm and, as they both had hoped, the temporary post had led to the offer of a full-time job after graduation. It was a coup: George would be the first Negro to work there as anything other than a cleaner.

George said with a touch of irritation: "The Freedom Riders are not lawbreakers. We're trying to get the law enforced. The segregationists are the criminals. I would have expected a lawyer such as Renshaw to understand that."

"He understands it. But all the same he can't hire a man who has been in trouble with the police. Believe me, it would be the same if you were white."

"But we're on the side of the law!"

"Life is unfair. Student days are over—welcome to the real world."

The leader called out: "Everybody, get your tickets and check your bags, please."

George stood up.

Greg said: "I can't talk you out of this, can I?"

He looked so forlorn that George longed to be able to give in, but he could not. "No, I've made up my mind," he said.

"Then please just try to be careful."

George was touched. "I'm lucky to have people who worry about me," he said. "I know that."

Greg squeezed his arm and left quietly.

George stood in line with the others at the window and bought a ticket to New Orleans. He walked to the blue-and-gray bus and handed over his bag to be loaded in the luggage compartment. Painted on the side of the bus were a large greyhound and the slogan: IT'S SUCH A COMFORT TO TAKE THE BUS . . . AND LEAVE THE DRIVING TO US. George got on board.

An organizer directed him to a seat near the front. Others were told to sit in interracial pairs. The driver paid no attention to the Riders, and the regular passengers seemed no more than mildly curious. George opened the book his mother had given him and read the first line.

A moment later the organizer directed one of the women to sit next to George. He nodded to her, pleased. He had met her a couple of times before and liked her. Her name was Maria Summers. She was demurely dressed in a pale gray cotton frock with a high neckline and a full skirt. She had skin the deep, dark color of George's mother's, a cute flat nose, and lips that made him think about kissing. He knew she was at the University of Chicago Law School, and like him was about to graduate, so they were probably the same age. He guessed she was not only smart but determined: she would have to be, to get into Chicago Law with two strikes against her, being both female and black.

He closed his book as the driver started the engine and pulled away. Maria looked down and said: "*To Kill a Mockingbird.* I was in Montgomery, Alabama, last summer."

Montgomery was the state capital. "What were you doing there?" George said.

"My father's a lawyer, and he had a client who sued the state. I was working for Daddy during the vacation."

"Did you win?"

"No. But don't let me keep you from reading."

"Are you kidding? I can read anytime. How often does a guy on a bus have a girl as pretty as you sit down next to him?"

"Oh, my," she said. "Someone warned me you were a smooth talker."

"I'll tell you my secret, if you want."

"Okay, what is it?"

"I'm sincere."

She laughed.

He said: "But please don't spread that around. It would spoil my reputation."

The bus crossed the Potomac and headed into Virginia on Route 1. "You're in the South, now, George," said Maria. "Are you scared yet?"

"You bet I am."

"Me, too."

The highway was a straight, narrow slash across miles of spring green forest. They passed through small towns where the men had so little to do that they stopped to watch the bus go by. George did not look out of the window much. He learned that Maria had been brought up in a strict churchgoing family, her grandfather a preacher. George said he went to church mainly to please his mother, and Maria confessed that she was the same. They talked all the way to Fredericksburg, fifty miles along the route.

The Riders went quiet as the bus entered the small historic town, where white supremacy still reigned. The Greyhound terminal was between two red-brick churches with white doors, but Christianity was not necessarily a good indication in the South. As the bus came to a halt, George saw the restrooms, and was surprised that there were no signs over the doors saying WHITES ONLY and COLORED ONLY.

The passengers got off the bus and stood blinking in the sunshine. Looking more closely, George saw light-colored patches over the toilet doors, and deduced that the segregation signs had been removed recently.

The Riders put their plan into operation anyway. First, a white organizer went into the scruffy restroom at the back, clearly intended for Negroes. He came out unharmed, but that was the easier part. George had already volunteered to be the black person who defied the rules. "Here goes," he said to Maria, and he walked into the clean, freshly painted restroom that had undoubtedly just had its WHITES ONLY sign removed.

There was a young white man inside, combing his pompadour. He glanced at George in the mirror, but said nothing. George was too scared to pee, but he could not just walk out again, so he washed his hands. The young man left and an older man came in and entered a cubicle. George dried his hands on the roller towel. Then there was nothing else to do, so he went out.

The others were waiting. He shrugged and said: "Nothing. Nobody tried to stop me—no one said anything."

Maria said: "I asked for a Coke at the counter and the waitress sold me one. I think someone here has decided to avoid trouble."

"Is this how it's going to be, all the way to New Orleans?" said George. "Will they just act as if nothing has happened? Then, when we've gone, impose segregation again? That would kind of cut the ground from under our feet!"

"Don't worry," said Maria. "I've met the people who run Alabama. Believe me, they're not that smart."

Walli Franck was playing the piano in the upstairs drawing room. The instrument was a full-size Steinway grand, and Walli's father kept it tuned for Grandma Maud to play. Walli was remembering the riff to Elvis Presley's record "A Mess of Blues." It was in the key of C, which made it easier.

His grandmother sat reading the obituaries in the *Berliner Zeitung*. She was seventy, a slim, straight figure in a dark blue cashmere dress. "You can play that sort of thing well," she said without looking up from the paper. "You've got my ear, as well as my green eyes. Your grandfather Walter, after whom you were named, never could play ragtime, rest his soul. I tried to teach him, but it was hopeless."

"You played ragtime?" Walli was surprised. "I've never heard you do anything but classical music."

"Ragtime saved us from starving when your mother was a baby. After the First World War, I played in a club called Nachtleben right here in Berlin. I was paid billions of marks a night, which was barely enough to buy bread; but sometimes I'd get tips in foreign currency, and we could live well for a week on two dollars."

"Wow." Walli could not imagine his silver-haired grandmother playing the piano for tips in a nightclub.

Walli's sister came into the room. Lili was almost three years younger, and these days he was not sure how to treat her. For as long as he could remember she had been a pain in the neck, like a younger boy but sillier. However, lately she had become more sensible and, to complicate matters, some of her friends had breasts.

He turned from the piano and picked up his guitar. He had bought it a year ago in a pawnshop in West Berlin. It had probably been pledged by an American soldier against a loan that was never repaid. The brand name was Martin and, although it had been cheap, it seemed to Walli a very good instrument. He guessed that neither the pawnbroker nor the soldier had realized its worth.

"Listen to this," he said to Lili, and he began to sing a Bahamian tune called "All My Trials" with lyrics in English. He had heard it on Western radio stations: it was popular with American folk groups. The minor chords made it a melancholy song, and he was pleased with the plaintive fingerpicking accompaniment he had devised.

When he had finished, Grandma Maud looked over the top of the newspaper and said in English: "Your accent is perfectly dreadful, Walli, dear."

"Sorry."

She reverted to German. "But you sing nicely."

"Thank you." Walli turned to Lili. "What do you think of the song?"

"It's a bit dreary," she said. "Maybe I'll like it more when I've heard it a few times."

"That's no good," he said. "I want to play it tonight at the Minnesänger." This was a folk club just off the Kurfürstendamm in West Berlin. The name meant "troubadour."

Lili was impressed. "You're playing at the Minnesänger?"

"It's a special night. They're having a contest. Anybody can play. The winner gets a chance of a regular gig."

"I didn't know clubs did that."

"They don't usually. This is a one-off."

Grandma Maud said: "Don't you have to be older to go to such a place?"

"Yes, but I've got in before."

Lili said: "Walli looks older than he is."

"Hmm."

Lili said to Walli: "You've never sung in public. Are you nervous?"

"You bet."

"You should play something more cheerful."

"I guess you're right."

"How about 'This Land Is Your Land'? I love that one."

Walli played it, and Lili sang along.

While they were singing, their older sister, Rebecca, came in. Walli adored Rebecca. After the war, when their parents had been desperately working all hours to feed the family, Rebecca had often been left in charge of Walli and Lili. She was like a second mother, but not so strict.

And she had such guts! He had watched with awe as she threw her husband's matchstick model out of the window. Walli had never liked Hans, and was secretly glad to see him go.

All the neighbors were talking about how Rebecca had unknowingly married a Stasi officer. It had given Walli status in school: no one had previously imagined there was anything special about the Francks. Girls especially were fascinated by the thought that everything said and done in his house had been reported to the police for almost a year.

Even though Rebecca was his sister, Walli could see that she was gorgeous. She had a fabulous figure and a lovely face that showed both kindness and strength. But now he noticed that she looked as if someone had died. He stopped playing and said: "What's the matter?"

"I've been fired," she said.

Grandma Maud put down the newspaper.

"That's crazy!" Walli said. "The boys in your school say you're their best teacher!"

"I know."

"Why did they sack you?"

"I think it was Hans's revenge."

Walli recalled Hans's reaction when he had seen his model smashed, thousands of little matchsticks scattered across the wet pavement. "You'll regret this," Hans had yelled, looking up through the rain. Walli had regarded that as bluster, but a moment's thought would have told him that an agent of the secret police had the power to carry out such a threat. "You and your family," Hans had screamed, and Walli was included in the curse. He shivered.

Grandma Maud said: "Aren't they desperate for teachers?"

"Bernd Held is frantic," Rebecca said. "But he was given orders from above."

Lili said: "What will you do?"

"Get another job. It shouldn't be difficult. Bernd has given me a glowing reference. And every school in East Germany is short of teachers, because so many have moved to the West."

"You should move west," said Lili.

"We should all move west," said Walli.

"Mother won't, you know that," said Rebecca. "She says we must solve our problems, not run away from them."

Walli's father came in, dressed in a dark blue suit with a waistcoat, old-fashioned but elegant. Grandma Maud said: "Good evening, Werner, dear. Rebecca needs a drink. She's been fired." Grandma often suggested that someone needed a drink. Then she would have one, too.

"I know about Rebecca," Father said shortly. "I've talked to her."

He was in a bad mood: he had to be, to speak ungraciously to his mother-in-law, whom he loved and admired. Walli wondered what had happened to upset the old man.

He soon found out.

"Come into my study, Walli," said Father. "I want a word." He went through the double doors into the smaller drawing room, which he used as his home office. Walli followed him. Father sat behind the desk. Walli knew he was to remain standing. "We had a conversation a month ago about smoking," Father said.

Walli immediately felt guilty. He had started smoking to look older, but he had grown to like it, and now it was a habit.

"You promised to give it up," his father said.

In Walli's opinion it was none of his father's business whether he smoked or not.

"Did you give it up?"

"Yes," Walli lied.

"Don't you know that it smells?"

"I suppose I do."

"I could smell it on you as soon as I walked into the drawing room."

Now Walli felt a fool. He had been caught out in a childish lie. This did not make him feel any more friendly toward his father.

"So I know you haven't given it up."

"Why did you ask me the question, then?" Walli hated the petulant note he heard in his own voice.

"I was hoping you'd tell the truth."

"You were hoping to catch me out."

"Believe that if you wish. I suppose you've got a pack in your pocket now."

"Yes."

"Put it on my desk."

Walli took the pack from his trouser pocket and angrily threw it onto the desk. His father picked up the pack and casually tossed it into a drawer. They were Lucky Strikes, not the inferior East German brand called f6, and it was almost a full packet, too.

"You'll stay in every evening for a month," his father said. "At least you won't be visiting bars where people play the banjo and smoke all the time."

Panic made Walli's stomach cramp. He struggled to remain calm and reasonable. "It's not a banjo—it's a guitar. And I can't possibly stay in for a month."

"Don't be ridiculous. You'll do as I say."

"All right," Walli said desperately. "But not starting tonight."

"Starting now."

"But I have to go to the Minnesänger club tonight."

"That's just the kind of place I want you to keep away from."

The old man was impossible! "I'll stay in every night for a month from tomorrow, okay?"

"Your quarantine will not be adjusted to suit your plans. That would defeat the purpose. It is intended to inconvenience you."

In this mood Father could not be shaken from his resolution, but Walli was mad with frustration, and he tried anyway. "You don't understand! Tonight I'm entering a contest at the Minnesänger—it's a unique opportunity."

"I'm not postponing your punishment to permit you to play the banjo!"

"It's a guitar, you stupid old fool! A guitar!" Walli stormed out.

The three women in the next room had obviously heard everything, and they stared at him. Rebecca said: "Oh, Walli . . ."

He picked up his guitar and left the room.

Until he got downstairs he had no plan, just rage; but when he saw the front door he knew what to do. With his guitar in his hand he walked out of the house and slammed the door so hard the house shook.

An upstairs window was thrown up and he heard his father shout: "Come back, do you hear me? Come back this minute, or you'll be in even worse trouble."

Walli walked on.

At first he was just angry, but after a while he felt exhilarated. He had defied his father and even called him a stupid old fool! He headed west, walking with a jaunty step. But soon his euphoria faded and he began to wonder what the consequences would be. His father did not take disobedience lightly. He commanded his children and his employees, and he expected them to comply. But what would he do? For two or three years now Walli had been too big to be spanked. Today Father had tried to keep him in the house as if it were a jail, but that had failed. Sometimes Father threatened to take him out of school and make him work in the business, but Walli considered that an empty threat: his father would not be comfortable with a resentful adolescent roaming around his precious factory. All the same, Walli had a feeling the old man would think of something.

The street he was on passed from East Berlin to West Berlin at a crossroads. Lounging on the corner, smoking, were three Vopos, East German cops. They had the right to challenge anyone crossing the invisible border. They could not possibly speak to everyone, because so many thousands of people went over every day, including many *Grenzgänger*, East Berliners who worked in the West for higher wages paid in valuable deutschmarks. Walli's father was a *Grenzgänger*, though he worked for profits, not wages. Walli himself crossed over at least once a week, usually to go with his friends to West Berlin cinemas, which showed sexy, violent American films that were more exciting than the preachy fables in Communist movie houses.

In practice the Vopos stopped anyone who caught their eye. Entire families crossing together, parents and children, were almost certain to be challenged on suspicion of trying to leave the East permanently, especially if they had luggage. The other types the Vopos liked to harass were adolescents, particularly those wearing Western fashions. Many East Berlin boys belonged to antiestablishment gangs: the Texas Gang, the Jeans Gang, the Elvis Presley Appreciation Society, and others. They hated the police and the police hated them.

Walli was wearing plain black pants, a white T-shirt, and a tan Windbreaker. He looked cool, he thought, a little like James Dean, but not a gang member. However, the guitar might get him noticed. It was the ultimate symbol of what they called "American unculture"—even worse than a Superman comic.

He crossed the road, careful not to look at the Vopos. Out of the corner of his eye he thought he saw one staring at him. But nothing was said, and he passed without stopping into the free world.

He caught a tram along the south side of the park to the Ku'damm. The best thing about West Berlin, he thought, was that *all* the girls wore stockings.

He made his way to the Minnesänger club, a cellar in a side street off the Ku'damm where they sold weak beer and frankfurter sausages. He was early, but the place was already filling up. Walli spoke to the club's young owner, Danni Hausmann, and put his name down on the list of competitors. He bought a beer without being questioned about his age. There were lots of boys like himself carrying guitars, almost as many girls, and a few older people.

An hour later the contest began. Each act did two songs. Some of the competitors were hopeless beginners strumming simple chords but, to Walli's consternation, several guitarists were more accomplished than he. Most looked like the American artists whose material they copied. Three men dressed like the Kingston Trio sang "Tom Dooley," and a girl with long black hair and a guitar sang "The House of the Rising Sun" just like Joan Baez, and got loud applause and cheers.

An older couple in corduroys got up and did a song about farming called "Im Märzen der Bauer" to the accompaniment of a piano-accordion. It was folk music, but not the kind this audience wanted. They got an ironic cheer, but they were out-of-date.

While Walli was waiting his turn, getting impatient, he was approached by a pretty girl. This happened to him a lot. He thought he had a peculiar face, with high cheekbones and almond eyes, as if he might be half Japanese; but many girls thought he was dishy. The girl introduced herself as Karolin. She looked a year or two older than Walli. She had long, straight fair hair parted in the middle, framing an oval face. At first he thought she was like all the other folkie girls, but she had a big wide smile that made his heart misfire. She said: "I was going to enter this contest with my brother playing guitar, but he's let me down—I don't suppose you'd care to team up with me?"

Walli's first impulse was to refuse. He had a repertoire of songs and none were duets. But Karolin was enchanting, and he wanted a reason to continue to talk to her. "We'd have to rehearse," he said doubtfully.

"We could step outside. What songs were you thinking of?"

"I was going to do 'All My Trials,' then 'This Land Is Your Land.'"

"How about 'Noch Einen Tanz'?"

It was not part of Walli's repertoire, but he knew the tune and it was easy to play. "I never thought of doing a comic song," he said.

"The audience would love it. You could sing the man's part, where he tells her to go home to her sick husband. Then I'd sing, 'Just one more dance,' and we could do the last line together."

"Let's try it."

They went outside. It was early summer, and still light. They sat on a doorstep and tried out the song. They sounded good together, and Walli improvised a harmony on the last line.

Karolin had a pure contralto voice that he thought could sound thrilling, and he suggested that their second number could be a sad song, for contrast. She rejected "All My Trials" as too depressing, but she liked "Nobody's Fault but Mine," a slow spiritual. When they ran through it, the hairs stood up on the back of Walli's neck.

An American soldier entering the club smiled at them and said in English: "My God, it's the Bobbsey Twins."

Karolin laughed and said to Walli: "I guess we do look alike—fair hair and green eyes. Who are the Bobbsey Twins?"

Walli had not noticed the color of her eyes, and he was flattered that she was aware of his. "I've never heard of them," he said.

"All the same, it sounds like a good name for a duo. Like the Everly Brothers."

"Do we need a name?"

"We do if we win."

"Okay. Let's go back in. It must be almost our turn."

"One more thing," she said. "When we do 'Noch Einen Tanz,' we should look at one another now and again, and smile."

"Okay."

"Almost as if we're boyfriend and girlfriend, you know? It will look good onstage."

"Sure." It would not be difficult to smile at Karolin as if she were his girlfriend.

Back inside, a blond girl was strumming a guitar and singing "Freight Train." She was not as beautiful as Karolin, but she was pretty in a more obvious way. Next, a virtuoso guitarist played a complicated fingerpicking blues. Then Danni Hausmann called Walli's name.

He felt tense as he faced the audience. Most of the guitarists had fancy leather straps, but Walli had never bothered to get one, and his instrument was held around his neck by a piece of string. Now, suddenly, he wished he had a strap.

Karolin said: "Good evening, we're the Bobbsey Twins."

Walli played a chord and began to sing, and found he no longer cared about a strap. The song was a waltz, and he strummed it jauntily. Karolin pretended to be a wanton strumpet, and Walli responded by becoming a stiff Prussian lieutenant.

The audience laughed.

Something happened to Walli then. There were only a hundred or so people in the place, and the sound they made was no more than an appreciative collective chuckle, but it gave him a feeling that he had not experienced before, a feeling a bit like the kick from the first puff of a cigarette.

They laughed several more times, and at the end of the song they applauded loudly.

Walli liked that even better.

"They love us!" Karolin said in an excited whisper.

Walli began to play "Nobody's Fault but Mine," plucking the steel strings with his fingernails to sharpen the drama of the plangent sevenths, and the crowd went quiet. Karolin changed and became a fallen woman in despair. Walli watched the audience. No one was talking. One woman had tears in her eyes, and he wondered if she had lived through what Karolin was singing about.

Their hushed concentration was even better than the laughter.

At the end they cheered and called for more.

The rule was two numbers each, so Walli and Karolin came down off the stage, ignoring the cries for an encore, but Hausmann told them to go back. They had not rehearsed a third song, and they looked at one another in panic. Then Walli said: "Do you know 'This Land Is Your Land'?" and Karolin nodded.

The audience joined in, which made Karolin sing louder, and Walli was surprised by the power of her voice. He sang a high harmony, and their two voices soared above the sound of the crowd.

When finally they left the stage he felt exhilarated. Karolin's eyes were shining. "We were really good!" she said. "You're better than my brother."

Walli said: "Have you got any cigarettes?"

They sat through another hour of the contest, smoking. "I think we were the best," Walli said.

Karolin was more cautious. "They liked the blond girl who sang 'Freight Train,'" she said.

At last the result was announced.

The Bobbsey Twins came second.

The winner was the Joan Baez look-alike.

Walli was angry. "She could hardly play!" he said.

Karolin was more philosophical. "People love Joan Baez."

The club began to empty, and Walli and Karolin headed for the door. Walli felt dejected. As they were leaving, Danni Hausmann stopped them. He was in his early twenties, and dressed in modern casual clothes, a black roll-neck sweater and jeans. "Could you two do half an hour next Monday?" he said.

Walli was too surprised to reply, but Karolin quickly said: "Sure!"

"But the Joan Baez imitator won," said Walli, then he thought: Why am I arguing?

Danni said: "You two seem to have the range to keep an audience happy for more than one or two numbers. Have you got enough songs for a set?"

Once again Walli hesitated, and again Karolin jumped in. "We will by Monday," she said.

Walli remembered that his father planned to imprison him in the house for a month of evenings, but he decided not to mention that.

"Thanks," said Danni. "You get the early slot, eight thirty. Be here by seven thirty."

They were elated as they walked out into the lamplit street. Walli had no idea what he would do about his father, but he felt optimistic that everything would work out.

It turned out that Karolin, too, lived in East Berlin. They caught a bus and began to talk about which numbers they would do next week. There were lots of folk songs they both knew.

They got off the bus and headed into the park. Karolin frowned and said: "The guy behind."

Walli looked back. There was a man in a cap thirty or forty yards behind them, smoking as he walked. "What about him?"

"Wasn't he in the Minnesänger?"

The man did not meet Walli's eye, even though Walli stared at him. "I don't think so," said Walli. "Do you like the Everly Brothers?"

"Yes!"

As they walked, Walli started to play "All I Have to Do Is Dream," strumming the guitar that hung around his neck on its string. Karolin joined in eagerly. They sang together as they crossed the park. He played the Chuck Berry hit "Back in the USA."

They were belting out the refrain, "I'm so glad I'm living in the USA," when Karolin halted suddenly and said: "Hush!" Walli realized they had reached the border, and saw three Vopos under a streetlight glaring at them malevolently.

He shut up immediately, and hoped they had stopped soon enough.

One of the cops was a sergeant, and he looked past Walli. Walli glanced back and saw the man in the cap give a curt nod. The sergeant took a step toward Walli and Karolin and said: "Papers." The man in the cap spoke into a walkie-talkie.

Walli frowned. It seemed Karolin had been right, and they had been followed.

It occurred to him that Hans might be behind this.

Could he possibly be so petty and vengeful?

Yes, he could.

The sergeant looked at Walli's identity card and said: "You're only fifteen. You shouldn't be out this late."

Walli bit his tongue. There was no point in arguing with them.

The sergeant looked at Karolin's card and said: "You're seventeen! What are you doing with this child?"

This made Walli recall the row with his father, and he said angrily: "I'm not a child."

The sergeant ignored him. "You could go out with me," he said to Karolin. "I'm a real man." The other two Vopos laughed appreciatively.

Karolin said nothing, but the sergeant persisted. "How about it?" he said.

"You must be out of your mind," Karolin said quietly.

The man was stung. "Now that's just rude," he said.

Walli had noticed this about some men. If a girl gave them the brush-off they became indignant, but any other response was taken as encouragement. What were women supposed to do?

Karolin said: "Give me back my card, please."

The sergeant said: "Are you a virgin?"

Karolin blushed.

Once again the other two cops sniggered.

"They ought to put that on women's identity cards," said the man. "Virgin, or not."

"Knock it off," Walli said.

"I'm gentle with virgins."

Walli was boiling. "That uniform doesn't give you the right to pester girls!"

"Oh, doesn't it?" The sergeant did not give back their identity cards.

A tan Trabant 500 pulled up and Hans Hoffmann got out. Walli began to feel frightened. How could he be in this much trouble? All he had done was sing in the park.

Hans approached and said: "Show me that thing you have around your neck."

Walli summoned up the nerve to say: "Why?"

"Because I suspect it is being used to smuggle capitalist-imperialist propaganda into the German Democratic Republic. Give it here."

The guitar was so precious that Walli still did not comply, scared as he was. "What if I don't?" he said. "Will I be arrested?"

The sergeant rubbed the knuckles of his right hand with the palm of his left.

Hans said: "Yes, eventually."

Walli ran out of courage. He pulled the string over his head and gave Hans the guitar.

Hans held the guitar as if to play it, hit the strings, and sang in

English: "You ain't nothing but a hound dog." The Vopos laughed hysterically.

Even the cops listened to pop radio, it seemed.

Hans pushed his hand under the strings and tried to feel inside the sound hole.

Walli said: "Be careful!"

The top E string broke with a ping.

"It's a delicate musical instrument!" Walli said despairingly.

Hans's reach was constrained by the strings. He said: "Anyone got a knife?"

The sergeant put his hand inside his jacket and pulled out a knife with a wide blade—not part of his standard-issue gear, Walli felt sure.

Hans tried to cut the strings with the blade, but they were tougher than he thought. He managed to snap the B and the G, but could not saw through the thicker ones.

"There's nothing inside," Walli said pleadingly. "You can tell by the weight."

Hans looked at him, smiled, then brought the knife down hard, point first, on the soundboard near the bridge.

The blade went straight through the wood, and Walli cried out in pain.

Pleased by this response, Hans repeated the action, smashing holes in the guitar. With the surface weakened, the tension in the strings pulled the bridge and the wood surrounding it away from the body of the instrument. He prized away the rest of it, revealing the inside like an empty coffin.

"No propaganda," he said. "Congratulations—you are innocent." He handed Walli the wrecked guitar, and Walli took it.

The sergeant handed back their identity cards with a grin.

Karolin took Walli's arm and drew him away. "Come on," she said in a low voice. "Let's get out of here."

Walli let her lead him. He could hardly see where he was going. He could not stop crying.

CHAPTER FOUR

Georgie Jakes boarded a Greyhound bus in Atlanta, Georgia, on
Sunday, May 14, 1961. It was Mother's Day.

He was scared.

Maria Summers sat next to him. They always sat together.
It had become a regular thing: everyone assumed that the empty seat
next to George was reserved for Maria.

To hide his nervousness, he made conversation with Maria. "So,
what did you think of Martin Luther King?"

King was head of the Southern Christian Leadership Conference,
one of the more important civil rights groups. They had met him last
night at a dinner in one of Atlanta's black-owned restaurants.

"He's an amazing man," said Maria.

George was not so sure. "He said wonderful things about the
Freedom Riders, but he's not here on the bus with us."

"Put yourself in his place," Maria said reasonably. "He's the leader
of a different civil rights group. A general can't become a foot soldier
in someone else's regiment."

George had not looked at it that way. Maria was very smart.

George was half in love with her. He was desperate for an opportunity
to be alone with her, but the people in whose homes the Riders stayed
were solid, respectable black citizens, many of them devout Christians,
who would not have allowed their guest rooms to be used for smooching.
And Maria, alluring though she was, did nothing more than sit next to
George and talk to him and laugh at his wisecracks. She never did the little
physical things that said a woman wanted to be more than friends: she did
not touch his arm, or take his hand getting off the bus, or press close to
him in a crowd. She did not flirt. She might even be a virgin at twenty-five.

"You talked to King for a long time," he said.

"If he wasn't a preacher, I'd say he was coming on to me," she said.

George was not sure how to respond to that. It would be no surprise to him if a preacher made a pass at a girl as enchanting as Maria. But she was naïve about men, he thought. "I talked to King a bit."

"What did he say to you?"

George hesitated. It was King's words that had scared George. He decided to tell Maria anyway: she had a right to know. "He says we're not going to make it through Alabama."

Maria blanched. "Did he really say that?"

"He said exactly that."

Now they were both scared.

The Greyhound pulled out of the bus station.

For the first few days George had feared that the Freedom Ride would be too peaceful. Regular bus passengers did not react to the black people sitting in the wrong seats, and sometimes joined in their songs. Nothing had happened when the Riders defied WHITES ONLY and COLORED notices in bus stations. Some towns had even painted over the signs. George feared the segregationists had devised the perfect strategy. There was no trouble and no publicity, and colored Riders were served politely in the white restaurants. Every evening they got off the buses and attended meetings unmolested, usually in churches, then stayed overnight with sympathizers. But George felt sure that as they left each town the signs would be restored, and segregation would return; and the Freedom Ride would have been a waste of time.

The irony was striking. For as long as he could remember, George had been wounded and infuriated by the repeated message, sometimes implicit but often spoken aloud, that he was inferior. It made no difference that he was smarter than 99 percent of white Americans. Nor that he was hardworking, polite, and well dressed. He was looked down upon by ugly white people too stupid or too lazy to do anything harder than pour drinks or pump gas. He could not walk into a department store, sit down in a restaurant, or apply for a job without wondering whether he would be ignored, asked to leave, or rejected because of his color. It made him burn with resentment. But now, paradoxically, he was disappointed that it was not happening.

Meanwhile the White House dithered. On the third day of the

Ride the attorney general, Robert Kennedy, had made a speech at the University of Georgia promising to enforce civil rights in the South. Then, three days later, his brother the president had backtracked, withdrawing support from two civil rights bills.

Was this how the segregationists would win? George had wondered. By avoiding confrontation, then carrying on as usual?

It was not. Peace had lasted just four days.

On the fifth day of the Ride one of their number had been jailed for insisting on his right to a shoeshine.

Violence had broken out on the sixth.

The victim had been John Lewis, the theology student. He had been attacked by thugs in a white restroom in Rock Hill, South Carolina. Lewis had allowed himself to be punched and kicked without retaliation. George had not seen the incident, which was probably a good thing, for he was not sure he could have matched Lewis's Gandhian self-restraint.

George had read short reports of the violence in the next day's papers, but he was disappointed to see the story overshadowed by the rocket flight of Alan Shepard, the first American in space. Who cares? George thought sourly. The Soviet cosmonaut Yuri Gagarin had been the first man in space, less than a month ago. The Russians beat us to it. A white American can orbit the earth, but a black American can't enter a restroom.

Then, in Atlanta, the Riders had been cheered by a welcoming crowd as they got off the bus, and George's spirits had lifted again.

But that was Georgia, and now they were headed for Alabama.

"Why did King say we're not going to make it through Alabama?" Maria asked.

"There's a rumor the Ku Klux Klan are planning something in Birmingham," George said grimly. "Apparently the FBI knows all about it but they haven't done anything to stop it."

"And the local police?"

"The police are *in* the damn Klan."

"What about those two?" With a jerk of her head Maria indicated the seats across the aisle and a row back.

George looked over his shoulder at two burly white men sitting together. "What about them?"

"Don't you smell cop?"

He saw what she meant. "Do you think they're FBI?"

"Their clothes are too cheap for the Bureau. My guess is they're Alabama Highway Patrol, undercover."

George was impressed. "How did you get to be so smart?"

"My mother made me eat my vegetables. And my father's a lawyer in Chicago, the gangster capital of the USA."

"So what do you think those two are doing?"

"I'm not sure, but I don't think they're here to defend our civil rights. Do you?"

George glanced out of the window and saw a sign that read ENTERING ALABAMA. He checked his wristwatch. It was one P.M. The sun was shining out of a blue sky. It's a beautiful day to die, he thought.

Maria wanted to work in politics or public service. "Protesters can have a big impact, but in the end it's governments that reshape the world," she said. George thought about that, wondering whether he agreed. Maria had applied for a job in the White House press office, and had been called for an interview, but she had not got the job. "They don't hire many black lawyers in Washington," she had said ruefully to George. "I'll probably stay in Chicago and join my father's law firm."

Across the aisle from George was a middle-aged white woman in a coat and hat, holding on her lap a large white plastic handbag. George smiled at her and said: "Lovely weather for a bus ride."

"I'm going to visit my daughter in Birmingham," she said, though he had not asked.

"That's nice. I'm George Jakes."

"Cora Jones. Mrs. Jones. My daughter's baby is due in a week."

"Her first?"

"Third."

"Well, you seem too young to be a grandmother, if you don't mind my saying so."

She purred a little. "I'm forty-nine years old."

"I would never have guessed that!"

A Greyhound coming in the opposite direction flashed its lights, and the Riders' bus slowed to a halt. A white man came to the driver's window and George heard him say: "There's a crowd gathered at the bus station in Anniston." The driver said something in reply that George could not hear. "Just be careful," said the man at the window.

The bus pulled away.

"What does that mean, a crowd?" said Maria anxiously. "It could be twenty people or a thousand. They could be a welcoming committee or an angry mob. Why didn't he tell us more?"

George guessed her irritation masked fear.

He recalled his mother's words: "I'm just so afraid they'll kill you." Some people in the movement said they were ready to die in the cause of freedom. George was not sure he was willing to be a martyr. There were too many other things he wanted to do, like maybe sleep with Maria.

A minute later they entered Anniston, a small town like any other in the South: low buildings, streets in a grid, dusty and hot. The roadside was lined with people as if for a parade. Many were dressed up, the women in hats, the children scrubbed, no doubt having been to church. "What are they expecting to see, people with horns?" George said. "Here we are, folks, real Northern Negroes, wearing shoes and all." He spoke as if addressing them, although only Maria could hear. "We've come to take away your guns and teach you Communism. Where do the white girls go swimming?"

Maria giggled. "If they could hear you, they wouldn't know you were joking."

He wasn't really joking; it was more like whistling past the graveyard. He was trying to ignore the spasm of fear in his guts.

The bus turned into the station, which was strangely deserted. The buildings looked shut up and locked. To George it felt creepy.

The driver opened the door of the bus.

George did not see where the mob came from. Suddenly they were all around the bus. They were white men, some in work clothes, others in Sunday suits. They carried baseball bats, metal pipes, and lengths of iron chain. And they were screaming. Most of it was inchoate, but George heard some words of hate, including *Sieg heil!*

George stood up, his first impulse to close the bus door; but the two men Maria had identified as state troopers were faster, and they slammed it shut. Perhaps they are here to defend us, George thought; or maybe they're just defending themselves.

He looked through the windows all around him. There were no police outside. How could the local police not know that an armed mob had gathered at the bus station? They had to be in collusion with the Klan. No surprise there.

A second later the men attacked the bus with their weapons. There was a frightening cacophony as chains and crowbars dented the bodywork. Glass shattered, and Mrs. Jones screamed. The driver started the bus, but one of the mob lay down in front of it. George thought the driver might just roll over the man, but he stopped.

A rock came through the window, smashing it, and George felt a sharp pain in his cheek like a bee sting. He had been hit by a flying shard. Maria was sitting by a window: she was in danger. George grabbed her arm, pulling her toward him. "Kneel down in the aisle!" he shouted.

A grinning man wearing knuckle-dusters put his fist through the window next to Mrs. Jones. "Get down here with me!" Maria shouted, and she pulled Mrs. Jones down next to her and wrapped her arms protectively around the older woman.

The yelling got louder. "Communists!" they screamed. "Cowards!"

Maria said: "Duck, George!"

George could not bring himself to cower before these hooligans.

Suddenly the noise diminished. The banging on the bus sides stopped and there was no more breaking glass. George spotted a police officer.

About time, he thought.

The cop was swinging a nightstick but talking amiably to the grinning man with the knuckle-dusters.

Then George saw three more cops. They had calmed the crowd but, to George's indignation, they were doing no more. They acted as if no crime had been committed. They chatted casually to the rioters, who seemed to be their friends.

The two highway patrolmen were sitting back in their seats, looking bewildered. George guessed their assignment was to spy on the Riders, and they had not reckoned on becoming victims of mob violence. They had been forced to join the Riders' side in self-defense. They might learn to see things from a new point of view.

The bus moved. George saw, through the windshield, that a cop was urging men out of the way and another was waving the driver forward. Outside the station, a patrol car moved in front of the bus and led it onto the road out of town.

George began to feel better. "I think we got away," he said.

Maria got to her feet, apparently unhurt. She took the handkerchief out of the breast pocket of George's suit coat and mopped his face gently. The white cotton came away red with blood. "It's a nasty little gash," she said.

"I'll live."

"You won't be so pretty, though."

"I'm pretty?"

"You used to be, but now . . ."

The moment of normality did not last. George glanced behind and saw a long line of pickup trucks and cars following the bus. They seemed to be full of shouting men. He groaned. "We didn't get away," he said.

Maria said: "Back in Washington, before we got on the bus, you were talking to a young white guy."

"Joseph Hugo," George said. "He's at Harvard Law. Why?"

"I thought I saw him in the mob back there."

"Joseph Hugo? No. He's on our side. You must be mistaken." But Hugo was from Alabama, George recalled.

Maria said: "He had bulging blue eyes."

"If he's with the mob, that would mean that all this time he's been pretending to support civil rights . . . while spying on us. He can't be a snitch."

"Can't he?"

George looked behind again.

The police escort turned back at the city line, but the other vehicles did not.

The men in the cars were shrieking so loud they could be heard over the sound of all the engines.

Beyond the suburbs, on a long, lonely stretch of Highway 202, two cars overtook the bus, then slowed down, forcing the driver to brake. He tried to pass, but they swerved from side to side, blocking his way.

Cora Jones was white-faced and shaking, and she clutched her plastic handbag like a life preserver. George said: "I'm sorry we got you into this, Mrs. Jones."

"So am I," she replied.

The cars ahead pulled aside at last and the bus passed them. But the ordeal was not ended: the convoy was still behind. Then George heard a familiar popping sound. When the bus began to weave all over the road he realized it was a burst tire. The driver slowed to a halt near a roadside grocery store. George read the name: Forsyth & Son.

The driver jumped out. George heard him say: "*Two* flats?" Then he went into the store, presumably to phone for help.

George was as tense as a bowstring. One flat tire was just a puncture; two was an ambush.

Sure enough, the cars in the convoy were stopping and a dozen white men in their Sunday suits were piling out, yelling curses and waving their weapons, savages on the warpath. George's stomach cramped again as he saw them running toward the bus, ugly faces twisted with hatred, and he knew why his mother's eyes had filled with tears when she talked about Southern whites.

At the head of the pack was an adolescent boy who raised a crowbar and gleefully smashed a window.

The next man tried to enter the bus. One of the two burly white passengers stood at the top of the steps and drew a revolver, confirming Maria's theory that they were state troopers in plain clothes. The intruder backed off and the trooper locked the door.

George feared that might be a mistake. What if the Riders needed to get out in a hurry?

The men outside began to rock the bus, as if trying to turn it over, all the while yelling: "Kill the niggers! Kill the niggers!" Women passengers were screaming. Maria clung to George in a way that might have pleased him if he had not been in fear of his life.

Outside, he saw two uniformed patrolmen arrive, and his hopes lifted; but, to his fury, they did nothing to restrain the mob. He looked at the two plainclothesmen on the bus: they looked foolish and scared. Obviously the uniformed men did not know about their undercover colleagues. The Alabama Highway Patrol was evidently disorganized as well as racist.

George cast around desperately for something he could do to protect Maria and himself. Get out of the bus and run? Lie down on the floor?

Grab a gun from a state trooper and shoot some white men? Every possibility seemed even worse than doing nothing.

He stared in fury at the two highway patrolmen outside, watching as if nothing wrong was happening. They were cops, for Christ's sake! What did they think they were doing? If they would not enforce the law, what right did they have to wear that uniform?

Then he saw Joseph Hugo. There was no possibility of mistake: George knew well those bulging blue eyes. Hugo approached a patrolman and spoke to him, then the two of them laughed.

He was a snitch.

If I get out of here alive, George thought, that creep is going to be sorry.

The men outside shouted at the Riders to get off. George heard: "Come out here and get what's coming to you, nigger lovers!" That made him think he was safer on the bus.

But not for long.

One of the mob had returned to his car and opened the trunk, and now the man came running toward the bus with something burning in his hands. He hurled a blazing bundle through a smashed window. Seconds later the bundle exploded in gray smoke. But the weapon was not just a smoke bomb. It set fire to the upholstery, and in moments thick black fumes began to choke the passengers. A woman screamed: "Is there any air up front?"

From outside, George heard: "Burn the niggers! Fry them!"

Everyone tried to get out of the door. The aisle was jammed with gasping people. Some were pressing forward, but there seemed to be a blockage. George yelled: "Get off the bus! Everybody get off!"

From the front, someone shouted back: "The door won't open!"

George recalled that the state trooper with the gun had locked the door to keep the mob out. "We'll have to jump out the windows!" he yelled. "Come on!"

He stood on a seat and kicked most of the remaining glass out of the window. Then he pulled off his suit coat and draped it over the sill, to provide some protection from the jagged shards still remaining stuck in the window frame.

Maria was coughing helplessly. George said: "I'll go first and catch you as you jump." Grasping the back of the seat for balance, he stood on the sill, bent double, and jumped. He heard his shirt tear on a snag, but felt no pain, and concluded that he had escaped injury. He landed on the roadside grass. The mob had backed off from the burning bus in fear. George turned and held his arms up to Maria. "Climb through, like I did!" he shouted.

Her pumps were flimsy compared with his toe-capped oxfords, and he was glad he had sacrificed his jacket when he saw her small feet on the sill. She was shorter than he, but her womanly figure made her wider. He winced when her hip brushed a shard of glass as she squeezed through, but it did not tear the fabric of her dress, and a moment later she fell into his arms.

He held her easily. She was not heavy, and he was in good shape. He set her on her feet, but she dropped to her knees, gasping for air.

He glanced around. The thugs were still keeping their distance. He looked inside the bus. Cora Jones was standing in the aisle, coughing, turning round and round, too shocked and bewildered to save herself. "Cora, come here!" he yelled. She heard her name and looked at him. "Come through the window, like we did!" he shouted. "I'll help you!" She seemed to understand. With difficulty, she stood on the seat, still clutching her handbag. She hesitated, looking at the jagged bits of glass all around the window frame; but she had on a thick coat, and she seemed to decide a cut was a better risk than choking to death. She put one foot on the sill. George reached through the window, grabbed her arm, and pulled. She tore her coat but did no harm to herself, and he lifted her down. She staggered away, calling for water.

"We have to get away from the bus!" he yelled to Maria. "The fuel tank might explode." But Maria was so racked by coughing that she seemed helpless to move. He put one arm around her back and the other behind her knees and picked her up. He carried her toward the grocery store and set her down when he thought they were at a safe distance.

He looked back and saw that the bus was now emptying rapidly. The door had at last been opened, and people were stumbling through as well as jumping from the windows.

The flames grew. As the last passengers got out, the inside of the vehicle became a furnace. George heard a man shout something about the fuel tank, and the mob took up the cry, shouting: "She's gonna blow! She's gonna blow!" Everyone scattered in fear, getting farther away. Then there was a deep thump and a sudden fierce gout of flame, and the vehicle rocked with the explosion.

George was pretty sure no one was left inside, and he thought: At least no one is dead—yet.

The detonation seemed to have sated the mob's hunger for violence. They stood around, watching the bus burn.

A small crowd of what appeared to be local people had gathered outside the grocery store, many cheering the mob; but now a young girl came out of the building with a pail of water and some plastic cups. She gave a drink to Mrs. Jones, then came to Maria, who gratefully downed a cup of water and asked for another.

A young white man approached with a look of concern. He had a face like a rodent, forehead and chin angling back from a sharp nose and buck teeth, red-brown hair slicked back with pomade. "How are you doing, darling?" he said to Maria. But he was concealing something, and as Maria started to reply he raised a crowbar high in the air and brought it down, aiming at the top of her head. George flung out an arm to protect her, and the bar came down hard on his left forearm. The pain was agonizing, and he roared. The man lifted the crowbar again. Despite his arm George lunged forward, leading with his right shoulder, and barged into the man so hard that he went flying.

George turned back to Maria and saw three more of the mob running at him, evidently bent on revenging their ratlike friend. George had been premature in thinking the segregationists had had their fill of violence.

He was used to combat. He had been on the Harvard wrestling team as an undergraduate, and had coached the team while getting his law degree. But this was not going to be a fair fight with rules. And he had only one working arm.

On the other hand, he had gone to grade school in a Washington slum, and he knew about fighting dirty.

They were coming at him three abreast, so he moved sideways. This not only took them away from Maria, but turned them so that they were now advancing in single file.

The first man swung an iron chain at him wildly.

George danced back, and the chain missed him. The momentum of the swing threw the man off balance. As he staggered, George kicked his legs from under him, and he crashed to the ground. He lost hold of his chain.

The second man stumbled over the first. George stepped forward, turned his back, and hit the man in the face with his right elbow, hoping to dislocate his jaw. The man gave a strangled scream and fell down, dropping his tire iron.

The third man stopped, suddenly scared. George stepped toward him and punched him in the face with all his might. George's fist caught the man full on the nose. Bones crunched and blood spurted, and the man screamed in agony. It was the most satisfying blow George had ever struck in his life. To hell with Gandhi, he thought.

Two shots rang out. Everyone stopped what they were doing and looked toward the noise. One of the uniformed state troopers was holding a revolver high in the air. "Okay, boys, you've had your fun," he said. "Let's move out."

George was furious. Fun? The cop had been a witness to attempted murder, and he called it fun? George was beginning to see that a police uniform did not mean much in Alabama.

The mob returned to their cars. George noticed angrily that none of the four police officers troubled to write down any license plates. Nor did they take any names, though they probably knew everyone anyway.

Joseph Hugo had vanished.

There was another explosion in the wreckage of the bus, and George guessed there must be a second fuel tank; but at this point no one was near enough to be in danger. The fire then seemed to burn itself out.

Several people lay on the ground, many still gasping for breath after inhaling smoke. Others were bleeding from various injuries. Some were Riders, some regular passengers, black and white. George himself was clutching his left arm with his right hand, holding it against his side, trying to keep it motionless because every movement was excruciatingly painful. The four men he had tangled with were helping one another limp back to their cars.

He managed to walk to where the patrolmen stood. "We need an ambulance," he said. "Maybe two."

The younger of the two uniformed men glared at him. "What did you say?"

"These people need medical attention," George said. "Call an ambulance!"

The man looked furious, and George realized he had made the mistake of telling a white man what to do. But the older patrolman said to his colleague: "Leave it, leave it." Then he said to George: "Ambulance is on its way, boy."

A few minutes later, an ambulance the size of a small bus arrived, and the Riders began to help each other aboard. But when George and Maria approached, the driver said: "Not you."

George stared at him in disbelief. "What?"

"This here's a white folks' ambulance," the driver said. "It ain't for nigras."

"The hell you say."

"Don't you sass me, boy."

A white Rider who was already on board came back out. "You have to take everyone to the hospital," he said to the driver. "Black and white."

"This ain't a nigra ambulance," the driver said stubbornly.

"Well, we're not going without our friends." With that the white Riders began to leave the ambulance one by one.

The driver was taken aback. He would look foolish, George guessed, if he returned from the scene with no patients.

The older patrolman came over and said: "Better take 'em, Roy."

"If you say so," said the driver.

George and Maria boarded the ambulance.

As they drove away, George looked back at the bus. Nothing remained but a drift of smoke and a blackened hulk, with a row of scorched roof struts sticking up like the ribs of a martyr burned at the stake.

Tanya Dvorkin left Yakutsk, Siberia—the coldest city in the world—after an early breakfast. She flew to Moscow, a distance of a little over three thousand miles, in a Tupolev Tu-16 of the Red Air Force. The cabin was configured for half a dozen military men, and the designer had not wasted time thinking of their comfort: the seats were made of pierced aluminum and there was no soundproofing. The journey took eight hours with one refueling stop. Because Moscow was six hours behind Yakutsk, Tanya arrived in time for another breakfast.

It was summer in Moscow, and she carried her heavy coat and fur hat. She took a taxi to Government House, the apartment building for Moscow's privileged elite. She shared a flat with her mother, Anya, and her twin brother, Dmitri, always called Dimka. It was a big place, with three bedrooms, though Mother said it was spacious only by Soviet standards: the Berlin apartment she had lived in as a child, when Grandfather Grigori had been a diplomat, had been much more grand.

This morning the place was silent and empty: Mother and Dimka had both left for work already. Their coats were hanging in the hall, on nails knocked in by Tanya's father a quarter of a century ago: Dimka's black raincoat and Mother's brown tweed, left at home in the warm weather. Tanya hung up her own coat beside them and put her suitcase in her bedroom. She had not expected them to be in, but all the same she felt a twinge of regret that Mother was not here to make her tea, nor Dimka to listen to her adventures in Siberia. She thought of going to see her grandparents Grigori and Katerina Peshkov, who lived on another floor in the same building, but decided she did not really have the time.

She showered and changed her clothes, then took a bus to the headquarters of TASS, the Soviet news agency. She was one of more than a thousand reporters working for the agency, but not many were flown around in air force jets. She was a rising star, able to produce lively and interesting articles that appealed to young people but nevertheless adhered to the party line. It was a mixed blessing: she was often given difficult high-profile assignments.

In the canteen she had a bowl of buckwheat kasha with sour cream, then she went to the features department, where she worked. Although she was a star, she did not yet merit an office of her own. She greeted her colleagues, then sat at a desk, put paper and carbons into a typewriter, and began to write.

The flight had been too bumpy even to make notes, but she had planned her articles in her head, and now she was able to write fluently, referring occasionally to her notebook for details. Her brief was to encourage young Soviet families to migrate to Siberia to work in the boom industries of mining and drilling: not an easy task. The prison camps provided plenty of unskilled labor, but the region needed geologists, engineers, surveyors, architects, chemists, and managers. However, Tanya in her article ignored the men and wrote about their wives. She began with an attractive young mother called Klara who had talked with enthusiasm and humor about coping with life at sub-zero temperatures.

Halfway through the morning Tanya's editor, Daniil Antonov, picked up the sheets of paper from her tray and began to read. He was a small man with a gentle manner that was unusual in the world of journalism. "This is great," he said after a while. "When can I have the rest?"

"I'm typing as fast as I can."

He lingered. "While you were in Siberia, did you hear anything about Ustin Bodian?" Bodian was an opera singer who had been caught smuggling in two copies of *Doctor Zhivago* he had obtained while singing in Italy. He was now in a labor camp.

Tanya's heart raced guiltily. Did Daniil suspect her? He was unusually intuitive for a man. "No," she lied. "Why do you ask? Have you heard something?"

"Nothing." Daniil returned to his desk.

Tanya had almost finished the third article when Pyotr Opotkin stopped beside her desk and began to read her copy with a cigarette dangling from his lips. A stout man with bad skin, Opotkin was editor in chief for features. Unlike Daniil he was not a trained journalist but a commissar, a political appointee. His job was to make sure features did not violate Kremlin guidelines, and his only qualification for the job was rigid orthodoxy.

He read Tanya's first few pages and said: "I told you not to write about the weather." He came from a village north of Moscow and still had the north-Russian accent.

Tanya sighed. "Pyotr, the series is about Siberia. People already know it's cold there. Nobody would be fooled."

"But this is *all* about the weather."

"It's about how a resourceful young woman from Moscow is raising her family in challenging conditions—and having a great adventure."

Daniil joined the conversation. "She's right, Pyotr," he said. "If we avoid all mention of the cold, people will know the article is shit, and they won't believe a word of it."

"I don't like it," Opotkin said stubbornly.

"You have to admit," Daniil persisted, "Tanya makes it sound exciting."

Opotkin looked thoughtful. "Maybe you're right," he said, and dropped the copy back into the tray. "I'm having a party at my house on Saturday night," he said to Tanya. "My daughter graduated college. I was wondering if you and your brother would like to come?"

Opotkin was an unsuccessful social climber who gave agonizingly boring parties. Tanya knew she could speak for her brother. "I'd love to, and I'm sure Dimka would too, but it's our mother's birthday. I'm so sorry."

Opotkin looked offended. "Too bad," he said, and walked on.

When he was out of earshot Daniil said: "It's not your mother's birthday, is it?"

"No."

"He'll check."

"Then he'll realize I made a polite excuse because I didn't want to go."

"You should go to his parties."

Tanya did not want to have this argument. There were more important things on her mind. She needed to write her articles, get out of there, and save the life of Ustin Bodian. But Daniil was a good boss and liberal minded, so she suppressed her impatience. "Pyotr doesn't care whether I attend his party or not," she said. "He wants my brother, who works for Khrushchev." Tanya was used to people trying to befriend her because of her influential family. Her late father had been a colonel in the KGB, the secret police; and her uncle Volodya was a general in Red Army Intelligence.

Daniil had a journalist's persistence. "Pyotr gave in to us over the Siberia articles. You should show that you're grateful."

"I hate his parties. His friends get drunk and paw each other's wives."

"I don't want him to bear a grudge against you."

"Why would he do that?"

"You're very attractive." Daniil was not coming on to Tanya. He lived with a male friend and she was sure he was one of those men not drawn to women. He spoke in a matter-of-fact tone. "Beautiful, and talented, and—worst of all—young. Pyotr won't find it difficult to hate you. Try a little harder with him." Daniil drifted away.

Tanya realized he was probably right, but she decided to think about it later, and returned her attention to her typewriter.

At midday she got a plate of potato salad with pickled herrings from the canteen and ate at her desk.

She finished her third article soon afterward. She handed the sheets of paper to Daniil. "I'm going home to bed," she said. "Please don't call."

"Good work," he said. "Sleep well."

She put her notebook in her shoulder bag and left the building.

Now she had to make sure she was not being followed. She was tired, and that meant she was likely to make foolish mistakes. She felt worried.

She went past the bus stop, walked several blocks to the previous stop on the route, and caught the bus there. It made no sense, which meant that anyone who did the same had to be following her.

No one was.

She got off near a grand pre-revolutionary palace now converted to apartments. She walked around the block, but no one appeared to be watching the building. Anxiously she went around again to make sure. Then she entered the gloomy hall and climbed the cracked marble staircase to the apartment of Vasili Yenkov.

Just as she was about to put her key in the lock the door opened, and a slim blond girl of about eighteen stood there. Vasili was behind her. Tanya cursed inwardly. It was too late for her to run away or pretend she was going to a different apartment.

The blonde gave Tanya a hard, appraising stare, taking in her hairstyle, her figure, and her clothes. Then she kissed Vasili on the mouth, threw a triumphant look at Tanya, and went down the staircase.

Vasili was thirty but he liked girls young. They yielded to him because he was tall and dashing, with carved good looks and thick dark hair always a little too long and soft brown bedroom eyes. Tanya admired him for a completely different set of reasons: because he was bright, brave, and a world-class writer.

She walked into his study and dropped her bag on a chair. Vasili worked as a radio script editor and was a naturally untidy man. Papers covered his desk, and books were stacked on the floor. He seemed to be working on a radio adaptation of Maxim Gorky's first play, *The Philistines.* His gray cat, Mademoiselle, was sleeping on the couch. Tanya pushed her off and sat down. "Who was that little tart?" she said.

"That was my mother."

Tanya laughed despite her annoyance.

"I'm sorry she was here," Vasili said, though he did not look very sad about it.

"You knew I was coming today."

"I thought you'd be later."

"She saw my face. No one is supposed to know there is a connection between you and me."

"She works at the GUM department store. Her name is Varvara. She won't suspect anything."

"Please, Vasili, don't let it happen again. What we're doing is dangerous enough. We shouldn't take additional risks. You can screw a teenager any day."

"You're right, and it won't happen again. Let me make you some tea. You look tired." Vasili busied himself at the samovar.

"I am tired. But Ustin Bodian is dying."

"Hell. What of?"

"Pneumonia."

Tanya did not know Bodian personally, but she had interviewed him, before he got into trouble. As well as being extraordinarily talented, he was a warm and kindhearted man. A Soviet artist admired all over the world, he had lived a life of great privilege, but he was still able to get publicly angry about injustice done to people less fortunate than himself—which was why they had sent him to Siberia.

Vasili said: "Are they still making him work?"

Tanya shook her head. "He can't. But they won't send him to the hospital. He just lies on his bunk all day, getting worse."

"Did you see him?"

"Hell, no. Asking about him was dangerous enough. If I'd gone to the prison camp they would have kept me there."

Vasili handed her tea and sugar. "Is he getting any medical treatment at all?"

"No."

"Did you get any idea of how long he might have to live?"

Tanya shook her head. "You now know everything I know."

"We have to spread this news."

Tanya agreed. "The only way to save his life is to publicize his illness and hope that the government will have the grace to be embarrassed."

"Shall we put out a special edition?"

"Yes," said Tanya. "Today."

Vasili and Tanya together produced an illegal news sheet called *Dissidence.* They reported on censorship, demonstrations, trials, and political prisoners. In his office at Radio Moscow, Vasili had his own stencil duplicator, normally used for making multiple copies of scripts. Secretly he printed fifty copies of each issue of *Dissidence.* Most of the people who received one made more copies on their own typewriters, or even by hand, and circulation mushroomed. This self-publishing system was called *samizdat* in Russian and was widespread: whole novels had been distributed the same way.

"I'll write it." Tanya went to the cupboard and pulled out a large cardboard box full of dry cat food. Pushing her hands into the pellets, she drew out a typewriter in a cover. This was the one they used for *Dissidence.*

Typing was as unique as handwriting. Every machine had its own characteristics. The letters were never perfectly aligned: some were a little raised, some off center. Individual letters became worn or damaged in distinctive ways. In consequence, police experts could match a typewriter to its product. If *Dissidence* had been typed on the same machine as Vasili's scripts, someone might have noticed. So Vasili had stolen an old machine from the scheduling department, brought it home, and buried it in the cat's food to hide it from casual observation. A determined search would find it, but if there should be a determined search Vasili would be finished anyway.

Also in the box were sheets of the special waxed paper used in the duplicating machine. The typewriter had no ribbon: instead, its letters pierced the paper, and the duplicator worked by forcing ink through the letter-shaped holes.

Tanya wrote a report on Bodian, saying that General Secretary Nikita Khrushchev would be personally responsible if one of the USSR's greatest tenors died in a prison camp. She recapitulated the main points of Bodian's trial for anti-Soviet activity, including his impassioned defense of artistic freedom. To divert suspicion away from herself, she misleadingly credited the information about Bodian's illness to an imaginary opera lover in the KGB.

When she had done, she handed two sheets of stencil paper to Vasili. "I've made it concise," she said.

"Concision is the sister of talent. Chekov said that." He read the report slowly, then nodded approval. "I'll go in to Radio Moscow now and make copies," he said. "Then we should take them to Mayakovsky Square."

Tanya was not surprised, but she was uneasy. "Is it safe?"

"Of course not. It's a cultural event that isn't organized by the government. Which is why it suits our purpose."

Earlier in the year, young Muscovites had started to gather informally around the statue of Bolshevik poet Vladimir Mayakovsky. Some would read poems aloud, attracting more people. A permanent rolling poetry festival had come into being, and some of the works declaimed from the monument were obliquely critical of the government.

Such a phenomenon would have lasted ten minutes under Stalin, but Khrushchev was a reformer. His program included a limited degree of cultural tolerance, and so far no action had been taken against the poetry readings. But liberalization proceeded by two steps forward and one back. Tanya's brother said it depended on whether Khrushchev was doing well, and felt strong politically, or was suffering setbacks, and feared a coup by his conservative enemies within the Kremlin. Whatever the reason, there was no predicting what the authorities would do.

Tanya was too tired to think about this, and she guessed that any alternative location would be as dangerous. "While you're at the radio station, I'm going to sleep."

She went into the bedroom. The sheets were rumpled: she guessed Vasili and Varvara had spent the morning in bed. She pulled the coverlet over the top, removed her boots, and stretched out.

Her body was tired but her mind was busy. She was afraid, but she still wanted to go to Mayakovsky Square. *Dissidence* was an important publication, despite its amateurish production and small circulation. It proved the Communist government was not all-powerful. It showed dissidents they were not alone. Religious leaders struggling against persecution read about folksingers arrested for protest songs, and vice versa. Instead of feeling like a single voice in a monolithic society, the dissident realized that he or she was part of a great network, thousands of people who wanted a government that was different and better.

And it could save the life of Ustin Bodian.

At last Tanya fell asleep.

She was awakened by someone stroking her cheek. She opened her eyes to see Vasili stretched out beside her. "Get lost," she said.

"It's my bed."

She sat upright. "I'm twenty-two—far too old to interest you."

"For you, I'll make an exception."

"When I want to join a harem, I'll let you know."

"I'd give up all the others for you."

"No, you wouldn't."

"I would, really."

"For five minutes, maybe."

"Forever."

"Do it for six months, and I'll reconsider."

"Six months?"

"See? If you can't be chaste for half a year, how can you promise forever? What the hell time is it?"

"You slept all afternoon. Don't get up. I'll just take off my clothes and slip into bed with you."

Tanya stood up. "We have to leave now."

Vasili gave up. He probably had not been serious. He felt compelled to proposition young women. Having gone through the motions he would now forget about it, for a while at least. He handed her a small bundle of about twenty-five sheets of paper, printed on both sides with slightly blurred letters: copies of the new issue of *Dissidence.* He wound a red cotton scarf around his neck, despite the fine weather. It made him look artistic. "Let's go, then," he said.

Tanya made him wait while she went to the bathroom. The face in the mirror looked at her with an intense blue-eyed stare framed by pale-blond hair in a short gamine crop. She put on sunglasses to hide her eyes and tied a nondescript brown scarf around her hair. Now she could have been any youngish woman.

She went into the kitchen, ignoring Vasili's impatient foot-tapping, and drew a glass of water from the tap. She drank it all, then said: "I'm ready."

They walked to the Metro station. The train was crowded with workers heading home. They went to Mayakovsky Station on the Garden Ring orbital road. They would not linger here: as soon as they had given out all fifty copies of their news sheet they would leave. "If there should be any trouble," Vasili said, "just remember, we don't know each other." They separated and emerged aboveground a minute apart. The sun was low and the summer day was cooling.

Vladimir Mayakovsky had been a poet of international stature as well as a Bolshevik, and the Soviet Union was proud of him. His heroic statue stood twenty feet high in the middle of the square named after him. Several hundred people milled about on the grass, mostly young, some dressed in vaguely Western fashions, blue jeans and roll-neck sweaters. A boy in a cap was selling his own novel, carbon-copy pages hole-punched and tied with string. It was called *Growing Up Backward.* A long-haired girl carried a guitar but made no attempt to play it: perhaps it was an accessory, like a handbag. There was only one uniformed cop, but the secret policemen were comically obvious, wearing leather jackets in the mild air to conceal their guns. Tanya avoided their eyes, though: they were not that funny.

People were taking turns to stand up and speak one or two poems each. Most were men but there was a sprinkling of women. A boy with an impish grin read a piece about a clumsy farmer trying to herd a flock of geese, which the crowd quickly realized was a metaphor for the Communist Party organizing the nation. Soon everyone was roaring with laughter except the KGB men, who just looked puzzled.

Tanya drifted inconspicuously through the crowd, half-listening to a poem of adolescent angst in Mayakovsky's futurist style, drawing the sheets of paper one at a time from her pocket and discreetly slipping them to anyone who looked friendly. She kept an eye on Vasili as he did the same. Right away she heard exclamations of shock and concern as people started to talk about Bodian: in a crowd such as this, most people would know who he was and why he had been imprisoned. She gave the sheets away as fast as she could, eager to get rid of them all before the police got wind of what was going on.

A man with short hair who looked ex-army stood at the front and, instead of reciting a poem, began to read aloud Tanya's article about Bodian. Tanya was pleased: the news was getting around even faster than she had hoped. There were shouts of indignation as he got to the part about Bodian not getting medical attention. But the men in the leather jackets noticed the change in atmosphere and looked more alert. She spotted one speaking urgently into a walkie-talkie.

She had five sheets left and they were burning a hole in her pocket.

The secret police had been on the edges of the crowd, but now they moved in, converging on the speaker. He waved his copy of *Dissidence* defiantly, shouting about Bodian as the cops came closer. Some in the audience crowded the plinth, making it difficult for the police to get near. In response the KGB men got rough, shoving people out of the way. This was how riots started. Tanya nervously backed away toward the fringe of the crowd. She had one more copy of *Dissidence*. She dropped it on the ground.

Suddenly half a dozen uniformed police arrived. Wondering fearfully where they had come from, Tanya looked across the road to the nearest building and saw more running out through its door: they must have been concealed within, waiting in case they were needed. They drew their nightsticks and pushed through the crowd, hitting people indiscriminately. Tanya saw Vasili turn and walk away, moving through the throng as fast as he could, and she did the same. Then a panicking teenager cannoned into her, and she fell to the ground.

She was dazed for a moment. When her vision cleared she saw more people running. She got to her knees, but she felt dizzy. Someone tripped over her, knocking her flat again. Then suddenly Vasili was there, grabbing her with both hands, lifting her to her feet. She had a moment of surprise: she would not have expected him to risk his own safety to help her.

Then a cop hit Vasili over the head with a truncheon and he fell. The cop knelt down, pulled Vasili's arms behind his back and handcuffed him with swift, practiced movements. Vasili looked up, caught Tanya's eye, and mouthed: "Run!"

She turned and ran but, an instant later, she collided with a uniformed policeman. He grabbed her by the arm. She tried to pull away, screaming: "Let me go!"

He tightened his grip and said: "You're under arrest, bitch."

The Nina Onilova Room in the Kremlin was named after a female machine-gunner killed at the Battle of Sevastopol. On the wall was a framed black-and-white photo of a Red Army general placing the Order of the Red Banner medal on her tombstone. The picture hung over a white marble fireplace that was stained like a smoker's fingers. All around the room, elaborate plaster moldings framed squares of light paintwork where other pictures had once hung, suggesting that the walls had not been painted since the revolution. Perhaps the room had once been an elegant salon. Now it was furnished with canteen tables pushed together to form a long rectangle and twenty or so cheap chairs. On the tables were ceramic ashtrays that looked as if they were emptied daily but never wiped.

Dimka Dvorkin walked in with his mind in a whirl and his stomach in knots.

The room was the regular meeting place of aides to the ministers and secretaries who formed the Presidium of the Supreme Soviet, the governing body of the USSR.

Dimka was an aide to Nikita Khrushchev, first secretary and chairman of the Presidium, but all the same he felt he should not be here.

The Vienna Summit was a few weeks away. It would be the dramatic first encounter between Khrushchev and the new American president, John Kennedy. Tomorrow, at the most important Presidium of the year, the leaders of the USSR would decide strategy for the summit. Today, the aides were gathering to prepare for the Presidium. It was a planning meeting for a planning meeting.

Khrushchev's representative had to present the leader's thinking so that the other aides could prepare their bosses for tomorrow. His unspoken task was to uncover any latent opposition to Khrushchev's ideas and, if possible, quash it. It was his solemn duty to ensure that tomorrow's discussion went smoothly for the leader.

Dimka was familiar with Khrushchev's thinking about the summit, but all the same he felt he could not possibly cope with this meeting. He was the youngest and most inexperienced of Khrushchev's aides. He was only a year out of university. He had never been to the pre-Presidium meeting before: he was too junior. But ten minutes ago his secretary had informed him that one of the senior aides had called in sick and the other two had just been in a car crash, so he, Dimka, had to stand in.

Dimka had got a job working for Khrushchev for two reasons. One was that he had come top of every class he had ever attended, from nursery school through university. The other was that his uncle was a general. He did not know which factor was the more important.

The Kremlin presented a monolithic appearance to the outside world but, in truth, it was a battlefield. Khrushchev's hold on power was not strong. He was a Communist heart and soul, but he was also a reformer who saw failings in the Soviet system and wanted to implement new ideas. But the old Stalinists in the Kremlin were not yet defeated. They were alert for any opportunity to weaken Khrushchev and roll back his reforms.

The meeting was informal, the aides drinking tea and smoking with their jackets off and their ties undone—most were men, though not all. Dimka spotted a friendly face: Natalya Smotrov, aide to Foreign Minister Andrei Gromyko. She was in her midtwenties, and attractive despite a drab black dress. Dimka did not know her well but he had spoken to her a few times. Now he sat down next to her. She looked surprised to see him. "Konstantinov and Pajari have been in a car crash," he explained.

"Are they hurt?"

"Not badly."

"What about Alkaev?"

"Off sick with shingles."

"Nasty. So you're the leader's representative."

"I'm terrified."

"You'll be fine."

He looked around. They all seemed to be waiting for something. In a low voice he said to Natalya: "Who chairs this meeting?"

One of the others heard him. It was Yevgeny Filipov, who worked for conservative defense minister Rodion Malinovsky. Filipov was in his thirties but dressed older, in a baggy postwar suit and a gray flannel shirt. He repeated Dimka's question loudly, in a scornful tone. "Who chairs this meeting? You do, of course. You're aide to the chairman of the Presidium, aren't you? Get on with it, college boy."

Dimka felt himself redden. For a moment he was lost for words. Then inspiration struck, and he said: "Thanks to Major Yuri Gagarin's remarkable space flight, Comrade Khrushchev will go to Vienna with the congratulations of the world ringing in his ears." Last month Gagarin had been the first human being to travel into outer space in a rocket, beating the Americans by just a few weeks, in a stunning scientific and propaganda coup for the Soviet Union and for Nikita Khrushchev.

The aides around the table clapped, and Dimka began to feel better.

Then Filipov spoke again. "The first secretary might do better to have ringing in his ears the inaugural speech of President Kennedy," he said. He seemed incapable of speaking without a sneer. "In case comrades around the table have forgotten, Kennedy accused us of planning world domination, and he vowed to pay any price to stop us. After all the friendly moves we have made—unwisely, in the opinion of some experienced comrades—Kennedy could hardly have made clearer his aggressive intentions." He raised his arm with a finger in the air, like a schoolteacher. "Only one response is possible from us: increased military strength."

Dimka was still thinking up a rejoinder when Natalya beat him to it. "That's a race we can't win," she said with a brisk commonsense air. "The United States is richer than the Soviet Union, and they can easily match any increase in our military forces."

She was more sensible than her conservative boss, Dimka inferred. He shot her a grateful look and followed up. "Hence Khrushchev's policy of peaceful coexistence, which enables us to spend less on the army, and instead invest in agriculture and industry." Kremlin conservatives hated peaceful coexistence. For them, the conflict with capitalist imperialism was a war to the death.

Out of the corner of his eye, Dimka saw his secretary, Vera, a bright, nervy woman of forty, enter the room. He waved her away.

Filipov was not so easily disposed of. "Let's not permit a naïve view of world politics to encourage us to reduce our army too fast," he said scornfully. "We can hardly claim to be winning on the international stage. Look at how the Chinese defy us. That weakens us at Vienna."

Why was Filipov trying so hard to prove that Dimka was a fool? Dimka suddenly recalled that Filipov had wanted a job in Khrushchev's office—the job that Dimka had got.

"As the Bay of Pigs weakened Kennedy," Dimka replied. The American president had authorized a crackpot CIA plan for an invasion of Cuba at a place called the Bay of Pigs: the scheme had gone wrong and Kennedy had been humiliated. "I think our leader's position is stronger."

"All the same, Khrushchev has failed—" Filipov stopped, realizing he was going too far. These premeeting discussions were frank, but there were limits.

Dimka seized on the moment of weakness. "What has Khrushchev failed to do, comrade?" he said. "Please enlighten us all."

Filipov amended quickly. "We have failed to achieve our main foreign policy objective: a permanent resolution of the Berlin situation. East Germany is our frontier post in Europe. Its borders secure the borders of Poland and Czechoslovakia. Its unresolved status is intolerable."

"All right," Dimka said, and he was surprised to hear a note of confidence in his own voice. "I think that's enough discussion of general principles. Before I close the meeting I will explain the trend of the first secretary's current thinking on the problem."

Filipov opened his mouth to protest against this abrupt termination, but Dimka cut him off. "Comrades will speak when invited by the chair," he said, deliberately making his voice a harsh grind; and they all went quiet.

"In Vienna, Khrushchev will tell Kennedy we can wait no longer. We have made reasonable proposals for regulating the situation in Berlin, and all we hear from the Americans is that they want no changes." Around the table, several men nodded. "If they will not agree to a plan, Khrushchev will say, then we will take unilateral action; and if the Americans try to stop us, we will meet force with force."

There was a long moment of silence. Dimka took advantage of it by standing up. "Thank you for your attendance," he said.

Natalya said what everyone was thinking. "Does that mean we are willing to go to war with the Americans over Berlin?"

"The first secretary does not believe there will be a war," said Dimka, giving them the evasive answer that Khrushchev had given him. "Kennedy is not mad."

He caught a look of mingled surprise and admiration from Natalya as he walked away from the table. He could not believe he had been so tough. He had never been a pussycat, but this was a powerful and smart group of men, and he had bullied them. His position helped: new though he was, his desk in the first secretary's suite of offices gave him power. And, paradoxically, Filipov's hostility had helped. They could all sympathize with the need to come down hard on someone who was trying to undermine the leader.

Vera was hovering in the anteroom. She was an experienced political assistant who would not panic unnecessarily. Dimka had a flash of intuition. "It's my sister, isn't it?" he said.

Vera was spooked. Her eyes widened. "How do you do that?" she said in awe.

It was not supernatural. He had feared for some time that Tanya was heading for trouble. He said: "What has she done?"

"She's been arrested."

"Oh, hell."

Vera pointed to a phone off the hook on a side table and Dimka picked it up. His mother, Anya, was on the line. "Tanya's in the Lubyanka!" she said, using the shorthand name for KGB headquarters in Lubyanka Square. She was close to hysteria.

Dimka was not taken totally by surprise. His twin sister and he agreed that there was a lot wrong with the Soviet Union, but whereas he believed reform was needed, she thought Communism should be abolished. It was an intellectual disagreement that made no difference to their affection for one another. Each was the other's best friend. It had always been that way.

You could be arrested for thinking as Tanya did—which was one of the things that was wrong. "Be calm, Mother, I can get her out of there," Dimka said. He hoped he would be able to justify that assurance. "Do you know what happened?"

"There was a riot at some poetry meeting!"

"I bet she went to Mayakovsky Square. If that's all . . ." He did not know everything his sister got up to, but he suspected her of worse than poetry.

"You have to do something, Dimka! Before they . . ."

"I know." Before they start to interrogate her, Mother meant. A chill of fear passed over him like a shadow. The prospect of interrogation in the notorious basement cells of KGB headquarters terrified every Soviet citizen.

His first instinct had been to say he would get on the phone, but now he decided that would not be enough. He had to show up in person. He hesitated momentarily: it could harm his career, if people knew he had gone to the Lubyanka to spring his sister. But that thought barely gave him pause. She came before himself and Khrushchev and the entire Soviet Union. "I'm on my way, Mother," he said. "Call Uncle Volodya and tell him what's happened."

"Oh, yes, good idea! My brother will know what to do."

Dimka hung up. "Phone the Lubyanka," he said to Vera. "Tell them very clearly that you're calling from the office of the first secretary, who is concerned about the arrest of leading journalist Tanya Dvorkin. Tell them that Comrade Khrushchev's aide is on his way to question them about it, and they should do nothing until he arrives."

She was making notes. "Shall I order up a car?"

Lubyanka Square was less than a mile from the Kremlin compound. "I have my motorcycle downstairs. That will be quicker." Dimka was privileged to own a Voskhod 175 bike with a five-speed gearbox and twin tailpipes.

He had known Tanya was heading for trouble because, paradoxically, she had ceased to tell him everything, he reflected as he rode. Normally they had no secrets from one another. Dimka had an intimacy with his twin that they shared with no one else. When Mother was away, and they were alone, Tanya would walk through the flat naked, to fetch clean underwear from the airing cupboard, and Dimka would pee without bothering to close the bathroom door. Occasionally Dimka's male friends would sniggeringly suggest that their closeness was erotic, but in fact it was the opposite. They could be so intimate only because there was no sexual spark.

But for the past year he had known she was hiding something from him. He did not know what it was, but he could guess. Not a boyfriend, he felt sure: they told each other everything about their romantic lives, comparing notes, sympathizing. Almost certainly it was political, he thought. The only reason she might keep something from him would be to protect him.

He drew up outside the dreaded building, a yellow brick palace erected before the revolution as the headquarters of an insurance company. The thought of his sister imprisoned in this place made him feel ill. For a moment he was afraid he was going to puke.

He parked right in front of the main entrance, took a moment to recover his self-possession, and walked inside.

Tanya's editor, Daniil Antonov, was already there, arguing with a KGB man in the lobby. Daniil was a small man, slightly built, and Dimka thought of him as harmless, but he was being assertive. "I want to see Tanya Dvorkin, and I want to see her *right now*," he said.

The KGB man wore an expression of mulish obstinacy. "That may not be possible."

Dimka butted in. "I'm from the office of the first secretary," he said.

The KGB man refused to be impressed. "And what do you do there, son—make the tea?" he said rudely. "What's your name?" It was an intimidating question: people were terrified to give their names to the KGB.

"Dmitri Dvorkin, and I'm here to tell you that Comrade Khrushchev is personally interested in this case."

"Fuck off, Dvorkin," said the man. "Comrade Khrushchev knows nothing about this case. You're here to get your sister out of trouble."

Dimka was taken aback by the man's confident rudeness. He guessed that many people trying to spring family or friends from KGB arrest would claim personal connections with powerful people. But he renewed his attack. "What's your name?"

"Captain Mets."

"And what are you accusing Tanya Dvorkin of?"

"Assaulting an officer."

"Did a girl beat up one of your goons in leather jackets?" Dimka said jeeringly. "She must have taken his gun from him first. Come off it, Mets, don't be a prick."

"She was attending a seditious meeting. Anti-Soviet literature was circulated." Mets handed Dimka a crumpled sheet of paper. "The meeting became a riot."

Dimka looked at the paper. It was headed *Dissidence.* He had heard of this subversive news sheet. Tanya might easily have something to do with it. This edition was about Ustin Bodian, the opera singer. Dimka was momentarily distracted by the shocking allegation that Bodian was dying of pneumonia in a Siberian labor camp. Then he recalled that Tanya had returned from Siberia today, and realized she must have written this. She could be in real trouble. "Are you alleging that Tanya had this paper in her possession?" he demanded. He saw Mets hesitate and said: "I thought not."

"She should not have been there at all."

Daniil put in: "She's a reporter, you fool. She was observing the event, just as your officers were."

"She's not an officer."

"All TASS reporters cooperate with the KGB, you know that."

"You can't prove she was there officially."

"Yes, I can. I'm her editor. I sent her."

Dimka wondered whether that was true. He doubted it. He felt grateful to Daniil for sticking his neck out in defense of Tanya.

Mets was losing confidence. "She was with a man called Vasili Yenkov, who had five copies of that sheet in his pocket."

"She doesn't know anyone called Vasili Yenkov," said Dimka. It might have been true: certainly he had never heard the name. "If it was a riot, how could you tell who was with whom?"

"I'll have to talk to my superiors," said Mets, and he turned away.

Dimka made his voice harsh. "Don't be long," he barked. "The next person you see from the Kremlin may not be the boy who makes the tea."

Mets went down a staircase. Dimka shuddered: everyone knew the basement contained the interrogation rooms.

A moment later Dimka and Daniil were joined in the lobby by an older man with a cigarette dangling from his mouth. He had an ugly, fleshy face with an aggressively jutting chin. Daniil did not seem pleased to see him. He introduced him as Pyotr Opotkin, features editor in chief.

Opotkin looked at Dimka with eyes screwed up to keep out the smoke. "So, your sister got herself arrested at a protest meeting," he said. His tone was angry, but Dimka sensed that underneath it Opotkin was for some reason pleased.

"A poetry reading," Dimka corrected him.

"Not much difference."

Daniil put in: "I sent her there."

"On the day she got back from Siberia?" said Opotkin skeptically.

"It wasn't really an assignment. I suggested she drop by sometime to see what was going on, that's all."

"Don't lie to me," said Opotkin. "You're just trying to protect her."

Daniil raised his chin and gave a challenging look. "Isn't that what you're here to do?"

Before Opotkin could reply, Captain Mets returned. "The case is still under consideration," he said.

Opotkin introduced himself and showed Mets his identity card. "The question is not whether Tanya Dvorkin should be punished, but how," he said.

"Exactly, sir," said Mets deferentially. "Would you like to come with me?"

Opotkin nodded and Mets led him down the stairs.

Dimka said in a quiet voice: "He won't let them torture her, will he?"

"Opotkin was mad at Tanya already," Daniil said worriedly.

"What for? I thought she was a good journalist."

"She's brilliant. But she turned down an invitation to a party at his house on Saturday. He wanted you to go, too. Pyotr loves important people. A snub really hurts him."

"Oh, shit."

"I told her she should have accepted."

"Did you really send her to Mayakovsky Square?"

"No. We could never do a story about such an unofficial gathering."

"Thanks for trying to protect her."

"My privilege—but I don't think it's working."

"What do you think will happen?"

"She might be fired. More likely, she'll be posted somewhere disagreeable, such as Kazakhstan." Daniil frowned. "I must think of some compromise that will satisfy Opotkin but not be too hard on Tanya."

Dimka glanced at the entrance door and saw a man in his forties with a brutally short military haircut and wearing the uniform of a Red Army general. "At last, Uncle Volodya," he said.

Volodya Peshkov had the same intense blue-eyed stare as Tanya. "What is this shit?" he said angrily.

Dimka filled him in. As he was finishing, Opotkin reappeared. He spoke obsequiously to Volodya. "General, I have discussed this problem of your niece with our friends in the KGB and they are content for me to deal with it as an internal TASS matter."

Dimka slumped with relief. Then he wondered whether Opotkin's entire approach had been to maneuver himself into a position where he could appear to do a favor for Volodya.

"Allow me to make a suggestion," said Volodya. "You might mark the incident as serious, without attaching blame to anyone, simply by transferring Tanya to another post."

That was the punishment Daniil had mentioned a moment ago.

Opotkin nodded thoughtfully, as if considering this idea; though Dimka was sure he would eagerly comply with any "suggestion" from General Peshkov.

Daniil said: "Perhaps a foreign posting. She speaks German and English."

This was an exaggeration, Dimka knew. Tanya had studied both languages in school, but that was not the same as speaking them. Daniil was trying to save her from banishment to some remote Soviet region.

Daniil added: "And she could still write features for my department. I'd rather not lose her to news—she's too good."

Opotkin looked dubious. "We can't send her to London or Bonn. That would seem like a reward."

It was true. Assignments in the capitalist countries were prized. The living allowances were colossal and, even though they did not buy as much as in the USSR, Soviet citizens still lived much better in the West than at home.

Volodya said: "East Berlin, perhaps, or Warsaw."

Opotkin nodded. A move to another Communist country was more like a punishment.

Volodya said: "I'm glad we've been able to resolve this."

Opotkin said to Dimka: "I'm having a party on Saturday evening. Perhaps you would like to come?"

Dimka guessed this would seal the deal. He nodded. "Tanya told me about it," he said with false enthusiasm. "We'll both be there. Thank you."

Opotkin beamed.

Daniil said: "I happen to know of a post in a Communist country that's vacant right now. We need someone there urgently. She could go tomorrow."

"Where's that?" said Dimka.

"Cuba."

Opotkin, now in a sunny frame of mind, said: "That might be acceptable."

It was certainly better than Kazakhstan, Dimka thought.

Mets reappeared in the lobby with Tanya beside him. Dimka's heart lurched: she looked pale and scared, but unharmed. Mets spoke with a mixture of deference and defiance, like a dog that barks because it is frightened. "Allow me to suggest that young Tanya stay away from poetry readings in future," he said.

Uncle Volodya looked as if he could strangle the fool, but he put on a smile. "Very sound advice, I'm sure."

They all went out. Darkness had fallen. Dimka said to Tanya: "I've got my bike—I'll take you home."

"Yes, please," she said. She obviously wanted to talk to Dimka.

Uncle Volodya could not read her mind as Dimka could, and he said: "Let me take you in my car—you look too shaken for a motorcycle ride."

To Volodya's surprise, Tanya said: "Thank you, Uncle, but I'll go with Dimka."

Volodya shrugged and got into a waiting ZIL limousine. Daniil and Opotkin said good-bye.

As soon as they were all out of earshot, Tanya turned to Dimka with a frantic look. "Did they say anything about Vasili Yenkov?"

"Yes. They said you were with him. Is that true?"

"Yes."

"Oh, shit. But he's not your boyfriend, is he?"

"No. Do you know what happened to him?"

"He had five copies of *Dissidence* in his pocket, so he's not getting out of the Lubyanka soon, even if he has friends in high places."

"Hell! Do you think they will investigate him?"

"I'm sure of it. They'll want to know whether he merely hands out *Dissidence,* or actually produces it, which would be much more serious."

"Will they search his flat?"

"They would be remiss if they didn't. Why—what will they find there?"

She looked around, but no one was near. All the same she lowered her voice. "The typewriter on which *Dissidence* is written."

"Then I'm glad that Vasili isn't your boyfriend, because he's going to spend the next twenty-five years in Siberia."

"Don't say that!"

Dimka frowned. "You're not in love with him, I can tell . . . but you're not wholly indifferent to him, either."

"Look, he's a brave man, and a wonderful poet, but our relationship is not a romance. I've never even kissed him. He's one of those men who has to have lots of different women."

"Like my friend Valentin." Dimka's roommate at university, Valentin Lebedev, had been a real Lothario.

"Exactly like Valentin, yes."

"So . . . how much do you care if they search Vasili's apartment and find this typewriter?"

"A lot. We produced *Dissidence* together. I wrote today's edition."

"Shit. I was afraid of that." Now Dimka knew the secret she had been keeping from him for the past year.

Tanya said: "We have to go to the apartment, now, and take that typewriter and get rid of it."

Dimka took a step back from her. "Absolutely not. Forget it."

"We must!"

"No. I'd risk anything for you, and I might risk a lot for someone you loved, but I'm not going to stick my neck out for this guy. We could all end up in fucking Siberia."

"I'll do it on my own, then."

Dimka frowned, trying to evaluate the risks of different actions. "Who else knows about you and Vasili?"

"No one. We were careful. I made sure I wasn't followed when I went to his place. We never met in public."

"So the KGB investigation will not link you to him."

She hesitated, and at that point he knew they were in deep trouble.

"What?" he said.

"It depends how thorough the KGB are."

"Why?"

"This morning, when I went to Vasili's flat, there was a girl there— Varvara."

"Oh, fuck."

"She was just going out. She doesn't know my name."

"But, if the KGB shows her photographs of people arrested at Mayakovsky Square today, will she pick you out?"

Tanya looked distraught. "She gave me a real up-and-down look, assuming I might be a rival. Yes, she would know my face again."

"Oh, God, then we have to get the typewriter. Without that, they'll think Vasili is no more than a distributor of *Dissidence*, so they probably won't track down his every casual girlfriend, especially as there seem to be a lot. You may get away with it. But if they find the typewriter, you're finished."

"I'll do it alone. You're right, I can't put you in this much danger."

"But I can't leave you in this much danger," he said. "What's the address?"

She told him.

"Not too far," he said. "Get on the bike." He climbed on and kicked the engine into life.

Tanya hesitated, then got on behind him.

Dimka switched on the headlight and they pulled away.

As he drove, he wondered if the KGB might already be at Vasili's place, searching the apartment. It was a possibility, he decided, but unlikely. Assuming they had arrested forty or fifty people, it would take them most of the night to do initial interviews, get names and addresses, and decide whom to prioritize. All the same, it would be wise to be cautious.

When he reached the address Tanya had given him he drove past it without slowing down. The streetlights showed a grand nineteenth-century house. All such buildings were now either converted to government offices or divided into apartments. There were no cars parked outside and no leather-coated KGB men lurking at the entrance. He drove all around the block without seeing anything suspicious. Then he parked a couple of hundred yards from the door.

They got off the bike. A woman walking a dog said: "Good evening," and passed on. They went into the building.

Its lobby had once been an imposing hall. Now a lone electric bulb revealed a marble floor that was chipped and scratched, and a grand staircase with several balusters missing from the banister.

They went up the stairs. Tanya took out a key and opened the apartment door. They stepped inside and closed the door.

Tanya led the way into the living room. A gray cat observed them warily. Tanya took a large box from a cupboard. It was half full of cat food pellets. She rummaged inside and pulled out a typewriter in a cover. Then she withdrew some sheets of stencil paper.

She ripped up the sheets of paper, threw them in the fireplace, and put a match to them. Watching them burn, Dimka said angrily: "Why the hell do you risk everything for the sake of an empty protest?"

"We live in a brutal tyranny," she said. "We have to do something to keep hope alive."

"We live in a society that is developing Communism," Dimka rejoined. "It's difficult and we have problems. But you should help solve those problems instead of inflaming discontent."

"How can you have solutions if no one is allowed to talk about the problems?"

"In the Kremlin we talk about the problems all the time."

"And the same few narrow-minded men always decide not to make any major changes."

"They're not all narrow-minded. Some are working hard to change things. Give us time."

"The revolution was forty years ago. How much time do you need before you finally admit that Communism is a failure?"

The sheets in the fireplace had quickly burned to black ashes. Dimka turned away in frustration. "We've had this argument so many times. We need to get out of here." He picked up the typewriter.

Tanya scooped up the cat and they went out.

As they were leaving, a man with a briefcase came into the lobby. He nodded as he passed them on the stairs. Dimka hoped the light was too dim for him to have seen their faces properly.

Outside the door, Tanya put the cat down on the pavement. "You're on your own, now, Mademoiselle," she said.

The cat walked off disdainfully.

They hurried along the street to the corner, Dimka trying ineffectually to conceal the typewriter under his jacket. The moon had risen, to his dismay, and they were clearly visible. They reached the motorcycle.

Dimka handed her the typewriter. "How are we going to get rid of it?" he whispered.

"The river?"

He racked his brains, then recalled a spot on the riverbank where he and some fellow students had gone, a couple of times, to stay up all night drinking vodka. "I know somewhere."

They got on the bike and Dimka drove out of the city center toward the south. The place he had in mind was on the outskirts of the city, but that was all to the good: they were less likely to be noticed.

He drove fast for twenty minutes and pulled up outside the Nikolo-Perervinsky Monastery.

The ancient institution, with its magnificent cathedral, was now a ruin, disused for decades and stripped of its treasures. It was located on a neck of land between the main southbound railway line and the Moskva River. The fields around it were being turned into building sites for new high-rise apartment buildings, but at night the neighborhood was deserted. There was no one in sight.

Dimka wheeled the bike off the road into a clump of trees and parked it on its stand. Then he led Tanya through the copse to the ruined monastery. The derelict buildings were eerily white in the moonlight. The onion domes of the cathedral were falling in, but the green tiled roofs of the monastery buildings were mostly intact. Dimka could not shake the feeling that the ghosts of generations of monks were watching him through the smashed windows.

He headed west across a swampy field to the river.

Tanya said: "How do you know about this place?"

"We came here when we were students. We used to get drunk and watch the sun rise over the water."

They reached the edge of the river. This was a sluggish channel in a wide bend, and the water was placid in the moonlight. But Dimka knew it was deep enough for the purpose.

Tanya hesitated. "What a waste," she said.

Dimka shrugged. "Typewriters are expensive."

"It's not just money. It's a dissident voice, an alternative view of the world, a different way of thinking. A typewriter is freedom of speech."

"Then you're better off without it."

She handed it to him.

He moved the roller rightward to its maximum extension, giving himself a handle by which to hold the machine. "Here goes," he said. He swung his arm back, then with all his might he flung the typewriter out over the river. It did not go far, but it landed with a satisfying splash and immediately disappeared from sight.

They both stood and watched the ripples in the moonlight.

"Thank you," said Tanya. "Especially as you don't believe in what I'm doing."

He put his arm around her shoulders, and together they walked away.

George Jakes was in a sour mood. His arm still hurt like hell although it was encased in plaster and supported by a sling around his neck. He had lost his coveted job before starting it: just as Greg had predicted, the law firm of Fawcett Renshaw had withdrawn its offer after he appeared in the newspapers as an injured Freedom Rider. Now he did not know what he was going to do with the rest of his life.

The graduation ceremony, called commencement, was held in Harvard University's Old Yard, a grassy plaza surrounded by gracious redbrick university buildings. Members of the Board of Overseers wore top hats and cutaway tailcoats. Honorary degrees were presented to the British foreign secretary, a chinless aristocrat called Lord Home, and to the oddly named McGeorge Bundy, one of President Kennedy's White House team. Despite his mood, George felt a mild sadness at leaving Harvard. He had been here seven years, first as an undergraduate, then as a law student. He had met some extraordinary people, and made a few good friends. He had passed every exam he took. He had dated many women and slept with three. He had got drunk once, and hated the feeling of being out of control.

But today he was too angry to indulge in nostalgia. After the mob violence in Anniston, he had expected a strong response from the Kennedy administration. Jack Kennedy had presented himself to the American people as a liberal, and had won the black vote. Bobby Kennedy was attorney general, the highest law enforcement officer in the land. George had expected Bobby to say, loud and clear, that the Constitution of the United States was in force in Alabama the same as everywhere else.

He had not.

No one had been arrested for attacking the Freedom Riders. Neither the local police nor the FBI had investigated any of the many violent crimes that had been committed. In America in 1961, while the police looked on, white racists could attack civil rights protesters, break their bones, try to burn them to death—and get away with it.

George had last seen Maria Summers in a doctor's office. The wounded Freedom Riders had been turned away from the nearest hospital, but eventually they had found people willing to treat them. George had been with a nurse, having his broken arm treated, when Maria had come to say that she had got a flight to Chicago. He would have got up and thrown his arms around her if he could. As it was she had kissed his cheek and vanished.

He wondered if he would ever see her again. I could have fallen hard for her, he thought. Maybe I already did. In ten days of nonstop conversation he had never once felt bored: she was at least as smart as he was, maybe smarter. And although she seemed innocent, she had velvet brown eyes that made him picture her in candlelight.

The commencement ceremony came to an end at eleven thirty. Students, parents, and alumni began to drift away through the shadows of the tall elms, heading for the formal lunches at which graduating students would be given their degrees. George looked out for his family but did not at first see them.

However, he did see Joseph Hugo.

Hugo was alone, standing by the bronze statue of John Harvard, lighting one of his long cigarettes. In the black ceremonial robe his white skin looked even more pasty. George clenched his fists. He wanted to beat the crap out of that rat. But his left arm was useless and, anyway, if he and Hugo had a fistfight in the Old Yard, today of all days, there would be hell to pay. They might even lose their degrees. George was already in enough trouble. He would be wise to ignore Hugo and walk on.

Instead he said: "Hugo, you piece of shit."

Hugo looked scared, despite George's injured arm. He was the same size as George, and probably as strong, but George had rage on his side, and Joseph knew it. He looked away and tried to walk around George, muttering: "I don't wish to speak to you."

"I'm not surprised." George moved to stand in his way. "You watched while a crazed mob attacked me. Those thugs broke my goddamned arm."

Hugo took a step back. "You had no business going to Alabama."

"And you had no business pretending to be a civil rights activist when all the time you were spying for the other side. Who was paying you, the Ku Klux Klan?"

Hugo lifted his chin defensively, and George wanted to punch it. "I volunteered to give information to the FBI," Hugo said.

"So you did it without pay! I don't know whether that makes it better or worse."

"But I won't be a volunteer much longer. I start work for the Bureau next week." He said it in the half-embarrassed, half-defiant tone of someone admitting that he belongs to a religious sect.

"You were such a good snitch that they gave you a job."

"I always wanted to work in law enforcement."

"That's not what you were doing in Anniston. You were on the side of the criminals there."

"You people are Communists. I've heard you talking about Karl Marx."

"And Hegel, and Voltaire, and Gandhi, and Jesus Christ. Come on, Hugo, even you aren't that stupid."

"I hate disorder."

And that was the problem, George reflected bitterly. People hated disorder. Press coverage had blamed the Riders for stirring up trouble, not the segregationists with their baseball bats and their bombs. It drove him mad with frustration: did no one in America think about what was *right*?

Across the grass he spotted Verena Marquand, waving at him. He abruptly lost interest in Joseph Hugo.

Verena was graduating from the English Department. However, there were so few people of color at Harvard that they all knew one another. And she was so gorgeous that he would have noticed her if she had been one of a thousand colored girls at Harvard. She had green eyes and skin the color of toffee ice cream. Under her robe she was wearing a green dress with a short skirt that showed off long, smooth legs. The mortarboard was perched on her head at a cute angle. She was dynamite.

People said she and George were a good match, but they had never dated. Whenever he had been unattached, she had been in a relationship, and vice versa. Now it was too late.

Verena was an ardent civil rights campaigner, and was going to work for Martin Luther King in Atlanta after graduation. Now she said enthusiastically: "You really started something with that Freedom Ride!"

It was true. After the firebombing at Anniston, George had left Alabama by plane with his arm in plaster; but others had taken up the challenge. Ten students from Nashville had caught a bus to Birmingham, where they had been arrested. New Riders had replaced the first group. There had been more mob violence by white racists. Freedom Riding had become a mass movement.

"But I lost my job," George said.

"Come to Atlanta and work for King," Verena said immediately.

George was startled. "Did he tell you to ask me?"

"No, but he needs a lawyer, and no one half as bright as you has applied."

George was intrigued. He had almost fallen in love with Maria Summers, but he would do well to forget her: he would probably never see her again. He wondered whether Verena would go out with him if they were both working for King. "That's an idea," he said. But he wanted to think about it.

He changed the subject. "Are your folks here today?"

"Of course, come and meet them."

Verena's parents were celebrity supporters of Kennedy. George was hoping they would now come out and criticize the president for his feeble reaction to segregationist violence. Perhaps George and Verena together could persuade them to make a public statement. That would do a lot to ease the pain of his arm.

He walked across the lawn beside Verena.

"Mom, Dad, this is my friend George Jakes," said Verena.

Her parents were a tall, well-dressed black man and a white woman with an elaborate blond coiffure. George had seen their photographs many times: they were a famous interracial couple. Percy Marquand was "the Negro Bing Crosby," a movie star as well as a smooth crooner. Babe Lee was a theater actress specializing in gutsy female roles.

Percy spoke in a warm baritone familiar from a dozen hit records. "Mr. Jakes, down there in Alabama you took that broken arm for all of us. I'm honored to shake your hand."

"Thank you, sir, but please call me George."

Babe Lee held his hand and looked into his eyes as if she wanted to marry him. "We're so grateful to you, George, and proud, too." Her manner was so seductive that George glanced uneasily at her husband, thinking he might be angered, but neither Percy nor Verena showed any reaction, and George wondered whether Babe did this to every man she met.

As soon as he could free his hand from Babe's grasp, George turned to Percy. "I know you campaigned for Kennedy in the presidential election last year," he said. "Aren't you angry now about his record on civil rights?"

"We're all disappointed," Percy said.

Verena broke in. "I should think so! Bobby Kennedy asked the Riders for a cooling-off period. Can you imagine? Of course CORE refused. America is ruled by laws, not mobs!"

"A point that should have been made by the attorney general," George said.

Percy nodded, unperturbed by this two-person attack. "I hear the administration has made a deal with the Southern states," he said. George pricked up his ears: this had not been in the newspapers. "The state governors have agreed to restrain the mobs, which is what the Kennedy brothers want."

George knew that in politics no one ever gave something for nothing. "What was the quid pro quo?"

"The attorney general will turn a blind eye to the illegal arrest of Freedom Riders."

Verena was outraged, and irritated with her father. "I wish you had told me about this before, Daddy," she said sharply.

"I knew it would make you mad, honey."

Verena's face darkened at this condescension, and she looked away.

George concentrated on the key question: "Will you protest publicly, Mr. Marquand?"

"I've thought about it," said Percy. "But I don't think it would have much impact."

"It might influence black voters against Kennedy in 1964."

"Are we sure we want to do that? We'd all be worse off with someone like Dick Nixon in the White House."

Verena said indignantly: "Then what *can* we do?"

"What's happened in the South in the past month has proved, beyond doubt, that the law as it stands is too weak. We need a new civil rights bill."

George said: "Amen to that."

Percy went on: "I might be able to help make that happen. Right now I have a little influence in the White House. If I criticize the Kennedys I'll have none."

George felt Percy should speak out. Verena voiced the same thought. "You ought to say what's right," she said. "America is full of people being judicious. That's how we got into this mess."

Her mother was offended. "Your daddy is famous for saying what's right," she said indignantly. "He has stuck his neck out again and again."

George saw that Percy was not to be persuaded. But perhaps he was right. A new civil rights bill, making it impossible for the Southern states to oppress Negroes, might be the only real solution.

"I'd better find my folks," George said. "An honor to meet you both."

"Think about working for Martin," Verena called after him as he walked away.

He went to the park where law degrees would be presented. A temporary stage had been built, and trestle tables had been set up in tents for the lunch afterward. He found his parents right away.

His mother had a new yellow dress. She must have saved up for it: she was proud, and would not allow the rich Peshkovs to buy things for her, only for George. She looked him up and down, in his academic robe and mortarboard. "This is the happiest day of my life," she said. Then, to his astonishment, she burst into tears.

George was surprised. This was unusual. She had spent the last twenty-five years refusing to show weakness. He put his arms around her and hugged her. "I'm so lucky to have you, Mom," he said.

He detached himself gently from her embrace and blotted her tears with a clean white handkerchief. Then he turned to his father. Like most of the alumni, Greg was wearing a straw boater that had a hatband printed with the year of his graduation from Harvard—in his case, 1942. "Congratulations, my boy," he said, shaking George's hand. Well, George thought, he's here, which is something.

George's grandparents appeared a moment later. Both were Russian immigrants. His grandfather, Lev Peshkov, had started out running bars and nightclubs in Buffalo, and now owned a Hollywood studio. Grandfather had always been a dandy, and today he wore a white suit. George never knew what to think of him. People said he was a ruthless businessman with little respect for the law. On the other hand, he had been kind to his black grandson, giving him a generous allowance as well as paying his tuition.

Now he took George's arm and said confidentially: "I have one piece of advice for you in your law career. Don't represent criminals."

"Why not?"

"Because they're losers," Grandfather chuckled.

Lev Peshkov was widely believed to have been a criminal himself, a bootlegger in the days of Prohibition. George said: "Are *all* criminals losers?"

"The ones who get caught are," said Lev. "The rest don't need lawyers." He laughed heartily.

George's grandmother, Marga, kissed him warmly. "Don't you listen to your grandfather," she said.

"I have to listen," George said. "He paid for my education."

Lev pointed a finger at George. "I'm glad you don't forget that."

Marga ignored him. "Just look at you," she said to George in a voice full of affection. "So handsome, and a lawyer now!"

George was Marga's only grandchild, and she doted on him. She would probably slip him fifty bucks before the end of the afternoon.

Marga had been a nightclub singer, and at sixty-five she still moved as if she were going onstage in a slinky dress. Her black hair was probably dyed that color nowadays. She was wearing more jewelry than was appropriate for an outdoor occasion, George knew; but he guessed that as the mistress, rather than the wife, she felt the need for status symbols.

Marga had been Lev's lover for almost fifty years. Greg was the only child they had had together.

Lev also had a wife, Olga, in Buffalo, and a daughter, Daisy, who was married to an Englishman and lived in London. So George had English cousins he had never met—white, he assumed.

Marga kissed Jacky, and George noticed people nearby giving them looks of surprise and disapproval. Even at liberal Harvard it was unusual to see a white person embrace a Negro. But George's family always drew stares on the rare occasions when they all appeared in public together. Even in places where all races were accepted, a mixed family could still bring out white people's latent prejudices. He knew that before the end of the day he would hear someone mutter the word *mongrel.* He would ignore the insult. His black grandparents were long dead, and this was his entire family. To have these four people bursting with pride at his graduation was worth any price.

Greg said: "I had lunch with old Renshaw yesterday. I talked him into renewing Fawcett Renshaw's job offer."

Marga said: "Oh, that's wonderful! George, you'll be a Washington lawyer after all!"

Jacky gave Greg a rare smile. "Thank you, Greg," she said.

Greg lifted a warning finger. "There are conditions," he said.

Marga said: "Oh, George will agree to anything reasonable. This is such a great opportunity for him."

She meant *for a black kid,* George knew, but he did not protest. Anyway, she was right. "What conditions?" he said guardedly.

"Nothing that doesn't apply to every lawyer in the world," Greg replied. "You have to stay out of trouble, is all. A lawyer can't get on the wrong side of the authorities."

George was suspicious. "Stay out of trouble?"

"Just take no further part in any kind of protest movement, marches, demonstrations, like that. As a first-year associate, you'll have no time for that stuff anyway."

The proposal angered George. "So I would begin my working life by vowing never to do anything in the cause of freedom."

"Don't look at it that way," said his father.

George bit back an irate retort. His family only wanted what was best for him, he knew. Trying to keep his voice neutral, he said: "Which way should I look at it?"

"Your role in the civil rights movement won't be as a frontline soldier, that's all. Be a supporter. Send a check once a year to the NAACP." The National Association for the Advancement of Colored People was the oldest and most conservative civil rights group: they had opposed Freedom Rides as being too provocative. "Just keep your head down. Let someone else go on the bus."

"There might be another way," said George.

"What's that?"

"I could work for Martin Luther King."

"Has he offered you a job?"

"I've received an approach."

"What would he pay you?"

"Not much, I'm guessing."

Lev said: "Don't think you can turn down a perfectly good job, then come to me for an allowance."

"Okay, Grandfather," said George, although that was exactly what he had been thinking. "But I believe I'll take the job anyway."

His mother joined the argument. "Oh, George, don't," she said. She was going to say more, but the graduating students were called to line up for their degrees. "Go," she said. "We'll talk more later."

George left the family group and found his place in line. The ceremony began, and he shuffled forward. He recalled working at Fawcett Renshaw last summer. Mr. Renshaw had thought himself heroically liberal for hiring a black law clerk. But George had been given work that was demeaningly easy even for an intern. He had been patient and looked for an opportunity, and one had come. He had done a piece of legal research that won a case for the firm, and they had offered him a job on graduation.

This kind of thing happened to him a lot. The world assumed that a student at Harvard must be intelligent and capable—unless he was black, in which case all bets were off. All his life George had had to prove that he was not an idiot. It made him resentful. If he ever had children, his hope was that they would grow up in a different world.

His turn came to go onstage. As he mounted the short flight of steps, he was astonished to hear hissing.

Hissing was a Harvard tradition, normally used against professors who lectured badly or were rude to students. George was so horrified that he paused on the steps and looked back. He caught the eye of Joseph Hugo. Hugo was not the only one—the hissing was too loud for that—but George felt sure Hugo had orchestrated this.

George felt hated. He was too humiliated to mount the stage. He stood there, frozen, and the blood rushed to his face.

Then someone began clapping. Looking across the rows of seats, George saw a professor standing up. It was Merv West, one of the younger faculty. Others joined him in applauding, and they quickly drowned out the hissing. Several more people stood up. George imagined that even people who did not know him had guessed who he was by the plaster cast on his arm.

He found his courage again and walked onto the stage. A cheer went up as he was handed his certificate. He turned slowly to face the audience and acknowledged the applause with a modest bow of his head. Then he went off.

His heart was hammering as he joined the other students. Several men shook his hand silently. He was horrified by the hissing, and at the same time elated by the applause. He realized he was perspiring, and he wiped his face with a handkerchief. What an ordeal.

He watched the rest of the ceremony in a daze, glad to have time to recover. As the shock of the hissing wore off, he could see that it had been done by Hugo and a handful of right-wing lunatics, and the rest of liberal Harvard had honored him. He should feel proud, he told himself.

The students rejoined their families for lunch. George's mother hugged him. "They cheered you," she said.

"Yes," Greg said. "Though for a moment there it looked as if it was going to be something else."

George spread his hands in a gesture of appeal. "How can I not be part of this struggle?" he said. "I really want the job at Fawcett Renshaw, and I want to please the family that has supported me through all these years of education—but that's not all. What if I have children?"

Marga put in: "That would be nice!"

"But, Grandmother, my children will be colored. What kind of world will they grow up in? Will they be second-class Americans?"

The conversation was interrupted by Merv West, who shook George's hand and congratulated him on getting his degree. Professor West was a little underdressed in a tweed suit and a button-down collar.

George said: "Thank you for starting the applause, Professor."

"Don't thank me, you deserved it."

George introduced his family. "We were just talking about my future."

"I hope you haven't made any final decisions."

George's curiosity was piqued. What did that mean? "Not yet," he said. "Why?"

"I've been talking to the attorney general, Bobby Kennedy—a Harvard graduate, as you know."

"I hope you told him that his handling of what happened in Alabama was a national disgrace."

West smiled regretfully. "Not in those words, not quite. But he and I agreed that the administration's response was inadequate."

"Very. I can't imagine he . . ." George trailed off as he was struck by a thought. "What does this have to do with decisions about my future?"

"Bobby has decided to hire a young black lawyer to give the attorney general's team a Negro perspective on civil rights. And he asked me if there was anyone I could recommend."

George was momentarily stunned. "Are you saying . . ."

West raised a warning hand. "I'm not offering you the job—only Bobby can do that. But I can get you an interview . . . if you want it."

Jacky said: "George! A job with Bobby Kennedy! That would be fantastic."

"Mother, the Kennedys have let us down so badly."

"Then go to work for Bobby and change things!"

George hesitated. He looked at the eager faces around him: his mother, his father, his grandmother, his grandfather, and back to his mother again.

"Maybe I will," he said at last.

CHAPTER EIGHT

D imka Dvorkin was abashed to be a virgin at the age of twenty-two.

He had dated several girls while at university, but none of them had let him go all the way. Anyway, he was not sure he should. No one had actually told him that sex should be part of a long-term loving relationship, but he sort of felt it anyway. He had never been in a frantic hurry to do it, the way some boys were. However, his lack of experience was now becoming an embarrassment.

His friend Valentin Lebedev was the opposite. Tall and confident, he had black hair and blue eyes and buckets of charm. By the end of their first year at Moscow State University he had bedded most of the girl students in the Politics Department and one of the teachers.

Early on in their friendship, Dimka had said to him: "What do you do about, you know, avoiding pregnancy?"

"That's the girl's problem, isn't it?" Valentin had said carelessly. "Worse comes to the worst, it's not that difficult to get an abortion."

Talking to others, Dimka found out that many Soviet boys took the same attitude. Men did not get pregnant, so it was not their problem. And abortion was available on demand during the first twelve weeks. But Dimka could not get comfortable with Valentin's approach, perhaps because his sister was so scornful about it.

Sex was Valentin's main interest, and studying took second place. With Dimka it had been the other way around—which was why Dimka was now an aide in the Kremlin and Valentin worked for the Moscow City Parks Department.

It was through his connections in Parks that Valentin had been able to arrange for the two of them to spend a week at the V. I. Lenin Holiday Camp for Young Communists in July 1961.

The camp was a bit military, with tents pitched in ruler-straight rows and a curfew at ten thirty, but it had a swimming pool and a boating lake and loads of girls, and a week there was a privilege much sought after.

Dimka felt he deserved a holiday. The Vienna Summit had been a victory for the Soviet Union, and he shared the credit.

Vienna had actually begun badly for Khrushchev. Kennedy and his dazzling wife had entered Vienna in a fleet of limousines flying dozens of stars-and-stripes flags. When the two leaders met, television viewers all over the world saw that Kennedy was several inches taller, towering over Khrushchev, looking down his patrician nose at the bald top of Khrushchev's head. Kennedy's tailored jackets and skinny ties made Khrushchev look like a farmer in his Sunday suit. America had won a glamour contest that the Soviet Union had not even known it was entering.

But once the talks began, Khrushchev had dominated. When Kennedy tried to have an amiable discussion, as between two reasonable men, Khrushchev became loudly aggressive. Kennedy suggested it was not logical for the Soviet Union to encourage Communism in Third World countries, then protest indignantly about American efforts to roll back Communism in the Soviet sphere. Khrushchev replied scornfully that the spread of Communism was a historic inevitability, and nothing that either leader did could stand in its way. Kennedy's grasp of Marxist philosophy was weak, and he had not known what to say.

The strategy developed by Dimka and other advisers had triumphed. When Khrushchev returned to Moscow he ordered dozens of copies of the summit minutes to be distributed, not only to the Soviet bloc, but to the leaders of countries as far away as Cambodia and Mexico. Since then Kennedy had been silent, not even responding to Khrushchev's threat to take over West Berlin. And Dimka went on holiday.

On the first day Dimka put on his new clothes, a checked short-sleeved shirt and a pair of shorts his mother had sewn from the trousers of a worn-out blue serge suit. "Are shorts like that fashionable in the West?" Valentin said.

Dimka laughed. "Not as far as I know."

While Valentin was shaving, Dimka went for supplies.

When he emerged he was pleased to see, right next door, a young woman lighting the small portable stove that was provided with each tent. She was a little older than Dimka; he guessed twenty-seven. She had thick red-brown hair cut in a bob, and an attractive scatter of freckles. She looked alarmingly fashionable in an orange blouse and a pair of tight black pants that ended just below the knee.

"Hello!" Dimka said with a smile. She looked up at him. He said: "Do you need a hand with that?"

She lit the gas with a match, then went inside her tent without speaking.

Well, I'm not going to lose my virginity with her, Dimka thought, and he walked on.

He bought eggs and bread in the store next to the communal bathroom block. When he got back there were two girls outside the next tent: the one he had spoken to, and a pretty blonde with a trim figure. The blonde wore the same style of black pants, but with a pink blouse. Valentin was talking to them, and they were laughing.

He introduced them to Dimka. The redhead was called Nina, and she made no reference to their earlier encounter, though she still seemed reserved. The blonde was Anna, and she was obviously the outgoing one, smiling and pushing her hair back with a graceful gesture.

Dimka and Valentin had brought with them one iron saucepan in which they planned to do all the cooking, and Dimka had filled it with water to boil the eggs; but the girls were better equipped, and Nina took the eggs from him to make blinis.

Things were looking up, Dimka thought.

Dimka studied Nina while they ate. Her narrow nose, small mouth, and daintily protruding chin gave her a guarded look, as if she were perpetually weighing things up. But she was voluptuous, and when Dimka realized he might see her in a swimsuit, his throat went dry.

Valentin said: "Dimka and I are going to take a boat and row across to the other side of the lake." This was the first Dimka had heard of such a plan, but he said nothing. "Why don't the four of us go together?" Valentin went on. "We could take a picnic lunch."

It could not possibly be that easy, Dimka thought. They had only just met!

The girls looked at one another for a telepathic moment, then Nina said briskly: "We'll see. Let's clear away." She began to pick up plates and cutlery.

That was disappointing, but perhaps not the end of the matter.

Dimka volunteered to carry the dirty dishes to the bathroom block.

"Where did you get those shorts?" Nina asked while they were walking.

"My mother sewed them."

She laughed. "Sweet."

Dimka asked himself what his sister would have implied by calling a man sweet, and he decided it meant he was kind but not attractive.

A concrete blockhouse contained toilets, showers, and large communal sinks. Dimka watched while Nina washed the dishes. He tried to think of things to say, but nothing came. If she had asked him about the crisis in Berlin he could have talked all day. But he had no gift for the mildly amusing nonsense that Valentin produced in an effortless stream. Eventually he managed: "Have you and Anna been friends long?"

"We work together," she said. "We're both administrators at the steel union headquarters in Moscow. I got divorced a year ago, and Anna was looking for someone to share her apartment, so now we live together."

Divorced, Dimka thought; that meant she was sexually experienced. He felt intimidated. "What was your husband like?"

"He's a shit," said Nina. "I don't like talking about him."

"Okay." Dimka searched desperately for something bland to say. "Anna seems like a really nice person," he tried.

"She's well connected."

That seemed an odd remark to make about your friend. "How so?"

"Her father got us this holiday. He's Moscow district secretary of the union." Nina seemed proud of this.

Dimka carried the clean dishes back to the tents. When they arrived, Valentin said cheerily: "We've made sandwiches—ham and cheese." Anna looked at Nina and made a gesture of helplessness, as if to say that she had been unable to halt the Valentin steamroller; but it was clear to Dimka that she had not really wanted to. Nina shrugged, and so it was settled that they would picnic.

They had to stand in line an hour for a boat, but Muscovites were accustomed to queuing, and by late morning they were out on the clear, cold water. Valentin and Dimka took turns rowing, and the girls soaked up the sun. No one seemed to feel the need for small talk.

On the far side of the lake they tied up the boat at a small beach. Valentin pulled off his shirt, and Dimka followed suit. Anna took off her blouse and pants. Underneath she was wearing a sky blue two-piece swimsuit. Dimka knew it was called a bikini, and was fashionable in the West, but he had never actually seen one, and he was embarrassed by how aroused he felt. He could hardly take his eyes off her smooth, flat stomach and her navel.

To his disappointment, Nina kept her clothes on.

They ate their sandwiches, and Valentin produced a bottle of vodka. No alcohol was sold in the camp store, Dimka knew. Valentin explained: "I bought it from the boat supervisor. He has a small capitalist enterprise going." Dimka was not surprised: most things people really wanted were sold on the black market, from television sets to blue jeans.

They passed the bottle around, and both girls took a long swallow.

Nina wiped her mouth on the back of her hand. "So, you two work together in the Parks Department?"

"No," Valentin laughed. "Dimka's too clever for that."

Dimka said: "I work at the Kremlin."

Nina was impressed. "What do you do?"

Dimka did not really like to say, because it sounded like boasting. "I'm an assistant to the first secretary."

"You mean to Comrade Khrushchev!" Nina said in astonishment.

"Yes."

"How the hell did you get a job like that?"

Valentin put in: "I told you, he's smart. He was top of every class."

"You don't land a job like that just by getting top marks," Nina said crisply. "Who do you know?"

"My grandfather, Grigori Peshkov, stormed the Winter Palace in the October Revolution."

"That doesn't get you a good job."

"Well, my father was in the KGB—he died last year. My uncle is a general. *And* I'm smart."

"Modest, too," she said, but her sarcasm was genial. "What's your uncle's name?"

"Vladimir Peshkov. We call him Volodya."

"I've heard of General Peshkov. So he's your uncle. With a family like that, how come you wear homemade shorts?"

Dimka was confused now. She was interested in him for the first time, but he could not make out whether she was admiring or scornful. Perhaps it was just her manner.

Valentin stood up. "Come and explore with me," he said to Anna. "We'll leave these two here to discuss Dimka's shorts." He held out his hand. Anna took it and let him pull her to her feet. Then they walked off into the woods, holding hands.

"Your friend doesn't like me," said Nina.

"He likes Anna, though."

"She's pretty."

Dimka said quietly: "You're beautiful." He had not planned to say it: it just came out. But he meant it.

Nina looked at him thoughtfully, as if reappraising him. Then she said: "Do you want to swim?"

Dimka did not care much for water, but he was keen to see her in her swimsuit. He pulled off his clothes: he was wearing swimming trunks under his shorts.

Nina had on a brown nylon one-piece, rather than a bikini, but she filled it out so well that Dimka was not disappointed. She was the opposite of slim Anna. Nina had deep breasts and wide hips, and there were freckles on her throat. She saw his gaze on her body, and she turned away and ran into the water.

Dimka followed.

It was bitingly cold despite the sun, yet Dimka enjoyed the sensual feel of the water all over his body. They both swam energetically to keep warm. They went out into the lake, then returned more slowly to the shore. They stopped short of the beach, and Dimka let his feet drift to the bottom. The water came to their waists. Dimka looked at Nina's breasts. The cold water made her nipples stick out, showing through her swimsuit.

"Stop staring," she said, and playfully splashed his face.

He splashed her back.

"Right!" she said, and grabbed his head, trying to duck him.

Dimka struggled and caught her around the waist. They wrestled in the water. Nina's body was heavy but firm, and he relished its solidity. He got both arms around her and lifted her feet off the bottom. When she thrashed, laughing and trying to free herself, he pulled her more firmly to him, and felt her soft breasts pressing against his face.

"I give in!" she yelled.

Reluctantly he put her down. For a moment they looked at one another. In her eyes he saw a gleam of desire. Something had changed her attitude to him: the vodka, the realization that he was a high-powered apparatchik, the exhilaration of horseplay in the water, or perhaps all three. He hardly cared. He saw the invitation in her smile, and kissed her mouth.

She kissed him back with enthusiasm.

He forgot the cold water, lost in the sensations of her lips and tongue, but after a few minutes she shivered and said: "Let's get out."

He held her hand as they waded through the shallows onto dry ground. They lay on the grass side by side and started kissing again. Dimka touched her breasts, and began to wonder whether this was the day he would lose his virginity.

Then they were interrupted by a harsh voice speaking through a megaphone: "Return your boat to the dock! Your time is up!"

Nina murmured: "It's the sex police."

Dimka chuckled, despite his disappointment.

He looked up to see a small rubber dinghy with an outboard motor passing a hundred yards offshore.

He waved acknowledgment. They were supposed to keep the boat for two hours. He guessed that a bribe to the supervisor would have secured an extension but he had not thought of it. Indeed, he had hardly dreamed that his relationship with Nina would progress so fast.

"We can't go back without the others," Nina said; but a moment later Valentin and Anna emerged from the woods. They had been only just out of sight, Dimka guessed, and had heard the megaphone summons.

The boys moved a little apart from the girls and they all put on their outer clothes over their swimsuits. Dimka heard Nina and Anna talking in low voices, Anna speaking urgently and Nina giggling and nodding agreement.

Then Anna gave Valentin a meaningful look. It seemed to be a prearranged signal. Valentin nodded and turned to Dimka. Quietly he said: "The four of us are going to the folk-dancing evening tonight. When we come back, Anna will come into our tent with me. You're to go with Nina in their tent. Okay?"

It was more than okay, it was thrilling. Dimka said: "You've arranged it all with Anna?"

"Yes, and Nina has just agreed."

Dimka could hardly believe it. He would be able to spend all night embracing Nina's firm body. "She likes me!"

"Must be the shorts."

They got into the boat and rowed back. The girls announced that they wanted to shower as soon as they returned. Dimka wondered how he could make the time pass quickly until evening.

When they reached the dock, they saw a man in a black suit waiting.

Dimka knew instinctively that this was a messenger for him. I might have known, he thought regretfully; things were going too well.

They all got out of the boat. Nina looked at the man sweating in his suit and said: "Are we going to be arrested for keeping the boat too long?" She was only half joking.

Dimka said: "Are you here for me? I'm Dmitri Dvorkin."

"Yes, Dmitri Ilich," the man said, respectfully using his patronymic. "I'm your driver. I'm here to take you to the airport."

"What's the emergency?"

The driver shrugged. "The first secretary wants you."

"I'll get my bag," said Dimka regretfully.

By way of a small consolation, Nina looked awestruck.

· · ·

The car took Dimka to Vnukovo airport, southwest of Moscow, where Vera Pletner was waiting with a large envelope and a ticket to Tbilisi, capital of the Georgian Soviet Socialist Republic.

Khrushchev was not in Moscow but at his dacha, or second home, in Pitsunda, a resort for top government officials on the Black Sea, and that was where Dimka was headed.

He had never flown before.

He was not the only aide whose holiday had been cut short. In the departure lounge, about to open the envelope, he was approached by Yevgeny Filipov, wearing a gray flannel shirt as usual despite the summer weather. Filipov looked pleased, which had to be a bad sign.

"Your strategy has failed," he said to Dimka with evident satisfaction.

"What's happened?"

"President Kennedy has made a television speech."

Kennedy had said nothing for seven weeks, since the Vienna Summit. The United States had not responded to Khrushchev's threat to sign a treaty with East Germany and take West Berlin back. Dimka had assumed that the American president was too cowed to stand up to Khrushchev. "What was the speech about?"

"He told the American people to prepare for war."

So that was the emergency.

They were called to board. Dimka said to Filipov: "What did Kennedy say, exactly?"

"Speaking of Berlin, he said: 'An attack upon that city will be regarded as an attack upon us all.' The full transcript is in your envelope."

They went on board, Dimka still wearing his holiday shorts. The plane was a Tupolev Tu-104 jetliner. Dimka looked out of the window as they took off. He knew how aircraft worked, the curved upper surface of the wing creating an air-pressure difference, but all the same it seemed like magic when the plane lifted into the air.

At last he tore his gaze away and opened the envelope.

Filipov had not exaggerated.

Kennedy was not merely making threatening noises. He proposed to triple the draft, call up reservists, and increase the American army to a million men. He was preparing a new Berlin airlift, moving six divisions to Europe, and planning economic sanctions on Warsaw Pact countries.

And he had increased the military budget by more than three *billion* dollars.

Dimka realized that the strategy Khrushchev and his advisers had mapped out had failed catastrophically. They had all underestimated the handsome young president. He could not be bullied, after all.

What could Khrushchev do?

He might have to resign. No Soviet leader had ever done that—both

Lenin and Stalin had died in office—but there was a first time for everything in revolutionary politics.

Dimka read the speech twice and mulled it for the rest of the two-hour journey. There was only one alternative to Khrushchev's resignation, he thought: the leader could sack all his aides, take on new advisers, and reshuffle the Presidium, giving his enemies more power, as an acknowledgment that he had been wrong and a promise to seek wiser counsel in the future.

Either way, Dimka's short career in the Kremlin was over. Perhaps it had been too ambitious, he thought dismally. No doubt a more modest future awaited him.

He wondered whether the voluptuous Nina would still want to spend a night with him.

The flight landed at Tbilisi and a small military aircraft shuttled Dimka and Filipov to an airstrip on the coast.

Natalya Smotrov from the Foreign Ministry was waiting for them there. The humid seaside air had curled her hair, giving her a wanton air. "There's bad news from Pervukhin," she said as she drove them away from the plane. Mikhail Pervukhin was the Soviet ambassador to East Germany. "The flow of emigrants to the West has turned into a flood."

Filipov looked annoyed, probably because he had not received this news before Natalya. "What numbers are we talking about?"

"It's approaching a thousand people a day."

Dimka was flabbergasted. "A thousand a *day*?"

Natalya nodded. "Pervukhin says the East German government is no longer stable. The country is approaching collapse. There could be a popular uprising."

"You see?" Filipov said to Dimka. "This is what your policy has led to."

Dimka had no answer.

Natalya drove along the coast road to a forested peninsula and turned in at a massive iron gate in a long stucco wall. Set amid immaculate lawns was a white villa with a long balcony on the upper floor. Beside the house was a full-size swimming pool. Dimka had never seen a home with its own pool.

"He's down by the sea," a guard told Dimka, jerking his head toward the far side of the house.

Dimka found his way through the trees to a shingle beach. A soldier with a submachine gun looked hard at him, then waved him on.

He found Khrushchev under a palm tree. The second-most powerful man in the world was short, fat, bald, and ugly. He wore the trousers of a suit, held up by suspenders, and a white shirt with the sleeves rolled. He was sitting on a wicker beach chair, and on a small table in front of him were a jug of water and a glass tumbler. He seemed to be doing nothing.

He looked at Dimka and said: "Where did you get those shorts?"

"My mother made them."

"I should have a pair of shorts."

Dimka said the words he had rehearsed. "Comrade First Secretary, I offer you my immediate resignation."

Khrushchev ignored that. "We will overtake the United States, in military might and economic prosperity, within the next twenty years," he said, as if he were continuing an ongoing discussion. "But, meanwhile, how do we prevent the stronger power from dominating global politics and holding back the spread of world Communism?"

"I don't know," said Dimka.

"Watch this," said Khrushchev. "I am the Soviet Union." He picked up the jug and poured water slowly into the glass until it was full to the brim. Then he handed the jug to Dimka. "You are the United States," he said. "Now you pour water into the glass."

Dimka did as he was told. The glass overflowed, and water soaked into the white tablecloth.

"You see?" said Khrushchev as if he had proved a point. "When the glass is full, no more can be added without making a mess."

Dimka was mystified. He asked the expected question. "What's the significance of this, Nikita Sergeyevich?"

"International politics is like a glass. Aggressive moves by either side pour water in. The overflow is war."

Dimka saw the point. "When tension is at its maximum, no one can make a move without causing a war."

"Well done. And the Americans do not want war, any more than we do. So, if we maintain international tension at the maximum—full to the brim—the American president is helpless. He cannot do anything without causing war, so he must do nothing!"

Dimka realized this was brilliant. It showed how the weaker power could dominate. "So Kennedy is now powerless?" he said.

"Because his next move is war!"

Had this been Khrushchev's long-term plan? Dimka wondered. Or had he just made it up as a hindsight justification? He was nothing if not an improviser. But it hardly mattered. "So, what are we going to do about the crisis in Berlin?" he said.

"We're going to build a wall," said Khrushchev.

CHAPTER NINE

George Jakes took Verena Marquand to the Jockey Club for lunch. It was not a club, but a swanky new restaurant in the Fairfax Hotel that had found favor with the Kennedy crowd. George and Verena were the best-dressed couple in the room, she ravishing in a gingham check frock with a wide red belt, he in a tailored dark blue linen blazer with a striped tie. Nevertheless, they were given a table by the kitchen door. Washington was integrated, but not unprejudiced. George did not let it get to him.

Verena was in town with her parents. They had been invited to the White House later today for a cocktail party being given to thank high-profile supporters such as the Marquands—and, George knew, to keep their goodwill for the next campaign.

Verena looked around appreciatively. "It's a long time since I was in a decent restaurant," she said. "Atlanta is a desert." With parents who were Hollywood stars, she had been raised to think lavish was normal.

"You should move here," George told her, looking into her startling green eyes. The sleeveless dress showed off the perfection of her café-au-lait skin, and she surely knew it. If she were to move to Washington, he would ask her for a date.

George was trying to forget Maria Summers. He was dating Norine Latimer, a history graduate who worked as a secretary at the National Museum of American History. She was attractive and intelligent, but it was not working: he still thought about Maria all the time. Perhaps Verena might be a more effective cure.

He kept all that to himself, naturally. "You're out of the swim, all the way down there in Georgia," he said.

"Don't be so sure," she said. "I'm working for Martin Luther King. He's going to change America more than John F. Kennedy."

"That's because Dr. King has only one issue, civil rights. The president has a hundred. He's the defender of the free world. Right now his major worry is Berlin."

"Curious, isn't it?" she said. "He believes in freedom and democracy for German people in East Berlin, but not for American Negroes in the South."

George smiled. She was always combative. "It's not just about what he believes," he said. "It's what he can achieve."

She shrugged. "So how much difference can *you* make?"

"The Justice Department employs nine hundred and fifty lawyers. Before I arrived, only ten were black. Already I'm a ten percent improvement."

"So what have you achieved?"

"Justice is taking a tough line with the Interstate Commerce Commission. Bobby has asked them to ban segregation in the bus service."

"And what makes you think this ruling will be enforced any better than all the previous ones?"

"Not much, so far." George was frustrated, but he wanted to hide the full extent of that from Verena. "There's a guy called Dennis Wilson, a young white lawyer on Bobby's personal team, who sees me as a threat, and keeps me out of the really important meetings."

"How can he do that? You were hired by Robert Kennedy—doesn't he want your input?"

"I need to win Bobby's confidence."

"You're cosmetic," she said scornfully. "With you there, Bobby can tell the world he's got a Negro advising him on civil rights. He doesn't have to listen to you."

George feared she might be right, but he did not admit it. "That depends on me. I have to make him listen."

"Come to Atlanta," she said. "The job with Dr. King is still open."

George shook his head. "My career is here." He remembered what Maria had said, and repeated it. "Protesters can have a big impact but, in the end, it's governments that reshape the world."

"Some do, some don't," said Verena.

When they left, they found George's mother waiting in the hotel lobby. George had arranged to meet her here, but had not expected her to wait outside the restaurant. "Why didn't you join us?" he asked.

She ignored his question and spoke to Verena. "We met briefly at the Harvard commencement," she said. "How are you, Verena?" She was going out of her way to be polite, which was a sign, George knew, that she did not really like Verena.

George saw Verena to a taxi and kissed her cheek. "It was great to see you again," he said.

He and his mother went on foot, heading for the Justice Department. Jacky Jakes wanted to see where her son worked. George had arranged for her to visit on a quiet day, when Bobby Kennedy was at CIA headquarters at Langley, Virginia, seven or eight miles out of town.

Jacky had taken a day off work. She was dressed for the occasion in a hat and gloves, as if she were going to church. As they walked he said: "What do you think of Verena?"

"She's a beautiful girl," Jacky replied promptly.

"You'd like her politics," George said. "You and Khrushchev." He was exaggerating, but both Verena and Jacky were ultraliberal. "She thinks the Cubans have the right to be Communists if they want."

"And so they do," Jacky said, proving his point.

"So what don't you like?"

"Nothing."

"Mom, we men aren't very intuitive, but I've been studying you all my life, and I know when you have reservations."

She smiled and touched his arm affectionately. "You're attracted to her, and I can see why. She's irresistible. I don't want to badmouth a girl you like, but . . ."

"But what?"

"It might be difficult to be married to Verena. I get the feeling she considers her own inclinations first, last, and in between."

"You think she's selfish."

"We're all selfish. I think she's spoiled."

George nodded and tried not to be offended. His mother was probably right. "You don't need to worry," he said. "She's determined to stay down there in Atlanta."

"Well, perhaps that's for the best. I only want you to be happy."

The Department of Justice was housed in a grand classical building across the street from the White House. Jacky seemed to swell a little with pride as they walked in. It pleased her that her son worked in such a prestigious place. George enjoyed her reaction. She was entitled: she had devoted her life to him, and this was her reward.

They entered the Great Hall. Jacky liked the famous murals showing scenes of American life, but she looked askance at the aluminum statue *Spirit of Justice*, which depicted a woman showing one breast. "I'm not a prude, but I don't see why Justice has to have her bosom uncovered," she said. "What's the reason for that?"

George considered. "To show that Justice has nothing to hide?"

She laughed. "Nice try."

They went up in the elevator. "How is your arm?" Jacky asked.

The plaster was off, and George no longer needed a sling. "It still hurts," he said. "I find it helps to keep my left hand in my pocket. Gives the arm a little support."

They got off at the fifth floor. George took Jacky to the room he shared with Dennis Wilson and several others. The attorney general's office was next door.

Dennis was at his desk near the door. He was a pale man whose blond hair was receding prematurely. George said to him: "When's he coming back?"

Dennis knew he meant Bobby. "Not for an hour, at least."

George said to his mother: "Come and see Bobby Kennedy's office."

"Are you sure it's okay?"

"He's not there. He wouldn't mind."

George led Jacky through an anteroom, nodding to two secretaries, and into the attorney general's office. It looked more like the drawing room of a large country house, with walnut paneling, a massive stone fireplace, patterned carpet and curtains, and lamps on occasional tables. It was a huge room, but Bobby had managed to make it look cluttered. The furnishings included an aquarium and a stuffed tiger. His enormous desk was a litter of papers, ashtrays, and family photographs. On a shelf behind the desk chair were four telephones.

Jacky said: "Remember that place by Union Station where we lived when you were a little boy?"

"Of course I do."

"You could fit the whole house in here."

George looked around. "You could, I guess."

"And that desk is bigger than the bed where you and I used to sleep until you were four."

"Both of us and the dog, too."

On the desk was a green beret, headgear of the U.S. Army Special Forces that Bobby admired so much. But Jacky was more interested in the photographs. George picked up a framed picture of Bobby and Ethel sitting on a lawn in front of a big house, surrounded by their seven children. "This is taken outside Hickory Hill, their home in McLean, Virginia." He handed it to her.

"I like that," she said, studying the photo. "He cares for his family."

A confident voice with a Boston accent said: "Who cares for his family?"

George spun round to see Bobby Kennedy walking into the room. He wore a crumpled light gray summer suit. His tie was loose and his shirt collar unbuttoned. He was not as handsome as his older brother, mainly because of his large rabbity front teeth.

George was flustered. "I'm sorry, sir," he said. "I thought you were out for the afternoon."

"That's all right," said Bobby, though George was not sure he meant it. "This place is owned by the American people—they can look at it if they like."

"This is my mother, Jacky Jakes," George said.

Bobby shook her hand vigorously. "Mrs. Jakes, you have a fine son," he said, turning on the charm, as he did whenever talking to a voter.

Jacky's face had darkened with embarrassment, but she spoke without hesitation. "Thank you," she said. "You have several—I was looking at them in this picture."

"Four sons and three daughters. They're all wonderful, and I speak with complete objectivity."

They all laughed.

Bobby said: "It was a pleasure to meet you, Mrs. Jakes. Come and see us anytime."

Though he was gracious, that was clearly a dismissal, and George and his mother left the room.

They walked along the corridor to the elevator. Jacky said: "That was embarrassing, but Bobby was kind."

"It was also planned," George said angrily. "Bobby's never early for anything. Dennis deliberately misled us. He wanted to make me look uppity."

His mother patted his arm. "If that's the worst thing that happens today, we'll be in good shape."

"I don't know." George recalled Verena's accusation, that his job was cosmetic. "Do you think my role here could be just to make Bobby look like he's listening to Negroes when he's not?"

Jacky considered. "Maybe."

"I might do more good working for Martin Luther King in Atlanta."

"I understand how you feel, but I think you should stay here."

"I knew you'd say that."

He saw her out of the building. "How is your apartment?" she said. "I have to see that next."

"It's great." George had rented the top floor of a high, narrow Victorian row house in the Capitol Hill neighborhood. "Come over on Sunday."

"So I can cook you dinner in your kitchen?"

"What a kind offer."

"Will I meet your girlfriend?"

"I'll invite Norine."

They kissed good-bye. Jacky would get a commuter train to her home in Prince George's County. Before she walked away she said: "Remember this. There are a thousand smart young men willing to work for Martin Luther King. But there's only one Negro sitting in the office next to Bobby Kennedy's."

She was right, he thought. She usually was.

When he returned to the office he said nothing to Dennis, but sat at his desk and wrote a summary for Bobby of a report on school integration.

At five o'clock Bobby and his aides jumped into limousines for the short ride to the White House, where Bobby was scheduled to meet with the president. This was the first time George had been taken along to a White House meeting, and he wondered whether that was a sign that he was becoming more trusted—or just that the meeting was less important.

They entered the West Wing and went to the Cabinet Room. It was a long room with four tall windows on one side. Twenty or so dark blue leather chairs stood around a coffin-shaped table. World-shaking decisions were made in this room, George thought solemnly.

After fifteen minutes there was no sign of President Kennedy. Dennis said to George: "Go and make certain Dave Powers knows where we are, will you?" Powers was the president's personal assistant.

"Sure," said George. Seven years at Harvard and I'm a messenger boy, he thought.

Before the meeting with Bobby, the president had been due to drop in on a cocktail party for celebrity supporters. George made his way to the main house and followed the noise. Under the massive chandeliers in the East Room, a hundred people were into their second hour of drinking. George waved to Verena's parents, Percy Marquand and Babe Lee, who were talking to someone from the Democratic National Committee.

The president was not in the room.

George looked around and spotted a kitchen entrance. He had learned that the president often used staff doors and back corridors, to avoid constantly being buttonholed and delayed.

He went through the staff door and found the presidential party right outside. The handsome, tanned president, only forty-four years old, wore a navy blue suit with a white shirt and a skinny tie. He looked tired and edgy. "I can't be photographed with an interracial couple!" he said in a frustrated tone, as if forced to repeat himself. "I'd lose ten million votes!"

George had seen only one interracial couple in the ballroom: Percy Marquand and Babe Lee. He felt outraged. So the liberal president was scared to be photographed with them!

Dave Powers was an amiable middle-aged man with a big nose and a bald head, about as different from his boss as could be imagined. He said to the president: "What am I supposed to do?"

"Get them out of there!"

Dave was a personal friend, and not scared to let Kennedy know when he was irritated. "What am I going to tell them, for Christ's sake?"

Suddenly George stopped being angry and started to think. Was this an opportunity for him? Without forming any definite plan, he said: "Mr. President, I'm George Jakes. I work for the attorney general. May I take care of this problem for you?"

He watched their faces and knew what they were thinking. If Percy Marquand was going to be insulted in the White House, how much better it would be if the offender were black.

"Hell, yes," said Kennedy. "I'd appreciate that, George."

"Yes, sir," said George, and he went back into the ballroom.

But what was he going to do? He racked his brains as he crossed the polished floor toward where Percy and Babe stood. He had to get them out of the room for fifteen or twenty minutes, that was all. What could he tell them?

Anything but the truth, he guessed.

When he reached the conversational group, and touched Percy Marquand gently on the arm, he still didn't know what he was going to say.

Percy turned, recognized him, smiled, and shook his hand. "Everybody!" he said to the people around him. "Meet a Freedom Rider!"

Babe Lee grabbed his arm with both hands, as if afraid someone was going to steal him. "You're a hero, George," she said.

At that moment George realized what he had to say. "Mr. Marquand, Miss Lee, I work for Bobby Kennedy now, and he would like to talk to you for a few minutes about civil rights. May I take you to him?"

"Of course," said Percy, and a few seconds later they were out of the room.

George regretted his words immediately. His heart thumped as he walked them to the West Wing. How was Bobby going to take this? He might say *Hell, no, I don't have time.* If an embarrassing incident resulted, George would be to blame. Why had he not kept his mouth shut?

"I had lunch with Verena," he said, making small talk.

Babe Lee said: "She loves her job in Atlanta. The Southern Christian Leadership Conference has a small headquarters organization, but they're doing great things."

Percy said: "Dr. King is a great man. Of all the civil rights leaders I've met, he's the most impressive."

They reached the Cabinet Room and went in. The half-dozen men there were sitting at one end of the long table, chatting, some smoking. They looked in surprise at the newcomers. George located Bobby and watched his face. He looked puzzled and irritated. George said: "Bobby, you know Percy Marquand and Babe Lee. They would be happy to talk to us about civil rights for a few minutes."

For a moment Bobby's face darkened with rage. George realized this was the second time today he had surprised his boss with an uninvited guest. Then Bobby smiled. "What a privilege!" he said. "Sit down, folks, and thank you for supporting my brother's election campaign."

George was relieved, for the moment. There would be no embarrassment. Bobby had switched to automatic charm. He asked Percy and Babe their views, and talked candidly about the difficulties the Kennedys were having with Southern Democrats in Congress. The guests were flattered.

A few minutes later the president came in. He shook hands with Percy and Babe, then asked Dave Powers to take them back to the party.

As soon as the door closed behind them, Bobby rounded on George. "Never do that to me again!" he said. His face showed the strength of his pent-up fury.

George saw Dennis Wilson smother a grin.

"Who the fuck do you think you are?" Bobby stormed.

George thought Bobby was going to hit him. He balanced on the balls of his feet, ready to dodge a blow. He said desperately: "The president wanted them out of the room! He didn't want to be photographed with Percy and Babe."

Bobby looked at his brother, who nodded.

George said: "I had thirty seconds to think of a pretext that wouldn't insult them. I told them you wanted to meet them. And it worked, didn't it? They're not offended—in fact they think they got VIP treatment!"

The president said: "It's true, Bob. George here got us out of a tight situation."

George said: "I wanted to make sure we didn't lose their support for the reelection campaign."

Bobby looked blank for a moment, taking it in. "So," he said, "you told them I wanted to talk to them, just as a way of keeping them out of the presidential photographs."

"Yes," said George.

The president said: "That was quick thinking."

Bobby's face changed. After a moment he started to laugh. His brother joined in, then the other men in the room followed suit.

Bobby put his arm around George's shoulders.

George still felt shaky. He had feared he would be fired.

Bobby said: "Georgie boy, you're one of us!"

George realized he had been accepted into the inner circle. He slumped with relief.

He was not as proud as he might have been. He had carried out a shabby little deception, and helped the president to pander to racial prejudice. He wanted to wash his hands.

Then he saw the look of rage on Dennis Wilson's face, and he felt better.

That August, Rebecca was summoned to secret police headquarters for a second time.

She wondered fearfully what the Stasi wanted now. They had already ruined her life. She had been tricked into a sham marriage, and now she could not get a job, no doubt because they were ordering schools not to hire her. What else could they do to her? Surely they could not put her in jail just because she had been their victim?

But they could do anything they liked.

She took the bus across town on a hot Berlin day. The new headquarters building was as ugly as the organization it represented, a rectilinear concrete box for people whose minds were all straight edges. Once again she was escorted up in the lift and along the sickly yellow corridors, but this time she was taken to a different office. Waiting for her there she found her husband, Hans. When she saw him, her fear was displaced by even stronger rage. Even though he had the power to hurt her, she was too angry to kowtow to him.

He was wearing a new blue-gray suit that she had not seen before. He had a large room with two windows and new modern furniture: he was more senior than she had thought.

Needing time to gather her wits, she said: "I was expecting to see Sergeant Scholz."

Hans looked away. "He was not suitable for security work."

Rebecca could see that Hans was hiding something. Presumably Scholz had been fired, or perhaps demoted to the traffic police. "I suppose he made a mistake in interviewing me here, rather than at the local police station."

"He should not have interviewed you at all. Sit there." He pointed to a chair in front of his big, ugly desk.

The chair was made of metal tubing and hard orange plastic—designed to make his victims even more uncomfortable, Rebecca guessed. Her suppressed fury gave her the strength to defy him. Instead of sitting, she went to the window and looked out over the car park. "You wasted your time, didn't you?" she said. "You went to all that trouble to watch my family, and you didn't find a single spy or saboteur." She turned to look at him. "Your bosses must be angry with you."

"On the contrary," he said. "This is considered one of the most successful operations the Stasi has ever conducted."

Rebecca could not imagine how that could be possible. "You can't have learned anything very interesting."

"My team has produced a chart showing every Social Democrat in East Germany, and the links between them," he said proudly. "And the key information was obtained in your house. Your parents know all the most important reactionaries, and many came to visit."

Rebecca frowned. It was true that most of the people who came to the house were former Social Democrats: that was only natural. "But they're just friends," she said.

Hans let out a mocking hoot of laughter. "Just friends!" he jeered. "Please, I know you think we're not very bright—you said so, many times, when I was living with you—but we're not completely brainless."

It occurred to Rebecca that Hans and all secret policemen were obliged to believe—or at least, to pretend to believe—in fantastic conspiracies against the government. Otherwise their work was a waste of time. So Hans had constructed an imaginary network of Social Democrats based on the Franck family house, all plotting to bring down the Communist government.

If only it were true.

Hans said: "Of course, it was never intended that I should marry you. A flirtation, just enough to get me into the house, was all that we planned."

"My proposal of marriage must have presented you with a problem."

"Our project was going so well. The information I was getting was crucial. Each person I saw at your house led us to more Social Democrats. If I declined your proposal the tap would have been turned off."

"How brave you were," Rebecca said. "You must be proud."

He stared at her. For a moment she could not read him. Something was going on in his mind, and she did not know what it was. It crossed her mind that he might want to touch her or kiss her. The thought made her flesh creep. Then he shook his head as if to clear it. "We're not here to talk about the marriage," he said with irritation.

"Why are we here?"

"You caused an incident at the employment exchange."

"An incident? I asked the man standing in front of me in the line how long he had been unemployed. The woman behind the counter stood up and yelled at me. 'There is no unemployment in Communist countries!' she screeched. I looked at the queue in front of me and behind, and I laughed. That's an incident?"

"You laughed hysterically and refused to stop, and you were ejected from the building."

"It's true that I couldn't stop laughing. What she said was so absurd."

"It was not absurd!" Hans fumbled a cigarette from a packet of f6. Like all bullies, he became nervous when someone stood up to him. "She was right," he said. "No one is out of work in East Germany. Communism has solved the problem of unemployment."

"Don't, please," said Rebecca. "You'll make me laugh again, and then I'll have to be ejected from this building as well."

"Sarcasm will do you no good."

She looked at a framed photograph on the wall showing Hans shaking hands with Walter Ulbricht, the East German leader. Ulbricht had a bald dome, and he cultivated a Vandyke beard and mustache: the resemblance to Lenin was faintly comic. Rebecca asked: "What did Ulbricht say to you?"

"He congratulated me on my promotion to captain."

"Also part of your reward for cruelly misleading your wife. So, tell me, if I'm not unemployed, what am I?"

"You are under investigation as a social parasite."

"That's outrageous! I have worked continuously since graduating. Eight years without a day of sick leave. I've been promoted and given extra responsibilities, including the supervision of new teachers. And then one day I discovered my husband was a Stasi spy, and soon afterward I was fired. Since then I have been to six job interviews. Each time, the school was desperate for me to start as soon as possible.

And yet—for no reason they could give me—each time they wrote afterward telling me they were not able to offer me the post. Do you know why?"

"No one wants you."

"Everyone wants me. I am a good teacher."

"You are ideologically unreliable. You would be a bad influence on impressionable youngsters."

"I have a glowing reference from my last employer."

"From Bernd Held, you mean. He, too, is under investigation for ideological unreliability."

Rebecca felt a chill of dread deep in her chest. She tried to keep her face expressionless. How terrible it would be if kind, capable Bernd were to get into trouble on her account. I must warn him, she thought.

She failed to hide her feelings from Hans. "That's rocked you, hasn't it?" he said. "I always had my suspicions about him. You were fond of him."

"He wanted to have an affair with me," Rebecca said. "But I was unwilling to deceive you. Just fancy that."

"I would have found you out."

"Instead of which, I found you out."

"I was doing my duty."

"So, you're making sure I can't get a job, and accusing me of social parasitism. What do you expect me to do—go west?"

"Emigration without permission is a crime."

"And yet so many people do it! I hear the number has risen to almost a thousand a day. Teachers, doctors, engineers—even police officers. Oh!" She was struck by an insight. "Is that what happened to Sergeant Scholz?"

Hans looked shifty. "None of your business."

"I can tell by your face. So Scholz went west. Why do all these respectable people turn criminal, do you suppose? Is it because they want to live in a country that has free elections, and so on?"

Hans raised his voice angrily. "Free elections gave us Hitler—is that what they want?"

"Perhaps they don't like living in a place where the secret police can do anything they like. You can imagine how uneasy that makes people."

"Only those who have guilty secrets!"

"And what's my secret, Hans? Come on, you must know."

"You are a social parasite."

"So you prevent my getting a job, then you threaten to jail me for not having a job. I suppose I'd be sent to a work camp, would I? Then I would have a job, except that I wouldn't be paid. I love Communism. It's so logical! Why are people so desperate to escape from it? I wonder."

"Your mother told me many times that she would never emigrate to the West. She would consider it running away."

Rebecca wondered what he was getting at. "So . . . ?"

"If you commit the crime of illegal emigration, you will never be able to come back."

Rebecca saw what was coming, and she was filled with despair.

Hans said triumphantly: "You would never see your family again."

·　·　·

Rebecca was crushed. She left the building and stood at the bus stop. Whichever way she looked at it, she was forced to either lose her family or lose her freedom.

Despondent, she took the bus to the school where she used to work. She was unprepared for the nostalgia that struck her like a blow when she walked in: the sound of young people's chatter, the smell of chalk dust and cleaning fluid, the notice boards and football boots and signs saying: NO RUNNING. She realized how happy she had been as a teacher. It was vitally important work, and she was good at it. She could not bear the thought of giving it up.

Bernd was in the head teacher's office, wearing a black corduroy suit. The cloth was worn but the color flattered him. He beamed happily when she opened the door. "Have they made you head?" she asked, although she could guess the answer.

"That will never happen," he replied. "But I'm doing the job anyway, and loving it. Meanwhile our old boss, Anselm, is head of a big school in Hamburg—and making double the salary. How about you? Take a seat."

She sat down and told him about her job interviews. "It's Hans's revenge," she said. "I never should have thrown his damn matchstick model out of the window."

"It may not be that," Bernd said. "I've seen this before. A man hates the person he has wronged, paradoxically. I think it's because the victim is a perpetual reminder that he behaved shamefully."

Bernd was very smart. She missed him. "I'm afraid Hans may hate you, too," she said. "He told me you're being investigated for ideological unreliability, because you wrote me a reference."

"Oh, hell." He rubbed the scar on his forehead, always a sign that he was worried. Involvement with the Stasi never had a happy ending.

"I'm sorry."

"Don't be. I'm glad I wrote that reference. I'd do it again. Someone has to tell the truth in this damn country."

"Hans also figured out, somehow, that you were . . . attracted to me."

"And he's jealous?"

"Hard to imagine, isn't it?"

"Not in the least. Even a spy couldn't fail to fall for you."

"Don't be absurd."

"Is that why you came?" Bernd said. "To warn me?"

"And to say . . ." She had to be discreet, even with Bernd. "To say that I probably won't see you for some time."

"Ah." He nodded understanding.

People rarely said they were going to the West. You could be arrested just for planning it. And someone who found out that you were intending to go was committing a crime if he failed to inform the police. So no one but your immediate family wanted the guilty knowledge.

Rebecca stood up. "So, thank you for your friendship."

He came around the desk and took both her hands. "No, thank *you*. And good luck."

"To you, too."

She realized that in her unconscious mind she had already made the decision to go west; and she was thinking of that, with surprise and anxiety, when unexpectedly Bernd bent his head and kissed her.

She was not expecting this. It was a gentle kiss. He let his lips linger on hers, but did not open his mouth. She closed her eyes. After a year of fake marriage it was good to know that someone genuinely found her desirable, even lovable. She felt an urge to throw her arms around him, but suppressed it. It would be madness now to start a doomed relationship. After a few moments she broke away.

She felt herself near to tears. She did not want Bernd to see her cry. She managed to say: "Good-bye." Then she turned away and quickly left the room.

. . .

She decided she would leave two days later, early on Sunday morning.

Everyone got up to see her off.

She could not eat any breakfast. She was too upset. "I'll probably go to Hamburg," she said, faking good spirits. "Anselm Weber is head of a school there now, and I'm sure he'll hire me."

Her grandmother Maud, in a purple silk robe, said: "You could get a job anywhere in West Germany."

"But it will be nice to know at least one person in the city," Rebecca said forlornly.

Walli chipped in: "There's supposed to be a great music scene in Hamburg. I'm going to join you as soon as I can leave school."

"If you leave school, you'll have to work," their father said to Walli in a sarcastic tone. "That will be a new experience for you."

"No quarreling this morning," said Rebecca.

Father gave her an envelope of money. "As soon as you're on the other side, get a taxi," he said. "Go straight to Marienfelde." There was a refugee center at Marienfelde, in the south of the city near Tempelhof airport. "Start the process of emigration. I'm sure you'll have to wait in line for hours, maybe days. As soon as you have everything in order, come to the factory. I'll set you up with a West German bank account, and so on."

Her mother was in tears. "We *will* see you," she said. "You can fly to West Berlin any time you want, and we can just walk across the border and meet you. We'll have picnics on the beach at the Wannsee."

Rebecca was trying not to cry. She put the money in a small shoulder bag that was all she was taking. Anything more in the way of luggage might get her arrested by the Vopos at the border. She wanted to linger, but she was afraid she might lose her nerve altogether. She kissed and hugged each of them: Grandmother Maud; her adoptive father, Werner; her adoptive brother and sister, Lili and Walli; and last of all Carla, the woman who had saved her life, the mother who was not her mother, and was for that reason even the more precious.

Then, her eyes full of tears, she left the house.

It was a bright summer morning, the sky blue and cloudless. She tried to feel optimistic: she was beginning a new life, away from the grim repression of a Communist regime. And she would see her family again, one way or another.

She walked briskly, threading through the streets of the old city center. She passed the sprawling campus of the Charité hospital and turned on to Invaliden Strasse. To her left was the Sandkrug Bridge, which carried traffic over the Berlin-Spandau Ship Canal to West Berlin.

Except that today it did not.

At first Rebecca was not sure what she was looking at. There was a line of cars that stopped short of the bridge. Beyond the cars, a crowd of people stood looking at something. Perhaps there had been a crash on the bridge. But to her right, in the Platz vor dem Neuen Tor, twenty or thirty East German soldiers stood around doing nothing. Behind them were two Soviet tanks.

It was puzzling and frightening.

She pushed through the crowd. Now she could see the problem. A crude barbed-wire fence had been erected across the near end of the bridge. A small gap in the fence was manned by police who seemed to be refusing to let anyone through.

Rebecca was tempted to ask what was going on, but she did not want to draw attention to herself. She was not far from Friedrich Strasse Station: from there she could go by subway directly to Marienfelde.

She turned south, walking faster now, and took a zigzag course around a series of university buildings to the station.

There was something wrong here, too.

Several dozen people were crowded around the entrance. Rebecca fought her way to the front and read a notice pasted to the wall that said only what was obvious: the station was closed. At the top of the steps, a line of police with guns formed a barrier. No one was being admitted to the platforms.

Rebecca began to be fearful. Perhaps it was a coincidence that the first two crossing places she had chosen were blocked. And perhaps not.

There were eighty-one places where people could cross from East to West Berlin. The next nearest was the Brandenburg Gate, where the broad Unter den Linden passed through the monumental arch into the Tiergarten. She walked south on Friedrich Strasse.

As soon as she turned west on Unter den Linden she knew she was in trouble. Here again there were tanks and soldiers. Hundreds of people were gathered in front of the famous gateway. When she got to the front of the crowd, Rebecca saw another barbed-wire fence. It was strung across wooden sawhorses and guarded by East German police.

Young men who looked like Walli—leather jackets, narrow trousers, Elvis hairstyles—were shouting insults from a safe distance. On the West Berlin side, similar types were yelling angrily, and occasionally throwing stones at the police.

Looking more closely, Rebecca saw that the various policemen— Vopos, border police, and factory militia—were making holes in the road, planting tall concrete posts, and stringing barbed wire from post to post in a more permanent arrangement.

Permanent, she thought, and her spirits sank into an abyss.

She spoke to a man next to her. "Is it everywhere?" she said. "This fence?"

"Everywhere," he said. "The bastards."

The East German regime had done what everyone said could not be done: they had built a wall across the middle of Berlin.

And Rebecca was on the wrong side.

PART TWO

BUG

1961–1962

CHAPTER ELEVEN

George felt wary when he went to lunch with Larry Mawhinney at the Electric Diner. George was not sure why Larry had suggested this, but he agreed out of curiosity. He and Larry were the same age and had similar jobs: Larry was an aide in the office of air force chief of staff General Curtis LeMay. But their bosses were at loggerheads: the Kennedy brothers mistrusted the military.

Larry wore the uniform of an air force lieutenant. He was all soldier: clean shaven, with buzz-cut fair hair, his tie knotted tightly, his shoes shiny. "The Pentagon hates segregation," he said.

George raised his eyebrows. "Really? I thought the army was traditionally reluctant to trust Negroes with guns."

Mawhinney lifted a placatory hand. "I know what you mean. But, one, that attitude was always overtaken by necessity: Negroes have fought in every conflict since the War of Independence. And two, it's history. The Pentagon today needs men of color in the military. And we don't want the expense and inefficiency of segregation: two sets of bathrooms, two sets of barracks, prejudice and hatred between men who are supposed to be fighting side by side."

"Okay, I buy that," said George.

Larry cut into his grilled-cheese sandwich and George took a forkful of chili con carne. Larry said: "So, Khrushchev got what he wanted in Berlin."

George sensed that this was the real subject of the lunch. "Thank God we don't have to go to war with the Soviets," he said.

"Kennedy chickened out," Larry said. "The East German regime was close to collapse. There might have been a counterrevolution, if the president had taken a tougher line. But the Wall has stopped the flood of refugees to the West, and now the Soviets can do anything they like in East Berlin. Our West German allies are mad as hell about it."

George bristled. "The president avoided World War Three!"

"At the cost of letting the Soviets tighten their grip. It's not exactly a triumph."

"Is that the Pentagon's view?"

"Pretty much."

Of course it was, George thought irritably. He now understood: Mawhinney was here to argue the Pentagon's line, in the hope of winning George as a supporter. I should be flattered, he told himself: it shows that people now see me as part of Bobby's inner circle.

But he was not going to listen to an attack on President Kennedy without hitting back. "I suppose I should expect nothing less of General LeMay. Don't they call him 'Bombs Away' LeMay?"

Mawhinney frowned. If he found his boss's nickname funny, he was not going to show it.

George thought the overbearing, cigar-chewing LeMay deserved mockery. "I believe he once said that if there's a nuclear war, and at the end of it there are two Americans and one Russian left, then we've won."

"I never heard him say anything like that."

"Apparently President Kennedy told him: 'You better hope the Americans are a man and a woman.'"

"We have to be strong!" Mawhinney said, beginning to get riled. "We've lost Cuba and Laos and East Berlin, and we're in danger of losing Vietnam."

"What do you imagine we can do about Vietnam?"

"Send in the army," Larry said promptly.

"Don't we already have thousands of military advisers there?"

"It's not enough. The Pentagon has asked the president again and again to send in ground combat troops. It seems he doesn't have the guts."

That annoyed George because it was so unfair. "President Kennedy does not lack courage," he snapped.

"Then why won't he attack the Communists in Vietnam?"

"He doesn't believe we can win."

"He should listen to experienced and knowledgeable generals."

"Should he? They told him to back the stupid Bay of Pigs invasion. If the Joint Chiefs are experienced and knowledgeable, how come they didn't tell the president that an invasion by Cuban exiles was bound to fail?"

"We *told* him to send air cover—"

"Excuse me, Larry, but the whole idea was to avoid involving Americans. Yet as soon as it went wrong, the Pentagon wanted to send in the marines. The Kennedy brothers suspect you people of a sucker punch. You led him into a doomed invasion by exiles because you wanted to force him to send in U.S. troops."

"That's not true."

"Maybe, but he thinks that now you're trying to lure him into Vietnam by the same method. And he's determined not to be fooled a second time."

"Okay, so he's got a grudge against us because of the Bay of Pigs. Seriously, George, is that a good enough reason to let Vietnam go Communist?"

"We'll have to agree to disagree."

Mawhinney put down his knife and fork. "Do you want dessert?" He had realized he was wasting his time: George was never going to be a Pentagon ally.

"No dessert, thanks," George said. He was in Bobby's office to fight for justice, so that his children could grow up as American citizens with equal rights. Someone else would have to fight Communism in Asia.

Mawhinney's face changed and he waved across the restaurant. George glanced back over his own shoulder and got a shock.

The person Mawhinney was waving at was Maria Summers.

She did not see him. She was already turning back to her companion, a white girl of about the same age.

"Is that Maria Summers?" he said incredulously.

"Yeah."

"You know her."

"Sure. We were at Chicago Law together."

"What's she doing in Washington?"

"Funny story. She was originally turned down for a job in the White

House press office. Then the person they appointed didn't work out, and she was the second choice."

George was thrilled. Maria was in Washington—permanently! He made up his mind to speak to her before leaving the restaurant.

It occurred to him that he might find out more about her from Mawhinney. "Did you date her at law school?"

"No. She only went out with colored guys, and not many of them. She was known as an iceberg."

George did not take that remark at face value. Any girl who said no was an iceberg, to some men. "Did she have anyone special?"

"There was one guy she was seeing for about a year, but he dumped her because she wouldn't put out."

"I'm not surprised," George said. "She comes from a strict family."

"How do you know that?"

"We were on the first Freedom Ride together. I talked to her a bit."

"She's pretty."

"That's the truth."

They got the check and split it. On the way out George stopped at Maria's table. "Welcome to Washington," he said.

She smiled warmly. "Hello, George. I've been wondering how soon I'd run into you."

Larry said: "Hi, Maria. I was just telling George how you were known as an iceberg at Chicago Law." Larry laughed.

It was a typical male jibe, nothing unusual, but Maria flushed.

Larry walked out of the restaurant, but George stayed behind. "I'm sorry he said that, Maria. And I'm embarrassed that I heard it. It was really crass."

"Thank you." She gestured toward the other woman. "This is Antonia Capel. She's a lawyer, too."

Antonia was a thin, intense woman with hair severely drawn back. "Good to know you," George said.

Maria said to Antonia: "George got a broken arm protecting me from an Alabama segregationist with a crowbar."

Antonia was impressed. "George, you're a real gentleman," she said.

George saw that the girls were ready to leave: their check was on the table in a saucer, covered with a few bills. He said to Maria: "Can I walk you back to the White House?"

"Sure," she said.

Antonia said: "I have to run to the drugstore."

They stepped out into the mild air of a Washington autumn. Antonia waved good-bye. George and Maria headed for the White House.

George studied her out of the corner of his eye as they crossed Pennsylvania Avenue. She wore a smart black raincoat over a white turtleneck, clothing for a serious political operator, but she could not cover up her warm smile. She was pretty, with a small nose and chin, and her big brown eyes and soft lips were sexy.

"I was arguing with Mawhinney about Vietnam," George said. "I think he hoped to persuade me as a way of indirectly getting to Bobby."

"I'm sure of it," said Maria. "But the president isn't going to give in to the Pentagon on this."

"How do you know?"

"He's making a speech tonight saying that there are limits to what we can achieve in foreign policy. We cannot right every wrong or reverse every adversity. I've just written the press release for the speech."

"I'm glad he's going to stand firm."

"George, you didn't hear what I said. I wrote a press release! Don't you understand how unusual that is? Normally the men write them. The women just type them out."

George grinned. "Congratulations." He was happy to be with her, and they had quickly slipped back into their friendly relationship.

"Mind you, I'll find out what they think of it when I get back to the office. What's happening at Justice?"

"It looks like our Freedom Ride really achieved something," George said eagerly. "Soon all interstate buses will have a sign saying: 'Seating aboard this vehicle is without regard to race, color, creed, or national origin.' The same words have to be printed on bus tickets." He was proud of this achievement. "How about that?"

"Well done." But Maria asked the key question. "Will the ruling be enforced?"

"That's up to us in Justice, and we're trying harder than ever before. We've already acted several times to oppose the authorities in Mississippi and Alabama. And a surprising number of towns in other states are just giving in."

"It's hard to believe we're really winning. The segregationists always seem to have another dirty trick in reserve."

"Voter registration is our next campaign. Martin Luther King wants to double the number of black voters in the South by the end of the year."

Maria said thoughtfully: "What we really need is a new civil rights bill that makes it difficult for Southern states to defy the law."

"We're working on that."

"So you're telling me Bobby Kennedy is a civil rights supporter?"

"Hell, no. A year ago the issue wasn't even on his agenda. But Bobby and the president hated those photographs of white mob violence in the South. They made the Kennedys look bad on the front pages of newspapers all over the world."

"And global politics is what they really care about."

"Exactly."

George wanted to ask her for a date, but he held back. He was going to break up with Norine Latimer as soon as possible: that was inevitable, now that Maria was here. But he felt he had to tell Norine their romance was over before he asked Maria out. Anything else would seem dishonest. And the delay would not be long: he would see Norine within a few days.

They entered the West Wing. Black faces in the White House were unusual enough for people to stare at them. They went to the press office. George was surprised to find it a small room jammed with desks. Half a dozen people worked intently with gray Remington typewriters and phones with rows of flashing lights. From an adjoining room came the chatter of teletype machines, punctuated by the bells they rang to herald particularly important messages. There was an inner office that George presumed must belong to press secretary Pierre Salinger.

Everyone seemed to be concentrating hard, no one chatting or looking out of the window.

Maria showed him her desk and introduced the woman at the next typewriter, an attractive redhead in her midthirties. "George, this is my friend Miss Fordham. Nelly, why is everyone so quiet?"

Before Nelly could answer, Salinger came out of his office, a small, chubby man in a tailored European-style suit. With him was President Kennedy.

The president smiled at everyone, nodded to George, and spoke to Maria. "You must be Maria Summers," he said. "You've written a good press release—clear and emphatic. Well done."

Maria flushed with pleasure. "Thank you, Mr. President."

He seemed in no hurry. "What were you doing before you came here?" He asked the question as if there was nothing in the world more interesting.

"I was at Chicago Law."

"Do you like it in the press office?"

"Oh, yes, it's exciting."

"Well, I appreciate your good work. Keep it up."

"I'll do my very best."

The president went out, and Salinger followed.

George looked at Maria with amusement. She seemed dazed.

After a moment, Nelly Fordham spoke. "Yeah, it takes you like that," she said. "For a minute there, you were the most beautiful woman in the world."

Maria looked at her. "Yes," she said. "That's exactly how I felt."

. . .

Maria was a little lonely, but otherwise happy.

She loved working at the White House, surrounded by bright, sincere people who wanted only to make the world a better place. She felt she could achieve a lot in government. She knew she would have to struggle with prejudice—against women and against Negroes—but she believed she could overcome that with intelligence and determination.

Her family had a history of prevailing against the odds. Her grandfather Saul Summers had walked to Chicago from his hometown of Golgotha, Alabama. On the way he had been arrested for "vagrancy" and sentenced to thirty days' labor in a coal mine. While there, he saw a man clubbed to death by guards for trying to escape. After thirty days he was not released, and when he complained he was flogged. He risked his life, escaped, and made it to Chicago. There he eventually became pastor of the Bethlehem Full Gospel Church. Now eighty years old, he was semiretired, still preaching occasionally.

Maria's father, Daniel, had gone to a Negro college and law school. In 1930, in the Depression, he had opened a storefront law firm in the

South Side neighborhood, where no one could afford a postage stamp, let alone a lawyer. Maria had often heard him reminisce about how his clients had paid him in kind: homemade cakes, eggs from their backyard hens, a free haircut, some carpentry around his office. By the time Roosevelt's New Deal kicked in and the economy improved, he was the most popular black lawyer in Chicago.

So Maria was not afraid of adversity. But she was lonely. Everyone around her was white. Grandfather Summers often said: "There's nothing wrong with white people. They just ain't black." She knew what he meant. White people did not know about "vagrancy." Somehow it slipped their minds that Alabama had continued to send Negroes to forced labor camps until 1927. If she spoke about such things, they looked sad for a moment, then turned away, and she knew they thought she was exaggerating. Black people who talked about prejudice were boring to whites, like sick people who recited their symptoms.

She had been delighted to see George Jakes again. She would have sought him out as soon as she got to Washington, except that a modest girl did not chase after a man, no matter how charming he was; and anyway she would not have known what to say. She liked George more than any man she had met since she broke up with Frank Baker two years ago. She would have married Frank if he had asked her, but he wanted sex without marriage, a proposal she had rejected. When George had walked her back to the press office, she had felt sure he was about to ask her for a date, and she had been disappointed when he had not.

She shared an apartment with two black girls, but did not have much in common with them. Both were secretaries, and mainly interested in fashions and movies.

Maria was used to being exceptional. There had not been many black women at her college, and at law school she had been the only one. Now she was the only black woman in the White House, not counting cleaners and cooks. She had no complaints: everyone was friendly. But she was lonely.

On the morning after she met George she was studying a speech by Fidel Castro, looking for nuggets the press office could use, when her phone rang and a man said: "Would you like to go swimming?"

The flat Boston accent was familiar, but she could not identify it for a moment. "Who is this?"

"Dave."

It was Dave Powers, the president's personal aide, sometimes called the First Friend. Maria had spoken to him two or three times. Like most people in the White House, he was amiable and charming.

But now Maria was taken by surprise. "Where?" she said.

He laughed. "Here in the White House, of course."

She recalled that there was a pool in the west gallery, between the White House and the West Wing. She had never seen it, but she knew it had been built for President Roosevelt. She had heard that President Kennedy liked to swim at least once a day because the water relieved the pressure on his bad back.

Dave added: "There will be some other girls."

Maria's first thought was of her hair. Just about every black woman in an office job wore a hairpiece or a wig to work. Blacks and whites alike felt that the natural look of black hair just was not businesslike. Today Maria had a beehive, with a hairpiece carefully braided into her own hair, which itself had been relaxed with chemicals to mimic the smooth, straight texture of white women's hair. It was not a secret: it would be obvious to every black woman who glanced at her. But a white man such as Dave would never even notice.

How could she go swimming? If she got her hair wet it would turn into a mess that she would not be able to rescue.

She was too embarrassed to say what the problem was, but she quickly thought of an excuse. "I don't have a swimsuit."

"We have swimsuits," Dave replied. "I'll pick you up at noon." He hung up.

Maria looked at her watch. It was ten to twelve.

What was she going to do? Would she be allowed to ease herself carefully into the water at the shallow end, and keep her hair dry?

She had asked all the wrong questions, she realized. She really needed to know why she had been invited and what might be expected of her—and whether the president would be there.

She looked at the woman at the next desk. Nelly Fordham was a single woman who had worked at the White House for a decade. She hinted that years ago she had been disappointed in love. She had been helpful to Maria from the start. Now she was looking curious. "'I don't have a swimsuit'?" she quoted.

"I'm invited to the president's pool," Maria said. "Should I go?"

"Of course! Just as long as you tell me all about it when you come back."

Maria lowered her voice. "He said there will be some other girls. Do you think the president will be there?"

Nelly looked around, but no one was listening. "Does Jack Kennedy like to swim surrounded by pretty girls?" she said. "No prizes for answering that one."

Maria still was not sure whether to go. Then she remembered Larry Mawhinney calling her an iceberg. That had stung. She was not an iceberg. She was a virgin at twenty-five because she had never met a man to whom she wanted to give herself body and soul, but she was not frigid.

Dave Powers appeared at the door and said: "Coming?"

"Heck, yes," said Maria.

Dave walked her along the arcade at the edge of the Rose Garden to the pool entrance. Two other girls arrived at the same time. Maria had seen them before, always together: both were White House secretaries. Dave introduced them. "Meet Jennifer and Geraldine, known as Jenny and Jerry," he said.

The girls led Maria into a changing room where a dozen or more swimsuits hung on hooks. Jenny and Jerry stripped off quickly. Maria noticed that both had superb figures. She did not often see white girls naked. Although blondes, both had dark pubic hair in a neat triangle. Maria wondered whether they trimmed it with scissors. She had never thought of doing that.

The swimsuits were all one-pieces and made of cotton. Maria rejected the more flamboyant colors and picked a modest dark navy. Then she followed Jenny and Jerry to the pool.

The walls on three sides were painted with Caribbean scenes, palm trees and sailing ships. The fourth wall was mirrored, and Maria checked her reflection. She was not too fat, she thought, except for her ass, which was too big. The navy blue looked good against her dark brown skin.

She noticed a table of drinks and sandwiches to one side. She was too nervous to eat.

Dave was sitting on the edge, barefoot with his pants rolled up, paddling his feet in the water. Jenny and Jerry were bobbing around, talking and laughing. Maria sat opposite Dave and put her feet in. The pool was as warm as a bath.

A minute later, President Kennedy appeared, and Maria's heart beat faster.

He was wearing the usual dark suit, white shirt, and narrow tie. He stood at the edge, smiling at the girls. Maria caught a lemon whiff of his 4711 cologne. He said: "Mind if I join you?" just as if it was their pool, not his.

Jenny said: "Please do!" She and Jerry were not surprised to see him, and Maria deduced that this was not the first time they had swum with the president.

He went into the dressing room and came out again wearing blue swimming trunks. He was lean and tanned, in great shape for a man of forty-four, probably on account of all the sailing he did at Hyannis Port on Cape Cod, where he had a holiday home. He sat on the edge, then eased himself into the water with a sigh.

He swam for a few minutes. Maria wondered what her mother would say. Ma would disapprove of her daughter going swimming with a married man if he were anyone other than the president. But surely nothing bad could happen here, in the White House, in front of Dave Powers and Jenny and Jerry?

The president swam over to where she sat. "How are you getting on in the press office, Maria?" He asked this as if it were the most important question in the world.

"Fine, thank you, sir."

"Is Pierre a good boss?"

"Very good. Everyone likes him."

"I like him, too."

This close, Maria could see the faint wrinkles at the corners of his eyes and mouth, and the touch of gray in his thick red-brown hair. His eyes were not quite blue, she saw, more like hazel.

He knew she was scrutinizing him, she thought, and he did not mind. Perhaps he was used to it. Perhaps he liked it. He smiled and said: "What kind of work are you doing?"

"A mixture." She was overwhelmingly flattered. Maybe he was just being nice, but he seemed genuinely interested in her. "Mostly I do research for Pierre. This morning I've been combing through a speech by Castro."

"Rather you than me. His speeches are long!"

Maria laughed. In the back of her mind a voice said, *The president is joking with me about Fidel Castro! In a swimming pool!* She said: "Sometimes Pierre asks me to write a press release, which is the part I like best."

"Tell him to give you more releases to write. You're good at it."

"Thank you, Mr. President. I can't tell you how much that means to me."

"You're from Chicago—is that right?"

"Yes, sir."

"Where are you living now?"

"In Georgetown. I share an apartment with two girls who work in the State Department."

"Sounds good. Well, I'm glad you're settled. I value your work, and I know Pierre does too."

He turned and talked to Jenny, but Maria did not hear what he said. She was too excited. The president remembered her name; he knew she was from Chicago; he thought highly of her work. And he was *so* attractive. She felt light enough to float up to the moon.

Dave looked at his watch and said: "Twelve thirty, Mr. President."

Maria could not believe she had been here for half an hour. It seemed like two minutes. But the president got out of the pool and went into the changing room.

The three girls got out. "Have a sandwich," Dave said. They all went to the table. Maria tried to eat something—this was her lunch break—but her stomach seemed to have shrunk to nothing. She drank a bottle of sugary soda pop.

Dave left, and the three girls changed back into their work clothes. Maria looked in the mirror. Her hair was a little damp, from the humidity, but it was still perfectly in place.

She said good-bye to Jenny and Jerry, then went back to the press office. On her desk was a thick report on health care and a note from Salinger asking for a two-page summary in an hour.

She caught the eye of Nelly, who said: "Well? What was that all about?"

Maria thought for a moment, then said: "I have no idea."

. . .

George Jakes got a message asking him to drop in on Joseph Hugo at FBI headquarters. Hugo was now working as personal assistant to FBI director J. Edgar Hoover. The message said that the Bureau had important information about Martin Luther King that Hugo wished to share with the attorney general's staff.

Hoover hated Martin Luther King. Not a single FBI agent was black. Hoover hated Bobby Kennedy, too. He hated a lot of people.

George considered refusing to go. The last thing he wanted was to speak to that creep Hugo, who had betrayed the civil rights movement and George personally. George's arm still hurt occasionally from the injury he had received in Anniston while Hugo looked on, chatting to the police and smoking.

On the other hand, if it was bad news George wanted to hear it first. Perhaps the FBI had caught King out in an extramarital affair, or something of that kind. George would welcome the chance to manage the dissemination of any negative information about the civil rights movement. He did not want someone such as Dennis Wilson spreading the word. For that reason he would have to see Hugo, and probably suffer his gloating.

FBI headquarters was on another floor of the Justice Department building. George found Hugo in a small office near the director's suite of rooms. Hugo had a short FBI haircut and wore a plain midgray suit with a white nylon shirt and a navy blue tie. On his desk was a pack of menthol cigarettes and a file folder.

"What do you want?" said George.

Hugo grinned. He could not conceal his pleasure. He said: "One of Martin Luther King's advisers is a Communist."

George was shocked. This accusation could blight the entire civil rights movement. He felt cold with worry. You could never prove that someone was *not* a Communist—and anyway, the truth hardly mattered: just the suggestion was deadly. Like the accusation of witchcraft in the Middle Ages, it was an easy way to stir up hatred among stupid and ignorant people.

"Who is this adviser?" George asked Hugo.

Hugo looked at a file, as if he had to refresh his memory. "Stanley Levison," he said.

"That doesn't sound like a Negro name."

"He's a Jew." Hugo took a photograph from the file and handed it over.

George saw an undistinguished white face with receding hair and large spectacles. The man was wearing a bow tie. George had met King and his people in Atlanta, and none of them looked like this. "Are you sure he works for the Southern Christian Leadership Conference?"

"I didn't say he *worked* for King. He's a New York attorney. Also a successful businessman."

"So in what sense is he an 'adviser' to Dr. King?"

"He helped King get his book published, and defended him from a tax-evasion lawsuit in Alabama. They don't meet often, but they talk on the phone."

George sat upright. "How would you know a thing like that?"

"Sources," Hugo said smugly.

"So, you claim that Dr. King sometimes telephones a New York attorney and gets advice on tax and publishing matters."

"From a Communist."

"How do you know he's a Communist?"

"Sources."

"What sources?"

"We can't reveal the identities of informants."

"You can to the attorney general."

"You're not the attorney general."

"Do you know Levison's card number?"

"What?" Hugo was momentarily flustered.

"Communist Party members have a card, as you know. Each card has a number. What's Levison's card number?"

Hugo pretended to search for it. "I don't think that's in this file."

"So you can't prove Levison is a Communist."

"We don't need *proof*," Hugo said, showing irritation. "We're not going to prosecute him. We're simply informing the attorney general of our suspicions, as is our duty."

George's voice rose. "You're blackening Dr. King's name by claiming that a lawyer he consulted is a Communist—and you offer no evidence whatsoever?"

"You're right," said Hugo, surprising George. "We need more evidence. That's why we'll be asking for a wiretap on Levison's phone." The attorney general had to authorize wiretaps. "The file is for you." He proffered it.

George did not take it. "If you wiretap Levison you'll be listening to some of Dr. King's calls."

Hugo shrugged. "People who talk to Communists take the risk of being wiretapped. Anything wrong with that?"

George thought there *was* something wrong with that, in a free country, but he did not say so. "We don't know that Levison is a Communist."

"So we need to find out."

George took the file, stood up, and opened the door.

Hugo said: "Hoover will undoubtedly mention this next time he meets with Bobby. So don't try to keep it to yourself."

That thought had crossed George's mind, but now he said: "Of course not." It had been a bad idea anyway.

"So what will you do?"

"I'll tell Bobby," George said. "He'll decide." He left the room.

He went up in the elevator to the fifth floor. Several Justice Department officials were just coming out of Bobby's office. George looked in. As usual, Bobby had his jacket off, his shirtsleeves rolled, and his glasses on. He had evidently just finished a meeting. George checked his watch: he had a few minutes before his next meeting. He walked in.

Bobby greeted him warmly. "Hi, George, how are things with you?"

It had been like this ever since the day George had imagined Bobby was about to hit him. Bobby treated him like a bosom pal. George wondered if that was a pattern. Maybe Bobby had to quarrel with someone before becoming close.

"Bad news," George said.

"Sit down and tell me."

George closed the door. "Hoover says he's found a Communist in Martin Luther King's circle."

"Hoover is a troublemaking cocksucker," said Bobby.

George was startled. Did Bobby mean that Hoover was queer? It seemed impossible. Maybe Bobby was just being insulting. "Name of Stanley Levison," George said.

"Who is he?"

"A lawyer Dr. King has consulted about tax and other matters."

"In Atlanta?"

"No, Levison is based in New York."

"It doesn't sound like he's really close to King."

"I don't believe he is."

"But that hardly matters," Bobby said wearily. "Hoover can always make it sound worse than it is."

"The FBI says Levison is a Communist, but they won't tell me what evidence they have, though they might tell you."

"I don't want to know anything about their sources of information." Bobby held up his hands, palms outward, in a defensive gesture. "I'd be blamed for every goddamn leak forever after."

"They don't even have Levison's party card number."

"They don't fucking know," Bobby said. "They're just guessing. But it makes no difference. People will believe it."

"What are we going to do?"

"King has to break with Levison," Bobby said decisively. "Otherwise Hoover will leak this, King will be damaged, and the whole civil rights mess will just get worse."

George did not think of the civil rights campaign as a "mess," but the Kennedy brothers did. However, that was not the point. Hoover's accusation was a threat that had to be dealt with, and Bobby was right: the simplest solution was for King to break with Levison. "But how are we going to get Dr. King to do that?" George asked.

Bobby said: "You're going to fly down to Atlanta and tell him to."

George was daunted. Martin Luther King was famous for defying authority, and George knew from Verena that in private as well as in public King could not easily be talked into anything. But George hid his apprehension behind a calm veneer. "I'll call now and make an appointment." He went to the door.

"Thank you, George," Bobby said with evident relief. "It's so great to be able to rely on you."

. . .

The day after she went swimming with the president, Maria picked up the phone and heard the voice of Dave Powers again. "There's a staff get-together at five thirty," he said. "Would you like to come?"

Maria and her flatmates had plans to see Audrey Hepburn and the dishy George Peppard in *Breakfast at Tiffany's*. But junior White House staffers did not say no to Dave Powers. The girls would have to drool over Peppard without her. "Where do I go?" she said.

"Upstairs."

"Upstairs?" That usually meant the president's private residence.

"I'll pick you up." Dave hung up.

Maria immediately wished she had put on a more fancy outfit today. She was wearing a plaid pleated skirt and a plain white blouse with little gold-colored buttons. Her hairpiece was a simple bob, short in the back with long scimitars of hair either side of her chin, in the current fashion. She feared she looked like every other office girl in Washington.

She spoke to Nelly. "Have you been invited to a staff get-together this evening?"

"Not me," said Nelly. "Where is it?"

"Upstairs."

"Lucky you."

At five fifteen, Maria went to the ladies' room to adjust her hair and makeup. She noticed that none of the other women was making any special effort, and she deduced that they had not been invited. Perhaps the get-together was for the newest recruits.

At five thirty, Nelly picked up her handbag to leave. "You take care of yourself, now," she said to Maria.

"You, too."

"No, I mean it," said Nelly, and she walked out before Maria could ask what she meant by that.

Dave Powers appeared a minute later. He led her out of doors, along the West Colonnade, past the entrance to the pool, then back inside and up in an elevator.

The doors opened on a grand hallway with two chandeliers. The walls were painted a color between blue and green that Maria thought might be called *eau de nil*. She hardly had time to take it in. "We're in the West Sitting Hall," Dave said, and led her through an open doorway into an informal room with a scatter of comfortable couches and a large arched window facing the sunset.

The same two secretaries were here, Jenny and Jerry, but no one else. Maria sat down, wondering whether others were going to join them. On the coffee table was a tray with cocktail glasses and a jug. "Have a daiquiri," Dave said, and poured it without waiting for her answer. Maria did not drink alcohol often, but she sipped it and liked it. She took a cheese puff from the tray of snacks. What was this all about?

"Will the First Lady be joining us?" she asked. "I'm longing to meet her."

There was a moment of silence, making her feel as if she had said something tactless; then Dave said: "Jackie's gone to Glen Ora."

Glen Ora was a farm in Middleburg, Virginia, where Jackie Kennedy kept horses and rode with the Orange County Hunt. It was about an hour from Washington.

Jenny said: "She's taken Caroline and John John."

Caroline Kennedy was four and John John was one.

If I were married to him, Maria thought, I wouldn't leave him to ride my horse.

Suddenly he walked in, and they all stood up.

He looked tired and strained, but his smile was as warm as ever. He took off his jacket, threw it over the back of a chair, sat on the couch, leaned back, and put his feet on the coffee table.

Maria felt she had been admitted to the most exclusive social group in the world. She was in the president's home, having drinks and snacks while he put his feet up. Whatever else happened, she would always have the memory of this.

She drained her glass, and Dave topped it up.

Why was she thinking, Whatever else happened? There was something off here. She was just a researcher, hoping for an early promotion to assistant press officer. The atmosphere was relaxed, but she was not really among friends. None of these people knew anything about her. What was she doing here?

The president stood up and said: "Maria, would you like a tour of the residence?"

A tour of the residence? From the president himself? Who would say no?

"Of course." She stood up. The daiquiri went to her head, and for a moment she felt dizzy, but it passed.

The president went through a side door, and she followed.

"This used to be a guest bedroom, but Mrs. Kennedy has converted it into a dining room," he said. The room was papered with battle scenes from the American Revolution. The square table in the middle looked too small for the room, Maria thought, and the chandelier too big for the table. But mostly she thought: I'm alone with the president in the White House residence—me! Maria Summers!

He smiled and looked into her eyes. "What do you think?" he said, as if he could not make up his own mind until he had heard her opinion.

"I love it," she said, wishing she could think of a more intelligent compliment.

"This way." He led her back across the West Sitting Hall and through the opposite door. "This is Mrs. Kennedy's bedroom," he said, and he closed the door behind them.

"It's beautiful," Maria breathed.

Opposite the door were two long windows with light blue drapes. To Maria's left was a fireplace with a couch placed on a rug patterned with the same blue. Over the mantel was a collection of framed drawings that looked tasteful and highbrow, just like Jackie. At the other end, the bedcovers and the canopy also matched, as did the cloth that covered the round occasional table in the corner. Maria had never seen a room like it, even in magazines.

But she was thinking: Why did he call it "Mrs. Kennedy's bedroom"?

Did he not sleep here? The big double bed was made up in two separate halves, and Maria recalled that the president had to have a hard mattress because of his back.

He led her to the window and they looked out. The evening light was soft over the South Lawn and the fountain where the Kennedy children sometimes paddled. "So beautiful," Maria said.

He put a hand on her shoulder. It was the first time he had touched her, and she trembled a little with the thrill. She smelled his cologne, close enough now to pick up the rosemary and musk under the citrus. He looked at her with the faint smile that was so alluring. "This is a very private room," he murmured.

She looked into his eyes. "Yes," she whispered. She felt a deep sense of intimacy with him, as if she had known him all her life, as if she knew beyond doubt that she could trust and love him without limit. She had a momentary guilty thought about George Jakes. But George had not even asked her for a date. She put him out of her mind.

The president put his other hand on the opposite shoulder and gently pushed her back. When her legs touched the bed she sat down.

He pushed her farther back, until she had to lean on her elbows. Still gazing into her eyes, he began to undo her blouse. For a moment she felt ashamed of those cheap gold-colored buttons, here in this unspeakably elegant room. Then he put his hands on her breasts.

Suddenly she hated the nylon brassiere that came between his skin and hers. Swiftly she undid the rest of the buttons, slipped her blouse off, reached behind her back to undo her bra, and threw that aside too. He gazed adoringly at her breasts, then took them in his soft hands, stroking them gently at first, then grasping them firmly.

He reached under her plaid skirt and pulled down her panties. She wished she had remembered to trim her pubic hair, as Jenny and Jerry did.

He was breathing hard, and so was she. He unfastened his suit pants and dropped them, then he lay on top of her.

Was it always this quick? She did not know.

He entered her smoothly. Then, feeling resistance, he stopped. "Haven't you done this before?" he said with surprise.

"No."

"Are you okay?"

"Yes." She was more than okay. She was happy, eager, yearning.

He pushed more gently. Something gave way, and she felt a sharp pain. She could not suppress a soft cry.

"Are you okay?" he repeated.

"Yes." She did not want him to stop.

He continued with closed eyes. She studied his face, the look of concentration, the smile of pleasure. Then he gave a sigh of satisfaction, and it was over.

He stood upright and pulled up his pants.

Smiling, he said: "The bathroom is through there." He pointed to a door in the corner, then did up his fly.

Suddenly Maria felt embarrassed, lying on the bed with her nakedness exposed to view. She stood up quickly. She grabbed her blouse and bra, stooped to pick up her panties, and ran into the bathroom.

She looked in the mirror and said: "What just happened?"

I lost my virginity, she thought. I had intercourse with a wonderful man. He happens to be the president of the United States. I enjoyed it.

She put her clothes on, then adjusted her makeup. Fortunately he had not mussed her hair.

This is Jackie's bathroom, she thought guiltily; and suddenly she wanted to leave.

The bedroom was empty. She went to the door, then turned and looked back at the bed.

She realized he had not once kissed her.

She went into the West Sitting Hall. The president sat there alone, his feet up on the coffee table. Dave and the girls had gone, leaving behind a tray of used glasses and the remains of the snacks. Kennedy seemed relaxed, as if nothing momentous had happened. Was this an everyday occurrence for him?

"Would you like something to eat?" he said. "The kitchen's right here."

"No, thank you, Mr. President."

She thought: He just fucked me, and I'm still calling him Mr. President.

He stood up. "There's a car at the South Portico waiting to take you home," he said. He walked her out into the main hall. "Are you okay?" he said for the third time.

"Yes."

The elevator came. She wondered if he would kiss her good night.

He did not. She got into the elevator.

"Good night, Maria," he said.

"Good night," she said, and the doors closed.

. . .

It took a while for George to tell Norine Latimer that their affair was over.

He was dreading it.

He had broken up with girls before, of course. After one or two dates it was easy: you just didn't call. After a longer relationship, in his experience, the feeling was usually mutual: both of you knew that the thrill had gone. But Norine fell between the two extremes. He had been seeing her only for a few months, and they were getting on fine. He had been hoping that they would spend a night together soon. She would not be expecting the brush-off.

He met her for lunch. She asked to be taken to the restaurant in the basement of the White House, known as the mess, but women were not allowed in. George did not want to take her somewhere swanky such as the Jockey Club, for fear she would imagine he was about to propose. In the end they went to Old Ebbitt's, a traditional politicians' restaurant that had seen better days.

Norine looked more Arabic than African. She was dramatically handsome, with wavy black hair and olive skin and a curved nose. She wore a fluffy sweater that really did not suit her: George guessed she was trying not to intimidate her boss. Men were uncomfortable with authoritative-looking women in their offices.

"I'm really sorry about canceling last night," he said when they had ordered. "I was summoned to a meeting with the president."

"Well, I can't compete with the president," she said.

That struck him as kind of a dumb thing to say. Of course she couldn't compete with the president; no one could. But he did not want to get into that discussion. He went right to the point. "Something's happened," he said. "Before I met you, there was another girl."

"I know," said Norine.

"What do you mean?"

"I like you, George," Norine said: "You're smart and funny and kind. And you're handsome, apart from that ear."

"But . . ."

"But I can tell when a man is carrying a torch for someone else."

"You can?"

"I guess it's Maria," said Norine.

George was astonished. "How the heck did you know that?"

"You've mentioned the name four or five times. And you've never talked about any other girl from your past. So it doesn't take a genius to figure out that she's still important to you. But she's in Chicago, so I thought maybe I could win you away from her." Norine suddenly looked sad.

George said: "She's come to Washington."

"Smart girl."

"Not for me. For a job."

"Whichever, you're dumping me for her."

He could hardly say yes to that. But it was true, so he said nothing.

Their food came, but Norine did not pick up her fork. "I wish you well, George," she said. "Take care of yourself."

It seemed very sudden. "Uh . . . you too."

She stood up. "Good-bye."

There was only one thing to say. "Good-bye, Norine."

"You can have my salad," she said, and she walked out.

George toyed with his food for a few minutes, feeling bad. Norine had been gracious, in her own way. She had made it easy for him. He hoped she was okay. She did not deserve to be hurt.

He went from the restaurant to the White House. He had to attend the President's Committee on Equal Employment Opportunity, chaired by Vice President Lyndon Johnson. George had formed an alliance with one of Johnson's advisers, Skip Dickerson. But he had half an hour to spare before the meeting started, so he went to the press office in search of Maria.

Today she was wearing a polka-dot dress with a matching hair band. The band was probably holding in place a wig: Maria's cute bob was definitely not natural.

When she asked him how he was, he did not know how to answer. He felt guilty about Norine; but now he could ask Maria out with a good conscience. "Pretty good, on balance," he said. "You?"

She lowered her voice. "Some days I just hate white people."

"What brought this on?"

"You haven't met my grandfather."

"Never met any of your family."

"Grandpa still preaches in Chicago now and again, but he spends most of his time in his hometown, Golgotha, Alabama. Says he never really got used to the cold wind in the Midwest. But he's still feisty. He put on his best suit and went down to the Golgotha courthouse to register to vote."

"What happened?"

"They humiliated him." She shook her head. "You know their tricks. They give people a literacy test: you have to read part of the state constitution aloud, explain it, then write it down. The registrar picks which clause you have to read. He gives whites a simple sentence, like: 'No person shall be imprisoned for debt.' But Negroes get a long, complicated paragraph that only a lawyer could understand. Then it's up to the registrar to say whether you're literate or not, and of course he always decides the whites are literate and the Negroes aren't."

"Sons of bitches."

"That's not all. Negroes who try to register get fired from their jobs, as a punishment, but they couldn't do that to Grandpa because he's retired. So, as he was leaving the courthouse, they arrested him for loitering. He spent the night in jail—no picnic when you're eighty." There were tears in her eyes.

The story hardened George's resolve. What did he have to complain about? So, some of the things he had to do made him want to wash his hands. Working for Bobby was still the most effective thing he could do for people like Grandpa Summers. One day those Southern racists would be smashed.

He looked at his watch. "I have a meeting with Lyndon."

"Tell him about my grandpa."

"Maybe I will." The time George spent with Maria always seemed too short. "I'm sorry to hurry away, but do you want to meet up after work?" he said. "We could have drinks, maybe go for dinner somewhere?"

She smiled. "Thank you, George, but I have a date tonight."

"Oh." George was taken aback. Somehow it had not occurred to him that she might already be dating. "Uh, I have to go to Atlanta tomorrow, but I'll be back in two or three days. Maybe over the weekend?"

"No, thanks." She hesitated, then explained: "I'm kind of going steady."

George was devastated—which was stupid: why would a girl as attractive as Maria *not* have a steady date? He had been a fool. He felt disoriented, as if he had lost his footing. He managed to say: "Lucky guy."

She smiled. "It's nice of you to say so."

George wanted to know about the competition. "Who is he?"

"You don't know him."

No, but I will as soon as I can learn his name. "Try me."

She shook her head. "I prefer not to say."

George was frustrated beyond measure. He had a rival and did not even know the man's name. He wanted to press her, but he was wary of acting like a bully: girls hated that. "Okay," he said reluctantly. With massive insincerity he added: "Have a great evening."

"I sure will."

They separated, Maria heading for the press office and George toward the vice president's rooms.

George was heartsick. He liked Maria more than any girl he had ever met, and he had lost her to someone else.

He thought: I wonder who he is?

. . .

Maria took off her clothes and got into the bath with President Kennedy.

Jack Kennedy took pills all day but nothing relieved his back pain like being in water. He even shaved in the tub in the mornings. He would have slept in a pool if he could.

This was his bathtub, in his bathroom, with his turquoise-and-gold bottle of 4711 cologne on the shelf over the washbasin. Since the first time, Maria had never been back inside Jackie's quarters. The president had a separate bedroom and bathroom, connected to Jackie's suite by a short corridor where—for some reason—the record player was housed.

Jackie was out of town, again. Maria had learned not to torture herself with thoughts of her lover's wife. Maria knew she was cruelly betraying a decent woman, and it grieved her, so she did not think about it.

Maria loved the bathroom, which was luxurious beyond dreams, with soft towels and white bathrobes and expensive soap—and a family of yellow rubber ducks.

They had slipped into a routine. Whenever Dave Powers invited her, which was about once a week, she would take the elevator up to the residence after work. There was always a pitcher of daiquiris and a tray of snacks waiting in the West Sitting Hall. Sometimes Dave was there, sometimes Jenny and Jerry, sometimes no one. Maria would pour a drink and wait, eager but patient, until the president arrived.

Soon afterward they would move to the bedroom. It was Maria's favorite place in the world. It had a four-poster bed with a blue canopy, two chairs in front of a real fire, and piles of books, magazines, and newspapers everywhere. She felt she could cheerfully live in this room for the rest of her life.

He had gently taught her to give oral sex. She had been an eager pupil. That was usually what he wanted when he arrived. He was often in a hurry for it, almost desperate; and there was something arousing about his urgency. But she liked him best afterward, when he would relax and become warmer, more affectionate.

Sometimes he put a record on. He liked Sinatra and Tony Bennett and Percy Marquand. He had never heard of the Miracles or the Shirelles.

There was always a cold supper in the kitchen: chicken, shrimp, sandwiches, salad. After they ate they would undress and get into the bath.

She sat at the opposite end of the tub. He put two ducks in the water and said: "Bet you a quarter my duck can go faster than yours." In his Boston accent he said *quarter* like an Englishman, not pronouncing the letter *r*.

She picked up a duck. She loved him most when he was like this:

playful, silly, childish. "Okay, Mr. President," she said. "But make it a dollar, if you got the moxie."

She still called him Mr. President most of the time. His wife called him Jack; his brothers sometimes called him Johnny. Maria called him Johnny only at moments of great passion.

"I can't afford to lose a dollar," he said, laughing. But he was sensitive, and he could tell she was not in the right mood. "What's the matter?"

"I don't know." She shrugged. "I don't usually talk to you about politics."

"Why not? Politics is my life, and yours, too."

"You get pestered all day. Our time together is about relaxing and having fun."

"Make an exception." He picked up her foot, lying alongside his thigh in the water, and stroked her toes. She had beautiful feet, she knew; and she always put varnish on her toenails. "Something has upset you," he said quietly. "Tell me what it is."

When he looked at her so intensely, with his hazel eyes and his wry smile, she was helpless. She said: "The day before yesterday, my grandfather was jailed for trying to register to vote."

"Jailed? They can't do that. What was the charge?"

"Loitering."

"Oh. This happened somewhere in the South."

"Golgotha, Alabama, his hometown." She hesitated, but decided to tell him the whole truth, although he would not like it. "Do you want to know what he said when he came out of jail?"

"What?"

"He said: 'With President Kennedy in the White House, I thought I could vote, but I guess I was wrong.' That's what Grandma told me."

"Hell," said the president. "He believed in me, and I failed him."

"That's what he thinks, I guess."

"What do you think, Maria?" He was still stroking her toes.

She hesitated again, looking at her dark foot in his white hands. She feared that this discussion could become acrimonious. He was touchy about the least suggestion that he was insincere or untrustworthy, or that he failed to keep his promises as a politician. If she pushed him too hard, he might end their relationship. And then she would die.

But she had to be honest. She took a deep breath and tried to remain calm. "Far as I can see, the issue is not complicated," she began. "Southerners do this because they can. The law, as it stands, lets them get away with it, despite the Constitution."

"Not entirely," he interrupted. "My brother Bob has stepped up the number of lawsuits brought by the Justice Department for voting rights violations. He has a bright young Negro lawyer working with him."

She nodded. "George Jakes. I know him. But what they're doing isn't enough."

He shrugged. "I can't deny that."

She pressed on. "Everyone agrees that we have to change the law by bringing in a new civil rights act. A lot of people thought you promised that in your election campaign. And . . . nobody understands why you haven't done it yet." She bit her lip, then risked the ultimate. "Including me."

His face hardened.

She immediately regretted being so candid. "Don't be mad," she pleaded. "I wouldn't upset you for the world—but you asked me the question, and I wanted to be honest." Tears came to her eyes. "And my poor grandpa spent all night in jail, in his best suit."

He forced a smile. "I'm not mad, Maria. Not at you, anyway."

"You can tell me anything," she said. "I adore you. I would never sit in judgment on you—you must know that. Just say how you feel."

"I'm angry because I'm weak, I guess," he said. "We have a majority in Congress only if we include conservative Southern Democrats. If I bring in a civil rights bill, they'll sabotage it—and that's not all. In revenge, they'll vote against all the rest of my domestic legislation program, including Medicare. Now, Medicare could improve the lives of colored Americans even more than civil rights legislation."

"Does that mean you've given up on civil rights?"

"No. We have midterm elections next November. I'll be asking the American people to send more Democrats to Congress so that I can fulfill my campaign promises."

"Will they?"

"Probably not. The Republicans are attacking me on foreign policy. We've lost Cuba, we've lost Laos, and we're losing Vietnam. I had to let Khrushchev put up a barbed-wire fence right across the middle of Berlin. Right now my back is up against the goddamn wall."

"How strange," Maria reflected. "You can't let Southern Negroes vote because you're vulnerable on foreign policy."

"Every leader has to look strong on the world stage, otherwise he can't get anything done."

"Couldn't you just try? Bring in a civil rights bill, even though you'll probably lose it. At least then people would know how sincere you are."

He shook his head. "If I bring in a bill and get defeated I'll look weak, and that will jeopardize everything else. And I'd never get a second chance on civil rights."

"So what should I tell Grandpa?"

"That doing the right thing is not as easy as it looks, even when you're president."

He stood up, and she did the same. They toweled each other dry, then went into his bedroom. Maria put on one of his soft blue cotton nightshirts.

They made love again. If he was tired, it was brief, like the very first time; but tonight he was at ease. He reverted to a playful mood, and they lay back on the bed, toying with one another, as if nothing else in the world mattered.

Afterward he went to sleep quickly. She lay beside him, blissfully happy. She did not want the morning to come, when she would have to get dressed and go to the press office and begin her day's work. She lived in the real world as if it were a dream, waiting only for the call from Dave Powers that meant she could wake up and come back to the only reality that mattered.

She knew that some of her colleagues must have guessed what she was doing. She knew he was never going to leave his wife for her. She knew she should be worried about getting pregnant. She knew that everything she was doing was foolish and wrong and could not possibly have a happy ending.

And she was too much in love to care.

. . .

George understood why Bobby was so pleased to be able to send him to talk to King. When Bobby needed to put pressure on the civil rights movement, he had more chance of success using a black messenger. George thought Bobby was right about Levison but, nevertheless, he was not entirely comfortable with his role—a feeling that was beginning to be familiar.

Atlanta was cold and rainy. Verena met George at the airport, wearing a tan coat with a black fur collar. She looked beautiful, but George was still hurting too much from Maria's rejection to be attracted. "I know Stanley Levison," Verena said, driving George through the urban sprawl of the city. "A very sincere guy."

"He's a lawyer, right?"

"More than that. He helped Martin with the writing of *Stride Toward Freedom*. They're close."

"The FBI says Levison is a Communist."

"Anyone who disagrees with J. Edgar Hoover is a Communist, according to the FBI."

"Bobby referred to Hoover as a cocksucker."

Verena laughed. "Do you think he meant it?"

"I don't know."

"Hoover, a powder puff?" She shook her head in disbelief. "It's too good to be true. Real life is never that funny."

She drove through the rain to the Old Fourth Ward neighborhood, where there were hundreds of black-owned businesses. There seemed to be a church on every block. Auburn Avenue had once been called the most prosperous Negro street in America. The Southern Christian Leadership Conference had its headquarters at number 320. Verena pulled up at a long two-story building of red brick.

George said: "Bobby thinks Dr. King is arrogant."

Verena shrugged. "Martin thinks Bobby is arrogant."

"What do you think?"

"They're both right."

George laughed. He liked Verena's sharp wit.

They hurried across the wet sidewalk and went inside. They waited outside King's office for fifteen minutes, then they were called.

Martin Luther King was a handsome man of thirty-three, with a mustache and prematurely receding black hair. He was short, George guessed about five foot six, and a little plump. He wore a well-pressed dark-gray suit with a white shirt and a narrow black satin tie. There was a white silk handkerchief in his breast pocket, and he had large cuff links. George caught a whiff of cologne. He got the impression of a man whose dignity was important to him. George sympathized: he felt the same.

King shook George's hand and said: "Last time we met, you were on the Freedom Ride, heading for Anniston. How's the arm?"

"It's completely healed, thank you," George said. "I've given up competitive wrestling, but I was ready to do that anyway. Now I coach a high school team in Ivy City." Ivy City was a black neighborhood in Washington.

"That's a good thing," King said. "To teach Negro boys to use their strength in a disciplined sport, with rules. Please have a seat." He waved at a chair and retreated behind his desk. "Tell me why the attorney general has sent you to speak to me." There was a hint of injured pride in his voice. Perhaps King thought Bobby should have come himself. George recalled that King's nickname within the civil rights movement was De Lawd.

George outlined the Stanley Levison problem briskly, leaving out nothing but the wiretap request. "Bobby sent me here to urge you, as strongly as I can, to break all ties with Mr. Levison," he said in conclusion. "It's the only way to protect yourself from the charge of being a fellow traveler with the Communists—an accusation that can do untold harm to the movement that you and I both believe in."

When he had finished, King said: "Stanley Levison is not a Communist."

George opened his mouth to ask a question.

King held up a hand to silence him: he was not a man to tolerate interruption. "Stanley has never been a member of the Communist Party. Communism is atheistical, and I as a follower of the Lord Jesus Christ would find it impossible to be the close friend of an atheist. But—" He leaned forward across the desk. "That is not the whole truth."

He was silent for a few moments, but George knew that he was not supposed to speak.

"Let me tell you the whole truth about Stanley Levison," King went on at last, and George felt he was about to hear a sermon. "Stanley is good at making money. This embarrasses him. He feels he should spend his life helping others. So, when he was young, he became . . . entranced.

Yes, that's the word. He was entranced by the ideals of Communism. Although he never joined, he used his remarkable talents to help the Communist Party of the USA in various ways. Soon he saw how wrong he was, broke the association, and gave his support to the cause of freedom and equality for the Negro. And so he became my friend."

George waited until he was sure King had finished, then he said: "I'm deeply sorry to hear this, Reverend. If Levison has been a financial adviser to the Communist Party, he is forever tainted."

"But he has changed."

"I believe you, but others will not. By continuing a relationship with Levison you will be giving ammunition to our enemies."

"So be it," said King.

George was flabbergasted. "What do you mean?"

"Moral rules must be obeyed when it doesn't suit us. Otherwise, why would we need rules?"

"But if you balance—"

"We don't balance," King said. "Stanley did wrong to help the Communists. He has repented and is making amends. I'm a preacher in the service of the Lord. I must forgive as Jesus does and welcome Stanley with open arms. Joy shall be in heaven over one sinner that repenteth, more than over ninety and nine just persons. I myself am too often in need of God's grace to refuse mercy to another."

"But the cost—"

"I'm a Christian pastor, George. The doctrine of forgiveness goes deep into my soul, deeper even than freedom and justice. I could not go back on it for any prize."

George realized his mission was doomed. King was completely sincere. There was no prospect of changing his mind.

George stood up. "Thank you for taking the time to explain your point of view. I appreciate it, and so does the attorney general."

"God bless you," said King.

George and Verena left the office and walked outside. Without speaking, they got into Verena's car. "I'll drop you at your hotel," she said.

George nodded. He was thinking about King's words. He did not want to talk.

They drove in silence until she pulled up at the hotel entrance. Then she said: "Well?"

He said: "King made me ashamed of myself."

. . .

"That's what preachers do," said his mother. "It's their job. It's good for you." She poured a glass of milk for George and gave him a slice of cake. He did not want either.

He had told her the whole thing, sitting in her kitchen. "He was so strong," George said. "Once he knew what was right, he was going to do it, no matter what."

"Don't set him up too high," Jacky said. "No one's an angel— especially if he's a man." It was late afternoon, and she was still wearing her work clothes, a plain black dress and flat shoes.

"I know that. But there I was, trying to persuade him to break with a loyal friend for cynical political reasons, and he just talked about right and wrong."

"How was Verena?"

"I wish you could have seen her, in that coat with a black fur collar."

"Did you take her out?"

"We had dinner." He had not kissed her good night.

Out of the blue, Jacky said: "I like that Maria Summers."

George was startled. "How do you know her?"

"She belongs to the club." Jacky was supervisor of the colored staff at the University Women's Club. "It doesn't have many black members, so of course we talk. She mentioned she worked at the White House. I told her about you, and we realized you two already know each other. She has a nice family."

George was amused. "How do you know *that*?"

"She brought her parents in for lunch. Her father's a big lawyer in Chicago. He knows Mayor Daley there." Daley was a big Kennedy supporter.

"You know more about her than I do!"

"Women listen. Men talk."

"I like Maria, too."

"Good." Jacky frowned, remembering the original topic of

conversation. "What did Bobby Kennedy say when you got back from Atlanta?"

"He's going to okay the wiretap on Levison. That means the FBI will be listening to some of Dr. King's phone calls."

"How much does that matter? Everything King does is intended to be publicized."

"They may find out, in advance, what King is going to do next. If they do, they'll tip off the segregationists, who will be able to plan ahead, and may find ways to undermine what King does."

"It's bad, but it's not the end of the world."

"I could tip King off about the wiretap. Tell Verena to warn King to be careful what he says on the phone to Levison."

"You'd be betraying the trust of your work colleagues."

"That's what bothers me."

"In fact, you'd probably have to resign."

"Exactly. Because I'd feel a traitor."

"Besides, they might find out about the tip-off, and when they looked around for the culprit they'd see one black face in the room—yours."

"Maybe I should do it anyway, if it's the right thing."

"If you leave, George, there's *no* black face in Bobby Kennedy's inner circle."

"I knew you'd say I should shut up and stay."

"It's hard, but yes, I think you should."

"So do I," said George.

CHAPTER TWELVE

Y ou live in an amazing house," Beep Dewar said to Dave Williams.

Dave was thirteen years old; he had lived here as long as he could remember; and he had never really noticed the house. He looked up at the brick façade of the garden front, with its regular rows of Georgian windows. "Amazing?" he said.

"It's so old."

"It's eighteenth century, I think. So it's only about two hundred years old."

"Only!" She laughed. "In San Francisco, nothing is two hundred years old!"

The house was in Great Peter Street, London, a couple of minutes' walk from Parliament. Most of the houses in the neighborhood were eighteenth century, and Dave knew vaguely that they had been built for members of Parliament and peers who had to attend the House of Commons and the House of Lords. Dave's father, Lloyd Williams, was an M.P.

"Do you smoke cigarettes?" said Beep, taking out a packet.

"Only when I get the chance."

She gave him one and they both lit up.

Ursula Dewar, known as Beep, was also thirteen, but she seemed older than Dave. She wore nifty American clothes, tight sweaters and narrow jeans and boots. She claimed she could drive. She said British radio was square: only three stations, none playing rock and roll—and they went off the air at midnight! When she caught Dave staring at the small bumps her breasts made in the front of her black turtleneck, she was not even embarrassed; she just smiled. But she never quite gave him an opportunity to kiss her.

She would not be the first girl he had kissed. He would have liked to let her know that, just in case she thought he was inexperienced. She would be the third, counting Linda Robertson, whom he did count even though she had not actually kissed him back. The point was, he knew what to do.

But he had not managed it with Beep, not yet.

He had come close. He had discreetly put his arm around her shoulders in the back of his father's Humber Hawk, but she had turned her face away and looked out at the lamplit streets. She did not giggle when tickled. They had jived to the Dansette record player in the bedroom of his fifteen-year-old sister, Evie; but Beep had declined to slow-dance when Dave put on Elvis singing "Are You Lonesome Tonight?"

Still he lived in hope. Sadly, this was not the moment, standing in the small garden on a winter afternoon, Beep hugging herself to keep warm, both of them stiffly dressed in their best clothes. They were off to a formal family occasion. But there would be a party later. Beep had a quarter bottle of vodka in her handbag to spike the soft drinks they would be given while their parents hypocritically glugged whisky and gin. And then anything might happen. He stared at her pink lips closing around the filter tip of her Chesterfield, and imagined yearningly what it would be like.

His mother's American accent called from the house: "Get in here, you kids—we're leaving!" They dropped their cigarettes into the flower bed and went inside.

The two families were assembling in the hall. Dave's grandmother Eth Leckwith was to be "introduced" to the House of Lords. This meant she would become a baroness, be addressed as Lady Leckwith, and sit as a Labour peer in the upper chamber of Parliament. Dave's parents, Lloyd and Daisy, were waiting, with his sister, Evie, and a young family friend, Jasper Murray. The Dewars, wartime friends, were here too. Woody Dewar was a photographer on a one-year assignment in London, and had brought his wife, Bella, and their children, Cameron and Beep. All Americans seemed fascinated by the pantomime of British public life, so the Dewars were joining in the celebration. They formed a large group as they left the house and headed for Parliament Square.

Walking through the misty London streets, Beep transferred her attention from Dave to Jasper Murray. He was eighteen and a Viking, tall and broad with blond hair. He wore a heavy tweed jacket. Dave longed to be so grown-up and masculine, and to have Beep look up at him with that expression of admiration and desire.

Dave treated Jasper like an older brother, and asked his advice. He had confessed to Jasper that he adored Beep and could not figure out how to win her heart. "Keep trying," Jasper had said. "Sometimes sheer persistence works."

Dave could hear their conversation. "So you're Dave's cousin?" Beep said to Jasper as they crossed Parliament Square.

"Not really," Jasper replied. "We're no relation."

"So how come you live here rent-free and everything?"

"My mother was at school with Dave's mother in Buffalo. That's where they met your father. Since then they've all been friends."

There was more to it than that, Dave knew. Jasper's mother, Eva, had been a refugee from Nazi Germany and Dave's mother, Daisy, had taken her in, with characteristic generosity. But Jasper preferred to underplay the extent to which his family was indebted to the Williamses.

Beep said: "What are you studying?"

"French and German. I'm at St. Julian's, which is one of the larger colleges of London University. But mostly I write for the student newspaper. I'm going to be a journalist."

Dave was envious. He would never learn French or go to university. He was bottom of the class at everything. His father despaired.

Beep said to Jasper: "Where are your parents?"

"Germany. They move around the world with the army. My father's a colonel."

"A colonel!" said Beep admiringly.

Dave's sister, Evie, muttered in his ear: "Little tart, what does she think she's doing? First she flutters her eyelashes at you, then she flirts with a man five years older!"

Dave made no comment. He knew that his sister had a massive crush on Jasper. He could have taunted her, but he refrained. He liked Evie and, besides, it was better to save up stuff like this and use it next time she was mean to him.

"Don't you have to be born an aristocrat?" Beep was saying.

"Even in the oldest families there has to be a first one," Jasper said. "But nowadays we have life peers, who don't pass the title to their heirs. Mrs. Leckwith will be a life peer."

"Will we have to curtsey to her?"

Jasper laughed. "No, idiot."

"Will the queen be there for the ceremony?"

"No."

"How disappointing!"

Evie whispered: "Stupid bitch."

They went into the Palace of Westminster by the Lords Entrance. They were greeted by a man in court dress, including knee breeches and silk stockings. Dave heard his grandmother say in her lilting Welsh accent: "Obsolete uniforms are a sure sign of an institution in need of reform."

Dave and Evie had been coming to the Parliament building all their lives, but it was a new experience for the Dewars, and they marveled. Beep forgot to be charmingly dizzy and said: "Every surface is decorated! Floor tiles, patterned carpets, wallpaper, wood paneling, stained glass, and carved stone!"

Jasper looked at her with more interest. "It's typical Victorian Gothic."

"Oh, really?"

Dave was beginning to get irritated with the way Jasper was impressing Beep.

The party split, most of them following an usher up several flights to a gallery overlooking the debating chamber. Ethel's friends were already there. Beep sat next to Jasper, but Dave managed to sit the other side of her, and Evie slid in beside him. Dave had often visited the House of Commons, at the other end of the same palace, but this was more ornate, and had red leather benches instead of green.

After a long wait there was a stir of activity below and his grandmother came in, walking in line with four other people, all dressed in funny hats and extremely silly robes with fur trimmings. Beep said: "This is amazing!" but Dave and Evie giggled.

The procession stopped in front of a throne, and Grandmam knelt down, not without difficulty—she was sixty-eight. There was a lot of passing round of scrolls that had to be read aloud. Dave's mother, Daisy, was explaining the ceremony in a low voice to Beep's parents, tall Woody and plump Bella, but Dave tuned her out. It was all bollocks really.

After a while Ethel and two of her escorts went and sat on one of the benches. Then followed the funniest part of all.

They sat down, then immediately stood up again. They took off their hats and bowed. They sat down and put their hats back on again. Then they went through the whole thing again, looking for all the world like three marionettes on strings: stand up, hats off, bow, sit down, hats on. By this time Dave and Evie were helpless with suppressed laughter. Then they did it a third time. Dave heard his sister splutter: "Stop, please stop!" which made him giggle even more. Daisy directed a stern blue-eyed glare at them, but she was too full of fun herself not to see the funny side, and in the end she grinned too.

At last it was over and Ethel left the chamber. Her family and friends stood up. Dave's mother led them through a maze of corridors and staircases to a basement room for the party. Dave checked that his guitar was safe in a corner. He and Evie were going to perform, though she was the star: he was merely her accompanist.

Within a few minutes there were about a hundred people in the room.

Evie buttonholed Jasper and started asking him about the student newspaper. The subject was close to his heart, and he answered with enthusiasm, but Dave was sure Evie was onto a loser. Jasper was a boy who knew how to look after his own interests. Right now he had luxurious lodgings, rent-free, a short bus ride from his college. He was not likely to destabilize that comfortable situation by beginning a romance with the daughter of the house, in Dave's cynical opinion.

However, Evie took Jasper's attention away from Beep, leaving the field clear for Dave. He got her a ginger beer and asked her what she thought of the ceremony. Surreptitiously, she poured vodka into their soft drinks. A minute later everyone applauded as Ethel came in, dressed now in normal clothes, a red dress and matching coat with a small hat perched on her silver curls. Beep whispered: "She must have been drop-dead gorgeous, once upon a time."

Dave found it creepy to think about his grandmother as an attractive woman.

Ethel began to speak. "It's such a pleasure to share this occasion with all of you," she said. "I'm only sorry my beloved Bernie didn't live to see this day. He was the wisest man I ever knew."

Granddad Bernie had died a year ago.

"It is strange to be addressed as 'my lady,' especially for a lifelong socialist," she went on, and everyone laughed. "Bernie would ask me whether I had beaten my enemies or just joined them. So let me assure you that I have joined the peerage in order to abolish it."

They applauded.

"Seriously, comrades, I gave up being the member of Parliament for Aldgate because I felt it was time to let someone younger take over, but I haven't retired. There is too much injustice in our society, too much bad housing and poverty, too much hunger in the world—and I may have only twenty or thirty campaigning years left!"

That got another laugh.

"I've been advised that here in the House of Lords it's wise to take up one issue and make it your own, and I've decided what my issue will be."

They went quiet. People were always keen to know what Eth Leckwith would do next.

"Last week my dear old friend Robert von Ulrich died. He fought in the First World War, got in trouble with the Nazis in the thirties, and ended up running the best restaurant in Cambridge. Once, when I was a young seamstress working in a sweatshop in the East End, he bought me a new dress and took me to dinner at the Ritz. And . . ." She lifted her chin defiantly. "And he was a homosexual."

There was an audible susurration of surprise in the room.

Dave muttered: "Blimey!"

Beep said: "I like your grandmother."

People were not used to hearing this subject discussed so openly, especially by a woman. Dave grinned. Good old Grandmam, still making trouble after all these years.

"Don't mutter—you're not really shocked," she said crisply. "You all know there are men who love men. Such people do no harm to anyone— in fact, in my experience they tend to be gentler than other men—yet what they do is a crime according to the laws of our country. Even worse, plainclothes police detectives pretending to be men of the same sort entrap them, arrest them, and put them in jail. In my opinion this is as bad as persecuting people for being Jewish or pacifist or Catholic. So my main campaign here in the House of Lords will be homosexual law reform. I hope you will all wish me luck. Thank you."

She got an enthusiastic round of applause. Dave figured that almost everyone in the room genuinely did wish her luck. He was impressed. He thought jailing queers was stupid. The House of Lords went up in his estimation: if you could campaign for that sort of change here, maybe the place was not completely ludicrous.

Finally Ethel said: "And now, in honor of our American relatives and friends, a song."

Evie went to the front and Dave followed her. "Trust Grandmam to give them something to think about," Evie murmured to Dave. "I bet she'll succeed, too."

"She generally gets what she wants." He picked up his guitar and strummed the chord of G.

Evie began immediately:

O say can you see, by the dawn's early light,

Most of the people in the room were British, not American, but Evie's voice made them all listen.

What so proudly we hail'd at the twilight's last gleaming,

Dave thought nationalist pride was bollocks, really, but despite himself he felt a little choked up. It was the song.

Whose broad stripes and bright stars through the perilous fight
O'er the ramparts we'd watch'd were so gallantly streaming?

The room was so quiet that Dave could hear his own breathing. Evie could do this. When she was onstage, everyone watched.

And the rocket's red glare, the bombs bursting in air,
Gave proof through the night that our flag was still there,

Dave looked at his mother and saw her wipe away a tear.

O say does that star-spangled banner yet wave
O'er the land of the free and the home of the brave?

They clapped and cheered. Dave had to give his sister credit: she was a pain in the neck at times, but she could hold an audience spellbound.

He got another ginger beer, then looked around for Beep, but she was not in the room. He saw her older brother, Cameron, who was a creep. "Hey, Cam, where did Beep go?"

"Out for a smoke, I guess," he said.

Dave wondered if he could find her. He decided to go and look. He put down his drink.

He approached the exit at the same time as his grandmother, so he held the door for her. She was probably heading for the ladies' room: he had a vague notion that old women had to go a lot. She smiled at him and turned up a red-carpeted staircase. He had no idea where he was so he followed her.

On the half landing she was stopped by an elderly man leaning on a cane. Dave noticed that he was wearing an elegant suit in a pale gray material with a chalk stripe. A patterned silk handkerchief spilled out of the breast pocket. His face was mottled and his hair was white, but obviously he had once been a good-looking man. He said: "Congratulations, Ethel," and shook her hand.

"Thank you, Fitz." They seemed to know each other well.

He held on to her hand. "So you're a baroness now."

She smiled. "Isn't life strange?"

"Baffles me."

They were blocking the way, and Dave hovered, waiting. Although their words were trivial, their conversation had an undertone of passion. Dave could not put his finger on what it was.

Ethel said: "You don't mind that your housekeeper has been elevated to the peerage?"

Housekeeper? Dave knew that Ethel had started out as a maid in a big house in Wales. This man must have been her employer.

"I stopped minding that sort of thing a long time ago," the man said. He patted her hand and released it. "During the Attlee government, to be precise."

She laughed. Clearly she liked talking to him. There was a powerful undertone to their conversation, neither love nor hate, but something else. If they had not been so old, Dave would have thought it was sex.

Getting impatient, Dave coughed.

Ethel said: "This is my grandson, David Williams. If you really have stopped minding, you might shake his hand. Dave, this is Earl Fitzherbert."

The earl hesitated, and for a moment Dave thought he was going to refuse to shake; then he seemed to make up his mind, and stuck out his hand. Dave shook it and said: "How do you do?"

Ethel said: "Thank you, Fitz." Or, rather, she almost said it, but seemed to choke before finishing the sentence. Without saying anything more, she walked on. Dave nodded politely at the old earl and followed.

A moment later Ethel disappeared through a door marked LADIES.

Dave guessed there was some history between Ethel and Fitz. He decided to ask his mother about it. Then he spotted an exit that might lead outside, and forgot all about the old folk.

He stepped through the door and found himself in an irregular-shaped internal courtyard with rubbish bins. This would be the perfect place for a surreptitious smooch, he thought. It was not a thoroughfare, no windows overlooked it, and there were odd little corners. His hopes rose.

There was no sign of Beep, but he smelled tobacco smoke.

He stepped past the bins and looked around the corner.

She was there, as he had hoped, and there was a cigarette in her left hand. But she was with Jasper, and they were locked in an embrace. Dave stared at them. Their bodies seemed glued together, and they were kissing passionately, her right hand in his hair, his right hand on her breast.

"You're a treacherous bastard, Jasper Murray," said Dave, then he turned and went back into the building.

. . .

In the school production of *Hamlet*, Evie Williams proposed to play Ophelia's mad scene in the nude.

Just the idea made Cameron Dewar feel uncomfortably warm.

Cameron adored Evie. He just hated her views. She joined every bleeding-heart cause in the news, from animal cruelty to nuclear disarmament, and she talked as if people who did not do the same must be brutal and stupid. But Cameron was used to this: he disagreed with most people his age, and all of his family. His parents were hopelessly liberal, and his grandmother had once been editor of a newspaper with the unlikely title *The Buffalo Anarchist*.

The Williamses were just as bad, leftists every one. The only halfway sensible resident of the house in Great Peter Street was the sponger Jasper Murray, who was more or less cynical about everything. London was a nest of subversives, even worse than Cameron's hometown of San Francisco. He would be glad when his father's assignment was over and they could go back to America.

Except that he would miss Evie. Cameron was fifteen years old and in love for the first time. He did not *want* a romance: he had too much to do. But as he sat at his school desk trying to memorize French and Latin vocabulary, he found himself remembering Evie singing "The Star-Spangled Banner."

She liked him, he felt sure. She realized he was clever, and asked him earnest questions: How did nuclear power stations work? Was Hollywood an actual place? How were Negroes treated in California? Better still, she listened attentively to his answers. She was not making small talk: like him, she had no interest in chitchat. They would be a well-known intellectual couple, in Cameron's fantasy.

For this year Cameron and Beep were going to the school Evie and Dave attended, a progressive London establishment where—as far as Cameron could see—most of the teachers were Communists. The controversy about Evie's mad scene went all around the school in a flash. The drama teacher, Jeremy Faulkner, a beardie in a striped college scarf, actually approved of the idea. However, the head teacher was not so foolish, and he stamped on it decisively.

This was one instance in which Cameron would have been glad to see liberal decadence prevail.

The Williams and Dewar families went together to see the play. Cameron hated Shakespeare but he was looking forward eagerly to seeing what Evie would do onstage. She had an air of intensity that seemed to be brought out by an audience. She was like her great-grandfather Dai Williams, the pioneering trade unionist and evangelical preacher, according to Ethel, Dai's daughter. Ethel had said: "My father had the same bound-for-glory light in his eyes."

Cameron had studied *Hamlet* conscientiously—the way he studied everything, in order to get good marks—and he knew that Ophelia was a notoriously difficult part. Supposedly pathetic, she could easily become comic, with her obscene songs. How was a fifteen-year-old going to play this role and carry an audience with her? Cameron did not want to see her fall on her face (although there was, in the back of his mind, a little fantasy in which he put his arms around her delicate shoulders and comforted her as she wept for her humiliating failure).

With his parents and his kid sister, Beep, he filed into the school hall, which doubled as the gym, so that it smelled equally of dusty hymn books and sweaty sneakers. They took their seats next to the Williams family: Lloyd Williams, the Labour M.P.; his American wife, Daisy; Eth Leckwith, the grandmother; and Jasper Murray, the lodger. Young Dave, Evie's kid brother, was somewhere else, organizing an intermission bar.

Several times in the past few months Cameron had heard the story of how his mother and father had first met here in London, during the war, at a party given by Daisy. Papa had walked Mama home: when he told the story, a strange light came into his eye, and Mama gave him a look that said *Shut the hell up right now,* and he said no more. Cameron and Beep wondered pruriently what their parents had done on the walk home.

A few days later Papa had parachuted into Normandy, and Mama had thought she would never see him again; but all the same she had broken off her engagement to another man. "My mother was furious," Mama said. "She never forgave me."

Cameron found the school hall seats uncomfortable even for the half hour of morning assembly. Tonight was going to be purgatory. He knew all too well that the full play was five hours long. Evie had assured him that this was a shortened version. Cameron wondered how short.

He spoke to Jasper, sitting next to him. "What's Evie going to wear for the mad scene?"

"I don't know," said Jasper. "She won't tell anyone."

The lights went down and the curtain rose on the battlements of Elsinore.

The painted backdrops that formed the scenery were Cameron's work. He had a strong visual sense, presumably inherited from his father, the photographer. He was particularly pleased with the way the painted moon concealed a spotlight that picked out the sentry.

There was not much else to like. Every school play Cameron had ever seen had been dreadful, and this was no exception. The seventeen-year-old boy playing Hamlet tried to seem enigmatic but succeeded only in being wooden. However, Evie was something else.

In her first scene Ophelia had little to do other than listen to her condescending brother and her pompous father, until at the end she cautioned her brother against hypocrisy in a short speech that Evie delivered with waspish delight. But in her second scene, telling her father about Hamlet's crazy invasion of her private room, she blossomed. At the start she was frantic, then she became calmer, quieter, and more concentrated, until it seemed the audience hardly dared to breathe while she said: "He raised a sigh so piteous and profound." And then, in her next scene, when the enraged Hamlet raved at her about joining a nunnery, she seemed so bewildered and hurt that Cameron wanted to leap onstage and punch him out. Jeremy Faulkner had wisely decided to end the first half at that point, and the applause was tremendous.

Dave was presiding over an intermission bar selling soft drinks and candy. He had a dozen friends serving as fast as they could. Cameron was impressed: he had never seen school pupils work so hard. "Did you give them pep pills?" he asked Dave as he got a glass of cherry pop.

"Nope," said Dave. "Just twenty percent commission on everything they sell."

Cameron was hoping Evie might come and talk to her family during the intermission, but she still had not appeared when the bell rang for the second half, and he returned to his seat, disappointed but eager to see what she would do next.

Hamlet improved when he had to badger Ophelia with dirty jokes in front of everyone. Perhaps it came naturally to the actor, Cameron thought unkindly. Ophelia's embarrassment and distress increased until it bordered on hysteria.

But it was her mad scene that brought the house down.

She entered looking like an inmate of an asylum, in a stained and torn nightdress of thin cotton that reached only to midthigh. So far from being pitiable, she was jeering and aggressive, like a drunk whore on the street. When she said: "The owl was a baker's daughter," a sentence that in Cameron's opinion meant nothing at all, she made it sound like a vile taunt.

Cameron heard his mother murmur to his father: "I can't believe that girl is only fifteen."

On the line "Young men may do it if they come to it, by cock they are to blame," Ophelia made a grab for the king's genitals that provoked a nervous titter from the audience.

Then came a sudden change. Tears rolled down her cheeks, and her voice sank almost to a whisper as she spoke of her dead father. The audience fell silent. She was a child again as she said: "I cannot choose but weep, to think they should lay him in the cold ground."

Cameron wanted to cry too.

Then she rolled her eyes, staggered, and cackled like an old witch. "Come, my coach!" she cried insanely. She put both hands to the neckline of her dress and ripped it down the front. The audience gasped. "Good night, ladies!" she cried, letting the garment fall to the floor. Stark naked, she cried: "Good night, good night, good night!" Then she ran off.

After that the play was dead. The gravedigger was not funny and the sword fight at the end so artificial as to be boring. Cameron could think of nothing but the naked Ophelia raving at the front of the stage, her small breasts proud, the hair at her groin a flaming auburn; a beautiful girl driven insane. He guessed every man in the audience felt the same. No one cared about Hamlet.

At the curtain call the biggest applause was for Evie. But the head teacher did not come onstage to offer the lavish praise and extensive thanks normally given to the most hopeless of amateur dramatic productions.

As they left the hall, everyone looked at Evie's family. Daisy chatted brightly to other parents, putting a brave face on it. Lloyd, in a severe dark-gray suit with a waistcoat, said nothing but looked grim. Evie's grandmother Eth Leckwith smiled faintly: perhaps she had reservations, but she was not going to complain.

Cameron's family also had mixed reactions. His mother's lips were pursed in disapproval. His father wore a smile of tolerant amusement. Beep was bursting with admiration.

Cameron said to Dave: "Your sister's brilliant."

"I like yours, too," said Dave with a grin.

"Ophelia stole the show from Hamlet!"

"Evie's a genius," Dave replied. "Drives our parents up the wall."

"Why?"

"They don't believe show business is serious work. They want us both to go into politics." He rolled his eyes.

Cameron's father, Woody Dewar, overheard. "I had the same problem," he said. "My father was a United States senator, and so was my grandfather. They couldn't understand why I wanted to be a photographer. It just didn't seem like a real job to them." Woody worked for *Life* magazine, probably the best photo journal in the world after *Paris Match*.

Both families went backstage. Evie emerged from the girls' dressing room looking demure in a twinset and a below-the-knee skirt, an outfit obviously chosen to say *I am not a sexual exhibitionist, that was Ophelia*. But she also wore an expression of quiet triumph. Whatever people said about her nudity, no one could deny that her acting had captivated the audience.

Her father was the first to speak. Lloyd said: "I just hope you don't get arrested for indecent exposure."

"I didn't really plan it," Evie said as if he had paid her a compliment. "It was kind of a last-minute thing. I wasn't even sure the nightdress would rip."

Crap, thought Cameron.

Jeremy Faulkner appeared in his trademark college scarf. He was the only teacher who allowed pupils to call him by his first name. "That was fabulous!" he raved. "A peak moment!" His eyes were bright with excitement. The thought occurred to Cameron that Jeremy, too, was in love with Evie.

Evie said: "Jerry, these are my parents, Lloyd and Daisy Williams."

For a moment the teacher looked scared, but he recovered quickly. "Mr. and Mrs. Williams, you must be even more surprised than I was," he said, deftly disclaiming responsibility. "You should know that Evie is the most brilliant pupil I have ever taught." He shook hands with Daisy, then with a visibly reluctant Lloyd.

Evie spoke to Jasper. "You're invited to the cast party," she said. "My special guest."

Lloyd frowned. "Party?" he said. "After that?" Clearly he felt a celebration was not appropriate.

Daisy touched his arm. "It's okay," she said.

Lloyd shrugged.

Jeremy said brightly: "Just for an hour. School in the morning!"

Jasper said: "I'm too old. I'd feel out of place."

Evie protested: "You're only a year older than the sixth-formers."

Cameron wondered why the hell she wanted him there. He *was* too old. He was a university student: he did not belong at a high school party.

Fortunately, Jasper agreed. "I'll see you back at the house," he said firmly.

Daisy put in: "No later than eleven o'clock, please."

The parents left. Cameron said: "My God, you got away with it!"

Evie grinned. "I know."

They celebrated with coffee and cake. Cameron wished Beep was there to put some vodka into the coffee, but she had not taken part in the production so she had gone home, as had Dave.

Evie was the center of attention. Even the boy playing Hamlet admitted she was the star of the evening. Jeremy Faulkner could not stop talking about how her nakedness had expressed Ophelia's vulnerability. His praise for Evie became embarrassing and eventually kind of creepy.

Cameron waited patiently, letting them monopolize her, knowing that he had the ultimate advantage: he would be taking her home.

At ten thirty they left. "I'm glad my father got this assignment in

London," Cameron said as they zigzagged through the back streets. "I hated leaving San Francisco, but it's pretty cool here."

"That's good," she said without enthusiasm.

"The best part is getting to know you."

"How sweet. Thank you."

"It's really changed my life."

"Surely not."

This was not going the way Cameron had imagined. They were alone in the deserted streets, speaking in low voices as they walked close together through circles of lamplight and pools of darkness, but there was no feeling of intimacy. They were more like people making small talk. All the same he was not giving up. "I want us to be close friends," he said.

"We already are," she replied with a touch of impatience.

They reached Great Peter Street and still he had not said what he wanted to say. As they approached the house he stopped. She took another step forward, so he grabbed her arm and held her back. "Evie," he said, "I'm in love with you."

"Oh, Cam, don't be ridiculous."

Cameron felt as if he had been punched.

Evie tried to walk on. Cameron gripped her arm more tightly, not caring now if he hurt her. "Ridiculous?" he said. There was an embarrassing quaver in his voice, and he spoke again more firmly. "Why should it be ridiculous?"

"You don't know anything," she said in a tone of exasperation.

This was a particularly hurtful reproach. Cameron prided himself on knowing a great deal, and he had imagined she liked him for that. "What don't I know?" he said.

She pulled her arm out of his grasp with a vigorous jerk. "I'm in love with Jasper, you idiot," she said, and she went into the house.

CHAPTER THIRTEEN

I n the morning, while it was still dark, Rebecca and Bernd made
love again.

They had been living together three months, in the old town
house in Berlin-Mitte. It was a big house, which was fortunate, for
they shared it with her parents, Werner and Carla, plus her brother,
Walli, and her sister, Lili, and Grandmother Maud.

For a while, love had consoled them for all they had lost. Both were
out of work, prevented from getting jobs by the secret police—despite
East Germany's desperate shortage of schoolteachers.

But both were under investigation for social parasitism, the crime of
being unemployed in a Communist country. Sooner or later they would
be convicted and jailed. Bernd would go to a prison labor camp, where
he would probably die.

So they were going to escape.

Today was their last full day in East Berlin.

When Bernd slid his hand gently up Rebecca's nightdress, she said:
"I'm too nervous."

"We may not have many more chances," he said.

She grabbed him and clung to him. She knew he was right. They
might both die attempting to flee.

Worse, one might die and one might live.

Bernd reached for a condom. They had agreed that they would
marry when they reached the free world, and avoid pregnancy until
then. If their plans should go wrong, Rebecca did not want to raise a
child in East Germany.

Despite all the fears that troubled her, Rebecca was overcome by
desire, and responded energetically to Bernd's touch. Passion was a

recent discovery for her. She had mildly enjoyed sex with Hans, most of the time, and with two previous lovers, but she had never before been flooded with desire, possessed by it so completely that for a while she forgot everything else. Now the thought that this could be the last time made her desire even more intense.

After it was over he said: "You're a tiger."

She laughed. "I never was before. It's you."

"It's us," he said. "We're right."

When she had caught her breath, she said: "People escape every day."

"No one knows how many."

Escapers swam across canals and rivers, they climbed barbed wire, or they hid in cars and trucks. West Germans, who were allowed into East Berlin, brought forged West German passports for their relatives. Allied troops could go anywhere, so one East German man bought a U.S. army uniform at a theatrical costume shop and walked through a checkpoint unchallenged.

Rebecca said: "And many die."

The border guards showed no mercy and no shame. They shot to kill. They sometimes left the wounded to bleed to death in no-man's-land, as a lesson to others. Death was the penalty for trying to leave the Communist paradise.

Rebecca and Bernd were planning to escape via Bernauer Strasse.

One of the grim ironies of the Wall was that in some streets the buildings were in East Berlin but the sidewalk was in the West. Residents of the east side of Bernauer Strasse had opened their front doors on Sunday, August 13, 1961, to find a barbed-wire fence preventing them from stepping outside. At first, many leaped from upstairs windows to freedom—some injuring themselves, others jumping onto a blanket held by West Berlin firemen. Now all those buildings had been evacuated, their doors and windows boarded up.

Rebecca and Bernd had a different plan.

They got dressed and went down to breakfast with the family— probably their last for a long time. It was a tense repeat of the same meal on August 13 last year. On that occasion the family had been sad and anxious: Rebecca had been planning to leave, but not at the risk of her life. This time they were scared.

Rebecca tried to be cheerful. "Maybe you'll all follow us across the border one day," she said.

Carla said: "You know we aren't going to do that. You *must* go—you have no life left here. But we're staying."

"What about Father's work?"

"For now, I carry on," Werner said. He was no longer able to go to the factory he owned because it was in West Berlin. He was trying to manage it remotely, but that was nearly impossible. There was no telephone service between the two Berlins, so he had to do everything by mail, which was always liable to be delayed by the censors.

This was agony for Rebecca. Her family was the most important thing in the world to her, but she was being forced to leave them. "Well, no wall lasts forever," she said. "One day Berlin will be reunited, and then we can be together again."

There was a ring at the doorbell, and Lili jumped up from the table. Werner said: "I hope that's the postman with the factory accounts."

Walli said: "I'm going to cross the Wall as soon as I can. I'm not going to spend my life in the East, with some old Communist telling me what music to play."

Carla said: "You can make your own decision—as soon as you're an adult."

Lili came back into the kitchen looking scared. "It's not the postman," she said. "It's Hans."

Rebecca let out a small scream. Surely her estranged husband could not know about her escape plan?

Werner said: "Is he alone?"

"I think so."

Grandma Maud said to Carla: "Remember how we dealt with Joachim Koch?"

Carla looked at the children. Obviously they were not supposed to know how Joachim Koch had been dealt with.

Werner went to the kitchen cupboard and opened the bottom drawer. It contained heavy pans. He pulled the drawer all the way out and set it on the floor. Then he reached deep into the cavity and brought out a black pistol with a brown grip and a small box of ammunition.

Bernd said: "Jesus."

Rebecca did not know much about guns, but she thought it was a Walther P38. Werner must have kept it after the war.

What had happened to Joachim Koch? Rebecca wondered. Had he been killed?

By Mother? And *Grandma*?

Werner said to Rebecca: "If Hans Hoffmann takes you out of this house we will never see you again." Then he began to load the gun.

Carla said: "He may not be here to arrest Rebecca."

"True," said Werner. He said to Rebecca: "Talk to him. Find out what he wants. Scream if you need to."

Rebecca stood up. Bernd did the same. "Not you," Werner said to Bernd. "The sight of you might anger him."

"But—"

Rebecca said: "Father's right. Just be ready to come if I call."

"All right."

Rebecca took a deep breath, made herself calm, and went into the hall.

Hans stood there in his new blue-gray suit, wearing a striped tie that Rebecca had given him for his last birthday. He said: "I got the divorce papers."

Rebecca nodded. "You were expecting them, of course."

"Can we talk about it?"

"Is there anything to say?"

"Perhaps."

She opened the door of the dining room, used occasionally for formal dinners and otherwise for doing homework. They went in and sat down. Rebecca did not close the door.

"Are you sure you want to do this?" Hans said.

Rebecca was scared. Did he mean escape? Did he know? She managed to say: "Do what?"

"Get divorced," he said.

She was confused. "Why not?" she said. "It's what you want, too."

"Is it?"

"Hans, what are you trying to say?"

"That we don't have to be divorced. We could start again. This time there would be no deceptions. Now that you know I am an officer of the Stasi, there would be no need for lies."

This felt like a stupid dream in which impossible things happen. "But why?" she said.

Hans leaned forward across the table. "Don't you know? Can't you at least guess?"

"No, I can't!" she said, although she had the glimmering of a creepy suspicion.

"I love you," said Hans.

"For God's sake!" Rebecca shouted. "How can you say such a thing? After all you've done!"

"I mean it," he said. "I was faking it at first. But I realized after a while what a wonderful woman you are. I *wanted* to marry you—that wasn't just work. You're beautiful, and smart, and dedicated to teaching—I admire dedication. I've never met a woman like you. Come back to me, Rebecca—please."

"No!" she shouted.

"Think about it. Take a day. Take a week."

"No!"

She was yelling her refusal at the top of her voice, but he acted as if she were coyly pretending reluctance. "We'll talk again," he said with a smile.

"No!" she yelled. "Never! Never! Never!" And she ran from the room.

They were all at the open door of the kitchen, looking scared. Bernd said: "What? What happened?"

"He doesn't want a divorce," Rebecca wailed. "He says he loves me. He wants to start again—give it another chance!"

Bernd said: "I'm going to fucking strangle him."

But there was no need to restrain Bernd. At that moment they heard the front door slam.

"He's gone," Rebecca said. "Thank God."

Bernd put his arms around her and she buried her face in his shoulder.

"Well," said Carla in a shaky voice, "I wasn't expecting *that*."

Werner unloaded the pistol.

Grandma Maud said: "That's not the end of it. Hans will come back. Stasi officers do not believe that ordinary people can say no to them."

"And they're right," said Werner. "Rebecca, you have to leave today."

She detached herself from Bernd's embrace. "Oh, no—today?"

"Now," her father said. "You're in terrible danger."

Bernd said: "He's right. Hans may come back with reinforcements. We have to do now what we planned to do tomorrow morning."

"All right," said Rebecca.

Rebecca and Bernd ran upstairs to their room. Bernd put on his black corduroy suit with a white shirt and a black tie, as if going to a funeral. Rebecca, too, dressed all in black. They both put on black gym shoes. From under the bed Bernd took a coiled washing line he had bought last week. He slung it across his body like a bandolier, then put on a brown leather jacket to hide it. Rebecca donned a dark short coat over her black roll-neck sweater and black pants.

They were ready in a few short minutes.

The family was waiting in the hall. Rebecca hugged and kissed them all. Lili was crying. "Don't get killed," she sobbed.

Bernd and Rebecca put on leather gloves and went to the door.

They waved to the family one more time, then they went out.

. . .

Walli followed them at a distance.

He wanted to see how they did it. They had not told anyone their plan, not even the family. Mother said the only way to keep a secret was to tell nobody. She and Father were ardent about this, leading Walli to suspect that it came from those mysterious wartime experiences that they never explained.

Walli had told the family he was going to play the guitar in his room. He had an electric instrument now. Hearing no noise, his parents would assume he was practicing without plugging in.

He slipped out through the back door.

Rebecca and Bernd walked arm in arm. Their pace was brisk, but not hurried enough to attract attention. It was half past eight, and the morning mist was beginning to lift. Walli could easily follow the two figures, the washing line making a bulge on Bernd's shoulder. They did not look back, and his sneakers made no sound as he walked. He noticed that they, too, were wearing sneakers, and he wondered why.

Walli was excited and scared. What an amazing morning. He had almost fallen over when Father pulled out that drawer and revealed a damn pistol. The old man had been ready to shoot Hans Hoffmann! Maybe Father was not such a doddery old fool after all.

Walli was frightened for his beloved sister. She might be killed within the next few minutes. But he was also thrilled. If she could escape, so could he.

Walli was still determined to escape. After he had defied his father by going to the Minnesänger club against orders, he had not after all got into trouble: his father had said that the destruction of his guitar was punishment enough. But all the same he was suffering under two tyrants, Werner Franck and General Secretary Walter Ulbricht, and he intended to be free of both at the first opportunity.

Rebecca and Bernd came to a street that led directly to the Wall. Two border guards were visible at the far end, stamping their boots in the morning chill. Slung from their shoulders they had Soviet PPSh-41 submachine guns with drum magazines. Walli saw no chance of anyone getting over the barbed wire with those two watching.

But Rebecca and Bernd turned off the street and entered a cemetery.

Walli could not follow them along the paths through the graves: he would be too conspicuous in that open space. He walked quickly at a right angle to their route until he was behind the chapel in the middle of the cemetery. He peeped around the corner of the building. They evidently had not seen him.

He watched them walk to the northwest corner of the graveyard.

There was a chicken-wire fence and, beyond that, the backyard of a house.

Rebecca and Bernd climbed over the fence.

That explains the sneakers, Walli thought.

What about the washing line?

. . .

The buildings on Bernauer Strasse were derelict, but the side streets were still occupied normally. Rebecca and Bernd, tense and fearful, crept across the backyard of a row house on such a side street, five doors from the end of the road where the Wall blocked it off. They climbed a second fence, then a third, each time moving closer to the Wall. Rebecca was thirty years of age, and agile. Bernd was older at forty, but he was in good shape: he had coached the school soccer team. They reached the back of the house third from the end.

They had visited the cemetery once before, again dressed in black to pose as mourners, their true purpose to study these houses. Their view had not been perfect—and they could not risk using binoculars—but they were fairly sure the third house offered a possible route up to the roof.

One roof led to another, eventually connecting with the empty buildings on Bernauer Strasse.

Now that Rebecca was closer, she was even more apprehensive.

They had planned their ascent by way of a low coal bunker, then an outhouse with a flat roof, and finally a gable end with a jutting windowsill. But all the heights had looked smaller from the cemetery. Close up, the climb appeared formidable.

They could not go inside the house. The occupants might raise the alarm: if they did not, they would be punished severely later.

The roofs were damp with mist, and would be slippery, but at least it was not raining.

Bernd said: "Are you ready?"

She was not. She was terrified. "Hell, yes," she said.

"You're a tiger," he said.

The coal bunker was chest height. They climbed onto it. Their soft shoes made little sound.

From there, Bernd got both elbows over the edge of the flat outhouse roof and scrambled up. Lying on his belly, he reached down and hauled Rebecca up. They both stood on the roof. Rebecca felt dizzyingly conspicuous, but when she looked around she saw no one but a single distant figure back in the cemetery.

The next part was forbidding. Bernd got one knee up on the window ledge, but it was narrow. Fortunately the curtains were drawn, so that if there were people in the room they would not see anything—unless they heard a noise and came to investigate. With some difficulty he got his other knee on the sill. Leaning on Rebecca's shoulder for support, he contrived to stand upright. With his feet now firmly planted, albeit on a narrow footing, he helped Rebecca up.

She knelt on the ledge and tried not to look down.

Bernd reached out to the sloping edge of the pitched roof, their next step up. He could not climb onto the roof from where he was: there was nothing to grab but the edge of a slate. They had already discussed this problem. Still kneeling, Rebecca braced herself. Bernd put one foot on her right shoulder. Holding the roof edge for balance, he put all his weight on her. It hurt, but she took the strain. A moment later his left foot was on her left shoulder. Evenly balanced, she could hold him—for a few moments.

A second later he cocked his leg over the edge of the slates and rolled up onto the roof.

He splayed his body out, for maximum traction, then reached down. With one gloved hand he grabbed the collar of Rebecca's coat, and she grasped his upper arm.

The curtains were suddenly pulled apart, and a woman's face stared at Rebecca from a distance of a few inches.

The woman screamed.

With an effort, Bernd lifted Rebecca until she was able to get her leg over the sloping edge of the roof; then he pulled her toward him until she was safe.

But they both lost control and started to slide down.

Rebecca spread her arms and pressed the palms of her gloved hands to the slates, trying to brake her slide. Bernd did the same. But they continued to slip, slowly but relentlessly—then Rebecca's sneakers touched an iron gutter. It did not feel sturdy, but it held, and they both came to a stop.

"What was that scream?" Bernd asked urgently.

"A woman in the bedroom saw me. I don't think she could have been heard on the street, though."

"But she might raise the alarm."

"Nothing we can do. Let's keep going."

They edged crabwise across the pitched roof. The houses were old and some of the roof slates were broken. Rebecca tried not to put weight on the gutter that her feet were touching. Their progress was painfully slow.

She imagined the woman at the window talking to her husband. "If we do nothing we'll be accused of collaborating. We could say we were fast asleep and didn't hear anything, but they'll probably arrest us anyway. And even if we call the police they might arrest us on suspicion. When things go wrong they arrest everyone in sight. Best just to keep our heads down. I'll draw the curtains again."

Ordinary people avoided any contact with the police—but the woman at the window might not be ordinary. If she or her husband was a party member, with a soft job and privileges, they would have a degree of immunity from police harassment, and in those circumstances they would undoubtedly raise a hue and cry.

But the seconds ticked by, and Rebecca heard no sound of a commotion. Perhaps she and Bernd had got away with it.

They came to an angle in the roof. Bracing his feet on the opposing sides, Bernd was able to crawl upward until he got his hands over the roof ridge. Now he had a safer grip, though he ran the risk that his dark-gloved fingertips might be noticed by the police on the street.

He turned the angle and crawled on, every second getting nearer to Bernauer Strasse and freedom.

Rebecca followed. She glanced over her shoulder, wondering if anyone could see her and Bernd. Their dark clothing was inconspicuous against the gray slates, but they were not invisible. Was anyone watching? She could see the backyards and the cemetery. The dark figure she had noticed a minute ago was now running from the chapel toward the cemetery gate. A leaden fear made her stomach cold. Had he seen them, and was he hurrying to warn the police?

She suffered a moment of panic, then she realized the figure was familiar.

"Walli?" she said.

What the hell was he up to? Obviously he had followed her and Bernd. But to what end? And where was he heading in such a hurry?

There was nothing she could do but worry.

They came to the back wall of the apartment building on Bernauer Strasse.

The windows were boarded up. Bernd and Rebecca had talked about breaking through the boards to get in, then breaking through another set at the front to get out, but they had decided it would be too noisy, time-consuming, and difficult. Easier, they guessed, to go over the top.

The ridge of the roof they were on was at the level of the gutters of the high adjacent building, so they could easily step from one roof to the next.

From then on they would be clearly visible to the guards with the machine guns on the side street below.

This was their most vulnerable moment.

Bernd crawled up the house roof to the ridge, straddled it, then scrambled up onto the higher roof of the apartment building, heading for the top.

Rebecca followed. She was breathing hard now. Her knees were bruised and her shoulders ached where Bernd had stood on them.

When she was straddling the lower roof she took a look down. She was alarmingly close to the policemen on the street. They were lighting cigarettes: if one should glance upward, all would be lost. Both she and Bernd would be easy targets for their submachine guns.

But they were only a few steps from freedom.

She braced herself to wriggle onto the roof in front of her. Beneath her left foot something moved. Her sneaker slipped, and she fell. She was still astride the ridge, and the impact hurt her groin. She gave a muffled cry, leaned vertiginously sideways for a horrifying moment, then regained her balance.

Unfortunately the cause of her stumble, a loose slate, slipped down the roof, tumbled over the gutter, and fell to the street, where it shattered noisily.

The cops heard the sound and looked at the fragments on the pavement.

Rebecca froze.

The police looked around. Any second now it would occur to them that the slate must have fallen from the roof, and they would look up. But, before they did, one was hit by a flung stone. A second later, Rebecca heard her brother's voice yelling: "All cops are cunts!"

. . .

Walli picked up another stone and threw it at the police. This one missed.

Baiting East German policemen was suicidally stupid—he knew that. He was likely to be arrested, beaten up, and jailed. But he had to do it.

He could see that Bernd and Rebecca were hopelessly exposed. The police would spot them any second now. They never hesitated to shoot escapers. The range was short, about fifty feet. Both fugitives would be riddled with machine-gun bullets in a few seconds.

Unless the cops could be distracted.

They were not much older than Walli. He was sixteen; they seemed about twenty. They were looking around in confusion, their newly lit cigarettes between their lips, unable to figure out why a slate had shattered and two stones had been thrown.

"Pig-faces!" Walli yelled. "Shitheads! Your mothers are whores!"

They saw him then. He was a hundred yards away, visible despite the mist. As soon as they set eyes on him they started to move toward him.

He backed away.

They started to run.

Walli turned and fled.

At the cemetery gate he looked back. One of the men had stopped, no doubt realizing they should not both leave their post at the Wall to chase someone who had merely thrown stones. They had not yet got around to wondering why anyone would do something so rash.

The second cop knelt down and aimed his gun.

Walli slipped into the cemetery.

.   .   .

Bernd looped the clothesline around a brick chimney, pulled it tight, and tied a secure knot.

Rebecca lay flat on the roof ridge, looking down, panting. She could see one cop pounding along the street after Walli, and Walli running across the cemetery. The second cop was returning to his post, but—luckily—he kept looking back, watching his colleague. Rebecca did not know whether to be relieved or horrified that her brother was risking his life to divert the attention of the police for the next few crucial seconds.

She looked the other way, into the free world. In Bernauer Strasse, on the far side of the street, a man and a woman stood watching her and talking excitedly.

Holding the rope, Bernd sat down, then slid on his bottom down the west slope of the roof to the edge. Next he wound the rope twice around his chest under his arms, leaving a long tail of fifty or so feet. He could now lean out over the edge, supported by the rope tied to the chimney.

He returned to Rebecca and straddled the ridge. "Sit upright," he said. He tied the free end of the clothesline around her and tied a knot. He held the rope firmly in his leather-gloved hands.

Rebecca took a last look into East Berlin. She saw Walli nimbly scaling the fence at the far end of the cemetery. His figure crossed a road and vanished into a side street. The cop gave up and turned back.

Then the man happened to look up, toward the roof of the apartment building, and his jaw dropped in astonishment.

Rebecca was in no doubt about what he had seen. She and Bernd were perched on top of the roof, clear against the skyline.

The cop shouted and pointed, then broke into a run.

Rebecca rolled off the ridge and slowly slid down the slope of the roof until her sneakers touched the gutter at the front.

She heard a burst of machine-gun fire.

Bernd stood upright beside her, bracing himself with the rope tied to the chimney.

Rebecca felt him take her weight.

Here goes, she thought.

She rolled over the gutter and slid into thin air.

The rope pulled painfully around her chest, above her breasts. She dangled in the air for a moment, then Bernd played out the rope and she began to descend in short jerks.

They had practiced this at her parents' house. Bernd had let her down from the highest window all the way to the backyard. It hurt his hands, he said, but he could do it, if he had good gloves. All the same, she was instructed to pause briefly anytime she could rest her weight on a window surround to give him a moment's respite.

She heard shouts of encouragement, and guessed that a crowd had now gathered down on Bernauer Strasse, on the west side of the Wall.

Below her she could see the pavement and the barbed wire that ran along the façade of the building. Was she in West Berlin yet? The frontier police would shoot anyone on the east side, but they had strict instructions not to fire into the West, for the Soviets did not want any diplomatic incidents. But she was dangling immediately above the barbed wire, neither in one country nor the other.

She heard another burst of machine-gun fire. Where were the cops, and who were they shooting at? She guessed they would try to get up on the roof and shoot her and Bernd before it was too late. If they followed the same laborious route as their quarry they would not catch up in time. But they could probably save time by entering the building and simply running up the stairs.

She was almost there. Her feet touched the barbed wire. She pushed away from the building, but her legs did not quite clear the wire. She felt the barbs rip her trousers and tear her skin painfully. Then a crowd gathered around and helped her, taking her weight, disentangling her from the barbed wire, unwinding the rope around her chest, and setting her on the ground.

As soon as she was steady on her feet, she looked up. Bernd was on the edge of the roof, loosening the rope around his chest. She stepped backward across the road so that she could see better. The policemen had not yet reached the roof.

Bernd got the rope firmly in both hands, then stepped backward off the roof. He rappelled slowly down the wall, slipping the rope through his hands as he went. This was extremely difficult, because all his weight was supported by his grip on the rope. He had practiced at home, walking down the back wall of the town house at night when he would not be seen. But this building was taller.

The crowd in the street cheered him.

Then a cop appeared on the roof.

Bernd came down faster, risking his grip on the rope for more speed.

Someone shouted: "Get a blanket!"

Rebecca knew there was not enough time for that.

The cop aimed his submachine gun at Bernd, but hesitated. He could not fire into West Germany. He might well hit people other than the escapers. It was the kind of incident that could start a war.

The man turned and looked at the rope around the chimney. He might have untied it, but Bernd would reach the ground first.

Did the cop have a knife?

Apparently not.

Then he was inspired. He put the barrel of his gun against the taut rope and fired a single round.

Rebecca screamed.

The rope split, its end flying into the air over Bernauer Strasse.

Bernd fell like a stone.

The crowd scattered.

Bernd hit the sidewalk with a sickening thump.

Then he lay still.

. . .

Three days later Bernd opened his eyes, looked at Rebecca, and said: "Hello."

Rebecca said: "Oh, thank God."

She had been out of her mind with worry. The doctors had told her that he would recover consciousness, but she had not been able to believe it until she saw it. He had undergone several operations, and in between he had been heavily drugged. This was the first time she had seen the light of intelligence in his face.

Trying not to cry, she leaned over the hospital bed and kissed his lips. "You're back," she said. "I'm so glad."

He said: "What happened?"

"You fell."

He nodded. "The roof. I remember. But . . ."

"The policeman broke your rope."

He looked along the length of his body. "Am I in plaster?"

She had been longing for him to come round, but she had also been dreading this moment. "From the waist down," she said.

"I . . . I can't move my legs. I can't feel them." He looked panicky. "Have my legs been amputated?"

"No." Rebecca took a deep breath. "You've broken most of the bones in your legs, but you can't feel them because your spinal cord is partially severed."

He was thoughtful for a long moment. Then he said: "Will it heal?"

"The doctors say that nerves may heal, albeit slowly."

"So . . ."

"So you may get some below-the-waist functions back, eventually. But you will be in a wheelchair when you leave this hospital."

"Do they say how long?"

"They say . . ." She had to make an effort not to cry. "You must prepare for the possibility that it may be permanent."

He looked away. "I'm a cripple."

"But we're free. You're in West Berlin. We've escaped."

"Escaped to a wheelchair."

"Don't think of it that way."

"What the hell am I going to do?"

"I've thought about this." She made her voice firm and confident, more so than she felt. "You're going to marry me and return to teaching."

"That's not likely."

"I've already phoned Anselm Weber. You'll remember that he's now head of a school in Hamburg. He has jobs for both of us, starting in September."

"A teacher in a wheelchair?"

"What difference will that make? You'll still be able to explain physics so that the dullest child in the class understands. You don't need legs for that."

"You don't want to marry a cripple."

"No," she said. "But I want to marry you. And I will."

His tone became bitter. "You can't marry a man with no below-the-waist functions."

"Listen to me," she said fiercely. "Three months ago I didn't know what love was. I've only just found you, and I'm not going to lose you. We've escaped, we've survived, and we're going to live. We'll get married, we'll teach school, and we'll love each other."

"I don't know."

"I want only one thing from you," she said. "You must not lose hope. We'll confront all difficulties together, and we'll solve all problems together. I can put up with any hardship as long as I've got you. Promise me, now, Bernd Held, that you'll never give up. Never."

There was a long pause.

"Promise," she said.

He smiled. "You're a tiger," he said.

PART THREE

ISLAND

1962

CHAPTER FOURTEEN

D imka and Valentin rode the Ferris wheel in Gorky Park with Nina and Anna.

After Dimka had been called away from the holiday camp, Nina had taken up with an engineer and had dated him for several months, but then they broke up, so now she was free again. Meanwhile, Valentin and Anna had become a couple: he slept over at the girls' apartment most weekends. Also, significantly, Valentin had told Dimka a couple of times that having sex with one woman after another was just a phase men went through when they were young.

I should be so lucky, Dimka thought.

On the first warm weekend of the short Moscow summer, Valentin proposed a double date. Dimka agreed eagerly. Nina was smart and strong-minded, and she challenged him: he liked that. But mainly she was sexy. He often thought about how enthusiastically she had kissed him. He wanted very much to do that again. He recalled how her nipples had stuck out in the cold water. He wondered whether she ever thought about that day on the lake.

His problem was that he could not share Valentin's cheerfully exploitative attitude to girls. Valentin, at least until he met Anna, would say anything to get a girl into bed. Dimka felt it was wrong to manipulate or bully people. He also believed that if someone said no, you should accept it, whereas Valentin always took no to mean "Maybe not yet."

Gorky Park was an oasis in the desert of earnest Communism, a place Muscovites could go simply to have fun. People put on their best clothes, bought ice cream and candy, flirted with strangers, and kissed in the bushes.

Anna pretended to be scared on the Ferris wheel, and Valentin went along with the charade, putting his arm around her and telling her it was perfectly safe. Nina looked comfortable and unworried, which Dimka preferred to phony terror, but it gave him no chance to get intimate.

Nina looked good in a cotton shirtwaist dress with orange and green stripes. The back view was particularly alluring, Dimka thought as they climbed off the wheel. For this date he had managed to get a pair of American jeans and a blue checked shirt. In exchange he had given two ballet tickets that Khrushchev did not want: *Romeo and Juliet* at the Bolshoi.

"What have you been doing since I saw you last?" Nina asked him as they strolled around the park, drinking lukewarm orange cordial bought from a stall.

"Working," he said.

"Is that all?"

"I usually get to the office an hour before Khrushchev, to make sure everything is ready for him: the documents he needs, the foreign newspapers, any files he might want. He often works until late into the evening, and I rarely go home before he does." He wished he could make his job sound as exciting as it really was. "I don't have much time for anything else."

Valentin said: "Dimka was the same at university—work, work, work."

Happily, Nina did not seem to think that Dimka's life was dull. "You're really with Comrade Khrushchev every day?"

"Most days."

"Where do you live?"

"Government House." It was an elite apartment building not far from the Kremlin.

"Very nice."

"With my mother," he added.

"I'd live with my mother for the sake of a place in that building."

"My twin sister normally lives with us, also, but she's gone to Cuba— she's a reporter with TASS."

"I'd like to go to Cuba," Nina said wistfully.

"It's a poor country."

"I could live with that, in a climate where there's no winter. Imagine dancing on the beach in January."

Dimka nodded. He was thrilled by Cuba in a different way. Castro's revolution showed that rigid Soviet orthodoxy was not the only possible form of Communism. Castro had new, different ideas. "I hope Castro survives," he said.

"Why shouldn't he?"

"The Americans have invaded once already. The Bay of Pigs was a disaster, but they will try again, with a bigger army—probably in 1964, while President Kennedy is running for reelection."

"That's terrible! Can't something be done?"

"Castro is trying to make peace with Kennedy."

"Will he succeed?"

"The Pentagon is against it, and conservative congressmen are making a fuss, so the whole idea is getting nowhere."

"We have to support the Cuban revolution!"

"I agree—but our conservatives don't like Castro either. They're not sure he's a real Communist."

"What will happen?"

"It depends on the Americans. They may leave Cuba alone. But I don't think they're that smart. My guess is they'll keep harassing Castro until he feels the only place he can look for help is the Soviet Union. So he'll end up asking us for protection, sooner or later."

"What can we do?"

"Good question."

Valentin interrupted them. "I'm hungry. Have you girls got any food at home?"

"Of course," said Nina. "I bought a knuckle of bacon for a stew."

"Then what are we waiting for? Dimka and I will buy some beer on the way."

They took the Metro. The girls had an apartment in a building controlled by the steel union, their employer. Their place was small: a bedroom with two single beds, a living room with a couch in front of a television set, a kitchen with a tiny dining table, and a bathroom. Dimka guessed that Anna was responsible for the lacy cushions on the couch and the plastic flowers in the vase on top of the TV, and Nina had bought the striped curtains and the posters on the wall showing mountain scenery.

Dimka worried about the shared bedroom. If Nina wanted to sleep with him, would the two couples make love in the same room? Such arrangements had not been unknown when Dimka was a university student in crowded accommodations. All the same he did not like the idea. Apart from anything else, he did not want Valentin to know just how inexpert he was.

He wondered where Nina slept when Valentin stayed over. Then he noticed a small stack of blankets on the living room floor, and he deduced that she slept on the couch.

Nina put the joint in a big saucepan; Anna chopped up a large turnip; Valentin put out cutlery and plates; and Dimka poured the beer. Everyone but Dimka seemed to know what was going to happen next. He was a little unnerved, but he went along.

Nina made a tray of snacks: pickled mushrooms, blinis, sausage, and cheese. While the stew was cooking they went into the living room. Nina sat on the couch and patted the place beside her to indicate that Dimka should sit there. Valentin took the easy chair and Anna sat on the floor at his feet. They listened to music on the radio while they drank their beer. Nina had put some herbs in the pot, and the aroma from the kitchen made Dimka hungry.

They talked about their parents. Nina's were divorced, Valentin's were separated, and Anna's hated one another. "My mother didn't like my father," said Dimka. "Nor did I. Nobody likes a KGB man."

"I've been married once—never again," Nina said. "Do you know anyone who is happily married?"

"Yes," said Dimka. "My uncle Volodya. Mind you, my aunt Zoya is gorgeous. She's a physicist, but she looks like a film star. When I was little I called her Magazine Auntie, because she resembled the impossibly beautiful women in magazine photos."

Valentin stroked Anna's hair, and she laid her head on his thigh in a way Dimka found sexy. He wanted to touch Nina, and surely she would not mind—why else had she invited him to her apartment?—but he felt awkward and embarrassed. He wished she would do something: she was the experienced one. But she seemed content to listen to the music and sip beer, a faint smile on her face.

At last supper was ready. The stew was delicious: Nina was a good cook. They ate it with black bread.

When they had finished and cleared away, Valentin and Anna went into the bedroom and closed the door.

Dimka went to the bathroom. The face in the mirror over the washbasin was not handsome. His best feature was a pair of large blue eyes. His dark brown hair was cut short in the military style approved for young apparatchiks. He looked like a serious young man whose thoughts were far above sex.

He checked the condom in his pocket. Such things were in short supply and he had gone to a lot of trouble to get some. However, he did not agree with Valentin's contention that pregnancy was the woman's problem. He felt sure he would not enjoy sex if he felt he might be forcing the girl to go through either childbirth or abortion.

He returned to the living room. To his surprise, Nina had her coat on.

"I thought I'd walk you to the Metro station," she said.

Dimka was baffled. "Why?"

"I don't think you know this neighborhood—I wouldn't like you to get lost."

"I mean, why do you want me to leave?"

"What else would you do?"

"I'd like to stay here and kiss you," he said.

Nina laughed. "What you lack in sophistication, you make up for in enthusiasm." She took off her coat and sat down.

Dimka sat beside her and kissed her hesitantly.

She kissed him back with reassuring enthusiasm. He realized with mounting excitement that she did not care if he was inexpert. Soon he was eagerly fumbling with the buttons of her shirtwaist. She had wonderfully large breasts. They were encased in a formidable utilitarian brassiere, but she took that off, then offered them to be kissed.

Things moved quickly after that.

When the big moment arrived, she lay on the couch with her head on the armrest and one foot on the floor, a position she assumed so readily that Dimka thought she must have done it before.

He hastily took out his condom and fumbled it out of the packet, but she said: "No need for that."

He was startled. "What do you mean?"

"I can't bear children. I've been told by doctors. It's why my husband divorced me."

He dropped the condom on the floor and lay on top of her.

"Easy does it," she said, guiding him inside.

I've done it, Dimka thought; I've lost my virginity at last.

· · ·

The speedboat was the kind once known as a rumrunner: long and narrow, extremely fast, and painfully uncomfortable to ride in. It crossed the Straits of Florida at eighty knots, hitting every wave with the impact of a car knocking down a wooden fence. The six men aboard were strapped in, the only way to be halfway safe in an open boat at such a speed. In the small cargo hold they had M3 submachine guns, pistols, and incendiary bombs. They were going to Cuba.

George Jakes really should not have been with them.

He stared across the moonlit water, feeling seasick. Four of the men were Cubans living in exile in Miami: George knew only their first names. They hated Communism, hated Castro, and hated everyone who did not agree with them. The sixth man was Tim Tedder.

It had started when Tedder walked into the office at the Justice Department. He was vaguely familiar, and George had placed him as a CIA man, although he was officially "retired" and working as a freelance security consultant.

George had been on his own in the room. "Help you?" he had said politely.

"I'm here for the Mongoose meeting."

George had heard of Operation Mongoose, a project that the untrustworthy Dennis Wilson was involved in, but he did not know the full details. "Come in," he had said, waving at a chair. Tedder had walked in with a cardboard folder under his arm. He was about ten years older than George, but looked as if he had got dressed in the 1940s: he wore a double-breasted suit and his wavy hair was brilliantined with a high side parting. George said: "Dennis will be back any second."

"Thanks."

"How's it going? Mongoose, I mean."

Tedder looked guarded and said: "I'll report at the meeting."

"I won't be there." George looked at his wristwatch. He was deceitfully implying that he had been invited, which he had not; but he was curious. "I have a meeting at the White House."

"Too bad."

George recalled a fragment of information. "According to the original plan, you should now be in phase two, the buildup."

Tedder's face cleared as he inferred that George was in the loop. "Here's the report," he said, opening the cardboard folder.

George was pretending to know more than he did. Mongoose was a project to help anti-Communist Cubans foment a counterrevolution. The plan had a timetable whose climax was the overthrow of Castro in October of this year, just before the midterm congressional elections. CIA-trained infiltration teams were supposed to undertake political organization and anti-Castro propaganda.

Tedder handed George two sheets of paper. Pretending to be less interested than he was, George said: "Are we keeping to our timetable?"

Tedder avoided the question. "It's time to pile on the pressure," he said. "Furtively circulating leaflets that poke fun at Castro is not achieving what we want."

"How can we increase the pressure?"

"It's all in there," Tedder said, pointing at the paper.

George looked down. What he read was worse than he expected. The CIA was proposing to sabotage bridges, oil refineries, power plants, sugar mills, and shipping.

At that moment Dennis Wilson walked in. He had his shirt collar undone, his tie loose, and his sleeves rolled, just like Bobby, George noticed, although his receding hairline would never rival Bobby's vigorous thatch. When Wilson saw Tedder talking to George he looked surprised, then anxious.

George said to Tedder: "If you blow up an oil refinery, and people are killed, then anyone here in Washington who approved the project is guilty of murder."

Dennis Wilson spoke angrily to Tedder. "What have you told him?"

"I thought he was cleared!" said Tedder.

"I am cleared," said George. "My security clearance is the same as

Dennis's." He turned to Wilson. "So why have you been so careful to keep this from me?"

"Because I knew you'd make a fuss."

"And you were right. We're not at war with Cuba. Killing Cubans is murder."

"We are at war," said Tedder.

"Oh?" said George. "So, if Castro sent agents here to Washington, and they bombed a factory and killed your wife, that wouldn't be a crime?"

"Don't be ridiculous."

"Apart from the fact that it's murder, can't you imagine the stink if this gets out? There would be an international scandal! Picture Khrushchev at the United Nations, calling on our president to stop financing international terrorism. Think of the articles in *The New York Times*. Bobby might have to resign. And what about the president's reelection campaign? Has no one even thought about the politics of all this?"

"Of course we have. That's why it's top secret."

"And how's that working out?" George turned a page. "Am I really reading this?" he said. "We're trying to assassinate Fidel Castro with poisoned cigars?"

"You're not on the team for this project," said Wilson. "So just forget about it, okay?"

"Hell, no. I'm going straight to Bobby with this."

Wilson laughed. "You asshole. Don't you realize? Bobby's in charge of it!"

George was flattened.

All the same, he had gone to Bobby, who had said calmly: "Go down to Miami and take a look at the operation, George. Have Tedder show you around. Come back and tell me what you think."

So George had visited the large new CIA camp in Florida where Cuban exiles were trained for their infiltration missions. Then Tedder had said: "Maybe you should come on a mission. See for yourself."

It was a dare, and Tedder had not expected George to accept it. But George felt that if he refused he would be putting himself in a weak position. Right now he had the high ground: he was against Mongoose on moral and political grounds. If he refused to go on a raid, he would be seen as timid. And perhaps there was a part of him that could not resist the challenge of proving his courage. So, foolishly, he had said: "Yes. Will you be coming along?"

That had surprised Tedder, and George had seen clearly that Tedder wished he could withdraw the offer. But now he, too, had been challenged. It was what Greg Peshkov would call a pissing contest. And Tedder, too, had felt unable to back down; although he had said, as an afterthought: "Of course, we can't tell Bobby you came."

So here they were. It was a pity, George reflected, that President Kennedy was so fond of the spy novels of the British writer Ian Fleming. The president seemed to think the world could be saved by James Bond in reality as well as in thrillers. Bond was "licensed to kill." That was crap. No one was licensed to kill.

Their target was a small town called La Isabela. It lay along a narrow peninsula that stuck like a finger out of Cuba's north coast. It was a port, and had no business other than trade. Their aim was to damage the harbor facilities.

Their arrival was timed for first light. The sky to the east was turning gray when the skipper, Sanchez, throttled back the powerful engine, and its roar faded to a low burble. Sanchez knew this stretch of coast well: his father had owned a sugar plantation in the neighborhood, before the revolution. The silhouette of a town began to emerge on the dim horizon, and he killed the engine and unshipped a pair of oars.

The tide took them toward the town; the oars were mainly for steering. Sanchez had judged his approach perfectly. A line of concrete piers came into view. Behind the piers, George could dimly see large warehouses with pitched roofs. There were no big ships in port: farther along the coast, a few small fishing boats were moored. A low surf whispered on the beach; otherwise the world was hushed. The silent speedboat bumped against a pier.

The hatch was opened and the men armed themselves. Tedder offered George a pistol. George shook his head. "Take it," Tedder said. "This is dangerous."

George knew what Tedder was up to. Tedder wanted him to get blood on his hands. That way he would lose the ability to criticize

Mongoose. But George was not so easy to manipulate. "No, thanks," he said. "I'm strictly an observer."

"I'm in charge of this mission, and I'm ordering you."

"And I'm telling you to fuck off."

Tedder gave in.

Sanchez tied up the boat and they all disembarked. No one spoke. Sanchez pointed to the nearest warehouse, which also seemed to be the largest. They all ran toward it. George brought up the rear.

No one else was in sight. George could see a row of houses that looked little more than timber shacks. A tethered ass was cropping the sparse grass at the side of the dirt road. The only vehicle in sight was a rusty pickup truck of 1940s vintage. This was a very poor place, he realized. Clearly it had once been a busy port. George guessed it had been ruined by President Eisenhower, who had imposed an embargo on trade between the USA and Cuba in 1960.

Somewhere, a dog started barking.

The warehouse had timber sides and a corrugated-iron roof, but no windows. Sanchez found a small door and kicked it in. They all ran inside. The place was empty but for packaging litter: broken packing cases, cardboard boxes, short lengths of rope and string, discarded sacks and torn netting.

"Perfect," said Sanchez.

The four Cubans threw incendiary bombs around the floor. A moment later they flamed up. The litter caught fire immediately. The timber walls would light in moments. They all ran outside again.

A voice said in Spanish: "Hey! What's this?"

George turned to see a white-haired Cuban man in some kind of uniform. He was too old to be a cop or a soldier, so George guessed he was the night watchman. He wore sandals. However, he had a handgun on his belt, and he was fumbling to open the holster.

Before he could get his gun out, Sanchez shot him. Blood bloomed from the breast of his white uniform shirt and he fell backward.

"Let's go!" Sanchez said, and the five men ran toward the speedboat.

George knelt over the old man. The eyes stared up at the brightening sky, seeing nothing.

Behind him, Tedder yelled: "George! Let's go!"

Blood pumped from the chest wound for a few moments, then slowed to a trickle. George felt for a pulse, but there was none. At least the man had died fast.

The blaze in the warehouse was spreading rapidly, and George could feel its heat.

Tedder said: "George! We'll leave you behind!"

The speedboat's engine started with a roar.

George closed the dead man's eyes. He stood up. For a few seconds he remained standing, head bowed. Then he ran for the speedboat.

As soon as he was aboard, the boat veered away from the dock and headed across the bay. George strapped himself in.

Tedder yelled in his ear: "What the fuck did you think you were doing?"

"We killed an innocent man," George said. "I thought he deserved a moment of respect."

"He was working for the Communists!"

"He was the night watchman—he probably didn't know Communism from cheesecake."

"You're a goddamn pussy."

George looked back. The warehouse was now a giant bonfire. People were swarming around it, presumably trying to put out the blaze. He returned his gaze to the sea in front, and did not look back again.

When at last they reached Miami and stood on solid ground again, George said to Tedder: "While we were at sea, you called me a pussy." He knew this was stupid, almost as stupid as going on the raid, but he was too proud to let it pass. "We're on dry land, now, with no safety issues. Why don't you say it again, here?"

Tedder stared at him. Tedder was taller than George, but not so broad. He must have had some kind of training in unarmed combat, and George could see him weighing the odds, while the Cubans looked on with neutral interest.

Tedder's gaze flicked to George's cauliflower ear and back again and he said: "I think we'll just forget it."

"I thought so," said George.

On the plane back to Washington he drafted a short report for Bobby, saying that in his opinion Operation Mongoose was ineffective,

ISLAND

as there was no sign that people in Cuba (as opposed to exiles) wanted to overthrow Castro. It was also a threat to the global prestige of the United States, as it would cause anti-American hostility if it ever became public. When he handed Bobby the report, he said succinctly: "Mongoose is useless, and it's dangerous."

"I know," Bobby said. "But we have to do something."

. . .

Dimka was seeing all women differently.

He and Valentin spent most weekends with Nina and Anna at the girls' apartment, the couples taking turns to sleep in the bed or on the floor of the living room. In the course of a night he and Nina would have sex twice and even three times. He knew, in more detail than he had ever dreamed of, how a woman's body looked and smelled and tasted.

Consequently he looked at other women in a new, more knowing way. He could imagine them naked, speculate how their breasts curved, visualize their body hair, imagine their faces when they made love. In a way he knew all women, knowing one.

He felt a little disloyal to Nina when he admired Natalya Smotrov on the beach at Pitsunda, wearing a canary yellow swimsuit, with wet hair and sandy feet. Her trim figure was not as curvy as Nina's, but it was no less delightful. Perhaps his interest was pardonable: he had been here on the Black Sea coast for two weeks with Khrushchev, living the life of a monk. Anyway, he was not seriously courting temptation, for Natalya wore a wedding ring.

She was reading a typed report while he took a midday swim, and then she slipped a dress on over her swimsuit at the same time as he changed into his homemade shorts, so they walked together from the beach up to what they called the Barracks.

It was an ugly new building with bedrooms for relatively low-status visitors such as themselves. They met with the other aides in the empty dining room, which smelled of boiled pork and cabbage.

This was a jockeying-for-position meeting ahead of next week's Politburo. The purpose, as always, was to identify controversial issues and assess the support for one side or another. Then an aide could save his boss from the embarrassment of arguing in favor of a proposal that would be subsequently rejected.

Dimka went on the attack right away. "Why is the Defense Ministry so slow in sending arms to our comrades in Cuba?" he said. "Cuba is the only revolutionary state in the American continent. It is proof that Marxism applies all over the world, not just in the East."

Dimka's fondness for the Cuban revolution was more than ideological. He was thrilled by the bearded heroes with their combat fatigues and their cigars—such a contrast to the grim-faced Soviet leaders in their gray suits. Communism was supposed to be a joyous crusade to make a better world. Sometimes the Soviet Union was more like a medieval monastery where everyone had taken vows of poverty and obedience.

Yevgeny Filipov was aide to the defense minister, and he bristled. "Castro is not a true Marxist," he said. "He ignores the correct line laid down by the Popular Socialist Party of Cuba." The PSP was the pro-Moscow party. "He goes his own revisionist way."

Communism was badly in need of revision, in Dimka's opinion, but he did not say that. "The Cuban revolution is a massive blow to capitalist imperialism. We should support it if only because the Kennedy brothers so hate Castro!"

"Do they?" said Filipov. "I don't know so much. The Bay of Pigs invasion happened a year ago. What have the Americans done since?"

"They have spurned Castro's peace feelers."

"True: the conservatives in Congress would not let Kennedy make a pact with Castro even if he wanted to. But that doesn't mean he's going to war."

Dimka looked around the room at the assembled aides in their short-sleeved shirts and sandals. They were watching him and Filipov, discreetly remaining silent until they could tell who was going to win this gladiatorial contest. Dimka said: "We have to make sure the Cuban revolution is not overthrown. Comrade Khrushchev believes there will be another American invasion, this one better organized and more lavishly financed."

"But where is your evidence?"

Dimka was defeated. He had been aggressive and done his best, but his position was weak. "We don't have evidence either way," he admitted. "We have to argue from probabilities."

"Or we could delay arming Castro until the position becomes clearer."

Around the table several people nodded agreement. Filipov had scored heavily against Dimka.

At that moment Natalya spoke. "As a matter of fact, there is some evidence," she said. She passed Dimka the typed pages she had been reading on the beach.

Dimka scanned the document. It was a report from the KGB station chief in the USA, and it was headed: "Operation Mongoose."

While he was rapidly reading the pages, Natalya said: "Contrary to what Comrade Filipov from the Defense Ministry argues, the KGB is sure the Americans have *not* given up on Cuba."

Filipov was furious. "Why has this document not been circulated to us all?"

"It's only just in from Washington," Natalya said coolly. "You'll get a copy this afternoon, I'm sure."

Natalya always seemed to get hold of key information a little ahead of everyone else, Dimka reflected. It was a great skill for an aide. Clearly she must be very valuable to her boss, Foreign Minister Gromyko. No doubt that was why she had such a high-powered job.

Dimka was astonished by what he was reading. It meant he would win today's argument, thanks to Natalya, but it was bad news for Cuba's revolution. "This is even worse than Comrade Khrushchev feared!" he said. "The CIA has sabotage teams in Cuba ready to destroy sugar mills and power stations. It's guerrilla warfare! And they're plotting to assassinate Castro!"

Filipov said desperately: "Can we rely on this information?"

Dimka looked at him. "What's your opinion of the KGB, comrade?"

Filipov shut up.

Dimka got to his feet. "I'm sorry to draw this meeting to a premature close," he said. "But I think the first secretary needs to see this right away." He left the building.

He followed a path through the pine forest to Khrushchev's white stucco villa. Inside, it was strikingly furnished with white curtains and furniture made of timber bleached like driftwood. He wondered who had picked such a radically contemporary style: certainly not the peasant Khrushchev, who, if he noticed decor at all, would probably have preferred velvet upholstery and flower-patterned carpets.

Dimka found the leader on the upstairs balcony that looked over the bay. Khrushchev was holding a pair of powerful Komz binoculars.

Dimka was not nervous. Khrushchev had taken a liking to him, he knew. The boss was pleased with the way he stood up to the other aides. "I thought you would want to see this report right away," Dimka said. "Operation Mongoose—"

"I just read it," Khrushchev interrupted. He handed the binoculars to Dimka. "Look over there," he said, pointing across the water toward Turkey.

Dimka put the binoculars to his eyes.

"American nuclear missiles," said Khrushchev. "Aimed at my dacha!"

Dimka could not see any missiles. He could not see Turkey, which was one hundred fifty miles away in that direction. But he knew that this characteristically theatrical gesture by Khrushchev was essentially right. In Turkey the USA had deployed Jupiter missiles, obsolete but certainly not harmless: Dimka had this information from his uncle Volodya in Red Army Intelligence.

Dimka was not sure what to do. Should he pretend he could see the missiles through the binoculars? But Khrushchev must know he could not.

Khrushchev solved the problem by snatching the binoculars back. "And do you know what I'm going to do?" he said.

"Please tell me."

"I'm going to let Kennedy know how it feels. I will deploy nuclear missiles in Cuba—aimed at *his* dacha!"

Dimka was speechless. He had not been expecting this. And he could not see it as a good idea. He agreed with his boss in wanting more military aid for Cuba, and he had been battling the Defense Ministry over that issue—but now Khrushchev was going too far. "Nuclear missiles?" he repeated, trying to gain time to think.

"Exactly!" Khrushchev pointed to the KGB report on Operation Mongoose that Dimka was still clutching. "And that will convince the Politburo to support me. Poisoned cigars. Ha!"

"Our official line has been that we will not deploy nuclear weapons in Cuba," Dimka said, in the manner of one who presents incidental information, rather than in an argumentative tone. "We have given the Americans that reassurance several times, and publicly."

Khrushchev grinned with impish delight. "Then Kennedy will be all the more surprised!"

Khrushchev scared Dimka in this mood. The first secretary was not a fool, but he was a gambler. If this scheme went wrong it could lead to a diplomatic humiliation that might bring about Khrushchev's downfall as leader—and, by way of collateral damage, end Dimka's career. Worse, it might provoke the American invasion of Cuba that it was intended to prevent—and his beloved sister was in Cuba. There was even a chance that it would spark the nuclear war that would end capitalism, Communism, and quite possibly the human race.

On the other hand, Dimka could not help feeling excited. What a tremendous blow would be struck against the rich, smug Kennedy boys, against the global bully that was the United States, and against the whole capitalist-imperialist power bloc. If the gamble paid off, what a triumph it would be for the USSR and Khrushchev.

What should he do? He switched to practical mode and strained to think of ways to reduce the apocalyptic risks of the scheme. "We could start by signing a peace treaty with Cuba," he said. "The Americans could hardly object to that without admitting that they were planning to attack a poor Third World country." Khrushchev looked unenthusiastic but said nothing, so Dimka went on. "Then we could step up the supply of conventional weapons. Again it would be awkward for Kennedy to protest: why shouldn't a country buy guns for its army? Finally we could send the missiles—"

"No," said Khrushchev abruptly. He never liked gradualism, Dimka reflected. "This is what we'll do," Khrushchev went on. "We'll ship the missiles secretly. We'll put them in boxes labeled 'drainage pipes,' anything. Even the ships' captains won't know what's inside. We'll send our artillerymen over to Cuba to assemble the launchers. The Americans won't have any idea what we're up to."

Dimka felt a little sick, with both fear and exhilaration. It would be extraordinarily difficult to keep such a big project secret, even in the Soviet Union. Thousands of men would be involved in crating the weapons, sending them by train to the ports, opening them in Cuba, and deploying them. Was it even possible to keep them all quiet?

However, he said nothing.

Khrushchev went on: "And then, when the weapons are launch-ready, we'll make an announcement. It will be a fait accompli—the Americans will be helpless to do anything about it."

It was just the kind of grand dramatic gesture Khrushchev loved, and Dimka realized he would never talk him out of it. He said cautiously: "I wonder how President Kennedy will react to such an announcement."

Khrushchev made a scornful noise. "He's a boy—inexperienced, timid, weak."

"Of course," said Dimka, though he feared Khrushchev might be underestimating the young president. "But they have midterm elections on November sixth. If we revealed the missiles during the campaign, Kennedy would come under heavy pressure to do something drastic, to avoid humiliation at the polls."

"Then you have to keep the secret until November sixth."

Dimka said: "Who does?"

"You do. I'm putting you in charge of this project. You'll be my liaison with the Defense Ministry, who will have to carry it out. It will be your job to make sure they don't let the secret leak before we're ready."

Dimka was shocked enough to blurt out: "Why me?"

"You hate that prick Filipov. Therefore I can trust you to ride him hard."

Dimka was too aghast to wonder how Khrushchev knew he hated Filipov. The army was being given a near-impossible task—and Dimka would get the blame if it went wrong. This was a catastrophe.

But he knew better than to say so. "Thank you, Nikita Sergeyevich," he said formally. "You can rely on me."

T he GAZ-13 limousine was called a Seagull because of its streamlined American-style rear wings. It could reach one hundred miles per hour, just, although it was uncomfortable at such speeds on Soviet roads. It was available in two-tone burgundy and cream with whitewall tires, but Dimka's was black.

He sat in the back as it drove onto the quayside at Sevastopol, Ukraine. The town stood on the tip of the Crimean Peninsula, where it poked out into the Black Sea. Twenty years ago it had been flattened by German bombing and artillery fire. After the war it had been rebuilt as a cheerful seaside resort with Mediterranean balconies and Venetian arches.

Dimka got out and looked at the ship moored at the dock, a timber freighter with oversize hatches designed to take tree trunks. Under the hot summer sun, stevedores were loading skis and clearly labeled cartons of cold-weather clothing, to give the impression that the ship was headed to the frozen north. Dimka had devised the deliberately misleading code name Operation Anadyr, after a town in Siberia.

A second Seagull pulled onto the dock and parked behind Dimka's. Four men in Red Army Intelligence uniforms got out and stood waiting for his instructions.

A railway line ran alongside the dock, and a massive gantry straddled the line, positioned to shift cargo directly from railcar to ship. Dimka looked at his wristwatch. "The fucking train should be here by now."

Dimka was wound up tight. He had never been so tense in all his life. He had not even known what stress was until he started this project.

The senior Red Army man was a colonel called Pankov. Despite his rank, he addressed Dimka with formal respect. "You want me to make a call, Dmitri Ilich?"

A second officer, Lieutenant Meyer, said: "I think it's coming."

Dimka looked along the track. In the distance he could see, approaching slowly, a line of low-slung open railcars loaded with long wooden crates.

Dimka said: "Why does everyone think it's all right to be fifteen fucking minutes late?"

Dimka was worried about spies. He had visited the chief of the local KGB station and reviewed his list of suspected people in the area. They were all dissidents: poets, priests, painters of abstract art, and Jews who wanted to go to Israel—typical Soviet malcontents, about as threatening as a cycling club. Dimka had them all arrested anyway, but not one looked dangerous. Almost certainly there were real CIA agents in Sevastopol, but the KGB did not know who they were.

A man in captain's uniform came from the ship across the gangway and addressed Pankov. "Are you in charge here, Colonel?"

Pankov inclined his head toward Dimka.

The captain became less deferential. "My ship can't go to Siberia," he said.

"Your destination is classified information," Dimka said. "Do not speak of it." In Dimka's pocket was a sealed envelope that the captain was to open after he had sailed from the Black Sea into the Mediterranean. At that point he would learn he was going to Cuba.

"I need cold-weather lubricating oil, antifreeze, deicing equipment—"

Dimka said: "Shut the fuck up."

"But I have to protest. Siberian conditions—"

Dimka said to Lieutenant Meyer: "Punch him in the mouth."

Meyer was a big man and he hit hard. The captain fell back, his lips bleeding.

Dimka said: "Go back aboard your ship, wait for orders, and keep your stupid mouth shut."

The captain left, and the men on the quay turned their attention back to the approaching train.

Operation Anadyr was huge. The approaching train was the first of nineteen similar, all required to bring just this first missile regiment to Sevastopol. Altogether, Dimka was sending fifty thousand men and two hundred thirty thousand tons of equipment to Cuba. He had a fleet of eighty-five ships.

He still did not see how he was to keep the whole thing secret.

Many of the men in authority in the Soviet Union were careless, lazy, drunk, and just plain stupid. They misunderstood their instructions, they forgot, they approached challenging tasks halfheartedly and then gave up, and sometimes they just decided they knew better. Reasoning with them was useless; charm was worse. Being nice to them made them think you were a fool who could be ignored.

The train inched alongside the ship, its steel-on-steel brakes squealing. Each purpose-built railcar carried just one wooden crate eighty feet long and nine feet square. A crane operator mounted the gantry and entered its control cabin. Stevedores leaped onto the railcars and began readying the crates for loading. A company of soldiers had traveled with the train, and now they began to help the stevedores. Dimka was relieved to see that the missile regiment flashes had been removed from their uniforms, in accordance with his instructions.

A man in a civilian suit jumped down off a car, and Dimka was irritated to see that it was Yevgeny Filipov, his opposite number at the Defense Ministry. Filipov approached Pankov, as the captain had, but Pankov said: "Comrade Dvorkin is in command here."

Filipov shrugged. "Just a few minutes late," he said with a satisfied air. "We were delayed—"

Dimka noticed something. "Oh, no," he said. "Fuck it."

Filipov said: "Something wrong?"

Dimka stamped his foot on the concrete quay. "Fuck, fuck, fuck!"

"What is it?"

Dimka looked at him in fury. "Who's in charge on the train?"

"Colonel Kats is with us."

"Bring the dumb bastard here to me right away."

Filipov did not like to do Dimka's bidding, but he could hardly refuse such a request, and he went away.

Pankov looked an inquiry at Dimka.

Dimka said with weary rage: "Do you see what is stenciled on the side of each crate?"

Pankov nodded. "It's an army code number."

"Exactly," Dimka said bitterly. "It means: 'R-12 ballistic missile.'"

"Oh, shit," said Pankov.

Dimka shook his head in impotent fury. "Torture is too good for some people."

He had feared that sooner or later he would have a showdown with the army, and on balance it suited him to have it now, over the very first shipment. And he was prepared for it.

Filipov returned with a colonel and a major. The senior man said: "Good morning, comrades. I'm Colonel Kats. Slight delay, but otherwise everything is going smoothly—"

"No, it's not, you dimwitted prick," said Dimka.

Kats was incredulous. "What did you say?"

Filipov said: "Look here, Dvorkin, you can't talk to an army officer like that."

Dimka ignored Filipov and spoke to Kats. "You have endangered the security of this entire operation by your disobedience. Your orders were to paint over the army numbers on the crates. You were provided with new stencils reading 'Construction-Grade Plastic Pipe.' You were to paint new markings on all the crates."

Kats said indignantly: "There wasn't time."

Filipov said: "Be reasonable, Dvorkin."

Dimka suspected Filipov might be happy for the secret to leak, for then Khrushchev would be discredited and might even fall from power.

Dimka pointed south, out to sea. "There is a NATO country just one hundred and fifty miles in that direction, Kats, you fucking idiot. Don't you know that the Americans have spies? And that they send them to places such as Sevastopol, which is a naval base and a major Soviet port?"

"The markings are in code—"

"In code? What is your brain made of, dog shit? What training do you imagine is given to capitalist-imperialist spies? They are taught to recognize uniform badges—such as the missile regiment flash you are wearing on your collar, also against orders—as well as other military insignia and equipment markings. You stupid turd, every traitor and CIA informant in Europe can read the army code on these crates."

Kats tried standing on his dignity. "Who do you think you are?" he said. "Don't you dare speak to me like that. I've got children older than you."

"You are relieved of your command," said Dimka.

"Don't be ridiculous."

"Show him, please."

Colonel Pankov took a sheet of paper from his pocket and handed it to Kats.

Dimka said: "As you see from the document, I have the necessary authority."

Filipov's jaw was hanging open, Dimka saw.

Dimka said to Kats: "You are under arrest as a traitor. Go with these men."

Lieutenant Meyer and another of Pankov's group smoothly positioned themselves either side of Kats, took his arms, and marched him to the limousine.

Filipov recovered his wits. "Dvorkin, for God's sake—"

"If you can't say anything helpful, shut your fucking mouth," Dimka said to him. He turned to the missile regiment major, who had not said a word so far. "Are you Kats's second-in-command?"

The man looked terrified. "Yes, comrade. Major Spektor at your service."

"You are now in command."

"Thank you."

"Take this train away. North of here is a large complex of train sheds. Arrange with the railway management to stop there for twelve hours while you repaint the crates. Bring the train back here tomorrow."

"Yes, comrade."

"Colonel Kats is going to a labor camp in Siberia for the rest of his life, which will not be very long. So, Major Spektor, don't make a mistake."

"I won't."

Dimka got into his limousine. As he drove away, he passed Filipov standing on the quay, looking as if he was not sure what had just happened.

. . .

Tanya Dvorkin stood on the dock at Mariel, on Cuba's north coast, twenty-five miles from Havana, where a narrow inlet opened into a huge natural harbor hidden among hills. She looked anxiously at a Soviet ship moored at a concrete pier. Parked on the pier was a Soviet ZIL-130 truck pulling an eighty-foot trailer. A crane was lifting a long wooden crate from the ship's hold and moving it through the air, with painful slowness, toward the truck. The crate was marked in Russian: CONSTRUCTION-GRADE PLASTIC PIPE.

She saw all this by floodlights. The ships had to be unloaded at night, by order of her brother. All other shipping had been cleared out of the harbor. Patrol boats had closed the inlet. Frogmen searched the waters around the ship to guard against an underwater threat. Dimka's name was mentioned in tones of fear: his word was law and his wrath terrible to behold, they said.

Tanya was writing articles for TASS that told how the Soviet Union was helping Cuba, and how grateful the Cuban people were for the friendship of their ally on the far side of the globe. But she reserved the real truth for the coded cables she sent, via the KGB's telegraph system, to Dimka in the Kremlin. And now Dimka had given her the unofficial task of making sure his instructions were carried out without fail. That was why she was anxious.

With Tanya was General Paz Oliva, the most beautiful man she had ever met.

Paz was breathtakingly attractive: tall and strong and a little scary, until he smiled and spoke in a soft bass voice that made her think of the strings of a cello being caressed by a bow. He was in his thirties: most of Castro's military men were young. With his dark skin and soft curls he looked more Negro than Hispanic. He was a poster boy for Castro's policy of racial equality, such a contrast with Kennedy's.

Tanya loved Cuba, but it had taken a while. She missed Vasili more than she had expected. She realized how fond she was of him, even though they had never been lovers. She worried about him in his Siberian labor camp, hungry and cold. The campaign for which he had been punished—publicizing the illness of Ustin Bodian, the opera singer—had been successful, sort of: Bodian had been released from prison, though he had died soon afterward in a Moscow hospital. Vasili would find the irony telling.

Some things she could not get used to. She still put on a coat to go out, although the weather was never cold. She got bored with beans and rice and, to her surprise, found herself longing for a bowl of kasha with sour cream. After endless days of hot summer sun, she sometimes hoped for a downpour to freshen the streets.

Cuban peasants were as poor as Soviet peasants, but they seemed happier, perhaps because of the weather. And eventually the Cuban people's irrepressible joie de vivre bewitched Tanya. She smoked cigars and drank rum with tuKola, the local substitute for Coke. She loved to dance with Paz to the irresistibly sexy rhythms of the traditional music they called *trova*. Castro had closed most of the nightclubs, but no one could prevent Cubans playing guitars, and the musicians had moved to small bars called *casas de la trova*.

But she worried for the Cuban people. They had defied their giant neighbor, the United States, only ninety miles away across the Straits of Florida, and she knew that one day they might be punished. When she thought about it, Tanya felt like the crocodile bird, bravely perched between the open jaws of the great beast, pecking food from a row of teeth like broken knives.

Was the Cubans' defiance worth the price? Only time would tell. Tanya was pessimistic about the prospects for reforming Communism, but some of the things Castro had done were admirable. In 1961, the Year of Education, ten thousand students had flocked to the countryside to teach farmers to read, a heroic crusade to wipe out illiteracy in one campaign. The first sentence in the primer was "The peasants work in the cooperative," but so what? People who could read were better equipped to recognize government propaganda for what it was.

Castro was no Bolshevik. He scorned orthodoxy and restlessly sought out new ideas. That was why he annoyed the Kremlin. But he was no democrat either. Tanya had been saddened when he had announced that the revolution had made elections unnecessary. And there was one area in which he had imitated the Soviet Union slavishly: with advice from the KGB he had created a ruthlessly efficient secret police force to stamp out dissent.

On balance, Tanya wished the revolution well. Cuba had to escape from underdevelopment and colonialism. No one wanted the Americans back, with their casinos and their prostitutes. But Tanya wondered whether Cubans would ever be allowed to make their own decisions. American hostility drove them into the arms of the Soviets; but as Castro moved closer to the USSR, it became increasingly likely that the Americans would invade. What Cuba really needed was to be left alone.

But perhaps now it had a chance. She and Paz were among a mere handful of people who knew what was in these long wooden crates. She was reporting directly to Dimka on the effectiveness of the security blanket. If the plan worked it might protect Cuba permanently from the danger of an American invasion, and give the country breathing space in which to find its own way into the future.

That was her hope, anyway.

She had known Paz a year. "You never talk about your family," she said as they watched the crate being positioned in the trailer. She addressed him in Spanish: she was now fairly fluent. She had also picked up a smattering of the American-accented English that many Cubans used occasionally.

"The revolution is my family," he said.

Bullshit, she thought.

All the same, she was probably going to sleep with him.

Paz might turn out to be a dark-skinned version of Vasili, handsome and charming and faithless. There was probably a string of lissome Cuban girls with flashing eyes taking turns to fall into his bed.

She told herself not to be cynical. Just because a man was gorgeous he did not have to be a mindless Lothario. Perhaps Paz was simply waiting for the right woman to become his life partner and toil alongside him in the mission to build a new Cuba.

The missile in its crate was lashed to the bed of the trailer. Paz was approached by a small, obsequious lieutenant called Lorenzo, who said: "Ready to move out, General."

"Carry on," said Paz.

The truck moved slowly away from the dock. A herd of motorcycles roared into life and went ahead of the truck to clear the road. Tanya and Paz got into his army car, a green Buick LeSabre station wagon, and followed the convoy.

Cuba's roads had not been designed for eighty-foot trucks. In the last three months, Red Army engineers had built new bridges and reconfigured hairpin bends, but still the convoy moved at walking pace much of the time. Tanya noted with relief that all other vehicles had been cleared from the roads. In the villages through which they passed, the low-built two-room wooden houses were dark, and the bars were shut. Dimka would be satisfied.

Tanya knew that back at the dockside another missile was already being eased onto another truck. The process would go on until first light. Unloading the entire cargo would take two nights.

So far, Dimka's strategy was working. It seemed no one suspected what the Soviet Union was up to in Cuba. There was no whisper of it on the diplomatic circuit or in the uncontrolled pages of Western newspapers. The feared explosion of outrage in the White House had not yet happened.

But there were still two months to go before the American midterm elections; two more months during which these huge missiles had to be made launch-ready in total secrecy. Tanya did not know whether it could be done.

After two hours they drove into a broad valley that had been taken over by the Red Army. Here engineers were building a launch site. This was one of more than a dozen tucked away out of sight in the folds of the mountains all across the 777-mile-long island of Cuba.

Tanya and Paz got out of the car to watch the crate being off-loaded from the truck, again under floodlights. "We did it," said Paz in a tone of satisfaction. "We now have nuclear weapons." He took out a cigar and lit it.

Sounding a note of caution, Tanya said: "How long will it take to deploy them?"

"Not long," he said dismissively. "A couple of weeks."

He was not in the mood to think about problems, but to Tanya the task looked as if it might take more than two weeks. The valley was a dusty construction site where little had so far been achieved. All the same, Paz was right: they had done the hard part, which was bringing nuclear weapons into Cuba without the Americans finding out.

"Look at that baby," Paz said. "One day it could land in the middle of Miami. Bang."

Tanya shuddered at the thought. "I hope not."

"Why?"

Did he really need to be told? "These weapons are meant to be a threat. They're supposed to make the Americans afraid to invade Cuba. If ever they are used, they will have failed."

"Perhaps," he said. "But if they do attack us, we will be able to wipe out entire American cities."

Tanya was unnerved by the evident relish with which he contemplated this dreadful prospect. "What good would that do?"

He seemed surprised by the question. "It will maintain the pride of the Cuban nation." He uttered the Spanish word *dignidad* as if it were sacred.

She could hardly believe what she was hearing. "So you would start a nuclear war for the sake of your pride?"

"Of course. What could be more important?"

Indignantly she said: "The survival of the human race, for one thing!"

He waved his lighted cigar in a dismissive gesture. "You worry about the human race," he said. "My concern is my honor."

"Shit," said Tanya. "Are you mad?"

Paz looked at her. "President Kennedy is prepared to use nuclear weapons if the United States is attacked," he said. "Secretary Khrushchev will use them if the Soviet Union is attacked. The same for De Gaulle of France and whoever is the leader of Great Britain. If one of them said anything different he would be deposed within hours." He drew on his cigar, making the end glow red, then blew out smoke. "If I'm mad," he said, "they all are."

. . .

George Jakes did not know what the emergency was. Bobby Kennedy summoned him and Dennis Wilson to a crisis meeting in the White House on the morning of Tuesday, October 16. His best guess was that the subject would be on the front page of today's *New York Times*, with the headline:

Eisenhower Calls President
Weak on Foreign Policy

The unwritten rule was that ex-presidents did not attack their successors. However, George was not surprised that Eisenhower had flouted the convention. Jack Kennedy had won by calling Eisenhower weak and inventing a nonexistent "missile gap" in the Soviets' favor. Clearly Ike was still hurting from this punch below the belt. Now that Kennedy was vulnerable to a similar charge, Eisenhower was getting his revenge—exactly three weeks before the midterm elections.

The other possibility was worse. George's great fear was that Operation Mongoose might have leaked. The revelation that the president and his brother were organizing international terrorism would be ammunition for every Republican candidate. They would say the Kennedys were criminals for doing it and fools for letting the secret out. And what reprisals might Khrushchev dream up?

George could see that his boss was furious. Bobby was not good at hiding his feelings. Rage showed in the set of his jaw and the hunch of his shoulders and the arctic blast of his blue-eyed gaze.

George liked Bobby for the openness of his emotions. People who worked with Bobby saw into his heart, frequently. It made him more vulnerable but also more lovable.

When they walked into the Cabinet Room, President Kennedy was already there. He sat on the other side of the long table, on which were several large ashtrays. He was in the center, with the presidential seal on the wall above and behind him. Either side of the seal, tall arched windows looked out onto the Rose Garden.

With him was a little girl in a white dress who was obviously his daughter, Caroline, not quite five years old. She had short light brown hair parted at the side—like her father's—and held back with a simple clip. She was speaking to him, solemnly explaining something, and he was listening raptly, as if her words were as vital as anything else said in this room of power. George was profoundly struck by the intensity of the connection between parent and child. If ever I have a daughter, he thought, I will listen like that, so that she will know she is the most important person in the world.

The aides took their seats against the wall. George sat next to Skip Dickerson, who worked for Vice President Lyndon Johnson. Skip had very fair straight hair and pale skin, almost like an albino. He pushed his blond forelock out of his eyes and spoke in a Southern accent. "Any idea where the fire is?"

"Bobby isn't saying," George replied.

A woman George did not know came into the room and took Caroline away. "The CIA has some news for us," the president said. "Let's begin."

At one end of the room, in front of the fireplace, stood an easel displaying a large monochrome photograph. The man standing next to it introduced himself as an expert photointerpreter. George had not known that such a profession existed. "The pictures you are about to see were taken on Sunday by a high-altitude U-2 aircraft of the CIA flying over Cuba."

Everyone knew about the CIA's spy planes. The Soviets had shot one down over Siberia two years ago, and had put the pilot on trial for espionage.

Everyone peered at the photo on the easel. It seemed blurred and grainy, and showed nothing that George could recognize except maybe trees. They needed an interpreter to tell them what they were looking at.

"This is a valley in Cuba about twenty miles inland from the port of Mariel," the CIA man said. He pointed with a little baton. "A good-quality new road leads to a large open field. These small shapes scattered around are construction vehicles: bulldozers, backhoes, and dump trucks. And here"—he tapped the photo for emphasis—"here, in the middle, you see a group of shapes like planks of wood in a row. They are in fact crates eighty feet long by nine feet across. That is exactly the right size and shape to contain a Soviet R-12 intermediate-range ballistic missile, designed to carry a nuclear warhead."

George just managed to stop himself from saying *Holy shit,* but others were not so restrained, and for a moment the room was full of astonished curses.

Someone said: "Are you sure?"

The photointerpreter replied: "Sir, I have been studying air reconnaissance photographs for many years, and I can assure you of two things: one, this is exactly what nuclear missiles look like, and two, nothing else looks like this."

God save us, George thought fearfully; the goddamn Cubans have nukes.

Someone said: "How the hell did they get there?"

The photointerpreter said: "Clearly the Soviets transported them to Cuba in conditions of utter secrecy."

"Snuck them in under our fucking noses," said the questioner.

Someone else asked: "What is the range of those missiles?"

"More than a thousand miles."

"So they could hit . . ."

"This building, sir."

George had to repress an impulse to get up and leave right away.

"And how long would it take?"

"To get here from Cuba? Thirteen minutes, we calculate."

Involuntarily, George glanced at the windows, as if he might see a missile coming across the Rose Garden.

The president said: "That son of a bitch Khrushchev lied to me. He told me he would not deploy nuclear missiles in Cuba."

Bobby added: "And the CIA told us to believe him."

Someone else said: "This is bound to dominate the rest of the election campaign—three more weeks."

With relief, George turned his mind to the domestic political consequences: the possibility of nuclear war was somehow too terrible to contemplate. He thought of this morning's *New York Times.* How much more Eisenhower could say now! At least when he was president he had not allowed the USSR to turn Cuba into a Communist nuclear base.

This was a disaster, and not just for foreign policy. A Republican landslide in November would mean that Kennedy was hamstrung for the last two years of his presidency, and that would be the end of the civil rights agenda. With more Republicans joining Southern Democrats in opposing equality for Negroes, Kennedy would have no chance of bringing in a civil rights bill. How long would it be then before Maria's grandfather would be allowed to register to vote without getting arrested?

In politics, everything was connected.

We have to do something about the missiles, George thought.

He had no idea what.

Fortunately Jack Kennedy did.

"First, we need to step up U-2 surveillance of Cuba," the president said. "We have to know how many missiles they have and where they are. And then, by God, we're going to take them out."

George perked up. Suddenly the problem did not seem so great. The USA had hundreds of aircraft and thousands of bombs. And President Kennedy taking decisive, violent action to protect America would do no harm to the Democrats in the midterms.

Everyone looked at General Maxwell Taylor, chairman of the Joint Chiefs of Staff and America's most senior military commander after the president. His wavy hair, slick with brilliantine and parted high on his head, made George think he might be vain. He was trusted by both Jack and Bobby, though George was not sure why. "An air strike would need to be followed by a full-scale invasion of Cuba," Taylor said.

"And we have a contingency plan for that."

"We can land one hundred fifty thousand men there within a week of the bombing."

Kennedy was still thinking about taking out the Soviet missiles. "Could we guarantee to destroy every launch site in Cuba?" he asked.

Taylor replied: "It will never be one hundred percent, Mr. President."

George had not thought of that snag. Cuba was 777 miles long. The air force might not be able to find every site, let alone destroy them all.

President Kennedy said: "And I guess any missiles remaining after our air strike would be fired at the USA immediately."

"We would have to assume that, sir," said Taylor.

The president looked bleak, and George had a sudden vivid sense of the dreadful weight of responsibility he bore. "Tell me this," said Kennedy. "If one missile landed on a medium-size American city, how bad would that be?"

Election politics were driven from George's mind, and once again his heart was chilled by the dreaded thought of nuclear war.

General Taylor conferred with his aides for a few moments, then turned back to the table. "Mr. President," he said, "our calculation is that six hundred thousand people would die."

D imka's mother, Anya, wanted to meet Nina. This surprised him. His relationship with Nina was exciting, and he slept with her every chance he got, but what did that have to do with his mother?

He put that to her, and she answered in tones of exasperation. "You were the cleverest boy in school, but you're such a fool sometimes," she said. "Listen. Every weekend that you're not away somewhere with Khrushchev, you're with this woman. Obviously she's important. You've been seeing her for three months. Of course your mother wants to know what she's like! How can you even ask?"

He supposed she was right. Nina was not just a date nor even merely a girlfriend. She was his lover. She had become part of his life.

He loved his mother, but he did not obey her in everything: she disapproved of the motorcycle, the blue jeans, and Valentin. However, he would do anything reasonable to please her, so he invited Nina to the apartment.

At first Nina refused. "I'm not going to be inspected by your family, like a used car you're thinking of buying," she said resentfully. "Tell your mother I don't want to get married. She'll soon lose interest in me."

"It's not my family, it's just her," Dimka told her. "My father's dead and my sister's in Cuba. Anyway, what have you got against marriage?"

"Why, are you proposing to me?"

Dimka was embarrassed. Nina was thrilling and sexy, and he had never been anywhere near so deeply involved with a woman, but he had not thought about marriage. Did he want to spend the rest of his life with her?

He dodged the question. "I'm just trying to understand you."

"I've tried marriage, and I didn't like it," she said. "Satisfied?"

Challenge was her default setting. He did not mind. It was part of what made her so exciting. "You prefer being single," he said.

"Obviously."

"What's so great about it?"

"I don't have to please a man, so I can please myself. And when I want something else I can see you."

"I fit neatly into the slot."

She grinned at the double meaning. "Exactly."

However, she was thoughtful for a while; then she said: "Oh, hell, I don't want to make an enemy of your mother. I'll go."

On the day, Dimka felt nervous. Nina was unpredictable. When something happened to displease her—a plate carelessly broken, a real or imagined slight, a note of reproof in Dimka's voice—her disapproval was a blast like Moscow's north wind in January. He hoped she would get on with his mother.

Nina had not previously been inside Government House. She was impressed by the lobby, which was the size of a small ballroom. The apartment was not large but it was luxuriously finished, by comparison with most Moscow homes, having thick rugs and expensive wallpaper and a radiogram—a walnut cabinet containing a record player and a radio. These were the privileges of senior KGB officers such as Dimka's father.

Anya had prepared a lavish spread of snacks, which Muscovites preferred to a formal dinner: smoked mackerel and hard-boiled eggs with red pepper on white bread; little rye bread sandwiches with cucumber and tomatoes; and her pièce de résistance, a plate of "sailboats," ovals of toast with triangles of cheese held upright by a toothpick like a mast.

Anya wore a new dress and put on a touch of makeup. She had gained a little weight since the death of Dimka's father, and it suited her. Dimka felt his mother was happier since her husband had died. Maybe Nina was right about marriage.

The first thing Anya said to Nina was: "Twenty-three years old, and this is the first time my Dimka has ever brought a girl home."

He wished his mother had not told her that. It made him seem a beginner. He *was* a beginner, and Nina had figured that out long ago, but all the same he did not need her to be reminded. Anyway, he was learning fast. Nina said he was a good lover, better than her husband, though she would not go into details.

To his surprise, Nina went out of her way to be pleasant to his mother, politely calling her Anya Grigorivitch, helping in the kitchen, asking her where she got her dress.

When they had had some vodka, Anya felt relaxed enough to say: "So, Nina, my Dimka tells me you don't want to get married."

Dimka groaned. "Mother, that's too personal!"

But Nina did not seem to mind. "I'm like you. I've already been married," she said.

"But I'm an old woman."

Anya was forty-five, which was generally considered too old for remarriage. Women of that age were thought to have left desire behind—and, if they had not, they were regarded with distaste. A respectable widow who remarried in middle age would be careful to tell everyone it was "just for companionship."

"You don't look old, Anya Grigorivitch," Nina said. "You might be Dimka's big sister."

This was rubbish, but Anya liked it all the same. Perhaps women always enjoyed such flattery, regardless of whether it was credible. Anyway, she did not deny it. "I'm too old to have more children, anyway."

"I can't have children, either."

"Oh!" Anya was shaken by that revelation. It upturned all her fantasies. For a moment she forgot to be tactful. "Why not?" she asked bluntly.

"Medical reasons."

"Oh."

Clearly Anya would have liked to know more. Dimka had noticed that medical details were of great interest to many women. But Nina clammed up, as she always did on this subject.

There was a knock at the door. Dimka sighed: he could guess who it was. He opened up.

On the doorstep were his grandparents, who lived in the same building. "Oh! Dimka—you're here!" said his grandfather Grigori

Peshkov, feigning surprise. He was in uniform. He was nearly seventy-four, but he would not retire. Old men who did not know when to quit were a major problem in the Soviet Union, in Dimka's opinion.

Dimka's grandmother Katerina had had her hair done. "We brought you some caviar," she said. Clearly this was not the casual drop-in they were pretending. They had found out that Nina was coming and they were here to check her out. Nina was being inspected by the family, just as she had feared.

Dimka introduced them. Grandmother kissed Nina and Grandfather held her hand longer than necessary. To Dimka's relief, Nina continued to be charming. She called Grandfather "comrade General." Realizing immediately that he was susceptible to attractive girls, she flirted with him, to his delight, at the same time giving Grandmother a woman-to-woman look that said *You and I know what men are like.*

Grandfather asked her about her job. She had recently been promoted, she told him, and now she was publishing manager, organizing the printing of the steel union's various newsletters. Grandmother asked about her family, and she said she did not see much of them as they all lived in her hometown of Perm, a twenty-four-hour train journey eastward.

She soon got Grandfather onto his favorite subject, historical inaccuracies in Eisenstein's film *October,* especially the scenes depicting the storming of the Winter Palace, in which Grandfather had participated.

Dimka was pleased they were all getting on so well, yet at the same time he had the uneasy sensation that he was not in control of whatever was happening here. He felt as if he were on a ship sailing through calm waters to an unknown destination: all was well for the moment, but what lay ahead?

The phone rang, and Dimka answered. He always did in the evenings: it was usually the Kremlin calling for him. The voice of Natalya Smotrov said: "I've just heard from the KGB station in Washington."

Talking to her while Nina was in the room made Dimka feel awkward. He told himself not to be stupid: he had never touched Natalya. He had thought about it, though. But surely a man need not feel guilty for his thoughts? "What's happened?" he asked.

"President Kennedy has booked television time this evening to talk to the American people."

As usual, she had the hot news first. "Why?"

"They don't know."

Dimka thought immediately of Cuba. Most of his missiles were there now, and the nuclear warheads to go with them. Tons of ancillary equipment and thousands of troops had arrived. In a few days the weapons would be launch-ready. The mission was almost complete.

But two weeks remained before the American midterm elections. Dimka had been considering flying to Cuba—there was a scheduled air service from Prague to Havana—to make sure the lid was screwed on tight for a few more days. It was vital that the secret be kept just a little longer.

He prayed that Kennedy's surprise TV appearance would be about something else: Berlin, perhaps, or Vietnam.

"What time is the broadcast?" Dimka asked Natalya.

"Seven in the evening, Eastern time."

That would be two o'clock tomorrow morning in Moscow. "I'll phone him right away," he said. "Thank you." He broke the connection, then dialed Khrushchev's residence.

The phone was answered by Ivan Tepper, head of the household staff, the equivalent of a butler. "Hello, Ivan," said Dimka. "Is he there?"

"On his way to bed," said Ivan.

"Tell him to put his trousers back on. Kennedy is going to speak on television at two A.M. our time."

"Just a minute, he's right here."

Dimka heard a muttered conversation, then Khrushchev's voice. "They have found your missiles!"

Dimka's heart sank. Khrushchev's spontaneous intuition was usually right. The secret was out—and Dimka was going to take the blame. "Good evening, comrade First Secretary," he said, and the four people in the room with him went silent. "We don't yet know what Kennedy will be speaking about."

"It's the missiles, bound to be. Call an emergency meeting of the Presidium."

"What time?"

"In an hour."

"Very good."

Khrushchev hung up.

Dimka dialed the home of his secretary. "Hello, Vera," he said. "Emergency Presidium at ten tonight. He's on his way to the Kremlin."

"I'll start calling people," she said.

"You have the numbers at your home?"

"Yes."

"Of course you do. Thank you. I'll be at the office in a few minutes." He hung up.

They were all staring at him. They had heard him say "Good evening, comrade First Secretary." Grandfather looked proud, Grandmother and Mother were concerned, and Nina had a gleam of excitement in her eye. "I've got to go to work," Dimka said unnecessarily.

Grandfather said: "What's the emergency?"

"We don't know yet."

Grandfather patted him on the shoulder and looked sentimental. "With men such as you and my son, Volodya, in charge, I know the revolution is safe."

Dimka was tempted to say he wished he felt so confident. Instead he said: "Grandfather, will you get an army car to take Nina home?"

"Of course."

"Sorry to break up the party . . ."

"Don't worry," said Grandfather. "Your work is more important. Go, go."

Dimka put on his coat, kissed Nina, and left.

Going down in the elevator, he wondered despairingly whether he had somehow let out the secret of the Cuban missiles, despite all his efforts. He had run the entire operation with formidable security. He had been brutally efficient. He had been a tyrant, punishing mistakes severely, humiliating fools, ruining the careers of men who failed to follow orders meticulously. What more could he have done?

Outside, a nighttime rehearsal was in progress for the military parade scheduled for Revolution Day, in two weeks' time. An endless line of tanks, artillery, and soldiers rumbled along the embankment of the Moskva River. *None of this will do us any good if there's a nuclear* war, he thought. The Americans did not know it, but the Soviet Union had few nuclear weapons, nowhere near the numbers the USA had. The Soviets could hurt the Americans, yes, but the Americans could wipe the Soviet Union off the face of the earth.

As the road was blocked by the procession, and the Kremlin was less than a mile away, Dimka left his motorcycle at home and walked.

The Kremlin was a triangular fortress on the north side of the river. Within were several palaces now converted to government buildings. Dimka went to the senate building, yellow with white pillars, and took the elevator to the third floor. He followed a red carpet along a high-ceilinged corridor to Khrushchev's office. The first secretary had not yet arrived. Dimka went two doors farther along to the Presidium Room. Fortunately, it was clean and tidy.

The Presidium of the Supreme Soviet was in practice the ruling body of the Soviet Union. Khrushchev was its chairman. This was where the power lay. What would Khrushchev do?

Dimka was first, but soon Presidium members and their aides began to trickle in. No one knew what Kennedy was going to say. Yevgeny Filipov arrived with his boss, Defense Minister Rodion Malinovsky. "This is a fuckup," Filipov said, hardly able to hide his glee. Dimka ignored him.

Natalya came in with the black-haired, dapper foreign minister Andrei Gromyko. She had decided that the late hour licensed casual clothing, and she looked cute in tight American-style blue jeans and a loose-fitting wool sweater with a big rolled collar.

"Thank you for the early warning," Dimka murmured to her. "I really appreciate it."

She touched his arm. "I'm on your side," she said. "You know that."

Khrushchev arrived and opened the meeting by saying: "I believe Kennedy's television address will be about Cuba."

Dimka sat up against the wall behind Khrushchev, ready to run errands. The leader might need a file, a newspaper, or a report; he might ask for tea or beer or a sandwich. Two other Khrushchev aides sat with Dimka. None of them knew the answers to the big questions. Had the Americans found the missiles? And, if they had, who had let the secret out? The future of the world hung in the balance but Dimka, somewhat to his shame, was equally worried about the future of Dimka.

Impatience was driving him mad. Kennedy would speak four hours from now. Surely the Presidium could learn the content of his speech before then? What was the KGB for?

Defense Minister Malinovsky looked like a veteran movie star, with his regular features and thick silver hair. He argued that the USA was not about to invade Cuba. Red Army Intelligence had people in Florida. There was a buildup of troops there, but nowhere near enough for an invasion, he thought. "This is some kind of election campaign trick," he said. Dimka thought he sounded overconfident.

Khrushchev, too, was skeptical. Perhaps it was true that Kennedy did not want war with Cuba, but was he free to act as he wished? Khrushchev believed that the American president was at least partly under the control of the Pentagon and capitalist-imperialists such as the Rockefeller family. "We must have a contingency plan in case the Americans do invade," he said. "Our troops must be prepared for every eventuality." He ordered a ten-minute break for committee members to consider the options.

Dimka was horrified by the rapidity with which the Presidium had begun to discuss war. This was never the plan! When Khrushchev decided to send missiles to Cuba, he had not intended to provoke combat. How did we get here from there? Dimka thought despairingly.

He saw Filipov in an ominous huddle with Malinovsky and several others. Filipov was writing something down. When they reconvened, Malinovsky read a draft order for the Soviet commander in Cuba, General Issa Pliyev, authorizing him to use "all available means" to defend Cuba.

Dimka wanted to say: *Are you mad?*

Khrushchev felt the same. "We would be giving Pliyev the authority to start a nuclear war!" he said angrily.

To Dimka's relief Anastas Mikoyan backed Khrushchev. Always a peacemaker, Mikoyan looked like a lawyer in a country town, with a neat mustache and receding hair. But he was the man who could talk Khrushchev out of his most reckless schemes. Now he opposed Malinovsky. Mikoyan had extra authority because he had visited Cuba shortly after its revolution.

"What about handing over control of the missiles to Castro?" said Khrushchev.

Dimka had heard his boss say some crazy things, especially during hypothetical discussions, but this was irresponsible even by his standards. What was he thinking?

"May I counsel against?" said Mikoyan mildly. "The Americans know that we don't want nuclear war, and as long as we control the weapons they will try to solve this problem by diplomacy. But they will not trust Castro. If they know he has his finger on the trigger they may try to destroy all the missiles in Cuba with one massive first strike."

Khrushchev accepted that, but he was not prepared to rule out nuclear weapons altogether. "That would mean the Americans can have Cuba back!" he said indignantly.

At that point, Alexei Kosygin spoke up. He was Khrushchev's closest ally, though ten years younger. His receding hair had left a gray quiff on top of his head like the prow of a ship. He had the red face of a drinker, but Dimka thought he was the smartest man in the Kremlin. "We should not be thinking about when to use nuclear weapons," Kosygin said. "If we get to that point, we will have failed catastrophically. The question to discuss is this: What moves can we make today to ensure that the situation does not deteriorate into nuclear war?"

Thank God, Dimka thought, someone talking sense at last.

Kosygin went on: "I propose that General Pliyev be authorized to defend Cuba by all means *short of* nuclear weapons."

Malinovsky had doubts, fearing that U.S. intelligence might somehow learn of this order; but despite his reservations the proposal was agreed on, to Dimka's great relief, and the message was sent. The danger of a nuclear holocaust still loomed, but at least the Presidium was focused on avoiding a war rather than fighting it.

Soon afterward, Vera Pletner looked into the room and beckoned Dimka. He slipped out. In the broad corridor she handed him six sheets of paper. "This is Kennedy's speech," she said quietly.

"Thank heaven!" He looked at his watch. It was one fifteen A.M., forty-five minutes before the American president was due to go on television. "How did we get this?"

"The American government kindly provided our Washington embassy with advance copies, and the Foreign Ministry has quickly translated it."

Standing in the corridor, alone but for Vera, Dimka read fast. "This government, as promised, has maintained the closest surveillance of the Soviet military buildup on the island of Cuba."

Kennedy called Cuba an island, Dimka noticed, as if it did not count as a real country.

"Within the past week, unmistakable evidence has established the fact that a series of offensive missile sites is now in preparation on that imprisoned island."

Evidence, Dimka thought; what evidence?

"The purpose of these bases can be none other than to provide a nuclear strike capability against the Western Hemisphere."

Dimka read on but, infuriatingly, Kennedy did not say how he had come by the information, whether from traitors or spies, in the Soviet Union or Cuba, or by some other means. Dimka still did not know whether this crisis was his fault.

Kennedy made much of Soviet secrecy, calling it deception. That was fair, Dimka thought; Khrushchev would have made the same accusation in the reverse situation. But what was the American president going to do? Dimka skipped pages until he came to the important part.

"First, to halt this offensive buildup, a strict quarantine on all offensive military equipment under shipment to Cuba is being initiated."

Ah, Dimka thought; a blockade. That was against international law, which was why Kennedy was calling it a quarantine, as if he were combating some plague.

"All ships of any kind bound for Cuba from whatever nation or port will, if found to contain cargoes of offensive weapons, be turned back."

Dimka saw immediately that this was just a preliminary. The quarantine would make no difference: most of the missiles were already in place and nearly ready to be fired—and Kennedy must know that, if his intelligence was as good as it seemed. The blockade was symbolic.

There was also a threat. "It shall be the policy of this nation to regard any nuclear missile, launched from Cuba, against any nation in the Western Hemisphere, as an attack by the Soviet Union on the United States, requiring a full retaliatory response upon the Soviet Union."

Dimka felt as if something cold and heavy had settled in his stomach. This was a terrible threat. Kennedy would not trouble to find out whether the missile had been launched by the Cubans or the Red Army; it was all the same to him. Nor would he care what the target was. If they bombed Chile it would be the same as bombing New York.

Any time one of Dimka's nukes was fired, the USA would turn the Soviet Union into a radioactive desert.

Dimka saw in his mind the picture everyone knew, the mushroom cloud of a nuclear bomb; and in his imagination it rose over the center of Moscow, where the Kremlin and his home and every familiar building lay in ruins, and scorched corpses floated like a hideous scum on the poisoned water of the Moskva River.

Another sentence caught his eye. "It is difficult to settle or even discuss these problems in an atmosphere of intimidation." The hypocrisy of the Americans took Dimka's breath away. What was Operation Mongoose if not intimidation?

It was Mongoose that had persuaded a reluctant Presidium to send the missiles in the first place. Dimka was beginning to suspect that aggression was self-defeating in international politics.

He had read enough. He went back into the Presidium Room, walked quickly up to Khrushchev, and handed him the sheaf of papers. "Kennedy's television speech," he said, clearly enough for everyone to hear. "An advance copy, provided by the USA."

Khrushchev snatched the papers and began to read. The room fell silent. There was no point in saying anything until they knew what was in the document.

Khrushchev took his time reading the formal, abstract language. Now and again he snorted with derision or grunted with surprise. As he progressed through the pages, Dimka sensed that his mood was changing from anxiety to relief.

After several minutes he put down the last page. Still he said nothing, thinking. At last he looked up. A smile broke over his lumpy peasant face as he looked around the table at his colleagues. "Comrades," he said, "we have saved Cuba!"

·   ·   ·

As usual, Jacky interrogated George about his love life. "Are you dating anyone?"

"I only just broke up with Norine."

"Only just? That was almost a year ago."

"Oh . . . I guess it was."

She had made fried chicken with okra and the deep-fried cornmeal dumplings she called hush puppies. This had been his favorite meal when he was a boy. Now at twenty-six he preferred rare beef and salad, or pasta with clam sauce. Also, he normally had dinner at eight in the evening, not six. But he tucked in and did not tell her any of this. He preferred not to spoil the pleasure she took in feeding him.

She sat opposite him at the kitchen table, as she always had. "How is that nice Maria Summers?"

George tried not to wince. He had lost Maria to another man. "Maria has a steady," he said.

"Oh? Who is he?"

"I don't know."

Jacky made a frustrated noise. "Didn't you ask?"

"I sure did. She wouldn't tell me."

"Why not?"

George shrugged.

"It's a married man," his mother said confidently.

"Mom, you can't possibly know that," George said, but he had a horrible suspicion she might be right.

"Normally a girl boasts about the man she's seeing. If she clams up, she's ashamed."

"There could be another reason."

"Such as?"

For the moment George could not think of one.

Jacky went on: "He's probably someone she works with. I sure hope her preacher grandfather doesn't find out."

George thought of another possibility. "Maybe he's white."

"Married and white too, I'll bet. What is that press officer like, Pierre Salinger?"

"An affable guy in his thirties, good French clothes, a little heavy. He's married, and I hear he's up to no good with his secretary, so I'm not sure he has time for another girlfriend."

"He might, if he's French."

George grinned. "Have you ever met a French person?"

"No, but they have a reputation."

"And Negroes have a reputation for being lazy."

"You're right. I shouldn't talk that way, people are individuals."

"That's what you always taught me."

George had only half his mind on the conversation. The news about the missiles in Cuba had been kept secret from the American people for a week, but it was about to be revealed. It had been a week of intense debate within the small circle who knew, but little had been resolved. Looking back, George realized that when he had first heard he had underreacted. He had thought mainly of the imminent midterm elections and their effect on the civil rights campaign. For a moment he had even relished the prospect of American retaliation. Only later had the truth sunk in: that civil rights would no longer matter, and no more elections would ever be held, if there was a nuclear war.

Jacky changed the subject. "The chef where I work has a lovely daughter."

"Is that so?"

"Cindy Bell."

"What is Cindy short for, Cinderella?"

"Lucinda. She graduated this year from Georgetown University."

Georgetown was a neighborhood of Washington, but few of the city's black majority attended its prestigious university. "She white?"

"No."

"Must be bright, then."

"Very."

"Catholic?" Georgetown University was a Jesuit foundation.

"Nothing wrong with Catholics," Jacky said with a touch of defiance. Jacky attended Bethel Evangelical Church, but she was broad-minded. "Catholics believe in the Lord, too."

"Catholics don't believe in birth control, though."

"I'm not sure I do."

"What? You're not serious."

"If I'd used birth control, I wouldn't have you."

"But you don't want to deny other women the right to a choice."

"Oh, don't be so argumentative. I don't want to ban birth control."

She smiled fondly. "I'm just glad I was ignorant and reckless when I was sixteen." She stood up. "I'll put some coffee on." The doorbell rang. "Would you see who that is?"

George opened the front door to an attractive black girl in her early twenties, wearing tight Capri pants and a loose sweater. She was surprised to see him. "Oh!" she said. "I'm sorry, I thought this was Mrs. Jakes's house."

"It is," said George. "I'm visiting."

"My father asked me to drop this off as I was passing." She handed him a book called *Ship of Fools.* He had heard the title before: it was a bestseller. "I guess Dad borrowed it from Mrs. Jakes."

"Thank you," George said, taking the book. Politely he added: "Won't you come in?"

She hesitated.

Jacky came to the kitchen door. From there she could see who was outside: it was not a large house. "Hello, Cindy," she said. "I was just talking about you. Come in, I've made fresh coffee."

"It sure smells good," said Cindy, and she crossed the threshold.

George said: "Can we have coffee in the living room, Mom? It's almost time for the president."

"You don't want to watch TV, do you? Sit and talk to Cindy."

George opened the living room door. He said to Cindy: "Would you mind if we watched the president? He's going to say something important."

"How do you know?"

"I helped write his speech."

"Then I have to watch," she said.

They went in. George's grandfather Lev Peshkov had bought and furnished this house for Jacky and George in 1949. After that Jacky proudly refused to take anything more from Lev except George's school and college costs. On her modest salary she could not afford to redecorate, so the living room had changed little in thirteen years. George liked it this way: fringed upholstery, an Oriental rug, a china cabinet. It was old-fashioned, but homey.

The main innovation was the RCA Victor television set. George turned it on, and they waited for the green screen to warm up.

Cindy said: "Your mom works at the University Women's Club with my dad, doesn't she?"

"That's right."

"So he didn't really need me to drop off the book. He could have given it back to her tomorrow at work."

"Yes."

"We've been set up."

"I know."

She giggled. "Oh, well, what the heck."

He liked her for that.

Jacky brought in a tray. By the time she had poured coffee, President Kennedy was on the monochrome screen, saying: "Good evening, my fellow citizens." He was sitting at a desk. In front of him was a small lectern with two microphones. He wore a dark suit, white shirt, and narrow tie. George knew that the shadows of terrible strain on his face had been concealed by television makeup.

When he said Cuba had "a nuclear strike capability against the Western Hemisphere," Jacky gasped and Cindy said: "Oh, my Lord!"

He read from sheets of paper on the lectern in his flat Boston accent, *hard* pronounced "haad," and *report* pronounced "repoat." His delivery was deadpan, almost boring, but his words were electrifying. "Each of these missiles, in short, is capable of striking Washington, DC—"

Jacky gave a little scream.

"—the Panama Canal, Cape Canaveral, Mexico City—"

Cindy said: "What are we going to do?"

"Wait," said George. "You'll see."

Jacky said: "How could this happen?"

"The Soviets are sneaky," George said.

Kennedy said: "We have no desire to dominate or conquer any other nation or impose our system on its people." At that point, normally Jacky would have made a derisive remark about the Bay of Pigs invasion; but she was beyond political point-scoring now.

The camera zoomed in for a close-up as Kennedy said: "To halt this offensive buildup, a strict quarantine on all offensive military equipment under shipment to Cuba is being initiated."

"What use is that?" said Jacky. "The missiles are there already—he just said so!"

Slowly and deliberately, the president said: "It shall be the policy of this nation to regard any nuclear missile, launched from Cuba, against any nation in the Western Hemisphere, as an attack by the Soviet Union on the United States, requiring a full retaliatory response upon the Soviet Union."

"Oh, my Lord," said Cindy again. "So if Cuba launches just one missile, it's all-out nuclear war."

"That's right," said George, who had attended the meetings where this had been thrashed out.

As soon as the president said, "Thank you and good night," Jacky turned off the set and rounded on George. "What is going to happen to us?"

He longed to reassure her, to make her feel safe, but he could not. "I don't know, Mom."

Cindy said: "This quarantine makes no difference to anything, even I can see that."

"It's just a preliminary."

"So what comes next?"

"We don't know."

Jacky said: "George, tell me the truth, now. Is there going to be war?"

George hesitated. Nuclear weapons were being loaded on jets and flown around the country, to ensure that some at least would survive a Soviet first strike. The invasion plan for Cuba was being refined, and the State Department was sifting candidates to lead the pro-American government that would take charge of Cuba afterward.

Strategic Air Command had moved its alert status to DEFCON 3—Defense Condition Three, ready to start a nuclear attack in fifteen minutes.

On balance, what was the likeliest outcome of all this?

With a heavy heart, George said: "Yes, Mom. I think there will be war."

.   .   .

In the end the Presidium ordered all Soviet missile ships still on their way to Cuba to turn around and come home.

Khrushchev reckoned he lost little by this, and Dimka agreed. Cuba had nukes now; it hardly mattered how many. The Soviet Union would avoid a confrontation on the high seas, claim to be a peacemaker in this crisis—and still have a nuclear base ninety miles from the USA.

Everyone knew that would not be the end of the matter. The two superpowers had not yet addressed the real question, what to do about the nuclear weapons already in Cuba. All Kennedy's options were still open, and as far as Dimka could see, most of them led to war.

Khrushchev decided not to go home tonight. It was too dangerous to be even a few minutes' car journey away: if war broke out he had to be here, ready to make instant decisions.

Next to his grand office was a small room with a comfortable couch. The first secretary lay down there in his clothes. Most of the Presidium made the same decision, and the leaders of the world's second-most powerful country settled down to an uneasy sleep in their offices.

Dimka had a small cubbyhole down the corridor. There was no couch in his office: just a hard chair, a utilitarian desk, and a file cabinet. He was trying to figure out where would be the least uncomfortable place to lay his head when there was a tap at the door and Natalya came in. She brought with her a light fragrance unlike any Soviet perfume.

She had been wise to dress casually, Dimka realized: they were all going to sleep in their clothes. "I like your sweater," he said.

"It's called a Sloppy Joe." She used the English words.

"What does that mean?"

"I don't know, but I like how it sounds."

He laughed. "I was just trying to figure out where to sleep."

"Me, too."

"On the other hand, I'm not sure I'll be able to sleep."

"You mean, knowing you might never wake up?"

"Exactly."

"I feel the same."

Dimka thought for a moment. Even if he spent the night awake, worrying, he might as well find somewhere to be comfortable. "This is a palace, and it's empty," he said. He hesitated, then added: "Shall we explore?" He was not sure why he said that. It was the kind of thing his lady-killer friend Valentin might come out with.

"Okay," said Natalya.

Dimka picked up his overcoat, to use as a blanket.

The spacious bedrooms and boudoirs of the palace had been inelegantly subdivided into offices for bureaucrats and typists, and filled with cheap furniture made of pine and plastic. There were upholstered chairs in a few of the larger rooms for the most important men, but nothing you could sleep on. Dimka began to think of ways to make a bed on the floor. Then, at the far end of the wing, they passed along a corridor cluttered with buckets and mops and came to a grand room full of stored furniture.

The room was unheated, and their breath turned to white vapor. The large windows were frosted over. The gilded wall lights and chandeliers had sockets for candles, all empty. A dim light came from two naked bulbs hanging from the painted ceiling.

The stacked furniture looked as if it had been here since the revolution. There were chipped tables with spindly legs, chairs with rotting brocade upholstery, and carved bookcases with empty shelves. Here were the treasures of the tsars, turned to junk.

The furniture was rotting away here because it was too ancien régime to be used in the offices of commissars, although Dimka guessed it was the kind of stuff that might sell for fortunes in the antique auctions of the West.

And there was a four-poster bed.

Its hangings were full of dust but the faded blue coverlet appeared intact and it even had a mattress and pillows.

"Well," said Dimka, "here's one bed."

"We may have to share," said Natalya.

That thought had crossed Dimka's mind, but he had dismissed it. Pretty girls sometimes casually offered to share a bed with him in his fantasies, but never in real life.

Until now.

But did he want to? He was not married to Nina, but she undoubtedly wanted him to be faithful to her, and he certainly expected the same of her. On the other hand, Nina was not here, and Natalya was.

Foolishly, he said, "Are you suggesting we sleep together?"

"Just for warmth," she said. "I can trust you, can't I?"

"Of course," he said. That made it all right, he supposed.

Natalya drew back the ancient coverlet. Dust rose, making her sneeze. The sheets beneath had yellowed with age, but seemed intact. "Moths don't like cotton," she remarked.

"I didn't know that."

She stepped out of her shoes. In her jeans and sweater she slipped between the sheets. She shivered. "Come on," she said. "Don't be shy."

Dimka put his coat over her. Then he unlaced his shoes and pulled them off. This was strange but exciting. Natalya wanted to sleep with him, but without sex.

Nina would never believe it.

But he had to sleep somewhere.

He took off his tie and got into bed. The sheets were icy. He put his arms around Natalya. She laid her head against his shoulder and pressed her body to his. Her bulky sweater and his suit coat made it impossible for him to feel the contours of her body, but all the same he got an erection. If she felt it, she did not react.

In a few minutes they stopped shivering and felt warmer. Dimka's face was pressed into her hair, which was wavy and abundant and smelled of lemon soap. His hands were on her back, but he got no sense of her skin through the chunky sweater. He could feel her breath on his neck. The rhythm of her breathing changed, becoming regular and shallow. He kissed the top of her head, but she made no response.

He could not figure Natalya out. She was just an aide, like Dimka, and not more than three or four years his senior, but she drove a Mercedes, twelve years old and beautifully preserved. She usually dressed in conventionally dowdy Kremlin clothes yet she wore costly imported perfume. She was charming to the point of flirtatiousness, but she went home and cooked dinner for her husband.

She had inveigled Dimka into bed with her, then she had fallen asleep.

He was sure he would not sleep, lying in bed with a warm girl in his arms.

But he did.

It was still dark outside when he woke up.

Natalya mumbled: "What's the time?"

She was still in his arms. He craned his neck to look at his wrist, which was behind her left shoulder. "Six thirty."

"And we're still alive."

"The Americans didn't bomb us."

"Not yet."

"We'd better get up," Dimka said; and he immediately regretted it. Khrushchev would not be awake yet. And even if he was, Dimka did not have to bring this delicious moment to a premature end. He was bewildered, but happy. Why the hell had he suggested getting up?

But she was not ready. "In a minute," she said.

He was pleased by the thought that she liked lying in his arms.

Then she kissed his neck.

It was the lightest possible touch of her lips on his skin, as if a moth had flown out of the ancient hangings and brushed him with its wings; but he had not imagined it.

She had kissed him.

He stroked her hair.

She tilted her head back and looked at him. Her mouth was slightly open, the full lips a little parted, and she was smiling faintly, as if at a pleasant surprise. Dimka was no expert on women but even he could not mistake the invitation. Still he hesitated to kiss her.

Then she said: "Today we're probably going to be bombed to oblivion."

So Dimka kissed her.

The kiss heated up in a flash. She bit his lip and pushed her tongue into his mouth. He rolled her onto her back and put his hands up inside her baggy sweater. She unfastened her brassiere with a swift movement. Her breasts were delightfully small and firm, with big pointed nipples that were already hard to his fingertips. When he sucked them she gasped with pleasure.

He tried to take off her jeans, but she had another idea. She pushed him onto his back and feverishly undid his trousers. He was afraid he would come right away—something that happened to a lot of men, according to Nina—but he did not. Natalya pulled his cock out of his underwear. She stroked it with both hands, pressed it to her cheek, and kissed it, then put it in her mouth.

When he felt himself about to explode he tried to withdraw, pushing her head away: this was how Nina preferred it. But Natalya made a protesting noise, then rubbed and sucked harder, so that he lost control and came in her mouth.

After a minute she kissed him. He tasted his semen on her lips. Was that peculiar? It felt simply affectionate.

She pulled off her jeans and underwear, and he realized it was his turn to please her. Fortunately Nina had tutored him in this.

Natalya's hair was as curly and plentiful here as on her head. He buried his face, longing to return the delight she had given him. She guided him with her hands on his head, indicating by slight pressure when his kisses should be lighter or heavier, moving her hips up or down to tell him where to concentrate his attention. She was only the second woman he had done this to, and he luxuriated in the taste and the smell of her.

With Nina this was only a preliminary, but in a surprisingly short time Natalya cried out, first pressing his head hard against her, then, as if the pleasure were too much, pushing him away.

They lay side by side, catching their breath. This had been a totally new experience for Dimka, and he said reflectively: "This whole question of sex is more complicated than I thought."

To his surprise, this made her laugh heartily.

"What did I say?" he said.

She laughed all the more, and all she would say was: "Oh, Dimka, I adore you."

.   .   .

La Isabela was a ghost town, Tanya saw. Once a thriving Cuban port, it had been hit hard by Eisenhower's trade embargo. It was miles from anywhere, and surrounded by salt marshes and mangrove swamps. Scraggy goats roamed the streets. Its harbor hosted a few shabby fishing boats—and the *Aleksandrovsk*, a fifty-four-hundred-ton Soviet freighter packed to the gunwales with nuclear warheads.

The ship had been headed for Mariel. After President Kennedy announced the blockade, most of the Soviet ships had turned back, but a few that were only hours from landfall had been ordered to make a dash for the nearest Cuban port.

Tanya and Paz watched the ship inch up to the concrete dock in a shower of rain. The antiaircraft guns on deck were concealed beneath coils of rope.

Tanya was terrified. She had no idea what was going to happen. All her brother's efforts had failed to stop the secret getting out before the American midterm elections—and the trouble Dimka might be in as a result was only the least of her worries. Clearly the blockade was no more than an opening shot. Now Kennedy had to appear strong. And with Kennedy being strong and the Cubans defending their precious *dignidad* anything could happen, from an American invasion to a worldwide nuclear holocaust.

Tanya and Paz had become more intimate. They had told one another about their childhoods and their families and their past lovers. They touched each other frequently. They often laughed. But they held back from romance. Tanya was tempted, but she resisted. The idea of having sex with a man just because he was so beautiful seemed wrong. She liked Paz—despite his *dignidad*—but she did not love him. In the past she had kissed men she did not love, especially while she was at university, but she had not had sex with them. She had gone to bed with only one man, and she had loved him, or at least she had thought she did at the time. But she might sleep with Paz, if only to have someone's arms around her when the bombs fell.

The largest of the dockside warehouses was burned out. "I wonder how that happened," Tanya said, pointing.

"The CIA set fire to it," said Paz. "We get a lot of terrorist attacks here."

Tanya looked around. The quayside buildings were empty and derelict. Most of the homes were one-story wooden shacks. Rain pooled on the dirt roads. The Americans could blow the whole place up without doing noticeable damage to the Castro regime. "Why?" she said.

Paz shrugged. "It's an easy target, here on the end of the peninsula. They come over from Florida in a speedboat, sneak ashore, blow something up, shoot one or two innocent people, and go back to America." In English he added: "Fuckin' cowards."

Tanya wondered if all governments were the same. The Kennedy brothers spoke of freedom and democracy yet they sent armed gangs across the water to terrorize the Cuban people. The Soviet Communists talked of liberating the proletariat while they imprisoned or murdered everyone who disagreed with them, and they sent Vasili to Siberia for protesting. Was there an honest regime anywhere in the world?

"Let's go," said Tanya. "It's a long way back to Havana, and I need to tell Dimka that this ship has arrived safely." Moscow had decided the *Aleksandrovsk* was close enough to reach port, but Dimka was anxious for confirmation.

They got into Paz's Buick and drove out of town. On either side of the road were tall thickets of sugarcane. Turkey vultures floated above, hunting the fat rats in the fields. In the distance, the high chimney of a sugar mill pointed like a missile at the sky. The flat landscape of central Cuba was crosshatched with single-track railway lines built to transport cane from the fields to the mills. Where the land was uncultivated it was mostly tropical jungle, flame trees and jacarandas and towering royal palms; or rough scrub grazed by cattle. The slim white egrets that followed the cows were grace notes on the dun landscape.

Transport in rural Cuba was still mostly horse-drawn, but as they approached Havana the roads became crowded with military trucks and buses taking reservists to their bases. Castro had declared a full combat alert. The nation was on a war footing. As Paz's Buick sped by, the men waved and called out: "*Patria o muerte!* Motherland or death! *Cuba sí, yanqui no!*"

On the outskirts of the capital she saw that a new poster had appeared overnight and now blanketed every wall. In simple black and white, it showed a hand clutching a machine gun and the words A LAS ARMAS—"To Arms." Castro really understood propaganda, she reflected, unlike the old men in the Kremlin, whose idea of a slogan was: "Implement the resolutions of the twentieth party congress!"

Tanya had written and encoded her message earlier, and had only to fill in the exact time that the *Aleksandrovsk* had docked. She took the message into the Soviet embassy and gave it to the KGB communications officer, whom she knew well.

Dimka would be relieved, but Tanya was still fearful. Was it really good news that Cuba had another shipload of nuclear weapons? Might not the Cuban people—and Tanya herself—be safer with none?

"Do you have other duties today?" Tanya asked Paz when she came out.

"My job is liaison with you."

"But in this crisis . . ."

"In this crisis, nothing is more important than clear communication with our Soviet allies."

"Then let's walk along the Malecón together."

They drove to the sea front. Paz parked at the Hotel Nacional. Soldiers were stationing an antiaircraft gun outside the famous hotel.

Tanya and Paz left the car and walked along the promenade. A wind from the north whipped the sea into angry surges that crashed against the stone wall, throwing up explosions of spray that fell on the promenade like rain. This was a popular place to stroll, but today there were more people than usual, and their mood was not leisurely. They clustered in small crowds, sometimes talking but often silent. They were not flirting or telling jokes or showing off their best clothes. Everyone was looking in the same direction, north, toward the United States. They were watching for the *yanquis.*

Tanya and Paz watched with them for a while. She felt in her heart that the invasion had to happen. Destroyers would come slicing through the waves; submarines would surface a few yards away; and the gray planes with the blue-and-white stars would appear out of the clouds, loaded with bombs to drop on the Cuban people and their Soviet friends.

At last Tanya took Paz's hand in her own. He squeezed gently. She looked up into his deep brown eyes. "I think we're going to die," she said calmly.

"Yes," he said.

"Do you want to go to bed with me first?"

"Yes," he said again.

"Shall we go to my apartment?"

"Yes."

They returned to the car and drove to a narrow street in the old town, near the cathedral, where Tanya had upstairs rooms in a colonial building.

Tanya's first and only lover had been Petr Iloyan, a lecturer at her university. He had worshipped her young body, gazing at her breasts and touching her skin and kissing her hair as if he had never come across anything so marvelous. Paz was the same age as Petr but, Tanya quickly realized, making love with him was going to be different. It was *his* body that was the center of attention. He took his clothes off slowly, as if teasing her, then stood naked in front of her, giving her time to take in his perfect skin and the curves of his muscles. Tanya was happy to sit on the edge of the bed and admire him. The display seemed to excite him, for his penis was already fat with arousal and half erect, and Tanya could hardly wait to get her hands on it.

Petr had been a slow, gentle lover. He had been able to work Tanya up into a fever of anticipation, then hold back tantalizingly. He would change positions several times, rolling her on top, then kneeling behind her, then getting her to straddle him. Paz was not rough but he was vigorous, and Tanya gave herself up to excitement and pleasure.

Afterward Tanya made eggs and coffee. Paz turned on the TV and they watched Castro's speech while they ate.

Castro sat in front of a Cuban national flag, its bold blue and white stripes appearing black and white in the monochrome television picture. As always, he wore battle-dress drab, the only sign of rank a single star on the epaulet: Tanya had never seen him in a civilian suit, nor in the kind of pompous medal-encrusted uniform beloved of Communist leaders elsewhere.

Tanya felt a rush of optimism. Castro was no fool. He knew he could not defeat the United States in a war, even with the Soviet Union on his side. Surely he would come up with some dramatic gesture of reconciliation, some initiative that would transform the situation and defuse the time bomb.

His voice was high and reedy, but he spoke with overwhelming passion. The bushy beard gave him the air of a messiah crying in the wilderness, even though he was obviously in a studio. His black eyebrows moved expressively in a high forehead. He gestured with his big hands, sometimes raising a schoolmasterly forefinger to forbid dissent, often clenching a fist. At times he grasped the arms of his chair as if to prevent himself taking off like a rocket. He appeared to have no script, not even any notes. His expression showed indignation, pride, scorn, rage—but never doubt. Castro lived in a universe of certainty.

Point by point, Castro attacked Kennedy's television speech, which had been broadcast on live radio beamed at Cuba. He scorned Kennedy's appeal to the "captive people of Cuba." "We are not sovereign by the grace of the *yanquis*," he said contemptuously.

But he said nothing about the Soviet Union and nothing about nuclear weapons.

The speech lasted ninety minutes. It was a performance of Churchillian magnetism: brave little Cuba would defy big bullying America and would never give in. It must have boosted the morale of the Cuban people. But otherwise it changed nothing. Tanya was bitterly disappointed and even more scared. Castro had not even tried to prevent war.

At the end he cried: "Motherland or death, we will win!" Then he jumped out of the chair and rushed out as if he had not a minute to lose on his way to save Cuba.

Tanya looked at Paz. His eyes were glistening with tears.

She kissed him, then they made love again, on the couch in front of the flickering screen. This time it was slower and more satisfying. She treated him the way Petr had treated her. It was not difficult to adore his body, and he undoubtedly liked adoration. She squeezed his arms and kissed his nipples and pushed her fingers into his curls. "You're so beautiful," she murmured as she sucked his earlobe.

Afterward, as they lay sharing a cigar, they heard noises from outside. Tanya opened the door leading to the balcony. The city had been quiet while Castro was on television, but now people were coming out onto the narrow streets. Night had fallen, and some were carrying candles and torches. Tanya's journalistic instincts returned. "I have to go out there," she said to Paz. "This is a big story."

"I'll come with you."

They pulled on their clothes and left the building. The streets were wet but the rain had stopped. More and more people appeared. There was a carnival atmosphere. Everyone was cheering and shouting slogans. Many were singing the national anthem, "La Bayamesa." There was nothing Latin about the tune—it sounded more like a German drinking song—but the singers meant every word.

> *To live in chains is to live*
> *In dishonor and ignominy*

Hear the call of the bugle:
Hasten, brave ones, to arms!

As Tanya and Paz marched through the alleys of the old city with the crowd, Tanya noticed that many of the men had armed themselves. Lacking guns, they carried garden tools and machetes, and had kitchen knives and meat cleavers in their belts, as if they were going to fight the Americans hand-to-hand on the Malecón.

Tanya recalled that one Boeing B-52 Stratofortress of the United States Air Force carried seventy thousand pounds of bombs.

You poor fools, she thought bitterly, how much use do you think your knives will be against that?

CHAPTER SEVENTEEN

George had never felt nearer death than he did in the Cabinet Room of the White House on Wednesday, October 24.

The morning meeting began at ten, and George thought war would break out before eleven.

Technically this was the Executive Committee of the National Security Council, called ExComm for short. In practice President Kennedy summoned anyone he felt could help in the crisis. His brother Bobby was always among them.

The advisers sat on leather chairs around the long table. Their aides sat on similar chairs up against the walls. The tension in the room was suffocating.

The alert status of the Strategic Air Command had moved to DEFCON 2, the level just below imminent war. Every bomber of the air force was ready. Many were continuously in the air, loaded with nukes, patrolling over Canada, Greenland, and Turkey, as close as they could get to the borders of the USSR. Every bomber had a preassigned Soviet target.

If war broke out, the Americans would unleash a nuclear firestorm that would flatten every major town in the Soviet Union. Millions would die. Russia would not recover in a hundred years.

And the Soviets had to have something similar planned for the United States.

Ten o'clock was the moment the blockade went into effect. Any Soviet vessel within five hundred miles of Cuba was now fair game. The first interception of a Soviet missile ship, by the USS *Essex*, was expected between ten thirty and eleven. By eleven they might all be dead.

CIA chief John McCone began by reviewing all Soviet shipping en route to Cuba. He spoke in a drone that heightened the tension by making everyone impatient. Which Soviet ships should the navy intercept first? What would happen then? Would the Soviets allow their ships to be inspected? Would they fire on American ships? What should the navy do then?

While the group tried to second-guess their opposite numbers in Moscow, an aide brought McCone a note. McCone was a dapper, white-haired man of sixty. He was a businessman, and George suspected that the CIA career professionals did not tell him everything they were doing.

Now McCone peered through his rimless glasses at the note, which seemed to puzzle him. Eventually he said: "Mr. President, we've just received information from the Office of Naval Intelligence that all six Soviet ships currently in Cuban waters have either stopped or reversed course."

George thought: What the hell does that mean?

Dean Rusk, the bald, pug-nosed secretary of state, asked: "What do you mean, Cuban waters?"

McCone did not know.

Bob McNamara, the Ford president whom Kennedy had made secretary of defense, said: "Most of these ships are outbound, from Cuba to the Soviet Union—"

"Why don't we find out?" the president interrupted tetchily. "Are we talking about ships leaving Cuba or ships coming in?"

McCone said: "I'll find out," and he left the room.

The tension rose another notch.

George had always imagined that crisis meetings in the White House would be supernaturally high-powered, with everyone supplying the president with accurate information so that he could make a wise judgment. But this was the greatest crisis ever, and all was confusion and misunderstanding. That made George even more afraid.

When McCone came back in he said: "These ships are all westbound, all inbound for Cuba." He listed the six vessels by name.

McNamara spoke next. He was forty-six, and the phrase *whiz kid* had been invented for him when he turned the Ford Motor Company from loss to profit. President Kennedy trusted him more than anyone else in the room except Bobby. Now from memory McNamara reeled off the positions of all six ships. Most were still hundreds of miles from Cuba.

The president was impatient. "Now, what do they say they're doing with those, John?"

McCone replied: "They either stopped or reversed direction."

"Is this *all* the Soviet ships, or just selected ones?"

"This is a selected bunch. There are twenty-four altogether."

Once again McNamara interrupted with the key information. "It looks as though these are the ships closest to the quarantine barrier."

George whispered to Skip Dickerson, sitting next to him: "The Soviets seem to be pulling back from the brink."

"I sure hope you're right," Skip murmured.

The president said: "We're not planning to grab any of those, are we?"

McNamara said: "We're not planning to grab any ship that is not proceeding to Cuba."

General Maxwell Taylor, the chairman of the Joint Chiefs, picked up a phone and said: "Get me George Anderson." Admiral Anderson was the chief of naval operations and was in charge of the blockade. After a few seconds Taylor began speaking quietly.

There was a pause. Everyone was trying to absorb the news and figure out what it meant. Were the Soviets giving in?

The president said: "We ought to check first. How do we find out if six ships are simultaneously turning? General, what does the navy say about this report?"

General Taylor looked up and said: "Three ships are definitely turning back."

"Be in touch with the *Essex* and tell them to wait an hour. We have to move quickly because they're going to intercept between ten thirty and eleven."

Every man in the room looked at his watch.

It was ten thirty-two.

George got a glimpse of Bobby's face. He looked like a man reprieved from a death sentence.

The immediate crisis was over, but George realized over the next few minutes that nothing had been resolved. While the Soviets were clearly moving to avoid confrontation at sea, their nuclear missiles were still in Cuba. The clock had been turned back an hour, but it was still ticking.

ExComm discussed Germany. The president feared Khrushchev might announce a blockade of West Berlin to parallel the American blockade of Cuba. There was nothing they could do about that, either.

The meeting broke up. George was not needed at Bobby's next appointment. He left with Skip Dickerson, who said: "How's your friend Maria?"

"Fine, I think."

"I was in the press office yesterday. She called in sick."

George's heart missed a beat. He had given up all hope of a romance with Maria, but all the same the news that she was ill made him feel panicky. He frowned. "I didn't know that."

"None of my business, George, but she's a nice gal, and I thought maybe someone should check up on her."

George squeezed Skip's arm. "Thanks for letting me know," he said. "You're a pal."

White House staffers did not call in sick in the middle of the greatest crisis of the Cold War, George reflected, not unless they were seriously ill. His anxiety deepened.

He hurried to the press office. Maria's chair was empty. Nelly Fordham, the friendly woman at the next desk, said: "Maria's not well."

"I heard. Did she say what the trouble was?"

"No."

George frowned. "I wonder if I could get away for an hour and go see her."

"I wish you would," Nelly said. "I'm worried too."

George looked at his watch. He was pretty sure Bobby would not need him until after lunch. "I guess I could manage it. She lives in Georgetown, doesn't she?"

"Yes, but she moved from her old place."

"Why?"

"Said her flatmates were too nosy."

That made sense to George. Other girls would be desperate to learn the identity of a clandestine lover. Maria was so determined to keep the secret that she had moved out. That indicated how serious she was about the guy.

Nelly was flicking through her Rolodex. "I'll write down the address for you."

"Thanks."

She handed him a piece of paper and said: "You're Georgy Jakes, aren't you?"

"Yes." He smiled. "It's a long time since anyone called me Georgy, though."

"I used to know Senator Peshkov."

The fact that she mentioned Greg meant, almost certainly, that she knew he was George's father. "Really?" George said. "How did you know him?"

"We dated, if you want to know the truth. But nothing came of it. How is he?"

"Pretty well. I have lunch with him about once a month."

"I guess he never married."

"Not yet."

"And he must be past forty."

"I believe there is a lady in his life."

"Oh, don't worry. I'm not after him. I made that decision a long time ago. All the same, I wish him well."

"I'll tell him that. Now I'm going to jump in a cab and go check on Maria."

"Thank you, Georgy—or George, I should say."

George hurried out. Nelly was an attractive woman with a kind heart. Why had Greg not married her? Perhaps it suited him to be a bachelor.

George's taxi driver said: "You work in the White House?"

"I work for Bobby Kennedy. I'm a lawyer."

"No kidding!" The driver did not trouble to hide his surprise that a Negro should be a lawyer with a high-powered job. "You tell Bobby we ought to bomb Cuba to dust. That's what we ought to do. Bomb them to goddamn dust."

"Do you know how big Cuba is, end to end?" George said.

"What is this, a quiz show?" the driver said resentfully.

George shrugged and said no more. Nowadays he avoided political discussions with outsiders. They usually had easy answers: send all the Mexicans home, put Hells Angels in the army, castrate the queers. The greater their ignorance, the stronger their opinions.

Georgetown was only a few minutes away, but the journey seemed long. George imagined Maria collapsed on the floor, or lying in bed on the edge of death, or in a coma.

The address Nelly had given George turned out to be a gracious old house divided into studio apartments. Maria did not answer her downstairs doorbell, but a black girl who looked like a student let George in and pointed out Maria's room.

Maria came to the door in a bathrobe. She certainly looked sick. Her face was bloodless and her expression dejected. She did not say *Come in,* but she walked away, leaving the door open, and he entered. At least she was ambulatory, he thought with relief: he had feared worse.

It was a tiny place, one room with a kitchenette. He guessed she shared the bathroom down the hall.

He looked hard at her. It pained him to see her this way, not just sick, but miserable. He longed to take her in his arms, but he knew that would be unwelcome. "Maria, what's the matter?" he said. "You look terrible!"

"Just feminine problems, that's all."

That phrase was normally code for a menstrual period, but he was pretty sure this was something else.

"Let me make you a cup of coffee—or maybe tea?" He took off his coat.

"No, thanks," she said.

He decided to make it anyway, just to show her that he cared. But then he glanced at the chair she was about to sit on, and saw that the seat was stained with blood.

She noticed it at the same time, blushed, and said: "Oh, hell."

George knew a little about women's bodies. Several possibilities passed through his mind. He said: "Maria, have you suffered a miscarriage?"

"No," she said tonelessly. She hesitated.

George waited patiently.

At last Maria said: "An abortion."

"You poor thing." He grabbed a towel from the kitchenette, folded it, and placed it on the bloodstain. "Sit on this, for now," he said. "Rest." He looked at the shelf over the refrigerator and saw a packet of jasmine tea. Figuring that must be what she liked, he put water on to heat. He said no more until he had made the tea.

Abortion law varied from state to state. George knew that in DC it was legal for the purpose of protecting the health of the mother. Many doctors interpreted this liberally, to include the woman's health and general well-being. In practice, anyone who had the money could find a doctor willing to perform an abortion.

Although she had said she did not want tea, she took a cup.

He sat opposite her with a cup for himself. "Your secret lover," he said. "I guess he's the father."

She nodded. "Thank you for the tea. I presume World War Three hasn't started yet, otherwise you wouldn't be here."

"The Soviets turned their ships back, so the danger of a showdown at sea has receded. But the Cubans still have nukes, aimed at us."

Maria seemed too depressed to care.

George said: "He wouldn't marry you."

"No."

"Because he's already married?"

She did not answer.

"So he found you a doctor and paid the bill."

She nodded.

George thought that was a despicable way to behave, but if he said so she would probably throw him out for insulting the man she loved. Trying to control his anger, George said: "Where is he now?"

"He'll call." She glanced at the clock. "Soon, probably."

George decided not to ask any more questions. It would be unkind to interrogate her. And she did not need to be told how foolish she had been. What *did* she need? He decided to ask. "Is there anything you need? Anything I can do for you?"

She started to cry. Between sobs she said: "I hardly know you! How come you're my only real friend in the whole city?"

He knew the answer to that question. She had a secret that she would not share. That made it difficult for others to be close to her.

She said: "Lucky for me you're so kind."

Her gratitude embarrassed him. "Does it hurt?" he said.

"Yes, it hurts like hell."

"Should I call a doctor?"

"It's not that bad. They told me to expect this."

"Do you have any aspirin?"

"No."

"Why don't I step out and get you some?"

"Would you? I hate to ask a man to run errands."

"It's okay, this is an emergency."

"There's a drugstore right on the corner of the block."

George put down his cup and shrugged on his coat.

Maria said: "Could I ask you an even bigger favor?"

"Sure."

"I need sanitary napkins. Do you think you could buy a box?"

He hesitated. A man, buying sanitary napkins?

She said: "No, it's too much to ask, forget it."

"Hell, what are they going to do, arrest me?"

"The brand name is Kotex."

George nodded. "I'll be right back."

His bravado did not last long. When he reached the drugstore he felt stricken with embarrassment. He told himself to shape up. So, it was uncomfortable. Men his age were risking their lives in the jungles of Vietnam. How bad could this be?

The store had three self-service aisles and a counter. Aspirins were not displayed on the open shelves, but sold from the counter.

To George's dismay, feminine sanitary products were the same.

He picked up a cardboard container with six bottles of Coke. She was bleeding, so she needed fluids. But he could not postpone the moment of mortification for long.

He went up to the counter.

The pharmacist was a middle-aged white woman. Just my luck, he thought.

He put the Cokes on the counter and said: "I need some aspirin, please."

"What size? We have small, medium, and large bottles."

George was thrown. What if she asked him what size sanitary towels he wanted? "Uh, large, I guess," he said.

The pharmacist put a large bottle of aspirin on the counter. "Anything else?"

A young woman shopper came and stood behind him, holding a wire basket containing cosmetics. She was obviously going to hear everything.

"Anything else?" the pharmacist repeated.

Come on, George, be a man, he thought. "I need a box of sanitary napkins," he said. "Kotex."

The young woman behind him stifled a giggle.

The pharmacist looked at him over her spectacles. "Young man, are you doing this for a bet?"

"No, ma'am!" he said indignantly. "They are for a lady who is too sick to come to the store."

She looked him up and down, taking in the dark gray suit, the white shirt, the plain tie, and the folded white handkerchief in the breast pocket of the jacket. He was glad he did not look like a student involved in a jape. "All right, I believe you," she said. She reached below the counter and picked up a box.

George stared at it in horror. The word *Kotex* was printed on the side in large letters. Was he going to have to carry that out in the street?

The pharmacist read his mind. "I guess you'd like me to wrap this for you."

"Yes, please."

With quick, practiced movements she wrapped the box in brown paper, then she put it in a bag with the aspirin.

George paid.

The pharmacist gave him a hard look, then seemed to relent. "I'm sorry I doubted you," she said. "You must be a good friend to some girl."

"Thank you," he said, and he hurried out.

Despite the October cold, he was perspiring.

He returned to Maria's place. She took three aspirins, then went along the corridor to the bathroom, clutching the wrapped box.

George put the Cokes in the refrigerator, then looked around. He saw a shelf of law books over a small desk with framed photographs. A family group showed her parents, he presumed, and an elderly clergyman who must have been her distinguished grandfather. Another showed Maria in graduation robes. There was also a picture of President

Kennedy. She had a television set, a radio, and a record player. He looked through her discs. She liked the latest pop music, he saw: the Crystals; Little Eva; Booker T and the MGs. On the table beside her bed was the novel *Ship of Fools*.

While she was out, the phone rang.

George picked it up. "This is Maria's phone."

A man's voice said: "May I speak with Maria, please?"

The voice was vaguely familiar, but George could not place it. "She stepped out," he said. "Who is—wait a minute, she just walked in."

Maria snatched the phone from him. "Hello? Oh, hi . . . He's a friend, he brought me some aspirins . . . Oh, not too bad, I'll get by . . ."

George said: "I'll step outside, give you some privacy."

He strongly disapproved of Maria's lover. Even if the jerk was married he should have been here. He had made her pregnant, so he should have taken care of her after the abortion.

That voice . . . George had heard it before. Had he actually met Maria's lover? It would not be surprising, if the man was a work colleague, as George's mother surmised. But the voice on the phone was not Pierre Salinger's.

The girl who had let him in now walked by, on her way out again. She grinned at him standing outside the door like a naughty boy. "Have you been misbehaving in class?" she said.

"No such luck," said George.

She laughed and walked on.

Maria opened the door and he went back inside. "I really have to get back to work," he said.

"I know. You came to visit me in the middle of the Cuba crisis. I'll never forget that." She was visibly happier now that she had talked to her man.

Suddenly George had a flash of realization. "That voice!" he said. "On the phone."

"You recognized it?"

He was astonished. "Are you having an affair with Dave Powers?"

To George's consternation, Maria laughed out loud. "Please!" she said.

He saw right away how unlikely it was. Dave, the president's personal assistant, was a homely-looking man of about fifty who still wore a hat. He was not likely to win the heart of a beautiful and lively young woman.

A moment later, George realized who Maria *was* having an affair with.

"Oh, my God," he said, staring. He was astonished at what he had just figured out.

Maria said nothing.

"You're sleeping with President Kennedy," George said in amazement.

"Please don't tell!" she begged. "If you do, he'll leave me. Promise, please!"

"I promise," said George.

.   .   .

For the first time in his adult life, Dimka had done something truly, indisputably, shamefully wrong.

He was not married to Nina, but she expected him to be faithful, and he assumed she was faithful to him; so there was no question that he had betrayed her trust by spending the night with Natalya.

He had thought it might be the last night of his life but, since it had not been, the excuse seemed feeble.

He had not had sexual intercourse with Natalya, but that, too, was a lousy excuse. What they had done was, if anything, even more intimate and loving than regular sex. He felt wretchedly guilty. Never before had he seen himself as untrustworthy, dishonest, and unreliable.

His friend Valentin would probably handle this situation by cheerfully carrying on affairs with both women until he was found out. Dimka did not even consider that option. He felt bad enough after one night of deception: he could not possibly do it on a regular basis. He would end up throwing himself in the Moskva River.

He had to either tell Nina, or break up with her, or both. He could not live with such a mammoth deception. But he found that he was scared. This was ludicrous. He was Dmitri Ilich Dvorkin, hatchet man to Khrushchev, hated by some, feared by many. How could he be afraid of a girl? But he was.

And what about Natalya?

He had a hundred questions for Natalya. He wanted to know how she felt about her husband. Dimka knew nothing about him except his name, Nik. Was she getting divorced? If so, did the breakdown of the marriage have anything to do with Dimka? Most importantly, did Natalya see Dimka playing any role in her future?

He kept seeing her around the Kremlin, but there was no chance for them to be alone. The Presidium met three times on Tuesday—morning, afternoon, and evening—and the aides were even busier during the meal breaks. Each time Dimka looked at Natalya she seemed more wonderful. He was still wearing the suit he had slept in, as were all the men, but Natalya had changed into a dark blue dress with a matching jacket that made her look both authoritative and alluring at the same time. Dimka had trouble concentrating on the meetings, even though their task was to prevent World War III. He would gaze at her, remember what they had done to one another, and look away in embarrassment; then, a minute later, he would stare at her again.

But the pace of work was so intense that he was not able to talk privately to her even for a few seconds.

Khrushchev went home to his own bed late on Tuesday night, so everyone else did the same. First thing on Wednesday, Dimka gave Khrushchev the glad news—hot from his sister in Cuba—that the *Aleksandrovsk* had docked safely at La Isabela. The rest of the day was equally busy. He saw Natalya constantly, but neither of them had a minute to spare.

By this time Dimka was asking himself questions. What did *he* think Monday night meant? What did he want in the future? If any of them were alive in a week's time, did he want to spend the rest of his life with Natalya, or Nina—or neither?

By Thursday he was desperate for some answers. He felt, irrationally, that he did not want to be killed in a nuclear war before he had resolved this.

He had a date with Nina that evening: they were to go to a movie with Valentin and Anna. If he could get away from the Kremlin, and keep the date, what would he say to Nina?

The morning Presidium normally began at ten, so the aides got together informally at eight in the Onilova Room. On Thursday morning Dimka had a new proposal from Khrushchev to put to the others. He was also hoping for a private talk with Natalya. He was about to approach her when Yevgeny Filipov appeared with the early editions of the European newspapers. "The front pages are all equally bad," he said. He was pretending to be distraught with grief, but Dimka knew he was feeling the opposite. "The turning back of our ships is portrayed as a humiliating climb-down by the Soviet Union!"

He was hardly exaggerating, Dimka saw, looking at the papers spread on the cheap modern tables.

Natalya sprang to Khrushchev's defense. "Of course they say that," she countered. "All those newspapers are owned by capitalists. Did you expect them to praise our leader's wisdom and restraint? How naïve are you?"

"How naïve are *you*? The London *Times*, the Italian *Corriere della Sera*, and *Le Monde* of Paris—these are the papers read and believed by the leaders of the Third World countries whom we hope to win to our side."

That was true. Unfair though it was, people around the world trusted the capitalist press more than Communist publications.

Natalya replied: "We cannot decide our foreign policy based on the probable reactions of Western newspapers."

"This operation was supposed to be top secret," Filipov said. "Yet the Americans found out about it. We all know who was responsible for security." He meant Dimka. "Why is that person sitting at this table? Should he not be under interrogation?"

Dimka said: "Army security may be to blame." Filipov worked for the defense minister. "When we know how the secret got out, then we will be able to decide who should be interrogated." It was feeble, he knew, but he still had no idea what had gone wrong.

Filipov changed his tack. "At this morning's Presidium, the KGB will report that the Americans have massively stepped up their mobilization in Florida. The railroad tracks are jammed with railcars carrying tanks and artillery. The racetrack in Hallandale has been taken over by the 1st Armored Division, thousands of men sleeping in the grandstands. Ammunition factories are working twenty-four hours a day producing bullets for their planes to strafe Soviet and Cuban troops. Napalm bombs—"

Natalya interrupted him. "This, too, was expected."

"But what will we do when they invade Cuba?" Filipov said. "If we respond using only conventional weapons, we cannot win: the Americans are too strong. Will we respond with nuclear weapons? President Kennedy has stated that if one nuclear weapon is launched from Cuba he will bomb the Soviet Union."

"He cannot mean it," said Natalya.

"Read the reports from Red Army Intelligence. The American bombers are circling us now!" He pointed at the ceiling, as if they might look up and see the planes. "There are only two possible outcomes for us: international humiliation, if we're lucky, and nuclear death if we're not."

Natalya fell silent. No one around the table had an answer to that.

Except Dimka.

"Comrade Khrushchev has a solution," he said.

They all looked at him in surprise.

He went on: "At this morning's meeting, the first secretary will propose making an offer to the United States." There was dead silence. "We will dismantle our missiles in Cuba—"

He was interrupted by a chorus of reaction around the table, from gasps of surprise to cries of protest. He held up a hand for quiet.

"We will dismantle our missiles *in exchange* for a guarantee of what we have wanted all along. The Americans must promise not to invade Cuba."

They took a few moments to digest this.

Natalya was the quickest to get it. "This is brilliant," she said. "How can Kennedy refuse? He would be admitting his intention to invade a poor Third World country. He would be universally condemned for colonialism. And he would be proving our point that Cuba needs nuclear missiles to defend itself." She was the smartest person at the table, as well as the prettiest.

Filipov said: "But if Kennedy accepts, we have to bring the missiles home."

"They will no longer be necessary!" Natalya said. "The Cuban revolution will be safe."

Dimka could see that Filipov wanted to argue against this but could not. Khrushchev had got the Soviet Union into a fix, but he had devised an honorable way out.

When the meeting broke up, Dimka at last managed to grab Natalya. "We need a minute to discuss the wording of Khrushchev's offer to Kennedy," he said.

They retreated to a corner of the room and sat down. He gazed at the front of her dress, remembering her little breasts with their pointed nipples.

She said: "You have to stop staring at me."

He felt foolish. "I wasn't staring at you," he said, though it was obviously not true.

She ignored that. "If you keep it up even the men will notice."

"I'm sorry, I can't help it." Dimka was downcast. This was not the intimate, happy conversation he had foreseen.

"No one must know what we did." She looked scared.

Dimka felt as if he were talking to a different person from the cheerfully sexy girl who had seduced him only the day before yesterday. He said: "Well, I'm not planning to go around telling people, but I didn't know it was a state secret."

"I'm married!"

"Are you planning to stay with Nik?"

"What kind of question is that?"

"Do you have any children?"

"No."

"People get divorced."

"My husband would never agree to a divorce."

Dimka stared at her. Obviously that was not the end of the matter: a woman might get a divorce against her husband's will. But this discussion was not really about the legal situation. Natalya was in some kind of panic. Dimka said: "Why did you do it, anyway?"

"I thought we were all going to die!"

"And now you regret it?"

"I'm married!" she said again.

That did not answer his question, but he guessed he was not going to get any more from her.

Boris Kozlov, another of Khrushchev's aides, called across the canteen: "Dimka! Come on!"

Dimka stood up. "Can we talk again soon?" he murmured.

Natalya looked down and said nothing.

Boris said: "Dimka, let's go!"

He left.

The Presidium discussed Khrushchev's proposal for most of the day. There were complications. Would the Americans insist on inspecting the launch sites to verify that they had been deactivated? Would Castro accept inspection? Would Castro promise not to accept nuclear weapons from any other source, for example China? Still Dimka thought it represented the best yet hope of peace.

Meanwhile, Dimka thought about Nina and Natalya. Before this morning's conversation, he had thought it was up to him which of the two women he wanted. He now realized he had deluded himself into thinking the choice was his to make.

Natalya was not going to leave her husband.

He realized he was crazy for Natalya in a way he had never been for Nina. Every time there was a tap on his office door he hoped it was Natalya. In his memory he replayed their time together over and over, obsessively hearing again everything she said, up to the unforgettable words: "Oh, Dimka, I adore you."

It was not *I love you* but it was close.

But she would not get a divorce.

All the same, Natalya was the one he wanted.

That meant he had to tell Nina their affair was over. He could not carry on an affair with a girl he liked second best: it would be dishonest. In his imagination he could hear Valentin mocking his scruples, but he could not help them.

But Natalya intended to stay with her husband. So Dimka would have no one.

He would tell Nina tonight. The four were due to meet at the girls' apartment. He would take Nina aside and tell her . . . what? It seemed more difficult when he tried to think of the actual words. Come on, he told himself; you've written speeches for Khrushchev, you can write one for yourself.

Our affair is over . . . I don't want to see you anymore . . . I thought I was in love with you, but I've realized I'm not . . . It was fun while it lasted . . .

Everything he thought of sounded cruel. Was there no kind way to say this? Perhaps not. What about the naked truth? I've met someone else, and I really love her . . .

That sounded worst of all.

At the end of the afternoon, Khrushchev decided the Presidium should put on a public display of international goodwill by going en masse to the Bolshoi Theater, where the American Jerome Hines was singing *Boris Godunov*, the most popular of Russian operas. Aides were invited too. Dimka thought it was a stupid idea. Who was going to be fooled? On the other hand, he found himself relieved to have to call off his date with Nina, which he was now dreading.

He phoned her place of work and caught her just before she left. "I can't make it tonight," he said. "I've got to go to the Bolshoi with the boss."

"Can't you get out of it?" she said.

"Are you joking?" A man who worked for the first secretary would miss his mother's funeral rather than disobey.

"I want to see you."

"It's out of the question."

"Come after the opera."

"It will be late."

"No matter how late it is, come to my place. I'll be up, if I have to wait all night."

He was puzzled. She was not normally so insistent. She almost sounded needy, and that was not like her. "Is anything wrong?"

"There's something we have to discuss."

"What?"

"I'll tell you tonight."

"Tell me now."

Nina hung up.

Dimka put on his overcoat and walked to the theater, which was only a few steps from the Kremlin.

Jerome Hines was six foot six, and wore a crown with a cross on top: his presence was immense. His astonishingly powerful bass filled the theater and made its echoing spaces seem small. Yet Dimka sat through Mussorgsky's opera without hearing much. He ignored the spectacle onstage. He spent the evening worrying alternately about how the

Americans would respond to Khrushchev's peace proposal and how
Nina would respond to his ending their affair.

When at last Khrushchev said good night, Dimka walked to the
girls' apartment, which was a mile or so from the theater. On the way
he tried to guess what Nina wanted to talk about. Perhaps she was going
to end their relationship: that would be a relief. She might have been
offered a promotion that required her to move to Leningrad. She might
even have met someone else, as he had, and decided the new man was
Mr. Right. Or she could be ill: a fatal disease, perhaps connected with
the mysterious reasons why she could not get pregnant. All these
possibilities offered Dimka an easy way out, and he realized he would
be gladdened by any one, perhaps even—to his shame—the fatal illness.

No, he thought, I don't really wish her dead.

As promised, Nina was waiting for him.

She was wearing a green silk robe, as if about to go to bed, but her
hair was perfect and she wore a little light makeup. She kissed him on
the lips, and he kissed her back with shame in his heart. He was
betraying Natalya by relishing the kiss, and betraying Nina by thinking
of Natalya. The double guilt gave him a pain in his stomach.

Nina poured a glass of beer and he drank half of it quickly, eager for
some Dutch courage.

She sat beside him on the couch. He was pretty sure she had nothing
on under the robe. Desire stirred in him, and the picture of Natalya in
his mind began to fade a little.

"We're not at war yet," he said. "That's my news. What's yours?"

Nina took the beer from him and set it on the coffee table, then she
held his hand. "I'm pregnant," she said.

Dimka felt as if he had been punched. He stared at her in
uncomprehending shock. "Pregnant," he said stupidly.

"Two months and a bit."

"Are you sure?"

"I've missed two consecutive periods."

"Even so . . ."

"Look." She opened her robe to show him her breasts. "They're
bigger."

They were, he saw, feeling a mixture of desire and dismay.

"And they hurt." She closed the robe, but not very tight. "And smoking makes me sick to my stomach. Damn it, I *feel* pregnant."

This could not be true. "But you said . . ."

"That I couldn't have children." She looked away. "That's what my doctor told me."

"Have you seen him?"

"Yes. It's confirmed."

Incredulously, Dimka said: "What does he say now?"

"That it's a miracle."

"Doctors don't believe in miracles."

"That's what I thought."

Dimka tried to stop the room spinning around him. He swallowed hard and struggled to get over the shock. He had to be practical. "You don't want to get married, and I sure as hell don't," he said. "What are you going to do about it?"

"You have to give me the money for an abortion."

Dimka swallowed. "All right." Abortions were readily available in Moscow, but they were not free. Dimka considered how he would get the money. He had been planning to trade in his motorcycle and buy a used car. If he postponed that he could probably manage it. He might borrow from his grandparents. "I can do that," he said.

She immediately relented. "We should pay half each. We made this baby together."

Suddenly Dimka felt different. It was her use of the word *baby*. He found himself conflicted. He pictured himself holding a baby, watching a child take its first steps, teaching it to read, taking it to school. He said: "Are you sure an abortion is what you want?"

"How do *you* feel?"

"Uncomfortable." He asked himself why he felt this way. "I don't think it's a sin, or anything like that. I just started imagining, you know, a little baby." He was not sure where these feelings had come from. "Could we have the child adopted?"

"Give birth, and then hand the baby over to strangers?"

"I know, I don't like it either. But it's hard, to raise a child on your own. I'd help you, though."

"Why?"

"It will be my child, too."

She took his hand. "Thank you for saying that." She looked very vulnerable suddenly, and his heart lurched. She said: "We love each other, don't we?"

"Yes." At that moment he did. He thought of Natalya, but somehow his picture of her was vague and distant, whereas Nina was here—in the flesh, he thought, and that phrase seemed more vivid than usual.

"We'll both love the child, won't we?"

"Yes."

"Well, then . . ."

"But you don't want to get married."

"I didn't."

"Past tense."

"I felt that way when I wasn't pregnant."

"Have you changed your mind?"

"Everything feels different now."

Dimka was bewildered. Were they talking about getting married? Desperate for something to say, he tried a joke. "If you're proposing to me, where's the bread and salt?" The traditional betrothal ceremony required the exchange of gifts of bread and salt.

To his astonishment, she burst into tears.

His heart melted. He put his arms around her. At first she resisted, but after a moment she allowed herself to be hugged. Her tears wet his shirt. He stroked her hair.

She lifted her head to be kissed. After a minute she broke away. "Will you make love to me, before I get too fat and hideous?" Her robe gaped, and he could see one soft breast, charmingly freckled.

"Yes," he said recklessly, pushing the picture of Natalya even farther back in his mind.

Nina kissed him again. He grasped her breast: it felt even heavier than before.

She pulled away again. "You didn't mean what you said at the start, did you?"

"What did I say?"

"That you sure as hell didn't want to get married."

He smiled, still holding her breast. "No," he said. "I didn't mean it."

. . .

On Thursday afternoon George Jakes felt a faint optimism.

The pot was boiling, but the lid was still on. The quarantine was in force, the Soviet missile ships had turned back, and there had been no showdown on the high seas. The United States had not invaded Cuba and no one had fired any nuclear weapons. Perhaps World War III could be averted after all.

The feeling lasted just a little longer.

Bobby Kennedy's aides had a television set in their office at the Justice Department, and at five o'clock they watched a broadcast from United Nations headquarters in New York. The Security Council was in session, twenty chairs around a horseshoe table. Inside the horseshoe sat interpreters wearing headphones. The rest of the room was crowded with aides and other observers, watching the head-to-head confrontation between the two superpowers.

The American ambassador to the UN was Adlai Stevenson, a bald intellectual who had sought the Democratic presidential nomination in 1960 and been defeated by the more telegenic Jack Kennedy.

The Soviet representative, the colorless Valerian Zorin, was speaking in his usual drone, denying that there were any nuclear weapons in Cuba.

Watching on television in Washington, George said in exasperation: "He's a goddamn liar! Stevenson should just produce the photographs."

"That's what the president told him to do."

"Then why doesn't he?"

Wilson shrugged. "Men like Stevenson always think they know best."

On-screen, Stevenson stood up. "Let me ask one simple question," he said. "Do you, Ambassador Zorin, deny that the USSR has placed and is placing medium- and intermediate-range missiles and sites in Cuba? Yes or no?"

George said: "Attaboy, Adlai," and there was a murmur of agreement from the men watching TV with him.

In New York, Stevenson looked at Zorin, who was sitting just a few seats away from him around the horseshoe. Zorin continued to write notes on his pad.

Impatiently, Stevenson said: "Don't wait for the translation—yes or no?"

The aides in Washington laughed.

Eventually Zorin replied in Russian, and the interpreter translated: "Mr. Stevenson, continue your statement, please, you will receive the answer in due course, do not worry."

"I am prepared to wait for my answer until hell freezes over," said Stevenson.

Bobby Kennedy's aides cheered. At last, America was giving them what for!

Then Stevenson said: "And I'm also prepared to present the evidence in this room."

George said: "Yes!" and punched the air.

"If you will indulge me for a moment," Stevenson went on, "we will set up an easel here at the back of the room where I hope it will be visible to everyone."

The camera moved in to focus on half a dozen men in suits who were swiftly mounting a display of large blow-up photographs.

"Now we've got the bastards!" said George.

Stevenson's voice continued, measured and dry, but somehow infused with aggression. "The first of these exhibits shows an area north of the village of Candelaria, near San Cristobal, southwest of Havana. The first photograph shows the area in late August 1962; it was then only peaceful countryside."

Delegates and others were crowding around the easels, trying to see what Stevenson was referring to.

"The second photograph shows the same area one day last week. A few tents and vehicles had come into the area, new spur roads had appeared, and the main road had been improved."

Stevenson paused, and the room was quiet. "The third photograph, taken only twenty-four hours later, shows facilities for a medium-range missile battalion," he said.

Exclamations from the delegates combined into a hum of surprise.

Stevenson went on. More photographs were put up. Until this moment some national leaders had believed the Soviet ambassador's denial. Now everyone knew the truth.

Zorin sat stone-faced, saying nothing.

George glanced up from the TV to see Larry Mawhinney enter the room. George looked askance at him: the one time they had talked, Larry had got angry with him. But now he seemed friendly. "Hi, George," he said, as if they had never exchanged harsh words.

George said neutrally: "What's the news from the Pentagon?"

"I came to warn you that we're going to board a Soviet ship," Larry said. "The president made the decision a few minutes ago."

George's heartbeat quickened. "Shit," he said. "Just when I thought things might be calming down."

Mawhinney went on: "Apparently he thinks the quarantine means nothing if we don't intercept and inspect at least one suspicious vessel. He's already getting flak because we let an oil tanker through."

"What kind of ship are we going to arrest?"

"The *Marucla*, a Lebanese freighter with a Greek crew, under charter to the Soviet government. She left from Riga, ostensibly carrying paper, sulfur, and spare parts for Soviet trucks."

"I can't imagine the Soviets entrusting their missiles to a Greek crew."

"If you're right, there'll be no trouble."

George looked at his watch. "When will it happen?"

"It's dark in the Atlantic now. They'll have to wait until morning."

Larry left, and George wondered how dangerous this was. It was hard to know. If the *Marucla* were as innocent as she pretended to be, perhaps the interception would go off without violence. But if she were carrying nuclear weapons, what would happen? President Kennedy had made another knife-edge decision.

And he had seduced Maria Summers.

George was not very surprised that Kennedy was having an affair with a black girl. If half the gossip were true, the president was not in any way picky about his women. Quite the contrary: he liked mature women and teenagers, blondes and brunettes, socialites who were his equal and empty-headed typists.

George wondered for a moment whether Maria had any idea that she was one among so many.

President Kennedy had no strong feelings about race, always

considering it as a purely political issue. Although he had not wanted to be photographed with Percy Marquand and Babe Lee, fearing it would lose him votes, George had seen him cheerfully shaking hands with black men and women, chatting and laughing, relaxed and comfortable. George had also been told that Kennedy attended parties where there were prostitutes of all colors, though he did not know whether those rumors were true.

But the president's callousness had shocked George. It was not the procedure she had undergone—though that was unpleasant enough—but the fact that she had been alone. The man who made her pregnant should have picked her up after the operation and driven her home and stayed with her until he was sure she was okay. A phone call was not enough. His being president was not a sufficient excuse. Jack Kennedy had fallen a long way in George's estimation.

Just as he was thinking about men who irresponsibly get girls pregnant, his own father walked in.

George was startled. Greg had never before visited this office.

"Hello, George," he said, and they shook hands just as if they were not father and son. Greg was wearing a rumpled suit made of a soft blue pinstripe fabric that looked as if it had some cashmere in the mix. If I could afford a suit like that, George thought, I'd keep it pressed. He often thought that when he looked at Greg.

George said: "This is unexpected. How are you?"

"I was just passing your door. Do you want to get a cup of coffee?"

They went to the cafeteria. Greg ordered tea and George got a bottle of Coke and a straw. As they sat down, George said: "Someone was asking after you the other day. A lady in the press office."

"What's her name?"

"Nell something. I'm trying to remember. Nelly Ford?"

"Nelly Fordham." Greg looked into the distance, his expression showing nostalgia for half-forgotten delights.

George was amused. "A girlfriend, evidently."

"More than that. We were engaged."

"But you didn't get married."

"She broke it off."

George hesitated. "This may be none of my business . . . but why?"

"Well . . . if you want to know the truth, she found out about you, and she said she didn't want to marry a man who already had a family."

George was fascinated. His father rarely opened up about those days.

Greg looked thoughtful. "Nelly was probably right," he said. "You and your mother were my family. But I couldn't marry your mom—couldn't have a career in politics and a black wife. So I chose the career. I can't say it's made me happy."

"You've never talked to me about this."

"I know. It's taken the threat of World War Three to make me tell you the truth. How do you think things are going, anyway?"

"Wait a minute. Was it ever really in the cards that you might marry Mom?"

"When I was fifteen I wanted to, more than anything else in the world. But my father made damn sure it didn't happen. I had another chance, a decade later, but at that point I was old enough to see what a crazy idea it was. Listen, mixed-race couples have a hard enough time of it now, in the sixties. Imagine what it would have been like in the forties. All three of us would probably have been miserable." He looked sad. "Besides, I didn't have the guts—and *that's* the truth. Now tell me about the crisis."

With an effort, George turned his mind to the Cuban missiles. "An hour ago I was beginning to believe we might get through this—but now the president has ordered the navy to intercept a Soviet ship tomorrow morning." He told Greg about the *Marucla*.

Greg said: "If she's genuine, there should be no problem."

"Correct. Our people will go aboard and look at the cargo, then give out some candy bars and leave."

"Candy?"

"Each interception vessel has been allocated two hundred dollars for 'people-to-people materials'—that means candy, magazines, and cheap cigarette lighters."

"God bless America. But . . ."

"But if the crew is Soviet military and the cargo is nuclear warheads, the ship probably won't stop when requested. Then the shooting starts."

"I better let you get back to saving the world."

They got up and left the cafeteria. In the hall they shook hands again. Greg said: "The reason I came by . . ."

George waited.

"We may all die this weekend, and before we do there's something I want you to know."

"Okay." George wondered what the hell was coming.

"You are the best thing that ever happened to me."

"Wow," George said quietly.

"I haven't been much of a father, and I wasn't kind to your mother, and . . . you know all that. But I'm proud of you, George. I don't deserve any credit, I know, but, my God, I'm proud." He had tears in his eyes.

George had had no idea Greg felt so strongly. He was stunned. He did not know what to say in response to such unexpected emotions. In the end he just said: "Thank you."

"Good-bye, George."

"Good-bye."

"God bless and keep you," said Greg, and he walked away.

.   .   .

Early Friday morning George went to the White House Situation Room.

President Kennedy had created this suite in the West Wing basement where previously there had been a bowling alley. Its ostensible purpose was to speed communications in a crisis. The truth was that Kennedy believed the military had kept information from him during the Bay of Pigs crisis, and he wanted to make sure they never got another chance to do that.

This morning the walls were covered with large-scale maps of Cuba and its sea approaches. The teletype machines chattered like cicadas on a warm night. Pentagon telegrams were copied here. The president could listen in to military communications. The quarantine operation was being run from a room in the Pentagon known as Navy Flag Plot, but radio conversations between that room and the ships could be overheard here.

The military hated the Situation Room.

George sat on an uncomfortable modern chair at a cheap dining table and listened. He was still mulling over last night's conversation with Greg. Had Greg expected George to throw his arms around him and cry: "Daddy!" Probably not. Greg seemed comfortable with his avuncular role. George had no wish to change that. At the age of twenty-six he could not suddenly start treating Greg like a regular father. All the same, George *was* kind of happy about what Greg had said. My father loves me, he thought; that can't be bad.

The USS *Joseph P. Kennedy* hailed the *Marucla* at dawn.

The *Kennedy* was a twenty-four-hundred-ton destroyer armed with eight missiles, an antisubmarine rocket launcher, six torpedo tubes, and twin five-inch gun mounts. It also had nuclear depth charge capability.

The *Marucla* immediately cut its engines, and George breathed easier.

The *Kennedy* lowered a boat and six men crossed to the *Marucla*. The sea was rough, but the crew of the *Marucla* obligingly threw a rope ladder over the side. All the same, the chop made it difficult to board. The officer in charge did not want to look ridiculous by falling in the water, but eventually he took a chance, leaped for the ladder, and boarded the ship. His men followed.

The Greek crew offered them coffee.

They were delighted to open the hatches for the Americans to inspect their cargo, which was pretty much what they had said. There was a tense moment when the Americans insisted on opening a crate labeled SCIENTIFIC INSTRUMENTS, but it turned out to contain laboratory equipment no more sophisticated than what might be found in a high school.

The Americans left and the *Marucla* resumed course for Havana.

George reported the good news to Bobby Kennedy by phone, then hopped a cab.

He told the driver to take him to the corner of Fifth and K Streets, in one of the city's worst slum neighborhoods. Here, above a car showroom, was the CIA's National Photographic Interpretation Center. George wanted to understand this art and had asked for a special briefing, and since he worked for Bobby, he got it. He picked his way across a sidewalk littered with beer bottles, entered the building, and passed through a security turnstile; then he was escorted to the fourth floor.

He was shown around by a gray-haired photointerpreter called Claud Henry, who had learned his trade in the Second World War, analyzing aerial photographs of bomb damage from Germany.

Claud told George: "Yesterday the navy sent Crusader jets over Cuba, so we now have low-level photographs, much easier to read."

George did not find it so easy. To him the photos pinned up around Claud's room still looked like abstract art, meaningless shapes arranged in a random pattern. "This is a Soviet military base," Claud said, pointing at a photo.

"How do you know?"

"Here's a soccer pitch. Cuban soldiers don't play soccer. If it was a Cuban camp it would have a baseball diamond."

George nodded. Clever, he thought.

"Here's a row of T-54 tanks."

They just looked like dark squares to George.

"These tents are missile shelters," Claud said. "According to our tentologists."

"Tentologists?"

"Yes. I'm actually a cratologist. I wrote the CIA handbook on crates."

George smiled. "You're not kidding, are you?"

"When the Soviets are shipping very large items such as fighter aircraft, they have to be carried on deck. They disguise them by putting them in crates. But we can usually work out the dimensions of the crate. And a MiG-15 comes in a different-size crate than a MiG-21."

"Tell me something," said George. "Do the Soviets have this kind of expertise?"

"We don't think so. Consider this. They shot down a U-2 plane, so they know we have high-altitude planes with cameras. Yet they thought they could send missiles to Cuba without us finding out. They were still denying the existence of the missiles until yesterday, when we showed them the photos. So, they know about the spy planes and they know about the cameras, but until now they didn't know we could see their missiles from the stratosphere. That leads me to think they're behind us in photointerpretation."

"That sounds right."

"But here's last night's big revelation." Claud pointed to an object with fins in one of the photos. "My boss will be briefing the president about this within the hour. It's thirty-five feet long. We call it a Frog, for Free Rocket over Ground. It's a short-range missile, intended for battlefield situations."

"So this will be used against American troops if we invade Cuba."

"Yes. And it's designed to carry a nuclear warhead."

"Oh, shit," said George.

"That's probably what President Kennedy is going to say," said Claud.

The radio was on in the kitchen of the house in Great Peter Street on Friday evening. All over the world, people were keeping their radios on, listening fearfully for news flashes.

It was a big kitchen, with a long scrubbed-pine table in the center. Jasper Murray was making toast and reading the newspapers. Lloyd and Daisy Williams got all the London papers and several Continental ones as well. Lloyd's main interest as a member of Parliament was foreign affairs, and had been ever since he fought in the Spanish Civil War. Jasper was scanning the pages for some reason to hope.

Tomorrow, Saturday, there would be a protest march in London, if London was still standing in the morning. Jasper would be there as a reporter for *St. Julian's News*, the student paper. Jasper did not really like doing news reports: he preferred features, longer, more reflective pieces, in which the writing could be a little more fancy. He hoped one day to work in magazines, or maybe even television.

But first he wanted to be editor of *St. Julian's News.* The post came with a small salary and a sabbatical year off studies. It was much coveted, as it practically guaranteed the student a good job in journalism after graduation. Jasper had applied but had been defeated by Sam Cakebread. The Cakebread name was famous in British journalism: Sam's father was assistant editor of *The Times* and his uncle was a much-loved radio commentator. He had a younger sister at St. Julian's College who had interned with *Vogue* magazine. Jasper suspected that it was Sam's name, not his ability, that had won him the job.

But ability was never enough in Britain. Jasper's grandfather had been a general, and his father had been on course for a similar career, until he made the mistake of marrying a Jewish girl, and in consequence had never been promoted above the rank of colonel. The British establishment never forgave people who broke their rules. Jasper had heard it was different in the United States.

Evie Williams was in the kitchen with Jasper, sitting at the table, making a placard that read HANDS OFF CUBA.

Evie no longer had a schoolgirl crush on Jasper. He was relieved. She was sixteen now, and beautiful in a pale, ethereal way; but she was too solemn and intense for his taste. Anyone who dated her would have to share her passionate commitment to a wide range of campaigns against cruelty and injustice, from apartheid in South Africa to experiments on animals. Jasper had no commitment to anything, and anyway he preferred girls like the impish Beep Dewar, who even at the age of thirteen had put her tongue in his mouth and rubbed herself against his erection.

As Jasper watched, Evie inscribed, inside the *O* of OFF, the four-branched symbol of the Campaign for Nuclear Disarmament. Jasper said: "So your slogan supports two idealistic causes for the price of one!"

"There's nothing idealistic about it," she said sharply. "If war breaks out tonight, do you know what the first target of Soviet nuclear bombs will be? Britain. That's because we have nuclear weapons, which they need to eliminate before they attack the United States. They won't be bombing Norway, or Portugal, or any country that has the sense to stay out of the nuclear competition. Anyone who thinks logically about the defense of our country knows that nuclear weapons don't protect us—they put us in danger."

Jasper had not intended his remark to be taken seriously, but Evie took everything seriously.

Evie's fourteen-year-old brother, Dave, was also at the table, making miniature Cuban flags. He had used a stencil to paint the stripes onto sheets of heavy paper, and now he was attaching the sheets to small sticks of plywood with a borrowed staple gun. Jasper resented Dave's privileged life, with wealthy, easygoing parents, but he worked hard to be friendly. "How many are you making?" he asked.

Dave said: "Three hundred and sixty."

"Not a random number, presumably."

"If we don't all get killed by bombs tonight, I'm going to sell them at the demonstration tomorrow for sixpence each. Three hundred and sixty sixpences are one hundred and eighty shillings, or nine pounds, which is the price of the guitar amplifier I want to buy."

Dave had a nose for business. Jasper remembered his soft drinks stall at the school play, staffed by teenage boys who worked at top speed because Dave was paying them a commission. But Dave did badly at his lessons, coming at or near the bottom of the class in all academic subjects. It drove his father wild, for in other respects Dave seemed bright. Lloyd accused Dave of laziness, but Jasper thought it was more complicated. Dave had trouble making sense of anything written down. His own writing was dire, full of spelling mistakes and even reversed letters. It reminded Jasper of his best friend at school, who had been incapable of singing the school song, and found it hard to hear the difference between his one-note drone and the melody the other boys were singing. Likewise, Dave had to make an effort of concentration to see the difference between the letters *d* and *b*. He longed to fulfill the expectations of his high-achieving parents, but always fell short.

As he stapled his sixpenny flags together, his mind evidently wandered, for apropos of nothing he said: "Your mother and mine can't have had much in common when they first met."

"No," said Jasper. "Daisy Peshkov was the child of a Russian-American gangster. Eva Rothmann was a doctor's daughter from a middle-class Jewish family in Berlin, sent to America to escape the Nazis. Your mother took my mother in."

Evie, who had been named after Eva, said: "My mother just has a big heart."

Jasper said half to himself: "I wish someone would send me to America."

"Why don't you just go?" said Evie. "You could tell them to leave the Cuban people alone."

Jasper did not care a damn about the Cubans. "I can't afford it." Even living rent-free he was too broke to buy a ticket to the United States.

At that moment the woman with the big heart walked into the room. Daisy Williams at forty-six was still attractive, with big blue eyes and fair curls: when she was young she must have been irresistible, Jasper thought. Tonight she was dressed modestly, in a midblue skirt with matching jacket and no jewelry; hiding her wealth, Jasper thought sardonically, the better to play the part of a politician's wife. Her figure was still trim, though not as slim as it used to be. Picturing her naked, he thought she would be better in bed than her daughter, Evie. Daisy would be like Beep, ready for anything. He was surprised to catch himself in such a fantasy about someone his mother's age. It was a good thing women could not read men's minds.

"What a nice picture," she said fondly. "Three kids working quietly." She still had a distinctive American accent, though its edges had been worn smooth by her living in London for a quarter of a century. She looked with surprise at Dave's flags. "You don't often take an interest in world affairs."

"I'm going to sell them for sixpence each."

"I might have guessed your efforts had nothing to do with world peace."

"I leave world peace to Evie."

Evie said with spirit: "Someone has to worry about it. We could all be dead before this march begins, you know—just because Americans are such hypocrites."

Jasper looked at Daisy, but she was not offended. She was used to her daughter's abrasive ethical pronouncements. Mildly, she said: "I guess Americans have been badly scared by the missiles in Cuba."

"Then they should imagine how other people feel, and take their missiles out of Turkey."

"I think you're right, and it was a mistake for President Kennedy to put them there. All the same, there's a difference. Here in Europe we're used to having missiles pointed at us—on both sides of the Iron Curtain. But when Khrushchev secretly sent missiles to Cuba he made a shocking change in the status quo."

"Justice is justice."

"And practical politics is something else. But look how history repeats itself. My son is like my father, always alert for an opportunity to make a few bucks, even on the brink of World War Three. My daughter is like my Bolshevik uncle Grigori, determined to change the world."

Evie looked up. "If he was a Bolshevik, he did change the world."

"But was it for the better?"

Lloyd came in. Like his coal-mining ancestors, he was short in stature with broad shoulders. Something about the way he walked reminded Jasper that he had once been a champion boxer. He was dressed with old-fashioned flair, in a black suit with a faint herringbone stripe, a crisp white linen handkerchief in his breast pocket. The two parents were obviously going to a political event. "I'm ready if you are, my darling," he said to Daisy.

Evie said: "What's your meeting about?"

"Cuba," said her father. "What else?" He noticed her placard. "I see you've already made up your mind about the issue."

"It's not complicated, is it?" she said. "The Cuban people should be allowed to choose their own destiny—isn't that a basic democratic principle?"

Jasper saw a row looming. In this family, half the rows were about politics. Bored by Evie's idealism, he interrupted. "Hank Remington is going to sing 'Poison Rain' in Trafalgar Square tomorrow." Remington, an Irish boy whose real name was Harry Riley, was leader of a pop group called the Kords. The song was about nuclear fallout.

"He's wonderful," said Evie. "So clear thinking." Hank was one of her heroes.

"He came to see me," said Lloyd.

Evie immediately changed her tone. "You didn't tell me!"

"It happened only today."

"What did you think of him?"

"He's a genuine working-class genius."

"What did he want?"

"He wanted me to stand up in the House of Commons and denounce President Kennedy as a warmonger."

"So you should!"

"And what happens if Labour wins the next general election? Suppose I become foreign secretary. I might have to go to the White House and ask the president's support for something the Labour government wants to do, perhaps a resolution in the United Nations against racial discrimination in South Africa. Kennedy might remember how I insulted him, and tell me to drop dead."

Evie said: "You should do it anyway."

"Calling someone a warmonger usually doesn't help. If I thought it would resolve the current crisis, I would do it. But it's a card you can play only once, and I prefer to save it for a winning hand."

Jasper reflected that Lloyd was a pragmatic politician. He approved.

Evie did not. "I believe that people should stand up and tell the truth," she said.

Lloyd smiled. "I'm proud to have such a daughter," he said. "I hope you will hold on to that belief all your life. But now I must go and explain the crisis to my supporters in the East End."

Daisy said: "Bye, kids. See you later."

They went out.

Evie said: "Who won that argument?"

Your father did, Jasper thought, hands down; but he did not say so.

. . .

George returned to downtown Washington in a state of high anxiety. Everyone had been working on the assumption that an invasion of Cuba was bound to succeed. The Frogs changed everything. U.S. troops would now face battlefield nuclear weapons. Perhaps the Americans would still prevail, but the war would be harder and would cost more lives, and the result was no longer a foregone conclusion.

He got out of his taxi at the White House and stopped by the press office. Maria was at her desk. He was happy to see that she looked much better than she had three days earlier. "I'm fine, thank you," she said in answer to George's query. A small weight of worry lifted from his heart, leaving the larger still heavy on him. She was recovering physically, but he did not know what spiritual damage was being caused by her secret love affair.

He was not able to ask her more intimate questions because she had company. With her was a young black man in a tweed jacket. "Meet Leopold Montgomery," she said. "He's with Reuters. He came by to pick up a press release."

"Call me Lee," the man said.

George said: "I guess there aren't many colored reporters covering Washington."

"I'm the only one," Lee said.

Maria said: "George Jakes works with Bobby Kennedy."

Lee suddenly became more interested. "What's he like?"

"It's a great job," George said, avoiding the question. "Mainly I advise on civil rights. We take legal action against Southern states that prevent Negroes from voting."

"But we need a new civil rights act."

"Say that, brother." George turned to Maria. "I can't stay. I'm glad you're feeling better."

Lee said: "I'll walk with you, if you're going over to Justice."

George avoided the company of newsmen, but he felt a camaraderie with Lee, who was trying to make it in white Washington just as George was, so he said: "Okay."

Maria said: "Thanks for dropping by, Lee. Please call me if you need any clarification on that release."

"Sure will," he said.

George and Lee left the building and went along Pennsylvania Avenue. George said: "What's in your press release?"

"Although the ships have turned around, the Soviets are still constructing missile launch sites in Cuba, and they're doing it at top speed."

George thought of the aerial reconnaissance photographs he had just seen. He was tempted to tell Lee about them. He would have liked to give a scoop to a young black reporter. However, it would have been a breach of security, and he resisted the impulse. "I guess that's so," he said noncommittally.

Lee said: "The administration seems to be doing nothing."

"What do you mean?"

"The quarantine is clearly ineffective, and the president isn't doing anything else."

George was stung. He was part of the administration, albeit a small part, and he felt unjustly accused. "In his television speech on Monday the president said the quarantine was just the beginning."

"So he will be taking further action?"

"That's obviously what he meant."

"But what will he do?"

George smiled, realizing he was being pumped. "Watch this space," he said.

When he got back to Justice, Bobby was in a rage. It was not Bobby's way to yell and curse and throw objects across the room. His fury was cold and mean. People talked about his terrifying blue-eyed stare.

"Who's he mad at?" George asked Dennis Wilson.

"Tim Tedder. He's sent three infiltration teams into Cuba, six men to a team. More are waiting to go."

"What? Why? Who told the CIA to do that?"

"It's part of Operation Mongoose, and apparently no one told them to *stop*."

"But they might start World War Three all on their own!"

"That's why Bobby's spitting nails. Also, they sent in a two-man team to blow up a copper mine—and, unfortunately, they've lost contact."

"So those two guys are probably in jail now, drawing floor plans of the CIA station in Miami for their Soviet interrogators."

"Yeah."

"This is a stupid time to do that stuff for so many reasons," George said. "Cuba's preparing for war. Castro's security is always good, but right now it must be on high alert."

"Exactly. Bobby's going to a Mongoose meeting at the Pentagon in a few minutes, and I expect he will nail Tedder to a cross."

George did not go with Bobby to the Pentagon. He still was not invited to Mongoose meetings—somewhat to his relief: his trip to La Isabela had convinced him that the whole operation was criminal, and he wanted nothing more to do with it.

He sat at his desk, but found it difficult to concentrate. Civil rights had taken a backseat anyway: no one was thinking about equality for Negroes this week.

George felt the crisis was slipping out of President Kennedy's control. Against his better judgment the president had ordered the *Marucla* to be boarded. The event had gone off without trouble, but what would happen next time? Now there were battlefield nuclear weapons in Cuba: America might still invade, but the price would be high. And just to add an extra element of risk, the CIA was playing its own games.

Everyone was desperate to cool the temperature, but the opposite kept happening, a nightmarish escalation of the crisis that no one wanted.

Later in the afternoon, Bobby came back from the Pentagon with a wire service report in his hand. "What the hell is this?" he said to the aides. He began to read: "In response to the speeded-up campaign to build missile launch sites in Cuba, fresh action by President Kennedy is expected imminently"—he held his hand in the air, finger pointing up—"according to sources close to the attorney general." Bobby looked around the room. "Who blabbed?"

George said: "Oh, fuck."

Everyone looked at him.

Bobby said: "Do you have something to tell me, George?"

George wanted to sink through the floor. "I'm sorry," he said. "All I did was quote the president's speech, saying the quarantine was only the beginning."

"You can't say that sort of thing to reporters! You've given him a new story."

"Oh, boy, I know that now."

"And you've escalated the crisis just when we were all trying to calm things down. The next story will speculate what action the president has in mind. Then if he does nothing they'll say he's dithering."

"Yes, sir."

"Why were you talking to him at all?"

"He was introduced to me at the White House and he walked along Pennsylvania Avenue with me."

Dennis Wilson said to Bobby: "Is that a Reuters report?"

"Yes, why?"

"It was probably written by Lee Montgomery."

George groaned inwardly. He knew what was coming next. Wilson was deliberately making the incident look worse.

Bobby said: "What makes you say that, Dennis?"

Wilson hesitated, so George answered the question. "Montgomery is a Negro."

Bobby said: "Is that why you talked to him, George?"

"I guess I didn't want to tell him to drop dead."

"Next time, that's exactly what you say to him, and to any other reporter who tries to get a story out of you, no matter what his color."

George was relieved to hear the words *next time.* It meant that he was not going to be fired. "Thank you," he said. "I'll remember that."

"You'd better." Bobby went into his office.

"You got away with it," Wilson said to George. "Lucky bastard."

"Yeah," said George. He added sarcastically: "Thanks for your help, Dennis."

Everyone returned to their work. George could hardly believe what he had done. He, too, had inadvertently poured fuel on the flames.

He was still feeling depressed when the switchboard put through a long-distance call from Atlanta. "Hi, George, this is Verena Marquand."

Her voice cheered him up. "How are you?"

"Worried."

"You and the whole world."

"Dr. King asked me to call you and find out what's happening."

"You probably know as much as we do," George said. He was still smarting from Bobby's reprimand, and he was not about to risk another indiscretion. "Pretty much everything is in the newspapers."

"Are we really going to invade Cuba?"

"Only the president knows that."

"Will there be a nuclear war?"

"Even the president doesn't know that."

"I miss you, George. I wish I could sit down with you and just, you know, talk."

That surprised him. He had not known her well at Harvard, and he had not seen her for a half a year. He was not aware that she was fond enough of him to miss him. He did not know what to say.

She said: "What am I going to tell Dr. King?"

"Tell him . . ." George paused. He thought of all the people around President Kennedy: the hotheaded generals who wanted war now, the CIA men trying to be James Bond, the reporters who complained of inaction when the president was being cautious. "Tell him the smartest man in the United States is in charge, and we can't ask for better than that."

"Okay," said Verena, and she hung up.

George asked himself if he believed what he had said. He wanted to hate Jack Kennedy for the way he had treated Maria. But could anyone else handle this crisis better than Kennedy? No. George could not think of another man with the right combination of courage, wisdom, restraint, and calm.

Late in the afternoon, Wilson took a phone call, then said to everyone in the room: "We're getting a letter from Khrushchev. It's coming through to the State Department."

Someone asked: "What does it say?"

"Not much, so far," Wilson said. He looked at his notebook. "We don't have it all yet. 'You are threatening us with war, but you well know that the least you would receive in reply would be to experience the same consequences . . .' It was delivered to our embassy in Moscow just before ten this morning, our time."

George said: "Ten o'clock! It's six in the evening now. What's taking so long?"

Wilson answered with weary condescension, as if tired of explaining elementary procedures to beginners. "Our people in Moscow have to translate the letter into English, then encrypt it, then key it. After it's received here in Washington, State Department officials must decrypt it and then type it. And every word must be triple-checked before the president acts. It's a long process."

"Thank you," said George. Wilson was a smug prick. However, he knew a lot.

It was Friday night, but no one was going home.

Khrushchev's message arrived in bits. Predictably, the important part was at the end. If the United States would promise not to invade Cuba, Khrushchev said, "the necessity for the presence of our military specialists would disappear."

It was a compromise proposal, and that had to be good news. But what, exactly, did it mean?

Presumably the Soviets would withdraw their nuclear weapons from Cuba. Nothing less would count for anything.

But could the United States promise never to invade Cuba? Would President Kennedy even consider tying his own hands like that? George thought he would be loath to give up all hope of getting rid of Castro.

And how would the world react to such a deal? Would they see it as a foreign policy coup for Khrushchev? Or would they say Kennedy had forced the Soviets to back down?

Was this good news? George could not decide.

Larry Mawhinney put his buzz-cut head around the door. "Cuba has short-range nuclear weapons now," he said.

"We know," said George. "The CIA found them yesterday."

"That means we have to have the same," said Larry.

"What do you mean?"

"The Cuba invasion force must be equipped with battlefield nukes."

"Must it?"

"Of course! The Joint Chiefs are about to demand them. Would you send our men into battle less well armed than the enemy?"

He had a point, George saw; but there was a terrible consequence. "So now any war with Cuba must be a nuclear war, from the start."

"Damn right," said Larry, and he left.

.   .   .

Last thing, George dropped by his mother's house. Jacky made coffee and put a plate of cookies in front of him. He did not take one. "I saw Greg yesterday," he said.

"How is he?"

"Same as ever. Except . . . Except that he told me I was the best thing that ever happened to him."

"Hm!" she said in a disparaging tone. "What brought that on?"

"He wanted me to know how proud he is of me."

"Well, well. There is still some good in that man."

"How long is it since you last saw Lev and Marga?"

Jacky narrowed her eyes in suspicion. "What kind of question is that?"

"You get along well with Grandmother Marga."

"That's because she loves you. When a person loves your child, it's endearing. You'll find that out when you have kids."

"You haven't seen her since Harvard commencement, more than a year ago."

"That's true."

"You don't work on the weekend."

"The club is closed Saturdays and Sundays. When you were small I had to have weekends off, to take care of you when you weren't in school."

"The First Lady has taken Caroline and John Junior to Glen Ora."

"Oh, and I suppose you think I ought to go to my country house in Virginia and spend a couple of days riding my horses?"

"You could go and see Marga and Lev in Buffalo."

"Go to Buffalo for the weekend?" she said incredulously. "For pity's sake, child! I'd spend all Saturday on the train there and all Sunday on the train back."

"You could fly."

"I can't afford to."

"I'll buy you a ticket."

"Oh, my good Lord," she said. "You think the Russians are going to bomb us this weekend, don't you?"

"It's never been closer than this. Go to Buffalo."

She drained her cup, then got up and went to the sink to wash it. After a moment she said: "And what about you?"

"I have to stay here and do what I can to prevent it happening."

Jacky shook her head decisively. "I'm not going to Buffalo."

"It would ease my heart mightily, Mom."

"If you want to ease your heart, pray to the Lord."

"You know what the Arabs say? 'Trust in Allah, but tether your camel.' I'll pray if you'll go to Buffalo."

"How do you know the Russians won't bomb Buffalo?"

"I don't know for sure. But I'd guess it's a secondary target. And it may be out of range of those missiles in Cuba."

"You make a weak case, for a lawyer."

"I'm serious, Mom."

"So am I," she said. "And you're a good son, to worry about your mother. But listen to me, now. From the age of sixteen I've given my life to nothing but raising you. If everything I've done is going to be wiped out in a nuclear flash, I don't want to be alive afterward to know about it. I'm staying where you are."

"Either we'll both survive, or we'll both die."

"'The Lord giveth, and the Lord taketh away,'" she quoted. "'Blessed be the name of the Lord.'"

. . .

The United States had more than two hundred nuclear missiles that could reach the Soviet Union, according to Dimka's uncle Volodya in Red Army Intelligence. The Americans believed the Soviet Union had about half that many intercontinental missiles, Volodya said. In truth, the USSR had precisely forty-two.

And some of them were obsolete.

When the United States did not immediately reply to the Soviet Union's compromise offer, Khrushchev ordered even the oldest and most unreliable missiles to be made launch-ready.

In the early hours of Saturday morning, Dimka telephoned the missile testing range at Baikonur in Kazakhstan. The army base there had two five-engined Semyorkas, obsolete R-7 rockets of the type that had taken the *Sputnik* into orbit five years ago. They were being readied for a Mars probe.

Dimka called off the Mars expedition. The Semyorkas were included in the Soviet Union's forty-two intercontinental missiles. They were needed for World War III.

He ordered the scientists to fit both rockets with nuclear warheads and fuel them.

Preparation for launch would take twenty hours. The Semyorkas used an unstable liquid propellant, and they could not be kept on alert for more than a day. They would be used this weekend or not at all.

Semyorka rockets often exploded on takeoff. However, if they did not, they could reach Chicago.

Each was to be fitted with a 2.8-megaton bomb.

If one managed to hit its target, it would destroy everything within seven miles of the center of Chicago, from the lake shore to Oak Park, according to Dimka's atlas.

When he was sure the commanding officer had understood the orders, Dimka went to bed.

The phone woke Dimka. His heart pounded: was it war? How many minutes did he have to live? He snatched up the receiver. It was Natalya. First with the news, as usual, she said: "There's a flash from Pliyev."

General Pliyev was in command of Soviet forces in Cuba.

"What?" said Dimka. "What does it say?"

"They think the Americans are going to attack today, at dawn their time."

It was still dark in Moscow. Dimka turned on the bedside light and looked at his watch. It was eight in the morning: he should be at the Kremlin. But dawn in Cuba was still five and a half hours away. His heart slowed a little. "How do they know?"

"That's not the point," she said impatiently.

"What is the point?"

"I'll read you the last sentence. 'We have decided that in the event of a U.S. attack on our installations, we will employ all available means of air defense.' They will use nuclear weapons."

"They can't do that without our permission!"

"But that's exactly what they're proposing."

"Malinovsky won't let them."

"Don't bet on that."

Dimka cursed under his breath. Sometimes the military seemed actually to want nuclear annihilation. "I'll meet you in the canteen."

"Give me half an hour."

Dimka showered fast. His mother offered him breakfast, but he refused, so she gave him a piece of black rye bread to take with him. "Don't forget there's a party for your grandfather today," Anya said.

It was Grigori's birthday: he was seventy-four. There would be a big lunch at his apartment. Dimka had promised to bring Nina. They were planning to surprise everyone by announcing their engagement.

But there would be no party if the Americans attacked Cuba.

As Dimka was leaving, Anya stopped him. "Tell me the truth," she said. "What's going to happen?"

He put his arms around her. "I'm sorry, Mother, I don't know."

"Your sister's over there in Cuba."

"I know."

"She's right in the line of fire."

"The Americans have intercontinental missiles, Mother. We're all in the line of fire."

She hugged him, then turned away.

Dimka drove to the Kremlin on his motorcycle. When he got to the Presidium building, Natalya was waiting in the canteen. Like Dimka, she had dressed in a hurry, and she looked a little disheveled. Her untidy hair fell over her face in a way he found charming. I must stop thinking like this, he told himself: I'm going to do the right thing, and marry Nina and raise our child.

He wondered what Natalya would say when he told her that.

But this was not the moment. He took his piece of rye bread from his pocket. "I wish I could get some tea," he said. The canteen doors were open but no one was serving yet.

"I've heard that restaurants in the United States open when people want food and drinks, not when the staff wants to work," said Natalya. "Do you think it's true?"

"Probably just propaganda," said Dimka. He sat down.

"Let's draft a reply to Pliyev," she said, and opened a notebook.

Chewing, Dimka concentrated on the issue. "The Presidium should forbid Pliyev to launch nuclear weapons without specific orders from Moscow."

"I'd rather forbid him even to mount the warheads on the rockets. Then they can't be fired by accident."

"Good thinking."

Yevgeny Filipov came into the room. He was wearing a brown pullover under a gray suit jacket. Dimka said: "Good morning, Filipov, have you come to apologize to me?"

"For what?"

"You accused me of allowing the secret of our Cuban missiles to leak out. You even said I should be arrested. Now we know the missiles were photographed by a spy plane of the CIA. Obviously you owe me a groveling apology."

"Don't be ridiculous," Filipov blustered. "We didn't think their high-altitude photographs would show something as small as a missile. What are you two plotting?"

Natalya answered with the truth. "We're discussing this morning's flash message from Pliyev."

"I've already spoken to Malinovsky about it." Filipov worked for Defense Minister Malinovsky. "He is in agreement with Pliyev."

Dimka was horrified. "Pliyev can't be allowed to start World War Three on his own initiative!"

"He won't be starting it. He'll be defending our troops from American aggression."

"The level of response can't be a local decision."

"There may be no time for anything else."

"Pliyev must make time, rather than trigger a nuclear exchange."

"Malinovsky believes we must protect the weapons we have in Cuba. If they were destroyed by the Americans, it would weaken our ability to defend the USSR."

Dimka had not thought of that. A significant part of the Soviet nuclear stockpile was now in Cuba. The Americans could wipe out all those costly weapons, leaving the Soviets seriously weakened.

"No," said Natalya. "Our whole strategy must be based on *not* using nuclear weapons. Why? Because we have so few, by comparison with the American arsenal." She leaned forward across the canteen table. "Listen to me, Yevgeny. If it comes to all-out nuclear war, *they win.*" She sat back. "So we may brag, we may bluster, we may threaten, but we may not fire our weapons. For us, nuclear war is suicide."

"That's not how the Defense Ministry sees it."

Natalya hesitated. "You speak as if a decision has already been made."

"It has. Malinovsky has endorsed Pliyev's proposal."

Dimka said: "Khrushchev won't like that."

"On the contrary," said Filipov. "He agreed with it."

Dimka realized he had missed out on early-morning discussions because he had been up so late last night. That put him at a disadvantage. He stood up. "Let's go," he said to Natalya.

They left the cafeteria. Waiting for the elevator, Dimka said: "Damn. We've got to reverse that decision."

"I'm sure Kosygin will want to raise it at the Presidium today."

"Why don't you type the order we drafted and suggest Kosygin bring it to the meeting? I'll try to soften Khrushchev up."

"All right."

They parted and Dimka went to Khrushchev's office. The first secretary was reading translations of Western newspaper articles, each one stapled to the original clipping. "Have you read Walter Lippmann's article?"

Lippmann was a syndicated American columnist of liberal views. He was said to be close to President Kennedy.

"No." Dimka had not yet looked at the papers.

"Lippmann proposes a swap: we withdraw our missiles from Cuba, and they remove theirs from Turkey. It's a message to me from Kennedy!"

"Lippmann is only a journalist—"

"No, no. He's a mouthpiece for the president."

Dimka doubted that American democracy worked that way, but he said nothing.

Khrushchev went on: "It means that if we propose this swap, Kennedy will accept."

"But we have already demanded something different—their promise not to invade Cuba."

"So, we will keep Kennedy guessing!"

We'll certainly keep him confused, Dimka thought. But that was Khrushchev's way. Why be consistent? It only made life easier for the enemy.

Dimka changed the subject. "There will be questions at the Presidium about Pliyev's message. Giving him the power to fire nuclear weapons—"

"Don't worry," said Khrushchev with a deprecating wave. "The Americans are not going to attack now. They're even talking to the United Nations general secretary. They want peace."

"Of course," said Dimka deferentially. "So long as you know it's going to come up."

"Yes, yes."

The leaders of the Soviet Union gathered in the paneled Presidium Room a few minutes later. Khrushchev opened the meeting with a long speech arguing that the time for an American attack had passed. Then he raised what he called the Lippmann Proposal. There was little enthusiasm for it around the long table, but no one opposed him. Most people realized the leader had to conduct diplomacy in his own style.

Khrushchev was so excited about the new idea that he dictated his letter to Kennedy there and then, while the others listened. Then he ordered that it should be read out on Radio Moscow. That way the American embassy here could forward it to Washington without the time-consuming chore of encoding it.

Finally Kosygin raised the issue of Pliyev's flash. He argued that control of nuclear weapons must remain in Moscow, and read out the order to Pliyev that Dimka and Natalya had drafted.

"Yes, yes, send it," said Khrushchev impatiently; and Dimka breathed easier.

An hour later Dimka was with Nina, going up in the elevator at Government House. "Let's try to forget our woes for a while," he said to her. "We won't talk about Cuba. We're going to a party. Let's enjoy ourselves."

"That suits me," Nina said.

They went to the apartment of Dimka's grandparents. Katerina opened the door in a red dress. Dimka was startled to see that it was knee length, in the latest Western fashion, and that his grandmother still had slim legs. She had lived in the West, while her husband was on the diplomatic circuit, and she had learned to dress more stylishly than most Soviet women.

She looked Nina up and down with the unapologetic curiosity of old people. "You look well," she said, and Dimka wondered why her tone of voice sounded a little odd.

Nina took it as a compliment. "Thank you, so do you. Where did you get that dress?"

Katerina led them into the living room. Dimka remembered coming here as a boy. His grandmother had always given him *belev* candy, a traditional Russian kind of apple confection. His mouth watered: he would have liked a piece right then.

Katerina seemed a little unsteady in her high-heeled shoes. Grigori was sitting in the easy chair opposite the television, as always, though the set was off. He had already opened a bottle of vodka. Perhaps that was why Grandmother was wobbling a little.

"Birthday greetings, Grandfather," said Dimka.

"Have a drink," said Grigori.

Dimka had to be careful. He would be no use to Khrushchev drunk. He knocked back the vodka Grigori gave him, then put the glass down out of Grandfather's reach, to avoid a refill.

Dimka's mother was already there, helping Katerina. She came out of the kitchen carrying a plate of crackers with red caviar. Anya had not inherited Katerina's stylishness. She always looked comfortably dumpy, whatever she wore.

She kissed Nina.

The doorbell rang and Uncle Volodya came in with his family. He was forty-eight, and his close-cropped hair was now gray. He was in uniform: he might be called to duty at any moment. Aunt Zoya followed him, approaching fifty but still a pale Russian goddess. Behind her trailed their two teenagers, Dimka's cousins, Kotya and Galina.

Dimka introduced Nina. Both Volodya and Zoya greeted her warmly.

"Now we're all here!" said Katerina.

Dimka looked around: at the old couple who had started it all; at his plain mother and her handsome blue-eyed brother; at his beautiful aunt and his teenage cousins; and at the voluptuous redhead he was going to marry. This was his family. And it was the most precious part of everything that would be lost today if his fears came true. They all lived within a mile of the Kremlin. If the Americans fired their nuclear weapons at Moscow tonight, the people in this room would all be lying dead in the morning, their brains boiled, their bodies crushed, their skin burned black. And the only consolation was that he would not have to mourn them because he, too, would be dead.

They all drank to Grigori's birthday.

"I wish my little brother, Lev, could be with us," said Grigori.

"And Tanya," said Anya.

Volodya said: "Lev Peshkov is not so little anymore, Father. He's sixty-seven years old and a millionaire in America."

"I wonder if he has grandchildren in America."

"Not in America, no," said Volodya. Red Army Intelligence could find out this sort of thing easily, Dimka knew. "Lev's illegitimate son, Greg, the senator, is a bachelor. But his legitimate daughter, Daisy, who lives in London, has two adolescents, a boy and a girl, about the same age as Kotya and Galina."

"So, I'm a great-uncle to two British kids," Grigori said, musing in a pleased tone. "What are they called? Jane and Bill, perhaps." The others laughed at the odd sounds of the English names.

"David and Evie," said Volodya.

"You know, I was supposed to be the one to go to America," Grigori said. "But at the last minute I had to give my ticket to Lev." He went into a reminiscence. His family had heard the story before, but they listened again, happy to indulge him on his birthday.

After a moment, Volodya took Dimka aside and said: "How was this morning's Presidium?"

"They ordered Pliyev not to fire nuclear weapons without specific orders from the Kremlin."

Volodya grunted disparagingly. "Waste of time."

Dimka was surprised. "Why?"

"It will make no difference."

"Are you saying Pliyev will disobey orders?"

"I think any commander would. You haven't been in battle, have you?" Volodya gave Dimka a searching look with those intense blue eyes. "When you're under attack, fighting for your life, you defend yourself with any means that come to hand. It's visceral, you can't help it. If the Americans invade Cuba, our forces there will throw everything at them, regardless of orders from Moscow."

"Shit," said Dimka. All this morning's efforts had been wasted, if Volodya was right.

Grandfather's story wound down, and Nina touched Dimka's arm. "Now might be a good moment."

Dimka addressed the assembled family. "Now that we have honored my grandfather's birthday, I have an announcement. Quiet, please." He waited for the teenagers to stop talking. "I have asked Nina to marry me, and she has accepted."

They all cheered.

Another round of vodka was poured, but Dimka managed not to drink this one.

Anya kissed Dimka. "Well done, my son," she said. "She didn't want to get married—until she met you!"

"Maybe I'll have great-grandchildren soon!" said Grigori, and he winked broadly at Nina.

Volodya said: "Father, don't embarrass the poor girl."

"Embarrass? Rubbish. Nina and I are friends."

"Don't worry about that," said Katerina, who was now drunk. "She's already pregnant."

Volodya protested: "Mother!"

Katerina shrugged. "A woman can tell."

So that was why Grandmother looked Nina up and down so hard when we arrived, Dimka thought. He saw a glance pass between Volodya and Zoya: Volodya raised an eyebrow, Zoya gave a slight nod, and Volodya made a momentary "Oh!" with his mouth.

Anya looked shocked. She said to Nina: "But you told me . . ."

Dimka said: "I know. We thought Nina couldn't have children. But the doctors were wrong!"

Grigori raised yet another glass. "Hooray for wrong doctors! I want a boy, Nina—a great-grandson to carry on the Peshkov-Dvorkin line!"

Nina smiled. "I'll do my best, Grigori Sergeivitch."

Anya still looked troubled. "The doctors made a mistake?"

"You know doctors, they never admit to mistakes," said Nina. "They say it's a miracle."

"I just hope I live to see my great-grandchild," said Grigori. "Damn the Americans to hell." He drank.

Kotya, the sixteen-year-old boy, spoke up. "Why do the Americans have more missiles than we do?"

Zoya answered: "When we scientists began to work on nuclear energy, back in 1940, and we told the government that it could be used to create a super-powerful bomb, Stalin did not believe us. So the West got ahead of the USSR, and they're still ahead. That's what happens when governments don't listen to scientists."

Volodya added: "But don't repeat what your mother says when you go to school, okay?"

Anya said: "Who cares? Stalin killed half of us, now Khrushchev will kill the other half."

"Anya!" protested Volodya. "Not in front of the children!"

"I feel for Tanya," said Anya, ignoring her brother's remonstrances. "Over there in Cuba, waiting for the Americans to attack." She began to weep. "I wish I could have seen my pretty little girl again," she said, sudden tears streaming down her cheeks. "Just once more, before we die."

. . .

By Saturday morning the U.S. was ready to attack Cuba.

Larry Mawhinney gave George the details in the basement Situation Room at the White House. President Kennedy called this area a pigpen, because he found it cramped; but he had been raised in grand spacious homes: the suite was larger than George's apartment.

According to Mawhinney, the air force had five hundred seventy-six planes at five different bases ready for the air strike that would turn Cuba into a smoking wasteland. The army had mobilized one hundred fifty thousand troops for the invasion that would follow. The navy had twenty-six destroyers and three aircraft carriers circling the island nation. Mawhinney said all this proudly, as if it were his own personal achievement.

George thought Mawhinney was too glib. "None of that will be any use against nuclear missiles," George said.

"Fortunately, we have nukes of our own," Mawhinney replied.

Like that made everything all right.

"How do we fire them, exactly?" said George. "I mean, what does the president do, physically?"

"He has to call the Joint War Room at the Pentagon. His phone in the Oval Office has a red button that connects him instantly."

"And what would he say?"

"He has a black leather briefcase containing a set of codes that he has to use. The briefcase goes everywhere with him."

"And then . . . ?"

"It's automatic. There's a program called the Single Integrated Operational Plan. Our bombers and missiles take off with about three thousand nuclear weapons, and head for a thousand targets in the

Communist bloc." Mawhinney made a flattening motion with his hand. "Wipe them out," he said with relish.

George was not buying this attitude. "And they do the same to us."

Mawhinney looked annoyed. "Listen, if we get the first punch in, we can destroy most of their weapons before they get off the ground."

"But we're not likely to get the first punch in, because we're not barbarians, and we don't want to start a nuclear war that would kill millions."

"That's where you politicians go wrong. A first strike is the way to win."

"Even if we do what you want, we'll only destroy *most* of their weapons, you said."

"Obviously, we won't get a hundred percent."

"So, whatever happens, the USA gets nuked."

"War is not a picnic," Mawhinney said angrily.

"If we avoid war, we can carry on having picnics."

Larry looked at his watch. "ExComm at ten," he said.

They left the Situation Room and went upstairs to the Cabinet Room. The president's senior advisers were gathering, with their aides. President Kennedy entered a few minutes after ten. This was the first time George had seen him since Maria's abortion. He stared at the president with new eyes. This middle-aged man in the dark suit with the faint stripe had fucked a young woman, then let her go to the abortion doctor on her own. George felt a momentary flash of pure vitriolic rage. At that moment he could have killed Jack Kennedy.

All the same, the president did not look evil. He was bearing the strain of the cares of the world, literally, and George, against his will, felt a pang of sympathy, too.

As usual, CIA chief McCone opened the meeting with an intelligence summary. In his customary soporific drone he announced news frightening enough to keep everyone wide awake. Five medium-range missile sites in Cuba were now fully operational. Each had four missiles, so there were now twenty nuclear weapons pointed at the United States and ready to be fired.

At least one had to be targeted on this building, George thought grimly, and his stomach cramped in fear.

McCone proposed round-the-clock surveillance of the sites. Eight

U.S. Navy jets were ready to take off from Key West to overfly the launchpads at low level. Another eight would travel the same circuit this afternoon. When it got dark they would go again, illuminating the sites with flares. In addition, high-altitude reconnaissance flights by U-2 spy planes would continue.

George wondered what good that would do. The overflights might detect prelaunch activity, but what could the U.S. do about that? Even if the American bombers took off immediately, they would not reach Cuba before the missiles were fired.

And there was another problem. As well as nuclear missiles aimed at the USA, the Red Army in Cuba had SAMs, surface-to-air missiles designed to bring down aircraft. All twenty-four SAM batteries were operational, McCone reported, and their radar equipment had been switched on. So American planes overflying Cuba would now be tracked and targeted.

An aide came into the room with a long sheet of paper torn off a teletype machine. He gave it to President Kennedy. "This is from the Associated Press in Moscow," said the president, and he read it aloud. "'Premier Khrushchev told President Kennedy yesterday he would withdraw offensive weapons from Cuba if the United States withdrew its rockets from Turkey.'"

Mac Bundy, the national security adviser, said: "He did not."

George was as puzzled as everyone else. Khrushchev's letter yesterday had demanded that the USA promise not to invade Cuba. It had said nothing about Turkey. Had the Associated Press made a mistake? Or was Khrushchev up to his usual tricks?

The president said: "He may be putting out another letter."

That turned out to be the truth. In the next few minutes, further reports made the situation clearer. Khrushchev was making a completely separate new proposal, and had broadcast it on Radio Moscow.

"He's got us in a pretty good spot here," said President Kennedy. "Most people would regard this as not an unreasonable proposal."

Mac Bundy did not like that idea. "What 'most people,' Mr. President?"

The president said: "I think you're going to find it difficult to explain why we want to take hostile military action in Cuba when he's saying:

'Get yours out of Turkey and we'll get ours out of Cuba.' I think you've
got a very touchy point there."

Bundy argued for going back to Khrushchev's first offer. "Why pick
that track when he's offered us the other track in the last twenty-four
hours?"

Impatiently, the president said: "This is their new and latest
position—and it's a public one." The press did not yet know about
Khrushchev's letter, but this new proposal had been made through the
media.

Bundy persisted. America's NATO allies would feel betrayed if
the U.S. traded missiles, he said.

Defense Secretary Bob McNamara expressed the bewilderment and
fear that they all felt. "We had one deal in the letter, now we've got a
different one," he said. "How can we negotiate with somebody who
changes his deal before we even get a chance to reply?"

No one knew the answer.

· · ·

That Saturday, the royal poinsettia trees in the streets of Havana
blossomed with brilliant red flowers like bloodstains on the sky.

Early in the morning Tanya went to the store and grimly laid in
provisions for the end of the world: smoked meat, canned milk,
processed cheese, a carton of cigarettes, a bottle of rum, and fresh
batteries for her flashlight. Although it was daybreak there was a line,
but she waited only fifteen minutes, which was nothing to someone
accustomed to Moscow queues.

There was a doomsday air in the narrow streets of the old town.
Habaneros were no longer waving machetes and singing the national
anthem. They were collecting sand in buckets for putting out fires,
sticking gummed paper over their windows to minimize flying shards,
toting sacks of flour. They had been so foolish as to defy their superpower
neighbor, and now they were going to be punished. They should have
known better.

Were they right? Was war unavoidable now? Tanya felt sure no
world leader really wanted it, not even Castro, who was beginning to
sound borderline crazy. But it could happen anyway. She thought

gloomily of the events of 1914. No one had wanted war then. But the Austrian emperor had seen Serbian independence as a threat, in the same way that Kennedy saw Cuban independence as a threat. And once Austria declared war on Serbia the dominoes fell with deadly inevitability until half the planet was involved in a conflict more cruel and bloody than any the world had previously known. But surely that could be avoided this time?

She thought of Vasili Yenkov, in a prison camp in Siberia. Ironically, he might have a chance of surviving a nuclear war. His punishment might save his life. She hoped so.

When she got back to her apartment she turned on the radio. It was tuned to one of the American stations broadcasting from Florida. The news was that Khrushchev had offered Kennedy a deal. He would withdraw the missiles from Cuba if Kennedy would do the same in Turkey.

She looked at her canned milk with a feeling of overwhelming relief. Maybe she would not need emergency rations after all.

She told herself it was too soon to feel safe. Would Kennedy accept? Would he prove wiser than the ultraconservative Emperor Franz Joseph of Austria?

A car honked outside. She had a long-standing date to fly to the eastern end of Cuba with Paz today to write about a Soviet antiaircraft battery. She had not really expected him to show up, but when she looked out of the window she saw his Buick station wagon at the curb, its wipers struggling to cope with a tropical rainstorm. She picked up her raincoat and bag and went out.

"Have you seen what your leader has done?" he asked angrily as soon as she got into the car.

She was surprised by his rage. "You mean the Turkey offer?"

"He didn't even consult us!" Paz pulled away, driving too fast along the narrow streets.

Tanya had not even thought about whether the Cuban leaders should be part of the negotiation. Obviously Khrushchev, too, had overlooked the need for this courtesy. The world saw the crisis as a conflict of superpowers, but naturally the Cubans still imagined it was about them. And this faint prospect of a peace deal seemed to them a betrayal.

She needed to calm Paz down, if only to prevent a road accident. "What would you have said, if Khrushchev had asked you?"

"That we will not trade our security for Turkey's!" he said, and banged the steering wheel with the heel of his hand.

Nuclear weapons had not brought security to Cuba, Tanya reflected. They had done the opposite. Cuba's sovereignty was more threatened today than ever. But she decided not to enrage Paz further by pointing this out.

He drove to a military airstrip outside Havana where their plane was waiting, a Yakovlev Yak-16 propeller-driven Soviet light transport aircraft. Tanya looked at it with interest. She had never intended to be a war correspondent but, to avoid appearing ignorant, she had taken pains to learn the stuff men knew, especially how to identify aircraft, tanks, and ships. This was the military modification of the Yak, she saw, with a machine gun mounted in a ball turret on top of the fuselage.

They shared the ten-seat cabin with two majors of the 32nd Guards air fighter regiment, dressed in the loud check shirts and peg-top pants that had been issued in a clumsy attempt to disguise Soviet troops as Cubans.

Takeoff was a little too exciting: it was the rainy season in the Caribbean, and there were gusty winds, too. When they could see the land below, through gaps in the clouds, they glimpsed a collage of brown and green patches crazed with crooked yellow lines of dirt road. The little plane was tossed around in a storm for two hours. Then the sky cleared, with the rapidity characteristic of tropical weather changes, and they landed smoothly near the town of Banes.

They were met by a Red Army colonel called Ivanov who already knew all about Tanya and the article she was writing. He drove them to an antiaircraft base. They arrived at ten A.M., Cuban time.

The site was laid out as a six-pointed star, with the command post in the center and the launchers at the points. Beside each launcher stood a transporter trailer bearing a single surface-to-air missile. The troops looked miserable in their waterlogged trenches. Inside the command post, officers stared intently at green radar screens that beeped monotonously.

Ivanov introduced them to the major in command of the battery. He was obviously tense. No doubt he would have preferred not to have visiting VIPs on a day such as this.

A few minutes after they arrived, a foreign aircraft was sighted at high altitude entering Cuban airspace two hundred miles west. It was given the tag Target No. 33.

Everyone was speaking Russian, so Tanya had to translate for Paz. "It must be a U-2 spy plane," he said. "Nothing else flies that high."

Tanya was suspicious. "Is this a drill?" she asked Ivanov.

"We were planning to fake something, for your benefit," he said. "But actually this is the real thing."

He looked so worried that Tanya believed him. "We're not going to shoot it down, are we?" she said.

"I don't know."

"The arrogance of these Americans!" Paz raved. "Flying right above us! What would they say if a Cuban plane overflew Fort Bragg? Imagine their indignation!"

The major ordered a combat alert, and Soviet troops began to move missiles from transporters to launchers, and to attach the cables. They did it with calm efficiency, and Tanya guessed they had practised many times.

A captain was plotting the course of the U-2 on a map. Cuba was long and thin, 777 miles from east to west but only fifty to a hundred miles from north to south. Tanya saw that the spy plane was already fifty miles inside Cuba. "How fast do they fly?" she asked.

Ivanov answered: "Five hundred miles an hour."

"How high?"

"Seventy thousand feet, roughly double the altitude of a regular jet airline flight."

"Can we really hit a target that far away and moving so fast?"

"We don't need a direct hit. The missile has a proximity fuse. It explodes when it gets close."

"I know we're targeting this plane," she said. "But please tell me we're not actually going to fire at it."

"The major is calling for instructions."

"But the Americans might retaliate."

"Not my decision."

The radar was tracking the intruder plane, and a lieutenant reading from a screen called out its height, speed, and distance. Outside the command post, the Soviet artillerymen adjusted the aim of the launchers to follow Target No. 33. The U-2 crossed Cuba from north to south, then turned east, following the coast, coming closer to Banes. Outside, the missile launchers turned slowly on their pivoting bases, tracking the target like wolves sniffing the air. Tanya said to Paz: "What if they fire by accident?"

That was not what he was thinking about. "It's taking pictures of our positions!" he said. "Those photographs will be used to guide their army when they invade—which could be in a few hours' time."

"The invasion is much more likely to happen if you kill an American pilot!"

The major had the phone to his ear while he watched the fire-control radar. He looked up at Ivanov and said: "They're checking with Pliyev." Tanya knew that Pliyev was the Soviet commander in chief in Cuba. But surely Pliyev would not shoot down an American plane without authorization from Moscow?

The U-2 reached the southernmost tip of Cuba and turned, following the north coast. Banes was near the coast. The U-2's course would bring it directly overhead. But at any instant it could turn north—and then, traveling at about a mile a second, it could quickly be out of range.

"Shoot it down!" said Paz. "Now!"

Everyone ignored him.

The plane turned north. It was almost directly above the battery, though thirteen miles high.

Just a few more seconds, please, Tanya thought, praying to she knew not what god.

Tanya, Paz, and Ivanov stared at the major, who stared at the screen. The room was silent but for the beeping of the radar.

Then the major said: "Yes, sir."

What was it—reprieve or doom?

Without putting down the phone, he spoke to the men in the room. "Destroy Target No. 33. Fire two missiles."

"No!" said Tanya.

There was a roar of sound. Tanya looked through the window. A missile rose from its launcher and was gone in a blink. Another followed seconds later. Tanya put her hand to her mouth, feeling she might vomit in fear.

They would take about a minute to reach an altitude of thirteen miles.

Something might go wrong, Tanya thought. The missiles could malfunction, veer off course, and land harmlessly in the sea.

On the radar screen, two small dots approached a larger one.

Tanya prayed they would miss.

They went fast, then all three dots merged.

Paz let out a yell of triumph.

Then a scatter of smaller dots sprayed across the screen.

Speaking into the phone, the major said: "Target No. 33 is destroyed."

Tanya looked out of the window, as if she might see the U-2 crashing to earth.

The major raised his voice. "It's a kill. Well done, everyone."

Tanya said: "And what will President Kennedy do to us now?"

. . .

George was full of hope on Saturday afternoon. Khrushchev's messages were inconsistent and confusing, but the Soviet leader seemed to be seeking a way out of the crisis. And President Kennedy certainly did not want war. Given goodwill on both sides, it seemed inconceivable that they would fail.

On his way to the Cabinet Room, George stopped by the press office and found Maria at her desk. She was wearing a smart gray dress, but she had on a bright pink headband, as if to announce to the world that she was well and happy. George decided not to ask how she was: clearly she did not want to be treated as an invalid. "Are you busy?" he said.

"We're waiting for the president's reply to Khrushchev," she said. "The Soviet offer was made publicly, so we're assuming the American response will be released to the press."

"That's the meeting I'm going to with Bobby," George said. "To draft the response."

"Swapping missiles in Cuba for missiles in Turkey seems like a reasonable proposal," she said. "Especially as it may save all our lives."

"Praise be."

"Your mom says that."

He laughed and moved on. In the Cabinet Room, advisers and their aides were gathering for the four o'clock meeting of ExComm. Among a knot of military aides by the door, Larry Mawhinney was saying: "We have to stop them giving Turkey to the Communists!"

George groaned. The military saw everything as a fight to the death. In truth, nobody was going to give Turkey away. The proposal was to scrap some missiles that were obsolete anyway. Was the Pentagon really going to oppose a peace deal? He could hardly believe it.

President Kennedy came in and took his usual place, in the middle of the long table with the windows behind him. They all had copies of a draft response put together earlier. It said that the USA could not discuss missiles in Turkey until the Cuba crisis had been resolved. The president did not like the wording of this reply to Khrushchev. "We're rejecting his message," he complained. "He" was always Khrushchev: Kennedy saw this as a personal conflict. "This is not going to be successful. He's going to announce that we've rejected his proposal. Our position ought to be that we're *glad* to discuss this matter—once we get a positive indication that they have ceased their work in Cuba."

Someone said: "That really injects Turkey as a quid pro quo."

National Security Adviser Mac Bundy chimed in: "That's my worry." Bundy, whose hair was receding although he was only forty-three, came from a Republican family and tended to be hard-line. "If we sound, to NATO and other allies, as if we want to make this trade, then we're in real trouble."

George was disheartened: Bundy was lining up with the Pentagon, against a deal.

Bundy went on: "If we appear to be trading the defense of Turkey for a threat to Cuba, we'll just have to face a radical decline in the effectiveness of the alliance."

That was the problem, George realized. The Jupiter missiles might have been obsolete, but they symbolized American determination to resist the spread of Communism.

The president was not convinced by Bundy. "The situation is moving there, Mac."

Bundy persisted. "The justification for this message is that we expect it to be turned down."

Really? thought George. He was pretty sure President Kennedy and his brother did not see it that way.

"We expect to be acting against Cuba tomorrow or the next day," Bundy went on. "What's our military plan?"

This was not how George had thought the meeting would go. They should be talking about peace, not war.

Defense Secretary Bob McNamara, the whiz kid from Ford, answered the question. "A large air strike leading to invasion." Then he turned the argument back to Turkey. "To minimize the Soviet response against NATO following a U.S. attack on Cuba, we get those Jupiters out of Turkey before the Cuban attack—and let the Soviets know. On that basis, I don't believe the Soviets would strike Turkey."

That was ironic, George thought: to protect Turkey, it was necessary to take away its nuclear weapons.

Secretary of State Dean Rusk, who George thought was one of the smarter men in the room, warned: "They might take some other action—in Berlin."

George marveled that the American president could not attack a Caribbean island without calculating the repercussions five thousand miles away in Eastern Europe. It showed how the entire planet was a chess board for the two superpowers.

McNamara said: "I'm not prepared at this moment to recommend air attacks on Cuba. I'm just saying we must now begin to look at it more realistically."

General Maxwell Taylor spoke. He had been in touch with the Joint Chiefs of Staff. "The recommendation they give is that the big strike, Operations Plan 312, be executed no later than Monday morning, unless there is irrefutable evidence in the meantime that offensive weapons are being dismantled."

Sitting behind Taylor, Mawhinney and his friends looked pleased. Just like the military, George thought: they could hardly wait to go into battle, even though it might mean the end of the world. He prayed that the politicians in the room would not be guided by the soldiers.

Taylor continued: "And that the execution of this strike plan be followed by the execution of 316, the invasion plan, seven days later."

Bobby Kennedy said sarcastically: "Well, I'm surprised."

There was loud laughter around the table. Everyone thought the military's recommendations were absurdly predictable, it seemed. George felt relieved.

But the mood became grim again when McNamara, reading a note passed to him by an aide, suddenly said: "The U-2 was shot down."

George gasped. He knew that a CIA spy plane had gone silent during a mission over Cuba, but everyone was hoping it had suffered a radio problem and was on its way home.

President Kennedy evidently had not been briefed about the missing plane. "A U-2 was shot down?" he said, and there was fear in his voice.

George knew why the president was appalled. Until this moment, the superpowers had been nose to nose, but all they had done was threaten one another. Now the first shot had been fired. From this point on, it would be much more difficult to avoid war.

"Wright just said it was found shot down," McNamara said. Colonel John Wright was with the Defense Intelligence Agency.

Bobby said: "Was the pilot killed?"

As so often, he had asked the key question.

General Taylor said: "The pilot's body is in the plane."

President Kennedy said: "Did anyone see the pilot?"

"Yes, sir," Taylor replied. "The wreckage is on the ground and the pilot's dead."

The room went quiet. This changed everything. An American was dead, shot down in Cuba by Soviet guns.

Taylor said: "That raises the question of retaliation."

It certainly did. The American people would demand revenge. George felt the same. Suddenly he yearned for the president to launch the massive air attack that the Pentagon had demanded. In his mind he saw hundreds of bombers in close formation sweeping across the Florida Straits and dropping their deadly payload on Cuba like a hailstorm. He wanted every missile launcher blown up, all the Soviet troops slaughtered, Castro killed. If the entire Cuban nation suffered, so be it: that would teach them not to kill Americans.

The meeting had been going on for two hours, and the room was foggy with tobacco smoke. The president announced a break. It was a good idea, George thought. George himself certainly needed to calm down. If the others were feeling as bloodthirsty as he was, they were in no state to make rational decisions.

The more important reason for the break, George knew, was that President Kennedy had to take his medicine. Most people knew he had a bad back, but few understood that he fought a constant battle against a whole range of ailments, including Addison's disease and colitis. Twice a day the doctors shot him up with a cocktail of steroids and antibiotics to keep him functioning.

Bobby undertook to redraft the letter to Khrushchev, with the help of the president's cheerful young speechwriter Ted Sorensen. The two of them went with their aides to the president's study, a cramped room next to the Oval Office. George took a pen and yellow pad and wrote down everything Bobby told him to. With only two people discussing it, the draft was done quickly.

The key paragraphs were:

1. You would agree to remove these weapons systems from Cuba under appropriate United Nations observation and supervision; and undertake, with suitable safeguards, to halt the further introduction of such weapons systems into Cuba.
2. We, on our part, would agree—upon the establishment of adequate arrangements through the United Nations to ensure the carrying out and continuation of these commitments—(a) to remove promptly the quarantine arrangements now in effect and (b) to give assurances against an invasion of Cuba and I am confident that other nations of the Western Hemisphere would be prepared to do likewise.

The USA was accepting Khrushchev's first offer. But what about his second? Bobby and Sorensen agreed to say:

The effect of such a settlement on easing world tensions would enable us to work toward a more general arrangement regarding "other armaments" as proposed in your second letter.

It was not much, just a hint of a promise to discuss something, but it was probably the most that ExComm would allow.

George privately wondered how this could possibly be enough.

He gave his handwritten draft to one of the president's secretaries and asked her to get it typed. A few minutes later, Bobby was summoned to the Oval Office, where a smaller group was gathering: the president, Dean Rusk, Mac Bundy, and two or three others, with their closest aides. Vice President Lyndon Johnson was excluded: he was a smart political operator, in George's opinion, but his rough Texas manners grated on the refined Boston Kennedy brothers.

The president wanted Bobby to carry the letter personally to the Soviet ambassador in Washington, Anatoly Dobrynin. Bobby and Dobrynin had had several informal meetings in the last few days. They did not much like one another, but they were able to speak frankly, and had formed a useful back channel that bypassed the Washington bureaucracy. In a face-to-face meeting, perhaps Bobby could expand on the hint of a promise to discuss the missiles in Turkey—without getting prior approval from ExComm.

Dean Rusk suggested that Bobby could go a little further with Dobrynin. In today's meetings it had become clear that no one really wanted the Jupiter missiles to remain in Turkey. From a strictly military point of view they were useless. The problem was cosmetic: the Turkish government and the other NATO allies would be angered if the USA traded those missiles in a Cuba settlement. Rusk suggested a solution that George thought was very smart. "Offer to pull the Jupiters out later—say, in five or six months' time," said Rusk. "Then we can do it quietly, with the agreement of our allies, and step up the Mediterranean activity of our nuclear-armed submarines to compensate. But the Soviets have to promise to keep that deal deadly secret."

It was a startling suggestion, but brilliant, George thought.

Everyone agreed with remarkable speed. ExComm discussions had rambled all over the globe for most of the day, but this smaller group here in the Oval Office had suddenly become decisive. Bobby said to George: "Call Dobrynin." He looked at his watch, and George did the same: it was seven fifteen P.M. "Ask him to meet me at the Justice Department in half an hour," Bobby said.

The president added: "And release the letter to the press fifteen minutes later."

George stepped into the secretaries' office next to the Oval Office and picked up a phone. "Get me the Soviet embassy," he said to the switchboard operator.

The ambassador agreed instantly to the meeting.

George took the typed letter to Maria and told her the president wanted it released to the press at eight P.M.

She looked anxiously at her watch, then said: "Okay, girls, we'd better go to work."

Bobby and George left the White House and a car drove them the few blocks to the Justice Department. In the gloomy weekend lighting, the statues in the Great Hall seemed to watch the two men suspiciously. George explained to the security staff that an important visitor would shortly arrive to see Bobby.

They went up in the elevator. George thought Bobby looked exhausted, and undoubtedly he was. The corridors of the huge building echoed emptily. Bobby's cavernous office was dimly lit, but he did not bother to switch on more lamps. He slumped behind his wide desk and rubbed his eyes.

George looked out of the window at the streetlights. The center of Washington was a pretty park full of monuments and palaces, but the rest of it was a densely populated metropolis with five million residents, more than half of them black. Would the city be here this time tomorrow? George had seen pictures of Hiroshima: miles of buildings flattened to rubble, and burned and maimed survivors on the outskirts, staring with uncomprehending eyes at the unrecognizable world around them. Would Washington look like that in the morning?

Ambassador Dobrynin was shown in at exactly a quarter to eight. He was a bald man in his early forties, and he clearly relished his informal meetings with the president's brother.

"I want to lay out the current alarming situation the way the president sees it," Bobby said. "One of our planes has been shot down over Cuba and the pilot is dead."

"Your planes have no right to fly over Cuba," Dobrynin said quickly.

Bobby's discussions with Dobrynin could be combative, but today the attorney general was in a different mood. "I want you to understand the political realities," he said. "There is now strong pressure on the president to respond with fire. We can't stop these overflights: it's the only way we can check the state of construction of your missile bases. But if the Cubans shoot at our planes, we're going to shoot back."

Bobby told Dobrynin what was in the letter from President Kennedy to Secretary Khrushchev.

"And what about Turkey?" Dobrynin said sharply.

Bobby replied carefully. "If that is the only obstacle to achieving the regulation I mentioned earlier, the president doesn't see any insurmountable difficulties. The greatest difficulty for the president is the public discussion of the issue. If such a decision were announced now it would tear NATO apart. We need four to five months to remove the missiles from Turkey. But this is extremely confidential: only a handful of people know that I am saying this to you."

George watched Dobrynin's face carefully. Was it his imagination, or was the diplomat concealing a rush of excitement?

Bobby said: "George, give the ambassador the phone numbers we use to get to the president directly."

George grabbed a pad, wrote down three numbers, tore off the sheet, and handed it to Dobrynin.

Bobby stood up, and the ambassador did the same. "I need an answer tomorrow," Bobby said. "That's not an ultimatum, it's the reality. Our generals are itching for a fight. And don't send us one of those long Khrushchev letters that take all day to translate. We need a clear, businesslike answer from you, Mr. Ambassador. And we need it fast."

"Very well," said the Russian, and he went out.

· · ·

On Sunday morning, the KGB station chief in Havana reported to the Kremlin that the Cubans now thought an American attack was inevitable.

Dimka was at a government dacha at Novo-Ogaryevo, a picturesque village on the outskirts of Moscow. The dacha was a small place with white columns that made it look a bit like the White House in Washington. Dimka was preparing for the Presidium meeting to be held here in a few minutes, at twelve noon. He went around the long oak table with eighteen briefing folders, putting one in each place. They contained President Kennedy's latest message to Khrushchev, translated into Russian.

Dimka felt hopeful. The American president had agreed to everything Khrushchev had originally demanded. If this letter had arrived, miraculously, minutes after Khrushchev's first message had been sent, the crisis would have been over instantly. But the delay had permitted Khrushchev to add to his demands. And, unfortunately, Kennedy's letter did not directly mention Turkey. Dimka did not know whether that would be a sticking point for his boss.

The Presidium members were assembling when Natalya Smotrov came into the room. Dimka noticed first that her curly hair was getting longer and sexier, and second that she looked scared. He had been trying to get a few minutes with her to tell her about his engagement. He felt he could not give the news to anyone in the Kremlin until he had told Natalya. But once again this was not a good moment. He needed her alone.

She came straight to him and said: "Those imbeciles have shot down an American plane."

"Oh, no!"

She nodded. "A U-2 spy plane. The pilot is dead."

"Shit! Who did it, us or the Cubans?"

"No one will say, which means it was probably us."

"But no such order was given!"

"Exactly."

This was what they had both feared: that someone would start the shooting without authorization.

The members were taking their seats, aides behind them as usual. "I'll go and tell him," Dimka said but, as he spoke, Khrushchev came in. Dimka hurried to his side and murmured the news in the leader's ear as he sat down. Khrushchev did not reply, but looked grim.

He opened the meeting with what was clearly a prepared speech. "There was a time when we advanced, as in October 1917; but in March 1918 we had to retreat, having signed the Brest-Litovsk agreement with the Germans," he began. "Now we find ourselves face-to-face with the danger of war and nuclear catastrophe, with the possible result of destroying the human race. In order to save the world, we must retreat."

That sounded like the beginning of an argument for compromise, Dimka thought.

But Khrushchev quickly turned to military considerations. What should the Soviet Union do if the Americans were to attack Cuba today, as the Cubans themselves fully expected? General Pliyev must be instructed to defend Soviet forces in Cuba. But he should ask permission before using nuclear weapons.

While the Presidium was discussing that possibility, Dimka was called out of the room by Vera Pletner, his secretary. There was a phone call for him.

Natalya followed him out.

The Foreign Ministry had news that must be passed to Khrushchev immediately—yes, in the middle of the meeting. A cable had just been received from the Soviet ambassador in Washington. Bobby Kennedy had told him the missiles in Turkey would be removed in four or five months—but this must be kept deadly secret.

"This is good news!" Dimka said delightedly. "I'll tell him right away."

"One more thing," said the Foreign Ministry official. "Bobby kept stressing the need for speed. Apparently the American president is under severe pressure from the Pentagon to attack Cuba."

"Just as we thought."

"Bobby kept saying there is very little time. They must have their answer today."

"I'll tell him."

He hung up. Natalya was standing beside him, looking expectant. She had a nose for news. He told her: "Bobby Kennedy offered to remove the missiles from Turkey."

She smiled broadly. "It's over!" she said. "We've won!" Then she kissed him on the lips.

Dimka went back into the room in high excitement. Malinovsky, the defense minister, was speaking. Dimka went up to Khrushchev and said in a low voice: "A cable from Dobrynin—he's received a new offer from Bobby Kennedy."

"Tell everyone," Khrushchev said, interrupting the speaker.

Dimka repeated what he had been told.

Presidium members rarely smiled, but Dimka now saw broad grins around the table. Kennedy had given them everything they had asked for! It was a triumph for the Soviet Union and for Khrushchev personally.

"We must accept as quickly as possible," Khrushchev said. "Bring in a stenographer. I will dictate our letter of acceptance immediately, and it must be broadcast on Radio Moscow."

Malinovsky said: "When should I instruct Pliyev to start dismantling the missile launchers?"

Khrushchev looked at him as if he were stupid. "Now," he said.

.   .   .

After the Presidium, Dimka at last got Natalya alone. She was sitting in an anteroom, going through her notes of the meeting. "I have something to tell you," he said. For some reason he had a feeling of discomfort in his stomach, though he had nothing to be nervous about.

"Go ahead." She turned a page in her notebook.

He hesitated, feeling he did not have her attention.

Natalya put down the book and smiled.

Now or never.

Dimka said: "Nina and I are engaged to be married."

Natalya went pale and her mouth dropped open in shock.

Dimka felt the need to say something else. "We told my family yesterday," he said. "At my grandfather's birthday party." Stop gabbling, shut up, he told himself. "He's seventy-four."

When Natalya spoke, her words shocked him. "What about me?" she said.

He hardly understood what she meant. "You?" he said.

Her voice dropped to a whisper. "We spent a night together."

"I'll never forget it." Dimka was baffled. "But afterward, all you would say to me was that you were married."

"I was scared."

"Of what?"

Her face showed genuine distress. Her wide mouth was twisted in a grimace, almost as if she were in pain. "Don't get married, please!"

"Why not?"

"Because I don't want you to."

Dimka was flabbergasted. "Why didn't you tell me?"

"I didn't know what to do."

"But now it's too late."

"Is it?" She looked at him with pleading eyes. "You can break off an engagement . . . if you want to."

"Nina is going to have a baby."

Natalya gasped.

Dimka said: "You should have said something . . . before . . ."

"And if I had?"

He shook his head. "There is no point in discussing it."

"No," she said. "I see that."

"Well," said Dimka, "at least we avoided a nuclear war."

"Yes," she said. "We're alive. That's something."

T he smell of coffee woke Maria. She opened her eyes. President Kennedy was in bed beside her, sitting upright with several pillows propping him, drinking coffee and reading the Sunday edition of *The New York Times*. He was wearing a light-blue nightshirt, as was she. "Oh!" she said.

He smiled. "You sound surprised."

"I am," she said. "To be alive. I thought we might die in the night."

"Not this time."

She had gone to sleep half-hoping it would happen. She dreaded the end of their love affair. She knew it had no future. For him to leave his wife would destroy him politically; to do so for a black woman was unthinkable. Anyway, he did not even want to leave Jackie: he loved her, and he loved their children. He was happily married. Maria was his mistress, and when he tired of her he would discard her. Sometimes she felt she would prefer to die before that came to pass—especially if death could come while she was at his side, in bed, in a flash of nuclear destruction that would be over before they knew what was happening.

She said none of this: her role was to make him happy, not sad. She sat upright, kissed his ear, looked over his shoulder at the newspaper, took his cup from his hand, and drank some of his coffee. Despite everything, she was glad she was still alive.

He had not mentioned her abortion. It was almost as if he had forgotten about it. She had never raised it with him. She had called Dave Powers and said she was pregnant; and Dave had given her a phone number and said he would take care of the doctor's fee. The only time the president had spoken about it had been when he phoned her after the procedure. He had bigger worries on his mind.

Maria thought about raising the subject herself, but quickly decided against it. Like Dave, she wanted to shield the president from care, not give him additional burdens. She felt sure this was the right decision, though she could not help feeling sorry, and even hurt, that she was not able to talk to him about something so important.

She had feared that sex might be painful after the procedure. However, when Dave had asked her to go to the residence last night, she had been so reluctant to decline the invitation that she had decided to take the risk; and it had been fine—wonderful, in fact.

"I'd better move," the president said. "I'm going to church this morning."

He was about to get up when the bedside phone rang. He picked it up. "Good morning, Mac," he said.

Maria guessed he was talking to McGeorge Bundy, the national security adviser. She jumped out of bed and went to the bathroom.

Kennedy often took calls in bed in the morning. Maria assumed that the people who phoned either did not know or did not care whether he had company. She saved the president embarrassment by making herself scarce during such conversations, just in case they were top secret.

She peeped out of the door in time to see him hang up the phone. "Great news!" he said. "Moscow Radio announced that Khrushchev is dismantling the Cuban missiles and sending them back to the USSR."

Maria had to restrain herself from shouting for joy. It was over!

"I feel like a new man," said the president.

She threw her arms around him and kissed him. "You saved the world, Johnny," she said.

He looked reflective. After a minute he said: "Yeah, I guess I did."

. . .

Tanya was standing on her balcony, leaning on the wrought-iron parapet, breathing deeply of the damp Havana morning air, when Paz's Buick pulled up below, completely blocking the narrow street. He jumped out of the car, looked up, saw her, and yelled: "You betrayed me!"

"What?" She was astonished. "How?"

"You know."

He was a passionate and mercurial character, but she had never seen him this angry, and she was glad he had not come up the stairs to the apartment. However, she was baffled as to the reason for his rage. "I've told no secrets, and I haven't slept with another man," she said. "So I'm sure I haven't betrayed you."

"Then why are they dismantling the missile launchers?"

"Are they?" If that was so, the crisis was over. "Are you sure?"

"Don't pretend you don't know."

"I'm not pretending anything. But if it's true, we're saved." Out of the corner of her eye she noticed neighbors opening windows and doors, to watch the row with unabashed curiosity. She ignored them. "Why are you angry?"

"Because Khrushchev made a deal with the *yanquis*—and never even discussed it with Castro!"

The neighbors made disapproving noises.

"Of course I didn't know," she said with annoyance. "Do you imagine Khrushchev talks to me about such things?"

"He sent you here."

"Not personally."

"He talks to your brother."

"You really believe I'm some kind of special emissary of Khrushchev?"

"Why do you suppose I have gone everywhere with you for months?"

In a quieter voice, she replied: "I imagined it was because you liked me."

The listening women made sympathetic cooing sounds.

"You're not welcome here any longer," he yelled. "Pack your suitcase. You are to leave Cuba immediately. Today!"

With that he jumped back into his car and roared away.

"It was nice knowing you," said Tanya.

. . .

Dimka and Nina celebrated by going to a bar near her apartment that evening.

Dimka was determined not to think about his unsettling conversation with Natalya. It changed nothing. He put her to the back of his mind. They had had a brief fling and it was over. He loved Nina, and she was going to be his wife.

He bought a couple of bottles of weak Russian beer and sat beside her on a bench. "We're going to be married," he said tenderly. "I want you to have a wonderful dress."

"I don't want a lot of fuss," Nina said.

"Nor do I, for myself, but that could be a problem," Dimka said with a frown. "I'm the first of my generation to get married. My mother and grandparents will want to throw a big party. What about your family?" He knew that Nina's father had died in the war, but her mother was still alive, and she had a brother a couple of years younger than she.

"I hope Mother will be well enough to come." Nina's mother lived in Perm, nine hundred miles east of Moscow. But something told Dimka that Nina did not really want her mother to come.

"What about your brother?"

"He'll ask for leave, but I don't know if he'll get it." Nina's brother was in the Red Army. "I have no idea where he's stationed. He could be in Cuba, for all I know."

"I'll find out," Dimka said. "Uncle Volodya can pull a few strings."

"Don't go to too much trouble."

"I want to. This will probably be my only wedding!"

She snapped: "What do you mean by that?"

"Nothing." He had meant it lightheartedly, and he was sorry to have irritated her. "Forget I said it."

"Do you think I'm going to divorce you as I did my first husband?"

"I said exactly the opposite, didn't I? What's the matter with you?" He forced a smile. "We should be happy today. We're getting married, we're having a baby, and Khrushchev has saved the world."

"You don't understand. I'm not a virgin."

"I guessed that."

"Will you be serious?"

"All right."

"A wedding is normally two young people promising to love one another forever. You can't say that twice. Don't you see that I'm embarrassed to be doing this again because I've already failed at it once?"

"Oh!" he said. "Yes, I do see, now that you've explained it." Nina's attitude was a little old-fashioned—lots of people got divorced nowadays—but perhaps that was because she came from a provincial town. "So you want a celebration appropriate to a second marriage: no extravagant promises, no newlywed jokes, an adult awareness that life doesn't always go according to plan."

"Exactly."

"Well, my beloved, if that's what you want, I will make sure you have it."

"Will you, really?"

"Whatever made you think I wouldn't?"

"I don't know," she said. "Sometimes I forget what a good man you are."

. . .

That morning, at the last ExComm of the crisis, George heard Mac Bundy invent a new way of describing the opposite sides among the president's advisers. "Everyone knows who were the hawks and who were the doves," he said. Bundy himself was a hawk. "Today was the day of the doves."

But there were few hawks this morning: everyone was full of praise for President Kennedy's handling of the crisis, even some who had recently argued that he was being dangerously weak, and had pressed him to commit the United States to a war.

George summoned up the nerve to banter with the president. "Maybe you should solve the India-China border war next, Mr. President."

"I don't think either of them, or anyone else, wants me to."

"But today you're ten feet tall."

President Kennedy laughed. "That'll last about a week."

Bobby Kennedy was pleased at the prospect of seeing more of his family. "I've almost forgotten my way home," he said.

The only unhappy people were the generals. The Joint Chiefs of Staff, meeting at the Pentagon to finalize plans for the air attack on Cuba, were furious. They sent the president an urgent message saying that Khrushchev's acceptance was a trick to gain time. Curtis LeMay said this was the greatest defeat in American history. No one took any notice.

George had learned something, and he felt it was going to take him a while to digest it. Political issues were interlinked more closely than he had previously imagined. He had always thought that problems such as Berlin and Cuba were separate from each other and had little connection with such issues as civil rights and health care. But President Kennedy had been unable to deal with the Cuban missile crisis without thinking of the repercussions in Germany. And if he had failed to deal with Cuba, the imminent midterm elections would have crippled his domestic program, and made it impossible for him to pass a civil rights bill. Everything was connected. This realization had implications for George's career that he needed to mull over.

When ExComm broke up George kept his suit on and went to his mother's house. It was a sunny autumn day, and the leaves had turned red and gold. She cooked him supper, as she loved to do. She made steak and mashed potatoes. The steak was overdone: he could not persuade her to serve it in the French style, medium rare. He enjoyed the food anyway, because of the love with which it was made.

Afterward she washed the dishes and he dried, then they got ready to go to the evening service at Bethel Evangelical Church. "We must thank the Lord for saving us all," she said as she stood in front of the mirror by the door, putting on her hat.

"You thank the Lord, Mom," George said amiably. "I'll thank President Kennedy."

"Why don't we just agree to be grateful to both?"

"I'll buy that," said George, and they went out.

PART FOUR

GUN

1963

J oe Henry's Dance Band had a regular Saturday night gig in the restaurant of the Europe Hotel in East Berlin, playing jazz standards and show tunes for the East German elite and their wives. Joe, whose real name was Josef Heinried, was not much of a drummer, in Walli's opinion; but he could keep the beat, even when drunk, and besides, he was an official of the musicians' union, so he could not be fired.

Joe arrived at the staff entrance of the hotel at six P.M. in an old black Framo V901 van with his precious drums in the back packed tight with cushions. While Joe sat at the bar drinking beer, it was Walli's job to carry the drums from the van to the stage, unpack them from their leather cases, and set up the kit the way Joe liked it. There was a bass drum with a kick pedal, two tom-toms, a snare drum, a high hat, a crash cymbal, and a cowbell. Walli handled them as gently as if they were eggs: they were American Slingerland drums that Joe had won from a GI in a card game back in the 1940s, and he would never get another set like it.

The pay was lousy, but as part of the deal Walli and Karolin performed for twenty minutes in the interval, as the Bobbsey Twins, and, most importantly, they got musicians' union cards, even though Walli at seventeen was too young.

Walli's English grandmother, Maud, had chortled when he told her the name of the duo. "Are you Flossie and Freddie, or Bert and Nan?" she had said. "Oh, Walli, you do make me laugh." It turned out that the Bobbsey Twins were not a bit like the Everly Brothers. There was a series of old-fashioned books for children about the impossibly perfect

Bobbsey family with two sets of beautiful rosy-cheeked twins. Walli and Karolin had decided to stick with the name anyway.

Joe was an idiot but Walli was learning from him just the same. Joe made sure the band was too loud to be ignored, though not so loud that people complained they could not converse. He gave each band member the spotlight in one number, keeping the musicians happy. He always opened with a well-known number, and he liked to finish while the dance floor was packed, leaving people wanting more.

Walli did not know what the future held, but he knew what he wanted. He was going to be a musician, the leader of a band, popular and famous; and he was going to play rock music. Perhaps the Communists would soften their attitude to American culture, and permit pop groups. Maybe Communism would fall. Best of all, Walli might find a way to go to America.

All that was a long way off. Right now his ambition was that the Bobbsey Twins would become popular enough for him and Karolin to become full-time professionals.

Joe's musicians drifted in while Walli was setting up, and they began to play at seven sharp.

Communists were ambivalent about jazz. They were suspicious of everything American, but the Nazis had banned jazz, which made jazz anti-Fascist. In the end they permitted it because so many people liked it. Joe's band had no vocalist, so there was no problem about songs that celebrated bourgeois values, such as "Top Hat, White Tie and Tails" or "Puttin' on the Ritz."

Karolin arrived a minute later, and her presence lit up the shabby backstage area with a glow like candlelight, bathing the gray walls in a rosy wash and making the grimy corners vanish into shadow.

For the first time, there was something in Walli's life that mattered as much as music. He had had girlfriends before; in fact they came without much effort by him. And they had usually been willing to have sex with him, so intercourse for Walli was not the unattainable dream it was for most of his schoolmates. But he had experienced nothing like the overwhelming love and passion he felt for Karolin. "We think the same way—we even say the same thing sometimes," he had told Grandmother Maud, and she had said: "Ah—soul mates." Walli and

Karolin could talk about sex as easily as they talked about music, confiding what they liked and did not like—though there was not much that Karolin did not like.

The band would play for another hour. Walli and Karolin got into the back of Joe's van and lay down. It became a boudoir, dimly lit by the yellow glow from the car park lights; Joe's cushions were a velvet divan, and Karolin a languorous odalisque, opening her robes to offer her body to Walli's kisses.

They had tried sex using a condom, but neither of them liked it. Sometimes they had intercourse without a condom, and Walli withdrew at the last moment, but Karolin said that was not really safe. Tonight they used their hands. After Walli had come into Karolin's handkerchief, she showed him how to please her, guiding his fingers, and she came with a little "Oh!" that sounded more like surprise than anything else.

"Sex with the one you love is the second-best thing in the world," Maud had said to Walli. Somehow a grandmother could say things that a mother could not.

"If that's second best, what's first?" he had asked.

"Seeing your children happy."

"I thought you were going to say: 'Playing ragtime,'" Walli had said, and she had laughed.

As always, Walli and Karolin went from sex to music with no break, as if it were all one. Walli taught Karolin a new song. He had a radio in his bedroom and he listened to American stations broadcasting from West Berlin, so he knew all the popular numbers. This one was called "If I Had a Hammer," and it was a hit for an American trio called Peter, Paul and Mary. It had a compelling beat, and he felt sure the audience would love it.

Karolin was doubtful about the lyrics, which mentioned justice and freedom.

Walli said: "In America, Pete Seeger is called a Communist for writing it! I think it annoys bullies everywhere."

"How does that help us?" Karolin said with remorseless practicality.

"No one here will understand the English words."

"All right," she said, giving in reluctantly. Then she said: "I have to stop doing this, anyway."

Walli was shocked. "What do you mean?"

She looked somber. She had saved some piece of bad news so that it would not spoil the sex, Walli realized. Karolin had impressive self-control. She said: "My father has been questioned by the Stasi."

Karolin's father was a supervisor at a bus station. He seemed uninterested in politics, and was an unlikely suspect for the secret police. "Why?" said Walli. "What did they question him about?"

"You," she said.

"Oh, shit."

"They told him you were ideologically unreliable."

"What was the name of the man who interrogated him? Was it Hans Hoffmann?"

"I don't know."

"I bet it was." If Hans was not the actual interviewer, he was surely responsible, Walli thought.

"They said Dad would lose his job if I continued to be seen in public singing with you."

"Do you have to do what your parents say? You're nineteen."

"I'm still living with them, though." Karolin had left school but was at a technical college studying to be a bookkeeper. "Anyway, I can't be responsible for my father getting the sack."

Walli was devastated. This blighted his dream. "But . . . we're so good! People love us!"

"I know. I'm so sorry."

"How do the Stasi even know about your singing?"

"Do you remember the man in the cap who followed us the night we met? I see him occasionally."

"Do you think he follows me all the time?"

"Not all the time," she said in a lowered voice. People always spoke quietly when mentioning the Stasi, even if there was no one to overhear. "Maybe just now and again. But I suppose that sooner or later he noticed me with you, and started tailing me, and found out my name and address, and that's how they got to my father."

Walli refused to accept what was happening. "We'll go to the West," he said.

Karolin looked agonized. "Oh, God, I wish we could."

"People escape all the time."

Walli and Karolin had talked of this often. Escapers swam canals, obtained false papers, hid themselves in truckloads of produce, or just sprinted across. Sometimes their stories were told on West German radio stations; more often there were all kinds of rumors.

Karolin said: "People die all the time, too."

At the same time as Walli was eager to leave, he was tortured by the possibility that Karolin would be hurt, or worse, in the escape. The border guards shot to kill. And the Wall changed constantly, becoming more and more formidable. Originally it had been a barbed-wire fence. Now in many places it was a double barrier of concrete slabs with a broad floodlit middle patrolled by dogs and guarded by watchtowers. It even had tank traps. No one had ever tried to cross in a tank, though border guards fled frequently.

Walli said: "My sister escaped."

"But her husband was crippled."

Rebecca and Bernd were married now and living in Hamburg. Both were schoolteachers, even though Bernd was in a wheelchair: he had not yet recovered completely from his fall. Their letters to Carla and Werner were always delayed by the censors, but they got through in the end.

"I don't want to live here, anyway," said Walli derisively. "I'll spend my life singing songs that are approved by the Communist Party, and you'll be a bookkeeper so that your father can keep his job in the bus garage. I'd rather be dead."

"Communism can't last forever."

"Why not? It's lasted since 1917. And what if we have children?"

"What makes you say that?" she asked sharply.

"If we stay here, we're not just condemning ourselves to a life in prison. Our children will suffer, too."

"Do you want to have children?"

Walli had not intended to raise this subject. He did not know whether he wanted children. First he needed to save his own life. "Well, I don't want to have children in East Germany," he said. He had not thought of this before, but now that he had said it he felt sure of it.

Karolin looked serious. "Then maybe we should escape," she said. "But how?"

Walli had toyed with many ideas, but he had a favorite. "Have you seen the checkpoint near my school?"

"I've never really looked."

"It's used by vehicles carrying goods to West Berlin—meat, vegetables, cheese, and so on." The East German government did not like feeding West Berlin, but they needed the money, according to Walli's father.

"And . . . ?"

Walli had worked out some details in his fantasy. "The barrier is a single length of timber about six inches thick. You show your papers, then the guard swings up the barrier to let your truck in. They inspect your load in the compound, then there's another similar barrier to the exit."

"Yes, I recall the setup."

Walli made his voice more confident than he felt. "It strikes me that a driver who had trouble with the guards could probably crash through both barriers."

"Oh, Walli, it's so dangerous!"

"There's no safe way to get out."

"You don't have a truck."

"We'll steal this van." After the show, Joe always sat in the bar while Walli packed up the drum kit and loaded the van. By the time Walli was finished, Joe was more or less drunk, and Walli would drive him home. Walli did not have a license, but Joe did not know that, and he had never been sober enough to notice Walli's erratic driving. After helping Joe into his apartment, Walli had to stash the kit in the hallway, then garage the van. "I could take it tonight, after the show," he said to Karolin. "We could go across first thing in the morning, as soon as the checkpoint opens."

"If I'm late home my father will come looking for me."

"Go home, go to bed, and get up early. I'll wait for you outside the school. Joe won't surface before midday. By the time he realizes his van is missing, we'll be strolling in the Tiergarten."

Karolin kissed him. "I'm scared, but I love you," she said.

Walli heard the band playing "Avalon," the closing number of the first set, and he realized they had been talking a long time. "We're on in five minutes," he said. "Let's go."

The band left the stage and the dance floor emptied. It took Walli less than a minute to set up the microphones and the small guitar amplifier. The audience returned to their drinks and their conversations. Then the Bobbsey Twins came on. Some customers took no notice; others looked on with interest: Walli and Karolin made an attractive couple, and that was always a good start.

As usual they began with "Noch Einen Tanz," which got people's attention and made them laugh. They sang some folk songs, two Everly Brothers numbers, and "Hey Paula," a hit for an American duo very like themselves called Paul and Paula. Walli had a high voice, and sang harmonies over Karolin's tune. He had developed a fingerpicking guitar style that was rhythmic as well as melodic.

They finished with "If I Had a Hammer." Most of the audience loved it, clapping along with the beat, though there were a few stern faces at the words *justice* and *freedom* in the refrain.

They came off to loud applause. Walli's head swam with the euphoria of knowing he had enchanted an audience. It was better than being drunk. He was flying.

Passing them in the wings, Joe said: "If you ever sing that song again, you're fired."

Walli's elation was punctured. He felt as if he had been slapped. Furious, he said to Karolin: "That settles it. I'm leaving tonight."

They returned to the van. Often they made love a second time, but tonight both were too tense. Walli was boiling with rage. "What's the earliest you could meet me in the morning?" he said to Karolin.

She thought for a minute. "I'll go home now and tell them I need an early night, because I have to get up early in the morning . . . for a rehearsal of my college's May Day parade."

"Good," he said.

"I could be with you by seven without arousing suspicion."

"That's perfect. There won't be much traffic through the checkpoint at that hour on a Sunday morning."

"Kiss me again, then."

They kissed long and hard. Walli touched her breasts, then pulled away. "Next time we make love, we'll be free," he said.

They got out of the van. "Seven o'clock," Walli repeated.

Karolin waved and disappeared into the night.

Walli got through the rest of the evening on a wave of hope mingled with rage. He was constantly tempted to show his scorn for Joe, but also fearful that for some reason he would not be able to steal the van. However, if he showed his feelings Joe did not notice, and by one o'clock Walli was parked in the street outside his school. He was out of sight of the checkpoint, around two corners, which was good: he did not want the guards to see him and get suspicious.

He lay on the cushions in the back of the van with his eyes shut, but it was too cold to sleep. He spent much of the night thinking about his family. His father had been bad-tempered for more than a year. Father no longer owned the television factory in West Berlin: he had made it over to Rebecca, so that the East German government could not find a way to take it from the family. He was still trying to run the place, even though he could not go there. He had hired a Danish accountant to be his liaison. As a foreigner, Enok Andersen was able to cross between West and East Berlin once a week for a meeting with Father. It was no way to run a business, and it drove Father crazy.

Walli did not think his mother was happy either. She was mostly absorbed in her work, as head of nursing at a large hospital. She hated the Communists as much as the Nazis, but there was nothing she could do about it.

Grandmother Maud was as stoical as ever. Germany had been fighting Russia for as long as she could remember, she said, and she only hoped to live long enough to see who won. She thought that playing the guitar was an achievement, unlike Walli's parents, who saw it as a waste of time.

The one Walli would miss most was Lili. She was fourteen now, and he liked her a lot better than he had when they were kids and she was a pest.

He tried not to think too much about the dangers ahead of him. He did not want to lose his nerve. In the small hours, when he felt his determination weakening, he thought of Joe's words: "If you ever sing that song again, you're fired." The recollection stoked Walli's rage. If he stayed in East Germany he would spend his life being told what to play by numbskulls such as Joe. It would be no life at all; it would be hell; it would be impossible. He had to leave, whatever else happened. The alternative was unthinkable.

That thought gave him courage.

At six o'clock he left the van and went in search of a hot drink and something to eat. However, there was nothing open, even at the railway stations, and he returned to the van hungrier than ever. The walking had warmed him, though.

Daylight took the chill off. He sat in the driving seat, so that he could look out for Karolin. She would find him without difficulty: she knew the vehicle, and anyway there were no other vans parked near the school.

Over and over again he visualized what he was about to do. He would take the guards by surprise. It would be several seconds before they realized what was happening. Then, presumably, they would shoot.

With any luck, by that time the guards would be behind Walli and Karolin, shooting at the back of the van. How dangerous was that? Walli really had no idea. He had never been shot at. He had never seen anyone fire a gun, for any reason. He did not know whether bullets could pass through cars or not. He recalled his father saying that hitting someone with a firearm was not as easy as it seemed in the movies. That was the extent of Walli's knowledge.

He suffered an anxious moment when a police car drove past. The cop in the passenger seat gave Walli a hard stare. If they asked to see his driving license he was done for. He cursed his foolishness in not staying in the back of the van. But they drove on without stopping.

In Walli's imagination, both he and Karolin would be killed by the guards if something went wrong. But now for the first time it occurred to him that one might be hit while the other survived. That was a terrible prospect. They often said "I love you" to one another, but Walli was feeling it in a different way. To love someone, he now realized, was to have something so precious that you could not bear to lose it.

An even worse possibility struck him: one of them might be crippled, like Bernd. How would Walli feel if Karolin were paralyzed and it was his fault? He would want to commit suicide.

At last his watch said seven o'clock. He wondered if any of these thoughts had occurred to her. Almost certainly they had. What else would she have been thinking of in the night? Would she come walking along the street, sit next to him in the van, and quietly tell him she was not willing to take the risk? What would he do then? He could not give up, and live out his life behind the Iron Curtain. But could he leave her and go alone?

He was disappointed when seven fifteen came around and she had not appeared.

By seven thirty he was worried, and by eight he was in despair.

What had gone wrong?

Had Karolin's father discovered there was no rehearsal tomorrow for the college's May Day parade? Why would he trouble to check a thing like that?

Was Karolin ill? She had been perfectly well last night.

Had she changed her mind?

She might have.

She had never been as sure as he of the need to escape. She voiced doubts and foresaw difficulties. When they had talked about it last night, he had suspected she was against the whole idea until he mentioned raising their children in East Germany. That was when she had come round to Walli's way of thinking. But now it looked as if she had had second thoughts.

He decided to give her until nine o'clock.

Then what? Go alone?

He no longer felt hungry. The tension in his guts was such that he knew he could not eat. He was thirsty, though. He would almost have given his guitar for hot coffee with cream in it.

At eight forty-five, a slim girl with long fair hair came walking along the street toward the van, and Walli's heart beat faster; but as she came closer he saw that she had dark eyebrows and a small mouth and an overbite. It was not Karolin.

At nine Karolin still had not appeared.

Go or stay?

If you ever sing that song again, you're fired.

Walli started the engine.

He moved forward slowly and turned the first corner.

He would need to be traveling fast to bust through the timber barrier. On the other hand, if he approached at top speed the guards would be forewarned. He needed to begin at normal speed, slow down a little to lull them, then stamp on the gas.

Unfortunately, not much happened when you stamped on the gas in this vehicle. The Framo had a 900 cc three-cylinder two-stroke engine. Walli thought maybe he should have kept the drums on board, so that their weight would give the van more impetus when it hit.

He turned a second corner, and the checkpoint stood ahead of him. About three hundred yards away, the road was blocked by a barrier that lifted to give access to a compound with a guardhouse. The compound was about fifty yards long. Another wooden barrier blocked the exit. Beyond that, the road was bare for thirty yards, then turned into a regular West Berlin street.

West Berlin, he thought; then West Germany; then America.

There was a truck waiting at the near barrier. Walli hurriedly stopped the van. If he got into a queue he was in trouble, for he would have little opportunity to build up speed.

As the truck passed through the barrier, a second vehicle pulled up. Walli waited. But he saw a guard staring his way, and realized his presence had been noted. In an attempt to cover up, he got out of the van, went around to the back, and opened the rear door. From there he could see through the windscreen. As soon as the second vehicle passed into the compound, he returned to the driving seat.

He put the van in gear and hesitated. It was not too late to turn around. He could take the van back to Joe's garage, leave it there, and walk home, his only problem to explain to his parents why he had been out all night.

Life or death.

If he waited now, another truck might come along and block his way; and then a guard might stroll along the street and ask him what the hell he thought he was doing, loitering within sight of a checkpoint; and his opportunity would be lost.

If you ever sing that song again . . .

He let out the clutch and moved forward.

He reached thirty miles an hour, then slowed down a little. The guard standing by the barrier was watching him. He touched the brake. The guard looked away.

Walli floored the accelerator pedal.

The guard heard the change in the engine note and turned around, wearing a slight frown of puzzlement. As the van picked up speed, he waved at Walli with a *Slow down* gesture. Pointlessly, Walli pressed harder on the pedal. The Framo gained pace lumberingly, like an elephant. Walli saw the guard's expression change in slow motion, from curiosity to disapproval to alarm. Then the man panicked. Even though he was not in the way of the van, he took three steps backward and flattened himself against a wall.

Walli let out a yell that was half war cry, half sheer terror.

The van hit the barrier with a crash of deforming metal. The impact threw Walli forward onto the steering wheel, which struck his ribs painfully. He had not anticipated that. Suddenly it was hard to catch his breath. But the timber bar fractured with a crack like a gunshot, and the van moved on, its pace only a little reduced by the impact.

Walli changed into first gear and accelerated. The two vehicles ahead of him had both pulled over for inspection, leaving a clear path to the exit. The other people in the compound, three guards and two drivers, turned to see what the noise was. The Framo picked up speed.

Walli experienced a rush of confidence. He was going to make it! Then a guard with more than average presence of mind knelt down and aimed his submachine gun.

He was just to one side of Walli's route to the exit. In a flash Walli realized he would pass the guard at point-blank range. He was sure to be shot and killed.

Without thinking, he swung the wheel and drove straight at the guard.

The guard fired a burst. The windscreen shattered, but to Walli's astonishment he was not hit. Then he was almost on top of the man. He was suddenly struck by the horror of driving a vehicle over a living human body, and he swung the wheel again to avoid the guard. But he was too late, and the front of the van hit the man with a sickening thump, knocking him down. Walli cried: "No!" The vehicle lurched as its front offside wheel rolled over the guard. "Oh, Christ!" Walli wailed. He had never wanted to hurt anyone.

The van slowed as Walli yielded to despair. He wanted to jump out and see if the guard was alive, and if so help him. Then gunfire broke out again, and he realized they were going to kill him now if they could. Behind him, he heard bullets hit the metal of the van.

He pressed the pedal down and swung the wheel again, trying to get back on track. He had lost momentum. He managed to steer toward the exit barrier. He did not know whether he was going fast enough to break it. Resisting the impulse to change gear, he let the engine shriek in first.

He felt a sudden pain as if someone had stuck a knife in his leg. He shouted out in shock and agony. His foot came up off the pedal, and the van immediately slowed. He had to force himself to press down again, despite how it hurt. He screamed in pain. He felt hot blood run down his calf into his shoe.

The van hit the second timber barrier. Again Walli was thrown forward; again the wheel bruised his ribs; again the wooden bar splintered and fell away; and again the van kept going.

The van crossed a patch of concrete. The gunfire ceased. Walli saw a street with shops, advertisements for Lucky Strike and Coca-Cola, shiny new cars, and, best of all, a small group of startled soldiers in American uniforms. He took his foot off the accelerator and tried to brake. Suddenly the pain was too much. His leg felt paralyzed, and he was unable to press down on the brake pedal. In desperation he steered the van into a lamppost.

The soldiers rushed to the van and one threw open the door. "Well done, kid, you made it!" he said.

I made it, Walli thought. I'm alive, and I'm free. But without Karolin.

"Hell of a ride," the soldier said admiringly. He was not much older than Walli.

As Walli relaxed, the pain became overwhelming. "My leg hurts," he managed to say.

The soldier looked down. "Jeez, look at all that blood." He turned and spoke to someone behind him. "Hey, call an ambulance."

Walli passed out.

. . .

Walli got his bullet wound stitched up and was discharged from hospital the next day with bruised ribs and a bandage around the calf of his right leg.

According to the newspapers, the border guard he had run over had died.

Limping, Walli went to the Franck television factory and told his story to the Danish accountant, Enok Andersen, who undertook to tell Werner and Carla that he was all right. Enok gave Walli some West German deutschmarks, and Walli got a room at the YMCA.

His ribs hurt every time he turned over in bed, and he slept badly.

Next day he retrieved his guitar from the van. The instrument had survived the crossing without damage, unlike Walli. However, the vehicle was a write-off.

Walli applied for a West German passport, granted automatically to escapers.

He was free. He had escaped from the suffocating puritanism of Walter Ulbricht's Communist regime. He could play and sing anything he chose.

And he was miserable.

He missed Karolin. He felt as if he had lost a hand. He kept thinking of things he would tell her or ask her tonight or tomorrow, then suddenly remember that he could not speak to her; and the dreadful recollection hit him every time like a kick in the stomach. He would see a pretty girl on the street, and think about what he and Karolin might do next Saturday in the back of Joe's van; then he would realize that there would be no more evenings in the back of the van, and he would feel stricken by grief. He walked past clubs where he might get a gig, then wondered if he could bear to perform without Karolin at his side.

He spoke on the phone to his sister Rebecca, who urged him to come and live in Hamburg with her and her husband; but he thanked her and declined. He could not bring himself to leave Berlin while Karolin was still in the East.

Missing her grievously, he took his guitar a week later to the Minnesänger folk club, where he had met her two years ago. A sign outside said it was not open on Mondays, but the door stood ajar, so he went in anyway.

Sitting at the bar, adding up figures in a ledger, was the club's young compere and owner, Danni Hausmann. "I remember you," said Danni. "The Bobbsey Twins. You were great. Why did you never come back?"

"The Vopos smashed up my guitar," Walli explained.

"But now you have another, I see."

Walli nodded. "But I've lost Karolin."

"That was careless. She was a pretty girl."

"We both lived in the East. She's still there, but I escaped."

"How?"

"I drove a van through the barrier."

"That was you? I read about it in the newspapers. Hey, man, cool! But why didn't you bring the chick?"

"She didn't show up at the rendezvous."

"Too bad. Want a drink?" Danni went behind the bar.

"Thanks. I'd like to go back for her, but I'm wanted for murder there now."

Danni pumped two glasses of draft beer. "The Communists made a huge fuss about that. They're calling you a violent criminal."

They had also demanded Walli's extradition. The government of West Germany had refused, saying that the guard had shot at a German citizen who merely wanted to go from one Berlin street to the next, and responsibility for his death lay with the unelected East German regime that illegally imprisoned its population.

In his head Walli did not believe that he had done wrong, but in his heart he could not get used to the idea that he had killed a man.

He said to Danni: "If I crossed the border they would arrest me."

"Man, you're fucked."

"And I still don't know why Karolin didn't come."

"And you can't go back to ask her. Unless . . ."

Walli pricked up his ears. "Unless what?"

Danni hesitated. "Nothing."

Walli put down his glass. He was not going to let a thing like that pass him by. "Come on, man—what?"

Danni said thoughtfully: "Of all the people in Berlin, I guess the one I could trust is a guy who killed an East German border guard."

This was maddening. "What are you talking about?"

Danni made up his mind. "Oh, just something I heard."

If it were just something he had heard, he would not be so secretive about it, Walli thought. "What did you hear?"

"There might be a way to go back without passing through a checkpoint."

"How?"

"I can't tell you."

Walli was angered. Danni seemed to be toying with him. "Then why the fuck did you say it?"

"Take it easy, okay? I can't tell you, but I could take you to see someone."

"When?"

Danni thought for a minute, then answered the question with a question. "Are you willing to go back today? Like, now?"

Walli was scared, but he did not hesitate. "Yes. But why the rush?"

"So that you have no chance to tell anyone. They're not exactly professional about security, but they're not completely stupid either."

He was talking about an organized group. It sounded promising. Walli got off his stool. "Can I leave my guitar here?"

"I'll put it in the store." Danni picked up the instrument in its case and locked it in a cupboard with several other instruments and some amplification gear. "Let's go," he said.

The club was just off the Ku'damm. Danni closed up and they walked to the nearest subway station. Danni noticed his limp. "You were shot in the leg, according to the newspapers."

"Yeah. Hurts like fuck."

"I guess I can trust you. A Stasi undercover agent wouldn't go so far as to wound himself."

Walli did not know whether to be thrilled or terrified. Might he really be able to return to East Berlin—today? It seemed too much to hope for. Yet it also filled him with dread. East Germany still had the death penalty. If he were caught, he would probably be executed by guillotine.

Walli and Danni took the subway across the city. It occurred to Walli that this could be a trap. The Stasi probably had agents in West Berlin, and the owner of the Minnesänger could be one. Would they go to so much trouble to catch Walli? It was a stretch; but, knowing how vengeful Hans Hoffmann was, Walli thought it was possible.

He studied Danni covertly as they rode the underground train. Could *he* be a Stasi agent? It was hard to imagine. Danni was about twenty-five, and had longish hair combed forward in the latest style. He wore elastic-sided boots with pointed toes. He had a successful club. He was too cool to be a cop.

On the other hand, he was perfectly placed to spy on West Berlin's young anti-Communists. Most of them probably came to his club. He must know just about every student leader in West Berlin. Did the Stasi care about what such young people were doing?

Of course they did. They were obsessed, like medieval priests hunting witches.

Yet Walli could not pass up this opportunity, if it meant he might speak to Karolin just one more time.

He vowed to be alert.

The sun was going down when they came out of the subway in the district called Wedding. They walked south, and Walli quickly realized they were heading for Bernauer Strasse, where Rebecca had escaped.

The street had changed, he saw in the fading daylight. On the south side, in place of the barbed-wire fence, there was now a concrete wall; and the buildings on the Communist side were in the process of being demolished. On the free side, where Walli and Danni were, the street seemed blighted. The ground-floor shops in the apartment buildings looked run-down. Walli guessed that nobody wanted to live so close to the Wall, repellent to the eye and to the heart.

Danni led him to the back of a building and they went in by the rear entrance of a disused shop. It seemed to have been a grocery store, for on the walls were enamel advertisements for canned salmon and cocoa. However, the shop and the rooms around it were full of loose earth, piled high, leaving only a narrow passage through; and Walli began to guess what was going on here.

Danni opened a door and went down a concrete stair lit by an electric bulb. Walli followed. Danni called out a phrase that might have been code: "Submariners coming in!" At the foot of the stairs was a large cellar, undoubtedly used by the grocer for storage. Now there was a hole a yard square in the floor, and a surprisingly professional-looking hoist over it.

They had dug a tunnel.

"How long has this been here?" Walli asked. If his sister had known about it last year she might have escaped this way, and avoided Bernd's crippling injury.

"Too long," said Danni. "We finished it a week ago."

"Oh." That was too late to have been any use to Rebecca.

Danni added: "We only use it in twilight. In daytime we would be too visible, and at night we would have to use flashlights, which might call attention to us. All the same, the risk of discovery increases every time we bring people across."

A young man in jeans came up a ladder out of the hole: presumably one of the student tunnelers. He looked hard at Walli, then said: "Who's this, Danni?"

"I vouch for him, Becker," said Danni. "I've known him since before the Wall went up."

"Why is he here?" Becker was hostile and suspicious.

"To go across."

"He wants to go to the East?"

Walli explained: "I escaped last week, but I need to go back for my girlfriend. I can't cross by a regular checkpoint because I killed a border guard, so I'm wanted for murder."

"You're that guy?" Becker looked at him again. "Yeah, I recognize you from the photograph in the paper." His attitude changed. "You can go, but you haven't got much time." He looked at his watch. "They'll start coming through from the East in ten minutes exactly. There's hardly room to pass someone in the tunnel, and I don't want you to cause a traffic jam and slow down the escapers."

Walli was scared, but he did not want to lose this chance. "I'll go right away," he said, concealing his fear.

"Okay, go."

He shook Danni's hand. "Thanks," he said. "I'll be back for my guitar."

"Good luck with your girl."

Walli scrambled down the ladder.

The shaft was three yards deep. At the bottom was the entrance to a tunnel about a yard square. It was neatly built, Walli saw immediately. There was a plank floor, and the roof was propped at intervals. He dropped to his hands and knees and began to crawl.

After a few seconds he realized there were no lights. He kept crawling as it became completely dark. He felt viscerally scared. He knew that the real danger would come when he emerged into East Germany at the other end of the tunnel, but his animal instincts told him to be frightened now, as he crawled forward unable to see an inch in front of his face.

To distract himself, he tried to picture the streetscape above. He was passing beneath the road, then the Wall, then the half-demolished houses on the Communist side; but he did not know how much farther the tunnel went, nor where it terminated.

He was breathing hard with the effort, his hands and knees were sore from crawling on planks, and the bullet wound in his calf was burning with pain; but all he could do was grit his teeth and go on.

The tunnel could not be infinite. It must end eventually. He just had to keep crawling. The sense that he was lost in endless darkness was just childish panic. He had to stay calm. He could do that. Karolin was at the end of this tunnel—not literally, but all the same the thought of her sexy, wide-mouthed smile gave him strength to combat his fear.

Was there a glimmer ahead, or did he imagine it? For a long time it remained too faint to be sure of; but at last it strengthened, and a couple of seconds later he emerged into electric light.

There was another shaft above his head. He went up a ladder and found himself in another basement. Three people stood staring at him. Two had luggage: he guessed they were escapers. The third, presumably one of the student organizers, looked at him and said: "I don't know you!"

"Danni brought me," he said. "I'm Walli Franck."

"Too many people know about this tunnel!" the man said. His voice was shrill with anxiety.

Well, of course, Walli thought; everyone who escapes through it obviously knows the secret. He understood why Danni had said that the danger increased every time it was used. He wondered whether it would still be open when he wanted to return. The thought of being trapped in East Germany again almost made him want to turn around and crawl all the way back.

The man turned to the two with bags. "Go," he said. They went down the shaft. Returning his attention to Walli, he pointed to a flight of stone steps. "Go to the top and wait," he said. "When the coast is clear, Cristina will open the hatch from the outside. You get out. Then you're on your own."

"Thanks." Walli went up the steps until his head came up against an iron trapdoor in the ceiling. This had originally been used for deliveries of some kind, he guessed. He crouched on the steps and forced himself to be patient. Lucky for him there was someone keeping watch on the outside, otherwise he might be seen leaving.

After a couple of minutes, the hatch opened. In the evening light, Walli saw a young woman in a gray head scarf. He scrambled out, and two more people with bags hurried down the steps. The young woman called Cristina closed the hatch. She had a pistol stuffed into her belt, he saw with surprise.

Walli looked around. He was in a small walled yard at the back of a derelict apartment building. Cristina pointed to a wooden door in the wall. "Go that way," she said.

"Thank you."

"Get lost," she said. "Fast."

They were all too stressed to be polite.

Walli opened the door and passed through to the street. To his left, a few yards away, was the Wall. He turned right and started walking.

At first he looked around constantly, expecting to see a police car screech up. Then he tried to act normally and saunter along the pavement as he had used to. No matter how he tried, he could not lose the limp: his leg hurt too much.

His first impulse was to go straight to Karolin's house. But he could not knock on her door. Her father would call the police.

He had not thought this out.

Perhaps it would be better if he met her leaving class tomorrow afternoon. There was nothing suspicious about a boy waiting outside the college for his girlfriend, and Walli had done it often. Somehow he would have to make sure none of her classmates saw his face. He was agonizingly impatient to see her, but he would be mad not to take precautions.

What would he do in the meantime?

The tunnel had come out in Strelitzer Strasse, which ran southward into the old city center, Berlin-Mitte, where his family lived. He was only a few blocks from his parents' house. He could go home.

They might even be pleased to see him.

As he approached their street, he wondered whether the house might be under surveillance. If that was so, he could not go there. He thought again about changing his appearance, but he had nothing with which to disguise himself: when he left his room at the YMCA this morning he had not dreamed he might be back in East Berlin by nightfall. At his family home there would be hats and scarves and other useful items of attire—but first he had to get there safely.

Happily it was now dark. He walked along his parents' street on the opposite side, scanning for people who might be Stasi snoops. He saw no loiterers, no one sitting in a parked car, no one stationed at a window. All the same he went to the end of the street and walked around the block. Coming back, he ducked down the alley that led to the backyards. He opened a gate, crossed his parents' yard, and came to the kitchen entrance. It was nine thirty: his father had not yet locked up the house. Walli opened the door and stepped inside.

The light was on but the kitchen was empty. Dinner was long over and his family would be upstairs in the drawing room. Walli crossed the hall and went up. The drawing room door was open, and he stepped inside. His mother, father, sister, and grandmother were watching television. Walli said: "Hello, everyone."

Lili screamed.

Grandmother Maud said in English: "Oh, my goodness!"

Carla went pale and her hands flew to her mouth.

Werner stood up. "My boy," he said. In two strides he crossed the room and folded Walli into his arms. "My boy, thank God."

In Walli's heart a dam of pent-up feeling burst, and he wept.

His mother hugged him next, tears flowing freely. Then Lili, then Grandmother Maud. Walli wiped his eyes with the sleeve of his denim shirt, but more kept coming. His overwhelming emotion had taken him by surprise. He had thought himself hardened, at the age of seventeen, to being alone and separated from his family. Now he saw that he had only been postponing the tears.

At last they all calmed down and dried their eyes. Mother rebandaged

Walli's bullet wound, which had bled while he was in the tunnel. Then she made coffee and brought some cake, and Walli realized he was starving. When he had eaten and drunk his fill, he told them the story. Then, when they had asked all their questions, he went to bed.

· · ·

Next day at half past three he was leaning against a wall across the street from Karolin's college, wearing a cap and sunglasses. He was early: the girls came out at four.

The sun was shining optimistically on Berlin. The city was a mixture of grand old buildings, hard-edged modern concrete, and slowly disappearing vacant lots where bombs had fallen during the war.

Walli's heart was full of longing. In a few minutes he would see Karolin's face, framed by long curtains of fair hair, the wide mouth smiling. He would kiss her hello, and feel the soft roundness of her lips on his. Perhaps they would lie down together, before the night was over, and make love.

He was also consumed by curiosity. Why had she not turned up at their rendezvous, nine days ago, to escape with him? He was almost certain something had happened to spoil their plan: her father had somehow divined what was afoot and locked her in her room, or a similar stroke of bad luck. But he also suffered a fear, faint but not negligible, that she had changed her mind about coming with him. He could hardly contemplate the possible reason why. Did she still love him? People could change. In the East German media he had been portrayed as a heartless killer. Had that affected her?

Soon he would know.

His parents were devastated by what had happened, but they had not tried to make him change his plans. They had not wanted him to leave home, feeling that he was much too young, but they knew that now he could not stay in the East without being jailed. They had asked what he was going to do in the West—study, or work—and he had said he could not make any decisions until he had talked to Karolin. They had accepted that, and for the first time his father had not tried to tell him what to do. They were treating him like a grown-up. He had been demanding this for years, but now that it had happened he felt lost and scared.

People began to come out of the college.

The building was an old bank converted into classrooms. The students were all girls in their late teens, learning to be typists and secretaries and bookkeepers and travel agents. They carried bags and books and folders. They wore spring sweater-and-skirt combinations, a bit old-fashioned: trainee secretaries were expected to dress modestly.

At last Karolin emerged, wearing a green twinset, carrying her books in an old leather briefcase.

She looked different, Walli thought; a bit more round-faced. She could not have put on much weight in a week, could she? She was with two other girls, chatting, though she did not laugh when they did. Walli feared that if he spoke to her now the other girls would notice him. That would be dangerous: even though he was disguised, they might know that the notorious murderer and escaper Walli Franck had been Karolin's boyfriend, and suspect that this boy in dark glasses was he.

He felt panic rise: surely his purpose could not be so easily frustrated, now at the last moment, after all he had been through? Then the two friends turned left and waved good-bye, and Karolin crossed the street on her own.

As she came near, Walli took off his sunglasses and said: "Hello, baby."

She looked, recognized him, and gave a squeal of shock, stopping in her tracks. He saw astonishment and fear on her face, and something else—could it be guilt? Then she ran to him, dropped her briefcase, and threw herself into his arms. They hugged and kissed, and Walli was swamped by relief and happiness. His first question was answered: she still loved him.

After a minute he realized passersby were staring—some smiling, others looking with disapproval. He put his sunglasses back on. "Let's go," he said. "I don't want people to recognize me." He picked up her dropped briefcase.

They walked away from the college, holding hands. "How did you get back?" she said. "Is it safe? What are you going to do? Does anyone know you're here?"

"We've got so much to talk about," he said. "We need a place to sit down and be private." Across the street he spotted a church. Perhaps it would be open for people seeking spiritual calm.

He led Karolin to the door. "You're limping," she said.

"That border guard shot me in the leg."

"Does it hurt?"

"You bet it does."

The church door was unlocked, and they went in.

It was a plain Protestant hall, dimly lit, with rows of hard benches. At the far end a woman in a head scarf was dusting the lectern. Walli and Karolin sat in the back row and spoke in low voices.

"I love you," Walli said.

"I love you, too."

"What happened on Sunday morning? You were supposed to meet me."

"I got scared," she said.

This was not the answer he had been expecting, and he found it hard to understand. "I was scared, too," he said. "But we made each other a promise."

"I know."

He could see that she was in an agony of remorse; but there was something else. He did not want to torture her, but he had to know the truth. "I took a terrible risk," he said. "You shouldn't have backed out without a word."

"I'm sorry."

"I wouldn't have done it to you," he said. Then he added accusingly: "I love you too much."

She flinched as if he had struck her. But her answer was spirited. "I'm not a coward," she said.

"If you love me, how could you have let me down?"

"I'd give my life for you."

"If that was true, you would have come with me. How can you say it, now?"

"Because it's not just my life at risk."

"It's mine, too."

"And someone else's."

Walli was baffled. "Whose, for God's sake?"

"I'm talking about the life of our child."

"What?"

"We're going to have a baby. I'm pregnant, Walli."

Walli's mouth fell open. He could not speak. His world turned upside down in an instant. Karolin was pregnant. A baby was coming into their lives.

His child.

"Oh, my God," he said at last.

"I was so torn, Walli," she said in anguish. "You have to try to understand that. I wanted to go with you, but I couldn't put the baby in danger. I couldn't get in the van, knowing you were going to crash through the barrier. I wouldn't care if I got injured, but not the child." She was pleading with him. "Say you understand."

"I understand," he said. "I think."

"Thank you."

He took her hand. "All right, let's talk about what we're going to do."

"I know what I'm going to do," she said firmly. "I already love this baby. I'm not going to get rid of it."

She had been living with the knowledge for some weeks, he guessed, and she had thought long and hard. All the same he was taken aback by her strength of purpose. "You speak as if it's nothing to do with me," he said.

"This is my body!" she said fiercely. The cleaner looked round, and Karolin lowered her voice, though she continued to speak forcefully. "I will not be told what to do with my body by any man, you or my father!"

Walli guessed that her father had tried to persuade her to have an abortion. "I'm not your father," Walli said. "I'm not going to tell you what to do, and I don't want to talk you into an abortion."

"I'm sorry."

"But is this our baby, or just yours?"

She began to cry. "Ours," she said.

"Then shall we talk about what we're going to do—together?"

She squeezed his hand. "You're so grown-up," she said. "It's a good thing—you're going to be a father before you're eighteen."

That was a shocking thought. He pictured his own father, with his short haircut and his waistcoats. Now Walli would be required to play that role: commanding, authoritative, reliable, always able to provide for the family. He was not ready, no matter what Karolin said.

But he had to do it, anyway.

"When?" he said.

"November."

"Do you want to get married?"

She smiled through her tears. "Do you want to marry me?"

"More than anything in the world."

"Thank you." She hugged him.

The cleaner coughed reprovingly. Conversation was permitted, but physical contact was not.

Walli said: "You know I can't stay here in the East."

"Couldn't your father get a lawyer?" she said. "Or exert some political pressure? The government might issue a pardon, if all the circumstances were explained."

Karolin's family was not political. Walli's was, and he knew with total certainty that he was never going to receive a pardon for killing a border guard. "It's impossible," he said. "If I stay here they'll execute me for murder."

"So what can you do?"

"I have to go back to the West, and I have to stay there, unless Communism collapses, and I don't see that happening in my lifetime."

"No."

"You'll have to come with me to West Berlin."

"How?"

"We'll go out the way I came in. Some students have dug a tunnel under Bernauer Strasse." He looked at his watch. Time was passing quickly. "We need to be there around sundown."

She looked horrified. "Today?"

"Yes, right away."

"Oh, God."

"Wouldn't you prefer our child to grow up in a free country?"

She grimaced as if in pain at the conflict within her. "I'd prefer not to take terrible risks."

"So would I. But we have no choice."

She looked away from him, at the rows of pews and the assiduous cleaner, and at a plaque on the wall saying I AM THE WAY, THE TRUTH, AND THE LIFE. It was not helpful, Walli thought, but Karolin made up her mind. "Then let's go," she said, and she stood up.

They left the church. Walli headed north. Karolin was subdued, and he tried to cheer her up. "The Bobbsey Twins are having an adventure," he said. She smiled briefly.

Walli considered whether they might be under surveillance. He was pretty sure no one had seen him leave his parents' house this morning: he had gone out the back way and no one had followed him. But did Karolin have a tail? Perhaps there had been another man waiting outside her college for her to emerge, someone expert at making himself inconspicuous.

Walli started to look behind him every minute or so to check whether there might be one person always in view. He did not see anyone suspicious, but he succeeded in spooking Karolin. "What are you doing?" she said fearfully.

"Checking for a tail."

"You mean the man in the cap?"

"Maybe. Let's catch a bus." They were passing a stop, and Walli pulled Karolin to the end of the queue.

"Why?"

"To see if anyone gets on and off with us."

Unfortunately it was rush hour, and millions of Berliners were catching buses and trains home. By the time a bus came, there were several people in line behind Walli and Karolin. As they boarded he looked hard at each of them. There was a woman in a raincoat, a pretty girl, a man in blue overalls, a man in a suit with a trilby hat, and two teenagers.

They rode the bus three stops east, then got off. The woman in the raincoat and the man in overalls got off behind them. Walli headed west, going back the way they had come, figuring that anyone who followed them on such an illogical route must be suspicious.

But no one did.

"I'm pretty sure we're not being tailed," he said to Karolin.

"I'm so scared," she said.

The sun was going down. They needed to hurry. They turned north, heading for Wedding. Walli checked behind him again. He saw a middle-aged man in the brown canvas coat of a warehouseman, but no one he had noticed earlier. "I think we're all right," he said.

"I'm not going to see my family again, am I?" Karolin said.

"Not for a while," Walli replied. "Unless they escape, too."

"My father would never leave. He loves his buses."

"They have buses in the West."

"You don't know him."

Walli did know him, and Karolin was right. Her father was as different as could be from the clever, strong-willed Werner. Karolin's father had no political or religious ideas and cared nothing for freedom of speech. If he lived in a democracy he probably would not bother to vote. He liked his work and his family and his pub. His favorite food was bread. Communism gave him everything he needed. He would never escape to the West.

It was twilight when Walli and Karolin reached Strelitzer Strasse.

Karolin became increasingly jumpy as they walked along the street toward where it dead-ended at the Wall.

Ahead Walli noticed a young couple with a child. He wondered if they, too, were escaping. Yes, they were: they opened the door to the yard and disappeared.

Walli and Karolin reached the place, and Walli said: "We go in here."

Karolin said: "I want my mother with me when I have the baby."

"We're almost there!" Walli said. "Through this door there's a yard with a hatch. We go down the shaft and along the tunnel to freedom!"

"I'm not scared of escaping," she said. "I'm scared of giving birth."

"You'll be fine," Walli said desperately. "They have great hospitals in the West. You'll be surrounded by doctors and nurses."

"I want my mother," she said.

Over her shoulder Walli saw, four hundred yards away at the corner of the street, the man in the brown canvas coat talking to a policeman. "Shit!" he said. "We *were* followed." He looked at the door, then at Karolin. "It's now or never," he said. "I have no choice, I have to go. Are you coming with me, or not?"

She was crying. "I want to, but I can't," she said.

A car came around the corner, traveling fast. It stopped beside the policeman and the tail. A familiar figure jumped out of the car, a tall man with a stoop: Hans Hoffmann. He spoke to the man in the brown coat.

Walli said to Karolin: "Either follow me, or walk quickly away from here. There's going to be trouble." He stared at her. "I love you," he said. Then he dashed through the door.

Standing over the hatch was Cristina, still wearing the head scarf and the gun in her belt. When she saw Walli she threw the iron doors open. "You may need that gun," Walli said to her. "The police are coming."

He took one look back. The wooden door in the wall remained shut. Karolin had not followed him. Pain twisted in his stomach: it was the end.

He scrambled down the steps.

In the cellar the young couple with the child were standing with one of the students. "Hurry!" Walli yelled. "The police are coming!"

They went down the shaft: mother first, then child, then father. The child was slow on the ladder.

Cristina came down the steps and shut the iron trapdoor behind her with a clang. "How did the police get onto us?" she said.

"The Stasi were following my girlfriend."

"You stupid fool, you've betrayed us all."

"Then I'll go last," Walli said.

The male student went down the shaft, and Cristina made to follow.

"Give me your gun," Walli said.

She hesitated.

Walli said: "If I'm behind you, you won't be able to use it."

She handed it to him.

He took it gingerly. It looked exactly like the pistol his father had pulled from its hiding place in the kitchen, the day Rebecca and Bernd had escaped.

Cristina noticed his unease. "Have you ever fired a gun?" she said.

"Never."

She took it back from him and moved a lever near the hammer. "Now the safety catch is off," she said. "All you do is point it and pull the trigger." She put the safety catch on again and handed the gun back to him. Then she went down the ladder.

Walli could hear shouts and car engines outside. He could not guess what the police were doing, but it was clear he was running out of time.

He saw how things had gone wrong. Hans Hoffmann had had Karolin under surveillance, no doubt hoping that Walli might come back for her. The tail had seen her meet a boy and go off with him. Someone had decided not to arrest them immediately, but to see whether they would lead their watchers to a group of coconspirators. There had been a slick change of personnel after they got off the bus, and a new follower had taken over, the man in the brown coat. At some point he had realized they were heading for the Wall, and had pressed the panic button.

Now the police and the Stasi were outside, searching the rear of the derelict buildings, trying to figure out where Walli and Karolin had gone. They would find the trapdoor any second now.

With the pistol in his hand Walli went down the shaft, following the others.

As he reached the foot of the ladder he heard the clang of the iron hatch. The police had located the entrance. A moment later there were gruff shouts of surprise and triumph as they saw the hole in the floor.

Walli had to wait a long, agonizing moment at the mouth of the tunnel, until Cristina disappeared inside. He followed her, then stopped. He was slim, and he was just about able to turn in the narrow passage. He peeked out, looking up the shaft, and saw the bulk of a policeman stepping onto the ladder.

This was hopeless. The police were too close. All they had to do was point their guns into the tunnel and fire. Walli himself would be shot, and when he fell the bullets would pass over him and hit the next in line—and so on: the slaughter would be bloody. And he knew they would not hesitate to shoot, for no mercy was shown to escapers, ever. It would be carnage.

He had to keep them out of the shaft.

But he did not want to kill another man.

Kneeling just inside the mouth of the tunnel, he moved the safety catch of the Walther. Then he put his hand holding the gun outside the tunnel, pointed it upward, and pulled the trigger.

The gun kicked in his hand. The bang was very loud in the confined space. Immediately afterward he heard shouts of dismay and fear, but not of pain, and he guessed he had scared them without actually hitting anyone. He peeped out and saw the cop scrambling back up the ladder and out of the shaft.

He waited. He knew the escapers ahead of him would be slow, because of the child. He could hear the cops discussing in angry tones what they were going to do. None of them was willing to go down the shaft: it was suicide, one said. But they could not just let people escape!

To reinforce the danger to them, Walli fired the gun again. He heard sudden panic movements as if they had all pulled back from the shaft. He thought he had succeeded in scaring them off. He turned to crawl away.

Then he heard a voice he knew well. Hans Hoffmann said: "We need grenades."

"Oh, fuck," said Walli.

He stuck the gun in his belt and began to crawl along the tunnel. There was nothing for it now but to get as far along as possible. In no time he felt Cristina's shoes in front of him. "Hurry up!" he yelled. "The cops are getting grenades!"

"I can't go faster than the guy in front of me!" she yelled back.

All Walli could do was follow. It was dark now. He heard no sound from the cellar to his rear. Regular cops were not normally equipped with grenades, he guessed, but Hans could get some from nearby border guards in a couple of minutes.

Walli could see nothing, but he could hear the panting of his fellow fugitives, and the scrape of their knees on the boards. The child began to cry. Yesterday Walli would have cursed it for a dangerous nuisance, but today he was a father-to-be, and he felt only pity for the frightened kid.

What would the police do with their grenades? Would they play safe, and drop one into the shaft, where it might do little damage? Or would one have the nerve to climb down the ladder and throw one lethally into the tunnel? That might kill all the escapers.

Walli decided he had to do more to discourage the cops. He lay down, rolled over, pulled the gun, and raised himself on his left elbow. He could see nothing, but he pointed the gun back along the tunnel and pulled the trigger.

Several people screamed.

Cristina said: "What was that?"

Walli put the gun away and resumed crawling. "I was just discouraging the cops."

"Warn us next time, for Christ's sake."

He saw light ahead. The tunnel seemed shorter going back. He heard cries of relief as people realized they were at the end. He found himself going faster, pushing up against Cristina's shoes.

Behind him, there was an explosion.

He felt the shock wave, but it was weak, and he knew immediately that they had dropped the first grenade into the down shaft. He had never paid enough attention to physics in school, but he guessed that in those circumstances nearly all the explosive force would go upward.

However, he could foresee what Hans would do next. Having made sure there was no longer someone lying in wait inside the tunnel entrance, he would now send a cop down the ladder to throw a grenade into the tunnel.

Ahead the group was emerging into the cellar of the disused grocery. "Quickly!" Walli yelled. "Climb the ladder fast!"

Cristina exited the tunnel and stood in the shaft, smiling. "Relax," she said. "This is the West. We're out—we're free!"

"Grenades!" Walli yelled. "Go up, fast as you can!"

The couple with the child was climbing the ladder with painful slowness. The male student and Cristina followed. Walli stood at the foot of the ladder, trembling with impatience and fear. He went up right behind Cristina, his face at her knees. He reached the top and saw them all standing around, laughing and hugging. "Lie flat!" he yelled. "Grenades!" He threw himself to the floor.

There was a terrific boom. The shock wave seemed to rock the cellar. Then there was a gushing sound like a fountain, and he guessed that earth was spurting from the mouth of the tunnel. Confirming his guess, a rain of mud and small stones fell on him. The hoist over the shaft collapsed and fell into the hole.

The noise died away. The cellar was quiet except for the sobbing of the child. Walli looked around. The kid had a nosebleed, but seemed otherwise unhurt, and no one else appeared injured. He looked over the lip of the shaft and saw that the tunnel had fallen in.

He stood upright, shakily. He had made it. He was alive and free.

And alone.

. . .

Rebecca had spent a lot of her father's money on the apartment in Hamburg. The place was the ground floor of a grand old merchant's house. All the rooms were big enough to allow Bernd to turn the wheelchair—even the bathroom. She had installed every known aid for a man paralyzed from the waist down. Walls and ceilings were festooned with ropes and grab handles that enabled him to wash and dress himself and get in and out of bed. He could even cook in the kitchen, if he wanted to, though like most men he could not prepare anything more complicated than eggs.

She was determined—furiously determined—that she and Bernd were going to live as normal an existence as possible, despite his injury. They would enjoy their marriage and their work and their freedom. Life for them would be busy and varied and satisfying. Anything less would give the victory to the tyrants on the other side of the Wall.

Bernd's condition had not changed since he left the hospital. The doctors said he might improve, and he should keep hoping. One day, they insisted, he might be able to father children. Rebecca should never stop trying.

She felt she had a lot to be happy about. She was teaching again, doing what she was good at, opening the minds of young people to the intellectual riches of the world they lived in. She was in love with Bernd, whose kindness and humor made every day a pleasure. They were free to read what they liked, think what they liked, and say what they liked, without having to worry about police spies.

Rebecca had a long-term aim, too. She yearned to be reunited with her family one day. Not her original family: the memory of her biological parents was poignant, but distant and vague. However, Carla had rescued her from the hell of war, and had made her feel safe and loved, even when they were all hungry and cold and scared. Over the years the house in Mitte had filled with people to love and be loved by Rebecca: baby Walli; then her new father, Werner; then a baby girl, Lili. Even Grandmother Maud, that impossibly dignified old English lady, had loved and cared for Rebecca.

She would be reunited with them when all West Germans were reunited with all East Germans. Many people thought that day might never come. Perhaps they were right. But Carla and Werner had taught Rebecca that if you wanted change you had to take political action to get it. "In my family, apathy isn't an option," Rebecca had said to Bernd. So they had joined the Free Democratic Party, which was liberal, though not as socialist as Willy Brandt's Social Democratic Party. Rebecca was branch secretary and Bernd was treasurer.

In West Germany you could join any party you liked except the Communist Party, which was banned. Rebecca disapproved of that prohibition. She hated Communism, but banning it was the kind of thing Communists did, not democrats.

Rebecca and Bernd drove to work together every day. They came home after school, and Bernd laid the table while Rebecca prepared dinner. Some days, after they had eaten, Bernd's masseur came. Because Bernd could not move his legs, they had to be massaged regularly to improve the circulation and prevent, or at least slow, the wasting of nerves and muscles. Rebecca cleared away while Bernd went into the bedroom with the masseur, Heinz.

This evening she sat down with a pile of exercise books and began marking. She had asked her pupils to write an imaginary advertisement about the attractions of Moscow as a holiday destination. They liked tongue-in-cheek assignments.

After an hour Heinz departed, and Rebecca went into the bedroom.

Bernd lay naked on the bed. His upper body was strongly muscular, because he constantly had to use his arms to move himself. His legs looked like those of an old man, thin and pale.

He usually felt good, physically and mentally, after massage. Rebecca leaned over him and kissed his lips, long and slow. "I love you," she said. "I'm so happy to be with you." She said it often, because it was true, and because he needed reassurance: she knew that sometimes he wondered how she could love a cripple.

She stood facing him and took off her clothes. He liked her to do this, he said, even though it never gave him a hard-on. She had learned that paralyzed men rarely got psychogenic erections, the kind caused by sexy sights or thoughts. All the same his eyes followed her with evident enjoyment as she unfastened her bra, slid her stockings off, and stepped out of her panties.

"You look great," he said.

"And I'm all yours."

"Lucky me."

She lay beside him and they caressed each other languorously. Sex with Bernd, before and after his accident, had always been about soft kisses and murmured endearments, not just fucking. In that way he was different from her first husband. Hans had had a program: kiss, undress, get hard, come. Bernd's philosophy was anything you like, in any order.

After a while she straddled him, then maneuvered so that he could kiss her breasts and suck her nipples. He had adored her breasts right from the start, and now he enjoyed them with the same intensity and relish as before the accident; and that aroused her more than anything.

When she was ready, she said: "Do you want to try?"

"Sure," he said. "We should always try."

She moved back, so that she was astride his withered legs, and bent over his penis. She manipulated it with her hand. It grew a little, and he got what was called a reflex erection. For a few moments it was hard enough to go inside her, then it quickly subsided. "Never mind," she said.

"I don't mind," he said, but she knew it was not true. He would have liked to have an orgasm. He wanted children, too.

She lay beside him, took his hand, and placed it on her vagina. He positioned his fingers in the way she had taught him, then she pressed his hand with her own and moved rhythmically. It was like masturbation, but using his hand. He stroked her hair fondly with his other hand. It worked, as it always did, and she had a delightful orgasm.

Lying beside him afterward, she said: "Thank you."

"You're welcome."

"Not just for that."

"What, then?"

"For coming with me. For escaping. I can never tell you enough how grateful I am."

"Good."

The doorbell rang. They looked at one another in puzzlement: they expected no one. Bernd said: "Maybe Heinz left something behind."

Rebecca was mildly annoyed. Her euphoria had been shattered. She put on a robe and went to the door, feeling grumpy.

There stood Walli. He looked thin and smelled ripe. He wore

jeans, American baseball shoes, and a grubby shirt—no coat. He was carrying a guitar and nothing else.

"Hello, Rebecca," he said.

Her grumpiness evaporated in a flash. She smiled broadly. "Walli!" she said. "What a wonderful surprise! I'm so happy to see you!"

She stood back and he stepped into the hallway.

"What are you doing here?" she said.

"I've come to live with you," he said.

The most racist city in America was probably Birmingham, Alabama. George Jakes flew there in April 1963.

Last time he came to Alabama, he recalled vividly, they had tried to kill him.

Birmingham was a dirty industrial city, and from the plane it had a delicate rose-pink aura of pollution, like the chiffon scarf around the neck of an old prostitute.

George felt the hostility as he walked through the terminal. He was the only colored man in a suit. He remembered the attack on him and Maria and the Freedom Riders in Anniston, just sixty miles away: the bombs, the baseball bats, the whirling lengths of iron chain, and most of all the faces, twisted and deformed into masks of hatred and madness.

He walked out of the airport, located the taxi stand, and got into the first car in line.

"Get out of the car, boy," said the driver.

"I beg your pardon?"

"I don't drive for no goddamn nigras."

George sighed. He was reluctant to get out. He felt like sitting there in protest. He did not like to make things easy for racists. But he had a job to do in Birmingham, and he could not do it in jail. So he got out.

Standing by the open door, he looked down the line. The car behind had a white driver: he assumed he would get the same treatment again. Then, three cars back, a dark brown arm came out of the window and waved at him.

He stepped away from the first cab.

"Close the door!" the driver yelled.

George hesitated, then said: "I don't close doors for no goddamn segregationists." It was not a very good line, but it gave him some small satisfaction, and he walked away leaving the door wide open.

He jumped into the cab with the black driver. "I know where you're going," the man said. "Sixteenth Street Baptist Church."

The church was the base of fiery preacher Fred Shuttlesworth. He had founded the Alabama Christian Movement for Human Rights, after the state courts outlawed the moderate National Association for the Advancement of Colored People. Clearly, George thought, any Negro arriving at the airport was assumed to be a civil rights campaigner.

But George was not going to the church. "Take me to the Gaston Motel, please," he said.

"I know the Gaston," said the driver. "I saw Little Stevie Wonder in the lounge there. It's just a block from the church."

It was a hot day and the cab had no air-conditioning. George wound down the window and let the slipstream cool his perspiring skin.

He had been sent by Bobby Kennedy with a message for Martin Luther King. The message was stop pushing, calm things down, end your protests, things are changing. George had a feeling that Dr. King was not going to like it.

The Gaston was a low-built modern hotel. Its owner, A. G. Gaston, was a coal miner who had become Birmingham's leading black businessman. George knew that Gaston was nervous about the disruption being brought to Birmingham by King's campaign, but gave his qualified support nonetheless. George's taxi drove through the entrance into a motor court.

Martin Luther King was in Room 30, the motel's only suite; but before seeing him George had lunch with Verena Marquand in the nearby Jockey Boy Restaurant. When he asked for his hamburger medium rare, the waitress looked at him as if he were speaking a foreign language.

Verena ordered a salad. She looked more alluring than ever in white pants and a black blouse. George wondered if she had a boyfriend. "You're on a downhill slope," he said to her while they were waiting for their food. "First Atlanta, now Birmingham. Come to Washington, before you find yourself stuck in Mudslide, Mississippi." He was teasing, but he did think that if she came to Washington he might ask her out on a date.

"I go where the movement takes me," she replied seriously.

Their lunch arrived. "Why did King decide to target this town?" George asked while they were eating.

"The commissioner of public safety—effectively the chief of police—is a vicious white racist called Eugene 'Bull' Connor."

"I've seen his name in the papers."

"The nickname tells you all you need to know about him. As if that were not enough, Birmingham also has the most violent chapter of the Ku Klux Klan."

"Any idea why?"

"This is a steel town, and the industry is in decline. Skilled, high-wage jobs have always been reserved for white men, while blacks do low-paid work such as cleaning. Now the whites are desperately trying to maintain their prosperity and privileges—just at the moment when blacks are asking for their fair share."

It was a crisp analysis, and George's respect for Verena went up a notch. "How does that show itself?"

"Klan members throw homemade bombs at the homes of prosperous Negroes in mixed neighborhoods. Some people call this town Bombingham. Needless to say, the police never arrest anyone for the bombings, and the FBI somehow just can't seem to figure out who might be doing it."

"No surprise there. J. Edgar Hoover can't find the Mafia, either. But he knows the name of every Communist in America."

"However, white rule is weakening here. Some people are beginning to realize it does the town no good. Bull Connor just lost an election for mayor."

"I know. The White House view is that Birmingham's Negroes will get what they want in due course, if they're patient."

"Dr. King's view is that now is the time to pile on the pressure."

"And how is that working out?"

"To be frank, we're disappointed. When we sit in at a lunch counter, the waitresses turn out the lights and say sorry, they're closing."

"A clever move. Some towns did something similar to the Freedom

Riders. Instead of making a fuss, they just ignored what was happening. But that level of restraint is too much for most segregationists, and they soon reverted to beating people up."

"Bull Connor won't give us a permit to demonstrate, so our marches are illegal, and the protesters are usually jailed; but they're too few to make the national news."

"So maybe it's time for another change of tactics."

A young black woman came into the café and approached their table. "The Reverend Dr. King is free to see you now, Mr. Jakes."

George and Verena left their lunches half-eaten. As with the president, you did not ask Dr. King to wait while you finished what you were doing.

They returned to the Gaston and went upstairs to King's suite. As always, he was dressed in a dark business suit: the heat seemed to make little difference to him. George was struck again by how small he was, and how handsome. This time King was less wary, more welcoming. "Sit down, please," he said, waving to a couch. His voice was mild even when his words were barbed: "What has the attorney general got to tell me that he can't say over the phone?"

"He wants you to consider delaying your campaign here in Alabama."

"Somehow I'm not surprised."

"He supports what you're trying to achieve, but he feels the protest may be ill timed."

"Tell me why."

"Bull Connor has just lost the election for mayor to Albert Boutwell. There's a new city government. Boutwell is a reformer."

"Some people feel Boutwell is just a more dignified version of Bull Connor."

"Reverend, that may be so; but Bobby would like you to give Boutwell the chance to prove himself—one way or the other."

"I see. So that message is: Wait."

"Yes, sir."

King looked at Verena, as if inviting her to comment, but she said nothing.

After a moment King said: "Last September, Birmingham businessmen promised to remove humiliating WHITES ONLY signs from their stores and, in return, Fred Shuttlesworth agreed to a moratorium on demonstrations. We kept our promise, but the businessmen broke theirs. As has happened so many times, our hopes were blasted."

"I'm sorry to hear that," said George. "But—"

King ignored the interruption. "Nonviolent direct action seeks to create so much tension, and sense of crisis, that a community is forced to confront the issue and open the door to sincere negotiation. You ask me to give Boutwell time to show his true colors. Boutwell may be less of a brute than Connor, but he is a segregationist, dedicated to keeping the status quo. He needs to be prodded to act."

This was so reasonable that George could not even pretend to disagree, though the likelihood of his changing King's mind seemed to be fading rapidly.

"We have never made a gain, in civil rights, without pressure," King went on. "Frankly, George, I have yet to engage in a campaign that was 'well timed' in the eyes of men such as Bobby Kennedy. For years now I have heard the word 'Wait.' It rings in my ears with piercing familiarity. This 'Wait' always means 'Never.' We have waited three hundred and forty years for our rights. African nations are moving with jetlike speed toward independence, but we still creep at horse-and-buggy pace toward gaining a cup of coffee at a lunch counter."

George realized now that he was hearing a sermon being rehearsed, but he was no less mesmerized. He had abandoned all hope of fulfilling his mission for Bobby.

"Our great stumbling block, in our stride toward freedom, is not the White Citizens' Councilor or the Ku Klux Klanner. It's the white moderate who is more devoted to order than to justice; who constantly says, like Bobby Kennedy: 'I agree with the goal you seek, but I cannot condone your methods.' He paternalistically believes he can set the timetable for another man's freedom."

Now George felt ashamed, for he was Bobby's messenger.

"We will have to repent, in this generation, not merely for the hateful words and actions of bad people, but for the appalling silence of the good," King said, and George had to struggle against tears. "The time is always ripe to do right. 'Let justice roll down like waters, and righteousness like an ever flowing stream,' said the prophet Amos. You tell Bobby Kennedy that, George."

"Yes, sir, I will," said George.

. . .

When George got back to Washington he called Cindy Bell, the girl his mother had tried to fix him up with, and asked her for a date. She said: "Why not?"

It would be his first date since he had dumped Norine Latimer in the doomed hope of romancing Maria Summers.

He took a taxi to Cindy's place the following Saturday evening. She was still living at her parents' home, a small working-class house. Her father opened the door. He had a bushy beard: George guessed a chef did not need to look neat. "I'm glad to meet you, George," he said. "Your mother is one of the finest people I've ever known. I hope you don't mind me saying something so personal."

"Thank you, Mr. Bell," said George. "I agree with you."

"Come in, Cindy's almost ready."

George noticed a small crucifix on the wall in the hallway, and remembered that the Bells were Catholic. He recalled being told, as a teenager, that convent schoolgirls were the hottest.

Cindy appeared in a tight sweater and a short skirt that made her father frown a little, though he said nothing. George had to smother a smile. She was curvy and did not want to hide it. A small silver cross on a chain hung between her generous breasts—for protection, perhaps?

George handed her a small box of chocolates tied up with a blue ribbon.

Outside, she raised her eyebrows at the taxi.

"I'm going to buy a car," George said. "I just haven't had time."

As they drove downtown, Cindy said: "My father admires your mother for raising you on her own, and making such a good job of it."

"And they lend each other books," said George. "Is your mom okay with all that?"

Cindy giggled. The idea of sexual jealousy in the parental generation was naturally comical. "You're sharp. Mom knows nothing else is going on—but all the same she's on her guard."

George felt glad he had asked her out. She was intelligent and warm, and he was beginning to think how pleasant it would be to kiss her. The thought of Maria became dim in his mind.

They went to an Italian restaurant. Cindy confessed that she loved all kinds of pasta. They had tagliatelle with mushrooms, then veal escalopes in a sherry sauce.

She had a degree from Georgetown University, but she told him she was working as a secretary to a black insurance broker. "Girls get hired as secretaries, even after college," she said. "I'd like to do government work. I know people think it's dull, but Washington runs this whole country. Unfortunately, the government hires mostly white people for the important jobs."

"That's true."

"How did you break in?"

"Bobby Kennedy wanted a black face on his team, to make him look sincere about civil rights."

"So you're a symbol."

"I was, at the start. It's better now."

After dinner they went to see Tippi Hedren and Rod Taylor in Alfred Hitchcock's latest film, *The Birds.* During the scary scenes, Cindy clung to George in a way he found delightful.

On the way out, they disagreed amiably about the ending of the movie. Cindy hated it. "I was so disappointed!" she said. "I was looking forward to the explanation."

George shrugged. "Not everything in life has an explanation."

"Yes, it does, but sometimes we just don't know it."

They went to the bar of the Fairfax Hotel for a nightcap. He ordered Scotch and she had a daiquiri. Her silver cross caught his eye. "Is that just jewelry, or something more?" he said.

"Something more," she replied. "It makes me feel safe."

"Safe from . . . anything in particular?"

"No. It just guards me, generally."

George was skeptical. "You don't believe that."

"Why not?"

"Uh . . . I don't want to offend you, if you're sincere, but it seems superstitious to me."

"I thought you were religious. You go to church, don't you?"

"I go with my mother because it's important to her, and I love her. To make her happy, I'll sing hymns and listen to prayers and hear a sermon, all of which seem to me to be just . . . mumbo jumbo."

"Don't you believe in God?"

"I think there's probably a controlling intelligence in the universe, a being that decided the rules, such as E equals MC squared, and the value of pi. But that being isn't likely to care whether we sing its praise or not, I doubt whether its decisions can be manipulated by praying to a statue of the Virgin Mary, and I don't believe it will organize special treatment for you on account of what you have around your neck."

"Oh."

He saw that he had shocked her. He realized he had been arguing as if at a White House meeting, where the issues were too important for anyone to care about other people's feelings. "I probably shouldn't be so direct," he said. "Are you offended?"

"No," she said. "I'm glad you told me." She finished her drink.

George put some money down on the bar and slid off his stool. "I've enjoyed talking to you," he said.

"Nice movie, disappointing ending," she said.

That summed up the evening. She was likable and attractive, but he could not see himself falling for a woman whose beliefs about the universe were so much at odds with his own.

They went outside and got a cab.

On the ride back, George realized that in his heart of hearts he was not sorry the date had not worked out. He still had not fully got over Maria. He wondered how much longer it was going to take.

When they reached Cindy's house she said: "Thank you for a lovely evening." She kissed his cheek and got out of the car.

Next day Bobby sent George back to Alabama.

．　．　．

George and Verena stood in Kelly Ingram Park, in the heart of black Birmingham, at twelve noon on Friday, May 3, 1963. Across the road was the famous Sixteenth Street Baptist Church, a magnificent redbrick Byzantine building designed by a black architect. The park was crowded with civil rights campaigners, bystanders, and anxious parents.

They could hear singing from inside the church: "Ain't Gonna Let Nobody Turn Me Round." A thousand black high school students were getting ready to march.

To the east of the park, the avenues leading downtown were blocked by hundreds of police. Bull Connor had commandeered school buses to take the marchers to jail, and he had attack dogs in case anyone refused to go. The police were backed up by firemen with hoses.

There were no colored men in the police force or the fire brigade.

The civil rights campaigners always applied, in the correct way, for permission to march. Every time, they were refused. When they marched nevertheless, they were arrested and sent to jail.

In consequence, most of Birmingham's Negroes were reluctant to join the demonstrations—permitting the all-white city government to claim that Martin Luther King's movement had little support.

King himself had gone to jail here exactly three weeks ago, on Good Friday. George had marveled at how crass the segregationists were: did they not know who else had been arrested on Good Friday? King had been put in solitary confinement, for no reason other than sheer malice.

But King's jailing had hardly made the papers. A Negro being mistreated for demanding his rights as an American was not news. King had been criticized by white clergymen in a letter that got big publicity. From the jail he had written a reply that smoldered with righteousness. No newspapers had printed it, though perhaps they yet would. Overall, the campaign had got little publicity.

Birmingham's black teenagers clamored to join the demonstrations, and at last King agreed to permit schoolchildren to march, but nothing changed: Bull Connor just jailed the children, and no one cared.

The sound of the hymns from inside the church was thrilling, but that was not enough. Martin Luther King's campaign in Birmingham was going nowhere, just like George's love life.

George was studying the firemen on the streets to the east of the park. They had a new type of weapon. The device appeared to take water from two inlet hoses and force it out through a single nozzle. Presumably that gave the jet supercharged force. It was mounted on a tripod, suggesting that it was too powerful for a man to hold. George was glad he was strictly an observer, and would not be taking part in the march. He suspected that the jet would do more than soak you.

The doors of the church flew open and a group of students emerged through the triple arches, dressed in their Sunday best, singing. They marched down the long, broad flight of steps to the street. There were about sixty of them, but George knew that this was only the first contingent: there were hundreds more inside. Most were high school seniors, with a sprinkling of younger kids.

George and Verena followed them at a distance. The watching crowd in the park cheered and clapped as the marchers paraded down Sixteenth, passing mostly black-owned stores and businesses. They turned east along Fifth Avenue and came to the corner of Seventeenth, where their way was blocked by police barricades.

A police captain spoke through a bullhorn. "Disperse, get off the street," he said. He pointed to the firemen behind him. "Otherwise you're going to get wet."

On previous occasions the police had simply herded demonstrators into paddy wagons and buses and taken them to jail. But, George knew, the jails were now full and overcrowded, and Bull Connor was hoping to minimize arrests today: he would prefer them all to go home.

Which was the last thing they were going to do. The sixty kids stood in the road, facing the massed ranks of white authority, and sang at the tops of their voices.

The police captain made a signal to the firemen, who turned on the water. George noted that they deployed regular hoses, not the tripod-mounted water cannon. Nevertheless the spray drove most of the marchers back, and sent the bystanders scurrying across the park and into doorways. Through his bullhorn the captain kept repeating: "Evacuate the area! Evacuate the area!"

Most of the marchers retreated—but not all. Ten simply sat down. Already soaked to the skin, they ignored the water and continued singing.

That was when the firemen turned on the water cannon.

The effect was instant. Instead of a spurt of water, unpleasant but harmless, the seated pupils were blasted with a high-powered jet. They were knocked backward and cried out in pain. Their hymn turned to screams of fright.

The smallest of them was a little girl. The water lifted her physically from the ground and blasted her backward. She rolled along the street like a blown leaf. Her arms and legs flailed helplessly. Bystanders began yelling and cursing.

George swore and ran into the street.

The firemen relentlessly directed their tripod-mounted hose to follow the child, so that she could not escape from its force. They were trying to wash her away like a scrap of litter. George was the first of several men to reach her. He got between the hose and her, and turned his back.

It was like being punched.

The jet knocked him to his knees. But the little girl was now protected, and she got to her feet and ran toward the park. However, the fire hose followed her and tumbled her down again.

George was enraged. The firemen were like hunting dogs bringing down a young deer. Shouts of protest from bystanders told him that they, too, were infuriated.

George ran after the girl and shielded her again. This time he was prepared for the impact of the jet, and he managed to keep his balance. He knelt and picked up the child. Her pink churchgoing dress was sodden. Carrying her, he staggered toward the sidewalk. The firemen chased him with the jet, trying to knock him down again, but he stayed on his feet long enough to get to the other side of a parked car.

He set the girl on her feet. She was screaming in terror. "It's okay, you're safe now," George told her, but she could not be consoled. Then a distraught woman rushed to her and picked her up. The girl clung to the woman, and George guessed that this was her mother. Weeping, the mother carried her away.

George was bruised and sodden. He turned around to see what was happening. The marchers had all been trained in nonviolent protest, but the furious onlookers had not, and now they were retaliating, he saw, throwing rocks at the firemen. This was turning into a riot.

He could not see Verena.

Police and firemen advanced along Fifth Avenue, trying to disperse the crowd, but their progress was slowed by the hail of missiles. Several men went into the buildings along the south side of the street and bombarded the police from upstairs windows, throwing stones, bottles, and garbage. George hurried away from the fracas. He stopped on the next corner, outside the Jockey Boy Restaurant, and stood with a small group of reporters and spectators, black and white.

Looking north, he saw that more contingents of young marchers were coming out of the church and taking different southbound streets to avoid the violence. That would create a problem for Bull Connor by splitting his forces.

Connor responded by deploying the dogs.

They came out of the vans snarling, baring their teeth, and straining against their leather leashes. Their handlers looked just as vicious: thickset white men in police caps and sunglasses. Dogs and handlers alike were animals eager to attack.

Cops and dogs rushed forward in a pack. Marchers and bystanders tried to flee, but the crowd on the street was now tightly packed, and many people could not get away. The dogs were hysterical with excitement, snapping and biting and drawing blood from people's legs and arms.

Some people fled west, into the depths of the black neighborhood, chased by cops. Others took sanctuary in the church. No more marchers were emerging from the triple arches, George saw: the demonstration was coming to an end.

But the police had not yet had enough.

From nowhere, two cops with dogs appeared beside George. One grabbed hold of a tall young Negro: George had noticed him because he was wearing an expensive-looking cardigan sweater. The boy was about fifteen, and had taken no part in the demonstration other than to watch. Nevertheless the cop spun him round, and the dog leaped up and sunk its teeth into the boy's middle. He cried out in fear and pain. One of the reporters snapped a picture.

George was about to intervene when the cop pulled the dog off. Then he arrested the boy for parading without a permit.

George noticed a big-bellied white man, dressed in a shirt and no jacket, watching the arrest. From photographs in the newspapers he recognized Bull Connor. "Why didn't you bring a meaner dog?" Connor said to the arresting officer.

George felt like remonstrating with the man. He was supposed to be the commissioner of public safety, but he was acting like a street hoodlum.

But George realized he was in danger of getting arrested himself, especially now that his smart suit was a drenched rag. Bobby Kennedy would not be pleased if George ended up in jail.

With an effort, George suppressed his anger, clamped his mouth shut, turned, and walked briskly back to the Gaston.

Fortunately he had a spare pair of pants in his luggage. He took a shower, dressed again in dry clothes, and sent his suit for pressing. He called the Justice Department and dictated to a secretary his report on the day's events for Bobby Kennedy. He made his report dry and unemotional, and left out the fact that he had been fire-hosed.

He found Verena again in the lounge of the hotel. She had escaped without injury, but she looked shaken. "They can do anything they like to us!" she said, and there was a note of hysteria in her voice. He felt the same, but it was worse for her. Unlike George, she had not been a Freedom Rider, and he guessed this might be the first time she had seen violent racial hatred in its naked horror.

"Let me buy you a drink," he said, and they went to the bar.

Over the next hour he talked her down. Mostly he just listened; every now and again he said something sympathetic or reassuring; he helped her become calm by being calm himself. The effort brought his own boiling passions under control.

They had dinner together quietly in the hotel restaurant. It was just dark when they went upstairs. In the corridor Verena said: "Will you come to my room?"

He was surprised. It had not been a romantic or sexy evening, and he had not regarded it as a date. They were just two fellow-campaigners commiserating.

She saw his hesitation. "I just want someone to hold me," she said. "Is that all right?"

He was not sure he understood, but he nodded.

The image of Maria flashed into his mind. He suppressed it. It was time he forgot her.

When they were in the room she closed the door and put her arms around him. He pressed her body to his and kissed her forehead. She turned her face away and laid her cheek against his shoulder. Okay, he thought, you want to hug but you don't want to kiss. He made up his mind to simply follow her cues. Whatever she wanted would be all right with him.

After a minute she said: "I don't want to sleep alone."

"Okay," he said neutrally.

"Can we just cuddle?"

"Yes," he said, though he could not believe it would happen that way.

She drew away from his embrace. Then, quickly, she stepped out of her shoes and pulled her dress over her head. She was wearing a white brassiere and panties. He stared at her perfect creamy skin. She took off her underwear in a couple of seconds. Her breasts were flat and firm with tiny nipples. Her pubic hair had an auburn tinge. She was the most beautiful woman he had ever seen naked—by far.

He took it all in at a glance, for she immediately got into bed.

George turned away and took off his shirt.

Verena said: "Your back! Oh, God—it's awful!"

George felt sore from the fire hose, but it had not occurred to him that the damage would show. He stood with his back to the mirror by the door and looked over his shoulder. He saw what Verena meant: his skin was a mass of purple bruises.

He took off his shoes and socks slowly. He had an erection, and he was hoping it would go down, but it did not. He could not help it. He stood up and took off his pants and undershorts, then he got into bed as quickly as she had.

They hugged. His erection pressed into her belly, but she showed no reaction. Her hair tickled his neck and her breasts were squashed against his chest. He was madly aroused, but instinct told him to be still, and he obeyed it.

Verena began to cry. At first she made small moaning noises, and George was not sure whether they indicated sexual feelings. Then he felt her warm tears on his chest, and she began to shake with sobbing. He patted her back in the primal gesture of comfort.

A part of his mind marveled at what he was doing. He was naked in bed with a beautiful woman and all he could do was pat her back. But on a deeper level it made sense. He had a vague but sure feeling that they were giving one another a kind of comfort stronger than sex. They were both in the grip of an intense emotion, albeit one for which George did not have a name.

Verena's sobs gradually eased. After a while her body relaxed, her breathing became regular and shallow, and she drifted into the helplessness of sleep.

George's erection subsided. He closed his eyes and concentrated on the warmth of her body against his, and the light feminine aroma that rose from her skin and her hair. With such a girl in his arms he felt sure he would not sleep.

But he did.

When he woke up in the morning, she was gone.

. . .

On that Saturday morning Maria Summers went to work in a pessimistic mood.

While Martin Luther King had been in jail in Alabama, the Commission on Civil Rights had produced a horrifying report on abuse of Negroes in Mississippi. But the Kennedy administration had cleverly undermined the report. A Justice Department lawyer called Burke Marshall had written a memo quibbling with its findings; Maria's boss, Pierre Salinger, had portrayed its proposals as extremist; and the American press had been fooled.

And the man Maria loved was in charge. President Kennedy had a good heart, she believed, but his eye was always on the next election. He had done well in last year's midterms: his coolheaded handling of the Cuban missile crisis had won him popularity, and the expected Republican landslide had been averted. But now he was worrying about his reelection contest next year. He did not like Southern segregationists, but he was not willing to sacrifice himself in the battle against them.

So the civil rights campaign was fizzling out.

Maria's brother had four children of whom she was very fond. They, and any children Maria herself might have in the future, were going to grow up to be second-class Americans. If they traveled in the South they would have trouble finding a hotel willing to take them in. If they went to a white church they would be turned away, unless the pastor considered himself a liberal and directed them to a special roped-off seating area for Negroes. They would see a sign saying WHITES ONLY outside public toilets, and a sign directing COLOREDS to a bucket in the backyard. They would ask why there were no black people on television, and their parents would not know how to answer them.

Then she reached the office and saw the newspapers.

On the front page of *The New York Times* was a photograph from Birmingham that made Maria gasp with horror. It showed a white policeman with a savage German shepherd dog. The dog was biting a harmless-looking Negro teenager while the cop held the boy by his cardigan sweater. The cop's teeth were bared in a grin of eager malice, as if he wanted to bite someone too.

Nelly Fordham heard Maria's gasp and looked up from *The Washington Post*. "Ugly, ain't it?" she commented.

The same picture was on the front of many other American newspapers, and the airmail editions of foreign papers too.

Maria sat at her desk and began to read. The tone had altered, she noticed with a gleam of hope. It was no longer possible for the press to point the finger of blame at Martin Luther King and say that his campaign was ill timed and Negroes should be patient. The story had changed, with the unstoppable chemistry of media coverage, a mysterious process that Maria had learned to respect and fear.

Her excitement grew as she began to suspect that the white Southerners had gone too far. The press was now talking about violence against children on the streets of America. They still quoted men who said it was all the fault of King and his agitators, but the segregationists' customary tone of confident deprecation had gone, and now there was a note of desperate denial. Was it possible that one photograph could change everything?

Salinger came into the room. "Everybody," he said. "The president looked at the papers this morning, saw the photographs from Birmingham, and felt sickened—and he would like the press to know it. This is not an official statement, but it is an off-the-record briefing. The key word is *sickened.* Put it out right away, please."

Maria looked at Nelly and they both raised their eyebrows. This was a change.

Maria picked up the phone.

.   .   .

By Monday morning, George was moving like an old man, cautiously, trying to minimize the twinges of pain. The Birmingham Fire Department's water cannon produced a pressure of one hundred pounds per square inch, according to the newspapers, and George could feel every pound on every inch of his back.

He was not the only one hurting on Monday morning. Hundreds of demonstrators were bruised. Some had been dog-bitten badly enough to need stitches. Thousands of schoolchildren were still in jail.

George prayed their sufferings would prove worthwhile.

There was hope now. The wealthy white businessmen of Birmingham wanted to end the conflict. No one was shopping: a black boycott of downtown stores had been made more effective by the fear of whites that they might get caught up in a riot. Even the hard-nosed owners of steel mills and factories felt that their businesses were being damaged by the city's reputation as the world capital of violent racism.

And the White House hated the continuing global headlines. Foreign newspapers, taking for granted the Negroes' right to justice and democracy, could not understand why the American president seemed unable to enforce his own laws.

Bobby Kennedy sent Burke Marshall to try to make a deal with Birmingham's leading citizens. Dennis Wilson was his aide. George did not trust either. Marshall had undermined the Commission on Civil Rights report with legal quibbles, and Dennis had always been jealous of George.

Birmingham's white elite would not negotiate directly with Martin Luther King, so Dennis and George had to act as go-betweens, with Verena representing King.

Burke Marshall wanted King to call off Monday's demonstration. "And take the pressure off, just when we're gaining the advantage?" said Verena incredulously to Dennis Wilson in the swanky lounge of the Gaston Motel. George nodded agreement.

"The city government can't do anything right now anyway," Dennis responded.

The city government was going through a separate but related crisis: Bull Connor had mounted a legal challenge to the election he had lost, so there were two men claiming to be mayor. Verena said: "So they're divided and weakened—good! If we wait for them to resolve their differences, they'll come back stronger and more determined. Don't you White House people know anything about politics?"

Dennis pretended that the civil rights campaigners were muddled about what they wanted. That, too, infuriated Verena. "We have four simple demands," she said. "One: immediate desegregation of lunch counters, restrooms, water fountains, all facilities in stores. Two: nondiscriminatory hiring and promotion of black employees in the stores. Three: all demonstrators to be released from jail, and charges dropped. Four: for the future, a biracial committee to negotiate desegregation of the police, schools, parks, movie theaters, and hotels." She glared at Dennis. "Anything muddled there?"

King was asking for things that should have been taken for granted, but all the same it was too much for the whites. That evening, Dennis came back to the Gaston and told George and Verena the counterproposals. The store owners were willing to desegregate fitting rooms immediately, other facilities after a delay. Five or six black employees could be promoted to "tie jobs" as soon as the demonstrations ended. The businessmen could do nothing about the prisoners, because that was a matter for the courts. Segregation of schools and other city facilities had to be referred to the mayor and the city council.

Dennis was pleased. For the first time ever, the whites were negotiating!

But Verena was scornful. "This is nothing," she said. "They never ask two women to share a fitting room, so they're hardly segregated in the first place. And there are more than five Negro men in Birmingham capable of putting on a tie. As for the rest—"

"They say they have no power to reverse the decisions of the courts or change the laws."

"How naïve are you?" said Verena. "In this town, the courts and the city government do what the businessmen ask them to do."

Bobby Kennedy asked George to put together a list of the most influential white businessmen in town, with their phone numbers. The president was going to call them personally and tell them they needed to compromise.

George noted other exciting signs. Mass meetings in Birmingham churches on Monday evening collected an amazing $40,000 in donations to the campaign: it took King's people most of the night to count it all, which they did in a motel room rented for the purpose. Even more money was pouring in by mail. The movement normally lived from hand to mouth, but Bull Connor and his dogs had brought a massive windfall.

Verena and King's people settled in for a late-night session in the sitting room of King's suite, discussing how to keep the pressure on. George was not invited—he did not want to learn things he might feel obliged to report to Bobby—so he went to bed.

In the morning he put on his suit and went downstairs to King's ten o'clock press conference. He found the motel courtyard crammed with more than a hundred journalists from all over the world, sweating under the Alabama sun. King's Birmingham campaign was hot news— again thanks to Bull Connor. "The activities which have taken place in Birmingham over the last few days mark the nonviolent movement's coming of age," King said. "This is the fulfillment of a dream."

George could not see Verena anywhere, and the suspicion grew in him that the real action might be elsewhere. He left the motel and went around the corner to the church. He did not find Verena, but he did notice schoolchildren coming out of the church basement and getting into cars parked in a line along Fifth Avenue. He sensed an air of forced nonchalance about the adults supervising them.

He ran into Dennis Wilson, who had news. "The Senior Citizens Committee is having an emergency meeting at the chamber of commerce."

George had heard of this unofficial group, nicknamed the Big Mules. They were the men who held the real power in the town. If they were panicking, something would have to change.

Dennis said: "What are King's people planning?"

George was glad he did not know. "I wasn't invited to the meeting," he said. "But they've cooked up something."

He parted from Dennis and walked downtown. Even strolling alone he knew he might be arrested for parading without a permit, but he had to take the risk: he would be of no use to Bobby if he hid in the Gaston.

In ten minutes he reached Birmingham's typical Southern-town business district: department stores, cinemas, civic buildings, and a railway line running through the middle.

George figured out what King's plan was only when he saw it going into operation.

Suddenly Negroes walking alone, or in twos and threes, began to congregate, brandishing placards that they had until now kept hidden. Some sat down, blocking the sidewalk; others knelt to pray on the steps of the massive art deco city hall. Conga lines of hymn-singing teenagers wove in and out of segregated stores. Traffic slowed to a halt.

The police were caught unawares: they were concentrated around Kelly Ingram Park, half a mile away, and the demonstrators had blindsided them. But George felt sure that this air of good-natured protest could last only as long as Bull Connor remained off balance.

As morning turned into afternoon he returned to the Gaston. He found Verena looking worried. "This is great, but it's out of control," she said. "Our people are trained in nonviolent protest, but thousands of others are just joining in, and they have no discipline."

"It's increasing the pressure on the Big Mules," George said.

"But we don't want the governor to declare martial law." The governor of Alabama was George Wallace, an unyielding segregationist.

"Martial law means federal control," George pointed out. "Then the president would have to order at least partial integration."

"If it's forced on the Big Mules from the outside they'll find ways to undermine it. Better that it's their decision."

Verena was a subtle political thinker, George could tell. No doubt she had learned a lot from King. But he was not sure whether she was right on this point.

He ate a ham sandwich and went out again. The atmosphere around Kelly Ingram Park was now more tense. There were hundreds of police in the park, swinging their nightsticks and restraining their eager dogs. The fire brigade hosed anyone headed downtown. The Negroes, resenting the hoses, began to throw stones and Coke bottles at the police. Verena and others of King's team moved through the crowd, begging people to stay calm and refrain from violence, but they had little effect. A strange white vehicle that people called the Tank drove up and down Sixteenth Street, with Bull Connor bellowing through a loudspeaker: "Disperse! Get off the streets!" It was not a tank, George had been told, but an army surplus armored car Connor had bought.

George saw Fred Shuttlesworth, King's rival as leader of the campaign. At forty-one he was a wiry, tough-looking man, smartly dressed with a trim mustache. He had survived two bombings, and his wife had been stabbed by a Ku Klux Klansman, but he seemed to have no fear, and refused to leave town. "I wasn't saved to run," he liked to say. Although a fighter by nature, he was now trying to marshal some of the youngsters. "You mustn't taunt the police," he was saying. "Don't act like you intend to strike them." It was good advice, George figured.

Kids gathered around Shuttlesworth and he led them, like the Pied Piper, back toward his church, waving a white handkerchief in the air in an attempt to show the police his peaceful intent.

It almost worked.

Shuttlesworth led the kids past the fire trucks outside the church to the basement entrance, which was at street level, and ushered them inside and down the stairs. When they were all in, he turned to follow. At that moment George heard a voice say: "Let's put some water on the reverend."

Shuttlesworth turned, frowning, to look back. A jet from a water cannon hit him squarely in the chest. He staggered and fell backward down the stairs with a clatter and a roar.

Someone yelled: "Oh, my God, Shuttlesworth is struck!"

George rushed in. Shuttlesworth lay at the foot of the stairs, gasping. "Are you okay?" George yelled, but Shuttlesworth could not answer. "Get an ambulance, somebody, fast!" George shouted.

George was astonished that the authorities had been so stupid. Shuttlesworth was a hugely popular figure. Did they actually *want* to provoke a riot?

Ambulances were near at hand, and it was only a minute or two later that two men came in with a stretcher and carried Shuttlesworth out.

George followed them up to the sidewalk. Black bystanders and white police were milling around dangerously. Reporters had gathered and press photographers clicked as the stretcher was eased into the ambulance. They all watched it drive away.

A moment later, Bull Connor appeared. "I waited a week to see Shuttlesworth hit by a hose," he said jovially. "I'm sorry I missed it."

George was furious. He hoped one of the bystanders would punch Connor's fat face.

A white newspaper reporter said: "He left in an ambulance."

"I wish it was a hearse," said Connor.

George had to turn away to control his fury. He was saved by Dennis Wilson, who appeared from nowhere and grabbed his arm. "Good news!" he said. "The Big Mules caved!"

George spun around. "What do you mean, they caved?"

"They formed a committee to negotiate with the campaigners."

That *was* good news. Something had changed them: the demonstrations, or the phone calls from the president, or the threat of martial law. Whatever the reason, they were now desperate enough to sit down with black people and discuss a truce. Perhaps it could be agreed before the rioting turned seriously nasty.

"But they need someplace to meet," Dennis added.

"Verena will know. Let's go find her." George turned to leave, then paused and looked back at Bull Connor. He was becoming irrelevant, George now saw. Connor was on the streets, jeering at civil rights campaigners, but at the chamber of commerce the city's most powerful men had changed course—and they had done so without consulting Connor. Maybe the time was coming when fat white bullies would no longer rule the South.

And then again, maybe not.

.   .   .

The compromise was announced at a press conference on Friday. Fred Shuttlesworth attended, with cracked ribs from the water cannon, and announced: "Birmingham reached an accord with its conscience today!" Shortly afterward he fainted and had to be carried out. Martin Luther King declared a victory and flew home to Atlanta.

Birmingham's white elite had at last agreed to some measure of desegregation. Verena complained that it was not much, and in a way she was right: they were making a few minor concessions. But George believed that a huge change of principle had occurred: the whites had accepted that they needed to negotiate with the Negroes about segregation. They could no longer simply lay down the law. Those negotiations would continue, and they could go in only one direction.

Whether this was a small advance or a major turning point, every colored person in Birmingham was celebrating on Saturday night, and Verena invited George to her room.

He soon learned that she was not one of those girls who liked the man to take charge in bed. She knew what she wanted and she was comfortable asking for it. That was fine with George.

Almost anything would have been fine with him. He was enchanted by her lovely pale body and her witchy green eyes. She talked a lot while they made love, telling him how she felt, asking him if this pleased him or that embarrassed him; and the talk heightened their intimacy. He realized, more strongly than ever, how sex could be a way of getting to know the other person's character as well as her body.

Near the end she wanted to get on top. This, too, was new: no woman had done that with him before. She knelt astride him, and he held her hips and moved with her. She closed her eyes, but he did not. He watched her face, fascinated and enthralled, and when at last she reached her climax, he did too.

A few minutes before midnight he stood at the window in a robe, looking down on the streetlights of Fifth Avenue, while Verena was in the bathroom. His mind returned to the agreement King had struck with Birmingham's whites. If it was a triumph for the civil rights movement, die-hard segregationists would not accept defeat, he guessed; but what *would* they do? Bull Connor undoubtedly had a plan for sabotaging the agreement. So presumably did George Wallace, the racist governor.

That day the Ku Klux Klan had held a rally at Bessemer, a small town eighteen miles from Birmingham. According to Bobby Kennedy's intelligence, supporters had come from Georgia, Tennessee, South Carolina, and Mississippi. No doubt their speakers had spent the evening working them up into a frenzy of indignation about Birmingham giving in to the blacks. By now the women and children must have gone home, but the men would have started drinking and bragging to one another about what they were going to do.

Tomorrow would be Mother's Day, Sunday, May 12. George recalled Mother's Day two years ago, when white people had tried to kill him and other Freedom Riders by firebombing their bus at Anniston, sixty miles from here.

Verena emerged from the bathroom. "Come back to bed," she said, getting under the sheet.

George was eager. He hoped to make love to her at least once more before dawn. But just as he was about to turn away from the window, something caught his eye. The headlights of two cars were approaching along Fifth Avenue. The first vehicle was a white Birmingham Police Department patrol car, clearly marked with the number 25. It was followed by an old round-nosed Chevrolet from the early fifties. Both cars slowed as they drew level with the Gaston.

George suddenly noticed that the cops and state troopers who had been patrolling the streets around the motel had vanished. There was no one on the sidewalk.

What the hell . . . ?

A second later something was thrown from the open rear window of the Chevrolet, across the sidewalk, to the wall of the motel. The object landed right underneath the windows of the corner suite, Room 30, which Martin Luther King had occupied until he left earlier today.

Then both cars accelerated.

George turned from the window, crossed the room in two strides, and threw himself on top of Verena.

Her yell of protest was just beginning when it was drowned by a tremendous boom. The entire building shook as if in an earthquake. The air filled with the sounds of smashing glass and the rumble of falling masonry. The window of their room shattered with a tinkling noise like death chimes. There was a creepy moment of quiet. As the sound of the two cars faded, George heard shouts and screams from within the building.

He said to Verena: "Are you okay?"

She said: "What the fuck happened?"

"Someone threw a bomb from a car." He frowned. "The car had a police escort. Can you believe that?"

"In this goddamn town? You bet I can."

George rolled off her and looked around the room. He saw broken glass all over the floor. A piece of green cloth was draped over the end of the bed, and after a moment he realized it was the curtain. A picture of President Roosevelt had been blown off the wall by the force of the blast, and lay faceup on the carpet, crazed glass over the president's smile.

Verena said: "We have to go downstairs. People may be hurt."

"Wait a minute," George said. "I'll get your shoes." He put his feet down on a clear patch of the rug. To cross the room he had to pick up shards of glass and throw them aside. His shoes and hers were side by side in the closet: he liked that. He put his feet into his black leather oxfords, then picked up Verena's white kitten-heels and took them to her.

The lights went out.

They both dressed quickly in the dark. They discovered there was no water in the bathroom. They went downstairs.

The darkened lobby was full of panicking hotel staff and guests. Several people were bleeding but it seemed no one was dead. George pushed his way outside. By the streetlights he saw a hole five feet across in the wall of the building, and a spill of heavyweight rubble across the sidewalk. Trailers parked in the adjacent lot had been wrecked by the force of the blast. But, by a miracle, no one had been badly injured.

A cop arrived with a dog, then an ambulance drew up, then more police. Ominously, groups of Negroes began to gather outside the motel and in Kelly Ingram Park on the next block. These people were not the nonviolent Christians who had marched joyfully out of the Sixteenth Street Baptist Church singing hymns, George noted anxiously. This crowd had spent Saturday evening drinking in bars and pool halls and juke joints, and they did not subscribe to the Gandhian philosophy of passive resistance favored by Martin Luther King.

Someone said there had been another bomb, a few blocks away, at the parsonage occupied by Martin Luther King's brother, Alfred, always known as A. D. King. An eyewitness had seen a uniformed cop place a package on the porch a few seconds before the blast. Clearly the Birmingham police had tried to murder both King brothers at the same time.

The crowd got angrier.

Soon they were throwing bottles and rocks. Dogs and water cannon were the favorite targets. George went back inside the motel. Verena was helping to rescue an elderly black woman from a wrecked ground-floor room by flashlight.

"It's getting nasty out there," George said to Verena. "They're throwing rocks at the police."

"So they damn well should. The police are the bombers."

"Think about this," George said urgently. "Why do the whites want a riot tonight? To sabotage the agreement."

She wiped plaster dust off her forehead. George watched her face and saw rage replaced by calculation. "Damn, you're right," she said.

"We can't let them do it."

"But how can we stop it?"

"We have to get all the movement leaders out there calming people down."

She nodded. "Hell, yes. I'll start rounding people up."

George went back outside. The riot had escalated fast. A taxicab had been overturned and torched, and was blazing in the middle of the road. A block away, a grocery store was alight. Squad cars approaching from downtown were halted at Seventeenth Street by a hail of missiles.

George grabbed a megaphone and addressed the crowd. "Everybody stay calm!" he said. "Don't jeopardize our deal! The segregationists are trying to provoke a riot—don't give them what they want! Go home to bed!"

A black man standing nearby said to him: "How come *we* have to go home every time *they* start violence!"

George jumped on the hood of a parked car and stood on the roof. "This is not helping us!" he said. "Our movement is nonviolent! Everybody go home!"

Someone yelled: "We're nonviolent, but they ain't!"

Then an empty whisky bottle flew through the air and hit George's forehead. He climbed down from the roof of the car. He touched his head. It hurt, but it was not bleeding.

Others took up his cry. Verena appeared with several movement leaders and preachers, and they all mingled with the crowd, trying to talk people down. A. D. King got up on a car. "Our home was just bombed," he cried. "We say, Father, forgive them, for they know not what they do. But you are not helping—you are hurting us! Please, clear this park!"

Slowly, it began to work. Bull Connor was nowhere to be seen, George noted: the man in charge was Chief of Police Jamie Moore—a law enforcement professional rather than a political appointee—and that helped. The police attitude seemed to have changed. Dog handlers and firemen no longer seemed eager for a fight. George heard a cop saying to a group of Negroes: "We're your friends!" It was bullshit, but a new kind of bullshit.

There were hawks and doves among the segregationists, George realized. Martin Luther King had allied himself with the doves, and thereby outflanked the hawks. Now the hawks were trying to reignite the fires of hatred. They could not be allowed to succeed.

Lacking the stimulus of police aggression, the crowd lost the will to riot. George began to hear a different kind of comment. When the burning grocery store collapsed, people sounded penitent. "That's a doggone shame," said one man, and another said: "We gone too far."

At last the preachers got them singing, and George relaxed. It was all over, he felt.

He found Chief Moore on the corner of Fifth Avenue and Seventeenth Street. "We need to get repair crews to the motel, Chief," he said politely. "Power and water are out, and it's going to get unsanitary in there pretty quickly."

"I'll see what I can do," said Moore, and put his walkie-talkie to his ear.

But before he could speak into it, the state troopers arrived.

They wore blue helmets and they carried carbines and double-barreled shotguns. They arrived in a rush, most in cars, some on horseback. Within seconds there were two hundred or more. George stared in horror. This was a catastrophe—they would restart the riot. But that was what Governor George Wallace wanted, he realized. Wallace, like Bull Connor and the bombers, saw that the only hope now for the segregationists was a complete breakdown of law and order.

A car drew up and Wallace's director of public safety, Colonel Al Lingo, jumped out, toting a shotgun. Two men with him, apparently bodyguards, had Thompson submachine guns.

Chief Moore holstered his walkie-talkie. He spoke softly, but carefully did not address Lingo by his military rank. "If you'd leave, Mr. Lingo, I'd appreciate it."

Lingo did not trouble to be courteous. "Get your cowardly ass back to your office," he said. "I'm in charge now, and my orders are to put those black bastards to bed."

George expected them to tell him to get lost, but they were too intent on their argument to care about him.

"Those guns are not needed," said Moore. "Will you please put them up? Somebody's going to get killed."

"You're damn right!" said Lingo.

George walked away quickly, heading back to the motel.

Just before he went inside he turned to look, just in time to see the state troopers charge the crowd.

Then the riot started all over again.

George found Verena in the motel courtyard. "I have to go to Washington," he said.

He did not want to go. He wanted to spend time with Verena, talking to her, deepening their newfound intimacy. He wanted to make her fall in love with him. But that would have to wait.

She said: "What are you going to do in Washington?"

"Make sure the Kennedy brothers understand what's happening. They have to be told that Governor Wallace is provoking violence in order to undermine the deal."

"It's three o'clock in the morning."

"I'd like to get to the airport as early as possible and catch the first flight out. I might have to go via Atlanta."

"How will you get to the airport?"

"I'm going to look for a taxi."

"No cab will pick up a black man tonight—especially one with a lump on his forehead."

George touched his face exploratively and found a bump just where she said. "How did that happen?" he said.

"I seem to remember seeing a bottle hit you."

"Oh, yes. Well, it may be dumb, but I have to try to get to the airport."

"What about your luggage?"

"I can't pack in the dark. Besides, I don't have much. I'm just going to go."

"Be careful," she said.

He kissed her. She put her arms around his neck and pressed her slim body to his. "It was great," she whispered. Then she let him go.

He left the motel. The avenues heading directly downtown were blocked to the east: he would have to take a circuitous route. He walked west, then north, then turned east when he felt he was well clear of the rioting. He did not see any taxis. He might have to wait for the first bus of Sunday morning.

A faint light was showing in the eastern sky when a car screeched to a halt alongside him. He got ready to run, fearing white vigilantes, then changed his mind when three state troopers got out, rifles at the ready.

They won't need much of an excuse to kill me, he thought fearfully.

The leader was a short man with a swagger. George noticed he had a sergeant's chevrons on his sleeve. "Where are you going, boy?" the sergeant said.

"I'm trying to get to the airport, Sarge," George said. "Maybe you can tell me where I can find a taxicab."

The leader turned to the others with a grin. "He's trying to get to the airport," he repeated, as if the idea were risible. "He thinks we can help him find a taxi!"

His subordinates laughed appreciatively.

"What are you going to do at the airport?" the sergeant asked George. "Clean the toilets?"

"I'm going to catch a plane to Washington. I work at the Department of Justice. I'm a lawyer."

"Is that so? Well, I work for George Wallace, the governor of Alabama, and we don't pay too much mind to Washington, down here. So get in the goddamn car before I break your woolly head."

"What are you arresting me for?"

"Don't get smart with me, boy."

"If you seize me without good cause, you're a criminal, not a trooper."

With a sudden quick motion the sergeant swung his rifle, butt first. George ducked and instinctively raised his hand to protect his face. The wooden butt of the rifle struck his left wrist painfully. The other two troopers seized his arms. He offered no resistance, but they dragged him along as if he were struggling. The sergeant opened the rear door of the car and they threw him on the backseat. They slammed the door before he was fully inside, and it jammed his leg, causing him to shout in pain. They opened the door again, shoved his injured leg inside, and closed the door.

He lay slumped on the backseat. His leg hurt but his wrist was worse. They can do anything they like to us, he thought, because we're black. At that moment he wished he had thrown rocks and bottles at the police instead of running around telling people to calm down and go home.

The troopers drove to the Gaston. There they opened the back door of the car and pushed George out. Holding his left wrist in his right hand, he limped back into the courtyard.

. . .

Later that Sunday morning George at last found a working taxi with a black driver and went to the airport, where he caught a flight to Washington. His left wrist hurt so badly that he could not use his arm, and he kept his hand in his pocket for support. The wrist was swollen, and to ease the pain he took off his watch and unbuttoned his shirt cuff.

From a pay phone at National Airport he called the Department of Justice and learned that there would be an emergency meeting at the White House at six P.M. The president was flying in from Camp David, and Burke Marshall had been helicoptered in from West Virginia. Bobby was on his way to Justice and urgently required a briefing, and no, there was no time for George to go home and change his clothes.

Vowing to keep a clean shirt in his desk drawer from now on, George got a taxi to the Justice Department and went straight to Bobby's office.

George insisted that his injuries were too trivial to require medical treatment, though he winced every time he tried to move his left arm. He summarized the night's events for the attorney general and a group of advisers including Marshall. For some reason Bobby's huge black Newfoundland dog, Brumus, was there too.

"The truce that was agreed on with such difficulty this week is now in jeopardy," George told them in conclusion. "The bombings, and the brutality of the state troopers, have weakened the Negroes' commitment to nonviolence. On the other side, the riots threaten to undermine the position of the whites who negotiated with Martin Luther King. The enemies of integration, George Wallace and Bull Connor, hope that one side or both will renounce the agreement. Somehow we have to prevent that happening."

"Well, that's pretty clear," said Bobby.

They all got into Bobby's car, a Ford Galaxie 500. It was spring, and he had the top down. They drove the short distance to the White House. Brumus enjoyed the ride.

Several thousand demonstrators were outside the White House, noticeably a mixture of black and white, carrying placards that said SAVE THE SCHOOLCHILDREN OF BIRMINGHAM.

President Kennedy was in the Oval Office, sitting in his favorite chair, a rocker, waiting for the group from Justice. With him was a powerful trio of military men: Bob McNamara, the whiz kid secretary of defense, plus the army secretary and the army chief of staff.

This group had gathered here today, George realized, because the Negroes of Birmingham had started fires and thrown bottles last night. Such an emergency meeting had never been called during all the years of nonviolent civil rights protest, even when the Ku Klux Klan bombed the homes of Negroes. Rioting brought results.

The military men were present to discuss sending the army into Birmingham. Bobby focused as always on the political reality. "People are going to be calling for the president to take action," he said. "But here's the problem. We can't admit that we're sending federal troops to control the state troopers—that would be the White House declaring war on the state of Alabama. So we'd have to say it was to control the rioters—and that would be the White House declaring war on Negroes."

President Kennedy got it right away. "Once the white people have the protection of federal troops, they might just tear up the agreement they just made," he said.

In other words, George thought, the threat of Negro riots is keeping the agreement alive. He did not like this conclusion, but it was hard to escape.

Burke Marshall spoke up. He saw the agreement as his baby. "If that agreement blows up," he said wearily, "the Negroes will be, uh . . ."

The president finished his sentence. "Uncontrollable," he said.

Marshall added: "And not only in Birmingham."

The room went quiet as they all contemplated the prospect of similar riots in other American cities.

President Kennedy said: "What is King doing today?"

George said: "Flying back to Birmingham." He had learned this just before leaving the Gaston. "By now, I have no doubt, he's making the rounds of the big churches, urging people to go home peacefully after the service and stay indoors tonight."

"Will they do what he says?"

"Yes, provided there are no further bombings, and the state troopers are brought under control."

"How can we guarantee that?"

"Could you deploy U.S. troops *near* Birmingham, but not actually *in* the city? That would demonstrate support for the agreement. Connor and Wallace would know that if they misbehave, they will forfeit their power. But it would not give the whites the chance to renege on the deal."

They talked it up and down for a while, and in the end that was what they decided to do.

George and a small subgroup moved to the Cabinet Room to draft a statement for the press. The president's secretary typed it. Press conferences were usually held in Pierre Salinger's office, but today there were too many reporters and television cameras for that room, and it was a warm spring evening, so the announcement was made in the Rose Garden. George watched President Kennedy step outside, stand in front of the world's press, and say: "The Birmingham agreement was and is a just accord. The federal government will not permit it to be sabotaged by a few extremists on either side."

Two steps forward, one step back, and two more forward, George thought; but we make progress.

Dave Williams had a plan for Saturday night. Three girls from his class at school were going to the Jump Club in Soho, and Dave and two other boys had said, casually, that they might meet the girls there. Linda Robertson was one of the girls. Dave thought she liked him. Most people assumed he was thick, because he always came bottom of the class in exams, but Linda talked to him intelligently about politics, which he knew about because of his family.

Dave was going to wear a new shirt with startlingly long collar points. He was a good dancer—even his male friends conceded that he had a stylish way of doing the Twist. He thought he had a good chance of starting a romance with Linda.

Dave was fifteen but, to his intense annoyance, most girls of his age preferred older boys. He still winced when he remembered how, more than a year ago, he had followed the enchanting Beep Dewar, hoping to steal a kiss, and had found her locked in a passionate embrace with eighteen-year-old Jasper Murray.

On Saturday mornings the Williams children went to their father's study to receive their weekly allowances. Evie, who was seventeen, was given a pound; Dave got ten shillings. Like Victorian paupers, they often had to listen to a sermon first. Today Evie was given her money and dismissed, but Dave was told to wait. When the door closed, his father, Lloyd, said: "Your exam results are very bad."

Dave knew that. In ten years of schooling he had failed every written test he had ever taken. "I'm sorry," he said. He did not want to get into an argument: he just wanted to take his money and go.

Dad was wearing a check shirt and a cardigan, his Saturday morning outfit. "But you're not stupid," he said.

"The teachers think I'm thick," Dave said.

"I don't believe that. You're intelligent, but lazy."

"I'm not lazy."

"What are you, then?"

Dave did not have an answer. He was a slow reader, but worse than that he always forgot what he had read as soon as he turned the page. He was a poor writer, too: when he wanted to put "bread" his pen would write "beard" and he would not notice the difference. His spelling was atrocious. "I got top marks in oral French and German," he said.

"Which only proves you can do it when you try."

It did not prove any such thing, but Dave did not know how to explain that.

Lloyd said: "I've thought long and hard about what to do, and your mother and I have talked about it endlessly."

This sounded ominous to Dave. What the hell was coming now?

"You're too old to be spanked, and anyway we never had much faith in physical punishment."

That was true. Most kids were smacked when they misbehaved, but Dave's mother had not struck him for years; his father, never. What bothered Dave now, however, was the word *punishment*. Clearly he was in for it.

"The only thing I can think of, to force you to concentrate on your studies, is to withdraw your allowance."

Dave could not believe what he was hearing. "What do you mean, withdraw?"

"I'm not giving you any more money until I see an improvement in your schoolwork."

Dave had not seen this coming. "But how am I supposed to get around London?" And buy cigarettes, and get into the Jump Club, he thought in a panic.

"You walk to school anyway. If you want to go anywhere else, you'll have to do better in your lessons."

"I can't live like that!"

"You get fed for nothing, and you have a wardrobe full of clothes, so you won't lack for much. Just remember that if you don't study, you'll never have the money to get around."

Dave was outraged. His plan for this evening was ruined. He felt helpless and infantile. "So that's it?"

"Yes."

"I'm wasting my time here, then."

"You're listening to your father trying to guide you as best he can."

"Same bloody thing," Dave said, and he stamped out.

He took his leather jacket off the hook in the hall and left the house. It was a mild spring morning. What was he going to do? His plan for the day had been to meet some friends in Piccadilly Circus, stroll along Denmark Street looking at guitars, have a pint of beer in a pub, then come home and put on the shirt with the long collar points.

He had some change in his pocket—enough for half a pint of beer. How could he get the money for admission to the Jump Club? Perhaps he could work. Who would employ him at short notice? Some of his friends had jobs on Saturday or Sunday, working in shops and restaurants that needed extra people at the weekend. He considered walking into a café and offering to wash up in the kitchen. It was worth a try. He turned his steps toward the West End.

Then he had another idea.

He had relatives who might employ him. His father's sister, Millie, was in the fashion business, with three shops in affluent north London suburbs: Harrow, Golders Green, and Hampstead. She might give him a Saturday job, though he did not know how good he would be at selling frocks to ladies. Millie was married to a leather wholesaler, Abie Avery, and his warehouse in east London might be a better bet. But both Auntie Millie and Uncle Abie would probably check with Lloyd, who would tell them that Dave was supposed to be studying, not working. However, Millie and Abie had a son, Lenny, aged twenty-three, who was a small-time businessman and hustler. On Saturdays Lenny operated a market stall in Aldgate, in the East End. He sold Chanel No. 5 and other expensive perfumes at ludicrously low prices. He whispered to his customers that they were stolen, but in fact they were simple fakes, cheap scent in expensive-looking bottles.

Lenny might give Dave a day's work.

Dave had just enough money for the Tube fare. He turned into the nearest station and bought his ticket. If Lenny turned him down he did not know how he was going to get back. He guessed he could walk a few miles if necessary.

The train took him underneath London from the affluent west to the working-class east. The market was already crowded with shoppers eager to buy at prices lower than those in the regular stores. Some of the goods *were* stolen, Dave guessed: electric kettles, shavers, irons, and radio sets slipped out of the back door of the factory. Others were surplus production sold off cheaply by the makers: records no one wanted, books that had failed to become bestsellers, ugly photo frames, ashtrays in the shape of seashells. But most were defective. There were boxes of stale chocolates, striped scarves with a flaw in the weave, piebald leather boots that had been unevenly dyed, china plates decorated with half a flower.

Lenny resembled his and Dave's grandfather, the late Bernie Leckwith, with thick dark hair and brown eyes. Lenny's hair was oiled and combed into an Elvis Presley pompadour. His greeting was warm. "Hello, young Dave! Want some scent for the girlfriend? Try Fleur Sauvage." He pronounced it "flewer savidge." "Guaranteed to make her knickers fall down, yours for two shillings and sixpence."

"I need a job, Lenny," said Dave. "Can I work for you?"

"Need a job? Your mother's a millionaire, ain't she?" said Lenny evasively.

"Dad cut off my allowance."

"Why did he do that?"

"Because my schoolwork is poor. So I'm broke. I just want to earn enough money to go out tonight."

For the third time, Lenny replied with a question. "What am I, the Labour Exchange?"

"Give me a chance. I bet I could sell perfume."

Lenny turned to a customer. "You, madam, have got very good taste. Yardley perfumes are the classiest on the market—yet that bottle in your hand is only three shillings, and I had to pay two-and-six to the bloke that stole it, I mean to say supplied it to me."

The woman giggled and bought the perfume.

"I can't pay you a wage," Lenny said to Dave. "But I tell you what I'll do: I'll give you ten percent of everything you take."

"It's a deal," said Dave, and he joined Lenny behind the display.

"Keep the money in your pockets and we'll settle up later." Lenny gave him a "float" of a pound in coins to make change.

Dave picked up a bottle of Yardley, hesitated, smiled at a passing woman, and said: "The classiest perfume on the market."

She smiled back and walked on.

He kept trying, imitating Lenny's patter, and after a few minutes he sold a bottle of Joy by Patou for two-and-six. He soon knew all Lenny's lines: "Not every woman has the flair to wear this one, but you . . . Only buy this if there's a man you *really* want to please . . . Discontinued line, the government banned this scent because it's too sexy . . ."

The crowds were cheerful and always ready to laugh. They dressed up to come to the market: it was a social event. Dave learned a whole range of new slang for money: a sixpenny piece was a Tilbury, five shillings was a dollar, and a ten-shilling note was half a knicker.

The time passed quickly. A waitress from a nearby café brought two sandwiches of thick white bread with fried bacon and ketchup, and Lenny paid her and gave one of the sandwiches to Dave, who was surprised to learn that it was lunchtime. The pockets of his drainpipe jeans grew heavy with coins, and he recalled with pleasure that 10 percent of the money was his. At midafternoon he noticed that there were hardly any men on the streets, and Lenny explained that they had all gone to a football match.

Toward the end of the afternoon, business slowed to almost nothing. Dave thought the money in his pockets might amount to as much as five pounds, in which case he had made ten shillings, the amount of his normal allowance—and he could go to the Jump Club.

At five o'clock Lenny began to dismantle the stall, and Dave helped to put the unsold goods in cardboard boxes, then they loaded everything into Lenny's yellow Bedford van.

When they counted Dave's money, he had taken just over nine pounds. Lenny gave him a pound, a little more than the agreed ten percent, "because you helped me pack up." Dave was delighted: he had made twice the amount his father should have given him this morning. He would gladly do this every Saturday, he thought, especially if it meant he did not have to listen to his father's preaching.

They went to the nearest pub and got pint glasses of beer. "You play the guitar a bit, don't you?" Lenny said as they sat at a grimy table with a full ashtray.

"Yes."

"What sort of instrument have you got?"

"An Eko. It's a cheap copy of a Gibson."

"Electric?"

"It's semihollow."

Lenny looked impatient: perhaps he did not know much about guitars. "Can you plug it in, is what I'm asking."

"Yes—why?"

"Because I need a rhythm guitarist for my group."

That was exciting. Dave had not thought of joining a group, but the idea appealed to him instantly. "I didn't know you had a group," he said.

"The Guardsmen. I play piano and do most of the singing."

"What kind of music?"

"Rock and roll—the only kind."

"By which you mean . . ."

"Elvis, Chuck Berry, Johnny Cash . . . All the greats."

Dave could play three-chord songs without difficulty. "What about the Beatles?" Their chords were more difficult.

Lenny said: "Who?"

"A new group. They're fab."

"Never heard of them."

"Well, anyway, I can play rhythm guitar on old rock songs."

Lenny looked mildly offended at the phrase, but he said: "So, do you want to audition for the Guardsmen?"

"I'd love to!"

Lenny looked at his watch. "How long will it take you to go home and get your guitar?"

"Half an hour, and half an hour to get back."

"Meet me at the Aldgate Workingmen's Club at seven. We'll be setting up. We can audition you before we play. Have you got an amplifier?"

"Small one."

"It'll have to do."

Dave got the Tube. His success as a salesman, and the beer he had drunk, gave him an inner glow. He smoked a cigarette on the train, rejoicing at his victory over his father. He imagined saying casually to Linda Robertson: "I play guitar in a beat group." That could hardly fail to impress her.

He arrived home and entered the house by the back door. He managed to slip up to his room without seeing either of his parents. It took him only a few moments to put his guitar in its carrying case and pick up his amplifier.

He was about to leave when his sister, Evie, came into his room, dressed up for Saturday night. She wore a short skirt and knee boots, and her hair was back-combed in a beehive. She had heavy eye makeup in the panda style made fashionable by Dusty Springfield. She looked older than seventeen. "Where are you going?" Dave asked her.

"To a party. Hank Remington is supposed to be there."

Remington, lead singer of the Kords, sympathized with some of Evie's causes, and had said so in interviews.

"You've caused a stir today," Evie said. She was not accusing him: she always took his side in arguments with the parents, and he did the same for her.

"What makes you say that?"

"Dad's really upset."

"Upset?" Dave was not sure what to make of that. His father could be angry, disappointed, stern, authoritarian, or tyrannical, and he knew how to react; but upset? "Why?"

"I gather you and he had a row."

"He wouldn't give me my allowance because I failed all my exams."

"What did you do?"

"Nothing. I walked out. I probably slammed the door."

"Where have you been all day?"

"I worked on Lenny Avery's market stall and earned a pound."

"Good for you! Where are you off to now, with your guitar?"

"Lenny has a beat group. He wants me to play rhythm guitar." That was an exaggeration: Dave did not have the job yet.

"Good luck!"

"I suppose you'll tell Mum and Dad where I've gone."

"Only if you want me to."

"I don't care." Dave went to the door, then hesitated. "He's upset?"

"Yes."

Dave shrugged and left.

He got out of the house without being seen.

He was looking forward to the audition. He played and sang a lot with his sister, but he had never sat in with a real group that had a drummer. He hoped he was good enough—though rhythm guitar was not difficult.

On the Tube his thoughts kept wandering back to his father. He was a bit shocked to learn that he could upset Dad. Fathers were supposed to be invulnerable—but that attitude was childish, he now saw. Irritatingly, he might have to change his outlook. He could no longer be merely indignant and resentful. He was not the only sufferer. Dad had hurt him, but he had hurt Dad as well, and they were both responsible. Feeling responsible was not as comfortable as feeling outraged.

He found the Aldgate Workingmen's Club and carried his guitar and amplifier inside. It was a drab place, with bright neon strips throwing a harsh light on Formica tables and tubular chairs lined up in rows that made him think of a factory canteen: hardly the place for rock and roll.

The Guardsmen were onstage, tuning up. As well as Lenny on piano there was Lew on drums, Buzz on bass, and Geoffrey on lead guitar. Geoffrey had a microphone in front of him, so presumably he also did some singing. All three were older than Dave, in their early twenties, and he feared they might be much better musicians than he was. Suddenly, playing rhythm did not seem so easy.

He tuned his guitar to the piano and plugged into his amplifier. Lenny said: "Do you know 'Mess of Blues'?"

Dave did, and he felt relieved. It was a rock-steady number in the key of C, led by a rolling piano part, easy to accompany on the guitar. He strummed along with it effortlessly, and found a special kick in playing with others that he had never experienced on his own.

Lenny sang well, Dave thought. Buzz and Lew made a solid rhythm section, very steady. Geoff had some fancy licks on lead guitar. The group was competent, if a bit unimaginative.

At the end of the song, Lenny said: "The chords round out the sound of the group nicely, but can you play more rhythmically?"

Dave was surprised to be criticized. He thought he had done well. "Okay," he said.

The next number was "Shake, Rattle and Roll," a Jerry Lee Lewis hit that was also piano-led. Geoffrey sang in unison with Lenny on the chorus. Dave played choppy chords on the offbeat, and Lenny seemed to like that better.

Lenny announced "Johnny B. Goode," and without being asked Dave enthusiastically played the Chuck Berry introduction. When he got to the fifth bar he expected the group to join in, as on the record, but the Guardsmen remained silent. Dave stopped, and Lenny said: "I usually play the intro on the piano."

"Sorry," Dave said, and Lenny restarted the number.

Dave felt dispirited. He was not doing well.

The next number was "Wake Up, Little Susie." To Dave's surprise, Geoffrey did not sing the Everly Brothers harmony. After the first verse, Dave moved to Geoffrey's microphone and began to sing with Lenny. A minute later, two young waitresses who were putting ashtrays out on the tables stopped their work to listen. At the end of the song they clapped. Dave grinned with pleasure. It was the first time he had been applauded by anyone outside his family.

One of the girls said to Dave: "What's your group called?"

Dave pointed at Lenny. "It's his group, and they're called the Guardsmen."

"Oh." She seemed mildly disappointed.

Lenny's last choice was "Take Good Care of My Baby," and again Dave sang the harmony. The waitresses danced along the aisles between the rows of tables.

Afterward, Lenny got up from the piano. "Well, you're not much of a guitarist," he said to Dave. "But you sing nicely, and those girls really went for it."

"So am I in, or out?"

"Can you play tonight?"

"Tonight!" Dave was pleased, but he had not expected to start immediately. He was looking forward to seeing Linda Robertson later.

"You got something better to do?" Lenny looked a bit offended that Dave had not accepted instantly.

"Well, I was going to see a girl, but she'll just have to wait. What time will we be through?"

"This is a workingmen's club. They don't stay up late. We come offstage at half past ten."

Dave calculated that he could be at the Jump Club by eleven. "That's okay," he said.

"Good," said Lenny. "Welcome to the group."

· · ·

Jasper Murray still could not afford to go to America. At St. Julian's College, London, there was a group called the North America Club that chartered flights and sold cheap tickets. Late one afternoon he went to their little office in the student union and inquired about prices. He learned that he could go to New York for ninety pounds. It was too much, and he left disconsolate.

He spotted Sam Cakebread in the coffee bar. For several days he had been looking for a chance to speak to Sam outside the office of the student newspaper, *St. Julian's News.* Sam was the paper's editor, Jasper its news editor.

With Sam was his younger sister, Valerie, also a student at St. Julian's, wearing a tweed cap and a minidress. She wrote articles about fashion for the paper. She was attractive: in other circumstances Jasper would have flirted with her, but today he had other matters on his mind. He would have preferred to talk to Sam on his own, but he decided that Valerie's presence was no real problem.

He carried his coffee to Sam's table. "I want your advice," he said. He wanted information, not advice, but people were sometimes reluctant to share information, whereas they were always flattered to be asked for advice.

Sam was wearing a herringbone jacket with a tie and smoking a pipe: perhaps he wanted to look older. "Take a seat," he said, folding the paper he had been reading.

Jasper sat down. His relationship with Sam was awkward. They had been rivals for the post of editor, and Sam had won. Jasper had concealed his resentment, and Sam had made him news editor. They had become colleagues, but not friends. "I want to be next year's editor," Jasper said. He hoped that Sam would help him, either because he was the right man for the job—which he was—or out of guilt.

"That's up to Lord Jane," said Sam evasively. Jane was provost of the college.

"Lord Jane will ask your opinion."

"There's a whole appointment committee."

"But you and the provost are the members who count."

Sam did not argue with that. "So you want my advice."

"Who else is in the running?"

"Toby, obviously."

"Really?" Toby Jenkins was the features editor, a plodder who had commissioned a dull series of worthy articles about the work of university officials such as the registrar and the treasurer.

"He will apply."

Sam himself had got the job partly because of the distinguished journalists among his relations. Lord Jane was impressed by such connections. This irritated Jasper, but he did not mention it.

Jasper said: "Toby's stuff is pedestrian."

"He's an accurate reporter, if unimaginative."

Jasper recognized this remark as a dig at himself. He was the opposite of Toby. He prized sensation over accuracy. In his reports a scuffle always became a fight, a plan was a conspiracy, and a slip of the tongue was never less than a blatant lie. He knew that people read newspapers for excitement, not information.

Cakebread added: "And he did write that piece about rats in the refectory."

"So he did." Jasper had forgotten. The article had caused an uproar. It had been luck, really: Toby's father worked for the local council and knew about the efforts of the pest control department to eradicate vermin in the eighteenth-century cellars of St. Julian's College. Nevertheless the article had secured the job of features editor for Toby, who had written nothing half as good since. "So I need a scoop," Jasper said thoughtfully.

"Perhaps."

"You mean, like, revealing that the provost is skimming off university funds to pay his gambling debts."

"I doubt that Lord Jane gambles." Sam did not have a great sense of humor.

Jasper thought about Lloyd Williams. Might he provide some kind of tip-off? Lloyd was frightfully discreet, unfortunately.

Then he thought of Evie. She had applied to attend the Irving School of Drama, which was part of St. Julian's College, so she was of interest to the student newspaper. She had just got her first acting job, in a film called *All Around Miranda.* And she was going out with Hank Remington, of the Kords. Perhaps . . .

Jasper stood up. "Thanks for your help, Sam. I really appreciate it."

"Anytime," said Sam.

Jasper caught the Tube home. The more he thought about interviewing Evie, the more excited he became.

Jasper knew the truth about Evie and Hank. They were not just dating, they were having a passionate affair. Her parents knew she went out with Hank two or three evenings a week, and came home at midnight on Saturdays. But Jasper and Dave also knew that most days after school Evie went to Hank's flat in Chelsea and had sex with him. Hank had already written a song about her, "Too Young to Smoke."

But would she give Jasper an interview?

When he got home to the house in Great Peter Street, Evie was in the red-tiled kitchen, learning lines. Her hair was pinned up untidily, and she wore a faded old shirt, but she still looked fabulous. Jasper's relationship with her was warm. Throughout her girlish crush on him, he had always been kind, though never encouraging. His motive for being so careful was that he did not want a crisis that would cause a rift between him and her generously hospitable parents. Now he was even more glad he had kept her goodwill. "How's it going?" he said with a nod at her script.

She shrugged. "The part isn't difficult, but film will be a new challenge."

"Maybe I should interview you."

She looked troubled. "I'm supposed to do only the publicity arranged by the studio."

Jasper felt a mild panic. What kind of journalist would he make if he failed to secure an interview with Evie even though he lived in her house? "It's only for the student paper," he said.

"I suppose that doesn't really count."

His hopes rose. "I'm sure not. And it might help you get accepted by the Irving drama school."

She put down the script. "All right. What do you want to know?"

Jasper suppressed his feeling of triumph. Coolly he said: "How did you get the part in *All Around Miranda*?"

"I went to an audition."

"Tell me about that." Jasper took out a notebook and started writing.

He was careful not to mention her nude scene in *Hamlet*. He feared she would tell him not to mention it. Fortunately he did not need to question her about it, for he had seen it himself. Instead he asked her about the stars of the movie, and other famous people she had met, and gradually worked around to Hank Remington.

When Jasper mentioned Hank, Evie's eyes lit up with a characteristic intensity of feeling. "Hank is the most courageous and dedicated person I know," she said. "I admire him so much."

"But you don't just admire him."

"I adore him."

"And you are dating."

"Yes, but I don't want to say too much about that."

"Of course, no problem." She had said "Yes," and that was enough.

Dave came in from school and made instant coffee with boiling milk. "I thought you weren't supposed to do publicity," he said to Evie.

Jasper thought: Shut your mouth, you overprivileged little shit.

Evie replied to Dave. "This is only for *St. Julian's News*," she said.

Jasper wrote the article that evening.

As soon as he saw it typed out, he realized it could be more than just a piece for the student paper. Hank was a star, Evie was a minor actress, and Lloyd was a member of Parliament: this could be a big story, he thought with mounting excitement. If he could get something published in a national newspaper it would give his career prospects a major boost.

It could also get him in trouble with the Williams family.

He gave his article to Sam Cakebread the next day.

Then, with trepidation, he phoned the tabloid *Daily Echo*.

He asked for the news editor. He did not get the news editor, but he was put through to a reporter called Barry Pugh. "I'm a student journalist, and I've got a story for you," he said.

"Okay, go ahead," said Pugh.

Jasper hesitated only a moment. He was betraying Evie and the entire Williams family, he knew; but he plunged on anyway. "It's about the daughter of a member of Parliament who is sleeping with a pop star."

"Good," said Pugh. "Who are they?"

"Could we meet?"

"I suppose you want some money?"

"Yes, but that's not all."

"What else?"

"I want my name on the article when it appears."

"Let's get the story down first, then we'll see."

Pugh was trying to employ the kind of blandishments Jasper had used on Evie. "No, thanks," Jasper said firmly. "If you don't like the story, you don't have to print it, but if you do use it you must put my name on it."

"All right," said Pugh. "When can we meet?"

.   .   .

Two days later, at breakfast in Great Peter Street, Jasper read in the *Guardian* that Martin Luther King was planning a massive demonstration of civil disobedience in Washington in support of a civil rights bill. King was forecasting that there would be one hundred thousand people. "Boy, I'd love to see that," said Jasper.

Evie said: "Me, too."

It was to take place in August, during the university vacation, so Jasper would be free. But he could not afford ninety pounds for the fare to the USA.

Daisy Williams opened an envelope and said: "My goodness! Lloyd, here's a letter from your German cousin Rebecca!"

Dave, the youngest, swallowed a mouthful of Sugar Puffs and said: "Who the heck is Rebecca?"

His father had been leafing through newspapers with the speed of a professional politician. Now he looked up and said: "Not really a cousin. She was adopted by some distant relations of mine after her parents died in the war."

"I'd forgotten we had German relatives," Dave said. "*Gott im Himmel!*"

Jasper had noticed that Lloyd was suspiciously vague about his relatives. The late Bernie Leckwith had been his stepfather, but no one ever mentioned his real father. Jasper felt sure Lloyd had been illegitimate.

It was not quite a tabloid story: bastardy was not as much of a disgrace as formerly. All the same, Lloyd never gave details.

Lloyd went on: "Last time I saw Rebecca was in 1948. She was about seventeen. By then she had been adopted by my relation Carla Franck. They lived in Berlin-Mitte, so now their house must be on the wrong side of the Wall. What's become of her?"

Daisy answered: "She's obviously got out of East Germany, somehow, and moved to Hamburg. Oh . . . her husband was injured escaping, and he's in a wheelchair."

"What prompted her to write to us?"

"She's trying to trace Hannelore Rothmann." Daisy looked at Jasper. "She was your grandmother. Apparently she was kind to Rebecca in the war, the day Rebecca's real parents were killed."

Jasper had never met his mother's family. "We don't know exactly what happened to my German grandparents, but Mother is sure they're dead," he said.

Daisy said: "I'll show this letter to your mother. She should write to Rebecca."

Lloyd opened the *Daily Echo* and said: "Bloody hell, what's this?"

Jasper had been waiting for this moment. He clasped his hands together in his lap to stop them shaking.

Lloyd spread the newspaper on the table. On page three was a photograph of Evie coming out of a nightclub with Hank Remington, and the headline:

Kords Star Hank
& Labour MP's
Nudie Daughter, 17

by Barry Pugh and Jasper Murray

"I didn't write that!" Jasper lied. His indignation sounded forced, to him; what he really felt was elation at the sight of his own name over a report in a national newspaper. The others did not seem to notice his mixed emotions.

Lloyd read aloud: "'Pop star Hank Remington's latest flame is the just-seventeen daughter of Lloyd Williams, member of Parliament for Hoxton. Movie starlet Evie Williams is famous for appearing nude onstage at Lambeth Grammar, the posh school for top people's children.'"

Daisy said: "Oh, dear, how embarrassing."

Lloyd read on: "'Evie said: "Hank is the most courageous and dedicated person I have ever known." Both Evie and Hank support the Campaign for Nuclear Disarmament, despite the disapproval of her father, who is Labour spokesman on military affairs.'" Lloyd looked at Evie severely. "You know a lot of courageous and dedicated people, including your mother, who drove an ambulance during the Blitz, and your great-uncle Billy Williams, who fought at the Somme. Hank must be remarkable, to overshadow them."

"Never mind that," said Daisy. "I thought you weren't supposed to do interviews without asking the studio, Evie."

"Oh, God, this is my fault," Jasper said. They all looked at him. He had known there would be a scene like this, and he was ready for it. He had no difficulty looking distraught: he felt horribly guilty. "I interviewed Evie for the student paper. The *Echo* must have lifted my story—and rewritten it to make it sensational." He had prepared this fiction in advance.

"First lesson of public life," Lloyd said. "Journalists are treacherous."

That's me, Jasper thought—treacherous. But the Williams family seemed to accept that he had not intended the *Echo* to run the story.

Evie was close to tears. "I might lose the part."

Daisy said: "I can't imagine this will do the movie any damage—quite the reverse."

"I hope you're right," said Evie.

"I'm so sorry, Evie," said Jasper, with all the sincerity he could muster. "I feel I've really let you down."

"You didn't mean to," Evie said.

Jasper had got away with it. Around the table, no one was looking accusingly at him. They saw the *Echo* report as nobody's fault. The only one he was not sure of was Daisy, who wore a slight frown and avoided his eye. But she loved Jasper for his mother's sake, and she would not accuse him of duplicity.

Jasper stood up. "I'm going to the *Daily Echo* office," he said. "I want to meet this Pugh bastard and see what explanation he can offer."

He was glad to get out of the house. He had successfully lied his way through a difficult scene, and the release of tension was enormous.

An hour later he was in the newsroom of the *Echo*. He was thrilled to be there. This was what he wanted: the news desk, the typewriters, the ringing phones, the pneumatic tubes carrying copy across the room, the air of excitement.

Barry Pugh was about twenty-five, a small man with a squint, wearing a rumpled suit and scuffed suede shoes. "You did well," he said.

"Evie still doesn't know I gave the story to you."

Pugh had little time for Jasper's scruples. "Bloody few stories would ever be published if we asked permission every time."

"She was supposed to refuse all interviews except those arranged by the studio publicist."

"Publicists are your enemies. Be proud you outwitted one."

"I am."

Pugh handed him an envelope. Jasper tore it open. It contained a check. "Your payment," Pugh said. "That's what you get for a page three lead."

Jasper looked at the amount. It was ninety pounds.

He remembered the march on Washington. Ninety pounds was the fare to the USA. Now he could go to America.

His heart lifted.

He put the check in his pocket. "Thank you very much," he said.

Barry nodded. "Let us know if you have any more stories like that."

. . .

Dave Williams was nervous about playing the Jump Club. It was a deeply cool central London venue, just off Oxford Street. It had a reputation for breaking new stars, and had launched several groups now in the hit parade. Famous musicians went there to listen to new talent.

Not that it looked special. There was a small stage at one end and a bar at the other. In between was room for a couple of hundred people to dance buttock-to-buttock. The floor was an ashtray. The only decoration consisted of a few tattered posters of famous acts that had played there in the past—except in the dressing room, where the walls bore the most obscene graffiti Dave had ever come across.

Dave's performance with the Guardsmen had improved, thanks in part to helpful advice from his cousin. Lenny had a soft spot for Dave, and talked like an uncle to him, although he was only eight years older. "Listen to the drummer," Lenny had told him. "Then you'll always be on the beat." And: "Learn to play without looking at your guitar, so that you can meet the eyes of people in the audience." Dave was grateful for any tips he could get, but he knew he was still far short of seeming professional. All the same he felt wonderful onstage. There was nothing to read or write, so he was no longer a dunce; in fact, he was competent, and getting better. He had even fantasized about becoming a musician, and never having to study, ever again; but he knew the chances were small.

The group was improving, however. When Dave sang in harmony with Lenny they sounded modern, more like the Beatles. And Dave had persuaded Lenny to try some different material, authentic Chicago blues and danceable Detroit soul, the kind of thing the younger groups were playing. As a result they were getting more dates. Instead of once a fortnight, they were now booked every Friday and Saturday night.

But Dave had another reason for anxiety. He had got this gig by asking Evie's boyfriend, Hank Remington, to recommend the group. But Hank had turned his nose up at their name. "The Guardsmen sounds old-fashioned, like the Four Aces, and the Jordanaires," he had said.

"We might change it," Dave had said, willing to do anything for a booking at the Jump Club.

"The latest vogue is a name from an old blues, like the Rolling Stones."

Dave recalled a track by Booker T. and the MGs that he had heard a few days earlier. He had been struck by its oddball name. "How about Plum Nellie?" he had said.

Hank had liked that, and told the club they should try out a new group called Plum Nellie. A suggestion from someone as famous as Hank was like a command, and the group got the gig.

But when Dave had proposed the name change, Lenny had turned it down flat. "The Guardsmen we are, and the Guardsmen we stay," he had said mulishly, and started talking about something else. Dave had not dared to tell him the Jump Club already thought they were called Plum Nellie.

Now the crisis was approaching.

At the sound check they played "Lucille." After the first verse, Dave stopped and turned to the lead guitarist, Geoffrey. "What the fuck was that?" Dave said.

"What?"

"You played something weird halfway through."

Geoffrey gave a knowing smile. "Nothing. It's just a passing chord."

"It's not on the record."

"What's the matter, can't you play C sharp diminished?"

Dave knew exactly what was going on. Geoffrey was trying to show him up as a beginner. But unfortunately Dave had never heard of a diminished chord.

Lenny said: "Known to pub pianists as a double minor, Dave."

Swallowing his pride, Dave said to Geoffrey: "Show me."

Geoffrey rolled up his eyes and sighed, but he demonstrated the chord shape. "Like that, all right?" he said wearily, as if tired of dealing with amateurs.

Dave copied the chord. It was not difficult. "Next time, tell me before we play the fucking song," he said.

After that it went well. Phil Burleigh, the owner of the club, entered in the middle and listened. Being prematurely bald, he was naturally known as Curly Burleigh. At the end he nodded approval. "Thank you, Plum Nellie," he said.

Lenny shot a filthy look at Dave. "The group is called the Guardsmen," he said firmly.

Dave said: "We discussed changing it."

"You discussed it. I said no."

Curly said: "The Guardsmen is a terrible name, mate."

"It's what we're called."

"Listen, Byron Chesterfield is coming in tonight," Curly said with a note of desperation. "He's the most important promoter in London—in Europe, probably. You might get work from him—but not with that name."

"Byron Chesterfield?" said Lenny, laughing. "I've known him all my life. His real name is Brian Chesnowitz. His brother's got a stall in Aldgate Market."

Curly said: "It's your name I'm worried about, not his."

"Our name is fine."

"I can't put on a group called the Guardsmen. I've got a reputation." Curly stood up. "I'm sorry, lads," he said. "Pack up your gear."

Dave said: "Come on, Curly, you don't want to piss off Hank Remington."

"Hank's an old mate," said Curly. "We played skiffle together at the 2i's Coffee Bar in the fifties. But he recommended me a group called Plum Nellie, not the Guardsmen."

Dave was distraught. "All my friends are coming!" he said. He was thinking of Linda Robertson in particular.

Curly said: "I'm sorry about that."

Dave turned to Lenny. "Be reasonable," he said. "What's in a name?"

"It's my group, not yours," said Lenny stubbornly.

So that was the issue. "Of course it's your group," said Dave. "But you taught me that the customer is always right." He was struck by inspiration. "And you can change the name back to the Guardsmen tomorrow morning, if you want."

Lenny said: "Naah," but he was weakening.

"Better than not playing," said Dave, pressing his advantage. "It would be a real comedown to go home now."

"Oh, fuck it, all right," said Lenny.

And the crisis was over, to Dave's intense relief and pleasure.

They stood at the bar drinking beer while the first customers trickled in. Dave limited himself to one pint: enough to relax him, not enough to make him fumble the chords. Lenny had two pints, Geoffrey three.

Linda Robertson showed up, to Dave's delight, in a short purple dress and white knee boots. She and all Dave's friends were legally too young to drink alcohol in bars, but they went to great lengths to look older, and anyway the law was not enforced strictly.

Linda's attitude to Dave had changed. In the past she had treated him like a bright kid brother, even though they were the same age. The fact that he was playing at the Jump Club turned him into a different person in her eyes. Now she saw him as a sophisticated grown-up, and asked him excited questions about the group. If this was what he got for being in Lenny's crummy outfit, Dave thought, what must it be like to be a real pop star?

With the others he returned to the dressing room to change. Professional groups usually appeared wearing identical suits, but that was expensive. Lenny compromised with red shirts for everyone. Dave thought that group uniforms were going out of fashion: the anarchic Rolling Stones dressed individually.

Plum Nellie was bottom of the bill, and played first. Lenny, as leader of the group, introduced the songs. He was seated at the side of the stage, with the upright piano angled so that he could look at the audience. Dave stood in the middle, playing and singing, and most eyes were on him. Now that the worry about the group's name was out of the way—at least for the moment—he could relax. He moved as he played, swinging the guitar as if it were his dance partner; and when he sang he imagined he was speaking to the audience, emphasizing the words with his facial expressions and the movements of his head. As always, the girls responded to that, watching him and smiling as they danced to the beat.

After the set, Byron Chesterfield came to the dressing room.

He was about forty, and wore a beautiful light blue suit with a waistcoat. His tie had a pattern of daisies. His hair was receding either side of an old-fashioned brilliantined quiff. He brought a cloud of cologne into the room.

He spoke to Dave. "Your group is not bad," he said.

Dave pointed to Lenny. "Thank you, Mr. Chesterfield, but it's Lenny's group."

Lenny said: "Hello, Brian, don't you remember me?"

Byron hesitated a moment, then said: "My life! It's Lenny Avery." His London accent became broader. "I never recognized you. How's the stall?"

"Doing great, never better."

"The group is good, Lenny: bass and drums solid, nice guitars and piano. I like the vocal harmonies." He jerked a thumb at Dave. "And the girls love the kid. You getting much work?"

Dave was excited. Byron Chesterfield liked the group!

Lenny said: "We're busy every weekend."

"I might be able to get you an out-of-town gig for six weeks in the summer, if you're interested," Byron said. "Five nights a week, Tuesday to Saturday."

"I don't know," said Lenny with indifference. "I'd have to get my sister to run the stall for me while I was away."

"Ninety pound a week in your hand, no deductions."

That was more than they had ever been paid, Dave calculated. And with luck it would fall in the school holiday.

Dave was annoyed to see Lenny still looking dubious. "What about board and lodging?" he said. Dave realized he was not uninterested, he was negotiating.

"You get lodging but not board," Byron said.

Dave wondered if this was at a seaside resort, where there was seasonal work for entertainers.

Lenny said: "I couldn't leave the stall for that kind of money, Brian. Pity it's not a hundred and twenty pound a week. Then I could consider it."

"The venue might go to ninety-five, as a personal favor to me."

"Say a hundred and ten."

"If I forgo my own fee I can make it a hundred."

Lenny looked at the rest of the group. "What do you say, lads?"

They all wanted to take the job.

"What's the venue?" Lenny said.

"A club called the Dive."

Lenny shook his head. "Never heard of it. Where is it?"

"Didn't I mention that?" said Byron Chesterfield. "It's in Hamburg."

. . .

Dave could hardly contain his excitement. A six-week gig—in Germany! Legally, he was old enough to quit school. Was there a chance he might become a professional musician?

In exuberant mood, he took his guitar and amplifier and Linda Robertson to the house in Great Peter Street, intending to drop off his gear before walking her home to her parents' place in Chelsea. Unfortunately his parents were still up, and his mother waylaid him in the hall. "How did it go?" she asked brightly.

"Great," he said. "I'm just dropping off my gear, and I'm going to walk Linda home."

"Hello, Linda," said Daisy. "How nice to see you again."

"How do you do?" Linda said politely, morphing into a demure schoolgirl; but Dave could see his mother taking in the short dress and the sexy boots.

"Will the club hire you again?" Daisy asked.

"Well, a promoter called Byron Chesterfield offered us a summer job at another club. It's great because it's all during the school holiday."

His father came out of the drawing room, still wearing his suit from whatever Saturday night political meeting he had attended. "What's happening in the school holiday?"

"Our group has a six-week engagement."

Lloyd frowned. "You need to do some revision in the vacation. Next year you have the all-important O-level exams. To date, your grades are nowhere near good enough to permit you to take the whole summer off."

"I can study in the day. We'll be playing in the evenings."

"Hmm. You obviously don't care about missing the annual holiday with your family in Tenby."

"I do," Dave lied. "I love Tenby. But this is a great opportunity."

"Well, I don't see how we can leave you alone in this house for two weeks while we're in Wales. You're still only fifteen."

"Er, the club isn't in London," Dave said.

"Where is it?"

"Hamburg."

Daisy said: "What?"

Lloyd said: "Don't be ridiculous. Do you imagine we're going to allow you to do that at your age? It must be illegal under German employment law, for one thing."

"Not all laws are strictly enforced," Dave argued. "I bet you illegally bought drinks in pubs before you were eighteen."

"I went to Germany with my mother when I was eighteen. I certainly never spent six weeks unsupervised in a foreign country at the age of fifteen."

"I won't be unsupervised. Cousin Lenny will be with me."

"I don't see him as a reliable chaperone."

"Chaperone?" said Dave indignantly. "What am I, a Victorian maiden?"

"You're a child, according to the law, and an adolescent, in reality. You're certainly not an adult."

"You've got a cousin in Hamburg," Dave said desperately. "Rebecca. She wrote to Mam. You could ask her to look after me."

"She's a distant cousin by adoption, and I haven't seen her for sixteen years. That's not a sufficiently close connection for me to dump an unruly teenager on her for the summer. I'd hesitate to do it to my sister."

Daisy adopted a conciliatory tone. "From her letter I got the impression of a kind person, Lloyd, dear. And I don't think she has children of her own. She might not mind being asked."

Lloyd looked annoyed. "Do you actually want Dave to do this?"

"No, of course not. If I had my wish, he would come to Tenby with us. But he is growing up, and we may have to loosen the apron strings." She looked at Dave. "He's going to find it harder work and less fun than he imagines, but he may learn some life lessons from it."

"No," said Lloyd with an air of finality. "If he were eighteen, perhaps I'd agree. But he's too young, much too young."

Dave wanted to scream with rage and burst into tears at the same time. Surely they would not spoil this opportunity?

"It's late," said Daisy. "Let's talk about it in the morning. Dave needs to get Linda home before her parents start to worry."

Dave hesitated, reluctant to leave the argument unresolved.

Lloyd went to the foot of the stairs. "Don't get your hopes up," he said to Dave. "It isn't going to happen."

Dave opened the front door. If he walked out now, without saying anything else, he would leave them with the wrong impression. He needed them to know they could not stop him going to Hamburg easily. "Listen to me," he said, and his father looked startled. Dave made up his mind. "For the first time in my life, I'm a success at something, Dad," he said. "Just understand me. If you try to take this from me, I'll leave home. And, I swear, if I leave I will never, ever, come back."

He led Linda out and slammed the door.

Tanya Dvorkin was back in Moscow, but Vasili Yenkov was not. After the two of them had been arrested at the poetry reading in Mayakovsky Square, Vasili had been convicted of "anti-Soviet activities and propaganda" and sentenced to two years in a Siberian labor camp. Tanya felt guilty: she had been Vasili's partner in crime, but she had got away with it.

Tanya assumed Vasili had been beaten and interrogated. But she was still free and working as a journalist, therefore he had not given her away. Perhaps he had refused to talk. More likely, he might have named plausible fictitious collaborators who the KGB believed were simply difficult to track down.

By the spring of 1963 Vasili had served his sentence. If he was alive—if he had survived the cold, hunger, and disease that killed many prisoners in labor camps—he should be free now. Ominously, he had not reappeared.

Prisoners were normally allowed to send and receive one letter per month, heavily censored; but Vasili could not write to Tanya, for that would betray her to the KGB; so she had no information; and no doubt the same applied to most of his friends. Perhaps he wrote to his mother in Leningrad. Tanya had never met her: Vasili's association with Tanya was secret even from his mother.

Vasili had been Tanya's closest friend. She lay awake nights worrying about him. Was he ill, or even dead? Perhaps he had been convicted of another crime, and had his sentence extended. Tanya was tortured by the uncertainty. It gave her a headache.

One afternoon she took the risk of mentioning Vasili to her boss, Daniil Antonov. The features department of TASS was a large, noisy room, with journalists typing, talking on the phone, reading newspapers, and walking in and out of the reference library. If she spoke quietly she would not be overheard. She began by saying: "What happened about Ustin Bodian, in the end?" The ill treatment of Bodian, a dissident opera singer, was the subject of the edition of *Dissidence* Vasili had been giving out when arrested—an issue written by Tanya.

"Bodian died of pneumonia," Daniil said.

Tanya knew that. She was pretending ignorance only to bring the conversation around to Vasili. "There was a writer arrested with me that day—Vasili Yenkov," she said in a musing tone. "Any idea what happened to him?"

"The script editor. He got two years."

"Then he must be free by now."

"Perhaps. I haven't heard. He won't get his old job back, so I'm not sure where he'd go."

He would come to Moscow, Tanya felt sure. But she shrugged, pretending indifference, and went back to typing an article about a woman bricklayer.

She had made several discreet inquiries among people who would have known if Vasili had returned. The answer had been the same in all cases: no one had heard anything.

Then, that afternoon, Tanya got word.

Leaving the TASS building at the end of the working day, she was accosted by a stranger. A voice said: "Tanya Dvorkin?" and she turned to see a pale, thin man in dirty clothes.

"Yes?" she said, a little anxiously: she could not imagine what such a man would want with her.

"Vasili Yenkov saved my life," he said.

It was so unexpected that for a moment she did not know how to respond. Too many questions raced through her mind: How do you know Vasili? Where and when did he save your life? Why have you come to me?

He thrust into her hand a grubby envelope the size of a regular sheet of paper, then he turned away.

It took Tanya a moment to gather her wits. At last she realized there was one question more important than all the rest. While the man was still within earshot she said: "Is Vasili alive?"

The stranger stopped and looked back. The pause struck fear into Tanya's heart. Then he said: "Yes," and she felt the sudden lightness of relief.

The man walked away.

"Wait!" Tanya called, but he quickened his pace, turned a corner, and disappeared from view.

The envelope was not sealed. Tanya looked inside. She saw several sheets of paper covered with handwriting that she recognized as Vasili's. She pulled them halfway out. The first sheet was headed:

Frostbite

by Ivan Kuznetsov

She pushed the sheets back into the envelope and walked on to the bus stop. She felt scared and excited at the same time. "Ivan Kuznetsov" was an obvious pseudonym, the commonest name imaginable, like Hans Schmidt in German or Jean Lefevre in French. Vasili had written something, an article or a story. She could hardly wait to read it, yet at the same time she had to resist the impulse to hurl it away from her like something contaminated, for it was sure to be subversive.

She shoved it into her shoulder bag. When the bus came it was crowded—this was the evening rush hour—so she could not look at the manuscript on her way home without the risk that someone would read it over her shoulder. She had to suppress her impatience.

She thought about the man who had handed it to her. He had been badly dressed, half starved, and in poor health, with a look of permanent wary fearfulness: just like a man recently released from jail, she thought. He had seemed glad to get rid of the envelope, and reluctant to say more to her than he had to. But he had at least explained why he had undertaken his dangerous errand. He was repaying a debt. "Vasili Yenkov saved my life," he had said. Again she wondered how.

She got off the bus and walked to Government House. On her return from Cuba she had moved back into her mother's flat. She had no reason to get her own apartment and, if she had, it would have been a lot less luxurious.

She spoke briefly to Anya, then went to her bedroom and sat down on the bed to read what Vasili had written.

His handwriting had altered. The letters were smaller, the risers shorter, the loops less flamboyant. Did that reflect a change of personality, she wondered, or just a shortage of writing paper?

She began to read.

Josef Ivanovich Maslov, called Soso, was overjoyed when the food arrived spoiled.

Normally, the guards stole most of the consignment and sold it. The prisoners were left with plain gruel in the morning and turnip soup at night. Food rarely went bad in Siberia, where the ambient temperature was usually below freezing—but Communism could work miracles. So when, occasionally, the meat was crawling with maggots and the fat rancid, the cook threw it all into the pot, and the prisoners rejoiced. Soso gobbled down kasha that was oily with stinking lard, and longed for more.

Tanya was nauseated, but at the same time she had to read on.

With each page she was more impressed. The story was about an unusual relationship between two prisoners, one an intellectual dissident, the other an uneducated gangster. Vasili had a simple, direct style that was remarkably effective. Life in the camp was described in brutally vivid language. But there was more than just description. Perhaps because of his experience in radio drama, Vasili knew how to keep a story moving, and Tanya found that her interest never flagged.

The fictional camp was located in a forest of Siberian larch, and its work was chopping down the trees. There were no safety rules and no protective clothing or equipment, so accidents were frequent. Tanya particularly noted an episode in which the gangster severed an artery in his arm with a saw and was saved by the intellectual, who tied a tourniquet around his arm. Was that how Vasili had saved the life of the messenger who had brought his manuscript to Moscow from Siberia?

Tanya read the story twice. It was almost like talking to Vasili: the phrasing was familiar from a hundred discussions and arguments, and she recognized the kinds of things he found funny or dramatic or ironic. It made her heart ache with missing him.

Now that she knew Vasili was alive, she had to find out why he had not returned to Moscow. The story contained no clue to that. But Tanya knew someone who could find out almost anything: her brother.

She put the manuscript in the drawer of her bedside table. She left the bedroom and said to her mother: "I have to go and see Dimka—I won't be long." She went down in the elevator to the floor on which her brother lived.

The door was opened by his wife, Nina, nine months pregnant. "You look well!" Tanya said.

It was not true. Nina was long past the stage when people said a pregnant woman looked "blooming." She was huge, her breasts pendulous, her belly stretched taut. Her fair skin was pale under the freckles, and her red-brown hair was greasy. She looked older than twenty-nine. "Come in," she said in a tired voice.

Dimka was watching the news. He turned off the television, kissed Tanya, and offered her a beer.

Nina's mother, Masha, was there, having come from Perm by train to help her daughter with the baby. Masha was a small, prematurely wrinkled peasant woman dressed in black, visibly proud of her citified daughter in her swanky apartment. Tanya had been surprised when she first met Masha, having previously got the impression that Nina's mother was a schoolteacher; but it turned out that she merely worked in the village school, cleaning it in fact. Nina had pretended that her parents were somewhat higher in status—a practice so common as to be almost universal, Tanya supposed.

They talked about Nina's pregnancy. Tanya wondered how to get Dimka alone. There was no way she was going to talk about Vasili in front of Nina or her mother. Instinctively she mistrusted her brother's wife.

Why did she feel that so strongly, she wondered guiltily? It was because of the pregnancy, she decided. Nina was not intellectual, but she was clever: not the type to suffer an accidental pregnancy. Tanya had a suspicion, never voiced, that Nina had manipulated Dimka into the marriage. Tanya knew that her brother was sophisticated and savvy about almost everything: he was naïve and romantic only about women. Why would Nina have wanted to entrap him? Because the Dvorkins were an elite family, and Nina was ambitious?

Don't be such a bitch, Tanya told herself.

She made small talk for half an hour, then got up to go.

There was nothing supernatural about the twins' relationship, but they knew each other so well that each could usually guess what the other was thinking, and Dimka intuited that Tanya had not come to talk about Nina's pregnancy. Now he stood up too. "I've got to take out the garbage," he said. "Give me a hand, would you, Tanya?"

They went down in the elevator, each carrying a bucket of rubbish. When they were outside, at the back of the building, with no one else around, Dimka said: "What is it?"

"Vasili Yenkov's sentence is up, but he hasn't come back to Moscow."

Dimka's face hardened. He loved Tanya, she knew, but he disagreed with her politics. "Yenkov did his best to undermine the government I work for. Why would I care what happens to him?"

"He believes in freedom and justice, as you do."

"That kind of subversive activity just gives the hard-liners an excuse to resist reform."

Tanya knew she was defending herself, as well as Vasili. "If it were not for people like Vasili, the hard-liners would say everything was all right, and there would be no pressure for change. How would anyone know that they killed Ustin Bodian, for example?"

"Bodian died of pneumonia."

"Dimka, that's not worthy of you. He died of neglect, and you know it."

"True." Dimka looked chastened. In a softer voice he said: "Are you in love with Vasili Yenkov?"

"No. I *like* him. He's funny and smart and brave. But he's the kind of man that needs a succession of young girls."

"Or he *was*. There are no nymphets in a prison camp."

"Anyway, he is a friend, and he's served his sentence."

"The world is full of injustice."

"I want to know what has happened to him, and you can find out for me. If you will."

Dimka sighed. "What about my career? In the Kremlin, compassion for dissidents unjustly treated is not considered admirable."

Tanya's hopes rose. He was weakening. "Please. It means a lot to me."

"I can't make any promises."

"Just do your best."

"All right."

Tanya felt overcome by gratitude, and kissed his cheek. "You're a good brother," she said. "Thank you."

. . .

Just as the Eskimos were said to have numerous different words for snow, so the citizens of Moscow had many phrases for the black market. Everything other than life's most basic necessities had to be bought "on the left." Many such purchases were straightforwardly criminal: you found a man who smuggled blue jeans from the West and you paid him an enormous price. Others were neither legal nor illegal. To buy a radio or a rug, you might have to put your name down on a waiting list; but you could leap to the top of the list "through pull," by being a person of influence and having the power to return the favor; or "through friends," by having a relative or pal in a position to manipulate the list. So widespread was queue-jumping that most Muscovites believed no one *ever* got to the top of a list just by waiting.

One day Natalya Smotrov asked Dimka to go with her to buy something on the black market. "Normally I'd ask Nik," she said. Nikolai was her husband. "But it's a present for his birthday, and I want it to be a surprise."

Dimka knew little about Natalya's life outside the Kremlin. She was married with no children, but that was about the extent of his knowledge. Kremlin apparatchiks were part of the Soviet elite, but Natalya's Mercedes and her imported perfume indicated some other source of privilege and money. However, if there was a Nikolai Smotrov in the upper reaches of the Communist hierarchy, Dimka had never heard of him.

Dimka asked: "What are you going to give him?"

"A tape recorder. He wants a Grundig—that's a German brand."

Only on the black market could a Soviet citizen buy a German tape recorder. Dimka wondered how Natalya could afford such an expensive gift. "Where are you going to find one?" he asked.

"There's a guy called Max at the Central Market." This bazaar, in Sadovaya-Samotyochnaya, was a lawful alternative to state stores. Produce from private gardens was sold at higher prices. Instead of long queues and unattractive displays, there were mountains of colorful vegetables—for those who could afford them. And the sale of legitimate produce masked even more profitable illegal business at many of the stalls.

Dimka understood why Natalya wanted company. Some of the men who did this kind of work were thugs, and a woman had reason to be wary.

Dimka hoped that was her only motive. He did not want to be led into temptation. He felt close to Nina just now, her time being near. They had not had sex for a couple of months, which made him more vulnerable to Natalya's charms. But that paled beside the drama of pregnancy. The last thing Dimka wanted was a dalliance with Natalya. But he could hardly refuse her this simple favor.

They went in the lunch hour. Natalya drove Dimka to the market in her ancient Mercedes. Despite its age it was fast and comfortable. How did she get parts for it? he wondered.

On the way she asked him about Nina. "The baby is due any day," he said.

"Let me know if you need baby supplies," Natalya said. "Nik's sister has a three-year-old who no longer needs feeding bottles and suchlike."

Dimka was surprised. Baby feeding bottles were a luxury more rare than tape recorders. "Thank you, I will."

They parked and walked through the market to a shop selling secondhand furniture. This was a semilegal business. People were allowed to sell their own possessions, but it was against the law to be a middleman, which made the trade cumbersome and inefficient. To Dimka, the difficulties of imposing such Communist rules illustrated the practical necessity of many capitalist practices—hence the need for liberalization.

Max was a heavy man in his thirties dressed American style in blue jeans and a white T-shirt. He sat at a pine kitchen table, drinking tea and smoking. He was surrounded by cheap used couches and cabinets and beds, mostly elderly and damaged. "What do you want?" he said brusquely.

"I spoke to you last Wednesday about a Grundig tape recorder," said Natalya. "You said to come back in a week."

"Tape recorders are difficult to get hold of," he said.

Dimka intervened. "Don't piss about, Max," he said, making his voice as harsh and contemptuous as Max's. "Have you got one or not?"

Men such as Max considered it a sign of weakness to give a direct answer to a simple question. He said: "You'll have to pay in American dollars."

Natalya said: "I agreed to your price. I've brought exactly that much. No more."

"Show me the money."

Natalya took a wad of American bills from the pocket of her dress.

Max held out his hand.

Dimka took Natalya's wrist to prevent her handing over the money prematurely. He said: "Where is the tape recorder?"

Max spoke over his shoulder. "Josef!"

There was a movement in the back room. "Yes?"

"Tape recorder."

"Yes."

Josef came out, carrying a plain cardboard box. He was a younger man, maybe nineteen, with a cigarette dangling from his lip. Although small, he was muscular. He put the box down on a table. "It's heavy," he said. "Have you got a car?"

"Around the corner."

Natalya counted out the cash.

Max said: "It cost me more than I expected."

"I don't have any more money," Natalya said.

Max picked up the bills and counted them. "All right," he said resentfully. "It's yours." He stood up and stuffed the wad into the pocket of his jeans. "Josef will carry it to your car." He went into the back room.

Josef grasped the box to pick it up.

Dimka said: "Just a minute."

Josef said: "What? I haven't got time to waste."

"Open the box," said Dimka.

Josef took the weight of the box, ignoring him, but Dimka put his hand on it and leaned on it, making it impossible for Josef to lift it. Josef gave him a look of blazing fury, and for a moment Dimka wondered if there would be violence. Then Josef stood back and said: "Open the damn thing yourself."

The lid was stapled and taped. Dimka and Natalya got it open with some difficulty. Inside was a reel-to-reel tape recorder. The brand name was Magic Tone.

"This is not a Grundig," Natalya said.

"These are better than Grundigs," Josef said. "Nicer sound."

"I paid for a Grundig," she said. "This is a cheap Japanese imitation."

"You can't get Grundigs these days."

"Then I'll have the money back."

"You can't, not once you've opened the box."

"Until we opened the box, we didn't know you were trying to defraud us."

"Nobody defrauded you. You wanted a tape recorder."

Dimka said: "Bugger this." He went to the door of the back room.

Josef said: "You can't go in there!"

Dimka ignored him and went in. The room was full of cardboard boxes. A few were open, showing television sets, record players, and radios, all foreign brands. But Max was not there. Dimka saw a back door.

He returned to the front room. "Max has run off with your money," he told Natalya.

Josef said: "He's a busy man. He has a lot of customers."

"Don't be so fucking stupid," Dimka said to him. "Max is a thief, and so are you."

Josef pointed a finger close to Dimka's face. "Don't you call me stupid," he said in a threatening tone.

"Give her the money back," Dimka said. "Before you get into real trouble."

Josef grinned. "What are you going to do—call the police?"

They could not do that. They were engaged in an illegal transaction. And the police would probably arrest Dimka and Natalya but not Josef and Max, who were undoubtedly paying bribes to protect their business.

"There's nothing we can do," Natalya said. "Let's go."

Josef said: "Take your tape recorder."

"No, thanks," Natalya said. "It's not what I want." She went to the door.

Dimka said. "We're coming back—for the money."

Josef laughed. "What are you going to do?"

"You'll see," Dimka said weakly, and he followed Natalya out.

He was seething with frustration as Natalya drove back to the Kremlin. "I'm going to get your money back," he said to her.

"Please don't," she said. "Those men are dangerous. I don't want you to get hurt. Just leave it."

He was not going to leave it, but he said no more.

When he got to his office, the KGB file on Vasili Yenkov was on his desk.

It was not thick. Yenkov was a script editor who had never been in trouble nor even under suspicion until the day in May 1961 when he had been arrested carrying five copies of a subversive news sheet called *Dissidence*. Under interrogation he claimed he had been handed a dozen copies a few minutes earlier and had begun to pass them out under a sudden impulse of compassion for the opera singer who had pneumonia. A thorough search of his apartment had revealed nothing to contradict his story. His typewriter did not match the one used to produce the newsletter. With electrical terminals attached to his lips and his fingertips, he had given the names of other subversives, but innocent and guilty people alike did that under torture. As was usual, some of the people named had been impeccable Communist Party members, while others the KGB had failed to trace. On balance, the secret police were inclined to believe Yenkov was not the illegal publisher of *Dissidence*.

Dimka had to admire the grit of a man who could maintain a lie under KGB interrogation. Yenkov had protected Tanya even while suffering agonizing torture. Perhaps he deserved his freedom.

Dimka knew the truth that Yenkov had kept hidden. On the night of Yenkov's arrest, Dimka had driven Tanya on his motorcycle to Yenkov's apartment, where she had picked up a typewriter, undoubtedly the machine used to produce *Dissidence*. Dimka had hurled it into the Moskva River half an hour later. Typewriters did not float. He and Tanya had saved Yenkov from a longer sentence.

Yenkov was no longer at the logging camp in the larch forest, according to the file. Someone had discovered that he had a little technical expertise. His first job at Radio Moscow had been studio production assistant, so he knew about microphones and electrical connections. The shortage of technicians in Siberia was so chronic that this had been enough to get him a job as an electrician in a power station.

He had probably been pleased, at first, to move to inside work at which he did not have to risk losing a limb to a careless axe. But there was a downside. The authorities were reluctant to permit a competent technician to leave Siberia. When his sentence was up, he had applied in the usual way for a travel visa to return to Moscow. And his application had been refused. That left him no choice but to continue in his job. He was stuck.

It was unjust; but injustice was everywhere, as Dimka had pointed out to Tanya.

Dimka studied the photograph in the file. Yenkov looked like a movie star, with a sensual face, fleshy lips, black eyebrows, and thick dark hair. But there seemed more to him than that. A faint expression of wry amusement around the corners of his eyes suggested that he did not take himself too seriously. It would not be surprising if Tanya were in love with this man, despite her denials.

Anyway, Dimka would try to get him released for her sake.

He would speak to Khrushchev about the case. However, he needed to wait until the boss was in a good mood. He put the file in his desk drawer.

He did not get an opportunity that afternoon. Khrushchev left early, and Dimka was getting ready to go home when Natalya put her head around his door. "Come for a drink," she said. "We need one after our horrible experience in the Central Market."

Dimka hesitated. "I need to get home to Nina. Her time is near."

"Just a quick one."

"Okay." He screwed the cap onto his fountain pen and spoke to his secretary. "We can go, Vera."

"I've got a few more things to do," she said. She was conscientious.

The Riverside Bar was patronized by the young Kremlin elite, so it was not as dismal as the average Moscow drinking hole. The chairs were comfortable, the snacks were edible, and for the better-paid apparatchik with exotic tastes there were bottles of Scotch and bourbon behind the bar. Tonight it was crowded with people whom Dimka and Natalya knew, mostly aides like themselves. Someone thrust a glass of beer into Dimka's hand and he drank gratefully. The mood was boisterous. Boris Kozlov, a Khrushchev aide like Dimka, told a risky joke. "Everybody! What will happen when Communism comes to Saudi Arabia?"

They all cheered and begged him to tell them.

"After a while there will be a shortage of sand!"

Everyone laughed. The people in this group were keen workers for Soviet Communism, as Dimka was, but they were not blind to its faults. The gap between party aspirations and Soviet reality bothered them all, and jokes released the tension.

Dimka finished his beer and got another.

Natalya raised her glass as if about to give a toast. "The best hope for world revolution is an American company called United Fruit," she said. The people around her laughed. "No, seriously," she said, though she was smiling. "They persuade the United States government to support brutal right-wing dictatorships all over Central and South America. If United Fruit had any sense they would foster gradual progress toward bourgeois freedoms—the rule of law, freedom of speech, trade unions—but, happily for world Communism, they're too dumb to see that. They stamp ruthlessly on reform movements, so the people have nowhere to turn but to Communism—just as Karl Marx predicted." She clinked glasses with the nearest person. "Long live United Fruit!"

Dimka laughed. Natalya was one of the smartest people in the Kremlin, as well as the prettiest. Flushed with gaiety, her wide mouth open in a laugh, she was enchanting. Dimka could not help comparing her with the weary, bulging, sex-averse woman at home, though he knew the thought was cruelly unjust.

Natalya went to the bar to order snacks. Dimka realized he had been here more than an hour: he had to leave. He went up to Natalya with the intention of saying good-bye. But the beer was just enough to make him incautious and, when Natalya smiled warmly at him, he kissed her.

She kissed him back, enthusiastically.

Dimka did not understand her. She had spent a night with him; then she yelled at him that she was married; then she asked him to go for a drink with her; then she kissed him. What next? But he hardly cared about her inconsistency when her warm mouth was on his and the tip of her tongue was teasing his lips.

She broke the embrace, and Dimka saw his secretary standing beside them.

Vera's expression was severely judgmental. "I've been looking for you," she said with a note of accusation. "There was a phone call just after you left."

"I'm sorry," said Dimka, not sure whether he was apologizing for being hard to find or for kissing Natalya.

Natalya took a plate of pickled cucumbers from the bartender and returned to the group.

"Your mother-in-law called," Vera went on.

Dimka's euphoria had now evaporated.

"Your wife has gone into labor," Vera said. "All is well, but you should join her at the hospital."

"Thank you," said Dimka, feeling that he was the worst kind of faithless husband.

"Good night," said Vera, and she left the bar.

Dimka followed her out. He stood breathing the cool night air for a moment. Then he got on his motorcycle and headed for the hospital. What a moment to be caught kissing a colleague. He deserved to feel humiliated: he had done something stupid.

He parked his bike in the hospital car park and went in. He found Nina in the maternity ward, sitting up in bed. Masha was on a chair beside the bed, holding a baby wrapped in a white shawl. "Congratulations," Masha said to Dimka. "It's a boy."

"A boy," Dimka said. He looked at Nina. She smiled, weary but triumphant.

He looked at the baby. He had a lot of damp dark hair. His eyes were a shade of blue that made Dimka think of his grandfather Grigori. All babies had blue eyes, he recalled. Was it his imagination that this baby seemed already to look at the world with Grandfather Grigori's intense stare?

Masha held the baby out to Dimka. He took the little bundle as if handling a large eggshell. In the presence of this miracle, the day's dramas faded to nothing.

I have a son, he thought, and tears came to his eyes.

"He's beautiful," Dimka said. "Let's call him Grigor."

. . .

Two things kept Dimka awake that night. One was guilt: just when his wife was giving birth in bloodshed and agony, he had been kissing Natalya. The other was rage at the way he had been outwitted and humiliated by Max and Josef. It was not he but Natalya who had been robbed, but he felt no less indignant and resentful.

Next morning on the way to work he drove his motorcycle to the Central Market. For half the night he had rehearsed what he would say to Max. "My name is Dmitri Ilich Dvorkin. Check who I am. Check who I work for. Check who my uncle is and who my father was. Then meet me here tomorrow with Natalya's money, and beg me not to take the revenge you deserve." He wondered whether he had the nerve to say all that; whether Max would be impressed or scornful; whether the speech would be threatening enough to retrieve Natalya's money and Dimka's pride.

Max was not sitting at the pine table. He was not in the room. Dimka did not know whether to be disappointed or relieved.

Josef was standing by the door to the back room. Dimka wondered whether to unleash his speech on the youngster. He probably did not have the power to get the money back, but it might relieve Dimka's feelings. While Dimka hesitated he noticed that Josef had lost the threatening arrogance he had displayed yesterday. To Dimka's astonishment, before he had a chance to open his mouth Josef backed away from him, looking scared. "I'm sorry!" Josef said. "I'm sorry!"

Dimka could not account for this transformation. If Josef had found out, overnight, that Dimka worked in the Kremlin and came from a politically powerful family, he might be apologetic and conciliatory, and he might even give the money back, but he would not look as if he were afraid for his life. "I just want Natalya's money," Dimka said.

"We gave it back! We already did!"

Dimka was puzzled. Had Natalya been here before him? "Who did you give it to?"

"Those two men."

Dimka could not make sense of this. "Where is Max?" he said.

"In the hospital," said Josef. "They broke both his arms? Isn't that enough for you?"

Dimka reflected for a moment. Unless this was all some charade, it seemed that two unknown men had beaten Max severely and forced him to give them the money he had taken from Natalya. Who were they? And why had they done this?

Clearly Josef knew no more. Bemused, Dimka turned and left the store.

It was not the police who had done this, he reasoned as he walked back to his bike, nor the army nor the KGB. Anyone official would have arrested Max and taken him to prison and broken his arms in private. Someone unofficial, then.

Unofficial meant gangland. So there were nasty criminals among Natalya's friends or family.

No wonder she never said much about her private life.

Dimka drove fast to the Kremlin but still he was dismayed to find that Khrushchev had got there before him. However, the boss was in a good mood: Dimka could hear him laughing. Perhaps this was the moment to mention Vasili Yenkov. He opened his desk drawer and took out Yenkov's KGB file. He picked up a folder of documents for Khrushchev to sign, then he hesitated. He was a fool to do this, even for his beloved sister. But he suppressed his anxiety and went into the main office.

The first secretary sat behind a big desk speaking on the telephone. He did not much like the phone, preferring face-to-face contact: that way, he said, he could tell when people were lying. However, this conversation was jovial. Dimka put the letters in front of him, and he began to sign while continuing to talk and laugh into the mouthpiece.

When he hung up, Khrushchev said: "What's that in your hand? Looks like a KGB file."

"Vasili Yenkov. Sentenced to two years in a labor camp for possessing a leaflet about Ustin Bodian, the dissident singer. He's served his time, but they're keeping him there."

Khrushchev stopped signing and looked up. "Do you have some personal interest?"

Dimka felt a chill of fear. "None whatsoever," he lied, managing to keep the anxiety out of his voice. If he revealed his sister's link to a convicted subversive it could end his career and hers.

Khrushchev narrowed his eyes. "So why should we let him come home?"

Dimka wished he had refused Tanya. He should have known Khrushchev would see through him: a man did not become leader of the Soviet Union without being suspicious to the point of paranoia. Dimka backpedaled desperately. "I don't say we should bring him home," he said as calmly as he could. "I just thought you might like to know about him. His crime was trivial, he has suffered his punishment, and for you to grant justice to a minor dissident would accord with your general policy of cautious liberalization."

Khrushchev was not fooled. "Someone has asked you for a favor." Dimka opened his mouth to protest his innocence, but Khrushchev held up a hand to silence him. "Don't deny it, I don't mind. Influence is your reward for hard work."

Dimka felt as if a death sentence had been lifted. "Thank you," he said, sounding more pathetically grateful than he wished.

"What job is Yenkov doing in Siberia?" Khrushchev asked.

Dimka realized that the hand holding the file was trembling. He pressed his arm against his side to stop it. "He's an electrician in a power station. He's not qualified, but he used to work in radio."

"What was his job in Moscow?"

"He was a script editor."

"Oh, for fuck's sake!" Khrushchev threw down his pen. "A script editor? What the hell use is a script editor? They're desperate for electricians in Siberia. Leave him there. He's doing something useful."

Dimka stared at him in dismay. He did not know what to say.

Khrushchev picked up his pen and resumed signing. "A script editor," he muttered. "My arse."

. . .

Tanya typed out Vasili's short story, "Frostbite," with two carbon copies.

But it was too good merely for samizdat publication. Vasili evoked the world of the prison camps with brutal vividness—but he did more. Copying it, she had realized, with an ache in her heart, that the camp stood for the Soviet Union, and the story was a savage critique of Soviet society. Vasili was telling the truth in a way that Tanya could not, and she burned with remorse. Every day she wrote articles that were published in newspapers and magazines all over the USSR; every day she carefully avoided reality. She did not tell outright lies, but she always skirted around the poverty, injustice, repression, and waste that were the actual characteristics of her country. Vasili's writing showed her that her life was a fraud.

She took the typescript to her editor, Daniil Antonov. "This came to me in the mail, anonymously," she said. He might well guess that she was lying, but he would not betray her. "It's a short story set in a prison camp."

"We can't publish it," he said quickly.

"I know. But it's very good—the work of a great writer, I think."

"Why are you showing it to me?"

"You know the editor of *New World* magazine."

Daniil looked thoughtful. "He occasionally publishes something unorthodox."

Tanya lowered her voice. "I don't know how far Khrushchev's liberalization is intended to go."

"The policy has vacillated, but the overall instruction is that the excesses of the past should be discussed and condemned."

"Would you read it and, if you like it, show it to the editor?"

"Sure." Daniil read a few lines. "Why do you think it was sent to *you*?"

"It's probably written by someone I met when I went to Siberia two years ago."

"Ah." He nodded. "That would explain it." He meant *Not a bad cover.*

"The author will probably reveal his identity if the story is accepted for publication."

"Okay," said Daniil. "I'll do my best."

The University of Alabama was the last all-white state university in the USA. On Tuesday, June 11, two young Negroes arrived at the campus in Tuscaloosa to register as students. George Wallace, the diminutive governor of Alabama, stood at the doors of the university with his arms folded and his legs astride, and vowed to keep them out.

At the Department of Justice in Washington, George Jakes sat with Bobby Kennedy and others listening to telephone reports from people at the university. The television was on, but for the moment none of the networks was showing the scene live.

Less than a year ago, two people had been shot dead during riots at the University of Mississippi after its first colored student enrolled. The Kennedy brothers were determined to prevent a repeat.

George had been to Tuscaloosa, and had seen the university's leafy campus. He had been frowned at as he walked across the green lawns, the only dark face among the pretty girls in bobby socks and the smart young men in blazers. He had drawn for Bobby a sketch of the grand portico of the Foster Auditorium, with its three doors, in front of which Governor Wallace now stood, at a portable lectern, surrounded by highway patrolmen. The June temperature in Tuscaloosa was rising toward a hundred degrees. George could visualize the reporters and photographers crowded in front of Wallace, sweating in the sun, waiting for violence to break out.

The confrontation had long been anticipated and planned by both sides.

George Wallace was a Southern Democrat. Abraham Lincoln, who freed the slaves, had been a Republican, while proslavery Southerners had been Democrats. Those Southerners were still in the party, helping Democratic presidents get elected, then undermining them once in office.

Wallace was a small, ugly man, going bald except for a patch at the front of his head that he greased and combed into a ludicrous quiff. But he was cunning, and George Jakes could not figure out what he was up to today. What result did Wallace hope for? Mayhem—or something more subtle?

The civil rights movement, which had seemed moribund two months ago, had taken wing after the Birmingham riots. Money was pouring in: at a Hollywood fund-raiser, movie stars such as Paul Newman and Tony Franciosa had written checks for a thousand dollars each. The White House was terrified of more disorder, and desperate to appease the protesters.

Bobby Kennedy had at last come round to the belief that there must be a new civil rights bill. He now admitted that the time had come for Congress to outlaw segregation in all public places—hotels, restaurants, buses, restrooms—and to protect the right of Negroes to vote. But he had not yet convinced his brother the president.

Bobby was pretending to be calm and in charge this morning. A television crew was filming him, and three of his seven children were running around the office. But George knew how fast Bobby's relaxed openness could turn to cold fury when things went wrong.

Bobby was resolved that there would be no rioting—but he was equally determined to get the two students enrolled. A judge had issued a court order to admit the students, and Bobby, as attorney general, could not let himself be defeated by a state governor intent on flouting the law. He was ready to send in troops to remove Wallace by force—but that, too, would be an unhappy ending, Washington bullying the South.

Bobby was in his shirtsleeves, bent over the speakerphone on his wide desk, with wet marks of perspiration under his arms. The army had set up mobile communications, and someone in the crowd was telling Bobby what was happening. "Nick has arrived," the voice on the speaker said. Nicholas Katzenbach was deputy attorney general, and Bobby's representative on the scene. "He's going up to Wallace . . . he's handing him the cease-and-desist." Katzenbach was armed with a presidential proclamation ordering Wallace to cease illegally defying a court order. "Now Wallace is making a speech."

George Jakes's left arm was in a discreet black silk sling. State troopers had cracked a bone in his wrist in Birmingham, Alabama. Two years earlier a racist rioter had broken the same arm in Anniston, which was also in Alabama. George hoped never to go to Alabama again.

"Wallace isn't talking about segregation," said the voice on the speaker. "He's talking about states' rights. He says Washington doesn't have the right to interfere in Alabama schools. I'm going to try to get close enough so you can hear him."

George frowned. In his inaugural speech as governor, Wallace had said: "Segregation now, segregation tomorrow, segregation forever." But then he had been speaking to white Alabamans. Who was he trying to impress today? Something was going on here that the Kennedy brothers and their advisers had not yet understood.

Wallace's speech was long. When at last it was over, Katzenbach once again demanded that Wallace obey the court, and Wallace refused. Stalemate.

Katzenbach then left the scene—but the drama was not over. The two students, Vivian Malone and James Hood, were waiting in a car. By prior arrangement, Katzenbach escorted Vivian to her dormitory, and another Justice Department lawyer did the same for James. This was only temporary. To register formally, they had to enter the Foster Auditorium.

The lunchtime news came on television, and in Bobby Kennedy's office someone turned up the sound. Wallace stood at the lectern, looking taller than he was in real life. He said nothing about colored people or segregation or civil rights. He talked of the might of central government oppressing the sovereignty of the state of Alabama. He spoke indignantly about freedom and democracy, as if there were no Negroes being denied the vote. He quoted the American Constitution as if he did not spurn it every day of his life. It was a bravura performance, and it worried George.

Burke Marshall, the white lawyer who headed the civil rights division, was in Bobby's office. George still did not trust him, but Marshall had become more radical since Birmingham, and now he proposed resolving the stalemate in Tuscaloosa by sending troops in. "Why don't we just go ahead and do it?" he said to Bobby.

Bobby agreed.

It took time. Bobby's aides ordered sandwiches and coffee. On the campus, everyone held their positions.

News came in from Vietnam. At a road junction in Saigon a Buddhist monk called Thich Quang Duc, doused in five gallons of gasoline, had calmly struck a match and set himself alight. His suicide was a protest at the persecution of the Buddhist majority by the American-sponsored president Ngo Dinh Diem, who was a Catholic.

There was no end to the travails of President Kennedy.

At last the voice on Bobby's speakerphone said: "General Graham has arrived . . . with four soldiers."

"Four?" said George. "That's our show of force?"

They heard a new voice, presumably that of the general addressing Wallace. He said: "Sir, it is my sad duty to ask you to step aside under orders from the president of the United States."

Graham was the commander of the Alabama National Guard, and he was clearly doing his duty against his inclination.

But the voice on the phone now said: "Wallace is walking away . . . Wallace is leaving! Wallace is leaving! It's over!"

There was cheering and handshaking in the office.

After a minute the others noticed that George was not joining in. Dennis Wilson said: "What's the matter with you?"

In George's opinion, the people around him were not thinking hard enough. "Wallace planned this," he said. "All along, he intended to give in as soon as we called in the troops."

"But why?" said Dennis.

"That's the question that's been bothering me. All morning, I've had this suspicion that we're being used."

"So what did Wallace gain by this charade?"

"A showcase. He's just been on television, posing as the ordinary man standing up to a bullying government."

"Governor Wallace, complaining about being bullied?" said Wilson. "That's a joke!"

Bobby had been following the argument, and now he intervened. "Listen to George," he said. "He's asking the right questions."

"It's a joke to you and me," said George. "But many working-class Americans feel that integration is being shoved down their throats by Washington do-gooders such as all of us in this room."

"I know," said Wilson. "Though it's unusual to hear that from . . ." He was going to say from a Negro, but changed his mind. "From someone who campaigns for civil rights. What's your point?"

"What Wallace was doing, today, was talking to those white working-class voters. They'll remember him standing there, defying Nick Katzenbach—a typical East Coast liberal, they'll say—and they'll remember the soldiers making Governor Wallace withdraw."

"Wallace is the governor of Alabama. Why would he need to address the nation?"

"I suspect he will oppose Jack Kennedy in next year's Democratic primaries. He's running for president, folks. And he opened his campaign today on national television—with our help."

There was a moment of quiet in the office as that sank in. George could tell that they were convinced by his argument, and worried by its implications.

"Right now, Wallace leads the news, and he looks like a hero," George finished. "Maybe President Kennedy needs to seize back the initiative."

Bobby touched the intercom on his desk and said: "Get me the president." He lit a cigar.

Dennis Wilson took a call on another phone and said: "The two students have entered the auditorium and registered."

A few moments later Bobby picked up the phone to talk to his brother. He reported a nonviolent victory. Then he began to listen. "Yes!" he said at one stage. "George Jakes said the same thing . . ." There was another long pause. "Tonight? But there's no speech . . . Of course it can be written. No, I think you've made the right decision. Let's do it." He hung up and looked around the room. "The president is going to introduce a new civil rights bill," he said.

George's heart leaped. That was what he and Martin Luther King and everyone in the civil rights movement had been asking for.

Bobby went on: "And he's going to announce it on live television—tonight."

"Tonight?" said George in surprise.

"In a few hours' time."

That made sense, George thought, though it would be a rush. The president would be back at the top of the news, where he belonged—ahead of both George Wallace and Thich Quang Duc.

Bobby added: "And he wants you to go over there and work on the speech with Ted."

"Yes, sir," said George.

He left the Justice Department in a state of high excitement. He walked so fast that he was panting when he reached the White House. He took a minute to catch his breath on the ground floor of the West Wing. Then he went upstairs. He found Ted Sorensen in his office with a group of colleagues. George took off his jacket and sat down.

Among the papers scattered on the table was a telegram from Martin Luther King to President Kennedy. In Danville, Virginia, when sixty-five Negroes had protested segregation, forty-eight of them had been so badly beaten by the police that they had ended up in the hospital. "The Negro's endurance may be at breaking point," King's cable said. George underlined that sentence.

The group worked intensely on the speech. It would begin with a reference to the day's events in Alabama, emphasizing that the troops had been enforcing a court order. However, the president would not linger on the details of this particular squabble, but move quickly to a strong appeal to the moral values of all decent Americans. At intervals, Sorensen took handwritten pages to the secretaries to be typed.

George felt frustrated that something so important had to be done in a last-minute rush, but he understood why. Drafting legislation was a rational process; politics, by contrast, was an intuitive game. Jack Kennedy had good instincts, and his gut feelings told him that he needed to take the initiative today.

Time passed too quickly. The speech was still being written when the TV crews moved into the Oval Office and began to set up their lights. President Kennedy walked along the corridor to Sorensen's room and asked how it was coming. Sorensen showed him some pages, and the president did not like them. They moved into the secretaries' office, and Kennedy started dictating changes to be typed. Then it was eight o'clock, and the speech was unfinished, but the president was on the air.

George watched the TV in Sorensen's room, biting his nails.

And President Kennedy gave the performance of his life.

He started off a little too formally, but he warmed up when he spoke of the life prospects of a Negro baby: half as much chance of completing high school, one-third of the chance of graduating college, twice as much chance of being unemployed, and a life expectancy seven years shorter than that of a white baby.

"We are confronted primarily with a moral issue," he said. "It is as old as the scriptures and as clear as the American Constitution."

George marveled. Much of this was unscripted, and it showed a new Jack Kennedy. The slick modern president had discovered the power of sounding biblical. Perhaps he had learned from the preacher Martin Luther King. "Who among us would be content to have the color of his skin changed?" he said, reverting to short, plain words. "Who among us would then be content with the counsels of patience and delay?"

It was Jack Kennedy and his brother Bobby who had counseled patience and delay, George reflected. He rejoiced that now at last they had seen the painful inadequacy of such advice.

"We preach freedom around the world," the president said. He was about to go to Europe, George knew. "But are we to say to the world, and much more importantly to each other, that this is the land of the free—except for the Negroes? That we have no second-class citizens—except Negroes? That we have no class or caste system, no ghettoes, no master race—except with respect to Negroes?"

George exulted. This was strong stuff—especially the reference to the master race, which called the Nazis to mind. It was the kind of speech he had always wanted the president to make.

"The fires of frustration are burning in every city, north and south, where legal remedies are not at hand," Kennedy said. "Next week I shall ask the Congress of the United States to act, to make a commitment it has not fully made this century, to the proposition that"—he had gone formal, but now he reverted to plain language—"race has no place in American life or law."

That was a quote for the newspapers, George thought immediately: race has no place in American life or law. He was excited beyond measure. America was changing, right now, minute by minute, and he was part of that change.

"Those who do nothing are inviting shame as well as violence," the president said, and George thought he meant it, even though doing nothing had been his policy until a few hours ago.

"I ask the support of all our citizens," Kennedy finished.

The broadcast ended. Along the corridor, the TV lights were switched off and the crews began to pack their gear. Sorensen congratulated the president.

George was euphoric but exhausted. He went home to his apartment, ate scrambled eggs, and watched the news. As he had hoped, the president's broadcast was the main item. He went to bed and fell asleep.

The phone woke him. It was Verena Marquand. She was weeping and barely coherent. "What happened?" George asked her.

"Medgar," she said, and then something he could not understand.

"Are you talking about Medgar Evers?" George knew the man, a black activist in Jackson, Mississippi. He was a full-time employee of the National Association for the Advancement of Colored People, the most moderate of the civil rights groups. He had investigated the murder of Emmett Till and organized a boycott of white stores. His work had made him a national figure.

"They shot him," Verena sobbed. "Right outside his house."

"Is he dead?"

"Yes. He has three children, George—three! His kids heard the shot and went out and found their father bleeding to death on their driveway."

"Oh, Christ."

"What is *wrong* with these white people? Why do they do this to us, George? Why?"

"I don't know, baby," said George. "I just don't know."

·   ·   ·

Once again, Bobby Kennedy sent George to Atlanta with a message for Martin Luther King.

When George called Verena to make the appointment, he said: "I'd love to see your apartment."

He could not figure Verena out. That night in Birmingham they had made love and survived a racist bomb, and he had felt very close to her. But days had gone by, then weeks, without another opportunity to make love, and their intimacy had evaporated. Yet, when she had been distraught with the news of the murder of Medgar Evers, she had not phoned Martin Luther King, nor her father, but George. Now he did not know what their relationship was.

"Sure," she said. "Why not?"

"I'll bring a bottle of vodka." He had learned that vodka was her favorite booze.

"I share the place with another girl."

"Shall I bring two bottles?"

She laughed. "Easy, tiger. Laura will be happy to go out for the evening. I've done it often enough for her."

"Does that mean you'll make dinner?"

"I'm not much of a cook."

"How about if you fry a couple of steaks and I make a salad?"

"You have sophisticated taste."

"That's why I like *you*."

"Smooth talker."

He flew there the next day. He was hoping to spend the night with her, but he did not want her to feel taken for granted, so he checked into a hotel, then got a taxi to her place.

He had more than seduction on his mind. Last time he had brought a message from Bobby to King, he had felt ambivalent about it. This time Bobby was right and King was wrong, and George was determined to change King's mind. So first he would try to change Verena's.

Atlanta in June was hot, and she greeted him wearing a sleeveless tennis dress that showed her long light tan arms. Her feet were bare, and that made him wonder whether she had anything on under the dress. She kissed him on the lips, but briefly, so that he was not sure what it meant.

She had a classy modern apartment with contemporary furniture. She could not afford it on the salary Martin Luther King was giving her, George guessed. Percy Marquand's record royalties must have been paying the rent.

He put the vodka down on the kitchen counter and she handed him a bottle of vermouth and a cocktail shaker. Before making the drinks he said: "I want to be sure you understand something. President Kennedy is in the greatest trouble of his political career. This is much worse than the Bay of Pigs."

She was shocked, as he had intended. "Tell me why," she said.

"Because of his civil rights bill. The morning after his television broadcast—the morning after you called to tell me that Medgar had been murdered—the House majority leader telephoned the president. He said it was going to be impossible to pass the farm bill, mass-transit funding, foreign aid, and the space budget. Kennedy's program of legislation has been completely derailed. Just as we feared, those Southern Democrats are taking their revenge. And the president's rating in the opinion polls dropped ten points overnight."

"It's done him good internationally, though," she pointed out. "You may just have to tough it out at home."

"Believe me, we are," George said. "Lyndon Johnson has come into his own."

"Johnson? Are you kidding me?"

"No, I'm not." George was friendly with one of the vice president's aides, Skip Dickerson. "Did you know that the city of Houston shut off dockside electricity to protest the navy's new policy on shore leave integration?"

"Yes, the bastards."

"Lyndon solved that problem."

"How?"

"NASA is planning to build a tracking station worth millions of dollars in Houston. Lyndon just threatened to cancel it. The city turned the power back on seconds later. Never underestimate Lyndon Johnson."

"We could do with more of that attitude in the administration."

"True." But the Kennedy brothers were fastidious. They did not want to dirty their hands. They preferred to win the argument by sweet reason. Consequently, they did not make much use of Johnson; in fact they looked down on him for his arm-twisting skills.

George filled the cocktail shaker with ice, then poured in some vodka and shook it up. Verena opened the refrigerator and took out two cocktail glasses. George poured a teaspoonful of vermouth into each frosted glass, swirled it around to coat the sides, then added the cold vodka. Verena dropped an olive into each glass.

George liked the feeling of doing something together. "We make a good team, don't we?" he said.

Verena raised her glass and drank. "You make a good martini," she said.

George smiled ruefully. He had been hoping for a different answer, one that affirmed their relationship. He sipped and said: "Yeah, I do."

Verena got out lettuce and tomatoes and two sirloin steaks. George began to wash the lettuce. As he did so he turned the conversation to the real purpose of his visit. "I know that we've talked about this before, but it doesn't help the White House that Dr. King has Communist associates."

"Who says he does?"

"The FBI."

Verena snorted contemptuously. "That famously reliable source of information on the civil rights movement. Knock it off, George. You know that J. Edgar Hoover believes that anyone who disagrees with him is a Communist, including Bobby Kennedy. Where's the evidence?"

"Apparently the FBI has evidence."

"Apparently? So you haven't seen any. Has Bobby?"

George felt embarrassed. "Hoover says the source is sensitive."

"Hoover has refused to show the evidence to the attorney general? Who does Hoover think he's working for?" She sipped her drink thoughtfully. "Has the *president* seen the evidence?"

George said nothing.

Verena's incredulity mounted. "Hoover can't say no to the president."

"I believe the president decided not to push the matter to a confrontation."

"How naïve are you people? George, listen to me. *There is no evidence.*"

George decided to concede the point. "You're probably right. I don't believe that Jack O'Dell and Stanley Levison are Communists, though probably they used to be; but don't you see that the truth doesn't matter? There are grounds for suspicion, and that's enough to discredit the civil rights movement. And, now that the president has proposed a civil rights bill, he gets discredited too." George wrapped the washed lettuce in a towel and windmilled his arm to dry the leaves. Irritation made him do it more energetically than necessary. "Jack Kennedy has put his political life on the line for civil rights, and we can't let him be brought down by charges of Communist association." He tipped the lettuce into a bowl. "Just get rid of those two guys, and solve the problem!"

Verena spoke patiently. "O'Dell is an employee of Martin Luther King's organization, just as I am, but Levison isn't even on the payroll. He's just a friend and adviser to Martin. Do you really want to give J. Edgar Hoover the power to choose Martin's friends?"

"Verena, they're standing in the way of the civil rights bill. Just tell Dr. King to get rid of them—please."

Verena sighed. "I think he will. It's taking a while for his Christian conscience to get around to the idea of spurning loyal longtime supporters, but in the end he'll do it."

"Thank the Lord for that." George's spirits lifted: for once he could go back to Bobby with good news.

Verena salted the steaks and put them in a frying pan. "And now I'll tell you something," she said. "It won't make any goddamn difference. Hoover will continue to leak stories to the press about how the civil rights movement is a Communist front. He would do it if we were all lifelong Republicans. J. Edgar Hoover is a pathological liar who hates Negroes, and it's a damn shame your boss doesn't have the balls to fire him."

George wanted to protest but unfortunately the accusation was true. He sliced a tomato into the salad.

Verena said: "Do you like your steak well cooked?"

"Not too much."

"The French way? So do I."

George made a couple more drinks and they sat at the small table to eat. George embarked on the second half of his message. "It would help the president if Dr. King would call off this damn Washington sit-in."

"That isn't going to happen."

King had called for a "massive, militant, and monumental sit-in demonstration" in Washington, coinciding with nationwide acts of civil disobedience. The Kennedy brothers were appalled. "Consider this," George said. "In Congress, there are some people who will always vote for civil rights and some who never will. The ones who matter are those who could go either way."

"Swing voters," said Verena, using a phrase that had come into vogue.

"Exactly. They know that the bill is morally right but politically unpopular, and they're looking for excuses to vote against it. Your demonstration will give them the chance to say: 'I'm for civil rights, but not at the point of a gun.' The timing is wrong."

"As Martin says, the timing is always wrong for white people."

George grinned. "You're whiter than I am."

She tossed her head. "And prettier."

"That's the truth. You're just about the prettiest sight I've ever seen."

"Thank you. Eat up."

George picked up his knife and fork. They ate mostly in silence. George complimented Verena on the steaks, and she said he made a good salad, for a man.

When they had finished they carried their drinks into the living room and sat on the couch, and George resumed the argument. "It's different, now, don't you see? The administration is on our side. The president is trying his best to pass the bill we've been demanding for years."

She shook her head. "If we've learned one thing, it's that change comes faster when we keep up the pressure. Did you know that Negroes are getting served by white waitresses in Birmingham restaurants now?"

"Yes, I did know that. What an incredible turnaround."

"And it wasn't achieved by waiting patiently. It happened because they threw rocks and started fires."

"The situation has changed."

"Martin won't cancel the demonstration."

"Would he modify it?"

"What do you mean?"

This was George's Plan B. "Could it become a simple law-abiding march, rather than a sit-in? Congressmen might feel less threatened."

"I don't know. Martin might consider that."

"Hold it on a Wednesday, to discourage people from staying in the city all weekend, and end it early so that the marchers leave well before nightfall."

"You're trying to draw the sting."

"If we must have a demonstration, we should do everything possible to make sure the occasion is nonviolent and makes a good impression, especially on television."

"In that case, how about stationing portable toilets all along the route? I guess Bobby can get that done, even if he can't fire Hoover."

"Great idea."

"And how about rounding up some white supporters? The whole thing will look better on TV if there are white marchers as well as black."

George considered. "I bet Bobby could get the unions to send contingents."

"If you can promise both of those things as sweeteners, I think we have a chance of changing Martin's mind."

George saw that Verena had come around to his point of view and was now discussing how to persuade King. That was half a victory. He said: "And if you can persuade Dr. King to change the sit-in to a march, I think we might get the president to endorse it." He was sticking his neck out, but it was possible.

"I'll do my best," she said.

George put his arm around her. "See, we *are* a good team," he said. She smiled and said nothing. He persisted. "Don't you agree?"

She kissed him. It was the same as the last kiss: more than just friendly, less than sexy. She said thoughtfully: "After that bomb smashed the window of my hotel room, you crossed the room barefoot to fetch my shoes."

"I remember," he said. "There was broken glass all over the floor."

"That was it," she said. "That was your mistake."

George frowned. "I don't get it. I thought I was being nice."

"Exactly. You're too good for me, George."

"What? That's insane!"

She was serious. "I sleep around, George. I get drunk. I'm unfaithful. I had sex with Martin, once."

George raised his eyebrows but said nothing.

"You deserve better," Verena went on. "You're going to have a wonderful career. You might be our first Negro president. You need a wife who will be true to you and work alongside you and support you and be a credit to you. That's not me."

George was bemused. "I wasn't looking that far ahead," he said. "I was just hoping to kiss you some more."

She smiled. "That, I can do," she said.

He kissed her long and slow. After a while he stroked the outside of her thigh, up inside the skirt of her tennis dress. His hand went as far as her hip. He had been right: no underwear.

She knew what he was thinking. "See?" she said. "Bad girl."

"I know," he said. "I'm crazy about you anyway."

It had been hard for Walli to leave Berlin. Karolin was there, and he wanted to be near her. But that made no sense when they were separated by the Wall. Although they had been only a mile apart he could never see her. He could not risk crossing the border again: it was only by luck that he had not been killed last time. All the same it had been hard for him to move to Hamburg.

Walli told himself he understood why Karolin had chosen to stay with her family to have the baby. Who was best qualified to help her when she gave birth—her mother, or a seventeen-year-old guitar player? But the logic of her decision was small consolation to him.

He thought about her when he went to bed at night and as soon as he woke up in the morning. When he saw a pretty girl in the street it just made him sad about Karolin. He wondered how she was. Did the pregnancy make her uncomfortable and nauseous, or was she glowing? Were her parents angry with her, or thrilled at the prospect of a grandchild?

They exchanged letters, and both always wrote "I love you." But they hesitated to say more about their emotions, knowing that every word would be scrutinized by a secret policeman in the censorship office, perhaps someone they knew, such as Hans Hoffmann. It was like declaring your feelings in front of a scornful audience.

They were on opposite sides of the Wall, and they might as well have been a thousand miles apart.

So Walli came to Hamburg and moved into his sister's spacious apartment.

Rebecca never nagged him. His parents, in their letters, badgered him to go back to school, or perhaps college. Their stupid suggestions had included that he should study to become an electrician, a lawyer, and a schoolteacher like Rebecca and Bernd. But Rebecca herself said nothing. If he spent all day in his room practicing the guitar, she made no objection, just asked him to wash up his coffee cup instead of leaving it dirty in the sink. If ever he talked to her about his future, she said: "What's the rush? You're seventeen. Do what you want, and see what happens." Bernd was equally tolerant. Walli adored Rebecca and liked Bernd more every day.

He had not yet got used to West Germany. People had bigger cars and newer clothes and nicer homes. The government was openly criticized in the newspapers and even on television. Reading some attack on the aging Chancellor Adenauer, Walli would find himself looking guiltily over his shoulder, fearful that someone might observe him reading subversive material; and he would have to remind himself that this was the West, where he had freedom of speech.

He was sad to move away from Berlin but, he now discovered to his delight, Hamburg was the pounding heart of the German music scene. It was a port city, entertaining sailors from all over the world. A street called the Reeperbahn was the center of the red-light district, with bars, strip joints, semi-secret homosexual clubs, and many music venues.

Walli longed for only two things in life: to live with Karolin, and to be a professional musician.

One day soon after moving to Hamburg he walked along the Reeperbahn with his guitar slung over his shoulder and went into every bar to ask if they would like a singer-guitarist to entertain their customers. He believed he was good. He could sing, he could play, and he could please an audience. All he needed was a chance.

After a dozen or so rejections he struck lucky at a beer cellar called El Paso. The decor was evidently intended to be American, with the skull of a longhorn steer over the door and posters of cowboy films on the walls. The proprietor wore a Stetson, but his name was Dieter and he spoke with a Low German accent. "Can you play American music?" he said.

"You betcha," said Walli in English.

"Come back at seven thirty. I'll give you a trial."

"How much would you pay me?" said Walli. Although he still got an allowance from Enok Andersen, the accountant at his father's factory, he was desperate to prove he could be financially independent, and justify his refusal to follow his parents' career advice.

But Dieter looked mildly offended, as if Walli had said something impolite. "Play for half an hour or so," he said airily. "If I like you, then we can talk about money."

Walli was inexperienced, but not stupid, and he felt sure that such evasiveness was a sign that the money would be low. However, this was the only offer he had got in two hours, and he accepted it.

He went home and spent the afternoon putting together half an hour of American songs. He would start with "If I Had a Hammer," he decided; the audience at the Europe Hotel had liked it. He would do "This Land Is Your Land" and "A Mess of Blues." He practiced all his choices several times, though he hardly needed to.

When Rebecca and Bernd came home from work and heard his news, Rebecca announced that she would go with him. "I've never seen you play to an audience," she said. "I've just heard you messing about at home and never finishing the song you started."

It was kind of her, particularly as tonight she and Bernd were excited about something else: the visit to Germany of President Kennedy.

Walli and Rebecca's parents believed that only American firmness had prevented the Soviet Union from taking over West Berlin and incorporating it into East Germany. Kennedy was a hero to them. Walli himself liked anyone who gave the tyrannical East German government a hard time.

Walli laid the table while Rebecca prepared supper. "Mother always taught us that if you want something you join a political party and campaign for it," she said. "Bernd and I want East and West Germany to be reunited, so that we and thousands more Germans can be with their families again. That's why we've joined the Free Democratic Party."

Walli wanted the same thing, with all his heart, but he could not imagine how it might happen. "What do you think Kennedy will do?" he asked.

"He may say that we have to learn to live with East Germany, at least for now. That's true, but it's not what we want to hear. I'm hoping he'll give the Communists a poke in the eye, if you want to know the truth."

They watched the news after they ate. The picture was in clear shades of gray on the screen of their up-to-the-minute Franck television—not blurred green like the old sets.

Today Kennedy had been in West Berlin.

He had made a speech from the steps of Schöneberg town hall. In front of the building was a vast plaza that was jam-packed with spectators. According to the newsreader, there were four hundred fifty thousand people in the crowd.

The handsome young president spoke in the open air, a huge stars-and-stripes flag behind him, the breeze tousling his thick hair. He came out fighting. "There are some who say that Communism is the wave of the future," he said. "Let them come to Berlin!" The audience roared their agreement. The cheers were even louder when he repeated the sentence in German. *"Lass' sie nach Berlin kommen!"*

Walli saw that Rebecca and Bernd were delighted by this. "He's not talking about normalization, or realistically accepting the status quo," Rebecca said approvingly.

Kennedy was defiant. "Freedom has many difficulties, and democracy is not perfect," he said.

Bernd commented: "He's referring to the Negroes."

Then Kennedy said scornfully: "But we have never had to put up a wall to keep our people in!"

"Right!" Walli shouted.

The June sun shone down on the president's head. "All free men, wherever they live, are citizens of Berlin," he said. "And therefore, as a free man, I take pride in the words: *Ich bin ein Berliner!*"

The crowd went wild. Kennedy stepped back from the microphone and slid his notes into his jacket pocket.

Bernd was smiling broadly. "I think the Soviets will get that message," he said.

Rebecca said: "Khrushchev is going to be mad as hell."

Walli said: "The madder the better."

He and Rebecca were in an upbeat mood as they drove to the Reeperbahn in the van she had adapted for Bernd and his wheelchair. El Paso had been empty during the afternoon, and now it had only a handful of customers. Dieter in the Stetson had been less than friendly earlier, and this evening he was grumpy. He pretended to have forgotten to ask Walli to come back, and Walli feared he was going to withdraw the offer of a tryout; but then he jerked his thumb toward a tiny stage in the corner.

As well as Dieter there was a middle-aged barmaid with a big bust wearing a check shirt and a bandanna: Dieter's wife, Walli guessed. Clearly they wanted to give their bar a distinctive character, but neither had much charm, and they were not attracting many customers, American or otherwise.

Walli hoped that he might be the magic ingredient that pulled in the crowds.

Rebecca bought two beers. Walli plugged in his amplifier and switched the microphone on. He felt excited. This was what he loved, and what he was good at. He looked at Dieter and his wife, wondering when they wanted him to begin, but neither showed any interest in him, so he strummed a chord and started singing "If I Had a Hammer."

The few customers glanced at him with curiosity for a moment, then went back to their conversations. Rebecca clapped along with the beat enthusiastically, but no one else did. Nevertheless Walli gave it everything, strumming rhythmically and singing loudly. It might take two or three numbers, but he could win this crowd over, he told himself.

Halfway through the song, the microphone went dead. So did Walli's amplifier. The power to the stage had obviously failed. Walli finished the song without amplification, figuring that was slightly less embarrassing than stopping in the middle.

He put down his guitar and went to the bar. "The power's gone dead onstage," he said to Dieter.

"I know," said Dieter. "I switched it off."

Walli was baffled. "Why?"

"I don't want to listen to that rubbish."

Walli felt as if he had been slapped. Every time he had ever performed in public, people had liked what he did. He had never been told that his music was rubbish. His stomach went cold with shock. He hardly knew what to do or say.

Dieter added: "I asked for American music."

That made no sense. Walli said indignantly: "That song was a number one hit in America!"

"This place is named after 'El Paso' by Marty Robbins—the greatest song ever written. I thought you would play that sort of thing. 'Tennessee Waltz,' or 'On Top of Old Smoky,' songs by Johnny Cash, Hank Williams, Jim Reeves."

Jim Reeves was the most boring musician the world had ever known. "You're talking about country-and-western music," Walli said.

Dieter did not feel he needed to be enlightened. "I'm talking about American music," he said with the confidence of ignorance.

There was no point in arguing with such a fool. Even if Walli had realized what was wanted, he would not have played it. He was not going into the music business to play "On Top of Old Smoky."

He returned to the stage and put his guitar in its case.

Rebecca looked bewildered. "What happened?" she said.

"The landlord didn't like my repertoire."

"But he didn't even listen to one song all through!"

"He feels he knows a lot about music."

"Poor Walli!"

Walli could deal with Dieter's boneheaded scorn, but Rebecca's sympathy made him want to cry. "It doesn't matter," he said. "I wouldn't want to work for such an asshole."

"I'm going to give him a piece of my mind," said Rebecca.

"No, please don't," Walli said. "It won't help to have my big sister tell him off."

"I suppose not," she said.

"Come on." Walli picked up his guitar and amplifier. "Let's go home."

.   .   .

Dave Williams and Plum Nellie arrived in Hamburg with high hopes. They were on a roll. They were becoming popular in London, and now they were going to wow Germany.

The manager of the Dive was called Herr Fluck, which Plum Nellie found hilarious. Not so funny was the fact that he did not like Plum Nellie much. Even worse, after two evenings Dave thought he was right. The group was not giving the punters what they wanted.

"Make dance!" Herr Fluck said in English. "Make dance!" The people in the club, all in their teens and twenties, were mainly interested in dancing. The most successful numbers were the ones that got the girls out on the floor, bopping with one another, so that the men could then cut in and get paired off.

But mostly the group fell short of generating the kind of excitement that got everyone moving. Dave was appalled. This was their big chance and they were fluffing it. If they did not improve, they would be sent home. "For the first time in my life, I'm a success at something," he had said to his skeptical father; and in the end his father had let him come to Hamburg. Would he have to go home and admit that he had failed at this, too?

He could not figure out what the problem was, but Lenny could. "It's Geoff," he said. Geoffrey was the lead guitarist. "He's homesick."

"Does that make him play badly?"

"No, it makes him drink, and the drink makes him play badly."

Dave took to standing right next to the drum kit and hitting his guitar strings harder and more rhythmically, but it did not make much difference. He realized that when one musician underperformed, it brought down the whole group.

On his fourth day he went to visit Rebecca.

He was delighted to discover that he had not one but two relations in Hamburg, and the second was a guitar-playing seventeen-year-old boy. Dave had schoolboy German, and Walli had picked up some English from his grandmother Maud; but they both spoke the language of music, and they spent an afternoon trading chords and guitar licks. That evening Dave took Walli to the Dive, and suggested that the club hire Walli to play in the intervals between Plum Nellie's sets. Walli played a new American hit called "Blowin' in the Wind," which the manager liked, and he got the job.

A week later, Rebecca and Bernd invited the group for a meal. Walli explained to her that the boys worked late into the night and got up at midday, so they liked to eat at around six in the evening, before going onstage. That was fine with Rebecca.

Four of the five accepted the invitation: Geoff would not come.

Rebecca had cooked a pile of pork chops in a rich sauce, with great bowls of fried potatoes, mushrooms, and cabbage. Dave guessed she wanted, in a motherly way, to make sure they got one good meal in the course of a week. She was right to worry: they were living mainly on beer and cigarettes.

Her husband, Bernd, helped with the cooking and serving, moving himself around with surprising agility. Dave was struck by how happy Rebecca was, and how much in love with Bernd.

The group tucked into the food eagerly. They all talked in mixed English and German, and the atmosphere was amiable even if they did not understand everything that was said.

After eating they all thanked Rebecca profusely, then got the bus to the Reeperbahn.

Hamburg's red-light district was like London's Soho but more open, less discreet. Until he came here, Dave had not known that there were male prostitutes as well as female.

The Dive was a grubby basement. By comparison, the Jump Club was plush. At the Dive the furniture was broken, there was no heating or ventilation, and the toilets were in the backyard.

When they arrived, still full of Rebecca's food, they found Geoff in the bar, drinking beer.

The group went onstage at eight. With breaks, they would play until three in the morning. Every night they played every song they knew at least once, and their favorites three times. Herr Fluck made them work hard.

Tonight they played worse than ever.

Throughout the first set Geoff was all over the place, playing wrong notes and fumbling his solos; and that put everyone else off. Instead of concentrating on entertaining people, they were struggling to cover Geoff's mistakes. By the end of the set Lenny was angry.

In the interval, Walli sat on a stool, front of stage, and played the guitar and sang Bob Dylan songs. Dave sat and watched. Walli had a cheap harmonica on a rack that fitted around his neck, so that he could blow and strum at the same time, just as Dylan did. Walli was a good musician, Dave thought, and smart enough to recognize that Dylan was the latest craze. The clientele of the Dive mostly preferred rock and roll, but some listened, and when Walli went offstage he got a round of enthusiastic applause from a table of girls in the corner.

Dave accompanied Walli to the dressing room, and there they discovered a full-scale crisis.

Geoff was on the floor, drunk and incapable of standing upright without assistance. Lenny, kneeling over him, slapped his face hard every now and again. That probably relieved Lenny's feelings, but it did not bring Geoff round. Dave got a mug of black coffee from the bar, and they forced Geoff to drink some, but that made no difference either.

"We'll have to go on without no fucking lead guitarist," said Lenny. "Unless you can play Geoff's solos, Dave."

"I can do the Chuck Berry stuff, but that's all," said Dave.

"We'll just have to leave the rest out. This fucking audience probably won't notice."

Dave was not sure Lenny was right. Guitar solos were part of the dynamic of good dance music, creating light and shade and preventing the repetitive pop tunes from becoming boring.

Walli said: "I can play Geoff's part."

Lenny looked scornful. "You've never played with us."

"I hear your whole act three nights," Walli said. "I can play all those songs."

Dave looked at Walli and saw in his eyes an eagerness that was touching. He was evidently yearning for this opportunity.

Lenny was skeptical. "Really?"

"I can play. Is not difficult."

"Oh, isn't it?" Lenny was a bit miffed.

Dave was keen to give Walli a chance. "He's a better guitarist than I am, Lenny."

"That's not saying fucking much."

"He's better than Geoff, too."

"Has he ever been in a group?"

Walli understood the question. "In a duo. With a girl singer."

"He hasn't worked with a drummer, then."

That was a key point, Dave knew. He recalled how startled he had been, the first time he played with the Guardsmen, to discover the tight discipline imposed on his playing by the drumbeat. But he had managed, and Walli could surely do the same. "Let him try, Lenny," Dave pleaded. "If you don't like what he does, you can send him off after the first number."

Herr Fluck put his head around the door and said: *"Raus! Raus!* It's showtime!"

"All right, all right, *wir kommen,*" Lenny replied. He stood up. "Pick up your axe and get onstage, Walli."

Walli went on.

The opening number of the second set was "Dizzy, Miss Lizzy," which was guitar-led. Dave said to Walli: "Do you want to warm up with an easier one?"

"No, thanks," said Walli.

Dave hoped his confidence was justified.

Lew, the drummer, counted: "Three, four, *one.*"

Walli came in right on cue and played the riff.

The group came in a bar later. They played the intro. Just before Lenny started to sing, Dave caught his eye, and Lenny nodded approvingly.

Walli played the guitar part perfectly without apparent effort.

At the end of the song, Dave gave Walli a wink.

They did the set. Walli played every number well, and even joined in some of the backing vocals. His performance lifted the group's energy and they got the girls out on the floor.

It was the best set they had played since they got to Germany.

As they went off, Lenny put his arm around Walli and said: "Welcome to the group."

. . .

Walli hardly slept that night. Playing with Plum Nellie, he had felt he belonged, musically, and that he enhanced the group. It had made him so happy that he began to fear it might not last. Had Lenny really meant it when he said: "Welcome to the group"?

Next day Walli went to the cheap boardinghouse in the St. Pauli district where the group lodged. He arrived at midday, just as they were getting up.

He hung out for a couple of hours with Dave and Buzz, the bass player, going through the group's repertoire, polishing up beginnings and endings of songs. They seemed to assume he would be playing with them again. He wanted confirmation.

Lenny and Lew, the drummer, surfaced around three in the

afternoon. Lenny was direct. "Do you definitely want to join this group?"

"Yes," Walli said.

"That's it, then," said Lenny. "You're in."

Walli was not convinced. "What about Geoff?"

"I'll talk to him when he gets up."

They went to a café called Harald's on Grosse Freiheit and had coffee and cigarettes for an hour, then they came back and woke Geoff. He looked ill, which was not surprising after drinking so much that he had passed out. He sat on the edge of his bed while Lenny talked to him and the others listened from the doorway. "You're out of the group," Lenny said. "I'm sorry about it, but you let us down badly last night. You were too drunk to stand up, let alone play. Walli took your place and I'm making him permanent."

"He's just a punk kid," Geoff managed.

Lenny said: "Not only is he sober, he's a better guitarist than you."

"I need coffee," said Geoff.

"Go to Harald's."

They did not see Geoff again before they left for the club.

They were setting up onstage just before eight when Geoff walked in, sober, guitar in hand.

Walli stared at him in consternation. Earlier he had got the impression Geoff had accepted that he was fired. Maybe he had just been too hungover to argue.

Whatever the reason, he had not packed his bag and left, and Walli became anxious. He had suffered so many setbacks: the police smashing up his guitar so that he could not appear at the Minnesänger; Karolin withdrawing from the gig at the Europe Hotel; and the proprietor of El Paso pulling the plug halfway through his first song. Surely this would not turn into another disappointment?

They all stopped what they were doing and watched as Geoff climbed onstage and opened his guitar case.

At that point Lenny said: "What are you doing, Geoff?"

"I'm going to show you that I'm the best guitarist you've ever heard."

"For Pete's sake! You're fired and that's that. Just fuck off to the station and catch a train to Hook."

Geoff changed his tone and became wheedling. "We've been playing together for six years, Lenny. That has to count for something. You have to give me one chance."

This seemed so reasonable that Walli, to his alarm, felt sure Lenny would agree. But Lenny shook his head. "You're an all-right guitar player, but you're no genius, and you're an awkward bastard too. Since we got here you've been playing so badly that we were on the point of being fired last night when Walli joined us."

Geoff looked around. "What do the others think?" he said.

"Who told you this group was a democracy?" Lenny said.

"Who told you it's not?" Geoff turned to Lew, the drummer, who was adjusting a foot pedal. "What do you think?"

Lew was Geoff's cousin. "Give him another chance," Lew said.

Geoff addressed the bassist. "What about you, Buzz?"

Buzz was an easygoing character who would go along with whoever shouted loudest. "I'd give him a chance."

Geoff looked triumphant. "That makes three of us against one of you, Lenny."

Dave put in: "No, it doesn't. In a democracy, you have to be able to count. It's you three against Lenny, me, and Walli—which makes it even."

Lenny said: "Don't bother about the votes. This is my group and I make the decisions. Geoff is fired. Put your instrument away, Geoff, or I'll sling it right out the fucking door."

At this point Geoff seemed to accept that Lenny was serious. He put his guitar back in its case and slammed the lid. Picking it up, he said: "I'll promise you something, you bastards. If I go, you'll all go."

Walli wondered what that meant. Perhaps it was just an empty threat. Anyway, there was no time to think about it. A couple of minutes later they started to play.

All Walli's fears departed. He could tell he was good and the group was good with him in it. Time passed quickly. In the interval, he went back onstage alone and sang Bob Dylan songs. He included a number he had written himself, called "Karolin." The audience seemed to like it. Afterward he went straight back onstage to open the second set with "Dizzy, Miss Lizzy."

While he was playing "You Can't Catch Me" he saw a couple of uniformed policemen at the back talking to the proprietor, Herr Fluck, but he thought nothing of it.

When they came off at midnight, Herr Fluck was waiting in their dressing room. Without preamble he said to Dave: "How old are you?"

"Twenty-one," said Dave.

"Don't give me that shit."

"What do you care?"

"In Germany we have laws about employing minors in bars."

"I'm eighteen."

"The police say you're fifteen."

"What do the police know about it?"

"They've been talking to the guitar player you just fired—Geoff."

Lenny said: "The bastard, he's shopped us."

Herr Fluck said: "I run a nightclub. Prostitutes come in here, drug dealers, criminals of all kinds. I must constantly prove to the police that I do my best to obey the law. They say I have to send you home—all of you. So, good-bye."

Lenny said: "When do we have to go?"

"You leave the club now. You leave Germany tomorrow."

Lenny said: "That's outrageous!"

"When you're a club owner, you do as the police tell you." He pointed at Walli. "He does not have to leave the country, being German."

"Fuck it," said Lenny. "I've lost two guitarists in one day."

"No, you haven't," said Walli. "I'm coming with you."

J asper Murray fell in love with the USA. They had all-night radio and three channels of television and a different morning newspaper in every city. The people were generous and their houses were spacious and their manners were relaxed and informal. Back home, English people acted as if they were perpetually taking tea in a Victorian drawing room, even when they were doing business deals or giving television interviews or playing sports. Jasper's father, an army officer, could not see this, but his German-Jewish mother did. Here in the States, people were direct. In restaurants, waiters were efficient and helpful without bowing and scraping. No one was obsequious.

Jasper was planning a series of articles about his travels for *St. Julian's News,* but he also had a higher ambition. Before leaving London, he had spoken to Barry Pugh and asked if the *Daily Echo* might be interested to see what he wrote. "Yeah, sure, if you come across something, you know, special," Pugh had said without enthusiasm. Last week in Detroit, Jasper had got an interview with Smokey Robinson, lead singer of the Miracles, and had sent the article to the *Echo* by express post. He reckoned it should have got there by now. He had given the Dewars' number, but Pugh had not phoned. Jasper was still hopeful, though, and he would call Pugh today.

He was staying at the Dewar family apartment in Washington. It was a big place in a swanky building a few blocks from the White House. "My grandfather Cameron Dewar bought this before the First World War," Woody Dewar explained to Jasper at the breakfast table. "Both he and my father were senators."

A colored maid called Miss Betsy poured orange juice for Jasper and asked if he would like some eggs. "No, thanks, just coffee," he said. "I'm meeting a family friend for breakfast in an hour."

Jasper had met the Dewars at the house in Great Peter Street during the year the family had spent in London. He had not been close to them except, briefly, to Beep, but all the same they had welcomed him to their home, more than a year later, with open-handed hospitality. Like the Williamses, they were casually generous, especially toward young people. Lloyd and Daisy were always happy to accommodate stray teenagers for a night or a week—or, in Jasper's case, several years. The Dewars seemed the same. "It's so kind of you to let me stay here," Jasper said to Bella.

"Oh, you're welcome, it's nothing," she said, and she meant it.

Jasper turned to Woody. "I assume you'll be photographing today's civil rights march for *Life* magazine?"

"That's right," said Woody. "I'll mingle with the crowd, taking discreet candid shots with a small thirty-five-millimeter camera. Someone else will do the essential formal pictures of the celebrities on the platform."

He was dressed casually, in chinos and a short-sleeved shirt, but all the same it would be difficult for such a tall man to be inconspicuous. However, Woody's revealing news photographs were world famous. "I'm familiar with your work, as is everyone who's interested in journalism," said Jasper.

"Does any particular subject attract you?" Woody asked. "Crime, politics, war?"

"No. I'd be happy to cover everything—as you seem to."

"I'm interested in faces. Whatever the story—a funeral, a football game, a murder investigation—I photograph faces."

"What do you expect today?"

"No one knows. Martin Luther King is predicting a hundred thousand people. If he gets that many, it will be the biggest civil rights march ever. We all hope it will be happy and peaceful, but we're not counting on it. Look what happened in Birmingham."

"Washington is different," Bella put in. "We have colored police officers here."

"Not many," Woody said. "Although you can bet they will all be at the forefront today."

Beep Dewar came into the dining room. She was fifteen and petite. "Who's going to be at the forefront?" she said.

"Not you, I hope," said her mother. "You stay clear of trouble, please."

"Of course, Mama."

Jasper noted that Beep had learned a measure of discretion in the two years since he had last seen her. Today she looked cute, but not especially sexy, in tan jeans and a loose-fitting cowboy shirt—a sensible outfit for a day that might turn disorderly.

She acted toward Jasper as if she had completely forgotten about their flirtation in London. She was signaling that he should not expect to take up where he had left off. No doubt she had had boyfriends since then. For his part, he was relieved that she did not feel he belonged to her.

The last member of the Dewar family to appear at breakfast was Cameron, Beep's older brother by two years. He was dressed like a middle-aged man, in a linen jacket with a white shirt and a tie. "You stay out of trouble too, Cam," said his mother.

"I have no intention of going anywhere near the march," he said prissily. "I'm planning to visit the Smithsonian."

Beep said: "Don't you believe colored people should be able to vote?"

"I don't believe they should cause trouble."

"If they were allowed to vote, they wouldn't need to make their point in other ways."

Bella said: "That's enough, you two."

Jasper finished his coffee. "I need to make a transatlantic phone call," he said. He felt obliged to add: "I'll pay for it, of course," though he was not sure he had enough money.

"Go right ahead," Bella said. "Use the phone in the study. And please don't trouble about paying."

Jasper was relieved. "You're so kind," he said.

Bella waved that aside. "I think *Life* magazine probably takes care of our phone bill, anyway," she said vaguely.

Jasper went into the study. He called the *Daily Echo* in London and reached Barry Pugh, who said: "Hi, Jasper, how are you enjoying the USA?"

"It's great." Jasper swallowed nervously. "Did you get my Smokey Robinson piece?"

"Yes, thanks. Well written, Jasper, but it doesn't make it for the *Echo*. Try the *New Musical Express*."

Jasper was disheartened. He had no interest in writing for the pop press. "Okay," he said. Not ready to give up, he added: "I thought the fact that Smokey is the Beatles' favorite singer might give the interview extra interest."

"Not enough. Nice try, though."

Jasper tried hard to keep the disappointment out of his voice. "Thanks."

Pugh said: "Isn't there some kind of demonstration in Washington today?"

"Yes, civil rights." Jasper's hopes rose again. "I'll be there—if you'd like a report?"

"Hmm . . . Give us a ring if it gets violent."

And not otherwise, Jasper inferred. Disappointed, he said: "Okay, will do."

Jasper cradled the phone and stared at it pensively. He had worked hard on the Smokey Robinson piece and he felt the Beatles connection made it special. But he had been wrong, and all he could do was try again.

He returned to the dining room. "I must go," he said. "I'm meeting Senator Peshkov at the Willard Hotel."

Woody said: "The Willard is where Martin Luther King stays."

Jasper brightened. "Maybe I could get an interview." The *Echo* would surely be interested in that.

Woody smiled. "There will be several hundred reporters hoping for an interview with King today."

Jasper turned to Beep. "Will I see you later?"

"We're meeting at the Washington Monument at ten," she said. "There's a rumor that Joan Baez is going to sing."

"I'll look for you there."

Woody said: "Did you say you're meeting Greg Peshkov?"

"Yes. He's the half brother of Daisy Williams."

"I know. The domestic arrangements of Greg's father, Lev Peshkov, were hot gossip when your mother and I were teenagers in Buffalo. Please give Greg my regards."

"Of course," said Jasper, and he went out.

. . .

George Jakes entered the coffee shop at the Willard and looked around for Verena, but she had not yet arrived. However, he saw his father, Greg Peshkov, having breakfast with a good-looking man of about twenty who had a blond Beatle haircut. George sat at their table and said: "Good morning."

Greg said: "This is Jasper Murray, a student from London, England. He's the son of an old friend. Jasper, meet George Jakes."

They shook hands. Jasper looked faintly startled, as people often did when they saw Greg and George together; but, like most people, he was too polite to ask for an explanation.

Greg said to George: "Jasper's mother was a refugee from Nazi Germany."

Jasper said: "My mother has never forgotten how the American people welcomed her that summer."

George said to Jasper: "So the subject of racial discrimination is familiar to you, I guess."

"Not really. My mother doesn't like to talk about the old days too much." He smiled engagingly. "At school in England I was called Jasper Jewboy for a while, but it didn't stick. Are you involved in today's march, George?"

"Kind of. I work for Bobby Kennedy. Our concern is to make sure the day goes smoothly."

Jasper was interested. "How are you able to do that?"

"The Mall is full of temporary drinking fountains, first aid stations, portable toilets, and even a check-cashing facility. A church in New York has made eighty thousand sandwich lunches for the organizers to distribute free. All speeches are limited to seven minutes, so that the event will end on time and visitors can leave town well before dark. And Washington has banned the sale of liquor for the day."

"Will it work?"

George did not know. "Frankly, everything depends on the white people. It only takes a few cops to start throwing their weight around, using billy clubs or fire hoses or attack dogs, to turn a prayer meeting into a riot."

Greg said: "Washington isn't the Deep South."

"It isn't the North, either," said George. "So there's no telling what will happen."

Jasper persisted with his questions. "And if there is a riot?"

Greg answered him. "There are four thousand troops stationed in the suburbs, and fifteen thousand paratroopers close by in North Carolina. Washington hospitals have canceled all nonurgent surgery to make room for the wounded."

"Blimey," said Jasper. "You're serious."

George frowned. These precautions were not public knowledge. Greg had been briefed, as a senator; but he should not have told Jasper.

Verena appeared and came to their table. All three men stood up. She spoke to Greg. "Good morning, Senator. Good to see you again."

Greg introduced her to Jasper, whose eyes were popping out. Verena had that effect on white and black men. "Verena works for Martin Luther King," Greg said.

Jasper turned a hundred-watt smile on Verena. "Could you get me an interview with him?"

George snapped: "Why?"

"I'm a student journalist. Didn't I mention that?"

"No, you did not," George said with irritation.

"I'm sorry."

Verena was not immune to Jasper's charm. "I'm so sorry," she said with a rueful smile. "An interview with the Reverend Dr. King is out of the question today."

George was annoyed. Greg should have warned him that Jasper was a journalist. Last time George talked to a reporter he had embarrassed Bobby Kennedy. He hoped he had not said anything indiscreet today.

Verena turned to George, and her tone changed to annoyance. "I just talked to Charlton Heston. FBI agents are phoning our celebrity supporters this morning, telling them to stay in their hotel rooms for the day because there's going to be violence."

George made a disgusted noise. "The FBI is worried, not that the march will be violent, but that it will be a success."

Verena was not satisfied with that. "Can't you stop them trying to sabotage the whole event?"

"I'll speak to Bobby, but I don't think he'll want to cross swords with

J. Edgar Hoover on something so minor." George touched Greg's arm. "Verena and I have to talk. Excuse us, please."

Verena said: "My table is over there."

They crossed the room. George forgot about the sneaky Jasper Murray. As they sat down, he said to Verena: "What's the situation?"

She leaned across the table and spoke in a low voice, but she was bursting with excitement. "It's going to be bigger than we thought," she said, her eyes shining. "A hundred thousand people is an underestimate."

"How do you know?"

"Every scheduled bus, train, and plane to Washington today is full," she said. "At least twenty chartered trains arrived this morning. At Union Station you can't hear yourself think for the people singing 'We Shall Not Be Moved.' Special buses are coming through the Baltimore tunnel at the rate of one hundred per hour. My father chartered a plane from Los Angeles for all the movie stars. Marlon Brando is here, and James Garner. CBS is broadcasting the whole thing live."

"How many people do you think will show up altogether?"

"Right now we're guessing double the original estimate."

George was flabbergasted. "Two hundred thousand people?"

"That's what we think now. It could go higher."

"I don't know whether that's good or bad."

She frowned in irritation. "How could it be bad?"

"We just haven't planned for that many. I don't want trouble."

"George, this is a protest movement—it's *about* trouble."

"I wanted us to show that a hundred thousand Negroes could meet in a park without starting a goddamn fight."

"We're in a fight already, and the whites started it. Hell, George, they broke your wrist for trying to go to the airport."

George touched his left arm reflexively. The doctor said it had healed, but it still gave him a twinge sometimes. "Did you see *Meet the Press*?" he asked her. Dr. King had been questioned by a panel of journalists on the NBC news show.

"Of course I did."

"Every question was about either Negro violence or Communists in the civil rights movement. We must not let these become the issues!"

"We can't let our strategy be dictated by *Meet the Press*. What do you think those white journalists are going to talk about? Don't expect them to ask Martin about violent white cops, dishonest Southern juries, corrupt white judges, and the Ku Klux Klan!"

"Let me put it to you another way," George said calmly. "Suppose today goes off peacefully, but Congress rejects the civil rights bill, and *then* there are riots. Dr. King will be able to say: 'A hundred thousand Negroes came here in peace, singing hymns, giving you the chance to do the right thing—but you spurned the opportunity we offered, and now you see the consequences of your obstinacy. If there are riots now, you have no one to blame but yourselves.' How about that?"

Verena smiled reluctantly and nodded assent. "You're pretty smart, George," she said. "Did you know that?"

. . .

The National Mall was a three-hundred-acre park, long and narrow, stretching for two miles from the Capitol at one end to the Lincoln Memorial at the other. The marchers assembled in the middle, at the Washington Monument, an obelisk more than five hundred feet tall. A stage had been set up and, when George arrived, the pure, thrilling voice of Joan Baez was ringing out "Oh, Freedom."

Jasper looked for Beep Dewar, but the crowd was already at least fifty thousand strong, and not surprisingly he could not see her.

He was having the most interesting day of his life, and it was not yet eleven in the morning. Greg Peshkov and George Jakes were Washington insiders who had casually given him exclusive information: how he wished the *Daily Echo* was interested. And green-eyed Verena Marquand was possibly the most beautiful woman Jasper had ever seen. Was George sleeping with her? Lucky man, if so.

Joan Baez was followed by Odetta and Josh White, but the crowd went wild when Peter, Paul and Mary appeared. Jasper could hardly believe he was seeing these huge stars live onstage without even buying a ticket. Peter, Paul and Mary sang their latest hit, "Blowin' in the Wind," a song written by Bob Dylan. It seemed to be about the civil rights movement, and included the line: "How many years can some people exist before they're allowed to be free?"

The audience became even more madly enthusiastic when Dylan

himself walked on. He sang a new song about the murder of Medgar Evers, called "Only a Pawn in Their Game." The song sounded enigmatic to Jasper, but the listeners were oblivious to ambiguity, and rejoiced that the hottest new music star in America seemed to be on their side.

The throng was swelling minute by minute. Jasper was tall, and could look over most heads, but he could no longer see the edge of the multitude. To the west, the famous long reflecting pool led to the Greek temple commemorating Abraham Lincoln. The demonstrators were supposed to march to the Lincoln Memorial later, but Jasper could see that many were already migrating to the western end of the park, probably intent on securing the best seats for the speeches.

So far there had been no hint of violence, despite media pessimism— or had it been media wishful thinking?

There seemed to be news photographers and television cameras everywhere. They often focused on Jasper, perhaps because of his pop-star haircut.

He started to write an article in his head. The event was a picnic in a forest, he decided, with revelers lunching in a sunlit glade while bloodthirsty predators skulked in the deep shade of the surrounding woods.

He strolled west with the crowd. The Negroes were dressed in their Sunday best, he noticed, the men in ties and straw hats, the women in bright print dresses and head scarves, whereas the whites were casual. The issue had widened from segregation, and the placards called for votes, jobs, and housing. There were delegations from trade unions, churches, and synagogues.

Near the Lincoln Memorial he ran into Beep. She was with a group of girls heading in the same direction. They found a spot where they had a clear view of the stage that had been set up on the steps.

The girls passed around a large bottle of warm Coca-Cola. Some of them were Beep's friends, Jasper discovered; others had simply tagged along. They were interested in him as an exotic foreigner. He lay in the August sun chatting idly to them until the speeches began. By that time the crowd stretched farther than Jasper could see. He felt sure there were more than the one hundred thousand expected.

The lectern stood in front of the giant statue of the brooding

President Lincoln, seated on a huge marble throne, his massive hands on the arms of the chair, his beetle brows drawn, his expression stern.

Most of the speakers were black, but there were a few whites, including a rabbi. Marlon Brando was on the platform, brandishing an electric cattle prod of the kind used on Negroes by the police in Gadsden, Alabama. Jasper liked the sharp-tongued union leader Walter Reuther, who said scathingly: "We cannot defend freedom in Berlin as long as we deny freedom in Birmingham."

But the crowd grew restless and began to shout for Martin Luther King.

He was almost the last speaker.

King was a preacher, and a good one, Jasper knew immediately. His diction was crisp, his voice a vibrant baritone. He had the power to move the crowd's emotions, a valuable skill that Jasper admired.

However, King had probably never before preached to so many people. Few men had.

He cautioned that the demonstration, triumphant though it was, meant nothing if it did not lead to real change. "Those who hope that the Negro needed to blow off steam, and will now be content, will have a rude awakening if the nation returns to business as usual." The audience cheered and whooped at every resonant phrase. "There will be neither rest nor tranquillity in America until the Negro is granted his citizenship rights," King warned. "The whirlwinds of revolt will continue to shake the foundations of our nation until the bright day of justice emerges."

As he drew near to the end of his seven minutes, King became more biblical. "We can never be satisfied as long as our children are stripped of their selfhood, and robbed of their dignity, by signs stating 'For Whites Only,'" he said. "We will not be satisfied until justice runs down like waters, and righteousness like a mighty stream."

On the platform behind him, the gospel singer Mahalia Jackson cried: "My Lord! My Lord!"

"Even though we face the difficulties of today and tomorrow, I still have a dream," he said.

Jasper sensed that King had thrown away his prepared speech, for he was no longer manipulating his audience emotionally. Instead, he seemed to be drawing his words from a deep, cold well of suffering and pain, a well created by centuries of cruelty. Jasper realized that Negroes described their suffering in the words of the Old Testament prophets, and bore their pain with the consolation of Jesus's gospel of hope.

King's voice shook with emotion as he said: "I have a dream that one day this nation will rise up and live out the true meaning of its creed: 'We hold these truths to be self-evident, that all men are created equal.'

"I have a dream that one day, on the red hills of Georgia, the sons of former slaves and the sons of former slave owners will be able to sit down together at the table of brotherhood—I have a dream.

"That one day even the state of Mississippi—a state sweltering with the heat of injustice, sweltering with the heat of oppression—will be transformed into an oasis of freedom and justice. I have a dream."

He had hit a rhythm, and two hundred thousand people felt it sway their souls. It was more than a speech: it was a poem and a canticle and a prayer as deep as the grave. The heartbreaking phrase "I have a dream" came like an amen at the end of each ringing sentence.

"That my four little children will one day live in a nation where they will not be judged by the color of their skin but by the content of their character—I have a dream today.

"I have a dream that one day down in Alabama—with its vicious racists, with its governor having his lips dripping with the words of interposition and nullification—one day right there in Alabama, little black boys and black girls will be able to join hands with little white boys and white girls as sisters and brothers—I have a dream today.

"With this faith we will be able to hew, out of the mountain of despair, a stone of hope.

"With this faith we will be able to transform the jangling discords of our nation into a beautiful symphony of brotherhood.

"With this faith we will be able to work together, to pray together, to struggle together, to go to jail together, to stand up for freedom together, knowing that we will be free one day."

Looking around, Jasper saw that black and white faces alike were running with tears. Even he felt moved, and he had thought himself immune to this kind of thing.

"And when this happens; when we allow freedom to ring; when we let it ring from every village and every hamlet, from every state and every city; we will be able to speed up that day when *all* of God's children, black men and white men, Jews and Gentiles, Protestants and Catholics, will be able to join hands . . ."

Here he slowed down, and the crowd was almost silent.

King's voice trembled with the earthquake force of his passion. ". . . and sing, in the words of the old Negro spiritual:

"Free at last!

"Free at last!

"Thank God Almighty, we are free at last!"

He stepped back from the microphone.

The crowd gave a roar such as Jasper had never heard. They rose to their feet in a surge of rapturous hope. The applause rolled on, seeming as endless as the ocean waves.

It went on until King's distinguished white-haired mentor, Benjamin Mays, stepped up to the microphone and pronounced a blessing. Then people knew it was over, and at last they turned away reluctantly from the stage to go home.

Jasper felt as if he had come through a storm, or a battle, or a love affair: he was spent but jubilant.

He and Beep headed for the Dewar apartment, hardly speaking. Surely, Jasper thought, the *Echo* would be interested in this? Hundreds of thousands of people had heard a heart-stopping plea for justice. Surely British politics, with its dismal sex scandals, could not compete with this for space on the front page of a newspaper?

He was right.

Beep's mother, Bella, was sitting at the kitchen table, shelling peas, while Miss Betsy peeled potatoes. As soon as Jasper walked in, Bella said to him: "The *Daily Echo* in London has called twice for you. A Mr. Pugh."

"Thank you," said Jasper, his heart beating faster. "Do you mind if I return the call?"

"Of course not, go right ahead."

Jasper went to the study and phoned Pugh. "Did you take part in the march?" said Pugh. "Did you hear the speech?"

"Yes, and yes," said Jasper. "It was incredible—"

"I know. We're going all out with it. Can you give us an I-was-there piece? As personal and impressionistic as you like. Don't worry too much about facts and figures, we'll have all those in the main report."

"I'd be happy to," said Jasper. It was an understatement: he was ecstatic.

"Let it run. About a thousand words. We can always cut if necessary."

"All right."

"Call me in half an hour and I'll put you through to a copy taker."

"Couldn't I have longer?" said Jasper; but Pugh had already hung up.

"Blimey," said Jasper to the wall.

There was an American-style yellow legal pad on Woody Dewar's desk. Jasper pulled it toward him and picked up a pencil. He thought for a minute, then wrote:

"Today I stood in a crowd of two hundred thousand people and heard Martin Luther King redefine what it means to be American."

. . .

Maria Summers felt high.

The television set had been on in the press office, and she had stopped work to watch Martin Luther King, as had just about everyone else in the White House, including President Kennedy.

When it ended she was walking on air. She could hardly wait to hear what the president thought of the speech. A few minutes later she was summoned to the Oval Office. The temptation to hug Kennedy was even harder for her to resist than usual. "He's damn good," was Kennedy's slightly detached reaction. Then he said: "He's on his way here now," and Maria was overjoyed.

Jack Kennedy had changed. When Maria had first fallen in love with him, he had been in favor of civil rights intellectually, but not emotionally. The change was not due to their affair. Rather, it was the relentless brutality and lawlessness of the segregationists that had shocked him into a heartfelt personal commitment. And he had risked everything by bringing forward the new civil rights bill. She knew better than anyone how worried he was about it.

George Jakes came in, immaculately dressed as always, today in a dark blue suit with a pale gray shirt and a striped tie. He smiled warmly at her. She was fond of him: he had been a friend in need. He was, she thought, the second-most attractive man she had ever met.

Maria knew that she and George were here for show, because they were among the small number of colored people in the administration. They were both reconciled to being used as symbols. It was not dishonest: though their number was small, Kennedy had appointed more Negroes to high-level posts than any previous president.

When Martin Luther King walked in, President Kennedy shook his hand and said: "I have a dream!"

It was meant well, Maria knew, but she felt it was ill judged. King's dream came from the depths of vicious repression. Jack Kennedy had been born into America's privileged elite, powerful and rich: how could he claim to have a dream of freedom and equality? Dr. King obviously felt this too, for he looked embarrassed and changed the subject. Later, in bed, the president would ask Maria where he had taken a wrong step, she knew; and she would have to find a loving and reassuring way to explain it to him.

King and the other civil rights leaders had not eaten since breakfast. When the president realized this, he ordered coffee and sandwiches for them from the White House kitchen.

Maria got them all to line up for a formal photograph, then the discussion began.

King and the others were riding a wave of elation. After today's demonstration, they told the president, the civil rights bill could be toughened up. There should be a new section banning racial discrimination in employment. Young black men were dropping out of school at an alarming rate, seeing no future.

President Kennedy suggested that Negroes should copy the Jews, who valued education and made their kids study. Maria came from a Negro family who did exactly that, and she agreed with him. If black kids dropped out of school, was that the government's problem? But she also saw how cleverly Kennedy had shifted the discussion away from the real issue, which was millions of jobs that were reserved for whites only.

They asked Kennedy to lead the crusade for civil rights. Maria knew that he was thinking something he could not say: that if he became too strongly identified with the Negro cause, then all the white people would vote Republican.

The shrewd Walter Reuther offered different advice. Identify the businessmen behind the Republican party and pick them off in small groups, he said. Tell them that if they don't cooperate, their profits will suffer. Maria knew this as the Lyndon Johnson approach, a combination of cajolery and threats. The advice went over the president's head: it just was not his style.

Kennedy went through the voting intentions of congressmen and senators, ticking off on his fingers those likely to oppose the civil rights bill. It was a dismal register of prejudice, apathy, and timidity. He was going to have trouble passing even a watered-down version of the bill, he made clear; anything tougher was doomed.

Gloom seemed to fall on Maria like a funeral shawl. She felt tired, depressed, and pessimistic. Her head ached and she wanted to go home.

The meeting lasted more than an hour. By the time it finished, all the euphoria had evaporated. The civil rights leaders filed out, their faces showing disenchantment and frustration. It was all very well for King to have a dream, but it seemed the American people did not share it.

Maria could hardly believe it but, despite all that had happened today, it seemed the great cause of equality and freedom was no farther forward.

J asper Murray felt confident he would get the post of editor of *St. Julian's News*. With his application he had sent in a clipping of his article in the *Daily Echo* about Martin Luther King's "I have a dream" speech. Everyone said it was a great piece. He had been paid twenty-five pounds, less than he had got for the interview with Evie: politics was not as lucrative as celebrity scandal.

"Toby Jenkins has never had a paragraph published anywhere outside the student press," Jasper told Daisy Williams, sitting in the kitchen in Great Peter Street.

"Is he your only rival?" she asked.

"As far as I know, yes."

"When will you hear the decision?"

Jasper looked at his watch, although he knew the time. "The committee is meeting now. They'll put up a notice outside Lord Jane's office when they break for lunch at twelve thirty. My friend Pete Donegan is there. He'll be my deputy editor. He's going to phone me immediately."

"Why do you want the post so badly?"

Because I know how bloody good I am, Jasper thought; twice as good as Cakebread and ten times better than Toby Jenkins. I deserve this job. But he did not open his heart to Daisy Williams. He was a little wary of her. She loved his mother, not him. When the interview with Evie had appeared in the *Echo*, and Jasper had pretended to be dismayed, it had seemed to him that Daisy had not been completely deceived. He worried that she saw through him. However, she always treated him kindly, for his mother's sake.

Now he gave her a softened version of the truth. "I can turn *St.*

Julian's News into a better paper. Right now it's like a parish magazine. It tells you what's going on, but it's frightened of conflict and controversy." He thought of something that would appeal to Daisy's ideals. "For example, St. Julian's College has a board of governors, some of whom have investments in apartheid South Africa. I'd publish that information and ask what such men are doing governing a famous liberal college."

"Good idea," Daisy said with relish. "That'll stir them up."

Walli Franck came into the kitchen. It was midday, but he had evidently just got up: he kept rock-and-roll hours.

Daisy said to him: "Now that Dave's back in school, what are you going to do?"

Walli put instant coffee into a cup. "Practice the guitar," he said.

Daisy smiled. "If your mother were here, I guess she would ask if you shouldn't try to earn some money."

"I don't want to earn money. But I must. That's why I have a job."

Walli's grammar was sometimes so correct that it was hard to understand. Daisy said: "You don't want money, but you do have a job?"

"Washing beer glasses at the Jump Club."

"Well done!"

The doorbell rang, and a minute later a maid showed Hank Remington into the kitchen. He had classic Irish charm. He was a chirpy redhead with a big smile for everyone. "Hello, Mrs. Williams," he said. "I've come to take your daughter out to lunch—unless you're available!"

Women enjoyed Hank's flattery. "Hello, Hank," Daisy said warmly. She turned to the maid and said: "Make sure Evie knows Mr. Remington is here."

"Is it *Mr.* Remington, now?" said Hank. "Don't give people the idea that I'm respectable—it could ruin my reputation." He shook hands with Jasper. "Evie showed me your article about Martin Luther King— that was great, well done." Then he turned to Walli. "Hi, I'm Hank Remington."

Walli was awestruck, but managed to introduce himself. "I'm Dave's cousin, and I play guitar in Plum Nellie."

"How was Hamburg?"

"Great, until we got thrown out because Dave was too young."

"The Kords used to play in Hamburg," Hank said. "It was great. I was born in Dublin but I grew up on the Reeperbahn, if you know what I mean."

Jasper found Hank fascinating. He was rich and famous, one of the biggest pop stars in the world, yet he was working hard to be nice to everyone in the room. Did he have an insatiable desire to be liked—and was that the secret of his success?

Evie came in looking great. Her hair had been cut in a short bob that mimicked the Beatles, and she wore a simple Mary Quant A-line dress that showed off her legs. Hank pretended to be bowled over. "Jesus, I'll have to take you somewhere posh, looking like that," he said. "I was thinking of a Wimpy bar."

"Wherever we go, it will have to be quick," Evie said. "I've got an audition at three thirty."

"What for?"

"A new play called *A Woman's Trial.* It's a courtroom drama."

Hank was pleased. "You'll be making your stage debut!"

"If I get the part."

"Oh, you'll get it. Come on, we'd better go, my Mini's parked on a yellow line."

They went out and Walli returned to his room. Jasper looked at his watch: it was twelve thirty. The editor would be announced any minute now.

Making conversation, he said: "I loved the States."

"Would you like to live there?" Daisy asked.

"More than anything. And I want to work in television. *St. Julian's News* will be a great first step, but basically newspapers are obsolete. TV news is the thing now."

"America is my home," Daisy said musingly, "but I found love in London."

The phone rang. The editor had been chosen. Was it Jasper, or Toby Jenkins?

Daisy answered. "He's right here," she said, and handed the receiver to Jasper, whose heart was thudding.

The caller was Pete Donegan. He said: "Valerie Cakebread got it."

At first Jasper did not understand. "What?" he said. "Who?"

"Valerie Cakebread is the new editor of *St. Julian's News.* Sam Cakebread fixed it for his sister."

"Valerie?" When Jasper understood he was flabbergasted. "She's never written anything but fashion puffs!"

"And she made the tea at *Vogue* magazine."

"How could they do this?"

"Beats me."

"I knew Lord Jane was a prick, but this . . ."

"Shall I come to your place?"

"What for?"

"We should go out and drown our sorrows."

"Okay." Jasper hung up the phone.

Daisy said: "Bad news, obviously. I'm sorry."

Jasper was rocked. "They gave the job to the current editor's sister! I never saw that coming." He recalled his conversation with Sam and Valerie in the coffee bar of the student union. The treacherous pair, neither had even hinted that Valerie was in the running.

He had been outmaneuvered by someone more guileful than himself, he realized bitterly.

Daisy said: "What a shame."

It was the British way, Jasper thought resentfully; family connections were more important than talent. His father had fallen victim to the same syndrome, and in consequence was still only a colonel.

"What will you do?" Daisy said.

"Emigrate," Jasper said. His resolve was now stronger than ever.

"Finish college first," Daisy said. "Americans value education."

"I suppose you're right," Jasper said. But his studies had always come second to his journalism. "I can't work for *St. Julian's News* under Valerie. I gave in gracefully last year, after Sam beat me to the job, but I can't do it again."

"I agree," Daisy said. "It makes you look like a second-rater."

Jasper was struck by a thought. A plan began to form in his mind. He said: "The worst of it is that now there won't be a newspaper to expose such things as the scandal of college governors having investments in South Africa."

Daisy took the bait. "Maybe someone will start a rival newspaper."

Jasper pretended to be skeptical. "I doubt it."

"It's what Dave's grandmother and Walli's grandmother did in 1916. It was called *The Soldier's Wife*. If they could do it . . ."

Jasper put on an innocent face and asked the key question. "Where did they get the money?"

"Maud's family was rich. But it can't cost much to print a couple of thousand copies. Then you pay for the second issue with the income from the first."

"I got twenty-five pounds from the *Echo* for my piece on Martin Luther King. But I don't think that would be enough . . ."

"I might help."

Jasper pretended reluctance. "You might never get your money back."

"Draw up a budget."

"Jack's on his way over here now. We can make some calls."

"If you put in your own money, I'll match it."

"Thank you!" Jasper had no intention of spending his own money. But a budget was like a newspaper gossip column: most of it could be fiction, because no one ever knew the truth. "We could get the first issue together for the beginning of term, if we're quick."

"You should run that story about South African investments on the front page."

Jasper's spirits had lifted again. This might even be better. "Yeah . . . *St. Julian's News* will have a bland front page saying 'Welcome to London,' or something. Ours will be the real newspaper." He began to feel excited.

"Show me your budget as soon as you can," Daisy said. "I'm sure we can work something out."

"Thank you," said Jasper.

I n September of 1963 George Jakes bought a car. He could afford it and he liked the idea, even though in Washington it was easy enough to get around on public transport. He preferred foreign cars: he thought they were more stylish. He found a dark blue five-year-old two-door Mercedes-Benz 220S convertible that had a classy look. On the third Sunday in September he drove to Prince George's County, Maryland, to visit his mother. She would cook him dinner, then they would drive together to Bethel Evangelical Church for the evening service. These days it was not often he had time to visit her, even on a Sunday.

Driving along Suitland Parkway with the top down in the mild September sunshine, he thought about all the questions she would ask him and what answers he would give. First, she would want to know about Verena. "She says she's not good enough for me, Mom," he would say. "What do you think of that?"

"She's right," his mother would probably say. Not many girls were good enough for her son, in her opinion.

She would ask how he was getting on with Bobby Kennedy. The truth was that Bobby was a man of extremes. There were people he hated implacably: J. Edgar Hoover was one. That was fine by George: Hoover was contemptible. But Lyndon Johnson was another. George thought it was a pity that Bobby hated Johnson, who could have been a powerful ally. Sadly, they were oil and water. George tried to imagine the big, boisterous vice president hanging out with the ultrachic Kennedy clan on a boat at Hyannis Port. The image made him smile: Lyndon would be like a rhinoceros in a ballet class.

Bobby liked as hard as he hated, and fortunately George was someone he liked. George was one of a small inner group who were trusted so much that even when they made mistakes it was assumed they were well intentioned and so they were forgiven. What would George say to his mother about Bobby? "He's a smart man who sincerely wants to make America a better country."

She would want to know why the Kennedy brothers were moving so slowly on civil rights. George would say: "If they push harder there will be a white backlash, and that will have two results. One, we'll lose the civil rights bill in Congress. Two, Jack Kennedy will lose the 1964 presidential election. And if Kennedy loses, who will win? Dick Nixon? Barry Goldwater? It could even be George Wallace, heaven forbid."

These were his musings as he parked in the driveway of Jacky Jakes's small, pleasant ranch-style house and let himself in at the front door.

All those thoughts fled his mind instantly when he heard the sound of his mother weeping.

He suffered a moment of childish fear. He had not often known his mother to cry: she had always been a tower of strength in the landscape of his youth. But, on the few occasions when she had given in, and howled her grief and fear uncontrollably, little Georgy had been bewildered and terrified. And now, just for a second, he had to suppress the revival of that boyhood terror, and remind himself that he was a grown man, not to be scared by a mother's tears.

He slammed the door and strode across the little hallway into the living room. Jacky was sitting on the tan velvet couch in front of the television set. Her hands were pressed to her cheeks as if to hold her head on. Tears streamed down her face. Her mouth was open, and she was wailing. She was staring wide-eyed at the TV.

George said: "Mama, what is it, for God's sake, what happened?"

"Four little girls!" she sobbed.

George looked at the monochrome picture on the screen. He saw two cars that looked as if they had been in a smash. Then the camera moved to a building and panned along damaged walls and broken windows. It pulled back, and he recognized the building. His heart lurched. "My God, that's the Sixteenth Street Baptist Church in Birmingham!" he said. "What did they do?"

His mother said: "The whites bombed the Sunday school!"

"No! No!" George's mind refused to accept it. Even in Alabama, men would not bomb a Sunday school.

"They killed four girls," Jacky said. "Why did God let this happen?"

On television, a newsreader's voice-over said: "The dead have been identified as Denise McNair, aged eleven—"

"Eleven!" said George. "This can't be true!"

"—Addie Mae Collins, fourteen; Carole Robertson, fourteen; and Cynthia Wesley, fourteen."

"But they're children!" said George.

"More than twenty other people were injured by the blast," the newsreader intoned in a voice devoid of emotion, and the camera showed an ambulance pulling away from the scene.

George sat down next to his mother and put his arms around her. "What are we going to do?" he said.

"Pray," she replied.

The newsreader continued remorselessly. "This was the twenty-first bomb attack on Negroes in Birmingham in the last eight years," he said. "The city police have never brought any perpetrators to justice for any of the bombings."

"Pray?" said George, his voice trembling with grief.

Right then he wanted to kill someone.

. . .

The Sunday school bomb horrified the world. As far away as Wales, a group of coal miners started a collection to pay for a new stained-glass window to replace one smashed in the Sixteenth Street Baptist Church.

At the funeral, Martin Luther King said: "In spite of the darkness of this hour, we must not lose faith in our white brothers." George tried to follow that counsel, but he found it hard.

For a while George felt public opinion swinging toward civil rights. A congressional committee toughened Kennedy's bill, adding the ban on employment discrimination that the campaigners wanted so badly.

But a few weeks later the segregationists came out of their corner fighting.

In mid-October an envelope was delivered to the Justice Department and passed to George. It contained a slim bound report from the FBI entitled:

COMMUNISM AND THE NEGRO MOVEMENT
A CURRENT ANALYSIS

"What the fuck?" George murmured to himself.

He read it quickly. The report was eleven pages long and devastating. It called Martin Luther King "an unprincipled man." It claimed that he took advice from Communists "knowingly, willingly and regularly." With an assured air of inside knowledge it said: "Communist Party officials visualize the possibility of creating a situation whereby it could be said that, as the Communist Party goes, so goes Martin Luther King."

These confident assertions were not backed up by a single scrap of evidence.

George picked up the phone and called Joe Hugo at FBI headquarters, which was on another floor in the same Justice Department building. "What is this shit?" he said.

Joe knew immediately what he was talking about and did not bother to pretend otherwise. "It's not my fault your friends are Commies," he said. "Don't shoot the messenger."

"This is not a report. It's a smear of unsupported allegations."

"We have evidence."

"Evidence that can't be produced is not evidence, Joe, it's hearsay—weren't you listening in law school?"

"Sources of intelligence have to be protected."

"Who have you sent this crap to?"

"Let me check. Ah . . . the White House, the secretary of state, the defense secretary, the CIA, the army, the navy, and the air force."

"So it's all over Washington, you asshole."

"Obviously we don't try to *conceal* information about our nation's enemies."

"This is a deliberate attempt to sabotage the president's civil rights bill."

"We would never do a thing like that, George. We're just a law enforcement agency." Joe hung up.

George took a few minutes to recover his temper. Then he went through the report underlining the most outrageous allegations. He typed a note listing the government departments to which the report had been sent, according to Joe. Then he took the document in to Bobby.

As always, Bobby sat at his desk with his jacket off, his tie loosened, and his glasses on. He was smoking a cigar. "You're not going to like this," George said. He handed over the report, then summarized it.

"That cocksucker Hoover," said Bobby.

It was the second time George had heard Bobby call Hoover a cocksucker. "You don't mean that literally," George said.

"Don't I?"

George was startled. "Is Hoover a homo?" It was hard to imagine. Hoover was a short, overweight man with thinning hair, a squashed nose, lopsided features, and a thick neck. He was the opposite of a fairy.

Bobby said: "I hear the Mob has photos of him in a woman's dress."

"Is that why he goes around saying there is no such thing as the Mafia?"

"It's one theory."

"Jesus."

"Make an appointment for me to see him tomorrow."

"Okay. In the meantime, let me go through the Levison wiretaps. If Levison is influencing King toward Communism, there must be evidence in those phone calls. Levison would have to talk about the bourgeoisie, the masses, class struggle, revolution, the dictatorship of the proletariat, Lenin, Marx, the Soviet Union, like that. I'll make a note of every such reference and see what they add up to."

"That's not a bad idea. Let me have a memo before I meet with Hoover."

George returned to his office and sent for the transcripts of the wiretap on Stanley Levison's phone—faithfully copied to the Justice Department by Hoover's FBI. Half an hour later a file clerk wheeled a cart into the room.

George started work. Next time he looked up was when a cleaner opened his door and asked if she could sweep his office. He stayed at his desk while she worked around him. He remembered "pulling all-nighters" at Harvard Law, especially during the absurdly demanding first year.

Long before he finished, it was clear to him that Levison's

conversations with King had nothing to do with Communism. They did not use a single one of George's key words, from *alienation* to *Zapata*. They talked about a book King was writing; they discussed fund-raising; they planned the march on Washington. King admitted fears and doubts to his friend: even though he advocated nonviolence, was he to blame for riots and bombings provoked by peaceful demonstrations? They rarely touched on wider political issues, never on the Cold War conflicts that obsessed every Communist: Berlin, Cuba, Vietnam.

At four A.M. George put his head down on the desk and napped. At eight he took a clean shirt from his desk drawer, still in its laundry wrapper, and went to the men's room to wash. Then he typed the note Bobby had requested, saying that in two years of phone calls Stanley Levison and Martin Luther King had never spoken about Communism or any subject remotely associated therewith. "If Levison is a Moscow propagandist, he must be the worst one in history," George finished.

Later that day, Bobby went to see Hoover at the FBI. When he came back he said to George: "He agreed to withdraw the report. Tomorrow his liaison men will go to every recipient and retrieve all copies, saying it needs to be revised."

"Good," George said. "But it's too late, isn't it?"

"Yes," said Bobby. "The damage is done."

. . .

As if President Kennedy did not have enough to worry about in the autumn of 1963, the crisis in Vietnam boiled over on the first Saturday in November.

Encouraged by Kennedy, the South Vietnamese military deposed their unpopular president, Ngo Dinh Diem. In Washington, National Security Adviser McGeorge Bundy woke Kennedy at three A.M. to tell him the coup he had authorized had now taken place. Diem and his brother, Nhu, had been arrested. Kennedy ordered that Diem and his family be given safe passage to exile.

Bobby summoned George to go with him to a meeting in the Cabinet Room at ten A.M.

During the meeting an aide came in with a cable announcing that both Ngo Dinh brothers had committed suicide.

President Kennedy was more shocked than George had ever seen him. He looked stricken. He paled beneath his tan, jumped to his feet, and rushed from the room.

"They didn't commit suicide," Bobby said to George after the meeting. "They're devout Catholics."

George knew that Tim Tedder was in Saigon, liaising between the CIA and the Army of the Republic of Vietnam, the ARVN, pronounced "Arvin." No one would be surprised if it turned out that Tedder had fouled up.

Around midday a CIA cable revealed that the Ngo Dinh brothers had been executed in the back of an army personnel carrier.

"We can't control anything over there," George said to Bobby in frustration. "We're trying to help those people find their way to freedom and democracy, but nothing we do works."

"Just hang on another year," said Bobby. "We can't lose Vietnam to the Communists now—my brother would be defeated in the presidential election next November. But as soon as he's reelected, he'll pull out faster than you can blink. You'll see."

. . .

A gloomy group of aides sat in the office next to Bobby's one evening that November. Hoover's intervention had worked, and the civil rights bill was in trouble. Congressmen who were ashamed to be racists were looking for a pretext to vote against the bill, and Hoover had given them one.

The bill had been routinely passed to the Committee on Rules, whose chair, Howard W. Smith, from Virginia, was one of the more rabid conservative Southern Democrats. Emboldened by the FBI's accusations of Communism in the civil rights movement, Smith had announced that his committee would keep the bill bottled up indefinitely.

It made George furious. Could these men not see that their attitudes had led to the murder of the Sunday school girls? As long as respectable people said it was all right to treat Negroes as if they were not quite human, ignorant thugs would think they had permission to kill children.

And there was worse. With a year to go before the presidential election, Jack Kennedy was losing popularity. He and Bobby were especially worried about Texas. Kennedy had won Texas in 1960 because he had a popular Texan running mate, Lyndon Johnson. Unfortunately, three years of association with the liberal Kennedy administration had just about destroyed Johnson's credibility with the conservative business elite.

"It's not just civil rights," George argued. "We're proposing to abolish the oil depletion allowance. Texas oilmen haven't paid the taxes they ought to for decades, and they hate us for wanting to scrap their privileges."

"Whatever it is," said Dennis Wilson, "thousands of Texas conservatives have left the Democrats and joined the Republicans. And they love Senator Goldwater." Barry Goldwater was a right-wing Republican who wanted to scrap Social Security and drop nuclear bombs on Vietnam. "If Barry runs for president, he's going to take Texas."

Another aide said: "We need the president to go down there and romance those shitkickers."

"He will," said Dennis. "And Jackie's going with him."

"When?"

"They're going to Houston on November twenty-first," Dennis replied. "And then, the next day, they'll go to Dallas."

Maria Summers was watching on TV, in the White House press office, as Air Force One touched down in brilliant sunshine at the Dallas airport called Love Field.

A ramp was maneuvered into place at the rear door. Vice President Lyndon Johnson and his wife, Lady Bird Johnson, took up their positions at the foot of the ramp, waiting to greet the president. A chain-link fence kept back a crowd of two thousand.

The aircraft door opened. There was a suspenseful pause, then Jackie Kennedy emerged, wearing a Chanel suit and a matching pillbox hat. Right behind her was her husband, Maria's lover, President John F. Kennedy. Secretly, Maria thought of him as Johnny, the name his brothers occasionally used.

The television commentator, a local man, said: "I can see his suntan all the way from here!" He was a novice, Maria guessed: although the television picture was monochrome he failed to tell his audience the colors of things. Every woman watching would have been interested to know that Jackie's outfit was pink.

Maria asked herself whether she would change places with Jackie, given the chance. In her heart Maria yearned to own him, to tell people she loved him, to point to him and say: "That's my husband." But there would be sadness as well as pleasure in the marriage. President Kennedy betrayed his wife constantly, and not just with Maria. Although he never admitted it, Maria had gradually realized that she was only one of a number of girlfriends, maybe dozens. It was hard enough to be his mistress and share him: how much more painful it must be to be his wife, knowing that he was intimate with other women, that he kissed them and touched their private parts and put his cock in their mouths every chance he got. Maria had to be content: she got what a mistress was entitled to. But Jackie did *not* have what a wife was entitled to. Maria did not know which was worse.

The presidential couple descended the ramp and began to shake hands with the Texas bigwigs waiting for them. Maria wondered how many of the people who were so pleased to be seen with Kennedy today would support him in next year's election—and how many were already planning, behind their smiles, to betray him.

The Texas press was hostile. *The Dallas Morning News,* owned by a rabid conservative, had in the past two years called Kennedy a crook, a Communist sympathizer, a thief, and "fifty times a fool." This morning it was struggling to find something negative to say about the triumphant tour by Jack and Jackie. It had settled for the feeble STORM OF POLITICAL CONTROVERSY SWIRLS AROUND KENNEDY ON VISIT. Inside, however, there was a pugnacious full-page advertisement paid for by "the American Fact-Finding Committee" with a list of sinister questions addressed to the president, such as: "Why has Gus Hall, head of the U.S. Communist Party, praised almost every one of your policies?" The political ideas were about as stupid as could be, Maria thought. Anyone who believed that President Kennedy was a secret Communist had to be certifiably insane, in her opinion. But the tone was deeply nasty, and she shivered.

A press officer interrupted her thoughts. "Maria, if you're not busy . . ."

She was not, evidently, since she was watching television. "What can I do for you?" she said.

"I want you to run down to the archives." The National Archives building was less than a mile from the White House. "Here's what I need." He handed her a sheet of paper.

Maria often wrote press releases, or at least drafted them, but she had not been promoted to press officer: no woman ever had. She was still a researcher after more than two years. She would have moved on long ago, were it not for her love affair. She looked at the list and said: "I'll get on it right away."

"Thanks."

She took a last glance at the television. The president moved away from the official party and went to the crowd, reaching over the fence to shake hands, Jackie behind him in her pillbox hat. The people roared with excitement at the prospect of actually touching the golden couple. Maria could see the Secret Service men she knew well trying to stay close to the president, hard eyes scanning the throng, alert for trouble.

In her mind she said: *Please take good care of my Johnny.*

Then she left.

. . .

That morning George Jakes drove his Mercedes convertible out to McLean, Virginia, eight miles from the White House. Bobby Kennedy lived there with his large family in a thirteen-bedroom white-painted brick house called Hickory Hill. The attorney general had scheduled a lunch meeting there to discuss organized crime. This subject was outside George's area of expertise, but he was getting invited to a wider range of meetings as he became closer to Bobby.

George stood in the living room with his rival Dennis Wilson, watching the TV coverage from Dallas. The president and Jackie were doing what George and everyone else in the administration wanted them to do, charming the socks off the Texans, chatting with them and touching them, Jackie giving her famous irresistible smile and extending a gloved hand to shake.

George glimpsed his friend Skip Dickerson in the background, close to Vice President Johnson.

At last the Kennedys retreated to their limousine. It was a stretched Lincoln Continental four-door convertible, and the top was down. The people were going to see their president in the flesh, without even a window intervening. Texas governor John Connally stood at the open door wearing a white ten-gallon hat. The president and Jackie got into the rear seat. Kennedy rested his right elbow on the edge, looking relaxed and happy. The car pulled away slowly, and the motorcade followed. Three buses of reporters brought up the rear.

The convoy drove out of the airport and onto the road, and the television coverage came to an end. George switched off the set.

It was a fine day in Washington, too, and Bobby had decided to have the meeting outside, so they all trooped through the back door and across the lawn to the pool patio, where chairs and tables had been set out ready. Looking back toward the house, George saw that a new wing had been built. It was not finished, for some workmen were painting it, and they had a transistor radio playing, its sound a mere susurration at this distance.

George admired what Bobby had done about organized crime. He had different government departments working together to target individual heads of crime families. The Federal Bureau of Narcotics had been gingered up. The Bureau of Alcohol, Tobacco and Firearms had been enlisted. Bobby had ordered the Internal Revenue Service to investigate mobsters' tax returns. He had got the Immigration and Naturalization Service to deport those who were not citizens. It all amounted to the most effective attack ever on American crime.

Only the FBI let him down. The man who should have been the attorney general's staunchest ally in the fight, J. Edgar Hoover, stood aloof, claiming there was no such thing as the Mafia, perhaps—George now knew—because the Mob was blackmailing him over his homosexuality.

Bobby's crusade, like so much that the Kennedy administration did, was disdained in Texas. Illegal gambling, prostitution, and drug use were popular among many leading citizens. *The Dallas Morning News* had attacked Bobby for making the federal government too powerful, and argued that crime should remain the responsibility of local law enforcement authorities—who were mostly incompetent or corrupt, as everyone knew.

The meeting was interrupted when Bobby's wife, Ethel, brought out lunch: tuna sandwiches and chowder. George looked at her with admiration. She was a slim, attractive woman of thirty-five, and it was hard to believe that four months ago she had given birth to their eighth child. She was dressed with the understated chic that George now recognized as the trademark of the Kennedy women.

A phone beside the pool rang and Ethel picked it up. "Yes," she said, and she carried the phone on its long lead to Bobby. "It's J. Edgar Hoover," she said.

George was startled. Was it possible that Hoover *knew* they were discussing organized crime without him, and was calling to reprimand them? Could he have bugged Bobby's patio?

Bobby took the phone from Ethel. "Hello?"

Across the grass, George noticed one of the house painters behaving oddly. He picked up his portable radio, spun around, and started running toward Bobby and the group on the patio.

George looked again at the attorney general. A look of horror came over Bobby's face, and suddenly George felt scared. Bobby turned away from the group and clasped his hand over his mouth. George thought, What is that bastard Hoover saying to him?

Then Bobby turned back to the group eating lunch and cried: "Jack's been shot! It might be fatal!"

George's thoughts moved with underwater slowness. Jack. That means the president. He's been shot. Shot in Dallas, it must be. It might be fatal. He might be dead.

The president might be dead.

Ethel ran to Bobby. All the men jumped to their feet. The painter arrived at the poolside, holding up his radio, unable to speak.

Then everyone began talking at the same time.

George still felt submerged. He thought of the important people in his life. Verena was in Atlanta, and she would hear the news on the radio. His mother was at work, in the University Women's Club; she would hear in minutes. Congress was in session, and Greg would be there. Maria—

Maria Summers. Her secret lover had been shot. She would be grief-stricken—and she would have no one to comfort her.

George had to go to her.

He ran across the lawn and through the house to the parking lot in front, jumped into his open Mercedes, and drove off at top speed.

. . .

It was just before two in the afternoon in Washington, one in Dallas, and eleven in the morning in San Francisco, where Cam Dewar was in a math class, studying differential equations and finding them hard to understand—a new experience for him, for until now all schoolwork had been easy.

His year in a London school had done him no harm. In fact the English kids were a little ahead, because they started school younger. Only his ego had been damaged, by Evie Williams's scornful rejection.

Cameron had little respect for the hip young math teacher, Mark "Fabian" Fanshore, with his crew cut and his knitted ties. He wanted to be the pupils' friend. Cameron thought a teacher should be authoritative.

The principal, Dr. Douglas, stepped into the room. Cameron liked him better. The school's leader was a dry, aloof academic, who did not care whether people liked him or not as long as they did what he told them.

"Fabian" looked up in surprise: Dr. Douglas was not often seen in classrooms. Douglas said something to him in a low voice. It must have been shocking, for Fabian's handsome face paled beneath his tan. They talked for a minute, then Fabian nodded and Douglas walked out.

The bell rang for the midmorning break, but Fabian said firmly: "Stay in your seats, please, and listen to me in silence, all right?" He had the odd speech habit of muttering "All right?" and "Okay?" with unnecessary frequency. "I've got some bad news for you," he went on. "Terribly bad news, in fact, okay? There has been a dreadful event in Dallas, Texas."

Cameron said: "The president is in Dallas today."

"Correct, but don't interrupt me, okay? The very shocking news is that our president has been shot. We don't yet know if he's dead, all right?"

Someone said: "Fuck!" out loud but, astonishingly, Fabian ignored it.

"Now I want you to keep calm. Some of the girls in the school may be very upset." There were no girls in the math class. "The younger children will need reassurance. I expect you to behave like the young men you are and help others who may be more vulnerable, okay? Take your break now as usual, and look out for alterations in the school timetable later. Off you go."

Cameron picked up his books and walked out into the corridor, where all hope of quiet and order evaporated in seconds. The voices of children and adolescents pouring out of classrooms rose to a roar. Some kids were running, some standing dumbstruck, some crying, most shouting.

Everyone was asking whether the president was dead.

Cam did not like Jack Kennedy's liberal politics, but suddenly that did not matter. If Cam had been old enough, he would have voted for

Nixon, but all the same he felt personally outraged. Kennedy was the American president, elected by the American people, and an attack on him was an attack on them.

Who shot my president? he thought. Was it the Russians? Fidel Castro? The Mafia? The Ku Klux Klan?

He spotted his younger sister, Beep. She yelled: "Is the president dead?"

"Nobody knows," Cam said. "Who's got a radio?"

She thought for a moment. "Dr. Duggie has one."

That was true, there was an old-fashioned mahogany wireless set in the head's study. "I'm going to see him," Cam said.

He made his way through the corridors to the head's room and knocked on the door. Dr. Douglas's voice called: "Come!" Cameron went in. The head was there with three other teachers, listening to the radio. "What do you want, Dewar?" said Douglas in his customary irritated tone.

"Sir, everyone in the school would like to listen to the radio."

"Well, we can't get them all in here, boy."

"I thought you might put the radio in the school hall and turn up the volume."

"Oh, did you, now?" Douglas looked about to issue a scornful dismissal.

But his deputy, Mrs. Elcot, murmured: "Not a bad idea."

Douglas hesitated a moment, then nodded. "All right, Dewar. Good thinking. Go to the hall and I'll bring the radio."

"Thank you, sir," said Cameron.

.　.　.

Jasper Murray was invited to the opening night of *A Woman's Trial* at the King's Theatre in London's West End. Student journalists did not normally get such invitations, but Evie Williams was in the cast, and she had made sure he was on the list.

Jasper's newspaper, *The Real Thing*, was going well, so well that he had dropped out of classes to run it for a year. The first issue had sold out after Lord Jane attacked it, in an uncharacteristically incontinent outburst during Freshers' Week, for smearing members of the governing body. Jasper was delighted to have enraged Lord Jane, who was a pillar of the British establishment that disfavored people such as Jasper and his father. The second issue, containing further revelations about college bigwigs and their dubious investments, had broken even financially, and the third had made a profit. Jasper had been obliged to conceal the extent of his success from Daisy Williams, who might have wanted her loan repaid.

The fourth issue would go to the printer tomorrow. He was not so happy with this one: there was no big controversy.

He put that out of his mind for the moment and settled in his seat. Evie's career had overtaken her education: there was no point in going to drama school when you were already getting film parts and West End roles. The girl who had once had an adolescent crush on Jasper was now a confident adult, still discovering her powers but in no doubt about where she was going.

Her distinguished boyfriend sat next to Jasper. Hank Remington was the same age as Jasper. Although Hank was a millionaire and world famous, he did not look down on a mere student. In fact, having left school at the age of fifteen, he was inclined to defer to people he thought were educated. This pleased Jasper, who did not say what he knew to be true, that Hank's raw genius counted for a lot more than school exams.

Evie's parents were in the same row, as was her grandmother Eth Leckwith. The major absence was her brother, Dave, whose group had a gig.

The curtain went up. The play was a legal drama. Jasper had heard Evie learning her lines, and he knew that the third act took place in a courtroom; but the action started in the prosecuting barrister's chambers. Evie, playing his daughter, came in halfway through the first act and had an argument with her father.

Jasper was awestruck by Evie's confidence and the authority of her performance. He had to keep reminding himself that this was the kid who lived in the same house as he. He found himself resenting the father's smug condescension and sharing the daughter's indignation and frustration. Evie's anger grew and, as the end of the act drew near, she began an impassioned plea for mercy that had the audience silently mesmerized.

Then something happened.

People began to mutter.

At first the actors onstage did not notice. Jasper looked around, wondering whether someone had fainted or thrown up, but he could see nothing to explain the talking. On the other side of the auditorium two people left their seats and walked out with a third man who appeared to have come to summon them. Hank, sitting beside Jasper, hissed: "Why don't these bastards keep quiet?"

After a minute Evie's magisterial performance faltered, and Jasper knew that she had become aware of something going on. She tried to win back the attention of the audience by becoming more histrionic: she spoke louder, her voice cracked with emotion, and she strode about the stage, making large gestures. It was a brave effort, and Jasper's admiration rose even higher; but it did not work. The murmur of conversation rose to a buzz, then to a roar.

Hank stood up, turned around, and said to the people behind him: "Will you lot just bloody well shut up?"

Onstage, Evie stumbled. "Think of what that woman . . ." She hesitated. "Think of how that woman has lived—has suffered—has been through . . ." She fell silent.

The veteran actor playing her barrister father got up from behind his desk, saying, "There, there, dear," a line that might or might not have been in the script. He came downstage to where Evie was standing and put his arm around her shoulder. Then he turned, squinting into the spotlights, and spoke directly to the audience.

"If you please, ladies and gentlemen," he said in the fruity baritone for which he was famous, "will someone kindly tell us what on earth has happened?"

. . .

Rebecca Held was in a hurry. She came home from work with Bernd, made supper for them both, and got ready to go to a meeting while Bernd cleared away. She had recently been elected to the parliament that governed the Hamburg city-state—one of a growing number of female members. "Are you sure you don't mind me rushing out?" she said to Bernd.

He spun his wheelchair around to face her. "Never give anything up for me," he said. "Never sacrifice anything. Never say you can't go somewhere or do something because you have to take care of your crippled husband. I want you to have a full life that gives you everything you ever hoped for. That way you'll be happy, you'll stay with me, and you'll go on loving me."

Rebecca's question had been little more than a courtesy, but clearly Bernd had been thinking about this. His speech moved her. "You're so good," she said. "You're like Werner, my father. You're strong. And you must be right, because I do love you, now more than ever."

"Speaking of Werner," he said, "what do you make of Carla's letter?"

All post in East Germany was liable to be read by the secret police. The sender could be jailed for saying the wrong thing, especially in letters to the West. Any mention of hardship, shortages, unemployment, or the secret police themselves would get you in trouble. So Carla wrote in hints. "She says that Karolin is now living with her and Werner," Rebecca said. "So I think we have to infer that the poor girl was thrown out by her parents—probably under pressure from the Stasi, maybe from Hans himself."

"Is there no end to that man's vengefulness?" said Bernd.

"Anyway, Karolin has been befriended by Lili, who is almost fifteen, just the right age to be fascinated by a pregnancy. And the mother-to-be will get plenty of good advice from Grandma Maud. That house will be a safe haven for Karolin, the way it was for me when my parents were killed."

Bernd nodded. "Are you not tempted to get back in touch with your roots?" he asked. "You never talk about being Jewish."

She shook her head. "My parents were secular. I know that Walter and Maud used to go to church, but Carla got out of the habit, and religion has never meant anything to me. And race is best forgotten. I want to honor my parents' memory by working for democracy and freedom throughout Germany, East and West." She smiled wryly. "Sorry to make a speech. I should save it for the parliament." She picked up her briefcase with the papers for the meeting.

Bernd looked at his watch. "Check the news before you go, in case there's something you need to know about."

Rebecca turned on the TV. The bulletin was just beginning. The newsreader said: "The American president, John F. Kennedy, was shot and killed today in Dallas, Texas."

"No!" Rebecca's exclamation was almost a scream.

"The young president and his wife, Jackie, were driving through the city in an open car when a gunman fired several shots, hitting the president, who was pronounced dead minutes later at a local hospital."

"His poor wife!" said Rebecca. "His children!"

"Vice President Lyndon B. Johnson, who was in the motorcade, is believed to be on his way back to Washington to take over as the new president."

"Kennedy was the defender of West Berlin," said Rebecca, distraught. "He said: 'I am a Berliner.' He was our champion."

"He was," said Bernd.

"What will happen to us now?"

. . .

"I made a terrible mistake," said Karolin to Lili, sitting in the kitchen of the town house in Berlin-Mitte. "I should have gone with Walli. Would you fill a hottie for me? I've got a backache again."

Lili took a rubber bottle from the cupboard and filled it at the hot tap. She felt Karolin was too hard on herself. She said: "You did what you thought was best for your baby."

"I was timid," Karolin said.

Lili arranged the bottle behind Karolin. "Would you like some warm milk?"

"Yes, please."

Lili poured milk into a pan and put it on to heat.

"I acted from fear," Karolin went on. "I thought Walli was too young to be trustworthy. I thought my parents could be relied upon. It was the reverse of the truth."

Karolin's father had thrown her out after the Stasi threatened to get him fired from his job as a bus station supervisor. Lili had been shocked. She had not known there were parents who would do such things. "I can't imagine my parents turning on me," Lili said.

"They never would," Karolin said. "And when I turned up on their doorstep, homeless and penniless and six months pregnant, they took me in without a moment's hesitation." She winced at another pang.

Lili poured warm milk into a cup and gave it to Karolin.

Karolin took a sip and said: "I'm so grateful to you and your family. But the truth is I'll never trust anyone again. The only person you can rely upon in this life is yourself. That's what I've learned." She frowned, then she said: "Oh, God!"

"What?"

"I've wet myself." A damp patch spread across the front of her skirt.

"Your waters have broken," Lili said. "That means the baby is coming."

"I've got to clean myself up." Karolin stood up, then groaned. "I don't think I can make it to the bathroom," she said.

Lili heard the front door open, then shut. "Mother's home," she said. "Thank God!" A moment later Carla came into the kitchen. She took in the scene at a glance and said: "How often are the pains coming?"

"Every minute or two," Karolin replied.

"Goodness, we don't have much time," said Carla. "I'm not even going to try to get you upstairs." Briskly, she started putting towels on the floor. "Lie down right here," she said. "I gave birth to Walli on this floor," she added brightly, "so I expect it will do for you." Karolin lay down, and Carla pulled off the soaked underwear.

Lili was frightened, even though her competent mother was now here. Lili could not imagine how a whole baby could emerge through such a tiny opening. Her fear grew worse, not better, a few minutes later when she saw the opening begin to enlarge.

"This is nice and quick," said Carla calmly. "Lucky you."

Karolin's groans of agony seemed restrained: Lili felt she would have been screaming her head off.

Carla said to Lili: "Put your hand here, and hold the head when it comes out." Lili hesitated, and Carla said: "Go on, it will be all right."

The kitchen door opened, and Lili's father appeared. "Have you heard the news?" he said.

"This is no place for men," Carla said without looking at him. "Go to the bedroom, open the bottom drawer of the chest, and bring me the light blue cashmere shawl."

"All right," Werner said. "But someone shot President Kennedy. He's dead."

"Tell me later," said Carla. "Bring me that shawl."

Werner disappeared.

"What did he say about Kennedy?" Carla asked a minute later.

"I think the baby's coming out," Lili said fearfully.

Karolin gave a huge wail of pain and effort, and the baby's head squeezed out. Lili supported it with one hand. It was wet and slimy and warm. "It's alive!" she said. She found herself overflowing with an emotion of love and protectiveness for the tiny scrap of new life.

And she was no longer frightened.

. . .

Jasper's newspaper was produced in a tiny office in the student union building. The room contained one desk, two phones, and three chairs. Jasper met Pete Donegan there half an hour after leaving the theater.

"There are five thousand students in this college and another twenty thousand or more at other London colleges, and a lot are American," Jasper said as soon as Pete walked in. "We need to call all our writers and get them working straightaway. They must talk to every American student they can think of, preferably tonight, tomorrow morning at the latest. If we do this right we can make a huge profit."

"What's the splash?"

"Probably HEARTBREAK OF U.S. STUDENTS. Get a mug shot of anyone who gives a good quote. I'll do the American teachers: Heslop in English, Rawlings in engineering . . . Cooper in philosophy will say something outrageous, he always does."

"We ought to have a biography of Kennedy as a sidebar," said Donegan. "And maybe a page of pictures of his life—Harvard, the navy, his wedding to Jackie—"

"Wait a minute," said Jasper. "Didn't he study in London at one point? His father was American ambassador here—a right-wing Hitler-supporting bastard, apparently—but I seem to recall that the son went to the London School of Economics."

"That's right, it comes back to me now," said Donegan. "But his studies were cut short, after only a few weeks."

"It doesn't matter," said Jasper excitedly. "Someone there must have met him. It makes no difference if they spoke to him for less than five minutes. We just need one quote, I don't care if it's only: 'He was quite tall.' Our splash is THE STUDENT JFK I KNEW, BY LSE PROF."

"I'll get on it right away," said Donegan.

. . .

When George Jakes was a mile from the White House, traffic slowed to a stop for no apparent reason. He banged on his steering wheel in frustration. He pictured Maria weeping alone somewhere.

People started to blare their horns. Several cars ahead, a driver got out and spoke to someone on the sidewalk. At the corner, half a dozen people were gathered around a parked car with its windows open, listening, presumably to the car radio. George saw a well-dressed woman clap her hand to her mouth in horror.

In front of George's Mercedes was a new white Chevrolet Impala. The door opened and the driver got out. He was wearing a suit and hat, and might have been a salesman making calls. He looked around, saw George in his open-top car, and said: "Is it true?"

"Yes," George said. "The president has been shot."

"Is he dead?"

"I don't know." There was no radio in George's car.

The salesman approached the open window of a Buick. "Is the president dead?"

George did not hear the reply.

The traffic was not moving.

George turned off his engine, jumped out of the car, and started to run.

He was dismayed to realize that he had got out of shape. He always seemed too busy to work out. He tried to think when was the last time he had done some vigorous exercise, and he could not remember. He found himself perspiring and breathing hard. Despite his impatience, he had to alternate jogging with fast walking.

His shirt was soaked with sweat when he reached the White House. Maria was not in the press office. "She went to the National Archives Building to do some research," said Nelly Fordham, whose face was wet with tears. "She probably hasn't even heard the news yet."

"Do we know whether the president is dead?"

"Yes, he is," said Nelly, and she sobbed afresh.

"I don't want Maria to hear it from a stranger," George said, and he left the building and ran along Pennsylvania Avenue toward the National Archives.

. . .

Dimka had been married to Nina for a year, and their child, Grigor, was six months old, when he finally admitted to himself that he was in love with Natalya.

She and her friends frequently went for a drink at the Riverside Bar after work, and Dimka got into the habit of joining the group when Khrushchev did not keep him late. Sometimes it was more than one drink, and often Dimka and Natalya were the last two left.

He found he was able to make her laugh. He was not generally considered a comedian, but he relished the many ironies of Soviet life, and so did she. "A worker showed how a bicycle factory could make mudguards more quickly by molding one long strip of tin, then cutting it, instead of cutting it first, then bending the pieces one by one. He was reprimanded and disciplined for endangering the five-year plan."

Natalya laughed, opening her wide mouth and showing her teeth. The way she laughed suggested a potential for reckless abandon that made Dimka's heart beat faster. He imagined her throwing her head back like that while they were making love. Then he imagined seeing her laugh like that every day for the next fifty years, and he realized that was the life he wanted.

He did not tell her, though. She had a husband, and seemed to be happy with him; at least, she said nothing bad about him, although she was never in a hurry to go home to him. More importantly, Dimka had a wife and a child, and he owed them his loyalty.

He wanted to say: *I love you. I'm going to leave my family. Will you leave your husband, live with me, and be my friend and lover for the rest of our lives?*

Instead he said: "It's late, I'd better go."

"Let me drive you," she said. "It's too cold for your motorcycle."

She pulled up at the corner near Government House. He leaned across to kiss her good night. She let him kiss her lips, briefly, then pulled back. He got out of the car and went into the building.

On the way up in the elevator he thought about the excuse he would make to Nina for being late. There was a genuine crisis at the Kremlin: this year's grain harvest had been a catastrophe, and the Soviet government was desperately trying to buy foreign wheat to feed its people.

When he entered the apartment, Grigor was asleep and Nina was watching TV. He kissed her forehead and said: "I was kept late at the office, sorry. We had to finish a report on the bad harvest."

"You shit-faced liar," said Nina. "Your office has been calling here every ten minutes, trying to find you, to tell you that President Kennedy has been killed."

. . .

Maria's tummy rumbled. She looked at her watch and realized she had forgotten to have lunch. The work she was doing had absorbed her, and for two or three hours no one had come into this area to disturb her. But she was almost done, so she decided to finish off, then get a sandwich.

She bent her head over the old-fashioned ledger she was reading, then looked up again when she heard a noise. She was astonished to see George Jakes come in, panting, his suit jacket wet with perspiration, his eyes a little wild. "George!" she said. "What the heck . . . ?" She stood up.

"Maria," he said, "I'm so sorry." He came around the table and put his hands on her shoulders, a gesture that was a little too intimate for their strictly platonic friendship.

"Why are you sorry?" she said. "What have you done?"

"Nothing." She tried to pull back, but he tightened his grip. "They shot him," he said.

Maria saw that George was close to tears. She stopped resisting him and stepped closer. "Who was shot?" she said.

"In Dallas," he said.

Then she began to understand, and a terrible dread rose inside her. "No," she said.

George nodded. In a quiet voice he said: "The president is dead. I'm so sorry."

"Dead," Maria said. "He can't be dead." Her legs felt weak, and she sank to her knees. George knelt with her and folded her in his arms. "Not my Johnny," she said, and a huge sob erupted from inside her. "Johnny, my Johnny," she moaned. "Don't leave me, please. Please, Johnny. Please don't leave." She saw the world turn gray, she slumped helplessly, then her eyes closed and she lost consciousness.

.   .   .

Onstage at the Jump Club in London, Plum Nellie performed a storming version of "Dizzy, Miss Lizzy" and came off to shouts of: "More!"

Backstage, Lenny said: "That was great, lads, best we've ever played!"

Dave looked at Walli and they both grinned. The group was getting better fast, and every gig was the best ever.

Dave was surprised to find his sister waiting in the dressing room. "How did the play go?" he said. "I'm sorry I couldn't be there."

"It stopped in the first act," she said. "President Kennedy has been shot dead."

"The president!" said Dave. "When did this happen?"

"A couple of hours ago."

Dave thought of their American mother. "Is Mam upset?"

"Terribly."

"Who shot him?"

"No one knows. He was in Texas, in a place called Dallas."

"Never heard of it."

Buzz, the bass player, said: "What shall we do for an encore?"

Lenny said: "We can't do an encore, it would be disrespectful. President Kennedy has been assassinated. We have to do a minute's silence, or something."

Walli said: "Or a sad song."

Evie said: "Dave, you know what we should do."

"Do I?" He thought for a second, then said: "Oh, yeah."

"Come on, then."

Dave went onstage with Evie and plugged in his guitar. They stood at the microphone together. The rest of the group watched from the wings.

Dave spoke into the microphone. "My sister and I are half British, half American, but we feel very American tonight." He paused. "Most of you probably know by now that President Kennedy has been shot dead."

He heard several gasps from the audience, indicating that some had not heard, and the room went quiet. "We would like to play a special song now, a song for all of us, but especially for Americans."

He played a G chord.

Evie sang:

> *O say can you see, by the dawn's early light,*
> *What so proudly we hail'd at the twilight's last gleaming,*

The room was dead silent.

> *Whose broad stripes and bright stars through the perilous fight*
> *O'er the ramparts we watch'd were so gallantly streaming?*

Evie's voice rose thrillingly.

> *And the rocket's red glare, the bombs bursting in air,*
> *Gave proof through the night that our flag was still there,*

Several people in the audience were crying openly now, Dave saw.

> *O say does that star-spangled banner yet wave*
> *O'er the land of the free and the home of the brave?*

"Thank you for listening," said Dave. "And God bless America."

PART FIVE

SONG

1963–1967

CHAPTER THIRTY-ONE

Maria was not allowed to go to the funeral.

The day after the assassination was a Saturday, but like most White House staff she went into work, performing her duties in the press office with tears streaming down her face. It was not noticed: half the people there were crying.

She was better off here than at home alone. Work distracted her a little from her grief, and there was no end of work: the world's press wanted to know every detail of the funeral arrangements.

Everything was on TV. Millions of American families sat in front of their sets all weekend. The three networks canceled all their regular programs. The news consisted entirely of stories linked to the assassination, and between bulletins there were documentaries about John F. Kennedy, his life, his family, his career, and his presidency. With merciless pathos they reran the happy footage of Jack and Jackie greeting the crowds at Love Field on Friday morning, an hour before his death. Maria recalled how she had idly asked herself if she would change places with Jackie. Now both of them had lost him.

At midday on Sunday, in the basement of the Dallas police station, the prime suspect, Lee Harvey Oswald, was himself murdered, live on television, by a minor mobster called Jack Ruby; a sinister mystery piled on top of an insupportable tragedy.

On Sunday afternoon Maria asked Nelly Fordham if they needed tickets for the funeral. "Oh, honey, I'm sorry, no one from this office is invited," Nelly said gently. "Only Pierre Salinger."

Maria felt panicky. Her heart fluttered. How could she not be there when they lowered the man she loved into his grave? "I have to go!" she said. "I'll speak to Pierre."

"Maria, you can't go," Nelly said. "You absolutely can't."

Something in Nelly's tone rang an alarm bell. She was not just giving advice. She almost sounded scared.

Maria said: "Why not?"

Nelly lowered her voice. "Jackie knows about you."

This was the first time anyone in the office had acknowledged that Maria had had a relationship with the president; but in her distress Maria hardly noticed that milestone. "She can't possibly know! I was always careful."

"Don't ask me how, I have no idea."

"I don't believe you."

Nelly might have been offended, but she just shook her head sadly. "From what little I understand of such things, I believe the wife always knows."

Maria wanted to deny it indignantly, but then she thought of the secretaries Jenny and Jerry, and the socialites Mary Meyer and Judith Campbell, and others. Maria was sure they all had sexual relations with President Kennedy. She had no proof, but when she saw them with him she just sort of knew. And Jackie had feminine intuition too.

Which meant Maria could not go to the funeral. She saw that now. The widow could not be forced to face her husband's mistress at such a time. Maria understood that with total, miserable certainty.

So she stayed at home on Monday to watch it on TV.

The body had been lying in state in the rotunda at the Capitol. At half past ten the flag-draped coffin was carried out of the building and placed on a caisson, a type of gun carriage, drawn by six white horses. The procession then headed toward the White House.

Two men stood out in the funeral cortege, being inches taller than the rest: French president Charles de Gaulle, and the new American president, Lyndon Johnson.

Maria was all cried out. She had been sobbing for almost three days. Now when she looked at the television she just saw a pageant, a show organized for the benefit of the world. For her this was not about drums and flags and uniforms. She had lost a man; a warm, smiling, sexy man; a man with a bad back and faint wrinkles in the corners of his hazel eyes and a set of rubber ducks on the edge of his bathtub. She would never look at him again. Life without him stretched long and empty ahead of her.

When the cameras zoomed in on Jackie, her beautiful face visible despite the veil, Maria thought that she, too, looked numb. "I wronged you," Maria said to the face on the screen. "God forgive me."

She was startled by a ring at the door. It was George Jakes. He said: "You shouldn't be alone for this."

She felt a surge of helpless gratitude. When she really needed a friend, George was there. "Come in," she said. "I'm sorry I look like a slattern." She was wearing a nightdress and an old bathrobe.

"You look fine to me." George had seen her worse than shabby.

He had brought a bag of Danish pastries. Maria put them on a plate. She had not had breakfast but, all the same, she did not eat a pastry. She did not feel hungry.

A million people lined the route, according to the television commentary. The coffin was taken from the White House to St. Matthew's Cathedral, where there was a mass.

At twelve noon there was a five-minute silence, and traffic stopped all over America. The cameras showed crowds standing silent on city streets. It was strange to be in Washington and hear no cars outside. Maria and George stood in front of the TV set in her little apartment. They bowed their heads. George took her hand and held it. She felt a wave of affection for him.

When the five-minute silence ended, Maria made coffee. Her appetite returned, and they ate the pastries. No cameras were allowed in the church, so for a while there was nothing to watch. George talked to distract her, and she appreciated it. He said: "Will you stay in the press office?"

She had hardly thought about it, but she knew the answer. "No. I'm going to leave the White House."

"Good idea."

"Apart from everything else, I don't see a future for myself in the press office. They never promote women, and I'm not going to spend my life as a researcher. I'm in government because I want to get things done."

"There's an opening in the Justice Department that might suit you." George spoke as if the thought had just occurred to him, but Maria suspected he had planned to say this. "Dealing with corporations that disobey government regulations. They call it compliance. Could be interesting."

"Do you think I'd have a chance?"

"With a degree from Chicago Law and two years' experience in the White House? Absolutely."

"They don't hire many Negroes, though."

"You know something? I think Lyndon may change that."

"Really? He's a Southerner!"

"Don't prejudge him. To be honest, our people have treated him badly. Bobby hates him, don't ask me why. Maybe because he calls his dick Jumbo."

Maria giggled for the first time in three days. "You're kidding."

"Apparently it's large. If he wants to intimidate someone, he pulls it out and says: 'Meet Jumbo.' That's what people say."

Men told such stories, Maria knew. It might be true and it might not. She grew serious again. "Everyone in the White House thinks Johnson's behavior has been callous, especially toward the Kennedys."

"I don't buy that. Look, when the president had just died and no one knew what to do next, America was terribly vulnerable. What if the Soviets had chosen that moment to take over West Berlin? We are the government of the most powerful country in the world, and we have to do our job, without a second's pause, no matter how deep our sadness. Lyndon picked up the reins immediately, and a darn good thing he did, because no one else was thinking about it."

"Not even Bobby?"

"Least of all Bobby. I love the man, you know that, but he surrendered to his grief. He's comforting Jackie and he's organizing his brother's funeral, and he's not governing America. Frankly, most of our people are just as bad. They may think Lyndon is being callous. I think he's being presidential."

At the end of the mass, the coffin was brought out of the church and again placed on the caisson for the journey to Arlington National Cemetery. This time the mourners traveled in a long line of black limousines. The procession passed the Lincoln Memorial and crossed the Potomac River.

Maria said: "What will Johnson do about the civil rights bill?"

"That's the big question. Right now the bill is doomed. It's with the rules committee, whose chairman, Howard Smith, won't even say when they will begin discussing it."

Maria thought of the Sunday school bombing. How could anyone side with those Southern racists? "Can't his committee overrule him?"

"Theoretically, yes, but when the Republicans ally with the Southern Democrats they have a majority, and they always defeat civil rights, no matter what the public thinks. I don't know how these people can pretend they believe in democracy."

On television, Jackie Kennedy lit an eternal flame to burn perpetually over the grave. George took Maria's hand again, and she saw tears in his eyes. They watched in silence as the casket was slowly lowered into the ground.

Jack Kennedy was gone.

Maria said: "Oh, God, what will happen to us all now?"

"I don't know," said George.

.   .   .

George left Maria reluctantly. She was sexier than she knew in her cotton nightdress and her old velvet bathrobe, with her hair naturally curly and untidy instead of laboriously straightened. But she no longer needed him: she was planning to meet Nelly Fordham and some other girls from the White House at a Chinese restaurant that evening for a private wake, so she would not be alone.

George had dinner with Greg. They ate at the dark-paneled Occidental Grill, a stone's throw from the White House. George smiled at his father's appearance: as always, he wore expensive clothes as if they were rags. His slim black satin tie was awry, his shirt cuffs were unbuttoned, and there was a whitish mark on the lapel of his black suit. Fortunately, George had not inherited his slovenliness.

"I thought we might need cheering up," said Greg. He loved high-class restaurants and refined cuisine, and this was a trait George *had* inherited. They ordered lobster and Chablis.

George had felt closer to his father since the Cuban missile crisis, when the threat of imminent annihilation had caused Greg to open his heart. George had always felt, as an illegitimate child, that he was an embarrassment, and that when Greg played the role of father he did so dutifully but without enthusiasm. However, since that surprising conversation he had understood that Greg really loved him. Their relationship continued to be unusual and rather distant, but George now believed it was founded on something genuine and lasting.

While they were waiting for their food, George's friend Skip Dickerson approached their table. He was dressed for the funeral in a dark suit and a black tie, which looked dramatic against his white-blond hair and pale skin. In his Southern accent, he drawled: "Hi, George. Good evening, Senator. May I join you for just a minute?"

George said: "This is Skip Dickerson, who works for Lyndon. For the president, I should say."

"Pull up a chair," said Greg.

Skip drew up a red leather chair, leaned forward, and spoke intensely to Greg. "The president knows you're a scientist."

Now, thought George, what the heck is this about? Skip never wasted time in small talk.

Greg smiled. "My major in college was physics, yes."

"You graduated summa cum laude from Harvard."

"Lyndon is more impressed by that sort of thing than he should be."

"But you were one of the scientists who developed the atom bomb."

"I worked on the Manhattan Project, that's true."

"President Johnson wants to make sure you approve of the plans for the Lake Erie study."

George knew what Skip was talking about. The federal government was financing a waterfront study for the city of Buffalo that would probably lead to a major harbor construction project. It was worth millions of dollars to several companies in upstate New York.

Greg said: "Well, Skip, we'd like to be sure the study isn't going to be pruned in the budget."

"You can count on that, sir. The president feels this project is top priority."

"I'm glad to hear that, thank you."

The conversation had nothing to do with science, George felt sure. It was about what congressmen called "pork"—the allocation of federal spending projects to favored states.

Skip said: "You're welcome, and enjoy your dinner. Oh, before I go— can we count on you to support the president on this darn wheat bill?"

The Soviets had had a bad harvest, and they were desperate for grain. As part of the process of trying to get along a little better with the Soviet Union, President Kennedy had sold them surplus American wheat on credit.

Greg sat back and spoke thoughtfully. "Members of Congress feel that if the Communists can't feed their people it's not up to us to help them out. Senator Mundt's wheat bill would cancel Kennedy's deal, and I kind of think Mundt is right."

"And President Johnson agrees with you!" said Skip. "He sure doesn't want to help Communists. But this will be the first vote after the funeral. Do we really want it to be a slap in the face for the dead president?"

George put in: "Is that really President Johnson's concern? Or does he want to send a message saying that he's in charge of foreign policy now, and he's not going to have Congress second-guess every nickel-and-dime decision he makes?"

Greg chuckled. "Sometimes I forget how smart you are, George. That's exactly what Lyndon wants."

Skip said: "The president wants to work hand in glove with Congress on foreign policy. But he would really appreciate being able to count on your support tomorrow. He feels it would be a terrible dishonor to the memory of President Kennedy if the wheat bill passes."

Neither man was willing to say what was really going on here, George noted. The simple truth was that Johnson was threatening to cancel the Buffalo dock project if Greg voted for the wheat bill.

And Greg caved. "Please tell the president that I understand his concern and he can count on my vote," he said.

Skip stood up. "Thank you, Senator," he said. "He'll be very pleased."

George said: "Before you go, Skip . . . I know the new president has a lot on his mind, but sometime in the next few days he's going to turn his thoughts to the civil rights bill. Please call me if you think I can help in any way at all."

"Thanks, George. I appreciate that." Skip left.

Greg said: "Nicely done."

"Just making sure he knows the door is open."

"That kind of thing is so important in politics."

Their food came. When the waiters had retreated, George picked up his knife and fork. "I'm a Bobby Kennedy man, through and through," he said as he began to carve his lobster. "But Johnson shouldn't be underestimated."

"You're right, but don't overestimate him either."

"What does that mean?"

"Lyndon has two failings. He's intellectually weak. Oh, listen, he's as cunning as a Texas polecat, but that's not the same thing. He went to schoolteacher college, and never learned abstract thinking. He feels inferior to us Harvard-educated types, and he's right. His grasp of international politics is feeble. The Chinese, the Buddhists, Cubans, Bolsheviks—such people have different ways of thinking that he will never understand."

"What's his other failing?"

"He's morally weak, too. He has no principles. His support of civil rights is genuine, but it's not ethical. He sympathizes with colored people as underdogs, and he thinks he's an underdog, too, because he comes from a poor Texas family. It's a gut reaction."

George smiled: "He just got you to do exactly what he wanted."

"Correct. Lyndon knows how to manipulate people one at a time. He's the most skillful parliamentary politician I've ever met. But he's not a statesman. Jack Kennedy was the opposite: hopelessly incompetent at managing Congress, superb on the international stage. Lyndon will deal with Congress masterfully, but as leader of the free world? I don't know."

"Do you think he has any chance of getting the civil rights bill past Congressman Howard Smith's committee?"

Greg grinned. "I can't wait to see what Lyndon will do. Eat your lobster."

Next day Senator Mundt's wheat bill was defeated by fifty-seven votes to thirty-six.

The headline on the day after read:

Wheat Bill—First Johnson Victory

. . .

The funeral was over. Kennedy was gone, and Johnson was president. The world had changed, but George did not know what that meant, and nor did anyone else. What kind of president would Johnson be? How would he be different? A man most people did not know had suddenly become leader of the free world and ruler of its most powerful country. What was he going to do?

He was about to say.

The chamber of the House of Representatives was packed full. Television lights glared on the assembled congressmen and senators. The justices of the Supreme Court wore their black robes, and the Joint Chiefs of Staff glittered with medals.

George was seated next to Skip Dickerson in the gallery, which was equally full, with people sitting on the steps in the aisles. George studied Bobby Kennedy, down below at one end of the cabinet row, head bent, staring at the floor. Bobby had got thinner in the five days since the assassination. Also, he had taken to wearing his dead brother's clothes, which did not fit him, and added to the impression of a man who had shrunk.

In the presidential box sat Lady Bird Johnson with her two daughters, one plain, one pretty, all three women having old-fashioned hairstyles. With them in the box were several Democratic Party luminaries: Mayor Daley of Chicago, Governor Lawrence of Pennsylvania, and Arthur Schlesinger, the Kennedys' in-house intellectual, who—George happened to know—was already conspiring to unseat Johnson in next year's presidential race. Surprisingly, there were also two black faces in the box. George knew who they were: Zephyr and Sammy Wright, cook and chauffeur to the Johnson family. Was that a good sign?

The big double doors swung open. A doorkeeper with the comic name of Fishbait Miller shouted: "Mr. Speaker! The president of the United States!" Then Lyndon Johnson walked in, and everyone stood up and applauded.

George had two worrying questions about Lyndon Johnson, and both would be answered today. The first was: Would he abandon the troublesome civil rights bill? Pragmatists in the Democratic Party were urging him to do just that. Johnson would have a good excuse, if he wanted one: President Kennedy had failed to get congressional support for the bill and it was doomed to failure. The new president was entitled to give it up as a bad job. Johnson could say that legislation on the crippling, divisive issue of segregation must wait until after the election.

If he did say that, the civil rights movement would be set back years.

The racists would celebrate victory, the Ku Klux Klan would feel that everything they had done was justified, and the corrupt white police, judges, church leaders, and politicians of the South would know they could carry on persecuting and beating and torturing and murdering Negroes with no fear of justice.

But if Johnson did not say that, if he affirmed his support for civil rights, there was another question: Would he have the authority to fill Kennedy's shoes? That question, too, would be answered in the next hour, and the prospects were poor. Lyndon was a smooth operator one-on-one; he was at his least impressive when speaking to large groups on formal occasions—which was precisely what he had to do in a few moments' time. For the American people, this was his first major appearance as their leader, and it would define him, for better or worse.

Skip Dickerson was biting his nails. George said to him: "Did you write the speech?"

"A few lines of it. It was a team effort."

"What's he going to say?"

Skip shook his head anxiously. "Wait and see."

Washington insiders expected Johnson to screw up. He was a bad public speaker, tedious and stiff. Sometimes he rushed his words, sometimes he sounded ponderous. When he wanted to emphasize something he just shouted. His gestures were embarrassingly awkward: he would lift one hand and jab a finger in the air, or raise both arms and wave his fists. Speeches generally revealed Lyndon at his worst.

George could not read anything in Johnson's demeanor as he walked through the applauding crowd, went up to the dais, stood at the lectern, and opened a black loose-leaf notebook. He showed neither confidence nor nervousness as he put on a pair of rimless spectacles, then waited patiently until the applause died down and the audience settled in their seats.

At last he spoke. In an even, measured tone of voice he said: "All I have I would have given, gladly, not to be standing here today."

The chamber became hushed. He had struck exactly the right note of sorrowful humility. It was a good start, George thought.

Johnson continued in the same vein, speaking with slow dignity. If he felt the impulse to rush, he was controlling it firmly. He wore a dark blue suit and tie, and a shirt with a tab-fastened collar, a style considered formal in the South. He looked occasionally from one side to the other, speaking to the whole of the chamber and at the same time seeming to command it.

Echoing Martin Luther King, he talked of dreams: Kennedy's dreams of conquering space, of education for all children, of the Peace Corps. "This is our challenge," he said. "Not to hesitate, not to pause, not to turn about and linger over this evil moment, but to continue on our course so that we may fulfill the destiny that history has set for us."

He had to stop, then, because of the applause.

Then he said: "Our most immediate tasks are here on this hill."

This was the crunch. Capitol Hill, where Congress sat, had been at war with the president for most of 1963. Congress had the power to delay legislation, and used it often, even when the president had campaigned and won public support for his plans. But since John Kennedy announced his civil rights bill they had gone on strike, like a factory full of militant workers, delaying everything, mulishly refusing to pass even routine bills, scorning public opinion and the democratic process.

"First," said Johnson, and George held his breath while he waited to hear what the new president would put first.

"No memorial oration or eulogy could more eloquently honor President Kennedy's memory than the earliest possible passage of the civil rights bill for which he fought so long."

George leaped to his feet, clapping for joy. He was not the only one: the applause burst out again, and this time went on longer than previously.

Johnson waited for it to die down, then said: "We have talked long enough in this country about civil rights. We have talked for one hundred years or more. It is time, *now*, to write the next chapter—and to write it in the books of law."

They applauded again.

Euphoric, George looked at the few black faces in the chamber: five Negro congressmen, including Gus Hawkins of California, who actually looked white; Mr. and Mrs. Wright in the presidential box, clapping; a scatter of dark faces among the spectators in the gallery. Their expressions showed relief, hope, and gladness.

Then his eye fell on the rows of seats behind the cabinet, where the senior senators sat, most of them Southerners, sullen and resentful.

Not a single one was joining in the applause.

. . .

Skip Dickerson laid it out to George six days later in the small study next to the Oval Office. "Our only chance is a discharge petition."

"What's that?"

Dickerson pushed his blond forelock out of his eyes. "It's a resolution passed by Congress discharging the rules committee from control of the bill and forcing it to be sent to the floor for debate."

George felt frustrated that these arcane procedures had to be gone through so that Maria's grandfather would not be thrown in jail for registering to vote. "I've never heard of that," he said.

"We need a majority vote. Southern Democrats will be against us, so I calculate we're fifty-eight votes short."

"Shit. We need fifty-eight Republicans to support us before we can do the right thing?"

"Yes. And that's where you come in."

"Me?"

"A lot of Republicans claim to support civil rights. After all, theirs is the party of Abraham Lincoln, who freed the slaves. We want Martin Luther King and all the Negro leaders to call their Republican supporters, explain this situation to them, and tell them to vote for the petition. The message is that you can't be in favor of civil rights unless you're in favor of the petition."

George nodded. "That's good."

"Some will say they're in favor of civil rights but they don't like this procedural hurry-up. They need to understand that Senator Howard Smith is a hard-core segregationist who will make sure his committee debates the rules until it's too late to pass the bill. What he's doing is not *delay,* it's *sabotage.*"

"Okay."

A secretary put her head around the door and said: "He's ready for you."

The two young men stood up and walked into the Oval Office.

As always, George was struck by the sheer size of Lyndon Johnson.

He was six foot three, but height was only part of it. His head was big, his nose was long, his earlobes were like pancakes. He shook George's hand, then held on to it, grasping George's shoulder with his other hand, standing close enough to make George feel uncomfortable at the intimacy.

Johnson said: "George, I've asked all the Kennedy people to stay on at the White House and help me. You're all Harvard educated and I went to Southwest Texas State Teachers' College. See, I need y'all more than he did."

George did not know what to say. This level of humility was embarrassing. After a hesitation he said: "I'm here to help you any way I can, Mr. President."

By now a thousand people must have said that or something similar, but Johnson reacted as if he had never heard it before. "I sure appreciate you saying that, George," he said fervently. "Thank you." Then he got down to business. "A lot of people have asked me to soften up the civil rights bill to make it easier for Southerners to swallow. They've suggested taking out the prohibition against segregation in public accommodations. I'm not willing to do that, George, for two reasons. The first is that they're going to hate the bill regardless of how hard or soft it is, and I don't believe they'll support it no matter how much I draw its teeth."

That sounded right to George. "If you're going to have a fight, you might as well fight for what you really want."

"Exactly. And I'll tell you the second reason. I have a friend and employee called Mrs. Zephyr Wright."

George recalled Mr. and Mrs. Wright, who had been in the presidential box at the House of Representatives.

Johnson went on: "One time when she was about to drive to Texas I asked her to take my dog with her. She said: 'Please don't ask me to do that.' I had to ask why. 'Driving through the South is tough enough just being black,' she said. 'You can't find a place to eat or sleep or even go to the bathroom. With a dog it's going to be just impossible.' That hurt me, George; it almost brought me to tears. Mrs. Wright is a college graduate, you know. That was when I realized how important public accommodations are when we're talking about segregation. I know what it is to be looked down on, George, and I sure don't wish it on anyone else."

"It's good to hear that," said George.

He knew he was being romanced. Johnson still had hold of his hand and shoulder, was still leaning in a little too close, his dark eyes looking at George with remarkable intensity. George knew what Johnson was doing—but it was working just the same. George felt moved by the story about Zephyr, and believed Johnson when he said he knew what it was to be looked down upon. He felt a surge of admiration and affection for this big, awkward, emotional man who seemed to be on the side of the Negroes.

"It's going to be tough, but I think we can win it," said Johnson. "Do your best, George."

"Yes, sir," said George. "I will."

. . .

George explained President Johnson's strategy to Verena Marquand shortly before Martin Luther King went to the Oval Office. She looked stunning in a bright red PVC raincoat but, for once, George was not distracted by her beauty. "We have to put everything we've got into this effort," he said urgently. "If the petition fails, the bill fails, and Southern Negroes will be back where they started."

He gave Verena a list of Republican congressmen who had not yet signed the petition.

She was impressed. "President Kennedy talked to us about votes, but he never had a list like this," she said.

"That's Lyndon," said George. "If the whips tell him how many votes they think they've got, he says: 'Thinking isn't good enough—I need to know!' He has to have the names. And he's right. This is too important for guesswork."

He told her that civil rights leaders had to put pressure on liberal Republicans. "Every one of these men must get a call from someone whose approval he cares about."

"Is that what the president is going to tell Dr. King this morning?"

"Precisely." Johnson had seen all the most important civil rights leaders one by one. Jack Kennedy would have had them all in a room together, but Lyndon could not work his magic so well in large groups.

"Does Johnson think the civil rights leaders can turn all these Republicans around?" Verena said skeptically.

"Not on their own, but he's enlisting others. He's seeing all the union leaders. He had breakfast with George Meany this morning."

Verena shook her beautiful head in wonder. "You have to give him credit for energy." She looked thoughtful. "Why couldn't President Kennedy do this?"

"Same reason Lyndon can't sail a yacht—he doesn't know how."

Johnson's meeting with King went well. But next morning George's optimism was punctured by a segregationist backlash.

Leading Republicans denounced the petition. McCulloch of Ohio said it had irritated people who might otherwise have supported the civil rights bill. Gerald Ford told reporters that the rules committee should be allowed time to hold hearings, which was rubbish: everyone knew that Smith wanted to kill the bill, not debate it. All the same, reporters were briefed that the petition had failed.

But Johnson was not discouraged. Wednesday morning he spoke to the Business Advisory Council, eighty-nine of the most important American businessmen, and he said: "I am the only president you have; if you would have me fail, then you fail, for the country fails."

Then he addressed the executive council of the AFL-CIO, the largest federation of unions, and said: "I need you, I want you, and I believe you should be at my side." He got a standing ovation, and the Steelworkers' thirty-three lobbyists stormed Capitol Hill.

George was sitting down to dinner with Verena in one of the restaurants there when Skip Dickerson passed their table and hissed: "Clarence Brown has gone to see Howard Smith."

George explained to Verena: "Brown is the senior Republican on Smith's committee. Either he's telling Smith to tough it out, and ignore the lobbying . . . or he's saying that Republicans can't take this pressure much longer. If two people on the committee turn against Smith, his decisions can be overturned by a majority vote."

"Could it all be over so quickly?" Verena marveled.

"Smith may jump before he's pushed. It looks more dignified." George moved his plate away. Tension had ruined his appetite.

Half an hour later Dickerson came by again. "Smith caved," he crowed. "There will be a formal statement tomorrow." He walked on, spreading the news.

George and Verena grinned at one another. Verena said: "Well, God bless Lyndon Johnson."

"Amen," said George. "We have to celebrate."

"What shall we do?"

"Come to my apartment," said George. "I'll think of something."

There was no uniform at Dave's school, but boys were mocked for being overdressed. Dave took some ribbing on the day he showed up in a four-button jacket, a white shirt with long collar points, a paisley tie, and blue hipster trousers with a white plastic belt. He did not care about the teasing. He had a mission.

Lenny's group had been on the fringes of show business for years. As things stood, they could spend another decade playing rock and roll in clubs and pubs. Dave wanted more than that in 1964. And the way forward was to make a record.

After school he took the Tube to Tottenham Court Road and walked from there to an address in Denmark Street. On the ground floor of the building was a guitar shop, but beside it was a door leading to an office above, and a nameplate that said CLASSIC RECORDS.

Dave had spoken to Lenny about getting a recording contract, but Lenny had been discouraging. "I've tried that," he had said. "You can't get through the door. It's a closed circle."

That made no sense. There had to be a way in, otherwise no one would ever make records. But Dave knew better than to chop logic with Lenny. So he decided to do it on his own.

He had begun by studying the names of the record companies in the hit parade. It was a complicated exercise, because there were many labels, all owned by a few companies. The phone book had helped him sort them out, and he had picked Classic as his target.

He had called their number and said: "This is British Railways Lost Property. We have a tape in a box marked: 'Head of Artists and Recording, Classic Records.' Who should we send it to?" The girl who answered the phone had given him a name and this address in Denmark Street.

At the top of the stairs he found a receptionist, probably the one he had spoken to on the phone. Assuming a confident air, he used the name she had given him. "I'm here to see Eric Chapman," he said.

"What name shall I say?"

"Dave Williams. Tell him Byron Chesterfield sent me."

This was a lie, but Dave had nothing to lose.

The receptionist disappeared through a door. Dave looked around. The lobby was decorated with framed gold and silver discs. A photograph of Percy Marquand, the Negro Bing Crosby, was inscribed: "To Eric, with thanks for everything." Dave noticed that all the discs were at least five years old. Eric needed fresh talent.

Dave felt nervous. He was not accustomed to deception. He told himself not to be timid. He was not breaking the law. If he were found out, the worst that could happen was that he would be told to get out and stop wasting people's time. It was worth risking that.

The secretary came out, and a middle-aged man stood in the doorway. He wore a green cardigan over a white shirt and a nondescript tie. He had thinning gray hair. He leaned on the doorpost, looking Dave up and down. After a moment he said: "So Byron sent you to me, did he?"

His tone was skeptical: obviously he did not believe the story. Dave avoided repeating the lie by telling another. "Byron said: 'EMI has the Beatles, Decca has the Rolling Stones, Classic needs Plum Nellie.'" Byron had said nothing of the kind. Dave had figured it out for himself, reading the music press.

"Plum what?"

Dave handed Chapman a photo of the group. "We've done a stint at the Dive in Hamburg, as the Beatles did, and we've played the Jump Club in London, like the Stones." He was surprised he had not yet been thrown out, and he wondered how much longer his luck would hold.

"How do you know Byron?"

"He's our manager." Another lie.

"What sort of music?"

"Rock and roll, but with a lot of vocal harmonies."

"Just like every other pop group at the moment."

"But we're better."

There was a long pause. Dave was pleased that Chapman was even talking to him. Lenny had said: "You can't get through the door." Dave had proved him wrong there.

Then Chapman said: "You're a bloody liar."

Dave opened his mouth to protest, but Chapman held up a hand to silence him. "Don't tell me any more whoppers. Byron isn't your manager and he didn't send you here. You might have met him, but he didn't say Classic Records needs Plum Nellie."

Dave said nothing. He had been caught out. This was humiliating. He had tried to bluff his way into a record company and he had failed.

Chapman said: "What's your name, again?"

"Dave Williams."

"What do you want from me, Dave?"

"A recording contract."

"There's a surprise."

"Give us an audition. I promise you won't regret it."

"I'll tell you a secret, Dave. When I was eighteen, I got my first job in a recording studio by saying I was a qualified electrician. I lied. The only qualification I had was grade seven piano."

Dave's heart leaped in hope.

"I like your cheek," Chapman said. A little sadly, he added: "If I could turn back the clock, I wouldn't mind being a young chancer all over again."

Dave held his breath.

"I'll audition you."

"Thanks!"

"Come into the recording studio after Christmas." He jerked a thumb at the receptionist. "Cherry will give you an appointment." He went back into his room and closed the door.

Dave could hardly believe his luck. He had been caught out in his silly lies—but he had got an audition just the same!

He made a provisional appointment with Cherry, and said he would phone to confirm when he had checked with the rest of the group. Then he went home, walking on air.

As soon as he got back to the house in Great Peter Street he picked up the phone in the hall and called Lenny. "I got us an audition with Classic Records!" he said triumphantly.

Lenny was not as enthusiastic as Dave expected. "Who told you to do that?" He was miffed because Dave had taken the initiative.

Dave refused to be deflated. "What have we got to lose?"

"How did you manage it?"

"Bluffed my way in. I saw Eric Chapman, and he said okay."

"Blind luck," said Lenny. "It happens sometimes."

"Yeah," said Dave, though he was thinking: I wouldn't have got lucky if I'd stayed home sitting on my arse.

"Classic isn't really a pop label," Lenny said.

"That's why they need us." Dave was running out of patience. "Lenny, how can this be bad?"

"No, it's fine, we'll see if it comes to anything."

"Now we have to decide what to play at the audition. The secretary told me we'll get to record two songs."

"Well, we should do 'Shake, Rattle and Roll,' obviously."

Dave's heart sank. "Why?"

"It's our best number. Always goes down well."

"You don't think it's a bit old-fashioned?"

"It's a classic."

Dave knew he could not fight Lenny about this, not right now. Lenny had already swallowed his pride once. He could be pushed, but not too far. However, they could do two songs: perhaps the second could be more distinctive. "How about a blues?" Dave said desperately. "For a contrast. Show our range."

"Yeah. 'Hoochie Coochie Man.'"

That was a bit better, more like the material the Rolling Stones were doing. "Okay," said Dave.

He went into the drawing room. Walli was there with a guitar on his knee. He had been living with the Williams family ever since coming from Hamburg with the group. He and Dave often sat in this room, playing and singing, between school and dinner.

Dave told him the news. Walli was pleased, but worried about Lenny's choice of material. "Two songs that were hits in the fifties," he said. His English was improving fast.

"It's Lenny's group," said Dave helplessly. "If you think you can change his mind, please try."

Walli shrugged. He was a great musician but a bit passive, Dave found. Evie said everyone was passive by comparison with the Williams family.

They were pondering Lenny's taste when Evie came in with Hank Remington. *A Woman's Trial* was a hit, despite the catastrophic opening on the day President Kennedy was killed. Hank was recording a new album with the Kords. They spent their afternoons together, then went off to their separate jobs.

Hank was wearing crushed-velvet hipster trousers and a polka-dot shirt. He sat with Dave and Walli while Evie went upstairs to change. As always he was charming and amusing, telling stories about the Kords on tour.

He picked up Walli's guitar and strummed some chords absentmindedly, then said: "Do you want to hear a new song?"

They did, of course.

It was a sentimental ballad called "Love Is It." The appeal was instant. It was a lovely melody with a little shuffle in the beat. They asked him to play it again, and he did.

Walli said: "What was that chord at the start of the bridge?"

"C sharp minor." Hank showed him, then passed him the guitar.

Walli played the chords, and Hank sang it a third time. Dave improvised a harmony.

"That sounded nice," Hank said. "Such a pity we're not going to record it."

"What?" Dave was incredulous. "It's beautiful!"

"The Kords think it's soppy. We're a rock outfit, they say; we don't want to sound like Peter, Paul and Mary."

"I think it's a number one hit," said Dave.

His mother put her head around the door. "Walli," she said. "Phone call for you—from Germany."

It would be Walli's sister Rebecca in Hamburg, Dave guessed. Walli's family in East Berlin could not phone him: the regime there did not allow phone calls to the West.

While Walli was out of the room, Evie reappeared. She had put her hair up and wore jeans and a T-shirt, ready for makeup and wardrobe artists to go to work on her. Hank was going to drop her at the theater on his way to the recording studio.

Dave was distracted, thinking about "Love Is It," a great song that the Kords did not want.

Walli came back in, followed by Daisy. He said: "That was Rebecca."

"I like Rebecca," said Dave, remembering pork chops and fried potatoes.

"She just received a letter, very delayed, from Karolin in East Berlin." Walli paused. He seemed to be in the grip of some emotion. At last he managed to say: "Karolin had the baby. It's a girl."

Everyone jumped up and congratulated him. Daisy and Evie kissed him. Daisy said: "When did this happen?"

"The twenty-second of November. Easy to remember: it was the day Kennedy was shot."

"How much did she weigh?" Daisy asked.

"Weigh?" said Walli as if that was an incomprehensible question.

Daisy laughed. "It's something people always tell you about new babies."

"I didn't ask what she weighed."

"Never mind. What about her name?"

"Karolin suggests Alice."

"That's lovely," said Daisy.

"Karolin will send me a photograph," said Walli. "Of my daughter," he added dazedly. "But she sends it via Rebecca, because letters to England are even more held up in the censor's office."

Daisy said: "I can't wait to see the picture!"

Hank rattled his car keys impatiently. Maybe he found baby talk boring. Or, Dave thought, perhaps he did not like the baby taking the spotlight away from him.

Evie said: "Oh, my God, look at the time. Bye, everyone. Congratulations again, Walli."

As they were leaving, Dave said: "Hank, are the Kords really not going to record 'Love Is It'?"

"Really. When they take against something, they're a stubborn lot."

"In that case . . . could Walli and I have the song for Plum Nellie? We've got an audition in January with Classic Records."

"Sure," said Hank with a shrug. "Why not?"

. . .

Lloyd Williams asked Dave to step into his study on Saturday morning.

Dave was about to go out. He was wearing a horizontally striped blue-and-white sweater, jeans, and a leather jacket. "Why?" he said pugnaciously. "You're no longer giving me an allowance." The money he earned playing with Plum Nellie was not much, but it was enough for Tube fares, drinks, and occasionally a shirt or a new pair of boots.

"Is money the only reason for speaking to your father?"

Dave shrugged and followed him into the room. It had an antique desk and some leather chairs. A fire smoldered in the grate. On the wall was a picture of Lloyd at Cambridge in the thirties. The room was a shrine to everything that was out-of-date. It seemed to smell of obsolescence.

Lloyd said: "I ran into Will Furbelow at the Reform Club yesterday."

Will Furbelow was the head of Dave's school. Being bald, he was inevitably known as None Above.

"He says you're in danger of failing all your exams."

"He's never been my biggest fan."

"If you fail, you will not be allowed to continue at the school. That will be the end of your formal education."

"Thank God for that."

Lloyd was not going to be riled. "Every profession will be closed to you, from accountant to zoologist. They all require you to pass exams. The next possibility, for you, is an apprenticeship. You could learn to do something useful, and you should think about what you might like: bricklaying, cooking, motor mechanics . . ."

Dave wondered whether Dad was out of his mind. "Bricklaying?" he said. "Do you even *know* me? I'm Dave."

"Don't sound incredulous. These are the jobs people do if they can't pass exams. Below that level, you could be a shop assistant or a factory hand."

"I can't believe I'm hearing this."

"I was afraid you would do this, close your eyes to reality."

Dad was the one closing his eyes, Dave thought.

"I realize you're getting beyond the age where I can expect you to obey me."

Dave was startled. This was a new approach. He said nothing.

"But I want you to be clear about where we stand. When you leave school, I expect you to work."

"I am working, quite hard. I play three or four nights a week, and Walli and I have started trying to write songs."

"I mean that I expect you to support yourself. Although your mother has inherited wealth, we agreed long ago that we would never support our children in idleness."

"I'm not idle."

"You think that what you do is work, but the world may not see it that way. In any event, if you want to continue living here you'll have to pay your share."

"You mean rent?"

"If you want to call it that, yes."

"Jasper's never paid rent, and he's lived here for years!"

"He's still a student. And he passes his exams."

"What about Walli?"

"A special case, because of his background; but sooner or later he must pay his share, too."

Dave was working out the implications. "So, if I don't become a bricklayer or a shop assistant, and I don't make enough money with the group to pay your rent, then . . ."

"Then you will have to look for alternative accommodation."

"You'll throw me out."

Lloyd looked pained. "All your life, you've had the best of everything handed to you on a plate: a lovely home, a great school, the best food, toys and books, piano lessons, skiing holidays. But that was when you were a child. Now you're almost an adult, and you have to face reality."

"My reality, not yours."

"You scorn the kind of work that ordinary people do. You're different, you're a rebel. Fine. Rebels pay a price. Sooner or later, you have to learn that. That's all."

Dave sat thoughtful for a minute. Then he stood up. "Okay," he said. "I get the message." He went to the door.

As he left, he glanced back, and saw his father watching him with an odd expression.

He thought about that as he went out of the house and slammed the front door. What was that look? What did it mean?

He was still thinking about it as he bought his Tube ticket. Going down on the escalator, he saw an advertisement for a play called *Heartbreak House.* That was it, he thought. That was his father's facial expression.

He had looked heartbroken.

. . .

A small color photograph of Alice arrived in the post, and Walli studied it eagerly. It showed a baby like any other: a tiny pink face with alert blue eyes, a cap of thin dark brown hair, a blotchy throat. The rest of her was tightly wrapped in a sky-blue blanket. All the same Walli felt an upsurge of love and a sudden need to protect and care for the helpless creature he had made.

He wondered if he would ever see her.

With the picture was a note from Karolin. She said that she loved Walli and missed him, and she was going to apply to the East German government for permission to emigrate to the West.

In the picture, Karolin was holding Alice and looking at the camera. Karolin had put on weight, and her face was more round. Her hair was pulled back, instead of framing her face like curtains. She no longer resembled all the other pretty girls in the Minnesänger folk club. She was a mother now. It made her even more desirable in Walli's eyes.

He showed the photograph to Dave's mother, Daisy. "Well, now, what a beautiful baby!" she said.

Walli smiled, though in his opinion no babies were beautiful, not even his own.

"I think she has your eyes, Walli," Daisy went on.

Walli's eyes had a slight Oriental look. He figured some long-ago ancestor must have been Chinese. He could not tell whether or not Alice's eyes were similar.

Daisy continued to gush. "And this is Karolin." Daisy had not seen her before: Walli had no photos. "What a pretty young woman."

"Wait till you see her dressed up," Walli said proudly. "People stop and stare."

"I hope we will see her, sometime."

A shadow fell over Walli's happiness, as if a cloud had hidden the sun. "So do I," he said.

He followed the news from East Berlin, reading the German newspapers in the public library, and he often questioned Lloyd Williams, whose specialty as a politician was foreign affairs. Walli knew that getting out of East Germany was ever more difficult: the Wall was being made larger and more formidable, with more guards and more towers. Karolin would never try to escape, especially now that she had a child. However, there might be another way. Officially, the East German government would not say whether legal emigration was possible; indeed, they would not even say which department dealt with applications. But Lloyd had learned, from the British embassy in Bonn, that about ten thousand people a year were given permission. Perhaps Karolin would be one of them.

"One day, I feel certain," said Daisy; but she was just being nice.

Walli showed the picture to Evie and Hank Remington, who were sitting in the drawing room, reading a script. The Kords were hoping to make a movie, and Hank wanted Evie to be in it. They put down their papers to coo over the baby.

"We have our audition with Classic Records today," Walli told Hank. "I'm meeting Dave after school."

"Hey, good luck with that," Hank said. "Are you going to do 'Love Is It'?"

"I hope so. Lenny wants to do 'Shake, Rattle and Roll.'"

Hank shook his head, making his long red hair swirl in a way that had caused a million adolescent girls to scream for joy. "Too old-fashioned."

"I know."

People were constantly coming and going at the house in Great Peter Street, and now Jasper came in with a woman Walli had not seen before. "This is my sister, Anna," he said.

Anna was a dark-eyed beauty in her middle twenties. Jasper was good-looking, too: they must be a handsome family, Walli thought. Anna had a generously rounded figure, unfashionable now that all models were flat-chested like Jean "the Shrimp" Shrimpton.

Jasper introduced everyone. Hank stood up to shake hands with Anna and said: "I've been hoping to meet you. Jasper tells me you're a book editor."

"That's right."

"I'm thinking of writing my life story."

Walli thought Hank was a bit young, at twenty, to be writing his autobiography; but Anna had a different view. "What a wonderful idea," she said. "Millions of people would want to read it."

"Oh, do you think so?"

"I know it, even though biography isn't my field—I specialize in translations of German and East European literature."

"I had a Polish uncle, would that help?"

Anna laughed, a rich chuckle, and Walli warmed to her. So did Hank, and they sat down to discuss the book.

Carrying two guitars, Walli left the house.

He had found Hamburg a startling contrast to East Germany, but London was unnervingly different, an anarchic riot. People wore all styles of clothing, from bowler hats to miniskirts. Boys with long hair were too commonplace even to be stared at. Political commentary was not just free, it was outrageous: Walli had been shocked to see a man on television impersonating Prime Minister Harold Macmillan, talking in his voice and wearing a little silver mustache and making idiotic pronouncements, though the Williams family had laughed heartily.

Walli was also struck by the number of dark faces. Germany had a few coffee-colored Turkish immigrants, but London had thousands of people from the Caribbean islands and the Indian subcontinent. They came to work in hospitals and factories and on the buses and trains. Walli noticed that the Caribbean girls were very stylishly dressed and sexy.

He met Dave at the school gates and they took the Tube to north London.

Dave was nervous, Walli could tell. Walli was not nervous. He knew he was a good musician. Working at the Jump Club every night he heard dozens of guitarists, and it was rare to come across one who was more accomplished than he. Most got by with a few chords and a lot of enthusiasm. When he did hear someone good he would stop washing glasses and watch the group, studying the guitarist's technique, until the boss told him to get back to work; then, when he got home, he would sit in his room and imitate what he had heard until he could play it perfectly.

Unfortunately, virtuosity did not make you a pop star. There was more to it than that: charm, good looks, the right clothes, publicity, clever management, and, most of all, good songs.

And Plum Nellie had a good song. Walli and Dave had played "Love Is It" to the rest of the group, and they had performed it at several gigs over the busy Christmas season. It went down well, although—as Lenny pointed out—you could not dance to it.

But Lenny did not want to audition it. "Not our type of material," he had said. He felt the same as the Kords: it was too pretty and sentimental for a rock group.

From the Tube station, Walli and Dave walked to a big old house that had been soundproofed and converted into recording studios. They waited in the hall. The others turned up a few minutes later. A receptionist asked them all to sign a piece of paper that she said was "for insurance." To Walli it looked more like a contract. Dave frowned as he read it, but they all signed.

After a few minutes, an inner door opened and an unprepossessing young man slouched out. He wore a V-neck sweater with a shirt and tie, and he was smoking a hand-rolled cigarette. "Right," he said by way of introduction, and pushed his hair out of his eyes. "We're almost ready for you. Is this your first time in a recording studio?"

They admitted that it was.

"Well, our job is to make you sound your best, so just follow our guidance, okay?" He seemed to feel he was granting them a great favor. "Come into the studio and plug in, and we'll take it from there."

Dave said: "What's your name?"

"Laurence Grant." He did not say exactly what his role was, and Walli guessed he was a lowly assistant trying to make himself seem important.

Dave introduced himself and the group, which made Laurence fidget impatiently; then they went in.

The studio was a large room with low lighting. At one side was a full-size Steinway piano, very like the one in Walli's home in East Berlin.

It had a padded cover and was partly hidden by a screen draped in blankets. Lenny sat at it and played a series of chords all the way up the keyboard. It had the warm tone characteristic of Steinways. Lenny looked impressed.

A drum kit was set up ready. Lew had brought his own snare drum, and he set about making the change.

Laurence said: "Something wrong with our drums?"

"No, it's just that I'm used to the feel of my own snare."

"Ours is more suitable for recording."

"Oh, okay." Lew removed his own drum and put the studio snare back on its stand.

Three amplifiers stood on the floor, their lights showing that they were on and ready. Walli and Dave plugged into the two Vox AC30 models and Buzz took the larger Ampeg bass amp. They tuned to the piano.

Lenny said: "I can't see the rest of the group. Do we have to have this screen?"

"Yeah, we do," said Laurence.

"What's it for?"

"It's a baffle."

Walli could tell, from Lenny's expression, that he was none the wiser; but he let it drop.

A middle-aged man in a cardigan entered through a different door. He was smoking. He shook hands with Dave, who obviously had met him before, then introduced himself to the rest of the group. "I'm Eric Chapman, and I'll be producing your audition," he said.

This is the man who holds our future in his hands, Walli thought. If he thinks we're good, we'll make records. If not, there's no court of appeal. I wonder what he likes. He doesn't look like a rock-and-roller. More the Frank Sinatra type.

"I gather you haven't done this before," Eric said. "But there's really not much to it. At first it's best to ignore the equipment, and try to relax and play as if this was a regular gig. If you make a minor mistake, just play through." He pointed at Laurence. "Larry here is our general dogsbody, so ask him for anything you need: tea, coffee, extra leads, whatever."

Walli had not heard the English word *dogsbody* before, but he could guess what it meant.

Dave said: "There is one thing, Eric. Our drummer, Lew, brought his own snare, because he's more comfortable with it."

"What type is it?"

Lew answered. "Ludwig Oyster Black Pearl."

"Should be fine," Eric said. "Go ahead and switch."

Lenny said: "Do we have to have this baffle here?"

"I'm afraid we do," Eric said. "It keeps the piano mike from picking up too much drum sound."

So, Walli thought, Eric knows what he's talking about, and Larry is full of shit.

Eric said: "If I like you, we'll talk about what to do next. If not, I won't beat about the bush: I'll tell you straight that you're not what I'm looking for. Is that okay with everybody?"

They all said it was.

"All right, let's give it a whirl."

Eric and Larry retreated through a soundproofed door and reappeared behind an internal window. Eric put on headphones and spoke into a microphone, and the group heard his voice coming from a small speaker on the wall. "Are you ready?"

They were ready.

"Tape is rolling. Plum Nellie audition, take one. In your own time, lads."

Lenny started to play boogie-woogie piano. It sounded wonderful on the Steinway. After four bars the group came in like clockwork. They played this number at every gig: they could do it in their sleep. Lenny went all out, doing the Jerry Lee Lewis vocal flourishes. When they had finished, Eric played back the recording without comment.

Walli thought it sounded good. But what did Eric think?

"You play that well," he said over the intercom when they had finished. "Now, have you got something more modern?"

They played "Hoochie Coochie Man." Once again the piano sounded marvelous to Walli, the minor chords thundering out.

Eric asked them to play both songs again, and they did so. Then he came out of the control booth. He sat on an amplifier and lit a cigarette. "I said I would tell you straight, and I will," he said, and Walli knew then that he was going to reject them. "You play well, but you're old-fashioned.

The world doesn't need another Jerry Lee Lewis or Muddy Waters. I'm looking for the next greatest thing, and you're not it. I'm sorry." He took a long drag on his cigarette and blew out smoke. "You can have the tape, and do what you like with it. Thanks for coming in." He stood up.

They all looked at one another. Disappointment was written on every face.

Eric went back into the control room, and Walli saw him, through the glass, taking the reel-to-reel tape off the machine.

Walli stood up, about to pack his guitar away.

Dave blew on his microphone, and the sound was amplified: everything was still on. He strummed a chord. Walli hesitated. What was Dave up to?

Dave began to sing "Love Is It."

Walli joined in immediately, and they sang in harmony. Lew came in with a quiet drum pattern, and Buzz played a simple walking bass. Finally Lenny joined in on the piano.

They played for two minutes, then Larry switched everything off, and the group was silenced.

It was all over, and they had failed. Walli was more disappointed than he would have expected. He was so sure the group was good. Why could Eric not see it? He undid the strap of his guitar.

Then Eric came back. "What the fuck was that?" he said.

Dave said: "A new song we've just learned. Did you like it?"

"It's completely different," Eric said. "Why did you stop?"

"Larry turned us off."

"Turn them on again, Larry, you prick," said Eric. He turned back to Dave. "Where did you get the song?"

"Hank Remington wrote it for us," said Dave.

"Of the Kords?" Eric was frankly skeptical. "Why would he write a song for you?"

Dave was equally candid. "Because he's going out with my sister."

"Oh. That explains it."

Before going back into the booth, Eric spoke quietly to Larry. "Go and phone Paulo Conti," he said. "He only lives around the corner. If he's at home, ask him to pop in right away."

Larry left the studio.

Eric went back into the booth. "Tape rolling," he said over the intercom. "Whenever you're ready."

They did the song again.

All Eric said was: "Again, please."

After the second time he came out again. Walli feared he would say it was not good enough after all. "Let's do it again," he said. "This time we'll record the backing first time around, and the vocals after."

Dave said: "Why?"

"Because you play better when you don't have to sing, and you sing better when you don't have to play."

They recorded the instruments, then they sang the song while the recording was played to them through headphones. Afterward Eric came out of the booth to listen with them. They were joined by a well-dressed young man with a Beatle haircut: Paulo Conti, Walli presumed. Why was he here?

They listened to the combined track, Eric sitting on an amp and smoking.

When it ended, Paulo said in a London accent: "I like it. Nice song."

He seemed confident and authoritative, though he was only about twenty. Walli wondered what right he had to an opinion.

Eric dragged on his cigarette. "Now, we might have something here," he said. "But there's a problem. The piano part is wrong. No offense, Lenny, but the Jerry Lee Lewis style is a bit heavy-handed. Paulo is here to show you what I mean. Let's record it again with Paulo on the piano."

Walli looked at Lenny. He was angry, Walli could tell; but he was keeping it under control. He remained sitting on the piano stool and said: "Let's get something straight, Eric. This is my group. You can't shove me out and bring Paulo in."

"I wouldn't worry too much about that if I were you, Lenny," said Eric. "Paulo plays with the Royal National Symphony Orchestra and he's released three albums of Beethoven sonatas. He doesn't want to join a pop group. I wish he did—I know half a dozen outfits that would take him on quicker than you can say *hit parade*."

Lenny looked foolish and said aggressively: "All right, so long as we understand each other."

They played the song again, and Walli could see immediately what

Eric meant. Paulo played light trills with his right hand and simple chords with his left, and it suited the song much better.

They recorded it again with Lenny. He tried to play like Paulo, and made a decent job of it, but he did not really have the touch.

They recorded the backing twice more, once with Paulo and once with Lenny; then they recorded the vocal part three times. Finally Eric was satisfied. "Now," he said, "we need a B side. What have you got that's similar?"

"Wait a minute," Dave said. "Does that mean that we've passed the audition?"

"Of course you have," said Eric. "Do you think I go to this much trouble with groups I'm about to turn down?"

"So . . . 'Love Is It' by Plum Nellie will be released as a record?"

"I bloody well hope so. If my boss turns it down I'll quit."

Walli was surprised to learn that Eric had a boss. Until now he had given the impression that he *was* the boss. It was a trivial deception, but Walli marked it.

Dave said: "Do you think it will be a hit?"

"I don't make predictions—I've been in this business too long. But if I thought it was going to be a miss, I wouldn't be here talking to you, I'd be down the pub."

Dave looked around at the group, grinning. "We passed the audition," he said.

"You did," Eric said impatiently. "Now, what have you got for the B side?"

. . .

"Are you ready for some good news?" said Eric Chapman over the phone to Dave Williams a month later. "You're going to Birmingham."

At first Dave did not know what he meant. "Why?" he said. Birmingham was an industrial city one hundred twenty miles north of London. "What's in Birmingham?"

"The television studio where they make *It's Fab!*, you idiot."

"Oh!" Dave suddenly felt breathless with excitement. Eric was talking about a popular show that featured pop groups miming to their records. "Are we on it?"

"Of course you are! 'Love Is It' will be their Hot Tip for the week."

The record had been out five days. It had been played on the BBC Light Programme once, and several times on Radio Luxembourg. To Dave's surprise, Eric did not know how many copies had actually been bought: the record business was not that good at tracking sales.

Eric had released the version with Paulo on the piano. Lenny had pretended not to notice.

Eric treated Dave as the leader of the group, despite what Lenny had told him. Now he said: "Have you got decent outfits to wear?"

"We normally wear red shirts and black jeans."

"It's black-and-white television, so that'll probably look fine. Make sure you all wash your hair."

"When are we going?"

"Day after tomorrow."

"I'll have to get off school," Dave said worriedly. There might be trouble about that.

"You may have to *leave* school, Dave."

Dave gulped. He wondered if that was true.

Eric finished: "Meet me at Euston station at ten in the morning. I'll have your tickets."

Dave hung up the phone and stared at it. He was going to be on *It's Fab!*

It was beginning to look as if he might actually make a living by singing and playing the guitar. As that prospect came to seem more real, his dread of the alternatives grew. What a comedown it would be now, if he had to get a regular job after all.

He called the rest of the group immediately, but he decided not to tell his family until afterward. There was too much risk that his father would try to stop him going.

He kept the exciting secret to himself all evening. Next day at lunchtime he asked to see the head teacher, old None Above.

Dave felt intimidated in the headmaster's study. In his early days at school he had been caned in this office several times for such offenses as running in the corridor.

He explained the situation and pretended there had not been time to get a note from his father.

"It seems to me you have to choose between getting a decent education and becoming a pop singer," said Mr. Furbelow, pronouncing the words *pop singer* with a grimace of distaste. He looked as if he had been asked to eat a can of cold dog food.

Dave thought of saying: *Actually, my ambition is to become a prostitute's minder,* but Furbelow's sense of humor was as scant as his hair. "You told my father I'm going to fail all my exams and be thrown out of the school."

"If your work does not improve rapidly, and if you consequently fail to gain any O-level qualifications, you will not be admitted to the sixth form," the head said with prissy exactness. "All the more reason why you may not take days off school to appear on trashy television programs."

Dave thought of arguing about "trashy" and decided it was a lost cause. "I thought you might regard a trip to a television studio as an educational experience," he said reasonably.

"No. There is far too much talk nowadays about educational 'experiences.' Education takes place in the classroom."

Despite Furbelow's mulish obstinacy, Dave continued to try to reason with him. "I'd like to have a career in music."

"But you don't even belong to the school orchestra."

"They don't use any instruments invented in the last hundred years."

"And all the better for it."

Dave was finding it harder and harder to keep his temper. "I play the electric guitar quite well."

"I don't call that a musical instrument."

Against his better judgment, Dave allowed his voice to rise in a challenge. "What is it, then?"

Furbelow's chin lifted and he looked superior. "More a sort of nigger noisemaker."

For a moment, Dave was silenced. Then he lost his cool. "This is just willful ignorance!" he said.

"Don't you dare speak to me like that."

"Not only are you ignorant, you're a racist!"

Furbelow stood up. "Get out this instant."

"You think it's all right for you to come out with your crude prejudices, just because you're the burned-out head of a school for rich kids!"

"Be silent!"

"Never," said Dave, and he left the room.

In the corridor outside the head's study, it occurred to him that he could not now go to class.

A moment later he realized he could not stay in the school.

He had not planned this, but in a moment of madness he had, in fact, left school.

So be it, he thought; and he left the building.

He went to a café nearby and ordered eggs and chips. He had burned his boats. After he had called the head ignorant and burned-out and a racist they would not have him back, no matter what. He felt scared as well as liberated.

But he did not regret what he had done. He had a chance of becoming a pop star—and the school had wanted him to let it slip by!

Ironically, he was at a loss to know what to do with his newfound freedom. He wandered around the streets for a couple of hours, then returned to the school gates to wait for Linda Robertson.

He walked her home after school. Naturally the whole class had noticed his absence, but the teachers had said nothing. When Dave told her what had happened, she was awestruck. "So you're going to Birmingham anyway?"

"You bet."

"You'll have to leave school."

"I've left."

"What will you do?"

"If the record is a hit, I'll be able to afford to get a flat with Walli."

"Wow. And if it's not?"

"Then I'm in trouble."

She invited him in. Her parents were out, so they went to her bedroom, as they had done before. They kissed, and she let him feel her breasts; but he could tell she was troubled. "What's the matter?" he said.

"You're going to be a star," she said. "I know it."

"Aren't you glad?"

"You'll be mobbed by dolly birds who will let you go all the way."

"I hope so!"

She burst into tears.

"I was kidding," he said. "I'm sorry!"

She said: "You used to be this cute little kid I liked to talk to. None of the girls even wanted to kiss you. Then you joined a group and turned into the coolest boy in school, and they all envied me. Now you'll be famous and I'll lose you."

He thought she wanted him to say that he would be faithful to her, no matter what, and he was tempted to swear undying love; but he held back. He really liked her, but he was not yet sixteen, and he knew he was too young to be tied down. However, he did not want to hurt her feelings, so he said: "Let's just see what happens, okay?"

He saw the disappointment on her face, though she covered it up quickly. "Good idea," she said. She dried her tears, then they went down to the kitchen and had tea and chocolate biscuits until her mother came home.

When he got back to Great Peter Street there was no sign of anything unusual, so he deduced that the school had not telephoned his parents. No doubt None Above would prefer to write a letter. That gave Dave a day of grace.

He said nothing to his parents until the following morning. His father left at eight. Then Dave spoke to his mother. "I'm not going to school," he said.

She did not fly off the handle. "Try to understand the journey that your father has made," she said. "He was illegitimate, as you know. His mother worked in a sweatshop in the East End, before she went into politics. His grandfather was a coal miner. Yet your father went to one of the world's great universities, and by the time he was thirty-one he was a minister in the British government."

"But I'm different!"

"Of course you are, but to him it looks as if you just want to throw away everything he and his parents and grandparents have achieved."

"I have to live my own life."

"I know."

"I've left school. I had a row with old None Above. You'll probably get a letter from him today."

"Oh, dear. Your father will find that hard to forgive."

"I know. I'm leaving home, too."

She began to cry. "Where will you go?"

Dave felt tearful, too, but he kept control. "I'll stay at the YMCA for a few days, then get a flat with Walli."

She put a hand on his arm. "Just don't be angry with your father. He loves you so much."

"I'm not angry," said Dave, though he was, really. "I'm just not going to be held back by him, that's all."

"Oh, God," she said. "You're as wild as I was, and just as pigheaded."

Dave was surprised. He knew she had made an unhappy first marriage, but all the same he could not imagine his mother being wild.

She added: "I hope your mistakes won't be as bad as mine."

As he was leaving, she gave him all the money in her purse.

Walli was waiting in the hall. They left the house carrying their guitars. As soon as they were outside in the street all feelings of regret vanished, and Dave began to feel both excited and apprehensive. He was going to be on television! But he had gambled everything. He felt a little dizzy every time he remembered that he had left home and school.

They got the Tube to Euston. Dave had to ensure the television appearance was a success. This was paramount. If the record did not sell, he thought fearfully, and Plum Nellie was a failure, what then? He might have to wash glasses at the Jump Club, like Walli.

What could he do that would make people buy the record?

He had no idea.

Eric Chapman was waiting at the railway station in a pin-striped suit. Buzz, Lew, and Lenny were already there. They loaded their guitars onto the train. The drums and amplifiers were going separately, being driven in a van to Birmingham by Larry Grant; but no one would trust him with the precious guitars.

On the train, Dave said to Eric: "Thanks for buying our tickets."

"Don't thank me. The cost will be deducted from your fee."

"So . . . the television company will pay our fee to you?"

"Yes, and I'll deduct twenty-five percent, plus expenses, and pay you the rest."

"Why?" said Dave.

"Because I'm your manager, that's why."

"Are you? I didn't know."

"Well, you signed the contract."

"Did I?"

"Yes. I wouldn't have recorded you otherwise. Do I look like a charity worker?"

"Oh—that piece of paper we signed before the audition?"

"Yes."

"She said it was for insurance."

"Among other things."

Dave had a feeling he had been tricked.

Lenny said: "The show's on Saturday, Eric. How come we're going on a Thursday?"

"Most of it's prerecorded. Just one or two of the acts perform live on the day."

Dave was surprised. The show gave the impression of a fun party full of kids dancing and having a great time. He said: "Will there be an audience?"

"Not today. You've got to pretend you're singing to a thousand screaming girls all wetting their knickers for you."

Buzz, the bass player, said: "That's easy. I've been performing for imaginary girls since I was thirteen."

It was a joke, but Eric said: "No, he's right. Look at the camera and picture the prettiest girl you know standing right there taking her bra off. I promise you, it will put just the right sort of smile on your face."

Dave realized he was smiling already. Maybe Eric's trick worked.

They reached the studio at one. It was not very smart. Much of it was dingy, like a factory. The parts that appeared on camera had a tawdry glamour, but everything out of shot was scuffed and grubby. Busy people walked around ignoring Plum Nellie. Dave felt as though everyone knew he was a beginner.

A group called Billy and the Kids was onstage when they arrived. A record was playing loudly, and they were singing and playing along, but they had no microphones and their guitars were not plugged in. Dave knew, from his friends, that most viewers did not realize the acts were miming, and he wondered how people could be so dumb.

Lenny was scornful of the jolly Billy and the Kids record, but Dave was impressed. They smiled and gestured to the nonexistent audience, and when the song came to an end they bowed and waved as if acknowledging gales of applause. Then they did the whole thing all over again, with no less energy and charm. That was the professional way, Dave realized.

Plum Nellie's dressing room was large and clean, with big mirrors surrounded by Hollywood lights, and a fridge full of soft drinks. "This is better than what we're used to," said Lenny. "There's even a toilet roll in the bog!"

Dave put on his red shirt, then went back to watch the filming. Mickie McFee was performing now. She had had a string of hits in the fifties and was making a comeback. She was at least thirty, Dave guessed, but she looked sexy in a pink sweater stretched tight across her breasts. She had a great voice. She did a soul ballad called "It Hurts Too Much," and she sounded like a black girl. What must it be like, Dave wondered, to have so much confidence? He was so anxious he felt as if his stomach was full of worms.

The cameramen and technicians liked Mickie—they were mostly the older generation—and they clapped when she finished.

She came down off the stage and saw Dave. "Hello, kid," she said.

"You were great," Dave said, and introduced himself.

She asked him about the group. He was telling her about Hamburg when they were interrupted by a man in an Argyle sweater. "Plum Nellie onstage, please," the man said in a soft voice. "Sorry to butt in, Mickie, darling." He turned to Dave. "I'm Kelly Jones, producer." He looked Dave up and down. "You look fab. Get your guitar." He turned back to Mickie. "You can eat him up later."

She protested: "Give a girl a chance to play hard to get."

"That'll be the day, duckie."

Mickie waved a good-bye and disappeared.

Dave wondered whether they had meant a single word they had said.

He had little time to think about it. The group got onstage and were shown their places. As usual, Lenny turned up his shirt collar, the way Elvis did. Dave told himself not to be nervous: he would be miming, so he didn't even have to play the song right! Then they were into it and Walli was fingering the introduction as the record began.

Dave looked at the rows of empty seats and imagined Mickie McFee pulling the pink sweater off over her head to reveal a black brassiere. He grinned happily into the camera and sang the harmony.

The record was two minutes long, but it seemed to be over in five seconds.

He expected to be asked to do it again. They all waited onstage. Kelly Jones was talking earnestly to Eric. After a minute they both came over to the group. Eric said: "Technical problem, lads."

Dave feared there was something wrong with their performance, and the television appearance might be canceled.

Lenny said: "What technical problem?"

Eric said: "It's you, Lenny, I'm sorry."

"What are you talking about?"

Eric looked at Kelly, who said: "This show is about kids with groovy clothes and Beatle haircuts raving to the latest hits. I'm sorry, Lenny, but you're not a kid, and your haircut is five years out-of-date."

Lenny said angrily: "Well, I'm very sorry."

Eric said: "They want the group to appear without you, Lenny."

"Forget it," said Lenny. "It's my group."

Dave was terrified. He had sacrificed everything for this! He said: "Listen, what if Lenny combs his hair forward and turns down the collar of his shirt?"

Lenny said: "I'm not doing it."

Kelly said: "And he would still look too old."

"I don't care," said Lenny. "It's all of us or none of us." He looked around the group. "Right, lads?"

No one said anything.

"Right?" Lenny repeated.

Dave felt scared, but forced himself to speak. "I'm sorry, Lenny, but we can't miss this chance."

"You bastards," Lenny said furiously. "I should never have let you change the name. The Guardsmen were a great little rock-and-roll combo. Now it's a schoolboy group called Plum fucking Nellie."

"So," Kelly said impatiently. "You'll go back onstage without Lenny and do the number again."

Lenny said: "Am I being fired from my own group?"

Dave felt like a traitor. He said: "It's only for today."

"No, it's not," said Lenny. "How can I tell my friends that my group is on telly but I'm not in it? Fuck that. It's all or nothing. If I leave now, I leave forever."

No one said anything.

"Right, then," said Lenny, and he walked out of the studio.

They all looked shamefaced.

Buzz said: "That was brutal."

Eric said: "That's show business."

Kelly said: "Let's go for another take, please."

Dave feared he would not be able to jig about merrily, after such a traumatic row, but to his surprise he managed fine.

They went through the song twice, and Kelly said he loved their performance. He thanked them for their understanding, and hoped they would come back on the show soon.

When the group returned to the dressing room, Dave hung back in the studio and sat in the empty audience section for a few minutes. He was emotionally exhausted. He had made his television debut, and he had betrayed his cousin. He could not help remembering all the helpful advice Lenny had given him. I'm an ungrateful rotter, he thought.

Heading back to join the others, he looked in at an open door and saw Mickie McFee in her dressing room, holding a glass in her hand. "Do you like vodka?" she said.

"I don't know what it tastes like," said Dave.

"I'll show you." She kicked the door shut, put her arms around his neck, and kissed him with her mouth open. Her tongue had a booze taste a bit like gin. Dave kissed her back enthusiastically.

She broke the embrace and poured more vodka into her glass, then offered it to him.

"No, you drink it," he said. "I prefer it that way."

She emptied the glass, then kissed him again. After a minute she said: "Oh, boy, you are a living doll."

She stepped back, then, to Dave's astonishment and delight, she pulled her tight pink sweater over her head and threw it aside.

She was wearing a black bra.

Dimka's grandmother, Katerina, died of a heart attack at the age of seventy. She was buried in Novodevichy Cemetery, a small park full of monuments and little chapels. The tombstones were prettily topped with snow, like slices of iced cake.

This prestigious resting place was reserved for leading citizens: Katerina was here because one day Grandfather Grigori, a hero of the October Revolution, would be buried in the same grave. They had been married almost fifty years. Dimka's grandfather seemed dazed and uncomprehending as his lifelong companion was lowered into the frozen ground.

Dimka wondered what it must be like, to love a woman for half a century and then lose her, suddenly, between one beat of the heart and the next. Grigori kept saying: "I was so lucky to have her. I was so lucky."

A marriage such as that was probably the best thing in the world, Dimka thought. They had loved one another and had been happy together. Their love had survived two world wars and a revolution. They had had children and grandchildren.

What would people say about Dimka's marriage, he wondered, when he was lowered into the Moscow earth, perhaps fifty years from now? "Call no man happy until he is dead," said the playwright Aeschylus: Dimka had heard that quote at university and always remembered it. Youthful promise could be blighted by later tragedy; suffering was often rewarded by wisdom. According to family legend, the young Katerina had preferred Grigori's gangster brother, Lev, who had fled to America, leaving her pregnant. Grigori had married her and raised Volodya as his son. Their happiness had had an inauspicious beginning, proving Aeschylus's point.

Another surprise pregnancy had triggered Dimka's own marriage. Perhaps he and Nina could end up as happy as Grigori and Katerina. It was what he longed for, despite his feelings for Natalya. He wished he could forget her.

He looked across the grave at his uncle Volodya and aunt Zoya and their two teenagers. Zoya at fifty was serenely beautiful. There was another marriage that seemed to have brought lasting happiness.

He was not sure about his own parents. His late father had been a cold man. Perhaps that was a consequence of being in the secret police: how could people who did such cruel work be loving and sympathetic? Dimka looked at his mother, Anya, weeping for the loss of her own mother. She had seemed happier since his father died.

Out of the corner of his eye he looked at Nina. She was solemn but dry-eyed. Was she happy being married to him? She had been divorced once, and when Dimka met her she had said she never wanted to marry again and was unable to have children. Now she stood beside him as his wife and carried Grigor, their nine-month-old son, wrapped in a bearskin blanket. Dimka sometimes felt he had no idea what was going on in her mind.

Because Grandfather Grigori had stormed the Winter Palace in 1917, a lot of people had showed up to say a last farewell to his wife. Some were important Soviet dignitaries. Here was the bushy-eyebrowed Leonid Brezhnev, secretary of the Central Committee, glad-handing the mourners. There was Marshal Mikhail Pushnoy, who had been a young protégé of Grigori's in the Second World War. Pushnoy, an overweight Lothario, was stroking his luxuriant gray mustache and turning his charm on Aunt Zoya.

Anticipating this crowd, Uncle Volodya had paid for a reception in a restaurant just off Red Square. Restaurants were dismal places, with surly waiters and poor food. Dimka had heard, from both Grigori and Volodya, that they were different in the West. However, this one was typically Soviet. The ashtrays were full when they arrived. The snacks were stale: dry blinis and curling old pieces of toast with perfunctory slices of boiled egg and smoked fish. Fortunately, even Russians could not spoil vodka, and there was plenty of that.

The Soviet food crisis was over. Khrushchev had succeeded in buying grain from the United States and elsewhere, and there would be no famine this winter. But the emergency had highlighted a long-term disappointment. Khrushchev had pinned his hopes on making Soviet agriculture modern and productive—and he had failed. He ranted about inefficiency, ignorance, and clumsiness, but he had made no headway against such problems. And agriculture symbolized the general miscarriage of his reforms. For all his maverick ideas and sudden radical changes, the USSR was still decades behind the West in everything except military might.

Worst of all, the opposition to Khrushchev within the Kremlin came from men who wanted not more reform but less, hidebound conservatives such as preening Marshal Pushnoy and back-slapping Brezhnev, both now roaring with laughter at one of Grigori's war stories. Dimka had never been so worried about the future of his country, his leader, and his own career.

Nina handed the baby to Dimka and got a drink. A minute later she was with Brezhnev and Marshal Pushnoy, joining in their laughter. People always laughed a lot at funeral wakes, Dimka had noticed: it was the reaction after the solemnity of the burial.

Nina was entitled to party, he felt: she had carried Grigor and given birth to him and breast-fed him, so she had not had much fun for a year.

She had got over her anger with Dimka for lying to her on the night Kennedy died. Dimka had calmed her with another lie. "I did work late, but then I went for a drink with some colleagues." She had remained angry for a while, but less so, and now she seemed to have forgotten the incident. He was pretty sure she had no suspicion of his illicit feelings for Natalya.

Dimka took Grigor around the family, proudly showing people his first tooth. The restaurant was in an old house, with tables spread through several ground-floor rooms of different sizes. Dimka ended up in the farthest room with his uncle Volodya and aunt Zoya.

That was where his sister cornered him. "Have you seen how Nina is behaving?" Tanya said.

Dimka laughed. "Is she getting drunk?"

"And flirting."

Dimka was not perturbed. Anyway, he was in no position to

condemn Nina: he did the same when he went to the Riverside Bar with Natalya. He said: "It is a party."

Tanya had no inhibitions about what she said to her twin. "I noticed that she went straight for the most high-ranking men in the room. Brezhnev just left, but she's still making eyes at Marshal Pushnoy—who must be twenty years older than her."

"Some women find power attractive."

"Did you know that her first husband brought her to Moscow from Perm and got her the job with the steel union?"

"No, I didn't."

"Then she left him."

"How do you know?"

"Her mother told me."

"All Nina got from me was a baby."

"And an apartment in Government House."

"You think she's some kind of gold digger?"

"I worry about you. You're so smart about everything—except women."

"Nina is a little materialistic. It's not the worst of sins."

"So you don't mind."

"No, I don't."

"Okay. But if she hurts my brother I'll scratch her eyes out."

. . .

Daniil came and sat opposite Tanya in the canteen at the TASS building. He put down his tray and tucked a handkerchief into his shirt collar to protect his tie. Then he said: "The people at *New World* like 'Frostbite.'"

Tanya was thrilled. "Good!" she said. "It took them long enough—it must be at least six months. But that's great news!"

Daniil poured water into a plastic tumbler. "It will be one of the most daring things they've ever printed."

"So they're going to publish?"

"Yes."

She wished she could tell Vasili. But he would have to find out on his own. She wondered if he was able to get the magazine. It must be available at libraries in Siberia. "When?"

"They haven't decided. But they don't do anything in a hurry."

"I'll be patient."

. . .

Dimka was awakened by the phone. A woman's voice said: "You don't know me, but I have information for you."

Dimka was confused. The voice belonged to Natalya. He threw a guilty look at his wife, Nina, lying beside him. Her eyes were still closed. He looked at the clock: it was five thirty in the morning.

Natalya said: "Don't ask questions."

Dimka's brain started to work. Why was Natalya pretending to be a stranger? She wanted him to do the same, obviously. Was it for fear that his tone of voice would betray his fondness for her to the wife beside him in bed?

He played along. "Who are you?"

"They're plotting against your boss," she said.

Dimka realized that his first interpretation had been wrong. What Natalya feared was that the phone might be tapped. She wanted to be sure Dimka did not say anything to reveal her identity to the listening KGB.

He felt the chill of fear. True or false, this meant trouble for him. He said: "Who is plotting?"

Beside him, Nina opened her eyes.

Dimka shrugged helplessly, miming: *I have no idea what is going on.*

"Leonid Brezhnev is approaching other Presidium members about a coup."

"Shit." Brezhnev was one of the half-dozen most powerful men under Khrushchev. He was also conservative and unimaginative.

"He has Podgorny and Shelepin on his side already."

"When?" said Dimka, disobeying the instruction not to ask questions. "When will they strike?"

"They will arrest Comrade Khrushchev when he returns from Sweden." Khrushchev was planning a trip to Scandinavia in June.

"But why?"

"They think he's losing his mind," said Natalya, and then the connection was broken.

Dimka hung up and said *Shit* again.

"What is it?" Nina said sleepily.

"Just work problems," Dimka said. "Go back to sleep."

Khrushchev was not losing his mind, though he was depressed, seesawing between manic cheerfulness and deep gloom. At the root of his disquiet was the agricultural crisis. Unfortunately, he was easily seduced by quick-fix solutions: miracle fertilizers, special pollination, new strains. The one proposal he would not consider was relaxing central control. All the same, he was the Soviet Union's best hope. Brezhnev was no reformer. If he became leader the country would go backward.

It was not just Khrushchev's future that worried Dimka now: it was his own. He had to reveal this phone call to Khrushchev: on balance that was less dangerous than concealing it. But Khrushchev was still enough of a peasant to punish the bringer of bad news.

Dimka asked himself whether this was the moment to jump ship, and leave Khrushchev's service. It would not be easy: apparatchiks generally went where they were told. But there were ways. Another senior figure could be persuaded to request that a young aide be transferred to his office, perhaps because the aide's special skills were needed. It could be arranged. Dimka could try for a job with one of the conspirators, Brezhnev perhaps. But what was the point of that? It might save his career, but to no purpose. Dimka was not going to spend his life helping Brezhnev hold back progress.

However, if he was to survive, he and Khrushchev needed to be ahead of this conspiracy. The worst thing they could do would be to wait and see what happened.

Today was April 17, 1964, Khrushchev's seventieth birthday. Dimka would be the first to congratulate him.

In the next room, Grigor began to cry.

Dimka said: "The phone woke him."

Nina sighed and got up.

Dimka washed and dressed quickly, then wheeled his motorcycle out of the garage and rode fast to Khrushchev's residence in the suburb called Lenin Hills.

He arrived at the same time as a van bringing a birthday present. He watched as security men carried into the living room a huge new radio-television console with a metal plaque inscribed:

FROM YOUR COMRADES AT WORK

IN THE CENTRAL COMMITTEE

AND THE COUNCIL OF MINISTERS

Khrushchev often grumpily told people not to waste public money buying him presents, but everyone knew he was secretly happy to receive them.

Ivan Tepper, the butler, showed Dimka upstairs to Khrushchev's dressing room. A new dark suit hung ready to be put on for the day of congratulatory ceremonies. Khrushchev's three Hero of Socialist Labor stars were already pinned to the breast of the jacket. Khrushchev sat in a robe drinking tea and looking at the newspapers.

Dimka told him about the phone call while Ivan helped Khrushchev on with his shirt and tie. The KGB wiretap on Dimka's phone, if there was one, would confirm his story that the call was anonymous, supposing that Khrushchev checked. Natalya had been clever, as always.

"I don't know whether it's important or not, and I didn't think it was for me to decide," Dimka said cautiously.

Khrushchev was dismissive. "Aleksandr Shelepin isn't ready to be leader," he said. Shelepin was a deputy prime minister and former head of the KGB. "Nikolai Podgorny is narrow. And Brezhnev isn't suited either. Do you know they used to call him the Ballerina?"

"No," said Dimka. It was hard to imagine anyone less like a dancer than the stocky, graceless Brezhnev.

"Before the war, when he was secretary of Dnepropetrovsk Province."

Dimka saw that he was supposed to ask the obvious question. "Why?"

"Because anyone could turn him round!" said Khrushchev. He laughed heartily and put his jacket on.

So the threatened coup was dismissed with a joke. Dimka was relieved that he was not being condemned for crediting stupid reports. But one worry was replaced by another. Was Khrushchev's intuition right? His instincts had proved reliable in the past. But Natalya always got news first, and Dimka had never known her to be wrong.

Then Khrushchev picked up another thread. His sly peasant eyes narrowed and he said: "Do these petty plotters have a reason for their discontent? The anonymous caller must have told you."

This was an embarrassing question. Dimka did not dare tell Khrushchev that people thought he was mad. Desperately improvising, he said: "The harvest. They blame you for last year's drought." He hoped this was so implausible it would be inoffensive.

Khrushchev was not offended, but irritated. "We need new methods!" he said angrily. "They must listen to Lysenko!" He fumbled his jacket buttons, then let Tepper do them up.

Dimka kept his face expressionless. Trofim Lysenko was a scientific charlatan, a clever self-promoter who had won Khrushchev's favor even though his research was worthless. He promised improved yields that never materialized, but he managed to persuade political leaders that his opponents were "antiprogress," an accusation that was as fatal in the USSR as "Communist" was in the USA.

"Lysenko performs experiments on cows," Khrushchev went on. "His rivals use fruit flies! Who gives a shit about fruit flies?"

Dimka recalled his aunt Zoya talking about scientific research. "I believe the genes evolve faster in fruit flies—"

"Genes?" said Khrushchev. "Rubbish! No one has ever seen a gene."

"No one has ever seen an atom, but that bomb destroyed Hiroshima." Dimka regretted the words as soon as they were out of his mouth.

"What do you know about it?" Khrushchev roared. "You're just repeating what you've heard, parrot-fashion! Unscrupulous people use innocents like you to spread their lies." He shook his fist. "We will get improved yields. You'll see! Get out of my way."

Khrushchev pushed past Dimka and left the room.

Ivan Tepper gave Dimka an apologetic shrug.

"Don't worry," said Dimka. "He's got mad at me before. He won't remember this tomorrow." He hoped it was true.

Khrushchev's rage was not as worrying as his misapprehensions. He was wrong about agriculture. Alexei Kosygin, who was the best economist in the Presidium, had plans for reform that involved loosening the grip that ministries held on agriculture and other industries. That was the way to go, in Dimka's opinion; not miracle cures.

Was Khrushchev just as wrong about the plotters? Dimka did not know. He had done his best to warn his boss. He could not start a countercoup on his own.

Going down the stairs, he heard applause from the open door of the dining room. Khrushchev was receiving congratulations from the Presidium. Dimka paused in the hall. When the applause died down, he heard the slow bass voice of Brezhnev. "Dear Nikita Sergeyevitch! We, your close comrades in arms, members and candidate members of the Presidium and secretaries of the Central Committee, extend special greetings and fervently congratulate you, our closest personal friend and comrade, on your seventieth birthday."

It was fulsome even by Soviet standards.

Which was a bad sign.

. . .

A few days later, Dimka was given a dacha.

He had to pay, but the rent was nominal. As with most luxuries in the Soviet Union, the difficulty was not the price but getting to the head of the queue.

A dacha—a weekend home or holiday villa—was the first ambition of upwardly mobile Soviet couples. (The second was a car.) Dachas were normally granted only to Communist Party members, naturally.

"I wonder how we got it," Dimka mused after opening the letter.

Nina thought there was no mystery. "You work for Khrushchev," she said. "You should have been given one long ago."

"Not necessarily. It generally takes a few more years of service. I can't think of anything I've done recently that has been especially pleasing to him." He recalled the argument about genes. "In fact just the opposite."

"He likes you. Someone handed him a list of vacant dachas and he put your name next to one. He didn't think about it for longer than five seconds."

"You're probably right."

A dacha could be anything from a palace by the sea to a hut in a field. The following Sunday, Dimka and Nina went to find out what theirs was like. They packed a picnic lunch, then, with baby Grigor, took the train to a village thirty miles outside Moscow. They were full of eager curiosity. A station attendant gave them directions to their place, which was called the Lodge. It took them fifteen minutes to walk there.

The house was a one-story timber cabin. It had a large kitchen-cum-living-room and two bedrooms. It was set in a small garden that ran down to a stream. Dimka thought it was paradise. He wondered again what he had done to get so lucky.

Nina liked it, too. She was excited, moving through the rooms and opening cupboards. Dimka had not seen her so happy for months.

Grigor, who was not so much walking as staggering, seemed delighted to have a new place in which to stumble and fall.

Dimka was imbued with optimism. He envisioned a future in which he and Nina came here on summer weekends year after year. Every season they would marvel over how different Grigor was from last year. Their son's growth would be measured in summers: he would talk next season, count the summer after, then catch a ball, then read, then swim. He would be a toddler here at the dacha, then a boy climbing a tree in the garden, then an adolescent with spots, then a young man charming the girls in the village.

The place had not been used for a year or more, and they threw open all the windows, then set about dusting surfaces and sweeping floors. It was partly furnished, and they started a list of things they would bring next time: a radio, a samovar, a bucket.

"I could come here with Grigor on Friday mornings in the summer," Nina said. She was washing pottery bowls in the sink. "You could join me on Friday night, or Saturday morning if you have to work late."

"You wouldn't mind being here on your own at night?" said Dimka as he scrubbed ancient grease off the kitchen range. "It's a bit lonely."

"I'm not nervous, you know that."

Grigor cried for his lunch, and Nina sat down to feed him. Dimka took a look around outside. He would have to erect a fence at the bottom of the garden, he saw, to prevent Grigor falling into the stream. It was not deep, but Dimka had read somewhere that a child could drown in three inches of water.

A gate in a wall led to a larger garden beyond. Dimka wondered who his neighbors were. The gate was not locked, so he opened it and went through. He found himself in a small wood. Exploring, he came within sight of a larger house. He speculated that his dacha might once have been the home of the gardener at the big house.

Not wanting to intrude on someone's privacy, he turned back—and came face-to-face with a soldier in uniform.

"Who are you?" said the man.

"Dmitri Dvorkin. I'm moving into the little house next door."

"Lucky you—it's a jewel."

"I was just exploring. I hope I haven't trespassed."

"You'd better stay on your own side of that wall. This place belongs to Marshal Pushnoy."

"Oh!" said Dimka. "Pushnoy? He's a friend of my grandfather."

"Then that's how you got the dacha," said the soldier.

"Yes," said Dimka, and he felt vaguely troubled. "I suppose it is."

CHAPTER THIRTY-FOUR

George's apartment was the top floor of a high, narrow Victorian row house in the Capitol Hill neighborhood. He preferred this to a modern building: he liked the proportions of the nineteenth-century rooms. He had leather chairs, a high-fidelity record player, plenty of bookshelves, and plain canvas blinds at the windows instead of fussy drapes.

It looked even better with Verena in it.

He loved to see her doing everyday things in his home: sitting on the couch and kicking off her shoes, making coffee in her bra and panties, standing naked in the bathroom brushing her perfect teeth. Best of all he liked to see her asleep in his bed, as she was now, her soft lips slightly parted, her lovely face in repose, one long, slender arm thrown back to reveal the strangely sexy armpit. He leaned over her and kissed her armpit. She made a noise in her throat but did not wake up.

Verena stayed here every time she came to Washington, which was about once a month. It was driving George crazy. He wanted her all the time. But she was not willing to give up her job with Martin Luther King in Atlanta, and George could not leave Bobby Kennedy. So they were stuck.

George got up and walked naked into the kitchen. He started a pot of coffee and thought about Bobby, who was wearing his brother's clothes, spending too much time at the graveside holding hands with Jackie, and letting his political career go to hell.

Bobby was the public's favorite choice for vice president. President Johnson had not asked Bobby to be his running mate in November, nor had he ruled him out. The two men disliked one another, but that did not necessarily prevent their teaming up for a Democratic victory.

Anyway, Bobby needed to make only a small effort to become Johnson's friend. A little sucking up went a long way with Lyndon. George had planned it with his friend Skip Dickerson, who was close to Johnson. A dinner party for Johnson at Bobby and Ethel's Virginia mansion, Hickory Hill; a few warm handshakes in full view in the corridors of the Capitol; a speech in which Bobby said Lyndon was a worthy successor to his brother; it could be easily done.

George hoped it would happen. A campaign might bring Bobby out of his grief-stricken torpor. And George himself relished the prospect of working in a presidential election campaign.

Bobby could make something special of the normally insignificant post of vice president, just as he had revolutionized the role of attorney general. He would become a high-profile advocate for the things he believed in, such as civil rights.

But first Bobby needed somehow to be reanimated.

George poured two mugs of coffee and returned to the bedroom. Before getting back under the covers he turned on the television. He had a TV set in every room, like Elvis: he felt uneasy if he was away from the news too long. "Let's see who won the California Republican primary," he said.

Verena said sleepily: "You so romantic, baby, I like to die."

George laughed. Verena often made him laugh. It was one of the best things about her. "Who are you trying to kid?" he said. "You want to watch the news, too."

"Okay, you're right." She sat up and sipped coffee. The sheet fell off her, and George had to tear his gaze away to look at the screen.

The leading candidates for the Republican nomination were Barry Goldwater, the right-wing senator from Arizona, and Nelson Rockefeller, the liberal governor of New York. Goldwater was an extremist who hated labor unions, welfare, the Soviet Union, and—most of all—civil rights. Rockefeller was an integrationist and an admirer of Martin Luther King.

They had fought a close contest so far, but the result of yesterday's California primary would be decisive. The winner would take all the state's delegates, about 15 percent of the total attending the Republican convention. Whoever had won last night would almost certainly be the Republican candidate for president.

The commercial break ended, the news came on, and the primary was the top story. Goldwater had won. It was a narrow victory—52 percent to 48 percent—but Goldwater had all the California delegates.

"Hell," said George.

"Amen to that," said Verena.

"This is really bad news. A serious racist is going to be one of the two presidential candidates."

"Maybe it's good news," Verena argued. "Could be all the sensible Republicans will vote Democrat to keep Goldwater out."

"That's worth hoping for."

The phone rang and George picked up the bedside extension. He immediately recognized the Southern drawl of Skip Dickerson, saying: "Did you see the result?"

"Fucking Goldwater won," said George.

"We think it's good news," said Skip. "Rockefeller might have beaten our man, but Goldwater is too conservative. Johnson will wipe the floor with him in November."

"That's what Martin Luther King's people think."

"How do you know that?"

George knew because Verena had told him. "I talked to . . . some of them."

"Already? The result has only just been announced. You're not actually in bed with Dr. King, are you, George?"

George laughed. "Never mind who I'm in bed with. What did Johnson say when you told him the result?"

Skip hesitated. "You won't like it."

"Now I *have* to know."

"Well, he said: 'Now I can win without the help of that little runt.' I apologize, but you did ask."

"Damn."

The little runt was Bobby. George saw immediately the political calculation Johnson had made. If Rockefeller had been his opponent, Johnson would have had to work hard for liberal votes, and having Bobby on the ticket would have helped him win them. But running against Goldwater he could automatically count on all the liberal Democrats and many liberal Republicans too. His problem now would be securing the votes of the white working class, many of whom were racist. So he no longer needed Bobby—in fact, Bobby would now be a liability.

Skip said: "I'm sorry, George, but it's, you know, realpolitik."

"Yeah. I'll tell Bobby. Though he's probably guessed. Thanks for letting me know."

"You bet."

George hung up and said to Verena: "Johnson doesn't want Bobby for his running mate now."

"It makes sense. He doesn't like Bobby, and now he doesn't need him. Who will he pick instead?"

"Gene McCarthy, Hubert Humphrey, or Thomas Dodd."

"Where does this leave Bobby?"

"That's the problem." George got up and turned the volume of the television down to a murmur, then returned to bed. "Bobby's been useless as attorney general since the assassination. I still push on with lawsuits against Southern states that prevent Negroes from voting, but he's not really interested. He's also forgotten all about organized crime—and he was doing so well! We got Jimmy Hoffa convicted, and Bobby hardly noticed."

Shrewdly, Verena asked: "Where does that leave *you*?" She was one of only a few people who thought ahead as fast as George himself.

"I may quit," George said.

"Wow."

"I've been treading water for six months, and I'm not going to do it much longer. If Bobby really is a spent force I'll move on. I admire him more than any man, but I'm not going to sacrifice my life to him."

"What will you do?"

"I could probably get a great job with a Washington law firm. I've had three years' experience in the Department of Justice, and that's worth a lot."

"They don't hire many Negroes."

"That's true, and a lot of firms wouldn't even give me an interview. But others might hire me just to prove they're liberal."

"Really?"

"Things are changing. Lyndon is really hot on equal opportunities.

He sent Bobby a note complaining about how few female lawyers the Justice Department hires."

"Good for Johnson!"

"Bobby was mad as hell."

"So you'll work for a law firm."

"If I stay in Washington."

"Where else would you go?"

"Atlanta. If Dr. King still wants me."

"You'd move to Atlanta," Verena said thoughtfully.

"I could."

There was a silence. They both looked at the screen. Ringo Starr had tonsillitis, the newsreader told them. George said: "If I moved to Atlanta, we could be together all the time."

She looked pensive.

"Would you like that?" he asked her.

Still she said nothing.

He knew why. He had not said *how* they would be together. He had not planned this, but they had got to the point where they had to decide whether to get married.

Verena was waiting for him to propose.

An image of Maria Summers came into his mind, unbidden, unwanted. He hesitated.

The phone rang.

George picked it up. It was Bobby. "Hey, George, wake up," he said jocularly.

George concentrated, trying to put the thought of marriage out of his mind for a minute. Bobby sounded happier than he had for a long time. George said: "Did you see the California result?"

"Yes. It means Lyndon doesn't need me. So I'm going to run for senator. What do you think of that?"

George was startled. "Senator! For what state?"

"New York."

So Bobby would be in the Senate. Maybe he could shake up those crusty old conservatives, with their filibusters and their delaying tactics. "That's great!" said George.

"I want you to join my campaign team. What do you say?"

George looked at Verena. He had been on the brink of proposing marriage. But now he was not moving to Atlanta. He was going on the campaign trail, and if Bobby won he would be back in Washington, working for Senator Kennedy. Everything had changed, again.

"I say yes," George said. "When do we start?"

D imka was with Khrushchev at the Black Sea holiday resort of Pitsunda, on Monday, October 12, 1964, when Brezhnev called.

Khrushchev was not at his best. He lacked energy and talked about the need for old men to retire and make way for the next generation. Dimka missed the old Khrushchev, the podgy gnome full of mischievous ideas, and wondered when he would come back.

The study was a paneled room with an Oriental rug and a bank of telephones on a mahogany desk. The phone that rang was a special high-frequency instrument connecting party and government offices. Dimka picked it up, heard the subterranean rumble of Brezhnev's voice, and handed the phone to Khrushchev.

Dimka heard only Khrushchev's half of the conversation. Whatever Brezhnev was saying, it caused the leader to say: "Why? . . . On what issue? . . . I'm on vacation, what could be so urgent? What do you mean, you all got together? . . . Tomorrow? . . . All right!"

After he hung up, he explained. The Presidium wanted him to return to Moscow to discuss urgent agricultural problems. Brezhnev had been insistent.

Khrushchev sat thoughtfully for a long time. He did not dismiss Dimka. Eventually he said: "They haven't got any urgent agricultural problems. This is what you warned me of six months ago, on my birthday. They're going to throw me out."

Dimka was shocked. So Natalya had been right.

Dimka had believed Khrushchev's reassurances, and his faith had seemed justified in June, when Khrushchev came back from Scandinavia and the threatened arrest did not take place. At that point, Natalya had admitted that she no longer knew what was happening. Dimka assumed the plot had come to nothing.

Now it seemed that it had merely been postponed.

Khrushchev had always been a fighter. "What will you do?" Dimka asked him.

"Nothing," said Khrushchev.

That was even more shocking.

Khrushchev went on: "If Brezhnev thinks he can do better, let him try, the big turd."

"But what will happen with him in charge? He doesn't have the imagination and energy to drive reforms through the bureaucracy."

"He doesn't even see much need for change," the old man said. "Maybe he's right."

Dimka was aghast.

Back in April he had considered whether to leave Khrushchev and try for a job with another senior Kremlin figure, but he had decided against it. Now that was beginning to look like a mistake.

Khrushchev became practical. "We'll leave tomorrow. Cancel my lunch with the French minister of state."

Beneath a thundercloud of gloom Dimka set about making the arrangements: getting the French delegation to come earlier, ensuring the plane and Khrushchev's personal pilot would be ready, and altering tomorrow's diary. But he did it all as if in a trance. How could the end come so easily?

No previous Soviet leader had retired. Both Lenin and Stalin had died in office. Would Khrushchev be killed now? What about his aides?

Dimka asked himself how much longer he had to live.

He wondered if they would even let him see little Grigor again.

He pushed the thought to the back of his mind. He could not operate if he were paralyzed by fear.

They took off at one the following afternoon.

The flight to Moscow took two and a half hours, with no change of time zone. Dimka had no idea what awaited them at the end of the trip.

They flew to Vnukovo-2, south of Moscow, the airport for official flights. When Dimka got off the plane behind Khrushchev, a small group of minor officials greeted them, instead of the usual crowd of top government ministers. At that point, Dimka knew for sure that it was all over.

Two cars were parked on the runway: a ZIL-111 limousine and a five-seater Moskvitch 403. Khrushchev walked to the limousine, and Dimka was ushered to the modest saloon.

Khrushchev realized they were being separated. Before getting into his car, he turned and said: "Dimka."

Dimka felt close to tears. "Yes, comrade First Secretary?"

"I may not see you again."

"Surely that cannot be!"

"Something I should tell you."

"Yes, comrade?"

"Your wife is fucking Pushnoy."

Dimka stared at him, speechless.

"Better you should know," Khrushchev said. "Good-bye." He got into his car and it pulled away.

Dimka sat in the back of the Moskvitch, dazed. He might never see the impish Nikita Khrushchev again. And Nina was sleeping with a stout middle-aged general with a gray mustache. It was all too much to take in.

After a minute, the driver said: "Home or office?"

Dimka was surprised he had a choice. That meant he was not being taken to the basement prison of the Lubyanka, at least not today. He was reprieved.

He considered his options. He could hardly work. There was no point in making appointments and preparing briefings for a leader who was about to fall. "Home," he said.

When he got there, he found himself surprisingly reluctant to accuse Nina. He was embarrassed, as if he were the wrongdoer.

And he *was* guilty. One night of oral sex with Natalya was not the same as the ongoing affair that Khrushchev's words implied, but it was bad enough.

Dimka said nothing while Nina fed Grigor. Then Dimka bathed him and put him to bed, and Nina made supper. While they ate, he told her that Khrushchev would resign tonight or tomorrow. It would be in the newspapers in a couple of days, he guessed.

Nina was alarmed. "What about your job?"

"I don't know what will happen," he said anxiously. "Right now no one is worrying about aides. They're probably deciding whether or not to kill Khrushchev. They'll deal with the small fry later."

"You'll be all right," she said after a moment's reflection. "Your family is influential."

Dimka was not so sure.

They cleared away. She noticed he had not eaten much. "Don't you like the stew?"

"I'm on edge," he said. Then he blurted it out. "Are you Marshal Pushnoy's mistress?"

"Don't be stupid," she said.

"No, I'm serious," Dimka said. "Are you?"

She put the plates in the sink with a bang. "What gave you that stupid idea?"

"Comrade Khrushchev told me. I assume he got the information from the KGB."

"How would they know?"

Dimka noticed that she was answering questions with questions, usually a sign of deceit. "They watch the movements of all senior government figures, looking for nonconformist behavior."

"Don't be ridiculous," she said again. She sat down and took out her cigarettes.

"You flirted with Pushnoy at my grandmother's funeral."

"Flirting is one thing—"

"And then we got a dacha right next to his."

She put a cigarette in her mouth and struck a match, but it went out. "That did seem a coincidence—"

"You're a cool one, Nina, but your hands are shaking."

She threw the dead match on the floor. "Well, how do you think I feel?" she said angrily. "I'm in this apartment all day with nobody to talk to but a baby and your mother. I wanted a dacha and you weren't going to get us one!"

Dimka was taken aback. "So you admit that you prostituted yourself?"

"Oh, be realistic, how else does anyone get anything in Moscow?"

She got the cigarette alight and drew on it hard. "You work for a general secretary who is mad. I open my legs for a marshal who is horny. There's not much difference."

"So why did you open your legs for me?"

She said nothing, but involuntarily looked around the room.

He understood instantly. "For an apartment in Government House?"

She did not deny it.

"I thought you loved me," he said.

"Oh, I was fond of you, but since when was that enough? Don't be such a baby. This is the real world. If you want something, you pay the price."

He felt a hypocrite, accusing her, so he confessed. "Well, I might as well tell you that I've been unfaithful too."

"Ha!" she said. "I didn't think you had the nerve. Who with?"

"I'd rather not say."

"Some little typist in the Kremlin, of course."

"It was just one night, and we didn't have intercourse, but I don't feel that makes it much better."

"Oh, for God's sake, do you think I care? Go ahead—enjoy it!"

Was Nina raving in her anger, or revealing her true feelings? Dimka felt bewildered. He said: "I never foresaw that kind of marriage for us."

"Take it from me, there's no other kind."

"Yes, there is," he said.

"You dream your dreams, I'll dream mine." She switched on the television.

Dimka sat staring at the screen for a while, not seeing or hearing the program. After a while he went to bed, but he did not sleep. Later, Nina got into bed next to him, but they did not touch.

Next day Nikita Khrushchev left the Kremlin forever.

Dimka continued to go into work every morning. Yevgeny Filipov, walking around in a new blue suit, had been promoted. Obviously he had been part of the plot against Khrushchev, and had earned his reward.

Two days later, on Friday, the newspaper *Pravda* announced Khrushchev's resignation.

Sitting in his office with little to do, Dimka noticed that Western newspapers for the same day announced that the British prime minister had also been deposed. Upper-class Conservative Sir Alec Douglas-Home had been replaced by Harold Wilson, leader of the Labour Party, in a national election.

To Dimka in a cynical mood there was something askew when a rampantly capitalist country could fire its aristocratic premier and install a social democrat at the will of the people, whereas in the world's leading Communist state such things were plotted in secrecy by a tiny ruling elite and then announced, days later, to an impotent and docile population.

The British did not even ban Communism. Thirty-six Communist candidates had stood for Parliament. None had been elected.

A week ago, Dimka would have balanced these thoughts against the overwhelming superiority of the Communist system, especially as it would be when reformed. But now the hope of reform had withered, and the Soviet Union had been preserved with all its flaws for the foreseeable future. He knew what his sister would say: barriers to change were an integral part of the system, just another of its faults. But he could not bring himself to accept that.

The following day *Pravda* condemned subjectivism and drift, harebrained scheming, bragging and bluster, and several other sins of Khrushchev's. All that was crap, in Dimka's opinion. What was happening was a lurch backward. The Soviet elite was rejecting progress and opting for what they knew best: rigid control of the economy, repression of dissenting voices, avoidance of experiment. It would make them feel comfortable—and keep the Soviet Union trailing behind the West in wealth, power, and global influence.

Dimka was given minor tasks to perform for Brezhnev. Within a few days he was sharing his small office with one of Brezhnev's aides. It was only a matter of time before he was ousted. However, Khrushchev was still in the Lenin Hills residence, so Dimka began to feel that his boss and he might live.

After a week Dimka was reassigned.

Vera Pletner brought him his orders in a sealed envelope, but she looked so sad that Dimka knew the envelope contained bad news before he opened it. He read it immediately. The letter congratulated him on being appointed assistant secretary of the Kharkov Communist Party.

"Kharkov," he said. "Fuck it."

His association with the disgraced leader had clearly outweighed the influence of his distinguished family. This was a serious demotion. There would be a salary increase, but money was not worth much in the Soviet Union. He would be assigned an apartment and a car, but he would be in Ukraine, a long way from the center of power and privilege.

Worst of all, he would be living four hundred fifty miles from Natalya.

Sitting at his desk, he sank into a depression. Khrushchev was finished, Dimka's career had gone backward, the Soviet Union was heading downhill, his marriage to Nina was a train wreck, and he was to be sent away from Natalya, the bright spot in his life. Where had he gone wrong?

There was not much drinking in the Riverside Bar these days, but that evening he met Natalya there for the first time since coming back from Pitsunda. Her boss, Andrei Gromyko, was unaffected by the coup, and remained foreign minister, so she had kept her job.

"Khrushchev gave me a parting gift," Dimka said to her.

"What?"

"He told me Nina is having an affair with Marshal Pushnoy."

"Do you believe it?"

"I presume the KGB told Khrushchev."

"Still, it might be a mistake."

Dimka shook his head. "She admitted it. That wonderful dacha we got is right next door to Pushnoy's place."

"Oh, Dimka, I'm sorry."

"I wonder who watches Grigor while they're in bed."

"What are you going to do?"

"I can't feel very indignant. I'd be having an affair with you if I had the nerve."

Natalya looked troubled. "Don't talk like that," she said. Her face showed different emotions in quick succession: sympathy, sadness, longing, fear, and uncertainty. She pushed back her unruly hair in a nervous gesture.

"Too late now, anyhow," said Dimka. "I've been posted to Kharkov."

"What?"

"I heard today. Assistant secretary of the Kharkov Communist Party."

"But when will I see you?"

"Never, I imagine."

Her eyes filled with tears. "I can't live without you," she said.

Dimka was astonished. She liked him, he knew that, but she had never spoken this way, even during the single night they had spent together. "What do you mean?" he said idiotically.

"I love you, didn't you know that?"

"No, I didn't," he said, stupefied.

"I've loved you for a long time."

"Why did you never tell me?"

"I'm frightened."

"Of . . . ?"

"My husband."

Dimka had suspected something like this. He assumed, though he had no proof, that Nik was responsible for the savage beating of the black-marketeer who had tried to cheat Natalya. It was no surprise if Nik's wife was terrified of declaring her love for another man. This was the reason for Natalya's changeability, from sexy warmth one day to cold distance the next. "I guess I'm frightened of Nik, too," he said.

"When do you leave?"

"The furniture van will come on Friday."

"So soon!"

"In the office, I'm a loose cannon. They don't know what I might do. They want me out of the way."

She took out a white handkerchief and touched her eyes with it. Then she leaned closer to him across the little table. "Do you remember that room with all the old Tsarist furniture?"

He smiled. "I'll never forget it."

"And the four-poster bed?"

"Of course."

"It was so dusty."

"And cold."

Her mood had changed again, and now she was playful, teasing. "What do you remember most?"

An answer sprang to mind instantly: her little breasts with their big pointed nipples. But he suppressed it.

She said: "Go on, you can tell me."

What did he have to lose? "Your nipples," he said. He was half embarrassed, half inflamed.

She giggled. "Do you want to see them again?"

Dimka swallowed hard. Trying to match her light mood, he said: "Guess."

She stood up, suddenly looking decisive. "Meet me there at seven," she said. Then she walked out.

. . .

Nina was furious. "Kharkov?" she yelled. "What am I supposed to do in fucking Kharkov?"

Nina did not normally use bad language: she felt it was coarse. She had risen above such low habits. Her lapse was a sign of how strongly she felt.

Dimka was unsympathetic. "I'm sure the steel union there will give you a job." In any case it was time she sent Grigor to a day nursery and returned to work, something that was expected of Soviet mothers.

"I don't want to be exiled to a provincial city."

"Nor do I. Do you imagine I volunteered?"

"Didn't you see this coming?"

"I did, and I even considered switching jobs, but I thought the putsch had been canceled, when it had only been postponed. Naturally the plotters did all they could to keep me in the dark."

She gave him a calculating look. "I suppose you spent last night saying good-bye to your typist."

"You told me you didn't care."

"All right, smart mouth. When do we have to go?"

"Friday."

"Hell." Looking furious, Nina started packing.

On Wednesday, Dimka spoke to his uncle Volodya about the move. "It's not just about my career," he said. "I'm not in government for myself. I want to prove that Communism can work. But that means it has to change and improve. Now I'm afraid we could go backward."

"We'll get you back to Moscow as soon as we can," Volodya said.

"Thank you," Dimka said with fervent gratitude. His uncle had always been supportive.

"You deserve it," Volodya said warmly. "You're smart and you get things done, and we don't have a surplus of such people. I wish I had you in my office."

"I was never the military type."

"But, listen. After something like this has happened, you have to prove your loyalty by working hard and not complaining—and, most of all, not constantly begging to be sent back to Moscow. If you do all that for five years, I can start working on your return."

"Five years?"

"Until I can *start*. Don't count on less than ten. In fact, don't count on anything. We don't know how Brezhnev is going to work out."

In ten years the Soviet Union could slide back all the way to poverty and underdevelopment, Dimka thought. But there was no point in saying so. Volodya was not just his best chance—he was his only chance.

Dimka saw Natalya again on Thursday. She had a split lip. "Did Nik do that?" said Dimka angrily.

"I slipped on icy steps and fell on my face," she said.

"I don't believe you."

"It's true," she said, but she would not meet him in the furniture storeroom again.

On Friday morning a ZIL-130 panel truck arrived and parked outside Government House, and two men in overalls began to carry Dimka's and Nina's possessions down in the elevator.

When the truck was almost full, they stopped for a break. Nina made them sandwiches and tea. The phone rang, and the doorman said: "There's a messenger here from the Kremlin, has to deliver personally."

"Send him up," said Dimka.

Two minutes later, Natalya appeared at the door in a coat of champagne-colored mink. With her damaged lip, she looked like a ravaged goddess.

Dimka stared at her uncomprehendingly. Then he glanced at Nina.

She caught his guilty look, and glared at Natalya. Dimka wondered if the two women would fly at one another. He got ready to intervene.

Nina folded her arms across her chest. "So, Dimka," she said, "I suppose this is your little typist."

What was Dimka supposed to say? *Yes*? *No*? *She's my lover*?

Natalya looked defiant. "I'm not a typist," she said.

"Don't worry," said Nina. "I know exactly what you are."

That jibe was rich, Dimka thought, coming from the woman who had slept with a fat old general in order to get a dacha. But he did not say so.

Natalya looked haughty and handed him an official-looking envelope.

He tore it open. It was from Alexei Kosygin, the reforming economist. He had a strong power base so, despite his radical ideas, he had been made chairman of the Council of Ministers in the Brezhnev government.

Dimka's heart leaped. The letter offered him a job as aide to Kosygin—here in Moscow.

"How did you manage this?" he said to Natalya.

"Long story."

"Well, thank you." He wanted to throw his arms around her and kiss her, but refrained. He turned to Nina. "I'm saved," he said. "I can stay in Moscow. Natalya has got me a job with Kosygin."

The two women stared at one another, each hating the other. No one knew what to say.

After a long pause, one of the removal men said: "Does that mean we have to unload the truck?"

· · ·

Tanya flew Aeroflot to Siberia, touching down at Omsk on the way to Irkutsk. The plane was a comfortable Tupolev Tu-104 jet. The overnight flight took eight hours, and she dozed most of the way.

Officially, she was on assignment for TASS. Secretly, she was going to look for Vasili.

Two weeks ago Daniil Antonov had come to her desk and discreetly handed her the typescript of "Frostbite." "*New World* can't publish this after all," he had said. "Brezhnev is clamping down. Orthodoxy is the watchword now."

Tanya had shoved the sheets of paper into a drawer. She was disappointed, but she had been half prepared for this. She said: "Do you remember the articles I wrote three years ago about life in Siberia?"

"Of course," he said. "It was one of the most popular series we ever did—and the government got a surge of applications from families wanting to go there."

"Maybe I should do a follow-up. Talk to some of the same people and ask how they're getting on. Also interview some newcomers."

"Great idea." Daniil lowered his voice. "Do you know where he is?"

So he had guessed. It was not surprising. "No," she said. "But I can find out."

Tanya was still living at Government House. She and her mother had moved up a floor into the grandparents' large apartment, after the death of Katerina, so that they could look after Grandfather Grigori. He claimed he did not need looking after: he had cooked and cleaned for himself and his kid brother, Lev, when they were factory workers before the First World War and living in one room in a St. Petersburg slum, he said proudly. But the truth was that he was seventy-six, and he had not cooked a meal nor swept a floor since the revolution.

That evening Tanya went down in the elevator and knocked on the door of her brother's apartment.

Nina opened up. "Oh," she said rudely. She retreated into the apartment, leaving the door open. She and Tanya had never liked one another.

Tanya stepped into the little hallway. Dimka appeared from the bedroom. He smiled, pleased to see her. She said: "A quiet word?"

He picked up his keys from a small table and led her outside, closing the apartment door. They went down in the elevator and sat on a bench in the spacious lobby. Tanya said: "I want you to find out where Vasili is."

He shook his head. "No."

Tanya almost cried. "Why not?"

"I've just avoided being exiled to Kharkov, by the skin of my teeth. I'm in a new job. What impression will I give if I start making inquiries about a criminal dissident?"

"I have to talk to Vasili!"

"I don't see why."

"Imagine how he must feel. He finished his sentence more than a year ago, yet he's still there. He may fear being forced to remain there the rest of his life! I have to tell him that we haven't forgotten about him."

Dimka took her hand. "I'm sorry, Tanya. I know you're fond of him. But what good will it do to put myself at risk?"

"On the strength of 'Frostbite,' he could be a great author. And he writes about our country in a way that encapsulates everything that's wrong. I have to tell him to write more."

"So what?"

"You work in the Kremlin: you can't change anything. Brezhnev is never going to reform Communism."

"I know. I'm in despair."

"Politics in this country is finished. Literature could be our only hope, now."

"Is a short story going to make any difference?"

"Who knows? But what else can we do? Come on, Dimka. We've always disagreed about whether Communism should be reformed or abolished, but neither of us has ever just given up."

"I don't know."

"Check where Vasili Yenkov lives and works. Say it's a confidential political inquiry for a report you're working on."

Dimka sighed. "You're right, we can't just give up."

"Thank you."

He got the information two days later. Vasili had been released from the prison camp but for some reason there was no new address on file. However, he was working at a power station a few miles outside Irkutsk. The recommendation of the authorities was that he should be refused a travel visa for the foreseeable future.

Tanya was met at the airport by a representative of the Siberian recruitment agency, a woman in her thirties called Irina. Tanya would have preferred a man. Women were intuitive: Irina might suspect Tanya's true mission.

"I thought we could start at the Central Department Store," Irina said brightly. "We have a lot of things you can't easily buy in Moscow, you know!"

Tanya forced enthusiasm. "Great!"

Irina drove her into the town in a four-wheel-drive Moskvitch 410.

Tanya dropped her bag at the Central Hotel, then let herself be shown around the store. Curbing her impatience, she interviewed the manager and a counter assistant.

Then she said: "I want to see the Chenkov power station."

"Oh!" said Irina. "But why?"

"I went there last time I was here." This was a lie, but Irina would not know that. "One of my themes will be how things have changed. Also, I'm hoping to reinterview people I saw last time."

"But the power station has not been forewarned of your visit."

"That's all right. I'd prefer not to disrupt their work. We'll look around, then I'll talk to people during the lunch break."

"As you wish." Irina did not like it, but she was obliged to do everything possible to please an important journalist. "I'll just call ahead."

The Chenkov was an old coal-fired electricity-generating station, built in the thirties when cleanliness was not a consideration. The smell of coal was in the air, and its dust coated all surfaces, turning white to gray and gray to black. They were greeted by the manager, in a suit and a dirty shirt, clearly taken by surprise.

As Tanya was shown around she looked for Vasili. He should be easy to spot, a tall man with thick dark hair and movie-star looks. But she must not reveal, to Irina or anyone else nearby, that she knew him well and had come to Siberia to look for him. "You seem familiar," she would say. "I believe I must have interviewed you last time I was here." Vasili was quick-witted, and he would readily understand what was going on, but she would keep talking as long as possible, to give him time to get over his shock at seeing her.

An electrician would probably work in the control room, or on the furnace floor, she speculated; then she realized he could be fixing a power outlet or a lighting circuit anywhere in the complex.

She wondered how he might have changed in the intervening years. Presumably he still felt she was a friend: he had sent his story to her. No doubt he had a girlfriend here—perhaps several, knowing him. Would he be philosophical about his extended imprisonment, or enraged by the injustice done to him? Would he be pathetic, or rail at her for not getting him out?

She did her job thoroughly, asking workers how they and their families felt about life in Siberia. They all mentioned the high salaries and rapid promotion consequent on the shortage of skilled people. Many spoke cheerfully of the hardships: there was a spirit of pioneering camaraderie.

By midday she still had not seen Vasili. It was frustrating: he could not be far away.

Irina took her to the management dining room, but Tanya insisted on having lunch in the canteen with the workers. People relaxed while they were eating, and they spoke more honestly and colorfully. Tanya made notes of what they said, and kept looking around the room, choosing the next interviewee and at the same time keeping an eye out for Vasili.

However, the lunch hour went by and he did not appear. The canteen began to empty out. Irina proposed moving on to their next appointment, a visit to a school where Tanya would be able to speak to young mothers. Tanya could not think of a reason for refusing.

She would have to ask for him by name. She imagined saying: *I seem to remember an interesting man I met last time, an electrician, I think, called Vasili . . . Vasili, um, Yenkov? Could you find out whether he still works here?* It was barely plausible. Irina would make the inquiry, but she was not stupid, and she was sure to wonder what was Tanya's special interest in this man. It would not take her long to find out that Vasili had come to Siberia as a political prisoner. Then the question would be whether Irina decided to shut up and mind her own business—often the preferred way in the Soviet Union—or to curry favor by mentioning Tanya's query to someone above her in the Communist Party hierarchy.

For years no one had known of the friendship between Tanya and Vasili. That was their protection. It was why they had not been sentenced to life imprisonment for publishing a subversive magazine. After Vasili's arrest, Tanya had let one person into the secret, her twin brother. And Daniil had guessed. But now she was in danger of arousing the suspicions of a stranger.

She steeled her nerve to speak, and then Vasili appeared.

Tanya clamped her hand over her mouth to stop herself screaming. Vasili looked like an old man. He was thin and bent. His hair was long and straggly and streaked with gray. His formerly fleshy, sensual face was drawn and lined. He wore grubby overalls with screwdrivers in the pockets. He dragged his feet as he walked.

Irina said: "Is something wrong, Comrade Tanya?"

"Toothache," said Tanya, improvising.

"I'm so sorry."

Tanya could not tell whether Irina believed her.

Her heart was thudding. She was overjoyed to have found Vasili, but horrified by his ravaged appearance. And she had to conceal this storm of emotions from Irina.

She stood up, letting Vasili see her. Few people were left in the canteen, so he could not miss her. She turned her face aside, not looking at him, to divert Irina's suspicion. She picked up her bag as if to go. "I must see a dentist as soon as I get home," she said.

Out of the corner of her eye she saw Vasili stop suddenly, staring at her. So that Irina would not notice, she said: "Tell me about the school we're going to. What age are the pupils?"

They began walking toward the door as Irina answered her question. Tanya tried to observe Vasili without looking directly at him. He remained frozen staring, for several moments. As the two women approached him, Irina gave him a quizzical look.

Tanya then looked directly at Vasili again.

His sunken face was now looking stunned. His mouth hung open and he stared unblinkingly at her. But there was something in his eyes other than shock. Tanya realized it was hope—astonished, incredulous, yearning hope. He was not completely defeated: something had given this wreck of a man the strength to write that wonderful story.

She remembered the words she had prepared. "You look familiar— did I talk to you last time I was here, three years ago? My name is Tanya Dvorkin and I work for TASS."

Vasili closed his mouth and started to collect himself, but still he seemed dumbstruck.

Tanya kept on talking. "I'm writing a follow-up to my series on emigrants to Siberia. I'm afraid I don't remember your name, though— I've interviewed hundreds of people in the last three years!"

"Yenkov," he said at last. "Vasili Yenkov."

"We had a most interesting talk," Tanya said. "It's coming back to me. I must interview you again."

Irina looked at her watch. "We're short of time. The schools close early here."

Tanya nodded at her and said to Vasili: "Could we meet this evening? Would you mind coming to the Central Hotel? Perhaps we could have a drink together."

"At the Central Hotel," Vasili repeated.

"At six?"

"Six o'clock at the Central Hotel."

"I'll see you then," Tanya said, and she went out.

. . .

Tanya wanted to reassure Vasili that he had not been forgotten. She had done that already, but was it enough? Could she offer him any hope? She also wanted to tell him that his story was wonderful and he should write more, but again she had no encouragement to offer him: "Frostbite" could not be published and the same would probably be true of anything else he produced. She feared she might end up making him feel worse, not better.

She waited for him in the bar. The hotel was not bad. All visitors to Siberia were VIPs—no one came here for a holiday—so the place had the level of luxury expected by the Communist elite.

Vasili came in, looking a bit better than he had earlier. He had combed his hair and put on a clean shirt. He still looked like a man recovering from an illness, but the light of intelligence shone in his eyes.

He took both her hands in his. "Thank you for coming here," he said, his voice trembling with emotion. "I can't begin to tell you how much it means to me. You're a friend, a solid-gold friend."

She kissed his cheek.

They ordered beer. Vasili ate the free peanuts like a starving man.

"Your story is wonderful," Tanya said. "Not just good, but extraordinary."

He smiled. "Thank you. Perhaps something worthwhile can come out of this terrible place."

"I'm not the only person who admires it. The editors of *New World* accepted it for publication." He lit up with gladness, and she had to bring him down again. "But they changed their minds when Khrushchev was deposed."

Vasili looked crestfallen, then he took another handful of nuts. "I'm not surprised," he said, recovering his equanimity. "At least they liked it—that's the important thing. It was worth writing."

"I've made a few copies and mailed them—anonymously, of course—to some of the people who used to receive *Dissidence*," she added. She hesitated. What she planned to say next was bold. Once said, it could not be retracted. She took the plunge. "The only other thing I could do is try to get a copy out to the West."

She saw the light of optimism in his eyes, but he pretended to be dubious. "That would be dangerous for you."

"And for you."

Vasili shrugged. "What are they going to do to me—send me to Siberia? But you could lose everything."

"Could you write some more stories?"

From underneath his jacket he took a large used envelope. "I have already," he said, and he gave the envelope to her. He drank some beer, emptying his glass.

She glanced into the envelope. The pages were covered with Vasili's small, neat handwriting. "Why," she said with elation, "it's enough for a book!" Then she realized that if she were caught with this material she, too, could end up stuck in Siberia. She slipped the envelope into her shoulder bag quickly.

"What will you do with them?" he asked.

Tanya had given this some thought. "There's an annual book fair in Leipzig, in East Germany. I could arrange to cover it for TASS—I speak German, after a fashion. Western publishers attend the fair—editors from Paris and London and New York. I might be able to get your work published in translation."

His face lit up. "Do you think so?"

"I believe 'Frostbite' is good enough."

"That would be so wonderful. But you would be taking a terrible risk."

She nodded. "So would you. If somehow the Soviet authorities found out who the author was, you'd be in trouble."

He laughed. "Look at me—starving, dressed in rags, living alone in a hostel for men that is always cold—I'm not worried."

It had not occurred to her that he might not be getting enough to eat. "There's a restaurant here," she said. "Shall we have dinner?"

"Yes, please."

Vasili ordered beef Stroganoff with boiled potatoes. The waitress put a small bowl of bread rolls on the table, as was done at banquets. Vasili ate all the rolls. After the Stroganoff he ordered pirozhki, a fried bun filled with stewed plums. He also ate everything Tanya left on her plate.

She said: "I thought skilled people were highly paid here."

"Volunteers are, yes. Not ex-prisoners. The authorities submit to the price mechanism only when forced."

"Can I send you food?"

He shook his head. "Everything is stolen by the KGB. Parcels arrive ripped open, marked 'Suspicious package, officially inspected,' and everything decent is gone. The guy in the room next to mine received six jars of jam, all empty."

Tanya signed the bill for dinner.

Vasili said: "Does your hotel room have its own bathroom?"

"Yes."

"Does it have hot water?"

"Of course."

"Can I take a shower? At the hostel we get hot water only once a week, and then we have to rush before it runs out."

They went upstairs.

Vasili was a long time in the bathroom. Tanya sat on the bed, looking out at the grimy snow. She felt stunned. She knew, in a vague way, what labor camps were like, but seeing Vasili had brought it home to her in a devastatingly vivid way. Her imagination had not previously stretched to the extent of the prisoners' suffering. And yet, despite everything, Vasili had not succumbed to despair. In fact, he had summoned, from somewhere, the strength and courage to write about his experiences with passion and humor. She admired him more than ever.

When at last he emerged from the bathroom, they said good-bye. In the old days he would have made a pass at her, but today the thought did not seem to cross his mind.

She gave him all the money in her purse, a bar of chocolate, and two pairs of long underwear that would be too short but otherwise would fit him. "They might be better than what you've got," she said.

"They certainly are," he said. "I don't have any underwear."

After he left, she cried.

CHAPTER THIRTY-SIX

E very time they played "Love Is It" on Radio Luxembourg, Karolin cried.

Lili, now sixteen, thought she knew how Karolin felt. It was like having Walli back home, singing and playing in the next room, except that they could not walk in and see him and tell him how good it sounded.

If Alice was awake they would sit her close to the radio and say: "That's your daddy!" She did not understand, but she knew it was something exciting. Sometimes Karolin sang the song to her, and Lili accompanied her on the guitar and sang the harmony.

Lili's mission in life was to help Karolin and Alice emigrate to the West and be reunited with Walli.

Karolin was still living at the Franck family house in Berlin-Mitte. Her parents would have nothing to do with her. They said she had disgraced them by giving birth to an illegitimate child. But the truth was that the Stasi had told her father he would lose his job as a bus station supervisor because of Karolin's involvement with Walli. So they had thrown her out, and she had moved in with Walli's family.

Lili was glad to have her there. Karolin was like an older sister to replace Rebecca. And Lili adored the baby. Every day when she came home from school she watched Alice for a couple of hours, to give Karolin a break.

Today was Alice's first birthday, and Lili made a cake. Alice sat in her high chair and happily banged a bowl with a wooden spoon while Lili mixed a light sponge cake that the baby could eat.

Karolin was upstairs in her room, listening to Radio Luxembourg.

Alice's birthday was also the anniversary of the assassination. West

German radio and television had programs about President Kennedy and the impact of his death. East German stations were playing it down.

Lyndon Johnson had been president by default for almost a year, but three weeks ago he had won an election by a landslide, defeating the Republican ultraconservative Barry Goldwater. Lili was glad. Although Hitler had died before she was born, she knew her country's history, and she was frightened by politicians who made excuses for racial hatred.

Johnson was not as inspiring as Kennedy, but he seemed equally determined to defend West Berlin, which was what mattered most to Germans on both sides of the Wall.

As Lili was taking the cake out of the oven, her mother arrived home from work. Carla had managed to keep her job as nursing manager in a large hospital, even though she was known to have been a Social Democrat. One time when a rumor had gone around that she was to be fired, the nurses had threatened to go on strike, and the hospital director had been obliged to avert trouble by reassuring them that Carla would continue to be their boss.

Lili's father had been forced to take a job, even though he was still trying to run his business in West Berlin by remote control. He had to work as an engineer in a state-owned factory in East Berlin, making televisions that were far inferior to the West German sets. At the outset he had made some suggestions for improving the product, but this was seen as a way of criticizing his superiors, so he stopped. This evening as soon as he arrived home from work he came into the kitchen and they all sang "Hoch Soll Sie Leben," the traditional German birthday song meaning: "Long may she live."

Then they sat around the kitchen table and talked about whether Alice would ever see her father.

Karolin had applied to emigrate. Escape was becoming more difficult every year: Karolin might have tried to cross, all the same, had she been alone; but she was not willing to risk Alice's life. Every year a few people were allowed out legally. No one could find out the grounds on which applications were judged, but it seemed that most of those allowed to leave were unproductive dependents, children and old people.

Karolin and Alice were unproductive dependents, but their application had been refused.

As always, no reason was given.

Naturally, the government would not say whether any appeal was possible. Once again, rumor filled the information gap. People said you could petition the country's leader, Walter Ulbricht.

He seemed an unlikely savior, a short man with a beard that imitated Lenin's, slavishly orthodox in everything. He was rumored to be happy about the coup in Moscow because he had thought Khrushchev insufficiently doctrinaire. All the same, Karolin had written him a personal letter, explaining that she needed to emigrate in order to marry the father of her child.

"They say he's a believer in old-fashioned family morality," Karolin said. "If that's true, he ought to help a woman who only wants her child to have a father."

People in East Germany spent half their lives trying to guess what the government planned or wanted or thought. The regime was unpredictable. They would allow a few rock-and-roll records to be played in youth clubs, then suddenly ban them altogether. For a while they would be tolerant about clothing, then they would start arresting boys in blue jeans. The country's constitution guaranteed the right to travel, but very few people got permission to visit their relatives in West Germany.

Grandmother Maud joined in the conversation. "You can't tell what a tyrant is going to do," she said. "Uncertainty is one of their weapons. I've lived under the Nazis as well as the Communists. They're depressingly similar."

There was a knock at the front door. Lili opened it and was horrified to see, standing on the doorstep, her former brother-in-law, Hans Hoffmann.

Lili held the door a few inches ajar and said: "What do you want, Hans?"

He was a big man, and could easily have shoved her out of the way, but he did not. "Open up, Lili," he said in a voice of weary impatience. "I'm with the police, you can't keep me out."

Lili's heart was pounding, but she stayed where she was and shouted over her shoulder: "Mother! Hans Hoffmann is at the door!"

Carla came running. "Did you say Hans?"

"Yes."

Carla took Lili's place at the door. "You're not welcome here, Hans," she said. She spoke with calm defiance, but Lili could hear her breathing, fast and anxious.

"Is that so?" Hans said coolly. "All the same, I need to speak to Karolin Koontz."

Lili gave a small cry of fear. Why Karolin?

Carla asked the question. "Why?"

"She has written a letter to the comrade general secretary, Walter Ulbricht."

"Is that a crime?"

"On the contrary. He is the leader of the people. Anyone may write to him. He is glad to hear from them."

"So why have you come here to bully and frighten Karolin?"

"I'll explain my purpose to Fräulein Koontz. Don't you think you'd better ask me in?"

Carla murmured to Lili: "He might have something to tell us about her application to emigrate. We'd better find out." She opened the door wide.

Hans stepped into the hall. He was in his late thirties, a big man who stooped slightly. He wore a heavy double-breasted dark blue coat of a quality not generally available in East German shops. It made him look larger and more menacing. Lili instinctively moved away from him.

He knew the house, and now he acted as if he still lived here. He took off his coat and hung it on a hook in the hall, then without invitation he walked into the kitchen.

Lili and Carla followed him.

Werner was standing up. Lili wondered fearfully if he had taken his pistol from its hiding place behind the saucepan drawer. Perhaps Carla had been arguing on the doorstep in order to give him time to do just that. Lili tried to stop her hands shaking.

Werner did not hide his hostility. "I'm surprised to see you in this house," he said to Hans. "After what you did, you should be ashamed to show your face."

Karolin was looking puzzled and anxious, and Lili realized she did not know who Hans was. In an aside Lili explained: "He's with the Stasi. He married my sister and lived here for a year, spying on us."

Karolin's hand went to her mouth and she gasped. "That's him?" she whispered. "Walli told me. How could he do such a thing?"

Hans heard them whispering. "You must be Karolin," he said. "You wrote to the comrade general secretary."

Karolin looked scared but defiant. "I want to marry the father of my child. Are you going to let me?"

Hans looked at Alice in her high chair. "Such a lovely baby," he said. "Boy or girl?"

It made Lili shake with fear just that Hans was looking at Alice.

Reluctantly, Karolin said: "Girl."

"And what's her name?"

"Alice."

"Alice. Yes, I think you said that in your letter."

Somehow this pretense of being nice about the baby was even more frightening than a threat.

Hans pulled out a chair and sat at the kitchen table. "So, Karolin, you seem to want to leave your country."

"I should think you'd be glad—the government disapproves of my music."

"But why do you want to play decadent American pop songs?"

"Rock and roll was invented by American Negroes. It's the music of oppressed people. It's revolutionary. That's why it's so strange to me that Comrade Ulbricht hates rock and roll."

When Hans was defeated by an argument he always just ignored it. "But Germany has such a wealth of beautiful traditional music," he said.

"I love traditional German songs. I'm sure I know more than you do. But music is international."

Grandmother Maud leaned forward and said waspishly: "Like socialism, comrade."

Hans ignored her.

Karolin said: "And my parents threw me out of the house."

"Because of your immoral way of life."

Lili was outraged. "They threw her out because you, Hans, threatened her father!"

"Not at all," he said blandly. "What are respectable parents to do when their daughter becomes antisocial and promiscuous?"

Angry tears came to Karolin's eyes. "I have never been promiscuous."

"But you have an illegitimate child."

Maud spoke again. "You seem a little confused about biology, Hans. Only one man is required to make a baby, legitimate or otherwise. Promiscuity has nothing to do with it."

Hans looked stung, but once again he refused to rise to the bait. Still addressing Karolin, he said: "The man you wish to marry is wanted for murder. He killed a border guard and fled to the West."

"I love him."

"So, Karolin, you beg the general secretary to grant you the privilege of emigration."

Carla said: "It's not a privilege, it's a right. Free people may go where they like."

That got to Hans. "You people think you can do anything! You don't realize that you belong to a society that has to act as one. Even fish in the sea know enough to swim in schools!"

"We're not fish."

Hans ignored that and turned back to Karolin. "You are an immoral woman who has been rejected by her family because of outrageous behavior. You have taken refuge in a family with known antisocial tendencies. And you wish to marry a murderer."

"He's not a murderer," Karolin whispered.

"When people write to Ulbricht, their letters are passed to the Stasi for evaluation," Hans said. "Yours, Karolin, was given to a junior officer. Being young and inexperienced, he took pity on an unmarried mother, and recommended that permission be granted." This sounded like good news, Lili thought, but she felt sure there would be a twist in the tail. She was right. Hans went on: "Fortunately, his superior passed his report to me, recalling that I have had previous dealings with this"—he looked around with an expression of disgust—"with this undisciplined, nonconformist, troublemaking group."

Lili knew what he was going to say now. It was heartbreaking. Hans had come here to tell them that he had been responsible for the rejection of Karolin's application—and to rub it in personally.

"You will receive a formal reply—everyone does," he said. "But I can tell you now that you will not be permitted to emigrate."

"Can I visit Walli?" Karolin begged. "Just for a few days? Alice has never even her father!"

"No," said Hans with a tight smile. "People who have applied for emigration are never subsequently allowed to take holidays abroad." His hatred showed through momentarily as he added: "What do you think we are, stupid?"

"I will apply again in a year's time," said Karolin.

Hans stood up, a smile of triumphant superiority playing around his lips. "The answer will be the same next year, and the year after, and always." He looked around at all of them. "None of you will be given permission to leave. Ever. I promise you."

With that he left.

.   .   .

Dave Williams phoned Classic Records. "Hello, Cherry, this is Dave," he said. "Can I speak to Eric?"

"He's out at the moment," she said.

Dave was disappointed and indignant. "This is the third time I've phoned!"

"Unlucky."

"He could phone me back."

"I'll ask him."

Dave hung up.

He was not unlucky. Something was wrong.

Plum Nellie had had a great 1964. "Love Is It" had gone to number one on the hit parade, and the group—without Lenny—had done a tour of Britain with a package of pop stars including the legendary Chuck Berry. Dave and Walli had moved into a two-bedroom apartment in the theater district.

But things had now cooled right down. It was frustrating.

Plum Nellie had a second record out. Classic had released "Shake, Rattle and Roll," with "Hoochie Coochie Man" on the B side, rushing it out for Christmas. Eric had not consulted the group, and Dave would have preferred to record a new song.

Dave had proved right. "Shake, Rattle and Roll" had flopped. Now it was January 1965, and as Dave thought about the year ahead he had a sense of panic. At night he had dreams about falling—from a roof, out of a plane, off a ladder—and woke up feeling that his life was about to end. The same sensation came over him when he contemplated his future.

He had allowed himself to believe that he was going to be a musician. He had left his parents' home and his school. He was sixteen, old enough to get married and pay taxes. He had thought he had a career. And suddenly it was all falling apart. He did not know what to do. He was no good at anything other than music. He could not face the humiliation of going back to live in his parents' house. In old-fashioned stories the boy hero would "run away to sea." Dave loved the idea of disappearing, then returning five years later, bronzed and bearded and telling tales of faraway places. But in his heart he knew he would hate the discipline of the navy. It would be worse than school.

He did not even have a girlfriend. When he left school he had ended his romance with Linda Robertson. She said she had been expecting it, though she cried all the same. When he received the money from Plum Nellie's appearance on *It's Fab!* he had got Mickie McFee's phone number from Eric and asked her if she wanted to go out with him, maybe to dinner and a movie. She had thought for a long moment, then said: "No. You're really sweet, but I can't be seen out with a sixteen-year-old. I already have a bad reputation, but I don't want to look quite such a fool." Dave had been hurt.

Walli was sitting next to Dave now, guitar in hand as usual. He was playing with a metal tube fitted over the middle finger of his left hand, and singing: "Woke up this morning, believe I'll dust my broom."

Dave frowned. "That's the Elmore James sound!" he said after a minute.

"It's called bottleneck guitar," Walli said. "They used to do it with the neck of a broken bottle, but now someone makes these metal things."

"It sounds great."

"Why do you keep phoning Eric?"

"I want to know how many copies we sold of 'Shake, Rattle and Roll,' what's happening about the American release of 'Love Is It,' and whether we've got any tour dates coming up—and our manager won't speak to me!"

"Fire him," said Walli. "He is a breast."

Walli's English was almost perfect now. "A tit, you mean," Dave said. "We say he's a tit, not a breast."

"Thank you."

"How can I fire him if I can't get him on the phone?" Dave said gloomily.

"Go round to his office."

Dave looked at Walli. "You know, you're not as dumb as you sound." Dave began to feel better. "That's exactly what I'm going to do."

The downhearted feeling left him as he stepped outside. Something about the streets of London always cheered him. This was one of the world's great cities: anything could happen.

Denmark Street was less than a mile away. Dave was there in fifteen minutes. He went up the stairs to the office of Classic Records. "Eric is out," Cherry said.

"Are you sure?" said Dave. Feeling bold, he opened Eric's door.

Eric was there, behind the desk. He looked a bit foolish, having been caught out in deceit. Then his expression changed to anger and he said: "What do you want?"

Dave did not say anything immediately. His father sometimes said: "Just because someone asks you a question, don't think you have to answer. I've learned that in politics." Dave just stepped into the room and closed the door behind him.

If he remained standing, he thought, it would look as if he expected to be told to leave at any moment. So he sat on the chair in front of Eric's desk and crossed his legs.

Then he said: "Why are you avoiding me?"

"I've been busy, you arrogant little sod. What is it?"

"Oh, all kinds of things," Dave said expansively. "What's happening to 'Shake, Rattle and Roll'? What are we doing in the New Year? What news from America?"

"Nothing, nothing, and nothing," said Eric. "Satisfied?"

"Why would I be satisfied with that?"

"Look." Eric put his hand in his pocket and took out a roll of bills. "Here's twenty quid. That's what you've got coming for 'Shake, Rattle and Roll.'" He threw four five-pound notes on the desk. "Now are you satisfied?"

"I'd like to see the figures."

Eric laughed. "The figures? Who do you think you are?"

"I'm your client, and you're my manager."

"Manager? There's nothing to manage, you twerp. You were a one-hit wonder. We have them all the time in our business. You had a stroke of luck. Hank Remington gave you a song, but you never had real talent. It's over, forget it, go back to school."

"I can't go back to school."

"Why ever not? What are you, sixteen, seventeen?"

"I failed every exam I ever took."

"Then get a job."

"Plum Nellie is going to be one of the most successful acts in the world, and I'm going to be a musician for the rest of my life."

"Keep dreaming, son."

"I will." Dave stood up. He was about to leave when he thought of a snag. He had signed a contract with Eric. If the group really did do well, Eric might claim a percentage. He said: "So, Eric, you're not Plum Nellie's manager anymore, is that what you're telling me?"

"Hallelujah! He's got the message at last."

"I'll take back that contract, then."

Eric suddenly looked suspicious. "What? Why?"

"The contract we signed, the day we recorded 'Love Is It.' You don't want to keep it, do you?"

Eric hesitated. "Why do you want it back?"

"You've just told me I have no talent. Of course, if you see a great future for the group—"

"Don't make me laugh." Eric picked up the phone. "Cherry, my love, get the Plum Nellie contract out of the file and give it to young Dave on his way out." He cradled the handset.

Dave picked up the money from the desk. "One of us is a fool, Eric," he said. "I wonder which?"

. . .

Walli loved London. There was music everywhere: folk clubs, beat clubs, theaters, concert halls, and opera houses. Every night Plum Nellie was not playing he went out to hear music, sometimes with Dave, sometimes alone. Every now and again he went to a classical recital, where he would hear new chords.

The English were strange. When he said he was German, they always started talking about the Second World War. They thought they had won the war, and they got offended if he pointed out that it was actually the Soviets who had defeated the Germans. Sometimes he said he was Polish, just to avoid having the same boring conversation again.

But half the people in London were not English anyway: they were Irish, Scottish, Welsh, Caribbean, Indian, and Chinese. All the drug dealers came from islands: Maltese men sold pep pills, heroin pushers were from Hong Kong, and you could buy marijuana from Jamaicans. Walli liked to go to Caribbean clubs, where they played music with a different beat. He was approached by lots of girls at all these places, but he always told them he was engaged.

One day the phone rang, while Dave was out, and the caller said: "May I speak to Walter Franck?"

Walli almost replied that his grandfather had been dead for more than twenty years. "I am Walli," he said after a hesitation.

The caller switched to German. "This is Enok Andersen calling from West Berlin."

Andersen was the Danish accountant who managed Walli's father's factory. Walli recalled a bald man with glasses and a ballpoint pen in the breast pocket of his jacket. "Is something wrong?"

"All your family is well, but I am the bringer of disappointing news. Karolin and Alice have been refused permission to emigrate."

Walli felt as if he had been punched. He sat down heavily. "Why?" he said. "What reason?"

"The government of East Germany does not give reasons for their decisions. However, a Stasi man visited the house—Hans Hoffmann, whom you know."

"A jackal."

"He told the family that none of them would ever get permission to emigrate or travel to the West."

Walli covered his eyes with his hand. "Never?"

"That's what he said. Your father asked me to convey this to you. I'm very sorry."

"Thank you."

"Is there any message I can give your family? I cross to East Berlin once a week still."

"Say I love them all, please." Walli choked up.

"Very well."

Walli swallowed. "And say that I *will* see them all again one day. I feel sure of it."

"I'll tell them that. Good-bye."

"Good-bye." Walli hung up, feeling desolate.

After a minute he picked up his guitar and played a minor chord. Music was consoling. It was abstract, just notes and their relationships. There were no spies, no traitors, no policemen, no walls. He sang: "I miss you, Alice . . ."

.   .   .

Dave was glad to see his sister again. He met her outside the office of her agency, International Stars. Evie was wearing a purple derby hat. She said: "Home is pretty dull without you."

"Nobody has rows with Dad?" said Dave with a grin.

"He's so busy, since Labour won the election. He's in the cabinet now."

"And you?"

"I'm doing a new film."

"Congratulations!"

"But you fired your manager."

"Eric felt Plum Nellie was a one-hit wonder. But we haven't given up. However, we must get some more gigs. All we've got in the diary is a few nights at the Jump Club, and that won't even pay the rent."

"I can't promise that International Stars will take you on," Evie said. "They agreed to talk to you, that's all."

"I know." But agents did not meet people just to blow them off, Dave figured. And clearly the agency wanted to be nice to Evie Williams, the hottest young actress in London. So he had high hopes.

They went inside. The place was different from Eric Chapman's office. The receptionist was not chewing gum. There were no trophies on the lobby walls, just some tasteful watercolors. It was classy, though not very rock-and-roll.

They did not have to wait. The receptionist took them into the office of Mark Batchelor, a tall man in his twenties wearing a shirt with a fashionable tab collar and a knitted tie. His secretary brought coffee on a tray. "We love Evie, and we'd like to help her brother," Batchelor said when the initial pleasantries were out of the way. "But I'm not sure we can. 'Shake, Rattle and Roll' has damaged Plum Nellie."

Dave said: "I don't disagree, but tell me exactly what you mean."

"If I may be frank . . ."

"Of course," said Dave, thinking how different this was from a conversation with Eric Chapman.

"You look like an average pop group who had the good luck to get your hands on a Hank Remington song. People think the song was great, not you. We live in a small world—a few record companies, a handful of tour promoters, two television shows—and everyone thinks the same. I can't sell you to any of them."

Dave swallowed. He had not expected Batchelor to be this candid. He tried not to show his disappointment. "We *were* lucky to get a Hank Remington song," he admitted. "But we're not an average pop group. We have a first-class rhythm section and a virtuoso lead guitarist, and we look good, too."

"Then you have to prove to people that you're not one-hit wonders."

"I know. But with no recording contract and no big gigs I'm not sure how we do that."

"You need another great song. Can you get another from Hank Remington?"

Dave shook his head. "Hank doesn't write songs for other people. 'Love Is It' was a one-off, a ballad that the Kords didn't want to record."

"Perhaps he could write another ballad." Batchelor spread his hands in a who-knows gesture. "I'm not creative, that's why I'm an agent, but I know enough to realize that Hank is a prodigy."

"Well . . ." Dave looked at Evie. "I suppose I could ask him."

Batchelor said breezily: "What harm could it do?"

Evie shrugged. "I don't mind," she said.

"All right, then," said Dave.

Batchelor stood up and put out his hand to shake. "Good luck," he said.

As they left the building, Dave said to Evie: "Can we go and see Hank now?"

"I've got some shopping to do," Evie said. "I told him I'd see him tonight."

"This is really important, Evie. My whole life is in ruins."

"All right," she said. "My car's around the corner."

They drove to Chelsea in Evie's Sunbeam Alpine. Dave chewed his lip. Batchelor had done him the favor of being brutally honest. But Batchelor did not believe in Plum Nellie's talent—just Hank Remington's. All the same, if Dave could get just one more good song from Hank, the group would be back on course.

What was he going to say?

Hi, Hank, got any more ballads? That was too casual.

Hank, I'm in a fix. Too needy.

Our record company made a real mistake releasing 'Shake, Rattle and Roll.' But we could rescue the situation—with a little help from you. Dave did not like any of these approaches, mainly because he hated to beg.

But he would do it.

Hank had an apartment by the river. Evie led the way into a big old house and up in a creaking elevator. She spent most nights here now. She opened the apartment door with her own key. "Hank!" she called out. "It's only me."

Dave walked in behind her. There was a hallway with a splashy modern painting. They passed a gleaming kitchen and looked into a living room with a grand piano. No one was there.

"He's out," Dave said despondently.

Evie said: "He might be taking an afternoon nap."

Another door opened, and Hank emerged from what was obviously the bedroom, pulling his jeans on. He closed the door behind him. "Hello, love," he said. "I was in bed. Hello, Dave, what are you doing here?"

"Evie brought me to ask you a really big favor," said Dave.

"Yeah," said Hank, looking at Evie. "I was expecting you later."

"Dave couldn't wait."

Dave said: "We need a new song."

"It's not a good time, Dave," said Hank. Dave expected him to explain, but he did not.

Evie said: "Hank, is something wrong?"

"Yeah, actually," said Hank.

Dave was startled. No one ever answered yes to that question.

Evie's feminine intuition was far ahead of Dave. "Is there someone in the bedroom?"

"I'm sorry, love," said Hank. "I wasn't expecting you back."

At that point the bedroom door opened and Anna Murray came out.

Dave's mouth fell open in shock. Jasper's sister had been in bed with Evie's boyfriend!

Anna was fully dressed in business clothes, including stockings and high heels, but her hair was mussed and her jacket buttons were misaligned. She did not speak and avoided meeting anyone's eye. She went into the living room and came back out carrying a briefcase. She went to the apartment door, lifted a coat off the hook, and went out without speaking a word.

Hank said: "She came round to talk about my autobiography, and one thing led to another . . ."

Evie was crying. "Hank, how could you?"

"I didn't plan it," he said. "It just happened."

"I thought you loved me."

"I did. I do. This was just . . ."

"Just what?"

Hank looked to Dave for support. "There are some temptations a man can't resist."

Dave thought of Mickie McFee, and nodded.

Evie said angrily: "Dave's a boy. I thought you were a man, Hank."

"Now," he said, suddenly looking aggressive, "watch your mouth."

Evie was incredulous. "Watch my mouth? I've just caught you in bed with another girl, and you're telling me to watch my mouth?"

"I mean it," he said threateningly. "Don't go too far."

Dave was suddenly scared. Hank looked as if he might punch Evie. Was that what working-class Irish people did? And what was Dave supposed to do—protect his sister from her lover? Would Dave be expected to fight the greatest musical genius since Elvis Presley?

"Too far?" Evie said angrily. "I'm going too far now—right out of the fucking door. How's that?" She turned and marched away.

Dave looked at Hank. "Erm . . . about that song . . ."

Hank shook his head silently.

"Okay," said Dave. "Right." He could not think of a way to continue the conversation.

Hank held the door for him and he went out.

Evie cried in the car for five minutes, then dried her eyes. "I'll drive you home," she said.

When they got back to the West End, Dave said: "Come up to the flat. I'll make you a cup of coffee."

"Thanks," she said.

Walli was on the couch, playing the guitar. "Evie's a bit upset," Dave told him. "She broke up with Hank." He went into the kitchen and put the kettle on.

Walli said: "In English, the phrase 'a bit upset' means very unhappy. If you were only a little unhappy, say because I forgot your birthday, you would say you were 'terribly upset,' wouldn't you?"

Evie smiled. "Bless you, Walli, you're so logical."

"Creative, too," said Walli. "I'll cheer you up. Listen to this." He started to play, then he sang: "I miss ya, Alicia."

Dave came in from the kitchen to listen. Walli sang a sad ballad in D minor, with a couple of chords Dave did not recognize.

When it ended, Dave said: "It's a beautiful song. Did you hear it on the radio? Who's it by?"

"It's by me," Walli said. "I made it up."

"Wow," said Dave. "Play it again."

This time, Dave improvised a harmony.

Evie said: "You two are great. You didn't need that bastard Hank."

Dave said: "I want to sing this song to Mark Batchelor." He looked at his watch. It was half past five. He picked up the phone and called International Stars. Batchelor was still at his desk. "We have a song," Dave said. "Can we come to your office and play it to you?"

"I'd love to hear it, but I was just leaving for the day."

"Can you drop in at Henrietta Street on your way home?"

There was a hesitation, then Batchelor said: "Yes, I could, it's near my train station."

"What's your drink?"

"Gin and tonic, please."

Twenty minutes later Batchelor was on the sofa with a glass in his hand, and Dave and Walli were playing the song on two guitars and singing in harmony, with Evie joining in on the chorus.

When the song ended he said: "Play it again."

After the second time they looked at him expectantly. There was a pause. Then he said: "I wouldn't be in this business if I didn't know a hit when I heard it. This is a hit."

Dave and Walli grinned. Dave said: "That's what I thought."

"I love it," Batchelor said. "With this, I can get you a recording contract."

Dave put down his guitar, stood up, and shook hands with Batchelor to seal the deal. "We're in business," he said.

Mark took a long sip of his drink. "Did Hank just write the song on the spot, or did he have it in a drawer somewhere?"

Dave grinned. Now that they had shaken hands, he could level with Batchelor. "It's not a Hank Remington song," he said.

Batchelor raised his eyebrows.

Dave said: "You assumed it was, and I apologize for not correcting you, but I wanted you to have an open mind."

"It's a good song, and that's all that matters. But where did you get it?"

"Walli wrote it," said Dave. "This afternoon, while I was in your office."

"Great," said Batchelor. He turned to Walli. "What have you got for the B side?"

. . .

"You ought to go out," Lili Franck said to Karolin.

This was not Lili's own idea. In fact it was her mother's. Carla was worried about Karolin's health. Since Hans Hoffmann's visit, Karolin had lost weight. She looked pale and listless. Carla had said: "Karolin is only twenty years old. She can't shut herself up like a nun for the rest of her life. Can't you take her out somewhere?"

They were in Karolin's room, now, playing their guitars and singing to Alice, who was sitting on the floor surrounded by toys. Occasionally she clapped her hands enthusiastically, but mostly she ignored them. The song she liked best was "Love Is It."

Karolin said: "I can't go out, I've got Alice to look after."

Lili was prepared to deal with objections. "My mother can watch her," she said. "Or even Grandmother Maud. Alice's not much trouble in the evenings." Alice was now fourteen months and sleeping all night.

"I don't know. It wouldn't feel right."

"You haven't had a night out for years—literally."

"But what would Walli think?"

"He doesn't expect you to hide away and never enjoy yourself, does he?"

"I don't know."

"I'm going to the St. Gertrud Youth Club tonight. Why don't you come with me? There's music and dancing and usually a discussion—I don't think Walli would mind."

The East German leader, Walter Ulbricht, knew that young people needed entertainment, but he had a problem. Everything they liked— pop music, fashion, comics, Hollywood movies—was either unavailable or banned. Sports were approved of, but usually involved separating the boys from the girls.

Lili knew that most people of her age hated the government. Teenagers did not care much about Communism or capitalism, but they were passionate about haircuts, fashion, and pop music. Ulbricht's puritan dislike of everything they held dear had alienated Lili's generation. Worse, they had developed a fantasy, probably wholly unrealistic, about the lives of their contemporaries in the West, whom they imagined to have record players in their bedrooms and cupboards full of hip new clothes and ice cream every day.

Church youth clubs were permitted as a feeble attempt to fill the gap in the lives of adolescents. Such clubs were safely uncontroversial, but not as suffocatingly righteous as the Communist Party youth organization, the Young Pioneers.

Karolin looked thoughtful. "Perhaps you're right," she said. "I can't spend my life being a victim. I've had bad luck, but I mustn't let that define me. The Stasi think I'm just the girl whose boyfriend killed a border guard, but I don't have to accept what they say."

"Exactly!" Lili was pleased.

"I'm going to write to Walli and tell him all about it. But I'll go with you."

"Then let's get changed."

Lili went to her own room and put on a short skirt—not quite a miniskirt, as worn by girls on the Western television shows watched by everyone in East Germany, but above the knee. Now that Karolin had agreed, Lili asked herself whether this was the right course. Karolin certainly needed a life of her own: she had been dead right in what she said about not letting the Stasi define her. But what would Walli think, when he found out? Would he worry that Karolin was forgetting him? Lili had not seen her brother for almost two years. He was nineteen now, and a pop star. She did not know what he might think.

Karolin borrowed Lili's blue jeans, then they made up their faces together. Lili's older sister, Rebecca, had sent them black eyeliner and blue eye shadow from Hamburg, and by a miracle the Stasi had not stolen it.

They went to the kitchen to take their leave. Carla was feeding Alice, who waved good-bye to her mother so cheerfully that Karolin was a little put out.

They walked to a Protestant church a few streets away. Only Grandmother Maud was a regular churchgoer, but Lili had been twice previously to the youth club held in the crypt. It was run by a new young pastor called Odo Vossler, who wore his hair like the Beatles. He was dishy, though he was too old for Lili, at least twenty-five.

For music Odo had a piano, two guitars, and a record player. They started with a folk dance, something the government could not possibly disapprove of. Lili was paired with Berthold, a boy of about her own age, sixteen. He was nice but not sexy. Lili had her eye on Thorsten, who was a bit older and looked like Paul McCartney.

The dance steps were energetic, with much clapping and twirling. Lili was pleased to see Karolin entering into the spirit of the dance, smiling and laughing. She already looked better.

But the folk dancing was only a token, something to talk about in response to hostile inquiries. Someone put on "I Feel Fine" by the Beatles, and they all started to do the Twist.

After an hour they paused for a rest and a glass of Vita Cola, the East German Coke. To Lili's great satisfaction, Karolin looked flushed and happy. Odo went around talking to each person. His message was that if anyone had any problems, including issues about personal relationships and sex, he was there to listen and give advice. Karolin said to him: "My problem is that the father of my child is in the West," and they got into a deep discussion until the dancing started again.

At ten, when the record player was switched off, Karolin surprised Lili by picking up one of the guitars. She gestured to Lili to take the other. The two had been playing and singing together at home, but Lili had never imagined doing it in public. Now Karolin started an Everly Brothers number, "Wake Up, Little Susie." The two guitars sounded good together, and Karolin and Lili sang in harmony. Before they got to the end, everyone in the crypt was jiving. At the end of the song, the dancers called for more.

They played "I Want to Hold Your Hand" and "If I Had a Hammer," then for a slow dance they did "Love Is It." The kids did not want them to stop, but Odo asked them to play one more number, then go home before the police came and arrested him. He said it with a smile, but he meant it.

For a finale they played "Back in the USA."

Early in 1965, as Jasper Murray prepared for his final university exams, he wrote to every broadcasting organization in the USA whose address he could find.

They all got the same letter. He sent them his article about Evie dating Hank, his piece on Martin Luther King, and the assassination special edition of *The Real Thing*. And he asked for a job. Any job, as long as it was in American television.

He had never wanted anything this much. Television news was better than print—faster, more engaging, more vivid—and American television was better than British. And he knew he would be good at it. All he needed was a start. He wanted it so much it hurt.

When he had mailed the letters—at considerable expense—he let his sister, Anna, buy him lunch. They went to the Gay Hussar, a Hungarian restaurant favored by left-wing writers and politicians. "What will you do if you don't get a job in the States?" Anna asked him after they had ordered.

The prospect depressed him. "I really don't know. In this country, you're expected to work for provincial newspapers first, covering cat shows and the funerals of long-serving aldermen, but I don't think I can face that."

Anna got the restaurant's signature cold cherry soup. Jasper had fried mushrooms with tartar sauce. Anna said: "Listen, I owe you an apology."

"Yes," said Jasper. "You damn well do."

"Look, Hank and Evie weren't even engaged, let alone married."

"But you knew perfectly well that they were a couple."

"Yes, and I was wrong to go to bed with him."

"You were."

"There's no need for you to be so bloody sanctimonious. It's uncharacteristic for me, but it's just the kind of thing you'd do."

He did not argue with that because it was true. He had on occasion gone to bed with women who were married or engaged. Instead he said: "Does Mother know?"

"Yes, and she's furious. Daisy Williams has been her best friend for thirty years, and has also been extraordinarily kind to you, letting you live there rent-free—and now I've done this to her daughter. What did Daisy say to you?"

"She's angry, because you caused her daughter such pain. But she also said that when she fell in love with Lloyd she was already married to someone else, so she does not feel entitled to too much moral indignation."

"Well, anyway, I'm sorry."

"Thank you."

"Except that I'm not really sorry."

"What do you mean?"

"I went to bed with Hank because I fell in love with him. Since that first time, I've spent almost every night with him. He's the most wonderful man I've ever met, and I'm going to marry him, if ever I can nail his foot to the floor."

"As your brother, I'm entitled to ask what on earth he sees in you."

"Other than big tits, you mean?" She laughed.

"Not that you aren't good-looking, but you are a few years older than Hank, and there are about a million nubile maidens in England who would jump into his bed at a snap of his fingers."

She nodded. "Two things. First, he's clever but undereducated. I'm his tour guide to the world of the mind: art, theater, politics, literature. He's enchanted by someone who talks to him about that stuff without condescending."

Jasper was not surprised. "He used to love to talk to Daisy and Lloyd about all that. But what's the other thing?"

"You know he's my second lover."

Jasper nodded. Girls were not supposed to admit this sort of thing, but he and Anna had always known about each other's exploits.

She went on: "Well, I was with Sebastian almost four years. In that length of time, a girl learns a lot. Hank knows very little about sex, because he's never kept a girlfriend long enough to develop real intimacy. Evie was his longest relationship, and she was too young to teach a man much."

"I see." Jasper had never thought this way about relationships, but it made sense. He was a bit like Hank. He wondered whether women thought him unsophisticated in bed.

"Hank learned a lot from a singer called Mickie McFee, but he only slept with her twice."

"Really? Dave Williams shagged her in a dressing room."

"And Dave told you?"

"I think he told everyone. It may have been his first shag."

"Mickie McFee gets around."

"So, you're Hank's love tutor."

"He learns fast. And he's growing up quickly. What he did to Evie, he will never do again."

Jasper was not sure he believed that, but he did not voice his misgivings.

. . .

Dimka Dvorkin flew to Vietnam in February 1965 along with a large group of Foreign Ministry officials and aides, including Natalya Smotrov.

It was Dimka's first trip outside the Soviet Union. But he was even more excited about being with Natalya. He was not sure what was going to happen, but he had an exhilarating sense of liberation, and he could tell she felt the same. They were far away from Moscow, out of range of his wife and Natalya's husband. Anything could happen.

Dimka was feeling more optimistic in general. Kosygin, his boss since the fall of Khrushchev, understood that the Soviet Union was losing the Cold War because of its economy. Soviet industry was inefficient, and Soviet citizens were poor. Kosygin's aim was to make the USSR more productive. The Soviets had to learn how to manufacture things that people of other countries might want to buy. They had to compete with the Americans in prosperity, not just in tanks and missiles. Only then would they have a hope of converting the world to their way of life. This attitude heartened Dimka. Brezhnev, the leader, was woefully conservative, but perhaps Kosygin could reform Communism.

Part of the economic problem was that so much of the national income was spent on the military. In the hope of reducing this crippling expense, Khrushchev had come up with the policy of peaceful coexistence, living side by side with the capitalists without fighting wars. Khrushchev had not done much to implement the idea: his quarrels in Berlin and Cuba had required more military expenditure, not less. But progressive thinkers in the Kremlin still believed in the strategy.

Vietnam would be a severe test.

On stepping out of the plane, Dimka was assailed by a warm, wet atmosphere unlike anything he had experienced. Hanoi was the ancient capital of an ancient country, long oppressed by foreigners, first the Chinese, then the French, then the Americans. Vietnam was more crowded and more colorful than any place Dimka had ever seen.

It was also split in two.

Vietnamese leader Ho Chi Minh had defeated France in the anticolonial war of the fifties. But Ho was an undemocratic Communist, and the Americans refused to accept his authority. President Eisenhower had sponsored a puppet government in the south, based in the provincial capital of Saigon. The unelected Saigon regime was tyrannical and unpopular, and was under attack by resistance fighters called the Vietcong. The South Vietnamese army was so weak that now, in 1965, it had to be propped up by twenty-three thousand American troops.

The Americans were pretending that South Vietnam was a separate country, just as the Soviet Union pretended that East Germany was a country. Vietnam was a mirror image of Germany, though Dimka would never dare say that aloud.

While the ministers attended a banquet with North Vietnamese leaders, the Soviet aides ate a less formal dinner with their Vietnamese opposite numbers—all of whom spoke Russian, some having visited Moscow. The food was mostly vegetables and rice, with small amounts of fish and meat, but it was tasty. There were no female Vietnamese staffers, and the men seemed surprised to see Natalya and the two other Soviet women.

Dimka sat next to a dour middle-aged apparatchik called Pham An. Natalya, sitting opposite, asked the man what he hoped to get from the talks.

An replied with a shopping list. "We need aircraft, artillery, radar, air defense systems, small arms, ammunition, and medical supplies," he said.

This was exactly what the Soviets were hoping to avoid. Natalya said: "But you won't need those things if the war comes to an end."

"When we have defeated the American imperialists our needs will be different."

"We would all like to see a smashing victory for the Vietcong," said Natalya. "But there might be other possible outcomes." She was trying to broach the idea of peaceful coexistence.

"Victory is the only possibility," said Pham An dismissively.

Dimka was dismayed. An was stubbornly refusing to engage in the discussion for which the Soviets had come here. Perhaps he felt it was beneath his dignity to argue with a woman. Dimka hoped that was the only reason for his obstinacy. If the Vietnamese would not talk about alternatives to war, the Soviet mission would fail.

Natalya was not easily deflected from her purpose. She now said: "Military victory most certainly is *not* the only possible outcome." Dimka found himself feeling proud of her gutsy persistence.

"You speak of defeat?" said An, bristling—or at least pretending to bristle.

"No," she said calmly. "But war is not the only road to victory. Negotiations are an alternative."

"We negotiated with the French many times," An said angrily. "Every agreement was designed only to gain time while they prepared further aggression. This was a lesson to our people, a lesson on dealing with imperialists, a lesson we will never forget."

Dimka had read the history of Vietnam and knew that An's anger was justified. The French had been as dishonest and perfidious as any other colonialists. But that was not the end of the story.

Natalya persisted—quite rightly, since this was the message Kosygin was undoubtedly giving Ho Chi Minh. "Imperialists are treacherous, we all know that. But negotiations can also be used by revolutionaries. Lenin negotiated at Brest-Litovsk. He made concessions, stayed in power, and reversed all those concessions when he was stronger."

An parroted Ho Chi Minh's line. "We will not consider negotiations until there is a neutral coalition government in Saigon that includes Vietcong representatives."

"Be reasonable," Natalya said mildly. "To make major demands as preconditions is just a way of avoiding negotiations. You must consider compromise."

An said angrily: "When the Germans invaded Russia and marched all the way to the gates of Moscow, did you compromise?" He banged the table with his fist, a gesture that surprised Dimka coming from a supposedly subtle Oriental. "No! No negotiations, no compromise—and no Americans!"

Soon after that the banquet ended.

Dimka and Natalya returned to their hotel. He walked with her to her room. At the door, she said simply: "Come in."

It would be only their third night together. The first two they had spent on a four-poster bed in a dusty storeroom full of old furniture at the Kremlin. But somehow being together in a bedroom seemed as natural as if they had been lovers for years.

They kissed and took off their shoes, and kissed again and brushed their teeth, and kissed again. They were not crazed with uncontrollable lust: rather, they were relaxed and playful. "We've got all night to do anything we like," Natalya said, and Dimka thought those were the sexiest words he had ever heard.

They made love, then had some caviar and vodka she had brought with her, then made love again.

Afterward, lying on the twisted sheets, looking up at the slow-moving ceiling fan, Natalya said: "I assume someone is eavesdropping on us."

"I hope so," Dimka said. "We sent a KGB team over here at great expense to teach them how to bug hotel rooms."

"Perhaps it's Pham An listening," Natalya said, and giggled.

"If so, I hope he enjoyed it more than the dinner."

"Hmm. That was kind of a disaster."

"They'll have to change their attitude to get weapons from us. Even Brezhnev doesn't want us involved in a massive war in Southeast Asia."

"But if we refuse to arm them, they could go to the Chinese."

"They hate the Chinese."

"I know. Still . . ."

"Yes."

They drifted off to sleep and were awakened by the phone. Natalya picked it up and gave her name. She listened for a while, then said: "Hell." Another minute went by and she hung up. "News from South Vietnam," she said. "The Vietcong attacked an American base last night."

"Last night? Only hours after Kosygin arrived in Hanoi? That's no coincidence. Where?"

"A place called Pleiku. Eight Americans were killed and a hundred or so wounded. And they destroyed ten U.S. aircraft on the ground."

"How many Vietcong casualties?"

"Only one body was left behind in the compound."

Dimka shook his head in amazement. "You've got to give it to the Vietnamese, they're terrific fighters."

"The Vietcong are. The South Vietnamese army is hopeless. That's why they need the Americans to fight for them."

Dimka frowned. "Isn't there some American big shot in South Vietnam right now?"

"McGeorge Bundy, national security adviser, one of the worst of the capitalist-imperialist warmongers."

"He'll be on the phone to President Johnson right now."

"Yes," said Natalya. "I wonder what he's saying."

She had her answer later the same day.

American planes from the aircraft carrier USS *Ranger* bombed an army camp called Dong Hoi on the coast of North Vietnam. It was the first time the Americans had bombed the north, and it began a new phase in the conflict.

Dimka watched in despair as Kosygin's position crumbled, bit by bit, during the course of the day.

After the bombing, American aggression was condemned by Communist and nonaligned countries around the world.

Third World leaders now expected Moscow to come to the aid of Vietnam, a Communist country being directly attacked by American imperialism.

Kosygin did not want to escalate the Vietnam War, and the Kremlin could not afford to give massive military aid to Ho Chi Minh, but that was exactly what they now did.

They had no choice. If they drew back the Chinese would step in, eager to supplant the USSR as the mighty friend of small Communist countries. The position of the Soviet Union as defender of world Communism was now at stake, and everyone knew it.

All talk of peaceful coexistence was forgotten.

Dimka and Natalya were thrown into gloom, as was the entire Soviet delegation. Their negotiating position with the Vietnamese was fatally undermined. Kosygin had no cards to play: he had to grant everything Ho Chi Minh asked for.

They remained in Hanoi three more days. Dimka and Natalya made love all night, but during the daytime all they did was make detailed notes of Pham An's shopping list. Even before they left, a consignment of Soviet surface-to-air missiles was on its way.

Dimka and Natalya sat together on the plane home. Dimka dozed, delightfully recalling four humid nights of love under a lazy ceiling fan.

"What are you smiling about?" Natalya said.

He opened his eyes. "You know."

She giggled. "Apart from that . . ."

"What?"

"When you review this trip in your mind, don't you get a feeling . . . ?"

"That we were totally managed and exploited? Yes, from the first day."

"In fact, that Ho Chi Minh deftly manipulated the two most powerful countries in the world, and ended up getting everything he wanted."

"Yes," said Dimka. "That's exactly the feeling I get."

. . .

Tanya went to the airport with Vasili's subversive typescript in her suitcase. She was scared.

She had done dangerous things before. She had published a seditious newspaper; she had been arrested in Mayakovsky Square and dragged off to the notorious basement of the KGB's Lubyanka building; and she had made contact with a dissident in Siberia. But this was the most frightening.

Communicating with the West was a crime of a higher order. She was taking Vasili's typescript to Leipzig, where she hoped to place it with a Western publisher.

The news sheet that she and Vasili had published had been distributed only in the USSR. The authorities would be much angrier about dissident material that found its way to the West. Those responsible would be considered not just rebels but traitors.

Thinking about the danger, sitting in the back of the taxi, she felt nauseated by fear, and clamped her hand over her mouth in a panic until the sensation faded.

On arrival she almost told the driver to turn around and take her home. Then she remembered Vasili in Siberia, hungry and cold, and she steeled her nerve and carried her case into the terminal.

The Siberia trip had changed her. Before, she had thought of Communism as a well-intentioned experiment that had failed and ought to be scrapped. Now, she saw it as a brutal tyranny whose leaders were evil. Every time she thought of Vasili, her heart was filled with hatred for the people who had done this to him. She even had trouble talking to her twin brother, who still hoped that Communism could be improved rather than abolished. She loved Dimka, but he was closing his eyes to reality. And she had realized that wherever there was cruel oppression—in the Deep South of the USA, in British Northern Ireland, and in East Germany—there had to be many nice ordinary people like her family who looked away from the grisly truth. But Tanya would not be one of them. She was going to fight it to the end.

Whatever the risk.

At the desk she handed over her papers and placed her case on the scale. If she had believed in God, she would have prayed.

Check-in staff were all KGB. This one was a man in his thirties with the blue shadow of a heavy beard. Tanya sometimes assessed people by imagining what they would be like to interview. This one would be assertive to the point of aggression, she thought, answering neutral questions as if they were hostile, constantly on the lookout for hidden implications and veiled accusations.

He looked hard at her face, comparing it with her photograph. She tried not to seem scared. However, she told herself, even innocent Soviet citizens were scared when KGB men looked at them.

He put her passport down on his desk and said: "Open the bag."

There was no knowing why. They might do it because you appeared suspicious or because they had nothing better to do or because they liked pawing through women's underwear. They did not have to give a reason.

Heart pounding, Tanya opened her case.

The clerk knelt down and began to rifle through her things. It took him less than a minute to discover Vasili's typescript. He took it out and read the title page: *Stalag: A Novel of the Nazi Concentration Camps* by Klaus Holstein.

This was fake, as was the contents list, the preface, and the prologue.

The clerk said: "What is this?"

"A partial translation of an East German work. I'm going to the Leipzig Book Fair."

"Has this been approved?"

"In East Germany, of course, otherwise it would not have been published."

"And in the Soviet Union?"

"Not yet. Works may not be submitted for approval before they are finished, obviously."

She tried to breathe normally as the clerk flicked through the pages.

"These people have Russian names," he said.

"There were many Russians in the Nazi camps, as you know," Tanya said.

If her story were to be checked it would fall flat in no time, she knew. If the clerk took the time to read more than the first few pages he would see that the stories were not about the Nazis but about the Gulag; and then it would take the KGB only a few hours to learn that there was no East German book nor a publisher, at which point Tanya would be taken back to that cellar in the Lubyanka.

He riffled the pages idly, as if wondering whether to make a fuss about this or not. Then there was a commotion at the next desk: a passenger was objecting to the confiscation of an icon. Tanya's clerk returned her papers with her boarding card and waved her away, then went to assist his colleague.

Her legs felt so weak she feared she might not be able to walk away.

She recovered her strength and made it through the rest of the formalities. The plane was the familiar Tupolev Tu-104, this one configured for civilian passengers, a bit cramped with six seats abreast. The flight to Leipzig was a thousand miles, and took a little over three hours.

When Tanya picked up her suitcase at the other end she looked carefully at it but saw no signs that it had been opened. But she was not yet in the clear. She carried it into the customs and immigration zone, feeling as if she were holding something radioactive. She recalled that the East German government was said to be harsher than the Soviet regime. The Stasi was even more omnipresent than the KGB.

She showed her papers. An official studied them carefully, then dismissed her with a discourteous gesture.

She headed for the exit, not looking at the faces of the uniformed officials, all men, who stood scrutinizing passengers.

Then one of them stepped in front of her. "Tanya Dvorkin?"

She almost burst into guilty tears. "Y-yes."

He addressed her in German. "Please come with me."

This is it, she thought; my life is over.

She followed him through a side door. To her surprise, it led to a parking area. "The director of the book fair has sent a car for you," the official said.

A driver was waiting. He introduced himself and put the incriminating suitcase into the trunk of a two-tone green-and-white Wartburg 311 limousine.

Tanya fell into the backseat and slumped, as helpless as if she were drunk.

She began to recover as the car took her into the city center. Leipzig was an ancient crossroads that had hosted trade fairs since the Middle Ages. Its railway station was the biggest in Europe. In her article Tanya would mention the city's strong Communist tradition, and its resistance to Nazism, which continued into the 1940s. She would not include the thought that occurred to her now, that Leipzig's grand nineteenth-century buildings looked even more gracious beside the brutalist Soviet-era architecture.

The taxi took her to the fair. In a large hall like a warehouse, publishers from Germany and abroad had erected stalls where they displayed their books. Tanya was shown around by the director. He explained to her that the main business of the fair was the buying and selling, not of physical books, but of licenses to translate them and publish them in other countries.

Toward the end of the afternoon she managed to get away from him and look around on her own.

She was astonished by the enormous number and bewildering variety of books: car manuals, scientific journals, almanacs, children's stories, Bibles, art books, atlases, dictionaries, school textbooks, and the complete works of Marx and Lenin in every major European language.

She was looking for someone who might want to translate Russian literature and publish it in the West.

She began to scan the stalls for Russian novels in other languages.

The Western alphabet was different from the Russian, but Tanya had learned German and English at school, and had studied German at university, so she could read the names of the authors and generally guess at the titles.

She spoke to several publishers, telling them she was a journalist for TASS and asking them how they were benefiting from the fair. She got some quotes useful for her article. She did not even hint that she had a Russian book to offer them.

At the stall of a London publisher called Rowley she picked up an English translation of *The Young Guard,* a popular Soviet novel by Alexander Fadeyev. She knew it well, and amused herself by deciphering the English of the first page until she was interrupted. An attractive woman of about her own age addressed her in German. "Please let me know if I can answer any questions."

Tanya introduced herself and interviewed the woman about the fair. They quickly discovered that the editor spoke Russian better than Tanya spoke German, so they switched. Tanya asked about English translations of Russian novels. "I'd like to publish more of them," said the editor. "But many contemporary Soviet novels—including the one you're holding in your hand—are too slavishly pro-Communist."

Tanya pretended to be prickly. "You wish to publish anti-Soviet propaganda?"

"Not at all," the editor said with a tolerant smile. "Writers are permitted to like their governments. My company publishes many books that celebrate the British Empire and its triumphs. But an author who sees nothing at all wrong in the society around him may not be taken seriously. It's wiser to throw in a soupçon of criticism, if only for the sake of credibility."

Tanya liked this woman. "Can we meet again?"

The editor hesitated. "Do you have something for me?"

Tanya did not answer the question. "Where are you staying?"

"The Europa."

Tanya had a room reserved at the same hotel. That was convenient. "What's your name?"

"Anna Murray. What's yours?"

"We'll talk again," said Tanya, and she walked away.

She felt drawn to Anna Murray on instinct, an instinct refined by a quarter of a century of life in the Soviet Union; but her feeling was supported by evidence. First, Anna was clearly British, not a Russian or East German posing as British. Second, she was neither Communist nor strenuously pretending to be the opposite. Her relaxed neutrality was impossible for a KGB spy to fake. Third, she used no jargon. People brought up in Soviet orthodoxy could not help talking about party, class, cadres, and ideology. Anna used none of the key words.

The green-and-white Wartburg was waiting outside. The driver took her to the Europa, where she checked in. Almost immediately she left her room and returned to the lobby.

She did not want to draw attention to herself even by merely asking at reception for Anna Murray's room number. At least one of the desk clerks would be an informant for the Stasi, and might make a note of a Soviet journalist seeking out an English publisher.

However, behind the reception desk was a bank of numbered pigeonholes where the staff deposited room keys and messages. Tanya simply sealed an empty envelope, wrote on it "Frau Anna Murray," and handed it in without speaking. The clerk immediately put it in the pigeonhole for Room 305.

There was a key in the space, which meant that Anna Murray was not in her room right now.

Tanya went into the bar. Anna was not there. Tanya sat for an hour, sipping a beer, roughing out her article on a notepad. Then she went into the restaurant. Anna was not there either. She had probably gone out to dinner with colleagues at a restaurant in the city. Tanya sat alone and ordered the local speciality, *allerlei,* a vegetable dish. She sat over her coffee for an hour, then left.

Passing through the lobby, she looked again at the pigeonholes. The key for 305 had gone.

Tanya returned to her own room, picked up the typescript, and walked to the door of Room 305.

There she hesitated. Once she had done this, she was committed. No cover story would explain or excuse her action. She was distributing anti-Soviet propaganda to the West. If she were caught, her life would be over.

She knocked on the door.

Anna opened it. She was barefoot and there was a toothbrush in her hand: clearly she had been getting ready for bed.

Tanya put her finger on her lips, indicating silence. Then she handed Anna the typescript. She whispered: "I'll come back in two hours." Then she walked away.

She returned to her own room and sat on the bed, shaking.

If Anna simply rejected the work, that would be bad enough. But if Tanya had misjudged her, Anna might feel obliged to tell someone in authority that she had been offered a dissident book. She might fear that, if she kept quiet about it, she could be accused of taking part in a conspiracy. She might think that the only sensible thing to do was to report the illicit approach that had been made to her.

But Tanya believed most Westerners did not think that way. Despite Tanya's dramatic precautions, Anna would have no real sense that she was guilty of a crime just by reading a typescript.

So the main question was whether Anna would like Vasili's work.

Daniil had, and so had the editors of *New World*. But they were the only people who had read the stories, and they were all Russian. How would a foreigner react? Tanya felt confident that Anna would see that the material was well written, but would it move her? Would it break her heart?

At a few minutes past eleven, Tanya returned to Room 305.

Anna opened the door with the typescript in her hand.

Her face was wet with tears.

She spoke in a whisper. "It's unbearable," she said. "We have to tell the world."

. . .

One Friday night Dave found out that Lew, the drummer in Plum Nellie, was homosexual.

Until then he had thought that Lew was just shy. A lot of girls wanted to have sex with boys who played in pop groups, and the dressing room was sometimes like a brothel, but Lew never took advantage. This was not astonishing: some did, some did not. Walli never went with "groupies." Dave occasionally did, and Buzz, the bass player, never said no.

Plum Nellie was getting gigs again. "I Miss Ya, Alicia" was in the top twenty at number nineteen, and rising. Dave and Walli were writing songs together, and hoping to make a long-playing record. Late one afternoon they went to the BBC studios in Portland Place and prerecorded a radio performance. The money was peanuts but it was an opportunity to promote "I Miss Ya, Alicia." Maybe the song would go to number one. And, as Dave sometimes said, you could live on peanuts.

They came out blinking into the evening sunshine and decided to go for a drink at a nearby pub called the Golden Horn.

"I don't fancy a drink," said Lew.

"Don't be daft," Buzz said. "When have you ever said no to a pint of beer?"

"Let's go to a different pub, then," said Lew.

"Why?"

"I don't like the look of that one."

"If you're afraid of being pestered, put your sunglasses on."

They had been on television several times, and they were sometimes recognized by fans in restaurants and bars, but there was rarely any trouble. They had learned to stay away from places where young teenagers might gather, such as coffee bars near schools, for that could lead to a mob scene; but they were all right in grown-up pubs.

They went into the Golden Horn and approached the bar. The bartender smiled at Lew and said: "Hello, Lucy, dear, what'll it be, vod and ton?"

The group looked at Lew in surprise.

Buzz said: "So you're a regular here?"

Walli said: "What's a vod and ton?"

Dave said: "Lucy?"

The barman looked nervous. "Who are your friends, Lucy?"

Lew looked at the other three and said: "You bastards, you've found me out."

Buzz said: "Are you queer?"

Having been found out, Lew threw caution to the winds. "I'm as queer as a clockwork orange, a three-pound note, a purple unicorn, or a football bat. If you weren't all blind as well as stupid you would have figured it out years ago. Yes, I kiss men and go to bed with them whenever I can without getting caught. But please don't worry that I might make advances to you: you're all much too fucking ugly. Now let's have a drink."

Dave cheered and clapped, and after a moment of shocked hesitation Buzz and Walli followed his lead.

Dave was intrigued. He knew about queers, but only in a theoretical way. He had never had a homosexual friend, as far as he knew—though most of them kept it secret, as Lew had, because what they did was a crime. Dave's grandmother Lady Leckwith was campaigning for the law to be changed, but so far she had not succeeded.

Dave was in favor of his grandmother's campaign, mainly because he hated the kind of people who opposed her: pompous clergymen, indignant Tories, and retired colonels. He had never really thought about the law as something that might affect his friends.

They had a second round of drinks, and a third. Dave's money was running low, but he had high hopes. "I Miss Ya, Alicia" was going to be released in the USA. If it was a hit there the group would be made. And he would never again have to worry about spelling.

The pub filled up quickly. Most of the men had something in

common: a way of walking and talking that was a bit theatrical. They called one another "lovey" and "precious." After a while it became easy to tell who was queer and who was not. Perhaps that was why they did it. There were also a few girls in couples, most with short haircuts and trousers. Dave felt he was seeing a new world.

However, they were not exclusive, and seemed happy to share their favorite pub with heterosexual men and women. About half the people there knew Lew, and the group found themselves at the center of a conversational cluster. The queers bantered in a distinctive way that made Dave laugh. A man in a shirt similar to Lew's said: "Ooh, Lucy, you're wearing the same shirt as me! How nice." Then he added in a stage whisper: "Unimaginative bitch," and the others laughed, including Lew.

Dave was approached by a tall man who said in a low voice: "Listen, mate, do you know who could sell me some pills?"

Dave knew what he was talking about. A lot of musicians took pep pills. Various kinds could be bought at places such as the Jump Club. Dave had tried some but did not really like the effect.

He looked hard at the stranger. Although he was dressed in jeans and a striped sweater, the jeans were cheap and did not go with the sweater, and the man had a short military-style haircut. Dave had an uneasy feeling. "No," he said curtly, and turned away.

In one corner stood a tiny stage with a microphone. At nine o'clock a comedian came on, to enthusiastic applause. It was a man dressed as a woman, although the hair and makeup were so good that in a different setting Dave might not have twigged.

"Could I have everybody's attention, please?" the comic said. "I'd just like to make an important public announcement. Jerry Robertson's got VD."

They all laughed. Walli said to Dave: "What's VD?"

"Venereal disease," Dave said. "Spots on your cock."

The comedian paused, then added: "I know, because I gave it to him."

This got another laugh, then there was a commotion at the door. Dave looked that way and saw several uniformed policemen coming in, pushing people out of the way.

The comic said: "Ooh, it's the law! I do like a uniform. The police come here a lot, have you noticed? I wonder what attracts them?"

He was making a joke of it, but the police were unpleasantly serious. They shoved their way through the crowd, seeming to enjoy being unnecessarily rough. Four went into the men's toilets. "Perhaps they've just come for a pee," said the comic. An officer got up on the stage. "You're an inspector, aren't you?" the comic said flirtatiously. "Have you come to inspect me?"

Two more cops dragged the comic away. "Don't worry!" he cried. "I'll come quietly!"

The inspector grabbed the microphone. "Right, you filthy pansies," he said. "I have information that illegal drugs are being sold on these premises. If you don't want to get hurt, stand face to the wall and get ready to be searched."

The police were still pouring in. Dave looked around for a way out, but all the doors were blocked by blue uniforms. Some of the customers moved to the edges of the room and stood facing the walls, looking resigned, as if all this had happened to them before. The police never raided the Jump Club, Dave reflected, even though drugs were sold there almost openly.

The cops who had gone into the toilet came out frog-marching two men, one of whom was bleeding from the nose. One of the cops said to the inspector: "They were in the same cubicle, governor."

"Charge them with public indecency."

"Right you are, guv."

Dave was struck painfully in the back, and cried out. A policeman wielding a nightstick said: "Get over by the wall."

Dave said: "What did you do that for?"

The cop stuck the club close to Dave's nose. "Shut your mouth, queer boy, or I'll shut it with my truncheon."

"I'm not a—" Dave stopped himself. Let them believe what they like, he thought. I'd rather be with the queers than with the police. He stepped to the wall and stood as ordered, rubbing the painful spot in his back.

He found himself next to Lew, who said: "Are you all right?"

"Just a bit bruised. You?"

"Nothing much."

Dave was learning about why his grandmother wanted to change the law. He felt ashamed for having lived so long in ignorance.

Lew said in a low voice: "At least the cops haven't recognized the group."

Dave nodded. "They're not the type to be familiar with the faces of pop stars."

Out of the corner of his eye he saw the inspector talking to the badly dressed man who had asked about buying pills. Now he understood the cheap jeans and the military haircut: the man was an undercover detective, poorly disguised. He was shrugging his shoulders and spreading his arms in a helpless gesture, and Dave guessed he had failed to find anyone selling drugs.

The police searched everyone, making them turn out their pockets. The one who examined Dave felt his crotch a good deal longer than was necessary. Are these cops queer too? Dave wondered. Is that why they do this?

Several men objected to the intimate searching. They were beaten with truncheons, then arrested for assaulting the police. Another man had a packet of pills he said were prescribed by his doctor, but he was arrested all the same.

Eventually the police left. The barman announced drinks on the house, but few people took up the offer. The members of Plum Nellie left the pub. Dave decided to go home for an early night.

"Does that sort of thing happen a lot to you queers?" he asked Lew as they were saying good-bye.

"All the time, mate," said Lew. "All the fucking time."

.   .   .

Jasper went to visit his sister at Hank Remington's Chelsea flat one evening at seven o'clock, when he was sure Anna would be home from work but the couple would not yet have gone out. He felt nervous. He wanted something from Anna and Hank, something vital to his future.

He sat in the kitchen and watched Anna make Hank his favorite food, a fried-potato sandwich. "How's your work?" he asked her, making small talk.

"Wonderful," she said, and her eyes gleamed with enthusiasm. "I've discovered a new writer, a Russian dissident. I don't even know his real name, but he's a genius. I'm publishing his stories set in a Siberian prison camp. The title is *Frostbite*."

"Doesn't sound like much of a laugh."

"It is funny in parts, but it will break your heart. I'm having it translated right now."

Jasper was skeptical. "Who wants to read about people in a prison camp?"

"The whole world," said Anna. "You wait and see. How about you— do you know what you'll do after graduation?"

"I've been offered a job as junior reporter on the *Western Mail*, but I don't want to take it. I've been editor and publisher of my own paper, for Christ's sake."

"Did you get any replies from America?"

"One," said Jasper.

"Only one? What did they say?"

Jasper took the letter out of his pocket and showed it to her. It was from a television news show called *This Day*.

Anna read it. "It just says they don't hire people without an interview. How disappointing."

"I plan to take them at their word."

"What do you mean?"

Jasper pointed to the address on the letterhead. "I'm going to show up at their office with this letter in my hand and say: 'I've come for my interview.'"

Anna laughed. "They'll have to admire your cheek."

"There's only one snag." Jasper swallowed. "I need ninety pounds for the airfare. And I've only got twenty."

She lifted a basket of potatoes out of the fryer and set them to drain. Then she looked at Jasper. "Is that why you've come here?"

He nodded. "Can you lend me seventy pounds?"

"Certainly not," she said. "I don't have seventy pounds. I'm a book editor. That's almost a month's salary."

Jasper had known that would be the answer. But it was not the end of the conversation. He gritted his teeth and said: "Can you get it from Hank?"

Anna layered the fried potatoes on a slice of buttered white bread.

She sprinkled malt vinegar over them, then salted them heavily. She put a second slice of bread on top, then cut the sandwich in halves.

Hank walked in, tucking his shirt into a pair of orange corduroy hipster trousers. His long red hair was wet from the shower. "Hi, Jasper," he said with his usual cordiality. Then he kissed Anna and said: "Wow, baby, something smells good."

Anna said: "Hank, this could be the most expensive sandwich you will ever eat."

Dave Williams was looking forward to meeting his notorious grandfather, Lev Peshkov.

Plum Nellie was on the road in the States in the autumn of 1965. The All-Star Touring Beat Revue gave performers a hotel room every second night. Alternate nights were spent on the bus.

They would do a show, get on the bus at midnight, and drive to the next city. Dave never slept properly on the bus. The seats were uncomfortable and there was a smelly toilet at the back. The only refreshment was a cooler full of sugary soda pop supplied free by Dr Pepper, the sponsor of the tour. A soul group from Philadelphia called the Topspins ran a poker game on the bus: Dave lost ten dollars one night and never played again.

In the morning they would arrive at a hotel. If they were lucky, they could check in right away. If not, they had to hang around the lobby, bad-tempered and unwashed, waiting for last night's guests to vacate their rooms. They would do the next evening's show, spend the night at the hotel, and get back on the bus in the morning.

Plum Nellie loved it.

The money was not much, but they were touring America: they would have done it for nothing.

And there were the girls.

Buzz, the bass player, often had several fans in his hotel bedroom during the course of a single day and night. Lew was enthusiastically exploring the queer scene—though Americans preferred the word *gay* to *queer*. Walli remained faithful to Karolin, but even he was happy, living his dream of being a pop star.

Dave did not much like sex with groupies, but there were several terrific girls on the tour. He made a play for blond Joleen Johnson from the Tamettes, who turned him down, explaining that she had been happily married since she was thirteen. Then he tried Little Lulu Small, who was flirty but would not go to his room. Finally one evening he got talking to Mandy Love from the Love Factory, a black girl group from Chicago. She had big brown eyes and a wide mouth and smooth midbrown skin that felt like silk under Dave's fingertips. She introduced him to marijuana, which he liked better than beer. They spent every hotel night together after Indianapolis, though they had to be discreet: interracial sex was a crime in some states.

The bus rolled into Washington, DC, on a Wednesday morning. Dave had an appointment for lunch with Grandfather Peshkov. This had been arranged by his mother, Daisy.

He dressed for the engagement like the pop star he was: a red shirt, blue hipster trousers, a gray tweed jacket with a red overcheck, and narrow-toed boots with a Cuban heel. He got a cab from the cheap hotel where the groups were staying to the swankier place where his grandfather had a suite.

Dave was intrigued. He had heard so many bad things about this old man. If the family legends were true, Lev had killed a policeman in St. Petersburg, then fled Russia, leaving a pregnant girlfriend behind. In Buffalo he made his boss's daughter pregnant, married her, and inherited a fortune. He had been suspected of murdering his father-in-law, but never charged. During Prohibition he had been a bootlegger. While married to Daisy's mother he had had numerous mistresses, including the movie star Gladys Angelus. It went on and on.

Waiting in the hotel lobby, Dave wondered what Lev looked like. They had never met. Apparently Lev had visited London once, for Daisy's wedding to her first husband, Boy Fitzherbert; but he had never returned.

Daisy and Lloyd came to the USA about every five years, mainly to see her mother, Olga, now in a retirement home in Buffalo. Dave knew that Daisy did not have much love for her father. Lev had been absent most of Daisy's childhood. He had had a second family in the same city—a mistress, Marga, and an illegitimate son, Greg—and apparently he had always preferred them to Daisy and her mother.

Across the lobby Dave saw a man in his early seventies dressed in a silver-gray suit with a red-and-white-striped tie. He recalled his mother saying that her father had always been a dandy. Dave smiled and said: "Are you Grandfather Peshkov?"

They shook hands, and Lev said: "Don't you have a tie?"

Dave got this sort of thing all the time. For some reason the older generation felt they had the right to be rude about young people's clothes. Dave had a number of stock replies, ranging from charming to hostile. Now he said: "When you were a teenager in St. Petersburg, Grandfather, what did cool kids like you wear?"

Lev's stern expression broke into a grin. "I had a jacket with mother-of-pearl buttons, a waistcoat and a brass watch chain, and a velvet cap. And my hair was long and parted in the middle, just like yours."

"So we're alike," Dave said. "Except that I've never killed anyone."

Lev was startled for a moment, then he laughed. "You're a smart kid," he said. "You've inherited my brains."

A woman in a chic blue coat and hat came to Lev's side, walking like a fashion model although she had to be near Lev's age. Lev said: "This is Marga. She ain't your grandma."

The mistress, Dave thought. "You're obviously too young to be anyone's grandmother," he said with a smile. "What should I call you?"

"You are a charmer!" she replied. "You can call me Marga. I used to be a singer, too, you know, though I never had your kind of success." She looked nostalgic. "In those days I ate handsome boys like you for breakfast."

Girl singers haven't changed, Dave thought, remembering Mickie McFee.

They went into the restaurant. Marga asked a lot of questions about Daisy, Lloyd, and Evie. They were excited to hear about Evie's acting career, especially as Lev owned a Hollywood studio. But Lev was most interested in Dave and his business. "They say you're a millionaire, Dave," he said.

"They lie," said Dave. "We're selling a lot of records, but there's not as much money in it as people imagine. We get about a penny a record. So if we sell a million copies, we earn enough maybe for each of us to buy a small car."

"Someone's robbing you," said Lev.

"I wouldn't be surprised," Dave said. "But I don't know what to do about it. I fired our first manager, and this one is much better, but I still can't afford to buy a house."

"I'm in the movie business, and sometimes we sell records of our soundtrack music, so I've seen how music people work. You want some advice?"

"Yes, please."

"Set up your own record company."

Dave was intrigued. He had been thinking along the same lines, but it seemed like a fantasy. "Do you think that's possible?"

"You can rent a recording studio, I guess, for a day or two, or however long it takes."

"We can record the music, and I suppose we can get a factory to make the discs, but I'm not so sure about selling them. I wouldn't want to spend time managing a team of sales representatives, even if I knew how."

"You don't need to do that. Get the big record company to do sales and distribution for you on a percentage basis. They'll get the peanuts and you'll get the profits."

"I wonder if they would agree to that."

"They won't like it, but they'll do it, because they can't afford to lose you."

"I guess."

Dave found himself drawn to this shrewd old man, despite his criminal reputation.

Lev had not finished. "What about publishing? You write the songs, don't you?"

"Walli and I do it together, usually." Walli was the one who actually put the songs down on paper, for Dave's handwriting and spelling were so bad that no one could ever read what he wrote; but the creative act was a collaboration. "We make a little extra from songwriting royalties."

"A little? You should make a lot. I bet your publisher employs a foreign agent who takes a cut."

"True."

"If you look into it, you'll find the foreign agent also employs a subagent who takes another cut, and so on. And all the people taking cuts are part of the same corporation. By the time they've taken twenty-five percent three or four times you got zip." Lev shook his head in disgust. "Set up your own publishing company. You'll never make money until you're in control."

Marga said: "How old are you, Dave?"

"Seventeen."

"So young. But at least you're smart enough to pay attention to business."

"I wish I was smarter."

After lunch they went into the lounge. "Your uncle Greg is going to join us for coffee," Lev said. "He's your mother's half brother."

Dave recalled that Daisy spoke fondly of Greg. He had done some foolish things in his youth, she said, but so had she. Greg was a Republican senator, but she even forgave him that.

Marga said: "My son, Greg, never married, but he has a son of his own, called George."

Lev said: "It's kind of an open secret. Nobody mentions it, but everyone in Washington knows. Greg ain't the only congressman with a bastard kid."

Dave knew about George. His mother had told him, and Jasper Murray had actually met George. Dave felt it was cool to have a colored cousin.

Dave said: "So George and I are your two grandsons."

"Yeah."

Marga said: "Here come Greg and George now."

Dave looked up. Walking across the lounge was a middle-aged man wearing a stylish gray flannel suit that needed a good brush and press. Beside him was a handsome Negro of about thirty, immaculately dressed in a dark gray mohair suit and a narrow tie.

They came up to the table. Both men kissed Marga. Lev said: "Greg, this is your nephew, Dave Williams. George, meet your English cousin."

They sat down. Dave noticed that George was poised and confident, despite being the only dark-skinned person in the room. Negro pop stars were growing their hair longer, like everyone else in show business, but George still had a short crop, probably because he was in politics.

Greg said: "Well, Daddy, did you ever imagine a family like this?"

Lev said: "Listen to me, I'll tell you something. If you could go back in time, to when I was the age Dave is now, and you could meet the young Lev Peshkov, and tell him how his life was going to turn out, do you know what he'd do? He'd say you were out of your goddamn mind."

. . .

That evening George took Maria Summers out to dinner for her twenty-ninth birthday.

He was worried about her. Maria had changed her job and moved to a different apartment, but she did not yet have a boyfriend. She socialized with girls from the State Department about once a week, and she went out with George now and again, but she had no romantic life. George feared she was still mourning. The assassination was almost two years ago, but a person could easily take longer than that to recover from the murder of her lover.

His affection for Maria was definitely not that of a brother. He found her sexy and alluring, and had ever since that bus ride to Alabama. He felt about her the way he felt about Skip Dickerson's wife, who was gorgeous and charming. Like his best friend's wife, Maria was simply not available. If life had turned out differently, he felt sure he might be happily married to her. But he had Verena; and Maria wanted no one.

They went to the Jockey Club. Maria wore a gray wool dress, smart but plain. She had no jewelry on, and wore her glasses all the time. Her hairpiece was a little old-fashioned. She had a pretty face and a sexy mouth, and—more importantly—she had a warm heart: she could have found a man easily, if only she had tried. However, people were beginning to say that she was a career girl, a woman whose job was the most important thing in her life. George did not really think that could make her happy, and he fretted about her.

"I just got a promotion," she said as they sat down at the restaurant table.

"Congratulations!" said George. "Let's have champagne."

"Oh, no, thank you, I have to work tomorrow."

"It's your birthday!"

"All the same, I won't. I might have a small brandy later, to help me sleep."

George shrugged. "Well, I guess your seriousness explains your promotion. I know you're intelligent, capable, and extremely well educated, but none of that counts, normally, if your skin is dark."

"Absolutely. It's always been next to impossible for people of color to get high posts in government."

"Well done for overcoming that prejudice. It's quite an achievement."

"Things have changed since you left the Justice Department—and you know why? The government is trying to persuade Southern police forces to hire Negroes, but the Southerners say: 'Look at your own staff—they're all white!' So senior officials are under pressure. To prove they're not prejudiced, they need to promote people of color."

"They probably think one example is enough."

Maria laughed. "Plenty."

They ordered. George reflected that both he and Maria had succeeded in breaking the color bar, but that did not show that it was not there. On the contrary, they were the exceptions that proved the rule.

Maria was thinking along the same lines. "Bobby Kennedy seems all right," she said.

"When I first met him he regarded civil rights as a distraction from more important issues. But the great thing about Bobby is that he'll see reason, and change his mind if necessary."

"How's he doing?"

"Early days yet," George said evasively. Bobby had been elected as the senator from New York, and George was one of his close aides. George felt that Bobby was not adjusting well to his new role. He had been through so many changes—leading adviser to his brother the president, then sidelined by President Johnson, and now a junior senator—that he was in danger of losing track of who he was.

"He ought to speak out against the Vietnam War!" Maria clearly felt passionately about this, and George sensed that she had been planning to lobby him. "President Kennedy was *reducing* our effort in Vietnam, and he refused again and again to send ground combat troops," she said. "But as soon as Johnson was elected he sent thirty-five hundred marines, and the Pentagon immediately asked for more. In June, they demanded another one hundred seventy-five thousand troops—and

General Westmoreland said it probably wouldn't be enough! But Johnson just lies about it all the time."

"I know. And the bombing of the north was supposed to bring Ho Chi Minh to the negotiating table, but it just seems to have made the Communists more resolute."

"Which is exactly what was predicted when the Pentagon war-gamed it."

"Did they? I don't think Bobby knows that." George would tell him tomorrow.

"It's not generally known, but they ran two war games on the effect of bombing North Vietnam. Both showed the same result: an *increase* in Vietcong attacks in the south."

"This is exactly the spiral of failure and escalation that Jack Kennedy feared."

"And my brother's eldest boy is coming up to draft age." Maria's face showed her fear for her nephew. "I don't want Stevie to be killed! Why doesn't Senator Kennedy speak out?"

"He knows it will make him unpopular."

Maria was not willing to accept that. "Will it? People don't like this war."

"People don't like politicians who undermine our troops by criticizing the war."

"He can't let public opinion dictate to him."

"Men who ignore public opinion don't remain in politics long, not in a democracy."

Maria raised her voice in frustration. "So no one can ever oppose a war?"

"Maybe that's why we have so many of them."

Their food came, and Maria changed the subject. "How is Verena?"

George felt he knew Maria well enough to be frank. "I adore her," he said. "She stays at my apartment every time she comes to town, which is about once a month. But she doesn't seem to want to settle down."

"If she settled down with you, she'd have to live in Washington."

"Is that so bad?"

"Her job is in Atlanta."

George did not see the problem. "Most women live where their husband's job is."

"Things are changing. If Negroes can be equal, why not women?"

"Oh, come on!" George said indignantly. "It's not the same."

"It certainly is not. Sexism is worse. Half the human race are enslaved."

"Enslaved?"

"Think how many housewives work hard all day for no pay! And in most parts of the world, a woman who leaves her husband is liable to be arrested and brought home by the police. Someone who works for nothing and can't leave the job is called a slave, George."

George was annoyed by this argument, the more so as Maria seemed to be winning it. But he saw an opportunity to bring up the subject that was really worrying him. He said: "Is this why you're single?"

Maria looked uncomfortable. "Partly," she said, not meeting his eye.

"When do you think you might start dating again?"

"Soon, I guess."

"Don't you want to?"

"Yes, but I work hard, and don't have much spare time."

George did not buy this. "You think no one can ever live up to the man you lost."

She did not deny it. "Am I wrong?" she said.

"I believe you could find someone who would be kinder to you than he was. Someone smart and sexy and also faithful."

"Maybe."

"Would you go out on a blind date?"

"I might."

"Do you care if he's black or white?"

"Black. It's too much trouble, dating white guys."

"Okay." George was thinking of Leopold Montgomery, the reporter. But he did not say so yet. "How was your steak?"

"It melted in the mouth. Thank you for bringing me here. And for remembering my birthday."

They ate dessert, then had brandy with coffee. "I have a white cousin," said George. "How about that? Dave Williams. I met him today."

"How come you haven't seen him before?"

"He's a British pop singer, here on tour with his group, Plum Nellie."

Maria had never heard of them. "Ten years ago I knew every act in the hit parade. Am I growing old?"

George smiled. "You're twenty-nine today."

"Only a year off thirty! Where did the time go?"

"Their big hit was called 'I Miss Ya, Alicia.'"

"Oh, sure, I've heard that song on the radio. So your cousin is in that group?"

"Yeah."

"Do you like him?"

"I do. He's young, not yet eighteen, but he's mature, and he charmed our cantankerous Russian grandfather."

"Have you seen him perform?"

"No. He offered me a free ticket, but they're in town tonight only, and I already had a date."

"Oh, George, you could have canceled me."

"On your birthday? Heck, no." He called for the check.

He drove her home in his old-fashioned Mercedes. She had moved to a larger apartment in the same neighborhood, Georgetown.

They were surprised to see a police car outside the building with its lights flashing.

George walked Maria to the door. A white cop was standing outside. George said: "Is there something wrong, Officer?"

"Three apartments in this building were burglarized this evening," the cop said. "Do you live here?"

"I do!" said Maria. "Was number four robbed?"

"Let's go look."

They entered the building. Maria's door had been forced open. Her face looked bloodless as she walked into the apartment. George and the cop followed.

Maria looked around, bewildered. "It looks the way I left it." After a second she added: "Except that all the drawers are open."

"You need to check what's missing."

"I don't own anything worth stealing."

"They generally take money, jewelry, liquor, and firearms."

"I'm wearing my watch and ring, I don't drink, and I sure don't own a gun." She went into the kitchen, and George watched through the open door. She opened a coffee tin. "I had eighty dollars in here," she told the cop. "It's gone."

He wrote in his notebook. "Exactly eighty?"

"Three twenties and two tens."

There was one more room. George crossed the living room and opened the door to the bedroom.

Maria cried: "George! Don't go in there!"

She was too late.

George stood in the doorway, looking around the bedroom in amazement. "Oh, my God," he said. Now he saw why she was not dating.

Maria turned away, mortified with embarrassment.

The cop went past George into the bedroom. "Wow," he said. "You must have a hundred pictures of President Kennedy in here! I guess you were a fan of his, right?"

Maria struggled to speak. "Yes," she said, sounding choked up. "A fan."

"I mean, with the candles, and flowers, and like that, it's amazing."

George turned away from the sight. "Maria, I'm sorry I looked," he said quietly.

She shook her head, meaning he had no need to apologize: it had been an accident. But George knew he had violated a secret, sacred place. He wanted to kick himself.

The cop was still talking. "It's almost like a, what do you call it, in a Catholic church? A shrine, is the word."

"That's right," said Maria. "It's a shrine."

. . .

The program *This Day* was part of a network of television and radio stations and studios, some of which were housed in a downtown skyscraper. In the personnel department was an attractive middle-aged woman called Mrs. Salzman who fell victim to Jasper Murray's charm. She crossed her shapely legs and looked at him archly over the top of her blue-framed spectacles and called him Mr. Murray. He lit her cigarettes and called her Blue Eyes.

She felt sorry for him. He had come all the way from Britain in the hope of being interviewed for a job that did not exist. *This Day* never hired beginners: all its staff was experienced television reporters, producers, cameramen, and researchers. Several of them were distinguished in their profession. Even the secretaries were news veterans. In vain Jasper protested that he was not a beginner: he had been editor of his own paper. The student press did not count, Mrs. Salzman told him, oozing compassion.

He could not go back to London: it would be too humiliating. He would do anything to stay in the USA. His job on the *Western Mail* would have been filled by someone else by now.

He begged Mrs. Salzman to find him a job, any job, no matter how menial, somewhere in the network of which *This Day* was a part. He showed her his green card, obtained from the American embassy in London, which meant he had permission to seek employment in the States. She told him to come back in a week.

He was staying at an international student hostel on the Lower East Side, paying a dollar a night. He spent a week exploring New York, walking everywhere to save cash. Then he went back to see Mrs. Salzman, taking with him a single rose. And she gave him a job.

It was *very* menial. He was a clerk-typist on a local radio station, his task to listen to the radio all day and log everything that happened: which advertisements were aired, which records were played, who was interviewed, the length of the news bulletins and the weather forecasts and the traffic reports. Jasper did not care. He had got a foot in the door. He was working in America.

The personnel office, the radio station, and the *This Day* studio were all in the same skyscraper, and Jasper hoped he might get to know the people on *This Day* socially, but it never happened. They were an elite group who kept themselves separate.

One morning Jasper found himself in the elevator with Herb Gould, editor of *This Day*, a man of about forty with the permanent shadow of a blue-black beard. Jasper introduced himself and said: "I'm a great admirer of your show."

"Thank you," Gould said politely.

"It's my ambition to work for you," Jasper went on.

"We don't need anyone right now," Gould said.

"One day if you have time I'd like to show you my articles for British national newspapers." The elevator came to a halt. Desperately, Jasper kept going. "I've written—"

Gould held up a hand to silence him and stepped out of the lift. "Thanks all the same," he said, and he walked away.

A few days later, Jasper was at his typewriter with his headphones on and heard the mellifluous voice of Chris Gardner, the host of the midmorning show, say: "The British group Plum Nellie is in the city today for a show tonight with the All-Star Touring Beat Revue." Jasper pricked up his ears. "We were hoping to bring you an interview with these guys, who are being called the new Beatles, but the promoter said they wouldn't have time. Here instead is their latest hit, written by Dave and Walli: 'Good-bye London Town.'"

As the record began, Jasper tore off his headphones, jumped up from his desk—in a little booth in the corridor—and went into the studio. "I can get an interview with Plum Nellie," he said.

On air, Gardner sounded like the kind of movie star who always played the romantic lead, but in fact he was a homely-looking man with dandruff on the shoulders of his cardigan. "How would you manage that, Jasper?" he said with mild skepticism.

"I know the group. I grew up with Dave Williams. My mother and his are best friends."

"Can you get the group to come into the studio?"

Jasper probably could, but that was not what he wanted. "No," he said. "But if you give me a microphone and a tape recorder I'll guarantee to interview them in their dressing room."

There was a certain amount of bureaucratic fuss—the station manager was reluctant to let an expensive tape recorder leave the building—but at six that evening Jasper was backstage at the theater with the group.

Chris Gardner wanted no more than a few minutes of bland remarks from the group: how they liked the United States, what they thought about girls screaming at their concerts, whether they felt homesick. But Jasper hoped to give the radio station more than that. He intended this interview to be his passport to a real job in television. It had to be a sensation that rocked America.

First he interviewed them all together, doing the vanilla questions, talking about the early days back in London, getting them relaxed. He told them the station wanted to show them as fully rounded human beings: this was journalists' code for intrusive personal questions, but they were too young and inexperienced to know that. They were open with him, except for Dave, who was guarded, perhaps remembering the fuss caused by Jasper's article about Evie and Hank Remington. The others trusted him. Something else they had yet to learn was that no journalist could be trusted.

Then he asked them for individual interviews. He did Dave first, knowing that he was the leader. He gave Dave an easy ride, avoiding probing questions, not challenging any of the answers. Dave returned to the dressing room looking tranquil, and that gave the others confidence.

Jasper interviewed Walli last.

Walli was the one with a real story to tell. But would he open up? All Jasper's preparations were aimed at that result.

Jasper placed their chairs close together, and spoke to Walli in a low voice, to create the illusion of privacy, even though their words would be heard by millions. He put an ashtray next to Walli's chair to encourage him to smoke, guessing that a cigarette would make him feel more at ease. Walli lit up.

"What kind of child were you?" Jasper said, smiling as if this was just a lighthearted conversation. "Well-behaved, or naughty?"

Walli grinned. "Naughty," he said, and laughed.

They were off to a good start.

Walli talked about his childhood in Berlin after the war and his early interest in music, then about going to the Minnesänger club, where he came second in the contest. This brought Karolin into the conversation in a natural way, as she and Walli had paired up that night. Walli became passionate as he spoke about the two of them as a musical duo, their choice of material and the way they performed together, and it was clear how much he loved her, even though he did not say it.

This was great stuff, a lot better than the average pop star interview, but still not enough for Jasper.

"You were enjoying yourselves, you were making good music, and you were pleasing audiences," Jasper said. "What went wrong?"

"We sang 'If I Had a Hammer.'"

"Explain to me why that was a mistake."

"The police didn't like it. Karolin's father was afraid he would lose his job because of us, so he made her quit."

"So, in the end, the only place you could play your music was the West."

"Yes," Walli said briefly.

Jasper sensed that Walli was trying to dam the flow of passion.

Sure enough, after a moment's hesitation Walli added: "I don't want to say too much about Karolin—it could get her into trouble."

"I don't think the East German secret police listen to our radio station," Jasper said with a smile.

"No, but still . . ."

"I won't broadcast anything risky, I guarantee."

It was a worthless promise, but Walli accepted it. "Thanks," he said.

Jasper moved on quickly. "I believe the only thing you took with you, when you left, was your guitar."

"That's right. It was a sudden decision."

"You stole a vehicle."

"I was roadying for the bandleader. I used his van."

Jasper knew that this story, although big in the German press, had not been widely reported in the United States. "You drove to the checkpoint . . ."

"And smashed through the wooden barrier."

"And the guards shot at you."

Walli just nodded.

Jasper lowered his voice. "And the van hit a guard."

Walli nodded again. Jasper wanted to yell at him: *This is radio—stop nodding!* Instead he said: "And . . ."

"I killed him," Walli said at last. "I killed the guy."

"But he was trying to kill you."

Walli shook his head, as if Jasper were missing the point. "He was my age," Walli said. "I read about him in the newspapers later. He had a girlfriend."

"And that's important to you . . ."

Walli nodded again.

Jasper said: "What does that signify?"

"He was similar to me," Walli said. "Except that I liked guitars and he liked guns."

"But he was working for the regime that imprisoned you in East Germany."

"We were just two boys. I escaped because I had to. He shot me because he had to. It's the Wall that is evil."

That was such a great quote that Jasper had to suppress his elation. In his head he was already writing the article he would offer to the tabloid *New York Post*. He could see the headline:

Secret Anguish of
Pop Star Walli

But he wanted yet more. "Karolin didn't leave with you."

"She didn't show up. I had no idea why. I was so disappointed, and I couldn't understand it. So I escaped anyway." In the pain of remembering, Walli had lost sight of the need to be cautious.

Jasper prompted him again. "But you went back for her."

"I met some people who were digging a tunnel for escapers. I had to know why she had not shown up. So I went through the tunnel the wrong way, into the East."

"That was dangerous."

"If I had been caught, yes."

"And you met up with Karolin, then . . ."

"She told me she was pregnant."

"And she didn't want to escape with you."

"She was afraid for the baby."

"Alicia."

"Her name is Alice. I changed it in the song. For the rhyme, you know?"

"I understand. And what is your situation now, Walli?"

Walli choked up. "Karolin can't get permission to leave East Germany, not even for a short visit; and I can't go back."

"So you are a family split in two by the Berlin Wall."

"Yes." Walli let out a sob. "I may never see Alice."

Jasper thought: *Gotcha.*

.   .   .

Dave Williams had not seen Beep Dewar since her visit to London four years ago. He was eager to meet her again.

The last date of the Beat Revue tour was in San Francisco, where Beep lived. Dave had got the Dewars' address from his mother, and had sent them four tickets and a note inviting them to come backstage afterward. They had not been able to reply, for he was in a different city every day, so he did not know whether they were going to turn up.

He was no longer sleeping with Mandy Love—much to his regret. She had taught him a lot, including oral sex. But she had never really felt comfortable walking around with a white British boyfriend, and she had now gone back to her long-term lover, a piano player. They would probably get married when the tour was over, Dave thought.

Since then Dave had had no one.

By now Dave knew what kinds of sex he did and did not like. In bed girls could be intense, or slutty, or soulful, or sweetly submissive, or briskly practical. Dave was happiest when they were playful.

He had a feeling Beep would be playful.

He wondered what would happen if Beep showed up tonight.

He recalled her at thirteen, smoking Chesterfield cigarettes in the garden in Great Peter Street. She had been pretty and petite, and sexier than anyone had a right to be at that age. To Dave at thirteen, hypersensitized by adolescent hormones, she had been impossibly alluring. He had been flat crazy for her. However, although they had got on well, she had not been interested in him romantically. To his immense frustration, she had preferred the older Jasper Murray.

His thoughts drifted to Jasper. Walli had been upset when the interview was broadcast on the radio. Even worse had been the story in the *New York Post,* headlined:

**"I May Never
See My Kid"
—Pop Star Dad**

by Jasper Murray

Walli was afraid the publicity might cause trouble for Karolin in East Germany. Dave recalled Jasper's interview with Evie, and made a mental note never to trust a word Jasper said.

He wondered how much Beep might have changed in four years. She might be taller, or she might have grown fat. Would he still find her overwhelmingly desirable? Would she be more interested in him now that he was older?

She might have a boyfriend, of course. She might go out with that guy tonight instead of coming to the gig.

Before the show, Plum Nellie had a couple of hours to look around. They quickly realized that San Francisco was the coolest city of them all. It was full of young people in radically stylish clothes. Miniskirts were out. The girls wore dresses that trailed the floor, flowers in their hair, and tiny bells that tinkled as they moved. The men's hair was longer here than anywhere else, even London. Some of the young black men and women had grown it into a huge fuzzy cloud that looked amazing.

Walli in particular loved the town. He said he felt as if he could do anything here. It was at the opposite end of the universe from East Berlin.

There were twelve acts in the Beat Revue. Most of them played two or three songs, then went off. The top-of-the-bill act had twenty minutes at the end. Plum Nellie was big enough stars to close the first half with fifteen minutes, during which they played five short songs. No amplifiers were carried on tour: they played through whatever was available at the venue, often primitive speakers designed for sports announcements. The audience, almost all teenage girls, screamed loudly all the way through, so that the group could not hear themselves. It hardly mattered: no one was listening.

The thrill of working in the USA was wearing off. The group was getting bored, and looking forward to going back to London, where they were due to record a new album.

After the performance they returned backstage. The venue was a theater, so their dressing room was large enough, and the toilet was clean—quite different from the beat clubs in London and Hamburg. The only refreshment available was the free Dr Pepper from the sponsor, but the doorman was usually willing to send out for beer.

Dave told the group that friends of his parents might come backstage, so they had to behave. They all groaned: that meant no drugs and no fumbling with groupies until the old people had gone.

During the second half, Dave saw the doorman at the artists' entrance and made sure he had the names of the guests: Mr. Woody Dewar, Mrs. Bella Dewar, Mr. Cameron Dewar, and Miss Ursula "Beep" Dewar.

Fifteen minutes after the end of the show, they appeared in the doorway of his dressing room.

Beep had hardly changed at all, Dave saw with delight. She was still petite, no taller than she had been at thirteen, although she was curvier. Her jeans were tight around her hips but flared below the knee, the latest fashion, and she wore a closely fitting sweater with broad blue and white stripes.

Had she dressed up for Dave? Not necessarily. What teenage girl would *not* dress up to go backstage at a pop concert?

He shook hands with all four visitors and introduced them to the rest of the group. He was afraid the other guys might disgrace him, but in fact they were on their best behavior. They all invited family guests occasionally, and each appreciated the others being restrained in the presence of older relatives and friends of their parents.

Dave had to force himself to stop staring at Beep. She still had that look in her eye. Mandy Love had it, too. People called it sex appeal or je ne sais quoi or just "It." Beep had an impish grin, a sway in her walk, and an air of lively curiosity. Dave was as consumed with desperate desire as he had been when he was a thirteen-year-old virgin.

He tried to talk to Cameron, who was two years older than Beep and already studying at the University of California at Berkeley, just outside San Francisco. But Cam was difficult. He was in favor of the Vietnam War, he thought civil rights should progress more gradually, and he felt it was right that homosexual acts should be crimes. He also preferred jazz.

Dave gave the Dewars fifteen minutes, then said: "This is the last night of our tour. There's a farewell get-together at the hotel starting in a few minutes. Beep and Cam, would you like to come?"

"Not me," said Cameron immediately. "Thanks all the same."

"Shame," said Dave with polite insincerity. "What about you, Beep?"

"I'd love to come," said Beep, and looked at her mother.

"In by midnight," said Bella.

Woody said: "Use our taxi service to get home, please."

"I'll make sure of it," Dave reassured them.

The parents and Cameron left, and the musicians got on the bus with their guests for the short ride to the hotel.

The party was in the hotel bar, but in the lobby Dave murmured in Beep's ear: "Have you ever tried smoking marijuana?"

"You mean pot?" she said. "You bet!"

"Not so loud—it's against the law!"

"Have you got some?"

"Yes. We should probably smoke it in my room. Then we can join the party."

"Okay."

They went to his room. Dave rolled a joint while Beep found a rock station on the radio. They sat on the bed, passing the roach back and forth. Mellowing out, Dave smiled and said: "When you came to London . . ."

"What?"

"You weren't interested in me."

"I liked you, but you were too young."

"*You* were too young, for the things I wanted to do to you."

She grinned mischievously. "What did you want to do to me?"

"There was a long list."

"What came first?"

"First?" Dave was not going to tell her. Then he thought: Why not? So he said: "I wanted to see your tits."

She handed him the joint, then pulled the striped sweater over her head with a swift movement. She had nothing on underneath it.

Dave was astounded and overjoyed. He got a hard-on just looking. "They're so beautiful," he said.

"Yes, they are," she said dreamily. "So pretty I sometimes have to touch them myself."

"Oh, my God," Dave groaned.

"On your list," Beep said, "what was second?"

.   .   .

Dave changed his flight to a week later and stayed on at the hotel. He saw Beep after school every weekday and all day Saturday and Sunday.

They went to movies, they shopped for cool clothes, and they walked around the zoo. They made love two or three times a day, always using condoms.

One evening while he was undressing she said: "Take off your jeans."

He looked at her, lying on the hotel bed wearing just her panties and a denim cap. "What are you talking about?"

"Tonight you're my slave. Do as you're told. Take off your jeans."

He was already taking them off, and he was about to say so when he realized that this was a fantasy. The thought amused him, and he decided to play along. He pretended to be reluctant, and said: "Aw, do I have to?"

"You have to do everything I say, because you belong to me," she said. "Take off your goddamn jeans."

"Yes, ma'am," Dave said.

She sat upright, watching him. He saw the mischievous lust in her faint smile. "Very good," she said.

Dave said: "What should I do next?"

Dave knew why he had fallen so hard for Beep, both when he was thirteen and again a few days ago. She was full of fun, ready to try anything, hungry for new experiences. With some girls, Dave had been bored after two fucks. He felt he could never get bored with Beep.

They made love, Dave pretending reluctance while Beep ordered him to do things he was already longing for. It was weirdly exciting.

Afterward he said idly: "Where did you get your nickname, anyway?"

"Have I never told you?"

"No. There's so much I don't know about you. Yet I feel as if we've been close for years."

"When I was little I had a toy car, the kind you sit in and pedal. I don't even remember it, but apparently I loved it. I spent hours driving it, and I used to say: 'Beep! Beep!'"

They got dressed and went for hamburgers. Dave saw her bite into hers, watched the juice run down her chin, and realized that he was in love.

"I don't want to go back to London," he said.

She swallowed and said: "Then stay."

"I can't. Plum Nellie has to make a new album. Then we go on tour in Australia and New Zealand."

"I adore you," she said. "When you go, I'll cry. But I'm not going to spoil today by being miserable about tomorrow. Eat your hamburger. You need the protein."

"I feel we're soul mates. I know I'm young, but I've had a lot of different girls."

"No need to brag. I've done pretty well, too."

"I didn't mean to brag. I'm not even proud of it—it's too easy when you're a pop singer. I'm trying to explain, to myself as well as to you, why I feel so sure."

She dipped a French fry into ketchup. "Sure of what?"

"That I want this to be permanent."

She froze with the French fry halfway to her mouth, then put it back on the plate. "What do you mean?"

"I want us to be together always. I want us to live together."

"Live together . . . how?"

"Beep," he said.

"Still here."

He reached across the table and took her hand. "Would you think about maybe getting married?"

"Oh, my God," she said.

"I know it's crazy, I know."

"It's not crazy," she said. "But it's sudden."

"Does that mean you want to? Get married?"

"You're right. We're soul mates. I've never had half this much fun with a boyfriend."

She was still not answering the question. He said slowly and distinctly: "I love you. Will you marry me?"

She hesitated for a long moment, then she said: "Hell, yes."

.   .   .

"Don't even ask me," said Woody Dewar angrily. "You two are not getting married."

He was a tall man, dressed in a tweed jacket with a button-down shirt and a tie. Dave had to work hard not to be intimidated.

Beep said: "How did you know?"

"It doesn't matter."

"My creep of a brother told you," Beep said. "What a dick I was to confide in him."

"There's no need for bad language."

They were in the drawing room of the Dewars' Victorian mansion on Gough Street in the Nob Hill district. The handsome old furniture and expensive but faded curtains reminded Dave of the house in Great Peter Street. Dave and Beep sat together on the red velvet couch, Bella was in an antique leather chair, and Woody stood in front of the carved stone fireplace.

Dave said: "I know it's sudden, but I have obligations: recording in London, a tour of Australia, and more."

"Sudden?" said Woody. "It's totally irresponsible! The mere fact that you can make the suggestion at all, after a week of dating, proves that you're nowhere near mature enough for marriage."

Dave said: "I hate to boast, but you force me to say that I've been living independently from my parents for two years; in that time I've built up a multimillion-dollar international business; and although I'm not as rich as people imagine, I am able to keep your daughter in comfort."

"Beep is seventeen! And so are you. She can't marry without my permission, and I'm not giving it. And I'm betting Lloyd and Daisy will take the same attitude to you, young Dave."

Beep said: "In some states you can get married at eighteen."

"You're not going anywhere like that."

"What are you going to do, Daddy, put me in a nunnery?"

"Are you threatening to elope?"

"Just pointing out that, in the end, you don't really have the power to stop us."

She was right. Dave had checked, at the San Francisco public library on Larkin Street. The age of majority was twenty-one, but several states allowed women to marry at eighteen without parental consent. And in Scotland the age was sixteen. In practice it was difficult for parents to prevent the marriage of two people who were determined.

But Woody said: "Don't you bet on that. This is not going to happen."

Dave said mildly: "We don't want to quarrel with you about this, but I think Beep's just saying that yours is not the only opinion that counts here."

He thought his words were inoffensive, and he had spoken in a courteous tone of voice, but that seemed to infuriate Woody more. "Get out of this house before I throw you out."

Bella intervened for the first time. "Stay where you are, Dave."

Dave had not moved. Woody had a bad leg from a war wound: he was not throwing anyone anywhere.

Bella turned to her husband. "Darling, twenty-one years ago you sat in this room and confronted my mother."

"I wasn't seventeen, I was twenty-five."

"Mother accused you of causing the breaking-off of my engagement to Victor Rolandson. She was right: you were the cause of it, though at that point you and I had spent only one evening together. We had met at Dave's mother's party, after which you went off to invade Normandy and I didn't see you for a year."

Beep said: "One evening? What did you do to him, Mom?"

Bella looked at her daughter, hesitated, then said: "I blew him in a park, honey."

Dave was astonished. Bella and Woody? It was unimaginable!

Woody protested: "Bella!"

"This is no time to mince words, Woody, dear."

Beep said: "On the first date? Wow, Mom! Way to go!"

Woody said: "For God's sake . . ."

Bella said: "My darling, I'm just trying to remind you of what it was like to be young."

"I didn't propose marriage right away!"

"That's true, you were painfully slow."

Beep giggled and Dave smiled.

Woody said to Bella: "Why are you undermining me?"

"Because you're being just a little pompous." She took his hand, smiled, and said: "We were in love. So are they. Lucky us, lucky them."

Woody became a little less angry. "So we should let them do anything they like?"

"Certainly not. But perhaps we can compromise."

"I don't see how."

"Suppose we tell them to ask us again in a year. In the meantime, Dave will be welcome to come and live here, in our house, whenever he can get a break from working with the group. While he's here he can share Beep's bed, if that's what they want."

"Certainly not!"

"They're going to do it, either here or elsewhere. Don't fight battles you can't win. And don't be a hypocrite. You slept with me before we were married, and you slept with Joanne Rouzrokh before you met me."

Woody got up. "I'll think about it," he said, and he walked out of the room.

Bella turned to Dave. "I'm not giving orders, Dave, either to you or to Beep. I'm asking you—begging you—to be patient. You're a good man from a fine family, and I will be happy when you marry my daughter. But please wait a year."

Dave looked at Beep. She nodded.

"All right," said Dave. "A year."

.   .   .

On the way out of the hostel in the morning, Jasper checked his pigeonhole. There were two letters. One was a blue airmail envelope addressed in his mother's graceful handwriting. The other had a typed address. Before he could open them he was called. "Telephone for Jasper Murray!" He stuffed both envelopes into the inside pocket of his jacket.

The caller was Mrs. Salzman. "Good morning, Mr. Murray."

"Hello, Blue Eyes."

"Are you wearing a tie, Mr. Murray?" she said.

Ties had become unfashionable, and anyway a clerk-typist was not required to be smart. "No," he said.

"Put one on. Herb Gould wants to see you at ten."

"He does? Why?"

"There's a vacancy for a researcher on *This Day*. I showed him your clippings."

"Thank you—you're an angel!"

"Put on a tie." Mrs. Salzman hung up.

Jasper returned to his room and put on a clean white shirt and a sober dark tie. Then he put his jacket and topcoat back on and went to work.

At the newsstand in the lobby of the skyscraper, he bought a small box of chocolates for Mrs. Salzman.

He went to the offices of *This Day* at ten minutes to ten. Fifteen minutes later, a secretary took him to Gould's office.

"Good to meet you," Gould said. "Thanks for coming in."

"I'm glad to be here." Jasper guessed that Gould had no memory of their conversation in the elevator.

Gould was reading the assassination edition of *The Real Thing*. "In your résumé it says you started this newspaper."

"Yes."

"How did that come about?"

"I was working on the official university student newspaper, *St. Julian's News*." Jasper's nervousness receded as he began to talk. "I applied for the post of editor, but it went to the sister of the previous editor."

"So you did it in a fit of pique."

Jasper grinned. "Partly, yes, though I felt sure I could do a better job than Valerie. So I borrowed twenty-five pounds and started a rival paper."

"And how did it work out?"

"After three issues we were selling more than *St. Julian's News*. And we made a profit, whereas *St. Julian's News* was subsidized." This was only slightly exaggerated. *The Real Thing* had just about broken even over a year.

"That's a real achievement."

"Thank you."

Gould held up the *New York Post* clipping of the interview with Walli. "How did you get this story?"

"What had happened to Walli wasn't a secret. It had already appeared in the German press. But in those days he was not a pop star. If I may say so . . ."

"Go on."

"I believe the art of journalism is not always finding out facts. Sometimes it's *realizing* that certain already-known facts, written up the right way, add up to a big story."

Gould nodded agreement. "All right. Why do you want to switch from print to television?"

"We know that a good photograph on the front page sells more copies than the best headline. Moving pictures are even better. No doubt there will always be a market for long in-depth newspaper articles, but for the foreseeable future most people are going to get their news from television."

Gould smiled. "No argument here."

The speaker on his desk beeped and his secretary said: "Mr. Thomas is calling from the Washington bureau."

"Thanks, sweetie. Jasper, good talking to you. We'll be in touch." He picked up the phone. "Hey, Larry, what's up?"

Jasper left the office. The interview had gone well, but it had ended with frustrating suddenness. He wished he had had the chance to ask how soon he would hear. But he was a supplicant: no one was worried about how he felt.

He returned to the radio station. While he was at the interview, his job had been done by the secretary who regularly relieved him at lunchtime. Now he thanked her and took over. He took off his jacket, and remembered the mail in his pocket. He put on his headphones and sat at the little desk. On the radio, a sports reporter was previewing a ball game. Jasper took out his letters and opened the one with the typewritten address.

It was from the president of the United States.

It was a form letter, with his name handwritten in a box.

It read:

> *Greeting:*
> *You are hereby ordered for induction into the Armed*
> *Forces of the United States*

Jasper said aloud: "What?"

> *and to report at the address below on January 20, 1966, at*
> *7 A.M. for forwarding to an Armed Forces Induction*
> *Station.*

Jasper fought down panic. This was obviously a bureaucratic foul-up. He was British: the U.S. Army surely would not conscript foreign citizens.

But he needed to get this sorted out as soon as possible. American bureaucrats were as maddeningly incompetent as any, and equally capable of causing endless unnecessary trouble. You had to pretend to take them seriously, like a red light at a deserted crossroads.

The reporting station was just a few blocks from the radio station. When the secretary came back to relieve him for lunch, he put on his jacket and topcoat and walked out of the building.

He turned up his collar against the cold New York wind and hurried through the streets to the federal building. There he entered an army office on the third floor and found a man in a captain's uniform sitting at a desk. The short-back-and-sides haircut looked more ridiculous than ever, now that even middle-aged men were growing their hair longer.

"Help you?" said the captain.

"I'm pretty sure this letter has been sent to me in error," Jasper said, and he handed over the envelope.

The captain scanned it. "You know there's a lottery system?" he said. "The number of men liable for service is greater than the number of soldiers required, so the recruits are selected randomly." He handed the letter back.

Jasper smiled. "I don't think I'm eligible for service, do you?"

"And why would that be?"

Perhaps the captain had not noticed his accent. "I'm not an American citizen," Jasper said. "I'm British."

"What are you doing in the United States?"

"I'm a journalist. I work for a radio station."

"And you have a work permit, I presume."

"Yes."

"You're a resident alien."

"Exactly."

"Then you are liable to be drafted."

"But I'm not American!"

"Makes no difference."

This was becoming exasperating. The army had screwed up, Jasper was almost certain. The captain, like many petty officials, was simply unwilling to admit a mistake. "Are you telling me that the United States army conscripts foreigners?"

The captain was unperturbed. "Conscription is based on residence, not citizenship."

"That can't be right."

The captain began to look irritated. "If you don't believe me, check it out."

"That's exactly what I'm going to do."

Jasper left the building and returned to the office. The personnel department would know about this kind of thing. He would go and see Mrs. Salzman.

He gave her the box of chocolates.

"You're sweet," she said. "Mr. Gould likes you, too."

"What did he say?"

"Just thanked me for sending you to him. He hasn't made up his mind yet. But I don't know of anyone else under consideration."

"That's great news! But I have a little problem you might be able to help me with." He showed her the letter from the army. "This must be a mistake, surely?"

Mrs. Salzman put her glasses on and read the letter. "Oh, dear," she said. "How unlucky. And just when you were getting along so well!"

Jasper could hardly believe his ears. "You're not saying I'm really liable for military service?"

"You are," she said sadly. "We've had this trouble before with foreign employees. The government says that if you want to live and work in the United States, you ought to help defend the country from Communist aggression."

"Are you telling me I'm going in the army?"

"Not necessarily."

Jasper's heart leaped with hope. "What's the alternative?"

"You can go home. They won't try to stop you from leaving the country."

"This is outrageous! Can't you get me out of it?"

"Do you have a hidden medical condition of any kind? Flat feet, tuberculosis, a hole in the heart?"

"Never been ill."

She lowered her voice. "And I presume you're not homosexual."

"No!"

"Your family doesn't belong to a religion that forbids military service?"

"My father's a colonel in the British army."

"I'm so sorry."

Jasper began to believe it. "I'm really leaving. Even if I get the job on *This Day*, I won't be able to take it up." He was struck by a thought. "Don't they have to give you your job back when you've finished your military service?"

"Only if you've held the job for a year."

"So I might not even be able to return to my job as clerk-typist on the radio station!"

"There's no guarantee."

"Whereas if I leave the United States now . . ."

"You can just go home. But you'll never work in the USA again."

"Jesus."

"What will you do? Leave, or join the army?"

"I really don't know," he said. "Thank you for your help."

"Thank you for the chocolates, Mr. Murray."

Jasper left her office in a daze. He could not return to his desk: he had to think. He went outside again. Normally he loved the streets of New York: the high buildings, the mighty Mack trucks, the extravagantly styled cars, the glittering window displays of the fabulous stores. Today it had all turned sour.

He walked toward the East River and sat in a park from which he could see the Brooklyn Bridge. He thought about leaving all this and going home to London with his tail between his legs. He thought about spending two long years working for a provincial British newspaper. He thought about never again being able to work in the USA.

Then he thought about the army: short hair, marching, bullying sergeants, violence. He thought about the hot jungles of Southeast Asia. He might have to shoot small, thin peasant men in pajamas. He might be killed, or crippled.

He thought of all the people he knew in London who had envied his going to the States. Anna and Hank had taken him to dinner at the

Savoy to celebrate. Daisy had given a farewell party for him at the house in Great Peter Street. His mother had cried.

He would be like a bride who comes home from the honeymoon and announces a divorce. The humiliation seemed worse than the risk of death in Vietnam.

What was he going to do?

CHAPTER THIRTY-NINE

The St. Gertrud Youth Club had changed.

    It had started out more or less harmless, Lili recalled. The East German government approved of traditional dancing, even if it took place in the basement of a church. And the government was happy for a Protestant pastor such as Odo Vossler to chat to youngsters about relationships and sex, since his views were likely to be as puritanical as their own.

Two years later the club was not so innocent. They no longer began the evening with a folk dance. They played rock music and danced in the energetic individualist style that youngsters all over the world called freaking out. Later, Lili and Karolin would play guitars and sing songs about freedom. The evening always ended with a discussion, led by Pastor Odo; and these discussions regularly strayed into forbidden territory: democracy, religion, the shortcomings of the East German government, and the overwhelming attraction of life in the West.

Such talk was commonplace at Lili's home, but for some of the kids it was a new and liberating experience to hear the government criticized and the ideas of Communism challenged.

This was not the only place where such things went on. Three or four evenings a week, Lili and Karolin took their guitars to a different church hall or a private house in or near Berlin. They knew that what they were doing was dangerous, but both felt they had little to lose. Karolin knew that she would never be reunited with Walli while the Berlin Wall remained standing. After the American newspapers ran stories about Walli and Karolin, the Stasi had punished the family by having Lili expelled from college: now she worked as a waitress in the canteen of the Ministry of Transport. Both young women had been determined not to let the government stifle them. Now they were famous among young people who secretly opposed the Communists. They made tape recordings of their songs that were passed around from one fan to another. Lili felt they were keeping the flame alight.

For Lili there was another attraction at St. Gertrud's: Thorsten Greiner. He was twenty-two, but he had a baby face like Paul McCartney's that made him look younger. He shared Lili's passion for music. He had recently broken up with a girl called Helga who was just not intelligent enough for him—in Lili's opinion.

One evening in 1967 Thorsten brought to the club the latest record by the Beatles. On one side was a bouncingly happy number called "Penny Lane," which they all danced to energetically; on the other a weirdly fascinating song, "Strawberry Fields Forever," to which Lili and others did a kind of slow dream-dance, swaying to the music and waving their arms and hands like underwater plants. They played both sides of the disc again and again.

When people asked Thorsten how he got the record, he tapped the side of his nose in a mysterious gesture and said nothing. But Lili knew the truth. Once a week Thorsten's uncle Horst drove across the border into West Berlin in a van full of bolts of cloth and cheap clothing, the East's largest export. Horst always gave the border guards a share of the comic books, pop records, makeup, and fashionable clothes he brought back.

Lili's parents thought the music was frivolous. For them only politics was serious. But they failed to understand that for Lili and her generation the music was political, even when the songs were about love. New ways of playing guitars and singing were all tied up with long hair and different clothes, racial tolerance and sexual freedom. Every song by the Beatles or Bob Dylan said to the older generation: "We don't do things your way." For teenagers in East Germany that was a stridently political message, and the government knew it and banned the records.

They were all freaking out to "Strawberry Fields Forever" when the police arrived.

Lili was dancing opposite Thorsten. She understood English, and she was intrigued by John Lennon singing: "Living is easy with eyes closed, misunderstanding all you see." It so vividly described most people in East Germany, she thought.

Lili was among the first to spot the uniforms coming through the street door. She knew right away that the Stasi had at last caught up with the St. Gertrud Youth Club. It was inevitable: young people were bound to talk about exciting things they did. No one knew how many East German citizens were informers for the secret police, but Lili's mother said it was more than the Gestapo had. "We couldn't do now what we did in the war," Carla had said; though when Lili had asked what she did in the war her mother had clammed up, as always. Anyway, it had been likely all along that sooner or later the Stasi would get wind of what was going on in the basement of St. Gertrud's Church.

Lili immediately stopped dancing and looked around for Karolin, but could not see her. Odo was not in sight either. They must have left the basement. In the corner opposite the street door was a staircase that led directly to the pastor's house alongside the church. They had probably gone out that way for some reason.

Lili said to Thorsten: "I'm going to fetch Odo."

She was able to push through the crowd of dancers and slip away before most people realized they were being raided. Thorsten followed her. They got to the top of the staircase before Lennon sang: "Let me take you down—" and stopped abruptly.

The harsh voice of a police officer began to give orders below as they crossed the hall of the pastor's residence. It was a large house for a single man: Odo was lucky. Lili had not been here often, but she knew he had a study on the ground floor at the front, and she guessed this was the likeliest place to find him. The door was ajar, and she pushed it wide and stepped inside.

There, in an oak-paneled room with bookshelves full of works of biblical scholarship, Odo and Karolin were locked in a passionate embrace. They were kissing with their mouths open. Karolin's hands were on Odo's head, her fingers buried in his long, thick hair. Odo was stroking and squeezing Karolin's breasts. She pressed against him, her body curved tautly like an archer's bow.

Lili was shocked silent. She thought of Karolin as her brother's wife, the fact that they were not actually married a mere technicality. It had never occurred to her that Karolin could become fond of another man—let alone the pastor! For a moment her mind searched wildly for some alternative explanation: they were rehearsing a play, or doing calisthenics.

Then Thorsten said: "My God!"

Odo and Karolin jumped apart with a suddenness that was almost comic. Shock and guilt showed on their faces. After a moment they spoke together. Odo said: "We were going to tell you." At the same time Karolin said: "Oh, Lili, I'm so sorry . . ."

For a frozen moment, Lili was vividly conscious of details: the check pattern of Odo's jacket, Karolin's nipples poking through her dress, Odo's theological degree in a brass frame on the wall, the old-fashioned flowered carpet with a threadbare patch in front of the fireplace.

Then she remembered the emergency that had brought her upstairs. "The police have come," she said. "They're in the basement."

Odo said: "Hell!" He strode out and Lili heard him hurrying down the stairs.

Karolin stared at Lili. Neither woman knew what to say. Then Karolin broke the spell. "I must go with him," she said, and followed Odo.

Lili and Thorsten were left in the study. It was a nice place for kissing, Lili thought sadly: the oak paneling, the fireplace, the books, the carpet. She wondered how often Odo and Karolin had done this, and when it had started. She thought about Walli. Poor Walli.

She heard shouting from downstairs, and that energized her. She had no reason to return to the basement, she realized. Her coat was down there but the evening was not bitterly cold: she could manage without it. She might escape.

The front door of the house was on the opposite side of the building from the basement entrance. She wondered whether the police had the whole place surrounded, and decided probably not.

She crossed the hall and opened the front door. There were no police in sight.

She said to Thorsten: "Shall we leave?"

"Yes, quickly."

They went out, closing the door quietly.

"I'll see you home," Thorsten said.

They hurried around the corner, then slowed their pace when they were out of sight of the church. Thorsten said: "That must have been a shock for you."

"I thought she loved Walli!" Lili wailed. "How could she do this to him?" She began to cry.

Thorsten put his arm around her shoulders as they walked along. "When was it that Walli left?"

"Almost four years ago."

"Have Karolin's prospects of emigrating got any better?"

Lili shook her head. "Worse."

"She needs someone to help her raise Alice."

"She has me, and my family!"

"Perhaps she feels that Alice needs a father."

"But . . . the pastor!"

"Most men wouldn't even think about taking on an unmarried mother. Odo is different just because he is a pastor."

At the house, Lili had to ring the doorbell because her key was in her coat. Her mother came to the door, saw her face, and said: "What on earth has happened?"

Lili and Thorsten stepped inside. Lili said: "The police raided the church, and I went to warn Karolin and found her kissing Odo!" She burst into fresh tears.

Carla closed the front door. "You mean *really* kissing him?"

"Yes, like mad!" said Lili.

"Come into the kitchen and have a cup of coffee, both of you."

As soon as they had told their story, Lili's father left, intending to do what he could to ensure that Karolin did not spend the night in jail. Carla then pointed out that Thorsten probably ought to go home in case his parents had heard of the raid and were worrying about him. Lili saw him to the door and he kissed her on the lips, briefly but delightfully, before walking away.

Then the three women were alone in the kitchen: Lili, Carla, and Grandmother Maud. Alice, now three years old, was asleep upstairs.

Carla said to Lili: "Don't be too hard on Karolin."

"Why not?" said Lili. "She's betrayed Walli!"

"It's been four years—"

"Grandmother waited four years for Grandfather Walter," Lili said. "And she didn't even have a baby!"

"That's true," said Maud. "Although I thought about Gus Dewar."

"Woody's father?" said Carla, surprised. "I didn't know that."

"Walter was tempted, too," Maud went on, with the cheerful indiscretion characteristic of people too old to be embarrassed. "By Monika von der Helbard. But nothing happened."

The way she made light of this annoyed Lili. "It's easy for you, Grandmother," she said. "Everything is so far in the past."

Carla said: "I'm sad about this, Lili, but I don't see how we can be angry. Walli may never come home, and Karolin may never leave East Germany. Can we really expect her to spend her life waiting for someone she may never see again?"

"I thought that was what she was going to do. I thought she was committed." Though Lili realized she could not remember Karolin actually saying it.

"I think she's already waited a long time."

"Is four years a long time?"

"It's long enough for a young woman to start asking herself whether she wants to sacrifice her life to a memory."

Both Carla and Maud sympathized with Karolin, Lili realized with dismay.

They discussed the matter until midnight, when Werner came home, accompanied by Karolin—and Odo.

Werner said: "Two of the boys managed to get into fights with police officers, but other than them nobody went to jail, I'm happy to say. However, the youth club is closed."

Everyone sat at the kitchen table. Odo sat beside Karolin. To Lili's horror, he held Karolin's hand in front of everybody. He said: "Lili, I'm sorry you found out by accident just when we were getting ready to tell you."

"Tell me what?" she said aggressively, though she thought grimly that she could guess.

"We love each other," Odo said. "I expect this is hard for you to accept, and we're sorry about that. But we have thought and prayed about it."

"Prayed?" Lili said incredulously. "I've never known Karolin to pray for anything!"

"People change."

Weak women change to please men, Lili thought. But before she could say it her mother spoke up. "This is hard for us all, Odo. Walli loves Karolin and the baby he's never seen. We know that from his letters. And we could guess it from Plum Nellie's songs: so many of them are about separation and loss."

Karolin said: "If you wish, I will leave this house tonight."

Carla shook her head. "It's hard for us, but it's harder for you, Karolin. I can't ask a normal young woman to dedicate her life to someone she may never see again—even though that person is our beloved son. Werner and I have talked about this. We knew it was coming sooner or later."

Lili was shocked. Her parents had foreseen this! They had said nothing to her. How could they be so heartless?

Or were they just more sensible? She did not want to believe that.

Odo said: "We want to get married."

Lili stood up. "No!" she cried.

Odo said: "And we hope you will all give us your blessing: Maud, Werner, Carla, and most of all Lili, who has been such a great friend to Karolin through her years of trouble."

"Go to hell," said Lili, and she left the room.

. . .

Dave Williams pushed his grandmother around Parliament Square in her wheelchair, followed by a flock of photographers. Plum Nellie's publicist had tipped off the newspapers, so Dave and Ethel had expected the cameras, and they posed cooperatively for ten minutes. Then Dave said: "Thank you, gentlemen," and turned into the car park of the Palace of Westminster. He paused at the Peers' Entrance, waved for one more shot, then pushed the chair into the House of Lords.

The usher said: "Good afternoon, m'lady."

Grandmam Ethel, Baroness Leckwith, had lung cancer. She was taking powerful drugs to control the pain, but her mind was clear. She could still walk a little way, though she quickly became breathless.

She had every reason to retire from active politics. But today the Lords were discussing the Sexual Offences Bill 1967.

Ethel felt strongly about this partly because of her gay friend Robert. To Dave's surprise his father, whom Dave considered an old stick-in-the-mud, was also passionately in favor of reforming the law. Apparently Lloyd had witnessed the Nazi persecution of homosexuals and had never forgotten it, although he refused to discuss the details.

Ethel would not speak in the debate—she was too ill for that—but she was determined to vote. And when Eth Leckwith was determined, there was no stopping her.

Dave pushed her along the entrance hall, which was a cloakroom, each coat hook having a pink ribbon loop on which members were supposed to hang their swords. The House of Lords did not even pretend to move with the times.

It was a crime in Britain for a man to have sex with another man, and every year hundreds of men who did so were prosecuted, jailed, and—worst of all—humiliated in the newspapers. The bill under discussion today would legalize homosexual acts by consenting adults in private.

The issue was controversial, and the bill was unpopular with much of the general public; but the tide was running in favor of reform. The Church of England had decided not to oppose a change in the law. They still said homosexuality was a sin, but they agreed it should not be a crime. The bill had a good chance, but its supporters feared a last-minute backlash—hence Ethel's determination to vote.

Ethel asked Dave: "Why are you so keen to be the one who takes me to this debate? You've never shown much interest in politics."

"Our drummer, Lew, is gay," Dave said, using the American word. "I was with him once in a pub called the Golden Horn when the police raided it. I was so disgusted with the way the cops behaved that I've been looking, ever since, for a way to show that I'm on the side of the homosexuals."

"Good for you," Ethel said; then she added, with the waspishness characteristic of her later years: "I'm glad to see that the crusading spirit of your forebears hasn't been entirely obliterated by rock and roll."

Plum Nellie was more successful than ever. They had released a "concept album" called *For Your Pleasure Tonight* that pretended to be a recording of a show featuring groups of different kinds: old-time music hall, folk, blues, swing, gospel, Motown—all in fact Plum Nellie. It was selling millions all over the world.

A policeman helped Dave carry the wheelchair up a flight of steps. Dave thanked him, wondering whether he had ever raided a gay pub. They reached the Peers' Lobby and Dave wheeled Ethel as far as the threshold of the debating chamber.

Ethel had planned this and got the agreement of the leader of the Lords to her appearing in her wheelchair. But Dave himself was not allowed to push her into the chamber, so they waited for one of her friends to notice her and take over.

The debate was already under way, with the peers sitting on red leather benches either side of a room whose decorations seemed ludicrously rich, like a palace in a Disney movie.

A peer was speaking, and Dave listened. "The bill is a queers' charter and will encourage that most loathsome creature, the male prostitute," the man said pompously. "It will increase the temptations that lie in the path of adolescents." That was strange, Dave thought. Did this guy believe that all men were queer, but most simply resisted temptation? "It is not that I lack compassion for the unfortunate homosexual—I am also not lacking in compassion for those who are dragged into his net."

Dragged into his net? What a lot of rubbish, Dave thought.

A man got up from the Labour side and took the handles of Ethel's wheelchair. Dave left the chamber and went up a staircase to the spectators' gallery.

When he got there another peer was speaking. "In one of the more popular Sunday newspapers last week there appeared an account, which some of Your Lordships may have seen, of a homosexual wedding in a Continental country." Dave had read this story in the *News of the World.* "I think the newspaper concerned is to be congratulated on highlighting this very nasty happening." How could a wedding be a nasty happening? "I only hope that, if this bill becomes law, the most vigilant eye will be kept on practices of this kind. I do not think these things could happen in this country, but it is possible."

Dave thought: Where do they dig up these dinosaurs?

Fortunately not all the peers were this bad. A formidable-looking woman with silver hair got up. Dave had met her at his mother's house: her name was Dora Gaitskell. She said: "As a society, we gloss over many perversions between men and women in private. The law, and society, are very tolerant towards these and turn a blind eye." Dave was astonished. What did she know about perversions between men and women? "Those men who are born, conditioned, or tempted irrevocably into homosexuality should have extended to them the same degree of tolerance as is extended to any other so-called perversion between men and women." Good for you, Dora, thought Dave.

But Dave's favorite was another white-haired old woman, this one with a twinkle in her eye. She, too, had been a guest at the house in Great Peter Street: her name was Barbara Wootton. After one of the men had gone on at great length about sodomy, she struck a note of irony. "I ask myself: What are the opponents of this bill afraid of?" she said. "They cannot be afraid that disgusting practices will be thrown upon their attention, because these acts are legalized only if they are performed in private. They cannot be afraid that there will be a corruption of youth, because these acts will be legalized only if they are performed by consenting adults. I can only suppose that the opponents of the bill will be afraid that their imagination will be tormented by visions of what will be going on elsewhere." The clear implication was that men who tried to keep homosexuality criminal did so as a way of policing their own fantasy life, and Dave laughed out loud—and was quickly told to keep quiet by an usher.

The vote was taken at half past six. It seemed to Dave that more people had spoken against than for the bill. The process of voting took an inordinately long time. Instead of putting slips of paper in a box, or pressing buttons, the peers had to get up and leave the chamber, passing through one of two lobbies, for either the "Contents" or the "Not Contents." Ethel's wheelchair was pushed into the "Content" lobby by another peer.

The bill was passed by one hundred eleven votes to forty-eight. Dave wanted to cheer, but it would have seemed wrong, like applauding in church.

Dave met Ethel at the entrance to the chamber and took over the wheelchair from one of her friends. She looked triumphant but exhausted, and he could not help wondering how long she had to live.

What a life she had had, he thought as he pushed her through the ornate corridors toward the exit. His own transformation from class dunce to pop star was nothing by comparison with her journey, from a two-bedroom cottage beside the slag heap in Aberowen all the way to the gilded debating chamber of the House of Lords. And she had transformed her country as well as herself. She had fought and won political battles—for votes for women, for welfare, for free health care, for girls' education, and now freedom for the persecuted minority of homosexual men. Dave had written songs that were loved around the world, but that seemed nothing compared with what his grandmother had achieved.

An elderly man walking with two canes stopped them in a paneled hallway. His air of decrepit elegance rang a bell, and Dave recalled seeing him once before, here in the House of Lords, on the day Ethel had become a baroness, about five years ago. The man said amiably: "Well, Ethel, I see you got your buggery bill passed. Congratulations."

"Thank you, Fitz," she said.

Dave remembered, now. This was Earl Fitzherbert, who had once owned a big house in Aberowen called Tŷ Gwyn, now the College of Further Education.

"I'm sorry to hear you've been ill, my dear," said Fitz. He seemed fond of her.

"I won't mince words with you," Ethel said. "I haven't got long to go. You'll probably never see me again."

"That makes me terribly sad." To Dave's surprise, tears rolled down the old earl's wrinkled face, and he pulled a large white handkerchief from his breast pocket to wipe his eyes. And now Dave recalled that the previous time he had witnessed a meeting between them he had been struck by an undercurrent of intense emotion, barely controlled.

"I'm glad I knew you, Fitz," Ethel said, in a tone that suggested he might have assumed the opposite.

"Are you?" Fitz said. Then to Dave's astonishment he added: "I never loved anyone the way I loved you."

"I feel the same," she said, doubling Dave's amazement. "I can say it now that my dear Bernie's gone. He was my soul mate, but you were something else."

"I'm so glad."

"I have only one regret," Ethel said.

"I know what it is," said Fitz. "The boy."

"Yes. If I have a dying wish, it is that you will shake his hand."

Dave wondered who "the boy" might be. Not himself, presumably.

The earl said: "I knew you would ask me that."

"Please, Fitz."

He nodded. "At my age, I ought to be able to admit when I've been wrong."

"Thank you," she said. "Knowing that, I can die happy."

"I hope there's an afterlife," he said.

"I have no idea," said Ethel. "Good-bye, Fitz."

The old man bent over the wheelchair, with difficulty, and kissed her lips. He pulled himself upright again and said: "Farewell, Ethel."

Dave pushed the wheelchair away.

After a minute he said: "That was Earl Fitzherbert, wasn't it?"

"Yes," said Ethel. "He's your grandfather."

. . .

The girls were Walli's only problem.

Young, pretty, and sexy in a wholesome way that seemed to him uniquely American, they trooped through his front door in dozens, all eager to have sex with him. The fact that he was remaining faithful to his girlfriend in East Berlin seemed only to make him more desirable.

"Buy a house," Dave had said to the members of the group. "Then, when the bubble bursts and nobody wants Plum Nellie anymore, at least you'll have somewhere to live."

Walli was beginning to realize that Dave was very smart. Since he had set up the two companies, Nellie Records and Plum Publishing, the group was making a lot more money. Walli was still not the millionaire people thought he was, though he would be when the royalties started to come in from *For Your Pleasure Tonight.* Meanwhile, he could at last afford to buy a home of his own.

Early in 1967 he bought a bow-fronted Victorian house in San

Francisco, on Haight Street near the corner of Ashbury. In this neighborhood, property values had been blighted by a years-long battle over a proposed freeway that was never built. Low rents drew students and other young people, who created a laid-back ambience that then attracted musicians and actors. Members of the Grateful Dead and Jefferson Airplane lived there. It was common to see rock stars, and Walli could walk around almost like a normal person.

The Dewars, the only people Walli knew in San Francisco, expected him to gut the house and modernize it; but he thought the old-fashioned coffered ceilings and wood paneling were cool, and he kept everything, though he had it all painted white.

He installed two luxurious bathrooms and a custom kitchen with a dishwashing machine. He shopped for a television set and a state-of-the-art record player. Otherwise he bought little normal furniture. He put rugs and cushions on the polished wood floors, mattresses and coat rails in the bedrooms. He had no chairs other than six stools of the kind used by guitarists in recording studios.

Both Cameron and Beep Dewar were students at Berkeley, the San Francisco branch of the University of California. Cam was a weirdo who dressed like a middle-aged man and was more conservative than Barry Goldwater. But Beep was cool, and she introduced Walli to her friends, some of whom lived in his neighborhood.

Walli lived here when he was not touring with the group or recording in London. While here, he spent most of his time playing the guitar. To play as apparently effortlessly as he did onstage required a high order of skill, and he never let a day go by without practicing for at least a couple of hours. After that he would work on songs: trying out chords, putting together fragments of melody, struggling to decide which were wonderful and which merely tuneful.

He wrote to Karolin once a week. It was difficult to think of things to say. It seemed unkind to tell her about movies and concerts and restaurants of the kind that she could never enjoy.

With Werner's help he had arranged to send monthly payments so that Karolin could support herself and Alice. A modest allowance in a foreign currency bought a lot in East Germany.

Karolin wrote back once a month. She had learned guitar and

formed a duo with Lili. They did protest songs and circulated tapes of their music. Otherwise her life seemed empty in comparison with his own, and most of her news was about Alice.

Like most people in the neighborhood, Walli did not lock his doors. Friends and strangers wandered in and out. He kept his favorite guitars in a locked room at the top of the house: otherwise he owned little worth stealing. Once a week, a local store filled his refrigerator and food cupboard with groceries. Guests helped themselves, and when the food ran out Walli went to restaurants.

In the evenings he saw movies and plays, went to hear bands, or hung out with other musicians, drinking beer and smoking marijuana, in their homes or his own. There was a lot to see on the street: impromptu gigs, street theater, and performance art events that people called "happenings." In the summer of 1967 the neighborhood suddenly became famous as the world center of the hippie movement. When schools and colleges closed for the vacation, youngsters from all over America hitchhiked to San Francisco and headed for the corner of Haight and Ashbury. The police decided to turn a blind eye to the widespread use of marijuana and LSD, and to people having sex more or less publicly in Buena Vista Park. And all the girls were taking the contraceptive pill.

The girls were Walli's only problem.

Tammy and Lisa were typical. They came from Dallas, Texas, on a Greyhound bus. Tammy was blond; Lisa was Hispanic; both were eighteen. They had planned just to ask for Walli's autograph and had been amazed to find his door open and him sitting on a giant cushion on the floor playing an acoustic guitar.

After their bus ride they needed a shower, they said, and he told them to go right ahead. They had showered together without closing the bathroom door, as Walli discovered in an absentminded moment, thinking about harmonies, when he went in there to pee. Was it coincidence that at that very moment Tammy was soaping Lisa's olive-skinned little breasts with her white hands?

Walli left and used the other bathroom, but it took all his strength.

The postman brought his mail, including letters forwarded from London by Mark Batchelor, Plum Nellie's manager. One was addressed in Karolin's handwriting and had an East German stamp. Walli set it aside to read later.

It was a normal day in Haight-Ashbury. A musician friend strolled in and they started writing a song together, but it came to nothing. Dave Williams and Beep Dewar stopped by: Dave was living at her parents' house and looking for a property to buy. A dealer called Jesus dropped off a pound of marijuana and Walli hid most of it in the cabinet of a guitar amplifier. He did not mind sharing; but, if he did not ration it, all of it would be gone by nightfall.

In the evening Walli went to a diner with a few friends, taking Tammy and Lisa. Four years after leaving the Soviet bloc he still marveled at the abundance of food in America: big steaks, juicy hamburgers, piles of French fries, mountainous crisp salads, thick milk shakes, all for next to nothing, and coffee with free refills! Not that such food was expensive in East Germany—it just did not exist there at all. Butchers were always short of the best cuts of meat, and restaurants grumpily served mean portions of unappealing food. Walli had never seen a milk shake there.

Over dinner Walli learned that Lisa's father was a doctor serving the Mexican community in Dallas, and that she hoped to study medicine and follow in his footsteps. Tammy's family ran a profitable gas station, but her brothers would take it over, and she was going to art school to study fashion design with the aim of opening a clothing store. They were ordinary girls, but this was 1967 and they were taking the pill and they wanted to get laid.

It was a warm night. After eating they all went to the park. They sat down with a group of people singing gospel songs. Walli joined in, and no one recognized him in the dark. Tammy was tired after the bus journey, and she lay down with her head in his lap. He stroked her long blond hair and she went to sleep.

A little after midnight, people began to leave. Walli strolled home, not noticing until he got there that Tammy and Lisa were still with him. "Do you to have a place to spend the night?" he said.

Tammy said in her Texas accent: "We could sleep in the park."

Walli said: "You can crash on my floor if you want."

Lisa said: "Would you like to sleep with one of us?"

Tammy said: "Or both?"

Walli smiled. "No, I have a girlfriend, Karolin, back in Berlin."

"Is that true?" said Lisa. "I read it in the paper, but . . ."

"It's true."

"And you have a baby daughter?"

"She's three years old, now. Her name is Alice."

"But no one still believes in fidelity, and all that crap, do they? Especially not in San Francisco. All you need is love, right?"

"Good night, girls."

He went upstairs to the bedroom he normally used and got undressed. He could hear the girls moving around downstairs. It was just after one thirty when he got into bed—an early night for a musician.

This was the time of day when he liked to read and reread Karolin's letters. It soothed him to think about her, and he often fell asleep imagining that she was in his arms. He settled on his mattress, sitting upright with his back to a pillow propped against the wall, and pulled the sheet up under his chin. Then he opened the envelope.

He read:

> *Dear Walli—*

That was strange. She normally wrote "My beloved Walli" or "My love."

> *I know this letter will bring you pain and distress, and for that I am so sorry that my heart is almost breaking.*

What on earth could have happened? He read on fast.

> *You left four years ago and there is no hope of us being together in the foreseeable future. I'm weak, and I cannot face a lifetime alone.*

She was ending their affair—she was breaking up with him. It was the last thing he expected.

> *I have met someone, a good man who loves me.*

She had a boyfriend! This was even worse. She had betrayed Walli. He began to feel angry. Lisa had been right: no one still believed in fidelity and all that crap.

Odo is the pastor of St. Gertrud's Church in Berlin-Mitte.

Walli said aloud: "A fucking clergyman!"

He will love and care for my baby.

"She calls her 'my baby'—but Alice is my baby too!"

We are going to get married. Your parents are upset but they have not ceased to be kind to me, as they always are to everyone. Even your sister Lili tries to understand, though she finds it difficult.

I bet she does, thought Walli. Lili would hold out longest.

You made me happy for a short while, and you gave me my precious Alice, and for that I will always love you.

Walli felt hot tears on his cheeks.

I hope that in years to come you will find it in your heart to forgive me and Odo, and that one day we may meet as friends, perhaps when we are old and gray.

"In hell, maybe," said Walli.

> *With love,*
> *Karolin*

The door opened and Tammy and Lisa came in.

Walli's vision was blurred with tears, but it seemed to him that they were both naked.

Lisa said: "What's the matter?"

Tammy said: "Why are you crying?"

Walli said: "Karolin broke up with me. She's going to marry the pastor."

Tammy said: "I'm so sorry," and Lisa said: "Poor you."

Walli was ashamed of his tears but he could not stop them. He threw the letter down, rolled sideways, and pulled the sheet over his head.

They got into bed either side of him. He opened his eyes. Tammy, facing him, touched the tears on his face with a gentle finger. Behind him, Lisa pressed her warm body against his back.

He managed to say: "I don't want this."

Tammy said: "You shouldn't be alone, feeling so sad. We'll just cuddle you. Close your eyes."

He yielded, and shut his eyes. Slowly his anguish turned to numbness. His mind emptied and he drifted into a doze.

When he woke up, Tammy was kissing his mouth and Lisa was sucking his penis.

He made love to each of them in turn. Tammy was gentle and sweet; Lisa was energetic and passionate. He was grateful to them for consoling him in his grief.

But, for all that, no matter how he tried, he could not come.

CHAPTER FORTY

The mine dog was getting tired.

He was a thin Vietnamese boy wearing nothing but cotton shorts. He had to be about thirteen years old, Jasper Murray guessed. The boy had been so foolish as to go into the jungle to gather nuts this morning just when a platoon of D Company—"Desperadoes"—was setting out on its mission.

His hands were tied behind his back and attached by a string, thirty yards long, to a corporal's web belt. The boy walked along the path ahead of the company. But it had been a long morning, and he was still a kid, and now his steps were faltering, causing the men to catch up with him inadvertently. When that happened, Sergeant Smithy threw a bullet at him, hitting him on the head or back, and the kid would cry out and go faster.

The jungle trails were mined and booby-trapped by the resistance, the Vietcong insurgents, usually called Charlie. The mines were all improvised: reloaded American artillery shells; old U.S. Army Bouncing Betties; dud bombs turned into real ones; even French army pressure mines left over from the fifties.

Using a Vietnamese peasant as a mine dog was not very unusual, although no one would admit it back in the States. Sometimes the slants knew which stretches of the trail had been mined. Other times they were somehow able to see warning signs invisible to the grunts. And if the mine dog failed to spot the trap he would get killed instead of them. No downside.

Jasper was disgusted, but he had seen worse things in the six months he had so far spent in Vietnam. In Jasper's opinion, men of all nations were capable of savage cruelty, especially when they were scared. He knew that the British army had committed gruesome atrocities in Kenya: his father had been there, and now, whenever Kenya was mentioned, Dad looked pale and muttered something feeble about brutality on both sides.

However, D Company was special.

It was part of Tiger Force, the Special Forces unit of the 101st Airborne Division. Supreme commander General William Westmoreland proudly called them "my fire brigade." Instead of regular uniforms they wore tiger-striped battle dress without insignia. They were allowed to grow beards and carry handguns openly. Their specialty was pacification.

Jasper had joined D Company a week ago. The assignment was probably a bureaucratic error: he did not particularly belong here, but Tiger Force mixed men from many different units and divisions. This was his first mission with them. In this platoon there were twenty-five men, about half black and half white.

They did not know Jasper was British. Most GIs had never met a Brit, and he had got bored with being an object of curiosity. He had changed his accent, and to them he sounded Canadian, or something. Never again did he want to explain that he did not actually know the Beatles.

Their mission today was to "cleanse" a village.

They were in Quang Ngai Province, in the northern part of South Vietnam known to the army as I Corps Tactical Zone, or just "the northern region." Like about half of South Vietnam, it was ruled not by the regime in Saigon but by the Vietcong guerrillas, who organized village government and even collected taxes.

"The Vietnamese people just don't understand the American way," said the man walking alongside Jasper. He was Neville, a tall Texan with an ironic sense of humor. "When the Vietcong took over this region there was a lot of uncultivated land, owned by rich people in Saigon who couldn't be bothered to farm it, so Charlie gave it to the peasants. Then, when we started to win territory back, the Saigon government returned the land to the original owners. Now the peasants are mad at us, can you believe that? They don't get the concept of private property. That tells you how dumb they are."

Corporal John Donellan, a black soldier known as Donny, overheard and said: "You're just a fucking Communist, Neville."

"I am not—I voted for Goldwater," Neville said mildly. "He promised to keep uppity Negroes in their place."

The others within earshot laughed: this kind of banter was enjoyed by soldiers. It helped them deal with their fear.

Jasper, too, liked Neville's subversive sarcasm. But during their first rest stop this morning he had noticed Neville rolling a joint, and sprinkling into the marijuana some of the unrefined heroin they called brown sugar. If Neville was not a junkie, he soon would be.

Guerrilla fighters moved among the people as fish swam in the sea, according to the Chinese Communist leader Chairman Mao. General Westmoreland's strategy for defeating the Vietcong fish was to take away their sea. Three hundred thousand peasants in Quang Ngai were being rounded up and moved to sixty-eight fortified concentration camps, to leave the landscape deserted but for the Vietcong.

Except that it was not working. As Neville said: "These people! They act as if we have no right to come to their country and order them to leave their homes and their fields and go live in a prison camp. What is wrong with them?" Many peasants evaded the roundup and stayed close to their land. Others went, then escaped from the crowded, unsanitary camps and came home. Either way, they were now legitimate targets in the eyes of the army. "If there are people who are out there— and not in the camps—they're pink as far as we're concerned," General Westmoreland said. "They're Communist sympathizers." The lieutenant briefing the platoon had put it even more clearly. "There are no friendlies," he had said. "Do you hear me? There are no friendlies. No one is supposed to be here. Shoot anything that moves."

The target this morning was a village that had been evacuated and then reoccupied. Their job was to clean it out and level it.

First they had to find it. Navigation was difficult in the jungle. Landmarks were few and visibility was restricted.

And Charlie could be anywhere, maybe a yard away. The knowledge kept them all on edge. Jasper had learned to look *through* the foliage, from one layer to the next, scanning for a color, a shape, or a texture that did not fit. It was difficult to stay vigilant when you were tired, dripping with sweat, and pestered by bugs, but men who let their guard down at the wrong moment got killed.

There were different kinds of jungle, too. Bamboo thickets and elephant grass were impassable in practice, though the army high command refused to admit it. Canopy forests were easier, for the dim light restricted the undergrowth. Rubber plantations were best: the trees in neat rows, the undergrowth kept down, usable roads. Today Jasper was in a mixed forest, with banyan, mangrove, and jackfruit trees, the green backdrop splashed with the bright colors of tropical forest flowers, orchids and arums and chrysanthemums. Hell has never looked so pretty, Jasper was thinking when the bomb went off.

He was deafened by a bang and thrown to the ground. His shock did not last long. He rolled away from the trail, stopped in the flimsy shelter of a bush, deployed his M16 rifle, and looked around.

At the head of the line of men, five bodies lay on the ground. None was moving. Jasper had seen death in combat several times since arriving in Vietnam, but he would never get used to it. A moment ago there had been five walking, talking human beings, men who had told him a joke or bought him a drink or given him a hand scrambling over a deadfall; and now there was just a mess of mangled bloody chunks of meat on the ground.

He could guess what had happened. Someone had stepped on a hidden pressure mine. Why had the mine dog not set it off? The boy must have spotted it and had the presence of mind to keep quiet and walk around it. Now he was nowhere to be seen. He had got the better of his captors in the end.

Another of the men came to the same conclusion. He was Mad Jack Baxter, a tall Midwesterner with a black beard. Screaming, "That fucking slant led us into it!" he ran forward, firing his rifle, sending rounds uselessly into the greenery, wasting ammunition. "I'll kill the motherfucker!" he screamed. Then his twenty-round magazine was empty and he stopped.

They were all angry, but others were more sensible. Sergeant Smithy was already on the radio, calling in medevac. Corporal Donny was kneeling down, optimistically looking for a pulse in one of the prone bodies. Jasper saw that a chopper could not possibly land on this narrow trail. He jumped up and yelled to Smithy: "I'll look for a clearing!"

Smithy nodded. "McCain and Frazer, go with Murray," he shouted.

Jasper checked that he had a couple of Willie Petes, white phosphorus grenades, then struck out from the path, followed by the other two.

He looked for signs that the terrain might be turning rocky or sandy so that the vegetation might thin out and form a clearing. He was careful to note what landmarks he could, so as not to get lost. After a couple of minutes they emerged from the jungle onto the banked edge of a rice paddy.

At the far side of the field Jasper saw three or four figures wearing the thin cotton pajamas that were the everyday clothing of peasants. Before he could count them they had spotted him and melted into the jungle.

He wondered whether they were from the target village. If so, he had inadvertently warned them of the company's approach. Well, that was too bad: saving the injured took priority.

McCain and Frazer ran around the edge of the paddy, securing the perimeter. Jasper exploded a Willie Pete. It set fire to the rice, but the shoots were green and the flames soon went out. However, a column of thick white phosphorus smoke rose into the air, signaling his location.

Jasper looked around. Charlie knew that when the Americans were preoccupied with their dead and wounded it was a good time to attack them. Jasper held his M16 in two hands and scanned the jungle, ready to drop to the ground and shoot back if they were fired on. McCain and Frazer were doing the same, he saw. In all probability none of them would get the chance to duck. A sniper in the trees would have all the time in the world to draw a bead and fire an accurate deadly shot. It was always like that in this fucking war, Jasper thought. Charlie sees us but we don't see him. He hits and runs. Next day the sniper is pulling up weeds in a rice paddy and pretending to be a simple farmer who wouldn't know one end of a Kalashnikov from the other.

While he waited he thought of home. I could be working for the *Western Mail* now, he mused, sitting in a comfortable council chamber, dozing while an alderman drones on about the dangers of inadequate street lighting, instead of sweating in a rice paddy wondering if I'll take a bullet in the next few seconds.

He thought of his family and friends. His sister, Anna, had become a big shot in the book world after discovering a brilliant Russian dissident writer who went under the pseudonym of Ivan Kuznetsov. Evie Williams, who had once had an adolescent crush on Jasper, was now a movie star living in Los Angeles. Dave and Walli were millionaire rock stars. But Jasper was a foot soldier on the losing side in a cruel, stupid war a thousand miles from nowhere.

He wondered about the antiwar movement in the States. Were they making headway? Or were people still fooled by the propaganda that protesters were all Communists and drug addicts who wanted to undermine America? There would be a presidential election next year, 1968. Would Johnson be defeated? Would the winner stop the war?

The chopper landed and Jasper led the stretcher team through the jungle to the site of the explosion. He remembered his landmarks and found the platoon without difficulty. As soon as he arrived he could see, from the attitudes of the men standing around, that all the casualties were dead. The medevac team would be taking back five body bags.

The survivors were fuming. "That slant led us right into a goddamn trap," said Corporal Donny. "Ain't that some kind of fuckin' us around?"

"Fuckin'-A," said Mad Jack.

As always, Neville pretended to agree while implying the contrary. "Fool kid probably thought we might kill him when we had no more use for him," he said. "Too dumb to realize that Sergeant Smithy was planning to take him home to Philadelphia and put him through college." No one laughed.

Jasper told Smithy about the peasants he had seen in the rice paddy. "Our village must be in that direction," Smithy said.

The company went with the bodies back to the chopper. After it took off, Donny deployed an M2 flamethrower to napalm the rice field, burning the entire crop in a few minutes. "Good work," said Smithy. "Now they know that if they come back they won't have anything to eat."

Jasper said to him: "I guess the chopper will have warned the villagers. We'll probably find the place empty." Or, Jasper thought, there could be an ambush; but he did not say that.

"Empty is okay," said Smithy. "We'll flatten the place anyway. And intelligence says there are tunnels. We have to find those and destroy them."

The Vietnamese had been digging tunnels since the start of their war against the French colonists in 1946. Beneath the jungle were literally hundreds of miles of passageways, ammunition dumps, dormitories, kitchens, workshops, and even hospitals. They were difficult to destroy. Water traps at regular intervals protected the inhabitants from being smoked out. Aerial bombing usually missed the target. The only way to damage them was from the inside.

But first the tunnel had to be found.

Sergeant Smithy led the platoon along a trail from the rice field into a small plantation of coconut palms. When they emerged from the palms they could see the village, about a hundred houses overlooking cultivated fields. There was no sign of life, but all the same they entered cautiously.

The place appeared deserted.

The men went from house to house, yelling: *"Didi mau!"* which was Vietnamese for "Get out!" Jasper looked into a house and saw the shrine that was the center of most Vietnamese homes: a display of candles, scrolls, incense pots, and tapestries dedicated to the family's ancestors. Then Corporal Donny deployed the flamethrower. The building had walls of woven bamboo daubed with mud, and a roof of palm leaves, and the napalm quickly set the whole place blazing.

Walking toward the center of the village, rifle at the ready, Jasper was surprised to hear a rhythmic thumping noise. He realized he was listening to the beat of a drum, probably a *mo,* a hollow wooden instrument struck with a stick. He guessed that someone had used the *mo* to warn the villagers to flee. But why was he still drumming?

With the others he followed the noise to the middle of the village. There they found a ceremonial pond with lotus flowers in front of a small *dinh,* the building that was the center of village life: temple, meeting hall, and schoolroom.

Inside, sitting cross-legged on a floor of beaten earth, they found a shaven-headed Buddhist monk drumming on a wooden fish about eighteen inches long. He saw them enter but did not stop.

The company had one soldier who spoke a little Vietnamese. He was a white American from Iowa, but they called him Slope. Now Smith said: "Slope, ask the slant where the tunnels are."

Slope shouted at the monk in Vietnamese. The man ignored him and continued drumming.

Smithy nodded to Mad Jack, who stepped forward and kicked the monk in the face with a heavyweight U.S. Army M-1966 jungle combat boot. The man fell backward, blood coming from his mouth and nose, and his drum and stick flew in opposite directions. Creepily, he made no sound.

Jasper swallowed. He had seen Vietcong guerrillas tortured for information: it was commonplace. Though he did not like it, he thought it was reasonable; they were men who wanted to kill him. Any man in his early twenties captured in this zone was probably one of the guerrillas or someone who actively supported them, and Jasper was reconciled to such men being tortured even when there was no proof they had ever fought against the Americans. This monk might have looked like a noncombatant, but Jasper had seen a ten-year-old girl throw a grenade into a parked helicopter.

Smithy picked up the monk and held him upright, facing the soldiers. His eyes were closed but he was breathing. Slope asked him the question again.

The monk made no response.

Mad Jack picked up the wooden fish, held it by its tail, and started to beat the monk with it. He hit the man on the head, shoulders, chest, groin, and knees, pausing every now and again for Slope to ask the question.

Jasper was really uncomfortable now. Just by watching this he was committing a war crime, but it was not so much the illegality that bothered him: he knew that when U.S. Army investigators looked into allegations of atrocities they always found insufficient evidence. He just did not see that this monk deserved it. Jasper was sickened, and turned away.

He did not blame the men. In every place, in every time, in every country there were men who would do this kind of thing, given the right circumstances. Jasper blamed the officers who knew what was happening and did nothing, the generals who lied to the press and the people back in Washington, and most of all the politicians who did not have the courage to stand up and say: "This is wrong."

A moment later Slope said: "Give it up, Jack, the fucker's dead."

Smithy said: "Shit." He let go of the monk, who fell lifeless to the ground. "We have to find the fucking tunnels."

Corporal Donny and four others came into the temple dragging three Vietnamese: a man and a woman of middle age, and a girl of about fifteen. "This family thought they could hide from us in the coconut shed," said Donny.

The three Vietnamese stared in horror at the body of the monk, his robes soaked in blood, his face a pulpy mass that hardly looked human.

Smithy said: "Tell them they're going to look like that unless they show us the tunnels."

Slope translated. The peasant man answered him. Slope said: "He says there are no tunnels in this village."

"Lying motherfucker," said Smithy.

Jack said: "Shall I . . . ?"

Smithy looked thoughtful. "Do the girl, Jack," he said. "Make the parents watch."

Jack looked eager. He ripped the girl's pajamas off, causing her to scream. He threw her to the ground. Her body was pale and slender. Donny held her down. Jack pulled out his penis, already half erect, and rubbed it to stiffen it.

Once again Jasper was horrified but not surprised. Rape was not commonplace, but it happened too frequently. Men occasionally reported it, usually when they were new to Vietnam. The army would investigate and find the allegations unsupported by evidence, meaning that all the other soldiers said they did not want any trouble and anyway they had seen nothing, and the matter would end there.

The older woman started talking, a stream of hysterical, pleading words. Slope said: "She says the girl is a virgin and really only a child."

"She's no child," said Smithy. "Look at the black fur on that little snatch."

"The mother swears by all the gods that there are no tunnels here. She says she doesn't support the Vietcong because she used to be the village moneylender but Charlie stopped her."

Smithy said: "Do it, Jack."

Jack lay on the girl, his big frame hiding most of her slight body. He seemed to be having difficulty penetrating. The other men shouted encouragement and made jokes. Jack gave a powerful thrust, and the girl screamed.

He pumped vigorously for a minute. The mother continued to plead, though Slope did not bother to translate. The father was silent, but Jasper saw tears streaming down his face. Jack grunted a couple of times, then stopped and withdrew. There was blood on the girl's thighs, bright red on her ivory skin.

Smithy said: "Who's next?"

"I'll do her," said Donny, unzipping.

Jasper left the temple.

This was not normal. Any pretext of getting the father to talk was now redundant: if he had known anything he would have revealed it before the rape began. Jasper had run out of excuses for the men of this platoon. They were out of control. General Westmoreland had created a monster and deliberately let it loose. They were beyond sanity. They were not even animals; they were worse than that; they were mad, evil fiends.

Neville followed him out. "Remember, Jasper," he said, "this is necessary to win the hearts and minds of the Vietnamese people."

Jasper knew that this was Neville's way of bearing the unbearable, but all the same he could not stomach Neville's humor at this moment. "Why don't you shut the fuck up?" he said, and walked away.

He was not the only one sickened by the scene in the temple. About half the platoon was out here, watching the village burn. A pall of black smoke lay over the village like a shroud. Jasper could hear the girl screaming in the temple, but after a while she stopped. Minutes later, he heard a shot, then another.

But what was he going to do about it? If he made a complaint, nothing would be done except that the army would find ways to punish him for stirring up trouble. But maybe, he thought, he should do it anyway. In any case, he vowed to go back to the States and spend the rest of his life exposing the liars and fools who made this kind of atrocity happen.

Then Donny came out of the temple and approached him. "Smithy wants you," he said.

Jasper followed the corporal back into the temple.

The girl lay splayed on the floor, a bullet hole in her forehead. Jasper also noticed a bleeding bite mark on her small breast.

The father was dead, too.

The mother was on her knees, begging, presumably, for mercy.

Smithy said: "You haven't lost your cherry yet, Murray."

He meant that Jasper had not yet committed a war crime.

Jasper knew what was coming.

Smithy said: "Shoot the old woman."

"Fuck you, Smithy," said Jasper. "Shoot her yourself."

Mad Jack raised his rifle and pressed the end of the barrel into the side of Jasper's neck.

Suddenly everyone was silent and still.

Smithy said: "Shoot the old woman, or Jack will shoot you."

Jasper had no doubt that Smithy was willing to give the order, and that Jack would obey. And he understood why. They needed him to be complicit. Once he had killed the woman he would be as guilty as any of them, and that would prevent him making trouble.

He looked around. All eyes were on him. No one protested or even looked uneasy. This was a rite they had performed before, he could tell. No doubt they did it with every newcomer to the company. Jasper wondered how many men had refused the order, and died. They would have been recorded as killed by enemy fire. No downside.

Smithy said: "Don't take too long making up your mind, we have work to do."

They were going to kill the woman anyway, Jasper knew. He would not save her by refusing to do it himself. He would be sacrificing his own life for nothing.

Jack prodded him with the rifle.

Jasper raised his M16 and pointed it at the woman's forehead. She had dark brown eyes, he saw, and a little gray in her black hair. She did not move away from his gun, or even flinch, but continued pleading in words he could not comprehend.

Jasper touched the selector lever on the left side of the gun, moving it from "Safe" to "Semi," allowing it to fire a single round.

His hands were quite steady.

He pulled the trigger.

PART SIX

FLOWER

1968

Jasper Murray spent two years in the army, one year of training in the USA and one of combat in Vietnam. He was discharged in January 1968 without ever having been wounded. He felt lucky.

Daisy Williams paid for him to fly to London to see his family. His sister, Anna, was now editorial director of Rowley Publishing. She had at last married Hank Remington, who was proving to be more enduring than most pop stars. The house in Great Peter Street was strangely quiet: the youngsters had all moved out, leaving only Lloyd and Daisy in residence. Lloyd was now a minister in the Labour government and therefore rarely home. Ethel died that January, and her funeral was held a few hours before Jasper was due to fly to New York.

The service was at the Calvary Gospel Hall in Aldgate, a small wooden shack where she had married Bernie Leckwith fifty years earlier, when her brother, Billy, and countless boys like him were fighting in the frozen mud trenches of the First World War.

The little chapel could seat a hundred or so worshippers, with another twenty or thirty standing at the back; but more than a thousand people turned up to say good-bye to Eth Leckwith.

The pastor moved the service outside and the police closed the street to cars. The speakers got up on chairs to address the crowd. Ethel's two children, Lloyd Williams and Millie Avery, both in their fifties, stood at the front with most of her grandchildren and a handful of great-grandchildren.

Evie Williams read the parable of the Good Samaritan from the Gospel of Luke. Dave and Walli brought guitars and sang "I Miss Ya, Alicia." Half the cabinet were there. So was Earl Fitzherbert. Two buses from Aberowen brought a hundred Welsh voices to swell the hymn singing.

But most of the mourners were ordinary Londoners whose lives had been touched by Ethel. They stood in the January cold, the men holding their caps in their hands, the women shushing their children, the old people shivering in their cheap coats; and when the pastor prayed for Ethel to rest in peace, they all said amen.

. . .

George Jakes had a simple plan for 1968: Bobby Kennedy would become president and stop the war.

Not all of Bobby's aides were in favor. Dennis Wilson was happy for Bobby to remain simply the senator from New York. "People will say that we already have a Democratic president and Bobby should support Lyndon Johnson, not run against him," he said. "It's unheard-of."

They were at the National Press Club in Washington on January 30, 1968, waiting for Bobby, who was about to have breakfast with fifteen reporters.

"That's not true," George said. "Truman was opposed by Strom Thurmond and Henry Wallace."

"That was twenty years ago. Anyway, Bobby can't win the Democratic nomination."

"I think he'll be more popular than Johnson."

"Popularity has nothing to do with it," Wilson said. "Most of the convention delegates are controlled by the party's power brokers: labor leaders, state governors, and city mayors. Men like Daley." The mayor of Chicago, Richard Daley, was the worst kind of old-fashioned politician, ruthless and corrupt. "And the one thing Johnson is good at is infighting."

George shook his head in disgust. He was in politics to defy those old power structures, not give in to them. So was Bobby, in his heart. "Bobby will get such a bandwagon rolling in the country that the power brokers won't be able to ignore him."

"Haven't you talked to him about this?" Wilson was pretending to be incredulous. "Haven't you heard him say that people will see him as selfish and ambitious if he runs against a Democratic incumbent?"

"More people think he's the natural heir to his brother."

"When he spoke at Brooklyn College, the students had a placard that said: HAWK, DOVE—OR CHICKEN?"

This jibe had stung Bobby and dismayed George. But now George tried to put it in an optimistic light. "That means they want him to run!" he said. "They know that he's the only contender who can unite old and young, black and white, and rich and poor, and can get everyone working together to end the war and give blacks the justice they deserve."

Wilson's mouth twisted in a sneer but, before he could pour scorn on George's idealism, Bobby walked in, and everyone sat down to breakfast.

George's feelings about Lyndon Johnson had undergone a reverse. Johnson had started so well, passing the Civil Rights Act of 1964 and the Voting Rights Act of 1965, and planning the War on Poverty. But Johnson failed to understand foreign policy, as George's father, Greg, had forecast. All Johnson knew was that he did not want to be the president who lost Vietnam to the Communists. Consequently he was now hopelessly mired in a dirty war and dishonestly telling the American people he was winning it.

The words had also changed. When George was young, *black* was a vulgar term, *colored* was more dainty, and *Negro* was the polite word, used by the liberal *New York Times,* always with a capital letter, like *Jew.* Now *Negro* was considered condescending and *colored* evasive, and everyone talked about black people, the black community, black pride, and even black power. Black is beautiful, they said. George was not sure how much difference the words made.

He did not eat much breakfast: he was too busy making notes of the questions and Bobby's answers in preparation for a press release.

One of the journalists asked: "How do you feel about the pressure on you to run for president?"

George looked up from his notes and saw Bobby give a brief, humorless grin, then say: "Badly. Badly."

George tensed. Bobby was too damn honest sometimes.

The journalist said: "What do you think about Senator McCarthy's campaign?"

He was talking not about the notorious Senator Joe McCarthy, who had hunted down Communists in the fifties, but a completely opposite character, Senator Eugene McCarthy, a liberal who was a poet as well as a politician. Two months ago Gene McCarthy had declared his intention of seeking the Democratic nomination, running as the antiwar candidate against Johnson. He had already been dismissed as a no-hoper by the press.

Now Bobby replied: "I think McCarthy's campaign is going to help Johnson." Bobby still would not call Lyndon the president. George's friend Skip Dickerson, who worked for Johnson, was scornful about this.

"Well, will you run?"

Bobby had lots of ways of not answering this question, a whole repertoire of evasive responses; but today he did not use any of them. "No," he said.

George dropped his pencil. Where the hell had that come from?

Bobby added: "In no conceivable circumstances would I run."

George wanted to say: *In that case, what the fuck are we all doing here?*

He noticed Dennis Wilson smirking.

He was tempted to walk out there and then. But he was too polite. He stayed in his seat and carried on making notes until the breakfast ended.

Back in Bobby's office on Capitol Hill, he wrote the press release, working like an automaton. He changed Bobby's quote to: "In no foreseeable circumstances would I run," but it made little difference.

Three staffers resigned from Bobby's team that afternoon. They had not come to Washington to work for a loser.

George was angry enough to quit, but he kept his mouth shut. He wanted to think. And he wanted to talk to Verena.

She was in town, and staying at his apartment as always. She now had her own closet in his bedroom, where she kept cold-weather clothes she never needed in Atlanta.

She was so upset she was near tears that evening. "He's all we have!" she said. "Do you know how many casualties we suffered in Vietnam last year?"

"Of course I do," said George. "Eighty thousand. I put it in one of Bobby's speeches, but he didn't use that part."

"Eighty thousand men killed or wounded or missing," Verena said. "It's awful—and now it will go on."

"Casualties will certainly be higher this year."

"Bobby has missed his shot at greatness. But why? Why did he do it?"

"I'm too angry to talk to him about it, but I believe he genuinely suspects his own motives. He's asking himself whether he wants this for the sake of his country, or his ego. He's tormented by such questions."

"Martin is too," Verena said. "He asks himself whether inner-city riots are his fault."

"But Dr. King keeps those doubts to himself. You have to, as a leader."

"Do you think Bobby planned this announcement?"

"No, he did it on impulse, I'm sure. That's one of the things that make him difficult to work for."

"What will you do?"

"Quit, probably. I'm still thinking about it."

They were getting changed to go out for a quiet dinner, and at the same time waiting for the news to come on TV. Tying a wide tie with bold stripes, George watched Verena in the mirror as she put on her underwear. Her body had changed in the five years since he had first seen her naked. She would be twenty-nine this year, and she no longer had the leggy charm of a foal. Instead she had gained poise and grace. George thought her mature look was even more beautiful. She had grown her hair in the bushy style called a "natural," which somehow emphasized the allure of her green eyes.

Now she sat in front of his shaving mirror to do her eye makeup. "If you quit, you could come to Atlanta and work for Martin," she said.

"No," said George. "Dr. King is a single-issue campaigner. Protesters protest, but politicians change the world."

"So what would you do?"

"Run for Congress, probably."

Verena put down her mascara brush and turned to look directly at him. "Wow," she said. "That came out of left field."

"I came to Washington to fight for civil rights, but the injustice suffered by blacks isn't just a matter of rights," George said. He had been thinking about this a long time. "It's about housing and unemployment and the Vietnam War, where young black men are being killed every day. Black people's lives are affected even by events in Moscow and Peking, in the long term. A man like Dr. King inspires people, but you have to be an all-around politician in order to do any real good."

"I guess we need both," Verena said, and went back to doing her eyes.

George put on his best suit, which always made him feel better. He would have a martini later, maybe two. For seven years his life had been bound up inextricably with Robert Kennedy's. Maybe it was time to move on.

He said: "Does it ever occur to you that our relationship is peculiar?"

She laughed. "Of course! We live apart and meet every month or two for mad passionate sex. And we've being doing this for years!"

"A man might do what you do, and meet his mistress on business trips," George said. "Especially if he were married. That would be normal."

"I kind of like that idea," she said. "Meat and potatoes at home, and a little caviar when away."

"I'm glad to be the caviar, anyway."

She licked her lips. "Mm, salty."

George smiled. He would not think about Bobby anymore this evening, he decided.

The news came on TV, and George turned up the volume. He expected Bobby's announcement to be the first report, but there was a bigger story. During the New Year holiday that the Vietnamese called Tet, the Vietcong had launched a massive offensive. They had attacked five of the six largest cities, thirty-six provincial capitals, and sixty small towns. The assault had astounded the U.S. military by its size: no one had imagined the guerrillas capable of such a large-scale operation.

The Pentagon said the Vietcong forces had been repelled, but George did not believe it.

The newscaster said further major attacks were expected tomorrow.

George said to Verena: "I wonder what this will do for Gene McCarthy's campaign."

. . .

Beep Dewar persuaded Walli Franck to make a political speech.

At first he refused. He was a guitar player, and he feared he would make a fool of himself, like a senator singing pop songs in public. But he came from a political family, and his upbringing would not allow him to be apathetic. He remembered his parents' scorn for those West Germans who failed to protest about the Berlin Wall and the repressive East German government. They were as guilty as the Communists, his mother said. Now Walli realized that if he turned down a chance to speak a few words in favor of peace, he was as bad as Lyndon Johnson.

Plus he found Beep pretty much irresistible.

So he said yes.

She picked him up in Dave's red Dodge Charger and drove him to Gene McCarthy's San Francisco campaign headquarters, where he talked to a small army of young enthusiasts who had spent the day knocking on doors.

He felt nervous when he stood up in front of the audience. He had prepared his opening line. He spoke slowly, but informally. "Some people told me I should stay out of politics because I'm not American," he said in a conversational tone. Then he gave a little shrug and said: "But those people think it's okay if Americans go to Vietnam and kill people, so I guess it's not so bad for a German to come to San Francisco and just talk . . ."

To his surprise there was a howl of laughter and a round of applause. Maybe this would be all right.

Young people had been flocking to support McCarthy's campaign since the Tet Offensive. They were all neatly dressed. The boys were clean shaven and had midlength hair. The girls wore twinsets and saddle shoes. They had changed their appearance to persuade voters that McCarthy was the right president not just for hippies but for middle Americans too. Their slogan was: "Neat and clean for Gene."

Walli paused, making them wait, then he touched his shoulder-length blond locks and said: "Sorry about my hair."

They laughed and clapped again. This was just like show business, Walli realized. If you were a star, they would love you just for being more or less normal. At a Plum Nellie concert, the audience would cheer wildly at literally anything Walli or Dave said into the microphone. And a joke became ten times as funny when told by a celebrity.

"I'm not a politician. I can't make a political speech . . . but I guess you guys hear as many of those as you want."

"Right on!" shouted one of the boys, and they laughed again.

"But I have some experience, you know? I used to live in a Communist country. One day the police caught me singing a Chuck Berry song called 'Back in the USA.' So they smashed up my guitar."

The audience went quiet.

"It was my first guitar. In those days I had only one. Broke my guitar, broke my heart. So, you see, I know about Communism. I probably know more about it than Lyndon Johnson. I hate Communism." He raised his voice a little. "And I'm *still* against the war."

They broke out into cheers again.

"You know some people believe Jesus is coming back to earth one day. I don't know if that's true." They were uneasy with this, not sure how to take it. Then Walli said: "If he comes to America he'll probably be called a Communist."

He glanced sideways at Beep, who was laughing along with the rest. She was wearing a sweater and a short but respectable skirt. Her hair was cut in a neat bob. She was still sexy, though: she could not hide that.

"Jesus will probably be arrested by the FBI for un-American activities," Walli went on. "But he won't be surprised: it's pretty similar to what happened to him the first time he came to earth."

Walli had hardly planned beyond his first sentence, and now he was making it up as he went along, but they were delighted. However, he decided to quit while he was ahead.

He had prepared his ending. "I just came here to say one thing to you, and that's: Thank you. Thank you on behalf of millions of people all over the world who want to end this evil war. We appreciate the hard work you're doing here. Keep it up, and I hope to God you win. Good night."

He stepped back from the microphone. Beep came up to him and took his arm, and together they left by the back door, with cheers and applause still ringing out. As soon as they were in Dave's car, Beep said: "My God—you were brilliant! You should run for president!"

He smiled and shrugged. "People are always pleased to find that a pop star is a human being. That's really all it is."

"But you spoke sincerely—and you were so witty!"

"Thanks."

"Maybe you get it from your mother. Didn't you tell me she was in politics?"

"Not really. There's no normal politics in East Germany. She was a city councilor, before the Communists cracked down. By the way, did you notice my accent?"

"Just a little bit."

"I was afraid of that." He was sensitive about his accent. People associated it with Nazis in war movies. He tried to speak like an American, but it was difficult.

"Actually it's charming," Beep said. "I wish Dave could have heard you."

"Where is he, anyway?"

"London, I think. I imagined you would know."

Walli shrugged. "I know he's taking care of business somewhere. He'll show up as soon as we need to write some songs, or make a film, or go on the road again. I thought you two were going to get married."

"We are. We just haven't gotten around to it yet, he's been so busy. And, you know, my parents are cool about us sharing a bedroom when he's here, so it's not like we're desperate to get away from them."

"Nice." They reached Haight-Ashbury and Beep stopped the car outside Walli's house. "You want a cup of coffee or something?" Walli did not know why he said that: it just came out.

"Sure." Beep turned off the throaty engine.

The house was empty. Tammy and Lisa had helped Walli deal with his grief about Karolin's engagement, and he would always be grateful to them, but they had been living a fantasy life that had lasted only as long as the vacation. When summer turned to fall they had left San Francisco and gone home to attend college, like most of the hippies of 1967.

While it lasted, it had been an idyllic time.

Walli put on the new Beatles album, *Magical Mystery Tour*, then made coffee and rolled a joint. They sat on a giant cushion, Walli cross-legged, Beep with her feet tucked under her, and passed the roach. Soon Walli drifted into the mellow mood he liked so much. "I hate the Beatles," he said after a while. "They are so fucking good."

Beep giggled.

Walli said: "Weird lyrics."

"I know!"

"What does that line mean? 'Four of fish and finger pies.' It sounds like, you know, cannibalism."

"Dave explained that to me," Beep said. "In England they have seafood restaurants that sell fish in batter with French fries to go. They call it 'fish and chips.' And 'four of fish' means four pennies' worth."

"What about 'finger pie'?"

"Okay, that's when a boy puts his finger up a girl's, you know, vagina."

"And the connection?"

"It means that if you bought fish and chips for a girl she would let you finger her."

"Remember the days when that was daring?" Walli said nostalgically.

"Everything's different now, thank God," said Beep. "The old rules don't apply anymore. Love is free."

"Now it's oral sex on the first date."

"What do you like best?" Beep mused. "Giving oral sex, or receiving?"

"What a difficult question!" Walli was not sure he ought to be talking about this with his best friend's fiancée. "But I think I like receiving." He could not resist the temptation to add: "What about you?"

"I prefer giving," she said.

"Why?"

She hesitated. For a moment she looked guilty: perhaps she, too, was not sure they should be discussing this, despite her hippie talk about free love. She took a long draw on the joint and blew out smoke. Her face cleared, and she said: "Most boys are so bad at oral sex that receiving is never as exciting as it should be."

Walli took the joint from her. "If you could tell the boys of America what they need to know about giving oral sex, what would you say?"

She laughed. "Well, first of all, don't start licking right away."

"No?" Walli was surprised. "I thought it was all about licking."

"Not at all. You should be gentle at first. Just kiss it!"

Walli knew, then, that he was lost.

He looked down at Beep's legs. Her knees were pressed close together. Was that defensive? Or a sign of excitement?

Or both?

"No girl ever told me that," he said. He gave her back the joint.

He was feeling an irresistible rush of sexual excitement. Was she feeling it, too, or just playing a game with him?

She sucked the last of the smoke from the roach and dropped it in the ashtray. "Most girls are too shy to talk about what they like," she said. "The truth is that even a kiss can be too much, right at the start. In fact . . ." She gave him a direct look, and at that moment he knew that she, too, was lost. She said in a lower voice: "In fact, you can give her a thrill just by breathing on it."

"Oh, my God."

"Even better," she said, "is to breathe on it through the cotton of her underwear."

She moved slightly, parting her knees at last, and he saw that under her short skirt she was wearing white panties.

"That's amazing," he said hoarsely.

"Do you want to try it?" she said.

"Yes," said Walli. "Please."

. . .

When Jasper Murray returned to New York he went to see Mrs. Salzman. She got him an interview with Herb Gould, for a job as a researcher on the television news show *This Day*.

He was now a different proposition. Two years ago he had been a supplicant, a student journalist desperate for a job, someone to whom nobody owed anything. Now he was a veteran who had risked his life for the USA. He was older and wiser, and he was owed a debt, especially by men who had not fought. He got the job.

It was strange. He had forgotten what cold weather felt like. His clothes bothered him: a suit and a white shirt with a button-down collar and a tie. His regular business oxford shoes were so light in weight he kept thinking he was barefoot. Walking from his apartment to the office he found himself scanning the sidewalk for concealed mines.

On the other hand, he was busy. The civilian world had few of the long, infuriating periods of inactivity that characterized army life: waiting for orders, waiting for transport, waiting for the enemy. From his first day back Jasper was making phone calls, checking files, looking up information in libraries, and conducting preinterviews.

In the office of *This Day* a mild shock awaited Jasper. Sam Cakebread, his old rival on the student newspaper, was now working for the program. He was a fully fledged reporter, not having had to take time out to fight a war. Irksomely, Jasper often had to do preparatory research for stories that Sam would then report on camera.

Jasper worked on fashion, crime, music, literature, and business. He researched a story about his sister's bestseller, *Frostbite,* and its pseudonymous author, speculating about which of the known Soviet dissidents might have written it, based on writing style and prison camp experiences; concluding it was probably someone nobody had heard of.

Then they decided to do a show about the astonishing Vietcong operation that had been dubbed the Tet Offensive.

Jasper was still angry about Vietnam. His rage burned low in his guts like a damped furnace, but he had forgotten nothing, least of all his vow to expose men who lied to the American people.

When the fighting began to die down, during the second week of February, Herb Gould told Sam Cakebread to plan a summing-up report, assessing how the offensive had changed the course of the war. Sam presented his preliminary conclusions to an editorial meeting attended by the whole team, including researchers.

Sam said the Tet Offensive had been a failure for the North Vietnamese in three ways. "First, Communist forces were given the general order: 'Move forward to achieve final victory.' We know this from documents found on captured enemy troops. Second: although fighting is still going on in Hue and Khe Sanh, the Vietcong have proved unable to hold a single city. And third, they have lost more than twenty thousand men, all for nothing."

Herb Gould looked around for comment.

Jasper was very junior in this group, but he was unable to keep quiet. "I have one question for Sam," he said.

"Go ahead, Jasper," said Herb.

"What fucking planet are you living on?"

There was a moment of shocked silence at his rudeness. Then Herb said mildly: "A lot of people are skeptical about this, Jasper, but explain why—maybe without the profanity?"

"Sam has just given us President Johnson's line on Tet. Since when did this program become a propaganda agency for the White House? Shouldn't we be challenging the government's view?"

Herb did not disagree. "How would you challenge it?"

"First, documents found on captured troops cannot be taken at face value. The written orders given to soldiers are not a reliable guide to the enemy's strategic objectives. I have a translation here: 'Display to the utmost your revolutionary heroism by surmounting all hardships and difficulties.' This is not strategy, it's a pep talk."

Herb said: "So what *was* their objective?"

"To demonstrate their power and reach, and thereby to demoralize the South Vietnam regime, our troops, and the American people. And they have succeeded."

Sam said: "They still didn't take any cities."

"They don't need to hold cities—they're already there. How do you think they got to the American embassy in Saigon? They didn't parachute in, they walked around the corner! They were probably living on the next block. They don't *take* cities because they already *have* them."

Herb said: "What about Sam's third point—their casualties?"

"No Pentagon figures on enemy casualties are trustworthy," Jasper said.

"It would be a big step, for our show to tell the American people that the government lies to us about this."

"Everyone from Lyndon Johnson to the grunt on patrol in the jungle is lying about this, because they all need high kill figures to justify what they're doing. But I know the truth because I was there. In Vietnam, any dead person counts as an enemy casualty. Throw a grenade into a bomb shelter, kill everyone inside—two young men, four women, an old man, and a baby—that's eight Vietcong dead, in the official report."

Herb was dubious. "How can we be sure this is true?"

"Ask any veteran," said Jasper.

"It's hard to credit."

Jasper was right and Herb knew it, but Herb was anxious about taking such a strong line. However, Jasper judged he was ready to be talked round. "Look," said Jasper. "It's now four years since we sent the first ground combat troops to South Vietnam. Throughout that period, the Pentagon has been reporting one victory after another, and *This Day* has been repeating their statements to the American people. If we've had four years of victory, how come the enemy can penetrate to the heart of the capital city and surround the U.S. embassy? Open your eyes, will you?"

Herb was thoughtful. "So, Jasper, if you're right, and Sam's wrong, what's our story?"

"That's easy," said Jasper. "The story is the administration's credibility after the Tet Offensive. Last November Vice President Humphrey told us we're winning. In December General Palmer said the Vietcong had been defeated. In January Secretary of Defense McNamara told us the North Vietnamese were losing their will to fight. General Westmoreland himself told reporters the Communists were unable to mount a major offensive. Then one morning the Vietcong attacked almost every major city and town in South Vietnam."

Sam said: "We've never questioned the president's honesty. No television show ever has."

Jasper said: "Now's the time. Is the president lying? Half of America is asking that."

Everyone looked at Herb. It was his decision. He was silent for a long moment. Then he said: "All right. That's the title of our report. 'Is the President Lying?' Let's do it."

.   .   .

Dave Williams got an early flight from New York to San Francisco and ate an American breakfast of pancakes with bacon in first class.

Life was good. Plum Nellie was successful and he would never have to take another exam for the rest of his life. He loved Beep and he was going to marry her as soon as he could find the time.

He was the only member of the group who had not yet bought a house, but he hoped to do so today. It would be more than a house, though. His idea was to buy a place in the country, with some land, and build a recording studio. The whole group could live there while they were making an album, which took several months nowadays. Dave often recalled with a smile how they had recorded their first album in one day.

Dave was excited: he had never bought a house before. He was looking forward eagerly to seeing Beep, but he had decided to take care of business first, so that his time with her would be uninterrupted. He was met at the airport by his business manager, Mortimer Schulman. Dave had hired Morty to take care of his personal finances separately from those of the group. Morty was a middle-aged man in relaxed California clothes, a navy blazer with a blue shirt open at the neck. Because Dave was only twenty he often found that lawyers and accountants condescended to him and tried to give him instructions rather than information. Morty treated him as the boss, which he was, and laid out options, knowing that it was up to Dave himself to make the decisions.

They got into Morty's Cadillac, drove across the Bay Bridge, and headed north, passing the university town of Berkeley, where Beep was a student. As he drove, Mort said: "I received a proposition for you. It's not really my role, but I guess they thought I was the nearest thing to your personal agent."

"What proposition?"

"A television producer called Charlie Lacklow wants to talk to you about doing your own TV show."

Dave was surprised: he had not seen that one coming. "What kind of show?"

"You know, like *The Danny Kaye Show* or *The Dean Martin Show*."

"No kidding?" This was big news. Sometimes it seemed to Dave that success was falling on him like rain: hit songs, platinum albums, sellout tours, successful movies—and now this.

There were a dozen or more variety shows on American television every week, most of them headlined by a movie star or a comic. The host would introduce a guest and chat for a minute, then the guest would sing his or her latest hit, or do a comedy routine. The group had appeared as guests on many such programs, but Dave did not see how they could fit into that format as hosts. "So it would be *The Plum Nellie Show*?"

"No. *Dave Williams and Friends*. They don't want the group, just you."

Dave was dubious. "That's flattering, but . . ."

"It's a major opportunity, if you ask me. Pop groups generally have a short life, but this is your chance to become an all-around family entertainer—which is a role you can play until you're seventy."

That struck a chord. Dave had thought about what he might do when Plum Nellie were no longer popular. It happened to most pop acts, though there were exceptions—Elvis was still big. Dave was planning to marry Beep and have children, a prospect he found daunting. The time might come when he needed another way to earn a living. He had thought about becoming a record producer and artist manager: he had done well in both roles for Plum Nellie.

But this was too soon. The group was hugely popular and now, at last, making real money. "I can't do it," he said to Morty. "It might break up the group, and I can't risk that while we're doing so well."

"Should I tell Charlie Lacklow you're not interested?"

"Yeah. With regrets."

They crossed another long bridge and entered hilly country with orchards on the lower slopes, the plum and almond trees frothing pink and white blossoms. "We're in the valley of the Napa River," said Morty. He turned onto a dusty side road that wound upward. After a mile he drove through an open gate and pulled up outside a big ranch house.

"This is the first one on my list, and the nearest to San Francisco," Morty said. "I don't know if it's the kind of thing you had in mind."

They got out of the car. The place was a rambling timber-framed building that went on forever. It looked as if two or three outbuildings had been joined to the main residence at different times. Walking around to the far side, they came upon a spectacular view across the valley. "Wow," said Dave. "Beep is going to love this."

Cultivated fields fell away from the grounds of the house. "What do they grow here?" said Dave.

"Grapes."

"I don't want to be a farmer."

"You'd be a landlord. Thirty acres are rented out."

They went inside. The place was barely furnished with ill-assorted tables and chairs. There were no beds. "Does anyone live here?" Dave asked.

"No. For a few weeks every fall the grape pickers use it as a dormitory."

"And if I move in . . ."

"The farmer will find other accommodation for his seasonal workers."

Dave looked around. The place was ramshackle and derelict, but beautiful. The woodwork seemed solid. The main house had high ceilings and an elegant staircase. "I can't wait for Beep to see it," he said.

The main bedroom had the same spectacular view over the valley. He pictured himself and Beep getting up in the morning and looking out together, making coffee, and having breakfast with two or three barefoot children. It was perfect.

There was space for half a dozen guest rooms. The large detached barn, currently full of agricultural machinery, was the right size for a recording studio.

Dave wanted to buy it immediately. He told himself not to get enthusiastic too soon. He said: "What's the asking price?"

"Sixty thousand dollars."

"That's a lot."

"Two thousand dollars an acre is about the market price for a producing vineyard," Morty said. "They'll throw in the house for free."

"Plus it wants a lot of work."

"You said it. Central heating, electrical rewiring, insulation, new bathrooms . . . You could spend almost as much again fixing it up."

"Say a hundred thousand dollars, not including recording equipment."

"It's a lot of money."

Dave grinned. "Fortunately, I can afford it."

"You certainly can."

When they went outside, a pickup truck was parking. The man who got out had broad shoulders and a weathered face. He looked Mexican but he spoke without an accent. "I'm Danny Medina, the farmer here," he said. He wiped his hands on his dungarees before shaking.

"I'm thinking of buying the place," Dave said.

"Good. It will be nice to have a neighbor."

"Where do you live, Mr. Medina?"

"I have a cottage at the other end of the vineyard, just out of sight over the lip of the ridge. Are you European?"

"Yes, British."

"Europeans usually like wine."

"Do you make wine here?"

"A little. We sell most of the grapes. Americans don't like wine, except for Italian Americans, and they import it. Most people prefer cocktails or beer. But our wine is good."

"White or red?"

"Red. Would you like a couple of bottles to try?"

"Sure."

Danny reached into the cab of the pickup, pulled out two bottles, and handed them to Dave.

Dave looked at the label. "Daisy Farm Red?" he said.

Morty said: "That's the name of the place, didn't I tell you? Daisy Farm."

"Daisy is my mother's name."

Danny said: "Maybe it's an omen." He climbed back into the vehicle. "Good luck!"

As Danny drove away, Dave said: "I like this place. Let's buy it."

Morty protested: "I have five more to show you!"

"I'm in a hurry to see my fiancée."

"You might like one of the other places even more than this."

Dave gestured over the vine fields. "Do any of them have this view?"

"No."

"Let's go back to San Francisco."

"You're the boss."

On the way back, Dave began to feel daunted by the project he had embarked on. "I guess I need to find a builder," he said.

"Or an architect," said Morty.

"Really? Just to fix a place up?"

"An architect would talk to you about what you want, draw up plans, then get bids from a number of builders. He would also supervise the work, in theory—though in my experience they tend to lose interest."

"Okay," said Dave. "Do you know anyone?"

"Do you want an old established firm, or someone young and hip?"

Dave considered. "How about someone young and hip who works for an old established firm?"

Morty laughed. "I'll ask around."

They drove back to San Francisco and, shortly after midday, Morty dropped Dave off at the Dewar family house on Nob Hill.

Beep's mother let Dave in. "Welcome!" she said. "You're early—which is great, except that Beep's not here."

Dave was disappointed, but not surprised. He had anticipated spending the whole day looking at properties with Morty, and had told Beep to expect him at the end of the afternoon. "I guess she's gone to school," Dave said. She was a sophomore at Berkeley. Dave knew—though her parents did not—that she studied very little, and was in danger of failing her exams and getting expelled.

He went to the bedroom they shared and put down his suitcase. Beep's contraceptive pills were on the bedside table. She was careless, and sometimes forgot to take the tablet, but Dave did not mind. If she got pregnant, they would just get married in a hurry.

He returned downstairs and sat in the kitchen with Bella, telling her all about Daisy Farm. She was infected by his enthusiasm and eager to view the place.

"Would you like some lunch?" she offered. "I was about to make soup and a sandwich."

"No, thanks, I had a huge breakfast on the plane." Dave was hyped up. "I'll go and tell Walli about Daisy Farm."

"Your car's in the garage."

Dave got in his red Dodge Charger and zigzagged across San Francisco from its wealthiest neighborhood to its poorest.

Walli was going to love the idea of a farmhouse where they could all live and make music, Dave thought. They would have all the time they wanted to perfect their recordings. Walli was itching to work with one of the new eight-track tape recorders—and people were already talking about even bigger sixteen-track machines—but today's more complex music took longer to make. Studio time was costly, and musicians sometimes felt rushed. Dave believed he had found the solution.

As Dave drove, a fragment of a tune came into his head, and he sang: "We're all going to Daisy Farm." He smiled. Perhaps it would be a song. "Daisy Farm Red" would be a good title. It could be a girl or a color or a type of marijuana. He sang: "We're all going to see Daisy Farm Red, where the fruit hangs on the vine."

He parked outside Walli's house in Haight-Ashbury. The front door was unlocked, as always. The living room on the ground floor was empty, but littered with the debris of the previous night: pizza boxes, dirty coffee cups, full ashtrays, and empty beer bottles.

Dave was disappointed not to find Walli up. He was itching to discuss Daisy Farm. He decided to wake Walli.

He went upstairs. The house was quiet. It was possible Walli had got up earlier and gone out without cleaning up.

The bedroom door was closed. Dave knocked and opened it. Walking in, he sang: "We're all going to Daisy Farm," then he stopped dead.

Walli was in bed, half sitting up, clearly startled.

Next to him on the mattress was Beep.

For a moment Dave was too shocked to speak.

Walli said: "Hey, man . . ."

Dave's stomach lurched, as if he were in an elevator that had dropped too fast. He suffered a feeling of panicky weightlessness. Beep was in bed with Walli, and there was no ground beneath Dave's feet. Stupidly, he said: "What the fuck is this?"

"It's nothing, man . . ."

Shock turned to anger. "What are you talking about? You're in bed with my fiancée! How can it be *nothing*?"

Beep sat upright. Her hair was tousled. The sheet fell away from her breasts. "Dave, let us explain," she said.

"Okay, explain," said Dave, folding his arms.

She got up. She was naked, and the perfect beauty of her body brought home to Dave, with the force and shock of a punch in the face, that he had lost her. He wanted to weep.

Beep said: "Let's all have coffee and—"

"No coffee," Dave said, speaking harshly to save himself from the humiliation of tears. "Just explain."

"I don't have any clothes on!"

"That's because you've been fucking your fiancé's best friend." Dave found that angry words masked his pain. "You said you were going to explain that to me. I'm still waiting."

Beep pushed her hair out of her eyes. "Look, jealousy is out-of-date, okay?"

"And what does that mean?"

"I love you and I want to marry you, but I like Walli too, and I like going to bed with him, and love is free, isn't it? So why lie about it?"

"That's it?" said Dave incredulously. "That's your explanation?"

Walli said: "Take it easy, man, I think I'm still tripping a little."

"You two took acid last night—is that how this happened?" Dave felt a glimmer of hope. If they had only done it once . . .

"She loves you, man. She just passes the time with me, while you're away, you know?"

Dave's hope was dashed. This was not the only time. It was a regular thing.

Walli stood up and pulled on a pair of jeans. "My feet grew bigger in the night," he said. "Weird."

Dave ignored the druggy talk. "You haven't even said you're sorry—either of you!"

"We're not sorry," said Walli. "We felt like screwing, so we did. It doesn't change anything. No one is faithful anymore. All you need is love—didn't you understand that song?" He stared at Dave intently. "Did you know you have an aura? Kind of like a halo. I never noticed that before. It's blue, I think."

Dave had taken LSD himself, and he knew there was little prospect of getting any sense out of Walli in this state. He turned to Beep, who seemed to be coming down from the high. "Are you sorry?"

"I don't believe that what we did was wrong. I've grown past that mentality."

"So you'd do it again?"

"Dave, don't break up with me."

"What's to break up?" Dave said wildly. "We don't have a relationship. You screw anyone you fancy. Live that way if you want, but it's not marriage."

"You have to leave those old ideas behind."

"I have to get out of this house." Dave's rage was turning to grief. He realized he had lost Beep: lost her to drugs and free love, lost her to the hippie culture his music had helped to create. "I have to get away from you." He turned away.

"Don't go," she said. "Please."

Dave went out.

He ran down the stairs and out of the house. He jumped into his car and roared away. He almost ran over a long-haired boy staggering across Ashbury Street, smiling vacantly, stoned out of his mind in the afternoon. To hell with all hippies, Dave thought, especially Walli and Beep. He did not want to see either of them again.

Plum Nellie was finished, he realized. He and Walli were the essence of the group, and now that they had quarreled there was no group. Well, so be it, Dave thought. He would start his solo career today.

He saw a phone booth and pulled up. He opened the glove box and took out the roll of quarters he kept there. He dialed Morty's office.

Morty said: "Hey, Dave, I talked to the Realtor already. I offered fifty grand and we settled on fifty-five, how's that?"

"Great news, Morty," said Dave. He would need the recording studio for his solo work. "Listen, what was the name of that TV producer?"

"Charlie Lacklow. But I thought you were worried about breaking up the group."

"Suddenly I'm not so worried about it," Dave said. "Set up a meeting."

.   .   .

By March the future was looking bleak for George and for America.

George was in New York with Bobby Kennedy on Tuesday, March 12, the day of the New Hampshire primary, the first major clash between rival Democratic hopefuls. Bobby had a late supper with old friends at the fashionable "21" restaurant on Fifty-second Street. While Bobby was upstairs, George and the other aides ate downstairs.

George had not resigned. Bobby seemed liberated by announcing that he would not run for president. After the Tet Offensive, George wrote a speech that openly attacked President Johnson, and for the first time Bobby did not censor himself, but used every coruscating phrase. "Half a million American soldiers with seven hundred thousand Vietnamese allies, backed by huge resources and the most modern weapons, are unable to secure even a single city from the attacks of an enemy whose strength is about two hundred and fifty thousand!"

Just as Bobby seemed to be getting his fire back, George's disillusionment with President Johnson had been completed by the president's reaction to the Kerner Commission, appointed to examine the causes of racial unrest during the long, hot summer of 1967. Their report pulled no punches: the cause of the rioting was white racism, it said. It was sharply critical of government, the media, and the police, and it called for radical action on housing, jobs, and segregation. It was published as a paperback and sold two million copies. But Johnson simply rejected the report. The man who had heroically championed the Civil Rights Act of 1964 and the Voting Rights Act of 1965—the keystones of Negro advancement—had given up the fight.

Bobby, having made the decision not to run, continued to torment himself with worry about whether he had done the right thing—as was his characteristic way. He talked about it to his oldest friends and his most casual acquaintances, his closest advisers—including George— and newspaper reporters. Rumors began to circulate that he had changed his mind. George would not believe it unless he heard it from Bobby's own lips.

Primaries were local races between people from the same party who wanted to be that party's presidential candidate. The first Democratic primary was held in New Hampshire. Gene McCarthy was the hope of the young, but he was doing badly in opinion polls, trailing a long way behind President Johnson, who wanted to run for reelection. McCarthy had little money. Ten thousand enthusiastic young volunteers had arrived in New Hampshire to campaign for him, but George and the other aides around the table at "21" confidently expected tonight's result to be a victory for Johnson by a huge margin.

George looked forward to the presidential election in November with trepidation. On the Republican side the leading moderate, George Romney, had dropped out of the race, leaving the field clear for the flaky conservative Richard Nixon. So the presidential election would almost certainly be fought between Johnson and Nixon, both pro-war.

Toward the end of the gloomy meal George was summoned to the phone by a staffer who had the New Hampshire result.

Everyone had been wrong. The result was completely unexpected.

McCarthy had gained 42 percent of the vote, astonishingly close to Johnson's 49.

George realized that Johnson could be beaten after all.

He rushed upstairs and gave Bobby the news.

Bobby's reaction was downbeat. "It's too much!" he said. "Now how am I going to get McCarthy to drop out?"

That was when George understood that, after all, Bobby was going to run.

. . .

Walli and Beep went to Bobby Kennedy's rally to disrupt it.

Both were angry at Bobby. For months he had refused to declare himself a presidential candidate. He did not think he could win, and—they believed—he had not had the guts to try. So Gene McCarthy had stuck his neck out, and had done so well that he now had a real chance of beating President Johnson.

Until now. For Bobby Kennedy had declared his candidacy and stepped in to exploit all the work McCarthy's supporters had done and snatch the victory for himself. They thought he was a cynical opportunist.

Walli was contemptuous, Beep was incandescent. Walli's response was more moderate because he saw the political reality behind the personal morality. McCarthy's base consisted mostly of students and intellectuals. His masterstroke had been to conscript his young followers into a volunteer army of election campaigners, and that had given him a burst of success no one had expected. But would those volunteers be enough to take him all the way to the White House? All through his youth Walli had heard his parents making judgments like this, talking about elections—not those in East Germany, which were a sham, but in West Germany and France and the United States.

Bobby's support was broader. He pulled in the Negroes, who believed he was on their side, and the vast Catholic working class—Irish, Polish, Italian, and Hispanic. Walli hated Bobby's moral shallowness, but he had to admit—though it made Beep angry—that Bobby had a better chance than Gene of beating President Johnson.

All the same, they agreed that the right thing to do was to boo Bobby Kennedy tonight.

The audience included a lot of people like themselves: young men with long hair and beards, hippie girls with bare feet. Walli wondered how many of them had come to jeer. There were also blacks of all ages, the young ones with their hair in the style now called an Afro, their parents in the colorful dresses and smart suits they wore to church. The breadth of Bobby's appeal was shown by a substantial minority of middle-class, middle-aged white people, dressed in chinos and sweaters in the chill of a San Francisco spring.

Walli himself had his hair tucked up inside a denim cap, and wore sunglasses to hide his identity.

The stage was surprisingly bare. Walli had been expecting flags, streamers, posters, and giant photographs of the candidate, such as he had seen on television for other campaign rallies. Bobby just had a bare stage with a lectern and a microphone. In another candidate that would have been a sign that he had run out of money, but everyone knew Bobby had unlimited access to the Kennedy fortune. So what did it mean? To Walli it said: "No bullshit, this is the real me." Interesting, he thought.

Right now the lectern was occupied by a local Democrat who was warming up the crowd for the big star. It was a lot like show business, Walli reflected. The audience was getting used to laughing and clapping, and at the same time becoming more eager for the appearance of the act they had come to see. For the same reason, Plum Nellie concerts featured a lesser group as support.

But Plum Nellie no longer existed. The group should by now have been working on a new album for Christmas, and Walli had a few songs that had reached the stage where he wanted to play them for Dave, so that Dave could write a bridge or change a chord or say: "Great, let's call it 'Soul Kiss.'" But Dave had dropped out of sight.

He had sent a coldly polite note to Beep's mother, thanking her for letting him stay at the house and asking her to pack his clothes and have them ready to be picked up by an assistant. Walli knew, from a phone call to Daisy in London, that Dave was renovating a farmhouse in Napa Valley and planning a recording studio there. And Jasper Murray had phoned Walli, trying to check a rumor that Dave was making a television special without the group.

Dave was suffering from old-fashioned jealousy, quite out-of-date now according to hippie thinking. He needed to realize that people could not be tied down, they should make love to anyone they wanted. Strongly as Walli believed this he could not help feeling guilty. He and Dave had been close, they liked and trusted one another, they had stuck together all the way from the Reeperbahn. Walli was unhappy about having wounded his friend.

It was not as if Beep was the love of Walli's life. He liked her a lot— she was beautiful and fun and great in the sack, and they were a much-admired couple—but she was not the only girl in the world. Walli probably would not have screwed her if he had known it would destroy the group. But he had not been thinking about consequences; he had instead been living for the moment, the way people should. It was especially easy to give in to such careless impulses when you were stoned.

She was still shaken from having been dumped by Dave. Perhaps that was why she and Walli were comfortable together: she had lost Dave and he had lost Karolin.

Walli's mind was wandering, but he was jerked back to the present moment when Bobby Kennedy was announced.

Bobby was smaller than Walli had imagined, and less confident. He walked up to the lectern with a half smile and a wave that was almost shy. He put his hand in the pocket of his suit jacket, and Walli recalled President Kennedy doing exactly the same.

Several people in the audience immediately held up signs. Walli saw KISS ME, BOBBY! and BOBBY IS GROOVY. Beep now drew a rolled-up sheet of paper from her pants leg, and she and Walli held it up. It read simply: TRAITOR.

Bobby began to speak, referring to a small pack of file cards he took from his inside pocket. "Let me begin with an apology," he said. "I was involved in many of the early decisions on Vietnam, decisions which set us on our present path."

Beep yelled out: "Too damn right!" and the people around her laughed.

Bobby went on in his flat Boston accent. "I am willing to bear my share of the responsibility. But past error is no excuse for its own perpetuation. Tragedy is a tool for the living to gain wisdom. 'All men make mistakes,' said the ancient Greek Sophocles. 'But a good man yields when he knows his course is wrong, and repairs the evil. The only sin is pride.'"

The audience liked that, and applauded. As they did so, Bobby looked down at his notes, and Walli saw that he was making a theatrical mistake. This should be a two-way exchange. The crowd wanted their star to look at them and acknowledge their praise. Bobby seemed embarrassed by them. This kind of political rally did not come easily to him, Walli realized.

Bobby continued on the subject of Vietnam but, despite the initial success of his opening confession, he did not do well. He was tentative, he stammered, and he repeated himself. He stood still, looking wooden, seeming reluctant to move his body or gesture with his hands.

A few opponents in the hall heckled him, but Walli and Beep did not join in. There was no need. Bobby was killing himself without assistance.

During a quiet moment, a baby cried. Out of the corner of his eye, Walli saw a woman get up and move toward the exit. Bobby stopped in midsentence and said: "Please don't leave, ma'am!"

The audience tittered. The woman turned in the aisle and looked at Bobby up on the stage.

He said: "I'm used to the sound of babies crying."

They laughed at that: everyone knew he had ten children.

"Besides," he added, "if you go the newspapers will say that I ruthlessly threw a mother and baby out of the hall."

They cheered at that: many young people hated the press for its biased coverage of demonstrations.

The woman smiled and returned to her seat.

Bobby looked down at his notes. For a moment he had come across as a warm human being. At that point he might have turned the crowd. But he would lose them again by returning to his prepared speech. Walli thought he had missed his opportunity.

Then Bobby seemed to realize the same thing. He looked up again and said: "I'm cold in here. Are you cold?"

They roared their agreement.

"Clap," he said. "Come on, that'll warm us up." He began to clap his hands, and the audience did the same, laughing.

After a minute he stopped and said: "I feel better now. Do you?" And they shouted their assent again.

"I want to talk about decency," he said. He was back to his speech, but now he was not referring to his notes. "Some people think that long hair is indecent, and bare feet, and smooching in the park. I'll tell you what I think." He raised his voice. "Poverty is indecent!" The crowd shouted approval. "Illiteracy is indecent!" They applauded again. "And I say, right here in California, that it is indecent for a man to work in the fields with his back and his hands without ever having hope of sending his son to college."

No one in the room could doubt that Bobby believed what he was saying. He had put away his file cards. He became passionate, waving his arms, pointing, banging the lectern with a fist; and the listeners responded to the strength of his emotion, acclaiming every fervent phrase. Walli looked at their faces and recognized the expressions he saw when he himself was up onstage: young men and women staring in rapture, eyes wide, mouths open, faces shining with adoration.

No one ever looked at Gene McCarthy that way.

At some point, Walli realized, he and Beep had quietly dropped their TRAITOR banner to the floor.

Bobby was speaking about poverty. "In the Mississippi Delta I have seen children with distended stomachs and facial sores from starvation." He raised his voice. "I don't think that's acceptable!

"Indians living on their bare and meager reservations have so little hope for the future that the greatest cause of death among teenagers is suicide. I believe we can do better!

"The people of the black ghettoes listen to ever greater promises of equality and justice as they sit in the same decaying schools and huddle in the same filthy rooms warding off the rats. I am convinced that America can do better than that!"

He was building up to the climax, Walli saw. "I come here today to ask for your help over the next few months," Bobby said. "If you, too, believe that poverty is indecent, give me your support."

They yelled that they would.

"If you, too, think it is unacceptable that children starve in our country, work for my campaign."

They hurrahed again.

"Do you believe, as I do, that America can do better?"

They roared their agreement.

"Then join me—and America *will* do better!"

He stepped back from the lectern, and the crowd went wild.

Walli looked at Beep. He could tell that she felt the way he did. "He's going to win, isn't he?" said Walli.

"Yes," said Beep. "He's going all the way to the White House."

. . .

Bobby's ten-day tour took him to thirteen states. At the end of the last day, he and his entourage boarded a plane in Phoenix to fly to New York. By then George Jakes was sure Bobby was going to be president.

The public response had been overwhelming. Thousands mobbed Bobby at airports. They crowded the streets to watch his motorcade go by, Bobby always standing on the backseat of a convertible, with George and others sitting on the floor holding his legs so that the people could not pull him out of the car. Gangs of children ran alongside shouting: "Bobby!" Whenever the car stopped, people flung themselves at him. They ripped off his cuff links and his tie pins and the buttons on his suits.

On the plane, Bobby sat down and emptied his pockets. Out came a snowstorm of paper like confetti. George picked up some of the scraps from the carpet. They were notes, dozens of them, neatly written and carefully folded small and thrust into Bobby's pockets. They begged him to attend college graduations or visit sick children in city hospitals, and they told him that prayers were being said for him in suburban homes, and candles lit in country churches.

Bobby took off his suit coat and rolled up his sleeves, as was his habit. That was when George noticed his arms. Bobby had hairy forearms, but that was not what struck George. His hands were swollen and his skin was webbed with angry red scratches. It happened when the crowds were touching him, George realized. They did not want to injure him, but they adored him so much that they drew blood.

The people had found the hero they needed—but Bobby, too, had found himself. That was why George and the other aides called it the

Free at Last tour. Bobby had struck a style that was all his own. He had a new version of the Kennedy charisma. His brother had been charming but contained, self-possessed, private—the right manner for 1963. Bobby was more open. At his best, he gave the audience the feeling that he was laying bare his own soul, confessing himself to be a flawed human being who wanted to do the right thing but was not always certain what it was. The catchphrase of 1968 was: "Let it all hang out." Bobby felt comfortable doing that, and they loved him for it.

Half the people on the plane flying back to New York were newsmen. For ten days they had been photographing and filming the ecstatic crowds, and filing reports on how the new, reborn Bobby Kennedy was winning voters' hearts. The power brokers of the Democratic Party might not like Bobby's youthful liberalism, but they would not be able to ignore the phenomenon of his popularity. How could they blandly select Lyndon Johnson to run a second time when the American people were clamoring for Bobby? And if they ran an alternative pro-war candidate—Vice President Hubert Humphrey, say, or Senator Muskie—he would take votes from Johnson without denting Bobby's support. George did not see how Bobby could fail to get the nomination.

And Bobby would beat the Republican. It would almost certainly be "Tricky" Dick Nixon, a has-been who had been beaten by a Kennedy once already.

The road to the White House seemed clear of obstacles.

As the plane approached John F. Kennedy airport in New York, George wondered what Bobby's opponents would do to try to stop him. President Johnson had been scheduled to make a national television broadcast this evening while the plane was in the air. George looked forward to finding out what Johnson had said. He could not think of anything that would make a difference.

"It must be quite something," one of the journalists said to Bobby, "to land at an airport named for your brother."

It was an unkind, intrusive question from a reporter hoping to spark an intemperate response that would make a story. But Bobby was used to this. All he said was: "I wish it was still called Idlewild."

The plane taxied to the gate. Before the seat belt sign was switched off, a familiar figure came on board and ran down the aisle to Bobby. It was the New York State chairman of the Democratic Party. Before he reached Bobby he shouted: "The president is not going to run! The president is not going to run!"

Bobby said: "Say that again."

"The president is not going to run!"

"You must be kidding."

George was stunned. Lyndon Johnson, who hated the Kennedys, had realized that he could not win the Democratic nomination, doubtless for all the reasons that had occurred to George. But he hoped that another pro-war Democrat could beat Bobby. Johnson had figured, then, that the only way he could sabotage Bobby's run for the presidency was to withdraw from the race himself.

And now all bets were off.

CHAPTER FORTY-TWO

Dave Williams knew that his sister was up to something.

He was making the pilot of *Dave Williams and Friends*, his own television show. When first it was proposed he had taken the idea lightly: it seemed a superfluous augmentation of the tidal wave of Plum Nellie's success. Now the group had split and Dave needed the show. It was the beginning of his solo career. It had to be good.

The producer had suggested inviting Dave's movie-star sister to appear as a guest. Evie was hotter than ever. Her latest film, a comedy about a snobby girl who hired a black lawyer, was a huge hit.

Evie proposed to sing a duet with her costar in the movie, Percy Marquand. The producer, Charlie Lacklow, loved the idea but worried about the choice of song. Charlie was a small, belligerent man with a grating voice. "It has to be a comedy song," he said. "They can't sing 'True Love' or 'Baby, It's Cold Outside.'"

"Easier said than done," said Dave. "Most duets are romantic."

Charlie had shaken his head. "Forget it. This is television. We can't even hint at sex between a white woman and a black man."

"They could sing 'Anything You Can Do, I Can Do Better.' That's comic."

"No. People will think it's a comment on civil rights."

Charlie Lacklow was smart, but Dave did not like him. Nobody did. He was a bad-tempered bully, and his occasional attempts to be ingratiatingly nice only made it worse.

Dave tried: "How about 'Mockingbird'?"

Charlie thought for a minute. "'If that mockingbird don't sing, he's gonna buy me a diamond ring,'" he sang. He reverted to speech. "I guess we can get away with that."

"Sure we can," Dave said. "The original recording was by a brother-and-sister duo, Inez and Charlie Foxx. No one thought it suggested incest."

"Okay."

Dave discussed the sensitivities of the American television audience with Evie, and explained the choice of song, and she agreed—except that she had a gleam in her eye that Dave knew too well. It meant trouble. It was how she had looked just before the school production of *Hamlet,* when she had played Ophelia in the nude.

They also discussed his breakup with Beep. "Everybody reacts as if it was just a typical teenage romance that didn't last," Dave complained. "But I stopped having teenage romances long before I stopped being a teenager, and I never much liked screwing around. I was serious about Beep. I wanted kids."

"You grew up faster than Beep," Evie said. "And I grew up faster than Hank Remington. Hank has settled down with Anna Murray—I hear he doesn't screw around anymore. Maybe Beep will do the same."

"And it will be too late for me, just as it was for you," Dave said bitterly.

Now the orchestra was tuning up, Evie was in makeup, and Percy was putting on his costume. Meanwhile the director, Tony Peterson, asked Dave to record his introduction.

The show was in color, and Dave was dressed in a burgundy velvet suit. He looked into the camera, imagined Beep walking back into his life with her arms reaching out to embrace him, and smiled warmly. "Now, fans, a special kick. We have both stars of the hit movie *My Client and I:* Percy Marquand, and my very own sister, Evie Williams!" He clapped his hands. The studio was quiet, but the sound of an audience applauding would be dubbed onto the soundtrack before the show was broadcast.

"I love the smile, Dave," said Tony. "Do it again."

Dave did it three times, and Tony pronounced himself satisfied.

At that point Charlie came in with a gray-suited man in his forties. Dave saw immediately that Charlie was in obsequious mode. "Dave, I want you to meet our sponsor," he said. "This is Albert Wharton, the top man at National Soap and one of the leading businessmen in America. He's flown here all the way from Cleveland, Ohio, to meet you, isn't that great of him?"

"It sure is," said Dave. People flew halfway around the world to see him every time he did a concert, but he always acted pleased.

Wharton said: "I have two teenage children, a boy and a girl. They're going to be envious that I met you."

Dave was trying to concentrate on making a great show, and the last thing he needed was to talk to a laundry detergent magnate; but he realized he had to be polite to this man. "I should sign a couple of autographs for your kids," he said.

"That would give them a thrill."

Charlie snapped his fingers at Miss Pritchard, his secretary, who was following behind him. "Jenny, sweetie," he said, even though she was a prim forty-year-old. "Get a couple of Dave's photos from the office."

Wharton looked like a typical conservative businessman with short hair and boring clothes. That prompted Dave to say: "What made you decide to sponsor my show, Mr. Wharton?"

"Our leading product is a detergent called Foam," Wharton began.

"I've seen the ads," Dave said with a smile. "'Foam washes cleaner than white!'"

Wharton nodded. Probably everyone he met quoted his advertising to him. "Foam is well known and trusted, and has been for many years," he said. "For that reason, it's also a bit fuddy-duddy. Young housewives tend to say: 'Foam, yes, my mother always used it.' Which is nice, but it has its dangers."

Dave was amused to hear him talk about the character of a box of detergent as if it were a person. But Wharton spoke with no hint of humor or irony, and Dave suppressed the impulse to take it lightly. He said: "So I'm here to let them know that Foam is young and groovy."

"Exactly," said Wharton. Then he smiled at last. "And, at the same time, to bring some popular music and wholesome humor into American homes."

Dave grinned. "It's a good thing I'm not in the Rolling Stones!"

"It certainly is," said Wharton in deadly earnest.

Jenny came back with two eight-by-ten color photographs of Dave, and a felt-tipped pen.

Dave said to Wharton: "What are your children called?"

"Caroline and Edward."

Dave dedicated one photo to each child and signed.

Tony Peterson said: "Ready for the 'Mockingbird' segment."

A little set had been built for this number. It looked like a corner of a swanky store, with glass cupboards full of glittery luxuries. Percy came on in a dark suit and a silver tie, like a floorwalker. Evie was a wealthy shopper with hat, gloves, and handbag. They took their positions either side of a counter. Dave smiled at the pains Charlie had taken to make sure their relationship was not seen as amorous.

They rehearsed with the orchestra. The song was upbeat and lighthearted. Percy's baritone and Evie's contralto harmonized nicely. At the appropriate moments, Percy produced from under the counter a caged bird and a tray of rings. "We'll add canned laughter at that point, to let the audience know it's intended to be funny," said Charlie.

They did it for the cameras. The first take was perfect, but they did it again for safety, as always.

As they were coming to the end, Dave felt good. This was ideal family entertainment for the American audience. He began to believe that his show would succeed.

In the last bar of the song, Evie leaned across the counter, stood on tiptoe, and kissed Percy's cheek.

"Wonderful!" said Tony, walking onto the set. "Thank you, everybody. Set up for Dave's next introduction, please." He had a distinct air of embarrassed haste, and Dave wondered why.

Evie and Percy stepped off the set.

Beside Dave, Mr. Wharton said: "We can't broadcast that kiss."

Before Dave could say anything, Charlie Lacklow said fawningly: "Of course not, don't worry, Mr. Wharton, we can lose it, we'll cut to Dave applauding, probably."

Dave said mildly: "I thought the kiss was charming and kind of innocent."

"Did you?" said Wharton severely.

Dave wondered apprehensively if this was going to become an issue.

Charlie said: "Drop it, Dave. We can't show an interracial kiss on American television."

Dave was surprised. But, thinking about it, he realized that those few black people who appeared on TV were rarely if ever touched by white people. "Is that, like, a policy, or something?" he asked.

"More of an unwritten rule," Charlie said. "Unwritten, and unbreakable," he added firmly.

Evie heard the exchange and said challengingly: "Why is that?"

Dave saw the look on her face and groaned inwardly. Evie was not going to let this pass. She wanted a fight.

But for a few moments there was silence. No one was sure what to say, especially with Percy right there.

Eventually Wharton answered Evie's question in his dry accountant's tone. "The audience would disapprove," he said. "Most Americans believe the races should not intermarry."

Charlie Lacklow added: "Exactly. What happens on television is happening in your home, in your living room, with your kids watching, and your mother-in-law."

Wharton looked at Percy and remembered that he was married to Babe Lee, a white woman. "I'm sorry if this offends you, Mr. Marquand," he said.

"I'm used to it," Percy said mildly; not denying that he was offended, but declining to make a big deal of it. Dave thought that was remarkably gracious.

Evie said indignantly: "Maybe television should work to alter people's prejudices."

"Don't be naïve," Charlie said rudely. "If we show them something they don't like, they'll just change the goddamn channel."

"Then *all* the networks should do the same, and portray America as a place where all men are equal."

"It won't work," said Charlie.

"Perhaps it won't," said Evie. "But we have to try, don't we? We have a responsibility." She looked around the group: Charlie, Tony, Dave, Percy, and Wharton. Dave felt guilty when he met her eye, for he knew she was right. "All of us," she went on. "We make television programs, which influence how people think."

Charlie said: "Not necessarily—"

Dave interrupted him. "Knock it off, Charlie. We influence people. If we didn't, Mr. Wharton would be wasting his money."

Charlie looked angry, but he had no answer.

"Now we have a chance, today, to make the world a better place," Evie went on. "Nobody would mind if I kissed Bing Crosby on prime-time television. Let's help people to see that it's no different if the cheek I kiss is a little darker in color."

They all looked at Mr. Wharton.

Dave felt perspiration break out under his skintight frilled shirt. He did not want Wharton to be offended.

"You argue well, young lady," said Wharton. "But my duty is to my shareholders and my employees. I'm not here to make the world a better place, I'm here to sell Foam to housewives. And I won't achieve that if I associate my product with interracial sex, with all due respect to Mr. Marquand. I'm a big fan, by the way, Percy—I have all your records."

Dave found himself thinking of Mandy Love. He had been crazy about her. She was black—not golden tan like Percy, but a beautiful deep coaly brown. Dave had kissed her skin until his lips were sore. He might have proposed to her, if she had not gone back to her old boyfriend. And Dave would now be in Percy's position, straining to tolerate a conversation that insulted his marriage.

Charlie said: "I think the duet works as a beautiful symbol of interracial harmony without hinting at the prickly topic of sex between the races. I believe we've done a wonderful job here—provided we leave out the kiss."

Evie said: "Nice try, Charlie, but that's bullshit, and you know it."

"It's the reality."

Trying to lighten the mood, Dave said: "Did you call sex a 'prickly topic,' Charlie? That's funny."

No one laughed.

Evie looked at Dave. "Aside from making jokes, what are you going to do, Dave?" she said, almost taunting him. "You and I were raised to stand up for what's right. Our father fought in the Spanish Civil War. Our grandmother won women the right to vote. Are you going to give in?"

Percy Marquand said: "You're the talent, Dave. They need you. Without you they don't have a show. You have power. Use it to do good."

Charlie said: "Get real. There's no show without National Soap. We'll have trouble finding a new sponsor—especially after people find out why Mr. Wharton pulled out."

Wharton had not actually said he would withdraw his sponsorship over the kiss, Dave noted. Nor had Charlie said that finding a new sponsor would be impossible—just difficult. If Dave insisted on keeping the kiss, the show might go on, and Dave's television career might survive.

Perhaps.

"Is this really my decision?" he said.

Evie said: "Looks like it."

Was he prepared to take the risk?

No, he was not.

"The kiss comes out," he said.

.   .   .

Jasper Murray flew to Memphis in April to check out a strike by sanitation workers that was becoming violent.

Jasper knew about violence. All men, including himself, had it in them to be either peaceable or vicious, according to circumstances, he believed. Their natural inclination was to lead a quiet, law-abiding life; but given the right sort of encouragement most of them were capable of committing torture, rape, and murder. He knew.

So when he came to Memphis he listened to both sides. The city hall spokesman said that outside agitators were inciting the strikers to violent behavior. The campaigners blamed police brutality.

Jasper asked: "Who is in charge?"

The answer was Henry Loeb.

Loeb, the Democrat mayor of Memphis, was openly racist, Jasper learned. He believed in segregation, supported "separate but equal" facilities for whites and blacks, and publicly railed against court-ordered integration.

And almost all the sanitation workers were black.

Their wages were so low that many qualified for welfare. They had to do compulsory unpaid overtime. And the city would not recognize their union.

But it was the issue of safety that started the strike. Two men had been crushed to death by a malfunctioning truck. Loeb refused to retire obsolete trucks or tighten safety rules.

The city council voted to end the strike by recognizing the union, but Loeb overrode the council.

The protest spread.

It got national attention when Martin Luther King weighed in on the side of the sanitation men.

King flew in for his second visit on the same day as Jasper, April 3, 1968, a Wednesday. That evening a storm darkened the city. In pounding rain, Jasper went to hear King speak to a rally at the Mason Temple.

Ralph Abernathy was the warm-up man. Taller and darker than King, less handsome and more aggressive, he was—according to gossip—King's drinking and womanizing buddy as well as his closest ally and friend.

The audience consisted of sanitation workers and their families and supporters. Looking at their worn shoes and their old coats and hats, Jasper realized that these were some of the poorest people in America. They were ill-educated and they did dirty jobs and they lived in a city that called them second-class citizens, nigras, boys. But they had spirit. They were not going to take it any longer. They believed in a better life. They had a dream.

And they had Martin Luther King.

King was thirty-nine, but he looked older. He had been a little chubby when Jasper saw him speak in Washington, but he had put on weight in the five years since then, and now he looked plump. If his suit had not been so smart he might have been a shopkeeper. But that was before he opened his mouth. When he spoke, he became a giant.

Tonight he was in an apocalyptic mood. As lightning flashed outside the windows, and the crash of thunder interrupted his speech, he told the audience that his plane that morning had been delayed by a bomb threat. "But it doesn't matter with me, now, because I've been to the mountaintop," he said, and they cheered. "I just want to do God's will." And then he was seized by the emotion of his own words, and his voice trembled with urgency the way it had on the steps of the Lincoln Memorial. "And he's allowed me to go up to the mountain," he cried.

"And I've looked over." His voice rose again. "And I've *seen* the Promised Land!"

King was genuinely moved, Jasper could see. He was perspiring heavily and shedding tears. The crowd shared his passion and responded, shouting out: "Yes!" and "Amen!"

"I may not get there with you," King said, his voice shaking with feeling, and Jasper recalled that in the Bible, Moses had never reached Canaan. "But I want you to know, tonight, that we as a people will get to the Promised Land." Two thousand listeners erupted in applause and amens. "And so I'm happy tonight. I'm not worried about anything. I'm not fearing any man." He paused, then said slowly: "Mine eyes have seen the glory of the coming of the Lord."

With that he seemed to stagger back from the pulpit. Ralph Abernathy, behind him, leaped up to support him, and led him to his seat amid a hurricane of approbation that rivaled the storm outside.

Jasper spent the next day covering a legal dispute. The city was trying to get the courts to ban a demonstration King had planned for the following Monday, and King was working on a compromise that would guarantee a small, peaceful march.

At the end of the afternoon, Jasper talked to Herb Gould in New York. They agreed that Jasper would try to arrange for Sam Cakebread to interview both Loeb and King on Saturday or Sunday, and Herb would send a crew to get footage of Monday's demonstration, for a report to be broadcast on Monday evening.

After talking to Gould, Jasper went to the Lorraine Motel, where King was staying. It was a low two-story building with balconies overlooking the parking lot. Jasper spotted a white Cadillac that, he knew, was loaned to King, along with a chauffeur, by a black-owned Memphis funeral home. Near the car was a group of King's aides, and among them Jasper spotted Verena Marquand.

She was as breathtakingly gorgeous as she had been five years ago, but she looked different. Her hairdo was an Afro, and she wore beads and a caftan. Jasper saw tiny lines of strain around her eyes, and wondered what it was like working for a man who was so passionately adored and at the same time so bitterly hated as Martin Luther King.

Jasper gave her his most winning smile, introduced himself, and said: "We've met before."

She looked suspicious. "I don't think so."

"Sure we have. But you could be forgiven for not remembering. The date was the twenty-eighth of August, 1963. A lot else happened on that day."

"Especially Martin's 'I have a dream' speech."

"I was a student reporter and I asked you to get me an interview with Dr. King. You gave me the brush-off." Jasper also remembered how mesmerized he had been by Verena's beauty. He was feeling the same enchantment now.

She softened. With a smile she said: "And I guess you still want that interview."

"Sam Cakebread will be here at the weekend. He's going to talk to Herb Loeb. He really should interview Dr. King as well."

"I'll do my best, Mr. Murray."

"Please call me Jasper."

She hesitated. "Satisfy my curiosity. How did we come to meet, that day in Washington?"

"I was having breakfast with Congressman Greg Peshkov, a family friend. You were with George Jakes."

"And where have you been since then?"

"Vietnam, some of the time."

"You fought?"

"Saw some action, yes." He hated talking about that. "May I ask you a personal question?"

"Try me. I don't promise to answer."

"Are you and George still an item?"

"I'm not going to answer."

At that moment they both heard King's voice, and looked up. He was standing on the balcony outside his room, looking down, saying something to one of the aides near Jasper and Verena in the parking lot. King was tucking his shirt in, as if dressing after a shower. He was probably getting ready to go out for dinner, Jasper thought.

King put both hands on the rail and leaned over, joshing with someone below. "Ben, I want you to sing 'My Precious Lord' for me tonight like you've never sung it before—want you to sing it real pretty."

The driver of the white Cadillac called up to him: "The air's turning cool, Reverend. You might want a topcoat tonight."

King said: "Okay, Jonesy." He straightened up from the rail.

A shot rang out.

King staggered back, threw up his arms like a man on a cross, hit the wall behind him, and fell.

Verena screamed.

King's aides took cover around the white Cadillac.

Jasper dropped to one knee. Verena crouched down in front of him. He put both arms around her, pulling her head to his chest protectively, and looked for the source of the shot. There was a building across the street that might be a rooming house.

There was no second shot.

Jasper was torn for a moment. He released Verena from his protective embrace. "Are you okay?" he asked her.

"Oh, Martin!" she said, looking up at the balcony.

They both stood up warily, but the shooting seemed to have stopped.

Without speaking, they both dashed up the exterior staircase to the balcony.

King lay on his back, his feet up against the railing. Ralph Abernathy was bent over him, as was another campaigner, the amiable, bespectacled Billy Kyles. Screams and moans were coming from the people in the parking lot who had seen the shooting.

The bullet had smashed King's neck and jaw and ripped off his necktie. The wound was terrible, and Jasper knew immediately that King had been struck by an expanding slug known as a dumdum. Blood was pooling around King's shoulders.

Abernathy was yelling: "Martin! Martin! Martin!" He patted King's cheek. Jasper thought he saw a faint sign of awareness on King's face. Abernathy said: "Martin, this is Ralph, don't worry, it's going to be all right." King's lips moved but there was no sound.

Kyles was first to the phone in the room. He picked it up, but apparently there was no one at the switchboard. Kyles started banging on the wall with his fist, shouting: "Answer the phone! Answer the phone! Answer the phone!"

Then he gave up and ran back out to the balcony. He shouted to the people in the parking lot: "Call an ambulance, Dr. King has been shot!"

Someone wrapped King's shattered head in a towel from the bathroom.

Kyles took an orange-colored spread from the bed and put it over King, covering his body up to his destroyed neck.

Jasper knew wounds. He knew how much blood a man could lose, and what a man could and could not recover from.

He had no hope for Martin Luther King.

Kyles lifted King's hand, prized open his fingers, and took away a pack of cigarettes. Jasper had never seen King smoking: obviously he did it only in private. Even now Kyles was protecting his friend. The gesture touched Jasper's heart.

Abernathy was still talking to King. "Can you hear me?" he said. "Can you hear me?"

Jasper saw the color of King's face alter dramatically. The brown skin paled and turned a grayish tan. The handsome features became unnaturally still.

Jasper knew death, too, and this was it.

Verena saw the same thing. She turned away and stepped inside the room, sobbing.

Jasper put his arms around her.

She slumped against him, weeping, and her hot tears soaked into his white shirt.

"I'm so sorry," Jasper whispered. "So sorry." Sorry for Verena, he thought. Sorry for Martin Luther King.

Sorry for America.

. . .

That night, the inner cities of the United States exploded.

Dave Williams, in the bungalow at the Beverly Hills Hotel where he was living, watched the television coverage with horror. There were riots in one hundred ten cities. In Washington, twenty thousand people overwhelmed the police and set fire to buildings. In Baltimore, six people died and seven hundred were injured. In Chicago, two miles of West Madison Street were reduced to rubble.

All the next day Dave stayed in his room, sitting on the couch in front of the TV, smoking cigarettes. Who was to blame? It was not just the gunman. It was all the white racists who stirred up hatred. And it was all the people who did nothing about cruel injustice.

People such as Dave.

In his life he had been given one chance to stand up against racism. It had happened a few days ago in a television studio in Burbank. He had been told that a white woman could not kiss a black man on American television. His sister had demanded that he challenge that racist rule. But he had caved in to prejudice.

He had killed Martin Luther King, as surely as Henry Loeb and Barry Goldwater and George Wallace had killed him.

The show would be broadcast tomorrow, Saturday, at eight in the evening, without the kiss.

Dave ordered a bottle of bourbon from room service and fell asleep on the couch.

In the morning he woke up early, knowing what he had to do.

He showered, took a couple of aspirins for his hangover, and dressed in his most conservative outfit, a green check suit with broad lapels and flared pants. He ordered a limousine and went to the studio in Burbank, arriving at ten.

He knew Charlie Lacklow would be in his office, even though it was the weekend, because Saturday was broadcast day, and there were sure to be last-minute panics—just like the one Dave was about to create.

Charlie's middle-aged secretary, Jenny, was at her desk in the outer office. "Good morning, Miss Pritchard," Dave said. He treated her with extra respect because Charlie was so rude to her. In consequence she adored Dave and would do anything for him. "Would you please check flights to Cleveland?"

"In Ohio?"

He grinned. "Is there another Cleveland?"

"You want to go there today?"

"As soon as possible."

"Do you know how far it is?"

"About two thousand miles."

She picked up her phone.

Dave added: "Order a limousine to meet me at the airport there."

She made a note, then spoke into the phone. "When is the next flight to Cleveland? . . . Thank you, I'll hold." She looked at Dave again. "Where in Cleveland do you want to go?"

"Give the driver Albert Wharton's home address."

"Is Mr. Wharton expecting you?"

"It's going to be a surprise." He winked at her and went into the inner office.

Charlie was behind the desk. In honor of Saturday he was wearing a tweed jacket and no tie. "Could you make two edits of the show?" Dave said. "One with the kiss and one without?"

"Easily," said Charlie. "We already have an edit without the kiss, ready to broadcast. We could make the alternative this morning. But we're not going to do it."

"Later today you're going to get a phone call from Albert Wharton, asking you to leave the kiss in. I just want you to be ready. You wouldn't want to disappoint our sponsor."

"Of course not. But what makes you so sure he's going to change his mind?"

Dave was not at all sure, but he did not tell Charlie that. "Having both versions ready, what would be the latest time you could make the change?"

"About ten minutes to eight, Eastern time."

Jenny Pritchard put her head around the door. "You're booked on the eleven o'clock plane, Dave. The airport is seven miles from here, so you need to leave now."

"I'm on my way."

"The flight takes four and a half hours, and there's a three-hour time difference, so you land at six thirty." She handed him a slip of paper with Mr. Wharton's address. "You should be there by seven."

"That gives me just enough time," said Dave. He waved a good-bye at Charlie and said: "Stay by the phone."

Charlie looked bemused. He was not used to being pushed around. "I'm not going anywhere," he said.

In the outer office, Miss Pritchard said: "His wife is Susan and his children are Caroline and Edward."

"Thank you." Dave closed Charlie's door. "Miss Pritchard, if you ever get fed up with working for Charlie, I need a secretary."

"I'm fed up now," she said. "When do I start?"

"Monday."

"Should I come to the Beverly Hills Hotel at nine?"

"Make it ten."

The hotel limousine took Dave to LAX. Miss Pritchard had called the airline, and there was a stewardess waiting to take him through the VIP channel, to avoid mob scenes in the departure lounge.

He had had nothing but aspirins for breakfast, so he was glad of the in-flight lunch. As the plane came down toward the flat city by Lake Erie, he ruminated over what he was going to say to Mr. Wharton. This was going to be difficult. But if he handled it well perhaps he could turn Wharton around. That would make up for his earlier cowardice. He longed to tell his sister that he had redeemed himself.

Miss Pritchard's arrangements worked well, and a car was waiting for him at Hopkins International Airport. It took him to a leafy suburb not far away. A few minutes after seven the limousine pulled into the driveway of a large but unostentatious ranch-style house. Dave walked up to the entrance and rang the bell.

He felt nervous.

Wharton himself came to the door in a gray V-neck sweater and slacks. "Dave Williams?" he said. "What the hey . . . ?"

"Good evening, Mr. Wharton," Dave said. "I'm sorry to intrude, but I'd really like to speak to you."

When he got over his surprise, Wharton seemed pleased. "Come on in," he said. "Meet the family."

Wharton ushered Dave into the dining room. The family appeared to be finishing dinner. Wharton had a pretty wife in her thirties, a daughter of about sixteen, and a spotty son a couple of years younger. "We have a surprise visitor," Wharton said. "This is Mr. Dave Williams, of Plum Nellie."

Mrs. Wharton put a small white hand to her mouth and said: "Oh my golly gosh."

Dave shook hands with her, then turned to the youngsters. "You must be Caroline and Edward."

Wharton looked pleased that Dave had remembered his children's names.

The kids were awestruck to get a surprise visit from a real pop star they had seen on TV. Edward could hardly speak. Caroline pulled back her shoulders, making her breasts stick out, and gave Dave a look that he had seen before in a thousand teenage girls. It said: *You can do anything you like to me.*

Dave pretended not to notice.

Mr. Wharton said: "Sit down, Dave, please. Join us."

Mrs. Wharton said: "Would you like some dessert? We're having strawberry shortcake."

"Yes, please," Dave said. "I'm living in a hotel—some home cooking would be a real treat."

"Oh, you poor thing," she said, and she went off to the kitchen.

"Have you come from Los Angeles today?" Wharton asked.

"Yes."

"Not just to call on me, I'm sure."

"Actually, yes. I want to talk to you one more time about tonight's show."

"Okay," Wharton said dubiously.

Mrs. Wharton returned with the dessert on a platter and began to serve.

Dave wanted the children on his side. He said to them: "In the show that your dad and I made, there's a part where Percy Marquand does a duet with my sister, Evie Williams."

Edward said: "I saw their movie—it was a blast!"

"At the end of the song, Evie kisses Percy on the cheek." Dave paused.

Caroline said: "So? Big deal!"

Mrs. Wharton raised a flirtatious eyebrow as she passed Dave a large wedge of strawberry shortcake.

Dave went on: "Mr. Wharton and I talked about whether this would offend our audience—something neither of us wants to do. We decided to leave out the kiss."

Wharton said: "I think it was a wise choice."

Dave said: "I've come here to see you today, Mr. Wharton, because I believe that, since we made that decision, the situation has changed."

"You're talking about the assassination of Martin Luther King."

"Dr. King was killed, but America is still bleeding." That

sentence came into Dave's head from nowhere, the way song lyrics sometimes did.

Wharton shook his head, and his mouth set in a stubborn line. Dave's optimism lost its fizz. Wharton said ponderously: "I have more than a thousand employees—many of them Negroes, by the way. If sales of Foam plummet because we offended viewers, some of those people will lose their jobs. I can't risk that."

"We would both be taking a risk," Dave said. "My own popularity is also at stake. But I want to do something to help this country heal."

Wharton smiled indulgently, as he might have if one of his children said something hopelessly idealistic. "And you think a kiss can do that?"

Dave made his voice lower and harsher. "It's Saturday night, Albert. Picture this: all over America, young black men are wondering whether to go out tonight and start fires and smash windows, or kick back and stay out of trouble. Before making up their minds, a lot of them will watch *Dave Williams and Friends*, just because it's hosted by a rock star. How do you want them feeling at the end of the show?"

"Well, obviously—"

"Think of how we built that set for Percy and Evie. Everything about the scene says that white and black have to be kept apart: their costumes, the roles they're playing, and the counter between them."

"That was the intention," said Wharton.

"We emphasized their separateness, and I don't want to throw that in black people's faces, especially not tonight, when their great hero has been murdered. But Evie's kiss, right at the end, undermines the whole setup. The kiss says we don't have to exploit one another and beat one another and murder one another. It says we *can* touch one another. That shouldn't be a big thing, but it is."

Dave held his breath. In truth he was not sure the kiss was going to stop many riots. He wanted the kiss left in just because it stood for right against wrong. But he thought maybe this argument might convince Wharton.

Caroline said: "Dave's so right, Dad. You really ought to do it."

"Yeah," said Edward.

Wharton was not much moved by his children's opinions, but he turned to his wife, somewhat to Dave's surprise, and asked: "What do you think, dear?"

"I wouldn't tell you to do anything that would harm the company," she said. "You know that. But I think this could even benefit National Soap. If you're criticized, tell them you did it because of Martin Luther King. You could end up a hero."

Dave said: "It's seven forty-five, Mr. Wharton. Charlie Lacklow is waiting by the phone. If you call him in the next five minutes, he'll have time to switch the tapes. The decision is yours."

The room went quiet. Wharton thought for a minute. Then he got up. "Heck, I think you might be right," he said.

He went out into the hall.

They all heard him dialing. Dave bit his lip. "Mr. Lacklow, please . . . Hello, Charlie . . . Yes, he's here, having dessert with us . . . We've had a long discussion about it, and I'm calling to ask you to put the kiss back in the show . . . Yes, that's what I said. Thank you, Charlie. Good night."

Dave heard the sound of the phone being cradled, and allowed a warm sense of triumph to suffuse him.

Mr. Wharton came back into the room. "Well, it's done," he said.

Dave said: "Thank you, Mr. Wharton."

.　.　.

"The kiss got huge publicity, nearly all of it good," Dave said to Evie over lunch in the Polo Lounge on Tuesday.

"So National Soap benefited?"

"That's what my new friend Mr. Wharton tells me. Sales of Foam have gone up, not down."

"And the show?"

"Also a success. They have already commissioned a season."

"And all because you did the right thing."

"My solo career is off to a great start. Not bad for a kid who failed all his exams."

Charlie Lacklow joined them at their table. "Sorry I'm late," he said insincerely. "I've been working on a joint press release with National Soap. A bit late, three days after the show, but they want to capitalize on the good publicity." He handed two sheets of paper to Dave.

Evie said: "May I see?" She knew Dave had trouble reading. He handed the papers to her. After a minute she said: "Dave! They have you saying: 'I wish to pay tribute to the managing director of National Soap,

Mr. Albert Wharton, for his courage and vision in insisting that the show be broadcast including the controversial kiss.' The nerve!"

Dave took back the paper.

Charlie handed him a ballpoint pen.

Dave wrote: "OK" at the top of the sheet, then signed it and handed it to Charlie.

Evie was apoplectic. "It's outrageous!" she said.

"Of course it is," said Dave. "That's show business."

CHAPTER FORTY-THREE

On the day Dimka's divorce became final, there was a meeting of top Kremlin aides to discuss the crisis in Czechoslovakia.

Dimka was bucked. He longed to marry Natalya, and now one major obstacle was out of the way. He could hardly wait to tell her the news, but when he arrived at the Nina Onilova Room several other aides were already there, and he had to wait.

When she came in, with her curly hair falling around her face in the way he found so enchanting, he gave her a big smile. She did not know what it was for, but she smiled back happily.

Dimka was almost as happy about Czechoslovakia. The new leader in Prague, Alexander Dubček, had turned out to be a reformer after Dimka's own heart. For the first time since Dimka had been working in the Kremlin, a Soviet satellite had announced that its version of Communism might not be exactly the same as the Soviet model. On April 5 Dubček had announced an action program that included freedom of speech, the right to travel to the West, an end to arbitrary arrests, and greater independence for industrial enterprises.

And if it worked in Czechoslovakia it might work in the USSR too.

Dimka had always thought that Communism could be reformed— unlike his sister and the dissidents, who believed it should be scrapped.

The meeting began, and Yevgeny Filipov presented a KGB report that said bourgeois elements were attempting to undermine the Czech revolution.

Dimka sighed heavily. This was typical of the Kremlin under Brezhnev. When people resisted their authority, they never asked whether there were legitimate reasons, but always looked for—or invented—malign motives.

Dimka's response was scornful. "I doubt if there are many bourgeois elements left in Czechoslovakia, after twenty years of Communism," he said.

As evidence Filipov produced two pieces of paper. One was a letter from Simon Wiesenthal, director of the Jewish Documentation Center in Vienna, praising the work of Zionist colleagues in Prague. The other was a leaflet printed in Czechoslovakia calling for Ukraine to secede from the USSR.

Across the table, Natalya Smotrov was derisive. "These documents are such obvious forgeries as to be laughable! It's not remotely plausible that Simon Wiesenthal is organizing a counterrevolution in Prague. Surely the KGB can do better than this?"

Filipov said angrily: "Dubček has turned out to be a snake in the grass!"

There was a grain of truth in that. When the previous Czech leader became unpopular, Dubček had been approved by Brezhnev as a replacement because he seemed dull and reliable. His radicalism had come as a nasty shock to Kremlin conservatives.

Filipov went on. "Dubček has allowed newspapers to attack Communist leaders!" he said indignantly.

Filipov was on weak ground here. Dubček's predecessor, Antonín Novotný, had been a crook. Now Dimka said: "The newly liberated newspapers revealed that Novotný was using government import licenses to buy Jaguar cars that he then sold to his party colleagues at a huge profit." He pretended incredulity. "Do you really want to protect such men, Comrade Filipov?"

"I want Communist countries to be governed in a disciplined and rigorous way," Filipov replied. "Subversive newspapers will soon start demanding Western-style so-called democracy, in which political parties representing rival bourgeois factions create the illusion of choice but unite to repress the working class."

"Nobody wants that," said Natalya. "But we do want Czechoslovakia to be a culturally advanced country attractive to Western tourists. If we crack down and tourism declines, the Soviet Union will be forced to pay out even more money to support the Czech economy."

Filipov sneered: "Is that the Foreign Ministry view?"

"The Foreign Ministry wants a negotiation with Dubček to ensure that the country remains Communist, not a crude intervention that will alienate capitalist and Communist countries alike."

In the end the economic arguments prevailed with the majority around the table. The aides recommended to the Politburo that Dubček be questioned by other Warsaw Pact members at their next meeting in Dresden, East Germany. Dimka was exultant: the threat of a hard-line purge had been warded off, at least for the moment. The thrilling Czech experiment in reformed Communism could continue.

Outside the room, Dimka said to Natalya: "My divorce has come through. I am no longer married to Nina, and that's official."

Her response was muted. "Good," she said, but she looked anxious.

Dimka had been living apart from Nina and little Grigor for a year. He had his own small place, where he and Natalya snatched a few hours of togetherness once or twice a week. It was unsatisfactory to both of them. "I want to marry you," he said.

"I want the same."

"Will you talk to Nik?"

"Yes."

"Tonight?"

"Soon."

"What are you scared of?"

"I'm not frightened for myself," she said. "I don't care what he does to me." Dimka winced, remembering her split lip. "It's you I'm worried about," she went on. "Remember the tape recorder man."

Dimka remembered. The black market trader who had cheated Natalya had been so badly beaten that he ended up in hospital. Natalya's implication was that the same might happen to Dimka if she asked Nik for a divorce.

Dimka did not believe this. "I'm not some lowlife criminal, I'm right-hand man to the premier. Nik can't touch me." He was 99 percent sure of this.

"I don't know," Natalya said unhappily. "Nik has high-up contacts too."

Dimka spoke more quietly. "Do you still have sex with him?"

"Not often. He has other girls."

"Do you enjoy it?"

"No!"

"Does he?"

"Not much."

"Then what's the problem?"

"His pride. He'll be angry to think I could prefer another man."

"I'm not afraid of his anger."

"I am. But I will talk to him. I promise."

"Thank you." Dimka lowered his voice to a whisper. "I love you."

"I love you, too."

Dimka returned to his office and summarized the aides' meeting for his boss, Alexei Kosygin.

"I don't believe the KGB, either," Kosygin said. "Andropov wants to suppress Dubček's reforms, and he's fabricating evidence to support that move." Yuri Andropov was the new head of the KGB, and a fanatical hard-liner. Kosygin went on: "But I need reliable intelligence from Czechoslovakia. If the KGB is untrustworthy, who can I turn to?"

"Send my sister there," said Dimka. "She's a reporter for TASS. In the Cuban missile crisis she sent Khrushchev superb intelligence from Havana via the Red Army telegraph. She can do the same for you from Prague.

"Good idea," said Kosygin. "Organize it, will you?"

.   .   .

Dimka did not see Natalya the next day, but the day after that she phoned just as he was leaving the office at seven.

"Did you talk to Nik?" he asked her.

"Not yet." Before Dimka could express his disappointment she went on: "But something else happened. Filipov came to see him."

"Filipov?" Dimka was astonished. "What does a Defense Ministry official want with your husband?"

"Mischief. I think he told Nik about you and me."

"Why would he do that? I know we're always clashing in meetings, but still . . ."

"There's something I haven't told you. Filipov made a pass at me."

"The stupid prick. When?"

"Two months ago, at the Riverside Bar. You were away with Kosygin."

"Incredible. He thought you might go to bed with him just because I was out of town?"

"Something like that. It was embarrassing. I told him I wouldn't sleep with him if he were the last man in Moscow. I probably should have been gentler."

"You think he talked to Nik for revenge?"

"I'm sure of it."

"What did Nik say to you?"

"Nothing. That's what worries me. I wish he'd bust my lip again."

"Don't say that."

"I'm afraid for you."

"I'll be fine, don't worry."

"Be careful."

"I will."

"Don't walk home, drive."

"I always do."

They said good-bye and hung up. Dimka put on his heavy coat and fur hat and left the building. His Moskvitch 408 was in the Kremlin car park, so he was safe there. He drove home, wondering whether Nik would have the nerve to ram his car, but nothing happened.

He reached his building and parked on the street a block away. This was the moment of greatest vulnerability. He had to walk from the car door to the building door under the streetlights. If they were going to beat him up they might do it here.

There was no one in sight, but they might be hiding.

Nik himself would not be the one to carry out the attack, Dimka presumed. He would send some of his thugs. Dimka wondered how many. Should he fight back? Against two he might have a chance: he was no pussy. If there were three or more he might as well lie down and take it.

He got out of the car and locked it.

He walked along the pavement. Would they burst out of the back of that parked van? Come around the corner of the next building? Be lurking in this doorway?

He reached his building and went inside. Perhaps they would be in the lobby.

He had to wait a long time for the elevator.

When it arrived and the doors closed he wondered if they would be in his apartment.

He unlocked his front door. The place was silent and still. He looked into the bedroom, the living room, the kitchen, and the bathroom.

The place was empty.

He bolted the door.

. . .

For two weeks Dimka walked around fearing he could be attacked at any minute. Eventually he decided it was not going to happen. Perhaps Nik did not care that his wife was having an affair; or perhaps he was too wise to make an enemy of someone who worked in the Kremlin. Either way, Dimka began to feel safer.

He still wondered at the spite of Yevgeny Filipov. How could the man even have been surprised that Natalya rejected him? He was dull and conservative and homely-looking and badly dressed: what did he imagine he had to tempt an attractive woman who already had a lover as well as a husband? But clearly Filipov's feelings had been deeply wounded. However, his revenge seemed not to have worked.

But the main thing on Dimka's mind was the Czech reform movement that was being called the Prague Spring. It had caused the most bitter Kremlin split since the Cuban missile crisis. Dimka's boss, Soviet premier Alexei Kosygin, was the leader of the optimists, who hoped the Czechs could find a way out of the bog of inefficiency and waste that was the typical Communist economy. Muting their enthusiasm for tactical reasons, they proposed that Dubček be watched carefully, but that confrontation should be avoided if possible. However, conservatives such as Filipov's boss, Defense Minister Andrei Grechko, and KGB chief Andropov were unnerved by Prague. They feared that radical ideas would undermine their authority, infect other countries, and subvert the Warsaw Pact military alliance. They wanted to send in the tanks, depose Dubček, and install a rigid Communist regime slavishly loyal to Moscow.

The real boss, Leonid Brezhnev, was sitting on the fence, as he so often did, waiting for a consensus to emerge.

Despite being some of the most powerful people in the world, the top men in the Kremlin were scared of stepping out of line. Marxism-Leninism answered all questions, so the eventual decision would be infallibly correct. Anyone who had argued for a different outcome was therefore revealed to be culpably out of touch with orthodox thinking. Dimka sometimes wondered if it was this bad in the Vatican.

Because no one wanted to be the first to express an opinion on the record, as always they had to get their aides to thrash things out informally ahead of any Politburo meeting.

"It's not just Dubček's revisionist ideas about freedom of the press," said Yevgeny Filipov to Dimka one afternoon in the broad corridor outside the Presidium Room. "He's a Slovak who wants to give more rights to the oppressed minority he comes from. Imagine if *that* idea starts to get around places such as Ukraine and Belarus."

As always, Filipov looked ten years out-of-date. Nowadays almost everyone was wearing their hair longer, but he still had an army crop. Dimka tried to forget for a moment that he was a malicious troublemaking bastard. "These dangers are remote," Dimka argued. "There's no immediate threat to the Soviet Union—certainly nothing to justify ham-fisted military intervention."

"Dubček has undermined the KGB. He's expelled several agents from Prague and authorized an investigation into the death of the old foreign minister Jan Masaryk."

"Is the KGB entitled to murder ministers in friendly governments?" Dimka asked. "Is that the message you want to send to Hungary and East Germany? That would make the KGB worse than the CIA. At least the Americans only murder people in enemy countries such as Cuba."

Filipov became petulant. "What is to be gained by allowing this foolishness in Prague?"

"If we invade Czechoslovakia, there will be a diplomatic freeze—you know that."

"So what?"

"It will damage our relations with the West. We're trying to reduce tension with the United States, so that we can spend less on our military. That whole effort could be sabotaged. An invasion might even help Richard Nixon get elected president—and he could *increase* American defense spending. Think what that could cost us!"

Filipov tried to interrupt, but Dimka overrode him. "The invasion will also shock the Third World. We're trying to strengthen our ties with nonaligned countries in the face of rivalry from China, which wants to replace us as leader of global Communism. That's why we're organizing the World Communist Conference in November. That conference could become a humiliating failure if we invade Czechoslovakia."

Filipov sneered: "So you would simply let Dubček do what he likes?"

"On the contrary." Dimka now revealed the proposal favored by his boss. "Kosygin will go to Prague and negotiate a compromise—a nonmilitary solution."

Filipov in his turn put his cards on the table. "The Defense Ministry will support that plan in the Politburo—on condition that we immediately begin preparations for an invasion in case the negotiation should fail."

"Agreed," said Dimka, who felt sure the military would make such preparations anyway.

The decision made, they went in opposite directions. Dimka returned to his office just as his secretary, Vera Pletner, was picking up the phone. He saw her face turn the color of the paper in her typewriter. "Has something happened?" he said.

She gave him the receiver. "Your ex-wife," she said.

Suppressing a groan, Dimka took the instrument and spoke into it. "What is it, Nina?"

"Come at once!" she screamed. "Grisha's gone!"

Dimka's heart seemed to stop. Grigor, whom they called Grisha, was not quite five years old, and had not yet started school. "What do you mean, gone?"

"I can't find him, he's disappeared, I've looked everywhere!"

There was a pain in Dimka's chest. He struggled to remain calm. "When and where did you last see him?"

"He went upstairs to see your mother. I let him go on his own—I always do, it's only three floors in the lift."

"When was that?"

"Less than an hour ago—you have to come!"

"I'm coming. Phone the police."

"Come quickly!"

"Phone the police, okay?"

"Okay."

Dimka dropped the phone and left the room. He raced out of the building. He had not paused to put on his coat, but he hardly noticed the cold Moscow air. He jumped into his Moskvitch, shoved the steering-column gearshift into first, and tore out of the compound. Even with his foot flat to the floor, the little car did not go fast.

Nina still had the apartment they had lived in together at Government House, less than a mile from the Kremlin. Dimka double-parked and ran in.

There was a KGB doorman in the lobby. "Good afternoon, Dmitri Ilich," the man said politely.

"Have you seen Grisha, my little boy?" said Dimka.

"Not today."

"He's disappeared—could he have gone out?"

"Not since I came back from my lunch break at one."

"Have any strangers entered the building today?"

"Several, as always. I have a list—"

"I'll look at it later. If you see Grisha, call the apartment immediately."

"Yes, of course."

"The police will be here any minute."

"I'll send them right up."

Dimka waited for the elevator. He was slick with perspiration. He was so jumpy he pressed the wrong button and had to wait while the lift stopped at an intermediate floor. When he reached Nina's floor she was in the corridor with Dimka's mother, Anya.

Anya was wiping her hands compulsively in her flower-print apron. She said: "He never reached my apartment. I don't understand what happened!"

"Could he have got lost?" said Dimka.

Nina said: "He's gone there twenty times before—he knows the way—but yes, he could have got distracted by something and gone to the wrong place, he's five years old."

"The doorman is sure he hasn't left the building. So we just have to search. We'll knock at every apartment door. No, wait, most of the residents have telephones. I'll go down and use the doorman's phone to call them."

Anya said: "He might not be in an apartment."

"You two search every corridor and staircase and cleaning closet."

"All right," said Anya. "We'll take the elevator to the top floor and work down."

They got in the lift and Dimka ran down the stairs. In the lobby he told the doorman what was happening and began to phone apartments. He was not sure how many there were in the building: maybe a hundred? "A little boy is lost, have you seen him?" he said each time his call was answered. As soon as he heard "No" he hung up and dialed the next apartment. He made a note of the apartments where there was no answer or no phone.

He had done four floors without a glimmer of hope when the police arrived, a fat sergeant and a young constable. They were maddeningly calm. "We'll take a look around," the sergeant said. "We know this building."

"It'll need more than two of you to search properly!" Dimka said.

"We'll send for reinforcements if necessary, sir," the sergeant said.

Dimka did not want to spend time arguing with them. He went back to phoning, but he was beginning to think that Nina and Anya had the best chance of finding Grisha. If the boy had wandered into the wrong apartment, surely the occupier would have phoned the doorman by now. Grisha might be going up and down staircases, lost. Dimka wanted to weep when he thought of how scared the little boy would be.

After he had been phoning for another ten minutes, the two policemen came up the stairs from the basement with Grisha walking between them, holding the sergeant's hand.

Dimka dropped the phone and ran to him.

Grisha said: "I couldn't open the door, and I cried!"

Dimka picked him up and hugged him, striving not to weep with relief.

After a minute he said: "What happened, Grisha?"

"The policemen found me," he said.

Anya and Nina appeared from the stairwell and came running, ecstatic with relief. Nina snatched Grisha from Dimka and crushed the boy to her bosom.

Dimka turned to the sergeant. "Where did you find him?"

The man looked pleased with himself. "Down in the cellar, in a storeroom. The door wasn't locked, but he couldn't reach the handle. He's had a scare, but otherwise he seems to have come to no harm."

Dimka addressed the boy. "Tell me, Grisha, why did you go down to the basement?"

"The man said there was a puppy—but I couldn't find the puppy!"

"The man?"

"Yes."

"Someone you know?"

Grisha shook his head.

The sergeant put his cap on to leave. "All's well that ends well, then."

"Just a minute," Dimka said. "You heard the boy. A man lured him down there with talk of a puppy."

"Yes, sir, he told me that. But no crime seems to have been committed, as far as I can see."

"The child was abducted!"

"Difficult to know exactly what happened, especially when the information comes from one so young."

"It's not difficult at all. A man inveigled the child down to the cellar, then abandoned him there."

"But what would be the point of that?"

"Look, I'm grateful to you for finding him, but don't you think you're taking the whole thing rather lightly?"

"Children do go astray every day."

Dimka began to be suspicious. "How did you know where to look?"

"A lucky guess. As I say, we're familiar with this building."

Dimka decided not to voice his suspicions while he was still in a state of high emotion. He turned away from the officer and spoke to Grisha again. "Did the man tell you his name?"

"Yes," said Grisha. "His name is Nik."

. . .

Next morning, Dimka sent for the KGB file on Nik Smotrov.

He was in a rage. He wanted to get a gun and kill Nik. He had to keep telling himself to remain calm.

It would not have been difficult for Nik to get past the doorman yesterday. He could have faked a delivery, entered close behind some

760 I FLOWER

legitimate residents so that he looked part of the group, or just flashed a Communist Party card. Dimka found it a little more difficult to figure out how Nik could have known that Grisha would be moving from one part of the building to another on his own, but on reflection he decided Nik had probably reconnoitered the building a few days earlier. He could have chatted to some neighbors, figured out the child's daily schedule, and picked the best opportunity. He had probably paid off those local policemen, too. His aim was to scare Dimka half to death.

He had succeeded.

But he was going to regret it.

In theory, Alexei Kosygin as premier could look at any file he liked. In practice, KGB chief Yuri Andropov would decide what Kosygin could and could not see. However, Dimka felt sure that Nik's activities, though criminal, had no political dimension, so there was no reason for the file to be withheld. Sure enough, it arrived on his desk that afternoon.

It was thick.

As Dimka suspected, Nik was a black market trader. Like most such men, he was an opportunist. He would buy and sell whatever came his way: flowered shirts, costly perfume, electric guitars, lingerie, Scotch whisky—any illegally imported luxury difficult to obtain in the Soviet Union. Dimka went carefully through the reports, looking for something he could use to destroy Nik.

The KGB dealt in rumors, and Dimka needed something definite. He could go to the police, report what the KGB file said, and demand an investigation. But Nik was sure to be bribing the police—otherwise he could not have got away with his crimes for so long. And his protectors would naturally want the bribes to continue. So they would make sure the investigation got nowhere.

The file contained plenty of material on Nik's personal life. He had a mistress and several girlfriends, including one with whom he smoked marijuana. Dimka wondered how much Natalya knew about the girlfriends. Nik met business associates most afternoons at the Bar Madrid near the Central Market. He had a pretty wife, who—

Dimka was shocked to read that Nik's wife was having a long-term affair with Dmitri Ilich "Dimka" Dvorkin, aide to Premier Kosygin.

Seeing his own name felt horrible. Nothing was private, it seemed.

At least there were no pictures or tape recordings.

There was, however, a photo of Nik, whom Dimka had never seen. He was a good-looking man with a charming smile. In the picture he wore a jacket with epaulets, a high-fashion item. According to the notes he was just under six feet tall with an athletic build.

Dimka wanted to pound him into jelly.

He put revenge fantasies out of his mind and read on.

Soon he struck gold.

Nik was buying television sets from the Red Army.

The Soviet military had a colossal budget that no one dared question for fear of being thought unpatriotic. Some of the money was spent on high-technology equipment bought from the West. In particular, every year the Red Army bought hundreds of expensive televisions. Their preferred brand was Franck, of West Berlin, whose sets had a superior picture and great sound. According to the file, most of these TVs were not needed by the army. They were ordered by a small group of midranking officers, who were named in the file. The officers then declared the televisions obsolete and sold them cheaply to Nik, who resold them at a huge price on the black market and shared out the profits.

Most of Nik's dealings were penny-ante, but this scam had been making him serious money for years.

There was no proof that the story was true, but it made total sense to Dimka. The KGB had reported the story to the army, but an army investigation had turned up no proof. Most likely, Dimka thought, the investigator had been cut in on the deal.

He phoned Natalya's office. "Quick question," he said. "What brand of TV do you have at home?"

"Franck," she said immediately. "It's great. I can get you one, if you like."

"No, thanks."

"Why do you ask?"

"I'll explain later." Dimka hung up.

He looked at his watch. It was five. He left the Kremlin and drove to the street called Sadovaya-Samotyochnaya.

He had to scare Nik. It would not be easy, but he had to do it. Nik had to be made to understand that he must never, ever, threaten Dimka's family.

He parked his Moskvitch but did not get out immediately. He

recalled the frame of mind he had been in throughout the Cuban missile project, when he had to keep the mission secret at all costs. He had destroyed men's careers and ruined their lives without hesitation, because the job had to be done. Now he was going to ruin Nik.

He locked his car and walked to the Bar Madrid.

He pushed open the door and stepped inside. He stood still and looked around. It was a bleak modern place, cold and plastic, insufficiently warmed by an electric fire and some photographs of flamenco dancers on the walls. The handful of customers gazed at him with interest. They looked like petty crooks. None resembled the photo of Nik in the file.

At the far end of the room was a corner bar with a door next to it marked PRIVATE.

Dimka strode through the room as if he owned it. Without stopping he spoke to the man behind the bar. "Nik in the back?"

The man looked as if he might be about to tell Dimka to stop and wait, but then he looked again at Dimka's face and changed his mind. "Yes," he said.

Dimka pushed open the door.

In a small back room four men were playing cards. There was a lot of money on the table. To one side, on a couch, two young women in cocktail dresses and heavy makeup were smoking long American cigarettes and looking bored.

Dimka recognized Nik immediately. The face was as handsome as the photograph had suggested, but the camera had failed to capture the cold expression. Nik looked up and said: "This is a private room. Piss off."

Dimka said: "I've got a message for you."

Nik put his cards facedown on the table and sat back. "Who the fuck are you?"

"Something bad is going to happen."

Two of the card players stood up and turned to face Dimka. One reached inside his jacket. Dimka thought he might be about to draw a weapon. But Nik held up a cautionary hand, and the man hesitated.

Nik kept his eyes on Dimka. "What are you talking about?"

"When the bad thing happens, you'll ask who's causing it."

"And you'll tell me?"

"I'm telling you now. It's Dmitri Ilich Dvorkin. He's the cause of your problems."

"I don't have any problems, asshole."

"You didn't, until yesterday. Then you made a mistake—asshole."

The men around Nik tensed, but he remained calm. "Yesterday?" His eyes narrowed. "Are you the creep she's fucking?"

"When you find yourself in so much trouble that you don't know what to do, remember my name."

"You're Dimka!"

"You'll see me again," said Dimka, and he turned slowly and walked out of the room.

As he walked through the bar, all eyes were on him. He looked straight ahead, expecting a bullet in the back at any moment.

He reached the door and went out.

He grinned to himself. I got away with it, he thought.

Now he had to make good on his threat.

He drove six miles from the city center to the Khodynka airfield and parked at the headquarters of Red Army Intelligence. The old building was a bizarre piece of Stalin-era architecture, a nine-story tower surrounded by a two-story outer ring. The directorate had expanded into a newer fifteen-story building nearby: intelligence organizations never got smaller.

Carrying the KGB file on Nik, Dimka went into the old building and asked for General Volodya Peshkov.

A guard said: "Do you have an appointment?"

Dimka raised his voice. "Don't fuck around, son. Just call the general's secretary and say I'm here."

After a flurry of anxious activity—few people dropped by this place without a summons—he was directed through a metal detector and led up in the lift to an office on the top floor.

This was the highest building around and it had a fine view over the roofs of Moscow. Volodya welcomed Dimka and offered him tea. Dimka had always liked his uncle. Now in his midfifties, Volodya had silver-gray hair. Despite the hard blue-eyed stare, he was a reformer—unusual among the generally conservative military. But he had been to America.

"What's on your mind?" said Volodya. "You look ready to kill someone."

"I've got a problem," Dimka told him. "I've made an enemy."

"Not unusual, in the circles within which you work."

"This is nothing to do with politics. Nik Smotrov is a gangster."

"How did you come to fall foul of such a man?"

"I'm sleeping with his wife."

Volodya looked disapproving. "And he's threatening you."

Volodya had probably never been unfaithful to Zoya, his scientist wife, who was as beautiful as she was brilliant. But that meant he had scant sympathy for Dimka. Volodya might have felt differently if he had been so foolish as to marry someone like Nina.

Dimka said: "Nik kidnapped Grisha."

Volodya sat upright. "What? When?"

"Yesterday. We got him back. He was only shut in the cellar of Government House. But it was a warning."

"You have to give up this woman!"

Dimka ignored that. "There's a particular reason why I've come to you, Uncle. There's a way you could help me and do the army some good at the same time."

"Go on."

"Nik is behind a fraud that costs the army millions every year." Dimka explained about the TV sets. When he had finished he put the file on Volodya's desk. "It's all in there—including the names of the officers who are organizing the whole thing."

Volodya did not pick up the file. "I'm not a policeman. I can't arrest this Nik. And if he's bribing police officers, there's not much I can do about it."

"But you can arrest the army officers involved."

"Oh, yes. They will all be in army jails within twenty-four hours."

"And you can shut down the whole business."

"Very quickly."

And then Nik will be ruined, Dimka thought. "Thank you, Uncle," he said. "That's very helpful."

· · ·

Dimka was in his apartment, packing for Czechoslovakia, when Nik came to see him.

The Politburo had approved Kosygin's plan. Dimka was flying with him to Prague to negotiate a nonmilitary solution to the crisis. They would find a way to allow the liberalization experiment to continue while at the same time reassuring the diehards that there was no fundamental threat to the Soviet system. But what Dimka hoped was that in the long term the Soviet system *would* change.

Prague in May would be mild and wet. Dimka was folding his raincoat when the doorbell rang.

There was no doorman in his building, and no intercom system. The street door was permanently unlocked and visitors walked upstairs to the apartments unannounced. It was not as luxurious as Government House, where his ex-wife was living in their old apartment. Dimka occasionally felt resentful, but he was glad Grisha was near his grandmother.

Dimka opened the door and was shocked to see his lover's husband standing there.

Nik was an inch taller than Dimka, and heavier, but Dimka was ready to take him on. He stepped back a pace and picked up the nearest heavy object, a glass ashtray, to use as a weapon.

"No need for that," said Nik, but he stepped into the hall and shut the door behind him.

"Piss off," said Dimka. "Go now, before you get into any more trouble." He managed to sound more confident than he felt.

Nik glared at him with hot hatred in his eyes. "You've made your point," he said. "You're not afraid of me. You're powerful enough to turn my life to shit. I should be scared of you. All right, I get it. I'm scared."

He did not sound it.

Dimka said: "What have you come here for?"

"I don't give a toss for the bitch. I only married her to please my mother, who's dead now. But a man's pride is hurt when another man pokes his fire. You know what I mean."

"Get to the point."

"My business is ruined. No one in the army will speak to me, let alone sell me TV sets. Men who have built four-bedroom dachas from the money I've made for them now walk past me in the street without speaking—those who aren't in jail."

"You shouldn't have threatened my son."

"I know it now. I thought my wife was opening her legs for some little apparatchik. I didn't know he was a fucking warlord. I underestimated you."

"So bugger off home and lick your wounds."

"I have to make a living."

"Try working."

"No jokes, please. I've found another source of Western TV sets—nothing to do with the army."

"Why should I care?"

"I can rebuild the business you destroyed."

"So what?"

"Can I come in and sit down?"

"Don't be so fucking stupid."

Rage flared again in Nik's eyes, and Dimka feared he had gone too far, but the flame died down, and Nik said meekly: "Okay, here's the deal. I'll give you ten percent of the profits."

"You want me to go into business with you? In a criminal enterprise? You must be mad."

"All right, twenty percent. And you don't have to do anything except leave me alone."

"I don't want your money, you fool. This is the Soviet Union. You can't just buy anything you want, like in America. My connections are worth far more than you could ever pay me."

"There must be something you want."

Until this moment Dimka had been arguing with Nik just to keep him off balance, but now he saw an opportunity. "Oh, yes," he said. "There is something I want."

"Name it."

"Divorce your wife."

"What?"

"I want you to get a divorce."

"Divorce Natalya?"

"Divorce your wife," Dimka said again. "Which of those three words are you having trouble understanding?"

"Fuck me, is that all?"

"Yes."

"You can marry her. I wouldn't touch her now anyway."

"If you divorce her, I'll leave you alone. I'm not a cop, and I'm not running a crusade against corruption in the USSR. I have more important work to do."

"It's a deal." Nik opened the door. "I'll send her up."

That took Dimka by surprise. "She's here?"

"Waiting in the car. I'll have her things packed up and sent around tomorrow. I don't want her in my place ever again."

Dimka raised his voice. "Don't you dare hurt her. If she's even bruised, the whole deal is off."

Nik turned in the doorway and pointed a threatening finger. "And don't you renege. If you try to screw me I'll cut off her nipples with the kitchen scissors."

Dimka believed he would. He suppressed a shudder. "Get out of my flat."

Nik left without closing the door.

Dimka was breathing hard, as if he had been running. He stood still in the small hall of the apartment. He heard Nik clattering down the stairs. He put the ashtray down on the hall table. His fingers were slippery with perspiration, and he almost dropped it.

What just happened seemed like a dream. Had Nik really stood in this hallway and agreed to a divorce? Had Dimka really scared him off?

A minute later he heard footsteps of a different kind on the stairs: lighter, faster, coming up. He did not go out of the apartment: he felt stuck where he was.

Natalya appeared in the doorway, her broad smile lighting up the whole place. She threw herself into his arms. He buried his face in her mass of curls. "You're here," he said.

"Yes," she said. "And I'm never going to leave."

CHAPTER FORTY-FOUR

Rebecca was tempted to be unfaithful to Bernd. But she could not lie to him. So she told him everything in a convulsion of repentance. "I've met someone I really like," she said. "And I've kissed him. Twice. I'm so sorry. I'll never do it again."

She was scared of what he would say next. He might immediately ask for a divorce. Most men would. Bernd was better than most men, though. But it would break her heart if he were not angry but simply humiliated. She would have hurt the person she loved most in the world.

However, Bernd's response to her confession was shockingly different from anything she had expected. "You should go ahead," he said. "Have an affair with the guy."

They were in bed, last thing at night, and she turned over and stared at him. "How can you say that?"

"This is 1968, the age of free love. Everyone is having sex with everyone else. Why should you miss out?"

"You don't mean that."

"I didn't mean it to sound so trivial."

"What did you mean?"

"I know you love me," he said, "and I know you like having sex with me, but you mustn't go through the rest of your life without experiencing the real thing."

"I don't believe in the real thing," she said. "It's different for everyone. It's much better with you than it was with Hans."

"It will always be good, because we love each other. But I think you need a really good fuck."

And he was right, she thought. She loved Bernd and she liked the peculiar sex they had, but when she thought about Claus lying on top of her, kissing her and moving inside her, and how she would lift her hips to meet his thrusts, she immediately got wet. She was ashamed of this feeling. Was she an animal? Perhaps she was, but Bernd was right about what she needed.

"I think I'm weird," she said. "Maybe it's because of what happened to me in the war." She had told Bernd—but no one else, ever—how Red Army soldiers had been about to rape her when Carla had offered herself instead. German women rarely spoke of that time, even to one another. But Rebecca would never forget the sight of Carla going up that staircase, head held high, with the Soviet soldiers following her like eager dogs. Rebecca, thirteen years old, had known what they were going to do, and she had wept with relief that it was not happening to her.

Bernd asked perceptively: "Do you also feel guilty that you escaped while Carla suffered?"

"Yes, isn't that strange?" she said. "I was a child, and a victim, but I feel as if I did something shameful."

"It's not unusual," Bernd said. "Men who survive battles feel remorse because others died and not them." Bernd had got the scar on his forehead during the battle of Seelow Heights.

"I felt better after Carla and Werner adopted me," Rebecca said. "Somehow that made it all right. Parents make sacrifices for their children, don't they? Women suffer to bring children into the world. Perhaps it doesn't make much sense, but once I became Carla's daughter I felt entitled."

"It makes sense."

"Do you really want me to go to bed with another man?"

"Yes."

"But why?"

"Because the alternative is worse. If you don't do it, you'll always feel, in your heart, that you missed out on something because of me, that you made a sacrifice for my sake. I'd rather you went ahead and tried it. You don't have to reveal the details: just come home and tell me you love me."

"I don't know," Rebecca said, and she slept uneasily that night.

On the evening of the next day she was sitting next to the man who wanted to become her lover, Claus Krohn, in a meeting room in Hamburg's enormous green-roofed neo-Renaissance town hall. Rebecca was a member of the parliament that ran the Hamburg city-state. The committee was discussing a proposal to demolish a slum and build a new shopping center. But all she could think about was Claus.

She was sure that after tonight's meeting Claus would invite her to a bar for a drink. This would be the third time. After the first he had kissed her good night. The second had ended with a passionate clinch in a car park, when they had kissed with mouths open and he had touched her breasts. Tonight, she felt sure, he would ask her to go to his apartment.

She did not know what to do. She could not concentrate on the debate. She doodled on her agenda. She was both bored and anxious: the meeting was tedious but she did not want it to end because she was scared of what would happen next.

Claus was an attractive man: intelligent, kind, charming, and exactly her age, thirty-seven. His wife had died in a car crash two years ago, and he had no children. He was not good-looking in the movie-star sense, but he had a warm smile. Tonight he was wearing a politician's blue suit, but he was the only man in the room with a shirt open at the neck. Rebecca wanted to make love to him, wanted it badly. And at the same time she dreaded it.

The meeting came to an end and, as she expected, Claus asked her if she would like to meet him at the Yacht Bar, a quiet place well away from city hall. They drove there in their separate cars.

The bar was small and dark, busiest in the daytime, when it was used by people who had sailboats, quiet and almost deserted now. Claus ordered a beer, Rebecca asked for a glass of Sekt. As soon as they were settled she said: "I told my husband about us."

Claus was startled. "Why?" he said. Then he added: "Not that there's much to tell." All the same he looked guilty.

"I can't lie to Bernd," she said. "I love him."

"And you obviously can't lie to me, either," Claus said.

"I'm sorry."

"It isn't something to apologize for—just the opposite. Thank you for being honest. I appreciate it." Claus looked crestfallen, and amid all her other emotions Rebecca felt pleased that he liked her enough to be so disappointed. He said ruefully: "If you've confessed to your husband, why are you here with me now?"

"Bernd told me to go ahead," she said.

"Your husband wants you to kiss me?"

"He wants me to become your lover."

"That's creepy. Is it to do with his paralysis?"

"No," she lied. "Bernd's condition makes no difference to our sex life." This was the story she had told her mother and a few other women whom she was really close to. She deceived them for Bernd's sake: she felt it would be humiliating for him if people knew the truth.

"Well," said Claus, "if this is my lucky day, shall we go straight to my apartment?"

"Let's not rush, if you don't mind."

He put his hand over hers. "It's okay to be nervous."

"I haven't done this often."

He smiled. "That's not a bad thing, you know, even if we are living in the age of free love."

"I slept with two boys at university. Then I married Hans, who turned out to be a police spy. Then I fell in love with Bernd and we escaped together. There, that's my entire love life."

"Let's talk about something else for a while," he said. "Are your parents still in the East?"

"Yes, they'll never get permission to leave. Once you make an enemy of someone like Hans Hoffmann—my first husband—he never forgets."

"You must miss them."

She could not express how much she missed her family. The Communists had blocked calls to the West the day they built the Wall, so she could not even speak to her parents on the phone. All she had was letters—opened and read by the Stasi, usually delayed, often censored, any enclosure of value stolen by the police. A few photos had got through, and Rebecca had them next to her bed: her father turning gray, her mother getting heavier, Lili growing into a beautiful woman.

Instead of trying to explain her grief she said: "Tell me about yourself. What happened to you in the war?"

"Nothing much, except that I starved, like most kids," he said. "The house next door was destroyed and everyone in it killed, but we were all right. My father is a surveyor: he spent much of the war assessing bomb damage and making buildings safe."

"Do you have brothers and sisters?"

"One of each. You?"

"My sister, Lili, is still in East Berlin. My brother, Walli, escaped soon after I did. He's a guitar player in a group called Plum Nellie."

"That Walli? He's your brother?"

"Yes. I was there when he was born, on the floor of our kitchen, which was the only warm room in the house. Quite an experience for a fourteen-year-old girl."

"So he escaped."

"And came to live with me, here in Hamburg. He joined the group when they were playing some grimy club on the Reeperbahn."

"And now he's a pop star. Do you see him?"

"Of course. Every time Plum Nellie plays in West Germany."

"What a thrill!" Claus looked at her glass and saw that it was empty. "Would you like another Sekt?"

Rebecca felt a tightness in her chest. "No, thanks, I don't think so."

"Listen," he said. "Something I want you to understand. I'm desperate to make love to you, but I know you're torn. Just remember that you can change your mind at any moment. There's no such thing as the point of no return. If you feel uncomfortable, just say so. I won't be angry or insistent, I promise. I would hate to feel I'd pushed you into something you weren't ready for."

It was exactly the right thing for him to say. The tightness eased. Rebecca had been afraid of getting in too deep, realizing she had made the wrong decision, and feeling unable to back out. Claus's promise set her mind at rest. "Let's go," she said.

They got into their cars and Rebecca followed Claus. Driving along she felt a wild exhilaration. She was about to give herself to Claus. She pictured his face as she took off her blouse: she was wearing a new bra, black with lace trimming. She thought of how they would kiss— frantically before, lovingly after. She imagined his sigh as she took his penis in her mouth. She felt she had never wanted anything so badly, and she had to clamp her teeth together to prevent herself crying out.

Claus had a small apartment in a modern building. Going up in the elevator, Rebecca was assailed by doubts again. What if he didn't like what he saw when she took off her clothes? She was thirty-seven: she no longer had the firm breasts and perfect skin of her teenage years. What if he had a hidden dark side? He might produce handcuffs and a whip, then lock the door—

She told herself not to be silly. She had the normal woman's ability to know when she was with a weirdo, and Claus was delightfully normal. All the same, she felt apprehensive as he opened the apartment door and ushered her in.

It was a typical man's home, a bit bare of ornament, with utilitarian furniture except for a large television and an expensive record player. Rebecca said: "How long have you lived here?"

"A year."

As she had guessed, it was not the home he had shared with his late wife.

He had undoubtedly planned what to do next. Moving quickly, he ignited the gas fire, put a Mozart string quartet on the record deck, and assembled a tray with a bottle of schnapps, two glasses, and a bowl of salted nuts.

They sat side by side on the couch.

She wanted to ask him how many other girls he had seduced on this couch. It would have struck a wrong note, but all the same she wondered. Was he enjoying being single, or did he long to marry again? Another question she was not going to ask.

He poured drinks and she took a sip just for something to do.

He said: "If we kiss now, we'll taste the liquor on each other's tongues."

She grinned. "All right."

He leaned toward her. "I don't like to waste money," he murmured.

She said: "I'm so glad you're frugal."

For a moment they could not kiss because they were giggling too much.

Then they did.

. . .

People thought Cameron Dewar was mad when he invited Richard Nixon to speak at Berkeley. It was the most famously radical campus in the country. Nixon would be crucified, they said. There would be a riot. Cam did not care.

Cam thought Nixon was the only hope for America. Nixon was strong and determined. People said he was unscrupulous and sly: so what? America needed such a leader. God forbid that the president should be a man such as Bobby Kennedy who could not stop asking himself what was right and what was wrong. The next president had to destroy the rioters in the ghettos and the Vietcong in the jungle, not search his own conscience.

In his letter to Nixon, Cam said that the liberals and the crypto-Communists on campus got all the attention in the left-leaning media, but in truth most students were conservative and law-abiding, and there would be a huge turnout for Nixon.

Cam's family was furious. His grandfather and his great-grandfather had both been Democratic senators. His parents had always voted Democrat. His sister was so outraged she could barely speak. "How can you campaign for injustice and dishonesty and war?" Beep said.

"There's no justice without order on the streets, and there's no peace while we're threatened by international Communism."

"Where have you *been* the last few years? When the blacks were nonviolent they just got attacked with nightsticks and dogs! Governor Reagan praises the police for beating up student demonstrators!"

"You're so against the police."

"No, I'm not. I'm against criminals. Cops who beat up demonstrators are criminals, and they should go to jail."

"There, that's why I support such men as Nixon and Reagan: because their opponents want to put cops in jail instead of troublemakers."

Cam was pleased when Vice President Hubert Humphrey declared that he would seek the Democratic nomination. Humphrey had been Johnson's yes-man for four years, and no one would trust him either to win the war or to negotiate peace, so he was unlikely to be elected, but he might spoil things for the more dangerous Bobby Kennedy.

Cam's letter to Nixon got a reply from one of the campaign team, John Ehrlichman, suggesting a meeting. Cam was thrilled. He wanted to work in politics: maybe this was the beginning!

Ehrlichman was Nixon's advance man. He was intimidatingly tall, six foot two, with black eyebrows and receding hair. "Dick loved your letter," he said.

They met at a fragrant coffee shop on Telegraph Avenue and sat outside under a tree in new leaf, watching students go by on bicycles in the sunshine. "A nice place to study," Ehrlichman said. "I went to UCLA."

He asked Cam a lot of questions. He was intrigued by Cam's Democratic forebears. "My grandmother was editor of a newspaper called the *Buffalo Anarchist*," Cam admitted.

"It's a sign of how America is becoming more conservative," Ehrlichman said.

Cam was relieved to learn that his family would not be an obstruction to a career in the Republican Party.

"Dick won't speak on the Berkeley campus," Ehrlichman said. "It's too risky."

Cam was disappointed. He thought Ehrlichman was wrong: the event could be a big success.

He was about to argue when Ehrlichman said: "But he wants you to start a group called Berkeley Students for Nixon. It will show that not all young people are fooled by Gene McCarthy or in love with Bobby Kennedy."

Cam was flattered to be taken so seriously by a presidential campaigner, and he quickly agreed to do what Ehrlichman asked.

His closest friend on campus was Jamie Mulgrove, who like Cam was majoring in Russian and a member of the Young Republicans. They announced the formation of the group, and got some publicity in *The Daily Californian*, the student newspaper, but only ten people joined.

Cam and Jamie organized a lunchtime meeting to attract members. With Ehrlichman's help, Cam got three prominent California Republicans to speak. He booked a hall that would hold two hundred fifty.

He sent out a press release and this time got a wider response from local newspapers and radio stations intrigued by the counterintuitive idea of Berkeley students supporting Nixon. Several ran stories about the meeting and promised to send reporters.

776 | F L O W E R

Sharon McIsaac from the *San Francisco Examiner* called Cam. "How many members do you have so far?" she asked.

Cam took an instinctive dislike to her pushy tone. "I can't tell you that," he said. "It's like a military secret. Before a battle, you don't let the enemy know how many guns you've got."

"Not many, then," she said sarcastically.

The meeting was shaping up to be a minor media event.

Unfortunately, they could not sell the tickets.

They could have given them away, but that was risky: it could attract left-wing students who would heckle.

Cam still believed that thousands of students were conservative, but he realized they were unwilling to admit it in today's atmosphere. That was cowardly, but politics did not matter much to most people, he knew.

But what was he going to do?

The day before the meeting he had more than two hundred tickets left—and Ehrlichman called. "Just checking, Cam," he said. "How's it shaping up?"

"It's going to be terrific, John," Cam lied.

"Any press interest?"

"Some. I'm expecting a few reporters."

"Sold many tickets?" It was almost as if Ehrlichman could read Cam's mind over the phone.

Cam was caught in his deception and could not backtrack. "A few more to go and we'll be sold out." With luck, Ehrlichman would never know.

Then Ehrlichman dropped his bombshell. "I'll be in San Francisco tomorrow, so I'll come along."

"Great!" said Cam, his heart sinking.

"See you then."

That afternoon, after a class on Dostoevsky, Cam and Jamie stayed in the lecture theater and scratched their heads. Where could they find two hundred Republican students?

"They don't have to be real students," Cam said.

"We don't want the press saying the meeting was packed with stooges," Jamie said anxiously.

"Not stooges. Just Republicans who don't happen to be students."

"I still think it's risky."

"I know. But better than a flop."

"Where are we going to get the bodies?"

"Do you have a number for the Oakland Young Republicans?"

"I do."

They went to a pay phone and Cam called. "I need two hundred people just to make the event look like a success," he confessed.

"I'll see what I can do," the man said.

"Tell them not to speak to reporters, though. We don't want the press finding out that Berkeley Students for Nixon consists mainly of people who aren't students."

After Cam hung up, Jamie said: "Isn't this kind of dishonest?"

"What do you mean?" Cam knew exactly what he meant, but he was not going to admit it. He was not willing to jeopardize his big chance with Ehrlichman just for the sake of a petty lie.

Jamie said: "Well, we're telling people that Berkeley students support Nixon, but we're faking it."

"But we can't back out now!" Cameron was scared that Jamie would want to cancel the whole thing.

"I guess not," Jamie said dubiously.

Cam was in suspense all the next morning. At half past twelve there were only seven people in the hall. When the speakers arrived Cam took them to a side room and offered them coffee and cookies baked by Jamie's mother. At a quarter to one the place was still almost deserted. But then at ten to one, people started to trickle in. By one the room was almost full, and Cam breathed a little easier.

He invited Ehrlichman to chair the meeting. "No," said Ehrlichman. "It looks better if a student does it."

Cam introduced the speakers but hardly heard what they said. His meeting was a success, and Ehrlichman was impressed—but it could still go wrong.

At the end he summed up and said that the popularity of the meeting was a sign of a student backlash against demonstrations, liberalism, and drugs. He got an enthusiastic round of applause.

When it was over he could hardly wait to get them all out the door.

The reporter Sharon McIsaac was there. She had a crusading look, reminding him of Evie Williams, who had spurned his adolescent love. Sharon was approaching students. A couple declined to speak to her; then, to Cam's relief, she buttonholed one of the few genuine Berkeley Republicans. By the time the interview was over, everyone else had left.

At two thirty Cam and Ehrlichman stood in an empty room. "Well done," said Ehrlichman. "Are you sure all those people were students?"

Cam hesitated. "Are we on the record?"

Ehrlichman laughed. "Listen," he said. "When the semester ends, do you want to come and work on Dick's presidential election campaign? We could use a guy like you."

Cam's heart leaped. "I'd love to," he said.

. . .

Dave was in London, staying with his parents in Great Peter Street, when Fitz knocked on the door.

The family was in the kitchen: Lloyd, Daisy, and Dave—Evie was in Los Angeles. It was six, the hour at which the children had used to eat their evening meal, which they called "tea," when they were small. In those days the parents would sit with them for a while and talk about the day, before going out for the evening, usually to some political meeting. Daisy would smoke and Lloyd would sometimes make cocktails. The habit of meeting in the kitchen to chat at that hour had persisted long after the children grew too old to have "tea."

Dave was talking to his parents about his breakup with Beep when the maid came in and said: "It's Earl Fitzherbert."

Dave saw his father tense up.

Daisy put her hand on Lloyd's arm and said: "It will be all right."

Dave was consumed with curiosity. He knew, now, that the earl had seduced Ethel when she was his housekeeper, and that Lloyd was the illegitimate child of their affair. He knew, too, that Fitz had angrily refused to acknowledge Lloyd as his son for more than half a century. So what was the earl doing here tonight?

Fitz walked into the room using two canes and said: "My sister, Maud, has died."

Daisy sprang up. "I'm so sorry to hear that, Fitz," she said. "Come and sit down." She took his arm.

But Fitz hesitated and looked at Lloyd. "I have no right to sit down in this house," he said.

Dave could tell that humility did not come naturally to Fitz.

Lloyd was controlling intense emotion. This was the father who had rejected him all his life. "Please sit down," Lloyd said stiffly.

Dave pulled out a kitchen chair and Fitz sat at the table. "I'm going to her funeral," he said. "It's in two days' time."

Lloyd said: "She was living in East Germany, wasn't she? How did you hear that she had died?"

"Maud has a daughter, Carla. She telephoned the British embassy in East Berlin. They were so kind as to phone me and give me the news. I was a minister in the Foreign Office until 1945, and that still counts for something, I'm glad to say."

Without being asked, Daisy took a bottle of Scotch from a cupboard, poured an inch into a glass, and put it in front of Fitz with a small jug of tap water. Fitz poured a little water into the whisky and took a sip. "How kind of you to remember, Daisy," he said. Dave recalled that Daisy had lived with Fitz for a while, when she was married to his son, Boy Fitzherbert. That was why she knew how he liked his whisky.

Lloyd said: "Lady Maud was my late mother's best friend." He sounded a little less uptight. "I last saw her when Mam took me to Berlin in 1933. At that time Maud was a journalist, writing articles that annoyed Hitler."

Fitz said: "I haven't seen my sister or spoken to her since 1919. I was angry with her for marrying without my permission, and marrying a German, too; and I stayed angry for almost fifty years." His discolored old face showed profound sadness. "Now it's too late for me to forgive her. What a fool I was." He looked directly at Lloyd. "A fool about that, and other things."

Lloyd gave a brief, silent nod of acknowledgment.

Dave caught his mother's eye. He felt that something important had just happened, and her expression confirmed it. Fitz's regret was so deep it could hardly be spoken, but he had come as near as he could to apologizing.

It was hard to imagine that this feeble old man had once been swept by tidal waves of passion. But Fitz had loved Ethel, and Dave knew that Ethel had felt the same, for he had heard her say it. Fitz had rejected their child and now, after a lifetime of denial, he was looking back and comprehending how much he had lost. It was unbearably sad.

"I'll go with you," Dave said impulsively.

"What?"

"To the funeral. I'll go to Berlin with you." Dave was not sure why he wanted to do this, except he sensed it might have a healing effect.

"You're very kind, young Dave," said Fitz.

Daisy said: "That would be a wonderful thing to do, Dave."

Dave glanced at his father, nervous that Lloyd would disapprove; but there were surprising tears in Lloyd's eyes.

Next day Dave and Fitz flew to Berlin. They stayed overnight at a hotel on the west side.

"Do you mind if I call you Fitz?" Dave said over dinner. "We always called Bernie Leckwith 'Grandpa,' even though we knew he was my father's stepfather. And as a child I never met you. So it feels, like, too late to change."

"I'm in no position to dictate to you," said Fitz. "And anyway, I really don't mind."

They talked about politics. "We Conservatives were right about Communism," said Fitz. "We said it wouldn't work, and it doesn't. But we were wrong about social democracy. When Ethel said we should give everyone free education and free health care and unemployment insurance, I told her she was living in a dream world. But now look: everything she campaigned for has come to pass, and yet England is still England."

Fitz had a charming ability to admit his mistakes, Dave thought. Clearly the earl had not always been this way: his quarrels with his family had lasted decades. Perhaps it was a quality that came with old age.

The following morning a black Mercedes with a driver, ordered by Dave's secretary, Jenny Pritchard, was waiting to take them across the border and into the East.

They drove to Checkpoint Charlie.

They went through a barrier and into a long shed where they had to hand over their passports. Then they were asked to wait.

The border guard who had taken their passports went away. After a while a tall, stooped man in a civilian suit ordered them to get out of their Mercedes and follow him.

The man strode ahead, then looked around, irritated at Fitz's slowness. "Please hurry," he said in English.

Dave remembered the German he had learned in school and improved in Hamburg. "My grandfather is old," he said indignantly.

Fitz spoke in a low voice. "Don't argue," he said to Dave. "This arrogant bastard is with the Stasi." Dave raised an eyebrow: he had not previously heard Fitz use bad language. "They're like the KGB, only not so softhearted," Fitz added.

They were taken to a bare office with a metal table and hard wooden chairs. They were not asked to sit, but Dave held a chair for Fitz, who sank into it gratefully.

The tall man spoke German to an interpreter, who smoked cigarettes as he translated the questions. "Why do you wish to enter East Germany?"

"To attend the funeral of a close relative at eleven this morning," Fitz answered. He looked at his wristwatch, a gold Omega. "It's ten now. I hope this won't take long."

"It will take as long as necessary. What is your sister's name?"

"Why do you ask that?"

"You say you wish to attend the funeral of your sister. What is her name?"

"I said I wanted to attend the funeral of a close relative. I did not say it was my sister. You obviously know all about it already."

This secret policeman had been waiting for them, Dave realized. It was hard to imagine why.

"Answer the question. What is your sister's name?"

"She was Frau Maud von Ulrich, as your spies have obviously informed you."

Dave noticed that Fitz was getting annoyed, and breaking his own injunction to say as little as possible.

The man said: "How is it that Lord Fitzherbert has a German sister?"

"She married a friend of mine called Walter von Ulrich, who was a German diplomat in London. He was killed by the Gestapo during the Second World War. What did you do in the war?"

Dave saw, from the look of fury on the tall man's face, that he had understood; but he did not answer the question. Instead he turned to Dave. "Where is Walli Franck?"

Dave was astonished. "I don't know."

"Of course you know. He is in your music group."

"The group has split. I haven't seen Walli for months. I don't know where he is."

"This is not believable. You are partners."

"Partners fall out."

"What is the reason for your quarrel?"

"Personal and musical differences." In truth the differences were purely personal. Dave and Walli had never had any musical differences.

"Yet now you wish to attend the funeral of his grandmother."

"She was my great-aunt."

"Where did you last see Walli Franck?"

"In San Francisco."

"The address, please."

Dave hesitated. This was getting nasty.

"Answer, please. Walli Franck is wanted for murder."

"I last saw him in Buena Vista Park. That's on Haight Street. I don't know where he lives."

"Do you realize that it is a crime to obstruct the police in the course of their duty?"

"Of course."

"And that if you commit such a crime in East Germany, you may be arrested and tried and put in jail here?"

Dave was suddenly frightened, but he tried to remain calm. "And then millions of fans all over the world would demand my release."

"They will not be allowed to interfere with justice."

Fitz put in: "Are you sure your comrades in Moscow would be pleased with you for creating a major international diplomatic incident over this?"

The tall man laughed scornfully, but he was not convincing.

Dave had a flash of insight. "You're Hans Hoffmann, aren't you?"

The interpreter did not translate this, but instead said quickly: "His name is of no concern to you."

But Dave could tell by the tall man's face that his guess had been right. He said: "Walli told me about you. His sister threw you out, and you've been taking revenge on her family ever since."

"Just answer the question."

"Is this part of your revenge? Harassing two innocent men on their way to a funeral? Is that the kind of people you Communists are?"

"Wait here, please." Hans and his interpreter left the room, and Dave heard from the other side of the door the sound of a bolt being shot.

"I'm sorry," Dave said. "This seems to be about Walli. You would have been better off on your own."

"Not your fault. I just hope we don't miss the funeral." Fitz took out his cigar case. "You don't smoke, Dave, do you?"

Dave shook his head. "Not tobacco, anyhow."

"Marijuana is bad for you."

"And I suppose cigars are healthy?"

Fitz smiled. "Touché."

"I've had this argument with my father. He drinks Scotch. You parliamentarians have a clear policy: all dangerous drugs are illegal, except the ones you like. And then you complain that young people won't listen."

"You're right, of course."

It was a big cigar, and Fitz smoked it all and dropped the stub in a stamped-tin ashtray. Eleven o'clock came and went. They had missed the funeral for which they had flown from London.

At half past eleven the door opened again. Hans Hoffmann stood there. With a little smile he said: "You may enter East Germany." Then he walked away.

Dave and Fitz found their car. "We'd better go straight to the house, now," said Fitz. He gave the driver the address.

They drove along Friedrich Strasse to Unter den Linden. The old government buildings were fine but the sidewalks were deserted. "My God," said Fitz. "This used to be one of the busiest shopping streets in Europe. Look at it now. Merthyr Tydfil on a Monday."

The car pulled up outside a town house in better condition than the other homes. "Maud's daughter seems to be more affluent than her neighbors," Fitz remarked.

Dave explained. "Walli's father owns a television factory in West Berlin. Somehow he manages to run it from here. I guess it still makes money."

They went into the house. The family introduced themselves. Walli's parents were Werner and Carla, a handsome man and a plain woman with strong features. Walli's sister, Lili, was nineteen and attractive, and did not look like Walli at all. Dave was intrigued to meet Karolin, who had long fair hair parted in the center and forming curtains either side of her face. With her was Alice, the inspiration for the song, a shy four-year-old with a black ribbon in her hair for mourning. Karolin's husband, Odo, was a little older, about thirty. He had fashionably long hair but wore a clerical collar.

Dave explained why they had missed the funeral. They mixed languages, though the Germans spoke English better than the English spoke German. Dave sensed that the family's attitude to Fitz was equivocal. It was understandable: he had after all been harsh to Maud, and her daughter might think it was too late to make amends. However, it was also too late to remonstrate, and no one spoke of the fifty-year estrangement.

A dozen friends and neighbors who had attended the funeral were having coffee and snacks served by Carla and Lili. Dave talked to Karolin about guitars. It turned out she and Lili were underground stars. They were not allowed to make records, because their songs were about freedom, but people made tape recordings of their performances and loaned them to one another. It was a bit like samizdat publishing in the Soviet Union. They discussed cassette tapes, a new format, more convenient though with poor sound quality. Dave offered to send Karolin some cassettes and a deck, but she said they would only be stolen by the secret police.

Dave had assumed Karolin must be a hard-hearted woman, to break off her relationship with Walli and marry Odo, but to his surprise he liked her. She seemed kind and smart. She spoke of Walli with great affection and wanted to know all about his life.

Dave told her how he and Walli had quarreled. She was distressed by the story. "It's not like him," she said. "Walli was never the type to fool around. Girls used to fall for him all the time, and he could have had a different one every weekend, but he never did."

Dave shrugged. "He's changed."

"What about your former fiancée? What's her name?"

"Ursula, but everyone calls her Beep. To be honest, it's not surprising that she should be unfaithful. She's kind of wild. It's part of what makes her so attractive."

"I think you still have feelings for her."

"I was crazy about her." Dave gave an evasive answer because he did not know how he felt now. He was angry with Beep, enraged by her betrayal, but if she wanted to come back to him he was not sure what he would do.

Fitz came over to where the two of them were sitting. "Dave," he said, "I'd like to see the grave before we return to West Berlin. Would you mind?"

"Of course not." Dave stood up. "We should probably go soon."

Karolin said to Dave: "If you do speak to Walli, please give him my love. Tell him I long for the day when he can meet Alice. I will tell her all about him when she's old enough."

They all had messages for Walli: Werner, Carla, and Lili. Dave guessed he would have to speak to Walli just to pass them on.

As they were leaving, Carla said to Fitz: "You should have something of Maud's."

"I'd like that."

"I know just the thing." She disappeared for a minute and came back with an old leather-bound photograph album. Fitz opened it. The pictures were all monochrome, some sepia, many faded. They had captions in large, loopy handwriting, presumably Maud's. The oldest had been taken in a grand country house. Dave read: "Tŷ Gwyn, 1905." That was the Fitzherbert country residence, now Aberowen College of Further Education.

Seeing photos of himself and Maud as young people made Fitz cry. Tears rolled down the papery old skin of his wrinkled face and soaked into the collar of his immaculate white shirt. He spoke with difficulty. "Good times never come back," he said.

They took their leave. The chauffeur drove them to a large and charmless municipal cemetery, and they found Maud's grave. The earth had already been returned to the pit, forming a small mound that was, pathetically, the size and approximate shape of a human being. They stood side by side for a few minutes, saying nothing. The only sound was birdsong.

Fitz wiped his face with a large white handkerchief. "Let's go," he said.

At the checkpoint they were again detained. Hans Hoffmann watched, smiling, while they and their cars were thoroughly searched.

"What are you looking for?" Dave asked. "Why would we smuggle something out of East Germany? You don't have anything here that anyone wants!" No one answered him.

A uniformed officer seized on the photograph album and handed it to Hoffmann.

Hoffmann looked through it casually and said: "This will have to be examined by our forensic department."

"Of course," Fitz said sadly.

They had to leave without it.

As they drove away, Dave looked back and saw Hans drop the album into a rubbish bin.

.   .   .

George Jakes flew from Portland to Los Angeles to meet Verena with a diamond ring in his pocket.

He had been on the road with Bobby Kennedy, and had not seen Verena since the funeral of Martin Luther King in Atlanta seven weeks earlier.

George was devastated by the assassination. Dr. King had been the bright burning hope of black Americans, and now he was gone, murdered by a white racist with a hunting rifle. President Kennedy had given hope to blacks and he, too, had been killed by a white man with a gun. What was the point of politics if great men could be so easily wiped out? But, George thought, at least we still have Bobby.

Verena was even harder hit. At the funeral she had been bewildered, angry, and lost. The man she had admired, cherished, and served for seven years was gone.

To George's consternation she had not wanted him to console her. He was hurt deeply by this. They lived six hundred miles apart, but he was the man in her life. He figured that her rejection was part of her grief, and would pass.

There was nothing for her in Atlanta—she did not want to work for King's successor, Ralph Abernathy—so she had resigned. George had thought she might move into his apartment in Washington. However, without explanation she had gone back to her parents' home in Los Angeles. Perhaps she needed time alone to grieve.

Or perhaps she wanted something more than just an invitation to move into his place.

Hence the ring.

The next primary was California, which gave George a chance to visit Verena.

At LAX he rented a white Plymouth Valiant, a cheap compact—the campaign was paying—and drove to North Roxbury Drive in Beverly Hills.

He passed through tall gates and parked in front of a Tudor-style brick house that he guessed was the size of five genuine Tudor houses. Verena's parents, Percy Marquand and Babe Lee, lived like the stars they were.

A maid let him in and showed him into a living room that had nothing Tudor about it: a white carpet, air-conditioning, and a floor-to-ceiling window that looked out onto a swimming pool. The maid asked if he would like a drink. "A soda, please," he said. "Any kind."

When Verena came in he suffered a shock.

She had cut off her wonderful Afro, and her hair was now cropped close to her head, as short as his. She wore black pants, a blue shirt, a leather blazer, and a black beret. It was the uniform of the Black Panther Party for Self-Defense.

George suppressed his outrage in order to kiss her. She gave him her lips, but only briefly, and he knew right away that she had not moved on from her mood at the funeral. He hoped his proposal would bring her out of it.

They sat on a couch covered in a swirly pattern of burnt orange, primrose yellow, and chocolate brown. The maid brought George a

Coke with ice in a tall glass on a silver tray. When she had gone he took Verena's hand. Holding in his anger, he said as gently as he could: "Why are you wearing that uniform?"

"Isn't it obvious?"

"Not to me."

"Martin Luther King led a nonviolent campaign, and they shot him."

George was disappointed in her. He had expected a better argument than that. He said: "Abraham Lincoln fought a civil war, and they shot him, too."

"Blacks have a right to defend themselves. No one else will—especially not the police."

George could barely conceal his contempt for these ideas. "You just want to scare whitey. Nothing has ever been achieved by this kind of grandstanding."

"What has nonviolence achieved? Hundreds of black people lynched and murdered, thousands beaten and jailed."

George did not want to fight with her—on the contrary, he wanted to bring her back to normal—but he could not help raising his voice. "Plus the Civil Rights Act of 1964, the Voting Rights Act of 1965, and six black congressmen and a senator!"

"And now white people are saying it's gone far enough. No one has been able to pass a law against housing discrimination."

"Maybe the whites are afraid they'll have Panthers in Gestapo outfits walking around their nice suburbs carrying guns."

"The police have guns. We need them too."

George realized that this argument, which seemed to be about politics, was really about their relationship. And he was losing her. If he could not talk her out of the Black Panthers, he could not bring her back into his life. "Look, I know that police forces all over America are full of violent racists. But the solution to that problem is to improve the police, not shoot them. We have to get rid of politicians such as Ronald Reagan who encourage police brutality."

"I refuse to accept a situation where the whites have guns and we don't."

"Then campaign for gun control and more black cops in senior positions."

"Martin believed in that and he's dead." Verena's words were defiant, but she could not keep it up, and she began to cry.

George tried to embrace her, but she pushed him away. Nevertheless he strove to make her see reason. "If you want to protect black people, come and work on our campaign," he said. "Bobby is going to be president."

"Even if he wins, Congress won't let him do anything."

"They'll try to stop him, and we'll have a political battle, and one side will win and the other will lose. It's how we change things in America. It's a lousy system, but all the others are worse. And shooting each other is the worst of all."

"We're not going to agree."

"Okay." He lowered his voice. "We've disagreed before, but always kept on loving each other, haven't we?"

"This is different."

"Don't say that."

"My whole life has changed."

George looked hard at her face, and saw there a mixture of defiance and guilt that gave him a clue to what was going on. "You're sleeping with one of the Panthers, aren't you?"

"Yes."

George had a heavy feeling in his guts, as if he had drunk a tankard of cold ale. "You should have told me."

"I'm telling you now."

"My God." George was sad. He fingered the ring in his pocket. Was it going to stay there? "Do you realize it's seven years since we graduated from Harvard?" He fought back tears.

"I know."

"Police dogs in Birmingham, 'I have a dream' in Washington, President Johnson backing civil rights, two assassinations . . ."

"And blacks are still the poorest Americans, living in the lousiest houses, getting the most perfunctory health care—and doing more than their share of the fighting in Vietnam."

"Bobby's going to change all that."

"No, he's not."

"Yes, he is. And I'm going to invite you to the White House to admit that you were wrong."

Verena went to the door. "Good-bye, George."

"I can't believe it ends like this."

"The maid will see you out."

George found it difficult to think straight. He had loved Verena for years, and had assumed they would marry sooner or later. Now she had ditched him for a Black Panther. He felt lost. Although they had lived apart, he had always been able to think about what he would say to her and how he would caress her next time they were together. Now he was alone.

The maid came in and said: "This way, Mr. Jakes, if you please."

Automatically he followed her to the hall. She opened the front door.

"Thank you," he said.

"Good-bye, Mr. Jakes."

George got into his rented car and drove away.

. . .

On voting day in the California primary, George was with Bobby Kennedy at the Malibu beach home of John Frankenheimer, the movie director. The weather was overcast that morning, but nevertheless Bobby swam in the ocean with his twelve-year-old son, David. They both got caught in the undertow and emerged with scratches and scrapes from being dragged over the pebbles. After lunch Bobby fell asleep beside the pool, stretched out across two chairs, his mouth open. Looking through the glass patio doors, George noticed an angry mark on Bobby's forehead from the swimming incident.

He had not told Bobby that he had broken up with Verena. He had told only his mother. He barely had time to think on the campaign trail, and California had been nonstop: airport mob scenes, motorcades, hysterical crowds, and packed meetings. George was glad to be so busy. He had the luxury of feeling sad only for a few minutes every night before falling asleep. Even then he found himself imagining conversations with Verena in which he persuaded her to return to legitimate politics and campaign for Bobby. Perhaps their different approaches had always been a manifestation of fundamental incompatibility. He had never wanted to believe that.

At three o'clock the results of the first exit poll were broadcast on

TV. Bobby led Gene McCarthy 49 percentage points to 41. George was elated. I can't win my girl, but I can win elections, he thought.

Bobby showered and shaved and put on a blue pin-striped suit and a white shirt. Either the suit, or perhaps his increased confidence, made him seem more presidential than ever before, George thought.

The bruise on Bobby's forehead was unsightly, but John Frankenheimer found some professional movie makeup in the house and covered up the mark.

At half past six the Kennedy entourage got into cars and drove into Los Angeles. They went to the Ambassador Hotel, where the victory celebration was already getting under way in the ballroom. George went with Bobby to the Royal Suite on the fifth floor. There in a large living room a hundred or more friends, advisers, and privileged journalists were downing cocktails and congratulating one another. Every TV set in the suite was on.

George and the closest advisers followed Bobby through the living room and into one of the bedrooms. As always, Bobby mixed partying with hard political talk. Today, as well as California, he had won a low-profile primary in South Dakota, birthplace of Hubert Humphrey. After California he felt confident of winning New York, where he had the advantage of being one of the state's senators. "We're beating McCarthy, damn it," he said exultantly, sitting on the floor in a corner of the room, keeping an eye on the TV.

George was beginning to worry about the convention. How could he make sure that Bobby's popularity was reflected in the votes of delegates from states where there were no primaries? "Humphrey is working hard on states such as Illinois, where Mayor Daley controls the delegate votes."

"Yeah," said Bobby. "But in the end men like Daley can't ignore popular feeling. They want to win. Hubert can't beat Dick Nixon, and I can."

"It's true, but do the Democratic power brokers know that?"

"They will by August."

George shared Bobby's sense that they were riding a wave, but he saw the dangers ahead all too clearly. "We need McCarthy to withdraw so that we can concentrate on beating Humphrey. We have to make a deal with McCarthy."

Bobby shook his head. "I can't offer him the vice presidency. He's a Catholic. Protestants might vote for one Catholic, but not two."

"You could offer him the top job in cabinet."

"Secretary of State?"

"If he pulls out now."

Bobby frowned. "It's hard to imagine working with him in the White House."

"If you don't win, you won't be in the White House. Should I put out feelers?"

"Let me think about it some more."

"Of course."

"You know something else, George?" Bobby said. "For the first time I don't feel I'm here as Jack's brother."

George smiled. That was a big step.

George went into the main room to talk to reporters, but he did not get a drink. When he was with Bobby he preferred to stay sharp. Bobby himself liked bourbon. But incompetence on his team infuriated him, and he could lacerate someone who let him down. George felt comfortable drinking alcohol only when Bobby was far away.

He was still stone-cold sober a few minutes before midnight when he accompanied Bobby down to the ballroom to give his victory speech. Bobby's wife, Ethel, looked groovy in an orange-and-white minidress with white tights, despite being pregnant with their eleventh child.

The crowd went wild, as always. The boys all wore Kennedy straw hats. The girls had a uniform: blue skirt, white blouse, and red Kennedy sash. A band blared a campaign song. Powerful television lights added to the heat in the room. Led by bodyguard Bill Barry, Bobby and Ethel pushed through the crowd, their young supporters reaching out to touch them and pull their clothes, until they reached a small platform. Jostling photographers added to the chaos.

The crowd hysteria was a problem for George and others, but it was Bobby's strength. His ability to get this emotional reaction from people was going to take him to the White House.

Bobby stood behind a bouquet of microphones. He had not asked for a written speech, just some notes. His performance was lackluster, but no one cared. "We are a great country, an unselfish country, and a compassionate country," he said. "I intend to make that my basis for running." These were not inspiring words, but the crowd adored him too much to care.

George decided he would not go with Bobby to the Factory discotheque afterward. Seeing couples dance would only remind him that he was alone. He would get a good night's sleep before flying to New York in the morning to launch the campaign there. Work was the cure for his heartache.

"I thank all of you who made this possible this evening," Bobby said. He flashed the Churchillian V-for-victory sign, and around the room hundreds of young people repeated the gesture. He reached down from the platform to shake some of the outstretched hands.

Then there was a glitch. His next appointment was with the press in a nearby room. The plan was for him to pass through the crowd as he left, but George could see that Bill Barry was unable to clear a path between the hysterical teenage girls shouting: "We want Bobby! We want Bobby!"

A hotel employee in the uniform of a maître d'hôtel solved the problem, pointing Bobby to a pair of swinging doors that evidently led through staff quarters to the press room. Bobby and Ethel followed the man into a dim corridor, and George and Bill Barry and the rest of the entourage hurried after them.

George was wondering how soon he could again raise with Bobby the need to make a deal with Gene McCarthy. It was the strategic priority, in George's opinion. But personal relationships were so important to the Kennedys. If Bobby could have made a friend of Lyndon Johnson everything would have been different.

The corridor led to a brightly lit pantry zone with gleaming stainless-steel steam tables and a huge ice maker. A radio reporter was interviewing Bobby as they walked, saying: "Senator, how are you going to counter Mr. Humphrey?" Bobby shook hands with smiling staff on his way through. A young kitchen worker turned from a tray stacker as if to greet Bobby.

Then, in a lightning flash of terror, George saw a gun in the young man's hand.

It was a small black revolver with a short barrel.

The man pointed the gun at Bobby's head.

George opened his mouth to yell but the shot came first.

The little weapon made a noise that was more of a pop than a bang.

Bobby threw his hands up to his face, staggered back, then fell to the concrete floor.

George roared: "No! No!" It could not be happening—it could not be happening again!

A moment later came a volley of shots like a Chinese firecracker. Something stung George's arm, but he ignored it.

Bobby lay on his back beside the ice machine, hands above his head, feet apart. His eyes were open.

People were yelling and screaming. The radio reporter was babbling into his microphone: "Senator Kennedy has been shot! Senator Kennedy has been shot! Is that possible? Is that possible?"

Several men jumped on the gunman. Someone was shouting: "Get the gun! Get the gun!" George saw Bill Barry punch the shooter in the face.

George knelt by Bobby. He was alive, but bleeding from a wound just behind his ear. He looked bad. George loosened his tie to help him breathe. Someone else put a folded coat under Bobby's head.

A man's voice was moaning: "God, no . . . Christ, no . . ."

Ethel pushed through the crowd, knelt beside George, and spoke to her husband. There was a flicker of recognition in Bobby's face, and he tried to speak. George thought he said: "Is everyone else all right?" Ethel stroked his face.

George looked around. He could not tell whether anyone else had been hit by the volley of bullets. Then he noticed his own forearm. The sleeve of his suit was ripped and blood was seeping from a wound. He had been hit. Now that he noticed, it hurt like hell.

The far door opened, and reporters and photographers from the press room burst through. The cameramen mobbed the group around Bobby, shoving each other and climbing on the stoves and sinks to get better shots of the bleeding victim and his stricken wife. Ethel pleaded: "Give him some air, please! Let him breathe!"

An ambulance crew arrived with a stretcher. They took Bobby by the shoulders and feet. Bobby cried weakly: "Oh, no, don't . . ."

"Gently!" Ethel begged the crew. "Gently."

They lifted him onto the stretcher and strapped him in.

Bobby's eyes closed.

He never opened them again.

CHAPTER FORTY-FIVE

That summer Dimka and Natalya painted the apartment, with the sun shining through the open windows. It took longer than necessary because they kept stopping for sex. Her glorious hair was tied up and hidden in a rag, and she wore an old shirt of his with a frayed collar; but her shorts were tight, and every time he saw her up a ladder he had to kiss her. He pulled down her shorts so often that after a while she just wore the shirt; and then they had even more sex.

They could not marry until her divorce was finalized, and for the sake of appearances Natalya had her own tiny apartment nearby, but unofficially they were already embarking on their new life together in Dimka's place. They rearranged the furniture to Natalya's liking and bought a couch. They developed routines: he made breakfast, she cooked dinner; he polished her shoes, she ironed his shirts; he shopped for meat, she for fish.

They never saw Nik, but Natalya began to establish a relationship with Nina. Dimka's ex-wife was now the accepted lover of Marshal Pushnoy, and spent many weekends with him at his dacha, hosting dinners with his intimate friends, some of whom brought *their* mistresses. Dimka did not know how Pushnoy arranged matters with his wife, a pleasant-looking elderly woman who always appeared at his side on formal state occasions. During Nina's country weekends, Dimka and Natalya looked after Grisha. At first Natalya was nervous, never having had children of her own—Nik hated kids. But she quickly became fond of Grisha, who looked a lot like Dimka; and, not surprisingly, she turned out to have the usual maternal instincts.

Their private life was happy but their public life was not. The diehards in the Kremlin only pretended to accept the Czechoslovakia compromise. As soon as Kosygin and Dimka got back from Prague the conservatives went to work to undermine the agreement, pressing for an invasion that would crush Dubček and his reforms. The argument raged through June and July in the heat of Moscow and in the Black Sea breezes at the dachas to which the Communist Party elite migrated for their summer holidays.

For Dimka this was not really about Czechoslovakia. It was about his son and the world in which he would grow up. In fifteen years Grisha would be at university; in twenty he would be working; in twenty-five he might have children of his own. Would Russia have a better system, something like Dubček's idea of Communism with a human face? Or would the Soviet Union still be a tyranny in which the unchallengeable authority of the party was brutally enforced by the KGB?

Infuriatingly Leonid Brezhnev, general secretary, sat on the fence. Dimka had come to despise him. Terrified of being caught on the losing side, Brezhnev would never make up his mind until he knew which way the collective decision was likely to go. He had no vision, no courage, no plan for making the Soviet Union a better country. He was no leader.

The conflict came to a head at a two-day meeting of the Politburo starting on Thursday, August 15. As always, the formal meeting consisted mostly of polite interchanges of platitudes, while the real battles were fought outside.

It was in the plaza that Dimka had his face-off with Yevgeny Filipov, standing in the sunshine outside the yellow-and-white palace of the senate building among the parked cars and waiting limousines. "Look at the KGB reports from Prague," Filipov said. "Counterrevolutionary student rallies! Clubs where the overthrow of Communism is openly discussed! Secret weapons caches!"

"I don't believe all the stories," Dimka said. "True, there is discussion of reform, but the dangers are being exaggerated by the failed leaders of the past who are now being pushed aside." The truth was that Andropov, the hard-line head of the KGB, was fabricating sensational intelligence reports to bolster the conservatives; but Dimka was not foolhardy enough to say so out loud.

Dimka had a source of reliable intelligence: his twin sister. Tanya was in Prague, sending carefully noncommittal articles to TASS and, at the same time, supplying Dimka and Kosygin with reports saying that Dubček was a hero to all Czechs except the old party apparatchiks.

It was almost impossible for people to get at the truth in a closed society. Russians told so many lies. In the Soviet Union almost every document was deceitful: production figures, foreign policy assessments, police interviews with suspects, economic forecasts. Behind their hands people murmured that the only true page in the newspaper was the one with the radio and television programs.

"I can't tell which way it's going to go," Natalya said to Dimka on Thursday night. She still worked for Foreign Minister Andrei Gromyko. "All the signals from Washington say President Johnson will do nothing if we invade Czechoslovakia. He has too many problems of his own— riots, assassinations, Vietnam, and a presidential election."

They had finished painting for the evening and were sitting on the floor sharing a bottle of beer. Natalya had a single smudge of yellow paint on her forehead. For some reason that made Dimka want to fuck her. He was wondering whether to do it now or get washed and go to bed first when she said: "Before we get married . . ."

That was ominous. "Yes?"

"We should talk about children."

"We probably should have done that before we spent all summer screwing our brains out." They had never used birth control.

"Yes. But you already have a child."

"We have a child. He's ours. You'll be his stepmother."

"And I'm very fond of him. It's easy to love a boy who looks so much like you. But how do you feel about having more?"

Dimka could see that for some reason she was worried about this, and he needed to reassure her. He put down the beer and embraced her. "I adore you," he said. "And I would love to have children with you."

"Oh, thank God," she said. "Because I'm pregnant."

. . .

It was difficult to get newspapers in Prague, Tanya found. This was an ironic consequence of Dubček's abolition of censorship. Previously, few people had bothered to read the anodyne and dishonest reports in the state-controlled press. Now that the papers could tell the truth, they could never print enough copies to keep up with the demand. She had to get up early in the morning to buy them before they sold out.

Television had been freed, too. On current affairs programs, workers and students questioned and criticized government ministers. Released political prisoners were allowed to confront the secret policemen who had thrown them in jail. Around the television set in the lobby of any large hotel there was often a small crowd of eager viewers watching the discussion on the screen.

Similar exchanges were taking place in every café, works canteen, and town hall. People who had suppressed their true feelings for twenty years were suddenly allowed to say what was in their hearts.

The air of liberation was infectious. Tanya was tempted to believe that the old days were over and there was no danger. She had to keep reminding herself that Czechoslovakia was still a Communist country with secret police and torture basements.

She had with her the typescript of Vasili's first novel.

It had arrived, shortly before she left Moscow, in the same way as his first short story, handed to her in the street outside her office by a stranger who was unwilling to answer questions. As before, it was written in small handwriting—no doubt to save paper. Its sardonic title was *A Free Man.*

Tanya had typed it out on airmail paper. She had to assume that her luggage would be opened. Although she was a trusted reporter for TASS, it was still possible that any hotel room she stayed in would be turned over, and the apartment allocated to her in the old town of Prague would be thoroughly searched. But she had devised a clever hiding place, she thought. All the same she lived in fear. It was like possessing a nuclear bomb. She was desperate to pass it on as soon as possible.

She had befriended the Prague correspondent of a British newspaper, and at the first opportunity she had said to him: "There's a book editor in London who specializes in translations of East European novels— Anna Murray, of Rowley Publishing. I'd love to interview her about Czech literature. Do you think you could get a message to her?"

This was dangerous, for it established a traceable connection between Tanya and Anna; but Tanya had to take some risks, and it seemed to her that this one was minimal.

Two weeks later the British journalist had said: "Anna Murray's coming to Prague next Tuesday. I couldn't give her your phone number because I don't have it, but she'll be at the Palace Hotel."

On Tuesday Tanya called the hotel and left a message for Anna saying: "Meet Jakub at the Jan Hus monument at four." Jan Hus was a medieval philosopher burned at the stake by the Pope for arguing that mass should be said in the local language. He remained a symbol of Czech resistance to foreign control. His memorial was in Old Town Square.

The secret police agents in all hotels took special interest in guests from the West, and Tanya had to assume that they were shown all messages, therefore they might stake out the monument to see whom Anna was meeting. So Tanya did not go to the rendezvous. Instead she intercepted Anna on the street and slipped her a card with the address of a restaurant in the Old Town and the message: "Eight P.M. tonight. Table booked in the name of Jakub."

There was still the possibility that Anna would be followed from her hotel to the restaurant. It was unlikely: the secret police did not have enough men to tail every foreigner all the time. Nevertheless Tanya continued to take precautions. That evening she put on a loose-fitting leather jacket, despite the warm weather, and went to the restaurant early. She sat at a different table from the one she had reserved. She kept her head down when Anna arrived, and watched as Anna was seated.

Anna was unmistakably foreign. No one in Eastern Europe was that well dressed. She had a dark-red pantsuit tailored to her voluptuous figure. She wore it with a glorious multicolored scarf that had to come from Paris. Anna had dark hair and eyes that probably came from her German-Jewish mother. She must be close to thirty, Tanya calculated, but she was one of those women who became more beautiful as they left their youth behind.

No one followed Anna into the restaurant. Tanya stayed put for fifteen minutes, watching the arrivals, while Anna ordered a bottle of Hungarian Riesling and sipped a glass. Four people came in, an elderly married couple and two youngsters on a date: none looked remotely like police. Finally Tanya got up and joined Anna at the reserved table, draping her jacket over the back of her chair.

"Thank you for coming," Tanya said.

"Please don't mention it. I'm glad to."

"It's a long way."

"I'd travel ten times as far to meet the woman who gave me *Frostbite*."

"He's written a novel."

Anna sat back with a satisfied sigh. "That's what I was hoping you'd say." She poured wine into Tanya's glass. "Where is it?"

"Hidden. I'll give it to you before we leave."

"Okay." Anna was puzzled, for she could see no sign of a typescript, but she accepted what Tanya said. "You've made me very happy."

"I always knew that *Frostbite* was brilliant," Tanya said reflectively. "But even I didn't anticipate the international success you've had. In the Kremlin they're furious about it, especially as they still can't figure out who the author is."

"You should know that there's a fortune in royalties due to him."

Tanya shook her head. "If he received money from overseas that would give the game away."

"Well, maybe one day. I've asked the largest London firm of literary agents to represent him."

"What is a literary agent?"

"Someone who looks after the author's interests, negotiates contracts, and makes sure the publisher pays on time."

"I never heard of that."

"They've opened a bank account in the name of Ivan Kuznetsov. But you should think about whether the money should be invested somehow."

"How much is it?"

"More than a million pounds."

Tanya was shocked. Vasili would be the richest man in Russia if he could get his hands on the money.

They ordered dinner. Prague restaurants had improved in recent months, but the food was still traditional. Their beef and sliced dumplings came in a rich gravy garnished with whipped cream and a spoonful of cranberry jam.

Anna asked: "What's going to happen here in Prague?"

"Dubček is a sincere Communist who wants the country to remain part of the Warsaw Pact, so he presents no fundamental threat to Moscow; but the dinosaurs in the Kremlin don't see it that way. No one knows what's going to happen."

"Do you have children?"

Tanya smiled. "Key question. Perhaps we may choose to suffer the Soviet system, for the sake of a quiet life; but do we have the right to bequeath such misery and oppression to the next generation? No, I don't have children. I have a nephew, Grisha, whom I love, the son of my twin brother. And this morning in a letter my brother told me that the woman who will soon be his second wife is already pregnant, so I'll have another nephew or a niece. For their sakes, I have to hope that Dubček will succeed, and other Communist countries will follow the Czech example. But the Soviet system is inherently conservative, much more resistant to change than capitalism. That may be its most fundamental flaw, in the long run."

When they had finished, Anna said: "If we can't pay our author, can we perhaps give you a present to pass to him? Is there anything from the West he would like?"

A typewriter was what he needed, but that would blow his cover. "A sweater," she said. "A really thick warm sweater. He's always cold. And some underwear, the kind with long sleeves and long legs."

Anna looked aghast at this peep into the life of Ivan Kuznetsov. "I'll go to Vienna tomorrow and get him the best quality."

Anna nodded, pleased. "Shall we meet again here on Friday?"

"Yes."

Tanya stood up. "We should leave separately."

A look of panic crossed Anna's face. "What about the typescript?"

"Wear my jacket," said Tanya. It might be a bit small for Anna, who was heavier than Tanya; but she could get it on. "When you reach Vienna, unpick the lining." She shook Anna's hand. "Don't lose it," she said. "I don't have a copy."

. . .

In the middle of the night Tanya was awakened by her bed shaking. She sat up, terrified, thinking the secret police had come to arrest her.

When she turned on the light she saw that she was alone, but the shaking had not been a dream. The framed photograph of Grisha on her bedside table seemed to be dancing, and she could hear the tinkling sound of small jars of makeup vibrating on the glass top of her dressing table.

She jumped out of bed and went to the open window. It was first light. There was a loud rumbling noise coming from the nearby main street, but she could not see what was causing it. She was filled with a vague dread.

She looked for her leather jacket, and remembered that she had given it to Anna. She quickly pulled on blue jeans and a sweater, stepped into her shoes, and hurried out. Despite the early hour there were people on the street. She walked swiftly in the direction of the noise.

As soon as she reached the main street she knew what had happened.

The noise was caused by tanks. They were rolling along the street, slowly but unstoppably, their caterpillar tracks making a hideous din. Riding on the tanks were soldiers in Soviet uniforms, most young, just boys. Looking along the street in the gentle light of dawn, Tanya saw that there were dozens of tanks, perhaps hundreds, the incoming line stretching all the way to the Charles Bridge and beyond. Along the sidewalks small groups of Czech men and women stood, many in their nightwear, watching with dismay and stupefaction as their city was overrun.

The conservatives in the Kremlin had won, Tanya realized. Czechoslovakia had been invaded by the Soviet Union. The brief season of reform and hope was over.

Tanya caught the eye of a middle-aged woman standing next to her. The woman wore an old-fashioned hairnet like the one Tanya's mother put on every night. Her face was streaming with tears.

That was when Tanya felt the wetness on her own cheeks and realized that she, too, was weeping.

. . .

A week after the tanks rolled into Prague, George Jakes was sitting on his couch in Washington, in his underwear, watching television coverage of the Democratic convention in Chicago.

For lunch he had heated a can of tomato soup and eaten it straight from the pan, which now stood on the coffee table, with the red remains of the glutinous liquid congealing inside.

He knew what he ought to do. He should put on a suit and go out and get himself a new job and a new girlfriend and a new life.

Somehow he just could not see the point.

He had heard of depression and he knew this was it.

He was only mildly diverted by the spectacle of the Chicago police running amok. A few hundred demonstrators were peacefully sitting down in the road outside the convention center. The police were wading into them with nightsticks, savagely beating everyone, as if they did not realize they were committing criminal assault live on television—or, more likely, they knew but did not care.

Someone, presumably Mayor Richard Daley, had let the dogs off the leash.

George idly speculated on the political consequences. It was the end of nonviolence as a political strategy, he guessed. Martin Luther King and Bobby Kennedy had both been wrong, and now they were dead. The Black Panthers were right. Mayor Daley, Governor Ronald Reagan, presidential candidate George Wallace, and all their racist police chiefs would use violence against anyone whose ideas they found distasteful. Black people needed guns to protect themselves. So did anyone else who wanted to challenge the bull elephants of American society. Right now in Chicago the police were treating middle-class white kids the way they had always treated blacks. That had to change attitudes.

There was a ring at his doorbell. He frowned, puzzled. He was not expecting a visitor and did not want to talk to anyone. He ignored the sound, hoping the caller would go away. The bell rang again. I might be out, he thought; how do they know I'm here? It rang a third time, long and insistently, and he realized the person was not going to give up.

He went to the door. It was his mother. She was carrying a covered casserole dish.

Jacky looked him up and down. "I thought so," she said, and she walked in uninvited.

She put her casserole in his oven and turned on the heat. "Take a shower," she ordered him. "Shave your sorry face and put on some decent clothing."

He thought of arguing but did not have the energy. It seemed easier just to do as she said.

She began clearing up the room, putting his soup pan in the kitchen sink, folding newspapers, opening windows.

George retired to his room. He took off his underwear, showered, and shaved. It would make no difference. He would slob out again tomorrow.

He put on chinos and a blue button-down shirt, then returned to the living room. The casserole smelled good, he could not deny that. Jacky had laid the dining table. "Sit down," she said. "Supper's ready."

She had made King Ranch chicken in a tomato-cream sauce with green chilies and a cheese crust. George could not resist it, and he had two platefuls. Afterward his mother washed up and he dried the dishes.

She sat with him to watch the convention coverage. Senator Abraham Ribicoff was speaking, nominating George McGovern, a last-minute alternative peace candidate. He caused a stir by saying: "With George McGovern as president of the United States, we would not have to have Gestapo tactics in the streets of Chicago."

Jacky said: "My, that's telling them."

The convention hall went quiet. The television director cut to a shot of Mayor Daley. He looked like a giant frog, with bulging eyes, a jowly face, and a neck that was all rolls of fat. For a moment he forgot he was on television—just like his cops—and yelled vituperatively at Ribicoff.

The microphones did not pick up his words. "I wonder what he said," George mused.

"I can tell you," said Jacky. "I can lip-read."

"I never knew that."

"When I was nine years old I went deaf. Took them a long time to figure out what was wrong. Eventually I had an operation that restored my hearing. But I never forgot how to lip-read."

"Okay, Mom, prove it. What did Mayor Daley say to Abe Ribicoff?"

"He said: 'Fuck you, you Jew son of a bitch,' that's what he said."

. . .

Walli and Beep were staying in the Chicago Hilton, on the fifteenth floor, where the McCarthy campaign had its headquarters. They were tired and dispirited when they went to their room at midnight on the last day of the convention, Thursday. They had lost: Hubert Humphrey, Johnson's vice president, had been chosen as the Democratic candidate. The presidential election would be fought between two men who supported the Vietnam War.

They did not even have any dope to smoke. They had given that up, temporarily, for fear of giving the press a chance to smear McCarthy. They watched TV for a while, then went to bed, too miserable to make love.

Beep said: "Shit, I'll be back in class in a couple of weeks. I don't know if I can face it."

"I guess I'll make a record," Walli said. "I've got some new songs."

Beep was dubious. "You think you can patch things up with Dave?"

"No. I'd like to, but he won't. When he called me to tell me he had seen my folks in East Berlin, he was real cold, even though he was doing a nice thing."

"Oh, God, we really hurt him," Beep said sadly.

"Besides, he's doing fine on his own, with his TV show and everything."

"So how will you make an album?"

"I'll go to London. I know Lew will drum for me, and Buzz will play bass: they're both pissed at Dave for breaking up the group. I'll lay down the basic tracks with them, then record the vocals on my own, and spend some time adding overdubs, guitar licks, and vocal harmonies and maybe even strings and horns."

"Wow, you've really thought about this."

"I've had time. I haven't been inside a studio for half a year."

There was a bang and a crash and the room was flooded with light from the hall. Walli realized with incredulity and terror that someone had beaten the door in. He threw back the sheets and jumped out of bed, yelling: "What the fuck?"

The room lights came on and he saw two uniformed Chicago policemen entering through the wreckage of the door. He said: "What the hell is going on?"

By way of reply one of them hit him with a nightstick.

Walli managed to dodge, and instead of hitting his head the

truncheon landed painfully on his shoulder. He yelled in agony and Beep screamed.

Grasping his injured shoulder, Walli backed toward the bed. The cop swung his stick again. Walli jumped back, falling on the bed, and the club hit his leg. He roared in pain.

Both cops lifted their clubs. Walli rolled over, covering Beep. One nightstick smashed into his back and the other his hip. Beep screamed: "Stop it, please, stop, we haven't done anything wrong, stop hitting him!"

Walli felt two more excruciating blows and thought he would pass out. Then suddenly it stopped, and two pairs of heavily booted footsteps sounded across the room and out.

Walli rolled off Beep. "Ah, fuck, it hurts," he said.

Beep knelt up, trying to see his injuries. "Why did they do it?" she said.

Walli heard, from outside the room, sounds of more doors being broken down and more screaming people being dragged from their beds and beaten. "The Chicago police can do anything they like," he said. "It's worse than East Berlin."

. . .

In October, on a plane to Nashville, Dave Williams sat next to a Nixon supporter.

Dave was going to Nashville to make a record. His own studio in Napa, Daisy Farm, was still under construction. Besides, some of the best musicians in the business were in Nashville. Dave felt that rock music was becoming too cerebral, with psychedelic sounds and twenty-minute guitar solos, so he planned an album of classic two-minute pop songs, "The Girl of My Best Friend" and "I Heard It Through the Grapevine" and "Woolly Bully." Besides, he knew that Walli was making a solo album in London and he did not want to be left behind.

And he had another reason. Little Lulu Small, who had flirted with him on the All-Star Touring Beat Revue, now lived in Nashville and worked as a backing singer. He needed someone to help him forget Beep.

On the front page of his newspaper was a photograph from the

Olympic Games in Mexico City. It was of the medal ceremony for the two hundred meters race. The gold medal winner was Tommie Smith, a black American, who had broken the world record. A white Australian took silver, and another black American bronze. All three men wore human rights badges on their Olympic jackets. While "The Star-Spangled Banner" was being played, the two American athletes had bowed their heads and raised their fists in the Black Power salute, and that was the photo in all the papers.

"Disgraceful," said the man sitting next to Dave in first class.

He looked about forty, and was dressed in a business suit with a white shirt and a tie. He had taken from his briefcase a thick typed document and was annotating it with a ballpoint pen.

Dave normally avoided talking to people on planes. The conversation usually turned into an interview about what it was really like to be a pop star, and that was boring. But this guy did not appear to know who Dave was. And Dave was curious to know what went on in the head of such a man.

His neighbor went on: "I see that the president of the International Olympic Committee has thrown them out of the games. Damn right."

"The president's name is Avery Brundage," Dave said. "It says in my paper that back in 1936, when the games were held in Berlin, he defended the right of the Germans to give the Nazi salute."

"I don't agree with that either," said the businessman. "The games are nonpolitical. Our athletes compete as Americans."

"They're Americans when they win races, and when they get conscripted into the army," Dave said. "But they're Negroes when they want to buy the house next door to yours."

"Well, I'm for equality, but slow change is usually better than fast."

"Maybe we should have an all-white army in Vietnam, just until we're sure American society is ready for complete equality."

"I'm against the war, too," the man said. "If the Vietnamese are dumb enough to want to be Communists, let them. It's Communists in America we should be worried about."

He was from a distant planet, Dave felt. "What line of business are you in?"

"I sell advertising for radio stations." He offered his hand to shake. "Ron Jones."

"Dave Williams. I'm in the music business. If you don't mind my asking, who will you vote for in November?"

"Nixon," said Jones without hesitation.

"But you're against the war, and you favor civil rights for Negroes, albeit not too soon; so you agree with Humphrey on the issues."

"To hell with the issues. I have a wife and three kids, a mortgage and a car loan; they're my issues. I've fought my way up to regional sales manager and I have a shot at national sales director in a few years' time. I've worked my socks off for this and no one's going to take it away from me: not rioting Negroes, not drug-taking hippies, not Communists working for Moscow, and certainly not a softhearted liberal like Hubert Humphrey. I don't care what you say about Nixon, he stands for people like me."

At that moment Dave felt, with an overwhelming sense of impending doom, that Nixon was going to win.

.　.　.

George Jakes put on a suit and a white shirt and a tie, for the first time in months, and went for lunch with Maria Summers at the Jockey Club. It was her invitation.

He could guess what was going to happen. Maria had been talking to his mother. Jacky had told Maria that George spent all day moping in his apartment, doing nothing. Maria was going to tell him to pull himself together.

He could not see the point. His life was wrecked. Bobby was dead and the next president would be either Humphrey or Nixon. Nothing could be done, now, to end the war or to bring equality for blacks or even to stop the police beating up anyone they took a dislike to.

All the same he agreed to have lunch with Maria. They went back a long way.

Maria was looking attractive in a mature way. She wore a black dress with a matching jacket and a row of pearls. She projected confidence and authority. She looked like what she was, a successful midlevel bureaucrat at the Department of Justice. She refused a cocktail and they ordered lunch.

When the waiter had gone, she said to George: "You never get over it."

He understood that she was comparing his grief for Bobby to her own bereavement over Jack.

"There's a hole in your heart, and it doesn't go away," she said.

George nodded. She was so right that it was difficult not to cry.

"Work is the best cure," she said. "That and time."

She had survived, George realized. Her loss was the greater, for Jack Kennedy had been her lover, not just her friend.

"You helped me," she said. "You got me the job at Justice. That was my salvation: a new environment, a new challenge."

"But not a new boyfriend."

"No."

"You still live alone?"

"I have two cats," she said. "Julius and Loopy."

George nodded. Her being single would have helped her at the Justice Department. They hesitated to promote a married woman who might get pregnant and leave, but a confirmed spinster had a better chance.

Their food came and they ate in silence for a few minutes. Then Maria put down her fork. "I want you to go back to work, George."

George was moved by her loving concern, and he admired the steady determination with which she had rebuilt her life. But he could not work up any enthusiasm. He gave a helpless shrug. "Bobby's gone, McCarthy lost the nomination. Who would I work for?"

Maria surprised him by saying: "Fawcett Renshaw."

"Those bastards?" Fawcett Renshaw was the Washington law firm that had offered George a job when he graduated, only to withdraw the offer because he went on the Freedom Ride.

"You'd be their civil rights expert," she added.

George relished the irony. Seven years ago, involvement with civil rights had debarred him from working at Fawcett Renshaw; now it qualified him. We have won some victories, he thought, despite everything. He began to feel better.

"You've worked at Justice and on Capitol Hill, so you have priceless inside knowledge," she went on. "And, you know what? Suddenly it's become fashionable for a Washington law firm to have one black lawyer on the team."

"How do you know what Fawcett Renshaw wants?" he asked.

"At the Justice Department we have a lot to do with them. Usually trying to get their clients to comply with government legislation."

"I'd end up defending corporations who violate civil rights legislation."

"Think of it as a learning experience. You'll gain firsthand knowledge of how equalities legislation works on the ground. That would be valuable if ever you returned to politics. Meanwhile you'll be making good money."

George wondered if he ever would return to politics.

He looked up to see his father approaching across the restaurant. Greg said: "I've just finished lunch—may I join you for coffee?"

George wondered whether this apparently accidental meeting had in fact been planned by Maria. He also recalled that old Renshaw, the senior partner at the law firm, was a boyhood friend of Greg's.

Maria said to Greg: "We were just talking about George going back to work. Fawcett Renshaw wants him."

"Renshaw mentioned it to me. You'll be invaluable to them. Your contacts are matchless."

"Nixon looks like he's winning," George said dubiously. "Most of my contacts are with the Democrats."

"They're still useful. Anyway, I don't expect Nixon to last long. He'll crash and burn."

George raised his eyebrows. Greg was a liberal Republican who would have preferred someone such as Nelson Rockefeller as presidential candidate. Even so, he was being surprisingly disloyal to his party. "You think the peace movement will destroy Nixon?" George asked.

"In your dreams. The other way around, more likely. Nixon isn't Lyndon Johnson. Nixon understands foreign policy—better than most people in Washington, probably. Don't be fooled by his dumb-ass talk about Commies, that's just for the benefit of his supporters in the trailer parks." Greg was a snob. "Nixon will get us out of Vietnam, and he'll say we lost the war because the peace movement undermined the military."

"So what will bring him down?"

"Dick Nixon lies," Greg said. "He lies just about every time he opens his damn mouth. When a Republican administration came into office in 1952, Nixon claimed we had discovered thousands of subversives in the government."

"How many had you found?"

"None. Not a single one. I know, I was a young congressman. Then he told the press we had come across a blueprint for socializing America in the files of the outgoing Democratic administration. Reporters asked to see it."

"He didn't have a copy."

"Correct. He also said he had a secret Communist memorandum about how they planned to work through the Democratic Party. No one ever saw that, either. I suspect that Dick's mother never told him it's a sin to tell a lie."

"There's a lot of dishonesty in politics," George said.

"And in many other walks of life. But few people lie as much and as shamelessly as Nixon. He's a cheat and a crook. He's gotten away with it until now. People do. But it's different when you're president. Reporters know they've been lied to about Vietnam, and more and more they scrutinize everything the government says. Dick will get caught out, and then he'll fall. And you know something else? He'll never understand why. He'll say the press was out to get him all along."

"I sure hope you're right."

"Take the job, George," Greg pleaded. "There's so much to be done."

George nodded. "Maybe I will."

. . .

Claus Krohn was a redhead. On his head, his hair was a dark reddish-brown, but on the rest of his body it was ginger. Rebecca was particularly fond of the triangle that grew from his groin up to a point near his navel. It was what she looked at when she was giving him oral sex, which she enjoyed at least as much as he did.

Now she lay with her head on his belly and tangled her fingernails idly in the curls. They were in his apartment on a Monday night. Rebecca had no meetings on Monday nights, but she pretended she did, and her husband pretended to believe her.

The physical arrangements were easy. Her feelings were harder to manage. It was so difficult to keep these two men in separate compartments in her head that she often wanted to give up. She felt miserably guilty about being unfaithful to Bernd. But her reward was passionate and satisfying sex with a charming man who adored her. And Bernd had given her permission. She reminded herself of that again and again.

This year everyone was doing it. Love was all you needed. Rebecca was no hippie—she was a schoolteacher and a respected city politician—but all the same she was affected by the atmosphere of promiscuity, almost as if she were inadvertently inhaling some of the marijuana in the air. Why not? she asked herself. What's the harm?

When she looked back on the thirty-seven years of her life so far, all her regrets were for things she had *not* done: she had not been unfaithful to her rotten first husband; she had not got pregnant with Bernd's child while it was still possible; she had not escaped from the East German tyranny years earlier.

At least she would never look back and regret not having fucked Claus.

Claus said: "Are you happy?"

Yes, she thought, when I forget about Bernd for a few minutes. "Of course," she said. "I wouldn't be toying with your pubic hair otherwise."

"I love our time together, except that it's always too short."

"I know. I'd like to have a second life, so that I could spend it all with you."

"I'd settle for a weekend."

Too late, Rebecca saw where the conversation was going. For a moment, she stopped breathing.

She had been afraid of this. Monday evenings were not enough. Perhaps there had never really been a chance that Claus would be satisfied with once a week. "I wish you hadn't said that," she said.

"You could get a nurse to take care of Bernd."

"I know I could."

"We could drive to Denmark, where nobody knows us. Stay in a small seaside hotel. Walk along one of those endless beaches and breathe the salt air."

"I knew this would happen." Rebecca stood up. Distractedly, she looked for her underwear. "It was only a question of when."

"Hey, slow down! I'm not forcing you."

"I know you're not, you sweet, kind man."

"If you're not comfortable taking a weekend away, we won't do it."

"We won't do it." She found her panties and pulled them on, then reached for her bra.

"Then why are you getting dressed? We have another half hour at least."

"When we began doing this I swore I'd stop before it got serious."

"Listen! I'm sorry I wanted a weekend away with you. I'll never mention it again, I promise."

"That's not the problem."

"Then what is?"

"I *want* to go away with you. That's what bothers me. I want it more than you do."

He looked baffled. "Then . . . ?"

"So I have to choose. I can't love you both any longer." She zipped her dress and stepped into her shoes.

"Choose me," he pleaded. "You've given six long years to Bernd. Isn't that enough? How could he be dissatisfied?"

"I made a promise to him."

"Break it."

"A person who breaks a promise diminishes herself. It's like losing a finger. It's worse than being paralyzed, which is merely physical. Someone whose promises are worthless has a disabled soul."

He looked ashamed. "You're right."

"Thank you for loving me, Claus. I'll never forget a single second of our Monday evenings."

"I can't believe I'm losing you." He turned away.

She wanted to kiss him one more time, but she decided not to.

"Good-bye," she said, and she went out.

· · ·

In the end, the election was nail-bitingly close.

In September Cam had been ecstatically confident that Richard Nixon would win. He was far ahead in the polls. The police riot in Democratic Chicago, fresh in the minds of television viewers, tainted his opponent, Hubert Humphrey. Then, through September and October, Cam learned that voters' memories were maddeningly short. To Cam's horror, Humphrey began to close the gap. On the Friday before the election, the Harris poll had Nixon ahead 40–37; on Monday, Gallup said Nixon 42–40; on election day, Harris put Humphrey ahead "by a nose."

On election night, Nixon checked into a suite in the Waldorf Towers in New York. Cam and other key volunteers gathered in a more modest room with a TV and a refrigerator full of beer. Cam looked around the room and wondered excitedly how many of them would get jobs in the White House if Nixon won tonight.

Cam had got to know a plain, serious girl called Stephanie Maple, and he was hoping she might go to bed with him, either to celebrate Nixon's victory or for consolation in defeat.

At half past eleven they saw longtime Nixon press aide Herb Klein speaking from the cavernous press room several floors below them. "We still think we can win by three to five million, but it looks closer to three million at this point." Cam caught Stephanie's eye and raised his eyebrows. They knew Herb was bullshitting. By midnight Humphrey was ahead, in the votes already counted, by six hundred thousand. Then, at ten minutes past midnight, came news that deflated Cam's hopes: CBS reported that Humphrey had won New York—not by a whisker, but by half a million votes.

All eyes turned to California, where voting went on for three more hours after the polls closed in the East. But California went to Nixon, and it all came down to Illinois.

No one could predict the Illinois result. Mayor Daley's Democratic Party machine always cheated brazenly. But had Daley's power been diminished by the sight of his police bludgeoning kids on live television? Was his support of Humphrey even reliable? Humphrey had uttered the mildest of veiled criticism of Daley, saying: "Chicago last August was filled with pain," but bullies were thin-skinned, and there were rumors that Daley was so disgruntled that his backing for Humphrey was halfhearted.

Whatever the reason, in the end Daley did not deliver Illinois for Humphrey.

When the TV announced that Nixon had taken the state by one hundred forty thousand votes, the Nixon volunteers erupted with joy. It was over, and they had won.

They congratulated one another for a while, then the party broke up and they headed for their rooms, to get a few hours' sleep before Nixon's victory speech in the morning. Cam said quietly to Stephanie: "How about one more drink? I have a bottle in my room."

"Oh, gosh, no, thanks," she said. "I'm beat."

He hid his disappointment. "Maybe another time."

"Sure."

On his way to his room Cam ran into John Ehrlichman. "Congratulations, sir!"

"And to you, too, Cam."

"Thank you."

"When do you graduate?"

"June."

"Come and see me then. I might be able to offer you a job."

It was what Cam dreamed of. "Thank you!"

He entered his room in high spirits, despite Stephanie's refusal. He set his alarm and fell on the bed, exhausted but triumphant. Nixon had won. The decadent, liberal sixties were coming to an end. From now on people would have to work for what they wanted, not demand it by going on demonstrations. America was once again going to become strong, disciplined, conservative, and rich. There would be a new regime in Washington.

And Cam would be part of it.

PART SEVEN

TAPE

1972–1974

J acky Jakes cooked fried chicken, sweet potatoes, collard greens, and corn bread. "To heck with my diet," said Maria Summers, and tucked in. She loved this kind of food. She noticed that George ate sparingly, a little chicken and some greens, no bread. He had always had refined tastes.

It was Sunday. Maria visited the Jakes house almost as if she were family. It had started four years ago, after Maria helped George get his job at Fawcett Renshaw. That Thanksgiving, he had invited Maria to his mother's house for the traditional turkey dinner, in an attempt to cheer them all up after their hopes had crashed in Nixon's election victory. Maria had been missing her own family, so far away in Chicago, and had been grateful. She loved Jacky's combination of warmth and feistiness, and Jacky had seemed to take to her, too. Since then Maria had visited every couple of months.

After dinner they sat in the living room. When George was out of the room, Jacky said: "Something's eating you, child. What's on your mind?"

Maria sighed. Jacky was perceptive. "I've got a hard decision to make," Maria said.

"Romance, or work?"

"Work. You know, at first it seemed President Nixon wouldn't be as bad as we all feared. He's done more for black people than anyone ever expected." She ticked off items on her fingers. "One: He forced the construction unions to accept more blacks in their industry. The unions fought him hard on that but he held out. Two: He helped minority businesses. In three years, minorities' share of government contracts has gone from eight million dollars to two hundred forty-two million dollars. Three: He desegregated our schools. We had the laws in place already, but Nixon enforced them. By the time Nixon's first term ends, the proportion of children in all-black schools in the South will be below ten percent, down from sixty-eight percent."

"Okay, I'm convinced. What's the problem?"

"The administration *also* does things that are just plain wrong—I mean criminal. The president acts as if the law doesn't apply to him!"

"Believe me, honey, all criminals think that."

"But we public servants are supposed to be discreet. Silence is part of our code. We don't rat on the politicians, even when we disagree with what they're doing."

"Hmm. Two moral principles in conflict. Your duty to your boss contradicts your duty to your country."

"I could just resign. I'd probably earn more outside the government anyway. But Nixon and his people would just carry on, like Mafia hoodlums. And I don't *want* to work in the private sector. I want to make America a better society, especially for blacks. I've dedicated my life to that. Why should I give it up just because Nixon's a crook?"

"Plenty of government people talk to the press. I read stories all the time about what 'sources' are telling reporters."

"We're so shocked because Nixon and Agnew got elected by promising law and order. The blatant hypocrisy of it all makes us kind of furious."

"So, you have to decide whether to 'leak' to the media."

"I guess that's what I'm thinking."

"If you do," said Jacky anxiously, "please be careful."

Maria and George went with Jacky to the evening service at Bethel Evangelical Church, then George drove Maria home. He still had the old dark blue Mercedes convertible he had bought when he first came to Washington. "Just about every part of this car has been replaced," he said. "Cost me a fortune."

"Then it's a good thing you're earning a fortune at Fawcett Renshaw."

"I do okay."

Maria realized she was holding her shoulders so rigidly that her back hurt. She tried to relax her muscles. "George, I have something serious to talk about."

"All right."

She hesitated. Now or never. "In the past month, in the Justice Department, antitrust investigations into three separate corporations have been canceled on the direct orders of the White House."

"Any reason?"

"None given. But all three were major donors to Nixon's campaign in 1968, and are expected to finance his reelection campaign this year."

"But that's straightforward perverting the course of justice! It's a crime."

"Exactly."

"I knew Nixon was a liar, but I didn't think he was an actual crook."

"It's hard to believe, I know."

"Why are you telling me?"

"I want to give the story to the press."

"Wow, Maria, that's kind of dangerous."

"I'm prepared to take the risk. But I'm going to be very, very careful."

"Good."

"Do you know any reporters?"

"Of course. There's Lee Montgomery, for a start."

Maria smiled. "I dated him a few times."

"I know—I fixed you up."

"But that means he knows of the connection between you and me. Think of someone who's never met me."

"You're right, bad idea. How about Jasper Murray?"

"Head of the Washington bureau of *This Day*? He'd be ideal. How do you know him?"

"I met him years ago, when he was a student journalist, pestering Verena for an interview with Martin Luther King. Then, six months ago, he approached me at a press conference given by one of my clients. Turns out he was at that motel in Memphis, talking to Verena, when they both saw Dr. King shot. He asked me what had become of her. I had to tell him I had no idea. I think he was kind of taken with her."

"Most men are."

"Including me."

"Will you go see Murray?" Maria was tense, fearing that George would refuse, saying he did not want to get involved. "Will you tell him what I've told you?"

"So I would be, like, your cutout. There would be no direct connection between you and Jasper."

"Yes."

"It's like a James Bond movie."

"But will you do it?" She held her breath.

He grinned. "Absolutely," he said.

. . .

President Nixon was mad as hell.

He stood behind his large two-pedestal desk in the Oval Office, framed by the gold window drapes. His back was hunched, his head down, his bushy eyebrows drawn together in a frown. His jowly face was dark, as always, with the shadow of a beard he could never quite shave off. His lower lip was thrust out in his most characteristic expression, defiance that always seemed on the point of turning into self-pity.

His voice was deep, grating, gravelly. "I don't give a damn how it's done," he said. "Do whatever has to be done to stop these leaks and prevent further unauthorized disclosures."

Cam Dewar and his boss, John Ehrlichman, stood listening. Cam was tall, like his father and grandfather, but Ehrlichman was taller. Ehrlichman was domestic affairs assistant to the president. His modest job title was misleading: he was one of Nixon's closest advisers.

Cam knew why the president was angry. They had all watched *This Day* the evening before. Jasper Murray had turned the lens of his prying camera on Nixon's financial backers. He claimed that Nixon had canceled antitrust investigations into three large corporations, all of which had made substantial donations to his campaign.

It was true.

Worse, Murray had implied that any company that needed to divert an investigation in this presidential election year only had to make a large enough contribution to the Committee to Reelect the President, known as CREEP.

Cam guessed that was probably true, too.

Nixon used the power of the presidency to help his friends. He also attacked his enemies, directing tax audits and other investigations at corporations that donated to the Democrats.

Cam had found Murray's report sickening in its hypocrisy. Everybody knew this was how politics worked. Where did they think the money for election campaigns would come from otherwise? The Kennedy brothers would have done the same, if they had not already had more money than God.

Leaks to the press had plagued Nixon's presidency. *The New York Times* had exposed Nixon's top secret bombing raids on Vietnam's neighbor Cambodia, citing anonymous White House sources. Syndicated reporter Seymour Hersh had revealed that U.S. troops had murdered hundreds of innocent people at a Vietnamese village called My Lai—an atrocity the Pentagon had tried desperately to cover up. Now, in January 1972, Nixon's popularity was at an all-time low.

Dick Nixon took it personally. He took everything personally. This morning he looked hurt, betrayed, outraged. He believed the world was full of people who had it in for him, and the leaks confirmed his paranoia.

Cam, too, was enraged. When he got the White House job he had hoped to be part of a group that would change America. But everything the Nixon administration tried to do was undermined by liberals in the media and their traitorous "sources" within the government. It was agonizingly frustrating.

"This Jasper Murray," said Nixon.

Cam remembered Jasper. The man had been living at the Williams house in London a decade ago when the Dewar family visited. Now *there* was a nest of crypto-Communists.

Nixon said: "Is he a Jew?"

Cam felt impatient, and kept his face rigidly expressionless. Nixon had some crackpot ideas, and one was that Jews were natural spies.

Ehrlichman said: "I don't think so."

Cam said: "I met Murray years ago in London. His mother is half Jewish. His father is a British army officer."

"Murray is British?"

"Yes, but we can't use that against him because he served with the U.S. Army in Vietnam. Saw action, has the medals to prove it."

"Well, find a way to stop these leaks. I don't want to be told why it can't be done. I don't want excuses. I want results. I want it done, whatever the cost."

This was the kind of fighting talk Cam liked to hear. He felt bucked.

Ehrlichman said: "Thank you, Mr. President," and they went out.

"Well, that's clear enough!" Cam said eagerly as soon as they were outside the Oval Office.

"We need surveillance on Murray," Ehrlichman said decisively.

"I'll get on it," said Cam.

Ehrlichman headed for his office. Cam left the White House and walked along Pennsylvania Avenue toward the Department of Justice.

"Surveillance" meant a lot of things. It was not against the law to "bug" a room by placing a hidden recording device. However, getting into the room secretly to place the bug almost always involved the crime of breaking and entering, or burglary. And wiretapping, recording telephone conversations, *was* illegal—with exceptions. The Nixon administration believed wiretapping was legal if approved by the attorney general. In the last two years the White House had placed a total of seventeen wiretaps, all approved by the attorney general on grounds of national security and installed by the FBI. Cam was on his way to get authorization for number eighteen.

His memory of Jasper Murray as a youngster was vague, but he vividly recollected the beautiful Evie Williams, who had brutally spurned the advances of fifteen-year-old Cam. When he had told her that he was in love with her she had said: "Don't be ridiculous." And then, when he pressed her for a reason, she had said: "I'm in love with Jasper, you idiot."

He told himself these were silly adolescent dramas. Evie was a movie star now, and a supporter of every Communist cause from civil rights to sex education. In a famous incident on her brother's television show she had kissed Percy Marquand, scandalizing an audience who was not used to seeing whites even touch blacks. And she was certainly no longer in love with Jasper. She had dated pop star Hank Remington for a long time, though they were not together now.

But the memory of her scornful rebuff stung Cam like a burn. And women were still rejecting him. Even Stephanie Maple, who was not beautiful at all, had turned him down on the night of Nixon's victory.

Later, when they both came to Washington to work, Stephanie had at last agreed to go to bed with Cam; but she had ended the romance after one night, which in a way was worse.

Cam knew he was tall and awkward, but so was his father, who apparently had never had trouble attracting women. Cam had talked to his mother about this indirectly. "How come you fell for Dad?" he had said. "He's not handsome or anything."

"Oh, but he was so *nice,*" she had said.

Cam had no idea what she was talking about.

He arrived at the Department of Justice and entered the high Great Hall with its art deco aluminum light fixtures. He anticipated no problem with the authorization: the attorney general, John Mitchell, was a Nixon crony, and had been Nixon's campaign manager in 1968.

The elevator's aluminum door opened. Cam got in and pressed the button for the fifth floor.

·   ·   ·

In ten years in the Washington bureaucracy, Maria had learned to be watchful. Her office was in the corridor leading to the attorney general's suite of rooms, and she kept her door open, so that she could see who came and went. She was especially alert on the day after the broadcast of the edition of *This Day* based on her leak. She knew there would be an explosive reaction from the White House, and she was waiting to see what form it would take.

As soon as she saw one of John Ehrlichman's aides go by, she jumped out of her chair.

"The attorney general is in a meeting and can't be disturbed," she said, catching him up. She had seen him before. He was an awkward, gangling white boy, tall and thin, his shoulders like a wire coat hanger for his suit. She knew the type: he would be clever and naïve at the same time. She put on her most friendly smile. "Perhaps I can do something for you?"

"It's not the kind of thing that can be discussed with a secretary," he said irritably.

Maria's antennae quivered. She sensed danger. But she pretended to be eager to help. "Then it's a good thing I'm not a secretary," she said. "I'm an attorney. My name is Maria Summers."

He clearly had difficulty with the concept of a black woman lawyer. "Where did you study?" he asked skeptically.

He probably expected her to name an obscure Negro college, so she took pleasure in saying casually: "Chicago Law." But she could not resist asking: "How about you?"

"I'm not a lawyer," he admitted. "I majored in Russian at Berkeley. Cam Dewar."

"I've heard of you. You work for John Ehrlichman. Why don't we talk in my office?"

"I'll wait for the attorney general."

"Is this about that TV show last night?"

Cam glanced around furtively. No one was listening.

"We have to do something about that," Maria said emphatically. "The business of government can't go on with these leaks all the time," she went on, feigning indignation. "It's impossible!"

The young man's attitude warmed. "That's what the president thinks."

"But what are we going to do about it?"

"We need a wiretap on Jasper Murray."

Maria swallowed. Thank God I found out about this, she thought. But she said: "Great—some tough action at last."

"A journalist who admits to receiving confidential information from within the government is clearly a danger to national security."

"Absolutely. Now don't you worry about the paperwork. I'll put an authorization form in front of Mitchell today. He'll be glad to sign it, I know."

"Thank you."

She caught him looking at her chest. Having seen her first as a secretary and then as a Negro, he was now regarding her as a pair of breasts. Young men were so predictable. "This will be what they call a black bag job," she said. The phrase meant illegal breaking and entering. "Joe Hugo is in charge of that for the FBI."

"I'll go and see him now." The headquarters of the Bureau was in the same building. "Thank you for your help, Maria."

"You're welcome, Mr. Dewar."

She watched him retreat down the corridor, then she closed her office door. She picked up the phone and dialed Fawcett Renshaw. "I'd like to leave a message for George Jakes," she said.

. . .

Joe Hugo was a pale man with prominent blue eyes. He was somewhere in his thirties. Like all FBI agents he wore excruciatingly conservative clothes: a plain gray suit, a white shirt, a nondescript tie, black toe-capped shoes. Cam himself was conventional in his tastes, but his unremarkable brown chalk-stripe suit with wide lapels and flared trousers suddenly seemed radical.

Cam told Hugo he worked for Ehrlichman and said right out: "I need a wiretap on Jasper Murray, the television journalist."

Joe frowned. "Tap the office of *This Day*? If *that* story got out . . ."

"Not his office, his home. The leakers we're talking about most likely sneak out late in the evening and go to a pay phone and call him at home."

"Either way it's a problem. The FBI doesn't do black bag jobs anymore."

"What? Why?"

"Mr. Hoover feels the Bureau is in danger of taking the rap for other people in government."

Cam could not contradict that. If the FBI was caught burglarizing the home of a journalist, naturally the president would deny all knowledge. That was how things worked. J. Edgar Hoover had been breaking the law for years, but now for some reason he had got a bug up his ass about it. There was no telling with Hoover, seventy-seven years old and no saner than he had ever been.

Cam raised his voice. "The president has asked for this wiretap, and the attorney general is happy to authorize it. Are you going to refuse?"

"Relax," said Hugo. "There's always a way to give the president what he needs."

"You mean you'll do it?"

"I mean there's a way." Hugo wrote something on a pad and tore off the sheet. "Call this guy. He used to do these jobs officially. He's retired now, which just means he does them unofficially."

Cam was uncomfortable with the idea of doing things unofficially.

What did that mean? he wondered. But he sensed this was not the moment to quibble.

He took the piece of paper. It bore the name "Tim Tedder" and a phone number. "I'll call him today," Cam said.

"From a pay phone," said Hugo.

.   .   .

The mayor of Roath, Mississippi, sat in George Jakes's office at Fawcett Renshaw. His name was Robert Denny, but he said: "Call me Denny. Everyone knows Denny. Even my little lady wife calls me Denny." He was the kind of man George had been fighting for a decade: an ugly, fat, foul-mouthed, stupid white racist.

His city was building an airport, with help from the government. But recipients of federal funding had to be equal-opportunity employers. And Maria in the Justice Department had learned that the new airport would have no black staff other than skycaps.

This was typical of the kind of work George got.

Denny was as condescending as a man could be. "We do things a little differently in the South, George," he said.

Don't I fucking know it, George thought; you thugs broke my arm eleven years ago, and it still aches like a bastard on a cold day.

"People in Roath wouldn't have confidence in an airport run by coloreds," Denny went on. "They would fear things might not be done right, you know, from a safety point of view. I'm sure you understand me."

You bet I do, you racist fool.

"Old Renshaw is a good friend of mine."

Renshaw was not a friend of Denny's, George knew. The senior partner had met this client just twice. But Denny was hoping to make George nervous. *If you mess up, your boss is going to be real mad at you.*

Denny went on: "He tells me that you're the best person in Washington to get the Justice Department off my back."

George said: "Mr. Renshaw is right. I am."

With Denny were two city councilors and three aides, all white. Now they sat back, showing relief. George had reassured them that their problem could be solved.

"Now," George said, "there are two ways we could achieve this. We could go to court and challenge the Justice Department's ruling. They're not that smart over there, and we can find flaws in their methodology, mistakes in their reports, and bias. Litigation is good for my firm, because our fees would be high."

"We can pay," said Denny. The airport was clearly a lucrative project.

"Two snags with litigation," George said. "One, there are always delays—and you want to get your airport built and operating as soon as you can. Two, no lawyer can put his hand on his heart and tell you what the court's decision will be. You never know."

"Not here in Washington, anyhow," said Denny.

Clearly the courts in Roath were more amenable to Denny's wishes.

"Alternatively," George said, "we could negotiate."

"What would that involve?"

"A phased introduction of more black employees at all levels."

"Promise them anything!" said Denny.

"They're not completely stupid, and payments would be tied to compliance."

"What do you think they'll want?"

"The Justice Department doesn't really care, so long as they can say they've made a difference. But they will consult with black organizations in your town." George glanced down at the file on his desk. "This case was brought to the Justice Department by Roath Christians for Equal Rights."

"Fucking Communists," said Denny.

"The Justice Department will probably agree to any compromise that has the approval of that group. It gets them and you out of the department's hair."

Denny reddened. "You better not be telling me I have to negotiate with the goddamn Roath Christians."

"It's the smart way to go if you want a quick solution to your problem."

Denny bristled.

George added: "But you don't have to see them personally. In fact I recommend you don't speak to them at all."

"Then who will negotiate with them?"

"I will," said George. "I'll fly down there tomorrow."

The mayor grinned. "And you being, you know, the color you are, you'll be able to talk them into backing down."

George wanted to strangle the dumb prick. "I don't want you to misunderstand me, Mr. Mayor—Denny, I should say. You will have to make some real changes. My job is to make sure they're as painless as possible. But you're an experienced political leader, and you know the importance of public relations."

"That's the truth."

"If there's any talk of the Roath Christians backing down, it could sabotage the whole deal. Better for you to take the line that you've graciously made some small concessions, much against your will, in order to get your airport built for the good of the town."

"Gotcha," Denny said with a wink.

Without realizing it, Denny had agreed to reverse a decades-old practice and employ more blacks at his airport. This was a small victory, but George relished it. However, Denny would not be happy unless he could tell himself and others that he had pulled a fast one. Best, perhaps, to go along with the delusion.

George winked back.

As the delegation from Mississippi was leaving the office, George's secretary gave him a strange look and a slip of paper.

It was a typed phone message: "There will be a prayer meeting at the Barney Circle Full Gospel Church tomorrow at six."

The secretary's look said this was a strange way for a high-powered Washington lawyer to spend the cocktail hour.

George knew the message was from Maria.

.   .   .

Cam did not like Tim Tedder. He wore a safari suit and had a soldier's short haircut. He had no sideburns, at a time when almost everyone wore sideburns. Cam felt Tedder was too gung ho. He clearly relished everything clandestine. Cam wondered what Tedder would have said if asked to kill Jasper Murray rather than just wiretap him.

Tedder had no scruples about breaking the law, but he was used to working with the government, and within twenty-four hours he appeared in Cam's office with a written plan and a budget.

The plan provided for three men to watch Jasper Murray's apartment over two days to determine his routine. Then they would enter at a time they knew to be safe and plant a transmitter in his phone. They would also place a tape recorder nearby, probably on the roof of the building, in a casing marked 50,000 VOLTS—DO NOT TOUCH to discourage investigation. Then they would change the tapes once every twenty-four hours for a month, and Tedder would provide transcripts of all conversations.

The price for all this was five thousand dollars. Cam would get the money from the slush fund operated by the Committee to Reelect the President.

Cam took the proposal to Ehrlichman, sharply conscious that he was crossing a line. He had never done anything criminal in his life. Now he was about to become a conspirator in a burglary. It was necessary: the leaks had to be stopped, and the president had said: "I don't give a damn how it's done." All the same, Cameron did not feel good about it. He was jumping off a diving board in the dark, and could not see the water below.

John Ehrlichman wrote "E" in the approve box.

Then he added an anxious little note: "If done under your assurance that it is not traceable."

Cam knew what that meant.

If it all went wrong, he was to take the blame.

. . .

George left his office at five thirty and drove to Barney Circle, a low-rent residential neighborhood east of Capitol Hill. The church was a shack on a lot surrounded by a high chicken-wire fence. Inside, the rows of hard chairs were half full. The worshippers were all black, mostly women. It was a good place for a clandestine meeting: an FBI agent in here would be as conspicuous as a turd on a tablecloth.

One of the women turned around, and George recognized Maria Summers. He sat next to her.

"What is it?" he whispered. "What's the emergency?"

She put her finger to her lips. "Afterward," she said.

He smiled wryly. He would have to sit through an hour of prayers. Well, it would probably do his soul good.

George was delighted to be part of this cloak-and-dagger plot with Maria. His work at Fawcett Renshaw did not satisfy his passion for justice. He was helping to advance the cause of equality for blacks, but piecemeal, and slowly. He was now thirty-six, old enough to know that youthful dreams of a better world are rarely fulfilled, but all the same he thought he ought to be able to do more than get a few extra blacks hired at Roath airport.

A robed pastor entered and began with an extempore prayer that lasted ten or fifteen minutes. Then he invited the congregation to sit in silence and hold their own conversations with God. "We will be glad to hear the voice of any man who feels moved by the Holy Spirit to share his prayers with the rest of us. In accordance with the teaching of the Apostle Paul, women remain silent in the church."

George nudged Maria, knowing she would be bristling at that piece of sanctified sexism.

George's mother adored Maria. George suspected that Jacky thought she might have been like Maria, if she had been born a generation later. She might have had a good education and a high-powered job and a black dress with a row of pearls.

During the prayers George's thoughts wandered to Verena. She had disappeared into the Black Panthers. He would have liked to believe that she was responsible for the more humane side of their mission, such as cooking free breakfasts for inner-city schoolchildren whose mothers spent the early mornings cleaning white people's offices. But, knowing Verena, she might just as easily be robbing banks.

The pastor closed the meeting with another long prayer. As soon as he said amen, the members of the congregation turned to one another and began to chat. The hum of their conversations was loud, and George felt he could talk to Maria without fear of being overheard.

Maria said immediately: "They're going to tap Jasper Murray's home phone. One of Ehrlichman's boys came over from the White House."

"Obviously Jasper's last TV show triggered this."

"You bet your socks."

"And it's not really Jasper they're after."

"I know. It's the person who's giving him information. It's me."

"I'll see Jasper tonight and warn him to be careful what he says on his home phone."

"Thanks." She looked around. "We're not as unobtrusive as I'd hoped."

"Why not?"

"We're too well dressed. We obviously don't belong here."

"And my secretary now thinks I'm born again. Let's get out of here."

"We can't leave together. You go first."

George left the little church and drove back toward the White House.

Maria was not the only insider leaking to the press, he reflected: there were many. George figured that the president's casual disregard of the law had shocked some government workers into breaking a lifelong discretion. Nixon's criminality was particularly horrifying in a president who had campaigned on a law-and-order ticket. George felt as if the American people were victims of a gigantic hoax.

George tried to think where would be the best place to meet Jasper. Last time he had simply gone to the office of *This Day*. Doing that once might not have been dangerous, but he should avoid a repeat visit. He did not want to be seen with Jasper too often by Washington insiders. On the other hand, their meeting had to seem casual, not furtive, just in case they were spotted.

He drove to the parking garage nearest to Jasper's office. A block of spaces on the third floor was reserved for the staff of *This Day*. George parked nearby and went to a pay phone.

Jasper was at his desk.

George did not give his name. "It's Friday night," he said without preamble. "When were you thinking of leaving the office?"

"Soon."

"Now would be good."

"Okay."

George hung up.

A few minutes later Jasper came out of the elevator, a big man with a mane of fair hair, carrying a raincoat. He walked to his vehicle, a bronze Lincoln Continental with a black fabric roof.

George got into the Lincoln beside him and told him about the wiretap.

Jasper said: "I'll have to take the phone to pieces, and remove the bug."

George shook his head. "If you do that they'll know, because they won't get any transmissions."

"So what?"

"So they'll find another way to bug you, and next time we might not be so lucky as to find out about it."

"Shit. I take all my most important calls at home. What am I going to do?"

"When an important source calls, say you're busy and you'll call back; then go out to a pay phone."

"I guess I'll figure something out. Thanks for the tip. Does it come from the usual source?"

"Yes."

"He's well informed."

"Yes," said George, "he is."

CHAPTER FORTY-SEVEN

Beep Dewar came to see Dave Williams at Daisy Farm, his recording studio in Napa Valley.

The rooms were plain yet comfortable, but there was nothing plain about the studio, which had state-of-the-art equipment. Several hit albums had been made here, and renting the place to bands had turned into a small but profitable business. Sometimes they asked Dave to be their producer, and he found that he seemed to have a talent for helping them achieve the sounds they wanted.

Which was just as well, for Dave was not making as much money as he once had. Since the breakup of Plum Nellie there had been a greatest hits album, a live album, and an album of outtakes and alternate versions. Each had sold less than the previous one. Solo albums by former members had done modestly well. Dave was not in trouble, but he was no longer buying a new Ferrari every year. And the trend was down.

When Beep called and asked if she could drive up and see him the next day he had been so surprised that he had not asked whether she had some special reason.

That morning he shampooed his beard in the shower, put on clean jeans, and picked out a bright blue shirt. Then he asked himself why he was making a fuss. He was no longer in love with Beep. Why did he care what she thought of his appearance? He realized that he wanted her to look at him and regret jilting him. "Bloody fool," he said aloud to himself, and put on an old T-shirt.

All the same, he wondered what she wanted.

He was in the studio, working with a young singer-songwriter making his first album, when the gate phone flashed silently. He left the artist working on the middle eight and stepped outside. Beep drove up to the house in a red Mercury Cougar with the top down.

He expected her to have changed, and was intrigued to see what she would look like, but in fact she was the same: small and pretty with an impish look in her eye. She hardly seemed different from when he had first met her, a decade ago, when she had been a disturbingly sexy thirteen-year-old. Today she wore blue matador pants and a striped tank top, and her hair was cut in a short bob.

First he took her to the back of the house and showed her the view across the valley. It was winter, and the vines were bare, but the sun was shining, and the rows of brown plants threw blue shadows, making curvilinear patterns like brushstrokes.

She said: "What kind of grapes do you grow?"

"Cabernet sauvignon, the classic red grape. It's hardy, and this stony soil suits it."

"Do you make wine?"

"Yes. It's not great, but it's improving. Come inside and try a glass."

She liked the all-wood kitchen, which looked traditional despite having all the latest gadgets. The cabinets were natural hand-scraped pine, washed with a light stain to give the wood a golden glow. Dave had removed the flat ceiling, opening up the height of the room to the underside of the pitched roof.

He had spent a lot of time designing this room because he wanted it to be like the kitchen of the house in Great Peter Street, a room where everyone came to hang out, eat and drink and talk.

They sat at the antique pine table and Dave opened a bottle of Daisy Farm Red 1969, the first one he and Danny Medina had produced as partners. It was still too tannic, and Beep made a face. Dave laughed. "I guess you have to appreciate its potential."

"I'll take your word for that."

She took out a pack of Chesterfields. Dave said: "You were smoking Chesterfields when you were thirteen."

"I ought to give it up."

"I had never seen such long cigarettes."

"You were sweet at that age."

"And the sight of your lips sucking on a Chesterfield was strangely arousing to me, though I could not have said why."

She laughed. "I could have told you."

He took another sip of the wine. It might be better in a couple more years. He said: "How is Walli?"

"Fine. He does more dope than he should, but what can I tell you? He's a rock star."

Dave smiled. "I smoke a joint most evenings myself."

"Are you dating anyone?"

"Sally Dasilva."

"The actress. I saw a picture of the two of you, arriving at some premiere, but I didn't know if it was serious."

It was not very serious. "She's in LA, and we both work a lot. But we get a weekend together once in a while."

"By the way, I have to tell you how much I admire your sister."

"Evie's a good actress."

"She made me weep with laughter in that movie where she played a rookie cop. But it's her activism that makes her a hero. A lot of people oppose the war, but not many have the guts to go to North Vietnam."

"She was scared shitless."

"I bet."

Dave put down his glass and gave Beep a direct look. He could not contain his curiosity any longer. "What's really on your mind, Beep?"

"First, thanks for seeing me. You didn't have to, and I appreciate it."

"You're welcome." He had almost said no, but inquisitiveness had overcome resentment.

"Second, I apologize for what I did back in 1968. I'm sorry I hurt you. It was cruel, and I'll never cease to be ashamed."

Dave nodded. He was not going to disagree. To let her fiancé find her in bed with his best friend was about as cruel as a girl could be, and the fact that she had been only twenty at the time was not enough of an excuse.

"Third, Walli is sorry too. He and I still love each other, don't get me wrong, but we know what we did. Walli will tell you so himself, if you ever give him the chance."

"Okay." She was beginning to churn up Dave's emotions. He felt echoes of long-forgotten passions: anger, resentment, loss. He was impatient to find out where this was leading.

Beep said: "Could you ever forgive us?"

He was unprepared for the question. "I don't know, I haven't thought about it," he said weakly. Before today he might have said that he no longer cared, but somehow Beep's questions were reawakening dormant grief. "What would forgiving you involve?"

Beep took a breath. "Walli wants to re-form the group."

"Oh!" Dave had not been expecting that.

"He misses working with you."

Dave found that gratifying, in a mean-minded sort of way.

Beep added: "The solo albums haven't done so well."

"His sold better than mine."

"But it's not even the sales that bother him. He doesn't care about the money, doesn't spend half of what he earns. What matters to him is that the music was better when the two of you made it together."

"I can't disagree with that," said Dave.

"He's got some songs he'd like to share with you. You could get Lew and Buzz over from London. We could all live here at Daisy Farm. Then, when the album comes out, maybe you could do a reunion concert, even a tour."

Against his will Dave felt excited. Nothing had ever been as thrilling as the Plum Nellie years, all the way from Hamburg to Haight-Ashbury. The group had been exploited and cheated and ripped off, and they had loved every minute of it. Now he was respected and fairly paid, a television personality, a family entertainer, a show business entrepreneur. But it was not half so much fun.

"Go back on the road?" he mused. "I don't know."

"Think about it," Beep pleaded. "Don't say yes or no."

"Okay," Dave said. "I'll think about it."

But he already knew the answer.

He walked her out to her car. There was a newspaper lying on the passenger seat. Beep picked it up and handed it to him. "Have you seen this?" she said. "It's a photo of your sister."

. . .

The picture showed Evie Williams in camouflage fatigues.

The first thing that struck Cam Dewar was how alluring she looked. The baggy clothing only reminded him that underneath was the perfect body the world had seen in the movie *The Artist's Model*. The heavy boots and the utilitarian cap just made her more cute.

She was sitting on a tank. Cam did not know much about armaments, but the caption told him this was a Soviet T-54 with a 100 mm gun.

All around her were uniformed soldiers of the North Vietnamese army. She seemed to be telling them something amusing, and her face was alight with animation and humor. They were smiling and laughing the way people anywhere in the world did around a Hollywood celebrity.

She was on a peace mission, according to the accompanying article. She had learned that Vietnamese people did not wish to be at war with the United States. "There's a fucking surprise," Cam said sarcastically. All they wanted was to be left alone, Evie said.

The picture was a public relations triumph for the antiwar movement. Half the girls in America wanted to be Evie Williams, half the boys wanted to marry her, and they all admired her courage in going to North Vietnam. Worse yet, the Communists were doing her no harm. They were talking to her and telling her that they wanted to be friends with the American people.

How could the wicked president drop bombs on these nice folks?

It made Cam want to puke.

But the White House was not taking this lying down.

Cam was working the phones, calling sympathetic journalists. There were not too many of those: the liberal media hated Nixon, and a part of the conservative media found him too moderate. But there were enough supporters, Cam thought, to start a backlash, if only they would play along.

Cam had in front of him a list of points to make, and he chose from the list depending on whom he was talking to. "How many American boys do you think have been killed by that tank?" he asked a writer for a talk show.

"I don't know, you tell me," the man replied.

The correct answer was probably none, since North Vietnamese tanks generally did not meet American forces, but engaged the South Vietnamese army. However, that was not the point. "It's a question liberals ought to be asked on your show," Cam said.

"You're right, it's a good question."

Speaking to a columnist for a right-wing tabloid he asked: "Did you know that Evie Williams is British?"

"Her mother is American," the journalist pointed out.

"Her mother hates America so much that she left in 1936 and has never lived here since."

"Good point!"

Speaking to a liberal journalist who often attacked Nixon, Cam said: "Even you have to admit she's naïve, to let herself be used like this by the North Vietnamese for anti-American propaganda. Or do you take her peace mission seriously?"

The results were spectacular. Next day began a backlash against Evie Williams that was larger in scale than her original triumph. She became public enemy number one, replacing Eldridge Cleaver, the serial rapist and Black Panther leader. Letters vilifying her poured into the White House—and not all of them were whipped up by local Republican Parties around the country. She became a hate figure to the people who had voted for Nixon, people who clung to the simple belief that you were either for America or against it.

Cam found the whole thing deeply gratifying. Every time he read another tabloid diatribe against her, he remembered how she had called his love ridiculous.

But he was not through with her yet.

When the backlash was at its height, he called Melton Faulkner, a pro-Nixon businessman who was on the board of one of the television networks. He got the switchboard to dial the call, so that Faulkner's secretary would say to him: "The White House is on the line!"

When he reached Faulkner he gave his name and said: "The president has asked me to call you, sir, about a special the network is planning on Jane Addams."

Jane Addams, who died in 1935, had been a progressive campaigner, suffragette, and winner of the Nobel Peace Prize.

"That's right," said Faulkner. "Is the president a fan of hers?"

The hell he is, Cam thought; Jane Addams was just the kind of woolly-minded liberal he hated. "Yes, he is," Cam said. "But *The Hollywood Reporter* says you're thinking of casting Evie Williams as Jane."

"That's right."

"You probably saw the recent news about Evie Williams and the way she let herself be exploited for propaganda by America's enemies."

"Sure, I read that story."

"Are you sure this anti-American British actress with socialist views is the right person to play an American hero?"

"As a board member, I don't have any say in casting . . ."

"The president has no power to take any action about this, heaven forbid, but he thought you might be interested to hear his opinion."

"I most certainly am."

"Good to talk to you, Mr. Faulkner." Cam hung up.

He had heard people say that revenge is sweet. But no one had told him how sweet.

. . .

Dave and Walli sat in the recording studio on high stools, holding guitars. They had a song called "Back Together Again." It was in two parts, the different parts in different keys, and they needed a hinge chord for the transition. They sang the song over and over, trying different things.

Dave was happy. They still had it. Walli was an original, coming up with melodies and harmonic progressions that no one else used. They bounced ideas off one another and the result was better than anything either did alone. They were going to make a triumphant comeback.

Beep had not changed, but Walli had. He was gaunt. His high cheekbones and almond eyes were accentuated by his thinness, and he looked vampirishly handsome.

Buzz and Lew sat nearby, smoking, listening, waiting. They were patient. As soon as Dave and Walli had the song figured out, Buzz and Lew would move to their instruments and work out the drum and bass parts.

It was ten in the evening, and they had been working for three hours. They would keep going until three or four in the morning, then sleep until midday. Those were rock-and-roll hours.

This was their third day in the studio. They had spent the first jamming, playing old favorites, enjoying getting used to one another again. Walli had played wonderful melodic guitar lines. Unfortunately, on the second day Walli had suffered a stomach upset and retired early. So this was their first day of serious work.

On an amplifier beside Walli stood a bottle of Jack Daniel's and a tall glass with ice cubes. In the old days they had often drunk booze or smoked joints while they worked on songs. It had been part of the fun. These days Dave preferred to work straight, but Walli had not changed his habits.

Beep came in with four beers on a tray. Dave guessed she wanted Walli to drink beer instead of whisky. She often brought food into the studio: blueberries with ice cream, chocolate cake, bowls of peanuts, bananas. She wanted Walli to live on something other than booze. He would take a spoonful of ice cream or a handful of peanuts, then return to his Jack Daniel's.

Fortunately he was still brilliant, as the new song showed. However, he was getting irritated with their inability to come up with the right transition chord. "Fuck," he said. "I have it in my head, you know? But it won't come out."

Buzz said: "Musical constipation, mate. You need a rock laxative. What would be the equivalent of a bowl of prunes?"

Dave said: "A Schoenberg opera."

Lew said: "A drum solo by Dave Clark."

Walli said: "A Demis Roussos album."

The phone flashed and Beep picked it up. "Come on in," she said, and hung up. Then she said to Walli: "It's Hilton."

"Okay." Walli got off his stool, put his guitar in a stand, and went out.

Dave looked inquiringly at Beep, who said: "A dealer."

Dave kept playing the song. There was nothing unusual about a dope dealer calling at a recording studio. He did not know why musicians used drugs so much more than the general population, but it had always been so: Charlie Parker had been a heroin addict, and he was the generation before last.

While Dave strummed, Buzz picked up his bass and played along, and Lew sat behind the kit and began to drum quietly, looking for the groove. They had been improvising for fifteen or twenty minutes when Dave stopped and said: "What the fuck has happened to Walli?"

He left the studio, followed by the others, and returned to the main house.

They found Walli in the kitchen. He was stretched out on the floor, stoned, with a hypodermic syringe still stuck in his arm. He had shot up as soon as his supply arrived.

Beep bent over him and gently pulled out the needle. "He'll be out now until morning," she said. "I'm sorry."

Dave cursed. That was the end of the day's work.

Buzz said to Lew: "Shall we go to the cantina?"

There was a bar at the bottom of the hill, mostly used by Mexican farm workers. It had the ridiculous name of the Mayfair Lounge, so they referred to it as the cantina.

"Might as well," said Lew.

The rhythm section left.

Beep said: "Help me get him to bed."

Dave picked up Walli by the shoulders, Beep took his legs, and they carried him to the bedroom. Then they returned to the kitchen. Beep leaned against the counter while Dave put on coffee.

"He's an addict, isn't he?" Dave said, fiddling with a paper filter.

Beep nodded.

"Do you think we can even make this album?"

"Yes!" she said. "Please don't give up on him. I'm afraid . . ."

"Okay, stay calm." He switched the machine on.

"I can manage him," she said desperately. "He maintains in the evenings, just keeping going on small amounts while he works, then in the early hours he shoots up and nods out. This was unusual, today. He doesn't often just crash like that. Normally I score the stuff and ration it."

Dave was appalled. He looked at her. "You've become nursemaid to a junkie."

"We make these decisions when we're too young to know better, then we have to live with them," she said, and she started to cry.

Dave put his arms around her, and she wept on his chest. He gave her time, while the front of his shirt got wet and the kitchen filled with the aroma of coffee. Then he gently disengaged himself and poured two cups.

"Don't worry," he said. "Now that we know about the problem, we can work around it. While Walli's at his best we'll do the difficult stuff: writing the songs, the guitar solos, the vocal harmonies. When he's not around we'll lay down backing tracks and do a rough mix. We can get it together."

"Oh, thank you. You've saved his life. I can't tell you how relieved I am. You're such a good man." She stood on tiptoe and kissed his lips.

Dave felt weird. She was thanking him for saving her boyfriend's life and, at the same time, kissing him.

Then she said: "I was such a fool to give you up."

That was disloyal to the man in the bedroom. But loyalty had never been her strength.

She put her arms around his waist and pressed her body to his.

For a moment he held his hands in the air, away from her; then he gave in, and put his arms around her again. Perhaps loyalty was not his strength either.

"Junkies don't have much sex," she said. "It's been a while."

Dave felt shaky. At some level, he realized, he had known this was going to happen, from the moment she drove up in that red convertible.

He was shaking because he wanted her so badly.

Still he said nothing.

"Take me to bed, Dave," she said. "Let's fuck like we used to, just once, for old times' sake."

"No," he said.

But he did.

.   .   .

They finished the album the day FBI director J. Edgar Hoover died.

Over breakfast at noon the following day, in the kitchen of Daisy Farm, Beep said: "My grandfather is a senator, and he says J. Edgar liked to suck cock."

They were all amazed.

Dave grinned. He was pretty sure old Gus Dewar had never said "suck cock" to his granddaughter. But Beep liked to talk that way in front of guys. She knew it turned them on. She was mischievous. It was one of the things that made her exciting.

She went on: "Grandpapa told me Hoover lived with his associate director, a guy called Tolson. They went everywhere together, like husband and wife."

Lew said: "It's people like Hoover give us queers a bad name."

Walli, up unusually early, said: "Hey, listen, we're going to do a reunion concert when the album comes out, right?"

Dave said: "Yeah. What's on your mind?"

"Let's make it a fund-raiser for George McGovern."

The idea of rock bands raising money for liberal politicians was catching on, and McGovern was the leading contender for the Democratic nomination in this year's presidential election, running as a peace candidate.

Dave said: "Great idea. Doubles our publicity, and helps to end the war as well."

Lew said: "I'm for it."

Buzz said: "Okay, I'm outvoted, I concede."

Lew and Buzz left soon after to catch a plane to London. Walli went into the studio to pack his guitars into their cases, a job he did not like to leave to roadies.

Dave said to Beep: "You can't just go."

"Why not?"

"Because for the last six weeks we've been fucking our brains out every time Walli nodded out."

She grinned. "Been great, hasn't it?"

"And because we love each other." Dave waited to see whether she would confirm or deny this.

She did neither.

He repeated: "You can't just go."

"What else am I going to do?"

"Talk to Walli. Tell him to get a new nursemaid. Come and live here with me."

Beep shook her head.

"I met you a decade ago," Dave said. "We've been lovers. We were engaged to get married. I think I know you."

"So?"

"You're fond of Walli, you care for him, you want him to be okay. But you rarely have sex with him and, what's even more telling, you don't mind that. Which tells me you don't love him."

Once again she did not confirm or deny what he said.

Dave said: "I think you love me."

She looked into her empty coffee cup, as if she might see answers there in the dregs.

"Shall we get married?" Dave said. "Is that why you're hesitating— you want me to propose? Then I will. Marry me, Beep. I love you. I loved you when we were thirteen years old and I don't think I ever stopped."

"What, not even when you were in bed with Mandy Love?"

He smiled ruefully. "I might have forgotten about you just for a few moments now and again."

She grinned. "Now I believe you."

"What about children? Would you like to have kids? I would."

She said nothing.

Dave said: "I'm pouring my heart out here, and I'm getting nothing back. What's going on in your head?"

She looked up, and he saw that she was crying. She said: "If I leave Walli, he'll die."

"I don't believe he will," Dave said.

Beep held up a hand to silence him. "You asked me what's going on in my head. If you really want to know, don't contradict what I say."

Dave shut up.

"I've done a lot of selfish bad things in my life. Some you know about, but there are more."

Dave could believe that. But he wanted to tell her that she had also brought joy and laughter into many people's lives, including his own. However, she had asked him just to listen, so he did.

"I hold Walli's life in my hands."

Dave bit back a retort, but Beep said what had been on the tip of his tongue. "Okay, it's not my fault he's a junkie, I'm not his mother, I don't have to save him."

Dave thought Walli might be tougher than Beep reckoned. On the other hand Jimi Hendrix had died, Janis Joplin had died, Jim Morrison had died . . .

"I want to change," Beep said. "More, I want to make up for my mistakes. It's time for me to do something that isn't just what grabs me at the moment. It's time for me to do something good. So I'm going to stay with Walli."

"Is that your last word?"

"Yes."

"Good-bye, then," said Dave, and he hurried out of the room so that she would not see him cry.

CHAPTER FORTY-EIGHT

The Kremlin is in a panic about Nixon's visit to China," said Dimka to Tanya.

They were in Dimka's apartment. His three-year-old daughter, Katya, was on Tanya's knee, and they were looking through a book with pictures of farm animals.

Dimka and Natalya had moved back into Government House. The Peshkov-Dvorkin clan now occupied three apartments in the same building. Grandfather Grigori was still in his original place, living now with his daughter, Anya, and granddaughter, Tanya. Dimka's ex-wife, Nina, lived there with Grisha, eight years old and a little schoolboy. And now Dimka and Natalya and little Katya had moved in. Tanya adored her nephew and niece and was always happy to babysit. Government House was almost like a peasant village, Tanya sometimes thought, with the extended family minding the children.

People often asked Tanya whether she did not want children of her own. "There's plenty of time," she always answered. She was still only thirty-two. But she did not feel she was free to marry. Vasili was not her lover, but she had dedicated her life to the undercover work they did together, first in publishing *Dissidence*, then in smuggling Vasili's books to the West. Occasionally she was courted by one of the diminishing number of eligible bachelors her age, and sometimes she would go on a few dates and even go to bed with one of them. But she could not let them into her clandestine life.

And Vasili's life was now more important than her own. With the publication of *A Free Man* he had become one of the world's leading writers. He interpreted the Soviet Union to the rest of the planet. After his third book, *The Age of Stagnation*, there was talk of a Nobel Prize, except that apparently they could not award it to a pseudonym. Tanya was the conduit by which his work reached the West, and it would be impossible to keep such a big, terrible secret from a husband.

The Communists hated "Ivan Kuznetsov." The whole world knew that he could not reveal his real name for fear that his work would be suppressed, and this made the Kremlin leaders look like the Philistines they were. Every time his work was mentioned in the Western media, people pointed out that it had never been published in Russian, the language in which it had been written, because of Soviet censorship. It drove the Kremlin mad.

"Nixon's trip was a big success," Tanya said to Dimka. "In our office we get news feeds from the West. People can't stop congratulating Nixon on his vision. This is a giant leap forward for the stability of the world, they say. Also, his poll ratings have jumped—and this is election year in the United States."

The idea that the capitalist-imperialists might link with the maverick Chinese Communists to gang up on the USSR was a terrifying prospect to the Soviet leadership. They immediately invited Nixon to Moscow in an attempt to redress the balance.

"Now they're desperate to make sure Nixon's visit here is also a success," Dimka said. "They'll do anything to keep the USA from siding with China."

Tanya was struck by a thought. "Anything?"

"I exaggerate. But what did you have in mind?"

Tanya felt her heart beat faster. "Would they release dissidents?"

"Ah." Dimka knew, but would not say, that Tanya was thinking of Vasili. Dimka was one of a very few people who knew of Tanya's connection to a dissident. He was too cautious to mention it casually. "The KGB is proposing the opposite—a clampdown. They want to jail everyone who might possibly wave a protest placard at the American president's passing limousine."

"That's stupid," said Tanya. "If we suddenly put hundreds of people in jail, the Americans will find out—they have spies, too—and they won't like it."

Dimka nodded. "Nixon doesn't want his critics saying that he came here and ignored the whole issue of human rights—not in an election year."

"Exactly."

Dimka looked thoughtful. "We must make the most of this opportunity. I have a meeting tomorrow with some people from the U.S. embassy. I wonder if I can use that . . ."

. . .

Dimka had changed. The invasion of Czechoslovakia had done it. Until that moment he had clung stubbornly to the belief that Communism could be reformed. But he had seen, in 1968, that as soon as a few people began to make progress in changing the nature of Communist government, their efforts would be crushed by those who had a stake in keeping things just the same. Men such as Brezhnev and Andropov enjoyed power, status, and privilege: why would they risk all that? Dimka now agreed with his sister: Communism's biggest problem was that the all-embracing authority of the party always stifled change. The Soviet system was helplessly frozen in a terrified conservatism, just as the regime of the tsars had been sixty years earlier, when his grandfather had been a foreman at the Putilov Machine Works in St. Petersburg.

How ironic that was, Dimka reflected, when the first philosopher to explain the phenomenon of social change had been Karl Marx.

Next day Dimka chaired another in a long series of discussions about Nixon's visit to Moscow. Natalya was there, but unfortunately so was Yevgeny Filipov. The American team was led by Ed Markham, a middle-aged career diplomat. Everyone spoke through interpreters.

Nixon and Brezhnev would sign two arms limitation treaties and an environmental protection agreement. "The environment" was not an issue in Soviet politics, but apparently Nixon felt strongly about it, and had promoted pioneering legislation in the States. Those three documents would be sufficient to guarantee that the visit would be hailed as a historic triumph, and go a long way toward guarding against the dangers of a Chinese-American alliance. Mrs. Nixon would visit schools and hospitals. Nixon was insisting on having a meeting with a dissident poet, Yevgeny Yevtushenko, whom he had met previously in Washington.

At today's meeting the Soviets and the Americans discussed security and protocol, as always. In the middle of the meeting Natalya said the words she had previously agreed on with Dimka. Speaking in a casual tone to the Americans, she said: "We have been carefully considering your demand that we release a large number of so-called political prisoners, as a token gesture toward what you call human rights."

Ed Markham threw a startled look at Dimka, who was chair of the meeting. Markham knew nothing of this. That was because the Americans had made no such demand. Dimka made a quick, surreptitious brushing-away gesture, indicating that Markham should keep quiet. A skilled and experienced negotiator, the American said nothing.

Filipov was equally surprised. "I have no knowledge of any such—"

Dimka raised his voice. "Please, Yevgeny Davidovitch, do not interrupt Comrade Smotrov! I insist that one person speaks at a time."

Filipov looked furious, but his Communist Party training forced him to follow the rules.

Natalya went on: "We have no political prisoners in the Soviet Union, and we cannot see the logic of releasing criminals onto the streets to coincide with the visit of a foreign head of state."

"Quite," said Dimka.

Markham was clearly mystified. Why raise a fictitious demand only to refuse it? But he waited in silence to see where Natalya was going. Meanwhile Filipov drummed his fingers on his writing pad in frustration.

Natalya said: "However, a small number of persons are denied internal travel visas because of connections with antisocial groups and troublemakers."

That was precisely the situation of Tanya's friend Vasili. Dimka had tried once before to get him released, but had failed. Perhaps he would have more luck this time.

Dimka watched Markham intently. Would he realize what was going on and play his part? Dimka needed the Americans to pretend they had made demands about releasing dissidents. He could then go back to the Kremlin and say the USA was insisting on this as a precondition of Nixon's visit. At that point any objections from the KGB or any other group would fall away, for everyone in the Kremlin was desperate to get Nixon here to woo him away from the hated Chinese.

Natalya went on: "As these people have not actually been sentenced by the courts, there is no legal bar to action by the government, so we offer to ease the restraints, permitting them to travel, as a gesture of goodwill."

Dimka said to the Americans: "Would that action on our part satisfy your president?"

Markham's face had cleared, and he had now understood the game Natalya and Dimka were playing. He was happy to be used that way, and he said: "Yes, I think that might be sufficient."

"That's agreed, then," said Dimka, and sat back in his chair with a profound sense of accomplishment.

. . .

President Nixon came to Moscow in May, when the snow had thawed and the sun shone.

Tanya had been hoping to see a large-scale release of political prisoners to coincide with the visit, but she had been disappointed. This was the best chance in years to get Vasili out of his hovel in Siberia and back to Moscow. Tanya knew that her brother had tried, but it seemed he had failed. It made her want to weep.

Her boss, Daniil Antonov, said: "Follow the president's wife around today, please, Tanya."

"Fuck off," she said. "Just because I'm a woman doesn't mean I have to do stories about women all the time."

Throughout her career Tanya had fought against being given "feminine" assignments. Sometimes she won, sometimes she lost.

Today she lost.

Daniil was a good guy, but he was not a pushover. "I'm not asking you to cover women all the time, and I never have, so don't talk shit. I'm asking you to cover Pat Nixon today. Now just do as you're told."

Daniil was actually a great boss. Tanya gave in.

Today Pat Nixon was taken to Moscow State University, a thirty-two-story yellow stone building with thousands of rooms. It seemed mostly empty.

Mrs. Nixon said: "Where are all the students?"

The rector of the university, speaking through interpreters, said: "It's exam time, they're all studying."

"I'm not getting to meet the Russian people," Mrs. Nixon complained.

Tanya wanted to say: *You bet you're not meeting the people—they might tell you the truth.*

Mrs. Nixon looked conservative even by Moscow standards. Her hair was piled high and sprayed rigid, like a Viking helmet and almost as hard. She wore clothes that were too young-looking for her and at the same time out of fashion. She had a fixed smile that rarely faltered, even when the press corps following her became unruly.

She was taken into a study room where three students sat at tables. They seemed surprised to see her and clearly did not know who she was. It was evident they did not want to meet her.

Poor Mrs. Nixon probably had no idea that any contact with Westerners was dangerous for ordinary Soviet citizens. They were liable to be arrested afterward and interrogated about what was said and whether the meeting was prearranged. Only the most foolhardy Muscovites wanted to exchange words with foreign visitors.

Tanya composed her article in her head while she followed the visitor around. *Mrs. Nixon was clearly impressed by the new modern Moscow State University. The USA does not have a university building of comparable size.*

The real story was in the Kremlin, which was why Tanya had been bad-tempered with Daniil. Nixon and Brezhnev were signing treaties that would make the world a safer place. That was the story Tanya wanted to cover.

She knew from reading the foreign press that Nixon's China visit and this Moscow trip had transformed his prospects in the November presidential election. From a January low, his approval rating had soared. He now had a strong chance of getting reelected.

Mrs. Nixon was dressed in a two-piece check suit with a short jacket and discreetly below-the-knee skirt. Her white shoes had a low heel. A chiffon neck scarf completed her outfit. Tanya hated doing fashion. She had covered the Cuban missile crisis, for God's sake—from Cuba!

At last the First Lady was whisked away in a Chrysler LeBaron limousine, and the press pack dispersed.

In the car park Tanya saw a tall man wearing a long, threadbare coat in the spring sunshine. He had unkempt iron gray hair, and his lined face looked as if it might once have been handsome.

It was Vasili.

She stuffed her fist into her mouth and bit her hand to suppress the scream that bubbled up in her throat.

He saw that she had recognized him, and he smiled, showing gaps where he had lost teeth.

She walked slowly over to where he stood, hands in the pockets of his coat. He had no hat, and he squinted because of the sun.

"They let you out," Tanya said.

"To please the American president," he said. "Thank you, Dick Nixon."

He should have thanked Dimka Dvorkin. But it was probably better not to tell anyone that, not even Vasili.

She looked around warily, but there was no one else in sight.

"Don't worry," said Vasili. "For two weeks this place has been crawling with security police, but they all left five minutes ago."

She could restrain herself no longer, and threw herself into his arms. He patted her back as if to comfort her. She hugged him hard.

"My," he said, "you smell good."

She broke the embrace. She was bursting with a hundred questions and had to restrain her enthusiasm and pick one. "Where are you living?"

"They gave me a Stalin apartment—old, but nice."

Apartments from the Stalin era had bigger rooms and higher ceilings than the more compact flats built in the late fifties and sixties.

She was overflowing with exhilaration. "Shall I visit you there?"

"Not yet. Let's find out how closely they're watching me."

"Do you have work?" It was a favorite trick of the Communists to make sure a man could not get a job, then accuse him of being a social parasite.

"I'm at the Agriculture Ministry. I write pamphlets for peasants explaining new farming techniques. Don't pity me: it's important work, and I'm good at it."

"And your health?"

"I'm fat!" He opened his coat to show her.

She laughed happily. He was not fat, but perhaps he was not as thin as he had been. "You're wearing the sweater I sent you. I'm amazed it reached you." It was the one Anna Murray had bought in Vienna. Tanya would now have to explain all that to him. She did not know where to start.

"I've hardly taken this off for four years. I don't need it, in Moscow in May, but it's hard to get used to the idea that the weather is not always freezing."

"I can get you another sweater."

"You must be making big money!"

"No, I'm not," she said with a wide smile. "But you are."

He frowned, puzzled. "How come?"

"Let's go to a bar," she said, taking his arm. "I've got such a lot to tell you."

. . .

The front page of *The Washington Post* carried an odd story on the morning of Sunday, June 18. To most readers it was a bit baffling. To a handful it was utterly unnerving.

5 Held in Plot to Bug Democrats' Office Here

by Alfred E. Lewis
Washington Post Staff Writer

Five men, one of whom said he is a former employee of the Central Intelligence Agency, were arrested at 2:30 A.M. yesterday in what authorities described as an elaborate plot to bug the offices of the Democratic National Committee here.

Three of the men were native-born Cubans and another was said to have trained Cuban exiles for guerrilla activity after the 1961 Bay of Pigs invasion.

They were surprised at gunpoint by three plain-clothes officers of the metropolitan police department in a sixth floor office at the plush Watergate, 2600 Virginia Ave., NW, where the Democratic National Committee occupies the entire floor.

There was no immediate explanation as to why the five suspects would want to bug the Democratic National Committee offices or whether or not they were working for any other individuals or organizations.

Cameron Dewar read the story and said: "Oh, shit."

He pushed away his cornflakes, too tense now to eat. He knew exactly what this was about, and it presented a terrible threat to President Nixon. If people knew or believed that the law-and-order president had ordered a burglary, it could even derail his reelection.

Cam scanned the paragraphs until he came to the names of the accused men. He feared that Tim Tedder would be among them. To Cam's relief, Tedder was not mentioned.

But most of the men named were Tedder's friends and associates.

Tedder and a group of former FBI and CIA agents formed the White House Special Investigations Unit. They had a high-security office on the ground floor of the Executive Office Building, across the street from the White House. Taped to their door was a piece of paper marked: PLUMBERS. It was a joke: their job was to stop leaks.

Cam had not known they planned to bug the Democrats' offices. However, he was not surprised: it was quite a good idea, and might lead to information about sources of leaks.

But the stupid idiots were not supposed to get themselves arrested by the Washington fucking police.

The president was in the Bahamas, due back tomorrow.

Cam called the Plumbers' office. Tim Tedder answered. "What are you doing?" Cam said.

"Weeding files."

In the background, Cam heard the whine of a shredder. "Good," he said.

Then he got dressed and went to the White House.

At first it seemed that none of the burglars had any direct connection with the president, and throughout Sunday Cam thought the scandal might be managed. Then it turned out that one of them had given a false name. "Edward Martin" was in fact James McCord, a retired CIA agent employed full-time by CREEP, the Committee to Reelect the President.

"That does it," Cam said. He felt crushed and devastated. This was terrible.

Monday's *Washington Post* carried the information about McCord in a story bylined Bob Woodward and Carl Bernstein.

Still Cam hoped the president's involvement might be covered up.

Then the FBI stepped in. The Bureau began to investigate the five burglars. In the old days, Cam thought regretfully, J. Edgar Hoover would have done no such thing; but Hoover was dead. Nixon had installed a crony, Patrick Gray, as acting director, but Gray did not know the Bureau and was struggling to control it. The upshot was that the FBI was beginning to act like a law enforcement agency.

The burglars had been found in possession of large amounts of cash, new bills with sequential numbers. This meant that sooner or later the FBI would be able to trace the money and find out who had given it to them.

Cam already knew. This money, like the payments for all the administration's undercover projects, came from the CREEP slush fund.

The FBI inquiry had to be shut down.

. . .

When Cam Dewar walked into Maria Summers's office at the Department of Justice, she suffered a moment of fear. Had she been found out? Had the White House somehow discovered that she was Jasper Murray's source of inside information? She was standing at her file cabinet, and for a moment her legs felt so weak she feared she might fall.

But Cam was friendly, and she calmed down. He smiled, took a seat, and gave her the adolescent up-and-down look that indicated he found her attractive.

Keep on dreaming, white boy, she thought.

What was he up to now? She sat at her desk, took off her glasses, and gave him a warm smile. "Hi, Mr. Dewar," she said. "How did that wiretap work out?"

"In the end it didn't give us much information," Cam said. "We think Murray may have a secure phone somewhere else that he uses for confidential calls."

Thank God, she thought. "That's too bad," she said.

"We appreciate your help, all the same."

"You're very kind. Is there something else I can do for you?"

"Yes. The president wants the attorney general to order the FBI to stop investigating the Watergate burglary."

Maria tried to conceal her shock as her mind reeled with the implications. So it *was* a White House caper. She was amazed. No president other than Nixon would have been so arrogant and stupid.

Once again, she would find out the most if she pretended to be supportive. "Okay," she said, "let's think about this. Kleindienst isn't Mitchell, you know." John Mitchell had resigned as attorney general in order to run CREEP. His replacement, Richard Kleindienst, was another Nixon crony, but not as biddable. "Kleindienst will want a reason," Maria said.

"We can give him one. The FBI investigation may lead to confidential matters of foreign policy. In particular, it may reveal damaging information about CIA involvement in President Kennedy's Bay of Pigs invasion."

That was typical of Tricky Dick, Maria thought with disgust. Everyone would pretend they were protecting American interests when in reality they were saving the president's sorry ass. "So it's a matter of national security."

"Yes."

"Good. That will justify the attorney general in ordering the FBI to back off." But Maria did not want it to be so easy for the White House. "However, Kleindienst may want concrete assurance."

"We can provide that. The CIA is prepared to make a formal request. Walters will do it." General Vernon Walters was deputy director of the CIA.

"If the request is formal, I think we can go ahead and do exactly what the president wants."

"Thank you, Maria." The boy stood up. "You've been very helpful, again."

"You're welcome, Mr. Dewar."

Cam left the room.

Maria stared thoughtfully at the chair he had vacated. The president must have authorized this burglary, or at least turned a blind eye to it. That was the only possible reason for Cam Dewar to be working so hard on a cover-up. If someone in the administration had okayed the burglary in defiance of Nixon's wishes, that person would by now have been named and shamed and fired. Nixon was not squeamish about getting rid of embarrassing colleagues. The only person he cared to protect was himself.

Was she going to let him get away with it?

Like hell she was.

She picked up the phone and said: "Call Fawcett Renshaw, please."

CHAPTER FORTY-NINE

D ave Williams was nervous. It was almost five years since Plum Nellie had played to a live audience. Now they were about to face sixty thousand fans at Candlestick Park in San Francisco.

Performing in a studio was not the same at all. The tape recorder was forgiving: if you played a bum note or your voice cracked or you forgot the lyrics, you could just erase the error and try again.

Anything that went wrong here tonight would be heard by everyone in the stadium and never corrected.

Dave told himself not to be silly. He had done this a hundred times. He recalled playing with the Guardsmen in pubs in the East End of London, when he had known only a handful of chords. Looking back, he marveled at his youthful audacity. He remembered the night Geoffrey had passed out, dead drunk, at the Dive in Hamburg, and Walli had come onstage and played lead guitar throughout the set with no rehearsal. Happy-go-lucky days.

Dave now had nine years' experience. That was longer than the entire career of many pop stars. All the same, as the fans streamed in, buying beer and T-shirts and hot dogs, all trusting Dave to ensure they would have a great evening, he felt shaky.

A young woman from the music company that distributed Nellie Records came into his dressing room to ask if there was anything he needed. She wore loon pants and a crop top, showing off a perfect figure. "No, thanks, darling," he said. All the dressing rooms had a small bar with beer and liquor, soft drinks and ice, and a carton of cigarettes.

"If you want a little something to relax you, I have supplies," she said.

He shook his head. He did not want drugs right now. He might smoke a joint afterward.

She persisted. "Or if I can, you know, do anything . . ."

She was offering him sex. She was as gorgeous as a slim California blonde could be, which was very beautiful indeed, but he was not in the mood.

He had not been in the mood since the last time he saw Beep.

"Maybe after the show," he said. If I get drunk enough, he thought. "I appreciate the offer, but right now I want you to get lost," he said firmly.

She was not offended. "Let me know if you change your mind!" she said cheerfully, and she went out.

Tonight's gig was a benefit for George McGovern. His election campaign had succeeded in bringing young people back into politics. In Europe he would have been middle-of-the-road, Dave knew, but here he was considered left-wing. His tough criticism of the Vietnam War delighted liberals, and he spoke with authority because of his combat experience in World War II.

Dave's sister, Evie, came to his dressing room to wish him luck. She was dressed to avoid recognition, with her hair pinned up under a tweed cap, sunglasses, and a biker jacket. "I'm going back to England," she said.

That surprised him. "I know you've had some bad press since that Hanoi photo, but . . ."

She shook her head. "It's worse than bad press. I'm hated today as passionately as I was loved a year ago. It's the phenomenon Oscar Wilde noticed: one turns to the other with bewildering suddenness."

"I thought you might ride it out."

"So did I, for a while. But I haven't been offered a decent part in six months. I could play the plucky girl in a spaghetti Western, a stripper in an off-Broadway improvisation, or any part I like in the Australian tour of *Jesus Christ Superstar*."

"I'm sorry—I had no idea."

"It wasn't exactly spontaneous."

"What do you mean?"

"A couple of journalists told me they got calls from the White House."

"This was organized?"

"I think so. Look, I was a popular celebrity who attacked Nixon at every opportunity. It's not surprising that he stuck the knife in me when I was foolish enough to give him a chance. It isn't even unfair: I'm doing my best to put *him* out of a job."

"That's pretty big of you."

"And it might not even be Nixon. Who do we know who works at the White House?"

"Beep's brother?" Dave was incredulous. "Cam did this to you?"

"He fell for me, all those years ago in London, and I turned him down kind of roughly."

"And he's held a grudge all these years?"

"I could never prove it."

"The bastard!"

"So, I've put my swanky Hollywood home on the market, sold my convertible, and packed up my collection of modern art."

"What will you do?"

"Lady Macbeth, for a start."

"You'll be terrifying. Where?"

"Stratford-upon-Avon. I'm joining the Royal Shakespeare Company."

"One door closes and another opens."

"I'm so happy to be doing Shakespeare again. It's ten years since I played Ophelia at school."

"In the nude."

Evie smiled ruefully. "What a little show-off I was."

"You were also a good actor, even then."

She stood up. "I'll leave you to get ready. Enjoy yourself tonight, little brother. I'll be in the audience, bopping."

"When are you leaving for England?"

"I'm on a plane tomorrow."

"Let me know when *Macbeth* opens. I'll come and see you."

"That would be nice."

Dave walked out with Evie. The stage had been built on a temporary scaffold at one end of the field. Behind the stage, a crowd of roadies, sound men, record company people, and privileged journalists milled on the grass. The dressing rooms were tents pitched in a roped-off area.

Buzz and Lew had arrived, but there was no sign of Walli. Dave was relying on Beep to get Walli here on time. He wondered anxiously where they were.

Soon after Evie left, Beep's parents came backstage. Dave was again on good terms with Bella and Woody. He decided not to tell them what Evie had said about Cam stirring up the press against her. Lifelong Democrats, they were already annoyed that their son was working for Nixon.

Dave wanted to know what Woody thought of McGovern's chances. "George McGovern has a problem," Woody said. "In order to defeat Hubert Humphrey and get the nomination, he had to break the power of the old Democratic Party barons, the city mayors and the state governors and the union bosses."

Dave had not followed this closely. "How did he manage that?"

"After the mess of Chicago 1968 the party rewrote the rules, and McGovern chaired the commission that did that."

"Why's that a problem?"

"Because the old power brokers won't work for him. Some detest him so much that they started a movement called Democrats for Nixon."

"Young people like him."

"We have to hope that will be enough."

At last Beep arrived with Walli. The Dewar parents went off to Walli's dressing room. Dave put on his stage outfit, a red one-piece jumpsuit and engineer boots. He did some exercises to warm up his voice. While he was singing scales, Beep came in.

She gave him a sunny smile and kissed his cheek. As always, she lit up the room just by walking in. I should never have let her go, Dave thought. What kind of an idiot am I?

"How is Walli?" he said worriedly.

"He's had a hit of dope, just enough to get him through the gig. He'll shoot up when he comes offstage. He's all right to play."

"Thank God."

She was wearing satin hot pants and a sequined bra top. She had put on a little weight since the recording sessions, Dave saw: her bust seemed bigger and she even had a cute tummy bulge. He offered her a drink. She asked for a Coke. "Help yourself to a cigarette," he said.

"I quit."

"That's why you've put on weight."

"No, it's not."

"That wasn't a put-down. You look fabulous."

"I'm leaving Walli."

That shocked him. He turned from the bar and stared at her. "Wow," he said. "Does he know yet?"

"I'm going to tell him after tonight's show."

"That's a relief. But what about all that stuff you told me about being a less selfish person and saving Walli's life?"

"I have a more important life to save."

"Your own?"

"My baby's."

"Christ." Dave sat down. "You're pregnant."

"Three months."

"That's why your shape has changed."

"And smoking makes me puke. I don't even use pot anymore."

The dressing room PA crackled, and a voice said: "Five minutes to showtime, everybody. All stage technicians should now be in performance positions."

Dave said: "If you're pregnant, why are you leaving Walli?"

"I'm not bringing up a child in that environment. It's one thing to sacrifice myself, something else to do it to a kid. This child is going to have a normal life."

"Where will you go?"

"I'm moving back in with my mom and dad." She shook her head in a gesture of wonder. "It's incredible. For ten years I've done everything I could to piss them off, but when I needed their help they just said yes. Fucking amazing."

The PA said: "One minute, everybody. The band is kindly invited to move to the wings whenever they're ready."

Dave was struck by a thought. "Three months . . ."

"I don't know whose baby it is," Beep said. "I conceived while you were making the album. I was on the pill, but sometimes I used to forget to take it, especially if I was stoned."

"But you told me that Walli and you seldom had sex."

"Seldom isn't never. I'd say there's a ten percent chance it's Walli's baby."

"So ninety percent mine."

Lew looked into Dave's tent. "Here we go," he said.

"I'm coming," Dave said.

Lew went, and Dave said to Beep: "Live with me."

She stared at him. "Do you mean it?"

"Yes."

"Even if it's not your baby?"

"I'm sure I'll love your baby. I love you. Hell, I love Walli. Live with me, please."

"Oh, God," she said, and she started to cry. "I was hoping and praying you'd say this."

"Does that mean you will?"

"Of course. It's what I'm longing for."

Dave felt as if the sun had risen. "Well, then, that's what we'll do," he said.

"What are we going to do about Walli? I don't want him to die."

"I have an idea about that," Dave said. "I'll tell you after the show."

"Go onstage, they're waiting for you."

"I know." He kissed her mouth softly. She put her arms around him and hugged him. "I love you," he said.

"I love you, too, and I was crazy to ever let you go."

"Don't do it again."

"Never."

Dave went out. He ran across the grass and up the steps to where the rest of the band was waiting in the wings. Then he was struck by a thought. "I forgot something," he said.

Buzz said irritably: "What? The guitars are onstage."

Dave did not answer. He ran back to his dressing room. Beep was still there, sitting down, wiping her eyes.

Dave said: "Shall we get married?"

"Okay," she said.

"Good."

He ran back to the scaffold.

"Everyone okay?" he said.

Everyone was okay.

Dave led the band onto the stage.

. . .

Claus Krohn asked Rebecca to have a drink after a meeting of the Hamburg parliament.

She was taken aback. It was four years since she had ended their love affair. For the past twelve months, she knew, Claus had been seeing an attractive woman who was the membership officer of a trade union. Claus meanwhile was an increasingly powerful figure in the Free Democratic Party, to which Rebecca also belonged. Claus and his girlfriend were a good match. In fact, Rebecca had heard they were planning to get married.

So she gave him a discouraging look.

"Not at the Yacht Bar," Claus added hastily. "Somewhere less furtive."

She laughed, reassured.

They went to a bar in the town center not far from the city hall. For old times' sake, Rebecca asked for a glass of Sekt. "I'll come right to the point," Claus said as soon as they had their drinks. "We want you to stand for election to the national parliament."

"Oh!" she said. "I would have been less surprised if you'd made a pass at me."

He smiled. "Don't be surprised. You're intelligent and attractive, you speak well, and people like you. You're respected by men of all parties here in Hamburg. You have almost a decade of experience in politics. You'd be an asset."

"But it's so sudden."

"Elections always seem sudden."

The chancellor, Willy Brandt, had engineered a snap election, to be held in eight weeks' time. If Rebecca agreed, she could be a member of parliament before Christmas.

When she got over the surprise, Rebecca felt eager. Her passionate desire was for the reunification of Germany, so that she and thousands more Germans could be reunited with their families. She would never achieve that in local politics—but as a member of the national parliament she might have some influence.

Her party, the FDP, was in a coalition government with the Social Democrats led by Willy Brandt. Rebecca agreed with Brandt's "Ostpolitik," trying to have contact with the East despite the Wall. She believed this was the quickest way to undermine the East German regime.

"I'll have to talk to my husband," she said.

"I knew you'd say that. Women always do."

"It will mean leaving him alone a lot."

"This happens to all spouses of members of parliament."

"But my husband is special."

"Indeed."

"I'll talk to him this evening." Rebecca stood up.

Claus stood too. "On a personal note . . ."

"What?"

"We know each other quite well."

"Yes . . ."

"This is your destiny." He was serious. "You were meant to be a national politician. Anything less would be a waste of your talents. A criminal waste. I mean it."

She was surprised by his intensity. "Thank you," she said.

She felt both elated and dazed as she drove home. A new future had suddenly opened up. She had thought about national politics, but had feared it would be too difficult, as a woman and as the wife of a disabled husband. But now that the prospect was more than a fantasy she felt eager.

On the other hand, what would Bernd do?

She parked the car and hurried into their apartment. Bernd was at the kitchen table in his wheelchair, marking school essays with a sharp red pencil. He was undressed and wearing a bathrobe, which he could manage to put on himself. The most difficult garment, for him, was a pair of trousers.

She told him immediately about Claus's proposition. "Before you speak, let me say one more thing," she said. "If you don't want me to do this, I won't. No argument, no regrets, no recriminations. We're a partnership, and that means neither of us has the right to change our life unilaterally."

"Thank you," he said. "But let's talk about the details."

"The Bundestag sits from Monday to Friday about twenty weeks of the year, and attendance is compulsory."

"So you'd spend about eighty nights away in an average year. I can cope with that, especially if we get a nurse to come in and help me in the mornings."

"Would you mind?"

"Of course. But no doubt your nights at home would be all the sweeter."

"Bernd, you're so good."

"You have to do this," he said. "It's your destiny."

She gave a little laugh. "That's what Claus said."

"I'm not surprised."

Her husband and her ex-lover both thought that this was what she should do. She thought so too. She felt apprehensive: she believed she could do it, but it would be a challenge. National politics was tougher and nastier than local government. The press could be vicious.

Her mother would be proud, she thought. Carla ought to have been a leader, and probably would have been if she had not got trapped in the prison of East Germany. She would be thrilled that her daughter was fulfilling her defeated aspiration.

They talked it over for the next three evenings, then, on the fourth, Dave Williams arrived.

They were not expecting him. Rebecca was astonished to see him on the doorstep, wearing a brown suede coat and carrying a small suitcase with a Hamburg airport tag. "You could have called!" she said in English.

"I lost your number," he replied in German.

She kissed his cheek. "What a wonderful surprise!" She had liked Dave back in the days when Plum Nellie was playing on the Reeperbahn, and the boys had come to this apartment for their only square meal of the week. Dave had been good for Walli, whose talent had flowered in the partnership.

Dave came into the kitchen, set down his suitcase, and shook hands with Bernd. "Have you just flown in from London?" Bernd asked.

"From San Francisco. I've been traveling twenty-four hours." They spoke their usual mixture of English and German.

Rebecca put coffee on. As she got over her surprise, it occurred to her that Dave must have some special reason for this visit, and she felt anxious. Dave was explaining to Bernd about his recording studio, but Rebecca interrupted him. "Why are you here, Dave? Is something wrong?"

"Yes," said Dave. "It's Walli."

Rebecca's heart missed a beat. "What's the matter? Tell me! He's not dead . . ."

"No, he's alive. But he's a heroin addict."

"Oh, no." Rebecca sat down heavily. "Oh, no." She buried her face in her hands.

"There's more," said Dave. "Beep is leaving him. She's pregnant, and she doesn't want to raise a child in the drug scene."

"Oh, my poor little brother."

Bernd said: "What is Beep going to do?"

"She's moving into Daisy Farm with me."

"Oh." Rebecca saw that Dave looked embarrassed. He had resumed his romance with Beep, she guessed. That could only make things worse for her brother. "What can we do about Walli?"

"He needs to give up heroin, obviously."

"Do you think he can?"

"With the right kind of help. There are programs, in the States and here in Europe, that combine therapy with a chemical substitute, usually methadone. But Walli lives in Haight-Ashbury. There's a dealer on every corner, and if he doesn't go out and score, one of them will knock on his door. It's just too easy for him to lapse."

"So he has to move?"

"I think he has to move here."

"Oh, my goodness."

"Living with you, I think he could kick the habit."

Rebecca looked at Bernd.

"I'm concerned about you," Bernd said to her. "You have a job and a political career. I'm fond of Walli, not least because you love him. But I don't want you to sacrifice your life to him."

"It's not forever," Dave put in quickly. "But if you could keep him clean and sober for a year . . ."

Rebecca was still looking at Bernd. "I won't sacrifice my life. But I might have to put it on hold for a year."

"If you turn down a Bundestag seat now, the offer might never be renewed."

"I know."

Dave said to Rebecca: "I want you to come with me back to San Francisco and persuade Walli."

"When?"

"Tomorrow would be good. I've already made flight reservations."

"Tomorrow!"

But there was really no choice, Rebecca thought. Walli's life was at stake. Nothing compared with that. She would put him first; of course she would. She hardly needed to think about it.

All the same, she felt sad about turning down the thrilling prospect that had been so briefly held out to her.

Dave said: "What did you say, a moment ago, about the Bundestag?"

"Nothing," Rebecca said. "Just something else I was thinking of doing. But I'll come with you to San Francisco. Of course I will."

"Tomorrow?"

"Yes."

"Thank you."

Rebecca stood up. "I'll pack a bag," she said.

CHAPTER FIFTY

J asper Murray was depressed. President Nixon—liar, cheat, and crook—was reelected by a huge majority. He won forty-nine states. George McGovern, one of the most unsuccessful candidates in American history, got only Massachusetts and the District of Columbia.

Worse, as new revelations about Watergate scandalized the liberal intelligentsia, Nixon's popularity remained strong. Five months after the election, in April 1973, the president's approval rating stood at 60–33.

"What do we have to do?" Jasper said frustratedly to anyone who would listen. The media, led by *The Washington Post*, revealed one presidential crime after another as Nixon scrambled desperately to cover up his involvement in a break-in. One of the Watergate burglars had written a letter, which the judge read out in court, complaining that the defendants had been subjected to political pressure to plead guilty and remain silent. If this was true, it meant the president was trying to pervert the course of justice. But voters seemed not to care.

Jasper was in the White House briefing room on Tuesday, April 17, when the tide turned.

The room had a slightly raised stage at one end. A lectern stood in front of a backdrop curtain that was colored a television-friendly shade of blue-gray. There were never enough chairs, and some reporters sat on the tan carpet while cameramen jostled for space.

The White House had announced that the president would make a brief statement but take no questions. The reporters had assembled at three o'clock. It was now half past four and nothing had happened.

Nixon appeared at four forty-two. Jasper noticed that his hands seemed to be shaking. Nixon announced the resolution of a dispute between the White House and Sam Ervin, chair of the Senate committee that was investigating Watergate. White House staff would now be allowed to testify to the Ervin Committee, although they might refuse to answer any question. It was not much of a concession, Jasper thought. But surely an innocent president would not even be having this argument.

Then Nixon said: "No individual holding, in the past or present, a position of major importance in the administration should be given immunity from prosecution."

Jasper frowned. What did this mean? Someone must have been demanding immunity, someone close to Nixon. Now Nixon was publicly refusing it. He was hanging someone out to dry. But who?

"I condemn any attempts to cover up, no matter who is involved," said the president, who had tried to shut down the FBI investigation; and then he left the room.

Press secretary Ron Ziegler mounted the podium to a storm of questions. Jasper did not ask any. He was intrigued by the statement about immunity.

Ziegler now said that the announcement just made by the president was the "operative" statement. Jasper immediately recognized that as a weasel word, deliberately vague, intended to obscure the truth rather than to clarify it. The other journalists in the room saw it too.

It was Johnny Apple of *The New York Times* who asked whether that implied all previous statements were inoperative.

"Yes," said Ziegler.

The press corps were furious. This meant they had been lied to. For years they had been faithfully reporting Nixon's statements, giving them the credence due to the leader of the nation. They had been taken for fools.

They would never trust him again.

Jasper went back to the office of *This Day*, still wondering who had been the real target of Nixon's statement about immunity.

He got the answer two days later. He picked up the phone to hear a woman say, in a trembling voice, that she was secretary to White House counsel John Dean, and she was calling senior reporters in Washington to read a statement from him.

This in itself was bizarre. If the president's legal adviser wanted to say something to the press, he should have done so through Ron Ziegler. Clearly there was a rift.

"'Some may hope or think that I will become a scapegoat in the Watergate case,'" the secretary read. "'Anyone who believes that does not know me . . .'"

Ah, thought Jasper, the first rat abandons the sinking ship.

. . .

Maria was amazed by Nixon. He had no dignity. As more and more people realized what a fraud he was, he did not resign, but stayed in the White House, blustering and obfuscating and threatening and lying, lying, lying.

At the end of April, John Ehrlichman and Bob Haldeman resigned together. Both had been close to Nixon. Because of their German names they had been dubbed "the Berlin Wall" by those who felt shut out by them. They had organized criminal activities such as burglary and perjury for the president: could anyone possibly believe that they had done those things against his will and without telling him? The idea was laughable.

Next day, the Senate voted unanimously for a special prosecutor to be appointed, independent of the tainted Justice Department, to investigate whether the president should be charged with crimes.

Ten days later, Nixon's approval rating fell to 44–45—the first time he had ever scored negative.

The special prosecutor went to work fast. He began to hire a team of lawyers. Maria knew one of them, a former Justice Department official called Antonia Capel. Antonia lived in Georgetown, not far from Maria's apartment, and one evening Maria rang her doorbell.

Antonia opened the door and looked surprised.

"Don't say my name," said Maria.

Antonia was puzzled, but she was quick-witted. "Okay," she said.

"Could we talk?"

"Of course—come in."

"Would you meet me at the coffee shop along the block?"

Antonia looked bewildered but said: "Sure. I'll ask my husband to bathe the kids . . . um, give me fifteen minutes?"

"You bet."

When Antonia arrived at the coffee shop she said: "Is my apartment bugged?"

"I don't know, but it might be, now that you're working for the special prosecutor."

"Wow."

"Here's the thing," said Maria. "I don't work for Dick Nixon. My loyalty is to the Justice Department and to the American people."

"Okay . . ."

"I don't have anything particular to tell you right now, but I want you to know that if there is any way I can help the special prosecutor, I will."

Antonia was smart enough to know that she was being offered a spy inside Justice. "That could be really important," she said. "But how will we stay in contact without giving the game away?"

"Call me from a pay phone. Don't give your name. Say anything about a cup of coffee. I'll meet you here the same day. Is this a good time?"

"Perfect."

"How are things going?"

"We're just getting started. We're looking for the right lawyers to join the team."

"On that subject, I have a suggestion: George Jakes."

"I think I've met him. Remind me who he is."

"He worked for Bobby Kennedy for seven years, first at Justice when Bobby was attorney general, then in the Senate. After Bobby was killed, George went to work at Fawcett Renshaw."

"He sounds ideal. I'll give him a call."

Maria stood up. "Let's leave separately. Reduces the chance of our being seen together."

"Isn't it terrible that we have to act so furtively when we're doing the right thing?"

"I know."

"Thank you for coming to see me, Maria. I really appreciate it."

"Good-bye," said Maria. "Don't tell your boss my name."

. . .

Cameron Dewar had a television set in his office. When the Ervin Committee hearings were being broadcast from the Senate, Cam's TV was on continuously—as was just about every other set in downtown Washington.

On the afternoon of Monday, July 16, Cam was working on a report for his new boss, Al Haig, who had replaced Bob Haldeman as White House chief of staff. Cam was not paying close attention to the televised testimony of Alexander Butterfield, a midlevel White House figure who had organized the president's daily schedule during Nixon's first term, then left to run the Federal Aviation Administration.

A committee lawyer called Fred Thompson was questioning Butterfield. "Were you aware of the installation of any listening devices in the Oval Office of the president?"

Cam looked up. That was unexpected. Listening devices—commonly called bugs—in the Oval Office? Surely not.

Butterfield was silent for a long time. The committee room went quiet. Cam whispered: "Jesus."

At last Butterfield said: "I was aware of listening devices, yes, sir."

Cam stood up. "Fuck, no!" he shouted.

On TV, Thompson said: "When were those devices placed in the Oval Office?"

Butterfield hesitated, sighed, swallowed, and said: "Approximately the summer of 1970."

"Christ almighty!" Cam yelled to his empty room. "How could this happen? How could the president be so stupid?"

Thompson said: "Tell us a little bit about how those devices worked— how they were activated, for example."

Cam yelled: "Shut up! Shut the fuck up!"

Butterfield went into a long explanation of the system, and eventually revealed that it was voice-activated.

Cam sat down again. This was a catastrophe. Nixon had secretly recorded everything that went on in the Oval Office. He had talked about burglaries and bribes and blackmail, all the time knowing that his incriminating words were being taped. "Stupid, stupid, stupid!" Cam said out loud.

Cam could guess what would happen next. Both the Ervin Committee and the special prosecutor would demand to hear the tapes. Almost certainly, they would succeed in forcing the president to hand them over: they were key evidence in several criminal investigations. Then the whole world would know the truth.

Nixon might succeed in keeping the tapes to himself, or perhaps

876 | T A P E

destroying them; but that was almost as bad. For if he were innocent, the tapes would vindicate him, so why should he hide them? Destroying them would be seen as an admission of guilt—as well as one more in a lengthening list of crimes for which he could be prosecuted.

Nixon's presidency was over.

He would probably cling on. Cam knew him well by now. Nixon did not know when he was beaten—he never had. Once upon a time this had been a strength. Now it might lead him to suffer weeks, perhaps months of diminishing credibility and growing humiliation before he finally gave in.

Cam was not going to be part of that.

He picked up the phone and called Tim Tedder. They met an hour later at the Electric Diner, an old-fashioned luncheonette. "You're not worried about being seen with me?" said Tedder.

"It doesn't matter anymore. I'm leaving the White House."

"Why?"

"Haven't you been watching TV?"

"Not today."

"There's a voice-activated recording system in the Oval Office. It's taped everything that has been said in that room for the past three years. This is the end. Nixon is finished."

"Wait a minute. All the time he was arranging this stuff, he was bugging *himself*?"

"Yes."

"Incriminating himself."

"Yes."

"What kind of idiot does that?"

"I thought he was smart. I guess he had us all fooled. He sure had me fooled."

"What are you going to do?"

"That's why I called you. I'm making a new start in life. I want a new job."

"You want to work for my security firm? I'm the only employee—"

"No, no. Listen. I'm twenty-seven. I have five years' experience in the White House. I speak Russian."

"So you want to work for . . . ?"

"The CIA. I'm well qualified."

"You are. You'd have to go through their basic training."

"No problem. Part of my new start."

"I'm happy to call my friends there, put in a good word."

"I appreciate that. And there's one other thing."

"What?"

"I don't want to make a big deal of this, but I do know where the bodies are buried. The CIA has broken some rules in this whole Watergate affair. I know all about the CIA's involvement."

"I know."

"That last thing I want to do is blackmail anyone. You know where my loyalties lie. But you might hint to your friends in the Agency that, naturally, I wouldn't spill the beans on my employer."

"I get it."

"So, what do you think?"

"I think you're a shoo-in."

. . .

George was happy and proud to be on the special prosecutor's team. He felt he was part of the group leading American politics, as he had been when working for Bobby Kennedy. His only problem was that he did not know how he could ever go back to the kind of penny-ante cases he had been working at Fawcett Renshaw.

It took five months, but in the end Nixon was forced to hand over to the special prosecutor three raw tapes from the Oval Office recording system.

George Jakes was in the office with the rest of the team when they listened to the tape from June 23, 1972, less than a week after the Watergate burglary.

He heard the voice of Bob Haldeman. "The FBI is not under control because Gray doesn't exactly know how to control it."

The recording was echoey but Haldeman's cultured baritone was fairly clear.

Someone said: "Why would the president need to have the FBI under control?" It was a rhetorical question, George thought. The only reason was to stop the Bureau investigating the president's own crimes.

On the tape, Haldeman went on: "Their investigation is now leading into some productive areas because they have been able to trace the money."

George recalled that the Watergate burglars had had a lot of cash in new bills with sequential numbers. That meant that sooner or later the FBI would be able to find out who had given them the money.

Everyone now knew that this money came from CREEP. However, Nixon was still denying that he had known anything about it. Yet here he was talking about it six days after the burglary!

The gravelly bass voice of Nixon interrupted. "The people who donated money could just say they gave it to the Cubans."

George heard someone in the room say: "Holy crap!"

The special prosecutor stopped the tape.

George said: "Unless I'm mistaken, the president is proposing to ask his donors to perjure themselves."

The special prosecutor said dazedly: "Can you imagine that?"

He pressed the button and Haldeman resumed. "We don't want to be relying on too many people. The way to handle this now is for us to have Walters call Pat Gray and just say: 'Stay the hell out of this.'"

This was close to a story Jasper Murray had run based on a leak from Maria. General Vernon Walters was the deputy director of the CIA. The Agency had a long-standing agreement with the FBI: if an investigation by one threatened to expose secret operations of the other, that investigation could be halted by a simple request. Haldeman's idea seemed to be to get the CIA to pretend that the FBI's investigation into the Watergate burglars was somehow a threat to national security.

Which would be perversion of the course of justice.

On the tape, President Nixon said: "Right, fine."

The prosecutor stopped the tape again.

"Did you hear that?" George said incredulously. "Nixon said: 'Right, fine.'"

Nixon went on: "It's likely to blow the whole Bay of Pigs thing, which we think would be very unfortunate for the CIA and for the country and for American foreign policy." He seemed to be spinning a story that the CIA might tell the FBI, George thought.

"Yeah," said Haldeman. "That's the basis we'll do it on."

The prosecutor said: "The president of the United States sitting in his office telling his staff how to commit perjury!"

Everyone in the room was stunned. The president was a criminal, and they had the proof in their hands.

George said: "The lying bastard, we've got him."

On the tape, Nixon said: "I don't want them to get any ideas we're doing it because our concern is political."

Haldeman said: "Right."

In the room, gathered around the tape player, the assembled lawyers burst out laughing.

. . .

Maria was at her desk in the Justice Department when George called. "I just heard from our friend," he said. She knew he meant Jasper. He was speaking in code in case the phones were tapped. "The White House press office called the networks and booked air time for the president. Nine o'clock tonight."

It was Thursday, August 8, 1974.

Maria's heart leaped. Could this be the end at last? "Maybe he's going to resign," she said.

"Maybe."

"God, I hope so."

"It's either that or he'll just profess his innocence again."

Maria did not want to be alone when this happened. "Do you want to come over?" she said. "We'll watch it together."

"Yeah, okay."

"I'll make supper."

"Nothing too fattening."

"George Jakes, you're vain."

"Make a salad."

"Come at seven thirty."

"I'll bring the wine."

Maria went out to shop for dinner in the heat of Washington in August. She no longer cared much about her work. She had lost faith in the Justice Department. If Nixon resigned today, she would start looking for another job. She still wanted to be in government service:

only the government had the muscle to make the world a better place. But she was sick of crime and the excuses of criminals. She wanted a change. She thought she might try for the State Department.

She bought salad, but she also got some pasta and Parmesan cheese and olives. George had refined tastes, and he was getting worse as he grew into middle age. But he certainly was not fat. Maria herself was not fat but, on the other hand, she was not thin. As she approached forty she was just getting, well, more like her mother, especially around the hips.

She left for the day a few minutes before five. A crowd had gathered outside the White House. They were chanting, "Jail to the Chief," a pun on the anthem "Hail to the Chief."

Maria caught the bus to Georgetown.

As her salary had improved over the years she had moved apartments, always to a larger place in the same neighborhood. She had got rid of all but one of the photos of President Kennedy during her last move. Her current place had a comfortable feel. Where George had always had rectilinear modern furniture and plain decor, Maria liked patterned fabrics and curved lines and lots of cushions.

Her gray cat Loopy came to greet her, as always, and rubbed her head against Maria's leg. Julius, the boy cat, was more aloof: he would show up later.

She set the table and washed the salad and grated the Parmesan cheese. Then she took a shower and put on a cotton summer dress in her favorite shade, turquoise. She thought about putting on lipstick and decided not to.

The evening news on TV was mostly speculation. Nixon had had a meeting with Vice President Gerald Ford, who might be president tomorrow. Press secretary Ziegler had announced to the White House reporters that the president would address the nation at nine, then had left the press briefing room without answering questions on what he would speak about.

George arrived at seven thirty, wearing slacks and loafers and a blue chambray shirt open at the neck. Maria tossed the salad and put the pasta in boiling water while he opened a bottle of Chianti.

Her bedroom door was open, and George looked inside. "No shrine," he said.

"I threw away most of the photographs."

They sat at her small dining table to eat.

They had been friends for thirteen years, and each had seen the other in the depths of despair. Each had had one overwhelming lover who had gone: Verena Marquand to the Black Panthers, President Kennedy into the hereafter. In different ways, both George and Maria had been left. They shared so much that they were comfortable together.

Maria said: "The heart is a map of the world, did you know that?"

"I don't even know what it means," he said.

"I saw a medieval map once. It showed the earth as a flat disc with Jerusalem in the center. Rome was bigger than Africa, and America was not even shown, of course. The heart is that kind of map. The self is in the middle and everything else is out of proportion. You draw the friends of your youth large, then later it's impossible to rescale them when other more important people need to be added. Anyone who has done you wrong is shown too big, and so is anyone you loved."

"Okay, I get it, but . . ."

"I've thrown out my photos of Jack Kennedy. But he will always be drawn too large on the map in my heart. That's all I mean."

After dinner they washed up, then sat on a large, soft couch in front of the TV with the last of the wine. The cats went to sleep on the rug.

Nixon came on at nine.

Please, Maria thought, let the torment end now.

Nixon was sitting in the Oval Office, a blue curtain behind him, the Stars and Stripes on his right and the president's flag on his left. The deep, gravelly voice began immediately. "This is the thirty-seventh time I have spoken to you from this office, where so many decisions have been made that shaped the history of this nation."

The camera began a slow zoom in. The president was wearing a familiar blue suit and tie. "Throughout the long and difficult period of Watergate, I have felt it was my duty to persevere, to make every possible effort to complete the term of office to which you elected me. In the past few days, however, it has become evident to me that I no longer have a strong enough political base in the Congress to justify continuing that effort."

George said excitedly: "That's it! He's resigning!"

Maria grabbed his arm in excitement.

The cameras pulled in for a close-up. "I have never been a quitter," Nixon said.

"Oh, shit," said George, "is he going back on it?"

"But, as president, I must put the interests of America first."

"No," said Maria, "he's not going back."

"Therefore I shall resign the presidency effective at noon tomorrow. Vice President Ford will be sworn in as president at that hour in this office."

"Yes!" George punched the air. "He's done it! He's gone!"

What Maria felt was not so much triumph as relief. She had woken up from a nightmare. In the dream, the highest officers in the land had been crooks, and no one could do anything to stop them.

But in real life they had been found out and shamed and deposed. She had a sense of safety, and realized that for two years now she had not felt that America was a secure place to be.

Nixon admitted no faults. He did not say that he had committed crimes, told lies, and tried to put the blame on other people. Turning the pages of his speech, he referred to his triumphs: China, arms limitation talks, Middle East diplomacy. He finished on a defiant note of pride.

"It's over," Maria said in a tone of incredulity.

"We won," said George, and he put his arms around her.

Then, without thinking about it, they were kissing.

It felt like the most natural thing in the world.

It was not a sudden burst of passion. They kissed playfully, exploring each other's lips and tongues. George tasted of wine. It was like discovering a fascinating topic of conversation they had previously overlooked. Maria found herself smiling and kissing at the same time.

However, their embrace soon turned passionate. Maria's pleasure became so intense it made her breathe hard. She unbuttoned George's blue shirt so that she could feel his chest. She had almost forgotten what it was like to have a man's bony frame in her arms. She relished his big hands touching the private places of her body, so different from her own small, soft fingers.

Out of the corner of her eye, she saw both cats leave the room.

George caressed her for a surprisingly long time. She had had only one previous lover, and he had not been so patient: by now he would have been on top of her. She was torn between pleasure in what George was doing and an almost panicky need to feel him inside her.

Then at last it happened. She had forgotten how good it felt. She crushed his chest to hers and lifted her legs to pull him farther in. She said his name again and again until she was overwhelmed by spasms of pleasure, and cried out. A moment later she felt him ejaculate inside her, and that made her convulse one more time.

They lay fused together, breathing hard. Maria could not touch him enough. She pressed one hand into his back, the other on his head, feeling his body, almost fearing that he might not be real, this could be a dream. She kissed his deformed ear. His panting breath was hot on her neck.

Slowly her breathing returned to normal. The world around became real again. The TV was still on, broadcasting reactions to the resignation. She heard a commentator say: "This has been a truly momentous day."

Maria sighed. "It sure has," she said.

. . .

George thought the ex-president should go to jail. Many people did. Nixon had committed more than enough crimes to justify a prison sentence. This was not medieval Europe, where kings were above the law: this was America, and justice was the same for everyone. The House Judiciary Committee had ruled that Nixon should be impeached, and Congress had endorsed the committee's report by a remarkable majority of 412 votes to 3. The public favored impeachment by 66 percent to 27. John Ehrlichman had already been sentenced to twenty months in prison for his crimes: it would be unfair if the man who had given him his orders were to escape punishment.

A month after the resignation, President Ford pardoned Nixon.

George was outraged, and so was just about everyone else. Ford's press secretary resigned. *The New York Times* said the pardon was "a profoundly unwise, divisive and unjust act" that had destroyed the new president's credibility at a stroke. Everyone assumed Nixon had cut a deal with Ford before handing power over to him.

"I can't take much more of this," said George to Maria in the kitchen of his apartment. He was mixing olive oil and red wine vinegar in a jug to make salad dressing. "Sitting behind a desk at Fawcett Renshaw while the country goes to hell."

"What are you going to do?"

"I've been thinking about it a lot. I want to go back into politics."

She turned to face him, and he was puzzled to see disapproval on her face. "What do you mean?" she said.

"The congressman for my mother's district, the Ninth Maryland, is retiring in two years. I think I can get nominated for the seat. In fact I know I can."

"So you've already talked to the Democratic Party there."

She was definitely angry with him, but he had no idea why. "Just exploratory discussions, yes," he said.

"Before you talked to me."

George was startled. Their romance was only a month old. Did he already have to clear everything with Maria? He almost said that, but bit back the words and tried something softer. "Maybe I should have talked to you first, but it didn't occur to me." He poured the dressing over the salad and started to toss it.

"You know I just applied for a really good job in the State Department."

"Of course."

"I think you know I want to go all the way to the top."

"And I bet you'll do it."

"Not with you, I won't."

"What are you talking about?"

"Senior State Department officials have to be nonpolitical. They must serve Democratic and Republican congressmen with equal diligence. If I'm known to be with a congressman I'll never get a promotion. They will always say: 'You can't really trust Maria Summers, she sleeps with Congressman Jakes.' They'd assume my loyalty was to you, not them."

George had not thought of that. "I'm really sorry," he said. "But what can I do?"

"How much does this relationship matter to you?" she said.

George thought her challenging words masked a plea. "Well," he said, "it's a little early to talk of marriage—"

"Early?" she said, getting angry. "I'm thirty-eight years old and you're only my second lover. Did you think I was looking for a casual fling?"

"I was going to say," he said patiently, "that if we do get married I assume we'll have children and you'll stay home and take care of them."

Her face was flushed with outrage. "Oh, is that what you assume? Not only do you plan to prevent me getting any further promotions, you actually expect me to give up my career altogether!"

"Well, that's what women usually do when they marry."

"The hell it is! Wake up, George. I realize that your mother devoted herself from the age of sixteen exclusively to caring for you, but you were born in 1936, for Christ's sake. We're in the seventies now. Feminism has arrived. Work is no longer something a woman does merely to pass the time until some man condescends to make her his domestic slave."

George was bewildered. This had come out of the blue. He had done something normal and reasonable, and she was spitting with rage. "I don't know why you're so goddamn ornery," he said. "I haven't ruined your career or made you a domestic slave, and I haven't actually asked you to marry me."

Her voice went quiet. "You asshole," she said. "You total asshole."

She left the room.

"Don't go," he said.

He heard the apartment door slam.

"Hell," he said.

He smelled smoke. The steaks were burning. He turned off the heat under the pan. The meat was charred black, inedible. He tipped the steaks into the garbage bin.

"Hell," he said again.

PART EIGHT

YARD

1976–1983

Grigori Peshkov was dying. The old warrior was eighty-seven, and his heart was failing.

Tanya had managed to get a message to his brother. Lev Peshkov was eighty-two but he had announced that he was coming to Moscow, in a private jet. Tanya had wondered if he would get permission to visit, but he had managed it. He had arrived yesterday and was due to visit Grigori today.

Grigori lay in bed in his apartment, pale and still. He was sensitive to pressure, and could not bear the weight of the bedclothes on his feet, so Tanya's mother, Anya, had placed two boxes in the bed, tenting the blankets so that they warmed without touching him.

Though he was weak, Tanya still felt the power of his presence. Even in repose his chin jutted pugnaciously. When he opened his eyes, he revealed that intense blue-eyed stare that had so often struck fear into the hearts of the enemies of the working class.

It was a Sunday, and family and friends came to visit. They were saying good-bye, though naturally they pretended otherwise. Tanya's twin, Dimka, and his wife, Natalya, brought Katya, their pretty seven-year-old. Dimka's ex-wife, Nina, turned up with the twelve-year-old Grisha, who had the beginnings of his great-grandfather's formidable intensity, despite his youth. Grigori smiled benignly on them all. "I fought in two revolutions and two world wars," he said. "It's a miracle I lasted this long."

He fell asleep, then, and most of the family went out, leaving Tanya and Dimka sitting at the bedside. Dimka's career had advanced: he was now an official of the State Planning Committee and a candidate member of the Politburo. He was still a close associate of Kosygin, but their attempts to reform the Soviet economy were always blocked by Kremlin conservatives. Dimka's wife, Natalya, was chair of the Analytical Department at the Foreign Ministry.

Tanya began to tell her brother about the latest feature she had written for TASS. At the suggestion of Vasili, who worked now in the Agriculture Ministry, she had flown to Stavropol, a fertile southern region where the collective farms were experimenting with a bonus system based on results. "Harvests are up," she told Dimka. "The reform is a big success."

"The Kremlin won't like bonuses," Dimka said. "They'll say the system smacks of revisionism."

"The system has been operating for years," she said. "The regional first secretary there is a real live wire. A man called Mikhail Gorbachev."

"He must have friends in high places."

"He knows Andropov, who goes to a spa in the region to take the waters." The KGB chief suffered from kidney stones, an agonizing ailment. If ever a man deserved such pain, Tanya thought, Yuri Andropov did.

Dimka was intrigued. "So this Gorbachev is a reformer who is friendly with Andropov?" he said. "That makes him an unusual man. I must keep an eye on him."

"I found him refreshingly commonsensical."

"We certainly need new ideas. Do you remember Khrushchev, back in 1961, forecasting that the USSR would overtake the USA in both production and military strength in twenty years?"

Tanya smiled. "At the time he was thought pessimistic."

"Now fifteen years have passed and we're farther behind than ever. And Natalya tells me the East European countries have also fallen behind their neighbors. They're kept quiet only by massive subsidies from us."

Tanya nodded. "It's a good thing we have huge exports of oil and other raw materials to help us pay the bills."

"But it's not enough. Look at East Germany. We have to have a damn wall to stop people escaping to capitalism."

Grigori stirred. Tanya felt guilty. She had been questioning her grandfather's fundamental beliefs while sitting at his deathbed.

The door opened and a stranger walked in. He was an old man, thin and bent but immaculately dressed. He had on a dark-gray suit that was molded to his body like something worn by the hero in a movie. His white shirt gleamed and his red tie glowed. Such clothes could only come from the West. Tanya had never met him, but all the same there was something familiar about him. This must be Lev.

He ignored Tanya and Dimka and looked at the man in the bed.

Grandfather Grigori gave him a look that said he knew the visitor but could not quite place him.

"Grigori," the newcomer said. "My brother. How did we get so old?" He spoke a queer old-fashioned dialect of Russian with the harsh accent of a Leningrad factory worker.

"Lev," said Grigori. "Is it really you? You used to be so handsome!"

Lev leaned over and kissed his brother on both cheeks, then they embraced.

Grigori said: "You got here just in time. I'm about done for."

A woman about eighty years old followed Lev in. She was dressed, Tanya thought, like a prostitute, in a stylish black dress and high heels, makeup and jewelry. Tanya wondered whether it was normal for old women to dress that way in America.

"I saw some of your grandchildren in the next room," Lev said. "They're a fine bunch."

Grigori smiled. "The joy of my life. How about you?"

"I have a daughter by Olga, the wife I never much liked, and a son by Marga here, who I preferred. I wasn't much of a father to either of my children. I never had your sense of responsibility."

"Any grandchildren?"

"Three," Lev said. "One's a movie star, one's a pop singer, and one's black."

"Black?" said Grigori. "How did that happen?"

"It happened the usual way, idiot. My son, Greg—named for his uncle, by the way—he fucked a black girl."

"Well, that's more than his uncle ever did," said Grigori, and the two old men chuckled.

Grigori said: "What a life I've had, Lev. I stormed the Winter Palace. We destroyed the tsars and built the first Communist country. I defended Moscow against the Nazis. I'm a general and Volodya is a general. I feel so guilty about you."

"Guilty about me?"

"You went to America and missed it all," Grigori said.

"I have no complaints," said Lev.

"I even got Katerina, though she preferred you."

Lev smiled. "And all I got was a hundred million dollars."

"Yes," said Grigori. "You got the worst of the deal. I'm sorry, Lev."

"It's okay," said Lev. "I forgive you." He was being ironic but, Tanya thought, Grigori did not seem to realize that.

Uncle Volodya came in. He was on his way to some army ceremony, wearing his general's uniform. Tanya realized with a sudden shock that this was the first time he had seen his real father. Lev stared at the son he had never met. "My God," Lev said. "He looks like you, Grigori."

"He's yours, though," said Grigori.

Father and son shook hands.

Volodya said nothing, seeming in the grip of an emotion so powerful that he could not speak.

Lev said: "When you lost me as a father, Volodya, you didn't lose much." Keeping hold of his son's hand, he looked him up and down: gleaming boots, Red Army uniform, combat medals, piercing blue eyes, iron gray hair. "I did, though," Lev said. "I guess I lost a lot."

.   .   .

As she left the apartment Tanya found herself wondering where the Bolsheviks had gone wrong, where Grandfather Grigori's idealism and energy had been perverted into tyranny. She went to the bus stop, heading for a rendezvous with Vasili. On the bus, thinking over the early years of the Russian Revolution, she wondered whether Lenin's decision to close all newspapers except the Bolshevik ones had been the key error. It meant that right from the start alternative ideas had had no circulation and the conventional wisdom could never be challenged. Gorbachev in Stavropol was exceptional in having been allowed to try something different. Such people were generally stifled. Tanya was a journalist, and suspected herself of egocentrically overrating the importance of a free press, but it seemed to her that the lack of critical newspapers made it much easier for other forms of oppression to flourish.

It was now four years since Vasili had been released. In that time he had shrewdly rehabilitated himself. At the Agriculture Ministry he had devised an educational radio serial set on a collective farm. As well as the dramas about unfaithful wives and disobedient children, the characters discussed agricultural techniques. Naturally the peasants who ignored advice from Moscow were lazy and shiftless, and the wayward teenagers who questioned the Communist Party's authority were the ones who were jilted by their boyfriends or failed their exams. The serial was a huge success. Vasili returned to Radio Moscow and was given an apartment in a block occupied by writers approved by the government.

Their meetings were clandestine, but Tanya also ran into him occasionally at union events or private parties. He was no longer the walking cadaver that had returned from Siberia in 1972. He had put on weight and regained some of his former presence. Now in his midforties, he would never again be movie-star handsome; but the lines of strain on his face somehow added to his allure. And he still had buckets of charm. Each time Tanya saw him he was with a different woman. They were not the nubile teenagers who had adored him in his thirties, though perhaps they were the middle-aged women those teenagers had become: smart females in chic clothes and high-heeled shoes who always seemed able to get hold of scarce nail varnish, hair dye, and stockings.

Tanya met him secretly once a month.

Each time he would bring her the latest installment of the book he was working on, written in the small, neat handwriting he had developed in Siberia to save paper. She would type it for him, correcting his spelling and punctuation where necessary. At their next meeting she would hand him the typescript for review and discuss it with him.

Millions of people around the world bought Vasili's books, but he never met any of them. He could not even read the reviews, which were written in foreign languages and published in Western newspapers. So Tanya was the only person with whom he could discuss his work, and he listened hungrily to everything she had to say. She was his editor.

Tanya went to Leipzig every March to cover the book fair there, and each time she met with Anna Murray. She always came back with a present for Vasili from Anna—an electric typewriter, a cashmere overcoat—and news of even more money piling up in his London bank account. He would probably never get to spend any of it.

She still took careful precautions when meeting him. Today she got off the bus a mile from the rendezvous, and made sure she was not being followed while she walked to the café, called Josef's. Vasili was already there, sitting at a table with a vodka glass in front of him. On the chair beside him was a large buff envelope. Tanya waved casually, as if they were acquaintances meeting by chance. She got a beer from the bar, then sat opposite Vasili.

She was happy to see him looking so well. His face had a dignity he had not possessed fifteen years earlier. He still had soft brown eyes, but nowadays they were keenly perceptive as often as they twinkled with mischief. She realized there was no one, outside her family, whom she knew better. She knew his strengths: imagination, intelligence, charm, and the gritty determination that had enabled him to survive and keep writing for a decade in Siberia. She also knew his weaknesses, the main one of which was an irresistible urge to seduce.

"Thanks for the tip about Stavropol," she said. "I've done a nice piece."

"Good. Let's just hope the whole experiment doesn't get stamped on."

She handed Vasili the last episode, typed out, and nodded at the envelope. "Another chapter?"

"The last." He gave it to her.

"Anna Murray will be happy." Vasili's new novel was called *First Lady.* In it the American president's wife—as it might be, Pat Nixon— gets lost in Moscow for twenty-four hours. Tanya marveled at Vasili's power of invention. Seeing life in the USSR through the eyes of a well-meaning conservative American was a richly comic way to criticize Soviet society. She slipped the envelope into her shoulder bag.

Vasili said: "When can you take the whole thing to the publisher?"

"As soon as I get a foreign trip. At the latest, next March, in Leipzig."

"March?" Vasili was disappointed. "That's six months away," he said in a tone of reproof.

"I'll try to get an assignment where I could meet her."

"Please do."

Tanya was offended. "Vasili, I risk my damn life to do this for you. Get someone else, if you can, or do the job yourself. Hell, I wouldn't mind."

"Of course." He was immediately contrite. "I'm sorry. I have so much invested in it—three years' work, all in the evenings after I come home from my job. But I have no right to be impatient with you." He reached across the table and put his hand over hers. "You've been my lifeline, more than once."

She nodded. It was true.

All the same, she still felt cross with him as she walked away from the café with the ending of his novel in her bag. What was bugging her? It was those women in high-heeled shoes, she decided. She felt that Vasili should have grown out of that phase. Promiscuity was adolescent. He demeaned himself by showing up at every literary party with a different date. By now he should have settled down in a serious relationship with a woman who was his equal. She could be younger, perhaps, but she should be able to match his intelligence and appreciate his work, perhaps even help him with it. He needed a partner, not a series of trophies.

She went to the TASS office. Before she reached her desk she was accosted by Pyotr Opotkin, the editor in chief for features, the department's political overseer. As always a cigarette dangled from his lips. "I've had a call from the Agriculture Ministry. Your piece on Stavropol can't go out," he said.

"What? Why not? The bonus system has been passed by the ministry. And it works."

"Wrong." Opotkin liked to tell people they were wrong. "It's been scrapped. There's a new approach, the Ipatovo Method. They send fleets of combine harvesters all over the region."

"Central control again, instead of individual responsibility."

"Exactly." He took the cigarette from his mouth. "You'll have to write a completely new article about the Ipatovo Method."

"What does the regional first secretary say?"

"Young Gorbachev? He's implementing the new system."

Of course he was, Tanya reflected. He was an intelligent man. He knew when to shut up and do as he was told. Otherwise he would not have become first secretary.

"All right," she said, stifling her anger. "I'll write a new piece."

Opotkin nodded and walked away.

It had been too good to be true, Tanya thought: a new idea, bonuses paid for good results, improved harvests in consequence, no input required from Moscow. It was a miracle the system had been permitted for a few years. In the long run, such a system was totally out of the question.

Of course it was.

CHAPTER FIFTY-TWO

George Jakes wore a new tuxedo. He looked pretty good in it, he thought. At forty-two he no longer had the wrestler's physique he had been so proud of in his youth, but he was still slim and straight, and the black-and-white wedding uniform flattered him.

He stood in Bethel Evangelical Church, which his mother had been attending for decades, in the Washington suburb he now represented as congressman. It was a low brick building, small and plain, and normally it was decorated only with a few framed quotations from the Bible: THE LORD IS MY SHEPHERD and IN THE BEGINNING WAS THE WORD. But today it was decked out for a celebration, with streamers and ribbons and masses of white flowers. The choir was belting out "Soon Come" while George waited for his bride.

In the front row, his mother wore a new dark blue suit and a matching pillbox hat with a little veil. "Well, I'm glad," Jacky had said when George told her he was getting married. "I'm fifty-eight years old, and I'm sorry you waited so gosh-darn long, but I'm happy you got here in the end." Her tongue was always sharp, but today she could not keep the proud smile from her face. Her son was getting married in her church, in front of all her friends and neighbors, and on top of that he was a congressman.

Next to her was George's father, Senator Greg Peshkov. Somehow he was able to make even a tuxedo look like creased pajamas. He had forgotten to put cuff links in his shirt, and his bow tie looked like a dead moth. No one minded.

Also in the front row were George's Russian grandparents, Lev and Marga, now in their eighties. Both looked frail, but they had flown from Buffalo for the wedding of their grandson.

By showing up at the wedding, and sitting in the front row, George's white father and grandparents were admitting the truth to the world; but no one cared. This was 1978, and what had once been a secret disgrace now hardly mattered.

The choir began to sing "You Are So Beautiful" and everyone turned and looked back toward the church door.

Verena came in on the arm of her father, Percy Marquand. George gasped when he saw her, and so did several people in the congregation. She wore a daring off-the-shoulder white dress that was tight to midthigh, then flared to a train. The caramel skin of her bare shoulders was as soft and smooth as the satin of her dress. She looked so wonderful it hurt. George felt tears sting his eyes.

The service passed in a blur. George managed to make the right responses, but all he could think was that Verena was his, now, forever.

The ceremony was folksy, but there was nothing modest about the wedding breakfast thrown afterward by the bride's father. Percy rented Pisces, a Georgetown nightclub that featured a twenty-foot waterfall at the entrance emptying into a giant goldfish pond on the floor below, and an aquarium in the middle of the dance floor.

George and Verena's first dance was to the Bee Gees' "Stayin' Alive." George was not much of a dancer, but it hardly mattered: everyone was looking at Verena, holding up her train with one hand while disco-dancing. George was so happy he wanted to hug everyone.

The second person to dance with the bride was Ted Kennedy, who had come without his wife, Joan: there were rumors that they had split. Jacky grabbed the handsome Percy Marquand. Verena's mother, Babe Lee, danced with Greg.

George's cousin Dave Williams, the pop star, was there with his sexy wife, Beep, and their five-year-old son, John Lee, named after the blues singer John Lee Hooker. The boy danced with his mother, and strutted so expertly that he made everyone laugh: he must have seen *Saturday Night Fever.*

Elizabeth Taylor danced with her latest husband, the millionaire would-be senator John Warner. Liz was wearing the famous square-cut thirty-three-carat Krupp diamond on the ring finger of her right hand. Seeing all this through a mist of euphoria, George realized dazedly that his wedding had turned into one of the outstanding social events of the year.

George had invited Maria Summers, but she had declined. After their brief love affair had ended in a quarrel, they had not spoken for a year. George had been hurt and bewildered. He did not know how he was supposed to live his life: the rules had changed. He also felt resentful. Women wanted a new deal, and they expected him to know, without being told, what the deal was, and to agree to it without negotiation.

Then Verena had emerged from seven years of obscurity. She had started her own lobbying company in Washington, specializing in civil rights and other equality issues. Her initial clients were small pressure groups who could not afford to employ their own full-time lobbyist. The rumor that Verena had once been a Black Panther seemed only to give her greater credibility. Before long she and George were an item again.

Verena seemed to have changed. One evening she said: "Dramatic gestures have their place in politics, but in the end advances are made by patient legwork: drafting legislation and talking to the media and winning votes." You've grown up, George thought, and he only just stopped himself from saying it.

The new Verena wanted marriage and children, and felt sure she could have both and a career too. Once burned, George did not again put his hand in the fire: if that was what she thought, it was not up to him to argue.

George had written a tactful letter to Maria, beginning: "I don't want you to hear this from someone else." He had told her that he and Verena were together again and talking about marriage. Maria had replied in tones of warm friendship, and their relationship had reverted to what it had been before Nixon resigned. But she remained single, and did not come to the wedding.

Taking a break from dancing, George sat down with his father and grandfather. Lev was downing champagne with relish and telling jokes. A Polish cardinal had been made Pope, and Lev had a fund of bad-taste Polish Pope jokes. "He did a miracle—made a blind man deaf!"

Greg said: "I think this is a highly aggressive political move by the Vatican."

George was surprised by that, but Greg usually had grounds for what he said. "How so?" said George.

"Catholicism is more popular in Poland than elsewhere in Eastern Europe, and the Communists aren't strong enough to repress religion there as they have in all other countries. There's a Polish religious press, a Catholic university, and various charities that get away with sheltering dissidents and noting human rights abuses."

George said: "So what is the Vatican up to?"

"Mischief. I believe they see Poland as the Soviet Union's weak spot. This Polish Pope will do more than wave at tourists from the balcony—you watch."

George was about to ask what the Pope *would* do when the room went quiet and he realized that President Carter had arrived.

Everyone applauded, even the Republicans. The president kissed the bride, shook hands with George, and accepted a glass of pink champagne, although he took only one sip.

While Carter was talking to Percy and Babe, who were long-term Democratic fund-raisers, one of the president's aides approached George. After a few pleasantries the man said: "Would you consider serving on the House Permanent Select Committee on Intelligence?"

George was flattered. Congressional committees were important. A seat on a committee was a source of power. "I've been in Congress only two years," he said.

The aide nodded. "The president is keen to advance black congressmen, and Tip O'Neill agrees." Tip O'Neill was the House majority leader, who had the prerogative of granting committee seats.

George said: "I'll be glad to serve the president any way I can—but intelligence?"

The CIA and other intelligence agencies reported to the president and the Pentagon, but they were authorized, funded, and in theory controlled by Congress. For security, control was delegated to two committees, one in the House and one in the Senate.

"I know what you're thinking," said the aide. "Intelligence committees are usually packed with conservative friends of the military. You're a liberal who has criticized the Pentagon over Vietnam and the CIA over Watergate. But that's why we want you. At present those committees don't oversee, they just applaud. And intelligence agencies that think they can get away with murder will commit murder. So we need someone in there asking tough questions."

"The intelligence community is going to be horrified."

"Good," said the aide. "After the way they behaved in the Nixon era, they need to be shaken up." He glanced across the dance floor. Following his gaze, George saw that President Carter was leaving. "I have to go," the aide said. "Do you want time to think?"

"Hell, no," said George. "I'll do it."

. . .

"Godmother? Me?" said Maria Summers. "Are you serious?"

George Jakes smiled. "I know you're not very religious. We're not, either, not really. I go to church to please my mother. Verena has been once in the last ten years, and that was for our wedding. But we like the idea of godparents."

They were having lunch in the Members' Dining Room of the House of Representatives, on the ground floor of the Capitol building, sitting in front of the famous fresco *Cornwallis Sues for Cessation of Hostilities.* Maria was eating meat loaf; George had a salad.

Maria said: "When's the baby due?"

"A month or so—early April."

"How is Verena feeling?"

"Terrible. Lethargic and impatient at the same time. And tired, always tired."

"It will soon be over."

George brought her back to the question. "Will you be godmother?"

She evaded it again. "Why have you asked me?"

He thought for a moment. "Because I trust you, I guess. I probably trust you more than anyone outside my family. If Verena and I died in a plane crash, and our parents were too old or dead, I feel confident that you would make sure my children were cared for, somehow."

Maria was evidently moved. "It's kind of wonderful to be told that."

George thought, but did not say, that it was now unlikely Maria would have children of her own—she would be forty-four this year, he calculated—and that meant she had a lot of spare maternal affection to give to the children of her friends.

She was already like family. His friendship with her had lasted almost twenty years. She still went to see Jacky several times a year. Greg liked Maria, too, as did Lev and Marga. It was hard not to like her.

George did not give voice to any of these considerations, but instead said: "It would mean a lot to Verena and me if you would do it."

"Is it really what Verena wants?"

George smiled. "Yes. She knows that you and I had a relationship, but she's not the jealous type. Matter of fact, she admires you for what you've achieved in your career."

Maria looked at the men in the fresco, with their eighteenth-century coats and boots, and said: "Well, I guess I'll be like General Cornwallis, and surrender."

"Thank you!" said George. "I'm very happy. I'd order champagne, but I know you wouldn't drink it in the middle of a working day."

"Maybe when the baby is born."

The waitress picked up their plates and they asked for coffee. "How are things in the State Department?" George asked. Maria was now a big shot there. Her title was deputy assistant secretary, a post more influential than it sounded.

"We're trying to figure out what's happening in Poland," she said. "It's not easy. We think there's a lot of criticism of the government from inside the United Workers' Party, which is the Communist Party. Workers are poor, the elite are too privileged, and the 'propaganda of success' just calls attention to the reality of failure. National income actually fell last year."

"You know I'm on the House intelligence committee."

"Of course."

"Are you getting good information from the agencies?"

"It's good, as far as we know, but there's not enough of it."

"Would you like me to ask about that in the committee?"

"Yes, please."

"It may be that we need additional intelligence personnel in Warsaw."

"I think we do. Poland could be important."

George nodded. "That's what Greg said when the Vatican elected a Polish Pope. And he's usually right."

. . .

At the age of forty, Tanya became dissatisfied with her life.

She asked herself what she wanted to do with her next forty years, and found that she did not want to spend them as an acolyte to Vasili Yenkov. She had risked her freedom to share his genius with the world, but that had done nothing for her. It was time she focused on her own needs, she decided. What that meant, she did not know.

Her discontent came to a head at a party to celebrate the award of the Lenin Prize in literature to Leonid Brezhnev's memoirs. The award was risible: the three volumes of the Soviet leader's autobiography were not well written, not true, and not even by Brezhnev, having been ghostwritten. But the writers' union saw the prize as a useful pretext for a shindig.

Getting ready for the party, Tanya put her hair in a ponytail like Olivia Newton-John's in the movie *Grease*, which she had seen on an illicit videotape. The new hairstyle did not cheer her up as much as she had hoped.

As she was leaving the building, she ran into her brother in the lobby, and told him where she was going. "I see that your protégé, Gorbachev, made a fulsome speech in praise of Comrade Brezhnev's literary genius," she said.

"Mikhail knows when to kiss ass," Dimka said.

"You did well to get him onto the Central Committee."

"He already had the support of Andropov, who likes him," Dimka explained. "All I had to do was persuade Kosygin that Gorbachev is a genuine reformer." Andropov, the KGB chief, was increasingly the leader of the conservative faction in the Kremlin; Kosygin the champion of the reformers.

Tanya said: "Gaining the approval of both sides is unusual."

"He's an unusual man. Enjoy your party."

The do was held in the utilitarian offices of the writers' union, but they had managed to get hold of several cases of Bagrationi, the Georgian champagne. Under its influence, Tanya got into an argument with Pyotr Opotkin, from TASS. No one liked Opotkin, who was not a journalist but a political supervisor, but he had to be invited to social events because he was too powerful to offend. He buttonholed Tanya and said accusingly: "The Pope's visit to Warsaw is a catastrophe!"

Opotkin was right about that. No one had imagined how it would be. Pope John Paul II turned out to be a talented propagandist. When he got off the plane at Okecie military airport he fell to his knees and kissed the Polish ground. The picture was on the front pages of the Western press next morning, and Tanya knew—as the Pope must have known—that the image would find its way back into Poland by underground routes. Tanya secretly rejoiced.

Daniil, Tanya's boss, was listening, and he interjected: "Driving into Warsaw in an open car, the Pope was cheered by two million people."

Tanya said: "Two *million*?" She had not seen this statistic. "Is that possible? It must be something like five percent of the entire population—one in every twenty Poles!"

Opotkin said angrily: "What is the point of the party controlling television coverage when people can see the Pope for themselves?"

Control was everything for men such as Opotkin.

He was not done. "He celebrated mass in Victory Square in the presence of two hundred and fifty thousand people!"

Tanya knew that. It was a shocking figure, even to her, for it starkly revealed the extent to which Communism had failed to win the hearts of the Polish people. Thirty-five years of life under the Soviet system had converted nobody but the privileged elite. She made the point in appropriate Communist jargon. "The Polish working class reasserted their reactionary old loyalties at the first opportunity."

Poking Tanya's shoulder with an accusing forefinger, Opotkin said: "It was reformists like you who insisted on letting the Pope go there."

"Rubbish," said Tanya scornfully. Kremlin liberals such as Dimka had urged letting the Pope in, but they had lost the argument, and Moscow had told Warsaw to ban the Pope—but the Polish Communists had disobeyed orders. In a display of independence unusual for a Soviet satellite, the Polish leader Edward Gierek had defied Brezhnev. "It was the Polish leadership that made the decision," Tanya said. "They feared there would be an uprising if they forbade the Pope's visit."

"We know how to deal with uprisings," said Opotkin.

Tanya knew she was only damaging her career by contradicting Opotkin, but she was forty and sick of kowtowing to idiots. "Financial pressures made the Polish decision inevitable," she said. "Poland gets huge subsidies from us, but it needs loans from the West as well. President Carter was very tough when he went to Warsaw. He made it clear that financial aid was linked to what they call human rights. If you want to blame someone for the Pope's triumph, Jimmy Carter is the culprit."

Opotkin must have known this was true, but he was not going to admit it. "I always said it was a mistake to let Communist countries borrow from Western banks."

Tanya should have left it there, and allowed Opotkin to save face, but she could not restrain herself. "Then you face a dilemma, don't you?" she said. "The alternative to Western finance is to liberalize Polish agriculture so that they can produce enough of their own food."

"More reforms!" Opotkin said angrily. "That is always your solution!"

"The Polish people have always had cheap food: that's what keeps them quiet. Whenever the government puts up prices, they riot."

"We know how to deal with riots," said Opotkin, and he walked away.

Daniil looked bemused. "Good for you," he said to Tanya. "Though he may make you pay."

Tanya said: "I want some more of that champagne."

At the bar she ran into Vasili. He was alone. Tanya realized that lately he had been showing up to events like this without a floozie on his arm, and she wondered why. But she was focused on herself tonight. "I can't do this much longer," she said.

Vasili handed her a glass. "Do what?"

"You know."

"I suppose I can guess."

"I'm forty. I have to live my own life."

"What do you want to do?"

"I don't know, that's the trouble."

"I'm forty-eight," he said. "And I feel something similar."

"What?"

"I don't chase girls anymore. Or women."

She was in a cynical mood. "Don't chase them—or just don't catch them?"

"I detect a note of skepticism."

"Perceptive of you."

"Listen," he said, "I've been thinking. I'm not sure we need to continue the pretense that we barely know one another."

"What makes you say that?"

He leaned closer and lowered his voice, so that she had to strain to hear him over the noise of the party. "Everyone knows that Anna Murray is the publisher of Ivan Kuznetsov, yet no one has ever connected her to you."

"That's because we're ultracautious. We never let anyone see us together."

"That being the case, there's no danger in people knowing that you and I are friends."

She was not sure. "Maybe. So what?"

Vasili tried a roguish smile. "You once told me you'd go to bed with me if I would give up the rest of my harem."

"I don't believe I ever said that."

"Perhaps you implied it."

"And anyway, that must have been eighteen years ago."

"Is it too late now to accept the offer?"

She stared at him, speechless.

He filled the silence. "You're the only woman who ever really mattered to me. Everyone else was just a conquest. Some I didn't even like. If I had never slept with her before, that was enough reason for me to seduce her."

"Is this supposed to make you more attractive to me?"

"When I got out of Siberia I tried to resume that life. It's taken me a long time, but I've realized the truth at last: it doesn't make me happy."

"Is that so?" Tanya was getting angrier.

Vasili did not notice. "You and I have been friends for a long time. We're soul mates. We belong together. When we sleep together, it will just be a natural progression."

"Oh, I see."

He was oblivious to her sarcasm. "You're single, I'm single. Why are we single? We should be together. We should be married."

"So, to sum up," Tanya said, "you've spent your life seducing women you never really cared for. Now you're pushing fifty and they don't really attract you—or perhaps you no longer attract them—so, at this point, you're condescending to offer me marriage."

"I may not have put this very well. I'm better at writing things down."

"You bet you haven't put it well. I'm the last resort of a fading Casanova!"

"Oh, hell, you're upset with me, aren't you?"

"*Upset* comes nowhere near it."

"This is the opposite of what I intended."

Over his shoulder, she caught the eye of Daniil. On impulse she left Vasili and crossed the room. "Daniil," she said. "I'd like to go abroad again. Is there any chance I could get a foreign posting?"

"Of course," he said. "You're my best writer. I'll do anything I can, within reason, to keep you happy."

"Thank you."

"And, coincidentally, I've been thinking that we need to strengthen our bureau in one particular foreign country."

"Which one?"

"Poland."

"You'd send me to Warsaw?"

"That's where it's all happening."

"All right," she said. "Poland it is."

. . .

Cam Dewar was fed up with Jimmy Carter. He thought the Carter administration was timid, especially in its dealings with the USSR. Cam worked on the Moscow desk at CIA headquarters in Langley, nine miles from the White House. National Security Adviser Zbigniew Brzezinski was a tough anti-Communist, but Carter was cautious.

However, it was election year, and Cam hoped Ronald Reagan would get in. Reagan was aggressive on foreign policy, and promised to liberate intelligence agencies from Carter's milk-and-water ethical constraints. He would be more like Nixon, Cam hoped.

Early in 1980 Cam was surprised to be summoned by the deputy head of the Soviet bloc section, Florence Geary. She was an attractive woman a few years older than Cam: he was thirty-three, she was probably about thirty-eight. He knew her story. She had been hired as a trainee, used as a secretary for years, and given training only when she kicked up a stink. Now she was a highly competent intelligence officer, but she was still disliked by many of the men because of the trouble she had caused.

Today she was wearing a plaid skirt and a green sweater. She looked like a schoolteacher, Cam thought; a sexy schoolteacher, with good breasts.

"Sit down," she said. "The House intelligence committee thinks our information out of Poland is poor."

Cameron took a seat. He looked out of the window to avoid staring at her chest. "Then they know who to blame," he said.

"Who?"

"The director of the CIA, Admiral Turner, and the man who appointed him, President Carter."

"Why, exactly?"

"Because Turner doesn't believe in HUMINT." Human intelligence, or HUMINT, was what you got from spies. Turner preferred SIGINT, signals intelligence, obtained by monitoring communications.

"Do *you* believe in HUMINT?"

She had a nice mouth, he realized; pink lips, even teeth. He forced himself to concentrate on answering the question. "It's inherently unreliable, because all traitors are liars, by definition. If they're telling us the truth they must be lying to their own side. But that doesn't make HUMINT worthless, especially if it's assessed against data from other sources."

"I'm glad you think so. We need to beef up our HUMINT. How do you feel about working overseas?"

Cameron's hopes leaped. "Ever since I joined the Agency, six years ago, I've been asking for a foreign posting."

"Good."

"I speak Russian fluently. I'd love to go to Moscow."

"Well, life's a funny thing. You're going to Warsaw."

"No kidding."

"I don't kid."

"I don't speak Polish."

"You'll find your Russian useful. Polish schoolchildren have been learning Russian for thirty-five years. But you should learn some Polish too."

"Okay."

"That's all."

Cameron stood up. "Thanks." He went to the door. "Could we discuss this some more, Florence?" he said. "Maybe over dinner?"

"No," she said firmly. Then, just in case he had not got the message, she added: "Definitely not."

He went out and closed the door. Warsaw! On balance, he was pleased. It was a foreign posting. He felt optimistic. He was disappointed she had turned down his invitation to dinner, but he knew what to do about that.

He picked up his coat and went outside to his car, a silver Mercury Capri. He drove into Washington and threaded through the traffic to the Adams Morgan district. There he parked a block away from a storefront massage parlor called Silken Hands.

The woman at the reception desk said: "Hi, Christopher, how are you today?"

"Fine, thanks. Is Suzy free?"

"You're in luck, she is. Room Three."

"Great." Cam handed over a bill and went farther inside.

He pushed aside a curtain and entered a booth containing a narrow bed. Beside the bed, sitting on a plastic chair, was a heavyset woman in her twenties reading a magazine. She wore a bikini. "Hello, Chris," she said, putting down the magazine and standing up. "Would you like a hand job, as usual?"

Cam never had full intercourse with prostitutes. "Yes, please, Suzy." He gave her a bill and started taking off his clothes.

"It'll be my pleasure," she said, tucking the money away. She helped him undress, then said: "You just lie down and relax, baby."

Cam lay on the bed and closed his eyes while Suzy went to work. He pictured Florence Geary in her office. In his mind, she pulled the green sweater over her head and unzipped her plaid skirt. "Oh, Cam, I just can't resist you," she said in Cam's imagination. Wearing only her underwear, she came around her desk and embraced him. "Do anything you like to me, Cam," she said. "But please, do it hard."

In the massage parlor booth, Cam said aloud: "Yeah, baby."

. . .

Tanya looked in the mirror. She was holding a small container of blue eye shadow and a brush. Makeup was more easily available in Warsaw than in Moscow. Tanya did not have much experience with eye shadow, and she had noticed that some women applied it badly. On her dressing table was a magazine open at a photograph of Bianca Jagger. Glancing frequently at the picture, Tanya began to color her eyelids.

The effect was pretty good, she thought.

Stanislaw Pawlak sat on her bed in his uniform, with his boots on a newspaper to keep the covers clean, smoking and watching her. He was tall and handsome and intelligent, and she was crazy about him.

She had met him soon after arriving in Poland, on a tour of army headquarters. He was part of a group called the Gold Fund, able young officers selected by the defense minister, General Jaruzelski, for rapid advancement. They were frequently rotated to new assignments, to give them the breadth of experience necessary for the high command to which they were destined.

She had noticed Staz, as he was called, partly because he was so good-looking, and partly because he was obviously taken with her. He spoke Russian fluently. Having talked to her about his own unit, which handled liaison with the Red Army, he had then accompanied her on the rest of the tour, which was otherwise dull.

Next day he had turned up on her doorstep at six in the evening, having got her address from the SB, the Polish secret police. He had taken her to dinner at a hot new restaurant called the Duck. She quickly realized that he was as skeptical about Communism as she was. A week later she slept with him.

She still thought about Vasili, wondering how his writing was going, and whether he missed their monthly meetings. She was viscerally angry with him, though she was not sure why. He had been crass, but men *were* crass, especially the handsome ones. What she was really seething about was the years before his proposal. Somehow she felt that what she had done for him during that long time had been dishonored. Did he believe she had just been waiting, year after year, until he was ready to be her husband? That thought still infuriated her.

Staz was now spending two or three nights a week at her apartment.

They never went to his place: he said it was little better than a barracks. But they were having a great time. And all along, in the back of her mind, she had been wondering if his anti-Communism might one day lead to action.

She turned to face him. "How do you like my eyes?"

"I adore them," he said. "They have enslaved me. Your eyes are like—"

"I mean my makeup, idiot."

"Are you wearing makeup?"

"Men are blind. How are you going to defend your country with such poor powers of observation?"

His mood became dark again. "We make no provision for defending our own country," he said. "The Polish army is totally subservient to the USSR. All our planning is about supporting the Red Army in an invasion of Western Europe."

Staz often talked like this, complaining about Soviet domination of the Polish military. It was a sign of how much he trusted her. In addition, Tanya had found that Poles spoke boldly about the failings of Communist governments. They felt entitled to complain in a way that other Soviet subjects did not. Most people in the Soviet bloc treated Communism as a religion that was a sin to question. The Poles tolerated Communism as long as it served them, and protested as soon as it fell short of their expectations.

All the same, Tanya now switched on her bedside radio. She did not think her apartment was bugged—the SB had their hands full spying on Western journalists, and probably left Soviet ones alone—but caution was an ingrained habit.

"We are all traitors," Staz finished.

Tanya frowned. He had never before called himself a traitor. This was serious. She said: "What on earth do you mean?"

"The Soviet Union has a contingency plan to invade Western Europe with a force called the Second Strategic Echelon. Most of the Red Army tanks and personnel carriers headed for West Germany, France, Holland, and Belgium will pass through Poland on their way. The United States will use nuclear bombs to try to destroy those forces before they reach the West—that is, while they are still crossing Poland. We estimate that four hundred to six hundred nuclear weapons will be exploded in our country. There will be nothing left but a nuclear wasteland. Poland will have disappeared. If we cooperate in the planning of this event, how can we not be traitors?"

Tanya shuddered. It was a nightmare scenario—but terrifyingly logical.

"America is not the enemy of the Polish people," said Staz. "If the USSR and the USA go to war in Europe, we should side with the Americans, and liberate ourselves from the tyranny of Moscow."

Was he just blowing off steam, or something more? Tanya said carefully: "Is it just you who thinks like this, Staz?"

"Certainly not. Most officers my age feel the same. They pay lip service to Communism, but if you talk to them when they're drunk you'll hear another story."

"In that case, you have a problem," she said. "By the time the war begins, it will be too late for you to win the trust of the Americans."

"This is our dilemma."

"The solution is obvious. You have to open a channel of communication now."

He gave her a cool look. The thought crossed her mind that he might be an agent provocateur, assigned to provoke her into subversive remarks so that she could be arrested. But she could not imagine that a faker would be such a good lover.

Staz said: "Are we just talking, now, or are we having a serious discussion?"

Tanya took a breath. "I'm as serious as life and death," she said.

"Do you really think it could be done?"

"I know it," she said emphatically. She had been engaging in clandestine subversion for two decades. "It's the easiest thing in the world—but keeping it secret, and getting away with it, is more difficult. You would have to exercise the most extreme caution."

"Do you think I *should* do it?"

"Yes!" she said passionately. "I don't want another generation of Soviet children—or Polish children—to grow up under this stifling tyranny."

He nodded. "I can tell that you really mean it."

"I do."

"Will you help me?"

"Of course I will."

. . .

Cameron Dewar was not sure he would make a good spy. The undercover stuff he had done for President Nixon had been amateurish, and he was lucky not to have gone to jail with his boss, John Ehrlichman. When he joined the CIA he had been trained in the tradecraft of dead drops and brush passes, but he had never actually used such tricks. After six years at CIA headquarters in Langley he had at last been posted to a foreign capital, but he still had not done clandestine work.

The U.S. embassy in Warsaw was a proud white marble building on a street called Aleje Ujazdowskie. The CIA occupied a single office near the ambassador's suite of rooms. Off the office was a windowless storeroom that was used for developing photographic film. The staff was four spies and a secretary. It was a small operation because they had few informants.

Cam did not have much to do. He read the Warsaw newspapers, with the aid of a dictionary. He reported the graffiti he saw: LONG LIVE THE POPE and WE WANT GOD. He talked to men like himself who worked for the intelligence services of other countries in the North Atlantic Treaty Organization, NATO, especially those of West Germany, France, and Britain. He drove a used lime green Polski Fiat whose battery was so undersize that it had to be recharged every night or the car would not start in the morning. He tried to find a girlfriend among the embassy secretaries, and failed.

He felt a loser. His life had once seemed full of promise. He had been a star student at school and university, and his first job had been in the White House. Then it had all gone wrong. He was determined not to let his life be blighted by Nixon. But he needed a success. He wanted to be top of the class again.

Instead he went to parties.

Embassy staff who had wives and children were happy to go home in the evenings and watch American movies on videotape, so the single men got to go to all the less important receptions. Tonight Cam was heading to the Egyptian embassy for a gathering to welcome a new deputy ambassador.

When he started the Polski, the radio came on. He kept it tuned to the SB wavelength. Reception was often weak, but sometimes he could hear the secret police talking as they tailed people around the city.

Sometimes they were tailing him. The cars changed but it was usually the same two men, a swarthy one he called Mario and a fat guy he thought of as Ollie. There seemed to be no pattern to the surveillance, so he just assumed he was more or less always being watched. That was probably what they wanted. Maybe they deliberately randomized their surveillance precisely in order to keep him permanently on edge.

But he, too, had been trained. Surveillance should never be avoided in an obvious way, he had learned, for that is a signal, to the other side, that you are up to something. Form regular habits, he had been told: go to Restaurant A every Monday, Bar B every Tuesday. Lull them into a false sense of security. But look for gaps in their watchfulness, times when their attention lapses. That will be when you can do something unobserved.

As he drove away from the U.S. embassy he saw a blue Skoda 105 tuck into the traffic two cars behind him.

The Skoda trailed him across the city. He saw Mario at the wheel and Ollie in the front passenger seat.

Cam parked in Alzacka Street and saw the blue Skoda pull up a hundred yards past him.

He was sometimes tempted to talk to Mario and Ollie, as they were so much part of his life, but he had been warned never to do that, for then the SB would switch personnel and it would take him time to recognize the new people.

He entered the Egyptian embassy and took a cocktail from a tray. It was so diluted he could hardly taste the gin. He talked to an Austrian diplomat about the difficulty of buying comfortable men's underwear in Warsaw. When the Austrian drifted away, Cam looked around and saw a blond woman in her twenties standing alone. She caught his eye and smiled, so he went to speak to her.

He swiftly found out that she was Polish, her name was Lidka, and she worked as a secretary in the Canadian embassy. She was wearing a tight pink sweater and a short black skirt that showed off her long legs. She spoke good English, and listened to Cam with an intensity of concentration that he found flattering.

Then a man in a pin-striped suit summoned her peremptorily, making Cam think he must be her boss, and the conversation broke up. Almost immediately Cam was approached by another attractive woman, and he began to think it was his lucky day. This one was older, about forty, but prettier, with short pale blond hair and bright blue eyes enhanced by blue eye shadow. She spoke to him in Russian. "I've met you before," she said. "Your name is Cameron Dewar. I'm Tanya Dvorkin."

"I remember," he said, glad of the chance to show off his fluency in Russian. "You're a reporter for TASS."

"And you're a CIA agent."

He certainly would not have told her that, so she must have guessed. Routinely, he denied it. "Nothing so glamorous," he said. "Just a humble cultural attaché."

"Cultural?" she said. "Then you can help me. What kind of painter is Jan Matejko?"

"I'm not sure," he said. "Impressionist, I think. Why?"

"Art really not your thing?"

"I'm more a music person," he said, feeling cornered.

"You probably love Szpilman, the Polish violinist."

"Absolutely. Such technique with the bow!"

"What do you think of the poet Wislawa Szymborska?"

"I haven't read much of his work, sadly. Is this a test?"

"Yes, and you failed. Szymborska is a woman. Szpilman is a pianist, not a violinist. Matejko was a conventional painter of court scenes and battles, not an impressionist. And you're no cultural attaché."

Cam was mortified to have been found out so easily. What a hopeless undercover agent he was! He tried to brush it off with humor. "I might just be a very bad cultural attaché."

She lowered her voice. "If a Polish army officer wanted to talk to a representative of the USA, you could arrange it, I guess."

Suddenly the conversation had taken a serious turn. Cam felt nervous. This could be some kind of trap.

Or it could be a genuine approach—in which case, it might represent a great opportunity for him.

He answered cautiously. "I can arrange for anyone to talk to the American government, naturally."

"In secret?"

What the hell was this? "Yes."

"Good," she said, and walked away.

Cam got another drink. What had that been about? Was it real, or had she been mocking him?

The party was coming to an end. He wondered what to do with the rest of the evening. He thought of going to the bar in the Australian embassy, where he sometimes played darts with amiable spooks from Oz. Then he saw Lidka standing nearby, again on her own. She really was very sexy. He said to her: "Do you have plans for dinner?"

She looked puzzled. "You mean recipes?"

He smiled. She had not come across the phrase *plans for dinner*. He said: "I meant, would you like to have dinner with me?"

"Oh, yes," she said immediately. "Could we go to the Duck?"

"Of course." It was an expensive restaurant, though not if you were paying in American dollars. He looked at his watch. "Shall we leave now?"

Lidka surveyed the room. There was no sign of the man in the pinstriped suit. "I'm free," she said.

They headed for the exit. As they were passing through the door the Soviet journalist, Tanya, reappeared and spoke to Lidka in bad Polish. "You dropped this," she said, holding out a red scarf.

"It's not mine," said Lidka.

"I saw it fall from your hand."

Someone touched Cam's elbow. He turned away from the confused conversation and saw a tall, good-looking man of about forty dressed in the uniform of a colonel in the People's Army of Poland. In fluent Russian the man said: "I want to talk to you."

Cam replied in the same language. "All right."

"I will find a safe place."

Cam could do nothing but say: "Okay."

"Tanya will tell you where and when."

"Fine."

The man turned away.

Cameron turned his attention back to Lidka. Tanya was saying: "My mistake, how silly." She walked quickly away. Clearly she had wanted to distract Lidka for the few moments the soldier was talking to Cam.

Lidka was puzzled. "That was a bit strange," she said as they left the building.

Cam was excited, but he pretended to be equally mystified. "Peculiar," he said.

Lidka persisted. "Who was that Polish officer who spoke to you?"

"No idea," Cam said. "My car's this way."

"Oh!" she said. "You have a car?"

"Yes."

"Nice," said Lidka, looking pleased.

. . .

A week later, Cam woke up in bed in Lidka's apartment.

It was more of a studio: one room with a bed, a TV, and a kitchen sink. She shared the shower and toilet down the hall with three other people.

For Cam, it was paradise.

He sat upright. She was standing at the counter making coffee— with his beans: she could not afford real coffee. She was naked. She turned and walked to the bed, carrying a cup. She had wiry brown pubic hair and small pointed breasts with mulberry dark nipples.

At first he had been embarrassed about her walking around naked, because it made him want to stare, which was rude. When he confessed this she had said: "Look all you want, I like it." He still felt bashful, but not as much as before.

He had seen Lidka every night for a week.

He had had sex with her seven times, which was more than in his entire life up to that point, not counting hand jobs in massage parlors.

One day she had asked if he wanted to do it again in the morning.

He had said: "What are you, a sex maniac?"

She had been offended, but they had made it up.

While she brushed her hair, he sipped his coffee and thought about the day ahead. He had not yet heard from Tanya Dvorkin. He had reported the exchanges at the Egyptian embassy to his boss, Keith Dorset, and they had agreed there was nothing to do but wait and see.

He had a bigger issue on his mind. He knew the expression *honey trap*. Only a fool would fail to wonder whether Lidka had an ulterior motive in going to bed with him. He had to consider the possibility that she was working under orders from the SB. He sighed and said: "I have to tell my boss about you."

"Do you?" She did not seem alarmed. "Why?"

"American diplomats are supposed to date only nationals of NATO countries. We call it the 'fuck NATO rule.' They don't want us falling in love with Communists." He had not told her that he was a spy rather than a diplomat.

She sat on the bed beside him with a sad face. "Are you breaking up with me?"

"No, no!" The idea almost panicked him. "But I have to tell them, and they will check you out."

Now she looked worried. "What does that mean?"

"They'll investigate whether you could be an agent of the Polish secret police, or something."

She shrugged. "Oh, well, that's all right. They'll soon find out I'm nothing of the kind."

She seemed relaxed about it. "I'm sorry, but it has to be done," Cam said. "One-night stands don't matter, but we're obliged to report if it gets to be more than that, you know, a real loving relationship."

"Okay."

"We do have that, don't we?" Cam said nervously. "A real loving relationship?"

Lidka smiled. "Oh, yes," she said. "We do."

CHAPTER FIFTY-THREE

The Franck family traveled to Hungary in two Trabant cars. They were going on holiday. Hungary was a popular summer destination for East Germans who could afford the petrol.

As far as they could tell, they were not followed.

They had booked their holiday through the tourist office of the East German government. They had half-expected to be refused visas, even though Hungary was a Soviet bloc country; but they had been pleasantly surprised. Hans Hoffmann had missed an opportunity to persecute them: perhaps he was busy.

They needed two cars because they were taking Karolin and her family. Werner and Carla were madly fond of their granddaughter, Alice, now sixteen. Lili loved Karolin, but not Karolin's husband, Odo. He was a good man, and he had got Lili her present job, as administrator of a church orphanage; but there was something forced about his affection for Karolin and Alice, as if loving them was a good deed. Lili thought a man's love should be a helpless passion, not a moral duty.

Karolin felt the same. She and Lili were close enough to share secrets, and Karolin had confessed that her marriage had been a mistake. She was not miserable with Odo, but nor was she in love with him. He was kind and gentle, but not sexy: they made love about once a month.

So the holiday group was six people. Werner, Carla, and Lili took the bronze car and Karolin, Odo, and Alice went in the white one.

It was a long drive, especially in a Trabi with a 600 cc two-stroke engine: six hundred miles all across Czechoslovakia. The first day took them to Prague, where they stayed overnight. When they left their hotel, on the morning of the second day, Werner said: "I'm pretty sure no one is following us. We seem to have got away with it."

They drove to Lake Balaton, fifty miles long, the largest lake in Central Europe. It was tantalizingly close to Austria, a free country. However, the entire border was fortified by one hundred fifty miles of electric fence, to prevent people escaping from the workers' paradise.

They pitched two tents side by side at a campsite on the southern shore.

They had a secret purpose: they were going to meet Rebecca.

It was Rebecca's idea. She had spent a year of her life looking after Walli, and he had succeeded in giving up drugs. He now had his own apartment near Rebecca's in Hamburg. In order to care for him, she had turned down a chance to stand for the Bundestag, the national parliament; but when he got well the offer had been renewed. Now she was an elected member, specializing in foreign policy. She had traveled to Hungary on an official trip, and seen that Hungary was deliberately attracting Western holidaymakers: tourism and cheap Riesling were the country's only means of earning foreign currency and reducing its massive trade deficit. The Westerners went to special, segregated holiday camps, but outside the camps there was nothing to stop fraternization.

So there was no law against what the Francks were doing. Their trip was permitted, and so was Rebecca's. Like them, she was coming to Hungary for a budget holiday. They would rendezvous as if by accident.

But the law was merely cosmetic in Communist countries. The Francks knew there would be terrible trouble if the secret police found out what they were up to. So Rebecca had arranged everything clandestinely, through Enok Andersen, the Danish accountant who still frequently crossed the border from West Berlin to East to see Werner. Nothing had been written down and there were no phone calls. Their greatest fear was that Rebecca would somehow be arrested—or even just kidnapped by the Stasi—and taken to a prison in East Germany. It would be a diplomatic incident, but the Stasi might do it anyway.

Rebecca's husband, Bernd, was not coming. His condition had deteriorated and his kidneys were malfunctioning. He was working only part-time, and could not travel far.

Werner straightened up from hammering in a tent peg to say quietly to Lili: "Take a look around. They didn't follow us here, but maybe they felt they didn't need to, because they had sent people on ahead."

Lili strolled around the site as if exploring. The campers at Lake Balaton were cheerful and friendly. As an attractive young woman, Lili was greeted and offered coffee or beer and snacks. Most tents were occupied by families, but there were some groups of men and a few of girls. No doubt the singles would find one another over the next few days.

Lili was single. She liked sex and had had several love affairs— including one with a woman, which her family did not know about. She had the same maternal instincts as other women, she supposed, and she adored Walli's child, Alice. But Lili was put off by the idea of having children of her own by the dismal prospect of raising them in East Germany.

She had been refused a place at university, because of her family's politics, so she had trained as a nursery nurse. She would never have been promoted if the authorities had had their way, but Odo had helped her get a job with the church, where hiring was not controlled by the Communist Party.

However, her real work was music. Along with Karolin, she continued to sing and play guitar in small bars and youth clubs, often in church halls. Their songs protested against industrial pollution, destruction of ancient buildings and monuments, clearing of natural forests, and ugly architecture. The government hated them, and they had both been arrested and cautioned for spreading propaganda. However, the Communists could not actually be *in favor* of poisoning rivers with factory effluent, so they found it difficult to take drastic action against environmentalists, and in fact usually tried to co-opt them into the toothless official Society for Nature and Environmental Protection.

In the USA, Lili's father said, conservatives accused environment campaigners of being antibusiness. It was more difficult for Soviet bloc conservatives to accuse them of being anti-Communist. After all, the whole point of Communism was to make industry work for the people rather than for the bosses.

One night Lili and Karolin had sneaked into a recording studio and made an album. It was not officially released, but cassette tapes of it in unmarked boxes had sold by the thousand.

Lili made a circuit of the campsite, which was occupied almost exclusively by East Germans: the camp for Westerners was a mile away. As she was returning to her family she noticed, outside a tent close to theirs, two men of about her own age drinking beer. One had receding fair hair, the other was dark with a Beatle haircut fifteen years out of date. The fair one met her eye and looked quickly away, which aroused her suspicion: young men did not generally avoid her eye. These two did not offer her a drink or ask her to join them. "Oh, no," she muttered.

Stasi men were not hard to spot. They were brutal, not smart. It was a career for people who craved prestige and power but had little intelligence and no talents. Rebecca's first husband, Hans, was typical. He was little more than a nasty bully, but he had risen steadily and now seemed to be one of their top commanders, driving around in a limousine and living in a large villa surrounded by a high wall.

Lili was reluctant to call attention to herself, but she decided she needed to verify her suspicion, so she had to be brazen. "Hello, guys!" she said amiably.

Both men grunted a perfunctory greeting.

Lili was not going to let them off easily. "Are you here with your wives?" she said. They could hardly fail to recognize that as a come-on.

The fair one shook his head and the other just said: "No." They were not clever enough to pretend.

"Really?" This was almost confirmation enough, she thought. What were two single men doing at a holiday camp if not looking for girls? And they were too badly dressed to be homosexual. "Tell me," said Lili, forcing a bright tone, "where do you go for a good time in the evenings here? Is there anywhere to dance?"

"I don't know."

That was enough. If these two are on holiday, I'm Mrs. Brezhnev, she thought. She walked away.

This was a problem. How could the Francks meet Rebecca without the Stasi men finding out?

Lili returned to her family. Both tents were now up. "Bad news," she told her father. "Two Stasi men. One row south and three tents east of us."

"I was afraid of that," said Werner.

. . .

They were to meet Rebecca two days later at a restaurant she had visited on her first trip. But before going there the Francks would have to shake off the secret police. Lili was worried, but her parents seemed unreasonably calm.

On the first day, Werner and Carla left early in the bronze Trabi, saying they were going to reconnoiter. The Stasi men followed them in a green Skoda. Werner and Carla were out all day and returned looking confident.

Next morning, Werner told Lili he was taking her for a hike. They stood outside the tent with rucksacks, helping each other adjust them. They put on stout boots and wide-brimmed hats. It was clear to anyone who looked that they were setting out for a long walk.

At the same time, Carla prepared to depart with shopping bags, making a list and saying loudly: "Ham, cheese, bread . . . anything else?"

Lili worried that they were being too obvious.

They were watched by the secret policemen, who were sitting outside their tent, smoking.

They set off in opposite directions, Carla heading for the car park, Lili and Werner for the beach. The Stasi agent with the Beatle haircut went after Carla, and the fair one followed Werner and Lili.

"So far, so good," said Werner. "We've split them."

When Lili and Werner got to the lake Werner turned west, following the shoreline. He had obviously scouted this the day before. The ground was intermittently rough. The fair-haired Stasi agent followed them at a distance, not without difficulty: he was not dressed for hiking. Sometimes they paused, pretending they needed a rest, to let him catch up.

They walked for two hours, then came to a long, deserted beach. Partway along, a rough track emerged from the trees to dead-end at the high-tide mark.

Parked there was the bronze Trabant with Carla at the wheel.

There was no one else in sight.

Werner and Lili got into the car and Carla drove off, leaving the Stasi man stranded.

Lili resisted the temptation to wave good-bye.

Werner said to Carla: "You shook off the other guy."

"Yes," said Carla. "I created a diversion outside the grocery store by setting fire to a rubbish bin."

Werner grinned. "A trick you learned from me many years ago."

"Absolutely. Naturally he got out of his car and went to see what was happening."

"And then . . ."

"While he was distracted, I put a nail in his tire. Left him changing the wheel."

"Nice."

Lili said: "You two did this stuff in the war, didn't you?"

There was a pause. They never spoke much about the war. Eventually Carla said: "Yes, we did a little bit, nothing worth boasting about."

That was all they ever said.

They drove to a village and slowed down at a small house with a sign in English saying BAR. A man standing outside directed them to park in a field at the back, out of sight.

They went inside to a small bar too charming to be a government enterprise. Right away Lili saw her sister, Rebecca, and threw her arms around her. They had not been together for eighteen years. Lili tried to look at Rebecca's face but could not see for tears. Carla and Werner hugged Rebecca in turn.

When at last Lili's vision cleared she saw that Rebecca looked middle-aged, which was no surprise: she would be fifty next birthday. She was heavier than Lili remembered.

But the most striking thing was how smart she looked. She wore a blue summer dress with a pattern of small dots, and a matching jacket. Around her neck was a silver chain with a single large pearl, and she had a chunky silver bracelet on her arm. Her smart sandals had a cork heel. Slung over her shoulder was a navy blue leather bag. Politics was not notably well paid, as far as Lili knew. Could it be that *everyone* in West Germany was this well dressed?

Rebecca led them through the bar to a private room at the back where a long table was already laid with cold meat platters, bowls of salad, and bottles of wine. Standing by the table was a thin, handsome, wasted-looking man in a white T-shirt and skinny black jeans. He might have been in his forties, or perhaps younger if he had suffered an illness. Lili assumed he must be an employee of the bar.

Carla gasped, and Werner said, "Oh, my God."

Lili saw that the thin man was gazing expectantly at her. She suddenly noticed his almond-shaped eyes and realized that she was looking at her brother, Walli. She let out a small scream of shock: he looked so old!

Carla embraced Walli, saying: "My little boy! My poor little boy!"

Lili hugged and kissed him, crying all over again. "You look so different," she sobbed. "What happened to you?"

"Rock and roll," he replied with a laugh. "But I'm getting over it." He looked at his older sister. "Rebecca sacrificed a year of her life—and a great career opportunity—to save me."

"Of course I did," said Rebecca. "I'm your sister."

Lili felt sure Rebecca had not hesitated. For her, nothing came before family. Lili had a theory that it was because she was adopted that she felt so strongly.

Werner held Walli in his arms a long time. "We didn't know," he said, his voice thick with emotion. "We didn't know you were coming."

Rebecca said: "I decided to keep it a complete secret."

Carla said: "Isn't it dangerous?"

"It certainly is," said Rebecca. "But Walli wanted to take the risk."

Then Karolin walked in with her family. Like the others, she took a few moments to recognize Walli, then she gave a cry of shock.

"Hello, Karolin," he said. He took her hands and kissed her on both cheeks. "It's so good to see you again."

Odo said: "I'm Odo, Karolin's husband. I'm very glad to meet you at last."

Something flashed across Walli's face. It was gone in a split second, but Lili knew that Walli had seen and understood something about Odo that had shocked him, and had then covered up his shock instantly. The two men shook hands amiably.

Karolin said: "And this is Alice."

"Alice?" said Walli. He looked dazedly at the tall sixteen-year-old girl with long fair hair draping her face like curtains. "I wrote a song about you," he said. "When you were little."

"I know," she said, and kissed his cheek.

Odo said: "Alice knows her history. We told her everything, as soon as she was old enough to understand."

Lili wondered whether Walli heard the note of righteousness in Odo's voice. Or was she being oversensitive?

Walli said to Alice: "I love you, but Odo raised you. I'll never forget that, and I'm sure you won't either."

For a minute he choked up. Then he regained control and said: "Everybody, let's sit down and eat. This is a happy day." Lili realized that Walli had probably paid for everything.

They all sat around the table. For a few moments they were like strangers, feeling awkward, trying to think of something to say. Then several people spoke at once, all asking Walli questions. Everyone laughed. "One at a time!" Walli said, and they all relaxed.

Walli told them he had a penthouse in Hamburg. He was not married, though he had a girlfriend. About every eighteen months or two years he went to California, moved into Dave Williams's farmhouse for four months, and made a new album with Plum Nellie. "I'm an addict," he said. "But I've been clean for seven years, eight come September. When I do a gig with the band, I have a guard outside my dressing room to search people for drugs." He shrugged. "It seems extreme, I know, but there it is."

Walli had questions, too, especially for Alice. While she was answering them, Lili looked around the table. This was her family: her parents, her sister, her brother, her niece, and her oldest friend and singing partner. How lucky she was to have them all together in the same room, eating and talking and drinking wine.

The thought occurred to her that some families did this every week, and took it for granted.

Karolin was sitting next to Walli, and Lili watched them together. They were having a good time. They still made one another laugh, she noticed. If things had been different—if the Berlin Wall had fallen—might their romance have been rekindled? They were still young: Walli was thirty-three, Karolin thirty-five. Lili pushed the thought away: it was an idle speculation, a foolish fantasy.

Walli retold the story of his escape from Berlin for Alice's benefit. When he got to the part where he sat all night waiting for Karolin, who did not show up, she interrupted him. "I was frightened," she said. "Frightened for myself, and for the baby inside me."

"I don't blame you," Walli said. "You did nothing wrong. I did nothing wrong. The only wrong was the Wall."

He described how he had driven through the checkpoint, busting the barrier. "I'll never forget that man I killed," he said.

Carla said: "It wasn't your fault—he was shooting at you!"

"I know," Walli said, and Lili knew from his tone of voice that at last he was at peace about this. "I feel sorry, but I don't feel guilty. I wasn't wrong to escape; he wasn't wrong to shoot at me."

"Like you said," Lili put in, "the only wrong is the Wall."

CHAPTER FIFTY-FOUR

C am Dewar's boss, Keith Dorset, was a podgy man with sandy hair. Like a lot of CIA men, he dressed badly. Today he wore a brown tweed jacket, gray flannel trousers, a white shirt with brown pencil stripes, and a dull green tie. Seeing him walking down the street, the eye would slide over him while the brain dismissed him as a person of no account. Perhaps this was the effect he sought, Cameron thought. Or perhaps he just had bad taste.

"About your girlfriend, Lidka," Keith said, sitting behind a large desk in the American embassy.

Cam was pretty sure Lidka was free of any sinister associations, but he looked forward to having this confirmed.

Keith said: "Your request is denied."

Cam was astonished. "What are you talking about?"

"Your request is denied. Which of those four words are you having trouble understanding?"

CIA men sometimes behaved as if they were in the army, and able to bark orders at everyone below them in rank. But Cam was not that easily intimidated. He had worked at the White House. "Denied for what reason?" he said.

"I don't have to give reasons."

At the age of thirty-four, Cam had his first real girlfriend. After twenty years of rejection he was sleeping with a woman who seemed to want nothing but to make him happy. Panic at the prospect of losing her made him foolhardy. "You don't *have* to be an asshole, either," he snapped.

"Don't you dare speak to me like that. One more smart-ass remark and you're on a plane home."

Cam did not want to be sent home. He backed off. "I apologize. But I'd still like to know the reasons for your denial, if I may."

"You have what we call 'close and continuing contact' with her, don't you?"

"Of course. I told you that myself. Why is it a problem?"

"Statistics. Most of the traitors we catch spying against the United States turn out to have relatives or close friends who are foreigners."

Cam had suspected something like this. "I'm not willing to give her up for statistical reasons. Do you have anything specific against her?"

"What makes you think you have the right to cross-examine me?"

"I'll take that as a no."

"I warned you about wisecracks."

They were interrupted by another agent, Tony Savino, who approached with a sheet of paper in his hand. "I'm just looking at the acceptance list for this morning's press conference," he said. "Tanya Dvorkin is coming for TASS." He looked at Cam. "She's the woman who spoke to you at the Egyptian embassy, isn't she?"

"She sure is," Cam said.

Keith said: "What's the subject of the press conference?"

"The launch of a new, streamlined protocol for Polish and American museums to loan each other works of art, it says here." Tony looked up from the paper. "Not the kind of thing to attract TASS's star writer, is it?"

Cam said: "She must be coming to see me."

.   .   .

Tanya spotted Cam Dewar as soon as she walked into the briefing room at the American embassy. A tall, thin figure, he was standing at the back like a lamppost. If he had not been here, she would have sought him out after the press conference, but this was better, less noticeable.

However, she did not want to look too purposeful when she approached him, so she decided to listen to the announcement first. She sat next to a Polish journalist whom she liked: Danuta Gorski, a feisty brunette with a big toothy grin. Danuta was a member of a semi-underground movement called the Defense Committee that produced pamphlets about workers' grievances and human rights violations.

These illegal publications were called *bibula*. Danuta lived in the same building as Tanya.

While the American press officer was reading out the announcement he had already given them in printed form, Danuta murmured to Tanya: "You might want to take a trip to Gdańsk."

"Why?"

"There's going to be a strike at the Lenin Shipyard."

"There are strikes everywhere." Workers were demanding pay rises to compensate for a massive government increase in food prices. Tanya reported these as "work stoppages," for strikes happened only in capitalist countries.

"Believe me," said Danuta, "this one could be different."

The Polish government was dealing with each strike swiftly, granting pay rises and other concessions on a local basis, keen to shut down protests before they could spread like stains on a cloth. The nightmare of the ruling elite—and the dream of dissidents—was that the stains would join up until the cloth was entirely a new color.

"Different how?"

"They fired a crane operator who is a member of our committee—but they picked the wrong person to victimize. Anna Walentynowicz is a woman, a widow, and fifty-one years old."

"So she attracts a lot of sympathy from chivalrous Polish men."

"And she's a popular figure. They call her Pani Ania, Mrs. Annie."

"I might take a look." Dimka wanted to hear about any protest that promised to become serious, in case he might need to discourage a Kremlin crackdown.

As the press conference was breaking up, Tanya passed Cam Dewar and spoke to him quietly in Russian. "Go to the Cathedral of St. John on Friday at two and look at the Baryczkowski Crucifix."

"That's not a good place," the young man hissed.

"Take it or leave it," Tanya said.

"You have to tell me what this is about," Cam said firmly.

Tanya realized she had to risk talking to him for another minute. "A line of communication in case the Soviet Union should invade Western Europe," she said. "The possibility of forming a group of Polish officers who would switch sides."

The American's jaw dropped. "Oh . . . Oh . . ." he stuttered. "Right, yes."

She smiled at him. "Satisfied?"

"What's his name?"

Tanya hesitated.

Cam said: "He knows mine."

Tanya decided she had to trust this man. She had already placed her own life in his hands. "Stanislaw Pawlak," she said. "Known as Staz."

"Tell Staz that for security reasons he should never speak to anyone here at the embassy except me."

"Okay." Tanya walked quickly out of the building.

She gave Staz the message that evening. Next day she kissed him good-bye and drove two hundred miles north to the Baltic Sea. She had an old but reliable Mercedes-Benz 280S with vertically aligned twin headlamps. In the late afternoon she checked into a hotel in the old town of Gdańsk, directly across the river from the wharves and dry docks of the shipyard, which was on Ostrow Island.

On the following day it was one week exactly since the firing of Anna Walentynowicz.

Tanya got up early, put on canvas overalls, crossed the bridge to the island, reached the shipyard gate before sunrise, and strolled in with a group of young workers.

It was her lucky day.

The shipyard was plastered with newly pasted posters calling for Pani Ania to be given her job back. Small groups were gathering around the posters. A few people were handing out leaflets. Tanya took one and deciphered the Polish.

Anna Walentynowicz became an embarrassment because her example motivated others. She became an embarrassment because she stood up for others and was able to organize her coworkers. The authorities always try to isolate those who have leadership qualities. If we do not fight against this, then we will have no one to stand up for us when they raise work quotas, when health and safety regulations are broken, or when we are forced to work overtime.

Tanya was struck by that. This was not about more pay or shorter hours: it was about the right of Polish workers to organize for themselves, independently of the Communist hierarchy. She had a feeling this was a significant development. It started a small glow of hope in her belly.

She walked around the yard as the daylight strengthened. The sheer scale of shipbuilding was awesome: the thousands of workers, the kilotons of steel, the millions of rivets. The high sides of half-built ships rose far above her head, their mountainous weight perilously balanced by spiderweb scaffolding. Immense cranes bowed their heads over each ship, like adoring Magi around a giant manger.

Everywhere she went, workers were downing tools to read the leaflet and discuss the case.

A few men started a march, and Tanya followed them. They went in procession around the yard, carrying makeshift placards, handing out leaflets, calling on others to join them, growing in numbers. Eventually they came to the main gate, where they began telling arriving workers that they were on strike.

They closed the factory gate, sounded the siren, and flew the Polish national flag from the nearest building.

Then they elected a strike committee.

While that was going on they were interrupted. A man in a suit clambered up on an excavator and began to shout at the crowd. Tanya could not understand everything he said, but he seemed to be arguing against the formation of a strike committee—and the workers were listening to him. Tanya asked the nearest man who he was. "Klemens Gniech, the director of the shipyard," she was told. "Not a bad guy."

Tanya was aghast. How weak people were!

Gniech was offering negotiations if the strikers would first go back to work. To Tanya this seemed a transparent trick. Many people booed and jeered Gniech, but others nodded agreement, and a few drifted away, apparently headed for their workplaces. Surely it could not fall apart so fast?

Then someone jumped up on the excavator and tapped the director on the shoulder. The newcomer was a small, square-shouldered man with a bushy mustache. Although he seemed to Tanya an unimpressive figure, the crowd recognized him and cheered. They evidently knew who he was. "Remember me?" he yelled at the director in a voice loud enough for everyone to hear. "I worked here for ten years—then you fired me!"

"Who's that?" Tanya asked her neighbor.

"Lech Wałęsa. He's only an electrician, but everyone knows him."

The director tried to argue with Wałęsa in front of the crowd, but the little man with the big mustache gave him no leeway. "I declare an occupation strike!" he roared, and the crowd shouted their agreement.

Both the director and Wałęsa stepped down from the excavator. Wałęsa took command, something everyone seemed to accept without question. When he ordered the director's chauffeur to drive in his limousine and fetch Anna Walentynowicz, the chauffeur did as he was told and, even more astonishing, the director made no objection.

Wałęsa organized the election of a strike committee. The limousine returned with Anna, who was greeted by a storm of applause. She was a small woman with hair as short as a man's. She had round glasses and wore a blouse with bold horizontal stripes.

The strike committee and the director went in the Health and Safety Center to negotiate. Tanya was tempted to try to insinuate herself in there with them, but she decided not to push her luck: she was fortunate to have got inside the gates. The workers were welcoming the Western media, but Tanya's press card showed that she was a Soviet reporter for TASS, and if the strikers discovered that they would throw her out.

However, the negotiators must have had microphones on their tables, for their entire discussion was broadcast over loudspeakers to the crowd outside—which struck Tanya as democratic in the extreme. The strikers could instantly express their feelings about what was said by booing or cheering.

She figured out that the strikers now had several demands in addition to the reinstatement of Anna, including security from reprisals. The one that the director could not accept, surprisingly, was for a monument outside the factory gates to commemorate the massacre by police of shipyard workers protesting against food price rises in 1970.

Tanya wondered whether this strike would also end in a massacre. If it did, she realized with a chill, she was right in the firing line.

Gniech explained that the area in front of the gates had been designated for a hospital.

The strikers said they preferred a monument.

The director offered a commemorative plaque somewhere else in the shipyard.

They declined.

A worker said disgustedly into the microphone: "We're haggling over dead heroes like beggars under a lamppost!"

The people outside applauded.

Another negotiator appealed directly to the crowd: Did they want a monument?

They roared their answer.

The director retired to consult with his superiors.

There were now thousands of supporters outside the gates. People had been collecting donations of food for the strikers. Few Polish families could afford to give food away, but dozens of sacks of provisions were now passed through the gates for the men and women inside, and the strikers ate lunch.

The director came back in the afternoon and announced that the highest authorities had approved the monument in principle.

Wałęsa declared that the strike would go on until all the demands had been met.

And then, almost as an afterthought, he added that the strikers also wanted to discuss the formation of free independent trade unions.

Now, Tanya thought, this is getting *really* interesting.

. . .

On Friday after lunch Cam Dewar drove to the Old Town of Warsaw.

He was followed there by Mario and Ollie.

Most of Warsaw had been flattened in the war. The town had been reconstructed with straight roads and sidewalks and modern buildings. Such a cityscape was not suitable for clandestine meetings and furtive exchanges. However, the planners had striven to re-create the original Old Town with its cobbled streets and little alleys and irregular houses. It was done a little too well: the straight edges and regular patterns and fresh colors looked too new, like a movie set. Nevertheless, it provided a more congenial environment for secret agents than did the rest of the city.

Cam parked and walked to a high town house. There on the first floor was the Warsaw equivalent of Silken Hands. Cam had been a regular customer until he met Lidka.

In the main room of the apartment, the girls were sitting around in lingerie, watching television and smoking. A voluptuous blonde stood up immediately, letting her robe fall open briefly to give him a glimpse of plump thighs and lacy underwear. "Hello, Crystek, we haven't seen you for a couple of weeks!"

"Hi, Pela." Cam went to the window and looked down at the street. As usual, Mario and Ollie were sitting outside the bar opposite, drinking beer and watching the girls in summer dresses go by. They would expect him to remain inside for at least half an hour, maybe an hour.

So far, so good.

Pela said: "What's the matter, is your wife following you?"

The other girls laughed.

Cam took out his money and gave Pela the usual fee for a hand job. "I need a favor today," he said. "Do you mind if I slip out the back door?"

"Is your wife going to come up here and make a fuss?"

"It's not my wife," he said. "It's my girlfriend's husband. If he makes trouble, offer him a free blow job. I'll pay."

Pela shrugged.

Cam went down the back stairs and out through the yard, feeling good. He had shaken off his followers—and they did not realize it. He would be back in under an hour, and he would go out by the front door. They would never know he had left the apartment.

He hurried across Old Town Market Square and along a street called Swietojanska to the Cathedral of St. John, a church devastated in the war and rebuilt since. The SB were no longer following him—but they might be following Stanislaw Pawlak.

The CIA station in Warsaw had held a long meeting to decide how to handle this contact. Every step had been planned.

Outside the church, Cam saw his boss, Keith Dorset. Today he had on a boxy gray suit from a Polish store, something he wore only for surveillance jobs. There was a cap stuffed into his jacket pocket. That was the all clear. If he had been wearing the hat, it would have meant that the SB were inside the church and the rendezvous should be aborted.

Cam entered by the Gothic main door in the west front. The awesome architecture and the atmosphere of sanctity amplified his feeling of portent. He was about to make contact with an enemy informant. It was a crucial moment.

If this went well, he would be firmly set on his career as a CIA agent. If not, he would be back behind a desk in Langley in no time.

Cam was pretending that Staz would not meet anyone but him. The purpose of this lie was to make it difficult for Keith to send Cam home. Keith was making trouble about Lidka, even though investigation had revealed that she had no connection with the SB and was not even a member of the Communist Party. However, if Cam could succeed in recruiting a Polish colonel as a spy for the CIA, such a triumph would put him in a strong position to defy Keith.

He looked around, scanning for secret policemen, but all he saw were tourists, worshippers, and priests.

He walked up the north aisle until he came to the chapel containing the famous sixteenth-century crucifix. The handsome Polish officer was standing in front of it, staring at the expression on the face of Christ. Cam stood beside him. They were alone.

Cam spoke in Russian. "This is the last time we'll talk."

Stanislaw replied in the same language. "Why?"

"Too dangerous."

"For you?"

"No, for you."

"How will we communicate? Through Tanya?"

"No. In fact, from now on please don't tell her anything about your relationship with me. Cut her out of the loop. You can still sleep with her, if that's what you're doing."

"Thank you," Stanislaw said ironically.

Cam ignored that. "What kind of car do you drive?"

"A green 1975 Saab 99." He recited the license plate number.

Cameron memorized it. "Where do you keep the car at night?"

"On Jana Olbrachta Street, near the apartment block where I live."

"When you park it, leave the window open a crack. We will slip an envelope through."

"Dangerous. What if someone else reads the note?"

"Don't worry. The envelope will contain a typed advertisement from someone who offers to wash your car at a low price. But when you pass a warm iron over the paper, a message will be revealed. It will tell you when and where to meet us. If you're not able to make the rendezvous, for any reason, it doesn't matter: we'll just send you another envelope."

"What will happen at these meetings?"

"I'll get to that." Cam had a list of things to say, agreed on by his colleagues at the planning meeting, and he needed to get through them as fast as possible. "About your group of friends."

"Yes?"

"Don't form a conspiracy."

"Why not?"

"You'll be found out. Conspirators always are. You have to wait until the last minute."

"So what can we do?"

"Two things. One, get ready. Make a list in your head of people you trust. Decide exactly how each one will turn against the Soviets if war breaks out. Make yourself known to dissident leaders such as Lech Wałęsa, but give them no hint of what you're up to. Reconnoiter the television station and plan how you'll take it over. But keep everything in your head."

"And the second thing?"

"Give us information." Cam tried not to show how tense he felt. This was the big ask, the one Stanislaw might refuse. "The order of battle of Soviet and other Warsaw Pact armies: numbers of men, tanks, aircraft—"

"I know what is meant by *order of battle*."

"And their war plans in the event of a crisis."

There was a long pause, then at last Stanislaw said: "I can get those."

"Good," Cam said with feeling.

"And what do I get in return?"

"I'm going to give you a phone number and a code word. You must use it only in the event of a Soviet invasion of Western Europe. When you call the number you will be answered by a senior commander in the Pentagon who speaks Polish. He will treat you as the representative of the Polish resistance to the Soviet invasion. You will be, for all practical purposes, the leader of free Poland."

Stanislaw nodded thoughtfully, but Cam could tell he was attracted by the offer. After a few moments he said: "If I agree to this, I will be placing my life in your hands."

"You already have," said Cam.

. . .

The Gdańsk Shipyard strikers were careful to keep the international media fully briefed on their activities. Ironically, this was the best way to communicate with the Polish people. The Polish media were censored, but Western newspaper reports were picked up by the American-funded Radio Free Europe and broadcast right back into Poland. It was the main way Poles learned the truth about what was happening in their country.

Lili Franck followed events in Poland on the West German television news, which everyone in East Berlin could watch if they angled their aerials the right way.

The strike spread, to Lili's delight, despite all the government's efforts. The Gdynia shipyard came out, and public transport workers struck in sympathy. They formed the Interfactory Strike Committee (MKS), with its headquarters in the Lenin Shipyard. Its number one demand was the right to form free trade unions.

Like many others in East Germany, the Franck family discussed all this avidly, sitting in the upstairs drawing room of the town house in Berlin-Mitte, in front of their Franck television set. A rent was showing in the Iron Curtain, and they speculated eagerly about what it might lead to. If Poles could rebel, perhaps Germans could too.

The Polish government tried to negotiate factory by factory, offering generous raises to strikers who split from MKS and settled. The tactic failed.

Within a week, three hundred striking enterprises had joined the MKS.

The tottering Polish economy could not stand many days of this. The government at last accepted reality. The deputy prime minister was sent to Gdańsk.

A week later a deal was agreed on. The strikers were given the right to form free trade unions. It was a triumph that astonished the world.

If the Poles could win freedom, would the Germans be next?

. . .

Keith said to Cam: "You're still seeing that Polish girl."

Cam said nothing. Of course he was still seeing her. He was as happy as a kid in a candy store. Lidka was eager to have sex with him whenever he wanted it. Until now, few girls had wanted to have sex with him at all. "Do you like this?" she would say as she caressed him; and if he admitted he did, she would say: "But do you like it a little bit, do you like it a lot, or do you like it so much you want to die?"

Keith said: "I've told you that your request has been denied."

"But you haven't said why."

Keith looked angry. "I've made a decision."

"But is it the right decision?"

"Are you challenging my authority?"

"No, you're challenging my girlfriend."

Keith became angrier. "You think you have me over a barrel because Stanislaw won't speak to anyone else."

That was exactly what Cam thought, but he denied it. "It has nothing to do with Staz. I'm not willing to give her up for no reason."

"I may have to fire you."

"I still won't give her up. In fact—" Cam hesitated. The words that came into his mind were not what he had planned. But he said them anyway. "In fact, I'm hoping to marry her."

Keith changed his tone. "Cam," he said, "she may not be an agent of the SB, but she could still have an ulterior motive for sleeping with you."

Cam bristled. "If it's nothing to do with intelligence, it's nothing to do with you."

Keith persisted, speaking gently, as if trying not to hurt Cam's feelings. "A lot of Polish girls would like to go to America, you know that."

Cam did know that. The thought had occurred to him long ago. He felt embarrassed and humiliated that Keith should say it. He kept his face wooden. "I know," he said.

"Forgive me for saying it, but she could be deceiving you for that reason," Keith said. "Have you considered that possibility?"

"Yes, I've considered it," said Cam. "And I don't care."

. . .

In Moscow, the big question was whether to invade Poland.

The day before the Politburo debate, Dimka and Natalya clashed with Yevgeny Filipov at a preparatory meeting in the Nina Onilova Room. Filipov said: "Our Polish comrades require military assistance urgently, to resist the attacks of traitors in the employ of the capitalist-imperialist powers."

Natalya said: "You want an invasion, as in Czechoslovakia in 1968 and Hungary in 1956."

Filipov did not deny it. "The Soviet Union has the right to invade any country when the interests of Communism are under threat. That's the Brezhnev Doctrine."

Dimka said: "I'm against military action."

"There's a surprise," said Filipov sarcastically.

Dimka ignored that. "In both Hungary and Czechoslovakia, the counterrevolution was led by revisionist elements within the Communist Party ruling cadres," he said. "It was therefore possible to remove them, like chopping the head off a chicken. They had little popular support."

"Why should this crisis be different?"

"Because in Poland the counterrevolutionaries are working-class leaders with working-class backing. Lech Wałęsa is an electrician. Anna Walentynowicz is a crane driver. And hundreds of factories are on strike. We're dealing with a mass movement."

"We have to crush it all the same. Are you seriously suggesting that we abandon Polish Communism?"

"There's another problem," Natalya put in. "Money. Back in 1968 the Soviet bloc did not owe billions of dollars in foreign debt. Today we are totally dependent on loans from the West. You heard what President Carter said in Warsaw. Credit from the West is linked to human rights."

"So . . . ?"

"If we send the tanks into Poland, they will withdraw our line of credit. So, Comrade Filipov, your invasion will ruin the economy of the entire Soviet bloc."

There was a silence in the room.

Dimka said: "Does anyone have any other suggestions?"

. . .

To Cam it seemed an omen that a Polish officer had turned against the Red Army at the same time as Polish workers were rejecting Communist tyranny. Both events were signs of the same change. As he headed for his rendezvous with Stanislaw, he felt he might be part of a historic earthquake.

He left the embassy and got into his car. As he hoped, Mario and Ollie followed him. It was important that they had him under surveillance while he met with Stanislaw. If the interaction went as planned, Mario and Ollie would faithfully report that nothing suspicious had taken place.

Cam hoped Stanislaw had received and understood his instructions.

Cam parked in Old Town Market Square. Carrying a copy of today's *Trybuna Ludu*, the official government newspaper, he strolled across the square. Mario got out of his car and walked after him. Half a minute later, Ollie followed at a distance.

Cam headed down a side street with the two secret policemen in train.

He went into a bar, sat near the window, and asked for a beer. He could see his shadows loitering nearby. He paid for his drink as soon as it came, so that he would be able to leave quickly.

He checked his watch frequently while he drank his beer.

At one minute to three he went out.

He had practised this maneuver over and over at Camp Peary, the CIA's training center near Williamsburg, Virginia. He had been able to do it perfectly there. But this would be the first time he did it for real.

He quickened his pace a little as he approached the end of the block. Turning the corner, he glanced back and saw that Mario was about thirty yards behind.

Just around the corner was a shop selling cigarettes and tobacco. Stanislaw was exactly where Cam expected him to be, standing outside the shop, looking in the window. Cam had about thirty seconds before Mario turned the corner—plenty of time to execute a simple brush pass.

All he had to do was exchange the newspaper he was carrying for the one in Stanislaw's hand, which was identical except that—all being well—it should contain the photocopies Stanislaw had made of documents in his safe at army headquarters.

There was only one snag.

Stanislaw was not carrying a newspaper.

Instead he had a large buff-colored envelope.

He had not followed his instructions to the letter. Either he had misunderstood, or he had imagined that the exact details did not matter.

Whatever the reason, things had gone wrong.

Panic froze Cam's brain. His step faltered. He did not know what to do. He wanted to scream abuse at Staz.

Then he controlled himself. He forced himself to be calm. He made a split-second decision. He would not abort the exchange. He would go through with it.

He walked straight toward Stanislaw.

As they brushed past one another, they exchanged the newspaper for the envelope.

Immediately, Stanislaw walked into the shop, carrying the newspaper, and disappeared from sight.

Cam walked on, carrying the envelope, which was an inch thick with the documents inside.

At the next corner he again glanced back and got a glimpse of Mario. The secret policeman was about twenty yards behind, apparently relaxed and confident. He had no notion of what had just happened. He had not even seen Stanislaw.

Would he notice that Cam was no longer carrying a newspaper, but held an envelope instead? If he did, he might arrest Cam and confiscate the envelope. That would be the end of Cam's triumph—and the end of Stanislaw's life.

It was summer. Cam had no coat under which to conceal the envelope. Besides, hiding it could be worse: Mario might be *more* likely to notice if Cam was suddenly empty-handed.

He passed a street newsstand, but realized he could not stop and buy a newspaper within Mario's sight, for that would draw attention to the fact that he no longer had his original paper.

He realized he had made a foolish mistake. He had been so mesmerized by the brush-past routine that he had not thought of the simplest way out. He should have taken the envelope and *kept* the newspaper.

Too late now.

He felt trapped. It was so frustrating he wanted to scream. Everything had gone perfectly but for one small detail!

He could step into a store and buy another newspaper. He looked for a newsagent's shop. But this was Poland, not America, and there was not a store on every block.

He turned another corner and sighted a rubbish bin. Hallelujah! He quickened his pace and looked inside. His luck was out: there were no newspapers. He spotted a magazine with a colorful cover. He snatched it up and walked on. As he walked, he surreptitiously folded the magazine so that the cover was inside and a page of plain black-and-white print was on the outside. He wrinkled his nose: there had been something disgusting in the bin, and the smell clung to the magazine. He tried not to breathe deeply as he slid the envelope between the pages.

He felt better. He now looked almost the same as he had before.

He returned to his car and took out his keys. This perhaps would be the moment they stopped him. He imagined Mario saying: "Just a minute, let me see that envelope you're trying to hide." As quickly as he could, he unlocked the door.

He saw Mario a few paces away.

Cam got into his car and placed the magazine in the footwell on the passenger side.

Glancing up, he saw Mario and Ollie getting into their car.

It looked like he had got away with it.

For a moment, he felt too weak to move.

Then he started his engine and drove back to the embassy.

. . .

Cam Dewar sat in Lidka's bedsitting room, waiting for her to come home.

She had a photograph of him on her dressing table. Cam found that so pleasing that it almost made him cry. No girl had ever wanted a photo of him, let alone framed it and kept it by her mirror.

The room expressed her personality. Her favorite color was bright pink, and that was the shade of the bedcovers and the tablecloth and the cushions. The closet held few clothes, but they all flattered her: short skirts, V-necked dresses, pretty costume jewelry, prints with small flowers and bows and butterflies. Her bookshelf held all of Jane Austen in English and Tolstoy's *Anna Karenina* in Polish. In a box under the bed, like a secret stash of pornography, she had a collection of American magazines about home decoration, full of photographs of sunlit kitchens painted in bright colors.

Today Lidka had begun the tedious process of being vetted by the CIA as a potential wife. This was much more thorough than the investigation of a mere girlfriend. She had to write her life story, undergo days of interrogation, and take an extended lie-detector test. All this had been going on somewhere else in the embassy while Cam did his normal day's work. He was not allowed to see her until she came home.

It was going to be difficult for Keith Dorset to fire Cam now. The information Staz was producing was solid gold.

Cam had given Staz a compact thirty-five-millimeter camera, a Zorki, which was a Soviet-made copy of a Leica, so that he could photograph documents in his office with the door shut instead of feeding them through the photocopying machine in the secretaries' bullpen. He could pass Cam hundreds of pages of documents in a handful of rolls of film.

The latest question the Warsaw CIA station had asked Staz was: What would trigger a westward attack by the Red Army's Second Strategic Echelon? The files he had provided in answer had been so comprehensive that Keith Dorset had received a rare written compliment from Langley.

And still Mario and Ollie had never seen Staz.

So Cam was confident that he would not be fired, and his marriage would not be forbidden, unless Lidka turned out to be an actual agent of the KGB.

Meanwhile, Poland was lurching toward freedom. Ten million people had joined the first free trade union, called Solidarity. That was one in every three Polish workers. Poland's biggest problem now was not the Soviet Union but money. The strikes, and the consequent paralysis of Communist Party leadership, had crippled an already weak economy. The result was a shortage of everything. The government rationed meat, butter, and flour. Workers who had won generous pay rises found they could not buy anything with their money. The black market exchange rate for the dollar more than doubled, from one hundred twenty zlotys to two hundred fifty. First Secretary Gierek was succeeded by Kania, who was then replaced by General Jaruzelski, which made no difference.

Tantalizingly, Lech Wałęsa and Solidarity hesitated on the brink of overthrowing Communism. A general strike was prepared, then called off at the last minute, on the advice of the Pope and the new American president, Ronald Reagan, both of whom feared bloodshed. Cam was disappointed by Reagan's timidity.

He got off the bed and laid the table with cutlery and plates. He had brought home two steaks. Naturally diplomats were not subject to the shortages that afflicted the Poles. They were paying in desperately needed dollars: they could have anything they wanted. Lidka was probably eating better than even the Communist Party elite.

Cam wondered whether to make love to her before or after eating the steaks. Sometimes it was good to savor the anticipation. Other times he was in too much of a hurry. Lidka never minded either way.

At last she arrived home. She kissed his cheek, put down her bag, took off her coat, and went along the hall to the bathroom.

When she came back he showed her the steaks. "Very nice," she said. Still she did not look at him.

"Something's wrong, isn't it?" Cam said. He had never known her to be ill-tempered. This was unique.

"I don't think I can be a CIA wife," she said.

Cam fought down panic. "Tell me what's happened."

"I'm not going back tomorrow. I won't put up with it."

"What's the problem?"

"I feel like a criminal."

"Why, what did they do?"

At last she looked directly at him. "Do you believe I'm just using you to get to America?"

"No, I don't!"

"Then why did they ask me that?"

"I don't know."

"Does the question have anything to do with national security?"

"Nothing at all."

"They accused me of lying."

"Did you lie?"

She shrugged. "I didn't tell them everything. I'm not a nun, I've had lovers. I left one or two out—but your horrible CIA knew! They must have gone to my old school!"

"I know you've had lovers, I have too." Though not many, Cam thought, but he did not say it. "I don't mind."

"They made me feel like a prostitute."

"I'm sorry. But it really doesn't matter what they think of us, so long as they give you a security clearance."

"They're going to tell you a lot of nasty stories about me. Things they've been told by people who hate me—girls who are jealous, and boys I wouldn't sleep with."

"I won't believe them."

"Do you promise?"

"I promise."

She sat on his lap. "I'm sorry I was grouchy."

"I forgive you."

"I love you, Cam."

"I love you, too."

"I feel better now."

"Good."

"Do you want me to make *you* feel better?"

This kind of talk made Cam's mouth dry. "Yes, please."

"Okay." She stood up. "You just lie back and relax, baby," she said.

. . .

Dave Williams flew to Warsaw with his wife, Beep, and their son, John Lee, for the marriage of his brother-in-law, Cam Dewar.

John Lee could not read, although he was an intelligent eight-year-old and went to a fine school. Dave and Beep had taken him to an educational psychologist, and had learned that the boy suffered from a common condition called dyslexia, or word-blindness. John Lee would learn to read, but he would need special help and he would have to work extra hard at it. Dyslexia ran in families and afflicted boys more than girls.

That was when Dave realized what his own problem was.

"I believed I was dumb, all through school," he told Beep that evening, in the pine kitchen of Daisy Farm, after they had put John Lee to bed. "The teachers said the same. My parents knew I wasn't dumb, so they assumed I must be lazy."

"You're not lazy," she said. "You're the hardest-working person I know."

"Something was wrong with me, but we didn't know what it was. Now we do."

"And we'll be able to make sure John Lee doesn't suffer the way you did."

Dave's lifelong struggle with writing and reading was explained. It had not oppressed him for many years, not since he had become a songwriter whose lyrics were on the lips of millions. All the same he felt enormously relieved. A mystery had been unraveled, a cruel disability accounted for. Most important of all, he knew how to make sure it did not afflict the next generation.

"And you know what else?" Beep had said, pouring a glass of Daisy Farm cabernet sauvignon.

"Yeah," said Dave. "He's probably mine."

Beep had never been sure whether Dave or Walli was the father of John Lee. As the boy grew and changed and looked more and more like Dave, neither of them had known whether the likenesses were inherited or acquired: hand gestures, turns of phrase, enthusiasms, all could have been learned by a boy who adored his daddy. But dyslexia could not be learned. "It's not conclusive," Beep said. "But it's strong evidence."

"And anyway, we don't care," said Dave.

However, they had vowed never to speak of this doubt to anyone else, including John Lee himself.

Cam's wedding took place at a modern Catholic church in the small town of Otwock, on the outskirts of Warsaw. Cam had embraced Catholicism. Dave had no doubt the conversion was entirely cynical.

The bride wore a white dress that her mother had got married in: Polish people had to recycle clothing.

Lidka was slim and attractive, Dave thought, with long legs and a nice bust, but there was something about her mouth that suggested ruthlessness to him. Perhaps he was being harsh: fifteen years as a rock star had made him cynical about girls. They went to bed with men to seek some advantage for themselves more often than most people thought, in his experience.

The three bridesmaids had made themselves short summery dresses in bright pink cotton.

The reception was held at the American embassy. Woody Dewar paid for it, but the embassy was able to secure plentiful supplies of food, and something other than vodka to drink.

Lidka's father told a joke, half in Polish and half in English. A man walks into a government-owned butcher's shop and asks for a pound of beef.

"*Nie ma*—we don't have any."

"Pork, then."

"*Nie ma.*"

"Veal?"

"*Nie ma.*"

"Chicken."

"*Nie ma.*"

The customer leaves. The butcher's wife says: "The guy is crazy."

"Of course," says the butcher. "But what a memory!"

The Americans looked awkward, but the Poles laughed heartily.

Dave had asked Cam not to tell anyone that his brother-in-law was in Plum Nellie, but the news had got out, as it usually did, and Dave was besieged by Lidka's friends. The bridesmaids made a big fuss of him, and it was clear that Dave could go to bed with any of them, or even—one hinted—with all three at the same time, if he was so inclined.

"You should meet my bass player," Dave said.

While Cam and Lidka were doing their first dance, Beep said quietly to Dave: "I know he's a creep, but he's my brother, and I can't help feeling pleased he's found someone at last."

Dave said: "Are you sure Lidka isn't a gold digger who just wants an American passport?"

"That's what my parents are afraid of. But Cam's thirty-four and single."

"I guess you're right," Dave said. "What has he got to lose?"

. . .

Tanya Dvorkin was full of fear when she attended Solidarity's first national convention in September 1981.

The proceedings began in the cathedral at Oliwa, a northern suburb of Gdańsk. Two sharp stiletto towers menacingly flanked a low baroque portal through which the delegates entered the church. Tanya sat with Danuta Gorski, her Warsaw neighbor, the journalist and Solidarity organizer. Like Tanya, Danuta wrote blandly orthodox reports for the official press while privately pursuing her own agenda.

The archbishop gave a don't-make-trouble sermon about peace and love of the fatherland. Although the Pope was gung ho, the Polish clergy was conflicted about Solidarity. They hated Communism, but they were natural authoritarians, hostile to democracy. Some priests were heroically brave in defying the regime, but what the church hierarchy wanted was to replace a godless tyranny with a Christian tyranny.

However, it was not the church that bothered Tanya, nor any of the other forces tending to divide the movement. Much more ominous were the threatening maneuvers by the Soviet navy in the Gulf of Gdańsk, together with "land exercises" by one hundred thousand Red Army troops on Poland's eastern border. According to the article by Danuta in today's *Trybuna Ludu*, this military muscle-flexing was a response to increased American aggression. No one was fooled. The Soviet Union wanted to tell everyone that it was poised to invade if Solidarity made the wrong noises.

After the service the nine hundred delegates moved in buses to the campus of the University of Gdańsk, where the convention was to be held in the massive Olivia Sports Hall.

All this was highly provocative. The Kremlin hated Solidarity. Nothing so dangerous had happened in a Soviet bloc country in more than a decade. Democratically elected delegates from all over Poland were gathering to hold debates and pass resolutions by voting, and the Communist Party had no control whatsoever. It was a national parliament in all but name. It would have been called revolutionary, if that word had not been besmirched by the Bolsheviks. No wonder the Soviets were frantic.

The sports hall was equipped with an electronic scoreboard. As Lech Wałęsa stood to speak, it lit up with a cross and the Latin slogan POLONIA SEMPER FIDELIS, "Poland ever faithful."

Tanya went outside to her car and turned on the radio. Programs were normal all across the dial. The Soviets had not invaded yet.

The rest of Saturday passed without major drama. It was not until Tuesday that Tanya began to feel scared again.

The government had published a draft bill on workers' self-government that gave employees the right to be consulted about management appointments. Tanya reflected wryly that President Reagan would never for one minute consider giving such rights to Americans. Even so, the bill was not radical enough for Solidarity, for it stopped short of giving the workforce the power to hire and fire; so they proposed a national referendum on the issue.

Lenin must have turned in his mausoleum.

Worse, they added a clause saying that if the government refused a referendum, the union would organize one itself.

Tanya again felt the needle of fear. The union was beginning to play the leadership role normally reserved for the Communist Party. The atheists were taking over the church. The Soviet Union would never accept this.

The resolution was passed with only one vote against, and the delegates stood and applauded themselves.

But that was not all.

Someone proposed sending a message to workers in Czechoslovakia, Hungary, East Germany, and "all the nations of the Soviet Union." Among other things, it said: "We support those among you who have decided on the difficult road of struggle for free trade unions." It was passed by a show of hands.

They had gone too far, Tanya felt sure.

The Soviets' worst fear was that the Polish crusade for freedom would spread to other Iron Curtain countries—and the delegates were rashly encouraging just that! The invasion now seemed inevitable.

Next day the press was full of Soviet outrage. Solidarity was interfering in the internal affairs of sovereign states, they screeched.

But still they did not invade.

. . .

Soviet leader Leonid Brezhnev did not want to invade Poland. He could not afford to lose credit with Western banks. He had a different plan. Cam Dewar found out from Staz what it was.

It always took a few days to process the raw material that Staz produced. Picking up his rolls of film in a dangerous clandestine brush pass was only the beginning. The film had to be developed in the darkroom at the American embassy, and the documents printed and photocopied. Then a translator with a high-level security clearance sat down and converted the material from Polish and Russian to English. If there were a hundred or more pages—as was frequent—it took days. The result had to be typed up and photocopied, again. Then at last Cam could see what kind of fish he had netted.

As the Warsaw winter freeze set in, Cam pored over the latest batch and found a well-worked-out and detailed scheme for a clampdown by the Polish government. Martial law would be declared, all freedoms would be suspended, and all agreements made with Solidarity would be reversed.

It was only a contingency plan. But Cam was astonished to learn that Jaruzelski had war-gamed it within a week of taking office. Clearly he had had this in mind right from the start.

And Brezhnev was relentlessly pressing him to go ahead.

Jaruzelski had resisted the pressure earlier in the year. Then, Solidarity had been well positioned to fight back, with workers occupying factories all over the country and preparations well advanced for a general strike.

At that time, Solidarity had prevailed, and the Communists had appeared to yield. But now the workers were off guard.

They were also hungry, tired, and cold. Everything was scarce, inflation was rampant, and food distribution was sabotaged by Communist bureaucrats who wanted the old days back. Jaruzelski calculated that the people would take only so much hardship before they began to feel that the return of authoritarian government might be a blessing.

Jaruzelski *wanted* a Soviet invasion. He had sent a message to the Kremlin, asking bluntly: "Can we count on military assistance from Moscow?"

The reply he received had been equally blunt: "No troops will be sent."

This was good news for Poland, Cam reflected. The Soviets might bully and bluster, but they were not willing to take the ultimate step. Whatever happened, it would be done by Polish people.

However, Jaruzelski might yet clamp down, even without the backup of Soviet tanks. His plan was right there on Staz's film. Staz himself clearly feared that the plan would be carried out, for he had included a handwritten note. This was unusual enough for Cam to pay it serious attention. Staz had written: "Reagan can prevent this happening if he threatens to cut off financial aid."

Cam thought that was shrewd. Loans from Western governments and Western banks were keeping Poland afloat. The one thing worse than democracy would be bankruptcy.

Cam had voted for Reagan because he promised to be more aggressive in foreign policy. Now was his chance. If he acted quickly, Reagan could stop Poland taking a giant step backward.

. . .

George and Verena had a pleasant suburban home in Prince George's County, Maryland, just outside the Washington city limits, in the suburb he represented as congressman. He had to go to church every week now, a different denomination each Sunday, to worship with his voters. His job involved a few such chores, but most of the time he was passionately engaged. Jimmy Carter was out and Ronald Reagan was in the White House, and George was able to fight for the poorest people in America, many of whom were black.

Every month or two Maria Summers came to see her godson, Jack, now eighteen months old and showing some of the feistiness of his grandmother Jacky. She usually brought him a book. After brunch George would wash the dishes and Maria would dry, and they would talk about intelligence and foreign policy.

Maria was still working at the State Department. Her boss was now Secretary of State Alexander Haig. George asked whether State was getting better information on Poland. "Much better," she said. "I don't know what you did, but the CIA really smartened up its act."

George passed her a bowl to dry. "So what's happening in Warsaw?"

"The Soviets will not invade. We know that. The Polish Communists asked them to, and they refused point-blank. But Brezhnev is pressing Jaruzelski to declare martial law and abolish Solidarity."

"That would be a shame."

"That's what the State Department thinks."

George hesitated. "I hear the word *but* coming along . . ."

"You know me too well." She smiled. "We have the power to stamp on the martial law plan. President Reagan would only have to say that future economic aid depends on human rights."

"Why doesn't he?"

"He and Al Haig don't really believe the Poles will impose martial law on themselves."

"Who knows? It might be smart to issue the warning anyway."

"That's what I think."

"So why don't they?"

"They don't want the other side to realize just how good our intelligence is."

"There's no point in having intelligence unless you use it."

"Maybe they will," said Maria. "But right now they're dithering."

. . .

Snow was falling in Warsaw two weekends before Christmas. Tanya spent Saturday night alone. Staz never explained why he was or was not free to stay at her apartment. She had never been to his place, though she knew where he lived. Since she had introduced him to Cam Dewar, Staz had been closemouthed about everything to do with the army. Tanya assumed this was because he was revealing secrets to the

Americans. He was like a prisoner who is on good behavior all day while digging an escape tunnel at night.

But this was the second Saturday Tanya had spent without him. She was not sure why. Was he tiring of her? Men did. The only man who had remained a permanent part of her life was Vasili, and she had never slept with him.

She found she was missing Vasili. She had never allowed herself to fall in love with him, because he was promiscuous, but she felt drawn to him. What she liked in men, she was beginning to realize, was courage. The three most important men in her life had been Paz Oliva, Staz Pawlak, and Vasili. As it happened they were all terrifically handsome. But they were also brave. Paz had stood up to the might of the USA, Staz had betrayed the secrets of the Red Army, and Vasili had defied the power of the Kremlin. Of the three, Vasili was the one who most thrilled her imagination, for he had written devastating stories about the Soviet Union while starved and half-frozen in Siberia. She wondered how he was, and wished she knew what he was writing now. She wondered if he had gone back to his old Casanova ways, or had genuinely settled down.

She went to bed and read *Doctor Zhivago* in German—it still had not been published in Russian—until she felt sleepy and turned out the light.

She was awakened by banging. She sat upright and turned on the light. It was half past two in the morning. Someone was pounding on a door, though not her door.

She got up and looked out of the window. The cars parked on either side of the street were covered with a fresh layer of snow. In the middle of the road were two police cars and a BTR-60 armored personnel carrier, carelessly parked at random angles in the manner of cops who knew they could do anything they liked.

The noise from outside her apartment changed from banging to crashing. It sounded as if someone was trying to demolish the building with a sledgehammer.

Tanya put on a bathrobe and went to the hall. She picked up her TASS press card, which was lying on a hall table with her car keys and change. She opened her door and looked into the corridor. Nothing was happening, except that two of her neighbors were also nervously peeping out.

Tanya propped her door open with a chair and went out. The noise was coming from the next floor down. She looked over the banisters and saw a group of men in the military camouflage uniform of the ZOMO, the notorious security police. Wielding crowbars and hammers, they were breaking down the door of Tanya's friend Danuta Gorski.

Tanya yelled: "What are you doing? What's happening?"

Some of her neighbors also shouted questions. The police took no notice.

The door was opened from inside, and Danuta's husband stood there, a frightened man in pajamas and glasses. "What do you want?" he said. From within the apartment came the sound of children crying.

The cops strode in, shoving him out of the way.

Tanya ran down the stairs. "You can't do this!" she yelled. "You have to identify yourselves!"

Two big policemen came out of the apartment dragging Danuta, her abundant hair in disarray, wearing a nightdress and a white candlewick dressing gown.

Tanya stood in front of them, blocking the staircase. She held up her press card. "I am a Soviet reporter!" she shouted.

"Then get the fuck out of the way," one replied. He lashed out at her with a crowbar he held in his left hand. It was not a calculated blow, for he was striving to control the struggling Danuta with the other hand, but the iron bar caught Tanya across the face. She felt a blaze of pain and staggered back. The two police pushed past her and hauled Danuta down the stairs.

Tanya had blood in her right eye but she could see with her left. Another cop emerged from the apartment carrying a typewriter and a telephone answering device.

Danuta's husband reappeared with a child in his arms. "Where are you taking her?" he shouted. The police did not reply.

Tanya said to him: "I'm going to call the army right now and find out." Holding one hand to her injured face, she went back up the stairs.

She glanced in the hall mirror. She had a gash on her forehead and her cheek was red and already swelling with a bruise, but she thought the blow had not broken any bones.

She picked up the phone to call Staz.

It was dead.

She turned on the television and the radio. The TV was blank, the radio silent.

This was not just about Danuta, then.

A neighbor followed her in. "Let me call a doctor," the woman said.

"I don't have time." Tanya stepped into her little bathroom, held a towel under the tap, and washed her face gingerly. Then she returned to her bedroom and dressed quickly in thermal underwear, jeans and a heavy sweater, and a big, thick coat with a fur lining.

She ran down the stairs and got into her car. Snow was falling again but the main roads were clear, and she soon saw why. Tanks and army trucks were everywhere. With a growing apprehension of doom she realized that the arrest of Danuta was just a small part of something ominously massive.

The troops swarming into the center of Warsaw were not Russians, however. This was not like Prague in 1968. The vehicles had Polish army markings and the soldiers wore Polish uniforms. The Poles had invaded their own capital.

They were setting up roadblocks, but they had only just started, and for the moment it was possible to circumvent them. Tanya drove her Mercedes fast, pushing her luck on slippery bends, to Jana Olbrachta Street, in the west of the city. She parked outside Staz's building. She knew the address but she had never been here before: he always said it was little better than a barracks.

She ran inside. It took her a couple of minutes to find the right apartment. She banged on the door, praying he would be in, though she feared the overwhelming likelihood was that he was out on the streets with the rest of the army.

The door was opened by a woman.

Tanya was shocked into silence. Did Staz have another girlfriend?

The woman was blond and pleasant-looking, wearing a pink nylon nightdress. She stared at Tanya's face in consternation. "You've been hurt!" she said in Polish.

Tanya noticed, in the hallway behind the woman, a small red tricycle. This woman was not his girlfriend, she was his wife, and they had a child.

Tanya felt a jolt of guilt like an electric shock. She had been taking Staz away from his family. And he had been lying to her.

With an effort, she wrenched her mind back to the present emergency. "I need to speak to Colonel Pawlak," she said. "It's urgent."

The woman heard her Russian accent, and her attitude changed in an instant. She glared angrily at Tanya. "So you're the Russian whore," she said.

Evidently Staz had not succeeded in keeping his love affair entirely secret from his wife. Tanya wanted to explain that she had not known he was married, but this was not the moment. "There's no time for that!" she said desperately. "They're taking over the city! Where is he?"

"He's not here."

"Will you help me find him?"

"No. Now fuck off and die." The woman slammed the door.

"Shit," said Tanya.

She stood outside the apartment door. She put her hand to her aching cheek: it seemed to be swelling grotesquely. She did not know what to do next.

The other person who might know what was going on was Cam Dewar. She probably could not phone him: she guessed all the civilian phones in the city had been cut off. However, Cam might go to the American embassy.

She ran outside, jumped back into her car, and headed for the south of the city. She cut across the outskirts, avoiding the city center, where there would be roadblocks.

So Staz had a wife. He had been deceiving both women. He was a smooth liar, Tanya thought bitterly: he was probably a good spy. Tanya was so angry that she felt like giving up on men. They were all the damn same.

She saw a group of soldiers putting up a placard on a lamppost. She stopped to look, though she did not risk getting out of her car. It was a decree issued by something called the Military Council for National Salvation. There was no such council: it had just been invented, no doubt by Jaruzelski. She read it with horror. Martial law was in force. Civil rights were suspended, the frontiers were closed, travel between cities was prohibited, all public gatherings were banned, there was a curfew from ten P.M. to six A.M., and the armed forces were authorized to use coercion to restore law and order.

This was the clampdown. And it had been carefully planned—that poster had been printed in advance. The plan was being carried out with ruthless efficiency. Was there any hope?

She drove off again. In a dark street two ZOMO men stepped into the light of her twin headlights, and one held up a hand to stop her. At that moment Tanya felt a stab of pain in her cheek, and made a split-second decision. She floored the accelerator pedal. She thanked the stars for her powerful German engine as the car leaped forward, startling the men, who jumped aside. She screeched around a corner and was out of their sight before they could deploy their guns.

A few minutes later she pulled up outside the white marble embassy. All the lights were on: they, too, would be trying to find out what was happening. She sprang out of her car and ran to the U.S. marine at the gate. "I have important information for Cam Dewar," she said in English.

The marine pointed behind her. "That looks like him now."

Tanya turned to see a lime green Polski Fiat pulling up. Cam was at the wheel. Tanya ran to the car, and Cam rolled down his window. He addressed her in Russian, as always. "My God, what did you do to your face?"

"I had a conversation with the ZOMO," she said. "Do you know what's happening?"

"The government has arrested just about every Solidarity leader and organizer—thousands of them," Cam said grimly. "All phone lines are dead. There are massive roadblocks on every major road in the country."

"But I see no Russians!"

"No. The Poles have done this to themselves."

"Did the American government know this was going to happen? Did Staz tell you?"

Cam said nothing.

Tanya took that for a yes. "Couldn't Reagan do something to stop it?"

Cam looked as perplexed and disappointed as Tanya felt. "I thought he could," he said.

Tanya could hear her own voice rising to a screech of frustration. "Then, for God's sake, why didn't he?"

"I don't know," said Cam. "I just don't know."

· · ·

When Tanya got home to Moscow, there was a bunch of flowers from Vasili waiting for her in her mother's apartment. How had he found roses in Moscow in January?

The flowers were a spot of brightness in a desolate landscape. Tanya had suffered two shocks: Staz had deceived her, and General Jaruzelski had betrayed the Polish people. Staz was no better than Paz Oliva, and she had to wonder what was wrong with her judgment. Perhaps she was wrong about Communism, too. She had always believed it could not last. She had been a schoolgirl in 1956 when the Hungarian people's rebellion had been crushed. Twelve years later the same had happened to the Prague Spring, and after another thirteen years Solidarity had gone the same way. Maybe Communism really was the way of the future, as Grandfather Grigori had died believing. If so, a grim life was ahead for her nephew and niece, Dimka's children, Grisha and Katya.

Soon after Tanya arrived home, Vasili invited her to dinner.

They could be friends openly now, they agreed. He had been rehabilitated. His radio show was a long-running success, and he was a star of the writers' union. No one knew that he was also Ivan Kuznetsov, dissident author of *Frostbite* and other anti-Communist books that had been bestsellers in the West. It was remarkable, Tanya thought, that she and he had succeeded in keeping the secret so long.

She was getting ready to leave the office and go to Vasili's place when she was accosted by Pyotr Opotkin, screwing up his eyes against the smoke from the cigarette between his lips. "You've done it again," he said. "We're getting complaints at the highest level about your article on cows."

Tanya had visited the Vladimir Region, where Communist Party officials were so inefficient that cattle were dying on a huge scale while their feed rotted in barns. She had written an angry piece, and Daniil had sent it out. Now she said: "I suppose the corrupt and lazy bastards who let the cows die have complained to you."

"Never mind them," Opotkin said. "I've had a letter from the Central Committee secretary responsible for ideology!"

"He knows about cows, does he?"

Opotkin thrust a piece of paper at her. "We're going to have to publish a retraction."

Tanya took it from him but did not read it. "Why are you so concerned to defend people who are destroying our country?"

"We cannot undermine Communist Party cadres!"

The phone on Tanya's desk rang, and she picked it up. "Tanya Dvorkin."

A vaguely familiar voice said: "You wrote the article about cows dying in Vladimir."

Tanya sighed. "Yes, I did, and I have already been reprimanded. Who is this calling?"

"I am the secretary responsible for agriculture. My name is Mikhail Gorbachev. You interviewed me in 1976."

"So I did." Gorbachev was obviously going to add his condemnation to Opotkin's, Tanya assumed.

Gorbachev said: "I called to congratulate you on your excellent analysis."

Tanya was astonished. "I . . . uh, thank you, comrade!"

"It is desperately important that we eliminate such inefficiency on our farms."

"Uh, comrade Secretary, would you mind saying that to my editor in chief? We were just discussing the article, and he was talking of a retraction."

"Retraction? Rubbish. Put him on the phone."

Grinning, Tanya said to Opotkin: "Secretary Gorbachev would like to talk to you."

At first Opotkin did not believe her. He took the phone and said: "To whom am I speaking, please?"

From then on he was silent but for the occasional: "Yes, comrade."

At last he put down the phone. He walked away without speaking to Tanya.

It gave her profound satisfaction to crumple the retraction and toss it into the bin.

She went to Vasili's apartment not knowing what to expect. She hoped he was not going to ask her to join his harem. Just in case, she was wearing unsexy serge trousers and a drab gray sweater, to discourage him. All the same, she found herself looking forward to the evening.

He opened the door, wearing a blue sweater and a white shirt, both new-looking. She kissed his cheek, then studied him. His hair was gray, now, but still luxuriant and wavy. At fifty he was upright and slim.

He opened a bottle of Georgian champagne and put snacks on the table, squares of toast with egg salad and tomato, and fish roes on cucumber. Tanya wondered who had made them. It would not be beyond him to have one of his girlfriends do it.

The apartment was comfortable, full of books and pictures. Vasili had a tape deck that played cassettes. He was affluent now, even without the fortune in foreign royalties that he could not receive.

He wanted to know all about Poland. How had the Kremlin defeated Solidarity without an invasion? Why had Jaruzelski betrayed the Polish people? He did not think his apartment was bugged, but he played a Tchaikovsky cassette just in case.

Tanya told him that Solidarity was not dead. It had gone underground. Many of the men arrested under martial law were still in jail, but the sexist secret police had failed to appreciate the major role played by women. Almost all the female organizers were still at large, including Danuta, who had been arrested, then released. She was again working undercover, producing illegal newspapers and pamphlets, rebuilding lines of communication.

All the same, Tanya had no hope. If they rebelled again, they would be crushed again. Vasili was more optimistic. "It was a near thing," he said. "In half a century, no one has come so close to defeating Communism."

This was like the old days, Tanya thought, feeling comfortable as the champagne relaxed her. Back in the early sixties, before Vasili was jailed, they had often sat around like this, talking and arguing about politics and literature and art.

She told him about the phone call from Mikhail Gorbachev. "He's an odd one," Vasili said. "We in the agriculture ministry see a lot of him. He's Yuri Andropov's pet, and he seems to be a rock-solid Communist. His wife is even worse. Yet he backs reformist ideas, whenever he can do it without offending his superiors."

"My brother thinks highly of him."

"When Brezhnev dies—which can't be far distant now, please, God—Andropov will make a bid for the leadership, and Gorbachev will back him. If the bid fails, both men will be finished. They'll be sent to the provinces. But if Andropov succeeds, Gorbachev has a bright future."

"In any other country Gorbachev, at fifty, would be just the right age to become leader. Here, he's too young."

"The Kremlin is a geriatric ward."

Vasili served borsch, beetroot soup with beef. "This is good," Tanya said. She could not help asking: "Who made it?"

"I did, of course. Who else?"

"I don't know. Do you have a housekeeper?"

"Just a babushka who comes to clean the apartment and iron my shirts."

"One of your girlfriends, then?"

"I don't have a girlfriend at the moment."

Tanya was intrigued. She recalled the last conversation they had had before she went to Warsaw. He had claimed to have changed, and grown up. She had felt he needed to show that, not just say it. She had been sure it was just another line of chat intended to get her into bed. Could she have been wrong? She doubted it.

After they had eaten, she asked him how he felt about those royalties piling up in London.

"You should have the money," he said.

"Don't be silly. You wrote the books."

"I had little to lose—I was already in Siberia. They couldn't do much more to me, except kill me, and I would have been relieved to die. But you risked everything—your career, your freedom, your life. You deserve the money more than I do."

"Well, I wouldn't take it, even if you could give it to me."

"Then it will stay there until I die, probably."

"You wouldn't be tempted to escape to the West?"

"No."

"You sound sure."

"I am sure."

"Why? You'd be free to write whatever you like, all the time. No more radio serials."

"I wouldn't go . . . unless you went, too."

"You don't mean that."

He shrugged. "I don't expect you to believe me. Why should you? But you're the most important person in my life. You came to Siberia to find me—no one else did. You tried to get me released. You smuggled my work out to the free world. For twenty years, you've been the best friend a person could have."

She was moved. She had never looked at it that way. "Thank you for saying that," she said.

"It's no more than the truth. I'm not leaving." Then he added: "Unless, of course, you go with me."

She stared at him. Was he making a serious suggestion? She was frightened to ask. She looked out of the window at the snowflakes whirling in the lamplight.

Vasili said: "Twenty years, and we've never even kissed."

"True."

"Yet still you think I'm a heartless Casanova."

In truth she no longer knew what to think. Had he changed? Did people ever really change? She said: "After all this time, it would be a shame to spoil our record."

"And yet I want to, with all my heart."

She changed the subject. "Given the chance, would you defect to the West?"

"With you, yes. Not otherwise."

"I always wanted to make the Soviet Union a better place, not leave it. But after the defeat of Solidarity I find it difficult to believe in a better future. Communism could last a thousand years."

"It could last longer than me or you, at least."

Tanya hesitated on the brink. She was surprised by how much she wanted to kiss him. And more: she wanted to stay here, talking to him, on this couch in this warm apartment with those snowflakes falling outside the window, for a long, long time. What a strange feeling that was, she thought. Perhaps it was love.

So she kissed him.

After a while, they went into the bedroom.

. . .

Natalya was always first with the news. She came to Dimka's office in the Kremlin on Christmas Eve, looking anxious. "Andropov is not going to be at the Politburo meeting," she said. "He's too ill to leave the hospital."

The next Politburo meeting was scheduled for the day after Christmas.

"Damn," said Dimka. "That's dangerous."

Strangely, Yuri Andropov had turned out to be a good Soviet leader. For the previous fifteen years he had been the efficient head of a cruel and brutal secret service, the KGB. And now, as general secretary of the Communist Party of the Soviet Union, he continued to repress dissidents ruthlessly. But within the party he was astonishingly tolerant of new ideas and reforms. Like a medieval Pope who tortured heretics yet discussed with his cardinals arguments against the existence of God, Andropov talked freely to his inner circle—which included both Dimka and Natalya—about the shortcomings of the Soviet system. And the talk led to action. Gorbachev's brief was extended from agriculture to the entire economy, and he produced a program to decentralize the Soviet economy, taking some of the power of decision away from Moscow and giving it to managers closer to the problems.

Unfortunately Andropov fell ill shortly before Christmas 1983, having been leader for barely a year. This worried Dimka and Natalya. Andropov's stick-in-the-mud rival for the leadership had been Konstantin Chernenko, who was still number two in the hierarchy. Dimka feared that Chernenko would take advantage of Andropov's illness to regain the ascendancy.

Now Natalya said: "Andropov has written a speech to be read out."

Dimka shook his head. "That's not enough. In Andropov's absence, Chernenko will chair the meeting, and once that happens everyone will accept him as leader-in-waiting. And then the whole country will go backward." The prospect was too depressing to contemplate.

"Obviously we want Gorbachev to chair the meeting."

"But Chernenko is number two. I wish he'd go to hospital."

"He will soon—he's not a well man."

"But probably not soon enough. Is there any way we can bypass him?"

Natalya considered. "Well, the Politburo must do what Andropov tells it to do."

"So he could just issue an order saying Gorbachev will chair the meeting?"

"Yes, he could. He's still the boss."

"He could add a paragraph to his speech."

"Perfect. I'll call him and suggest it."

Later that afternoon Dimka got a message summoning him to Natalya's office. When he got there he saw that her eyes were gleaming with excitement and triumph. With her was Arkady Volsky, Andropov's personal aide. Andropov had summoned Volsky to the hospital and had given him a handwritten addendum to the speech. Volsky now gave it to Dimka.

The last paragraph read:

For reasons which you understand, I will not be able to chair meetings of the Politburo and Secretariat in the near future. I would therefore request members of the central committee to examine the question of entrusting the leadership of the Politburo and secretariat to Mikhail Sergeyevich Gorbachev.

It was expressed as a suggestion, but in the Kremlin a suggestion from the leader was the same thing as a direct order.

"This is dynamite," said Dimka. "They can't possibly disobey."

"What should I do with it?" said Volsky.

Dimka said: "First, make several photocopies, so that there's no point in anyone tearing it up. Then . . ." Dimka hesitated.

Natalya said: "Don't tell anyone. Just give it to Bogolyubov." Klavdii Bogolyubov was in charge of preparing the papers for Politburo meetings. "Be low-key. Just tell him to add the extra material to the red folder containing Andropov's speech."

They agreed that was the best plan.

Christmas Day was not a big festival. The Communists disliked its religious nature. They changed Santa Claus to Father Frost and the Virgin Mary to the Snow Maiden, and moved the celebration to New Year. That was when the children would get their gifts. Grisha, who was now twenty, was getting a cassette player, and Katya, fourteen, a new dress. Dimka and Natalya, as senior Communist politicians, did not dream of celebrating Christmas, regardless of their personal beliefs. Both went to work as usual.

The day after, Dimka went to the Presidium Room for the Politburo meeting. He was met at the door by Natalya, who had got there earlier. She looked distraught. She was holding open the red folder containing Andropov's speech. "They left it out!" she said. "They left out the last paragraph!"

Dimka sat down heavily. "I never imagined Chernenko would have the guts," he said.

There was nothing they could do, he realized. Andropov was in hospital. If he had stormed into the room and yelled at everyone, his authority would have been reasserted; but he could not. Chernenko had correctly estimated Andropov's weakness.

"They've won, haven't they?" said Natalya.

"Yes," said Dimka. "The Age of Stagnation begins again."

PART NINE

BOMB

1984–1987

George Jakes went to the opening of an exhibition of African American art in downtown Washington. He was not very interested in art, but a black congressman had to support such things. Most of his work as a congressman was more important.

President Reagan had enormously increased government spending on the military, but who was going to pay? Not the wealthy, who had received a big tax cut.

There was a joke that George often repeated. A reporter asked Reagan how he was going to reduce tax and increase spending at the same time. "I'm going to keep two sets of books," was the answer.

In reality Reagan's plan was to cut Social Security and Medicare. If he had his way, unemployed men and welfare mothers would lose out to finance the boom in the defense industry. The idea made George mad with rage. However, George and others in Congress were struggling to prevent this, and so far they had succeeded.

The upshot was a rise in government borrowing. Reagan had increased the deficit. All those shiny new weapons for the Pentagon would be paid for by future generations.

George took a glass of white wine from a tray held by a waiter and looked around the exhibits, then spoke briefly to a reporter. He did not have much time. Verena needed to go out tonight, to a Georgetown political dinner, so he would be in charge of their son, Jack, who was now four. They had a nanny—they had to, for they both had demanding jobs—but one of them was always on duty as backup in case the nanny should fail to show up.

He set his glass down untasted. Free wine was never worth drinking. He put on his coat and left. A cold rain had started, and he held the exhibition catalogue over his head as he hurried to his car. His elegant old Mercedes was long gone: a politician had to drive an American vehicle. He now had a silver Lincoln Town Car.

He got in, switched on the windshield wipers, and set off for Prince George's County. He crossed the South Capitol Street Bridge and took Suitland Parkway east. He cursed when he saw how heavy the traffic was: he was going to be late.

When he got home, Verena's red Jaguar stood in the driveway, nose out, ready to go. The car had been a present from her father on her fortieth birthday. George parked next to it and walked into the house, carrying a briefcase full of papers, his evening's work.

Verena was in the hallway, looking spectacularly glamorous in a black cocktail dress and patent high-heeled pumps. She was as mad as a polecat. "You're late!" she yelled.

"I'm really sorry," George said. "The traffic on Suitland Parkway is crazy today."

"This dinner party is really important to me—three members of Reagan's cabinet will be there, and I'm going to be late!"

George understood her irritation. For a lobbyist, the chance to meet powerful people socially was priceless. "I'm here now," he said.

"I am not the maid! When we make an arrangement you have to keep it!"

This tirade was not unusual. She often got angry and screamed at him. He always tried to take it calmly. "Is Nanny Tiffany here?"

"No, she's not, she went home sick, that's why I had to wait for you."

"Where's Jack?"

"Watching TV in the den."

"Okay, I'll go and sit with him now. You go on out."

She made a furious noise and stalked off.

He kind of envied whoever was going to sit next to her at dinner. She was still the sexiest woman he had ever met. However, he now knew that being her long-distance lover, as he had for many years, was better than being her husband. In the old days they had had sex more times in a weekend than they did now in a month. Since they got married their frequent and furious rows, usually about child care, had eroded their affection for one another like a slow drip of strong vitriol. They lived together, they took care of their son, and they pursued their careers. Did they love one another? George no longer knew.

He went into the den. Jack was on the couch in front of the TV. The boy was George's great consolation. He sat next to him and put his arm around his small shoulders. Jack snuggled up.

The show featured a group of high school pupils involved in some kind of adventure. "What are you watching?" George asked.

"*Whiz Kids.* It's great."

"What's it about?"

"They catch crooks with their computers."

One of the child geniuses was black, George noticed, and he thought: How the world turns.

. . .

"We're really lucky to be invited to this dinner," said Cam Dewar to his wife, Lidka, as their cab pulled up outside a grand mansion on R Street near the Georgetown Library. "I want us both to make a good impression."

Lidka was scornful. "You are an important person in the secret police," she said. "I think *they* need to impress *you*."

Lidka did not understand how America worked. "The CIA is not the secret police," Cam said. "And I'm not a very important person by the standards of these people."

Cam was not exactly a nobody, all the same. Because of his past experience in the White House, he was now the CIA's liaison man with the Reagan administration. He was thrilled to have the job.

He had got over his disappointment with Reagan's failure in Poland. He put that down to inexperience. Reagan had been president for less than a year when Solidarity was crushed.

In the back of Cam's mind, a devil's advocate said that a president ought to be smart enough and knowledgeable enough to make confident decisions from the moment he takes office. He recalled Nixon saying: "Reagan is a nice guy, but he doesn't know what the Christ is going on in foreign policy."

But Reagan's heart was in the right place, that was the main thing. He was passionately anti-Communist.

Lidka said: "And your grandfather was a senator!"

That did not count for much either. Gus Dewar was in his nineties. After Grandmama died he had moved from Buffalo to San Francisco to be near Woody, Beep, and his great-grandson, John Lee. He was long retired from politics. Besides, he was a Democrat, and by Reaganite standards an extreme liberal.

Cam and Lidka walked up a short flight of steps to a red-brick house that looked like a small French château, with dormer windows in the slate roof and a white stone entrance topped by a small Greek pediment. This was the home of Frank and Marybell Lindeman, heavyweight donors to Reagan's campaign funds and multimillion-dollar beneficiaries of his tax cut. Marybell was one of half a dozen women who dominated Washington social life. She entertained the men who ran America. That was why Cam felt lucky to be here.

Although the Lindemans were Republicans, Marybell's dinners were cross-party affairs, and Cam was expecting to see senior men from both sides here tonight.

A butler took their coats. Looking around the grand hall, Lidka said: "Why do they have these terrible paintings?"

"It's called Western art," Cam said. "That's a Remington—very valuable."

"If I had all that money, I wouldn't buy pictures of cowboys and Indians."

"They're making a point. The impressionists were not necessarily the best painters ever. American artists are just as good."

"No, they're not—everyone knows that."

"Matter of opinion."

Lidka shrugged: another mystery of American life.

The butler showed them into a wide drawing room. It looked like an eighteenth-century salon, with a Chinese dragon carpet and a scatter of spindly chairs upholstered in yellow silk. Cam realized they were the first guests to arrive. A moment later, Marybell appeared through another door. She was a statuesque woman with a mass of red hair that might or might not have been its natural color. She was wearing a necklace of what looked, to Cam, like unusually large diamonds. "How kind of you to come early!" she said.

Cam knew this was a reproof, but Lidka was oblivious. "I couldn't wait to see your wonderful house," she gushed.

"And how do you like living in America?" Marybell asked her. "Tell me, what is the best thing about this country, in your opinion?"

Lidka thought for a moment. "You have all these black people," she said.

Cam suppressed a groan. What the hell was she saying?

Marybell was surprised into silence.

Lidka waved a hand to indicate the waiter holding a tray of champagne flutes, the maid bringing canapés, and the butler, all of whom were African American. "They do everything, like opening doors and serving drinks and sweeping the floor. In Poland we have no one to do that work—everyone has to do it themselves!"

Marybell looked a little frantic. Such talk was incorrect even in Reagan's Washington. Then she looked over Lidka's shoulder and saw another guest hovering. "Karim, darling!" she screeched. She embraced a handsome dark-skinned man in an immaculate pin-striped suit. "Meet Cam Dewar and his wife, Lidka. This is Karim Abdullah, from the Saudi embassy."

Karim shook hands. "I've heard of you, Cam," he said. "I work closely with some of your colleagues in Langley."

Karim was letting Cam know he was in Saudi intelligence.

Karim turned to Lidka. She was looking startled. Cam knew why. She had not expected to see someone as dark as Karim at Marybell's party.

However, Karim charmed her. "I have been told that Polish women are the most beautiful in the world," he said. "But I didn't believe it— until this moment." He kissed her hand.

Lidka could take any amount of that sort of bullshit.

"I heard what you were saying about black people," Karim said. "I agree with you. We have none in Saudi Arabia—so we have to import them from India!"

Cam could see that Lidka was bewildered by the fine distinctions of Karim's racism. To him, Indians were black but Arabs were not. Fortunately, Lidka knew when to shut up and listen to a man.

More guests came in. Karim lowered his voice. "However," he said conspiratorially, "we must be careful what we say—some of the guests may be liberals."

As if to illustrate his point, a tall, athletic-looking man with thick fair hair came in. He looked like a movie star. It was Jasper Murray.

Cam was not pleased. He had hated Jasper since they were teenagers. Then Jasper had become an investigative reporter and had helped to bring President Nixon down. His book about Nixon, *Tricky Dick*, had been a bestseller and a successful movie. He had been relatively quiet during the Carter administration, but had returned to the attack as soon as Reagan took over. He was now one of the most popular figures on television, up there with Peter Jennings and Barbara Walters. Only last night his show, *This Day*, had devoted half an hour to the American-backed military dictatorship in El Salvador. Murray had repeated claims by human rights groups that government death squads there had murdered thirty thousand people.

The network that broadcast *This Day* was owned by Frank Lindeman, Marybell's husband; so Jasper had probably felt unable to decline the invitation to dinner. The White House had put pressure on Frank to get rid of Jasper, but so far Frank had refused. Although he held a majority of shares, he had a board to answer to, and investors who could make trouble if he fired one of his biggest stars.

Marybell seemed to be anxiously waiting for something. Then one more guest arrived, rather late. She was a stunningly glamorous black woman lobbyist called Verena Marquand. Cam had not met her, but recognized her from photographs.

The butler announced dinner and they all moved through a double doorway to the dining room. The women made appreciative noises when they saw the long table decked with gleaming glassware and silver bowls of yellow hothouse roses. Cam saw that Lidka was wide-eyed. This outdid all the photographs in her home decorating magazines, he guessed. She had surely never seen or even imagined anything so lavish.

There were eighteen people around the table, but the conversation was immediately dominated by one person. She was Suzy Cannon, a vituperative gossip reporter. Half of what she wrote turned out to be untrue, but she had a jackal's nose for weakness. She was conservative, but more interested in scandal than politics. Nothing was private to her. Cam prayed that Lidka would keep her mouth shut. Anything said tonight might appear in tomorrow's newspaper.

But Suzy turned her gimlet eyes on Cam, to his surprise. "I believe you and Jasper know each other," she said.

"Not really," said Cam. "We met in London many years ago."

"But I hear that you both fell in love with the same girl."

How the hell did she know that? "I was fifteen, Suzy," Cam said. "I probably fell in love with half the girls in London."

Suzy turned to Jasper. "How about you? Do you remember this rivalry?"

Jasper had been deep in conversation with Verena Marquand, sitting next to him. Now he looked irritated. "If you're planning to write an article about teenage romances that took place more than twenty years ago, and call it news, Suzy, all I can say is you must be sleeping with your editor."

Everyone laughed: Suzy was in fact married to the news editor of her paper.

Cam noticed that Suzy's laugh was forced, and her eyes glared hatred at Jasper. He recalled that Suzy as a young journalist had been fired from *This Day* after a series of wildly inaccurate reports.

Now she said: "You must have been interested to watch Jasper's show on TV last night, Cam."

Cam said: "Not interested so much as dismayed. The president and the CIA are trying to support the anti-Communist government in El Salvador."

Suzy said: "And Jasper seems to be on the other side, doesn't he?"

Jasper said: "I'm on the side of truth, Suzy. I know this is hard for you to grasp." Cam noticed that no trace of his British accent remained.

Cam said: "I was sorry to see such propaganda on a major network."

Jasper snapped: "How would *you* report on a government that murders thirty thousand of its own citizens?"

"We don't accept that figure."

"Then how many citizens of El Salvador do *you* think have been murdered by their government? Give us the CIA estimate."

"You should have asked that before broadcasting your show."

"Oh, I did. I got no answer."

"No Central American government is perfect. You focus on the ones we support. I think you're simply anti-American."

Suzy smiled. "You're British, aren't you, Jasper?" she said with poisonous sweetness.

Jasper looked riled. "I became a U.S. citizen more than a decade ago. I'm so pro-American that I risked my damn life for this country. I spent two years in the United States Army—one of those in Vietnam. And I wasn't sitting on my ass behind a desk in Saigon, either. I saw action, and I killed people. You've never done that, Suzy. And how about you, Cam? What did you do in Vietnam?"

"I wasn't called up."

"Then maybe you should just shut the fuck up."

Marybell interrupted. "I think that's enough about Jasper and Cam." She turned to a congressman from New York sitting next to her. "I see that your city has banned discrimination against homosexuals. Are you in favor of that?"

The conversation turned to gay rights, and Cameron relaxed—too soon.

A question was asked about legislation in other countries, and Suzy said: "What's the law in Poland, Lidka?"

"Poland is a Catholic country," said Lidka. "We have no homosexuals there." A moment of silence ensued, and she added: "Thank God."

.   .   .

Jasper Murray left the Lindeman house at the same time as Verena Marquand. "Suzy Cannon is a real troublemaker," he said as they went down the steps.

Verena laughed, showing white teeth in the lamplight. "That's the truth."

They reached the sidewalk. The taxi Jasper had ordered was nowhere in sight. He walked with Verena to her car. "Suzy's got it in for me," he said.

"She can't do you much harm, can she? You're such a big shot now."

"On the contrary. There's a serious campaign against me in

Washington right now. It's election year, and the administration doesn't want television programs like the one I did last night." He felt comfortable confiding in her. They had been thrown together the day they watched Martin Luther King die. That sense of intimacy had never really gone away.

Verena said: "I'm sure you can fight off a gossip attack."

"I don't know. My boss is an old rival called Sam Cakebread who has never liked me. And Frank Lindeman, who owns the network, would dearly love to get rid of me if he could find a pretext. Right now the board is afraid they'll be accused of biasing the news if they fire me. But one mistake and I'm out."

"You should be like Suzy, and marry the boss."

"I would if I could." He looked up and down the street. "I ordered a taxi for eleven o'clock, but I don't see it. The show won't pay for limousines."

"Do you want a ride?"

"That'd be great."

They got into her Jaguar.

She took off her high-heeled shoes and handed them to him. "Put these on the floor on your side, would you?" She drove in her stockings. Jasper felt a sexy frisson. He had always found Verena devastatingly alluring. He watched her as she pulled into the late-night traffic and accelerated down the street. She was a good driver, if a little too fast: no surprise there.

"There aren't many people I trust," he said. "I'm one of the most well-known people in America, and I feel more alone now than I ever have. But I trust you."

"I feel the same. I have since that awful day in Memphis. I've never felt more terrifyingly vulnerable than the moment I heard that shot. You covered my head with your arms. A person doesn't forget something like that."

"I wish I'd found you before George did."

She glanced over at him and smiled.

He was not sure what that meant.

They reached his building and she pulled up on the left side of the one-way street. "Thanks for the ride," Jasper said. He got out. Leaning back into the car, he picked up her shoes from the floor and placed them on the passenger seat. "Great shoes," he said. He slammed the door.

He walked around the car to the sidewalk and came to her window. She lowered the glass. "I forgot to kiss you good night," he said. He leaned into the car and kissed her lips. She opened her mouth immediately. The kiss became passionate in an instant. Verena reached behind his neck and pulled his head inside the car. They kissed with frantic eagerness. Jasper reached into the car and pushed his hand up inside the skirt of her cocktail dress until he could cup the soft cotton-covered triangle between her legs. She moaned and thrust her hips upward against his grasp.

Breathless, he broke the kiss. "Come inside."

"No." She moved his hand away from her groin.

"Meet me tomorrow."

She did not reply, but pushed him away until his head and shoulders were outside the car.

He said again: "Meet me tomorrow?"

She put the shift into gear. "Call me," she said. Then she put her foot down and roared away.

. . .

George Jakes was not sure whether to believe Jasper Murray's TV show. Even to George it seemed unlikely that President Reagan would support a government that murdered thousands of its own people. Then, four weeks later, *The New York Times* sensationally revealed that the head of El Salvador's death squad, Colonel Nicolás Carranza, was a CIA agent receiving $90,000 a year from American taxpayers.

Voters were furious. They had thought that after Watergate the CIA had been whipped into line. But it was clearly out of control, paying a monster to commit mass murder.

In his study at home, George finished the papers in his briefcase a few minutes before ten. He screwed the cap back onto his fountain pen, but sat there a few more minutes, reflecting.

No one on the House intelligence committee had known about Colonel Carranza, nor had any member of the equivalent Senate committee. Caught off guard, they were all embarrassed. They were supposed to supervise the CIA. People thought this mess was their fault. But what could they do if spooks lied to them?

He sighed and stood up. He left his study, turning out the light, and stepped into Jack's room. The boy was fast asleep. When he saw his child like this, so peaceful, George felt as if his heart would burst. Jack's soft skin was surprisingly dark, like Jacky's, even though he had two white grandparents. Light-skinned people were still favored in the African American community, despite all the talk about black being beautiful. But Jack was beautiful to George. His head lay on his teddy bear at what looked like an uncomfortable angle. George slipped a hand under the boy's head, feeling soft curls just like his own. He lifted Jack's head a fraction, gently slid the bear out, then carefully rested the head back on the pillow. Jack slept on, oblivious.

George went to the kitchen and poured a glass of milk, then carried it into the bedroom. Verena was already in bed, wearing a nightdress, with a pile of magazines beside her, reading and watching TV at the same time. George drank the milk, then went into the bathroom and brushed his teeth.

They seemed to be getting on a little better. They rarely made love, these days, but Verena was more even-tempered. In fact she had not erupted for a month or so. She was working hard, often late into the evenings: perhaps she was happier when her job was more demanding.

George took off his shirt and lifted the lid of the laundry hamper. He was about to drop his shirt in when his eye was caught by Verena's underwear. He saw a lacy black brassiere and matching panties. The set looked new, and he did not recall seeing it on her. If she was buying sexy underwear, why was she not letting him view it? She sure as hell was not shy about such things.

Looking more closely, he saw something even more strange: a blond hair.

He was possessed by a terrible fear. His stomach cramped. He picked the garments out of the hamper.

Carrying them into the bedroom, he said: "Tell me I'm crazy."

"You're crazy," she said; then she saw what he had in his hand. "Are you going to do my laundry?" she quipped, but he could tell she was nervous.

"Nice underwear," he said.

"Lucky you."

"Except that I haven't seen it on you."

"Unlucky you."

"But someone has."

"Sure. Dr. Bernstein."

"Dr. Bernstein is bald. There's a blond hair in your underpants."

Her cappuccino skin went paler, but she remained defiant. "Well, Sherlock Holmes, what do you deduce from that?"

"That you had sex with a man with long blond hair."

"Why does it have to be a man?"

"Because you like men."

"I might like girls too. It's the fashion. Everyone is bisexual now."

George felt profoundly sad. "I note you're not denying that you're having an affair."

"Well, George, ya got me."

He shook his head incredulously. "Are you making light of this?"

"I guess I am."

"So you admit it. Who are you fucking?"

"I'm not going to tell you, so don't ask again."

George was having more and more difficulty suppressing his anger. "You act as if you've done nothing wrong!"

"I'm not going to pretend. Yes, I'm seeing someone I like. I'm sorry to hurt your feelings."

George was bewildered. "How did this happen so quickly?"

"It happened slowly. We've been married more than five years. The thrill is gone, like the song says."

"What did I do wrong?"

"You married me."

"When did you become so angry?"

"Am I angry? I thought I was just bored."

"What do you want to do?"

"I'm not giving him up for the sake of a marriage that hardly exists any longer."

"You know I can't accept that."

"So, leave. You're not a prisoner."

George sat down on her dressing table stool and buried his face in his hands. He was swamped by a wave of intense emotion, and found himself suddenly taken back to childhood. He recalled the embarrassment of being the only boy in the class who did not have a father. He felt again the agonies of envy he had suffered when he saw other boys with their fathers, throwing a ball, fixing a punctured bicycle tire, buying a baseball bat, trying on shoes. He boiled anew with rage at the man who had, in his eyes, abandoned his mother and him, caring nothing for the woman who had given herself to him, nor for the child that had been born of their love. He wanted to scream, he wanted to punch Verena, he wanted to weep.

He managed to speak at last. "I'm not leaving Jack," he said.

"Your choice," said Verena. She switched off the TV, threw her magazines to the floor, turned out the bedside light, and lay down, facing away from him.

"Is that it?" George said amazedly. "Is that all you have to say?"

"I'm going to sleep. I have a breakfast meeting."

He stared at her. Had he ever known her?

Of course he had. In his heart he had understood that there were two Verenas: one a dedicated activist for civil rights, the other a party girl. He loved them both, and he had believed that with his help they could become one happy, well-adjusted person. And he had been wrong.

He remained there for several minutes, looking at her in the dim light from the streetlamp on the corner. I waited so long for you, he thought; all those years of long-distance love. Then, at last, you married me, and we had Jack, and I thought everything would be all right, forever.

At last he stood up. He took off his clothes and put on pajamas.

He could not bring himself to get into bed beside her.

There was a bed in the guest room, but it was not made up. He went to the hall and got his warmest coat from the closet. He went to the guest room and lay down with the coat over him.

But he did not sleep.

. . .

George had noticed, some time ago, that Verena sometimes wore clothes that did not suit her. She had a pretty flower-print dress that she put on when she wanted to seem like an innocent girl, though in fact it made her look ridiculous. She had a brown suit that drained her face of color, but she had paid so much for it that she was not willing to admit it was a mistake. She had a mustard-colored sweater that made her wonderful green eyes go muddy and dull.

Everyone did the same, George reckoned. He himself had three cream-colored shirts that he wished would fray at the collars soon so that he could throw them away. For all sorts of reasons, people wore clothes they hated.

But never when meeting a lover.

When Verena put on the black Armani suit with the turquoise blouse and the black coral necklace, she looked like a movie star, and she knew it.

She had to be going to see her paramour.

George felt so humiliated that it was like a gnawing pain in his stomach. He could not subject himself to this much longer. It made him feel like jumping off a bridge.

Verena left early, and said she would be home early, so George figured they were going to meet for lunch. He had breakfast with Jack, then left him with Nanny Tiffany. He went to his rooms in the Cannon House Office Building, near the Capitol, and canceled his appointments for the day.

At twelve noon, Verena's red Jaguar was parked as usual in the lot near her downtown office. George waited down the block in his silver Lincoln, watching the exit. The red car appeared at half past twelve. He pulled into the traffic and followed her.

She crossed the Potomac and headed out into the Virginia countryside. As the traffic thinned he fell back. It would be embarrassing if she spotted him. He hoped she would not notice something as common as a silver Lincoln. He could not have done this in his distinctive old Mercedes.

A few minutes before one she pulled off the road at a country restaurant called the Worcester Sauce. George sped by, then U-turned a mile down the road and came back. He drove into the restaurant parking lot and took a slot from which he could see the Jaguar. Then he settled down to wait.

He brooded. He knew he was being stupid. He knew this could end in embarrassment or worse. He knew he should drive away.

But he had to know who his wife's lover was.

They came out at three.

He could tell by the way Verena walked that she had had a glass or two of wine with her lunch. They came across the lot hand in hand, she giggling at something the man said, and hot fury boiled inside George.

The man was tall and broad, with thick fair hair, quite long.

As they came closer, George recognized Jasper Murray.

"You son of a bitch," he said aloud.

Jasper had always had a yen for Verena, right from the first time they had met, at the Willard Hotel on the day of Martin Luther King's "I have a dream" speech. But lots of men had a yen for Verena. George had never imagined that Jasper, of all of them, would be the betrayer.

They walked to the Jaguar and kissed.

George knew he should start his car and drive away. He had learned what he needed to know. There was nothing else to be done.

Verena's mouth was open, George could see. She leaned into Jasper with her hips. Both had their eyes closed.

George got out of his car.

Jasper grasped Verena's breast.

George slammed the car door and strode across the tarmac toward them.

Jasper was too absorbed in what he was doing but Verena heard the slam and opened her eyes. She saw George, pushed Jasper away, and screamed.

She was too late.

George reached back with his right arm then hit Jasper with a punch that had all the force of his back and shoulders in it. His fist connected with the left side of Jasper's face. George felt the deeply satisfying squish of soft flesh, then, a split second later, the hardness of teeth and bones. Then pain blazed in his hand.

Jasper staggered backward and fell to the ground.

Verena yelled: "George! What have you done?" She knelt beside Jasper, careless of her stockings.

Jasper lifted himself on one elbow and felt his face. "Fucking animal," he said to George.

George wanted Jasper to get up off the ground and hit back. He wanted more violence, more pain, more blood. He stared at Jasper for a long moment, seeing through a red mist. Then the fog cleared, and he realized Jasper was not going to get up and fight.

George turned around, went back to his car, and drove away.

When he got home, Jack was in his bedroom, playing with his collection of toy cars. George closed the door, so that Nanny Tiffany could not hear. He sat on the bed, which was covered by a counterpane that looked like a racing car. "I've got something very difficult to tell you," he said.

"What happened to your hand?" Jack said. "It's all red and puffed up."

"I banged it on something. You have to listen to me."

"Okay."

This was going to be hard for a four-year-old to understand. "You know I'll always love you," George said. "Just like Grandma Jacky loves me, even though I'm not a little boy anymore."

"Is Grandma coming today?"

"Maybe tomorrow."

"She brings cookies."

"Listen. Sometimes mommies and daddies stop loving each other. Did you know that?"

"Yeah. Pete Robbins's daddy doesn't love his mommy anymore." Jack's voice became solemn. "They got *divorced*."

"I'm glad you understand that, because your mom and I don't love each other anymore."

George watched Jack's face, trying to see whether he understood or not. The boy looked bewildered, as if something apparently impossible seemed to be happening. The look on his face wrenched George's heart. He thought: How can I be doing something this cruel to the person I love most in the world?

How did I get here?

"You know I've been sleeping in the guest room."

"Yeah."

Here comes the hard part. "Well, I'm going to sleep at Grandma's house tonight."

"Why?"

"It's because Mom and I don't love each other."

"Okay, then, I'll see you tomorrow."

"I'm going to be sleeping at Grandma's a lot from now on."

Jack began to see that this would affect him. "Will you read my bedtime story?"

"Every night, if you like." George vowed to keep this promise.

Jack was still working out the implications. "Will you make my warm milk for breakfast?"

"Sometimes. Or Mom will. Or Nanny Tiffany."

Jack knew prevarication when he heard it. "I don't know," he said. "I think you better not sleep at Grandma's."

George ran out of courage. "Well, we'll see," he said. "Hey, how about some ice cream?"

"Yeah!"

It was the worst day of George's life.

. . .

Driving from the Capitol homeward to Prince George's County, George brooded on hostages. This year in Lebanon, four Americans and a Frenchman had been kidnapped. One of the Americans had been released, but the rest were languishing in some prison, unless they were already dead. George knew that one of the Americans was the CIA head of station in Beirut.

The kidnappers were almost certainly a militant Muslim group called Hezbollah, "the Party of God," founded in response to the Israeli invasion of Lebanon in 1982. They had been bankrolled by Iran and trained by Iranian Revolutionary Guards. The United States regarded Hezbollah as an arm of the Iranian government, and classified Iran as a sponsor of terrorism, therefore a country that should not be allowed to buy weapons. George found that ironic, given that President Reagan was sponsoring terrorism in Nicaragua by funding the Contras, a brutal antigovernment group that carried out assassinations and kidnappings.

All the same, George was angry about what was happening in Lebanon. He wanted to send the marines into Beirut with all guns blazing. People should be taught the cost of abducting American citizens! He felt this strongly, but he knew it was an infantile response. Just as the Israeli invasion had bred Hezbollah, so a violent American attack on Hezbollah would spawn more terrorism. Another generation of young Middle Eastern men would grow up swearing revenge upon America, the great Satan. George and all thinking people realized, when the blood cooled, that revenge was self-defeating. The only answer was to break the chain.

Which was easier said than done.

George was also aware that he had personally failed that test. He had punched Jasper Murray. Jasper was no wimp, but he had sensibly resisted the temptation to fight back. As a result the damage had been limited—no credit to George.

George was living with his mother again—at the age of forty-eight! Verena was still in the family home with little Jack. George presumed that Jasper spent nights there, but he did not know for sure. He was struggling to find a way to live with divorce—just like millions of other men and women.

It was Friday night, and he turned his mind to the weekend. He was on his way to Verena's house. They had settled into a routine. George picked up Jack on Friday evening and took him to Grandma Jacky's house for the weekend, then brought him back home on Monday morning. It was not how George had wanted to raise his child, but it was the best he could manage.

He thought about what they would do. Tomorrow maybe they would go to the public library together and get some bedtime storybooks. Church on Sunday, of course.

He arrived at the ranch-style house that used to be his home. Verena's car was not in the driveway: she was not home yet. George parked and went to the front door. From politeness he rang the bell, then let himself in with his key.

The house was quiet. "It's only me," he called out. There was no one in the kitchen. He found Jack sitting in front of the TV, alone. "Hi, buddy," he said. He sat down and put his arm around Jack's shoulders. "Where's Nanny Tiffany?"

"She had to go home," Jack said. "Mommy's late."

George controlled his anger. "So you're on your own here?"

"Tiffany said it's a mergency."

"How long ago was that?"

"I don't know." Jack still could not reckon time.

George was furious. His son had been left alone in the house at the age of four. What was Verena thinking of?

He got up and looked around. Jack's weekend case stood in the hall. George checked inside and saw everything necessary: pajamas, clean clothes, teddy bear. Nanny Tiffany had done that before she left to deal with what Jack called her mergency.

He went into the kitchen and wrote a note: "I found Jack alone in the house. Call me."

Then he got Jack and went out to the car.

Jacky's house was less than a mile away. When they arrived, Jacky gave Jack a glass of milk and a homemade cookie. He told her all about the cat next door, which came to visit and got a saucer of milk. Then Jacky looked at George and said: "All right, what's eating you?"

"Step into the living room and I'll tell you." They moved to the next room, and George said: "Jack was on his own in the house."

"Oh, that should not happen."

"Damn right."

She overlooked the bad language for once. "Any idea why?"

"Verena didn't come home at the appointed time, and the nanny had to leave."

At that moment they heard a squeal of tires outside. They both looked out of the window and saw Verena getting out of her red Jaguar and running up the path to the door.

George said: "I'm going to kill her."

Jacky let her in. She ran to the kitchen and kissed Jack. "Oh, baby, are you okay?" she said tearfully.

"Yeah," said Jack nonchalantly. "I had a cookie."

"Grandma's cookies are great, aren't they?"

"You bet."

George said: "Verena, you'd better come in here and explain yourself."

She was panting and perspiring. For once she did not appear arrogantly in control. "I was only a few minutes late!" she cried. "I don't know why that goddamn nanny ran out on me!"

"You can't be late when you're looking after Jack," George said severely.

She resented that. "Oh, like you never were?"

"I never left him alone."

"It's very difficult on my own!"

"It's your damn fault you're on your own."

Jacky said: "George, you're in the wrong here."

"Stay out of this, Mom."

"No. It's my house and my grandson, and I won't stay out of anything."

"I can't overlook this, Mom! She did wrong."

"If I'd never done anything wrong, I wouldn't have you."

"That's nothing to do with it."

"I'm just saying we all make mistakes, and sometimes things turn out all right anyway. So stop beating Verena up. It won't do any good."

Reluctantly, George saw that she was right. "But what are we going to do?"

Verena said: "I'm sorry, George, but I just can't cope." She started to cry.

Jacky said: "Well, now that we've stopped yelling, maybe we can start thinking. This nanny of yours is no good."

Verena said: "You don't know how difficult it is to get a nanny! And it's worse for us than for most people. Everyone else hires illegal immigrants and pays them cash, but politicians have to have someone with a green card who pays taxes, so no one wants the job!"

"All right, calm down, I'm not blaming you," Jacky said to Verena. "Maybe I can help."

George and Verena stared at Jacky.

Jacky said: "I'm sixty-four, I'm about to retire, and I need something to do. I'll be your backup. If your nanny lets you down, just bring Jack here. Leave him here overnight when you need to."

"Boy," said George, "that sounds like a solution to me."

Verena said: "Jacky, that would be wonderful!"

"Don't thank me, honey, I'm being selfish. I'll get to see my grandson more."

George said: "Are you sure it won't be too much work, Mom?"

Jacky made a contemptuous noise. "When was the last time something was too much work for me?"

George smiled. "Never, I guess."

And that settled it.

CHAPTER FIFTY-SIX

Rebecca's tears were cold on her cheeks.

It was October, and a biting wind from the North Sea was blowing across Ohlsdorf Cemetery in Hamburg. This graveyard was one of the largest in the world, a thousand acres of sadness and mourning. It had a monument to victims of Nazi persecution, a walled grove for resistance fighters, and a mass grave for the thirty-eight thousand Hamburg men, women, and children killed in ten days by Operation Gomorrah, the Allied bombing campaign of summer 1943.

There was no special area for victims of the Wall.

Rebecca knelt down and picked up the dead leaves scattered over her husband's grave. Then she placed a single red rose on the earth.

She stood still, looking at the tombstone, remembering him.

Bernd had been dead a year. He had lived to sixty-two, which was good for a man with a spinal cord injury. In the end his kidneys had failed, a common cause of death in such cases.

Rebecca thought about his life. It had been blighted by the Wall, and by the injury he had received escaping from East Germany, but despite that he had lived well. He had been a good schoolteacher, perhaps a great one. He had defied the tyranny of East German Communism and escaped to freedom. His first marriage had ended in divorce, but he and Rebecca had loved each other passionately for twenty years.

She did not need to come here to remember him. She thought about him every day. His death was an amputation: she was constantly surprised to find he was not there. Alone in the flat they had shared for so long, she often talked to him, telling him about her day, commenting on the news, saying how she felt, hungry or tired or restless. She had not altered the place, and it still had the ropes and handles that had enabled him to move himself around. His wheelchair stood at the side of the bed as if ready for him to sit upright and haul himself into it. When she masturbated, she imagined him lying beside her, one arm around her, the warmth of his body, his lips on hers.

Fortunately her work was constantly absorbing and challenging. She was now a junior minister in the foreign affairs department of the West German government. Because she spoke Russian and had lived in East Germany she specialized in Eastern Europe. She had little free time.

Tragically, the reunification of Germany seemed ever farther away. Die-hard East German leader Erich Honecker appeared unassailable. People were still being killed trying to escape across the Wall. And in the Soviet Union the death of Andropov had only brought in yet another ailing septuagenarian leader, Konstantin Chernenko. From Berlin to Vladivostok, the Soviet empire was a bog in which its citizens struggled and often sank but never made progress.

Rebecca realized her mind had wandered from Bernd. It was time to go. "Good-bye, my love," she said softly, and she walked slowly away from the grave.

She pulled her heavy coat around her and folded her arms as she crossed the cold cemetery. She gratefully got into her vehicle and turned on the engine. She was still driving the van with the wheelchair hoist. It was time she traded it in for a normal car.

She drove to her apartment. Outside her building was a shiny black Mercedes S500, with a chauffeur in a cap standing beside it. Her spirits lifted. As she expected, she found that Walli had let himself into the apartment with his own key. He was sitting at the kitchen table with the radio on, tapping his foot to a pop song. On the table was a copy of Plum Nellie's latest album, *The Interpretation of Dreams.* "I'm glad I caught you," he said. "I'm on my way to the airport. I'm flying to San Francisco." He stood up to kiss her.

He would be forty in a couple of years, and he looked great. He still smoked, but he never took drugs or alcohol. He was wearing a tan leather jacket over a blue denim shirt. Some girl ought to snap him up, Rebecca thought; but although he had girlfriends he seemed in no hurry to settle down.

When she kissed him she touched his arm and noticed that the leather of his jacket was as soft as silk. It had probably cost a fortune. She said: "But you've only just finished your album."

"We're doing a tour of the States. I'm going to Daisy Farm for three weeks of rehearsal. We open in Philadelphia in a month."

"Give the boys my love."

"Sure will."

"It's a while since you toured."

"Three years. Hence the long rehearsal. But stadium gigs are where it's at now. It's not like the All-Star Touring Beat Revue, with twelve bands playing two or three songs each to a couple of thousand people in a theater or gymnasium. It's just fifty thousand people and us."

"Will you do some European dates?"

"Yes, but they haven't been fixed yet."

"Any in Germany?"

"Almost certainly."

"Let me know."

"Of course. I may be able to get you a free ticket."

Rebecca laughed. As Walli's sister she was treated like royalty whenever she went backstage at a Plum Nellie gig. The band had often talked in interviews about the old days in Hamburg, and how Walli's big sister used to give them their only good meal of the week. For that she was famous in the world of rock and roll.

"Have a great tour," she said.

"You're about to fly to Budapest, aren't you?"

"For a trade conference, yes."

"Will there be some East Germans there?"

"Yes, why?"

"Do you think one of them might be able to get an album to Alice?"

Rebecca grimaced. "I don't know. My relations with East German politicians are not warm. They think I'm a lackey of the capitalist-imperialists, and I think they are unelected thugs who rule by terror and keep their people imprisoned."

Walli smiled. "So, not much common ground, then."

"No. But I'll try."

"Thanks." He handed her the disc.

Rebecca looked at the photograph on the sleeve, of four middle-aged men with long hair and blue jeans. Buzz, the randy bass player, was overweight. The gay drummer, Lew, was losing his hair. Dave, the leader of the band, had a touch of gray in his hair. They were established, successful, and rich. She remembered the hungry kids who had come here to this apartment: thin, scruffy, witty, charming, and full of hopes and dreams. "You've done well," she said.

"Yeah," said Walli. "We have."

. . .

On the last evening of the Budapest conference, Rebecca and the other delegates were given a tasting of Tokaj wines. They were taken to a cellar owned by the Hungarian government bottling organization. It was in the Pest district, east of the Danube River. They were offered several different kinds of white wine: dry; strong; the lightly alcoholic nectar called *eszencia;* and the famous slow-fermented *aszú.*

All over the world, government officials were bad at throwing parties, and Rebecca feared this would be a dull occasion. However, the old cellar with its arched ceilings and stacked cases of booze had a cozy feel, and there were spicy Hungarian snacks of dumplings, stuffed mushrooms, and sausages.

Rebecca picked out one of the East German delegates and gave him her most engaging smile. "Our German wines are superior, don't you think?" she said.

She chatted flirtatiously with him for a few minutes, then asked him the question. "I have a niece in East Berlin, and I want to send her a pop record, but I'm afraid it might get damaged in the mail. Would you take it for me?"

"Yes, I suppose I could," he said dubiously.

"I'll give it to you tomorrow at breakfast, if I may. You're very kind."

"Okay." He looked troubled, and Rebecca thought there was a chance he might hand over the disc to the Stasi. But all she could do was try.

When the wine had relaxed everyone, Rebecca was approached by Frederik Bíró, a Hungarian politician of her own age whom she liked. He specialized in foreign policy, as she did. "What's the truth about this country?" she asked him. "How is it doing, really?"

He looked at his watch. "We're about a mile from your hotel," he said. He spoke good German, like most educated Hungarians. "Would you like to walk back with me?"

They got their coats and left. Their route followed the broad, dark river. On the far bank, the lights of the medieval town of Buda rose romantically to a hilltop palace.

"The Communists promised prosperity, and the people are disappointed," Bíró said as they walked. "Even Communist Party members complain about the Kádár government." Rebecca guessed that he felt freer to talk out in the open air where they could not be bugged.

She said: "And the solution?"

"The strange thing is that everyone knows the answer. We need to decentralize decisions, introduce limited markets, and legitimize the semi-illegal gray economy so that it can grow."

"Who stands in the way of this?" She realized she was firing questions at him like a courtroom lawyer. "Forgive me," she said. "I don't mean to interrogate you."

"Not at all," he said with a smile. "I like people who speak in a direct way. It saves time."

"Men often resent being spoken to that way by a woman."

"Not me. You could say that I have a weakness for assertive women."

"Are you married to one?"

"I was. I'm divorced now."

Rebecca realized this was none of her business. "You were about to tell me who stands in the way of reform."

"About fifteen thousand bureaucrats who would lose their power and their jobs; fifty thousand top Communist Party officials who make almost all the decisions; and János Kádár, who has been our leader since 1956."

Rebecca raised her eyebrows. Bíró was being remarkably frank. The thought crossed her mind that Bíró's candid remarks may not have been totally spontaneous. Had this conversation perhaps been planned? She said: "Does Kádár have an alternative solution?"

"Yes," said Bíró. "To maintain the standard of living of Hungarian workers, he is borrowing more and more money from Western banks, including German ones."

"And how will you pay the interest on those loans?"

"What a good question," said Bíró.

They drew level with Rebecca's hotel, across the street from the river. She stopped and leaned on the embankment wall. "Is Kádár a permanent fixture?"

"Not necessarily. I'm close to a promising young man called Miklós Németh."

Ah, Rebecca thought, so this is the point of the conversation: to tell the German government, quietly and informally, that Németh is the reformist rival to Kádár.

"He's in his thirties, and very bright," Bíró continued. "But we fear a Hungarian repeat of the Soviet situation: Brezhnev replaced by Andropov and then Chernenko. It's like the queue for the toilet in a home for old men."

Rebecca laughed. She liked Bíró.

He bent his head and kissed her.

She was only half surprised. She had sensed that he was attracted to her. What surprised her was how excited she felt to be kissed. She kissed him back eagerly.

Then she drew back. She put her hands on his chest and pushed him away a little. She studied him in the lamplight. No man of fifty looked like Adonis, but Frederik had a face that suggested intelligence and compassion and the ability to smile wryly at life's ironies. He had gray hair cut short and blue eyes. He was wearing a dark blue coat and a bright red scarf, conservatism with a touch of gaiety.

She said: "Why did you get divorced?"

"I had an affair, and my wife left me. Feel free to condemn me."

"No," she said. "I've made mistakes."

"I regretted it, when it was too late."

"Children?"

"Two, grown up. They have forgiven me. Marta has remarried, but I'm still single. What's your story?"

"I divorced my first husband when I discovered he worked for the Stasi. My second husband was injured escaping over the Berlin Wall. He was in a wheelchair, but we were happy together for twenty years. He died a year ago."

"My word, you're about due for some good luck."

"Perhaps I am. Would you walk me to the hotel entrance, please?"

They crossed the road. On the corner of the block, where the streetlights were less glaring, she kissed him again. She enjoyed it even more this time, and pressed her body against his.

"Spend the night with me," he said.

She was sorely tempted. "No," she said. "It's too soon. I hardly know you."

"But you're going home tomorrow."

"I know."

"We may never meet again."

"I'm sure we will."

"We could go to my apartment. Or I'll come to your room."

"No, though I'm flattered by your persistence. Good night."

"Good night, then."

She turned away.

He said: "I travel often to Bonn. I'll be there in ten days' time."

She turned back, smiling.

He said: "Will you have dinner with me?"

"I'd love to," she said. "Call me."

"Okay."

She walked into the hotel lobby, smiling.

.   .   .

Lili was at home in Berlin-Mitte one afternoon when her niece, Alice, came, in a rainstorm, to borrow books. Alice had been refused admission to university, despite her outstanding grades, because of her mother's underground career as a protest singer. However, Alice was determined to educate herself, so she was studying English in the evenings after she finished her shift at the factory. Carla had a small collection of English-language novels inherited from Grandmother Maud. They went upstairs to the drawing room and looked through the books together while the rain drummed on the windows. They were old editions, prewar, Lili guessed. Alice picked out a collection of Sherlock Holmes stories. She would be the fourth generation to read them, Lili calculated.

Alice said: "We've applied for permission to go to West Germany." She was all youthful eagerness.

"We?" Lili asked.

"Helmut and I."

Helmut Kappel was her boyfriend. He was a year older, twenty-two, and studying at university.

"Any special reason?"

"I've said we want to visit my father in Hamburg. Helmut's grandparents are in Frankfurt. But Plum Nellie is doing a world tour, and we really want to see my father onstage. Maybe we can time our visit to coincide with his German gig, if he does one."

"I'm sure he will."

"Do you think they'll let us go?"

"You may be lucky." Lili did not want to discourage youthful optimism, but she was doubtful. She herself had always been refused permission. Very few people were allowed to go. The authorities would suspect that people as young as Alice and Helmut did not intend to come back.

Lili suspected it herself. Alice had often talked wistfully of living in West Germany. Like most young people, she wanted to read uncensored books and newspapers, see new films and plays, and listen to music regardless of whether it was approved by the seventy-two-year-old Erich Honecker. If she managed to get out of East Germany, why would she come back?

Alice said: "You know, most of the things that got this family into bad odor with the authorities actually happened before I was born. They shouldn't be punishing me."

But her mother, Karolin, was still singing those songs, Lili thought.

The doorbell sounded, and a minute later they heard agitated voices in the hall. They went downstairs to investigate, and found Karolin standing there in a wet raincoat. Inexplicably, she was carrying a suitcase. She had been let in by Carla, who stood beside her in the hall, wearing an apron over her formal work clothes.

Karolin's face was red and puffy with crying.

Alice said: "Mother . . . ?"

Lili said: "Has something happened?"

Karolin said: "Alice, your stepfather has left me."

Lili was flabbergasted. Odo Vossler? It was surprising to her that mild Odo had the guts to leave his wife.

Alice put her arms around her mother, saying nothing.

Carla said: "When did this happen?"

Karolin wiped her nose with a handkerchief. "He told me three hours ago. He wants a divorce."

Lili thought: Poor Alice, left by two fathers.

Carla said indignantly: "But pastors are not supposed to get divorced."

"He's leaving the clergy, too."

"Good grief."

Lili realized that an earthquake had struck the family.

Carla became practical. "You'd better sit down. We'll go in the kitchen. Alice, take your mother's coat and hang it up to dry. Lili, make coffee."

Lili put water on to boil and took a cake out of the cupboard. Carla said: "Karolin, whatever has come over Odo?"

She looked down. "He is . . ." She obviously found this difficult to say. Averting her eyes, she said quietly: "Odo tells me he has realized that he is homosexual."

Alice gave a little scream.

Carla said: "What a terrible shock!"

Lili had a sudden flash of memory. Five years ago, when they had all met up in Hungary, and Walli had met Odo for the first time, she had seen a startled reaction pass over Walli's face, brief but vivid. Had Walli intuited the truth about Odo in that moment?

Lili herself had always suspected that Odo's love for Karolin was not a grand passion but more of a Christian mission. If a man should ever propose to Lili, she did not want him to do it out of the kindness of his heart. He should desire her so much he could hardly keep his hands off her: that was a good reason for a proposal of marriage.

Karolin looked up. Now that the awful truth was out, she was able to meet Carla's eye. "It's not a shock, really," she said quietly. "I sort of knew."

"How?"

"When we were first married, there was a young man called Paul, very good-looking. He was invited for supper a couple of times a week, and Bible study in the vestry, and on Saturday afternoons they would go for long, invigorating walks in Treptower Park. Perhaps they never did anything—Odo is not a deceiving man. But, when he made love to me, somehow I felt sure he was thinking about Paul."

"What happened? How did it end?"

Lili cut the cake into slices while she listened. She put the slices on a plate. No one ate any.

Karolin said: "I never knew the full story. Paul stopped coming to the house and to church. Odo never explained why. Perhaps they both pulled back from physical love."

Carla said: "Being a pastor, Odo must have suffered a terrible conflict."

"I know. I'm so sorry for him, when I'm not feeling angry."

"Poor Odo."

"But Paul was only the first of half a dozen boys, all very similar, terribly good-looking and sincere Christians."

"And now?"

"Now Odo has found real love. He is abjectly apologetic to me, but he has made up his mind to face what he truly is. He's moving in with a man called Eugen Freud."

"What will he do?"

"He wants to be a teacher in a theological college. He says it's his real vocation."

Lili poured boiling water on the ground coffee in the jug. Now that Odo and Karolin had split up, she wondered how Walli would feel. Of course he could not be reunited with Karolin and Alice because of the accursed Berlin Wall. But would he want to? He had not settled permanently with another woman. It seemed to Lili that Karolin really was the love of his life.

But all that was academic. The Communists had decreed that they could not be together.

Carla said: "If Odo has resigned as pastor, you'll have to leave your house."

"Yes. I'm homeless."

"Don't be silly. You'll always have a home here."

"I knew you'd say that," said Karolin, and she burst into tears.

The doorbell rang.

"I'll go," said Lili.

There were two men on the doorstep. One wore a chauffeur's uniform and held an umbrella over the other man, who was Hans Hoffmann.

"May I come in?" said Hans, but he walked into the hall without waiting for an answer. He was holding a package about a foot square.

His driver returned to the black ZIL limousine parked at the curb.

Lili spoke with distaste. "What do you want?"

"To speak to your niece, Alice."

"How did you know she was here?"

Hans smiled and did not bother to answer. The Stasi knew everything.

Lili went into the kitchen. "It's Hans Hoffmann. He wants Alice."

Alice stood up, pale with fear.

Carla said: "Take him upstairs, Lili. Stay with them."

Karolin half-rose out of her chair. "I should go with her."

Carla put a restraining hand on Karolin's arm. "You're in no state to deal with the Stasi."

Karolin accepted that and sat back down again. Lili held the door for Alice, who came out of the kitchen into the hall. The two women went upstairs, followed by Hans.

Lili almost offered Hans a cup of coffee, from automatic politeness, but she stopped herself. He could die of thirst first.

Hans picked up the Sherlock Holmes book Alice had left on the table. "English," he commented, as if that confirmed a suspicion. He sat down, tugging on the knees of his fine wool trousers to prevent creasing. He put the square packet on the floor beside his chair. He said: "So, young Alice, you wish to travel to West Germany. Why?"

He was a big shot now. Lili did not know what his exact title was, but he was more than just a secret policeman. He made speeches at national meetings and spoke to the press. However, he was not too important to persecute the Franck family.

"My father lives in Hamburg," Alice said in answer to his question. "So does my aunt Rebecca."

"Your father is a murderer."

"It happened before I was born. Are you punishing me for it? That isn't what you mean by Communist justice . . . is it?"

Hans gave that smug I-thought-so nod again. "A smart mouth, just like your grandmother. This family will never learn."

Lili said angrily: "We have learned that Communism means petty officials can take their revenge, without regard to justice or the law."

"Do you imagine that such talk is the way to persuade me to grant Alice permission to travel?"

"You've made up your mind already," Lili said wearily. "You're going to refuse. You wouldn't have come here to say yes to her. You just want to gloat."

Alice said: "Where in the writings of Karl Marx do we read that in the Communist state workers are not allowed to travel to other countries?"

"Restrictions are made necessary by the conditions prevailing."

"No, they're not. I want to see my father. You prevent me. Why? Just because you can! That has nothing to do with socialism and everything to do with tyranny."

Hans's mouth twisted. "You bourgeois people," he said in tones of disgust. "You can't bear it when others have power over you."

"Bourgeois?" said Lili. "I don't have a uniformed chauffeur to hold an umbrella over me while I walk from the car to the house. Nor does Alice. There's only one bourgeois in this room, Hans."

He picked up the package and handed it to Alice. "Open it," he said.

Alice took off the brown paper wrapping. Inside was a copy of Plum Nellie's latest album, *The Interpretation of Dreams.* Her face lit up.

Lili wondered what trick Hans was up to now.

"Why don't you play your father's record?" Hans said.

Alice withdrew the inner white envelope from the colored sleeve. Then with finger and thumb she took the black plastic disc from the envelope.

It came out in two pieces.

Hans said: "It seems to be broken. What a shame."

Alice began to cry.

Hans stood up. "I know the way out," he said, and he left.

. . .

Unter den Linden was the broad boulevard through East Berlin to the
Brandenburg Gate. Under another name, the street continued into
West Berlin through the park called the Tiergarten. Since 1961, though,
Unter den Linden had dead-ended at the Brandenburg Gate, blocked by
the Berlin Wall. From the park on the west side, the view of the
Brandenburg Gate was disfigured by a high, ugly, gray-green fence
covered with graffiti, and a sign in German that said:

WARNING

YOU ARE NOW LEAVING

WEST BERLIN

Beyond the fence was the killing field of the Wall.

Plum Nellie's road crew built a stage right up against the ugly fence
and stacked a mighty wall of loudspeakers facing out into the park. On
Walli's instructions, equally powerful speakers faced the other way, into
East Berlin. He wanted Alice to hear him. A reporter had told him that
the East German government objected to the speakers. "Tell them that
if they take their wall down, I'll do the same with mine," Walli had said,
and the quote was in all the papers.

Originally they had thought to do the German gig in Hamburg, but
then Walli had heard about Hans Hoffmann breaking Alice's disc, and
in retaliation he had asked Dave to reschedule in Berlin, so that a
million East Germans would be able to hear the songs Hoffmann had
attempted to deny to Alice. Dave had loved the idea.

Now they stood together, looking at the stage from the side as
thousands of fans gathered in the park. "This is going to be the loudest
we've ever been," said Dave.

"Good," said Walli. "I want them to hear my guitar all the way to
fucking Leipzig."

"Remember the old days?" Dave said. "Those tinny little speakers
they had in baseball stadiums?"

"No one could hear us—we couldn't hear ourselves!"

"Now a hundred thousand people can listen to music that sounds
the way we intended."

"It's kind of a miracle."

When Walli returned to his dressing room, Rebecca was there. "This is fantastic," she said. "There must be a hundred thousand people in the park!"

She was with a gray-haired man of about her own age. "This is my friend Fred Bíró," she said.

Walli shook his hand, and Fred said: "It's an honor to meet you." He spoke German with a Hungarian accent.

Walli was amused. So his sister was dating at the age of fifty-three! Well, good for her. The guy seemed to be her type, intellectual but not too solemn. And she looked younger, with a Princess Diana hairstyle and a purple dress.

They chatted for a while, then left him to get ready. Walli changed into clean blue jeans and a flame red shirt. Peering into the mirror, he put on eyeliner so that the crowd could read his expression better. He remembered with disgust the times when he had had to manage his drug intake so carefully: a small amount to keep him level during the performance, and a big hit afterward as his reward. He was not for one second tempted to return to those habits.

He was called to go onstage. He joined up with Dave, Buzz, and Lew. Dave's whole family was there to wish them well: his wife, Beep; their eleven-year-old son, John Lee; Dave's parents, Daisy and Lloyd; and even his sister, Evie; all looking proud of their Dave. Walli was glad to see them all, but their presence reminded him poignantly that he was not able to see his own family: Werner and Carla, Lili, Karolin and Alice.

But with any luck they would be listening on the other side of the Wall.

The band went onstage and the crowd roared their welcome.

.   .   .

Unter den Linden was jammed with thousands of Plum Nellie fans, old and young. Lili and her family, including Karolin, Alice, and Alice's boyfriend, Helmut, had been there since early morning. They had secured a position close to the barrier the police had set up to keep the crowd at a distance from the Wall. As the crowd had grown through the day, the street had developed a festival atmosphere, with people talking to strangers and sharing their picnics and playing Plum Nellie tapes on portable boom boxes. As darkness fell they opened bottles of beer and wine.

Then the band came on, and the crowd went wild.

East Berliners could see nothing but the four bronze horses pulling Victory's chariot atop the arch. But they could hear everything loud and clear: Lew's drumming; Buzz's thudding bass; Dave's rhythm guitar and high harmonies; and, best of all, Walli's perfect pop baritone and lyrical guitar lines. The familiar songs soared out of the speaker stacks and thrilled the moving, dancing crowd. That's my brother, Lili kept thinking; my big brother, singing to the world. Werner and Carla looked proud, Karolin was smiling, and Alice's eyes were shining.

Lili glanced up at a government office building nearby. Standing on a small balcony were half a dozen men in ties and dark coats, clearly visible by the streetlights. They were not dancing. One was taking photographs of the crowd. They must be Stasi, Lili realized. They were making a record of traitors disloyal to the Honecker regime—which was, nowadays, almost everyone.

Looking more closely, she thought she recognized one of the secret policemen. It was Hans Hoffmann, she was almost sure. He was tall and slightly stooped. He seemed to be speaking angrily, moving his right arm in a violent hammering gesture. Walli had said in an interview that the band wanted to play here because East Germans were not allowed to listen to their records. Hans must have known that his breaking Alice's disc was the reason for this concert and this crowd. No wonder he was angry.

She saw Hans throw up his hands in despair, turn, and leave the balcony, disappearing into the building. One song ended and another began. The crowd yelled their approval as they recognized the opening chords of one of Plum Nellie's biggest hits. Walli's voice came through the speakers: "This one is for my little girl."

Then he sang "I Miss Ya, Alicia."

Lili looked at Alice. Tears were streaming down her face, but she was smiling.

CHAPTER FIFTY-SEVEN

William Buckley, the American kidnapped in Lebanon by Hezbollah on March 16, 1984, was officially described as a political officer at the U.S. embassy in Beirut. In fact he was the CIA head of station.

Cam Dewar knew Bill Buckley and thought he was a good guy. Bill was a slight figure in conservative Brooks Brothers suits. He had a head of thick graying hair and matinee-idol looks. A career soldier, he had fought in Korea and served with the Special Forces in Vietnam, ending with the rank of colonel. In the sixties he had joined the Special Activities Division of the CIA. That was the division that carried out assassinations.

Bill was single at fifty-seven. According to Langley gossip, he had a long-distance relationship with a woman called Candace in Farmer, North Carolina. She wrote him love letters and he telephoned her from all over the world. When he was in the USA, they were lovers. Or so people said.

Like everyone else at Langley, Cam was angry about the kidnapping and desperate to get Bill released. But all efforts failed.

And there was worse news. One by one, Bill's agents and informers in Beirut began to disappear. Hezbollah had to be getting their names from Bill. That meant he was being tortured.

The CIA knew Hezbollah's methods, and they could guess what was happening to Bill. He would be permanently blindfolded, chained at the ankles and wrists, and kept in a box like a coffin, day after day, week after week. After a few months of this he would be literally insane: drooling, gibbering, trembling, rolling his eyes, and letting out sudden random screams of terror.

So Cam was savagely pleased when at last someone came up with a plan of action against the kidnappers.

The plan originated not with the CIA, but with the president's national security adviser, Bud McFarlane. On his staff Bud had a gung-ho marine lieutenant colonel called Oliver North, known as Ollie. Among the men North had recruited to help him was Tim Tedder, and it was Tim who told Cam of McFarlane's plan.

Cam eagerly took Tim into the office of Florence Geary. Tim was a former CIA agent and an old acquaintance of Florence's. As always, he had his hair cut as if he were still in the army, and today he wore a safari suit that was as close to a military uniform as civilian dress could get.

"We're going to work with foreign nationals," Tim explained. "There will be three teams, each of five men. They won't be CIA employees and they won't even be Americans. But the Agency will train them, equip them, and arrange finance."

Florence nodded. "And what will these teams do?" she said neutrally.

"The idea is to get to the kidnappers before they strike," Tim said. "When we know that they're planning a kidnapping, or a bombing, or any other kind of terrorist act—we will direct one of the teams to go in and eliminate the perpetrators."

"Let me get this straight," said Florence. "These teams will kill terrorists *before* they commit crimes."

She was not as excited by the plan as Cam was, evidently, and he had a bad feeling.

"Exactly," said Tim.

"I have one question," said Florence. "Are you two out of your fucking minds?"

Cam was outraged. How could Florence be against this?

Tim said indignantly: "I know it's unconventional—"

"Unconventional?" Florence interrupted. "By the laws of every civilized country it's *murder*. There is no due process, there is no requirement of proof, and by your own admission the people you're targeting may have done nothing more than merely *think* about committing crimes."

Cam said: "Actually, it's not murder. We'd be acting like a cop who gets off an early shot at a criminal who is pointing a gun at him. It's called preemptive self-defense."

"So you're a lawyer, now, Cam."

"That's not my opinion, it's Sporkin's." Stanley Sporkin was the CIA general counsel.

"Well, Stan's wrong," said Florence. "Because we never see a pointed gun. We have no way of knowing who is about to commit a terrorist act. We don't have intelligence of that quality in Lebanon—we never have. So we'll end up killing people who we *think* might be planning terrorism."

"Perhaps we can improve the reliability of our information."

"What about the reliability of the foreign nationals? Who will be on these five-man teams? Local Beirut bad guys? Mercenaries? International-security-company Eurotrash? How can you trust them? How can you *control* them? Yet whatever they do will be our responsibility—especially if they kill innocent people!"

Tim said: "No, no—the whole operation will be arm's length and deniable."

"It doesn't sound very deniable to me. The CIA is going to train and equip them and finance their activities. And have you thought of the political consequences?"

"Fewer kidnappings and bombings."

"How can you be so naïve? If we strike at Hezbollah this way, you think they will sit back and say: 'Gosh, the Americans are tougher than we thought, maybe we'd better give up this whole terrorism idea.' No, no. They will be screaming for revenge! In the Middle East, violence always begets more violence—haven't you learned that yet? Hezbollah bombed the marine corps barracks in Beirut—why? According to Colonel Geraghty, who was the marine commander at the time, it was in response to the U.S. Sixth Fleet shelling innocent Muslims in the village of Suq al-Gharb. One atrocity brings another."

"So you're just going to give in and say nothing can be done?"

"Nothing *easy* can be done, just hard political work. We lower the temperature, we restrain both sides, and we bring them to the negotiating table, again and again, no matter how many times they walk out. We don't give up and, whatever happens, we don't escalate the violence."

"I think we can—"

But Florence was not yet done. "This plan is criminal, it's impractical, it has horrendous political consequences in the Middle East, and it endangers the reputations of the CIA, the president, and the USA. But that is not all. There is yet one more thing that completely rules it out."

She paused, and Cam was forced to say: "What?"

"We are forbidden *by the president* to carry out assassinations. 'No person employed by or acting on behalf of the United States Government shall engage in, or conspire to engage in, assassination.' Executive Order 12333. Ronald Reagan signed it in 1981."

"I think he's forgotten that," said Cam.

. . .

Maria met Florence Geary in downtown Washington at the Woodward and Lothrop department store, which everyone called Woodies. Their rendezvous was in the brassiere department. Most agents were men, and any man who followed them in here would be conspicuous. He might even get arrested.

"I used to be size thirty-four A," said Florence. "Now I'm thirty-six C. What happened?"

Maria chuckled. At forty-eight she was a little older than Florence. "Join the club of middle-aged women," she said. "I always had a big ass, but I used to have cute little boobs that stood up all on their own. Now I need serious support."

In two decades in Washington, Maria had assiduously cultivated contacts. She had learned early on how much was achieved—for good or ill—through personal acquaintance. Back in the days when the CIA had been using Florence as a secretary, instead of training her to be an agent as they had promised, Maria had sympathized with her plight, woman to woman. Maria's contacts were usually women, always liberal. She exchanged information with them, giving early warning of threatening moves by political opponents, and helped them discreetly, often by assigning higher priority to projects that might otherwise be sidelined by conservative men. The men did much the same.

They each picked out half a dozen bras and went to try them on. It was a Tuesday morning, and the changing room was empty. Nevertheless, Florence kept her voice low. "Bud McFarlane has come up with a plan that is complete madness," she said as she unbuttoned her blouse. "But Bill Casey committed the CIA." Casey, a crony of President Reagan's, was head of the CIA. "And the president said yes."

"What plan?"

"We're training assassination squads of foreign nationals to kill terrorists in Beirut. They call it preemptive counterterrorism."

Maria was shocked. "But that's a crime, by the laws of this country. If they succeed, McFarlane and Casey and Ronald Reagan will all be murderers."

"Exactly."

The two women took off the bras they were wearing and stood side by side in front of the mirror. "You see?" said Florence. "They've lost that sit-up-and-beg look."

"Mine, too."

There was a time, Maria reflected, when she would have been too embarrassed to do this with a white woman. Maybe things really were changing.

They started to try on the bras. Maria said: "Has Casey briefed the intelligence committees?"

"No. Reagan decided he could just inform the chair and vice chair of each committee, and the Republican and Democratic leaders of the House and Senate."

That explained why George Jakes had not heard about this, Maria deduced. Reagan had made a sly move. The intelligence committees had a quota of liberals, to ensure that at least some critical questions were asked. Reagan had found a way to sideline the critics and inform only those he knew would be supportive.

Florence said: "One of the teams is here in the States right now, on a two-week training course."

"So the whole thing is quite far advanced."

"Right." Florence looked at herself in a black bra. "My Frank is pleased that my bust has changed. He always wanted a wife with big tits. He claims he's going to church to thank God."

Maria laughed. "You have a nice husband. I hope he likes your new bras."

"And what about you? Who will appreciate your underwear?"

"You know me, I'm a career girl."

"Were you always?"

"There was a guy, a long time ago, but he died."

"I'm so sorry."

"Thank you."

"And no one else since?"

She hardly hesitated. "One near miss. You know, I like men, and I like sex, but I'm not prepared to give up my whole life and become an appendage to some guy. Your Frank obviously understands that, but not many men do."

Florence nodded. "Honey, you got that right."

Maria frowned. "What do you want me to do about these murder squads?" The thought occurred to her that Florence was a secret agent, after all, and she might have found out, or guessed, that Maria had leaked stories to Jasper Murray. Did she want Maria to leak this one?

But Florence said: "I don't want you to do anything, right now. The plan is still a stupid idea that may be nipped in the bud. I just want to be sure that someone outside the intelligence community knows about it. If the shit hits the fan, and Reagan starts lying about murder the way Nixon lied about burglary, at least you will know the truth."

"Meanwhile, we just pray that it never happens."

"Amen."

. . .

"We've selected our first target," said Tim Tedder to Cam. "We're going for the big guy."

"Fadlallah?"

"Himself."

Cam nodded. Muhammad Hussein Fadlallah was a leading Muslim scholar and a grand ayatollah. In his sermons he called for armed resistance to the Israeli occupation of Lebanon. Hezbollah said he was their inspiration, no more, but the CIA was convinced he was the mastermind behind the kidnapping campaign. Cam would be glad to see him dead.

Cam and Tim were sitting in Cam's office at Langley. On his desk was a framed photograph of himself with President Nixon, deep in conversation. Langley was one of the few places where a man could still be proud of having worked for Nixon. "Is Fadlallah planning more kidnappings?" Cam asked.

Tim said: "Is the Pope planning more baptisms?"

"What about the team? Are they trustworthy? Are they under control?" Florence Geary's objections had been overruled, but her misgivings had not been stupid, and Cam was now remembering what she had said.

Tim sighed. "Cam, if they were trustworthy, responsible people who respected legitimate authority, they wouldn't be available for hire as paid assassins. They are as reliable as such people ever are. And we have them more or less under control, for now."

"Well, at least we're not financing them. I got the money from the Saudis—three million dollars."

Tim raised his eyebrows. "That was well done."

"Thanks."

"We might consider putting the whole project technically under the control of Saudi intelligence, to improve deniability."

"Good idea. But even then we'll need a cover story, after Fadlallah is killed."

Tim thought for a minute, then said: "Let's blame Israel."

"Yeah."

"Everyone will readily believe the Mossad did a thing like this."

Cam frowned uneasily. "I'm still worried. I wish I knew exactly how they were going to do it."

"Better if you don't know."

"I have to know. I might go to Lebanon. Get a closer look."

"If you do," said Tim, "go carefully."

. . .

Cam rented a white Toyota Corolla and drove south from the center of Beirut to the mostly Muslim suburb of Bir el-Abed. It was a jungle of ugly concrete apartment buildings interspersed with handsome mosques, each mosque on its broad lot, like a gracious specimen tree carefully cultivated in a clearing amid a crowded forest of rough pines. Poor though the country was, the traffic in the narrow streets was heavy, and the shops and street stalls were besieged by crowds. It was hot, and the Toyota had no air-conditioning, but Cam drove with the windows closed, fearful of contact with the unruly population.

He had visited the district once before, with a CIA guide, and he quickly found the street where Ayatollah Fadlallah lived. Cam drove slowly past the high-rise apartment building, then went all around the block and parked a hundred yards before the building on the opposite side of the road.

On the same street were several more apartment buildings, a cinema, and, most importantly, a mosque. Every afternoon at the same time, Fadlallah walked from his apartment building to the mosque for prayers.

That was when they would kill him.

No foul-ups, please, God, Cam prayed.

Along the short stretch of street Fadlallah would have to follow, cars were parked nose to tail at the curb. One of those cars contained a bomb. Cam did not know which.

Somewhere nearby the trigger man was concealed, watching the street like Cam, waiting for the ayatollah. Cam scanned the cars and the overlooking windows. He did not spot the trigger man. That was good. The assassin was well concealed, as he should be.

Cam had been assured by the Saudis that no innocent bystanders would be hurt. Fadlallah was always surrounded by bodyguards: some of them would undoubtedly suffer injury, but they always kept the general public well away from their leader.

Cam worried whether the bomb's effects could be predicted so accurately. But civilians were sometimes hurt in a war. Look at all the Japanese women and children killed at Hiroshima and Nagasaki. Of course, the United States had been at war with Japan, which it was not with Lebanon; but Cam told himself that the same principle applied. If a few passersby suffered cuts and bruises, the end surely justified the means.

Still, he was alarmed by the number of pedestrians. A car bomb was more suited to a lonely location. Here, a marksman with a high-powered rifle would have been a better choice.

Too late now.

He looked at his watch. Fadlallah was behind schedule. That was unnerving. Cam wished he would hurry.

There seemed to be a lot of women and girls on the street, and Cam wondered why. A minute later he figured out that they were coming out of the mosque. There must have been some special event for females, the Muslim equivalent of a mothers' meeting. Unfortunately they were crowding the damn street. The squad might have to abort the explosion.

Now Cam hoped that Fadlallah would be even later.

He scanned the cityscape again, looking for an alert man concealing some kind of radio-operated triggering mechanism. This time he thought he spotted the man. Three hundred yards away, opposite the mosque, a first-floor window stood open in the side wall of a tenement. Cam would not have noticed the man but that the afternoon sun, moving down the western sky, had shifted the shadows to reveal the figure. Cam could not make out the man's features but recognized his body language: tense, poised, waiting, scared, two hands grasping something that might have been a transistor radio with a long retractable aerial, except that no one held on to a transistor radio for dear life.

More and more women came out of the mosque, some wearing only the hijab head scarf, others in the all-concealing burqa. They thronged the sidewalks in both directions. Soon, Cam hoped, the rush would be over.

He looked toward Fadlallah's building and saw, to his horror, that the ayatollah was coming out, surrounded by six or seven other men.

Fadlallah was a small old man with a long white beard. He wore a round black hat and white robes. His face had an alert, intelligent expression, and he was smiling slightly at something a companion was saying as they left the building and turned into the street.

"No," said Cam aloud. "Not now. Not now!"

He looked along the street. The sidewalks were still crowded with women and girls, talking, laughing, showing in their smiles and gestures the relief felt by people on leaving a holy place after a solemn service. Their duty was done, their souls were refreshed, and they were ready to resume the worldly life, looking forward to the evening ahead, to supper, conversation, amusement, family, and friends.

Except that some of them were going to die.

Cam jumped out of his car.

He waved frantically toward the tenement window where the trigger man lurked, but there was no response. It was hardly surprising: Cam was too far away, and the man was concentrating on Fadlallah.

Cam looked across the street. Fadlallah was walking away from Cam, toward the mosque and the assassin's lair, at a brisk pace. The explosion had to be seconds away.

Cam ran along the street toward the tenement building, but his progress was slow because of the crowds of women. He drew curious and hostile looks, an obvious American running through a throng of Muslim women. He drew level with Fadlallah and saw one of the bodyguards point him out to another. Before many more seconds passed, someone would accost him.

He ran on, throwing caution to the winds. Fifty feet from the tenement he stopped, shouted, and waved at the assassin in the window. He could see the man clearly now, a young Arab with a wispy beard and a terrified expression. "Don't do it!" Cam yelled, knowing he was now hazarding his own life. "Abort, abort! For the love of God, abort!"

From behind, someone seized him by the shoulder and said something aggressive in harsh Arabic.

Then there was a tremendous bang.

Cam was thrown flat.

He was breathless, as if someone had hit him on the back with a plank. His head hurt. He could hear screams, men cursing, and the sliding sound of falling rubble. He rolled over, gasping, and struggled to his feet. He was alive, and as far as he could tell not seriously hurt. An Arab man lay motionless at his feet, probably the person who had grabbed him by the shoulder. The man had taken the full force of the blast, his body shielding Cam, it seemed.

He looked across the street.

"Oh, my Jesus," he said.

There were bodies everywhere, horribly twisted and bloodied and broken. Those not lying still were staggering, stanching wounds, screaming, and looking for their loved ones. Some people's loose Middle Eastern clothing had been blown away, and many of the women were half-naked in the true obscenity of violent death.

Two apartment buildings had their fronts destroyed, and masonry and household objects were still falling into the street, massive chunks of concrete alongside chairs and TV sets. Several buildings were burning. The road was littered with damaged cars, as if all the vehicles had been dropped from a height and had landed haphazard.

Cam knew immediately that the bomb had been too large, far too large.

On the other side of the street he saw the white beard and black hat of Fadlallah, who was being rushed back toward his building by his bodyguards. He appeared unhurt.

The mission had failed.

Cam stared at the carnage around him. How many had died? He guessed fifty, sixty, even seventy. And hundreds were injured.

He had to get out of there. In not many seconds people would start to think about who had done this. Even though his face was bruised and his suit was ripped, they would know he was American. He had to leave before it occurred to anyone that they had a chance of instant revenge.

He hurried back to his car. All the windows were smashed, but it looked as if it might go. He threw open the door. The seat was covered with broken glass. He pulled off his jacket and used it to sweep the seat free of shards. Then, in case he had missed any, he folded the jacket and placed it on the seat. He got in and turned the key.

The car started.

He pulled out, made a U-turn, and drove away.

He recalled Florence Geary's statement, which at the time he had thought hysterically exaggerated. "By the laws of every civilized country it's *murder*," she had said.

But it was not just murder. It was mass murder.

President Ronald Reagan was guilty.

And so was Cam Dewar.

. . .

On a small table in the living room, Jack was doing a jigsaw puzzle with his godmother, Maria, while his father, George, looked on. It was Sunday afternoon at Jacky Jakes's house in Prince George's County. They had all gone to Bethel Evangelical Church together, then had eaten Jacky's smothered pork chops—in onion gravy—with black-eyed peas. Then Maria had brought out the puzzle, carefully chosen to be neither too easy nor too hard for a five-year-old. Soon Maria would leave and George would drive Jack back to Verena's house. Then George would sit down at the kitchen table with his files for a couple of hours and prepare for the week ahead in Congress.

But this was a moment of stillness, when no engagements pressed. The afternoon light fell on the two heads bent over the puzzle. Jack was going to be handsome, George thought. He had a high forehead, wide-apart eyes, a cute flat nose, a smiling mouth, a neat chin, all in proportion. Already his expressions showed his character. He was completely absorbed in the intellectual challenge of the puzzle, then when he or Maria placed a piece correctly he would smile with satisfaction, his small face lighting up. George had never known anything as fascinating and moving as this, the growth of his own child's mind, the daily dawning of new understanding, numbers and letters, mechanisms and people and social groups. Seeing Jack run and jump and throw a ball seemed a miracle, but George was even more heart-struck by this look of intense mental concentration. It brought to his eyes tears of pride and gratitude and awe.

He was grateful to Maria, too. She visited about once a month, always bringing a gift, always spending time with her godson, patiently reading with him or talking to him or playing games. Maria and Jacky had given Jack stability through the trauma of his parents' divorce. It was a year now since George had left the marital home. Jack was no longer waking up in the middle of the night and crying. He seemed to be settling into the new way of life—though George could not help feeling apprehensive about possible long-term effects.

They finished the jigsaw. Grandma Jacky was called in to admire the completed work, then she took Jack into the kitchen for a glass of milk and a cookie.

George said to Maria: "Thank you for all you do for Jack. You're the greatest godmother ever."

"It's no sacrifice," she said. "It's a joy to know him."

Maria was going to be fifty next year. She would never have a child of her own. She had nieces and nephews in Chicago, but the main object of her maternal love was Jack.

"I have something to tell you," Maria said. "Something important."

She got up and closed the living room door, and George wondered what was coming.

She sat down again and said: "That car bomb in Beirut the day before yesterday."

"That was awful," George said. "It killed eighty people and wounded two hundred, mostly women and girls."

"The bomb was not placed by the Israelis."

"Who did it, then?"

"We did."

"What the hell are you talking about?"

"It was a counterterrorism initiative by President Reagan. The perpetrators were Lebanese nationals, but they were trained, financed, and controlled by the CIA."

"Jesus. But the president is obliged by law to tell my committee about covert actions."

"I think you'll find he informed the chairman and vice chairman."

"This is horrible," George said. "But you sound pretty sure of it."

"I was told by a senior CIA person. A lot of Agency veterans were against this whole program. But the president wanted it and Bill Casey forced it through."

"What on earth got into them?" George wondered. "They committed mass murder!"

"They're desperate to put a stop to the kidnappings. They think Fadlallah is the mastermind. They were trying to take him out."

"And they fucked it up."

"But good."

"This has to come out."

"That's what I think."

Jacky came in. "Our young man is ready to go back to his mother."

"I'm coming." George stood up. "All right," he said to Maria. "I'll take care of it."

"Thanks."

George got into the car with Jack and drove slowly through the suburban streets to Verena's house. Jasper Murray's bronze Cadillac was in the driveway beside Verena's red Jaguar. That was opportune, if it meant Jasper was there.

Verena came to the door in a black T-shirt and faded blue jeans. George went inside and Verena took Jack away for his bath. Jasper came out of the kitchen, and George said: "A word with you, if I may."

Jasper looked wary, but said: "Sure."

"Shall we go into"—George almost said *my study,* but corrected himself—"the study?"

"Okay."

He saw with a pang that Jasper's typewriter was on his old desk, along with a stack of reference books a journalist might need: *Who's Who in America, Atlas of the World, Pears' Cyclopaedia, The Almanac of American Politics.*

The study was a small room with one armchair. Neither man wanted to take the chair behind the desk. After an awkward hesitation, Jasper pulled out the desk chair and placed it opposite the armchair, and they both sat down.

George told him what Maria had said, without naming her. As he talked, in the back of his mind he wondered why Verena preferred Jasper to him. Jasper had a hard edge of self-interested ruthlessness, in George's opinion. George had put this question to his mother, who had said: "Jasper's a TV star. Verena's father is a movie star. She spent seven years working for Martin Luther King, who was the star of the civil rights movement. Maybe she needs her man to be a star. But what do I know?"

"This is dynamite," Jasper said when George had told him the whole story. "Are you sure of your source?"

"It's the same as my source for the other stories I've given you. Completely trustworthy."

"This makes President Reagan a mass murderer."

"Yes," said George. "I know."

CHAPTER FIFTY-EIGHT

On that Sunday, while Jacky and George and Maria and little Jack were in church, singing "Shall We Gather at the River," Konstantin Chernenko died in Moscow.

It happened at twenty minutes past seven in the evening, Moscow time. Dimka and Natalya were at home, eating bean soup for supper with their daughter, Katya, a schoolgirl of fifteen, and Dimka's son, Grisha, a university student of twenty-one. The phone rang at seven thirty. Natalya picked it up. As soon as she said: "Hello, Andrei," Dimka guessed what had happened.

Chernenko had been dying ever since he became leader, a mere thirteen months ago. Now he was in the hospital with cirrhosis and emphysema. All Moscow was waiting impatiently for him to expire. Natalya had bribed Andrei, a nurse at the hospital, to call her as soon as Chernenko breathed his last. Now she hung up the phone and confirmed it. "He's dead," she said.

This was the moment of hope. For the third time in less than three years, a tired old conservative leader had died. Once again there was a chance for a new young man to step in and change the Soviet Union into the kind of country in which Dimka wanted Grisha and Katya to live and raise his grandchildren. But that hope had been disappointed twice before. Would the same happen again?

Dimka pushed his plate away. "We have to act now," he said. "The succession will be decided in the next few hours."

Natalya nodded agreement. "The only thing that matters is who chairs the next meeting of the Politburo," she said.

Dimka thought she was right. That was how things worked in the Soviet Union. As soon as one contender nosed ahead, no one would bet on any other horse in the race.

Mikhail Gorbachev was second secretary, and therefore officially deputy to the late leader. However, his appointment to that position had been hotly contested by the old guard, who had wanted Moscow party boss Viktor Grishin, seventy years old and no reformer. Gorbachev had won that race by only one vote.

Dimka and Natalya left the dining table and went into the bedroom, not wanting to discuss this in front of the children. Dimka stood at the window, looking out at the lights of Moscow, while Natalya sat on the edge of the bed. They did not have much time.

Dimka said: "With Chernenko dead, there are exactly ten full members of the Politburo, including Gorbachev and Grishin." The full members were the inner circle of Soviet power. "By my calculation, they divide right down the middle: Gorbachev has four supporters and Grishin has the same."

"But they aren't all in town," Natalya pointed out. "Two of Grishin's men are away: Shcherbitsky is in the United States, and Kunayev is at home in Kazakhstan, a five-hour flight away."

"And one of Gorbachev's men: Vorotnikov is in Yugoslavia."

"Still, that gives us a majority of three against two—for the next few hours."

"Gorbachev must call a meeting of full members tonight. I'll suggest he says it's to plan the funeral. Having called the meeting, he can chair it. And once he's chaired that meeting, it will seem automatic that he chairs all subsequent meetings and then becomes leader."

Natalya frowned. "You're right, but I'd like to nail it down. I don't want the absentees to fly in tomorrow and say everything has to be discussed all over again because they weren't here."

Dimka thought for a minute. "I don't know what else we can do," he said.

Dimka called Gorbachev on the bedroom phone. Gorbachev already knew that Chernenko was dead—he, too, had his spies. He agreed with Dimka that he should call the meeting immediately.

Dimka and Natalya put on their heavy winter coats and boots and drove to the Kremlin.

An hour later the most powerful men in the Soviet Union were gathering in the Presidium Room. Dimka was still worrying.

Gorbachev's group needed a masterstroke that would make Gorbachev the leader irrevocably.

Just before the meeting, Gorbachev pulled a rabbit out of the hat. He approached his archrival, Viktor Grishin, and said formally: "Viktor Vasilyevich, would you like to chair this meeting?"

Dimka, standing close enough to hear, was astounded. What the hell was Gorbachev doing—conceding defeat?

But Natalya, right next to Dimka, was smiling triumphantly. "Brilliant!" she said with quiet elation. "If Grishin is proposed as chair the others will vote him down anyway. It's a false offer, an empty gift box."

Grishin thought for a moment and obviously came to the same conclusion. "No, comrade," he said. "You should chair this meeting."

And then Dimka realized, with growing jubilation, that Gorbachev had closed a trap. Now that Grishin had refused, it would be difficult for him to change his mind and demand the chairmanship tomorrow, when his supporters arrived. Any proposal to make Grishin chair would meet the argument that he had already turned down the position. And if he resisted that argument he would look like a ditherer anyway.

So, Dimka concluded, smiling broadly, Gorbachev would become the new leader of the Soviet Union.

And that was exactly what happened.

. . .

Tanya came home eager to tell Vasili her plan.

They had been more or less living together, unofficially, for two years. They were not married: once they became a legal couple they would never be allowed to leave the USSR together. And they were determined to get out of the Soviet bloc. Both felt trapped. Tanya continued to write reports for TASS that followed the party line slavishly. Vasili was now lead writer on a television show in which square-jawed KGB heroes outwitted stupid sadistic American spies. And both of them longed to tell the world that Vasili was the acclaimed novelist Ivan Kuznetsov, whose latest book, *The Geriatric Ward*—a savage satire on Brezhnev, Andropov, and Chernenko—was currently a bestseller in the West. Sometimes Vasili said all that mattered was that he had written the truth about the Soviet Union in stories that were read all over the world. But Tanya knew he wanted to take credit for his work, proudly, instead of fearfully concealing what he had done like a secret perversion.

But even though Tanya was bursting with enthusiasm, she took the trouble to turn on the radio in the kitchen before speaking. She did not really think their apartment was bugged, but it was an old habit, and there was no need to take chances.

A radio commentator was describing a visit by Gorbachev and his wife to a jeans factory in Leningrad. Tanya noted the significance. Previous Soviet leaders had visited steel mills and shipyards. Gorbachev celebrated consumer goods. Soviet manufactures ought to be as good as those of the West, he always said—something that had not even been a pipe dream for his predecessors.

And he took his wife with him. Unlike earlier leaders' wives, Raisa was not just an appendage. She was attractive and well-dressed, like an American first lady. She was intelligent, too: she had worked as a university lecturer until her husband became first secretary.

All this was hopeful but little more than symbolic, Tanya thought. Whether it came to anything would depend on the West. If the Germans and the Americans recognized liberalization in the USSR and worked to encourage change, Gorbachev might achieve something. But if the hawks in Bonn and Washington saw this as weakness, and made threatening or aggressive moves, the Soviet ruling elite would retreat back into its shell of orthodox Communism and military overkill. Then Gorbachev would join Kosygin and Khrushchev in the graveyard of failed Kremlin reformers.

"There's a conference of scriptwriters in Naples," Tanya said to Vasili, as the radio burbled in the background.

"Ah!" Vasili saw the significance immediately. The city of Naples had an elected Communist government.

They sat together on the couch. Tanya said: "They want to invite writers from the Soviet bloc, to prove that Hollywood is not the only place where television shows are made."

"Of course."

"You're the most successful writer of television drama in the USSR. You ought to go."

"The writers' union will decide who will be the lucky ones."

"With advice from the KGB, obviously."

"Do you think I have a chance?"

"Make an application, and I'll ask Dimka to put in a good word."

"Will you be able to come?"

"I'll ask Daniil to assign me to cover the conference for TASS."

"And then we'll both be in the free world."

"Yes."

"And then what?"

"I haven't worked out all the details, but that should be the easy part. From our hotel room we can phone Anna Murray in London. As soon as she finds out we're in Italy she'll catch the next plane. We'll give our KGB minders the slip and go with her to Rome. She will tell the world that Ivan Kuznetsov is really Vasili Yenkov, and he and his girlfriend are applying for political asylum in Great Britain."

Vasili was quiet. "Could it really happen, do you think?" he said, sounding almost like a child talking about a fairy tale.

Tanya took both his hands in hers. "I don't know," she said, "but I want to try."

. . .

Dimka had a big office in the Kremlin now. There was a large desk with two phones, a small conference table, and a couple of couches in front of a fireplace. On the wall was a full-size print of a famous Soviet painting, *The Mobilization Against Yudenich at the Putilov Machine Factory*.

His guest was Frederik Bíró, a Hungarian government minister with progressive ideas. He was two or three years older than Dimka, but he looked scared as he sat on the couch and asked Dimka's secretary for a glass of water. "Am I here to be reprimanded?" he said with a forced smile.

"Why do you ask that?"

"I'm one of a group of men who think Hungarian Communism has become stuck in a rut. That's no secret."

"I have no intention of reprimanding you for that or anything else."

"I'm to be praised, then?"

"Not that either. I assume you and your friends will form the new

Hungarian regime as soon as János Kádár dies or resigns, and I wish you luck, but I didn't ask you here to tell you that."

Bíró put down his water without tasting it. "Now I'm really scared."

"Let me put you out of your misery. Gorbachev's priority is to improve the Soviet economy by reducing military expenditure and producing more consumer goods."

"A fine plan," Bíró said in a wary tone. "Many people would like to do the same in Hungary."

"Our only problem is that it isn't working. Or, to be exact, it isn't working fast enough, which comes to the same thing. The Soviet Union is bust, bankrupt, broke. The falling price of oil is the cause of the immediate crisis, but the long-term problem is the crippling underperformance of the planned economy. And it's too severe to be cured by canceling orders for missiles and making more blue jeans."

"What is the answer?"

"We're going to stop subsidizing you."

"Hungary?"

"All the East European states. You've never paid for your standard of living. We finance it, by selling you oil and other raw materials below market prices, and buying your crappy manufactures that no one else wants."

"It's true, of course," Bíró acknowledged. "But that's the only way to keep the population quiet and the Communist Party in power. If their standard of living falls, it won't be long before they start asking why they have to be Communists."

"I know."

"Then what are we supposed to do?"

Dimka shrugged deliberately. "That's not my problem, it's yours."

"It's our problem?" Bíró said incredulously. "What the fuck are you talking about?"

"It means you have to find the solution."

"And what if the Kremlin doesn't like the solution we find?"

"It doesn't matter," Dimka said. "You're on your own now."

Bíró was scornful. "Are you telling me that forty years of Soviet domination of Eastern Europe is coming to an end, and we are going to be independent countries?"

"Exactly."

Bíró looked at Dimka long and hard. Then he said: "I don't believe you."

.   .   .

Tanya and Vasili went to the hospital to visit Tanya's aunt Zoya, the physicist. Zoya was seventy-four and had breast cancer. As the wife of a general, she had a private room. Visitors were allowed in two at a time, so Tanya and Vasili waited outside with other family members.

After a while Uncle Volodya came out, holding the arm of his thirty-nine-year-old son, Kotya. A strong man with a heroic war record, Volodya was now as helpless as a child, following where he was led, sobbing uncontrollably into a handkerchief that was already sodden with tears. They had been married forty years.

Tanya went in with her cousin Galina, the daughter of Volodya and Zoya. She was shocked by her aunt's appearance. Zoya had been head-turningly beautiful, even into her sixties, but now she was cadaverously thin, almost bald, and clearly only days or perhaps hours from the end. However, she was drifting in and out of sleep, and did not seem to be in pain. Tanya guessed she was dosed with morphine.

"Volodya went to America after the war, to find out how they had made the Hiroshima bomb," Zoya said, contentedly indiscreet under the influence of the drug. Tanya thought of telling her to say no more, then reflected that these secrets no longer mattered to anyone. "He brought back a Sears Roebuck Catalogue," Zoya went on, smiling at the memory. "It was full of beautiful things that any American could buy: dresses, bicycles, records, warm coats for children, even tractors for farmers. I wouldn't have believed it—I would have taken it for propaganda—but Volodya had been there and knew it was true. Ever since then I've wanted to go to America, just to see it. Just to look at all that plenty. I don't think I'll make it now, though." She closed her eyes again. "Never mind," she murmured, and she seemed to sleep again.

After a few minutes, Tanya and Galina went out, and two of the grandchildren took their places at the bedside.

Dimka had arrived and joined the group waiting in the corridor. He took Tanya and Vasili aside and spoke to them in a low voice. "I recommended you for the conference in Naples," he said to Vasili.

"Thank you—"

"Don't thank me. I was unsuccessful. I had a conversation today with the unpleasant Yevgeny Filipov. He's in charge of this kind of thing now, and he knows that you were sent to Siberia for subversive activities back in 1961."

Tanya said: "But Vasili has been rehabilitated!"

"Filipov knows that. Rehabilitation is one thing, he said, and going abroad is another. It's out of the question." Dimka touched Tanya's arm. "I'm sorry, sister."

"We're stuck here, then," Tanya said.

Vasili said bitterly: "A leaflet at a poetry reading, a quarter of a century ago, and I'm still being punished. We keep thinking that our country is changing, but it never really does."

Tanya said: "Like Aunt Zoya, we're never going to see the world outside."

"Don't give up yet," said Dimka.

PART TEN

WALL

1988–1989

CHAPTER FIFTY-NINE

asper Murray was fired in the fall of 1988.

He was not surprised. The atmosphere in Washington was different. President Reagan remained popular, despite having committed crimes far worse than those that had brought Nixon down: financing terrorism in Nicaragua, trading weapons for hostages with Iran, and turning women and girls into mangled corpses on the streets of Beirut. Reagan's collaborator Vice President George H. W. Bush looked likely to become the next president. Somehow—and Jasper could not figure out how this trick had been worked—people who challenged the president and caught him out cheating and lying were no longer heroes, as they had been in the seventies, but instead were considered disloyal and even anti-American.

So Jasper was not shocked, but he was deeply hurt. He had joined *This Day* twenty years ago, and he had helped make it a hugely respected news show. To be fired seemed like a negation of his life's work. His generous severance package did nothing to soothe the pain.

He probably should not have made a crack about Reagan at the end of his last broadcast. After telling the audience he was leaving, he had said: "And remember: if the president tells you it's raining, and he seems really, really sincere—take a look out of the window anyway . . . just to make sure." Frank Lindeman had been livid.

Jasper's colleagues threw a farewell party in the Old Ebbitt Grill that was attended by most of Washington's movers and shakers. Leaning against the bar, late in the evening, Jasper made a speech. Wounded, sad, and defiant, he said: "I love this country. I loved it the first time I came here, back in 1963. I love it because it's free. My mother escaped from Nazi Germany; the rest of her family never made it. The first thing Hitler did was take over the press and make it subservient to the government. Lenin did the same." Jasper had drunk a few glasses of wine, and as a result he was a shade more candid. "America is free because it has disrespectful newspapers and television shows to expose and shame presidents who fuck the Constitution up the ass." He raised his glass. "Here's to the free press. Here's to disrespect. And God bless America."

Next day Suzy Cannon, always eager to kick a man when he was down, published a long, vitriolic profile of Jasper. She managed to suggest that both his service in Vietnam and his naturalization as an American citizen were desperate attempts to conceal a virulent hatred of the United States. She also portrayed him as a ruthless sexual predator who had taken Verena away from George Jakes just as he had stolen Evie Williams from Cam Dewar back in the sixties.

The result was that he found it difficult to get another job. After several weeks of trying, at last another network offered him a position as European correspondent—based in Bonn.

"Surely you can do better than that," Verena said. She had no time for losers.

"No network will hire me as an anchor."

They were in the living room late in the evening, having just watched the news and about to get ready for bed.

"But Germany?" Verena said. "Isn't that a post for a kid on his way up the ladder?"

"Not necessarily. Eastern Europe is in turmoil. There could be some interesting stories coming out of that part of the world in the next year or two."

She was not going to let him make the best of it. "There are better jobs," she said. "Didn't *The Washington Post* offer you your own comment column?"

"I've worked in television all my life."

"You haven't applied to local TV," she said. "You could be a big fish in a small pond."

"No, I couldn't. I'd be a has-been on his way down." The prospect made Jasper shudder with humiliation. "I'm not going to do that."

Her face took on a defiant look. "Well, don't ask me to go to Germany with you."

He had been anticipating this, but he was taken aback by her blunt determination. "Why not?"

"You speak German, I don't."

Jasper did not speak very good German, but that was not his best argument. "It would be an adventure," he said.

"Get real," Verena said harshly. "I have a son."

"It would be an adventure for Jack, too. He'd grow up bilingual."

"George would go to court to stop me from taking Jack out of the country. We have joint custody. And I wouldn't do it anyway. Jack needs his father and his grandmother. And what about my work? I'm a big success, Jasper—I have twelve people working for me, all lobbying the government for liberal causes. You can't seriously ask me to give that up."

"Well, I guess I'll come home for the holidays."

"Are you serious? What kind of a relationship would we have? How long will it be before you're bouncing on a bed with a plump Rhinemaiden in blond plaits?"

It was true that Jasper had been promiscuous most of his life, but he had never cheated on Verena. The prospect of losing her suddenly seemed insupportable. "I can be faithful," he said desperately.

Verena saw his distress, and her tone softened. "Jasper, that's touching. I think you even mean it. But I know what you're like, and you know what I'm like. Neither of us can remain celibate for long."

"Listen," he pleaded. "Everyone in American television knows I'm looking for a job, and this is the only one I've been offered. Don't you understand? My back is up against the goddamn wall. I don't have an alternative!"

"I do understand, and I'm sorry. But we have to be realistic."

Jasper found her sympathy worse than her scorn. "Anyway, it won't be forever," he said defiantly.

"Won't it?"

"Oh, no. I'm going to make a comeback."

"In Bonn?"

"There will be more European stories leading the American television news than ever before. You just fucking watch me."

Verena's face turned sad. "Shit, you're really going, aren't you?"

"I told you, I have to."

"Well," she said regretfully, "don't expect me to be here when you come back."

. . .

Jasper had never been to Budapest. As a young man he had always looked west, toward America. Besides, all his life Hungary had been overcast by the gray clouds of Communism. But in November 1988, with the economy in ruins, something astonishing happened. A small group of young reform-minded Communists took control of the government and one of them, Miklós Németh, became prime minister. Among other changes, he opened a stock market.

Jasper thought this was astounding.

Only six months earlier Karoly Grosz, the thuggish chief of the Hungarian Communist Party, had told *Newsweek* magazine that multiparty democracy was "an historic impossibility" in Hungary. But Németh had enacted a new law allowing independent political "clubs."

This was a big story. But were the changes permanent? Or would Moscow soon clamp down?

Jasper flew into Budapest in a January blizzard. Beside the Danube, snow lay thick on the neo-Gothic turrets of the vast parliament building. It was in that building that Jasper met Miklós Németh.

Jasper had got the interview with the help of Rebecca Held. Although he had not previously met her, he knew about her from Dave Williams and Walli Franck. As soon as he got to Bonn he had looked her up: she was the nearest thing he had to a German contact. She was now an important figure in the German Foreign Office. Even better, she was a friend—perhaps a lover, Jasper guessed—of Frederik Bíró, aide to Miklós Németh. Bíró had fixed up the interview.

It was Bíró who now met Jasper in the lobby and escorted him through a maze of corridors and passageways to the office of the prime minister.

Németh was just forty-one. He was a short man with thick brown hair that fell over his forehead in a kiss curl. His face showed intelligence and determination, but also anxiety. For the interview he sat behind an oak table and nervously surrounded himself with aides. No doubt he was vividly aware that he was speaking not just to Jasper, but to the United States government—and that Moscow would be watching, too.

Like any prime minister, he talked mostly in predictable clichés. There would be hard times ahead, but the country would emerge stronger in the long run. *And yadda yadda yadda,* thought Jasper. He needed something better than this.

He asked whether the new political "clubs" could ever become free political parties.

Németh gave Jasper a hard, direct look, and said in a firm, clear voice: "That is one of our greatest ambitions."

Jasper concealed his astonishment. No Iron Curtain country had ever had independent political parties. Did Németh really mean it?

Jasper asked whether the Communist Party would ever give up its "leading role" in Hungarian society.

Németh gave him that look again. "In two years I could imagine that the head of government might not be a Politburo member," he said.

Jasper had to stop himself saying *Jesus Christ!*

He was on a roll, and it was time for the big one. "Might the Soviets intervene to stop these changes, as they did in 1956?"

Németh gave him the look for the third time. "Gorbachev has taken the lid off a boiling pot," he said, slowly and distinctly. Then he added: "The steam may be painful, but change is irreversible."

And Jasper knew he had his first great story from Europe.

. . .

A few days later he watched a videotape of his report as it had appeared on American television. Rebecca sat beside him, a poised, confident woman in her fifties, friendly but with an air of authority. "Yes, I think Németh means every word," she said in answer to Jasper's question.

Jasper had ended the report speaking to the camera in front of the parliament building, with snowflakes landing in his hair. "The ground is frozen hard here in this Eastern European country," he said on the screen. "But, as always, the seeds of spring are stirring underground. Clearly the Hungarian people want change. But will their Moscow overlords permit it? Miklós Németh believes there is a new mood of tolerance in the Kremlin. Only time will tell whether he is right."

That had been Jasper's sign-off, but now to his surprise he saw that another clip had been added to his piece. A spokesman for James Baker, secretary of state to newly inaugurated President George H. W. Bush, spoke to an invisible interviewer. "Signs of softening in Communist attitudes are not to be trusted," the spokesman said. "The Soviets are attempting to lull the United States into a false sense of security. There is no reason to doubt the Kremlin's willingness to intervene in Eastern Europe the minute they feel threatened. The urgent necessity now is to underscore the credibility of NATO's nuclear deterrent."

"Good God," said Rebecca. "What planet are they on?"

. . .

Tanya Dvorkin returned to Warsaw in February 1989.

She was sorry to leave Vasili on his own in Moscow, mainly because she would miss him, but also because she still nursed a faint anxiety that he would fill the apartment with nubile teenagers. She did not really believe it would happen. Those days were over. All the same the worry nagged at her a little.

However, Warsaw was a great assignment. Poland was in a ferment. Solidarity had somehow risen from its grave. Amazingly, General Jaruzelski—the dictator who had cracked down on freedom only seven years previously, breaking every promise and stamping on the independent trade union—had in desperation agreed to round-table talks with opposition groups.

In Tanya's opinion, Jaruzelski had not changed—the Kremlin had. Jaruzelski was the same old tyrant, but he was no longer confident of Soviet support. According to Dimka, Jaruzelski had been told that Poland must solve its own problems, without help from Moscow. When Mikhail Gorbachev first said this, Jaruzelski had not believed it. None of the East European leaders had. But that had been three years ago, and at last the message was beginning to sink in.

Tanya did not know what would happen. No one did. Never in her life had she heard so much talk of change, liberalization, and freedom. But the Communists were still in control in the Soviet bloc. Was the day coming nearer when she and Vasili could reveal their secret, and tell the world the true identity of the author Ivan Kuznetsov? In the past such hopes had always ended up crushed beneath the caterpillar tracks of Soviet tanks.

As soon as Tanya arrived in Warsaw, she was invited to dinner at the apartment of Danuta Gorski.

Standing at the door, ringing the bell, she remembered the last time she had seen Danuta, being dragged out of this very apartment by the brutish ZOMO security police in their camouflage uniforms, on the night seven years ago when Jaruzelski had declared martial law.

Now Danuta opened the door, grinning broadly, all teeth and hair. She hugged Tanya, then led her into the dining room of the small apartment. Her husband, Marek, was opening a bottle of Hungarian Riesling, and there was a plate of snack-size sausages on the table with a small dish of mustard.

"I was in jail for eighteen days," Danuta said. "I think they let me out because I was radicalizing the other inmates." She laughed, throwing back her head.

Tanya admired her guts. If I were a lesbian I could fall for Danuta, she thought. All the men Tanya had loved had been courageous.

"Now I'm part of this Round Table," Danuta went on. "Every day, all day."

"It is really a round table?"

"Yes, a huge one. The theory is that no one is in charge. But, in practice, Lech Wałęsa chairs the meetings."

Tanya marveled. An uneducated electrician was dominating the debate on the future of Poland. This kind of thing had been the dream of her grandfather the Bolshevik factory worker Grigori Peshkov. Yet Wałęsa was the anti-Communist. In a way she was glad Grandfather Grigori had not lived to see this irony. It might have broken his heart.

"Will anything come of the Round Table?" Tanya asked.

Before Danuta could answer, Marek said: "It's a trick. Jaruzelski wants to cripple the opposition by co-opting its leaders, making them part of the Communist government without changing the system. It's his strategy for staying in power."

Danuta said: "Marek is probably right. But the trick is not going to work. We're demanding independent trade unions, a free press, and real elections."

Tanya was shocked. "Jaruzelski is actually discussing free elections?" Poland already had phony elections, in which only Communist parties and their allies were allowed to field candidates.

"The talks keep breaking down. But he needs to stop the strikes, so he reconvenes the Round Table, and we demand elections again."

"What's behind the strikes?" Tanya said. "I mean, fundamentally?"

Marek interrupted again. "You know what people are saying? 'Forty-five years of Communism, and still there's no toilet paper.' We're poor! Communism doesn't work."

"Marek is right," said Danuta again. "A few weeks ago a store here in Warsaw announced that it would be accepting down payments for television sets on the following Monday. It didn't have any TVs, mind you, it was just hoping to get some. People started queuing on the Friday beforehand. By Monday morning there were fifteen thousand people in line—just to put their names on a list!"

Danuta stepped into the kitchen and returned with a fragrant bowl of *zupa ogórkowa,* the sour cucumber soup that Tanya loved. "So what will happen?" Tanya asked as she tucked in. "Will there be real elections?"

"No," said Marek.

"Maybe," said Danuta. "The latest proposal is that two-thirds of the seats in parliament should be reserved for the Communist Party, and there should be free elections for the remainder."

Marek said: "So we would still have phony elections!"

Danuta said: "But this would be better than what we have now! Don't you agree, Tanya?"

"I don't know," said Tanya.

. . .

The spring thaw had not arrived, and Moscow was still under its duvet of snow, when the new Hungarian prime minister came to see Mikhail Gorbachev.

Yevgeny Filipov knew that Miklós Németh was coming, and he buttonholed Dimka outside the leader's office a few minutes before the meeting. "This nonsense must be stopped!" he said.

These days, Filipov was looking increasingly frantic, Dimka

observed. His gray hair was untidy, and he went everywhere in a rush. He was now in his early sixties, and his face was permanently set in the disapproving frown he had worn for so much of his life. His baggy suits and ultrashort haircut were back in fashion: kids in the West called the look retro.

Filipov hated Gorbachev. The Soviet leader stood for everything Filipov had been fighting against all his life: relaxation of rules instead of strict party discipline; individual initiative as opposed to central planning; friendship with the West rather than war against capitalist imperialism. Dimka could almost sympathize with a man who had wasted his days fighting a losing battle.

At least, Dimka hoped it had been a losing battle. The conflict was not over yet.

"What nonsense in particular are we talking about?" Dimka said wearily.

"Independent political parties!" Filipov said as if he were mentioning an atrocity. "The Hungarians have started a dangerous trend. Jaruzelski is now talking about the same thing in Poland. Jaruzelski!"

Dimka understood Filipov's incredulity. It was, indeed, astonishing that the Polish tyrant was now talking of making Solidarity a part of the nation's future, and of allowing political parties to compete in a Western-style election.

And Filipov did not know it all. Dimka's sister, in Warsaw for TASS, was sending him accurate information. Jaruzelski was up against the wall, and Solidarity was adamant. They were not just talking, they were planning an election.

This was what Filipov and the Kremlin conservatives were fighting to prevent.

"These developments are highly dangerous!" Filipov said. "They open the door to counterrevolutionary and revisionist tendencies. What is the point of that?"

"The point is that we no longer have the money to subsidize our satellites—"

"We have no satellites. We have allies."

"Whatever they are, they're not willing to do what we say if we can't pay for their obedience."

"We used to have an army to defend Communism—but not anymore."

There was some truth in that exaggeration. Gorbachev had announced the withdrawal from Eastern Europe of a quarter of a million troops and ten thousand tanks—an essential economy measure, but also a peace gesture. "We can't afford such an army," said Dimka.

Filipov was so indignant he looked as if he might burst. "Can't you see that you're talking about the end of everything we have worked for since 1917?"

"Khrushchev said it would take us twenty years to catch up with the Americans in wealth and military strength. It's now twenty-eight years, and we're farther behind than we were in 1961 when Khrushchev said it. Yevgeny, what are you fighting to preserve?"

"The Soviet Union! What do you imagine the Americans are thinking, as we run down our army and permit creeping revisionism among our allies? They're laughing up their sleeves! President Bush is a Cold Warrior, intent on overthrowing us. Don't fool yourself."

"I disagree," said Dimka. "The more we disarm, the less reason the Americans will have for building up their nuclear stockpile."

"I hope you're right," said Filipov. "For all our sakes." He walked away.

Dimka, too, hoped he was right. Filipov had put his finger on the flaw in Gorbachev's strategy. It relied upon President Bush being reasonable. If the Americans responded to disarmament with reciprocal measures, Gorbachev would be vindicated, and his Kremlin rivals would look foolish. But if Bush failed to respond—or, even worse, increased military spending—then it would be Gorbachev who looked a fool. He would be undermined, and his opponents might seize the opportunity to overthrow him and return to the good old days of superpower confrontation.

Dimka went to Gorbachev's suite of rooms. He was looking forward to meeting Németh. What was happening in Hungary was exciting. Dimka was also eager to find out what Gorbachev would say to Németh.

The Soviet leader was not predictable. He was a lifelong Communist who was nevertheless unwilling to impose Communism on other countries. His strategy was clear: glasnost and perestroika, openness and restructuring. His tactics were less obvious, and on any particular issue it was hard to know which way he would jump. He kept Dimka on his toes.

Gorbachev was not warm toward Németh. The Hungarian prime minister had asked for an hour and had been offered twenty minutes. It could be a difficult meeting.

Németh arrived with Frederik Bíró, whom Dimka already knew. Gorbachev's secretary immediately took the three of them into the grand office. It was a vast high-ceilinged room with paneled walls painted a creamy yellow. Gorbachev was behind a contemporary black-stained wood desk that stood in a corner. There was nothing on the desk but a phone and a lamp. The visitors sat down on stylish black leather chairs. Everything symbolized modernity.

Németh got down to business with few courtesies. He was about to announce free elections, he said. Free meant free: the result could be a non-Communist government. How would Moscow feel about that?

Gorbachev flushed, and the purple birthmark on his bald dome darkened. "The proper path is to return to the roots of Leninism," he said.

This did not mean much. Everyone who tried to change the Soviet Union claimed to be returning to the roots of Leninism.

Gorbachev went on: "Communism can find its way again, by going back to the time before Stalin."

"No, it can't," said Németh bluntly.

"Only the party can create a just society! This cannot be left to chance."

"We disagree." Németh was beginning to look ill. His face was pale and his voice was shaky. He was a cardinal challenging the authority of the Pope. "I must ask you one question very directly," he said. "If we hold an election and the Communist Party is voted out of power, will the Soviet Union intervene with military force as it did in 1956?"

The room went dead silent. Even Dimka did not know how Gorbachev would respond.

Then Gorbachev said one Russian word: "Nyet." No.

Németh looked like a man whose death sentence had been repealed.

Gorbachev added: "At least, not as long as I'm sitting in this chair."

Németh laughed. He did not think Gorbachev was in danger of being deposed.

He was wrong. The Kremlin always presented a united front to the world, but it was never as harmonious as it pretended. People had no idea how shaky was Gorbachev's grip. Németh was satisfied to know what Gorbachev's own intentions were, but Dimka knew better.

However, Németh was not finished. He had won from Gorbachev a huge concession—a promise that the USSR would not intervene to prevent the overthrow of Communism in Hungary! Yet now, with surprising audacity, Németh pressed for a further guarantee. "The fence is dilapidated," he said. "It has to be either renewed or abandoned."

Dimka knew what Németh was talking about. The border between Communist Hungary and capitalist Austria was secured by a stainless steel electric fence one hundred and fifty miles long. It was naturally very expensive to maintain. To renew the whole thing would cost millions.

Gorbachev said: "If it needs renewing, then renew it."

"No," said Németh. He might have been nervous, but he was determined. Dimka admired his guts. "I don't have the money, and I don't need the fence," Németh went on. "It's a Warsaw Pact installation. If you want it, you should renew it."

"That isn't going to happen," said Gorbachev. "The Soviet Union no longer has that kind of money. A decade ago, oil was forty dollars a barrel and we could do anything. Now it's what, nine dollars? We're broke."

"Let me make sure we understand one another," said Németh. He was perspiring, and he wiped his face with a handkerchief. "If you do not pay, we will not renew the fence, and it will cease to operate as an effective barrier. People will be able to go to Austria, and we will not stop them."

There was another pregnant silence. Then at last Gorbachev sighed and said: "So be it."

That was the end of the meeting. The farewell courtesies were perfunctory. The Hungarians could not get away quickly enough. They had got everything they asked for. They shook hands with Gorbachev and left the room at a fast walk. It was as if they wanted to get back on the plane before Gorbachev had time to change his mind.

Dimka returned to his own office in a reflective mood. Gorbachev had surprised him twice: first by being unexpectedly hostile to Németh's reforms, and second by offering no real resistance to them.

Would the Hungarians abandon the fence? It was an essential part of the Iron Curtain. If suddenly people were allowed to walk over the border and into the West, that could be a change even more momentous than free elections.

But Filipov and the conservatives had not yet surrendered. They were on the alert for the least sign of weakness in Gorbachev. Dimka did not doubt that they had contingency plans for a coup.

He was looking thoughtfully at the large revolutionary picture on his office wall when Natalya called. "You know what a Lance missile is, don't you?" she said without preamble.

"A short-range surface-to-surface tactical nuclear weapon," he replied. "The Americans have about seven hundred in Germany. Fortunately their range is only about seventy-five miles."

"Not any longer," she said. "President Bush wants to upgrade them. The new ones will fly two hundred eighty miles."

"Hell." This was what Dimka feared and Filipov had predicted. "But this is illogical. It's not that long ago that Reagan and Gorbachev *withdrew* intermediate-range ballistic missiles."

"Bush thinks Reagan went too far with disarmament."

"How definite is this plan?"

"Bush has surrounded himself with Cold War hawks, according to the KGB station in Washington. Defense Secretary Cheney is gung ho. So is Scowcroft." Brent Scowcroft was the national security adviser. "And there's a woman called Condoleezza Rice, who is just as bad."

Dimka despaired. "Filipov is going to say: 'I told you so.'"

"Filipov and others. It's a dangerous development for Gorbachev."

"What's the Americans' timetable?"

"They're going to put pressure on the West Europeans at the NATO meeting in May."

"Shit," said Dimka. "Now we're in trouble."

. . .

Rebecca Held was at her apartment in Hamburg, late in the evening, working, with papers spread over the round table in the kitchen. On the counter were a dirty coffee cup and a plate with the crumbs of the ham sandwich she had eaten for supper. She had taken off her smart working clothes, removed her makeup, showered, and put on baggy old underwear and an ancient silk wrap.

She was preparing for her first visit to the United States. She was going with her boss, Hans-Dietrich Genscher, who was vice chancellor of Germany, foreign minister, and head of the Free Democratic Party, to which she belonged. Their mission was to explain to the Americans why they did not want any more nuclear weapons. The Soviet Union was becoming less threatening under Gorbachev. Upgraded nukes were not merely unnecessary: they might actually be counterproductive, undermining Gorbachev's peace moves and strengthening the hand of hawks in Moscow.

She was reading a German intelligence appraisal of the power struggle in the Kremlin when the doorbell rang.

She looked at her watch. It was half past nine. She was not expecting a visitor and she certainly was not dressed to receive one. However, it was probably a neighbor in the same building on some trivial errand, needing to borrow a carton of milk.

She did not merit a full-time bodyguard: she was not important enough to attract terrorists, thank God. All the same her door had a peephole so that she could check before opening up.

She was surprised to see Frederik Bíró outside.

She had mixed feelings. A surprise visit from her lover was a delight—but she looked a perfect fright. At the age of fifty-seven any woman wanted time to prepare before she showed herself to her man.

But she could hardly ask him to wait in the hall while she made up her face and changed her underwear.

She opened the door.

"My darling," he said, and kissed her.

"I'm pleased to see you, but you've caught me unawares," she said. "I'm a mess."

He stepped inside and she closed the door. He held her at arm's length and studied her. "Tousled hair, glasses, dressing gown, bare feet," he said. "You look adorable."

She laughed and led him into the kitchen. "Have you had dinner?" she said. "Shall I make you an omelette?"

"Just some coffee, please. I ate on the plane."

"What are you doing in Hamburg?"

"My boss sent me." Fred sat at the table. "Prime Minister Németh is coming to Germany next week to see Chancellor Kohl. He's going to ask Kohl a question. Like all politicians, he wants to know the answer before he asks it."

"What question?"

"I need to explain."

She put a cup of coffee in front of Fred. "Go ahead, I've got all night."

"I'm hoping it won't take that long." He ran a hand up her leg inside her robe. "I have other plans." He reached her underwear. "Oh!" he said. "Roomy panties."

She blushed. "I wasn't expecting you!"

He grinned. "I could get both hands inside there—both arms, maybe."

She pushed his hands away and moved to the other side of the table. "Tomorrow I'm going to throw out all my old underwear." She sat opposite him. "Stop embarrassing me and tell me why you're here."

"Hungary is going to open its border with Austria."

Rebecca did not think she had heard him right. "What are you talking about?"

"We're going to open our border. Let the fence fall into disrepair. Free our people to go where they want."

"You can't be serious."

"It's an economic decision as much as a political one. The fence is collapsing and we can't afford to rebuild it."

Rebecca was beginning to understand. "But if the Hungarians can get out, so can everyone else. How will you stop Czechs, Yugoslavs, Poles . . ."

"We won't."

". . . and East Germans. Oh, my goodness, my family will be able to leave!"

"Yes."

"It can't happen. The Soviets won't allow it."

"Németh went to Moscow and told Gorbachev."

"What did Gorbi say?"

"Nothing. He's not happy, but he won't intervene. He can't afford to renew the fence either."

"But . . ."

"I was there, at the meeting in the Kremlin. Németh asked him straight out, would the Soviets invade as they did in 1956? His answer was *nyet*."

"Do you believe him?"

"Yes."

This was world-changing news. Rebecca had been working for this all her political life, but she could not believe it was really going to happen: her family, able to travel from East to West Germany! Freedom!

Then Fred said: "There is one possible snag."

"I was afraid of that."

"Gorbachev promised no military intervention, but he did not rule out economic sanctions."

Rebecca thought that was the least of their problems. "Hungary's economy will become west-facing, and it will grow."

"That's what we want. But it will take time. People may face hardship. The Kremlin may hope to push us into an economic collapse before the economy has time to adjust. Then there could be a counterrevolution."

He was right, Rebecca saw. This was a serious danger. "I knew it was too good to be true," she said despondently.

"Don't despair. We have a solution. That's why I'm here."

"What's your plan?"

"We need support from the richest country in Europe. If we can have a big line of credit from German banks, we can resist Soviet pressure. Next week, Németh will ask Kohl for a loan. I know you can't authorize such a thing on your own, but I was hoping you could give me a steer. What will Kohl say?"

"I can't imagine he'll say no, if the reward is open borders. Apart from the political gain, think what this could mean to the German economy."

"We may need a lot of money."

"How much?"

"Possibly a billion deutschmarks."

"Don't worry," Rebecca said. "You've got it."

. . .

The Soviet economy was getting worse and worse, according to the CIA report in front of Congressman George Jakes. Gorbachev's reforms—decentralization, more consumer goods, fewer weapons—were not enough.

There was pressure on the East European satellites to follow the USSR by liberalizing their own economies, but any changes would be minor and gradual, the Agency forecast. If any country rejected Communism outright, then Gorbachev would send in the tanks.

That did not sound right to George, sitting in a meeting of the House intelligence oversight committee. Poland, Hungary, and Czechoslovakia were running ahead of the USSR, moving toward free enterprise and democracy, and Gorbachev was doing nothing to hold them back.

But President Bush and Defense Secretary Cheney believed passionately in the Soviet menace, and as always the CIA was under pressure to tell the president what he wanted to hear.

The meeting left George feeling dissatisfied and anxious. He took the dinky Capitol subway train back to the Cannon House Office Building, where he had a suite of three crowded rooms. The lobby had a reception desk, a couch for waiting visitors, and a round table for meetings. To one side was the administration office, crammed with staff desks and bookshelves and filing cabinets. On the opposite side was George's own room, with a desk and a conference table and a picture of Bobby Kennedy.

He was intrigued to see, on his list of afternoon appointments, a clergyman from Anniston, Alabama, the Reverend Clarence Bowyer, who wanted to talk to him about civil rights.

George would never forget Anniston. It was the town where the Freedom Riders had been attacked by a mob and their bus firebombed. It was the only time someone had tried seriously to kill George.

He must have said yes to the man's request for a meeting, though he could not now remember why. He assumed that a preacher from Alabama who wanted to see him would be African American, and he was startled when his assistant ushered in a white man. The Reverend Bowyer was about George's age, dressed in a gray suit with a white shirt and a dark tie, but wearing trainers, perhaps because he had to do a lot of walking in Washington. He had large front teeth and a receding chin, and salt-and-pepper hair that accentuated the resemblance to a red squirrel. There was something vaguely familiar about him. With him was a teenage boy who looked just like him.

"I try to bring the gospel of Jesus Christ to soldiers and others working at the Anniston army depot," Bowyer said, introducing himself. "Many of my congregation are African Americans."

Bowyer was sincere, George thought; and he had a mixed-race church, which was unusual. "What's your interest in civil rights, Reverend?"

"Well, sir, I was a segregationist as a young man."

"Many people were," George said. "We've all learned a lot."

"I've done more than learn," said Bowyer. "I have spent decades in deep repentance."

That seemed a little strong. Some of the people who asked for meetings with congressmen were more or less crazy. George's staff did their best to filter out the lunatics, but now and again one would slip through the net. However, Bowyer struck George as pretty sane. "Repentance," George repeated, playing for time.

"Congressman Jakes," said Bowyer solemnly, "I have come here to apologize to you."

"What for, exactly?"

"In 1961 I hit you with a crowbar. I believe I broke your arm."

In a flash George understood why the man looked familiar. He had been in the mob at Anniston. He had tried to hit Maria, but George had put his arm in the way. It still hurt in cold weather. George stared in astonishment at this earnest clergyman. "So that was you," he said.

"Yes, sir. I don't have any excuses to offer. I knew what I was doing, and I did wrong. But I have never forgotten you. I just would like you to know how sorry I am, and I wanted my son, Clam, to witness my confession of evildoing."

George was nonplussed. Nothing like this had ever happened to him. "So you became a preacher," he said.

"At first I became a drinker. Because of whisky, I lost my job and my home and my car. Then one Sunday the Lord led my footsteps to a little mission in a shack in a poor neighborhood. The preacher, who happened to be black, took as his text the twenty-fifth chapter of Matthew's gospel, especially verse forty: 'Inasmuch as ye have done it unto one of these the least of my brethren, ye have done it unto me.'"

George had heard more than one sermon on that verse. Its message was that a wrong done to anyone was a wrong done to Jesus. African Americans, who had more wrongs done to them than most citizens, gained strong consolation from that notion. The verse was even quoted on the Wales Window at the Sixteenth Street Baptist Church in Birmingham.

Bowyer said: "I went into that church to mock, and I came out saved."

George said: "I'm glad to hear of your change of heart, Reverend."

"I do not deserve your forgiveness, Congressman, but I hope for God's." Bowyer stood up. "I will not take up any more of your valuable time. Thank you."

George stood too. He felt that he had not responded adequately to a man in the grip of powerful emotion. "Before you go," he said, "let us shake hands." He took Bowyer's hand in both of his. "If God can forgive you, Clarence, I guess I should too."

Bowyer choked up. Tears came to his eyes as he shook George's hand.

On impulse, George embraced him. The man was shaking with sobs.

After a minute, George broke the hug and stepped back. Bowyer tried to speak but was unable to. Weeping, he turned and left the room.

His son shook George's hand. "Thank you, Congressman," the boy said in a shaky voice. "I can't express how much your forgiveness means to my father. You are a great man, sir." He followed Bowyer out of the room.

George sat back down, feeling dazed. Well, he thought, how about that?

. . .

He told Maria about it that evening.

Her reaction was unsympathetic. "I guess you're entitled to forgive them, it was your arm that got broken," she said. "Me, I'm not big on mercy for segregationists. I'd like to see Reverend Bowyer serve a couple of years in jail, or maybe on a chain gang. *Then* perhaps I'd accept his apology. All those corrupt judges and brutal cops and bomb makers are still walking around free, you know. They've never been brought to justice for what they did. Some are probably drawing their damn pensions. And they want forgiveness, too? I'm not going to help them feel comfortable. If their guilt makes them miserable, I'm glad. It's the least they deserve."

George smiled. Maria was getting feistier in her fifties. She was one of the most senior people in the State Department, respected by Republicans and Democrats alike. She carried herself with confidence and authority.

They were in her apartment, and she was making dinner, sea bass stuffed with herbs, while George laid the table. A delicate aroma filled the room, making George's mouth water. Maria topped up his glass of Lynmar Chardonnay, then put broccoli into a steamer. She was a little heavier than she used to be, and she was trying to adopt George's lean cuisine tastes.

After dinner they took their coffee to the couch. Maria was in a mellow mood. "I want to be able to look back and say that the world was a safer place when I left the State Department than when I arrived," she said. "I want my nephews and nieces, and my godson, Jack, to raise their children without the threat of a superpower holocaust hanging over them. Then I'll be able to say that my life was well spent."

"I understand how you feel," said George. "But it seems like a pipe dream. Is it possible?"

"Maybe. The Soviet bloc is nearer to collapse than at any time since the Second World War. Our ambassador to Moscow believes that the Brezhnev Doctrine is dead."

The Brezhnev Doctrine said that the Soviet Union controlled Eastern Europe, just as the Monroe Doctrine gave the same rights to the USA in South America.

George nodded. "If Gorbachev no longer wants to boss the Communist empire, that's a huge geopolitical gain for the USA."

"And we should be doing everything we can to help Gorbachev stay in power. But we're not, because President Bush believes the whole thing is a confidence trick by Gorbachev. So he's actually planning to *increase* our nuclear weapons in Europe."

"Which is guaranteed to undermine Gorbachev and encourage the hawks in the Kremlin."

"Exactly. Anyway, I have a bunch of Germans coming tomorrow to try and set him straight."

"Good luck with that," George said skeptically.

"Yeah."

George finished his coffee but he did not want to go. He felt comfortable, full of good food and wine, and he always enjoyed talking to Maria. "You know something?" he said. "Aside from my son and my mother, I like you better than anyone else in the world."

"How is Verena?" Maria said sharply.

George smiled. "She's seeing your old boyfriend Lee Montgomery. He's a *Washington Post* editor now. I think it's serious."

"Good."

"Do you remember . . ." He probably should not say this, but he had drunk half a bottle of wine, and he thought, What the hell? "Do you remember the time we had sex on this couch?"

"George," she said, "I don't do it often enough to forget."

"Unfortunately, neither do I."

She laughed, but said: "I'm glad."

He felt nostalgic. "How long ago was that?"

"It was the night Nixon resigned, fifteen years ago. You were young and handsome."

"And you were almost as beautiful as you are today."

"Why, you smooth talker."

"It was nice, wasn't it? The sex, I mean."

"Nice?" She pretended to be offended. "Is that all?"

"It was great."

"Yeah."

He was possessed by a feeling of regret for missed opportunities. "What happened to us?"

"We had separate paths to follow."

"I guess." There was a silence, then George said: "Do you want to do it again?"

"I thought you'd never ask."

They kissed, and immediately he remembered how it had been the first time: so relaxed, so natural, so right.

Her body had changed. It was softer, less taut, the skin dryer to his touch. He guessed the same was true of his own body: the wrestling muscles had gone long ago. But it made no difference. Her lips and tongue were fervently busy on his, and he felt the same eager pleasure at being drawn into the arms of a sensual and loving woman.

She unbuttoned his shirt. While he was taking it off, she stood up and quickly slipped out of her dress.

George said: "Before we go any farther . . ."

"What?" She sat down again. "Are you having second thoughts?"

"On the contrary. That's a pretty bra, by the way."

"Thank you. You can take it off me in a minute." She unbuckled his belt.

"But there's something I want to say. At the risk of spoiling everything . . ."

"Go ahead," she said. "Take a chance."

"I'm realizing something. I guess I should have figured it out before."

She watched him, smiling a little, saying nothing, and he had the strangest feeling that she knew exactly what was coming.

"I'm realizing that I love you," he said.

"Do you, really?"

"Yes. Do you mind? Is it okay? Have I ruined the atmosphere?"

"You fool," she said. "I've been in love with you for years."

. . .

Rebecca arrived at the State Department in Washington on a warm spring day. There were daffodils in the flower beds, and she was full of hope. The Soviet empire was weakening, perhaps fatally. Germany had the chance to become united and free. The Americans just needed a nudge in the right direction.

Rebecca reflected that it was because of Carla, her adoptive mother, that she was here in Washington, representing her country, negotiating with the most powerful men in the world. Carla had taken a terrified thirteen-year-old Jewish girl in wartime Berlin and had given her the confidence to become an international stateswoman. I must get a photograph to send her, Rebecca thought.

With her boss, Hans-Dietrich Genscher, and a handful of aides, she went into the art-moderne State Department building. The two-story lobby featured a huge mural called *The Defense of Human Freedoms,* which showed the five freedoms being protected by the American military.

The Germans were greeted by a woman whom Rebecca had known, until now, only as a warm, intelligent voice on the phone: Maria Summers. Rebecca was surprised to see that Maria was African American. Then she felt guilty at being surprised: there was no reason why an African American should not hold a high post in the State Department. Finally, Rebecca realized there were very few other dark faces in the building. Maria was unusual and Rebecca's surprise was, after all, justified.

Maria was friendly and welcoming, but it soon became clear that Secretary of State James Baker did not feel the same. The Germans waited outside his office for five minutes, then ten. Maria was clearly mortified. Rebecca began to worry. This could not be an accident. To keep the German vice chancellor waiting was a calculated insult. Baker must be hostile.

Rebecca had heard before of the Americans doing this kind of thing. Afterward they would tell the media that the visitors had been snubbed because of their views, and embarrassing stories would appear in the press back home. Ronald Reagan had done the same to the British opposition leader, Neil Kinnock, because he, too, was a disarmer.

Rebecca hardly cared about the insult as such. Male politicians postured a lot. It was just boys waving their dicks around. But it meant the meeting was likely to be unproductive, and that was bad news for detente.

After fifteen minutes they were shown in. Baker was a lanky, athletic man with a Texas accent, but there was nothing of the country bumpkin about him: he was immaculately barbered and tailored. He gave Hans-Dietrich Genscher a notably brief handshake and said: "We are deeply disappointed in your attitude."

Fortunately, Genscher was no pussycat. He had been vice chancellor of Germany and foreign minister for fifteen years, and he knew how to ignore bad manners. A balding man in glasses, he had a fleshy, pugnacious face. "We feel that your policy is out-of-date," he said calmly. "The situation in Europe has changed, and you need to take that into account."

"We have to maintain the strength of the NATO nuclear deterrent," Baker said as if repeating a mantra.

Genscher controlled his impatience with a visible effort. "We disagree—and so do our people. Four out of five Germans want all nuclear weapons withdrawn from Europe."

"They are being duped by Kremlin propaganda!"

"We live in a democracy. In the end, the people decide."

Dick Cheney, the American secretary of defense, was also in the room. "One of the Kremlin's primary goals is to denuclearize Europe," he said. "We must not fall into their trap!"

Genscher was clearly irritated to be lectured on European politics by men who knew a good deal less about the subject than he did. He looked like a schoolteacher trying in vain to explain something to pupils who were deliberately being obtuse. "The Cold War is over," he said.

Rebecca was aghast to see that the discussion was going to be completely profitless. No one was listening: they had all made up their minds beforehand.

She was right. The two sides traded irritable remarks for a few more minutes, then the meeting broke up.

There was no photo opportunity.

As the Germans were leaving, Rebecca racked her brains for some way to rescue this, but came up with nothing.

In the lobby, Maria Summers said to Rebecca: "That didn't go the way I expected."

It was not an apology, but it was as near to one as Maria was permitted, by her position, to offer. "That's okay," said Rebecca. "I'm sorry there wasn't more dialogue and less point-scoring."

"Is there anything we can do to move the senior people closer together on this issue?"

Rebecca was about to say that she did not know, then she was struck by a thought. "Maybe there is," she said. "Why don't you bring President Bush to Europe? Let him see for himself. Have him talk to the Poles and the Hungarians. I believe he might change his mind."

"You're right," said Maria. "I'm going to suggest it. Thank you."

"Good luck," said Rebecca.

CHAPTER SIXTY

Lili Franck and her family were astonished.

They were watching the news on West German television. Everyone in East Germany watched West German television, even the Communist Party apparatchiks: you could tell by the angle of the aerials on their roofs.

Lili's parents were there, Carla and Werner, plus Karolin and Alice, and Alice's fiancé, Helmut.

Today, May 2, the Hungarians had opened their border with Austria.

They did not do it discreetly. The government held a press conference at Hegyeshalom, the place where the road from Budapest to Vienna crossed the border. They might almost have been *trying* to provoke the Soviets into a reaction. With great ceremony, in front of hundreds of foreign cameras, the electronic alarm and surveillance system were switched off along the entire frontier.

The Franck family stared in incredulity.

Border guards with giant wire cutters began to slice up the fence, pick up great rectangles of barbed wire, carry them away, and throw them carelessly into a pile.

Lili said: "My God, that's the Iron Curtain coming down."

Werner said: "The Soviets won't stand for this."

Lili was not so sure. She was not certain of anything these days. "Surely the Hungarians wouldn't have done this unless they expected the Soviets to accept it, would they?"

Her father shook his head. "They may *think* they can get away with it . . ."

Alice was bright-eyed with hope. "But this means Helmut and I can leave!" she said. She and her fiancé were desperate to get out of East

Germany. "We can just drive to Hungary, as if we're going on holiday, then walk across the border!"

Lili sympathized: she yearned for Alice to have the opportunities in life that she herself had missed. But it could not possibly be that easy.

Helmut said: "Can we? Really?"

"No, you cannot," said Werner firmly. He pointed at the television set. "First of all, I don't see anyone actually walking across the border yet. Let's see if it really happens. Second, the Hungarian government could change its mind at any time and start arresting people. Third, if the Hungarians really do start to let people leave, the Soviets will send in the tanks and put a stop to it."

Lili thought her father might be too pessimistic. Now seventy, he was becoming timid in his old age. She had noticed it in business. He had scorned the idea of remote controls for television sets, and when they rapidly became indispensable his factory had had to scramble to catch up. "We'll see," Lili said. "In the next few days, some people are bound to try to escape. Then we'll find out whether anyone stops them."

Alice said excitedly: "What if Grandfather Werner is wrong? We can't just ignore a chance like this! What should we do?"

Her mother, Karolin, said anxiously: "It sounds dangerous."

Werner said to Lili: "What makes you think the East German government will continue to allow us to go to Hungary?"

"They'll have to," Lili argued. "If they canceled the summer holidays of thousands of families, there really would be a revolution."

"Even if it turns out to be safe for others, it may be different for us."

"Why?"

"Because we're the Franck family," Werner said in a tone of exasperation. "Your mother was a Social Democrat city councilor, your sister humiliated Hans Hoffmann, Walli killed a border guard, and you and Karolin sing protest songs. And our family business is in West Berlin, so they can't confiscate it. We've always been an irritant to the Communists. In consequence, unfortunately, we get special treatment."

Lili said: "So we have to take special precautions, that's all. Alice and Helmut will be extra cautious."

"I want to go, whatever the danger," Alice said emphatically. "I understand the risk, and I'm prepared to take it." She looked accusingly at her grandfather. "You've raised two generations under Communism. It's mean, it's brutal, it's stupid, and it's broke—yet it's still here. I want to live in the West. So does Helmut. We want our children to grow up in freedom and prosperity." She turned to her fiancé. "Don't we?"

"Yes," he said, though Lili sensed he was more wary than Alice.

"It's mad," said Werner.

Carla spoke for the first time. "It's not mad, my darling," she said forcefully to Werner. "It's dangerous, yes. But remember the things we did, the risks we took for freedom."

"Some of our number died."

Carla would not let up. "But we thought it was worth the risk."

"There was a war on. We had to defeat the Nazis."

"This is Alice and Helmut's war—the Cold War."

Werner hesitated, then sighed. "Perhaps you're right," he said reluctantly.

"Okay," said Carla. "In that case, let's make a plan."

Lili looked at the TV again. In Hungary, they were still dismantling the fence.

. . .

On election day in Poland, Tanya went to church with Danuta, who was a candidate.

It was a sunny Sunday, June 4, with a few puffy clouds in a blue sky. Danuta dressed her two children in their best clothes and brushed their hair. Marek put on a tie in the red and white colors of Solidarity, which were also the colors of the Polish flag. Danuta wore a hat, a white straw bowler with a red feather.

Tanya was in an agony of doubt. Was all this really happening? An election, in Poland? The fence coming down in Hungary? Disarmament in Europe? Did Gorbachev really mean it about openness and restructuring?

Tanya dreamed of freedom with Vasili. The two of them would tour the world: Paris, New York, Rio de Janeiro, Delhi. Vasili would be interviewed on television and talk about his work and the long years of secrecy. Tanya would write travel articles, maybe a book of her own.

But when she woke up from her daydream she waited, hour by hour, for the bad news: the roadblocks, the tanks, the arrests, the curfew, and the bald men in bad suits coming on television to announce that they had foiled a counterrevolutionary plot financed by the capitalist-imperialists.

The priest told his congregation to vote for the most godly candidates. As all Communists were in principle atheists, that was a clear steer. The authoritarian Polish clergy did not much like the liberal Solidarity movement, but they knew who their real enemies were.

The election had come sooner than Solidarity expected. The union had rushed to raise money, rent offices, hire staff, and mount a national election campaign, all in a few weeks. Jaruzelski had done this deliberately, to wrong-foot Solidarity, knowing that the government had an organization firmly in place and ready to go.

However, that was the last smart thing Jaruzelski had done. Since then the Communists had been lethargic, as if they were so sure of winning that they could hardly be bothered to campaign. Their slogan was "With us it's safer," which sounded like a condom ad. Tanya had put that joke in her report for TASS, and to her surprise the editors had not taken it out.

In the people's minds this was a contest between General Jaruzelski, the country's brutal leader for almost a decade, and the troublemaking electrician Lech Wałęsa. Danuta had her photograph taken with Wałęsa, as did every other Solidarity candidate, and the photographs had been put up everywhere. Throughout the campaign the union published a daily newspaper, written mostly by Danuta and her women friends. Solidarity's most popular poster showed Gary Cooper as Marshal Will Kane, holding a ballot paper instead of a gun, with the slogan HIGH NOON, 4 JUNE 1989.

Perhaps the incompetence of the Communist campaign was to be expected, Tanya thought. After all, the idea of going cap in hand to the people and saying "Please vote for me" was totally alien to the Polish ruling elite.

The new upper chamber, called the senate, had one hundred seats, and the Communists expected to win most of those. The Polish people had their backs to the wall, economically, and they would probably vote for the familiar Jaruzelski rather than the maverick Wałęsa, Tanya expected. In the lower chamber, called the Sejm, the Communists could not lose, because 65 percent of the seats were reserved for them and their allies.

Solidarity's aspirations were modest. They figured that if they won a substantial minority of votes, the Communists would be forced to give them a voice in the government.

Tanya hoped they were right.

After mass, Danuta shook hands with everyone in the church.

Then Tanya and the Gorski family went to the polling station. The ballot paper was long and complicated, so Solidarity had set up a stall outside to show people how to vote. Instead of marking their preferred candidates, they had to put a line through the ones they did not like. The Solidarity campaigners gleefully showed model ballot papers with all the Communists crossed out.

Tanya watched people voting. For most this was their first experience of a free election. She observed a shabbily dressed woman moving her pencil down the list, giving a little grunt of fulfillment each time she identified a Communist, and running her pencil through the name with a smile of pleasure. Tanya suspected the government might have been unwise to choose a system of marking the paper in which rejection could feel so physically satisfying.

She talked to some of the voters, asking what was on their minds when they made their choices. "I voted Communist," said a woman in an expensive coat. "They made this election possible." But most seemed to have picked Solidarity candidates. Tanya's sample was of course completely unscientific.

She went to Danuta's place for lunch, then the two women left Marek in charge of the children and drove in Tanya's car to Solidarity headquarters, which was upstairs at the Café Surprise, in the city center.

The mood there was up. The opinion polls gave Solidarity a lead, but no one relied on that because almost 50 percent were don't-knows. However, reports coming in from all over the country said morale was high. Tanya herself felt cheerful and optimistic. Whatever the result, a real election seemed to be taking place in a Soviet bloc country, and that alone was reason to be glad.

After the polls closed that evening Tanya went with Danuta to see her votes being counted. This was a tense moment. If the authorities decided to cheat, there were a hundred ways they could fix the result. Solidarity scrutineers watched closely, but no one saw any serious irregularity. This in itself was amazing.

And Danuta won by a landslide.

She had not really been expecting it, Tanya could tell from her look of pale shock. "I'm a deputy," she said unbelievingly. "Elected by the people." Then her face broke into that huge toothy grin, and she began to accept everyone's congratulations. So many people kissed her that Tanya began to worry about hygiene.

As soon as they could get away they drove through the lamplit streets back to the Café Surprise, where everyone was gathered around the television sets. Danuta's result was not the only landslide: Solidarity candidates were doing better than anyone expected, by far. "This is wonderful!" said Tanya.

"No, it's not," said Danuta gloomily.

Tanya realized that the Solidarity people were subdued. She was baffled by this glum reaction to triumphant news. "What on earth is wrong?"

"We're doing too well," Danuta said. "The Communists can't accept this. There will be a reaction."

Tanya had not thought of that.

"So far the government hasn't won anything," Danuta went on. "Even where they're unopposed, some Communist candidates haven't even gained the minimum fifty percent. It's too degrading. Jaruzelski will have to disallow the result."

"I'm going to speak to my brother," Tanya said.

She had a special number that enabled her to get through to the Kremlin quickly. It was late, but Dimka was still at the office. "Yes, Jaruzelski just called here," he told her. "I gather the Communists are being humiliated."

"What did Jaruzelski say?"

"He wants to impose martial law again, exactly as he did eight years ago."

Tanya's heart sank. "Shit." She remembered Danuta being dragged off to jail by the ZOMO thugs while her children cried. "Not again."

"He proposes to declare the election null and void. 'We still hold the levers of power in our hands,' he said."

"It's true," Tanya said dismally. "They have all the guns."

"But Jaruzelski is scared of doing this on his own. He wants Gorbachev's support."

Tanya was heartened. "What did Gorbi say?"

"He hasn't responded yet. Someone's waking him up right now."

"What do you think he'll do?"

"He'll probably tell Jaruzelski to solve his own problems. That's what he's been saying for the last four years. But I can't be sure. To see the party rejected so completely in a free election . . . that could be too much even for Gorbachev."

"When will you know?"

"Gorbachev is just going to say yes or no, then go back to sleep. Call me in an hour."

Tanya hung up. She did not know what to think. Clearly Jaruzelski was ready to clamp down, arrest all the Solidarity activists, throw civil liberties out the window, and reimpose his dictatorship, just as he had in 1981. It was what always happened when Communist countries got the smell of freedom in their nostrils. But Gorbachev said the old days were over. Was it true?

Poland was about to find out.

Tanya stared at the phone in an agony of suspense. What should she tell Danuta? She did not want to panic everyone. But maybe they should be warned of Jaruzelski's intentions.

Danuta said to her: "Now you're looking glum, too. What did your brother say?"

Tanya hesitated, then decided to say that nothing had been decided, which was the simple truth. "Jaruzelski called Gorbachev but hasn't reached him yet."

They continued to watch the screens. Solidarity was winning everything. So far, the Communists had not won a single contested seat. More results just confirmed the early signs. *Landslide* was hardly a strong enough word: it was more like a tsunami.

In the room over the café, euphoria mingled with fear. The gradual shift in power for which they had hoped was now out of the question.

One of two things would happen in the next twenty-four hours. The Communists might again seize power by force. Or, if they did not, they were finished forever.

Tanya forced herself to wait a full hour before calling Moscow again.

"They talked," Dimka said. "Gorbachev refused to back a crackdown."

"Thank heaven," said Tanya. "So what is Jaruzelski going to do?"

"Backpedal just as fast as he can."

"Really?" Tanya could hardly believe such good news.

"He's out of options."

"I suppose he is."

"Enjoy the celebration."

Tanya hung up and spoke to Danuta. "There will be no violence," she said. "Gorbachev has ruled it out."

"Oh, my God," said Danuta in a voice that mingled incredulity with jubilation. "We really have won, haven't we?"

"Yes," said Tanya, with a feeling of satisfaction and hope that went all the way to the bottom of her heart. "This is the beginning of the end."

· · ·

It was high summer and sweltering hot in Bucharest on July 7. Dimka and Natalya were there with Gorbachev for a Warsaw Pact summit. Their host was Nicolae Ceaușescu, the mad dictator of Romania.

The most important item on the agenda was "the Hungary problem." Dimka knew it had been put on the list by the East German leader, Erich Honecker. Hungary's liberalization threatened all the other Warsaw Pact countries, by calling attention to the repressive nature of their unreformed regimes, but it was worst for East Germany. Hundreds of East Germans on holiday in Hungary were leaving their tents and walking into the woods and through holes in the old fence to Austria and freedom. The roads leading from Lake Balaton to the frontier were littered with their tinny Trabant and Wartburg cars, abandoned without regret. Most had no passports, but that did not matter: they were transported to West Germany, where they were automatically given citizenship and helped to settle. No doubt they soon replaced their old cars with more reliable and comfortable Volkswagens.

The Warsaw Pact leaders met in a large room with flag-draped tables arranged in a rectangle. As always, aides such as Dimka and Natalya sat around the edges of the room. Honecker was the driving force, but Ceaușescu led the charge. He stood up from his seat next to Gorbachev and began to attack the reformist policies of the Hungarian government. He was a small, bent man with bushy eyebrows and wild eyes. Although he was talking to a few dozen people in a conference room, he shouted and gesticulated as if addressing thousands in a stadium. His twisted lips spat as he ranted. He made no bones about what he wanted: a repeat of 1956. He called for a Warsaw Pact invasion of Hungary to oust Miklós Németh and return the country to orthodox Communist Party rule.

Dimka looked around the room. Honecker was nodding. Czech hard man Miloš Jakeš wore an expression of approval. Bulgaria's Todor Zhivkov clearly agreed. Only Poland's leader, General Jaruzelski, sat unmoving and expressionless, perhaps humbled by his election defeat.

All these men were brutal tyrants, torturers, and mass murderers. Stalin had not been exceptional, he had been typical of Communist leaders. Any political system that allowed such people to rule was evil, Dimka reflected. Why did it take us all so long to figure that out?

But Dimka, like most of the people in the room, was watching Gorbachev.

The rhetoric no longer mattered. It was of no consequence who was right and who was wrong. No one in the room had the power to do anything without the consent of the man with the port-wine stain on his bald head.

Dimka thought he knew what Gorbachev was going to do. But he could never be sure. Gorbachev was divided, like the empire he ruled, between conservative and reformist tendencies. No speeches were likely to change his mind. Most of the time he just looked bored.

Ceaușescu's voice rose almost to a scream. At that moment Gorbachev caught the eye of Miklós Németh. The Russian gave the Hungarian a slight smile as Ceaușescu sputtered saliva and vituperation.

Then, to Dimka's utter astonishment, Gorbachev winked.

Gorbachev held the smile a second longer, then looked away and resumed his bored expression.

. . .

Maria managed to avoid Jasper Murray almost until the end of President Bush's European visit.

She had never met Jasper. She knew what he looked like: she had seen him on television, as everyone had. He was taller in real life, that was all. Over the years she had been the secret source of some of his best stories, but he did not know that. He only met George Jakes, the intermediary. They were careful. It was why they had never been found out.

She knew the whole story of Jasper's being fired from *This Day.* The White House had put pressure on Frank Lindeman, the owner of the network. That was how a star reporter came to be exiled. Although with the turmoil in Eastern Europe, plus Jasper's nose for a good story, the assignment had turned out to be a hot one.

Bush and his entourage, including Maria, ended up in Paris. Maria was standing in the Champs-Élysées with the press corps on Bastille Day, July 14, watching an interminable parade of military might, and looking forward to going home and making love to George again, when Jasper spoke to her. He pointed to a huge poster of Evie Williams advertising face cream. "She had a crush on me when she was fifteen years old," he said.

Maria looked at the picture. Evie Williams had been blacklisted by Hollywood for her politics, but she was a big star in Europe, and Maria recalled reading that her personal line of organic beauty products was making her more money than movies ever had.

"You and I have never met," Jasper said. "But I got to know your godson, Jack Jakes, when I was living with Verena Marquand."

Maria shook his hand warily. Talking to reporters was always dangerous. No matter what you said, the mere fact that you had had a conversation put you in a weak position, for then there could always be an argument about what you had actually said. "I'm glad to meet you at last," she said.

"I admire you for your achievements," he said. "Your career would be remarkable for a white man. For an African American woman, it's astonishing."

Maria smiled. Of course Jasper was charming—that was how he got people to talk. He was also completely untrustworthy, and would betray his mother for the sake of a story. She said neutrally: "How are you enjoying Europe?"

"Right now it's the most exciting place in the world," he said. "Lucky me."

"That's great."

"By contrast," Jasper said, "this trip has not been a success for President Bush."

Here it comes, Maria thought. She was in a difficult position. She had to defend the president and the policies of the State Department, even though she agreed with Jasper's assessment. Bush had failed to take leadership of the freedom movement in Eastern Europe: he was too timid. But she said: "We think it's been something of a triumph."

"Well, you have to say that. But, off the record, was it right for Bush to urge Jaruzelski—a Communist tyrant of the old school—to run for president in Poland?"

"Jaruzelski may well be the best candidate to oversee gradual reform," Maria said, though she did not believe it.

"Bush infuriated Lech Wałęsa by offering a paltry aid package of a hundred million dollars, when Solidarity had asked for ten billion."

"President Bush believes in caution," Maria argued. "He thinks the Poles need to reform their economy first, then get aid. Otherwise the money will be wasted. The president is a conservative. You may not like that, Jasper, but the American people do. That's why they elected him."

Jasper smiled, acknowledging a point scored, but he pressed on. "In Hungary, Bush praised the Communist government for removing the fence, not the opposition who put the pressure on. He kept telling the Hungarians not to go too far, too fast! What kind of advice is that from the leader of the free world?"

Maria did not contradict Jasper. He was one hundred percent correct. She decided to deflect him. To give herself a moment to think, she watched a low-loader go by bearing a long missile with a French flag painted on its side. Then she said: "You're missing a better story."

He raised a skeptical eyebrow. That accusation was not often leveled at Jasper Murray. "Go on," he said in a tone of mild amusement.

"I can't talk to you on the record."

"Off it, then."

She gave him a hard look. "So long as we're clear on that."

"We are."

"Okay. You probably know that some of the advice the president has been getting suggests that Gorbachev is a fraud, glasnost and perestroika are Communist flummery, and the whole charade is no more than a way to trick the West into dropping its guard and disarming prematurely."

"Who gives him this advice?"

The answer was the CIA, the national security adviser, and the secretary of defense, but Maria was not going to run them down when talking to a journalist, even off the record, so she said: "Jasper, if you don't know that already, you're not the reporter we all think you are."

He grinned. "Okay. So what's the big story?"

"President Bush was inclined to accept that advice—before he came on this trip. The story is that he has seen the reality on the ground here in Europe, and has altered his view accordingly. In Poland he said: 'I have this heady feeling that I'm witnessing history being made on the spot.'"

"Can I use that quote?"

"You may. He said it to me."

"Thanks."

"The president now believes that change in the Communist world is real and permanent, and we need to give it guarded encouragement, instead of kidding ourselves that it isn't really happening."

Jasper gave Maria a long look that, she thought, had in it a measure of surprised respect. "You're right," he said at last. "That is a better story. Back in Washington the Cold Warriors, like Dick Cheney and Brent Scowcroft, are going to be mad as hell."

"You said that," Maria said. "I didn't."

. . .

Lili, Karolin, Alice, and Helmut drove from Berlin to Lake Balaton, in Hungary, in Lili's white Trabant. As usual, it took two days. On the way Lili and Karolin sang every song they knew.

They were singing to cover their fear. Alice and Helmut were going to try to escape to the West. No one knew what would happen.

Lili and Karolin would stay behind. Both were single but, all the same, their lives were in East Germany. They hated the regime, but they wanted to oppose it, not flee from it. It was different for Alice and Helmut, who had their lives in front of them.

Lili knew only two people who had tried to leave: Rebecca, and Walli. Rebecca's fiancé had fallen from a roof and been crippled for life. Walli had run over a border guard and killed him, a trauma that had haunted him for years. They were not happy precedents. But the situation had changed now—hadn't it?

On the first evening at the holiday camp they came across a middle-aged man called Berthold, sitting outside his tent, holding forth to half a dozen young people drinking beer from cans. "It's obvious, isn't it?" he said in a voice that was confidential but carrying. "The whole thing is a trap set by the Stasi. It's their new way of catching subversives."

A young man sitting on the ground, smoking a cigarette, seemed skeptical. "How does that work, then?"

"As soon as you cross the border, you're arrested by the Austrians. They hand you over to the Hungarian police, who send you back to East Germany in handcuffs. Then you go straight to the interrogation rooms in Stasi headquarters in Lichtenberg."

A girl standing nearby said: "How would you know a thing like that?"

"My cousin tried to cross the border here," said Berthold. "Last thing he said to me was: 'I'll send you a postcard from Vienna.' Now he's in a prison camp near Dresden, working in a uranium mine. It's the only way our government can get people to work in those mines, no one else will do it—the radiation gives you lung cancer."

The family discussed Berthold's theory in low voices before going to bed. Alice said scornfully: "Berthold is one of those men who know it all. How would he find out that his cousin is working in a uranium mine? The government doesn't admit to using prisoners that way."

But Helmut was worried. "He may be an idiot, but what if his story is true? The border could be a trap."

Alice said: "Why would the Austrians send escapers back? They have no love of Communism."

"They may not want the trouble and expense of dealing with them. Why should the Austrians care about East Germans?"

They argued for an hour and came to no conclusion. Lili lay awake for a long time, worrying.

Next morning in the communal dining room Lili spotted Berthold regaling a different group of young people with his theories, a large plate of ham and cheese in front of him. Was he genuine, or a Stasi faker? She felt she had to know. He looked as if he would be there some time. On impulse, she decided to search his tent. She left the room.

Tents were not secured: holidaymakers were simply advised not to leave money or valuables behind. All the same, Berthold's entrance was tightly laced.

Lili began to untie the strings, trying to appear relaxed, as if she had every right to do it. Her heart was like a drumbeat in her chest. She made an effort not to glance guiltily at people walking by. She was used to sneaking around—the gigs she played with Karolin were always semi-illegal—but she had never done anything quite like this. If Berthold should for some reason abandon his breakfast early and come back sooner than she expected, what would she say? "Oops, wrong tent, sorry!" The tents were all alike. He might not believe her—but what would he do, go to the police?

She opened the flap and stepped inside.

Berthold was neat, for a man. His clothes were folded in a suitcase, and there was a drawstring bag full of laundry. He had a sponge bag containing a safety razor and shaving soap. His bed was made of canvas stretched across metal tubing. Beside the bed was a small pile of magazines in German. It all looked innocent.

Don't rush, she told herself. Look carefully for clues. Who is this man and what is he doing here?

A sleeping bag was folded on top of the camp bed. When Lili picked it up she felt something heavy. She unzipped the bag and rummaged inside. She found a book of pornographic photos—and a gun.

It was a small black pistol with a short barrel. She did not know much about firearms, and she could not identify the make, but she thought it was what they called a nine-millimeter. It looked designed to be concealed.

She stuffed it into the pocket of her jeans.

She had the answer to her question. Berthold was not a know-all braggart. He was a Stasi agent, sent here to spread scare stories and discourage escapers.

Lili refolded the sleeping bag and stepped out of the tent. Berthold was not in sight. She quickly laced up the tent flap with trembling fingers. Another few seconds and she would be safe. As soon as Berthold looked for his gun, he would know that someone had been there, but if she could get away now he would never know who. Lili guessed he would not even report the theft to the Hungarian police, for they would surely disapprove of a German secret agent bringing a pistol to one of their holiday camps.

She walked briskly away.

Karolin was in Helmut and Alice's tent, and they were talking in low voices, still arguing about whether the border crossing might be a trap. Lili interrupted the discussion. "Berthold is a Stasi agent," she said. "I searched his tent." She drew the gun from her pocket.

"That's a Makarov," said Helmut, who had served in the army. "A Soviet-made semiautomatic pistol, standard issue for the Stasi."

Lili said: "If the border really were a trap, the Stasi would be keeping the fact secret. The way Berthold is telling everyone pretty much proves it's not true."

Helmut nodded. "That's good enough for me. We're going."

They all stood up. Helmut said to Lili: "Would you like me to get rid of the gun?"

"Yes, please." She handed it over, relieved to be rid of it.

"I'll find a secluded spot on the beach and throw it in the lake."

While Helmut was doing that, the women put towels and swimsuits and bottles of sun lotion into the trunk of the Trabi as if they were going off for a day's outing, maintaining the fiction of a family holiday. When Helmut came back, they drove to the grocery and bought cheese, bread, and wine for a picnic.

Then they headed west.

Lili kept looking behind, but as far as she could tell no one was following them.

They drove fifty miles and turned off the main road when they were close to the border. Alice had a map and a magnetic compass. As they wound around country roads, pretending to look for a picnic spot in the forest, they saw several cars with East German plates abandoned at the roadside, and knew they were in the right area.

There was no sign of officialdom, but Lili worried all the same. Clearly the East German secret police had an interest in escapers, but there was probably nothing they could do.

They were passing a small lake when Alice said: "I calculate we're less than a mile from the fence here."

A few seconds later Helmut, who was at the wheel, turned off the road onto an unpaved track through the trees. He stopped the car in a clearing a few steps from the water.

He turned off the engine. "Well," he said into the silence. "Are we going to pretend to have lunch?"

"No," said Alice, her voice high-pitched with tension. "I want to go, now."

They all got out of the car.

Alice led the way, checking the compass. The going was easy, with little undergrowth to slow their steps. Tall pines filtered the sunshine, throwing patches of gold onto the carpet of needles underfoot. The forest was quiet. Lili heard the cry of some kind of waterfowl, and occasionally the distant roar of a tractor.

They passed a yellow Wartburg Knight, half-hidden by low-hanging branches, its windows broken and its fenders already rusting. A bird flew out of its open trunk, and Lili wondered whether it had nested there.

She scanned the surroundings constantly, looking for the patch of green or gray wool that would betray a uniform, but she saw no one. Helmut was equally alert, she noticed.

They climbed a rise, then the forest ran out abruptly. They emerged onto a strip of cleared land and saw, a hundred yards away, the fence.

It was not impressive. The posts were of rough-hewn wood. There were several rows of wire, which presumably had once been electrified. The top row, at a height of six feet, was plain barbed wire. On the far side was a field of yellow grain ripening in the August sun.

They crossed the cleared strip and came to the fence.

Alice said: "We can climb over the fence right here."

Helmut said: "They have definitely switched off the electricity . . . ?"

"Yes," said Alice.

Impatiently, Karolin reached out and touched the wire. She touched all the wires, grasping each firmly in her hand. "Off," she said.

Alice kissed and hugged her mother and Lili. Helmut shook hands.

A hundred yards away, from over a rise, two soldiers appeared in the gray tunics and tall peaked caps of the Hungarian Border Guard Service.

Lili said: "Oh, no!"

Both men leveled their rifles.

"Stand still, everyone," said Helmut.

Alice said: "I can't believe we got this close!" She began to cry.

"Don't despair," said Helmut. "It's not over yet."

Coming closer, the guards lowered their rifles and spoke in German. No doubt they knew exactly what was going on. "What are you doing here?" one said.

"We came to picnic in the woods," Lili said.

"A picnic? Really?"

"We meant no harm!"

"You are not allowed here."

Lili was desperately afraid the soldiers would arrest them. "All right, all right," she said. "We'll go back!"

She feared that Helmut might put up a fight. They might be killed, all four of them. She felt shaky and her legs were weak.

The second guard spoke. "Be careful," he said. He pointed along the fence in the direction from which he had come. "A quarter of a mile from here is a gap in the fence. You might accidentally cross the border."

The two guards looked at one another and laughed heartily. Then they went on their way.

Lili stared in astonishment at their retreating backs. They kept on walking, not looking back. Lili and the others watched them until they were out of sight in silence.

Then Lili said: "They seemed to be telling us . . ."

"To find the gap in the fence!" Helmut said. "Let's do it, quick!"

They hurried in the direction in which the guard had pointed. They kept close to the edge of the forest, in case they needed to hide. Sure enough, after a quarter of a mile they came to a place where the fence was broken. The wooden posts had been uprooted and the wires, snapped in places, lay flat on the ground. It looked as if a heavy truck had driven through it. The earth all around was heavily trodden, the grass brown and sparse. Beyond the gap, a path between two fields led to a distant clump of trees with a few roofs showing: a village, or perhaps just a hamlet.

Freedom.

A small pine tree nearby was hung with key rings, thirty, forty, maybe fifty of them. People had left behind the keys to their apartments and cars, a defiant gesture to show that they were never coming back. As the branches were moved by a light breeze, the metal glittered in the sunlight. It looked like a Christmas tree.

"Don't hesitate," Lili said. "We said good-bye ten minutes ago. Just go."

Alice said: "I love you, Mother, and Lili."

"Go," said Karolin.

Alice took Helmut's hand.

Lili looked up and down the cleared strip alongside the fence. There was no one in sight.

The two young people walked through the gap, stepping carefully over the fallen fence.

On the other side, they stopped and waved, even though they were only ten feet away. "We're free!" Alice said.

Lili said: "Give my love to Walli."

"And mine," said Karolin.

Alice and Helmut walked on, hand in hand, up the path between the fields of grain.

At the far end they waved again.

Then they entered the little village and disappeared from sight.

Karolin's face was wet with tears. "I wonder if we'll ever see them again," she said.

CHAPTER SIXTY-ONE

West Berlin made Walli nostalgic. He remembered being a teenager with a guitar, playing Everly Brothers hits in the Minnesänger folk club just off the Ku'damm, and dreaming of going to America to be a pop star. I got what I wanted, he thought—and a lot that I didn't.

While he was checking into his hotel he ran into Jasper Murray. "I heard you were over here," said Walli. "I guess what's happening in Germany is exciting to cover."

"It is," said Jasper. "Americans aren't normally interested in European news, but this is special."

"Your show, *This Day*, isn't the same without you. I hear its ratings are down."

"I probably ought to pretend to be sorry. What are you up to these days?"

"Making a new album. I left Dave mixing it in California. He'll probably fuck it up with strings and a glockenspiel."

"What brings you to Berlin?"

"I'm meeting my daughter, Alice. She escaped from East Germany."

"Are your parents still there?"

"Yes, and my sister Lili." And Karolin, Walli thought, but he did not mention her. He longed for her to escape, too. Deep in his heart he still missed her, despite all the years that had passed. "Rebecca's here in the West," he added. "She's a big shot in the Foreign Office now."

"I know. She's been helpful to me. Maybe we could do a piece on a family divided by the Wall. It would show the human suffering caused by the Cold War."

"No," said Walli firmly. He had not forgotten the interview Jasper had done back in the sixties, which had caused so much trouble for the Francks in the East. "My family would be made to suffer by the East German government."

"Too bad. Good to see you, anyhow."

Walli checked into the Presidential Suite. He turned on the TV in the living room. The set was a Franck, made in his father's factory. The news was all about people fleeing East Germany via Hungary and, now, via Czechoslovakia too. He left the set on with the sound low. It was his habit to have the TV on when he was doing other things. He had been thrilled to learn that Elvis did the same.

He took a shower and put on fresh clothes. Then the desk called to say that Alice and Helmut were downstairs. "Send them up," Walli said.

He felt nervous, which was silly. This was his daughter. But he had seen her only once in her twenty-five years. At that time she had been a skinny teenager with long fair hair, reminding him of Karolin when he had first met her, back in the sixties.

A minute later the bell rang and he opened the door. Alice was now a young woman, with no teenage gawkiness. Her fair hair was cut in a bob, so she no longer looked so strikingly like the young Karolin, though she had Karolin's thousand-candlepower smile. She was dressed in shabby East German clothes and down-at-heel shoes, and Walli made a mental note to take her shopping.

He kissed her awkwardly on both cheeks and shook hands with Helmut.

Alice looked around the suite and said: "Wow, nice room."

It was nothing by comparison with hotels in Los Angeles, but Walli did not tell her that. She had a lot to learn, but there was plenty of time.

He ordered coffee and cakes from room service. They sat around the table in the living room. "This is weird," Walli said candidly. "You're my kid, but we're strangers."

"I know your songs, though," Alice said. "Every one. You weren't there, but you've been singing to me all my life."

"That's kind of awesome."

"Yeah."

They told him the story of their escape in detail. "Looking back, it was easy," Alice said. "But at the time I was scared to death."

They were living temporarily in an apartment rented for them by the Franck factory accountant, Enok Andersen. "What are you going to do, long term?" Walli asked.

Helmut said: "I'm an electrical engineer, but I'd like to learn about business. Next week I'm going on the road with one of the salesmen for Franck televisions. Your father, Werner, says that's the way to begin."

Alice said: "In the East I was working in a pharmacy. At first I'll probably do the same here, but one day I'd like to have my own shop."

Walli was pleased they were thinking about work. He had nursed a secret anxiety that they might want to live on his money, which would have been bad for them. He smiled and said: "I'm glad neither of you wants to be in the music business."

Alice said: "But the main thing we want to do is have children."

"I'm so glad. I can't wait to be a granddad rock star. Are you going to get married?"

"We've been talking about that," she said. "We never cared about it, living in the East, but now we kind of want to. How would you feel about that?"

"Marriage itself is not a big issue for me, but I'd be kind of thrilled if you decided to do it."

"Good. Daddy, would you sing at my wedding?"

That came from behind and knocked Walli over. It was all he could do not to cry. "Sure, honey," he managed to say. "I'd be glad to." To cover his emotion he turned to the television.

The screen was showing a demonstration the previous evening in Leipzig, in East Germany. Protesters carrying candles marched in silence from a church. They were peaceful, but police vans drove into the crowd, running over several people, then the cops jumped out and started arresting marchers.

Helmut said: "Those bastards."

Walli said: "What is the demonstration about?"

"The right to travel," said Helmut. "We've escaped, but we can't go back. Alice has you, now, but she can't visit her mother. And I'm separated from both my parents. We don't know if we'll ever see them again."

Alice said angrily: "People are demonstrating because there's no reason why we should live like this. I should be able to see my mother as well as my father. We should be allowed to go to and fro between East and West. Germany is one country. We should get rid of that Wall."

"Amen to that," said Walli.

．　．　．

Dimka liked his boss. Gorbachev in his deepest soul believed in the truth. Since Lenin died, every Soviet leader had been a liar. They had all glossed over what was wrong and declined to acknowledge reality. The most striking characteristic of Soviet leadership for the last sixty-five years was the refusal to face facts. Gorbachev was different. As he struggled to navigate through the storm that was battering the Soviet Union, he held on to that one guiding principle, that the truth must be told. Dimka was full of admiration.

Both Dimka and Gorbachev were pleased when Erich Honecker was deposed as leader of East Germany. Honecker had lost control of the country and the party. But they were disappointed by his successor. To Dimka's annoyance, Honecker's loyal deputy, Egon Krenz, took over. It was like replacing Tweedledum with Tweedledee.

All the same, Dimka thought Gorbachev would have to give Krenz a helping hand. The Soviet Union could not permit the collapse of East Germany. Perhaps the USSR could live with democratic elections in Poland and market forces in Hungary, but Germany was different. It was divided, like Europe, into East and West, Communist and capitalist; and if West Germany were to triumph that would signal the ascendancy of capitalism, and the end of the dream of Marx and Lenin. Even Gorbachev could not allow that—could he?

Krenz made the usual pilgrimage to Moscow two weeks later. Dimka shook the hand of a fleshy-faced man with thick gray hair and a look of smug satisfaction. He might have been a heartthrob in his youth.

In the grand office with the yellow-paneled walls, Gorbachev greeted him with cool courtesy.

Krenz brought with him a report by his chief economic planner saying that East Germany was bankrupt. The report had been suppressed by Honecker, Krenz claimed. Dimka knew that the truth about East Germany's economy had been hidden for decades. All the propaganda about economic growth had been lies. Productivity in factories and mines was as low as 50 percent of that in the West.

"We have kept going by borrowing," Krenz told Gorbachev, sitting on a black leather chair in the grand Kremlin room. "Ten billion deutschmarks a year."

Even Gorbachev was shocked. "Ten *billion*?"

"We have been taking out short-term loans to pay the interest on long-term loans."

Dimka put in: "Which is illegal. If the banks find out . . ."

"The interest on our debt is now four and a half billion dollars a year, which is two-thirds of our entire foreign currency earnings. We must have your help to deal with this crisis."

Gorbachev bristled. He hated it when East European leaders begged for money.

Krenz wheedled. "East Germany is in a sense the child of the Soviet Union." He tried a masculine joke. "One should acknowledge the paternity of one's children."

Gorbachev did not even smile. "We are in no position to offer you assistance," he said bluntly. "Not in the present condition of the USSR."

Dimka was surprised. He had not expected Gorbachev to be this tough.

Krenz was baffled. "Then what am I to do?"

"You must be honest with your people, and tell them that they cannot continue to live in the manner they have become used to."

"There will be trouble," Krenz said. "A state of emergency would have to be declared. Measures must be taken to prevent a mass breakthrough across the Wall."

Dimka thought this was approaching political blackmail. Gorbachev did, too, and he stiffened. "In that case, do not expect to be rescued by the Red Army," Gorbachev said. "You have to solve these problems yourself."

Did he really mean it? Was the USSR really going to wash its hands of East Germany? Dimka's excitement mounted with his astonishment. Was Gorbachev willing to go all the way?

Krenz looked like a priest who has realized there is no God. East Germany had been created by the Soviet Union, subsidized from the Kremlin's coffers, and protected by the strength of the Soviet military.

He could not take in the idea that that was all over. He clearly had absolutely no idea what to do next.

When he had gone, Gorbachev said to Dimka: "Issue a reminder to commanders of our forces in East Germany. They must not *under any circumstances* get involved in conflicts between the government there and its citizens. This is an absolute priority."

My God, Dimka thought, is this really the end?

. . .

By November there were demonstrations every week in major towns in East Germany. The numbers grew larger and the crowds grew bolder. They could not be crushed by brutal police baton charges.

Lili and Karolin were invited to play at a rally in the Alexander Platz, not far from their home. Several hundred thousand people showed up. Someone had painted a huge placard with the slogan WIR SIND DAS VOLK, "We are the people." All around the edges of the square were police in riot gear, waiting for the order to wade into the crowd with their truncheons. But the cops looked more frightened than the demonstrators.

Speaker after speaker denounced the Communist regime, and the police did nothing.

The organizers permitted pro-Communist speakers, too, and to Lili's astonishment the government's chosen defender was Hans Hoffmann. From her position in the wings, where she and Karolin were waiting for their turn onstage, she stared at the familiar, stooped figure of the man who had persecuted her family for a quarter of a century. Despite his expensive blue coat he was shivering from the cold—or perhaps it was fear.

When Hans tried to smile amiably, he succeeded only in looking like a vampire. "Comrades," he said, "the party has listened to the voices of the people, and new measures are on the way."

The crowd knew this was bullshit, and they began to hiss.

"But we must proceed in an orderly fashion, acknowledging the leading role of the party in developing Communism."

The hissing turned to booing.

Lili watched Hans closely. His expression showed rage and frustration. A year ago, one word from him could have destroyed any of the people in the crowd; but now, suddenly, they seemed to have the power. He could not even shut them up. He had to raise his voice to a shout in order to be heard, even with the help of the microphone. "In particular, we must not make every member of the state security organizations into scapegoats for whatever mistakes may have been made by the former leadership."

This was no less than a plea for sympathy on behalf of the bullies and sadists who had been oppressing the people for decades, and the crowd was outraged. They jeered and yelled: *"Stasi raus,"* "Stasi out."

Hans yelled at the top of his voice: "After all, they were only obeying orders!"

That brought a roar of incredulous laughter.

For Hans, to be laughed at was the worst fate. He flushed with rage. Suddenly Lili recalled the scene, twenty-eight years ago, when Rebecca had thrown Hans's shoes at him from the upstairs window. It had been the scornful laughter of the women neighbors that had driven Hans into a fury.

Now Hans remained at the microphone, unable to speak over the noise, but unwilling to give in. It was a battle of wills between him and the crowd, and he lost. His arrogant expression crumpled, and he seemed close to tears. At last he turned from the microphone and stepped away from the lectern.

He cast one more look at the crowd, laughing and jeering at him, and gave up. As he walked off, he saw Lili and recognized her. Their eyes met as she walked onstage with Karolin, both carrying guitars. In that instant he looked like a beaten dog, so tragic that Lili almost felt sorry for him.

Then she passed him and moved to center stage. Some of the crowd recognized Lili and Karolin, others knew their names, and they roared a welcome. Lili and Karolin went up to the microphones. They strummed a major chord, then together they launched into "This Land Is Your Land."

And the crowd went wild.

. . .

Bonn was a provincial town on the banks of the Rhine River. It was an unlikely choice for a national capital, and had been picked for precisely that reason, to symbolize its temporary nature, and the faith of the German people that one day Berlin would again be the capital of a reunited Germany. But that had been forty years ago, and Bonn was still the capital.

It was a boring place, but that suited Rebecca, for she worked too hard to have a social life, except when Fred Bíró was in town.

She was busy. Her area of expertise was Eastern Europe, which was in the throes of a revolution whose end no one could see. Most days she had working lunches, but today she took a break. She left the Foreign Office and walked on her own to an inexpensive restaurant where she ordered her favorite dish, *Himmel und Erde,* heaven and earth, made of potatoes and apples with bacon.

While she was eating, Hans Hoffmann appeared.

Rebecca pushed back her chair and stood up. Her first thought was that he had come to kill her. She was on the point of screaming for help when she noticed the expression on his face. He looked defeated and sad. Her fear vanished: he was no longer dangerous.

"Please don't be afraid, I mean no harm," he said.

She remained standing. "What do you want?"

"A few words. A minute or two, no more."

For a moment she wondered how he had managed to come from East to West Germany, then she realized that travel restrictions did not apply to senior officers in the secret police. They could do anything they liked. He had probably told his colleagues that he had an intelligence mission in Bonn. Perhaps he did.

The restaurant proprietor came over and said: "Is everything all right, Frau Held?"

Rebecca stared at Hans a moment longer. Then she said: "Yes, thank you, Günther, I think it's okay." She sat down again and Hans sat opposite.

She picked up her fork and put it down again. She had lost her appetite. "A minute or two, then."

"Help me," he said.

She could hardly believe her ears. "What?" she said. "Help *you?*"

"It's all falling apart. I have to get out. The crowds laugh at me. I'm afraid they'll kill me."

"What on earth do you imagine I might do for you?"

"I need a place to stay, money, papers."

"Are you out of your mind? After all you've done to me and my family?"

"Don't you understand why I did those things?"

"Because you hate us!"

"Because I love you."

"Don't be ridiculous."

"I was assigned to spy on you and your family, yes. I dated you in order to get inside the house. But then something happened. I fell in love with you."

He had said this once before, on the day she escaped over the Wall. He really meant it. He *was* out of his mind, she decided. She began to feel scared again.

"I told no one of my feelings," he said, smiling nostalgically, as if he were recalling an innocent youthful romance rather than a wicked deception. "I pretended to be exploiting you and manipulating your feelings. But I really loved you. Then you said we should get married. I was in heaven! I had the perfect excuse to give my superiors."

He was living in a dreamworld, but was that not true of the entire East German ruling elite?

"That year that we spent together, as man and wife, was the best time of my life," Hans said. "And your rejection broke my heart."

"How can you say that?"

"Why do you think I haven't remarried?"

She was stupefied. "I don't know," she said.

"I have no interest in other women. Rebecca, you are the love of my life."

She stared at him. She realized that this was not just a stupid story, a hopeless attempt to gain sympathy. Hans was sincere. He meant every word.

"Take me back," he pleaded.

"No."

"Please."

"The answer is no," she said. "It will always be no. Nothing you could say would change my mind. Please don't force me to use harsh words to make you understand." I don't know why I'm reluctant to hurt him, she thought; he never hesitated to be cruel to me. "Just accept what I have said to you and leave."

"All right," he said sadly. "I knew you'd say this, but I had to try." He stood up. "Thank you, Rebecca. Thank you for that year of happiness. I will always love you." He turned away and walked out of the restaurant.

Rebecca stared after him, still deep in shock. God in heaven, she thought; I wasn't expecting that.

CHAPTER SIXTY-TWO

I t was a cold November day in Berlin, with an obscuring mist and a brimstone smell of sulfur in the air from the smoky factories in the infernal East. Tanya, hastily transferred here from Warsaw to help cover the mounting crisis, felt that East Germany was about to have a heart attack. Everything was breaking down. In a remarkable repeat of what had happened in 1961 before the Wall went up, so many people had fled to the West that schools were closing for lack of teachers and hospitals were running on skeleton staffing. Those who remained behind became more and more angry and frustrated.

The new leader, Egon Krenz, was focusing on travel. He hoped that if he could satisfy people on that issue, other grievances would fade away. Tanya thought he was wrong: demanding more freedom was likely to become a habit with East Germans. Krenz had published new travel regulations on November 6 that would permit people to go abroad, with permission from the Interior Ministry, taking with them fifteen deutschmarks, about enough for a plate of sausages and a stein of beer in West Germany. This concession was scorned by the public. Today, November 9, the increasingly desperate leader had called a press conference to reveal yet another new travel law.

Tanya sympathized with the yearning of East Germans to be free to go where they wished. She longed for the same liberty for herself and Vasili. He was world famous, but he had to hide behind a pseudonym. He had never left the Soviet Union, where his books were not published. He should be able to go and accept in person the prizes his alter ego had won, and bask a little in the sunshine of acclaim—and she wanted to go with him.

Unfortunately she did not see how East Germany could ever set its people free. It could hardly exist as an independent state: that was why they had built the Wall in the first place. If they let their citizens travel, millions would leave permanently. West Germany might be a prissily conservative country, with old-fashioned attitudes on women's rights, but it was a paradise by comparison with the East. No country could survive the exodus of its most enterprising young people. Therefore Krenz would never willingly give East Germans the one thing they wanted above all else.

So it was with low expectations that Tanya went to the International Press Center on Mohren Strasse a few minutes before six in the evening. The room was packed with journalists, photographers, and television cameras. The rows of red seats were full, and Tanya had to join the crowd around the sides of the room. The international press corps was here in force: they could smell blood.

Krenz's press officer, Günter Schabowski, came into the room with three other officials at six sharp and sat at the table on the platform. He had gray hair and wore a gray suit and a gray tie. He was a competent bureaucrat whom Tanya liked and trusted. For an hour he announced ministerial changes and administrative reforms.

Tanya marveled at the sight of a Communist government scrambling to satisfy a public demand for change. It was almost unknown. And on the rare occasions when it had happened, the tanks had rolled in soon afterward. She recalled the agonizing disappointments of the Prague Spring in 1968 and Solidarity in 1981. But, according to her brother, the Soviet Union no longer had the power or the will to crush dissent. She hardly dared to hope it was true. She pictured a life in which she and Vasili could write the truth without fear. Freedom. It was hard to imagine.

At seven Schabowski announced the new travel law. "It will be possible for every citizen of East Germany to leave the country using border crossing points," he said. That was not very illuminating, and several journalists asked for clarification.

Schabowski himself seemed uncertain. He put on a pair of half-moon spectacles and read the decree aloud. "Private travel to foreign countries can be applied for without presentation of existing visa requirements or proving the need to travel or familial relationships."

It was all written in obfuscatory bureaucratic language, but it sounded good. Someone said: "When does this new regulation come into effect?"

Schabowski clearly did not know. Tanya noticed that he was perspiring. She guessed that the new law had been drafted in a rush. He shuffled the papers in front of him, looking for the answer. "As far as I know," he said, "immediately, without delay."

Tanya was bewildered. Something was effective immediately—but what? Could anyone just drive up to a checkpoint and cross? But the press conference came to an end without any further information.

Tanya wondered what to write as she walked the short distance back to the Hotel Metropol on Friedrich Strasse. In the grubby grandiosity of the marble lobby, Stasi agents in their customary leather jackets and blue jeans lounged around, smoking and watching a television set with a bad picture. It was showing film from the press conference. As Tanya got her room key, she heard one receptionist say to another: "What does that mean? Can we just go?"

No one knew.

.   .   .

Walli was in his West Berlin hotel suite, watching the news with Rebecca, who had flown in to see Alice and Helmut. They were all planning to have dinner together.

Walli and Rebecca puzzled over a low-key report on ZDF's seven o'clock *Today* program. There were new travel regulations for East Germans, but it was not clear what they meant. Walli could not figure out whether his family would be allowed to visit him in West Germany or not. "I wonder if I might even see Karolin again soon," he mused.

Alice and Helmut arrived a few minutes later, pulling off their cold-weather coats and scarves.

At eight Walli switched over to ARD's *Day Show*, but did not learn much more.

It seemed impossible that the Wall that had blighted Walli's life could be opened. In a flash of memory that was all too familiar, he relived those few traumatic seconds at the wheel of Joe Henry's old black Framo van. He recalled his terror as he saw the border guard kneel down and aim the submachine gun, his panic as he swung the wheel and drove at the guard, his confusion as bullets shattered his windscreen. He was sickened as he felt the sensation of his wheels bumping over a human being. Then he crashed through the barrier to freedom.

The Wall had taken his innocence. It had also taken Karolin from him. And his daughter's childhood.

That daughter, now a few days from her twenty-sixth birthday, was saying: "Is the Wall still the Wall, or not?"

Rebecca said: "I can't make it out. It's almost as if they've opened the border by mistake."

Walli said: "Shall we go out and see what's happening on the streets?"

. . .

Lili, Karolin, Werner, and Carla regularly watched ARD's *Day Show*, as did millions of people in East Germany. They thought it told the truth, unlike their own state-controlled news shows, which depicted a fantasy world no one believed in. All the same, they were puzzled by the ambiguous eight o'clock news. Carla said: "Is the border open or not?"

Werner said: "It can't be."

Lili stood up. "Well, I'm going to have a look."

In the end all four of them went.

As soon as they stepped out of the house and breathed the cold night air, they felt the emotional charge in the atmosphere. The streets of East Berlin, dimly lit by yellow lamps, were unusually busy with people and cars. Everyone was headed the same way, toward the Wall, mostly in groups. Some young men were trying to thumb a ride, a crime that would have got them arrested a week ago. People were talking to strangers, asking what they knew, whether it was really true that they could go to West Berlin now.

Karolin said to Lili: "Walli is in West Berlin. I heard it on the radio. He must have come to see Alice." She looked thoughtful. "I hope they like each other."

The Franck family walked south on Friedrich Strasse until they saw, in the distance, the powerful floodlights of Checkpoint Charlie, a compound that occupied the street for an entire block, from Zimmer Strasse on the near, Communist side, to Koch Strasse, which was free.

Coming closer, they saw people pouring out of the Stadtmitte subway station, swelling the crowd. There was also a line of cars, their drivers clearly unsure whether to approach the checkpoint or not. Lili sensed the feeling of celebration, but she was not sure they had anything to celebrate. As far as she could see, the gates were not open.

Many people held back, just out of range of the floodlights, afraid to show their faces; but the bolder ones approached nearer, committing the criminal offense of "unwarrantable intrusion into a border area," despite the risk of arrest and a sentence of three years in a labor camp.

The street narrowed as it approached the checkpoint, and the crowd thickened. Lili and her family pushed through to the front. Before them, under lights as bright as day, they could see the red-and-white gates for pedestrians and cars, the lounging border guards with their guns, the customs buildings, and the watchtowers rising over it all. Inside a glass-walled command post, an officer was talking on the telephone, making large, frustrated arm-waving gestures as he spoke.

To the left and right of the checkpoint, stretching away along Koch Strasse in both directions, was the hated Wall. Lili felt a sickening lurch in her stomach. This was the edifice that for most of her life had split her family into two halves that almost never met. She hated the Wall even more than she hated Hans Hoffmann.

Lili said aloud: "Has anyone tried to walk through?"

A woman next to her said angrily: "They turn you away. They say you need a visa from a police station. But I went to the police station and they didn't know anything about it."

A month ago, the woman would have shrugged her shoulders at this typical bureaucratic foul-up and gone home, but tonight things were different. She was still here, unsatisfied, protesting. No one was going home.

The people around Lili broke into a rhythmic chant: "Open up! Open up!"

When they trailed off, Lili thought she could hear chanting from the far side. She strained her ears. What were they saying? Eventually she made it out: "Come over! Come over!" She realized that West Berliners, too, must be gathering at checkpoints.

What was going to happen? How would this end?

A line of half a dozen vans came along Zimmer Strasse to the checkpoint, and fifty or sixty armed border guards got out.

Standing beside Lili, Werner said grimly: "Reinforcements."

. . .

Dimka and Natalya sat on the black leather chairs in Gorbachev's office feeling excited and tense. Gorbachev's strategy, of letting the Eastern European satellites go their own way, had led to a crisis that seemed about to boil over. This could be either dangerous or hopeful. Perhaps it was both.

For Dimka the issue was, as always, the sort of world his grandchildren would grow up in. Grigor, his son with Nina, was already married; Dimka's and Natalya's daughter, Katya, was at university; both would probably have children in the next few years. What did the future hold for those kids? Was old-fashioned Communism really finished? Dimka still did not know.

Dimka said to Gorbachev: "Thousands of people are gathering at the Berlin Wall checkpoints. If the East German government does not open the gates, there will be riots."

"That's not our problem," said Gorbachev. It was a litany. He always said it. "I want to speak to Chancellor Kohl of West Germany," he went on.

Natalya said: "He's in Poland tonight."

"Get him on the phone as soon as you can—not later than tomorrow. I don't want him to start talking about German reunification. That would escalate the crisis. The opening of the Wall is probably all the destabilization that East Germany can deal with right now."

He was dead right, Dimka thought. If the border was opened, a united Germany could not be far in the future; but it was better not to raise such an inflammatory issue right now.

"I'll get on to the West Germans right away," said Natalya. "Anything else?"

"No, thank you."

Natalya and Dimka stood up. Gorbachev still had not told them what to do about the immediate crisis. Dimka said: "What if Egon Krenz calls from East Berlin?"

"Don't wake me up."

Dimka and Natalya left the room.

Outside, Dimka said: "If he doesn't do something soon, it will be too late."

"Too late for what?" Natalya asked.

"Too late to save Communism."

. . .

Maria Summers was at Jacky Jakes's home in Prince George's County, having early supper with her godson, Jack. The TV was on, and she saw Jasper Murray, in a coat and scarf, reporting from Berlin. He was on the western, free side of Checkpoint Charlie, standing in a crowd near the little Allied guard post that had been built in the middle of Friedrich Strasse, beside a sign that said YOU ARE LEAVING THE AMERICAN SECTOR in four languages. Behind him she could see floodlights and watchtowers.

Jasper said: "The crisis of Communism is reaching a new peak of tension here tonight. After weeks of demonstrations, the East German government today announced the opening of the border with the West—but it seems no one has told the border guards or the passport police. So thousands of Berliners are gathering on both sides of the infamous Wall, demanding to exercise their brand-new right to cross over, while the government does nothing—and the armed guards grow increasingly nervous."

Jack finished his sandwich and went off for his bath. "He's nine years old, and newly shy," Jacky said with a wry smile. "He tells me he's too old to be bathed by his grandmother."

Maria was fascinated by the news from Berlin. She was remembering her lover, President Kennedy, saying to the world: *"Ich bin ein Berliner."*

"I've spent my life working for the American government," she said to Jacky. "All that time, our aim has been to defeat Communism. But, in the end, Communism defeated itself."

"Why is it happening?" said Jacky. "I can't make it out."

"A new generation of leaders came to power, most importantly Gorbachev. When they opened the books and looked at the numbers, they said: 'If this is the best we can do, what's the point of Communism?'

I feel as if I might as well never have joined the State Department—me and hundreds of other people."

"What else would you have done?"

Without thinking, Maria said: "Got married."

Jacky sat down. "George never told me your secrets," she said. "But I thought you must be in love with a married man, back in the sixties."

Maria nodded. "I've loved two men in my life," she said. "Him, and George."

Jacky said: "What happened? Did he go back to his wife? They usually do."

"No," said Maria. "He died."

"Oh, my goodness!" said Jacky. "Was it President Kennedy?"

Maria stared at her in astonishment. "How did you figure that out?"

"I didn't, I guessed."

"Please don't tell anyone! George knows, but no one else does."

"I can keep secrets." Jacky smiled. "Greg didn't know he was a father until George was six."

"Thank you. If it ever gets out I'll be all over those trashy supermarket newspapers. Goodness knows how much damage that would do to my career."

"Don't worry. But listen. George will be home soon. You two are practically living together now. You're so well matched." She lowered her voice. "I like you much better than Verena."

Maria laughed. "And my folks would have preferred George to President Kennedy, if they had known, you can bet on that."

"Do you think you and George might get married?"

"The problem is that I couldn't do my job if I were married to a congressman. I have to be bipartisan, or at least appear so."

"You'll retire one day."

"Another seven years and I'll be sixty."

"Will you marry him then?"

"If he asks me—yes."

. . .

Rebecca was at Checkpoint Charlie, on the western side, with Walli, plus Alice and Helmut. Rebecca was being careful to avoid Jasper

Murray and his television cameras. She felt that joining a street mob was not the right thing for a Bundestag deputy, let alone a government minister. But she was not going to miss this. It was the greatest ever demonstration against the Wall—the Wall that had crippled the man she loved and blighted her life. The East German government could not possibly survive it—could they?

The air was cold, but she was warmed by the crowd. There were several thousand people in the stretch of Friedrich Strasse leading to the checkpoint. Rebecca and the others were near the front. Just past the Allied hut, a white line was painted across the road where Friedrich Strasse intersected Koch Strasse. The line showed where West Berlin ended and East Berlin began. On the corner, the Café Adler was doing a roaring trade.

The Wall ran along the cross street, Koch Strasse. There were in fact two walls, both made of tall concrete panels, separated by a strip of cleared land. On the Western side, the concrete was covered with colorful graffiti. Opposite where Rebecca stood was a gap beyond which were several armed guards standing in front of three red-and-white gates, two for vehicles and one for pedestrians. Behind the gates were three watchtowers. Rebecca could see soldiers behind the glass windows, scanning the crowd malevolently through binoculars.

Some of the people near Rebecca were talking to the guards, imploring them to let the people through from the East. The guards did not respond. An officer came up to the crowd and tried to explain that there were as yet no new regulations about travel from the East. No one believed him: they had seen it on TV!

The press of the crowd was irresistible, and gradually Rebecca was forced forward until she crossed the white line and found herself technically in East Berlin. The guards looked on helplessly.

After a while the guards retreated behind the gates. Rebecca was astounded. East German soldiers did not normally withdraw from a crowd: they controlled it, using whatever brutality was necessary.

Now the crossroads was clear of guards, and the crowd continued to edge forward. Either side of them, the double wall dead-ended in a short cross-wall linking inner and outer barriers and blocking access to the cleared strip. To Rebecca's amazement, two bold protesters climbed the wall and sat on the rounded upper edges of the concrete panels.

Guards approached them and said: "Please come down."

The climbers politely refused.

Rebecca's heart was thudding. The climbers were in East Berlin—as was she—and so could be shot by the guards for transgressing the Wall, as so many others had been in the last twenty-eight years.

But there was no shooting. Instead, several other people climbed the Wall in different places and sat on top, dangling their legs either side, defying the guards to do something about it.

The guards returned to their positions behind the gates.

This was amazing. By Communist standards it was lawlessness, anarchy. But no one was doing anything to stop it.

Rebecca remembered that Sunday in August 1961, when she was thirty, and she had left home to walk to West Berlin and found all the crossing points blocked by barbed wire. The barrier had now been there for half her lifetime. Could that era be coming to an end at last? She longed for it with all her heart.

The crowd was now in open defiance of the Wall, the guards, and the East German regime. And the mood of the guards was changing, Rebecca saw. Some talked to the protesters, which was forbidden. One protester reached out and snatched a guard's cap, putting it on his own head. The guard said: "Please may I have it back? I need it or I'll be in trouble." The protester good-naturedly handed it back.

Rebecca looked at her wristwatch. It was almost midnight.

. . .

On the eastern side, the people around Lili were chanting: "Let us go! Let us go!"

From the west side of the checkpoint came an answering chant: "Come! Come! Come!"

The crowd had inched closer to the guards, minute by minute, until now they were within touching distance of the gates, and the guards had retreated inside the compound.

Behind Lili a throng of tens of thousands, and a line of cars, stretched along Friedrich Strasse farther than she could see.

Everyone knew the situation was dangerously unstable. Lili feared the guards would just start firing into the crowd. They did not have enough ammunition to protect themselves from ten thousand angry people. But what else could they do?

In the next instant, Lili found out.

Suddenly an officer appeared and shouted: *"Alles auf!"*

All the gates swung open at once.

A roar went up from the waiting crowd, and they surged forward. Lili struggled to stay near her family as everyone flooded through the pedestrian and vehicle gateways. Running, stumbling, shouting and screaming for joy, they passed through the compound. The gates on the far side were also open. They surged through, and East met West.

People were weeping, hugging, and kissing. The waiting crowd had bunches of flowers and bottles of champagne. The noise of rejoicing was deafening.

Lili looked around. Her parents were close behind her. Karolin was just in front. She said: "I wonder where Walli and Rebecca are?"

. . .

Evie Williams's return to America was a triumph. She got a standing ovation on the first night of *A Doll's House* on Broadway. Ibsen's bleak, introspective drama was perfect for the brooding intensity of her best acting.

When at last the audience tired of applauding and left the theater Dave, Beep, and their sixteen-year-old son, John Lee, made their way backstage to join the crowd of admirers. Evie's dressing room was full of people and flowers, and there were several bottles of champagne on ice. But, strangely, the people were silent and the champagne was unopened.

There was a TV set in one corner, and most of the cast were crowded around it, silent, watching the news from Berlin.

Dave said: "What is it? What's happening?"

. . .

Cam was in his office at Langley with Tim Tedder, watching television and drinking Scotch. Jasper Murray was on the screen, live from Berlin, yelling excitedly: "The gates are open and the East Germans are coming! They're flooding through in their hundreds, in their thousands! This is a historic day! The Berlin Wall has fallen down!"

Cam muted the sound. "Would you believe it?"

Tedder held up his glass in a toast. "The end of Communism."

"It's what we've been working toward all these years," said Cam.

Tedder shook his head skeptically. "Everything we did was completely ineffective. Despite all our efforts Vietnam, Cuba, and Nicaragua became Communist countries. Look at other places where we tried to prevent Communism: Iran, Guatemala, Chile, Cambodia, Laos . . . None of them does us much credit. And now Eastern Europe is abandoning Communism with no help from us."

"All the same we should think of a way to take the credit. Or let the president take it, at least."

"Bush has been in office less than a year, and he's been behind the curve all along," Tim said. "He can't claim to have caused this: if anything, he tried to slow it down."

"Reagan, maybe?" Cam mused.

"Be sensible," said Tedder. "Reagan didn't do this. Gorbachev did it. Him and the price of oil. And the fact that Communism never really worked anyway."

"What about Star Wars?"

"A weapons system that was never going to get beyond the science fiction stage, as everyone knew, including the Soviets."

"Reagan made that speech, though. 'Mr. Gorbachev, tear down this wall.' Remember?"

"I remember. Are you going to tell people that Communism collapsed because Reagan made a speech? They'll never believe that."

"Sure they will," said Cam.

.   .   .

The first person Rebecca saw was her father, a tall man with thinning fair hair, a neatly knotted tie visible in the V of his coat. He looked older. "Look!" she screamed at Walli. "It's Father!"

Walli's face broke into a wide grin. "So it is," he said. "I didn't think we'd find them in this multitude." He put his arm around Rebecca's shoulders and together they pushed through the crush. Helmut and Alice followed close behind.

Movement was frustratingly difficult. The crowd was thick, and everyone was dancing, jumping for joy, and embracing strangers.

Rebecca saw her mother next to her father, then Lili and Karolin. "They haven't seen us yet," she said to Walli. "Wave!"

There was no point in shouting. Everyone was shouting. Walli said: "This is the biggest street party in the world."

A woman with her hair in curlers cannoned into Rebecca, and she would have fallen but that Walli's arm supported her.

Then the two groups at last reached one another. Rebecca threw herself into her father's arms. She felt his lips on her forehead. The familiar kiss, the touch of his slightly bristly chin, the faint fragrance of his aftershave, filled her heart to bursting.

Walli hugged their mother. Then they swapped. Rebecca could not see for tears. They embraced Lili and Karolin. Karolin kissed Alice, saying: "I didn't think I'd see you again so soon. I didn't know if I'd see you again ever."

Rebecca looked at Walli as he greeted Karolin. He took both of her hands, and they smiled at one another. Walli said simply: "I'm so happy to see you again, Karolin. So happy."

"Me, too," she said.

They formed a ring, arms around each other, there in the middle of the street, in the middle of the night, in the middle of Europe. "Here we are," said Carla, looking around the circle at her family, smiling broadly, happy. "Together again, at last. After all that." She paused, then said it again. "After all that."

EPILOGUE

November 4, 2008

They were a strange family group, Maria reflected, looking around the living room of Jacky Jakes's house at a few seconds before midnight.

There was Jacky herself, Maria's mother-in-law, eighty-nine years old and feistier than ever.

There was George, Maria's husband for the last twelve years, now white-haired at seventy-two. Maria had been a bride for the first time at the age of sixty, which would have embarrassed her if she had not been so happy.

There was George's ex-wife, Verena, undoubtedly the most beautiful sixty-nine-year-old woman in America. She was with her second husband, Lee Montgomery.

Then there was George's son with Verena: Jack, a lawyer, age twenty-eight, with his wife and their pretty five-year-old daughter, Marga.

They were watching TV. The broadcast was coming from a park in Chicago where two hundred forty thousand ecstatically happy people had gathered.

Onstage was an African American family: a handsome father, a beautiful mother, and two sweet little girls. It was election night, and Barack Obama had won.

Michelle Obama and the girls left the stage, and the president-elect went to the microphone and said: "Hello, Chicago."

Jacky, the matriarch of the Jakes family, said: "Hush, now, everybody. Listen up." She turned up the volume.

Obama wore a dark gray suit and a burgundy tie. Behind him, rippling in a gentle breeze, were more American flags than Maria could count.

Speaking slowly, pausing after each phrase, Obama said: "If there is anyone out there who still doubts that America is a place where all things are possible, who still wonders if the dream of our founders is alive in our time, who still questions the power of our democracy—tonight is your answer."

Little Marga came up to Maria where she sat on the couch. "Granny Maria," she said.

Maria lifted the child onto her lap and said: "Hush, now, baby, everyone wants to listen to the new president."

Obama said: "It's the answer spoken by young and old, rich and poor, Democrat and Republican, black, white, Hispanic, Asian, Native American, gay, straight, disabled and not disabled—Americans who sent a message to the world that we have never been just a collection of individuals, or a collection of red states and blue states: we are, and always will be, the *United* States of America."

"Granny Maria," Marga whispered again. "Look at Granddad."

Maria looked at her husband, George. He was watching the television, but his lined brown face was streaming with tears. He was wiping them away with a big white handkerchief, but as soon as he dried his eyes the tears came again.

Marga said: "Why is Granddad crying?"

Maria knew why. He was crying for Bobby, and Martin, and Jack. For four Sunday school girls. For Medgar Evers. For all the freedom fighters, dead and alive.

"Why?" Marga said again.

"Honey," said Maria, "it's a long story."

Time's glory is to calm contending kings
To unmask falsehood and bring truth to light
To stamp the seal of time in aged things
To wake the morn and sentinel the night
To wrong the wronger till he render right

To ruinate proud buildings with thy hours
And smear with dust their glittering golden towers

—Shakespeare, *The Rape of Lucrece*

ACKNOWLEDGMENTS

My principal history adviser for The Century Trilogy has been Richard Overy. Other academic historians who helped with this volume were Clayborne Carson, Mary Fulbrook, Claire McCallum, and Matthias Reiss.

Numerous people who lived through the events of the era also helped me, either by checking my first draft or giving me interviews, especially: Mimi Alford on the Kennedy White House; Peter Asher on being a pop star; Jay Coburn and Howard Stringer on Vietnam; Frank Gannon on the Nixon White House, along with his colleagues Jim Cavanaugh, Tod Hullin, and Geoff Shephard; Congressman John Lewis on civil rights; and Angela Spizig and Annemarie Behnke on life in Germany. As always, Dan Starer of Research for Writers in New York City helped me find my advisers.

On my research trip to the American South my guides were: Barry McNealy in Birmingham, Alabama; Ron Flood in Atlanta, Georgia; and Ismail Naskai in Washington, DC. Ray Young at Fredericksburg's Greyhound station kindly dug out photographs from the sixties.

My friends Johnny Clare and Chris Manners read the first draft and made many useful criticisms. Charlotte Quelch corrected numerous errors.

My family helped me in immeasurable ways. Dr. Kim Turner advised me on many matters, especially medical. Jann Turner and Barbara Follett read the first draft and made perceptive and helpful comments.

Editors and agents who read the draft included Amy Berkower, Cherise Fisher, Leslie Gelbman, Phyllis Grann, Neil Nyren, Susan Opie, Jeremy Trevathan, and, as ever, Al Zuckerman.

ABOUT THE AUTHOR

Ken Follett burst into the book world with *Eye of the Needle,* an award-winning thriller and international bestseller. After several more successful thrillers, he surprised everyone with *The Pillars of the Earth* and its long-awaited sequel, *World Without End,* a national and international bestseller. Follett's new, magnificent historical epic, the Century Trilogy, opened with the bestselling *Fall of Giants.* He lives in England with his wife, Barbara.

CONNECT ONLINE

ken-follett.com